THE SERPENT'S CURSE

ALSO BY LISA MAXWELL

Unhooked

The Last Magician series
The Last Magician
The Devil's Thief

THE SERPENT'S CURSE

BOOK THREE IN THE LAST MAGICIAN SERIES

BY LISA MAXWELL

MARGARET K. McELDERRY BOOKS

NEW YORK   LONDON   TORONTO   SYDNEY   NEW DELHI

MARGARET K. McELDERRY BOOKS

An imprint of Simon & Schuster Children's Publishing Division

1230 Avenue of the Americas, New York, New York 10020

This book is a work of fiction. Any references to historical events, real people, or real places are used fictitiously. Other names, characters, places, and events are products of the author's imagination, and any resemblance to actual events or places or persons, living or dead, is entirely coincidental.

MARGARET K. McELDERRY BOOKS is a trademark of Simon & Schuster, Inc.

For information about special discounts for bulk purchases, please contact Simon & Schuster Special Sales at 1-866-506-1949 or business@simonandschuster.com.

The Simon & Schuster Speakers Bureau can bring authors to your live event. For more information or to book an event, contact the Simon & Schuster Speakers Bureau at 1-866-248-3049 or visit our website at www.simonspeakers.com.

Jacket designed by Russell Gordon

Interior designed by Brad Mead and Mike Rosamilia

The text for this book was set in Bembo Std.

Manufactured in the United States of America

First Edition

2 4 6 8 10 9 7 5 3 1

Library of Congress Cataloging-in-Publication Data

Names: Maxwell, Lisa, 1979- author.

Title: The serpent's curse / Lisa Maxwell.

Description: First edition. | New York : Margaret K. McElderry Books, [2021] | Series: The last magician ; 3 | Summary: "Esta and Harte race through time and across the country to steal back the remaining elemental stones needed to bind the book's power, stop the Order, and save the future of the Mageus"—Provided by publisher.

Identifiers: LCCN 2020025262 (print) | LCCN 2020025263 (ebook) | ISBN 9781481494489 (hardcover) | ISBN 9781481494502 (ebook)

Subjects: CYAC: Magic—Fiction. | Time travel—Fiction. | Demoniac possession—Fiction. | Gangs—Fiction. | New York (N.Y.)—History—20th century—Fiction.

Classification: LCC PZ7.M44656 Ser 2021 (print) | LCC PZ7.M44656 (ebook) | DDC [Fic]—dc23

LC record available at https://lccn.loc.gov/2020025262

LC ebook record available at https://lccn.loc.gov/2020025263

For Sarah,
whose fingerprints are on every page.
Thank you for making this story
immeasurably better.

~

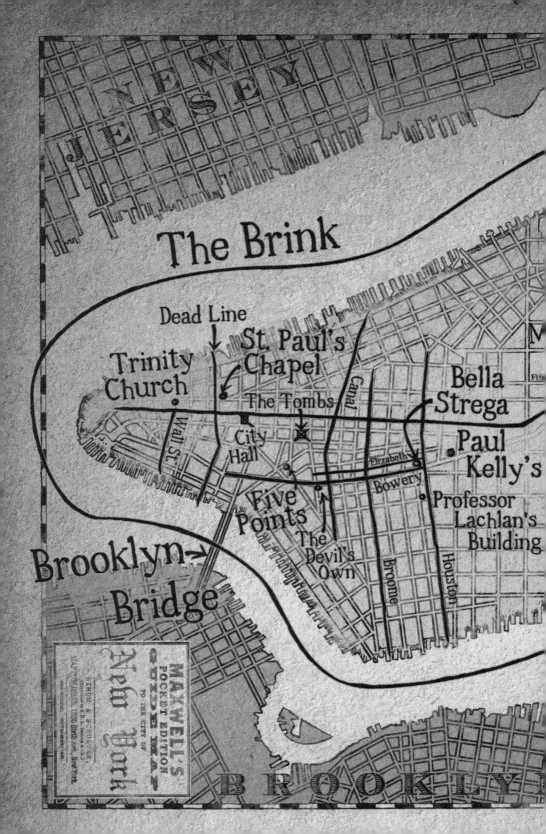

NEW JERSEY

The Brink

Dead Line

Trinity Church

St. Paul's Chapel

The Tombs

Bella Strega

City Hall

Paul Kelly's

Wall St.

Canal

Elizabeth

Bowery

Professor Lachlan's Building

Five Points

The Devil's Own

Broome

Houston

Brooklyn→ Bridge

MAXWELL'S
POCKET EDITION
GUIDE MAP
TO THE CITY OF
New York

SIMON & SCHUSTER,
MAP PUBLISHERS, 1230 Sixth Ave, New York

BROOKLY

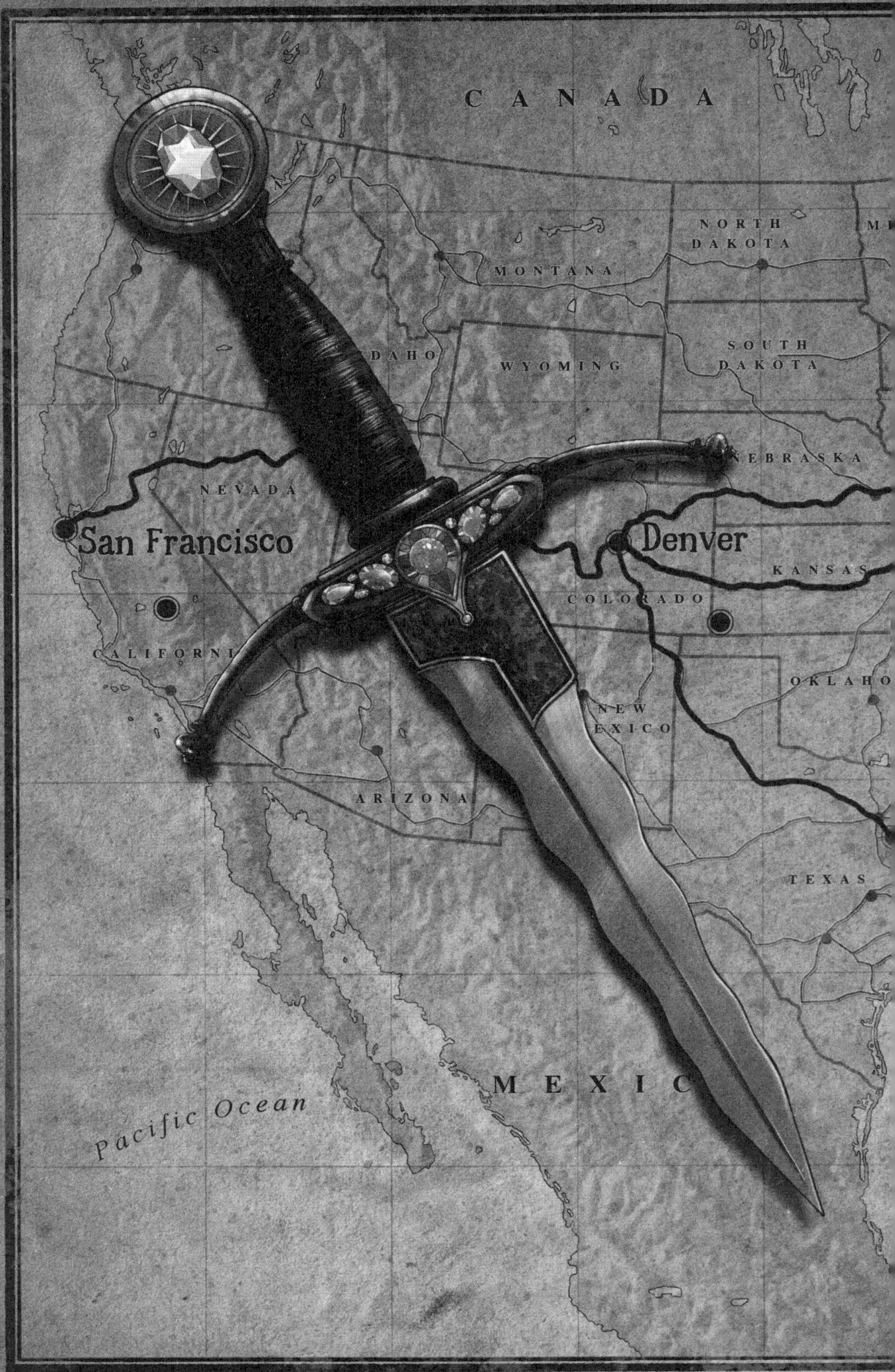
CANADA
NORTH DAKOTA
MONTANA
WYOMING
SOUTH DAKOTA
NEBRASKA
NEVADA
San Francisco
Denver
KANSAS
COLORADO
ARIZONA
TEXAS
Pacific Ocean

WISCONSIN

MICHIGAN

MAINE

VERMONT

NEW YORK

Chicago

PENNSYLVANIA

New York City

OHIO

NEW JERSEY

IOWA

INDIANA

ILLINOIS

WEST VIRGINIA

Atlantic Ocean

St. Louis

KENTUCKY

VIRGINIA

MISSOURI

TENNESSEE

NORTH CAROLINA

ARKANSAS

SOUTH CAROLINA

MISSISSIPPI

GEORGIA

ALABAMA

cana

LOUISIANA

FLORIDA

Gulf of Mexico

BROWN'S

RAILROAD

MAP OF THE

UNITED STATES

1904

Compiled from Latest Official Sources, showing carefully
selected list of Cities in readable type for quick reference.

PUBLISHED BY SIMON & SCHUSTER

THE SERPENT

1902—New York

The Serpent waited, concealed in the shadows of the city. His attention was focused on the bunching and shifting of the Aether around him . . . and on the estate just across Fifth Avenue from where he stood. The mansion, like its neighbors, glowed with electric light, an island of impossible luxury in the midst of a city that teemed with poverty and violence. But it was no safe haven, not even for the powerful men inside.

Despite all that had happened, the leaders of the Order still believed themselves to be inviolable. It did not matter that Khafre Hall was now a pile of ashes or that their artifacts and the Book of Mysteries had been taken from them. The Order of Ortus Aurea had continued on as though their greatest humiliation and defeat had been nothing more than a temporary embarrassment.

Let them parade around in their silken finery, the Serpent thought. Let them put on their airs and believe in the illusion of their superiority. No amount of wealth would protect them from what was coming—a new world, where those with the old magic would no longer be held back and beaten down. A world where *true* magic would be the key to power and where *he* would wield more than anyone.

As the Serpent waited, the Aether shifted around him again. Invisible to most, the Aether was the very quintessence of existence. To the Serpent, the world had a pulse. Soon his plans would begin to coalesce, and then *he* would be the one to make it race. To make it dance like a puppet on a string.

Certain as his victory seemed, though, the Serpent tempered his anticipation. After all, nearly two years before, he'd stood in that very place, expecting a victory that had never arrived.

The Aether lurched like an electric charge had sped through it, and the Serpent knew that the game was changing. If all went well, soon the cane he leaned against would be more than a crutch. Soon he would have the ring, and the cane would become a true weapon, just as it had once been for another. Once the power contained within the gorgon's head was fully unlocked, those who wore the mark would be his to command, and with them under his control, he would begin to rebuild the world anew.

By the time the door to the mansion opened to release a flood of people, the vibrations of the Aether had been whipped into a frenzy, and with it, the Serpent's certainty grew. Dressed in silks and satins and the dark wool of fine tuxedos and top hats, the rich poured screaming from the mansion like rats from a sinking ship.

The Serpent wasn't surprised. Humans were basically animals, stupid and instinctual. Easily led with the right incentives. No amount of money changed that. Let them scurry and flee—it would do them no good in the end. He had already made his plans, had already positioned his pieces on the board, and now he had only to wait. Soon one of the Order's artifacts would belong to him, and with it, *true* control over the Devil's Own . . . and then so much more.

LISA MAXWELL

THE GIRL WITH THE KNIFE

1902—New York

J. P. Morgan's ballroom was a riot of noise and violence. Viola Vaccarelli watched as the people around her erupted into panic. Jack Grew had tried to set a trap for her brother, but the moment Jack had given the word for the police to arrest him, Paolo's Five Pointers had revealed themselves and started to attack. As gunfire erupted in the ballroom, the members of the Order, along with their wives and rich friends, seemed suddenly to realize that their gala had turned deadly and that no amount of money would stop their blood from spilling. Tuxedoed men and silk-clad women toppled chairs and one another as they fled, but Viola cared for none of it. All she could see was the blood on her blade.

Jianyu's blood.

She had not been aiming for him. There had been a girl—one of Morgan's maids—with skin dark as any of the Turkish peddlers her father used to complain about back in the old country. The girl had been going for the ring. Viola had been sure of it.

Viola had not stopped to consider who the girl might be or whether she even understood the artifact's true value. She had simply pulled Libitina from its hidden sheath in a practiced fluid motion, as she'd done a hundred times before. Drawing back her arm, Viola had sent the knife flying. Then, out of nothing and nowhere, Jianyu had appeared, directly in the path between the girl and the blade.

She had named the knife for the goddess of funerals because it never missed. Because her blade always struck deadly and true. The ballroom had continued to roar around her, but Viola's eyes were fixed on Jianyu's shoulder, where Libitina was sheathed to the hilt in the flesh and muscle and bone of a man she had once considered a friend.

The brown-skinned girl had gone ashen with the sight, but Jianyu had paid her no attention. His eyes had been steady on Viola, despite the pain that had shadowed them. His mouth had formed careful words, but Viola heard only the roar of the room, the blood pounding behind her eyes, and her own shallow breathing.

Still, Jianyu's gaze had never wavered. His expression had creased with determination as he'd pulled Libitina from his shoulder. Blood had soaked the material of his tunic in response, and his hand had trembled as he held the dagger out to Viola. An offering. A truce. But all Viola could see was the blade, still sticky with his blood. It was a lurid stain on the shining metal and another dark mark on her soul.

Viola knew too well the weight of a soul. As Dolph Saunders' assassin, she'd taken so many lives. She'd accepted those black marks, one after another, in the hope that one day others like her would not have to struggle as she had. She'd made peace with her own certain damnation—had only hoped that it might have meaning. Now, staring at Jianyu's blood, Viola understood that she'd been a fool to ever hope for redemption.

Shame and guilt wrapped around her like a noose, but before her ears could clear, before she could understand Jianyu's words, his legs wobbled beneath him, and a man with skin as dark brown as the girl's scooped him up. Jianyu, who had always held himself with a determined strength, who had always seemed somehow apart from the rest of Dolph's gang, did not fight this man, and Viola understood immediately that they were friends—Jianyu, the girl, and this man. She realized in that instant the depth of her mistake.

Before Viola could say a word or take a step toward them, Jianyu's head lolled back. His body went slack in the man's arms, and his hand, which had been holding Libitina, went limp. Viola's dagger fell to the

LISA MAXWELL

floor, and the brown-skinned girl scooped the blade from the ground. She did not offer it, as Jianyu had, but instead lifted the knife in warning as she met Viola's eyes with a silent challenge. Judgment and anger and fear all burned at once in her dark eyes—and rightfully so.

Because Viola knew what the knife could do, she held steady. Even in the hands of a Sundren, a mere nick of the blade could be deadly.

Which is why I need to make them understand. She could fix this—all of it. The misunderstanding. Jianyu. The blood on the blade. Her curse was her gift as well. But Viola saw Jianyu's limp hand swinging listlessly—*lifelessly*—and felt a familiar heaviness pressing her down. For what she had done once again. For what she *was*.

When they began to back away, taking Jianyu with them, Viola could not seem to make her feet move or her mouth speak, even as the words waited on her tongue. Urgent. Necessary. The room was still rollicking, and Viola knew that she needed to go—with them, away, it did not matter. She could not stay there, and yet she seemed to be rooted in place.

Then a movement in the corner of her vision drew her attention back to her original destination, where a great stone beast sat upon a woman's chest. It looked like something from a nightmare, roughly hewn from rock or perhaps from clay, but the beast moved as though it were alive. It shifted, puffing itself up in warning to any that might approach. Guarding its treasure.

The ring.

Viola had only agreed to accompany her brother to the Order's gala because Nibsy Lorcan had told her that an artifact would be here. The last time she'd seen the ring was in the depths of the Order's Mysterium. Then, it had been on Krzysztof Zeranski's finger. The Order had taken the man, along with other powerful Mageus, and had bespelled him. They had been draining his affinity—killing Krzysztof and the others—with false magic, presumably to restore the power in the artifacts. Then, Viola had allowed Darrigan to get the better of her and slip away with the ring, but now Viola knew she had a second chance.

The ring was within her reach again, there upon the dead woman's hand. It was so close, this item that Dolph Saunders had desperately wanted. This artifact that Dolph had believed could help to free them all. Dolph had been her mentor and her friend. He'd given Viola a home and a purpose. He'd given her hope, too, that the world could be different.

But he'd lied.

Viola understood that now. She had seen the truth for herself, written in Dolph's own hand. He might have scooped Viola from the gutter and saved her from a life of misery under her brother's thumb, but she learned in the end that Dolph Saunders was a man of secrets. He'd done terrible things alongside the good.

Viola turned back to Jianyu, but the man carrying him had already disappeared into the crowd, and Viola felt a sharp pang of something too close to longing. She could simply walk away from all of this—from the danger swirling around her, from her brother with his anger and threats, and especially from the mad path that Dolph Saunders had set them all upon. She could leave the ring and follow Jianyu and his new friends, whoever they were. She could make right her mistake.

It's already too late. She had seen Jianyu's hand swinging lifelessly. She had no power over death.

Then the great beast shifted again, drawing Viola's attention back to the ring that glinted on the finger of the woman who lay dead beneath the heavy creature. The monstrous thing adjusted itself over the woman's lifeless body with a menacing lurch, and Viola was reminded that it was not only Dolph Saunders who had been after the Order's artifacts. Nibsy Lorcan had killed for his chance to possess them, and the Order would kill to retrieve them as well. Perhaps it already had. Perhaps this great stone beast was their work. Whatever Dolph Saunders might have been playing at, whatever his secrets or lies, Viola knew that neither Nibsy Lorcan nor the Order could be allowed to have the ring.

LISA MAXWELL

Viola had no idea where the couple was taking Jianyu, and with each passing second it was growing more impossible to follow, but the ring was *here*. She could not leave it. Letting her affinity unfurl a little, she sensed the lives of each person in the room. Their heartbeats surrounded her, but she felt nothing from the creature.

Because *this* was not life, she realized. The beast was nothing more than manipulation of matter, and Viola's affinity was for the blood of the living. It had no power over this creature.

Perhaps with her knife she could slay it. . . .

But Libitina was gone. It had disappeared into the crowd, along with Jianyu.

All around Viola, women still screamed and fainted, and men continued to run for cover as Paolo's scagnozzi stirred the confusion with their own violent glee. She ignored all of them. She moved slowly, cautiously slinking on satin slippers toward the dais where the woman lay. Viola knew the beast watched her. Still, she inched steadily closer. When she was little more than an arm's length away, the creature squared its shoulders in warning.

Viola didn't allow herself to hesitate or second-guess. She lunged for the woman, grabbed hold of her limp hand, and started to tug at the ring. But when Viola's fingers brushed against the cool smoothness of the ring's gemstone, suddenly the sound of blood became riotous in her ears. Her affinity flared, stirred by the power in the stone, and for a moment she felt the pulse of life in the room. Every beating heart. And she knew she could end them all.

But the beast was already moving toward Viola, and before she could move away, the force of its weight knocked into her. Her hand lost contact with the stone, and the clamoring rush of blood went silent.

The creature lurched again, and Viola thought her bones would crack beneath its weight as it shifted to press a broad clawed paw squarely on her throat. With the pressure, Viola could not draw breath, and she knew that with one more movement, the creature would snap her neck in two. Still, she reached for the woman's hand, careful not to touch the stone this time.

With the beast's weight crushing her, Viola's vision was starting to blur as she tugged at the ring until . . . *there*. Just as darkness pulled her under, the ring slipped free.

ANTICIPATION

1902—New York

Watching his gala dissolve into madness, Jack Grew felt the Book tremble against his chest. As gunfire rang throughout his uncle's ballroom, the most powerful men in New York revealed their cowardice. The leaders of the Order had lorded their power over him for so long. They'd thought him a failure—an *embarrassment*—but now they screamed like women as their fear exposed their truest selves.

The old men who led the Order were weak. *Impotent.* They had allowed their wealth and position to blind them to the truth—their days of power were nearing an end. Jack had seen their faces while he commanded the stage. All the demonstrations he'd performed upon that stage were mere parlor tricks compared to the power that was still undiscovered within the pages of the Book. Still, the old men of the Order had been shocked. They'd been awed by what they'd seen, and perhaps most gratifying of all, they'd been *afraid.* And that was *before* Paul Kelly and his men had turned the gala into a melee.

Jack's lips twitched as the Order debased themselves in front of common criminals. So much for their power. So much for the Order's great might. But the amusement of the moment could last for only so long. Across the room, Jack's beast waited, as did his prize.

The clay golem that Jack had formed with his own two hands and brought to life with knowledge he'd gleaned from the Book sat atop the broken and lifeless body of Evelyn DeMure. The harlot had tried to manipulate him with her siren's song, but in the end, her feral magic was no match for the gifts the Book had bestowed upon him. Her end was only the beginning for Jack. Her death would bring into being the world he would build, a world where every maggot who lurked in the shadows would finally be dealt with. Once he had the ring, he'd rebuild his machine, and there would be nowhere for them to hide.

Another shot rang out, but Jack barely heard it. The familiar bitterness of morphine lay on his tongue, emboldening him, and the power of the Book urged him on. Why should he bother to cower? What bullet could touch him now?

The Book trembled like a second heartbeat in the breast pocket of his jacket, and his blood answered, churning in anticipation. But then Jack saw that someone had reached Evelyn before him. A girl in purple, whose bright satin stood out amid the sea of dark suits. She was tugging at Evelyn's hand, trying to remove the ring.

With her cheap gown and swarthy skin, she certainly wasn't one of the fair porcelain dolls of society ballrooms. *She came with Paul Kelly*, Jack realized, remembering the girl from earlier in the evening. He'd dismissed her then as nothing but a trollop from the Bowery, but now he saw the determination in her dark features. Clearly, this girl knew what the ring was. The Book shuddered again, and Jack understood— she was one of *them*.

Ignoring the chaos around him, he stepped down from the small stage where he'd been presiding over the evening's events and pushed his way through the churning crowd. The Book beat an erratic tattoo against his chest as he clambered over toppled chairs, determined to reach Evelyn's body before Kelly's whore could take his victory. He was nearly there when another volley of shots rang out, and from nowhere, Jack found himself dragged down, pushed over, with the air knocked from his lungs.

"Get off, you damn—" Jack was already bringing his arm back to swing at his attacker.

"Now, just hold on there, Mr. Grew. It's not safe to—"

Jack stopped midswing, realizing it wasn't one of Kelly's men. It was instead one of the police who had been present to deal with Kelly. "This isn't necessary," he told the man through gritted teeth as he struggled against his would-be savior. "I'm perfectly fine."

"You need to stay down." The man pressed Jack to the floor again as more shots were exchanged.

He couldn't move the officer, but Jack wasn't without resources. His connection to the golem was stark and bright, and even pinned as he was, Jack's lips moved in a silent incantation. To protect the artifact. *To kill.* Against his chest, the Book felt like a brand.

Only when the gunshots ceased completely did the officer finally move and help Jack to his feet. From the corner of the room, Jack caught a flash of violet and saw the girl being carried away, limp and still, by one of Kelly's men.

He didn't bother to go after them. Instead, he went for the dais. There lay Evelyn, broken as a painted doll. Her lips were still a bright, unnatural red, and the rouge on her cheeks looked luridly pink against the pallor of her lifeless skin. Her hand was outstretched, but the ring was gone.

PART

I

AN UNFAMILIAR COUNTRY

1904—Texas

Esta Filosik stood on the open platform at the back of a train heading into the West. The wind tore at short strands of her hair, whipping them against her cheek as she took in the view. There was a wild beauty to the land, but the stark openness of the seemingly endless sky unnerved her. Despite the warmth in the air, a chill had sunk deep into her bones. It felt suspiciously like regret.

Harte was gone.

When she'd discovered his absence a little while ago, she hadn't even been surprised. Not *really*. His desertion felt strangely familiar. Almost expected. Maybe a part of her had been waiting for him to leave for weeks now, but it didn't hurt any less to know that she'd been right.

Not that she would ever admit *that*. Not even to herself.

It didn't seem to matter that he had a good reason to put distance between them. Back in New York, Harte had tried to warn her that the power that had once been within the Book of Mysteries was dangerous. In St. Louis, he'd tried to explain that it was growing stronger and becoming harder for him to control. But the night before, when that ancient power had overwhelmed him in the Festival Hall, Esta had finally understood. Harte's usual stormy eyes had gone black, and his expression had become so foreign that Esta had known instantly it wasn't Harte looking back at her.

And when she'd tried to help him—when she'd *touched* him? A shudder ran through her at the memory of the power she'd felt tearing at her.

No. Not a power. A person. Seshat.

Once, the ancient goddess had tried to save the old magic, but Seshat had been betrayed and trapped in the pages of the Ars Arcana. Now, after being imprisoned for so many years, she was furious and probably more than a little unhinged. To get her revenge, Seshat would destroy the world itself, and she would use Esta to do it.

So yes, maybe Harte had been right to leave, to put space between them until they had a way to control the goddess's power. But he should have discussed it with her. They could have made a plan. *Together.* Like the partners they were supposed to be. And he *certainly* shouldn't have taken the Key. It was, without a doubt, the bigger betrayal.

Esta wasn't *exactly* sure how time might unravel if she never returned to the city and gave her younger self the cuff with Ishtar's Key, as Professor Lachlan said she must. One thing was certain, though—Esta was undeniably connected to that small girl she had once been. She now wore the evidence of this link on her wrist, where a scar had appeared only days before.

Despite being new to Esta, the silvery letters looked like they'd been carved into her skin long ago, a single word in the Latin she'd learned as a child—the Latin that Professor Lachlan had taught her. *Redi.*

He'd used the imperative. It was a demand that she return to him.

The scar's sudden appearance was proof that however twisted and tangled time might be, the person Esta was now and the young girl Nibsy held captive were one and the same, as Nibsy and Professor Lachlan were one and the same. It was a sign—a warning—that Esta had no choice but to return the Key to her younger self and put her own life on its proper course. If she didn't, her present would become impossible. The person she was would cease to be.

Maybe that would be better.

Esta felt suddenly numb with a mixture of grief and exhaustion. Again and again she had tried to right the wrongs of history. She had tried to create a better future for those with the old magic, but she had failed—

No, Esta thought darkly. *I've made things even worse.*

When she and Harte had left New York weeks before, they'd only meant to find the artifacts before Nibsy could, but Esta had mistakenly brought them forward to 1904 and had destroyed a train in the process. Because of that mistake, the Devil's Thief and the Antistasi had been born. History had been set on a different path: the old magic had been deemed illegal, and *so many* had suffered because of it. And that was before they'd attacked the Society's ball—and the president. Esta could only imagine the ways history might continue to change because of what she'd done.

She should have listened to Harte and focused on collecting the stones. Instead, Esta had let her anger blind her, and she'd helped the Antistasi deploy a serum that turned out to be deadly. Worse, Jack Grew had still managed to slip away, taking the Book—and all of the secrets it held—with him. Without the Book, there was little chance of finding a way to use the stones to stop Seshat without Esta giving up her life.

But even sacrificing her life wasn't enough to right the wrongs she had created. Esta was willing to give up everything to stop Seshat here and now, but even if Harte could take the Key back to New York for her and give it to her younger self, the world was likely already changing in ways Esta couldn't predict and didn't want to think about.

She took a step toward the edge of the platform, ignoring how the wind lashed at her. Below, the ground rushed by in a blur of rock and brush. Maybe it would be better if she *didn't* return the stone. After all, without her meddling, the Book and its terrible power would have disappeared, as it had once before, and Seshat would never have been a threat. The world would be safe.

Safe. Esta looked out at the far-off horizon and tried to imagine that world, but she found she couldn't. Hadn't she learned long ago that safety was nothing but an illusion?

Her death was no solution. She *knew* that. If she never returned the Key, if history did unwind itself, the old magic would die, as Seshat had feared so long ago. Esta had grown up in that world, in a time far in the future, where magic was nothing but a fairy tale. And before magic faded away? There would be a century of fear and pain for those Mageus unlucky enough to have been born with a connection to the old magic. Removing herself from the equation wouldn't stop the Order or any of the Brotherhoods. It wouldn't end their hate or their violence or the power they held over the city she loved. It would simply leave the innocent as unprotected as they'd ever been. And Harte Darrigan would be gone as well, lost to history and memory, his life ended on a cold and lonely bridge.

It was that final thought that felt most impossible of all.

Esta's fingers brushed at the bracelet at her wrist. The cheap strand of beads was the only thing Harte had left her, but he'd used his affinity to make it something more. As soon as Esta touched it, she felt Harte there, like he was standing right beside her. His voice echoed softly through her mind, explaining where he would go, what he planned to do, and when his words died away, Esta thought she could almost feel the warm brush of lips against the column of her throat: a promise and a plea all at once.

To control Seshat and stop the ancient power from unmaking the world, they needed the other lost artifacts, but with Seshat's power growing, Harte's time was running out. The Dragon's Eye waited for him on a distant shore, but the Pharaoh's Heart was closer. It was where they would have traveled together if everything hadn't gone wrong in St. Louis. But with the threat of Seshat's power, they couldn't afford to waste time traveling together.

Find the dagger. Then meet me at the bridge. Together they would go back to the city and collect the final artifact.

It wasn't *exactly* a command. Harte hadn't used his affinity to take away Esta's will, as he could have. He'd left her behind, trusting that she would be able to do what he asked of her. Trusting that she'd be willing.

Or maybe he didn't trust her *completely*. . . . He'd taken her cuff, after all.

The land flew by around her, wide and open, a world filled with possibilities that were not for her. Would never be for her. Esta would do what Harte had asked. She would find the dagger and then meet him at the bridge, but she would not allow herself to forget where her path would inevitably lead. She would use her affinity to stop Seshat, and in doing so, she would lose her life. Once Seshat was no longer a threat, it would be left to Harte to take the Key to the small girl Esta had been and stop time from unwinding. There was nothing Esta could do about the tragedy she'd caused in St. Louis. There was no way she could see to take the stones back to 1902 without crossing them with themselves and losing them again. But she *could* still stop Seshat from unmaking the world. Perhaps with Seshat's power under control, Harte and the others they'd left in the city could fight the Order and create a different future for magic. Perhaps that could be enough.

Esta reached for the bracelet once more, the beads cool against her fingertips. Again Harte's voice came to her. She couldn't stop herself from closing her eyes as his words brushed against her and his presence surrounded her again. Nor could she stop her throat from going tight at the feel of his lips against her skin, but when she opened her eyes, she was alone in the middle of a wide sweep of unfamiliar country.

She tore the bracelet from her wrist, letting the tiny glass beads scatter like seeds in the wind. Esta wouldn't let herself rely on the comforting presence of Harte's voice, nor could she afford the distraction of his kiss. Both were only reminders of a future that could never be.

But first the dagger.

The air smelled faintly of the coal smoke expelled by the train, and the morning sky was a bright cornflower blue overhead. The train didn't seem to be slowing anytime soon, but that didn't mean that Esta couldn't get off. Far off in the distance, the jagged teeth of a town broke the endless stretch of the horizon. It was an opportunity.

Esta let her affinity flare until she could sense time hanging around her, but she'd barely started to reach for the seconds when she saw something else in the corner of her vision. A shadow lurked there, and the darkness had her drawing back and releasing her hold on time.

She'd seen darkness like that before. It had happened the first time, weeks ago, on the train out of New Jersey, and then again in St. Louis. Each time, destruction had followed. But every time it had happened before, Esta had been touching Harte; their connection had allowed Seshat's power to amplify her own. That couldn't be what was happening, though. Harte was gone, and Seshat's power with him.

Wasn't it?

Esta shook off the unease that had turned the warm summer wind suddenly cold against her skin. She took a deep breath to center herself, letting the rhythm of the train steady her, but before she could reach for her affinity again, she noticed that a small puff of smoke had appeared on the horizon. It was enough to make her pause.

Not smoke, Esta realized. It was a cloud of dust thrown up by a group of horses galloping toward the train. Even from that distance, she could tell they carried riders.

Esta took an instinctive step back from the railing, pulling herself out of sight. She didn't know who the riders were, but her instincts were screaming that their appearance was no coincidence.

The Order had found her.

A WHISPERING CERTAINTY

1904—St. Louis

I t was not yet six in the morning—an ungodly hour, to Jack Grew's thinking—when he found himself walking through the empty midway of the world's fair. Dark clouds hung heavy above, mirroring the mood of the whole city. As far as Jack was concerned, the gloom of the early morning suited him. His overcoat warded off the dampness of the day, and within a hidden inner pocket, the weight of the Book was a comfort, a ballast stone to keep him steady on his course. Within his mind, a new consciousness was taking form, a whispering certainty that he would prevail.

The grounds of the Exposition would not be open to the public today, not after the embarrassment at the ball that had happened the night before. The highest-ranking members of the Veiled Prophet Society—and consequently, all of St. Louis—had retreated to their individual mansions and boardrooms to lick their wounds and hide their fear, leaving the people of the city to fend for themselves.

Jack wasn't exactly surprised. The men who held power in the Society weren't any different from those who led the Order. Who could the men of the Veiled Prophet Society ever hope to be if they would not even reveal their faces?

Nothing. No one.

Luckily, Roosevelt was fine. The president had been removed from the Festival Hall moments before the attack, right before everything had erupted. Before leaving town late last night, Roosevelt had commended

Jack on his bravery, thanked him for his assistance and his loyalty, and given him a new position.

So, yes, perhaps Harte Darrigan and the girl had managed to slip through Jack's fingers, but the chaos they'd unleashed had worked in Jack's favor. Because of their actions, Jack had more authority than ever before. Because of their recklessness, the entire country understood exactly how dangerous feral magic was. The yellow journalists would sensationalize the events to sell their tawdry rags, and the fear and hate that was already spreading like a wildfire through the land would become the forge that could bring Jack's ultimate goals to fruition.

At the sound of steadily approaching footsteps, Jack turned to find Hendricks—one of the Jefferson Guard who had helped him in the previous weeks—approaching. *Right on time.*

Jack didn't bother calling out a greeting or lifting a hand in welcome. Instead, he kept his hands tucked into his jacket pockets, where his fingers brushed against the artifact he carried.

He'd found the piece years before, but after the events of the Conclave, he'd used the pages of the Ars Arcana to secret it away. To protect it. For the last two years, however, the Book had refused to return the artifact, stripping Jack of the power he might have otherwise wielded . . . until the night before. Now the familiar coolness of the stone in the artifact sent a thrill of anticipation through his blood, and the same whispering certainty rose within him again.

Hendricks' gaze shifted restlessly, as though he expected an attack. "Sir," he said in greeting. "Everything is ready. Just as you've required."

"Good," Jack said, ignoring the outstretched hand and withholding the praise he knew Hendricks craved. "Let's be on with it, then."

The two men made their way past the enormous sepulchral buildings, all quiet in the morning's gloom, until they came to a tower at least twenty stories high, as tall as the skyscrapers that were already starting to transform the skyline of Manhattan. The building at the base of the tower housed a mixture of working machinery and displays about the wonders of wireless telegraphy. Jack had already seen the exhibit—and the one in the Palace of Electricity, where the ever-present crackle of high-voltage electricity had signaled that the De Forest wireless machine was at work. He'd already watched the operators send messages to and from this very tower, through the air—as if by magic.

Jack wasn't as ignorant as the people whose eyes had goggled in wonder, though. He knew that it wasn't magic but *science* that accomplished the task, and he also knew that scientific thinking applied to the occult arts could reap great rewards.

Years before, Jack had worked in secret to create a machine that could cleanse the world of dangerous, feral magic. He had hoped to reveal his masterpiece at the Conclave. He had imagined his machine in the Wardenclyffe Tower, the wireless installation that J. P. Morgan had been financing for Tesla out on Long Island. Jack had planned to use the machine to lead the Order into the future. Now he had bigger dreams.

Here was evidence that Tesla's project had not been a waste of resources, as J. P. Morgan had eventually come to believe. Here, disguised as a novelty, was evidence that Jack's plan might one day be possible.

"How many know that we're here this morning?" Jack asked as the elevator began rising through the steel-framed tower. All around, the fairgrounds lay quiet and empty. Beyond, St. Louis looked as ragged and uninspiring as it did from the ground. It was nothing compared to New York, and thanks to the Society's inability to protect the fair—and to stop Esta and Darrigan from stealing the necklace—it never would be.

Hendricks' expression was like flint. "The bare minimum required, as you requested. They're all trustworthy."

"You're sure?" Jack asked, eyeing Hendricks. "This project is of the utmost importance, and secrecy is a necessity."

Hendricks glanced at Jack, a question in his eyes.

"By order of President Roosevelt himself, of course," Jack said easily. It wasn't a complete lie. Roosevelt *had* ordered him to take charge of the investigation into the incident at the ball, and the president had created the new cabinet position that granted Jack the power to do just that. "You know, I could use a good man like you on my staff."

"*You* could?" Hendricks asked, his brow wrinkling.

"On behalf of the president, of course," Jack amended humbly.

"Of course," Hendricks echoed. "It would be an honor to serve." He stood a little taller.

Even with his freshly starched uniform, Hendricks couldn't hide his softness. He was no soldier, honed for battle, but maybe he and the Guard could be useful nonetheless. The men who ran the Order and the Society were a minority too small to really wield power . . . unless the more insignificant members of the population yielded it voluntarily. With Hendricks, Jack might well be able to take control of the entire Jefferson Guard.

"The president will be honored by your commitment," Jack said solemnly as the elevator reached the top of the tower. "As am I."

Hendricks nodded and puffed out his chest even more.

The elevator shuddered to a stop, and the doors opened to reveal the observation platform. Windows encased the space. To the east, the Mississippi curved, muddy and dark, bisecting the country. To the west, endless possibility.

Hendricks made the introductions to the men who were waiting at the top and operating the tower. One sat at a long table that was cluttered with machinery. His concentration remained on the controls, as the other explained how the tower received signals.

"How far can you reach?" Jack asked, studying the machine, his mind whirling.

"So far we've managed to get messages from as far as Springfield, Illinois. A distance of over two hundred miles, sir," the operator told him.

Two hundred miles. It was twice what he had hoped to reach with the Wardenclyffe Tower. "I'd like to see the transformer," Jack said, wondering how they'd contained the enormous amount of electricity. It had been the singular problem of his original machine: the abundance of power it harvested could not be contained safely. Though the comforting weight of the artifact in his pocket reminded him that perhaps he already had an answer to that particular problem.

"Just through there, sir," the man told Jack, pointing to a partitioned area with only a small pane of glass to peer through.

Jack went closer and examined it. As he watched, the room lit with a dazzling brilliancy, and a muffled whoosh of sound carried through the heavy door.

"Open it," Jack told them.

"I'm not sure that's the best idea," the operator said hesitantly.

"I didn't ask if it was a good idea," Jack said, keeping his voice calm and even. "I asked you to open it."

"But the amount of voltage necessary to receive a message is quite dangerous," the operator hedged.

"I'm willing to assume that danger." Jack glanced at the man.

The operator blinked, clearly torn about what he should do, but eventually he relented. As he worked on unlocking the door of the partition, Jack took a vial from his pocket and placed a cube of morphine beneath his tongue, allowing the bitterness to flood his mouth slowly, so he could savor it. Just as he would savor this.

"Hendricks, you're free to wait outside if you'd like," Jack told the Guard, not bothering to look in his direction. He could sense Hendricks' hesitancy, but to the man's credit, he stayed.

Silence descended upon the observation tower as they all stood stock-still and waited for a message to arrive.

The flash of blinding light came without warning. The roar of a cannon surrounded him, as the hairs on the nape of Jack's neck lifted with the residual voltage that sifted through the air. The other men raised their hands to ward off the light, but Jack stared into the brightness, relishing the power that the tower managed to conduct. He gripped the artifact in his pocket, felt the coolness of the stone beneath his fingertips, the way it seemed to shudder and tremble at the power flooding through the room.

It seemed to Jack that the stone understood what it was meant for.

When the moment was over, Jack thanked the operator and indicated that he could reseal the transmitter behind the partition. The man was obviously relieved, and Hendricks did not bother to hide his nervous sigh. But none spoke against Jack. Not so long as he was the president's man.

They were nothing more than sheep. Expendable, stupid animals more concerned with their own meager lives than anything of real importance. Let them believe they were serving the president. It wasn't a lie, exactly, but the Guard—and the technology held within this tower—were just the beginning of Jack's plans.

SURROUNDED

1904—Texas

Esta watched the riders in the distance for another few seconds, and when it was clear that they were definitely heading toward the train, she made her decision. Even if she'd been willing to dismiss the shadow as a trick of her eyes—and she wasn't sure she should—she couldn't simply pull her affinity around herself and run, not if it meant leaving behind the two Antistasi who'd helped her escape from St. Louis. Instead, she went back into the car, rushing down the narrow corridor toward the berth she'd been sharing with North and Maggie. Before she could even grasp the handle, though, the door slid open to reveal more than six feet of irritated cowboy.

Jericho Northwood's mismatched eyes widened in surprise at the sight of her standing there, but then they narrowed. "Where do you think—"

The train lurched with a sudden burst of braking that made the car sway, but Esta didn't lose her footing. She pushed past North, tugging him inside the small Pullman berth and securing the door behind him. "We have a problem," she said, brushing off his clear irritation.

"You're damned right we have a problem," North blustered as Maggie crossed her arms over her chest. "We woke up and found the two of you gone, right along with our necklace."

"That's the least of our worries right now," Esta said, not bothering to correct him. The necklace was never going to be his, but she figured pointing out that fact wouldn't help. Instead, she moved past Maggie to peer out from a crack in the drapes that covered the windows. The train had slowed enough that the riders had come up to escort it into town. Most of the men wore the silver stars of law enforcement on their dark lapels. All of them carried guns.

"Where's Ben?" Maggie asked, using the name Harte had gone by in St. Louis. When Esta turned back, the other girl was peering through the thick lenses of her silver-rimmed spectacles, waiting for the answer— completely oblivious to the danger they were currently in.

"Gone," Esta told them.

"Gone *where*?" North demanded, stepping toward her.

"I don't know," she lied. It wasn't like she planned on taking the two Antistasi with her, anyway.

"Like hell," North said. "There's no way Ben went off without telling you where he was headed."

"That's what I would've thought too." Esta let her real disappointment and frustration infuse her tone. Even knowing he'd probably been right to go, she felt Harte's absence like a fresh bruise.

"But the necklace—" Maggie started.

"It's gone. He took my cuff as well," Esta told them, hoping that the bit of truth she was offering would be enough to distract them from their suspicion. She couldn't fight them and deal with the riders, too.

"You can't really expect us to believe you don't know where Ben went," North said.

"It won't matter what you believe if we can't figure out how to get out of the trouble we are currently in." Esta pulled the curtain back a little.

"What is all that?" Maggie moved toward the window, her brows bunching in confusion as she peered through the split in the curtain.

The riders had come up alongside the train now. Some of the marshals rode with their eyes forward, but others looked to the train cars, clearly searching for something.

Esta let the curtains fall back across the window to obscure their view.

"That ain't no welcoming committee," North told them, his voice dark.

Maggie's eyes were wide behind the lenses of her glasses. "But how could they have known we'd be here? No one saw us leave St. Louis."

"Maybe someone on the train recognized us," Esta said. It wasn't like they would have been easy to miss, with her and Harte barely conscious. "It wouldn't take much for someone to telegraph a message to the authorities."

North cursed under his breath. A moment ago, he'd been confident. Now he looked worried—scared, even—and he had good reason to be. The news of the attack they'd launched on the Veiled Prophets' ball would have spread quickly. Any news of the Devil's Thief would have, but an attack on the richest men in St. Louis—on *the president himself*? An attack like that wouldn't go unanswered.

"Where are we?" Esta asked North.

"We were heading toward Dallas, so we should be deep into Texas by now," North said.

"*Texas?*" That wasn't anywhere close to the dagger.

"It was the first train we could catch. I figured it would be far enough away from the mess we left in St. Louis. Plenty of wide-open spaces and people who usually mind their own business," North said. There was a challenge in his tone, daring her to contradict him. "It wasn't like you were in any shape to come up with something better."

"I didn't say I was." Esta barely remembered how Maggie and North had managed to get them away from the Festival Hall. "I'm grateful for all you did to get us out of St. Louis last night."

North snorted his contempt. "So grateful you and your partner decided to hightail it out of here without so much as a word."

"*I'm* still here," Esta reminded him, letting a chill settle over her words. *For now.*

Maggie stepped forward. "We don't have time for arguing. We'll sort everything out later—*after* we get out of this mess."

"There isn't any way out of this," North told Maggie. "Once this train stops, we'll be surrounded. Hell, we're *already* surrounded." He rubbed his hand over the coppery stubble on his jaw, his expression tight.

"There's always a way," Esta said, considering their options. "Give me a minute to think."

"Think all you want, but it won't help any," North said, trying to sound like he was in control of the situation, but there was a note in his voice that betrayed his fear. He swallowed hard, his throat working as his mismatched eyes met hers. "I've seen what happens with crowds like that. You can't reason with them, and you can't outrun them."

"After what we did . . ." Maggie's voice trailed off like she was remembering everything that had happened the night before. She grasped North's arm to steady herself. "When they find us—"

Esta understood Maggie's fear. Maggie had seen firsthand what had happened to the people they'd doused with Ruth's serum in St. Louis. She'd watched their magic awaken, and then she'd watched them die. She had every reason to be worried.

"There's no reason for them to find us," Esta said. They were still Mageus, weren't they? The two of them were *Antistasi*, for goodness' sake, and wasn't she the Devil's Thief? Maybe Esta didn't have her cuff, but they weren't powerless. They weren't without options. "You have your watch, don't you?" Esta asked North.

"What about it?" he said with a frown.

North's watch didn't tell time; it *changed* it. In St. Louis, they'd used his watch to try to undo the damage they'd done. It had all been too little and too late, but it didn't have to be too late now.

"Use it," Esta told North. "Take us forward, once this has all cleared out."

"That's not how the watch works." His mouth pressed itself into a flat line. "We're on a moving train. Even if we weren't, I can't go farther ahead than I've already been. I wouldn't know where I might land."

"You can't see where you'll end up when you use that thing?" Esta asked. It was a limit that Ishtar's Key didn't have. When Esta slipped through time with the cuff, she could see where she was going. She could find the right moment in the layers of years, like picking out a single word on the page of a book.

For a second Esta considered leaving, like she'd intended to before she'd seen the riders. Maybe North's watch couldn't save them, but there wasn't anything stopping Esta from pulling the seconds slow and slipping away. Maybe if she wasn't with them, North and Maggie would have a fighting chance. After all, Jack had only seen her and Harte in St. Louis. Without the necklace, there would be no proof that the two Antistasi had been involved in anything at all. Maybe without her they would be okay. But "maybe" wasn't enough for Esta to bet on.

If they had been seen together on the train, North and Maggie would still be targets. Esta couldn't walk away. She owed them too much—for standing against Ruth, for being willing to leave the Antistasi, for trying to help save the ball from Ruth's serum, and maybe most of all for saving Harte when Esta had been pulled under by Seshat's terrible power, helpless to do anything at all.

If North couldn't use his watch, there was only one way Esta could see to get out of the mess they were in. It meant breaking the rule that she lived by.

Never show them what you are. Never show them what you can do.

Professor Lachlan's words came back to Esta then, unwanted and unwelcome but true just the same. She hadn't even shown the truth of her affinity to Harte until that day on the bridge, when it had been a choice between revealing what she could do or letting a bullet take his life. There wasn't any bullet speeding toward them this time—not literally—but the danger was every bit as real.

The memory of the shadow she'd seen moments before rose, but Esta pushed it aside. It was only nerves or exhaustion. Nothing more. Seshat's power was in Harte, and Harte wasn't there.

Esta straightened her shoulders. "I can get us out," she told them. She only hoped they would all live long enough for her to regret what she was about to do.

THE COLD WITHIN

1904—A Train Heading West

H arte Darrigan leaned his head against the frame of the train's window and watched the continent pass by. He took every bit of it in—the long sweep of boundless plains that eventually climbed into mountainous terrain and then finally leveled itself out in the west. Once, he would have betrayed anyone and given up anything to have this view. Now, he knew that whatever possibility those wide-open spaces might hold, they were not for him. Maybe they never had been.

The bench seat beneath him was hard and nothing like the comfort of the Pullman berth he'd woken in the night before. Harte had been shaken from the soundness of sleep by the terrible dream he'd been having. In it, he'd been standing over a pit of vipers. He'd started to back away but had stopped short when he'd noticed something trapped within the writhing snakes: an arm. Then he'd realized the arm was Esta's. He hadn't thought or hesitated. He'd jumped into the pit with only one thought in his mind—to save her—but the snakes had quickly wrapped around him and began to pull him under as well.

When he woke, it had taken Harte a moment to realize that it wasn't a serpent wrapped around him but Esta's arms. Even once he understood that he was safe—that *she* was safe—his heart had continued to race. It was only as he focused on Esta—the warmth of her arms, the closeness of her face tucked into the crook of his neck—that Harte had started to breathe again. Esta had smelled lightly of sweat and the smoke from Maggie's devices, but beneath the grime of what they'd been through was an essence that was so undeniably *her*. For a moment Harte had simply lain there, willing away the vividness of the dream, but the second he'd started to truly relax into Esta's warmth, Seshat had lurched, rattling at the thin boundary that kept the ancient goddess from overtaking him completely.

Maybe he should have thrown himself from the speeding train and ended the danger Seshat posed right then and there, but Harte knew he couldn't, not yet. Not as long as the artifacts were out there, unprotected in the world, where Nibsy might retrieve them, and especially not when Jack Grew had the Book. Or rather, Harte remembered, the thing that lived *inside* Jack had it. *Thoth*. The very being that had trapped Seshat thousands of years ago in an attempt to take magic for himself was inside Jack now, pulling his strings in ways that Harte didn't yet understand.

It was Harte's own fault that the Book had ended up in Jack's hands—in *Thoth's* hands—and it was his responsibility to fix that mistake. But the danger Seshat posed to Esta was too real to ignore. Harte had known he couldn't stay. He couldn't risk losing her, not like that.

He had untangled himself from Esta's arms, and as the train slowed, pulling into some unknown station, he'd slipped the beaded bracelet onto Esta's wrist and touched her cheek softly, letting his affinity flare, just a little. He'd barely made contact when Seshat surged again, and it had taken everything Harte had to pull his magic back. His affinity had suddenly felt like something raw and untamed. Like something *apart* from himself that he could not completely control. He'd drawn back his hand, but not quickly enough. Esta had flinched in her sleep, pulling away from his touch.

Harte hadn't dared to touch her again. Even though Seshat seemed to recede, he could sense her anger at being denied once more.

He shook off the memory as the train sped along and told himself that leaving Esta had been the only way to protect her. He told himself that it would be faster this way. He would retrieve the Dragon's Eye for her, and then he'd meet her at the bridge. They would each find one of the missing stones, and then they'd find each other. Harte only hoped that Esta would come to understand, and that she wouldn't kill him when she found him.

It wasn't like she wouldn't have a good reason. The weight of her cuff tucked into his inside jacket pocket felt far heavier than the small piece of jewelry should have, as though his guilt was adding to its burden. It was, perhaps, the worst of all his betrayals.

He still didn't know why he'd taken it. Or maybe he simply didn't want to admit that he needed to know that she *would* come for him—even if it was only in wrath and fury. Because he couldn't bear to let her go, even if he would never deserve her.

Turning away from the window, Harte pulled his jacket around himself to ward off the chill. If there was any such thing as freedom—and he heartily doubted that there was—he knew now that it wasn't in the landscape that passed outside the train's windows. It was certainly nothing like the dream he'd once had to get out of Manhattan.

Now he had a different goal.

It wasn't a dream, exactly, because that word—"dream"—was for people who had a future in front of them, and Harte knew that he was already living on borrowed time.

Find the stones. Take back the Book. Save the girl. He repeated the words to himself like a mantra.

What makes you believe she's yours to save? The woman's voice echoing in his mind was low and soft with a breathiness that made him think of torn paper.

She's not mine. She never would be. But that didn't mean Harte wouldn't do everything in his power to save her just the same.

Seshat had been quiet since Harte had left Esta on the other train, but she laughed now, long and with a mocking edge that didn't seem quite sane. He pushed open the window, desperate for air as he tried to shove Seshat back into the cage of his own soul. It was July, but the mountain breeze coming in through the open window had a bite of coolness to it. Or perhaps the cold was within him, deep down in his bones, where he'd never be able to shake it free.

A REVELATION

1904—Texas

wo years had passed since Jericho Northwood had been in Texas, but it might as well have been yesterday for how familiar the sun and heat felt on his face. North had barely managed to get out of the state with his life, and this time wasn't turning out to be much different. Except now they had Esta. North's own eyes told him that what was happening—what Esta was doing—was real. But there was a part of him still struggling to believe what he was seeing.

Everything had all happened so fast. One second, at Maggie's urging—and against his better judgment—North had taken Esta by the hand, like she'd wanted. The next second, it was like he'd lost his hearing. It wasn't simply quiet, though. Everything had gone completely *silent*, like his ears had plum stopped working. But the second North opened his mouth, he could hear *himself* talking, so he'd known it wasn't his ears. It was everything else.

"What the—"

"We need to go," Esta said, her voice shaking a little as she cut off his question.

"Are you okay?" Maggie asked Esta.

North could see why Maggie was concerned—everything about Esta looked strung tight as a bow. Her jaw was clenched, she was holding her body like someone about to be slapped, and the color had all but drained from her face.

Esta gave a small nod. "I'm fine," she said in a strained voice that didn't sound fine at all. "But we have to move."

Before North could argue, Maggie was already reaching for the door. When she opened it and they stepped out into the corridor, North couldn't stop the curse that came out. "What did you do to him?"

The porter was standing at a berth two doors down, his hand poised to knock. Frozen like a statue. The man's face was lined, and there were tired circles beneath his eyes from his all-night shift. His dark-brown skin shone with sweat from the heat of the corridor, but though he was looking right at them, he didn't seem to be seeing them.

"I didn't do anything *to* him," Esta explained through gritted teeth. "I slowed things down *around* him."

"Time," Maggie said, without even a bit of fear. She sounded more curious than surprised. "You can manipulate time."

Esta's expression was still tight as she nodded. "We have to keep moving."

As they passed the porter, Maggie took something from her pocket and tossed it at him. A moment later, a violet-colored haze began to swirl around the man's head.

"What's that?" North asked. "Something new?"

"New-ish. It's a confounding solution," Maggie explained. "It won't hurt him," she added quickly. The color deepened on her cheeks, like she was embarrassed—maybe even a little ashamed—of the concoction. Or maybe she was embarrassed because she'd been caught trying to keep this one from him.

Maggie knew how he felt about some of her formulations. It was one thing to use a bit of smoke to get away from the Jefferson Guard or the Society, but when you started messing with people's minds—with their free will? Well, North didn't quite know what he thought of that. "What, exactly, does it do?"

Even with her furious blushing, at least Maggie had the courage not to look away from him as she explained. "The solution will confuse his memories for a few days. He won't be able to give anyone information about what happened or what he saw. Not for a while, at least. It will buy us some more time."

"Can you two talk about this later?" Esta asked, looking even more pale than she had a moment before. She gave a nod to indicate that they should keep moving, and from the look she was wearing, North decided not to argue.

Outside the train, nearly two dozen riders, maybe more, were frozen on horseback, exactly like the porter had been. They looked like stat-ues made of flesh and blood, defying the very laws of nature. Some of them were staring toward the train, and others had their mouths open, like they were caught in midshout. All of them were wearing a kind of angry determination North had seen in the eyes of Sundren too many times before.

Suddenly he understood the full significance of what Maggie had already realized. *Esta could manipulate time.* And she didn't need any watch to do it.

Maybe that revelation shouldn't have come as such a shock to him, but North had always thought the pocket watch his father had given him made him somehow exceptional. Now he understood that the watch—and his own affinity right along with it—wasn't much more than a parlor trick compared to what Esta Filosik could do. He'd been around a lot of Mageus during his time with the Antistasi in St. Louis, but North had never seen anything like this. Like *her*.

The Devil's Thief.

He'd helped Mother Ruth and the Antistasi use the legend of the Thief to undertake all manner of deeds as they fought against the Veiled Prophet Society, but North had never really imagined that there could be anything to the stories. He'd thought it was all a bunch of horseshit to pretend that any single person could be *that* powerful. Now he found himself thinking—and hoping—that he'd been wrong. Esta had better be every bit as powerful as all the papers believed, because if she let go of time now, they would be exposed.

They maybe could've tried to make it to the town, but who knew what was waiting for them there—probably more of the same marshals, since that was the direction the riders seemed to have come from. In the near distance, though, a cluster of wooden towers sprang up from the otherwise desolate landscape and gave them another option. They looked like oil rigs.

"If we can get over there," he told them, pointing toward the oil fields, "maybe we can lie low and figure out what to do next."

"Then let's go." Esta nodded for North to lead the way.

They took off together, with the two girls following North in an awkward, loping run. Each step drew them closer to safety, and North started to think that maybe they could get out of the mess they were in after all.

They were about fifty yards from the train when North felt Esta jerk him back, her grasp tightening like a vise around his hand. He looked back to find out what had happened, but what he saw didn't make any sense. Esta had stopped short, her expression twisting like she was in pain, but it was hard to look at her for very long. North could see her clearly enough when he didn't stare straight at her, but he couldn't quite *focus* on her. Beyond Esta, the world had gone all blurry-like. He couldn't make out much of anything at all, including Maggie.

North didn't have time even to begin processing what he was seeing before Esta's hand went suddenly slack. Her grip had been so steady, so determined, that the last thing he'd expected was for Esta to let go of him, so he wasn't prepared when her hand slipped from his and her legs collapsed beneath her. The second Esta released him, everything lurched into chaos. North was already moving, acting on instinct to scoop Esta into his arms before she hit the ground. Around them, the noise of the world felt suddenly deafening with the heavy roar of the train and the thunderous beats of the horses' hooves.

A shout went up, and North knew they'd been spotted. The shot ricocheting off the ground next to them a moment later confirmed it. With one look at Maggie's terrified expression, he began to shift his grip on Esta so that he could reach for his watch.

"Put me down," Esta demanded, wriggling to get free from his hold. From how feebly she was pushing at him, he wasn't sure she could walk on her own, but North let go. Sure enough, her legs wobbled a bit, and he had to catch her with one arm.

Maggie held out her hand to Esta. "We need more time."

But Esta didn't reach for Maggie's hand again, like North had expected. Esta's eyes were wide and her face had drained of all its color. She was shaking her head. "We need to go—the watch."

"What do you think I'm trying to do?" North ground out as he flipped open the cover. His hands shook as he adjusted the dial. "Grab hold of me," he told them.

Another volley of shots rang out, the clear report of them echoing through the hot Texas sky as he closed the watch's face. The world flashed white, the way it always did, but as the day shifted into the coolness of night, North felt an invisible fist punch him in the gut, knocking the air from him. He stumbled, leaning into Esta. His legs felt like they were going out from under him. Esta swayed under his weight, and they both went down.

At first North didn't feel any pain at all. He tried to sit upright, but he couldn't bring the air back into his lungs.

"Jericho—" Maggie's voice was shaking.

When Esta let out the kind of curse most women don't know, much less say, North knew it was bad. He wanted to tell them that he was fine, but all that came out was a ragged groan as pain erupted, hot and searing, through his side.

With the two girls panicking, North's mind was having trouble making sense of what had happened. The world was quiet now, dark as he'd intended. He'd taken them backward a few hours, and now above him, the Texas sky was swept with the brightness of stars he'd once marveled at. They lit the otherwise depthless night, but even the wonder of the stars couldn't take away the aching pain.

With his free hand, North reached for the source of that pain, grasping his side. He couldn't understand, at first, why his shirt should be wet. Then he looked down at his fingers and saw them coated with the dark stain of his own blood.

NO SUCH THING AS TOO LATE

1904—Texas

Esta staggered under North's weight, struggling to keep them both upright, as the reality of what had just happened slammed into her. From almost the moment she'd pulled time slow, the shadow of Seshat's power had been there, and the longer she'd held the seconds, the more intense it had become. By the time they'd run from the train, darkness had been swirling thick above her, like a storm threatening to break. And then it *had* broken, whole and complete, crashing over her until the world went dark. She didn't remember anything else until she'd come to, slung over North's shoulder like some kind of damsel who needed saving.

She'd dismissed the shadow she'd seen earlier, because she hadn't wanted to think there was any way Seshat's power could still affect her without Harte being close by. But Esta hadn't survived for so long by ignoring the truth when it was staring her in the face. Something had changed.

There wasn't time for her to consider what it meant, not when they were so exposed and not with the cowboy examining the blood on his fingertips like he didn't know who it belonged to. All the while, the dark spot on his light shirt continued to grow.

My fault. Esta had lost her grip on time, and they'd been seen. There was no escaping that fact. North had been shot because she'd failed to do what she'd promised.

"No," Maggie said, covering North's wound with her hands, trying to stop the bleeding. "No, no, no . . ."

40

"Can you walk?" Esta asked North, ignoring Maggie's growing panic. Even if the posse was gone and the night seemed quiet, they would be safer out of sight.

North's jaw tightened as he met Esta's eyes and nodded. Gently, he brushed Maggie's hands away. "I'm fine," he said, trying to straighten. He groaned when he moved, wincing with pain, but he managed to stay upright.

Clearly, he wasn't fine, but Esta wasn't about to argue if North was able—or at least willing—to walk on his own. North was tall, with a thin, rangy build, but he was solid beneath his clothing. She could help take some of his weight—and she did—but Esta doubted that even together she and Maggie would be able to carry him. The faster they found cover the better.

Esta suspected that North had taken them back a few hours, to the night before the train arrived, but she didn't know when the news of their impending arrival might have been sent to the marshals in town. There was no telling who might be watching for them. Before, she might have wrapped them in the cloak of her own affinity, but now she didn't dare risk using her magic again. Not until she understood why Seshat's darkness could touch her apart from Harte. After all, Esta knew too well what the darkness could do.

Trains derailed.

Elevator cables snapped.

Holes big enough to swallow horses split the ground.

It was more than bad luck. Seshat's ability to pull apart the Aether around them and unmake the order of existence was like Esta's own power, but stronger. Infinitely more potent.

"How far back did you take us?" she asked North.

"About six hours," he said with another pained groan.

It wasn't much time. Not nearly enough to get clear of the danger the marshals posed, even if North hadn't been injured.

"We need to get going," Esta told the two of them, hoping that her voice didn't give away her worry.

Thankfully, Esta didn't have to do more than support North's weight as they made their way toward the oil fields, where the enormous rigs stood like sentries against the night. The fields were two, maybe three hundred yards away, but they might as well have been in another country, especially since North seemed to be moving more slowly with each step.

Finally, they reached the edges of the oil fields and found an abandoned rig that had a small shed leaning close to its base. Inside, it smelled of dust and mold and a hint of something mechanical, but it was clear no one had been there for a while. The roof was only partially clinging to the walls, and moonlight streamed in from above, lighting the small space. Esta tried to help ease North down, but his legs went out from under him and he crumpled to the ground instead.

Maggie knelt next to him and started pulling away his jacket and shirt to see the wound beneath, but she went still when she exposed the small, jagged hole in his abdomen. She looked up at Esta with horror. "He needs a doctor."

Esta took one glance at the wound, ragged and still oozing blood, and knew the truth—a wound like that? A doctor wouldn't be able to help. Even if a doctor cleaned and bandaged him, the bullet would still be inside of North, and Esta knew that a shot to the gut like that one wouldn't heal. Without modern medicine, it would be a painful infection that would take North, rather than the loss of blood.

"No doctors," North said.

"Hush," Maggie whispered. "We'll find someone to get the bullet out of you and stitch you up and you'll be fine. We're going to take care of you."

North's eyes were steady on Esta, and she knew he understood. But she certainly wasn't going to be the one to tell Maggie, so she settled for the other reason. "He's right," Esta said. "You saw that posse. They rode out nearly at dawn. Chances are they're already expecting us. Finding a doctor would only bring them faster."

"I'd rather be in jail than know I could've tried to save him and didn't," Maggie told Esta.

Esta saw the determination in Maggie's eyes, but she knew the truth. "Why do you think we'd even make it to jail?" Esta asked softly.

"No doctor," North said again through gritted teeth. "No one's gonna be able to help me anyway."

"You don't know that," Maggie argued.

"I do," North said, grimacing again. He was looking worse now, paler, and his breathing seemed more ragged. "You two need to go while you can. It's not much, but six hours should give you a little room to get ahead of the marshals."

"We're not going anywhere," said Maggie, her voice cracking as she met Esta's gaze. "I won't leave him like this."

"Six hours won't make enough of a difference anyway," Esta agreed, her mind already furiously racing.

"You can't stay here," North told them.

"I won't just sit here and watch you die," Maggie said, stubborn as ever. "And I'm not leaving you behind." She glared at Esta, daring her to contradict this.

"We're not going to leave anyone behind," Esta told Maggie, pacing a little as she tried to think of some way out of the mess they were in. Absently, her fingers went to the scar at her wrist, and as she traced over the words, she had an idea. "We could use your formulations," she told Maggie.

"I don't have anything to heal a wound like that," Maggie said, stone-faced.

"Not to heal the wound," Esta said. "But maybe with a big enough distraction, we can get out of here and save North all at once."

"No," North told them. "You two need to go. It's too late for me."

"You of all people should know there's no such thing as too late," Esta told him. "But if we're lucky, maybe we'll be right on time."

IMPOSSIBLE CHOICES

1902—New York

With a strangled gasp, Viola jerked upright. Her eyes were wide open, but she saw nothing but inky blackness. The dream she'd been having lingered. She could still hear the roar of the crowded ballroom, still feel the beast's rough weight as it pressed the air from her lungs. Her mouth was dry with panic, and there was a dull roaring in her ears. Within her chest, her heartbeat felt unsteady, and for a long moment Viola did not remember where she was.

As the dream faded, the preceding days came back to her. Viola's eyes began to adjust, and soon she could make out the familiar slant of the low ceiling above her bed, the shape of the worn furniture, and the cold bare walls of the attic room closing her in. The air was warm and stuffy, but she rubbed her arms where gooseflesh still rose on her skin. Even without a window, Viola knew that it was nowhere near dawn. She also knew that she would find no more rest that night. If she closed her eyes again, she would only see Jianyu—the blood creeping across his shoulder, his lifeless hand dropping her knife—and she would feel the beast pressing down on her throat. She would dream of her bones cracking beneath the pressure of its grip and of her failure, as she had every night since the gala.

Instead of staying abed, Viola dressed quickly and, without lighting the lamp, pulled her hair back into a simple knot. Then she stepped soundlessly across the rough attic floorboards, making sure to miss the ones that would creak and alert her brother that she was stirring before a respectable hour. It would not do to rouse his suspicions, not now, when so much was at stake.

Paolo, he still watched her too closely—they all did—despite his claims that her actions at the gala had proven her loyalty to the family and to him. Since he'd rescued her from the beast's grip, Viola had continued to make sure that Paolo could find nothing of concern in her actions, even if that meant she had to remain small and meek. It did not matter that the weight of the role she played grew heavier with each passing day. She could not walk away from her brother or her mother or any of this—not until she knew for sure what had happened to the ring.

Though Viola remembered nothing after the great stone beast had crushed her beneath its weight, she was convinced that Paul or one of his men must have taken the artifact. When she'd come to in a carriage rattling toward the Bowery, her brother across from her and John Torrio's arms pinning her to him, no one had spoken of the artifact. Torrio's fingers had been rubbing against the underside of her breast, where her brother would not see, as the two gloated over their victory, and she knew it had not been the time to ask.

Viola shook off the memory of Torrio's wandering hands with a shudder and then headed downstairs. In the kitchen, the iron stove was waiting for her. It was a reminder of the tediousness sure to be found in the day ahead. Silently, she cursed it—and her own luck at being stuck once more under her brother's thumb. Viola was not made for chopping onions and baking bread. She knew that she had no talent for any of the domestic chores Paolo and their mother expected of her, but she would bide her time and do what she must to appease them . . . at least for a little while longer.

Again, her thoughts drifted to the night of the gala, but to her shame it wasn't Jianyu she thought of now, but Ruby Reynolds. The blond heiress had said dangerous things to Viola that night. But then, Ruby was rich enough to be brave and stupid all at once. In the quiet shadows of the kitchen, Viola could not stop herself from remembering how Ruby had looked that evening, draped in little more than a cloud of silk. Ruby had been dressed as Circe, the witch who turned men to swine, but with a mouthful of impossible words and a single kiss, the silly slip of a girl had done far worse to Viola.

Lifting her fingers to her lips, Viola stopped short of touching them. She forced herself to lower her hand. It did no good to think of things that could not be. Could *never* be. Pretty promises and the soft press of skin had simply given her a taste of a world that could never be hers. It had given her hope, the most dangerous of spells, but in the end Ruby's kiss had changed nothing at all.

Cursing softly, Viola slipped out the back door as noiselessly as she'd done everything else since waking. She muttered every vulgar word she could think of as she made her way to the outhouses behind the cafe, but by the time she was finished with her business there, she'd fallen silent. Not even the phrases that would make a sailor blush gave her any real satisfaction.

When Viola stepped back out into the cleaner night air, she knew she was not alone. She walked steadily toward the building, waiting for the intruder to show himself, and when she was nearly to the kitchen door, she paused.

"I know you're there," she said, her voice soft in the night. She missed the reassuring weight of Libitina—or any knife, really. Like a fool, she'd ventured out unarmed. In the distance, a dog howled, but no other sound reached her ear. "Whoever you are, show yourself. Only a coward hides in the shadows."

Viola waited, listening to the city rustling itself awake, a constant hum of life all around her. Just as she thought that maybe she'd been wrong, a man stepped from the alley that ran behind the row of buildings. He seemed enormous, with impossibly broad shoulders, dark, flashing eyes, and even darker skin.

Viola stepped back and instinctively drew on her affinity until the man was on his knees, but then she saw what he was holding in his hand—

Libitina.

She released her hold on his life at once, and the man slowly stumbled back to his feet, his free hand rubbing at his chest. "Where did you get that?" she asked, moving toward him. She realized that he wasn't so large as she had imagined him to be. He was simply a man, no taller than her brother or any other in the Bowery. His skin was not made of the darkness of night, but was instead a warm deep brown.

The man flinched, raising his hands in surrender, and she realized he was not a stranger. It was the same man she had seen at the gala, the one who had carried Jianyu away.

"He told me you would come if I showed you this," the man said, his eyes still wary as he held the knife to her, handle first. "Jianyu. He told us that you would believe me."

"Who are you?" Viola didn't reach for the blade, even as her palms itched to feel its weight.

"My name's Johnson. Abel Johnson," the man said again. His voice had gone tight with a fear that Viola recognized too well, but still this Abel Johnson offered her the knife—*Libitina*—once more. "Jianyu sent me to get you."

She was already reaching for her blade when she paused, the man's words—the significance of them—finally registering. Her heart felt suddenly lodged in her throat. "He's alive?"

"Only just," the man said, releasing the knife to Viola's keeping. "We've tried everything. Doctors and praying and every home remedy my mother ever knew, but nothing closes up the wound you gave him. He's been bleeding for days now." The man's jaw was clenched, but Viola could not tell whether it was fear or the usual male pride that he now held between his teeth. "He said that you would come, that you could do something about it. We have to go now. He doesn't have much time."

Viola felt herself torn in two. She could save Jianyu. She had thought him dead, already past healing, yet if his heart still beat, she could help him. But if she left now, she could not return. And if she did not return, she might never discover where her brother was keeping the ring.

"If you come with me now—"

Viola was shaking her head. "I can't."

"You can't come or you can't help him?" Abel asked, tucking his hands in his pockets.

"You don't understand. My brother—"

"I know all about your brother," Abel said, his mouth twisting as though he'd tasted something foul. "He's a dangerous man, and the men he surrounds himself with aren't much better. But Jianyu seemed to think that you were stronger than him."

Viola glanced back to the door. In a matter of an hour the sun would be up, and with it some of Paul's men. If she were discovered missing, and especially if anyone discovered who she had gone off with . . . "It's not so simple. Paul, he knows where the ring is."

Understanding flashed through Abel's expression. "Paul Kelly has it?"

"He must," Viola told him. "Right now he trusts me. If I leave without an excuse, he'll grow suspicious, and I won't be able to find out where it might be."

Abel Johnson looked like a man fighting with himself. "This ring—everyone keeps saying it's so important. But do you really believe it's worth a man's life? Your *friend's* life?"

Pressing her lips together, Viola met his eyes. "Jianyu knows how important the ring is. He wouldn't risk a chance to retrieve it for anything. Not even for his life."

Abel let out a frustrated breath. "Look, I don't pretend to know anything about this magic mumbo jumbo you all are involved in. It doesn't have anything at all to do with me. But Jianyu saved my sister's life twice now, so ring or not, I'm not leaving until you agree to come."

Viola wasn't sure what she should do. If Abel Johnson didn't leave, he'd get himself into trouble with Paul, and for what? Niente. It would only put them all in danger and make the ring even more difficult to locate. It certainly wouldn't save Jianyu.

LISA MAXWELL

She glanced back at the building. Her brother was an early riser. Soon he'd be stirring, and he'd expect her to be there. "There's no time for me to return before Paolo realizes I'm gone, but once the sun is up, I could make an excuse."

"I don't know if Jianyu has that long left," Abel told her. His expression was serious, and Viola could not tell if the look he wore was the truth or simply a bluff.

Guilt twisted her stomach, but she lifted her chin. Jianyu's life was in her hands, but she could not lose her chance to find the Delphi's Tear—to *protect* it from Nibsy, the Order, and even from her brother. Jianyu would not want that. He would understand. None of them were worthy of the power it contained. If any one of them had control of an artifact as powerful as the ring? Viola knew well the suffering that would follow. She could not allow that to happen.

"Come back at noon. Paul goes out after his lunch to check on his businesses around town. I should be able to slip away for a while then. Wait at the corner of Great Jones Street," she told him as she forced down her guilt. "If I can, I'll meet you there."

"That's not good enough," Abel said, his hands fisted at his sides.

"It has to be." Then Viola turned away from him, ignoring his protests as she walked toward the kitchen entrance of the Little Naples Cafe.

She did not look back as she closed the door behind her and leaned against it, pressing her back against the heavy wooden panel. She knew that every second that passed until noon would be a trial. If the ring weren't so important, if the others after it weren't so dangerous, her choice would have been easier.

When are choices ever easy? she thought darkly, and before she could stop herself, Viola was thinking of another choice—perhaps another mistake. What might have happened the night of the gala if she hadn't turned Ruby down? What if Viola had simply accepted the gift of Ruby's kiss, if the two of them had left the gala together, right then and there, for some impossible future? She would not have thrown her blade. She would not have hit Jianyu. She would not be in this position, stuck between the anvil and the hammer.

Viola lifted her fingers to her lips, and this time she touched them. But she could no longer feel the imprint of Ruby's mouth upon hers. Even the memory of it was beginning to turn hazy. Perhaps her refusal that night had been a mistake, but what other choice could she have made? Perhaps her refusal now was a mistake as well. She let her legs fold beneath her and began counting the minutes until Abel's return.

THE MOMENT APPROACHING

1904—Texas

The early-morning sun beat down from a crystalline sky as Esta finished placing the last vial of incendiary, and then, brushing her hands on her pants, she made her way back to where Maggie was waiting with North. He looked worse than before, his skin nearly gray and his breathing shallow.

"Is everything ready?" Maggie asked, looking up from where she sat cradling North.

"I think so," Esta said, glancing out to where she'd laid the charges.

"You really think this will work?" Maggie asked, her voice like glass.

Turning back, Esta saw Maggie sitting there, her skirts covered in the dust from the ground, her arms filled with North and her eyes filled with fear. "It has to."

Esta wasn't sure that Maggie heard, though. The other girl's attention was on North, and Esta wondered if the look on Maggie's face was the same one she herself had worn the day Harte nearly tumbled from the bridge, or the night before, when Jack Grew was choking the life out of him. She allowed herself a moment to wonder where Harte was, whether he'd made it off the train as he'd planned and was safely away, or if he too was trapped.

She wanted to believe that she would know if something had happened to him. She wanted to believe that maybe the fact that Seshat's power was still connected to her meant that Harte was as well, but Esta had never been one to spin fairy tales. And anyway, wanting a thing didn't make it so.

Far off in the distance, the keening whine of the train's whistle sounded. A few minutes later, it came into view, and the time for wondering was over.

Esta jogged to the place where the fuses she'd laid earlier all came together and ducked behind a row of scrubby bushes. She ignored the prickling brambles as she checked the position of the sun and wished she had a watch of her own. So much of the plan was dependent upon everything happening at exactly the right time, and yet she would have to rely only on instinct, hoping that she remembered and reacted when necessary.

The train was coming closer now, and when Esta turned, she saw that the posse was coming as well. A sense of déjà vu swept through her as she saw the horses at full gallop. Then she noticed that a small group of them had steered their mounts to the center of the tracks. The engineer must have seen the horses, because Esta heard the wailing screech of the brakes and the hiss of steam being released from the boiler as the train struggled to slow in time.

She remembered then how the train had swayed with the sudden braking, and she continued to watch the scene, waiting. Right now, the other versions of themselves should be leaving the Pullman berth. Soon they would make their way out of the train, as they had the first time. With the way Esta had used her affinity earlier, she wouldn't be able to see when her past self exited the train with Maggie and North. She wouldn't be able to tell when it was approaching—the moment she would lose hold of time and North would be shot. But if she could distract the posse right when it happened, if the men on horseback turned away instead of aiming for North, maybe she could rewrite what had happened.

She could only hope that there would be some sign of when to act once the train came to a stop. Because if she acted too late, all their plans would be for nothing. If North was shot as he was before, nothing would have changed.

As the horses' thundering hooves grew closer, Esta thought she saw the flicker of something—a wavering of her vision in the spot where they might have once stood a little ways off from the train. Her instincts told her that it was as good a sign as she'd ever get. She touched the scar at her wrist and hoped that her theories were right.

The igniter Maggie had given her was a strange contraption made from a glass vial that cracked in two to create a small explosion. It was easy enough to use, and Esta quickly activated the formula inside and set it on the fuses before pulling back under cover when the horses galloped past her.

A moment later, the entire landscape erupted as Maggie's incendiaries exploded, their flames consuming the small clutches of brush and shrubs where they'd been placed all along the landscape. The Flash and Bangs erupted next, like fireworks at close range. One by one they exploded at random intervals, drawing the riders' attention in multiple directions at once. The horses reared up, shying away from the noisy confusion despite their riders' commands. As Esta watched, the strange multicolored flames from the incendiaries that had set fire to the brush began to produce an ethereal fog. It wasn't the cloying smoke of a normal fire, but instead glowed a strange lavender as it swirled into the sky, a cyclone of power and flame that blocked the riders' way. It blocked their view as well. A few tried to shoot, but their leader held up a hand to stay them.

Esta waited, trying to remain calm, but she didn't know what was coming. If her theory was right, if they had been able to save North, then her present should become impossible. If time worked the way that Professor Lachlan had explained, her present self—the one crouching in the bushes and hoping—should no longer be. But what that meant, Esta didn't exactly know. . . .

As she continued to watch, the landscape around her fuzzed in and out of focus, and suddenly Esta felt a bolt of utter dread. She could sense time hanging around her, but the seconds had become erratic and unstable. The landscape flickered, and time felt suddenly dangerous. *Hungry.* She could almost feel the seconds turning toward her. Coming for her. She could sense their desire to devour her—to tear her from the world—but when she reached for her affinity, desperate to stop whatever was happening, Esta could no longer grasp the seconds. Her affinity slipped through her fingers like sand.

As the world around her shifted, she had the sudden, awful thought that she'd miscalculated. She'd wondered what would happen if she didn't return the cuff to her younger self. She'd wondered what it would feel like to disappear—whether it would hurt to be unmade or whether it would be soft, like sinking into darkness. She thought maybe it would be like forgetting—like nothing at all.

Now Esta understood. Now she knew how truly terrible it was to feel time pulling her—and everything she was—apart. Ripping her from existence.

Esta's mind raced for some solution, some way out of the trap she'd set for herself, but before she could do anything, she felt herself being unanchored from the present moment, torn away, torn back through the layers of time and place. Until she wasn't anything at all.

LISA MAXWELL

THE COVER OF NIGHT

1904—San Francisco

When Harte Darrigan finally disembarked from the train in California, he was still across the bay from the city he was trying to reach. He followed the line of railroad passengers to the long ferry boats and climbed aboard, the whole time trying not to look too overwhelmed by the sights around him. He'd lived his entire life on an island, but he'd never ventured close to the water's edge if he could help it. In California, though, there was no trace of the cold power that kept Mageus away from the shores of Manhattan. Harte felt only the briny dampness of the sea air and the strange coolness of the summer day as the wind ruffled his hair. He'd watched the continent unfold itself for the last few days, and now he'd reached its end.

Fog cloaked the sea as the ferry carried Harte onward, but as they drew closer to the opposite shore, San Francisco finally came into view. It was something to take it all in, the hills that flared up around the bustling docks, barely visible through the misty fog. Beyond the jut of land where the city sat, the bay emptied out into an endless sea, one that led to a world far wider and stranger than even Harte could imagine. Somehow, this view of San Francisco almost felt like enough to make up for the life he would never have.

Then the wind shifted, and suddenly Harte smelled himself instead of the sea—the days-old sweat and sourness rising up from his body and the other passengers' cigar smoke that had permeated his clothes on the train. His skin felt sticky, and his hair was a heavy, unwashed cap against his scalp. For a moment he had the ridiculous thought that he would give nearly anything to be back in New York, in his own apartment, sinking into the steaming water of the pristine porcelain tub he'd worked so long and so hard to call his own. But that life was gone now, and the apartment right along with it. There was no going back, not when he carried within his skin a power that could destroy the world itself.

As the ferry shuddered to a stop, Harte pulled his jacket closed to ward off the chill he felt and began to follow the other passengers once again. He told himself that it definitely wasn't stalling to clean up before he continued on. It wouldn't do to show up looking like a tramp when he went to retrieve the Dragon's Eye, the fanciful golden headpiece with an amber stone that seemed to glow from within. It would be hard enough to explain who he was and why he was there—*how* he was there—to a woman he'd never met. She probably hadn't even known Harte existed until the Dragon's Eye had arrived on her doorstep two years before.

It was early in the evening and the sun was already starting to set by the time Harte finally left the cheap boardinghouse and began to make his way up Market Street and into the heart of the city. The area near the docks was filled with squat rows of wooden buildings that housed saloons and worn-out hotels, along with cluttered shops that catered to travelers and sailors. But as Harte traveled away from the water, the city changed. The tumbled wooden structures near the water became well-made buildings of stone and brick that housed banks and offices. Instead of the workmen that had crowded the docks, filling the air with their raucous banter and all-too-human smells, the sidewalks in the business district were filled with men in suits who walked silently on, wearing serious, harried expressions.

Once, Harte might have relished every sight. Once, he might even have wished to be one of those men. Now, though, his only thought was for what came next—finding the Dragon's Eye. Meeting Esta. Defeating Seshat.

As though I would allow you to . . . Or didn't you learn your lesson, back on the train?

LISA MAXWELL

Harte shook off Seshat's voice and kept his pace steady and determined, but days with barely any sleep had taken their toll, and his steps felt as heavy as the artifacts weighing down his pockets. It didn't help that he knew that each step drew him closer to facing the past he'd been running from for so long.

When Harte turned onto California Street, he paused, confused by the grinding, growling whir he heard, until he realized it came from the cables that ran beneath the paved road. They sounded like some slumbering dragon waiting to rouse itself. Manhattan didn't have anything like the odd, open trollies that traversed the steep hills of this city. The thought of using one was briefly tempting, but Harte knew he needed to save his last few coins for the trip back to the bridge. Instead, he continued his hike, trying to prepare himself for what might come.

With his affinity, retrieving the headpiece shouldn't be difficult. A simple touch, skin to skin, and he could have it easily—and the person he was visiting would never even remember losing it. Nor would they remember him. Now, though, Harte wasn't sure that would be the wisest move. After he'd left Esta, he'd thought to use his affinity to board the next train, but when he'd tried, Seshat had lurched within him, making his magic feel like something apart from him, uncontrollable and dangerous. Harte had barely pulled back in time to stop her from doing whatever she'd planned, and after, he hadn't risked using his affinity again. Instead, he'd made the rest of the trip with nothing but his own cunning and what little money he had left.

It was clear that Seshat didn't like the other two artifacts he carried, and he imagined that the ancient goddess would do everything she could to prevent him from retrieving a third. Harte decided that it would be safer to depend on his wits and whatever was left of his charm. He would keep his affinity tucked away and use it only as a last resort.

Eventually you will need to rely on what you are, Seshat purred. *And when you do, I will be waiting.*

Harte shook off her voice. He didn't want to consider that Seshat might be right, especially since he didn't have much confidence in his charms. Maybe he would have had more if he'd known anything about the person who had the Dragon's Eye other than her name—Maria Lowe—and the address on Dawson Place, where she lived. He'd memorized both years ago, when he was still a boy and his mother had still been living with the man who had fathered him. That was before Molly O'Doherty had tossed Harte out into the streets, even though he was still a child. It was before Harte had taken up with Dolph Saunders and the Devil's Own and then, later, with Paul Kelly's gang. In those days, he'd still been Benedict O'Doherty, a name he'd only recently resurrected. He hadn't yet fashioned himself into Harte Darrigan or pulled himself out of the Bowery through sheer determination.

Harte still didn't want to look too closely at where the impulse to send the headpiece to the woman had come from. After everything that had happened at Khafre Hall—and with Seshat's voice newly echoing in his mind—he hadn't exactly been thinking straight when he sent the Order's artifacts out into the world. He'd only had the impulse that he needed to get them out of the city, because he knew that Nibsy Lorcan could never be allowed to retrieve them.

Back then, the country had seemed impossibly large to Harte. He'd thought that by separating the artifacts, by sending them out into the far corners of that enormous world, it would be impossible for *any* single person to bring them back together and harness their power. He'd been wrong, of course. Even if Nibsy Lorcan might not find the artifacts for decades, Harte's experience in St. Louis had shown him how easily they could fall into the wrong hands. Julian hadn't been able to resist wearing the necklace that contained the Djinni's Star, and the Society had found it. Harte had seen the discarded newspapers that littered the trains as he'd traveled; he already knew that Julian had paid the price for his naive stupidity. He only hoped that Maria Lowe had not been so unlucky.

Harte increased his pace, but walking faster couldn't turn back the years or undo the mistakes he'd made along the way. Already the sky was

LISA MAXWELL

growing darker and the city was beginning to come alive. Now that evening was falling over the streets, there was something about San Francisco that reminded Harte of New York. The two cities were nothing alike, but beneath the cover of night, they weren't so very different. He'd come thousands of miles only to find himself in the same place he'd started—a crowded, filthy cluster of buildings filled with work-weary souls who only wanted to make it to the next day. A trap dressed up like a dream.

The thought made Harte walk faster, not that he could ever outpace the memory of the boy he'd been. He was so deep in the darkness of his thoughts—so determined that whatever mistakes he'd made in the past, he would find the headpiece and make this one mistake right—that he almost didn't notice the fencing. Or the men who guarded it.

Harte pulled up short just before he crossed Kearny Street. On the other side of the intersection stood a trio of men. Each held a billy club as they watched the pedestrians with sharp eyes. They weren't police, or at least they weren't wearing the uniform of police, but behind them, a barricade of wood and barbed wire blocked the intersection. In the deep recesses of his mind, he heard Seshat laugh.

EXILED

1902—New York

R uby Reynolds barely cared that she was crumpling the sheet of paper in her hand as she stormed into the Barclays' library and slammed the door behind her. Theo didn't so much as look up as she propped her hands on his desk.

"Your sister said you were in here working," Ruby told him.

Theo continued annotating the notebook he'd been writing in, the words pouring from the tip of his pen in a slow, steady stream as ink transformed itself into his eminently readable hand. She knew that she was interrupting his studies, but she couldn't stop herself.

"Aren't you going to ask me why I've come?" Ruby demanded, her irritation growing by the second.

"I assumed you would tell me whether I asked or not," Theo told her with a small, impertinent smile.

"They've all refused me." Ruby threw herself into the nearby armchair. "It's now official. Every single reputable paper in town has rejected me. I just received the *Sun*'s rejection this afternoon. They publish the absolute rubbish that Sam Watson spouts on a regular basis, but they rejected my article about the gala outright. Can you imagine?"

"Not at all, darling. You're only going after the most powerful men in the city."

Ruby knew that Theo was her greatest supporter—had been since they were children—but his words still rankled. "Who are they to deny the people of this city the truth?" She felt her indignation rise once more.

"Who indeed?" He finished the line he was writing and set the pen on the table before looking up at her.

"They're a bunch of cowards. All of them," Ruby said, still stewing with anger. "And I told the editor, Mr. Bartleby, so myself."

Theo frowned at that piece of information. "You did *what*?"

"I marched straight into the *Sun's* office and demanded to see the editor. They told me I had to have an appointment," she muttered. "An *appointment*, if you can believe that!"

"What a novel idea," Theo mused.

"This isn't a joke to me, Theo." Ruby felt her shoulders sink right along with her spirits.

"I never said it was, darling," Theo said. "I'm merely imagining you storming into the offices of the *Sun* like an avenging Valkyrie. Did you finally manage to see Mr. Bartleby?"

Ruby deflated a little more. "No. He refused to meet with me, but I stood my ground. I told them exactly what I thought of their editorial choices."

"You didn't." His mouth kicked up a little.

"Do *not* mock me, Barclay." Then her temper faltered a little. "I couldn't bear it if you thought I was a joke too."

Theo's expression softened. "I would never think that of you. But you had to expect this would happen," he said, his smile fading. "I read your piece. It was wonderfully brave and honest, but the Order's reach is long."

Ruby let out a tired breath. The members of the Order might be some of the wealthiest and most powerful men in the city, but she had truly believed that publishers would want the truth. At the very least, she'd expected that Hearst and Pulitzer and all the rest would have craved the sales the headlines would have inspired. But one after another had slammed the door in her face.

"I'm not going to give up," she said, pulling her wits about her.

"That's my girl—"

"I'm going to try the *Spectacle*," she told him, glancing up to see what his reaction would be.

Theo's mouth fell open a little. "That's a terrible idea, Ruby."

She twisted her hands in her lap. "What choice do I have?"

"The *Spectacle* is nothing more than a gossip rag," Theo said as though Ruby needed to be reminded. "If they do accept your piece, you'll never be taken seriously again."

He was right, of course. Only the desperate or the stupid believed anything in the *Spectacle*, and once R. A. Reynolds was associated with it, her career would be over before it had even truly begun.

"Maybe I think it's worth the risk," she told him, trying to sound confident and failing miserably.

Theo's expression shifted, and his voice was softer when he spoke. "There are other ways to reach her, darling."

"I don't know what you're talking about," Ruby said, straightening a little.

"Ruby, when have you ever been able to hide anything from me?" Theo asked.

"This isn't about Viola," Ruby lied.

"Of course it is," Theo argued, coming around the desk so he could crouch in front of her. "I've read the piece. It more than stands on its own merit, but it's clear you wrote it for *her*."

Ruby lifted her chin, refusing to admit anything. "People should know the truth about the old magic," she said, her voice trembling more than she would have liked.

Hadn't Ruby recently discovered that for herself? Magic hadn't destroyed her family—that had been her father's fault, with his careless disregard for anything or anyone but himself. And magic hadn't destroyed whatever it was that Ruby might have been building with Viola. That had been all her *own* fault.

Theo took Ruby's hands in his. His grip was warm and steady, as always, like Theo himself. "Let me take you home," he said, pulling her to her feet. "You need time for this defeat to settle before you do something you'll regret. R. A. Reynolds has started to build a name for herself in this city. You can't throw it all away on the *Spectacle*. Not even for Viola Vaccarelli."

Ruby wanted to argue, but Theo was right. "Can we take the long way? I can't bear to deal with my family quite yet."

Outside, the heat of early summer was beginning to simmer. Even so, they took a route that meandered through the park, walking until Ruby's feet ached and the tightness in her chest had almost started to ease.

"Better?" Theo asked as they approached the front steps to her family's town house.

"A little," she admitted.

"It will all work out," Theo assured her.

She looked up at him, handsome as he ever was, and felt a rush of affection. Their whole lives, she'd felt that same affection, but it was nothing compared to the warmth she felt every time she remembered her lips on Viola's.

Ruby pushed that memory down where it belonged. "Would you like to come in?" she asked, forcing a brightness to her voice she didn't feel. But when Theo hesitated, she gave herself a shake. "Of course, you have your studies to get back to—"

"I have a few minutes," he said, his expression filled with something too close to pity for Ruby's liking. Still, she didn't send him on his way.

When she opened the door, it was clear that something was happening. Voices were coming from the front parlor, and the chattering of women could only mean that her sisters had assembled—*all* of her sisters. Ruby glanced at Theo, as if to tell him that he should go before it was too late. Heavens knew that once her mother and sisters started clucking about something, they wouldn't soon stop. But Theo, the dear, simply offered her his arm.

"Mother?" Ruby asked, stepping away from Theo a little when she saw who was assembled in the parlor. Two of her sisters had brought their husbands, and her uncle Archibald—her father's brother—was also there. "What is all of this? Has something happened?"

Her mother glanced at Ruby's older sister, Clara, who was the one to answer. "We've called the family to a meeting."

"Clearly," Ruby said, her unease growing. "But you seem to have forgotten my invitation."

"It was rather a last-minute decision," Clara said primly. "Still, we've made quite a lot of progress without you. We have your trip nearly planned."

Ruby understood the words coming from her sister's mouth, but they made little sense. She glanced up at Theo, who seemed equally as confused. "What trip?"

"We've decided that you will be accompanying Eleanor and Henry to the Continent this summer," Ruby's mother said, finally finding her voice.

"I've already been to the Continent. Just last spring," Ruby reminded them. "I've no wish to go again so soon."

"You have a trousseau to complete," her mother said, dismissing this concern. "You've put it off long enough."

"My trousseau can wait," Ruby told them. "I have work to do here, important work."

Clara's expression went stony, and her tone hardened. "Your *work* is exactly the problem."

Ruby blinked. "My work is not a *problem*." She knew that her family merely indulged her dreams to be a journalist, but they had never spoken outright against her vocation before.

Eleanor stepped forward, giving Clara a warning look. "You have to admit that what happened at the gala was quite . . . unsettling."

"Unsettling?" Clara said with her usual haughty laugh. "It was more than unsettling. It was downright improper. It's bad enough that you embarrassed the family at the Order's gala with your indecent display, but it's quite another thing to continue in your attempt to publicize that embarrassment for the entire world to see."

"Embarrassed?" Ruby couldn't make her mouth work to say anything else.

Her mother sighed. "You're no longer a girl, Ruby. And you cannot continue carrying on with such complete impropriety."

"I don't know what you could possibly mean." Ruby's head was still spinning when her uncle stepped forward.

"I received a call from Mr. Bartleby of the *Sun* a few hours ago," Uncle Archibald said. "It seems that you paid him a visit today. From what I understand, you made quite the spectacle of yourself this morning." He narrowed his eyes in her direction. "This cannot go on, my girl. Your family has been through enough."

"The *Constantina* departs on Thursday," Clara said.

"I won't be on it," Ruby told them, lifting her chin in a show of defiance.

"I'm afraid you have no choice in the matter," Ruby's mother said. "Your dear friend Emily Howald and her mother have graciously offered to host you at their London town house after you make your tour of the Paris dressmakers. You'll stay through the summer, of course. Possibly into the fall."

This was not a pleasure trip, Ruby realized suddenly. She was being exiled. When she spoke again, her voice sounded as hollow as she felt. "You would send me away for so long?"

"I would and I am," her mother said. "The summer will give you ample time to amass a respectable trousseau before the wedding."

"We've not even set a date yet," Ruby said, glancing at Theo, who looked every bit as taken off guard as she did.

"That is another problem that we have allowed to go on far too long. You'll be married when you return," her mother said. "It's all been arranged."

"You cannot simply *arrange* our lives, Mother," Ruby said, the panic rising hot and fast in her throat. "Shouldn't Theo and I have any say in the matter?"

"He's had his say. He has asked for your hand, and you consented. The family has given you ample time to set a date." Her mother's expression went carefully blank. "Perhaps I've not been as firm as I should have been with you, but I can no longer stand by while you ruin the chances of your younger sisters with your wild, reckless behavior."

"I hardly think—"

"That is the entire problem, my girl. You *don't* think. Do you know what I was told this morning?" her mother said, her tone turning suddenly icy. "Right now, at this very moment, all of society is atwitter with the rumor that *you* were seen kissing someone at the gala."

Ruby's stomach twisted as she pasted on a bright smile. "Surely Theo and I—"

"It was *not* Theo," her mother said. "Millicent St. Clair is being quite vocal about what she saw behind the curtains—particularly *who* it was that you were with." Her mother sank back into her chair, apparently too overwrought to remain upright.

Suddenly the air went out of the room. "Millicent St. Clair is nothing but a jealous harpy," Ruby said, but even she could hear the trembling in her voice. Someone had seen her kiss Viola.

"Of course she is," her mother said. "But the truth doesn't matter when gossip is involved."

"Mr. Bartleby had been doing his best to convince the other publishers to quash these rumors as a personal favor to me and to our family," Uncle Archibald said. "But after your performance in his offices today, he has reached the end of his patience."

Ruby's stomach turned with the understanding of what her uncle was saying. If that particular rumor found its way into the gossip columns, it would impact more than only herself. Her entire family—her two younger sisters especially—would be affected as well.

"I allowed you to put off setting a date for the wedding because of your father's *situation*," her mother said softly. "I had believed that we all needed time to heal. But this is too much, Ruby. I cannot allow you to ruin your younger sisters' chances at a good match. Not when they are so close to their debuts." Her mother put down the handkerchief she'd been crumpling into a ball with her fingers. "You'll go with Eleanor and her husband, as we have arranged. You will spend the summer in Europe while this whole mess blows over, and when you return, you will be married. With any luck, society will have put this vicious rumor to rest once and for all by then."

"That is assuming, of course, Barclay will still have you," Archibald said, lifting a brow in Theo's direction.

Ruby looked around the room, at the many pairs of eyes that were united in this against her. Theo seemed as shocked as she was.

You can throw me over, she wanted to say. But of course Theo would do no such thing.

"I've no wish to sever my engagement with Ruby. I'll have the notices sent to the papers immediately," he told them.

"Theo—"

He ignored the protest in Ruby's voice as he took her hand and placed a soft kiss upon her knuckles. Though he smiled at her, there was a sadness in his eyes that nearly broke her heart.

THE WHITE WOMAN

1902—New York

The pot on the stove was burning, but Viola didn't notice until it started to smoke. Not that she cared about the food inside. Her brother could eat his lunch burnt and bitter as far as she was concerned, but she removed it from the fire anyway. It wouldn't do to make Paul angry. Not when she'd already risked so much to keep his suspicions at bay.

Viola ladled some of the bitter greens and half-burned potatoes into two bowls, then added some thick slices of bread to the side. She took a moment to prepare the mask she wore around her family, and then she carried the tray into the dining room, where her brother and Torrio waited. She'd already made her excuses about leaving for the market. As soon as they were served, she could go, but she couldn't allow them to realize she was in a hurry, or they'd have questions.

"We'll need a third," Paolo told her, barely glancing up as he poked unhappily at the food she placed in front of him.

"You have another guest?" Viola asked, frowning. "Mama or—"

"If it were any of your business, I would have already explained," her brother said, glaring up at her in warning. He set the fork down and took a cigarette out of his silver case, his eyes steady on her while he lit it.

"Of course," she told him, letting her gaze drop. Not in deference, though he would certainly read it that way. No, Viola only lowered her eyes so her brother wouldn't see the hate burning in them. It was a trick that had served her well since she'd come to him for protection after the fiasco that was Khafre Hall.

Viola retreated to the kitchen, her cheeks burning in anger and shame all at once, silently cursing Paolo—and herself—as she violently scooped out another serving. Paul might have taken her from the grip of the demon at the gala, he might have commended her for attacking Jianyu, but that hadn't changed anything between the two of them.

When she returned to the front of the house with the third bowl, Viola's steps halted. Her brother's guest had arrived.

"Hello, Viola." Nibsy Lorcan's mouth curved in a small, satisfied smile as he took his place at the table with Paul. "I see you're still safe and well in your family's keeping."

At first Viola couldn't do more than stare in shocked confusion. After Mooch, one of the Devil's Own, had attacked Tammany's firehouse, she'd thought her brother had realized what a snake Nibsy Lorcan could be. "This one, *he's* your guest?" she asked, her words coming before she could think better of them.

One glance at Paolo, though, and Viola understood that something was happening here, some bigger game she'd not been made aware of. Her brother's expression narrowed ever so slightly—a warning. "Mr. Lorcan and I have business to discuss," Paul said, taking a final drag on his cigarette before stubbing it out.

Nibsy glanced over his spectacles. "You should join us," he said easily. "You might be interested in what I have to say as well. After all, we are old friends." He met her eyes, his gaze steady, as though reminding her of the last time they'd met—when he'd returned Libitina to her and revealed what Dolph had done to Leena.

"Viola has other things to attend to, I'm sure," Paul told Nibsy, cutting another meaningful look in her direction.

He wanted her to go, which made Viola want to stay all the more, but she didn't need to glance at the clock to know that the minutes, which had crept by all morning, were now racing toward the time when Abel would be waiting for her. Still, Nibsy Lorcan was dining with Paul, and Paul hadn't yet killed him. Something was happening.

THE SERPENT'S CURSE

69

"I thought you were on your way to the market," Paul said, raising his brows in question—another challenge. It only confirmed her suspicions.

As much as Viola wanted to stay and listen to their conversation, the clock would not wait. Abel, Jianyu, and the blood on her hands would not wait.

"I was just leaving," she said tightly as she placed the bowl in front of Nibsy. Then, still torn, she left her brother and Nibsy Lorcan to whatever business they had between them.

Outside, the summer day had turned hazy and humid. Viola glanced down the street toward the end of the block, where she'd expected Abel to be waiting, but there was no sign of him. As she began to feel the fear—the *relief*—that perhaps Abel hadn't come after all, he stepped from around the corner and glanced her way. Even from that distance, she could see his impatience.

"Something's happening," Viola said as soon as she was close enough. She motioned him to step around the corner and into a blind alleyway. When they were out of view of Paul's place, she tried to explain. "Nibsy Lorcan just arrived—"

"I don't know who that is," Abel said, interrupting her. "And I don't particularly care. You need to come now. Jianyu hasn't woken up all morning."

Viola froze. "He's worse?"

"This morning, not long after I left to find you, he closed his eyes and that was that." Abel's jaw went tight. "His skin feels like it's growing cooler."

Viola was shaking her head. Nibsy Lorcan was up to something—so was her brother—but she knew she could not stay to discover what it was. She could not have Jianyu's death added to the black marks against her soul.

"I can't go back to my sister again without you," Abel said. "I have a carriage waiting on the next block over. *Please.*" He started to offer her his hand—or maybe he meant to take her arm—but then his eyes shifted to something behind her, and he took a step back instead.

Viola turned, expecting Paul or one of his boys to be there, following her. Instead, she found Theo Barclay squaring his shoulders with suspicion and something strangely close to anger gleaming in his eye. Next to him, dressed in the most ridiculous mint-green frock of lace and chiffon, was Ruby Reynolds.

At the sight of her, Viola felt like her feet had been nailed to the ground and her tongue had been cut from her mouth. For a moment she could do nothing but stare at Ruby, there like some sort of apparition, with her cheeks flushed a becoming rose-petal pink and her eyes bright with some emotion Viola could not interpret.

"Are you okay, Miss Vaccarelli?" Theo's voice was tight, and his words were unusually clipped. Ruby clasped her hands silently next to him.

"Theo?" It took Viola a moment to realize she wasn't imagining them. Why had they come? "I'm fine," she said, realizing that she was staring and that Theo was wearing a look that indicated he viewed Abel as a threat. "Really, Theo. I'm okay."

"You don't look fine," Theo said, glowering at Abel. "Is he bothering you?"

She let out an impatient huff. "He's not bothering me. What are you doing here? I've told you it's not safe," she said, trying to draw Theo's attention back to herself.

"Ruby insisted we come," Theo said, glancing at the girl next to him.

"I needed to speak with you," Ruby said, stepping forward. Her voice was soft and breathy, as it always was, but there was that same thread of steel in it that had piqued Viola's interest in the weeks before.

Viola backed away. "I have nothing more to say."

"I'm leaving for Paris on Thursday with my sister. This was my only chance to come," Ruby told her.

"Paris?" Viola said, still not sure why either of them were there.

"I'm being exiled," Ruby said, her voice suddenly heavy with fury.

Viola frowned, not understanding.

"She'll be out of the city for a while—a few months," Theo explained. "Her family thought it best if she . . ." He shook his head. "It doesn't matter."

"Why would you bring her here?" Viola demanded.

Theo looked abashed. "She was quite insistent—"

"I threatened to come on my own if he didn't," Ruby clarified. "I couldn't leave without knowing—" She glanced at where Abel stood, waiting a few paces beyond Viola. "Could we could go somewhere more private to speak? Ferrara's, perhaps, or . . ."

"We have to go," Abel reminded Viola. "Jianyu can't wait."

Viola glanced at Abel and knew from the unease shadowing his voice that this was no lie or bluff. Still, she turned back to Ruby. "I'm sorry, but I have to go."

The color drained from Ruby's cheeks, but she didn't argue.

"With him?" Theo frowned at Abel. "Do you really think that's wise?"

"Yes," Viola said, but Theo's expression still remained creased with doubt. "Mr. Johnson is a friend."

"But we came all this way—"

"There is nothing to talk about," Viola said, her heart firmly in her throat and her eyes burning with unshed tears. "Good-bye, Theo. Good-bye, Miss Reynolds." She stepped around the two and started walking toward where she hoped Abel's carriage would be waiting.

She hadn't gone more than three paces, when someone grabbed her arm. Viola turned on her heel, expecting it to be Theo, but it was Ruby whose fingers were wrapped around her wrist. Suddenly the day felt too warm—her *skin* felt too warm. Suddenly Viola couldn't breathe.

"I know what you must think of me," Ruby said, pausing as though to steady her voice. "But please—" Her voice broke, and Viola realized that Ruby was pressing a folded piece of paper into her hand. "This is for you. Whatever you may think of me, read it? Please?"

Viola stood shocked and frozen. It would be so easy to reach for Ruby, to return the gentle pressure she felt as Ruby gripped her hand. Instead,

Viola pulled away—turned away—and as her heart ached, she walked on.

Abel had caught up to her a few seconds later. At first he didn't speak, but Viola could feel his interest. "He's not happy you're going with me," Abel said finally, tossing a glance behind them as they rounded a corner. "Neither of them is."

Viola felt strangely numb. The paper was still crumpled in her fist, the day was too warm, and yet she felt nothing at all. Nothing but an aching regret in the space where her heart had once beat steady and sure.

"You don't think he'll cause trouble, do you?" Abel asked.

Viola realized then that Abel was speaking to her and that he sounded strangely nervous. "Who? Theo?" She glanced up at Abel, who looked uncomfortable. "Why would he?"

"He seemed . . . concerned." Abel frowned.

"He's a man." Viola gave him an impatient look. "Isn't this what you men do? Interfere with the lives of women who aren't asking for your help?"

"I think he might be more concerned about the color of my skin." Abel's voice had a strange dullness to it. "And the color of yours."

Viola turned to him, understanding dawning, but she dismissed it with a wave of her hand. "I'm nothing to Theo Barclay. He's one of them—a rich boy, born con la camicia. And what am I? No one. An immigrant. An Italiana. And with the old magic as well."

"I don't think he sees it like that," Abel said.

"You know what they call us, don't you? Verme. Dagos. Filthy Guineas," Viola told him, snapping the words out. "No better than—" She stopped, her stomach twisting.

Abel's gaze was steady, as though he knew what she'd been about to say. "You sure look like a white woman to me. And whether you realize it or not, you become one to him the second we're together."

They stood there for a long moment, neither one looking away. Neither one willing to budge, even as the air grew tense between them.

"This was a bad idea," Abel said, finally glancing away. "I told Cela, but she wouldn't hear a word I was saying. We never should've gotten wrapped up in this. We have enough troubles without adding magic and white people to them."

Viola studied him. "I don't want to add to your troubles, Mr. Johnson."

"Maybe not, but tell me," Abel said. "What happens when this is all over? Where does that leave Cela or me—or any of us? Especially with your friends eyeing me like something the dog dragged out of the trash?"

Viola could only stare at him, because she had no answer— she had not even thought it a question until now. "I don't know," she told him, the raw honesty of that single statement making her feel suddenly exposed— suddenly too stupid for words. "I thought you said Jianyu couldn't wait?" she asked, shoving aside the uncomfortable emotion that had settled in the space below her rib cage.

Abel gave her an unreadable look before he climbed inside the hack. Viola could see Theo and Ruby over Abel's shoulder. Ruby had turned to him, but Theo was still watching with a look of concern on his face. Then the door closed and they were off, leaving behind Theo Barclay and Ruby Reynolds, as well as any chance Viola might have had to find out what Nibsy Lorcan and her brother were up to.

DÉJÀ VU

E sta awoke slumped over North's shoulder. The darkness that had overtaken her as they ran from the train was still shadowing her vision. At first she didn't know where she was.

Then she remembered—the train, the posse, and then . . . nothing but Seshat's power.

"What the hell?" North's voice sounded strangled, but she couldn't see what had put that emotion there. Actually, Esta couldn't see anything but his backside.

"Put me down," she demanded, trying to wriggle free of his hold, and he complied, letting her slide to the ground. She barely managed to catch herself on unsteady legs before she turned to see what the other two were looking at.

In the direction of the town, a cyclone was growing, but from the way it glowed with an eerie light, it didn't look like anything natural. It was a monster of a thing, a towering column of heat and light that wove itself along the ground between them and the men on horseback. Strange colors flashed within as it tracked back and forth, blocking the riders' path. In the distance, Esta heard explosions sounding, like firecrackers.

"Where did that come from?" she asked, her head still swirling. It was so enormous that, even from where they stood, she could feel the telltale warmth of magic in the air, soft and compelling. She knew in an instant that whoever had created the cyclone had used an affinity.

"I don't know," Maggie told her. "You fell and then, out of nowhere, fires started erupting. They looked like . . ." She shook her head, frowning. "I don't know how it's possible, but they looked like my incendiaries." Maggie glanced at North. "Do you think there are other Mageus here? Maybe even other Antistasi?"

"It's possible," North told Maggie. But he didn't sound like he thought it was likely.

Esta had the strangest premonition then, like a shiver of dread running down her spine. Something had happened that she couldn't quite remember. She was sure of it. "We need to go," she said, trying to shake off her unease. "Who knows how long that thing will keep those marshals occupied."

North took the lead as they started running for the oil fields, which had been their original destination, but Esta still felt off-kilter. Her vision remained tinged with the shadows that had darkened it before she passed out. With the posse occupied by the strange cyclone, they made good time, but when they finally reached the towers, they realized that the fields that had looked deserted from a distance were actually crawling with laborers.

Skirting around the edges of the area, the three of them moved from the shelter of one tower to another. Eventually they reached a place where they couldn't go any farther. Cutting through the center of the sprawling oil fields was another set of tracks, which held a line of massive tanker cars ready to transport the raw petroleum. There were men, too, lots of them. Beyond their hiding place, dozens of workers checked the pipes that were loading the tankers and prepped the shipment for travel. The engine stood waiting, its massive boilers releasing steam in a slow, lazy hiss.

The three of them pulled back, retreating to the shelter of an old, abandoned shed. Esta's skin crawled when they entered it. Something about the place felt . . . wrong, but it was also weirdly familiar in a way she couldn't explain.

"We're stuck," Maggie said. "There's no easy way around all those men."

"Even if there were, we don't know what's on the other side," Esta agreed.

"We could try for the town," North suggested. "Maybe we could blend in, lie low for a while."

Esta knew that would never work. "Once those marshals realize we're not on the train, they're going to start searching," she said. "In town or here, it doesn't matter. If they knew we were on that train, it means that someone recognized us. We're not going to be able to blend in."

"I could take us back," North said, reaching for his watch. "Maybe we could jump another train and get farther down the road, ahead of them."

Something in Esta recoiled at that idea, but she couldn't have said why. "No," she told him, going on nothing but instinct. "How much time could we possibly buy? Six hours, maybe twelve. The authorities already know we're headed in this direction. A few extra hours isn't going to help if we're spotted again—not when a telegram takes only a few seconds. They're going to keep hunting for us, and eventually they'll close in."

"We got off the train, didn't we?" North asked, frowning. "We can't just give up now. We have to keep going."

"Maybe there's someone here who'd be willing to help," Maggie said, biting at her lip. "Those fires didn't start themselves, and they didn't seem to be on the side of the riders."

"Maggie's right," North said. "Maybe there are Mageus here who could hide us. We might find ourselves some allies, maybe even a few Antistasi."

"Considering the way we left things with Ruth, any Antistasi we find might also be enemies," Esta reminded them. There was something about that strange cyclone of flame that just felt wrong to her, something that told her there was more to it than she understood. Not that she'd convince the two of them on a hunch. She went for logic instead. "Think about it," she pressed. "By now plenty of people know what we did in St. Louis. Just because there might be Mageus here doesn't mean they're necessarily friendly. Or maybe . . ." A thought occurred to her that seemed too ridiculous to be true.

"What?" North pressed.

Time was such a tricky thing, twisting and unpredictable, but Esta had never had to account for someone else who could manipulate it before. "You said those fires looked like your formulas, didn't you, Maggie?"

Maggie nodded. "Yes . . ."

"Is it possible that we *already* went back?" Esta asked. The two of them only stared at her, so she explained. "Maybe we're the ones who rescued *ourselves.*"

North was still frowning, but he wasn't disagreeing. His hand went to the pocket in his vest, where his watch waited. "It's not impossible," he admitted. "But even if that's the case, it doesn't help us to get out of here now. There's nowhere to go and too many damn witnesses."

Esta considered the men working the oil fields nearby, and an idea began to form. "Maybe we can use them to our advantage." She turned to Maggie. "Maybe we can use one of your formulations or devices."

"Of course," Maggie said, frowning. "But if we do that, they're going to know for sure that we're here."

"That's the point," Esta told her as she considered the waiting engine below. There was one thing necessary for a truly great trick—Harte had taught her that. *Misdirection.* "Those marshals wouldn't have been riding out to meet the train if they didn't already think we were on it, and thanks to whoever made that giant inferno of a cyclone, they know that *someone* has the old magic. So let's confirm their suspicions. And then let's disappear."

"Disappear?" Maggie said doubtfully.

"We'll need a distraction," Esta told her. "Something big enough for them not to notice us getting away. Something that will ensure they won't come looking for us later." She met their eyes, held their gaze. "I think it's time to kill the Devil's Thief."

A PARTNERSHIP OF SORTS

1902—New York

James Lorcan took another bite of the half-burned sludge from the bowl in front of him, but his awareness was still on Viola's departure, and on the way the Aether moved in response. His stomach turning at the taste of the food, he set the fork down and picked at the bread. Its flavor was familiar—a hearty rye with a hint of sweetness that had once been served in the kitchens of the Bella Strega. Despite her clear lack of talent for cooking, Viola, it seemed, had learned something from Tilly after all.

Which wasn't surprising. Dolph's assassin might be as sharp and unyielding as the blades she favored, but she'd always had a soft spot for Tilly Malkov. James hadn't missed the way Viola's eyes had followed the other girl around the kitchen in the Strega.

Kelly flashed a look at Torrio. "Follow her."

Torrio's mouth half fell open. "But I thought—"

"I don't pay you to think," Kelly said. "My sister is up to something, and I want to know what it is."

Torrio glanced at James, disgust clear on his face, but James was careful not to look too directly at him. There was no sense giving anything away here, in front of Paul Kelly.

"You don't think I should be here?" Torrio asked. "I thought we had business with—"

"*I* have business," Kelly said, cutting him off. "You have my sister to attend to."

"I ain't a nursemaid," Torrio told him, crossing his arms. Kelly slid a deadly look in Torrio's direction, but Torrio didn't so much as flinch. He returned the glare and allowed his lips to twitch with amusement. "And anyway . . . you sure you want me *tending* to Viola?"

Tension crackled across the table between the two Five Pointers. "I realize you *aren't* a nursemaid," Kelly said, keeping his voice dangerously even. "And I'm sure that *you* know how important my sister is to me. I send you because I trust you, Johnny. Don't tell me that trust is misplaced?"

Torrio's jaw was tight, and James sensed the Aether around him tremble. He kept his expression placid, watching the drama play out and making a note of this weakness as he planned all the while. Paul Kelly was a thorn in James' side, a danger as long as he held any real power in the Bowery. The trick would be to neutralize the danger of the Five Pointers in general, and even better if he could do so in a way that was *productive*.

With a violent thrust, Torrio was on his feet. He tore the napkin from where he'd tucked it into his shirtfront and stormed off. His anger would be useful, James thought . . . as long as it could be properly harnessed.

Once Torrio was gone and James knew for sure they were alone, he placed the bread on the table and dusted the crumbs from his fingers. "It's good to have people you can depend on," he said easily, keeping all trace of mockery from his voice.

Kelly glared at him. "What about you, Lorcan? Do *you* have people you can depend on?" he asked. "Or haven't you managed to take the Devil's Own in hand?"

It was a point of contention between them. Kelly would have happily taken the Strega and all who were loyal to Dolph by force, but James had managed to persuade Kelly of the benefits of coaxing the gang to his side first. It bought James time and provided access to—and protection from—the Five Pointers that he wouldn't have otherwise had. But James Lorcan knew Kelly's patience was running out. He'd have to figure out a way to take care of the threat Kelly posed soon.

"Without Saunders, the loyalty of the Devil's Own is already beginning

LISA MAXWELL

to wane, as I predicted. The desperate and fearful forget quickly," he told Kelly. It was true—mostly. As soon as he had the ring, it would be true in fact. Not that Kelly needed that information. "They'll be ready for you."

"Good." Kelly's eyes gleamed, clearly satisfied with this news.

Of course James had no intention of *ever* handing over the Bella Strega *or* the Devil's Own. Once the artifacts were his, Kelly would be no more than a fly to be swatted. And the Five Pointers? They'd make a fine addition to James' own numbers.

Paul Kelly gave him a knowing sort of look. "I'm sure it helps that you've seen no problems from Tammany. . . ."

Since Dolph's team had robbed the Order, Tammany's patrols had been ever present in the Bowery. Buildings had burned, beer halls had been destroyed. Any business that had even a pretense of association with the old magic had become a target. But Kelly had kept his end of their bargain—at least in that regard. The Bella Strega stood intact, untouched by Tammany's men.

"None," James admitted. "Although I'd point out that we've both benefited from our little arrangement," he said easily. "I trust you managed to enjoy yourself at the Order's gala."

He could tell by the slight tic in Kelly's jaw that his remark had hit its target. After all, without the warning that James had provided, Kelly and his men would have been sitting ducks, unprepared for Jack Grew's betrayal.

The ensuing fight should have provided the cover Logan Sullivan needed to retrieve the ring. Logan, who could find any magical object, had been a gift from James' future self, but so far the boy had failed to live up to his potential. The ring should have been easily obtained from the gala, but Logan had still managed to return empty-handed. Somewhere in the confusion, the artifact had disappeared, and since then, Logan hadn't been able to find any hint of it in the city. But then, Paul Kelly wasn't confined to the city, unlike James and every other Mageus.

"I didn't bring you here to talk about the gala," Kelly said, brushing the topic aside with a wave of his hand.

"Why *did* you call me here?" James asked. "I must admit I was surprised when I got your message."

It was a lie, of course. James had known almost immediately after Logan had returned from the gala empty-handed that he and Kelly would cross paths again—sooner rather than later. After all, they had an agreement. A partnership, of sorts. For now Kelly was useful. His men could go where James couldn't. They had the ability to move outside the city and search for the artifacts that Darrigan had managed to snatch right out of James' grasp, and James had something Kelly wanted—the Bella Strega and, with it, the Devil's Own. But Kelly's thirst for expanding his criminal empire made him vulnerable, and James had every intention of turning that against him when the time was right.

James considered Kelly. "Unless your little summons means that you have news for me?"

Kelly didn't rush to answer at first. Instead, he took another bite of greens and chewed without so much as grimacing. It was a tactic that James understood was meant to unnerve him, but he had no intention of filling the emptiness with unnecessary chatter. He simply waited as Kelly gracefully dabbed at his lips with the napkin from his lap.

Only after Kelly folded the napkin and set it aside did he finally speak. "I'm sure you're aware that the Order had some difficulties back in March," Kelly said with a sardonic lift of his heavy brows—a reminder of exactly how much he knew about the Khafre Hall job. "Word is that they've been looking for a new location to establish their headquarters."

"Oh?" James said, trying to cover his surprise. "They aren't simply going to rebuild Khafre Hall?"

The journal Logan brought him had made it clear—the Order wouldn't build a new headquarters in time for the Conclave. They would go into that gathering scattered and unorganized, weak enough that the Conclave would turn out to be a failure. They would not consolidate their power. They would not take control of the Brotherhoods, and because of that failure, the Order would never be the same. After, the journal had assured him, the Order and the other Brotherhoods would remain secretive organizations that worked in the shadows, always at odds with one another. They would still be a danger to Mageus, but after the failure of the Conclave, they would not be the threat they might have otherwise been.

"No," Kelly said. "Word is that something changed after Morgan's big gala."

A lot of things had changed after the gala—including the notebook Logan had brought him. After the gala, James found that his once clear, familiar handwriting seemed to have come alive, the letters flickering like a candle about to gutter, shifting into new arrangements that he could make neither heads nor tails of. When he first received the journal, he'd thought it would be the key to his victory, but after the gala—after Logan's failure to retrieve the ring—it had become all but worthless. Now he wondered if this was the reason.

"What do you think the cause for this change is?" James wondered.

"I can't be sure, but they have more confidence now," Kelly told him.

"You think they've retrieved an artifact," James realized.

Kelly squinted a little at James. "I don't know for sure, but I suspect that might be the case. So does Tammany. The Inner Circle is anxious to get into a new location, and soon."

If the Order had managed to retrieve one of their artifacts, if they suddenly had plans for a new headquarters, it meant that something had occurred that *hadn't* before. The entire future had been thrown into question. "How soon?"

Kelly took a cigarette from the gleaming case, rolling it a little between his thick fingers before placing it between his lips. "From what I hear, the Order already has a location picked out—the Fuller Building."

James frowned. The Fuller Building seemed an odd selection. While Khafre Hall had been a stately piece of old New York architecture, steeped in tradition and secrecy, the Fuller Building was a new landmark. Located across from Madison Square Park, it was an ostentatious thing, a blade of a building that the entire city had watched rise in a surprisingly short amount of time. With its strange, spindly skeleton of steel, everyone was sure that it would fall before it was finished. It was also one of the more exciting pieces of architecture in the city. It would be an enormous structure—if it stood. It would also be a landmark, James realized.

He supposed it made a sort of sense, especially if the Order had managed to retrieve the ring at the gala. The new skyscraper was a testament to science and demonstrated man's ability to rise up above the rabble of the streets, and it was situated in the beating heart of the modern city. Selecting the Fuller Building was tantamount to a declaration—the Order was not content to remain in the past. They were staking a new place, and they were declaring their continued importance.

"The building will be opening by the end of next month, won't it?" James asked.

Kelly lit the cigarette and took a long drag, letting the smoke enwreathe his head like some sort of demon. "Rumor has it, the Order will be moving what was left of their treasures into their new headquarters in a matter of weeks."

James frowned. "I hadn't realized they had much left after the fire." His mind was already whirling with the implications. Dolph had been so focused on the Book and the artifacts, could he have missed that the Order had something else of value?

"They have a couple of wagonloads, apparently," Kelly told him. "From what I've been able to learn, they've been storing them somewhere in Brooklyn—outside the Brink. Originally, they were going to rebuild Khafre Hall, but what happened at the gala made them anxious to move into their new headquarters and reestablish themselves as a force to be reckoned with in the city *now*, before their Conclave at the end of the year."

"That would be unfortunate for both of us," James said. "But perhaps it's also an opportunity?"

"I agree," Kelly told him. "Which is why I called you here. I want the Devil's Own on board."

"Certainly your Five Pointers can take care of a few wagons of goods," James said, the implication clear.

"You don't bring a knife to a gunfight, Lorcan, and the Order has weapons far beyond what my boys are equipped to handle."

James understood now. "You're afraid of their magic."

"I'm not afraid," Kelly said, his tone unyielding. "But I'll admit I don't have the specific skill set that you and your people do."

James knew this was the real reason Kelly wanted control over the Strega and Devil's Own. Kelly might have despised his sister—he despised everyone with the old magic—but he wasn't above using Viola or any other Mageus for his own means.

"Think of this as another way to solidify our partnership," Kelly said when James didn't immediately agree. "A show of continued good faith. After all, it would be a terrible shame if the Strega started having the same problems as some of the other saloons in the area."

James saw the threat for what it was, and he found that he had little interest in being Kelly's pawn. Still, he understood the opportunity that the situation presented.

"Of course," James said, pretending deference. "It does seem like it would be in *both* of our interests to make sure the Order can't regain a footing in the city."

James was glad suddenly that he hadn't simply allowed the Order to remove the threat of Paul Kelly at the gala. He'd wanted to, but the Aether had whispered otherwise, and once again his intuition had proven correct. Kelly, it seemed, could still be useful. When the time came, James would pit his two greatest enemies against each other and watch as they destroyed each other instead of him.

As he listened to the information Kelly offered, James' mind was already whirling with possibilities. The Aether bunched and shifted around him. He would retrieve the artifact he'd lost and take care of the problem Paul Kelly posed all at once. He'd help Kelly rob the Order, all right. Then he'd help the damned Five Pointer right into a noose.

MISDIRECTION

1904—Texas

North had done his damnedest to argue against Esta's plan, not only because it seemed like they were taking unnecessary risks, but also because it provided the Thief an opportunity to leave them in the dust, like her partner had. She assured them she wasn't interested in running, but North had a feeling that Esta could lie better than most. Still, it wasn't like he had a better idea, so there he was, right where he hadn't wanted to be, watching the train yard from a spot on an outcropping a little way off.

"It'll be okay," Maggie whispered from her place next to him. She could always read the direction of his thoughts too easily. "She's not going anywhere."

North grunted his disagreement.

From their vantage point, North could see the men going about their business, unaware of what was about to happen, and he didn't exactly envy them. Esta was below as well, inching toward the tracks. She'd wrapped some fabric they'd found in an empty shed around her waist as a makeshift skirt and covered her head with another strip of bright fabric to make it look like there was more hair beneath. She might have looked a mess, but Esta still moved with the kind of easy confidence that made you believe she could do practically anything. Which was exactly what North was worried about.

Together, they watched as Esta slunk around the edges of the train yard. When no one was looking, she climbed into the engine compartment.

None of the men seemed aware of what was happening. No one seemed to notice the girl pressing a gun against the engineer's spine, so they couldn't have seen her use Maggie's confounding solution on the poor guy. No one even looked up, not until the train's engines started humming and the wheels squealed as it began to move down the track. They paid attention then, because some of the tanker cars were still hooked to the pipes that fed them, and as the train pulled away, black liquid poured out onto the ground.

Before the train could pick up too much speed, North saw Esta push the engineer from the train. He rolled to his side, and some of the workers ran to him. As the engine continued away, the workers launched into action. Some were trying to stop the flood of crude oil that poured from the pipeline, but others were running after the train and trying to catch hold of one of the rails so they could climb up into the engine compartment. The sound of gunshots rang through the air, and North pulled Maggie back to protect her from any stray bullets.

"We need to go," he told her.

But Maggie shook him off. "We need to be sure." She turned back to the scene playing out before them.

A moment later, Esta emerged again from the back of the engine, the barrel of a pistol aimed toward the nearest tower.

One, two, three shots erupted from the pistol North had loaned to her, each echoing with the telltale puff of smoke from the firing. But nothing happened.

"Come on," Maggie whispered.

When the fourth puff of white smoke erupted from the gun, the tower exploded in a burst of blue flame. Two others followed in rapid succession, the sun-dried wooden frames burning so hot and so fast, North had to turn his face away. When he looked back again, flames were licking up into the sky. Blue and purple, green and orange and red, the inferno flickered with energy, like electricity gone feral. Like *magic*.

The crowd of men below were no longer focused only on the train.

Almost as one, they turned in horror. Some fled, while others started working to put out the fires before they could spread, but it was already too late. The buckets of water didn't touch the strange flames.

The explosions had done their job, just like Esta had thought they would. The posse of men who'd been investigating the other train arrived a few minutes later, charging in on mounts that became immediately skittish at the sight of the strange flames. The horses pranced uneasily beneath their riders, tossing their heads like they could shake away the heat.

A pair of men broke through the posse's ranks and came to the front. From the way they sat their horses and surveyed the destruction with a kind of stillness, North figured they must be the ones in charge. One of the men listened as the others in the yard all tried to talk at once, pointing and shouting in the direction the train was going, but the other man pushed back his hat and looked to the burning oil towers.

Beneath the brim of the hat, the sun revealed a face North hadn't seen in at least two years. A face he would never forget. *Jot Gunter.*

The man owned the ranch North had worked on years before, back in Crabapple, Texas. When Gunter had discovered the mark on North's wrist, he'd ordered North beaten, tossed from the ranch, and left for dead. Even from that distance, the rancher was easy to recognize, and North could tell that Gunter hadn't changed one bit. Same heavy white mustache. Same beady eyes. His presence there in the oil fields of Corsicana, Texas, though, was a variable North couldn't have predicted.

"We have to go. *Now*," he said again, this time taking Maggie by the hand and forcibly tugging her along.

"But Esta—"

"This whole crazy plan was her idea," North reminded Maggie. "She knows where to meet us." They needed to get away while they could.

As they went, North kept his eye on the engine picking up steam in the distance. But there was no sign of any change, no sign of Esta.

North wasn't sure what had worried him more—that Esta might run off on them, or that she might not be able to get free of the charging engine. The last time she'd used her affinity, it hadn't gone well. She wouldn't tell them what, exactly, had happened, and he hadn't been sure how smart it was for them to depend on her magic again.

When he'd brought up the issue earlier, she and Maggie had assured him that it would be fine. Esta would only have to hold on to time for a few seconds, long enough to make it off the train without breaking her neck. With luck, everyone else would believe that the Devil's Thief was still on the locomotive, while the three of them headed the other way. *Misdirection*, Esta had called it, but North suddenly had a sinking suspicion that the crowd wasn't the only audience she'd had in mind.

In the distance, the train was going faster. The smoke spewing from its smokestacks turned from a light gray to a darker, dangerous cloud of sooty black. Esta had accomplished what she'd planned to do, and now it was up to him and Maggie to get away from the crowd while they had the chance. North tugged Maggie on, and this time she came willingly, but as they reached the far edges of the oil fields, North felt the earth begin to rumble beneath his feet.

At first he didn't think much of it, but then he realized it was more than the train he was feeling. The vibrations under his boots were getting stronger even as the train was pulling farther away. It felt like the earth itself was about to split open.

"What's happening?" Maggie asked, her hand tightening around his as she tried to keep her footing. "My incendiaries wouldn't cause this."

"I don't know, but we need to keep moving."

He'd barely gotten the words out when the earth beneath the engine broke open into a long, jagged gash that swallowed the train whole. The chasm continued to travel in multiple directions from the place where the train disappeared, and moments later the locomotive itself exploded. Even from that distance, the force of the earth shaking nearly rocked them off their feet. Instinctively, North wrapped himself around Maggie, threw them both to the ground, and covered her with his body.

When the rumbling finally stopped and North allowed himself to look up, the dark iron body of the locomotive was gone. They could see nothing but a column of flames that rose from the broken ground, pouring black, sooty smoke into the sky that blotted out the blue. North cursed long and low as he looked over the terrible scene. He sensed Maggie trembling, and he understood what she was feeling. Something had gone terribly wrong.

When Maggie turned to him, her eyes were wide and her face had drained of color. "I didn't think—it wasn't supposed to explode yet. Not until it was farther down the track. Do you think Esta made it off before—" Maggie's voice broke. Her expression was so pained that his heart nearly cracked in two.

In the distance, fingers of fire reached high into the sky, and behind them, the oil fields looked like hell come to earth as another of the towers went up in flames. North and Maggie were stuck in the middle, lost in a thick haze that burned North's eyes and throat.

"I'm sure Esta's fine," he told Maggie, hoping he sounded more confident than he felt.

The riders had already gotten their horses under control. Half were stuck on the far side of the chasm, and some had tumbled into the split in the earth, but the remainder began to gallop toward the wreckage.

"Come on." North pulled Maggie gently along. "We need to get moving if we want to get to the meeting place on time."

"What if she doesn't show up, Jericho?" Maggie asked. "What if she got off the train too late? What if you were right to worry about her affinity and she's—"

"Esta Filosik has more lives than a cat," North said, even as his own stomach churned. "If she doesn't show up where she's supposed to, we can always go back and get her." His thumb rubbed across the worn metal cover of his pocket watch. Because, for Jericho Northwood, there was no such thing as too late.

LISA MAXWELL

PART

II

ON DAWSON PLACE

1904—San Francisco

Harte Darrigan pulled back into the empty doorway of a closed shop, out of view from the eagle-eyed guards at the barricade's entrance across the street. He wasn't sure what the men were looking for or why they were blocking the intersection. On the train, he'd read about the raids that were happening all over the country in retaliation for the Antistasi's attack in St. Louis. The barricade could be related to those actions.

Whatever the case, the address Harte was looking for was somewhere beyond that fencing. He supposed he could go around, but the barbed wire wasn't just across the one intersection. Blocks in either direction were cordoned off from the rest of the city. It was already growing late, and he didn't want to waste time on a detour, especially when there was no telling how far the blockade stretched.

As Harte tried to figure out how he could get past the guards without being seen or recognized, a pair of men approached the entrance. They were laughing and talking, their pale cheeks already bright pink from a night of drinking. After they spoke briefly with the guards, the gate was pulled back to allow them to pass.

So there was a way through.

After a few minutes more, it became clear who the guards were letting pass—men. That wasn't a surprise, though. Harte hadn't seen many women out on the streets since he'd arrived. San Francisco seemed like a city populated almost entirely by men. From the looks of it, the police were admitting a steady stream, mostly made up of white day laborers and sailors. If only he knew for sure what the sentries were looking for.

Harte noticed a driver leaning against a horse cart about halfway down the block. The man was smoking a thin cigar and reading a rumpled newspaper as he waited for his next fare. As Harte approached, the driver glanced up over the newsprint.

"You need a ride?" the man asked, as if to determine whether Harte was worth his time.

Harte shook his head. "Not at the moment. I have a question you might be able to answer."

The driver frowned and returned to reading with an annoyed snap of his paper. "That depends on what you want to know."

"What's going on over there?" Harte asked, tilting his head toward the barricade.

"Quarantine." A single, gruffly spoken word that didn't explain anything. "They have all of Chinatown cordoned off."

"Quarantine?" Harte repeated, relieved that it didn't have anything to do with Mageus or the Antistasi. "Why is there a quarantine?"

The man glanced up. "Plague, if you can believe that," he said with a grunt. "We haven't had a case of it in this town for three years, and now the Committee's saying they found multiple cases just this week."

"The Committee?" Harte asked.

"Vigilance Committee," the driver said, looking vaguely annoyed at the stream of questions. "Used to be the mayor who would determine quarantine, but now the Committee's got the bigger say. So maybe it's the plague, or maybe they're trying to root out some of the maggots that make trouble from time to time. What with the recent events, I'd expect it to be the latter." The man glanced up over his paper briefly. "Not that I'm complaining, mind you. No use taking any chances. If you ask me, the Committee'd be smarter to burn the whole damn Chinese quarter down."

Harte watched another man approach the checkpoint and then get ushered through. "People are still going in," he observed, an unspoken question in his tone.

"Quarantine don't stop people from their own stupidity." The driver turned the page without looking up. "If sailors who've been stuck on a boat for months don't care about their manhood falling off from some pox or another, a little thing like the plague ain't gonna scare them off either."

The idea that the actual *plague* was here seemed to be a bit far-fetched, but Harte knew how people could be, especially when it came to Chinese immigrants. He'd seen how they'd been treated in New York, and he couldn't imagine things were any better here in California. Not that he was going to risk pointing this fact out to the driver.

The man glanced up, clearly at the end of his patience. "Look, do you need a ride or not?"

"No," Harte said. "I was only—"

"If you don't need a ride, then shove off," the man said, jerking his thumb over his shoulder. "You're scaring away actual customers."

Harte thanked the man for his time before walking a bit farther down the sidewalk, toward the next intersection, where another entrance was guarded by another pair of armed men. Harte felt Seshat pacing like a caged tiger, but he wasn't sure what was making her so nervous—that he was getting closer to retrieving the artifact or the risk he might be taking by breaching the quarantine.

Plague or not, the Dragon's Eye was beyond the barricade. Maybe he could go around, but it would take more time and it was already getting late. Besides, he had no idea how far Chinatown stretched, and he didn't want to waste time figuring it out. Even now Esta might have the dagger. She might already be on her way to meet him at the bridge, and he would not leave her waiting. The faster he reached his destination, the better. He looked down the stretch of the street, considered the seemingly endless checkpoints, and decided to go through.

Harte approached the checkpoint like he belonged there, and his show of confidence seemed to work. The guard gave him only the briefest of glances before letting him pass. On the other side, the streets changed. The buildings were the same Italianate style as those throughout the city, but they dripped with red banners, hand-painted with the elegant, curling scrollwork of Chinese characters. Most were also canopied by wooden balconies that clung precariously to the walls of the buildings.

The sights and smells reminded Harte of Mott Street in New York, where dried shrimp would be piled in baskets along the sidewalk and roasted duck hung in the windows of the stalls. He found himself briefly, uncharacteristically homesick. But New York felt like a lifetime ago, and Harte couldn't afford to dwell on the past.

Pulling out the map he'd purchased earlier, he double-checked his direction and located the quickest route to the street name that he'd memorized as a boy. Then he set out, determined.

He wouldn't have discovered that such a place even existed if his father hadn't been so drunk that day. Usually, Samuel Lowe didn't return to the cramped two-room apartment that he shared with Harte's mother until late at night, when he was thoroughly drunk and ready for a fight. One day, though, Harte had come home to find the man who had fathered him sprawled out on the floor in the middle of the afternoon. His father had looked lifeless as he lay there in a puddle of his own vomit, and Harte's first thought had been, *It's over.* Then a snorting snore told Harte that his father wasn't dead, only unconscious.

It would have been safer to retreat and pretend he'd never seen that particular scene. But he *had* seen it. Harte had also noticed the loose papers on the table and the stack of letters tied with twine. The sheets were already soaking up the amber-colored whiskey that had spilled.

Harte had been barely twelve then, but he'd known what would happen if his father woke and found the papers soaked and damaged— Samuel Lowe never accepted responsibility for any of his misfortunes. Instead, he would take his frustration out on whoever happened to be closest. If Harte had left, he knew that person would have been his mother, and her bruises had barely started to heal from the last time.

Careful not to wake his father, Harte had taken the sopping papers and tried to shake the liquid from them before the ink smeared. He hadn't intended to look at the uneven scrawl on the damp pages, but the word "California" had shimmered up from the front of an envelope, drawing his attention as surely as a fairy tale.

When he was younger, Harte had never given any thought to who Samuel Lowe had been before he'd arrived in New York and started drinking himself into nightly stupors. Harte had spent so much energy avoiding his father's fists that it had never occurred to him that his father could possibly be the kind of person anyone would want to write letters to. He hadn't been able to stop himself from skimming over the contents, and the next thing he knew, he'd untied the other stack and was reading the correspondence in earnest.

As he read, Harte had discovered that his father had family in California, a mother he'd been sending money to. The more Harte read, the more his blood turned to fire. Samuel Lowe had never seen Molly O'Doherty as anything but a convenience. He'd used Harte's mother for the money she brought home each night, but he'd never planned to stay with her. It was all there, stark on the page. Molly O'Doherty had worked herself into exhaustion because she believed that Samuel Lowe loved her, never knowing that she was actually paying for his escape.

Harte had been so engrossed that he hadn't noticed when his father had started to stir. The old man's face had been blotchy with rage as he demanded the letters back. His father's demands always came with a raised fist, and that time had been no exception. But Harte had refused to take one more beating. Instead of cowering, he'd demanded answers. Of course, his old man had refused to give him any.

Maybe he should have simply taken the letters and left. Harte could have shown his mother the proof of his father's betrayal. But he was young and brash and filled with an anger that made it difficult to see straight. Instead, he'd used his affinity and issued a command, ordering

Samuel Lowe to leave the city and to forget that anyone was waiting for him in California.

It was only later that Harte understood the consequences of that decision. Instead of understanding—instead of *thanking* Harte for saving her—his mother had recoiled. She'd called Harte a liar and went after the man she loved. That choice ended up destroying her, leaving her a shell of who she'd once been.

For years Harte had carried the guilt of what he'd done. He knew that his choices that day proved beyond a doubt that he was truly his father's son—reckless and careless and undeserving. Once he was older, though, he had come to understand that the impact of those choices went far beyond what he'd done to his mother. Maria Lowe had been an innocent as well. She couldn't have known that the money her son sent belonged to someone else. She might even have been dependent on those funds, and she had likely imagined spending her old age with a son who would tend to her needs. Maybe that was why when Harte had been faced with the question of what to do with the stones, he'd sent the Dragon's Eye to her, hoping that it was enough to repay one more debt.

That was before Harte had understood that the artifacts were nothing but liabilities. Now he could only hope that the grandmother he'd never intended to claim still had the crown and that no one else had gotten to it—or to her—first.

After a few blocks, Harte passed through the barricade on the other side of the quarter and continued on a little farther before he finally arrived at the address that had loomed for so long in his imagination. Dawson Place was a small dead-end street that he would have missed if he hadn't been looking for it. Standing in front of the door, he was surprised at how plain and unremarkable it was. As a child, he'd imagined everything in California to be nothing short of fantastical, but this was simply a door—and a rather meager one at that. Still, his palms were damp from nerves, and he found himself wishing that Esta were standing next to him.

At first Harte couldn't even bring himself to knock. More than two years had passed for whoever waited behind the door. Two years when anything could have happened. *The Dragon's Eye might not even be here.*

He felt Seshat's amusement taunting him, but he brushed it aside. The crown *had* to be there. If it wasn't, maybe Maria Lowe could tell him where it had gone, and he would find it one way or another. Esta would be waiting for him soon enough, and Harte would not arrive without the artifact he'd promised her.

Once he knocked, Harte heard an immediate rustling from inside, and a moment later the door opened to reveal a small woman. Her hair was a dark, burnished blond shot through with ashy gray. It was pulled straight back from a round face, and her skin was smooth and unlined, except near the corners of her wide-set eyes. She looked younger than he'd expected, but he still hoped she was the woman he was seeking. Even though her expression was wary, Harte found himself searching for some trace of himself in her features.

"I'm looking for someone," he said to her, finally remembering that he was here for the Dragon's Eye and not to claim a family that didn't know he existed. "Are you Maria?"

The woman shook her head, frowning, and started to close the door, but Harte placed his foot in the jamb and tried again. "Maria Lowe," he repeated, this time more slowly. "Is she here? Do you know her?"

"There's no one here by that name." The woman again tried to push the door shut, this time with more force, but there was something in her expression that made Harte persist.

"If you aren't Maria, can you tell me where I could find her? She has something of mine," he said, his voice unsteady with the urgency he felt. "Something I sent her. A headpiece. Like a crown." With his foot still in the door, he motioned around the crown of her head. "With a large amber stone in it."

The woman's eyes widened.

She knew. Harte was sure of it.

It would only take a brush of skin against skin to find out, and it just might be worth risking whatever Seshat might do to retrieve the artifact. Harte reached for the woman, determined to use his affinity no matter the cost, but before he could touch her, he heard the sound of a pistol being cocked, and a voice came from the alleyway behind him.

"Don't even think about laying your hands on her."

Harte froze. His body reacted before his mind could catch up, steeling itself for the blow that it expected to feel.

"Put your hands up where I can see them," the man said. "And step back, or I will not regret putting a bullet in you."

Harte raised his hands so the man would know he meant no harm as he turned, slowly, his brain struggling to accept the truth. *It can't be.*

"Hello, Samuel," Harte said. He'd never called this man "Father" before, and he wasn't about to start now.

"Who are you?" The man narrowed his eyes and adjusted the gun, but Harte didn't miss the flash of unease in his father's eyes.

Harte's first thought was that the man before him was far too small to be the same terror he remembered from his childhood. But *of course* he would seem smaller. Harte had grown since then. It was more than the height that threw him off, though. There was something essentially changed about his father. Samuel Lowe was wearing a dark gray suit, nothing as precisely tailored as Harte had once bought himself, but well-made nonetheless. His eyes were sharper and clearer than Harte had ever seen them, and his skin was lined but not sallow or puffed from too much cheap gin. If Harte had met this man on the street, he might not have realized who he was.

"You *are* Samuel Lowe?" he pressed. "The same Samuel Lowe who once lived in New York with Molly O'Doherty."

"I don't know anyone by that name." He was still aiming the gun at Harte, but uncertainty flared in his expression. "Who *are* you?"

If Harte had any doubts about who this was, they evaporated. Even so many years later, his body still remembered the fear that tone used to inspire.

But Harte wasn't a child any longer. He was a few inches taller than his father, his body lean and strong from years of discipline and training, and he'd survived in a world that was bent on destroying him for too long to fear much of anything now. Instead of cowering, as he might have before, he straightened a little, jutting out his chin in an unmistakable challenge.

"You know exactly who I am," Harte said flatly, tossing the words out like a dropped gauntlet. "Or don't you recognize your own son?"

CORSICANA

1904—Texas

Jack Grew wiped the sweat from his brow as he directed his horse to follow along behind the sheriff of Corsicana, Texas. Once he'd received news that Esta had been spotted, Jack had taken the first train he could get out of St. Louis, but he'd still been too late. The Devil's Thief had evaded him again. Darrigan as well. And they'd left a trail of destruction in their wake.

Some of the men who had witnessed the events of the day before were with him. Riding behind Jack were Jot Gunter and other members of the Ranchers' Syndicate. Gunter was like many of the Syndicate's members: old, rich, and entirely too convinced of his own importance. But then, the ranchers in the Syndicate thought far too highly of themselves in general. They might own large swaths of the country, land where oil had been discovered a few years back, but they were still upstarts. Parvenus. Without breeding or history. The horses they rode had finer pedigrees than the men themselves, and the fact that the men seemed so proud of their backwater dump of a town only proved how pointless they were.

The last time Jack had seen Gunter was in New York at the Conclave, back in 1902. Gunter had been one of the representatives from the Syndicate. Like the men from the other Brotherhoods, he'd come to gloat. The members of the other Brotherhoods had believed the Order had been dealt a blow when Khafre Hall had burned, but they'd found out differently that cold December night two years before. Thanks to Jack, the Order had prevailed and would continue to lead the Brotherhoods through the new century.

Not that Jack would remind these men of this. He could pretend that they hadn't once been adversaries now that he had won. After all, it was always good to have allies, especially when they were weak men who could be controlled.

A quarter mile from the town itself was the site of the engine's explosion. There, the ground was scarred and split. Deep gashes spread from a larger chasm in the dusty earth, which was being guarded by a group of men with guns at the ready. As they got closer, a pair of men on horseback with bronze stars on their lapels rode out to meet the group. Other men, both on horseback and on foot, stood watch, probably to keep away the scavengers and newspapermen who swarmed around tragedies like vultures.

Federal marshals. Jack should know—he'd given the order for them to be there. The last thing anyone needed was for the locals to muck up the investigation.

Gunter and the mayor exchanged some words with the pair of marshals. Gunter made a show of puffing himself up as he spoke, but the two lawmen listened with uninterested silence, their faces shadowed by the broad brims of their hats. They simply shook their heads. Impatient with their lack of cooperation, the sheriff nudged his horse forward and tried to speak with the men. That didn't make any difference either. The two marshals only frowned at him as they exchanged words in low, hard tones, and the sheriff grew more agitated by the second.

Jack could feel the sweat rolling down his back as he allowed the sheriff and Syndicate men a little more time to display their own ineptitude. Then, growing bored, he urged his horse forward.

"Good afternoon, gentlemen," Jack drawled, giving the marshals a status they didn't quite deserve. "I've come to survey the site on behalf of Mr. Roosevelt."

The marshals recognized him immediately. To the sheriff's irritation—

and Jack's immense satisfaction—they moved quickly, so the group could pass. This time it was Jack who took the lead out toward the crevasse that had been torn into the earth by the explosion of the train.

The wreckage was still in place, but the engine itself was hardly recognizable, a twisted shell of metal and soot that might have at one time resembled a locomotive. But the destroyed engine wasn't what truly interested Jack. The deep hole that had been ripped into the ground and the gaping pit carved in the earth where the remains of the train lay were far more interesting. The medallion that Jack had taken from Hendricks and now wore on his own lapel began singing its high, dissonant warning call. Its blue glow indicated feral magic was nearby, and beneath his jacket, the Book seemed to almost shudder against his chest.

Jack had seen the same sort of scar carved into the earth before. It had been over two years now—the day Esta Filosik and Harte Darrigan destroyed a different train and escaped from his clutches. That day had set him on this new path in his life.

One look at the wreckage confirmed what Jack had suspected. Esta Filosik had been there. Probably Darrigan had as well. But whatever the sheriff of Corsicana or the men from the Syndicate thought, the wreckage didn't mean that the Thief was dead. Jack knew exactly how slippery Esta and Darrigan could be, and he wouldn't believe they were gone until he saw their bodies for himself.

ON THE HOOK

1904—Somewhere in the West

Esta surfaced slowly, the remnants of a strangely vivid dream clinging to her. The heat of a desert landscape still brushed against her skin, and her mouth felt dry, as if she'd actually spent the night running through blistering sand, trying to escape whatever beast slithered beneath. Her body was sore, and her head ached as the room swayed around her. It took her a moment to remember what had happened, and even then, it came back to her in disjointed bursts.

Slowly Esta realized that the motion of the room wasn't in her head. She was on a train, and from the rough, hard floor beneath her cheek, it wasn't a Pullman berth. The noise was deafening, and the air was stuffy and hot. At first she couldn't bring herself to do much more than lie with her cheek pressed to the floor, breathing in the dust and feeling the jarring vibrations of the track. When she finally opened her eyes, a shadow seemed to hang over her vision. She blinked, willing away the darkness, and tried to remember how she'd gotten there.

"Looks like Sleeping Beauty's coming to."

North. Esta rubbed at her eyes and forced herself to sit up.

She didn't know how North and Maggie had gotten her onto this train, and when she started to ask, the words wouldn't come. Her mouth felt like every bit of moisture had been drained from it, and all that came out was a hacking cough.

Maggie offered Esta some water and helped hold the canteen to her mouth so she could drink.

Esta only meant to take a swallow, just enough to be able to speak, but the water was like heaven, and she ended up nearly draining it. When she was done, she wiped her mouth with the back of her hand. "Where are we?"

"Not in Texas anymore," North said, like it was the only piece of information that mattered. When he finally spoke again, he didn't sound happy. "That was some show you put on back there. Causing an earthquake wasn't part of the plan."

"An earthquake?" Esta repeated, not bothering to hide her shock. "What are you talking about?" She remembered being on the locomotive now, remembered feeling a hesitancy that wasn't like her. But she'd pushed herself onward, believing that if the darkness rose again, she could simply release her hold on time before it could take her. But after that—

"You don't remember?" Maggie asked, her eyes soft with concern behind the lenses of her glasses.

"Everything happened so fast. . . ."

The darkness had come. Seshat's darkness. Esta struggled to remember more, and it came to her little by little, in flashes of memory. This time there hadn't been the slow seeping, like ink dropped in water. Instead, almost from the moment she'd pulled time slow, the blackness had rushed around her like a flood. She was only supposed to hold on to the seconds long enough to get off the train and out of sight, but too quickly she had been submerged beneath a different power. Esta had barely been able to push back the shadows, as her magic had turned into something wild and unhinged. The seconds had suddenly felt *alive*, and even as she'd climbed down from the engine and started to run from the train, she'd felt that time itself might turn on her. The darkness had pulsed and billowed, chasing her from the train like a phantom haunting her.

Hunting her.

It came back to her then, how the earth had started to quake. The ground had rippled beneath her as she'd sprinted away from the overheating engine, but before Esta could release her hold on time, darkness had pulled her under.

"The train . . . It *did* explode, though?" Esta asked. It was essential that the authorities believed the Thief was dead.

"Yes, but . . ." Maggie pressed her lips together and glanced at North.

"What happened back there was more than the boiler overheating," North said. "The ground shook clear out where we were, and the earth cracked as easy as an egg. Swallowed men and horses whole. It was a hell of a lot more than what you told us you had planned." His eyes narrowed. "Then you didn't show up like you were supposed to."

North wasn't exactly wrong to be suspicious. Esta *had* planned to use the distraction of the train exploding to slip away from the two Antistasi. She had a dagger to find, and once the Thief was presumed dead, they would have been safer without her.

"But you came back for me," Esta said. "Why risk that? Without the Thief, the two of you could have gone on and started over. You would have been safe."

"You and your partner still owe us a necklace," North told her.

"It wasn't only about the necklace." Maggie shot North a sharp look. "We couldn't leave you there," she said gently, touching Esta's arm. "You were willing to risk everything in St. Louis to help us try to stop the serum from deploying. I told you before, you're one of us now. The Antistasi take care of our own."

Esta wasn't sure how much she believed Maggie's explanation. North's statement about the necklace felt more like the truth. Still, without Maggie and North, the posse of marshals certainly would have found her, collapsed and unconscious somewhere between the train and safety. She owed them her life . . . again.

"You really don't have any idea what happened?" Maggie asked.

The two Antistasi were staring at her expectantly, and Esta knew she had a decision to make. Since finding Harte gone, every time she'd tried to use her affinity, she'd been surprised by a power she could not control. One thing was clear—if Seshat's power was somehow still affecting her, she might need the Antistasi's help more than she originally thought.

"I honestly don't know what happened back there," Esta said, using this truth as an anchor for the lies that were sure to come. "But I think it's tied to what happened back in St. Louis." She glanced up at them, trying to gauge their willingness to believe her. "Or maybe it began even before that."

Esta started slowly, picking her way through the minefield of her story, giving them enough of the truth to make her lies and omissions believable. She couldn't tell them about Harte or the other stones, but maybe she could tell them enough to ensure their continued help.

"The stories are true," she told them. "Two years ago, I did manage to break into the Order's vaults. We were trying to steal their most prized possessions, but instead, we unleashed something we weren't expecting. . . ." Esta told them about Seshat, about the power of the ancient goddess and how she had possessed Harte. And she told them about the threat that Seshat's power posed to the world itself.

"Maybe Ben thought leaving us was for the best," Esta said with a stiff shrug. "He must have believed he could use the stones to take care of the danger Seshat posed on his own. But maybe something more happened that night. Maybe part of Seshat's power is connected to *me* now."

She explained to them about the darkness that had appeared as they ran from the train, about how she'd lost hold of the seconds and woke up over North's shoulder. She told them, too, about the shadows that had pulled her under before the explosion. By the time Esta was finished speaking, Maggie's rapt and serious expression told Esta that she was on the hook. But North's mouth was still twisted with suspicion.

"That sure is some story you spun there," he said, not giving an inch.

"It's not a story," Esta assured him. *Not completely.* "You know what I can do with time. If I only wanted to distract you, I would have been long gone, not passed out cold waiting for the marshals and the rest of their posse to find me."

"She has a point," Maggie told him.

"You don't actually believe this story she's spinning?" North said to Maggie.

"I don't know what I believe." Maggie seemed to be measuring each of her words carefully. "But I know this much: Something *did* happen back in the Festival Hall. I was there. I *felt* it," she said before turning to Esta. "You're *sure* you don't have any idea where Ben went?"

"No," Esta lied. She paused, pretending to be nervous, and when she spoke again, she made her voice as soft as a secret. "But I do know where we might be able to find another artifact."

Maggie's expression brightened immediately, but North's brows bunched together, like he still didn't want to believe her. Still, Esta could sense the yearning behind his doubt, and she knew he was more interested than he wanted to be.

"You're telling us that you've known all along where *another* of the lost artifacts might be?" North asked.

"Possibly," Esta said. "Ben and I had a backup in case the necklace turned out to be a fake or in case we couldn't get it away from the Society. There's a dagger called the Pharaoh's Heart that holds a stone every bit as powerful as the Djinni's Star." She allowed the moment to settle around them, giving them the space to start believing that such a treasure could be theirs. "If you help me retrieve it, we can perform the ritual to break whatever connection I have with Seshat before she can do any more damage. Once we do that, the Pharaoh's Heart would be yours. I know it's not the necklace. . . ." She bit her lip a little, like she was sorry about this fact.

Maggie looked ready to accept, but North spoke first.

"You'd up and *give* this artifact to us?" He waved his hand dismissively. "Just like that?"

"The Antistasi need it more than I do," Esta said, telling them the exact thing she knew they wanted to hear. "And anyway . . ." She looked to Maggie now and spoke the words she knew would sink the hook. "Aren't we all on the same side?"

"Yes, of course," Maggie said, giving Esta a small, relieved smile. Then suddenly the pleasure drained from her expression. "But if you're telling us the truth about this Seshat creature and her possible connection to you, we have a bigger problem right now." She lifted her eyes to the ceiling of the boxcar as it rattled down the track before meeting Esta's gaze again. "If you weren't in control of *whatever* it was that happened back there in Texas, what makes you think you could stop it from happening again?"

Her meaning was clear to Esta. "You think I'd do something to this train while we're on it?"

Maggie shook her head. "I'm not saying you'd do it on purpose, but you have to admit, you don't have the best record. First the train in New Jersey and then the one in Texas. . . ."

"But if I don't use my affinity—"

"What makes you think you'll have a choice?" Maggie asked. "I *did* see Ben back in the Festival Hall. He had his hands around your neck. I believe you when you say that it wasn't him in control, but what will you do if this Seshat creature does the same to *you*?"

Esta's stomach twisted. She wanted to argue that it wasn't possible, but she couldn't make herself form the words to lie.

Maggie took Esta's hand. "If Seshat is as powerful as you say she is, what would stop her from using your affinity against you?" Her voice went even softer, like she was afraid Seshat herself might hear. "What if Seshat makes good on her threats before we can find the other artifact?"

Esta felt the train rumbling beneath her. The cadence of the wheels meeting the track was so much steadier than she felt. Maggie was right. Harte hadn't been in control back in St. Louis. If Seshat's power was still somehow affecting Esta's affinity, they had no idea what they were dealing with.

"You're right," Esta said softly. "I shouldn't be here. I'm a danger to both of you—to everyone." She wasn't sure why this clear way out of her entanglement with the Antistasi should feel so unsettling. And so depressing.

"Maybe you don't have to be," Maggie said, pulling a small leather pouch from her skirts.

"What do you mean?" Esta asked, frowning.

"Seshat wants your affinity, right?" Maggie asked, and Esta reluctantly nodded. "She can only use you through your magic."

"As far as we know," Esta admitted.

"It's a problem I might be able to take care of." Maggie took a small white pill from the leather pouch and held it up between her fingertips.

Esta knew all about Maggie's concoctions. She'd experienced some of the more potent ones back in St. Louis when she'd had her first run-in with the Antistasi, and she'd seen for herself what Maggie's serum was capable of. "What, *exactly*, is that?"

"It's sort of an oral version of Quellant," Maggie explained. "Unlike the fog we used back in St. Louis, this tablet can mute an affinity without leaving the person completely unconscious. It's also a lot more potent— it'll last close to twelve hours instead of the usual two." She held it out to Esta. "It stands to reason that if you can't reach your affinity, Seshat won't be able to either."

"You want to take my magic from me," Esta realized. Her body felt suddenly cold. She remembered what it was like to have her affinity stripped away by the Quellant back in St. Louis, especially the strange emptiness she'd felt.

"No," Maggie said, shaking her head. "I'm asking you to consider giving it up. Temporarily, at least. It would only be until we get the artifact."

Maggie's explanation seemed completely reasonable, but everything in Esta was screaming for her not to take the pill. The idea of willingly relinquishing her link to the old magic made her recoil. To give up the power that was so much a part of her—even for a short time . . .

But Maggie could be right about the danger Esta might pose to them. Esta had felt Seshat's furious determination back in St. Louis, and she had no other explanation for her inability to control her affinity now. If Seshat took her over the way she'd taken over Harte . . .

Reluctantly, Esta accepted the pill from Maggie. It was small and unimpressive, but she could feel the warm energy that spoke of old magic coming from within. Every instinct she had was screaming for her not to place it in her mouth, not to put herself at such a disadvantage. But she remembered the darkness, uncontrollable and absolute, as she'd run from that train. If Seshat actually did have a connection to her, it might happen again.

No. It would *happen again.* There was no denying that Seshat would keep trying. The ancient power wouldn't stop, not until they stopped her.

Still, Esta couldn't bring herself to do it. She was already starting to hand the tablet back, when another thought occurred to her—one that tipped the scales. If the Quellant could *truly* hold back Seshat's power, then perhaps it was an answer to a problem Esta had believed to be hopeless. Maybe with the Quellant, she and Harte could keep Seshat controlled enough to return to 1902 *together*.

It wouldn't do anything to protect the stones. If they returned to 1902 with the artifacts, they would likely lose the ones they currently had. But if they *could* return to the time they should have been in, Julian would never have given the necklace to the Society. The Devil's Thief never needed to exist. The Antistasi wouldn't have stoked the hatred of the Occult Brotherhoods with their violent deeds, the Defense Against Magic Act would not have been ratified, and the attack at the Festival Hall never would have happened. The serum wouldn't have been deployed— it might never be invented. Even if they couldn't find a way to bring the artifacts with them, she and Harte could fix the mistakes they'd made. They could start fresh.

They could have more time.

Going back wouldn't give Esta a future. She understood that. Seshat would still need to be dealt with, and if they couldn't retrieve the Book—if the Book didn't hold the answers they needed—Esta would willingly give her affinity and herself to control the ancient being. She would stop Seshat from taking her revenge on the world and save Harte from what that power would do to him. She would give him a future.

As she placed the pill in her mouth, Esta told herself that it was worth the risk. It was only temporary, and besides, she didn't need her affinity to steal the Pharaoh's Heart—and she still needed the dagger, especially if the Quellant didn't work. When she crushed the bitter pill between her teeth, she felt her affinity draw away from her almost immediately. Where her magic had once been, Esta felt only a strange, indescribable hollowness, but little else. There was no way to tell if it was enough to block Seshat's connection to her. There might never be, she realized. Not unless it didn't work. As the train rattled on, Esta could only hope that she'd made the right decision and that she hadn't just managed to hook herself.

FURY AND GRIEF

1902—New York

Cela Johnson didn't have any magic, and she hadn't ever particularly wanted any. But as she'd watched Jianyu grow paler and weaker over the past few days, the wound in his shoulder steadily seeping even as it had started to turn with infection, she had to admit that having *something* more than hot water and a few old herbs at her disposal might have been helpful. *Especially* when there wasn't anything natural about the wound itself.

She was fussing with the bandage and trying to ignore the way Jianyu's breathing had grown shallower since Abel had gone to get Viola a little while before. The house was mostly quiet now. A few of Abel's friends were in the kitchen, working on an article for the *New York Age*. The paper belonged to Timothy Thomas Fortune, the man who'd lent them the use of his house after their own had been burned to the ground by men from the railroad who'd wanted Abel to stop his organizing. But Cela couldn't hear the others from where she was in an upstairs bedroom. It might as well have been only her and Jianyu in that big old house, all alone.

Taking another blanket from the shelf, Cela layered it over Jianyu, knowing full well it wouldn't do a thing for the way his fingers had been growing colder. Still, if he was in there, she hoped that this bit of comfort might help.

"Just hold on a little longer, now," she murmured, tucking the blanket around his too-still body. "You said this friend of yours can help, and she's on her way."

Or she'd better be. Still, Cela couldn't help but think that they should've already been back.

A few minutes later, she felt her nerves unwind a bit at the sound of the door opening in the hallway below. The familiar rhythm of Abel's steps sounded on the stairs, and Cela turned from her vigil to see her brother standing in the doorway. Standing behind him was the white girl from the gala—the one who'd tried to kill her and who had created all this trouble in the first place. She wasn't overly tall, and Cela supposed there were those who might consider her pretty, but the uneven stitching of her hem and the rough material of her shirt made it clear she was as poor as everyone else.

Abel had been against getting mixed up with Jianyu from the start. Nothing good could come of messing with magic, he'd said, and he'd been right, like he usually was. But after all Cela had been through, she also knew that trouble had a way of following you just as soon as you tried to walk away from it.

"Is he—" Abel's voice was soft, and Cela could hear the worry in it. For all his blustering, he cared what happened to Jianyu as much as she did.

"He's still with us, but only just," Cela whispered, not quite stepping aside even as she could see the girl—Viola, Jianyu had called her—try to peer around her. From her deep olive skin and thick dark-brown hair, she looked to be one of the Italians who'd been filling the area around Mulberry Street since a few years before Cela was born.

Cela shifted her gaze to study the girl. At the gala, Cela had only seen a lady dressed in silken finery, but she'd known even then from the cut of the ready-made gown that the girl wasn't one of the Order's women. Now, Viola was dressed in a simple, serviceable navy skirt, her hair pulled back from a heart-shaped face. Her eyes were a strange shade of violet, but they were sharp, and a certain intelligence lurked behind them. If she attacked again, Cela was certain Jianyu wouldn't survive it.

"Even after what you did, he told us to send for you."

"We're friends," the girl said, her voice carrying the cadence of another land.

Cela only frowned, crossing her arms.

"Or we were once." The girl stepped forward, her face dappled in the shadows thrown by the lamp in the corner. "I didn't mean to hurt him."

"No," Cela said, still feeling a kind of prickly coolness. "You meant to hurt *me*."

Viola shook her head, but to Cela's surprise, it wasn't a denial that came out of her mouth. "I didn't know you were with him. I was trying to save the ring. I thought you were trying to steal it."

"Of *course* you did. You took one look at me and thought theft was the only possibility, but I can't steal something that belonged to me in the first place," Cela said, her words tart. When Viola's expression flashed with the disbelief and judgment Cela recognized too well, she gave Viola a cold smile in return. "Harte Darrigan gave that ring to me as payment for taking care of his mother. Not that I should have to explain myself to you."

"Darrigan?" The girl's eyes flashed. "You knew the magician?"

"I worked in the theater with Darrigan," Cela said. "Though I should have known better than to agree to help him, or to take anything he offered."

"That ring wasn't his to give," Viola said, her voice suddenly turning dangerous, and Cela was reminded that this girl was no innocent. At the gala, she'd let her knife fly, straight and true, with an intent to kill and an aim deadly enough to make good.

But Cela Johnson wouldn't let Viola see her nerves. "What Darrigan did or didn't have any right to doesn't matter now," Cela said, changing the subject. "Jianyu doesn't have much longer, and that's because of you. Can you help him or not?"

Viola's jaw went tight, like she was getting ready to argue, but when Cela stepped to the side, revealing Jianyu in the bed behind her, the girl's expression went slack with something that looked too similar to Cela's own grief. The way Viola took a halting step toward the bed, she could have been sleepwalking.

"Can you *help* him?" Cela repeated, placing herself between Jianyu and Viola. Her arms were crossed over her chest, but she was ready—to do what, she didn't know. But ready just the same. "Because I won't let you hurt him again."

Cela wasn't exactly sure where the nerve to speak so forcefully to a white girl had come from . . . but then Viola Vaccarelli wasn't *really* a white girl, was she? Maybe out in the wide world, Viola could pull on the protection of whiteness if she was standing next to Cela herself. But alone on the streets? She was a lowly immigrant. Not even a citizen. And here? In Mr. Fortune's house? Viola was only as important as what she could do for Jianyu.

"Cela," Abel warned gently from the doorway. He'd told her about what had happened earlier, the way his chest had ached like it was on fire and he'd thought his heart would explode. Viola had made it clear that she didn't need knives to kill.

Viola's only response to Cela's pointless threat was a quiet shake of her head. "I won't hurt him. I can help."

Cela didn't move away as Viola stepped toward the bed. She wasn't about to stand by if this little bit of a girl decided to finish the job she'd started at the gala.

"I thought I had killed him," Viola murmured as she knelt next to the bed. "I would have tried to find you sooner, but I thought it was too late." Pulling back the covers, she took one of Jianyu's hands in her own, shuddering a little, probably at the coolness of his skin. Then she glanced up at Cela, her strange plum-colored eyes brimming. "Thank you. For being his friend when I was not. For saving him."

Cela only nodded, glancing briefly over to where Abel stood in the doorway, as watchful as she felt. "I haven't saved him yet."

"You brought me here," Viola said. "It's not too late." Her lips pressed tightly together as she closed her eyes, her face tense with concentration.

Cela waited, but nothing seemed to happen. The minutes ticked by as the silence in the room spun itself around them. The city buzzed outside the open window, but it might as well have been another world altogether, because inside the room, they were all caught in a moment of dangerous hope. Viola's forehead wrinkled, her expression creased from some unseen exertion, her skin now damp with sweat. The hand that clutched Jianyu's trembled slightly.

Cela glanced up at Abel, who looked every bit as unsure as she felt.

It was taking too long. Certainly, something as powerful and dangerous as the old magic could have worked by now. Something was wrong.

Cela didn't know what she'd intended when she took a step toward the bed, but before she could touch the girl or pull her away from Jianyu, Viola gasped. Her eyes flew open as she released her hold on Jianyu and tumbled over, barely catching herself before she slumped to the floor.

"What is it?" Cela asked, stepping toward Jianyu. She took his hand and noticed that it felt warmer, but that could have been from Viola's grasp. He still wasn't moving. She squeezed Jianyu's hand slightly and touched his cheek to wake him. But nothing. Jianyu didn't so much as stir.

"Is he okay?" Abel asked from somewhere close behind her.

Cela didn't answer her brother. *Couldn't*. She turned on Viola, her throat tight with fury and grief all at once. "You said you could help him."

But Viola didn't respond. When she looked up at Cela, she was wearing an expression that could have been carved from stone, her eyes wide with something that might have been shock . . . or fear.

NOT COMPLETELY,
NOT ENOUGH

1902—New York

Viola felt the fury in Cela's voice as soundly as a slap across her face, and she welcomed it. Her hands were flat against the worn rag rug next to the bed, and her entire body trembled with the exertion to stay upright. But she wouldn't allow herself to grovel before these strangers. Instead, she pulled herself upright, back to her knees, and leaned against the bed. Jianyu's color looked a little better, and his breathing *had* improved. She took his hand again and felt that his skin was warmer now, but it wasn't enough.

She hadn't been enough.

Viola had allowed her affinity to unspool until she'd found the too-slow and too-unsteady beating of Jianyu's heart. He'd lost so much blood since the gala, and she found the reason—the tear made by her blade had not healed. It had continued to bleed, and because of that, Jianyu was still very far gone.

But not completely, she'd reminded herself. She'd bought him some more time.

She'd been barely aware of the two in the room—brother and sister, she'd finally realized. Not a couple, as she'd first assumed. It was an understandable mistake, considering that she herself had never seen that sort of easy affection between siblings before. Not in her own family, at least.

There had been no time for self-pity, though. No time to think of Paolo, his hatred or his fear. Instead, Viola had thrown herself into the work of saving her friend, pressing all of her affinity, all that she was, into

Jianyu's wound. She'd used her magic as it had always been intended to be used. For life, not death.

Viola was not—had never been—a gentle creature, but in this work, she was careful and soft. In this work, she sank herself more completely than perhaps ever before, until she and her affinity had become one. Until she'd felt overheated, slick with sweat from the exertion. Until the shame she'd carried for so long seemed to evaporate in the warmth building within her.

But it wasn't enough.

No matter how much of her affinity she'd channeled into Jianyu, his wound would not be healed. The flesh remained stubbornly insistent, fighting against her magic. She had done what she could, knitting together the tissue and bone, only to have them unravel again and again. So she'd changed direction and worked on the blood itself, urged it on until all that had been lost was replenished. Blood still seeped from the wound, but at least Jianyu was no longer in immediate danger of death. It had taken every bit of her strength.

"You said you could help him," Cela said again, her voice as wild as the fear in her eyes, as the panic Viola felt already churning within herself.

Viola looked up at Cela, accepting her judgment.

"He told us that you could *save* him," Cela demanded.

Viola was shaking her head, because she couldn't explain it. She didn't have words to counter the distrust in Cela's expression—distrust that she had more than earned.

Cela took a step toward Viola. "I don't know what you're playing at—"

Abel pulled his sister back, his hands steady on her shoulder. "I think what my sister is trying to say is that he doesn't look any better."

Viola glanced back at the bed, where Jianyu remained unmoving. His breathing looked steadier now, though, his color less faded. "He *is* better," she said softly.

"But not completely," Cela countered.

She turned back to them. "No. The wound wouldn't be healed." She tried to explain how her affinity worked, how she'd tried to knit the wound together and how it had resisted her.

"How is that possible?" Cela asked, her voice fraying a little at the edges. "You made the wound. Your knife did this. *You* should be able to *fix* it."

"Cela . . ." Abel's voice was a warning. He looked distinctly uneasy as he pulled his sister back gently.

Because he was afraid of her. Viola had given him a good enough reason to be.

Viola turned back to Jianyu and pulled herself to unsteady feet. She could feel their frustration, their suspicions, and she could not blame them. Placing Jianyu's hands back across his abdomen, she tucked the blankets around him gently.

The movement must have disturbed him, because his eyes fluttered open suddenly. Unfocused, they stared toward the ceiling until she leaned over him, hope caught in her throat, and then he looked at her.

Jianyu tried to speak, but his voice was a scuffed thing, rough and barely there. His brows pulled together, ever so slightly, but Viola couldn't tell if it was confusion or anger or pain that knitted them.

"I'm sorry," she whispered, hating the catch in her own throat and the way her eyes burned with tears. "I can't—" His mouth moved a little, but she shook her head. "You must rest," she said, pulling her hand back. She was suddenly afraid to touch him, because touching him meant facing her own failure.

His eyes were on her, still glassy and unfocused, when another unintelligible husk of a whisper came out. But she was already backing away.

Cela had gone to Jianyu's side and was already leaning over the bed and speaking in urgent, hushed tones as she held his hand. But Jianyu's eyes were following Viola.

"You can't just up and leave," Abel said.

Viola met his gaze and wondered what she would do if he tried to stop her.

"Vee—" Jianyu's mouth formed the first syllable of her name. From across the room, his eyes met hers, and she knew that he saw her standing there. Knew that he understood what she had done, and what she had failed to do.

She should have stepped toward him. She should have tried again, but Viola felt the weight of Cela's judgment and the unease in Abel's posture. She felt their distrust heavy in the room and knew that there was nothing more she could do for Jianyu, so she turned and she ran.

Outside, the early-summer heat was already starting to make the city air feel too close and too heavy, but Viola barely felt it. She was already overheated and chilled all at once, and the shift beneath her skirts was damp with her own sweat. She turned to look around the neighborhood, trying to figure out where she was in the city. She knew which direction she needed to go. South. Toward the Bowery.

THE BULLDOGGER

1904—Denver

Esta arrived in Colorado with Maggie and North two days after the mess in Texas. She'd taken dose after dose of the Quellant, but she still wasn't used to the gnawing emptiness where her connection to the old magic should have been. She doubted she ever would be. As unpleasant as the constant ache from her missing affinity was, at least nothing else had happened. The train had remained steady on its tracks, and no shadows had threatened the edges of her vision. And if Esta wanted to crawl out of her own skin from being so separated from such an essential part of herself? It was a small price to pay for the assurance that Seshat could not touch her.

Before they'd boarded a train for Denver, Esta had checked the headlines and found that the ruse in Texas seemed to have worked. The Devil's Thief was presumed dead, but any relief Esta might have felt was quickly erased by the sight of Julian Eltinge's picture looking up at her from the second page. Julian was among those who were already showing strange symptoms from being exposed to the serum in St. Louis. Esta knew what would eventually happen to those poor souls. First a connection to the old magic would awaken, and then a few days later they would die. They would not have easy deaths.

Esta tried not to think about Julian, with his whip-smart humor and sharp intelligence, suffering like that. He'd been nothing short of heroic at the parade, despite being cornered into a terrible situation, and the idea that he'd been doused with the serum gnawed at her. She couldn't stop herself from wondering what terrible affinity the serum might awaken in him, or whether he would have anyone at all to comfort him at the end. And as the train climbed into the mountains, she discovered the bitter taste of true regret.

When they finally arrived in Denver, Esta was completely on edge, but the sky that greeted them was wide and blue, and the mountain air didn't have the heavy blanket of humidity that had made Texas feel so oppressive. The Colorado air was thin, but she forced herself to focus on what lay ahead instead of the path of destruction she'd left behind.

The three of them had spent their time aboard the train planning, and as soon as they arrived, they headed directly for the edge of town, where the Curtis Brothers' Wild West Show—and with any luck, the Pharaoh's Heart—waited.

Even without her affinity, Esta was confident that she could retrieve the dagger quickly, but when they crested the hill and saw the Curtis Brothers' Wild West Show sprawling in the fields below, some of her confidence waned. This wasn't a simple rodeo. Instead, the grounds stretched over multiple acres, with an enormous tent of billowing white canvas holding court at the center and a large encampment of other tents sprawled around it.

"How will we ever find the dagger in all that?" Maggie asked, voicing Esta's own worry as they looked out over the grounds.

"One of those will belong to Bill Pickett," Esta said, pointing to the village of smaller tents clustered beyond the big top. "Once I figure out who he is, finding the dagger should be easy enough."

"You mean, once *we* figure it out," North corrected, eyeing her. He was still suspicious, and rightly so.

"Of course," she said easily. "But it will go faster if we split up."

"Like hell," North told her.

"It'll be safer, too," she added. "There's less chance of anyone recognizing us if we're not together. In case they're still looking for us."

"The Thief is dead," Maggie reminded her. "The headlines all said so."

"Just because the authorities *say* the Thief died in the crash doesn't mean the Order or any of the Brotherhoods have stopped looking," Esta argued. "The faster we get the dagger and the less we're seen together, the better."

"I don't like this," North grumbled. "You going off on your own is exactly the sort of thing you'd want to do if you were fixing to run."

Esta's patience was fraying. "I've taken the Quellant, haven't I? Besides, you have your watch. I can't outrun that."

It was a problem Esta had been considering, especially since her own affinity was out of reach at the moment. She didn't want to take the watch from North—it had been a gift from his late father—but she couldn't see any way around it. When the time was right, when she had the dagger in hand, she'd make sure they couldn't stop her from leaving.

North's eyes narrowed at her, like he could almost sense the path of her thoughts.

Esta let out a frustrated breath when she realized North was set on digging in his heels. They were wasting time arguing. "Look, you're welcome to come along with me. I'm sure Maggie can handle herself down there without you."

Her words had the desired effect. North might have hated to let Esta out of his sight, but he wasn't about to leave Maggie unprotected.

They split up, approaching the grounds of the show from opposite directions. Esta cut through a field that held horse-drawn wagons waiting for their drivers. It was peppered by the occasional motorcar, the past and future colliding. A little farther on, she passed corrals that held cattle and horses. There were people *everywhere*. Families and groups watched the ranch hands work. Couples wandered arm in arm, taking in the sights. Small children draped themselves over the fences to watch horses graze with a kind of bright-eyed excitement that Esta herself had never felt about much of anything, except maybe lifting a fat wallet or a diamond stickpin.

Or besting Harte.

Esta's chest felt suddenly tight at the thought. She almost wished she hadn't been so impulsive on the train and that the string of beads was still on her wrist. Surrounded by so many people, she felt strangely apart from them. The lies and omissions even kept her at arm's length from North and Maggie. It might have been nice to have Harte's voice in her ear right then, a sign that she wasn't truly alone.

A breeze kicked up, and Esta's nose wrinkled at the strange combination of fried food and popped corn and sawdust that assaulted her. But it was the scent of the animals that swept away all thoughts of Harte as another memory rose unexpectedly, as stark and clear as the sky above. The grief it brought with it nearly made her stumble.

Esta had grown up in the shadows of skyscrapers and spent her childhood navigating narrow canyons of brick and glass, breathing air laden with exhaust and the other smells of city life. But the scent of horses brought her back to the days when Dakari had taken her to see the tired-looking ponies that waited to cart tourists around Central Park. She would wander along, looking at the horses, while Dakari visited with old friends from when he was one of the drivers—back when he'd first come to the city, before the Professor had found him.

She'd been young then—no more than seven or eight—but the memory was so clear, it might as well have happened last week. Esta had never thanked Dakari properly for those trips. She'd never really thanked him for anything, she realized. Now it was too late.

The memory of the last time she'd seen him rose then, replacing that other, happier memory of those days near Central Park. When Esta had returned to her own time, when she'd discovered the truth about everything, she'd tried to fight. But Professor Lachlan had called Dakari into the library, and Dakari had come, unaware that he was about to be killed to teach Esta a lesson—another sacrificed pawn in Nibsy's deadly game. She drew in another deep breath, willing the scent of the horses to shove away the bloody image of Dakari's last moments. She refused to let *that* serve as her memory of the man who had been her trainer and healer, and also her friend.

The horses in the field nearby were nothing like the ponies from her youth, though. These beasts were tall and athletic, with well-muscled flanks and coats that gleamed in the midday sun. The horses of her childhood had always looked tired as they'd waited on the side of the busy street, silently resigned to their fates, chewing on grain from dirty plastic buckets amid the blaring traffic and noise. They didn't run or buck. With the blinders they wore, they couldn't even see much of the world around them. They simply followed the path set for them, driven on by the person who provided them food and water and a safe place to sleep. Maybe even then she had known that those horses' lives weren't so very different from her own, Esta thought ruefully, shoving the memory aside.

As she moved with the crowd toward the big top, she put her thoughts of the past behind her, right where they belonged. She needed to focus on the task at hand—finding the dagger and then figuring out a way to untangle herself from the two Antistasi, so she could get to Harte.

If she had hoped that getting the dagger from Pickett would be easy, that hope died at the sight of the two men standing on either side of the entrance to the big top. Each wore a serious expression on his face and the silver star of the US marshals pinned to his chest. *They could be looking for anyone. . . .* But Esta pulled the brim of her hat down anyway. Picking up her pace, she joined the tail end of a group entering the big top and made sure to keep her eyes ahead of her as she passed.

Once inside the enormous tent, Esta didn't bother to find a seat in the bleachers. There was an area to the left of the entrance, where men in cowboy hats and worn jeans leaned against the railing to watch the show. It was a standing room, and the men who filled it didn't look like the type to sit still long. They watched the horses and riders with a kind of critical squint, smoking hand-rolled cigarettes and commenting on the mounts each performer rode. A few who had positioned themselves closest to the arena's entrance hooted and hollered whenever a female rider went past or shouted slurs at the brown-skinned men who wore cavalry uniforms. The performers either didn't hear or pretended that they didn't care. They kept their shoulders back and their eyes forward as they kicked their horses into action and entered the arena to the cheers of the crowd.

Two men held court in the center of the arena. They looked like inverted images of each other—one fair and blond and the other with ruddier skin and dark hair—with horses to match. They were dressed in fringed leather that could have belonged in a Vegas show, and they took turns using a large, cone-shaped megaphone to announce each new act that rode into the arena. Esta figured they must be the Curtis brothers.

It quickly became apparent that, even with the clear skill of the riders, the Curtis brothers' version of the Wild West was about as authentic as Harte's old act as an expert in the mystical arts. She wondered briefly how it must feel for the buffalo soldiers to parade around for the same people who would keep them from sharing a table at a restaurant in town, or how the Lakota must feel about displaying their traditions in the same arena as the painted clowns who distracted the bulls. Esta wondered why any of them did it—if there was some benefit from being part of the Curtis brothers' entourage, or if the men and women were there in the ring because it was the lesser of the evils they could have chosen from. Maybe they thought they could change their fate.

Esta knew otherwise. In the end, history would march on toward a future where people would still be pushed down, kept away, and discarded. Maybe once she'd hoped that by destroying the Brink, she could change the future, but with everything that had happened, she wasn't so sure anymore. Fear and hatred and ignorance seemed so . . . *inevitable.*

Yet the future *had* changed, she reminded herself. The problem was that it had changed for the worse. She needed to concentrate on the job in front of her—finding the artifacts and containing Seshat's power—so there could be a future to worry about at all.

On posters at the train station, Pickett had been billed as a "bulldogger," whatever that meant. Esta didn't really care as long as the cowboy still had the dagger and didn't put up too much of a fight handing it over. With any luck, they'd never have to actually meet. Nothing good could come from that—especially not for Pickett himself. But for a long while, there was no sign of the cowboy. The show felt endless. Rider after rider, act after act, and Esta wondered if Pickett would ever make an appearance.

Nearly an hour in, the fairer of the two Curtis brothers announced the next act—a sharpshooter. At his signal, a woman rode into the arena, her horse kicking up dirt and dust. Esta couldn't help but be transfixed by the drama that filled the ring. In this time, before microphones and loudspeakers and in an arena filled with the chattering noise of a crowd, the woman relied on a sort of pantomime to create her act, flirting with the audience as she accomplished ever-more impressive feats by hitting impossible targets. Somehow Esta wasn't surprised to feel the warmth of magic sifting through the air whenever the woman took aim. Mageus had hidden among the theater folk back in New York. Why wouldn't they hide in plain sight here as well?

After the sharpshooter left the arena to thunderous applause, Esta's patience was finally rewarded.

"Ladies and gentlemen," the fairer of the brothers called. "We have a real treat for you today. Direct from the plains of Texas comes the dusky demon himself, a man who can subdue even the strongest steer with nothing but his force of will—Bill the Bulldogger Pickett!"

Pickett tore into the arena, a blur of speed on horseback, before he came to a dead stop mere inches from the Curtis brother who had announced him.

Esta had expected a giant of a man, a showman decked out in fringe and beadwork like the rest of the performers, but Pickett was dressed simply in the clothes of a working ranch hand: dark pants and a lighter shirt, with a hat that looked well loved and faded from days under the sun. She couldn't see much of his face beneath the brim, but his dark-brown skin had reddish undertones, and a heavy mustache shadowed his upper lip.

Pickett didn't turn when the men in the gallery around Esta whistled and shouted slurs. Under his command, his horse didn't so much as flinch when a bottle lobbed from the crowd shattered on the ground before him. Beneath the broad brim of his hat, his expression was placid, uninterested. Like he knew exactly who he was, even if everyone else was a fool. While the Curtis brothers droned on about Pickett's achievements, he busied himself with tying a rope into a lasso.

Esta admired confidence like that, and as she watched Pickett work—methodically, carefully—she thought she understood why Harte had entrusted the Pharaoh's Heart to this particular man. There was something steady about him. Something that set him apart from the others she'd seen prancing around the arena that day.

Once the Curtis brothers retreated, the mood in the arena changed again. The drums rolled once more, and at the sound of a rim shot, a steer was released into the ring. Pickett was off, faster than anything Esta could have expected. Faster than anyone she'd seen yet that day. In a matter of seconds, he chased the animal down and tossed a rope around its horns in one try, jumped from his horse and wrestled it to the ground in a single, fluid motion, and finished by tying up the animal's four legs. The entire process couldn't have even taken a whole minute, and then Pickett was back up on his horse, tearing around the arena again in a victory lap, while a couple of other men wrangled the steer away.

The audience cheered, whooping and hooting their approval, but the cheers were peppered with the same slurs from before. The men standing near Esta seemed more disgusted by Pickett's expertise than impressed, but Pickett continued to ignore them as he circled the ring, waving his hat but not letting so much as a smile curl beneath the heavy mustache. As he passed the standing gallery, Esta saw that Pickett's eyes were sharp, probably on the lookout for any others who might mean to cause him trouble.

Another drumroll rose, and another steer was released into the arena. Pickett kicked his horse into a gallop until he was next to the animal, but this time, instead of using the rope, which was still on the other animal, he swung himself out of his own saddle and leapt five, maybe six feet, onto the steer's back. The animal was more than twice Pickett's size, but that didn't seem to bother him. He grabbed it by the horns and then slid off so he could dig his boot heels into the ground to slow the beast. He twisted the horns until the steer's nose was pointing upward, and then he did something—Esta couldn't quite tell what it was, but she thought he might have latched onto the animal with his *mouth*—and a moment later Pickett's hands were in the air. He waved them in a victory wave as he was dragged along. The steer took maybe three or four more steps before, unbelievably, *impossibly*, it stumbled to its knees and went down. The bull writhed beneath Pickett's hold until, finally, it seemed to give up and remained there on the ground, completely subdued.

Esta searched for the feel of magic sifting through the air once more, but of course there wasn't any of the telltale warmth. Pickett never would have gotten out of Manhattan if he'd had the old magic. This was something else—talent, perhaps. Mastery, definitely. All born of a lifetime of work.

The crowd was strangely silent for a second before the arena exploded in shouts and cheers. As he stood and waved his hat to the crowd, Pickett looked even smaller than he had atop his horse. Next to the steer, he seemed utterly human.

It was the strangest and perhaps most impressive thing Esta had ever witnessed. Even once Pickett had released it, the steer remained on the ground, as shocked by what had happened as everyone else.

Esta was so taken by the display in the ring that she almost didn't notice the movement of the two men to her right. A pair of other performers were dragging the stunned animal out of the arena and Pickett was taking his final bow, but at the edge of the standing room, a group of marshals weren't watching the show. They had already started moving into the crowded standing-room area, and soon they were joined by others. Even if they weren't looking for her specifically, Esta realized they'd find her easily enough with the way they'd surrounded the crowd of men.

With her affinity, it would have been simple to slip away unseen, but the Quellant was still thick in her blood. Her affinity was out of reach.

The Thief is dead, Esta reminded herself. The marshals could be looking for anyone, but she wasn't going to take a chance of being accidentally found. Considering her options, she decided on the most expedient and gave the man in front of her a violent shove, which caused him to topple into the man next to him.

The effect was immediate. In a matter of seconds, the standing room erupted into angry shouting, and Esta ducked away from the heat of the growing brawl and slipped out the back of the big top as the marshals rushed in.

THE MARK OF THE ANTISTASI

1904—Texas

J ack Grew rolled the whiskey around in his cup and studied the way
it sloshed from side to side. Watery and sharp, it had definitely been
cut with something else, but the drink was doing its job, at least. The
tension of the day had started to ease after the first biting swallow, but it
wasn't gone. And it wasn't going fast enough.

The amber liquid stared back at him, mocking. The porter who'd first
reported seeing Esta on the train had been no help. The man had been
bewitched so resolutely that what came out of his mouth was nothing but
rubbish. Which meant that Jack was stuck. He couldn't leave Corsicana
without answers—not when the trail had gone cold. There was nothing
to do but wait until the haze of whatever spell the porter was under lifted.

He stared down into his cup, and it hit him suddenly that the color
of the whiskey reminded him of something . . . *Esta's eyes.* They'd been
the most unsettling shade of gold, much like whiskey. For a short time,
she'd made him believe that she wanted him. Even after all he'd lost in
Greece, even after all he should have learned there, Jack had let himself be
swayed once more by a set of round hips and a pretty pair of long lashes
batting in his direction. The memory of it was almost enough to turn his
stomach.

Jack lifted the tumbler, ready to throw it against the wall. He
wanted to watch the glass shatter, the amber liquid splatter and slide
down the wall. He wanted to imagine it was Esta he was destroying.
But he stopped himself. What was the use of wasting a perfectly good

drink, especially one that he'd already paid for? Instead of tossing the glass, Jack took one of the cubes of morphine—how was it that there were only three left?—and dissolved it in the whiskey, watching as the amber-colored liquid turned cloudy. Just as Esta's lovely eyes would when he finally finished her.

He was on his third drink and feeling *almost* calm again, when the saloon doors opened in a burst of noise. Jack turned to find Hendricks there, panting heavily with a shit-eating grin on his face.

"The spell is lifting."

Finally. Jack tossed a couple of coins on the countertop and followed without a word.

Back at Corsicana's jail, Gunter and a couple of other men from the Syndicate had already arrived. They all tipped their hats to Jack, a greeting that was becoming a familiar sign of their mutual respect.

"I hear things are changing?" Jack said, speaking to Gunter more than the others.

"Whatever they did to him, it's wearing off," Gunter said, nodding toward the barred cell.

"And?" Jack pressed.

"It's still slow going," Gunter told him with a frown. "But we expect that as the spell wanes, it'll work faster."

Behind the iron bars, the porter was sitting on the narrow cot, his elbows on his knees and his hands pressed on either side of his head. Next to him, a deputy held a heavy billy club, while the sheriff leaned lazily against the wall and asked another question.

"I told you," he said, sounding like a scared animal. "I don't remember."

The sheriff gave a nod, and the deputy jammed the club into the man's side. The porter let out another moan and tried to curl away from the attack, but he didn't drop his arms. They'd likely beat the sense out of him before the spell lifted.

Jack stepped toward them, but Jot Gunter snagged the sleeve of his coat. Jack looked down at the man's hand and then at the man himself.

"Have patience," Gunter said. "The sheriff is working on it. These things are delicate."

"Are they?" Jack asked, jerking away from Gunter and walking into the cell.

"If I may?" He glared at the sheriff, who shrugged and stepped out of the cell.

Once the man was gone, Jack spoke in a low, soothing voice, introducing himself to their prisoner. "Hello, George. My name is Jack Grew. I work for the president."

"My name isn't George," the man said, lifting his chin. "It's Johnson. Abel Johnson."

"Mr. Johnson," Jack acknowledged, pretending he cared. "We were told that you were the one who spotted the Thief on the train last night."

"I already told these men everything I remember," the porter said. His uniform was rumpled and stained. One sleeve had been ripped from his coat.

"If there's anything at all, any detail," Jack said softly, and then waited.

"Like I said—"

"Your record with the railroad is an interesting one," Jack said, his voice more clipped now. "You've been involved in labor strikes in the past, and you have a record of instigating unrest among the other porters."

"That was years ago," the man said, his eyes shifting away. Guilty. Nervous. Like he knew he'd been caught.

Jack repressed a satisfied smile. "I can understand you might be sympathetic to the Thief's cause, but—"

"I'm *not*," the porter said, his voice like a lash. He looked up then, one eye swollen shut. *The sheriff's work, no doubt.* "I don't have any sympathy at all for the Devil's Thief, and not for the rest of them either. My sister died because she got wrapped up with their kind." He grimaced. "I know they did something to my head. I can't put two thoughts together. When I try, everything gets all confused."

"So the Thief wasn't alone?" Jack asked, glancing up at the sheriff with satisfaction. "Can you describe the others? Even the smallest detail could help."

The man's face crumpled. "She was dressed in men's clothing, like the notices said she would be. And there was another woman too, I think. One wearing spectacles. And a man with them."

It didn't seem possible that a lead this promising might not pan out. "Did he have dark hair, nearly black?"

"No," the man said. "He had orangey hair poking out from beneath his hat and a tattoo of something on his wrist. A snake, maybe. But I can't remember anything else."

Not Darrigan.

Jot Gunter was already stepping toward the bars. "This man . . . did you happen to get a look at the color of his eyes?"

The porter held his head. "They might have been brown . . . or maybe green? Both feel right, but I don't see how that can be."

"Oh, it can be," Gunter said.

Jack turned to Gunter. "You know the man he's describing?"

Gunter looked far too pleased with himself. "I do. He's a maggot that should have been dead years ago—a ranch hand who once worked for me. He's a rather distinctive fella, actually—he has one green eye, one brown. And the mark of the Antistasi on his wrist."

LISA MAXWELL

A WRONG TURN

Once free of the crowd, Esta caught sight of Pickett moving away from the big top. He'd dismounted and was leading his horse toward a corral. After handing off his mount, he headed toward the village of tents. She tossed one more glance over her shoulder, to be sure she wasn't being followed, and then went in that direction as well.

Luckily, most of the other performers were still in the arena. Even without using her affinity, it wasn't difficult to follow Pickett through the grounds. Finally, he stopped at a cluster of smaller tents located at the back edge of the encampment. They were a little more faded and worn than some of the ones closer to the main big top. Outside, a couple of buffalo soldiers sat talking. Pickett greeted the pair before disappearing into his own tent for a few minutes. When he came out again, he was wearing fresh clothes—the jacket a bit more elaborate than the one he'd been wearing before. He joined up with the war veterans, and together they made their way back toward the main tent.

Esta waited a little longer to be sure no one was around before she slipped inside Pickett's tent. The cramped space held only a narrow folding cot for a bed, a small chest, and a table with clothes draped over the chair that stood nearby. It wouldn't take long to find out if the dagger was there. She started with the bed, but nothing was concealed under or within the thin mattress, so she moved on.

Her stomach sank when she saw the lock that secured the lid of the steamer trunk. It seemed too old and too simple to be the kind of lock that protected anything important. If the Pharaoh's Heart wasn't in the tent, it meant that Pickett was either carrying it with him . . . or it could already be gone.

Esta refused to think about that second option. Making short work of the lock, she started going through the contents of the trunk. Mostly it contained some clothing and papers, but the bottom seemed higher than it should have been. When she pushed aside the rest of the contents, she found that the floor of the trunk was actually a thin piece of wood that had been placed like a false bottom. Carefully, she pried it up, and when she saw what waited beneath, she felt the smallest spark of hope. A metal box was hidden there. It was secured with a combination lock—and it was about the same size as the dagger.

Her mouth was dry and her hands were shaking a little, but Esta examined the lock. She could have just taken the whole thing, but Bill Pickett was more likely to notice the missing box faster than he would notice if its contents went missing. It might take a little longer to open the box, but if Pickett didn't realize it was empty, she would have more time to get farther down the road.

Leaning her ear close, Esta began to rotate the tumbler to find the combination. She relaxed into the simple normalcy of the task. The first two numbers were easy enough, and she was well on her way to the third, when she realized that something was happening. Outside the tent, she heard voices. *Just a little farther . . .* and *there.* The final number snapped into place, but a new noise outside the tent stilled her hand. There was nowhere to hide, and without her affinity, Esta had no way to escape without being seen.

"Esta?" a familiar voice whispered from outside, and a second later Jericho Northwood stepped into the tent.

She let out the breath she'd been holding. "What are you doing here?"

North's expression was unreadable as he glanced down at the box she was holding. "Is that the dagger?"

"I don't know. I haven't gotten this open yet," she told him, scowling.

"Well, bring it with you. We have to go," North told her.

"I can't just take it," Esta explained.

"You're a thief, aren't you?" He peeked out from the flap of the tent without looking back at her.

"Yeah," Esta shot back. "But I don't usually tip off my mark by doing something as dumb as leaving a mess like this." She gestured to the contents of the trunk she'd piled on the ground to get to the box.

"You're going to have to," North said flatly, stepping toward her. "We have trouble."

"The marsh—"

Before she could finish the word, North held a finger to his lips. Then she heard it too. *Voices.* Men's voices, right outside the opening of the tent.

"Take the left side there, and I'll take the right," one man said, his voice a rough bark.

"It's some kind of raid," North whispered. "We saw a group of marshals arrive not long after we split up, but we couldn't find you in the crowd."

"They're looking for us," she said, certain.

North frowned like he didn't want to agree. "You saw the headlines, same as I did. But I don't think we should take any chances."

"Where's Maggie?" Esta whispered.

"Safe." He was already pulling his watch from his pocket. Despite the calmness in his voice, Esta didn't miss the way North's hands shook.

"I'll take this one," the first man said, closer now.

North was already extending his other hand to Esta as his thumb moved the dial of the watch. She reached for his hand without argument, but before she could take hold, an explosion sounded nearby. Both of them jumped, North nearly dropping his watch.

Outside the tent, the men started shouting as another explosion echoed. And then they were gone, off to deal with whatever had just happened.

Esta and North exchanged silent, uneasy looks, as though speaking might chase away this bit of luck that had managed to find them. In the distance, an alarm started to sound, the heavy metallic noise calling out its warning. Then the tent flap rustled, and Esta tensed again, but it was Maggie who'd stepped through the split in the canvas, her cheeks flushed pink.

"Mags?" North stepped toward Maggie. "What are you doing here? I told you to wait back outside the gate."

"You're lucky I didn't listen," Maggie said. "If I had, those men—"

Realization struck. "Tell me that explosion wasn't you," Esta said. "Tell me it wasn't an incendiary like back in Texas."

"It was a Flash and Bang," Maggie admitted, not quite meeting her eyes. "What else was I supposed to do? Let them find you in here?"

"You did fine," North told her, the new tremor in his voice betraying the truth. "But Esta's right. They're going to realize that wasn't any regular explosion soon enough. We have to get out of here. *Now.* And we're taking *that* with us." North grabbed the box before Esta could stop him. "We need to be gone before they *really* start looking for us. This way," North said, leading them toward the back side of the fairgrounds—away from the explosion Maggie had caused.

They made it past two more tents and were rounding the edge of a third, nearly to the back border of the encampment, when a woman stepped out, blocking their path. It was the sharpshooter Esta had seen in the show earlier.

"Y'all are an *awful* long way from the big top," the woman said, her voice carrying with it the cadence of the South.

This close, Esta realized that the woman wasn't as old as she'd seemed in the arena—she was maybe twenty, if that. Her plain dark hair was cut into a heavy fringe that framed her plain round face, and her nose was freckled beneath tight-set eyes of a cloudy blue. The sharpshooter wasn't exactly pretty and she wasn't exactly tall, but she certainly moved with an easy confidence that Esta might have admired if she hadn't been standing in the way of their escape.

"We must have taken a wrong turn when we were leaving the show," North said, stepping to shield Maggie.

"A wrong turn isn't all y'all seem to have taken." The woman's eyes were sharp on the box in North's hands. "That there don't look like it belongs to you."

A SERPENT MADE OF BONE

1904—Denver

North moved to block the woman's view of Maggie and Esta as he placed his hand in his pocket, ready to use his watch. It wouldn't take much to avoid this whole situation. A minute or two and they could miss the woman completely and slip out the back of the grounds.

The sharpshooter drew out one of her pistols and leveled it in his direction. "Keep your hands where I can see them. I don't want to shoot you," the woman said when North didn't immediately comply. "But I will. You should know right now that I never miss."

In the distance, an alarm was being sounded again, and North could smell smoke heavy in the air. Reluctantly, he took his hand from his pocket. He hadn't even managed to get the cover of the watch opened, and the body of the timepiece felt suddenly heavy, a useless weight in his pocket.

"Give it here," the woman said, holding out her free hand for the box.

North didn't make any move to comply. If the dagger was inside, he couldn't give it up. They'd already lost the necklace because he'd been stupid enough to fall asleep when he should have been keeping watch. He wouldn't be the cause of another powerful artifact slipping right out of the Antistasi's hands.

The woman raised the gun again, pulling back the hammer this time. "Whatever's in there ain't nothing to die over. Hand it over, and I'll let you go on your way. We can pretend all this never happened."

"You expect me to believe you're going to let us go?" North asked with a huff of disbelief.

"Don't do it, Jericho," Maggie said as she came up next to him. He tried to move back in front of her, but Maggie was too focused on the box in his hand.

"Y'all don't have much of a choice in the matter." Then the sharpshooter shifted the gun, aiming it at Maggie. "Like I said . . . I *never* miss."

North sensed Esta behind him, but he couldn't tell what she was doing—and he didn't dare take his eyes off this new danger to look. All he knew was that she'd been quiet so far, and he hoped she'd *stay* quiet and not do anything stupid. The last thing they needed was for someone to recognize her.

"You can't give it to her, Jericho," Maggie pleaded again. "She's not really going to shoot me."

"You willin' to bet your life on that?" the sharpshooter asked, her voice easy as the summer breeze.

North glanced between the gun and Maggie, who was shaking her head. Silently pleading for him not to hand it over. But he knew that the woman wasn't making an empty threat. "Mags, we don't have a choice."

He sensed Esta moving as he started to slowly offer the box, but he ignored her and Maggie both as he eased the box toward the woman's outstretched hands. The second he saw victory flash in the sharpshooter's eyes, North made his move, flinging the box toward her head with a violent shove. She did exactly what he'd hoped and lowered her gun in an attempt to catch the unwieldy package before it hit her flat in the face.

It gave him the opening he needed to lunge for her, pushing her down and pinning the hand holding the gun to the ground. He ripped the gun out of her hand and tossed it aside. Then he covered her mouth with his hand to keep her from making a racket that might give them away.

"Get the box," he told Maggie, who was already scurrying forward to retrieve it from where it had landed.

Esta went for the gun without having to be told.

Beneath him, the woman fought like a wildcat, and for a second North had the unpleasant realization that he had no idea what to do next. Even if she had cornered them and blocked their escape, he couldn't bring himself to knock out a female. But if he let her up, she was sure to alert the marshals, especially now that he'd attacked her. And he certainly didn't want to take her with them.

"Do you have anything for her?" he asked Maggie. "Quellant or—"

But the woman had gone completely still, her blue eyes wide as she stared at his wrist.

Inwardly, North cursed. He knew exactly what she was seeing. The edge of his shirt cuff had crept up his arm during the struggle, revealing the dark edge of his tattoo. Suddenly he felt a sharp pain in the palm of his hand, and he jerked away, looking at the red welts of teeth marks there with disgust, but the woman didn't scream as he'd expected her to.

"You're Antistasi," the woman said. It wasn't a question, and to North's surprise, it also didn't sound like an accusation. The woman looked up at Maggie. "You're the ones who set off the explosions." Understanding shifted quickly to concern. "You need to get out of here. If they find you—"

"That's what we were trying to do before you got in our way," North said, bristling with unease at the implication that this woman knew what they were.

Another shout sounded nearby. The group of men who were searching the tents were getting closer.

"If you get off me, I can help." The sharpshooter seemed younger and less battle-worn than she had a few minutes before. Not that it made North trust her.

"If I get off you, you're liable to turn on us," North said.

"Why would I do that, when we're on the same side?" Again the girl's eyes tracked to where Maggie and Esta stood behind him, and recognition lit her expression. "I wouldn't do anything that could help them catch the Thief."

"I don't know what you're—"

"Esta Filosik." The sharpshooter was ignoring North and speaking directly to Esta now. "I didn't recognize you at first, but now I ain't sure how I missed it. When the news came from Texas about your death, we all hoped it wasn't true. We knew it *had* to be a mistake, but then no one heard anything after."

There was a question in her statement, but Esta, thankfully, didn't respond. She met the woman's excited chatter with a long, cold silence. She seemed to be measuring the moment, the same as North was.

"You said 'we'?" North asked, still suspicious.

The woman's gaze returned to him. "Y'all didn't really think Mother Ruth's little band of Antistasi were the only ones interested in the Thief, did you? A lot of people paid attention to what happened in St. Louis. You must be Jericho Northwood." The sharpshooter's gaze flicked back to Maggie. "And Margaret Feltz, Ruth's baby sister. I'm surprised she let you go at all."

"I was never her prisoner." Maggie was at his side now.

"But you were most certainly her weapon," the woman said. "Everyone knows that. It was your affinity that kept Ruth in power."

North glanced up at Maggie, but he couldn't tell what was running through her pretty head. Maggie had been loyal to Ruth. She'd believed in her sister's vision and in the serum she created, but when that serum had turned out to be dangerous, when Ruth had refused to be swayed, Maggie had been brave enough to leave everything she'd ever known—and her only family—to do what she believed was right. And, somehow, this woman knew all about it.

"Who *are* you?" North asked, his instincts prickling. She knew too much about them for his liking.

"Cordelia Smith," the woman said. "I work here at the show, but I'm like y'all."

"What's that supposed to mean?" North demanded.

Esta came closer, still holding the pistol. "She's Mageus. I felt her affinity back in the arena."

"I'm *Antistasi*," the sharpshooter corrected. "Check my leg. You'll find your proof of my loyalty there."

"Go on," North said after a moment, refusing to let the woman's flirting throw him off. "Check her."

He kept focused on Cordelia Smith as Maggie pushed the woman's skirts high enough to check her leg.

"Higher," she said with a saucy curve of her lips, never breaking her gaze with North. "My left thigh."

North ignored the way his cheeks felt like embers and forced himself not to so much as blink. Whatever game this woman was playing, he wasn't interested.

"Let her up, Jericho," Maggie said, her voice soft but determined.

Making sure to keep his hold on the woman beneath him, he glanced back to see Maggie crouched over the woman's legs. Cordelia's skirt had been lifted to reveal long, slender legs covered in silk stockings, but above her garters, a tattoo wound itself around her thigh. A snake. Not a living serpent, like his, but an ouroboros just the same, its fanged skull devouring the delicate bones of its tail.

"She's not lying," Maggie said.

The sharpshooter only smiled at him, like a satisfied cat.

"It could still be a trap," North argued. He couldn't help but wonder why Cordelia had chosen to mark herself with death instead of the living serpent that was at the center of all the stories he'd heard as a child.

"Let her up, Jericho. If this were a trap, we'd already be caught," Maggie told him, lowering the woman's skirts. "She's not the one with the gun right now, anyway."

Another shout went up, closer still. The smell of smoke was thicker now, and North wondered what exactly Maggie had set on fire.

"Jericho . . ." Maggie's tone was firm, and she had that determined look she got sometimes when she wasn't going to be swayed. "If she says she can get us out of this mess, I don't think we have much choice but to give her a chance."

North didn't like the idea of letting the woman go, but he knew it was going to happen eventually. It wasn't like he could sit on her indefinitely, even if there weren't marshals searching the grounds. "Fine." Slowly he let go of Cordelia's arms, keeping himself ready for her counterattack, and when it didn't come, he rose from where he'd pinned her to the ground.

As the sharpshooter stood and readjusted her skirts, North backed away, edging closer to Maggie. He was already reaching in his pocket for his watch, in case he needed it, but Cordelia didn't attack or shout for help or try to run. She simply brushed herself off. She was still looking at the box, though, and—Antistasi or not—her expression was transparent enough that North could tell she was too interested for his liking.

"My gun," she said, holding out her hand to Esta.

"You said you could get us out of here," North said, stepping between the two. "You can have it back once we're safe. Until then, if you try anything at all, I won't be the least bit sad if she has to use it."

THE TRAITOR

1902—New York

The Bella Strega was crowded, the air filled with the usual cheap tobacco smoke and the scent of ale. Along with those common scents was the familiar warmth of the old magic. For James Lorcan, that warm energy signaled something more. It was a power that was filled with *possibility*. With the right tools, it could be molded and shaped. With the right choices, it was a power that he could someday *control*.

So far, though, *someday* remained elusive. The Aether moved in strange currents around him, teasing James with the promise of victory but holding it *just* out of reach. It was a curse to sense the future coming but be unable to see it clearly. Still, each day his plans grew more sure and the tenuous grasp he had on the Devil's Own grew stronger. Each day Dolph's people trusted him a little more, *depended* on him a little more, but James knew implicitly that nothing was guaranteed. Not yet. Not until he had the ring and could unlock the power in Dolph's cane. Then, and only then, would his control over the Devil's Own be absolute.

Seated near the rear of the saloon, his back against a wall, James watched his kingdom. He considered his options as he tried to read the message in the Aether.

"You really think the Order has the ring?" Logan asked. He was sitting to James' left, nervously picking at his nails as his eyes shifted uneasily around the room.

Clearly, Logan was still unsure about his new environment, but at least he was smart enough to keep his voice low. He'd have to be a complete fool not to see the way the others glared at him. They saw him as an interloper who'd taken an undeserved spot at James' side. Even now James sensed Werner watching them from across the barroom. He could practically feel Werner's annoyance. It couldn't be helped, though. Logan's ability to track objects would, no doubt, be useful, but James understood that the new boy could be dangerous, too, if his loyalty ever shifted. Better to keep him close, even if it caused those in the Strega to wonder. Better to make him believe that he had a home here, a friend.

"Paul Kelly's contacts at Tammany have all but confirmed it," James told Logan, tracing a circular stain on the table. "Considering that you've found no sign of the artifact in the city, it only makes sense that someone's taken it through the Brink and beyond our reach."

"It could be a setup, though," Logan said, frowning. "Kelly could have taken it just as well as the Order. This might be a trap to get rid of you and take the Strega without a fight."

"I've considered that," James told Logan, trying to keep the irritation out of his voice. Of *course* he'd considered it, but the Aether didn't lie. He had to play Kelly's games . . . at least for now. "No doubt Kelly will play dirty and try to turn the tables on us at some point, but I don't think his belief about what the Order is planning is a complete lie."

"What does the journal say?" Logan whispered.

"It remains as unreadable as ever." But with the new information from Paul Kelly, James found that the change in the journal no longer worried him. Instead, it *emboldened* him. Perhaps the future was no longer his to read, but that only meant that it was changeable. The future, it seemed, was his to *make*.

"There's no doubt that Kelly is up to something," James assured Logan. "Maybe he wants us to take the fall for what happened at Morgan's gala, or maybe this is all a distraction so he can take the ring for himself."

"But you won't let that happen," Logan said with smug satisfaction.

James couldn't help but smile softly at Logan's sureness. He'd been wary about Logan in the beginning, but Logan had proven himself—or at least, he'd proven his loyalty. Ever since his failure to retrieve the ring, he'd been *that* much more committed, and James was more than happy to use that commitment. It was so much easier than doling out threats.

"No," he told Logan. "That isn't going to happen. The stupid dago will get what he has coming to him."

The Aether in the barroom trembled suddenly. In the vibrations, James sensed a warning of approaching danger—but also something that felt like possibility. He barely had time to register the change before the doors of the Strega burst open with a violent crash. Everyone except the most inebriated turned to see what was happening, and the noise of the saloon died to a strangled whisper as they all realized who had entered. The smile that had been playing about James' mouth only broadened.

Viola had come home.

The customers parted as Dolph's assassin stalked toward the back of the barroom to the table where James sat, her dark skirts swishing around her legs and her violet eyes burning with fury. Werner, who'd been behind the bar, started to move, but James stayed him by lifting a hand.

"She's the girl from the gala," Logan said, his voice low and urgent. "The one who was going after the ring. I thought the beast crushed her."

"Such a shame it didn't," James told him, his words dripping with disdain.

He'd known all along that Viola was loyal to Dolph, but her little performance on the bridge a few weeks before had changed things. When she'd attacked James in defense of Esta, she'd made herself his enemy. He'd just as soon see her dead, except every instinct he had screamed that he couldn't take her out of the equation. *Not yet.* Now that she'd appeared in the Strega, the Aether was rearranging itself, suggesting a new way forward that he had not previously considered.

James himself didn't stand to greet the intruder. He simply leaned forward a little in his seat, as Dolph might have done, and tightened his grip on the gorgon-shaped topper of the cane he held. He could almost sense the power trapped within the silver. It was a reminder that everything that surrounded him—the bar, the people, and the power that came with them—was his now. *Not* Dolph Saunders'.

Without slowing her steps, Viola took her knife from her skirts and launched it at him. The air seemed to drain from the room as the blade sailed toward him and landed at the edge of the table, right in the center of the ring he'd been tracing earlier. But James didn't so much as flinch. Viola hadn't come to kill.

Not this time, at least. Not any other, if he had his way.

"Bastardo," Viola growled when she finally stood in front of him. She leaned down, her hands gripping the edge of the table until her knuckles flashed white. The stiletto knife was sunk into the table between them. "What have you done to my blade?"

"Hello, Viola," James said easily. "How delightful to see you've finally returned to us. You've made quite the entrance."

"I'll make more than that in a minute." She bared her teeth at him.

"You seem to be upset," James said, pretending surprise. "Strange, considering that *you're* the one who attacked me on the bridge." His gaze was steady, and he spoke only to her, but he made sure that his voice was loud enough for anyone nearby who happened to be listening to hear. "You remember the bridge, don't you? The day that you allowed Harte Darrigan to escape after he betrayed us all."

"You would have killed Esta," Viola reminded him through clenched teeth.

James leaned forward. "Esta would have deserved it." He did not stop the ice from flowing through his words. "She chose that traitor of a magician over us."

"It doesn't matter anymore." Viola's eyes narrowed. "Esta is gone and Darrigan is dead, Nibsy. As you will be if you don't tell me what you've done to my knife."

"Dead?" James let his mouth curve. "Certainly you've heard the reports by now, Viola. It's been in all the papers—Darrigan and Esta were seen *outside* the city. Alive and well. They betrayed us, and then she left with him *and* the treasures Dolph wanted so badly and you risked so much for." He watched the slight widening of her eyes, the way her breath caught. He enjoyed it, that moment of her distress. "Ah . . . So you *hadn't* heard."

Viola only stared, but James could see the indecision flickering in her expression. "I don't care about Esta or the damned magician. I want to know what you did to my knife."

"I kept it safe, and then I returned it to you," James said. "After I pulled it from my own leg, of course."

"No," Viola said, shaking her head. "You gave me Libitina after you let Mooch be taken by my brother, and like a fool I accepted it without looking for the trick. As though we were friends."

"We *were* friends once," he reminded her, ignoring the rustling unease that had gone through the Strega at her announcement about Mooch. There had been questions about what had happened to the boy ever since he'd helped James by setting one of Tammany's fire stations ablaze. James had pretended as much confusion—and dismay—as anyone, but now he barely cared if the whole barroom knew the truth. Now he cared only for the direction the Aether pushed him . . . *toward* Viola.

"I see exactly what your friendship is worth," Viola sneered. "Tell me, Nibsy, have you even tried to free Mooch from the Tombs?"

James only stared at her, feeling the world around him rearrange itself. Trying to discern the correct path, the correct words. "You can't really believe I would leave one of our own? I'm doing all I can. Mooch is a *friend.*"

The barroom eased back into its rhythm, apparently pleased enough with that answer.

"You were a friend to Dolph as well," Viola charged. "Now here you sit, in *his* seat, presiding over *his* home. Tell me, Nibsy, what have you done to avenge his murder?"

"What would you have me do?" he asked, pretending innocence. "You know the position we're all in now. You know how dangerous everything is because of *your* failure to retrieve the Book. You were the one who handed it to Darrigan, along with the artifacts, if I remember correctly. Not me."

Viola laughed, an ugly, hollow sound that had the people closest to them shuffling nervously back. "You were always slippery as a snake," she told him, her voice dangerous now. "Dolph trusted you, and this is how you repay him?"

"At least I'm here." James didn't so much as blink. "When the Bowery went mad, when Tammany's patrols started burning the homes of the innocent, what did *you* do? You *disappeared*." He paused then, because he knew that those around him were listening. "How is your brother doing, Viola? There are plenty here who've been marked by Kelly's men. I'm sure they'd like to know what it's like living under his protection."

"Perhaps you should tell them yourself," she huffed. "After all, you dined with him earlier, didn't you?"

"Business," James said with a cold smile. "I keep my friends close and my enemies closer, the same as Dolph did. All for the Devil's Own, Viola. *All* for the Devil's Own—"

He felt the sharpness of pain in his chest, but it was light enough that he knew she was only toying with him. If she'd wanted him dead, she could have killed him three times over by now. But then, if she'd wanted him dead, he would have known.

"Careful, Viola. My boys have orders should anything happen to me." The pain intensified so that his voice became strained. *Good. Let her dig her own grave.* "It would be a shame if something happened to your dear mother. Pasqualina, I believe her name is? She came by your brother's cafe after you left today. A lovely woman."

"My brother would kill you before her blood hit the ground," Viola snarled, but the threat had worked. The pain in his chest eased. "Tell me what you did to my knife," she demanded. "Why can't I heal the cut it made when you are just fine?" She gestured to him.

"You call this *fine*?" James asked, pretending to be more shocked than he was. He made a show of pulling himself to his feet, of leaning against the cane. Viola was a small woman, and even hunched against the cane, he was taller. "Because of what you did, I'll never walk on my own again."

"I could have killed you instead," Viola told him. "I should have."

"But you didn't *want* to," James told her, letting the sheer irony of it hang in the air between them. "I wonder why that is, Viola. Unless you knew even then, on the bridge, that I was right about Darrigan, and right about everything else as well."

Viola shook her head. But James knew that she could not dismiss the words that were already working into her mind, worming their way into her sureness. "Tell me what you did to Libitina. Why won't the wound heal?"

James could see the frantic fear in her eyes and he *savored* it. "You think I had something to do with *that*?"

"Who else?" she demanded.

"Have I had a hand in the others you've killed?" he asked. "You were Dolph's assassin, weren't you? How many did you use your blade on? How many have died by your hand, Viola?"

Her mouth was drawn tight, and James could see the guilt in her eyes, the *shame* of what she believed herself to be. It was a weakness that she hadn't yet accepted the choices she'd made or the power she held. It was a weakness that she still foolishly worried about a god who would never answer her cries. It was also a vulnerability that he could exploit.

"Who was it that you wanted dead this time?" James pressed, considering the question seriously for himself. Feeling the Aether bunch and shift. "Why try to save this poor soul now?"

Viola lifted her chin, her eyes narrowing. "It's none of your concern who I save."

James didn't agree. To his estimation, and based upon the way the Aether moved, the person Viola wanted to save had *everything* to do with him. The vibrations around him were moving in harmony now, urging him onward. *This* was what he needed—Viola's involvement *and* the involvement of the person she wanted to save.

Jianyu. The moment the name came to his mind, James knew he was right. Now he understood. He needed their affinities and their commitment to getting the ring. Could *use* them.

James had no idea what had caused Viola to cut Jianyu with her knife, but it was clear they were now aligned. He needed them both. Or rather, his plan did. But he couldn't make saving Jianyu too easy for her. *No.* That would raise her suspicions. Viola needed to hate him, and so James would gladly give her reason to. He would use that hatred to his own benefit, and then he would crush her and Jianyu both and take the victory that should have always been his.

A NEW ALLIANCE

1902—New York

Viola drew herself upright, refusing to let Nibsy see the way his words had affected her. "Tell me what you did to my knife, Nibsy." She let her affinity unfurl again, a small jolt this time. A clear reminder of what she could do. And what she was willing to risk.

"Do you truly not know?" Nibsy said. It looked as though he was trying to laugh, but all that came out was a weak cough. "Your knife. Libitina, you call it. It's not some random blade. It's the same as this cane, the same as any number of items floating through this city—it's been *changed* by magic. It's not natural magic, of course, but that sort of thing never really bothered Dolph, did it?" He eyed Viola, daring her to disagree.

But Viola couldn't. She knew about the cane, about what power it had over the marks they all wore when Dolph wielded it, and thanks to Nibsy, now she understood how the cane had been made. How Dolph had *taken* from Leena, had made an unwilling sacrifice of her power.

"I know this already," she said. "But you haven't explained why I can't heal the cut it made." She tried not to dwell too much on the fact that her knife had an origin like Dolph's cane.

"Viola . . ." Nibsy shook his head as though disappointed in her. "Dolph gave you a blade that could help you to kill because he knew you were too . . ." He waved a hand. "Let's be frank. Dolph knew you were too *weak* to use your affinity as it was meant to be used, and so he gave you the knife instead. Have you never wondered why your blade is so deadly? *Why you never miss?* It's ritual magic, Viola, crafted to work with what you *are*. It calls to blood, just as your magic does. If you intended to kill someone with that blade, they'll die. If someone is dying from your blade, that's not something I did. That, my old friend, is all your *own* doing. And it *always* has been."

Viola watched numbly as Nibsy took the knife from the tabletop in front of him. It was sunk inches deep, like the table was made of bread instead of wood. Then he placed it flat in front of him, the handle facing Viola.

At first all she could do was stare at it.

She'd known. *Of course* she'd known that the blade wasn't normal. It had a certain weight that seemed far heavier than its steel and an ability to do what no other could. But Viola had convinced herself that the lives Libitina took had nothing to do with her affinity. She'd believed that she could separate herself—what she was—from the things she did. As though that made any difference at all.

She'd been lying to herself. Willfully blind. *Because this is what I am. What I've always been.* Viola stared at Libitina, perhaps seeing it truly for the first time. Even now, even accepting what the knife was, her hands ached to hold the comforting weight once more.

"Nothing you can do with your affinity will save the person you've tried to kill, Viola." Nibsy gave her a rueful look. "False magic can only be broken by false magic. You know that."

"Tell me how to fix this." It took all of her effort to keep her voice from shaking. She glanced up from the blade, looking at him with fire in her eyes.

Nibsy's expression was unreadable. "Are we friends again, Viola? Because from your little display, I would have said you still consider me an enemy." He paused, letting the challenge filter through the nearly silent room. "I find that I have *very* few reasons to help an enemy."

Viola felt her temper spike. He was toying with her. Cat and mouse in front of an audience thirsty for blood—for *her* blood. But she would not give him the satisfaction. In the end, she would be the one to kill the snake.

She swiped the knife from the table and had it at Nibsy's throat before he could blink. Around her, the room contracted, and she sensed the boys she'd once seen as allies coming for her.

"Call them off, Nibsy." She nudged the point of the blade against his delicate skin. "You know what this can do, and I find that I have very few reasons to keep you alive if you won't help me. How do I fix this? I know you have the answer."

Nibsy raised his hand to stay the Devil's Own, but his gaze never left hers. "Dolph was hardly a fool," he told her, his eyes glinting over the rims of his lenses. "He would never have given you a weapon that strong unless he had some assurance that he could protect himself should you ever turn on him. Dolph knew how to reverse the effects of the knife," Nibsy said. "I'm sure he left instructions behind, along with the rest of his books and his things. You've seen for yourself how carefully he recorded the details of his work. . . ."

Viola ignored the amusement in Nibsy's tone as she thought of the sheet of paper he'd given to her just a few weeks before. A trick wrapped up in the truth. Viola had read over those notes countless times since then, hoping that she could find some sign that Dolph Saunders had not betrayed the one person he loved more than any other for something as small and as petty as power.

"You will give them to me now." Viola again increased the pressure of the knife against his throat. "Or I will take them myself."

Nibsy only laughed. Then he lowered his voice, so only the two of them could hear. "You can't fight them all, you know. Kill me if you must. Make me into a martyr." Nibsy's eyes shone with satisfaction. "You'll never make it out of this room. They're mine now, Viola. The Devil's Own, the Strega, and everything Dolph built. So have a care."

Her chest ached with the truth of his words. If she killed him, the people surrounding them in the barroom would not let her escape, and she could not kill them all—*would not* kill them all, even if she could. They were no more than pawns in Nibsy's game, the same as herself. But games were not something Viola had time for. Not when Jianyu was still so close to death. She'd done what she could, but his wound would continue to bleed. Unless she solved the problem, his death would be on her soul as well.

"Besides," Nibsy told her, "it's not only the instructions you need, Viola. Even if you killed me, even if you managed to find Dolph's notes and escape with your life, you'll need something more to reverse the effects of your knife." He took the blade of Libitina between his fingers delicately and moved it away from his own throat. "You need an object that contains false magic as powerful as that in your knife. A seal, perhaps, like the one we took from the Metropolitan, might do the trick. It's a pity it was lost that night, or you might already have the answer you need." He looked up at her over the rims of his spectacles. "It *was* lost?"

"Yes," Viola lied, her instincts screaming. "Along with the rest."

"Pity." He paused, the hesitation making her temper start to crack. "There's one place, of course, one organization rather, that might have another such piece."

"You mean the Order." She shook her head. "We took their treasures already. I watched the building burn myself."

"True, Khafre Hall burned, but you can't really imagine that the Order lost everything? After all, the Mysterium was far below ground level and well protected, physically and magically."

Viola disagreed. After all, she'd seen the walls of Khafre Hall crumble. She'd barely escaped them herself. If there was anything left, certainly it had been lost in the collapse.

"The Order still continues to persist," Nibsy pressed. "You were at their gala, so you know that they aren't completely powerless, and the entire city knows that their plans for the Conclave continue. That doesn't sound like an organization that has lost everything." He paused, picking at some dirt beneath his nails, but Viola knew he was baiting her. "I hear they have plans for a new headquarters. They'll be moving what was left of Khafre Hall there soon."

She lowered her knife, her mind spinning with the implications. "Why are you telling me this?"

Nibsy held her gaze. "Because the Order is still a threat."

"So am I," she growled, knowing there was something more Nibsy wasn't saying, some trick or trap he was setting for her.

"I've always appreciated that, Viola. Even if the rest of them didn't." She huffed her disbelief.

"You don't think I understand?" Nibsy asked, far too innocently. "I know how they looked at you, what they must have thought was between you and Dolph—"

"Nothing was between us but friendship," she said.

"As you insist . . ." Nibsy merely shrugged. "You think I don't know what it's like to have the Devil's Own suspect that you don't *truly* belong." He adjusted his grip on the cane—*on Dolph's cane.* "I know all too well. I can only imagine what it must be like for you now, though, to be under the thumb of your brother, a man who could not see your promise if it bit him on the nose. It doesn't have to be this way, Viola."

She was shaking her head, denying everything he said even as his words wrapped around her mind. "You know nothing."

"I know that your brother is planning on attacking the Order," Nibsy said, and when Viola couldn't stop her eyes from widening, his mouth twitched. "So Paul hasn't told you."

Of course he hadn't told her. Paolo never told Viola anything but what he wanted for dinner or how much of an embarrassment she was to him and to their family.

"Why would he do something so stupid?" she asked, trying to dismiss this tale even as her instincts jangled that it smacked of the truth. Paul might have saved her from the gala, but Viola had suspected that her brother still didn't trust her. Now she knew for sure.

"Jack Grew tried to kill him," Nibsy said with a shrug. "That alone makes it personal. But your brother's not a stupid man, Viola. Right now he enjoys the protection of Tammany, but he knows how inhospitable the city could become for him and his Five Pointers if the Order is able to rebuild their power. If the Order takes power away from Tammany, he would be at risk. He's asked me to help him destroy them."

"What should I care if he goes after the Order? Why should you?" Viola asked. She couldn't be drawn into his games. Not when she couldn't trust a word he said. "If Paolo wants to go after rich men, he's un idiota. One who will deserve whatever he gets."

"I have to admit, it wouldn't break my heart if the Order took care of Paul Kelly," Nibsy said. "But I'm afraid I can't stand by and not get involved. Not when your brother believes that the Order retrieved the ring at the gala."

"You don't mean . . ." She frowned. "Paul, he doesn't have it?" She'd assumed her brother or one of his men had taken it when the great stone beast had nearly killed her. Everything she'd done—every order she'd followed and meal she cooked for him—was because she'd been trying to figure out what Paul had done with the ring. But if Nibsy was to be believed, it had been for nothing.

"No," Nibsy said. "I don't believe he does."

Viola's thoughts were swirling, careening. "What do you want from me, Nibsy?" she asked, barely leashing her impatience.

"I want you to help me get the ring back," Nibsy said. "I don't trust Kelly to simply hand it over, as he's promised. I expect that he'll try to get rid of me instead. If he does, what will happen to the Strega? What will happen to the Devil's Own?"

Viola knew exactly what would happen—her brother would take everything Dolph Saunders had built. He would bend the Devil's Own until they broke, like he did to everything he touched.

"What do you think I can do?" Viola asked, wary.

"You can give me information," Nibsy told her. "I need to know what he's planning and what he's withholding. You can help me protect the Devil's Own from your brother's control."

Viola considered his proposal.

"I need your help, Viola," Nibsy said, looking somehow younger than he had a few minutes ago. Suddenly he wasn't the conniving snake that had greeted her but the boy she'd once known. "I know what you think of me. I know you don't trust my motives, but the Order cannot be allowed to keep the artifact. And your brother must not get the ring instead. An item like that holds power, even for Sundren. Think of what he would do with it."

It was far too easy to picture it. Even false magic in Paul's hands would be a nightmare, for Viola and for the entire city. "You are asking me to betray my family—my own *blood*."

"What has your blood ever done for you?" Nibsy asked. "They tossed you out and treated you like some scullery maid when you're more powerful by far. Because they have never understood you, and they will never accept you. Not like we do. Come back to the Devil's Own, Viola. If you're willing to put our past differences aside and start anew, we can end the Order once and for all. We can hit them now, before they're able to regroup for their Conclave. We can retrieve the artifact, like Dolph wanted us to, and in the process, you can save whoever it is you've hurt this time. Agree to pledge yourself to the Devil's Own once again, and I will hand over Dolph's notes. Help me, and I will help you as well."

Nibsy extended his hand across the table, but Viola did not take it. Nibsy Lorcan was a rat, and she'd be a fool to trust him. And yet, what was her alternative? She couldn't attack the Order alone, and she would never depend upon Paul to help her.

Viola did not sheath her knife as she considered the offer.

"We can begin to put Darrigan's betrayal to rights," Nibsy urged, his hand still extended. "We can avenge Dolph as well by driving Paul Kelly and his Five Pointers from the Bowery. I plan to go after the ring either way, but it would be easier together. If we were on the same side, we would have a real chance." He paused, a dramatic beat during which the entire room seemed to hold its collective breath. "It's what Dolph would have wanted."

It *was* what Dolph would have wanted, but Viola knew that Nibsy's words were all tricks and lies. She would be a fool to believe them without question. If she agreed to betray her brother, Nibsy would surely turn on her, like a viper turns to attack an intruder in its den. She *knew* that. But Jianyu's life was in the balance, the ring was within reach, and her teeth were every bit as sharp as Nibsy Lorcan's. If she was cunning, she would not have to battle Nibsy alone.

THE SUMMONS

1902—New York

Jack Grew strode into his uncle's mansion feeling every minute of sleep he'd lost since the gala. The ring had been there in the ballroom the night of the gala. He'd seen it sparkling on Evelyn's finger as she primped and teased him before the event. It had been there when she died as well, crushed beneath the great beast, and then . . . it was gone. In the weeks that had passed, there had been no sign of the artifact, no sign of the girl in the purple satin or what had become of her. And with Tammany still protecting Paul Kelly, Jack had no way to get to either of them. But the truth was clear—

He would find them *and* the ring, and when he did, he would make them all pay.

For now, though, Jack had other worries. He still wasn't sure why he'd been summoned to his uncle's home without warning or explanation. The Order had been quiet, and its members had been guarded after the gala. The event had been a success, of course, even with the mishap at the end. The papers had all marveled at the demonstrations, as Jack's aunt Fanny had hoped they would when the blasted event was arranged.

And yet, after all of the press they'd received, there had been only silence on the part of the Order. No one from the Inner Circle had congratulated Jack on his victory. No one had thanked him for the service he'd provided. Especially not his uncle. It was strange, then, for Jack to suddenly find himself so abruptly summoned. And so urgently.

The messenger had tracked him down earlier that morning. Jack had been on his way out and had planned to spend the day in his warehouse by the docks, trying to make sense of the pile of metal that had once been his machine. He was beginning to understand why it hadn't worked before. The stones he'd been using to focus the machine's power—expensive and precious as they might have been—weren't strong enough. He needed a stone imbued with a different type of power—a stone like the one in the ring.

The Delphi's Tear might have evaded him for now, but it was only a matter of time, Jack reasoned, before the artifact revealed itself to him. Or before the Book showed him another way.

Jack handed his hat to the maid who answered the door. He barely spared her a glance as he brushed past, ignoring the maid's sputtering protests, and made his own way back into the mansion, where his uncle's office lay in burnished silence.

If he'd expected a quiet family meeting, Jack was immediately disabused of that notion the second he turned into the west hall and heard low voices coming from Morgan's office. His steps faltered a little.

Jack allowed his hand to dip into his jacket pocket so that he could caress the cracked and worn leather of the Book's cover. It was a reminder to himself that he would ultimately prevail. Then Jack took one of the morphine cubes from the vial he always carried and let the bitterness of the drug drain away the slight pounding behind his eyes.

In the office, Jack found three men: his uncle, the High Princept, and another older man he didn't recognize. Each was richer and more pointless than the last. They stopped their conversation when he entered. When the maid came stumbling in directly behind Jack, apologizing and trying to explain how she had tried to stop him, Morgan himself glowered so darkly that Jack knew the girl would be working her fingers raw in the laundry before the end of the day.

"Your messenger told me that you required my presence," Jack said, ignoring the drama his unexpected entrance had created. "He said it was urgent and insisted that I come immediately, despite my being otherwise occupied."

Morgan harrumphed, his bulbous nose twitching with disdain. "Drinking and whoring does not constitute an occupation."

Jack fought the urge to sneer at his uncle. So this wasn't to be a commendation after all. He hadn't supposed it would be, but Morgan's words galled him nonetheless.

Still, he would not allow these men to goad him. "I would have thought I'd more than demonstrated my ability to *occupy* myself with something other than wine and women, Uncle," he said dryly.

"You did indeed." The High Princept stepped forward, placing himself between Morgan and Jack to defuse the situation. "It was an impressive display to be sure, my boy. Quite impressive."

"Except for certain complications," Morgan grumbled.

"Complications?" Jack lifted a single brow as he tried to read the tenor of the room. "It's true that the ending was somewhat . . . disorderly, but I'm sure you have ample funds to repair the damage to the ballroom. I imagine Aunt Fanny is beside herself, considering the opportunity she now has—"

"You killed a girl," Morgan said, throwing the fact like a gauntlet at his feet.

"She was a chorus girl. A common harlot," Jack told them, brushing away the issue.

"That may be, but Evelyn DeMure was a well-known performer in the city—unfortunately, one the public seems to have a certain amount of sympathy for," the Princept said. "There are a great many who are outraged by her death and who blame the Order."

"They're all fools, then. She was nothing but a maggot, one who would have used her feral powers to destroy the Order," Jack reminded them. "She was a siren, a threat. Now she is not."

"Have you no shame?" his uncle demanded.

"Why should I be ashamed when I am guilty of nothing?" Jack asked, his temper flaring. "Have I been charged with anything? *No.* The girl's death was deemed an accident."

"But the question remains—what kind of accident was it?" the Princept wondered.

Jack's instincts suddenly prickled. "I fail to understand your meaning."

"When did you learn that the girl had possession of the Delphi's Tear?" the High Princept asked, his gaze steady. Deadly calm.

Realization suddenly hit. They knew. Which meant that it wasn't Kelly's girl, nor Kelly himself, who'd managed to slip away with the ring. These men had it. The Delphi's Tear was back in the hands of the Order.

"I'm not certain what you mean," Jack hedged, weighing the moment—and his options—carefully.

"Let's cut through the bullshit," Morgan said, his mouth drawn into a flat, uncompromising line. "You're a constant disappointment, but despite what others have said, you're not an idiot. I don't give a fig about what the public thinks about the death of some showgirl, but I do care about loyalty, boy. And you've displayed an appalling lack of it. At some point, you knew that DeMure had one of the Order's most prized possessions, and still you kept that information from us."

"The question we've been asking ourselves is *when* you knew," the Princept said, his wizened old face not betraying any emotion.

"You think I *hid* this from you—that I was trying to take the artifact for my own?" Jack asked, changing tactics by pretending to be shocked.

"Why else keep it a secret?" Morgan blustered. "Why not tell the Inner Circle immediately, so the situation could be dealt with quickly and quietly—and most importantly, out of the public's view."

"Think carefully about your answer, boy," the Princept warned. "Your membership with our hallowed organization depends upon it."

His membership? Jack wanted to laugh in their faces. He wanted to *dare* them to revoke his membership, when he alone held the key to their future, but he knew that it would be a mistake. Without access to the Order, without the benefit of their trust, he might never be able to retrieve the ring from them. Certainly, there was no sense in making his task any more difficult.

"I admit that I had heard a rumor Evelyn had a ring resembling one of the lost artifacts," he started, choosing his words, careful to sound contrite and nervous. "But I didn't know for sure."

"You should have told us immediately," Morgan said.

"You of all people should understand my hesitance, Uncle." Jack bowed his head and tried to hide his fury behind a mask of remorse and humility. "After the mistakes I made in the past? I knew I couldn't afford another. I knew that retrieving one of the lost artifacts would be only one step toward atoning, but I was reluctant to give you false hope. I certainly never intended to keep the ring for my own," he lied. "Had I retrieved it, I would have given it to the Order immediately."

"How are we to believe you?" Morgan asked.

"Believe whatever you will," Jack told them, clenching his teeth to keep his anger from showing. "Revealing Evelyn's duplicity was to be a victory, but not for myself. It was to be a gift to the Inner Circle, to the Order itself, a grand moment when a maggot who had fooled so many would finally be held accountable for her crimes publicly, exposed for all the city—and the world—to see. After all, the gala was not for my benefit alone. Was it not meant to show the entire city that the Order had not been weakened by the fires of Khafre Hall? Apprehending Evelyn DeMure would have helped with that." Jack drew himself up, squared his shoulders. "But then Paul Kelly ruined everything. By the time I got to Evelyn, she was dead, and there was no sign of the ring."

"Still you didn't tell us, even after?" the Princept pressed.

"I didn't know for sure that she'd ever actually had it," Jack lied. "I thought that my instincts had proven false, and I was grateful that I hadn't exposed my mistakes once again." He glanced up, pretending an epiphany. "But how did you know? Unless—*did* she have it? Is the artifact back in the Order's possession once more?"

"It is," the Princept boasted, unable to hide his satisfaction.

"I'm glad to hear that," Jack said. It wasn't a complete lie. Now that he knew for sure where the Delphi's Tear was, he could set his sights on obtaining it. "I'm only happy to have helped, however small a role I might have played."

Morgan was clearly frustrated. "Your *role* in this could have ruined everything. Do you know what would have happened if the ring had fallen into the wrong hands?"

"But it didn't," Jack pressed, tired of being chastised like some misbehaving schoolboy. "The Order retrieved it, as I'd hoped they would."

"Enough." The Princept raised his hand to silence them both. "The Order currently stands at a great precipice," he said. "However, now that we have one of the lost artifacts back in our possession, our position is not quite so dire as it once was."

"Our situation is *still* tenuous," Morgan argued. "The Conclave at the end of the year was supposed to demonstrate our strengths—to the other Brotherhoods, to the entire country. The Brink was to be reconsecrated. *Expanded.* Instead, we've found ourselves far behind in our preparations. We may have retrieved the ring, but the rest of our most important artifacts remain missing. Khafre Hall still lies in ashes."

"Your new headquarters will make everyone forget that Khafre Hall ever burned," the third man said, breaking his silence. He had the kind of satisfied confidence that made Jack's teeth hurt.

"I don't believe we've been introduced," Jack said dully. "You are?"

"Harry Black." The man didn't bother to extend his hand.

Jack glanced at Morgan, wondering if he was supposed to know who this was. Wondering, suddenly, why this stranger was even here.

"Black is president of the Fuller Company," the Princept explained. "He's one of our newer initiates."

"I was at the gala, and I was impressed with what I saw," Black said, eyeing Jack. "*Very* impressed."

"He's offered the Order the top floors of his company's newest building for our headquarters," the Princept said, his mustache twitching.

"Which building is that?" Jack asked, though he had a feeling he already knew.

"The skyscraper being built on Fifth Avenue, across from Madison Square Park," Black said.

"The one that people have been taking bets on to see how far the debris will fall when it topples?" Jack said, incredulous. "What have the papers taken to calling it? The Flatiron?"

Black glared at him. "Only uneducated fools believe that the structure won't stand for an eternity. Steel construction is the future. With it, the city can grow to untold heights. The new building will be one of the tallest in the city when it's complete in a few weeks. Where better to house the Order? 'As above, so below,' after all."

"Certainly this won't be permanent. Khafre Hall will be rebuilt," Jack said. How could it not be? The old structure had been constructed on a site selected for its location over the confluence of two subterranean rivers. It was believed to be a powerful locus for elemental energy, water and earth coming together as they did. "The location alone—"

Morgan closed a ledger that had been open on his desk, closing the topic of conversation as well. "We didn't call you here today to hear your opinions. The matter has already been decided."

"Perhaps the location of Khafre Hall was important in the past," the Princept explained, "but the new headquarters has certain advantages that Khafre Hall does not." He glanced at Black.

"The building itself has been designed with principles of the occult arts in mind: the sacred triangle, the alignment of its sides with the sigil in the park and with the path of the stars." Black was clearly proud of this particular fact. "Even the height of the building will serve as a testament to the Order's power. Khafre Hall was the past—and a glorious past it was—but the new headquarters will serve the Order long into the future."

"We'll move into the building in a matter of weeks," the Princept explained. "During that time, the artifact will be installed in the new Mysterium, along with the rest of what was left from Khafre Hall. The building will be dedicated and warded with protections on the city's solstice. Which is why we asked you here today."

"This is a terrible idea," Morgan muttered.

"The boy has answered our questions," the Princept said, turning to Morgan. "I'm more than satisfied, and you know we could use his talent."

"I'd be happy to serve you and the Order in any way I can," Jack said, ignoring his uncle, who had clearly been overruled. He tried to hide his amusement at the situation, forced himself to appear humble and gracious.

"For now, the question of your membership to the Order will be set aside," the Princept said. "As I imagine you are aware, we had planned to use occasion of the Conclave to bolster the power of the Brink, as we must every century to maintain its power. But this centennial was to be different. This year, we were to do more than simply reconsecrate. We had planned to use the occasion of the Conclave to *build* on the work of those who came before us."

"The rumors were true, then?" Jack asked, knowing already that they were. It was no secret that the Inner Circle believed that the Brink could be made stronger, wider, but he hadn't known for sure that they'd managed it. "You found a way to expand the Brink?"

The High Princept nodded, a satisfied glimmer in his eyes. "Before the events of Khafre Hall, we'd already managed to bolster the power of the artifacts in preparation. With all five stones, we could have expanded the Brink's power and pushed out its reach. Ellis Island and the maggots who evade our inspectors there would no longer have been a problem. But now, with only one artifact in our possession, we must do what we can simply to *preserve* the Brink. Everything depends upon it."

"*Can* you perform the reconsecration ritual with a single stone?" Jack wondered.

"Thanks to the work we did before they were stolen, we believe we can," the Princept said. "But you can see why it is more essential than ever to protect that artifact at all costs. After your display at the gala, we believe you can be of help. It is essential that our new headquarters is impervious to any attack. If you're able to bring your considerable talents to aid us in the coming weeks, I believe we can put this whole unfortunate question of loyalty to rest. In fact, if all goes well, there will be a place for you in the Inner Circle."

"But if you screw this up," his uncle said, glaring. "If you think to betray our trust again—"

"You'll find no fault in my commitment to our cause," Jack told them with a small bow. "I will do all I can to ensure the safety of the artifact and our new headquarters."

They were the right words. The Princept's eyes glimmered with satisfaction.

By the time the three old goats finally dismissed him, the morphine had all but worn off. Jack could feel the ache building behind his eyes again, but he barely noticed. When he'd entered his uncle's mansion, he'd worried he might never find the ring, but he'd left with the Order's hopes—perhaps its very future—sitting in the palm of his hand. And if all went well, soon the artifact would be his.

LISA MAXWELL

BLOOD WILL TELL

1904—San Francisco

Maybe Harte Darrigan should have felt some satisfaction as he watched Samuel Lowe's expression shift from anger to confusion and then to disbelief. Instead, he felt nothing at all.

"Benedict?" the older man said, lowering his gun.

Harte had imagined this moment often enough—when he was a homeless urchin, struggling to survive alone in the New York streets, and later when he was a successful headliner on one of the biggest stages in the city. Even with the guilt he'd carried, Harte had wondered what it would be like to look his father in the eye and force the man to acknowledge him. He had imagined his old man discovering that Harte had survived—had *thrived*—without him. *In spite* of him.

"I don't go by that name anymore." Harte continued to glare at the man who had fathered him, but he felt only a dull emptiness where triumph should have been.

Samuel Lowe never should have been able to make it back to California, but he had. Worse, the years seemed to have been kind to him. True, his father had more gray at his temples, and lines now carved deep valleys across his forehead, but he looked healthier than Harte had ever seen him. From the clothes his father wore, he certainly wasn't destitute. On the smallest finger of his right hand, a gold ring glinted in the streetlight, yet another testament to his father's elevated station in life. While Harte had lived with the ever-present guilt of what he'd done to his mother, he'd never spared a second thought for his father. He'd assumed that Samuel Lowe would die drunk in a ditch somewhere. Harte had never considered that his father might have gone on to live his life without consequences.

The woman still standing in the doorway said something in a language that Harte could not understand—German, perhaps—but she no longer interested him. He took a step toward his father. He didn't care what Seshat might do to this man. Harte would finish what he'd started years before. But the movement of a small boy peeking out from behind his father's coat stopped him dead.

The child was dressed neatly in short pants with a well-fitting brown jacket over a clean white shirt. His dark-blond hair framed a round face, and there was a small scar that cut across the corner of his upper lip, but he had the same gray eyes Harte saw every time he looked in the mirror. Eyes he'd inherited from his father.

Harte wasn't sure how old the boy was—maybe seven? Perhaps a little younger?

His father—*their father*—stepped in front of the child, blocking him from Harte's view before he could decide. He bent down and said something close to the child's ear that Harte couldn't hear, then lifted his hand. Harte instinctively tensed, his muscles ready to protect the child—to protect *his brother*. But before Harte could take a step, his father's palm simply patted the boy on the back and pushed him along.

The child darted past Harte, toward the woman still waiting at the door behind him, but he pulled up short before he reached her. He turned back to Harte and examined him once more with a serious look on his face.

"Sammie," Harte's father warned. He said something in German—a language that Harte had never before heard his father use—that made the boy frown.

The sternness in Samuel Lowe's voice was like a slap to the face, bringing Harte back to himself, and the boy's eyes widened before he finally disappeared into the warmly lit interior of the home. The woman stared at Harte a beat longer with suspicion—and a warning—in her eyes. *A mother's eyes.* She likely wasn't Maria Lowe, then.

Whoever she was, the woman knew something about the Dragon's Eye, which meant that Harte's father probably also knew about the artifact. If that was the case—especially if Samuel Lowe had the Dragon's Eye—it would be much more difficult to get it back than Harte had anticipated.

Harte felt Seshat's pleasure at this discovery. *You could have your victory, and instead you hold back,* she whispered. *You could have everything you desire, but you will never defeat me. Your softness will be your undoing.* In the distant recesses of his mind, he sensed her satisfied amusement, but Harte shoved Seshat's taunting aside.

His father was saying something to the woman in short, clipped tones, and her mouth curved downward as she continued to examine Harte. She clearly wasn't happy, but eventually she pulled the door shut, closing off the light that had been spilling into the alley and leaving Harte alone with a ghost from his past.

"How are you even here?" his father demanded, turning on him. The gun wasn't raised, but it was still in his hand.

Harte didn't answer, and he refused to let any emotion show.

"You're supposed to be dead," his father said.

"I'd hoped the same about you," Harte said, keeping his tone bland.

His father's face creased with irritation, and Harte didn't miss the way his fist clenched. "You dare come here to my home and disrespect me after what you—" The sound of shouting nearby had Samuel Lowe pausing. His gaze slid beyond Harte, to the mouth of the alley. "It's the Committee's watchman. I won't let you ruin me again. You will go," his father ordered, a command that brought Harte back to his childhood.

"I'm afraid you lost the right to make demands of me a long time ago," Harte said, failing to keep his voice measured as he crossed his arms over his chest.

His father frowned, his nostrils flaring slightly in a strangely familiar sign of agitation. But there was something else in Samuel Lowe's eyes—something that looked gratifyingly like fear.

Harte allowed the corner of his mouth to curve. "I'm not going anywhere until I get what I—"

His father held up a hand to silence Harte when another shout sounded nearby. "We can't stay here arguing in the streets."

"I don't want to stay here at all," Harte told him, ignoring his own worry. He couldn't be caught there, but neither could he leave without the Dragon's Eye. "I'm perfectly happy to go—as soon as I get what I've come for."

"I don't owe you *anything*," his father sneered. "Not my time, not my wealth."

"I don't want either of those things," Harte told him, and he found that it was true. Maybe as a boy, he'd wished for his father's attention, but now Samuel Lowe was just a man like any other. A stranger. "Two years ago, I sent a package to Maria Lowe. Your mother. I've come to retrieve it."

Samuel Lowe's expression shuttered. "My mother is dead," he said flatly and without any emotion at all.

Harte frowned. "Her death doesn't change anything," he said. "I need the item I sent her—a headpiece made of gold that holds an amber stone."

"I don't know what you're talking about." His father feigned confusion, but Harte could tell he was lying. Samuel Lowe knew the Dragon's Eye. It was there, clear in the panic that colored his expression.

"That would be a problem for you," Harte told him. "There are men who want the crown, and when they come for it, you won't be able to protect yourself or the son you've claimed. Better you give it to me now, so I can draw them away. The piece isn't worth what keeping it will cost you."

"I think I'll take my chances," Samuel Lowe said, lifting his chin.

"I don't think you understand," Harte told him. "You don't have a choice. You can either give me what I've come for, or I will destroy this new life you've built for yourself piece by piece. I will destroy you, too, just as you destroyed my mother."

"And what about my son?" Samuel Lowe asked. "Would you leave him destitute and fatherless? Unprotected?"

Harte hesitated, thinking of the boy with the gray eyes so like his own, and that hesitation was enough.

Samuel Lowe's mouth twisted mockingly. "No . . . You won't hurt him," he said. "You don't have it in you."

Seshat laughed her dry, papery laugh, as though she agreed.

But Harte was sick of both of them. "Are you so sure?" He clenched his fists at his sides. "Blood will tell, after all, and it's your blood that runs in my veins."

His father blanched, but the second the words were out, Harte felt a wave of revulsion wash over him. He'd just threatened a child's life—his own *brother's* life—to get what he wanted. Could he really do it, if the moment arrived?

His father looked wary, and Harte hoped that the threat alone would be enough.

"You should go," his father said again, as another echoing shout sounded in the distance. "The Committee has eyes and ears everywhere, and you wouldn't want their watchmen to find you. Especially considering what you are. They make it their personal job to clean the city of filth like yours."

"If they take me, I'll be sure to direct them back to you," Harte said, without flinching. "You're better off to let me in."

Color climbed into the old man's cheeks, but he didn't take the bait.

"The woman who answered the door," Harte said. "She doesn't know about your life before, does she?" From the way his father's eyes shifted to the side, Harte knew he was right. "I bet you hadn't told her anything about New York. And the boy—I'd wager that he didn't know about me either."

His father's expression went tight, but Harte couldn't quite read the emotion. There was definitely anger there, but there was something more, something that couldn't possibly be regret clouding his father's eyes. After all, the man he'd known hadn't been capable of remorse.

"You can make all of this go away," Harte said again, more gently this time. "Simply give me what I came for, and I'll disappear. You'll never hear from me again, and you can go on pretending that I don't exist. It will be like this never happened."

Suddenly Samuel Lowe looked older and more exhausted. "It's not that easy," he told Harte, shaking his head.

It never is, Harte thought.

"I won't discuss this here. Not in the open. We'll go to a place not far from here, where it's safe. To talk." This time the old man didn't wait to see if Harte would follow. He simply started walking away, toward the streets beyond the narrow alley.

Why don't you take him now? Seshat whispered, taunting. *It would be so easy for you to reach out and take what is yours. What keeps you from it, other than weakness?*

What did keep him from reaching out and using his affinity against his father? It *would* be easy to command him to hand over the crown. . . . But Harte knew that if Seshat was urging him on, she was up to something. She would never allow him to retrieve the Dragon's Eye so easily, and now that he knew about the existence of his brother, there was more than one life at stake.

Weak, Seshat whispered, mocking. *It is the reason you cannot hope to win.*

Harte hesitated only a moment before, cursing to himself, he followed his father back into the heart of Chinatown.

CARELESS VIOLENCE

1904—San Francisco

It was growing late, but as Harte followed after his father, the sidewalks were still teeming with a mixture of Chinese men in traditional wear with queues down their backs and groups of white men in more Western-style clothing, who were clearly there for whatever amusement they could find.

The presence of those outsiders felt somehow different than in New York, where the rich from uptown would often go slumming on Mott Street to gawk at the Chinese people who were only trying to go about their day. Here the other white men didn't seem so much observers as participants, and the air was filled with the kind of electric anticipation that can happen only at night, when the world turns toward the shadows and revels in its baser instincts. The air was filled with the scent of grilled meats and heavy spices, garlic and liquor, all mixing together with the familiar smells of the city that Harte loved and hated at the same time.

They wound their way through the crowded streets and then exited the other side of Chinatown through the barricade. A few blocks away, they turned off the larger boulevard to find a stretch of blocks tucked away from the main thoroughfare. There, saloons and beer halls lined both sides of the streets. Women in various states of deshabille stood near some of the doorways, calling to the men who passed.

Harte's father paid little attention to the women as he walked, but eventually he stopped at a building with a large restaurant on the first floor. The doors were wide open to the night air, and Harte's stomach rumbled at the heavy scent of food. Inside, the noise of the streets gave way to the chatter of diners and the clinking of glasses. Waiters stood at the ready along the walls as a mixture of men dined in the main room. There were no women, at least not any that Harte could see.

His father lifted two fingers to get the attention of the waiter standing closest to the door, who clearly recognized him. After a quick exchange of words, they were shown to a table at the back of the restaurant. It was quieter there, but it wasn't exactly private. There were still other diners and waiters at tables nearby.

"Sit." His father took one of the seats on the other side of the table, clearly placing himself out of Harte's reach, as he had on their walk.

Harte could have argued, but creating a scene would not help him find the Dragon's Eye, so he took the seat across from his father. At first neither of them spoke. Harte understood that it was a test—impatience would be seen as a sign of weakness, so he kept silent. He refused to appear weak. Not before this man. *Not ever again.*

Deep within his skin, Seshat only laughed. It was the same papery thin laugh that set Harte's nerves on edge. But he shoved her down and focused on the man across from him . . . and on what would come next.

A little while into the uncomfortable silence, a waiter appeared with a tray of crabs and prawns along with an assortment of other side dishes. As the covers were removed from each plate, the fragrance of butter and garlic filled the air, reminding Harte that he hadn't eaten since he'd been on the train, hours before. Even then, he hadn't allowed himself to buy more than a stale sandwich and a mealy apple each day of his journey.

Samuel Lowe pointed at the tray of food. "It's been a hell of a long day, and I'm not dealing with you or your idiotic demands on an empty stomach, boy. You might as well eat."

"I'm not hungry," Harte said, despite the answering growl of his own stomach. After all that had happened between them, after all this man had done to Harte's mother, it seemed somehow wrong to break bread together like it was nothing.

On the other side of the broad table, Samuel Lowe ignored Harte's refusal. Even before the waiters were done serving, he'd started wielding an assortment of silver instruments to crack claws and withdraw the glistening meat from the various sea creatures on the table in front of them. The way his father worked with fluid, almost elegant movements made the gold ring on his finger flash. It also made Harte's stomach twist. The motion was familiar, but not because he remembered it from his childhood. It was familiar because it reminded Harte of *himself*. He used the same flick of his wrist as a distraction onstage during sleight-of-hand tricks.

Seeing this tiny echo of himself in his father's movements made Harte wonder again if all the stories he'd told himself about being something more than his father's son had ever been true. He'd betrayed so many people and hurt so many others. Not for the first time that night, Harte considered whether his intentions had ever mattered. Maybe the destruction he'd left in his wake—his mother, Julian, Esta, even Dolph—was evidence of the one thing he'd never wanted to accept: that his father's careless violence flowed in his own veins. That there was no escape from what he *was*.

Be glad if it gives you strength, Seshat hissed. *The world will drag you down and tear you apart for sport, but only if you allow it to. I do not understand your hesitation. Why do you fight what you* are? *Why not use it to your favor?*

Harte went still. Never before had her voice seemed so clear, so utterly logical to him.

I feel your hatred for this man, she urged. *Still you hold back. You could so easily make him pay for the pain he's caused you. Show him what you are. Make him understand how powerless he truly is . . . I will help you destroy him. You have only to promise me the girl.*

Never. Harte tried to shake Seshat's temptation from his mind. It would be so easy to do what she said, to use his affinity to destroy the life his father had built for himself. He could pay Samuel Lowe back for every black eye and every bruise the man had ever given him and for every time he'd ever touched Harte's mother.

Maybe once that decision would have been easier. After all, there was a time Harte had done *exactly* that, and his decision had left a trail of pain and tragedy in its wake. But Harte Darrigan wasn't the boy that Benedict O'Doherty had been. He'd made himself into something new—and he'd done it in spite of everything he'd come from and *despite* everything Samuel Lowe might have bequeathed to him in blood. Harte had to believe that his reluctance to take his revenge wasn't softness, as Seshat might think. He had to believe it was something else.

"I didn't come here to eat," Harte told his father, taking control of the situation. "And I don't have time for a pleasant visit. I only want the crown. Don't pretend you don't know what I'm talking about."

His father glanced up with a look of satisfaction as he dipped a prawn into a cup of melted butter and then, his fingertips slick and glistening, popped it whole into his mouth, but Harte didn't care that he'd lost this particular pissing contest. He'd stopped caring about this man's approval years before. All that mattered was retrieving the Dragon's Eye. *For Esta.*

His father wiped his mouth with the back of his wrist. "The fact of the matter is that I don't have the item you're looking for."

Harte had been watching for the lie, but as his father spoke, he found only truth. "But you must know where it is?"

"It's gone," his father told him with a wave of his hands. "When my mother died, I found the headpiece among her things. I didn't know why she had it, but I could tell immediately that it was valuable. About a year ago, I sold it to William Cooke and took the profit to buy my shop."

"Did you buy that piece of gold as well?" Harte asked, gesturing to the ring that glinted on his father's finger. He was close enough to see it more clearly now—its surface was etched with the image of an open eye that held a piece of onyx as a pupil.

His father's hand fisted, and without so much as blinking, he covered the ring with his other hand.

"I'll need an introduction to this William Cooke," Harte said. "If he doesn't still have the crown, he'll know where it went next."

His father shook his head. "You have no idea what you're asking."

"I'm a quick study," Harte told him.

His father couldn't hide his irritation, but then he relented and began to explain. "Cooke is a high-ranking official in the Vigilance Committee. He didn't keep the piece for himself. He used it to gain the highest-ranking office in the organization. They have the crown now, so you can just forget about getting it back. I won't allow you to go mucking around in things you can't understand. You could destroy everything I've built here, and I'm not about to let that happen after all I've been through to get where I am."

"I don't particularly care what you went through," Harte said. "As far as I'm concerned, you can keep your life and whatever it is you think you've built, as long as I get what I've come for."

Samuel Lowe considered him, and the calm intensity of the older man's stare made Harte suddenly uneasy. This man looked like his father, but the man Harte had known had been predictable in his violence—it had been a saving grace to be able to read Samuel Lowe's moods by the look in his eyes. But Harte couldn't tell what *this* man was thinking, and that felt more dangerous than his father's fists had ever been.

"You're very much your mother's son," Samuel Lowe said finally, but his tone made it clear that his words were not meant as a compliment.

"That's true enough," Harte agreed easily.

"You take pride in it?" his father asked. "Being the bastard of a whore. An *abomination*."

"In case you've forgotten, I'm *your* bastard as well," Harte said, clenching his teeth around the word.

Before his father could answer that charge, a waiter arrived with a pitcher of water, and an uneasy silence descended over the table while it was being poured. Harte's and his father's eyes remained locked, and after the waiter left, his father spoke again. "It's clear you don't even care about the hell you put me through."

"I certainly wouldn't hold your breath waiting for an apology," Harte said coldly.

"I would never expect one from the likes of you," his father said. "You know, I understood what you'd done the second you touched me that day." It confirmed Harte's suspicions about why he'd been keeping the distance between them. "I knew exactly what was happening, how you'd cursed me. I didn't want to leave New York. I wasn't ready yet, but I couldn't stop myself. Because of your evil spell, I was ranting like a madman when I crossed the bridge out of the city. The compulsion to keep moving didn't stop until I reached Brooklyn, but by then I'd already caught the notice of an officer, who thought I was drunk."

"You were," Harte reminded him. "In case you've forgotten, you'd passed out in your own vomit, a glass of liquor still in your hand."

His father ignored this fact. "They put me in jail rather than into a sanitarium, and they left me there for weeks."

"If you ask me, they should've left you longer," Harte said, unable to dredge up any sympathy at all.

His father glared at him. "You have no idea what I suffered in that place, how terrible it was to come off the drink with no help and no comfort. But by the time I was sober, I realized I was no longer compelled to return to your mother's side as I had been for years."

"My mother didn't compel you to stay and torture us."

"Didn't she?" Samuel gave a dry, ugly laugh. "Go on and tell yourself stories about what a saint she was, but Molly O'Doherty was nothing but a common bit of trash."

Harte's fists clenched. "Watch yourself, old man."

But his father ignored the not-so-veiled threat. "Once your mother had her claws in me, I couldn't break away. Only the liquor helped make any of it livable. But as soon as I crossed the bridge, I was free, well and truly—from the evils of drink and from the abomination that was your mother."

"You're lying," Harte spat, unwilling to believe that anything that came from this man's mouth could be the truth.

"In the end, my suffering proved the strength of my soul," his father said, lifting his chin as he ignored Harte's accusation. "My trials forged me, cleansed me of my sins, and made me into a new man. A man *worthy* of claiming a new life. Eventually I was released, and I returned here to take up the life that was waiting for me."

Harte still wasn't sure how that could be possible. He'd ordered his father away from California, ordered him to forget this life. . . . Unless Samuel Lowe *wasn't* lying about what Harte's mother had done. If that was the case, maybe there was something about the Brink that had broken through the compulsion Harte had tried to force upon his father, just as it had broken through whatever his mother's affinity might have done.

"My prosperity is evidence of my righteousness," his father went on, unaware of Harte's thoughts. "As I continue on the path, I continue to be rewarded—with my store, which prospers more every year. With a place in my city, and with a strong son who carries my name."

I'm your son. Harte shook off the thought. He'd never wanted to claim this man's name before, and he wasn't about to start now.

"I won't let you upset the life I've built here," his father continued.

"I'm only here for the Dragon's Eye," Harte reminded him. "Tell me where I can find it, and I'll leave you to your righteousness and your rewards."

"I told you. It's impossible." His father leaned forward, and there was panic in his eyes. "The Committee isn't a bunch of unorganized brutes, like the gang bosses you grew up around."

"You're afraid of them," Harte realized, not missing the way his father flinched at the accusation.

"My soul is blameless, my conscience clear," Samuel Lowe said, avoiding the question. "But I can't help you. I won't."

Harte kept his voice easy, but he made sure there was a note of menace in it as well. "I don't think you quite understand. I'm not asking."

Show him what you are, Seshat taunted, endlessly tempting. *Make him see you now as he never has before.*

It would be easy enough there, even with the prying eyes of the other diners, to reach across the table. It would be worth the risk to take his father by the hand—or by the *throat*.

The violence of the image shook Harte back to himself, and he looked at his outstretched hand, trying to remember when he'd raised it. His father had jerked back and was already reaching for his gun, when a commotion erupted on the other side of the restaurant—a clatter of dishes and metal serving plates. A waiter appeared suddenly, whispering an urgent rush of words to his father that Harte couldn't quite make out. His father's expression hardened as he nodded to the waiter.

Then Samuel Lowe turned to Harte. "We have to go. *Now.*"

A noise came from the front of the restaurant, and the waiter gestured urgently for them to follow. But Harte wasn't going to allow himself to be distracted. Not when he was so close.

"I'm not going anywhere," he said, crossing his arms and leaning back in his chair. "Not until I have what's mine."

"The Committee's watchmen are here. They're searching the restaurant," his father said, getting to his feet.

"What are they searching for?" Harte asked. He stood and prepared to block the old man's way if necessary.

"The same thing they're always searching for," his father said as he tried to skirt around Harte. "The Committee's main purpose is to eliminate the threat of creatures like you. If we stay here, you're likely to be swept up in the raid."

"Why would you help me?" Harte asked, suspicious. "Why not let them take me away? It would eliminate a problem for you."

"I can't risk being connected to you," his father said, and there was enough disgust in his expression that Harte believed him. "If they knew I didn't turn you in immediately, I'd be ruined."

The explanation contained enough of the truth that Harte stood and followed his father through the back of the restaurant toward a rear exit from the dining room, but before his father could disappear through it, Harte caught the older man's arm. "We're not done with our conversation."

"No," his father said, tearing his arm away. "We're nowhere near done."

The exit led to a passageway that ran behind the main dining room and through the kitchen. Around them, the cooks and waiters were in a panic, but their waiter led them through the confusion, toward a small door in the floor at the rear of the building. The waiter opened it, revealing a staircase that went down beneath the building, and then waved them through.

"Where are we going?" Harte asked, eyeing the dark space below.

"The tunnels. They connect various buildings in the city, if you know the right people. This one ends a couple of blocks from here. Far enough away to be safe." His father motioned that Harte should go first. When he didn't immediately move, his father raised one eyebrow, a challenge. "Unless you'd rather stay and deal with the watchmen on your own."

A crash came from the other side of the kitchen, followed by angry voices that signaled the watchmen were getting closer. There was no other exit that Harte could see. His only real choice was to accept the help his father was offering.

It was a mistake.

Harte was only three steps down into the gloom when he felt a sharp blow to the back of his skull. A blunt shove pushed him from behind and sent him tumbling down the steep steps. Harte tried to catch himself, but stars exploded across his vision, and he couldn't tell if the darkness that surrounded him came from the blow to his head or the lightless tunnels beneath.

COMPLICATIONS

1904—Denver

To Esta's relief, Cordelia Smith kept her word. The sharpshooter knew her way around the grounds and managed to avoid the marshals as she led them back toward the main entrance, but she didn't leave them once they were free from the show's grounds. Instead, Cordelia insisted on accompanying them into the city, where she took them to a small, barely furnished apartment. It was a safe house that she said was sometimes used by Antistasi who needed a place to lie low or meet with locals when traveling through the area. Clearly, no one had used it in a while, though. Dust covered everything, and the air had a kind of closed-up, musty smell.

Once they were inside and the door was secured, North placed the box they'd taken from Pickett on a rickety wooden table. Maggie went to open a window.

"Whatever's in there must be really something," Cordelia said, eyeing the box with too much interest for Esta's liking. "Especially considering the risk y'all took to get it."

Esta exchanged an uneasy glance with North and Maggie, who didn't look any more certain about Cordelia than she felt.

"Well?" Cordelia pressed. "Are you gonna open it or what?"

"We will," North said, clearly hedging. "But there's no rush."

Understanding, and then anger, flashed in Cordelia's eyes. "I think I have a right to know what y'all are up to, considering that you got me wrapped up in it as well."

"We didn't exactly ask for your help," Esta reminded her, which earned her a sharp look from Maggie.

"But y'all needed it, didn't you?" Cordelia asked. "Without me, you'd've been caught up back there in the middle of the raid."

Esta wasn't in any mood to admit that Cordelia was right. Maybe with the Quellant thick in her blood, she wouldn't have been able to slip past the marshals unseen, but she would have found another way out. She *always* found a way.

"We appreciate all you've done for us," North said before Esta had the chance to argue the point any further.

"But you still ain't gonna tell me what you're up to?" Cordelia paused, considering them. "It makes me think maybe the rumors I've been hearing were right."

"What rumors?" Maggie said.

"There's plenty that think you betrayed more than Ruth when y'all left St. Louis." Cordelia eyed Maggie, her expression suddenly suspicious. "And then after that train exploded? Seems like y'all should have contacted *someone*. Instead, you let everyone think the Thief was dead. Makes a body think maybe you've got something to hide."

"We didn't know who might be sympathetic to Ruth," North explained. "You said yourself that you couldn't believe she let Maggie go. We couldn't risk any of Ruth's followers coming after us."

Cordelia's expression shifted. "There's other rumors too, you know. Rumors that Ruth stole the real necklace from the Society, and that when y'all left St. Louis, you took the Djinni's Star right out of Ruth's grasp."

Maggie glanced at North, looking every bit as guilty as if she'd taken the necklace herself.

"It's true, isn't it?" Cordelia asked, excitement brightening her watery blue eyes.

North and Maggie exchanged an uneasy glance, but Esta decided to take control of the situation before the two of them could make things worse.

"We couldn't exactly let Ruth keep it, could we?" Esta asked, like this was obvious. Denying it would only make the sharpshooter more suspicious. The best she could hope for at this point was to keep Cordelia on their side and buy a little more time. Clearly, the other girl was loyal to the Antistasi. If Esta could make Cordelia believe that she, too, was loyal to the Antistasi's cause, the sharpshooter might be less of an obstacle. She might even be a help. "After what happened with the serum, we couldn't risk Ruth using the artifact against anyone else—other Antistasi, for instance. Could we?"

Cordelia turned to Maggie. "So when y'all left St. Louis, you were choosing the Antistasi over your sister?"

"My loyalty to the Antistasi didn't begin when I left St. Louis," Maggie told Cordelia, and Esta was surprised to see there wasn't even a hint of prevarication in her words.

Cordelia considered this for a long, uncomfortable moment before her expression cleared. "Well, where's it at?" she asked. "I'd sure like to take a look at it."

Which was, of course, impossible. The Djinni's Star was with Harte, traveling toward the other side of the continent. Not that any of them needed to know about that.

But North and Maggie looked uneasy, and Esta had the sense that the two Antistasi didn't want this woman to know they'd lost the necklace. Maggie opened her mouth and closed it again, like a fish gulping for air.

"We can't show you right now," Esta said, stepping in to save Maggie from another poorly told lie.

"Why not?" The suspicion returned to Cordelia's expression. "Y'all ain't fixin' to keep it for yourself, are you?"

"Of course not," Maggie said too quickly.

"Then it won't hurt to let me have a peek, as a show of good faith."

"We would," Esta told Cordelia, trying to draw the sharpshooter's attention away from Maggie, who apparently couldn't lie to save her soul. "Of *course* we would. But we don't have the necklace with us at the moment. You said yourself what a risk it was we were taking today," Esta reminded her. "You don't think we'd take the chance of putting something as important as the Djinni's Star in that kind of danger, do you?"

Cordelia frowned. She didn't want to agree with this logic, but she also couldn't find any fault in it. "Where is it?"

"Somewhere safe," Esta said. "We wouldn't want it to fall into the wrong hands, would we?"

"And that box there?" Cordelia said. "What was so important that y'all were willing to die for it?"

"Something that could help the Antistasi," Maggie offered.

Cordelia's brows drew together thoughtfully, and then realization seemed to strike. "You're talking about another artifact."

"Why would you think that?" Maggie said, unable to hide the anxious tremor in her voice.

But Cordelia only crossed her arms and stared at them. "That settles it. I'm not going anywhere until you show me what it is you took."

"Go on," North told Esta. "Open it."

"And try to be quick about it," Cordelia said, like she'd already guessed Esta's plan to delay. "I have another show this evening, and I don't need people noticing that I've gone missing."

"These things take time," Esta told them. She made a show of leaning her ear close to the lock and slowly working the tumbler.

A lock like this actually *didn't* take that much time—and she already had the combination—but none of the Antistasi watching her knew that. Esta wasn't in any hurry to box herself into a corner, though. Once the dagger was in play, things would become more complicated. Especially without her affinity to rely on.

"We should just break the damn thing open," North said, after a long few minutes of silence had ticked by while Esta pretended to listen to the lock.

"And risk damaging what's inside?" Esta asked.

North grumbled but didn't press any further. Still, with each turn of the tumbler, Esta could sense the impatience in the room swelling. But there was nothing she could think to do that would help her avoid opening the lock. She'd taken the Quellant, so there was no way to stop time, and even if she could, it wouldn't do her any good. As long as North had that watch of his, he could bring her right back. If that happened, Esta would have lost whatever trust she'd built with them.

"Almost—" Esta said, trying to stall as her mind continued to race. There had to be a way. . . .

She twisted the tumbler again, blinking, as she tried to focus on the numbers, but her vision was doing odd things. It looked like there were two of the box, two of the lock. Two of every number. Esta willed her vision to clear. "I've almost got it," she said, annoyed with the tremor in her voice.

Suddenly, the room wouldn't hold steady. One second everything was fine, and the next second, the room had shifted, transformed, before flickering back, and Esta went still, frozen by the strangeness of what she was seeing.

North and Cordelia and Maggie were all looking at her expectantly, but then her vision flickered again, and they were gone. It felt like all the layers of time that had ever been, all the layers that might ever be, were rising up around her. Even though she'd taken the Quellant, and even though her cuff, the one that held Ishtar's Key, was hundreds of miles away, Esta felt like she did right before she slipped through to a different time. Except now, time felt like a separate living thing. Time flexed and rose around her, pulsing with a strange energy. Unsteady. Unwieldy. And it felt *hungry*.

The three Antistasi were there again suddenly, and then, just as quickly, they weren't. Esta tried to keep herself upright as the room around her shifted and changed. She was standing in an empty room—and then her vision shifted again, and the room was filled with strangers dressed in clothes from her own time—then another shift, and the room changed again as reality faded in and out, like an old TV set blinking through a bad connection. The net of time that held the world in place—the very Aether that ordered reality—seemed to contract around her. It pressed in on her. Like it wanted to *devour* her.

The scar on Esta's wrist burned, and the word there felt like it had been freshly sliced into her skin. Then all at once, everything went still. The room stopped flickering, and the present moment seemed as ordinary and stable as ever.

"Well?" North demanded, apparently oblivious to what Esta had just experienced. One glance around the room told her that the others hadn't sensed anything at all.

"I'm working on it," Esta told him, her words sounding strangled even to herself. It took real concentration to keep her hands steady enough to move the tumbler into place, lining up the last number in the sequence that would open the lock.

What the hell was that? It had seemed like reality itself had splintered, like the seconds were trying to consume her. It had felt like time was trying to devour her whole, until she was . . . nothing. Esta rubbed absently at the scar on her arm as she opened the lock. The raised ridges of the Latin command ached beneath her touch.

She'd taken the Quellant. She had relinquished her affinity to protect herself—and everyone else—from Seshat, but Esta had the sense that whatever had happened *wasn't* Seshat. There had been no shadows, no darkness. Whatever that was felt more like time itself had tried to pull her under—like time had tried to *erase* her. Like Professor Lachlan had warned it would.

But why now? What changed? Esta had assumed that as long as the Key could be returned to her younger self, all would be well. Now, with the Quellant, she might even be able to go back to where time had splintered into a new future. She could still send her younger self forward. She should be okay, as long as that was all still a possibility.

Unless something has happened to Ishtar's Key.

The thought made Esta's breath catch. Harte knew how important the cuff was to her. He would never willingly let anything happen to it. She *knew* that. But maybe he hadn't been willing—

No. She wouldn't let herself think about that possibility. Harte was too smart and had survived too long to get caught now. The Key couldn't be lost. Maybe it was taking them too long to return it. Maybe time was simply running out of patience.

North clearly was. He grabbed the box from Esta when she didn't immediately open it, and she was still too unnerved to bother with fighting him.

Maggie moved closer to him. "Well?" she asked, her voice almost trembling, as North stared at the contents of the box.

After a few frozen seconds, North tossed the box on the table so violently that the coins and papers it held threatened to escape. "It's not here." Then he turned on Esta. "You told us it would be here. You promised that Pickett had the dagger."

"The dagger?" Cordelia asked, her eyes going wide. "You're talking about the Pharaoh's Heart."

North was still too busy glaring at Esta to answer.

"Y'all *are* going after the other artifacts," Cordelia said, excitement coloring her voice. "You're going to make the Sundren pay."

"No one is going to make anyone pay," Maggie said, sounding a little taken aback. "We're only here for the dagger. Or we were . . ."

Cordelia's excitement shifted to confusion. "But why would y'all ever think Bill Pickett would have an artifact?"

"Because that's what *she* told us," North said.

"He's a simple cowpoke," Cordelia told North. "He ain't even Mageus, or I would've already recruited him."

"He *has* to have it." Esta forced herself to ignore the trembling in her limbs and the burning of the scar as she stepped closer to look through the box herself. Harte had sent her to Denver to retrieve the dagger. If it wasn't there, she didn't know what she would do next. But North was right. Inside was nothing but a pile of coins and some papers with scribbled IOUs.

"It must be somewhere else, then," Esta told them.

"You already searched Pickett's tent," North reminded her.

"So maybe it's not in his tent," Esta said, trying to keep her voice steady. "Maybe Pickett keeps the dagger on him."

"Or maybe he never had it in the first place," North said, his eyes narrowing with suspicion. "Maybe this was all a bunch of *misdirection*, like that crazy tale you told us on the train about ancient goddesses and the end of the world. I knew we shouldn't have trusted her," he told Maggie.

"The fact that my tale was so *crazy* should tell you that it's true. Why would I make something like that up when I could have left you in the dust? Pickett has the knife," Esta snapped. "I wasn't lying about that before, and I'm not lying now. We have to go back. We have to look again."

"You'd be nuts to go back there right now," Cordelia said. "Artifact or not, there'll be marshals crawling all over back there for hours. Syndicate, too."

"The *Syndicate's* here?" Maggie asked, glancing nervously at North.

"Who do y'all think was in charge of that raid today?" Cordelia frowned like this was something they should have already known. "They've been gathering up people suspected of illegal magic ever since what happened in St. Louis. All the Brotherhoods have."

"Do you two have experience with this Syndicate?" Esta asked. It was clear the Syndicate was another of the Brotherhoods, but that didn't account for the severity of Maggie's and North's reaction.

"They helped run me out of Texas a couple of years back," North said, apparently not wanting to tell the entire story. He was still looking at Maggie. "I didn't want to worry you before, but . . ." His mouth pressed into a hard line before he spoke again. "I saw Jot Gunter back in Texas."

At this news, the color drained from Maggie's face. "You're sure?"

North rubbed at the back of his neck. "He was with the men at the oil fields."

They traded a meaningful glance, and Esta understood that there was some bigger story there—something that they were not saying.

"How do y'all know Jot Gunter?" Cordelia asked, her thick brows bunching. "He's one of the Syndicate's highest-ranking members."

"We go way back," North said darkly. "But I'd rather not run into him again anytime soon if I can help it."

"Jericho, they're definitely going to realize that my explosions today were the same as the ones I set off in Texas, and when they do . . ." Maggie raised her hand to cover her mouth, as though she could hold back the truth of what she'd done.

"It doesn't matter," Esta told them. Jot Gunter or the Syndicate or whoever was in her way—none of it mattered. She didn't know why time had wavered around her, but the warning had been clear enough: Her time was running out. "We have to go back. Bill Pickett has the dagger, and I'm not leaving until I get it."

A TRUTH TOO TERRIBLE

1904—Denver

Maggie hadn't missed the way Esta had said "I" rather than "we," and she wondered, not for the first time, if Esta would leave them as Ben had, empty-handed and without explanation. True, Esta had taken the Quellant, but Maggie had seen her in action over the past couple of weeks, and she didn't believe that something as simple as a missing affinity would stop the Thief if she set her mind to something.

And yet . . . Esta didn't look quite right. For all the confidence in her voice, she looked almost green and her hands were trembling. Maybe the emptiness of the box had shaken her badly, or maybe Esta had been shocked by the news about the Syndicate being in Denver. Whatever the case, Maggie couldn't worry too much about Esta's state. Not when they still didn't have an artifact in their possession.

When Esta had told them about the dagger, Maggie had thought that maybe fate had given her a way to correct the mistakes she'd made. Maybe the necklace was gone, but with the possibility of collecting the Pharaoh's Heart, she still had hope. Now she wasn't so sure. The dagger hadn't been in the box, and they were still empty-handed.

"Esta's right," Maggie told the others. "Bill Pickett's the only lead we have. Even if the Syndicate *is* here, we need to put all of our focus into figuring out whether Pickett still has the dagger, and if he doesn't, we need to find out if he knows where it is."

Jericho clearly didn't feel the same. "I don't know, Mags—"

"We need the Pharaoh's Heart, Jericho," Maggie said, cutting him off before he could give her all the good reasons they shouldn't. They'd lost everything else. They couldn't lose this, too. Especially not with the Antistasi sharpshooter looking at them with suspicion.

Jericho didn't respond at first, and Maggie could see in his expression that he still wasn't sure. For a moment she worried that he might refuse.

"You promised," she reminded him gently. "When we left St. Louis, you told me you understood how important this was. You told me I could depend on you."

He let out a ragged, frustrated breath. "You can. You *know* that."

Somehow, though, Jericho's reluctant acceptance didn't feel like the victory it should have been.

"I've never seen Pickett with anything that could be mistaken for a lost artifact," Cordelia said.

"That doesn't necessarily mean Pickett doesn't have it," Esta said. "If he's smart, he wouldn't have shown it off."

"A piece *that* valuable? I'd expect he'd keep it somewhere safer than his tent," Cordelia said. "Might could be that he left it back with his family in Texas."

"I'm not going back to Texas," Jericho said with a frown. "I just managed to get out of that state alive for the second time. I'm not interested in trying for a third."

"Not unless we have to," Maggie promised. Then she glanced at Esta. "The first thing we need to figure out is whether Pickett has the dagger with him here in Denver. Then we can go from there." She turned to Cordelia. Maggie was still unsettled about Cordelia implying she hadn't been faithful to the Antistasi's cause, but she figured the best way to neutralize the threat Cordelia might pose was to include her. "Cordelia, you know your way around the show. . . . How well do you know Bill Pickett?"

"Not well enough to go asking about some priceless lost artifact," Cordelia said, arching a single brow. "Besides, even if Pickett is sympathetic to our cause, I can't imagine he'd tell me a thing, not with the marshals prowling around today."

Cordelia was right. With all that had happened, and with how quickly the news had spread about the theft of the Djinni's Star and the attack on the world's fair, it wasn't likely that Bill Pickett would admit that he was in possession of one of the Order's other lost artifacts. Not willingly.

The weight of the leather pouch Maggie had carried with her from St. Louis suddenly felt heavier than it had a moment before. If they could get close enough, there *was* a way to ensure that Pickett revealed everything, but using the concoction she had in mind meant divulging secrets she'd never intended to reveal. At least not like this.

"Maybe there's a way you could earn his trust?" Maggie said hopefully.

"It would take time we don't have," Esta said, dismissing the idea. "With those explosions you set off, someone is bound to start piecing things together. It's not going to be hard to figure out no one died in the train explosion back in Texas. Once they do, they're going to know to look for us. The faster we get the dagger and get out of town, the better."

Esta was right. It had been a mistake to use the Flash and Bangs, and now Maggie had to deal with the consequences. As much as she wasn't keen on revealing this *particular* secret, the artifact they were seeking was too important for Maggie to put her own personal worries before her duty to the Antistasi . . . especially considering that she was mostly responsible for the mess they were in. She wouldn't allow herself to fail again, even if it meant Jericho might never look at her the same.

"I *might* have a formulation that could help with Pickett," Maggie said slowly, knowing that what she was about to reveal would change everything.

North turned to her, clearly surprised. "You do?"

She hesitated, staring at a snag in her skirts because she couldn't meet Jericho's eyes. She knew what his reaction was going to be. "If we can give it to Pickett, he won't have any choice but to tell us the truth about the dagger."

"What, like a truth serum?" Esta asked, getting to the point far more quickly than Maggie would have liked.

"Something like that," she admitted.

"You've been busier than I realized," Jericho said with a low whistle. "First the confounding solution you used on that porter, and now this? How many new formulations have you been working on, anyway?"

Maggie could have let the omission lie, but she couldn't bear one more thing between them. Better to tell him now than have him discover she'd withheld the truth from him twice. "It's not new," she told Jericho, finally risking a glance in his direction.

She must have looked as guilty as she felt, because understanding registered in Jericho's expression immediately.

"You never told me you had anything like that," he said, an unspoken question looming behind his words.

Maggie knew how he felt about some of the formulations Ruth had directed her to make. Oh, he was fine with the ones that flashed and banged, the ones that they needed for protection against their enemies, but he'd been uncomfortable all along with the idea of the serum, and with any formulation that took away a person's free will.

"I haven't used it in a long time," Maggie told him. That, at least, was the truth.

Jericho looked a little sick. "Well, as long as you've never used it on me."

Maggie didn't respond. She couldn't bring herself to lie, but the truth seemed impossible to tell.

Jericho frowned at her silence. "You *haven't* used it on me, have you?" he asked pointedly. "Maggie?"

Maggie's cheeks heated. "It was a long time ago," she said softly, like that was any excuse at all.

The color drained from Jericho's face, leaving his freckles stark against his pale skin. "When?" he asked, his voice sounding strangely hollow.

"You have to understand . . . We didn't know you yet," she tried to explain.

"When did you use it on me, Maggie?" Jericho asked.

"When you first arrived in St. Louis." She stared at the ground, because she couldn't bear to face him. "Ruth never trusted newcomers, so she usually used it whenever someone wanted to join us. We never gave a full dose, only enough to loosen a newcomer's tongue but not so much that they'd realize what was happening. You were no exception, but I had a feeling you were going to be different. I knew it was a mistake as soon as I gave it to you."

For a long stretch of seconds, the room filled with the kind of silence that chafed. "You never told me. Even after all this time we've known each other?"

"I didn't know how." She glanced up then, and the look on his face was even worse than she'd imagined it might be.

"All those nights we sat up late, talking about all sorts of things. I thought we were—" Jericho let out a dark laugh. His eyes, usually so warm and soft, glinted with anger. "You let me prattle on like a fool, and all the while you already knew everything there was to know about me."

"It's not like that," Maggie said, stepping toward Jericho, reaching for him. But he pulled back, and she let her arm drop to her side. "The minute Ruth started asking you questions, I *left*. Don't you remember? I left because I didn't want to hear what you told her. I didn't want to take your secrets from you."

"You sure didn't stop your sister from taking them, though," North charged.

Esta and Cordelia were silent, but Maggie could feel their attention on her. This whole scene was bad enough, but somehow having these two witnesses made her shame burn that much hotter.

"You're right," Maggie admitted. There was no way around it, and no reason to pretend now. "I let Ruth pressure me, like I always did, but I knew the minute I met you that things were going to be different. I had the sense that you were going to change everything for me. I couldn't stop Ruth—" She paused, shaking her head. "No . . . I didn't even try. But making that mistake changed something in me."

"You left me alone with her," Jericho charged.

Maggie took his anger, without argument or complaint. "I left, because I didn't want to take anything else from you. I wanted you to *give* me your story, free and clear. I wanted to deserve it."

"I thought you did," North said, and somehow the way his voice had gone soft and hollow tore through her.

"I'm sorry, Jericho," Maggie told him, taking another step closer. "I was a different person then, but that's not an excuse. I've never stopped being sorry—"

"If you were so sorry, you would have told me," he said.

That made Maggie press her lips together. There was no excuse for what she'd done, but there was even less of an excuse for keeping the secret for so long. Still, she had to make him understand. "I can't go back and undo it. I wish I'd been brave enough to trust you. But I need you to know that making that mistake made me realize that Ruth wasn't perfect or infallible. And I never let her do it again. *Ever*. Not to you, not to anyone." She glanced at Esta, who was frowning thoughtfully at her. "Not even when it would have been easier."

"You're willing to do it now, though," Jericho pointed out. "You've kept it all this time, and now you're willing to take the choice from a man who's done nothing to you."

"If there were any other way . . ." *If getting the dagger weren't so important.* Maggie met his eyes then, her shoulders a little straighter. "I can't take back my past, Jericho. But with the dagger, we might have a real chance to make a different future for ourselves. For everyone with the old magic. So, *yes*. I'm willing to use the truth tablets again to make that future—for you. For *us*."

"Whatever happened in the past, Maggie's right—we need to focus on what we can do now," Esta said softly. "I don't love the idea of drugging someone, but the sooner we know if Pickett still has the dagger, the sooner we can either retrieve it from him or get on with finding it. I don't see any other way. Not with multiple Brotherhoods closing in."

Maggie was thankful for the support, but it didn't stop North from turning away from her. It was like he couldn't even look at her.

"Cordelia," Esta said. "What are the chances you could slip Pickett the formulation?"

Cordelia frowned. "We work together, but not *together*, you know? People mostly keep to their own, and it might draw attention if I'm cozying up to a man I've never shown any interest in before. Especially a man like Pickett." She let out a sigh. "Honestly, that alone might cause Pickett trouble with some of the others. Not everyone in the show was happy when the Curtises added him to the bill, mostly because of the color of his skin. A lot of the cowboys didn't like being upstaged by someone they see as beneath them."

"Then that won't work. We don't want to cause Pickett any more trouble than we absolutely have to," Esta said. "Is there anyone else that could help? Another of the Antistasi you might trust?"

"I can do it," Jericho said, his voice flat and dull as an old penny.

"Jericho—" Maggie started, but the look he shot in her direction had her going silent.

"There are too many people involved as it is. If Cordelia can get me onto the grounds, maybe get me a position in the show, I can get close to Pickett. I know my way around a horse well enough."

"But the Syndicate is there." Maggie's stomach dropped. Jot Gunter had almost killed North once before. If they found him now . . .

"I can handle myself around the Syndicate," Jericho told her. "At least with them, I know exactly what I'm dealing with."

Maggie felt his words land hard, and the look he gave her was worse than a fist to her gut.

"It might be tricky with the raid, but then, maybe that'll help. There's sure to be some positions open. I could introduce you to the manager and try to get you set up today?" Cordelia offered.

"Sounds fine to me," North said, grabbing his hat from the table as he ignored Maggie's fragile silence. It was almost like he couldn't wait to get free of her.

"What about us?" Maggie asked.

"It'll be safer for y'all to stay here," Cordelia told her flatly.

"But—" Maggie protested.

"No way. We're coming with you," Esta insisted.

"The grounds were crawling with federal marshals when we left," Cordelia reminded them. "With all that happened earlier, we can't risk someone recognizing you as easily as I did. And you"—Cordelia looked directly at Maggie—"what do *you* know about cattle?"

Maggie shook her head. "Nothing," she admitted. But she didn't want to let Jericho go off without the two of them patching things up.

"It's bad enough Pickett has probably already realized someone's robbed him," Cordelia told her. "We can't chance you sticking out like a sore thumb and drawing attention."

"Cordelia's right," Jericho told them, but he didn't look at Maggie when he spoke. "It'll be safer for both of you to stay here." His words felt like a door closing, and she didn't have the key.

"Then it's settled," Cordelia said, clearly satisfied. "The two of you will stay here, and I'll take Jericho back to the showgrounds with me and get him introduced to Aldo."

"I'll need the formulation," Jericho said.

"You think you can give it to him today?" Esta asked, clearly surprised.

"Probably not," he admitted. "But I might get lucky, and I want to be ready. No sense wasting any more time going back and forth. The sooner I'm done with all this, the better."

"Of course," Maggie said, forcing her voice to stay calm. She refused to let a single tear break free as she dug through the small pouch. Finally, she found what she was looking for.

Jericho reached for the tablets, but Cordelia held out her hand. "It'll be safer for me to hold on to them . . . in case they search you."

Maggie frowned. She trusted Jericho to hold the tablets. He had a sense of right and wrong that wouldn't allow him to abuse them, but Cordelia? Antistasi or not, it could be disastrous if she gave the tablets to the wrong person.

"You never know what to expect with the Syndicate," Cordelia said. "I'm a known performer. They're not likely to look at me. But if they search him . . ."

"I can handle myself just fine," Jericho said.

Maggie couldn't take that risk. "You only need one, but you'll have to dissolve it in something," she told them as she handed the tablets to Cordelia. "It'll have a bitterness to it, so alcohol is best if you can find some. To hide the taste."

"They were in the beer, weren't they?" Jericho asked.

Maggie turned to him, confused.

"When you gave it to me," he clarified. "You put them in the beer that first night."

She couldn't lie to him, wouldn't ever again. But she also couldn't bring herself to say the words, so she only nodded.

Disappointment flashed across Jericho's expression—or maybe it was something closer to hurt. He let out a resigned breath that made it seem like he was deflating, and then he gave Cordelia a nod. "Let's get this over with," he said, opening the door to escort the sharpshooter out. "I'll be back as soon as I can," he told Maggie, but he didn't give her cheek a kiss as he usually did before he left.

"Are you okay?" Esta asked when Maggie didn't do anything but stare blankly at the closed door. Now that Jericho was gone, the tears that had been threatening all along would not come.

The question shook Maggie back to the moment. "I'm fine," she said, swallowing hard past the knot of regret in her throat.

"You don't seem fine," Esta told her.

"Well, I am," Maggie said. "Or I will be once North and Cordelia come back with news of the Pharaoh's Heart." She told herself it would be enough. It *had* to be enough. Especially if retrieving it had cost her everything else.

Esta was frowning, her dark brows pulled together thoughtfully. "I'm still not sure how I feel about Cordelia knowing all of our business."

Me neither. "She's Antistasi," Maggie said instead. It meant that she was an ally, but it could also be a problem. If Cordelia found out that they had managed to lose the necklace, the entire network would know. From the sound of things, people had already started to doubt her loyalty, which was also a problem. Maggie couldn't afford anyone to know that she'd failed to keep hold of the artifact. Not until she had a replacement for it.

"I'm still not sure I like her," Esta grumbled.

"I'm not either," Maggie admitted, giving Esta a resigned shrug. "But it looks like we're stuck with her. If she can help us get the dagger—"

"As long as she *does* help," Esta said. "All that talk of making Sundren pay . . ."

Maggie hadn't liked that bit either. "If Cordelia tries anything, Jericho will take care of it. Even if he *is* furious with me right now."

Esta held her gaze. "If he loves you half as much as he pretends to, he'll get over it."

"I'm not sure that he will," Maggie said, remembering the way Jericho had looked away from her. She knew how much his pride meant to him.

"Then he's not the man you thought he was," Esta said.

Maggie frowned. "Jericho deserved better than what I did to him."

"Maybe he did." Esta shrugged. "But sometimes the choices life hands to us aren't that simple. *People* aren't that simple. Look at your sister."

"What about my sister?" Maggie asked, suddenly wary.

"The serum was a mistake, and you left because you had to. But that doesn't mean you hate Ruth. It doesn't mean you can't forgive her."

"No," Maggie said, meaning it. "I could never hate her." Ruth had

LISA MAXWELL

been like a mother to her. Whatever mistakes Ruth might have made, she was family, and Maggie would do almost anything to protect her— *had* done almost anything. Now she worried about the choices she'd made, because Maggie understood that choosing to protect Ruth might very well cost her Jericho in the end.

THE OUROBOROS

1902—New York

It was early afternoon, and the barroom two floors below James Lorcan's flat was probably already filling with those who needed something to make their day easier. A glass of Nitewein to blunt the edge of unused magic. A few moments of quiet solitude among their own, surrounded by the familiar warmth of power. No doubt the boy, Logan, was waiting uneasily for him to appear, but for now James craved solitude. The Aether had been trembling, anxious and unsteady, ever since Paul Kelly had revealed that the Order had retrieved the ring, but James hadn't been able to find the solution that would make it stop.

Unlike the saloon, the apartment was quiet. It had once been Dolph Saunders', and with its damask chaise and lace curtains, the rooms still held the mark of Leena's more feminine touch, which made it comfortable as well. But the apartment was so much more than a place to lay his head or calm his nerves—it was also the key to his eventual victory. The shelves lining the wall contained all of Dolph's research—all of his secrets.

It had been those books that had originally drawn James to Dolph a few years before. On the surface, the gang leader had seemed like any of the other players on the deadly game board that was the Bowery, but when James had seen that shelf of books—*real books*, bound in leather and smelling of the wisdom of centuries—he'd known immediately that Saunders was something different. Perhaps even something useful.

Compared to James' own father, Dolph Saunders was nothing, of course. A common criminal at best. Yet, unlike Niall Lorcan, Saunders had somehow managed to amass an entire *shelf* of books. The unfairness of it had almost been too much to bear.

When James was younger, his family had only one book—not the Bible, as so many of his countrymen might have owned, but a well-used volume of *Le Morte d'Arthur*. Ragged though it was, the volume was a prized enough possession to warrant a spot in his family's meager luggage when they came to this terrible new world. It was a story of heroes and traitors, of magic and those who would discount its power.

His father had believed in Arthur, the boy king who could unite a country and lead a people, just as he believed in a better world for his family and for all Mageus. Niall Lorcan had brought his family to America so that he could help build such a world. James, on the other hand, had always felt a certain secret kinship with Merlin, the sorcerer who could prophesy the future. Merlin, who should have been the hero all along.

James had been a child when his father had crossed the wrong ward boss. In retaliation, they'd arrested his father and burned his family's home—his mother and sisters still inside—leaving James orphaned and alone in a city that didn't care if he ended up dead.

Perhaps if James hadn't been so tired from his endless hours on the factory floor, his concentration only on the danger the machine press posed to his small fingers, he might have sensed the reason that the Aether had rippled and bunched that day. If he'd been paying more attention, James might have understood the danger that was approaching. Perhaps he would have fought the foreman, who'd held him over that extra hour, and he too would have been in the family's apartment when it caught fire.

They told James later that the wooden tenement where his family had lived in two cramped rooms had burned like a torch, too hot and too fast for anyone to escape. To his neighbors, it was simply another random tragedy, too common perhaps, but unavoidable in a city that cared little for the lives of the poor. James had known differently, though. With the combination of affinities his family had been keeping secret, they should have been able to get out of the burning building. To die like they had? They must have been trapped somehow, locked in or blocked from escaping. James couldn't help but think that it would have taken more than locks to hold his family back—possibly even magic.

Not that anyone cared to listen to him. Instead, every one of his neighbors turned away—Mageus and Sundren alike—afraid to see the truth of what was happening all around them. Afraid to disturb the fragile equilibrium that kept their own families safe.

In the end, he'd been left alone to watch the building smolder for days, and as the charred beams turned to ash, James Lorcan had transformed as well. He'd vowed to himself that he would never again be taken off guard. He would never allow himself to be as weak as his father had been, believing in fairy tales and heroes and the lie of righteousness. When he'd walked away from the ashes of his former life, James had promised himself that he would determine his own fate. He'd decided there and then that he would change the world. And he would never again be at someone else's mercy—neither Mageus nor Sundren.

James had been patient. He'd carefully plotted and planned, and now the shelf of leather and vellum—and all of the wisdom contained in Dolph's volumes—was his. He ran his fingers over the spines, caressing them with the reverence a lesser man might reserve for gemstones or gold. James understood exactly how precious those books were and what a victory it had been to take them from Dolph, perhaps even a greater victory than taking the Devil's Own. After all, the riffraff Dolph had surrounded himself with was expendable. The Bowery teemed with other Mageus just like them—desperate and easily led. But these books? The knowledge they contained? Irreplaceable.

Selecting one of the volumes from the shelf, James brought it to the desk and opened it. It was a small ledger, filled with handwritten notes in various languages, sketches of alchemical recipes, and collected scraps from other sources. He turned to one of the inked illustrations. James had been drawn to this particular page again and again over the last few weeks—ever since he'd seen the newspaper accounts of Esta's and Darrigan's supposed deaths, ever since he'd realized they were still out there in the world, still within his grasp. The figure on the page was the image of a snake eating its own tail. Wrought in brilliant ink, the gilded highlights made the snake seem like it was moving each time the page shifted.

James could tell that the image was important by the care that had been taken with it. He ran his fingers over the serpent, wondering what, exactly, it had signified for Dolph. In general, the ouroboros was an ancient symbol that represented the beginning and end of time. Chaos and order. Magic and its opposite. But Dolph had placed enormous importance on this ancient symbol. He'd adopted the symbol as the mark for his gang, doubling it to include two interlocking snakes—one living, one no more than a skeleton. Life and death, Dolph used to say. Two sides of the same coin. Inscribed into the skin of any who pledged Dolph Saunders loyalty, the mark stood as a signal to others in the Bowery, but it also served as a guarantee that they would not betray the gang.

No . . . the marks had been a guarantee that the Devil's Own would not betray *Dolph Saunders.*

Dolph had infused the gorgon's silver head with Leena's ability to nullify nearby power, and combined with Dolph's own particular ability to borrow the affinities of any Mageus he touched, the cane had been a uniquely devastating tool. While Dolph had lived, that smiling Medusa had the ability to tear the affinity from any who wore the mark—and in doing so, destroy its bearer. But the power in the cane was larger than Dolph Saunders, and the possibilities it held had not ended with his pathetic life. Like the snake in the image, forever devouring its tail, the magic within the silver gorgon head continued on—infinite. Like all magical objects, that power could be *used.* James had only to figure out a way to access it completely, and to align its power with his own.

He had been working tirelessly ever since he'd moved into Dolph's rooms, but the only thing he'd managed was to make his own mark tingle with awareness. Once, he'd managed to make Werner look almost unsettled. But to *use* the power in the cane? To direct it as easily, as *effortlessly* as Dolph had? He would need something more to amplify his affinity. He needed the ring.

It wasn't lost on James that had Logan not failed so spectacularly at the gala, he might already have complete, unbreakable control over the Devil's Own. As it was, there was still unease within their ranks. Everyone had been nervous since Dolph had been killed. Everyone had been on edge with the constant threat of Tammany's patrols and the Five Pointers' presence in the Bowery, but Viola's appearance the day before had only made things worse. She'd been an unwelcome reminder of the past, and the news she'd brought about Mooch's imprisonment was still filtering through his ranks.

If she'd only accepted his offer of a new partnership. Instead, she'd told James that she needed time—to consider, to think. She'd walked out that night without any promise to return.

Viola's departure might have meant that she was plotting against him, but it didn't matter. The movement of the Aether assured him that whatever Viola might attempt to do, she was only setting her own trap. All he needed to do was watch and wait. The answers would come to him soon enough.

Suddenly James felt the Aether tremble. He paused. Something was happening. Some new part of the game had begun.

He closed the notebook and placed it back on the shelf. It would be best to get back down to the Strega, to make his presence felt before his meeting with Kelly. Best to shore up his authority now, before he went.

At first everything seemed as it should in the saloon. Men and women curled around their drinks, and warm magic filtered through the air. The Aether still trembled uneasily, but it did not immediately reveal the danger.

Then James realized the change—near the bar, a boy with a shock of red hair was talking to Werner. The last he'd seen the boy, Mooch

LISA MAXWELL

had been unconscious on the street. He should have still been in the Tombs—or better, dead—not here in the Strega where he could tell the others how James had left him behind, ripe for the picking by Tammany's patrols. Mooch was a problem James would have to consider, but for the moment, the Aether gave him no answers.

Soon that would change, James thought as he gripped the cane's head and felt the power vibrating within it. Soon his plans would fall into place. He would no longer be forced to feel his way through darkness, and the Devil's Own—Mooch included—would be his to command. But for that future to arrive, James needed the ring, which meant he needed to keep Paul Kelly on the hook. He glanced at the clock and realized that, for now, the problem of Mooch would have to wait. Paul Kelly would not.

THE HEART OF THE MATTER

1902—New York

Viola waited behind a pushcart parked near the corner of Elizabeth Street, watching for the sign that was supposed to come from the back door of the Bella Strega. Next to her, looking every bit out of place, was Theo Barclay, who had refused to leave after he'd helped her free Mooch from the Tombs.

It had been a mistake to bring him into this. Viola knew that to the pit of her soul, but she hadn't known what else to do. When she'd returned to Paul's after confronting Nibsy, only to find Theo waiting for her at the corner, Viola had taken it as a sign. Ruby had sent him, or so he'd claimed. She'd wanted to make sure that Viola was safe and well, as if an assassin needed a soft schoolboy to keep her safe. But after failing to heal Jianyu, after confronting Nibsy, Viola hadn't had the strength to push him away. The next thing she'd known, she was in his carriage, telling him far more than she'd intended to, and he was agreeing to far more than was safe.

"Do you think your friend did what you've asked?" Theo wondered, examining a bin of candy that the peddler was selling. The man who owned the cart was eyeing them both, but Theo especially, with his well-cut suit and fair hair.

"If you're not going to buy that, you should leave it be," Viola told him, purposely ignoring his question. "And I wouldn't exactly call Mooch my friend."

The truth was that Viola felt like expecting Mooch to uphold his promise was like chasing butterflies. He was as hardened by the streets and his experience as any of the Devil's Own, and the Bella Strega—even with Nibsy Lorcan at its head—represented safety in a dangerous city. Mooch would be a fool to risk his place, his *home*, even for the favor Theo had done by getting him out of the Tombs.

Theo placed a couple of coins into the peddler's outstretched hand in exchange for a paper sack of the candy, and Viola pulled him onward. He offered her a piece, but she waved him off.

"I still don't know how you convinced the judge to let him go," she said, shaking her head in disbelief.

"Judge Harris knows my father," Theo said with a shrug. "Besides, there wasn't any real evidence against him. It was all circumstantial."

As if that ever matters, Viola thought.

"It's been too long," she said, growing more impatient. They'd already looked at all the carts, and if they went through the vendors again, it would certainly draw attention. If the firebrand of a boy was going to help them, he would have opened the back door of the Strega by now.

"Let's give it a minute more," Theo said, popping one of the hard candies into his mouth. "These are quite good. . . ." He sounded mystified.

"Confetti," Viola said, absently wondering how anyone so rich could have gone through life without tasting such a common bit of sweetness. "Let's go before—"

The door of the Strega opened, and Mooch appeared, his red hair gleaming in the summer sun. Theo pocketed the candy and started to move.

"No," Viola said, stopping him. "You are not coming with me. Not in there."

He blinked at her with the frown of a man unaccustomed to not getting his way. "Of course I am."

"No," she told him, shaking her head. "The Strega isn't simply some saloon filled with your common ubriaconi. Mooch, he can burn a house down around you, and others are more deadly still. They're not friends, not anymore, and I won't risk your life."

"I'm not sure that's your decision to make," Theo said, visibly bristling.

Mooch was growing impatient, but Viola would not give in. "I will not be the one to tell Ruby what became of you if this goes poorly. If not for me, please, go. For her. Ruby will need someone to come home to."

Theo's jaw tensed, but finally he relented. "I'll expect a full report."

"Bene," Viola said. "Whatever you want. But you must go. *Now.*"

She didn't wait for Theo's agreement this time, but turned and made her way toward the impatient boy waiting at the back entrance of the Strega.

"What took so long?" she asked Mooch. The meeting her brother had set up with Nibsy should have started already.

"You told me to wait until it was clear," Mooch said with a cocky shrug. "Nibsy didn't leave like you said he would. Not right away, at least."

"He's gone now?" she asked.

"Went out the front a few minutes ago."

Viola frowned. If Nibsy was late for his meeting with Paolo, her brother would be in a wretched mood later. But there was nothing she could do for that, and there was no time for her to worry about things she could not change.

"Thank you," she told Mooch, meeting his eyes and trying to soften her expression. "I wasn't sure if you'd—"

"I owed you one favor for getting me out of there. No one else came," Mooch said with a shrug, but his voice was empty of emotion, hollow as Theo said his expression had been when they'd brought him into the courtroom. Then Mooch's mouth went tight. "But don't think this means I've forgotten what you did to Nibs on that bridge. You took that damn lying thief's side over the Devil's Own, and you made sure that Nibsy'll never walk good again. This don't make us friends. It only makes us even."

"Of course," Viola told him, hiding her frustration. She didn't regret her actions on the bridge, but there was no way to convince Mooch—or any of the Devil's Own—that she'd been right to protect Esta. Not when Nibsy was whispering his lies into their ears.

It might have been less trouble to just kill him, but Viola understood that his death wouldn't be enough. *Make me a martyr,* Nibsy had taunted, and he'd been right. To break his control over the Devil's Own, Viola knew she had to expose Nibsy for what he was first, or else the vacuum of his death would destroy everything Dolph had tried to build.

"My loyalty is to Dolph—and to what he stood for," she told Mooch, lowering her voice. "I'm not your enemy, Mooch. I never was."

"Yeah, well . . . that remains to be seen." Mooch frowned, as though he was suddenly unsure about what he'd promised to do. But he relented a second later, stepping aside to let her in.

Viola hadn't been inside the private quarters in the back of the Bella Strega since the day when everything had fallen apart on the bridge. She'd assumed then that nothing could be worse than what had happened after Khafre Hall, when they'd realized all had been lost—the Book, the artifacts, and their leader. But a few days later, she'd lost even more. She'd lost her home. Her purpose.

Stepping into the back rooms of the building was like stepping back into a different part of her life. The Elizabeth Street entrance opened into a small vestibule, where the aromas of the kitchen had seeped into the wood. The air from outside brought with it the sharpness of the trash that littered the alley, and the mixture of the two was a scent as familiar to Viola as her mother's rose water. There was something missing, though. Something was off. Then she realized—she hadn't been greeted by the warm smell of bread baking, as she had been when Dolph sat in the barroom, holding court, and Tilly stood at the great iron stove making the food that knitted them together.

"You'd better get on with it," Mooch said. "The place is crawling with the boys, and I can't keep them occupied all by myself."

With a sure nod, Viola took the narrow staircase up two floors to the hallway she'd once called home. She didn't bother to enter the room that had been hers. There was no time, and she had no desire to feel more loss than that which already creased her heart. Instead, she went to the end of the hall, where Dolph and Leena—and then later, Dolph alone—had made a home.

The door was locked, a marked change from when the rooms had belonged to Dolph. He had never feared intrusion, not when his gang wore a mark that could unmake them. Viola doubted that anyone would have dared cross his sanctuary without an invitation, even without the marks. It simply wasn't done. The Devil's Own was a gang, yes. A rowdy, dangerous bunch. But Dolph Saunders had given them a place to build a home for themselves, and there was a certain honor among thieves.

A pin from her hair made short work of the lock, and Viola let herself into the quiet of the flat. Once inside the apartment, she paused, allowing the past to wash over her. She'd been Leena's friend before Dolph's, and together they'd spent hours in these rooms. How many times had she sat in that chair by the window, learning her letters or talking strategy? How often had the rooms been a haven, free of judgment and shame, filled with something that had felt like hope?

Dolph should still be here. Dolph, who had lied to her . . . or at least, who had hidden the truth about too many things. About his cane and how it came by the awful power it held. About Libitina.

Why had he not explained how the blade worked and let Viola make her choice?

She knew already the answer. It had been a trick, yes. One that perhaps a true friend should not have played, but then, Viola had not really *wanted* to know. She'd accepted the knife without question, used its deadly blade without considering, because she'd wanted to believe that an acquired skill was somehow different from the heart of a thing. Viola had wanted to imagine that she could refuse that essential part of what she was—and what she felt drawn to do with her affinity. Healing and death, two sides of life itself. One impossible without the other.

The truth was that her friend had deceived her. The truth was also that he had done her a kindness. Dolph had allowed her to *be*, without judgment, what she was made to be. If Libitina was only so deadly because

Viola was actually channeling her own magic through the knife, then it meant that Dolph had given her a way to use her affinity without wrestling with the shame of it. He had given her a way out of the torture that would have come from holding herself back, from denying her magic.

How many Mageus had Viola watched suffer as they tried to hide what they were? How many turned to Nitewein or worse to dull the ache of unused affinities? *Too many.* She'd seen them in the Strega and in the streets, desperate and aching. She'd thought she was different somehow—stronger—and she'd pitied them, not knowing how close she'd come to being in their shoes.

Viola looked around the apartment and realized that nothing had changed—not really—but even so, the rooms were different now. The feel of the space was colder, despite the warm breeze that came in through the lace curtains. The oil painting they'd stolen from Morgan's collection still hung on the wall over the bookshelf, and Viola took a moment to trace the strange design on the book Newton held, remembering the night Dolph had told her why the Ars Arcana was so important. Something about that painting sparked another memory. . . .

There had been something carved into the cover of the Ars Arcana, hadn't there? But Viola couldn't remember whether it had been this design or some other, not with whatever Harte Darrigan had done to her that night.

She would never know for sure. The Book was gone now, along with Esta and the Magician.

Viola turned away from the painting and the questions she had no answers to and focused on what she *could* find instead. Running her finger across the spines of the books on the shelf, she dismissed some immediately. Voltaire and Kierkegaard wouldn't have the answers she needed. There was the book they had taken from the Metropolitan, an ancient-looking thing that had once belonged to Newton himself, but the answers she was looking for wouldn't be there, either. Finally, she came across a simple volume, bound with stitched cloth instead of leather, and she pulled it from the shelf. Thumbing through it, she could not stop the emotion of seeing Dolph's familiar script from crashing over her—the warmth of the memories and the disappointment as well.

As she flipped through the pages, Viola realized there was too much there: notations about the Brink, notes about the stones and the Book, and pages filled with crude sketches done in scratches of ink. There were notes written in English and Italian, German and French. As she searched for what she needed, Viola heard voices in the hallway, and panic slid down her spine, but . . . *there*. A sketch of a familiar shape. It was clearly Libitina, with her thin, sharp blade and ornate handle, sketched onto the page. But Viola could not read the words. They were written in a language she did not know, as though Dolph had been purposely cautious and intended to keep this knowledge from her.

Viola shook off her disappointment as she tucked the notebook into her skirts. It was a risk, maybe even a mistake, but she could not be sure how many of the pages she needed, and she could not leave without the knowledge she'd come for.

The voices were closer now, just outside the door, and even if they weren't heading for Dolph's apartment, Viola knew that she could not leave the way she'd come. Without hesitating, she went for the window. The gauzy curtains fluttered in the breeze when she opened the window wider. She pulled herself over the sill to the fire escape, then pushed the window back to where it had been before, and began the climb down. She did not look behind her to see if she'd been spotted, and her heart did not stop racing until she was on the ground and far away from the one place that had ever felt like home.

TIME'S FANGED JAWS

1904—Denver

North and Cordelia didn't come back that first night—Esta hadn't really expected them to, but she could tell that Maggie had hoped. They waited up until late, and she helped as Maggie tried to keep herself busy by making more of the Quellant. By the time they finally finished, the city outside their window was quiet, but the thoughts running through Esta's mind were too loud to let her sleep.

She wondered if Harte had made it to California yet, and she hoped he was having better luck than she was. She still regretted getting rid of the bracelet he'd left her. Even traveling with the two Antistasi, she felt alone, but it was never worse than in the middle of the night, when the world was quiet and endless with sleep. In those deep hours, she would have welcomed the sound of Harte's voice in her ear, the feel of his lips against her skin. She should have appreciated the bracelet for the gift it was. Once they met up, it was likely they wouldn't have much time. At least with the bracelet, she could have had the illusion of him.

The sky was already lightening when Esta finally drifted off, but her dreams were not easy. She found herself in a desert where dangerous magic swirled through the air. Beneath the sand, a monstrous serpent slid along, chasing her across an endless stretch of emptiness. Ahead, silhouetted against the blazing sky, she saw Harte standing with his back to her. Her heart leapt at the sight of him, and in response, the serpentine monster changed course, aiming instead for him.

Esta shouted, but Harte didn't turn. She started to run, but she knew she would never reach him in time. When she reached for her affinity, her magic lay cold and dead, and in the end, the serpent rose from the sand and lunged for Harte, its fanged jaws wide. As the serpent's teeth clamped shut, Esta woke with a start, the scar on her wrist burning again.

Despite the warm breeze coming in through the window, she felt chilled. Across the room, Maggie snored softly, but Esta didn't even try to sleep again.

They spent the rest of the next two days keeping themselves busy while they waited for news that never came. Esta watched and helped Maggie when she could, but the days dragged on, and they both grew more impatient and anxious for word from North and Cordelia.

"I think you've killed it," Esta said. She couldn't take listening to the sound of the pestle grinding against the marble mortar anymore. It was the afternoon of the third day, and she'd been watching out the window, jealous of everyone who was free to go about their business in the streets below as she tried to distract herself, but now she turned back to look at Maggie.

"What?" Maggie paused and looked up over her glasses.

The room finally descended into blessed silence. Maggie's hair had been threatening to fall from its loosely pinned bun all morning, and now a long piece did fall in front of her face. Maggie pushed it back, blinking a little, like she'd been so preoccupied with her work that she'd forgotten about Esta completely.

"Whatever you're grinding up in there—it's dead," Esta said, trying to keep her voice pleasant and not as frayed as her nerves felt. "Completely and utterly. You can't do anything else to it."

Maggie glanced down and gave a small curse that might have been amusing in any other situation. "I overdid it," she said. "And it was the last of my camphor. I won't be able to make any more of the Quellant until I get more." She cursed again.

"So let's go get some," Esta suggested. She wasn't used to sitting still for so long, and being trapped inside the dingy apartment was doing nothing for her nerves. "I'm sure there's a pharmacy or a shop or *something* in this town."

Maggie chewed on her lip, considering Esta's proposal, but eventually she shook her head. "I'll start on something else instead. If Jericho happens to come back today, I don't want to miss him."

"I'm sure North would wait for you," Esta told Maggie. She actually *wasn't* sure, considering how angry he'd been about the truth tablets.

But Maggie ended the conversation by returning to her work.

A breeze stirred through the window, but it did nothing for the close stuffiness of the small apartment. "Or we could go to *them*," Esta offered. "We can head out to the show and see if they've learned anything or made any progress. Getting out of this apartment might be what we both need." After all, she couldn't steal the dagger from a distance, and she definitely didn't trust that Cordelia wouldn't take it for the Antistasi.

"We already agreed that it's safer for us to stay here," Maggie reminded Esta, but the yearning was clear in Maggie's expression.

"Did we?" Esta asked, her patience ragged. "Because I don't remember having much say in the matter."

"With those incendiaries I set off, they're probably already looking for you—for all of us," Maggie said. "Jericho and Cordelia were right to leave us here."

Esta let out a long, resigned breath. "Maybe, but I hate that we have no idea what's happening out there." And that fact, along with the gnawing absence of her affinity, was driving Esta mad.

"I trust Jericho," Maggie said, like he was the only variable.

"Sure . . . but do you trust Cordelia?" Esta pressed.

"She's Antistasi," Maggie said, and it sounded an awful lot like she was trying to convince herself.

"Maybe . . ." Esta frowned. "But it feels like we're putting a lot of faith in someone we don't really know."

"You saw that tattoo on Cordelia's leg." Maggie pushed her glasses back up on her nose. "It covered most of her thigh. Putting herself through that would have taken a real commitment to the Antistasi's cause."

"Ruth was committed too. Look how that turned out," Esta said, before she could think better of it.

She realized her misstep immediately when Maggie's brows drew together.

"I didn't mean—" Esta stopped, knowing from Maggie's expression that she needed a different approach. "I'm sorry," she said, backtracking. "It's not like you were the only one who was blind to Ruth's faults. I was right there with you, and I should have known better."

Maggie's expression softened a little. "It's not like she was *your* sister."

"No, she wasn't," Esta admitted, thanking her lucky stars for that fact. "But I knew someone a lot like her once. It's just . . . well, you'd think I would have learned by now."

Maggie was staring at Esta now, pestle still raised. Her expression had shifted from anger to interest. "What happened?"

"Nothing," Esta said, pretending to brush aside Maggie's interest. "It doesn't matter."

"You might try trusting me, you know," Maggie said. "After all we've been through at this point . . ."

Esta didn't immediately answer. She knew it would be better if Maggie had to work a little for the information. It would land better, hook her more completely.

Maggie frowned at her. "Never mind. Forget that I even asked. Clearly you're not ever going to trust me, no matter how many times I save your life."

Esta could have made up some lie or changed the subject, but she had the sense that she was being presented with an opportunity. Harte was hundreds of miles away, and she was without both her cuff and her affinity. Now that Cordelia had entered the picture, Esta was starting to understand that the Antistasi's influence might reach farther than she'd expected. She might need an ally, and Maggie seemed the most likely candidate.

"No," Esta said, the portrait of contriteness. "You're right. You *do* deserve to know. But it's hard for me to talk about my past."

"You don't have to," Maggie told her with a resigned sigh. "But it's not like we have anywhere to go."

Esta knew instinctively that the moment in front of her was delicate. Maggie was right there, ripe for the con, but any lie she told could be too easily unraveled. If she truly wanted Maggie on her side—if she wanted to *keep* her there—Esta knew she had to give Maggie something true.

Too bad the truth was a secret she often kept even from herself.

Esta studied the yellowed lace covering the windows for a long stretch of seconds, considering where she should start.

"I told you about what we did in New York—how we broke into Khafre Hall and stole the artifacts—but I didn't tell you about before that." She paused, gathering her courage. It felt monumental to reveal so much, even if she had a strategic reason for doing it. "Before I was the Devil's Thief, I was just *a* thief," she began, her voice shaking more than she'd expected. "It's what I was raised to be—nothing more and nothing less—and I was fine with my situation because I believed in the person I was following. In fact, I never questioned him. If he was hard on me, I dismissed it as his right." Esta shrugged, remembering the times Professor Lachlan had berated her for her impulsiveness, the small failures that he never let her forget. "After all, he'd raised me. I was willing to lie, steal, and betray whoever he asked me to, all because I wanted to prove myself worthy of the life he'd given me."

"That's completely understandable," Maggie said softly. "I didn't know my mother. Ruth was the only family I ever really had, and I understood exactly what she'd sacrificed to raise me. It's one of the reasons I didn't leave after what she did to Jericho. That, and what she was working toward seemed bigger than my own petty concerns."

Esta turned back to Maggie and wondered for the first time if maybe she wasn't as alone in this as she'd suspected. "It was the same for me," she admitted. "I wanted to earn my place, but maybe even more, I wanted the dream he offered," she told Maggie, meeting her eyes now. "He told me that I could help him destroy the Brink—that together we could save the old magic. I was so committed to that cause, I didn't see the truth." Esta took a breath before she forced herself to go on. "I found out eventually that the dream I'd committed myself to wasn't even possible. All his talk of bringing down the Brink and saving magic? It was a lie. He'd only ever wanted power for himself. And in the end, a lot of people got hurt because I realized that too late." Dakari and Dolph, and so many others she'd betrayed.

"The Antistasi's cause isn't a lie, Esta," Maggie said as ardently as a true believer. "I have to believe that making the world safe for those like us is possible."

"I hope you're right," Esta said honestly. "I want that every bit as much as you do. But I hope your commitment to that cause doesn't blind you to the danger Cordelia might pose." She held Maggie's gaze. "Or to the Antistasi's faults."

Maggie frowned, considering Esta carefully, and Esta couldn't tell what she was thinking. She wondered if she'd gone too far.

"This person you're talking about—the one you were following," Maggie ventured. "It's Harte, isn't it?"

At first Esta didn't realize what Maggie had just said. But then understanding struck fast and hard. "What did you call him?" The words seemed stuck in her throat.

Maggie hadn't said "Ben," the name Harte had given the Antistasi in St. Louis. She'd said "Harte," which meant that she knew.

"Were you ever going to tell us who Ben really was?" Maggie asked, her expression unreadable.

Maggie's mouth was still moving, but suddenly Esta could no longer hear her. All of the sound in the room drained away. At first it felt like shock, but when Esta shook her head, trying to dislodge the silence, it didn't work.

Then Esta's vision flickered.

The world around her began fuzzing in and out of focus, and again it reminded her of the picture on one of those old TVs, and she understood instantly that this was more than simple panic. Whatever had happened to her before was happening again.

But so much worse.

Maggie must have already realized that something was wrong. She was moving across the space between them, holding out her hand to Esta. She hadn't taken more than three steps before Esta's vision flickered again, and then Maggie was gone.

The room looked suddenly different. It was the same apartment, but a family was gathered around a table eating together. Another flicker and she saw an empty room. Then a room with three men playing cards. Then Maggie. And then Esta could see everything at once, the different versions of the room layered one on top of another, superimposed. It felt like all of the possible realities were vying for prominence.

Esta felt the seconds sliding around her, slithering across her skin like the serpent from her dream. The scar on her wrist was burning as she tried to grasp hold of the present, where Maggie was still trying to reach her, but reality blurred and flickered, and then time opened its fanged jaws and swallowed her whole.

GONE

1904—San Francisco

In the moment before sleep gave way to waking, when the world was still obscured by the haze of dreams and the shadows of night, Harte Darrigan thought he was back on his couch in New York. At first he thought it was still weeks before, when he'd been forced to sleep in his parlor because Esta had taken over his bed. Before everything came rushing back to him, he could imagine her there, sleeping a few feet away behind his closed bedroom door, her scent on his sheets in the home he had made for himself from nothing more than determination and a dream for something more.

Then Harte felt a sharp, burning itch on his leg, and when he went to reach for it, he found that he couldn't. His arms had been pinned behind his back and secured at his wrists. He opened his eyes, not to his apartment, but to darkness as the scent of dust and dampness burned away the rest of the dream. All the events of the past few weeks and days and hours came rushing back in a dizzying, horrible flood.

The headpiece. His father. *Esta.* She would be waiting for him.

The thought of her had Harte sitting up with a sudden lurch that made his head spin again. His ears were ringing, and his stomach flipped at the movement, but he swallowed down any nausea. He wouldn't be sick. He *wouldn't.*

How long has it been?

Now that his eyes had adjusted to the dim light, Harte saw he was in some kind of cellar. Across the way, a door was fitted so poorly that light came in around the edges and kept the room from being pitch-black. It was cold like a cellar too, and Harte started to shiver.

As he waited for the room to stop spinning, he used the toe of one foot to rub the back of his ankle, trying to satisfy the aching itch that had woken him. The spot was tender to the touch, and he felt more pain than satisfaction when he scratched it. He tried not to think about the vermin that had been crawling all over him while he'd been unconscious, but he'd spent enough time sleeping on the streets or in flea-infested boardinghouses to know when he'd been bitten by something. Even though it hurt, he couldn't stop himself from scratching, but at least the pain of the bite was distracting him a little from the more persistent ache throbbing through his head.

His father, or whoever had hit him back at the restaurant, had done a thorough job of it. His eyes still weren't quite focusing correctly, but Harte could almost begin to make out the features of the room. One wall was lined with shelving that contained boxes and glass bottles. On the other was a row of large burlap sacks filled with dry goods. Harte realized then that the uneven pallet he was currently sitting on was a pile of those sacks, which had been emptied and stacked along the third wall. His father had mentioned that he owned a store—maybe he'd brought Harte there?

In the corner, Harte could hear something scratching and rustling—a rat, probably. Maybe a couple of them. But otherwise, the room was silent as a grave. The wide, rough floorboards that made up the ceiling above were quiet. If anyone was up there, he couldn't tell. He didn't plan on sticking around to find out.

With effort, he managed to get to his feet. He took one step and then two, and just as he thought he might be able to make it to the door, the room tilted again. Harte felt his legs going out from under him, and then the floor gave way and he collapsed. Since his hands were still tied behind him, he couldn't catch himself, and he landed hard, rattling his already-throbbing head again.

The earthen floor felt cool and damp against his cheek, and Harte couldn't do much more than breathe in the scent of dirt as he tried to keep his stomach from revolting.

He needed to get out of the ropes. It should have been easy enough—already he could tell that they weren't tied with any kind of expertise. He writhed a little, twisting his hands and shoulders to work at them, but every movement made his head spin and his stomach rebel. The only thing that helped was to close his eyes and hold perfectly still. His head was pounding so sharply within his skull that Harte was sure he could actually see his heartbeat.

It was a long time later when he realized that his position on the floor should have been more uncomfortable. The necklace with the Djinni's Star and Esta's cuff had been secured beneath his shirt. He'd wrapped the two artifacts close to his skin with a length of material, because he wanted to make sure that no one could lift them from his pockets—and because Seshat seemed to retreat when they were close to his body. They should have been poking into him—uncomfortable lumps between his body and the hard, earthen ground. But they weren't.

Harte sensed Seshat laughing then, a low rumble of mockery. *I told you,* she said. *You were soft and let an old man get the best of you. How could you ever expect to stop* me?

Harte rolled to one side and then the other, pressing his torso against the floor in a desperate bid to find some sign that the artifacts had simply shifted. But the movement made him dizzy, and panic made his vision blur and darken around the edges, and as he slipped back into unconsciousness, Harte knew that no amount of wishing or anything else would change the fact that the two stones that had been in his possession were gone.

THE TRIALS OF OTHERS

1904—Denver

O nce he was officially hired, North immediately threw himself into his new position with the Curtis Brothers' Show. He mucked stalls, brushed down horses, and lifted bale after bale of hay. By the end of that first night, his muscles ached something fierce. As long as he was working, he wasn't thinking, which was fine by him. Because if he started thinking, he'd have to make a decision—whether to forgive Maggie for what she'd done to him. Or for keeping it from him for so long. Whether he even could.

He didn't go back to town that first night or the next. Instead, he finished each day by collapsing into his assigned bunk and letting himself be pulled into a dreamless sleep. Then he rose early the following morning to start all over again. He'd figure things out with Maggie soon enough, he reasoned. It wasn't like he had anything to tell her yet, anyway. Three days in, and he'd only managed to see Bill Pickett from a distance. Cordelia had been right—the bulldogger kept to his own work and minded his business.

But then, everyone around the grounds was keeping to themselves. A few of the hands had been arrested during the raid, and no one was much interested in getting to know the newcomer who'd taken their place. North's experience in the mess tent had been the worst part, at first. There, men sat in small groups arranged by position and race, their backs turned and their heads down to ward off any intrusion.

Pretending not to notice the unspoken boundaries between the various groups, North sat directly in the space left between a couple of sullen-looking white cowboys and a couple of older gentlemen with skin even darker brown than Pickett's.

The older men turned out to be soldiers, veterans of the 10th Cavalry, who'd mostly served after the Civil War and out in the western territories, where they'd worked to maintain the peace by fighting against some of the same Lakota they now shared the arena with each afternoon. At first the men were pleasant if distant, but after a bit they warmed up enough to start regaling North with stories of their days in the cavalry. The stories grew more fantastic as each man tried to outdo the one who'd spoken before. Their good-natured competition wasn't exactly a chore to listen to, and North's enjoyment of—and growing respect for—the men wasn't an act, even if he was still angling for an introduction to Bill Pickett.

North felt a certain camaraderie with a sergeant named George, an older man with a long, narrow face capped by heavy brows. His brown eyes were speckled with amber, deep-set over a hooked nose, and his droll mouth drooped a little on one side when he talked. It was the result of a fever, he explained, after the army's hospital wouldn't admit him for treatment even with his many years of service. George didn't say it outright, but North understood—it was because of the color of his skin.

George looked far older than his fifty-odd years, but when he talked, his eyes lit with humor, and North could almost see the younger man George must once have been: the man who'd been born on a plantation and had run away and taken his freedom for himself when he wasn't more than twelve. George had taught himself to read so he could take up command of his own battalion instead of taking orders from the white sergeants who refused to see him and his men as their equals. He'd joined the Curtis Brothers' Show after his wife, Letty, had died a few years before. After she'd passed, George couldn't bring himself to stay in the house they'd shared. Too many memories, he'd told North.

North could appreciate the way George talked about his Letty, like she had been and still was the one and only light in his life. That kind of sentiment North understood deep to his core—it was exactly how he'd felt about Maggie, almost from the moment he'd met her. It was how he *still* felt about her, he realized, *despite everything.* And he found himself telling George about Maggie in turn.

Listening to their stories got North to thinking, though. He'd never known many people of color before—not in Chicago or Texas or even in St. Louis. It wasn't that he'd ever had any poor feelings about a person because of their skin, though he knew plenty who did. It was more that he simply hadn't thought to step outside his own steady path. Even on Gunter's ranch, he'd stuck to the group of Anglo cowhands and hadn't bothered much with the vaqueros unless he was working with them. He'd certainly never socialized with them.

Talking to George and his friends, though, and taking their easy company for the gift it was, North started to think that maybe he'd spent too much of his life only worrying about himself—and about the magic that flowed in his veins. He'd been so focused on how the world saw those with the old magic, he'd never considered that there were a lot of other folks with trials of their own.

The next morning, North was leading one of the horses in from the field to saddle it for the show, when he realized that his body hadn't felt so well used and sore from a good, solid day's work in a long, long time. The jobs he'd done in St. Louis for Mother Ruth and her Antistasi were often dangerous, but they'd never been all that physically taxing. Now North was starting to remember what it felt like to use his body the way it was intended. His skin was tender from the sun, and he knew he smelled of horse and sweat, but he felt happier than he had in years.

He patted the side of the horse he was leading, a pretty dappled Appaloosa mare the color of caramel. Out in the field, she'd rolled herself in a nice patch of mud, and while it might have made *her* feel better, it meant more work for North. He'd have to get her light, speckled hindquarters clean before the evening's show.

The sun was already low in the sky as North looped the mecate reins through his belt and started to fill a bucket of water from the pump. The mare seemed biddable and good-natured, from what he could tell. Maybe that was why he let himself get distracted by someone watching him from the edge of the corral. North thought he saw something on the man's lapel glinting in the sun. It wasn't the silver star of a marshal, but a round medallion that looked like a type he'd seen too many times before.

But that couldn't be right. There was no reason for the Society to be so far from St. Louis, way out in the mountains of Colorado.

North was so busy trying to get a look at the man without really looking that he wasn't paying attention to the mare like he should have been. Without warning or reason, the horse spooked, and before North knew what was happening, the animal's body was slamming into him. Nearly a thousand pounds of horseflesh pushed him into the fence as her hind leg kicked out.

He managed to dodge the worst of it. The hoof only caught the back of his thigh as he tumbled to the ground. But then the mare reared up, screaming her disapproval, and North knew he was in trouble. He barely had time to turn away, and he only had his arms to shield himself from the pummeling that was about to happen as the horse rose above him. Before her hooves could do any damage, though, someone else was there, standing between him and the Appaloosa. At first North only saw the shadow of a man silhouetted against the bright sun. He'd turned away from North as he walked the horse back, clicking and cooing at her until she stopped huffing her fear and finally calmed down.

North was still trying to catch his breath when the man turned. For a second he was too stunned to believe it could be Bill Pickett standing over him. It took Pickett extending a hand to him before North managed to pull himself together.

Pickett's grip was strong and sure, and the other cowboy hoisted North up to his feet like he weighed nothing at all.

"You okay there?" Pickett asked, squinting a little. He offered North the leading rope again.

"I think I'll live," North said, taking the rope. "Probably'll have a bruise on my leg to show off tomorrow, but it could have been a lot worse. 'Specially if you hadn't been there."

Pickett's brows went up in what looked to be amusement, and the heavy mustache over his mouth twitched. "Worse? You would've been *dead* if I hadn't been here. Can't get much worse than that."

Pickett was maybe in his early thirties, a decade or more older than North. His tightly curling dark-brown hair was clipped close to his head beneath his hat, and he carried himself with the confidence and self-possession of a man who knew what he was about. North had heard someone comment that Pickett's mother had been Choctaw. It hadn't been a compliment, but now North wondered if maybe they were right. Pickett's dark russet skin looked like it was permanently being warmed by the sun.

Then he decided it didn't matter. "Seems like I owe you my life, then," he told Pickett. "You didn't have to put yourself at risk like that."

"Yeah, well . . . I wasn't in any real danger. From the way you were walking when I saw you leading the mare in from the fields, I figured no one had warned you that she spooks easy around people she don't know." Pickett patted the horse's nose affectionately. "Steady as anything for Jimmy when he's riding her, but anyone else? She acts like she's still barely green broke."

"Well, you have my thanks," North told Pickett as he held out his hand. "I'm Jeric—" He stumbled a bit, tripping on his own tongue to keep himself from saying his actual name instead of the one Cordelia had given to the show's manager.

Pickett's brows went up again, until they were completely hidden by the brim of his hat. "Don't you know your own name?"

"Sorry. Must still be a little spooked myself," North said, trying to play off the slip with humor. "I'm Jerry. Jerry Robertson."

"One of the new ones," Pickett said with a tone that seemed more resigned than anything else. "You from here in Denver, then?"

"No, sir," North told him.

"No?" Pickett looked surprised.

"Originally, I'm from back east. Near around Chicago. But I've been traveling out around these parts for a while, looking for work here and there," he said.

"Well, watch yourself around this pretty girl," Pickett told him. "Last thing you want is to get your head kicked in."

The whole exchange lasted a couple of minutes, and before North could even consider what to do with the opportunity, Pickett was on his way. North turned back to the Appaloosa, more than a little shaken. The man on the other side of the fence was gone, but North realized suddenly where he'd seen the man before. It had been in St. Louis. The man had been wearing the uniform of the Jefferson Guard at the hotel the night the Antistasi had rescued the Thief.

If he was right, it meant that the Society was here, and if that was the case, there was a good chance that they'd been followed all the way from St. Louis.

It was hell to wait until his shift was over, but leaving sooner would only draw attention. As soon as North was done in the barn, though, he walked right past the mess tent toward the exit to the grounds. He hadn't gotten far when he ran into Cordelia.

"Where are you headed?" she asked, her dark brows bunching like caterpillars as she frowned. He could see the suspicion in her eyes and in the tightness around her mouth.

"We have a problem," he told her, explaining what he'd seen and who he thought the ruddy-faced man was. "It was probably the explosions Maggie set off. They would have been a dead giveaway to anyone familiar with her work in St. Louis." *And in Texas.*

Cordelia's frown deepened. "What about Pickett?"

"Pickett can wait. I *told* you—I need to talk to Maggie," North said, moving to go around the sharpshooter. He'd already waited too long. "I need to warn her."

236   LISA MAXWELL

Cordelia stepped in front of him. "*You* need to get the dagger from Pickett."

"You don't understand," North said. "The Jefferson Guard are the Society's own private police force. If they're here, it means they know we're here too."

"Then it's even more important that we get the dagger before they find you," Cordelia said.

"But Maggie—"

"Is safe right now," Cordelia told him. "I was headed into town anyway. I'll take care of warning the others." She pulled something from her pocket—one of the white tablets Maggie had given her—and placed it in his hand. All North could do was stare at it. Pickett had saved his life. Could he really do what he'd promised?

"Go on," Cordelia said, shooing North on when he didn't move immediately. "If you're right about what you saw, the sooner you find the dagger and get out of town, the better."

FRIENDS IN HIGH PLACES

1904—Denver

*S*he's gone.

It was all Maggie could seem to think as she stared in shock at the place where Esta had been sitting a few minutes before. If Maggie hadn't seen it for herself, she never would have believed it. Esta had flickered, looking oddly like a moving picture Maggie had seen once at a traveling dime museum. Then Esta's whole body had gone nearly transparent. Maggie had been able to see straight through the silhouette of her, to the room beyond. One second Esta had been there, whole and real, and the next she was gone.

No . . . No, no, no . . . First the necklace and now the Thief?

Maggie never should have pushed. She shouldn't have questioned Esta or revealed what she knew about Harte Darrigan. She should have kept playing along, but Esta had seemed so sincere talking about her childhood that Maggie had thought maybe they could finally trust each other. She hadn't been able to stop herself from asking, and because Maggie had pushed too far, Esta had run, the same as Maggie had feared from the very beginning.

Except . . . that wasn't *possible*. Esta had taken a dose of the Quellant earlier that morning. She shouldn't have been able to use her affinity to evade them. And yet . . .

Maggie stared at the spot where Esta had been and willed her back, but though the minutes ticked by, Esta never returned. Instead, a little while later the door to the apartment opened without warning, and Cordelia entered.

The sharpshooter took one look around, and her expression hardened. "Where's Esta?"

"Gone," Maggie said, realizing how completely insipid she sounded the second the word was out of her mouth. She knew exactly how bad it looked that Esta wasn't there.

"You let her go out alone?" Cordelia asked.

Maggie was shaking her head. "I didn't *let* her do anything."

"Well, she's clearly not *here*."

Maggie didn't know how to explain other than to say, "She disappeared."

"Disappeared?" It was clear Cordelia either didn't understand or didn't believe her.

"Like a ghost. One second Esta was sitting right there. We were talking, and . . ." Maggie didn't want to admit that maybe she'd been the cause. "It was like she'd never been there at all."

"She can't be gone," Cordelia said, sounding suddenly every bit as worried as Maggie felt. "Losing the Thief would be a terrible mess for the Antistasi"—her eyes narrowed—"and for you."

Something in Cordelia's tone struck a chord of warning in Maggie. "What's that supposed to mean?"

"It means that you ain't the only one with friends in high places, Margaret," Cordelia said, not quite answering her question.

Panic buzzed through Maggie like a swarm of angry bees. She couldn't get herself to think clearly. She had to *think*.

"I gave her the Quellant," she said as much to herself as to Cordelia. That fact alone should have *meant* something, but Esta had still managed to get away from her. Fear was starting to claw at Maggie now. "She shouldn't have been able to go anywhere."

A knock came at the door, and Maggie had a rush of hope that Esta had returned. But it wasn't Esta. Jericho walked in, and for a second the buzzing stopped, the fear receded, and everything fell away—everything but Jericho Northwood.

He came back. All Maggie could do was take in every inch of him, grateful and happy that Jericho was there despite what she'd done to him. She could only hope it meant that maybe he'd started to forgive her, but before Maggie could say even a word of welcome, Cordelia piped up.

"What are *you* doing here?" Cordelia sounded more angry than surprised. "I thought we agreed that you'd stay where you were."

"Maybe you agreed, but I told you I needed to talk to Maggie," he said, stepping past Cordelia without even looking at her, but he'd only partially closed the distance between them when he stopped short. "Where's Esta?"

"Gone," Cordelia said, her nostrils flaring. "She managed to slip away from Margaret."

"She *disappeared*," Maggie corrected.

Jericho frowned. "Weren't you still giving her the Quellant?"

"She took a dose this morning," Maggie assured him. Then another thought struck her. The idea had been rustling in the back of her brain for some time, but it had grown louder when she saw Esta vanish. Now she could no longer ignore it. "You don't think the whole story Esta told us about Seshat could have actually had some truth to it, do you?"

"No," Jericho said. "Of course not." But he didn't look as sure as he was trying to sound.

Maggie could sense Cordelia's unspoken questions, but she couldn't worry about them. Not right then. She couldn't let go of the idea that maybe Esta hadn't been lying, as they'd originally suspected. The story she'd told them in that boxcar as they were leaving Texas had seemed ridiculous. Neither of them had *really* believed her, but Maggie had been happy to use Esta's tale to her own advantage. Now she couldn't help but worry that maybe she'd been wrong. "Still, if the story about that ancient goddess was real—"

"It's *not*," North told her. "We're still here, aren't we? The world hasn't ended like she claimed it would."

He had a point. They *were* all still there, whole and real. The world was still spinning on, seemingly untouched. If Seshat was real, the goddess certainly hadn't followed through on her threat.

"Maybe this is all for the best," North said, looking almost thoughtful. Almost relieved.

"I don't know what either of you is going on about, but there ain't no way this could *possibly* be for the best," Cordelia said. "The Antistasi need Esta Filosik. She's necessary to our cause."

But Jericho wasn't looking at Cordelia or paying her any attention. His gaze was on Maggie, and there was a light in his eyes that made her stomach flip a little. "Maybe Esta doesn't have to be necessary to *our* plans," he said softly. "To yours and mine."

"What are you talking about?" Maggie asked, not quite understanding. The Antistasi's plans *were* their plans. *Weren't they?*

Jericho came over to take Maggie's hands in his. She could feel how rough they'd already become. "I've been doing a lot of thinking over the last few days, Mags. Maybe we should let this whole business go. The Antistasi. Esta Filosik. We could leave it all behind. We could start a life somewhere before we run out of chances."

Maggie's whole body suddenly felt cold. "Even if Esta's gone, we still have a chance to get one of the artifacts."

"One of them?" Cordelia asked. "But y'all said you have the necklace."

Maggie exchanged a nervous glance with Jericho.

"You said you had the Djinni's Star," Cordelia repeated. "Y'all told me the necklace was safe."

"We did have it," Jericho told Cordelia. "But her partner took the necklace and ran off as we were leaving St. Louis."

"Y'all are telling me you lost the artifact *and* the Thief?" Cordelia said, her expression unreadable. "That's the real reason y'all disappeared after the train explosion, ain't it? You were hiding your failure. I bet you wouldn't have even bothered to return to the Antistasi if I hadn't found you."

"Of course we would have!" Maggie exclaimed. Her stomach churned at the way Cordelia was staring at her, but she had to stay calm. She had to figure this out. "I thought if we could get the dagger, it would make up for losing the necklace," she explained. "We hoped it would be

THE SERPENT'S CURSE

241

enough." She turned back to Jericho. "Which is why we *have* to get the Pharaoh's Heart. We can't give up now. Not when there's still a chance that we could help the Antistasi to change things—*really* change things—for Mageus in this country."

North pushed back a piece of hair that had fallen into her face. The motion was so gentle, and the look on his face was tender enough to make Maggie want to cry. "If the Antistasi haven't changed anything in a thousand years, what makes you think that *we're* the ones who can finally get the job done?"

Because I have to, Maggie thought, the buzzing panic swarming through her again now.

"Who else will do it, Jericho?" she asked instead.

"Let Cordelia here take over," he said. "Let's get out of here. You and me. Right now."

Jericho didn't understand. How could he, when she hadn't told him everything?

Maggie's head was shaking already, as though her body knew what the answer had to be. "You found me because of the Antistasi. Who am I if I'm not this?" she asked him. "Who am I if I walk away without even trying to make it right?"

Jericho let out a ragged breath, and she could sense his growing frustration. "I found Ruth's organization because I was young and hot-headed, but you have to know by now that I only ever really stayed for you, Mags. Maybe Esta disappearing is the sign we needed. Let's go somewhere new and start a life together. We could stop running and fighting and just *be.* We don't have to stop helping people. *You* could help a lot of people with those formulas of yours, if you wanted to. We could build a little home and maybe even have us a couple of kids. We could be *happy.*"

Maggie could practically see them already, the children the two of them might have one day. Carrot-colored hair and freckles and impish, dimpled smiles. She could see them running and playing in this fairy tale he was building for her out of nothing but his words, and her heart clenched. Because she wanted it so *desperately*.

But it could never be hers if she walked away from this.

"And what then?" Maggie asked, her voice hollow as she turned the dream against him. "If these children you're imagining are born with the old magic, will we teach them to hide themselves away, as we were taught? Will we teach them to push down whatever affinity they might have and tell them that the old magic is a secret no one can know?"

North's expression softened. "I don't know, Mags. I don't have all the answers, but we're not the only ones with hardships in this world. There are plenty of Sundren who carry their own burdens through life, and they don't let those problems stop them from loving and living."

Maggie was aware of Cordelia standing nearby, watching and listening to every word they said. The sharpshooter had contacts in the network, but Maggie was only truly worried about one.

You're not the only one with friends in high places. Cordelia's words ricocheted through her brain, stirring up fear. Hardening her resolve.

Maggie wished she could set her responsibilities aside and step into Jericho's arms, but her burdens weren't so easy to set down, not when they were shaped like the lives of the people she loved. For her, stepping away from the path she'd been on her whole life would be more like walking off a cliff.

"I can't give up now," Maggie whispered, almost wishing that it wasn't true.

"It's not giving up to reach out and claim a life for ourselves, Mags," North said, squeezing her hand gently. In his eyes was the hope for a future she'd never thought to imagine.

She might have said yes. The word was pressing at her mouth, willing her to let it out, but before she could, a noise drew her attention. A moaning sound that soon solidified into a girl.

Esta was back.

A SIMPLE TRICK

1904—San Francisco

The next time Harte woke, there was no delay between returning to consciousness and remembering everything that had happened. The pain in his head, the ache in his shoulder, and the maddening, burning itch on his ankle reminded him immediately of where he was—and of the reality of his situation. His failures washed over him in an icy flood of shame. He'd been outmaneuvered by his sham of a father, and the artifacts in his possession, the necklace and the cuff—*Esta's cuff*—were gone.

Because you are weak, Seshat whispered. *I warned you, and still you allowed a powerless rat to best you.* Her voice was threaded with the same mockery that Harte was so used to. But there was a trembling energy to her words, except, *no*—the trembling was coming from *him*. His limbs were shaking a little, and the chill in the air made him feel almost feverish.

Maybe he *was* feverish. His body ached, and despite being unconscious for so long, he wanted nothing more than to close his eyes again.

Foolish boy, Seshat hissed. *You would accept your failure so easily? You are too soft and far too pitiful to be worthy of the girl or the power she holds within her.*

That was probably true, but Harte wasn't ready to accept it. Certainly, he wasn't going to lie there and wait for whatever his father had planned for him. But he felt so incredibly *awful*.

Get up, Seshat urged. *Or you will die here, and the girl—and every possibility she contains—will be lost.*

The tremulous energy in Seshat's voice struck a nerve. *If I die, what happens to you?*

Seshat didn't respond.

Harte realized then what emotion had colored Seshat's words—*fear*. It was so uncharacteristic of her usual rage and fury that it was almost enough to distract him from trying to figure out whether his shaking was from exhaustion or fever. He and Seshat had been locked in a battle of wills ever since the moment he'd touched the Ars Arcana and she'd used his affinity to channel herself into him. If Seshat was well and truly afraid now, it meant that Harte was in more trouble than he'd realized.

A single word floated through his mind—*plague*.

Before the wave of panic that thought brought with it could overwhelm him, Harte realized suddenly that he wasn't alone. He could hear breathing close by that didn't belong to him. It was either the biggest rat he'd ever seen—and there had been plenty of those in New York—or . . . He rolled over to his other side and found a small face framed by a cap of close-cropped dark-blond hair sitting on the floor next to him. Curious and too-familiar gray eyes sat above a button nose. They widened, and the child scrambled to his feet when he saw Harte looking at him.

It was the same child who had been with Harte's father. *My brother.* All thoughts of sickness were replaced with the strange and unsettling realization that he was not completely without connections in the world. Whether he would claim them, though, was a different matter altogether.

With some effort, Harte rocked himself upright. As he tried to make the room stop spinning—and tried to keep from heaving up the contents of his stomach—the boy backed up a little more. The child didn't shout or call for anyone, though. His eyes were still curious, but also wary now.

As he sat up, Harte realized his head felt a bit clearer. His ankle still itched and burned, and now when he scratched at it with his toe, the bites there ached sharply. It wasn't the first time he'd dealt with vermin, though, and he knew there was little he could do until the irritation ran its course. Still, they hurt more than most bites he'd had before—his entire leg ached—and he hoped that they hadn't become infected. Or maybe he hoped that they were infected, since that would be a lot easier to deal with than the plague that had quarantined Chinatown.

Seshat remained quiet, still withdrawn and far away, but Harte knew she was watching . . . and waiting. He wasn't sure how much time had passed since he'd last awoken. There were no windows in the cellar, so he couldn't even tell what time of day it was. It could have been the next morning or days later. Esta might already have found the dagger. She might be traveling back toward the bridge, or she might have already arrived. Maybe she was waiting there for him, wondering if he had deserted her again. If she thought he'd truly betrayed her, she might not wait long.

No . . . she would wait, because he had her cuff.

Or, he'd *had* it. Harte needed to get it back, which meant that he needed to get out of that dank basement, even if he'd rather curl up and go to sleep.

Harte's arms were still tied behind him, and his shoulders ached from being in that position for so long. With the small boy's eyes upon him, he tested the ropes again and found they hadn't been secured any better than they had been before. It wouldn't be hard to free himself, but the boy posed a problem. With the child there, Harte would have a witness to his escape. Possibly, the kid might even sound an alarm if Harte tried to leave.

"Where am I?" he asked the boy as he considered his options.

The boy didn't respond. He just stared at Harte without any indication that he'd understood.

"Do you speak English?" Harte asked, searching his brother's face for some indication that the child comprehended. "Can you understand me?"

The boy's brows drew together a little, but still he didn't respond. He just kept staring.

It was possible that the boy *didn't* know English. His father had spoken something that sounded like German to him before. It was likely that his brother had no idea what Harte was saying. At least he hadn't yet made any move to alert someone that Harte had awoken.

"Can you tell me where I am?" he asked the boy, trying again. "Is this your father's store?"

Nothing.

Harte tested the ropes again. They'd grown a bit looser from his earlier movements, and he could be out of them without much trouble. He *needed* to get out of them—and out of that cellar. He felt sore and tired and, well, he felt outright *sick*. But he pushed the thoughts of plague out of his mind. He had a feeling that the longer he stayed trapped in that dank cellar, the less chance he'd have of escaping successfully. Besides, he'd worked through illnesses before. He'd survived New York winters on the street; he would survive this as well. He had to. He had a promise to keep. But first he needed to get free.

"Would you like to see a magic trick?" Harte asked, trying to stop shivering long enough to give the boy a conspiratorial smile.

The boy's expression shifted then, a slight widening of the eyes. A spark of interest warred with the caution and curiosity that were already there.

He understands, Harte realized, grateful for this small mercy.

"I bet you *would* like to see a magic trick," he told the child, brushing away any misgiving he might have had about using the boy. "I'm a magician, you know. Did your father tell you that?"

The boy didn't speak, but he shook his head ever so slightly. His small, bright eyes burned with interest.

"I'm a rather famous one, actually." Harte was already working the ropes on his wrists, making small, refined movements that would have been imperceptible to the boy. "Have you ever seen a magician?"

"Magic is an a-a-bomb-bli-nation," the boy said, parsing out the difficult word slowly and carefully. His small voice was clear as a bell and uninflected with any emotion at all. The words came like they were something he'd memorized without understanding the meaning.

"Abomination," Harte said softly, not missing the way the boy flinched at the gentle correction. He'd heard the echo of his father's intonation in the boy's voice, and he understood what that flinch likely meant. But Harte wouldn't let himself be distracted. There was nothing he could do for this child. He was no hero—had never wanted to be. He was a liar. A bastard and a con, and he would not let himself forget that again. "That's an impressive word for such a small fellow. Do you know what that means?" Harte continued working the ropes—he nearly had it now.

"It is against the path of rightless—" He paused, his young eyes widening a little in something that looked like fear before he corrected himself. *"Righteousness,"* the boy finished. He looked relieved to have gotten the word out.

Harte would have bet enough money to fill his porcelain tub that the child had no idea what he was saying. "I see," he told the boy, careful to keep his voice gentle. "Well, I know some people see things that way. Perhaps your father does?" He paused, noting that the boy looked a bit more nervous. "But not everyone feels the same, you know. I, for one, happen to believe that magic isn't an abomination at all. Magic can be beautiful or exciting, and sometimes, magic is nothing more than a skill that comes from a lot of practice," he told the boy, and with a flourish, Harte drew the rope from behind his back with his now-freed hands.

The boy's eyes were as wide as saucers now, and he started to scurry back, clearly afraid. But he didn't yell or sound any alarm.

"Wait!" Harte said, putting his hands up to show he was harmless and offering the rope to the boy. "It's okay. Go ahead and have a look. No abomination there. It's only a simple trick I learned when I wasn't that much older than you." He offered the rope again. "Go on."

Fear warred with desire in the boy's expression, and Harte rubbed at his arms as he waited, trying to dispel the chill that had sunk into his bones. His skin was tender and his muscles ached when he touched them, but he couldn't worry about what that might mean. Infection or worse, it didn't matter. For now he needed to focus on the boy, to draw him in and earn his trust.

LISA MAXWELL

Finally, the boy inched forward and snatched the rope from his hands.

"See?" Harte said gently, hating himself a little for what he was about to do. "It's nothing more than a regular old rope."

The boy continued studying the length of rope with a serious little frown.

Now that his arms were free, Harte turned to the ropes around his ankles. As he'd expected, there was a series of angry red welts on his calf—flea bites, from the way they were clustered. They didn't look particularly infected, but his entire leg ached. If they were infected, it might explain the way he felt. He *hoped* that explained the way he felt.

"Would you like to see another trick?" he asked, trying to ignore the burning itch and the way his body ached.

The boy considered this question seriously, but to Harte's relief, the boy eventually nodded.

"My name's Harte," he said softly, tentative as he began the introductions. "Harte Darrigan. What's your name?"

The boy stared at him for a long, thoughtful moment. Then his small face screwed up with determination, and he spoke, his voice barely more than a whisper. "Sammie."

"It's nice to meet you, Sammie," Harte said, and once the words were spoken, he felt the truth of them. He was somehow almost happy to know this child, a brother he'd never thought to want.

A brother who could never know him.

Use him, Seshat whispered. *The faster you are free, the faster you can find the girl.*

Harte tried to brush off her words, but Seshat had a point. He hadn't traveled to California to find a family. He'd come for the lost artifact that held the Dragon's Eye. He *would* find it, and he would only stay long enough to retrieve Esta's cuff. He would use this boy if that was required, and he wouldn't allow himself to give in to sentimentality. He would not hesitate. *Not again.*

He felt Seshat stirring in his depths, still far off from the boundary between them, but now there was a shivering anticipation to her waiting.

The boy simply stared at him with the look Harte had seen countless times in the eyes of children he'd grown up with on the streets, children who had learned young that adults couldn't be trusted. Children who would never know a childhood free from the terror of living unprotected. It was a look Harte had probably worn too often himself. But there was nothing he could do for this boy, he reminded himself. He knew how his father—*their* father—would react when he learned that Harte had escaped. This child would pay the price. Harte couldn't take a child with him, and he certainly couldn't change the kind of man their father was. The most he could offer was a bit of happiness.

"Are you ready to see another trick?" he asked.

When the boy nodded eagerly, Harte gave Sammie—his *brother*—a few minutes of wonder. He offered a few simple tricks and illusions that could never make up for the nest of hornets Harte was about to overturn in his life. By the time he'd run through the tricks he could pull together from the supplies in the room, Sammie had become transformed. His serious little face was bright now, his gray eyes smiling in a way that Harte's maybe never had. Not even when he was young.

Harte took an elaborate bow, making it into a ridiculous gesture that had his hands nearly brushing the ceiling of the cramped and musty cellar. His brother applauded, and Harte hated himself even more than he had a moment before. He had the sudden thought that there must be another way. Maybe he *could* take the boy with him—

The sound of footsteps and voices above him drew Harte's attention, and he realized how stupid a thought that had been. He'd wasted enough time, and he needed to remember what was truly important—and what he still had to accomplish. It was time to go talk to his father.

REVELATIONS

W hen Esta finally came back to herself, it wasn't quick, and it wasn't easy. She had to fight to regain her body, wrestling it away from the pull of time, until she emerged from the Aether—*through* the Aether—wrung out and feeling completely untethered to the world around her.

At first she felt as if she were viewing the world through a fog. She could see Maggie and Cordelia and North in the room, but she didn't know them. They were nothing to her, and she, herself, was also nothing. But eventually the fog began to lift. Esta started to feel her body again—the ache of her muscles, the burning of her scar—and soon everything else came back to her as well. She remembered then who she was and what she was meant to do. Even then, fear vibrated through her body, and the scar on her wrist burned.

The aching scar seemed the surest sign that whatever had just happened was connected to her link with her younger self. The way time itself seemed to have devoured her—along with the fact that her affinity was still deadened by the Quellant—made Esta think, once again, that it hadn't been Seshat's doing. It felt more like a sign that her time to return her cuff might be running out.

Or maybe something happened to Harte.

She dismissed that thought immediately. Harte was too smart and too experienced to get himself into trouble he couldn't get out of. He was fine—so was her cuff. *He had to be.*

Maggie helped her to sit up, but Esta was only tangentially aware that it was trembling and not the world itself. It took a while for the quivering to die down enough to accept the cup of water Cordelia brought over. Maggie helped, but when Esta tried to drink, the water tasted bitter and her mouth felt like it was filled with sand. She could barely choke the liquid down.

"What happened?" Maggie asked.

"I don't know," Esta told them. "I was here, and then I . . . I wasn't." She explained what it had felt like, the way the room had shifted and reality had flickered and how time itself felt like it would swallow her whole. "How long was I gone?"

"Nearly an hour," Maggie told her. "We thought you'd left for good."

"We assumed you ran," North said, glaring at her.

"No." Esta was shaking her head. "It wasn't me. I didn't do anything to make that happen."

"But you will run," Cordelia said, the flatness of her voice sending a shiver of unease up Esta's spine. "The minute you have the dagger, you'll leave. You'll take it, like your partner took the necklace. Won't you?"

Esta meant to say *no*. But that wasn't what came out when she opened her mouth. "Of *course*," she blurted, the words tumbling out like they'd been *pulled* from her. Shocked, she clasped her hand over her mouth to stop herself from saying anything else.

North looked every bit as taken aback by her outburst as Esta felt, but his surprise quickly turned to irritation. "I knew it," he huffed, turning to Maggie. "Didn't I tell you? She's not even trying to hide it now."

Maggie's eyes had gone wide. "Esta? You said you'd give us the dagger. You *promised*."

"I lied." Esta was shaking her head to deny the words even as she spoke them, but there was a warmth flooding through her, a strange compulsion that made her want to tell them whatever they asked. "You gave me something," she realized, and then she turned on Maggie. "You used the truth tablets on me?"

"No," Maggie told her, frowning.

Cordelia took the glass that Esta had just drunk from and dumped the contents onto the floor. "We don't have time for any more games."

"Cordelia?" Maggie still looked like she was having trouble catching up. "What have you done?"

"What *you* should have done the second you lost the necklace," she told Maggie. "Clearly, she's bamboozled you into thinking she's on your side, but it's past time we have some answers."

North shifted a little, like he was suddenly uneasy, but he didn't say a word against what Cordelia had done.

So much for his lofty principles. Apparently they only applied when *he* was the one being drugged.

Esta was trying to school her features, but she was failing. No amount of training or self-possession was helping her to fight the effects of the drug she'd been given. How many tablets had Cordelia given her? How long had Maggie said the truth serum lasted? Esta couldn't be sure, but she knew her best chance was to delay. Maybe if she could hold out long enough, she'd be able to fight it.

"Does Pickett really have the Pharaoh's Heart?" Cordelia asked. "Or is this all nothing but a ruse to waste our time?"

"He has it," Esta said through gritted teeth. The more she tried to withhold, the more she felt compelled to speak. "Or he did."

"How do you know?" Cordelia demanded.

Again Esta tried to keep back the words, but Maggie's formulation was too strong. "Harte told me. He sent the dagger to Pickett himself."

Cordelia's eyes widened. "Does he know where the other artifacts are as well?"

Esta closed her eyes against the pain that was building in her head, the ache in her throat. She could handle a little pain, but she couldn't fight Maggie's formulation. "Yes." She looked up to Maggie, silently pleading with her to understand—to stop this—but Maggie only turned away from her.

"Do *you* know where the other artifacts are?" Cordelia asked.

Esta shook her head, but the word *yes* slipped from her lips, and when Cordelia pressed her for more information, she could not stop herself from answering. In the end, Esta told them everything she'd been trying so hard to hide: where Harte was going, what he was doing, and where they planned to meet. She might not have known every detail, but she knew enough to be dangerous. By the time Cordelia was done interrogating her, Esta's chest was heaving, and she felt like she'd been running for miles.

Maggie and North both looked overwhelmed, but Cordelia looked extremely pleased with herself.

Esta glared at the sharpshooter. She was furious, but anger was only part of what she felt. Fear also coursed through her, because she understood exactly how much she'd given away—and she had no way to warn Harte that he might be in danger.

"I knew you were hiding something," Maggie said softly. "But I thought you understood. Any one of those artifacts could have helped so many people—so many Mageus all over this country."

"One artifact alone wouldn't have done anything," Esta told Maggie, feeling too wrung out to bother trying to stop her words now.

"But you know where the others are," Maggie pressed. "The Antistasi could have used them."

"The Antistasi won't even exist if Seshat gets her way. Nothing will," Esta reminded them.

"You truly believe Seshat's real," Maggie said, frowning, like she had not considered that an actual possibility. "She's not just a story you made up to play on our sympathy?"

"I *did* use her to play on your sympathy," Esta admitted. "But that doesn't mean she's not as real as I am. Seshat's not some figment of my imagination or some delusion. She was betrayed by Thoth and trapped in the Book of Mysteries eons ago, and now she's in Harte—I didn't lie about that back on the train, and I'm not lying about it now. You were there in the Festival Hall, Maggie. You *saw*—" Esta didn't finish. She didn't want to remember the vacant, alien expression on Harte's face, or how close she'd come to losing him and to being lost herself. Then another thought occurred to her. "Why would you give me the Quellant if you didn't believe I was telling the truth about Seshat trying to use my power?"

"What if you do manage to get the five artifacts?" Maggie asked, ignoring the question. But she didn't have to answer, because Esta understood. Esta had let her fear lead her, and she'd been conned. "If you do manage to use the stones to control Seshat's power," Maggie pressed, "would you hand over the artifacts and give that power to the Antistasi?"

Esta hesitated, trying to choke back the truth, but in the end a single word escaped. "No," she whispered.

"I'm not exactly surprised," North grumbled.

"Why, Esta?" Maggie asked, looking more hurt and confused. "With that sort of power, the Antistasi could put an end to the Brotherhoods once and for all."

"Ending the Brotherhoods was never supposed to be the Antistasi's job," Esta said, fighting against every word that broke free, trying to choose the words that would work in her favor. "I have to try to make things right."

"If you gave Seshat's power to the Antistasi, you *could*," Maggie said.

"It's not that simple." Esta was shaking her head, but the words came anyway. "We didn't attack some random Sundren in St. Louis. We attacked the leaders of the Veiled Prophet Society, and more than that, we attacked the president of the United States. No one is going to forget that. Because of the serum, people who didn't give Mageus a second thought will be more aware of us than ever now. Regular people—*Sundren*—who never thought about the old magic before are going to be afraid now."

She paused, trying to figure out how to explain without making things worse. "This isn't about the Brotherhoods anymore, Maggie. Because we couldn't stop the serum from deploying, we have changed things in ways we can't even begin to predict. I have to try to fix that."

"But all that's done," Maggie told her. "It's over. We can't go back—"

"Maybe *you* can't," Esta said, clenching her jaw, but the serum was still thick in her blood, and there was little she could do to stop herself.

"You can?" North was frowning.

"With my cuff, yes," she admitted.

"How far can you go?" North asked, looking distinctly uneasy.

She met his gaze. "A lot farther than your watch."

Maggie's eyes widened. "Could you stop the parade?" She sounded interested despite herself.

"Much farther," Esta said.

"Why would you *need* to go farther than that?" Maggie asked. "If you could stop the parade, you could stop the serum from deploying."

"It's not enough," she told them.

"Seems like more than enough, if you ask me," North said.

"Because you don't understand . . . The Devil's Thief never should have existed," Esta told them. It was too much effort to hold back, so she decided to use the truth serum for her own purposes. She told them about the train leaving New Jersey back in 1902, the damage she'd done because of Seshat's power, and the way she'd been unable to control slipping through time. "Don't you see? If the Thief hadn't been created, there wouldn't be a Defense Against Magic Act. The Act shouldn't exist. Without the Thief, things were different. The *world* was different. It wasn't perfect, but it was easier. For a while, I didn't think I *could* go back—not with Harte. I didn't think it was possible with the way Seshat's power affected my affinity, but the Quellant changed all that. I think it's enough to block Seshat's power, and if I'm right, then I *have* to go back. I have to take Harte and the artifacts and try to put history back on the course it should have taken."

And if the stones disappear? It was possible they might not find an answer for the problem of the artifacts crossing with themselves when she slipped them back through time . . . but Esta would deal with that worry later. It was more important that they *could* go back. They could stop *this* future from becoming.

As silence descended on the room, Esta thought that maybe, just *maybe*, Maggie would understand. That she would agree.

"But without the Thief, there wouldn't be any Antistasi," Cordelia said, her voice cold with the truth of the matter.

Maggie's expression was suddenly unreadable. She was staring at Esta, as though seeing her for the first time.

"Where, exactly, would that leave us?" North asked, breaking his silence.

"I don't know. Wherever you should have been," Esta told him. "Not fighting a war you can't win."

"Maybe I'm already right where I'm supposed to be." North took a step closer to Maggie, as if to protect her. "Maybe I don't need you messing with that."

"You don't understand," Esta told him.

"I understand enough," he drawled. "You're not only talking about fixing what happened with the serum in St. Louis. You're talking about messing around with time itself. You could destroy our very *lives*."

"We've *already* destroyed lives," Esta said. "Plenty of them. Or have you forgotten the people in St. Louis who died from the serum? Have you forgotten *all* of the innocent people who have been caught up in the Antistasi's actions over the last couple of years? Is your life worth so much more than any of theirs?"

None of them looked ready to concede the point, and Esta understood their reluctance. Going back meant the possibility of saving some, but there was no way to predict how many other lives might be changed—or *how* they might be changed. Weighing one set of lives against another was an impossible arithmetic, one Esta didn't feel worthy to calculate.

But the Antistasi had no idea how different *this* version of 1904 was from the one that had once been—the one that was *supposed* to have been. Nothing she could say would give them a true sense of what life without the Defense Against Magic Act was like. More importantly, none of them—Esta included—could really know how different the future might *still* be because of what they'd done in St. Louis.

"You would risk destroying everything we worked for?" Cordelia said. "All of the progress we've made against the Brotherhoods? All that the Antistasi have become—you would endanger it?"

"Possibly," Esta admitted.

"What makes you think we would let you?" North asked as he drew out a pistol and leveled it directly at her chest.

THERE'S ALWAYS A CHOICE

1904—Denver

Maggie looked at the pistol in North's hand with a strange sense of detachment. She had known all along that Esta had been lying about who Ben—*Harte*—really was, even before they'd left St. Louis. She'd suspected that the two had been hiding their true motives as well, but her orders had been to bring them both to the Antistasi's side. Maggie had worried, of course, about whether she'd been doing enough, but now she saw how tenuous her control over the situation had been all along.

"Put down the gun, Jericho," she said, taking a slow, careful step toward him. He looked more afraid than angry, but fear could make people do things they normally wouldn't.

"I won't let her undo all that we have." The pistol shook, unsteady in his hand.

"You don't want to do this." Maggie kept her voice soft as she took another step. "We aren't killers."

"You heard what she said," Jericho told her. "She'd undo our lives if we let her."

"It's not going to come to that," Maggie said gently, sidling closer. "Put the gun down, Jericho. *Please.*" But he didn't respond to her request.

"Killing me won't save you, anyway," Esta told him. She looked drained, but her voice was steady.

"It sure might be worth a try," Jericho said.

Esta shook her head. "You don't understand. If you kill me now, it won't help. You won't get to keep this version of the present."

"You can't know that," Jericho said.

"I told you about the man who raised me," Esta said, looking to Maggie now. "But I didn't tell you everything. The man who trained me didn't only lie about what he wanted. He lied about *everything*. He killed my parents to get to me when I was a baby. I was born in 1899. But he sent me forward when I was a toddler, and I lived most of my life a hundred years from now, in the twenty-first century. I only came back to 1902 recently, a few months ago. But by coming back, I've changed things."

Maggie could tell that Esta was choosing her words, still fighting against the pull of the truth serum, but the tale Esta wove for them was nothing short of astounding. If Maggie didn't know what North was capable of with his watch, and if she didn't have so much faith in her own truth serum, she might not have accepted a word Esta was saying. To believe that Esta came from some time far beyond their own seemed too incredible to countenance. But Maggie knew that events could be changed. She'd seen North do it more than once. She didn't doubt her own abilities either. It hadn't been long enough for the effects of the truth tablets to wear off, which meant that this time—no matter how impossible her story seemed—Esta wasn't lying.

"If I don't take Ishtar's Key back to the girl in New York, time will unspool," Esta explained. "The world will go back to how it was before I stole the artifacts from the Order and before the Thief destroyed the train. This version of the present won't exist, and neither will the Antistasi—at least not as you are right now."

North turned to Maggie, to Cordelia, like he was looking for some sign that this was another trick. "That can't be right."

"She can't lie right now," Maggie reminded him, wishing it were otherwise.

"Put down that gun, Jericho," Cordelia commanded. She took out a small revolver of her own and pointed it at him.

The gun was still in Jericho's hand when he turned to Cordelia. "Don't tell me you're on her side too. I can't believe you'd sit here and let her destroy everything the Antistasi have done—everything that we are?"

"It doesn't matter what you believe or what you think," Cordelia told him. "The Thief is essential. *You* are not."

Panic skittered through Maggie. She didn't think that Cordelia was making an empty threat. "*Please*, Jericho."

He turned to her, his expression shadowed. "You want me to stand by and help her rearrange our lives? She'll destroy everything we have."

"I don't think even Esta Filosik has that kind of power," Maggie told him, the words coming before she could stop them, but they felt right somehow.

"She sure thinks she does," Jericho said, glaring at Cordelia.

"You showed up in St. Louis wearing a snake around your wrist and carrying the Antistasi's name in your mouth," Maggie reminded him. "You of all people should know that the Antistasi are older and bigger than any one group of us. They existed long before the Thief, and they'll exist long after, whatever changes Esta *thinks* she can make."

"Margaret's right," Cordelia said. "Fate itself brought the Antistasi into being, and it will preserve us, whatever time—or this Thief—might have in store." Her expression glowed with a kind of beatific fervor.

"Please, Jericho," Maggie said again, pleading. "The Antistasi can survive this. They're so much larger than one moment."

"I wasn't talking about the Antistasi," he said softly. The pistol in his hand lowered a little, and the sadness in his eyes made Maggie's throat go tight.

Too late, she realized his true meaning, and she stood, unable to move. Unable to speak. Stuck between two impossible choices.

"Let's just *go*, Maggie," Jericho pleaded as he lowered the gun completely. "Let Cordelia stay and deal with Esta if she wants, but if *this* life might disappear like it never was, why not enjoy what we have now? However long we might have left together." He held out his hand to her.

"I wish I could," Maggie whispered. She did not bother to stop the tear that broke free.

Jericho's eyes shuttered. "But you won't."

"I have to see this through," she told him, dashing at the wetness on her cheeks. Her throat was tight with everything she could not say, and her heart felt like lead. "You promised once that you would help me, Jericho. I'm asking you now to keep that promise."

Jericho stared at her for a long moment, and Maggie worried that he would refuse. Cordelia still hadn't lowered her gun, and Maggie wasn't sure that the sharpshooter was in any mood to be forgiving. For the first time in a long time, Maggie could not tell what Jericho Northwood was thinking.

"This is really what you want, Mags?" Jericho asked.

Maggie only knew it was what had to be. "Please . . ." She wasn't exactly sure what it was she was asking for.

Her plea hung in the air, and the silence that followed opened a chasm between them. In that moment, Maggie sensed that Jericho would turn from her, and after all she'd done to him—all her lies and evasions—it would be what she deserved. All she could do was stand there and hope, because she knew if Jericho turned away from her now, he would not come back. It would signal the end of something, and until that moment, she hadn't quite understood how much she needed the dream of a future with them together.

"In that case, I suppose I should be getting back," Jericho said finally. His voice rang as hollow as Maggie felt. "It appears I have a promise to keep." He tucked away his pistol and gave Esta another cold, appraising look. But he wouldn't look at Maggie, no matter how much she wanted him to.

Maggie didn't feel like she had any right to ask Jericho for anything more, so she didn't make any other plea. He left without another word between them, and she could not stop herself from flinching as the door closed behind him. With his leaving, something important had changed between them, and Maggie suspected that she would live to regret the choice she had made.

Cordelia stepped forward, but Maggie barely seemed to notice until the sharpshooter spoke. "You made the right choice, Margaret."

"Did I?" Maggie asked, still staring at the closed door. She wished there was a way she could go after him and take it all back. "Because I'm not so sure."

"You put your commitment to our cause—to the Antistasi—before your own personal gain," Cordelia said. "It is what we all gotta do. We all make sacrifices for the greater good."

But Maggie didn't see Cordelia making any such sacrifice. All she could think about was the way the light had gone from Jericho's eyes when she'd turned him down for the final time. She'd never forgive herself for being the one who'd dimmed it.

Cordelia turned to Esta. "Once we have the dagger, you'll take us to the other artifacts. I'm sure you understand what a waste of time and energy it would be for you to try to run."

Esta stared at her without replying, but even Maggie could read the defiance in her expression.

"We already know where y'all are going and what your plans are," Cordelia reminded Esta. "If you try to leave, there ain't no train you could take that's faster than the telegram I'll send to the network. Antistasi all across this country'll be waiting for you and searching for your magician friend. Something just might happen before you could reach him."

Esta's eyes lit with fury. "If you do anything—"

"What?" Cordelia gave her a small, amused smile. "You ain't in any position to make threats right now. I get that Ruth's actions made you suspicious, but Ruth Feltz ain't the Antistasi. We're not your enemy, Esta. Help us, and there ain't no reason Harte Darrigan needs to come to any harm."

Esta didn't immediately respond, but Maggie thought she likely understood exactly how stuck she was. "It doesn't seem like I have much choice," Esta said finally.

"There's always a choice," Cordelia told her, looking eminently pleased with herself. "But you gotta make the right one."

"If I help you?" Esta asked, her voice tight. "If I commit myself to the Antistasi's cause?"

"Once we have the artifacts, we'll be unstoppable. We can end the Brotherhoods' power once and for all. All the Sundren who've forced us into the shadows will live to regret their hatred."

No, Maggie thought as confusion flashed through her. *That isn't right.* Revenge *wasn't what any of the Antistasi's work had been about.* . . . *Was it?*

"We don't want to treat you like an enemy," Cordelia told Esta. "Not when you could be our ally." Then she turned to Maggie with a serious look. "I guess I should be getting back. If nothing else, we need to find the dagger, and soon. Especially if Jericho was right about seeing some kind of guard from St. Louis at the show."

"What?" Maggie's head whipped around. "You don't mean Jefferson Guard?"

"May could be that's what he called them," Cordelia said. "It happened earlier today. It must have slipped his mind to tell you, considering everything else that's happened." She finally tucked the small pistol away.

"If there are Guardsmen in Denver, it means the Society knows we're here," Maggie said. Suddenly nothing seemed as important as getting to Jericho. She turned to her table and started collecting as many of the devices and formulations as she could. She might need them all to get him out of there safely.

"What're you doing?" Cordelia asked.

"I just pushed Jericho out the door and straight into a trap," Maggie said, counting the incendiaries as she filled her pouch. "I'm coming with you."

"*I'll* take care of Jericho," Cordelia said.

Maggie looked up. "No, I have to—"

"I know my way around the show. No one will notice me. You, on the other hand . . ." Cordelia looked her up and down, and Maggie felt her cheeks warm with the implication that the sharpshooter found her wanting. "You'd only draw attention and make things even more dangerous for him."

"But—"

"No. You'll stay here and make sure Esta doesn't forget where her loyalties should lie," Cordelia decided. "*If* you think you can handle that much."

"I can handle it," Maggie said through clenched teeth.

"Good." Cordelia adjusted her hat in the hazy mirror. "You know, Margaret, for a second there, I really thought you might accept Jericho's offer to up and leave. I thought maybe you'd forgotten what you have at stake in all of this."

Something in Cordelia's voice sent a trickle of foreboding down Maggie's spine. "What is that supposed to mean?"

"Nothing much," Cordelia said. "But I'd watch yourself, if I were you. The Professor has already started to wonder if his trust in you has been misplaced."

"The *professor*?" Esta sat up a little straighter. "What professor?"

Maggie ignored Esta. "I didn't realize you were in contact with him," Maggie told Cordelia, trying to remain calm. But the room swam a little as she realized what that meant. What the Professor might already know.

"He ain't too happy with your recent silence," Cordelia said, looking far too satisfied with herself. "Don't worry, though. I've assured him that all's well." She gave a small shrug. "Of course, that was before I learned that y'all had lost the necklace. If I were you? I wouldn't give me any other reason to doubt your loyalty—not unless you'd like him knowing. Now, if you'll pardon me, I need to be getting back. We wouldn't want to let Jericho go off unsupervised. He might start thinking about leaving again or doing something else you'd regret."

HIS FATHER'S SON

1904—San Francisco

Harte ignored the ache in his head and in his leg as he considered what to do with the boy—his brother—and how to get out of the basement storeroom. He had to get back the artifacts that had been taken from him, and to do that, he had to find his father. Maybe the boy could help with that.

Squatting down until he was eye level with the child, Harte leaned in as though he had a secret. "You know, I could do a really wonderful trick if I had more space," he said, hating himself for the duplicity. But it would be far easier to have the child show him the way out than to risk taking a wrong turn in the building. For now the child seemed to like him. He'd use that—even if the boy ended up hating him later. "Would you like to see another one?"

The child nodded, his expression bright and hopeful.

"Do you know where we might find a little more room?" Harte asked. "This cellar's awfully cramped. There's no way an elephant would fit in here."

"An elephant?" the boy breathed.

Harte ignored the pang of guilt he felt and leaned in a little to sink the hook. "I think I might manage to conjure one up, *if* I had the room for it." He paused, pretending to think. "We would need to get outside, but I don't know the way. . . ."

"I do!" The boy took Harte's hand and began tugging him out into a corridor that was little more than a dirt-packed tunnel lined with dry

266

goods and supplies. There was no real light there, except the daylight that spilled from the open doorway at the top of a steep set of steps.

At the foot of the steps, Harte had to pause to catch his breath. If he'd been denying his situation before, the fact that he felt winded and tired from walking such a short distance forced him to realize the truth. He was sick. He could have happily climbed back onto that filthy makeshift pallet and rested, but he knew implicitly that this was his one chance at freedom.

Sammie put his finger to his mouth to quiet Harte, who hadn't said a word since they'd stepped out of the storage room.

"Is your father up there?" Harte whispered, straining his ears for some sign of what might be waiting for him above as he gathered his strength. His whole body felt hot and cold at the same time, and his muscles ached.

The boy nodded, and his expression was suddenly shadowed. "In his shop." His small, feathery brows drew together in an expression of worry. "I wasn't supposed to talk to you. He'll be angry when he finds out. Especially about the"—Sammie paused, clearly still nervous—"about the *magic*."

"He never has to know," Harte told the boy solemnly. "If you don't tell him, neither will I." He made a cross over his heart and held up a hand in an oath.

The boy looked doubtful, but interest seemed to win over caution.

At the top of the steps, Harte found himself in a short hallway that connected the store at the front of the building to the exit at the rear. Sammie motioned that Harte should follow him toward the back of the building, where the exit waited. Harte started to follow, but voices from the store drew his attention.

Hearing his father's voice made Harte pause, but when his father began to laugh, it flipped a switch of sorts. Before Harte even realized what he was doing, his feet were carrying him toward the storefront and the source of his father's voice. The boy tried to tug Harte back, whispering urgently that it was the wrong direction, but Harte wasn't listening.

He didn't bother with stealth. He simply stepped into the main room of the store like he owned it.

Immediately, Harte was surrounded by the scent of dry goods and dust. The walls were lined with wooden shelves that held glass jars filled with flour and sugar. One wall was taken up by a large cabinet that held a variety of tools and bolts of fabric.

This was no doubt his father's store, and from the look of things—the gleaming glass and wood in the shop, the shelves stocked with all manner of expensive inventory—the old man had a well-established business. A *thriving* business. This realization only stoked the fire of Harte's anger that much more. He felt like he was looking through a haze, though the blurring of his vision might also have been from the fever. Even with his entire body aching, he took another brazen step into the shop, daring the two men at the counter to ignore his presence.

At first Samuel Lowe didn't realize that he and his customer were no longer alone. He was weighing out some dark sugar on a large scale, and it was only when the customer he was helping lifted his gaze toward the rear of the shop that his father looked as well. When he saw Harte standing there, his face drained of color.

His father's shock lasted for only a moment. As soon as he saw Sammie standing behind Harte, Samuel Lowe's nostrils flared and his eyes narrowed. But Harte was no longer a child, and the instinctive, reflexive fear that sparked within him drained away quickly. He moved squarely into the center of the shop, daring his father to ignore him.

To Harte's surprise, his father did just that. Samuel Lowe turned back to the customer, an older man with silvery hair, and continued to wrap up the contents of the scale. His father took his time as he finished securing the parcel before handing it over, then waved the customer off without taking payment. Once the customer was gone, he finally returned his attention to Harte, and his expression had transformed into something more familiar—a mask of barely leashed rage.

Harte had seen that expression on his father's face too many times as a child. Then, he had never known what would be the right move—to run and hide, or to stand and protect his mother. Now, he didn't so much as blink. He doubted there was anything this man could threaten to take from him that Harte hadn't already given up, tossed away, or lost for himself.

"You shouldn't be here," his father said, but he wasn't addressing Harte. His gaze had focused on the spot behind Harte, where Sammie stood. "You were to wait in my office, practicing your figures."

"Don't blame the boy," Harte said, putting a protective arm around the child. "If someone hadn't done such an abysmal job of tying the ropes, I'd probably still be secured in that cellar you put me in. Was it one of your lackeys at the restaurant who tied me up? Or was that particular incompetence all yours?"

His father didn't answer, but Harte saw when the barb hit its mark. "It was for your own good." A line Harte had heard far too many times as a child. "If the Committee found you—"

"Nothing you ever did to me or my mother was for our good. Last night wasn't any different," Harte said, cutting the old man off.

"Last night?" His father looked confused. "The raid on the restaurant happened two days ago." The coldness in his father's eyes gave Harte the uncomfortable feeling that he wasn't lying.

Two days? He'd lost two days.

"You should be grateful I didn't let the watchmen take you," he sneered.

"Somehow, I doubt that," Harte said. He took a moment to look around the shop. "What was your plan, anyway?" he wondered. "I'm surprised you didn't already dispose of me."

His father clenched his jaw. "Merchant ships are always in need of new crew, and there was one about to leave. But then you came down with the fever."

"How very caring of you to let me recover before sending me anyway," Harte mocked, even as he felt his skin ache. The very mention of the fever seemed to have reminded his body of how terrible he felt.

"They don't take sickness on board." His father ground the words between his teeth. "I couldn't risk anyone tracing you back to me. The Vigilance Committee has the whole city on edge with talk of the plague, but at least right now they're focused on blaming the Chinese. I wasn't about to give them the opportunity to quarantine this building. It would ruin me."

"So you were planning to keep me down there indefinitely?"

"You would improve or you wouldn't," he said with a shrug.

"Well, I'm afraid you won't be able to ship me off now," Harte said, trying not to look half as awful as he felt. "I'm not going anywhere without the Dragon's Eye, and I'm *definitely* not leaving without the other items you stole from me."

"I stole nothing," the old man said. "Those items do not belong to you. They simply confirmed what I have known since you were a boy— you were never going to be anything more than a common criminal. When I figure out who you've taken them from, I'm sure I'll be handsomely rewarded for their return."

"You will return what belongs to me, and you will hand over the Dragon's Eye, or I will take *everything* from you." Harte put his hand on the boy's shoulder and felt an echo of Seshat's satisfaction when his father's eyes widened.

"If you think I'd let you—"

"Try me." Harte felt the boy trembling now, the birdlike bones of his shoulder fragile beneath his hand. "Or . . . you could help me retrieve the item I came for. Help me, and for your son's sake, I will let you keep your pathetic life and all you've built."

"Even if I believed your lies, I can't help you. The Committee won't give up the crown."

"I wasn't planning on asking for it."

"I won't help you steal it either," Samuel Lowe said. "If that piece goes missing, and they trace what you've done back to me, I'll lose everything anyway."

"What if I can keep you safe?" Harte asked. "I can make sure the Committee won't ever touch you. Your pathetic little life can continue on as it is now."

His father's expression flashed with understanding, and Harte could see the hatred warring with indecision. "You can't make such assurances. . . ."

"You of all people know that I can," Harte told him. Even though he wanted nothing more than to destroy Samuel Lowe, Harte would keep his word. Harte would leave his father untouched if it meant protecting the boy. "You know what I'm capable of. Help me, and I can make sure you keep the life you've built here. Or don't, and I will gladly tear it apart. Either way, I *will* get what I came here for."

Harte saw the exact moment when his father relented. "Fine. I'll take you to the crown, and then you'll see how impossible it is."

"You'll also give back the belongings you took from me," Harte added.

"After," his father said.

"No—" Harte began to argue, but his father held up a hand.

"Once I'm assured that you haven't done anything foolish to put me at risk, we'll discuss those other pieces. Until then, I'll keep them as insurance against you double-crossing me," his father said. "This is my offer. Take it or leave it."

Harte considered his options. Perhaps it was another trap, but accepting his father's terms would get him one step closer to retrieving the Dragon's Eye. Even if it was a trap, Harte had some insurance of his own.

He put his hand on the boy's shoulder. "Fine," he agreed. He would win one way or the other.

"Leave my son," Samuel Lowe commanded, eyeing Harte's grip on the boy. "He's not to be a part of this."

"I'm afraid he's already a part of this, and I find that I require some insurance of my own." Harte glanced down at the boy, and when he noticed the fear in the child's too-familiar gray eyes, he knew himself for what he truly was. A bastard. An abomination.

Truly his father's son.

And if Harte felt his resolve softening as he looked at the boy? If he felt the beginnings of regret for what would happen to the child once he was gone? He would not give in. He *couldn't*. This time, he would not allow himself to lose sight of what was most important: Retrieving the artifacts. Finding Jack and the Book. Giving Esta a chance at a different future.

Even with the small victory of his father's agreement, though, Harte still worried. He didn't like how quiet Seshat had become. He was used to her mockery and to her constantly testing the boundary between them. He'd expected it, especially as he drew closer to obtaining the artifacts that could end her, but instead, she remained silent.

With every passing second, Harte's legs felt heavier, and he was having more trouble holding back the shivering that threatened to rack his body. He'd grown so weak over the past couple of days of confinement. It would have been easy enough for Seshat to rise up and breach his defenses. But she hadn't. Because Seshat knew she had to allow this—to allow *him*—to find the stones. Because his promise to Esta was the only thing keeping Harte from curling up somewhere, from *giving* up and letting whatever this illness was take him—and Seshat along with him.

Harte did not mistake Seshat's silence for acquiescence, though. He didn't trust it. Instead, he reminded himself—and Seshat—that he needed the artifacts. Without them, he would not return to Esta . . . and that was the thing they *both* desired most of all.

THE PROFESSOR

1904—Denver

Only once before had Esta ever been in a situation that had seemed impossible to escape. She'd been lashed to a chair in Professor Lachlan's penthouse library, adorned with the five artifacts, and everything she'd once believed about her life had been crumbling around her. Maybe the Antistasi in Denver hadn't tied her to a chair, but she still felt every bit as trapped. Her free will had been obliterated by Maggie's formulation, and there was nothing Esta could do to take the information back now that she'd given it to them. Worse, she could not let go of one word Cordelia had said before she'd left.

"Who is the Professor, Maggie?"

Maggie turned to Esta. "What?"

"Cordelia said that there was a professor you've been in contact with," Esta pressed. "Who is he?"

For a second it looked like Maggie would try to lie to her, but then she relented. "I don't know who he is, exactly. I don't think he's actually a professor." She frowned. "Not like you're *actually* a thief. It's what everyone calls him because he knows so much about the old magic."

"He's in New York, isn't he?" Esta asked, knowing already what the answer would be.

"Yes, but . . ." Maggie looked suddenly more alarmed. "You know of him?"

Esta ran her finger along the scar on the inside of her wrist once more. Its sudden appearance had told her that Nibsy still planned on using her, but she hadn't considered that Nibsy could be involved with the Antistasi.

But I should have.

"What does he have on you?" Esta asked, instead of answering Maggie's question.

Immediately, Maggie's eyes widened and fear darkened her expression. "I don't know what you mean."

"Yes, you do." Esta took a step toward Maggie. "He's holding something over you, something so big that you decided to stay here with Cordelia and me instead of going off with North like I *know* you wanted to."

"I didn't—" Maggie's voice broke, betraying her once more.

"You *did*," Esta said, looking almost sympathetic. "It was right there, plain as day on your face, how much you *wanted* to say yes to him. But you didn't. You let Cordelia threaten you. Why?"

Maggie was shaking her head. "I can't . . . I'm not supposed to—not even Jericho knows about it."

"But Cordelia does," Esta pressed. "You didn't know that, though. Did you?"

Maggie looked completely miserable. She lifted her eyes to Esta, but still didn't explain.

"If Cordelia is working with this professor of yours, Maggie, you're in bigger trouble than you think."

"You can't know—"

"I *do* know. The man I told you about, the one who raised me?" Esta said, interrupting. "We called him Professor Lachlan. I would bet everything that they're the same person." Maggie was still shaking her head to deny it, but Esta wouldn't allow her to. "Think about it, Maggie. Two people who call themselves Professor, who both have deep knowledge about the old magic, and who both happen to live in Manhattan? You know I'm not lying about this," she pressed, using her situation to her advantage. "Cordelia made sure of that."

Maggie stared at her for a long, terrible moment before her face crumpled.

"Whatever he's holding over you, there has to be a way around it," Esta promised.

"There's not," Maggie whispered. "I thought I was helping, but I've made everything worse. You couldn't possibly understand."

"I *do* understand, Maggie," Esta said gently. "I know exactly how persuasive he is. He makes you feel important, like you're the only one who can help him, the only one capable of doing whatever he needs done. But he was only ever using you. It's what he does. He manipulates people, and when he's done with them, he discards them." She thought of Dolph, cold on the bar top, and Dakari falling lifeless and bloodied to the floor. But Esta pushed those memories away because she had to focus on *this* moment and especially on making Maggie understand. "He'll discard you, and he'll discard North as well." She took another step toward Maggie. "You don't have to let him, though. I can help you. We can do this—"

"I can't," Maggie moaned, cutting her off. "If I don't do what I've promised and bring you and the artifacts to New York, he'll kill Ruth and everyone else we left back in St. Louis."

"How?" Esta challenged. "He's trapped behind the Brink."

"But the Antistasi aren't," Maggie told her. "They're *his*."

"What do you mean?" Esta asked, trying to make sense of Maggie's fear. "The Antistasi are ancient—you said that yourself."

"The stories are, yes, but the network Cordelia's been talking about? *He's* the one who organized it," Maggie explained. "Maybe once the Antistasi were a loose organization, but that hasn't been the case for a couple of years now. The whole network is loyal to him. The Professor doesn't need to be anywhere close to St. Louis to hurt the people I care about there. He has plenty of others who will gladly follow his orders."

"Was Ruth following his orders too?"

"For a while," Maggie admitted. "But she grew tired of the arrangement.

She thought there was a better way to fight the Brotherhoods, so she cut him out. I was worried about her plan to break away from the larger network, so I agreed to be his eyes—his *spy*. I thought I was helping her." Maggie paused, clearly gathering her thoughts. "When you arrived in St. Louis, the Professor promised he would forgive Ruth *and* her followers if I could bring you to our side. I sent him a message when we left St. Louis to let him know I was with you and that we had two of the artifacts. But after Harte took the stones, I didn't tell him they were gone. I thought I could get the dagger instead. I hoped it would be enough to replace what I'd lost. When Cordelia tells him—"

"We can stop her before that happens," Esta said.

"It's probably already too late," Maggie said, sounding deflated and resigned. "Cordelia probably went straight to the telegraph office. He might already know—" Her voice broke, and she buried her face in her hands.

"Maybe, but I don't think so. Cordelia wouldn't put herself at risk by telling the Professor anything before she has the dagger in hand," Esta said. "What if she failed to retrieve it? She'd be in the same position you're in right now."

"I don't know," Maggie said.

"Fine. What if it *is* already too late?" Esta asked. "If that's the case, we don't have anything else to lose. But if I'm right? We still have time, Maggie. We can get ahead of this."

Maggie didn't answer immediately. She turned away and went to the window, looking out over the city streets instead of at Esta.

"Help me," Esta pleaded. "I wasn't lying about Seshat, Maggie. If I can't bring the artifacts together, if I can't control her power, then Seshat *will* destroy the world. She almost succeeded back in St. Louis. If we can stop Cordelia from alerting the network, we can get the stones. Help me, and I'll do whatever I can to make sure the Professor can't hurt you or anyone you love. I promise."

Esta waited a moment, but Maggie didn't respond. *"Maggie?"*

"Something's happening." She waved Esta over. "I *know* that guy. I saw him in St. Louis. He was there that night of the ball, in the Festival Hall."

Beneath the window was a long line of carriages and police wagons. With them were a half dozen of the Jefferson Guard and a group of marshals.

And watching over them all was Jack Grew.

As though he sensed them watching, Jack went very still and then turned to look up at their window. Esta pulled Maggie out of sight and motioned for her to be quiet. She eased the curtains back again, just enough to take another look. The last time she'd seen Jack had been in the Festival Hall. He'd been attacking Harte. Or, rather, the thing inside of him had been attacking the power inside of Harte. *Thoth.*

If Jack was there, it meant trouble. *Big trouble.* But it also meant a second chance, Esta thought suddenly. If Jack was in Denver, then so was the Book, and that meant there was a possibility she could leave Denver with both the Book *and* the Pharaoh's Heart in her possession. It would take finesse—and it would take convincing Maggie to abandon her commitment to the Antistasi and join her.

"If Jack Grew is here, he knows the Thief isn't dead," Esta said. Then she looked Maggie straight in the eye. "I know you care about your sister, and I know you don't want to believe anything I told you today, but if Jack Grew and the Jefferson Guard are here, things are worse than we suspected. They're here for us. Whatever threat the Professor might be holding over you, North is definitely in danger right now. We *have* to get to the show before they do," Esta said, telling Maggie the one thing she knew the other girl needed to hear. Luckily, it also happened to be true.

A WICKED BIT OF MAGIC

1902—New York

Cela Johnson had been trying to take in the dart of a dress for the last thirty minutes. It should have been an easy enough job, simple compared to the intricate beadwork on the costumes she'd once worked on at Wallack's. *Before all this.* But *before* felt like a lifetime ago. Considering how she'd up and taken off without notice, Cela knew she'd never work there—or in any of the white theaters—again.

The needle slipped and pierced her thumb, and Cela hissed in a breath, sucking at the wound for a second or two and tasting the copper of her own blood. She was never clumsy with a needle and thread, but it had been nearly impossible to concentrate ever since that Italian girl had come sweeping in—and then right back out—without saving Jianyu, as they all had hoped she would.

Though Cela had to admit that he did look a little better since Viola had used her magic on him. His color wasn't so ashen and his skin wasn't as cool to the touch, but Jianyu still wouldn't wake. Viola hadn't said that she would return, and there'd been no sign of her for days. And Cela had so many questions. . . .

Neither Cela nor Abel were quite sure what they should be doing about the ring Jianyu had been looking for. Somehow it didn't seem quite their business, and yet Cela couldn't shake the notion that she was supposed to keep looking for it. She was already involved, after all, even if she still couldn't remember why she'd agreed to take Darrigan's mother. She'd accepted the ring as payment, and she'd done so without questioning how a stage magician—even one as popular as Harte Darrigan—could have afforded such a thing.

Jianyu was only hurt now because Cela had accepted the ring and he'd been sent to watch out for her. But for Cela it was more than a simple case of what was owed. Before Abel had come back from the dead, Jianyu had become a friend. He'd trusted her with the truth of the ring when he could have lied about its power, and she'd promised him that she would help him find it in return. Cela Johnson wasn't going to back out now. Hadn't her Nan always said a promise spoken had to be kept? Well, she'd spoken all right. She just didn't know what she was supposed to do next, and she especially didn't know what she was supposed to do if Jianyu never woke up.

Outside the open window, a carriage rattled by, but instead of proceeding down the road, it came to a stop a little ways beyond the house. There wasn't anything special about the sound of it, but something stirred in Cela. She put aside the mending she'd been trying to do and went to the window, but the carriage had stopped beyond her view.

Rubbing at the back of her neck, Cela gave herself a moment to stretch. The room was too warm, and the scent of sickness was thick in the air, but she didn't trust leaving Jianyu alone, even if he wasn't in any shape to go moving on his own. If he woke, she wanted to be there. If he didn't wake, well, she wanted to be there for that as well.

A moment later she heard voices from below, soft and urgent, and then footsteps sounded on the stairs. Cela stepped in front of the bed, even though she couldn't have done much more than poke at the intruder with her needle, but the door opened to reveal Viola. The girl was dressed every bit as plainly as she'd been the first time she visited, but now her eyes were ringed with dark circles, like maybe she hadn't slept since she'd failed to save Jianyu either. When she stepped into the doorway, a white man filled the space she'd just vacated. He had hair the color of straw, slicked back in waves around his broad forehead, and was wearing a casual day suit tailored so precisely it practically screamed money. And money usually meant problems.

Cela nodded toward the stranger in the doorway. "Who is he?"

"Theo Barclay, miss. I'm a friend of Viola's." The man held his hat in his hands, and his mouth formed something that looked like it was trying to be a smile, but his expression remained tight and guarded. He looked every bit as uncomfortable as Cela felt with him crowding into the room.

"Why would you bring him here?" Cela asked Viola. Abel was out for the day, but he'd have a fit if he knew she'd brought a stranger to Mr. Fortune's house when they were supposed to be lying low.

"I tried to leave him behind, but you know how men get when they decide you need their help." Viola let out a frustrated sigh and gave Cela a long-suffering look, one that Cela sympathized with despite herself. "It's even worse when they have money."

Cela wasn't sure what Viola was going on about, but she had a feeling that this man's appearance couldn't mean anything good. "I thought we'd never see you again after the way you tore out of here last time. It's been two days without so much as a word." She didn't bother to stop herself from scowling.

Viola's eyes shifted toward the floor. "I'm sorry." It looked like she was swallowing her own tongue as she tried to force out the words.

"Why did you come back, anyway?" Cela demanded, her hands crossed over her chest. "It's clear you can't do him any good."

"Maybe not before," Viola said. "But now I think I can."

"What's changed?" Cela asked, trying to ignore the hope that made her feel light-headed.

"This," Viola said, pulling a small object from her skirts. She held it up for Cela to see. It was about the size of a thin cigar, halfway smoked, and seemed to be made of clay or stone. Or maybe some kind of dark-red rock.

"What is it?" Cela eyed the object, trying to figure out how it could help anything.

The white man's eyes lit up. "Where did you get—"

"Where is not important," Viola said, cutting him off with her words and a look. "What is important is this—Libitina, she's not a normal knife." Viola's full mouth pinched tight, but then she explained that the knife's blade was a wicked bit of magic—false magic, she called it, though it seemed to Cela true enough if it could cause a man's death so easily. "I was trying to heal him with my affinity, but it won't work alone. We need false magic to break false magic."

"And what about this one?" Cela glanced at the man who was blocking the doorway. "Is he some kind of wizard or something to help with your 'false magic'?"

"No," Theo Barclay said with an uneasy smile. It was the sort of wobbly smile men who hadn't grown into themselves still used on their mothers. "I'm a student, actually. Art history."

Cela couldn't stop her brows from rising. "That sounds . . ." She was about to say *pointless*, but nothing good came from speaking ugly, so she simply shook her head instead. "If you think there's something you can do, then you best get to it," she said reluctantly. She wouldn't let herself hope. Not yet.

Viola started toward the bed, but Cela suddenly had a wave of apprehension and stopped her. "You're sure this won't hurt him?"

"It shouldn't." But Viola's strange violet eyes looked unsure. She glanced up at the white man again, like she needed the confirmation.

"I've done the translations twice," he said. "It will work."

This was another gamble, Cela realized. Another shot in the dark. She hesitated a moment longer, torn and frustrated at her own powerlessness, before she finally relented and let Viola pass. It wasn't as if there was anything more she or any of Abel's friends could do for Jianyu. If Viola thought she could help, then who was Cela to stand in her way?

"You ever done this before?" Cela asked as Viola approached the bed.

"Once," Viola told her, but she didn't elaborate. "Help me get his shirt off?"

They worked together to carefully remove the shirt until Jianyu's bare chest was open to their view. When Cela removed the bandage, she saw that the wound in his shoulder hadn't changed. It was still raw and angry, still seeping blood after so many days. Behind her, Cela could sense Theo Barclay inching closer, but she tried to put him out of her mind—she only hoped he was gone before Abel returned. And that he wouldn't cause any trouble for them later.

At first Viola didn't move. She stood, staring at Jianyu. But if just looking at him could fix him, he would've been well already.

"Now what?" Cela asked, prodding Viola.

Viola glanced at her. "Now we try . . ."

The object was the shape of a cylinder, and now that she was closer, Cela could see that its surface was carved with a series of strange markings. When Viola rolled the object through the dark blood oozing from Jianyu's wound, it acted like a stamp and created a lurid trail of scarlet inscriptions across his shoulder and down over his chest.

Cela thought she had understood what it meant that Jianyu was Mageus. She'd been with him when he'd cloaked them both in his magic to escape a Bowery saloon. Back in Evelyn's apartment, she'd been caught in a siren's spell. But this was different. A strange energy filled the room, lifting the hairs on the nape of Cela's neck. Theo Barclay didn't seem as shaken as she felt, though. He was watching Viola work with bright interest, but Cela felt only deep unease. She steadied herself as Viola traced the small amulet in strange looping patterns over Jianyu's chest, and as Cela watched, the bloody runes began to glow.

PLANS TO MAKE

1902—New York

Coming back to life was not at all like waking up. There was no gentle stirring or warm satisfaction to be found in the comfort of a safe bed. Coming back to life was like surfacing through concrete. It was like being trapped in the maze of Diyu, lost between the levels of torments, unable to find the way back.

Jianyu's chest burned as though he were being flayed alive. His limbs felt like fire was running through his veins, but he was not yet at the surface. Darkness surrounded him, strangled him, even as he struggled against it. But soon the pain was nothing but noise. Soon, even through the terrible weight of it, he could begin to feel something other than the absolute certainty of death.

His eyes opened, but at first he could not see. It took minutes, maybe hours, for the world to come back to him, dim and blurred. He heard voices. Felt the pain recede as worried hands touched his skin. A pair of eyes appeared above him, and he found that he knew them.

"Viola?" Jianyu tried to form the shape of her name, but his mouth was still missing.

He had asked for Viola, had told Cela and Abel that she alone might be able to help him, but he had not been sure that she would come. Not when she had no idea of anything that had happened—not about how Dolph had been murdered or why Darrigan had done what he did. If she was here . . . If she had saved him, then truly, they might still have a chance.

"He needs water." Another voice, soft and sure. *Cela.* In the darkness between life and death, he had heard her voice coming to him from a distance, but he had not been sure whether it was real or a dream. He would likely never be able to repay her for all that she had done.

Jianyu felt something wet and cool against his face, liquid trickling down over his chin, and then his body seemed to understand what needed to be done. Suddenly he was swallowing. Gulping down the bright, cool liquid like it was the source of life itself, until he realized his body's mistake—or perhaps his body realized his—and he began coughing it back up. He barely cared that the two women leapt to fuss over him, like he was a very old or very incompetent fool of a man. His embarrassment at their fussing did not matter. He was not *dead*.

Perhaps he had wondered once or twice before what the future could possibly hold for him, trapped as he was in this country—on this island— so far from his homeland. He had wondered when he realized the truth of the Brink, and when a group of men had held him down and cut his queue, making it certain he could never return home. Often Jianyu had questioned whether the constant struggle of simply existing was worth the seemingly endless exhaustion, the endless battle. He had continued on, but he had wondered many times before what it was all for.

Jianyu had found the answer to that question as soon as he realized how desperate his injury was. As he had grown weaker, the wound constantly seeping with his blood and his life, and then later, when he fought against the ceaseless undertow that pulled him toward nothingness, Jianyu had understood that the struggle had always been worth it. Always, even in its darkest moments.

He was not *dead*. He had somehow survived, and these two women— Viola and Cela, who were so different from one another, so different from Jianyu himself—were the reason. He allowed them to cluck and fuss because he understood they needed to. He could only be grateful.

A while later, when he was dry and clothed and propped back up in the bed, Viola explained how they had solved the problem of the wound her knife had made, and Jianyu finally told her everything about what had happened in those days after the bridge. Eventually, they came to other things that needed to be said. Difficult things that belonged only between the two of them.

The atmosphere in the small room shifted, and Cela seemed to understand. She excused herself, pulling Theo Barclay out of the room along with her, so Jianyu could speak with Viola alone.

"When I told them to send for you, I was not sure that you would come," Jianyu admitted, forcing himself to meet Viola's eyes.

Viola frowned. "Why would you think something so stupid?"

"You were so angry at the gala, and I had not the time to explain." He paused, knowing these were excuses. "I also wondered if you had ever forgiven me . . . for Tilly."

Viola stiffened slightly. "What happened to Tilly wasn't your fault," she told him.

"The others were never so sure. I heard what they whispered about me, even after Dolph gave me his support," Jianyu told her, remembering those dark days after the Bella Strega's cook had been struck down by some unseen power. He had never felt as if he truly belonged to the Devil's Own, but after Tilly . . . it had felt even more impossible. He had stayed only for Dolph, because of Dolph.

"The others were fools," Viola told him, taking his hand in hers.

"Perhaps, but there were days after when you looked at me with fire in your eyes. There were days I wondered if the moment would come when my heart would seize in my chest." Jianyu squeezed her hand gently. "I know what Tilly meant to you. We all did."

Viola's gaze broke away to study their intertwined hands, and her throat worked like someone who was holding back tears. "I wouldn't have harmed you—I never blamed you."

Jianyu accepted her words, allowed the relief of them to wash over him before he spoke again. "And I do not lay any blame on you for what happened at the gala."

"I nearly killed you," Viola said, looking back up at him.

"Nearly is a great distance when it comes to dying," Jianyu reminded her. "You saved me. Now there is truly nothing to forgive."

"Tell that to the one downstairs," Viola told him, nodding toward the door. "She has knives in her eyes every bit as sharp as the one I carry."

"Both of you must lay them down," Jianyu said, feeling suddenly tired.

Viola gave an indelicate snort that reminded Jianyu of so many days sitting around the kitchen table at the Bella Strega, talking like friends—almost like family.

"Lay down your knives, Viola," Jianyu repeated. "Dolph Saunders believed that the only way to win against the Order, the only way to free the old magic, was to do so together." The memory of his old friend sent a wave of sadness through him. "You went back to the Strega?" he asked. "To get the information that saved me?"

"A few days ago, yes." Viola frowned.

"How did you find it to be?"

"Not the same, of course." Her expression darkened. "Nibsy sits at Dolph's table, and the Devil's Own look to him now."

"It is all as he planned," Jianyu told her. He'd seen it for himself when he'd been taken to the Strega as a prisoner by Mock Duck a few weeks before the gala.

"I still can't believe the little snake could have done all of this on his own," Viola said. "I still say that if Darrigan hadn't—"

"Dolph trusted Darrigan," Jianyu reminded her. "*Especially* at the end. Dolph's trust is enough for me, and so it should be enough for you as well."

Viola snorted her disagreement. "You trust too easily. So did Dolph, it seems. Now Darrigan is gone, and the artifacts with him."

Jianyu pushed away the blanket and swung his legs over the side of the bed. With each passing minute, he felt a little stronger. A little more like himself. He had wasted far too much time lying on his back. When he thought about all that had happened, all that had been lost and betrayed, fury coursed through him. He accepted the heat of his anger, let it buoy him. Gathering his strength, he placed his feet upon the rough rug and tested his strength.

"It was the only way," Jianyu said. "He and Esta will find the artifacts, and they shall return to us. Then we will end Nibsy together."

With some effort he pulled himself up, wobbling a little on his unsteady legs. Viola was there in an instant, offering her arm. Jianyu took it gladly, but only for a moment. Only long enough to regain his balance.

"Will we also end the Devil's Own?" Viola wondered, frowning at him. "They follow Nibsy because they believe him. They don't understand any of this."

"The Devil's Own follow Nibsy because he fills a need, *not* because they believe in him or in the world he wishes to build. They do not have the same loyalty to him as they once had to Dolph. We can use that knowledge to our advantage when the time comes." He would use his fury then as well.

"You need to rest," Viola said.

"I have rested enough," he told her. "The Order will not wait, and we have plans to make."

COMPLICIT

As Harte followed his father through the city, he tried to formulate a plan even as he struggled to hide how awful he felt. He wasn't sure where they were, or how far from the restaurant his father's shop was, but Harte realized quickly that he was weaker than he'd first suspected, and there was a particular pain in his left thigh that shot through his hip, growing worse with every step he took. The summer breeze felt like ice against his too-tender skin, and his heart was racing unevenly in his chest. He knew that the illness was something more than a simple infection, but he pushed that worry aside to save his strength as he followed his father through the unfamiliar streets.

At first, every time his father nodded silently to someone they passed, Harte tensed, but after a few blocks, he realized that his father's reputation seemed to matter to him far too much to risk drawing attention. Besides, Harte had hold of Sammie for a reason. If he felt guilty for using the boy—his own brother—as a hostage? He pushed that guilt down deep.

They stopped at the corner of Jackson Street and Montgomery, an area defined by wide thoroughfares lined with low, two- or three-story brick buildings. Many had iron shutters thrown open to bring in the summer breezes. These were not the same tumbledown wooden structures near the docks. Nor were they surrounded by the busy open-air market stalls or rickety-looking balconies of Chinatown. This, Harte could tell, was a place where men of means did business. Neat awnings capped a few of the shops, and signs were painted in ornately curling letters to declare their proprietors.

Harte's father came to a stop in front of a large brick building. It was a bank—Lucas, Turner, & Co.—and at three stories, it was taller than some of the others that surrounded it. The first floor was made from large, light-colored stone blocks. The two floors above were brick. Wooden fire escapes ringed the top two floors, and over the arched doorway, a bronze medallion depicted Lady Justice holding her scales aloft. But she was not blindfolded. Her eyes were open, and they seemed to stare down in judgment of the people on the sidewalk below.

"The Committee's offices are on the second floor," his father said, turning to Harte. "They keep the crown in their temple on the top floor, under lock and key. It's impossible to get into if you're not a member. You'd have to get through the bank's security and then make it past the men who work in the offices above. By then, the men inside would stop you before you could even hope to open the chamber on the top floor. So you see, *impossible*. You can let the boy go now. You won't be getting the crown."

Sammie looked up at Harte with a question in his eyes—and now the fear that Harte had inspired back at the shop had grown more complete.

I'm not going to hurt you, Harte wanted to tell the child, but he couldn't make that promise. He'd already hurt the boy by using him as a pawn. He'd promised his brother magic, but in the end he would betray him, just as he'd betrayed everyone else. Harte told himself that this was how it had to be. He could not turn back, not now. He had made a promise to Esta that he would die to keep, but even Harte Darrigan couldn't convince himself that he wouldn't have regrets in the end.

"Maybe it would be impossible if I were here alone," Harte said, hardening his resolve. "But I'm not. I have you—a member—to help me."

His father blanched, confirming what Harte suspected. "You don't know—"

"But I do. Maybe if you hadn't been wearing that ring, I wouldn't have put it together, but of course you wouldn't be able to resist showing everyone the mark of your status. You didn't simply sell Cooke the crown for cash. You got yourself into their little club. It's why you were so worried that the Committee might find out you didn't turn me in immediately."

Samuel Lowe's nostrils flared slightly, the only sign that anything Harte said had struck a nerve.

"You want your son back? I want the Dragon's Eye," Harte told him. "Take me to the crown, and I'll consider handing him over."

"You'll *consider*—"

"You still have items that belong to me," Harte reminded him. "It seems only fair that I keep something of yours until mine are returned."

"Father?" The boy's voice was a question and a plea all at once.

"Enough, Sammie," his father said, snapping at the child.

Harte felt the child flinch at the sharpness of their father's tone. He bent down so that he was eye level with Sammie. "Would you like to see another trick? Perhaps I could make something disappear?" he asked, infusing mischief into his tone.

The boy looked wary, but he screwed up enough courage to jut out his stubborn little chin as he met Harte's eyes. "I *want* to see the elephant."

Harte had to choke back a laugh at the boy's insistence. "Yes, well . . ." He glanced up at the sky, which was shrouded with the same clouds that had greeted his arrival to the city, and transformed his expression into regretful disappointment. "I'm afraid it doesn't look like elephant weather today after all. Perhaps a different trick? One that your father might help us with?"

"No," Samuel Lowe said, trying to imbue his voice with its usual authority and failing to hide the tremor of fear vibrating through it.

"No?" Harte asked, a warning in his voice. "You agreed—"

"I will show you where the crown is kept, but you will make no move to retrieve it," his father said. "Not now. Not when I or my son could be considered complicit. You will give me your word. Or I will make certain that you *never* see the other items again."

Harte didn't let the threat sway him. "You're not in any position to make threats," he told his father as he stepped closer to the boy, ignoring the pang of guilt he felt. "Enough with the stalling. I'm going in one way or the other. I can either make a scene and bring you down with me, or you can help me and make this easier for everyone."

Samuel Lowe seemed to know when he'd been outmaneuvered. "You will keep your mouth shut and remain silent once we're inside. Don't draw any attention to yourself. You're an outsider here," he told Harte. "This city is nothing like the streets you grew up running wild in."

Harte doubted there was much difference. Already, he saw the similarities—secret organizations that required loyalty and gave protection for a price, residents who were afraid to cross the wrong lines. And the Vigilance Committee, a group of men who seemed as determined to root out the old magic as any of the other Brotherhoods.

He followed his father through the arched doorway and was instantly surrounded by the opulence of the bank's lobby. The walls were polished wood that gleamed in the dim light, and the floors were inlaid with marble. A high counter ran along the back side of the room, where three men dressed in crisp dark suits sat behind brass bars, working steadily.

One of the men glanced up as Harte's father approached. The two spoke in low whispers, and Harte had to stop himself from gripping the boy's shoulders too tightly. He tried to steady himself, preparing for the betrayal that was likely to come as he waited in the stuffy quiet. It felt like being inside a tomb.

The clerk kept tossing glances in Harte's direction. When the clerk's brows drew together, Harte had the sinking feeling that he'd let himself walk into a trap, but after a moment the two seemed to have come to some understanding. The clerk gave a small nod finally, and his father directed Harte to a door just left of the counter. Still unsure, Harte followed, gently tugging the boy along with him for protection.

On the other side of the doorway, a steep staircase led upward. With his leg throbbing and his entire body aching, the climb felt impossible, but Harte did what he could to keep pace. He didn't want his father to know how winded he was or how dizzy he felt when he looked up the seemingly endless stretch of steps. *Esta will be waiting,* he reminded himself as he lifted his foot to the next step.

When they reached the third floor, they came to a heavy brass door inscribed with an unusual design. The etchings in the metal reminded him of some of the alchemical symbols he'd learned in the preparation of his stage act, but he didn't recognize any specifically. His father withdrew a brass key from his vest pocket and used it to unlock the door.

Beyond the door, a darkened antechamber led into a larger space. It looked like some kind of temple.

If Harte had thought that the lobby was beautiful, this room made it seem downright plain. The chamber was a large, octagonal space capped with a high, peaked ceiling. Beneath the ceiling, a line of transom windows let in daylight, and the floor was wood, patterned in the shape of the same opened eye that Harte had seen on the ring Samuel Lowe wore. The center of the eye was inlaid with precious stones, bright blue lapis lazuli and onyx. Gilded columns surrounded the room, and they were carved into human shapes, like sentinels. Harte thought he recognized the image of Washington in one, possibly Jefferson in another, but the rest were unfamiliar to him. The chamber was like stepping into another world, and in the center of that world, atop a carved altar of granite and gold, was the Dragon's Eye.

Harte moved toward the altar, pulling the boy along with him, but his father stepped in front of him, blocking his path to the crown. "You gave me your word."

The absurdity of this statement snapped the temper Harte had been holding back. "You don't deserve my word," he said, glaring at his father. "You stole everything from my mother. You don't deserve to keep this life. You don't deserve your reputation—or your son."

The boy whimpered, clearly misunderstanding Harte's meaning, but Harte ignored him.

"You understand *nothing.*" His father shook his head, disgust clear in his eyes. "You cannot take this piece. It would ruin me. It would destroy all I've built here—and anyone who depends upon me."

"I don't particularly care," Harte told him, but his conscience had already been tugging at him, and his father's words only served to make it worse.

"Do you have any idea how difficult it was for me to get a real start in this town? New money isn't taken seriously. Even though I gave Cooke everything by selling this crown to him, I'm still pushed aside and kept from my true potential," his father told him.

"You think you're the only one who has had to build a life from nothing?" Harte asked, incredulous. "You're not the only one who has people depending on him."

"It's not the same thing," his father sneered. "You're unnatural. An abomination, and anyone who depends on you is a fool who deserves what he gets."

That was probably true enough . . . but it wouldn't keep Harte from his objective.

Harte leaned down, eye level now with Sammie. "I think it's time for our magic trick," he told the child. "Are you ready?"

"Ben—" his father warned.

"That isn't my name," Harte said, never looking up at his father. His eyes were on the boy. "Do you know that magic tricks have certain requirements?"

The boy shook his head.

"I'll tell you the one thing that no trick can work without." Harte paused for a second, because everything depended on what would happen next—and also because he'd always liked a bit of drama. He lowered his voice. "The most important part of any magic trick is the *misdirection*. Do you know what that is?"

"Don't listen to him, son," Samuel Lowe commanded.

But the boy—his *brother*—was already drawn in, entranced. His eyes had grown wide with wonder, and again Harte felt the shame of what he was about to do—but he could not turn back now. He would not allow himself to soften.

"Would you like me to show you?" Harte asked, and when the boy nodded, he began to count. "One . . . two . . ."

On the count of "three," he released the boy, giving him a gentle push straight toward his father. It worked exactly as he'd planned. As Samuel Lowe caught the child, Harte gathered all of his remaining strength and sprinted for the crown.

It was in his hands in an instant, and because he could—because Sammie was still watching with bright, inquisitive eyes—Harte made the Dragon's Eye disappear with a flourish, tucking it securely into his jacket. He barely had time to see the smile light Sammie's serious little expression before he ran for the door, but it took every last bit of his strength to keep upright as he tried not to tumble down the steps to the floors below.

A PROMISE KEPT

1904—Denver

Jericho Northwood knew that playing with time came with consequences. He'd seen that for himself. Sometimes the consequences weren't all that noticeable, but other times they were—like when he saved a man's life in Oklahoma only to have that same man try to kill him a year later. Jot Gunter should be dead, but because North had been naive enough to save him, the rancher had lived to become an enemy.

What Esta was talking about doing, though, was a lot more than the handful of hours North's watch could give him. If she was truly able to go back years, she could change a whole lot of things. The effects of her meddling could ripple out in ways none of them could predict. North might have liked to think of his concerns as noble, but in truth, there were parts of his life that Jericho Northwood didn't want changed.

But he'd made Maggie a promise. If she wanted him to get the dagger from Pickett, then that was exactly what he'd do. As for after? He still wasn't sure.

Pickett's tent was on the far end of the performers' encampment, which suited North just fine. It meant fewer people would notice his visit and there was less of a chance that someone would interrupt. He snagged the half pint of whiskey he'd kept in his bunk, and when he was sure no one was looking, he put in the tablet Cordelia had given him earlier, so it would have time to dissolve. Then he gave the bottle a shake to be sure. He'd probably only get one chance at this.

If Pickett was surprised by North's visit, he didn't show it. The cowboy offered North a seat and welcomed his offer of a swig of whiskey. North told Pickett that it was a thank-you for saving his life. If he had any misgivings at all, he focused on Maggie instead.

After Pickett was done, North lifted the bottle to his own mouth and pretended to drink. By the time he'd lowered it and wiped his mouth with the back of his hand, the change in Pickett's expression told North the drug was working.

North allowed Pickett to talk for a few minutes about pointless things—horses and the weather. When their conversation turned to how Pickett felt every time he had to enter the arena to catcalls and slurs, how every performance he had to prove that he was more than the names they called him, North knew the other cowboy was ready.

Still, North wasn't completely without feeling. He'd seen the effect the formulation had on Esta. Taking a man's self-control was about the lowest thing a person could do. *You promised,* North told himself as he leaned forward and propped his elbows on the table between them.

"So I hear tell that you have a piece that's pretty impressive to see. . . ."

North left Pickett's tent not long after, with his legs feeling unsteady beneath him. He probably should've stayed with Pickett until the drug wore off completely, but he had to get to Maggie. It didn't matter that he'd left angry and hurt, not with what he'd just learned. He had to warn her.

North was so focused on getting back to his girl that he didn't even hear the person shouting his name at first. Even once he realized that one voice was louder than the rest of the usual background buzz of the grounds, it didn't register that the voice was calling for him, especially since the name they were calling wasn't the one he'd been born with. But then it clicked. For a moment North considered ignoring whoever it was. But the voice was getting louder and more insistent, which meant whoever wanted him wasn't giving up. When he glanced over his shoulder, North saw Aldo, the manager of the grounds, scurrying after him, waving for him to stop.

North had the sudden, uncanny sense that he needed to get out of there, but the grounds manager was one of the few people he couldn't easily ignore, and the person with Aldo was definitely one of the others: Clem Curtis, one of the brothers who owned the show. North cursed silently to himself, but he slowed his steps to get the meeting over with.

"Mr. Aldo," North said, lifting a finger to the brim of his hat and trying not to look half as impatient and frustrated—or nervous—as he felt.

Aldo was a broad-shouldered man whose paunch had won the battle against the waistband of his trousers years ago. His light hair curled around the base of his neck, and sandy stubble shadowed his jawline. North hadn't liked Aldo when he'd been forced to ingratiate himself with the man to get hired, and he liked him even less now.

"Something I can help you gentlemen with?" North asked, trying to appear indifferent at their interruption.

"Mr. Curtis here wanted to meet you," Aldo said.

"Me?" North asked, confused. He tried to make his surprise appear as interest, but mostly he felt uneasy. He would have preferred to remain unnoticed. "Can't imagine why," he said, falling into an affable, aw-shucks persona that he hoped would get him by.

"I've been hearing good things about you, Robertson," Curtis said, using North's assumed identity. "Aldo here says you've made quite a mark for yourself as a hard worker since you started."

"It's only been a couple of days now," North said, feigning humility.

In actuality, he was getting more nervous with each passing second. There was no reason for anyone to have noticed him. He hadn't been working any harder than anyone else—he'd made sure of it, so as not to stick out.

Tucking his hands into his pockets, he lifted his shoulders, clearly embarrassed by the attention. He used the movement to mask what he was really doing—maneuvering his pocket watch, flipping open the glass face . . . in case.

"But you've done well," Curtis said. "I probably don't need to tell you how hard it is to find good workers these days. I thought maybe you'd want to stay on with us permanently."

"Oh, I don't know," North said, not yet sure whether to feel relieved. His thumb hesitated over the dial of the watch. "That's a fine offer, but I'd have to consider—"

"What's there to consider?" the Curtis brother asked. "You don't already have another job lined up, do you?"

"Not exactly," North told him.

"A wife to support?"

"Mr. Robertson here isn't married," Aldo confirmed, looping his thumbs through his suspenders as he rocked on his heels. "He already assured me of that."

"Then what's holding you back?" Curtis asked.

"I can't think of anything at all," North admitted. There was a part of him that could almost imagine the life Curtis was proposing—traveling from place to place. Seeing the country while he spent his days with the horses he loved. Living out in the fresh, clean country air . . .

But it was an impossible dream. North was already on a path, and it didn't lead out into the wide world. It led to Maggie, which meant it would be guided by principles he'd already committed himself to long ago, maybe even before he could have possibly understood what they were.

Curtis didn't need to know that, either, though.

"I guess I'd be a fool not to accept," North told the men. It didn't matter that he wasn't planning on following through.

"Then it's settled." Curtis extended his hand. "I'll have Aldo draw up a contract, and we'll make it official."

It took everything North had to return Curtis' smile. He'd never have a life like the one Curtis proposed, one where all a man had to do was shake a hand, make a deal, earn a living doing what he loved. Without questions. Without fear. The best North could hope for was to keep fighting for the life he might have one day with Maggie, if he was lucky enough. He took Curtis' hand, shaking on the deal he'd never keep.

　　　　　　　　　　　　　　　LISA MAXWELL

He wasn't really surprised at how tightly Curtis grasped his hand. There were a lot of men who thought they could prove themselves through the strength of their handshake. North was surprised, though, when Curtis' other hand whipped out to latch onto his wrist. Before North could stop him or pull away, Curtis was ripping back the sleeve, exposing the dark snake inked into the skin of his wrist. He tried to fight free, but Aldo already had a pistol out and was aiming it directly at him.

"Good work, Aldo," Curtis said as a trio of other men came seemingly out of nowhere to take North by the arms. They pulled his hands from his pockets and wrenched them behind his back. In the process North's watch slipped from his fingers and landed on the ground as the men restrained him.

He looked at Aldo, pleading silently, but the other man turned away.

"I think we have the fella you were looking for," Curtis said.

"Nice work, Curtis." The voice was familiar . . . but North couldn't place why at first. Then Jot Gunter was there in front of him, shaking Clem Curtis' hand like they were old friends. He noticed the watch on the ground, and with a smile tugging up the edges of his heavy mustache, he crushed it beneath the heel of his boot.

No. No. No. No. No—

But it was too late. The watch was beyond his reach.

"He's been going by the name Jerry Robertson," Curtis told the men. "I noticed him around the other day, and when I heard about the Syndicate looking for a redheaded cowboy with two different-colored eyes, I had a feeling this might be the one."

Gunter came a little closer and examined North with squinted eyes. North refused to blink, but he couldn't help noticing that Gunter had a silver medallion on his lapel. It looked familiar—like the ones the Jefferson Guard wore back in St. Louis to detect illegal magic in the area.

"I believe it's him all right," Gunter said. "Jericho Northwood. You're supposed to be dead."

North let the pain and anger of losing his father's watch chase away the fear, and he gave his old boss a cold look. "Sorry to disappoint, Mr. Gunter, but it appears I'm a hard man to kill."

Gunter only stared at him. "We'll see about that." Then he turned to Clem Curtis. "Good work finding him for us."

"It was an honor to be of service," Aldo said, inserting himself between the two men.

Gunter glanced at the grounds manager and then dismissed him in the next breath as he returned his attention to Curtis. "The Syndicate won't forget this. We take care of our own."

The blond Curtis brother puffed up beneath the praise.

"Does anyone else know of this situation?" Gunter asked.

"Only a few people I trust implicitly," Curtis assured him. "Like you requested."

"Good," Gunter said. "And the arrangements for this evening's performance?"

"Your men will have complete access to the grounds," Aldo assured him.

Gunter gave Aldo a dismissive glance. "The president's man will be here this evening to supervise the raid personally. I trust we won't have any trouble."

"Of course not," Curtis told Gunter. "What would you like us to do with this one?"

"The secretary is set to arrive any minute now. I expect he'll want to interview this maggot for himself. I'll let him decide what's to be done with him after," Gunter said with a satisfied smile.

North struggled against the hold the other two men had on him, but it wasn't any use. They were too strong, and he was too outmanned.

Curtis glanced at the men holding North. "Take him over to the supply tent and keep him contained there. No one talks to him until the secretary arrives."

SIGILLUM

Viola paused on the small landing outside Jianyu's door, not quite sure what she was supposed to do next. From the way he'd pushed her out of the room, she doubted he wanted her to wait. He wanted to dress himself, and she had the sense that he needed to be left alone, to walk on his own power down the stairs. She'd been around enough men to know that they usually preferred not to test their weaknesses with an audience.

She realized suddenly that she still had the seal in her hand. Even once the bloody printed runes had started to glow, even once Jianyu woke and began looking more like himself, Viola had kept it tight in her fist, as though releasing it might somehow break the strange power it held. The small stone cylinder still felt oddly cool against her palm—a mark of the corrupted ritual magic it contained.

Thank the heavens it worked.

Viola hadn't been completely sure that it would. She'd hoped, of course, because she hadn't wanted to go back to Nibsy Lorcan, but knowing such things wasn't Viola's strength—it had been Dolph's.

Her old friend hadn't been like the other Bowery bosses, who attacked first and considered later. They'd taken the seal and many other objects from J. P. Morgan at the Metropolitan because Dolph had known that this small, unassuming object would be needed to steal the Book. He made a study of such things, because for Dolph Saunders, *knowing* had been the most important part of the battle.

But Dolph hadn't known about Nibsy, Viola thought, as a wave of grief and fury rose within her. If Jianyu's story was to be believed—and she had no reason to doubt it—not even Dolph Saunders had seen Nibsy's betrayal coming. He'd trusted the boy, and he'd paid the price. They all had.

Viola examined the stone seal, the markings on it still darkened by Jianyu's blood, and then she tucked it away as she said a silent prayer of thanks that she had kept it. She said one more prayer for Jianyu's continued health, and then she made her way down the stairs.

In the kitchen, Viola found that Theo had not yet left, as she had expected him to. He was sitting at the small table, studying the volume she'd taken from Dolph's apartment earlier that day—Dolph's notebook. Viola still couldn't believe Theo was there at all, much less that he'd waited so long. He *shouldn't* be there. It was a sweet sort of torture to be near him, to both feel closer to Ruby through his presence and to be reminded of what she could never have.

Cela was sitting next to Theo, peering over at the notebook as he turned the pages. Her hands were wrapped around a cup of something warm and steaming. At the sound of Viola's entrance, she looked up and stood all at once, a small burst of panic breaking out in her expression. "Is he—"

"He's up," Viola said. "He'll be down soon."

"I should go help him," Cela said, already moving in the direction of the stairs.

Viola caught her arm gently, felt her flinch at the touch. "He's well now, Cela. Let him be strong enough for this."

Cela looked like she disagreed, but she relented. "You want some coffee?" she asked, pulling away from Viola. "I put some on already."

"Please," Viola said gratefully.

She went to the table and took a seat near Theo. "You find anything interesting?"

Cela offered her the cup of steaming coffee before returning to her own seat on the other side of Theo.

"This journal is remarkable," Theo told her, frowning. "The collection of languages here alone—French, German, Spanish, even Latin. It's astounding that these are all in the same hand." He glanced up at her. "It doesn't seem possible that your friend could have written all of this on his own."

"Dolph Saunders had many talents," Viola said tightly, trying not to bristle at Theo's presumptions. She took a sip of the coffee to keep herself from saying anything else. It was burnt and bitter, but the bite of it settled something inside her.

Theo turned another page. "From the looks of it, he was brilliant," Theo said, sounding more than a little surprised by this.

"And why wouldn't he be?" Viola asked, this time unable to keep the reproach from her tone.

"I don't know," Theo said, frowning. "He lived in the Bowery and owned a saloon. I hadn't expected a scholar."

"Dolph Saunders lived in the Bowery because he was unwilling to hide what he was." Viola's heart clenched with the memory of her old friend. "He chose to live among the people who needed him." Outside the law. Outside of safety.

"I would have liked to meet him," Theo told her, and she had the sense that this was more than simple politeness.

"He was a complicated man," Viola admitted, wondering if any of them—including Leena—had ever really known Dolph.

"Most of them are," Cela said, sharing a knowing look with Viola, and for the moment, some of the tension between the two of them eased. "Or at least, a lot of them like to *believe* they are."

Viola could not stop her mouth from curving in agreement.

"Methodical, too," Theo told her, seemingly unaware of the small joke they'd made at his expense. "The amount of detail in some of these notes is astounding."

Something on one of the pages caught her eye. "I know this," she murmured, touching a finger to the illustration before he could turn to the next page.

"You've seen this before?" Theo frowned up at her, looking surprised.

"Sì." Viola had seen that same strange design earlier that day in Dolph's apartment. It had been part of the painting they'd stolen from Morgan's collection, depicted clearly—though maybe in not so much detail as this—on the cover of the book Newton held beneath the tree, under a sky with two moons.

"It's some kind of sigil," Theo told her, studying the illustration. "They're fairly common in ancient art, but this is one of the most intricate I've ever seen. You're sure *this* is the one you've seen?"

"Yes," Viola murmured. "In a painting . . ." *And somewhere else?* Again, it seemed strangely familiar, and she wondered if her memory of the Book of Mysteries—hazy as it might be—had any truth to it. "In the painting, it wasn't so clear as this one," she told them.

It *was* intricate. Looking at the diagram was enough to make Viola's eyes hurt. It felt impossible to follow the lines of the various shapes as they wove into one another, interlocking and then doubling back. They seemed to have no beginning, no end. They seemed almost alive on the page.

"What's a sigil, anyway?" Cela asked, sipping her coffee and peering over to look at the page. "I've never heard of such a thing."

"Traditionally, a sigil is nothing more than a symbol, usually something like a small diagram," Theo explained. "It comes from the Latin 'sigillum,' or 'seal.'"

"It doesn't look like the seal you all used to help Jianyu, though," Cela said.

"No," Theo agreed. "Sigils are more like written emblems than objects. I've seen some before in old illuminated manuscripts—especially medieval ones—but nothing like this." He squinted as though he was also having trouble focusing on the pattern. "Often, they're meant to represent the true name of an angel or a demon."

Viola was frowning now. "Why would anyone want such a thing?"

"Because names have power," Cela said softly. Her eyes were focused on the page, thoughtful now. "Naming is a way of claiming, isn't it?

LISA MAXWELL

Claiming yourself, claiming what you are. Names are powerful things, even without any magic attached."

"Exactly," Theo said. "If you knew the name of a demon or an angel— the true name of it—you could control it. Or so groups like the Order would believe."

"Che pazzo," Viola said, crossing herself. Only a madman would want such a thing.

"The Order really believes they can control a demon?" Cela sounded uneasy about this idea, and for once Viola agreed with her completely.

"Maybe not an *actual* demon." Theo's mouth curved a bit, though Viola couldn't begin to see what was amusing about any of this. "Over the centuries, people have used the word 'demon' to describe pretty much anything they couldn't explain or control . . . including those with magic."

Unease made Viola pause. "Someone could use this . . . this *sigil*," she said, the word tasting heavy on her tongue, "and they could control a person's magic?"

"Possibly," Theo said, frowning. "Though I only know the theory behind these as pieces of art. I'm less familiar with their actual use."

Hadn't the notes Nibsy gave her weeks ago indicated something similar? Dolph had taken part of Leena's magic and placed it into the head of his cane to use it. To control it. He'd taken a part of *her* to control for his own. It seemed to Viola the worst sort of betrayal, and she would not have believed it of her friend if she'd not seen the evidence written out in his own hand.

Dolph's cane and Viola's blade were only two examples of ordinary objects infused with power. She'd heard tales of many more, but Viola had never understood where those objects came from. Was this strange diagram what was needed to take the magic from a person? And if so, how did it work?

"What does that say?" Viola asked, pointing to the strange markings on the page near the sigil.

"I'm not sure," Theo admitted. "I've never seen this particular language before. It could be some kind of cuneiform, or some kind of code? I'm not exactly a student of languages."

"Dolph was," Viola said, more to herself than to any of them. She couldn't help but wonder why her old friend had chosen to inscribe this page with such strange figures when he could have used any one of his other tongues. *Unless he didn't want anyone else to be able to read what he wrote.*

Perhaps Dolph had known about the coming betrayal, but the question remained: What, exactly, had Dolph Saunders been trying to hide about this image? And why had he felt the need to hide it so thoroughly?

They would never know, Viola realized. Dolph was gone, and with him the answers to this puzzle.

"There are more notes on the back," Theo said. "It seems as though someone—possibly your friend—had the same idea. There are some notes here about the plan for an experiment, but . . . the next page seems to be missing." He flipped the page over to show Viola the place where one or more pages had been torn from the binding of the notebook.

"Sounds like nothing but a bunch of trouble, if you ask me," Cela said. "Whoever wants to go stirring up demons is nothing but a fool. Some things aren't meant to be messed with." She took her mug of coffee to the sink, done with the conversation.

Viola, though, could not take her eyes from the place where pages were missing from the book, or from the writing on the back of the page that held the strange illustration. Familiar writing, and this was in English. She took a piece of paper that she'd tucked for safety in Libitina's sheath and slowly, carefully unfolded it. On the surface was Dolph's hand, clear as day, describing what he'd done to Leena, or at least describing the aftermath of his efforts.

It was the same size—the same type of paper—and when she held it up to examine it, Theo's brows drew together.

"Nibsy gave this to me," she told him, answering his unspoken question. "Before the gala. He wanted to show me proof that Dolph wasn't who I believed him to be. He wanted to turn me against him."

A movement in the doorway drew Viola's attention.

Jianyu was standing there, a frown on his narrow face. "That is what Nibsy Lorcan wanted from everyone."

A DEVIL'S BARGAIN

1902—New York

Cela turned at the sound of Jianyu's voice to find him standing in the doorway, looking nearly like himself, if only a little thinner. She stepped toward him immediately, almost reflexively, but then she stopped herself. Suddenly she wasn't sure if she was *supposed* to go to him. She'd been taking care of him for days now, but Jianyu hadn't exactly had a choice about it. He hadn't been in any position to accept or reject her help.

Now he moved into the kitchen slowly, but he was holding himself upright in a way that had Cela hesitating. As much as Cela didn't want to admit it, maybe Viola had been right to stop her from going up to him a few minutes before—it was clear he needed this moment. It was there in his eyes, the quiet satisfaction—the *relief*—he must have felt in no longer being unable. This wasn't the same man Cela had tended to in the bed upstairs, but the Jianyu she had known from before. The one who had thrown himself in front of a knife to save her life. The one who had pulled a blade from his own shoulder without so much as wincing at the pain of it.

"Where is Abel?" Jianyu asked, taking a seat next to Theo Barclay at the table.

"He's out with his friend Joshua, working on some project or another for the union they're trying to get established," Cela told him. "He should be arriving anytime now, and he'll be glad to see that you're up and about."

Jianyu's shoulders relaxed a little as Cela placed a mug of the coffee she'd made in front of him. When he hesitated, staring down at the dark liquid, Cela realized that she didn't know if Jianyu even *liked* coffee.

She started to reach for the mug. "I could boil some water for tea—"

He put his hand on her arm to stop her. "Thank you." For a long moment they just kind of looked at each other.

It felt like his thank-you was for more than the coffee. He didn't say anything, but Cela felt it nonetheless. *Thank you for not leaving me. Thank you for caring for me. Thank you . . .* It was all there.

Or maybe it wasn't. Maybe she was spinning stories in her head.

Jianyu's hand was larger than she remembered it being—*he* was larger and more solid than she'd remembered him being as well. Somehow, over the past week or so, the idea of him seemed to have shrunk in her mind as he lay sick and unmoving in that bed. Now she remembered again how tall he was, how his slenderness belied his strength.

Now Jianyu's skin felt warm against hers, and with his hand steady on her arm, Cela realized that she had not expected him to wake again. Not *really*. She certainly hadn't expected that he'd recover so quickly.

Magic, she reminded herself. It was easy to forget the truth of that when she was with him—with all of them, really. They didn't seem any different from Abel or herself—or anyone else—until they did something strange and uncanny that made the hair on her neck rise to know that there was power she didn't really understand at work in the world.

Then again, there were a lot of things Cela Johnson didn't understand about the world. Who would have guessed that the strange gathering taking place in this house's too-small kitchen would have even been possible? The Italian girl with her glittering eyes and sharp tongue, Theo Barclay, whose suit declared that he was every inch Fifth Avenue, and then Jianyu with his short-cropped hair, and herself. None of them would have ever met if not for Harte Darrigan and the blasted ring. Their worlds should have remained separate, as neatly divided as the streets of the city were, each with their small enclaves and communities. Each keeping to themselves, because *that* was how you were supposed to keep yourself and the ones you loved safe and secure. So many different worlds were colliding in that tiny room, and not a single one of those worlds was safe *or* secure, and Cela couldn't help but wonder what would come of it.

"We need to discuss what will happen next," Jianyu said, almost as though he'd been thinking the same thing. He pulled back his hand and lifted the chipped mug of coffee. He didn't ask for any cream or sugar, just took a small sip, black as it was.

It had to be bitter—probably burnt, too, considering that it had been on the stove for too long now. But Jianyu's eyes fluttered closed for a second and he smiled, the barest curve of his lips. It was a private, inward-type smile, the sort of smile that told Cela that he maybe felt the same way about coming back, like maybe he hadn't really believed it would happen either, but now that it had, he was grateful.

"Thank you," he said again, and again Cela felt those two little words held a whole lot more than what he was saying. Then he set the chipped mug back onto the tabletop, and she wondered if the moment had even happened or if she'd only been imagining that something new was building between them.

"The only thing that *needs* to happen next is for you to rest," Cela told him, her voice sounding too tart, even to herself. "Everything else can wait until you're stronger."

"Do I look so weak?" Jianyu asked, lifting his brows in a challenge.

Cela frowned. "You look . . ." He looked fine, she admitted to herself. He looked healthy and whole and better than he had in days. She let out a sigh, already knowing she was going to lose this particular battle. "Not even an hour ago, you were two steps away from death. You need to rest."

"I have already rested more than enough for an entire lifetime," Jianyu said, dismissing her concern. "The Order cannot wait, not if they truly have the Delphi's Tear in their possession." He looked to Viola.

"Nibsy believes they have it," she confirmed. "My brother must

LISA MAXWELL

believe it too. I can't see any other reason he would be willing to include Nibsy Lorcan in whatever it is he's planning."

"You're going off the word of people that none of you even trust," Cela said, her instincts prickling. Jianyu was barely well and already he was going to toss himself into danger, and for what? For the girl who hadn't thought twice about skewering him with a knife. "This Nibsy person could be lying, for all you know. So could Paul Kelly. Either one of them could be setting you up."

"It is possible, but the fact remains that neither can be permitted to take possession of the ring," Jianyu told her—told all of them—and there was such a strength and sureness in his voice that even Cela, who would have rather seen him climb back into bed, couldn't argue with it. "We must retrieve it from the Order before they can use it to reestablish their power. Darrigan and Esta will return to us, and we must not be empty-handed."

"What, exactly, do you think you're going to do?" Cela asked, with no small amount of disbelief and more than a little worry. "Even if you *can* turn yourself into a ghost, I was at that gala. I saw what the Order's capable of."

"I agree," Theo said. "I know those men—too well, in some ways. They have money and power that make them nearly untouchable."

"We touched them before," Viola challenged. "We burned Khafre Hall to the ground and took their most precious treasures."

"You sure didn't manage to hold on to them long, though," Cela said, earning herself a sharp look from Viola.

Viola's eyes flashed, but Cela didn't care, exactly. Viola's confidence irritated her in ways she couldn't explain. Maybe it was the absolute sureness in her voice and the way she carried herself, like the world couldn't touch her. Or maybe it was that she seemed to assume all was forgiven for what had happened at the gala. As though Viola's healing Jianyu should've been enough to forgive her from nearly taking his life in the first place.

Maybe it *should* have been enough. But for Cela, who had sat by Jianyu's bed for days, who had fretted over his cooling skin and sluggish breathing, it didn't *feel* like enough. The only problem was that Cela wasn't exactly sure what *would* be.

"Cela is right. Before, we were more than two," Jianyu reminded Viola. "When we went to Khafre Hall, we had an entire team we trusted, and a leader to guide us. We can't hope to retrieve the ring as we are now. We still do not know when or where or how the ring may appear again, but clearly Nibsy and your brother know something more. We should use them as we can."

"My brother has told me nothing," Viola said stiffly, like she was almost embarrassed by this fact. "I doubt he will be any help at all."

"But Nibsy Lorcan might be," Jianyu offered.

"No," Viola said, shaking her head. "Better we kill that snake now before he can cause any more trouble."

"Funny how that seems to be your answer to everything," Cela said dryly, cutting her eyes in Viola's direction. Cela always tried to give people the benefit of the doubt. She knew too well what it was like to be judged for what she looked like instead of who she was, but Viola wasn't making the best case against the common idea that Italians couldn't be trusted with their tempers. "Throw your knife. Slice someone open. It's always the same with you."

"Cela," Jianyu said gently, but Cela could hear the reproach in his tone.

"You really forgive her so easily?" Cela asked, her throat suddenly tight. "You nearly *died*." She was more than a little mortified to hear how her voice broke.

"There is nothing to forgive," Jianyu told her. His dark eyes held such a soft sureness, a clear conviction, that Cela realized he really *wasn't* angry at Viola. More, she saw that he wanted *her* not to be angry as well.

Maybe he was right, but Cela was finding it awful hard to forgive Viola when she understood the truth of the matter—that knife hadn't been intended for Jianyu. It had been intended for *her*, and Cela doubted that Viola would've cared if *she'd* have been the one to die.

"Don't you ever get tired of being so . . ." Cela let her hand wave vaguely. "You're so damn unflappable all the time. Don't you *ever* get angry? Don't you ever just want to *scream?*"

Jianyu's mouth turned down. "Always. I am always angry." But he didn't say anything more. He didn't bother to explain, only met her eyes, willing her to understand.

Then, all at once, she did. Of course he couldn't rage and spout off. *Of course.* Jianyu was too visible in this city, just as she often was—even more so. Anger was a dangerous luxury when you had no one to stand with you, no safe place to fall.

"I didn't mean—" Cela stopped short, not knowing what she could possibly say.

"Cela's right," Jianyu said to Viola, mercifully changing the subject. "We cannot trust Nibsy, but neither can we simply remove him."

"Maybe *you* can't," Viola told him, but her gaze cut to Cela—a clear challenge. "For me, it wouldn't be so hard."

"Patience, Viola," Jianyu said. "Death is always easy. It is what comes after that is difficult. Think . . . what would happen to the Devil's Own without Nibsy's leadership? Would they follow you? Certainly they will not follow *me.* You may have forgiven me for what happened to Tilly, but for many of Dolph's numbers, it only proved that I never belonged."

Cela heard the note of something larger than sadness in his voice, and she thought that maybe she understood what had put it there. After all, she knew what it felt like to not belong where you were *supposed* to belong. She'd been reminded of that during the short stay with her aunt, and she thanked her lucky stars that Abel had come back, because he was maybe the one place where she felt she always belonged.

Here, too, she thought suddenly. She shouldn't feel that way at all, not with the strange mix of people all sitting around this table—especially not with Viola still staring daggers into her heart—but for some reason Cela felt more comfortable sitting next to Jianyu, talking through this strange business of magic, than she maybe had even with her own family at times.

Cela took Jianyu's hand before she realized what she was doing. It seemed natural somehow to reach for his hand. She told herself that it was because she still couldn't believe he was really sitting there, whole and healthy. She felt the need to touch him, if only to make sure the moment was real.

A flash of surprise and a question lit Jianyu's eyes, but then his fingers tightened around hers, and Cela realized that touching him—that reaching for him so easily—had been a mistake. She'd touched him a thousand times while he was sick without even thinking about it. But this? The small squeeze of his hand, the warmth of his skin against hers, and the sure strength of him made her too aware of things she hadn't realized she felt. Dangerous things that she had no business feeling.

She had to force herself not to pull away. She had to work hard to sit there and pretend that everything was exactly the same as it had been before.

"If we remove Nibsy now, the Devil's Own will fracture and crumble," Jianyu said, finally turning back to Viola. "You know this is true. The various powers in the Bowery will come for what is left, scavengers on the carcass of all Dolph built. We cannot allow that to happen."

Jianyu released Cela's hand then, and she felt relieved and bereft all at once. She pulled her hand back from the table, tucked it into the skirts that pooled in her lap, and ignored the way her heart felt like it might fly clean out of her chest.

"I know." Viola sighed. "I hate it, but you're not wrong. Even Mooch, even with what we did to help him, he doesn't trust me. He won't trust you, either."

"Nibsy has already offered you a new partnership," Jianyu told Viola. "It is a way back in."

"No," Viola said, all fire and vinegar. "He offered me a devil's bargain, not a partnership."

"Devil's bargain or not, I believe you must accept his offer," Jianyu said. "Allow Nibsy to believe that you are with him once more. Feed him enough information to keep him happy, and when the time is right, we shall pull back his mask and reveal him for what he truly is."

"It's too dangerous," Theo said, drawing their attention to him. He'd been so quietly watchful, and Jianyu's hand around hers had been such a distraction, that Cela had almost forgotten he was sitting right there.

"I can handle Nibsy Lorcan," Viola said, sounding suddenly insulted, where a moment before she'd been making the same argument herself.

"I'm sure you can handle damn near anything," Theo told her. "But you'd all be foolish to depend on this Nibsy fellow's information—or your brother's for that matter, Viola. If you do, you'll always be working blind, three steps behind the others. You need someone on the inside of the Order, someone who could make sure that you know more than either of them."

Jianyu tilted his head, clearly taking Theo's measure. "Where do you propose we find such a person?"

Cela knew what Theo Barclay would say even before the words were out of his mouth, because of course he would volunteer. Putting himself in such unnecessary danger was exactly the sort of thing someone would volunteer for when the world had never touched them and when they had no idea how much there was to lose.

"I can help," Theo said. "I know people. With the right incentives, it wouldn't be that difficult for me to find a contact in the Order—maybe even earn their trust."

"No," Viola said. "Assolutamente *no*. You're not getting involved with this."

"He's *already* involved," Cela pointed out. Her heart was still unsteady in her chest, and her skin felt too hot, because she understood that they were all tied up in this inextricably.

Whether they wanted to be or not.

THE EVENING SHOW

1904—Denver

The sound of the sirens clanging in the distance spurred Esta on as she and Maggie rushed toward the Curtis Brothers' Show. Jack Grew was in Denver. That was bad enough, but maybe even worse was the fact that Nibsy had been aware all along that she and Harte were in St. Louis. He'd been pulling strings that Esta hadn't even known existed. He was *still* pulling those strings, and if they didn't get to Cordelia first, Nibsy would send his network of Antistasi after the artifacts, and there was no way for Esta to warn Harte.

As awful as those developments were, the knowledge that Jack was in Denver urged Esta onward. The Book would *certainly* be with him, because there was no way Jack—or the thing that lived inside of him—would ever let the Ars Arcana out of sight. If Esta had any hope of finding a way of controlling Seshat's power without giving up her own life, it would be in the Book of Mysteries. If she could get it back from Jack, maybe she could begin to imagine a future for herself after all.

Esta pushed herself and Maggie along with her, nearly jogging the entire way to the show's grounds, but the thin mountain air made it hard to breathe. By the time they reached the edge of town, where the city fell away to the fields and mountains beyond, Esta's head was spinning.

"There are so many people," Maggie said, looking more than a little overwhelmed by the view of the crowded grounds. The evening show was clearly more popular than the afternoon.

"North was going after Pickett, so let's start with the performers' encampment," Esta told her.

Once they were on the grounds, it was easy enough for Esta to pretend confidence and blend in with the crowd that had come to watch the show, but Maggie couldn't help but look guilty. *No . . .* Maggie looked *scared*, which amounted to the same thing. While everyone else around them was smiling and appeared excited, Maggie's unease stood out like a beacon.

Esta was still wearing men's clothing, so she looped Maggie's arm through hers to escort her and offer some more support. "Relax," she murmured, pretending to be interested in the crowds and excitement. "We're going to find him. But you need to breathe."

They continued through the crowd, but as they went, Esta noticed a number of men trying to blend in among the families and couples. They were way too serious-looking for being out for a pleasant evening at the show, and if the men weren't actual marshals, they certainly moved like them.

"We need to keep moving," Esta said, pulling Maggie along steadily through the crowd.

They'd gone only a little farther, though, when Maggie stopped short. "Look at the medallions those men are wearing on their coats," she murmured. "To the left of the tent there."

Esta glanced at the trio of cowboys that Maggie had nodded toward. They all wore broad hats and the work clothes that were common for ranch hands around Denver. They also wore matching silver medallions on their jackets.

"Those men are wearing the Jefferson Guard's badges," Maggie said. "The ones they used to detect illegal magic at the fair."

"They aren't dressed like the Guard, though," Esta told her.

"Maybe they don't want to be recognized," Maggie said.

"Or maybe they're not Guard at all." Esta studied the men. "Didn't Cordelia say that more men from the Syndicate arrived today? It's possible that the Brotherhoods are working together now, maybe even sharing resources."

"That doesn't make sense," Maggie said. "The whole point of the Society wanting the necklace—the whole point of their stupid ball—was to make a show of their supremacy and put the other Brotherhoods in their place."

"I told you before, the attack on the Society likely changed things," Esta told her, considering the men. "If the two groups are working together, it means that what we did in St. Louis didn't weaken the Brotherhoods."

"You're saying that we made things worse by attacking the ball," Maggie whispered, horrified. "Our actions brought the Brotherhoods together."

"It looks like it. But we can deal with all that later," Esta said, trying to draw Maggie's attention back to the situation in front of them. "Right now we need to find North before anyone else does."

The walk to Pickett's tent seemed endless, but Esta knew they couldn't rush, not unless they wanted to draw attention. Once they were past the public areas, they picked up their pace a little, until they finally made it to the back of the encampment, where Pickett's tent was located.

When they were close, Esta heard voices coming from within and pulled Maggie back behind a nearby tent.

"What is it?" Maggie asked.

"Pickett has a visitor."

"Jericho?" Maggie asked.

Esta shook her head. "It doesn't sound like him."

She'd no sooner realized why the voice seemed so familiar when the flap of Pickett's tent opened and Jack Grew walked out. He had another man with him, the ruddy-faced blond Esta had seen that first day patrolling the show. Neither of them looked happy.

Esta cursed softly. If Jack was visiting Pickett, it meant there was a good chance he knew about the Pharaoh's Heart. Esta could only hope that if Jack had actually *found* the dagger, he would look more pleased with himself.

"Can I help you?" a voice said from behind them.

Esta and Maggie turned to find one of the buffalo soldiers standing there with a rifle slung over his shoulder. The older man's curling hair was graying around the temples of his long face, and he wore his mouth screwed up into a serious scowl.

"No, thank you," Esta said, pulling an air of confidence around her and wishing she'd thought to change into a skirt. Two women might have seemed less like a threat. "We're fine."

"You're not supposed to be here," the man said. "This here area's for performers only. Not for spectators."

"We were looking for someone," Maggie said. "A friend of ours."

His eyes were still suspicious as he turned his attention on Maggie. "Were you, now?"

"My . . . Uh . . ." She paused, like she suddenly didn't know what to call North. "My fiancé," she said finally. "He's new here, and I wanted to surprise him. My . . ." She glanced at Esta. "My brother and I wanted to say a quick hello before the show."

As lies went, it wasn't as bad as it could've been, but the man looked at Maggie, letting the silence grow uncomfortable between them. Then his expression shifted. "You don't by any chance go by the name of Margaret Jane?"

Maggie's eyes widened, and her cheeks went a little more pink. "My friends call me Maggie," she said, the words slow and careful.

"You're Jerry's girl, aren't you?"

"*Yes,*" she said, her voice coming in a rush. "Yes, I am."

The older man's expression softened. "I've heard a lot about you," he told Maggie. "He told us all about how pretty you were . . . and how smart. I'm George."

Maggie shook the soldier's outstretched hand, still looking a little shell-shocked by this turn of events, but Esta wasn't letting her guard down, no matter how friendly this man seemed.

"You don't by any chance know where we could find Jerry?" Esta asked, getting to the point.

George frowned, his entire expression darkening with something that looked like regret. "I'm afraid he's gone. They took him 'bout an hour ago."

"*Who* took him?" Esta asked as Maggie went deathly still beside her.

"Aldo, the grounds manager, and Clem Curtis himself, along with a couple of other fellas I didn't recognize," George told them, shaking his head. "I'm sorry, miss. I hate to be the bearer of bad news. You know, I liked Jerry right from the start. He seemed like a good man."

"He is," Maggie whispered. "The *best* man."

"That might be," George said, "but he must have done something awful wrong to have those men acting like they were."

"He existed," Esta said darkly, realizing exactly how difficult things had become.

George met her eyes, and she saw by his expression that he understood. After a long pause he gave a small nod, like he'd come to some decision. "Let me show you where they put him."

THE END OF THE LINE

1904—Denver

North swallowed down the blood that was pooling in his mouth as he tested his front incisor with his tongue. It was loose all right, but maybe if he let it be, it wouldn't fall out. Clem Curtis' men had done a number on him before they tied him up and dumped him in one of the supply tents to wait for whoever it was that would be interrogating him next. His left eye was swelling shut already, and from the feel of it, they'd split his lip as well.

As far as North could see, there wasn't a clear way out of the mess he'd found himself in. No one knew where he was, and he doubted anyone would find him in time. So when he heard voices outside the tent, he thought the knocks to his head had him imagining things. But his chest felt tight with panic when he understood it *wasn't* his imagination after all.

No. Maggie can't be here.

North struggled against the ropes, but Maggie and Esta had already stepped into the tent before he'd managed to do anything but make his wrists raw. Still, even with his fear and panic scooping his heart plum out of his chest, the sight of Maggie standing there, her hair falling from its pins and worry shadowing her face, made North feel like he could finally breathe again. She might have turned him down earlier, but she'd come for him now—and that fact made him both the happiest man who'd ever walked the earth and also unbearably afraid.

"What the hell are you doing here?" he asked, panic sharpening his tone more than he intended, as Maggie knelt in front of him and lifted her hands to his face.

"Oh, Jericho." From the horror in her expression, he must have looked even worse than he felt. "What did they do to you?"

It didn't matter what they'd done to him; he couldn't let them touch her. "You have to go," he told her, trying to pull his head away from the gentle touch of her hands. "And you gotta go *now*. It isn't safe here. Jot Gunter's here, and the Jefferson Guard is too."

"It's worse than that," Esta said, already working on his ropes while Maggie pulled some salve from her pouch. "They're working together—the Guard and the Syndicate. We saw men wearing the Guard's medallions just now on the grounds."

North batted away Maggie's fussing. "Even more reason for you to get out of here right now."

"I'm not going anywhere without you," Maggie told him, her voice shot through with steel.

North tried to focus on her with the eye that wasn't swelling shut. All he wanted to do was look at her, because whatever danger they might be in—whatever might happen next—she'd come back for him. That *had* to mean something. "I shouldn't be glad that you're here. . . ."

Maggie's eyes softened a little. "I never should've let you walk out that door."

Something loosened in North's chest. "I never should've asked you to choose."

"There are things I have to tell you—"

"You can tell me later," North told Maggie. "Right now you have to get out of here. When they dumped me here, they were talking about some kind of raid. You have to leave before you get caught up in it. Esta, you have to take her and—"

"We're not leaving without you," Esta said. "But you're right. We *do* have to get moving. George is working on distracting your guards, but he's not going to be able to hold their attention for long. Can you walk?"

"George?" North was trying to keep up. "How could you possibly know George?"

"He found us when we were outside Pickett's tent," Maggie explained. "When he told us they'd taken you—" Her voice broke before she could finish.

"Mags?" North reached up to cup her face gently with his hands. "Come on, sweetheart. Don't you go crying over me. I'm fine." He'd be a lot better when she was safe.

She lifted her glasses enough so that she could wipe the tears from her eyes; then, with a sniff, she looked at him, serious as she'd ever been. "I didn't mean it, you know. I want that life you were talking about. I want to find a place where we can start over. I want all of it, and I'd do anything to have it—"

"It's okay, Mags," he said. "We're going to figure this out."

"Did you manage to give Pickett the serum?" Esta asked as she worked on the ropes.

North met Maggie's eyes and saw hope burning there so bright it nearly blinded him. How was he supposed to tell her?

"Well?" Esta asked when he didn't immediately answer. "Is the dagger here, or—"

"It's gone," North said, the frustration of the discovery still churning in his belly. "Pickett hasn't had the piece for more than a year." He tossed the ropes off his legs and tried to get to his feet, but his right ankle screamed under his weight.

"Did he say what he did with it?" Maggie asked. She glanced at Esta with some silent meaning that North didn't understand.

"He sold it a while back. . . ." North explained what he'd learned from the cowboy. Pickett hadn't wanted to part with the piece, but he wasn't given much of a choice when he'd been approached by a young white businessman from out east. The way Pickett told it, he was given the choice to sell the dagger to the guy for a pittance, or the guy would have him arrested for stealing it.

Pickett had known his word wouldn't mean anything against the easterner's, considering the colors of their respective skins. He'd wanted to do right by the old friend who'd sent it to him for safekeeping, but he hadn't been able to see how spending his life in prison was going to help anyone.

"Did Pickett get the guy's name?" Esta asked.

North frowned. "Some New Yorker. John or Jack something."

"Jack?" Esta asked, her voice going oddly hollow. "Tell me it wasn't Jack Grew."

"That might be it," North said.

"Jack Grew isn't 'some New Yorker,'" Esta told them. "He's the one in St. Louis who attacked Harte. He also happens to be here. In Denver— we saw him coming out of Pickett's tent a few minutes ago."

Every inch of North's body felt like it had been battered and bruised, but his mind was clear and his determination steady. "If this Jack Grew character is here, then we can get the dagger from him."

But Maggie shook her head. "No, Jericho."

"*Yes*, Mags. Don't you see? We have another shot at getting an artifact, just like you wanted," he said. Now that she'd come back for him, there wasn't anything he wouldn't do to keep her. "Let me do this—for you."

"Jericho, *look* at you." Maggie's voice broke again, and she pressed her lips together, pausing to collect herself before she went on. "None of this ever would have happened if I'd listened to you earlier. You and I could be on a train to somewhere safe, a place where no one knows us and no one is looking for us. You were right. We could have gone off and spent whatever time we had together. Instead, we're here, with you beaten and bruised near to death. When I think about what could've happened—" Her voice broke.

The tears were welling in her eyes, and all North wanted was to make them stop.

"What if I hadn't run into George?" Maggie asked. "You might have disappeared tonight, and I would never have known what happened to you. And for what? *Nothing*. Because I'm chasing a dream that isn't even mine. It hasn't been mine for some time." She wiped her eyes and looked straight at him. "When you walked into my life, that was it for me, Jericho Northwood. The only dream I'm going to chase now is the life I can build with you."

"That's all fine and good, but what about Cordelia?" Esta said, shattering the perfection of the moment into a million pieces.

"What *about* Cordelia?" North asked. The sharp-mouthed sharpshooter wasn't his concern, not when all he wanted to do was take what Maggie was offering and never look back. "Cordelia's a smart girl who can shoot better than anyone I've ever seen."

"Which is unfortunate for you," Cordelia said as she stepped into the tent, her gun already drawn. "Margaret . . ." There was a gleam in her eye that North didn't like the look of. "I thought we went over this. You know what will happen to your sister if you leave."

"What does Ruth have to do with any of this?" North asked through clenched teeth. He'd seen the glimmering possibility of a future with Maggie, and he'd be damned if this woman would brush it away like some desert mirage by reminding Maggie about her sister.

"Maggie has responsibilities. She's made promises to the Antistasi," Cordelia said, her voice deadly even and calm. "She can't walk away . . . not without facing the *consequences*. It ain't just your lives at stake here. If she walks away—"

"I know," Maggie said, cutting Cordelia off. "But my sister made her choices. I've done what I could to protect her, but I can't do that forever."

Cordelia's expression hardened, and panic sparked in her eyes. "You can't walk away from the Antistasi, Margaret."

"I'm not walking away," Maggie told the sharpshooter as she tightened her grip on North. "I'm walking toward something else. Something more important."

North wasn't exactly sure what they were going on about, but as far as he was concerned, the discussion was over. They needed to get out of that tent and away from the showgrounds while they still could—*if* they still could.

"Maggie's done more than anyone could have asked. She's given up everything for the Antistasi—her home, her sister. If she's ready to walk away, you're not going to stop her." North ignored the pain in his leg as he put an arm around Maggie. "We're leaving. *Now.* Considering the situation out there, I'd suggest you do the same. You can go on and get whatever artifacts you want, and we wish you the best, but this is the end of the line for us."

He turned away from Cordelia, leaning into Maggie for support more than he would've liked.

"Well, at least y'all got that much right," Cordelia said, and as she spoke, North heard the hammer of her pistol click into place.

SURROUNDED

1904—Denver

The moment that Cordelia cocked her pistol, Esta knew things had become more complicated. It was clear that the sharpshooter didn't have any intention of letting them go, but there was more than pure fury in Cordelia's eyes. Fear was there too.

"You don't have to do this, Cordelia," Esta said, trying to draw her attention in a new direction. "Whatever the Professor has on you, we can help. *I* can help you fight him."

Cordelia only stared at her. Then the sharpshooter's mouth twisted into a sneer. "He told me you'd say that. He warned me that you would try to win me over with false promises, but it ain't gonna work. I won't let your lies turn my head."

"They're not lies, Cordelia. The Professor doesn't care about you. He doesn't even care about the Antistasi," Esta said. "You're nothing but a means to an end for him. He's using you to get to me."

Cordelia aimed the pistol at Esta. Her eyes had gone wide and more than a little wild. "That's where you're wrong. The Professor ain't *using* me. He *chose* me because he trusts me, and I will not betray that trust. We are so close to a different future. So close to freeing the old magic, like he promised." She was shaking her head. "I can't go back—I *won't* go back—to hiding myself away and living in fear of people who ain't got any kind of real power."

"You can't kill me," Esta reminded Cordelia, trying to ignore the way her heart skipped at seeing the gun's barrel pointed directly at her. "You might want to, but you know what will happen if you do. You know I wasn't lying."

"You're right." Cordelia's mouth went flat, but her eyes were more furious than ever.

Esta saw what was coming even before Cordelia swung the gun toward Maggie and North. She didn't have her affinity to reach for, so she couldn't pull the seconds slow or move the bullet out of its path. She only had herself. Before she considered what the consequences might be, Esta leapt at Cordelia, hitting the sharpshooter at the same moment the gun went off. The sound of it firing rang in Esta's ears as she pushed Cordelia to the ground and knocked the pistol from her hand.

Cordelia blinked, but her surprise lasted only a heartbeat, before she pushed Esta away and scrambled for the gun. Esta wasn't about to let Cordelia get it, though. She lunged, and in a matter of seconds, she'd straddled the sharpshooter, pinning Cordelia to the ground.

But then Esta heard North make a keening, wailing sound like some kind of wounded animal on the other side of the tent, and Cordelia began to laugh.

"I told y'all before," she said. "I never, *ever* miss."

Esta looked back to see that Maggie's eyes were wide and her face had drained of color. She was clutching her hands to her side, and North's hands were pressed over them as well, but blood was already seeping from beneath their fingers. For a moment all Esta could do was stare numbly, while Cordelia's unhinged laughter continued to vibrate beneath her. Then suddenly Cordelia wrenched herself to the side, throwing Esta off-balance.

Cordelia was on Esta before she'd even hit the ground. The sharpshooter's hands grabbed Esta's neck and started to squeeze, even as Esta tried to fight her off.

"That's enough," a voice said, accompanied by the second click of a pistol being primed. "Get off her now."

Cordelia went still at the sound of the voice, which was enough for

Esta to throw her off. She looked up to find George standing over them with Cordelia's gun in his hand.

"What in the Sam Hill is going on in here?" he asked. He took in the scene, and his mouth opened in a kind of disbelief when he saw Maggie bleeding in the corner of the tent. Then he looked back to Cordelia, and understanding dawned. "You did this?" he asked her.

Cordelia started to cackle.

"Hand me that rope," Esta said. They didn't have time for long explanations, and she doubted Cordelia was in any mind to give them anyway. "We need to get her secured before she can hurt anyone else."

On the other side of the tent, North was still cradling Maggie as he tried to stop the bleeding. "Maggie . . . Stay with me, honey," he pleaded. "Come on now, darlin'. Just keep looking here in my eyes. Right here, Mags . . ."

As George finished securing Cordelia's arms, Esta went over to help North with Maggie. He was cradling her in his arms, and Esta suddenly had the strangest sense that this scene had already played out. Maybe not quite like this, but . . . She shook away the thought. North was trying to get Maggie to focus on him, but she kept blinking and staring off, like she was seeing something in the distance.

"You can go back," Esta told him, feeling the full horror of what had happened. "A minute or two is all you'd need to fix this. You can use your watch—"

North was shaking his head. "It's gone. Gunter destroyed it when they got me earlier."

George had finished securing Cordelia and crouched next to them. "Let me?" he asked. When neither of them moved, he gently took North's and Maggie's hands away from the wound in her side. "It looks like the bullet went clean through. Maybe with a doctor—"

"Too much of a risk," Maggie said. "They'll realize—" She gasped in pain.

"The doctor I have in mind won't care," George said. "And she won't talk."

"Is she Mageus?" Esta asked.

"No, but Dr. Ford would be understanding," George said. "You'd be able to trust her."

"No, Jericho—" Maggie gasped.

"If there's a chance of saving Maggie, we should take it," Esta told North. "But we need to go now. Someone will have heard that shot, and with so many people swarming around looking for us—"

"Leave me and go," Maggie said, each word coming with visible effort. "While you can."

"No." North shook his head again. "I'm not going anywhere without you." He was already arranging her skirts so he could lift her in his arms.

But Esta had gone to check the flap of the tent, and what she saw outside made her stomach sink. "It doesn't look like we're going anywhere," she said. "We're surrounded."

THE HANDS THAT
HELD HIM DOWN

1904—San Francisco

Harte struggled to stay on his feet as he took the steps down from the temple two at a time. The weight of the Dragon's Eye was secure within the inner pocket of his coat, and deep within him, Seshat was rioting, pressing at the boundary between them. He couldn't tell if she was trying to stop him or urging him on, so he ignored her. He had enough to worry about with the feverish haze that coated his vision and the ache in his upper thigh that made each step feel like he was being stabbed. When he got to the second-floor landing, he paused long enough to catch his breath and to consider his options. The clerks in the bank lobby below would probably already know what happened. It was possible that his father might have even warned them. There was no way he was going to be able to walk out the front door.

Then Harte remembered the fire escape he'd seen from the street below.

Instead of continuing down the staircase, he went down the hall cutting through the middle of the building. Taking a chance, he opened one of the doors to find a small office with a pair of surprised clerks sitting behind desks piled high with stacks of papers and ledgers. The room was plain, nothing like the grandeur of the temple above, but there was a portrait of Lady Justice, her eyes wide and accusing, hanging on the wall behind them that told Harte these must be more of the Committee's offices. The men glanced up when Harte burst in, but his attention was on the open window on the other side of the room.

He pulled on his most charming smile. "Pardon the interruption, gentlemen. I need to do a routine check. I'll be out of your hair in a few minutes."

He was nearly through the window when the door opened again and another pair of men burst through, yelling orders at two office workers. Their surprise turned to action, and the closer of the two clerks lunged for Harte, catching him by his coat.

The man cocked his arm, ready to swing, but Harte had grown up in the streets and new how to fight fast and dirty. He blocked the blow and then shoved the man, pushing him into the others. As they stumbled back, Harte was out the window and onto the fire escape, which creaked under his weight. He'd almost made it to the ladder when he was pulled backward again. His head spun with the motion, and this time he didn't manage to dodge. Instead, he took the blow straight to his temple. The instant the fist connected with the side of his face, Harte's vision flickered.

Then came another blow, and another before Harte could fend them off. He felt the crunch of his nose breaking, followed by the warmth of blood running down his face. The coppery tang of it on his lips shook him into action. He finally managed to fend off the next fist, but before Harte could regain his balance completely, the man had bent him backward over the railing of the fire escape, holding him by the throat. The structure creaked under the pressure of their combined weight, but Harte couldn't do much to fight the man off—especially not with the world tilting and his vision blurring.

Inside of him, Seshat had gone strangely, uncomfortably quiet. Harte reached for his affinity, but his body was so weary and weak, and his mind so unsteady from the combination of fever and the battering he'd taken, that he could barely grasp the edges of his magic.

Help me, he pleaded, desperate for air. *Do something.*

Why should I help you, when you have done nothing but fight me? Even now you plan to use that stone to destroy me, Seshat told him, her voice a hollow whisper.

I wouldn't—

LISA MAXWELL

I know your heart, boy.

Harte's vision was beginning to go dark around the edges. *If they kill me, you die as well.*

Seshat rustled at that, clearly amused. *You were willing to die to destroy me before,* she taunted. *Why should this be any different?*

Because it *was.* True, Harte had been willing to give up his life if it meant saving Esta—he still was willing, if it came to that—but to die at the hands of these men? For *nothing?*

No. Not like this. Harte wanted to live. Even with the fever raging and shaking his limbs, he wanted to see tomorrow. He wanted to take the Book back from Jack and force its pages to give up their secrets. He wanted to find another path—another way. Most of all, he wanted to see Esta again.

Pulling on all of his remaining strength, Harte tried again to break free of the man's arms.

"You're not going anywhere," the man growled. He leaned in close, and Harte could smell the sourness of his breath. "You didn't really think the Vigilance Committee would allow you to walk away with a treasure as priceless as the Dragon's Eye?"

"If they didn't want it stolen," Harte rasped, writhing and trying to jerk away as he choked out the words, "they . . . shouldn't have left . . . it . . . unguarded."

The man only laughed—at Harte's words and at his unsuccessful attempt to free himself. "Who said it was unguarded? You walked right into our trap, just like we expected you to."

"Trap?" Harte realized his mistake. It made a sickening sort of sense now—the long conversation his father had with the man at the entrance, the ease with which they gained access to the temple, and the way the crown wasn't even in a case.

"You really think we'd keep something like that unprotected?" The man laughed again. "It was only on display because we were hoping to catch the Devil's Thief."

"Sorry to disappoint." Harte could barely choke out the words, but he refused to let the man know that he and Esta were connected. "But you have the wrong person."

"You don't disappoint," the man said, giving Harte another hard jerk that had his vision swimming. "Not completely, Mr. Darrigan."

Harte went suddenly still. They knew his name. He doubted that his father would have told them—he wouldn't have risked it. But still, they knew who he was. They'd been expecting him.

"Secretary Grew should be just as happy with you when he arrives."

Secretary Grew? There was only one person that could be.

Within his skin, Harte felt Seshat shudder. Still, he could not grasp his affinity. He was too exhausted, too feverish, and too unsteady to pull his magic around him. He needed help, and there was only one place he could turn.

Help me, he pleaded again.

He could sense Seshat there, watching and waiting. But she did not reply.

Harte understood that she was toying with him. *You heard him. Once Jack arrives, we'll be his prisoners. You know I won't be able to fight him. I won't be able to stop Thoth from taking your power. Not as weak as I am.*

Seshat remained silent as Harte continued to writhe against his captor's grip.

Thoth will finally have his victory, Harte told Seshat as he struggled to focus on his affinity, but again his magic slipped through his fingers. *He will take your power and use it for his own. He will destroy you.*

Isn't that what you would do as well? Seshat asked. *What makes you any different?*

Harte couldn't disagree, and he knew there wasn't a lie he could tell that Seshat wouldn't see right through, not when she lived inside his skin. Not when she knew his every whim and desire. *Because I don't want it for myself. Help me,* he pleaded. *For Esta.*

The girl. She is the only way. With her, I can unmake the world and destroy

Thoth once and for all. Seshat's voice came to him then, clear and close to the surface. *Will you promise not to stand in my way?*

You know I won't promise you that, Harte told her. *I will do anything to keep you from harming her. You* know *that. But help me now, and together we can destroy Thoth. Help me now, and I swear to you, I will do anything in my power to make him pay.*

Harte felt the skin of the man's palms against his tender neck. Everything ached. Every particle in his being hurt, but he didn't care. He focused everything he was on gathering his affinity . . . only to feel it slip away. Water between his fingers. Again.

Seshat remained silent. Distant.

Harte felt as though he were drowning and Seshat was standing on the shore, close enough to help but refusing to touch even a toe to the water. His vision was already starting to go dark at the edges, and his lungs were burning, and he knew—*knew*—that he had failed.

Harte knew that when Jack arrived, there would be no way to stop him from finally claiming Seshat. Thoth would have everything he'd ever wanted—all of the power he'd schemed and lied and betrayed for. Thoth would win, and the world would be remade under his control.

Suddenly Harte felt the goddess lurch, rousing herself unexpectedly. Her power rose alongside the familiar warmth of his own magic, and before his vision went completely dark, he used what was left of his strength to shove his affinity toward the man holding his neck. *Commanding* him.

The man holding him screamed. He released Harte and grabbed at his own head like he was trying to hold himself together. It was enough to let Harte drag in a deep breath, enough for the darkness in his vision to start to lift. He took a moment to get his legs steady beneath him. The man was still screaming and writhing, and the whites of his eyes had been all but obliterated by a swirling darkness. Harte backed away, horrified at what Seshat had done—what *his own* affinity had done. The man let out one more manic scream before turning to attack the others.

Harte swayed a little, gripping the railing for balance. He wasn't sure whether he could make it down the ladder, not with the way he currently felt, but he knew implicitly that if he didn't try now, he wouldn't get another chance. He wiped the blood that was still dribbling from his nose with the back of his sleeve and moved toward the fire escape again.

The world was still swimming, his limbs were trembling, and his balance was unstable, but somehow Harte managed to shimmy down the rickety ladder to the sidewalk below. When he was nearly there, his foot missed a rail and he stumbled, gripping the rungs so hard to keep from falling that he knew he'd have to pry splinters from his palms later. It didn't matter. Not when he was so close to being free.

Harte's feet hit the pavement, and he pulled himself upright, steadying himself on the side of the building for a moment. He'd barely started to move again, though, when the front door of the building opened, bringing with it the noisy clang of an alarm bell and a group of men. Behind him, another group had come out of the building next door, and Harte found himself surrounded. He turned in a slow circle, the horizon tilting and pitching as he tried to stay on his feet. His body shook from the exertion and from the fever, but he managed to keep himself upright.

There were twelve, maybe fifteen, people surrounding him now, but they were mostly soft-looking men dressed in rumpled, ill-fitting suits. Bank clerks and merchants, from the looks of them. If his vision hadn't still been blurry and his stomach hadn't been threatening to turn itself out onto the sidewalk, Harte might have considered fighting his way out. But that wasn't an option, not even with Seshat prowling within his skin, her power buoying him up and urging him on. He'd have to try running.

Then Harte heard the whimper.

It was such an insignificant noise, but he knew immediately what the sound was. He turned back to the entrance of the bank to find a man holding the boy—his *brother*—by the child's hair. The blade of a dagger was poised at the boy's throat, but Harte's father—*their* father—was standing off to the side with his arms crossed, doing nothing to free his son.

"You have something that belongs to us," the man said, pushing the boy forward. The knife never left the boy's throat.

"You'd let them kill your own son?" Harte asked Samuel Lowe, fear making him shudder more than even the fever could.

He already knew the answer. Of *course* his father would sacrifice the boy, especially if it meant saving his own reputation and the comfortable life he'd built.

Samuel Lowe only glared at him.

"He's a *child*," Harte said, his head still swimming from the blows. "He's *your* child."

"My wife is still young enough to bear me more sons," his father replied, with a cold sureness to his voice. "This one is a disappointment anyway—he proved that when he allowed you to escape." Sam Lowe's expression was deadly in its sincerity.

"The Dragon's Eye," the other man ordered as he pressed the knife against the pale skin of the boy's throat. "You will give us back the crown, or the boy will die."

Sammie whimpered again. A line of blood trickled from the knife's blade, and the boy began to cry in earnest. His eyes were locked with Harte's, and they shone with fear and the too-mature understanding of this betrayal.

Run, Seshat commanded, her whispering urging him on. *Why do you stand here like a lamb at the slaughter? Go while you can!*

His father stepped forward. "Why put the boy through this? You won't allow him to die. You're too weak. You always have been."

Harte had the crown secured in his jacket. With Seshat's help, he knew he could likely make it far enough to disappear into the city. He knew where his father lived; he might even be able to find the other artifacts before the fever took him completely. He could send them to Esta. He could keep his promises.

He should leave now, while he could. Even if it meant letting the boy die. After all, what was a single life measured against the many lives that could be helped by the artifacts?

Everything.

But the voice that came to Harte with such startling clarity was not Seshat's. It was the voice he'd stopped listening to years before. His own.

Go! Seshat commanded. *You cannot allow your weakness to destroy us both.*

She was right. If Harte stayed, if he gave up the Dragon's Eye, he might not escape again. Esta would never know what happened to him, and her cuff would be lost. If he left now, the boy might die but Harte could avoid Jack finding him. He could keep Thoth from claiming Seshat. The world would have a chance. *Esta* would have a chance. It would be so easy to add this boy's life to the scrap heap of his past. He only had to walk away.

But he couldn't. He never should have left the boy behind with their father. He'd convinced himself that there was nothing he could do for the kid—for his own brother—because *he* was no better than his father. After all, everything he'd accomplished in his life had been built from scheming and lies, grift and larceny—all qualities he'd believed he'd inherited from the man who had refused to claim him. He was his father's son, wasn't he? Whatever success he might have found had always felt tainted with that truth. It was why Harte pushed everyone away, including Esta.

But the boy was *also* his father's son, and the child was an innocent. As Harte had once been. Suddenly he saw the truth that he'd been denying for too long. The blood in his veins meant *nothing.* The rot at the center of his life had always been his father, but the choices Harte had made through the years, those were his own. They always had been.

With a flourish of his hands that had the men tensing to attack, Harte produced the crown, seemingly out of thin air. He saw Sammie's wonder—and his relief. The small body seemed to shudder at the sight of the Dragon's Eye, as though he understood that he'd somehow been given a reprieve.

Harte ignored the swirling spots in his vision and the way his muscles quaked with exhaustion as he held the crown over his head, making sure that everyone who had surrounded him could see it. Even in the overcast day, the gold seemed to glow, and the stone in the center of the headpiece shone with a peculiar light.

Seshat rattled the bars of her cage as she understood what he meant to do.

His father smiled cruelly, elbowing the man next to him. "I told you he would give in, with the right pressure."

Harte didn't pay any attention to the man who'd fathered him. Not his father, just a man, and a meager excuse for one at that. His attention was on the boy. On his *brother*. Blood dampened the collar of the boy's shirt, and fear was stark in his expression, but Harte would not allow the child to be harmed. He would give his brother a chance at a different life.

"It will be okay," he told Sammie, who had started crying. "I won't let them hurt you." It was a promise he would go to any length to keep.

"Put the crown on the ground in front of you and step back," the man holding Sammie said. "Carefully now."

Harte lowered the crown, struggling against the fury of Seshat's rage and his own weakened body to keep himself from toppling over. Before he placed it on the ground, he spoke directly to the boy. "I'm sorry," he told Sammie. "You didn't deserve any of this. You don't deserve his fists or his anger. They come from *his* failings. *Not* yours. Remember that. Whatever happens, I want you to remember that you're a thousand times better than he'll ever be."

Harte had barely gotten the final word out when he was tackled from behind. The crown fell from his hands, and before he could fight his way free, he was pinned to the ground, his face pressed into the dirty street with a boot to the back. He looked up to see his brother staring at him, his eyes wide. Sammie was still being held in place, but the man had lowered the knife from his throat.

"I think I can manage one more trick," Harte said, barely able to get out the words. "Would you like to see it?"

The boy's chin trembled, but he nodded ever so slightly.

"Remember what I told you," Harte said, and he managed to hold on to consciousness long enough to gather the strength he needed to grab tight to his affinity and push it into the hands that held him down.

FATED

1904—Denver

Esta took one more look before she eased the canvas back over the tent's entrance. All around the tent, people had gathered, Guard and Syndicate alike. Among the crowd Esta spotted the glint of the marshal's stars and silvery medallions that glowed an eerie blue in the twilight.

"It was Cordelia's shot," she realized. "It must have triggered the Guard's medallions."

"We have to get her to a doctor." North adjusted Maggie in his arms.

"There's no way out," Esta said. "It's as bad as when we were trapped on the train."

"You got us out of that mess," North said, his voice rising with his desperation.

"I had my affinity then," she reminded him. "With the Quellant—"

Maggie was trying to say something, but the pain was twisting her words.

"Shhh, sweetheart," North crooned. "We're going to figure this out."

But Maggie was shaking her head. "She can do it. . . ." She met Esta's eyes. "There's an antidote. In my pouch."

North dug into Maggie's pouch and came up with a red tablet that looked similar in size and shape to the Quellant that Esta had been taking ever since Texas and offered it to her. She felt the warmth of its energy wash over her palm, but she didn't raise it to her lips.

"Go on," North said, frowning. "Maggie's running out of time. We all are."

George was eyeing them with an uneasy curiosity, but Esta couldn't be concerned with him.

"What about Seshat?" she asked.

"What about her?" North growled.

"You know what happened before, in Corsicana and with the train. You still might not believe I'm telling the truth about her, but I know I am."

"Wasn't Seshat," Maggie said, coughing the words with some effort.

"You don't know that—"

"I *do*." Maggie gasped, like a bolt of pain had shot through her, but then she recovered herself. Her eyes were serious as she looked at Esta. "My fault," Maggie whispered. "Not Seshat. *Tell her,*" she directed North.

"She gave you something when we left St. Louis," North explained. "Some new concoction she was working on. To disrupt affinities."

"More in Texas," Maggie said, grimacing. "Before the explosion . . ."

"I don't understand," Esta said.

"Leaving St. Louis, we didn't know exactly what side you were on, and we didn't know what you could do. Maggie gave you something to make your magic unstable, so you wouldn't be tempted to use it against us," North said. "The darkness you saw back in Texas—that wasn't from any ancient creature. It was because of Maggie."

"I know what I saw," Esta argued. The darkness, the way the earth shattered from her affinity. It had to have been Seshat.

"It's the same," Maggie said, struggling with the words. "Always *you*."

"Seshat used my affinity—she amplified it," Esta said as understanding dawned on her. "That's what your formula did as well?"

"Unstable," Maggie rasped, closing her eyes against the pain.

"And the Quellant?" Esta demanded.

"Used your fear," Maggie told her softly.

"Why have me take it at all? You could have just stopped drugging me."

"Because I knew what you could do," Maggie admitted, grimacing. "The Professor warned me. Before we left St. Louis . . . I knew."

"Maggie used your worry to get you to agree to the Quellant," North explained. "Her new formulation seemed too risky, considering what happened in Texas, but we knew for sure that the Quellant would stop you from leaving us in the dust like your partner did. Or at least it would give us a fighting chance."

"You really are Ruth's sister, ain't yeh?" Cordelia asked Maggie. Then she started laughing again.

But Esta was impressed despite herself. For all Maggie's failures with lying, she'd managed to keep this secret. Still, if what they were saying was true, Esta had been a fool. She could have used her affinity all along, but she'd been trapped by her own fear instead. Well, she certainly wasn't going to be trapped by it any longer.

For a moment she considered leaving. After what North and Maggie had done to her, they almost deserved to be caught there by the Brotherhoods. *But George doesn't.* He was an innocent in all of this, a bystander who'd tried to help—who was still trying to help. And if the Syndicate found him here with the other three? Esta doubted they'd believe in George's innocence.

Esta took the antidote from North and crushed it between her teeth. The effect was almost immediate. Her affinity flooded back to her, warm and real and secure, and Esta could have wept from the relief of it. But she didn't have time for relief. They still had to get through the mob that had surrounded them.

It took a second to get everyone situated, so that each one of them had some grip on her. "Whatever you do, don't let go," she said as she pulled the seconds slow. She waited, but there was no darkness, no shadow over her vision. There was only the absolute rightness of having such an essential part of herself back, the exhilaration of flexing her affinity and letting it unfurl.

When they left the tent, Esta heard George's sharp intake of breath as he saw the crowd outside nearly frozen in time. He let out a curse—or maybe it was a prayer—but Esta kept her grip tight on his wrist so he couldn't slip out of her control.

"It's fine," she said. "We need to get past the perimeter."

To her left, she saw a familiar blond head of hair: Jack Grew was there, talking to a man with a white mustache. One of the Jefferson Guard was at his side, as the rest of the crowd waited for his orders. Esta made herself a promise that she'd come back for Jack and the Book, once the others were safe.

The group moved as quickly as they could, a many-headed hydra maneuvering through the crowd that had surrounded the tent. Finally, they made it through the grounds to the field where wagons and horses stood right alongside motorcars.

"Do any of you know how to drive one of those?" Esta asked, pointing to the cars, and when no one answered, she settled for a wagon with a pair of horses.

She had to release her hold on time so they could set Maggie in the back of the wagon. As George climbed into the driver's seat, Esta helped North make Maggie comfortable. Maggie looked bad, and North looked completely shell-shocked, but Esta hoped that everything would work out. They'd find the doctor for Maggie, and with any luck, she would survive. But Esta couldn't go with them. Not while Jack Grew was so close—and with him, the Book of Mysteries.

Esta started to back out of the wagon's bed, but North grabbed her by the wrist. "Where do you think you're going?"

"If Jack Grew is here, so is the dagger," she told him, starting to pull away. "And Harte will be waiting for me."

North was shaking his head as his grip on her wrist tightened. "No," he said. "You're coming with us. No way am I letting you run off to destroy our lives."

"I have to go," Esta told him, trying to keep her voice steady and calm. "You *know* that. If I don't find Harte before the Professor does, if I can't retrieve the cuff, you lose everything anyway."

He was still shaking his head, still holding on to her like it was the only thing that mattered.

"Let her go," Maggie whispered.

"It's going to be okay," North soothed. "Don't you concern yourself with any of this, Mags. You focus on staying awake until we can get you to this Dr. Ford, and I'll worry about Esta."

"No, Jericho. You have to let her go." Maggie coughed, a wet, groaning cough. "It's the only way."

"The only way for what? If I let her go, she'll go back and change everything," North said, his eyes burning with a kind of unholy fire. "I only just got you back."

Maggie was shaking her head, or she was trying to, but the effort of it seemed nearly too much for her. "There's nothing that could keep me from you, Jericho Northwood. Call it what you want. Fate. Destiny. Some things are meant. *We're* meant. Time can't unmake what we are. Even if this bullet is the end of me."

"It's not gonna be," North said, clutching Esta more tightly to him.

"Might," Maggie whispered, her eyes fluttering closed.

"She'll have a better chance to survive this if you get her to George's doctor," Esta told him. "You don't need me for that."

"I can't let you go," North said, turning his grief on her. It wasn't anger in his expression now, but pain and sorrow and fear.

"Yes," Esta said. "You can. Go on and release my wrist and take care of your girl."

North seemed frozen with indecision. "She's the best part of my life. I can't let you take her from me."

"I'm not going to take her from you, but that bullet might," Esta told him. "Maggie's right. Nothing is going to stop the two of you." If that wasn't the truth, Esta would do whatever she could to *make* it the truth. "Let me go, North. You're wasting time. We all are."

North stared at Esta, his eyes brimming. Still, he didn't release her.

"What if she doesn't make it?" Esta asked. "If I go back, this never has to happen. Maggie never has to be here. She never has to get wrapped up with me. She could *live*. She could spend her whole life safe and sound in St. Louis."

"Without me . . . ," North whispered.

"You'd risk her life to keep her?" Esta asked softly.

North seemed torn between the different ways he could lose her, stuck in his indecision.

"If I make it back, like I'm planning to, I'll do everything I can to make sure the two of you find each other," Esta promised. "But I don't think I'll need to. I think Maggie's right. I think there are some things that time itself doesn't have any power over." At least, she hoped there were.

North looked like a man being split in two. "I'm betting my whole world on you keeping your word," he said, before he finally released her.

"I will do *everything* in my power to keep it," Esta told him. One way or another, she would make this right. "Now get going before they realize we're gone."

Esta watched the wagon drive off into the night, heading in the direction of town. She didn't know what would happen to Maggie. The wound had looked bad, but Esta's concerns now had to be on Jack and on retrieving the Book that could change her fate. She pulled time around herself, familiar and comfortable as her own skin, and started back.

Slipping through the crowd was easy enough, especially with her affinity clear and steady. No darkness tinged her vision, and the knowledge that it had never been Seshat was both a comfort and a source of bitterness. She'd wasted so much time with fear and hesitation—for *nothing*. She wouldn't waste another second.

Jack wasn't there with the rest of the crowd, but from the tableau of people all looking in the direction of the supply tent where they'd found North, Esta had a feeling where he would be. She wasn't wrong. Inside the tent, she found Jack and two other men. Cordelia was slumped against the pole where they'd tied her, but her face had been bloodied. She looked to be unconscious, but Esta wasn't interested in wasting time on the sharpshooter now. Her focus was only on Jack.

The days that had passed since she'd seen him in St. Louis had clearly taken their toll. He had his hand in the air, his finger pointed toward one of the Curtis brothers, and his face had turned a dangerous shade of red. The way his jacket tugged to one side made it painfully obvious that Jack was concealing something there—at least, it was obvious to a thief.

She was so close. *So close.* It was a simple matter of easing up next to Jack, of dipping her fingers into his inside jacket pocket—careful not to touch any part of him—and . . . *yes.*

Esta's fingers brushed the worn leather of the Ars Arcana, and she carefully started to pull the small volume from Jack's pocket. Little by little, she worked it free, and then, after what felt like an eternity, she had it. The Book dangled from her fingertips, and Esta could barely breathe from the relief of it all. But when she adjusted for a more secure hold of the Book, Jack's hand grabbed her wrist. His fingers felt like iron, and for a second Esta didn't quite understand what was happening. The world was still silent, still suspended in time. . . .

But Jack was not.

FROM THE DEPTHS

1904—San Francisco

By the time Harte had been deposited into a windowless cell, the fever had him well in its clutches. He didn't regret the choice he'd made, even if Seshat continued to rail at him. Maybe he *could* have saved himself, but he'd used his last bit of strength to try to save his brother instead.

Seshat rattled the bars of her cage, raging at his stupidity and weakness, but Harte couldn't remain conscious. Even with the goddess screaming within him, a dark and empty sleep pulled Harte under. He'd already broken too many promises anyway.

He surfaced a while later, confused and lost. Something had happened. *Esta.* She'd changed the illusion, switched out her gown for a costume that barely covered her in a sprinkling of stars.

No . . . that wasn't right.

A brightness appeared. It disappeared and then came back once again, each time bringing with it pain that throbbed with each beat of his heart.

Voices. He couldn't make sense of what they were saying.

The crown. He reached for where he'd placed it in his coat but found it gone. He'd been in the chamber of a heart, a cold fire . . . and the crown had been there.

No . . . Something happened.

His thoughts were jumbled, unclear. Gray eyes and dark-blond hair. The boy.

Where was the Dragon's Eye?

It's gone, you fool. You gave it up for the boy, Seshat said, her voice the only steady thing in his world. *You doomed us both to save him.*

Gone. She was right. The crown was gone. Harte remembered now. He'd given it up for a chance that the boy could escape. *His brother.*

You could have escaped, and instead you let them take you. It was an accusation, but there was a question in Seshat's voice as well. It felt like she was trying to understand the puzzle before her. *You had the crown. You had everything you needed, and you let it all go. For a* child.

For my brother, Harte agreed.

He will grow to hate you and all that you are, she told him. *They always do. Even the ones we trust.*

Maybe he will. His heart broke a little at the thought. He would deserve at least part of Sammie's hate for how he'd used the boy. But Harte hoped it would be otherwise. He'd done what he could to try to make it right.

Now they will take everything you have and destroy everything you love. For a meaningless child. Confusion and frustration colored her words.

Not meaningless. Sammie was innocent, as Harte had once been. He would have the chance at a life that Harte had never had. *I didn't have a choice,* he said, a truth that could not be denied. It had been the right thing to do. He knew that still. *The only thing I could do.*

It was the last thing he thought before sleep pulled him under once more.

The seconds ticked by like hours. Hours passed like seconds. The cuffs that bound his wrists and the locked chain that attached his ankles to a bolt in the wall would have been easy enough to break out of, but the room wouldn't stop spinning, and the pain throbbing through his body felt like too much. He was so incredibly weak. All he could do was allow his eyes to close, allow the darkness to pull him down. . . .

Wake up. Seshat's voice was louder now. Urgent.

Harte stirred a little, wondering how long he'd been out, when an unexpected brightness seared his eyes. The blinding light pulled him from the depths, making his head swirl again.

People were close by. With him in the cell. Unseen hands touching him. If only he could remember where he was . . . or why he was there, pinned to a rough blanket and secured hand and foot.

Harte lay perfectly still, feigning sleep or unconsciousness as he tried to remember. It was easy enough, since it hurt too much to move. Body and soul, *everything* hurt too much.

The hands went away, but the voices did not, and a moment later Harte felt himself being hoisted upright, propped against a hard surface. Someone grasped his face, shaking him, smacking his cheeks until he couldn't stand the pain of it any longer and opened his eyes.

A man stood there. Dark hair. Dark eyes set into a blur of a face. Harte couldn't tell who it was. His eyes wouldn't focus. Even propped against the wall, his body felt heavy, dense. Weak.

"You will eat," the face said.

A gloved hand pulled down Harte's jaw. A spoon was placed at his lips. The salt of beef broth flooded his dry mouth.

Harte choked and sputtered. His throat was so raw it had forgotten how to swallow. He turned his head, closing his eyes to refuse more, but his captors were insistent. Again the hand, the spoon. Again the wash of salt and blandness of the beef. Over and over, until Harte stopped fighting it and simply closed his useless eyes and allowed it to happen.

In the end, the front of his shirt was soaked with broth, and they left him damp, smelling of old meat. The thin broth felt heavy in his stomach, and Harte felt nauseous again, but he knew that if he was sick, there was a good chance he would have to sit in his own filth. So he forced himself to take steady breaths and managed to keep the food down. He felt exhausted and aching, and oddly . . . better. But when he felt Seshat curling inside of him, when he remembered that Jack Grew might already be on his way to California, he wondered if *better* was really what he wanted to be.

Sometime later, the door of his cell opened and a group of people entered. Two men held him down, even though he didn't have the strength to move, as an older man entered.

"See what you can do to keep him alive," a voice said. "Secretary

Grew arrives in two days. He only has to last until then."

The older man took the order in silence. Moving forward, he pressed at the underside of Harte's wrists, moving his fingers and varying the pressure as though palpitating to sense something beneath his skin. The man's hands were gloved, like the hands of those who had fed him, but Harte was too weak to reach for his affinity anyway. And after what had happened on the fire escape, he didn't trust Seshat to help.

A moment later the others were cutting away Harte's shirt. It was stiff from the broth, and as they pulled it off, it felt like they were peeling away his skin as well.

Harte barely cared about the pain. Jack Grew was coming—soon—and with him Thoth. At that thought, Seshat lurched inside of Harte. He could feel her anger and panic and, again, her fear. It reminded him, suddenly, of a desert night beneath a star-swept sky that Seshat had shown him once. He'd felt the fear that had coursed through her when she'd realized what Thoth's intentions were. He felt that same fear, that same desperation now.

The man began to mark Harte's body with a brush dipped in dark ink. He drew strange figures at various points: his wrists, his breastbone, down the center of his abdomen. The man's expression was serious as he worked, and Seshat remained quiet, almost thoughtful, as Harte tried to struggle away from the hold the two younger men had on him, but he was too weak.

The doctor ignored Harte's protests and concentrated instead on positioning small clear crystals over the various inked figures. When the last was in place, Harte felt a sharp jolt, a burst of cold energy that coursed through his body, followed by a dull throbbing that wasn't exactly painful even if it wasn't pleasant.

He felt Seshat pacing, felt her interest in what was happening to him. But she remained silent.

Finally, the doctor seemed satisfied. "He should last for a few days more now."

The other men seemed relieved.

As the older man retrieved his crystals and wiped the ink from Harte's skin, the dull throbbing eased, and in its absence, Harte thought that perhaps he felt a tiny bit better. His leg still throbbed with pain, but he was no longer shivering *quite* as much from the fever.

Harte remained perfectly still, completely docile as the men left, locking the cell behind them. He knew as soon as they were gone that he had to get out of there. Even if he had plague, even if he couldn't make it to Esta, he could not lie there and wait for Jack Grew—or Thoth—to take Seshat's power for their own. He wasn't cured, not completely, but he could move now. He could *try*. He would do what he could to give Esta the weapons she needed in the fight that lay ahead, even if he didn't live to see her victory.

Harte's body still ached, and his skin felt like it was on fire. He still felt *so* weak, but he would not simply allow himself to wait around for Jack Grew and the creature that lived inside of him. Once the men left him, Harte pulled himself upright. His head still spun, but deep within his skin, he felt Seshat urging him on. He ignored her anticipation as he started working at the lock of his cuffs.

TIME AND ITS OPPOSITE

1904—Denver

Before Esta had time to react to the fact that Jack Grew was not constrained by her affinity, he'd already plucked the Book from her hand. The world remained silent and still around her, but somehow Jack wasn't stuck in the hold of time as he should have been. Instinctively, Esta wrenched her arm around to break Jack's hold, but his fingers were unbelievably strong as they dug deeper into her skin. He gave a violent jerk of her arm, pulling her closer. His eyes were wild with anger, and Esta knew that it wasn't only Jack looking at her. There was something far more ancient there, lurking in the darkness of his expanding pupils.

"Thoth," Esta whispered.

Jack's mouth curved into what might have been a smile, but his eyes were so dead and vacant that it looked more like something was manipulating him from within. "Yes?" said the thing inside of Jack.

It wasn't Jack's voice that came from his mouth. It was that otherworldly voice Esta had heard in the Festival Hall when Jack had Harte pinned to the ground and was trying to tear Seshat's power out of him.

"Let me go," Esta growled, trying to rip herself away from his grip and again failing.

"Did you think I wouldn't protect what is mine?" Thoth asked.

"The Book doesn't belong to you," Esta spat. "You stole it, just like you stole every bit of power you've ever pretended to have." She lifted her shoulder as she twisted, and this time it was enough of a distraction for her to wrench away.

The world remained frozen, held in the net of time and magic, but Jack was still free.

"That is a rather odd accusation coming from a thief," Jack mocked. When Esta didn't respond to his taunting, he began to circle slowly around her. "Isn't that what you are, Miss Filosik? A common criminal who pretends to be something more."

She wouldn't let his words distract her from her purpose—as long as the Book was within reach, it could still be hers. If she only knew where he was hiding the dagger . . .

"I've never pretended to be anything I'm not," Esta said, matching Jack step for step as he continued to circle her.

"But you do," he whispered, pausing as he considered her. "I've seen what you are, girl. I've seen everything you've ever been and everything you will never be. You may pretend to be some kind of savior, but in truth, you are nothing. An abomination." Jack moved then, faster than Esta had expected, and grabbed her arm. With a finger that felt like ice, he traced the word carved into her wrist, like he understood what it implied. "You are an *impossibility*, Esta Filosik. You believe that your life is your own, but you live on borrowed minutes. Soon time will take what it's owed. Time *always* takes what it is owed. Like a devouring serpent, it will claim you for its own, and you will not even be a memory. But I could save you from the jaws of time and help you become something more. You only need to give me what I want. Give me the key to controlling Seshat."

Esta ripped her hand away from him then, but she knew it was only because he allowed it. "Never."

"I see you, girl, even if you refuse to see yourself." Jack tilted his head, his lips pulling up as the two of them circled each other. "We're not so different, you and I."

"I am *nothing* like you," Esta told him.

"No?" Jack purred, unmoved by her emotion. "Do you not borrow power to become more than you are? Or do you truly believe that your use of Ishtar's Key—and the life it contains—is so innocent?"

Esta lifted her chin, ignoring the echo of unease at Thoth's words. She'd worried about that very thing ever since the Professor had told her how the stones were created, but she wouldn't allow Thoth to distract her now.

Jack—or the thing inside him—seemed amused. "It wasn't meant as a judgment, girl. Whatever people are careless enough to lose can be taken, and whatever can be taken can be made our own. Lives included."

"And power?" Esta pressed, her mind racing. She would not leave until she had the Book.

"*Especially* power," Thoth said, glowing from within Jack's eyes.

"Even if it destroys the people you take it from?" she asked. Esta wasn't sure how she was going to get out of this, but she knew she had to keep Thoth talking. As long as he was going on about himself, he wasn't trying to kill her, and as long as Jack was still standing there, she could try to get the Book.

"If a person isn't strong enough to protect what's theirs, they deserve to be destroyed," Thoth whispered. "So many are born with power they are unworthy of."

She turned a little more, keeping him squarely in front of her. "Like Seshat?"

Jack's eyes went darker still. "*Exactly* like Seshat. If she had been stronger, she would have protected herself . . . and her power."

"She didn't think she needed to," Esta said. "She considered you a friend—she trusted you."

"Which only proves my point. From the beginning, Seshat was far too weak. Far too *soft*. She relied on sentiment instead of strength," Thoth hissed. "She had the ability to touch the very strands of creation. She could have had endless power at her disposal, and instead, she allowed everything to slip through her fingers."

"So you betrayed her."

Jack's eyes narrowed, and the amusement drained from his expression.

"I gave Seshat every chance—I gave her a *choice*. I showed her the unfairness of the world. I showed her how those born without an affinity must suffer the capriciousness of fate in silent resignation. She could have helped me. Together we could have taken the beating heart of magic and made it our own. Instead, she refused to wield the power within these pages as it was meant to be used."

"She disagreed with you, so you destroyed her," Esta challenged.

"I did what was *required*." Jack grimaced as though struggling to control the muscles in his face. "Seshat tried to keep me from my fate, but she failed, as she was always destined to fail. She attempted to save the heart of magic by creating the Book, but it was *I* who transformed the Book into something more. Every page bears the mark of *my* work. Over eons I have collected the rituals and spells within those pages. Over centuries I have worked to fill each and every page with the very secrets of magic. Soon it will be complete."

Esta pretended to be unaffected by his claims. "But it's still nothing without Seshat, isn't it?"

An ancient laugh came from deep within Jack. "Even without her, it is so much more than a simple tome. With it, I have already gone far beyond the bounds of what anyone else has yet imagined."

"Maybe," Esta said. "But without Seshat's power, you're just Sundren. A ghost within a man. You're pretending to be more than you are, because you still need her power."

"That power belongs to *me*," Thoth growled, contorting the skin and muscles of Jack's face as he leaned toward her.

Esta held her ground. "How could Seshat's power *possibly* belong to you?"

"Did I not encourage her?" he snarled, closer now to her face. Nearly close enough for her to reach the Book. "It was I who gave her the idea of placing the last bit of pure magic in these pages. Because even then, I knew that one day I would be able to wield it. You see, girl, everything Seshat did, everything she created, was because of *me*."

Esta doubted that was true. "Without Seshat, the Book is nothing but some paper and vellum bound in a ratty old cover."

"Is it?" Thoth laughed from somewhere deep inside of Jack. With a flourish, he tossed it into the air, where it hung, suspended in the Aether.

Energy snaked around Esta, hot and cold alike, and the Book began to rotate and turn in midair, opening as it did so. Light poured from the surface of its pages as the Ars Arcana floated above Jack's outstretched hand. As Esta watched, something began to emerge from the opened pages—a hilt and then a bloodred stone.

"You recognize this dagger, don't you?" Jack had moved closer to her, and she felt Thoth's energy flowing through him, licking at her, like he was trying to taste her power. "You've been searching for it."

The Pharaoh's Heart. It was so close—an arm's length away—protruding from the pages of the Book.

Esta tried to understand what she was seeing. The dagger was rising from the pages like they were some sort of a portal.

"Any stage magician could do the same," Esta challenged, pretending to be unmoved. But she had the sense that she needed to understand what she was seeing. "It's a nice illusion, but that's all it is."

Jack pulled the dagger completely from the Book, and in a flash he had the tip of the knife poised at her throat. "Does *this* feel like an illusion?"

The blade pressed against her skin, so close to where it had once cut her before. She felt her affinity tremble as it sensed the icy, echoing power of the stone in the dagger's hilt, but she pretended indifference. "It doesn't seem any different than pulling a rabbit from a hat," she told him, schooling her features so he wouldn't see her fear.

"A rabbit from a hat?" Jack—or Thoth—seemed almost amused by her challenge. "A moment ago this dagger did not *exist*." His eyes flashed, the darkness growing in them.

"That isn't possible," Esta told him. "Things are or they aren't."

"Perhaps it's not possible for someone like you." Jack scoffed. "But then, magic this powerful demands a more sophisticated mind, one capable of understanding—of wielding it."

"One like yours?" she asked, not bothering to hide the scorn in her voice.

"Exactly," Thoth said, every bit as obtuse as Jack himself. "Do you know what magic is, child?"

"It's the possibility within chaos," Esta told him, remembering the words Seshat had used.

"Yes," the creature inside of Jack hissed close to her ear, seemingly impressed despite himself. "But do you *truly* understand? Chaos is ancient and endless. Timeless and eternal. In chaos, the power of the old magic was forged. It is the very *antithesis* of the order imposed by time." Jack smiled—or maybe it was Thoth. She could no longer tell them apart. "Do you not see? Seshat created this Book to save a piece of pure magic within these pages. She understood that the old magic and time could not coexist, because time is the *antithesis* of magic—the *destroyer* of magic—and so she used her affinity to take a piece of the old magic, breaking it from the whole, and use its power to create an object *outside* the ravages of time."

"That's impossible," Esta said, refusing to believe him. It was a trick, a lie. He was only trying to distract her.

"Is it? You of all people should know that with time, the old magic will fade, and eventually, those who once held an affinity for it will become ordinary—*weak* as any Sundren has ever been. Look at the Order. Look at what they have become over the centuries," Thoth said.

He wasn't wrong. Professor Lachlan had told Esta the same: once, the Order had themselves been Mageus. When they came to the New World, they noticed their affinities were waning, and they created the Brink to *protect* the strength of their power. But the Brink had been wrong from the start. Instead of providing protection, it had become a trap, and over time their affinities faded . . . and they forgot what they had once been. As time passed, their power became dependent on the magic they could steal through ritual.

"Seshat came to understand the truth of this paradox too late," Thoth continued. "She created writing because she thought to protect the old magic. Instead, she created a *new* type of magic, *ritual* magic. But Seshat hated that this new magic made power accessible to those souls cursed by the accident of birth to have no affinity for the old magic. She hated that unworthy Sundren could now claim what *she* wanted only for herself."

"No, she hated what *you* did with ritual magic," Esta charged, remembering the visions Seshat had revealed to her in the Festival Hall. "She understood you were perverting its possibilities for your own greed and gain. She wanted to protect that power from *you*, because she knew that you only cared about accruing more power for yourself."

"Perhaps she did," Thoth admitted. "But to keep that power from me, she had to keep it from time itself."

Still holding on to her, Jack whipped the knife from her throat and stabbed the blade into the Book, which was still hovering in the air. But it didn't tear the paper. It simply sank into the surface, and as it disappeared, the energy that had been coming from it faded. When he snapped his fingers, the Book clapped shut and fell into his hands.

"No, Esta Filosik. This is no simple illusion. The power locked within these pages is far stronger than you could possibly imagine. Because of the piece of pure magic within it, the Book can *transform* time, and once I finally unlock the beating heart of magic contained in these pages, I will be able to *use* that power. I will remake the world anew," he said, and the darkness in his eyes lit suddenly with strange lightning.

The idea was horrific. If Thoth could unlock and control the pure piece of magic, he could transform time itself. There would be no place to hide, no way to avoid his tyranny. But Esta could sense that there was something she was missing, something essential that Thoth wasn't saying. "But you still need Seshat to grasp that piece of pure magic, don't you? You need something more than you have right now to control it. If you didn't, you'd have taken that power for your own already."

Something shifted in Jack's expression. Annoyance, maybe.

"It's too much for you, isn't it?" Esta taunted. "You're not as strong as she was. You're not strong enough to control the beating heart of magic on your own."

"Thanks to your magician, I won't have to," Thoth said. "Seshat sealed her doom when she chose the boy to carry her power. He's allowed himself to become sloppy and weak. I recently received news from California, and it seems he's gotten himself captured by some of my associates. Soon he—and Seshat's power with him—will be mine."

Thoth's words landed like a blow, and before Esta could recover herself, Jack had moved—almost inhumanly fast—to capture her again. His arms were like a vise around her.

"You're lying," Esta said.

"Am I?" Thoth whispered. "As soon as I'm finished here, I'll board a train to California. Harte Darrigan and the bitch who lives within his skin will both be mine. But I could spare his life if you agree to help me."

"Never." Esta kept struggling.

"Why fight me, girl? Are you so eager to die?" Thoth asked. "I see your heart. I know your plans. You hope to control the goddess by giving everything you have—everything you are—to stop her from taking her revenge." The darkness in Jack's eyes seemed to swell then. "Give your power to *me* instead, and you can live. Give your affinity over willingly, like so many have before you. You need not die. With your affinity, I could control Seshat's power. With your magic, I could remove Seshat from the magician without destroying the boy who holds your heart. The world will spin on. I've no desire to destroy it, as Seshat does."

"No," she charged. "You want to control it."

Jack shrugged. "Would that not be better than ending it?" Esta could see Thoth's amusement in Jack's eyes.

Her mind raced. "But what of me? Won't time take what it's owed?"

"You've seen for yourself what the Book can do, what I can do with the Book," Thoth said.

"You could take me outside of time?" Esta asked.

"Or the child who will become you." Thoth shrugged. "Either way, you could live beyond the reach of time, and your magician with you. But make no mistake . . . I plan on taking your affinity either way. Fight me now, and I will destroy you and all that you hold dear."

"You expect me to trust you?" Esta asked, considering her options. His offer might have been more tempting if he hadn't also just revealed something important: She and Harte had assumed Seshat *was* the power within the Book, but Thoth's words confirmed that Seshat had succeeded in placing a piece of pure magic in those pages. If she and Harte could harness it, there was no telling what they might be able to do, all the people they might be able to save.

It felt more important than ever to get the Book. And to get it here and now, before Thoth could get away.

"Trust or not, it matters little," Thoth said. "One way or another, your affinity will belong to me, and so will Seshat's. I will no longer be beholden to the tedium of time. My power will truly be limitless."

"But not really," Esta told him. "There's only so much you can do without a body. After all, you needed Jack to get this far. Such a *glorious* specimen of manhood you've selected to do your bidding."

Jack's face twisted. "His weakness served my purposes, but soon I will be beyond the need for anything so pedestrian as a body."

"Maybe," she said. "But there's one thing you forgot when you hitched your entire plan for world domination to Jack Grew."

"I've forgotten *nothing*," Thoth sneered.

"The funny thing about bodies—especially male bodies—" Esta brought her knee up sharp, right between Jack's legs, and ancient demi-god or not, Jack crumpled at the impact. "They have a certain weakness."

She didn't stay to gloat. Snatching the Book from where it hovered in midair, and with time still pulled around her, she started to run, but she'd barely reached the opening of the tent when her vision flickered.

No. This can't be happening. Not now.

But as she moved, she felt time turning on her. The present moment was there, and then it wasn't, as the world around her flashed, cycling through the layers of time. Past. Present. And future. All at once. All terribly imminent. She felt herself start to fade, felt the Book fall through her fingers. She grabbed for it again, but it was like she was nothing but a shade, grasping for the reality she was no longer a part of.

PROMISES KEPT

1904—San Francisco

Harte Darrigan had once made a vow to himself that he would never again be tainted by the muck and filth of the streets. He'd spent too many nights curled in doorways with newspapers for warmth, fighting off rats and men alike. Now, though, standing across from the same door he'd approached when he'd first arrived in California, he felt so exhausted and worn down that he could have happily sunk right into whatever the slippery substance was under his feet. But he had the feeling that if he gave in to that longing to rest, he might never get up again.

He hadn't *truly* realized how weak he'd become until he'd made the decision to move. It still seemed incredible that he'd managed to get out of the hovel the Committee had kept him in at all. It was another mark of how bad he must have looked—they hadn't bothered really guarding him. As Harte freed himself and began navigating the streets of San Francisco, he realized that he was in serious trouble. With each new bout of feverish shivering, the mantle of dread he wore felt heavier.

He understood that he would not be able to make it back to the bridge, as he'd promised. He knew that he would never see Esta again, but Harte was determined to make right his biggest mistake. He would retrieve her cuff and return it to her—he would *try*.

What had he ever been thinking to take it from her in the first place?

He *hadn't* been thinking. He'd been desperate. Harte saw now that he hadn't been brave enough to stay after what had happened in St. Louis.

He'd been too afraid that Esta would turn away from him, disgusted by what lived inside his skin. He'd been a fool, and now it was too late.

Harte could only hope that Samuel Lowe hadn't had a chance to sell Ishtar's Key yet. Maybe he wouldn't be able to make it to their meeting at the bridge, but if the cuff was still somewhere in his father's home, Harte would find it. He could send it to Cela Johnson. Cela could leave the city. She could find Esta and explain. Harte had already asked far too much of the seamstress, but he would ask her for this one last thing as well. He would do everything he could to make sure that Esta knew he hadn't betrayed her on purpose.

Harte leaned against the damp brick of the building and watched the door across the alley for what felt like ages, until night fell over the city and lights glowed from within the windows around him. But no lights came on in his father's house. It remained dark and quiet, with no sign of anyone inside.

It was possible that the woman and the boy had left. Harte knew that his father wouldn't return. He'd made sure of it when he'd used the last of his strength to push his affinity into the men who'd wrestled him to the ground outside the bank. He could have used the opportunity to escape, but instead, he'd chosen to make the men believe they'd seen proof of his father's treachery. He'd ordered them to put Samuel Lowe on the first merchant ship they could find. It was the most he could do for the boy— one last trick to make the monster in Sammie's life disappear for good. He hoped it would be enough to give the kid a chance at a real future, a chance Harte had never had.

He closed his eyes and gathered his strength. In the darkness behind his eyelids, he could almost see the familiar lines of Esta's face, and in response, he felt Seshat stir with interest.

You can't have her, Harte said. *Neither of us can. But help me now, and we can both give her what she needs to defeat Thoth. Help me now, and we can end your enemy. You can have your revenge, even if neither of us lives to see it.*

He felt Seshat's frustration at his words, but he also sensed her

LISA MAXWELL

resignation. Harte didn't wait for her agreement. Instead, he started across the street and let himself into the darkened house.

The light from a streetlamp poured in through the small windows, casting an eerie pall over the home. It was a small space that held a living area and kitchen all together, but it was neat and tidy, with matched pieces of well-made furniture. On one wall was a large wardrobe cabinet flanked by a couple of low couches. In the opposite corner, a stove stood cold and waiting. It clearly hadn't been used in some time, but the air still held the smell of spices and oil.

Confident that no one seemed to be home, Harte leaned against the nearby table, but breathing only caused him to erupt into a fit of coughing, which shook his body and sent jolts of pain through him. He gripped one of the chairs, hunching over as he tried to brace himself. Finally, when the fit had passed, he gathered what little strength he had and turned back to his business. He had to find Esta's cuff.

He started with the wardrobe on the far side of the room. It was a large piece, solid and well made. Behind the closed doors, Harte found a combination of shelves and drawers. He started to open one of the drawers but stopped short. If it hadn't been so deathly quiet in the house, he might not have heard the noise, but in the muffled silence, the sound of a gun being cocked might as well have been as loud as a cannon. Harte froze.

"Your hands. Put them where I can see." It was a woman's voice, soft and accented, but confident just the same.

He turned slowly, raising his hands so that he could show he was no threat. On the other side of the room was the woman who had answered the door so many days before. His father's wife. She had seemed surprised then—maybe even afraid. Now she wore an expression both fierce and unwavering.

"Who are you?" she demanded. "Who sent you?"

"No one," he told her.

She shook her head. "I know what you are," she said, continuing to aim the gun at the center of his chest. "Committee rat. You've been sniffing around my home for days. I already told the other that I don't have what you're looking for."

"No," Harte said, feeling more light-headed than he had a moment before. "Not Committee."

"Then who sent you?" she demanded. Harte had no doubt that she would shoot if she didn't get the answer she wanted. "What do you want?"

"Please . . ." Harte stepped into the beam of light. "I'm not from the Committee. No one sent me. I only want the items your husband took from me—a necklace and a cuff," he told her, making a circular motion around his upper arm that had her leveling her gun at him again. "They weren't mine. I need to return them to their owner."

A blur darted from the back room, and it was all Harte could do to keep from falling over from the impact. *Sammie.* The woman put down the gun immediately and issued an urgent command to the child clinging to Harte's legs. But the boy argued back, refusing to let go.

"*You're* the one who gave yourself up for my son?" the woman said, surprise coloring her expression.

"It was the least I could do. I was the one who put him in danger in the first place," Harte said, gently pushing the child away from him.

"No," she said. "That was his father." The woman's expression shifted to concern, as though she'd finally taken stock of Harte. "You don't look well."

"I'm not," Harte admitted, swaying a little. "Which is why it's even more important that I retrieve what I came for. I need to return the pieces, and I don't know how much time I—"

"They're gone," she told him, her expression closed off.

"Gone." The word came out in a rush, and Harte felt like he'd been sucker punched.

"I'm sorry." The woman did not seem sorry.

"They can't be gone." He'd been having trouble staying upright before, but now the devastation of this information threatened to push him over completely.

"I had to. My husband's creditors would have taken the house if I hadn't paid them. It was the only way to save him, to save us from—"

A loud banging erupted on the other side of the door, followed by shouted commands that had the woman's eyes widening.

"Were you followed?" she demanded in a hushed whisper.

Harte shook his head, but in all honesty, he couldn't have known.

The woman seemed to sense this. She spoke to the child, who nodded obediently, before she looked back at Harte. "Go with Sammie and remain silent." Then she tucked the gun into the folds of her gown and shouted something to the people on the other side of the door.

"But—" Harte shook his head. Even as he wobbled on his feet, it seemed wrong to leave her to defend him.

"Go," she commanded. "You cannot be found here. Do you understand?"

The fear in her eyes told Harte everything he needed to know. He'd put this family in danger once again. This time he didn't argue when the boy took him by the hand and led him through a doorway to a bedroom. There Sammie pulled back the rug and opened a hatch in the floor to reveal a set of earthen steps leading down into a compartment that looked like a root cellar. There were blankets and pillows piled on the floor, along with a couple of carved wooden toys.

"Have you been staying down there?" Harte asked.

The boy nodded. "My father owed many people many debts, so my mother makes me hide when they come. She's been afraid for me ever since the Committee's men brought news that my father had been sent away."

"He's gone, then?" Harte asked, trying to keep himself awake.

"On a ship. He won't be returning," the boy said.

"Does that make you sad?" Harte asked, wondering if he'd made the wrong decision again.

"It should, but my father . . ." Sammie paused.

"It's okay," he told the boy. "You know it wasn't your fault?"

But Sammie only frowned, clearly unsure. Then his brows drew together. "It was you, wasn't it? This was your trick?"

Harte nodded, because he couldn't lie to the kid. "Does that make you angry with me?"

Sammie considered the question. "I don't think so. It will be harder for Mother with him gone, but she is strong, and she is smart." His eyes widened. "Your hand feels like fire."

"It's nothing," Harte said, pulling away from the boy's grasp. "I just need to rest for a while." His body suddenly felt every bit of the energy he'd exerted in escaping, in making it this far. "But there's something I need you to do for me—"

From the front of the house came a loud, clattering noise—Sammie's mother shouted something in German, which was followed by a crash.

The boy's eyes went wide, bright with fear and anger as he urged Harte toward the hideaway. *"Hurry."*

Without further argument, Harte stumbled down the handful of steps. His legs gave out before he reached the bottom, and he collapsed into the softness of the quilts as the boy began to replace the trapdoor that covered the hideaway.

"Wait," Harte told him, which made the boy pause. "I need you to do something for me. . . ."

Or that was what he'd intended to say, but his vision went dark, and the words felt cumbersome on his tongue.

There was something he had to tell the boy, something he needed the child to do for him. He had to get a message to Esta, but Harte was too exhausted for words, so he reached out his hand to the boy, pleading silently for Sammie to take hold. He tried to focus on his affinity, but the darkness was pulling him down again, and he didn't know how much longer he could fight it.

Why do you continue to lie to yourself? Seshat asked, suddenly closer now than she had been for days.

If we want to defeat Thoth, I need to make him understand. Harte was reaching for the boy, and his brother was leaning down to him, taking his hand, but Harte had so little strength left. His affinity felt so far from him. *Esta needs her cuff. He could send it to her. Or a message,* he thought frantically. There had to be a way to tell her. *Help me.*

I already have.

Seshat's power surged then, hot and sudden and so much stronger than Harte had expected. He felt his brother flinch and saw Sammie's eyes go wide with confusion. With an expression too much like pain.

No. This wasn't what he had intended at all. . . .

She will come for you, Seshat whispered as the power coursed through him. *You knew that. You made sure of it when you took her cuff. And when she finally arrives, you will be too weak to fight me. When she comes for you, she will be mine.*

THE RIGHT INCENTIVE

1904—Denver

Jack Grew crumpled to the ground, cupping his groin as pain radiated up through him and turned his stomach inside out. The world spun. The dingy walls of the tent tilted and swam, and all he could do was roll to his side and try not to retch as he watched Esta Filosik scoop up the Book of Mysteries from where he'd dropped it and begin to run.

Groaning, Jack gritted his teeth, willed himself up, but every movement was agony. His stomach churned, and the throbbing pain between his legs stole his breath.

But Esta didn't get far. She hadn't even made it to the opening of the tent when her steps faltered and then, right before his eyes, she disappeared. One moment she was there, destroying everything, and then it was like she was a ghost of a girl . . . and then, nothing at all.

The Book fell to the ground, its pages splayed open and the inscriptions upon the vellum glowing as though it understood how close it had come to being lost. The second she was gone, the silence that had plugged Jack's ears while they'd argued drained away, and a great roaring took its place. With it came the continued cackling laugh of the girl they'd found tied to the tent post in their prisoner's place.

"What the hell are you doing down there on the ground?" Clem Curtis asked, blinking in confusion at Jack's position on the ground. "What's wrong? You're breathin' all funny-like."

"I'm fine," Jack said, the wheeze in his voice betraying the lie as he tried to pull himself up.

"You don't look fine," Clem said, offering a hand, which Jack ignored. "You look practically apoplectic."

A moment before, Jack had been railing at the clown for losing the Antistasi cowboy who'd been slinking around the grounds of the Curtis Brothers' Show. They'd been so close to getting answers, and the Curtises had let the damn maggot get away. But Clem Curtis hadn't been privy to everything that had happened—*because Esta Filosik can control time.* Jack would have laughed at the idea of it, but his stones were screaming.

Get up.

Jack ignored Clem's question and listened instead to that voice inside him, that stronger part of himself that had guided him for years now. The voice had rarely been wrong, and so Jack obeyed. Forcing himself to his knees, despite the shooting pain that pulsed through his entire lower half every time he moved, he began the torturous crawl toward the Book.

Faster. Before Curtis realizes . . . Jack reached for the Book and felt an answering pulse of victory when his fingers wrapped around it. Ignoring the pain in his balls, he secured the Book of Mysteries inside his coat.

"Secretary Grew?" Curtis took a step toward him. "Are you going to explain what the hell is happening here?"

"It was an attack, or don't you remember?" Jack said, squeezing the words out through the pain as he pulled out his morphine tablets, placing two on his tongue. Then adding a third for good measure.

Clem looked around the tent, his expression suddenly anxious. "What attack?"

"The maggots got away," Jack sneered, pulling himself up to his feet. The world still swam every time he moved, and his balls felt like they'd been pushed up inside his body, but the quick-acting morphine had cut through some of the sharpest pain. "Tell your men to block every exit. No one gets off these grounds until I find the Antistasi bastards who are responsible."

The girl they'd found tied to the tent post had been cackling the whole time, a strange, unhinged laugh that sounded like something inside her was broken. Now she laughed harder.

"What is so goddamn funny?" Jack demanded, his temper finally fraying beyond any hope of control.

The girl went silent, pressing her lips together as hysterical mania lit her eyes. "You'll never catch them," she said before she cackled again. "The Antistasi will get to the Thief long before you do."

Jack glared at her, measuring her words. "You know Esta, don't you?" he asked. "You're one of them."

She only smiled at him, the wild smile of a woman gone mad.

He felt the weight of the Book and the dagger anchoring him.

"Who is this?" he asked Clem.

"Cordelia Smith," Clem told him. "She's our sharpshooter in the show."

"Did you know she's Mageus?" Jack asked.

Clem Curtis blustered and made excuses, but Jack's focus was on the sharpshooter, an ordinary-looking girl no one would miss.

"You are Mageus, aren't you, Cordelia? Feral magic runs in your veins," Jack said, feeling suddenly better about the situation. "Antistasi, too, from the sound of it."

The girl spat at him, but he was far enough away that she didn't even come close to hitting his shoes.

"I'll take her with me for questioning," Jack said, disgusted. "Perhaps with the right incentives, she can give us what we need to stop this plague of violence."

"I'll give you nothing." She bared her teeth like a feral cat.

"I think you'll find I can be quite *persuasive*," Jack told her, ignoring the hysterics. There was something about her that appealed to him—not her looks or her body, of course. But something inside of her that made him take notice.

Now that the Book had returned the Pharaoh's Heart, Jack had everything he needed to follow the instructions that Newton himself had left in the pages of the Book. With the ritual, he could create another artifact—a stone finally worthy of powering the machine he'd long dreamed of building. All he needed was a maggot with enough power worth harvesting.

Jack took the girl by the chin and couldn't help smiling when she jerked away and then tried to bite him. Cordelia Smith had a strength within her that might one day be useful.

"It doesn't matter what you do to me," Cordelia told him. "The Antistasi cannot be stopped. We are endless as a snake devouring its own tail. Infinite as time itself."

Jack only smiled. "Perhaps we should see how infinite *you* are?"

A RESCUE

1904—Denver

Once again, Esta felt herself returning long before she fully became a part of the world around her. First came the feel of the ground beneath her, the uneven and hard-packed earth that served as a floor for the tent. Then came the scent of smoke, which burned her throat and her nose until finally she could feel her body, her *self*, as something real and whole.

She pushed herself up from the ground, trying to make sense of the scene around her as she coughed. A moment ago she'd been certain of her victory, but now she remembered—Jack had been there. Thoth as well, and he'd told her about the Book before time had *unmade* her.

Time will take what it's owed, Thoth had told Esta. He'd called her an abomination, and now she wondered if there was any merit to his words. Maybe the two lives she led—the young girl back in New York and the girl she was now—couldn't coexist any more than copies of the stones could. Or maybe the reason time had tried to pull her apart again was even worse. Hadn't Jack told her that Harte had been captured in California? If that was true, maybe something had happened to Ishtar's Key. If Harte had lost the cuff, she wouldn't be able to take it back to the girl. It might explain the previous episodes—if Ishtar's Key was gone, her very present couldn't exist.

But she hadn't disappeared completely, which meant that there must still be a chance to retrieve Ishtar's Key—and with it, a chance to save

Harte. There might well come a day when time would not release her from its grip. A day when the darkness would win, and she would be unmade. But that day had not yet arrived.

Esta pulled herself upright. She didn't know how long she'd been gone this time. Seconds or minutes . . . or *more*? However long it had been, she didn't need to search the tent to know that Jack was gone, and with him, the Book. But she thought of Harte and what might be happening to him on the other side of the continent, and it was enough to shake her from her self-pity and to focus.

She pulled herself the rest of the way to her feet and staggered out of the tent into the cooler air of the summer night. At first she couldn't understand what she was seeing. All around her, the grounds of the Curtis Brothers' Wild West Show had devolved into confusion. She barely had time to jump out of the way of a trio of horses as they thundered by, nearly trampling her in the process. Another cowboy on horseback followed, already swinging a rope.

A pair of strong hands caught her from behind, and she turned to find the older man who'd helped them earlier. "This way, and keep your head down," George ordered as he pulled her through the chaos by the hand. "We gotta get you out of here."

"What's going on?" Esta asked, still feeling a little adrift, like she wasn't completely part of the world quite yet.

"All hell's breaking loose—that's what's going on," he said as though she should have figured that much out for herself. "A bunch of Antistasi troublemakers set half the horses loose, and the Syndicate's men are trying to round them all up—horses and men alike."

"I thought you went with North and Maggie," Esta said, following George without any argument.

"I got them all set up with Doc Ford a couple of hours ago. She'll take good care of the girl, but Jerry sent me back for you."

"Hours?" It had been more than a few minutes, then. "Why did he send you back?" she asked, suddenly uneasy.

"He said you might need a ride to the station."

"I do," Esta said, relaxing a little when she realized this was a rescue and not an attack.

George helped her into the wagon he had waiting for them at the far edge of the grounds, and they kept off the main roads as he drove her back to town. Once they saw the outskirts, where the streetlights glowed up ahead of them, he pulled the cart over.

"This is where we part ways," he told her. "I went around to the south, so if anyone's watching for people coming from the show, they shouldn't be looking in this direction. But it'll be safer for both of us if you go on foot from here." He pulled a familiar leather pouch from the underside of the driver's seat and offered it to her.

"Where'd you get this?"

"Miss Maggie sent it along for you," George explained. "She said you might need it."

Esta took the offered pouch, still heavy with the formulations that she'd helped Maggie prepare over the last few days. It contained a veritable arsenal that would surely come in handy in the days ahead—especially with whatever she would have to face in San Francisco.

"Thank you," she told him. "For everything."

"It wasn't much," George said. "Anyone would have done the same."

"No," she said, shaking her head. "That isn't even a little bit true. Could you do me one last favor, though?"

George raised his brows in a silent question.

"Check on Bill Pickett for me? Keep an eye out for him if you can. I have a feeling that the people who were after us might go for him next."

"You don't have anything to worry about when it comes to Bill. We'll make certain to keep an eye out."

Esta gave George a sure nod, wishing that she could give him something else—one of Maggie's concoctions or some protection or assurance beyond that. She was leaving him, Pickett, and everyone whose lives they'd touched in as much danger as they'd left Julian back in St. Louis. But there was nothing she could do except turn toward the city of Denver and the train that would carry her across the country to her magician. Esta picked up her pace, hoping that time wouldn't take her before she could reach him.

OUTMANEUVERED

Viola Vaccarelli barely trusted herself to speak as she walked alongside Theo, back to his carriage. She wasn't exactly sure how she'd lost the argument against him helping with the Order, but she had. Even Jianyu and Cela had agreed that if she wasn't willing to use Nibsy, they needed a way to get more information than what she might glean from her brother. And she *wasn't* willing to risk working with Nibsy. Viola knew her refusal to work with the little snake had confused them all—Viola included. But how could she explain to them why she was so afraid to take Nibsy's bargain when she couldn't even explain it to herself?

They thought her reluctance was because she hated Nibsy—and she did. But they did not understand that she could not give Nibsy what he wanted—information against Paul. Information that would likely destroy her brother. It didn't matter that Paolo could take care of himself or that he did not deserve her protection. Viola would have gladly destroyed Paul herself if it hadn't been for what that action would do to their mother.

Pasqualina Vaccarelli loved her son like she loved her saints. In her eyes, *Paolino* could do no wrong, and if he *had* done wrong, Viola's mother would never willingly admit it. Losing Paolo might well kill their mother. And if it didn't kill her? If Pasqualina ever found out that Viola had been involved in orchestrating Paolo's downfall? Certainly that would turn any love her mother might yet hold for Viola to hatred.

She wasn't sure why it mattered. Viola could not even explain to herself why she still cared, when her family had never been particularly kind or loving to her. They had never accepted her, not for the magic that lived beneath her skin nor for her headstrong temper nor for her unwillingness to find a nice boy and settle for the life she was *supposed* to want. They'd never looked at her with the clear affection that Abel had shown Cela, but they were still her family, weren't they? They were her blood, and she could not quite bring herself to betray them . . . not completely.

And if her mother had made life difficult for Viola, wasn't that only a mother's right? Pasqualina could not help having a daughter who refused to be meek and subservient, who would not take a man and settle down to a proper life. She could not help having a daughter born with the old magic, one who used that power to break the Lord's commandments with such impunity. Perhaps Pasqualina Vaccarelli had never shown Viola the patience that she reserved only for Paolo, but she *had* tried to show Viola what was right. That was surely a sign of her mother's love . . . *wasn't it?*

When they reached the carriage, Theo opened the door and offered Viola his hand, as he always did. Ever the gentleman, even if Viola was nothing like a lady. From the expression he wore, Theo was far too pleased with himself and far too sure as well.

Viola hated that he was right. Theo *could* gain access to the Order easier than any of them. He could verify the information from both Nibsy and Paul, and he could give her and Jianyu the upper hand, so that they could be the ones to retrieve the ring. But Viola could not accept the possibility that Theo might be hurt for helping her—not when he belonged to Ruby.

He was one more worry she had to add to her pile. One more life in her keeping.

"I still say that you don't need to do this," she told Theo, when they were finally secure in the carriage and on their way back to the Bowery.

"I believe it's already been decided," Theo said pleasantly. Always *pleasantly*. It was impossible to argue with him.

"You saw what happened at the gala," she said. "You understand what the Order is capable of. If they discover you're against them, your money and family name won't protect you."

"Perhaps," he admitted. "But I don't plan for them to find out."

She threw her hands up in exasperation. "No one *plans* for things to go wrong, Theo," Viola told him. "It's not worth risking yourself to help us. We have been living under the threat of the Order since we arrived in this city. Jianyu and I can handle ourselves."

"I'm not doing this for Jianyu," Theo told her. "I'm helping *you*, Viola. I'm helping my friend."

Her stomach twisted. "I am not worth your life."

"I don't think that's quite true," Theo said. "Neither does Ruby, or she wouldn't have made me promise to look after you. Blame her if you'd like, but I never break my promises."

Viola choked on a laugh. "I was sent to *kill* Ruby, or don't either of you remember how we met?"

"But you *didn't* kill her—or me," Theo pointed out.

That fact was irrelevant. "Every day you make me think that decision was a mistake," she muttered.

"Maybe it was," Theo agreed. "But it doesn't change the fact that you *did* spare us, and in sparing us, I believe you became stuck with us."

"What is one life spared when so many others were not so lucky?" He started to speak, to argue with her, but Viola shook her head and held up her hand to stop him. "*No.* You need to understand, Theo. Ruby, she has ideas—"

Viola's throat went tight suddenly as she remembered Ruby's ideas— how she had leaned in the night of the gala and kissed her. *Kissed* her.

Why did you do that? Viola had asked.

Because I saw you . . . and I wanted to.

As though anything could ever be so easy or simple. As though the press of lips, the stirring of breath didn't have to be worried over or fretted about or *earned*. As though it could just simply *be*. Without shame, without reservation.

What about Theo? Viola had asked.

He wouldn't care.

"Ruby always has ideas," Theo said with a sigh. "She doesn't always think them through, but she's also not often wrong."

He was looking at Viola with an unsettling softness in his expression. His light eyes and his pleasant face and his golden hair had no place in Viola's world, but Theo Barclay was looking at her like he understood something about her that even Viola did not have words for.

"She's wrong this time," Viola told him, wishing it were otherwise. "I need for you to *think*. I need for you to understand. Don't tell yourself stories about me, about my hidden goodness. I was *made* to be what I am. Every heart I stopped from beating was a choice. *My* choice. And I do not regret those choices."

Theo was still looking at her with an unreadable expression. "You didn't kill Ruby," he said finally. "You didn't allow me to die. You risked quite a lot to save Jianyu today, and it's clear from the way you speak of your friend Dolph that you would have gladly given your life if it could have saved his as well."

"It's not enough," Viola told him, feeling the truth of those words as clearly as she felt her own affinity. "One bit of good doesn't erase the rest."

"Maybe not," Theo agreed, his eyes soft with pity. "Maybe you are an assassin, by birth and by choice, but you are also my friend, Viola. You are *Ruby's* friend as well." He shrugged. "In my estimation, that's more than enough reason to help you, but in case you've forgotten, I have a stake in this too. Jack Grew was the one who ordered Ruby's death. For that reason alone, I will do whatever I can to help you bring down the Order, and Jack right along with it."

"Theo . . ." Viola sharpened her voice in warning.

"You might have saved me once before, Viola, but aside from that one unfortunate incident, I've done rather well at taking care of myself—and Ruby, too, for that matter. In fact, with her gone this summer, I won't have to constantly extricate her from problems of her own creation, and I would very much hate to find myself *bored*." He gave a mock shudder.

Viola realized then that there would be no talking Theo out of this. He had no affinity, no way to protect himself from the Order's magic or power. He had nothing at stake in this fight, but he was committed all the same.

"This is a terrible idea," she told him.

"Most amusing things are," Theo said, flashing an uneven smile as he patted her leg.

"The Order won't hesitate to make you disappear if they feel you're a threat," she told him. "They've had too much practice."

"I'll be fine," Theo said, looking far too pleased with himself. "You know, I believe this is the most excitement I've had in my life since Ruby decided to dress in men's clothing and infiltrate a Knights of Labor meeting. She practically caused a riot when her hair fell out of her hat and they discovered she was actually a woman." He laughed softly at the memory, his eyes gazing off into a past that Viola could not see.

Whatever Ruby might have said that night at the gala, Viola had the sense that Theo Barclay very much cared.

"You love her," she realized, her heart clenching a little at the thought.

"Of course." Theo gave her a small, sad smile. "Who wouldn't love Ruby Reynolds?" He winked before opening the carriage door, effectively ending their conversation.

Viola hadn't even noticed that they'd stopped, but now she saw that they'd arrived at the corner Theo usually dropped her at—one that was a safe enough distance from Paolo's building. After she'd alighted, she turned back to him. "I wish I could talk you out of this."

"I know," he told her. With a small, impertinent shrug, he closed the carriage door.

As she watched his carriage rattle away, Viola felt a sudden, inexplicable wave of sadness rush over her. *Who, indeed, wouldn't love Ruby Reynolds?*

She could not help but think of the moment at the gala when Ruby's lips had touched hers. It had been completely unexpected, but along with the shock of it, she'd had the strange sense of the world being right in a way it never had before. It was as though every bit of her life that hadn't *quite* fit together had rotated *solo un pó*, the pieces locking together in a way that finally made sense. Her affinity had never made her feel like that. Neither had her family or the hours she'd spent on her knees in church. But for the space of a heartbeat, the slice of a single moment, Viola had glimpsed a possibility that she had never imagined could be hers.

She'd immediately rejected it, of course. It was too unbelievably terrifying to think about what *real* happiness might look like—might *feel* like. It was too dangerous to even consider. She had the memory, though, and if it was all that she would ever have, Viola would take that memory and carry it with her—that perfect moment of happiness that was shaped precisely like Ruby's mouth.

The clanging of a nearby shop closing its shutters for the evening shook her back to herself. She didn't have time for dreams. There was too much work still ahead, too many lives she had to keep safe, and Paolo would be waiting for his supper.

A TWISTED KNOT

James Lorcan sat in the quiet of his rooms considering the telegram. Two years ago, he'd taken inspiration from one of Dolph's books to wrestle the loose, unorganized pockets of resistance into a network that was a true adversary to the Brotherhoods' power. For two years now, he'd plotted and planned and waited, certain that his patience would be rewarded. Certain the Antistasi would deliver Esta and Darrigan to him.

He turned the telegram over in his hand, but he knew that there was no secret message to be found in the ordinary sheet of paper. It simply confirmed what he'd suspected when he'd felt the Aether shudder the day before: Cordelia Smith was as good as dead. She'd been taken by Jack Grew and the Brotherhoods, and her capture had shaken the Antistasi's network. Badly. His contacts across the country were nervous.

The Antistasi were the least of James' worries, though. As their leader, James knew that the network could be brought in line easily enough once he took care of Ruth Feltz. Her death would send a message, and after he'd installed his own people in St. Louis, the Middle West would be back under his control. The bigger problem was Esta Filosik, and what he was going to do about her.

James took the notebook from his jacket pocket. He'd stopped worrying about the unreadable words years ago. What he needed wasn't on those pages anyway. He carefully pried loose the back cover and removed the small slip of paper he'd found months after everything had collapsed around him at the Conclave. It was impossibly old and impossibly fragile, but he understood that it was also the key to bringing Esta back to him, and with her, the artifacts and the Book.

If Cordelia had been captured, and if the Brotherhoods weren't crowing about apprehending the Devil's Thief, it meant that Esta had escaped. Already, she would be on her way to California, undoubtedly to find Darrigan and the other stones. He tested the Aether, considered his options. With his network in disarray, it would be more difficult to bring them to heel. Too much could go wrong, as it had already. No . . . a different tack was necessary. It was time, James thought, to remind Esta of what was at stake.

As he walked toward Orchard Street, the Bowery smelled of the coal smoke from the elevated trains and the sour rot of the vegetables and trash in the gutters. He'd been paying the rent on an apartment at the top floor of the building for more than three years now—ever since Leena had died on the bridge that night and Dolph had not. Three years of continuing to conceal Leena's darkest and most powerful secret. It was two years longer than he should have, based on what the notebook had originally told him. The timeline had changed, yet the girl was still there . . . and Esta was still alive.

Time was a twisted knot, as dangerous and impossible to untangle as a ball of snakes. Anyone who tried to pry it apart was liable to find time's venomous teeth sunk deep into their wrist. But James Lorcan believed himself up for the task.

The matron who lived on the top floor was an old woman with rheumy eyes and a voice like a rusted gate. She opened the door immediately at his knock, used to his oddly timed visits. He paid handsomely enough that she did not question him, never scolded or tried to turn him away, not even when he came in the dead of night.

She knew better.

"Where is she?" James asked.

The woman pointed toward the back bedroom. "She's napping, though."

"I don't care if she's spinning straw into gold," he said, brushing past the old lady and into the apartment.

He'd done what he could in the year after Leena's death to make the girl comfortable. Now the child must be close to seven, and each time James paid her a call, she reminded him more and more of who she would one day become—the viper who would betray him.

If only he could kill the child now, or rather, let the city do what it would with her. It would have been far easier than raising her. But before it had become worthless, the notebook had taught James that taking the girl's life would mean losing everything else. His only chance at regaining the destiny that had so far eluded him was through Leena's daughter. He hoped that with a firm enough hand, he could still mold the child into what she should have been if not for that damned magician. Either way, he would use her as he could.

The girl entered the room a moment later, holding tightly to the old woman's hand.

"Come here, child," he said.

The girl shrank from him, the same as she had each time since the night he'd first marked her two years before. James didn't blame the child for the fear in her golden eyes. It was another indication of how smart she was and how cunning she would become.

"We're going to play a little game," he told her, and held out his hand.

"Please, sir. No . . ." Her voice was no more than the mewing whine of a kitten, but he had no pity for her. Kittens grew into cats with claws, feral and dangerous if left unattended.

"Now, Carina," he said sternly, and she finally complied, slipping her trembling hand into his, even as her small mouth was pressed tight.

The mark on the underside of her wrist had long since scarred over into the shiny pink of new skin. The girl trembled in his grasp as James traced over the letters with his finger, and he wondered how close the connection was between this child and the girl she would become. Could Esta see his warnings? Could she feel the touch of his finger through the miles and the years? More importantly, would she understand?

He had not brought Viola's knife, but James doubted the make of the blade was what mattered. Tears were running down the apples of the girl's cheeks even before he touched the small pocketknife to her skin, and by the time it drew blood, she was crying in earnest.

James ignored the girl's tears.

As long as Esta Filosik was still in play, nothing was ever over. *Nothing was ever too late.*

PART

III

NEW ALLIANCES

1904—San Francisco

The air was oppressive with the fog that was coming in off the bay when Jack Grew arrived in San Francisco. He'd left Denver immediately after dealing with the maggot sharpshooter. Her affinity had been a welcome addition to the collection of power held within the Book. He had not bothered to stop and confer with Gunter or any of the others before he left. He brought Hendricks with him, but that was only because Jack had happened to see the Guardsman as he was leaving the grounds of the Curtis Brothers' Show.

Denver had been a fiasco, but at least it hadn't been a complete catastrophe. In Jack's pocket, the Book's power still throbbed in time with his own heart. Esta Filosik might have slipped away from him, but he knew exactly where she was heading, and he had allies already waiting.

When the ferry finally docked, Jack was met by one of the leaders of the Vigilance Committee. William Cooke was in his thirties—a decade older than Jack, but still young enough not to be part of the old guard. Jack remembered Cooke from the Conclave two years before. He'd been an attendee then—a junior delegate from the Vigilance Committee. Even then, Jack could sense a hunger in the other man, and in the time between, Cooke had apparently managed to rise through the ranks of his organization with impressive speed. He could be a rival for power unless Jack neutralized that threat right now.

Cooke seemed unaware of the direction of Jack's thoughts as he welcomed Jack on behalf of the entire organization to their "fair city" with a haughtiness that made Jack want to punch him. "Fair" was stretching things, in Jack's estimation. He'd traveled any number of places with the president, and even more on Roosevelt's behalf, but he'd never been this far west. Now he saw that he'd been missing nothing. The shores of San Francisco teemed with working-class miscreants, and the buildings along the waterfront were no better than shacks. Years before, New York had already made improvements in even its poorest neighborhoods that far surpassed these streets.

But he didn't tell Cooke any of this. There was no sense upsetting the man before he proved himself useful.

"I trust you've made the necessary arrangements," Jack said, lifting a handkerchief to his nose to ward off the smell as Cooke led him through the docks.

"After I received your telegram, the Committee doubled the watchmen's patrols."

"And the Thief?" Jack asked.

"So far there's been no sign of her," Cooke admitted.

"You've kept all of this quiet?" Jack asked. "We wouldn't want our quarry to get word that we're searching for her. If she has allies in this city, they might warn her off."

"We've kept everything in-house, like you wanted," Cooke assured him.

"There haven't been questions about the increased patrols?" Jack wondered.

Cooke shook his head, clearly self-satisfied with the job he'd done. "We're already dealing with a bit of an issue in Chinatown right now—a possible outbreak of plague." He shrugged. "It's been easy enough to explain the increased patrols throughout the city as being related to that. There's enough negative sentiment about the Chinese in the city that nobody has questioned our methods. If anything, the citizens approve of keeping a tighter watch on the foreigners, and they've welcomed the increased surveillance. They don't care who else we might be watching for."

Good. "President Roosevelt sends his heartfelt appreciation for all you and your men have done to help protect our great nation," Jack said solemnly. It wasn't *exactly* a lie. He was sure Roosevelt would have appreciated Cooke's assistance if he'd had any notion that Jack was still tracking the Thief. But while the president had been upset by the events at the world's fair, he didn't understand the true threat that feral magic posed to the country. Roosevelt cared about assimilation of the immigrants who brought the feral magic to the country, but he didn't understand that maggots with that sort of wild, dangerous power could never be truly American. Simply forcing a maggot to speak English would never be enough, not unless or until the power they carried was neutralized.

Cooke preened all the more. "Myself and my city are gratified to be of service to the president."

"You have my personal appreciation as well," Jack added. "I know that in the past our respective Brotherhoods have been at odds, but the events of the last few weeks have illustrated how important our mutual cooperation will be in this new century. I'm glad that men like yourself—modern men of action and intelligence—have the foresight to understand that our shared enemy requires new alliances."

"Alliances?" Cooke glanced at him.

"Unity against a common enemy," Jack clarified. He looked to Hendricks. "The medallions."

Hendricks gave a sure, obedient nod, removed a small linen pouch from his bag, and offered it to Cooke, who took it with some confusion.

"The Veiled Prophet Society and their Jefferson Guard offer you a token of our shared Brotherhood," Jack explained. "It is time to put our differences aside. It is time to act as one."

Cooke opened the pouch and removed one of the medallions to examine it. "What is this?"

"This is a device that the Jefferson Guard developed back in St. Louis. The Veiled Prophet Society uses them to detect feral magic," Hendricks explained. "And now . . . so shall the Vigilance Committee."

THE SERPENT'S CURSE

Cooke seemed suddenly more interested. "The Society sent this?" He frowned, turning the medallion over.

"As I said, we're stronger together against a common enemy. The Society believes this. I hope that the Vigilance Committee will come to believe it as well. Withholding from one another only weakens us all. Distribute them to your men with my compliments and thanks," Jack told Cooke. "They'll offer some protection against the Thief's feral magic and against any maggots who might think to help her. We can't let the Thief get away from us," he warned. "For the good of the country."

"For the good of the country," Cooke agreed.

They finally pushed through the crowds at the docks, and Cooke led them to an open-air carriage. The hills of San Francisco were barely visible through the murk of the cloudy day.

He would need to spend time with Cooke and the rest of the Vigilance Committee later, once this was all over, Jack thought. With Cooke under his influence, the Committee would likely be valuable allies in the future, but for now Jack was only interested in one thing—obtaining the artifact that was waiting for him, and making the damn magician sorry for ever crossing him.

"Now," Jack said. "About the other issue you wanted to discuss with me . . ." He took another cube of morphine and let it fortify him for what was to come.

A PREMONITION

The journey to California took Esta three interminable days. As the train cut through the country, she didn't know how much of a head start Jack might have had from Denver. She had no way of knowing if she'd be in time to reach Harte before anyone else could, but a new scar had appeared on her wrist. Considering that the scar had appeared somewhere in the middle of the Rocky Mountains, Esta figured Nibsy also knew that she'd managed to escape his reach in Denver. If he knew that, it was also likely that Cordelia had already notified Nibsy and the rest of the network about where Harte had been heading.

The scar formed a single word—*clavis*—but beneath that word there was a line of strange markings. Esta understood what the word meant— "key." It was Nibsy's way of ordering her to return with the cuff, but the markings were a puzzle. They seemed oddly familiar, but she couldn't remember where she might have seen them before, and she didn't know what they signified.

Even if Esta had any intention of bowing to Nibsy Lorcan's demands— and she definitely didn't—she didn't have Ishtar's Key. Until she found Harte, she *wouldn't* have Ishtar's Key, and she had a feeling that her arrival in California wouldn't go as easily as she hoped. After all, they'd left the sharpshooter behind, basically tied up like a gift for the Brotherhoods. If the Brotherhoods had Cordelia, it was possible that they already knew everything that Nibsy knew. They might have already found Harte. They might already be waiting for Esta as well. Even if she managed to slip past all of that danger and find Harte, Cordelia knew their final destination, which meant that the Brotherhoods probably would as well. If they could manage to make it out of San Francisco, returning to Manhattan to retrieve the final artifact had now become more dangerous.

Of course, none of that would matter if Esta couldn't reach Harte. From the way time had pulled her under, she now knew for sure that *nothing* would matter if she couldn't retrieve her cuff.

By the time Esta boarded the Pacific Railroad's ferry into San Francisco, she was both bone-tired and completely on edge. Each night she had tried to sleep on the train, but her dreams had taken her to the same tormented desert landscape, and every morning she awoke with the sand serpent rising, its fanged jaws wide to devour her. Surfacing from those dreams felt too much like coming back to herself after time had pulled her under in Denver. But the dreams also reminded her of Thoth's mocking threat: *You live on borrowed minutes. Time will take what it's owed.*

Esta no longer doubted that time itself had become a danger, like the serpent in her dreams, but as the train carried her onward, she realized that Thoth had given her an unexpected gift by revealing what the Book could do. The memory of Jack withdrawing the dagger from the pages of the Book had stuck with Esta as she'd run from Denver. She'd turned that image over in her mind instead of watching the landscape pass outside the train, and in the end she came to believe it was the solution that she had only dared to hope for.

The Ars Arcana was infused with a piece of pure magic. Seshat herself had revealed how she'd placed it there in those brittle pages an eon ago, but until Esta had watched Jack pull the dagger from the Book, she hadn't realized what that truly meant. Thoth's actions—his bragging—had demonstrated it more clearly than words could have possibly conveyed. The Book itself was a container of sorts. Its very pages could be used to take objects *out of time*. If she and Harte could get the Book, they could use it like Thoth had. They could place the artifacts outside of time and return back to 1902 without losing them.

And they *could* get the Book. Jack had told Esta that he was heading to California, hadn't he? They would be in the same city. She would have another chance to take the Ars Arcana from him—as long as she found Harte before Jack did.

Esta hadn't had any trouble at the station back in Oakland, but now that the ferry had finally shuddered to a stop, its engines rumbling beneath the steel decks as it came to rest next to the docks, she wondered if her luck would hold. The day was slightly overcast, but there was none of the famous fog she'd expected of the city. Even from that distance, she could see San Francisco huddled on the shore of the bay. It wasn't the city she was used to seeing in movies and pictures. There was no Coit Tower, no skyscrapers. Beyond the jut of land, the mouth of the bay lay wide open, devoid of the iconic Golden Gate Bridge, which wouldn't be built for decades to come.

As the other passengers began to move toward the exits, Esta wondered what she would find once she disembarked. Harte could already be gone. If she was wrong about what the episodes in Denver meant, he might not be in danger at all. He might already be traveling back to New York to find her. Even now he might be expecting her arrival, and when she didn't come . . .

He would wait for me, Esta thought. If this trip to California turned out to be nothing but a wild-goose chase, she could be back to the bridge in a few days. Harte wouldn't give up on her so quickly.

Esta tucked her coat around her and pulled the stolen hat farther down over her forehead as she followed the crush of people eager to leave the ship. She didn't check her pocket, where she'd secured Maggie's pouch, even though she wanted to. She wasn't green enough to make herself a mark for pickpockets who might be casing the crowd.

As the travelers from the ferry began to filter into a line down the gangplank, Esta searched the dock for any sign of trouble. She'd almost relaxed when the glint of metal on a dark lapel caught her eye. A pair of men were waiting not far from the exit to the ferry's dock, and they were both wearing medallions that looked too similar to the Jefferson Guard's to be a coincidence. Esta didn't know to which Brotherhood the men owed their allegiance, but it didn't really matter. If these men had medallions from the Society, it meant that the Brotherhoods' influence had already reached farther than she'd realized, all the way across the continent. Worse, it meant that they were expecting trouble—they were likely expecting *her*.

Esta hadn't thought the trip to California would be easy, but these two men definitely complicated things. Stuck in the line of passengers on the narrow path of the gangplank, though, there was little she could do without drawing attention. If she used her affinity to get past the men, it would trigger the medallions. She'd be past the danger, but the medallions would alert the men to the magic she'd used. If these men were waiting for her specifically, as she suspected they were, it would only confirm her arrival. She couldn't afford for the Brotherhoods to realize she'd arrived. Her affinity was always an option if push came to shove, but if she could avoid the men's notice without using it, she would.

But maybe these two men could help her. Esta had no idea where to find Harte. She'd boarded a train to California knowing only that she had no other choice. Thoth had told her that Harte had been captured by some associates of his. If the men were linked to the Brotherhoods, perhaps they could lead her to Harte.

Esta trailed behind a group of businessmen down the gangplank, and once they'd reached the dock, she kept close to the group, hoping that anyone who saw her would assume she was one of them. Once she was past the men with the medallions, she could get herself into a better position. They wouldn't wait at the docks forever, and when they left, she could follow them.

She was nearly past the men when a small boy appeared seemingly out of nowhere to tug on her jacket. She looked down at him, imagining him at first to be some kind of urchin trying to con travelers out of a few coins. His eyes were wide with an expression that looked strangely like surprise, considering he was the one who had approached her. There was something familiar about him, but she didn't have time to figure out what it was.

"I don't have anything," she said, pulling away. But the words were no sooner out of her mouth than Esta's vision blurred, and the boy flickered. He was there and then he wasn't. It happened so quickly that she might have dismissed it as a trick of her tired eyes, except that she knew it wasn't really the boy flickering. It was happening. Again.

Esta drew in an uneasy breath and held it, as though if she remained still for long enough, time would forget her debt. But her pulse was already racing, her skin clammy and damp with a cold sweat, and she felt the same panic she'd felt when she was chased by the sand serpent in her dreams, trying to outrun the impossible.

The world steadied a second later, but Esta didn't lie to herself about what had just happened. She understood and accepted the warning for what it was, and she knew she couldn't predict when time might open its jaws—like the serpent in her dream—and pull her under. She had the unmistakable premonition that there would be no waking from that if it happened again.

The boy was tugging at her again, but she jerked away once more and tried to push through the crowd to escape him.

"Miss Esta?" His small, high voice carried over the din of the crowded docks, but Esta didn't allow herself to turn back, not even when it registered what he had called her.

The scene in front of her flickered again. She saw the docks all around her and the shoreline beyond, cluttered with haphazard shack-like structures and teeming with people, and then they were gone. The city around it—past, present, and future—glimmered and flickered like a double-exposed image, unsteady and unmoored from her own moment in time.

Vaguely Esta was aware of someone shouting her name as the scene solidified again into the San Francisco of 1904. She turned, feeling like she was stuck in a dream as she watched the men with the medallions grab the boy. He was writhing and kicking as he tried to get away from them, and he was still shouting for her.

She didn't know how he knew her name, and she didn't care to wait around to figure it out. The men hadn't seen her yet. They were too busy wrestling the kid, and Esta knew that she should use the distraction to her advantage. She turned to go, but the second she turned away from the men and the boy, the world flickered again. And she knew—the boy was important. She didn't know who he was or how that could be, but she reached for her affinity anyway, pulling the seconds slow as she turned back. With each step she took toward him, her vision became clearer. The world became more stable and steady.

When she touched the boy and brought him into her net of time, he gasped and tried to pull away. Esta held tightly to his wrist as she dragged him away from the men and toward the mess of the city that lay beyond the docks. She didn't stop until they'd traveled far past the ramshackle buildings near the water and were well into the city proper. It was the San Francisco from before the earthquake that would level it. With the stink of the sewers and the trash heaped in the streets, it felt like an untamed outpost of humanity, and it made even Old New York seem practically clean and modern by comparison.

Finally, when Esta thought they were far enough away, she released her hold on the seconds. This time the boy didn't try to pull away again, but looked up at her, his eyes wide with something that might have been wonder. Or maybe it was fear, which would have made him smarter. He couldn't have been more than seven or eight. He had a tousled head of dark-blond hair, and beneath his button nose, his mouth was pressed in a flat line. But there was no fear in his expression.

"Who sent you?" she asked, trying to decide if the boy was a threat.

He simply stared at her, not answering. Perhaps he didn't know English?

"How did you know my name?" she demanded.

The child didn't move, but Esta knew he understood. Keen intelligence sparked in his eyes, but it looked like he was trying to figure out a difficult puzzle.

"How did you know who I was?" she pressed. After all, she was dressed in men's clothing. She didn't look like a "Miss" at all.

Again she had the thought that there was something about him that seemed familiar. Something that made her pause. "Did Harte send you?"

The boy's eyes widened as he nodded, and that was when Esta realized that his eyes were the same perfectly stormy gray as Harte's.

"Where is he?" she asked, her stomach turning at the shadow that crossed the boy's expression. "What's happened to him?"

But the child only shook his head. "You have to come with me."

TRUE POWER

1902—New York

When James Lorcan received yet another summons from Paul Kelly on a random Wednesday afternoon, he took his time about answering it. He knew that Kelly was only calling the meeting—a last-minute and unplanned meeting at that—to prove that he could. It was another volley in their battle of wills, and in return, James made sure to keep Kelly waiting, because James knew that *he* could.

Kelly might believe that he was the more powerful of the two of them—certainly, an argument could be made that Kelly's Five Pointers were the wildest and most dangerous of the gangs in the Bowery—but James knew otherwise. He understood that true power moved best in invisible currents, like electricity . . . or like magic. Those who knew how to wield it, to hold it firmly in the palm of their hand, didn't always require muscle and brawn. Often, they simply required a bit of patience— something Paul Kelly did not have.

Once he'd arrived at the Little Naples Cafe, James didn't miss that Kelly did not so much as offer him a glass of water. He didn't ask for one either, despite the growing warmth of the day. Instead, he waited for Kelly to finish the sandwich he'd been eating when James arrived and pretended that he hadn't been pulled away from his own business.

Kelly finished finally, dabbed at his mouth delicately with his napkin, and then pushed the plate aside. "I have news."

James inclined his head. "I figured as much."

"Things are moving faster than we expected," Kelly told him.

"How *much* faster?" James asked, allowing his affinity to unfurl a little to detect the way the Aether moved in response to this news. He might be working with Kelly, but James didn't trust the gangster. He had no plans to allow Kelly to obtain the upper hand in their dealings.

"We originally thought the plans were to move the goods during the summer solstice," Kelly said.

"They're not?" The solstice had made sense. Sundren, like those in the Order, often believed the movement of the planets and stars had important meaning, but then, maybe they did for false magic. "Why the change?"

"Not a change, exactly," Kelly said. "A misunderstanding. The Order *is* making their move on a solstice, but it's not the one on the calendar. It's a day they're calling the *Manhattan* Solstice, whatever that means."

"When?" James asked, because it was the only question that truly mattered.

"Not in late June, like we've been planning," Kelly said, looking almost annoyed. "They're planning on making the move on the twenty-eighth of May."

"That's only four days from now," James said. He had been operating under the assumption that he still had time to prepare. He'd planned to bring Viola to heel and align his forces *just so*.

"There's more," Kelly said.

There's always more, James thought with no little frustration. He didn't allow any of the concern he might have been feeling to show, though. Not in front of Kelly, where any display of weakness could be a weapon turned against him.

"Tell me," James said easily, as though they had not lost *weeks* of preparation.

"They're not bringing the goods across the bridge, like we originally thought." Kelly took out one of his small cigarettes and didn't bother to offer James one before he lit it. "They're bringing everything in by boat."

James tightened his grip on the gorgon's head. "You're sure?"

"Positive," Kelly said. "After the mess at Khafre Hall, the Order has decided that bringing the goods over the bridge would leave them too vulnerable. But by boat?" Kelly took a long drag on his cigarette, the tip glowing as he squinted through the smoke. "There are a lot of docks in the city. Word is, the Order figures that this plan will make it harder to predict where the boat will arrive."

"They're expecting an attack," James said, unsurprised. The Order would have been stupid not to expect some difficulty, especially after Khafre Hall.

"It seems that way," Kelly agreed.

It doesn't matter, James reminded himself, adjusting his grip on his cane. Beneath his hand, the sharp outlines of the serpents that formed the gorgon's hair pressed into his palm. The cool energy beneath the silvery surface was a balm to any anxiety he might feel. It was a reminder of the possibility that lay ahead. He'd been working diligently on accessing the magic held within the cane, and already he could sense the power there beginning to answer his call. Once he had the ring, he would have everything he needed to unlock that power completely.

"This change," James said. "It doesn't give us much time to plan."

Kelly shrugged. "It doesn't give *you* much time. My boys are ready to disable the Death Avenue train and lead the wagons right where we want them, but if we can't get our hands on the goods, the risk is all for nothing. Have you made any progress figuring out what the protections might be?"

They'd learned already that the Order was planning on using some kind of ritual to protect the wagon carrying their treasures, but James hadn't been able to quite figure out what it might entail. Maybe if Dolph's journal hadn't gone missing, he would have already had the answer.

Still, the information Kelly was providing might be of use, even if the new timeline was nothing short of a disaster. The Manhattan Solstice sounded like some kind of a fantasy that only the rich could devise, but

LISA MAXWELL

James had enough experience under his belt not to discount anything when it came to the Order. "I'll figure it out."

"I trust you'll let me know what you discover?" Kelly said.

"Of course," James lied, inclining his head. Once he figured out what the Order had planned, he'd tell Kelly just enough to let *that* particular problem take care of itself.

Outside the cafe, the streets were half in shadow, an effect of the slant of the sun and the tightly crowded buildings. There was still plenty of daylight left, but James didn't have any interest in lingering too long in Kelly's territory. Luckily, the man he needed to talk to was already waiting for him.

John Torrio was at the corner, talking with another of Kelly's lackeys, Razor Riley. The two had been more than helpful in manipulating Harte Darrigan into helping with the job at Khafre Hall, but James knew that Torrio was already chafing under Kelly's control. It was one thing to be taken in, trained, and groomed by one of the most powerful criminals in the city. It was another to remain his lackey when you'd outgrown that particular role.

James himself understood that feeling. It had been difficult to take orders from Dolph in those final few weeks, when James had known how close he was to his own victory. It had taken patience and fortitude to continue pretending, to hide what he was planning from Dolph, but his effort had paid off. Unlike James, Torrio was every bit as impatient and fiery as his boss. It was a convenient weakness that James had every intention of exploiting.

He gave Torrio a small nod of acknowledgment, but continued on, walking in the direction of the Strega. It took a few blocks for Torrio to finally come up beside him.

"You have news about Viola?" James asked, not pausing as the two strolled side by side.

Dolph's journal had gone missing the day after Viola had charged into the Strega, and James knew she'd been the one to take it. The loss hadn't

THE SERPENT'S CURSE

405

bothered him, not when the Aether suggested that the theft had been necessary. The journal was nothing more than a pawn to be sacrificed in order to move his game forward, and besides, James had already read over Dolph's nearly obsessive notes enough to no longer need them. But he still needed to understand *exactly* what Viola was up to, and the Aether didn't reveal those sorts of details.

"I got the information you asked for . . . if you have what *you* promised." Torrio jerked his head toward one of the basement bars that populated the area.

James decided it wasn't worth arguing about the meeting place. Not when their timeline had been cut so much shorter, and not when he needed Torrio on his side.

The saloon was like most of the basement bars in the city—dark and stuffy, smelling of sweat and stale lager. It was also the type of place where no one paid attention, and if they did, they certainly didn't talk.

"Your boss might not be smart enough to see that the world is far bigger than New York City, but I'm certainly glad that you are." James pulled the thin packet from inside his vest and held it out. Torrio grabbed for it, but James held firm. "Now, about Viola . . ."

"She's still spending her days up in Harlem," Torrio told him.

"With the same group as before?" James asked. He hadn't quite understood how Viola had come to know the person who owned the house—a colored man who operated a small newspaper in the city—but she'd been sneaking off from her brother's watch to meet people there fairly regularly.

Not people, James thought. *Sundren.* The same Sundren he'd seen with Jianyu at Evelyn DeMure's apartment before the gala. It wasn't a coincidence. It meant that he'd been right. With the missing journal and Viola's continued meetings, it indicated that Jianyu was likely in play now as well . . . and that it was past time for them to be brought to heel.

"That isn't news," James said, impatient. He still held firmly to the envelope. "Is there anything else?"

LISA MAXWELL

Torrio's eyes narrowed a little. "Maybe. If your information there is good." He nodded to the envelope.

"You won't know unless you share what you have on Viola," James told him, pulling the envelope back and moving to tuck it away again.

"There's nothing new about Viola," Torrio said. "But that toff she goes around with has been doing some interesting things lately. Seems he's been spending his days with Morgan and some of the Order types."

"Has he?" James asked, suddenly more interested. It began to make sense now why the Aether had insisted that Viola was so essential. If she had a link to the Order, that was likely a connection James could use to his favor. "You still haven't told Kelly anything about his sister's other activities?"

Torrio shook his head. "Not a word, like you insisted."

"Maybe it's time we let your boss know about where his dear little sister is going when he's not paying attention. Don't let him know anything about the toff, but I think it might be a good thing for Kelly to doubt his sister a little more." With the right pressure, Viola would be back where he'd wanted her—Jianyu as well. Both of them would be firmly under his control, and with a little luck, her connection to the Order would come with her.

James released the packet, handing it over to Torrio. "It's all there," he said when Torrio started to open it.

Torrio turned the envelope over like he wanted to pry inside of it. "It doesn't look like much."

"Looks can be deceiving." Then he gave Torrio a pat on the shoulder and headed out.

He had work to do and only four days to do it. Four days to bring Viola to heel, four days to discover what corrupt magic the Order might use, and four days to plan. The Aether bunched again, shifting with a shivering awareness of his certain victory. Four days, and the ring, along with all the power it contained, would be his.

THE TUNNELS

1904—San Francisco

Esta followed the boy through the streets of the city, leaving the confusion of the docks behind them. She wanted to ask him a million questions, but mostly, she didn't want to scare him into running, especially if he could provide some clue to Harte's whereabouts. Instead, she kept her affinity close, ready and waiting for her to grasp the seconds at a moment's notice, and she held a vial of incendiary laced with Quellant tucked in her fist, cool against her palm, because she knew that a pair of gray eyes meant very little. There were too many who might have known she would arrive in the city, and young as the boy seemed, Esta knew she might well be walking right into a trap.

The boy led her through the maze of the city, up roads that climbed so steeply that horses and wagons didn't even bother and along trolley routes that cut through the wild tumble of streets. She almost didn't realize that they were skirting Chinatown until she saw the signs painted with the Chinese characters hanging from the buildings beyond what looked like a barricade. But the boy didn't try to enter through the checkpoints, which was fine with Esta. Especially since the men guarding the entrances all had medallions glinting on their lapels.

"What's happening there?" she asked the boy.

"The Vigilance Committee." He glanced up at her, his small brow furrowed with determination. "Don't worry. We won't go that way."

He led her instead to a side street that turned into another alley. At the end of it, he opened a gate into a courtyard behind what appeared to be a restaurant. The bins of trash overflowed with rotten food that buzzed with flies and other vermin, but the boy didn't seem fazed, even when a rat scurried almost directly over his foot. He continued to the back of the courtyard, where he pulled open one of the wooden doors of a coal cellar.

"I'm not going down there," Esta told him, the darkness in the shaft below making her skin crawl. But the boy went first, disappearing into the shadows below, and Esta's only choices were to lose him completely or follow.

She followed. He'd already taken a candle from his pocket by the time she reached the bottom, where he waited, and a few seconds later he had it lit. That single flame was the only illumination they had as they traversed a series of tunnels that seemed to have been carved from the earth below the city. It wasn't long before Esta's boots were completely soaked from the layer of muck they had to walk through. From the smell of the place—earthy and rank at the same time—she didn't want to think too closely about what the mud might contain. She concerned herself instead with not slipping as she struggled to keep up with the sure-footed boy.

After a few minutes, though, Esta started to think she'd made a serious miscalculation. She'd been trying to memorize the twists and turns the boy had taken, but she soon lost track. Water trickled somewhere nearby, and the sounds of creatures scurrying and scratching followed them, but otherwise the tunnels were quiet. If this was a trap, if the tunnels opened into an ambush and she died here, it would be like she'd walked into her own grave. Still, despite the danger she might have been in, Esta felt stronger and steadier the farther she walked. Even in the darkened tunnel, her vision remained clear and focused. As far as she was concerned, that was even more confirmation that following the boy was the right decision.

Finally, the boy pushed aside a wooden board that exposed another branch of the tunnel. Once they were through, he replaced the board, then led her a little farther still, until they came to a short ladder. It didn't look overly sturdy, but the boy scaled it easily and rapped a short, staccato rhythm on the wooden ceiling above. A moment later, a panel moved aside, and a woman's face appeared. From the color of her hair and the shape of her nose, it was clear that she was the boy's mother and that she'd been expecting them.

The boy scrambled up through the opening, and Esta followed. As her eyes adjusted to the brightness, she found herself in a storage room lined with shelves of dry goods and ceramic jars. The woman stepped back to allow Esta through, then secured the door to the tunnel behind her, barring it with a length of wood as she scolded her son sharply in German, clearly assuming Esta wouldn't understand.

"I told you how dangerous it is for us now," the woman told him. "I told you to stay in your room. Every day I tell you the same, why can't you listen like a good boy would?"

The boy somehow looked even younger and smaller under his mother's reprimands. "I tried to stay, but I couldn't stop myself," he complained, tears making his eyes look damp and glassy. "I had to go."

"Lies on top of disobedience?"

"Not lies," the boy said, suddenly looking more stubborn. "See! This is the lady I had to find. This is Miss Esta."

The woman's eyes cut in Esta's direction. "You're not a man," she said in English.

"No," Esta agreed. "I'm not. My name's Esta. Esta Filosik."

"I know who you are," the woman said, but there was no heat and no fear in her voice.

"I'm looking for a friend of mine. Harte Darrigan. He's here, isn't he?"

The woman considered the question. Then she let out a long, tired-sounding breath. "I knew that one would be trouble."

Relief flashed through Esta. "Then you *do* know him? Do you know where he is?"

The woman nodded before turning back to the boy and instructing her son to finish setting the locks and the alarms. Finally, she gestured for Esta to come with her and led the way into the apartment proper.

"I didn't believe Sammie when he told me that he had to find someone—a lady from far away named Miss Esta," the woman said. When she spoke, her voice was soft, and her English had the sharp accent of her native German. "Sammie is usually such a good boy, but for the last few days, he has driven me mad with his disobedience. He kept trying to tell me, but I didn't believe that you could possibly exist, but now . . ." She closed her eyes, as though blinking would be enough to wake her from this awful dream, but when she finally opened them again, Esta could see the fear in her expression. "You have to understand. . . . My husband has been sent away. My child is all I have left."

"I'm not here to hurt either of you," Esta said softly. "I'm just looking for my friend. I think something might have happened to him. I'm hoping that your son finding me means that you can help me find him?"

The woman studied her, and Esta had the sense that it was not a matter of whether the woman could help her, but whether she *would*.

"Please," Esta said. "Do you have any idea what happened to him?"

At first the woman only sighed, like she had finally resigned herself to a fate she did not want. "Two days ago, your friend broke into my home, like a common thief, and I nearly shot him, thinking he was from the Committee. But then Sammie explained what your friend had done for him. He's sick, very sick," the woman told Esta, motioning that she should follow her toward a doorway at the back of the living area. "He practically collapsed at my feet that night. I've done what I could for him, to make him comfortable."

"Thank you . . ."

"Patience," the woman said. "Patience Lowe."

"Thank you, Patience. For helping him."

Patience shook her head sadly. "I couldn't call a doctor, not with the Committee's quarantine. But it would not have mattered. The sickness he has, it's not one that people recover from."

The woman stepped aside and waved Esta into the room beyond. There was a low platform bed and a large oak wardrobe in the corner. Harte wasn't there.

Before Esta could ask, Patience brushed past her into the room and rolled back the rug. Then she pulled up a panel of the wood flooring to reveal an indentation beneath. But nothing the woman had told her—or could have told her—prepared Esta for what she found below.

TO TOUCH HER ONCE MORE

1904—San Francisco

It wasn't the feverish chills that racked Harte's body, making every bone ache clear to the marrow, or even the pervading stench of vomit and sweat and sickness that he hated the most. Those things were awful, but Harte could have suffered them well enough. But the way his skin was so alive with pain that it felt like it was crawling with vermin every time he moved? *That* was true torture.

Not that he could have lifted his arm to scratch at his skin, even if he wanted to. Harte had become far too weak to bother with moving, and besides, there was barely room for him to fit head to toe in the makeshift cellar where Sammie and his mother had placed him. The hole where they'd hidden him smelled of dirt, a dark, damp scent that surrounded and overwhelmed. The walls had been dug from the earth, and the space, about the size of a small root cellar, clearly hadn't been part of the original building's plan.

The boy's mother had checked in on Harte often. Sometimes she would speak to him as she tried to spoon water past his cracked lips. She talked as she tried to help him, telling him about herself and explaining that her husband had created the hideaway. He'd dug it out by hand a few years before for when he needed to hide from the various people he owed money. The path of righteousness had apparently taken Samuel Lowe through the back room of more than one saloon, where he'd lost large sums of money playing cards with the wrong kind of people. Her husband's absence hadn't stopped his creditors from coming to the house, demanding their debts be repaid by a wife who had nothing to offer. It was one of many reasons Harte had to continue to remain hidden.

Sometimes, in the darkness of his burrow, Harte thought he could hear Seshat speaking to him. Once he even dreamed of her, dressed in blinding white, her eyes a black fire. Other times he dreamed of Esta. She would come to him, her soft mouth and devil's eyes sparking with anger and humor all at once. But Harte could never seem to reach her. He would've given damn near anything to touch her again and to tell her how sorry he was for being a fool by leaving her as he had.

In the darkness, Harte's other regrets came to him as well, one by one, along with the ghosts of all the people he had betrayed. His mother. Dolph Saunders. *Esta.* Countless others that he'd thrown aside for his own ends. Their faces rose up in the darkness, silent in their judgment, before fading away and leaving Harte alone once more.

The boy—his brother—never returned, though. Not after that first day when the child had led him to this hovel. He was likely afraid now. Harte hoped he was safe—he couldn't forget the way Seshat's power had surged through him, and he worried about the boy's absence and what it might mean. He also couldn't forget the threat Seshat had made about what she would do if Esta did finally find him.

Harte began to hope that death would take him—and the angry goddess inside his skin—before Esta could arrive. He came to realize that Seshat was right. Esta would never simply accept it if Harte didn't meet her at the bridge, as he'd promised. She might well come for him, even if it was only to make him pay for his betrayal. But Harte knew that if she did, he would not be able to hold the goddess back.

But perhaps he would not have to worry about that eventuality. He knew, the same way a wounded animal knows to find a quiet place to lie down for the last time, that he didn't have much longer. There was an ache in his inner thigh where a tumorlike growth had swelled hot and evil beneath the skin. It was so painful now that he couldn't even move his leg. His fever felt like a brand against his skin, and eventually even Seshat had abandoned him. She, too, had pulled inward, far beneath his surface, as though she had started to understand that her time was growing as short as his own. Trapped as she was inside of him, there was at least *some* consolation in the fact that Seshat's danger would pass when he did.

Harte only hoped that someone would remember him after he was gone. That someone could tell Esta what had become of him.

Esta.

In the darkness behind his eyes he could see her—the tilt of her full mouth when she smirked at him. The cut of her chin, sharp as her words. Her eyes, the color of whiskey and sunlight. The feel of her skin, softer than anything he'd ever held. And the scent of her. Clean and unsullied, like hope itself. From the very beginning, the very moment he'd seen her so many weeks ago in the Haymarket's ballroom, she'd called to him like a beacon. And he'd walked away. Again and again, he'd tossed her aside. Because he was too weak to trust. Too scared to stay.

If he concentrated, Harte could almost hear her voice. The deep, rough timbre. The irritation that colored it. Calling him.

He opened his eyes and could almost see her there, a dark vision above him, surrounded by brightness—Esta. *Like some saving, avenging angel.*

No. Not an angel. Esta couldn't be dead, and Harte's life certainly hadn't been pure enough for heaven.

But she seemed so *real.*

It was nothing but the delirium brought on by the pain and the fever. Or maybe he was dead already, and hell was nothing more and nothing less than this, being inches away from the girl he loved—

He *loved?* How ridiculous to discover that now, when it was far too late. When he would never be able to tell her. How painfully appropriate to fade away taunted by his greatest regret.

Harte tried to lift his hand, because maybe if he could only touch the angel looming above, it would be enough to pull him through to the other side and end this misery. But lifting his arm felt like trying to push through leaden waves. Still, the apparition floated above him, and he had the sense that if he could reach her, then maybe Esta would know how sorry he was for everything. If he could just touch her once more . . .

JAGGED HOPE

When Patience Lowe opened the trapdoor in the floor, the smell from below rose in a noxious wave, sick and stagnant and strong enough to make Esta gag. Below, a figure lay curled on his side.

At first Esta couldn't believe what she was seeing. Harte Darrigan, with his meticulous cleanliness. Harte, who hated to be dirty in any way. It was unthinkable that the wretch curled below could really be him. But it was. The space where he was lying was nothing more than a hole that had been clawed out of the earth, like the burrow of a rat beneath the city streets. It made Esta's chest hurt to see his skin slick with feverish sweat and his ragged clothes crusted over with his own sickness.

She couldn't tell at first if he was even breathing, but then Harte's eyes cracked open and his head turned toward the light. He seemed to be seeking out something other than the darkness he'd been buried in. His skin was sallow and grayish, and there were dark hollows beneath his eyes. His lips were cracked and scabbed over from bleeding, and the smell that wafted up to her carried with it the unmistakable reek of infection and death.

It was clear he wasn't seeing her. Not really. The whites of Harte's eyes were yellow and tinged with a feverish pink as he stared up, not quite focusing. His mouth was moving, like he wanted to speak, but all that came out was an indecipherable rattling. He tried to raise his hand like he was reaching for her, but the motion seemed labored, and he allowed his arm to fall back to rest on his abdomen again, his eyes closing from the effort.

"He needs help," she told Patience. "A doctor or—"

"No," the woman said, shaking her head. "There's no medicine that can help him now. The fever is too great. All we can do is wait."

Esta's temper spiked as the woman stood by. "How could you just leave him like this? It's like you put him in a grave to die."

"What else could I do?" Patience asked. "If I called for a doctor, they would have reported his illness to the Vigilance Committee, which is where he'd escaped from. Surely the Committee would have realized who he was. They would have taken everything I had left—my home, my child—and they would have used his illness as an excuse. They would have made an example of me, as they are making an example of the Chinese people in this city. My neighbors excuse the Committee's tactics—their patrols and their quarantine barricades—because it's happening to Chinatown and not to them. Because they already hate the Chinese people who live there. But most fool themselves into believing sickness can be held back with barbed wire. They are so terrified of the plague escaping those confines, they'll excuse any cruelty the Committee commits. Especially with my husband gone, there would have been no one to protect us."

"Plague?" Esta asked in disbelief. As in, *the* plague? Patience *had* to be overstating things.

"There has been news of cases in town recently," the boy's mother confirmed. "Because people fear catching the sickness, no one will speak against the Committee, no matter how terrible their tactics. What would you have had me do? The Committee has ruled this town with an iron fist, using the threat of magic to establish their power, for years now. How would you have me fight that power?"

Esta wasn't sure. It should have been enough that this woman had taken Harte in, had cared for him as much as she could, despite the apparent risk.

"His fever grows worse," Patience told her. "It will not be long now."

"I won't stand here and watch him die," Esta said. "People don't die of fevers—"

Except that they did. She *knew* that. In 1904, before modern medicine had given the world the miracle of antibiotics, a person could die from so much less than Harte was suffering from. It was astounding that he'd held on so long, considering the state he was in. In another time, he wouldn't have suffered so needlessly. In another age, he didn't need to die.

He doesn't *need to die.* . . . Not if she could get him to that other time.

Esta pulled the edge of her jacket up over her face, to ward off the smell, before she lowered herself down to where Harte lay. His skin felt like fire, and his limbs felt almost delicate as she moved them, checking for some sign of her cuff.

"Did he have anything with him?" Esta asked the woman. "A package or . . . *anything?*"

Patience shook her head. "He didn't have anything with him when he arrived."

Harte's hair was a tangled mess, and his clothes were filthy. Esta touched him, trying to wake him so she could speak to him, but he didn't stir. His breathing worried her even more than his lack of consciousness. The breaths he took were shallow and ragged, and there was a wet-sounding rattle in his chest. Esta had heard a sound like that before—back in New York, when she stood vigil with Viola and Dolph as Tilly took her final breaths.

No. She refused—*refused*—to accept this.

"It has to be here," she said, more to herself than to anyone else.

Harte knew what Ishtar's Key meant to her—to both of them. There was no way he would have taken her cuff and then lost it. The Harte she knew might be heavy-handed. He might be stupid and stubborn and predictably pigheaded, but he wasn't careless. She ignored the stench of him as well as the way he moaned as she tried to move him onto his side, to search beneath him.

But she didn't find anything. No cuff, no necklace. *Nothing.*

I'm still here, she reminded herself. If the Key were gone, she would be as well.

When Esta looked up again, Patience was shaking her head, and there was something that made Esta wonder if she knew more than she was saying.

"He should have had a silver cuff with him," Esta explained, making a circular motion around her own arm, where the cuff had once sat. "A bracelet that held a dark stone, and he should have been carrying a necklace as well. A *beautiful* necklace, with a bright-blue stone that looks like stars are trapped within it. But the cuff is what's really important. If I have the cuff, I can help him. I can take him away from here, and you and your son would no longer be in danger from someone discovering him."

The woman's eyes had widened slightly. She looked suddenly unsure, maybe even guilty.

"Please," Esta pleaded. "If you know what I'm talking about at all, if you saw anything like the pieces I described, you have to help me. I can pay you for them. I can give you whatever you want. I can *save* him if I have that cuff."

The woman didn't respond or react.

"If you do have the pieces I'm talking about, you can't keep them. There are people looking for them—dangerous people," Esta told her, trying another approach. "If you're worried about this Committee, they're nothing compared to the people who will be coming for you."

Patience hesitated a moment longer. When she finally spoke again, she made her voice no more than a whisper, like she was afraid the walls themselves might overhear. "My husband brought home pieces like you describe some days ago. But they're gone. I gave them to satisfy my husband's debts when his creditors came demanding payment," she said. "What could I do?"

Esta's stomach sank. "Tell me you didn't give away the cuff. *Tell me.*"

LISA MAXWELL

"I didn't have a choice," Patience explained, her voice filled with remorse. Then the woman's expression shifted. "You can't imagine what it is to live my life. Do you know that my father lost me in a card game? To be rid of his responsibility, he forced me to marry a man I would never have chosen. Now all I have is my child and this house. Our only chance to survive is to keep my husband's shop. Unlike you, I cannot pull on trousers and jaunt off and leave my responsibilities—my son—behind."

"I know," Esta told her softly. "You're right. I don't have a child to protect or a husband to find."

"I don't want to find my husband," she told Esta. "If he never returns, our lives will be hard, but in the end, they'll be better. A man like that can't be saved from himself. A man like that leaves only destruction in his wake."

"I'm sorry," Esta said, speaking truly. She had a feeling that the woman was on the cusp of some revelation, and she needed the right combination to unlock her willingness. "But this man, the one you were so good to tend to and comfort, even when it could have put you in danger? He *is* an honorable man. You must know something more."

Patience knew something about the artifacts, there was no question of that fact. Without her help, Harte would die. But even with the cuff, even if she could take him forward to a time where medicine might save him, Esta knew that it still might not be enough.

"Please," she said. She had never begged before. She had never felt desperate enough to beg, not even when she'd been tied to a chair at the mercy of a madman. *"Please,"* Esta repeated.

Because she could not imagine a world where Harte Darrigan didn't exist.

The woman's mouth pressed into a tight line, and Esta knew that everything was lost—Harte, the artifacts, herself. . . .

But then Patience relented.

"When my husband brought the pieces home, I sensed them, even before he showed them to me." She paused.

Esta waited silently, because it felt like something as simple as breathing might shatter the moment. But she immediately understood the implication of what Patience Lowe had just told her.

"I knew that my husband couldn't have obtained such pieces honestly, because I knew that they were too important for someone like *him* to have. When their true owner came for them, I didn't want to be empty-handed." She went to the bed and lifted the mattress, propping it on her shoulder so she could pull something from within the frame. Then Patience brought a small package wrapped in white linen and knelt next to the hole in the floor.

Esta's eyes were locked on the package that rested in the woman's lap. But she was afraid to lean too much into the hope that already made her feel light-headed.

"My husband never knew what I was or what I could do. He was too fond of talking about righteousness and abomination, and I knew from the beginning that it would be dangerous to reveal myself to him," Patience told Esta, her expression sour. "He thought these pieces were merely expensive, but I knew better."

"You knew they were powerful," Esta said. *Because Patience is Mageus.*

Patience unwrapped the package, and Esta almost sobbed in relief the second she saw the glint of silver and felt the power of the cuff's dark stone call out to her.

"You may be right about this one being a good man. He saved my boy when my husband would have sacrificed his only child for a bit of gold. If you truly believe you can save your friend, then I can't keep these from you." Patience held out the parcel, the necklace and cuff gleaming against the soft linen.

"Thank you," Esta said, taking them. The artifacts were delicate pieces, but they were heavy with the weight of magic, and when Esta touched them, she could feel their power calling to her. She slid on the cuff immediately and tucked the necklace into the leather pouch with Maggie's concoctions.

Esta had no sooner secured them and turned her energy to figuring out how she would get Harte up from the hole in the floor than bells began chiming. It was almost like the heavens themselves were celebrating, except that there was nothing celestial about the sound. It was a tinny, jagged noise that sounded every bit like a warning.

"Mama," the boy said, coming into the room with a look of panic.

The color had drained from the woman's face. "There's someone in the tunnel," Patience said, glancing back over her shoulder. She spoke to the boy in urgent, rapid German.

"Were you followed?"

"No. I was careful."

"Then how could they find us?"

She turned to Esta. "We must go. It is not safe here—"

"Not without him," Esta refused. She could save him. She *would*.

"No one should be in that tunnel. My husband built it as a way to escape from the enemies he made. If someone is there, they followed you. If they followed you through those tunnels, they are not friends."

"Help me carry him," Esta begged. "I know you have done so much already, but please, I need to get him outside."

Patience was shaking her head, backing away with her arms around the child. "I can't. If they find us here with you—" She shook her head again, then took her son's hand and disappeared through the door. They were gone before Esta could stop them.

THE WORLD CRUMBLES

1904—San Francisco

Esta couldn't blame Patience for running with her child. Not when she'd kept Harte alive long enough for Esta to find him, and especially not when she'd relinquished the cuff that could save them both. Esta had no idea what it must be like to have a child, the constant, urgent need to protect that small life, even at the cost of your own. She didn't really even know what it felt like to have a family. But she knew what she felt for Harte. She wouldn't let him go. She would not give up, not now.

If I can get him outside . . .

Esta didn't know San Francisco. She had no idea what she might find when she slipped ahead through the layers of time. She understood it would be dangerous with Seshat lurking beneath Harte's skin, but desperation made her reckless.

"Come on," she said, barely noticing how bad Harte smelled as she took him under the arms and started to pull him up out of the hole.

Harte had lost so much weight in the days since she'd seen him that he felt almost skeletal in her arms. With every tug, a terrible keening erupted from his throat. It sounded awful, painful—not quite human. Still Esta didn't stop. With the cuff on her arm and the necklace in the pouch tucked close to her body, she kept going. As she pulled him little by little through the apartment, the jangling bells became more insistent, and then she heard new sounds coming from the storeroom. Someone was pounding on the trapdoor in the floor.

Esta ignored that threat as well. If she could only get Harte outside the building, it would be safer to use Ishtar's Key. On she went, steadily tugging him along, until they were in the narrow alleyway outside the small apartment.

Night had not yet descended, but the alley was tucked far enough back from the larger street that it lay deep in shadows. Only the faintest hum from the city beyond reached her there. Exhausted, Esta lowered Harte to the ground and saw that he was looking at her. His mouth was moving again, and this time she recognized the whisper of her name hissing from his lips.

"See you," he whispered, each word a rattling breath. "Once more . . ." And then he reached for her, but before he could touch her, his eyes fluttered closed and his hand went limp, falling away.

Esta leaned over him and for a long, terrible moment, she thought it was too late. "Damn you, Darrigan," she said, her words choked with her tears. She gave him a not-so-gentle shake until his chest rose and fell again. "Don't you dare die on me until I make you pay for leaving me on that train. Do you hear me?"

He lay silent, his breath ragged.

They needed to get somewhere with more space, somewhere that might still be open in—*how many years*? She wasn't sure. The street would be safer. A park if she could get that far.

"You hold on a little while longer, and I'm going get us out of here," she said, talking to him and to herself at the same time. She was trembling with the fear of what would happen if he died as she considered which way they should go.

"No . . ." The word came out as barely a whisper. Harte's eyes opened halfway. "Too late."

He was right and he wasn't. Maybe in 1904 it was too late for him, but now that Esta had Ishtar's Key, Harte had a chance.

"It's not even close to too late," she told him, pulling him up so his head could rest on her lap.

Harte groaned at the movement, his face crumpling in pain. "Seshat . . . gone . . ."

"She's gone?" Esta asked.

"Not yet." Harte's eyes seemed unfocused as he stared up at the starless sky. "But when I die—"

"You're not going to die."

His eyes found hers then, the stormy gray so familiar and so intent as they finally focused on her. "Thoth is coming. . . . Go. Leave—"

Esta choked back tears she could not stop from falling. "When have I ever taken orders from you?"

She felt the vibrations of what might have been a laugh shuddering through his chest. But then he gasped and looked up at her again. "I die . . . Seshat dies."

The realization of what Harte was saying made Esta go cold. If she was being honest with herself, she'd known that this had always been one answer. Originally, before she'd returned to the past and changed everything, Harte had died on the Brooklyn Bridge. Originally, the Book had been lost, and Seshat had never been a threat. Harte wasn't wrong. If he died now, the ancient goddess would be finished. The world would be safe. She had her cuff. She could go back, set things right before Nibsy could collect the artifacts. With them, Esta could possibly even find Jack and take back the Book.

And Harte would be gone.

It was an impossible choice—a single person for the world itself.

But Esta had the Quellant now, and she had her cuff. She knew how to get the artifacts back and she knew how to subdue Seshat. There was still a chance to save Harte *and* go back and set things right. She would not choose if there was still a possibility that she could do both.

From within the house, Esta heard a crash that told her time was running out. She gripped Harte around the midsection and pulled her affinity close, concentrating on the seconds and then beyond them, to the layers of years that were and would be. Searching.

A man appeared in the doorway, a satisfied smile drawing his thin mouth into a cruel curve. "Esta Filosik," he said, apparently not realizing what she was doing.

She didn't even bother to look up. All of her concentration was on searching for the right year. Too close and there might not be medicine advanced enough to save him. Too far, and Esta risked any number of things—including crossing the stones with one of her many previous trips through time.

"Mr. Grew sent us for you," the man said.

Maybe she should have cared that this man could take her to the Book. Maybe she should have allowed him to lead her directly to Jack, but Esta knew Harte wouldn't make it if she did.

"You can tell Jack Grew that he can go to hell," Esta growled, finally finding the place she wanted—a clearing, a flash of chrome, and the whirling brightness of neon lights—and she closed her eyes and focused all her affinity on that time and place. On the *possibility* that waited there.

The man lunged for her, but she rolled them both away, through the layers of time to the city that waited beyond. As she slipped through, Esta felt the darkness rise in her. Around her. *Consuming* her. Seshat's power felt weaker than before, but it was still more than Esta could control. The ground began to shake, tossing the man back as it cracked beneath his feet.

Power slammed through Esta, hot and potent and *so* satisfying, and suddenly she lost hold of the layers of time. The ground was still shaking beneath her, more violently now. She heard someone scream, a crash.

She knew it was Seshat, but she could not give up. Not when Harte's life was at stake.

With all of the strength she had, Esta shoved Seshat's power back as she pulled on her own affinity again. She felt Ishtar's Key heat danger-ously against her arm as she pushed through the layers. Another power was sliding alongside her own. The ground continued to tremble, and as a chasm opened beneath them, Esta found herself falling, not into the gap in the earth but through time once more as darkness swelled and the world began to crumble around her.

A NEW ALLIANCE

1902—New York

Viola sat with Jianyu at the edge of the small room at the rear of the house, listening to Abel Johnson explain the situation they were facing to his friends. The back room was crowded with people, like too many sardines in a can. The air was hot and close, and tempers were beginning to fray. Though Viola remained quiet in the corner, she did not miss how some of Abel's friends often turned, giving her sideways glances without hiding their unease. She tried hard not to care.

She and Jianyu, along with Theo, Cela, and to some extent, Abel, had spent the last few weeks waiting and planning, but things had changed, and now everything was moving too quickly. Thanks to Theo, they knew that in a matter of days the Order would bring the Delphi's Tear back into the city and install it within the inner chambers of their new head-quarters. If that was allowed to happen, the chances of ever retrieving the ring would become much more unlikely—maybe impossible. With the shortened timeline, it had become obvious that they needed help.

Abel had finished his explanations, but he hadn't quite come to his point. Viola could read the mood in the room, though. Already she sensed that things would not go so easily as Cela and Abel had assured her.

When Cela glanced back at the two of them, her expression was guarded. Cela had been cordial ever since Jianyu had woken, but Viola knew that Cela had still not forgiven her for attacking Jianyu. *For attacking* her.

Cela's constant suspicion grated, but Viola accepted it as her due. It was no more than she was used to, after all. Hadn't she lived with looks just as sharp for as long as she could remember—from her own family, and later from those in the Devil's Own who did not understand why Dolph should put so much trust in a woman? If a lifetime of judgment had not broken her, neither would Cela Johnson's. No matter how deserved that judgment might be.

"The bottom line is that this isn't our fight, Abel," the one called Joshua said with a frustrated sigh. He was a stout man, whose shirt stretched tight across his stomach whenever he moved. He was maybe a year or two older than Abel and had a quietness about him that Viola had appreciated when they'd first met more than a week ago. This quietness gave his words more weight somehow. "We have pressure coming at us from all sides with the strike looming in Philadelphia, and now you're asking us to go stirring up trouble with the Order? If we do that, we'll be putting a mark on the back of every Negro in this city."

"We're already wearing that mark," Abel said.

"Well, I damn sure don't need to make the one on my back any bigger," another man argued. He was older still, and his face wore the kind of weariness of someone who worked too much and for too little. His hair was tightly curled about his head and had a reddish cast when the light hit it.

"I understand, Saul," Abel said. "But maybe by working together, we can make those targets a little smaller. Maybe we don't have to fight alone."

"Or maybe helping these folks does the opposite," another said. "We have families of our own to protect."

Saul's wife, a woman with skin as dark and smooth as ebony, placed her hand on Saul's knee. Her hair had been pulled back from her narrow face in a serviceable braid, but the humidity of the day had it curling around her temples, not much different from what Viola's own hair was doing at that moment. "We got children, Abe. Are you really asking us to put them at risk for a fight that isn't even ours? I'm sorry, but Joshua and my husband are right. We can't get involved." She sounded sorry for it, but unwilling to be moved.

Joshua leaned forward again. His deep-set eyes looked like they had already seen too much. "Look, Abe, I know that you and your sister like these folks, and I'm sure that you want to help, but we have *real* issues to solve right now. We have the meeting with the steel workers next week. If we can't get them to open their labor union to our men, it's going to set us back at least ten years. You should be focused on those problems, not some treasure hunt."

"It's not a treasure hunt," Cela told them, speaking for the first time since they'd gathered.

"You're right," Aaron said. "What you're talking about is robbery."

"Cela, honey, we'd like to help, but not like this," said another woman from the end of the table. She was older than the others, with a broad face and a bosom to match. "You know what they would do to us if we were caught helping with this crazy plan of yours, don't you? More than a hundred people—*our own people*—were murdered last year in cold blood for doing nothing but trying to live. We're barely through May, and this year's numbers look every bit as bad. This here city is *still* simmering with unsettled anger from what happened less than two years ago after that plainclothes officer got himself killed."

"Because we aren't even allowed to protect our own women when a white man attacks them," Aaron added.

The woman nodded in agreement. "*You* know what we lost during those days." She pursed her narrow mouth. "Can you really ask us to risk starting all that up again?"

Cela kept her tone even, her gaze steady. "Hattie, I know exactly what *we* lost," she told the other woman, emphasizing the word in a way that made it seem almost personal, and Viola couldn't help but wonder what Cela and Abel *had* lost.

"Then you should know better to start trouble where there wasn't none before," the older woman told her, sitting back in her chair with her arms crossed, like the point was irrefutable.

Viola remembered the unrest two years before. A plainclothes police officer had been killed, and his death had started a chain reaction of violence. The trouble had been mostly kept to the Tenderloin, though, because the police's violence had been focused on the colored people who lived there. It hadn't really touched the Bowery, and it certainly hadn't touched her. And anyway, Viola'd had her own troubles at the time.

Cela's brother, Abel, had been listening quietly to the conversation without saying much, but he spoke now. "I can't ask any of you to step up and put your lives at risk for a cause you don't believe in," he said quietly. "But for better or worse, Cela and I are committed. If you aren't, I'll understand, and we won't hold that decision against you one bit. But if you don't want to be involved, I think it's best if you go now."

Uneasy silence descended over the room as Abel's friends suddenly seemed unwilling to look at one another. Aaron and his wife were the first to stand and go, taking their leave without apology or explanation. Three others followed, until it was only Cela, her brother, and Joshua. A moment later, though, Joshua stood as well, his cap in his hands.

"I'm sorry, Abel. I'd like to help, but . . ." He didn't finish. Simply turned and left with the rest.

The three of them seemed stuck in the silence, until the sound of a carriage pulling up broke through their stunned disappointment.

"That'll be Theo," Viola murmured as the reality of what they'd failed to accomplish struck her. They would be alone against the Order, and they weren't ready.

Cela went to let Theo in, and when she returned with him, he looked more troubled than usual. "Tell me you have good news," he said.

"I'm afraid not," Abel told him. There was still a bit of tension there between the two, Viola noticed. Abel held himself a little straighter, kept his voice a little more formal when Theo was around. He clearly hadn't forgotten the first time they'd met, on the corner in the Bowery, even with Theo's willingness to act as their spy.

"They're all cowards," Cela said. Her voice seemed to echo in the now-empty room. "Every one of them."

Abel sighed and looked at his sister. "They're not cowards, Cela, and you know it. Those are some of the bravest men I know, but I can't blame them one bit for not wanting to put their necks on the line for this," he told her. "And you shouldn't either."

"Of course I should," Cela started, but Jianyu placed his hand on her knee to steady her.

"Why?" Abel asked, his brows raised. "What exactly has any Mageus ever done for us except get you wrapped up in their messes?"

"We are grateful for your help," Jianyu said. "We understand that your friends have lives to protect."

Abel nodded, looking even more exhausted. "They're good people," he told Jianyu. "I think they wanted to help, but Negroes all across this country have a hard enough time these days without inviting more trouble."

"As though they're the only ones who suffer," Viola huffed, her words coming before she could think better of it. Once they were spoken, she felt immediately shocked that she had said them at all. They were words she had heard a hundred times before—her mother's words and her brother's. They were her family's sentiments, but they'd surprised her by coming from her own mouth.

"Viola—" Jianyu's voice was a warning now.

She felt every pair of eyes in the room upon her, especially Cela's and Abel's. Their understanding—their judgment of her—was clear. More, she knew it was *deserved*.

"I didn't mean—" But Viola wasn't sure that there was anything she could possibly say to retract the words. She *had* meant them, even after all the Johnsons had done for her and for Jianyu, and suddenly her cheeks felt warm with that knowledge. Irritation and shame all mixed together.

"Oh, I think we all know *exactly* what you meant," Cela said, sounding even cooler than before.

"Cela . . ." Abel looked even more tired now.

"Don't *Cela* me, Abel Johnson," Cela said. "You put your reputation on the line to ask for help. The least this one here could do is be a little grateful for it."

"We *are* grateful," Jianyu said, stepping in before Viola could respond. He cut Viola a quelling look. "It does not stop our disappointment, though."

Abel leaned back into his chair, as though he was too exhausted to stay upright any longer. "You have to understand their perspective. . . . What happens if this goes badly? Who pays the price?"

"It's not a risk any of us takes lightly," Jianyu acknowledged.

"But we don't all take that risk equally," Abel reminded him. "The Order will come for all of us if we fail, yes, but Hattie wasn't wrong when she spoke of the lynchings."

"My countrymen are hated as well," Viola argued. "When I was a girl, eleven were hanged in New Orleans." Her family had prayed for weeks, for the men who had died and for their own safety.

"This conversation isn't about *you*, though," Cela said. "We aren't talking about how your countrymen have suffered. We're talking about what's at stake right now if my brother's friends offer their help."

"You're not wrong," Abel told Viola. "But what you need to understand is that the decision that my friends and I make to help you is a decision that impacts more than our small circle. More than a *hundred* of my brothers were lynched last year alone. *Citizens* of this country were killed in broad daylight, and the authorities looked the other way—or they helped—usually over some white woman." He eyed Viola pointedly. "Mrs. Wells exposed the truth about that particular kind of violence a decade ago in the very paper owned by the man whose house you're now standing in, and it *still* happens with impunity."

"There's little point in comparing suffering," Theo said, his tone verging on dismissive. "Terrible things happen every day to many different people."

"Spoken by a boy born with a silver spoon," Abel said. "Don't you see? It's all related. All of us are implicated. You included, Barclay."

"What is that supposed to mean?" Theo asked.

"You don't think I saw the way you looked at me when we first met?

Or don't you remember?" Abel asked. His voice was soft, pleasant even, but there was no mistaking the steel in it. "I knew exactly what was going through your mind when you saw Viola getting into my carriage."

"I didn't . . . That is to say, I didn't mean anything." Theo looked momentarily stunned.

Abel shook his head. "In the end, the numbers don't matter. One or one hundred, each is a life stolen—a promise wasted—all because of ignorance and hate. That, and that *alone*, is why I haven't put a stop to Cela's determination to help you."

Cela cut a sharp look at her brother, but she didn't say anything against him.

Silence swelled in the room again. Tension thick and palpable threatened to overwhelm, but it was Theo who surprised Viola by breaking it.

"I do believe I owe you an apology," he told Abel.

Abel straightened his shoulders, pulling himself up to his full height. Waiting. They were all waiting to see if this fragile alliance would crack or crumble beneath the pressure of their differences.

"You're right," Theo admitted, rubbing at the back of his neck. "When we first met, I behaved rather badly, I'm afraid. And for no reason at all. There was no reason for me to regard you with any suspicion. You're right to point that out now."

"I appreciate you saying that, but it doesn't change the facts. You reacted like you did, and others will react the same. They always do." Abel looked to Viola. "The bottom line is that a lot of people in the Bowery can hide what they are—they can tuck their magic away and lie low until the winds change. My friends can't. There's no hiding the color of our skin, and we wouldn't want to anyway. They have every right to say no to what we're asking of them, even without those reasons."

Theo's apology hadn't eased the tension in the room. If anything, there was even more now than there had been before. They all seemed to be looking to Viola, expecting something from her. Her instinct was to push back against that expectation and against their *judgment*.

LISA MAXWELL

But then, Viola's instinct was *always* to push back. She'd pushed back against the weight of her family's expectations since she was young, hadn't she? It was as natural to her as breathing. She'd rejected their hatred of her magic. She'd rejected their control over her. Their hatred and judgment had driven her from home and led her to the Devil's Own.

A thought settled over Viola then, one that left her more than a little shaken. How was her family's hatred toward her affinity any different from their other hatreds? The words that she had just spoken, the thoughts that had just overwhelmed her, those were her *family's* thoughts—her mother's and her brother's. They judged anyone who didn't fit into the small view of the world as they knew and understood it. They found anyone wanting who wasn't like them. It wasn't only her magic they rejected. They looked down upon the whole world outside their narrow community and their singular way of life. And she had accepted those views like mother's milk.

How had she not seen this about herself before? How had she, who had believed so much in what Dolph hoped and worked for, somehow still managed to carry her family's narrow-mindedness deep within her. Unexamined. She'd somehow missed that the seeds of something too close to hate grew already deep in her heart.

Had Dolph known that about her all along? Perhaps he'd been right not to trust her completely, not to take her into his complete confidence, as he apparently had Jianyu. Her words, still hanging in the air, shamed Viola more than her family had ever been able to, and suddenly she felt the fight drain out of her, leaving her hollowed out. Empty.

"I'm sorry," she said, feeling her cheeks burn and her throat go tight. "After all you've done, after all we've asked of you . . ." No. That wasn't it. "Even if you'd done nothing at all to help us, my words—my thoughts—they shame me."

Cela frowned, as though confused, but the anger in her expression eased a little.

"I would understand if you want to walk away from this now," Viola told Cela. "If either of you wanted to."

"We don't have any plans to back out now," Cela said. Her expression had softened a little, but she was still frowning. "Right, Abel?"

"My sister's right. We promised our help already," Abel agreed. "We'll keep that promise."

"But you said—" Viola started.

"Everything I said is true," Abel told her. "But our family doesn't go back on our word once it's given. What's more, I wouldn't want to. Even with the danger we might face, I can see that there's something bigger going on here than our differences." He glanced at his sister. "Cela was right when she made the commitment to help Jianyu. Maybe we can't change everything, but Cela and me, we're gonna try to help you change this *one* thing. Neither of us is walking away."

WAKING

1952—San Francisco

Harte Darrigan couldn't recall much about what had happened to him since the night he'd escaped from the Committee and made his way to his father's house for the second time. He remembered standing across from the door he'd knocked on that first day he'd arrived in San Francisco, before everything had gone wrong. And he remembered waiting to see if anyone was home so he could get Esta's cuff and the necklace back. Everything after that felt like a dream—or perhaps, more like a nightmare. All of it seemed too impossible and too awful to be real.

Now that he was beginning to wake, Harte realized he wasn't dreaming. And he certainly wasn't dead—he was in too much pain for that. It felt like he'd been beaten and bruised from head to toe, pummeled over and over until the agony had turned to monotony. But the pain seemed far too pedestrian for damnation, so Harte figured that he'd survived. He had the vague recollection that Esta had something to do with it.

Esta.

He remembered more then—she'd come for him, as Seshat had predicted. She'd done something. . . . Harte couldn't remember what had happened next. If he was still alive, he knew that it must have been Esta who'd saved him, like she had too many times before. But the memory of Seshat's promise was clear in his mind.

She will come for you, and when she does . . . she will be mine.

Harte lurched upright in a panic—or he tried to. His muscles screamed as he lifted his head from the pillow, and he found himself too weak to actually move. There was something covering his face, but he managed to tear it away, and then he saw her.

Close to his bed, Esta was sleeping in a straight-backed chair, alive and whole and seemingly untouched by Seshat's power. Harte was almost afraid to move. If he did, the moment might shatter and reveal itself as a dream. She looked impossibly perfect with her dark lashes resting on her cheeks. Her chest rose and fell in a slow, steady rhythm, and Harte couldn't remember having ever seen her so still or relaxed. She looked almost peaceful.

No, he realized. She looked *exhausted*. Maybe it was the shadows that the garish light was casting over the planes of her face, but her skin looked too pale, and there were dark circles beneath her eyes.

She was no longer dressed in the men's clothing she'd taken to wearing in St. Louis. Her hair now curled about her face in a way that looked unbearably feminine, even with its short length, and her wide mouth had been painted a soft coral pink that made her lips look like petals against her tawny skin. If she weren't so far away from him, Harte would have taken her hand in his, just to feel the warmth of her. Just to be sure that this wasn't another hallucination.

At that thought, Harte sensed Seshat rumble within him, and he knew that whatever had happened, the ancient power hadn't given up. He knew, too, that Esta saving him had been a mistake, but somehow he couldn't quite bring himself to be sorry about it.

Harte shifted a little, trying to sit up, and the movement was enough to alert Esta. Her eyes flew open as she woke with a start, but it took a second for her to realize where she was. The emotions that crashed through her expression made him blurt out a laugh.

Damn. It *hurt* to laugh.

"I can't imagine what you could possibly find funny," she said, trying hard to scowl at him as she moved closer to his bedside.

Esta didn't sound angry, though. She sounded like she was about to cry, which was impossible, because his girl was tough as nails.

He tried to casually shrug off her question, but it hurt too damn much to move even a little. Instead, Harte allowed his head to loll back against the pillow. He took his time memorizing every inch of her face, as Esta brushed a lock of sweat-damp hair away from his forehead. Then he remembered the rest of what had happened—ever single one of his failures—with a terrible rush of certainty.

"I lost your cuff," he told her.

She was adjusting his covers, even though they were perfectly fine. "Yes, you did."

"You should have let me die for that fact alone," Harte told her, unable to meet her eyes.

Esta tilted her head to the side and considered him. "Probably . . ."

But she didn't sound even a *fraction* as furious as he'd imagined she would be. "You aren't angry?"

"Oh no," she told him with a tired sigh. "I'm absolutely livid. Furious, even."

She didn't sound furious. Harte wasn't sure *what* emotion was coloring her voice, but he didn't think he'd ever heard it there before.

"I should never have taken it," he told her.

"No, you absolutely should not have." Her mouth turned down a little, but she looked more sad than angry. "You *definitely* shouldn't have left without discussing it with me first. I thought we'd moved past all that. I thought we were partners."

"I know." He sighed. Then he swallowed what little pride a man could have while wearing a gown without any drawers beneath and completely at the mercy of a woman he'd wronged so badly. A woman he *loved.* "I was scared."

"I can handle Seshat," she told him.

He didn't know that she was right about that. Harte had the feeling that the ancient goddess hadn't even begun to show them what she was capable of, but he wasn't talking about Seshat. "I didn't leave because of Seshat," he admitted. "She was an excuse."

Esta was silent, her steady gaze urging him on.

"It was what I had to do here—what I had to face. About my past. About *myself*." The rush of words must have taken more oxygen than he'd expected, because suddenly Harte felt dizzy. He closed his eyes and tried to draw in a steadying breath, but that hurt as well.

"*Did* you face it?" she asked.

Harte considered that. "Maybe," he told her, feeling incredibly tired.

Nothing had gone right, but he understood something now that he hadn't before. Seeing his father through older, more experienced eyes had changed him. Maybe not completely, but something inside of him had shifted nonetheless. Meeting his brother had changed him even more.

When he opened his eyes again, Esta was staring at him. "You'll tell me about it later." It was a command and a threat all at once.

"I didn't get the Dragon's Eye," he told her. Another failing. Another regret.

"I didn't get the Pharaoh's Heart," she said with a shrug. "I had the Book in my hands and I lost that, too."

"You had the Book?" Harte started to sit up again, but a wave of dizziness overtook him.

"It doesn't matter," Esta said as though their entire existence hadn't been focused on this one goal. "We'll get it. We'll get all of the artifacts. And we'll go back and fix our mistakes." Worry darkened her eyes once more. "But first you have to get well."

"So you *don't* want to murder me?" he asked carefully.

Esta let out a sigh that sounded like nothing more than simple weariness and exhaustion as she took his hand, rubbing her thumb in gentle circles. He felt so awful that the friction was almost painful, and Seshat's power still rustled softly, somewhere down in the depths. Perhaps he should have pulled away, but Seshat still felt very far off and every bit as weak as he was, and Esta was touching him—and she wasn't even strangling him.

"It's not exactly satisfying to kill someone who's already half-dead," Esta told him. A small smile curved at the corner of her full mouth, but her golden eyes still seemed far too sad. "I've decided to wait a while, until you're a little stronger. I want to make sure it's *really* worth the effort."

It wasn't the reaction Harte had expected, and he wondered if this was another dream—a feverish delusion brought on by desire and hope and desperation. "I'll deserve whatever you have planned for me."

He meant every word.

A noise from the hallway had Esta sitting up a little straighter.

"Someone's coming." She pulled her hand away from his, leaving the spot she'd been touching cold. "There's so much I haven't explained to you. . . . Don't tell them anything you don't need to. In fact, it might be easier if you pretend you can't remember what happened. I'll be back once they're gone."

Esta was gone before he could stop her—not that he actually could have stopped her. He wasn't exactly moving that quickly. Or at all.

A moment later, the curtain around his bed drew back to reveal a clean-shaven man in a white overcoat wearing thick, dark-rimmed spectacles. He was flanked by another man in a dark-green suit coat and a woman dressed in a light-blue gown with a white apron and a white, winged cap on the crown of her head. Her attire reminded him a little of something a nurse might wear, but he didn't think that could possibly be right, considering that her skirts were nearly up to her knees.

"I see you've decided to return to the living, Mr. Jones," the man in the white coat said in a kind of jocular tone. "I'm Dr. Calderone, and this is Mr. Fisk and Nurse Bagley. She's taken good care of you these past few weeks. Mr. Fisk here is a government man, but I suppose we won't hold that against him, will we?"

Harte wasn't sure what he was supposed to say to that, so he didn't respond.

The doctor looked over a clipboard that held a stack of papers, conferring with the other man as he flipped through them, while the nurse busied herself by tending to Harte. He tried to shoo her away, but he'd grown so weak that there wasn't much he could do besides suffer the indignity of having himself lifted and rolled as the sheets were changed out beneath him.

After a few long minutes, the doctor peered at Harte through his thick lenses. "You're a lucky man to still be here, you know."

"I can't say I feel particularly lucky," Harte grumbled, wishing the doctor would leave so that he could figure out where Esta had disappeared to. *She promised to come back,* he reminded himself. Seshat had not taken her, and he hadn't lost her. That thought alone would have to get him through the next few minutes.

"I suspect you feel like something dragged out of the bay," the doctor told him with a smile that didn't match the sentiment of his words. "Considering how close you were to death, I'd say that's to be expected. For a while there, I had my doubts you'd pull through. The whole thing was a crapshoot, trying to figure out how to treat you. Of course we read about certain diseases in medical school, but I'm not ashamed to admit that you're the first case of plague I've ever treated. Actually, I believe yours is the first case we've seen in the city for decades."

"Forty-six years," specified Mr. Fisk. "The Committee eradicated that particular disease in 1906."

Forty-six years.

Harte had to have misheard. . . .

Since he'd opened his eyes, his thoughts had been so focused on Esta and on the pain that he felt that he hadn't noticed his surroundings. Now the strangeness of everything started to sink in—the cut of the man's suit, the transparent tubes that hung around him, and the steady whirring of some electric machine next to his bed that looked like one of the futuristic exhibits at the world's fair.

The doctor was still prattling on about something, but Harte couldn't hear anything the man was saying. His mind was racing, an urgent jumbled mess of memories tumbling through it as he tried to remember, but the one thought that came to him again and again was *What did Esta do?*

BLOOD IN THE VEIN

After the unsettling discovery of her own craven weaknesses, Viola remained quiet for the rest of the day. She sat and she listened, but she didn't interject much as the others planned for the few remaining days ahead. What was there to say that could make anything better? They would get the ring because they had to. It would be harder without the help of Abel's friends, but if they positioned themselves just right, it might still be possible to sidestep Nibsy, and Paolo as well. To *win*.

It was late—far too late—by the time Viola realized how many hours had passed. The streets were already mostly empty of carriages and people, and night was beginning to fall. If she didn't hurry, her brother would miss her. He might have questions that she couldn't answer without ruining the tenuous grasp they had on the possibility of victory.

"I have to go," she told the others, gathering herself to leave.

"I'll take you," Theo said, also standing.

"No," she told him. "Stay. You should finish things here. You're needed."

"Take my carriage at least?"

Viola didn't want to. Every time she stepped into the soft interior of Theo's carriage, she thought of Ruby, and for now—while things were still so fragile—she couldn't be distracted. Still . . . without the carriage, she would certainly be late. "Thank you," she told him.

"I'll walk you out," Theo said.

"Let me," Cela told him. "You stay here and finish."

The two women had built a fragile truce between them in the weeks before this, but their argument earlier had shaken something loose in Viola, something that she couldn't put back in the place it had once been. Now that she was faced with the prospect of speaking with Cela alone, Viola felt suddenly nervous.

Cela led the way toward the front of the house in silence, and Viola wished she could find an excuse to avoid the conversation that was about to happen.

"You were awful quiet today," Cela said when they reached the small vestibule before the front door. "I mean, after we had words."

"It seemed better to listen," Viola said truthfully. *And to think . . .*

Cela nodded, as though agreeing. Then she let out a long sigh. "I don't know that I like you, exactly," Cela told her, "but I want you to know that I don't bear you any ill will. Jianyu trusts you, so I'm willing to trust you too. I'm willing to start again, if you are."

It was a bit of grace that Viola did not feel she deserved.

"I owe you an apology," she told Cela softly.

Cela simply stared at her, quiet and waiting, not giving so much as an inch.

When Viola had aimed Libitina back in Morgan's ballroom, she'd thought she was doing the right thing. Later, she'd told herself that she hadn't known who Cela was. How could she have known that Jianyu would be working with a brown-skinned girl? But now she wondered how she could have been so shortsighted. Now she wondered why she had aimed to kill. Had it been from desperation or the heat of the moment? Or had Viola taken one look at Cela in the rumpled servant's uniform and seen only the other girl's brown skin and curling hair? Had Viola heard her mother's voice in her ears, as she had earlier today?

She couldn't know for sure, but if Jianyu had not stepped in front of her blade, Viola might never have thought anything of what she'd done. If she had not heard Abel speak a little while before, she might never have wondered why she'd made that particular choice. And she would have been worse off for it.

"I can't take back the things I've done," Viola said finally.

In response, Cela's brows rose and her lips quirked as though to say, *That's not much of an apology.*

Viola bit back an answering smile at the other girl's backbone. Cela was right. "I *am* sorry for what I did," Viola told her. "For what I assumed about you, and for the ugliness in my heart that day. You and your brother," she said. "Your kindness and your bravery . . . it humbles me. I will work to be worthy of it."

"It's not about working for it," Cela said with a frown. "Everybody's worthy from the moment they're born, and maybe if more people understood that, we'd have a lot less ugliness in this world."

The words struck an odd chord in Viola, one that vibrated through her in ways she wasn't ready to hear.

Before Viola could respond, Cela frowned. "I'm betting everything I have on the two of you, you know. I'm trusting you to keep Abel safe."

"I will do anything in my power to see that you and your brother come to no harm," Viola said.

"I'm going to hold you to that." Cela gave Viola a small nod before she went back to join the others, a sign that maybe the future between the two of them didn't have to be so fraught with tension.

By the time Theo's driver finally dropped Viola off back in the Bowery that night, it was much later than she'd intended it to be, far later than was acceptable or easily explainable, and she could only hope that her brother was too busy to notice. Her hopes were dashed, though, when she stepped through the back kitchen entrance and saw her brother waiting. With him were Johnny the Fox and another of his lackeys, Razor Riley.

"So nice of you to finally join us, Viola," Paolo said. "I imagine you have a reasonable explanation for where you disappeared to for so long."

She lifted her chin, defiant. "I went out."

"Out . . ." Paolo's tone was dangerously amused. "I'm afraid you'll have to do better than that, little sister."

Torrio smirked at her. "She was probably with her friends on 127th Street."

Viola couldn't stop her eyes from widening. She'd thought she'd been careful, but the Fox was wearing a triumphant look on his ugly face. She'd thought she had everything under control—Nibsy and Paolo and the danger the Order posed. But if her brother knew about Cela and Abel . . .

"Ah yes, the eggplants you've been visiting." Paolo flicked his cigarette to the ground, then snuffed it out with the sole of his polished shoe. "When, *exactly*, were you planning to tell me about them?"

She took an instinctive step back.

It was such a stupid thing to say. *Eggplants.* It had been a joke in her family, a bit of absurdity that they'd used between themselves to pretend they were only having a bit of fun. It wasn't hatred. It wasn't the sort of evil you had to confess to Father McGean before you went to mass. It was a *joke*.

But it wasn't. It never had been.

It turned Viola's stomach now to realize how easily she'd been a part of that ugliness, how easily she'd allowed herself to use their hatred as a way to belong. When her family had arrived in this country, they'd had so many troubles—and for no reason at all. They'd been hated by the pale Germans who had long ago made themselves into members of the community, and by the freckled Irish who already spoke English when they stepped from the boat. They were too strange with their rosary beads, too dark, too unwanted, and so her family had reveled in the small knowledge that it could be worse. That at least they were better than some.

Viola had never thought anything of that reasoning, because when her mother and her brother were talking about others, they weren't focused on her. They weren't focused on *her* faults or the whispers that followed *her* through the streets, strange, unnatural girl that she was.

She'd been wrong to go along with their ugly joking. Viola saw that now so clearly, but there was nothing she could do. It wasn't the time to correct Paolo, because the word he used was nothing compared to the threat behind it—the knowledge it implied and the sure danger it meant for Cela and Abel.

"I don't know what you're talking about, Paolo. And anyway, you listen to this one now?" she asked, jerking her chin at Torrio in a show of defiance. Hoping that he didn't scent her terror. "I thought it was the other way around?"

Torrio's eyes glinted in a way she didn't like. *He knows too much.*

Paul ignored the slight. "Now, now, mia sorella, the time for lies is at its end. I've given you too much room to run free, I think, and now it's time we talk about how you're going to repay me."

"What is it you want from me?" Viola asked, fighting to keep her composure, even as her mind was already spinning.

"I want the thing that everyone wants, Viola. I want the ring James Lorcan is so keen to have." Paolo shrugged. "I also want to make Lorcan sorry for trying to double-cross me with that blaze in Tammany's firehouse, and I want the Order to pay for what they tried to do to me at the gala. I want their precious treasures, and I want their power, and unless you want your friends uptown to find their way into the river, you're going to help me get it."

Viola had been trying to protect her brother from Nibsy Lorcan because she'd still been holding on to what she'd been raised to think about family. Blood wasn't water. Blood was *important.* Family was all that a person could rely on when the world would rather see you dead. . . .

Except, that sentiment wasn't exactly true. Viola was more than the blood in her veins—she *would* be more. Perhaps she had been too late to save Dolph, but she would not let Paolo touch Cela or Abel. She would not let her brother touch Theo or Jianyu. Even if it broke her mother's heart in two, even if it severed any connection to her family or her past, Viola vowed that she would destroy Paolo herself.

NOT NEGOTIABLE

1952—San Francisco

Nearly *fifty years*. Esta had cost Harte almost half a century. It seemed an impossible amount of time to lose. Harte knew people who didn't even get to count that many years in a single lifetime.

"Mr. Jones?" The doctor was frowning down at him. "I asked whether you have any other questions for me."

Harte had a million questions, but none that this particular man could answer. He shook his head and closed his eyes, wishing they would leave him be. He needed to see Esta. He needed to understand. Eventually, the ruse worked. The two men left, but unfortunately, the *click-clack* of the nurse's heeled shoes remained.

"We'll have you fixed up in no time," she clucked. "More fluids and plenty of rest, and you'll be out of here before you know it."

Harte wanted to be out of there *now*.

Allowing his eyes to open a crack, he watched the nurse as she fluffed his pillow and checked on a tube that seemed to be attached to his arm. He hadn't noticed that before either. Now he could almost feel the ache from where a gleaming silver needle had been inserted into his bruised skin. It connected to translucent tubing that wound up to a glass bottle hanging above him.

"Would you like me to fetch your wife?" the nurse asked before she went.

"My *wha*—" Harte caught himself before he finished. "My *wife* . . ." The word felt strange in his mouth, especially when it was connected to Esta. And yet the *rightness* of it rocked through him. Considering what he was, what his affinity could do, the idea of ever being married had not seemed realistic. It *still* wasn't realistic, but somehow he couldn't stop the idea from taking root.

"Well, it's not visiting hours for a little while yet, but the poor lamb has been so worried about you that I think we could make an exception."

"Yes," Harte said, trying to keep his voice measured. "Please. I'd very much like to see my . . . my *wife*."

"Only for a few minutes, mind you," the nurse tutted, waggling her finger at him playfully. "Dr. Calderone has ordered plenty of rest, and we can't go against the doctor's orders."

It didn't take long for the nurse to return with Esta, but it might as well have been hours.

"Just a little while, now," Nurse Bagley reminded them as she escorted Esta to Harte's bedside.

Now that Esta was standing and Harte had the time to look, he allowed himself to really take in what she was wearing—her full skirt was a soft lavender blue that came only to midcalf, and her cream-colored blouse was capped by a soft-looking woolen cardigan that skimmed the curves of her body. It cut in at her waist and accentuated her figure better than any corset he'd ever seen her in. It was enough to make him completely lose his train of thought.

"Thank you," Esta told the nurse, her hands clasped demurely before her as she looked at him. But the tightness in her eyes didn't match her words.

Harte waited until he heard the *click* of the door closing behind Nurse Bagley before he trusted himself to speak. "You look—"

"We have to go," Esta said, launching into action. She was at his bedside in an instant.

"What's going on?" he asked. The warmth that had been curling inside of him went suddenly cold with the understanding that something was clearly wrong.

"I don't know, but something," she told him. "Three carloads of men in suits just arrived. I saw them pull up while the doctor was in here, and I don't think they're coming for visiting hours." She pulled back the covers for him and helped him sit up. "Do you think you can walk?"

"Honestly? I'm not certain." His weakness galled him, but Esta was gone before Harte could so much as complain, and before he could blink, she was back with a wheelchair. He tried to stand, but instead swayed on unsteady legs and ended up back where he started on the bed.

"Let me help you," she said, even as he tried to bat her away. She didn't leave him much choice, though. Before Harte could argue, Esta secured him under his arm like he was some sort of invalid, which he supposed he was. But the truth of the matter didn't make that fact any easier to swallow as she helped him into the chair.

Within him, he felt Seshat starting to rouse, stretching like a cat that had woken from a long nap. She felt like a shadow of herself, but Harte flinched away from Esta all the same.

"She's still there?" Esta asked.

Harte nodded as he pulled the needle from his arm. To his relief, it didn't bleed much, but it wasn't enough of a distraction. Within his skin, he felt Seshat growing ever more aware of Esta's presence, and Harte understood that nothing had changed. She might be weakened, as he was, but she wasn't gone. And she wouldn't stay weak for long.

"You should go," Harte told her, knowing that there was no way he could get out of the hospital under his own power and no way he could allow Esta to help him now that Seshat was waking.

Esta ignored him. She'd already taken a leather pouch from her handbag and was busy looking through it for something. Finally, she seemed to find it, and she withdrew a small white tablet that reminded him of the quinine he'd taken as a boy to ward off fever. She offered it to him. "This should help."

"What is that?" he asked, eyeing the tablet.

"You're not going to like it if I tell you, so maybe it's better if I don't," she said.

Harte narrowed his eyes at her—or he tried to. He suspected that he was currently too pathetic-looking to intimidate anyone, not that he'd ever managed to intimidate Esta anyway. "Why would I take something I'm not going to like?"

"Because you trust me."

He couldn't help but wonder if her earlier quip about waiting until he was well before she killed him had any merit to it.

She let out an impatient breath, clearly frustrated at his hesitation. "It's a type of Quellant."

That was a surprise. "Isn't that what the Antistasi used in St. Louis?"

"Yes," she told him. "But Maggie improved the formulation. This version won't knock you unconscious, but it will still block your affinity—and it should block Seshat's power as well."

Harte didn't like the idea of willingly giving up his affinity—however much a bother it had been for him—but the idea that the Quellant might mute Seshat's power? He tried to remember back to St. Louis. . . . He couldn't be sure, but it did seem like Seshat had gone silent when the Antistasi had doused him with the Quellant. If Esta was right, taking the tablet might protect her from Seshat. That alone would be worth the risk.

His instincts screamed against taking the tablet, but he ignored them and swallowed it down before he could allow himself to second-guess the idea. The effect was immediate and awful. It wasn't only the bitterness that filled his mouth but the cold numbness that flooded through him, drawing his affinity away until he felt hollowed out. But in that emptiness, he sensed . . . nothing. No stirring of power. No rasping, ancient laughter. It was almost a relief.

"Well?" Esta asked.

"It might have worked," Harte told her, afraid to be too sure in case he was wrong.

"There's one way to find out." Esta offered him her hand.

Harte hesitated. Every time he touched Esta, he was giving Seshat another opportunity to make good on her threat.

"Harte?" Esta asked, frowning.

"If we're wrong, I won't be able to hold her back," he admitted, hating himself for his weakness. "She wants you, Esta. She's not going to stop trying, and I can't—"

"It will be okay," Esta said, offering her hand again. "Trust me, Harte."

He wanted nothing more than to do just that—to reach for her, to take her hand. It seemed such a small thing, such a normal, inconsequential action, but for Harte Darrigan, touching someone had always been complicated. The goddess living within his skin made everything even more dangerous. Especially for Esta. He couldn't risk her life. He couldn't chance losing her—not now.

"You should go on without me," he said, still staring at her offered hand. Her fingers were long and graceful, the fingers of a pickpocket who'd never been caught. "It isn't worth the risk."

"You've already taken the Quellant," she said. "If it's not going to work, better to know now."

Before he could stop her, Esta grabbed his hand. Her skin felt warm and soft as her fingers closed around his, and then the sound of the room drained away, leaving the world silent, and then . . . nothing. Seshat didn't so much as shift inside of him. The emptiness grated against his already weak body, but for the first time in *ages*, he felt only himself.

"It worked," Harte whispered, barely able to believe it could be possible. It had been so long since he had touched *anyone* without holding back, but it had been especially too long since he'd touched Esta. He tightened his fingers around hers, afraid to let himself wonder what this new development meant for him. Maybe, *just maybe*, this was actually an answer. Maybe it could buy him a little more time, because now that he wasn't dead and gone, Harte Darrigan realized again how much he wanted to live.

Esta let out a shaking breath that made him suspect she'd been every bit as nervous and unsure. "You know what this means?" she asked.

It meant that he could kiss her again. . . .

"I can take you back to 1902," Esta said, apparently thinking of something else entirely. "We can stop the Thief and the Antistasi and the Defense Against Magic Act. We can set everything back the way it's supposed to be. We can make things *right*."

Harte tried to ignore the pang of disappointment he felt at her words. But Esta was right. They should be focusing on what they'd set out to do, not on what it would feel like to press his mouth against hers. But then another thought occurred to him.

"Esta, you know we can't cross the stones," he told her.

"If we can get the Book back from Jack, we won't have to," she told him. "We can use it to—"

"How are we even supposed to *find* Jack? It's been nearly fifty years!"

"You know about that," Esta said, looking suddenly uneasy.

"I know," Harte agreed. "But I don't understand why."

"I didn't have a choice," she explained. "You were so sick, and you needed antibiotics—penicillin. It's a type of drug that can cure infections, even really awful infections, like the one you had." Esta pressed her lips together before she spoke again, more determined now. "It was the only way, Harte."

"You could have left me there," he told her. "You *should* have. If I died, Seshat would have disappeared right along with me. It would have been so much easier—"

"Don't," Esta told him, her voice sharp now. "Don't you dare say that I should have just sat there and watched you die. You are *not* negotiable. Not for me."

He stared at her, shocked by the emotion in her voice, and fought the urge to argue that she was wrong. But he couldn't bring himself to do it. Greedy bastard that he was, Harte wanted her to feel for him even a small bit of what he felt for her. He wanted her to need him, wanted to *be needed*. Not for the cuff he'd taken, but for himself.

The truth was that no one had ever needed *him*—not his mother or Paul Kelly. Not even Dolph Saunders. They'd each needed his power.

They'd needed what he could do for them. He understood now that he'd taken Esta's cuff because he'd been worried that he, alone, wouldn't be enough to draw her back. But her words erased that worry. She hadn't come back for the cuff. She'd come back for *him*.

Harte wished that he could freeze this moment, or bottle the feeling bubbling up inside of him. Even for a little while. Because he knew it couldn't possibly last.

"That goes both ways, you know," he said when he finally trusted himself to speak without betraying everything he felt.

He thought that he'd succeeded in hiding the true depth of his emotions. His voice had been steady, easy even, but suddenly Esta's cheeks went pink and her eyes went soft.

"We'll figure it out," she told him. She was already pulling away from him, as though the terrible rawness of the moment had been too much for her. "Seshat and the Book and the artifacts—we'll figure out all of it. But first we need to get out of here."

Still holding his hand, Esta pushed the chair into the hallway and then through the hospital's corridors. Their gleaming white floors were filled with nurses in skirts so short that not even madams would have worn them in public. Esta released time long enough to take the elevator down, and Harte couldn't help but notice that there wasn't an operator in the empty car. Esta simply pressed one of the buttons that lined a panel near the door, and the machine began to move.

The nurses, the machinery, they were all indications of how much the world had changed in the years he'd lost. *In the years I've gained,* he thought ruefully. Forty-eight years. A lifetime.

As the doors opened at the bottom floor, the world went quiet again, and Esta pushed Harte through the still, silent lobby, dodging around people frozen in time. Harte didn't miss the men Esta had noticed arriving earlier. They were unmistakable with their dark suits. Familiar silver medallions gleamed on their lapels, and at the sight of them, Esta moved faster.

"Did you see them?" she asked, as she continued on toward the hospital's exit.

"You were right. They look like trouble."

"But did you see what they were *wearing*?" she asked. "Those medallions on their coats?"

"Like the Jefferson Guard," Harte realized. "Do you think it's the Society? It's been so long. . . ."

"Maybe, but it could be any one of the other Brotherhoods," Esta said. "What we did in St. Louis brought them together back in 1904. It doesn't look like much has changed in nearly fifty years," she told him, grimacing.

Then she pushed his chair out into the night air.

If Harte had thought he was ready for what waited for him beyond the hospital, he'd been wrong. The scene outside was like something that not even the inventors and scientists at the world's fair could have imagined. The streets were smooth ribbons of black, completely devoid of horses and packed instead with machines painted in every color imaginable. They were nothing like the motorcars he'd gawked at back in St. Louis at the Palace of Transportation. Those machines were as square and boxy as a wagon, but these machines? They seemed more like sculptures than vehicles, impossible art forged from metal as smooth as water and crystalline glass.

They *gleamed*. Bright silver glinted off each curve of them, and their bodies shone like the paint was still wet. And the buildings. In New York there had been one or two buildings that scraped at the sky, but they'd stood apart, like sentinels above the rest of the city—not like this. In the years that had passed, San Francisco had become enormous. The hospital itself was a massive brick structure that rose at least ten stories above him. *And the lights.* Broadway had glowed at night, but everywhere Harte looked, electric lights flashed and twinkled even more brightly.

It all felt like too much, and yet . . . it was *perfect*. All Harte could do was stare in wonder and horror and awe. The world around him was new and unknown and *perfect*. It was right there—so close to being *his*. So was Esta.

But only for a little while.

Harte reached back and put his hand over hers as he looked up at her, and Esta's expression flickered to concern as she inquired whether he was okay. He nodded but couldn't figure out how to put all the things he wanted to say in words that would make any sort of sense. Esta seemed to understand, though. Wordlessly, she paused to let their fingers intertwine as the city continued to spin around them. For a moment the world was distilled down to the two of them. Harte felt only the warmth of her skin, the strength beneath, and not any of the rumbling power that had dogged him since he'd touched the Ars Arcana in the Order's vaults.

Then something shifted in Esta's expression. Her eyes had softened and gone glassy, but now she blinked resolutely as her entire posture seemed to stiffen with resolve. He could feel her pulling away from him, even while their hands remained clasped. "We'll need to find somewhere to lie low," Esta told him. "Maybe a hotel or—"

"Esta." Harte squeezed her hand gently, and she went silent and stopped walking. "Thank you."

He felt her relax a bit. Her golden eyes softened, and she gave him a small nod. All the things that Harte wanted to say hung in the silence between them, but before he could figure out where to begin, the moment had passed.

"We should go," she said, blinking again as though to will away any hint of tears. "If those men back at the hospital were there for us, they'll have figured out that we've left by now, and the Quellant won't last forever." She released his hand and started pushing the chair again.

As they began to move again, Harte felt a wave of exhaustion sweep over him. Esta was right. Her words were a reminder that freedom wasn't possible anymore—not for him. Maybe it never had been. The men with medallions glinting on their lapels were sure signs that the wonders of the world around him would always remain out of reach. So, too, would

Esta. The Quellant she'd given him would soon wear off, and Seshat still prowled within his skin.

Now more than ever, perhaps, Harte knew that he would not allow the goddess to touch Esta. The time would come when they would run out of the Quellant, and if that happened before they managed to control Seshat, Harte would do whatever he had to in order to keep Esta safe and whole. He would give his life, and gladly, if it meant that Esta would be able to go on without the threat of Seshat's power. But as he watched the lights shine and listened to the automobiles slide along, as he caught the clean, floral scent of Esta's soap in the air, Harte Darrigan wondered how he would ever bear to let it all go.

INESCAPABLE

1952—Washington, DC

Jack Grew slammed the phone onto its receiver so hard that the bell within vibrated at the impact. The news he'd just received had anger curling hot and furious in his blood.

They'd managed to lose Darrigan and Esta. *Again.*

All the resources Jack had bestowed upon the various Brotherhoods— the Committee especially—all the investment he'd made in waiting so patiently for so long, and the idiots in California had managed to let Esta and the Magician escape. The patient in question had been admitted to the hospital weeks ago, but no one had noticed that the man matched Darrigan's description until earlier that day. Jack should have left immediately, but from all accounts, the patient was in no shape to go anywhere. Instead, he'd trusted the Committee's watchmen to do the work he'd been destined to do, and they'd let Darrigan escape. Again.

Jack walked across his office to the broad table that contained a map of the entire country. He studied the shoreline of California, tracing it with a single fingertip as though he could touch Darrigan from afar. It was too bad he couldn't transport himself there, through the power of his thoughts alone.

They were still there, he knew, looking at the curve of the bay as it cut into the California coastline. *Right there.* Somewhere in the hills of that city—waiting for him to discover them. He returned to his desk and made a quick call. The plane would be ready within the hour, and by evening, he would be in San Francisco taking care of things personally, once and for all.

Jack Grew had always known Darrigan and Esta would resurface. Even when his advisers had wanted to pull back from the project, even when the various chairmen of the various Brotherhoods had wondered if his ongoing surveillance program had persisted long enough, Jack understood what Esta Filosik was capable of, and he knew that the work he was doing would pay off. He hadn't expected to wait nearly fifty years, of course. But the sureness within him, the voice that guided his every victory, had counseled patience . . . and once again it had proven correct.

He walked around the large model, examining all that he had accomplished in the lifetime he'd lived so far. The country spread out before him, the hills and valleys, rivers and streams all in perfectly rendered relief, and among them a series of pins dotting the landscape in an inescapable net. His life's work. His final victory. Each pinpoint of blue was a tower already built and ready to be armed. Each pinpoint of red was a tower nearing completion. When they were finally connected, their power would create an impermeable net across the entire country, collecting feral magic better than the Brink ever could and destroying any maggots who still managed to hide themselves away from the righteousness of the law.

A knock came at the door, and Hendricks ducked his head through the opening. "The car is here for you, Mr. President."

"Good," Jack said, still relishing the way the title sounded after all these years. "I'll be there in a minute."

When Hendricks was gone, Jack turned back one last time to examine the map. Perhaps it was time, finally, to bring his great creation to life. Darrigan could try to run, but he would never escape. Wherever Seshat was hiding, her power would finally, *finally* be his.

PART

IV

THE CHANGED CITY

After they escaped from the hospital, Esta managed to find them a safe room at a decent hotel fairly quickly. It was easy enough to use her affinity to dodge behind the counter, lift a key, and adjust the paper ledgers to make it seem like they'd paid.

The next day, she searched the local paper for news of their escape from the hospital, but she found no mention of it. If the Brotherhoods knew that Esta and Harte were in the city, they hadn't publicized that knowledge. That fact didn't make Esta feel any better, though. The Society and the Syndicate had allowed the public to continue believing that the Thief was dead, even while they were searching for her at the Curtis Brothers' Show. Still, as long as the entire city wasn't searching for them, they had some time for Harte to recuperate. And he needed it.

For the next few weeks, they stuck close to the hotel as Harte grew stronger. As stir-crazy as she might have felt, Esta didn't go out for much more than food or supplies. At first, she'd been afraid to leave Harte for more than a couple of minutes because he'd still been so weak, and then later because there was a part of her that worried he would disappear again if she looked away. But as the days passed, their routine grew more familiar, and the room became a kind of den, a safe nest away from the dangers that had been dogging them for so long. Even Seshat had remained quiet. The goddess seemed to understand that her fate was tied to Harte's and that Harte needed to heal. In the peace of those long days, Esta found it too easy to imagine that the whole world was contained in that small room, and there were moments when she could almost forget what still lay ahead for them—and for her, especially.

Then, about three weeks later, everything changed.

She and Harte had been sitting together on the couch in an easy, companionable silence, when Esta woke from an unintended nap and discovered that it was later than she'd realized. Harte had dozed off too. She started to lift herself from the couch carefully, so as not to wake him, but his eyes fluttered open.

"I should get going," she told him. "We need dinner, and I—"

"Later," he said softly, tracing his finger across the back of her hand.

It was barely anything, the lightest fluttering of skin, warm and sure, against hers. But it was the first time he'd made a move to touch her on purpose since they'd settled in the hotel, and the shock of his skin made Esta's breath catch.

"Stay a while longer," he said, his gray eyes calm as the morning fog.

"The deli on the corner will close soon," she explained.

"I'm not really hungry."

"You will be, and even if you aren't, you'll need to eat," she told him. "I know you're feeling better, but you have a ways to go. You're still so thin."

"I'm not sick anymore, Esta," Harte murmured.

But Esta noticed the angles of his cheekbones and the way his collarbones jutted sharply beneath the soft cotton of his shirt, and she could only see how close she'd come to losing him.

"I'm okay," he told her gently. "You don't have to keep worrying about me."

"Fine." She tried to pull away, confused and embarrassed by the rush of emotions she felt, but he pinned her hand more firmly with his. He was right. She knew that. Harte didn't need her to take care of him anymore, not like he had in those early days. "Let me go, Harte," she said, her voice barely a whisper.

"Not yet," he said. He lifted his hand to cup her cheek. He might have said he wasn't hungry, but his eyes told a different story.

"Darrigan . . . ," she warned, but the catch in her voice betrayed her.

His face came closer, and Esta couldn't move. Didn't want to. In the days that had followed their escape, she'd barely thought about anything but making sure he stayed well, grew stronger. She'd cared for him like a nurse for a patient, never letting herself see him as a man—as himself. But now something essential seemed to have changed between them.

He paused, waiting for her consent, and she knew that if she let him come any closer, if she allowed him to press his lips against hers, there would be no turning back.

"We can't stay here forever," she told him, still not pulling away.

"But we can stay right now. We can for a little while longer," he replied, his breath warm against her lips.

"Can we?" she asked, and she found she really didn't know the answer. They had so much ahead of them to accomplish. And Esta had not forgotten what happened in Denver, the too-clear warnings time had issued.

In answer, Harte pressed his mouth against hers, soft and firm all at once, and every cell in her body seemed to sigh. It felt like she'd been swimming underwater, without air, for *so long*, and now she'd finally surfaced.

Esta could not stop herself from letting Harte pull her into the kiss. Her mouth opened slightly, and their breath intermingled, warm and sweet and so right that she thought she might shatter. She felt the warm slide of his tongue against her lips, and then, as she opened farther for him, it was over. He pulled away, his eyes wide with something that might have been pain or might have been fear.

"She's back," Esta said, knowing immediately what had put that expression on Harte's face. Seshat had been quiet, so they'd been saving the Quellant, but they should have known better. It had been too much to hope that Seshat's absence could have been permanent.

He scooted away from her, and then he stood and went to the window as he ran a shaking hand through his already rumpled hair. His eyes were stormy now. "I shouldn't have touched you. I should have known better."

"We both should have . . ." She never should have allowed it. They couldn't risk everything for something as silly as kissing—even if in that moment kissing felt more essential than anything.

The heat in Harte's eyes made Esta's throat go tight, and she knew they'd reached a turning point that couldn't be ignored. They couldn't stay there, in that room—in that time—avoiding their responsibilities any longer. Nibsy could still be out there searching for the stones. Jack certainly still had the Book. And hiding from the world wouldn't protect them . . . not when the greatest danger lived inside Harte's skin.

"Dinner," she told him, as if a simple errand could ever be enough to distract her.

The next morning, Esta stood at the window, watching the city wake as she contemplated her options. Below, a monochrome sea of gray and black suits made their way along the crowded sidewalks while trolleys and buses plodded through the streets. For the last few weeks, she'd been completely focused on Harte—on making sure he grew stronger every day. Now she looked at the world outside their room and wondered what their actions in 1904 might have done to this time, to *this* present. It was long past time to find out.

Harte was watching a variety show on the television, laughing at a comedian with a puppet, when Esta walked over and switched off the set.

He looked up at her, clearly annoyed.

She settled on the bed next to his feet, keeping far enough away that she wouldn't be tempted to touch him. "I think it's time we start figuring out what our next move should be. We need information. I'm thinking about going out. I could find the library or—"

"I have a better idea," Harte told her, already lifting himself from the bed.

Esta couldn't dissuade him, and within the hour, he was bathed and dressed in the clothes she'd stolen for him. The pants and shirt hung a little more than they should have from his thin frame, but with the way he'd been improving over the last couple of days, she knew it wouldn't be long before he filled them out.

LISA MAXWELL

With his dark hair slicked back, his face cleanly shaven again, and the modern cut of his pants and jacket, Harte almost looked like he'd stepped out of an episode of one of the old-fashioned shows he'd been watching. His color was better, and he couldn't hide his anticipation at the idea of leaving the hotel. As much as Esta wished she could convince him to stay and rest a little more, she couldn't really refuse.

Once they were out of the hotel and into the briskness of the late-fall day, Harte paused for a second to look around, his expression filled with something akin to wonder. He'd been watching the city from the windows of their fourth-floor room, but now that he was out in it, Esta wished she knew what he was thinking. She'd grown up in a world even louder and faster and more modern than this one, but since Harte had spent his life with gaslights and horse-drawn carriages, the cityscape before him must have felt like stepping onto another planet.

Harte didn't seem thrown off by it, though. Actually, Esta thought he was handling everything surprisingly well, considering. As he'd convalesced in the hotel room, he seemed to take the changes around him in stride.

They took a bus over to Grant Avenue, and from there they cut through the streets of Chinatown to reach the neighborhood known as Jackson Square. Chinatown was bustling with tourists and denizens alike. They walked along beneath buildings topped with pagoda-like roofs, while red lanterns hung on wires that crossed the streets and ornate dragons curled around streetlamps painted bright seafoam green. Harte stopped.

"What is it?" Esta asked, panic sliding through her. "Are you feeling okay?"

"What happened to this place?" Harte said with a hushed awe in his voice.

She hadn't noticed at first, but now that she really looked around, she understood what he was referring to. Grant Avenue was a wide street, filled with distinctive architecture and ornate flourishes. It was the Chinatown of movies and postcards, but it wouldn't have been there fifty years before. It certainly wasn't the Chinatown that Esta had seen from a distance, trapped behind a barbed-wire barricade.

"I'm not sure," she told him. "Time passes, I guess. Things change." It wasn't a good answer, but it was the only one she had to give.

Together, they walked up Grant Avenue, and Harte's worry eased into curiosity. Esta tried not to be too obviously amused at the way Harte marveled at the changed world. They turned onto Washington Street and then wandered north on Montgomery, until Harte came to a stop in front of a two-story brick building at the corner of Montgomery and Jackson Street. According to the historical marker out front, it had once been a bank built by William Tecumseh Sherman, the Civil War general. It wasn't a bank any longer. It seemed to house offices of some kind.

Harte stared up at it, frowning thoughtfully. "This was where the Committee's headquarters used to be," he said. "At least, I think it was. I thought the building was bigger."

"It might have been at one time," she told him. "At some point, there was an earthquake. It might have knocked part of this building down."

"Maybe . . ." He frowned, staring up at the building. "I'm sure this is it. I had the Dragon's Eye in my hands, and I was almost home free." His expression faltered.

"You did the right thing, Harte." She wanted to reach for him, but since the day before, he'd been careful to keep a certain amount of distance between them.

"I let it go." He turned to her, his expression bleak.

"You saved your brother's life," she said softly. "But, Harte, even if this is the same building, the crown can't still be here."

Harte looked like he wanted to argue, but Esta explained how she'd stolen the Dragon's Eye from the Chinatown in New York in the 1940s— nearly a decade before.

Harte listened, but she could sense his stubborn determination. "You said that St. Louis was different because of the train derailment we caused, right?"

"I'm not sure what that has to do with—"

He shrugged. "Maybe something has already changed the path of the Dragon's Eye."

"I guess it's possible," Esta admitted, even if she didn't think it was likely.

"I know you think I'm wrong," Harte told her. "But the fact is, we don't really know how this all works, do we?"

"How what works?" Esta asked.

"Time," he said. "We don't know how our actions affect the course of history. We've seen that they do, but we can't predict the effect of the things we've done—or might still do. Not *really*. Even trying to undo what happened in St. Louis . . . We don't know if it's actually even possible. You're just guessing and hoping you're right."

"I'm not *just* guessing," Esta told him, hating that he was closer to the truth than she wanted to admit.

"I didn't mean to start an argument." Harte let out a ragged breath. "But you have to admit . . . When I came here in 1904, I did something that hadn't been done before. It's possible that changed something. It's possible that the Dragon's Eye could still be here."

"It's been fifty years, Harte."

"If it's not here, then we haven't lost anything but time, and with the Quellant, you can always steal us more of that. But I think we should go in and take a look," he said, pointing to a sandwich-board sign sitting on the sidewalk that advertised an exhibition within. The offices seemed to be for some kind of historical society that had a museum open to the public.

Esta couldn't argue that it sounded promising.

"Even if the headpiece isn't in there, maybe the exhibition inside will have some clue about what happened to it," Harte said.

"Maybe," Esta said, still feeling uneasy. But Harte was already moving toward the arched front door, and she didn't have any choice but to follow.

THE DRAGON'S EYE

1952—San Francisco

Once Harte was inside the building, he realized he'd been bracing himself for an attack. Instead, he was met with nothing but silence in the cool marble lobby. He could see the echo of the bank it had once been, but now the room held a few large displays. The caged bank windows had been replaced by an open counter, where an older man sat. Harte sensed Esta entering behind him. When he turned to her, he was once again surprised by how pretty she looked in the strange clothing of this time, with her hair curling around her face and her lips painted a soft pink that made his mouth go dry. Within him, Seshat pressed at her cage, reminding Harte that he couldn't slip again, not like he had the day before.

Seshat had been so quiet as Harte recuperated that he'd started to believe she might have given up—maybe she was content with his promise to destroy Thoth and would not insist on using Esta to take her revenge on the world itself. The day before, Harte had woken from a nap and, for a moment, he'd forgotten the danger. All he'd seen was Esta, and he couldn't stop himself from touching her, from kissing her. But when his lips had touched Esta's, he'd let his guard down and Seshat had surged and reminded Harte of all that was at stake.

"Welcome," the man said. "I assume you're here for the exhibit?" He glanced between the two of them, and then, after taking their admission fees, pointed them in the direction of the rest of the exhibition.

The main displays were on the second floor of the building. They

470

started at the mouth of the staircase, and trailed through a series of small galleries that told the story of San Francisco from the beginning. Large, printed signs described the city's history, or at least the history that started with Spanish priests establishing missions, through to Mexico's surrender of the land to the United States. Along the way, various artifacts were spotlighted from above, their glass cases forming a winding path toward the back of the building.

As Harte and Esta went through the archway, they passed a young guard in a dark, ill-fitting suit. Harte sensed Esta tense as they passed him, but she continued on. When they were finally out of the guard's sight, Esta leaned so close that Harte felt Seshat lurch.

"Did you see the medallion on his lapel?" she whispered.

Harte frowned. He hadn't noticed, but he trusted Esta's instincts. "There must be something here they're trying to protect."

Together they wandered through the displays, and Harte didn't have to pretend that he was interested in the artifacts, especially the ones pertaining to the Vigilance Committee. It had apparently been started back in 1851 as a way to fight the lawlessness and corruption in the city. An etching depicted a building with two men hanging from nooses. There was a display with medallions that reminded Harte of the open-eyed ring his father wore, and a model of Lady Justice staring with her eyes wide open.

When they came to a display about earthquakes that had happened early in the century, they paused. Beneath a wall of photos was a model of the city, most of the streets destroyed by the quake. Chinatown had been flattened, as had most of the area around it. But the building they were currently in had remained standing . . . for the most part. It explained the missing top floor.

The level of sheer devastation made Harte pause. "The whole city was destroyed," he realized. *Twice.* He'd never seen anything like it. No wonder Chinatown seemed so changed from the streets that he'd walked only a few weeks before.

Esta was frowning. "I knew there was a big earthquake sometime early in the century, but I don't remember there being two. . . ."

"That's what it says," he read, running his finger along the words etched into the placard. "The first one was in July of 1904, and then there was another two years later, in April of 1906. It destroyed most of what had been rebuilt and burned the rest of the city to the ground."

Her brows were furrowed. "July?" Esta stepped closer and read the placard again. "That's when we were there, Harte. Look at this—the map. Look at where they think the epicenter was."

He leaned forward, but he knew already what he would find. On the other side of Chinatown, the small dead-end Dawson Place was marked with a red bull's-eye.

"I knew that Seshat was powerful, but I didn't realize—" She looked at the map again as though it might tell her some other story if she stared at it hard enough. "I did this." She lifted her hand and touched the spot on the map.

"You don't know that," Harte told her, wishing there was something more he could say.

"I do." She looked at him, her whiskey-colored eyes filled with certainty. "I felt her. When I slipped you forward. I thought I could hold her back, but I—"

The guard entered the room behind them, and Harte went on high alert. "Later," he told Esta as he nudged her along, ignoring the way Seshat rattled within.

As they rounded a corner and entered the next gallery, Harte noticed a glass case that glowed golden from within at the same time Esta grabbed for his arm. Seshat's power rustled at her closeness, but Harte barely noticed, because he'd already seen what had made Esta gasp. *The Dragon's Eye*. Miraculously, it was still there, every bit as ornate and fanciful as the day Harte had found it deep within the Order's vaults.

This time the crown wasn't sitting out in the open, but behind a thick case of glass that reminded Harte of the one that had contained the

Djinni's Star back in St. Louis. There was no hint of opium, as there had been at the fair, but he circled the case carefully, pretending to read over the information about the crown as he tried to figure out what security they would have to get through.

He looked up to find Esta staring at the headpiece, mouth pulled into a frown and her brows furrowed, like she was confused. He sidled up next to her. "The security seems minimal," he whispered. "We could try to take it now. . . ."

Esta shook her head ever so slightly. If he hadn't been looking for her answer, he wouldn't have realized she was telling him no. She glanced up at him, and he watched indecipherable emotions play across her features. She was about to say something, when the guard from before entered the room. This time he wasn't alone.

"Do you know, I think I've had enough touring for one day," Esta said. Her voice had a false brightness to it that couldn't mask her nerves. "I'm positively famished, though. Maybe we could find a place to eat?"

"Of course," he told her, playing along. He didn't allow himself to make eye contact with the guards, who were clearly following them.

Harte braced himself for an attack as they worked their way out of the exhibit and took the stairs back down to the lobby. They nodded to the man at the front desk, then let themselves out into the noise of the streets. Once they were outside, Esta picked up her pace, but a few blocks away, Harte tugged her to a stop. He leaned against one of the ornate lampposts.

"We need to keep moving," Esta told him. "I think we're being followed."

Before he could argue, she threaded her arm through his and began tugging him along. Even with the layers of clothing between them, Seshat pressed at Harte, writhing within him to get to Esta.

Soon, she whispered. *Soon the girl will be mine.*

No, he thought, shoving Seshat back into the farthest depths of what he was. *I will destroy us both before I ever let you touch her.*

Harte thought he could feel Seshat's mocking amusement, but he turned his attention back to Esta. "They were waiting for us. I should have expected it. I never should have brought you there—but it's been *fifty years*."

"Thoth's been waiting for centuries to get control of Seshat," Esta reminded him. "What's fifty years in the grand scheme of things?"

When they reached California Street, a cable car was stopped in the center of the intersection, blocking the flow of traffic. Just as the driver had finished collecting his fares and was returning his hand to the large hand brake in the center of the car, Esta tugged Harte into the street and urged him on. He didn't hesitate. Ignoring how exhausted and drained he felt, he sprinted alongside Esta to reach the trolley. They barely managed to hop on as it started moving—too late for anyone to follow. While Esta paid their fares, Harte collapsed into one of the empty seats. He didn't miss the two men standing at the corner, where they had been, watching the cable car pull away. Their frustration was clear, and on their lapels, silvery medallions gleamed.

Once the trolley car was underway, Esta settled into the seat next to Harte.

"We'll go back," he promised. "Tonight. We'll make a plan and then—"

She leaned in close, and suddenly Harte couldn't speak. She spoke low, so no one else could hear. "Are you sure that the headpiece you tried to steal was the real thing?"

Seshat prowled within his skin, and Harte pulled back, preserving the careful distance between himself and Esta.

"Of course . . ."

"You felt the power in the stone?"

"Yes—" But thinking back, Harte couldn't *actually* remember if he'd felt anything. He'd been so sick, and everything that day had happened so fast. "Honestly, I don't know," he admitted. Then he realized . . . "I didn't feel anything back there."

Esta glanced at him. "That wasn't the real Dragon's Eye. It was a replica—a damn good one, but a replica all the same," she told him. Strangely, she didn't seem upset by this news. "I wonder if they know?"

"What are you thinking?" he asked, trying to figure out her new mood.

"I'm thinking there's a good chance that you didn't lose the Dragon's Eye," she said, her golden eyes brightening. "I'm thinking that maybe the Committee never had the original to start with."

"Of course they did," Harte said, wishing it were otherwise. "My father told me that he sold it to them. He *gloated* about it. If he'd sold them a fake, he would have bragged about that, too."

Esta glanced at him. "But what if your father was wrong?"

Harte frowned. "What do you mean?"

"What if he only *thought* he sold the real Dragon's Eye to the Committee?" Esta asked. "What if they only *thought* they bought the real thing?"

Harte rubbed his hand over his face, tired in mind and body from trying to follow her and her logic. "You're not making a lot of sense."

"Remember how I told you that your stepmother, Patience, must have given your father's creditors replicas of the cuff and the necklace when they came to collect your father's debts—replicas that she'd probably used her affinity to make?" Esta asked.

Harte still remembered how shocked he'd been to learn that his father had been married to a woman who was Mageus without ever knowing it. "You think she made a replica of the Dragon's Eye, too?"

Esta nodded. "If Patience could sense the power in the cuff and the necklace, it stands to reason that she would have sensed the power in the Dragon's Eye as well."

Harte was glad he was already sitting down. "But she didn't tell you anything about the crown."

"Why would she? She didn't know me, and I didn't tell her I was looking for it," Esta said. "But I think it's absolutely possible that your father sold a fake crown to the Committee."

"It would have put him at risk if he'd been found out," Harte said, thinking through the implications. "You really think she would have done that to her husband?"

Esta shrugged. "From what she told me, she wasn't exactly fond of him. She seemed glad that he was gone."

"He wasn't the type of man *anyone* would be fond of," Harte said.

"It's likely that they *didn't* figure it out," Esta said. "If they had, they would have reacted long before you ever showed up to take the crown."

"But Jack would have realized—Thoth would have known," Harte said. "It's clear he's working with the Committee."

"Which only proves my theory. Think about it, Harte. If Jack discovered that the Committee had a real artifact, he would have taken it from them. There's no way it would still be on display nearly fifty years later. It's more likely he let them believe it was real because it served his purposes."

Harte couldn't argue with that logic. "So what do we do now?"

"Patience helped us once before," Esta said. "Maybe she would be willing to help us again. Even if she doesn't still have the crown, she might know where it is."

Hope warmed Harte as the cable car rattled along down California, cutting through a canyon of buildings. He was still a little short of breath, and his legs felt like he'd run for miles, but the cool, damp air brushed against his face, reviving him a little as they traveled along. With everything that had happened, could the Dragon's Eye truly still be within reach?

Then another thought occurred to him. "It's been nearly fifty years. I doubt she's still alive."

"What about your brother?" Esta asked. "He might know something. He might even have it."

"Sammie would be close to sixty by now himself." So much time had passed, Harte wasn't even sure that the boy would remember him. "He might be gone by now as well." The thought made his mood sink.

"It's possible," Esta agreed, but still, she seemed more determined than disheartened. "But we might as well look into it. If we can't find them, we'll be no worse off than we already are."

Harte felt every second of the day's excursion. "If Sammie is alive, I don't know where we'd even start to look for him. . . ."

Esta still didn't seem worried. Her mouth curled into a small smile. "Luckily, I do."

LISA MAXWELL

THE ARS ARCANA

1902—New York

J ack Grew was exhausted from the evening of arguing minutia with old men. It was later than he'd intended to stay at the Chandlers' dinner party, but he still ordered his driver to take him south instead of in the direction of his comfortable town house on the edge of Washington Square. It had been a long day of maneuvering and positioning and *pretending*, but his plans were progressing . . . and the evening was still ahead of him.

As the hack carried him through the city, he took a cube of morphine, then tipped his head back against the carriage's plush interior, closed his eyes, and enjoyed the familiar warmth spreading within his blood. His senses came alive, and he could feel within him that sureness that always grew sharper with the languid, dreamlike warmth of the drug. By the time the carriage arrived at the docks, Jack was relaxed and more than ready to begin the night of work ahead of him.

He unlocked the door of the warehouse and let himself inside its dark, musty interior. Lighting a lamp, he made quick work of securing the door to ensure he wouldn't be disturbed, then lit the other lamps he'd stationed at various points around the large room. The entire room smelled of axle grease and dust, and in the softly glowing light, he took account of his progress so far. A new machine was rising from the bits of bent metal and broken glass. Without an assistant, progress had been slower than Jack might have liked, but he had time. The Conclave was still months away.

On the far side of the room, a long table held his plans. After the mess at Khafre Hall, he'd found the entire warehouse ransacked. The table had been overturned, and little had been left of the blueprints and models but ash and dust. He'd managed to reproduce what had been lost, just as he would reproduce his machine. Jack smoothed out one of the few documents that had survived the carnage, a half-burned scrap of an illustration depicting the Philosopher's Hand. In the palm, a fish lay burning in mercurial flames, uniting the elements. It was the symbol for quintessence. Great alchemists understood the importance of this most powerful of all elements. Aether, it was often called, the substance that aligned all other elements. With quintessence, one could turn iron into gold. With quintessence, one could transmute matter—or magic.

Quintessence was the ingredient Jack had been missing before, when his first attempt at building the machine had failed so completely. His desperate desire to solve that problem had blinded him to Esta's and Darrigan's treachery, but in the end he'd discovered the solution despite them. Thanks to the Book of Mysteries, Jack now understood exactly what he needed to complete his machine—he needed an object infused with feral energy. As above, so below. Like to like. Not even the purest uncut diamond was durable enough to contain the dangerous power his machine would collect. He needed feral magic to capture feral magic, and he would have exactly what he needed once he obtained the ring he'd been so close to retrieving at the gala.

Jack took the Book from its place near his heart and set it on the table next to the Philosopher's Hand. With the morphine thick in his blood, he allowed his mind to wander free as he turned the pages. Sometime later, he realized he was staring at a page he'd never seen before, one written in English rather than the strange, unknown languages that filled so many of the other pages.

This wasn't a new experience. In the weeks since Jack had taken possession of the Ars Arcana, he'd discovered that it was rarely the same book twice. He had not yet come to understand how or why it revealed certain things to him but was grateful that it continued to do so. It had to be a signal of his continued worthiness, a sign that he was destined to prevail.

The writing on these new pages had been done in a cramped, sloping hand. The varying weight of the ink and the discoloration of the thick vellum told Jack that the page had likely been created long ago, before the smooth consistency of fountain pens was even an idea. He flipped through the next few pages, all in the same matching hand. His excitement only grew when he noticed a small notation at the bottom of one of the pages—*Is. Newton* had been inscribed there, in the same cramped style as the rest. With only a cursory glance, Jack understood *immediately* what this was. There on those pages, Newton had detailed his creation of the artifacts.

Righting a stool that had been knocked over in the destruction, Jack took another cube of morphine between his teeth and settled himself to read. On those pages, Newton had inscribed detailed illustrations of five precious gemstones, and alongside each drawing were notes about the gemstone's origin and the properties of the stone itself. Apparently, the old alchemist had carefully selected only the most perfect of materials, gem-stones prized for their purity and historical importance. The individual stones had been drawn from the five ancient mystical dynasties, and each was famed for the power that it held. Then Newton had used a ritual involving the Ars Arcana itself to imbue the stones with the feral magic of the most powerful Mageus he could find—each aligning with one of the five elements.

But something had changed. As the notes continued, Newton's hand grew more erratic and uneven. Later illustrations had been hastily scribbled onto the parchment, and still others had been blotted out. The content of the words matched their appearance. The clear English notes shifted into a confusing and often unintelligible series of arcane phrases. They were most likely coded alchemical recipes, metaphor layered upon metaphor, but Jack couldn't be sure of the meaning other than to understand that something had scared the old magician. Something had brought Newton to the brink of sanity before he'd managed to pull himself back.

Jack turned another page and found a diagram that looked very much like a copy of the symbol that was carved into the front of the Ars Arcana. The writing here was still erratic and clouded in metaphor, but the illustrations were clearer. The series of diagrams in the following pages seemed to depict the creation of what looked to be silver discs, each inscribed with the same strange design that graced the cover of the Ars Arcana, but when Jack turned the page, the information ceased. The next page was completely blank, as though the Book had decided to withhold its secrets. He couldn't tell what the purpose of the discs had been, or why Newton seemed so keen to create them.

Jack flipped back through the pages and examined Newton's notes once more, marveling at how close Newton had come to unlocking the true power within the Book, only to fail. The weight of what he'd been attempting had nearly driven him to madness. In the end, Newton had turned from the occult sciences and back to a safer and far more pedestrian path. Apparently, he had been too weak to handle the enormous potential of what he'd discovered. Instead, he'd given the Ars Arcana to the Order, along with the stones, for safekeeping.

As Jack closed the Book, his mind was still clouded with the haze of morphine. He considered the symbol carved into the cover, and as he meditated on it, he traced its intricate lines with the barest touch of his finger. In and out and around, following the figure as it doubled into itself over and out again, infinite. Impossible. Beyond his reach. Jack understood there was some larger secret here, but the Ars Arcana was not ready to reveal it.

It would soon enough. Jack had utter confidence that once he proved himself worthy, the Book would reveal everything. Until then he would focus on his machine and the destiny before him. Once he had the power contained within the Delphi's Tear, he would finally finish his great machine and show the world what could be achieved when power and science coalesced. Luckily, the old men of the Inner Circle had put Jack in the perfect position to make all of that possible.

THE DRAGON'S PEARL

1952—San Francisco

As the taxi glided through the streets of San Francisco, Harte tried to focus on the bright lights of the city instead of the gown Esta was wearing beneath the folds of the soft strip of cashmere she'd wrapped artfully around herself. All his life, Harte had wanted to see the world, to escape from Manhattan and explore the land beyond the Brink, but nothing could have prepared him for the amazement he felt seeing the sleek motorcars speed along. They flashed like schools of impossible fish beneath the city's lights. Nothing could have prepared him for the astounding wonder of it all. But somehow, nothing seemed half so astounding as the dress Esta was wearing.

From the front, the neckline of the frock skimmed her collarbones and was demure as anything she might have worn in his own time, but the back . . . Esta had asked him to pull the most ingenious little sliding fastener up to secure the dress, but even fastened, the back dipped nearly down to her waist, exposing an expanse of her smooth skin. The sight had been enough to rob him of words and make his palms sweat.

Her mouth had quirked a bit when she'd noticed his reaction, but Esta hadn't said anything as she'd tucked the leather pouch with Maggie's concoctions into her beaded evening bag. *Just to be safe,* she'd told him. Harte didn't argue with her logic. After they'd been followed earlier, it made sense not to take any chances. They might be followed again, and if that happened, they wouldn't be able to risk returning to the hotel.

Esta had used up most of the Quellant in those early days to be sure that Seshat would remain quiet while she'd taken care of Harte. Now there was only one tablet left, and they knew they had to save it until they were ready to return to 1902. Without the Quellant to leash her, though, Seshat prowled freely again beneath Harte's skin. She'd been mostly quiet, but he could tell that she was only waiting for an opportunity. He wasn't about to give her one, not when he was so close to protecting Esta for good.

Once they had the real crown and after they'd located the Book, they would use the last of the Quellant to go back to 1902 and retrieve the ring from Cela Johnson. Once Esta had all five of the artifacts, Harte would take care of Seshat so Esta wouldn't have to. She would be left with the Book and the power within it, and with that, she could defeat Nibsy Lorcan. She would be safe. For good.

And until then? Harte would be content with being an arm's length away from her, caught up in the sweetness of her perfume as they floated along in the plush comfort of this strange, quiet machine.

Without even thinking, Harte lifted his fingers to rub at his lips, but he could no longer resurrect the memory of the kiss they'd shared two days before. It felt like it had happened in another lifetime. He let his hand fall back into his lap and studied the passing streets as they rode on in silence until the taxi stopped at the address Esta had given the driver.

It had been far easier than Harte had expected to find his brother. Esta had located a telephone directory once they'd returned to the hotel the day before, and from there it had been a matter of sorting through the various entries to find Sammie. That had taken a while, but eventually they found a person who might be Harte's brother—a Sam Lowe, who owned a nightclub just outside of Chinatown.

Once out of the car, Harte felt the crisp snap of autumn's chill in the air. He could hear the sounds of an orchestra filter through the heavy golden doors each time they opened to admit another couple. On the enormous marquee above, the nightclub's name glimmered: THE DRAGON'S PEARL.

LISA MAXWELL

"It's too perfect not to have some connection." Esta glanced at Harte. "The crown is here. It *has* to be."

"Let's not get ahead of ourselves," Harte said, wanting her to be right and also not wanting to be disappointed. "First we need to see if the Sam Lowe who owns this place is really my brother."

Esta linked her arm through his and paused, as though to confirm that this was okay—that Seshat was calm.

"It's fine," he told her. "I can handle this." The power inside him was rumbling at Esta's closeness, but with the layers of fabric between their skin, Harte was able to push the ancient power back easily enough.

For now, Seshat whispered softly.

Harte grimaced in reply.

"I wish we had more of the Quellant," Esta said, noticing his discomfort.

"I'm fine." *At least for now.*

Besides, he hated the idea that he needed Maggie's formulation even to stand next to Esta. Even more, he hated the way the Quellant made him feel: cold and empty and incomplete. That aching hollowness was almost enough to have him yearning for something to take the pain away. He wondered if it was anything like what his mother felt after she'd ventured too close to the Brink. If so, Harte understood a little better why Molly O'Doherty had reached for the numbing lull of opium.

Together, Harte and Esta followed the crowd of people through the golden double doors and into the nightclub. Once they entered, they were surrounded by the sounds of the orchestra's music, crystal clinking, and couples speaking across linen-covered tabletops. The whole place was decorated in dark gleaming wood and gold accents. In the center of the room was a wide-open dance floor, which was anchored by a five-piece band that was playing a soft ballad. This wasn't the raucous Haymarket, with its painted ladies and packs of hungry young men roving for a night on the town. The clientele here was mostly couples—mostly older and mostly white, but the waitstaff and other workers all seemed to be Chinese people. Jewels glittered around every woman's neck as couples glided across the dance floor in smooth, looping circles or sat leaning close across tabletops, their quiet murmuring like the rustling of money.

The hostess was a Chinese woman wearing a red satin gown. Her dark hair had been cut nearly as short as Esta's and was curled and fluffed about her face in the style that seemed to be popular everywhere in the city. She led them to a table in the back corner of the club, away from the lights and bustle of the open dance floor, as they'd requested. Esta looked over the menu, which was divided into both American and Chinese offerings, but Harte could hardly concentrate on food. Instead, he scanned the room and the dance floor for any sign of the man who could be his brother.

"Are you sure he'll be here tonight?" Harte asked after they'd placed their order. He didn't know why, but he'd almost expected Sammie to be waiting for him at the door.

"That's what I was told by the person who answered the phone earlier," Esta said, looking around the room. "From what I understand, he's here every night."

"We should have come yesterday," he told her, frustrated at his own weakness.

"You needed to rest yesterday," Esta told him, her golden eyes flashing with something that looked too much like pity for Harte's liking.

He'd seen that look too many times since he'd woken in that damned hospital bed. As he'd recovered in the hotel, she'd been there by his side, watching over him as though he might disappear if she looked away. Harte didn't even want to think about the ways she had helped him. He would have been incinerated by the shame of his own weakness had he been well enough or strong enough to care at the time. And always, fear and pity had been stark in her expression—like he'd been some kind of wounded animal to save . . . except for that afternoon when he'd woken from an unintended nap and, not thinking about the consequences, had kissed her. It hadn't been pity in her eyes then. It had been hunger and hope as deep and unspeakable as his own.

Harte knew he should tell her how grateful he was. He could at least tell her how beautiful she looked that night, but he couldn't figure out where to start. He opened his mouth again and again—he probably looked like a fish—but the words wouldn't come.

Esta turned to him, and her expression shifted to concern. "Are you okay?"

"Fine," Harte mumbled, feeling stupid. Before he could pull himself together and try again, though, the orchestra trilled and the house lights began to dim. The dance floor was suddenly bathed in cool blues and pinks.

A line of chorus girls with their legs bare to the hip sashayed onto the floor. Their shoes clickety-clacked in rhythm as they came, and the scraps of their costumes threatened to come undone with every bounce and shimmy. Their act was followed by a Chinese couple. The woman was dressed in a diaphanous gown of silk and feathers that made her look like a bird of paradise, and the man, tall and slender in a topcoat and tails, spun her around the floor in a dreamlike waltz as easily as if she weighed no more than the feathers on her gown.

Their meals arrived, but Harte wasn't hungry. He picked haphazardly at the food on his plate as one act after another took the stage. Esta must have been as nervous as he was, because she didn't eat much either. By the time the waiter carried away their barely touched plates, the show was winding down, and there had been no sign of Sammie.

With the ringing of the piano, the entire club went dark, and a single beam of light flickered on to illuminate a girl in the center of the dance floor. She had hair the color of fire and was holding an enormous translucent sphere, like a giant soap bubble. The orchestra hummed softly, and she began to dance.

"She's not wearing anything at all," Harte murmured, feeling his cheeks heat in embarrassment. He'd seen plenty of bare arms and legs during his days onstage, but nothing like this.

Esta glanced at him, and Harte could tell she was trying not to laugh.

"I believe that's the point." But her expression shifted when the girl started dancing, and suddenly Harte felt the unmistakable warmth of magic—*natural* magic. "Did you feel that?" Esta whispered.

He nodded. "It can't be a coincidence."

In the center of the stage, the girl turned and dipped, holding the sphere so that it somehow never managed to reveal anything overly pertinent. But as lovely as the girl was with her willowy figure and softly waved dark hair falling around her shoulders, even the promise of seeing her entire body couldn't hold Harte's attention. It was nothing compared to the sight of the gentle slope of Esta's exposed back, the delicate pearls of her spine traveling down into the low dip of her dress.

When the floor show was over, he would ask her to dance. He would take the risk and hold her close. He could almost imagine what it would be like to rest his hand on the curve of her lower back, skin to skin . . .

Yes, Seshat purred.

No. Harte fisted his hands beneath the table to be sure that he did not reach for her. He couldn't allow himself to indulge in fantasies about being close to her again. He *wouldn't.*

He forced himself to look away from the smooth expanse of Esta's skin, ignoring the heat in his blood, and focused on studying the crowd instead. The people in the audience looked less titillated than vaguely interested in the girl on the floor, but Harte noticed one person watching the crowd instead of the floor show—an older man standing on the side of the dance floor with a scar that marred the corner of his mouth.

In a sharply cut black suit with satin lapels and a crimson tie, the man was dressed better than any of the other waitstaff. He held a set of menus in his arms, but he watched the room with the alertness of someone clearly in charge. He was older—*so much older*—but Harte would have recognized Sammie anywhere. Despite the man's lighter hair, Harte could see their father in Sammie's features, but Harte's brother wore them with a quiet dignity that Samuel Lowe had never quite managed.

Harte nudged Esta's arm, careful to limit their contact. "I think that's him." He nodded to where Sammie still watched over the room.

"It could be. . . ." She didn't sound as sure, but Harte knew.

The music was building, and before they could discuss it any further, the bubble burst and the girl pranced offstage to thunderous applause, exposing the pale globes of her bottom as she went. Sammie waited a second longer, but when a group of women in evening gowns emerged from the curtain behind him to begin circulating through the club, Harte's brother ducked into a back hallway.

"I'm going to follow him," Harte said, already on his feet.

"I'll come with you." Esta started to stand, but Harte was already shaking his head.

"I think it's better if I do this on my own."

Part of him didn't want to let Esta out of his sight, but with the dress she was wearing and the way Seshat seemed to sense his weakness, Harte knew it would be safer for everyone if he went alone.

Coward, Seshat mocked.

Harte didn't disagree. He *was* a coward. A braver man wouldn't have been afraid to keep Esta close, and a stronger one could have easily resisted touching her. But Harte Darrigan had never been anything but a bastard and a con, and now he was a desperate one at that. The Dragon's Eye *had* to be there. With the threat to his health behind him, he could already feel Seshat growing impatient. The sooner they had the crown, the sooner they could find the other artifacts, and the sooner he could put an end to the threat Seshat posed.

And until then? Harte wasn't so careless as to put everything at risk—especially not Esta—for something as insignificant as his pride.

WHAT CAME AFTER

1952—San Francisco

When Harte ducked through the curtain to follow Sammie, he found himself in a hallway that ran behind the stage. For a moment he was overwhelmed by the memories of another life: the feeling he'd get waiting in the darkened wings for the cue to enter the spotlight, his nerves jangling as the scent of greasepaint and powder filled his senses. But those days were long behind him.

Harte shook off his regret. If he didn't keep moving, someone was bound to notice that he didn't belong backstage. When a chorus girl's expression bunched with a question, he only nodded to her and kept walking like he was supposed to be there. Luckily, no one stopped him.

He passed by the dressing rooms and then turned into a long hallway that ran behind the stage. At the end of it, light spilled from an open doorway. Harte approached carefully and saw that it was an office. Behind a broad, cluttered desk, his brother was too focused on a stack of paper to notice him. Easing into the room, Harte pulled the door closed behind him. At the sound of it closing, Sammie finally looked up, irritated at the interruption. The irritation quickly turned to confusion, though . . . and then the color drained from his brother's face.

Harte felt suddenly, unaccountably embarrassed. He tucked his hands into his pockets and tried to force himself to appear at ease. "Hello, Sammie."

The man at the desk didn't respond at first. He only stared at Harte, shaking his head as his mouth moved without any sound coming out. Finally, Sammie seemed to find his voice. "It's not possible."

"It shouldn't be." Harte tried to ignore the nervousness he felt. He'd known Sammie only as a boy, after all, and then for only a very short time. They'd never discussed who they were to one another, and after everything Harte had put the kid through, he hadn't been sure what kind of reception he'd receive showing up so many years later.

Sammie stood and came around the desk, his hand reaching for Harte. "You look exactly like I remember you. Like a ghost—"

"I'm not a ghost," Harte told him, stepping back before his brother could poke him.

"Then how—" Sammie shook his head. "You haven't aged a day."

The weariness in Harte's body said otherwise. "It's a long story, and honestly, it's one you'd probably be better off not hearing." Harte hesitated, trying to figure out the best way to go about what he had to do, but in the end he found that he didn't have the stomach for anything but sincerity. He softened his voice. "How have you been, Sammie?"

At first his brother simply stared at him—in shock or disgust or sheer confusion, Harte couldn't tell. His stomach sank as he realized that maybe he'd miscalculated. He'd hoped that his brother would welcome seeing him, but now he wondered if he should have been more careful.

But then his brother seemed to come to terms with the situation he'd found himself a part of. "It's been a *long* time," Sammie said, giving Harte an expectant look. "A *lifetime* . . ." Then, when it was clear that Harte wasn't going to volunteer any real explanation, his brother shrugged. "You know how lifetimes go—there's good and there's bad mixed together. I'm lucky. I've had more good than bad."

"I'm glad to hear that," Harte told him, and he meant it.

"I have you to thank for it," his brother said, leaning against his desk.

Harte frowned. "I doubt that." He'd caused Sammie more trouble than anything else.

His brother's brows went up. "You don't think I remember that you saved my life that day?"

Harte shifted under the intensity of his brother's gaze. He wasn't any hero, and the last thing he wanted now was praise. *Especially* when he knew the danger he might be dragging Sammie back into. So he deflected. "Your father wouldn't have really let them—"

"Yes, he certainly would have," his brother interrupted. "You knew it, and I knew it too, even as young as I was back then. Our father would have let those men kill me if it meant saving himself and his precious reputation." Sammie lifted a single brow. "If you hadn't done what you did, I doubt I would have lived past that day."

At first Harte thought he must have misheard. "*Our* father?"

"She told me who you were," Sammie told him. "My mother, I mean. She said she knew the second you showed up at our home that you were his son. He'd never talked about having another child or another family, but Mother knew what kind of man she'd married."

Harte hadn't realized how still he'd been holding himself, fearing what Sammie might think or do. Now he felt only relief. It made his legs unsteady enough that he lowered himself to the leather sofa that stood against the wall. "I didn't realize she knew."

"She recognized him in you. She told me that it scared her at first— that *you* scared her with your intensity and your demands—but she realized that you weren't anything like him when you saved me that day. It's why she took care of you instead of returning you to the Committee." Sammie let out a breath, like he was letting go of part of the past he'd been carrying for too long. "He never came back, you know. Wherever he sailed off to, he stayed gone."

"I'm sorry . . ."

"Don't be," Sammie said, waving his hand in dismissal. "Our father was a weak and unhappy man, made all the worse because he thought he was being guided by some higher power. His disappearance was the beginning of my life, not the end of it."

LISA MAXWELL

Sammie's words were an unexpected balm. Even in the midst of the fever that had almost killed him, Harte had worried what his actions might have done to the boy and his father's wife. He'd worried about how they might have suffered for his impulsiveness, as his own mother had.

"It must be some life you've lived," Harte said softly. "You have quite the place here."

When Esta had discovered that Sammie owned a nightclub, Harte hadn't expected anything half as opulent as the Dragon's Pearl. How his brother had gone from the shy, skinny little kid to the man now sitting behind the desk, a golden bracelet glinting on his wrist, Harte couldn't imagine.

Or maybe he could. After all, hadn't he done the same for himself?

Sammie's expression turned a little smug. "I built it all myself."

"Really?" Harte asked, wondering if it had been built from the profit from a priceless lost artifact. "That must have been . . . difficult."

"No more difficult than anything else I've lived through," Sammie said. "Mother died when I was very young—not long after we met, actually. I was just a kid, and it was a struggle to stay alive for a long while."

"Was it one of the earthquakes that took her?" Harte asked, thinking of the exhibit they'd seen the day before.

"They were hard—terrible to live through—but no. Mother died because of what came after." Sammie got up from where he was leaning against the desk, went to a sideboard, and poured some amber-colored liquor into two crystal glasses. Then he handed one to Harte before downing his own in a single swallow.

"What came after?" Harte asked, not bothering to lift the cup to his lips. Instead, he watched the emotions play across Sammie's expression.

Sammie was old—older than Harte had ever imagined himself being. His dark-blond hair had already turned an ashy gray, and there were deep creases at the corners of his eyes that spoke of a lifetime filled with laughter. Even as old as he was, Sammie looked fit and healthy. He was about the same height as Harte, but he had a presence to him, a confidence and sense of self-possession that Harte had noticed from across the nightclub. With his hair slicked back and the sharp cut of his perfectly tailored suit, Sammie could have stood next to the richest and most powerful men in the country and not looked one bit out of place.

Sammie quirked a brow in Harte's direction as he poured himself another glass. "You know what came after. . . ." He gave Harte a pointed look.

"I've been away," Harte said, giving up nothing.

"Must have been a hell of a long time," Sammie said, again questioning without really asking.

"It was," Harte admitted. It was all that he would admit to. Slipping through time was Esta's to speak of, not his.

His brother's eyes narrowed a little, clearly trying to figure out another way to interrogate Harte, but finally Sammie seemed to relent. "If you know about the quakes, you must know that the Vigilance Committee determined that the first earthquake wasn't natural. They said it was some kind of attack by the Devil's Thief." He leaned against the desk again as he sipped the second glass of whiskey, this time more slowly than he had the first. "For the two years that followed, life in the city was nothing but raids and roundups. It was for our protection, the Committee said. They reasoned if the Devil's Thief had been hiding in the city, then there must be others with the illegal magic as well. They weren't wrong," he admitted with a shrug. "Back then, a lot of people had the old magic."

"Like your mother," Harte prodded. He wanted to see how much Sammie knew, or at least how much he was willing to admit.

Sammie nodded. "Yeah, like my mother. The period after the first quake was bad, but we survived it. The Committee took the opportunity the quake provided to focus their blame on the Chinese people for hiding the Devil's Thief—kind of a two-for-one. Chinatown dealt with the worst of it, so Mother was able to rebuild the shop without much trouble. We mostly managed to avoid the Committee's notice. But when the second quake came two years later, things got worse. That one was bigger, and it burned most of the city to the ground. Everyone was desperate to blame someone. The Committee took advantage of the devastation and blamed the Devil's Thief again."

"Did they have proof?"

"Who needs proof, when you run the city?" Sammie finished the last of the whiskey in his glass. "Anyway, after the second quake in '06, that's when the Committee built their tower."

Harte felt suddenly apprehensive. There was another tower once, another machine and another plan that was meant to attack the old magic. "What tower?"

"The one in Portsmouth Square. The Committee told the public that the tower would only *detect* magic," Sammie said. "It was supposed to serve as a warning in case someone like Miss Esta ever attacked again, and it was only supposed to target Chinatown. People were happy to go along with it, but a lot of us knew it was a lie. Stories of the Brink in New York had made their way across the country years before. No one really believed the Committee would be happy with simple *detection.*

"They built the thing right in the center of Portsmouth Square, and by 1908 it was ready—even before a lot of the other buildings were. I was still a kid then, but I knew things were bad. I should have done more to convince my mother to get out. . . ." Sammie paused, staring down at his empty glass. "The tower killed more people than either earthquake—people far outside Chinatown," he said. "It killed people—Mageus—all over the city."

"I'm sorry," Harte said. He didn't need Sammie to explain what had happened. He'd seen Jack's first machine for himself, and he understood too well what it was like to lose a mother. There was nothing he could say that would come close to making Sammie's loss any easier, even if it had happened years ago. But then Harte had another unpleasant thought. "This tower, it's not still operational, is it?"

"No," Sammie told him, blinking a little, as though clearing the memories from his mind. "Once Roosevelt heard what had happened—especially when news started spreading about exactly how many people died—he had the tower dismantled. But it was too late for too many, my mother included. I left San Francisco not long after that. I couldn't stomach staying. For a long time, I traveled around, looking for work where I could, busking on street corners for coins and begging when that didn't work.

"When we got dragged into the First World War, I signed up and served."

"The *first* world war?" Harte asked, suddenly struck by how much must have happened in the time he'd skipped over—and how much he didn't know.

Sammie nodded. "Somehow I didn't end up dead, so I came back to the States and started working in Chicago. It's where I met Mina. She was a Chinese woman who grew up here in San Francisco, but she toured all around as a singer on the Chop Suey Circuit. But traveling was starting to lose its shine for her." He shook his head with a tired-sounding laugh. "Mina was tired of dealing with backwater towns filled with people who'd never seen a Chinese person before, so we got married in Illinois, since it wasn't legal here in California. Still isn't. But San Francisco was always home to Mina. She wanted to come back here, where she'd grown up, and I loved her more than I feared my memories, so I agreed.

"I took all my savings and everything I had to start this place, but I did it for her. There were already a couple of Chinese clubs opening up in the city, but we wanted the Pearl to be a place where any performer could feel at home—Chinese or Mageus alike. That was around 1938. Mina died eight years ago, but I couldn't bear to get rid of the Pearl." Sammie smiled softly, and Harte didn't miss the sadness in his eyes. "The club reminds me of the good times we had, every single night." He set the glass on the desk and met Harte's eyes. "But you didn't really come back here to find out about my life, did you?" Sammie asked.

"No, I didn't," Harte admitted. "But I'm glad to hear it, nonetheless."

"I know why you're here," Sammie said, his expression never flickering. "My mother told me that someone might come for the crown one day. I've been ready for that eventuality for most of my life, but I never once imagined it would be you."

The surprise of Sammie's admission blindsided Harte, but somehow he choked out the question he needed to ask. "Do you still have it?"

Sammie shook his head. "I'm afraid you're a decade or so too late."

Harte was about to ask what had happened to the crown when Esta burst through the door. "We have a problem," she told Harte, already digging in her evening bag.

Sam gasped. "Miss Esta?"

She froze at the sound of her name, and then her expression brightened. "Hi, Sammie. It's good to see you again." Then the smile fell from her face as she looked to Harte. "I think they've found us."

"Who found you?" Sam asked.

"I'm not sure," Esta admitted. "But I'd bet money that they're with one of the Brotherhoods. A half-dozen men in dark suits came in a minute ago. They're standing at the back of the club, and I don't think they're here for the floor show."

She'd barely gotten the words out when a red light above the door began flashing. Sam looked up at it, and his expression turned flinty.

"That's trouble all right," he said, nodding toward the flashing light. "There are watchmen in the club."

THE RETICULUM

Y ou're sure they're watchmen?" Esta asked, frowning.

Sam nodded as he picked up the phone on his desk and lifted the receiver to his ear. "My people know how to pick out the Committee's men, even when they're trying to hide." He turned his attention to the phone. "Yeah . . . Li, send Gracie back, would you? And Paul and Dottie as well."

Sammie barked a few more orders into the phone, and once he'd ended the conversation and replaced the receiver, he turned to them. "You need to go. Maybe the watchmen followed you or maybe this is one of their usual checks. Either way, if the Committee finds you here, I could lose everything."

On the other side of the office, a large bookcase was built into the wall. Sam went over to it and ran his hand along the underside of the second shelf until an audible snap could be heard, and the bookcase hinged from the wall. Behind it was a heavy steel door secured by a series of combination locks.

Before Esta could gather her thoughts, the office door opened, and three people entered. One was the girl with the bubble. She was dressed now, but barely. The glimmering silver evening gown that clung to her lean body revealed almost as much as it covered. Up close, she looked older than she had onstage, where the footlights had washed out the fine lines around her mouth and eyes, but she was still strikingly pretty. Her dark-red hair was pinned up into a softly waved chignon, and her lips were painted a matching scarlet. Her beauty aside, there was a sharp perceptiveness in her wide-set eyes that hadn't been apparent during her act.

The other two were the Chinese dance team—Paul Wing and Dorothy Toy. They'd changed from their tails and evening gown and were dressed in street clothes. The husband was tall and slim, with a narrow face and eyes as sharp as his cheekbones, while the wife was willowy and petite. Her heart-shaped face was anchored by a narrow nose and a wide, generous mouth. When she performed earlier, her dreamy smile had betrayed a slight overbite, but she wasn't smiling now.

"What's the deal, Sam?" Paul asked.

"Watchmen," Sam said as he finished with the final lock and opened the heavy door to reveal a passageway.

"Any idea who they're looking for?" Dorothy asked, fear clear in her expression.

Sam glanced at Harte. "I don't know," he said, "but it'll be safer if you get out of here now. Better to be sure."

The bubble girl, Gracie, folded herself into Sam's arm, and Esta realized they were together. They made an odd couple, with him being so much older, but they still looked right somehow. Gracie appeared to have a backbone to match Sam's clear confidence.

Sam placed a soft kiss on her forehead. "Gracie, Paul, Dottie, this is Harte and Esta—they're old friends of mine. You all have a lot in common, if you catch my meaning."

Paul eyed Harte and Esta with a new appreciation. "I see . . ."

"Could you take them on over to the safe house, while I deal with the problem out front?"

"Of course, Sam," Paul said. "Thanks for the warning, as always." He'd already taken his wife's hand, and together they were ducking through the passageway.

Sam turned to Harte. "They'll show you the way. You'll be safe there until I get rid of the watchmen out front."

"But, Sam, honey, I'm not even dressed," Gracie told him.

"No time for that, sweetheart." Sam took off his tuxedo jacket and draped it around her shoulders. "Better safe than warm."

"You built your nightclub with an escape route?" Harte asked, frowning at the dark tunnel ahead of him.

"I didn't, but it serves my purposes. The building was modified by bootleggers during the early days of Prohibition," Sam explained. "But it was definitely one of the selling points for me when I decided to open the Pearl. A lot of the best performers have the old magic, and if I wanted the best, I needed to give them a way out in case we were raided."

Harte gave Esta a blank look, and she realized he wouldn't have any idea what Sam was talking about.

"The government outlawed alcohol in 1920," she explained to Harte.

"But you serve drinks here," Harte pointed out.

"Oh, Prohibition didn't last *that* long," Sammie said. "President Grew repealed the Volsted Act almost as soon as he took office after Harding died, back in '23."

Esta's heart practically stopped. "President Grew" was a phrase that felt as impossible as it was absurd. "I'm sorry, but did you just say *President Grew*?"

Sammie frowned. "Yeah. Why?"

"You don't mean *Jack* Grew?" Esta asked, feeling light-headed.

Sam was looking at her more strangely now than he had when she'd stepped into his office, appearing after fifty years and looking no older than the last time he'd seen her. "What other President Grew would I be talking about?"

"I don't know," Esta said weakly. "I'm just having trouble believing that Jack Grew was president."

"Still is," Sammie said with a confused frown.

"But that would mean he's been president since the twenties."

Sam sighed. "Unfortunately, there's no law against that. With the Brotherhoods on his side, it's been basically impossible for anyone to beat him."

Esta was having a hard time processing what Sammie had just told her. Jack Grew had somehow managed to become president. Worse, apparently Jack had been president for nearly thirty years . . . which meant that history had probably been rewritten in ways too overwhelming—too *terrible*—to comprehend.

"Figures that Jack would make sure liquor is still legal," Harte said, but his attempt at humor fell flat. He couldn't know how wrong this bit of news was, but he looked every bit as unsettled as Esta felt.

"Of course, Nitewein is still outlawed," Sam said. "Anything that pertains to old magic is. That part of Prohibition never really went away, which is why you all have to get going. I can't have the Committee discovering that I employ unregistered Mageus here in the club. Just listen to Gracie and the others, and I'll meet up with you later."

"Be careful," Gracie told Sam, giving him a kiss squarely on the lips and then straightening his tie. A second later, she ducked through the opening in the wall herself.

"We're not done talking about the crown," Harte told Sam.

"It's here?" Esta asked, eyeing the office, wondering if she might be able to pull time slow and take a look. . . .

"No," Sam told her, but his eyes cut to Harte. "I'll explain everything later. I promise. Right now I need you to get out of here."

Harte frowned like he wanted to argue, but Esta could see the worry and nervousness strung tight through Sam's entire body. He wasn't lying about the danger, and besides, it was clear what his relationship with Gracie was. As long as they were with her, Sam wasn't going anywhere.

Once they were both through the opening, Gracie handed Harte a heavy metal flashlight. He examined it with a puzzled expression as the safe door behind them sealed them into the darkness. Esta tried not to let her amusement show as she took it from him and demonstrated how to click on the beam of light.

They were all silent as they traveled through the series of corridors that stretched behind the wall of the nightclub and then down to a short tunnel that apparently connected it to the building at the rear. It opened into the storage room of a busy restaurant kitchen, which was filled with steam and the noise of clattering pans and orders barked in a blend of languages—Chinese, English, and Spanish all mixed together. Once they were outside, they followed an alley for two blocks, until they came to a set of steps that led to the door of a small studio apartment. The glass in the windows had been papered over to keep the light from escaping, and while Paul locked the door, Dottie made sure the coverings were secure before giving Gracie the okay to turn on the lights.

"How long has Sammie had this place?" Harte asked.

"Since he had to hide me during the war," Dottie explained as Gracie went over to the small kitchenette that was tucked into a corner and ran some water for the teapot that had been sitting on the stove. "There's a room behind the back wall, where I lived for about three years."

"You lived behind the wall?" Harte asked.

"I was doing a solo act at Sam's club back in '39—before I met Paul. But after Pearl Harbor, things changed fast. Once the authorities found out another one of the other girls was actually Japanese, they took her away. Took her right off the dance floor one night, and I think it really shook him up, you know?"

Esta could tell by the blank confusion in Harte's eyes that he didn't understand, but Dottie didn't seem to notice.

"I'd been pretty good friends with Mina before she passed, and Sammie already knew what I was . . . I mean, other than Japanese."

"Japanese?" Esta asked, her stomach sinking. She understood the implications of Dottie being Japanese during the Second World War. "I didn't realize . . ."

"Occidentals don't usually know the difference," Dottie said with a shrug. "A lot of the girls in the Chinese clubs aren't Chinese. Toy is just a stage name. My given name's Takahashi, but I haven't used it in a while."

When Esta had discovered that Sam owned the Dragon's Pearl, she also learned that it was only one of many clubs spread throughout the city that featured Chinese performers. Most of the other clubs, like the Forbidden City, were owned by Chinese proprietors and had completely Chinese casts, but Sammie's seemed to employ a mix of performers. The clubs all catered to white audiences, including the Dragon's Pearl.

"Anyhow," Dottie said, "Sam figured it was only a matter of time before the authorities found me, too. But he knew the stakes were a lot higher for me."

"Because you're Mageus," Esta realized.

Dottie nodded. "There's no way I could have hidden what I was in one of those camps. He bought this place and outfitted it. They never did find me. Now he keeps it in case someone needs to lie low for a while."

"It's too bad Ellie Wong didn't use it," Gracie said. "Did you hear that she disappeared last week?"

"No," Dottie said, her mouth falling open in uneasy surprise. "Was it the Committee?"

Paul grimaced. "From what I heard, there was a raid on the Forbidden City. Everybody split, like they do, but after, no one could find her. She hasn't been seen since."

"Maybe she's hiding somewhere, waiting things out," Dottie said, a faint hope tingeing her voice. "Or maybe she got the papers she needed to leave. A lot of people have been going north."

"Maybe . . ." Gracie didn't sound all that convinced. "But that's not what most people over at the Forbidden City think. Ellie hadn't been talking about leaving, and they're all nervous."

"They'd be stupid not to be," Paul said. "Every time things get too quiet, the watchmen get bored and people start disappearing. I don't know what the Committee is going to do when the Reticulum is finally finished. There won't be anyone left to harass."

"Oh, I doubt that'll ever happen," Gracie said dismissively as she returned her attention to the tea she'd been preparing. "If they were ever going to finish it, they would have by now."

But Esta didn't miss the nervous tremor to her voice, and from the look Harte gave her, neither did he.

"What's the Reticulum?" she asked, almost afraid to know the answer.

Suddenly an uneasy silence descended over the room that had the hair on Esta's neck rising as three pairs of eyes swiveled to her.

"The *Reticulum*," Dottie said, like Esta should already know this.

But when Esta simply shook her head to indicate she didn't understand, Gracie's brows drew together. "Who did you say you were again?"

"Friends of Sam's," Harte supplied. "*Old* friends. We've been away for a while."

Gracie's expression was doubtful, clearly suspicious. "You must've been on the moon," she said, but neither Esta nor Harte responded to the implied question. Gracie frowned as she glanced at the two dancers, who both gave a kind of shrug, but in the end they must have decided they trusted Sammie enough to let the impossibility go. "The Reticulum is President Grew's number one priority. Has been for years."

"He's used the promise of finishing it to keep himself in office," Paul said darkly.

"But what is it?" Esta pressed.

The three exchanged glances, almost like they were nervous even to talk about it. Finally, Dottie spoke. "It's a kind of magical net they're building over the entire country—from sea to shining sea, as they say. If they ever manage to finish the network, they'll be able to eliminate the old magic once and for all."

PAST FEARS MADE PRESENT

1952—San Francisco

As Gracie described the Reticulum in greater detail, Harte listened with a kind of horrified detachment. All at once he was both there in that tiny, cramped studio apartment and also back in a warehouse in Manhattan where Jack Grew had boasted to him about a machine that would eliminate magic better than the Brink ever could.

Harte had done what he could to destroy that machine before he'd left the city, but he should have expected that something like this would be possible, especially since he'd been stupid enough to literally hand Jack the Book. Even with all he'd experienced, though, Harte was having trouble imagining something on the scale of what Sammie's friends were describing.

"You're saying that the Reticulum could kill every Mageus in this country," he said, his voice sounding as hollow as he suddenly felt.

"I'm sure there will be places where a person could go," Paul said. "Remote, out-of-the-way places, but who can go live in the wilderness? Who would want to?"

"The Brotherhoods would probably just build another tower there once they found out about it, anyway," Gracie said dourly.

"The rest of the country has really *accepted* this?" Esta asked, sounding every bit as horrified as Harte felt.

"They haven't told people the truth," Paul explained. "According to all the official statements, the mechanisms in the towers simply detect and neutralize unregistered magic. If those who have the old magic turn themselves in and give up their power willingly, they wouldn't be affected at all."

"After what happened in San Francisco, people must know that's a lie," Harte said, thinking of Sammie and the mother he'd lost.

"Individual people might know," Gracie said. "But people in general? Crowds don't care about the details."

"Oh, people know," Dottie said bitterly. "People *always* know. But they don't care enough to stop it. The internments of American citizens during the last war certainly didn't concern them. Why should this? For most people, it's easier to look away. Even good people can convince themselves that something so terrible could only happen if the victims deserved it. 'If they had simply turned themselves in,' they'll say. 'If they had only given up their magic,' they'll say."

"It doesn't help that the Brotherhoods know how to keep the country scared," Paul agreed. "Anytime people in a community start questioning the need for the Reticulum, the Brotherhoods simply do a raid and show exactly how many unregistereds there are hiding in plain sight. They round them up and cart them off, and the community settles down."

"It's enough to keep everyone quiet," Dottie said.

By now the tea Gracie had been preparing had long since been forgotten. The discussion of the Reticulum and the danger they were all in had been enough to make the already-somber mood in the apartment practically funereal.

"There has to be something that can be done," Harte said.

"Oh, plenty *is* being done," Paul told him. "The Antistasi dismantle the towers almost as fast as the government can build them."

"They're still around?" Esta asked, sounding almost breathless.

Gracie nodded. "Of course. There's also the Quellant, if you can manage to get ahold of some. If there is a raid, it makes your affinity impossible to detect."

Harte glanced at Esta. Her lipstick had worn away, and she looked more tired than he'd first noticed. But her eyes had a new brightness, a hopefulness that he understood. After all, if they had more of the Quellant, he could protect Esta from Seshat. He could buy himself more time.

"How hard is it to find?" Harte asked.

"You can only get it on the Nitemarket," Paul said. "Though it's damn expensive these days, from what I've heard."

"It was a little easier to come by during the war," Dottie explained. "Sammie always made sure we all had a good supply of it, just in case."

"Do you still have some?" Esta asked, but the three performers shook their heads almost in unison.

"Sammie might," Gracie said. "I can ask when he gets here. . . . It sure is taking him a while, isn't it? He usually comes fairly quickly."

They all seemed to look at the clock on the wall at once, and suddenly it did feel like it had been a long time. Not long after, though, Sammie finally arrived, looking more than a little harried.

"I think I lost them," he said as he locked the door behind him, making sure to secure the extra latches.

"You always do." Gracie welcomed him back with a kiss, but Sam's posture didn't relax at all with the greeting.

"It wasn't as easy as it usually is," he told her. Then he turned to Dottie and Paul. "It should be safe enough now, but maybe take the long route home?"

"Will do," Paul said. "It's been . . . interesting," he told Harte and Esta with a quizzical smile. Then he turned to Sam. "You want us to drop Gracie off too?"

"Sam can take me home later," Gracie said, curling into Sam's side.

He gave her a quick squeeze but then released her. "I think it's better if you go with Paul and Dottie tonight, sweetheart."

"I thought you said you lost them?" Her nervousness was apparent, even to Harte. "What's going on, Sam?"

"Nothing I can't handle, but better not to take chances, right?" Sam chucked her affectionately on the chin. "You have two shows tomorrow, anyway."

Gracie frowned up at him. "But you're still coming by later?"

"I can't promise anything. Not tonight," Sam said, his expression faltering a little as he glanced in Harte and Esta's direction again. "I have a couple of things that need to be taken care of first."

Harte didn't like the sound of that at all. Neither, it seemed, did Gracie, but she didn't argue any further. A few minutes later, they finished saying their good-byes. Once the others were gone and the door was locked behind them, Sam located a bottle of whiskey in the cupboard above the stove and took a couple of long swallows before offering it to Harte.

Harte shook his head. "What happened after we left?"

Sam's expression was bleak, like he'd been wrung out and put up to dry. "The watchmen were on a tear, all right. They questioned me for a long time, and not particularly nicely." He took another long swallow straight from the bottle before pinning Harte with a knowing gaze. "They specifically wanted to know about you two."

Harte could feel the exhaustion of the day creeping over him, but he willed himself upright. "What did you tell them?"

"Nothing," Sam told Harte, lighting a cigarette and loosening his cuffs as he talked. "People always think that giving up information will save their sorry asses, but I've been around too long to make that kind of mistake. If you tell the Committee anything, they usually make sure you don't talk again."

Harte felt some of the tension drain from him. "Thank you," he said, trying to infuse his voice with all the sincerity he could.

"Don't thank me yet," Sammie said. "They're still looking for the two of you. They know you're in town, and they're not going to stop until they find you. As good as it is to see you again, the faster you get out of town, the easier it's going to be on everyone."

"We can't leave without the Dragon's Eye," Harte said.

"That's the thing. . . ." Sam took a long drag on the cigarette before expelling the smoke in a slow, steady stream. "Like I told you, I don't have it. I sold the crown at the Nitemarket years ago—back in '38. I needed the funds to start the Pearl."

"Who did you sell it to?" Harte pressed, thinking that maybe they could find the buyer.

"Who knows," Sam said. "No one uses real names when they're buying or selling at the Nitemarket. It's safer for everyone that way."

"But you know *when* you sold it." Esta gave Harte a look that made his stomach sink. He knew exactly what she was thinking.

"No, Esta . . ."

"Think about it, Harte. We know where Jack will be now. If we go back to 1920, we could get the Dragon's Eye, *and* we could take back the Pharaoh's Heart and the Book as well. We could stop Jack from taking office, and we could make it so this Reticulum nightmare never existed."

"You're talking like you have some kind of time machine," Sammie said, trying to laugh off the idea, but he grew serious when they didn't join him. "You're not *actually* talking about a time machine?"

"I think that the less you know, the safer you'll be," Esta said, choosing her words carefully.

The amusement drained from Sammie's expression. "You're not going to explain?"

"Esta's right," Harte agreed. "You've dealt with enough tonight. You've already put your business—your whole life here—in danger because of us."

"I'm more than strong enough to withstand whatever the Committee dishes out," Sam said, indignant. "I managed well enough during the last war. Dottie's still here, isn't she? Plenty of others, too."

"Yes, and we're going to make sure that you stay here too," Harte told him. Then he turned to Esta. "Say we do go back. Even if we can get the Book and the dagger from Jack, we only have one tablet of Quellant left," he reminded her. They would need that to get back to 1902.

"Maybe that doesn't have to be a problem," Esta said, glancing at Harte's brother. "Not if Sammie could find us some more."

"These days, the Nitemarket can be a little dodgy," Sammie hedged. "But if it's important—"

"No," Harte said. "You've done enough for us. I'm not having you take any more risks for our sake."

"He's not supposed to be president," Esta said softly. "This Reticulum they were talking about? It's not supposed to exist. None of this was supposed to happen."

"You're sure?" Harte asked, even though he knew already that Esta wouldn't have said it if she wasn't.

"Jack Grew isn't supposed to be *anyone* important. You said he's been in office since Prohibition?" she asked Sam, who was looking more than a little confused at their conversation.

"He was Harding's vice president," Sam explained. "He took office after Harding died, but he's won every election since."

"So much should have happened since then," Esta murmured. "Wars and a depression and presidents who changed the country and the world."

"Oh, we've had wars all right," Sam said, stubbing out the cigarette on the edge of the sink. "A depression, too. But President Grew has been at the helm the whole time, for better or for worse. A lot of the time, it's been worse."

"This Reticulum he's building," Harte asked Sammie. "How much of a reality is it?"

"It's getting close to completion, even with all the Antistasi have done to delay its progress," Sam said. "It's close enough that I keep telling Gracie to go—a lot of Mageus have already gotten false papers and left. I got her some too, but she won't leave without me, and I have too many people here depending on me."

"Harte, we can stop this," Esta said softly. "Jack. The Reticulum. All of it."

"How are *you* possibly going to stop it when an entire network of Antistasi hasn't been able to?" Sam wondered. "There are towers in every state and in every major town, and with television stations needing places to broadcast, they've only grown faster. There's no way you can dismantle the network now—I don't care how powerful you think you are."

"We can if the network was never built in the first place. . . ." Harte let out an unsteady breath, then turned back to Esta. "Just so you're aware, I hate this idea."

"I know," she told him. "But it could work. We could get the Book, the artifacts, *and* make sure Jack Grew never has the power to hurt anyone again."

TRAPPED IN TIME

1952—San Francisco

The next morning, Esta woke to the sound of rain. She pulled the window coverings back far enough to see that the sky was an impenetrable gray. The heaviness of the rain and overall gloom of the day might have seemed like some sort of premonition if Esta had been the type to believe in signs. She wasn't, but the weather cast a pall over her mood nonetheless.

Harte began stirring on the couch, where he'd insisted on sleeping. He needed the rest more than she did, but he'd refused to take the bed out of some kind of misplaced sense of chivalry, *the idiot*. His dark hair was sticking up in all directions like a disheveled chicken, and though Esta couldn't help but smile at the sight, she didn't miss the circles beneath his eyes.

They'd stayed up late into the night planning for what needed to be done. From what Esta could see, there was one place where they knew for sure they could find Jack in the past: the Republican National Convention of 1920. If Esta and Harte could get to the convention, they might be able to stop Jack and steal both the Book and the Pharaoh's Heart, all at the same time.

From what Sam explained, the event had been a turning point—the First World War had recently ended, and everyone had their opinion about what kind of nation the country should become. That year, Jack hadn't really been seen as a serious candidate, but the Antistasi had launched an attack on the convention, and Jack had seized the opportunity to activate a tower in retaliation. People weren't as horrified as they had been with his first tower in San Francisco. Instead, the success of that little exhibition allowed the Brotherhoods to rally the party and push Jack's nomination through for the vice presidency. Once Harding died unexpectedly in 1923, Jack took over.

They knew it would be difficult to steal the Book and the dagger from Jack in the middle of the convention, but if they could find him before the attack galvanized the public against those with the old magic, it might be possible to get close to him. It might be possible to *stop* him and save countless lives.

Harte still hated the idea, but Esta had held firm. History was long, and the country wide. They couldn't pass on this opportunity, not when it was the surest bet they'd had so far. And if they couldn't get more Quellant? If they could never return to 1902? They could at least take Jack Grew out of the equation. Even if they couldn't get the Book or the Pharaoh's Heart, they had to stop the threat of the Reticulum from ever materializing. And if they *did* manage to get both the Book and the Dagger? It was the best possible scenario. It was a risk they had to take.

Harte was pacing the floor by the time Sam finally arrived nearly twenty minutes late, looking tired and harried.

"The Nitemarket wasn't exactly hopping last night," he said. "There's rumors that the two of you have surfaced, and it seems that everyone's nervous about the Committee and what the Brotherhoods might do. I could only find a few more Quellant. Not as many as I'd hoped."

"Thank you," Esta said as she accepted the small wax envelope and glanced inside at the familiar tablets. *Only four.* Which was four more than they'd had before, she reminded herself as she tucked the packet into her leather pouch. It was enough to accomplish what they had to do. "They're exactly what we need."

"The bank opens in about forty minutes," Sam told them, handing over a parcel that contained a change of clothes for each of them. "The sooner we get this over with, the better, as far as I'm concerned."

Sam's car was waiting one block over—a red Mercedes with fenders that had more sleek curves than one of his chorus girls. Even with the umbrellas he'd brought, they were all sopping wet by the time they reached it. The bank where he'd kept the crown before he'd sold it was across the bay, in Oakland. They'd gone over the plan more than enough the night before. Maybe it was nerves or maybe there wasn't anything more to say, but they rode in silence in the plush, leather-lined interior as Sam navigated through the rain-splattered streets and across the massive steel bridge that connected the two cities.

Harte was sitting in the front with Sam, and he watched out the window, his eyes alert as they sped through a changed world. Esta could tell he was taking everything in, but she was more concerned with watching for signs that they were being followed. She didn't see any, but she wouldn't relax until the Dragon's Eye was safely in their possession.

Sam pulled the Mercedes into a spot about half a block from the bank. He cut the ignition and turned to Esta, draping one arm over the seat. "You're sure you don't need my help for this?"

Esta nodded. "We'll need your safety-deposit box number and the key."

He frowned as he held it up. "I'll get it back?"

"Of course," she lied, taking it from him and palming it. They hadn't explained everything. As far as Sam knew, they were only popping back long enough to get the crown. He thought they planned to return. "We're going to pay you back tenfold, I promise."

Sam gave her a doubtful look. "I can't help thinking I should be going in there with you," he told them. "It would be nothing at all for me to let you into the vault myself."

And then he'd have to explain how the people he'd been with had disappeared.

"It's really not necessary," Esta told him. "You have so much more to lose than we do if anything goes wrong."

"Just because I've got some years on you now doesn't mean I can't still handle myself," Sam said sourly.

"I don't doubt it. But you've already done more than anyone could have asked of you," Harte told him, speaking to Sam as if he were still a young boy and not the old man he'd become. "Remember, if we're not out in five minutes, you leave. Just go. Don't look back and don't worry about us. Whatever you do, *don't* come in after us."

Sam frowned, but he didn't fight them about the issue anymore.

Harte came around the car with the umbrella for Esta, and they started walking toward the entrance to the bank. She'd already removed her gloves. "Are you ready?" she asked, handing him one of the remaining tablets of Quellant.

"Not really." But he placed it into his mouth anyway and couldn't suppress a shudder. "That's terrible."

"I know." Esta remembered too well what it had been like to take Maggie's Quellant—to feel that essential part of herself sliding away. "Everything okay?" she asked when a strange look came over his face.

"I think so. . . ." Harte's brows were drawn together, like he was trying to figure something out. Then his expression relaxed a little. "The only positive thing about this whole situation is that I get to do this," he said, slipping his hand into hers.

His palm was warm, and Esta felt a shiver of awareness when his skin touched hers. She waited, her breath tight with something that felt too close to longing, but she didn't sense the vining warning of Seshat's energy. All she felt were the calluses on Harte's palms as their fingers intertwined. In that moment they were simply two people—a girl and a boy—walking together in the rain. For a moment, Esta allowed herself to imagine a life like this, where they could be . . . normal—whatever that meant. Safe, if there could be any such thing.

And if that life could not be? Could maybe *never* be? Esta would relish this stolen calm before the storm they were about to create.

The bank was housed in an unremarkable brick building with a large clock above the heavy double doors. "Ready?" Esta asked when Harte hesitated at the bottom of the steps leading up to the entrance.

He glanced over without bothering to hide his nerves. "What if we make things worse?"

Esta had the same worry, but she squeezed his hand gently. "If we don't try, they can never get better." Then she tilted her face up to him, and before she could allow herself to think through all the reasons why she shouldn't, she pressed her mouth against his.

Harte's lips felt cool against hers, soft with surprise, but he reacted almost immediately, deepening the kiss. His fingers closed around hers, and when she finally pulled away, the tightness around his jawline had softened and his stormy eyes looked hungry.

"Why did you do that?" Harte asked, still sounding a little breathless.

"Because you looked like you needed it," Esta told him. "And because I wanted to." She couldn't stop the smile that curved her lips. Before he could ruin the moment—before he started telling her all the ways that it had been a bad idea—she pulled him toward the bank. She tried not to let herself worry too much about the darkness she thought she noticed lurking in the depths of his eyes, a darkness that seemed to be waiting.

Inside the bank's vestibule, the steady patter of the rain went silent. People spoke in the hushed whispers usually reserved for funeral homes or churches or for being in the presence of large quantities of money. Esta didn't ask if Harte was ready, but instead simply pulled the seconds slow, until the soft sounds of the bank receded and the world went still.

They made their way into the cavernous marble and wood lobby. It was early enough that there were very few people around. Dodging behind the service counter, Esta carefully lifted a key ring from the belt of one of the tellers, and together they found the vault where the safety-deposit boxes waited. Luckily, the vault itself had already been opened for the day.

The vault was lined floor to ceiling with small, bronze-colored doors. The safety-deposit boxes would contain any number of things—important papers or keepsakes, but also gold and coins, cash and jewelry. Maybe it would have been safer to keep time completely still, but each box required two locks to be simultaneously unlocked—one with the master key they'd stolen from the teller and one that they needed to pick on their own. She couldn't do that *and* hold on to Harte, so Esta released time and started on the first lock. Beyond the entrance to the vault, she could hear the sounds of the bank coming back to life.

"I don't like this," Harte whispered.

"Me neither, but the faster we get to work, the faster we can get out of here," Esta said as she finished popping the lock she'd been working on.

Inside she found gold coins and a few pieces of jewelry, which she pocketed before moving on to the next and then the next. She couldn't let herself think about the people she was stealing from, or what these small treasures might mean to them, and in a matter of minutes she had quite a haul—cash and jewels, antique coins, and some old stock certificates as well. None of it would be traceable, because she was taking it all with them, back where no one would be looking for it.

Harte started working as well. His years of training for his act had made him a deft lockpick, and he worked almost as fast as she did with the master key. They replaced the boxes as they went, so that at first glance no one would notice anything had been taken. They were working so efficiently that in a matter of minutes they'd cleared enough to make Sam a very rich man.

Esta was finishing up when they heard footsteps approaching. She barely had time to lunge for Harte, who was on the other side of the vault, but before she could pull the seconds still, Sammie appeared in the doorway.

"The watchmen." His eyes were wide, and he was panting.

Esta understood immediately and reached for Sammie, but shots erupted and he shuddered, jerking violently—one, two, three, four times—and staggered out of her reach, falling sideways into Harte's arms.

Esta sprang into action, slamming the vault door closed and pulling the seconds slow all at once. The world went starkly, deafeningly silent.

At first all she could do was stand there, her heart pounding in her ears as she looked at the scene in front of her—the shocked anguish on

Harte's face, his arms outstretched to catch his brother, and the blood that had splattered the bronze doors from where Sam had been hit squarely in the back.

Esta was frozen with indecision. If she released time, the people who had shot Sammie would have the door to the vault opened in a matter of minutes—maybe even seconds. But she understood that she couldn't simply pull Harte and Sammie into the net of time with her. If she brought the two back into the regular march of seconds, Sammie's wounds would bleed and Harte's brother would die. All Esta could do was stand there between the seconds that separated life from death. Between the past that had been and the future she could remake, knowing that she couldn't stay there, trapped in time within an airless vault forever, but neither could she let go.

UNEXPECTED

1902—New York

Jack Grew was sitting in the back parlor of the Vanderbilt home with a group of other men, doing his level best to avoid the preening debutantes on the dance floor. The fact that the whiskey he was drinking seemed to be mostly water did nothing to help his growing irritation. It wasn't enough that the Order had decided he was worthy of trust. *No.* Jack's family had decided that he was in need of something more— namely, a wife. They had collectively decided that he should spend more time out in society and were determined that he suffer through every summer soiree since the gala.

It would be good for his reputation, his mother insisted. The more the important families of the city saw him, the less they would think of that girl's unfortunate death, his aunt had agreed. Marriage, the women had decided, would serve to help rehabilitate his image.

Rehabilitate. That was the actual word they'd used, as though Jack were some invalid convalescing with tuberculosis. Morgan, of course, was no help. Jack's uncle was clearly in the minority of opinions in the Inner Circle and was perfectly happy to allow the women of the family to arrange Jack's life. Morgan made it no secret that he would have preferred his nephew not be involved with the plans for their new headquarters, and he reminded Jack of this every time their paths crossed.

That night was like every other dinner party he'd been forced to attend. He made his required appearance to appease the cackling hens in his family, but that was Jack's limit. Instead of the crush of the ballroom, he found his usual spot with the men in the back parlor, far from the mothers with their sharp eyes and unwed daughters in tow. The last thing he needed was to be tied to one of those bits of muslin, not when he had more important things to accomplish.

Jack was playing a hand of rummy with a few of the older fellows, since they, at least, tended not to put much stock in gossip or marriage marts, when he noticed a familiar face—one he hadn't seen for weeks. Theo Barclay was walking through the parlor with the High Princept and two other men from the Inner Circle.

There was something about the group that bothered Jack. Maybe it was simply Barclay's appearance, or the ease with which Theo seemed to be conversing with the older men. Something was wrong with the portrait they made as the men cut through the back parlor, and Jack's instincts were prickling. He folded his hand and excused himself from the table, then made his way toward the trio.

"Barclay?" Jack called out. When Theo Barclay turned, a question—or was that a bit of panic—in his eyes, Jack pretended delight. "I thought that was you. But I thought I'd heard you were headed for the Continent with your lovely bride?"

Theo gave Jack a stiff excuse for a smile as the High Princept simply lifted his brows at the interruption.

"Ruby already departed, but I'm not set to leave quite yet, I'm afraid," Theo said, suddenly looking even more uncomfortable.

"But you *are* to be married?" Jack asked, wondering if the rumors he'd heard had any merit to them. He wouldn't be surprised, really. Reynolds, pretty as she might be, was nothing but a hoyden, and Barclay was hardly the type capable of bringing her to heel.

"Yes," Barclay said. "The wedding won't be until autumn, though. Ruby had her heart set on the colors of the season. Who was I to deny her?"

"Who indeed . . . other than her fiancé," Jack said, still considering Barclay's unexpected appearance that evening. "I hadn't realized that you knew each other." He motioned between Theo and the High Princept.

"Mr. Barclay is a new initiate," the old man said.

"Is he?" Jack stared at Theo, who was turning quite the shade of pink. "I hadn't realized you had any interest in the occult sciences, Barclay."

Theo blinked. "I, ah . . . Well, that is to say . . ." He was doing an absurdly bad job at covering his discomfort, which only proved to Jack that something was *certainly* amiss.

"Young Barclay here is quite an accomplished student of ancient art," the High Princept said. "He did your uncle a great service recently, returning one of the pieces lost in the robbery at the Metropolitan."

"Did he?" Jack's instincts were on alert, and in his jacket pocket, the Book's weight felt like an anchor. "How very . . . unexpected."

"Oh, not really," Theo said, looking distinctly uneasy. "I often frequent the auction houses looking for interesting pieces, and when I saw this *particular* piece come up, I knew immediately what it must be."

"Indeed?" Jack said, still eyeing him. "Can I inquire about which piece you returned?"

"An amulet," Theo told him. "From ancient Babylon, I believe."

Jack knew exactly what Theo was referring to—a bit of unpolished ruby carved into a seal. It had been one of the pieces Jack had been *particularly* interested in examining before the fiasco of the robbery had taken his opportunity. "My uncle must have been grateful for its return."

"He was," the Princept said. "Morgan himself recommended the boy's immediate initiation."

It was all too convenient and more than a little suspect, considering that Jack had never heard of Barclay's interest in the Order before this.

"Did he?" Jack said, considering Barclay anew.

Theo gave him a wobbly, unsettled smile. "Your uncle has been most gracious, but I was simply happy to be of service. He's quite well known as a collector in many art circles. Simply speaking with him about his holdings was an honor."

"I'm sure it was," Jack said dryly.

His uncle collected antiquities, rare art from the ancient world, including an array of pieces that were related to the occult sciences. Tablets and seals, amulets and figures carved with runelike markings. An entire portion of the collection had gone missing some months before, but there hadn't been any sign or clue since. Strange that Barclay, who was eminently *forgettable*, should be the one to return an item when any number of private investigators had been unable to do the same.

"Morgan was quite impressed with the extent of Barclay's knowledge and expertise when it came to certain pieces in the collection," the Princept said, turning to Theo. "It seems your art degrees weren't the frivolous waste that many of us originally believed them to be."

It was something closer to anger that flushed Theo's cheeks this time. "It seems not," he said evenly.

"Your family must be quite proud," Jack said.

"I'm sure yours feels the same after your resounding triumph at the gala," Theo replied, though his tone did not match his words. "I was there, you know."

"Oh, I'm aware," Jack drawled. "I had the pleasure of directing your lovely bride in her tableau, after all. She's turned out to be quite the beauty, hasn't she? Quite the hellion, too, from what I hear. She'll need a firm hand to rein her in. Are you sure you're up for such a job?"

Barclay's jaw had gone tight. "Unlike *some*, I'm not so insecure as to feel the need to treat my beloved like a broodmare."

Jack's fists clenched at the not-so-veiled insult, but the High Princept cleared his throat before he could so much as respond. "Yes, well. We have people waiting for us, Jack. I was going to introduce young Barclay here to some of our other members."

"Of course," Jack said, bowing his head slightly but keeping his eyes pinned to Theo Barclay.

It was no accident that the collection of ancient Ottoman art that his uncle had intended to display at the Metropolitan was stolen a few weeks before Khafre Hall was destroyed, Jack was sure of it. Just as he was certain that Theo Barclay had not found this piece from his uncle's collection by pure chance.

"Congratulations on your good fortune, Barclay." Jack extended his hand. "I'm sure you'll make a fine addition to our membership."

After a moment's hesitation, Theo took it, and they shook like gentlemen. But Jack held his grip for a heartbeat longer than necessary, relishing the way Theo's eyes widened ever so slightly.

Barclay was up to something—that much was certain. Jack had only to discover how he could best use that knowledge to his advantage.

TIME HELD ITS BREATH

1952—San Francisco

Harte stumbled under the weight of Sam's body. His brother was heavier than he looked, and as Sammie fell into him, Harte was barely able to break his fall. They both ended up on the cold metal floor of the vault. The next thing he knew, the vault door was being slammed closed, and Esta was standing over them with a look of quiet horror in her eyes.

"Sam?" Harte tried to maneuver to see if his brother was conscious. He could already feel blood soaking into his own clothing, but he refused to acknowledge the truth of it.

Sammie didn't respond. His face was slack and his eyes partially closed, but Harte couldn't process what had just happened. He looked up to find Esta with her hand clasped over her mouth. She was shaking her head, and Harte knew then, without her even saying a word. But he still didn't want to accept the truth of it.

"No," he told her, moving so that he could gently lay his brother out on the floor of the vault and try to shake him awake. He couldn't be the cause of another innocent life being snuffed out. Not again. Sammie couldn't die because of him.

Harte was still holding his brother, tapping gently at the face that now wore the years of an old man. Those years didn't seem to matter, though. All Harte could see was the boy beneath, the child he'd once given up everything to rescue and who'd then found Esta and rescued him in turn.

It can't end like this.

522

Their attackers were still outside, though. Dimly, Harte realized someone was already working the heavy tumbler of the vault door, and soon enough, the door would open once again and they would be trapped.

"He's gone, Harte," Esta said softly. Her voice trembled, even as the hand on his shoulder was firm as she tried to pull him away.

Harte ignored her and concentrated on Sam's face. *If he would only wake up . . .*

Esta tugged at him again. "We have to go," she said. "That lock will only keep them out for a couple more seconds."

"I'm not leaving him here," Harte told her. "I can't."

She crouched down and took his hand, but Harte refused to look at her. He couldn't leave his brother here to be found by their enemies. He *wouldn't.* "We're going to take him." As long as Harte had ahold of Sam, Esta couldn't leave him there.

"We can't," she told him. Her voice was soft, but the words still felt like a slap. "If Sammie disappears, they'll know for sure what happened here."

"I don't care about that," Harte told her.

"What happens when we get back to 1920, Harte?" Esta asked. "We can't stop guns that have already fired. We can't change what just happened by taking Sammie with us, but if we go now, it doesn't have to be like this." Her voice was more urgent now. "We can fix this, Harte, but we have to go. *Now.* You have to let Sammie go, because if they catch us here, this is how your brother's life ends. The Brotherhoods aren't going to let us get away again."

Harte was still shaking his head. He'd tried to save Sammie once before, and in the end it had come to this. "What if we can't change anything?" He looked up at her then. "What if we make it all *worse*?"

"I don't know," she told him. "But if we don't go now, everything ends right here. Including Sammie's life. Let go of him, Harte. Give me your hand."

Esta was right. Harte *knew* she was absolutely right about everything, but it felt impossible to let go of his brother. To leave him like this, alone on the cold floor of a darkened vault.

The turning of the lock on the vault had stopped, and Harte could hear the lever being depressed.

"Harte, please . . ." Esta's voice was gentle.

Before the door could open, she grabbed Harte's shoulder, and the sound drained from the vault as they were caught in the power of her magic. Finally, Harte made himself release his brother and left him there on the floor, outside of Esta's hold on time. Harte's legs seemed to move of their own accord, as he forced himself to his feet. Without another word, he took Esta's hand. She was trembling, he realized, the same as himself. But his legs were strangely solid beneath him.

Harte did not take his eyes from his brother's face. His body was cold, his brain numb, and every bit of himself felt as distant and dead as the Quellant had made Seshat's power. On the bloodstained floor of the vault, Sam stared up at them, sightless and silent.

"Let me . . ." Still holding Esta's hand, Harte bent down to close his brother's eyes. "This *has* to work," he told her.

Esta's face was dappled in shadow. "It will," she told him, her voice as determined as her expression. She wrapped her arms around him, pulling Harte into the warmth of her embrace. The vault was silent, and time seemed to be holding its breath. All at once the world felt like it was contracting around him, ripping itself apart in a great roaring, and then, suddenly, all was quiet again, and Harte found himself spinning through the endless darkness.

No . . . not *endless* darkness, and it was only his own head that was spinning. The floor was solid beneath him as Esta let go of his hand and the world righted itself. Nearby he could hear her breathing, soft and steady, as though the world itself hadn't been turned inside out.

Esta clicked on the flashlight that Sam had given them, and a beam illuminated the vault. Harte didn't need the light to know that Sammie was no longer there on the floor. He could only hope that Esta was right and that they could change the past so his brother would *never* be there.

Esta had already launched into action and had located Sammie's box. A moment later she opened the small metal door.

Harte felt the wash of power before Esta even lifted the golden crown from within Sammie's box and replaced it with everything they'd stolen from the other security boxes. He wondered how he hadn't recognized the fake Dragon's Eye for what it was. Still, standing there with the memory of his brother's body clear in his mind's eye, he didn't feel any relief. How could he, when obtaining the crown meant that he was one step closer to his inevitable end?

LOST

1920—A Train Heading East

Esta didn't know how she managed to guide Harte out of the bank vault and get him to the station in Oakland without anyone noticing the bloodstains on his clothes or his general state of shock, but she did. She bought two overnight tickets for a train to Chicago that left within the hour and sat silently by his side as they waited for the boarding call. Since the Quellant was still suppressing Seshat's power, she took the risk of taking his hand in hers, but he didn't respond. It was clear he was still reeling from the loss of his brother.

Esta thought she might almost understand what loss like that felt like. She'd lost too many people in her life—had herself been the cause of deaths and disappearances. There was the hollow shock of discovering too late that Dolph Saunders had been her true father and the pain of learning that her friend Mari had disappeared, erased from existence because of some change Esta had made in a seemingly unconnected past. Then there was Dakari. Esta still felt a numbing grief when she thought of her friend and mentor, and every time she did, the memory of him being murdered that night in Professor Lachlan's study rose in her mind.

Even once they were underway, safely ensconced inside the cramped quiet of the train berth, Harte remained distant and far too quiet. They barely talked through dinner, and Esta felt like she was looking at him through the wrong end of a spyglass. Harte was right there, an arm's length across the narrow table from her, and yet he felt too far away.

Worse, the air between them seemed to be charged with an

awkwardness that had *never* been there before. Esta felt like she was dining with a stranger instead of the one person who had always seemed to see her better than anyone ever had—even when they'd still been enemies. It felt like all of the intimacy they'd shared in the previous weeks, the long days and nights of his recovery—first at the hospital and especially at the hotel in San Francisco—had evaporated into nothing in the presence of his grief.

Or perhaps, the truth of that intimacy had finally come to the surface. Perhaps it had stripped bare each of their vulnerabilities far more than either of them had ever planned, exposing the soft, white underbellies they'd taken such pains to cover and protect for so long.

Still, Esta wanted to say something—*anything*—that could close the distance between them again. "It wasn't your fault, Harte," she whispered, finally breaking a silence that had grown too oppressive for her to bear.

He glanced up at her, his expression so dark that she knew it had been the wrong thing to say. "Sammie's dead, Esta."

"But you weren't the one who killed him."

His mouth went tight, and he stared down at his barely touched plate of food. "Is that how you feel about your friend Dakari?" he asked. His voice was gentle, but the question still felt like a slap.

"That's not the same," Esta argued, but she couldn't stop the guilt and shame from rising up within her, right alongside the memory of that night in Professor Lachlan's library.

"Isn't it?" Harte asked.

"Of course not," she said. Still, Esta couldn't blink away the image of Dakari's face when Professor Lachlan had aimed the gun at his chest. She would never forget the shock of betrayal and confusion that had flashed through Dakari's dark eyes as the bullet tore through him, nor the sound of his body hitting the floor. All because Professor Lachlan had been trying to bend Esta to his will.

"Sammie would never have been shot today if not for me dragging him into our troubles, Esta. He'd still be running his club and helping

Mageus like Gracie and Paul, and he could have lived to a ripe old age. I never should have walked into his life again. I should've learned after what happened with Julian. So please don't try to tell me this isn't my fault. It's as much my fault as if I'd pulled the trigger myself."

"Should I blame myself for Dakari's death, then?" Esta asked, feeling unbearably brittle.

"Of course not," he told her.

"It doesn't work both ways, Harte. If you caused Sammie's death, then I'm every bit as guilty of Dakari's," Esta said, letting the truth of that settle over her. "Dolph's too, for that matter."

"That's not what I'm saying." Harte raked a hand through his hair.

"But it is," she told him gently, tears burning in her eyes. "It's *exactly* what you're saying."

"No——" He reached for her hand.

She looked down at their fingers intertwined. "You're not wrong, though. Not really. Dakari did die because of me; that fact is irrefutable. So did Dolph. So did my mother and who knows how many other people."

Harte's voice was soft when he spoke again. Far gentler than she deserved. "You didn't kill any of them, Esta."

"That's my point," she whispered, feeling strangely lighter. "You're right . . . I *didn't* kill Dakari. It was Professor Lachlan who pulled the trigger." She felt something loosen within her and gave Harte's hand a gentle squeeze. "*You* didn't kill your brother, Harte. You saved him when he was just a boy. You gave him a long life, and you'll give him another one if everything goes as we hope it will."

"But we don't know for sure." Harte tried to pull away, but Esta didn't allow him to retreat.

"You're right," she admitted. "We can't know for sure right now. But we *have* to believe it. We have to keep going."

Harte pulled away from her then, and this time she let him. Before she could figure out how to make things better, though, the porter interrupted to clear away their plates and prepare the sleeping quarters. Harte wouldn't quite look at her as he announced that he would take the top bunk and climbed into it without another word.

Left with the choice between sitting up by herself or trying to sleep, Esta undressed, stripping down to the nylon slip she was wearing beneath the simple flared skirt, and climbed into her own bunk. She didn't know what the next few days would hold. If they were lucky, they would have the Book and four of the artifacts. If everything worked out, they would be one step closer to returning to the past and controlling Seshat once and for all. Even that promise didn't lift her spirits, though, not when her possible end was inching closer, and not when the distance that had sprung up between the two of them made her feel like she'd lost some-thing essential.

Esta had spent her whole life holding people back, pushing them away. Because it was what she'd been taught. Because it was *safer*. Even now she understood that she'd never really thanked Dakari, never told him what his friendship had meant to her, because she'd been scared. Scared that he would reject her, as she'd once thought her own parents had. Scared to admit that she needed someone to depend on, other than herself.

As the train hurtled eastward, carrying them toward whatever fate or time or luck held in store, Esta realized she was so *tired* of being alone. She was tired of being solitary and strong. Most of all, she was tired of holding herself away from *Harte*.

If the Book offered no other answers for controlling Seshat's power, Esta would have to give her affinity—her very *self*—to stop Seshat. That was fine. She could accept that end as her destiny. But she could not accept going to her death without Harte knowing what he meant to her. After all, Esta had never been one for regrets.

Easing herself out of the warmth of her own bed, she shivered as the cool air of the cabin made gooseflesh rise along her arms. She didn't let herself hesitate or second-guess but instead climbed directly up into the bunk above. Harte startled when she slid in beside him, but she ignored the way he tried to pull away from her. Instead, she curled around him, enjoying the warmth of his body and not allowing him to go. She was done hiding, finished with the endless push-pull between them.

You are not negotiable. She still felt her cheeks burn every time she thought about how the words had tumbled from her in the hospital before she could stop them.

That goes both ways, you know, he'd replied.

They hadn't talked about the exchange since, but Esta had convinced herself that Harte understood. His words proved it, didn't they? But then he'd pulled back, away from her.

"Esta—" Harte's voice was strained, a whispered plea between them, but she couldn't tell what he was asking for.

"You took the Quellant," she said simply. "We have a little time. . . ."

"I can't," he told her, even as she tucked her face into the place where his shoulder met his neck and pressed a kiss there.

"You could try," she whispered into the crook of his neck, breathing in the smell of him. Because, god, she just needed to feel something other than grief and pain and hopelessness.

No. Not *something.* She needed *him.*

"Esta . . ."

"Please, Harte," she whispered, not really knowing what she was asking for. All Esta knew was that she needed this, Harte's arms around her and the feel of their bodies pressed together.

He seemed to relent, and she felt his body relax little by little as they lay there. The train rocked and swayed beneath them as it carried them onward. Eventually, Harte turned to her, his face so close that she could smell on his breath the sweetness of the wine he'd sipped at dinner. "I have nothing to offer you," he whispered, his voice a hollow version if itself. "No past, no future."

I don't need a future. I might not even have one.

"You have right now," Esta said, the words coming without planning or any artifice. The moment they were free of her, she felt the truth of them. "I can steal all the time in the world, but right now is all that we've ever had."

"It's not enough." Harte's face turned away from her again, and he stared up at the ceiling. "You deserve more than that."

"Maybe . . . but I'm not asking for more." Esta placed a small, soft kiss on the underside of his jaw, just beneath his ear where his skin was smooth and smelled of whatever tonic he'd put on after shaving earlier that day. It was different from the scent he'd worn in New York, but it still seemed completely perfect for him. Warm with a hint of some spice, it was a scent that felt closer to home than any place she'd ever been.

A long stretch of minutes passed between them with nothing but the shuffling of the rails, the steady rocking of the car, and in the silence, Esta felt a quiet sureness that *this* was where she belonged, whatever might happen. She knew Harte would turn away from her again. She felt it coming, the shift in his body that would break the connection she needed so desperately, a connection that confirmed that she was still real and whole and alive, when everything else felt like it was crumbling around her.

Harte turned to her instead, surprising her. "I shouldn't," he said, his voice as raw as the look in his eyes.

Before Esta could prepare herself, before she could even feel the relief that shuttled through her when she realized what his words meant, his lips were on hers. And she was lost.

THE NIGHT-DARK COUNTRY

1920—A Train Heading East

Harte could no more have stopped himself from kissing Esta in that moment than he could have stopped his heart from beating. Ever since he'd left her on the train, he'd imagined what it would have been like to stay. To remain curled beside her in that narrow bunk and see her wake in the morning, her face soft with sleep and her eyes wanting him. Now he seemed to be handed a second chance, a gift he did not—*could not*—possibly deserve.

While he lay writhing in feverish pain back in San Francisco, the thought of Esta had been Harte's only comfort. The knowledge that he *had* to continue on, if only to make sure he made things right for her, had kept him fighting against the fever that had ravaged his body. How many hours had he spent in that limbo between life and death, holding on only because dying meant never seeing her again? In those dark, painful hours, how many times had he imagined this? Hoped beyond hope to be *worthy* of it.

Of *her*.

And then, after she'd saved him, he'd spent all of those days so close to her without ever touching her—not really—even though his fingers burned to feel her skin. To pull her close. He'd held back, because he knew he couldn't risk it. Because Harte understood too well the danger he was putting her in simply by existing. Because of Seshat.

But thanks to the terrible emptiness caused by the Quellant, Harte didn't have to worry about Seshat—not for a little while longer, at least.

The time would come when the goddess would rouse herself, push past the fog of the drug, and make her presence known. That he didn't doubt. But for now Seshat was silent. Absent. It was only himself and Esta, alone in the middle of the night-dark country, and the space between them brimmed with possibility.

He'd dreamed often of kissing her, of course. Even as he'd burned with the shame of all that she had to do for him as he had healed, each time Harte had collapsed into sleep, his traitorous brain had conjured Esta in his dreams. But with Seshat within him, he'd given up the possibility of ever having a moment like this.

You are not negotiable, not for me.

Had he been standing at the time, the words she'd spoken to him would have brought him to his knees, but once they were safely out of the hospital, neither of them had approached the issue again. In the hours and days since, he had not allowed himself to hope for the feel of Esta's hands cupping his face, the weight of her body pressing down on him, as it was now, as she moved over him and deepened the kiss, her legs on either side of his as she caged him in. But now he didn't have to hope. Now she was there in truth, over him. *With* him.

He wanted to tell Esta to wait, to slow down, because he wanted to remember every brush of her skin and taste on her lips. But her mouth was ravenous, her hands tugging at his shirt and pushing it up over his head, like she was driven by something more than need. Harte thought it felt too close to desperation, but then her cool palms ran across the bare skin of his chest, and he forgot about slow. He forgot about anything but the scent of her, softly clean and barely floral, and the feel of her, smooth and strong and *his*.

This time there was no echoing laughter. This time Seshat was locked away and could not mock or threaten.

Esta broke their kiss long enough to pull off the scrap of material she was wearing, and as she lifted her arms over her head to remove it, the moonlight sliced across her bare torso, illuminating the curves of her body. But she didn't give him nearly enough time to look or revel in the moment. She was kissing him again, hungry and insistent, pressing herself against him, the soft roundness of her body against the hard planes of his own.

Her hands were everywhere, like fire burning along his skin, and Harte was aware suddenly of what his illness had taken from him. His leanness was all bone and sinew without the strength he'd once had. But Esta didn't give him time to be self-conscious.

"Esta—" Her name was a prayer on his lips, and he could not have answered, even to himself, whether he meant for her to stop or to go on.

"I like the way it sounds when you say my name like that," she whispered against his neck, a smile in her voice as she nipped at his shoulder.

"Wait," he panted, as her lips explored the planes of his chest, farther down his torso.

Esta paused only long enough to look up at him, her golden eyes glinting in the darkness, as bright as the stone in the Dragon's Eye. "I want this, Harte. Tell me you want this too."

"Of course I do, but . . ." She moved again, and his words fell away, along with his reluctance.

What was the point of being chivalrous when her touch was turning his skin to flame? The heat of her mouth left a trail of fire across his skin. And when she rose up over him, burning as brightly as a phoenix, Harte knew for certain what he had perhaps always known, even from that first moment in the Haymarket, when he'd seen her across the ballroom and had felt instantly drawn to her. No one would ever match him so well. No one would ever fit with him as she did.

However much time they might have left, however much time Esta might steal for them—days or years or eternities—it would never be enough. There would never be anyone else for him but Esta. Not ever again.

The train lurched around a curve, and Esta lost her balance, falling onto him, her bare body like a brand against his. Somewhere in the distant recesses of his mind, Harte knew that it was too much, too fast. But he didn't stop. *Couldn't.* He shifted so they were side by side, equals as they'd ever been, hands roaming, mouths ravenous. An ecstatic fumbling need drove them onward toward some conclusion that they did not quite understand until it crashed over them, turning them both to ash.

When Harte finally came back to himself, his arms and legs were so tangled with Esta's that he could no longer tell where his body ended and where hers began. All he could do was lie there feeling slightly apart from everything. Finally, the sound of Esta's soft laughter brought Harte back to himself. He felt something dangerously close to happiness, and his mouth began to curve in answer. Then, all at once, he remembered everything that had happened. Sammie was dead. His brother was dead, and *this* was how he mourned him?

The memory of Sammie's body, bloodied and broken, rose in Harte's mind, and the shame of feeling anything close to happiness flooded through him. It was followed swiftly by a bolt of sheer panic as he realized what had just happened. What he'd *allowed* to happen.

He pulled away then, untangling himself from the warmth of Esta's arms so he could lie as far from her as possible in the narrow bunk. If she touched him now, he wouldn't be able to help himself.

"What is it?" Esta's eyes were soft and sleepy as she smiled at him. She looked utterly open, utterly *vulnerable.* Because she *was* vulnerable. Harte had allowed his control to slip, and his selfishness had put her in danger.

"I don't know what that was," he said, staring up at the ceiling of the berth. His voice sounded stiff and stilted, even to him. "But it can't happen again."

He could practically *feel* the smile slide from her lips as Esta propped herself up on her side to look down at him. "You don't know what *that* was?" she asked, her voice filled with humor, but it was tinged with wariness as well.

"Of course I know what *that* was," Harte said, feeling his cheeks burn. Her brows were drawn together and the emotion in her eyes was quickly giving way to something more alert. "We shouldn't have . . ." But Harte couldn't finish, because he was enough of a bastard to not want to take any of it back. Even though he knew he should.

Esta's voice was still soft, but there was a prickliness to her tone when she spoke again. "You said that you wanted—"

"I *did*," he admitted. Maybe he shouldn't have wanted her, and he definitely shouldn't have allowed himself to have her, but he wouldn't lie about the truth of the matter now.

"Then what's the problem?" Esta's words were clipped as she pulled away from him and sat up completely. She pulled the thin cotton sheet up along with her, as though she suddenly realized how bare she was and felt too exposed.

Harte couldn't bring himself to look at her. Even with the sheet covering her, he now knew every inch of the body hidden beneath. He wanted to know it better—wanted to trace his thumb over the scar on her shoulder that he hadn't noticed before. He wanted to press his lips there and take away the memory of whatever had caused it. He wanted to trace the silvery line at the base of her throat where Nibsy had cut her, until there was nothing in the world but the two of them again.

But it all felt too intimate . . . too *dangerous*. It was safer to let her establish this distance. Safer, too, if they were honest with each other about what this had been—what it could ever be. He thought of the nurse back at the hospital, the way the woman had called Esta his wife and how that had made him feel: terrified and awed and desperate all at once. With his body still warm and his mind still buzzing with pleasure, Harte wanted . . . He wasn't sure what he wanted other than Esta. But he was still a man without a future, without anything to offer her. He'd forgotten that for a moment, and he'd let himself take too much.

"It was a mistake."

"*Excuse me?*" Esta's voice had turned into a blade every bit as dangerous as Viola's.

Harte winced inwardly at the sharpness of her tone—the *hurt* in it as well—but there was something he had to say. He was going about this all wrong, but he was still so light-headed and overwhelmed, and he had to make her understand. "I never should have allowed it to happen."

"*Allowed?*" Esta's full mouth parted slightly.

Harte braced himself for her to finish, but where he'd prepared for fire, Esta gave him only ice. There was a long beat of silence, with the train car rocking and swaying beneath them, as though it were trying to convince them to return to the minutes before, when there had been only the rhythm of their bodies and mouths.

"You know, Darrigan, you are a complete and absolute *ass*." Esta's voice was devoid of all feeling or warmth.

Harte had the sudden and unpleasant premonition that he'd made a terrible mistake.

A sliver of moonlight cut through the space where the curtains had slid open, casting its glow over Esta's face—the soft mouth that had just been on his body, the sharp nose that he'd once thought made her striking more than classically pretty.

How had he ever thought that? Now he saw her, *all* of her. Not only her body, but the woman she was. He saw her strength *and* her vulnerability, her bravery *and* her fear. And when he saw her golden eyes glassy with unshed tears, he realized his utter stupidity. He'd spoken poorly, and because of that, she'd misunderstood.

But it was too late for him to take back his words or to repair the rift he'd created between them. A second later Esta slid out of his bunk without another word, leaving him with only the steady sound of the train beneath them and the empty comfort of his pride.

COMPLICATIONS

1920—A Train Heading East

Esta lay awake for the rest of the night. She could not silence the memory of Harte's words. They ran through her mind again and again, steady and constant as the train consuming the tracks beneath her.

It was a mistake.

I never should have allowed it to happen.

She could hear Harte's faint breathing above her, the soft not-quite snores he made as he slept the sleep of the righteous. She had thought he'd understood. When he'd laid his mouth on hers, when he'd pulled them both under, breaking through the casual stoicism they each wore like armor, she'd thought he was in agreement. Apparently, she'd been wrong.

She'd spent so much of her life trying—*trying*—so hard to be what she was supposed to be. The perfect thief. Loyal to her provider and mentor, loyal to her team. The perfect weapon. Honed and sharpened. Cast from steel. It didn't matter that Esta was *good* at all of those things. It didn't matter that her heart beat in time with the seconds when she lifted a wallet or found the final number in the tumbler of a lock. What mattered was that *none* of it had been a choice. Her life, her profession, her talent and drive . . . it had all been handed to her—*forced* upon her—and Esta had accepted each as her due. They had been nothing more and nothing less than the cost of belonging.

But Harte? He'd been a *choice*. From the first time she'd encountered him at the Haymarket, to when she'd saved him from the end he should

538

have met at the Brooklyn Bridge, to a few moments ago, when she'd let go of all propriety and control, Harte Darrigan was a choice Esta made again and again. Often against her better judgment. With him, she had never been anything more or anything less than who she truly was meant to be. And that *couldn't* be a mistake. Could it?

Esta wasn't sure what she was supposed to feel other than a biting disappointment and the sharp cut of something that she couldn't help but admit was hurt. Was she supposed to feel *different* somehow because of what had happened between them? Was she supposed to feel transformed?

She felt neither.

By the next morning, though, Esta managed to pull herself together. It wasn't like she had any other choice. She would not give the night before any more importance than Harte had. She would do what she'd always done—she would press onward, pretending confidence and hoping that she could spin its magic around her once more.

She would try.

They sat, too quiet and too awkward, barely picking at their breakfasts. Esta watched the land passing outside the train window so that she wouldn't have to look at him. Harte fidgeted with some dry toast, and she could tell he wanted to say something, but she didn't want to deal with any more excuses. Not now. Not in the bright light of morning, when everything about the night before made her feel like an utter fool. Harte apparently didn't understand that her silence meant that there was no need to discuss it.

"About what happened last night," he started.

Esta turned to him, ready. She gave him what she hoped was a calm and dignified smile. "I'd rather put it behind us."

"You can really do that?" Harte eyed her, his jaw suspiciously tight.

"Of course," she lied. She made a show of spearing a bit of potato and pretended to enjoy it, forcing herself to swallow it down.

"Just like that?" he asked, frowning. "You can act like last night never happened? Even after we—"

Esta slammed her fork down a bit more forcefully than she had intended, but at least it shut him up. She needed Harte to understand what she was about to say, and she needed him to understand it *now*. Because she didn't think she could handle it if he kept reminding her of what might have been . . . but what clearly wasn't.

"I will figure out a way to put last night behind me because I *have* to," she told him. "So do you. Whatever *mistakes* were made last night no longer matter. When we get to Chicago, we'll have *one* chance to steal the Book and the dagger from Jack. You know what the future holds, and we cannot allow the Reticulum or Jack Grew's presidency to become a reality. Last night was . . ." Her throat went tight. She suddenly had no idea how to finish that sentence.

"It was what?" Harte asked, and Esta wanted to believe that there was a note of longing in his voice that matched her own.

"It doesn't matter," she said, shoving aside the sentiment. "Last night can't figure into what happens next. We can't let it distract us."

Harte was silent, and Esta allowed herself to relax a bit, believing that everything was settled.

"And if there are . . . consequences?" Harte asked softly.

Consequences? It took a second, but then it hit her what he meant. "You mean . . ." She'd been so stupid. She hadn't even considered—

"There won't be," she told him, as though saying the words made it a fact.

Harte's dark brows drew together. "You can't know that for sure."

"I know that it doesn't matter," she told him, trying not to think about a future that could never be.

"How can it possibly not matter?" Harte was angry now, she could tell. But Esta was angry too. Or maybe she was hurt, and the two emotions felt close to the same when everything was so mixed up and desperate.

"Because it doesn't." She leaned over the plate of food that she no longer had any interest in. "Did you forget how this might well end?" she asked him. "There's only one way we know of to control the power of the Book—Seshat's power." She thought carefully about her words before she spoke again. She needed him to understand. "You know what Professor Lachlan tried to do to me when I returned to my own time. My affinity can unite the stones. We can use it to control Seshat's power. I've already accepted that I might not get to walk away from this, Harte."

As she'd spoken, Harte's face had gone pale. He was shaking his head like he didn't want to listen, or maybe like he didn't believe her. "The Book will have another answer," he said.

"It might not." The pain in his expression made Esta soften her voice. "Once we have the Book, we'll be able to get the stones back to 1902. The Quellant should hold off Seshat for the time being, at least. But we have only so much Quellant left, and you can't live with her inside your skin indefinitely, Harte. She has to be removed, and her power has to be controlled, and—right now, at least—there's only one way we know of to do that."

"Esta—"

"Maybe the Book *will* have some other answer. I hope it does. But if it doesn't, or if we can't *get* the Book, then I won't have any choice. I'll use my affinity to unite the stones, the same as Professor Lachlan would have. There's a good chance I'm not going to survive that, Harte."

"So last night," Harte said, swallowing hard. "It only happened because you felt like you had nothing to lose."

Esta stared at him in disbelief. How could he possibly be so blind? So *stupid*. "Last night happened because I have *everything* to lose."

"I should have thrown myself from the train leaving St. Louis," he said flatly.

She glared at him. "Martyrdom isn't a good look on you."

"But it works for you?" Harte asked, anger tingeing his voice. His hands were shaking a little, and he still looked practically colorless.

"It's not martyrdom. It's reality," Esta told him. "We have to find a way to control Seshat, and so far there is only one way we know of. I *can* do it, and I *will* if I have to. It's a reality we both need to accept."

"I *won't* accept that." Harte tossed his napkin onto the table. "There's no reason you have to give up your life to stop Seshat, not when there's an easier way."

"You don't get it, do you?" Esta asked. She shook her head, fighting back tears that she would *not* allow. "You weren't some itch I had to scratch last night, Harte. I have no interest in being some kind of hero. I don't want to die to save the world. But I'd happily give my life to save *you*."

Harte stared at her, and Esta immediately realized her mistake. With her words, she'd exposed far too much of her tender, beating heart, and the silence that filled the berth somehow felt more dangerous than any enemy she'd ever faced. She hadn't ever felt so exposed before.

Then Harte took her hand, and some of the panic receded. Her stomach flipped as his long, strong fingers intertwined with her own. His gray eyes were soft as he looked at her, and when he spoke, his voice was barely more than a whisper. "What makes you so certain I don't feel the exact same way?"

Esta couldn't move. She was afraid that if she did, the entire world around them would shatter and fall away. That *she* would shatter as well.

How had she not considered this? Last night, she'd been so angry at herself for thinking he hadn't understood, but now? She realized she'd been wrong. He *had* understood—*did* understand—and somehow that made it even worse. There was a raw openness in Harte's expression that was terrifying.

A realization settled over Esta that stole her breath, plucked it straight from her chest with fingers as nimble as her own. If Harte felt for her even half of what she felt for him, he would never allow her to do what she intended. If they could not find another way to stop Seshat—one that did not involve her using her affinity and giving up her life—Harte would take himself out of the equation to protect her, and his death would destroy her just the same.

LISA MAXWELL

PART

V

TRAFFIC AND LUCK

1902—New York

Cela Johnson decided that maybe she wasn't actually made for a life of crime right about the time that everyone else decided that *she* should be the one to sit on the rooftop of the tallest building on Thirteenth Avenue to watch for the Order's ship. She'd spent her share of evenings sitting on fire escapes, like everyone else born in a city that sizzled with the summer heat, but this was something different somehow.

To Cela's back, Manhattan's streets sprawled in all directions, an impossible stretch of humanity. Abel was out there somewhere, waiting like everyone else, for the signal she would send. In front of her, the Hudson River glinted, a chain of gold in the early-evening sun. Somewhere out beyond the river, the Order was making ready to move their goods, was maybe already moving them.

Cela lifted her spyglass to study the boats dotting the river, hoping that the sign she was looking for would come sooner rather than later. One of those boats held the ring that Darrigan had given her, the ring that had turned her life upside down. Soon a boat would start to inch its way toward one of the many busy docks that lined the western side of the island, and then the game would begin.

Noting the sun's low position in the sky, Cela checked her watch again. It was already 7:26. Not quite time, since nothing would happen until the sun was exactly at the right angle, nearly sitting on the horizon. But it was getting close.

The minutes felt like they were crawling by, but Cela didn't dare so much as look away or blink. The boat they were looking for would dock no earlier, and also probably no later, than 7:46, when the sun was exactly six degrees above the horizon. It was the beginning of a period the Order called the Golden Hour, when the sun was supposedly at its most powerful.

It wasn't when the sun was at its brightest, mind you, which would have been what any rational person might have assumed. Instead, it had something to do with astronomy. The Golden Hour, according to Theo's information, was marked by the sun's path, from six degrees above the horizon to six degrees below on this particular day—the Manhattan Solstice. Six because it was a powerful number. A sacred number, even, according to the men in the Order.

Maybe there was something to their beliefs, Cela thought as she watched the ships drifting in the distance. Six days for the good Lord to make the world, six points on the Star of David, and the devil himself loved the number so well he took it three times over.

The Order was depending upon the power of this false solstice, when the alignment of the sun would give their evil charms more power. Until the sun dipped below the horizon, the cargo would be untouchable. Literally untouchable, from what Theo told them.

Still, Cela thought this so-called Golden Hour was poorly named, especially since it wouldn't even last a whole hour. Fifty-two minutes was all the time the Order would have to take advantage of. In that time, the boat had to dock, and their treasures had to travel through the city streets and arrive at the Order's new quarters in the Flatiron Building. For those fifty-two minutes, some kind of strange magic would ensure their treasures would be safe. But if the wagons happened to be delayed, if they didn't reach their destination before the end of those fifty-two minutes, the shipment would be vulnerable.

It was essential that those wagons were delayed.

In a city that had more traffic snarls than pigeons most days, it seemed an easy enough thing to accomplish. If a train happened to be late, if it happened to find itself held up on Death Avenue—maybe by an over-turned cart, for instance—the wagon bearing the Order's goods wouldn't be able to take a direct route, straight across the island to reach the Flatiron Building. The wagons would have to be diverted around the chain of train cars and backed-up wagons, maybe for blocks in either direction.

With a little planning, the cluttered streets in the lower part of Manhattan would work in their favor. With a little luck, they would use Paul Kelly's men and Nibsy Lorcan's boys to divert the wagons and funnel them *away* from the Flatiron. If they could keep those wagons running until it was too late for the sun to provide its protection, it would be pos-sible for Jianyu to relieve the Order of their treasures before either Paul Kelly or Nibsy Lorcan could get to them. The ring could be retrieved.

If they managed to cut the Order's legs out from beneath them, maybe people would see that it *was* possible to rise up and topple the rich and the powerful. Maybe more things could change as well, and not only for Mageus.

Maybe. But Cela wasn't counting any chickens, especially not before they'd even gathered the eggs. There were too many things that could go wrong. For one, they still didn't know for sure where the ship would dock. For another, they were depending too much upon the capricious-ness of traffic and luck.

It didn't help that their planning had gone sideways a couple of days before. Somehow, Viola's brother had found out about his sister's trips to Harlem. He'd made demands, and then he'd made threats. Thank god, Viola had managed to warn them. It was a risk the Italian girl had taken, and one that Cela appreciated. She understood *exactly* how bad it was that Paul Kelly knew who she and Abel were. His Five Pointers had been causing trouble in the city for years, dangerous trouble. The kind of trouble that made people end up dead.

Cela might have understood why Viola and Jianyu had decided to use this Nibsy Lorcan fellow and try to play the two dangers off each other, but she still didn't like it. Everything she'd heard about Nibsy made Cela think he wasn't someone who could be easily duped or led. There was too much that could go wrong. For starters, Cela wasn't sure whether Viola had actually been able to convince Nibsy that she was on his side—not when Viola's eyes flashed with hate every time she heard his name. Cela also wasn't sure that a fifteen-year-old orphan could neutralize the threat of Paul Kelly, as Jianyu was hoping he would, even if the boy had managed to betray an entire gang and kill their leader to take power.

She only hoped that with Nibsy and Paul Kelly involved, there would be others to take the blame if things went wrong. Because if she or Abel were caught by the Order? Even the threat of the Five Pointers didn't worry Cela quite as much as what might happen if things went *that* wrong.

It was more than Cela's and Abel's lives at stake. Maybe Abel's friends had decided to sit this one out, but Cela knew that nothing was ever that easy. If word got out that the two of them had been involved and public sentiment turned against them, it could also turn against every Negro in the city—exactly like it had two years before, during the riots that killed her father.

Cela saw something then, far off on the Hudson. A small steamer ship that had been sitting in the middle of the river started to turn toward the shore, and when she checked her watch again, she had a sense that this was the ship she was looking for. She couldn't have been more certain if the ship had flown a banner declaring itself, but she watched a minute longer to be sure of the direction and the approximate location of the landing. When it was clear she'd been right, she tucked the spyglass under her arm and picked up the mirror.

Once the signal was given, it would be relayed along the rooftops, and their plan would be set in motion. Where the boat docked mattered, and the direction the wagon headed mattered even more. If the train was stopped too early, the Order would be able to avoid it. If they stopped it on the wrong part of Eleventh Avenue, the blockage would be useless.

Careful not to drop the mirror, she raised the spyglass again, prepared to send the first signal. Then something on the river drew her attention, and she stopped short. There were at least three ships moving now, each making a steady, even progression toward Manhattan. Each heading toward a dock evenly spaced along the island's edge.

Scanning the water, Cela looked for some indication of which ship was the right one, when realization struck. There wasn't a single ship, as they'd expected. The Order had sent *three* ships. And they were heading to three different docks. It was an eventuality that none of them had considered or prepared for.

Cela lifted the mirror and let it catch the light, sending a series of bright flashes. She hoped that the others would understand. *If they don't* . . . She pushed that thought aside and sent the message once again, to be sure. Even with this unexpected twist, their plans *had* to work. Too many lives hung in the balance.

NO REASON TO CHOOSE

1902—New York

James Lorcan had spent too many nights sleeping on the roof of the Bella Strega to let a little thing like the height of the building make him nervous, but he could tell that Paul Kelly didn't feel the same. The broad-faced gangster looked positively green and was doing his level best to stay as far from the edge as possible. James, on the other hand, had one foot perched on the cornice as he surveyed the streets below and the river beyond.

The sun was dropping quickly, falling ever steadily toward the horizon. Soon, the Order's boat would dock and the game would begin. Anticipation sizzled along his skin, brushed up by the frisson of energy stirring the Aether around him. Change was in the air, and the outcome would be his to command.

With Kelly was Viola, who still looked like she was ready to murder someone—mostly her brother. James suspected the only thing stopping her was the threat Kelly had made against the lives of her friends in Harlem. If Kelly ended up dead, orders had been given to end Cela Johnson and her brother, Abel, as well. It was a situation that had successfully positioned Viola right where James wanted her.

He ignored the tension radiating between the siblings and focused instead on the view through the spyglass. The river was crowded with boats, but he was too far inland to see much of the shoreline. Instead, he watched a dark figure on a rooftop about four blocks west.

"Can you see anything at all?" Kelly asked, clearly impatient for his own turn at the spyglass. Though why he hadn't thought to bring his own, James didn't know. "Is she where she's supposed to be?"

"She's there," Viola told her brother.

James watched a bit longer, until he could sense that Kelly was at the end of his patience, and then he waited a few seconds longer still before handing over the glass.

"She'd better *stay* there," Paul muttered, holding the glass to his eye.

Viola caught Nibsy's eye while Kelly was studying the skyline, her brows rising slightly in a question. He gave her a small nod, nothing noticeable, but enough to keep her leash loose. Viola had no guarantee that James would uphold his end of their bargain, but she had threatened to kill him—and happily—if he went back on his word. It was a promise she reminded him of now with a slight narrowing of her violet eyes.

Too bad that it was a promise she wouldn't live long enough to keep.

Paul Kelly, Viola, and the Order. Each posed a threat to James' plans. Kelly, because he wanted the Strega; Viola, because she wanted to avenge Dolph; and the Order, because they would destroy magic if they could. None would get their wish. If all went as James planned, the biggest threats to his control over the Devil's Own—and over the Bowery— would be taken care of by the end of the day.

He gave Viola an easy smile, glancing up over his glasses, but Viola only glared at him before she turned away.

When she'd come to him three days ago, James hadn't been surprised, of course. He'd ensured that Viola *had* to turn to him when he told Torrio to reveal Viola's jaunts to Harlem. James had known implicitly that Paul Kelly would not have been able to stand for his sister aligning herself with the people she'd chosen. Kelly might act the part of a gentleman, he might be all spit and polish, but at his heart, he was the same as anyone else—easily led by his hatred and fear.

How Viola had found Cela and Abel Johnson, James still didn't know. He didn't actually care as long as they remained useful for keeping Viola in line. After all, she might pretend to be the cold, calculating assassin, but James knew better. He'd seen her with Tilly, and he'd seen her with Dolph. Her fear for her friends was a weakness.

The Aether wasn't a scrying bowl or a crystal ball, but it had guided James nevertheless. He'd known that he needed Viola's help, even if he wasn't sure *why*, and once her involvement was secured, the vibrations in the Aether had changed—they'd become nearly *certain* of his victory.

"I think something is happening," Paul said, excitement coloring his voice. "One . . . two . . . three . . ." He counted the pattern, short and long, but then he frowned, pausing.

"What is it?" Viola asked, the nervous energy in her voice giving away her fear.

Kelly didn't respond at first. His lips moved in a silent count, but then he did finally turn on her. His face was red with temper, but his voice held a deadly calm. "Your friend is a dead woman."

"What are you talking about?" Viola asked, trying to take the spyglass from him. "Cela wouldn't do anything—"

"It's nothing but nonsense," Kelly snapped.

"Give me that," Viola said, finally taking the spyglass from her brother and lifting it to her eye. She was silent as she watched, her frown deepening. "I don't understand. Cela wouldn't risk such a thing. Something has happened."

James agreed. Against his skin, the Aether shifted, swirled, opened new possibilities. Something *was* happening, indeed.

"May I?" he asked, and reluctantly Viola handed over the glass.

Sure enough, James could clearly see the flash of Cela's mirror. He watched, counting the flashes—long and short—and then James started to laugh from the sheer absurdity.

"I can't imagine what you find funny, Lorcan," Kelly growled.

"I expect that you wouldn't, considering that it's *your* information that was wrong," Nibsy told him, lowering the spyglass. They'd depended on Kelly's sources to make their plan. One boat was supposed to dock at the specified time, and then the wagon carrying the Order's treasures would cut one clear path through the city before sundown. But apparently Kelly's sources had been wrong. "That girl isn't playing any game. She's using Morse code. She's doing exactly what she's supposed to be doing."

"Which dock will it be, then?" Kelly demanded. "Where will the boat land?"

"It's not a single boat as we expected," James said. "It appears that there are three."

"Three?" Viola asked. "You're sure?"

James raised the spyglass again. "Positive," he said, and he handed the spyglass back so Kelly could see for himself.

Kelly's jaw clenched as the seconds ticked by. When he'd seen enough, he lowered the glass. "Why would there be three?"

"Clearly, the Order must have been expecting an attack," James said. "They've made a move you didn't predict, and now we have to play their game."

"I'm not interested in any games," Kelly snarled.

"Don't worry," James said as he reveled in the way the Aether bunched. "We're not going to let them win." He took the mirror to signal back to the girl on the roof that they understood her message. "The Order believes themselves to be clever, but they've made a tactical error. We'll still win in the end."

"How?" Kelly demanded. "Any one of those ships could be carrying the goods."

"Or they all could," Viola said, suddenly sounding unsure.

"I don't think they'd take that risk," Nibsy said, letting the possibilities unfurl around him. "Multiple ships mean more to guard and additional chances that some of their treasures might go missing. They lost far too much when Khafre Hall burned. They won't want to sacrifice anything more." He paused, letting the Aether vibrate through him, listening. "No," he told them, feeling surer than ever. He understood then what he had to do to ensure his own victory. "The other ships are nothing but a distraction. The Order will keep the shipment together. One of those ships holds what we're after."

"But which one?" Viola asked, squinting toward the river. "What do we tell the others?"

"The train can't block enough of Eleventh Avenue to account for multiple routes," Kelly said, frowning. "If we choose the wrong place to stop it, the wagon we want could get through."

"There's three of us and three boats," Nibsy said. "There's no reason to choose."

THE DEVIL'S MARK

1902—New York

Viola gave Nibsy a cutting look. She'd been against Jianyu's idea that they go back to Nibsy for help. She'd come up with every possible reason why it was a terrible idea to trust Nibsy—Dolph's murderer—to neutralize the threat that her brother posed to Cela and Abel, because she'd known that he would turn against them—they both had. But at the time, there had been no other solution.

"You want us to go separately?" she asked Nibsy, suddenly more than suspicious.

"We could each follow one of the wagons," Nibsy said easily. "It's the only way to be sure."

But a single glance at the guileless expression on Nibsy's face told Viola that he was lying about something. Not about the ships. No, that particular trick made sense. Theo had warned them that the Order was nervous and that they should expect the unexpected. This new complication with so many ships certainly counted. But Nibsy's idea of each of them going a separate way? Viola didn't like it. It was too convenient that Nibsy would want to be away from the threat of her knife and her affinity.

"You seem far too eager to be off on your own," she said coldly as she narrowed her eyes at him.

"We'll have very little time once the boats land," Nibsy reminded them both. "We won't have room for hesitation or indecision. If the wagon, whichever boat it may be on, reaches the new headquarters before sundown, we won't be able to touch it. Splitting up makes the most sense. At least one of us is sure to reach the Order's goods."

Paolo had been silent for too long, a fact that made Viola wary. "And then what?" he asked now, his voice cold and calculating. "What assurance do I have that you won't go back on your word and take more than your share?"

"You think I would dare to cross *you*, Paul?" Nibsy said with a surprised blink.

More lies. More deception. Of course Nibsy would cross Paolo. It had been his plan from the start, and both Viola and her brother knew it. Why else would Paolo have been so willing to accept Viola's plan to go to Nibsy pretending friendship, if not for the fact that Paul thought he could use her to keep Nibsy Lorcan in line?

Both wanted the other out of the way. That fact seemed the only thing about the situation that worked to Viola's benefit. Let them have their little pissing contest. She had no intention of getting caught in the crossfire. Viola cared only about retrieving the ring and stopping the Order from regaining so much as a foothold in the city. She cared, too, about making sure that Cela and Abel were not harmed by their decision to commit themselves to this cause. Everything else—her brother and Nibsy, too, for that matter—could go to the devil as far as Viola was concerned.

"Of *course* you would try to cross me," Paolo said. "But you won't live for long after if you try."

"Enough," Viola told them. They didn't have time for this bickering. To the west, the boats churned toward shore. To the east, the tower waited, poised to solidify the Order's power once again. "We don't need to chase wagons," she told them. That had never been the plan anyway. "We know where they're going. We'll meet them there."

Nibsy's gaze slid to her. "And when they arrive?"

"We'll stop them from going any farther," she told them, wishing she felt surer than she sounded. "Together."

"We should still send the signals," Nibsy told Paul. "Any delays might help."

"No," Paul told him. "I want my people on Fifth Avenue waiting for the wagons, not running around the city like chickens after a fat worm."

"The Order is expecting an attack. It would be a shame to disappoint them," Nibsy argued. "If they don't run into any problems, they may start to believe that their plan to distract us hasn't worked. They might try something else we're not expecting."

Paul frowned. "Fine." But the tension strung between the two was enough to put Viola's teeth on edge.

Men. They were exhausting. And they were wasting time.

"What of the train?" Viola asked, drawing their attention back.

"Right across Twenty-Third," Paul said as though taking control of the situation. "We'll block their straightest route. If your people are ready to the south, mine will take the north," he told Nibsy. "And the three of us will take the building."

Nibsy took the mirror to send the signals as Paul inched closer to the edge of the roof, making sure not to get too close, and gave a sharp whistle. He listened, and then a moment later, he whistled again. "Where the hell is he?"

"Who?" Viola asked.

"Johnny. He's supposed to be waiting downstairs."

"We'll catch him on our way out," Nibsy told him, tucking the mirror away. He started for the rooftop door, but Paul grabbed his arm.

"Not so fast," her brother said. "I don't need you taking off and getting ahead of us."

"As if I could outrun you," Nibsy said. He gave a small flourish of his hand.

As Paul charged into the stairwell, Nibsy slid a glance to Viola. She couldn't tell what emotion was behind it. Satisfaction, maybe? Or perhaps amusement?

"After you," Nibsy said, and when Viola began to argue, he shrugged.

"I'd prefer to keep that knife of yours where I can see it, if you don't mind."

"I don't need a knife to stop your heart," she muttered as they began to descend the stairs, but she'd barely taken another step when the skin on her back felt suddenly cold. It was as though someone had slipped a piece of ice down her collar. Beneath her shift and her blouse, Viola felt the strange sensation of the mark she wore—*Dolph's* mark—trembling.

The feeling—the very *thought* of the mark coming to life—made her stumble, and she nearly missed the next step.

"Have a care, Viola," Nibsy said, but his voice was flat, without any hint of true concern.

It can't be. Viola glanced back up at him, but she couldn't read his expression. The glass of his spectacles flashed in the dim light, obscuring his eyes, but his mouth was soft. He seemed relaxed. Calm. But his hand gripped the cane that had once been Dolph's, and there was something possessive in the way his thumb traced the coils of the gorgon's serpentine hair. It made her shiver. It made her *wonder*.

"Is anything wrong?" Nibsy asked, his brows lifting above the wire rims of his glasses. "Something you wanted to say to me?"

"No," she said, shaking off her misgivings. She continued her descent, stepping more carefully now, even as she fought the urge to scratch at the ink in her skin.

Even in life, Dolph had never threatened her with the mark she wore. Not like he threatened others. He'd never needed to. Viola's loyalty had been absolute because Dolph had been, before all else, a trusted friend. But she'd heard stories about what happened to those who dared betray him or the Devil's Own. The fantastical stories about the curse of the serpents that were inscribed in their skin and the way Dolph Saunders could use those marks to unmake their bearers by taking their magic.

Viola hadn't wanted to believe those tales. They'd seemed too ridiculous to be true, but then, she hadn't known the man who'd written the journal entries about taking Leena's power. She hadn't known the version of Dolph Saunders who'd studied strange sigils to control demons and then hid his work behind unreadable markings. Viola had wondered many times in the days after Nibsy had shown her the sheets torn from Dolph's journal, notes written in Dolph's own hand, whether she had truly known Dolph Saunders at all.

But now, to think that Nibsy might be able to control the power Dolph had once claimed for himself, terrible and unnatural as it was? *Impossible.* Or so Viola hoped. She couldn't begin to contemplate what he might do with such power. She didn't want to.

She'd barely reached the next landing when a noise sounded from below. Gunshots rang out, and shouts echoed up the stairwell. On instinct, Viola started toward the sound, but Nibsy caught her by the wrist. "It would be more prudent to wait a minute or two," he said, completely unruffled by the commotion.

He wasn't at all surprised by the noise, she realized. "What have you done?"

"I've taken care of your brother . . . or rather, John Torrio has taken care of Paul for me," he told her. "That's what you wanted, wasn't it? To stop him from harming your friends?"

She frowned at him, but she was too smart to say anything.

"It's a funny thing, Viola. . . . The authorities were more than willing to turn a blind eye when your brother limited himself to simply terrorizing the poor urchins of the Bowery, but when he attacked the city's wealthiest men and their wives?" Nibsy shrugged. "They've been looking for Kelly for weeks now, and a certain sly Fox told them *exactly* where your brother could be found today."

"What of his Five Pointers?" she asked. "You know what will happen to Cela and her brother when Paolo doesn't call them off."

"They'll do whatever John Torrio tells them to do," Nibsy said. "Which will be what *I* tell him to do." He gave her a small, satisfied smile.

"And what is it that you'll tell him?" Viola asked, her fingers itching for her knife. She wished she could end this farce, but as long as Cela's and Abel's lives hung in the balance, she held her tongue.

"That all depends on how closely you stick to our agreement," Nibsy said easily.

"If anything happens to Cela or Abel Johnson, I *will* kill you," Viola promised. After all, if Paul was truly out of the way, she didn't need Nibsy. She certainly didn't need his threats. And if Jianyu would have counseled patience? Jianyu was nearly a mile away.

"I have no interest in harming your friends, Viola." Nibsy regarded her seriously through the thick lenses of his glasses. "Torrio, on the other hand, may not be so generous. Once we have the ring, I'll release them. But remember, if I die, so will they."

She could still kill him. She could kill Torrio, too, but Viola could not save Cela and her brother *and* help Jianyu get the ring. She could not be everywhere in the city at once. She would have to play Nibsy's game— for now, at least. She vowed, though, that she would not let him win.

"As long as they remain unharmed, you have nothing to fear," she said easily, refusing to allow herself to betray even a glimmer of the worry she felt churning in her stomach. "If you can't keep Torrio on his leash—"

"Torrio knows better than to cross me." Nibsy adjusted his grip on Dolph's cane. "But we should be going. After all, the Order's shipments won't wait."

It doesn't matter. Viola tried to tell herself as she continued down the stairs with Nibsy at her back. Even with this unexpected twist, things would work out. Hadn't they expected trouble from all sides? She would take back the ring, and then she would take her revenge on Nibsy Lorcan. She would stop his scheming before John Torrio could do anything to Cela or Abel. She *had* to. And if she couldn't?

She'd argued against Theo's involvement from the start. She'd tried to persuade him to be on a ship already sailing for the Continent by now, but she found herself suddenly grateful that he'd refused to budge in his determination to help them. If all else failed, Theo was positioned with the Order, there inside the new building, a last resort that they might very well need.

MINOR GODS

1902—New York

Jack Grew stood at the stone railing of the balcony on the eighteenth floor of the Flatiron Building, gazing out across the city. *His* city. Below, people scurried along like ants, unaware that he watched them like a god from above. The sun was low in the sky. Already it scraped at the tops of the buildings. Already the light was shifting into a golden haze, and soon the streets would glow with the power of the sun's rays, as they did only twice a year.

The ancients understood the solstice's importance. Each of the five mystical dynasties knew that the power could be harnessed simply by studying the movement of the stars. Pyramids and standing stones, towers and obelisks, each of the dynasties had their monuments to the sun, so why shouldn't this, the world's greatest city, have one as well?

But the men who built Manhattan had not been content to be directed by the stars. They had sought, instead, to bend the heavens to their will. The city's grid was only one example of the Order's influence on the island. The grid had been positioned, not along the arms of the compass rose, but with a careful attention to ley lines and numerology. This alignment of the city's streets was a tool to increase the Brink's power, but it meant that on the traditional solstice, the streets of Manhattan would remain as shadowed as ever. But on the *Manhattan* Solstice, dates known only to those in the Order—dates discernible only through careful study and mastery of the occult sciences—the streets would shine like gold, electric with the power of the sun.

On those days, the average citizen would wander on, eyes down and focused on the muck of their own life, as they always did. Most would never look up and notice the phenomenon, much less understand the potential. But Jack understood. When the Order had asked for his assistance, the Book had been only too willing to oblige by revealing even more of its secrets. Thanks to the Book, he knew how to tap into that power—to *direct* it. It was yet another sign that soon the old men who thought they ruled over him would be completely irrelevant.

Someone cleared their throat behind him, and Jack turned to find Theo Barclay standing with his hands clasped. Anticipation sizzled through Jack's veins.

"The High Princept said you had some use for me?" Barclay said, amiable as ever, though there was a tightness around his eyes as he stepped into the chamber. He carried into the room a wariness that Jack found more than satisfactory.

There was something about Barclay's face that always gave Jack the urge to lay a fist into it, to rearrange the other man's classically handsome features. Now, though, he held himself back. It wasn't the time. *Not yet.*

"Actually, yes. I do." Jack gave Barclay an easy smile, anticipation already building. He stepped back inside, leaving the door ajar so the summer winds could stir the warm air. "Well, what do you think?"

Theo looked around the chamber, his eyes widening a little as he looked around. "It's quite a lot to take in," Barclay murmured, running his finger along one of the carvings in the wall. "The detail is astounding."

Jack understood the awe that colored Barclay's expression. He'd felt it too, the first time he saw the walls of intricately carved sandstone blocks, inlaid as they were with gilding and marble and onyx. Now the walls glittered in the evening light that poured through the open balcony door. An elaborate golden staircase, delicate and intricately wrought, wound itself upward in the center of the room to a large, circular medallion carved with the Philosopher's Hand. Beyond that portal, an even more fabulous chamber waited.

All around the triangular chamber, burnished walnut shelves stood in rows precisely arranged to take advantage of the power derived from sacred geometry. Presently, those shelves were empty and waiting to be filled with the Order's remaining books and scrolls, which would be brought into this room as soon as the danger had passed. In the center of the room stood an altar that had been rescued from the charred remains of Khafre Hall.

"This room is actually modeled on one in an ancient Egyptian temple, you know."

"Is it?" Theo turned, his expression betraying his open interest as he dropped his guard.

"The Temple of Thoth had one of the greatest libraries in the world," Jack told him. The Book throbbed against Jack's chest—a reminder and a promise. "Some called it the Library of Life. It's said that writing was invented there, along with the same rituals we still practice today."

"Thoth?" Theo pursed his lips, his brow furrowing. "One of the more minor gods, wasn't he?"

"On the contrary," Jack said, forcing his voice to remain even. "To those who understand the history of the occult sciences, he is absolutely *peerless.*"

"Well, this room is certainly impressive, as is the entire arrangement, Jack. Five floors of the highest and most exclusive real estate in Manhattan," Barclay said. He gave Jack a half smile that looked tense. He was scared and clearly nervous but trying to play it off. "Everything is beautifully appointed. No one could doubt the Order's influence once they see this."

"It *is* rather impressive, but we had quite the bar to meet after what Khafre Hall had been," Jack told him, pretending not to notice how on edge Barclay was. "Though *you* were never invited, were you?"

"No," Barclay said with a shake of his head. "I never had the honor."

"It was a beautiful old building. Inside and out, Khafre Hall stood as a monument to the majesty of our civilization and to the wonder of the occult arts," Jack told him, feeling a wave of regret for his own hand in its demise. The regret, though, swiftly turned to anger.

Because I was tricked. Because Darrigan and that bitch of a girl made me look like a fool. But Jack wouldn't allow himself to be deceived again. Barclay would learn that soon enough.

"Khafre Hall was a marvel," Jack continued, running his fingers over the granite top of the tall, square altar that anchored the room. "We believed it to be impenetrable, with all of the various wards and protections placed around the building."

"It's a shame what happened to it," Theo said, still looking gratifyingly uneasy. "So much history and art . . . lost to a band of thieves."

"Lost to *maggots*," Jack corrected, allowing the fury to infuse his words before reining himself in once more. "But not *all* was lost. So much of this chamber was taken whole from the levels far beneath the city streets. This very altar once stood in the center of the old Mysterium."

"It's a beautiful piece. Fourth century, I believe?" Theo asked. He glanced up at Jack. "It's amazing any of it survived the fire."

"Not really so amazing. The Mysterium itself was warded with protections that other parts of Khafre Hall did not have." Protections that had kept Jack out, but he would be kept out no longer. He smiled at Barclay. "The old Mysterium was also far below ground level, carved into the very bedrock of the city and protected by the many rivers that still run beneath these streets. Of course, those rivers provided a means of escape for the maggots who attacked the Order this past spring. The new Mysterium won't have that particular weakness."

Theo looked around, far too interested for Jack's liking. "It does look well secured."

"This is simply an antechamber," Jack corrected, amused at the surprise in Barclay's expression. "The new Mysterium is above." He lifted his eyes to where the spiraling stairs disappeared into the ceiling. "The chamber above us is even more secure than this one, and far more so than its predecessor. Only the highest level of the Order has the privilege of entrance. If the alarms are triggered by an unworthy soul, the seal will engage, the air will drain from the space, and only the blood of the High Princept himself will be able to open it," Jack said.

Or at least, that's what the Inner Circle believes.

"But enough about that," Jack said, changing the topic to keep Barclay off-balance. He was enjoying the way Barclay's nerves were growing more frayed by the second. "Come, have a look at this view." He opened the glass door and stepped out onto the balcony, and when Barclay hesitated, he taunted him. "Don't tell me you're afraid?" He leapt up upon the wide stone railing so he could stand, a god above the men below. "It's incredible, this city. Come, see Manhattan as you've never seen it before."

"Come down from there, Jack," Barclay said, stepping out onto the small stone terrace. "There's no sense taking chances."

"What chances?" Jack laughed. "Don't you see? As above, so below. *We're* now the ones above, Barclay. *Far* above. We're practically in the clouds. Closer to heaven and the angels themselves. Closer, as well, to the power those divine beings will inevitably bestow upon those who are worthy." He could not stop himself from smiling as he felt the wind cutting against him, the Book anchoring him. "And those who are not worthy . . ." He withdrew the red blossom from his lapel and crushed it in his palm as he leaned out, holding his arm far over the edge.

"Jack . . . ," Theo warned, his eyes growing wider.

"We've designed these chambers with every attention to security. Walls within walls, chambers within chambers, each with fail-safes. If an intruder manages to get into the Mysterium this time?" Jack let the petals drop from his finger. "Unlike the defensive weakness of Khafre Hall, from here there's only one escape."

The wind gusted, taking the bits of the red petals into the air. Some swirled back onto the balcony and landed, like drops of blood, at Theo Barclay's feet. Jack hopped down from the railing. He kept his gaze steady as he enjoyed the play of nerves and indecision flashing through Barclay's expression. *Weak.* But he knew that already.

"*Was* there something that you needed from me, Jack?" Barclay asked, his voice noticeably tighter than it had been when he finally spoke again. "I was on my way out when the Princept said you wanted to see me."

"You aren't staying for the ceremony?" Jack asked, frowning. It was impossible that he'd been wrong about Barclay. . . .

"My ship leaves this evening," Theo told him.

"Ah yes. You're off to retrieve your bride." Jack smiled pleasantly as he began to circle to the left. Barclay, nervous as ever, matched his movement, never giving Jack his back.

"I'm only going for a visit for now. I'll be back next month, but Ruby won't be back until fall, closer to the wedding date."

"Still, it's a shame you can't attend this evening's events, especially after all you've done to help."

"I've been happy to be of service, and I appreciate the chance to see this. . . ." Theo nodded toward the view of the city as he tucked his hands in his pockets, still nervous. Still gratifyingly uneasy. "I wish you all the best of luck on the ceremony, though."

"Oh, we won't need luck," Jack said, coming up next to Theo. "Not when we have power on our side. Look there, you can see the Hudson River, more than a mile away."

"So you can," Theo said, glancing at Jack instead of in the direction of the river.

"The boats have probably already landed, and even now the wagons are making their way through the city," Jack told him with a smile, enjoying the moment when realization rippled through Barclay's features.

Barclay turned then, frowning deeply. "Was there to be more than one?"

"Oh," Jack said, feigning innocence. "Were you not told? The Inner Circle decided on a change in plans."

"A change." Barclay turned back to the view, suddenly looking rather unwell.

"The Order expected an attack, and there was concern that someone among our ranks wasn't as devoted to our cause as he should be," Jack said, never blinking. "Other arrangements were made. Three boats, each holding a single wagon. A diversion, if you will, for any who would try to stop our purpose."

"To give the one carrying the cargo a chance," Theo said. "Brilliant. Just . . ." He cleared his throat. "Brilliant."

"It is, rather." Jack took a moment to gloat. "The maggots who were planning to attack the shipment won't know which to follow. They thought to delay us, but instead, we'll keep them running . . . right into our trap." He took a step away from Theo. "Do you know the most brilliant part of all, though?" He waited until Theo had turned fully toward him, because Jack wanted to see the emotions that played across his face when he found out. "There's nothing in *any* of those wagons."

"Nothing?" Barclay's voice had a hollowness to it, like knocking on a tomb. It delighted Jack. "But we went to the trouble of warding them?"

"They're still warded, as we'd planned, but there's absolutely nothing inside."

Barclay blinked. "I don't understand."

"The story you were given about the boats was nothing but a test—a trap, if you will. The delivery isn't coming from the Hudson. It never was. The boat landed on the East River earlier today. The Order's most valuable treasures are already here, stowed in the Mysterium. Safe and protected from all dangers." Jack let his mouth curve. "Or that's what the rest of the Order believes. They're all downstairs, congratulating themselves on their superiority, unaware that the artifact they've attached all their hopes and dreams to is about to go missing."

By now Jack had maneuvered so that he stood between Barclay and any escape. He withdrew the pistol from his coat and leveled it at Theo.

"Jack?" Theo's hands went up without hesitation, but the confusion in his expression was priceless.

"This is where we say good-bye, I'm afraid, Barclay."

"What is all this, Jack?"

"It's the proper end for a thief," Jack said easily.

"I'm no thief." Theo took a step forward but stopped when Jack eased back the trigger. "I didn't take any artifact."

"You and I know that's only *barely* true," Jack said. "But the truth doesn't matter—especially not if your friends attack those wagons, as I expect they will. By the time tonight is finished, your treachery will be an established fact."

Theo let out a nervous, tittering laugh. It was the kind of involuntary noise people make when they realize they're in real danger and understand there's no way out. "I don't know what's going on here, Jack, but I assure you that this is all a misunderstanding. Whatever it is you think I've done—" He licked his lips. "Certainly, this is a mistake."

"No mistake, Barclay. Right now your friends are out there in the streets, chasing their own tails." Jack smiled. "By the time they realize that the wagons are empty, it will be too late. The sun will have set, and the Order will learn that they're under attack. When their precious artifact goes missing and they find you where you are not supposed to be, they'll assume that you are the cause."

"There will be no evidence," Barclay said.

Jack only laughed. "When has evidence ever mattered to embarrassed and fearful men? They will look for someone to blame. They'll *need* someone to hate, to *punish*. And when they find your body, broken and smashed on the walk below, they will point to you."

Barclay's expression was a mask of confusion. The fear in his eyes was *delicious*. "You can't make me jump, Jack."

"No?" Jack smiled pleasantly. He gave a shrug. "Perhaps not. But you'll fall one way or the other by the time the night's over, Barclay. Enjoy the view."

Jack was already back inside before Barclay could realize what was happening. He closed the door and locked it before Theo had even started to move, barring it with the combination of the heavy leaden locks and the runes the Book had given him for this very purpose. On the other side, Barclay pounded on the glass, his screaming made silent by the barrier between them. Jack watched with some amusement as Barclay tried jerking on the door, but when he grabbed the handle, he recoiled as pale-yellow smoke started pouring from the place he'd touched. A rather convenient little charm, Jack thought.

Desperate, Barclay slammed his fists against the pane of glass again and again, as though he would willingly slice his wrists to shreds if it meant escaping. But Jack knew that nothing Barclay tried would work. The glass and the door together were built to withhold any blow, and they were warded with the same magic that had once protected the Mysterium.

Jack turned toward the stairs in the center of the room, toward the next steps in the plan he'd devised to retrieve the Delphi's Tear. He left Theo Barclay to take care of himself.

With the enchantment layered into the smoke, Barclay was doomed anyway. The longer he stayed on that balcony, the better the ledge would begin to look. The wide-open expanse of sky would call to him, and by the time the sun had set, he would be so delirious that a different kind of exit would begin to look reasonable. Barclay would jump, and he would die, and in the chaos stirred by the events to come, Jack would walk away with the ring.

IN FOR A PENNY

Harte and Esta didn't discuss anything more about what had happened between them on the train, especially not once the Quellant faded and Seshat began to stir again. Instead, Harte couldn't stop thinking about what had happened—what he wanted it to mean—but he allowed the matter to drop, and they seemed to enter into an unspoken agreement, a fragile truce that was both a relief and a frustration.

What more was there to say about the matter? Wishing for a future or a long life with Esta wouldn't make it so.

Harte knew exactly how headstrong Esta was, and he knew it would be pointless to argue with her about using her affinity if it cost her life. He knew how he felt as well. He would do everything he could to retrieve the Book, but if the Ars Arcana didn't hold any answer to their dilemma—if it didn't show them a way to control Seshat while keeping Esta alive and whole—Harte still knew of one sure way to end the threat Seshat posed without harming Esta. He didn't need to argue with her about it. He would only need to *act*.

The truth of the matter was that Harte would not allow anyone else to lose their life for him or *because* of him. Not like Sammie had. He had been the one who had tried to steal the Book of Mysteries from the Order's vaults, and *he* would be the one to accept the consequences for the mistake of letting Seshat loose into the world. Not Esta.

And if she carries your child? Seshat whispered, a dark amusement curling in her voice.

The goddess felt stronger than she had before—more like she had back in St. Louis—except now Harte knew she was furious with being muzzled and chained by the effects of the Quellant. It was clearer than ever that taking Maggie's formulation had destroyed any hope of a truce, even with his continued promise to end Thoth.

Would you be so quick to sacrifice yourself and seek the easy escape of death? Seshat taunted. *Would you leave them unprotected and make your child a bastard, as you are? If you do, Thoth will destroy them both.*

Harte tried to push away Seshat's words. He knew what she was doing—trying to weaken him, trying to make him waver—but by the time they arrived in Chicago, he was exhausted from trying to ignore the unresolved issue between them. The train slowed into the station, all steam and grinding of brakes. Esta was looking out the window of their small Pullman berth, her expression a study of concentration, and Harte wondered if she was considering the same thing he was.

"Esta, when would you . . . ?" Harte hesitated, feeling unbearably, stupidly embarrassed.

"What?" Her dark brows drew together as she turned to him. "Are you okay? Is Seshat—"

"I'm fine," he said, cutting her off. The last thing he wanted to do was talk about Seshat. But Esta only gave him a questioning look. "I mean, she's still there, but that isn't what I wanted to discuss. We need to talk about what happened between us."

Esta grew wary. "What about it?"

"When might you know?" Harte asked, feeling his cheeks flame, and when she didn't understand, he was forced to spell it out for her. "If there were any . . . *complications.*"

"Complications," she repeated. Her expression had gone strangely, carefully blank. "Are we back to this, then?"

"You know I would never allow—"

"You wouldn't *allow*?" The wariness shifted to impatience now.

"That's not what I meant," he tried to say. "Only that if there *is* a child—"

"We are *not* talking about this right now, Harte," Esta snapped.

"I could marry you," he blurted.

Her mouth fell open, and for a moment, she looked as shocked as he felt from saying those words out loud. But then anger replaced shock. "Could you?"

Harte knew he was on precarious ground. It had come out all wrong.

"Esta—" He tried to collect his thoughts—tried to figure out how to say everything he felt—as she waited, dangerously quiet.

"Forget it, Harte," she said after a moment. "I think I'll pass on your generous offer to make an honest woman of me. I'm fine. We are getting off this train, and we are going to focus on finding Jack and the Book. We have enough to worry about without you inventing more problems."

She turned from him then to collect her bag with a cold determination, while Harte stood there wondering how he'd screwed everything up so absolutely. Again. Esta was already opening the door and heading out into the corridor before he could even begin to consider how to repair the fragile peace he'd broken, and then they were disembarking and the time for conversation had passed.

The station was packed and filled with an energy like something about to begin. It was because of the convention, Harte realized. Somewhere in the city, Antistasi were planning the attack that would set history on a different course, and somewhere in the city, Jack Grew was waiting with the Book. Still, even with so much at stake, Harte was painfully aware of Esta next to him—especially the anger that radiated from her stiffened spine and tight jaw. She refused to look at him.

With Esta resolutely ignoring him, Harte tried to push aside his hurt and his embarrassment. He needed to keep himself alert as they made their way through the station, watching for any sign of trouble. He didn't remember much about leaving the bank or catching the train in Oakland.

He'd been reeling still from the death of his brother, but now he saw that the world had changed once more. Chicago was all flash and energy, with boxy motorcars and bustling sidewalks and buildings that towered overhead. The air was thick with the scents of exhaust and bitter cigarettes and the noise of street vendors with their wares. Men in light-colored, slightly wrinkled-looking suits and groups of young women walking arm in arm without escorts filled the sidewalks. The women wore dresses that fit loose, with low waists that obscured the shape of their bodies and hemlines that exposed their ankles, and many wore hair cut bluntly at their chin, every bit as short as Esta's.

It didn't take them long to find lodging in a small hotel. Esta lifted a few wallets so they could purchase some new clothes, and eventually her icy demeanor began to thaw and she started to talk to him again. But they never regained the warm easiness of the truce they'd come to on the train. She was purposely holding herself back from him now, and Harte knew it was his fault.

Three days later, not much between them had improved, especially with Seshat pacing impatiently beneath his skin. But they'd uncovered a promising lead—whispers of a nightclub where Mageus were rumored to go. It wasn't much, but it was a start toward locating the Antistasi in the city, and so that evening Harte found himself standing beneath the brightly lit marquee of the Green Mill wearing one of his new ready-made suits and trying not to stare too hungrily at Esta. Her dress was ready-made as well, but it fit her like it had been tailored specifically for the long lines of her body. The fabric skimmed over her curves, a shimmering column that ended only slightly below the knee. It looked like it was made from dark, liquid gold, and Harte wanted nothing more than to reach out and touch the material—and the girl beneath.

He didn't have to worry about Seshat that night, because they'd decided to risk using one of the remaining Quellant tablets. For the first time in days, the goddess's mocking laughter and threatening whispers weren't echoing in Harte's mind, but he barely noticed. All his concentration was on Esta and the dress she was wearing, and the fact that she was still holding herself away from him. He might have so little time left, and he wanted to fix things between them before it was too late. He wanted to bring her back to him—to make sure she was safe and protected—but Harte understood that they had a job to do. He tucked his hands into his pockets and kept them—and his thoughts—to himself.

The convention had started the day before, and so far the ballots had been inconclusive, but they both knew it was only a matter of time until the presidential nominee would be decided. Once that happened, the Antistasi would attack, unless he and Esta got to them first and convinced them to abandon their plan.

Esta had described the Green Mill as a saloon, but that was underselling it a bit. The establishment took up nearly an entire city block. But unlike some of the German-run beer halls back in Manhattan, the Green Mill's many rooms and gardens were all polish and shine.

They passed through the crowded saloon in the front of the building, ignoring the mahogany bar that served a menu of seltzers and juice, then continued on to the sunken gardens that stood at the center of the complex. Open to the warm summer night air, the gardens were filled with people dancing and laughing. Harte still didn't quite understand the whole concept of Prohibition. He couldn't figure out why anyone thought it would be necessary—or even possible—to make alcohol illegal. From all appearances, his instincts were right—the people bouncing around the dance floor, their arms and legs flying in all directions, looked far less sober than the so-called dry gardens should have allowed.

"The entrance to the speakeasy is over there," Esta said, frowning at the crowded dance floor.

Her lips were a dark, deep red, and she'd done something to accent the peaked bow in the center, so her frowning only served to draw Harte's eyes to her mouth. Which only served to remind him how her lips had felt against his a few days before. Which reminded him how her whole body had felt against his. And that made him damn uncomfortable in a lot of different ways. It made him remember just how badly he wanted things that he could not have.

Harte realized suddenly that Esta was looking at him expectantly—he'd missed whatever she'd just said. "What?"

She let out a frustrated breath. "I said that we'll have to go around the dance floor. Do you have a preference which direction?"

In for a penny . . .

Harte took Esta's hand and, though she jumped at his touch, he didn't let her pull away as he led her toward the swirl of dancers. For the last few minutes, the couples crowding the dance floor had been doing some sort of dance that involved kicking and hopping, but now the music had shifted into something slower.

"What are you doing?" Esta asked as Harte swept her into a formal embrace and then whirled her onto the floor and into the crush of other couples.

"I'm dancing with you," he murmured.

"Clearly," she said dryly.

He felt sure she would pull away from him. She had every reason to, with how badly he'd mucked up everything a few days before. But when she didn't immediately, Harte moved a little closer.

"This isn't really the time or place," Esta told him, but she followed his lead, her feet tracing the easy loping circles of the waltz they were caught up in.

Harte leaned back and raised a single brow as he looked at her. "I'm not sure I could think of a much better one." Then he lifted his arm and pushed Esta gently into a twirling spin before closing the frame of their position again. "It reminds me a little of the night we met."

She gave him a smile that was all teeth. "I must remember things differently. How long did it take for your tongue to heal, anyway?"

He bit back a laugh at her tartness, glad to have something other than ice from her. "Nearly a week," he told her, remembering his surprise when their first kiss—a ruse he'd forced upon her to stop her from using magic where she shouldn't—had turned dangerous. At least for him. "I should have never let you go," he whispered, repeating the words he'd said that night.

"What?" Her steps faltered, but Harte kept her upright and continued their waltz.

"It's what I said to you that night. Back at the Haymarket. You were dancing with some old goat, and I was trying to get you away from him and warn you about how dangerous it was to use your magic with Corey's men watching. I had to distract you somehow. It worked well enough then." He looked into her eyes. "Is it working now?"

"Don't, Harte," she whispered, her words coming to him on the back of the melody that surrounded them.

But he wasn't listening. Or rather, he was, but he needed Esta to understand. "I thought it *was* all nothing but a ruse, you know." He twirled her again. They were near the middle of the floor now, making their way across to the far side of the gardens. "My ridiculous words. That kiss."

"We need to focus," Esta reminded him, but her voice caught as she spoke.

"You're right." He took a moment to really look at her, a golden flame among peacocks, an Amazonian *goddess* among bits of fluff. It was more than her beauty; there was a strength emanating from within her that was unmistakable. That was *irresistible*. It always had been.

"That's not what I meant," she said.

"I'd like to kiss you now," he told her. They'd stopped dancing for some reason, probably because he'd stopped, but the rest of the dancers continued to move around them.

Esta's brows drew together. "I'm not sure that's a good idea."

"It's probably a terrible idea," Harte told her. "But it's all I've been able to think about for *days*."

"Are you sure you weren't really thinking about *complications*?"

"I'd like to kiss you," he repeated, because there wasn't room for lies between them any longer, especially not there, embracing as they were on the swirling dance floor.

Her pink tongue darted out, licking her crimson lips, a clear sign she was every bit as nervous as he was. Her eyes, the same liquid gold as her dress, were serious as they studied him. Unreadable. Finally, as the song was winding down, she spoke. "I can't promise I won't bite you again."

"I think it's well worth the risk." He pulled her closer, his hand at her waist, skimming over the silky softness of her dress, and drew her toward him.

He took his time about it, because he wanted her to understand that what was between them—what had *always* been between them—was something rare. It wasn't perfect, not by a long shot, but it was real and alive and maybe it was even a little dangerous as well.

Leaning toward her, Harte paused before his mouth touched hers, letting himself enjoy this stolen moment. Letting Esta want it as much as he did. He could detect the faintly floral scent of her soap. Then, with his free hand, he gently tipped her chin up, reveling in the shiver of anticipation he felt course through her, and pressed his mouth against hers.

Once again, they were on a dance floor, surrounded by music and moving bodies, but this was nothing like their first kiss. That had been a taking, and a surprise for both of them. That first kiss—and so many others, including the ones on the train—had been a battle of wills. Harte wanted this one to be different, so he started as soft as a question. He didn't linger too long. He didn't part her lips with his tongue or force himself upon her. He held himself back as he drank in the truth of their connection and the small moan that escaped from her lips. Then he released her.

As kisses went, it was positively chaste, and yet when he pulled back, Esta had a dazed look in her whiskey-colored eyes that he rather liked. He was fairly certain he was wearing one to match.

"That was—"

She didn't get to finish her sentence before they were interrupted.

"Mr. Darrigan?" Two large men were suddenly beside them. Bouncers, probably. But how could they possibly know his name?

Harte turned to them and gave the two men his best confused look. "I'm sorry, but you have the wrong fellow."

They took a step closer, and the larger of the two spoke again. "I don't think we do, Mr. Darrigan. You can come easylike, or we can make this hard. Either way, Mr. Torrio wants a word with you."

Harte's stomach dropped clear to his feet. "Mr. Torrio?" It couldn't be. It wasn't possible.

The only Torrio Harte knew was John Torrio—Johnny the Fox—who'd worked for Paul Kelly. It couldn't be that his past had found him, not there, in that strange future. Not when he'd been so close to everything he'd never realized he needed.

"If you don't remember him, I'm sure we can find a way to remind you," the smaller of the two said with a leering smirk. "If you'd come this way . . . Your doll should come along too."

"Oh, she's not mine," Harte said, glancing at Esta. "I only took a turn with her on the dance floor. I'm sure she'll want to get back to the good time she came for."

"Still . . ." The big man inched up behind Esta, making it clear that she wasn't getting out of this meeting. "Mr. Torrio would like to meet you both."

THE CHICAGO OUTFIT

1920—Chicago

Esta kept her expression aloof as Harte argued with the two men who'd cornered them. He was clearly trying to give her an out, but it wasn't working. She didn't have any plans to go, anyway. If these two goons wanted her to play the role of some flighty arm candy, she'd give them what they expected, at least until a better opportunity presented itself.

Looping her arm through Harte's, Esta slid closer. "I don't mind saying a quick hello to your friend," she said with a vacant, airy smile. "But then I want to dance again."

The larger of the two gave her a once-over. As his cold eyes traced her body from head to toe, Esta's skin crawled. It was possible she'd gone a *little* overboard on her look for the night—her bobbed hair lay in finger waves around her face, her lips had been lacquered in a deep red, and her eyes were ringed with kohl. Maybe the dress *was* a little much, but looking in the mirror earlier, Esta had been more than satisfied that Harte would swallow his own tongue when he saw her.

Luckily, the guy's perusal didn't last long, and he didn't show any real interest. He was more concerned with taking them to Torrio—whoever he was.

Even with the two men shoving them along, Esta was having a hard time shaking the memory of Harte's lips upon hers. For the last three days, she and Harte had existed in a kind of limbo. They'd plotted and planned and, all the while, they'd made sure to keep at least an arm's distance between each other. They had not spoken any more about the train—not about Harte's question about *consequences* or his terrible forced proposal, if you could even call it that. And they definitely didn't talk about the fact that neither of them were willing to let the other sacrifice themselves. It seemed that they'd come to an agreement—they would do everything in their power to get the Book back from Jack, and they would hope against hope that it held some solution. And if it didn't? Or if they couldn't manage to retrieve it? Well, those were scenarios that they didn't need to argue about. *Not yet.*

Still, hours and days of Harte being just out of reach had been the worst kind of torture. Esta might have wanted to get his attention with her outfit that night, but the kiss had still been a surprise, and the effect of it even more so. She'd seen the hunger in his expression, and so she hadn't expected softness, but somehow, the teasing of his lips was exactly what she'd needed. It had felt like a balm against the frustration from the past couple of days. But the appearance of the two brutish-looking bouncers had quickly changed things.

It didn't help that the men looked like every gangster from every bad mafia movie she'd ever seen. They were big, broad guys dressed in sharp suits with noses that had been broken at some point. Their dark hair was slicked back from faces too rough to ever be considered handsome, but they moved through the Green Mill like they owned it.

"Who's Torrio?" Esta asked Harte, making sure to keep her voice too soft for the bruisers to hear her.

"He was one of Paul Kelly's guys back in New York."

"Paul Kelly? As in, the head of the Five Pointers?" Esta asked, frowning. Harte nodded.

Esta hadn't met Kelly, but she knew about him. The Five Pointers were one of the most famous gangs in the city. Once they'd even been backed by Tammany Hall. "I don't think Kelly's behind this," she told him, trying to remember any other details from the history that had been drilled into her by Professor Lachlan. "Paul Kelly's power faded when the bootleggers took over."

"You make it sound like that's bad news." Harte glanced at her, a question in his eyes.

"The thing is, what's interesting about the Five Pointers isn't the Five Pointers themselves. It's what came after. They recruited and trained gangsters who grew to become even more powerful and vicious than Paul Kelly ever was. People like Al Capone."

Harte shook his head. Of course he wouldn't know the name. In 1902, Capone was still two decades away from being a player. But now?

"Capone's probably the most famous bootlegger and gangster of the twentieth century . . . and he was based in Chicago."

By then they'd been escorted inside, through the darkened bar to the back corner, where a table of men sat in a plush velvet booth that had clearly been selected so they had a view of the entire room. Esta recognized only one of the three—a man with hooded eyes, swarthy skin, a wide nose and mouth, and three long horizontal scars that cut across the left side of his face. *Al Capone.* He was younger than most pictures she'd ever seen of him—maybe around twenty. Even this young, he wasn't a handsome man. His face hadn't quite filled out the way it would in his later years, and his dark hair hadn't receded yet from his round face. From his position at the table, he was clearly not the one in charge. Not yet.

The person who *was* in charge was seated at the center of the table, his back to a corner. He was an older man in his midforties. It had to be John Torrio.

Unlike Capone, Torrio didn't have the deep olive skin of the Sicilian mobsters who would take over in the popular imagination. He was smaller, or he seemed to be next to his young protégé, with a narrow face and small eyes that turned down at the corners. There was something about Torrio that reminded Esta of a rat or some other member of the rodent family. Everything about him, but especially his confidence, seemed dangerous.

When she hesitated to approach the table, one of the bouncers escorting them took her by the arm. She tried to pull away from him—she probably could have, if she'd wanted to make a scene—but his grip was too secure.

The other bouncer pushed Harte forward, until he was squarely in front of the booth that held the trio of men.

"Harte Darrigan," the man in the middle of the booth said, his eyes narrowing even more as he took them in. "I've heard of putting people on ice, but Jesus Christ, you haven't aged a day."

QUITE A PREDICAMENT

Harte could almost see the teenager he'd once run with in the older man sitting at the table in front of him. Same square face, same beady little eyes. But the skin of Torrio's neck had grown loose, and his hair had turned a dull gray. If he hadn't been expecting Torrio, Harte would have likely looked right past this older man—clearly, he *had* walked right past him without noticing already.

Still, when Torrio spoke, Harte was struck by how he hadn't really changed all that much. Worse, Torrio was pointing out a significant issue—Harte hadn't aged a day in comparison.

The larger guy next to Torrio, the one with the scars on his cheek, looked more interested in his drink than the newcomers his boss was talking to. "You really knew this guy back in the old days, Johnny?"

Torrio's gaze slid to the scar-faced guy next to him before returning to Harte. "Oh yeah. Darrigan and I go *way* back."

"It's been a long time, Johnny," Harte said, without so much as blinking. He wasn't about to let Torrio see exactly how nervous he was. He needed to get Esta out of there, and preferably as quickly as possible. "You still working for Paul Kelly?"

"I took care of Kelly years ago," Torrio said with a satisfied smirk. "Left New York for greener pastures not long after. This here is my club, and Chicago's my city." His expression turned even sharper. "Anything happens in my city, I know about it. So I gotta ask—what are you doing here, Darrigan?"

"I'm only here to take in the sights," Harte said easily, even as his skin crawled with apprehension. "I'd appreciate it if your guy there took his hands off the girl."

Torrio nudged the guy next to him. "You hear him? He's talking like he's in some kind of position to issue orders." The two guys gave Torrio questioning looks, but then Torrio's amusement drained away. "You think I'm dumb enough to believe that story? I ain't some easy mark, Darrigan. Like I don't know that you showing up here looking like some kind of ghost don't mean problems." His eyes narrowed. "You got one chance to tell me the truth—Why did Lorcan send you?"

"Lorcan?" Harte was too thrown off to hide the confusion he felt at hearing Nibsy's last name come from John Torrio's mouth. He only barely managed to pull himself together in the next breath. "I don't know any Lorcan," Harte lied. He didn't risk glancing at Esta, but he knew she must have noticed the name as well.

"Bullshit," Torrio spat. "You think I don't know what's what? You show up here, not even aged a day, and try to tell me it's not some kind of hocus-pocus from Lorcan? What does he want this time? A bigger cut? Well, he's sure as shit not getting any more from me. He sits safe in his little fortress back in New York and issues orders like I don't know when he's trying to pull my strings. James Lorcan might think that just because he's given me some good tips, he can keep me on a leash like some kind of pet, but you can tell him those days are done, you hear? You tell him I don't need his information anymore. I've been doing fine on my own. Or maybe I'll tell him myself," he said, his beady eyes narrowing, "once I get rid of you."

"Johnny, you got it all wrong," Harte said, holding up his hands in surrender. "I don't know any Lorcan, and I certainly don't work for him. I'm not here to cause you any trouble."

"I don't believe that for a second." Torrio studied Harte as though he could read the lie simply by looking at him. "But maybe we should find out for sure." He glanced at the two large security guys who'd ushered Harte and Esta to his table. "Take these two down to the tunnels and keep an eye on them. And have Mikey bring me the house phone. I have a call to make."

Harte heard Esta's gasp and turned to see the bruiser who had her by the arm already dragging her away. She was struggling against the guy, but he seemed to be able to counter every move she made.

"Enough," the other one said, pulling a dark pistol on Harte. "Tell the hellcat there to stop, or you both get it," he told Harte.

Esta froze at the bouncer's threat, and her kohl-rimmed eyes went wide when she saw the gun pointing at Harte.

"It's fine," Harte told her, trying to keep it together. But his blood felt hot from seeing the other man's hands digging into the bare skin of Esta's arm. He hated knowing that there was no way he could fight these men—not in the shape he was in, weak as he still felt, and definitely not with a gun pointing directly at his gut. "This is nothing but a big misunderstanding. Johnny here is going to make a call, and he'll see that we don't know any Lorcan."

Esta's jaw had gone tight, and he could see the fury that shimmered in her eyes—*and* the fear that shadowed them. If Torrio made that call, Nibsy would know exactly where—and *when*—they were.

"Let's go." The bruiser who had Harte shoved him toward the bar. "You too, doll. And don't try nothing."

If Harte hadn't taken the Quellant, maybe they could have escaped. A simple touch, a silent command, and they would have been free. It would have been worth the risk Seshat posed to get Esta away from John Torrio and his men. As it was, though, Harte's affinity lay far beyond his reach. Still, even with the mess they had fallen into, he couldn't really bring himself to regret taking it. Not when he still remembered how Esta had softened against him when he'd kissed her a few minutes before.

Maybe she had been right, back on the train. Maybe all they'd ever had was the moment in front of them. Harte had used that moment on the dance floor well, and now he would deal with the one they currently faced. Somehow.

When they reached the bar, the bartender gave them a small nod, and the guys led them around a corner into what looked like a storeroom. There was a heavy metal door in the back wall and, beyond it, a staircase. The guy who had ahold of Esta was already dragging her down the steps, while the one with the gun kept watch on Harte up top.

Harte had barely started descending the steps himself, when a commotion erupted in the room behind them. Men were shouting, and then came a series of loud crashes that sounded like bottles breaking. The bouncer who had Esta glanced back, but he seemed barely concerned as he dragged her.

The one who had Harte nudged him forward with the butt of the gun. "Let's go, unless you want to deal with the Feds."

At the bottom of the steps, the hall stretched into a dark tunnel that ran the length of the building. Esta had already been shoved through a narrow door as the other bouncer pushed Harte forward until he could see that they were being placed in a closet-size cell, with a dirt floor and damp brick walls. The door was heavy and looked to be made out of metal rather than wood. With the gun pressed close to his spine, Harte didn't have any choice but to join Esta inside.

He eyed the lock as he went and was relieved to see it wasn't anything complicated enough to keep them for long. Still, the sound of the heavy door closing shuddered through him as the two bouncers locked him and Esta into the dark, windowless prison.

Harte felt Esta slide closer, her hand finding his in the pitch-darkness.

"Are you okay?" she asked.

"Fine. You?"

"I'll be better when we get out of here," Esta told him. She released his hand, and then he heard her begin to rustle through her beaded evening bag.

"You don't happen to have a hairpin or something in there, do you?" he asked. "For the lock?"

"I have something better." A second later the *skritch* of a match sounded, and Esta held the flame up to show Harte the slim bronze pick they'd used in the bank vault. "Do you want to do the honors, or should I?"

"You're a wonder, you know that?" he mused, taking the pick from her as the flame of the match reached her fingertips.

Esta cursed and dropped the match to the ground, where it went dark. "I'd be more of a wonder if I had a flashlight," she grumbled.

He couldn't see her, but he could hear the frustration—and the nervousness—in her voice. Esta hated dark, tight places, probably the result of being locked in a closet by Nibsy when she was a toddler.

Luckily, it had been a long time since Harte had needed light to pick a lock. Years of practice in boxes and safes and cases of water had made him an expert in breaking any lock blind. This one was no exception. He could sense Esta close by him as he worked the pick into the lock, feeling for the pins inside the mechanism to give way. She wasn't crowding him, but in the darkness, that didn't matter. She could have been ten feet away; the lightless space made it feel like she was right there, next to him. The scent of her was a distraction, and the warmth of her both steadied him and made his nerves jangle.

"Esta . . ." He paused, not exactly knowing what he wanted to say. If he wanted her to be closer or to step back so that he could think.

She went very still.

"On the train . . ." He paused, feeling more than ridiculous, but it needed to be said. She had to understand. "You have to know—"

"It's fine," Esta told him, her clipped voice coming to him through the pitch-blackness.

"It absolutely isn't," he said. He stopped what he was doing and reached for her hand, feeling how it shook slightly—from the cold of the room or from nerves, he didn't know. "I was an idiot."

"You were," she said, and without being able to see her face, he could not sense what she was thinking. "But that isn't exactly a new development."

Harte barked out a surprised, grateful laugh, and as he moved closer,

Esta went suddenly still, as though she was waiting to see what would happen next. He paused, giving her room and time and an escape, if she needed one.

She was *so* close, and even without Seshat's constant prowling, Harte felt unsteady. He knew that if he kissed her, he would not want to stop.

"Are you going to take care of the lock, or do you need me to do it?" Esta asked finally. Her voice was breathy, and Harte understood he hadn't been alone in his desire, but it was also enough to shake him back to the moment at hand and to force him to focus.

"I can handle it," he said evenly, trying not to feel too disappointed. He worked carefully, letting the vibrations and the tension on the pick guide him, wishing Esta's feelings were as easy to unlock as the bit of metal beneath his hand.

He hadn't quite managed to release the lock when an explosion sounded on the other side of the door. Even with the thickness of the metal, Harte could hear the blast and feel the vibrations. It was enough to make him lose his concentration, and all the progress he'd made on the lock. Then a barrage of gunfire erupted, a muted *rat-a-tat-tat* that seemed impossibly fast, followed by more shouting. And then . . . silence.

Esta grabbed his arm. "What's going on out there?"

"I'm not sure, but maybe if we're lucky, it'll have taken care of Torrio for us," he told her, knowing that they couldn't possibly be *that* lucky. More likely, whatever was on the other side of the door would be another problem . . . and most likely a well-armed one.

For what seemed like an endless stretch of time, they stood together, Esta's hand on his arm, and they waited. Listening. They were concentrating so hard on trying to hear the danger that might be coming for them that they both jumped when a narrow window slid open in the door. The scent of gunpowder drifted in through the bright slash in the darkness. Then a set of mismatched eyes—one brown, one green—appeared in the window.

"Well, well . . . looks like the two of you have found yourselves in quite the predicament," a familiar voice said right before the lock clicked and the door swung open. On the other side, the hallway of the tunnel was filled with an unnatural fog that glowed with a bright lavender-and-yellow swirl, and Jericho Northwood stood grinning at the two of them, looking a few decades older and every bit as ornery as he ever had.

THE CITY'S SHADOWS

1902—New York

T he sounds of bells and sirens were already echoing through the city, fueling the anticipation and heating the blood in James Lorcan's veins. The Order knew for sure now that they were under attack, but James' plan was only beginning to unfold.

In the back of the open horse cart, Viola still looked a little stunned from what had happened a few minutes before. She'd watched her brother be carted off in a Black Maria, but James knew that she understood that she *still* wasn't free—not if she crossed James when he held the lives of her friends in his hands. She was clinging to the side of the cart's bed, trying to stay upright as they careered through the city. Off-balance, literally and figuratively, just as James preferred her.

In the distance, James heard the keening whine of a locomotive's whistle and the noise of a city stirring to find itself awash in confusion. *Finally*, it was beginning. As Werner urged the poor, bedraggled mare to move faster, only James himself knew how it was all destined to end.

Mooch and a few others from the Devil's Own rode cramped in the bed of the cart along with Viola. James had selected them each by hand—some for their particular abilities, and some, like Mooch, that he preferred to keep close. When the redhead exchanged an uneasy glance with Viola, his pale skin flushed so quickly and easily that James knew his suspicions had been right. There was something between the two—a connection had likely facilitated Viola's little bout of larceny and the disappearance of Dolph's journal. James figured that if the two were so happy to work together, they could die together as well.

The ride down Twenty-Third Street took only a handful of minutes, but with the sun ever lower in the sky, it might as well have been hours. Then, as the sun drew closer to the horizon, something odd began to happen. As the sky shifted closer to twilight, the streets began to light with a strange, almost ethereal glow. The drab red brick of buildings brightened in the odd light, and the puddles of water and troughs along the road turned to molten pots of gold. The city's shadows all stretched east, like nature itself was pointing their way. Urging them on.

It was a startling thing to see the road before them bathed in such a light, especially in a city where the streets were usually at least partially shaded by the ever-growing buildings that lined them. But for James, it was a sign that he'd been right. His plan would work. The Aether vibrated, dancing around him, and the sun warmed his skin as it lit their wagon in the eerie light.

"The Golden Hour," Viola murmured, lifting her hand as though she could catch the sunbeams and the power they supposedly held. Her drab, olive-toned skin suddenly looked almost bronze in the sun.

"It's beginning," James agreed. He looked back to see the sun descending right down the center of Twenty-Third Street. The fiery haze of the shimmering orb was framed perfectly by the buildings as it sank toward the river. It was an odd sight, and it might have even been beautiful if James had the time to appreciate beauty. As it was, they were racing the sun, and every minute was one fewer they had to stop the Order from securing the artifact. Because if the Order's delivery arrived before they did . . .

Block after block, the cart rattled over trolley tracks and uneven cobbles until finally the street emptied into the wide area in front of the wedge-shaped tower, but when they finally arrived, something was already happening. Police wagons stood in the plow-shaped plaza in front of the building. They were surrounding another plain wagon, and some of the dark-suited officers were trading fire with someone in the building on the other side of Fifth Avenue, while others were already tussling with men on the ground.

"Those are Five Pointers," Viola told him. "My brother's men."

"I'm aware," James said, satisfied with the way the Aether swirled around him. "It looks like Johnny the Fox hasn't turned into a rat. He's kept his promises."

"You knew the wagon would be here?" Viola asked, confusion swimming in her violet eyes.

"You've played three-card monte, haven't you, Viola?" Nibsy asked, faintly amused by her shock. "The shuffling of the cards is never anything more than a distraction. The money card is always already in the dealer's hand. The second we knew about the extra ships, I knew the goods wouldn't be on them."

"But if you knew there was nothing in the other wagons . . ." Viola frowned, finally piecing things together.

Too late, James thought. *Always too late.*

"Do you mean that Cela's brother and the rest, they are risking themselves for *nothing*?"

Nibsy shrugged, unbothered by her sudden worry. "They're doing what they're supposed to be doing—providing a necessary diversion so the Order doesn't realize we've caught on to their little game."

"And what of the Devil's Own?" she asked, clearly bristling. "Have you risked their lives as well?"

Nibsy turned to her then. He made sure that his gaze was unyielding. "The Devil's Own belong to me now, Viola. They do what *I* say."

"And if they're caught by the police, what then?" Viola pressed. "If they're killed?"

"Life and death." Nibsy tilted his head, trying to conceal his amusement as he considered her dismay. "Isn't that what our dear friend Dolph used to say? *Life and death.* Two sides of the same coin. It's what they all signed up for when they took his mark." Then he allowed his mouth to curve as Viola blanched, the color draining magnificently from her face.

"I never expected you, of all people, to be so squeamish about something so banal as a few deaths. People die every day in the Bowery. You *know* that. You've taken more than a few of those lives yourself."

One of the Five Pointers broke through the ranks of police suddenly, drawing everyone's attention. The man charged toward the back of the plain, waiting wagon, but the instant he grabbed hold of the rear door, strange markings on the wagon were illuminated, as though by electricity, and the man began to scream. The Aether trembled as the Five Pointer's face contorted in agony, but the man didn't release his hold.

Werner and Mooch, even Viola, turned away, repulsed by the sight, but Nibsy watched with a cool detachment.

"What the hell's happening to him?" Mooch asked, fear strangling his words.

"I told you the wagons would be protected," James said.

"But you never said they would do *that*," Werner argued.

"Didn't I?" James asked, masking his amusement.

"Any one of us could've been killed," Werner said, frowning.

"Not unless you had disobeyed my orders," James told him. He watched with some satisfaction as the Five Pointer continued to writhe and scream.

If Torrio had thought to cut James out, he'd thought wrong.

"You kept this information from me as well," Viola huffed, still visibly shaken by the sight.

He turned to her. "No one was supposed to touch the wagons, only to redirect them. Anyone who tried to change our agreed-upon plan and attempted to board one of the wagons would have deserved whatever happened to them," he said, making his voice cold as he eyed her. "But then, I'm confident in the loyalty of the Devil's Own. It's the other parties involved that I didn't trust."

"You still should have told me," she charged.

He shrugged. "There was no reason to."

Temper flashed in Viola's eyes. "You said we were partners."

"No," James told her. "I said you should come back to the Devil's

Own, that you should join *me*. I *never* said we would be equals."

Growing bored with Viola's display of temper—and with the conversation—James directed Werner to pull the cart into the park across from the building, far enough from the skirmish to be out of range and out of sight.

He turned his attention to Logan. "Is it there?"

"The wagon's already empty," the boy told him.

"How can he know this?" Viola demanded, as though she had any right to an answer.

"It's his job to know," James told her as he considered the building. "The Delphi's Tear will already be inside, then." *Unfortunate, but not catastrophic.* Not when he had yet another ace to play.

"Then it's impossible," Viola said, sounding far less devastated than she perhaps should have. But then, did she really believe he wouldn't see through her duplicity?

James glanced at her over his spectacles, and this time he did not bother to affect any look of innocence. "I will consider sparing the lives of your friends if you tell me everything you know about what waits for us inside that building. *Everything* Theo Barclay learned about the layout of the Order's new headquarters and what we might find inside."

Viola stared at him, disbelief coloring her cheeks. Fear, too, if he wasn't mistaken.

"Did you truly think I wouldn't find out that you had someone on the inside, Viola?" he asked, bored with her continued act. "Did you really think I wasn't aware you were trying to set your brother and me at odds with each other? You were never actually interested in coming back to the Devil's Own or pledging any *real* loyalty to me. I knew that for sure when I discovered that Dolph's journal had gone missing from my rooms a few weeks ago."

"You mean *Dolph's* rooms," she told him, confusion turning to anger. "You stole them from him, just as you stole his cane. As you stole his *life.*"

"It was your brother's Five Pointers who took Dolph's life," James lied.

"I simply stepped in to lead the Devil's Own when no one else would, including *you*."

"Lies," Viola seethed, and James felt a pain course through his chest. "I know what you did. It was *you* who murdered Dolph, not any Five Pointer. I should kill you now."

James ignored Werner's and Mooch's sudden interest. "Where did you get that information, Viola?" He tilted his head to one side, watching the emotions flicker across her face. "Let me guess. You believed tales whispered to you by Jianyu—though why you would trust him, I can't imagine. Not after what he did to Tilly."

"You have no business speaking her name," Viola snarled.

The tightness in his chest increased, and James couldn't repress his grimace. Logan was already moving to attack, but even with the pain near his heart, James held a hand up to stay him. Let Viola dig herself a deeper grave.

As the boys in the cart paused, waiting for his order, James clenched the head of the cane and tried to gather his strength. He felt the power beneath it. In the past weeks he'd grown so close to touching the promise of that power, and now he focused all that he was into it. He was gratified to hear Viola suck in a sharp breath, and he glanced up to see the confusion—the fear—in her eyes. He knew what had caused it, because he felt it himself, the echo of power in the mark he wore on his own skin. From the way the others shifted uneasily, he could tell they felt it as well. Which was fine. It would serve as a warning to all—that he was more than he seemed. That he should not be crossed.

"Have a *care*, Viola," James said, repeating his warning from a little while before through gritted teeth. "Your friends' lives still hang in the balance, and Torrio knows *exactly* how underhanded you can be. If I don't send the order to stop him, your friends will die."

He felt the pressure in his chest recede.

"Much better," he said, adjusting his grip on Dolph's cane. He held his focus on the marks for a few seconds longer, to show her he could, before he released them. "I only ever agreed to take you back because I knew you could provide additional information about what was inside that building. It seems my premonition was correct. You'll give me that information, and you'll give it now."

"It won't do you any good," Viola told him. "If the artifact is already inside, it will be impossible to take it back out."

Nibsy gave her a pitying look. "Come now, Viola. Nothing's ever impossible, especially not when your friends' lives are on the line." He saw her realization when it struck. She had made a play, and now she understood her loss. "I'm sure you'll figure out some way to retrieve the artifact. After all, sunset won't wait. And neither will my ring."

AN EXPECTED INTERRUPTION

1902—New York

After finishing with Theo Barclay, Jack Grew took the stairs down from the Library of Life room to the chambers below, whistling as he went. It was a strange little tune, and he realized as he reached the sixteenth floor that he couldn't recall where he'd heard it. Actually, he couldn't recall having *ever* heard it, except maybe in dreams, but Jack dismissed that idea at once. It didn't matter where he'd picked up the song. Things were going his way, and by the time night dropped her veil over the city, the Delphi's Tear would be his, and Theo Barclay would be no more.

The Order's ceremony to consecrate the top five floors of the Flatiron Building as their new headquarters was to be held in the more public chambers on the sixteenth floor. Here, a larger portion of the membership could be in attendance, as the upper floors were reserved for the wealthiest and most powerful members.

Like the library above, the more public sanctuary was also located at the front of the building so the members could take in the grandeur of the city. To enter, members were required to navigate a series of antechambers, each fortified with their own protections. Between each, narrow winding turns had been designed to disorient and confuse, so that by the time the member stepped into the space, he would immediately be overtaken by the view. Centered in front of the bank of windows was an angular altar. It had been carved from a single enormous piece of lapis lazuli, and the setting sun illuminated it, turning the altar as brilliant as the summer sky.

Jack entered behind a few of the other members, appreciating the warm glow of the phosphorus lamps that hung from gilded chains around the edges of the room and the ornate designs etched into the walls. With its windows, the entire space was bathed in the ethereal light of the Golden Hour. To the west, the sun had nearly reached the water. It would be only a little while longer now. Until the sun dipped below the horizon, Jack would enjoy the pageantry that was to come. And after . . . he would make his move.

Before the altar stood five women clad only in silken sarongs. Their bare skin had been painted in gold from head to toe, which made their bodies glisten in the strange light. Around each of their necks, a single large crystal dangled from a golden chain. Each pendant had been cut to symbolize one digit of the Philosopher's Hand: the key, the crown, the lantern, the star, and the moon. The elements necessary to transmute existence. The women were living statues; they barely blinked, even when the members inched forward to take a closer look. They'd been one of Jack's better ideas for the ceremony, but his best was yet to come.

While the other members swooned over the new surroundings, Jack felt nothing but satisfaction. Soon the Delphi's Tear would be his, and with it the ability to finally complete his machine. He would show the Order how wrong they had been to deny him for so long. He would show the Inner Circle the path down which their destiny must lead.

Jack took a seat close to the edge of the room as the lights went dim and the ceremony began. In the back of the chamber, a door opened that had not seemed to be there a moment before. It was a brilliant bit of illusion, and the men around Jack murmured appreciatively as four members of the Inner Circle made their way toward the altar. When they reached the front, they formed a line, and then one stepped forward and began to speak about the illustrious history of the Order of Ortus Aurea.

Jack barely paid attention to the old man's droning. What did he care about the past, when the future stretched in all its brilliant possibilities on the far horizon? On and on the speech went, and all the while Jack pictured what would come next and prepared himself. The old man prattled on for what seemed like an eternity, until finally bells could be heard from somewhere within the walls and the door at the back of the room opened once more.

This time it was the High Princept who appeared. He was flanked by two other men, each draped in white linen and wearing masks that obscured their identities. When the three reached the blue altar, the two masked men unrolled a scroll and held the wide swath of it upright, so the Princept could read an incantation. He invoked the gods and the angels, and he beseeched them to protect this place that would be a sanctuary for years to come. When he was finished, the masked men withdrew the scroll, and as one, the members in attendance stood and applauded.

Jack played his part, rising and clapping along with the rest. He would let them enjoy their moment, because he knew that his own plan was already unfolding.

In the preceding weeks, he'd worked long and hard to prepare for this night. He'd been forced to humble himself, bowing and pretending subservience, when he knew that the old men of the Inner Circle were nothing more than a past that hadn't realized it was over. In the end they'd trusted Jack enough to use him, but they hadn't allowed him to attend the ceremony to install the artifact into the Mysterium earlier that day. They said it was because he wasn't officially part of the Inner Circle—not yet. But Jack understood an excuse when he heard one. They were still holding him at arm's length.

No longer. The High Princept's arrival signaled that the time was finally at hand. He checked his watch and saw there were still a few minutes until the sun dipped farther than six degrees below the horizon, minutes during which the Order still would believe themselves to be protected by the power of the Golden Hour. But in those remaining minutes, they would find out how vulnerable they truly were.

An alarm sounded in the outer chamber, and Jack frowned down at his watch. It was a few minutes earlier than he'd planned, perhaps, but close enough. As the members began murmuring at the sudden interruption, the High Princept stood to reassure them.

"Gentlemen, we expected no less than an attack this evening, but please. Settle yourselves. Every precaution has been taken," he assured the room. "Every measure of possible protection has been put into place for this very eventuality, and the maggots who would try to disturb us this evening will find themselves sorry. As we sit here, safe in the sanctuary of our own making, the building is turning itself on our intruders."

As if on command, heavy shutters rolled down over the windows, leaving the entire sanctuary bathed only in the glow of the phosphorus lamps. It was exactly as Jack had hoped: The lamps cast enough light to throw the flickering shadows that would allow him to move through the crowd without being noticed.

"All of the chambers beyond this one will lock, making entrance or exit impossible," the Princept continued. "Even now security measures are being activated that will snuff out the threat any intruders might pose as easily as a candle."

The Princept didn't bother to tell the rest of the members that it had been Jack who had set up the entire system, which was, he supposed, probably for the best. It was unlikely any of the members would realize that the protections Jack had designed also contained an extra feature for this particular night: It would release a series of alchemical reactions that would appear to be an attack. The effect would doubtlessly cause enough confusion to keep the members of the Order distracted. In the end, it would seem that Jack's security system had worked and the building had been defended. In reality, the attack would be nothing more than smoke and mirrors. He'd learned that bit from Darrigan, back when he'd believed the magician had some real connection to the powers of the occult. The attack was nothing but misdirection—a diversion intended to keep the Order from realizing what was *actually* happening.

"As long as everyone is accounted for," the Princept called, "we are all safe here until the danger passes."

Jack waited, keeping his expression even as the men around him began looking over one another, counting among their ranks. He waited long enough to be sure that the room was already buzzing with confusion, and then he called out. "Barclay's missing! He was right here . . . but now he's gone."

It didn't matter that Barclay had never been there to begin with. The men around him reacted exactly as Jack had predicted they would. With confusion and then suspicion . . . and then, predictably, with *anger*.

Smiling to himself as the mood of the room shifted, Jack ducked behind a tapestry, depressed a lever hidden there, and let himself out into the hallway. The rest of the members would whip themselves into a fit while Jack retrieved the ring. In a matter of minutes, he would return to the sanctuary below, undetected, and when the Order discovered that the artifact was missing, Barclay would look like the culprit. The poor, desperate, *dead* culprit.

TIMES CHANGE

1920—Chicago

J ericho Northwood and his crew had only come to the Green Mill that night for the Nitewein that John Torrio and his lot sold to lure Mageus into the establishment. He hadn't expected to find a couple of familiar faces in addition. Now he had to figure out what he was going to do with them.

In truth, North had never expected to see hide nor hair of Esta Filosik, much less Harte Darrigan, again. He'd only expected that one day, when he was least expecting it, the life he had would simply disappear. He'd turned in each night thanking his lucky stars for the gift of one more day to be the man he was, living the life he had, and each morning he'd wake up with the grateful wonder that it was all still there, his life still intact and his family still whole and real in his arms. But now Esta was back, and with her, the threat she posed to him—to his life and to everything he'd built and everyone he loved.

He knew what Maggie would say. *Some things are destined,* his wife would tell him with that soft smile she always wore when she was somewhere between amused and exasperated. *There's no way around the two of us,* she'd say as she braided their youngest girl's hair. His Maggie had an absolute faith in the inevitability of the two of them and the little family they'd built for themselves, a belief that nothing—not time, nor magic—could shake. *Some things are meant to be.*

North didn't know that he quite agreed. He knew exactly how possible it was to change the course of things. Maggie could keep her faith, but North wasn't willing to chance everything he was and everything they'd built to the whimsy of fate. Not that he had any clue how to fight against something as slippery as destiny or as unyielding as time.

It didn't help any that the fear of what Esta could do to his life had only grown with each addition to his family. Their children were a spot of light in North's life, and he didn't trust fate to keep their lights aglow. But then, he had to admit that fate—fickle though she might be—had somehow seemed to smile on him far more than he'd ever deserved. He'd lost everything and then found Maggie. They'd made terrible mistakes with the Antistasi, and somehow still managed to make it through to the other side. Their life together, their children—if those were all gifts of fate, Jericho Northwood was damn lucky. Now, it seemed, fate had delivered Esta Filosik to him once more, but he wasn't sure what that meant.

"This way," North directed, leading the way through the eerie fog that filled the tunnel. "It'd be an awful big help if the two of you would each grab a case." He pointed to the stack of wooden crates that his guys were already carting out of the tunnels. "We don't have much time before the real agents show up."

Thankfully, Esta and Harte didn't argue or give him any trouble. Even dressed in some kind of slippery-looking scrap of a thing, Esta grabbed a crate and followed the line of men to the truck they'd parked out back. Once the crates of Nitewein were loaded up, North noticed Esta and Harte trading meaningful glances. Sirens were already singing in the distance.

North knew exactly what they were thinking, but he wasn't about to let them go so fast, not when he was still considering what he should do about them. "Why don't you hop on in? We can give you a lift."

"Oh, I think we can find our own way back," Harte said, and then offered his hand along with his thanks.

North didn't take the outstretched hand. "I wasn't really asking." He narrowed his eyes a bit, still considering his options if they didn't comply. There wasn't any way he was letting these two get away from him, not without figuring out what they were up to. "I think we ought to catch up a bit, don't you?" He let his gaze linger on Esta, a clear, if unspoken, challenge.

After a couple of seconds, she relented. "We *are* old friends, after all," she told Harte without even so much as blinking.

Old friends . . . North couldn't help but laugh, especially since they both looked like a couple of kids. Hell, it was hard to believe he'd ever been that young himself, even if he hadn't been all that much older the last time he'd seen the two of them. But their appearance—the smooth skin of their faces, devoid of the lines that already mapped his own life's joys and frustrations—was confirmation that Esta could do exactly what she'd threatened years ago in Denver. The question was whether North would give her that chance.

Reluctantly, Harte helped Esta up into the back of the truck, and then he hopped up himself. North followed, closing the rolling door behind them, then made his way between the crates that had been stacked along each side of the truck's bed and knocked a couple of times on the front wall. A second later, a window opened.

"Are we all set?" the driver, Floyd, asked.

"Let's get going," North told him, barely getting the words out before the truck was lurching into gear. "You okay up there, Rett?" North asked the passenger, who turned to look at him with familiar mismatched eyes. Floyd was one of the local guys who was helping out on the run, but Everett was his and Maggie's oldest boy.

Maggie had about wanted to skin North alive for taking Everett on this particular job. She still saw the boy as the fat, freckled toddler he'd once been, never mind that Everett was taller than North these days. He supposed it was a mother's prerogative to see the babe she'd once held in her arms, but a father understood when his boy was becoming a man. And he understood that men needed something more than their mother's apron strings. Everett spent too much time sitting in corners reading until his eyes crossed or tinkering at Maggie's side, and not enough time out in the world, as far as North was concerned.

Not that Maggie was wrong to have her worries. The jobs they did were always dangerous—always had been—and they usually did come with some complication or another. Right then, Chicago was riskier than usual, what with the Republican Convention in town. But of all the complications he could have worried about or prepared for, North hadn't expected this one.

Esta was studying the two of them, and North could practically feel her thinking. "He's yours," she said softly.

"He is," North said, beaming at his son with a pride he never bothered to repress. The boy shook his head in response, rolling his eyes a little like he was tired of the attention.

"Then Maggie . . ." Esta didn't finish, and North suspected that he understood why. Every time he thought of that night in Denver, his throat got a little tight, and he felt the fear of losing his girl all over again. It didn't matter that she was as hale and hearty now as she ever had been.

"Maggie came through okay," he told Esta. "The doctor George took us to saved her life."

"I'm glad to hear that," Esta told him, and North thought she might have even meant it. "I've been thinking about her these last few weeks . . . wondering."

Weeks? It was almost impossible to comprehend, considering that it had been years upon years for North.

"Cordelia was such a good shot," Esta said.

"Thankfully, the doctor was better. But you're right. Cordelia was good—too good. Maggie uses a chair now to get around." He couldn't stop the smile that came when he thought of his wife. "Not that it's slowed her down one bit."

"Then you've been happy?" Esta asked with a hopeful note.

"As much as anyone can be, I suspect," he told her. "I take it you never made it back?" He kept his words vague, but from the tightening of her lips, North knew Esta understood. He didn't miss the way Harte tensed at the question either.

Esta shook her head a little. "No. Not yet."

"But you will."

She didn't immediately respond.

"We have four kids," North told her. "Everett here's the oldest, then we got the twins, and little Ruthie is the youngest." He met her eyes, daring her to look away. Daring her to face what it meant if she carried through with her plan and took those lives from him.

"This lady knows Mama?" Everett asked, unaware of the tension in the back of the truck.

"I met your mother back in St. Louis," Esta confirmed. "Your father, too. We worked together for a while."

"That was years ago," North said. The last thing he needed was Everett getting some idea in his head that Esta was harmless. "Back before Denver."

From the way Everett's mouth went tight, North knew the boy understood his meaning.

"I'm glad to see that the two of you made a good life for yourselves," Esta said.

"We do okay," North said. "But that's mostly to do with Maggie. Once she healed up, she was a woman on a mission. News traveled fast about what happened, and it didn't take all that long for Maggie to wrestle control away from that Professor fellow. Especially since he was trapped behind the Brink."

"Maggie leads the Antistasi now?" Esta asked, and there was a note of something North couldn't decipher in her voice.

"No one person leads them anymore," North corrected. "Maggie saw what happened with Ruth and with the Professor. Even if she could have stepped up, she didn't think any one person should have that much power. Still doesn't. The Antistasi have gone back to being what they always were supposed to be—a loosely organized group of like-minded individuals. We still take action when it's warranted. Like tonight at the Green Mill."

"Because Torrio is working with the Professor?" Esta asked.

North was suddenly glad for the darkness of the truck. They'd been trying to figure out what Torrio and the rest of the Chicago Outfit had wanted with Mageus in the city for some time, but now that the words were out of Esta's mouth, the pieces came together. It was another of the Professor's ploys to wrestle back control.

"Actually, we were there for the Nitewein," he explained. "The Chicago Outfit tends to use more opium in theirs, which gets people hooked a lot faster. In the last few months, they've started using it to blackmail any Mageus who are unlucky enough to get caught up with them. We weren't aware of Torrio's connections," he admitted. "But that makes a helluva lot of sense, especially considering what the Outfit has forced people to do with their affinities."

"*Good* people," Everett added. "And they end up taking the fall when things go sideways, like they always do."

"What will you do with the Nitewein you've taken?" Harte asked.

"Probably we should destroy it," North admitted. "But I'm not one of the teetotalers who want to tell other people how to live their lives. It ain't exactly fair that Sundren get to buy their bootleg liquor and drown their troubles in relative safety but we don't. There're plenty who use the Nitewein to help them handle the effects of affinities they can't other-wise use." He paused, wondering how much the two of them knew . . . how much they'd missed. "It's gotten a lot worse, you know. The Defense Against Magic Act has only been strengthened these past years with Prohibition."

"It's going to get even worse still," Esta told him with a quiet certainty that made North feel more than a little uneasy.

"I'll have to take your word for it," he said. "Right now, though? There are plenty who need a bit of something to take off the edge, so we'll dilute the mixture and then unload it on the Nitemarket."

The truck rumbled to a stop, and North knew he had to make a choice about what to do with this new development. The back door lifted, and he jumped out, considering his options. "Why did you say you were in Chicago?" he asked, looking up at them.

"We didn't," Harte said, hopping out of the truck. He was dressed to the nines, sleek charcoal suit and crisp collar and cuffs—or it had been before the little dustup they'd found themselves in that night. Esta stood above them, looking like she was auditioning to be a hood ornament in that gold dress of hers. Harte helped her down.

By now a few others had come out of the warehouse to help them unload the Nitewein. North gave them a subtle nod, and they surrounded the truck. One of his guys stepped closer to Esta and took her by the arm, to keep her from shifting out before they could stop her.

"Maybe it would be best if you start explaining," North told them.

Harte seemed to suddenly realize they'd gone from being rescued to being trapped once again. He eyed the one who had ahold of Esta, looking like he wanted to kill the man himself. "Maybe you should call off your men."

North shook his head. "Not quite yet. Just because we might have worked together before doesn't mean I'm amenable to renewing our partnership. Especially when I know what it might eventually lead to." He focused on Esta, a reminder that he knew what her plans were.

"I know what you think of me," she said, her voice surprisingly calm considering her position. "And I know that if it weren't for Maggie, you probably wouldn't have let me leave Denver. But you trusted me once before, and I'm asking you to trust me again. Because we need your help."

"For what?" North asked.

"We need to find the Antistasi in Chicago. A group of them are planning some kind of attack on the convention, and we need to stop that from happening," she told him. "If they go through with the attack, it's going to change things in ways you can't even begin to comprehend."

North knew he shouldn't even ask. Every time these two had turned up, his life got flipped on its head. But he couldn't stop himself. "What is it that you think is going to happen?"

"If the Antistasi do what they're planning, the Brotherhoods are going to retaliate by activating some kind of a tower."

Everett had come up next to them and was listening. "Like the one on top of the Coliseum?"

"What's this you're talking about?" North turned to look at his oldest.

"It's a great big thing," Everett said. "Didn't you see it? We drove right by it last night."

North had been to Chicago enough times that he hadn't really been paying attention, but Everett was new to the city and had been taking everything in like the rube he was.

"If you remember, I was busy doing the driving," North told Everett, annoyed with himself for missing something like that.

"I'm not sure how you could've missed it," Everett said. "It was way up on top of the building's roof, and it was all lit up like a Christmas tree, with a great big American Steel sign and the Stars and Stripes spotlighted from below. I figured it was some sort of advertisement."

"That's J. P. Morgan's company," Esta said darkly as she traded another meaningful glance with Harte. "That tower isn't an advertisement. It's a weapon."

"What do you mean?" North asked.

"Just what I said. That tower isn't some decoration. It's a weapon, similar to the one that the Vigilance Committee used in California years ago," she told him. "You know about what happened there?"

"Of course." *Everyone* had heard about that. "It was a damn tragedy. The number of people who died . . ." North shook his head. "But it isn't possible that they'd build another. Roosevelt promised that the government wouldn't build anything like it, ever again. People wouldn't accept such a thing."

"American Steel isn't the government," Harte reminded North. Then he glanced briefly at Esta. "And as for people standing for it . . . times change."

North made his expression carefully blank. "You're saying you know for sure this will happen?"

Esta nodded. "If the Antistasi attack the convention, Jack Grew and the Brotherhoods are going to activate that tower. If that happens—"

"People will die," North said. "A lot of people. *Innocent* people."

"Didn't you know?" Harte said darkly. "There *are* no innocent Mageus. According to Jack and the Order and all of the Brotherhoods, there never were, and if they have their way, there never will be."

"Even if there are Antistasi here in the city planning some sort of deed . . . Even if the Brotherhoods retaliate, it won't work. Something like that, I can't believe the public will stand for it. They might not care if Mageus are rounded up and quietly deported or imprisoned. It's easy enough for people to ignore the things that they don't have to look straight at, but you're talking about a lot of people dying. Children and old people and everyone in between. You're talking about outright *murder*. If the Brotherhoods start up that tower, it'll backfire on them, same as it did in California."

"This time will be different," Esta said. Her face was partially shadowed, but even concealed by the darkness, her eyes were serious and filled with a sadness that even North couldn't possibly ignore. "The public will not only stand for it, but they'll reward Jack Grew—the person responsible for the tower and its effects—at the convention."

"Well, see, that's where you're wrong," North said, feeling a bit of relief. "They just decided on that Harding fella as the presidential nominee."

"When?" Esta demanded.

"Earlier this evening," he said, frowning at her tone. "An hour or so before we found you at the Green Mill. Seems to me your predictions are a little off this time."

"There's still the vice presidential nomination," Harte said.

"And then when Harding dies . . ." Esta didn't finish.

"How could you possibly know all that?" Everett asked Esta. "You're talking like you can prognosticate the future."

"It's not prognostication if you've seen it for yourself," North told his son, wishing it were otherwise.

"The bottom line is that if they voted to nominate Harding tonight, we're running shorter on time than we thought," Esta said. "We need to know what the Antistasi's plans are. We need to stop them."

"How do I know you're not just trying to scare me into cooperating?" North asked.

"I *am* trying to scare you," Esta told him. "Unless we do something, the attack *will* happen. The tower will be activated, and Jack Grew will become president. Once he's in power, Roosevelt's promises will be moot. Jack will build more towers—a whole network of them. Enough to wipe out every bit of the old magic in this country."

"We're going to figure this out with or without your help," Harte told him.

"With your help, we can maybe save even more lives, though. Including your own," Esta said. "Because if you stay here in the city, you're both going to die."

North wanted to argue that what they were saying was ridiculous. There was no way the events would unfold like that. But he knew better than to doubt Esta.

"It's like I said, the Antistasi aren't exactly organized these days," he said. "I've been in Chicago for nearly a week, and I haven't heard any rumors about anything happening at the convention. Whoever's planning it is keeping things quiet."

"But you *are* still involved with them. You could help us find out who's planning it," Esta said.

North hesitated. "Possibly," he admitted reluctantly. "I know someone who might know what's going on. We can find him at the Nitemarket."

THE GOLDEN HOUR

Jianyu Lee was stuck. He had positioned himself out of sight behind a cart parked on the outskirts of Madison Square, not quite a block away from where he'd intended to be, but he could not venture any closer. Not without being seen. *Especially* not with boys he recognized from the Devil's Own, boys who certainly would recognize him as well, prowling through the park. Jianyu had the sense that they were searching for something—possibly even for him—and so he stayed back, unable to do more than wait.

Everything had been going to plan until, quite suddenly, it was not.

Jianyu's first indication that something was amiss had been when the wagon, flanked by police on horseback, had arrived from the east nearly an hour before. He had known immediately what the wagon carried, even though it had been too early. *Far* too early, considering that sunset had still been minutes away. *All* of their information had indicated that the Order's boat would not even *land* until the Golden Hour began.

They had expected the Order to be prepared for an attack—Theo had warned them of the nervous energy among the old men of the Inner Circle—but they had not expected this.

Jianyu's reaction had been immediate. Without even hesitating, he had reached for the light, as he always did—then everything had changed. As the daylight took on a golden cast, the usual warmth of his affinity had transformed into a searing heat. The light had flashed around him, bright and impossibly *hot*. It had felt as though the sun itself had come down from the sky and had been attempting to consume him, and Jianyu could do nothing but release his affinity, even as the sunlight was still searing the surface of his skin. The truth was an unexpected blow. Something about the strange light on this strange day, during this strange hour, had changed the rules of his affinity.

They had expected the Order to use certain protections. They had known that the Order would use something about the power of this false solstice to keep what was left of their treasures safe, but they had all believed the protection would be only on the wagon carrying the goods. Perhaps even on the ring itself. Jianyu had not imagined—none of them had imagined—that the protections the Order used could also affect their affinities.

Or maybe it was only his that had been affected. Maybe because his magic aligned most closely with the light, Jianyu was more susceptible.

Whatever the case, his skin still stung, and though he wanted to pull the light around him and take the packages the men were beginning to unload from the wagon, he could not. He understood from the way the daylight had gone almost amber that there was no point even in trying. Apparently, the Golden Hour was more than a quaint description. It was a powerful type of ritual magic. All he could do was stand and watch as a group of men opened the wagon, removed a heavy crate, and took it, under armed guard, into the building.

It galled Jianyu to know how close he had been to the artifact. The ring had been *right there*, but as long as he could not wrap the light around himself, as long as he could not use his affinity, he could do nothing. He was far too conspicuous, especially in this part of town, far from the community of Chinese people who lived around Mott Street. Without his affinity to hide him, he would be immediately noticed. Immediately *targeted*.

Jianyu simmered with the frustration of being able to do *nothing* but wait, but then sirens had started to call through the city streets, and he had known it was truly beginning. He had known there was no way to warn Viola that all their careful scheming had been for nothing. He couldn't reach Cela or Abel to tell them that their plan was crumbling like ash.

Though it felt like he was stuck, drowning in a dragon's pool, in the end Jianyu had decided to stay where he was and to wait. He could only hope that whatever strange power was at work, it was only temporary. Certainly, as soon as the sun set and the Golden Hour waned, he would have access to his magic once again. *Certainly.* With his affinity, he could still hope to find the stone, even if it was behind thick iron walls or layers of protections.

It had been no easy task to remain unseen as the minutes crept on, especially once some of Dolph's boys had entered the park. Twice Jianyu had nearly been seen by one of the Devil's Own. Then, suddenly, things had changed once more. Two carts filled with Five Pointers had arrived and launched an attack on the now-empty wagon. Shots had been fired from buildings across the street as the plaza in front of the new skyscraper had erupted into a battle.

A few minutes later, Nibsy had arrived with a wagon of people. Viola had been there in the back, along with Mooch, Werner, and a light-haired boy who was not one of Dolph's, but Jianyu recognized him. The blond boy had been in Evelyn DeMure's apartment that night weeks before, when they'd almost retrieved the Delphi's Tear. They had failed that night. They could not fail again.

Jianyu moved closer to the wagon. If he could signal Viola, perhaps they could figure out a new direction. But there were too many people around, and the park itself was too open, with young trees and wide walkways that left nowhere for him to hide. Viola and Nibsy were arguing, and Viola turned to the park—Jianyu thought perhaps she saw him—but then she climbed down from the wagon and followed Nibsy's boys around the side of the building.

He had to stop her. He could not allow her to go into such danger alone.

Again Jianyu reached for his affinity, but before he could even grasp the light completely, he again felt the sun's power sear his skin, and once more, he was forced to release his affinity and the light with it.

By then it was too late. Viola was gone.

Nibsy turned, his head swiveling around toward the park. The lenses of his spectacles flashed golden in the setting sun, and Jianyu pulled back behind another carriage before he could be seen. When he chanced another look, Nibsy was still studying the park, his brow furrowed thoughtfully. Watching.

Frustrated with himself and the entire situation, Jianyu began walking away from Madison Square. He would take the long way around the building, cutting down a block or two east, far from the police and Nibsy. He would position himself to enter the building once the strange golden light eased. What else could he do? He only hoped that when the sun sank below the horizon, he would be able to touch his affinity. Until then, he could not simply stand there and wait.

THE TRUTH OF HISTORY

1920—Chicago

Esta couldn't help but study North and Everett as she and Harte followed the two toward the entrance of the Nitemarket. The father and son were of similar height and build, though Everett hadn't quite filled into his shoulders yet, and they moved alike with an easy, loping grace. In the yellowish glow of the streetlamps, North's reddish hair and Everett's ashy brown didn't look any different.

She understood from the way North glared at her that he hadn't forgotten her intention to go back and change the past. Now that he had not only Maggie to think of, but also Everett and his other children, the threat she posed was that much more dangerous. Esta couldn't fault him for worrying about that, but she also couldn't put everything aside for his fears . . . not when the truth of history lay before her, dangerous and demanding of her attentions.

Still . . . meeting Everett made things more real. Knowing what effects her actions might have now was different from thinking about some unknown future North and Maggie *might* have created. Everett was real and whole and every bit as vulnerable as any of the people Esta was trying to save by stopping Jack. Her returning to 1902 might negate his very existence. She would have to deal with that reality eventually, but not tonight. Not when the crescent moon hung like a scythe over the second city, a reminder of the reaping that would come if they couldn't stop the events that were about to unfold.

They took the L west until the tall buildings of the central part of

Chicago began to flatten out, and eventually they arrived at a station somewhere near Cicero. A few blocks from the stop, North led them to a lonely house in the center of an otherwise empty lot. It looked to be condemned.

"Once we're in the Nitemarket, it would be best if you leave the talking to me," he instructed. "That goes for you, too, Rett. Don't do anything stupid."

"It was only that one time—" the boy started.

"That *one time* was more than enough," North told him, sounding every bit like the father he was. "Your mother'll skin me alive if anything happens to you."

Esta bit back a smile at the two. In some ways, North still looked like the boy he'd once been, even beneath the lines of his face. He and Everett could have been mirror images, separated only by the passing of years.

The four of them went around the back of the building, where the lot was strewn with trash and old cigarette butts, and North led the way up the decaying steps to the back door. Inside, the house didn't reveal anything more. Plaster crumbled from the walls, and the floor was weak and rotted out in more than one spot, but once the door was closed, the noise of the outside world went suddenly silent—a lot more silent than the rickety old walls should have warranted.

"What kind of a game are you trying to play?" Harte growled.

North didn't answer, but a second later, a door on the other side of the room opened, and a small man emerged wearing enormous spectacles, with lenses so thick they made the eyes behind them look unnaturally small. Esta glanced at Harte, who looked every bit as unnerved as she felt by the guy's unexpected appearance.

"The weather doesn't look promising," the small man told them.

North stepped forward. "When the moon shines red, it's a nice enough night for a stroll."

The man eyed them before he finally nodded. Then he stepped aside so they could pass through the doorway that waited behind him.

Harte glanced at Esta, but she only shrugged in answer. It *could* be a trap, but considering that North knew what he had to lose if anything happened to her, she doubted it was.

North went first, moving toward the open doorway without hesitation, and Everett followed just as quickly. Esta gave Harte another small shrug and followed as well.

As she passed through the door, though, she felt the brush of magic— warm and cool all at once. Natural *and* ritual mixed together in a dizzying swirl of energy, and the world seemed to contract, pressing in on them. Moving forward felt like pushing through some impossibly thick substance, and then all at once the sound of the world came roaring back and Esta winced against the brightness of a brilliantly blinding light.

When she opened her eyes again, she found herself in a warehouse. It was a long, narrow building with a peaked metal roof, and the sound of rain pattering above caused a kind of quiet roar to surround them. Strings of flickering bulbs were draped overhead, providing the only light, and the long space was filled with various stalls, each displaying an assortment of ordinary-looking objects. It looked like some kind of flea market or junk sale, except the vendors eyed each of the shoppers with sharp suspicion and everyone spoke in low, hushed voices.

"This is the Nitemarket?" she asked, feeling unaccountably disappointed by how normal it seemed.

North nodded as he started to lead them through the aisles. "Keep your eyes down and your mouths closed."

"It's raining," Harte said, looking up at the ceiling.

In Chicago, the sky had been cloudless.

"I don't think we're in Kansas anymore," Esta murmured.

North glared at her with confused frustration. "Chicago never was in Kansas."

"It's just an expression," Esta told him as she shrugged off her mistake. "So what are we looking for? There's not a lot of anything but junk here."

"Junk that people would kill and die for," North said in a low whisper. "Pretty much everything sold here is illegal in about twenty different ways, but the one thing it all has in common is that it's infused with the old magic."

Esta glanced over at him. "Like your watch."

"Exactly." North's jaw was tight, and she realized he was nervous.

"Did you ever replace it?" she wondered, looking at the table they were passing. It looked like a collection of tools—hammers and awls, saws and vise clamps, each rusted and ordinary-looking.

"I thought about it for a while, but once I learned what it took to make a piece like that?" North shook his head. "I don't need that kind of power. No one does." His eyes cut in her direction, the judgment clear in them.

Esta found that she couldn't disagree.

Harte was examining a table covered with a display of knives and brass knuckles. "Someone must sure want that kind of power. A lot of some-ones, from the look of this place."

North pulled him away before he could pick up a pair of cuff links. "Doesn't mean they're right to. Come on," he told them. "I think I see Dominic over yonder."

Esta followed them down the narrow aisles. "Where did all of this come from?" She marveled at the sheer number of objects for sale. The variety as well. She'd assumed that magic-infused objects were rarer.

"From the same place as any magical object," North said. "Someone gave up their affinity to make each item you see here."

"Willingly?" Harte wondered.

"Does it matter?" North asked. "I imagine giving up even a part of your affinity would take a toll bigger than anyone could predict before they agreed. I don't want to think about what something like that would do to a body, even if they *had* been willing."

Esta didn't have to imagine. She *knew*. When Professor Lachlan had trapped her in New York and tried to use her affinity to unite the stones, she had felt the very beginnings of her magic being ripped away from her. She already knew the terror of feeling herself about to fly apart far too keenly. But now she wondered if that was also what Leena had experienced when Dolph Saunders had taken part of her affinity for his cane. Esta thought maybe she understood a little better Leena's decision to tell Dolph that their baby had died and to hide Esta away from him after she was born. Suddenly, the hall of goods around her seemed more sinister.

"Most of these are nothing but trinkets . . ." North was still talking, unaware of the direction of Esta's thoughts. "Nothing like the stones in the Order's artifacts. But even if someone thought they were making the decision freely, there's a lot of complications that could come up— whether they really understood what they were agreeing to, whether they were under duress. And that's if they were *actually* willing. Most of the time, the arrangements weren't as equitable as the sellers here would have everyone believe." He shook his head. "Once I realized what it took to make my watch, I found I didn't have any interest in finding another piece like it. I don't need that kind of weight on my conscience."

The stone in the cuff on Esta's arm felt somehow heavier than ever. Unlike the stones Seshat had made in her attempt to preserve the heart of magic—objects that she created willingly from her *own* power—the Order's artifacts drew their power from the affinities of Mageus that Newton had sacrificed in his attempt to control the Book.

From what Harte had witnessed, the lives of other innocent Mageus had been taken more recently to recharge the stones. He'd described for her the bodies of the missing Mageus he'd found in the Mysterium. They'd each been suspended in a web of dark, unnatural magic. All to preserve the Brink and the Order's power.

The origin of the Order's artifacts wasn't news to Esta. Someone had died, and because of that lost life, she could use the stone to slip through time. That was a fact. Every time Esta used the Key, she used that stolen power. Another fact. She'd tried to ignore those facts for a long time now. She'd told herself that she was using the stones for an honorable pur- pose, but standing there amid the swirling eddies of magic—natural and corrupt, hot and cold power alike—Esta wondered if she'd been conning herself all along. What did it mean that she was still willing to use power that wasn't rightfully hers? How did that make her any different from Thoth?

"It's not the same thing," Harte whispered, easily guessing the direction of Esta's thoughts. Her surprise must have shown, because he slid his palm against hers, tangling their fingers in a moment of stolen comfort.

She didn't even pretend to deny that he was right. "How is my using Ishtar's Key any different?"

"I don't know," he admitted. "Maybe it's not, but the world isn't black or white, good or evil. Ever since the day you came back for me, every choice you've made—right or wrong—has been because you believed it would help in some way."

"Not always. Not in St. Louis . . ."

"In St. Louis you made mistakes. We both did. We're trying to right those now." He squeezed her hand gently. "It's all we can do."

"I don't know if that's enough." Esta started to pull her hand away. She didn't deserve his comfort or his understanding.

But Harte caught her hand again and laid a kiss on her palm. "No one is blameless, Esta. Even saints had their sins. It isn't possible to live a perfect life, and even if you could, it wouldn't be very interesting." He released her hand then, and when he spoke again, his words came slowly. "You make mistakes. You learn. We all do. Sometimes it takes a little bad to cause an enormous amount of good. Dolph Saunders understood that. Would you blame him for the life he chose? For the sins he committed?"

Esta thought about the father she hadn't really known. She wasn't sure what to do with the goodness he'd shown to her and to the people in the Bowery, or with the terrible things he'd done as well—especially what he'd done to her mother. Finally, she shook her head. "I honestly don't know."

"That's fair enough," Harte said. "But it's like you told me back on the train—it's not your fault. Having the cuff, using it. You didn't create any of this. All you can do is figure out how you want to live in it."

He was right. The stone in her cuff had been made through the worst possible means. The mistakes she'd made in St. Louis had been terrible. But Esta wasn't walking away from her responsibilities. Not now. Not *ever*.

"Maybe you're right," she admitted. "But look at all of this, Harte. These are *Mageus* buying and selling power that isn't theirs to trade. How is this any different from what the Order does? It's all the same—people forgetting that the affinities we hold inside of us aren't separate from who we are. Maybe I didn't create any of this, but it'll be my fault if I allow it to remain."

Harte's mouth curved a little, and his eyes held promises that she wasn't sure he could keep. "Then by all means, let me be the one to help you tear the whole damn thing to the ground."

THE NITEMARKET

1920—Chicago

North didn't realize he'd lost Harte and Esta until Everett tapped on his arm.

"Your friends are still back there," his son said, giving North a look that reminded him of Maggie in its directness. And its impatience.

He knew Everett was itching to know more about the two strangers they'd picked up at the Green Mill, but the Nitemarket wasn't the time or the place to explain things—especially not to speak the name of the Thief. She was still something of a legend both loved and hated, depending on who you were talking to.

Since he didn't want to draw any more attention to their group than they already might have attracted, North retraced his steps rather than shouting for the two to pick up the pace. They were about twenty yards back, their heads close together as they spoke in voices too low for him to hear. Whatever they were talking about, their expressions were too serious for his liking.

"You two coming or what?"

Esta seemed startled by the interruption, but in a blink her expression transformed itself from surprise to her usual calm composure. She gave him a look so blandly disinterested that if North hadn't known better, he never would have thought she'd been lagging behind the group to start with. The problem was, he *did* know better.

Finally moving again, the four made their way deeper into the Nitemarket, looking for North's contact. They didn't talk much, and

Everett—thank heavens—did what North had told him: He kept his eyes down and his hands tucked into his pockets.

North had never been a fan of visiting the market, even if it did provide their family with a good living. Between Maggie's formulations—at least the ones she was willing to part with—and the goods North was able to liberate—like the Nitewein from that very night—the Nitemarket provided the Northwoods a steady stream of income, which helped augment whatever breeding horses on their ranch outside Kansas City brought in. *And* the market kept them connected to the Antistasi. Neither North nor Maggie had any desire to be drawn all the way back into the Antistasi, but if they kept one foot in the game, North hoped they could maybe see danger coming long before it arrived.

Like he'd told Esta and Harte, the Nitemarket wasn't a safe place. A person who knew where to look could usually find one of the many entrances in any good-size town—well, any town except New York City—but the market itself never seemed to be in the same location twice. It moved from place to place each night, presumably to avoid detection, but the market didn't limit entrance to Mageus, which made it even more dangerous in North's estimation. There were any number of Sundren who had managed to find their way into the cramped aisles of vendors and goods over the years. Usually, the outsiders were well-intentioned folk interested in family lore, or sympathetic souls looking for the thrill of brushing up against the old magic. Occasionally, though, there were Sundren who found the market specifically to cause problems. You never knew when you might run afoul of the occasional raid or groups of Sundren vigilantes playing at being heroes.

North probably shouldn't have brought Everett. Maggie certainly wouldn't have let the boy come if she'd been there to have a say. But with Esta's warnings about the tower—however unlikely they seemed—North felt better having his son by his side, even in a place as dangerous as the Nitemarket.

In one of the last stalls at the back of the long, cavernous hall, North finally found the contact he'd been looking for. Dominic Fusilli was an older man with a middle like pudding and hardly a white hair left to cover the mottled scalp of his head. They'd met about five years before, but North still didn't exactly trust Dom. Still, the older man had his uses.

"Northwood," Dom said, seeing the four of them approach. "I see you brought Junior."

"This is my oldest, Everett," North said, reluctantly making the introductions.

"He's the spitting image of you, isn't he?" Then Dom realized that Harte and Esta were also with them, and his eyes narrowed. "And a couple of others as well?"

North stepped in front of Esta, blocking the peddler from examining her too closely. It had been years since the Devil's Thief had disappeared, but it wasn't worth taking the chance that Dom might recognize Esta. The old guy pretended not to know what was going on, but North hadn't been green enough to buy that act five years ago. There wasn't any sense underestimating Dom now.

"Just some friends visiting from out of town," North said, dismissing the pair as he tried to change the subject to something safer. "I got a shipment recently that you might be interested in."

Dom was still trying to see around North without being too obvious about it, but the mention of more goods served as enough of a distraction to draw his attention back to their conversation. "That so?"

North nodded. "Nitewein. Prime vintage from what I can tell."

"Interesting." Dom scratched at the day-old stubble on his chin. "Word is the Chicago Outfit got raided earlier tonight. A lot of the product went missing. Turns out, though, it wasn't actually the Feds."

"Oh, I wouldn't know anything about that," North said easily, hooking his thumbs through the loops of his jeans. "I doubt the shipment I'm looking to unload is anything as powerful as the stuff from the Green Mill."

Dom's expression turned wry. "Especially not after you dilute it."

Since there wasn't any heat in his words, North took it to mean Dom was interested and that he didn't particularly care about the source. "I'll put you down for a case or two."

"Best make it three," Dom said. "Demand has been up lately. I assume we can discuss the price when you deliver? Or did you want to settle that now?" His gaze again traveled to the others with North.

"Later is fine," North said, trying to draw Dominic's attention back. They made a few quick arrangements for the delivery, and then North held out his hand and Dom took it, sealing the deal between them. "There is one other thing. . . ."

Dom's bushy brows rose a little. "Oh?"

"Everyone at the market knows that if there's something happening, you're the first to know," North said, laying it on thick. He could sense Esta and Harte growing impatient behind him, but he ignored the two of them and focused on Dom. North knew the old man well enough to handle him.

"I can't deny that I tend to know a thing or two," Dom preened.

"It's just that, well . . . usually I wouldn't pay rumors any mind, but since I brought my boy with me, I feel like maybe I should be a little more careful. Maggie'll be none too happy if I let anything happen to him. You know how she is."

"*Your* Maggie?" The old man shook his head, probably remembering the one run-in he'd had with North's wife. "I sure do."

That's what Dom got for trying to swindle his girl, though. Maggie had torn the old man up one side and down the other when she realized he'd been trying to get out of paying her for a delivery of some Quellant. After that, Dom wouldn't have anything to do with Maggie, and she didn't want North to have anything to do with him either. But Dom was too good a contact to cut out completely, so North dealt with the old man alone.

"Anyway, I've been hearing some whispers in Chicago about something big happening. I don't suppose you know what's in the works?" North asked.

Dom frowned, the bushy brows drawing together like woolly bears creeping over his eyes. "I haven't heard anything about anything. Things have been quiet all around."

"Are you sure?" Esta asked, breaking in like she was part of the conversation.

North stepped in front of her again. "She's not used to big cities," he explained when Dom looked suddenly wary from her interruption. "Gets nervous about things." He lowered his voice a little. "You know how women can be."

That seemed to mollify Dom a little, even if North could practically feel the heat of Esta's fuming behind him.

"So you haven't heard of any deeds in the works?" North asked again. "Because I'd hate to get in the middle of something unexpectedly, especially with my boy here."

"If anything is happening, it's not part of the usual network. No one would be stupid enough to start trouble with the convention in town— too much security and too much risk for anyone with any sense."

"That's what I suspected," North said, his mind churning at the implications. Esta had plenty of reasons to lie about the attack. She knew how he felt about her wanting to go back to change the past, and he had a sinking feeling this was another one of those *misdirections* of hers. "I appreciate your confirmation, anyway."

"Anytime," Dom told him, still trying to get a peek at the strangers with North. "Give Maggie my best."

"Will do," North said with a tip of his hat.

He wouldn't, of course. Maggie would have him by the short hairs if she knew he was dealing with Dom again. *Especially* if she knew he'd introduced the man to Everett.

With a jerk of his head, he got Everett and the other two moving, but all the while he could feel a headache building. North wasn't sure what Esta and Harte's game was, but he didn't plan to be a pawn in it, not this time.

He led them back toward the entrance of the market but ducked into a side aisle that was empty once they were well out of Dom's view. He closed the distance between himself and Esta, snagging her wrist so she couldn't get away from him.

"You got about two minutes to tell me what you're playing at," North hissed at Esta, using every inch of his height to tower over her.

"Back off," Harte said, the words coming out like a growl from low in his throat as he stepped toward them, but Everett had read the situation and was already between them, pistol drawn. Harte took another step forward, apparently not caring that he didn't have any chance against a gun.

"You might not want to mess with that," North warned Harte. "The boy has a way of tinkering with things to make them more effective."

"All of you, stop it," Esta said, not bothering to hide her frustration. North felt her tug at his wrist, but she didn't do more than test his grip. "I'm not playing at anything." Her voice was as calm and even as the liar she was born to be. "What I told you before was the truth. I can't help it if your contact hasn't heard anything."

"Dom's been with the Antistasi for a long time, and he knows things before anyone else. If the Antistasi had something planned—especially something as big as you're saying it'll be—he would know."

"The attack *will* happen," Esta insisted, not backing down one bit.

"Then it won't be done by the Antistasi," North told her.

Esta froze. For a second she looked like one of the hares that go stock-still when they get caught unaware out in the fields at the ranch, like not moving could save them from danger. "Then it's *not* the Antistasi." Her voice sounded unsteady, like she was shaken by this realization. She looked at Harte. "It's a setup," she told him.

"What?" Harte shook his head, clearly not following any better than North.

"It's a *setup*," she repeated, turning her attention back to North. "The whole attack . . . You could be right. Maybe the Antistasi *don't* have anything planned, but whoever *is* going to do the attack will set them up to take the fall for it."

"Nice try," North said. "But I'm not buying what you're selling, and I think we're finished—" There was a commotion at the other end of the hall, coming from the direction of the exit to Chicago. "What the—" But the string of curses that came out of North's mouth were lost in the noise of an explosion.

The Nitemarket was under attack.

ADESSO

Viola wasn't quite sure how everything had turned upside down so quickly.

She should have been smarter. She should have realized that the same boy who had betrayed Dolph—who had *killed* Dolph—would not be so easily defeated. A boy like that could do practically anything. But Viola hadn't imagined that skinny little Nibsy Lorcan could convince the Fox himself to move against her brother. It was unthinkable, but it had happened all the same.

Viola chanced a glance back at the park, wondering if Jianyu was nearby. The plan had been for Jianyu to wait near the building, a backup that neither Nibsy nor Paolo would know about, but that was before, when they believed that they could stop the wagon from arriving until after the Golden Hour's protection waned. But nothing else had gone to plan, and Viola could only hope that Jianyu was close. She hoped, too, that he'd heard Nibsy's threat and would understand that he must go to help Cela and Abel before John Torrio could harm them. She risked another look back toward the open spaces of Madison Square Park, but she could find no sign of Jianyu there or anywhere else.

"You're not thinking of running now, are you?" Nibsy asked, eyeing Viola and then glancing to the park.

"Of course not," she told him, cursing herself for being so careless. She had to focus. She couldn't make any more wrong steps, not when so much was at stake.

A few minutes later, Viola had little choice but to follow Mooch and Werner, along with the one called Logan, around the side of the building. With the Five Pointers occupying the police out front, it wasn't difficult to slip in through the back, not when Werner was quick to suffocate the few men who were waiting in the lobby. They'd fallen unconscious before they could so much as draw their guns.

Of course Nibsy himself didn't come along with them, the snake. He'd made excuses about his leg—he would only slow them down—but Viola saw the truth in his eyes. Nibsy Lorcan had never intended to put himself in danger, not when he had the lives of the Devil's Own to offer instead.

The new boy, Logan, was sent to lead them. Nibsy seemed to trust him above the others, but Viola couldn't understand why—she could tell that Mooch and Werner felt the same. Logan Sullivan had a look of fear in his eyes that made Viola nervous. She knew that fear could make people do stupid things, and she wasn't interested in dying—not today.

Beyond the entrance, the lobby's marble floors and walls shone in the evening's strange golden light. The ceiling was arched as gracefully as any church's and every bit as ornate. This wasn't the world of dirty tenements and crowded barrooms that all of them were used to. It was far grander than the cluttered shops and businesses they frequented south of Houston. They all seemed caught by the wonder of the sight—all except Logan.

"We need to get moving before the Order realizes we're in the building," Logan directed. He was jittery, this one, with shifty eyes and a tightness around his mouth that Viola didn't like. He was also carrying a lopsided satchel slung over his shoulder. *For the goods we find,* he'd explained when Viola had asked. But he glanced away, and she sensed there was something more about his plans that he wasn't revealing.

"Stairs or elevator?" Mooch asked.

"Stairs," Viola said immediately, but Logan disagreed.

"We'll be too exposed in a stairwell," he said. "The elevator gives us our best chance. It's faster, and we won't exhaust ourselves with the climb."

Viola had heard about elevators, but the tenements of the Bowery didn't have any need for them, so she'd never been in one herself. She stepped carefully across the threshold and into the glittering mirrored box, wary of every creak and groan. It felt too much like allowing herself to be trapped, but she didn't fully appreciate how terrible it would be until Logan pulled a gate over the entrance, caging them in like animals. With a push of a lever, the room suddenly lurched, and Viola grabbed for the gilded railing as they began to rumble upward.

The shining mirrors reflected her face back at her, and she saw that the weeks had not been kind. Dark smudges of exhaustion lay thick beneath her eyes. Her hair was pulled back from her face, but the heat and humidity of the day had it fuzzing up around her face. She looked *so* much like her mother, she realized—worn and tired. She wore the same expression as the women who worked morning until night to care for their families because it was their duty and their lot in life. Because they had no other choice.

Watching herself in the mirror, Viola could not help but think of Ruby, who always looked fresh and polished. Ruby, who would no doubt be completely at home in such a shining, beautiful place as this. It was more confirmation of what Viola already knew, of how impossible Ruby's words—her *kiss*—had been.

Viola's eyes met Werner's in the reflection of the mirror, and she saw that she wasn't alone in her apprehension about the elevator. Mooch, too, looked nervous. Only Logan seemed at ease.

"We're like fish waiting in a barrel," Viola muttered, looking away from the mirrored wall so she did not have to see her own fear. She cursed softly, trying to keep herself steady as the contraption jerked, but she could not force herself to relax as the elevator rattled onward, rising to whatever waited for them above. "As soon as these doors open, they'll be waiting. And then what will we do?"

"Fish don't have any weapons at their disposal," Logan said, unbothered. His eyes were focused on the dial over the door.

"I have only one knife," Viola told him. "Libitina, she's deadly, but she cuts one at a time, no more."

"You have more than a knife," Werner said, leveling a knowing look at her through the mirrored wall. "Same as me."

Viola could only stare at him. Here was a boy who could take the breath from a person's lungs. She'd seen how easily Werner had disposed of the men in the lobby. "It doesn't bother you?"

"Why should it?" Werner shrugged. "When we get to the top, whatever is waiting for us on the other side of this door won't hesitate to kill me. I don't know about you, but I'd prefer not to die." He grimaced, the nerves clear in his expression. "Not for a little while, at least."

The elevator rumbled to a halt on the eighteenth floor, and Logan turned to them. It was only the four of them standing there in uneasy silence, hearts in their throats, but the moment the cage doors opened, there would certainly be more.

"Ready?" Logan asked.

"Do we have a choice?" Sweat was glistening at Mooch's temples, and his hands were shaking.

"No," Logan admitted. They all held their collective breath as he pulled back the inner cage before depressing the lever that opened the outer door.

They had expected an ambush, but only an empty hall greeted them. They stepped into the gleaming silence, but there were no men with guns waiting—and no indication that any would come. There was only a polished grandeur that made the elevator look nearly shabby in comparison.

Viola had been inside Khafre Hall. She had seen the Mysterium for herself, but this one hallway surpassed anything she'd seen in that older building by far. Granite as deeply green as the trees in Central Park lined the walls. Golden sconces hung at even intervals along the walls, glowing with a warm, ethereal light. Inlaid gold glinted everywhere.

"Where is everyone?" Werner whispered as they eased their way down the hall.

"It's nearly sunset," Logan told them. "If our information was right, the members of the Order should be in their ceremonial chamber starting the consecration. They'll stay there, under the Golden Hour's protection, until the sun sets. We have to get moving. We won't have much time to take the ring once the sun is down and the power of the Golden Hour ends. This way."

Still on alert, they started down the hall, in the direction of the front of the building, where it pointed toward Madison Square Park. The Mysterium would be there somewhere, and with any luck, it would already hold the ring. It didn't matter that these other boys wanted the artifact. They had pledged themselves to Nibsy Lorcan, and Viola would not allow them to have it. She would wait until the time was right, and then she would take what she needed and be gone.

They were only halfway down the hall, though, when an alarm sounded.

"They know we're here," Werner said, licking his lips.

"We knew they would," Logan reminded him. "Let's go."

They'd taken a few steps more when the glowing lanterns suddenly went out. The windowless hallway went completely dark except for the square of daylight that shone through an open doorway at the end of the hall.

"Go!" Logan shouted, but no one needed to be told.

They tumbled through the entrance of the room as a steel door began to slide closed to cover the opening. Viola heard Mooch yelp and turned to find him caught by the door. With a flick of her blade, his jacket fell away. After the heavy door sealed them in, they could no longer hear the screams of the sirens.

The chamber they found themselves in was silent as a church. It was a large room lined with empty shelves. Its walls seemed to glimmer in the fading daylight, and Viola realized it was because there were veins of gold and precious stones set into the sandstone panels. The boys were studying the steel doors that had barricaded them in, but Viola was drawn to the center of the room, where a familiar table-like altar waited.

"I've seen this before," she said, her pulse racing.

This same table had been in the Mysterium, she was sure of it. When she and Darrigan had completed the puzzle of a lock in the vault far below the main levels of Khafre Hall, this very table had risen from the floor to expose the cabinet that had held the Ars Arcana. It had held a single bowl filled with a strange liquid. Now the bowl was gone. In its place was a box carved from some brilliant blue stone that had been polished to gleaming.

Viola reached carefully for the box, not really sure if she should touch the small chest, but when she ran her fingers across it, she sensed the cold of false magic . . . but nothing else.

"What's this?" Mooch asked, eyeing the box.

"I'm not sure." She used the tip of Libitina to flip open the golden latch and then the lid of the box itself. Nothing happened.

Werner had come up next to them as well. "Looks like junk," he said, clearly disappointed with the tarnished circlets of metal they found inside.

The two boys turned away, clearly unimpressed, but Viola paused at the sight of them. She remembered now—this very table had been sitting atop these same silver discs in the Mysterium those many weeks ago. But it wasn't only the *objects* that were familiar. They had been carved with a design that Viola had seen before—first on the book depicted in the painting of Newton that was hanging in Dolph Saunders' old rooms, and then later, with the unreadable notes in Dolph's journal.

Certainly, the marks inscribed into the surface of the metal discs were the same emblem, the *sigil*, as Theo had called it. She lifted the first disc and saw that there were more of the same beneath—four, in fact. There had been four in the Mysterium as well. It was too much a coincidence that she should find this symbol here, in the possession of the Order, when Dolph Saunders had thought to protect what he'd known about it.

Logan had already stepped beyond the altar and was looking up to where a golden staircase spiraled up to the ceiling. He scrambled up the steps and reached his hand toward the carving on the medallion in the ceiling where the staircase ended, tracing his finger along the lines inscribed there.

"It's up there," he told them. "The ring. I can feel it beyond this door." He pounded on the ceiling, but nothing happened.

Viola hesitated, but then she took one of the discs and examined it more closely. It was about the size of her palm and far heavier than she had expected from the nearly paper-thin bit of metal, but the cold energy felt like ice in her hands. It reminded her too much of the power of the Brink, but she tucked the four discs into her skirts. She imagined that Theo would be interested to examine them; perhaps he would have some idea of what the objects were. More than that, the etchings on these pieces reminded her of the drawings in Dolph's notebook. If Dolph had thought to conceal his notes about what they were, Viola had the sense that they must be important, even if she could not see why or how.

Werner had already lost interest and wandered away. He was staring at the wall of windows. "Who is that?"

Viola turned, following the direction of Werner's gaze, and for a moment it was as though he'd stolen her air. A man was standing on the balcony's ledge, silhouetted by the setting sun.

Not a man. *Theo.*

His arms were spread wide, but Viola couldn't tell if he was bracing himself on the enormous stone pillars or preparing to release them. She raced to the end of the room and grabbed the handle to the balcony door. It was stuck and impossible to open. She jerked at it, so desperate to open it that, at first, she did not feel the cold energy radiating from the latch. Withdrawing Libitina, she positioned the thin blade into the keyhole and pressed, letting the knife slice through the metal until the door swung open.

"Theo!" she said, stepping onto the balcony. "Come down from there! *Adesso!*" Her voice was shaking, and so was she as she moved toward him, trying to wave him down. At first he ignored her. "What are you doing up there? Sei pazzo? Theo!"

Theo turned finally at the sound of his name, but his eyes were blank.

It was as though he didn't know her. *No.* It was as though he didn't even *see* her.

"Do you feel that?" Mooch asked, coming up beside her. He shuddered.

Viola did feel it, the cold that seemed to have settled on the small balcony.

"He's under some kind of spell," Werner said.

"We have to get him down," Viola told them. Her heart pounded in her chest. They were so high up. There wasn't a single building in the Bowery even half so tall.

"We're not here for him," Logan said. "We're here for the ring. It's up there, and we have to find a way to get to it."

"The ring can wait," Viola said, turning back to Theo. She inched closer, careful not to disturb him. Considering the dazed and empty look in his eyes, Viola was afraid that anything she said or did might make him move in the wrong direction. "Theo, please. You have to listen to me."

"Look, if we get the ring, we can break whatever spell they put on him, right?" Logan asked, his voice betraying an urgency that Viola herself understood. She realized that perhaps his participation was no more voluntary than her own.

Werner frowned at Logan. "We can't leave him like that. He could jump any second now."

His words sent a bolt of panic through Viola that she had, until that moment, been keeping at bay. "Shut up," she told him sharply. "He's not going to jump." *He can't jump.*

"We don't have time for this," Logan told them. His voice was tighter now, more anxious. But Viola could tell that his worry was not for Theo. "The sun is already setting, and any minute now, someone is going to come. We have to figure out how to get that door open." He swallowed hard, the apple of his throat bobbing. "You know what will happen if we don't get the Delphi's Tear for James."

"You should know what will happen to you anyway if you follow a viper like Nibsy Lorcan," Viola told him.

"You don't know anything about James Lorcan," Logan said. His jaw was tight now, his voice angry.

"I know he'll put the knife in your back himself if it serves his purposes," Viola told him. "Ask this one." She gestured to Mooch, who only looked away. *The coward.*

"We're not leaving him up there. There's time for both," Werner said to Logan. Then he turned to Viola. "What should we do?"

"I don't know," she admitted. "I'm afraid that if we touch him, he might jump."

"Can you put him to sleep?" Werner asked. "I could try to take his breath, but that might make him panic. If you could—I don't know—relax him a bit?"

Viola frowned. "I think maybe, yes. That would work."

"When he collapses, we'll have to grab him before he tumbles," Werner told Mooch, who also inched closer.

"This is insane," Logan said. "You're wasting our time over a member of the *Order*?"

Viola ignored him. "If you're ready," she told the other two, aware that Logan was retreating into the empty library.

She closed her eyes and sent a quick prayer to any angel or saint who might be listening, and then she sent her affinity out. There was Theo's heartbeat, steady and true, and because Viola knew that it belonged to Ruby, she vowed that it would not stop. Then she tugged softly, slowing his pulse until finally he wobbled and started to go limp.

Theo didn't simply collapse, though. He bobbled, not backward, as she'd expected, but forward, toward the ground below.

A COLD ENERGY

1920—Chicago

Esta turned and saw that the source of the attack on the Nitemarket was a group of men dressed in long leather coats. They were covered from head to toe and were wearing masks and dark glasses that obscured their faces. There were only a handful of them, but three had machines that shot streams of green-tinged fire as they walked. One by one the booths went up in strange, crackling flames. Some of the vendors stayed and tried to rescue their goods, but the masked men ignored them. They continued working their way through the hall, and as they did, they began blocking the various entrances and exits. If they blocked the one to Chicago, Esta wasn't sure how she and the others would get back.

The heat of the flames and the icy coldness that came from the magic within them was thick in the air as Esta reached for North and Everett—Harte had already grabbed her arm—and yanked time to a screeching halt. The net of Aether that held the world in its grasp tugged uncharacteristically against her grip on it as she struggled to keep hold of three separate people and their affinities. Then she felt something else—an electric warmth that felt too much like Seshat's power—beginning to brush up her arm.

Esta looked to Harte, whose teeth were gritted, like he was struggling against himself.

"Those flames are doing something to the Quellant," he told her, confirming her fears. "It feels like it's being drained away."

Everett had startled from the sudden silence of the world, but now he looked at her with curiosity and interest. Esta wondered if she'd made a miscalculation in revealing the truth of her affinity to him, but North already knew anyway. And she didn't really have a choice, unless she was willing to leave North and his son behind to face the masked attackers alone.

Whoever the masked men were, it was clear that the attack was strategic and well organized. From the way they'd positioned themselves to cut the warehouse in two—and had immediately started herding the patrons like sheep—these men knew the market. The flames coming from their weapons burned with a cold energy that spoke of the type of ritualized magic used by the Brotherhoods. With their dark coats and masked faces, they looked like something out of an old sci-fi movie, but Esta knew that the creeping energy already vining itself up her arm was maybe even more of a threat. If the flames were eating away at the Quellant, she needed to get the four of them out of the Nitemarket now, before Seshat could do any real damage.

"We need to go," she told North and Everett. "*Now.* Whatever you do, don't let go."

"But the others," Everett argued. His expression was every bit as stubborn and mulish as North's had ever been, but it also bore the trace of Maggie's keen intelligence. And her kindness.

"We don't have time," Esta told him.

Everett was shaking his head, starting to pull away from her. "If we leave them here, they'll die."

Esta gripped him tighter, but she could already see darkness forming in the corner of her vision, and the ground was beginning to vibrate beneath them. She spoke to North, knowing he would understand without the explanation Everett seemed to require. "I won't be able to hold this much longer if we don't go now."

North's jaw went tight, and she knew he understood. "Let's go, son," he said, giving Everett a stern look.

"But, Pa—"

"It's not up for debate. You can't really expect me to explain to your mother what happened if you get hurt, can you? You know exactly what losing you would do to her." North's expression was stern, but his voice came out as barely a whisper.

"But all these people," Everett said, clearly torn.

"We can't save everyone," North told him, laying his free hand on his son's shoulder. "We never could."

Everett clearly didn't agree, but apparently he didn't have it in him to argue with his father—or maybe he didn't have it in him to break his mother's heart. He came, reluctantly, but he came.

The exit was still there, unmarked and seemingly undisturbed, but they all hesitated together before they went through.

"Do you think there's trouble waiting for us on the other side?" Everett asked.

"We'd be foolish not to expect it," North told him.

"It doesn't matter," Esta said, forming the words around clenched teeth. She could feel Seshat's power building, and already darkness was beginning to bleed into the world. Already she could feel the ground beneath her feet beginning to tremble. They had to go—*now*.

As they launched themselves through the doorway that led back to the shack in Cicero, Esta felt the same strange pressure of the passage, and as soon as they were through the doorway, she felt the fabric of time tearing from her fingers and from itself. She did the only thing she could do—she let go. Of Harte and the other two. Of time. Of *everything*. Together they tumbled through the doorway, into the dark dankness of the run-down shack.

And into the sights of three men with guns drawn.

The second Esta shook herself free of Harte, Seshat's darkness drained away. Immediately, she pulled the seconds slow again at the same instant that the waiting men fired at them. Time went still once more, but the bullet was already out of the gun and careening toward Everett. She pushed North's son out of the way, pulling him into the net of time with her only long enough for him to gasp in surprise before he hit the floor. Then Esta got back to her feet and ripped the guns from the men. When they were disarmed, she leveled the two pistols at the men and released time.

North had his own gun drawn a second later.

In the distance, sirens screamed. So many sirens. Something was happening, and from the sound of things even this far out from the city, it was something big.

"Who are you?" she demanded, shoving the dark nose of the pistol toward the men. "Who sent you?"

They weren't masked. They were maybe in their early twenties, dough-faced men who were barely more than boys, and they had the bland, pasty sameness of the midlevel businessmen who flooded the subways in New York twice a day in her own time. Esta doubted she would have been able to pick any one of them out of a lineup. The only thing remarkable about them at all was the silvery medallion that each wore on their lapel, medallions that were glowing a familiar eerie blue.

"We don't answer to maggots," the one on the left sneered. "And it's too late for you anyway. There's no stopping what the Brotherhoods have already set into motion." He gave her a cold smile, exposing a small black capsule held between his teeth. When he bit down, Esta heard a crackling snap, and blackness flooded the man's pupils.

Before she realized what was happening, there were two more snaps, as the others broke whatever they were holding between their teeth and joined the first. North moved for the men, but Harte pulled him back. It took only a few seconds for the darkness in their pupils to begin transforming the men, pulling them inward until suddenly they were gone with only a burst of numbing cold left behind in their wake.

"What the hell—" Harte swore as he scrubbed at his mouth. His eyes were wide with disbelief. "They're gone."

"I don't think those were the authorities," Everett said.

"I don't either," Esta agreed. "You saw their badges. . . ." She glanced at North and knew he'd recognized them as well.

"They were definitely from the Brotherhoods," North said. His face was caught in the shadows of the room, but Esta could tell that the truth of the situation was starting to become more real for him.

"Something's happened," she told them, her stomach sinking. "Those sirens—"

But North's attention was on Everett, who'd been moving toward the door that led back into the Nitemarket. He snagged his son by the collar. "Where do you think you're going?"

"If those men were from the Brotherhoods, the ones inside probably are too. If we don't go back, people are going to die in there," Everett told him, straightening so that he was taller than his father.

"And you think I'm going to let you go die with them?" North asked.

"I can stop this," Everett said, his face a mask of stubborn determination. "You know I can." He pulled a couple of small metal devices from his pocket.

"Maybe you can, and maybe you can't. But that's not a chance I'm willing to let you take," North told him. "Right now we're not going anywhere but back to the warehouse, where you'll be safe. Before anything else happens."

But Esta had a strong suspicion that North already knew his idea of safety was an illusion, especially if the attack had already happened.

"I can't leave now, not knowing I could've helped." Everett tried to pull away from his father, but North was still the stronger of the two. "You can't ask me to live with that."

"As long as you're alive, I can ask anything I want of you," North told him.

"What are those?" Esta asked, nodding toward the small objects Everett had in his hands. They didn't look like much—quarter-size bits of metal and wire that were clearly homemade.

"One of his inventions," North growled. "He's always tinkering with something or another."

"They're neutralizers," Everett told them. "They could stop those men and their weapons. Easily."

"It doesn't matter what they can do. You're not going back in there, and that's an order," North said, sounding every bit the old man he'd become.

Esta ignored North's blustering and studied Everett. The objects in his hand weren't the vials or concoctions Maggie had created. They looked much more advanced, well beyond the technology that should have existed in the twenties. "You really think those are enough to stop what's happening in there?"

"I *know* they are," he said.

"We don't have time for this," Harte argued. "I'm with North on this one. We need to go. Now."

Esta shook her head. "I think Everett's right. We have to go back. Especially if those sirens mean what I think they might."

"Like hell," North growled, stepping between Esta and his son. The action was sweet, but Everett was so far from being a boy that it was also a bit ridiculous.

"Think about it," she pressed. "If we allow the Brotherhoods to destroy the Nitemarket and get rid of everyone inside of it, who will be left to question the attack that's maybe already underway?"

"That might be, but if you're thinking of going back in there, you can do it without Everett," North said. "He's not—"

"What I'm *not* is a child," Everett cut in, his expression earnest and determined. "I know you think I'm too soft. I know you see me reading and tinkering and working by Mama's side, and that you want me to be more like you. But I already am, or I wouldn't care about this so much. I can do this. I *need* to do this."

"I can keep him safe," Esta told North.

"No." Now it was apparently Harte's turn to play the hero. "I'm not letting you go in there alone."

It took everything Esta had not to roll her eyes at him. As much as she was warmed by his concern, she knew they couldn't risk him going back in there. "Seshat isn't going to be any help if you come with me," she reminded him. "You stay here with North and keep watch in case anyone else does happen to show up. Everett and I will take care of the men in the Nitemarket."

Esta handed Harte the other pistol she'd been holding. With time pulled slow, she wouldn't need it. Then she held out her hand for Everett.

"I still don't like this," North said, stepping forward.

"That's because you got old," she told him dryly. "You've lost all your sense of adventure." But there was an emotion in his eyes—a fear that Esta knew she might never understand—and it made her soften a little. There wasn't really a version of her story that she could see ending with the sort of *consequences* that North and Maggie had to watch over. "I'll take care of him, North. I promise."

It felt like an odd promise to make since Everett was no child. He was a couple of years younger than Esta herself, but he was more than tall enough to feel like her equal.

"Ready?" she asked, and when Everett gave her a determined nod, she reached for her affinity and left the others suspended in time.

"It's quite a trick you can do there," Everett said, clearly trying to cover his unease with a little bravado.

"Yeah, well . . ." She shrugged off the unspoken question. "I'm more interested in seeing what sort of tricks *you* can do."

Once they were back inside the market, Esta saw that the destruction had progressed. More of the stalls were being consumed by the strange flames that filled the space both with the heat of fire's normal oxidation and the icy energy that was the mark of unnatural magic. It felt the same as standing too close to the Brink, and considering what the explosion had done to the Quellant that should have still been in Harte's system, she didn't have any desire to get close enough to the flames to test them.

Esta gave Everett a small jerk of her head, indicating that she'd follow his lead. Together they went to the first of the masked men, and she watched as he examined the weapon. He reached out to touch it, but she pulled him back.

"Don't," she warned. "We don't need company."

He gave her a small nod, like he understood, but paused to study the piece before carefully placing one of the small devices on the metal tank strapped to the first man's back. "I don't want to activate it now," he told her. "Not unless we want to get caught up in them going off—I mean, they won't hurt us, but they might make it more complicated. It would be best to set them off all at once and then get the hell out of the way."

"Sounds like a plan," she told him.

She studied the room as Everett led the way to the next masked figure. The flames were still undulating, slow and steady as they continued to burn, and all around, the Nitemarket was being consumed. People had started to flee almost immediately, or else they'd started to gather their merchandise in a feeble attempt to save what they could, but one person caught her eye.

Esta hadn't noticed him at first, but she recognized Dom standing not far from where the four of them had been when the attack originally broke out. He had a look of sheer fury on his face, and in his hand he held a bottle that looked like a Molotov cocktail. Apparently, he thought he could fight all five men with a single homemade bomb.

"How much does your dad like Dom?" Esta asked as Everett finished laying the last device. She pointed to where the rotund old man was standing, a portrait of rage and vengeance.

Everett shrugged. "From what I understand, he doesn't necessarily trust him, but Dom's a pretty dependable buyer. They go back quite a few years. My mom, on the other hand . . . she hates him."

Esta could see why. Something about Dom gnawed at her. She had the sense that he knew more than he was letting on, but she also had the feeling that leaving him behind would be a mistake. "Let's bring him with us."

She made sure to take the bottle from him before pulling him into the net of her affinity, which turned out to be a smart move, since he startled when she touched him. Thankfully, Dom didn't pester her with questions. His eyes narrowed as he took in his situation—her and Everett, the bomb now in her hands, and the world around them, silent and still—and seemed to accept it at once.

"I thought you looked familiar," he told her.

Esta shrugged off his comment. "I have a very ordinary face."

"You have a very *famous* face," Dom countered. But he didn't press. "I take it this is a rescue?"

"Of sorts," she agreed. "Follow along, and we'll be out of here in a second."

The three of them moved together—awkwardly at first and then increasingly with more coordination—until they reached the masked men. Once they were past them, Everett took another small device from his pocket—an object that looked like nothing more than an ordinary lighter.

"Is there a way to release time and get things moving again?" he asked.

"I promised your father I'd keep you safe," she reminded him.

"It'll only take a second. I want to be sure that the devices work," he added when she hesitated to answer.

She didn't love the idea. With the rest of the world frozen in the net of time, they were safe, but Everett had a point. It had been enough of a risk to come back that it made sense to make sure the risk had been worth it.

"Fine, but only for a second," Esta said, hoping that she didn't come to regret it. "Keep ahold of me, just in case."

Everett nodded, and carefully, Esta released the seconds. Confusion swarmed around them again, but neither Everett nor Dom so much as flinched. With a flick of his thumb, Everett struck the flint wheel of the lighter and a flame appeared. It took less than a second for the devices that he'd placed on the masked men to spark, and a second later the devices were crackling as blue-white smoke began to flow from them, billowing around them until they were almost obscured.

The masked men immediately realized that something had happened and turned, trying to find the source of the smoke, but before they could do more than twist, the smoke surrounding them began to solidify, and within seconds, they were each encased, head to toe, within a shell of hardened foam. The flames from their weapons died almost immediately, but not the flames that were still consuming the market itself.

"Will it kill them?" Esta asked, frowning at the ingeniousness—and deviousness—of the invention.

"No," Everett said, returning the lighter to the safety of his inside jacket pocket. "There's plenty of oxygen in there for them. But it'll drain any unnatural magic from the immediate area, and it'll hold them until someone else can deal with them."

Everett started back toward the men, but Esta held tight to him. "We need to go."

"I'm coming," he said, trying to pull away. "But I want one of those."

"No—"

"We need to know what we're up against," he told her.

The fire was still churning around them, and Esta knew that North would kill her for sure if anything happened to Everett, but she also saw his point. "Only if you can do it quickly."

It took him barely any time to break one of the flamethrowers from the pile of foam it protruded out of. "Got it," he told her, returning with a cocky smile and his eyes alight with interest as he looked at his new acquisition.

Beside her, Dom seemed far too quiet.

"Are you ready?" she asked, making her voice gentle. When he didn't answer at first, she asked if he was okay.

He looked around, taking in the extent of the destruction. "I can't believe it's gone," he said, his voice strangely hollow. "Everything I built."

"Everything *you* built?" Esta asked, eyeing him.

"You're not the only one with secrets," Dom said, finally glancing at her. He suddenly seemed somehow younger than his appearance would otherwise suggest, and Esta wondered whether the face Dom presented to the world was anything more than a mask. But that feeling lasted only a second, before her attention was drawn back to the danger around them.

The building that housed the Nitemarket was still burning. The fire had gone on long enough that it was clear there was no saving the building, but without the men and their flamethrowers, at least the people could escape. Everywhere she looked, the patrons and vendors alike were streaming toward other exits and returning to wherever they'd come from.

"I think I can put it out," Everett said, digging through his pockets.

"We need to go," Esta told him.

"But the market—"

Dom let out a long, tired-sounding breath. But then he shrugged. "It's fine."

"It's not fine," Everett argued, still trying to find something in the seemingly endless number of pockets he had tucked inside his jacket. He had to stop to cough, though, an indication that the smoke was getting to be too much.

"Now, Everett," Esta said, tugging on him.

"He built this. We can save it."

"I'll build it again," Dom told him, clapping his hand on Everett's shoulder. "*I'm* the market, boy. This is only a building. And buildings can always be rebuilt."

IMPOSSIBLE CHOICES

1902—New York

L ogan Sullivan dreamed of air-conditioning and flush toilets. He dreamed of street sweepers and automobiles, and especially, he dreamed of his smartphone, an object more powerful than the Mageus in this time, even with the surprising strength of their affinities, could imagine. He wanted to go home, back to *his* city and his own time, and the only way he was getting there was through Professor Lachlan.

Or rather, the way back was through the kid the Professor had once been, a kid named James Lorcan, with thick glasses and too much swagger for his wiry frame.

Logan knew that he had to keep James happy, or he was going to be out on his ass. Without the ring, Logan wasn't going anywhere. He'd be doomed to live out the rest of his—probably short—existence trapped in a past where people died of things like constipation. The way he saw it, there wasn't any choice. The Delphi's Tear was Logan's ticket out. With it, James assured him they could lure Esta back to the city, and once she was back, Esta could get Logan the hell out of there. Without it? Well . . . the ring was the only thing keeping James Lorcan interested in Logan, and James was the only thing between Logan and the many, *many* dangers of the city.

It didn't help that Logan should have already nabbed the stupid piece of jewelry weeks ago. James hadn't even bothered to hide his anger when Logan had let the Delphi's Tear slip away at Morgan's gala. Logan knew exactly how angry James had been because the kid had the exact same twitch near his right eye as Professor Lachlan. Logan had been on the wrong side of that anger enough times to know that it wasn't anything to mess with, but somehow the older Professor Lachlan seemed more reserved and polished—softer even—than this kid. James Lorcan looked like nothing, but he was all claws and teeth, and he had a whole gang to back him up. If Logan failed again, he doubted James would be so forgiving a second time.

Clearly, the ring was the only thing that should have mattered, but anyone could see that the dude on the balcony was in trouble. *Serious trouble.* A fall from that height? Without a parachute? Nobody could survive that. Logan tried to tell himself that the guy wasn't his problem. He tried to tell himself that he couldn't save everyone, but that he could help a hell of a lot of people if he got that artifact. If only he could figure out a way to get that door in the ceiling open so he could get to the ring. It was *right* there. . . .

Then he heard the girl scream.

From the first time Logan had met Viola, she'd seemed like a real ball-breaker. She was the last person he would have expected to make a sound like *that.* The scream was a high-pitched and utterly *female* noise, and it was so full of terror that he turned back. The three were leaning far over the railing, apparently holding on to the man, who had just jumped.

They have him. But Logan couldn't bring himself to turn away, not even when he saw the sun touching the water of the Hudson. Not even when it was clear that soon he would need to act.

Cursing himself and Esta and Professor Lachlan all at once, Logan ran to the balcony's edge. Whatever false magic the guy had been under had, apparently, broken. Now he was looking up in sheer terror at the people holding on to his arms.

"Help me," the guy screamed, his voice cracking with fear. His feet flailed so wildly to find some purchase on the medallion carved into the side of the building that Viola almost lost her grip on him.

Logan pushed her aside and took hold himself, cursing his stupidity all the while. Mooch glanced over at him, looking every bit as confused by Logan's involvement as he always looked, but Logan didn't care. He knew what they all thought of him. Every single one of the Devil's Own treated him like something that had crawled out of the latrines behind the Bella Strega. They'd been suspicious at first, and now that James kept putting him in charge of things, they hated him on sheer principle.

It wasn't a new experience, exactly. When he'd first been sent to New York to work under Professor Lachlan, Logan had suspected—at least at first—that Esta had hated him too. Luckily, she'd wanted the Professor's approval too much to let anyone know how she felt, and eventually she'd gotten over it. His situation now wasn't much different. To the Devil's Own, Logan was an outsider. An uninvited interloper who had moved up the ranks too quickly. He probably would've felt the same way in their position.

"If you let him go . . . ," Mooch warned, straining under the effort it was taking to hold tight.

"Don't let go of me," the guy pleaded.

"On three," Werner instructed. "We're all going to pull at the same time."

But the guy was freaking out so much that they were barely able to get his fingertips to the ledge.

"More," Mooch said. "We have to pull harder."

"He's gotta settle the hell down," Logan said. Sweat had broken out on his back and forehead, and with the gusting breeze, his skin felt clammy and slick beneath his clothes.

"Theo," Viola called. "You have to stop."

But Theo—apparently that was his name—wasn't listening to reason. The guy had already convinced himself he was a goner. "Please, you have to tell Ruby—"

"Tell her yourself," Viola snapped, sounding more like herself now.

Logan felt a burst of warmth filtering through the air. A moment later Theo's eyes drooped a little and the fight seemed to have drained out of him. He was deadweight now, but at least he wasn't actively fighting against them.

It had been a few weeks, but it was still unnerving how much stronger affinities were in this time. Logan had noticed it immediately, the way the old magic seemed to hang in the air, like cobwebs he was constantly surprised to walk into. Now he felt the telltale sign of Viola's power, and it lifted the hair on the back of his neck.

"One more time," Werner commanded, and started the count.

They pulled again, and this time they got Theo up and over the railing. He collapsed on the ground, conscious now, but visibly shaking. He might have been crying a little . . . or a lot, actually. He was gasping, and if he kept it up, he was going to pass out.

"Can't you do that thing to calm him down again?" Logan asked.

Viola glared at him. "Would you be so calm?"

Logan couldn't exactly say that he would be, so he didn't say anything else about the guy's whimpering. It didn't matter that he'd put everything on hold to help them save the guy. None of them had softened toward him.

"Fine," Logan said. "You're welcome, by the way."

It's not like I belong here, he reminded himself. He didn't need to worry about these people *or* what they thought of him. He only had to focus on what he'd been sent to do—the ring was still beyond his reach. He needed to figure out how to get that door in the ceiling open.

He'd barely stepped back into the library room and was about to head up the winding staircase again to take another look when he heard a grinding noise. The steel door that had trapped them was beginning to move. Slowly, it was retracting back into the wall, and Logan could already see a pair of legs waiting to enter on the other side.

Logan rushed back outside. "Someone's coming," he told the others, urging them to get out of view.

"We're trapped," Mooch said, his eyes wide.

"Shut up and get down," Logan ordered, pulling back to hide behind the half wall that ran beneath the windows as he closed the balcony door. Viola was on the other side, holding on to Theo, but he still looked like a mess.

Logan raised his fingers to his lips, and then he eased his head up, just enough to peer back into the library chamber. "There's only one," he told them. It was a younger guy with sandy hair, the guy from the gala—Jack Grew.

Jack had been facing toward the balcony the first time Logan looked, but now Logan chanced another peek and saw that Jack was already climbing the steps. He watched as Jack reached the top of the steps, took a pin from his lapel, and pricked his index finger. After he smeared the blood across the tips of his other fingers, Jack pressed his hand against the image of the Philosopher's Hand that was inscribed on the medallion. It wasn't even a second later when the heavy metal seal began to move, retracting into the ceiling and leaving an opening. Jack continued up the steps and disappeared into the chamber above.

Logan closed his eyes for a second and sent his affinity out to confirm . . . yes, the ring was there.

"He's gone," Logan said, standing now. He kept one eye on the opening in the ceiling, in case Jack Grew started to descend.

"We need to get Theo out of here," Viola told him. "Now, while we have a chance."

"No," Logan said. "We need to get the Delphi's Tear. That's what we were sent here to do, and that's what we're going to do. It's still up there." The round doorway was still gaping open like a portal, and the ring was *right there*. It was so close that Logan could not walk away from it—none of them could. Not when it would be so easy to climb the steps to overtake Jack Grew.

He could get the damn artifact, and he could go *home*.

Viola froze, and her dark brows drew together like she didn't believe him. "You can't know that for sure," she said.

"It's what I do," he explained. "If I want to find something, I can find it, especially if there's any trace of magic to it."

Werner let out a low, soft whistle. "No wonder Nibs keeps you around," he told Logan, giving him a newly appraising look.

"It takes some concentration," Logan admitted, shrugging off their sudden interest. "And I can only focus on one object at a time. But I know the ring is there. Even with all the other energy in the air right now, I can feel it, clear as day. We can't leave. Not when we can go up there right now and take it."

At first, though, none of them moved to agree. They all stood there stupidly, like the answer to so many of their problems wasn't sitting *right there*, like a fruit ripe for the picking. Logan wasn't sure what to make of their hesitation. It wasn't anything he'd ever experienced. Esta certainly wouldn't have hesitated. She would've closed her eyes and pulled time slow and the ring would have been theirs.

But Esta was gone, Logan reminded himself. She'd double-crossed him and left him alone in an unfriendly city with a pack of Lost Boy wannabes for company. Never mind that at the time this all happened, he'd technically been holding her hostage. But she'd betrayed Professor Lachlan and their whole mission first, hadn't she? Every bit of this situation was Esta's fault.

Logan looked at the two guys James had sent with him—the kid with the dirty-blond hair called Werner and the redhead, Mooch. They looked like they would cut someone without thinking twice, but now they were staring longingly at the freedom offered by the now-opened doorway. He didn't blame them, exactly. Now that the Order knew they were under attack, it would be a lot harder to get out of the building than it had been to get in. It would be a hell of a lot easier to walk away now, while they all still could.

Too bad walking away wasn't an option for Logan.

"You know how important this is to James," he told the two of them. "There's only one man up there. *One*. There are four of us, and I know what you all can do."

"You can't," Theo said. There was a little more color in his cheeks now, but his light eyes were still unfocused from the spell that had encouraged him to climb up on the ledge. "That chamber's protected."

Logan looked to the west, across the city that would someday climb far beyond the height of this building. The sun was sinking below the water now, its circle of orange beginning to melt into the Hudson. "The sun's already going down. Any minute now their protections will be worthless."

"You don't understand." Theo had managed to pull himself together a little, but he still looked dazed. "If that door closes while you're in there . . ." His voice was unsteady, like he was still trying to catch his breath. "No way out, except one."

No way out except one sounded about right to Logan. It was the ring or nothing. Whatever protections the Order might have in store, Logan was ready, and he was more than willing to risk them.

"It's right there, Viola," Logan said, willing her to understand. "We can't give up now. You could take out the guy upstairs without even *touching* him. So could you," he said to Werner. "Besides, you can't really be thinking about listening to this guy. He's one of them. *Of course* he doesn't want you to go up there."

"Theo's with us," Viola said. "But the ring . . . This one, he's right, Theo. We came for the ring. We have to *try.*"

"Not worth it." Theo was shaking his head now. "If you're locked in, you'll be trapped."

"Theo—"

"I know how important this is to you, Viola, and if there were any way to get the ring, I would help you in a heartbeat. But it's not possible. Jack told me everything. If you go up there, you won't be coming back down." Theo took Viola's hand. "I have to go, and so do you. I need to get out of here before Jack realizes I didn't jump like he planned." He seemed to be leaning on Viola more now, and her violet eyes were wide with indecision.

"Jack Grew?" Logan asked, his instincts buzzing at the sound of that name. "He's the one who opened the door up there. We can take him."

"You could help us," Viola told Theo. "If you did, we could be sure to win."

"I can't." Theo looked at Viola now, and there was a new desperation in his expression. "I can't risk being trapped up there. Don't you understand? Jack set all of this up because he wanted me to take the fall for the theft of the ring. When he discovers I didn't die, he'll do everything he can to pin the blame on me . . . and then he'll go after Ruby. You *know* he will. If I don't go now, there won't be anyone to protect her."

Something shifted in Viola's expression. An emotion lit her eyes that Logan didn't like the look of one bit.

"*Viola,*" Logan cautioned. He'd been waiting for something like this to happen. He'd been *warned*. "You know what will happen if we don't get that ring," he told her. "Your friends, the ones that Torrio guy is holding—what's going to happen to them if you walk away now? If you leave now without the ring, you'll never get across town in time to save them."

THE PROBLEM OF THE RING

Viola let Logan's threat roll off her back. She was too busy trying to keep Theo on his feet to worry about some too-soft boy with too-pretty eyes reminding her of what was at stake. She knew *exactly* what was at stake—the ring, to start. If they didn't retrieve it now, while the doorway in the ceiling was open, they likely never would. Or worse, *this* boy would, and if he survived, he would give it to Nibsy.

Somehow, though, the problem of the ring seemed suddenly small compared to her other problems. Viola had Theo to worry about, for one. Considering the way he was leaning on her, he wasn't going to walk out of the building on his own. If he didn't make it out of the building, if he didn't make it onto the ship that would carry him across the seas, who would be there to protect Ruby from Jack Grew? Certainly not Viola herself. She couldn't even leave the city, and Jack Grew could go anywhere.

And then there were Cela and Abel. . . .

Viola had treated them so poorly, and still they had risked so much. They had risked *everything*—all for a cause that was not even theirs. Logan was likely correct—she couldn't hope to reach Cela and Abel in time if she walked away now, but another question worried her.

"What happens if Theo is right and we do get trapped up there?" Viola asked Logan. "Yes, we can dispense with Jack Grew easily enough. He's a fly to be swatted. But if that door closes, if it locks us on the other side, what happens then?"

Logan eyed the opening in the ceiling, but he didn't answer.

"I'll tell you what happens," she told him, hating the truth of it. "No one will stop Johnny the Fox from hurting my friends. At least if I go now, I have a chance to save them, however slim it may be."

"I can't believe you're going to give up on the Delphi's Tear when it's *right there*," Logan said with clear disbelief. "If you walk away now, the Order will win. They will finish consecrating this chamber, and they will begin building their power, and they will never stop working to destroy magic. Someday, years from now, the old magic will be hardly anything but a myth, and it will be your fault."

Logan was not wrong. The ring was one of the artifacts Dolph Saunders had been willing to die for. Could Viola really walk away, knowing she was so close?

But she understood that Theo had not been lying, and she trusted him—perhaps as well as she trusted anyone. If Theo Barclay, who had risked his reputation and his life, said that there was no way out of the room above if that seal closed, she believed him.

"If we're trapped up there, the Order still wins," she told Logan.

"The halls are dark," Theo said. "It means the members are still secured in their sanctuary below. We can go now, before they've realized what happened here. We can leave now, and we can all live long enough to try again some other day."

Viola turned to Logan, not quite believing that everything had come to this, about to tell him that she had to go—that they *all* must go—when a familiar voice spoke close to her ear.

"We cannot leave the ring."

Viola turned to find Jianyu standing there. He'd appeared suddenly in the room, like an apparition.

Logan cursed from the surprise of Jianyu's appearance, and even the others jumped.

"What are you doing here?" Viola asked, her voice rising.

Jianyu gave her a bemused look at her spark of temper. "I saw you go into the building, and so I followed when I could," he said simply. "You would prefer I left you to accomplish this on your own?"

It wasn't that, but Viola understood that if Jianyu was there, then he had not heard Nibsy's threats as she'd hoped. If he was standing there, high above the city in the Order's most guarded rooms, no one was protecting Cela and Abel.

She shook her head. This wasn't the plan, but then, the plan had gone wrong nearly from the start. "Where were you before?" she demanded, even though it no longer mattered. Not when so much else had gone wrong.

"Delayed," Jianyu told her, and from the frustration in his expression, she suspected that something had happened—something they had not planned for. "That does not change what must happen next."

"If we're trapped up there, Cela and Abel will die," she told him. "Once Nibsy realizes we aren't coming out, he'll let Torrio kill them."

"Then go," Jianyu said. His expression was determined. "There will be some time before Nibsy knows for sure what has happened here. I will retrieve the artifact, as we planned, and you will go to protect our friends."

Viola hesitated. "But if Theo is correct and you're trapped when the door closes . . ."

"I will not be seen when it is opened again," Jianyu reassured her.

It was possible, she supposed, for Jianyu to make himself undetectable if he were locked into the room above. It was maybe possible that he could do what she could not. Perhaps they could still manage to succeed despite everything that had gone wrong during this terrible mess of a night.

"Go. Get to Cela and Abel," Jianyu told her again. "You are far better suited to handle that particular problem."

Jianyu was right. With her knife and with her affinity, she could neutralize Torrio's threat—as long as she arrived in time.

Viola gave Jianyu a nod. It was, it seemed, the only way. Then she turned to the others. "I'm going with Theo. Come with us?"

"You have your orders," Logan reminded Mooch and Werner. "We all do." He was glaring at Viola.

"He's right," Werner said. "Nibsy won't be happy if we come back without the ring."

"Will he be happier if you don't come back at all?" Viola asked him. "Will he even care?" When Werner didn't respond at first, she threw up her hands. "Nibsy can't expect so much of you if death is certain. Dolph never would have asked such a thing of you. He would not have asked it of *any* of us," she told them.

The invocation of Dolph's name sent an uneasiness through the group. It was Mooch who finally broke the momentary silence.

"Viola's right," Mooch agreed, stepping away from Logan. "I've already been to the Tombs once this month, and I don't have any plans to go back. I ain't interested in dying here either. Not for Nibsy Lorcan."

Viola gave him a nod of thanks.

Werner looked between Logan and Mooch. "I dunno, Mooch. Nibs gave us a job. . . ."

"It can't be done," Mooch argued. "Besides, you know what happened the last time he gave me a job to do."

Werner considered the issue.

"You can't walk away from this," Logan argued, but it was clear he'd lost control of the situation.

Werner ducked his head a little, meeting Logan's eyes. "I'm going with them," he said. "I'll take my chances with Nibsy. He ain't that tough, anyway."

"Come with us," Viola told Logan. "Jianyu can retrieve the artifact. There's no need to die here. Not for Nibsy."

"I don't have any plans to die," Logan told her, backing toward the staircase. His expression had hardened now, and his voice was stiff. "And I'm not about to let him walk off with the ring. If you're going, then go. But I'm staying." He glared at Jianyu.

Viola turned to Jianyu. "Are you sure about this?"

"I will get the ring," he told her, as though anything that day had been so easy as that. *I will keep it from this one.* He didn't say the words, but it was there in the silent sureness of his expression. "Go. Make certain that Cela is safe."

Viola didn't want to leave Jianyu, but they were out of time. Theo was already pulling at her hand, dragging her back into the library. She looked back only once, and Jianyu gave her a small nod. A silent promise. *Go,* his expression seemed to say. *Time is running out.*

He was not wrong. If Viola could make it back to the building where Cela was stationed before John Torrio made a move, she would be more than lucky. But she would try. *Madonna,* she would try.

"We should take the back staircase," Theo told them, leading the way to the other end of the building.

"The elevator worked last time," Mooch argued.

Viola hated the idea, but one look at Theo told her that Mooch was right. "Do you know how to work it?" she asked.

"I watched Logan," Werner said. "How hard could it be?"

In the end, it was Theo who depressed the lever to control their descent. They could still hear alarm bells ringing as the elevator vibrated around them. The small clocklike device above the door counted down to what might be an ambush.

When the doors opened, they were ready, but so, too, were the Order. When they stepped from the small cage, three men were waiting. Viola's knife was already drawn, but Mooch stepped in front of her. He closed his eyes, and flames erupted from the marble floors, first behind the men, who turned to see what had happened. Then the flames began to encircle them, holding them in place. The men drew guns, but the flames contracted suddenly, causing the men to press together, dropping their arms so they wouldn't be singed.

Mooch opened his eyes and gave Theo a smug, satisfied smile. "That should hold them."

Theo looked momentarily taken aback. "If it doesn't bring the whole building down."

"It won't," Mooch said, lifting his hand to show a small flame dancing at his fingertips. He let it weave between his fingers like a snake, but it didn't so much as singe his skin. "They do what I say." Then he closed his fist, extinguishing the flame.

Theo appeared briefly uneasy, but he blinked, and a look of utter concentration came over his face. "This way. We're close."

The four of them escaped through a service door. As they exited, Nibsy's boys started to leave, but Viola snagged Mooch by the arm.

"Nibsy can't know what happened in there," she told him. "Not yet. You have to buy me some time."

He pulled away. "I don't have to do nothing for you."

"You'd still be rotting in the Tombs if not for me," Viola reminded Mooch, but he was already walking away from her.

"We need to go," Theo urged. "I have to get to the ship if I want any chance of stopping the rumors that Jack has surely already started about me. He'll try to frame me when the ring disappears—especially if he's not the one who gets it. I can't be seen here. And *you* have to get to Cela and Abel before the Five Pointers can."

Viola looked up at the impossible building jutting like a blade against the deepening twilight of the evening sky. She sent up a prayer for Jianyu's safety, and then she and Theo melted into the crowd.

THE MYSTERIUM

1902—New York

J ack Grew stood in the center of the new Mysterium and paused long
enough to take in the wonder of his surroundings. The walls of the
room were lined with gilded sigils, the names of angels and demons
who lent their power to those worthy enough to carry out their will.

As above, so below.

Now Jack Grew was higher than any other—quite literally. The rest of
the men in attendance shivered and quaked in fear two floors below him,
and the rest of the city was lower still.

It had been almost too easy to reach this point. The old men in the
Inner Circle had been so taken with his demonstrations at the gala that
they had been more than willing to allow him the privacy to work on the
measures he'd proposed to seal the Mysterium—blood magic, as ancient
as the Nile itself. Guaranteed not to be corruptible or breakable. They
had been so excited about the enchantment, they'd never questioned his
truthfulness. Why would they, when they never doubted his desire to join
them? Who, after all, *wouldn't* want to become one of the chosen?

Only the man who had already surpassed them all.

The Inner Circle—the High Princept, especially—never considered
that membership in the Inner Circle meant nothing at all to Jack, so the
High Princept never suspected that Jack had also given *himself* a way into
the new Mysterium. A spare key, of sorts, that he had built into the very
enchantment he'd devised.

On instinct, Jack patted the place where the Book usually sat in his jacket pocket. His pulse jumped to find the pocket empty, but he reminded himself that this was for the best. He'd left the Ars Arcana back in his rooms, under lock and key in a heavily warded safe. It had been a hard decision—the temptation to keep it always with him was enormous—but Jack couldn't chance losing the Book, and he knew he couldn't be sure that the Inner Circle wouldn't have some surprise in store. He understood that some members still didn't completely trust him, so he had to be prepared in case they'd layered in some other protection that he was unaware of.

He could not allow anyone to discover that he had the Order's most prized and important artifact. Not now. Not when he was so close to retrieving the ring, and with it, to finally finishing his great machine. Still, the absence of the Book bothered him. Jack could almost feel the weight of it still there, a phantom limb.

So far everything was going to plan. It had been easy enough to duck out of the sanctuary without being seen, and when he'd arrived at the antechamber, the door opened easily, exactly as he'd planned. He'd found the balcony empty, as he'd hoped it would be.

Jack could have looked. There was part of him that wanted to. Seeing Barclay's broken body splayed on the pavement below would have given him *enormous* satisfaction, but he wouldn't be greedy. He would save that particular moment for after, when he would have the time to savor it.

Instead, he'd gone directly to the stairs, directly to the Mysterium above. There, the wall of windows at the end of the room made the streets of the city glow in an electrified gold, like an illuminated map through the crystalline glass. The windows had been specially designed and bespelled by the Inner Circle to reveal the truth of the Order's power. Through them, the men of the Inner Circle could be reminded that the city—every *inch* of the island—had been touched by the Order's power. The winding paths in Madison Square pulsed with a deep scarlet, and beyond the edge of the island, the Brink itself shimmered with ribbons of astounding colors, the only protection against the uncivilized threat of feral magic.

The strange threads of color looked different than they had earlier, though—the ribbons seemed more erratic, and now there was a shadowy darkness woven through their spaces. Jack wasn't sure what could be causing such an effect. He'd heard the worries the old men in the Order had about the Brink, concerns that it was waning in its power, but it was more likely that the difference was simply an effect of the solstice's power.

Either way, it didn't truly matter. The Brink was already becoming irrelevant. The Order might have been emboldened by retrieving the Delphi's Tear, but Jack knew that soon there would be more bridges and trains leading out of the city, maybe even a tunnel under the river. The Brink was a vestige of the past. It had served its purpose, but it would not be enough to stop the onslaught of maggots that insisted on coming to these shores. The Order must change to address that threat, or they, too, would fall into irrelevance, and their great nation—their *peerless civilization*—would fall to ruin.

Jack Grew would not allow that to happen.

In the center of the Mysterium was a replica of the Tree of Life wrought from iron and gold. Within the maze of its spindly branches were five open spaces, and in one of those spaces, the Delphi's Tear floated, suspended in the Aether. The entire piece seemed to glow from within. For the time being, it had an extra layer of protection upon it, charged as it was by the power of the Golden Hour. If the Order had been able to complete their ceremony, this protection could have been extended in time, recharged at each subsequent solstice.

If the Order had been able to complete the ceremony . . .

The air around the ring shimmered as Jack circled the sculpture and examined the artifact, waiting. With the Delphi's Tear, he would show the Order—no, the *country*—that there was a better way, a more modern and powerful approach to dealing with the threat of feral magic. He would show everyone how the occult sciences could change the world. He had only to wait for the golden light to dim, and with the confusion in the sanctuary below, the protections of the Golden Hour would fade. Jack would be able to take the ring and forge a new path toward a new future.

Once the sun had dipped below the horizon, Jack watched as the electrified streets began to dim. Far off, the Brink still lit the river with its strange colors, but the sculptural tree began to dim. Its protections began to wane. The Golden Hour had come to an end.

It was time.

Jack reached for the ring, certain of his victory, but he had not yet touched it when a pain erupted in the back of his head, sharp and *absolute*. His legs went out from under him at the impact, and he barely caught himself as he crumpled to the floor, his vision already blurring.

As Jack tried to gather his wits and focus through the pain, a masked figure stepped up behind him. Barely holding on to consciousness, Jack could only *just* make out the shape of a man. He realized then what had happened. Someone was there with him in the Mysterium. Someone had broken through every protection he'd created, throwing his plans into chaos.

No. This couldn't be happening. *Not again.*

Before Jack could even bring himself to his knees, the thief had already grabbed the ring, dislodging it from the Aether, and then turned to retreat. But the instant the thief's unworthy hands had touched the artifact, the protections Jack had put in place awoke. The medallion at the entrance of the Mysterium began to slide back into place, blocking the exit before the thief could reach it.

Jack couldn't help but laugh at the absurdity of the situation he found himself in as the thief darted around the room, looking for some other option. But there was no escape from a doorless room high above the city streets except one. Jack tried again to stand, but his head spun, and he collapsed again, unable to do more than simply lie there with the room swirling around him.

If he could make it to the doorway . . . perhaps he could pull himself across the floor and perform the ritual to open it—except that he knew that plan was pointless. Even if Jack could get *himself* out of this chamber, he was in no shape to stop the masked figure from also escaping. Better to be trapped there together. At least this way the bastard who'd hit him wouldn't be able to take the ring. At least this way Jack could make it appear that he was protecting the Order's treasures, and the old men would never know the truth.

Jack thought that he had planned so carefully. He'd been sure that he'd accounted for every possibility, and *still* this had happened. Soon the sanctuary below would open. Soon the Inner Circle would rush up to the Mysterium to check on the artifact, and the High Princept would use his blood to open the door. Soon they would find Jack here, and there would be questions.

It doesn't matter. Jack would have answers. When they finally discovered him, the perpetrator would already be disposed of. Perhaps he wouldn't get the ring that night, as he'd hoped, but Jack would be hailed a hero.

The thief pounded on the bronze seal on the floor, but after a few minutes, the thief seemed to understand that he was trapped. He ran to the end of the room and tore at the doorway that led to the balcony. The warm summer air gusted into the room, helping to clear Jack's head. His vision was still unsteady, but the pain was beginning to recede.

"There's no other way out, I'm afraid," Jack said, carefully pulling himself upright. He reached into his jacket and took out a pistol, aiming it at the intruder. "You're welcome to jump, but if you hand over the Delphi's Tear now, there's no need. I might even allow you to live."

The thief stepped out onto the balcony instead. Then, before Jack understood what he was doing, the figure threw himself off the ledge and disappeared into the wind.

STUBBORN TO A FAULT

1920—Chicago

J ericho Northwood took one look at the weapon his son was carrying when Everett returned from the Nitemarket with Esta and knew that things had gone too far. Esta might have kept her word by keeping Everett safe, but she'd clearly let the boy take too many risks. North had every mind to tell her so, except he didn't know how to without exploding or saying something that might embarrass Everett . . . or revealing something he'd regret, especially since they'd brought Dominic Fusilli with them. The last thing he needed was Dom any more entangled in the Northwood family's business, so North kept his mouth shut tight as they all tromped back to their warehouse.

As the elevated train rattled into the city, North tried to organize his thoughts. Everything seemed so much more complicated than he'd expected when he'd decided to bring Everett along for a quick bootlegging run. He'd only wanted to help toughen the boy up a little, not get him killed in the process. But with the sirens filling the city air, it was becoming more apparent that Esta might be right about the tower. It was an idea that made North's blood run cold.

He hadn't been much more than a kid himself when the tower in California had been activated, but he remembered the aftermath. The idea that something like that might happen again seemed completely impossible, but if Esta was right about the attacks, she was probably also right about the rest. The way North figured it, there was only one thing to do.

Once they were back at the warehouse, they were greeted by the man who'd driven the truck earlier. "There's been an attack," Floyd told him.

"We figured when we heard the sirens," North said. "What's the word?"

"It's the convention. According to what they're saying on the wireless, the delegates were in the middle of taking a vote on the vice presidential candidate—that easterner, Coolidge, was set to win—when everything went haywire. They're talking about monsters, and they're blaming the Antistasi."

"Monsters?" North asked.

Floyd nodded. "Great beasts, according to the descriptions of the people who made it out. This one guy, he was saying the creatures looked like they were made from shadow. They killed a bunch of people already, and as far as I can tell, the attack is still going on—there are still people trapped in the Coliseum."

North glanced at Esta, who gave him a dark look in return. *I told you,* she seemed to say.

"I want to hear for myself," North told Floyd.

"We have the wireless set up in the main room."

Together they went into the warehouse, where the other Antistasi North had hired were already gathered around the receiver, listening intently to the nonstop bulletins. They listened for a long time, trying to get a sense of what had happened. The attack had been violent. Already, they were starting to count the dead. But when the reports grew repetitive, North knew there was nothing more to learn, and he clicked off the receiver. In the end, fifty-three had been killed by some kind of magical beasts, and because the attacks were similar to what had happened at the Conclave back in 1902, they were already blaming the old magic.

Back then, the government had used the attacks on the Conclave to pass the Defense Against Magic Act. But that had been an attack on a private group of wealthy men. The convention was public, and the death toll was already horrifying. There was no telling what the Brotherhoods would do, no telling how much more they could turn the public against Mageus . . . except North already knew what came next. Esta had already told him what would happen.

At first no one moved or spoke. The group kept staring at the now-silent receiver, and then they began exchanging uneasy looks with one another.

"I know that they blamed the old magic for attacks like this before, but I've sure never heard of any Mageus with an affinity like *that*," one of the men said, finally breaking the silence.

"Because it wasn't Mageus," Esta told him. She looked to North. "It was a setup. And it worked. Coolidge should've been nominated tonight, but now . . ." She didn't finish. She didn't need to.

North launched into action. "The shipment I was telling you about is in the back," he told Dom. "We're going to be leaving town tonight. I'll give you whatever you want for a good price, if you help me get it off my hands."

Dom's eyes lit. "Mind if I take a look now, seeing as I'm here and all?"

"Be my guest," North said.

"You're leaving?" Esta asked once Dom had disappeared to find the promised crates of Nitewein.

"As soon as we can pack everything up and Dom hands over enough cash for me to pay the guys I hired for the job," he told her.

"You can't run from this," Harte said, stepping forward with fury in his eyes. "We told you what was going to happen."

Which was exactly why he was leaving. "I have my boy to consider," North said, refusing to feel even the smallest bit of guilt. "I'm not going to stay here and let him die."

"So that's it? You're not going to help us?" Harte asked, stepping even closer, as though he wanted to go toe-to-toe.

North lifted his chin. "I'm going to protect what's mine for as long as I can."

"I don't blame you," Esta told him, placing a hand on Harte's arm. She cut a warning look at him, before turning her attention back to North. "But I wish you'd reconsider. We could use the help."

North shook his head. "Not this time."

"The tower could go off as early as tomorrow night," Harte pressed. "You'd walk away from that, knowing how many people will be hurt?"

"If it meant my family was safe?" North glanced at Everett, the boy with his eyes and Maggie's heart. The boy who had made them a family. "I most certainly would."

"Safe." Esta gave him a sad shake of her head. "You say that like it's possible for people like us to be safe."

"For the last fifteen years or so, safe is *exactly* what I've been," North told her.

"Have you?" Her tone was unreadable.

"I have my ranch, my family," he told her. "I don't need this mess you're stirring up."

"We're not the ones doing the stirring," Harte told him.

"Mark my words," Esta added. "If that tower goes off, it won't only be Mageus in Chicago who will be harmed. When Jack Grew becomes president—*when*, not if—nothing is going to stop him from making life for those with the old magic worse than it's ever been. Even Mageus like you, who think they can run off to safety. They're going to build more towers. Eventually, they're going to come for your family, too."

"Eventually isn't today." North understood what was at stake. He wasn't an idiot, was he? Hadn't he lived through more deeds and fought long and hard for the promise of a future for his children and their children's children? But that future was still a ways off, and Everett was right here, real and whole. He couldn't set the boy's life aside for some distant possibility.

"We didn't stop the attack, but we can still stop Jack and the terrible future he's planning," Esta told him. "We can stop 'eventually' from ever arriving if we destroy that tower. Tonight. *Before* he sets it off. We can save the Mageus in the city *and* those who have no idea what's coming. Help us destroy the tower, and we can save your family."

"You can't destroy the tower tonight," Everett argued. "An attack like that wouldn't help your cause at all. You'd just be giving the Brotherhoods another reason to rally everyone against the old magic."

"Leave it be, Everett. This is none of our business," North told his son.

"The kid has a point," Harte said to Esta.

"No," North told them, stepping between his son and the other two. "He doesn't. He's not getting involved. Get your stuff," he told Everett, who had the weapon he'd brought back with him from the market on his lap. He was already starting to take it apart. "We're leaving as soon as we're packed."

Everett set the metal body of the flamethrower aside. "You can go if you want, but I'm not ready just yet."

Looking at his son, the boy's face a portrait of stubborn determination, North was struck immediately by how young Everett still was. It didn't matter that North himself had been even younger when his own father had died or that he'd been about Everett's age when he'd been jumping from place to place, getting into all sorts of trouble.

"I didn't ask if you were ready," North said.

"But I can help," Everett insisted. "I understand machines. I've studied everything I could about the California towers—at least in theory." Everett turned to Esta and Harte. "I can help," he repeated.

"Maybe you can," North told his son, "but you're not going to."

Everett frowned at him, and North saw the flicker of temper flash in his boy's eyes. That little show of backbone was what he'd wanted from his son all along, but North found himself now wishing he'd never started down this path.

"Son—"

But Everett stepped around North, ignoring the warning he'd infused in that single word, and spoke directly to Esta. "If you're going to go after that tower, you need to be smart about it," Everett said. "It's not enough to destroy it tonight. That would be another attack, and another reason for the Brotherhoods to retaliate. They might even be able to repair the tower in time to set it off like they're planning to, and you wouldn't have stopped anything. It would be better if we let the whole thing play out, but if we could disable the mechanism so no one realized . . . Or maybe if the machine didn't work like they expected . . . With a couple of adjustments to the tower, we could turn their whole plan into an enormous, embarrassing catastrophe. We could save the people in this city who have the old magic *and* make Jack Grew and the Brotherhoods look like incompetent, dangerous fools all at once."

"You don't by any chance have an idea for how to do that?" Esta asked, exchanging a silent look with Harte that North didn't like one bit.

"Yes," Everett told them.

"No," North said at the same time. "I told you—he is *not* getting involved. We're leaving tonight."

Everett met North's eyes. "I can help with this, Pa."

"What do you expect me to tell your mother if I have to go home without you?" North demanded.

"Tell her the truth," Everett said. "If I can help these people stop the Brotherhoods from succeeding with the massacre they have planned, then I'm gonna. I think she'll understand."

Esta's expression was unreadable as she studied Everett. Then her gaze lifted to North, and when her eyes met his, North put everything he could into the silent plea he sent her. *Leave me my son.*

"Your father's right," Esta said gently. "I can't ask you to risk your life. Your parents have done too much for us already for me to let you get caught up in this."

"I'm *already* caught up in it," Everett said, his jaw going tight. Then the boy turned to North. "I was born caught up in this. You can leave if you want. I wouldn't blame you, but I'm staying."

"Like hell you are," North growled, fear finally snapping his temper in two. "You're going to get your ass moving so I can get you back to your mother in one piece. One way or another we're pulling out of this city within the hour. If that means leaving all those books you brought with you behind, so be it."

"I'd like to see you make me go," Everett said. He squared his shoulders, like he wanted to remind North that soft as he might be, he was still already grown.

"You heard what I said," North ordered, ignoring his son's posturing. "Bring that contraption along if you'd like, but you're not staying here. You're coming back to the ranch with me. Tonight."

Everett met North's stare, and he didn't back down. "I am not going to leave every Mageus in this city to die because you're afraid."

The accusation rankled, but North saw that it wasn't the stubborn petulance of a child shining in his son's eyes. Everett looked every inch the man North had hoped his son would one day become, and he was struck suddenly with the irony of it all. He'd thought to toughen his son up, to transform him somehow, but the boy was already there. And North hadn't been smart enough to see it.

"Every Mageus in the city isn't your concern," North told him, but he knew already that this was a battle he was destined to lose.

"Of *course* they are," Everett said. "Isn't that what you and Ma have been going on about since I can remember? Helping others. Protecting those who can't protect themselves."

As much as the boy took after Maggie, he had too much of North's own stubbornness. How had North missed that before? Had he never really *seen* his own son? "I'm sure these two can take care of it well enough," North said, but there wasn't any real conviction in his words now. The truth was, he would have done the same years ago, back before he discovered what losing something really meant.

"You don't think I know why you brought me along this week?" his son asked. The Adam's apple in Everett's throat bobbed as he swallowed down the emotion that was swimming in his eyes. "You don't think I understand that you want me to be a little rougher and a little tougher—a little more like you?"

The look on Everett's face had North's heart clenching. "Son—"

Everett held up a hand to stop his father's protest. "Well, I'm *not* like you. I'm probably always going to choose a book over a horse and learning over brute strength, but there are times when a little book learning can come in handy, and this might be one of them."

Esta had been listening to everything Everett said, but her eyes were on North. In them was a question that North understood—it was up to him to answer.

"You know you're as bad as your mother sometimes, don't you?" he said, shaking his head at his son. "Always trying to save the world instead of your own tail."

Everett's smile was immediate and nearly incandescent in its hopefulness.

North chucked his arm around his boy, his heart aching with the helplessness he felt. He couldn't protect his child without destroying him in the process, and North wouldn't be the one to do that. "Your mother's going to murder me."

"I hate to interrupt such a lovely family moment . . ." Dom was back, and who knew how long the slippery old man had been listening. "But I'd like to get on with my night. If you're ready to sell, I'll take the lot. Nine fifty a case work for you?"

"Nine fifty?" That price was less than a third of what they usually took, but it would be enough to pay his men and send some back to Maggie and the kids as well. "That's basically robbery."

"If you have another buyer . . ." Dom shrugged with a knowing look, and North understood that there wouldn't be any other buyers—not if Dom had his way. He'd put word out that the goods were tainted, or worse, he'd tell people where they'd come from.

"Make it ten, and you have a deal," North threw back, because he knew that taking the first offer would only serve to make Dom suspicious. But his heart wasn't really in the negotiation.

"Done." Dom pulled out a thick stack of cash and counted out the amount before handing it over.

North tucked the money away without looking twice. Being short-changed was the least of his worries.

LISA MAXWELL

"I'll have some of my guys come by to pick up the goods by the end of the week," Dom said, offering North his hand.

"I won't be here," North told him as they shook, and he hoped it was because he was home with Maggie instead of dead and gone. "But I'll make sure the crates are waiting for you."

"Then I guess this is good-bye for now," Dom said. "It was an informative evening, Northwood." He eyed Harte and Esta, who had managed to keep quiet through the conversation. "I'll say one thing: You certainly do keep some interesting company."

"You're welcome to them," North grumbled.

Esta had come over by that time. "I'm hoping you can keep our little meeting between us," she said.

Dom tilted his head. "I make it a policy to never make promises I can't keep," he told her.

She didn't seem bothered by his refusal. "I understand . . . though it might make it harder for you to reestablish your business if anyone found out who really was in charge of running the Nitemarket."

"A threat?" Dom said, rubbing at his stubbled chin. "And not a very creative one at that. I expected better of you, Miss Filosik." He appeared to be suppressing a smile.

Esta's eyes narrowed a little. "You're a frustrating man, Mr. Fusilli."

"And a helpful one," Dom said with a slight twist of his mouth. "I couldn't help but overhear your discussion. I might have something that could help."

Esta didn't betray even an ounce of surprise. "Do you?"

Dom made a small flourish of his hand. "Walk me out, and maybe I can be persuaded to divulge it."

Esta glanced at Harte, who didn't look happy about the situation, but she only gave him a shrug before following Dom out.

"Do you really think you can disarm the machine in the tower without anyone realizing?" Harte asked Everett, part of his attention still on Esta and Dom as they left.

"I know how the California tower worked. I think we could do something even better than disarming it," Everett told Harte. Then his gaze shifted to North. "But I could probably use some help."

North knew when he was defeated. "It's not like I'm about to let you go climbing up there alone."

"Look on the bright side," Everett told him. "If we fail, you won't have to worry about Ma killing you."

North stared at his son. "You don't know your mother very well if you think she wouldn't drag me back from the dead just for the sake of killing me a second time."

ALREADY FALLING

1920—Chicago

The following evening, the June heat was thick and sticky as Harte stood next to Esta in the line of people waiting to enter the Chicago Coliseum. He felt the sweat already dampening the cotton of his shirt and the hair at his temples, but he was too exhausted to care. No one had slept much following the events at the Nitemarket. They all realized how little time they had to stop a deadly future from unfurling. Even with the short nap Esta had forced on him before they left, Harte felt every bit as old as North looked. Seshat might have been silenced by another tablet of the Quellant, but in his muscles and in his bones, Harte felt every second of every minute that he'd been awake.

The mood of the enormous crowd congregating around the building was boisterous. A group of women in white dresses held signs and shouted at every man passing, demanding women's suffrage. Other groups held signs supporting candidates, men whose names Harte didn't know and didn't particularly care to. Occasionally, a shout would go up—*America first!*—and in unison, the rest of the crowd would respond with raucous shouts and chants of *Harding! Harding!* There was an energy in the air despite the heat, an excitement that even Harte, who'd never cared for the often dirty dealings of the political machine in New York, could feel.

There was another emotion running through the crowd as well—fear. Or maybe it was anger. From the hushed whispers and anxious expressions many of the attendees wore, it was clear that the attack on the convention the night before was fresh in their minds. Many of the people in line to enter wore black armbands in solidarity with the fifty-three men who had been killed during the previous night's attack. Others held signs of support and shouted for an end to the threat of feral magic. None of them had any idea that the attack had been staged, and Harte wondered if they would care even if they *did* know—or if the attack had simply given them permission to put their truest and ugliest beliefs on display.

"It's exactly like Sammie described," he murmured to Esta. He realized then that he hadn't *quite* believed his brother's story. Not completely. Deep down, he'd hoped that Sammie had been exaggerating or had misremembered past events, but now Harte saw how naive that hope had been.

He understood fear, of course. He was well acquainted with the quiet, often unexamined hatred it inspired, and he knew as well what that hatred could do when channeled and directed. But he'd never imagined that it could unite *so* many people so quickly and absolutely. Short of standing in Khafre Hall that night so many weeks ago, Harte had never really seen the hatred against what he was—*who* he was—made quite so obvious.

"They've added security," Esta whispered. She nodded up toward the roofline, where men holding rifles lined the top of the building. "And that banner's new too."

The Coliseum was an enormous structure with a facade that reminded Harte of a castle with its multiple medieval-looking towers and arched entrances. The whole building was decorated with patriotic bunting and flags that hung limp and still in the windless air. In the center of the roofline, a tower rose, its steel frame a dark outline silhouetted by the setting sun. The tower bore a placard with the logo of American Steel at its apex, and hanging from that was an enormous silken banner. On it was an image Harte recognized: the Philosopher's Hand.

Harte had seen copies of this familiar alchemical formula many times before in his studies. He'd seen it in the warehouse where Jack Grew had built his first machine, and he'd seen it again in the bowels of Khafre Hall. But this version was different. The emblem on the banner reminded Harte a little of the moving picture box that had been in the San Francisco hotel room, because the image seemed almost *alive*. It had clearly been charmed in some way. The five elemental icons floated above the disembodied hand's fingers—crown, key, lantern, moon, and star—each rotating slowly, glowing with their own unique phosphorescence. The palm held the fish in a flame-bound sea with softly undulating waves. It was the symbolic representation of quintessence—Aether. But though the flames churned, the banner did not burn.

"Jack showed me a similar image back in New York," Harte told Esta. "This one appearing now can't be a coincidence."

"It's happening tonight." She sounded more worried than she had earlier. All day, she'd worn her usual air of confidence as they'd gone over the plans and preparations, until everything was excruciatingly clear and everyone was ready. Now she looked nervous.

Harte couldn't say anything to bolster her, though, because they'd finally reached the entrance. Esta fell silent as Harte handed over the tickets Dom had procured for them, and a man wearing a too-familiar silvery medallion on his lapel waved the two of them through.

"They're everywhere," Harte whispered, noticing that every few yards there was someone else wearing one of the medallions that served to detect illegal magic. Many wore badges bearing the enchanted image of the Philosopher's Hand as well.

"Of course they're everywhere. The Brotherhoods will be the reason Jack gets the nomination," Esta reminded him. "Unless we stop him."

Once inside the building, they allowed themselves to be carried with the crush of other attendees toward the main hall. Harte pulled the pocket watch Everett had given him from the inside pocket of his vest, but he was disappointed to see nothing but the time displayed by the hands. The watch was one of Everett's contraptions—not magic, because that would have been too dangerous in a hall filled with members from the Brotherhoods. Instead, the piece worked with some kind of radio signal. Apparently, where Maggie was adept with mixing formulas, her son had the same touch with machinery. When Everett and North were done with the tower, the watch would vibrate and its hands would begin to spin. So far they were holding maddeningly steady.

"I hope we weren't wrong to trust North and Everett," Harte said as he watched the steady ticking of the seconds, waiting for something to change.

"Rett was determined to help us," Esta reminded Harte, even as she scanned the crowded hall.

"He's not the one I'm worried about."

She glanced at him. "You think North would get in the way?"

"You and I both know that North has a family full of reasons to walk away from all this and to take his oldest son with him." Harte had seen the fear in the cowboy's eyes. His own father might never have looked at him with that same kind of concern, but after losing Sammie, Harte had at least a little understanding of what North might be feeling. "One good dose of one of Maggie's concoctions, and Everett wouldn't have much choice."

Esta's mouth went tight. "I don't think North would do that to Everett. Besides, if North was going to run, he would have last night."

"Maybe . . ." Harte hadn't forgotten the cowboy's reluctance to allow Everett to stay. "But if they left instead of heading to the tower, we'd never know. We're just assuming they're up there." He jerked his head toward the ceiling.

"If you were this worried, you should have let me go with Everett," Esta reminded him.

"We already went through this," Harte told her. "You can't be in two places at once."

"With my affinity, it would have been easy to—"

"Not with all these medallions. Besides, it's more important that we focus on getting the Book and the dagger from Jack," Harte said, cutting off the discussion. It hardly mattered that with her affinity, Esta practically *could* be in two places at once. He wanted her with him, though, because at least when she was near him, he knew she was safe. "Whatever happens with the tower, getting the Book and the dagger is more important anyway."

Esta frowned as though maybe she didn't agree.

"We cannot allow Jack or Thoth to keep that Book, Esta." Harte took her hand, tangling their fingers. He hated the Quellant and how empty it made him feel, but at least it allowed him to touch Esta while he still could. The Book was the best chance he had of saving Esta from herself—of maybe even saving them both—but if they couldn't get it back, he'd take whatever time he had left with her. "We need the secrets contained in those pages."

"You're right," Esta admitted. "I think we can trust North and Everett, though. This is going to work, Harte. It has to." She gave his hand a soft squeeze and then lowered her voice. "How is she?"

"Quiet," he said, knowing that Esta was talking about Seshat.

So far the power inside of him felt as absent and empty as his own. Still, he couldn't forget what had happened at the Nitemarket. Whatever those men had done during the attack had made the effects of the Quellant all but evaporate. Harte knew that he had to prepare for the possibility that it might happen again. As long as Seshat's power still lived inside him, he would continue to be a liability.

"Esta . . ." He wasn't exactly sure how he could make her understand.

She turned to him with a question in her eyes, her expression serious and guarded. There was so much he wanted to tell her, so much he wanted from her—with her—but he settled for the only thing he could do *for* her.

"If anything goes wrong tonight and you have a chance to escape, even if it's without me, I want you to promise that you will," he told her.

"We've been over this, Harte." Her eyes flashed with impatience, and she started to pull her hand away from him, but he caught it before she could pull away completely.

"Too many times," he admitted. Her fingers felt delicate entwined with his, but he knew they were strong and capable—just like Esta herself. "I still want your promise. If something happens, and it becomes too dangerous for you to take me with you, I need to know you won't hesitate. I *need* you to go on without me."

"And what about stopping Seshat?" Esta asked.

"I'll take care of her." He couldn't meet her eyes. "I've told you where you can find the ring—"

"No. Absolutely not," Esta told him with a determined tightness in her jaw.

"Think about what happened at the Nitemarket, Esta."

"I can fight off Seshat. I have before," she argued.

Harte hated everything about the conversation. "Maybe . . . But at what cost? The earthquakes we caused were all Jack needed to build the first tower. We can't risk something like that happening again, especially not here, where everyone is already scared and angry. Even if we are able to get away, the mess we leave behind could be devastating."

She shook her head, stubborn as she'd ever been. "I'm not going through all of this again with you, Harte. We will find Jack. We will get the Book. We will leave. *Together.* That's the plan, and that's what we're going to do."

Harte could feel himself clenching his teeth. He'd thought long and hard about this through the small hours of the night as they'd plotted and planned. If push came to shove, he'd do whatever he had to in order to give her a chance to go on—to survive.

"And what if there's no way to leave together?" Harte asked. "What if the choice is you going or both of us dying?"

Esta only stared at him. "It won't be."

"You don't know that," he said, wishing it were otherwise. "And it might not be only your life at risk. . . . What if what happened on the train—"

"*Nothing* happened on the train," Esta said, her words clipped and her cheeks an angry pink.

"You mean—"

"There were no *consequences*," Esta hissed. Her jaw was tight and her golden eyes flashed with anger. And with hurt. "Don't worry. There's no need for you to make an honest woman of me."

"That's not what I . . ." He paused, not knowing what he was supposed to say. Not knowing why he felt a twinge of disappointment mixed

LISA MAXWELL

in with the relief. There was nothing to stop him now from doing whatever he had to in order to keep Esta safe.

"Promise me, Darrigan," she told him, eyes narrowing as though she'd sensed the direction of his thoughts. "We leave together. Promise me that you won't do something stupid."

Harte didn't want to make any promises that he couldn't keep. He certainly didn't want to waste any more time arguing with her when he knew already what he was willing to do.

"You know, you look lovely tonight," he said instead.

Esta frowned at him, and it looked like she wanted to continue their argument, but then she seemed to sense that it was pointless. "I look like a boring old lady," she told him with a droll twist of her lips. They weren't painted the dark crimson of the night before, but that didn't make them any less distracting. "Just like every other boring old lady here."

She was right about the crowd—there were quite a few women in attendance, and they were definitely older for the most part—but Esta was utterly wrong about her appearance. True, her dress might have been a bit more sedate than the shimmering column of gold she'd worn to the Green Mill. Made from a dark olive linen, the color might have looked dowdy or utterly forgettable on anyone else. But not on Esta. The otherwise drab green somehow warmed the deep golds in her skin and made her whiskey-colored eyes look even brighter than usual.

The boxy frock had a low-set waist that obscured Esta's shape, but it didn't matter. With her height, the fit of the dress made her look willowy and graceful, and somehow its straight lines only drew more attention by hinting at the body hiding beneath it.

"Lovely," Harte repeated, lifting their joined hands and placing a soft kiss on the back of hers. He paused, their eyes locked, before he allowed his lips to brush across her knuckles again.

Esta's cheeks pinkened a little more, but this time it wasn't anger that colored them. "We need to focus on finding Jack," she whispered, gently pulling her hand away.

"I can focus on multiple things at once," he said, drawing his mouth into a wry grin, glad that however mad at him she might be, there was still something undeniable there between them. But the sadness in her eyes made Harte's smile falter. He wanted to know what had put that emotion there. "Esta—"

"We don't have to talk about this, Harte. We need to focus on the one thing that's important right now," she told him, brushing off the moment. "The rest can wait."

Harte wanted to argue. He wished they had a little more time and that he was a little less of a coward. There was so much he wanted to say— there were things he needed to tell her. He felt as though they were on the precipice of something he did not fully understand. It was somehow even more dangerous than the threat of the machine or the possibility of an unthinkable future. Whatever was between them felt bigger than the Order or the Brotherhoods and more powerful than the ancient being that waited deep within him.

It didn't seem to matter that Harte had escaped from death so many times—in chains and in water and in a feverish delirium. *This* moment felt infinitely more fraught. Like that step from the bridge he'd been willing to take so many months ago, Harte knew that with Esta, there would be no going back. He could retreat. He could take this exit that she was offering.

Except . . . it was already too late. He'd already jumped, was already falling, without any chance of returning to where he'd once been. Depthless water below, endless sky above, and all that mattered was the gold of Esta's eyes.

"What if I don't want to wait?" Harte asked softly, taking her hand again.

She gave him the smallest of shrugs and untangled her fingers from his. "That isn't your choice to make," she told him, and then she turned and began to lead him through the crowds to the enormous hall that waited beyond.

AN AWAKENING

1920—Chicago

Esta's knuckles still burned from where Harte had kissed them, and her cheeks felt like they were on fire. She didn't know why she'd just lied to Harte. It would be a week or more yet until she had to worry about whether what they'd done on the train—

No. She wasn't even going to think about *that.* Especially not there, surrounded by so many people wearing the Brotherhoods' medallions and a crowd who would happily cheer on their destruction. Not when Jack—the Book and the dagger as well—were so very close. She would figure all that out later, if there was even anything to figure out at all. Until then, Esta would do what she always did. She would pull the hard shell of self-discipline and focus around herself as she plunged onward toward the job ahead of her. And she would not let herself wonder whether Harte would have felt the same about a future together if the threat of *complications* hadn't been hanging over them.

The main hall of the Coliseum was an enormous arena with a vaulted ceiling running the length of the room and stadium seating ringing the main floor. Red, white, and blue buntings lined each level of the balconies, and flags were hanging in rows across the ceiling. Large signs with bold block letters demarcated the seating for the various states' delegates, and in the middle of the arena stood a main stage decorated in the colors of the flag. On it, a small woman had been speaking ever since they'd entered the arena. Her voice boomed out through the cavernous space, and periodically the crowd would erupt into cries and cheers when she made another point they agreed with.

"How is she doing that?" Harte asked Esta.

"It's a microphone," she told him.

"Magic?"

"Technology," she corrected. "It's electrified."

Heat swirled in the air, sultry and close, as the woman spoke. Her voice rose and fell, her words carefully crafted to condemn the women who would distract the men gathered there—*important men*—from the essential work of governing with inauspiciously timed demands for suffrage. Suffrage could wait, she cried, when the nation was whole and safe. When America put America first and took care of its own.

Women still couldn't vote, Esta realized. Perhaps suffrage would be granted soon—she didn't know *exactly* when that would happen or whether something they'd done might have changed that, too—but for now the women in the hall were nothing more than decorations on the arms of their men, without power or voice. And *this* woman was asking them to remain that way.

"I would remind you of Mr. Harding's words. Last night, in this very room among this very body of delegates, he accepted our party's nomination and reminded us all of our duty. In his great words, it is an 'inspiration to patriotic devotion—to safeguard America first . . . to stabilize America first . . . to prosper America first . . . to think of America first . . . to exalt America first . . . to live for and revere America first,'" she shouted, pausing so that the crowd could cheer after each beat of the speech. "So I say to my sisters, we must put our country before our own meager desires. The attack on our convention has illustrated that now is not the time to press the question of votes for women. Now is the time to focus only on the sanctity of our greatest institutions. The safety of our children and our very lives depends upon strong men who will enact strong policies to keep our families safe from the threat of those who would try to turn our country against the ideals of its founders."

The crowd's cheers grew overwhelming, and as the volume rose in a fevered pitch, the woman stepped back from the podium, clearly pleased with herself. Esta felt only disgust.

"We can change this," Harte murmured, like he'd read her thoughts. He brushed his hand against the back of hers, and Esta allowed the small intimacy of the contact. "We *will* change this. The world doesn't have to be this way."

"Doesn't it?" Esta asked, glancing at him.

Maybe they could stop the Reticulum, maybe they could even go back to where they'd started and try to set history back on its intended course. But what would it matter? Esta remembered what Thoth had told her back in Denver: Time and magic could not coexist. If he was telling the truth, it meant that no matter what she and Harte did, no matter how much they changed, the old magic would eventually die. It was also what Seshat had feared and was the reason she'd created the Book in the first place. The only question, it seemed, was how it would happen. And when.

"No," Harte said, his expression determined. "It *doesn't*."

Then Esta gave herself a shake. Maybe magic *would* die. Maybe one day it would fade away, but *how* the old magic met its final end mattered, she reminded herself. Maybe she couldn't stop the march of history. Maybe she couldn't stop the march of time, either, but she could stop this massacre. She could stop *this* future from unfolding. What they were doing there mattered—*it had to*—even with a sea of angry people around them that seemed to say otherwise.

The arena was sweltering, the temperature and mood both roiling and hot, as patriotism and excitement and anger all mixed together. The woman ended her speech with a rousing call for the nomination of Jack Grew, and a portion of the arena surged to their feet, cheering in response. But not all of the men in the crowd cheered, Esta noticed with a little relief. Large sections of the arena remained seated and unmoved, even as the announcer called for another ballot.

The time had not yet arrived, but with each new ballot, the moment when Jack would activate the tower drew closer. They needed to get the Book before that happened, but it would be far easier to take the Book when he was alone rather than in front of this crowd. To do that, they needed to find him.

"I think the speakers are coming from over there," Harte told her, pointing toward a small gap in the crowd where a man was approaching the stage.

"It's as good a place as any to start," Esta said, stepping away from him, so that she could focus.

They'd barely started making their way around the edge of the arena, toward the area where the speakers seemed to be entering and exiting the stage, when a man with dusty-blond hair and wearing a crooked boater hat trimmed in red and blue stepped into their path, blocking their way. Harte moved in front of Esta, to shield her from whatever might be coming.

But as Esta pushed Harte aside and took her place next to him, where she belonged, she realized the guy wasn't a threat—or at least not an immediate one. He was wearing a ridiculous smile and an even more ridiculous hat, which looked like the Fourth of July had thrown up on it. On his arm, he wore a black band emblazoned with the Philosopher's Hand, and his eyes were bright as he held out a pair of small silver pins.

"A vote for Grew is a vote to grow," he crowed.

It was a damn stupid slogan, as far as Esta was concerned. It didn't even make sense. "No thanks," she told the guy. "We're here for Coolidge."

"Mr. Grew offers these with his compliments, wherever your loyalties lie. We're all in this fight together," the guy said, practically glowing with righteousness and pride.

Esta was about to tell him where he could put the medallions when Harte took them instead. "Thank you," he said, tucking the pins into his pocket.

"Mr. Grew will be speaking later tonight, and I hope you'll give him a listen. He has a real plan for protecting our future," the guy said, even as Harte was pulling Esta along through the crowd, away from him.

"I can't believe you risked taking those," she told him, making sure to keep her voice low enough so as not to be overheard.

"Not much of a risk. Not with the Quellant I took. Anyway, I figured it would be worse to raise his suspicions," Harte said, shrugging off her worries. "Besides, if North and his kid manage to come through like they promised, Everett might want to take a look at how these work. Maybe it would help if the Antistasi knew what they're up against."

Esta couldn't fault that logic, even if she didn't like the idea of having the medallions so close.

They made their way around the arena's perimeter and were nearly in line with the stage, when another round of balloting began. The states were called one by one, and one by one representatives came to the floor of the hall to call out their votes. She and Harte paused to watch and listen, but in the end the voting was inconclusive. Jack had a good portion of the delegates, but not enough for the majority he needed. Not yet.

Harte checked the pocket watch Everett had given him.

"Anything?" Esta asked.

He shook his head and then tucked the watch away. "No. Nothing."

Esta could tell exactly what Harte was thinking—North and Everett were taking too long. She'd expected Everett's watch to have given some signal by now too. "We don't even know where Jack is," she told Harte, trying to stay positive. "Maybe he hasn't arrived yet. There's still time. . . ." She only wished that she knew how much.

Harte's eyes were serious as he searched the arena. Realizing the night wasn't over, the crowd was growing more unsettled, and a disconcerted rustling sifted through the arena as tempers rose to match the temperatures. "This crowd isn't going to hold," he said. "Not with this heat."

A little while later, the mood of the entire arena seemed to shift. An alertness went through the crowd like a wave crashing over the shore.

"There," Harte murmured as Jack Grew began to climb the steps to the stage. Harte had already pulled Everett's pocket watch out to check it again, but as he was opening it, Esta felt a cool energy course through the air.

"Did you feel that?"

Harte's eyes had gone a little wide as he stepped even farther away from her. "I did. And so did Seshat."

OUT OF TIME

1920—Chicago

Deep beneath Harte's skin, between what he was and what he could only ever hope to become, Seshat began to shift and move, awoken by whatever terrible magic had suddenly snaked through the air and drained the Quellant from his blood. The ancient goddess swelled, pushing at the boundary between them as she recognized the threat in their midst.

Thoth.

The sound of the name came to Harte as clearly as if Seshat had been standing right next to him and whispered it directly into his ear. All at once the arena fell away and Harte saw himself standing under a star-scattered sky, and the humid heat of the room turned into the dryness of the desert stretching all around him. A second later, though, the vision was gone. Once again Harte was back in the crowded Chicago arena, standing in the middle of the sweaty, sweltering crowd with Jack Grew holding the stage above.

Jack stepped up to the podium and accepted the cheers that greeted him. He let the crowd's applause grow and basked in their approval for a long while, before finally lifting his arms to quiet the crowd. After the arena went silent, he stepped closer to the podium and began to speak.

"Our convention occurs at a moment of crisis for our nation," Jack said, his familiar voice echoing through the cavernous room. "The recent attacks on this fine city—on this hallowed convention—are yet more evidence of the threats to our great nation's very way of life. There has been much talk about our party's chosen platform, our moral obligation to place our nation before the needs of an Old World, torn by a war that was not our creation. But the threat to our well-being lies not only outside our borders. As the events of last night showed us, the threat is already within our borders. It waits within our cities and towns, and any politician who does not grasp this danger is not fit to lead."

Much of the crowd roared again, and Jack accepted their approval, his chin tilted up to take it all in as a satisfied smile crept across his lips.

"Anything?" Esta asked.

Harte checked the watch and found nothing but the steady ticking progress of the second hand. "Not yet," he told her.

"They should be done by now," she murmured, echoing his own thoughts.

"We can't worry about that right now," Harte told her. If North and his look-alike son had abandoned them, it was too late to worry about it. If they were in trouble? "We need the Book. That's what we're here for."

Seshat chose that moment to lurch, and Harte couldn't stop himself from grimacing at the feel of her power beginning to grow.

"Seshat?" Esta asked, frowning.

He nodded.

Jack had started to speak again, his voice clear and his words painfully direct. "Those with feral magic are a blight on our great land. A disease that threatens the very fiber of our nation. For too long they have freely roamed our streets, threatening peaceful citizens. And now the opposition party would have us prostrate ourselves to foreign powers? The Democrats would have us join a so-called League of Nations and open our coffers to rebuild *other* lands, with no regard for the impact on public safety or the resources of our own great nation. Those are resources meant for the protection of our *own* people. Those are resources that should be used to fight the threat that already exists among us.

"Lenroot does not understand this threat. Allen does not understand this threat, and Coolidge *certainly* does not understand it. *None* of the other men who would ask for your vote understand the true danger. None have worked tirelessly to address the feral power that would have us kneel before it, that would destroy our very way of life . . . But *I* have."

As Jack droned on about his many accomplishments, it was clear where the other candidates' supporters were. The delegates from states that had not yet decided to throw their support behind Jack's candidacy sat quietly listening, barely clapping even at his more vociferous points, but the longer he spoke, the more delegates there were that began applauding.

"We all know the tragedy that befell this very convention hours ago," Jack said, his voice going low and sorrowful. "We have seen too many times the death and destruction that illegal power can generate. Too often, innocents have fallen victim to its terrible truth. But where is the other party's response to such a devastating attack? Where is Coolidge's?" Jack paused while the crowd shouted and booed. "You're right. They remain silent. They do *nothing*."

The crowd roared again, a mixture of anger and hissing disapproval for the other candidates' platforms and actions.

"And what has been done about those who perpetrated such a terrible crime upon the innocent? Upon the *just*? *Nothing.* They've been allowed to crawl back into the shadows, hidden and protected by those who would ask for your votes. Tonight, those with illegal, unregistered magic sleep soundly in their beds, unworried about their future, while the families of the fine men killed last night mourn and this city cowers in fear. Among our candidates, who will stand for those good, true Americans who want only to preserve our way of life?" He paused, letting the crowd swell. "*I* will. This is my promise. And I will make good on that promise this very night."

The crowd erupted again, some cheering while other sections rumbled with confused shouts, but it was clear that Jack had them in the palm of his hand.

Esta leaned her head toward Harte a little. "We're out of time. Are you sure there's no sign yet?"

He checked the watch again, but . . . *nothing*. It only read the time: nearly half past eight. He couldn't help but wonder if the world would make it to nine before everything changed.

Once, Harte had stopped Esta from killing Jack. He had believed that the benefit would not outweigh the price she would pay for the weight of Jack's life on her soul. But with all he'd gone through, all he knew about what was to come, Harte thought that it was possible he'd been wrong. For the right cause, perhaps it might even be worth the price.

You would kill the one but leave the rest? Seshat's voice curled in his mind again. *Look at them, so eager for blood to be spilled. So eager to prove themselves more powerful than they should ever hope to be. They are no better than Thoth. Yet you would absolve their sins? Why? With the girl, we could punish them all and rebuild the world anew.*

Harte watched the crowd, the anger in their faces. The righteousness in their expressions—and the excitement. They were like a pack of dogs drawn to an injured animal, ready to attack. He could not deny the truth of what Seshat said. . . . But he pushed away the temptation of her words.

"You would kill them all for the sake of the one who betrayed you," Harte said softly, speaking directly to Seshat.

"What?" Esta asked, turning to him, but Harte's focus was on Seshat, and especially on her power roiling and swelling within him.

They deserve *to be destroyed,* Seshat responded. *Their hearts are rot and ash, unworthy of the wonders this world could be if magic lived free once more.*

"It wasn't the world that betrayed you," Harte said.

Was it not?

"It was only one man," Harte argued. "A weak man, at that."

"Harte?" Esta's voice broke through the fog that Seshat's presence had created, and he realized that he'd been speaking aloud. She was trying to tell him something. "We have to go. *Now.* It's our only chance."

Seshat purred her encouragement, but Harte pressed her back, fighting against her power and the pull of her temptation.

"The second you use your affinity, every person wearing one of Jack's medallions will know what's happening," Harte argued. "And we don't have any idea if the machine is disabled."

"If I use my affinity, no one will be able to catch us. We can slip in, get the Book, and be gone in a blink, before they even know what's happening."

But Harte could feel Seshat prowling inside of him, ready to pounce. "I can't go with you."

Esta glared at him. "We've been through this."

"The Quellant is gone. We can't risk what Seshat might do." Esta was shaking her head, opening her mouth to argue, as she usually did, so Harte softened his voice. "If you're right, if everything goes well, you'll be back before I can even blink."

"No, Harte . . ."

"I'll be right here," he promised. "I'm not going anywhere."

Jack was still droning on, but above them the ceiling of the arena was moving, the large panels drawing back as the mechanism moving them groaned and creaked. The crowd was entranced as the night sky appeared above them, and topping the roof was the tower. It was capped with a small platform, but there was no sign of North or Everett, no sign that the job they'd been sent to do had been done.

"You have to go," Harte urged. "Jack has the Book, Esta. He's right *there*, and it's ripe for the picking. If we don't take it now, we might never have another chance."

She looked like she wanted to argue.

"We need the Ars Arcana, Esta. It's our best chance of finding a way to stop Seshat without destroying you."

Something in Esta's expression eased a little.

"You have to go. *Now.* And remember, if something goes wrong—if it's between getting the Book or coming back for me—you have to *keep* going."

"I am *not* leaving you behind." Esta lifted her chin and pressed her mouth against his. Her lips were firm, but Harte could feel her trembling, and in that moment it didn't take Esta's affinity to make time stand still, only the feel of her lips, warm and sweet and *his*.

Suddenly they were standing in a star-swept desert, the heat of the night brushing against them as a different heat built within. He heard a woman's laugh, low and throaty, and he pulled away, gasping. Suddenly it wasn't Esta in his arms, but another woman, one with hair braided like snakes, eyes ringed dark with kohl, and a hint of madness in her expression.

Then, all at once, the desert fell away and Esta was there, her eyes wide and her cheeks flushed. "I heard Seshat," she whispered. "Just now. I felt her." She shuddered.

"We need the Book, Esta." He grimaced as Seshat pressed against the boundary between them. "Go," he told her as the ceiling above came to a grinding halt.

Finally, she nodded. Fear was stark in her eyes as she pulled away from him, and Harte had to clench his hands into fists at his sides to keep from reaching for her. But he'd barely blinked, and Esta was gone.

BRITTLE BONES

1920—Chicago

Time hung still and silent around Esta, and she hardly felt the tug of the Aether as she allowed herself a moment to look at Harte. Every emotion—surprise and desire and *fear*—were all mixed together in his storm-colored eyes. The memory of his kiss was still on her lips, but the echo of Seshat's laughter rang in her ears.

Harte was right to urge her to do this without him. Esta knew that, and yet stepping away from him felt wrong. There was a part of her that worried that if she turned away now, he'd be gone. But she knew that fear was nothing more than the ghostly pain of a wound that had long since healed. Harte wasn't going anywhere. He wouldn't leave her behind again.

All around her, the arena had paused in a sultry silence, swamped with the humid heat of the summer night and caught in the net of her affinity. How long had Esta been nervous each time she'd reached for the seconds? Probably ever since they'd blown up a train leaving New York. Now, though, she felt the strength of her power, felt the way that Aether connected time and space, ordered the world.

I could tear this all apart.

The thought came to her stark and pure and clear. *If North and Everett failed . . . If the machine goes off, so many people will die. And no one here would mourn the loss.* Esta felt all of the hate and all of the fear, thick as the summer's heat that surrounded her. If North and Everett had not succeeded, she could bring down this entire arena to destroy the tower and the machine it held. And if it also destroyed the thousands of people who cheered on the destruction of innocents? *So be it.* She could eliminate the threat of Jack Grew once and for all. Esta felt the temptation stirring within her, felt herself pulling the strands of time a little more. . . .

She stopped, suddenly appalled at the direction of her thoughts. She was shaken by how tempting they had been, even though she didn't know where those thoughts had come from. Destroying the Coliseum wouldn't help. She *knew* that. Tearing this place in two might stop the machine, but it wouldn't stop the hate.

Esta realized she was hesitating, which was something she'd been doing too much of recently. Or maybe it was an improvement, since her impulsiveness had caused her so many problems before. But the memory of Denver was still fresh. Somehow, Thoth was not bound by her affinity, and Esta knew that what she was about to attempt might not be easy. But she would not fail again. This time she would be ready. She took one last look at Harte, and then she began moving toward the stage, where Jack Grew waited beneath the night sky.

When Esta finally made it to the center of the arena, she climbed the steps to the stage, careful to sense any possible disturbances in the Aether. Ready for whatever might happen.

Jack stood before her with his hand raised and his mouth open, caught in the middle of his ranting. Esta hadn't seen him since Denver. It had been only a matter of weeks for her, but for Jack it had been much, much longer. The years hadn't been kind to him. He looked even older now than the very first time she'd encountered him, back in Schwab's mansion in New York. His already-soft face now sagged with age, and his skin gleamed with sweat, pink and sallow all at once. If he'd ever been an attractive man, the years—and the drinking—had stolen his looks as deftly as any thief. Jack's eyes were the same, though. Watery blue, they still burned with righteousness and hatred, and looking at him, Esta knew that she would not be sorry for whatever happened to him tonight— whatever she had to do.

She took one final look around the room to see the world as Jack saw it. Patriotic bunting decorated the balconies and draped from rafters overhead, men wore boaters trimmed with red, and the crowd was entirely focused on the stage, so many of them with a feverish look in their eyes. *Because they believe in this.* Because their own lives were so narrow and pinched and *fearful* that Jack Grew was enough to represent a hope for something more—or at least, something different.

Slowly, Esta inched closer to Jack. His raised arm made what she had to do even easier, not that she really needed the assistance. She'd been lifting wallets and diamonds for as long as she could remember, and dipping her fingers into the concealed pocket within Jack's coat felt as natural as breathing to her.

The Ars Arcana was there, waiting for her, like she knew it would be. Her finger brushed against the crackled leather, and she swore that she felt a light frisson of energy, warm and cold mixed together. This time she would not lose it. This time there was no chance of her being pulled into the darkness of the void, not while the cuff was on her arm, ready and waiting.

Carefully, her fingers gripped the Book, and she started to pull. Little by little, inching it out from where it had been concealed, waiting for something to happen. Nothing did. When the Book was nearly free, she reached for it with her other hand, to steady the weighty mass of it.

Suddenly Jack's hand latched onto her wrist like an iron manacle, just like before. This time, though, Esta wasn't surprised, not like she'd been back in Denver. She acted immediately, using all of her weight and strength to wrench herself free. But it was impossible. Jack was so much stronger than he'd been before. No matter how she twisted or writhed, Esta couldn't break his grip. It was like wrestling with a marble statue, cold and completely unyielding. *Unnatural.* But she still had the Ars Arcana gripped tightly in her hand, and she vowed to herself that only death's fingers would pry it free.

The room was still frozen in time as Jack jerked Esta back to him, and when he opened his mouth, it was not Jack's voice she heard.

"Where is she?" Jack asked in a voice that reminded Esta of brittle bones and broken stone. He shook her, his strength impossible. "I know she's here. I can sense her power." His nostrils flared like he was scenting the air. "Seshat . . ." The name came out like a whispering hiss, long and soft, but the sound of it was like nails on glass to Esta. Then Jack turned on her, his eyes bleeding into blackness as the pupils grew and obliterated the watery blue, and the world slammed back into motion around her.

UNEXPECTED

1902—New York

Cela listened to the alarm bells bouncing off the sides of the city's building as the sun traveled toward the horizon. Soon it would set, and New Jersey would begin to grow dark with the first minutes of twilight. The evening creep would find its way to Manhattan's streets, and she would know—one way or the other—if their plan had worked.

After Cela packed up the spyglass and made sure there wasn't any evidence of her being up on that rooftop, she took one last look at the towering building to the east. It was something to see, even from that distance. The world was an impossible place sometimes—hate and love, science and magic, all wrapped up into one. It changed so fast, often in the blink of an eye, and yet . . . some things never changed at all.

She took the steps down to the street quickly. She'd be glad to have her feet on solid earth, where feet belonged, but when she came through the stairwell door into the bar that occupied the bottom floor of the building, the saloon was empty except for two men. It didn't take a genius to look at their broad, flat foreheads and swarthy skin to know that the Italians hadn't shown up at this particular bar for a random drink. Even if they hadn't reached for their guns as soon as she came through the door, Cela would've known they were Paul Kelly's men.

At first she thought maybe she could pretend she didn't understand why they were there, but she hadn't taken more than two steps before they closed ranks.

"Why don't you go ahead and have a seat?" the one said, kicking a chair so it slid across the floor in her direction.

She glanced up at the bartender, a West Indian man who was polishing a glass and who glanced away as soon as their eyes met.

No help at all.

It was clear—he didn't want any trouble, and she didn't blame him, exactly. Businesses like this depended on their owners making nice with all types. He didn't know her and didn't owe her a thing.

Straightening her spine, Cela faced the two Five Pointers. "Is there something you gentlemen needed?" she asked, pretending innocence.

The one with the scar across his eyebrow smirked. "Sit."

Reluctantly, she took the chair and did what he said. They'd expected problems, she told herself, but for the Five Pointers to have come after her so soon likely meant that something had gone very wrong.

Cela had known this would be a possibility the second she'd realized the Order had sent three ships instead of one, but she trusted Jianyu and Viola. She only had to wait this out, and they would come through for her. She *had* to believe that.

It wasn't like she had much choice.

A few minutes later, things got even worse when Abel was pushed through the door of the saloon by another pair of Five Pointers. He should've been clear on the other side of town, so the fact that he was there made Cela's stomach sink. It meant that things were worse than bad. It meant that things might even be beyond fixing.

She stood to go to Abel, but the one with the scar—and a gun—stepped between them. "Save the reunions for later," he said, waving his sidearm to instruct two of the others to lead Abel to a chair across the way.

"You okay, Rabbit?" Abel asked. "They didn't touch you?"

"I'm fine," she told him, which was a flat-out lie. There wasn't anything at all fine about this situation.

The minutes dragged on, one after another, until the city was shaded by night and the streetlights came on. The saloon was filled with the kind of uneasy silence that you find in funeral homes or hospital waiting rooms, where the news coming is sure to be bad.

"Johnny should've sent someone by now," one of the men said, his flat Bowery accent twisting the words.

"You know what he told us, Razor. These things take time. We're supposed to sit tight until we hear—no matter how long that takes."

The one called Razor—like that was any kind of name—thumbed at his nose. "I don't like it. If Paul finds out—"

"Paul ain't gonna find nothing out," the other guy said. "He got picked up earlier by the coppers. Saw it myself. He was all trussed up and carried off in a police wagon. The way I see it, he'll be in the Tombs for weeks. That is, if they don't transport him to Blackwell's Island for a longer stay."

Abel caught Cela's eyes from across the open space. Paul Kelly arrested? That answered one question but raised others—including why they were being held here by Kelly's men, especially if Kelly himself wasn't calling the shots anymore.

The doors of the saloon flew open, and a large, boisterous group of men burst through the door. They were clearly day laborers, probably from the docks nearby, and they'd clearly already been drinking. There were a couple of Negro men in their number, but Cela didn't recognize them.

Kelly's guys were on their feet in an instant, but the newcomers were already at the bar and causing all sorts of commotion. Out of nowhere, someone threw a punch, and their drunken noise transformed to an impromptu brawl. The barroom was suddenly a mess of confusion. Men were everywhere, wrestling and shoving one another, knocking over tables and chairs. There was nothing Kelly's guys could do but back up and try not to get caught up in it.

Abel was at Cela's side in a second. "You okay?"

"I told you I was," she said, flinching at the sound of a glass breaking. She glanced at Razor, but he was stuck behind a trio of men who were tussling in the corner.

"You all about ready to go?"

Cela looked up and realized it was Joshua standing there. "What—"

"Quick, now, before they realize," Joshua said.

Together they picked their way through the chaos. They were nearly at the door . . . and then they were there, and all they had to do was open it, and—

When the door swung open, another Five Pointer was there. He wasn't overly tall, but he had shoulders like a brick wall, and he had a gun pointed in their direction.

Abel started to step forward, but Cela caught his arm. She wasn't about to lose her only brother like that. From behind, she sensed movement, and when she turned, Razor and the other man were there, boxing them in.

"Where do you think you're going?" the guy at the door said with a smirk.

Her brother gave Joshua a look that Cela didn't like one bit. "Abel Johnson," she whispered. "Don't you do anything stupid."

"You should listen to the girl," the Five Pointer with the gun said, but the words were barely out of his mouth when his whole body jerked. He barked out a surprised yelp as his eyes went wide, and then he lunged for them.

Except he wasn't lunging . . . he was *falling*. A second later, he was laid out, face-first, on the ground, with a knife sticking out of his back. The too-familiar silver handle glinted in the light spilling out of the saloon's open door, and in the street beyond, Viola was there, looking ready for murder.

From behind her, Cela heard a strangled gasping noise, and when she turned, she saw the Five Pointers' faces contorted with pain. Razor crumpled to the floor, lifeless, and a second later, his friend followed.

Viola was already pulling her knife from the dead man's back. "Hurry," she told them, her eyes scanning for other dangers.

Cela didn't fight her brother when he grabbed her by the wrist and dragged her out into the night, with Joshua close behind. Her mind was still reeling. Outside, they picked up their pace, keeping to the shadows in case anyone else was watching. When they were a few blocks away from the saloon and it was clear that they hadn't been followed, they finally slowed to a stop.

"Thanks for the help," Abel said, taking Joshua by the hand and then pulling him in for a rough, brotherly embrace. "I hope the guys won't be in too much trouble for it."

"Seymour's gonna have a bill for you if they bust up too much of his stuff, but it'll be okay," Joshua assured Abel. "Another few minutes and they'll break it up."

"I don't understand," Cela said, looking between the two of them. "You planned this?"

"Not specifically," Joshua told her, glancing at Abel. "And it's not like I did all that much. We all would've been in hot water, if not for your friend there."

Cela followed Joshua's gaze to where Viola stood, her shoulders hunched and her usual defenses clearly in place. She looked away when Cela met her eyes.

"You said you didn't want to help," she said to Joshua, still not understanding. "No one wanted to help."

Joshua shrugged. "I didn't. I'm still not willing to get mixed up with any sort of magic, but you didn't really expect I'd leave my man here hanging, did you?"

Her brother was looking too smug for his own good.

"I didn't—" Cela didn't know what to say. "Thank you," she finished finally. It was all that seemed appropriate, and still it wasn't nearly enough.

"Come on, Rabbit," Abel said, once Joshua had gone off on his own way. "We need to get going. It's not going to take too long before Kelly's boys realize what happened."

Cela looked to Viola. The Italian girl had been standing apart from them, and now her arms were wrapped around herself, like she'd caught a chill despite the warm summer air. There was a lot that needed to be said, but Cela wasn't sure where to start, so she settled for the thing that seemed most important. "Thank you," she said softly, stepping closer to Viola. "We owe you our lives."

Viola's cheeks flushed, and she looked away. "It was nothing."

"That's not at all true," Cela said, laying a hand on Viola's arm. Jianyu had told her a little about how Viola felt using her affinity to kill. She had some sense of what the choice to take out the Five Pointers might have cost her. "You kept my brother safe. You came back for us. If you hadn't, we'd probably be dead."

Viola looked up finally. "I made a promise to you before."

Cela paused, remembering that night . . . the conversation they'd had in the darkened doorway of Mr. Fortune's house. Then, she hadn't been ready to give an inch, not after how ugly Viola had acted. Now? She wasn't sure what to think or where this put them, but she had the sense that they were somewhere new. "Thank you for keeping that promise." She let her hand fall away. "Where's Jianyu?"

"He'll come soon," Viola told Cela, but then her gaze rose.

When Cela turned, she could see the Flatiron Building rising above the city, slicing into the twilight sky.

She was about to turn back to Viola when she saw it—a man falling from the topmost point. He was no more than a speck plummeting to the ground, his arms spread like a bird's, as if he were about to take flight.

RIOTOUS FURY

1920—Chicago

The Chicago Coliseum had become a riot of noise and confusion. Harte had barely blinked, and suddenly Esta had appeared on the stage in the center of the room. She was holding the Book in her hand, but Jack Grew had her by the wrist. Seshat railed at the sight, but Harte barely noticed. All he was focused on was the way Jack was gripping Esta's arm and the fact that she hadn't already been able to wrestle away from him. Jack held on tightly to Esta despite her writhing, and within seconds he'd taken the Ars Arcana from her and shoved it back inside his jacket.

The Book hardly seemed to matter anymore, though, not when Harte saw the fear that was stark in Esta's expression. For once he understood Seshat's point. At that instant, he would have gladly destroyed everything just for the opportunity to kill the bastard.

Harte was already pushing his way through the riotous crowd to get to Esta when he felt another blast of cold energy shuttle through the room. Suddenly the doors to the arena clanged shut, and as the cold settled over him, Harte realized that he couldn't move. Struggle as he might, he could not take even one more step toward Esta. He was trapped in the eerie unnatural energy, locked in place and powerless.

"Help me," Harte said to Seshat, not caring who heard him. "If I can get to Jack, I will destroy Thoth."

I remember too well what happened the last time you made that promise. I gave you every chance, and you wasted it on an urchin.

This is different.

Is it? Seshat mused. *You had a chance already to kill him, or don't you remember? In the train station, weeks ago, the girl would have ended him. You stopped her then. Why should I trust you now? Why should I risk everything I am—everything the old magic could ever be—when you've allowed weakness to rule your actions again and again?*

It wasn't weakness to save my brother, and it wasn't weakness to spare Esta the horror of taking a life, Harte argued.

No?

No. *This time is different,* Harte promised. *This time, I will kill him with my own two hands.*

You have no chance, Seshat told him, her voice hollow. *Maybe before, you could have fought him. Perhaps you could have destroyed him years ago, when you stopped the girl from taking his life. Perhaps then . . . But now? Look around. Thoth has had far too long to reveal the secrets of the Book to the body that carries him. You should have let me have the girl. I would have ended Thoth and all of the hatred he has inspired before his power could grow. Look at what he has become. Look* what your weakness has done.

Harte did look—the entire hall was in an uproar. Those who had been sitting without making any judgment were now on their feet with the rest. Confusion swirled in the air, and stirring it was fear and hatred so thick that Harte could practically taste it, bitter on his tongue.

"So you're giving up?" he demanded. "You would let Thoth win?"

Seshat was silent, and Harte had the sense that she was waiting for something. But he couldn't understand her hesitation, not now when the danger—and the opportunity—were so clear.

Jack ignored the noise of the crowd and stepped to the microphone, dragging Esta along with him. His hand still locked around her wrist, he shouted, "As above!"

There were those in the crowd who answered, "So below!"

He shouted the phrase again and again, and each time he did so, Harte felt the cold energy swirl. Each time, more of the crowd answered back, until the discontent and confusion joined into a unified whole. "So below," the crowd responded. "So below."

"You need not fear feral magic," Jack thundered when he finally had most of the crowd on his side. "Not here in this place. Not when *I* stand before you." Esta was still struggling to get free, but Jack jerked her toward him and then took her by the chin with his free hand. "Do you recognize this woman?"

The crowd rustled and rumbled, until a cry split the steady noise. "The Thief! He has the Devil's Thief!"

"Impossible!" came shouts from delegates around the room.

"Not impossible," Jack crooned into the microphone. "Not when feral magic runs in her veins. Look at her! She appears to be nothing more than a girl, but many of you remember too well the terror she once inspired in the dark days before the Brotherhoods were united—before *I* worked to unite them. Look at her!" he shouted again, and Harte could hear the mania in his voice. "Look at how her face remains ageless. *Unnatural.* It is a mark against the very laws of nature and the known universe."

The crowd roared again. Jack had brought more of them under his thrall. With the cold energy radiating through the arena, its icy tendrils cutting through the sultry air, Harte wondered if Jack had actually put them under some spell. All around him, the medallions that had been distributed by the Brotherhoods were glowing a cold bright blue. Harte pulled the pair of medallions out of his own pocket and saw that they were also aglow, their eerie light caught like lightning in the palm of his hand.

On the stage, Jack had released Esta's throat so he could raise his hand to quiet the crowd. "But this abomination is not the only danger here tonight," he murmured. "There are others among us, others who refused the protection the Brotherhoods offered today. They pretend to be with us, pretend to have the care of our great nation in their hearts, but in truth they are enemies." Jack paused, his mouth curving with delight as the crowd began turning and searching for the traitors in their midst.

Then suddenly cold energy crackled around Harte, and all sound

LISA MAXWELL

drained from the room. It was like being caught in time with Esta, only no one was frozen. All around him, the people rioted, but Harte could hear only a single voice that carried to him over the silence.

"I know you're here, Darrigan," Jack said, his voice amplified without the help of any electronic augmentation. "You can end all of this if you'd only come forward."

All around Harte, people pointed and faces contorted with suspicion as men and women searched for those without the Brotherhoods' medallions. They called them out and began to pull them from their seats.

"Give yourself up," Jack said as he scanned the room from the safety of the stage. "Do you know how simple it would be for me to kill her right now? I could twist her delicate neck as easily as a bird's." His hand moved back to Esta's throat, but he didn't yet squeeze. "Maybe that's too easy, though. After all this time, I deserve more for my effort, don't you think?"

Harte's vision flickered then, and the sky began to fall through the opening in the ceiling. Stars tumbled into the arena, filling the entire space and transforming the world around Harte into a desert night. Suddenly Jack was a different man, one with his head shaved clean and his broad shoulders draped with white linen.

Seshat raged at the sight of Thoth, but Harte now sensed something more than fury—he felt her fear as well. She wanted to destroy Thoth, but she was *afraid* of him too. Harte realized then that it wasn't any spell of Jack's that was holding him in place. It was Seshat's doing.

She was *terrified*, and hers was a fear thick and cold enough to make Harte shudder.

As quickly as the vision appeared, the desert drained away, leaving simply Jack on the stage. "It will be such a joy to watch the power be stripped from her," he said. "I wonder what it will feel like when it happens. I wonder if I'll sense her suffering or only the thrill of what she gives me." Jack paused, searching the room again for Harte. "But it doesn't have to be this way. You *know* that Esta is not the one I want, Darrigan. You, on the other hand . . . I would gladly let her go free for the pleasure of watching *you* suffer as I destroy the evil inside of you. Bring me Seshat, and I'll let your precious little thief go. You can save her. But only if you show yourself."

Harte knew it was a lie. But even if he'd wanted to hand himself over, his feet were glued in place and his head was filled with the riotous fury of the angry goddess.

"Suit yourself," Jack murmured. "Seshat . . ." This time it was not Jack's voice, but a voice far more ancient and terrible that echoed through Harte's mind. "You think to escape my power?" Jack laughed, a cackling that sounded like the cracking of dry bones. "The boy cannot save you now. When my tower comes alive, you will have nowhere to hide. One way or another, before this night ends, your power will finally be mine."

The energy in the room crackled again, and suddenly the noise of the crowd returned. But Jack was lifting his arm to silence them. "There is no need to fear those who hide among us," he told the crowd. "Not any longer. Those who have attacked our city, those here in our noble ranks pretending goodwill when only evil lurks within their dark hearts, cannot escape our notice any longer. It begins here, with the final defeat of the Thief. Tonight, when we protect our cities and our people from the threat of feral magic once and for all."

The crowd was cheering, screaming its frenzied assent. They were with Jack now in the way only a crowd can be with someone—pushed on by an inertia impossible to harness or control.

"Years ago, we set about to protect our way of life. The tower in California demonstrated what might be done with enough fortitude, but Roosevelt bowed to the weakness of his party. Our own party will not bow. We *will* have our justice for those innocents brought low by the terrible danger of feral magic. Innocents like our brothers who were slain last evening." He ripped back a drape from what had appeared to be a table on the stage and revealed a lever-like mechanism. "And we will have our justice *now*."

The electricity that ran through the crowd had nothing to do with

LISA MAXWELL

magic. It was a miasma of hate and anticipation, righteousness and cowardice churning as one.

"The other candidates have not answered the question of how they will bring the illegal magic to heel once and for all, but I will answer that question for myself. *Tonight.* With your support, we will put an end to the danger feral magic presents to Chicago once and for all." Jack paused as the crowd cheered wildly, and then he leaned close to the microphone. "Are you with me?" he shouted. "Shall we put into action the promise of the great men who came before us?"

He had most of the room on his side as he held his hand to his ear, urging their cheers to grow, but not all. There were those who looked unsure. Others were already moving toward the still-locked doors. Either they didn't want to be part of this moment or they were afraid for their own lives.

It wasn't a surprise. Harte knew too well that there would always be those who would choose to side with the Order and the Brotherhoods even if the old magic flowed within them. But the illusion of safety was only that—an illusion—and as people reached the doors, they found them locked and guarded. Impassable.

Harte wanted to check the watch, but he couldn't move. He was frozen as solidly as if Esta had trapped him in time. Seshat held him still as she raged within him, pressing at the walls.

I can stop this, Harte begged her, fighting against her with all of the strength he had. *Let me go, and I'll kill Jack here and now. I will end Jack's life and Thoth's with him.*

Seshat remained silently pacing beneath his skin.

You know *what that tower is capable of,* Harte pressed. *You've seen my memories, and you've seen my fears. If Jack activates his machine, Thoth will win. He will take everything you are, everything you ever hoped to be, and you will be powerless against his control. Unless you let me go. It's our only chance. It's* your *only chance.*

The voice inside of him wailed, but suddenly Harte found that he could move. With his legs under his control once more, he sprinted toward the stage, shoving aside anyone he had to in order to reach Esta before Jack threw the lever. He was nearly to the steps of the stage—

"Tonight, it ends," Jack shouted, and Harte understood that he would be too late.

Before he could even reach the edge of the arena's floor, Jack pressed the lever, and the tower above began to crackle to life.

The crowd surged to their feet, stomping and whistling, and Jack's face was glowing with satisfaction. The lights in the arena hummed and flickered as the machine at the tower's apex started to glow.

CAUGHT BETWEEN

1920—Chicago

If North could have dragged Everett away from the mess of the convention, he would have. He would've risked most anything—drugging Everett into submission, tying him up, carrying him back to his mother . . . *anything.* He would have even risked Everett's hatred if he could have been sure that the boy would be safe. But North had been around a long time. He'd seen power come and go, and the one thing he'd learned through it all was that there were no guarantees of safety in this life, not when a meddling thief could slip back through time and unwind your whole existence in the blink of an eye.

In the last sixteen years, North had learned that all he could depend on was the present as it stood in front of him, in all its beauty and all its terror. The past and the future were nothing but stories people told themselves to feel like they had some control over their lives. So when he thought about taking away Everett's free will, even though he had the means, North found that he couldn't bring himself to do it. His boy had stood there with his shoulders back and asked North to treat him like the man he was becoming, and it would have been the gravest betrayal of that trust for North to do anything but agree.

Which is how North came to be standing on the roof of the Coliseum and discovering for maybe the first time exactly how much he hated being up high. Everett had taken to it like one of those little trained monkeys he'd seen once when the circus had come through Kansas City.

It was like the boy didn't realize how easy it would be to fall or how fragile his body actually was.

It took a lot longer to gain access to the roof than they'd been planning, even with the combination of Maggie's formulations and Everett's gadgets that they had on hand. They were running behind schedule, and by the time they made it up to the roof, the ceiling of the arena had already been drawn back. Above, the sky had turned dark, and all around them, as far as he could see, the city was lit up for the evening, like a million stars had fallen down from the heavens just for this occasion. North felt a sudden ache looking at it all, a yearning for his little house out on the lonesome prairie—for his wife and his children, too—all hundreds of miles away. There the sky was always spangled with stardust thick as milkweed in December.

"Ready?" Everett asked when a cheer erupted from the people assembled below. He looked up at the steel-framed structure that loomed over them, stretching stories into the night. He adjusted his pack of tools and other gear on his shoulder.

"Not really," North admitted, but he followed Everett across the roof and to the base of the tower anyway.

He let Everett go first and watched as the boy began to scale the steel frame with a graceful ease. He was about to start climbing himself when something stopped him. He had the oddest sense that he should wait a minute longer . . . and that sense made his skin prickle in warning.

Turning, he scanned the expanse of the rooftop for whatever it was he was waiting for, because he knew well enough to trust that sense he'd been born with. Even with his watch long since ground into trash, North wasn't helpless. The old magic that flowed through him had gotten him out of too many scrapes for him to ignore it now.

It wasn't even two minutes later when the threat appeared, like he'd suspected it would. A man stepped from the shadows wearing a medallion that flashed in the dim light. He was a great big bear of a guy, and he was wearing a long, dark duster jacket that reminded North of the

LISA MAXWELL

uniform worn by the Jefferson Guard years ago in St. Louis.

"You're not supposed to be here," the man said, already reaching for the weapon holstered beneath his long coat like some kind of cowboy from the Old West. But he'd barely had it out when something drew his attention. Instead of aiming the gun at North, he pointed it upward. *Toward Everett.*

North looked up to see that Everett had nearly reached the top of the tower. He was high enough that he was completely unaware of what was happening below, but not out of the range of that gun. His boy had a little farther to go before he would reach the safety of the platform at the top, where he could duck out of the line of fire. And Everett had no idea he was a target.

Without even considering the consequences, North ran for the man, slamming into him as the gun went off. The shot echoed through the nearby buildings. North felt a sharp burning in his side, but he ignored it and used all of his strength to shove the Guard to the ground. Right about when the Guard flipped him onto his back, North realized he was outmanned.

"Pa!" Everett called from above.

North looked up to see Everett starting to descend. "No!" he shouted. "I'll take care of this!"

It was a lie born of hopeful bravado and desperation. The Guard was stronger than he looked, and North doubted that he'd be able to do much more than buy Everett a little time, but if that was all he could do, that was what he would do. "Go on! You're almost—"

His words were cut short by the impact of the man's fist across his face.

North's vision doubled and blurred, but he held on to consciousness even as he tasted blood filling his mouth. North used his weight to shove the Guard off, rolling until they were nearly at the edge of the opening of the roof. Above, Everett was still hesitating, clearly torn and unsure about what to do, but the tower was beginning to crackle to life.

"You gotta go!" he shouted to his son, even as he struggled to keep the Guard from choking the life out of him. "You got once chance before this is all for nothing."

Still, Everett didn't move, and then, to North's horror, he began to descend.

No. If that tower came to life, they were all goners—every single one of them—and everything North had done, everything Everett had risked, would be wasted.

North could feel his body starting to fail him, could feel the years that he'd lived in every aching bone, in every shuddering beat of his heart. And he could feel the pain in his side, sharp and strangely familiar, even though he'd never been shot before. There would be no magic capable of bringing him back, and his death would be pointless if Everett didn't complete the job they'd come to do. No one would be safe if this tower activated—not Everett or Maggie or any of their kids waiting for him back at home. This had to be stopped here and now, and his boy was the only one who could do it.

North ignored the screaming pain in his side and wrenched himself free of the man's fists. It wasn't for long, but it was long enough. After all, he hadn't come so far or taken so many risks to let his son die from indecision—so he'd take the choice from him.

He looked up at Everett. "Give your mother a kiss for me."

North grabbed hold of the Guard and jerked to the right, throwing them both off-balance, and they tumbled through the opening together, falling away from the sound of Everett's screams and into the void of light and noise below.

LISA MAXWELL

FALLING INTO DARKNESS

1920—Chicago

E sta watched the crowd in the arena surge to its feet in response to Jack throwing the lever. They stomped and whistled their encouragement as the lights of the arena flickered overhead. She looked up to see bolts of energy circling around the apex of the tower like strange lightning pulsing in the night sky—a beacon and a warning all at once to anyone within sight of the Coliseum.

Suddenly, two figures were falling through the split in the ceiling, caught in a strange embrace as they plummeted to the ground. At first Esta couldn't understand what she was seeing—a stunt or a dummy? It had to be—but no. They were men. One had red hair—Esta was *sure* she saw red hair. *North,* she thought, her hope falling right along with him. Then the sound of their bodies hitting the ground seemed louder than anything. It was a dull, sickening thud that left the crowd gasping and Esta hollowed out by grief.

For North. For Everett. For them all.

Too late. Too late to run, too late to save themselves unless they stopped this. She *had* to find a way to stop it.

"You don't have to do this, Jack," Esta said, trying to speak to Jack instead of the demon that had possessed him.

Jack turned to Esta, and she saw that the watery blue had pushed aside the black. "Don't I?" he asked, his voice somewhere between Jack and Thoth.

"You can fight him," she pleaded. "Think of the people you're about to kill. Think of what he's turning you into."

There was more blue in his eyes now than black, more of Jack in his voice when he spoke. "That's *exactly* what I'm thinking of," he said, and he pushed the lever even farther, causing the power to surge once more.

In that instant, the darkness swelled again in Jack's eyes as well, overtaking the blue until only a deep blankness looked back at her. "Did you honestly think that anything he's done has been against his will?" Thoth asked, laughing. "I forced nothing upon him."

"You turned him into a monster," Esta said, still trying to pull away. If she could only reach the lever . . .

"You're telling yourself stories, girl. He dreamed of a machine that could create beautiful chaos—one that could destroy those who taunted him with their power—long before my servant in Greece found him. I didn't create his hatred or his fear. I simply used them to my advantage. They provided me an entrance to his mind and a willing body to bring my vision to light, and in return I bestowed upon him the power to make every one of his dreams come true."

A scream from the crowd suddenly tore through the room, punctuating Thoth's words. Jack threw his head back and laughed as another scream split through the noise of the hall, and another. "You thought you could defeat me?" Thoth laughed at her. "You thought you could escape me, and instead you ran straight into my arms. And now it's too late. There is no escape for you now. I will have your power—your life—at my disposal." The tower was glowing and crackling with energy above them. "And then I will take Seshat's power as well, and with it I will finally be able to control the beating heart of magic. I will become *infinite*."

He was right. Thoth, Jack, it didn't matter who was speaking to her now. It was too late to run, too late to stop the bright bolts of light streaming from the tip of the tower, searing like lightning into the night sky. But as the panic grew in the arena around her, Esta didn't feel the cold power she'd expected to come over her. Something else was happening instead in the crowd of delegates and spectators.

At first Esta couldn't make sense of what she was seeing, but then she

720   LISA MAXWELL

understood: The medallions the Brotherhoods had given out were starting to burst into flames. It wasn't the old magic that was being affected by the tower but the *corrupted* magic of the Brotherhood, and Esta could not repress her laugh at Everett's cunning. He'd explained to her how they could give the Brotherhoods a taste of their own poison, and his idea had *worked*.

As each medallion burst, the flames began to spread at an incendiary pace, and in a matter of seconds, the arena erupted in pandemonium. Flames from the medallions consumed the coats and shirts and dresses where they'd been pinned, and the people who'd willingly taken them were screaming, tearing their own garments from their bodies to escape.

They did it. The relief flashed through her bright and hot and complete, but it was short-lived. She still needed to get the Book away from Jack—and somewhere caught in the now-riotous crowd was Harte.

Everywhere, people were trying to escape from their burning garments and from the hall itself. The whole crowd was moving almost as one, pushing and climbing over one another as they tried desperately to reach the still-locked doors.

Slowly, Jack—or the thing inside of him—seemed to realize something had gone wrong. When the medallion Jack himself was wearing burst into flames, he released Esta to tear it from his coat. But even once the medallion was gone, smoke still poured from beneath his collar and cuffs. Jack pulled at the buttons of his shirt, tearing it open to reveal rows of strange symbols that glowed like embers on his skin. He seemed to scream more in rage than pain at first, but as he clawed at his skin, the markings only glowed brighter.

Esta was beginning to back away when Jack suddenly went strangely still. His head whipped around to look toward the steps that led up to the stage.

"Seshat," Thoth's voice hissed from Jack's mouth, its weathered rasp as old as time itself, and a serpent's smile crept across his face. His chest was still smoldering, but now Jack did not seem to be feeling the pain of the flames. "I thought you might join us."

The smell of burnt skin and sulfurous smoke was thick in the air as Esta turned to see Harte climbing the steps to the stage, his stormy eyes steady on her.

"No!" she screamed. But Jack had already leapt for Harte. It happened so fast—Jack lunged across the stage, pushing Harte back down the steps, until they were both on the ground, wrestling for control. In a blink, Jack had the advantage. His hands were around Harte's neck, strangling him.

Two of the men who had been onstage with them lunged for Esta, grabbing her by the arms to hold her in place. She twisted, catching one off guard as she kicked out viciously at the other's knee. In a fluid movement born from years of training under Dakari's watchful eye, Esta twisted again and again, meeting the men blow for blow until they were down and she had freed herself.

The men had been easy enough to dispatch, but she'd wasted precious time. Harte was no longer fighting, and Jack was looming over him, with his knee on Harte's chest. The Pharaoh's Heart was in his hand. Jack was already bringing the dagger down, directly toward Harte's chest, when Esta pulled time slow. Without hesitating, she was down the stairs, using all of her weight and all of her strength to knock Jack away from Harte.

Jack fell to the ground. His chest still glowed where the ritual magic he'd tattooed onto his skin continued to smolder, but the dagger clattered away and his coat lay open, revealing the Book. It was so close. Everything they'd fought for was right there, within reach, but Esta's eyes turned to Harte—

She wasn't thinking about Seshat or the danger of touching him when she made her choice. She wasn't thinking about anything other than how his lips had already gone blue, how his eyes already looked glassy and unfocused. She wouldn't lose him. Not now. Not after everything.

She pulled herself up and was at his side in an instant. "Harte," she said, cupping his face with her hands, drawing him into the net of her affinity.

He didn't move, but a shuddering breath was released from his lungs. "Harte, you have to wake up," she said, bringing her face close to his to

LISA MAXWELL

listen. "We have to go." But Harte lay as quiet and unmoving as if he was still frozen in time. He wasn't breathing.

Not knowing what else to do, she placed her mouth over his and filled his lungs with her own breath, but before she could pull back, his hands were on her arms, pinning her in place, and she felt herself falling into darkness.

THE SERPENT'S CURSE

1920—Chicago

Night fell from above, obscuring the confusion around her, and stars swirled around Esta until she found herself standing in an open chamber with stone-carved walls the color of sand. If she focused hard enough, she could almost look through the illusion and see the world as it was—the people still frozen in her hold of time and Jack lying nearby—but only just. And it was *so* difficult to focus beyond the illusion for very long. It was far easier to give in to it.

Above, the sky glimmered with an endless swath of stars, and along the edges of the room, flames climbed from great curved cauldrons of iron. Standing before Esta, a woman with hair coiled like snakes around her face and eyes like obsidian waited. *Seshat.*

"You came to me," Seshat whispered, anticipation thick in her papery voice. "You came to me *again*. As I knew you would."

Esta took a step back. She felt panic climbing inside her as she looked around the room, trying to see through the illusion Seshat had created, to find Harte. Even now he could be dying.

"I didn't come for you," she told Seshat. "I came for *him*."

Seshat reached out for Esta, as though she hadn't heard. "Take my hand, and together we will awaken the *true* heart of power, unleash the possibilities of chaos, and begin again. Together, we can unmake this world—all of its meagerness and hatred—and realize our fate."

Esta shook her head. "I don't want any of that. And neither do you."

"You think you know my heart?" Fires flashed in the depths of

Seshat's eyes as her hand dropped to her side in a fist. Suddenly she looked nearly inhuman in her rage. Esta had seen visions before; she'd seen Seshat in the throes of hope, but now the ancient goddess looked broken and twisted.

"Look what he's done to you," Esta whispered, unable to keep the horror and sorrow from her voice. "Look at what Thoth's made you into—"

"He's done *nothing* to make me. All I am I've claimed for myself."

"No," Esta protested, desperate to reach Harte. "You've *allowed* him to twist you and your plans into something else. You want to take your revenge on Thoth, fine. Take it. Death—worse than death—it's only what he deserves. Jack as well. But the whole world?" Esta's voice broke at the thought of it. She thought of Maggie, who would be waiting for North, not knowing what had happened. She thought of Everett, who'd been willing to risk everything and had lost even more. She thought of Viola and Jianyu—of all the Mageus in the city and across the land who would be destroyed by Seshat's anger. And the Sundren as well—deserving of such a fate or not. They were not hers—or Seshat's—to judge. To *condemn*. "The world doesn't deserve your wrath."

"Does it not? Once I felt as you do now. But can you not hear the cries of the people around you?" Seshat asked, her eyes narrowing. "You must see their hate here in this place, clear as the night above us. Do you not feel their loathing, hot and thick in this room, as they demand your end? And *still* you would save them?" There was a note in her voice, Esta realized. Anger, yes, but also something more. Something that sounded strangely like confusion. Maybe even curiosity. "They would kill you—each and every one of them would gladly take your life if given the chance." There was a question hanging in the air between them.

"Maybe they would," Esta admitted, still trying to sense Harte beneath the nearly impenetrable illusion Seshat had spun. "But this one room isn't the entire world. There are those who would stand by me, those who would give their lives to fight next to me—to protect me. North did. Just tonight he gave himself so others might live. He gave up *everything* for a chance at a different future. If you rip the world apart, his sacrifice was for nothing."

"What do I care of the sacrifice of one *man*?" she sneered.

"Why did you do it, then?" Esta asked, pleading. "I've seen your heart as well. I know that you were trying to save magic. Why do *any* of that if you only meant to tear the world apart in the end?"

"Because I did not understand until it was too late. There *is* no saving magic," Seshat said, her eyes flashing dark and eternal. "I thought to preserve the promise of the old magic through writing. By stabilizing its power, I thought to protect it from time's devouring jaws, but I only succeeded in weakening the old magic further—*faster*—instead. Magic was always destined to die away, but by taking a part of it, I made everything worse. Just as taking the affinity of a Mageus to create an object of power can destroy a person, taking a part of magic's own heart only served to hasten the end of *everything*—chaos and order, magic and reality alike."

"But you made the Book," Esta pressed, refusing to believe that this could be true. "You used your affinity to create an object outside of time to *protect* the beating heart of magic."

Seshat's eyes glinted, and something like sadness—maybe even regret— shadowed her expression. "But it did not work. Because of Thoth, I could not finish what I had started—I could not complete the ritual, could not reinsert the protected piece of magic back into the whole of creation, and those failures left the last piece of pure magic even more vulnerable. To time. To weak and craven souls who would use the power for their own. Maybe long ago, I could have corrected my mistakes. Now it is too late. Now there is only one answer. To preserve magic, we must destroy time. It is the only way."

But destroying time meant destroying reality itself. "Maybe it's magic that should die," Esta realized, her heart clenching at the thought. "Maybe it *should* simply fade away, and the world could keep spinning."

"Do you really think it's so easy?" Seshat scoffed. "You have seen the image of the serpent devouring its own tail. . . ."

"The ouroboros," Esta said. It was the symbol Dolph had taken, and the Antistasi as well.

"*Yes.* It's a representation of *balance*, but such balance comes at a price. It is the serpent's curse to continue on for infinity, devouring itself and holding all that is—and all that is not—in perfect equilibrium. Now it is my burden as well. You see, I disrupted that balance when I created writing, and in doing so, gave time a victory over the power of magic. My actions caused the old magic to die even faster. I created the Book because I thought I could replicate the balance of the ouroboros. I believed that if I took a piece of pure magic outside of time's grasp, then magic *could not* die."

"The Book," Esta realized. "Thoth showed me what it could do, the way it could hold the dagger. He said that the dagger existed and yet didn't all at once—that it was outside of time and reality."

"Yes," Seshat said. "I thought I could hold back time's fanged jaws with the creation of the Book, because I knew even then how essential the old magic was to the very existence of the world. *Everything* in the world—the sun and the stars and *even time itself*—it all begins and ends with magic. I knew that if the old magic dies, time is doomed as well, and the world with it. And it will not be an easy death. It will be a slow and terrible unmaking that will spare no one and nothing."

Esta thought she might understand what Seshat meant. Hadn't she herself felt the horror of being pulled out of time? Of nearly being unmade by time? But what Seshat was describing would be far larger, far more terrible. "But you stopped it by creating the Book. You did preserve that piece of pure magic. Why destroy *everything*, when we could destroy Thoth instead?"

"You still don't understand, do you, child?" Seshat's expression darkened, her eyes shuttered. "My creation of the Book was a mistake. By taking a piece of pure magic, I weakened the whole, and when Thoth stopped me from completing the ritual—when he destroyed the stones I had created to hold my fractured power—he made it impossible for me to return the heart of power to the whole. If I could have completed the ritual, I would have been able to protect magic without destroying time. If I had completed the ritual, time would no longer have had the power to touch magic, and all would have been preserved. Instead, both time and magic are at risk. If Thoth brings that piece of magic back into time's reach, it *will* die . . . and so will the whole. So, too, will time, and it will take the world with it."

It was like the Brink, then—they'd discovered not long ago that it couldn't be destroyed because it contained the affinities of all the Mageus it had killed. Bringing down the Brink would destroy magic itself—and if Seshat's words were true, then it would destroy the world as well. *But maybe it's never been about destroying the Brink.* Maybe they should have been trying to *fix* it instead.

"Do you see now?" Seshat pressed. "It would be a *mercy* to end this world compared to what will happen if time has its way—or if Thoth does. With my power, he would be able to use the beating heart of magic without risking time's wrath. Whatever power he gains over the part, he will have over the whole, and all I have done—all I have sacrificed—will have been for naught." Seshat leaned her face close so that Esta could feel the warmth of her breath, could smell her perfume, a scent like jasmine and old parchment and ancient books. "But if we destroy time . . . per-haps magic can begin again. Perhaps *everything* can begin again."

"There has to be another way, another solution," Esta said. "You can't actually *want* this?"

"I do not deny that I will take joy in Thoth's destruction—and the destruction of this ugly, meager world along with it. But what I *want* hasn't been of any consequence for eons. I will not be sad to give these last pieces of what I am to see this world unmade, and all the terrible souls it contains along with it—especially if it means that Thoth can never prevail."

"If you allow Thoth to make you into a monster, then he's already won." Esta was breathing hard, and her eyes were burning with tears she refused to shed. "He's twisted you into something worse than even himself. Your vengeance must have blinded you or you wouldn't be so willing to give up everything you were meant to be and become nothing more than a pawn to Thoth."

"Your life must be worth very little that you would insult me so," Seshat hissed. In a blink she'd latched onto Esta's already sore wrist. "You came to me. You chose *me*."

Esta could feel herself breaking apart. There was a moment when she considered how easy it would be to give in, to let go and allow Seshat's power to take her—especially if Harte was gone. But she didn't give in. Gathering all the strength she had left, she tore herself away from Seshat.

"No!" Esta snarled.

"You can't win, child," Seshat purred. "I saw your heart, your very soul. You understand what would happen if Thoth controlled my power. You know what he would do with the heart of magic trapped inside the Book. You want this as much as I—"

"No!" Esta roared again, and this time she focused her affinity, reached for the spaces between the seconds, and pulled, only a little, until the illusion began to waver like an earthquake rumbling beneath their feet. "There has to be another way. I will not sacrifice myself for your vengeance. I will fight you every second of every day, until time devours us both." Her chest was heaving, her heart pounding in her ears like a steady tattoo, urging her on. "But give me Harte, and I will tear Thoth from this world. I will *become* your vengeance." Esta struggled to hold her affinity steady, unsure of what Seshat would choose and unsure of what power she really had to stand against the goddess. "Give me Harte," she said again, softer this time. "Give me Harte, and once Thoth is no longer a danger, I will finish what you've started. The world deserves that chance. Give me Harte, and I will do what you could not. I will use what I am to finish what you started and save the old magic from the ravages of time and right the balance between them. I will take on the burden of the serpent's curse. But only for Harte's life. He's the one I came for. He's *always* the one I will come back for. *Not you.*"

Seshat's expression was unreadable as she stared at Esta. Seconds passed—or they could have been minutes or hours, since suddenly time seemed an empty promise. Finally she cocked her head a bit to the side, a painfully human gesture. "I wonder, child," Seshat whispered. "Would he do the same for you?"

Esta believed she knew the answer to that question, but she wasn't foolish enough to play Seshat's games.

"Fine," Seshat said. "But I will hold you to your promise. Destroy Thoth if you can. But if you cannot figure out a way to finish what I began—a way to bring magic and time back into balance—you *will* give yourself over to me. You will fight me no longer. And we will do what we must."

Suddenly the fires went out, and the room went completely dark, the only light coming from the stars above. Seshat sank back into the darkness. And then the illusion of the chamber faded, leaving only the arena—the chaos and smoke and hot fury in the air.

Beneath Esta's hands, Harte gasped, his lungs pulling in air and his eyes fluttering open, the stormy gray of his irises still unfocused.

"Destroy Thoth, as you've promised," Seshat whispered. It sounded like the goddess was there in the flesh. Esta could practically feel Seshat's warm breath close to her ear, but when Esta turned to look, she saw nothing but Jack lying on the floor nearby, his body still smoldering. "Fail and I will not be so merciful again."

"Esta?" Harte's voice rasped when he spoke, and his hands came to the bruised skin of his neck.

"I'm here," she said, her throat closing with an emotion she was not ready to face. And then she released him, leaving him back in the stillness of time.

The arena hung in silence around her as Esta stood, taking a moment to steady herself—to look at Harte, his eyes filled with a heartbreaking softness—and then she walked to where Jack lay on the ground, frozen in time.

Jack's eyes were wide, and his face was contorted in rage. The lapels of his jacket had flopped open, and the top edge of the Book was visibly peeking from its inside pocket. She knew that the second she touched the Book, Thoth would awaken—unless she took care of him first. She needed to act, before Thoth had a chance to understand what was happening. She would have to kill them both before Jack could fight back.

Esta's hands were surprisingly steady as she picked up the dagger from where it had fallen to the floor. Its weight was familiar, and when she held it in her hand, she thought she felt the answering call of the stones in the cuff and the necklace she wore beneath her clothes. But whether the echo of their power was a warning or encouragement, she didn't know. She ignored their warmth against her skin and took the dagger to where Jack lay.

He'd hurt so many, Esta reminded herself, even as her hands shook. Jack had taken life after life, and worse, he'd inspired the hate of so many. He hadn't created that hate—neither had Thoth—but together they had urged it on, given it purchase and light to grow, and because of him, so many had suffered. So many would suffer still.

Jack Grew was a vapid, insecure little man, and his death wouldn't be a loss for the world . . . not really.

It would be worth it—the dark stain she would claim for her own soul—to take his life. To save so many more. It was a weight Esta knew she could carry, one that she would happily bear, just as her father, Dolph, must have borne so many of his own sins. . . . And it didn't matter whether Harte would do the same for her. It did *not*.

Esta lifted the dagger and felt the power of the Pharaoh's Heart coursing through the air as she knelt by Jack, and then, before she could second-guess herself, she brought the dagger down, straight toward his heart.

The tip of the dagger hit bone, but then Esta felt the energy of the Pharaoh's Heart flare, and the dagger sank to the hilt in Jack's chest. Almost immediately, she felt Thoth's power rise up, awful and absolute, as it reached for her. But she held tight to the hilt of the dagger and pushed all of her affinity, all of herself toward Thoth.

She could feel Jack beneath her, but she could also feel something more pulling at the net of time—something less clear and less distinct lurking within him. Esta pushed her affinity toward Jack again, searching for the spaces between where he ended and Thoth began, and when she found the demigod, she used everything she was and everything she would ever be to tear at the shape of Thoth. To rip him from Jack, to tear him from that moment in time, until the darkness in the spaces between the world flooded through him.

A scream echoed from Jack's mouth—part human and part something that might once have been human long ago. As he screamed, a shadowy flood of dark energy poured out of his mouth and began to swarm in weaving tendrils through the room. It came together above them, a thick coil of inky black, and then all at once it burst open into a shower of ash like a terrible firework exploding above.

The power reverberating through the Aether knocked Esta back, and when she hit the floor, she lost her hold on the seconds. The world slammed back into motion, and the noise of the arena assaulted her as she watched the bits of darkness fall, descending onto the people in the arena. When they landed upon her skin, they felt like shards of ice that had the same cold energy and power as the Brink.

Esta brushed them away as she climbed to her feet and lunged for Jack. He was still writhing in agony as she took the Book from the inside of his coat, and when she looked into his eyes, she saw only watery blue. And fear.

She felt no victory as she took the Book from the pocket of his jacket.

He'd hurt so many people, but that didn't seem to matter as she watched him, weak and pathetic, with blood dribbling from the corner of his mouth. His hand was grasping for the knife that now protruded from his chest, but his fingers couldn't seem to take hold of it. Jack looked up at her again, pleading, and Esta felt an overwhelming sense of revulsion as the truth of what she'd done washed over her.

"Please . . ." Jack reached for her, his voice no more than a whisper as his eyes found the Book she held in her hand.

There wasn't time, though. Even if Esta had wanted to help him, police were already on their way through the frenzied crowd, which had finally managed to pry open the arena doors and was pushing to escape. She scrambled to her feet and reached for the hilt of the dagger. There was a sickening feel of bone grinding against metal and the wet suck of blood and muscle as she pulled the dagger from his chest.

The second the blade was free, Jack's arm went limp, falling to the floor next to him. His eyes were open and unseeing, a cloudy blue with no trace of black.

Esta turned back to Harte, who was still trying to right himself. She tried to pull the seconds slow, but her affinity slipped from her fingers as her legs wobbled beneath her. She'd given every bit of her energy to fighting Seshat and destroying Thoth, and now she was too exhausted to hold time for more than a second. Before she could reach Harte, they were surrounded by men in police uniforms, and Esta's arms were being wrenched behind her back.

Unable to do anything with her arms pinned, Esta watched as the men picked Harte up. Then they were moving, her barely able to keep on her feet and Harte half carried by the officers who'd surrounded them. Before the crowd could realize what had happened or could turn on them, they were whisked by the police down the back of the stage and then out through a hidden exit near the side of the arena.

Esta was too exhausted to struggle free of the police officers' hold on her. Instead of fighting, she let herself go limp and allowed them to carry her along. She hoped that she could collect enough strength to escape once they were no longer touching her, but the officers didn't release her as they led her and Harte outside to a waiting police van. Another officer with a face like a knife waited there, rifle at the ready. Deep-green eyes over a sharp nose met hers, and Esta had the oddest sense that she'd seen him before. She probably had, patrolling in the arena.

"Get them in the back," he growled as they approached.

When the van doors opened, Esta saw that Everett was already there, sitting on one of the benches with his head in his hands. Unceremoniously, she was hoisted up and shoved into the van, landing at his feet.

Harte was tossed in next, and immediately he reached for her. As he grabbed her hand, Esta realized that all she felt was the coolness of his skin. *No sign of Seshat.* But even with that knowledge, she still remembered Jack's watery eyes pleading with her, his lips foaming with blood. She'd killed him. Thoth was gone. But she would have to live with the memory of Jack's death—the memory of blade on bone and blood—for however long she had left.

The green-eyed officer jumped into the back with them, and Esta scrambled to her feet. Ready for whatever might come.

"Settle down," the officer ordered as the van doors closed, plunging them all into darkness.

Exhausted and weary as she was, Esta reached for Everett and prepared to slow time, but before she could grasp her affinity, she felt an odd push-pull that reminded her of the chamber they'd used to enter the Nitemarket.

The truck lurched into motion, and Esta stumbled backward, nearly falling. But a pair of arms caught her, and she realized that the darkness of the van was transforming itself. Suddenly, like she had with the entrance to the Nitemarket, she found herself somewhere else entirely.

The police officer who had climbed into the back with them started to laugh. He brushed at the mustache on his upper lip until it seemed to melt into his face. "You should see the looks on your faces," he said, slapping Harte on the back without any heat or malice. "You'd think you'd never seen a simple makeup powder before."

Harte looked too dazed to respond. Esta felt the same.

"What's going on?" she demanded.

The officer pushed his cap back on his head and crossed his leg like he was on some kind of pleasure tour. "I do believe this is what they call a rescue," the officer said.

"Why would you rescue us?" Harte asked, eyeing the officer's uniform. It looked damned authentic with its double row of buttons and the worn brass star on his chest. "You don't even know us."

"Don't I?" the officer asked, staring at Esta now. "I see the tickets I gave you worked."

Esta's mouth fell open a little. "Dom?"

"That isn't really my name, of course," he said. "But I guess it's as good as any of the others, if you need to call me something."

Harte didn't quite understand. "But you were—"

"Old? Fat?" The man dressed in the police uniform—Dom, if he was to be believed—shrugged. "And you dismissed me easily because of it, didn't you?"

"Why would you help us?" Esta asked. She had the sense that Dominic Fusilli never did anything unless he thought he could benefit from it.

"You saved my life," Dom said, rubbing at his chin. "I figured it's only right that I return the favor." When Esta stared at him in clear disbelief, he leveled an unreadable look in her direction. "And you might say I have a vested interest in your mission."

"How could you possibly know what my mission is?" Esta asked, not bothering to hide her suspicion.

"You want to destroy the Order, don't you? Bring down the Brink? Once New York is open and free, I can expand the Nitemarket." He gave her an impish smile. "I figured it was only good business to help you out however I could."

It was an answer, but she didn't think it was the entire answer.

"Are you going to tell us where we're going?" Harte asked.

"Isn't it obvious?" Dom pushed back a sliding panel in the wall of the truck, and warm air streamed through the opening.

Beyond, Esta saw the gleaming lights of an enormous city. Buildings climbed to impossible heights, even more than they had in either Chicago or San Francisco. At first she was too disoriented to recognize where she was, but then Esta saw the soaring stone towers of the Brooklyn Bridge.

ALL THAT MATTERS

1902—New York

When Jianyu came to, alarm bells were still clanging, and he understood exactly what had happened. He should have expected such a betrayal, and even now, with his head aching, he wondered how he had not. He should have suspected something was amiss when the one called Logan—Nibsy Lorcan's newest acquisition—waved him on and allowed him to lead the way up the narrow, winding steps to the Mysterium. He should never have turned his back on the other boy. He understood his mistake the moment Logan had attacked. Jianyu's legs had been taken out from beneath him. Pain had exploded through his head, and his vision had gone black.

From the look of things, he had been dragged behind one of the bookcases, but Jianyu refused to be grateful for the small mercy Logan had shown him. The doorway in the ceiling above had disappeared. In its place was the bronze seal that had been forged to depict a mystical hand. Jianyu had no way to tell whether Logan was still up there—whether he was trapped with the artifact he had sought or whether he had managed to escape with the ring before the chamber had been sealed.

The back of Jianyu's head continued to ache, and he felt more than a little unsteady as he pulled himself to his feet. He had no idea how long it had been, no sense of the time that had passed. What he did know was that he had to leave, *now*, before the Order was released from their sanctuary below. Before anything else could go wrong.

He also knew that he had failed again.

The sound of footsteps and shouting came to him suddenly from the hall beyond, and Jianyu understood something more—he was trapped. Without hesitation, he opened the light and managed to wrap it around himself before a group of robed white men entered the room. He recognized some of the men from the gala and, before the gala, from Khafre Hall and the Metropolitan. Then their numbers parted, and a white-haired man stepped through. It was the same man who had taken the stage that night in Khafre Hall, the same one who had trapped Esta. *The High Princept.*

The fact that they could not see him did not stop Jianyu from drawing farther back into the corner of the room. Outside, the night was already growing deeper. He no longer felt the heat of the strange ritual magic that had seared his skin during the Golden Hour, but his skin still felt raw. He should go—he should escape now, while the door was open and the way was clear—but something stayed him. He could not leave without the ring.

The Princept hurried up the steps and began some complicated ritual to open the portal overhead, as the others waited. Once the door was open, they climbed, one by one, disappearing into the chamber above. Again, Jianyu considered his options, and then he began to move toward the ladder himself. If Logan was still trapped with Jack Grew, there remained a chance to retrieve the Delphi's Tear. He would not leave such a chance untaken.

He climbed the staircase soundlessly, but when he entered the Mysterium, he saw no sign of Logan. The men were all red-faced and shouting.

"I don't know how the maggot managed to get the seal open!" Jack railed. Two of the robed men were flanking him and had taken him by the arms. "My designs were perfect. I accounted for every possibility." He tried to jerk away from the hold the men had on him.

"Clearly not *every* possibility," the Princept said. "The artifact is gone. We gave you our trust. You knew what regaining the Delphi's Tear meant to the Order—knew how essential it was for rejuvenating the Brink. Without the artifacts, we cannot perform the ritual at the Conclave. Without the ritual—"

"The ring couldn't have gone far," Jack said, cutting the Princept off. He nodded toward the open door of the balcony. "Even if the protections I placed failed, there was only one way for the maggot to escape. You should be able to collect the artifact easily enough from a dead man."

The Princept gave a small nod, and two of the men went out onto the open balcony to check. The other men all waited for their report.

"There's no one below," one of the robed men said, glaring.

"That's impossible," Jack said, still struggling against the other men's hold on him. "I saw the thief jump."

"Search him," the Princept demanded.

But Jack tore away from the men and shoved past the Princept to the balcony, where he leaned far over the stone railing. As the men followed, cornering Jack, Jianyu inched closer to examine the large golden tree that seemed to be growing in the center of the room. In its tangled gilded branches were five open spaces, likely for the five artifacts. He stepped out of range as the men dragged Jack back inside and began to search him for the missing ring. Jianyu waited, silent and ready to take the artifact the moment he could. He wished he could rush the men himself, wished that for once he could let the anger that burned within him spill out . . . but no. He would wait and he would remain patient, because he understood it was more important to *win*. It was as he had told Cela. Anger could wait. It would have to.

"It's not here," another of the robed men said finally, leaving Jack disheveled and panting.

Jack tore himself away from their grip. "I *told* you—"

But Jianyu did not wait to hear any more of their talk. If the ring was not there to be taken, if Logan's body was not below for all to see, then it was pointless to stay. He began to move back toward the staircase. He would go while he could. He would find Viola and Cela, and they would figure out what to do next. But he had barely reached the opening in the floor when another of the Order's robed men began to climb the stairs.

When the man entered the chamber, the others turned for the news.

"Did you find the maggots responsible?" the High Princept demanded.

"No . . ." The robed man's jaw clenched. "But we have another problem. Newton's sigils are gone."

By the time Jianyu extricated himself from the building, night had arrived. With the glare of the streetlights in this part of the city, it was simple now to keep the light open around him, but his feet could not seem to carry him fast enough. Once he found himself on the broad stretch of Fifth Avenue, though, he turned immediately west and began to run toward the building where Cela had been positioned. He did not allow himself to think about what might have happened to Cela or Abel if Viola had not made it in time. But if Paul Kelly's men had harmed his friends . . .

He was barely two blocks away when he saw them, standing on the corner of Twenty-Third Street. Viola, Abel, and Cela were all staring up at the building he had escaped from minutes before. Cela's deep-brown skin had taken on an almost silvery glow in the light thrown by the streetlamps, and Jianyu was struck suddenly by her beauty—the curve of her smooth cheek and the way her hair was curling around her temples, the strength in her narrow shoulders and the graceful, nimble fingers she had lifted to her mouth.

The direction of his thoughts made him nearly stumble and lose hold of the light.

Cela Johnson was not for him. He could offer her nothing—not safety, nor home, nor the promise of a future. He had his path set before him, and he would follow it through until the end. And if that thought made him feel suddenly more tired than he ever had been before? It did not matter. It *could* not matter.

Jianyu waited until he was closer to release his hold on the light. He did not let himself acknowledge—or revel in—the relief he saw in Cela's eyes. But he could not stop his heart from racing when she threw her arms around him, tucking her face close to his neck.

"I thought we'd lost you again," she whispered, hugging him a moment longer before she finally released him and stepped back.

Jianyu could still smell her perfume or her soap—a warm, sweet fragrance that made him suddenly unsteady. He glanced at Cela's brother, but if Abel thought anything of his sister's actions, he did not show it.

"We saw the man jumping from the building, and we thought . . ." Cela didn't finish.

"That was Logan," Jianyu said.

"What happened?" Viola asked. "Did you get the ring?"

Jianyu shook his head. There would be time later—to explain how Logan had attacked him and fled, to figure out what had happened to the boy and the artifact he had taken. "Did either of you take something from the Order's chambers?"

Viola frowned, but she took a package from her skirts no broader in diameter than a bowl of rice. She offered it to Jianyu, and when he peeled back the handkerchief she'd wrapped around it, cold energy filtered through the air.

He could not stop the smile that split his face. "We may not have the Delphi's Tear, but neither does the Order. Without the ring, they will not be able to reestablish their power. They need the artifacts to fortify the Brink, but even if they might retrieve them, without these sigils, they will no longer be able to control it."

NEARLY HOME

1920—Brooklyn

Esta watched the lights of the city—*her city*—grow closer and brighter as Dominic Fusilli's truck cut through the streets of Brooklyn. A moment before, she'd been in the heart of Chicago, but now, through whatever magic Dom used to create the entrances of the Nitemarket, she was home . . . or nearly home. She hadn't expected her heart to twist at the thought of returning. She hadn't realized how much she'd missed it, her city, with its tangled streets that never slept. For Esta, it had been only a matter of weeks since she'd left, but suddenly those weeks away felt so much longer.

Across the Hudson River, the Manhattan skyline wasn't *quite* the one she'd grown up with. There was no Chrysler Building with its Art Deco spire, no Empire State Building anchoring Midtown, and no Freedom Tower at the tip of the island. Those iconic landmarks wouldn't be built for years to come, but in this version of the skyline she could begin to see the promise of what the city would one day become. These streets glowed so much brighter than anyone could have imagined back in 1902, and the light the skyline threw off, the way it illuminated the atmosphere like a halo around the city, settled something in her chest.

She would not let herself think of the memory of the dagger plunging into Jack's chest, past bone and sinew, or of the memory of Jack's eyes—suddenly too human—pleading with her. She would not let herself wonder how she would go on living with blood on her hands, even if it had been necessary, even if Jack had deserved to die right alongside

Thoth. There would be time enough to think of that—to live with that—later.

Esta felt the tension vibrating from Harte, and she realized he was holding himself away from her. She didn't let go of her hold on the Book as she took one of their remaining Quellants and offered it to him.

"She's quiet," he said, hesitating.

"Take it anyway." She placed it in his hand. "Just in case."

He took the small white pill with shaking hands and placed it in his mouth. His eyes closed as he bit down, shuddering again as his throat worked to swallow. Little by little, the tension in his body eased, and eventually he opened his eyes. He stared at her as though testing himself.

"Better?" she asked after a long moment.

Harte nodded, though from his grimace—and from experience—Esta knew it was also worse.

"We won't need it for much longer," she assured him. "We're going to find a way to get her out of you. We're going to find a way to control her once and for all." *We have to.*

Harte didn't immediately agree. He leaned closer now, and there was something unsettling and almost resigned in his expression as he lifted his hand, tentative at first, to brush a lock of her hair back from where it had fallen into her eyes. Apparently he'd decided it was safe, because he cupped her face gently and tilted his own forward so he could rest his forehead against hers. "I saw Jack holding on to you up on the stage, and I thought I'd lost you."

"Not a chance," Esta said, feeling suddenly weak in the knees at the memory of Jack about to drive the dagger into Harte's chest.

But she couldn't let herself think about that, so she kissed him instead.

For a moment, the entire world narrowed to the feeling of her lips against his. For a moment, nothing else mattered. The dark blood that stained her dress, the way Everett rocked quietly in grief, even the difficult road that still lay ahead of them—it all melted away. There was only

Harte. His hands framing her face, his breath intermingling with hers. For a moment, she could forget. For a moment, she could hope.

Too soon, he broke the kiss with a sigh. But he didn't move away.

"I won't lose you," he told her softly.

She pulled back a little. "What makes you so certain I don't feel the exact same way?" she asked, giving his words back to him.

Esta knew they were standing at a crossroads, and the moment before them was far bigger than any single person, bigger even than she and Harte together. There was no way to save any one of them without saving the whole of magic, but they would be working against the snapping jaws of time itself. Still . . . they now had four of the lost artifacts. And they had the Book as well. The Ars Arcana was theirs again, and with the towers of the bridge awaiting them in the distance, and the promise of the city beyond, Esta would do whatever was necessary. She would find a way to to keep the promise she had made to Seshat. She would find a way to save them *all*.

WHAT WAS TO COME

1902—New York

James Lorcan waited in the shadows of Madison Square Park, watching the uppermost floors of the skyscraper for some sign of what had happened within. At the building's base, police clashed with Five Pointers. No one else was looking up, and so no one saw the figure that seemed no larger than a bird leap from the top floors. No one saw him tumble downward for less than a heartbeat, before a parachute emerged and carried him on the wind.

It had worked. James had barely believed it could be possible when Logan had suggested jumping to escape the top floor of the building. It seemed like a suicide mission to trust your life to a bit of silk, but the Aether had told James to go along with the other boy's idea, and so he had. Logan would either fly or fall, he'd figured. Either way, the ring would be his.

He watched for a long moment while Logan floated over Twenty-Third Street, and then he lost sight of him beyond the trees of the park. James waited a little longer before he snapped the reins and urged the horses onward down Madison Avenue. When he reached the corner of Twenty-Sixth Street, he stopped the wagon there and waited to see what would happen next. If Logan tried to run with the ring, he wouldn't get far. James had made sure that his own people lined the neighborhood around the Flatiron, just in case.

But Logan didn't try to run, as he might have. As perhaps he *should* have if he'd been a bit smarter. Instead, he emerged from the park a few minutes later. He'd already disposed of the parachute and the pack that had carried it. When he saw James in the wagon, relief flashed through his expression, and a moment later he was climbing inside.

"You have it?" James asked.

The boy's mouth kicked up on one side as he pulled something from his pocket and then dropped an enormous golden ring into James' outstretched hand. The setting held a stone as clear as a teardrop. *The Delphi's Tear.*

It was everything James had expected it to be and even more than he'd hoped. Almost immediately, he could sense the pull of the artifact calling to him. Whispering to him of its power, cool and steady and absolute. He felt the power within the cane vibrate, as though it knew what was to come.

"I found that for you once before," Logan said, his eagerness giving way to a cocky pride. But then his expression faltered, confusion replacing the confidence. "Or I will . . . someday. But maybe I won't have to if you hold on to it this time."

James didn't bother to respond. The future was nothing more than a story that was his to write—or to *rewrite*, as it were. The ring was heavy, and the gold of the setting had the deep burnished color of metal that was older and purer than the fashion of the day. It felt strangely warm in his hand, and for a moment he let himself marvel at it.

At the power it held within it—the kind of power that required a life sacrifice.

At the possibilities now before him.

Silently, he slid the ring onto his smallest finger, and he felt the Aether around him lurch again. It felt kinetic, exhilarating.

Right.

LISA MAXWELL

AUTHOR'S NOTE

~

The Last Magician series is, at heart, fantasy, but it is also a work of historical fiction. From the very beginning, I wanted to make it clear that this world is set in the real past, and that conceit has brought with it a host of complications beyond the usual worldbuilding of a fantasy series. Specifically, history is not pretty or sanitized, and historical fiction cannot be either, not if it is to be *true* in any sense of the word.

Looking back at our history, studying and recovering it, often brings to light a wealth of problematic incidents and issues—many of which are hurtful and offensive to modern readers. It is the job of the writer to make choices about what to include and what to leave out, and how to represent truthfully the often terrible events that have created our present. Writing fiction meant for entertainment, however, has allowed me freedom that the academic historian doesn't have. Fiction offers more flexibility in the choices I've made to position characters and events, and even in the language I use to represent the very real past.

Language has real power. If it didn't, ethnic slurs wouldn't be able to inflict such pain and violence, and people wouldn't use them to dehumanize others. But slurs aren't the only type of language that has power. The labels we place on each other and claim for ourselves also have power, but often labels that were once used in the past are later recognized as or become offensive to modern ears. One of those words is the label "Negro."

In previous books in the series, I've resisted using antiquated labels for groups. For example, historically, it would have been more accurate for the book to refer to Chinese Americans as "Oriental," a term that is now recognized as being offensive. Even in the 1950s, Sammie's friends in San Francisco would likely have referred to themselves with this term, just as they refer to the white patrons as "Occidentals." In the end, I decided against using that term, not only because it is offensive to modern readers, but also because it didn't add anything to the text other than historical accuracy. Because of the breadth of people and nations covered by the term, it wouldn't have helped me to describe more clearly any single, specific community. More importantly, using the term would not have contributed to Sammie's friends' agency in any way.

The term "Negro," and my use of it in this book, however, is somewhat different. Though the term may sound uncomfortable and problematic to modern ears, historically it was used by the African American community to claim an identity for themselves. In the late nineteenth century, "colored" would have been the common term, but by the early twentieth century, there had been a movement, led in part by Booker T. Washington and W. E. B. Du Bois, to replace "colored" with the term "Negro." Some historians see the increased use of "Negro" as a way that Black communities distinguished themselves from other immigrant groups and people of color. Other historians have suggested that the increased immigration during this period might have motivated the Black community to establish a group name, in the way the Italians or Polish immigrants had group names and corresponding identities.

Whatever the reasons the term began to grow in use and popularity, perhaps it is more important to recognize that by the early twentieth century, the term "Negro" came to stand for a new way of thinking—it signified the hopes for racial progress and aspirations of the Black community. During the first half of the twentieth century, "Negro" was the preferred term used to describe Black Americans. In 1928, Du Bois wrote that "etymologically and phonetically it is much better and more logical than 'African' or 'colored' or any of the various hyphenated circumlocutions."[1] According to one survey, before 1940, 74 percent of respondents self-identified as preferring the label "Negro" and 21 percent preferred the term "colored." Only 4 percent self-identified as "Black."[2] The label "Black" would not come into more common use until the 1960s, and "African American" even later—in the late 1980s.

My decision to have Cela and Abel claim the term "Negro" was intentional. Unlike "Oriental," which obscures individual ethnic identity, Cela's and Abel's use of the term "Negro" in this book does the opposite. The use of the label allows the Johnsons to align themselves with a historically specific identity and to claim agency as part of a larger community, just as their historical counterparts were doing at the time.

1. W. E. B. Du Bois, "The Name 'Negro,'" *The Crisis: 70th Anniversary Edition: Part I*, vol. 87, no. 9 (1980): 420-421.

2. Tom W. Smith, "Changing Racial Labels: From 'Colored' to 'Negro' to 'Black' to 'African American,'" *The Public Opinion Quarterly*, vol. 56, no. 4 (1992): 496–514.

ACKNOWLEDGMENTS

—

This book was not an easy one to write. Anyone who's been following me on social media knows that. If you've been waiting for the next installment of Esta and Harte's story, thanks for sticking around. You've been more than patient, and your support has buoyed me and humbled me. Thank you to each and every reader who sent me notes of encouragement, who told me that it was okay not to work myself sick, and who told me that you were willing to wait for it. I hope that *The Serpent's Curse* is everything that you hoped it would be. Thank you for sticking with me and these characters. I couldn't do any of this without you.

Thanks, too, to my long-suffering editor, Sarah McCabe, who dealt with more delays and missed deadlines than anyone should. From the very beginning, her keen insights have made this series immeasurably better. I am so lucky to be working with someone as supportive and patient as she is. Thank you to everyone at Simon & Schuster: Justin Chanda, Karen Wojtyla, Sarah Creech, Katherine Devendorf, Chelsea Morgan, Sara Berko, Penina Lopez, Valerie Shea, Jen Strada, Lauren Forte, Lauren Hoffman, Caitlin Sweeny, Chrissy Noh, Alissa Nigro, Anna Jarzab, Emily Ritter, Christina Pecorale and the rest of the S&S sales team, Michelle Leo and her education/library team, Nicole Russo, Cassie Malmo, and Ian Reilly. Thank you to Craig Howell for another incredible cover and Drew Willis for the gorgeous map designs. Thank you to Risikat Okedeyi and Shenwei Chang for their thoughtful readings and astute comments on earlier drafts of this book. Their insights made me a better writer, and any failings in this book are completely my own.

I owe an enormous debt of gratitude to my first home at S&S and the entire team at Simon Pulse. I feel fortunate to have had the opportunity to work with Mara Anastas and Liesa Abrams. Mara, especially, supported me and my books from the very beginning, and I will always be grateful to her for the career she helped me build. Thanks as well to my new home at McElderry, who have been awesomely welcoming and supportive as I've finished this book.

A million times a million thanks to the awesome readers of The Devil's Own street team, especially to Amanda Fink, Augustina Zanelli, Daria Covington, Davianna Nieto, Emily Howald, Julieta Ninno, Kayleigh Bowman, Kim McCarty, Sammira Rais-Rohani, and Alessandra Pelligrino. You are all rock stars.

Many thanks to my agent and friend Kathleen Rushall. I am so grateful to have you in my corner. Thank you for keeping me sane and always having my back, even when I don't have my own. Thank you especially for your patience as I figured out that I can't work like a machine—I got there eventually. Mostly. Your support and understanding mean everything. Thanks for being a better advocate for me than I am for myself.

To my writer friends who keep me sane in this bizarre business. To the Fiery Bitches: Jaye Robin Brown, Kristen Lippert-Martin, Angele McQuade, Shanna Beasely, Shannon Doleski, Sara Raasch, Olivia Hinebaugh, Danielle Stinson, Mary Thompson, and Anne Blankman. I hate this stupid virus for ruining our time together this spring, but I admire and miss the hell out of you ladies. Next year, or bust. To Helene Dunbar, Christina June, Scarlet Rose, Abbie Fine, Peternelle van Arsdale, Anna Brightly, Vivi Barnes, Flavia Brunetti, Lev C. Rosen, Jenny Pernovich, Kendal Kulper, and the whole community of kind, talented writers—in person and online—who make me better every day. Thank you to the booksellers and teachers and bloggers who have championed this series. I owe my every success to you.

Finally, to my guys. Jason, Max, and Harry. I'm sorry you had to live with this book right along with me for the last two years. You are patience and love and light, and I'm so glad you're mine. None of this would be worth anything without you.

LISA MAXWELL is the author of the Last Magician series and *Unhooked*. She grew up in Akron, Ohio, and has a PhD in English. She's worked as a teacher, scholar, bookseller, editor, and writer. When she's not writing books, she's a professor at a local college. She now lives in Virginia with her husband and two sons. You can follow her on Twitter and Instagram @LisaMaxwellYA or learn more about her upcoming books at Lisa-Maxwell.com.

THE DEVIL'S THIEF

ALSO BY LISA MAXWELL

The Last Magician
Unhooked

THE DEVIL'S THIEF

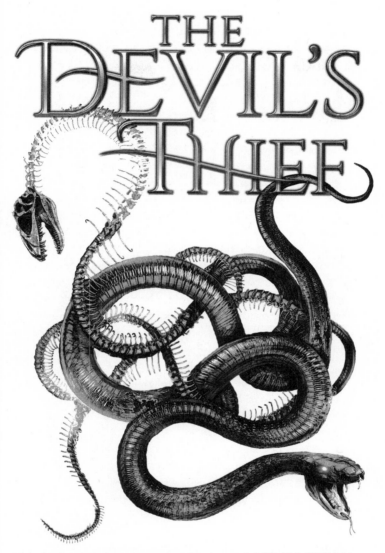

BOOK TWO IN THE *NEW YORK TIMES* BESTSELLING LAST MAGICIAN SERIES

BY LISA MAXWELL

SIMON PULSE

NEW YORK LONDON TORONTO SYDNEY NEW DELHI

SIMON PULSE

An imprint of Simon & Schuster Children's Publishing Division

1230 Avenue of the Americas, New York, New York 10020

First Simon Pulse hardcover edition October 2018

Text copyright © 2018 by Lisa Maxwell

Jacket title typography and photo-illustration copyright © 2018 by Craig Howell

Map illustrations copyright © 2017 (pages vi-vii) and 2018 (pages viii-ix) by Drew Willis

All rights reserved, including the right of reproduction in whole or in part in any form.

SIMON PULSE and colophon are registered trademarks of Simon & Schuster, Inc.

For information about special discounts for bulk purchases, please contact Simon & Schuster Special Sales at 1-866-506-1949 or business@simonandschuster.com.

The Simon & Schuster Speakers Bureau can bring authors to your live event. For more information or to book an event contact the Simon & Schuster Speakers Bureau at 1-866-248-3049 or visit our website at www.simonspeakers.com.

Jacket designed by Russell Gordon

Interior designed by Brad Mead

The text of this book was set in Bembo Std.

Manufactured in the United States of America

2 4 6 8 10 9 7 5 3 1

Library of Congress Cataloging-in-Publication Data

Names: Maxwell, Lisa, 1979- author.

Title: The devil's thief / by Lisa Maxwell.

Description: New York : Simon Pulse, [2018] | Series: The last magician ; 2 | Summary: "Esta and Harte set off on a cross-country chase through time to steal back the elemental stones they need to save the future of magic"—Provided by publisher.

Identifiers: LCCN 2018013470 (print) | LCCN 2018020872 (eBook) | ISBN 9781481494472 (eBook) | ISBN 9781481494458 (hardcover)

Subjects: | CYAC: Magic—Fiction. | Time travel—Fiction. | Stealing—Fiction. | Gangs—Fiction. | New York (N.Y.)—History—20th century—Fiction.

Classification: LCC PZ7.M44656 (eBook) | LCC PZ7.M44656 Dev 2018 (print) | DDC [Fic]—dc23

LC record available at https://lccn.loc.gov/2018013470

To Olivia and Danielle

~

*It is not often that someone comes along
who is a true friend and a good writer.*
—E. B. WHITE

HUDSON RIVER

Wallack's Theatre

Uncle Desmond's House

Broadway

Haymarket

CENTRAL PARK

←Satan's Circus

J. P. Morgan Mansion

Khafre Hall

Park

Third

23d

34th

42nd

59th

74th

BLACKWELL'S ISLAND

EAST RIVER

QUEENS

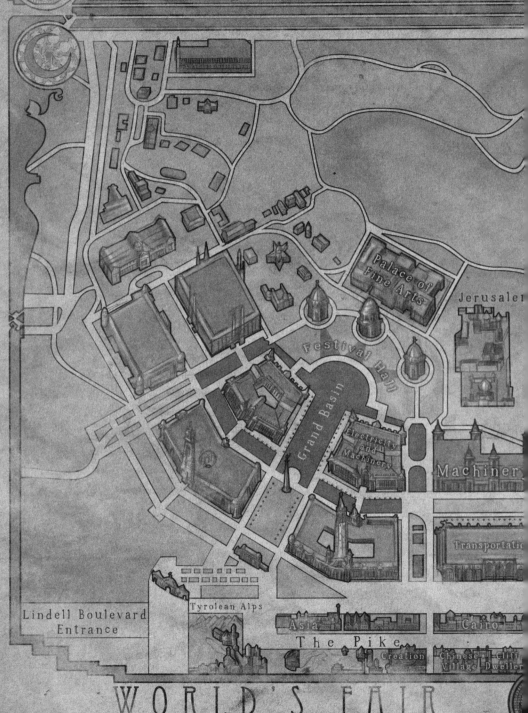

EXPOSITION UNIVERSELLE &

Palace of Fine Arts

Jerusalem

Festival Hall

Grand Basin

Electricity and Machinery

Machinery

Transportation

Lindell Boulevard Entrance

Tyrolean Alps

Asia

Cairo

The Pike

Creation

Chinese Village

Cliff Dweller

WORLD'S FAIR

TERNATIONALE DE ST. LOUIS

Agriculture

ST. LOUIS 1904

THE THIEF

1902—New York

The Thief turned her back on the city—on everything she had once been and on all the lies she had once believed. The ache of loss had honed her, and the weight of memory had pressed her into something new—hard and cold as a diamond. The Thief carried the memory of those losses as a weapon against what was to come as she faced the span of the great bridge.

The dark road spooled out before her, leading onward to where night had already bruised the horizon, its shadow falling over the low-slung buildings and the bare treetops of a land she'd never thought to visit. Measured in steps, the distance wasn't all that great, but between her and that other shore stood the Brink, with all its devastating power.

At her side stood the Magician. Once he had been her enemy. Always he had been her equal. Now he was her ally, and she had risked everything to come back for him. He shuddered, but whether it was from the cold evening air on his bare arms or from the reality of what they needed to do—the *impossibility* of it—the Thief couldn't be sure.

His voice came to her, a hushed whisper in the wind. "A day ago I had planned to die. I *thought* I was ready, but . . ." He glanced over at her, his storm-cloud eyes revealing everything he wasn't saying.

"This will work," she reassured him, not because she knew it was true but because there was no other option. She might not be able to change the past, might not be able to save the innocent or rewrite her mistakes and regrets, but she *would* change the future.

Behind them, a streetcar approached, sending vibrations through the track beneath their feet.

They couldn't be seen there.

"Give me your hand," the Thief commanded.

The Magician glanced at her, a question in his eyes, but she held out her bare hand, ready. With one touch he would be able read her every hope and fear. With one touch he could turn her from this path. Better to know where his heart stood now.

A moment later his hand caught hers, palm to palm.

The coolness of his skin barely registered, because when her skin touched his, power sizzled against her palm. She'd felt his affinity's warmth before, but what she felt now was something new. A wave of unfamiliar energy licked against her skin, testing her boundaries as though searching for a way *into* her.

The Book.

He'd tried to explain—tried to warn her after she had returned from the future he'd sent her to, a future he'd thought was safe. *All that power is in me,* he'd said.

She hadn't understood. Until now.

Now the familiar warmth of his affinity was overwhelmed by a stronger magic, a power that had once been contained in the pages of the Ars Arcana the Thief had tucked into her skirts—a book that people she loved had lied and fought and died for. Now its power was beginning to creep upward, wrapping around her wrist, solid and heavy as the silver cuff she wore on her arm.

At the edges of her consciousness, the Thief thought she heard voices whispering.

"Stop it," she told him through clenched teeth.

His response came out clipped, strained. "I'm trying."

When she looked over at him, his expression was pained, but his eyes were bright, their irises flashing with colors she could not have named. He drew in a breath, his nostrils flaring slightly with the effort, and a moment later the colors in his eyes faded until they were his usual stormy gray. The warmth vining around her arm receded, and the voices she'd heard scratching at the boundaries of her mind went quiet.

Together they began to walk. Away from their city, their only home. Away from her regrets and failures.

As they passed the first set of brick and steel arches, each step was one more toward their possible end. This close to the Brink, its cold energy warned anyone with an affinity for the old magic to stay away. The Thief could feel it, could sense those icy tendrils of corrupted power clawing at her, at the very heart of what she was.

But the warning didn't stop her.

Too much had happened. Too many people had been lost, and all because she had been willing to believe in the comfort of lies and too easily led. It was a mistake she wouldn't repeat. The truth of who and what she was had seared her, burning away all the lies she'd once accepted. About her world. About *herself*.

That blaze had cauterized her aching regrets and left her a girl of fire. A girl of ash and scars. She carried a taste in her mouth that made her think of vengeance. It stiffened her resolve and kept her feet moving. Because after everything that had happened, all that she had learned, she had nothing left to lose.

She had *everything* left to lose.

Brushing aside the dark thought, the Thief took a deep, steadying breath and found the spaces between the seconds that hung suspended around her. Once she had not thought of time, or her ability to manipulate it, as anything particularly special. She knew better now. Time was the quintessence of existence—Aether—the substance that held the world together. Now she appreciated the way she could sense *everything*—the air and the light, matter itself—tugging against the net of time.

How could she have missed this? It was all so startlingly clear.

The streetcar's bell clanged out its warning again, and this time she didn't hesitate to use her affinity to pull the seconds until they ran slow. As the world went still around her, the rumble of the streetcar died away into silence. And the Thief's breath caught in a strangled gasp.

"Esta?" the Magician asked, fear cracking his voice. "What's wrong?"

"Can't you see it?" she asked, not bothering to hide her wonder.

Before her the Brink shimmered in the light of the setting sun, its power fluctuating haphazardly in ribbons of energy. *Visible.* Almost solid. They were every color she had ever imagined and some she didn't have names for. Like the colors that had flashed in the Magician's eyes, they were beautiful. *Terrible.*

"Come on," she told the Magician, leading him toward the barrier. She could see the path they would take, the spaces between the coiling tendrils of power that would let them slide through untouched.

They were in the middle of the swirling colors, the Magician's hand like a vise around hers, cold and damp with his fear, when she noticed the darkness. It started at the edges of her vision, like the black spots you see after a flash of light. Nothing more than wisps at first, the darkness slowly bled into her vision like ink in water.

Before, the spaces between the seconds had been easy to find and grab hold of, but now they seemed to be slipping away, the substance of them dissolving as if eaten by the same darkness filling her vision.

"Run," she said as she felt her hold on time slipping.

"What?" The Magician looked over at her, his eyes now shadowed with the creeping blackness as well.

She stumbled, her legs suddenly like rubber beneath her. The cold power of the Brink was sliding against her skin like a blade. Everything was going dark, and the world around her was fading into nothing.

"Run!"

THE WHITE LADY

1902—New York

The white lady was dying, and there wasn't a thing that Cela Johnson could do about it. Cela's nose wrinkled as she approached the lump of rags and filth in the corner. The smell of sweat and piss and something like decay was thick in the air. It was the decay—the sweet ripeness of it—that told Cela the woman wouldn't make it through the week. Maybe not even through the night. Felt like Death himself had already arrived in the room and was just sitting around, waiting for the right moment.

Cela wished Death would hurry up already. Her brother, Abel, was due home the next evening, and if he found the woman in the house, there'd be hell to pay.

She'd been damned stupid for agreeing to keep the woman, not that she could fathom what had possessed her to accept Harte Darrigan's request two nights before. Cela liked the magician well enough—he was one of the few at the theater who bothered to looked her in the eye when he talked to her—and she supposed she did owe him for making Esta that gown of stars behind his back. But she certainly didn't owe him enough to be putting up with his dope fiend of a mother.

But Harte had always been too slick for his own good. He was like the paste stones she fixed to the performers' costumes: To the audience, her creations sparkled like they were covered in precious gems—but that was all lights and smoke. Her garments may have been well made, her seams straight and her stitching true, but there was nothing real about the sparkle and shine. Up close, you could tell easy enough that the stones were nothing but polished glass.

Harte was a little like that. The problem was, most people couldn't see past the shine.

Though she probably shouldn't think so uncharitably of the dead. She'd heard about what happened at the Brooklyn Bridge earlier that day. He'd attempted some fool trick and ended up jumping to his death instead. Which meant he wouldn't be coming back for his mother, as he'd told her he would.

Still . . . As much as Darrigan might have been all spit and polish on the surface, like the straight, evenly stitched seams in her costumes, there was something beneath that was sturdy and true. Cela had suspected that much all along, but she knew it for the truth when he'd appeared on her doorstep, cradling the filthy woman like she was the most precious of cargo. She supposed she owed it to him now to honor his last wishes by seeing his mother through to the other side.

Two days ago the woman had been so deep in an opium dream that nothing would rouse her. But it wasn't long before the opium had worn off and the moaning had begun. The laudanum-laced wine Harte had left had lasted less than a day, but the woman's pain had lasted far longer. At least she seemed to be peaceful now.

With a sigh, Cela knelt next to her, careful not to get her skirts too dirty on the cellar's floor. The old woman wasn't sleeping, as Cela had first thought. Her eyes were glassy, staring into the darkness of the ceiling above, and her chest rose and fell unevenly. There was a wet-sounding rattle in her shallow breaths that confirmed Cela's suspicions. Harte's mother would be dead by morning.

Maybe she should have felt worse about that, but she'd promised Harte that she'd look after the old woman and make her comfortable, not that she'd save her. After all, Cela was a seamstress, not a miracle worker, and Harte's mother—Molly O'Doherty, he'd called her—was far past saving. Anyone could see that.

LISA MAXWELL

Still, the woman—no matter how low life had laid her or how much she stank—deserved a bit of comfort in her final moments. Cela took the bowl of clean, warm water she'd brought with her to the cellar and gently mopped the woman's brow and the crusted spittle around her mouth, but the woman didn't so much as stir.

As Cela finished cleaning the woman up as well as she could without disturbing her, she heard footsteps at the top of the wooden stairs.

"Cela?" It was Abel, her older brother, who shouldn't have been home yet. He was a Pullman porter on the New York Central line, and he should have been on his way back from Chicago, not standing in their stairwell.

"That you, Abe?" she called, easing herself up from the floor and smoothing her hair back from her face. The dampness of the cellar was surely making it start to curl up around her temples. "I thought your train wasn't due until tomorrow?"

"Switched with someone for an earlier berth." She heard him start down the steps. "What're you doing down there?"

"I'm coming up now." She grabbed a jar of peaches—an excuse for being down in the cellar—and started up the steps before he could come all the way down. "I was just getting some fruit for tonight's dinner."

Above her, Abe was still dressed in his uniform. His eyes were ringed with fatigue—probably from taking a back-to-back shift to get home— but he was smiling at her with their father's smile.

Abel Johnson Sr. had been a tall, wiry man with the build of someone who used his hands for a living. He'd been killed in the summer of 1900, when the city had erupted in riots after Arthur Harris had been arrested for stabbing some white man who'd turned out to be a plainclothes policeman. Her father didn't have anything to do with it, but that hadn't stopped him from being caught up in the hate and the fury that had swept through the city during those hot months.

Some days Cela thought she could hardly remember her father's voice or the sound of his laugh, as though he was already fading from her memory. But it helped that Abe wore her father's smile almost every day.

Times like this, it struck her just how much her brother resembled her father. Same tall, wiry build. Same high forehead and square chin. Same lines of worry and exhaustion etched into his too-young face from the long hours of working on the rail lines. But he wasn't *exactly* the spitting image of his namesake. The deep-set eyes that were a warm chestnut brown flecked with gold, and the red undertones of his skin—those features were from their mother. Cela's own skin was a good bit darker, more like the burnished brown of her father's.

Abel's expression brightened at her mention of food. "You making me something good?"

She frowned. Because she'd been too wrapped up in caring for the old woman to go to the market, she didn't have anything but the jar of peaches in her hand. "Considering that I wasn't planning on you being home until tomorrow night? You'll have to settle for porridge with peaches, same as what I was planning on making for myself."

His expression fell, and he looked so forlorn that she had to hold back her laugh. She gathered up her skirts and took a few more steps. "Oh, don't look so—"

Before she could finish, a soft moaning came from the darkness of the cellar.

Abe went completely still. "You hear that?"

"What?" Cela asked, inwardly cursing herself and the old woman just the same. "I didn't hear nothing at all." She took another step up toward where Abel was waiting. But the stupid old woman let out another moan, which had Abel's expression bunching. Cela pretended that she didn't hear it. "You know this old building . . . probably just a rat or something."

Abel started to descend the narrow staircase. "Rats don't make that kind of noise."

"Abe," she called, but he already had the lamp out of her hand and was pushing past her. She closed her eyes and waited for the inevitable outburst, and when it came, she gave herself—and Abel—a moment before trudging back to the cellar.

"What the hell is going on, Cela?" he asked, crouched over the woman in the corner. The material of his navy porter's uniform was pulled tight across his shoulders, and he had his nose tucked into his shirt. She couldn't blame him—the woman stank. There was nothing for it.

"You don't need to worry about it," Cela told him, crossing her arms. Maybe it was a stupid decision to help out the magician, but it had been *her* decision. As much as Abe thought it was his duty to take up where their father left off, Cela wasn't a child anymore. She didn't need her older brother to approve every little thing she did, especially when five days of seven he wasn't even around.

"I don't need to worry about it?" Abe asked, incredulous. "There's a white woman unconscious in my cellar, and I don't need to *worry* about it? What have you gotten yourself into this time?"

"It's *our* cellar," she told him, emphasizing the word. Left to them *both* by their parents. "And I haven't gotten myself into anything. I'm helping a friend," she answered, her shoulders squared.

"She your friend?" Abe's face shadowed with disbelief.

"No. I promised a friend I'd keep her comfortable, until she . . ." But it seemed wrong, somehow, to speak Death's name when he was sitting in the room with them. "It's not like she's got much time left."

"That doesn't help anything, Cela. Do you know what could happen to us if someone found out she was here?" Abel asked. "How are we supposed to explain a white woman dying in our cellar? We could lose this building. We could lose *everything*."

"Nobody knows she's here," Cela said, even as her insides squirmed. *Why* had she agreed to do this? She wished she could go back and slap herself to the other side of tomorrow for even considering to help Harte. "You and I, we're the only ones with keys to the cellar. None of the tenants upstairs know anything about this. They don't *need* to know anything. She'll be gone before the night is over, and then you won't have to worry about it. You weren't even supposed to be home," she told him, as though that made any difference at all.

"So you were going behind my back?"

"It's my house too," Cela said, squaring her shoulders. "And I'm not a complete idiot. I got compensated for my trouble."

"You got compensated." Abe's voice was hollow.

She told him about the ring she had stitched into her skirts. The setting held an enormous clear stone, probably worth a fortune.

Abel was shaking his head. "You're just gonna walk up to some fancy East Side jeweler and sell it, are you?"

Cela's stomach sank. He was right. *How did I not think of that?* There was no way to sell the ring without raising suspicion. Not that she was going to admit it to him at that particular moment. "It's security. That's all."

"Security is this here building," Abel told her, lifting his eyes as though he could see through the ceiling above him, to the first floor where they lived, to the second floor the Brown family rented, clear up to the attic, which held a row of cots they leased out to down-on-their-luck single men in the dead of winter. "Security is what our parents gave us when they left us *this*."

He wasn't wrong. Their house had been bought and paid for with their father's hard work. It meant that no one could turn them away or raise their rent because of the color of their skin. More, it was a testament every day that their mother's choice in their father had been a good one, no matter what her mother's family had believed.

The woman moaned again, her breath rattling like Death himself was pulling the air from her chest. The sound had such a forlorn helplessness to it that Cela couldn't help but crouch over her.

"Cela, are you even hearing me?" Abel asked.

Somehow, the woman's skin was even more colorless. Her eyes were dull, lifeless. Cela reached out tentatively and touched the woman's cool hand, taking it in hers. The fingertips beneath the nails were already blue. "She's dying, Abe. This is her time, and whatever mistakes I might have made in bringing her here, I'm not leaving a dying woman alone, no matter what she is or what she isn't." Cela looked up at her brother. "Are you?"

His expression was creased in frustration, but a moment later his eyes closed and his shoulders sank. "No, Rabbit," he said softly, using her childhood nickname. "I suppose not." He opened his eyes again. "How long do you think she has?"

Cela frowned, staring at the fragile woman. She wasn't exactly sure. When their mother had passed on from consumption five years before, Cela had been barely twelve years old. Her father had kept her from the sickroom until the very last moments, trying to protect her. He'd always been trying to protect all of them.

"Can't you hear the death rattle? She's got hours . . . maybe minutes. I don't know. Not long, though." Because the rattle in the old woman's throat was the one thing she did remember of watching her mother pass on. That sickly, paper-thin rattle that sounded nothing like her sunshine-and-laughter mother. "She'll be gone before this night is through."

Together they waited silently for the moment when the woman's chest would cease to rise or fall.

"What are we going to do when she finally dies?" Abel asked after they'd watched for a long while. "We can't exactly call someone."

"When she passes, we'll wait for the dead of night, and then we'll take her to St. John's over on Christopher Street," Cela said, not really understanding where the impulse came from. But the moment the words were out, she felt sure they were right. "They can care for her there."

Abel was shaking his head, but he didn't argue. She could tell he was trying to think of a better option when a loud pounding sounded from the floor above.

Abel's dark eyes met hers in the flickering lamplight. It was well past ten, too late for a social call. "Someone's here," he said, as though Cela couldn't have figured that out on her own. But his voice held the same worry she felt.

"Maybe just a boarder needing a bed for the night," she told him.

"Weather's too nice for that," he said almost to himself as he stared up at the ceiling. The pounding came again, harder and more urgent than before.

"Just let it be," she told him. "They'll go away eventually."

But Abel shook his head. His eyes were tight. "You wait here, and I'll see what they want."

"Abe—"

He never did listen, she thought as he disappeared into the darkness of the staircase that led up to their apartment above. At least he'd left her the lamp.

Cela waited as Abe's footsteps crossed the floor above her. The pounding stopped, and she could just barely hear the low voices of men.

Then the voices grew into shouts.

The sudden sound of a scuffle had Cela on her feet. But before she could take even a step, the crack of a gun split the silence of the night and the thud of a body hitting the floor pressed the air from her lungs.

No.

There were more footsteps above now. Heavy footsteps made by heavy boots. There were men in their house. In *her* house.

Abel.

She started to go toward the steps, desperate to get to her brother, but something within her clicked, some primal urge that she could not understand and she could not fight. It was as though her feet had grown roots.

She had to get to her brother. But *she could not move.*

The papers had been filled with news of the patrols that were combing the city, ransacking private homes and burning them to the ground. The fires had been contained in the immigrant quarters close to the Bowery. The blocks west of Greenwich Village, where her father had bought the building they lived in, had been safe. But Cela knew enough about how quickly things could change that she understood last week's safety didn't mean anything today.

There were men in her house.

She could hear their voices, could feel their footfalls vibrating through her as they spread out like they were searching the rooms above. *Robbing us? Looking for something?*

Abe.

Cela didn't particularly care. She only needed to make sure Abel was okay. She needed to be upstairs, but her will no longer seemed to be her own.

Without knowing why she did it or what drove her, she turned from the steps that led up into the house her parents had bought ten years before with their hard-earned money and went to the white lady, now clearly lifeless. With the pads of her fingers, Cela closed the newly dead woman's eyes, saying a short prayer for both of their souls, and then she was climbing the short ramp to the coal chute.

Cela pushed open the doors and climbed out into the cool freshness of the night. Her feet were moving before she could make herself stop, before she could think *Abe* or *No* or any of the things that she *should* have been thinking. She couldn't have stopped herself from running if she tried, so she was already around the corner and out of sight when the flames started to lick from the windows of the only home she had ever known.

THE BOWERY AFIRE

1902—New York

By the time Jianyu Lee made it from the Brooklyn Bridge to the Bowery, his mind had turned to murder. Ironic that he was set on killing to avenge the man who had once saved him from a life of violence. Jianyu supposed that Dolph Saunders would have been amused by the turn of events. But Dolph was dead. The leader of the Devil's Own and the one sāi yàn who had never looked at Jianyu with the suspicion that shimmered in the eyes of so many others had been shot in the back by one of his own—by someone he had trusted. Someone they *all* had trusted.

Nibsy Lorcan.

For Jianyu, it did not matter whether Esta and Harte made it through the Brink, as they planned. If their wild scheme to get through its devastating power worked, he doubted they would ever return. Why should they, if they found freedom on the other side? If *he* were able to escape from this trap of a city, he would certainly never look back. He would find the first ship heading to the East, to the home he never should have left.

He would see the land that had borne him once again.

He would breathe the clean air of the village where his family lived in Sānnìng and forget his ambitions.

Once he had been *so* young. So innocent in his headstrong confidence. After his parents had died, his older brother, Siu-Kao, had raised him. Siu-Kao was nearly a decade older and had a wife who, though beautiful, was cunning as a fox. She had married his brother as much for the magic that ran in their family as for the benefit of the family's farmlands. But when their first child seemed not to have any affinity at all, she began to make clear that Jianyu was no longer welcome in her house. By the time he started to sprout hair beneath his arms, he was so angry at his place in his older brother's home, so desperate to strike out on his own, that he had decided to leave.

He saw now that his youth had blinded him and his magic had made him reckless. Drawn into one of the packs of roving bandits that were so common in the more impoverished villages throughout Gwóng-dūng, he had lived freely for a time, repudiating his older brother's control and choosing his own path. But then, he had lingered too long in one town, a tiny hamlet close to the banks of the Zyū Gōng, and had forgotten that magic was not a panacea for stupidity. He had been barely thirteen years of age when he was caught breaking into a local merchant's home.

Then, he could not have gone back to face his brother. He *refused*.

Then, he had believed that leaving his homeland and starting anew was his only recourse.

He had not realized that there were places in the world where magic was caged. Now, he knew too well. There was a safety in fealty that he had failed to understand and freedom in the constraints of family duty that he had not appreciated as a boy.

Once, he had thought that, given the chance, he would repent and live the life that had been demanded of him, a life he had once run from. He would not make the same mistakes again.

Why else would he have given his loyalty to Dolph Saunders if not for the promise that one day the Brink would be brought down? Why else would he have kept the queue so many others had already discarded, if not for the hope that one day he would find a way to return to his homeland? Certainly, it would have been easier to cut the long braid that drew curious glances and wary stares—many of his countrymen already had. But cutting his hair would mean a final admission that he would never return.

From what Esta had told him, though, going back to Sānnìng would be pointless if the danger she foresaw ever came to pass. If Nibsy Lorcan managed to obtain the Ars Arcana, the Book that contained the very source of magic, or if he retrieved the Order's five artifacts—ancient stones that the Order had used to create the Brink and maintain their power—the boy would be unstoppable. No land, no people—Mageus or Sundren—would be safe from the power Nibsy would wield. He would subjugate the Sundren, and he would use his control over Mageus to do so.

Jianyu saw it as his duty now to make sure that future could never be realized. If he could not return to his homeland, he would protect it from Nibsy Lorcan and his like.

Darrigan had left him with very specific instructions: Jianyu must protect the first of the Order's artifacts—and the woman who carried it. But he did not have much time. Soon the boy Esta had warned them about would arrive—a boy with the power to find lost objects and with knowledge of the future to come. A boy who was loyal to Nibsy. That boy could not be allowed to reach Nibsy, especially not so long as somewhere in the city, one of the Order's stones lay waiting to be found.

Jianyu would rather risk dying on foreign shores, his bones far from his ancestors, than allow Nibsy Lorcan to win. He would find the artifact and stop this "Logan." And then Jianyu would kill Nibsy and avenge his murdered friend. Or he would die trying.

As Jianyu made his way through the Bowery, toward his destination in the Village, the scent of ash and soot was heavy in the air. For the last week—ever since Dolph Saunders' team had robbed the Order of its most powerful artifacts and Khafre Hall had burned to the ground—much of the Lower East Side had been shrouded with smoke. In retaliation for the theft, one fire after another had erupted through the most impoverished neighborhoods of the city. The Order, after all, had a point to make.

Where Hester Street met the wide boulevard that was the Bowery, Jianyu passed the burned-out remains of a tenement. The sidewalk was heaped with the detritus of destroyed lives. The building had once housed Mageus, people who had lived under Dolph's care. Jianyu wondered where they had gone and who they would depend upon now that Dolph was dead.

As Jianyu walked, he noticed a clutch of dark shadows lurking just beyond the circle of lamplight across from the remains of the building. *Paul Kelly's men.* Sundren, all of them, the Five Pointers had nothing to fear from the Order.

Once, the Five Pointers wouldn't have dared cross Elizabeth Street or come within four blocks of the Bella Strega, Dolph's saloon. But now they walked the streets Dolph had once protected, their presence a declaration of their intent to occupy. To conquer.

It wasn't unexpected. As news of Dolph's death spread, the other gangs would begin to take the territory the Devil's Own once held. It was no more surprising to see the Five Pointers in the neighborhood than it would be to see Eastman's gang or any of the rest. If Jianyu had to guess, he suspected that even Tom Lee, the leader of the most powerful tong in Chinatown, would try to take what territory he could.

The Five Pointers were different, though. More dangerous. More ruthless.

They were a newer faction in the Bowery, and because of that they fought like they had something to prove. But unlike the other gangs, Kelly's boys had managed to procure the protection of Tammany Hall. The year before, the Five Pointers had broken heads and flooded polling places to elect a Tammany puppet to the city council, and ever since, the police overlooked whatever crimes the Five Pointers committed.

It had been bad enough that Kelly had been working in league with the corrupt bosses at Tammany, but during the days preceding Dolph's death, they had grown more brazen than ever. It had been an unmistakable sign that something was afoot. Everyone in the Strega had known that unrest was stirring in the Bowery, but it was a sign read too poorly and too late.

Feeling exposed, Jianyu drew on his affinity and opened the threads of light cast by the streetlamps. He bent them around himself like a cloak so that the Five Pointers wouldn't see him pass. Invisible to their predatory vigilance, he allowed himself to relax into the comfort of his magic, the certainty of it when everything else was so uncertain. Then he picked up his pace.

A few blocks later, the familiar golden-eyed witch on the Bella Strega's sign came into view. To the average person looking for warmth from the chill of the night or a glass of something to numb the pain of a life lived at the margins, the crowd of the Bella Strega might not have seemed any different from the other saloons and beer halls scattered throughout the city. Legal or illegal, those darkened rooms were a way for the city's poor to escape the disappointment and trials of their lives. But the Strega *was* different.

Or it had been.

Mageus of all types felt safe enough to gather within its walls without fear and without need to hide what they were, because Dolph Saunders had refused to appease the narrow-mindedness bred from fear and ignorance or to tolerate the usual divisions between the denizens of the Bowery. Going to the Strega meant the promise of welcome—of *safety*—in a dangerous city, even for one such as Jianyu. On any single night, the barroom would be filled with a mixture of languages and people, their common bond the old magic that flowed in their veins.

That was before a single bullet had put Dolph into a cold grave, Jianyu reminded himself as he passed under the witch's watchful gaze. Now that Nibsy Lorcan had control of the Devil's Own, there would be no guarantee of safety within those walls. Especially not for Jianyu.

According to Esta, Nibsy had the uncanny ability to see connections between events and to predict outcomes. Since Jianyu was determined to end Nibsy's reign, and his life, he couldn't risk returning to the Strega.

Still, Nibsy had not managed to predict how Dolph had changed the plans at Khafre Hall, nor how Jianyu had intended to help Harte Darrigan fake his own death on the bridge just hours before. Perhaps the

boy wasn't as powerful as Esta believed, or perhaps his affinity simply had limitations, as all affinities did. Finishing Nibsy might be difficult, but it would not be impossible. Especially since Viola could kill a man without touching him.

That would have to wait for another day, though. Jianyu still had to find Viola and tell her everything. She likely still believed that he had not been on the bridge and that Harte Darrigan had betrayed them all.

The Strega behind him, Jianyu continued on. He could have taken a streetcar or one of the elevated trains, but he preferred to walk so that he could think and plan. Gaining Cela's trust would be a delicate procedure, since Cela Johnson wouldn't be expecting him and few in the city trusted his countrymen. Protecting her and the stone might be even more difficult, since she was Sundren and had no idea what danger the ring posed. But he had promised Darrigan, and he understood all that was at stake. He would not fail.

By the time he reached the South Village, Jianyu detected smoke in the air. As he drew closer to Minetta Lane, where Miss Johnson lived, the scent grew stronger, filling his nostrils with its warning and his stomach with dread.

Jianyu knew somehow, before he was even in sight of the building, that it would be Cela Johnson's home that he found ablaze. Flames licked from windows, and the entire structure glowed from the fire within it. Even from across the street, the heat prickled his skin, making the wool coat he was wearing feel overwarm for the early spring night.

Nearby, the building's tenants watched as their home was devoured by the flames. Huddled together, they tried to protect the meager piles of belongings they'd been able to salvage, while a fire brigade's wagon stood by. The horses pawed at the ground, displaying their unease about the flickering light of the fire and the growing crowd. But the firemen did nothing.

It wasn't surprising.

Jianyu knew the fire brigade's current inaction was intentional. The brigades were mostly Irish, but being at least a generation removed from the boats and famine that had brought them to this land, they considered themselves natives. They looked with distaste on the newer waves of immigrants, from places to the east and the south, and on anyone whose skin wasn't as white as theirs, no matter how long their families had been in this land. When those homes burned, the brigades often moved slower and took fewer risks. Sometimes, if it suited their purposes, they ignored the flames altogether.

If asked, they would say it had been too late. They would tell the people weeping and wringing their hands that the fire had already consumed too much, that it was too dangerous even to try entering the building. Their lives could not be wasted on lost causes.

It didn't matter whether their words were true. The effect was the same. Even now, the men simply leaned against their wagon, their hands crossed over dark uniforms, impassive as the rows of brass buttons lining their chests. Their shining helmets reflected the light of the blaze, as the pale-faced men with long, narrow noses watched a home transform itself into ash. It had happened countless times before, and in the days to come, Jianyu knew that it would happen again.

Still under the cover of his magic, he approached the group of people slowly, listening for some indication that Cela was among them. For years now Jianyu had been Dolph Saunders' eyes and ears in the Bowery. It wasn't only that he was able to evade notice with his affinity. No, he also had a talent for understanding people and reading the words that remained unspoken, a skill he'd picked up when he'd traveled through Gwóng-dūng, before he was caught. He had wanted to start anew and to leave that life behind him, but because he hoped that the Brink could be destroyed, Jianyu had agreed to use his ability for Dolph, to warn him when danger was coming or to find those who needed help but didn't know where to ask.

He used that skill now, listening to the group that had congregated to comfort the family.

"... saw her take off like the hellhound was on her tail."

"Little Cela?"

"Mmm-hmm."

"*No . . .*"

"You don't think she started it?"

"She certainly didn't stay around to help, now, did she? Left the Browns upstairs without so much as a warning."

"Always thought there was something strange about that girl . . . Too uppity for her own good, if you ask me."

"Hush. You can't be telling lies about people like that. She was a good girl. A hard worker. She wouldn't burn down her own house."

"Abel wasn't in there, was he?"

"Can't be sure . . ."

"She wouldn't do anything to her brother. Say what you want about her, but Abe doted on that girl."

"Wouldn't be the first time a bitch bit the hand that fed her. Big house like that? She could sell it and go wherever she wanted."

"Abel never would've sold."

"That's what I'm *saying*. . . . They paid the insurance man, same as everyone."

"Carl Brown said there was a gunshot. . . ."

Jianyu turned away from the bitterness and jealousy that dripped like venom from their words. They knew nothing except that Cela was not inside the house.

The gunshot, the burning house. It could have been Cela's doing, but from the way the fire brigade stood silent and watchful rather than putting out the blaze, Jianyu thought otherwise. It was too much like what had happened in other parts of the city. It had the mark of the Order.

Which meant that someone, somehow, might already suspect that Cela had the Order's artifact. As long as she was alone in the city, without protection, she was in danger.

They all were.

THE TRUTH ABOUT POWER

1902—New York

From the table at the back of the Bella Strega, James Lorcan balanced the stiletto knife on its tip as he surveyed the barroom. The knife had once belonged to Viola, but considering that he'd found it lodged in his thigh, he'd decided he'd earned it. He watched the light flash off its deadly blade—a blade capable of slicing through any material—as he contemplated everything that had happened.

He was no longer relegated to a seat off to the side, as he had been when Dolph Saunders was alive. Now James occupied the head of the table—the space reserved for the leader of the Devil's Own—where he had always belonged, and Saunders occupied a small plot of land in a nearby churchyard, where *he* belonged. But it wasn't enough. It wasn't *nearly* enough.

At the table next to him were Mooch and Werner—Bowery toughs who had once taken Dolph Saunders' mark and pledged their loyalty to the Devil's Own. Now they, like the rest of Dolph's gang, looked to James for leadership. They were playing a hand of cards with a few others. From the way the Aether around them wavered and vibrated, one of them was bluffing about the hand he held—probably Mooch—and was about to lose. From what James could read, the others knew and were driving up the pot on purpose.

They hadn't invited James to join in, not that he would have anyway. He had never cared for games—not in that way. Take chess, for instance. Simpleminded people thought it was a challenge, but in reality the game was far too predictable. Every piece on the board had specific limitations, and every move led the player to a limited number of possibilities. Anyone with half a brain between their ears could learn the simple machinations to ensure victory. There was no true challenge there.

Life was so much more interesting a game. The players were more varied and the rules constantly changing. And the challenges those variables presented? They only served to sweeten the victory. Because there was *always* victory, at least for James Lorcan. People, after all, were not capable of untold depths. He didn't need his affinity to understand that at their heart, humans were no more than animals, driven by their hungers and fears.

Easily manipulated.

Predictable.

No, James didn't need his affinity to understand human nature, but it certainly helped. It sharpened and deepened his perceptions, which gave him an advantage over every other player on the board.

It wasn't that he could see the future exactly—he wasn't a fortune-teller. His affinity simply allowed him to recognize the possibilities fate held in a way most people couldn't fathom. After all, the world and everything in it was connected by Aether, just as words were connected on the pages of a book. There was a pattern to it all, like the grammar of a sentence or the structure of a story, and his affinity gave him the ability to read those patterns. But it was his *intelligence* that allowed him to *adjust* those patterns when it suited his needs. Change one word here, and the overall sentence adjusted. Cross out a sentence there, and a new meaning emerged. A new ending was written.

Just the day before, the future he had envisioned and planned for had been within his reach. With the Book's power, he could have restored magic and shown those like him what their *true* destinies were supposed to be—not cowering from ordinary, powerless Sundren, but *ruling* them. *Destroying* those who had tried to steal that power to make the world theirs. And he would have been the one to lead the Mageus into a new era.

But the Book was lost. He'd expected that Darrigan would fight—had even planned for the magician to run—but he hadn't predicted that Darrigan would be willing to *die*.

He hadn't predicted Esta's role either, though perhaps he should have. She'd always been slightly hazy to him, her connections to the Aether wavering and unsettled from the first. In the end, James had been wrong about her. In the end, she'd been as vulnerable and worthless as any of the other sheep that followed Dolph Saunders.

Without the Book, perhaps that particular dream could never be, but James Lorcan wasn't finished. As long as the future still held possibilities for anyone smart enough to take hold of them, his game was not at an end. Perhaps he could not take control of magic, as he'd once dreamed. Perhaps magic would fade from the earth, but there were *so* many other ways for him to win. So many other ways to make those who had taken his family—and his future—pay. So many ways to end up on top of them all.

After all, power wasn't always about obvious strength. Look what happened to James' own father, who had wanted nothing more than fairness for other workers like himself—safe conditions, a good wage. He'd tried to lead, and they'd crushed him. They'd burned James' house, killed his family, and taken everything from them. James had seen too many times what happened when you stepped up to lead.

You made yourself a target.

He didn't have any interest in following Dolph's fate, so he would do what he always did. He would bide his time. He would look to the long game while the small-minded tried to jump from space to space, knocking one another off the board while he watched from afar. It wouldn't take much—a suggestion here, a whisper there, and the leaders in the Bowery would be so focused on snuffing out one another over the scraps the Order left them that they wouldn't bother with James. Which would leave him free to focus on more important matters.

No, he certainly was no fortune-teller, but he could see the future on the horizon. Without the Book, magic would fade and the Brink would become nothing more than an antiquated curiosity. What power would the Order have then, especially without their most treasured possessions?

As their power waned, James would be moving his own pieces, preparing to meet them with a language they understood—the language of money. The language of political influence. Because he understood that without the Book, it would not be those like Dolph Saunders, trying to reclaim some lost past, who would win, but those willing to take hold of a brave and dangerous new future. People like Paul Kelly, who already understood how to use the politicians as his tools. And people like James himself, who knew that power—*true* power—didn't go to those who ruled by force but instead belonged to those who held the strings. True power was the ability to bend others to your will while they thought the bending was their own idea.

Perhaps James could no longer depend on the Book. Perhaps there was no way to save magic, but his game wasn't over. With a tug here and a push there, he would tie up the powers that be so securely, they would never realize where the true danger was coming from. And when the time was right, James Lorcan had a weapon of his own—a secret that Dolph had never known about.

A girl who would become the Order's undoing and the key to James Lorcan's final victory.

SANCTUARY

1902—New York

As she climbed aboard the late-night streetcar, Cela pulled her shawl up around her head to hide her face as she swallowed down a sob. The memory of the gunfire, a sound that had been so stark and clear and unmistakable in the quiet of the night, was still ringing in her ears. She couldn't forget how she'd *felt* the thud of a body slumping to the floor. It had echoed in her chest, and she felt like she would always hear that sound and feel the emptiness that had accompanied it.

Abe. She didn't know how she managed to find a seat when she couldn't hardly draw breath, and as the streetcar rumbled blindly on, it felt like her body would crumble in on itself to fill the gaping hole left in her chest.

She needed to go back. She couldn't leave Abe there, her brother and the closest family that she had left. She had to take care of his body and protect the property that her daddy had worked himself to the bone for . . . but she *couldn't.* Every time she thought about turning around, a wave of such utter fear would rise up in her that she felt physically ill.

As the streetcar rumbled on, she thought of going to her mother's family. They'd moved up to West Fifty-Second Street a few years back, but they'd never liked Cela's father all that much. Her uncles had always looked at him like he was beneath their sister—something the dog dragged in. Now that her grandmother had passed, there wasn't much buffer between the family's judgment and Cela's feelings. She'd end up there eventually—they'd have to be told, after all—but she didn't think she could handle them yet. Not while everything was so raw. Not while it was still too hard to think the words, much less say them out loud.

Especially not to people who would be thinking that Abe's death was his own fault, which was what they'd said about her father. Her uncles didn't know that Cela had been listening when they whispered to each other after the funeral, so they hadn't censored themselves. They'd complained that her father should've stayed inside the house where he belonged, instead of standing watch on the front porch for the angry mobs who had taken to the streets. They believed that her father should have known better than to stand up to them.

Her father had been trying to protect their family, just as Abe had been trying to protect her. Cela knew that she wouldn't be able even to look at her family at that moment without hearing the echoes of those insults. Not now, when her own guilt and grief were vines around her heart, piercing and alive, growing with each passing second.

Besides, as much as her family might have hurt her in the past, they were still her blood. She couldn't risk putting them in danger. Maybe the men who'd come pounding on their door that night weren't after anything more than their property. It wouldn't have been the first time someone thought they had a right to the house just because they wanted it. People had come with pretty promises and drawn up papers plenty of times, and first her father and then her brother had turned them away.

But they'd never come with guns.

And she'd never had a white lady up and die in her cellar before. Maybe those two things weren't at all related, but she had a feeling they were.

She should go to her family.

But it was too late to be waking people up.

But there was no way her uncle would open his door and not ask what the problem was, and there was no way Cela would be able to say the words, the ones that would make what just happened true. Not yet.

She wasn't ready. She wasn't sure if she'd ever really be ready, but she figured it would be a damn sight easier in the light of day. Though she was probably wrong about that, too.

Cela got off the streetcar at her usual stop, letting her body carry her along the streets through a combination of exhaustion and memory. The theater at least was a safe enough space, since it belonged to some rich white man. Nobody was gonna come and burn his property down, and she knew the ins and outs of the world behind the stage to get herself out of there if trouble did happen to find her again.

She let herself in through the back-alley stage door that nobody ever really used, except the people who kept things running from day to day. Inside the theater, it was silent. Even the last janitor would have gone home by now, which was fine. She didn't need to run into anyone anyway.

Her costume shop was in the basement, and since that was her domain, that was where she took herself. She was no stranger to working late to finish a project, but if she didn't want to break her neck on one of the ropes or props, she needed light. She decided on one of the oil lamps that they kept backstage in case of power outages rather than turning on the electric bulbs. The lamp threw a small halo of golden light around her, illuminating a step or two in front of her, but not much more than that. It was all she needed.

Down the stairs she went, counting as she always did so she could skip over the thirteenth riser. It was a habit of hers, but she felt the vines around her heart squeeze a little this time, remembering how Abe had made fun of her for it. She walked through the silent darkness of the cellar, wiping away the wetness on her cheeks before she unlocked the small storage room that had become her costume shop.

Inside, Cela set the lamp on the worktable and sat in the straight-backed chair in front of her heavy sewing machine, the one she spent most of her days in, sewing and cutting and stitching the masterpieces that made the stage come alive. For a moment she didn't feel anything

　　　　　　　　　　　　　　　LISA MAXWELL

at all—not fear or relief or even emptiness. For a moment she was just a breath in the night surrounded by the warmth of a body. But then the grief crashed into her, and a cry tore free of her throat.

My brother is dead.

She let the pain come, let it take her under into a dark place where not even the light of the lamp could reach her. All she had were the clothes on her back and a ring too fancy to fence without getting herself arrested or worse.

And her job . . .

And herself . . .

She wanted to stay down in that dark place, far below the waves of grief, but those thoughts buoyed her up, up, up . . . until she could feel the wetness on her cheeks again and see the oil lamp glowing softly in the small, cramped workshop room.

Abel would have hated to see her wallowing. After their father had been beaten and shot for trying to protect his own home, hadn't Abe been the one to put his arm around her and make her go on? She'd gone numb from the loss. The city she'd known as hers had become an unrecognizable, ugly place, and the life she'd once dreamed of had been buried with her father's body. But Abe had pulled Cela aside and told her that the choices their father had made needed to be honored with a life well and fully lived. It was the reason she'd gone out to look for work as a seamstress and then had pressed to get a position in one of the white theaters, where the pay was better, even if the respect from the performers was less. She'd *earned* their respect, however begrudgingly, because of her talent with a needle. Abel had pulled those dreams of hers out of the grave and handed them back, forcing her to carry on with them.

She still had that job, the one he'd been so proud of her for getting, and she still had herself. She had family in the city who would take her in if she really needed them, whatever they might think. And she had a ring, a gorgeous golden ring with a jewel as big as a robin's egg and as clear as a teardrop. It wasn't glass, Cela knew. Glass didn't glow like that or shine like a star when the light hit it. And glass wasn't that heavy. Even seated, she could feel the weight of it, tugging on her skirts from the secret pocket she'd stitched to hide it.

But her brother . . .

The vines tightened around her heart until they felt as though they would squeeze it down into nothing. But before she could let grief overtake her again, Cela heard something in the darkness: footsteps coming down the stairs. It was too late for anyone else to be around.

She picked up her shears. They weren't much of a weapon, true, but they were sharp as any blade and could cut just as deep.

"Hello?"

It was a woman's voice, and now that Cela really stopped to listen, she realized they were a woman's footsteps, too. Not that she put down the scissors.

Cela didn't answer. Silently, she willed the woman to go away.

"Hellooo . . . ?" the voice trilled. "Is someone down here?"

She knew that voice, Cela thought with a sinking feeling. She heard it often enough. Every time Evelyn DeMure had an idea for a new way to make her waist look trimmer or her bust look larger, Cela was the one who got to hear about it . . . and *boy* did she hear about it. Evelyn was the type of performer the workers backstage tried their best to avoid. Though she was undeniably talented, Evelyn thought she was more so, and she acted as though the world owed her something for her very presence.

Evelyn DeMure peered around the doorframe and found her. "Well, Cela Johnson . . ." Without her usual lipstick and rouge, Evelyn looked like a corpse in the dim lighting. "What *ever* are you doing here so late at night?"

Cela kept the scissors in her hands but picked up a piece of fabric to go with them. "I had some odds and ends to work on," she told Evelyn.

"At this hour?" Evelyn asked, eyeing her. "I would have expected you'd be home."

Home. Cela fought to keep her expression placid and to keep any trace of pain from her voice when she answered.

She intended to lie and brush Evelyn off, but suddenly Cela couldn't remember why she hadn't liked Evelyn. There was something soothing about the singer, like her very presence was enough to make all the pain and fear that Cela was carrying fade away. Cela hadn't wanted to face her family with all that had happened, but somehow she found herself telling Evelyn *everything*.

She told her about the white lady who'd died on her watch and the brother she would never see again . . . and about the ring, with its perfect, brilliant stone. It all came pouring out of her, and by the time she was done, she felt sleepy. So tired and relaxed now that she'd cried out all the tears left in her body.

"There, there," Evelyn cooed. "Just rest. Everything will be fine. Everything will be *just* fine."

Her eyes felt heavy . . . *so heavy*.

"That's it," Evelyn said, her voice soft and warm. "Just rest your head there. . . ."

Vaguely, Cela felt herself releasing the scissors. Her body, once wrung out with grief, felt soft now. Her chest a moment before had felt cold and empty. Hollow. Now she felt warm. Safe.

Her eyes fluttered shut, and when they opened again, Evelyn was gone. The lamp had long since gone out, and her workroom was as silent as a tomb.

With a groggy moan, Cela pulled herself upright, rubbing at her head, which still felt muddled and fuzzy. Evelyn's visit and the whole night before it felt like a dream. A *very* bad dream. For a moment she allowed herself to believe that it was.

Cela didn't need the light to make her way to the door. She knew her workroom well enough. But when she went to open it, she found it stuck. No. It was *locked*.

Not a dream, then.

Which meant it had happened—all of it had happened. Abe, her home. Evelyn.

Evelyn.

Cela was trapped, and she didn't need to feel her skirts to know that the ring Harte Darrigan had given her was gone.

COMMON RABBLE

J ack Grew smelled like shit. He'd been sitting in a stinking cell, surrounded by the foulest dregs of the city's worst denizens, for who knew how long. Since they'd taken his watch, he certainly didn't. There were no windows, no clock to mark the passing of time. It could have been hours or days for all he knew, and the whole while, he'd been surrounded by flea-bitten filth who were happy to wallow in their own excrement.

Most of them were asleep now, which was better than before. When he had first been tossed into the cell, the five other men had eyed him eagerly, and the largest of them, a tall, bearded man who didn't say much—probably because he didn't even speak English—had crowded him into a corner.

Touching his tongue to the space where a tooth had once been and wincing at the pain in his jaw, Jack told himself that he'd held his own. He'd managed to defend himself, at least. Maybe he hadn't stopped the man from taking his jacket, but he'd put up enough of a fight that the animal had given up and left him alone. They'd all left him alone eventually.

He lifted a hand to scratch at his hair. It had probably become infested with vermin the moment he'd entered the cell, but the movement caused a sharp ache in his shoulder. That damned policeman had nearly jerked it out of its socket on the bridge.

Not one of the idiots had understood what he'd been trying to tell them—that it was Harte Darrigan they should be arresting. That damned magician had been *right there*, and the police had done nothing.

They'd taken in Jack instead. And the worst part? He'd been arrested for *attempted* murder. He'd had a clear shot and was sure the bullet would hit its mark, but then . . . nothing. The bullet hadn't even grazed him. Darrigan was like a damned ghost evading death.

The filth of the cell and the stink of the slop bucket in the corner might have been easier to deal with if Darrigan were dead. The missing tooth and sore arm and hair filled with lice might even have been worth it if Jack had been the one to end the magician's useless life.

The echo of footsteps came from the darkened corridor outside the barred doors of the cell, and the inmates around him started to wake and rustle uncertainly. As the steps approached, men in other cells rattled their bars and called out curses. *Animals, all of them.* When the guard stopped outside the cell where Jack sat, the small barred window of the door was eclipsed by the guard's face, and then Jack heard his name being called as a small window slid open below.

Finally. He hadn't doubted that someone would come for him. He didn't belong there with the common rabble. He placed his hands through the opening, as expected of him.

"Enjoy your stay?" the policeman asked, his voice mocking as he handcuffed Jack through the door. "I s'pose them's not as fancy as the accommodations you're used to."

Jack ignored him. "Where are you taking me?" he asked as the guard pushed him toward the staircase at the end of the corridor.

"You're being arraigned," the guard told him. "Time to answer to the judge."

Once they made their way down the stairs, Jack was led through a heavy set of doors and found himself in a courtroom. A dour-looking judge sat at the high bench, listening to whatever the man in front of him was saying. At the sight of the man's back—the graying hair, the small patch of baldness at his crown, the fine wool of his overcoat—Jack's stomach sank. Not his father or cousin . . . This was worse. *Much worse.*

The man in front of the judge turned, and J. P. Morgan himself stood scowling at Jack as he approached the bench.

When that peasant bitch had caught Jack in her web of lies back in Greece last year, she'd wrapped him up so deeply that he'd practically lost himself. He still didn't remember most of the drunken days and nights he'd spent under her spell, but even then, the family had simply sent his cousin to round him up. If he found himself short of funds at closing time, one of the family's men would show up to pay the bill. His uncle didn't usually bother himself with the minutiae of the family's life, especially not the life of his wife's sister's oldest boy. But there was Morgan himself, in the flesh: his bulbous, cankerous nose, stooped shoulders, and a scowl on his face that meant trouble for Jack.

Shit.

Jack stood in front of the bench, trying to listen to whatever it was the judge was saying, but he couldn't concentrate. Not when his uncle was staring at him like he was something from the gutter.

The judge finished talking. "Do you understand?" he asked.

"Yes, sir," Jack answered, not really caring what he was answering to. He wasn't some damn little boy to be put into a corner. As long as it meant freedom, he would have agreed to anything.

Another officer stepped forward to remove the heavy cuffs, and Jack rubbed at his wrists.

"I expect that I won't have to see you here again," the judge told him. It wasn't a question.

"No, sir," Jack said, silently cursing the judge and his uncle and the whole lot of them put together.

Morgan didn't say anything until they were both in the private carriage, closed away from the prying eyes of the city. Outside, the sky was just beginning to go from the pale light of dawn to full day. He'd spent the whole night in that rotting cell.

After the carriage began to move, his uncle finally spoke. "You're damn lucky Judge Sinclair is up for election this fall, or it wouldn't have been so easy to get you out of there, boy. I don't know what the hell you were thinking, trying to shoot a man in broad daylight."

"I was trying to—"

"You can't possibly think I actually care?" Morgan snapped, his cold eyes silencing Jack as effectively as his words. "You had one job—to meet Darrigan and get the artifacts he stole. All you had to do was to stay out of the way so the Order—not *you*—could dispose of him."

"Darrigan made me look like a fool," Jack said, his temper barely leashed. "I couldn't let what he'd done to me stand."

"You made *yourself* look like a fool," Morgan said. "All that damned magician did was give you enough rope to hang yourself with. None in the Inner Circle wanted you on that bridge, but I convinced the Order to give you another chance, and what happens? You go off half-cocked, as usual. It's bad enough you brought those miscreants into our sanctuary, bad enough that Khafre Hall is in rubble and the Order's most important artifacts are missing. But to go and draw even more attention to the situation? You've embarrassed the entire family. You've embarrassed *me*."

You've embarrassed yourself. Jack, at least, had tried to do something. If the Order had given Jack the access he'd wanted months ago, Harte Darrigan wouldn't have been an issue. "I'll find Darrigan," he told Morgan. "I'll get back the Book and the artifacts."

"Darrigan is dead," Morgan said flatly.

"Dead?" *No. That couldn't be.* Not when Jack had plans to kill the magician himself.

"Jumped from the bridge right after you were taken away. If he had the Order's possessions, he either hid them or gave them to someone else. Not that it matters . . . We'll find the artifacts sooner or later."

"I'll help—"

"No," Morgan said bluntly, cutting him off. "You won't. You're finished. Your membership to the Order has been revoked."

The finality in his uncle's tone told Jack that it wasn't worth it to try explaining or apologizing. Especially not when his uncle had *that* look on his face. He would just have to bide his time, as he had after the fiasco in Greece. Eventually his uncle would cool off, and Jack would make them all understand.

"Further," Morgan continued, "you will be leaving the city *immediately*. Your bags have already been packed and are waiting at your mother's house. Once we arrive, you will have exactly thirty minutes to clean yourself up and say your good-byes. When you're presentable, you'll be taken to the train station."

Jack huffed. "You can't force me to leave."

Morgan's eyes narrowed. "Perhaps not. But tell me, how do you plan to live? Your parents have decided they will not be paying any more of your bills until and unless you prove yourself. The town house you leased will need to be paid for. The carousing you do—the drinking and the whoring—will now be yours to deal with. Who do you think will hire you in this town after the embarrassment of yesterday?"

Utter disbelief made Jack's head feel as though it were in a fog. His uncle had ruined him. Morgan had turned Jack's own parents against him, and with nothing more than a word, he could make sure no one in the city would have Jack. The truth of his own impotence burned. "And where will I be going?" he asked, his own voice sounding very far away from himself.

"Where you should have gone yesterday—the job is still waiting for you in Cleveland, just as it was before the fiasco on the bridge."

"And how long will I be working there?" Jack asked flatly.

"Indefinitely." Morgan picked up a newspaper that was sitting on the carriage bench next to him and opened it with a snap. The front-page headline glared darkly at him: THE MAGICIAN'S TRAGIC TUMBLE. Beneath the words was an etching of Darrigan himself, staring from the surface of the newsprint, his half smile mocking Jack.

Indefinitely. "That's it, then? I'm exiled."

"Don't be so damned dramatic," Morgan growled from behind the paper.

Once, Morgan's authority would have made Jack tremble, but now there was something about the sneering quality of J. P. Morgan's voice that made Jack bristle. *They still don't understand.* The Inner Circle of the Order, with their comfortable boardrooms and palatial mansions on Fifth Avenue, saw themselves as kings—as untouchable. They didn't realize that peasants start every revolution, and when the peasants rise up, royal heads are the first to roll.

But Jack knew. He understood.

"You're making a mistake," Jack said coldly. "You have no idea what these maggots are capable of. You have no idea the threats they pose."

With another violent snap, Morgan brought his newspaper down, practically tearing it across his lap, and glared at Jack. "Watch yourself, boy."

"I am *not* a boy," Jack said through gritted teeth. "I've been studying the occult arts, learning everything I can to understand the hermetical sciences and the threats the old magic poses, and still you refuse to recognize the progress I've made or to see me as an equal."

"That's because you are *not* an equal," Morgan said, his voice absolutely cold in its dismissal. "You imagine yourself the hero of some grand drama, but you are not even the fool. Do you honestly believe the Order is not aware of the growing threats? You're not the only one who has seen that Ellis Island has turned out to be a disappointment, that every new arrival threatens the very fabric of our society. Why do you think we've organized the Conclave?" Morgan shook his head, clearly disgusted. "You are nothing more than an insolent pup, too concerned with your own ego to see how little you know. The Inner Circle's work does not concern you, and yet your own arrogance and recklessness have cost more than you can even imagine."

"But the Mageus—"

"The Mageus are *our* concern, not yours. You think yourself somehow more aware, more *intelligent* than men who have years of experience beyond yours?" he scoffed.

"The Order is too focused on Manhattan. It doesn't realize—"

"The work of the Order goes *far* beyond keeping a few ragged immigrants in their place in the Bowery. You imagine me an old man, out of touch with the realities of the world, but *you* are the one who does not understand. The country is at a turning point. Not just our city, but the *country* as a whole, and there are more forces at work than you can comprehend, more forces than you are even *aware* of."

He leaned forward slightly, a movement more menacing than conspiratorial. "The Order has a plan—or we had one before Darrigan mangled it. The Conclave at the end of the year was to be our crowning achievement, a meeting to bring together all the branches of our brotherhood, and the Order was to prove our dominance—our readiness to lead—and once and for all to wipe the dangers of feral magic from our shores. But you brought vipers into our midst. Now, because of you, everything we have worked for is at risk."

"So let me stay," Jack demanded. "I have knowledge that could be useful. Let me help you. My machine—"

"Enough!" Morgan's bulbous nose twitched, as though he smelled something rotten. "You've done more than enough. Go to Cleveland. Keep your head down. Look around and learn a thing or two about how the world *really* works. And perhaps, if you manage not to make an even bigger ass of yourself, we'll let you come back and visit for Christmas."

BLOOD AND WATER

1902—New York

Viola Vaccarelli pretended to examine the produce of one of the Mott Street vendors as she watched the door of the church across the street. The shop's owner, an older man with his long, graying hair plaited neatly down his back, stood at the doorway watching her warily. She wondered if this was what Jianyu would look like as the years passed. But the memory of Jianyu, who Dolph had trusted to be his spy—and who had abandoned them all on the bridge—made Viola's thoughts turn dark.

When the shopkeeper took a step back, Viola realized that she had been scowling. To make amends, she pulled her mouth into a feeble attempt at a smile. The man blinked, his brow creasing even more, as though he knew her for the predator she was.

Basta. Let him be nervous. A tiger didn't apologize for its teeth, and Viola didn't have time to make nice with some stranger. She offered him a few coins for the ripe pear she'd selected, and he reached out tentatively to take them.

Across the street, the side door of the church opened and the first of the worshippers appeared. Viola stepped away from the old man, not bothering to wait for her change, and watched as a stream of women emerged from the side entrance of the church. They were mostly older, though there were a few younger women whose faces were already starting to show the same lines that mapped over their mothers'. They were the unmarried daughters—girls who had been unfortunate in their search for a husband and who still lived under their families' roof and rule. Viola had refused that future. She had turned her back on her family and on every expectation they held for her.

And now she would have to pay for it.

The older women wore the uniform of their generation: sturdy dark skirts, heavy, shapeless cloaks, and a fazzoletto copricapo made from lace or plain linen to cover their heads and preserve their modesty and humility before the lord and everyone else in the neighborhood. Viola had also pulled a scarf over her dark hair for the morning, but she had little interest in modesty. Concealment was her aim.

To anyone else, the line of Italian women might have seemed indistinguishable, but Viola could have picked out her mother in a crowd of a thousand such women. The way her mother's heavy body swayed as she turned west toward the blocks of Mulberry Street had been the rhythm of Viola's childhood.

It had been three years since Viola had spoken to her mother or had even *seen* any of her family, though they lived no more than a few blocks from the Bella Strega. But in the streets of the Bowery, a few blocks were the difference between the safety of home and crossing the wrong gang. Not that Viola worried too much about that . . . She could take care of herself and anyone else who might think to bother her.

Her mother's sturdy hands fluttered like birds as she spoke to the woman who walked beside her. Those hands could strangle a chicken or make the most delicate casarecce. They could wipe away a tear . . . or leave a mark that stung for days.

I should leave her be. She would find another way.

Without thinking, Viola reached for the blade she always kept at her side, the stiletto she'd named Libitina after the Roman goddess of funerals . . . and found it missing. She had launched it at Nibsy Lorcan the day before to protect Esta, the girl she had begrudgingly come to like. But in the confusion of the bridge, Viola had not been able to retrieve it. Now Esta was gone—the girl had disappeared as though she'd never existed—and so was Libitina, into Nibsy Lorcan's keeping. Viola was on her own, without friends or allies, but it was the absence of the knife she felt most acutely, as though she'd lost a part of herself.

She would get back her blade . . . eventually. For the time being, Libitina's replacement was secure in the sheath strapped against her thigh. It wasn't the same, though. The steel of *this* blade didn't speak to her in the same way, and the unfamiliar weight of the knife felt wrong, as though a matter of a few grams could leave Viola herself unbalanced.

But Viola had needed *something* to protect herself. The Bowery was in chaos. The already-corrupt police force had become more emboldened in the past few days. Under the direction of the Order, they'd been ransacking the lower part of Manhattan to find the Mageus who had stolen the Order's treasures from Khafre Hall. Viola had been part of that team. Led by Dolph Saunders, they had been on a mission to take the Ars Arcana, a book with untold power. Dolph had believed the Book could restore magic and free them all from the Order's control—and from the Brink.

Now Dolph was dead, and the thought of him laid out, pale and lifeless, on the bar top of the Strega still had the power to rob Viola of breath. He'd been a true friend to her, and she'd come to trust him—to depend upon his steadiness—even after her life had taught her never to trust. But Dolph was gone, along with the Book and any dream of freedom or a future different from the present's drudgery.

That double-crossing cazzo of a magician, Harte Darrigan, had ruined everything when he'd taken the Book from her in the bowels of Khafre Hall, leaving Viola looking the fool. Because of him, the Devil's Own had viewed her with suspicion shining in their eyes after they'd discovered that the sack she'd carried contained nothing of value. And there was no way to fix her mistakes. Darrigan had taken any hope of recovering the Book with him to his watery grave when he'd jumped from the bridge.

If that wasn't bad enough, on the bridge, Viola had made everything worse. She'd known that Nibsy suspected Esta of being in league with Darrigan. She had specific instructions to make sure *neither* of them got away, but when Nibsy raised a gun to Esta's throat, Viola had acted without thinking. She'd attacked the boy to save Esta—because it was what Tilly would have expected of her. And because it was what her own instincts screamed for her to do.

But her actions meant that she couldn't return to the Strega, not so long as Nibsy Lorcan had the loyalty of Dolph's crew.

Without Dolph, Viola had no one to stand between her and the dangers of the Bowery. Without the Book, she had no leverage with the Devil's Own. She certainly couldn't trust Nibsy to forgive her for skewering him.

Not that she particularly cared. She'd never liked the kid anyway.

But the Strega had been her home. The Devil's Own had been a family for her, one that had respected her skill and accepted her as she was. Perhaps the Book was gone, but she would do what she must to prove that she had not betrayed their trust. Even without the Book, she could finish what Dolph started. She would do everything in her power to destroy the Order.

To do that, she would need help. There was only one person she could think of who could protect her from the patrols—her older brother, Paolo. Going to Paolo had an added benefit: There were whispers in the streets that the Five Pointers were doing the Order's bidding now as well as Tammany's.

Paolo wasn't likely to forgive Viola for abandoning the family, and especially not for escaping his control and working for Dolph, a man he considered an enemy. Still, if her dear brother could help her get closer to the Order, she would suffer what she must. Which was why she had come to this place, to wait for her mother, the one person who might be able to protect her from Paolo's wrath.

Viola handed the pear she'd just purchased to a dirty-looking urchin on the corner and ran to catch up to her mother. "Mamma!" But the title was tossed around the streets of the Bowery so often that her mother didn't react, not until Viola used her first name:

"Pasqualina!"

Her mother turned then, at the sound of her name being shouted over the din of the street. It took a moment before her mother's dark eyes registered understanding, and Viola could read every emotion that flashed across her mother's face: shock, hope, then realization . . . and caution.

After murmuring something to her companion, who gave Viola a brooding, distrustful look before heading on her way alone, Viola's mother frowned at her. But she stopped walking and waited for Viola.

Her throat tight with a tenderness she thought she had long ago killed as surely as any life she'd taken with a blade, Viola approached her mother slowly until the two of them were standing an arm's distance apart.

"Viola?" Her mother lifted a hand as though to caress her daughter's cheek, but she did not finish bridging the distance between them. A moment passed, long and awful, and then her mother's hand dropped, limp at her side.

Viola nodded, unable to speak. For all her family had done, for all the anger Viola still felt, she'd missed her mother. Missed them all. Missed, even, the girl she had once been with them.

Her mother's expression faltered. "What do you want?" Spoken in the Sicilian of Viola's childhood, her mother's words sounded like a homecoming. But her mother's tone was like her eyes—flat and cold.

Viola had expected this. After all, she had committed the cardinal sin—she had abandoned her family. She had betrayed her brother and refused his authority, and maybe worst of all, she'd dared to claim a life that was more than any *good* woman would want for herself.

It didn't matter that Viola had long since considered herself a good woman. Her mother's judgment still stung. She had been on the receiving end of that same expression a hundred times as a girl, but she, who had learned to kill without regret, had never grown immune to it.

Viola dropped her eyes, forced herself to bow her head in the show of the submission expected of her. "I want to come home, Mamma."

"Home?"

Viola glanced up to find her mother's thick brows raised. "I want to come back to the family."

At first her mother didn't speak. She studied Viola instead with the same critical eye she often turned on a piece of bruised fruit at the market right before she haggled for a lower price.

"I was wrong," Viola said softly, keeping her head down, her shoulders bowed. "You were right about me—too headstrong and filled with my own importance. I've learned what it means to be without your family." The words tasted like ash in her mouth, but they were not a lie. Under Dolph's protection, Viola had learned what it meant to be without the expectations, demands, and restrictions her family imposed upon her.

"More like you got yourself in trouble," her mother said flatly, glancing down at Viola's belly. "Who is he?"

Viola frowned. "There is no man."

"I don't believe you."

"You see what's happening, no? The fires, the brawling in the streets? I see now how stupid I was to think I could go without my family—il sangue non é acqua."

Her mother's mouth pinched tight, and her eyes narrowed. "I tell you that your whole life, and now you listen? After it's too late?"

"I'm still your blood," Viola said softly, forcing a meekness into her voice that felt like a betrayal to everything she was.

Viola hadn't understood the truth of that phrase until she'd tried to leave her family behind. No matter the life she'd tried to claim for herself, she was always Paul Kelly's sister—and she always would be.

No, blood wasn't water. Blood left a stain.

"Why do you come to *me*? Why not go to Paolo, as you should? He's head of the family now," her mother said, crossing herself as she looked up to the sky, as though Viola's father might appear sanctified on the clouds above. "You need *his* blessing, not mine."

"I *want* to go to him," Viola said, twisting her hands in her skirts, making a show of nerves, and hating herself for it—not for the lie, but for the display of weakness when she had promised herself to always be strong. "But I'm not sure how to make amends for what I've done. Paolo listens to you, Mamma. You have his ear. If you tell him to forgive me, he will."

Her mother's jaw tightened, her face flushing red. "I see. . . . You come back to me because you need my help? After all you've done to us . . . to *me*—" Her mother's voice broke. "You make me a disgrace." Shaking her head, Viola's mother turned to go, but as she took a step down from the sidewalk into the street, she gasped and nearly tumbled to her knees.

Viola caught her mother before the older woman could hit the ground and pulled her to her feet. Pasqualina Vaccarelli was a stout, sturdy woman, but Viola could feel her mother's fragility, the aging that had taken some of her mother's vitality over the past three years.

It was a risk to use her affinity here, in the open—especially with how dangerous everything had become—but Viola pushed her power into her mother, feeling for the source of the pain and finding it immediately. The gout in her mother's joints had grown so much worse, and without hesitation, Viola directed her affinity toward it, clearing the joints that had gone stiff.

Her mother gasped, the old woman's dark eyes meeting her daughter's as Viola finished and withdrew her hands. Viola's blood felt warm, her skin alive with the flexing of her magic. *This* was what she had been meant for. Her god had given her this gift for life, not for the deaths her brother had forced upon her.

With a look of mingled surprised and relief, her mother raised a hand calloused by years of work and laid it against Viola's cheek. Her mouth was still turned down and her eyes were still stern, but there was gratitude in her mother's expression now as well. "I could have used you these past years."

"I know, Mamma," Viola said, placing her hand atop her mother's as she blinked back the prickling of tears. "I missed you, too."

This, at least, was no lie. She did miss the mother she'd once known, the woman who used to sing as she hung out the wash, who had tried to teach Viola how to knead dough until it became supple, and how to press linen with her bare hands until it was smooth. Those lessons had never stuck. No matter how she tried, Viola hadn't been built for that life. Her hands had been made to hold a blade, to wield magic. Her family had done everything they could to force her into the mold they believed was right. In the end, their expectations had just forced her away.

But now she was back. She would bend to their expectations, but she was older now. Stronger. She would not let them break her.

Her mother withdrew her hand. "I'll talk to your brother."

"Thank you—"

Her mother held up a hand to stop Viola's words. "Don't thank me. I make no guarantee. You'll have to be ready to take whatever penance Paolo gives you . . . *whatever* he demands of you."

Viola bowed her head to hide her disgust. Her mother had no idea what her *darling Paolino* was capable of. Viola's mother knew only that he ran a boxing club called the New Brighton and a restaurant called the Little Naples Cafe. She understood that he knew the big men in the city, but she had no idea that her son was one of the most powerful and dangerous gang bosses on the Lower East Side or what sins Viola's brother had demanded that Viola commit.

Viola wondered if her mother would have cared had she seen the split lip and blackened eyes she wore the first time she found her way into the safe haven of the Strega.

"Come." Without another word, Viola's mother began walking.

"Where are we going?" Viola asked, picturing the cramped rooms she had grown up in. But her mother was not heading in the direction of her childhood tenement.

Her mother turned back to her. "I thought you wanted me to speak with Paolo?"

"We're going now?"

Her mother gave her a dark look tinged with suspicion. "You want we should wait?"

Yes. Viola needed time to prepare, time to ready herself for whatever her sadist of a brother had in store. But it was clear that her mother would offer only once. "No. Of course not, Mamma. Now is perfect." She ducked her head in thanks. *Submissive.* "Thank you, Mamma."

"Don't thank me so quickly," her mother said with a frown. "You still have to talk to Paolo."

MOTHER OF EXILES

1902—New York

The early morning sky was heavy with clouds, and a thick mist coated the water as the ferry slouched through the Upper Bay that separated Brooklyn from New Jersey. At the stern of the ship, Esta Filosik looked like any other passenger. Her long, dark hair had been pulled back in an unremarkable style, and the worn skirt and heavy, faded traveling cloak were the sort of garments that encouraged the eye to glide past without noticing their wearer. She'd torn the hem out of the skirt to lengthen it, but otherwise the pieces fit well enough, considering that she'd liberated them from an unwatched clothesline that morning. But beneath the coarse material and rumpled wool, Esta carried a stone that could change time and a Book that could change the world itself.

She might have appeared at ease, uninterested in the far-off city sky-line, now no more than a shadow in the hazy distance behind them, but Esta's attention was sharp, aware of the few other passengers. She had positioned herself so that she could watch for any sign of danger and also so that no one could tell how much she needed the railing behind her for support.

The ship churned through the dark waters, coming up alongside Liberty Island—though it wouldn't be called that for another fifty years—and the lady herself loomed over them, a dark shadow of bur-nished copper. It was the closest Esta had ever been to the statue, but even this close, it was smaller than she'd expected. Unimpressive, considering how much it was supposed to symbolize. But then, Esta knew better than most that the symbolism was as hollow as the statue. For those like herself—those with the old magic—the lady's bright torch should have served as a warning, not a beacon, for what they'd find on these shores.

She wondered if her disappointment in the statue was an omen of things to come. Maybe the world she'd never thought to see would be equally small and unimpressive once she was finally in it.

Somehow, she doubted it would be that easy. The world was wide and vast and, for Esta, unknown. She knew everything about the city, but beyond it? She'd be working blind.

But she wouldn't be alone.

Standing beside her at the railing was Harte Darrigan, one-time magician and consummate con man. His cap covered his dark hair and shadowed his distinctive storm-gray eyes, making him look ordinary, unassuming . . . like any other traveler. He kept it pulled low over his forehead and turned his back to the other passengers so that no one would recognize him.

Without letting Harte know she was studying him, Esta watched him out of the corner of her eye. When the bottom had fallen out of her world, she'd made the choice to come back because she'd wanted to save him. Yes, she needed an ally, someone who would stand with her in the battles to come. But she'd come back here, to this time and place, because she'd wanted that ally to be *him*. Because of who he was and what he'd done for her. And because of who she was with him.

But his mood was as unreadable now as it had been ever since she'd woken in the early morning to find him watching her. He must have waited up all night, because when she'd finally awoken in that unfamiliar boardinghouse room in Brooklyn, he was sitting in a rickety chair at the end of the narrow bed, his elbows propped on his knees and his eyes ringed by dark circles and filled with worry. How he had managed to get them both through those final few yards of the Brink, she still didn't know.

She wanted to ask him. She wanted to ask so many things—about the darkness she had seen on the bridge, the way the inky black had seemed to bleed into everything. She wanted to know if he'd seen it too. Most of all, she wanted to lean into him and to take what support and warmth she could from his presence. But the way he had been looking at her had made her pause. She'd seen admiration in his eyes and frustration, distrust, and even disgust, but he'd never before looked at her like she was some fragile, broken thing.

At the moment he wasn't looking at her at all, though. As the boat churned onward, Harte's eyes were trained on the receding horizon and on the city that had been their prison for so long. Every lie he told, every con he ran, and every betrayal he'd committed had been to escape that island, yet there was no victory in his expression now that freedom was his. Instead, Harte's jaw was taut, his mouth pulled flat and hard, and his posture was rigid, as though waiting for the next attack.

Without warning, the somber note of the ferry broke the early morning calm, drowning out the noise of the rattling engines and the soft, steadily churning water. Esta flinched at the sound, and she couldn't stop herself from shivering a bit from the brisk wind—or from the memory of that darkness bleeding into the world, obliterating the light. Obliterating *everything*.

"You okay?" Harte asked, turning toward her with worry shadowing his features. His eyes searched over her, as though he was waiting for the moment he would need to catch her again when she collapsed.

But she wouldn't collapse. She wouldn't *allow* herself to be that weak. And she hated his hovering. "I'm just a little jumpy."

She thought Harte was about to reach for her. Before he could, she straightened and pulled back a little. If they were to be partners, they would be equals. She couldn't—*wouldn't*—allow her current weakness to be a liability.

Harte frowned and kept his hands at his sides, but Esta didn't miss the way his fingers curled into fists. Skilled liar that he was, he couldn't hide the hurt that flashed across his features any more than he could completely mask the worry etched into his expression every time he glanced at her.

Esta forced herself to ignore that, too, and focused on staying upright. On making herself appear stronger than she felt. *Confident.*

Harte gave her another long look before finally turning back to watch the land recede into the distance. She did the same, but her concentration was on what waited for them when the ship finally docked.

They had an impossible task ahead of them: to find four stones now scattered across a continent, thanks to Harte. Like Ishtar's Key—the stone Esta wore in a cuff around her upper arm—the stones had once been in the possession of the Order. The Dragon's Eye, the Djinni's Star, the Delphi's Tear, and the Pharaoh's Heart. They had been created when Isaac Newton imbued five ancient artifacts with the power of Mageus whose affinities happened to align with the elements. He'd been trying to control the power in the Book that was currently tucked into Esta's skirt, but he hadn't been able to. After Newton had suffered a nervous breakdown, he'd entrusted the artifacts and the Book to the Order, who later had used them to create the Brink and establish their power in the city—and to keep Mageus trapped on the island and sub-jugated under the Order's control. But Dolph Saunders and his gang had changed that.

Still, even if she and Harte managed to navigate the far-flung world, to find the stones and retrieve them, they still had to figure out how to *use* them to get the Book's power out of Harte and to free the Mageus of the city without destroying the Brink. Because, in the greatest of ironies, the Brink also kept the magic it took. If they destroyed the Brink, they risked destroying magic itself—and all Mageus along with it.

Esta was jarred from her thoughts when the boat lurched as it came up against the dock. Another blast of the horn, and the engines went silent. The few passengers around them began making their way toward the stairs.

"Ready?" Harte asked, his voice too soft, his eyes too concerned.

That worry sealed it for her. She took another moment to look at the skyline in the distance before turning to him. "I was thinking—"

"A dangerous proposition," he drawled. But his eyes weren't smiling. Not like they should have been. He was still too worried about her, and she knew enough to know that fear like that was a luxury they couldn't afford. Especially with all that was on the line.

"I think we should split up," Esta said.

"Split up?" he asked, surprised.

"I can't get us tickets to Chicago with you in the way. You keep looking at me like I'm about to fall over. People will notice."

"Maybe I keep looking at you like that because you look like you're having trouble staying upright."

"I'm fine," she said, not quite meeting his eyes.

"You think I don't know that you've been leaning on that railing like it's some kind of crutch?"

She ignored the truth—and the irritation—in his statement. "I can't lift a couple of tickets with you following me around."

Harte opened his mouth to argue, but she beat him to it.

"Besides, you're supposed to be dead," she reminded him. "The one thing we have going for us is that the Order isn't looking for you. We can't afford for someone to recognize either one of us in there, and that's more likely to happen if we're together."

He studied her for a moment. "You're probably right—"

"I usually am."

"—but I have one condition."

"What's that?" she asked, not at all liking the crafty expression in his eyes.

He held out his hand. "Give me the Book."

"What?" She pulled back. The Book was the reason he'd planned to double-cross Dolph's gang in the first place, and for a moment she wondered if she'd been stupid to think there was something between them.

"You want to split up, fine. We'll split up. But I get to carry the Book."

"You don't trust me," she said, ignoring the flicker of hurt. After all she'd risked for him . . . But what had she expected? He was a con man, a liar. It was part of what she admired in him, wasn't it? She wouldn't have wanted him to be anything else.

"I trust you as much as you trust me," he told her, a non-answer if ever there was one.

"After all I did for you . . ." She pretended to be more irritated than she felt. In truth, she couldn't blame him. She would have done the exact same thing. And there was something comforting in falling back into their old roles, that well-worn distrust that had kept them from falling too easily into each other.

"You have the cuff with the first stone," he told her. "If I'm holding the Book, we'll be even. Plus, if either one of us runs into trouble, we won't be putting both of the things we have at risk."

She could argue. She probably *should*. But Esta understood implicitly that agreeing to his demand would be a step toward solidifying their partnership. Whatever she might feel for Harte paled in comparison to all that they had left to do. Or so she told herself. Besides, if he already had the power of the Book inside of him, he didn't really need the Book itself, did he? What he needed was the stone she wore in the cuff beneath her sleeve, and he wasn't asking for that.

"Fine." She brushed off her disappointment as she slipped the Book from where she'd kept it within her cloak and held it out to him.

A small tome of dark, cracked leather, the Ars Arcana didn't look like much. Even with the strange geometric markings on the cover, there was nothing overtly remarkable about it. Maybe that was because the power of it was no longer held within its pages. Or maybe that was just the way of things—maybe power didn't always appear the way you expected it to.

Harte took it from her, and the moment his long fingers wrapped around the leather binding, she thought she saw the strange colors flash in his eyes again. But if they'd even been there at all, the colors were gone before she could decide.

He tucked the Book into his jacket and then adjusted the brim of his cap again. "You go first. I'll follow in a minute."

"We should decide on a place to meet."

"I'll find you." His eyes met hers, steady. "Get us a couple of tickets and wait for me on the platform of the first train to Chicago."

To keep the artifacts out of the hands of Nibsy Lorcan, Harte had sent most of them out of the city. To keep the Order from finding them, he'd scattered the artifacts. The first stone waited in Chicago, where one of Harte's old vaudeville friends, Julien Eltinge, was performing. They would be one day behind it, and there was a small chance they might even be able to get it before Julien received the package.

But Chicago was only the first of their stops. After Chicago, there was Bill Pickett, a cowboy in a traveling rodeo show who had the dagger. The crown had been sent to some distant family in San Francisco, which was an entire continent away. Worse, she and Harte weren't the only ones after the Order's artifacts or the only ones who needed the secrets of the Book. They would never be able to find them all before Logan appeared in New York in a week, where Esta had left him, and told Nibsy everything—about the future, about who Esta really was, and about every one of her weaknesses.

But they would go as quickly as they could. When they had the four, they would return to the city, where the last stone waited, protected by Jianyu, and then they would fight alongside those they'd left behind.

If there's anyone left.

"I guess I'll see you in a bit, then?" *God,* she hated how the rasp in her voice betrayed every worry that was running through her head and every hope that she was unwilling to admit.

Esta didn't do worry. She didn't do nerves or second-guessing or regrets. And she wasn't about to start, no matter how pretty Harte Darrigan's gray eyes might be or how weak she still felt from whatever had happened to her as she'd crossed the Brink. The only way through was through—and she didn't need anyone to carry her.

Proving that much to herself as well as to him, she started to go, but he caught her wrist gently. She could have pulled away from him if she'd wanted to, but the pressure of his hand gripping hers was reassuring, so she allowed herself the moment of comfort.

"I'm not going anywhere, Esta," he told her, his eyes serious. "Not until we finish this."

And then he'll be gone.

The unexpected sentimentality of the thought startled her. She couldn't allow herself to become so soft. Hadn't Harte just made that much clear? All that could matter now was fixing her mistakes—or the mistakes that she *could* fix, at least. The others—*and there have been so many*—she would just have to learn to live with. She would free the Book before its power could tear Harte apart, and then she would use it to destroy the Order, the rich men who preyed on the vulnerable. Esta would finish the job that Dolph Saunders had begun, even if she had to sacrifice herself to do it.

And before it was over, she would make Nibsy Lorcan pay—for Dakari, the one person who had always been a friend to her. For Dolph, the father she had not been allowed to know, and for Leena, the mother she would *never* know.

The first step was getting the stones back, and they would start in Chicago. *One step at a time. Nothing is more important than the job.*

Esta cringed at how quickly Professor Lachlan's words had come to her. *No,* she corrected herself. *Nibsy's words.* They were the words of a traitor, *not* a mentor and definitely not a father. She didn't have to live by them any longer, and she certainly didn't want them in her head.

Pulling her hand out of Harte's without another word, Esta set off across the upper deck. She kept her head down as she quickened her steps to catch up to the meager stream of early morning passengers making their way from the docks into the larger, busier train terminal. She glanced back just before she stepped through the wide doors, but Harte was nowhere in sight.

THE ARS ARCANA

Harte Darrigan had watched plenty of people walk away from him over the course of his brief life. He'd watched stage managers shut doors in his face and audiences stand up and leave when his act failed to impress them. He'd watched the guys he'd run wild with when he was just a kid turn away and pretend they didn't know him when he'd been forced to take the Five Pointers mark. He'd even watched his mother turn her back on him when he wasn't more than twelve . . . though he wouldn't deny that he'd deserved it. But somehow, watching Esta walk away made him want to howl, to run after her and tell her he'd changed his mind.

It was an impulse he didn't completely trust.

Yes, he admired Esta—for her talent and her determination. For the way she always met his eyes straight on, shoulders back, unafraid of what might come. His equal—his *better*, perhaps—in every way.

Of course, he *liked* her as well—for her sharp sense of humor and the flash in her eyes when she was angry. He liked her steadfastness and loyalty to those she cared about. And he liked that even when she was lying right to his face, she never pretended to be anything other than what she was.

He wouldn't say he loved her. No . . . He had seen what love had done to his mother and to Dolph. To Harte, the very word was a con—a lie that people told themselves and others to cover the truth. When people said love, what they really meant was dependency. Obsession. Weakness.

So no, he would not say he loved Esta, but he could admit that he wanted her. He could maybe, *maybe* even admit that he needed her. But he would only ever admit it to himself.

Now, though, that desire he felt for her—the wanting and needing—was a craving stronger, *darker* than it had ever been. Harte trusted it even less, because it wasn't entirely his own. In the furthest recesses of his mind, he could feel the power that had once been contained in the Book gathering its strength and pressing at his very soul, like some beaked and taloned creature about to hatch.

As Esta walked away from him, Harte's hands gripped the railing of the boat. He had to hold himself steady as he felt that power lash out within him, because it had already discovered the truth—it had already learned that *she* was his weakness.

If he released his hold on the railing, he would follow her, which was what the power trapped within him wanted more than anything. If he followed her as *he* wanted to, it would be that much harder to press the power down, to keep himself whole . . . and to keep Esta safe. Because if the power took hold of him, if he allowed it to reach for her—for all that she was and all that she could be—its razor-tipped claws would claim her. And it would destroy her.

Had Harte known what the Book was, he wouldn't have been so eager to get his hands on it. When Dolph Saunders had tempted him with the prospect of a way out of the city, he hadn't imagined that his own body and mind could become a prison more absolute than the island he'd been born on. He certainly hadn't expected the Book they stole from the Order to be a living thing—no one had. Because if any of the others—Dolph or Nibsy or the rest—had any idea of what the Book *really* contained, they never would have let him near it.

Days ago, everything had seemed clearer, simple even. In the bowels of Khafre Hall, his plan had been straightforward. If he took the Book from Dolph's gang, he would have the freedom he'd wanted for so long, and Nibsy Lorcan—the double-crossing rat—wouldn't be able to use it for his own ends. He'd seen Nibsy's plan, the way he would use the Book to control Mageus and use the Mageus under his control to eradicate Sundren. It would be a world safe for the old magic, but the only one with any freedom in it would be Nibsy himself.

But it hadn't only been Nibsy that Harte had been worried about. Stealing the Book from the Order also meant that Jack Grew would never be able to use it to finish the monstrous machine he was building, the one that could wipe magic from the earth. Too bad that the moment Harte's hands had brushed that crackled leather, all those plans had changed.

He was used to keeping himself away from others. Most people didn't realize how much of themselves they projected, so Harte had long become accustomed to pulling his affinity inward and keeping himself closed off. He hated being caught off guard by the onslaught of jumbled images and feelings and thoughts that most people shoved freely into the world. But he hadn't thought to prepare himself for the Book.

When his skin had made contact with the ancient, cracked cover, he'd realized his mistake. He'd felt a hot, searing energy enter him—a magic with a power like nothing he had ever experienced.

Then the screaming had started.

It had taken only seconds, but those seconds had felt like a never-ending barrage of sound and impressions, an incoherent jumble of languages he should not have been able to understand. But Harte never needed to know the words to understand a person's heart and mind, and touching the Book had been like reading a person.

Actually, it had been far easier. It was as though the power within the Book had been waiting for that moment—waiting for *him* to become its living body. He'd understood almost immediately that the Book was more than any one of them had predicted. It was power. It was wrath. It was the beating heart of magic in the world, and it wanted nothing more and nothing less than to be set free. To become. To *consume.*

And what it wanted most to consume was Esta.

Fortunately, the power he'd unwittingly freed was still weakened by centuries of imprisonment. Harte could still push it down and lock it away when he focused. But the power was growing stronger every day, and he knew that he wouldn't be able to suppress it forever. He hadn't *planned* to.

Harte had planned to die. He hadn't known for sure whether throwing himself from the bridge would silence the clamoring voices, but he'd figured that at least it would mean they couldn't use him as their pawn. But then Jianyu had shown up at the docks the night before the bridge and offered him another way.

By then Harte had already scattered the artifacts, sending most of them away from the city to keep them out of Nibsy's reach. He hadn't realized until it was too late that he could have used them to control the Book's power. He *certainly* hadn't expected Esta to return.

Now stopping Nibsy and the Order and keeping Esta safe depended on controlling it. To do that, they needed the artifacts. But retrieving them meant leaving people behind—his mother, for one. Jianyu, for another. And maybe most worrisome of all, it meant leaving one of the stones.

He'd given one to Cela because he didn't have any other way to repay her for what he'd done when he'd forced his dying mother upon her with his affinity. The ring had been the least obtrusive of the Order's pieces, other than maybe the cuff that he'd given to Esta. Harte had known even then that it wasn't a good enough trade, but now that Esta had returned, he truly understood the danger he'd put Cela in—especially if the boy Esta had brought back with her could find anything. He could only hope that the command he'd planted in her mind with his affinity would be enough to help Cela evade danger until Jianyu could protect her and the stone.

Harte waited a while before he released his hold on the railing, long enough that Esta was out of sight and the crewman on the ferry was beginning to pay more attention to him than was safe.

When he stepped from the boat onto the solidness of the New Jersey soil, he tested himself to make sure that the power within him was still quiet, pushed down deep. It was a new state, but for Harte, who had been trapped on the island of Manhattan his entire life, it might as well have been a new continent.

Around him, people bustled onward, gathering their bags and their children as they moved toward the terminal entrance. He joined them, keeping his cap low, his eyes down, allowing himself to be caught up in the current. He sensed the excitement of some heading off toward new places and the weariness of others making the same trip they'd made countless times before. All of them were oblivious to the miracle it was that they could choose to purchase a ticket, step onto a train, and arrive somewhere else. For Harte, that miracle was one he would never take for granted, however much time he had left.

As he was carried along by the crowd, he almost felt as though the world could be his. Perhaps their mission might actually work and a different future could be possible. But then he heard a whispering begin to grow louder in the recesses of his mind. The dark choir merged into a single voice, one that was speaking in a language he should not have recognized but understood nonetheless. A single word that held untold meaning.

Soon.

THE SIREN

1902—New York

The sun was already climbing into the sky as the streetcar rumbled north through the city. Jianyu kept himself tucked back into a corner, careful not to touch anyone and reveal his presence, until they reached the stop at Broadway, close to Wallack's Theatre, where Harte Darrigan had once performed. Cela's neighbors believed she'd fled from the house because she was guilty of the fire, but Jianyu suspected otherwise. He was not sure where she would go, but he hoped she would eventually return here, to the theater where she worked.

Keeping the light around him was easier now, with the morning sun providing ample threads for him to grasp and open around him. When he reached Wallack's, Jianyu looked up to find familiar eyes watching him from above.

It was only a painting, a large multistoried advertisement for the variety acts to be found inside, but Harte Darrigan's gaze seemed to be steady on Jianyu—though whether it felt like a warning or encouragement, he could not have said.

Still concealed by his affinity, Jianyu surveyed the theater from across the street. He could wait and watch for Cela to arrive, but he decided that inside there might be some hint of where else she would go. Keeping his affinity close, he crossed the street to the stage door. After picking the lock, he slipped into the darkened theater and began searching for some sign of Cela in the area backstage.

Inside, the theater waited, dark and silent. Jianyu had never set foot in Wallack's before, or any of the Broadway houses that advertised their shows on bright electric marquees. He had taken in a show at the Bowery Theatre once, when he had first arrived in the city, but it had been a noisy, raucous affair in a house tattered and broken by the usual crowd. Wallack's was different. It looked like a palace, and Jianyu had a feeling that it would still feel like one, even when the house was full.

He followed the narrow halls back, deeper into the theater, passing dressing room after dressing room. But Cela was not a performer. She would not be given her name on a door. No . . . she would be somewhere else, somewhere quieter. He continued on in the darkness until he came to steps that led down into the belly of the building.

The cellar smelled of dust and mold, of freshly cut wood and the sharpness of paint. It was darker there, but darkness was rarely without some strands of light within it. He took out the bronze mirror disks that helped him focus his affinity and used them to open the meager strands of light, keeping himself concealed as he moved through the cellar.

Jianyu saw the light that flickered behind him before he heard the voice that accompanied it. "Can I help you?"

He turned to find a woman with hair as bright as luck itself staring in his direction.

She cannot possibly see me. . . .

"I know you're there," she said, her eyes steady. Her face was pale as a ghost in the darkness. "I can feel you. You might as well show yourself before I call for someone."

Jianyu stayed still and quiet, barely allowing himself a breath as he considered his options.

"Just so you know, this staircase is the only way out." Her expression never shifted. "I know what you are," she told him, her eyes still not quite finding him. "I can *feel* you."

Without any warning, he felt the tendrils of warmth—of magic—brushing against him. She was Mageus, like him. He could try to escape as he was, but if she had magic, who knew what she was capable of? Better to face her now than to find himself trapped. Perhaps they might even be allies.

He released his hold on the light and watched as her eyes found him in the darkness of the basement.

"There. That wasn't so bad, was it?" she asked with a smile.

"I meant no harm," he told her, keeping his chin tipped down so that the brim of his hat would keep his features shadowed.

"You're here awful early," she said. Her magic was still brushing at him, like warm fingers running down the length of his neck, caressing his cheek and making his blood burn with something that felt suspiciously like desire.

"I am looking for someone," he said, trying to block the temptation of those warm tendrils.

"Well, it looks like you found someone," she said with a too-welcoming smile as she came the rest of the way down the stairs toward him.

He swallowed. Hard. "I am looking for a Miss Johnson . . . a Miss Cela Johnson," he said, fighting the urge to go to the woman. From the looks of it, she was wearing nothing more than a silken robe, and each movement she made threatened to expose more of the creamy flesh beneath.

"Who is it that's looking?" she asked, taking another step toward him.

The warm tendrils of magic were growing stronger now, and in the back of his mind Jianyu registered their danger. "She would not know me," he said, fighting the pull of the woman. "But we have a mutual friend."

The woman took another step toward him, her eyes glittering and her dark lips quirking with something that looked like amusement. He imagined it was the same sort of expression a mouse saw just before a cat pounced. "Does this mutual friend have a name?" she asked, taking yet another step. She was on the same level as he was now.

"I would prefer to keep that between Miss Johnson and myself," he said as she continued to walk toward him.

"Would you?" The woman *tsk*ed at him. "Well, that's a crying shame, seeing as there isn't any Cela Johnson here."

"I see. . . ." It was a lie. He could see it clear as day on the woman's pale face. In another two steps, she would be close enough to touch him, and he knew somehow that he could not let that happen. "Then I suppose I should take my leave—"

She lunged for him, but he pulled the mirrors from his pockets and, in a fluid motion, raised them as he spun away from her. The weak light wrapped around him and he ran, leaving the red-haired woman trying to catch herself as she tumbled to the floor.

If Cela Johnson was not there, the red-haired woman knew something about where she had gone, he thought as he took the steps two by two and sprinted for the theater's exit. He would retreat for the moment, but he would not leave until he searched the theater again. And he would not give up until he found her.

A BRUSH OF MAGIC

1902—New Jersey

Inside the train terminal, the noise of chattering voices was almost deafening under the canopy of glass and steel, but Esta barely noticed the racket. She was too busy bracing herself to do what needed to be done.

Though she had never been out of the city before, the New Jersey train station felt almost familiar. In her own time, she had often gone to Grand Central with Professor Lachlan as part of her training. Together they had studied the passengers as he instructed Esta about human nature. The tourists, overwhelmed by the speed and size of the city, would clutch their bags to them as though the devil himself would try to take their ratty luggage, but the locals had become accustomed to the rush and the noise, and the dangers no longer registered. He'd taught her how to case the commuters, too busy checking their phones to notice a thief watching their every move.

The schedule was displayed on a huge chalkboard over the far wall of the terminal's main hall. There was a train to Chicago departing at half past the hour from platform seven, but she still had to find two tickets. They had decided that buying tickets this close to the city, where they might be recognized, was too risky. The Order was most likely still looking for them—especially for her—and she didn't doubt they would have alerted all the transportation centers. Instead of buying two tickets, she'd have to steal them.

Before, Esta wouldn't have hesitated to pull time slow and slip unseen through the spaces between the seconds as she searched for a mark. But after what had happened on the bridge—after the blackness had bloomed in her vision and the way time felt as though it were dissolving around her—she felt unsure of herself . . . and she felt unsure of her affinity.

It was *not* a comfortable feeling.

But that darkness . . . Even the *memory* of it left her shaken. She didn't want to admit to herself that she was afraid—afraid of what that darkness meant and afraid that if she reached for her affinity now, she might find it missing or mangled in some way by the Brink's power.

So she did what anyone would do in that situation—she *didn't* admit it to herself or to anyone else. Instead, she relied on her bone-deep knowledge that she was a good enough thief to lift a couple of tickets from unsuspecting marks without any magic at all. Even if her legs felt unsteady beneath her.

She was still deciding on the best place to watch for a mark when she felt a shock of energy brush against her, warm and welcoming—the sign of the old magic. Frowning to herself, she searched the crowd for Harte. They had agreed to meet on the platform, but it would be just like him not to follow the plan. She couldn't afford for him to show up and get her caught, but as she scoured the crowd, she didn't find any sign of him. And, though she waited, she didn't feel the warmth of the magic again.

Maybe she'd been wrong. . . .

"There isn't time for breakfast. The train leaves in less than ten minutes, and we still have to find platform seven." The low male voice pulled Esta's attention back to the room around her. *Platform seven . . . the train to Chicago.*

Esta let go of her questions and searched for the source of the voice. Nearby, three men dressed in sharply tailored suits were examining their tickets. One was squinting up at the board, confirming the platform they needed, while another tucked his ticket into the outer pocket of his polished leather satchel. She listened a moment longer, and when she heard one of them say the number of their platform again, she began to walk.

It wouldn't do to follow them—that would be far too obvious. But there seemed to be only one entrance from the main terminal into the train shed. She could cut them off there. At least one ticket would be easy to lift. A second shouldn't be too much harder.

Feeling more like herself with every step, Esta pulled a cloak of confidence around her that was nearly as effective as Jianyu's invisibility. She kept the three men in her peripheral vision as she headed toward the entrance to the platforms. When she was about ten feet ahead of the men, she paused and pretended to read a poster advertising a variety show that had just arrived in town. She kept her expression calm and mildly interested in the sign in front of her, even as she kept her focus on the men. When they passed her, she waited one moment longer before turning to follow them. It would be easier to lift the tickets in the tunnel leading to the trains, where the flow of passengers was naturally constricted and where they wouldn't notice—or think anything of—her proximity to them. Or of being jostled by a fellow traveler.

They were just ahead of her, and she could still see the ticket peeking from the satchel. *Easy.*

As they approached the entrance to the platforms, she picked up her pace. A few steps more and she'd be able to sweep past them. Maybe she could trip and pretend to fall. One of them would probably be polite enough to stop and help her, giving her the opportunity to lift a second ticket. Then she'd be on to the platform and then the train—with Harte—before they even discovered their fare was missing.

Esta was nearly at their heels now—but out of nowhere, she felt another brush of warm energy that made her stumble. She caught herself before she fell and then had to scurry to keep up with the three men, scanning the narrowing passageway as she walked. *No sign of Harte.* And the men were almost to the place where the passage opened onto the platforms. She moved until she was barely an arm's reach away. Closer still . . . She was almost next to them, nearly close enough to slip the first of the tickets out of the satchel, when someone called her name.

"Esta?"

It wasn't the unexpectedness of hearing her name that made her pause, but the familiarity of the voice. Her first thought was *Harte*, but the moment she turned, she realized her error. It was a stupid move, a rookie mistake that she never would have made if she had been more on her game that morning.

Before she could completely register who had spoken, Jack Grew had her by the arm.

THE NEW BRIGHTON

1902—New York

Viola kept quiet as she walked with her mother the seven blocks to the small athletic club where her brother spent most of his days. The midmorning air was heavy with the threat of rain, and the smell of ash and soot mixed with the usual smells of the neighborhood—the overripe fruit and trash that lined the gutter and the baking of bread and the thick scent of garlic and spices that wafted from doorways. When they passed a still-smoldering building, Viola knew implicitly who was at fault for the tragedy.

She was.

Because she had let the magician outsmart her, she had failed Dolph. She had failed her kind, and she had failed herself. The Order should have been destroyed, but instead they had grown more oppressive than ever, taking revenge on the entire city for the deeds of a few.

She would kill them all if she could. But she needed to stay alive long enough to do it, and Paolo was her means to that end. First she had to survive whatever penance Paul had in store for her, and that would be trial enough, considering how she had betrayed the family by leaving them for the Devil's Own. Because for all intents and purposes, Paul *was* the family.

After their father died and the responsibility for the family had fallen on his shoulders, Paolo had supported them all as a bare-knuckle boxer. He'd anglicized his name to Paul Kelly because he thought it would pay better, and it had. But her dear brother hadn't stayed a boxer. Leading the

72

Five Pointers had turned out to be far more lucrative than getting his teeth knocked in every night. Because he was smart enough to grease the right palms at Tammany Hall, the police looked the other way.

Paul's deals with Tammany ensured the success of his athletic club, which was only a front for less legal activities. Come nightfall, the club hosted bare-knuckle matches, where beer flowed and bets were made— all with Paul taking his cut from the top, of course. Because Paul hid the truth of his work from their mother, she never knew what activities truly put bread on their table.

Unlike The Devil's Own, the boxing club Dolph had run, Paul's place didn't pulse with the warmth of magic. Paul, like their mother, was Sundren, without an affinity, and his gang was populated mostly by neighborhood boys whose childhood roughness had grown into a willing brutality. Viola was the black sheep of the family, an unexpected anomaly when her affinity appeared after generations of nothing. Her parents had seen it as a waste, bestowed as it was on a girl, but her brother had seen Viola's power as an opportunity—one that he felt he had every right to exploit.

Viola, of course, saw things differently, not that it had mattered to Paul or her mother at the time.

It was still too early in the day for Paul's usual crowd, so when her mother knocked at the unremarkable wooden door of the club, it was a boy about Viola's own age who answered and let them pass with barely a word. The main room of the club was mostly empty. A well-muscled man in the far corner pummeled a heavy bag that swung from the ceiling. He was bare-chested, and his left shoulder blade carried the angry red mark of the Five Pointers, an angular brand that was also a map of the neighborhood that gave her brother's gang its name. Another duo of men was sparring in the center of the floor, the heat and sweat from their bodies making the room feel too warm, too close. An older man smoked a thin cigar as he watched nearby.

As Viola and her mother entered, the man with the cigar glanced up, his face flashing with surprise to see her mother and then going flinty when he noticed Viola at her side. His hand went for the gun Viola knew would be hidden beneath his vest. The two men sparring and the other, larger man in the back of the room all paused to see what the interruption was.

"Get my son," her mother said, not paying any mind to the unease filtering through the room.

At first the older man didn't make any move to do as Viola's mother ordered. "What's she doing here?" he asked, nodding toward Viola.

Like Viola herself, Pasqualina Vaccarelli was not more than five feet tall. She might have been a broad, sturdy-looking woman, but her size should have put her at an immediate disadvantage. Viola's mother didn't so much as flinch, though. She gave the man the same look she'd given Viola and every one of her siblings—including Paolo—any time they were *truly* in trouble, the look that was usually accompanied by the sting of her wooden spoon. "Why do you think that is any of your business?"

The man's nostrils flared, but he waved off the two fighters, dismissing them, and then took himself off into the back room to find Paul. Viola's mother took the man's seat. Viola didn't join her. She would meet Paul on her feet.

They waited five minutes, ten, the time kept only by the smack of the other man's fist against the canvas bag. Finally, Paul appeared, dressed in his usual well-cut suit and with his dark hair slicked neatly into place, looking more like a banker than the thug he actually was. He embraced their mother and fawned over her for a minute or two, ignoring Viola completely. She wasn't fooled into thinking he hadn't seen her, though, so she wasn't surprised when he finally turned his attention to her.

Viola saw the attack coming—had expected it—and could have dropped Paul in his tracks to prevent it, but instead, she accepted the blow when the back of his hand collided with her left cheek. She stumbled and saw actual stars as her vision threatened to go black and she struggled to stay upright. But at least she had not so much as yelped at the pain. She wouldn't give him that satisfaction.

The next blow came before she was completely upright again. And then the next, until she felt the warmth of the blood trickling from her nose and tasted its coppery tang in her mouth. Her head spun too much for her to remain standing any longer, and she stumbled to her knees. It felt as though the world had narrowed to the pain her brother's fists had brought to the surface of her body.

Gingerly, Viola touched her mouth where her lip felt split. But she didn't look up at Paolo and she didn't say a word. She simply listened to the dull *thump . . . thump . . . thump* of fists hitting canvas, a sound that matched the beating of her own tired and scarred heart.

Paul pulled her to her feet, and Viola's head swirled as she tried to focus on him. His face was close to hers when she heard her mother's voice saying "basta."

"*I'll* decide what's enough, Mamma," Paul said, tightening his grip on Viola's arm where their mother couldn't see.

Viola could smell his expensive cologne, could feel the heat from his body as he crowded her with his size. He was trying to intimidate her, as he had when they were children. But she wasn't a child anymore. She hadn't been for a very long time.

"She needs to know her place," Paul said.

"You've shown her," their mother said, her tone indicating that nothing more was to be said about this. "Whatever she's done, she's still family."

Paul glared at Viola, who met his eyes without flinching. He held her a moment longer, though, his viselike grip on her arm painful, before he finally released her. Then he walked over and, placing his hands gently on his mother's shoulders, leaned down and gave her a kiss on the cheek. "Don't worry about it, Mamma. I know how to take care of family. I take care of you, don't I?"

Viola didn't have to look to know that her mother's eyes had softened and her stern mouth had tugged up at the corners. She could hear the fondness in her mother's voice. "You're a good boy, Paolo."

It took everything Viola had not to snort at that.

Paul called for one of his boys, and when two arrived, scurrying from the back room like rats, he told them to take his mother home.

Before she left, her mother came over and took Viola's chin with a sure grip. With an almost warm expression, her mother examined Viola's bloodied face. "Listen to your brother, mia figghia. Later we visit Father Lorenzo, and you can confess."

"Yes, Mamma," Viola murmured, lowering her eyes as the bitterness of the words mixed with the blood pooling in her mouth. She ignored the weariness that felt like a weight, the hurt that couldn't be brushed away any more than the tattoo inked between the blades of her shoulders.

After their mother left, Paul came over and looked at her face, disgust—and also jealousy—shining in his eyes. "I know why you're back." His wide mouth curled into a sneer. "Mamma, she thinks you came to your senses, but that's not it, is it?" He gave her still-sore cheek a less-than-friendly pat. "No . . . It's because the damn cripple isn't around to protect you now, isn't it?"

She wanted to spit in his face. She wanted to curse his name and tell him that Dolph Saunders had been more of a man than Paul would ever be. But Viola kept her mouth shut and tried to keep the hate from her eyes.

"What? Nothing to say for yourself?"

"What does it matter why I'm here?" she said, her words thick on her swollen lips. "I came back. I'm yours to use again, aren't I?"

His wide mouth turned down. "You're no good to me if I can't trust you."

"Who else would I be loyal to?" Viola asked. "You're right. Dolph Saunders *is* dead, and I'm not interested in dying or getting caught by some Order patrol. You think I haven't seen your boys working with them? You think I don't know you have friends in high places?" She shook her head. "I'm not an idiota, Paolo. I don't have nowhere else to go. I'll do what you need so long as you keep the Order away from me."

Paul didn't speak at first.

"I know what you want. . . . You want to control the Bowery," she persisted. "Everybody knows what I can do. *Everybody*. You don't think it will be a boon if they know I'm for you now?"

He considered her, his face so much like her late father's and yet so different. It was harder, less forgiving. Much, *much* more determined than her father's had ever been.

Paul stepped toward her, and before she realized what he'd planned, he had her by the throat, his large, meaty hands squeezing her neck so tightly she couldn't draw breath. Tight enough that she would wear the mark of them. "You were smart to go to Mamma, little sister. I'll take you on, for her sake. But if you go against me again, it will be the last time."

With every ounce of strength she had left, Viola pulled her affinity around her and pushed it toward her brother until his eyes went wide and he gasped, releasing her throat and bringing his hands up to his own. The man who had been punching the bag stopped his assault and started to approach them.

"Call him off," Viola told her brother.

Paul's eyes were filled with rage, but his face was turning purplish already from his inability to breathe. Finally, he lifted his hand, and the man halted.

"I didn't come back to hurt you, though the good lord knows I have every reason to, after what you've done. But you touch me again—if you let any of your men touch me—I will *end* you."

She released her hold on him, and he gasped, stumbling forward. "I'll kill you myself," he rasped.

Viola simply stared at him, unimpressed. "The bullet better be quick, Paolo."

He glared at her. "It will be."

"And how will you explain that to Mamma?" Her lips felt tight as she forced her mouth into the semblance of a cold smile. "Don't think

I haven't made arrangements to expose you if anything happens to me. Mamma will know all about your other activities, the whores and the criminals you depend on for your money." It was a lie, of course. If she'd had anyone else to turn to, she wouldn't be standing there, humiliating herself. "I need your protection, and in exchange I'll be your blade, but you and your scagnozzi can keep your damn hands off me."

The siblings studied each other in tense silence until, finally, Paul huffed out a hollow breath that sounded like he was vaguely amused.

Va bene. She needed him to respect her power, even if he didn't respect her.

"Go get yourself cleaned up." He gestured to the blood staining her shirt. "Can't have my blade tarnished, can I? You want my protection? You'll work for it."

"I wouldn't expect anything less." Viola was too tired, too jaded by the violence of her life to feel anything close to relief. But she did feel a certain satisfaction. Paul would have killed her already if he didn't mean to keep her. Until she figured out what she needed to do next, she'd be safe. Or as safe as any Mageus could be in this city.

But before she could go, the bell over the front door rang, signaling that someone else had come into the club.

"James," Paul said, stepping past Viola to greet the new arrival.

She turned to see who had arrived. Silhouetted by the morning light was a familiar face, a boy of no more than sixteen with dirty-blond hair and gold spectacles. *What is he doing here, when he's supposed to be leading the Devil's Own?* He was leaning against a familiar cane, one topped with a silver Medusa head that wore the face of Viola's friend Leena. It had once belonged to Dolph Saunders.

Viola took a step forward, ready to rip the cane from Nibsy's hands. *He has no right.* But the sharp look Paul gave her made her pause. It was too early to cross him. Too early for him to know where her true loyalties lay.

"Thanks for meeting with me, Paul."

"Of course. You know my sister," Paul said, gesturing absently toward Viola. "She's recently come back into the family."

"Has she?" Nibsy Lorcan said as he limped into the room.

She could see the questions in Nibsy's eyes, but she didn't say anything to answer them.

"Hello, Viola. I can't say it's a pleasure to see you again," Nibsy said, gesturing to his injured leg. His eyes glinted behind his glasses. "But it is certainly a surprise."

"I'll give you a surprise," she growled, taking a step toward him.

"You already did." Nibsy's voice was lower and more dangerous than she'd ever heard it. It was enough to make her pause. Then he looked at Paul. "If you can't control your sister, I'm not sure our arrangement will work out. Which would be a shame, since I brought the information you wanted." He pulled a small packet of paper from his coat pocket and held it up, drawing everyone's attention to it.

"Enough," Paul said, barely glancing in Viola's direction. "Go clean yourself up, like I said."

"I'm not leaving until he gives me what's mine." She met her brother's eyes, determined. "You want me to be your blade? It works better when I have a good knife."

Paul's expression barely flickered, but Viola had known her brother long enough to recognize the cold calculation in his eyes. "You forget, little sister, that I know you don't need a knife to kill. As far as I'm concerned, if Mr. Lorcan has something of yours, he can keep it . . . as a gift from me."

"You can't—"

"But I can," Paul said softly. "You're either back with the family or not. You're either loyal to me—*obedient to me*—or we are finished."

Viola glared at him. She thought briefly about ending the entire farce—about ending *Paolo*. But if she did, then what? She would never be able to face her mother, and she would be on her own again. The beating she'd just taken would have been for nothing. And she might never discover what was in the package that Nibsy had offered Paul.

She held Paul's gaze a moment longer, to make sure he understood that she wasn't afraid. This was a choice. She would bide her time and pretend to be dutiful, but when the moment came, she would make sure they regretted what they had done. Death was too easy for her brother. Family or not, first she would make him crawl.

A SERPENT'S SMILE

1902—New Jersey

I *knew* it was you," Jack said, his grip tight on Esta's arm.

He can't be here.

Shock paralyzed Esta for a moment—but only for a moment. Quickly on the heels of shock came the cold sureness of an emotion much darker than fear. *Of course* Jack Grew could be here. The nephew of J. P. Morgan, Jack was practically royalty in New York. His family would have simply paid the right people, whispered in the right ear, and Jack's little *indiscretion* on the bridge would have been brushed away like the morning's ashes. Never mind that the indiscretion was attempted murder.

If it hadn't been for Esta's quick thinking—and her ability to pull time still and move Harte out of the bullet's path—Jack would have killed him. With the terrible machine he'd been trying to build, Jack would have killed every Mageus in the city. Since he still had the same barely leashed wild-eyed look that he'd had the day before, Esta knew he was still dangerous, and she was not about to give him the chance to kill her, too.

Gathering her wits and swallowing down the sharp taste of hatred that had coated her mouth, she drew a serpent's smile across her lips and fell into the fake accent she'd used with Jack before. "Jack, darling," Esta purred, gently testing the strength of the grip he had on her arm. "Is it really you?"

"Surprised?" he asked, his mouth twisting into an answering smile that was all teeth and anticipation. His fingers on her arm just missed the cuff she wore beneath her sleeve.

Esta ignored the fury in his expression and stepped closer. "When the police took you, I was so worried."

Jack blinked, taken off guard by her words, just as she'd hoped. He almost seemed unsure about what to do next, but he did not loosen his hold on her. Then his expression went brittle and cold. "Somehow I doubt that," he said, his eyes narrowed. "You were the one who helped Darrigan make me look like a fool. You *ruined* me."

"No, Jack," she said, her eyes wide with feigned surprise. "You mustn't say such things."

"You think I haven't realized that you and Darrigan were in it together from the beginning?" Jack's fingers were digging into Esta's arm hard enough to leave a mark. "You don't think I know that everything you told me was a lie?"

Esta shook her head. "No . . . Darrigan *used* me," she said, forcing her voice to tremble a little. She had one chance to get this particular performance right. "I didn't know what he had planned that night. Don't you remember? He left me there, alone on that stage, to take the blame. You have to believe me. . . ."

"No. Actually, I don't." Jack glared at her. "If anything you just said was true, the Order would already have you. But you managed *miraculously* to get away—twice."

"I was afraid no one would believe me—"

"Because you don't deserve to be believed," he snapped. "Darrigan got you out of Khafre Hall somehow, and then you managed to get yourself off the bridge, which means you know more than you're saying." He started to yank her along, pulling her away from platform seven.

No. She wasn't going *anywhere* with Jack. Panic was making her pulse race, but Esta drew herself up, and even though fear put an edge to her voice, she leaned into the role she had perfected to hook Jack. "Let me go," she told him, using her most imperious voice as she tried to pull away.

If it weren't for the crowd, Esta would have dropped him in a second. Even with the crowd, a twist of her arm, a shifting of her weight, and Jack would be on his back. The problem was that if that happened, everyone in the terminal would be looking at her.

Any other time she might have risked it, because as soon as she was free, she could have pulled the seconds slow and been gone. But disappearing like that would mean revealing what she was to Jack, and if her affinity was as weak as she felt or if she lost her hold of it—as she had on the bridge—she would be stuck with more witnesses than she wanted. She'd be at the mercy of the crowd . . . and of Jack.

Esta's mind was racing as she stumbled along, doing everything she could to slow Jack's progress. The train nearby let off a hiss of steam, a sign that the boilers in the engines were nearly ready and a reminder that the train to Chicago would also leave soon. Other than the odd whispers of energy earlier, she hadn't seen any sign of Harte. She had to hope that he would still be waiting where they'd agreed, but Jack was dragging her in the wrong direction.

If she didn't show up, would Harte assume the worst and believe she'd betrayed him? It wouldn't be a stretch, considering their history. Would he come looking for her, or would he leave without her?

A cold thought struck her: *He can leave.* She'd given him the Book. She had the stone, true, but she'd given Harte the Book as an assurance that *she* wouldn't run. Why hadn't she considered that *he* might? After all, he was out of the city now. *Free.*

And she was trapped with Jack.

It doesn't matter. Whether Harte was waiting for her, as he'd promised, or had already abandoned her, she needed to focus. If she could just get away from Jack, she might still be able to get out of town. She knew where the first stone was. She could find it—and since she knew where Harte was headed, she could find him, too.

People around them were beginning to stare, so she decided to use that to her advantage and struggled more, putting up a fight to attract even more attention.

"Please, sir," she whimpered at a man in an ill-fitting vest and a scuffed derby hat, whose steps had slowed as he eyed the two of them. "I don't know this man," she pleaded.

But Jack jerked her back, putting himself between her and the person she was appealing to. "She knows *exactly* who I am," Jack told the confused stranger. "She's our maid. Tried to leave town with my mother's necklace."

The man eyed the two of them again, and Esta knew what he was seeing: Jack's expensively cut suit, contrasted with the rumpled skirts she'd lifted from a clothesline that morning. That, along with her fake accent, and the man in the vest paused only a second longer before making up his mind. He gave Jack a nod and kept walking toward the train platform, taking all hope Esta had of a rescue with him.

"Did you really think that would work?" Jack laughed.

Esta glared at him. "Did you really think I wouldn't try?"

"What did you think would happen—that the police would come and take *me* away?" He laughed. "Not likely, and not long after the police took you into custody, the Order would have made you wish you'd ended your life on that bridge with Darrigan."

"Like you aren't going to hand me over to them anyway."

The amusement that lit Jack's eyes made Esta go cold. "Maybe eventually I'll give you to my uncle and his friends . . . after I'm finished with you."

Her skin crawled. "If you think I'd let you touch me—"

"If you think you have a choice, you're not half as smart as you pretend to be," Jack told her. "But I don't want *you*. Women like you are a dime a dozen. I want what Darrigan took from the Order."

"I don't *know* what he took," she pleaded, playing dumb.

Jack gave her a mocking look. "I don't believe that for a second. We both know that Darrigan stole some very important pieces from the Order—a book called the Ars Arcana and the five ancient artifacts. I want them back."

"I'm sure you do, but I can't give you what I don't have," she said, meeting his eyes. "For all I know, the things you're looking for are at the bottom of the river—with him."

"Darrigan might be at the bottom of the river, but I don't believe the things he stole are." He leaned down so that his face was close to hers. With his strong patrician features and his shock of blond hair, he might have been handsome. But there was a detached arrogance in his icy blue eyes that made her skin crawl, and his skin had a sallow, puffy appearance, the effect of the whiskey already scenting his breath that morning. "No . . . I think there's a reason you were on the bridge yesterday. I think Darrigan told you where the Order's things are. Perhaps he even gave them to you."

She shook her head. "He didn't—"

He shook her into silence. "Then he told you *something*. He wouldn't have gone to all that trouble to steal them only to toss himself from a bridge. You know more than you're admitting. But don't worry. . . . I have ways to get the information out of you."

"You're welcome to try," she said, straightening her spine against the threat. He wouldn't get what she *did* have, either. As soon as he had her alone, she would do what she couldn't do here. She would make him regret touching her.

He cocked his head slightly at her boldness. "Do you know what's happening right now, as you stand here pretending innocence? The Order is turning the city inside out to find its lost treasures. And they will destroy anyone who stands in their way. The longer you delay the inevitable, the more who will suffer."

He was right. People were being punished because of her. Because of what she had failed to do. But she wouldn't allow him to use that against her. "To go to that kind of trouble, the Order must be awfully scared. They must know that without their little baubles, they're *nothing*."

His eyes raked over her, too perceptive. "They're the most powerful men in the country."

"They're cowards. Preying on the poor and the weak. I'm glad

Darrigan stole their precious trinkets. I'm glad the Order is afraid."

He did something then that she didn't expect—he *laughed*. "Even without their *trinkets*, they could destroy you." Then the amusement drained from his expression, and he pulled her close, his eyes not quite focused. He traced one finger down the side of her face. "But I could protect you from them. Once I have what Darrigan stole, you won't need to fear the Order any longer."

At first his words made no sense. Then realization struck. "You're not going to give any of it back to them, are you?"

"Why should I?" Jack's voice had gone bitter. "You're right. The Order is nothing more than a bunch of feeble old men. Look how easily trash from the gutter broke through their defenses. If they had only let me consult the Ars Arcana, I could have rid the entire city of the danger. Their precious Khafre Hall would still be standing. I could have *protected* them."

With the machine. Harte had told her everything about the dangerous invention Jack had been working on, a modern solution to expand the Brink's power and wipe out magic—and the people who had an affinity for it. "You would have killed innocent people."

"There are no innocent maggots," Jack sneered. "The old magic corrupts everyone the same." He paused, as though something almost humorous had occurred to him. "I suppose I owe Darrigan a debt of gratitude for liberating the Ars Arcana for me. With it I'll prove to the world who I really am and all that I can do, and the Order will come on their knees, begging."

The nearby train let off another hiss of steam, a reminder that she was running out of time.

"Because you're smarter than them," Esta said softly, infusing a breathiness into her voice as she tried another tactic. "You always have been."

Jack's eyes widened, just a bit, and his breath caught. For a moment he paused, and Esta thought her ploy had worked. But then his grip on her arm tightened again. "Did you really think I would fall for your lies again?"

She shook her head. She'd only hoped. "They weren't lies, Jack."

The flicker of uncertainty passed through Jack's expression.

Ignoring the scent of liquor on his breath, she leaned in closer. "I never lied about my feelings for you, darling." Then, before she could second-guess herself, she tipped her head up and pressed her lips against his.

Jack's mouth went stiff with surprise at first, but then he was kissing her. Or rather, he was mauling her, his lips overeager and without finesse, as though he could claim her simply by bruising her mouth with his. It took everything she had not to pull away or gag.

An eternity later, Jack came up for air, his blue eyes glazed with satisfaction, and she thought he might even loosen his hold on her, as she'd hoped. Instead, his grip only tightened. "If you're lying again—"

"No, Jack . . ." She fought to keep herself calm, but inside she was screaming. It hadn't worked, and now she had the stale taste of Jack coating her mouth. She began to gather her strength to fight him—to do anything she needed to do to get to platform seven before that train pulled away.

"If you betray me, I will kill you myself. And no one will miss you when you're gone. Not the trash in the Bowery and certainly not your con man of a magician." A dark amusement flashed in his cold eyes. "He's too busy feeding the fish in the Hudson."

"You sure about that, Jack?" a voice said, and Esta didn't need to look behind her to know that Harte had finally found her.

A VISION OF
LIGHT AND POWER

1902—New Jersey

Harte Darrigan knew he was a bastard in every sense of the word, but he couldn't stop the wave of possessiveness that flashed through him when he saw Esta tip her chin up and press her lips against Jack Grew's.

The train to Chicago was about to leave, and there had been no sign of her on the platform where they'd agreed to meet, so Harte had gone looking. He'd come around the corner and found her with Jack, and there was no mistaking what he saw—*she* had kissed *him*. On purpose. Even now, pinned against Jack, she wasn't struggling to get away. And if anyone could get away, it was Esta.

For a moment the only thing Harte could bring into focus was the way her fingers were curled around the lapels of Jack's coat. The voice inside of him had roared up, shrieking with a deafening pitch as it clawed at its confines, and by the time he had pushed it away and shoved it back down, Jack was speaking.

"... con man of a magician ... too busy feeding fish in the Hudson."

Rage had slammed through Harte, and the voice echoed in approval. "You sure about that, Jack?" he asked, gratified to see the surprise drain Jack's face of color. But in the space of a heartbeat, Jack's expression rearranged itself—surprise transformed to confusion and then to recognition—and he pulled Esta back against him, pinning her to him.

Harte took a step forward, but Esta shook her head.

For an instant the fury within him rose up again, but then he saw how wide her eyes were. There was a fear in them so uncharacteristic that Esta almost looked like a different person. Suddenly the station seemed to fall away, and it felt as though the entire world had narrowed down to the whiskey-colored irises of her eyes.

Her eyes were wide, and her expression was blank with terror. The stones around her glowed, a fiery circle of light and power. One by one the stones went dark, and then the blackness of her pupils seeped into the color, obliterating it, spreading to the whites of her eyes, until all that looked back was darkness. Emptiness. Nothing. And the darkness began to pour out of her. . . .

He stepped forward blindly, not knowing what he could possibly do. Not sure what he was even seeing.

"No!" she told him, the fear in her voice stopping him in his tracks. "Stay back."

All at once, the vision dissipated. They were in the station once more, and Esta's eyes were golden. They were still frightened, but there was none of the yawning blackness he'd seen just moments before. And Jack was smiling as though he'd already won.

"I'd listen to her if I were you," Jack said, his voice calm and level, as if they were discussing something as mundane as the weather or the price of bread. "Or don't listen. It doesn't much matter to me. If we're being honest with one another, I'll probably shoot her either way." Jack's eyes narrowed. "But then, honesty isn't something you're familiar with, is it, Darrigan?"

Honesty? The voice suddenly roared inside of him. *What could he know of honesty?*

Disoriented and filled with a combination of guilt and rage that he didn't quite understand, Harte tried to pull himself together. "Playing with guns again, Jack?" he asked, amazed that he managed to keep any tremor of fear out of his voice. "I'm sure the police over there would be interested in knowing about that."

"She'd have a bullet in her back before you finished calling them," Jack replied lazily.

The other passengers streamed around them like water parting for a rock in a stream, ignoring the tableau they must have made standing there, tense and clearly at odds. But then, wealth like Jack's granted a certain amount of invisibility, Harte thought. No one questioned you when you appeared to own the world.

Harte kept his focus on Jack so he wouldn't have to deal with the fear in Esta's eyes. "You don't really want to hurt her, Jack. Your family might own half the city, but murder is murder. There will be consequences for shooting a girl in the middle of a train station."

"Oh, I think you'll find that you're wrong about that," Jack said, and Harte didn't like the gleam in Jack's eyes. "Even if there are certain *inconveniences*, I think you'll find that I'm willing to deal with quite a lot to get what I want. I'm willing to do whatever it takes."

The determination in Jack's tone was a stone in the pit of Harte's stomach. "I know you are, Jack. But you don't have to—that's what I'm trying to tell you. We can make this easy. You don't *need* to hurt her. She doesn't have what you're looking for."

Jack's eyes narrowed, but Harte could read the anticipation and eagerness in his expression. *Just keep him interested.* Because without Esta . . .

He couldn't let himself think about that.

"And *you* do?" Jack asked.

"No—" Esta started to say, but another jerk from Jack had her gasping instead.

Harte tried to send Esta a silent message, what he hoped was an encouraging look to let her know everything would be fine. They'd get out of this mess. *He* would get them out.

"Of course I do," Harte answered lazily. He knew what Jack wanted. It was the same thing Jack—and everyone else—had wanted from the beginning: the Book. And all the knowledge and power it contained. Well . . . Jack could have one of those things.

"Where is it?" Jack demanded.

Harte didn't know whether the decision he was about to make was the right one or if it was his biggest mistake yet. But from the wild look in Jack's eyes, Harte knew that Jack would do everything he was threatening. After all, to Jack, Esta was expendable. Jack didn't know what she was, couldn't even begin to imagine how useful she might be to him, so Jack wouldn't hesitate to shoot her. And if that happened—if Esta died here and now—Harte would be lost as well.

He shuddered as the voice tried to claw its way to the surface of his mind. Pushing him forward. *Compelling* him.

Harte took the Book from inside his coat.

"You can't—" Esta said when she saw it, but Jack pushed her forward, silencing her with the threat of the gun in her back.

Jack's eyes widened slightly, and a hungry gleam shone within them. "Give it to me," he snapped.

"I know how much you want this, Jack," Harte said, pulling around him the familiar role he'd perfected over the past few years—the even-tempered, ever-confident magician. "How many times did you tell me about how your uncle and his friends kept you from everything you could be by refusing to let you have access to this Book? Well, here it is, Jack. You can have it—the power of the Ars Arcana and all the knowledge it contains. You simply have to release Esta, and it can be yours. *All* of it can be yours."

Jack's icy eyes were determined, and Harte could sense that Jack's desire for the Book burned hot and bright. He wanted to accept. . . .

Then Jack's expression shifted, and his lip curled slightly on one side. "Now I know you're lying. You expect me to believe you would give up all that for *her*? After all you've done to get it?" Jack shook his head. "No girl is worth *that*."

Harte let out a derisive chuckle, even as his stomach threatened to turn itself inside out. "Well, by all means . . . keep her, then—I'd rather have this anyway," he lied, making a show of tucking the Book back into his pocket as he turned to leave.

Ignoring the way Esta's body went tense, Harte shoved down the voice that roared its displeasure at the idea of leaving her behind. All around him, the station seemed to recede. The smell of coal smoke in the air and the noise of the early morning travelers. The hiss of steam from a train nearby and the final call of the conductor. None of the noise or sights of the station touched him, because all his energy was focused on walking away from Esta.

Harte got exactly three steps away before Jack did exactly what he had hoped.

"Wait!" Jack shouted.

Harte turned slowly, pretending to be annoyed at Jack's change of mind. "Yes?"

Jack lifted his chin, a sharp jerk that punctuated the demand in his words. "If it's really the Ars Arcana you have there, you should be able to prove it. Some demonstration of the Book's power will suffice."

Harte kept from showing any bit of the relief he felt at Jack's words. "Of course . . ." He withdrew the Book again. His heart was pounding away in his ears as loudly and as steadily as a train careening down the tracks.

Esta's eyes were determined, frantic to convey a single message that Harte was just as determined to ignore—*no.*

Trust me, he pleaded silently, but he couldn't be sure she understood.

He made a show of examining the Book, of riffling through its uneven pages and admiring it. "Despite its humble appearance, this Book is *quite* amazing. I've learned so much from it already," Harte told Jack, settling deeper into the role and taking comfort in that familiar, reliable part of himself. "I think you would be *very* impressed to see what I can do with it."

Jack only glared at him. "I doubt it. If that book had any *real* power, you wouldn't still be standing here talking."

Harte gave a conceding shrug. "You're right, Jack. So let's not talk any longer." He held the Book out in front of him.

Esta's face was creased in pain, her expression urgent with panic. "No, Harte. You can't—"

But before she could finish, Harte tossed the Book into the air, high over their heads.

THE CHOICE

1902—New Jersey

E sta had stopped worrying about the ache from the gun shoved against her lower back the moment she saw Harte take the Book from his coat and hold it out to Jack like an offering.

"No!" she screamed as Harte launched the Book into the air.

It felt like everything happened all at once: The moment the Book was airborne, Jack loosened his hold on her and leaped for it. In almost the same moment, Harte lunged toward her and took hold of Esta's wrist, urging, *"Now!"*

With a sudden flash of realization, she understood what Harte had intended all along, and with a speed and sureness that came from a combination of instinct and years of training, she drew on her own affinity and pulled time slow . . . just as the Book fell into Jack's outstretched hand.

Esta nearly crumpled in relief as the station around them went eerily silent—steam from the nearby engine hung in the air, an immovable cloud of vapor and dust that cloaked the figures trapped within it, and the people on the platform froze around them. Jack, too, had gone still mid-leap, his face fixed in a wild-eyed look of frenzy, while his fingertips had just barely grasped the small leather volume that was the root of all their problems.

Her affinity felt wobbly, unsure, but it was still there.

Almost immediately, she was being crushed to Harte's chest and surrounded by the familiar scent of him as he wrapped his arms around her.

"Thank god you understood." His breath was warm as he tucked his face into her neck, and she could feel him shaking.

His words barely registered. She hardly noticed the warmth of his body, strong and solid, because every ounce of her concentration was now on the shaky hold she had on the seconds around her.

Without releasing his grip on her, Harte pulled back and searched her face. There was a question in his gray eyes that she couldn't quite discern, and for a moment she thought she saw the flash of strange colors in his irises.

"Are you okay?" he asked finally.

"I've been better," she told him, shrugging off his concern with an instinct that years of training under the stern hand of Professor Lachlan had impressed upon her.

In truth, her legs felt like jelly, and the place where the gun had prodded her—just above her right kidney—still ached from the pressure. She'd have a bruise there later, but she would gladly take the bruise over the bullet that would have certainly been deadly.

All around her, the material net of time seemed to waver and vibrate . . . or maybe that was her own magic. Her power was there, but it felt slippery and too volatile, and she was concentrating harder than she usually had to. The more she focused on not losing hold of time, the more she felt a pain building behind her temples.

Part of her wanted to lean into Harte. He hadn't betrayed her or left her behind, and with the ache in her head and the shaky hold that she had on her affinity, she felt like she *needed* to take whatever comfort and strength she could from the sureness of his body.

But she'd no sooner had the thought than she dismissed it. That kind of need was nothing more than weakness. Instead, she drew on her *own* strength and took a step back, until the two of them were connected only by Harte's gentle grip on her. It was just enough of a connection to keep him linked to her, so he wasn't frozen like the rest of the station around them, and it was enough distance that some of the unsettling yearning she'd felt a heartbeat before eased. But with each second that passed, the struggle with her affinity only worsened.

"We should go," she told him.

Harte studied her a moment longer, his mouth turned down into a thoughtful frown that gave her the strangest urge to kiss him, if only to watch how his expression changed. If only to erase the memory of Jack. But she wouldn't act on her desire, not while her lips still felt fouled by the memory of Jack's punishing, whiskey-laced assault.

Together they approached Jack, who was suspended in the net of time. Harte reached up and easily took the Book from Jack's fingertips, then tucked it into his own coat again. "Ready?"

Jack was still suspended mid-lunge, his arm outstretched and reaching for something that was no longer there. His eyes, though—they burned with a hatred that made Esta hesitate, even as her grasp on time was slipping.

"We can't just leave him here," Esta told Harte, struggling to maintain her hold on the seconds. "He knows you're alive now. He knows you have the Book. When we disappear, he'll guess what we are."

Harte glanced at her, suddenly wary.

"He could tell the Order you're still alive or come after us himself." The pounding behind her temples had increased, and the periphery of her vision began to waver. She felt a darkness beginning to creep into the edges of her sight that mirrored the darkness of her thoughts, and she reached to pry the gun from Jack's hand. "As long as he's alive, he's a danger to us."

"We can't just kill him," Harte said, and his tone scraped against her nerves.

"He would have killed me." She looked down at the pistol she was now holding. Focusing on the weapon, she could almost ignore the way the blackness was teasing at the edges of her vision, growing to match the hate she felt building inside of her as she weighed the gun's solid body in her hands.

She hadn't only been trained to fight with her fists and with knives. A gun wasn't her first choice, but she knew how to use one. She also knew what it meant that the hammer was cocked and ready to fire, so she understood how close she'd come to having a bullet tear through her kidneys and guts—an irreparable wound that would have led to a painful death, especially in this time.

"He wasn't going to let either one of us go," she told Harte.

Harte took her by the wrist gently, as though to stop her, but then he paused. His eyes swirled with the strange colors as they had before, and she felt the beginnings of the same creeping energy that had climbed up her arm when they'd crossed the bridge. She thought he was about to agree, but then he blinked and his eyes cleared as he took the gun from her and eased the hammer back down.

His voice was tight when he finally spoke. "We're not like him, Esta."

"Aren't we?" she asked, thinking of all the people they had both been willing to betray in the weeks before to get the Book—to get what they wanted. She thought, too, of all the people who were innocent but who would suffer because of what she had done, because of the choices she had made. She could end this. She could stop Jack, if nothing else.

At the edges of her vision, the blackness was still growing, bleeding into the silent, still world. She wouldn't be able to hold on to her grasp of time much longer. "If we leave him here, how many more are going to die?"

"If you kill him in cold blood, it will change you," Harte told her firmly. "He isn't worth the price."

"Are you sure about that?" she asked, even as the blackness continued to grow. There was something strangely compelling about it, terrifying as it was. "Because *I'm* not."

She looked again at Jack. It was true that this puppy of a man wasn't the cause of her pain. He hadn't been the one to manipulate her, to murder her family, to strip away everything she thought she was until only the raw wound of a girl was left behind. But he certainly wasn't innocent.

There was so much evil in the world, so much more to come in the future. It might be worth it to trade her soul for a way to stop even a little of it. True, she could walk away and leave Jack here, alive and well—and able to hurt others. Or she could start here, now. She could become the vengeance that burned so hot in the pit of her stomach.

She started to reach for the gun, but Harte held it away from her.

"I *am* sure," he said as he ejected the revolving cylinder, emptied the bullets onto the ground, and placed the gun into Jack's coat pocket.

"Harte—" she started to argue.

"My soul, however, is already plenty stained," he interrupted, drawing back his fist.

The instant Harte's knuckles met Jack's face, the sickening crunch of bone echoed through the silent platform. Her affinity had already felt strained and uncertain with the darkness bleeding into her vision, and the moment Harte's fist made contact, Esta's already wavering affinity was disrupted by the connection between Harte and Jack. Jolted by the addition of another body to the circuit of magic between them, Esta's focus wavered and she lost her grip on time.

The world slammed back into motion at once. All around them the roar of the platform returned. Harte turned to look at her, confused about her failure, but she didn't have the words to explain it—or the time.

Behind Harte, Jack's head snapped back as the world around them lurched into motion, but he didn't go down.

"Come on!" Esta urged, tugging Harte along. She glanced back to see Jack, swaying on his feet as he dabbed at his bloodied nose and blinked in confusion. He was stunned, but he wouldn't be for long. "We need to get to a train."

"What happened?" Harte asked. "Why did you let go?"

"I didn't—" she started to say, but she didn't know how to begin describing the blackness she saw or the emptiness she felt. "Not now," she said, tugging him onward even as she struggled to find the threads of time, to focus enough to pull them slow.

Together they ran, pushing their way through the concerned crowd of people, dodging unaware travelers and carts of luggage as they sprinted toward their only chance at escape.

"I didn't get the tickets," she told him, lifting her skirts to keep up with his long strides.

"It doesn't matter." His hand gripped hers more securely as they ran. "We'll figure it out. We just need to get on a train. *Any* train at this point."

"Platform seven," she insisted, thinking of the stone waiting in Chicago. "We need to get to platform seven."

When they reached the platform, the shrill cry of a whistle split through the rustling commotion of the station. Esta looked over her shoulder to see Jack not far behind them, followed by a station officer. The train was already starting slowly down the track. A plume of its smoke canopied the platform with a heavy cloud of coal and sulfur as the steam hissed from the engines and the train began to pick up its pace.

"Go!" Harte shouted when her steps faltered. Ahead of them, two more policemen were racing toward them, their batons already raised as they shouted for people to get out of the way. He toppled a pile of luggage to create a roadblock for the people following them. But it wouldn't hold them for long. "We need more time," he told her, pulling her around an older man.

Her affinity felt more unsteady than ever, and her magic felt like something separate from her, untouchable. Her heart was pumping, her head was pounding, and time felt like the ragged ends of a scarf that had just been taken out of her reach by the breeze.

"I can't," she told him.

She saw the confusion in his eyes when he looked back at her, but Harte didn't hesitate. Running alongside the already-moving train, he reached the back of one of the cars and pulled her forward, boosting her onto the platform as he jogged alongside the train. He reached for the handle and was about to step up beside her when Esta saw Jack.

"Watch out!" Esta told him, but the warning came too late.

Before Harte could lift himself onto the train, Jack had him by the wrist, yanking him back.

"Harte!" Esta was already preparing to jump from the train when Harte shouted at her not to.

All around them, people had stopped to watch. The entire platform had taken on a strange, hushed atmosphere that had nothing to do with Esta's affinity and everything to do with the curiosity of the other travelers.

Harte jerked away from Jack, pulling his arm out of the coat to get free. Off-balance from losing his grip on Harte, Jack fell back, holding on to the coat. A moment later, Harte had boosted himself up into the train.

"Come on," he said, leading her toward the front of the nearly empty car. "We can't stay here—" he started. But before they could even reach the middle of the car, a station officer had come through the doorway. The moment he saw Harte and Esta, he drew out his billystick and blocked the entrance. The few passengers sitting in the car looked up, curious about what was happening.

Harte stepped in front of her, backing her toward the rear exit slightly. They'd had only a minute to catch their breath when the door of the car opened behind him. Esta turned to see Jack blocking their other means of escape.

"Get us out of this, Esta," Harte murmured as he kept his attention on both ends of the car and the approaching attackers.

"There's nowhere for you to go, Darrigan," Jack said, a satisfied smile sliding across his face.

"He's right, son. Put your hands up and get to your knees, and we can do this easy," the officer said from the front of the car.

They were trapped. Even if she could manage to pull time to a stop, there was nowhere to go—no way to escape.

Except one.

Esta had never tried to slip through time like that before—not in a moving vehicle. Time was connected to place, which meant she could only slip through if that place existed in the time she wanted to reach. But they didn't need to go very far—a day or two, maybe as much as a week—just long enough to be on a different version of this train, away from this danger.

She put all her effort, all her energy into focusing on the seconds around her. Ignoring the pounding in her temples, she drew deeper on her affinity than she ever had before. The stone on her arm, Ishtar's Key, grew uncomfortably warm as Esta focused on the spaces between the seconds and began reaching for the layered moments that make up the reality of a place. She riffled through those moments, hunting desperately to find what she was looking for.

Around them the train began to rattle, vibrating along the track violently enough to have the policeman grabbing at the back of a seat to stay on his feet.

"What's happening?" Harte asked.

But Esta didn't hear anything other than the roaring in her ears, searching and searching until she could see nothing but the multiplicity of moments stacked up around her, solid and real as the present one.

Usually, sifting through time was like riffling through the pages of a book, searching for some word, some detail to key into the right date and time. Usually, she had time to focus and sort through the layers to the precise point she wanted, to a *safe* point. But with the train picking up speed and the heat from the connection between her and Harte tugging at her attention, time itself felt loose and unmoored. Instead of finding a safe place, she found huge gaps where the train they were riding on didn't exist.

To find the same train, in the same place . . . at a different time . . .

She focused everything she had, everything she *was*, pushing against the impossibility of it. Ishtar's Key grew warmer and warmer, until it was nearly burning against her arm. And then, *there*. She saw a flash of possibility.

Even though it felt as though the world was collapsing in on them and the floor was falling out from under them, she didn't stop to be sure. Esta grabbed Harte's hand and dragged them both forward through time.

WALLACK'S THEATRE

1902—New York

Jianyu Lee understood the weight of failure. Its oppressiveness had chased him from his brother's house and later sent him, desperate to prove his worth, to a new land. Like the story of Kua Fu chasing the sun, Jianyu had tried to outrun the disappointments of his boyhood. Instead he'd carried them with him on the endless journey across sea and land, only to find more waiting when he arrived in this city and discovered that the promises of the Six Companies' agent had been lies.

He had tried to make the best of working for Wung Ah Ling, the man who fashioned himself as Tom Lee. With his diamond stickpin and stylish derby hat, the self-proclaimed "mayor" of Chinatown was well known throughout the city. He had been delighted to have a Mageus in his employ and had taken Jianyu under his tutelage. Lee had helped him perfect the English that Jianyu had been taught on his long journey, and Lee had explained that the work of the tong was to aid their brethren in navigating the strange ways of this strange land. To protect them. But the longer Jianyu collected bribe money from poor shopkeepers, living in the same rooms where they worked while Tom Lee lived in the palatial splendor of his three-floor apartment at 20 Mott Street, the more Jianyu realized that Lee was no different from the rich merchants back in Gwóng-dūng who ate well while the poor farmers starved.

The day Jianyu was sent by Lee to collect money from a laundryman whose rasping voice and well-lined skin reminded him of his long-deceased grandfather's was the day Jianyu realized he was still nothing more than a bandit. The new beginning he had hoped for was more of the same. After that, every day that he worked as Tom Lee's lackey, using his affinity against those who could not help themselves, he had added another stone to his burden. But Dolph Saunders had given him a way to lay some of that burden down when he'd offered Jianyu a place in the Devil's Own. The dream of destroying the Brink had given Jianyu hope for a different future—for himself and for each of his countrymen back home who carried an affinity, and who would be threatened if the Order's cancerous power were allowed to spread.

Jianyu had been so busy guarding against the danger of the Order that he had failed to see the danger in their midst. They all had, and Dolph's life had been the cost. In the days following Dolph's death, Jianyu felt the old familiar shame return, creeping in the shadows of too silent rooms, waiting for him to pick up the burden of his failures once again. Perhaps he might have. Perhaps one day he might still, but for now, Jianyu had work to do. Nibsy Lorcan was a danger perhaps even worse than the Order, who seemed focused on their power here in New York. If what Harte Darrigan told him was true, Nibsy's ambitions were much larger. If Nibsy controlled the stones, his power might stretch beyond the seas. Whatever might come, Nibsy Lorcan could not be allowed to win.

Jianyu had made Darrigan a promise to protect Cela Johnson and the stone she carried. It was the first step toward defeating Nibsy, and he would not fail.

First, however, he had to find her before anyone else did.

After the confrontation with the woman in the cellar of the theater, Jianyu knew he could not leave until he had determined whether Cela was inside. Which was why he spent the day watching the theater's doors from an alleyway across the street, wrapped in light, so no one noticed him as he waited. All morning, he passed the time by watching the comings and goings of those who did not have to worry about who or what they were, people who knew they belonged—or those who could pretend they belonged. How many among those who passed by that morning were also Mageus, able to blend in and become invisible within the crowd without using any magic at all? It was a comfort that Jianyu had not had since the day he left his own country.

But then, there magic had been different. There was no Order, no Brink. His affinity had not been a liability as it was here.

He was not sure when the exhaustion of nearly two days finally dragged him under, but it was growing dark by the time he was jolted awake by the toe of a policeman's boot. After producing the required identity papers—falsified documents that served as protection when he could not use his affinity—Jianyu pretended to move along as instructed. When the policeman had moved on, he drew his affinity close and returned to wait until the crowd from the last show had poured out of the front and the performers had finally stopped trickling out of the stage door.

Jianyu waited longer still, until he saw the woman from earlier leave, her hair a bright flame beneath the glow of the evening's marquee. Once she had turned the corner and was out of sight, Jianyu pulled the light around himself again and made his way back into the theater. Inside, he released his affinity, just in case there was anyone else left behind who could sense magic, and allowed his eyes to adjust. Again he began his search for some sign of Cela, hoping all the while that he had not missed her when he had failed to stay awake.

There hadn't been any sign of a costumer's shop backstage, so he went back to the cellar, where the woman had stopped his earlier search. Even if Cela herself wasn't below, perhaps her workroom would give him some clue to where she had gone or where she might be.

It was too dark to search properly without any light, so Jianyu took the chance of using the bronze mirrors in the pocket of his tunic. Focusing his affinity through them, he amplified the minuscule threads of light that surrounded him and wrapped them around the disk until it glowed. The soft halo of light guided him through the dusty space as he searched, looking for some sign that he had been correct—that Cela Johnson was, indeed, there.

Finally, he came to a room at the back of the cellar. The door was closed tight and locked, but he picked the lock cleanly and opened the door to find a workroom. The glow of his mirrors showed it to be a small space, but neat and tidy. Rolls of silks and bolts of fabric were piled all around. He ran his finger along the cool metal of the heavy sewing machine that stood in the corner and it came away clean. No dust had accumulated there or anywhere. It felt as though the room had been used . . . and recently.

"Cela?" he called softly into the emptiness. "Cela Johnson? Are you there?"

He listened, knowing that silence would be the only answer, before he tried once more. "My name is Jianyu Lee, and I've come to help you." He paused again, weighing the risks of divulging too much if someone else were listening, and then he decided to take the chance. "Harte Darrigan sent me to protect you."

He stood for a long time, his ears open and his focus sharp for any sign of life, any indication that Cela was still there. In the corner, he heard a rustling. . . .

But when he lifted his disk, the glowing light revealed the tail of some rodent just before it scurried away.

Cela Johnson had been there not long before. Jianyu was sure of it. But she wasn't there any longer. Only one question loomed larger than all the others—had she left this place of her own free will, or had someone else gotten to her first?

A HEARTFUL OF TROUBLE

1902—New York

Cela hated the darkness. She'd hated it ever since she'd been a little girl and Abel had locked her down in Old Man Robertson's coal cellar to punish her for eating the last of his peppermints. By the time he finally let her out, she'd cried so hard that snot was dripping out of her nose, her face was blotchy, and her voice was ragged. Trying to settle her down, he'd given her an awkward hug, the only kind that on-the-verge-of-manhood boys knew how to give, and he promised her he'd never do it again.

He'd kept that promise for as long as he could.

But Abel is gone.

Again, grief twisted around her heart so tightly that she thought it might stop altogether. She had to pause for a second just to force herself to breathe. But she couldn't stay there. It was up to Cela herself to make do, darkness or not.

She heard the man's voice calling her name again, and then she heard him say that Harte Darrigan had sent him. To protect her, of all things. Well, considering that Harte Darrigan had sent her nothing but a heartful of trouble, whoever was out there could just keep his help. She certainly didn't want anyone else's protection, either. She already had two lives on her conscience who had tried to protect her, and she'd carry those two souls with her for the rest of her days.

Even after she thought he was gone, she waited, just to be sure, before she unlatched the panel of the wall she'd been hiding behind and came out. She'd built herself the little hidey-hole to keep her sewing things safe when she needed to. Didn't matter that everyone at Wallack's got the costumes they needed. One person or another always had sticky fingers, wanting the best bits for themselves.

She'd never intended to hide herself there, but it worked just as well.

Her eyes were already used to the darkness, so she didn't have much trouble navigating the small area of her workroom. She was pleased when she discovered that her visitor had left the door open for her.

Cela didn't bother to gather anything with her but a scrap of fabric to use as a wrap. She closed the door to her workshop and locked that part of her life up behind her—she wasn't coming back. Not ever. Then on quick, sure feet, she followed the soft padding of the man's footsteps, up the steps, through the back halls to the stage door, and out into the night.

EMPTY STREETS

1902—New York

After his failure to find Cela at the theater, Jianyu had reached an impasse. He had no idea where to look for her next, but if the woman at the theater had her—or if someone else did—he would require help. He had to find Viola, which meant that he had to return to the Bowery.

The Bowery, he knew, was in chaos. And with Nibsy Lorcan in control of the Devil's Own, the streets around the Strega would no longer be safe for him, as they once had been.

There was one place in the city where Jianyu's countrymen were welcomed without hesitation—the blocks close to Mott Street known as the Chinese quarter. He might go there, but Jianyu had worn out his welcome more than two years before, when he'd broken his oath of loyalty to Tom Lee and the On Leong Tong by defecting to the Devil's Own.

If Jianyu was caught by the On Leongs now, he would be made to pay for his transgressions. The question was what the price would be. Tom Lee might use simple violence, or he might do more. Jianyu was Lee's nephew only on paper, after all. While Dolph was alive, the secrets he had collected had assured Jianyu's safety from Tom Lee, but the power of those secrets had died with Dolph. If Lee chose, he could alert the authorities to Jianyu's precarious position in the city—and to the falseness of his documents. If Jianyu were deported, it would be tantamount to a death sentence, because being removed from the city would mean passing through the Brink.

It did not seem worth the risk to attempt navigating those dangers in the dead of night, when it would be harder to pull on his affinity for concealment. Instead, he ventured east to Twenty-Fourth Street, just a few blocks from where the newest skyscraper was nearly complete. There, a friend from Jianyu's first days in the city had a small laundry he ran with his wife, a sturdy Irish girl with kind eyes and ruddy cheeks. Since it had been years, Ho Lai Ying was surprised to see him, but understood the reach of the tongs. Though he did not wake his wife or family, Lai Ying gave Jianyu a bowl of the family's leftover meal and a warm place to rest for the night. But Jianyu barely slept, and he was gone before daybreak, so as not to put his old friend in any danger.

As the morning began to warm, Jianyu's path finally brought him to the Bowery. He needed to speak with Viola, but he also needed to find Cela without rousing the interest of anyone else who might be hunting for her or the stone. He was so deep in thought considering his options that he failed to notice the pair of men who had started following him not long after he had crossed Houston. By the time he felt their presence, it was too late to open the light around himself—not without revealing what he was.

Picking up his pace, Jianyu headed down one of the busier thoroughfares. Perhaps they would be less likely to do anything to him if there were enough witnesses. It was a feeble, naive hope. The streets were nearly empty at that early hour, and even if they had been filled, witnesses were more likely to become part of an attack than to prevent one.

In an instant, the men were flanking him, and Jianyu knew that he had little choice. He turned, his hands up, ready for a fight, but the two men only looked at each other and laughed. They were dressed in the familiar uniform of Bowery toughs—brightly colored shirts and waistcoats in stripes or plaids, trim pants, and the ubiquitous bowler hats that they wore cocked over one eye. Their pale, pasty skin looked wan and sickly contrasted against their garish clothes.

"Whaddaya think you're gonna do?" the one said, laughing to the other. "I've seen how they fight . . . like chickens flapping their wings after you chop off their heads." He stepped forward, his narrow-set eyes so heavily hooded, they made him appear half-asleep. "Come on. Gimme the best you got. . . . Go ahead. Your first flap is free."

Jianyu kept his attention split evenly between the two of them as they circled him.

"Come on, you dirty bastard," the other taunted, laughing darkly all the while.

They were expecting something else from him, perhaps. Or maybe their mouths were smarter than they were, but Jianyu took their offer and launched himself at them. The larger of the two was too slow to ward off Jianyu's first blow. He went down easily, splayed in the dirt of the street and groaning with the damage Jianyu's fist had done to his face.

The other goggled for a moment, looking at his friend with a kind of horrified shock that gratified Jianyu to the very marrow of his bones. But Jianyu had spent too much time at The Devil's Own training with the rest of Dolph's crew to miss taking further advantage of the pair's surprise. He whipped around and drove his fist into the other boy's stomach, knocking the air from him, before the boy realized what was happening.

The first was climbing to his feet, his nose dripping with blood and his eyes filled with rage, but a strange calm had settled over Jianyu. With a slow, mocking smile, he raised his hand and motioned for the boy to come closer. He and the boy circled each other, dodging and ducking each other's fists as the second boy came to his feet. Without warning, the second boy ran at Jianyu, tackling him to the ground.

Jianyu's head cracked against the edge of the sidewalk, and for a moment his vision went white. That moment was enough for the two to take advantage. One was on him in an instant, and before Jianyu could protect himself, he felt a fist plow into his side. He lashed out, landing a glancing blow or two, but the other had already made it to his feet again and had joined in.

A vicious kick landed in Jianyu's back, sending a near-blinding pain through his body.

"That'll teach you," one of the boys growled as his fists plowed into Jianyu's stomach again. "Damn dirty—"

Jianyu did not need to hear the rest to know what the boy said. That word—or words like it—had followed him ever since he had stepped off the boat in Mexico. He had heard them as he had ridden the train in silence for days, first crossing the border and then a country that he knew could never be his. Those slurs had been his companion in the dead of night as their ferryman smuggled him into Manhattan. And once he had arrived, he had heard the slur—or some version of the same—every day in the city's streets, tossed about by filthy beggars who were not man enough to look him in the eye when they said it.

He struggled to his knees, but another vicious kick landed in his stomach, and he went over hard again, tasting the coppery blood in his mouth. His ears were ringing. He had to get up, had to get to his feet somehow if he wanted any chance to survive this.

". . . damned dirty . . ."

They had him by the hair. One of them was holding on to the long queue he wore braided down his back. There was a roaring in his ears, but he could not tell whether it was from their punches or from the fact that he knew what they were about to do even before he heard the *snick* of the switchblade opening. His head was pounding, and the sound of a thousand winds howled in his ears. He wanted to scream at them, but his mouth was filled with his own blood.

When it went off, Jianyu felt the gunshot as much as he heard it. It was so close that the echo of it rang through his head and rattled his bones, even though the bullet never touched him.

It took him a moment to realize he was still alive—to realize that he had not been struck by the bullet. He lay with his face pressed to the grime of the street, the sourness of his blood thick in his mouth, but he was still breathing. There was pain in his head, yes, but he was still breathing.

Footsteps came closer until he was looking at the scuffed toes of two brown boots.

"You are lucky I came along when I did," the voice said in the familiar tones of his own language. "They would have killed you once they were done scalping you."

Scalping... He knew without reaching for his hair that it was gone, and without it, returning to his own country would be impossible. Without it, the one feeble dream he had carried secretly in his heart for so long crumbled to ash.

"You should have let them kill me," he answered, the words a comfort on his tongue even though his lips were bloodied and swollen so much that they sounded garbled even to him.

"Now, why would I do a thing like that?" the voice said. "I've been waiting so long to talk to you."

IT COULD BE WORSE

New Jersey

Harte came to sprawled on the floor of the moving train car, but the officers were gone. So was Jack.

When he pulled himself up, his head spun so much that he was barely conscious of the soft pile of material he was sitting on or the legs that moved beneath it, but once he was upright, his stomach revolted. Lurching to his feet, he ran toward the door at the back of the train car, barely making it out onto the platform in time to empty his stomach over the railing to the tracks below.

He hung there with his mouth tasting sour, and the warm breeze blew across his clammy skin as the earth sped by beneath him. When the door of the train car slid open behind him not long after, he knew without looking that it was Esta. There was something about the way the air changed whenever she was around him. It had always been like that, but now the voice inside of him whispered *yes* every time she was close. *Soon.*

Harte shoved the voice away, and with what strength he had left, he locked it down tight. The effort it took made his head swim again.

"Are you okay?" Esta asked, coming to stand next to him at the railing.

He nodded, still feeling sick and too warm.

Because the weather *is too warm.*

The sky no longer had the gray heaviness of earlier that morning, and the crisp spring air had been transformed into the balmy heat of a summer's day. "What just happened?" he asked, closing his eyes against the motion of the train.

"You said to get us out. . . ."

Harte turned to her, comprehension already dawning on him, but before he could say anything, the door behind them opened and a uniformed conductor came out.

The man eyed Harte as he clung to the railing, but otherwise he gave no indication that anything was amiss. "Tickets, please."

They didn't have any tickets, but if he could just pull his head together and stay upright long enough to let go of the railing, he could fix this. One touch was all it would take. . . .

But Esta was speaking before he could manage. "I'm so sorry," she said, pulling a dark wallet from within the traveling cloak she wore. "We were in such a rush, and we didn't have time to purchase the tickets before we boarded. Can we pay now?"

"Sure, sure," the man said, pulling out a small booklet and punching two of the tickets with a small silver clamp. "End of the line . . . That'll be three fifty for each."

Harte should have been curious about where the stack of money had come from. He should have been interested to watch this new ritual, the purchasing of a ticket—the validation of his freedom. But it was all he could do to keep his stomach from revolting again and his mind from focusing too much on the reality of what Esta had done.

"Is a Pullman car available?" Esta asked the conductor, taking a couple of bills from the wallet and handing them over. Her voice was light and easy, but Harte could hear the edge in it. "My husband isn't feeling well. I think it might be best if he rested."

"No Pullman," the man said, raising a brow in their direction. "This train's only going as far as Baltimore. You can get a transfer to a Pullman at the next stop, if you're traveling farther."

"Of course. How silly of me," she said with a strained laugh. "Thank you anyway." She'd made her voice into something breathy and light, but she couldn't quite manage to keep a tremor of nervousness out of it.

Harte waited until the man had continued on through the next car before he let himself slide to the floor. His head was still spinning as he leaned back against the railing, and the way the train swayed made his already fragile stomach turn over again. He forced all of that aside too and focused on Esta. "The train on platform seven wasn't going to Baltimore."

She wasn't paying attention to him. Instead, she was trying to reach up her sleeve. Her mouth was a flat line of concentration—or was that pain?

"Esta—"

"Hold on," she said through gritted teeth, and a moment later she pulled the cuff from her arm with a hissing intake of breath. "There . . ." She held it delicately between her fingers, frowning as she examined it.

The cuff itself was a delicate piece of burnished silver, but the metal was less important than what it held—Ishtar's Key. It was one of the artifacts that gave the Order its power, but this particular stone was special because it allowed Esta to travel through time.

Through time . . .

Harte's empty stomach felt as though he'd swallowed a hot stone. "What did you do, Esta? This train was supposed to be going to *Chicago*."

"You told me to get us out of there, so I did," she told him, but her attention was on the stone in her hand—not on him.

"But this isn't the train we were on, is it?" he asked.

"Of course it is." She finally looked up from her examination of the cuff. "This is the same train—the *exact* same car. . . ." She hesitated, frowning a little. "It's just *slightly* ahead of when we were before."

"How slightly?" he asked, his stomach churning from the motion of the train and the idea of what she'd just done.

"I don't know. A day or two, nothing much mo—" But her words fell away as she glanced at the tickets the conductor had handed her.

"What is it?" he asked, swallowing down another round of nausea that had very little to do with the motion of the train.

She cursed as her face all but drained of color.

He had a very bad feeling that he was not going to like the answer to the question he had to ask: "How far ahead are we?"

"I was just trying to get us away from Jack and the police," she told him, never taking her eyes from the tickets.

"How far, Esta?"

She was practically chewing a hole into her lip. "I was looking for a day or two ahead. I didn't mean . . . I didn't—"

"*Esta.*" He cut her off and took a deep breath—both to calm himself and so he wouldn't be sick again. It could be worse. They could be in police custody right now. They could be at the mercy of Jack and the Order. "How bad is it?"

Silently, she handed him the tickets.

His eyes were still having trouble focusing from the strangely violent push-pulling sensation he'd experienced just moments before. It had felt like the world was collapsing in on him, twisting him about. It had felt awful—*wrong*. As he stared at the ticket, that feeling worsened, because there was no mistaking the date printed there.

"Two *years?*" He was going to be sick again.

Two years ago he was still struggling to climb out of the filth of the Bowery and doing his damnedest to survive. Two years ago he didn't have money in his pocket or a reputation on the stage. Two years ago he didn't even have the name he now wore. Two years was practically a lifetime in a world as capricious and dangerous as his, and she'd taken it from him without a second thought.

"I didn't do it on purpose," she whispered, her expression pained.

"How is that even possible?" he snapped, wincing inwardly at how sharply the words had come out.

But his sharpness was like a flint to a rock, sparking her temper. "Slipping through time isn't exactly easy, you know," she said, snatching the tickets back from him. "On a good day, it takes all my concentration to find the right minute to land, and that's when I'm *not* in a moving train cornered by the police. You're welcome, by the way. Seeing as we aren't currently in jail and all."

"*Two years*, Esta." But then he saw the way her hand holding the tickets was shaking, and his anger receded a little. "I meant for you to"—he waved vaguely—"to slow things down, so we could get off the train and get away."

"We got away, didn't we?" She gestured to the obvious absence of Jack.

He took a breath, trying to hold down the bile in his stomach along with his own temper. "You're right. We were in a tight spot, and you got us out," he told her, trying to mean it. "It'll be fine. You can fix this. You can take us back."

"Harte . . ." Her hesitation made his stomach twist all the more.

"You can *take us back*," he repeated.

Esta's expression was pained. "I have no idea what just happened. I meant to go two days and went two *years* instead."

"Because we were on a train—you said so yourself," he said slowly, trying to keep his composure. "We'll get off at the next station, and then you can—"

"It wasn't just the train," she said, not quite meeting his eyes.

The nausea somehow suddenly didn't seem so important. "What do you mean?"

"My affinity . . . it doesn't feel right. Ever since the Brink, it's felt off. *Unstable*."

He frowned at her. He'd known that the Brink had done a number on her, but he hadn't realized that it had affected her magic. "Why didn't you tell me? We could have waited another day."

"We needed to go—we have to get the stones," she snapped. "We're running out of time as it is. Soon Logan will be in the city and—" She broke off as though realizing what she was saying. It was already too late. Because of what she'd done, this Logan of hers had already been in the city for two years.

"And *nothing*. You should have *told me*," he said, maybe more forcefully than he'd intended. But his nerves were jangling, and his anger was the only thing that was keeping him from retching over the side of the train again.

"I *know*," she said, biting back at him, but then she closed her eyes and took a breath. "I know," she repeated, her voice softer now. "But everything was happening so fast. We had to find clothes and get out of Brooklyn, and I thought if I could just push through, it would be okay. That *I* would be okay."

"But you're not okay, are you?" he asked, and watched as a series of emotions flashed across her expression—denial, frustration, worry—all mixed together as one.

"You saw what happened at the station. I could barely hold on to time long enough to get us away from Jack," she told him, still staring out at the passing landscape as though she couldn't look at him. "You're right. I never should have tried slipping through time, but we were cornered on a moving train, and I thought, if I could just get us on the next train—if I could just get us to tomorrow—then we would be safe. But once I started to slip through, I couldn't control it. And then with you—"

"Me?" he interjected. "You're saying *I* caused this?"

"Not *you*," Esta said as she shook her head. "But whatever it is that's *inside* you now. I can feel it when you touch me, and when I'm trying to pull on my affinity, it's like trying to hold a live wire."

His stomach turned over again. "You think it's the Book?" At the very mention of it, the voice began to stir deep within him. On the bridge, he'd told her that the power of the Book was inside of him, but he hadn't told her everything. Before, he hadn't been able to find the words to explain what the Book wanted—and especially what it wanted of *her*. Now, with the questions and the *fear* that shone in her eyes, he couldn't make himself say them.

Her hair had come half undone and the dark strands of it were whipping about her face, but her expression was steady now. "I can't be sure. Maybe it wasn't you. Maybe something happened to me when we crossed the Brink."

Maybe he should have consoled her—forgiven her, even. But he was still too upset about the two years of his life that she'd carved away like nothing to give her any reprieve.

Esta sank down next to him, her skirts pooling over his legs. Gently, her hand touched his cheek, turning his head so that he was forced to look at her. "We will fix it," she told him, her eyes bright with determination. "*I* will fix this. But I don't think we should try to go back—not *yet*," she finished, before he could argue. "I don't know why we went so far. I don't know why I couldn't control where we landed. Usually I can. But if I try to take us back now and I miss again, we could be stuck. You saw what happened to the bag of stones I tried to bring back on the bridge."

"They were gone," he remembered. All that had been left were the charred remains of the settings. The stones themselves had turned to ash.

"I don't think the stones can exist at the same time with other versions of themselves. If I can't control my affinity again and we go back too far, Ishtar's Key will cross paths with itself, and it will be gone. We will be stuck whenever we land, with no way out of the city again and no way to stop Nibsy or the Order." She licked her lips. "And I don't know what will happen to *me* if the stone disappears."

"To you?" He shook his head, not understanding.

"Or to you. I told you what Nibsy did before we changed things," she said. "How he sent me forward?"

"When you were a baby . . ."

She nodded. "I think that still needs to happen. If I'm never sent forward, then I can't come back. If that happens, it means I wouldn't have been there to help with the heist at Khafre Hall or to save you—any of it. You'll die. Who knows what that would mean for the Order or Nibsy or magic." A shadow fell across her expression. "If I'm never sent forward as a baby, I'd grow up like I should have . . . in the past. I'm not sure that this version of me would even exist anymore."

Panic spiked inside of him. "You can't just disappear."

"Why not? The stones did, didn't they?" she asked, her gaze steady.

He considered that for a moment, a world without Esta. Everything he'd done to try to send her back to her own time had been to save her—from the past, from the power rollicking inside of him. But she'd come back, and in doing so, she'd given him another chance . . . one he didn't deserve. "Then you're right. We shouldn't chance it. We'll wait."

"You'd be okay with that?"

"The stones we're after still exist, don't they?" he asked. "It's only been two years. They can't have gone that far. We'll find them here . . . *now*."

She was still frowning at him. "And then what? We won't be able to take them back."

"Because they'll still exist in 1902," he realized.

They sat, speechless for a moment, as the *click-clack*ing of the track kept time beneath them.

"It doesn't matter," Esta said finally. "We'll worry about getting the stones back to 1902 when we're sure we *can* get back to 1902. First we get the Book's power under control. We need the stones for that. Maybe once we have them, there will be something in the Book itself to solve the problem. It got us through the Brink, didn't it? If there's not, two years isn't that long."

Two years is a lifetime. "It's not a great plan. . . ." Then he realized—*the Book.*

No.

Harte looked at Esta, unable for a moment to speak. "My coat" was all he could say.

"What about it?"

He saw the moment she understood what he meant, but he said the words anyway, because he had to face them. Because he knew that no amount of silence would make them any less real. "The Book was in the coat. The one I left behind—to get away from Jack."

SOME DISTANT STATION

1904—New Jersey

You should have let me kill him," Esta said, feeling herself go cold as she drew back from Harte. Because one thing was clear: None of this would have happened if he hadn't stopped her from killing Jack. They would still have the Book, for one. And they would still be in 1902, because Jack wouldn't have been chasing them.

She could have done it.

She could have gladly carried that burden with her for the rest of her life. She had no way of knowing what effect her inaction would have, but she knew one thing—nothing good could come from Jack getting ahold of the Book.

Harte was still sitting on the platform at the back of the train when she pulled herself to her feet. He looked pale and unsteady, but Esta was having a hard time finding any more sympathy.

"You shouldn't have stopped me," she continued.

"And then what?" Harte asked. "You would have just walked away, with his blood on your hands?"

"Better his blood than ours."

Harte scrubbed his hand down over his face, expelling a ragged breath as he closed his eyes for a moment. He looked as though he was about to be sick again. "I've done plenty of wrong in my life, but I don't want to be the type of man who can kill someone in cold blood." He opened his eyes to look at her. "Even someone who deserves it as much as Jack does."

There was something about the way his voice changed, the way it seemed to carry to her so clearly on the wind, even with the noise of the train and the tracks, that made Esta pause.

But only for a moment.

This world didn't allow for pausing or second-guessing. It wouldn't permit her to keep whatever delicate sensibilities Harte thought she should have.

All at once the memory of Professor Lachlan's library at the top of his building on Orchard Street arose in her mind. The dimmed lights. The smell of old books that had once meant safety. On her wrists, Esta could still feel the ache of bruises from the ropes that had held her to the chair. She could almost feel the heat of the stones Professor Lachlan had adorned her with, like the sacrifice he'd intended her to be. The man who had raised her would have used her affinity—used *her*—to unite the stones and take control of the Book's power. *You're just the vessel.* He would have killed her.

She lifted her hand to touch the still-healing wound just below her collarbone and closed her eyes against the memory of what had happened. . . . *These things do tend to work better with a little blood.*

That night had been less than twenty-four hours ago and was also still a hundred years to come. In the darkness behind her eyelids, another memory assaulted her—Dakari stepping into the room, unaware of what Professor Lachlan had planned. Unprepared for the bullet that came a few moments later.

The echo of the gun.

The sound of Dakari's body collapsing, deadweight, to the floor.

And the weight of the guilt she bore for his death.

Maybe she'd never had any real softness to start with. Or maybe the last bit of softness had been killed as surely as Dakari that day. Either way, Esta knew that if she could live with the memory of that night, she could bear anything. *Become* anything. Harte might not have believed that she was strong enough, but Esta had already survived the senseless loss of her friends, of her family—of her *father*. A little blood on her hands for the sake of their memory and for the sake of their lives was hardly anything.

Besides, she knew that she wouldn't have to carry any of it for very long. No matter what happened between now and the end, Professor Lachlan had already explained to her how the stones could be used to control the Book. She hadn't yet told Harte. She didn't know how he would react to learning that it would require sacrifice—her affinity and most likely her life—and they didn't have time for him to get all noble again or have second thoughts. But then, she was a girl without a past and without a future. She'd already resigned herself to the fact that she had little hope of walking out of this alive.

Now they would have to live with the consequences of *not* killing Jack when they'd had the chance. Two years had passed, and during that time the world had continued on, history unspooling itself each day. Who knew what had changed in the days and weeks since Jack Grew got his hands on the Book and all the knowledge contained in its pages? Who knew what might wait for them at the station at the end of the line?

Harte looked like he was going to be sick again. Not that Esta blamed him. When she thought of Jack with the Book, she felt like throwing up too.

"It'll be okay," she told him after a few minutes of tense silence, the wind whipping at them as the train sped onward. She wasn't sure that she believed it, but there didn't seem to be anything else to say as the train hurtled down the track, careening toward some distant station she had never thought to see and toward a future that she was determined to meet head-on—the same way she met everything else.

"You know what Jack could do with the Book." Harte turned from her, his eyes unfocused on the passing countryside. "The Order wouldn't let him have access to it because they knew how dangerous it was, and I *gave* it to him. He'll have secrets that even the Order was smart enough to keep away from him."

Every bit of what he'd said was true, but still . . . "If Jack had kept you from getting on the train, it would have been over anyway."

"I could have fought him," Harte said, his jaw tense. "I could have beat him."

"Sure. With the station police on your tail and all those people around *and* the train already leaving. A fistfight is exactly what would have worked." When Harte glanced back at her, irritation shadowing his expression, she continued. "You had to get on this train—*that* train—*whatever*. You made a choice, just like I did. You did what you had to do to get away. Besides, Jack doesn't really have all that much," she reminded him. "The Book's *power* is in you, right?"

Harte's jaw clenched. "There's still the information in its pages. That's more than enough for it to be dangerous."

"So we'll just have get it back." She pulled herself up to her feet again. "I'm a thief, aren't I? I'll steal it."

He looked up at her. "It might be too late for that already."

"If we can get control of my affinity, there is no such thing as too late." Still, there was a part of her that worried Harte was right.

She offered him a hand up. "We can get off at the next station and figure out what to do."

He ignored her offer of help. "We might as well wait until we get to Baltimore. We've already paid for the tickets," he told her. "No sense getting off until we're in a city that's big enough to give us our pick of routes. It's been two years," he said, an answer to her unspoken question. "I don't know where any of the people we need to find are now. I'll have to send out some telegrams, make some inquiries. If Julien is still performing, he shouldn't be that hard to find."

Already, the crowded industrial-looking buildings of the area around the station had given way to more open land. The smell of the coal burning in the train's engine was faint, and the air carried a scent she didn't recognize—something green and fresh and earthy that didn't exist in the city.

"We should probably get some seats," she told him. "It'll be a while before we reach Baltimore."

Harte pulled himself upright without her help but held tight to the railing for a moment to steady himself. "Where did you get the money for the tickets?" he asked as he reached for the door to the car. He held it open for her to enter.

"Compliments of Jack," she told him as she stepped through.

The car was almost entirely empty. In the front, an older man dozed with his head tucked into his own chest. He didn't stir at the sound of the door opening or the noise of the tracks. Still, Harte lowered his voice when he spoke.

"You took Jack's wallet?"

She shrugged. "He's good for it. And he was a little . . . distracted at the time." She slipped into an empty row of seats. When Harte didn't immediately sit next to her, she glanced up at him. He was staring at her with an unreadable expression on his face. "What?"

"That's why you were kissing him."

At first his words didn't make any sense. "Kissing . . . ?" Then she realized what was happening in that pretty little head of his. "You're an idiot. You know that, right?"

Harte had the grace to look a little embarrassed as he slid into the seat next to her. "Yeah," he muttered. "I'm aware."

Esta wanted to say something more, but Harte's attention had been drawn by the landscape speeding by. It was as though sitting on the platform of the train car, he hadn't even seen it, but now she could have disappeared altogether and he wouldn't have noticed. All Harte could see was the world outside the windows of the train—a world he had lied and stolen and cheated for.

She decided to let him have it. For now.

Through the seats, Esta could feel the vibrations of the rail, telegraphing the shape of the land they were crossing. She'd never thought she would leave the city—had never wanted to—but now she had to admit that the world was wider and more beautifully tempting than she could have expected. Already the towns were giving way to a landscape of fields carpeted with the lush green of summer crops, their stalks rippling in the breeze. The colors were more vibrant somehow. More raw and alive.

She wasn't supposed to be there, beyond the boundaries of the city she had called home for so long.

She should be dead by now, but she had survived Professor Lachlan's attempt to take her power—and her life. She had survived Jack's gun pressed against her back.

For a moment she let herself lean her head against Harte's shoulder and enjoy knowing that until the train pulled into the station, they were safe. Until the train arrived at their next station, it was just the two of them, the green of the landscape, and the steady cadence of the train.

But even as she allowed herself that one stolen moment of peace, Esta knew that her future was waiting. The world outside of that car might have changed in dangerous ways in the years they had skipped. There was only one thing she could be sure of when the train finally pulled into Baltimore: She would survive whatever came next. One step at a time, one moment and then another. Until she righted the wrongs that had been done . . . and made those who had caused them pay.

PART

II

SURFACING

1902—New York

When Jack opened his eyes, the light in the room was lavender. It was like being inside a damn flower. And he felt heavy . . . impossibly heavy, especially his left arm, which had been pinned across his abdomen with some sort of binding. He couldn't seem to move his fingers, but with the lavender light, he couldn't quite bring himself to care. Even if his head felt like it would split in two.

They must have given him something—some drug to dull the pain—because the room around him felt very far away, as though he were seeing it through a tunnel. But how did he get there?

There had been the ambulance. He remembered the bone-aching bumping of the carriage as it carried him to the hospital. . . . But this was not the hospital. Slowly but surely the room started to come more into focus. The walls were covered in a floral brocade, and above, the canopy of the bed dripped with lace.

It came to him then where he was—this was one of the spare guest rooms in his mother's house. Not ideal and yet also not terrible. Considering the temper his uncle had unleashed—how long ago had it been?—his family could just as well have left him alone in a cold, public hospital. Or worse, they could have kept to their word and shipped him westward, injured or not. It seemed that he'd been given a reprieve. A second chance of sorts. He would damn well use it.

Just as soon as he could move . . .

Jack lay there for a long while, his gaze tracing the looping patterns of the lace above his head, his brain feeling thick and heavy. Little by little, the events that had brought him to his mother's spare bedroom began to come back to him.

The train . . . Darrigan and the girl . . .

He remembered suddenly the moment when the medics had given him the coat that was not his and he had realized what was contained within its pocket. *The Book.*

With a start, he tried to sit up, but the smallest movement had his head splitting and his whole arm aching. He groaned and allowed his body to slump back into the softness of the bed. Jack couldn't remember the hospital or whatever had happened to him there, so he couldn't be sure of what had happened to the Book. *Did they find it in the coat? Did they take it?* He needed to know.

The door opened, and a young maid poked her head into the room. She was a bit skinnier than he usually preferred, but her skin was clear and her brown hair would probably float down over her shoulders if he unpinned it from the severe bun she wore.

Considering the state of his head and his arm, that would have to wait, he supposed.

"Mr. Grew?" The girl hesitated before she stepped fully into the room. When he didn't respond, she stepped closer to him. When she called his name again, he allowed his eyelids to flutter open, pretending that he was only just waking. "Are you awake, then? You've got visitors, if you're up for it today?"

"Water?" He was surprised at how hoarse he sounded.

"Of course," she said before she scurried off to get him a cup of water. When she returned, she held the cup out at arm's length, but he didn't bother to reach for it.

"My arm," he rasped. "If you could just . . ."

She regarded him warily, but stepped closer to the bedside to help him with the water. He could tell she was nervous, and it warmed something in him to know that even laid out on the bed as he was, she still understood him to be a threat.

Jack took his time sipping the water and enjoying the girl's nearness. She smelled of the soap they used on the bed linens and of the sweetness of fear. As he sipped, she kept her gaze trained on the glass she held in her slender fingers, refusing to meet his eyes. When he finished the last bit, just before she could pull the glass away, he used his free hand to grasp her wrist and was gratified to hear her sharp intake of breath.

Her wrist was as delicate as the rest of her. It felt temptingly fragile beneath his fingers, and he had the strangest idea that he could crush it as easily as the bones of a bird without much effort at all. But he did not tighten his grip, and she did not try to pull away. Instead, her cheeks flushed an attractive pink as her wide eyes met his.

"You must be feeling better if you're already accosting the help," a voice said from the entrance to the room.

The maid took the opportunity offered by Jack's momentary distraction to free herself from his grasp and scurry back from his bedside. Her movement revealed the source of the voice—it was one of the Barclay boys, the younger one, whom he'd been in school with. Thaddeus or Timothy or Theodore. "Theo . . ."

From Theo's flash of a smile, Jack had guessed right. Yes, it was Theo Barclay who had entered the room like they'd been friends all along, instead of bare acquaintances. And with him was a girl who put the maid completely out of Jack's mind.

"Glad to see that you're not half as bad as everyone made it sound," Theo said, stepping aside so the maid could get by. "You remember I told you about my fiancée?"

Jack didn't, of course, but even with the drugs leaving his mind heavy and dull, he still had enough social graces to lie. "Of course," he murmured, wondering why in the hell any man would bring his fiancée to another man's bedside.

"Theo heard that you'd been hurt, and he simply had to come see you," the girl said, her voice a soft fluttering thing, as utterly female as she was. "I hope you don't mind that I came along." She licked nervously at pink lips. "I know we haven't been formally introduced yet. . . ."

Jack decided that he didn't care *why* Theo had brought his fiancée, because the girl was a sight to behold. The purple light of the room complemented her creamy complexion and fair hair, as though it had been drawn just for her. She was dressed in what might have looked like an ordinary day dress on anyone else, but the high neck was made of a pale lace that looked so delicate, it was nearly sheer.

"I'm not overly interested in formalities," Jack said, wishing like hell he knew what he was wearing under the bedsheets. "I can't offer you any refreshments, since my maid seems to have absconded with the water glass, but feel free to have a seat anywhere you'd like."

"We won't be staying that long," Theo said with another good-humored smile. "We just wanted to check in on you. You had quite the luck, didn't you?"

"Did I?" Jack wondered aloud. Considering that he was stuck in a bed, his arm and head hurting like hell, he didn't feel particularly lucky.

"I'd say," Theo told him with a sure nod. "I've seen the pictures in the papers—the destruction was just incredible. After the stories that have been going around town, I half expected you to be at death's door."

"Stories?" Jack asked, trying to piece together the missing parts of his memory from Theo's words. *There was a train.*

"Rumors," Theo amended. "You know how our mothers can be when they sit around and gossip over tea."

Jack could only imagine what his mother and the other women who sat around clucking over the news of the day might have said about him. "I'm fine," he grumbled, trying to sit up again. But another sharp pain jolted through his arm, and he hissed as he sank back into bed. Like some feeble old man. *Weak.*

The girl took a step forward. "Is there anything we can do—"

"No," he growled, and then, realizing how her eyes had widened at the force of his tone, he softened his voice despite the pain that throbbed through his head. "No. I'm fine. The train derailed?" he asked, trying to remember.

"The authorities aren't entirely sure what happened," Theo said. "But from the pictures, it looked like the earth itself opened up. You're damn lucky—your car was turned on its side, but intact. The car after yours? It looked like the explosion ripped right through it. The tracks and everything else were just . . . *gone*. Some of the papers are calling you a hero for making it out alive."

"And the others?" Jack asked. Because there were always others.

"One of the papers got ahold of the doctor who treated you at the site of the wreckage," the girl told him. "He said that you had been conscious when they pulled you out and that you told him you knew who caused the derailment."

"I did?" Jack asked, trying to recall the moments after the crash. It was a blur of pain and confusion, but he did remember one thing more clearly now. *Darrigan and the girl.* Then it came to him—

"They disappeared," Jack said, talking to himself more than them. Which was impossible. People don't just *disappear*, unless . . .

No. How could he have missed it? But it made sense—a sick sort of sense. How else could Darrigan have duped him so easily? How else could the girl have fooled him with her lies? How could either of them have escaped from Khafre Hall without some sort of feral power? *They're Mageus.*

"Disappeared?" the girl asked. "Who disappeared?"

"Harte Darrigan and the girl," Jack said, his voice rough with the hatred he felt for them. They had taken his free will and used him, just as the witch in Greece had.

"Harte Darrigan . . . the magician?" the girl asked, stepping closer.

"He was on that train," Jack told them. "He was in the car with me before everything happened. I *saw* him. And the girl."

Jack saw the way Theo and his girl traded questioning glances. They didn't even bother to hide their skepticism. It was the same type of look people had traded when he'd been dragged back from Greece. They'd thought he'd simply been a lovesick fool then. He'd tried to explain that he hadn't been lovestruck but bespelled. There had been one night of drinking that he couldn't quite remember, and then . . . he hadn't been able to break apart from her after. Not until his cousin had shown up to remove him.

Jack's embarrassment had burned through any gratitude he might have felt for the rescue. Now his anger at being abused again was the glue holding him together.

"They're con artists and thieves, both of them," Jack told Theo, growing more and more agitated. "They ruined me when they destroyed Khafre Hall and took the Order's most prized treasures, and now they're trying to ruin me again."

"You do know that Darrigan is dead, don't you?" Theo asked, his voice careful. "It was all over the papers—he jumped from the Brooklyn Bridge the day before the accident."

"Did anyone find his body?" Jack asked.

"I'm not sure," Theo said, uncertain.

"Then how can you know he's dead?" Jack asked.

"They didn't find his body in the wreckage, either," Theo pointed out. "If he was in the same car as you, he would have been located." But his tone was too patient, too condescending, and it made Jack bristle.

"I told you," Jack said, his patience fraying. "He *disappeared*. They both did. There wouldn't have been a body to find."

The two traded glances again, and Jack felt fury building.

"I know what I saw—Darrigan and the girl were on the train with me. I'd just cornered them and was about to apprehend them. Ask the station police. . . . There was one of them on the car as well."

Theo frowned. "There was an officer on the same car as you, but he didn't make it."

"You truly think that Darrigan and this girl caused a massive train derailment?" the girl asked. There was less doubt than interest in her voice now. "And then you think he disappeared. The only way that could be true is if he were—"

"Mageus," Jack said, supplying the word.

"But the Brink," she pressed, taking yet another step toward Jack's bed. "There haven't been any verifiable reports of feral magic outside the city borders for years. If Darrigan is Mageus, he wouldn't have been able to pass through it."

"I told you, he stole the Order's artifacts. . . ." Jack considered this, turning the problem over in his mind as his head pounded. "Or the girl did."

"Who, exactly, was this girl?" Theo's fiancée asked.

"A con artist named Esta Filosik . . ." He hesitated. "Or that's what she *said* her name was. She was there the night Khafre Hall burned. She helped Darrigan then, and she helped him on the bridge."

"And the Order allowed the two of them into Khafre Hall?" the girl asked. "They didn't realize what Darrigan and the girl were—"

"No," he snapped, before she could finish her question. He glared at her, daring her to ask anything else. Daring her to judge him.

"We should be going, dear," Theo said to the girl, pulling her back.

"But I have more—"

"*Now*," Theo said more forcefully. "Can we get you anything before we go, Jack? Anything at all?"

He needed the Book.

"Pardon?" Theo said. "What book is it that you'd like?"

He hadn't intended to speak, and his voice broke as he tried to cover his mistake. "My coat," he corrected. "I meant that I'd like my coat."

"Are you cold?" the girl asked, her expression transforming itself again, this time from avid interest to concern. "I could stoke the fire a bit, or perhaps I could bring you another blank—"

"*No*," he said, not caring that she flinched. He didn't need her pity. "I don't want any damned blankets, and I'm not cold. I want my *coat*."

"Hold on there, Jack," Theo told him. "There's a pile of your things over here by the chest. Give me a moment to look."

Jack closed his eyes against the lavender light and the concern in the girl's eyes and the pain that still throbbed through him. But behind the darkness of his eyelids, all he could see was his own failure and impotence. He'd been a fool.

"Is this it?" Theo asked, and Jack opened his eyes to see Theo holding the rough woolen overcoat that Harte Darrigan had been wearing when he escaped.

Yes. Yes. Yes, yes, yes . . .

"Bring it to me," Jack demanded, not caring how he sounded. He didn't know where the sudden force in his voice came from or why he felt such an overwhelming desperation to hold that cracked leather in his hands once more.

Jack had to know if *they* had found it. He was in his mother's home, and there was a chance that someone from the Order would have gone through his things. There was a chance that they could have taken the Book before he had an opportunity to discover all its secrets.

"Would you like us to call someone?" Theo offered as he draped the coat over Jack's torso. "Or maybe I could get you something for the pain. There seem to be some bottles here on the bedside table. . . ."

"No—if I could just rest," Jack said, allowing his eyes to close again. Willing the two of them to leave already.

As the weight of the coat settled over him, Jack felt very far away from himself. He felt so drowsy and tired, and yet at the same time, unbearably alert. It must be the drugs they'd given him, the morphine the doctors must have used to set his arm.

"I'm glad to see that you're okay, Jack," Theo said. "Take care of yourself, now, won't you?"

"It was lovely to meet you," the girlish voice echoed.

Jack never opened his eyes. He pretended sleep until he heard the door latch when they closed it behind them. When he knew they were well and truly gone, he used his free hand to turn the ugly garment over. Ignoring the pain it caused, he searched for the opening to the pocket and then . . . *there.*

He held the Ars Arcana up and examined it in the soft light as victory coursed through his veins. It was difficult to flip through the pages while he was reclined, but sitting upright hurt too much. Grimacing from the effort it took to look, he found the small bottle of medicine that Theo had mentioned being on the table next to his bed. He reached for it, but the pain that shot through his arm was nearly blinding. For a moment he considered calling the maid back, but he couldn't risk her seeing the Book.

Bracing himself, Jack tried again, and this time his fingers brushed the glass bottle, knocking it within reach. He unstoppered it and took out two cubes without bothering to read the instructions. They dissolved into bitterness on his tongue, but the pain didn't immediately subside. He could still feel his heartbeat pounding in his very bones. So he tossed two more of the cubes into his mouth, grinding them between his teeth this time.

Slowly the pain started to recede, and as soon as he could breathe again, he opened the Book. The pages were brittle and not at all uniform. They looked like they had been taken from a number of different sources and then somehow bound seamlessly into the small tome. On their surface, they were filled with faded notes and writing—some in Latin, others in something that looked like Greek. Still others were in languages Jack had never seen.

He let his thumb run over the edges of the pages, and Jack couldn't tell if the warmth he felt was coming from the Book itself or from the morphine settling into his veins. After a moment he found that he didn't care, and he began to read.

A NEW CITY

1904—St. Louis

Compared to the brisk spring they'd left in New York, the St. Louis night felt sultry and close against Esta's skin as she walked next to Harte. None of the people crowding the sidewalks around them seemed to mind, though.

Esta and Harte had crossed the Mississippi and arrived in the city earlier that day. After sending a few telegrams in Baltimore, they discovered that Julien was no longer in Chicago. The vaudeville circuit Julien performed on had taken him to St. Louis, and the two of them had followed on the first overnight train they could find.

It had been something of a shock, arriving in the enormous train station filled with tourists in town for the world's fair, but together they'd managed to find their way to a hotel and to get themselves some clothes. Esta told herself that she and Harte were just partners and nothing more, but a night sharing the close quarters of a Pullman berth had left her feeling unsettled and restless. It had been a relief to get a few hours to herself. Now they were outside the theater where Julien Eltinge was performing, waiting to purchase tickets. The excited murmuring of the people out for the night felt electric.

St. Louis certainly wasn't New York. The streets were wider than in lower Manhattan, and most of them were paved with pounded gravel rather than cobblestones. The air hung thick with the coal smoke coming off the barges and riverboats down on the Mississippi. While the streets were lined with restaurants, their gilded names gracing plateglass windows, the lights seemed dim compared to those that shone on Broadway or even in the Bowery.

Esta wondered what Harte thought of it all. Ever since learning that she'd slipped them forward through time, he'd been keeping everything close to the vest. Even now his storm-gray eyes were steady as the line inched forward. But he was frowning slightly, as though he were weighing and measuring the world he was now a part of against expectations it could never live up to. Still, he looked calm, ready for whatever the evening held.

Actually, considering that he'd spent most of the trip green from motion sickness, he looked damn good, dressed in a sleek black evening suit with his dark hair combed back away from the sharp features of his face. Esta wasn't sure how he could possibly look so fresh, considering all the layers of linen and wool that he was wearing. He barely even looked warm, while she felt like she was wrapped in a blanket beneath the layers of corset and skirts. As a bead of sweat rolled down her back, she started to think that maybe picking the raw silk gown for the evening hadn't been the best idea.

It was too late to change now, though. Behind the walls of the theater in front of them, beyond the crowd with its champagne-tinged murmurs, was the first of the stones—the Djinni's Star.

"What time does Julien go on?" she asked as they stepped forward with the line.

"He'll be late in the show," Harte said, glancing up at the marquee, where Julien Eltinge's name was spelled out in the glow of electric lights. "Maybe around nine?"

"I still think it would be easier to slip into his apartment and take the necklace," she told him. They'd argued about it earlier on the train, but Harte had been insistent.

"Maybe—if we knew for sure that the stone was there. But it's not worth the risk of getting caught breaking in when I can just ask him for it."

"I never get caught," Esta said, cutting a look at him. "And do you really think using your affinity on him is the best idea?"

"It's the simplest way."

But Esta wasn't so sure. If *her* affinity felt off—shaky and unsettled—what must his be, with the Book's power inside of him?

The wind kicked up, providing some relief from the warmth of the night as it gusted between the buildings, rustling Esta's silken gown and taffeta wrap. It had a cool metallic scent to it that promised rain, and the clouds overhead, heavy and gray in the twilight sky, seemed to agree. But it also carried something else—a warm energy that was the unmistakable mark of magic.

"Did you feel that?" she asked, but Harte didn't seem to know what she was talking about. He stepped up to the ticket counter, and she focused her attention on the people around them. At first nothing seemed amiss, but then she saw the girl in blue.

If Esta herself hadn't been a thief, she would have thought nothing of the way the girl tripped or of the way the guy leaning near the lamppost reached out to keep the girl from falling. But Esta *was* a thief, so she didn't miss the flick of the girl's wrist or how the guy palmed the small package in the exchange, using the girl's clumsiness to cover for tucking it into his vest.

It took only a moment. The girl in blue thanked the guy and kept walking onward. The guy continued to lean against the lamppost, his broad-brimmed cowboy hat shielding his eyes and hiding most of his features except for a hard mouth. His shoulders had a slouch to them that Esta suspected couldn't be taught.

She was still trying to figure out what the girl might have given the guy when the shrill trilling of a whistle split the air. A moment later Esta turned to see a trio of men running toward the theater. They were wearing long, knee-length dark coats and had white bands with some sort of insignia wrapped around their right arms. On their lapels, golden medallions flashed in the lamplight. They were a bit smaller than normal police badges, but they had the same official look to them.

The guy with the broad hat glanced up at the commotion, but that

LISA MAXWELL

stiff mouth of his didn't betray any surprise or fear. Instead, the corner of it kicked up, like he'd been expecting them all along. He pulled out a pocket watch that flashed in the light cast by the lamp when he opened it. Lazily, he twisted the dial of the watch, like he had all the time in the world.

Then he tipped back the wide brim of his hat—and looked straight at Esta. He blinked, and then his eyes widened ever so slightly. The motion pulled the sleeve of his shirt back enough to expose a black circular tattoo that wound around his wrist. If he'd been surprised to see her staring, the moment passed quickly. He gave her a wink as he snapped the watch shut, and a burst of icy-hot energy ricocheted through the air . . . and he was *gone*.

She was still staring at the place where he'd disappeared when Harte pulled her back, knocking her off-balance as the three men burst through the line of people waiting. As they passed, Esta felt another wave of magic in their wake. Instinctively, she pulled her own affinity back as she caught herself against Harte.

She felt his arms tighten around her, and her skin burned from his closeness.

But if Harte noticed the same electric pull between them, he didn't show it. "I felt *that*," he said, frowning as he looked for any evidence of danger. "Come on . . ." He led her toward the entrance to the theater as the trio reached the lamppost and grabbed an unsuspecting man who'd been sitting on a bench near where the cowboy had been.

"But—" She was craning her neck, trying to see what was happening and looking for some sign of where the guy with the watch had disappeared to.

"We don't need to get wrapped up in whatever that is." Harte had his arm around her still as he led her into the lobby of the theater.

"*That* was magic," she said. "How can there be magic here?"

"I don't know," Harte told her, glancing back at the doorway of the theater. "But it didn't exactly feel natural."

"It felt . . . *off*, didn't it?" She should have pulled away from him now that they were inside, but she didn't. Even through the layers of material between them, she could feel the warmth of him, an antidote to the cold, unnatural energy that still sifted through the air. Instinctively, she shifted closer, wanting to dispel the unease the event had left in its wake. As she breathed in the warm scent of him, clean and crisp and so familiar, she leaned into him.

It was a mistake. Harte's posture went rigid, and his expression went carefully blank as he unwrapped his arms from her waist and stepped back. "It reminded me a little of the Brink," he said, his tone neutral and matter-of-fact, like he'd never touched her—or at least as though he hadn't meant anything by it. "But what caused it?"

Esta shook off the sting of his indifference. *If that's how it's going to be . . .* "From what I saw, they seemed to be after some cowboy wannabe with a magical pocket watch." She told him about the girl and the drop, and how the guy had looked right at her before he'd disappeared. "It was like he'd already known that they wouldn't catch him."

"But he saw *you*?" He frowned as though this was a problem.

"Looked right at me," she confirmed, remembering the way his expression had shifted slightly when he'd seen her. "But then, I'd been watching him first. Maybe he noticed."

"Do you think they could have been from the Order?" Harte asked.

"The way they were dressed?" The Order only admitted the richest and most exclusive men in the city—old money. "They didn't look the type."

"Then who were they?" Harte asked, frowning. "And who were the people who seemed to be after them?"

"I don't know. I don't like anything about this," she told him. When they had arrived in Baltimore the day before, nothing had seemed obviously different, and she'd breathed a little easier, hoping maybe it meant that Jack having the Book *hadn't* changed things too dramatically. But the cowboy with the watch and the uniformed men set off alarms. She'd never heard of anything like that before—not outside the Brink. "Let's just go. We can check out Julien's house tonight and come back here tomorrow, if we need to."

Harte looked back at the lobby doors and then at the street beyond like he was considering their options. "We're here already," he said after a moment. "Whatever that was seems to be over now, and no one out there was all that alarmed by it. We'll keep alert, but for now let's just get on with it and get out of this town before we run into anything else."

Esta didn't like it, but Harte was right. They'd come this far, and for her to back out now would mean admitting she was afraid. And she wasn't about to do that, especially when *he* didn't seem to be.

The theater's marbled lobby gave way to crimson carpet and walls dripping with crystal and gold. Compared to the spare brick exterior, the opulence of the theater itself was a surprise. When they made their way into the theater proper, the cavernous domed ceiling was painted with scenes of angels and gods, while crystal chandeliers lit the entire space with a soft, sparkling glow. Although the bill was vaudeville, the audience could have been attending a night at the opera as they sat in their velvet-lined seats draped in silks and furs and ornamented with jewels. Dressed in their finery, no one seemed bothered by the stuffy warmth of the air. Women lazily fanned themselves and men quietly dabbed at the beads of sweat on their foreheads without complaint.

Esta's fingers itched. In the dark, it would be so easy to take one or two of those jewels, especially since she didn't know what else lay ahead for them. The security that one emerald brooch might offer was more than tempting . . . but they still had to find Julien *and* get the necklace from him. Sticking around long enough to be caught was a rookie mistake, and Esta was anything but a rookie.

They'd only just gotten to their seats when the lights went down, leaving the theater in darkness except for the expanse of the crimson velvet curtain over the stage and making it impossible to talk anymore about what had happened. Next to her, Harte leaned forward ever so slightly, waiting for the curtain to rise. She used the cover afforded by the darkness in the theater to study him, his sharp features all shadow and light from the glow of the stage. His eyes were serious as the first act came on and split the silence with song.

For Esta, the next hour felt like it would never end. Stuck in the seat between Harte, who was leaning away from her like he didn't want to even bump her elbow, and an old woman whose furs smelled so strongly of mothballs that Esta's eyes watered, she couldn't manage to work up any interest in the acts. She didn't care about the troupe of dancers who kicked their bare legs to the ceiling or the small, goateed man who performed a monologue that at any other time might have had Esta in stitches. Not even the svelte woman dressed all in black who swallowed swords while telling bawdy jokes. It was more than an hour into the show when an act finally caught her attention—a woman who sang in a sultry contralto.

The woman wasn't classically pretty, but there was something completely compelling about her. She had an interesting face, with pale, milky skin and lightly flushed cheeks. Her wide mouth was painted in a bow, and she was dressed in a glittering aquamarine gown accented with pearls. The woman consumed the stage without moving more than a foot or two in either direction, and her voice . . . It was clear and resonant and contained all the pain and hope and wonder of the lyrics of the song.

"It's time," Harte whispered, leaning forward and gesturing for Esta to go.

"What?" She turned to him, confused. The plan was to leave while Julien was on the stage, so they could beat him to his dressing room.

"It's time," Harte repeated, nodding toward the woman on the stage.

"I thought we were going to wait for Julien's act," she whispered.

"We were." Amusement sparked in his eyes. "*That's* Julien."

INFAMOUS

1904—St. Louis

Harte knew that he should have prepared Esta for Julien's act, but the look of surprise on her face made keeping the secret worth it. The delight in her expression was also an enormous relief. The truth was, Harte hadn't exactly been sure how she would react to learning that Julien Eltinge had made a name for himself by impersonating women on the stage—not everyone accepted Julien's particular talent. But Esta took one more look toward the stage, her full mouth parted in a sort of awe as Julien hit a heartrending and impossibly high note, and she smiled. Then she gave Harte a sure nod and gathered her skirts in preparation to leave.

She was dressed in a gown of cloud gray, one she'd picked because she'd thought it was sedate enough to avoid notice. He didn't have the guts to tell her that it had the exact opposite effect. Made from a silk that looked almost liquid, it rippled against the ground as she walked, making her look like some sort of otherworldly apparition. It had drawn the eyes of men—and women—all the way from the hotel to the theater, and it had taken everything in him not to reach for her, to put a proprietary arm around her, so that every one of those onlookers—and Esta herself—knew who she was with.

But he didn't, because after he'd spent the last twenty-four hours in close quarters with her—first on the train and then as they navigated the unfamiliar city to find a hotel and buy evening clothes—what little self-control he had was fraying.

It had been a mistake to touch her earlier. He'd acted on instinct to pull her out of the way before those men in the dark coats had knocked her over, but the moment his arms had gone around her, he'd sensed her—the energy of her affinity, the heart of who and what she was—even through the thin leather of his gloves and the layers she was wearing. And then she'd settled into his arms as though she belonged there. He could have kissed her right there in the middle of the crowded lobby and damn all the repercussions.

The power inside of him had certainly wanted him to, but the way it had swelled at Esta's nearness had been enough to bring him back to himself, and he'd held it together. He had pushed the power and all of its wanting down and let go of her. He'd managed to keep his hands to himself ever since. He'd just have to *keep* managing.

"Harte?" Esta asked.

"What?" He blinked and realized she was staring at him. She'd been saying something, and he'd missed it.

"I said, which way?" she asked, unaware of the true direction of his thoughts.

Once they were back in the lobby, Harte could hear the rumble of applause within as Julien finished his first song, even through the closed theater doors. They'd have fifteen, maybe twenty minutes before his act was over—not much time considering that Harte hadn't had a chance to case the building.

But theaters were all pretty much the same, and Harte understood the rhythm of life on the stage and the way the world behind the curtain ticked like the gears of a clock, hidden and essential. He went with his instincts and led the way to an unremarkable door at the end of the lobby. Once through it, the lights were dimmer and the familiar energy of backstage enveloped him. He gave his eyes a moment to adjust as he took off his gloves—just in case. He prepared himself, making sure that the power inside of him was locked down tight as he took Esta's hand in his. Ignoring the surge of warmth and wanting that rose up within him, he led her through the maze that was backstage, toward where the dressing rooms were housed.

When they turned a corner, they ran into a woman with dark blond hair and an armful of fabric. From the look of it, she was a costumer, one of the backstage workers who took care of the performers in between acts, and for a moment Harte thought of Cela—of his mother—but when the woman's eyes went wide at the sight of them, Harte knew it meant trouble.

"You're not supposed to be back here," the woman said, her brows drawing together as she looked the two of them up and down, taking in the evening clothes they were wearing.

Esta's hand tightened around his, but Harte simply pasted on his most charming smile—the one that usually got him whatever he wanted. "No wrong turn at all," he said as he dropped Esta's hand and extended his now-free hand toward the woman. "Charlie Walbridge."

The woman only frowned at him as she looked down at his bare, out-stretched hand with brows bunched. Her nose scrunched up as though he were offering her a rotten piece of meat.

"Walbridge, as in the son of Cyrus P. Walbridge . . . the owner of this theater," he added, dropping his hand and infusing his voice with a hint of impatience. "This is my fiancée, Miss Ernestine Francis." It hadn't taken much effort earlier to figure out who the owner of the theater was, along with the names of a couple of the other more important men in town. He had no idea if Councilman Francis even had a daughter, but he knew that names—*certain* names—had power.

The gambit worked. The woman's eyes widened slightly, and she sputtered a hurried apology.

Harte gave her an appraising look. "Yes, well . . . mistakes do happen, don't they? I'll be sure to tell my father how dedicated his employees are to the theater's well-being, especially you, Miss . . ." He paused, waiting for her to supply her name.

"It's Mrs., actually, though my husband's been gone these past three years now. Mrs. Joy Konarske."

"Well, it's been a pleasure to meet you, Mrs. Konarske." He offered his hand again. "I'll be sure to tell my father how dutiful you've been. He'll be pleased to know his theater is being well looked after."

The woman's cheeks went a little pink as she paused to shift her burden of fabric so she could grasp Harte's outstretched hand. Her palm was rough and calloused from the work of laundering the costumes and tending to the performers' wardrobes each night, and Harte felt a flicker of guilt as he focused on pushing his affinity toward her, pulsing it gently—*just a little*—through the delicate boundary of flesh and into the very heart of who and what she was.

Her eyes widened, but she didn't pull away. *They never do,* he thought.

When Harte finally released the woman's hand a moment later, she had a slightly dazed look in her eyes. Giving the two of them a shaky smile, she wandered off, and Harte knew she would leave them be. She would forget having ever seen him—because he had ordered her to. And the moment she heard or saw a description of either Esta or himself, Mrs. Joy Konarske would feel a wave of such revulsion that she would do anything necessary to escape the person asking.

"Did you . . . ?" Esta asked, her voice low.

He met her eyes, expecting judgment but finding instead only worry. Or perhaps that was sadness? "Would you rather she tell someone she saw us here?" he whispered.

"Of course not," she whispered. "It's just . . . do you think it's safe? With the Book's power in you?"

He hadn't considered that. Why *hadn't* he considered that?

"I don't know." It wasn't like he'd had much choice. He'd done the only thing he could do, unless they wanted to be discovered before they even began.

Luckily, they didn't run into anyone else before they found Julien's dressing room and let themselves in. Despite the number of women's wigs and gowns that filled much of the room, it was a masculine space. Which, considering Julien, wasn't surprising. On the dressing table, an ashtray contained the remains of multiple cigars, and the cloying ghost of their smoke still hung thick in the air.

"How long do we have?" Esta asked.

"Maybe another ten minutes or so."

"I'll look here, if you check the dressing table," Esta said, turning to the large upright steamer trunk in the corner.

Harte knew it couldn't hurt to look. If they found the necklace, they could avoid Julien altogether. But he didn't really expect the necklace to be in the dressing room—Julien wasn't stupid. Even if Julien didn't know about the power the stone contained, he would be more careful than to leave it in an unlocked dressing room in a crowded theater. The heavy platinum collar was set with a turquoise-colored stone shot through with glittering veins of some silvery substance that made it look like a sky full of stars. It was singular, and clearly valuable, and Julien would keep something like that somewhere safe ... *especially* with the note Harte had sent along with it.

But Esta was right. It wouldn't hurt to look while they were there.

Before he'd even managed to sit at the dressing table, Esta had pulled a pin from her hair and popped the lock of the trunk. Harte paused to watch her as she began sorting through the drawers inside of it, and then he turned back to the dressing table.

For a moment he felt the shock of recognition. How many times had he sat at the same sort of table, the glow of the electric light over the mirror illuminating the familiar planes and angles of his own face? There were pots of stage paint and kohl on the tabletop, and their familiar scents came to him even beneath the staleness of the full ashtray, teasing at his memories and inspiring a pang of longing and loss so sharp, it surprised him.

He was never going to sit at a dressing table like this again. He was done with that life.

Even if he managed to get out of this mess alive—even if they could exorcise the power lurking beneath his skin *and* get away from the Order *and* stop Nibsy—Harte was supposed to be dead. He couldn't just resurrect himself. There would be no more applause, no more footlights. He would never again have the quiet solitude of a dressing room to call his own.

Maybe he would find a new name, a new life that he could be happy with, but it wouldn't be on the stage. And he would miss it—the rush of nerves before and the thrill of the applause after. He hadn't realized just how much until that moment.

"Find anything?" Esta asked, still rustling through papers in one of the trunk's drawers. It was enough to shake him out of his maudlin bout of self-pity and get to work.

"Not yet," he told her. He opened the first of the drawers, one filled with small pots of rouge and the powdery smell of talc. He didn't have to search through the items to see that the necklace wasn't there.

"What is all of this?" Esta murmured, and Harte turned to see what she had found.

She was holding a leather box, trimmed in gold and stamped with a gilded filigreed emblem that was inscribed with a stylized monogram of the letters *VP*. Harte came over to look as Esta pulled out a small golden medallion that hung from a green satin ribbon. It was the kind of medallion important dignitaries or generals wear when they dress for a parade. *Odd* . . .

He took the medal from her and examined it. Like the box itself, it was inscribed with an ornate *VP*, but the surface bore the portrait of a long-faced man with a full beard. The figure might have been a crusader or a saint, with his sharp cheekbones and solemn expression, but his face seemed to be partially obscured, as though a piece of fabric was hanging over it. Around the edge of the medallion were markings that could have been simple decorations or an unknown language—it was impossible to tell.

"I don't know," Harte said, frowning at the piece. The Julien he knew hadn't been involved with anything but the theater, and that medallion didn't look or feel like a prop.

"There's more," Esta told him, carefully lifting out a piece of scarlet silk that had been neatly folded into a square. It was a sash of some kind, and it, too, was pinned with another medallion. At the bottom of the box lay a small silver tray, ornately wrought with more of the strange symbols around the edges of an even more elaborate rendering of the same two letters—*VP*.

The light over the dressing table dimmed for a moment before returning to its normal brightness. "Put it away," he told Esta, handing back the medal. "That's the signal for the next act. Julien will be back any second now."

Esta worked to put the trunk back together and relocked it. She was just slipping the pin back into her hair when the dressing room door opened and the painted songstress from the stage entered the small confines of the dressing room.

It was always a shock to see Julien up close when he was dressed for his act. Even without the distance of the audience and the glare of the lights, he had mastered his art. His impersonation didn't rely on any of the camp that other female impersonators used. His stage persona wasn't a caricature of a woman. It wasn't clownish or overdone to get laughs. No, Julien's art—his true talent—was in his ability to become the thing itself. Had Harte passed Julien, dressed as he was now, on the streets, he wouldn't have seen anything other than the woman standing before him.

Not seeming to realize that he wasn't alone, Julien pulled off the perfectly coiffed blond wig and placed it on a wooden mannequin's head. Then he walked over to sit in front of the mirrored dressing table. Before he bothered with the makeup or the dress, Julien took a thick black cigar from a small tabletop humidor and lit it. He took a deep drag, allowing the smoke to wreathe his head as he reached for the decanter next to the ashtray and poured himself two fingers. He took a long drink before he put the cigar back between his teeth and began removing the elbow-length gloves he was wearing.

"You know, Darrigan . . ." Julien looked up and caught Harte's eye in the mirror. His deep, husky voice was completely at odds with the bright crimson paint on his mouth. "You're looking damn good for a dead man."

Harte gave a careless shrug. "I can't say that I feel all that dead."

Julien turned, a half smile curving at his mouth around the cigar as he shook his head. "I can't believe you are standing here. I can't believe you're in my dressing room."

"It's good to see you, Jules," Harte said, stepping forward to extend his hand in greeting.

Julien stood and took Harte's outstretched hand. "It's damn good to see you, too, Darrigan."

"Glad to hear it," Harte told him as he sent a small pulse of his affinity toward Julien.

Harte never saw thoughts clearly, just impressions and feelings. The most immediate of Julien's memories came first—the glare of the lights, the roar of the applause Julien had just received, the hot, sharp satisfaction that Julien had felt. Harte ignored his own yearning for those lights and for the warm rush that applause had always given him and concentrated instead on his purpose—some hint of the stone's fate. It came in an instant, the clear image of the necklace with its fantastical stone, and latching onto that image, Harte focused everything he was and sent another burst of magic toward Julien, transgressing the thin barrier between him and his friend and sending Julien a simple message. A single command.

Julien's expression faltered, his eyes slightly dazed and his brows creasing together momentarily. But then Harte released him, and Julien's expression cleared. Unaware of all that had just transpired, Julien turned back to his mirror and reached for his large jar of cold cream. He ignored Harte and Esta both as he spread the cream over one half of his face and then started wiping away the light base and bright rouge.

Esta had been watching all of this without saying a word, so Harte gestured for her to come forward. "Jules, I want you to meet someone," Harte said.

Julien's eyes lifted to Esta's in the mirror, and Harte knew exactly what his old friend was seeing—the way the silk gown she wore clung to every curve and the way she'd painted her mouth a subtle pink and pinned her hair into a style that looked artful and careless all at once. She looked like she came from money, proper and polished. But with her height and her confidence, she also looked dangerous, like a debutante on the verge of something more exciting.

A look of appreciation flashed over Julien's face as he examined Esta through the reflection of the mirror.

Mine, a voice inside Harte whispered in response, but he couldn't tell if it came from his own thoughts or that other power. Not caring all that much at the moment, he took Esta by the hand, so there was no mistaking who she was with.

"This is—"

"Oh, I know exactly who this is," Julien interrupted, turning Janus-faced to look at them both once again.

"You do?" Esta asked, glancing at Harte with a wary expression.

"Of course, Miss Filosik." Julien picked up the stub of the cigar again and gestured toward them before raising one brow in their direction. "I knew who you were the moment I walked into this room. After all . . . you're *infamous.*"

THE ANTIDOTE FOR GOSSIP

1902—New York

J ack could hear the commotion in his mother's parlor long before he made it to the bottom of the staircase. By the time he reached the lower steps, a cold sweat had broken out on his forehead and he wanted nothing more than to sit down, but the rumble of his uncle's voice told him that he should keep moving.

Thank god the mousy little maid had gotten over her initial fear of him. Without her mentioning his uncle's sudden arrival, Jack might have slept through the visit, completely unaware of how his family was arranging his future. It didn't matter if his head was swirling with the morphine he'd just taken or that his body still felt like . . . Well, it felt like he'd been hit by a train, didn't it? He would walk into the parlor under his own power and take the reins of his own fate.

". . . someone got to him," his uncle was roaring, waving a crumpled handful of newsprint at his mother.

"No one has been here," his mother said, her voice shaking as it often did when she was overwrought. "I think I would know if a newspaper-man came into my home."

"How else would they know any of this?" Morgan waved the paper at her again.

"Pierpont, dear—" His aunt Fanny was sitting next to Jack's mother, and her tone had a warning in it, not that his uncle seemed to care.

Jack's cousin was there as well, standing off to the side with his arms crossed and the same scowl on his face that he had worn the entire voyage back from Greece last year. It truly was a family affair, which always meant trouble for Jack.

It took a moment before any of them realized that he'd arrived. His mother saw him first, and she leaped to her feet at the sight of him. "Darling, what are you doing out of bed?" She wasn't three steps toward him before his uncle stepped in her path and waved the newspaper he'd been brandishing in Jack's face.

"What is the meaning of this, boy?"

The room was spinning a little, but Jack forced himself to stay upright. "The meaning of what? I've been abed for—" He looked to his mother. The days had all run together. "How long have I been up there?"

"Three days, dear," she said, a small, sad smile on her face as she beamed at him. "You should sit down. You're not well." She went over to the tufted chair closest to him and began arranging the pillows.

He couldn't stand her constant fussing, like he was still a child. It was how they all saw him, he knew. And they were all wrong. "I'm fine," he said, waving her off.

He wasn't fine, but he damned sure wasn't going to admit it in front of his uncle and his cousin. The last thing he would be was weak in front of them. "I've no idea what you're referring to," he told Morgan, meeting the old man's gaze. "Perhaps if you'd stop shouting and explained it, I could offer a response."

Morgan glared at him. "Who did you talk to?"

"Recently?" Jack asked. "No one but my mother and the ever-present parade of doctors and maids who insist on constantly intruding on my rest and recovery."

Most of the maids were pretty enough, but all the doctors had been a nuisance, constantly checking on him and telling him to rest, when all he wanted to do was study the Book he'd hidden beneath the mountain of pillows and blankets the maids piled onto the bed. Day and night, he wanted only to pore over the pages and unlock its secrets.

"Then how did the *Herald* manage to publish this story?" Morgan thrust the paper at him.

Jack swayed a little on his feet, but he opened the crumpled page to find a headline about himself. He let his eyes skim over it. "What of it?" he asked. Nothing seemed amiss. "None of this is untrue. Darrigan and the girl were on the train before it derailed. The authorities said that there wasn't a bomb, so it might well have been magic that caused the accident."

"None of that matters," Morgan said. "I don't care about some damn train derailment. I care about the fact that this reporter knows what happened at Khafre Hall—that the fire wasn't an accident of faulty wiring. Do you know what lengths the Inner Circle undertook to ensure that the truth of the Khafre Hall disaster did not become public? It was a delicate thing, to steer the press away from the real cause of the fire, and yet here it is, a full-page spread that reveals not only that we were robbed of our most important artifacts, but that we were robbed by common *trash*. This article knows everything. Who did you talk to?"

The past few days were a haze of pain and morphine . . . and the thrall of the Book. Jack could have talked to Roosevelt himself, and he wouldn't necessarily have remembered. Not that he would admit that now. "No one," he said instead. "I've no idea how this . . . Reynolds, whoever he is, knows any of this."

"Well, he does, and it's made a damn mess of things," Morgan said, ripping the paper from Jack's hands. "Do you know how *weak* this makes the Order look? We're already getting word from the other Brotherhoods that they're concerned about the state of the Conclave—about the Order's ability to host it. After all, if I can't control my own family, how can we possibly think to arrange an event as important as the Conclave?" He tossed the paper aside.

"I don't know why you assume it was my fault," Jack said, bristling at his uncle's tone.

"Because it usually *is* your fault," his cousin said. "It's one scheme after another with you, Jack, and none of them are reasonable. You don't think things through. Are you sure you didn't give this interview?"

Jack clenched his jaw to keep from railing at the snideness in his cousin's tone. Across the room, his mother was still looking at him with a sadness in her eyes that made him want to smash his fist into her precious collection of figurines. When he spoke, it took effort to make his words measured and calm. "This is the first I've even been out of bed."

But his cousin wasn't listening. "Maybe we should give Jack something of a holiday, to recuperate," his cousin suggested to his uncle. "Until this all blows over."

"It's not going to blow over," Morgan spat. "This isn't a private family matter, like the problem in Greece last year. That damn article is everywhere, and the other papers are picking up the story as well. If we send him off now, it's going to look like we have something to hide. That's the last thing we want—it would give credence to the story."

"What else can we do with him?" his cousin asked.

"I'm standing right here," Jack said darkly. He felt out of breath just standing there, but thankfully, the morphine he'd taken before he came down had eased the pain in his arm and in his head.

"As though that matters in the slightest," his uncle sneered. Then he turned back to his son, Jack's cousin. "We'll demand a retraction."

"From the *Herald*?" His cousin shook his head. "It's not much more than a gossip rag these days. They don't care whether the story's accurate, so long as it sells. It might be better to meet them on their own terms. Get another story out there, one that sheds some doubt on this one. I can talk to Sam Watson, if you want. You remember, I introduced you at the Metropolitan. He's been a great friend to the Order, first with the theft at the Met and then in the past few weeks with his editorials about the dangers of a certain criminal element. I'm sure he could do an interview with Jack and reframe the story."

"I don't want to do any damn interview," Jack said, but no one was listening.

"Do that," his uncle said, pacing. "It's a start, but it's not enough. Retracting the story doesn't change the fact that this Reynolds has made the Order look like old fools."

Which you are, Jack thought. But even with the morphine loosening his mind, he managed to keep his mouth shut tight. He didn't need to worry about his uncle or the Order any longer now that he had the Book.

"It sounds to me like what you need is an engagement," his aunt Fanny ventured.

Morgan turned to her, impatient. "Thank you, dearest, but this matter doesn't concern you."

His aunt ignored the dismissal. "If you're trying to neutralize unwanted gossip, you need something more exciting for the press to focus on than an interview, Pierpont. Trust me. The world of gossip is one I am intimately familiar with, and I have far more experience at controlling it than you do. When a girl's reputation is soiled, the best thing her family can do is to get her engaged, and quickly. There's nothing like a big society wedding to distract the gossips. Isn't that right, Mary?" she asked, turning to Jack's mother.

His mother, a small, weak woman who'd become even more so with age, looked troubled. "I don't think Jack's in any condition to court anyone," she said tentatively, "though I suppose the Stewart girl might be interested since she had such a dismal season."

"I am not being shackled to some failed debutante," Jack said. He certainly wasn't going to allow his mother and aunt to arrange a marriage to save his reputation, like they might for some ruined girl.

"No, dear," his aunt told his mother. "I would never do that to some poor girl."

Jack opened his mouth to argue, but he couldn't figure out what to say. He didn't want to be married off, but his aunt's flippant dismissal was insulting.

"We don't need an *actual* wedding. If you want to stop gossip, you give them something else to talk about. It must simply be an event. A *spectacular* event." His aunt turned to Morgan. "A party or a gala of some sort. The Order could host it, which would make it a show of your continued strength."

"It's hardly the time for a party, Fanny."

His aunt *tsk*ed. "One does not hide from the world when tongues begin to wag, Pierpont. One shows up at the opera wearing the finest gown one can find."

"It is also no time to think about shopping," Morgan growled.

"Mother has a point," Jack's cousin said, rubbing at his chin thoughtfully. "The Order could host a gala—something large and elaborate. Even better if it's an exclusive event. That would get the papers interested in covering it."

"And where would we host it?" Morgan asked darkly. "Khafre Hall is a pile of rubble and ash, if you remember correctly."

"Use our ballroom," his aunt said. "But you can't simply throw a ball. You need something more original than that." She considered the problem for a moment. "What about a tableau vivant?"

"Aren't they a bit risqué?" his mother asked.

"They're perfectly appropriate, if they're depicting great art," his aunt said primly. "But yes. They're often considered quite risqué, which is the entire point. News of it would cause a stir. There would be speculation for weeks about which artworks would be selected and who would be posing for each of the scenes."

"Not simply art," his cousin said, shaking his head. "Scenes from some flouncy rococo paintings won't do. If we're to restore the Order's reputation, we need to present great works that show the Order's strength and importance. Scenes of the dangers of feral magic and the power of science and enlightenment to protect the people. It could work."

"Possibly," Morgan said darkly, considering the proposition. "But we would have to make sure this one doesn't muck everything up again," he added, nodding toward Jack. "We'll have to make sure he's well out of sight."

"*This one* is standing right here," Jack muttered again. And again they ignored him. He'd had enough, he thought, and began to retreat to the relative sanity of his room. They could figure out whatever they wanted to do as long as it didn't include parading him around as a bridegroom. He had other, more important matters to attend to.

"Oh, no," his aunt said. "You can't hide him away."

"Why the hell not?" Morgan asked.

"Every society wedding needs a bride, Pierpont. That's the entire point," his aunt said.

Jack stopped in his tracks and turned back to the room.

"Everyone shows up to the church to see the chit dressed in white and redeemed," his aunt continued. "Everyone wants to know if it was truly a love match, or if the groom looks ready to dash. If you want to discredit this article, you need to show you've nothing to hide."

"I am not marrying some girl," Jack said again, his voice clipped and barely containing his frustration.

"I'm not talking about you taking a bride, dear. I'm talking about you *being* the bride," his aunt said with a dreamy smile.

"Like hell—" Jack started to say, but his aunt was still talking.

"You must make Jack the focus," she told his uncle.

"Absolutely not," Morgan growled, his nose twitching with disgust at the idea.

"It's the only way," his aunt said, looking at Jack with a dangerously thoughtful expression. Nothing good ever came of meddling women when they started to think. "Yes. I can see it now," she told Morgan. "You make Jack the man of the hour, the celebrant of the night. The event will show that the Order isn't afraid or weak or even laid low, and you can use this story to your advantage. You can't retract what's been written any more than a girl can reclaim her virginity, but you can use it to help your cause. Recast Jack as a hero who discovered the danger on the train, a danger that reveals the continued necessity of the Order."

"I don't like it," Morgan said.

"That's not the point, dear," his aunt told Morgan. "What poor girl likes being forced into marriage because of one little indiscretion when men get to have as many as they like? The point is in the necessity. You must take the story and make it your own. It's the surest way, and it will shore up the Order's power at the same time."

"I'm not some pawn to be used," Jack growled. His head felt light and heavy all at once from the morphine in his veins, but his anger felt like something pure. How dare they try to arrange his life. How *dare* they treat him like some stupid little chit being traded between men. "I deserve to have a say in this."

Morgan turned to him. "From the evidence in this article, you've already had your say. Now your choice is to listen or to leave. Do I make myself clear?"

He was clenching his teeth so tightly that he suspected they would crack at any moment, but Jack gave his uncle a tight nod. "Crystal."

They turned back to their planning as though he were no more than a misbehaving child, scolded and dismissed. *Fine.* Let them think that. Let them believe that he would bow and scrape to win their favor again. They didn't realize that already they were becoming unnecessary. The world was spinning on without them, and so would Jack. While they fussed like women over linens and china patterns, he would be learning and planning, and when the moment was right, he would step into their place and make the old men who thought they ruled the city obsolete.

But until then Morgan wasn't the only one who had contacts and people who could do him favors. Jack would use one of his to find this R. A. Reynolds. He'd met Paul Kelly a few weeks back, and from all he'd heard, Kelly wouldn't have a problem with delivering a message for him. He would make sure that damn newspaperman was sorry he ever crossed Jack Grew.

CONSEQUENCES

1904—St. Louis

Had Esta not been trained since she was a child to suppress every flicker of emotion when faced with some sudden danger, her jaw might have dropped at Julien Eltinge's words. Instead, she kept her features placid, the combination of boredom and cool poise that never failed to evade attention. As much as she now loathed the man who had raised her, she was grateful in that moment for her ability to hide her reaction so completely. But inside, her instincts were on high alert, and her stomach felt like she'd just been sucker punched.

"Infamous?" Esta asked. "I'm not sure what you've heard about me, but surely infamous is overstating things, Mr. Eltinge."

Julien's mouth hitched up around his cigar again. "Oh, I don't think it's overstating things at all," he replied, his dark eyes glittering. They were too sharp. Too perceptive—and she had a feeling that so was he. Setting the cigar back in the ashtray, Julien turned back to the mirror and began removing the makeup on the other side of his face. "After all, you can't destroy a train and not expect to get a reputation, you know," he said as calmly and easily as someone talking about the weather.

Destroy a train?

The dressing room seemed to fall away, and all at once Esta felt as though she were back on the train out of New Jersey. The stone that she was wearing against her arm almost felt warm at the memory of how hard it had been to grasp the seconds, to find the right moment to pull them through to get away from Jack. Though she was on solid ground, Esta's legs felt suddenly unsteady, just as they had when the ground beneath the train had seemed to quake, like the train was about to run itself off the rails. And even in the warmly lit dressing room, the darkness that had tugged at her vision and her consciousness haunted her.

No . . . that's impossible.

"But please, let's not stand on ceremony. You must call me Julien." He glanced up at Esta in the mirror, smiling slightly as he wiped more of the makeup from his face. "After all, a friend of Darrigan's is a friend of mine."

"What are you going on about, Julien?" Harte asked. "She didn't destroy anything—certainly not a train."

"I suppose it would be the sort of thing one *would* remember. . . ." Julien gave her another of those too-perceptive looks. "It's what all the papers claimed, though."

"And you believed them?" Harte asked, scorn coloring his tone. "You of all people should know not to trust those muckrakers."

Julien's affable expression flickered slightly, but he didn't immediately respond. Esta noticed that he was still watching her, and he continued to study her for a few moments longer, before turning back to the dressing table. He took his time wiping the rest of the cold cream and makeup from his face, erasing the woman who had commanded the stage until all that was left was the man beneath, a man who was no less compelling.

There was nothing remotely feminine about Julien's features without the light base or the brightness of the rouge on his cheeks and lips. Instead, he had a rugged, almost Mediterranean look to him, with olive-toned skin, sweat-damp black hair that held the hint of a curl, and coal-dark eyes that were as perceptive as a raven's. He picked up the cigar again—an affectation, Esta realized—wielding the thick stump of it like a sword.

Julien turned to face the two of them then, and his voice was serious when he spoke. "To be honest, Darrigan, I didn't pay attention to the story when it first happened. There's always some accident or another the papers are going on about. But then that one fellow claimed it *wasn't* an accident. The only reason I even noticed it really is because he claimed *you* were there."

"What fellow was that?" Harte asked.

"What's his name—the one who always runs with Roosevelt these days," Julien said, wagging the cigar in the air as he tried to think. "Grew, I think it is. Gerald or James . . ."

Esta's stomach went tight. "Jack."

"That's it." Julien pointed the cigar at her. "Jack Grew—one of the Morgans, isn't he?"

"J. P. Morgan's nephew," Harte supplied, but his voice sounded as hollow as Esta suddenly felt.

Julien nodded, apparently not noticing either of their reactions. "Yes, that one. He got caught up in the mess. A few days after it happened, one of the papers came out with this whole story about how the derailment wasn't an accident. Jack Grew claimed that the two of you were the ones who set some fire and burned down the headquarters of the Order of Ortus Aurea in New York to cover a theft and that he'd tracked you to the train and had almost apprehended you when you attacked him—"

"*I* attacked *him*?" Esta didn't even try to hide the disgust in her voice.

"And blew up half the train to escape," Julien finished. "A lot of people died in the crash, you know. After Grew claimed it wasn't an accident, the powers that be started paying attention—oh, don't look so offended, Darrigan. I'm just telling you what the papers said."

"You're accusing us of destroying a train, Jules," Harte said, his voice lower and more dangerous now. "Of killing innocent people."

"I'm not accusing *you* of anything. You're supposed to be dead, after all. Nasty fall off a bridge, from what I heard."

"So you're accusing me?" Esta asked, still trying to make sense of the strange person that was Julien Eltinge.

She knew men like him, men who used their good looks and easy confidence to get their way. Men like Logan, who she'd thought was a friend and a partner until he'd turned against her. Men like Harte, too, if she were honest with herself. Julien's charm was a warning of sorts—a sign that she had to be on alert. But there was something else beneath the charm, and that part of him was still a puzzle.

"I'm not accusing anyone," Julien said.

Harte let out an impatient breath. "You're trying my patience, Jules."

Julien gave Esta a wry look out of the corner of his eye. "You know, he can be a jackass sometimes." He paused to consider what he'd just said. "Actually, he's a jackass more often than not, isn't he? But I never knew him for a murderer. You, on the other hand . . ." He looked at Esta full on now, a question in his darkly perceptive eyes. "I don't know *you* at all."

"She's with me." Harte stepped forward, slightly in front of her, to assert himself physically as he spoke. "That's all you need to know."

Esta barely stopped herself from rolling her eyes in exasperation. Harte had pretty much ignored her since they'd left New York, and *now* he was suddenly interested? Typical. But in front of Julien, she let him have his little moment.

Jules gave Harte an inquiring look. "I see," he said, amusement brightening his expression when he finally looked at Esta again. Then he let out a soft chuckle. "Harte Darrigan . . . I never thought to see the day. . . ." He laughed again.

Esta lifted her chin slightly and affected what she hoped was a look of utter disinterest, even as she was still trying to process everything Julien had just told them. Something had happened to the train they were on after they had slipped through time—something that had never happened before.

"Tell me about the train," Esta demanded.

Julien held Esta's gaze a few moments longer before he began to speak. "There was a big derailment a couple of years ago. The accident tore a gaping hole into a section of track just outside the station in New Jersey. From the reports in the papers, the track was gone. Utterly *demolished*, and half the train with it. The inspectors said that damage like that could have only been the result of an explosion. At first they thought it was one of the anarchist groups that are always blowing things up when they don't get their way, but then a couple days after, the *Herald* broke the story about this Jack Grew character. Apparently, he claimed that the two of you were responsible. Of course, most people thought he was cracked, seeing as how Darrigan here was supposed to *already* be dead— no offense—"

"None taken," Harte said, but his jaw was tight, and Esta had a feeling he didn't like to be reminded.

"And then there was his claim that it wasn't a bomb. He said you used magic."

"Magic?" Esta asked, pretending to be surprised.

"Claimed that you were Mageus," Julien said, implying the unspoken question.

"We've known each other for ages, Jules. If I were Mageus, don't you think you would know?" Harte asked, bringing Julien's attention back to him. "If either one of us were Mageus, how would we have gotten out of the city?"

Esta tried not to hold her breath as she waited for Julien's answer.

"That was the question everyone was asking," Julien said finally. "Dangerous magic outside the protection of the Brink? It should have been impossible. But they never found your bodies in the wreckage, and Grew continued to swear you had both been there.

"Of course, his people used the whole thing as proof that the Order's work was still important. The Order denied that magic could escape the confines of the Brink, just as they denied that the fire at their headquarters had been anything but an accident—faulty wiring or some such thing. Nothing could have been stolen from them because only the devil's own thief could have broken into the Order of Ortus Aurea's vaults. As you can imagine, the public *loved* that. The Devil's Thief."

"The Devil's Thief?" Esta asked.

"That's what they started calling you," Julien said, stubbing out the cigar for good this time. "You were in all the papers for a while. Everyone was trying to figure out who you were and where you'd gone. Every reporter was trying to unmask the Devil's Thief."

"Damn stupid name," Harte muttered.

Julien laughed. "Maybe, but it made a helluva headline, if you ask me."

"I didn't," Harte said flatly.

Julien ignored him. "It has the right . . . je ne sais *something*. Really grabs attention." He glanced more directly at Esta. "It would play great onstage, if you're ever interested in the theater business?"

Harte spoke before she could answer. "She's not."

Esta shot Harte a look, but he didn't even see it. His focus was on Julien, and his impatience felt like a living, breathing thing.

Julien didn't seem to notice. Or maybe he didn't care. With a shrug, he continued. "Damn shame. Tall girl like you? I bet you've got a great set of legs under those skirts—"

"Julien . . . ," Harte ground out.

"I can't believe you really don't know *any* of this," Julien said, confusion replacing the amusement in his expression. "I figured that was why you'd gone to ground—that you were either dead or hiding out somewhere. Either way, I didn't ever expect to see you back here."

"We were . . ." Harte paused as though unsure of how to explain.

"Out of the country," Esta supplied easily.

Julien frowned, considering the two of them. "Still, you'd think that news like that would have reached—"

A knock sounded at the door, cutting Julien's words off midsentence.

The sudden alertness in Harte's posture mirrored Esta's own feeling of unease. There was only one entrance—and, therefore, only one exit—to the dressing room. If Julien was right about them being wanted and if *he* had recognized her so easily, it was possible that someone else had too. They couldn't be caught there. Not after how far they'd come, and not with all they still had left to do.

"You didn't—" Harte started, but Julien held up a hand to silence him.

"Who is it?" Julien shouted, not bothering to move to open the door. He, too, seemed suddenly on edge.

"It's Sal."

"The stage manager," he whispered to Harte.

"Well, what do you want?" he boomed. "I'm a little busy at the moment."

"There's some of the Jefferson Guard here. They're doing a sweep of the whole theater," the manager shouted through the closed door. "Thought I'd warn you in case you were . . . uh . . . indisposed."

"Well, I am." Julien's gaze moved between Harte and Esta. "Can you hold them off for a few minutes?"

"I can probably get you five," the voice called from the other side of the door.

"Do that and I'll owe you a bottle of something better than your usual swill."

The three of them waited in silence for Sal's footsteps to retreat. The moment they could no longer be heard, Julien was on his feet. "Come on. You two need to get out of here." He pushed aside a rack of beaded evening gowns that glimmered in the light as they moved.

"What's going on?" Esta asked Julien. "What's he talking about—the guards?"

"The Jefferson Guard. They're a private militia here in St. Louis." Julien began to work on loosening a panel on the back wall. "Their main job is to hunt down illegal magic, but they've been on higher alert than usual with the Exposition going on this year—especially since the Antistasi attacks that happened last October."

"Antistasi?" Harte asked at the same time Esta said, "What attacks?"

"The Antistasi are a group of anarchists, but instead of the usual dynamite and bullets, the Antistasi use magic to make trouble. They started cropping up after the Defense Against Magic Act went into effect last year, but you probably don't know about that, either." When they shook their heads, he continued. "Basically, it made all forms of unregulated, natural magic officially illegal," Julien explained as he continued to loosen the panel in the wall.

"The Antistasi . . . they're Mageus?" Esta asked.

"That's what they claim," Julien said. "Once the Act went into effect, they suddenly seemed to be *everywhere*, making all kinds of trouble. Actually, you and the train became something of an inspiration for them."

Harte's eyes met Esta's, and she knew he was thinking the same thing she was.

Mageus living outside the city—outside the Brink? The old magic wasn't supposed to exist anywhere else in the country. Wasn't that what she'd always been taught? It was what she'd been brought up to believe. But she'd felt it herself outside the theater. There was magic in the streets of St. Louis. Strange magic, but power just the same. Had something changed because of what they'd done back in New York when they stole from the Order and let Jack get the Book? Or had everything she'd known been a lie?

Once, Esta had been grateful for the education she'd been given. Her deep knowledge of New York allowed her to be a master of its streets no matter when she landed, but now she was even more aware of the holes in that education. Had Professor Lachlan withheld the information about Mageus outside the city from her on purpose to keep her blind? Or was this some new future she couldn't have been prepared for?

One thing *was* certain—in her own time, there hadn't been any Defense Against Magic Act.

"Don't worry, sweetheart," Julien said softly, misreading her concern. "We'll get you out of here." He worked at pulling the panel aside, to open a hole into the wall. "The Jefferson Guard might not be looking for you specifically, but I'm willing to bet the bounty on your pretty little head is a lot bigger than their usual price."

"There's a bounty?" Esta asked.

"Christ," Julien said, half-disgusted and half-astounded. "You really have been away for a while. *Of course* there's a bounty. J. P. Morgan

himself offered it. You can't just go blowing up trains without consequences, you know."

"I told you, she didn't do anything to that train," Harte ground out.

"And I've already said I'm inclined to believe you, but it will be harder
to convince the Guard if they find you here. They're not known for
fighting fair, so you'd have a hell of a time getting away."

"But—" Harte started to argue.

"He's right," Esta interrupted before he could delay them any more.
"Let's go while we can." She sent him a silent look that she hoped he
understood.

"Smart girl," Julien said.

She didn't bother to acknowledge the compliment. Her mind was
swirling with the implications of everything they'd just learned: She was
a wanted criminal and there was magic—maybe even Mageus—outside
the confines of the Brink.

By then Julien had completely removed the panel of the wall, exposing a passageway behind it. "I've used this in the past when I wanted
to slip out without dealing with the stage-door crowd." His expression
faltered, and Esta couldn't help but wonder what that meant. "Follow this
passage to the left," Julien instructed. "It'll bring you to the boiler room.
From there you should be able to find your way out easily enough."

"About that bounty, Jules . . ." Harte's expression was as sharp as the
part that split his dark hair. "You sure you don't have any interest in
claiming it for yourself?"

Julien looked legitimately taken aback. His voice held a warning
when he finally spoke. "I would have thought you knew me better than
that, Darrigan."

"Like you said, it *has* been a long time," Harte said, and there was
something unspoken, charged between them. "A lot seems to have
changed while I was gone. I just need to know whether you have too."

"I don't want their blood money," Julien said flatly as he nodded
toward the opening. From the look in his eyes, Esta could even believe

that he meant it. "Go on. When the Jefferson Guard comes through, I'll make sure they're distracted for a while so you can get well away from the theater."

"We still need to talk, Julien," Harte pressed.

"Sure, sure," Julien said, waving them onward. "I'll meet you at King's in a couple of hours."

"Where's King's?" Harte asked.

"It's a saloon down on Del Mar—a hole in the wall where nobody should recognize you, or care even if they do." Julien stepped back to allow them entrance to the tunnel behind the wall. "Go on, then. Before they come back."

A SKY DARK AND STARLESS

Harte hesitated only a second longer, searching Julien's face for any indication that the opening in front of them was some kind of trick or a trap, but he found none. Julien's eyes were steady, his expression seemingly sincere. Still, it wasn't worth taking any unnecessary chances.

Harte extended his hand. "Thanks, Jules."

Julien grasped Harte's hand without hesitation and gave the most fleeting squeeze of pressure before he drew it away. But skin to skin, it was enough. A pulse of power, and they'd be safe—from Julien, at least. Considering all they'd just learned, though, Harte wasn't sure how far that safety would extend.

Without another word, Harte followed Esta into the dark tunnel, which got even darker when Julien replaced the panel behind him. They waited in the gloom, listening to the scrape of the rack of dresses, as Julien hid the panel and their eyes accustomed themselves to the lack of light. Even without seeing her, Harte could sense Esta nearby. The warmth of her—and of her affinity—called to him, and to the power within him. For the moment that power was quiet, but he knew it was only watching and waiting for him to let down his guard.

"Come on," Harte whispered to Esta when he could almost see the shape of the passageway. "We should go while we can."

Eventually they came to the boiler room, a larger chamber that smelled faintly of coal and dust. Since it was summer, the room was silent and empty, the fires long since gone cold. The large steel tanks that heated the water before it was pumped to radiators throughout the theater loomed over them, shadowy shapes that made it impossible to see if anyone waited on the other side of the room. They moved carefully, as silently as they could, and soon enough they found the workman's entrance on the far side of the chamber.

"Are we sure this isn't a trap?" she asked as she looked at the window-less exit door.

"Not one that Julien set," he assured her. "I took care of it."

"We should still be careful. I've never heard anything about these patrols. I don't know if they're something new or . . ." She seemed lost for words. "I don't remember learning anything about them or the law against magic he was talking about. None of this existed in the future I knew."

Harte thought he understood the emotion in her voice. Back in Manhattan, there had been Mageus willing to sell out their own kind for a handful of coin, but the Jefferson Guard and whatever this act was that made magic illegal were dangers they hadn't expected.

"Even if these patrols are Mageus, they shouldn't be able to find us unless we're using our affinities. We don't need to use any magic to get back to the hotel," he told her, answering her unspoken worry that they would be discovered. "This isn't any different from Corey's boys back at the Haymarket. If we keep our heads down and our affinities cold, we'll be fine." He hoped.

Esta seemed to believe his false bravado—or she pretended to. She gave him a sure nod, and they eased themselves silently out into the back alley behind the theater, but as they went, Harte kept himself alert, just in case someone was waiting. The way seemed to be clear, and they walked toward the end of the alley as thunder rumbled in the distance.

"Slow down," Esta hissed. He opened his mouth to argue—to tell her that the faster they were away from those Guardsmen, the better—but she explained before he got out a single word. "You start scurrying and it'll draw more attention. You'll look guilty."

She was right. Even though every instinct in him wanted to run, Harte forced himself to slow his pace as they approached the mouth of the alley.

To the right, a Black Maria waited in front of the theater. Next to the windowless carriages stood more of the men dressed in dark coats. They must be the Jefferson Guard, from what Julien had said, which explained why they had been after the cowboy Esta had seen earlier. Stationed at the theater doors were four more similarly dressed men, all facing the theater and waiting for the audience to depart. Their posture was alert and clearly watchful.

"We can go back around the block," Harte suggested. "It's a bit farther, but at least we won't have to pass them."

"I thought you said they wouldn't be able to sense us."

He frowned, remembering the burst of cool energy that had accompanied the three Guardsmen when they'd rushed past outside the theater. It hadn't been completely natural magic, which would have felt only warm. "I don't think they'd be able to, but with the Book's power inside me and with what happened earlier . . ."

She nodded, her golden eyes serious. "You're right. It's not worth chancing it."

The theater was only a handful of blocks from the hotel they'd found, the Jefferson, which was close to the Mississippi River and nestled near the heart of downtown. The building was thirteen stories tall and capped with an ornate decorative cornice that sat like a crown on the top. It was clearly a new building, built for the crowds who would travel to the fair. Even in the overcrowded city, the dirt and grime of horse carts and the soot from the smokestacks of nearby riverboats hadn't yet marred the building.

Maybe they should have gone with something more inconspicuous, but it had been two years since they'd left New York. They'd assumed two years would be enough time and St. Louis would be enough distance that no one would be looking for them. Besides, the Jefferson featured private baths, and the promise of soaking away the grime of the previous days and the long train ride in his own room—away from Esta and the way she provoked the power inside of him—had proven too great a temptation to resist.

Now, with the clouds hanging even heavier in the sky, flickering with the warning of the storm to come, the hotel looked like a sanctuary. In their rooms, they'd be safe. They had a couple of hours before they were supposed to meet Julien, when he'd bring them the stone, as Harte had silently demanded before they parted ways. He needed that time to fortify himself. It took so much energy to keep the voice inside of him locked down, to keep a handle on the power that constantly threatened to bubble up—especially when Esta was so close.

When they entered the peacefulness of the lobby, it was a marked difference from the bustling and cramped city outside the front doors. The moment he was inside, Harte felt some of the evening's tension drain from him as he was enveloped in the hush of the hotel. A mezzanine balcony ran along all four sides of the lobby, and marble columns ringed the room, supporting an arched ceiling that was painted with the verdant green of lifelike palm trees, while crystal chandeliers threw their soft light through the fronds of *real* palm trees throughout the room. From somewhere far off—maybe the ballroom upstairs—music was playing, but despite the small groups of people still milling about, there was a sense of safety in the cavernous, two-story atrium.

They were barely across the lobby, heading for the bank of elevators, each encased in an ornate brass cage, when Harte caught a bit of motion out of the corner of his eye. When he turned, it looked as though the palm trees that were planted in small, private groves around the room were moving, as if blown by some invisible breeze. As he watched, puzzled, the music went silent so that all he could hear was the wind, and the lobby around him seemed to shift—to fade into a different place . . . a different time. . . .

It was night, the ceiling above had turned into a sky dark and starless, and the wind that rustled the palms carried upon its back the scent of betrayal, thick and metallic like old blood. . . . A friend turned foe who would destroy the heart of magic if he held it in his hands. He was coming. . . .

Harte blinked, and the vision faded.

Who is coming?

When he looked again, the palms were still, and he was surrounded once more by the opulence of the lobby, and in the air, there was only the tinkling of music from far off and the quiet murmur of conversation. But the power *inside* of him was rioting.

Esta's arm had tightened around his.

"What is it?" he asked, thinking that maybe she had just seen the same dark night and felt the same unsettling awareness that something awful was on its way.

"To your left, there by the large palm. Gray pants and a light-colored jacket," she said, and he knew in that instant that she wasn't talking about whatever it was he'd just seen.

"There's one leaning against the front desk—*no*! Don't actually look at them," she hissed.

"Who?" he asked, fighting the urge to crane his neck around and trying to ignore the way the voice inside of him was rumbling, its power churning and building.

"I don't know, but they're definitely not guests. I've known how to case a place since I was eight. I know what a cop looks like even when he's not in a uniform," she told him. "They just have this way of standing and a watchfulness about their eyes that isn't quite easy, no matter how good they are at being undercover." She finally glanced over at him. "You're *sure* Julien wouldn't go after the bounty?"

"I made sure," he said, bristling at her doubt. The memory of the vision had put him on edge, and Esta's questioning only made it worse.

"Well, maybe it didn't work—"

Before she could finish, he pulled her to the side, backing her against one of the large marble columns and positioning them both behind one of the palms, so she would have a view of the room behind him. Wrapping his arms around her, he leaned in, so his face was close to her neck. He was gratified to feel the hitch in her breath.

But the voice was seething with anticipation.

Her voice came soft and breathy. "What are you—"

"See how many there are," he whispered close to her ear, testing his self-control even as the power inside of him surged at her nearness.

He felt the moment she realized what he was doing. Her body went pliant against his and her arms reached up to wrap around his neck, joining in on the ruse. *It's just an act,* he told himself, ignoring the fact that he didn't care if it was.

She must have used the French-milled soap she'd found in a shop earlier that afternoon, when they'd purchased the evening wear, because she smelled different than she usually did. The scent was something darkly floral, but beneath the heady, flowery scent was still Esta, clean and real and so familiar that it took all of Harte's strength to not move closer.

The voice within him purred its encouragement, and he could feel the unnatural heat of it gathering and shifting, ready for the moment when he would be at his weakest. The moment he would forget to hold its power in check.

He wouldn't let that happen.

He thought of the vision he'd had at the train station—Esta with her eyes replaced by an endless darkness—and he vowed that he would never be that weak. If the power inside of him grew too strong, he'd leave. He would protect her, even if it meant losing all hope of reclaiming himself. He'd been willing to destroy himself once to quiet the Book. He would be willing to do it again, if it came to that.

But with Esta in his arms and the soft music in the distance and the scent of her surrounding him, thoughts of death faded. He couldn't quite stop himself from brushing his lips lightly against the warm column of her neck.

Her breath hitched again, and Harte felt the voice urging him on. So he pulled back, refusing both himself and the power any measure of real satisfaction.

"There are six, maybe seven in the lobby," she told him, sounding steady and sure. But this close, he could feel the rise and fall of her chest, and if nothing else, he knew she wasn't as unaffected as she pretended—he wasn't alone in how he felt.

"You're *sure* it's the police?" he asked.

"I'm pretty sure," she told him, her voice a low rasp. "The Jefferson Guards who were at the theater were all wearing armbands—they weren't hiding what they were."

"Maybe, whoever these men are, they aren't here for us," Harte said hopefully, pushing his luck and his self-control as he nuzzled his nose gently into her hair. The strands felt cool against his skin, like silk, and the voice hummed in anticipation. Instead, he pulled back again, proving to the power inside of him—and to himself—that he could. That he was in control—not his desire and certainly not the voice that was now ever-present in the recesses of his mind.

"Oh, they're here for us," Esta assured him. "Or maybe they're just here for me. . . . The one by the fern keeps throwing glances our way." She let out a sigh, her breath warm against his neck. "I can't believe how stupid I was to let you talk me into this place. Even with false names, it was too much of a risk. It's too big, too central."

"I know," he told her, feeling the guilt tug at him. She'd suggested somewhere more out of the way, but after the flea-ridden room in Brooklyn, he'd wanted hot running water and a bed without anything crawling in it. "But it's too late to go back. We need a way out of here now."

"Well, it's not going to be the way we came in," she said, leaning into him even more.

He couldn't tell if she was doing it on instinct or if it was part of the ruse, but he held himself back just the same. He could feel the power within him preparing itself, anticipating the moment he would cease to hold it back, and he could not let it win.

"There are too many of them," she said.

He wondered if she realized how perfectly they fit together, her softness against his own lean lines, or if she knew what it did to him to have her so close and not be able to let himself go any further. His heart pounded in his ears, but he kept himself composed. "Maybe there's a service exit?"

"Probably," she murmured, pulling back a bit. "But they'll be watching it, too."

He felt her shift in his arms. "What is it?" he asked.

"We have to go," she whispered. "They're starting to move. Just . . . act natural. We'll have at least some advantage if they don't know we've realized they're here."

Esta let out an airy laugh that he wouldn't have expected she had in her. Then she ducked her head away, a show of coyness that was all a display for those watching, before tucking her arm through his and starting to lead him away from their spot among the palms.

Harte saw immediately that it was hopeless. If the men hadn't looked like police before, they did now, arranged as they were across the room. There was no mistaking what they were doing—covering the exit, so the two of them had nowhere to go. "Now what?"

"I have an idea," she told him. "The elevator."

Again they started walking in the direction of the bronze cages, but now Harte was even more aware of how the men in the lobby were able to track them without so much as moving their heads. "Are you mad?" he said, slowing his steps and pulling her back. "If we get into an elevator, we'll be trapped."

"We'll also be out of their sight," she said. "That will buy us some time. . . . Unless you have a better plan?"

The elevator bank was only a few yards away. "We could run for it. If you think you can control your affinity, you could slow things down and give us a chance to slip out of here."

"Maybe . . ." Her focus was on the elevators just ahead of them. "But if I can't control it, we could be in worse trouble."

Before Harte was ready, they'd arrived at the elevator bank, and before he could stop her, Esta had reached out and pressed the button to call the elevator. Above them, the hand of the elevator's dial moved steadily toward the bottom, like a clock winding down their time as the men in the lobby began their approach.

THE POCKET WATCH

1904—St. Louis

J ericho Northwood—North to most people who knew him—startled
a couple of pigeons when he reappeared against the lamppost a few
hours past when the Guard had come tearing in after him, but it was
late enough that no one much was around to notice. His eyes were still
looking in the direction where the girl had been, but she was long gone.

He still couldn't quite believe she'd been there. She'd just been standing in line for tickets to the theater, like any of the other nobs in town.
Like she wasn't one of the most wanted Antistasi in the country.

The sketches the newspapers had published back when the first train
accident happened made her look like a wild harridan, an avenging
demon set to destroy all Sundren who offended her. The girl he'd seen
was every bit as tall as the reports claimed, but she was younger than
any of the pictures made her seem, and softer looking too. North had
recognized her just the same, though. There was no mistaking it. Esta
Filosik—the Devil's Thief—was in St. Louis.

North looked at his pocket watch again, the one his daddy had given
him when he'd turned eleven. Who knew where his daddy had gotten
it from—he'd always known, somehow, that he wasn't supposed to ask. It
was dangerous enough living with a secret like magic, even back before
they passed the Defense Against Magic Act right after the Great Conclave
of aught-two. But the trade in objects that could bolster a dying affinity?
Well, asking questions about that could be damn near deadly if the wrong
person caught wind of it. Even as a boy he'd known that.

The watch was a scratched-up bronze piece that might have once looked like gold, but the years had worn away the lie. The glass that covered its simple face had already been cracked when he'd received it, but seeing as how he didn't use it to *tell* time, that hadn't ever worried him none. He'd had it for near seven years now, and he hadn't bothered to fix it. Why should he, when it worked just fine? When he used it, he thought of his daddy, and for all the other moments, he kept his thoughts about his father and everything that had happened put away, where they belonged.

North tucked the watch back into his vest pocket—and the memories along with it—next to the package Maggie had given him a few minutes before. He didn't have to examine it to know what it was—a key to the chemist's down the block. He'd cursed Mother Ruth three times over for sending Maggie in to do such a dangerous job. The girl didn't have any business stealing keys when Ruth had plenty of others who could do it just as easily and with less risk. But North always had the suspicion that Ruth liked to test her baby sister—to make sure of where Maggie's loyalties lay and to keep her sharp.

From North's perspective, Maggie was more than sharp enough. The girl was a miracle of a genius when it came to creating serums and devices, and he would have thought Ruth would want to keep her out of harm's way, considering how important she was for their next deed.

They'd borrowed the idea of "propaganda of the deed"—using direct actions to inspire others—from the anarchists, but the Antistasi weren't sloppy enough to use bombs. They used magic instead. In the year since North had come into town and found Ruth, he'd helped with plenty of the Antistasi's deeds—including the one last October—but the one they were currently planning was different. It was more than a statement for attention; it was a demand for recognition. A deed so monumental, so dramatic, that it would transform the country.

It was also coming too soon. From North's view, there were still too many variables and too many unanswered questions. They had only a few more weeks to get them answered, because they would have only one chance to hit the biggest target of all.

But North was just a foot soldier. He wasn't the general. He didn't particularly want to be the general either.

Taking the packet from his pocket, North unwrapped the key it contained. The slip of paper had a list of items in Maggie's crooked scrawl. He knew Maggie needed the materials for her tests, but he also knew that Ruth would want to know about what he'd seen. He wasn't sure if having Esta Filosik in town was a good omen or not. Maybe she could help them. . . . But then, if anyone else knew of her appearance, it could mean trouble. The Guard would be more alert, and the whole town would be on edge.

Well, there wasn't a reason he had to do a thing about it right then. Maggie had a list of items for him to obtain, and he wasn't about to disappoint her.

North pulled his hat down low over his eyes as he turned into the alley next to the chemist's shop, making sure no one saw as he used the key to slip inside. When he was done, he'd have plenty of time to tell Ruth everything. He had his watch, after all.

DUST AND METAL

1904—St. Louis

While Harte watched the dial of the elevator creep steadily downward, he had the clear sense that their time was running out. Each second that ticked by was one closer to the moment when the police in the lobby would reach them. But after a string of seconds, nothing had happened.

"They're not coming," he said, when he realized the plainclothes officers had stopped approaching.

"If they already knew we were here, they probably have people stationed in our rooms," she told him, sounding far calmer than he was feeling. "There's no reason to create a public scene if they can get to us there."

Which didn't make him feel one bit better. "If we can't go to our rooms, where are we going?"

She glanced at him. "We're in a hotel, Harte. It's *filled* with rooms. We don't need our own."

Inside, the power of the Book felt unsettled, as though it were a caged animal pacing. "They'll be able to see which floor we stop at," he argued, his chest feeling tight as the hand of the dial reached the bottom and the elevator groaned to a stop.

"That's the idea," she said, leaning forward to press a soft kiss against his lips.

It was over before he'd realized what had just happened. He barely registered the shocking warmth and the softness of her mouth against his. If it weren't for the absolute torment of the voice's realization that he'd let her slip away again, he might have thought he'd imagined the whole thing.

The elevator doors opened, revealing an interior empty except for the operator. "What's the plan?" he murmured as they stepped inside the close quarters of the elevator.

Earlier that day, he'd admired the polished wood and gleaming mirrors of the interior. When they'd first checked in, Harte had thought the elevators were sleek and modern, a marvel of the age, but now the mirrored cage felt as airless and constricting as a prison cell. Once the doors closed and the elevator started moving, they would be even farther from any chance of escape.

"Seven, please," Esta told the operator, an older man with deep brown skin who was dressed in the pristine uniform of the hotel porters.

Harte realized that she had spoken loudly enough for the men in the lobby to hear.

"Yes, ma'am," the operator said as he set to closing the gate.

The moment the doors were closed and the operator had pressed the lever forward, causing the elevator to rise, Esta leaned over and whispered in his ear, "It would probably be better if he doesn't remember any of this, but we need the elevator to keep moving. Maybe a little more slowly." She nodded toward the operator. "Have him stop at seven . . . *nicely.*"

Harte gave her a small nod to let her know that he understood, even if he had no idea how she planned to get them out of the mess they were in once they reached the seventh floor.

The operator perched on a small stool, silent and stoic, facing the switch and monitoring the elevator's rise, ignoring the passengers in the car, as he'd presumably been trained to. If he'd heard any of their exchange, he pretended not to. If he sensed that anything was amiss, he didn't show it. But his uniform presented a problem. The operator was buttoned up to his neck, his hands and wrists covered with white gloves. Because Harte's affinity needed skin-to-skin contact, the only option he had was the strip of exposed skin between the high collar of the man's jacket and the straight edge of his hairline, a gap caused by the way his shoulders were hunched, probably the effect of the long hours he spent on shift.

Harte felt guilty for taking advantage of him, but he couldn't see any other way out of the mess they were in. He took a deep breath, focusing his affinity and preparing himself—he'd have only one chance to pull this off without having to resort to other, more violent measures. As the elevator passed the second floor, the bell in the car rang and the car itself vibrated slightly. Harte took the opportunity to reach forward and gently touch two fingers against the nape of the man's neck, pushing his affinity toward the boundary between flesh and soul all at once.

The operator went stiff for a moment, but he kept his hand on the lever, releasing the pressure only a little so the path of the elevator slowed slightly. Harte withdrew his fingers a moment later, and the operator didn't so much as flinch. The elevator kept climbing, though now more sluggishly, and the operator kept staring at the dial. He and Esta might have been two ghosts for all the poor man knew or cared.

"Boost me up," Esta said, staring at the wood paneling on the ceiling.

He realized then her intention—above them, the soft light thrown by the glass globe exposed a panel. "You can't be serious," he muttered, but he didn't bother to argue. It wasn't as though he had a better plan.

Girding himself against the usual rumbling excitement of the voice, he offered his hands so Esta could step into them and then lifted her toward the low ceiling. It took her only a moment to swing the panel open and pull herself up through it.

"Come on," she said, reaching her hand back for him.

The elevator was still progressing slowly and steadily upward. The bell dinged again as they passed the fourth floor.

"I can get it myself," he told her, and with a short leap, his fingertips grasped the edge of the opening. As the elevator continued to move, he pulled himself up into the darkness of the shaft. It smelled of dust and metal, and the moment Esta replaced the ceiling hatch, the only light they had to see by were the narrow beams that came through the brass grates marking each floor. The hotel had a bank of three elevators, and together the sound of the machinery driving the cables echoed around them as the individual cars stopped at the various floors.

"Now what?" he asked, reaching out to hold the cable of the still-moving lift to steady himself. The movement of the elevator reminded him too much of the swaying of the train. He took a deep breath and held on more tightly.

Esta didn't seem bothered by the movement, since she wasn't holding on to one of the cables. "With any luck, those guys from the lobby are running toward the seventh floor right now. But we won't be in the elevator when it stops."

"We can't stay here, either," he said. "Even if that operator can't tell them where we went, they'll figure it out eventually."

"Eventually," Esta agreed, speaking loudly enough that he could hear her over the mechanical clicks and groans. "I'm betting on that, too. They'll waste manpower and time stopping the elevators and looking for us. But we won't be here by then, either." She was peering over the edge of the car, far enough that he wanted to pull her back. "Give me your hand." She reached back without looking to see if he'd comply.

"What?" he hesitated.

"Your hand. Now!" She looked back at him then, determination flashing in her eyes. "Trust me, Harte."

Before he could think of all the reasons he shouldn't, Harte slipped his hand into hers.

Satisfied, she turned back to the edge. "Ready?" she asked, not looking back at him. "One . . ."

"No, Esta—"

"Two . . ." She wasn't listening.

The contents of his stomach were quickly working their way up his throat. "Don't—"

"Three!"

A TURNING OF THE TIDES

1902—New York

James Lorcan felt his view of the future rearrange itself as he laid the paper onto the worn desk in front of him. Once, it had been Dolph's desk, just as the apartment he was sitting in had belonged to Dolph as well.

The apartment was much better outfitted than the pair of cramped rooms above that James had called home before. But the comforts of the rooms were unimportant compared to what else James now had at his fingertips—all Dolph's notes, all his books, and all his *knowledge*.

And my, my . . . what Dolph had been hiding. James had used some of Dolph's secrets already to secure Paul Kelly's alliance. He would use more of them in the days to come to position the players in the Bowery exactly where he wanted them.

On the wall hung a portrait of Newton beneath a tree, a spoil from a heist Dolph's team had done at the Metropolitan. To the average viewer, the painting depicted nothing more than the most astounding revelation of the modern age—Newton's discovery of gravity. At the man's feet lay an apple, red and round, and above him the sun and moon shone, a pair of guardians in the sky.

But to someone more astute, the painting showed something more. The book Newton held in his hand was rumored to be the Book of Mysteries. The portrait depicted the point in history where Newton's two lives converged—Newton the magician who had nearly gone mad from his experiments with alchemy and Newton the scientist. Both were in search of eternal truth and untold knowledge, and in the portrait, both found it within the pages of the Ars Arcana.

Across the centuries there had been stories and myths about the fabled Book. Some said it was rumored to contain the very source of magic. Others thought it was the Book of Thoth, an ancient manuscript buried in the Nile River that held the knowledge of the gods, knowledge unfit for the feeble minds of men. Still others thought it was a fantastical grimoire, a book of the most powerful ritual magic ever developed. Many had hunted for it—James himself had hunted for it. Two days ago he had thought the Book gone, forever beyond his reach, but now . . .

James let his eyes scan over the newsprint once again, allowing his affinity to flare out, searching for new connections in the Aether as he considered this development.

He almost hadn't noticed. The papers were always filled with the trivial—stories meant to grab attention with lurid details of death and tragedy. James hadn't cared to read the story about the train and the carnage of its derailment. In fact, he'd already tossed the paper aside when Kelly told him about the reporter that he was sending Viola to kill.

Now his eyes caught on the name of a dead man.

Harte Darrigan.

If the papers could be believed—and, in truth, often they *couldn't*—Harte Darrigan wasn't dead. And neither was Esta. If the two had made it through the Brink, it meant that not only was the Book still out there and attainable, but that they were *using* it.

James took Viola's knife and balanced its point on the tabletop as he considered the possibilities. Two days ago he had believed that the fate of the world had already been inscribed: Magic would die. It would fade away until it was nothing but a memory and a superstition. The future would belong not to Mageus with their innate connections to the world, but to the Sundren. In the days following the mess on the bridge, James had accepted this fate. He'd considered his options and made adjustments to shore up his power, but this new information changed things again.

After all, the pages of a book could be torn out. A story could be rewritten. His affinity wasn't perfect, of course—or it wasn't perfect *yet*. But if this new information meant anything at all, it meant there was a very good possibility that he would get everything he wanted in the end.

James allowed the tip of the knife to sink into the page, carving out the names as one might carve out a heart. He tucked them into his vest pocket, talismans for the future, as he made his way down to the barroom to hold court over his new kingdom. He had a sense that something was coming, some change in the Aether that could mean a turning of the tides for him. There was much to consider, but Harte Darrigan and Esta Filosik would not escape him again. They would pay for their perfidy. James would make sure of it.

MOCK DUCK

Jianyu looked up from where he lay in the filth of the street, his head throbbing and his vision blurred, to find Sai Wing Mock, the leader of the Hip Sings and Tom Lee's rival in the Chinese quarter, standing over him. If Tom Lee and his On Leongs might occasionally take advantage, the Hip Sings were ruthless, and none was more so than the man who went by the name of Mock Duck.

Mock dressed like a dandy, his Western-style suit cut close and his queue tucked up under a slate-gray porkpie hat, but it was rumored that he wore chain mail beneath his clothes—a defense against the enemies he had made in the years since he had started the war between the On Leongs and the Hip Sings. His hand still held the gun he had used to scare off Jianyu's attackers, and his fingers were sharply tipped with long, polished nails—an overt sign of his wealth and position. No common laborer had fingertips as deadly as that.

At first the leader of the Hip Sings simply stared at Jianyu lying on the ground. His dark eyes were thoughtful. "I've heard stories about you, Mr. Lee," he said finally, again using the Cantonese they shared.

"Lee isn't my name," Jianyu told him, speaking before he had fully considered his words. It was stupid of him to provoke Mock, especially here, where he was alone and unarmed and at the mercy of a man who was rumored to have ordered any number of murders. But here, at the mercy of Tom Lee's rival, it seemed important to make it clear that he had no side in their bloody war.

Mock Duck's wide, full mouth twitched. "I have heard that, too."

Jianyu wanted to know why Mock Duck had been looking for him and what the tong leader might want of him, but he understood implicitly that silence was safer. When staring down a viper, surviving often meant not giving the snake a reason to strike. Instead, Jianyu focused on his affinity and tried to find the threads of light. But his head swirled from where it had cracked against the street. He was struggling to remain conscious, and he couldn't focus enough to keep the light from slipping through his fingers.

"Pick him up," Mock commanded, "and bring him."

Mock was not alone. *Of course not.* The boys who had jumped him would not have been scared off by a single man, gun or not.

Jianyu felt himself being roughly hoisted, and his head swam again with the movement. In response, his stomach, empty as it was, heaved, and it was all he could do to keep from retching, which would be taken as a further sign of weakness. Jerking away from their support, he forced himself to stay upright. He would walk under his own power, if he did nothing else.

Mock led the way as the group traveled through one of the tunnels that connected the various blocks around the Chinese quarter. The air underground was thick and stale, and the echoes of their footsteps were the only sounds. When they emerged, they were close to the Bowery, far from the Hip Sings' usual territory.

Jianyu knew where they were headed before he saw the golden-eyed witch on the sign over the Strega, so he was not exactly surprised when Mock Duck went through the saloon's front doors as though he owned the place, his highbinders escorting Jianyu behind him.

The barroom was mostly empty, since it was so early in the day, but Jianyu recognized a couple of Dolph's boys—Mooch and Werner were in the back, and Sylvan was wiping down the bar under the watchful eye of one who could only be a Five Pointer. They looked up when Mock Duck entered, but their expressions showed little more than curious interest.

There was no sign of Viola.

Once the Strega had been Jianyu's home, a sanctuary from the dangers of the city streets. Stepping into the familiar barroom as a prisoner felt somehow worse than all his injuries. His head felt like it would split open from where it had struck the pavement and his gut throbbed where it had taken a boot, but being treated like a stranger in this place that had once been a home made him feel lost in a way he had never felt before. With everything else, it was nearly too much, and the only thing that kept him steady was the sight of the traitor who had murdered Dolph.

At the back of the barroom, sitting in the seat that he had killed for, Nibsy Lorcan lifted his eyes to see what the commotion was. His spectacles flashed in the light, the blank lenses giving him the appearance of a button-eyed automaton Jianyu had once seen at a dime museum. Soulless. Driven by some mechanism within that Jianyu did not comprehend.

The two highbinders holding Jianyu shoved him forward as Mock Duck presented him.

"You found him," Nibsy said, and Jianyu could not decide if it was satisfaction or simple anticipation that colored the boy's voice.

"And you can have him as soon as I receive my fee," Mock said.

Nibsy shouted to the barkeep, and the boy brought a stack of bills wrapped in paper and a ledger. Mock Duck counted the money carefully and then flipped through the notebook, murmuring appreciatively. "This is all on Tom Lee?"

"And a few others who might cause you problems," Nibsy said.

Mock Dock gave Nibsy a small, satisfied nod as he closed the booklet. "I trust we will do business again, Mr. Lorcan." He held out his hand, and Nibsy took it.

"Likewise." Nibsy directed two men—Five Pointers, if Jianyu wasn't mistaken—to take hold of Jianyu. Then he waited until Mock Duck and his men left before he looked at Jianyu. "So . . . ," he drawled, bringing himself to his feet and using the cane that had once belonged to Dolph to make his way to where Jianyu stood. "The traitor returns."

With Jianyu's vision swirling, there were two of Nibsy, but Jianyu sneered at both of them. "You dare to call *me* the traitor?"

"We were all on the bridge, weren't we?" Nibsy asked, and Jianyu realized that his words were meant for the people watching warily throughout the Strega. "We were there for Dolph—for the Devil's Own—and *you* weren't. Your cowardice doomed us all."

His head was spinning and the edges of his vision were starting to dim. It was a struggle to stay conscious, but Jianyu forced himself to focus and allowed the corner of his mouth to curve. "Are you so certain that I was absent?"

He saw the realization flash behind the lenses of Nibsy's spectacles, but the boy's expression never so much as flickered. "If you were there, you didn't help us. You let the magician get away, and with it, our chances of defeating the Order. You betrayed everyone here."

The people in the barroom were murmuring now, an uneasy buzzing like a hive about to erupt. Jianyu understood what drama was playing out too well. Nibsy would use the Devil's Own against him. He would convince them of Jianyu's treachery, and in turn they would do Nibsy's dirty work. It would take very little. . . . It had been only Dolph who had held them back when Tilly was hurt, after all.

"I am not the traitor in this room," Jianyu said, his voice rough from a combination of pain and anger. "It was not my gun that ended Dolph's life. It was yours."

The barroom went still.

"The lies of a traitor." Nibsy laughed, but Jianyu could feel the questions still hanging in the air around them. "A feeble attempt to cover your own guilt," he said, stepping even closer. He pulled from his jacket a familiar knife—Viola's—and held it to Jianyu's face.

Where did he get Viola's knife? She prized it above all others and would not have willingly given it to anyone—even if she had believed them to be a friend. She could not be dead. Not Viola. Not when he needed her.

"Do you know what we do to traitors, Jianyu?"

The knife flashed in the light of the barroom, but Jianyu did not so much as flinch. "Traitors deserve death," Jianyu said, struggling to keep his voice even despite the pain of simply breathing. They must have broken a rib, maybe two. "Are you prepared to die, Nibsy?"

"My name is James," Nibsy said, bringing the knife closer until the tip of it was poised against the skin under Jianyu's chin. "And it's not me who is going to die today."

The air in the room was electric. Everyone was focused on Jianyu, Nibsy, and the point of the impossible blade held between them. But Jianyu simply stared at Nibsy, refusing to back down. Refusing to take back his accusations.

After a long, fraught moment, Nibsy smiled and pulled back. "I think a quick death is too easy for this one, don't you?" he asked the room, but the barroom returned nothing except uneasy silence. "I think he should tell us everything he knows—about where Darrigan is and what he's done with the Order's treasures. But not here. No, we wouldn't want to make a mess before the afternoon rush. Take him up to my rooms, would you, Mooch? I think we can continue our little conversation there."

Perhaps Jianyu should have fought once they were out of the main barroom and making their way up the familiar staircase. He didn't suspect it would take much. Though Mooch had trained under Dolph's watchful eye in the ring of the boxing club, the same as Jianyu, Mooch hadn't trained for nearly as long. But Jianyu was still too unsteady from the beating to risk it. One more hit to the head and he doubted he would remain conscious.

More important, he didn't think he would convince Mooch of anything by attacking him. Nibsy was playing a long game, and so must he.

MOTHER RUTH

1904—St. Louis

They called her Mother Ruth, but she was no one's mother. At least not by blood. Her arms had never held a babe of her own, nor had they ever yearned to, because she knew a simple truth—giving yourself over in that way was a weakness. She would never allow a man to take that freedom from her, because she'd had enough of her freedom taken already. Hadn't she watched her parents scrape by with barely enough to feed their family? Hadn't she seen with her own two eyes how her mother wasted away, babe after babe, until finally, her fourteenth had taken the last she had to give?

Or perhaps her own mother had wasted away for another reason. Ruth often wondered—was it truly the babes? Or was it that her mother had given away the part of herself that made her whole? Because Ruth had to imagine that what made her mother whole was the very thing that made Ruth herself whole—magic.

Ruth's father had been a small-minded man. Only heaven knew why her mother had made herself small to get a ring on her finger. But when her father had learned that his wife had the old magic, he'd done what he could to beat it out of her until she'd found ways to keep it hidden from him. But something like magic can't be pressed down forever.

Her mother had only kitchen magic, a kind of power she could weave into the food she made or the ale she brewed, but Ruth herself knew the power that something so seemingly simple could bestow because her own power was the same. She'd never understood it, a woman like her mother, cowering in fear of a man such as her father. But even as a small child, Ruth had been old enough and wise enough to know that some things in the world weren't meant to be comprehended. Ruth's mother had hidden her magic, and before she'd died giving birth to her fourteenth child, she'd taught the rest of her children who'd been born with affinities—Ruth included—how to hide theirs.

On the day they'd buried her mother, Ruth's father had told her in no uncertain terms that, as the oldest, the children were her responsibility now. Ruth might not have had a choice in the what, but she decided that day that she would chose the how. She taught her brothers and sisters how to stand on their own and how to cultivate their magic so that they couldn't ever be pressed small by anyone.

Maybe she could have run off. Maybe she should've.

After all, she was already more than twenty when her mother died, and in those days, she was still young and pretty enough that there were plenty of boys whose heads turned when she walked by. She could have picked any one of them, thick-skulled and easygoing as they were, but why trade one duty for another? Better the devil you knew, she reasoned.

So she'd managed to raise all her brothers and sisters to adulthood. Mother Ruth, they called her, even when she told them she wasn't their mother. Most of them took themselves far from the meagerness of their childhood, which was fine by Ruth. Fewer for her to worry about. They could do what they would with the world, and she would do the same.

Her whole life, Ruth had exactly one hour to herself each week—the hour she took to go to Mass. But on a fateful Sunday, she never made it. That Sunday she chanced to dart under the cover of a random livery stable for shelter from the rain on the way to St. Alban's. In addition to the soft rustling of horseflesh, she'd found herself interrupting a meeting, and it surprised even her that she'd stayed to listen to what was being said instead of continuing on. But there had been magic in the air, a warmth that she'd missed from her own mother's arms—a warmth that called to her in a way that nothing else ever had. And there was something else: a righteous anger that she felt an answering call to deep in her bones.

Instead of praying, she learned to shout. Instead of kneeling, she learned to rise. And she hadn't stopped since.

The Antistasi had been a new beginning for her. When she found the group that day, they were little more than a ragtag bunch hoping for companionship and an escape from their hard-scratched lives. They were disorganized and undisciplined, taking their name from bedtime stories about another time, when Mageus had fought fiercely against their annihilation during the Disenchantment.

But since the Great Conclave two years before, since the Defense Against Magic Act had made the very thing she was illegal, something had changed in the organization. And Ruth had changed right along with it.

She had given the movement everything she had, everything that she was. She used money from the brewery she had built for herself and her siblings, and she used the Feltz Brewery building in support of the Antistasi's cause as well. Now she walked through the rows of women cleaning and filling bottles, and she knew that she'd been put on this earth for a purpose. Not only to save the girls who worked for her from a lifetime of servitude for a moment's indiscretion, but for something much larger—a demonstration of the power those who lived in the shadows held. A demonstration that could change *everything* for those who still had a link to the old magic.

Her eyes were sharp on her workers as she walked toward the nursery, which was housed in the back of the brewery. The nursery was Maggie's doing. Ruth's youngest sister—and the one who had taken their mother's life—Maggie was already seventeen and was the last to remain with Ruth. They had no pictures, so Maggie couldn't have known that she was the image of their mother, with her ash-brown hair curling about her temples and the small pair of silver-rimmed spectacles perched on the end of her upturned nose. And her eyes . . . For Ruth, looking at Maggie was like seeing her mother peer at her from the beyond. Or it would have been, except that Maggie's eyes had a strength in them that Ruth had no memory of her mother ever possessing.

When Ruth entered the small nursery, Maggie was tending to the newest little one, a bundle of energy who had been abandoned by parents who either couldn't take care of him or didn't want to. It happened too often, Mageus born to parents after generations of affinities gone cold. Many of those children were seen as anomalies. Freaks. Abominations.

Some parents accepted their children as they were—but that was rare. Most of the time, when the parents' efforts to curtail their children's powers didn't work, they discarded them. Asylums or orphanages across the countryside were filled with these castoffs, strange children who didn't understand who or what they were. Those sent to the asylums rarely left whole—if they left at all—and at the orphanage, the rod wasn't spared. Those children left mean as junkyard dogs, dangerous and volatile, easy marks for the police or the Jefferson Guard.

The other children in the nursery were the victims of the Act. Their parents had been rounded up and imprisoned or sent away. The children who were left behind might be taken in by friends or neighbors, hidden away so that the Guard couldn't find them, but not everyone had some-one. Those who didn't were often brought to the brewery until they could be placed in homes where they would be safe.

It had been Maggie's idea to start taking in the urchins—to steal them from the children's homes and asylums when necessary—and to raise them with an understanding of what they were so they could be placed with families who would appreciate them. So they could thrive the way Ruth had allowed *her* to thrive, Maggie reasoned.

The girl was too innocent for her own good. She'd meet a hard end if she didn't look past that rosy tint she saw the world through. Ruth per-mitted the nursery because it seemed like good business. More children with magic meant that the Antistasi could grow rather than die. The Society and other organizations like them could do what they would to snuff out the old magic, but another generation was waiting to rise up behind.

Maggie glanced up from the child, who had just managed to set fire to the blanket he was holding, and gave Ruth a look of utter exasperation.

"I see this one is still causing you problems."

"He doesn't mean to," Maggie said, stomping out the last of the flames.

"If he burns down my brewery, it won't matter if he meant it or not," Ruth said.

"We're working on it," Maggie said, but her pale cheeks flushed with embarrassment, her emotions clear as day on her porcelain skin.

"Use the Nitewein if you need to."

"He's a baby," Maggie protested.

"He's a menace if he can't control his affinity. See that he's taken care of, or I'll do it for you. We're running too far behind schedule to have anything go wrong now."

"Yes, Mother Ruth," Maggie murmured, her eyes downcast.

Ruth sighed. This wasn't what she'd come for. "North just returned."

"Jericho's back already?" Maggie said, and Ruth could see the interest in her sister's expression.

Even as hardened as she was, Ruth understood the power of roguish eyes set into a lean face. North had the same appeal as a raggedy stray cat—you believed you could tame it and then it would love you forever. But Ruth didn't doubt that, like any stray, Jericho Northwood had claws.

From the way her sister's expression brightened, it was clear Maggie's interest in the boy hadn't faded. She'd deal with Maggie's little infatuation later, but for now . . . "He's brought the supplies you asked for."

But Maggie didn't pay her any mind. She was still fussing with the baby. "I'll get to them soon enough." Her tone offered no excuses.

The spine of steel her baby sister hid beneath her soft outer shell always did manage to surprise her. "You know how important the serum is," Ruth insisted.

Maggie nodded. "But it can wait until the little ones are in bed."

LISA MAXWELL

"Maybe it can, but the news North brought with him can't. You'll need to come."

The boy Maggie was tending picked up a small carved wooden horse, his fingertips flaring to a brilliant orange that caused the toy horse to smolder.

Ruth gave Maggie a warning look before she took her leave. There was an unexpected visitor in her city. Tonight the Antistasi had more important business to attend to than someone else's children.

THE RISK OF MAGIC

1904—St. Louis

In the dim light of the elevator shaft, Esta felt Harte's fear as clearly as the vibrations of the machine beneath their feet, but she didn't have time to explain.

As the car next to them descended, it created a rush of air warm with the scent of dust and axle grease that rustled the silk of her skirts and whipped at the hair coming loose around her face. Harte's hand was gripping hers tightly enough that she could feel the sizzle of energy between them creeping against her skin.

Not for the first time, she had the feeling that it wasn't him she was sensing. The energy wasn't the same brush of warmth she'd felt from him when he'd manipulated her in the theater weeks ago or tried to read her thoughts in the carriage on the way to Khafre Hall. This energy felt different. More potent. More *compelling*, which was a sure sign of danger if she ever felt one.

She didn't have time to worry too much about it at that moment, though. She would have one shot at this, one chance to get it right. And she might be making a huge mistake.

The moment the two elevator cars drew even with each other, Esta focused on her affinity and pulled time still. The vibrations beneath her feet stopped, and the noise in the shaft went silent. At the same time, she pulled Harte forward onto the roof of the next car and let go of her hold on time.

The elevators lurched back into motion as she released Harte's hand.

Relief flooded through her as Harte grabbed for the cable to steady himself. *It worked.* She hadn't known for sure what would happen when she used her affinity. She hadn't known if she'd even be able to. She'd thought about taking the jump without slowing the elevators, but the risk of using her magic for the briefest moment seemed preferable to falling to their deaths.

Her gamble had paid off. Together they watched the elevator they had just been on continue to rise above them as the car they now were on top of descended. She'd used her affinity and nothing odd had happened. It had worked, just as it always had worked—easy. *Right.* But it wasn't enough. They couldn't keep standing there, because every second brought them closer to the ground floor, where more police waited.

When the car they were riding on lurched to a stop at the fourth floor, Harte seemed to gather his wits about him. "We can't stay here," he said, echoing her thoughts.

She listened for the sound of the doors opening and felt the slight bounce as people entered the elevator. "We're not going to," she told him. "We're getting off."

"Esta, there are too many people in there." He gestured to the car below their feet.

The sound of the doors closing told her that they were about to move again. "We aren't leaving that way. Hold on," she said, just before the cables lurched back into motion.

Harte frowned at her, shadows thrown by the dim light of the shaft flickering across his face. "What's the plan?"

"The doors to the shaft," she said, pointing to the fourth-floor opening they were descending away from. "When we get to the second floor, I'm going to slow things down again long enough for us to open them. If anyone's watching in the lobby, the elevator won't look like it stopped."

"You really think you can?" he asked.

"It worked a minute ago. We'll just have to hope our luck holds." The second floor was quickly approaching, and any moment now, the police who were probably waiting for them on the seventh floor would discover the empty elevator car. "Give me your hand," she commanded, and this time he didn't argue.

When the car was halfway past the third floor's ornate brass grate, she focused on the seconds around her. Against her skin, she could feel the stirrings of the power simmering within Harte, but she ignored it and focused instead on the way time hung in the spaces around them, as real and as material as the cables that held the cars and the dust that tickled her nose. It would take longer than a few seconds to climb out of the elevator, and she wasn't completely sure what would happen—not with Harte and the Book's power making her own affinity feel so unstable again. But she didn't have any other ideas.

She found the spaces between the seconds, those moments that held within them reality and its opposite, and she pulled them apart until the elevator slowed and the world around her went silent. But with the heat of the Book's power prodding at her, it wasn't easy to keep her hold on time.

"Help me," she told him, grasping the metal grates with her free hand.

Understanding, Harte took the other side, and together they began to pull the doors apart. Once they were wide enough, Esta checked to make sure the way was clear. Standing a few feet away, at the opening to the stairs, was a man who could only be one of the plainclothes officers. He stood, staring sightlessly in their direction.

"Can you hold it?" Harte asked.

The tendrils of heat and power that had vibrated against her skin when she took Harte's hand were climbing her arm. The more they twisted themselves around her, the more slippery the spaces between the seconds felt. A moment ago those spaces had felt solid and real, but with every passing heartbeat, her hold on time—her hold on magic itself—grew murky, indistinct. As though neither the seconds nor her magic really even existed.

"Not much longer," she told him through gritted teeth as she fought to keep hold of her affinity.

"Then we'd better hurry." Harte climbed down from the roof of the elevator and into the hallway and then turned to help her.

Esta's feet had no sooner touched the ground than she realized the darkness of the elevator shaft had followed her into the well-lit hallway. It hung in the edges of her vision, threatening.

From inside the shaft, she heard a groaning of cables, a sound starkly out of place in the silent hush of the timeless moment. "Did you hear that?"

Harte frowned. "What?"

The groaning came again, louder this time. *"That,"* she told him. There shouldn't have been any sound, not now when she had slowed the seconds to a near stop and the rest of the world had gone still and silent. Fear pooling within her, Esta tried to pull away from Harte, but he held her tight. "I can't . . ."

"Esta?" He tightened his grip on her, his eyes stormy with confusion.

There were people in those elevators, people who had nothing to do with the officers chasing her. People who might die if the cables broke and the elevator plummeted to the ground below, just as people had died on the train. She didn't understand what was happening, but she knew she had to stop it.

Esta wrenched herself away from Harte, away from the unsettling energy that felt like it was trying to claim her, and allowed time to slam back into motion. Suddenly, the gears of the elevator began to churn and she could hear music coming from somewhere nearby.

"What—" Harte started, but before he could question her any further, the man at the stairway shouted.

"Hey!" He pointed at them, his eyes wide with disbelief that he hadn't noticed them standing there before. Lifting a whistle to his mouth, he reached for the golden medallion he wore on his lapel, but before he could touch it, Harte attacked, tackling the man and then knocking him out before he could do anything else.

"We have to get out of this hallway," he told her as he rubbed at the knuckles of his right hand. "Before someone comes."

Esta had already realized they'd need a hiding place. By the time Harte had pulled himself to his feet, she had one of the nearby rooms unlocked. "Bring him in here," she said, stepping aside. "If we leave him out there, they'll know."

The room was exactly like the one she had checked into earlier that day. The walls were papered in the same elegant chintz, the bed had been covered in the same fine linens, and the furniture had the same burnished wood and brass fixtures as hers. This room, though, clearly belonged to a man. There were trousers and socks strewn about the floor, and even with the window open, the smell of stale smoke and old sweat hung in the air.

"What are we supposed to do with him?" Harte asked as he locked the door behind him.

"Take him into the bathroom," Esta told him as she propped her leg up on the bed and hitched up her skirts.

Instead of moving, Harte was looking at her exposed leg.

She ignored the heated look he was giving her—and the answering warmth she felt stirring inside of her—as she unfastened the silk stocking she was wearing and pulled it down her leg. "Snap out of it, would you? Here," she said, tossing the stocking to Harte, who still looked stunned as he caught the scrap of fabric. "Tie him up with that." She rolled off the other stocking and tossed it to him as well.

If they weren't in such a bind, the way his ears went pink as he caught the bit of silk might almost have been adorable, but they needed to get out of the room and the hotel as fast as they could. The longer it took, the more likely they'd be caught. After all, it was only a matter of time before the police figured out what she and Harte had done and started searching rooms.

While Harte was in the bathroom tying up the watchman, Esta began stripping out of the gown she was wearing. The second she had slipped it on at the department store, she'd known it was perfect. She'd never been one to care all that much for clothes, but she'd loved the dress, despite knowing that she was in no position to be admiring silly, pretty things. She sighed a little as it tumbled to the floor in a puddle of silk the color of quicksilver. *The exact color of Harte's eyes.*

Esta shoved that unwanted thought aside as she stepped out of the pile of fabric and balled the gown up, the physical action reinforcing how unimportant the garment was. She kicked it under the bed.

"What are you *doing*?"

Esta turned to find Harte, his eyes wide and his cheeks pink.

"Getting rid of the dress," she told him.

"I see that," he said, and she didn't miss the way his hand clenched into a fist or the tightness in his voice. "But *why* are you getting rid of the dress?"

"It's too noticeable," she said, frowning. "And I'm too noticeable in it."

"You don't think *this* is going to be even more noticeable?" he asked as he gestured stiffly toward her, standing as she was in nothing more than a corset and a pair of drawers.

In her own time she saw people wearing less than this on the city streets. Not that Harte would understand. So often, she forgot how different they were—how much a product of his own time he was. Moments like this reminded her . . . but he was just going to have to get over it.

"I wasn't planning on going out there like this," she said, heading to the wardrobe. "There has to be something in here," she told him.

She gathered some of the men's clothing that was hanging clean and freshly pressed inside the wardrobe. When she saw the doubt in his expression, she ignored it.

"That is never going to work," he muttered, more to himself than to her.

"Look at how easily Julien recognized me, and he wasn't even looking for me—I'm too tall not to stand out," she told him. "At least for a woman."

He looked unconvinced. "You really think you look *anything* like a man?"

"I think people usually only see what they *expect* to see," she said as she slipped a stiffly pressed shirt on. It smelled of fresh linen and starch, scents that brought to mind memories of Professor Lachlan, of a childhood spent trying to please him, the days she'd spent studying next to him in the library that took up the top floor of the building.

But now the memory of that library brought with it a different image. *Dakari.* And the smell of linen and starch only served to remind her that lies often hid behind the faces you trusted.

Pushing aside the past, she buttoned the shirt, but not before she loosened the ties of her corset a little, so it didn't press her into such an hourglass shape. Finally able to breathe, she finished fastening the buttons.

"Let's hope they're all blind," Harte muttered. "Every single one of them." But he left her to finish getting dressed while he went and checked on the man in the bathroom one last time.

She tried not to be too pleased with his response as she found a top hat in the wardrobe and, smoothing out the stray strands around her face as best she could, tucked her hair up into it. Frowning at herself in the ornately beveled mirror, she wondered if Harte was right. Her face was still too soft looking, and she didn't have time to do much more than try to rub away the powder she'd put on earlier that night.

It will work. She'd dressed like a man before—when she'd helped Dolph Saunders rob Morgan's exhibit at the Metropolitan Museum of Art a few weeks back. She'd walked into a room filled with members of the Order—including J. P. Morgan himself—and no one had noticed that she was a woman. Of course, it might have only worked then because people never pay any attention to the servants.

"Ready?" she asked, giving her lapels one final tug to cover what evidence there was of the shape of her corset beneath the suit.

Harte turned and gave her a good long, appraising look. "We should just use your affinity and slip out without all"—he gestured toward her new outfit—"*this*."

"Didn't you see what happened in the hallway?" she asked, shuddering a little at the memory of the darkness. There was something about it that felt both empty and all-consuming at the same time, like if she stared at it straight on, she might lose herself in it. And then there were the sounds of the cables groaning. She didn't trust her affinity right now—at least not when it was linked to Harte.

"If you're still feeling weak, we can go in small spurts. You don't have to hold time for so long." The desire she'd seen in his eyes earlier was gone now. Instead, Harte was looking at her with the soft pity that made her skin crawl.

"I feel fine," she told him. It was a lie—she felt shaken and unsure of her affinity, but the darkness wasn't her fault . . . or was it? Had she brought something through the Brink—something dangerous and unexpected? She didn't know, and they didn't have time to figure it out. All she knew for sure was that she hated the worried emotion in his eyes. "There's no reason to push our luck. Let's just do this my way, okay?"

She didn't leave him much choice; she was in the hallway before he could argue.

Once again the sounds of an orchestra and the distant murmuring of a party came to them through the quiet. "If we can get to the ballroom, we can use the crowd to hide," Esta said, pointing in the direction of the music. "If there's a ballroom, there has to be a way to get to the kitchen—a service hall or something. From there maybe we can find a delivery entrance for the hotel."

"They'll be watching those doors too," Harte said, checking behind them as they continued onward down the hall.

"Probably." They paused only a moment before crossing in front of the stairwell the man in the bathroom had been guarding. "But if I have to chance using my magic, I'd rather wait until then," she said.

"*If* we get that far," he muttered under his breath.

She shot him a hard look. "They'll have discovered the empty elevator by now, and if they figure out that the guard on this floor is missing . . ."

"I'm not planning on standing here, waiting for them to find us,"

Harte finished, sweeping his arm to indicate that she should lead the way.

They followed the sound of the music to the mezzanine entrance of the ballroom, a narrow balcony that ringed the dance floor below on three sides. Inside, the glittering chandeliers were dimly lit, giving the ballroom a soft glow. On one end, a stage held a small orchestra that was playing a waltz, but no one on the dance floor below was dancing. Probably, Esta realized, because the room was filled with men. Even the servers, all dressed in white jackets and dark pants, were men. There wasn't a woman in sight.

Esta leaned close to Harte so she could speak in a low voice. "Feel free to admit I was right any time you'd like."

THE HANDS OF JUSTICE

1904—St. Louis

T hunder crackled in the sky as Jack Grew's carriage made its way through the streets of St. Louis. He'd come to this shithole of a city as part of the president's entourage to visit the world's fair, and also as the Order's representative for the meeting of the Brotherhoods that the Society was hosting in a couple of weeks. For the past two days, he'd been annoyed at being away from New York for so long, but now it seemed the trip had suddenly become more promising. Word had come only moments before. *They found her.*

Two years. Two years without a trace of her, and now Esta Filosik would be his.

Jack had been waiting for this moment long enough that he'd already run through many possibilities for their first reunion. He'd considered a quick sneer and a cold laugh as he watched her dragged away to rot in prison. But he'd also considered doing something she wouldn't expect— perhaps he would *thank* her for what she'd done, for what he'd become.

Of course, she hadn't been the one to give him the Book—Darrigan had done that. But the train accident that had left his arm broken had, ironically enough, created a new future for him. The girl had been a very convenient scapegoat, a target for the public's anger and evidence of the continued need for the Order and their like.

Once, the Order had been seen as a curiosity, unimportant to the average person. Since the day on the train, though, the tide had turned. If magic had once been a distant fairy tale, the train accident and all the attacks that followed had made it an immediate danger. The entire country was afraid, which worked just fine for Jack. With every new Antistasi attack, with every new tragedy committed in the name of the Devil's Thief, the Order's power—and Jack's along with it—had grown.

As the carriage rumbled along the final few blocks to the hotel, Jack couldn't help but chuckle to himself. Yes. When he finally came face-to-face with her, she would be in handcuffs, and he would *thank* her. In his mind's eye, he imagined her full mouth parting in confusion. She would, most likely, plead with him. Miss Filosik—if that was even her name—wasn't stupid. She would understand immediately that her life was, for all intents and purposes, *finished*. Over. But before she met with some untimely accident in the women's prison, Jack would take the opportunity to thank her for all her treachery. It had, after all, made him a star.

How could his family send him away when he was a hero who had tried to stop a madwoman? *They couldn't.* So they had publicly lauded his bravery, the whole lot of them. But despite all his success—all the power he'd attained and all he'd done to ensure the Order remained relevant enough that he could use it to his own ends—they whispered to one another about him. They still wondered if he'd imagined the events on the train or made them up.

But Jack had known he wasn't mad. He'd known that not only had Esta been on the train, but that she had *survived*.

He reached into his vest and let his fingers brush against the Book that he carried with him everywhere. He'd had all his clothes altered to conceal it, and he kept it on his person at all times. He would not leave it behind, no matter the event. Nor would he trust servants or safes, not when the Book had opened doors to a consciousness he had only dreamed of.

Unable to resist its call, he took the Book from its home close to his chest and thumbed through the pages. Greek and Latin he could read, thanks to the interminable schooling he'd had as a boy, but there were other, less comprehensible languages mixed with strange symbols that graced many of the pages. Those pages should have been impossible for him to understand, and yet he'd woken in his mother's house after being dosed with morphine that first time to discover that he'd somehow translated them just the same.

Now his own small, neat hand filled the pages with notes and translations, but looking at the writing in the jarring carriage caused his head to ache. He took a small vial from his waistcoat pocket and placed one of the cubes it contained on his tongue. It took only a moment for the bitterness to erupt, familiar and satisfying, in his mouth, and then only a few moments more before he felt the tension behind his eyes ease.

The notations came into focus as he searched for the page he wanted. A protection charm of sorts, or so he believed it to be. Alone in the carriage, he let the strange words roll from his mouth, filling the cramped space with the cool resonance of the power that would forevermore be his.

He had known the girl was alive all along. And now he would prove it to everyone else.

The carriage pulled up in front of the Jefferson, and Jack tucked the Book back into the safety of his waistcoat as he prepared himself. He would thank Miss Filosik, and if she wanted to beg for her life, he would accept whatever she offered. Then he would toss her back to the hands of justice—hands that were controlled, of course, by his family and others like them.

Jack's personal servant and bodyguard, Miles, opened the door for him and waited silently with an umbrella in hand. When he stepped from the carriage, Jack noticed the line of dark wagons manned by uniformed officers and smiled. *There will be no getting away this time.*

"Wait here," he commanded, brushing past Miles without bothering with the umbrella. What did a bit of dampness matter when Jack was so close to victory? He would have satisfaction. He knew it as surely as he felt the Book in his jacket, its familiar weight reminding him that he held all the cards.

THE TRAITOR

Jianyu did not fight Mooch as he was led up the familiar steps of the Strega.

"I am not a traitor," he said softly as he forced his legs to move through the pain of lifting himself one step at a time.

But if Mooch heard what Jianyu said, he didn't respond.

When they reached the second floor, Mooch opened a familiar door and pushed Jianyu through. Then he shoved him into one of the chairs Jianyu had sat in countless times before during conversations with Dolph.

"I am not a traitor," he repeated as Mooch tied Jianyu's arms behind him and his ankles to the chair legs. "The traitor is the one who has taken a fallen man's home, just as he took his life. The traitor is the one who carries Dolph's cane and commands his holdings as though he has any right."

Mooch eyed him. "You can't really expect me to believe that little Nibsy was the one to put a bullet in Dolph's back? He don't have it in him."

"Then why do you follow his orders?" Jianyu asked softly.

"Maybe Nibs ain't tough, but he's smart," Mooch said after a minute. "And anyway, who else am I gonna follow, you?"

"He will discard you the moment you're not of use to him," Jianyu said. "Look at what is already happening."

"Nothing is happening," Mooch said.

"Then why are there Five Pointers in the Strega?" Jianyu asked. When

Dolph was alive, it would have never happened. Every one of the Devil's Own knew what Paul Kelly's men were capable of. Every one of them had been furious when the Five Pointers attacked two of the Devil's Own not even a week before.

"We have an understanding now," Mooch said, but the edge in his tone told Jianyu that not everyone was happy with this understanding.

"Do you?" he asked softly. Every breath he took was a pain, but he continued. "Because Nibsy trusts Kelly?"

"Don't nobody here trust Kelly. We all know he's a snake, but Nibsy's explained it—Kelly's got connections we need. He's kept the Strega from burning, hasn't he?"

"So he has." Jianyu kept his voice low and as steady as he could. "But catching a snake by the tail will not keep him from striking you."

"You know what? Just shut your yap, okay?" Mooch told him, more agitated now. "If you didn't betray us, where was you on the bridge while we was getting our asses handed to us?"

"I was following Dolph's orders," Jianyu told him. It was nothing more or less than the truth.

"Dolph Saunders is *dead*," Mooch said, his voice breaking with something that sounded like pain and frustration all rolled into a single emotion. "He was already laid out and cold before we went to the bridge."

"His death did not invalidate the task he gave me," Jianyu said carefully. "*Me*. Not the traitor you follow now."

Mooch took a step back and began pacing. He wasn't the smartest of the Devil's Own, and what Jianyu had said was clearly having an effect on him.

Mooch was shaking his head as though the action might jar loose an errant thought. Then he stopped and glared at Jianyu. "No. I'm done listening to you and your lies right now. Just . . . You just keep your damned ugly mouth shut, you hear me?"

Jianyu didn't respond to the slur. He watched the boy who had once been loyal to Dolph pace with a nervous energy that told Jianyu that his words had struck a nerve. The boy's cheeks had gone blotchy with his consternation. If Jianyu could just keep himself upright and conscious for long enough, perhaps he could continue to pick at Mooch's doubt.

But there wasn't time. Before he could say anything else, Werner burst through the door.

Mooch turned in surprise, his fists already up like he was expecting an attack.

"You gotta come—"

"What the hell are you doing, bursting in here like—"

"The Strega's on fire." The other boy grabbed Mooch by the sleeve. "We gotta help."

The color drained from Mooch's face, but he didn't hesitate to follow Werner.

"You cannot leave me here!" Jianyu called, but they were already gone.

The Strega took up the first floor of the building. If the saloon was on fire, the building could go quickly, and Jianyu was stuck two stories above and tied to a chair. He jerked at the ropes binding his wrists and found that they were too tight to slip free of. The same with his feet.

Faintly, he could smell the evidence of the fire as the breeze blew in through the opened window. Perhaps if he could scoot the chair close enough, he could call for help.

With all the strength he had left, he swung his body forward, moving the chair inches in the direction he wanted to go. The motion made his head swirl again, and his stomach threatened to expel its contents, but he tried again. His skin felt clammy, damp with the exertion as he struggled to move the chair closer to the window, but when the door behind him swung open, Jianyu went still.

"There you are."

He turned to see a girl entering the room. She was about his age—perhaps seventeen—and of average height. Though her figure was trim, there was a softness in the curve of her hips and the swell of her bosom. Her heart-shaped face held expressive, deep-set eyes that were upturned at the corners, and her thick, dark hair had been parted in the middle and smoothed back into a chignon at the nape of her neck, a style recently fashionable in the city. But around her temples, fine wisps of hair had started to curl out of their style. The dress she was wearing was a sage green that complemented the deep burnt umber of her skin. Even as rumpled as it was and as dirty as the hem had become, the gown was so perfectly tailored that it might have come from the finest dressmaker's shop on Fifth Avenue, which told him who this must be.

"Cela Johnson?" he asked, sure that he could not be right. It was not possible that the girl he had been searching for was *here*, in the Strega.

Cela gave him a small nod, the only affirmation he would have for now, it seemed.

"What are you doing here?" he asked, trying to focus on her. His head ached so badly that it looked as though there were two of her.

"Saving you," she said with a tone that told him he should have figured that much out on his own. "Or can't you tell?" She was already working at the ropes around his wrist with her nimble fingers.

"But how did you find me?" he asked, wincing at the way she tugged at the ropes, jarring him.

"I followed you from the theater."

His wrists were free and she started on the ropes at his ankles. He should have helped her, but the very thought of movement made the room spin.

"But why—"

"Look, Mr. Lee—"

"Jianyu," he said, not wanting her to use a name that wasn't truly his.

"Mr. Jianyu—"

"Simply Jianyu. No mister."

She made an exasperated noise in the back of her throat. "We don't have time for this. They're going to figure out pretty quick that the fire I started isn't any real threat. We need to be gone by then."

Even through his pain, that surprised him. "*You* started the fire?"

"You have a lot of questions," she muttered as the last of the ropes came untied. "That's fine, because I have some of my own. But all that is gonna have to wait. We need to move. Can you walk okay?"

Jianyu gave her a sure nod, hoping it was not a lie as he got to his feet, using the table to steady himself. His eyes caught on a piece of newsprint sitting there. It had been cut unevenly, and when his eyes caught on the headline, he understood why. Crumpling the paper, he stuffed it into his tunic pockets.

"Come on," Cela urged, already at the door.

On unsteady feet, he followed, but the specter of smoke that signaled the burning of the Strega hung heavy in the air.

INTO THE FIRE

1902—New York

The moment Jianyu Lee told Cela that Harte Darrigan had sent him, she'd had a feeling that he would be trouble. Watching him try to keep himself upright as they made their escape from the building, she knew she'd been right.

She never should have followed him. Once she was freed from her workroom, she should have turned north and gone straight to her family, but curiosity had gotten the better of her when she'd watched him walking away from the theater late the night before, his long braid swinging down his back.

She hadn't known that Darrigan was friends with any Chinese men. She didn't know *anyone* who even knew any of the Chinese people, who mostly kept to themselves as they held on to their strange dress and stranger customs. So she couldn't help but wonder if Darrigan really had sent the man to help her, and if he had, why? Did he know who was responsible for her brother's murder?

If he knew anything about what had happened to Abe, it seemed worth the risk, so she'd followed him, keeping herself back a ways as he headed first to a Chinese laundry on Twenty-Fourth Street, at the southern edge of the area some called the Tenderloin and others called Satan's Circus. She probably should have left him there, but she'd felt almost safe hiding in the quiet side alley near the laundry. She'd only meant to rest for a little while, but she'd fallen asleep without meaning to and only woke when she heard the door of the laundry close sometime around dawn. Rousing herself, she'd followed him as he walked south, toward the Bowery.

She had seen the boys following before he did—stupid, rangy things who barely had hair sprouting on their pale, pimpled chins, and mean as rats. There wasn't even time to warn him before they had him cornered and on the ground, and she wasn't big enough or strong enough—or stupid enough—to jump into a fight she couldn't win. She'd thought to wait until they'd left to help him, but then that other one came.

Mock Duck, they called him, and everyone in the city had read about what he was capable of. The papers had been covering the war between the tongs on Mott Street and Pell Street the same way they covered the gossip of the people who lived in the mansions on Fifth Avenue—like it was some kind of sport. But while the people in the fancy mansions wore the wrong hats or went out dancing with people who might not be their own wives, the violence stirred up by Mock Duck and his highbinders killed innocent people.

Cela had almost left then, because she'd figured the guy she'd been following must've been one of Mock Duck's highbinders himself. They'd take care of their own, even if they wouldn't be able to put his hair back onto his head. But it was clear soon enough that Mock Duck wasn't saving him so much as taking him prisoner.

A smarter woman would have called it quits right then and there, maybe. A woman with some brains in her head wouldn't have followed them deeper into the Bowery. But she was a woman without much more to lose. Jianyu Lee had claimed that Darrigan had sent him to protect her. Her brother had already died doing that—just as her father had—and she would carry that knowledge with her all her days. She wasn't about to add another life to her load.

Out of the frying pan, she thought as she pulled the scrap of fabric she'd taken up over her head. She kept her distance as she followed them to some saloon on the Bowery. And then, when she needed a distraction to get Jianyu on his own, she made one.

She was in the fire now—literally, if they didn't get out of there, and fast. But from the way Jianyu was moving, it didn't seem like fast was an option.

They were nearly to the ground floor, nearly free, when they heard voices—angry voices—coming their way.

She looked back up at Jianyu, who was standing on the step above her, to see if he'd heard them. From the expression on his face, it was clear that he had. Maybe they could go back up. . . . But if the fire was still burning—she didn't think it would be, but if it *was*—she wasn't ready to die quite yet.

The boy didn't look half as concerned as Cela felt. With a smooth, practiced motion, he withdrew two dark disks from the inside pocket of his tunic.

"Step up here and hold on to me," he told her.

"Hold on to you?" she repeated, sure she must have misheard him.

"You're right. It would be better if you climbed onto my back." He maneuvered past her and then stooped slightly, waiting.

"I'm *not* climbing up onto you. I don't know you from Adam," she said, thinking that maybe she should take her chances with the fire. "You can barely walk as it is."

"I'm fine," he said, clipping out the words through clenched teeth.

She saw the way he was masking the hurt with the fire in his eyes. She'd done the same thing many times herself.

"It's nothing personal. I just—"

"Unless you would like to explain to the men coming up the steps who you are and what you're doing here, you would be wise to do as I say and climb onto my back."

The voices were getting closer.

"Fine," she said, hoping with every bit of her being that her mother wasn't watching from the hereafter as she used his shoulders to pull herself up and wrapped her legs around him.

The first thing she thought, and it was maybe the least sensible thing she could have picked to think, was that the guy beneath her was all muscle. He looked half-dead from the beating he'd gotten, but with her legs secure around his midsection and her arms around his neck, she could feel the strength beneath his loose clothes.

The second thing she thought, once she got over the idiotic first thought, was that the papers were wrong. But then, she should have known that the papers would be wrong. Weren't they usually when it came to anyone who wasn't white? She'd read all sorts of things about the Chinese men who made their home in the city—about their strange habits and the filthy conditions in which they lived, refusing to become good, solid Americans like everyone else. But this boy smelled like the earth, like something green and pleasant.

She was still thinking the second thought when Jianyu made a subtle movement of his hands, and she felt the world tilt.

"Hold on," he said, and started down the steps.

When they reached the landing below, he paused, listening. She could feel his labored breathing. "Stay still and be quiet," he commanded, as though he had some right to command *her* when she was the one who was doing the rescuing. But seeing how she was the one who'd climbed up onto him, however unwillingly, maybe he wasn't too far off the mark.

Men were coming up the steps—the same swarthy-skinned Italians who'd been standing around at the saloon. They were dressed in dark pants and coats and there was a meanness to the air around them, but the guy carrying her didn't do more than pull back against the wall.

And just like that, those men walked past them like they weren't even standing there. Like she wasn't nothing but a haint walking in the world.

The men were still too close and Cela was too unnerved to ask what had happened. She decided instead to take the blessings as they came and to hope that their luck held.

As the men continued up, Jianyu began to descend again, and a moment later they were out the back of the building and into the busy traffic of Elizabeth Street.

"Don't let go," he told her just as she started to release his neck.

She probably shouldn't have listened, but there was something about the way he said it—more desperate than commanding—that made her comply.

"They can't see us," he whispered, answering her unspoken question.

"None of them?"

"Not as long as you stay where you are," he said, hitching her up higher on his back and walking away from the building she'd rescued him from.

She understood then. "You're one of *them*," she said. But though his jaw went tight, he didn't answer.

He didn't put her down until they were two blocks away. In the distance, she could hear the clanging of a fire brigade's wagons as he released her. His face was turned, solemn and serious, toward the direction of the sound.

"What is it?" she asked.

"Dolph built the Strega from nothing. To see it burn . . ." His voice fell away.

"The bar, you mean? It won't burn," she assured him. "I only set a small fire in a waste can—one that would make a lot of smoke and look worse than it is. Besides," she said, pausing to listen to the approaching sirens, "it sounds like someone there has friends in high places if the brigades are already coming."

He turned to her. "Thank you for rescuing me, Miss Johnson." His straight, dark hair was hanging lank and uneven around his face from where it had been so unceremoniously chopped. It should have looked a mess, but instead it served to accent the sharp angles of him—his razorblade cheekbones and sharp chin, the wide, strong nose, and the finely knit brows over too-knowing eyes.

"You might as well call me Cela. Everyone else does."

"Cela," he repeated, swaying a bit on his feet.

"Whoa, there," she said, catching him up under the arm before he toppled over. "They messed you up good, didn't they?"

"I'm fine," Jianyu said, grimacing even as he said it.

"Sure you are." She helped him over to a shuttered doorway, where he could lean and rest.

"Come," he said. "We're still too close."

He led the way to a streetcar stop another block over, and he didn't speak again until they were heading uptown and away from the Bowery. "Is there somewhere you can go?" he asked her, still clutching his stomach as the car rattled along, like he was trying to hold it in. "Somewhere you would feel safe?"

"Safe?" Cela wanted to laugh from the sheer absurdity of the idea. "I'm not sure what safe even is anymore."

BEWARE THE DEVIL'S THIEF

1904—St. Louis

arte Darrigan was probably more likely to put on a dress himself than ever admit to Esta that her decision to wear the clothing she'd found in the hotel room was a good idea, even if the ballroom below *was* filled with nothing but men. For one thing, admitting that she had been right would only embolden her, but more important, maybe, it was taking everything he had not to be distracted by the shape of her legs in the trousers she was wearing. So he shot her a dark look instead and focused on the problem at hand—getting them out of the hotel before they were found.

"The kitchen entrance must be there," Harte said, ignoring her remark as he pointed toward the far end of the room, where a door periodically swung open as white-coated servers came and went at regular intervals. "There are steps in the corner there, by the stage. Then we'll keep to the edge of the room until we have to cut across. Stick close, but not too close," he said, "and try not to sway your hips so much."

"I do *not* sway my hips." She glared at him.

"You *do*," he told her flatly. He should know, since he'd just followed her down a hallway. She opened her mouth as if to argue, but he cut her off. "You walk like a woman." He took a moment to look her over for any other flaw that might give her away. "Pull your hat down lower," he told her as she stared at him. "Your eyes—they're too soft. Christ," he swore, his stomach twisting. There was no way she was going to make it through a room full of men without them noticing what she really was.

She might as well have worn just the corset. "We're dead."

"We'll be fine," she told him. "I've been around men my whole life."

"Yeah, well, in case you haven't noticed, I've actually *been* one," he grumbled.

"It would have been kind of hard for me to miss." Her mouth twitched, and he thought he saw something warmer than mere amusement flicker in her whiskey-colored eyes. At the sight of it, the power inside of him flared with anticipation. He was too busy pushing it back down to return her banter, and she let out a tired breath at his silence. "Oh, come on, Harte. Most of the people in here are drunk. They're not going to notice me."

"Let's hope not." But he didn't have a lot of confidence.

Once they'd descended to the main ballroom, the sounds of glasses clinking and the rumble of men amused at their own jokes surrounded them. As they skirted the edges of the ballroom, something in Harte's periphery drew his attention, and he glanced up to see that there were now a few men standing at the edge of the mezzanine, searching the crowd below. They were wearing the same dark coats and white armbands as the Guard outside the theater.

"Don't look up," he told Esta. He nodded to a bleary-eyed old man as he lifted a bowl of champagne from a passing tray.

"What—"

"I said, *don't look*," he said through clenched teeth as he raised the glass to his lips. He didn't drink, but instead used the motion to cover his survey of the room. "There are two men up on the mezzanine now—maybe more."

"Police?" she asked.

"The Guard." His gaze slid to her. "We're running out of time if they're already looking for us here."

"For me," Esta corrected. "They're looking for the Devil's Thief." Her eyes were steady and her jaw tight.

"Well, they're not going to find her." Harte glanced at Esta over the rim of the glass. "You could get us out of here right now."

She shook her head. "You saw what happened in the hallway. I could barely hold on to the seconds. We don't know what the Guard is capable of. And if they can track magic . . ."

She was probably right. If the Brink or the power of the Book inside of him had done something to her magic—or to his—it was better not to chance it until they knew more. "Let's go."

They left behind the relative safety of the mezzanine's overhang to cut a line across the ballroom floor. Directly across the room, the double doors to the kitchens swung loosely on their hinges every time a waiter appeared with another tray of champagne or canapés. Behind the doors, the light of the service hallway was a beacon, urging them on.

If Harte could have made a beeline to those doors, he would have, but too fast or too direct and it might draw the attention of the men watching from above. As much as everything in him was screaming to *Run. Go. Get out*, he forced himself to keep the interminable pace as he meandered through the crowded floor, stopping at random intervals to pretend to watch the orchestra or take one of the hors d'oeuvres from the white-coated servers circulating through the crowd.

It felt like they would never reach the other side . . . and then, all at once, they were there, nearly to the edges of the ballroom. Only a few feet more and they could duck into the safety of the back of the house. But just before they could slip through the doors, the orchestra abruptly went silent. All around them, there was a delayed reaction, a ripple of awareness that filtered through the crowd as the men in the room, drunk as they might have been, realized something had happened.

Harte turned too, just long enough to see that one of the plainclothes officers had taken the stage and was lifting his hands, telling the crowd to be patient as the lights on the chandeliers suddenly grew brighter.

"If I could have your attention, gentlemen," the officer shouted. "I'm Detective Sheehan of the St. Louis Police, and I'm sorry to interrupt your evening, but there's a wanted criminal on the loose. She was spotted entering the hotel a few minutes ago, and we believe she may still be in the building."

The rustling around them increased as the men craned their necks, searching for a woman among them. Next to him, Esta pulled the hat lower over her brow.

The officer continued. "We just need a moment of your time as my men secure the room and do a quick sweep."

"I'm here, Officer," a voice called over the din of the crowd.

Esta—and everyone else in the room—turned to look up at the balcony, where a figure stood dressed in a crimson gown. Her face was half covered by a red porcelain mask tipped with horns, and she stood on the edge of the railing with her arms lifted, as though she were about to dive into the crowd. The Guardsmen started charging around the mezzanine to where she stood. With a swirl of her arms, she took a sweeping bow, and in a sudden plume of scarlet smoke, the figure was gone.

"You'll have to be quicker than that if you want to catch me," another voice called from the other side of the ballroom. Again the heads in the room swiveled to find the source of the sound. This figure was wearing the same devilish mask, but she was dressed in a gown of midnight, and standing on the railing above, she looked like a shadow against the gilded walls.

"Or me," a voice bellowed. This one was dressed in ghostly white, her face masked as well.

"Or me." Another voice, again from a different corner of the mezzanine.

"Or me." The woman in red was back.

Their voices echoed off the walls as the sound of thunder rumbled through the ballroom, and the air seemed suddenly charged and electric. A strange, impossible wind began to swirl through the room, eliciting more nervous rustling from the men who'd been having fun only a moment before. A single word circulated through the ballroom, as quickly as a wildfire fed by the air: *Antistasi*.

The men in the ballroom were already running toward the door, but the police had blocked the exits.

"Who are they?" Esta whispered, her hand on Harte's arm.

"I don't know," he said, looking up at the women. Each was balanced precipitously on the balcony. "From the sound of it, we've found the Antistasi that Julien told us about."

"Beware the Devil's Thief," they chanted in unison as more smoke billowed from beneath them. "Her enemies, beware her wrath." With a flash of light, the figures were gone, but the trailing smoke was still moving steadily toward the ballroom floor, like something alive.

"They're incredible," Esta whispered, her voice filled with something like wonder.

But Harte didn't feel the awe that was clear in Esta's expression. There was something eerie about the apparitions. Something more than unsettling. And it didn't help that the masked women were using that damned name, the one the papers had pinned on Esta, which could only mean trouble for them as long as they stayed in this town.

Then Harte felt the icy heat of magic in the air and knew it had something to do with the fog of smoke hanging over their heads. He wasn't about to wait and see what that fog contained. "Let's go." He took Esta's hand and moved in the opposite direction of the rest of the now-panicking crowd.

He didn't bother to check if anyone noticed them crossing the final few feet toward the service doors. Once they were in the hallway beyond, they began to run.

"This way." Esta pointed at a narrow staircase that led down toward the first floor.

They took the steps at a sprint, and at the bottom they found themselves in another hall of linoleum floors and cream-colored walls. Harte could already hear noise coming from the stairs behind them. To the right, other voices seemed to be drawing closer. He didn't know whether it was more police or just the kitchen staff, but they couldn't stay to find out.

Harte tugged Esta down the hall in the opposite direction and through a doorway.

"It's a dead end," she said, looking around for some other exit.

It was a storage room. One wall was lined with gleaming silver serving ware, soup tureens, and domed platters. In the corner, two large wheeled carts were filled with clean linens.

From just outside the door came the sound of voices, and Harte went to lean against it, cracking it open so he could listen. "There's someone out there," he told her as he tried to make out what they were saying. "I think they're looking for whoever those women in the ballroom were. We need to get out of here."

"What about that?" she asked, pointing out a smaller door on the far wall. It was square, about halfway up the wall, and when she opened it, he could see it was some kind of chute. The space was just large enough for a person to fit through. "Looks like it goes down to the basement. Maybe it's the laundry?" she offered, indicating the carts filled with linens.

"It could just as easily be a trash chute leading to an incinerator." He walked over and poked his head into the dark opening for a moment.

Outside the door, the voices were growing louder. "I think we should risk it," she said, already lifting a leg to wedge herself into the chute. "If we get down to the basement, there has to be a way out."

"Esta, no," Harte said, pulling her back as they heard another door in the hallway bang open. "We don't know how far the drop might be or what's down there."

"But—" He scooped her up before she could finish her protest.

"We can't risk breaking a leg or something," he said as he carried her, squirming, over to the laundry bins.

He saw her eyes widen as she understood what he was about to do. "Harte, don't you even think about—"

But he was already dumping her into the rolling bin. "Cover up."

Esta struggled to right herself amid the slippery piles of fabric. "But—"

"We don't have time to argue," he said, pulling extra linens from one of the other bins. Whoever those women in the ballroom were, they'd bought Harte and Esta some time with their distraction. At least Harte hoped they had. "I trusted you in the elevator. Now it's your turn."

"Harte—"

"Get down and *stay* down," he snapped, and then piled another load of linens on top of her before she could argue any more.

Harte tied one of the white tablecloths around his waist, approximating the aprons he'd seen the servers wearing earlier. He wasn't dressed in one of the white jackets the other hotel workers wore, but he had to hope it was like Esta had said: No one ever noticed the help.

"Ready?" he asked the cart, and he got a string of muffled curses in reply. He figured that was as good as a yes.

Carefully, he backed out of the room, pulling the cart behind him. Turning away from the voices and trying to figure out where he was, Harte tried to look natural as he maneuvered the cart down the hall. He was nearly to the first turn when he heard someone calling out behind him.

"Hey! You there!"

Pretending that he hadn't heard them, Harte kept his pace brisk but steady as he headed for where the hall branched into a T.

"Hey!" The shout came again. "Stop!"

He took the first right and then broke into a run. He didn't bother to slow down for the set of swinging doors ahead, but instead took them at full speed and plunged into the kitchen. Surprised chefs raised their heads, pausing their work to watch him rush through. On the other side of the kitchen was an empty service hall. He didn't look back to see how close their pursuers were, but tore down the hallway and then out another set of doors that led to the lobby.

The front door of the hotel was ahead of them—just a few more yards and they would be out into the night—when the shrill screech of a whistle split the air, causing the tinkling of the piano to cut short and people all throughout the lobby to stare. And in front of him, blocking the one exit he had left, two uniformed policemen stepped into his path to stop him.

In that moment Harte knew they were done. There would be more police outside, and even if he got them through the front doors, they'd have no place to go. Not that he would go easily.

"Hold on," he told Esta as he picked up his speed.

"Harte, what are you—"

He'd expected the two men to move out of the way, but they held their ground, bracing for impact, so when the cart plowed into them, they all went over. Esta tumbled out of the cart, disoriented and with her hair falling from her hat, but Harte was already on his feet, taking her by the hand.

"Run!" he shouted, half dragging her as he sprinted toward the exit, but suddenly there were three more men blocking their way. He pulled up short as he realized there was no way to get through them—not without magic.

"Esta—" Her name was a question and demand all at once.

She tightened her hold on his hand as though she understood, but at first nothing happened.

"Any time now," he said as the men started to close in on them.

She blinked over at him. "Right—"

Harte almost stumbled when the men chasing them seemed to halt in midstride, and Esta let out a shaking breath. Together they wove through the men and out the front doors of the hotel. He'd been right: There were police wagons and a row of dark-suited police standing along the front of the hotel, waiting for them.

The storm that had threatened all evening had started, and the cold drops of rain, suspended midfall, felt needle-sharp against Harte's face as he and Esta continued to run from the hotel. Above, the sky glowed from a flash of lightning, the bright forks of the electric bolts frozen like cracks in an iced pond. They lit the night with their brilliance.

Next to him, Esta's breath hitched as she stumbled, nearly pulling him down with her. But he caught the two of them in time. "Esta?"

"I can't—" she said through gritted teeth. "It's too much." She was trying to pull away from him.

He realized then that where their hands were clasped, ribbons of energy, like miniatures of the lightning bolts that hung in the sky, were winding about, binding them together. These weren't frozen in time, though, like everything else around them. This energy was alive—hot and dangerous and creeping up her arm. The voice inside of him was howling in victory.

"We're too close," he said, looking at what was happening with a numb sort of horror. The hotel was still in sight. The police were still a danger. Everything they'd risked, everything they'd done to escape, would have been for nothing if they didn't get away. "I need you to hold on for just a few more minutes."

Esta's face was twisted with the effort of what she was doing. "It feels like fire." But she nodded, and without pausing or asking for permission, Harte scooped her over his shoulders, in a fireman's carry, and threaded his way through the now-still traffic. He ignored the needlelike cold of the raindrops. The power inside of him surged again, pulsing with satisfaction, but he gathered all his strength and pushed it down.

He was barely across the street, just out of view of the hotel, when Esta gasped and the world around them righted itself. Above, the sky went dark, and a moment later thunder crashed over the steady patter of raindrops. He ran for the cover of a doorway and lowered Esta to the ground.

"Did we make it?" she whispered.

"Yeah," he said, brushing back the hair from her face. "We made it. We have to keep going, though. I need you to help me here. You're going to have to walk."

She wasn't listening. Her gaze was glassy and unfocused as she stared up at the night sky. "Can you see that? It's like the darkness is eating the world."

Harte didn't bother to look. His attention was on Esta as her eyes fluttered closed and her limbs went limp.

AN UNEXPECTED CHALLENGE

1904—St. Louis

R uth waited beneath the cover of the brewery's wagon, across
from the Jefferson Hotel, watching for some sign of what was
happening within. Along the street near the front entrance, the
dark bodies of police wagons blocked her view of the front door. She had
more Antistasi stationed at the other entrances, just in case.

She wasn't sure what she was expecting. Ever since the legend of the
Devil's Thief was born after the train accident two years before, Ruth
had always assumed it was a lie perpetrated by the Order and the other
Occult Brotherhoods to stir up anger against her kind. Ruth had never
really believed that a girl, a simple *girl*, could have done what the reports
claimed she had. Which had not stopped Ruth and the other Antistasi
leaders from claiming the Devil's Thief as their own, or from using her
name to unify their cause.

All across the country, there were pockets of Mageus who lived quiet
lives, but something changed after the Defense Against Magic Act was
passed. Ordinary people who were happy living ordinary lives suddenly
realized they had never been safe. They began to look to the Thief for the
promise of a different future, and groups like Ruth's had been more than
happy to provide them with hope.

When other deeds—small and large, across the country—were done
by people claiming to be the Devil's Thief, Ruth had always assumed that
it was simply a group of Antistasi like her own. She'd never thought that
the same girl could have been involved. The Devil's Thief was nothing

but a myth, a folk hero like Paul Bunyan or John Henry. Maybe she'd been a real girl at some point, but the Thief had become something so much larger than any single person. She'd become an ideal. A calling.

But then, earlier that night, North had seen the girl, the one whose face had been in papers across the land, and Ruth had to accept the possibility that she'd been wrong. She also had to face the possibility of a challenge to her own power in St. Louis. After all, stories are often easier to tame than actual hearts.

Ruth had no idea who this girl was or what she wanted. She didn't even know if the girl *was* the Thief, though the police and the Guard certainly were treating her as such. At best, the girl's appearance was a minor distraction. At worst, the girl might have come to the city to take control of it. Ruth had worked too hard, had far too much planned, to allow that.

Still, it wouldn't do for the girl to be caught now. If she was, the specter of the Devil's Thief would be useless as a shield against any retaliation that Ruth's Antistasi might incur. There was too much at stake, so she'd brought her people to the Jefferson. They would provide a distraction for the girl to escape, and if possible, they would bring the girl to Ruth. As a competitor, the girl could be a problem, but as an ally—or better, a *subordinate* . . . Well, that idea held a certain attraction.

It had been too long. With North and his watch, time was flexible, but waiting was still interminable. As long as her people were inside, Ruth would worry.

She didn't have to worry for much longer, though. Lightning flashed in a brilliant arc overhead, illuminating the street and the facade of the hotel, and before the thunder could break, a pair appeared out of nowhere. Ruth squinted through the rain as the taller of the two scooped the other up and ran. And she felt the crash of warm magic sift through the air, unusually strong. Impossibly pure. Ruth hadn't felt power like *that* in her entire life.

A moment later four masked figures dressed in gowns appeared just out of the beam of the streetlamp nearby. They ran toward the wagon and were inside before anyone could see them. The back door of the wagon closed, and a window slid open near the driver's perch.

"Did you run into any problems?" Ruth asked, peering back into the darkness of the wagon's covered bed. North had already taken the mask from his face and was stripping out of the dark gown.

"Not one," North told her. "Maggie's devices worked like a charm."

"They usually do," Ruth said, a spark of pride for her youngest sister glowing within her.

"We didn't find the Thief inside. Do you think she got out?" Maggie asked, pulling her own mask from her face. It was always a moment of shock to see Maggie dressed in scarlet, when Ruth was used to the girl wearing more sedate colors. From the look on North's face—the open longing—Ruth suspected that he felt the same.

She looked back in the direction where the two people had appeared in the rain. "I think she did," Ruth told them. "But North was right. She's not alone."

"Do you want me to follow them?" North asked.

Ruth considered his offer—and the way her sister's expression filled with worry at the mention of it. With the power the Thief clearly had, having her on their side might be a boon, but she knew that if Maggie was worried about North, she would not be able to focus on the work necessary to complete the serum. Thief or no Thief, they were running out of time. "We have eyes enough in the city. If they surface again or cause any problems, we'll know. For now, I need you close."

RESPONSIBILITIES

1902—New York

As the streetcar rattled north toward Fifty-Second Street, where her uncle and his family lived, Cela couldn't stop her voice from cracking as she told Jianyu about how Abe had been killed in their own house. Tears fell down her cheeks as she explained how the theater workroom that had been her pride—her sanctuary—had been turned into her prison.

"I *knew* you were there," he said.

She nodded. "I heard you, but I didn't know who you were. With the night I'd had . . . Then you went on about Darrigan, and I didn't think it was smart to reveal myself, not after everything else."

"It is understandable after what happened to your brother and your house," Jianyu said simply, an acknowledgment that Cela didn't quite understand.

"I didn't say anything about my house," she told him, her stomach suddenly feeling like she'd swallowed molten lead.

"You do not know?" His expression faltered. "When I came to find you, it was burning."

Even sitting down as she was, it was her turn to sway and his turn to steady her. That house had been her daddy's pride and joy. It was his mark in the world, and if Jianyu was right, it was gone. Just like her brother. Just like everything she'd loved. All in a single night.

The vines around her heart grew thorns, and her breath felt like it was being pressed from her.

Has it already been two days?

Cela pulled away from the comfort of Jianyu's hand over hers.

He let her go, but his eyes narrowed thoughtfully.

"What?" she demanded, her very soul raw and weeping from the losses that had been piled one on another.

"Harte Darrigan lied about many things, but he did not lie about you," he told her softly. "He chose well."

"Well, he should've chosen somebody else," she told him, unable to keep the bitterness out of her voice.

Jianyu let out a ragged breath, a sigh that Cela took for agreement. They rode in silence for a while longer, but eventually he turned to her again. "Darrigan's mother?" he asked gently. "He told me that he left her with you. She was not in the house?"

"She died before I left," she assured him. *Before it burned.*

"Who was it that killed your brother?"

"I hoped that you would know," she said. "I was in the cellar when it happened. I heard the gunshot, and I ran. I don't even know *why* I ran. It's like I couldn't stop myself. I left Abe there. I left him like some coward."

Her voice hitched, and the memory of Abe—his laughing eyes and his strong features that were so much like their father's—threatened to overwhelm her. Threatened to pull her down so she'd never get back up.

"You are far from a coward, Cela Johnson." Jianyu reached over and gently wiped the tears from her cheeks. It was a strangely intimate gesture, a liberty that he didn't have any right to take with her. But she didn't stop him. She simply accepted his comfort as the gift she knew he'd intended.

"It's because of Darrigan, isn't it? Everything that happened to me—to Abe—it's all because I took his mother in and accepted that damn ring as payment."

"I cannot be sure, but . . ." He inclined his head, wincing a little at the movement.

"It's why Evelyn locked me in my workshop. She wanted the ring Darrigan left me," she told him. Cela still didn't understand how the stupid wench had managed to get it out of the seam of her skirt, or why she had given it up without so much as a fight.

"Do you still have it?" Jianyu asked, his eyes cutting to her and his voice suddenly urgent. "Did Evelyn get the ring?"

"She must've taken it," Cela said.

"No—"

"Good riddance to it, too. Evil old thing didn't bring me anything but bad luck."

Jianyu was looking paler than he had before. His skin had golden undertones before, but now the color all but drained from his face. "It'll bring worse luck if we do not retrieve it."

"We. There isn't gonna be any 'we,'" she told him. The streetcar was pulling to the curb and she wasn't going to continue on this ride. "This is my stop. I'm going to go to my family, heaven help them, and you can go wherever you'd like, but I don't want anything to do with that ring, or Harte Darrigan, or anything else. Now, I freed you, and you freed me, so I think we'd better call things even and part ways right here and now."

Jianyu frowned, but he didn't argue.

"I can't exactly say it was a pleasure, but it was interesting." She held out her hand. "God go with you, because lord knows that if you go after that ring, you're gonna need every bit of his protection."

He reached for her hand, but Jianyu's skin barely touched hers before she registered how cool it felt—too cool—and then he was collapsing as though the life had gone right out of him. It was only her quick reflexes that kept him from hitting his head a second time.

She hadn't realized he was in such bad shape. He'd seemed fine a moment before. Well, he wasn't her responsibility. Cela propped Jianyu back up onto the seat and then started to go. But she got only about four steps away before she turned back.

She couldn't leave him there. She *should*, but she couldn't.

With a sigh, she jostled Jianyu until he was conscious again, just enough to get himself up. Even then she had to support his weight—his arm draped over her shoulder—to get him down the aisle and off the streetcar, apologizing to the folks who were watching her with clear disapproval as she went. Once outside, Cela took a moment to get her bearings. Jianyu was barely conscious, but he was at least on his feet.

"Come on," she told him, heading deeper into the neighborhood. "Let's get you somewhere before you go and pass out again."

She hadn't been relishing the idea of going to her family to start with. If her uncle Desmond and his brood looked disapprovingly at her before, she could only imagine what he would do when she showed up on his doorstep, homeless, grieving, and with a half-dead Chinese man in tow.

MISSED OPPORTUNITIES

1904—St. Louis

It was madness inside the Jefferson Hotel. Jack stopped short not three steps into the lobby. Dark-suited police were everywhere. Some were talking to groups of people clad in evening finery—women in satin dripping with jewels and men in sharply cut tuxedoes that would have made even a Vanderbilt green with envy—while others had created a border around the room and watched any new arrivals with suspicious eyes.

"You can't come in here now," one of the officers barked at Jack, but the man's voice was enough to bring him back to attention. And the morphine he'd just ingested was enough to make him not care. He stepped past the man without bothering to argue.

The man took him by the arm and whipped him around. "I said you can't—"

"I was told to come," Jack said, cutting him off.

"By who?" the officer blustered, narrowing his eyes.

"By me," a voice said from behind the officer.

"Chief Matson, I presume?" Jack said, jerking free of the other officer's grasp. He held out his hand in greeting.

The chief was a short man, stout and sturdy with the eyes of a hawk. "It's good to finally meet you, Mr. Grew," the man said as he shook Jack's hand. "But I'm afraid it's been a waste of your time."

The man's words cooled some of the easy warmth the morphine had spread through Jack's veins. "You said they were here," Jack said, his voice clipped.

"They were, but they're gone now," the police chief said.

"Gone." The impossibility of the word was a punch in the stomach. "They can't be gone. Didn't you have men at all the exits?"

"Every one, regular and service alike. They didn't get out any of the exits."

"Then they have to be here," Jack said, trying to keep his tone level. "Have you searched the whole hotel?"

"We don't need to," Matson told him.

Jack could practically feel the vein in his neck throbbing. Even with the morphine to dampen the noise and confusion of the lobby, the chief's words sparked his temper. "Why the hell not?"

"What's the point? We saw them disappear," the chief said. "Hell, half the force saw it. Just about five minutes ago." The chief pointed to a spot not twenty yards from the front door. "We had them surrounded, all their escapes blocked. They were there one minute and then—boom—they were gone, just like that. Like they were ghosts."

I was right. They laughed behind my back and called me a fool, but I was right.

"'Course, I don't believe in ghosts," the chief of police said. "So I called the Guard."

"The Guard?" Jack felt like the world had narrowed until he could concentrate on only one thing.

"The Jefferson Guard. They take care of any problems we have round these parts with illegal magic."

"They didn't take care of this one," Jack said darkly. "This is unacceptable, Chief Matson. You assured me that you could secure the area for Roosevelt's arrival."

The chief bristled, his heavy jowls wobbling as his cheeks turned red. "I have the utmost faith in our people to make sure everything is secure when the president arrives. Hey, Hendricks, come on over here," the chief called.

Across the room, a ruddy-faced man with a high forehead and a mop of honey-colored hair lifted his head. "I'll be done in a second."

"You'll be done now," the chief snapped forcefully enough to draw the attention of everyone in the room. He turned back to Jack and huffed in annoyance. "The Guard thinks that because the city council has given them free rein, they've got some standing, but they're still just amateurs."

"Hendricks, meet Mr. Jack Grew," the chief said once the other man had come over. "He's here to help prepare for the president's visit at the gala. I was just assuring him that we have everything under control."

Hendricks kept his hands tucked behind his back and his chin lifted. Up close, the man was younger than Jack had expected. He couldn't have been more than twenty, but he had the kind of broad shoulders and lean, strong features that made Jack puff out his own chest a little more.

"Hendricks here is a colonel with the Guard," the chief explained. "He can explain everything we have set up. I'll leave Mr. Grew with you, Colonel?"

"Yes, sir," the guy said, his expression never flickering.

"Right, then. You'll be in good hands." He gave Jack a rough pat on the arm before he walked off to find another of his officers.

"You have questions about our security measures?" Hendricks asked.

"This Guard . . . What is it?" Jack asked.

"The Jefferson Guard is tasked with protecting St. Louis from illegal magic," Hendricks said, reciting the words as though from memory.

"What does that entail, exactly?" Jack asked, eyeing the man.

"We do what the normal police can't." The colonel's eyes were emotionless when they met his. "We use a specific set of skills and tools to hunt Mageus who refuse to assimilate themselves as productive members of society."

Even with the haze of morphine dulling the brightness and noise around him, Jack felt his attention peak. "Really? You hunt Mageus?"

Hendricks nodded. "We show them back to the gutters and the prisons where they belong. We eliminate the danger they pose to proper society."

"Excellent," Jack said, reaching for the vial of morphine cubes. "Absolutely outstanding."

DELMONICO'S

1902—New York

T he boning of the new corset was digging into the soft flesh of
Viola's hip, but there wasn't a thing she could do to adjust it, not
so long as her brother's scagnozzo had her by the arm. And also
not so long as she was supposed to be playing the part of a lady. It had
been four days since Viola had accepted her brother's beating as the cost
of using his protection. In four days, the split in her lip had healed itself
enough for her to be presentable in public. In those four days, she'd bided
her time and done everything her brother had asked of her, no matter
how insulting. She'd played the part of the dutiful, penitent sister, but
she'd kept her eyes and ears opened and she'd started to plan.

The maître d' was checking over his ledger, searching for their reservation. Occasionally, he'd glance up at Viola and her escort with a questioning look, as though he knew that neither of them belonged. The longer
they stood there, the more Viola felt the eyes of other people on them.
She wished the stuffed-shirt fool would hurry up. She was more than
ready to have a table between her and her escort for the night. Already
he'd been too free with his eyes . . . and his hands.

Paul didn't fool her one bit, arranging all of this just so she could
dispose of one stupid journalist for an *important friend*. There were a
hundred ways to kill a man, maybe more, and not one of them required
a fancy dress, with her tette pushed up to her chin and her breath
pressed out of her lungs. Nor did they require her to have dinner at a
fancy restaurant with John Torrio, the man all the Five Pointers called

the Fox. No, her brother had set this up because he didn't trust her yet. Torrio, or John, as he'd introduced himself, was nothing more than a nursemaid—though she doubted he'd appreciate being thought of as such. He was only there to keep an eye on her and to make sure she did what Paul had asked of her.

So what if a lady needed an escort to dine at a restaurant like Delmonico's? Killing a man in the middle of a crowded restaurant was a fool's errand. She could have killed him in the streets just as easily.

But Paul didn't want this Reynolds killed easily. Her brother was making a point. With so many witnesses, Viola would be forced to use her affinity—and in doing so, she would have to break the vow she had made to herself years ago. As long as she could get a clear view of this man, it would be easy enough to make it look like he'd died naturally, and with no obvious attack, it would be impossible for anyone to see the man's death as anything but a tragic misfortune. In the blink of an eye, Paul's friend would be rid of his little problem and Viola's soul would bear another black mark that could never be erased.

Even so, the act didn't require a fancy restaurant. Viola knew *exactly* what Paul was up to. It was no accident that he'd sent Torrio with her— her brother was matchmaking. His plan to marry her off had been the last straw to drive her away before. Now that she was back in the bosom of the family's control, he was testing her. The old goat he'd tried to tie her to the last time was probably dead by now, so it only made sense for Paul to try shackling her to the man he was grooming to be his second—all the better to keep them *both* under his control.

Out of the corner of her eye, Viola studied Torrio as they were shown to their table. He wasn't bad looking—a tall, striking boy from just outside Napoli with dark eyes and dark hair combed straight back from his face. He didn't have the characteristic crook in his nose that most who ran in the gangs wore as a badge of honor, but even dressed in a fancy dinner jacket, he didn't have Paul's polish. Torrio still looked like the streets.

And like all men, he walked through the world as though what he had in his pants was enough to make him a king. *But then,* she thought, watching Torrio snap out orders to the waitstaff, who all jumped to meet his demands, *maybe it is.*

Dinner was interminable. Viola tried to keep her mouth drawn into what she hoped was more smile than snarl as her escort droned on about all his accomplishments, but the task wore on her. He didn't stop his bragging to eat the first two courses. Instead he talked around the food in his mouth. When the steaks came, huge slices of meat that were dressed with herbed butter and creamed spinach, Torrio finally—thankfully—shut up.

Better he focus on his steak than continue to imagine that he had a chance with her. Men never took that news well, and she couldn't afford to maim or kill the guy when she was trying to convince Paul she could be trusted. He and Nibsy were planning something, and gaining Paul's trust was the first step in finding out what it was.

Viola shifted in her seat as she picked at her bloody steak and the gelatinous oysters, hating the entire situation she'd found herself in. The food was too rich for her, right along with everything else in the restaurant. Her whole life, she'd stuck close to what she knew—first her mother's kitchen and then the Strega, where she worked behind the bar, serving people of her own class and station. She had never really gone much farther than the streets of the Bowery, even when she left her family. But all around her, the dining room was filled with brilliantly white linen and gleaming crystal, candlelight and brightly polished silver. Delmonico's, with its gilded opulence, was evidence of how big the divide was between what she was and what the rest of the world held.

And the people . . . The men who could signal a waiter with a look instead of the roughly barked orders Torrio used and the ladies with their pretty manners and their tinkling, girlish voices all served to remind Viola of exactly *who* she was—and who she would never be. She hated them all almost as much as she hated the full corset biting into her skin and the ruffled flounce at her shoulders that pinned her arms down at her sides.

Worst of all, the longer they sat, the more she began to think that the entire evening had been pointless. Paul had been confident in the intelligence he had from his network of busboys and cooks that R. A. Reynolds dined at Delmonico's on Thursday nights at seven thirty. Reynolds always sat at the same table, a private corner booth, and Paul had arranged for Viola and Torrio to be seated at a table across the room with a clear view of the booth.

But seven thirty had come and gone, and there had been no sign of R. A. Reynolds or anyone else. The whole fiasco had been an absolute waste of time. As Torrio downed another glass of the expensive scotch that Paul was paying for and cut large pieces of beefsteak to shovel into his mouth, Viola picked at her food and counted the moments until she could go home and take off the ridiculous dress.

It was close to eight when a flurry of commotion erupted behind them. Viola turned to look and saw that a young couple had just arrived. They weren't much older than Viola herself, but they were clearly favorites. The girl, especially, seemed to know almost everyone, because she stopped and chatted at nearly every table they passed.

In a sea of lavish gowns, the girl stood out like a peacock among pigeons. She was dressed in a gown that looked, even to Viola, who knew very little about such trivial things, *expensive*. It was perfectly tailored to the girl's lithe body, and its color—a light blush that matched the flush of the girl's cheeks—would have looked ridiculously frivolous on anyone with less confidence. Instead, the pink hue only served to accent the glow of the girl's creamy skin and the dark fringe of lashes around her eyes.

She was as slender and delicate looking as a reed, with polished fingertips that had clearly never seen a day's worth of work. Her blond hair had just a touch of copper when the candlelight hit it, and the long, graceful column of her neck was ringed with a simple strand of pearls

LISA MAXWELL

that lay against the fragile notch at the base of her throat.

Her skin would be soft there, fragile and fragrant with whatever scent she wears. Lilies, maybe . . . or roses . . . something floral and as pink as she is.

Viola's cheeks felt warm suddenly, as she realized the direction her thoughts had gone. She'd been staring openly. She glanced at Torrio to make sure he hadn't noticed, but he was still busy shoveling the last of his potatoes into his mouth. Confident he wasn't paying her any attention, she allowed herself one more peek at the girl. At the very moment Viola looked up, the girl's eyes met hers. Dark blue, the color the sea had been in the middle of the Atlantic, and just as dangerous.

Viola looked away as a wave of shame crashed over her—it had been only a few weeks since she had lost Tilly, and there she was, so easily distracted by a girl whose every breath screamed of wealth that Viola could never begin to dream of. And to be distracted *here*, of all places, when she was clearly being watched by her brother's escort?

Merda. If Paul heard of it . . .

She knew exactly what would happen if Paul heard of it. He'd make sure Viola was either married or dead, because everyone knew her soul was already too blackened for the convent.

But Torrio hadn't noticed the entrance of the couple or the direction of Viola's thoughts. As he signaled the waiter for yet another drink, Viola couldn't help herself. She chanced one more peek at the girl just in time to see the maître d' pull back the curtain to open a private booth—the Reynolds booth—and let the couple in. The girl had already disappeared behind the velvet curtains, but her escort had stopped to speak with the maître d'.

Viola didn't allow herself to wonder about the way her heart sank the moment the girl was out of sight. Her focus was on the girl's escort, R. A. Reynolds. The man she was supposed to kill.

Viola pulled on her affinity and sent it outward, searching for the link to this R. A. Reynolds across the room. She found him easily, his heartbeat steady like the ticking of a clock, pulsing nearly in time with her own.

She could do this. It would be so easy to simply slow the flow of blood, to call to that living part of him and command it, to *stop* it.

Why should she care that Reynolds was so young?

Why should she care that he looked the maître d' in the eye when he spoke to him—as though they were old friends? Or that the girl in the booth would have to witness her escort crumpling into a lifeless heap?

She shouldn't care. She *didn't*.

Who was this Reynolds to her? Un pezzo grosso. A rich boy living off his father's money and name who had never worked—had never *slaved*—a day in his life. His hands would not have calluses beneath the gloves he wore. His stomach had never known the carving pain of true hunger. There were a hundred more like him, each less important than the one before. The world wouldn't miss this one.

Still, Viola hesitated.

She'd killed many times before, and her soul was, surely, already stained beyond reckoning with the blood of her victims. It *shouldn't* have mattered.

Viola was still staring at the velvet curtain of the booth long after the man had disappeared behind it and the tether she'd had to the steady beating of his heart went slack.

Torrio's foot nudged hers beneath the table. "That's them, ain't it?" Torrio asked. "Why didn't you . . . ?" He waggled his fingers at her.

Yes . . . why didn't I? Viola realized that Torrio was looking at her, his dark eyes sharp and far too suspicious. She'd just done exactly what Paul had been afraid of—she'd missed her opportunity to take out Reynolds when she could have. Now he was behind the velvet curtain, hidden from her sight and out of reach of her affinity.

"Paul didn't tell me Reynolds dined with other people," she told him, trying to pull herself back together. It was a feeble excuse, and the look on Torrio's face told her that he suspected what had happened. "I was thrown off by the other one."

"The girl?" Torrio's brows drew together.

"She's a witness," Viola said, knowing that the excuse was ridiculous. A witness to what? It wasn't like her magic could be seen.

"So take her out too," Torrio said with a shrug. "What do you care?"

"I don't," she lied. "But Paul might. We don't know who she is. What if she's the daughter of someone important? It could cause a lot of problems for Paul, killing the wrong person."

"It'll cause more problems if you don't take care of the *right* person. You had a clear shot there."

"It's not so simple."

He frowned as though he could see straight through the lie to the truth of her, and for a moment Viola wondered if he knew what she'd been thinking—if he understood the real reason for her hesitation.

Torrio leaned forward, his elbows on the table and his expression menacing. "Well, what are we supposed to do now?"

"We wait?" she offered, even though the last thing she wanted to do was spend another minute sitting across from Torrio in that oppressive restaurant. "Maybe the girl will leave. Or maybe it would be better to go."

"You want to go?" Torrio's brows flew up. "That ain't happening. This gets done tonight. We can do it your way and make your brother happy, or we can do it mine, and you can deal with Paul later," he told Viola, his tone sharp.

"No," she said, backtracking. She knew full well what was at risk if Paul was unhappy. "I only meant that we could wait and catch them outside. We don't know when they'll come out of there, and if we stay too much longer, we're gonna draw attention."

Torrio frowned. "We'll wait a little while longer." Then he barked at a passing waiter to get him another drink, and as he waited for it, he studied her from across the table. For most of the dinner, he'd ignored her, but now Viola felt the full weight of his perceptiveness. She could see exactly why Paul had selected Torrio and why Paul was also stupid for trusting him. It didn't matter that fancy ladies uptown prized the soft fur of the fox—Viola knew well enough that foxes were just overgrown rats.

"It must sting," Torrio said, leaning back in his chair.

Viola didn't take the bait his comment was intended to be.

"Being back under your brother's thumb, I mean."

"I know what you meant," she said, leveling her gaze at him so he would know she didn't care.

Amusement flickered across his expression, but on Torrio it only made him look like he was up to something. "What was it like working for the zoppo?"

Viola's skin felt hot, and she was struggling to keep her temper from erupting. But Torrio kept pushing.

"I hear Dolph let you lead him around like a dog on a chain."

"You mean like Paul leads you?" she retorted, keeping her voice flat, bored.

Her words hit their mark. Torrio's mouth twisted with a look of utter disgust.

"At least I wouldn't let a boy get the best of me."

"What boy?" Viola said.

"You didn't know?" Torrio laughed. "The one with the occhiali."

"Nibsy?" she said, and the moment the boy's name was past her lips, it felt like the first time she'd cut herself on Libitina's blade. At first she'd felt nothing at all, and then the bite of pain began to throb and ache. It was like that now. Numbness followed by a sharp, cutting pain.

But it made sense—the way Nibsy had taken over the Strega when the rest of them had been too shocked, too broken, to do more than make it through the next day. The way he'd attacked Esta on the bridge. Of *course* it had been Nibsy.

Dolph couldn't have known, and yet Viola didn't doubt that he had suspected. He'd been even more guarded in the weeks before the Khafre Hall job. He'd pulled away from her, but she hadn't been the one to betray him. If Torrio spoke the truth, it had been Nibsy.

"Face it, Viola. You chose the wrong man to follow. Dolph was as weak as his leg. Or maybe it wasn't only his leg that was weak, eh?" He leaned toward her as he laughed.

LISA MAXWELL

Her temper snapping, Viola reached for her steak knife, but Torrio didn't notice. His attention had been drawn by something else, and he jerked his chin, signaling her to look. "She's leaving."

The girl in the blush-colored gown had just exited the booth. "Where's she going?" Viola asked, balling her hand into a fist so she wouldn't take the knife and teach him the lesson he deserved.

"How should I know? But this is your chance," Torrio told her.

"My chance for what? Reynolds is still behind the curtains," she told him.

"Then you should get your pretty little ass behind the curtains too," he said, the impatience clear in his voice.

"You think nobody's gonna notice if I just walk into a private booth and leave a dead man when I walk out? You're pazzo, Johnny. Stupid and crazy."

Torrio ignored her use of the nickname. "I've been called worse, cara. Too bad I'm also the one in charge right now. I'll create a diversion," he told her. "I'll make sure nobody in this room is looking at you when you get close to Reynolds' booth."

"That is a terrible idea," Viola said through clenched teeth.

"It's not an idea. It's an order." John Torrio leaned over the table again. "Unless you want me to tell Paul that you aren't going to work out, you don't really have a choice in the matter. Now *go*."

Viola wanted nothing more than to spit at him. But she was dressed as a lady, so she decided to act the part. Letting her affinity unfurl, she found the slow beating of his heart, and she tugged—just a little. Torrio gasped, and Viola answered his strangled breath with a sharp-toothed smile.

"We need to get something clear, Johnny." She lowered her voice until it was the throaty purr that she knew men liked. "I *always* have a choice. For instance, I could choose to take your life right now, you miserable excuse for a man, but I won't because I promised my brother, and I've chosen my family. Now, I'm gonna do what you say, but not because I have to. Not because you talk to me like I'm no better than some dog.

I'm gonna go take care of Reynolds because right now I don't want to look at your ugly face no more. And once I'm done, I'm gonna tell my brother to keep you the hell away from me."

With a swish of her silken skirts, she released her hold on Torrio's life and started to walk toward the booth. It was a risk, she knew, turning her back on a rat like Torrio, especially after she'd embarrassed him. She wasn't so stupid as to think that he wasn't carrying a gun or to believe that he wasn't crazy enough to shoot her here, in front of the entire world and the reporter they were supposed to kill, just to prove what a man he was. But even if she had to lower herself to wallow in the muck of her brother's dealings, she wasn't ever going to crawl. Not for someone as pathetic as Johnny the Fox.

She took her time making her way past the white-topped tables glowing with candlelight and filled with the stomach-turning scents of roasted meat. But the sight of the rare beefsteaks only reminded her of flesh and of the life she was about to take. Of the promise to herself she was about to break.

REASONABLE

1904—St. Louis

Esta clawed her way back to consciousness, scrabbling up through the murky darkness that had pulled her under. Slowly, she became aware of the rattling movement of her seat. Vaguely, she realized that she wasn't alone. Her head was cushioned by a warm lap, and someone's fingers were gently stroking the hair at her temples. *Harte.*

Not again . . .

Swatting away his hand, she struggled to sit up.

"Careful," Harte said when she bobbled. His hands caught her before she could tumble over onto him, but she pulled away. She could damn well sit up on her own.

"What happened?" she asked as she rubbed at her eyes, blinking away the last of the darkness as she willed her vision to clear. She remembered the strange events in the ballroom and escaping the hotel, but the last thing she recalled was her vision fading behind a heavy fog of inky black and a sense that the world itself was flying apart. And then . . . nothing.

"You fainted," he told her. "Again. Don't worry, though. I managed to get us away safely while you took your little nap." But the lightness of his words didn't mask the worry in his voice. "You can show your appreciation later."

She bristled. She didn't need his worry. Didn't want it either. "In your dreams," she said, shooting him a dark look.

But he didn't throw back a reply, as she'd expected him to. Outside the carriage, lightning flickered, illuminating the planes of his face and exposing the concern in his eyes. A few moments later, farther off now, thunder rumbled, echoing in the distance. When the sound faded, the carriage descended into an uneasy silence.

"For a minute back there, I thought I'd lost you," Harte said softly.

"I'm fine," she said, brushing aside the emotion in his voice. She did not tell him that for a minute she had felt lost. That there was something about the darkness—the absoluteness of it—that made her think that if it gained too much ground, there wouldn't be any going back.

His eyes were steady. "You're lying."

The certainty in his voice struck a nerve. "I'll stop when you do."

Esta made sure that Harte was the first one to look away.

"Those people in the ballroom," she said, testing the silence that had grown between them.

"The Antistasi?" Harte said, frowning. "If that's who they were . . ."

"I've never seen anything like that," she told him. When she'd seen the first figure appear, the one dressed in red, she'd been shocked, but as more appeared, she'd felt a thrill coursing through her blood that she'd only ever felt before she lifted a diamond or cleaned out a safe.

"They're a damn menace," Harte said darkly.

"What?" She turned to look at him, confused. "They were *amazing*. The way they stood up to the police and the Guard."

"They were performing," he said, his tone skeptical. "That was a show."

She shrugged. "Well, at least they weren't cowering or hiding what they were."

"They were using *your* name," he said.

She crossed her arms and tried to figure out what his problem was. "I thought you didn't even like the name."

"I don't. But whether I like it isn't the point," he said, clearly frustrated. "Look at how easily Julien recognized you, Esta. What if other people recognize you as this Devil's Thief too? If these Antistasi are using your name, it means that more people will be looking for you. It makes everything we have to do more dangerous."

He was right. She knew he was right, and yet the sight of those four women, strong and powerful and *unafraid*? They'd sparked some small fire in Esta. She'd been running and hiding for so long—her whole life, covering up who and what she was. To have that kind of freedom? She would gladly take the danger that went along with it.

"Well, I think these Antistasi, whoever they might be, are admirable," Esta said. "If magic's illegal, like Julien told us, they're at least trying to do something."

"That's what I'm afraid of." Harte looked like he was about to say something more, but the carriage was slowing. "We can argue later," he said, peering out of the window as the cab rattled to a stop. "We're here, and I don't have any money to pay for this taxi. We're going to have to run for it—if you're feeling up to it?"

Esta gave him a scornful look. "*Thief*, remember?" She slipped a wallet from the inside pocket of her stolen jacket.

"In the ballroom?" he asked.

"I figured we'd need it eventually," she told him, giving him a couple of damp bills.

While Harte handed over the money and made sure that the driver forgot them, Esta dashed for an overhang to get out of the rain, and to prove to him—and to herself—that she could.

The lightning was more sporadic now, and the rain itself seemed to be slowing, but Harte was still damp by the time he made it to where she had propped herself against a wall to catch her breath. As he approached, she straightened a little to hide just how unsteady her legs actually felt, but from the expression on his face, she knew he understood.

Her hair had fallen, wet and lank, around her face, and Harte reached to brush one of the sodden clumps back. He let his hand cup her cheek, and for a second she forgot how annoyed she'd been with him and marveled at the warmth of his fingertips. She considered closing the distance between them to prove just how okay she was.

A step closer and it would be so easy to press her mouth against his, to let herself go. So much had happened in the last two days. So much had changed in the last two years. Esta only wanted one moment in the stretch of their past and future to put aside all that lay ahead—to forget the sacrifice she would make to ensure that *this* future, the one where magic was illegal and Guardsmen hunted Mageus, wouldn't be the one that lasted.

Harte pulled back from her, and the possibility that had been between them evaporated into the humid air of the summer night.

"We need to find somewhere to get dry," he told her, tucking his hands back into his pockets and making it clear that he hadn't felt the same as she had. "Your skin is like ice."

They found a boardinghouse a few blocks farther into the neighborhood. It was a run-down, semi-attached building about three blocks from King's Saloon. The matron who answered the door was dressed in a clean, plain shift, and her gray hair was tucked away under a dark kerchief. At first she eyed them suspiciously, her gaze lingering on Esta's disheveled hair and the suit she was wearing, but when Esta produced a stack of bills from the stolen wallet, the woman's eyes lit. She waved them inside and didn't ask any questions or bother with their names.

There was only one room left, the woman told them, leading them up the dark, narrow staircase and opening a door at the top. It was small, with a narrow bed and a desk with a rickety chair. A second chair stood near a squat stove in the corner. It certainly wasn't the plush luxury they'd had at the Jefferson, but at least it seemed clean. *Sort of.* The coverlet on the bed was stained, but the linens seemed to be freshly washed and the furniture was free from dust and grime.

The woman lit a small fire in the stove before she left them alone, closing the door behind her.

"We need to get you warmed up," Harte said.

"I'm fine," she said, trying to hold herself still so he wouldn't see her shivering.

"You're *not* fine, and it's only going to get worse if you don't get those wet clothes off." He went to her and helped slip the wet dinner jacket from her shoulders before she could argue. Turning his back to give her some privacy, he draped her jacket over the edge of the second chair and moved it so the warmth of the meager fire could dry it out. "Give me the rest."

"Harte," she warned.

"I won't look," he told her before she could argue any more.

She didn't really care, but it was clear he wasn't going to give in, so she unbuttoned the shirt she was wearing and took it off. She rolled it in a ball and threw it at the back of his head. "There."

"The pants, too, and then get into bed," he told her.

"We're supposed to be meeting Julien soon," she argued. But he was right about her clothes. They felt clammy and uncomfortable, so she stepped out of the soaked pants.

"*We're* not doing anything. You're going to stay here and warm your-self up before you end up sick. I'll go meet Julien alone."

His words chilled her faster than the rain had. "Excuse me?"

He turned then. "You heard me, Esta."

"You are *not* going without me," she said, but as she took a step toward him, her legs went out from under her.

He rushed to catch her before she hit the ground. "How are you plan-ning to meet Julien when you can barely keep yourself upright?"

"Get off," she said, and he let her go willingly and watched her stagger back from him. "I'm fine. I'm going with you."

"Esta, please. You have to be reasonable."

"*Reasonable?*" she said, not caring about the edge in her tone.

He didn't move any closer. "You need to rest."

"I should be there too," she argued. She took a step toward him and then another, testing her own strength. "I *need* to be there."

"Why?" he asked. "Unless you still don't trust me."

She wasn't sure how to answer that. She did—or she wanted to.

He pulled away from her. "There are people looking for you," he reminded her. "Those people in the ballroom didn't help with that."

"They think the Devil's Thief is a *girl*," she reminded him.

"A pair of trousers doesn't make you look any less like a girl." Harte let out a ragged breath when she glared at him. "Look at you," he said, pointing at her. "Your hair is . . ." His voice faltered. He started again. "And your eyes . . ."

"What about my eyes?" she asked, narrowing them at him.

"They're *pretty!*" he gasped in exasperation.

"They're just eyes, Harte."

"And you . . . your . . ." He waved his hand in the general direction of her whole body.

"My what?" She glared at him.

He groaned with frustration, his cheeks and the tips of his ears pink. "Look. *Please.* Just let me do this. I can run over to King's and wait for Julien. He should be bringing the stone with him," he said, and before she could interrupt, he added, "You can be here, warm. *Resting.* Getting stronger, so we can leave town before anything else happens."

"For the last time, I don't need to re—"

"Please," he said softly before she could finish. "*I* need you to. You saw what the Antistasi are capable of tonight. You saw the police and the Guard. We have no idea what might be waiting for us out there, and I can't keep you safe when you can hardly stay on your feet right now."

Esta flinched at the emotion behind his words. "It's not your job to keep me safe. I'm not some liability, Harte."

"I never said you were."

"You just did," she told him, not bothering to disguise the hurt and anger in her voice. "We're supposed to be in this together."

"We *are.*" He picked up the pants she'd left on the floor. "But this time, for once, just stay put and let me handle it." And without another word, he scooped up the rest of the damp garments she'd taken off—the only clothing that she had—and walked out the door.

KING'S SALOON

1904—St. Louis

Harte was nearly a block away from the boardinghouse when he realized what he'd just done. Esta was going to murder him—or worse—and he would deserve every bit of it.

When they'd first arrived at the boardinghouse, he hadn't intended to leave her there, but she looked so miserable and tired that he thought it would be better for her to rest. When he turned and saw her half-dressed, though, he had to get away. With her hair falling around her face like some sea nymph come to the surface to tempt him, the power inside of him urged him to go to her.

Or maybe he couldn't blame that impulse *entirely* on the Book. It had felt a little like the first time he'd seen her, that night at the Haymarket, when he'd found himself walking toward her even before he understood what he was doing. *That* particular decision had earned him a sore tongue, so he didn't trust his instincts one bit where Esta was concerned.

Nor would he let himself become some puppet for whatever was living inside of him. Not as long as he could fight it. If the voice was telling him to go to Esta, to let himself have her, then he would do the opposite.

But in truth, he'd left her there because he was a coward. And he probably could have used her at King's. After all, he hadn't been the one to notice the police at the hotel, and he doubted he'd be able to pick any out at King's, should they be waiting.

When Harte stepped into the saloon, there was no sign of Julien. He ordered a drink at the bar and found a table in the corner to wait—and to watch.

King's was about half the size of the Bella Strega, the bar Dolph Saunders had owned back in the Bowery. Like the Strega, smoke hung thick in the overwarm air and the customers crowded at the bar or around tables, hunched over their glasses as though the whiskey they had ordered would run off if they didn't stay watchful. But the Strega was always filled with the comforting warmth of magic, and that energy had marked Dolph's bar as a safe space for Mageus like Harte.

There was a different sort of magic floating through the air in King's Saloon—a jolt of energy that had nothing to do with the old magic Harte had an affinity for. This magic came from the notes of an upright piano in the corner, where a man wore a porkpie hat pushed back to reveal a wide forehead and a face completely enthralled by the song he was playing. Harte had heard the bouncing melodies of ragtime tunes before, but this man's fingers flew over the ivory keys with a trembling intensity like nothing Harte had ever experienced. When the man hit the song's minor chords, Harte felt their dissonance vibrate down into the very core of himself, stirring something he hadn't known was there. He wasn't the only one affected—on the tiny dance floor, couples swayed close together, driven by the moody chords and compelling rhythm, their bodies intimately intertwined.

Twenty minutes passed, maybe more, but each time the saloon's front door banged open, it wasn't Julien. The meager chunk of ice in Harte's drink had long since melted. Esta would be waiting, and she'd be mad enough as it was without Harte spending even more time. Maybe something had gone wrong—maybe Julien had gotten himself caught up with the Jefferson Guard or maybe Harte hadn't given the right suggestion.

Or maybe the Book interfered with my affinity, just as it did with Esta's.

But he shook off that thought. He felt fine, and in some ways his affinity felt even clearer and stronger than ever. Still, as the moments ticked by, Harte started to think that if Julien were coming, he would have arrived already.

Nearly an hour past the time when Julien should have arrived, Harte gave up and drank the now-warm whiskey, wincing as it burned down his throat. As a rule, he hated hard liquor—hated the way it made his head foggy and his reflexes sluggish—but he had a feeling he'd need some fortification for whatever Esta dished out when he went back to the boardinghouse. He was already on his feet, gathering his still-damp coat to leave, when the door opened once more and Julien appeared, silhouetted by the streetlight behind him.

Julien Eltinge entered the barroom the same way he'd entered the stage earlier that night—like someone who knew he was born to command attention. It wasn't that he made any fuss—the door didn't slam, and he didn't do anything obvious to draw attention to his arrival—but the energy in the air seemed to shift, and the entire barroom felt it.

Though he probably saw Harte immediately, Julien didn't come over right away. Instead, he took his time circulating through the room, shaking every hand that reached out to greet him, and then accepted a drink from the barkeeper, downing it in a single swallow. It wasn't an accident, Harte knew. Julien was making it clear whose turf they were on and who was going to take the lead.

Which was fine with Harte. He could just feel the whiskey starting to soften the world, and he needed a moment to gather his wits. When Julien finally decided to approach Harte's table, Harte got to his feet just long enough to greet him with a handshake.

Julien took the chair across from him without being asked and called for the bartender to bring another round of drinks. "I still can't believe you're here. Harte Darrigan, back from the dead and come to haunt me," he said, chuckling.

"Like I said, Jules, I was in Europe, not dead."

"You were gone an awfully long time." Though Julien's words were neutral, his expression held an unspoken question and, more worrisome, doubt.

"The tour was going well, and we found we liked European sensibilities," Harte told him, trying to keep his tone easy and carefree. "You know how it is when you find an audience. You milk them while you can. But eventually the money dried up, like it always does. I got tired of the scenery, so here we are."

"I'm surprised you came back at all." Julien eyed him. "It was a risk, considering who you're traveling with—the Devil's Thief."

"Don't start with that again," he said testily. After the strange women who'd appeared in the ballroom, he'd had enough of the Devil's Thief nonsense. "She has a name, you know."

"Yes," Julien said, studying Harte as though trying to determine the truth of his story. "There are plenty of people who are aware of her name."

Despite the way the whiskey was making him feel loose, Harte met Julien's gaze steadily. After a moment Julien seemed to relent. He pulled a case of cigars from his inside pocket and offered one to Harte. When Harte waved him off with a polite refusal, Julien shrugged.

"Your loss." He cupped his hand around the end of the thick cigar, inhaling as he held a match to its end to light it. Taking a couple of deep puffs, Julien leaned back in his chair, the picture of confidence as the bartender delivered their drinks. But there was still a question in his eyes. "We both know you're not really here to talk about your European holiday," Julien said.

Harte's unease grew, but he put on a mask of outward calm. "Not really, Jules."

"I didn't think so. From the company you're keeping these days, I'd be surprised if you weren't wrapped up in something big." He let his words trail off, allowing Harte an opening.

Harte didn't take it. *Just give me the stone, already.* "Look, Jules, I'd rather not have to lie to an old friend—"

Julien shrugged. "It wouldn't be the first time."

"Maybe I've turned over a new leaf," Harte said, with a calmness meant to mask his nerves.

Julien huffed out his contempt at that sentiment. "Like hell you have,

Darrigan. I know you too well to believe *you* could change."

"Maybe you knew me," Harte said gently. "But it's been an awful long time." It had been even longer for Julien, who hadn't had two years pass by in a matter of seconds. "Can we just leave it that there are some things you're better off not knowing?"

Julien studied him a moment longer, puffing out acrid clouds of yellowish smoke from the cigar clamped between his teeth. After a long, thoughtful moment, the corners of his mouth hitched up, and he let out a rusty-sounding laugh. "It's always something with you, isn't it, Darrigan? All the times I tried to take you under my wing and show you how *not* to get yourself in trouble, and here we are again."

"Did you really expect anything less from me, Jules?"

"Tell me this much, at least—is it the girl?" Julien asked.

"It usually is a girl, isn't it?" Harte said, trying to make light of Julien's question.

Julien's mouth kicked up at the joke. Then he leaned forward, his gaze darting around the room, as though concerned that someone might overhear. But his eyes glinted with mischief, and for a moment Harte could see in them the Julien he'd once known—the old friend who smiled his way through a fistfight and then walked into a barroom with his shoulders back and his head up just to prove no one could keep him down.

"Tell me straight, Darrigan," Julien said in low tones. "Did she do it? The train, I mean . . ."

Any warmth he might have felt drained away, and Harte was suddenly aware of the cold dampness of his clothes and the danger of the situation. "Esta had nothing to do with attacking any train. And if you ever knew me at all, you'll know I'm telling you the truth about that."

Julien stared at him as though considering what he'd just said. Finally, he sat up straight, a knowing look in his eyes as he clamped the cigar between his teeth again. "Because we were friends once, I'm willing to believe you . . . for now. But I'll tell you this—as a friend—if she *is* planning on causing some kind of problem here, especially at the Exposition, you'd best steer clear. The mood in the city right now? It's not good. With all the outsiders, there's been rumblings about Antistasi causing problems."

"What's the deal with them, anyway?" Harte asked. "I've never heard of them before."

"They're a fairly recent phenomenon," Julien explained. "Until the Act passed last year, Mageus hadn't been much of a problem outside New York. Everyone assumed that the Brink had taken care of them, but once the Act went into effect, the Antistasi started causing trouble *outside* the city. It got bad here in St. Louis when they were trying to build the grounds of the Exposition. A lot of people died."

"The Antistasi killed people?" Harte asked, his stomach twisting. It was one thing to dress up and set off smoke packets, but murder was something else entirely.

Julien nodded. "Last fall was the worst. Back in October, not long after the Act went into full effect, there was a major attack on the building crews of the Exposition. They used some kind of fog that ate up a good part of Lafayette Park. People who saw it from the outside said it was like a living thing—you could *feel* the evil coming off it—and the people who got trapped in it lost their minds. Masons destroyed walls they'd just built, electricians set fire to half a block of buildings, and fights—*nasty*, deadly fights—broke out between people who were friends. When the fog finally lifted, the whole area was covered in ice. People had frostbite—they lost fingers and toes—and water mains all over the site had burst. It set everything back months and nearly caused the Exposition to delay opening. The Antistasi claimed credit for it."

Harte's awareness was prickling. The people in the Jefferson had used the same sort of thing for their little performance in the ballroom. He hadn't stuck around long enough to see what the effect of it would be, but he'd felt the cold magic in that room. From what Julien was saying, they might have escaped more than they'd realized.

Harte had met plenty of Mageus in New York, but he'd never heard of anyone using a fog. Magic—true magic—didn't need any trick to make it work. It was just a connection with the very essence of the world itself. Now, ritual magic—*corrupt* magic—that was something different. Ritual magic was about separation. It was a breaking apart of the elements of existence in order to control them instead of working within their connections.

Ritual magic—like what the Order did when they'd created the Brink and what Dolph had done when he'd created the marks worn by the Devil's Own—always came with a price.

"Did they ever catch the people who did it—these Antistasi?" Harte asked.

Julien shook his head. "No. The Antistasi are damn good at evading capture. But ever since the attack last October, the Jefferson Guard was given as much authority as the actual police to stop them," he said. "If your girl is here to cause problems, she's going to have a hell of a time trying to get away after. The police and the Jefferson Guard both . . . none of them are taking any chances. Not with the world watching the Exposition."

"Esta's not here to cause any trouble," Harte told him, which was nearly the truth. Esta certainly wasn't an Antistasi or any other kind of anarchist. They just needed the necklace, and once they had it, they'd be gone.

"I guess I'll have to take your word for it," Julien said. "Where is the minx anyway?"

"I left her behind at our hotel. Told her to stay put," Harte said gruffly, inwardly glad that Esta wasn't there to hear him. But it was easier this way, to speak Julien's language—and to pretend that he had some actual control over the situation. In reality, the idea of anyone being able to control Esta was laughable. "I thought we could handle this between the two of us old friends."

"Ah," Julien said, stubbing out his cigar in the ashtray. "So we come to it at last . . . *old friend.*"

Harte shrugged. "You said yourself that I wasn't here to talk about my European vacation."

"I know this is about the package you sent me a couple years back," Julien said darkly. "That necklace."

Something about Julien's tone put Harte on edge. "So it is," he said carefully.

"When I got the damn thing, I told myself that it would come back to bite me." Julien leaned his elbows on the table. "The second I got the package and that ridiculous note of yours, I told myself, 'This is going to be trouble.' I wanted to send it back, but by then, I'd already heard about your leap from the bridge. I thought about just tossing it, but I couldn't bring myself to do that, either."

"I can solve that problem right now by taking it off your hands once and for all," Harte said easily.

"Don't I wish," Julien told him, more agitated now. "I'd like nothing better than to give the blasted thing back to you, but I can't."

"Of course you can," Harte said, urging him on.

But Julien was shaking his head, and Harte had the sinking feeling that he wasn't going to like what Julien had to say next.

"I don't have it," Julien told him, and at least he had the grace to look embarrassed.

Before Harte could say another word, a voice broke through the music and noise of the barroom. "What do you mean, you *don't have it?*"

Harte looked up, knowing already who would be standing there, knowing before his eyes took in the rumpled, dirty coat and the wide-brimmed hat that Esta would be glaring down at him. But he wasn't ready for how she looked or what she'd done to herself.

"Well, well," Julien said as he took her in, head to toe. He tossed a sardonic look Harte's way, and he knew Julien was laughing at him. "So much for telling her to stay put."

UNEXPECTED

1902—New York

Viola made her way across the restaurant toward the private booth where R. A. Reynolds waited, shoring up her resolve for what she was about to do. It wasn't that she was squeamish. She'd taken lives before and had still found a way to live with herself, but the men she had killed in the past had deserved their deaths, as much as anyone could deserve such a thing. At the very least, those men had each had a fighting chance, because she'd used skill, not magic. She hadn't taken a life with her affinity since she was just a child, back when she'd believed that duty to family was more important than her own soul. Before she'd understood that she was more than the blood that ran in her veins.

She knew what those in the Bowery believed about her—that she could kill without touching them. It was true enough, but she'd used their fear of her and her affinity as armor. She killed, yes, but only those who preyed on the weak. And she killed not with what she was—what her god had made her to be—but from choice and practiced skill. She killed with a blade.

But her favorite blade was in the hands of a traitor. All she had left was herself.

Her own heartbeat felt unsteady as she drew closer to the booth. She didn't know what Torrio would ultimately do—whether he would create a diversion, as he'd said, or whether he would attack her for what she'd done to him. But when she was only a few steps away from the velvet draperies that hid Reynolds from the prying eyes of the other diners, she heard Torrio erupt behind her.

"I asked for scotch, damn you!" he shouted.

Viola glanced over her shoulder just in time to see him throw a glass of scotch into the face of one of the waiters. With the eyes of the restaurant on the scene he was making, Viola took her chance and slipped behind the curtain of the booth.

The man in the small private dining room looked up from his soup, and Viola saw the moment when expectation became confusion.

"Yes?" he asked. "Can I help you?"

He has a nice face.

It was a ridiculous thought. She could see from across the room that Reynolds was a handsome man, but here in the muffled intimacy of the private dining booth, she saw that he had the kind of face that would grow old well.

"Are you Reynolds?"

"Excuse me?" The brows drew together, but there was no threat in his expression. Only interest.

"Are you R. A. Reynolds?" she repeated more slowly.

The man's face went blank, and he leaned forward in his seat. "Who is it that's asking?"

His confidence told the story of who he was. From his fine suit jacket to the look of boredom on his face, it was clear that this Reynolds came from money. He was no better than the rest of them, no better than the people in the dining room whose lives were so far above Viola's that she could barely imagine them.

She *could* kill him, she realized. It wouldn't really be so hard to let her affinity find the blood pumping in his veins again and stop it. Just as she'd healed her mother's gout, she could fell him in an instant, and no one would know. One less rich boy to grow into a rich man. One less danger for her kind in the future. She was already damned—what would one more mark on her soul matter in the end?

But there was a warmth in the way he was looking at her that made her hesitate.

"Is there something I can help you with?" he asked, and his expression didn't at all have the cool disinterest that most of his class carried.

"I come with a message," she said, stalking toward him.

"I see," he said, eyeing her as she approached. If he sensed the danger she posed to him, he didn't show it. "And who, exactly, is this message from?"

"Unimportant." She reached for the knife tucked into the folds of her gown even as she moved closer to him. "But he's a dangerous man. An important man in this city."

"Ah," the man said, and now a spark of humor glinted in his eyes. "I suppose you've come to warn me off."

Viola frowned, thrown by his response. He was not reacting the way he should. Perhaps because he didn't realize that Death could wear a woman's skirts.

"I imagine this is about the column in the *Herald*," he said, sounding more bored than concerned. "Let me guess. If I don't stop looking for trouble, trouble will find me, or some such thing?" He smiled at her, and she knew she had been right. The way his eyes crinkled at the corners, the dimple that softened his left cheek—as an old man, he would wear the traces of his happiness.

But he would not make it that far.

In a flash, Viola closed the distance between them and had her blade out at his throat. But he didn't so much as flinch. "I don't think you understand," she told him.

"Oh, I understand perfectly." The man's eyes met hers calmly. He was pazzo, this one, with a knife to his throat and not a worry on his face. "You intend to kill me to keep me from writing more columns that anger your employer, whoever that may be."

"You don't believe I'll kill you right here and now?" She pressed the tip of the knife in until it dented the skin just above the large vein that runs down the neck. Any more pressure and he'd be dead before anyone could help him.

He glanced at the blade poised at his throat and then back at her. "On the contrary," he said softly, "I'm quite convinced you could kill me. Though I'm a little surprised at the knife, to be honest. A gun would do the job just as easily, and there would be less chance of a mistake."

Viola glared at him. "With a knife, I never make a mistake."

The man seemed even more amused at this. "Still, I would advise against killing me right now. It wouldn't have the effect you're intending."

Confused, Viola pulled back. "And why is that?"

She heard the click of a pistol's hammer at the same time a woman's voice spoke: "Because he's not R. A. Reynolds."

Viola drew in a sharp breath and, keeping her knife pointed at the man's throat, she turned to find the girl in pink leveling a pistol steadily at her. The way the girl stood, confident and sure of the weapon in her hand, Viola knew she wasn't bluffing.

"I suppose that's who you've come looking for?" the girl asked, keeping the gun trained on Viola as she stepped closer.

"Yes," Viola said, considering her options. With the gun aimed at her, the hammer already back and ready to fire, she was trapped. She was accurate and deadly with a knife, but she wasn't faster than the bullet would be.

She could still kill them. A flare of magic and her affinity could snuff their lives as easily as a candle. "I have a message for R. A. Reynolds."

"They always do," the girl said, her airy tone more bored than truly annoyed. "I'm surprised your employer didn't do his homework—I'm assuming it's a him. Men with fewer brains than balls usually underestimate me."

The girl's brash words didn't match the flounce of silk or delicate air she had about her. "You?" Viola asked, trying to make sense of the girl's meaning as she let her affinity flare out into the room. She found the man easily, his familiar heartbeat steady and slow, and then the girl's, which was just as steady. But even as steady as it was, Viola could sense the satisfaction—and excitement—coursing through the girl's blood.

She'd assumed that the girl was nothing more than a bit of fluff, a pretty thing to amuse Reynolds, but she'd been wrong. *This one, she's more than she seems.*

"Yes," the girl said. "You see, he's not R. A. Reynolds. *I* am."

"You are the newspaperman?" Viola asked, forgetting her focus and letting her affinity go cold again.

"Do I look like a man?" the girl asked, her pink lips curving into a mocking smile.

Viola glanced between the man and the girl in frustration.

"I'm afraid she's telling the truth," the man said cheerfully, the point of the knife still pressed against his throat.

"Who are you?" the girl asked, leveling the gun in Viola's direction. "Who sent you?"

Viola could only stare, awed at the girl's confidence and shamed by her own shortsightedness. She had assumed that R. A. Reynolds was a man. She who knew well enough what it meant to do a man's work in a man's world, and all the while to do it better than most. She'd been a fool. And now she was trapped, because she knew then that she would never be able to take this particular girl's life.

"I asked you a question," the girl said, her eyes steady and her expression serious. "Let's see. It's usually Tammany and their goons making threats, but with my most recent column, I suspect it might be someone from the Order. I can't imagine they would have enjoyed that piece, and I can't see why anyone from Tammany would care about the train."

"The Order?" Viola spoke before she could stop herself. She wanted to destroy the Order, not to do its dirty work.

"You don't even know why you're here, do you?" the girl asked.

"I know enough," Viola said. "I know you should stop before something happens. Before you can't take it back."

"The one thing you should know about me, especially if you're so set on doing me harm, is that I never take anything back," the girl said, stepping forward. "Do I, darling?" she asked the man.

"Unfortunately for the rest of us, no, you never do. Even when you're wrong."

"Which is why I try never to be wrong." The girl took another step toward Viola. "I must not have been wrong about the train for your employer, whoever it is, to send you after me. The Order knows it was magic that destroyed those tracks, don't they? They're well aware that the people who stole their treasures are still out there, and they don't want anyone else to know. They're afraid of being seen as weak and ineffective. I'm right, aren't I?"

This one, she knew too much, but not so much as she thought. She didn't know that one of the people who stole the Order's treasures was standing in front of her. "Enough with the talking," Viola said.

"But you haven't answered my question." The girl's aim was as steady as her gaze. "And considering that you are currently threatening the life of my fiancé, I think the least you could do is provide me with some answers."

Her fiancé?

Before Viola could begin to think about why her chest had gone tight at the girl's words, there was a rustling of the curtains, and a moment later, Torrio appeared.

"Ah, more guests, darling," the still-seated man said lazily as Torrio took aim.

He definitely was pazzo, that one, acting as though her knife couldn't spill his blood before he could blink and as though Torrio's gun wasn't a threat at all.

But the girl—Reynolds—seemed to realize what her escort hadn't about the danger Torrio posed them. She took an instinctive step back. Her small silver pistol was still raised, but now she swiveled it to aim toward the newcomer.

"I know who you are," the girl said, her expression lighting with something suspiciously close to excitement. "John Torrio. You work for Kelly's gang."

They were both pazza, and the girl's mouth was going to get her killed.

Torrio's dark eyes met Viola's with a silent threat that was unmistakable—her way or his. It didn't matter that Torrio would assume that the guy at the tip of her blade was Reynolds; he would kill the girl in pink just for being there. One way or another, the couple would die.

So Viola did the only thing she could do. Allowing her affinity to unfurl, she found the now-familiar heartbeats of the man with a face that could have aged into kindness and the girl who looked no older or more serious than a debutante until she opened her smart mouth. Viola let her magic flare, pulling at the blood in their veins until the girl's eyes went wide a heartbeat before she crumpled to the floor. The man gasped, grabbing his chest before slumping over into his soup.

But even after the two were completely still, Torrio didn't lower his gun. Instead, he took a step forward and nudged the girl's body with his toe. His finger was still on the trigger of his revolver.

"Leave it," Viola hissed, putting her knife back in its sheath beneath her skirts.

"Just to be sure," Torrio said flatly as he took aim.

Viola came around the table and stepped between Torrio's gun and the girl's body. "If you shoot their bodies now, it can be traced back to you—and then back to Paul. Leave them be, and no one can prove anything," she said.

Torrio considered the two bodies, as though trying to decide if it was worth the risk.

"Let's just go before someone comes," Viola pleaded, taking a step closer to Torrio. "Before we're found."

He didn't answer immediately, probably just to make it clear that he was the one in charge of the situation. "Fine," he said as he eased the hammer back down and tucked the gun into the holster he wore beneath his jacket.

Viola didn't look back as Torrio dragged her from the privacy of the curtained booth. The dining room was still in chaos. The whole restaurant had erupted into a near brawl. Those who hadn't already fled were huddled in the corners of the restaurant, trapped by men in once-crisply pressed tuxedos who had turned the palatial dining room into a bare-knuckled ring.

"What did you do?" Viola asked. She pulled away from him as he headed toward the back of the room.

He didn't answer.

In the kitchens, the white-coated staff watched them silently pass into the alley behind the restaurant. It smelled of rotting trash, and the ground was coated with a layer of grease that had Viola slipping in her ridiculous heeled shoes, but Torrio held her firmly by the hand and practically shoved her into the carriage waiting at the end of the alleyway.

They were moving before Torrio had even latched the door, but he settled into the seat across from her with an unreadable look on his face.

"You weren't going to do it," he accused.

She met his dark, emotionless eyes and lifted her chin. "I don't know what you mean. They're dead, aren't they?"

"You hesitated," he told her flatly. "I could see it in your eyes. You were going soft."

"And you were going to make a mess of things," she told him, putting as much scorn into her tone as she could muster. "Men." She gave a disgusted harrumph. "Always thinking their *leetle* guns are the answer to everything. Going off half-cocked without thinking. *Too early.*" She held his gaze a moment longer to be sure he understood her meaning, and just as his cheeks started to turn red, she dismissed him by turning to look out the window of the carriage.

But Viola couldn't dismiss the memory of the girl—Reynolds—or how she'd had so much fire in her eyes . . . until Viola had snuffed it out.

A FINE SPECIMEN OF
MANHOOD

1904—St. Louis

E sta looked down at Harte, savoring the way his eyes had gone wide and the color had drained from his cheeks. "Is that what he told you?" she asked, giving the two boys a smile that was all teeth. "That I was supposed to *stay put*?"

Harte's mouth was still hanging open in shock, and he had "guilty" written all over him. But really, it served him right, leaving her like he had.

Julien, on the other hand, didn't looked surprised at all by her appearance. Instead, there was the glint of appreciation in his expression. "He might have said something to that effect." He nodded in her direction. "This getup—it's a good look on you. Join us?" he said, gesturing to the empty chair at the table.

Esta sent one more glare in Harte's direction before taking the offered seat. She removed her hat and faced him straight on, daring him to speak.

He closed his gaping mouth and then opened it again, as though he wanted to say something, but all he did was sputter.

"What is it, Harte?" she asked in a dangerously sweet voice. "You're not choking on your drink, are you?" She batted her eyes coyly. "Such a shame," she drawled, pausing for a beat. "Maybe next time."

Finally, he seemed to find his voice.

He could have asked any number of things—how she'd managed to get clothes when he'd left her half-naked in the room, or how she'd found King's on her own, for starters—but the first question he asked was the one that probably mattered least of all:

"What did you do to your hair?"

"Do you like it?" Esta asked, blinking mildly at him as she ran her hand down the nape of her bare neck.

"I . . ." Harte was trying to speak, but while his mouth was moving, no words were coming out.

She decided to take that maybe not as approval but as a success. Anyway, she didn't care much whether he approved or not—it was her head, her hair.

Maybe it *had* been a moment of madness on her part. At least, that was certainly how it started. When Harte had walked out on her—like he had any right to tell her what to do—weak as she'd felt, all she could do was rage. She *might* have knocked over the chair, and she'd definitely slammed her fist against the scarred surface of the desk . . . which had hurt more than she'd predicted. It had also jarred the drawer open and revealed a pair of old, rusted shears.

Maybe she hadn't really been thinking, and maybe she hadn't *really* considered the permanence of her actions when she took that first fistful of her hair and hacked through it with the dull blades. But she certainly didn't regret it.

She'd stood there for a moment with a handful of hair, shocked by her own impulsiveness. In a daze, she'd let the severed strands fall to the floor, and her stomach had fallen right along with them. But then she'd pulled herself together and finished the job—because, really, what else was there to do? She had resolutely ignored the twinge of fear that *maybe* she was making a mistake. Instead, she'd embraced the racing bite of adrenaline every time another clump of her dark hair fell at her feet.

It was a terrible haircut, ragged and uneven and slightly shorter than a bob, but the more hair that fell, the more weight she felt lifting from her and the more she'd hacked away. After all, it had been the Professor who'd made her keep it long. Growing up, it would have been so much easier to deal with a shorter style on a daily basis as she trained with Dakari or learned her way around the city. But Professor Lachlan didn't want her in wigs when she slipped through time. Too much of a risk, he'd said. Not authentic enough.

But there wasn't any Professor Lachlan. There was only Nibsy and the lies he'd built up like a prison around her childhood, hiding the truth of what he was. Of who *she* was. With every lock she snipped, she'd cut away the weight of her past, freeing herself more and more from those lies.

Then she'd found herself some clothes.

It had been a risk to use her affinity after all that had happened that night, but Harte had left her trapped in the room with nothing but a corset and a pair of lacy drawers. It was either take the risk to venture out or admit that he'd won. She'd been too livid to allow him to win, so she'd used her affinity to sneak out to a neighboring room. She'd waited for the blackness to appear again, but it never did. Which meant that it wasn't *her* who was the problem—it was *Harte*. Or maybe it was the power of the Book, but considering how irritated she was with him, it amounted to the same thing.

"How about you, Julien? Do you like it? I think it suits me." Esta raised her chin and dared Julien to disagree as the piano player in the corner crescendoed into a run of notes that filled the air with a feverish emotion. The song he was playing sounded the way wanting felt, and it stroked something inside of her, something dark and secret that had yearned for freedom without knowing what freedom truly was.

"It's a daring choice," Julien said, smiling into his glass as he took a drink and watching the two of them with obvious amusement.

In reply, Esta shot him a scathing look. She hadn't cut her hair and bound her breasts and found her own way to King's for Julien's entertainment. She was there because she was *supposed* to be there. Because it was her *right* to be there. She wasn't about to allow Harte to discard her like some kind of helpless damsel while he took care of the business that they were supposed to be attending to together. After all, it wasn't Harte who'd recognized the danger at the hotel earlier. It wasn't Harte who'd thought fast enough to evade the police waiting for them.

So what if she'd fainted a little after? She'd gotten them out of the Jefferson when Harte had miscalculated in the laundry room. Even with whatever was happening to her affinity, she wasn't weak. Harte should know that much about her by now. And she shouldn't have to prove herself—*especially* not to him.

Yet there she was, sitting in some run-down saloon doing just that. Because she had to send Harte—both of them, really—the message that she wasn't someone they could just push aside when the boys wanted to play.

Harte leaned over the table toward her and lowered his voice to where she could just barely hear it over the notes of the piano. "You can't really think this is going to work."

"I'm fairly certain it already has," she told him, reaching across to take the glass of amber liquid sitting in front of him. "You're the only one who seems to be bothered." Leaning back in her chair, she brought the glass to her lips, satisfied with the flash of irritation that crossed Harte's face. She took a sip of the tepid liquor, trying not to react as it burned down her throat, searing her resolve.

"She certainly has the bone structure to carry it off," Julien said, appraising her openly. "And the nerve, apparently."

"Don't," Harte warned Julien. "The last thing I need is for you to encourage this."

"It doesn't look like she needs any encouragement," Julien told Harte, sending a wink in Esta's direction.

She lifted her glass—a silent salute—in reply.

"If you need some pointers?" Julien said, offering Esta one of the thick black cigars from his inside jacket pocket. "I'd be happy to oblige."

She waved off the offer of the cigar—the sting of the whiskey was enough for one night. "Pointers?"

"Don't—" Harte warned again, but they both ignored him this time.

"If you're going to go through with this little impersonation, I could be of some assistance. You know, I'm something of an expert." Julien struck a match and let it flare for a second before he lit the cigar she'd just refused, puffing at it until smoke filled the air. He waved his hand to extinguish the flame and tossed the spent match carelessly into the ashtray on the table between them. "For instance, your legs."

"What's wrong with my legs?" Esta asked, frowning as she looked down at the dark trousers she'd lifted from the neighboring room. They fit well enough, she thought, examining them critically. They certainly were a lot more comfortable than the skirts she'd been wearing for the past few weeks.

"Men don't sit like that," Julien said, exhaling a cloud of smoke that had Esta's eyes watering. "Women make themselves small. It's pressed into them, I think. But little boys are taught from birth that the world is theirs. Spread your knees a bit more."

Esta raised her brows, doubtful. She didn't need *that* kind of help.

Understanding her point, he smiled. "Not like that. Like you deserve the space." He leaned forward, a spark of amusement in those raven's eyes of his. "Like it's *already* yours."

Julien was right. Even in her own time, the men she'd encountered on buses and in the subway claimed space around them like they had every right to it. That understanding—plus the expression on Harte's face that warned her not to—had her sliding her knees apart a little. "Like this?"

"Exactly," Julien said. "Better already."

"Julien, this is ridiculous," Harte said, his voice tight.

She had the feeling that if she looked, Harte's ears would be pink again, but Julien was still watching Esta, and she wasn't about to be the first one to look away. After a long moment, he turned to Harte. "She'll be fine. If I could turn *you* into"—he gestured vaguely in Harte's direction—"*this*, then I can teach her just as well."

"What do you mean?" Esta asked, not missing how Harte's lips were pressed in a flat line.

"He doesn't mean anything. Just ignore him," Harte said, eyeing what was left of the glass of whiskey in her hand like he wanted it.

Julien acted as though Harte hadn't spoken. "What I mean is that I taught Darrigan everything he knows about becoming the fine specimen of manhood that you see before you today. I even gave him his name."

"Did you really?" Esta asked, more than a little amused at the silent fury—and embarrassment—etched into Harte's expression. She tossed back the last of the liquor, just to irritate him.

"Where else do you think he learned it from? You should have seen him the first time he auditioned at the Lyceum. It wasn't even one of the better houses, you know. Catered mostly to the riffraff who could afford a step above the theaters in the Bowery, but not much more. I'd been working on my own act for a while then and was having a fair amount of success. I happened to be around for auditions one day, and I saw him—"

"Julien," Harte said under his breath.

"He wasn't any good?" she asked, leaning forward.

"Oh, the act itself was fine." Julien looked to Harte. "What was it you did, some sleight of hand or something?"

Harte didn't answer at first, but realizing that Julien wasn't going to let it go, he mumbled, "Sands of the Nile."

"That's right!" Julien said, snapping his fingers to punctuate his excitement. "He didn't get to finish, though. The stage manager let him have maybe a minute thirty before he got the hook. You couldn't blame the guy—anyone could tell what Darrigan was within a second or two of meeting him. You should have heard him then. His *Bow'ry bo-hoy* twang was as thick as the muck of a city sewer—I could hardly understand him. And it didn't help that he looked as rough as he sounded . . . like he'd punch the first person who looked sideways at him."

Esta glanced at Harte, who was quietly seething across the table. "He still looks like that if you know which buttons to push," she said. *Actually, he looks like that right now.* Which was fine with her.

"So you helped him?" she asked Julien. "Why?"

"That's the question, isn't it?" Julien took another long drag on the cigar, spouting smoke through his nose like some mischievous demon.

Esta suspected that he wasn't really thinking through the answer. The pauses were too purposeful. It was a fairly ingenious ploy, she had to admit, and one Julien was damn good at—pulling the listener along, making them want to hang on his every word. By the time he finally spoke, even she was aching for his answer.

"I could say that I'm just the sort of kind, benevolent soul that likes to help others—"

Harte huffed out a derisive laugh, but Julien paused long enough so that nothing distracted from the rest of his statement.

"I *could* say that, but I'll tell you the truth instead," he finished, his gaze darting momentarily to Harte. "That day I saw something in him that you can't teach—I saw *presence*. Even as untrained and uncouth as he was then, when Darrigan got up on that stage, he commanded it like he was born to walk the boards. There was something unmolded about his talent—something I wanted to have a hand in shaping."

"That's bullshit and you know it, Jules," Harte said, apparently unable to take any more. "You only helped me because you needed someone to take care of the Delancey brothers." Harte glanced at Esta. "They were a couple of wannabe gangsters in the neighborhood who didn't understand that Jules' act was just an act. They'd taken to stalking him after shows, trying to intimidate him to prove what big men they were."

"I held my own with them," Julien said stiffly.

"Sure you did, but the rules of the gentleman's boxing club don't exactly hold water in the Bowery, and swollen eyes are hard to cover up, even with all the face paint in the world." Harte shrugged. "So yeah, Jules here taught me how to not look and act like trash from the gutter, and I taught him how to fight dirty so he could get rid of the Delanceys. It's as simple as that."

Julien's expression was drawn. "You know how to ruin a good story, you know that, Darrigan?"

"I'm not here to tell stories," Harte told him, and then glared at Esta. "And neither is she. We're here for the necklace."

Julien frowned, and Esta didn't miss how he'd blanched a little. "I already told you, I don't have it."

"How could you get rid of it after that letter I sent you?" Harte said, his voice low. "Did you miss the part where I asked you to hold on to it for me? To keep it *safe*?"

"No," Julien said, his voice going tight. "I understood, but I also believed you'd jumped off a bridge and were supposed to be dead."

"So you decided to ignore my dying request?" Harte asked.

Julien looked slightly uncomfortable. "I held on to it for so long, and it's not like I thought you were ever coming back—"

"Enough drama, Jules. Just tell us where it is already," Harte demanded, a threat coloring his voice.

"Harte," Esta murmured. "Let him talk."

Julien sent her an appraising look, less grateful than interested. "Like I said, I *did* hold on to it. I kept it under lock and key, just like you told me to. But then last winter, Mrs. Konarske, the costume mistress at the theater, created a gown that was practically made for it."

Harte groaned. "You didn't."

"I figured you were dead and gone, and I couldn't resist." Julien snubbed what was left of the cigar into the ashtray. "I wore it for less than a week before someone offered to purchase it."

"You sold it?" Esta asked, her instincts prickling. If Julien had simply sold the necklace, it meant that it wasn't lost. She was a thief; she'd just steal it back.

"I didn't really have a choice." From Julien's uneasy expression, Esta knew there was something more he wasn't saying. "Anyway, if it makes you feel any better, I haven't worn the gown since." He sounded almost disappointed.

"I don't care about your costume, Jules. I need to know who you sold the necklace to." Harte's eyes were sharp and determined.

"That's the thing." Julien looked up at Harte, waiting a beat before he spoke again. "I have no idea."

Harte swore at him until Esta kicked him under the table. As frustrated as she was with Julien, they needed him on their side, and at the rate Harte was going, he was going to say something he wouldn't be able to take back.

"You must have some idea of who purchased it," she said more gently. "Even if you don't know who the buyer was, someone had to have given you the money and taken the stone."

"Oh, of course there was an exchange," Jules agreed. "But that doesn't mean I know who it was that made it."

Esta could practically feel Harte's impatience. "Stop talking nonsense, Jules."

"I didn't sell the necklace to a *person*." Julien's voice was calm and even, and he paused to take a long swallow of whiskey.

"I'm not getting any younger," Harte said through clenched teeth.

But Julien refused to be rushed. It was a master class of a confidence game. He leaned forward, his dark eyes ringed with the reflection of the lamp on the table between them. "If you're thinking of getting it back, you might as well forget it," he said softly, pausing to draw the moment out. "Because I sold it to the Veiled Prophet."

THE SOCIETY

1904—St. Louis

Harte felt the ends of his patience fraying as the power of the Book churned inside of him. It had started the moment he'd looked up and found Esta standing there, her hair shorn and her eyes bright with anger. He wasn't ready for her unexpected appearance, hadn't prepared himself to hold the power back, and when he felt the fury radiating from her, the voice reared up, pushing toward the feeble boundaries he'd erected in his mind.

He could feel the sweat at his temples from the exertion of keeping that power in check. He wanted to throttle Julien just for looking at Esta, and doubly for the meandering explanation, but Harte managed to keep his voice somewhat calm when he spoke. "Who, *exactly*, is the Veiled Prophet?"

Julien considered the question. "The Veiled Prophet isn't so much a who as a *what*."

"If you don't stop talking in riddles—" Harte started to growl, but he felt another sharp kick under the table. Across from him, Esta shot a warning look that had the power inside of him purring. It liked her anger—and it liked his even more so, because it distracted him. Made him weak. So he buttoned his temper back up the best he could.

"What Harte *means* to say," Esta cut in, shooting him another look, "is that we're in a bit of a bind. As you might have surmised from my new look, the police know I'm here in the city. We only took the risk of meeting you because we need the necklace. And since you don't have it, we need to find it and get out of town—and out of your hair—before they find me. If there's anything you can do to help, we'd be grateful."

"See, Darrigan, *this* is how you deal with a friend." Julien's mouth curved up before he turned back to Esta. "The Veiled Prophet isn't just a person. He's an institution in this town—a figurehead of sorts—and the person who plays him changes," he explained. "Each year the Society selects someone new to fill the role, but the identity of the Prophet himself is never revealed. So you see, the person I sold the necklace to could have been any number of people. I never saw his face."

"What's the Society?" Esta asked.

"The Veiled Prophet Society," Julien explained.

"Never heard of them," Harte told him, trying to keep his voice even.

"You're new in town, so that's not surprising," Julien said with a shrug. "But you know how it is—the rich always have their little clubs. The Society's not so different from the Order. Mostly, it's a bunch of bankers and politicians who see themselves as a sort of group of the city fathers, and just like the Order back in New York, they model themselves as a philanthropic organization. Each Independence Day, they put on a big parade and throw a fancy ball to crown a debutante. Nothing—and I mean *nothing*—happens in this city without the Society knowing or having a hand in it."

"Which is why you had to sell the necklace when they offered to buy it," Esta said.

She was right. With the kind of act Julien did, he'd be a target. He'd need the Society behind him, not against him.

Julien nodded. His jaw was tight as he took another long swig of the whiskey in front of him. "It wasn't just money they were offering," he told her. "The Veiled Prophet himself came to me after one of my shows—showed up in the dressing room without an invitation, a lot like you two," he said, but there was no real humor in his voice. "Said he'd pay a king's ransom for the necklace, and when I refused—because honest to god, Darrigan, I never intended to part with the stupid thing—when I didn't accept his offer right away, he made it clear that if I didn't sell, I wouldn't work in this town, maybe not in any other, ever again. But if I sold . . ."

"They offered you protection," Harte finished.

Julien nodded tightly. "I'm *this* close to making it big, Darrigan. I've had people from the Orpheum Circuit checking out my act multiple times now, and I've even been talking to this bigwig in New York about developing a whole show for me, maybe even opening back on Broadway. But they aren't completely sold on the idea yet. You know how it is. They're waiting to see how the rest of this run goes. With the Exposition and all the visitors in town, it could go pretty well, but if the Society decided to make things hard, I could lose everything I've worked for. You understand?"

Harte nodded. He *did* understand. He knew what it was like to be on the edge of success, one step away from the grime of your past. Sometimes you did what you had to do. How often had Harte himself ignored the coincidence of a lucky break that came not long after a "favor" he'd done for Paul Kelly? Too many. So yes, Harte understood, but . . .

"It doesn't change anything," he told Julien. "We still need the necklace."

"You have to understand, Darrigan. As much as I'd like to, I can't help you. Not if the Society's involved," Julien said. "There's too much at stake for me right now."

Harte almost felt sorry for him. He definitely felt the twinges of guilt for his own part in the mess Julien was in, and he probably would have felt more than just twinges had Julien not gone against his explicit directions. "I'm afraid, Jules, that you don't really have a choice."

Julien's brow furrowed. "You can't force me to help you."

He was wrong about that, of course. A simple handshake or tap, and Harte could force Julien to do whatever he wanted him to. From the tentative expression on Esta's face, that was what she expected to happen. But he didn't want to do things that way if he could help it. He didn't want to treat an old friend like a common mark.

Harte leaned over the table and lowered his voice. "Let me ask you a question—do you really think that J. P. Morgan gives a fig about some dead people on a train?"

Suddenly Julien looked wary and unsure. "What are you talking about?"

"The bounty on Esta's head," Harte told him. "It isn't because of any train derailment. It's because of what we took from the Order."

"The Order denied that anything was stolen," Julien said, but his voice wavered.

"They lied," Esta said. "They couldn't let anyone know what we did. It would have made them look like weak fools if word got out that they'd been taken so easily."

"Their headquarters at Khafre Hall was basically a fortress," Harte added, "and we still managed to relieve the Order of their most prized possessions, including the necklace."

"*No,*" Julien said, his voice rising.

"Settle down, Jules," Harte told him gently. His frustration had given way to pity—and to guilt. "People are starting to look."

"You *wouldn't* have put me at risk like that," Julien said, his voice shaking. "Not after all I did for you."

"I needed someone I could trust to keep the necklace safe for me," Harte said. *I needed someone good at keeping secrets.* "And if you remember, I gave you specific instructions to keep it hidden unless you needed it for an emergency. An *emergency*—as in life or death. I didn't tell you to go parading it out onstage because you got a new outfit."

Julien's hand trembled as he went for the cigars in his coat pocket. "I still don't see how any of that's my problem." He tried to light one, but after fumbling for a moment with the matches, he gave up.

"Oh, come on, Jules. Don't make me spell it out for you," Harte said. "These rich men are all alike—and they talk. You don't think eventually the Order is going to find out this Prophet has the necklace?"

"And if the Order finds out, they're going to wonder if you know where the other things are," Esta added. "They're going to come after you."

Julien's face had gone ashen. "I knew it. I knew the second you appeared in my dressing room that you were going to bring me nothing but trouble. I should have let the Jefferson Guard have you last night, friends or not."

"Maybe," Harte agreed. "But be glad that you didn't."

"I can't imagine why," Julien said with narrowed eyes. "I wouldn't be in this mess right now."

"You made this mess when you wore the necklace onstage, but if you want to get out of it, you're going to need to help us," Harte said, remembering the strange items Esta had found in Julien's dressing room. "We need someone on the inside, someone who knows the Society. You're going to help us figure out where this Prophet of yours has the necklace, and then you're going to help get us in so we can take it back before anyone else finds out."

THE SECRETS OF THE BOOK

J ack Grew let himself into his suite and locked the door behind him. Once he turned on the lamp, he was welcomed by the sight of rich mahogany and silk, plush Persian carpets, and the glint of brass, but it was the silence that soothed him. *Finally*, blessed silence.

The past few hours at the Jefferson Hotel had been a mess of noise and confusion, but in the end only one thing mattered: Esta had escaped. The police and the Guard had both had her cornered, trapped, and she had still managed to slip past them.

After checking the lock once more, just to be sure, and pulling the curtains closed, Jack loosened his tie and took the Book from the secret pocket of his waistcoat. Sitting in the wingback chair by the fireplace, he ran his fingers over the now-familiar design on the crackled cover. The Sigil of Ameth—the seal of truth. He took a moment, as he always did, to trace the lines carved into the leather. There was something mesmerizing about the design. The figures seemed distinct and separate—rhomboids and triangles laid one on top of another. Tracing them, however, revealed a different reality—the shapes were not separate, as they appeared, but infinitely interlocking. Much like the pages of the Book itself, there was no beginning or end to the lines, simply the endless circuit that drew him deeper and deeper into the truth.

Calmed by this ritual, he took the vial of morphine cubes from his pocket and placed two on his tongue, welcoming their bitterness like an old friend. He could already feel their effects as he opened the small tome. Little by little he felt the tension of the day drift away as the morphine pushed back the ache pounding in his temples. Little by little, his senses came to life, and he felt more aware than he had all evening.

For two years he'd studied the pages of the Ars Arcana, and still he had not unlocked all its secrets. Some days it seemed like he could turn the pages endlessly, never reaching the back cover. Other days the Book seemed smaller and more compact. It was never the same volume twice, and the surprise of what would greet him each evening when he opened it was his favorite part of the day.

Tonight the Book's pages numbered only thirty or so, and they were pages he'd seen many times before. His own handwriting annotated the incomprehensible markings on page after page, evidence of his devotion to the Book. Of his devotion to the craft and the *science* of magic. It didn't matter that he shouldn't have been able to read most of them. He never worried when he came out of the haze of morphine and scotch and found a new page deciphered, a new secret unlocked. It was simply part of the Book's power, a signal of his own worthiness as the Book revealed truth to him when his mind was clear and open and ready to receive it.

He crushed one more morphine cube between his teeth as he searched for the passage he had been working on a few days before, but his mind kept drifting away from the Book and back to the fact that Esta Filosik and Harte Darrigan were here, in this city.

It wasn't a surprise somehow. Almost from the moment he'd stepped off the train, he'd sensed that this trip wouldn't be like the others. He'd sensed the promise in the air, but he'd assumed it was a political victory on the horizon.

Two years had passed without any sign of her or Darrigan. Of course there had been claims that she was responsible for any number of tragedies. The Antistasi were keen to claim the so-called Devil's Thief as one of their own and to use her to further their aims. Which was just fine with Jack. The more the Antistasi tried to resist the march of history, the more they made themselves a target for the hatred and fear of the ordinary citizen. Every attack, no matter how small, had surely and steadily built support that allowed them to pass the Act. Every death the Antistasi caused had been another example of why the country couldn't allow magic to go unchecked. Yes, two years had gone by without Esta Filosik, but they had been two very fruitful years for Jack Grew.

Ever since the train derailment, Jack had used the publicity it had garnered to work his way up the rungs of power. He'd started with the Order, using the Book to obtain a place on their council at the Conclave, where he'd spoken of the dangers of feral magic outside the city. That oration had caught the ear of a senator, who had asked for Jack's help to accrue enough votes to pass an act outlawing magic. The president hadn't paid attention until the Antistasi had started their attacks, but considering that Roosevelt himself was in office because of the act of the anarchist who assassinated McKinley, he had a keen desire to see any additional threats quashed. Once Jack had Roosevelt's ear, he'd used it wisely, and it wasn't long before he was an advisor the president turned to often.

After all, who better to fight the outbreak of magic, the destruction of national unity, than someone who had been so hurt by it?

For nearly six months he'd been traveling as an attaché for President Roosevelt, combing the country to collect intelligence about what remained of the illegal magic and the maggots that continued to cling to it. It wasn't an official cabinet position—not yet at least—but Jack had hopes. No. Jack had *ambitions*. And he would not stop until they were met.

Flipping through the familiar pages, Jack relaxed into the clarity of the morphine and let his mind open to the possibility of the Book. He found the page he wanted—one that didn't always appear. It was a sign, he knew, that this was what he was meant to do. His fingers ran down the notes he'd made in the margins, but when he read the words on the page, it wasn't English he spoke but a language far more ancient.

Jack wasn't an idiot. He knew there was a reason Esta and Darrigan had surfaced here and now, and he knew that their appearance in St. Louis had everything to do with the Society's most recent acquisition: a necklace that they touted as an ancient treasure—a necklace that Jack had every intention of taking for himself. With it he would be one step closer to claiming the power within the Book as his own and wiping even the *memory* of the maggots who would try to stand against him from the face of the earth.

UNEXPLAINED DARKNESS

1904—St. Louis

Esta watched Julien's back as he made his way through the crowded barroom and then out into the night. "You're sure he won't just run to this Society of his and rat us out?" she asked Harte, turning back to him.

His brows drew together. "He won't tell anyone he's seen us."

"But that stuff in his dressing room—the medallions and the sashes," she pressed. "They were all inscribed with the letters *VP*. He's one of them."

"I know, but Julien's not stupid," he said. "He might not like it, but he'll give us the information we need to protect himself and his career."

Esta frowned as Harte called for another glass of whiskey, and when it arrived, he drank it down in a single long swallow. He didn't say anything else at first. He simply sat, staring sightlessly for a moment, his cheeks flushed from the drink as the piano's music wrapped the room in its hypnotic rhythm. It was a ragtime tune, a syncopated run of grace notes and black keys. It had been in the background all night, but now with the silence hanging between her and Harte, she couldn't help but listen. And as she did, she could practically hear the future in the rhythms and chords—the lazy, laid-back, just-behind-the-beat attitude that would eventually become the blues and jazz and then rollick through the twentieth century with chimerical transformations.

For now, though, it was simply a ragtime tune on the verge of something more, but it seemed to be a promise—or maybe a warning—that they, too, while safe for the moment, were on the verge of something they couldn't predict.

"So Julien is . . ." She wasn't sure what she wanted to say, not with the way Harte was looking at her, eyes stormy and unreadable.

"He's a damn genius," Harte said flatly. It did not sound like a compliment. "You saw him onstage earlier, and you saw him here tonight."

She had. Everything about Julien, from the sharp part dividing his dark hair to the way he used the thick cigars as props to punctuate his words, was the portrait of male confidence. If Esta hadn't seen Julien remove the blond wig and stage makeup with her own eyes in the dressing room earlier, she would have had trouble believing he was the same *woman* who had captivated the entire auditorium with her throaty, heartrending song.

"Which Julien is the real Julien?" she asked. "And which is the act?"

Harte frowned. "Honestly, I'm not sure it matters."

"No?"

He shook his head. "A long time ago I reached a point where I decided that Julien is whatever he wants to be. He *is* the woman who captivates audiences onstage *and* he's also the man he appears to be off the stage." Harte paused, like he was choosing his words carefully. "They're the same person, and that ability he has—to switch between the two without losing any of himself—he taught me how important it is not to lose the heart of who you are when you're becoming someone else."

Esta realized then what Julien had meant when he'd said he'd taught Harte everything he knew. She'd seen in Julien the echo of the same male swagger that Harte carried himself with. Or rather, she supposed, she saw the origin of it. But she couldn't help wondering who Harte became when he was with her.

"Look, don't worry about Julien," he said darkly. "*I'll* take care of him."

She narrowed her eyes at him. "You're not cutting me out of this, Harte."

"I'm not trying to cut you out," he told her. "I'm trying to keep you safe."

"Well, stop trying. I've been just fine on my own up until now. I don't need some knight in shining armor."

"I never said I wanted to be one." His voice was clipped. "We're supposed to be in this together, but you don't want me to worry about you or do anything to help you. What *do* you need, Esta?"

I need you to stop pulling away from me.

The unexpectedness of the thought surprised her. "I need you to back off and trust that I know my own limits," she said instead. She saw the hurt flicker across his features, but she didn't apologize. "I need you to trust *me*."

"You mean like you trust me?" He stared at her for a moment, shaking his head. "I left you alone for an hour and you cut off your hair."

"It's *my* hair, Harte. I can do what I want with it."

He frowned, his gaze sweeping over her face, down the nape of her neck, and taking in the too-large coat and the rumpled shirt beneath it. As much as she hated to admit it—even to herself—she couldn't have felt warmer if he'd used his hands instead.

"I would have brought you with me if I'd known you were going to do something so drastic," he said finally.

"You shouldn't have left me at all."

His eyes met hers, and she swore that they were filled with everything he wasn't saying. Then he blinked and glanced away as though he couldn't bear to look at her any longer.

She sighed, annoyed at his dramatics. "You're giving yourself way too much credit, Darrigan," she told him. When he didn't acknowledge her words, she rapped on the table between them to get his attention. "Did you hear me? This was *my* choice."

He still wouldn't look at her. "If I hadn't left you and made you angry—"

"I would have done it anyway," she said, interrupting him before he said anything even more stupid. "It was a *necessity*. I'm taller than most women. I stand out. But as a man, I'm average. Easy to overlook. And you saw what happened back at the Jefferson. A hat can fall off or hairpins can come loose. We can't risk that happening again—*I* couldn't risk it. It's just hair."

He frowned at her as though he didn't believe her—or maybe he just didn't want to believe her.

"Besides, I like it," she told him, lifting her chin in defiance. "Julien's right—I have the bones to pull it off . . . *and* the confidence."

His expression told her that he didn't agree, but there was some other emotion in his eyes. Something almost hungry. For a moment she felt caught by the intensity there.

"You're dangerous enough on your own without Julien's help."

Her cheeks felt suddenly warm. "You think I'm dangerous?" she said, fighting to keep her lips from curling into a smile. She liked the idea of him seeing her that way, liked the idea of keeping him on his toes even better.

"From the moment I saw you in the Haymarket. But you don't need me to tell you that." The stormy gray of his irises seemed somehow darker than it had been a moment before. Again she thought she saw the flash of unnamed colors in their depths. "You already *know* you're dangerous."

He was right. She'd trained her whole life to be a weapon, but him acknowledging it didn't delight her any less.

"This will work." She felt the truth of it now, deep inside. "Julien will help us get the necklace, and then we'll move on to the next stone. After all," she said with a self-satisfied smirk, "I am the Devil's Thief, aren't I?"

Something shifted in his expression. "I'm not sure that's a title you want to be claiming."

"You're not still worried about the people in the ballroom, are you?" she asked, remembering the thrill she'd felt at the sight of them—their masked faces and billowing skirts. Most of all, she remembered the way the mood in the ballroom had transformed from festive to fearful as the men surrounding them scurried like roaches to escape.

"If those were the Antistasi, we need to steer clear of them," Harte said. Then he told her what Julien had relayed to him, about the attacks on the Exposition and other places around town.

"They've hurt people?" Esta asked, feeling a tremor of unease—and, oddly, disappointment.

"And they've done it using the name of the Devil's Thief," Harte said darkly.

"Because of the train," she said, her mood falling. "Because I started this."

Harte's brows drew together. "You didn't blow up that train, Esta."

"Maybe not intentionally," she said. "But something happened to it. I slipped through time, and people died."

"Maybe. Or maybe you had nothing to do with it," Harte argued.

She shook her head. "You don't really believe that. Look what happened in the hotel, and in the station. Even on the bridge, when we were crossing the Brink. Something happens to me when I use my affinity around you. There's something about the power of the Book that changes it. Whenever I try to hold on to time, I see this darkness I can't explain."

"Darkness?" Harte asked. He'd gone very still.

"When I use my affinity, I can see the spaces between time, but when I'm touching you, it's like those spaces become nothing. Like time itself is disappearing. Didn't you hear those elevator cables? It sounded like they were about to snap." She licked her lips, forcing herself to go on. "What if that's what happened to the train?"

He was frowning at her again, and when he finally spoke, it sounded as though he was choosing his words carefully. "You don't know that. What we do know is that you didn't *intend* to do anything to that train. If these Antistasi are using whatever happened for their own benefit, they're nothing but opportunists."

"Or maybe they're just trying to make some good come of a tragedy," she argued. "You heard Julien. Jack used the derailment to drive fear and anger against Mageus. Maybe the Antistasi are just answering those lies."

Because *someone* had to. "These Antistasi might be opportunists, but they helped us escape tonight. Maybe that makes them our allies."

"We don't need allies," Harte argued. "We need to get the necklace and get out of town as quickly as possible. The sooner we get the necklace, the sooner we can collect the rest of the artifacts and get back to the city to help Jianyu."

"Fast might not be possible. We had a whole team going into Khafre Hall," she told him. "If there are a group of Mageus here in St. Louis who are actively working against the Guard, maybe we could use them."

"To do that we'd have to find them and convince them to trust us. And we'd have to figure out if *we* could trust *them*," Harte told her. "The police and the Guard already know you're here. The Order will know soon too. The faster we're out of this town, the better."

Esta couldn't disagree with that. Even though she was less recognizable with her new haircut and wearing a man's suit, the longer they stayed, the more dangerous it became. Finding the Antistasi *would* take time, but she wasn't sure that Harte was right about his reluctance to at least look into them.

By then the pianist was playing the final chords of his song and the people on the dance floor had started to thin. "We should go," he said, but she didn't miss the tightness in his voice or the way the muscle in his jaw ticked with frustration.

Fine. He could sulk all he wanted as far as she was concerned. What he couldn't do anymore was leave her out.

POPPIES

1902—New York

After Delmonico's, Viola knew she was being watched even more closely than before. She had not exactly failed Paul's little test, but her hesitation to kill the reporter had made her suspect. Her brother still didn't fully trust her—rightfully so, since her submissiveness was nothing more than a ploy. But his suspicions made things uncomfortable and inconvenient. Especially since he seemed to be working with Nibsy Lorcan, the rat.

She would have killed Nibsy already for his treachery, but she couldn't risk crossing her brother. Not until she discovered what he was doing with the boy. Paul was powerful enough and his Five Pointers were vicious enough that they could have crushed Nibsy and the remaining Devil's Own before now. Which meant that Nibsy had something Paul needed. Perhaps Nibsy was simply holding Paul at bay with the secrets Dolph had collected about the Five Pointers over the years, but from what Viola had seen, their interactions were more cordial than blackmail would suggest.

Staying under her brother's watchful eye meant subjecting herself to Nibsy *and* to the Order. Both were repugnant. Unthinkable. But staying where she was meant that neither Nibsy nor the Order were likely to touch her. She would bide her time and learn their weaknesses. She would use Paul against Nibsy, and she would get her knife back.

And when the moment was right, she would destroy the Order from the inside.

Unfortunately, biding her time meant pretending a meekness that was contrary to everything she was. In the days after Delmonico's, her hands had become dried and pruned from scrubbing dishes, and the only blade she'd been able to get close to was the small paring knife that she had tucked in her skirts. It was a pathetic thing—only about four inches long, made of flimsy steel that had long ago bent at the tip. In a fight, it would be of little use at all, but then, she had no opportunity to fight. She'd offered to be his weapon, but he'd made her into nothing more than a kitchen maid. Already, she could feel herself dulling, like a knife tossed into a drawer and forgotten, and she worried that the razor edge of what she had once been was starting to wear away.

The kitchen door of the Little Naples Cafe opened behind her, and Viola turned, her hand already reaching for her insignificant knife. But it was only her mother, coming to look over the pot that Viola was tending.

"'Giorno, Mamma," Viola said, her eyes cast down at the floor as she stepped back to give her mother access.

Her mother's expression was serious, her eyes appraising, as she took the spoon from Viola and gave the pot of lentils a stir. She made a non-committal sound as she brought the spoon to her mouth and tasted, but then her mouth turned down. "Not enough salt. Did you use the guanciale, like I told you?"

"Yes, Mamma," Viola answered, her eyes still trained on the floor so that her mother would not see the frustration in them. "Sliced thin, like you said."

"And you rendered it enough before you put in the beans?"

"Yes, Mamma." She clenched her teeth to keep from saying more.

"Well, I guess it will have to do, then," her mother said with a sigh. It was the same sigh Viola had heard nearly every day of her childhood. "For today . . . You'll do better tomorrow."

"Yes, Mamma." Viola tried to relax her jaw and glanced up at her mother, who was already picking at the potatoes Viola had sliced for the greens.

"Too thick," her mother was muttering as she examined Viola's work.

It didn't matter that the potatoes were perfectly cubed, uniform and even—Viola knew how to use a blade, after all—it was always the same. Too thick or too thin, too salty or not enough. Every day her mother came to inspect Viola's work, and nothing was ever good enough for her *Paolino*.

But for Viola?

She was too brazen, too prideful. *You want too much.*

Viola shook off the ghosts of the past. "Will you be eating with Paolo today, Mamma?" She asked, a feeble attempt to get her mother out of the kitchen before Viola said or did something she couldn't take back.

"Sì," her mother told her, and lifted a dish to examine its cleanness. "Bring me some of the bread, too."

Viola made up two dishes of the lentils and paired them with slices of bread. That, at least, her mother could find no fault with, because Viola had learned to make bread from a master. She'd watched Tilly day in and day out in the Strega's kitchen, as her friend transformed a pile of ingredients into the warm loaves that kept Dolph's people filled and happy. Viola had memorized the movement of Tilly's hands as she'd measured and stirred and kneaded—the way her nimble fingers had worked over the lump of flour and yeast until it turned smooth and supple as flesh. She'd been happy there, content to simply watch the girl she'd fallen in love with, the friend who had no idea what she meant to Viola.

Tilly had been brave. She'd died because she'd rushed in to help without thought of herself or of the danger she might have been in. Even after her magic had been stripped from her, Tilly had fought until the end. And so would Viola.

Viola wiped the dampness from her cheeks and picked up the two plates. She pasted on the smile that her brother liked to see her wear. As she pushed through the doorway, into the main room, she felt the eyes of Paul's boys on her, but she ignored their heated looks. She wasn't interested, and she knew that none would touch her so long as Paul acted as though she were his property. Her mother and her brother were sitting at a table in a corner, and she served them their lunch with a bowed head and a hardened heart, knowing that sometimes bravery must be soft and secret, just as Tilly's was.

She left the two of them to eat, and needing some air, she carried a bowl of scraps out to the rubbish pile in the back. The string of curses she muttered as she walked would have made even the most hardened Bowery Boy blush if any of them could've made out the Italian she used. Though she didn't use her mother tongue to save anyone's delicate sensibilities. She didn't care if a lady would know the words she was using—she'd stopped being a lady the first day her brother forced her to kill a man.

She'd just placed her scrap bowl on a bench outside the building when she realized she wasn't alone. Pretending to wipe her hands on her raggedy apron, she pulled the small knife from her skirts and continued to move toward the outhouses. When she sensed movement out of the corner of her eye, she didn't hesitate. With a single fluid motion, she whipped around and sent the knife flying at her target.

It hit true, as it always did, pinning the intruder by the edge of her sleeve to the wooden fence.

Her sleeve?

The girl's eyes had gone wide with fear—or was it simply surprise? But then fear gave way to pleasure, and her entire countenance lit. "Oh, bravo!"

It took a moment for the truth of what Viola was seeing to register. It was the girl from Delmonico's, but instead of the flouncy pink confection she'd been wearing before, she had on a dark skirt and what appeared to be a man's waistcoat. A cravat was tied neatly at the neck of her crisp white shirt, and she was wearing a gentleman's cap on her head. She looked ridiculous, like a child playing dress-up with her papà's clothes.

She looks perfect.

"What are you doing here?" Viola hissed, ignoring the warmth that had washed over her as she tossed a glance back toward the kitchen door. After all Viola had done to keep her alive, the girl had just walked straight into the den of the lion.

"Right now I'm trying to get myself free," the girl said as she tried to wiggle the knife out of the wood.

Viola stalked toward her, and with a jerk that made the girl flinch, she withdrew the knife and held it at the girl's throat. "You should not be here."

She heard the click of the pistol's hammer before she realized they were not alone. "And you shouldn't be threatening her again, Miss Vaccarelli."

He knows who I am. Viola glared at him to show that she didn't care, and she did not drop the knife.

"Yes, well, if you'll be so kind as to come along?" He motioned with the gun, which looked about as comfortable in his hand as a live fish would have.

Americani and their guns. They all thought they were cowboys. Too bad cows had more brains than half of them. "I'm not going with you," Viola said.

The girl frowned at her accomplice. "Theo, stop being an idiot and put that thing down." Then her midnight-blue eyes met Viola's and her cheeks went pink. "We've no intention of hurting you, whatever Theo might want you to believe. We simply want to talk."

Viola glanced back at the man—the same one from the restaurant. "I don't have nothing to say to you."

The girl sighed. "As you can see, we know who you are—Viola Vaccarelli, sister of Paul Vaccarelli, the owner of this fine establishment and also the leader of the gang of ruffians known as the Five Pointers, who have been terrorizing the Bowery ever since the elections last summer. Of course, with his alleged connections to Tammany—"

"*Shhh,*" Viola hissed, looking back over her shoulder again.

"She could go on for days like this," the man said jauntily. "I've found the best way to shut her up is to let her have her say."

"He's probably right about that," the girl said with a smile that wrinkled her nose.

It was the sort of simpering smile Viola should have wanted to smack off the girl's face, but for some reason it shot a bolt of heat straight to Viola's middle.

"Viola?" Torrio called from the kitchen. "You still out there?"

Viola froze. She had thought she'd made it clear she wanted nothing to do with Torrio, but since his courtship was being encouraged by Paul and since Torrio saw in Viola a way to solidify his influence in the Five Pointers, he kept coming back. Day after day. Like a rash.

She pushed the girl around the side of the building. "You have to go. *Now.*"

"Well, we're certainly not leaving after we've come all this way to talk with you," the girl said primly.

"Hey, V," Torrio called again. "You need some help or something?" His voice had an edge to it. Like he thought he had some claim over her.

"I'm fine," she called back, trying to make her voice nice. She sent the two a silent warning to keep quiet.

"What're you doing out there?" His voice was closer now.

Panic crept up Viola's spine. If Torrio saw the two here—alive and well—he would know that she hadn't killed them. Worse, he'd know that when she stopped him from shooting their bodies, she'd stood in the way of direct orders. She had to get rid of him. "I'll be there in a minute," she called. "I have to take a piss, all right? You can't help with that."

There was a moment of horrified silence. *Men. So delicate about simple things.*

Torrio's voice came a second later, gruffer and more demanding: "Your mother's leaving, so hurry up about it, eh?"

Viola let out another string of muttered curses as she waited to make sure that Torrio went back inside. When she turned back to her intruders, the girl was smirking at her.

"What's so funny?" Viola demanded, her hands on her hips.

The girl didn't look embarrassed. Instead she gave Viola a long, amused look, taking her in from head to toe and landing finally on Viola's face. Something in the girl's expression shifted, but Viola couldn't tell what it was. "Nothing," the girl told her, more serious now. "Nothing at all."

"If the two of you are ready, perhaps we should take our discussion elsewhere?" Theo suggested.

"Yes," the girl said. "Let's. We have so much to talk about."

Viola tossed another glance over her shoulder to make sure no one was looking for her. "Fine," she said, knowing it would be easier to get rid of the girl once and for all if she simply gave in now.

"Perhaps you'd fancy going on a short drive with us?" the man offered. "We've a carriage waiting just down the road."

"Fine, fine," Viola said. Anything to get them away from Torrio and her brother.

But as she walked next to the girl, away from Paul's building and toward a gleaming carriage at the end of the block, she realized the girl smelled not like the sweetness of lilies or the simpering softness of roses, as Viola had expected. Instead, she smelled of something far more earthy, like poppies. The moment that scent hit her nose and wrapped around her senses, Viola knew she was in bigger trouble than she'd bargained for.

CLOSE QUARTERS

Ruby Aurelea Reynolds knew she was in trouble the moment the carriage door shut, closing her and Theo in with the small Italian girl who took up all the air in the space. Ruby was rarely the type to feel out of her depth. She was the youngest of five girls and had survived a childhood of teacups and pinafores to become what she wanted to become—a published journalist who had carved out a career for herself despite her mother's protests and society's dismay. And if she'd caused a few scandals here or there? Well, scandal was an excellent way of dispensing with the nuisance of unwanted suitors, who were really only after the fortune her father had left behind.

She'd braved the slums of the city and the matrons of society, but sitting across from Viola Vaccarelli, their knees almost touching as the carriage jostled along, Ruby suddenly felt nervous. It wasn't because Ruby had been naive enough to believe that Viola wasn't dangerous. Of course she was. After all, the girl was the sister of a nefarious gang leader and had been holding poor Theo at knifepoint the first time they'd met. That, coupled with the deadly little trick Viola had just accomplished with an ordinary kitchen knife . . . No, Ruby had expected danger.

She just hadn't realized . . . not really.

It had all seemed so simple when she and Theo had set out that morning—they would find Viola, and then Ruby would charm her into giving up whatever information she might have that would bring the Order to its knees.

People in the city thought so highly of the Order of Ortus Aurea because they didn't know the truth. The Order pretended to be above the fray, blameless protectors of the city against an unenlightened horde. Maybe once they had been, but they certainly weren't any longer. Her sources revealed them to be in league now with the corrupt politicians at Tammany, and her recent experiences proved that they weren't above using common criminals like Paul Kelly to do their dirty work. All to shore up their power and protect their reputation. And for what? The city was no safer. And whatever story her family might have spread about her father's death, Ruby knew it was the Order's fault that he'd left his wife to raise five girls on her own.

But now that Viola was scowling at her in silence, Ruby was beginning to doubt her plan. Viola did not look as though she would be easily charmed. Still, there was so much at stake, so much good that Ruby could do if she were just brave enough to take the first step.

After a long silence accompanied only by the rumble of the wheels against the uneven streets, Ruby decided that she was hesitating, and she never hesitated.

"Perhaps we should begin with introductions," she said, mimicking her mother's brightest hostess voice. Her words came out too high, too false sounding. "I'm R. A. Reynolds, as you know. The R stands for Ruby. And this is my fiancé, Theodore Barclay."

"Please, call me Theo," he volunteered, the dear.

Viola didn't speak. She just continued to glower at them, and Ruby realized that her narrowed eyes were the most startling shade of violet, like the irises Ruby's mother grew in the greenhouse on their roof.

"Well, we already know who you are," Ruby said, chewing nervously on her lips. This wasn't going well at all. "Theo, darling, you need to put that thing away. How can anyone relax with you pointing a gun at them?"

Viola glanced at the weapon, but she didn't seem bothered by it. Nor did she seem any more relaxed when Theo finally tucked the pistol back under his coat.

"Truly . . ." Ruby's voice was low as a whisper. "Despite the little . . . um . . . *event* at Delmonico's, we don't mean you any harm. I know you didn't want to hurt us."

"You do?" Viola asked, her dark brows winging up in surprise.

The girl nodded. "Of course. It was the other one—John Torrio— who made you do it. I've been doing some investigating, and I've learned all about him and his more . . . *inventive* tactics. But I hadn't realized until the night at Delmonico's what he *is*."

Viola continued to frown, but otherwise she didn't react. She certainly didn't volunteer any information.

"You *know*," Ruby said expectantly, hoping that Viola would pick up her meaning. "One. Of. *Them*."

"Torrio, he's bad news, and that's all I know about him," Viola said, eyeing Ruby as though she were the worst sort of fool. Ruby understood that look—it was the same look everyone gave her when she tried to speak up about anything important. It was the look that meant she should go back to the sitting room and pick up some needlepoint and have babies and forget about any sort of real life.

"He's a Five Pointer, same as your brother, but that's not all that John Torrio is, is it?"

Viola gave her a look of disgust. "Look, Miss Reynolds—"

"Ruby—"

"*Miss Reynolds,*" Viola insisted, keeping a clear boundary between them even as their knees bumped. "I don't know what you're playing at, but you don't want to mess with John Torrio or my brother. They're not nice people. They don't play by any rules you would understand, and they won't think twice about getting rid of anyone who causes them a problem."

"I'm not afraid of them," Ruby said, lifting her chin. They couldn't possibly be worse than half of her sisters' friends, the jealous harpies who wouldn't hesitate to cut your reputation to shreds with a whisper just for looking at them the wrong way.

"Then you're an idiot. This isn't a game. My brother, Torrio, they *kill* people," Viola said, and there was something in the way her voice broke that made Ruby's heart clench. "They make people disappear."

"And Tammany Hall protects them," Ruby said, knowing even more surely that the path she was on was the right one. "The very people elected to serve everyone are protecting the . . . the . . . *criminals* that they're supposed to be stopping."

Theo patted Ruby on the knee, making her realize just how animated she'd become.

"She gets a bit overwrought sometimes," he told Viola.

"I am not overwrought," Ruby said tartly, pushing his hand away. She felt her cheeks flame and cursed her mother for giving her skin so fair it showed every emotion in the same color—pink.

"Of course you're not," he told her, but she knew that tone of voice. As much as she adored Theo, she couldn't stand it when he got all paternal.

Ruby cut him a sharp look, and he was smart enough to raise his hands in mock surrender. She turned back to Viola. "I'm *not* overwrought," she repeated. "I'm simply passionate about the causes I believe in. You see, I'm a journalist."

"This one, he's your fiancé?" Viola asked.

"Guilty, I'm afraid," Theo said with his usual lopsided smile.

"And you allow her to do this?" Viola asked, her expression incredulous. "You're an idiot too."

He laughed as the carriage bumped along.

"He doesn't *let* me do anything," Ruby cut in, her cheeks feeling even warmer than before.

"True," Theo agreed. "I merely follow along, cleaning up the chaos that ensues in her wake," he said cheerfully. "The things we do for love."

Enough. She tried to give him what she hoped was a scathing glare, but he just continued to grin at her. Probably because he knew exactly how much it would annoy her.

"I'd prefer not to be caught up in anybody's wake," Viola said. "I have troubles enough of my own. I don't need any of yours. If you could just let me out—"

"But we haven't even had a chance to talk," Ruby said with a sudden burst of panic. She reached over and clasped Viola's bare hand.

It didn't matter that she was wearing gloves—Ruby felt the warmth of Viola's skin even through the delicate leather. She wondered if Viola felt that same jolt of energy, because the moment after their hands met, Viola pulled away like she'd been burned.

"So talk," Viola said, her voice rougher than it had been a moment before. Her violet eyes seemed darker somehow.

"Talk . . ." It took Ruby a second to remember what she'd wanted to talk about. "Right." She pulled her small notebook and pencil from inside of her handbag to allow herself a moment to gather her wits again.

She flipped through the pages, each filled with her own familiar looping scrawl. Glancing over them, she focused, centering herself on the job at hand. Viola Vaccarelli was not some silly missish debutante, like most of the girls Ruby had grown up around. Her spine was too straight, her gaze too direct. It was as though she could see through all Ruby's posturing to every one of the doubts that lurked beneath.

Taking a steadying breath, Ruby set her own shoulders and began. "I'm working on a story about the corruption at the very heart of the city. I know the Five Pointers are in league with Tammany—"

"Everybody knows that," Viola said, crossing her arms over the fullness of her bosom.

She isn't wearing stays. It was an absurd thought, but the moment it occurred to Ruby, she couldn't dismiss it. There was nothing lascivious about Viola's dress, though. Nothing at all provocative. She simply looked . . . comfortable. Free.

Focus, Reynolds.

"As I was saying, people know about their connection to Tammany, but after our encounter at Delmonico's, I realized that your brother must also be working with the Order of Ortus Aurea."

"Why would anyone care about that?" Viola challenged, but her expression closed up so tightly that Ruby knew she was onto something.

"People might care that the organization that claims to be protecting the city is working with violent gang leaders like Paul Kelly, but I think they would care even more if they knew the Order was working with the very people they were trying to protect us *from*. I want to expose them, Miss Vaccarelli. I want everyone in the city to know that the Order isn't the benevolent force they believe but are instead harboring dangerous criminals."

"You can't," Viola said, shaking her head.

"Of course I can," Ruby said. "It's what I *do*."

"Not if you want to make it to your wedding day," Viola told her, and there was an odd tremor to her voice. "My brother and the Five Pointers, they won't want you messing in their business. That's what I was trying to tell you at the restaurant. You need to stop before they stop you."

"They can try, but it won't matter if I can expose them first," Ruby said, trying to imbue her words with the conviction that she felt so firmly. "But I need your help."

"What could you possibly think I can do for you?"

"Don't pretend that you don't know Paul Kelly has Mageus in his ranks."

Viola's face had gone pale, and she looked as though she wanted to leap from the rolling carriage. *Maybe she doesn't know.*

"John Torrio is Mageus," Ruby said in a hushed voice. Although why she bothered to lower her voice, she couldn't have said. It was only the three of them in the carriage.

"Torrio?" Viola's expression bunched in confusion.

"You must have known," Ruby insisted. "I knew it the second I woke up from whatever that was he did to us back at Delmonico's. For both of us to faint with no provocation whatever? And . . ." She lowered her voice. "It *felt* like magic, didn't it, Theo?"

Theo gave Ruby a long-suffering expression. "It felt like my head hit the table, darling."

Ruby shot him another annoyed look before she went back to ignoring him. "It felt positively *electric*."

"You think John Torrio has the old magic?" Viola said, her voice hollow with what could only be disbelief.

She didn't know, the poor dear.

"Yes. Oh, I realize this is all coming as a shock to you, but you see now why the story I'm working on is so important. If I can prove that Kelly's gang uses Mageus and that the Order is protecting the Five Pointers, then I can prove the Order is protecting the very thing they say they want to destroy. Can't you see?" She leaned forward and, without meaning to, took Viola's hand again. This time she ignored the bolt of heat she felt. It was adrenaline. Excitement. *Surely* Viola felt that as well. "With your help, I could end the Order."

UNEXPECTED BENEFITS

1902—New York

Viola was speechless. She took in the girl, this Ruby Reynolds, with her expression expectant and her eyes shining, and all Viola could do was gape. The girl thought *Torrio* was the Mageus?

"You understand how important this is, don't you?" Ruby asked. "You'll help me?"

"Why?" was all Viola could manage at first.

Ruby frowned. "Why what?"

"Why would you want to destroy the Order?" Viola asked. "They're like you—rich and white, native born. You have the world at your feet. Why do this?"

Ruby looked as though someone had struck her. "Maybe *I* don't want to be like *them*, Miss Vaccarelli."

Viola had not known that an expression could go quiet until that moment, but it wasn't an easy silence brought on by fear. It was a fierce stillness that she understood too well. In that instant, the painted bird turned into a tiger, silent and deadly.

"Yes," Ruby told her in a voice that was as brittle as broken glass, "I do have the world at my feet. I have a *wonderful* life filled with all the best people at all the best parties in the best city in the world." She leaned forward, her expression serious. "But I'm tired of pretending that everything about my life is as it should be. I'd rather be dead."

Viola refused to let herself be moved by the rich girl's pretty words. "You poke around Paul Kelly and you will be."

"Then at least I'll know I've lived well, won't I?"

The man, Theo, patted Ruby's leg gently, as though to comfort her, but even Viola could see that Ruby didn't need comfort. Her skin was flushed and her eyes were clear and determined. She was a strange creature—not half so fragile as Viola had first suspected. But perhaps every bit as spoiled if her people allowed her to flit about the city, chasing after every idea that entered her head.

"The Order is a menace to the city," Ruby said, her voice softer now, grave and serious. "They've grown weak, and they're afraid of that weakness. They're afraid of their own irrelevance in this new, modern age, so they've turned to Tammany to help shore up the power they've lost, and now they've turned to your brother. They've become the very thing they're supposed to be protecting the city from. Look at what they did, sending you and Torrio to scare me, all because I wrote a *story*. A story that was the truth. But it was a story that showed them to be weak and ineffective. They don't want anyone to know about what really happened at Khafre Hall. They don't want anyone to understand how pointless they are, so they will use any means—corrupt politicians and criminals, even Mageus—to protect themselves. To prop up their dying institution. And people will die."

"People already have," Viola said darkly.

"Then you understand?" Ruby asked, her voice tinged with hope.

The three of them sat in an uneasy silence for a long while before Theo finally spoke. "We can provide you with compensation for your testimony, of course. We can get you out of the city, if you're worried about your safety."

We. Because they were together. Because they would be married. And once they were, the girl would be like every other girl who gathered a bouquet and pledged herself to a man. Viola wondered what would happen to the girl's fire then. Would it sputter out, or would it explode, destroying the pretty picture of their lives together?

"I don't worry about my safety," Viola said, shaking her head. The girl was a menace to herself, to Mageus everywhere, and now, to Viola. And there was only one way to make sure that danger didn't go unchecked. And if it also helped Viola chip away at the Order's power? Then that was an unexpected benefit. They would make strange allies, these two. But they seemed sincere. "Fine," Viola told Ruby. "I'll help you."

"Thank you—" Ruby started to say, but Viola held up a hand to silence her.

"I have a condition."

"What type of condition?" Theo asked, looking at her now as though she were a roach that had just crawled out of the cupboard.

"You don't write no more articles until our arrangement is done. Not a one," she said, when the girl was about to argue.

"But I have to write," Ruby said. "It's my *profession*."

Viola shook her head. If the girl published anything else, everyone would know that Viola hadn't actually killed Reynolds.

"Can she write under a different name?" Theo asked.

"But, Theo—"

"It's only until you get the information you need," he said, and then glanced at Viola. "How long will that take?"

"It depends on what she wants from me."

"I need information," Ruby said. "From what I can tell, the Order is looking for the people who destroyed Khafre Hall. I need to know what they took. I need names, evidence of the Order's connection to your brother and the Five Pointers. I need incontrovertible proof that the Order isn't what it appears to be. That it is a danger to the city."

"You ask for a lot—too much maybe. It will take time," Viola said before Ruby could even open her smart mouth. "Paul, he doesn't trust me. To get the information will be a delicate thing." But it wouldn't be impossible. And if Viola could implicate Nibsy as well? She could take out two birds at once. "If you write more of your stories, it will make it harder for me to find what you're asking for. It will make it dangerous for me, too," she finished, playing on the girl's emotions.

"Well, she can't go on without writing indefinitely," Theo said. "There has to be some sort of limitation."

Until Libitina is in my hands again, Viola thought, but that wasn't anything she could say out loud. "Until I say so. That's my offer. Take it or figure out how to get access to the Five Pointers some other way."

Viola waited, half-convinced that her bluff would be called and that Ruby would reject the offer and continue on her reckless course alone and half hoping she wouldn't.

Finally, Ruby nodded. "Deal," she said, extending her hand.

Viola examined it for a moment, cursing herself for getting mixed up in all of this. She should walk away and wash her hands of everything. But if the girl helped her to destroy the Order and put her brother in his place all while making Nibsy a target? It was an opportunity she couldn't refuse.

She didn't like this Ruby Reynolds. She didn't like her perfectly white teeth or her pert nose or the way her cheeks turned pink every time someone spoke to her. Maybe Ruby wasn't so fragile as Viola had expected, but the girl was still too delicate for Viola's world. Whatever happened, Viola had tried to warn her.

Viola took Ruby's hand and shook, ignoring the warmth that washed through her body when her skin slid against the smooth, soft leather of Ruby's gloves. Their eyes met, and for some reason, Viola could only see Tilly looking back at her. And she hated Ruby Reynolds that much more.

The carriage had come to a stop without Viola even noticing it. Once she finally did, she pulled her hand away.

"When should we meet next?" Theo asked, breaking the silence.

Viola shook her head. "I'm not sure."

"That won't do—" he started, but Ruby stopped him.

"I'm sure she has responsibilities to tend to," Ruby told him, but her eyes didn't leave Viola's. "She'll send word when she has something. . . . Won't you?"

Just days ago she'd been stuck in the Bowery, where she would live and die. She'd been mourning Tilly, but she'd been content with her lot in life, with knowing what it was—what it would be. Now everything was uncertain. Now she didn't know where she would land. But she was determined that it would be on her feet. "I'll send word when I can."

Theo pulled a creamy white card from his jacket pocket and handed it to her. "You can contact us here," he said.

As she took it from him, she noticed his perfectly manicured nails, the smooth skin of his fingertips, and the Madison Avenue address. She had killed men far more dangerous than Theo Barclay, but for the first time in a long time, Viola felt the uneasy stirrings of a different type of fear.

Theo opened the door and let her alight from the carriage. She realized she was back where she'd started—all that had just happened, and they'd only circled a couple of blocks.

"We'll talk again soon," Ruby told her before the carriage door closed.

Viola watched the carriage drive away until it turned the corner, leaving the filth and the poverty of the Bowery behind without any evidence that it had ever been there.

Shaking off her foul mood, Viola started back toward Paul's building. Whatever she pretended to be, Ruby Reynolds was nothing but a poor little rich girl, having a good time as she played her little games. She was everything that Viola had grown to hate—privileged, careless, and ignorant of the realities of the world.

Or she was supposed to be. But Viola had seen the way her expression changed when she spoke of a different sort of life. Yes, Ruby Reynolds was everything that Viola was supposed to hate, but Viola knew without a doubt that she would do whatever she must to make sure that pretty, delicate Ruby Reynolds survived long enough to see the error of her ways.

FURIOUS

1904—St. Louis

O utside King's, the night air was damp and still held the coolness of the storm that had passed earlier. Esta pulled her cap down low over her eyes, but she kept her shoulders squared and her strides purposeful, remembering what Julien had told her. She was still annoyed with Harte, still thinking about the train and the Antistasi and about what all of it might mean, but as they walked, her annoyance eased.

Around her, the unfamiliar city felt strangely comfortable. Maybe it was that the energy of the city—the feeling of so many people living and breathing and fighting and loving all in a small parcel of land—was the same. Crowded. Eminently alive, even in the dead of night.

When they reached the boardinghouse, Harte hesitated. The sky had cleared and now moonlight cast its pall over his features.

"What is it?" Esta asked.

"Nothing. I just . . ." But he shook his head instead of finishing the sentence and led the way up the front porch steps and then up the narrow staircase to the room they'd rented a few hours before.

Once she'd unlocked their door, all she could think about was getting out of the stale-smelling clothes she was wearing. Everything reeked of the cigars Julien insisted on constantly smoking and the body odor of the clothes' previous owner. She stripped off the jacket and tossed it aside, then started unbuttoning the shirt before she realized that Harte still hadn't moved any farther into the room than just inside the doorway. He had his hands tucked into his pockets and a look on his face that made her pause.

"Aren't you coming in?" she asked, shrugging off the shirt.

His eyes drifted down to the strips of bedsheet that she'd torn to wrap around her torso, binding down her breasts to better hide her natural shape. "This isn't going to work," he said.

Not this again. "Julien thinks it'll work just fine. No one in that saloon even looked twice at me, and you know it." But he was shaking his head, disagreeing with her. He was always disagreeing with her. "You're just angry you didn't think of it first," she told him.

"You think I'm *angry?*" he said as he took a step toward her. There was something oddly hollow in his voice, something unreadable in his eyes.

"Aren't you?"

He took another step, then another, until he was close enough that she could feel the heat of his skin. "Furious." But he didn't sound it, not even a little.

There was an odd light in his eyes, but it wasn't the strange colors she'd seen in them before. Instead, it was a question, a spark of wanting and hope and need so fierce that she couldn't do more than simply tilt her chin up in an answer and invitation all at once.

Then his lips were on hers, firm and confident, without any space between them for more questions. She could have stopped him, could have stopped *herself* from wrapping her arms around his neck and pulling him closer, but she didn't want to. All the fear and frustration and worry of the night was still there, but suddenly it simply didn't matter. All that mattered at that moment was the feel of his lips against hers and the reality of Harte, solid and warm and wanting, as he deepened the kiss, pulling her into it. Losing himself as well.

And then all at once he backed away, breaking the connection between them. His eyes were brighter now, and she could see the unnameable colors shimmering there as his chest rose and fell with the effort of his breathing. She wanted to draw him back and kiss him again, but she waited, because she sensed that any movement would break the fragile hope spun out of the moment.

Slowly, tentatively, he reached out to brush the fringe of hair back from her face. "I can't believe you did this to your hair."

"It's just hair, Harte," she said, the warmth that had blossomed inside of her cooling a bit at his words. But his fingers sifting through her short locks were making it hard to stay angry at him. "I don't really care if you like it or not."

He frowned at her. "I never said I didn't like it," he told her softly.

"At the bar, I thought . . ." He was running his hand down the bare nape of her neck. "You looked so upset."

"Can you blame me?" he whispered, and then he leaned in until his forehead rested against hers. "You surprised me. I thought you were safe, and then you appeared . . . like this—"

She pulled back, about to snap at him again, but she stopped when she saw the expression on his face. The desire and *need* that matched her own.

He ran his hand down the side of her neck, and in its wake, she felt her affinity ripple and warm, felt herself warm as well. "You might as well have arrived completely naked, with your neck so exposed and the shape of your legs in those pants where every person in the bar could see them."

"No one was looking." She was frustrated and amused all at once at his prudishness.

"*I* was looking," he told her, and he drew her in to him again, kissing her with a desperation that made her lose her breath.

She was only partially aware that the door was still open behind him because all of her senses were taken up with the kiss. His hands ran down her neck, over her shoulders and her arms, smoothing away the anger and fear of the day, pressing aside the emptiness she'd felt when her affinity had slipped from her grasp and sparking something else—something warmer and brighter than she'd felt before. Then he was tugging at the bindings around her chest until they fell away completely and her bare skin brushed against the rough fabric of his coat. She could have stopped him at any moment, but she didn't *want* to. Instead, she threaded her fingers through his hair, drawing him closer, urging him on. Meeting him will for will, want for want.

It wasn't until the back of her legs hit the low bed that she realized they had been moving across the room, but then they toppled together onto the thin mattress, Harte's weight pressing down onto her and boxing her in. *Yes,* she wanted to say, but the second they were horizontal, Harte went completely still. He pulled back from her, and she watched his expression close up like a house before a storm, while the strange colors bloomed within his irises.

"Harte?" she whispered, touching his face when he didn't move other than the ragged rise and fall of his chest as he caught his breath. But even though his eyes were open, staring straight into hers, Esta had the sense that Harte wasn't really there.

THE WOMAN

1904—St. Louis

Harte was a breath away from Esta. He could feel her skin hot against his, the softness of her body against the firmness of his own, but it wasn't her he was seeing. The dingy room had fallen away as well, and he felt the oppressiveness of summer—a dry, baking heat that licked along his skin.

There was a woman dressed in white linen robes that draped the floor, and the woman was screaming. She was Esta and she was another woman all at the same time, and she was—*they* were—screaming. The sound echoed in his ears so loudly that he couldn't hear anything but the terror and agony and *rage* in her voice. The woman was looking at him, her face superimposed over Esta's, and though there was a part of Harte that dimly realized none of this was real—that this was some sort of vision or waking nightmare—he could not shake himself free of it.

He wanted to scream at Esta to get away. He needed to break the connection between them, but it was too late. The voice had swelled within him, blotting out Esta's face completely.

And then there was only darkness and it was as though he was the woman. As though he was seeing what she saw, feeling what she felt.

Ahead there was a light, and she went toward it until it grew brighter and brighter and became a chamber that was lined with scrolls and parchments piled high upon the shelves. Knowledge and power and all the secrets of the world.

She'd done this.

She'd created it all, but none of it had worked. There was still more to do, or the power in the world would fade as surely as moonlight in the brightness of dawn.

In the center of the room stood a long, low table, and upon its surface gleamed five gemstones—stones not hewed from the earth but made.

The power she wielded was dying. Magic had been fading for some time, growing weaker with each division, with each breaking apart. She had tried to stop its slow death. She had created something to suspend power, pure and whole. To preserve it. So she had created the word and the page. But it had not worked. It had been stolen from her, perverted and abused.

She had meant to save them all, and instead she had created magic's undoing. But she would stop that. Now. Here.

She ran her fingers over the stones that she had created, and he could feel the way they called to her. He could feel the pull of them, strong and sure and clear.

And then the vision tilted and changed again. The world tipped and there was a woman—or perhaps it was Esta? Her dark hair was wild around her face. Her eyes had gone black and empty and she was screaming. The stones were aglow, and she was trapped within their power. Pain and rage and fury whipped about the chamber. And fear. There was a fear thick in the air—fear, and the pain of betrayal.

"Harte?" He felt cool fingers touch his face, drawing him up from the depths, and he flinched away, surfacing from the nightmare that had intruded into his waking.

"Don't touch me," he said, his voice strained and sharp. He pulled back. Scuttled away from her with an awkward jerking step, falling out of the bed to get away. "Just—stay over there. Stay away."

The vision still haunted him. The woman and Esta, their faces alternating as he tried to shake the image of the woman screaming from his mind.

Esta turned on her side to look at him. "What is it?" she asked. "What's gotten into you?"

"I *want you*—" But he clapped his hands over his own mouth, because it wasn't him who'd spoken. The voice had taken advantage of his weakness and had forced itself up from within him, taking his body and using it as if he were nothing more than a puppet.

Her mouth curved and her golden eyes went dark. "Well, I think what just happened proves that you can have me," she said impishly.

"No!" he roared. And the word was his own. He was *himself*. Harte Darrigan, not whatever lived inside of him.

Esta flinched, and he saw hurt flash across her face. "Harte, what's wrong?" She was reaching for him and looking so beautiful and fragile and utterly breakable.

He knew what the vision meant—*he* would break her. The Book—the power inside of him, whatever it was—would break her and use her and it would be his fault. *All my fault.* He would break her like he broke his mother, but this time there would be nothing left afterward, nothing but the blackness that still haunted him long after the vision had faded.

The blackness, just like the darkness that Esta had told him she saw when their affinities connected.

Swallowing hard, he forced himself to look at her—to make sure that the blackness in her eyes wasn't real. Her hair was a mess, the short strands chopped in uneven lengths and falling around her face like some sort of fairy creature, but her eyes were her own. There was concern and pain and a question in their whiskey-colored depths. "I can't hold it back," he told her. He saw the flash of pleasure in her expression before he killed it with the words he said next. "It's the Book. . . ."

"The *Book*?" she asked.

"The power of whatever it is inside of me. I—" He stopped, corrected himself. "*It* wants you. It wants to use you, and if it does . . ." *The blackness was so empty, like nothing at all. Like it will bleed into the world and no one will be safe.*

"What are you saying?" she asked slowly, her tone cooling now. "Are you telling me that you didn't *want* to kiss me?"

"Yes," he said, shaking his head. But it didn't feel like the truth. "I don't know."

Esta sat up the rest of the way, frowning at him. She pulled the sheets around her, but not before he saw the flash of brownish pink and the smooth expanse of skin that had almost been his.

Yes . . . Mine . . .

"No!" he said. His voice was like the report of a gun in the tiny room, and she flinched again. But he would not let it have her. "I don't know what this is inside of me," he told her, his voice rough. "I don't know what this is between us. I don't know if I want you or if it's the power that does, but *this* can't happen. This can't *ever* happen."

"Harte . . ?" There was an ache in her voice that pierced him.

"I've seen things," he whispered, the memory of the visions crashing over him again.

"What are you talking about?" she asked.

"Visions. At the station, at the hotel, just now . . ." He looked at her, willed her to understand as he told her what he'd seen. "I'm going to hurt you. If I touch you, if I let myself go with you, I'll destroy you."

"You won't—"

He let out a ragged breath. "You can't know that."

"I'm not some fragile flower, Harte. We'll figure this out. We'll do it *together.*"

She reached for him, but he drew back, avoiding her touch. The voice was too near to the surface of him. Then he turned away, because he knew that if he looked at her now, saw the hurt in her eyes and her body bared to him as it was, his control would crumble. "I apologize," he said stiffly, his voice brittle and clipped.

"There's nothing to apologize for." She was on her feet now. He could hear her wrapping the blanket around herself. "In case you missed it, I was right there with you."

But he was already grabbing his coat, heading for the door, which was still open. *We didn't even close the door.* So much for control.

"You're seriously leaving?" she asked.

"I'm going to walk for a bit." He did turn back to her then, and her hair was rumpled and her lips were bruised red from their kissing. "I need some air."

"Harte—"

"And some space," he finished, striding out the open door. Once he was through it, he closed it behind him with an unmistakable finality.

His legs were shaking as he ran down the steps of the boardinghouse and out into the night. It was still warm, the air was damp from the rain, and the clouds had parted above to show the stars, but Harte didn't notice any of that. He didn't even notice which way he was going. He simply walked, as quickly and as doggedly as his feet would go.

He'd kissed her. He'd kissed her, touched her, and it had been *everything*—*more* than everything. More than he could have imagined.

He could have had her. She would have given herself to him, and he could have taken her there, on that narrow, dirty bed in that narrow, worn-out room. *And she would have hated him for it later.*

Onward he walked until the power inside of him receded and the soles of his feet felt as ragged as he did, as he vowed with every step he took that he would never let that happen.

THE REMAINS OF
WHAT HAD BEEN

1904—St. Louis

E sta looked at the crackled paint on the back of the closed door as the realization of what Harte had just done settled in her blood. She was holding the blanket up over her bare chest, and through the open window she could hear the sounds of dogs barking and the occasional rattle of a carriage in the distance. Her heart was galloping, and her skin felt flushed and warm from Harte's kisses, even as her fury mounted.

His words echoed in her mind: *I'm going to hurt you.*

At least he hadn't been lying about *that.*

She had known all along that uniting the stones and taking control of the Book might mean the end of her. Professor Lachlan had told her as much when he'd tried to take the power of the Book himself. *You're just the vessel.* Wasn't that what he'd said?

She had hoped that the Book would hold some key to changing that fate, but the Book was in the hands of Jack Grew, and who knew where he was? The only way to get back to the time and place where they lost it was to get Harte under control. But when she touched Harte, she could barely slow down the seconds. She wasn't about to trust slipping through time until they figured out how to control the power he had in him.

Power that, apparently, wanted her.

She shuddered at the thought of it. Suddenly the room felt too close— and at the same time, unbearably empty. Esta pulled on the chemise she'd worn earlier beneath her corset. For a moment she just stood in the silence, taking in the narrow, sagging bed with its stained cover rumpled and askew, the faded curtains looking so tired and worn that they would fall at any moment, and the pile of hair she'd left on the floor earlier.

She'd almost slept with Harte Darrigan. A few minutes ago she'd trusted him enough to lay down all her defenses. And he hadn't even been there. He hadn't even been the one—the *thing*—in control. Everything that had just happened—he wasn't even sure it had been him.

A coldness settled over her as she reached up to push what was left of her hair out of her eyes. Her fingers still remembered what it had felt like just hours before to run through the long strands, to tuck the locks that had fallen back behind her ears, but now her own hair felt foreign to her. Tentatively, she brushed at the nape of her neck, where the ragged ends of her hair felt coarse and sharp, but it only reminded her of the way Harte had touched her.

Across the room, she caught her reflection in the scarred mirror, and without thinking, she stepped closer. She barely recognized herself—the dark rings beneath her eyes, the way her short hair made her jaw seem sharper and her mouth harder, even as her mouth was still rouged from the friction of Harte's kisses. Her eyes were no longer softened by the makeup she'd used to darken her lashes. It was more than the haircut that had changed her. It was the fire in her eyes kindled by heartache and senseless tragedy. It was the determination in the hard set of her mouth.

For a moment she examined this new version of herself and realized the overwhelming reality of what she had done—to her hair, with Harte—of where they were and what was at stake. And of what might still lie ahead.

She didn't yet know the person looking back at her, but she liked what she saw. Or she would learn to. She would do what she must to make sure that Nibsy could never have the stones. She would make sure that the Book and its power were protected from the Order and others who might use them to harm those like her. But she would harden herself against Harte Darrigan. She would be his partner, would even save him if she could, but she would not allow herself to open her heart to him.

She would not make the same mistake again.

At her feet, the remains of what had once been her hair littered the floor. She considered it, the long strands soft beneath the leather soles of the men's shoes she still wore. That hair had belonged to a different girl. Esta could no more go back to being that girl than she could reattach the hair to her head. No more than she could wipe the memory of Harte's kisses from her lips. Gathering the pile of hair from the floor, Esta tossed it into the stove, but the fire had already gone cold and dead.

TOO LATE

The fog that had descended upon the Bowery was thick and murky as the night itself. The soft halo of the streetlamps barely cut through the gloom. The streets, wet with the day's rain, shone like the water that flooded the rice paddies around his village. For a moment Jianyu almost felt like he was there, standing on a hillside and looking over the endless sweep of fields around his family's home, the water-soaked ground drowning the weeds that would otherwise choke the life from the rice. But then the image flickered, and it was only the city he saw—the grimness of the streets, the sloshing puddles that would never be enough to wash away the filth and poverty that choked the life from the Bowery.

He was late. He had already failed Cela, and now he would fail again.

Picking up his pace, he did not bother with magic. His affinity would be of no help, not with the way his footsteps could be traced from puddle to puddle, but he kept to the shadows and moved faster. He could not be late. If the boy reached Nibsy, the results could be devastating. With the boy, Nibsy would hold knowledge of what was to come. It could make him unstoppable.

The streets were empty, a spot of luck in an otherwise dismal string of days. Lonely and silent, they offered no comfort. To be taken off guard, to have been beaten so soundly, and then to be handed over by Mock Duck for a handful of secrets? Perhaps he should have been grateful that he was alive. Certainly he should be grateful that Cela had been following him

334

and had risked her own life to rescue him. But it galled him to know that he had required *her* protection. He had failed her—just as he had failed Dolph—but he would not fail again. He would not allow the boy from another time to win. If that happened, if Nibsy became as powerful as Harte and Esta predicted, the impact would be felt far beyond the reaches of the city, perhaps even far across the seas.

A shadow on the other side of the street moved, drawing Jianyu's attention. As he turned, a man stepped from the darkness into the gloom of the lamplight.

Mock Duck. The silver buttons of his waistcoat glinted like eyes in the night.

Jianyu kept his head down and picked up his pace. He reached for his bronze mirrors but found his pockets empty. *No matter.* He called to his affinity and opened the light around him as he began to run, cutting down an alley to the next block. He did not turn to see if Mock's high-binders were following. Instead, he focused on avoiding the puddles that would expose his exact path.

Two more blocks and then another half a block west, and he would be where Esta said the boy would arrive . . . if he had not already missed him.

He turned onto Essex Street and pulled up short. Ahead, a group of men were surrounding another.

Too late.

Jianyu kept the light close to him as he edged nearer, careful to avoid the telltale ripples his shoes would cause in the puddles at his feet. When he was close enough to see, his stomach tightened. Tom Lee and a trio of On Leongs were standing over someone—a man or a boy—and the person on the ground was deathly still.

He should go. Tom Lee would not forgive Jianyu for abandoning his oath to the On Leongs. Perhaps Lee was not as violent as Mock Duck, but Jianyu knew that if Lee found him there, Lee would not hesitate to attack. But Jianyu needed to know—was the man they stood over the boy he was looking for? He edged closer, keeping his affinity tightly around him.

One of the On Leongs kicked the man with such violence that Jianyu felt an answering ache in his own gut. The man moaned in pain and rolled onto his back.

Jianyu's blood ran cold.

The person on the ground was not the blond boy Esta had described on the bridge. In the wan glow of the lamplight, Jianyu saw *himself* on the ground—it was not the boy's face but his own contorted in agony as Tom Lee's men prepared to attack again.

He stumbled back in stunned disbelief, splashing into stagnant water. In the shock of the moment, his affinity slipped.

Tom Lee and his men turned at the noise, and their eyes widened to see him there. Their expressions were a mixture of surprise and horror as they looked between Jianyu, standing as he was in the weak, flickering lamplight, and the body on the ground, barely moving. But Tom Lee showed no such fear. He stepped toward Jianyu, a gleam of anticipation in his expression as he pulled a pistol from inside his coat and raised it.

Jianyu turned to run, but the echo of the gun's explosion drowned out his footsteps. He felt the pain of the bullet tear through him, and then he was falling.

Falling toward the muck and wetness of the rain-slicked streets. Falling through them—on and on—as though death were nothing but a constant descent. Falling as though he would never stop, as though he would never land.

Until his body hit hard, and he jolted upright, struggling to get to his feet. He had to run—

"Just settle down there," a voice said, and it was not the Cantonese that he expected. It was in English, soft and rolling like none he had heard before. "Cela! Get in here, girl."

Jianyu's eyes opened, and the street melted away, leaving a small but comfortable room. The glow of a small lamp lit the space, and the air felt close and warm, smelling of sweat and stale bodies.

No, not the room. It was *he* who smelled of stale sweat. His clothes were damp with it, and he suddenly felt unbearably hot and cold all at once.

"What is it?" Cela was there in the doorway.

"He's waking up," a male voice said. It was the person holding him down, an older man with tawny-brown skin, his hair gray at the temples of his broad forehead. "Deal with him."

The hands were gone, and a moment later the bed dipped and Cela sat next to him. Her graceful hands felt cool against the skin of his forehead when she touched him.

"How long?" he asked, his voice coming out as a dry rasp as he struggled to sit up. His side still ached and his head pounded.

"Hold on," Cela said, reaching for a cup of water. She tried to put it in his hands, but he pushed it away.

"How long have I been here?" he asked again, his heart still racing from the dream of death.

"You've been in and out for nearly five days," Cela said.

No. He was late. *Too late.* He tried to swing his legs off the bed, but the motion made him dizzy.

"You have to sit down," Cela told him, holding him by the arm as he swayed.

"I have to go," he said, shaking her off.

"Go?" Vaguely he realized that her voice sounded very far away. "You can barely sit up. Where do you think you're going?"

He struggled to his feet. *Too late.* But his vision swam, and he stumbled backward.

"You're not going anywhere," Cela said. She pushed him gently back into bed, and his limbs felt so weak that he could not fight her. "You're going to drink this water, and if you keep that down, you can have some broth."

"I am too late," he told her, taking the cup. His hands were trembling from the weight of the water, and he could not seem to make them stop.

"You had the life half beaten out of you. Whatever it is can wait," she said, indicating that he should drink.

She was wrong. The boy would not wait to arrive, would not wait to find Nibsy. Jianyu drank the water reluctantly, but he was surprised at the coolness of it, at how parched he suddenly felt. It was gone before it even began to touch his thirst. "More," he asked, his voice a plea more than a command. *Five days.*

He took the second glass and drank, as much to prove that he could as for his thirst. *Five days.* He had lost five days. Which meant that he was already too late.

DISCARDED

1902—New York

For Logan Sullivan, traveling through time wasn't the romantic adventure the movies made it out to be. For one thing, he didn't get to sail along in a floating car or a magical police box. It wasn't an easy jump. It hurt. And another thing—it made his head spin, his guts feel like they were about to fall out, and his very *self* feel like it was about to shatter. There was always a moment just as Esta dragged Logan from one time to another when he swore that there was a chance they wouldn't make it at all, a point where it felt like he didn't even exist. In short, time travel was a difficult, dangerous, and frustrating pain in the ass.

But then again, so was Esta.

She was the one who had always been able to see right through him, and that was damn inconvenient for Logan Sullivan, considering he'd discovered a long time ago that it was easier to move through the world if you let your pretty face do the talking.

Still, pain in the ass or not, he'd felt bad about the gun he'd pressed to her side and even worse about the bullets Professor Lachlan had loaded into it. It wasn't that he didn't believe the Professor when he'd told Logan that Esta had turned on them and couldn't be trusted. It was that Logan might have been a lot of things, but he'd never thought of himself as a murderer. He didn't like the idea of having to put a bullet in her back. Even if she had done the same to Dakari.

So he'd been glad when she hadn't fought him as they'd walked to the departure point. He'd been relieved when he'd had to nudge her only once to get her moving, but he should have known it couldn't be that easy. Nothing with her ever was. One minute he felt like the whole world was being ripped apart, like his very soul was collapsing in on itself, and then he felt the solidness of the pavement beneath him again.

Before he could even pull himself upright, he'd felt a pain tear through his shoulder joint, and his hand had gone numb as Esta slid away from him. He'd stumbled, trying to get to his feet, but his vision was only *just* clear enough to see Esta scoop up the bag he'd been carrying and disappear.

Logan was trying to get his eyes to focus, when the reality of his situation hit him. The dampness of the cobbled street, the smell of coal smoke and soot in the air. The strange slant of light coming down through the overcast day, and the bustle of voices around him in languages he didn't understand. Professor Lachlan had tried to teach him, but he never had the head for words the way Esta had.

Esta. Who was always good at everything. Esta, who had definitely abandoned him.

In the past.

There was a scent in the air with the sootiness—a ripeness that indicated something alive. Or something that had once been alive. Animals or rotten food or shit. Yeah, definitely shit. In the cool morning air, the stench was muted, but Logan could imagine the smell would be thick enough to choke when the heat of the summer swept over the city.

He wasn't supposed to be there during the summer. Professor Lachlan had promised. Once Logan had delivered the bag and the notes, Esta was supposed to bring him back to his own time—*their* own time.

Where. He. Belonged.

The bag he'd been carrying was long gone, but at least he still had the notes, he thought as he patted the pocket of his jacket. *Yeah. Still there.*

Logan finally managed to sit up. His pants were damp from the puddle he'd landed in. *Rainwater . . . Let it be rainwater. . . .* Rubbing at his head where it had hit the concrete, he realized he was being watched. Two broad-shouldered guys with dark coats and hats tipped low over their eyes were stalking toward him. One had a stick of some sort—a club, but with a wicked spike at the end.

Scrambling to his feet, Logan put his hands up as he tried to back away, but he backed up instead into someone else.

"Whoa," he said, his head still swirling as he struggled to stay up.

"What do we have here?" the largest of the guys asked, taking another step toward Logan and penning him in. The guy smiled, a ruthless sort of grin that made Logan feel like he'd just swallowed a stone. He wasn't the fighter—that was Esta. He was more of a talk-your-way-out-of-the-situation type. But these guys didn't look like they were interested in listening.

"Where'd the girl go?" the other one said, his expression as flat as his broken nose. "She was just here and then—"

"Stuff it," the larger one said, jabbing at Logan with his stick. "She's one of them." He pinned Logan with a look. "Wasn't she? Does that mean you're one of them too?"

"Look, I don't want any problems," Logan told them.

"Too late for that now, ain't it?" the large one said as the man Logan had backed into took him by the arms. The other one picked up the gun Logan had been holding just moments earlier, his insurance against Esta's probable attempt at escape, and pocketed it. "I think you'd better come with us. The boss is going to want to see you."

Jerked and pressed along, there was no choice but to walk—walk and curse Esta and her damn treachery the whole way.

THE SIREN

1902—New York

Jack Grew had had enough of the constant coddling and fussing of his mother after two days. After five, he was finished completely, so he moved himself back into his own set of rooms. It had given him some peace, not having a constant parade of maids and doctors checking on him, and also some space from the rest of his family, who seemed always to be showing up to remind him about the next interview or appointment they'd arranged.

They were always doing the arranging. Never asking. Never consulting. Only demanding, and he was damn well sick of it. Now, at least, he had time to pour himself into deciphering the Ars Arcana.

When the clock struck eight, its long, sonorous chimes dragged Jack from his stupor. He blinked a few times, trying to remember where he was or what he had been doing. On the table in front of him, the Book was lying open, the page filled with symbols and markings in a language he didn't recognize.

Right. He'd been reading. Or he'd been trying to.

He rubbed at his eyes. He'd sat down not long after five to wade through a page of Greek and must have fallen asleep at some point. That was the thing he'd discovered about the Book—when he was studying it, time seemed to have no real meaning. He'd often wake in the morning, still dressed in the clothes he had been wearing the night before, his neck aching from sleeping upright in a chair, and the Book open in front of him.

Or perhaps that was simply an effect of the morphine, he thought dully, even as the ache in his head made him grimace. Taking the vial from his pocket, he removed a cube of the morphine and popped it into his mouth, cringing at the bitterness of it. But a few moments later the pain started to fade.

Not quickly enough, he thought, placing two more of the bitter cubes into his mouth. A little while longer, maybe, and he'd stop using the pain-killer. He wasn't some damn soldier who couldn't give it up. It hadn't been *that* long, he thought, his mind already softening and growing clearer. It simply took time, he told himself as he turned back to the Book.

It wasn't the ringing of the clock that brought him out of his stupor the second time. *No.* That was a different bell altogether.

He blinked, his head still swirling pleasantly and the pain in his head feeling very far away. He went to rub his eyes only to discover that his hand held a pen. The Book was still open, but now the page that had been completely incomprehensible before was filled with notations . . . and they were in his own hand.

Not just notations. Translations. And he didn't recall writing any of it.

The bell was still ringing.

The doorbell. Sam Watson. He'd almost completely forgotten about the appointment his uncle had made for another interview. The first one had been a complete waste of time, but apparently the Order felt that they needed to put a word in the ear of the press about the gala, and they were using Sam—and Jack—to do it.

Jack groaned as he closed the Book with a violent snap. The pages rippled, bouncing with the force of it. *The bell—and Watson—could damned well wait,* he thought as he took the Book into his bedroom and secured it in the safe. He took two more cubes of morphine to dampen the pain that was already shooting through his head from the incessant ringing of the bell. Then he went to the door.

It wasn't Watson.

"Miss DeMure," Jack said, surprised to see her standing in his doorway.

She was wearing a silk gown of the deepest emerald green, which contrasted with the red of her hair and lips.

She'd come with Sam before, to the first interview he'd had with the reporter. From the looks she'd given Jack during that interview, she'd been interested in Jack—*more* than interested. He'd hoped to see her again, but he hadn't expected her to arrive at his town house, unannounced and alone.

He looked past her, for some sign that Sam Watson was with her.

"Sam couldn't come," she said, stepping past him. "Regrettably, he was detained by something at the office. I thought you might enjoy my company instead." She tossed a smile over her shoulder, and Jack, who was not one to overlook a gift like this, shut the door behind her.

"Your company?" he asked expectantly, turning back to her.

She was running her gloved fingertips over the smooth, dark wood of the entry table. "Was I wrong?"

"No," he said, feeling a flush of warmth and satisfaction. "Not at all. Please, come in. Something to drink?"

The went into the parlor, and he poured them both glasses of sherry. She took the offered drink with a coy smile, but then she turned from him to examine one of the figurines on the sideboard.

He understood immediately the dance that she'd just started, and his gut went tight at the thought of what was to come—the give and take as they circled each other. The tease and the promise of it. And the moment he would triumph.

After a moment Evelyn turned to him, her eyes glittering in the soft light. "I knew Harte Darrigan, you know. . . ."

"Darrigan?" Irritation coursed through Jack as his mood went icy. The last thing he wanted to think about when he was entertaining a willing woman was that damned magician.

Evelyn nodded. "Some might say that I knew him *intimately.*"

"Did you?" he asked, not bothering to hide the disgust in his voice.

"Oh, don't be jealous, Jack," she said, and then she laughed, deep and throaty.

Despite his irritation, the sound tugged at his gut again, but the morphine was still in his blood, making his mind clear and his thoughts direct. She was toying with him.

But he was no mouse.

He stalked over to her slowly, so she wouldn't be afraid. So she wouldn't realize that it wasn't he who was the prey. "I wouldn't waste my time being jealous of trash like Darrigan," he told her.

Her red mouth drew up into a smile. "I didn't think you would. I knew from the moment I heard you speak to Sam the other day that you were too smart, too shrewd for an emotion as petty as jealousy. Which is why I thought you might be interested in information I have about him."

He took another step closer, until he could smell the cloying perfume that hung around her like a cloud, brash and loud—just like she was. "What information?"

"I was there that night, you know," she told him, sipping her sherry and never once breaking eye contact. *A challenge if ever there was one.* "I was at Khafre Hall the night everything happened. I know the Order is trying to cover the truth, that they're using you to distract the public from what actually happened. If you say Darrigan was on the train, I believe you."

"You do?" Jack asked, coming closer yet and placing his glass on the sideboard.

"Of course, Jack. I knew Darrigan, and I knew that bitch of an assistant he found. She's the one to blame for all of this, you know."

He took her by the arm and was gratified to see the flash of fear in her eyes. "I'm not interested in games. If you know where Darrigan or the girl are, you will tell me."

"I don't know where he is. I don't know if he even made it off the train—" He tightened his grip on her arm, and her eyes went wide. "But I do know that he might have left something behind . . . something that might interest you."

"Did he?" Jack asked, releasing his hold on her a little and then releasing her completely. The morphine had finally bloomed in his veins, softening everything and making him feel very present, like he was everywhere in the room at once. "What did he leave behind?"

"Information like that I could only share with my friends. My very *close* friends," she purred. "Are we friends, Jack?"

"Of course," he murmured.

His mouth curved up of its own accord as she stepped toward him, her eyes lighting with victory, clearly believing that she had won.

But oh, how very, very wrong she was.

THE EXPOSITION

1904—St. Louis

Harte waited with Esta at the corner of Lindell and Plaza, across from one of the main entrances to the world's fair. She hadn't spoken to him all morning, but it wasn't as though he had been willing to bring up what had happened between them the night before. They were both cowards, it seemed, but Harte didn't miss the way she had been careful not to touch him, not even allowing her arm to brush against his as the streetcar carried them through the town.

Standing outside the gates and watching the steady stream of visitors, Harte began to realize just how large the world's fair actually was. Lafayette Park, where the Exposition was being housed, stretched for miles in each direction. The scope of the event was astounding. In the distance, he could hear the roar of the crowds and the din of music coming from inside the gates, and every so often, the boom of a cannon or the sharp report of a gun echoed through the air.

"You need to relax," Esta said, her voice finally breaking through his thoughts. "Looking like that, you're going to draw attention."

"Like what?" he asked, risking a glance at her. It was, of course, a mistake. Her eyes were alert and her cheeks pink with the excitement of the day—or maybe it was just the heat—and at the sight of her, something clenched inside of him, something that had nothing to do with the power that had been rumbling ever since he'd kissed her the night before.

"Like you're about to attack someone," she said, cutting him an unreadable look out of the corner of her eye.

"I do not look like—" But he saw a familiar face approaching. "He's coming."

Despite being more than twenty minutes late, Julien strutted over to them as though nothing were amiss. "You're late," Harte told Julien, reaching out to shake hands in greeting.

"Unavoidable," Julien said with an affable shrug. But the expression in his eyes didn't match the ease of his words.

When Julien took Harte's hand in greeting, Harte thought briefly about using his affinity, just to be sure. But across the street, a troop of what was clearly the Jefferson Guard stood at attention near the gates. If Julien was right about them being able to sense magic, it wasn't worth the risk.

Esta held out her hand as well. "Good to see you again, Jules," she said, her voice pitched lower than usual.

"Well, well," Julien said, taking the greeting in stride.

Harte let out a muttered curse. "This is madness," he said. "There's no way someone isn't going to notice what she actually is."

"No one's going to be paying her any attention," Julien said, nodding toward the entrance across the street. "Not with the wonders that await them within."

"What wonders are those?" Esta asked, apparently enjoying herself. If she was mad about the night before, she hadn't said anything. Which meant she was definitely mad about it, and eventually he would have to face the consequences.

Not that he blamed her. He'd taken advantage of her and then he'd walked out on her. He deserved whatever she meted out.

Julien tucked his thumbs into his waistcoat pockets and rocked on his heels. "In there? Only the largest and most impressive fair the world has ever seen," he said. "Within those walls lie the evidence of our civilization's brilliance and the wonders of the wide world—all the innovations and discoveries this age has to offer."

"You can cut the drama any time now, Jules," Harte said, bristling at the way Esta's eyes were laughing at Julien's words. *She won't even look at me.* "All we want is the necklace. You said it was here?"

Julien shot Esta a conspiratorial look. "Patience, Darrigan." Then he started across the street, leaving them to follow.

"He's a little insufferable, isn't he?" Esta asked, making sure to keep her voice low enough that Julien wouldn't hear.

"More than a little," Harte said dryly.

"But I still like him."

Harte glanced at her. "Most people have that reaction. Try not to fall for it. Okay, Slim?"

"Slim?"

"Just trying it out," he told her with a shrug. "I need something to call you if you're going to insist on this getup."

She glared at him, and he felt almost relieved. "Well, it's not going to be Slim."

It was the way her cheeks flushed that sealed the deal for him. "I don't know," he said, his mouth twitching. "I think the name's already growing on me."

She started to argue, but he simply picked up his pace to walk next to Julien, leaving her to catch up with them.

They paid their entry fees and followed the crush of people through the ornate arches that acted as gateways into the fair. The crowd around them moved slowly, in part because directly in front of them was a band-stand where a full brass band was playing a bouncing march. As the three of them pushed their way through the crowd that had gathered to listen, Esta pointed to the big bass drum painted with the band's name.

"It's Sousa?" Esta asked Julien.

The band's conductor was dressed in military blue and his baton snapped out a pattern with almost mechanical precision to keep time for the music. Harte had heard of John Philip Sousa, of course—*who hadn't?*—but he wondered what it was about the bandleader that put a look of such serious concentration on Esta's face.

"I told you, they have the most famous performers, the most astounding displays from countries all over the world, and the most magnificent grounds ever built," Julien said. "The Society wants this Exposition to put St. Louis on the map—make it as important as Chicago, maybe even as important as Manhattan."

Esta glanced at Harte, and the look she gave him indicated that it wasn't going to happen. But the moment their eyes met, her expression faltered.

Harte's stomach sank as she turned away from him again. "I just want the necklace, Jules. Can we get to it?"

They had to push their way through the crowd around the bandstand. To their left, a tree-lined alley led deeper into the park, and Harte could see the sun glinting off a body of water. Julien continued to follow the path past administrative buildings and then onto an area with signage declaring it THE PIKE.

"Here we are," he said, gesturing toward the brick-paved path before them.

The wide boulevard led into a kind of surreal fantasy world. At the entrance, mountains at least ten stories high dwarfed a small alpine village, which sprouted up next to the replica of a castle that could have come from the stories of King Arthur. As far as the eye could see, the street was lined with a jumble of buildings painted in colors too bright to be real. In the distance, Harte heard the echo of gunfire again.

"What is that?" Esta asked.

"Probably the reenactment of the Second Boer War they stage twice a day," Julien said, checking his pocket watch. "Ah, yes. Nearly ten thirty, when the cavalry is usually set to attack."

"The cavalry?" Harte asked, wondering where the hell they were.

"Actors, mostly, but some were actually in the real fighting." Julien gave him a wink. "Welcome to the Pike. There's nothing that's ever been built like it. Here, you can take voyages anywhere in the world without ever leaving the city. You can travel to Hades or into the heavens. You can meet a geisha or ride to the North Pole and back. Amazing, isn't it?"

"It's something," Harte said doubtfully as he studied the wide boulevard in front of him.

He'd dreamed his whole life of escaping the city, and now it seemed that he had an opportunity to do more than escape—he could be transported—but somehow none of it felt right. Harte had never been anywhere but the island of Manhattan, but he knew at a glance that nothing they were about to see was real. Every building was too brightly painted and too perfect. With the electric signs and lampposts—lit even though the sun was overhead—and the noise of the barkers, each shouting to entice the fairgoers into paying another twenty-five cents to experience some new wonder, the Pike had a carnivalesque feel to it that he knew meant it was a poor approximation of the real wonders the world held.

Actually, the exhibitions of the Pike felt a little like the dime museums in the Bowery. The popularity of those tawdry little storefronts had always made Harte uncomfortable with the way they paraded people as oddities, as nothing more than objects to be viewed for a couple of coins.

From the half-horrified look on Esta's face, Harte could tell she must have felt the same.

The Pike was lined with *strangest* combination of buildings. A Japanese pagoda was the neighbor of a building meant to represent ancient Rome. A large man-made cavern with the words CLIFF DWELLERS stood butted up against a building that could have been something from St. Mark's Square in Venice.

"Those aren't actually Native Americans?" Esta asked Julien as they passed the Cliff Dwellers building and she noticed a pair of dark-haired women standing silently and offering beaded bracelets for sale.

"They're Indians, if that's what you mean," Julien said, giving her a strange look. "What else would they be?"

"Actors?" she asked, but Harte couldn't tell if it was hope or fear he heard in her tone.

"What would the point of that be?" Julien asked, and from the look of surprise on his face, he seemed legitimately confused.

"I don't know," Esta said vaguely. "Do they live here, on the grounds?"

"Who knows," Julien said dismissively. "They seem happy enough, don't they?"

But from the look on Esta's face, Harte could tell that she wasn't convinced. Her brows were furrowed, and there was concern—maybe even dismay—coloring her expression. "Do they force them to be here?" she asked.

"How should I know?" Julien said with a shrug. "But I'm sure they're compensated."

He didn't care, Harte realized, because it wasn't his problem. Julien had been born free to make his own choices, to pick his own paths—to go *wherever* he wanted, *whenever* he wanted. He couldn't understand what it might be like to live a different life.

One of the women caught Harte's eye and lifted her arm to offer him a bracelet. He shook his head in a gentle refusal, but not before he realized that Esta was right. Behind the placid expression the woman wore was something Harte recognized too easily—a frustration and disappointment with the world that she hadn't been able to hide, at least not from him. Because he felt it too keenly himself.

He pulled out a couple of coins and traded them for one of the bracelets. The woman showed no sign of pleasure as she pocketed the money and selected an item for him. Not even bothering to look at the bracelet, he ran his thumb over the smooth beads as he tucked it into the pocket of his waistcoat—a reminder that the world was wider than he had realized and there was no end to the troubles it contained.

The three of them made their way through the parade of grotesquely beautiful sights. The architecture might not be authentic, but it was still astounding. All along the brick-lined boulevard, average citizens mixed with people dressed in fanciful costumes. Whether they were authentic, Harte didn't know, but the embroidery and beading and detail of each costume had a certain beauty nonetheless.

Music poured out of the buildings, the different styles blending and clashing with the noise of the street. The fair's organizers had created a world where fantasies of far-off lands and exotic people could come to life for anyone willing to pay twenty-five cents. Maybe it wasn't real, but Harte understood implicitly that veracity didn't matter—to the fair or to the people who attended. Those who handed over their coins here were no different from the ones who had sat in the seats watching his act night after night. They didn't want reality, with all its messy complications and unpleasant truths; they wanted the fantasy—the possibility of escape. And even Harte, who knew better, couldn't help but be a little drawn in by the spectacle of it all.

"Here we are," Julien said, when they arrived at an enormous archway emblazoned with the words THE STREETS OF CAIRO.

Beyond the opening, the street led through a veritable city of sand-colored buildings, all with Arabic flourishes—a series of arches and minarets accented the flat-sided buildings. Above, domed rooftops blocked out the blue summer sky, and in the streets, men dressed in flowing robes called out, advertising camel and donkey rides through the streets of the reproduced city. It was clearly supposed to be Egypt, but it was a fanciful, stylized version of Egypt that was meant for those who would never travel there.

"This had better have something to do with the necklace, Jules," Harte told him.

"This is the Society's special offering for the fair," Julien told them, his voice barely audible above the noisy streets. "The centerpiece, from what I've been told, is a mystical artifact from the ancient world—a necklace with a stone that contains stars within it."

"It's here?" Esta asked.

"Not that it'll do you any good," Julien said. "The security is top-notch, and with the recent activity of the Antistasi, everyone is on high alert."

"We'll worry about that later," Harte said. "Let's make sure it's the necklace we're looking for."

Together they followed the maze of buildings past a makeshift bazaar, with stands selling reams of brightly woven material and small trinkets that looked like items that could have been taken from a pharaoh's tomb. There was an enormous restaurant that spilled the scent of roasting meats and heady spices out into the streets, tempting the people who passed. Finally, in the deepest heart of the attraction, they came to a building carved to look as though it had come directly from ancient Egypt.

A large, deep portico was flanked with striped sandstone columns, each painted with something that looked like hieroglyphics. It reminded Harte of Khafre Hall, with its gilded flourishes and bright cerulean accents. From the way Esta had gone very still, as though every cell in her body had come alert, he figured she thought the same.

"Are you ready to take a trip down the Nile?" Julien asked.

But Harte didn't have the patience for Julien's games. The heat of the day was getting to him, making his head pound and his vision swim, and suddenly he couldn't hear anything but a roaring in his mind.

The sun was high enough that the temple threw no shadow. It would be cool inside, welcoming and safe within the shade of its thick walls.

Just as quickly as the vision had submerged him in a different time and place, it drained away, leaving Harte's ears ringing and a cold sweat coating his skin.

"Harte?" Esta was saying his name, and when he met her eyes, he saw the worry in them. It should have felt better than the indifference she'd shown him all day, but the vision had left him shaken.

Pull yourself together.

"I'm fine, Slim," he told her with a wink.

Her eyes flashed with annoyance. "But you just—"

"Let it go," he told her. Then he directed his attention to Julien, who was watching him with a serious expression. "Let's get this done and see what we're dealing with."

Apparently, Julien wasn't being overly dramatic—inside the building they found a line of people waiting to board actual boats that were shaped like long, flat-bottomed canoes with upturned ends, meant to look like boats that had once sailed down the Nile. When it was their turn to board, Julien slipped the line attendant a few coins and managed to get them a boat to themselves.

"After you," he said to Esta, allowing her to step into the small craft first.

She took a bench in the middle, and Julien began to follow, but Harte grabbed his arm, to stop him.

"Youth before beauty," he told Julien as he took the opportunity to slide into the seat next to her. He ignored the knowing smirk playing at Julien's mouth and pretended that he didn't notice Esta's annoyance.

At the rear of the ship, an oarsman was dressed in a linen robe shot through with gold and the worst wig Harte had ever seen. The black coiled braids were ratty and matted, and they hung around the man's lean face, framing bright blue eyes that had been ringed with kohl. It looked like his skin had been turned tan with makeup as well—it was too russet colored to be natural. He probably was supposed to look like an Egyptian painting come to life, but unlike Julien's impersonation of a woman, the oarsman's costume was a caricature. Like the white vaudeville performers who blackened their faces with burnt cork for minstrel numbers, it was a mockery of the very people it was trying to depict.

The oarsman remained silent as the boat started moving. Slowly and steadily, he pushed the craft away from the loading dock and down a narrow channel of unnaturally blue water. Next to Harte, Esta was straight-backed and alert, taking in everything as the boat approached a darkened tunnel.

"Here we go," Julien murmured, tossing a mischievous look back to the two of them just as the boat glided into the tunnel.

The farther they went, the darker it became, until the boat was traveling through an artificial night, and the only noise was the soft lapping of the water as they moved onward.

"In the beginning there was only the sea, dark and infinite. . . ." The oarsman's voice came to them, deep and overly dramatic. "This primeval sea was made only of chaos. . . ."

The oarsman's voice fell silent again, leaving them to float along in the murky darkness, but Harte couldn't relax—not with Esta so close and not with the power inside of him stirring in the darkness.

Though they were out of the heat of the midmorning sun, the attraction felt close and muggy, almost like breathing through a blanket of dampness. The air tasted of mold and dust, like it might in an ancient tomb. Harte wondered if that effect was intentional as he swallowed against the tightness that had risen in his throat and fought the urge to loosen his collar.

He didn't need to see Esta to know how close she was, and neither did the voice inside of him. The darkness seemed to embolden it, and he struggled to ignore its echoing and unintelligible chorus, which was damn difficult when the oarsman was droning on about something behind him.

"The chaos was endless and it held no life until the waters split and the sun god Ra emerged to bring forth order and to create the world."

Ahead, a pinpoint of light appeared, which seemed to grow as they approached, until their boat passed into another room. The next chamber was painted in gold so that, with the light reflecting off the domed surface, it looked as though they were within the sun itself. The voice retreated, just a little, but it was enough that he felt like he could breathe again. Next to him, Esta's face was turned away. She was taking in the sights of the chamber they were passing through—or maybe she was still avoiding him, he couldn't tell.

Harte regretted ever touching her, and yet he couldn't regret it completely. Even now, even hours away from those stolen seconds when he could feel every inch of her body, strong and capable and *soft* beneath him, even in the bright, cleansing light of day, his lips still remembered the taste of her and his fingertips still held the memory of her skin's heat. If all he ever had of her was that memory, he would gladly take it.

He couldn't help but use the opportunity to study her: the graceful line of her neck where it met her shorn hair, the lips that were too pink and too soft to belong to any boy, and the shape of her legs—long and lithe and strong—outlined by the trousers she'd insisted on wearing. The oarsman was going on again, this time about the adventures of Ra and Osiris, Isis and Horus, and other deities Harte had learned of when he was preparing his old act, but he wasn't listening. Not really. He knew these stories already—had learned them as part of his so-called training in the occult arts. Instead, he ignored the oarsman and let his mind replay the handful of minutes from the night before when his world had felt unmoored and dangerous and perfect all at once.

As if responding to the memory of it, the power inside of him seemed to rouse itself, swelling until Harte could barely hear the soft swish of the water, and the oarsman's narrative was a sound coming from far off in the distance. Considering he hadn't slept more than a couple of hours the night before—and in an uncomfortable straight-backed chair, no less—it took every bit of his strength to press it back and keep it from growing. He was barely aware of the rooms they passed because his attention was focused on the power threatening to erupt within him. And on Esta, less than an arm's reach away.

After the boat passed through the third chamber—one filled with a makeshift temple—they entered a chamber lined with shelves filled with different tablets and piles of rolled parchments. All at once the voice inside of him went quiet. But it wasn't an easy quiet. The power that had been bunching and flexing within him seemed to fade until all he felt was a silent emptiness.

MAPPING THE FAIR

1904—St. Louis

North was watching the gondolas glide across the lagoon toward the Festival Hall, making notes about their timing, when he saw the guy. At first North couldn't figure out why he looked so darn familiar, but then it came to him. It was the same guy who'd been standing outside the theater the night before—and he'd been with the Thief.

Curious, he tucked away his notebook and started following from a distance.

Since he'd left Maggie at her building an hour before, he'd been doing what he did most days as he waited for her—learning everything he could about the Exposition. It was an enormous place, filled with people and passageways that could mean trouble, and they were running out of time to make sure they knew everything they could. So far he'd mapped out the entire eastern side: the display of the villages from the Philippines and most of the agriculture and forestry exhibits. He'd been slowly working his way westward, through the offering from Morocco and the replica of Jerusalem. He knew where the entrances and exits were, where the Guard often congregated when they were supposed to be watching the crowd, and when they changed shifts. He knew all the places where they could be exposed and all the places where someone could lie low if need be. Little by little he'd accounted for all the dangers, because Ruth wanted him to determine everything that might cause them trouble. North figured that this guy certainly counted—especially since he wasn't alone.

When the guy and his two companions turned onto the Pike, North used the noise and confusion around him to get a little closer. There was a pretty big crowd of people waiting to get into the Hereafter, which was a damn idiotic thing to want as far as North was concerned, but he used the cover they provided to maneuver around and get ahead of the three he'd been following. He cut across the boulevard to the deep overhand of Creation, where he could wait without being seen. A moment later they came through the crowd, and North barked out a laugh of surprise that startled a woman standing next to him.

One of the other guys wasn't a guy, after all. It was the Thief. She looked different in the suit and cap, and her hair had been chopped to just above her collar, but anyone with two eyes in their head—or at least anyone who was paying attention—would have known who it was.

But what's she doing here?

It was one thing to have the girl that all the papers called the Devil's Thief appear in town at the same time Ruth was close to the biggest— and most dangerous—deed the Antistasi had ever planned. Maybe it was just a coincidence. But having her appear at the fair—the same venue that Ruth had been eyeing for months? And just when everything was about to come together?

North didn't like it.

With his hat pulled low over his forehead, he kept as close as he could and followed the three down the Pike, until they came to the Streets of Cairo. He didn't like how they'd gone directly to the Society's attraction, passing everything else with barely a look.

Maybe he should have followed them in, but he'd already mapped it out—there was one way in and one way out—and he'd been through the darn boat ride enough already. There wasn't any reason to take the risk of being seen or recognized, because the last thing the Antistasi needed was for the Guard to start paying attention to North. He still had about a third of the fair left to map out, after all. Instead of following them into the attraction, he found a place under the Chinese archway across from Cairo to wait instead, watching for the three to exit.

Most of the fair didn't bother him, but North didn't much like the Pike. Everything about it was too big and too loud and too brash. Though, he had to admit, the horse they called Beautiful Jim Key had been a sight, all right. Smartest damn animal North had ever heard of, much less seen with his own eyes. But that was the fair for you—unbelievable. Above him, the arch was something to see too, painted in a red brighter than blood and gleaming with gold. Strange symbols in black and bright blue covered the surface, and at the tip of every roofline was a fanciful curlicued dragon, looking down upon the crowd like guardians.

But not even those guardians could stop what Ruth and the Antistasi had planned.

At the end of the month, the top representatives from all the Brotherhoods would be in the city. For one night they would be in one place, together. The perfect target.

If all went well, they wouldn't just make a statement to the Society; they would make a statement about magic and the world and what the future could be. The deed Ruth was planning was impossible and yet it was so obvious. If it worked, it would change everything—*absolutely everything*. The Society would crumble, the Brotherhoods would be left without their leaders, and magic itself would be free. *Restored*.

Legend or not, North wasn't about to let the Devil's Thief get in the Antistasi's way.

THE DJINNI'S STAR

1904—St. Louis

The oarsman was still talking, but all Esta could think about was how close Harte was and how he was pretending to ignore her. His silence grated on her. She hadn't slept all night because she'd been thinking about what had happened between them. He hadn't returned until it was almost morning, and by then she'd been too angry and frustrated—with him and with herself—to talk, so she'd turned away and pretended to be asleep.

But even once they'd gotten the message from Julien to meet at the Exposition, Harte had been sullen and silent. Since she wasn't the one who had stormed off, she wasn't about to be the first to offer an olive branch.

She could almost still feel him on her lips. She would probably always remember the weight of his body as it pressed her into the mattress. How could he sit there acting as though *nothing* had happened between them?

Unless it really *was* only the power of the Book that wanted her and not Harte. Which meant that she'd made a fool of herself over him for no reason at all.

Esta shoved those thoughts aside and turned farther away from Harte, pretending to concentrate on the ride. Each room the boat passed through was elaborately decorated to simulate some scene in ancient Egypt—or at least what people in the early twentieth century imagined ancient Egypt might look like—but Esta barely saw them. Her focus was constantly being drawn back to Harte—the stiff set of his spine and the way he smelled clean, like soap and linen, despite the heat of the day.

"Finally, we come to the House of Books," the oarsman said as they came to a chamber lined with shelves, each filled with different tablets and piles of rolled parchments. "Here the god Thoth, master of the Library of Life, invented the art of writing and gave it to the people."

Harte had held himself away from her, still and watchful for the entire ride, but when the oarsman spoke about Thoth, something changed. It felt like the moment before it rains, when the air has a specific quality that feels like a storm is coming. When Esta glanced over at Harte, he had the strangest look on his face.

"Is that what they say?" Harte asked, his words dripping with a scorn that seemed out of proportion to the moment. "Thoth, the *master* of the Library?" A dark laugh bubbled up from his chest.

He was acting so strangely that Esta forgot her irritation for a moment. "Harte?" She reached out to touch him, and the moment their skin met, he whipped his head around to face her. His hand snaked up to latch on to her wrist, and she felt a burst of heat that had nothing to do with Harte's magic. Still, she couldn't pull away, not without causing the boat to rock or tip.

"Thoth didn't invent anything," Harte told her. But his voice sounded off, and his eyes were all wrong. Like the night before, he was looking at her without seeing her, but now his pupils were enormous, dilated enough to obscure the color of his irises. Something peered out from within him, a darkness that reminded her of the inky blackness that had seeped into her vision at the train station and the hotel.

"Harte," she said softly, trying to call him back to himself. "What are you talking about?"

"Thoth was nothing but a *thief*." Harte practically spit the word with disgust. "He took knowledge that wasn't his, and when that didn't satisfy him, he took more." Again came that strange, deep, mirthless laugh, which had Julien sending a questioning look in Esta's direction.

She shook her head just slightly, to indicate that she didn't know what Harte was up to. "Shhh," she hissed, when his laughter didn't stop.

Before Esta could say anything more, the oarsman started up again, explaining how the ancients believed that whatever was written in the library in Cairo would be transcribed and made real in the world of the gods. "Thoth was one of the ancient civilization's most important gods. He gave the world not only writing, but science and magic," the oarsman continued. "He carved order from the chaos of the cosmos through the creation of the written word, and through the inscription of spells, he eliminated the wild danger of magic and made its power safe."

"Lies," Harte muttered. "All lies . . ."

"What is *wrong* with you?" Esta whispered, jabbing at him with her elbow.

Harte blinked. "What?" Frowning, he pulled back from her. His eyes were still wrong, but she could see the gray halo around the black returning. Maybe he'd been wrong to kiss her the night before. Maybe she'd been wrong in wanting him to. But looking at his strange, half-dazed expression, some of her anger cooled.

The oarsman was still going on and on with his sonorous narration. "Because he was a benevolent god, Thoth contained the cosmic dangers of that chaos within a book. He buried the Book of Thoth in the Nile, protected by serpents, and those who attempted to retrieve it paid a steep price, for the knowledge of the gods was never meant for mere mortals."

The Book of Thoth? Esta glanced at Harte. Whatever had come over him a moment before seemed to have passed. He was still tense, but he was listening to the oarsman now. Or if he wasn't, he was focused on something, since his expression was one of concentration rather than disgust.

They passed out of the library chamber and made their way into a brilliantly blue room that contained a large diorama. On a hill far off in the distance stood a white temple, shining under an artificial sun.

"As time passed and civilizations transformed into new empires," the oarsman explained, "Thoth became known as Hermes, but he continued in his quest for knowledge and his commitment to man. Myth tells us he stole knowledge from Olympus for humans, and so he became the patron of thieves. Later, he would become Hermes Trismegistus, inventor of the Emerald Tablets, which held the secrets of the philosopher's stone, the very foundation of alchemy.

"Through the secrets of the Emerald Tablets, the power to transform the very essence of the world was revealed to man," the oarsman told them as he navigated past what was obviously supposed to be Mount Olympus. "Through the careful study of the hermetical arts, we have learned to control the power that once posed a danger. And through alchemy and the occult arts, those who perfect themselves, like the Veiled Prophet himself, can stand against the wild dangers of uncontrolled power."

They glided into the darkness of another tunnel in silence, and on the other side, they found the end of the ride.

"And now," the oarsman said, "if you'll proceed along the Path of Righteousness to the Temple of Khorassan, the Veiled Prophet offers a view of one of his most prized treasures, a collar forged in the ancient world that contains a stone rumored to have been created by Thoth himself."

The hairs on the back of Esta's neck rose at his words. From the look on Harte's face, he'd shaken off whatever had happened back in the House of Books. But his expression didn't hold the same anticipation she felt. His eyes were still glassy and distant, his jaw was tight, and there was a sheen of sweat on his temples. It was like he hadn't even heard the oarsman.

The path was painted to look like it was paved in silver, but it was as fake as everything else on the Pike. As they walked along it with the other, completely oblivious tourists, the music changed to a softly driving melody that sounded vaguely Eastern. The path emptied into a smaller chamber that was already filled with people. In the center of the room, blocked from view, a glass case was illuminated from above.

Esta didn't need to see the case to know that it would contain the Djinni's Star. She could feel it calling to her, just as it had called to her in a posh Upper East Side jewelry store not long after the turn of the millennium—the last time she stole it.

If she could just slow time, perhaps she'd be able to take it here and now, but the closer she got to the case in the center of the room, the more she knew that using her affinity would be impossible. It wasn't only that they'd walked past a pair of Jefferson Guards to enter the chamber but also that there was something sickly sweet scenting the air.

"Opium," Harte whispered to her, his expression still distant, but more serious now as well.

"It's just a bit of fragrance," Julien told him, brushing aside Harte's concerns. "They wanted to give the whole sensory experience."

But Esta didn't doubt that Harte was right. She'd smelled that scent before and had experienced the numbing effects of the drug as it took her ability to pull time slow when she'd been captured at the Haymarket, back when she'd first arrived in Old New York. Even now her magic felt dulled, softened by the drug. It wasn't enough to harm anyone, but it was enough to make an affinity weaker.

Soon the three of them were standing in front of the glass case, and there, laid against midnight velvet, was the Djinni's Star. Set into the platinum collar, the stone was polished to a brilliant shine, and within its depths, it looked as though it contained galaxies.

"I hope you can see how impossible getting your necklace back is going to be," Julien said, leaning in close so no one else would hear. "The Streets of Cairo is the Veiled Prophet Society's offering at the fair, and that necklace is the centerpiece. They're never going to sell it back to you."

They hadn't exactly been planning to pay for it.

"Then I suppose we'll have to take it," Esta said with a shrug.

"Take it?" Julien's mouth fell open. He looked to Harte, who was staring at the stone with a thoughtful expression. "From the Society? You're completely mad."

"No," she whispered, giving Julien a smug smile. "I'm a thief."

THE STREETS OF CAIRO

1904—St. Louis

Harte's skin felt like it was on fire, even as the blood in his veins felt like ice. In front of him was the Djinni's Star, and the power inside of him was churning, but whether it was in approval or fear, he couldn't tell. Dimly, he realized that Esta and Julien were talking about the necklace, but he hadn't been following their conversation . . . until Esta said that she was a thief.

"Not here," he told her in a hushed voice. They were in a room filled with people, surrounded by Jefferson Guards. There was confidence, and then there was idiocy.

She gave him a scowl, but she closed her mouth.

"Come on," he said, needing air. There was only so long even he could hold his breath, and he was already feeling light-headed from whatever had happened on the boat ride. Without waiting to see if they were following, he pushed through the overcrowded room and out into the street so he could finally take a breath of air that wasn't filled with the cloying, dulling power of opium and could collect himself enough to push back the power that was rumbling excitedly inside of him.

Once he was outside, it took a moment for Harte's eyes to adjust to the brightness. He inhaled to clear his head, but his pulse was still pounding in his temples. Instead of exiting where they had entered the attraction, they had been dumped back out onto the main thoroughfare of the Pike. The noise was deafening, and the crowd all seemed to be surging in the same direction.

Harte turned to find Esta and Julien in the crowd and was relieved to see them there, right behind him.

Julien tugged at Harte's sleeve. "Come on," he said, trying to lead Harte in the direction everyone else seemed to be heading. "You can't just stand here in the middle of this mess. We'll get trampled."

As Julien pulled him back, a large flat-bedded wagon pulled by a team of matching gray horses passed by. A small hut made of what looked like dried palm fronds and lashed-together branches had been built at the back of the wagon's bed. In front of the hut, an older man with darkly tanned skin who was wearing nothing more than a swath of fabric around his waist sat on a stool, looking completely uninterested in any of the people who were staring or yelling around him. Other men who were similarly dressed stood at attention, while a gaggle of children sat in the center. They might have been singing or shouting—Harte couldn't tell because of the noise of the crowd.

"What is all of this, anyway?" Harte asked, following Julien and Esta closer to the shelter of the buildings, where the crowd wasn't as thick.

"It's a parade," Julien told him.

"I can see that, but *why*?" Harte asked, feeling unaccountably irritated. The power inside of him was still churning, and the heat of the day was starting to creep against his skin. "Isn't the fair itself enough?"

"It's all part of the fun, Darrigan," Julien told him. "How else will you know what exhibits to visit? That one that just passed, it's for the Igorot Village—fascinating stuff. They wear hardly anything. . . . Anyway, it'll be over soon enough. The parades never last very long, since they have at least two a day. This one's the midday offering. There will be another later, when the lights come on."

The three of them stood in the shade of the building for a few minutes, penned in by the crowd as the parade went by. After the wagon came a group of women dressed in silken robes, their faces painted white like geisha. Around them, the Jefferson Guard marched in straight lines, creating a boundary of protection so that the eager crowd couldn't get too close. Whenever someone—usually a man—tried to approach, the closest of the Guards would push him back with a kind of bored violence.

"Are you okay?" Esta asked, eyeing Harte with a worried frown.

"I'm fine," he said, shrugging off her concern.

"Because you look—"

A loud wailing split the air, and the parade erupted into chaos as three figures dressed in rumpled gowns and wearing odd, misshapen masks descended on the parade, attacking the Jefferson Guard. A sharp *pop* sounded, cutting through the noise and the confusion of the crowd, and colored smoke suddenly began streaming from one of the figures' fingertips.

The Guardsmen who had been surrounding the geisha sprang into action, countering the attack.

"The Antistasi," Julien said, and his voice contained a note of true fear. But Harte wasn't so sure. There was no trace of magic in the air, no indication that the smoke was anything but a distraction.

Other Guardsmen came out of the Nile exhibit and barreled through the crowd, pushing over anyone who happened to be in their way as they rushed toward the masked figures. A woman screamed as they knocked her aside, causing her to drop the child she'd been holding up for a better view of the passing floats. The child started to wail, but the Guardsmen didn't stop to help. With an urgency that bordered on violence, they began grabbing anyone trying to escape the fog. Man or woman, even children—it didn't seem to matter.

One of the figures had been caught by a group of the Guard, who'd already ripped the mask away. Beneath it was a boy who couldn't have been more than fourteen. He spit at the Guardsmen and shouted, "Forever reign the Antistasi!"

"Long live the Devil's Thief!" cried another in reply.

In response, one of the Guardsmen buried his fist in the boy's stomach.

Esta took a step toward them, but Harte caught her wrist. She turned to look at him, her eyes bright with fury. "They're *children*," she said, her voice breaking on the word.

"We can't help them," Harte told her.

"*I* can—"

"No," he said, cutting her off. If she used her affinity here, now, in the middle of this mess? There was no telling what might happen, especially considering the clear threat posed by the gates behind them.

"We can't just leave them," she told him, starting to pull away.

"If they catch us, things are going to get worse. We need to *go*."

But Esta was staring at him like he was her enemy, like she would tear the sun from the sky to stop what was happening. For a moment Harte thought he would have to carry her—or worse, betray everything they'd built between them by *forcing her*. But he couldn't risk it. Not only because it would be the worst kind of treachery, but also because he was already having enough trouble keeping the power inside of him in check while he held her arm.

He could feel it pressing at the most fragile parts of him—the parts that wanted Esta, the parts that *agreed* with her. Together they could destroy the Guard. They could help the boys, who clearly were no more Antistasi than anyone else in the crowd. He could see it, how easy it would be to make a different choice. A single touch, and he could make the Guardsman who was beating the child destroy *himself*.

The violence of the image, the sharpness of it, startled Harte enough that he gasped. Then he shook it off and focused on what was real. On what was *true*.

The power was still struggling to get closer to Esta—as though it craved her fury. He would not let it have her.

"Come on," Harte said, jerking her back and following Julien as his friend led them in the opposite direction of the parade, away from the noise of the Pike and toward one of the smaller side routes that led back into the main part of the fair.

Esta eventually came, looking back toward the Pike every few steps, until they came to where the entrance of the Pike met the regular walkways of the fair. The noise of the crowd was a low murmur here, and

Harte could barely hear the confusion of the Pike. Manicured pathways led to large, palatial buildings, and well-dressed people came and went from their entrances.

"We need to get out of here," Harte said, releasing Esta's arm and feeling the power inside of him rage.

"You might want to wait," Julien suggested. "With an Antistasi attack, they'll be checking all the exits."

"They weren't Antistasi," Esta said, her voice hollow as she looked back toward the Pike. From there they couldn't see anything but the outlines of the buildings. There was no way to know what was happening.

"It doesn't matter who they were," Julien said. "You saw how the Guard reacted. They'll be looking for anyone involved, and you don't want to get caught up in it."

"Jules is right," Harte said, needing that time to gather his wits and his strength. "We'll wait for a while—play the tourist until we're sure things have died down."

"I, unfortunately, cannot," Julien told them. "This, I believe, is where I say my good-byes."

"You're leaving?" Esta asked, turning back to them.

"*I'm* not a wanted fugitive," Julien told her. "I have nothing to fear from the Guard, and I also have a matinee today."

"We're not done," Harte said, trying to keep his voice level even as the power inside of him was still unsettled over his refusal to accommodate its wishes. He took another step back from Esta, just to be sure.

Julien frowned at them. "I've done what you asked—I've shown you the necklace."

"We don't *have* the necklace yet, though," Harte pointed out. "As long as it's on display like that, you're at risk."

Julien visibly bristled. "Then take care of it, Darrigan. She might be a thief, but I'm not."

"You want us to take care of it? We need information—about the security or any events that might be happening. We need to know whether the necklace is always there or if they move it at night."

"Why would you think I could get you that information?" Julien asked, clearly annoyed, and if Harte wasn't mistaken, more than a little uneasy.

"Because you're in the Society," Harte pressed, not caring when Julien blanched. "Did you think we didn't know, Jules?"

"It's just a courtesy membership," he said. "I'm no one to them. A *joke*."

Harte didn't miss the bitterness in his friend's voice, but he couldn't do anything about it. "You're closer to the Society than either of us," Harte told him. "You want to get rid of us? You'll get us the information."

"Fine," Julien said. "But it'll take time."

"The sooner we can get the necklace, the sooner we're out of your hair," Harte told him. "And the sooner you can go on with your life like none of this ever happened."

Julien let out a frustrated breath. "If I never had to see your face again, it wouldn't be soon enough, Darrigan."

Harte watched Julien walk off, keeping his eyes on his friend until he'd lost sight of him in the crowds.

"We could have helped those kids," Esta said, her voice low and angry.

He let out a tired breath and reluctantly turned back to her. "I know," he told her.

"Then why—"

"Because we have more important things to do," he said.

"They were kids, Harte. Those were smoke bombs and costumes," she said, her voice shaking. "They were dressed up as Antistasi—as *me*. The skirts and the masks. You saw it, didn't you? They were playing the Devil's Thief. And those Guardsmen were *vicious*. They had to see they were just kids, and it didn't matter."

"You're not responsible for that," he told her, and the moment he said the words, he knew that it had been the wrong thing to say. Her eyes flashed with fury, and the power inside of him warmed.

Her voice was cool and detached when she spoke again. "Aren't I? Maybe *you* can separate what you want from what everyone else is suffering through. God knows you have before. But I can't. I *won't.*"

Her words hit their mark, in part because of how true they were. The mess they were in was his doing, all because he'd wanted to be free of the city. Because he'd been willing to sacrifice almost *anything* for that one dream. But that didn't change the fact that they were on a mission, and if they didn't succeed, Mageus would have a lot more to worry about than the Guard.

"We have to find the stones, Esta," he said softly. "We need the necklace, and then we need to find Bill to get the dagger, and then we have the rest of the continent to cross for the crown, and we can't do that if we're in jail or *dead.*" He paused, gathering himself, pushing away the power that was poking at his weaknesses. Esta's eyes were still blazing at him, but he went on. "If we don't get the stones, Nibsy wins. Jack wins. I wanted to help those kids, but doing that would have put a great big target on our backs. You want to help those kids and countless others like them? We have to *win*. We have to find the stones and get the Book back." *I'm running out of time. And so are you.*

The thought came to him so clearly that he knew it was true.

Esta frowned at him, but some of the heat in her expression drained. "I hate them," she told him, her voice hollow. "I hate the Guard and I hate the Society—all of them."

"So do I," Harte said, meaning every word. "So let's not just beat up a few Guardsmen here and there. Let's bring them to their knees. We steal the necklace, we humiliate them, and then we move on and do it again until we have what we need. Until we can go back before any of this happened—before the Act, before the Guard—and stop it. *That's* how we're going to save those boys."

She let out a heavy breath and scrubbed her hand over her mouth. It was an utterly guileless gesture, and one that made her look every bit the man she was dressed as. "You're probably right," she said. "But that doesn't change how angry with you I am right now."

"Be as angry as you want," he said. "As long as you're angry here, and not in some jail."

"There isn't a jail that can hold me," she told him, cutting her eyes in his direction.

"I don't know. . . . Those bars on the Nile exhibit might do the trick."

Her expression faltered at the mention of them. "Speaking of the Nile, you want to tell me what happened on that boat?" she asked.

He took a breath. "I don't know," he said. "I was there, and then I wasn't."

"You were talking about Thoth like you knew him," she said, a question in her eyes. "You called him a liar."

Vaguely he remembered saying those words, but they felt like they were someone else's memories, someone else's words. "I think it's whatever—or whoever—was trapped in the Book. Every day it gets stronger. Every day it gains a little more control." *And being around you is making it worse.*

"Well, whatever it is, it sure doesn't like Thoth," she said, looking away from him.

"It's old," he told her, not sure where the words came from. "I get this sense that it's been waiting a very long time to be freed. . . . It's not going to wait much longer."

Esta glanced up at him, and for a moment the anger in her eyes was replaced by worry. "Well, it's gonna have to," she told him. "We're close. The necklace is right there." She pointed toward the Pike. "And opium or the Guard or whatever, that building isn't Khafre Hall. We can do this." She paused, thoughtful. "What if we used a parade as a distraction?"

A couple passed close by, the man eyeing the two of them with a serious frown. "Maybe, but let's not talk about it here," he said. "We don't know who might be listening."

"Fine," she said. "What do you want to do, then?"

"We need to waste a little time, but standing around like this is drawing attention. You want to go in there and see what's inside?" he asked, pointing to a nearby building. "It might be cooler, since we'll be out of the sun."

The building turned out to be the Palace of Transportation. The enormous hall was filled with all manner of machinery—sleek steam engines and automobiles that gleamed under the electric lights. As they walked through, pretending to be tourists until they could safely leave, Esta had a far-off, almost sad look in her eyes.

"Someday, everyone will have one of these," she told him as she ran her finger along the curved metal of an automobile. "No one really stays in one place unless they have to. You could get onto an airplane and fly anywhere you want. . . ."

"Fly?" It seemed impossible. "Like in an airship?"

She shook her head. "Faster. And higher. You can be across the country in a handful of hours." Her expression faltered. "Or some people can." She glanced over at him, a spark of hope in her eye. "When we get the stones and the Book—because we *will*—we have to do something with them. We have to figure out what to do about the Brink—fix it or destroy it. There's an entire future coming, and Mageus won't survive by being trapped in the city. Maybe they'd have a chance if things were different. Maybe that's why we ended up here, so we could see what might be. So we could understand that things *can* be changed. That *we* can change them, only this time, we can change them for the better. Even if we can't go back. We can start now."

He couldn't feel an answering hope. Standing in the Palace of Transportation, he was surrounded by machines built for speed, all ways for ordinary people to escape from their lives and travel wherever their hearts desired. They were machines of the future, machines that one day would be. But Harte Darrigan knew that they were not for him. He was a man without a future, and not one of those wondrous machines could move fast enough or go far enough to help him escape from the danger he carried within.

NEVER ENOUGH

1904—St. Louis

North had been trying to see past the spectacle of the parade to the Cairo exhibit when everything erupted. As soon as the Jefferson Guard went charging in, he gave up his attempt to follow the Thief and made his exit, working his way through the crowds that were all trying to flee in the same direction. They were Sundren, so they couldn't tell that the eruption was nothing more than smoke set off by some stupid kids trying to play Antistasi.

He didn't exactly blame them for trying. He'd spent his whole childhood hiding the bit of magic that flowed in his veins. His daddy had taught him how to keep it still, so that no one would know. But hiding away their magic hadn't improved their lives any. It certainly hadn't saved his father.

North had been seventeen and already two years on his own when that train derailed in New Jersey and the newspapers began spreading the fear that Mageus were beyond the Brink. Until then, most Sundren thought magic was something that the Brink had dealt with. They went through their ordinary lives not thinking that Mageus could be among them.

Until then, hiding had to be enough for people like him—a quiet life, a quiet death.

It had never really been enough. And sometimes death wasn't quiet or easy.

It had not been enough for his father, who'd withered away because of it. He'd done his best to raise North after his mother had run off, but by the time he died in the Chicago slaughterhouses where he worked, he'd become a small man, tired and far older than his years. The day North buried his father, he didn't have enough money even for the plainest of tombstones, and there was less than a week left before his landlord would knock on the door, demanding the rent. He could have gone to the same plant where his father had worked and died, and they would have taken him on, tall and strong as he was even then. But he'd decided to go west instead, hoping that in the wide-open spaces of the country, he could find some kind of life for himself.

He'd traveled to the endless sweeping plains and realized that no matter how far he went, no matter how big the sky above him, there wasn't really any way to live free. Not for someone like him.

The first time he'd heard of the Devil's Thief, North was working at a stockyard in Kansas. He'd looked at the picture of the girl staring up from a crumpled piece of newsprint and had felt a spark of hope that had set him off to search for others who were also tired of never having enough. He'd ended up in St. Louis before he finally found the Antistasi, and once he saw Maggie, that was about it for him.

If he'd been a little younger, he probably would have done something just as stupid as those kids. Had his daddy not been around to keep him in line for so long, he probably would have done something that stupid even *without* hearing about the Thief.

He wondered for a second if those kids had fathers who would tan their hides for getting caught up by the Guard, or if they were on their own, like so many kids were these days. North supposed he'd have to take care of them later—get them out of the holding cell the Guard were bound to put them in and either get them back to their parents or find them a safe place to go. But before he worried about those kids, he needed to get to Maggie.

Her building was a monstrosity of a thing, flanked by two enormous towers. Inside, a row of some mechanical contraptions helped to keep tiny infants alive. Ruth hadn't wanted Maggie to bother with working at the fair. They had plenty of people to do reconnaissance, and Ruth thought she would have been better served to keep working on the serum. But small and delicate as Maggie might look, his girl had a spine of steel when she wanted something. In the end, Maggie had won . . . mostly. North still escorted her to and from work, but she tended to the children and watched for any with an affinity all the while.

North moved along with the crowds until he came to the railing and could catch her attention. She looked up from her work and frowned when she saw him. They didn't need words. From just a look, he understood her point, and he maneuvered his way through the crowd of mostly women to the side hall. A moment later, Maggie was there.

"What is it?" she asked, clearly irritated that he'd interrupted her.

"We might have a problem." He told her about what he'd seen, about the Thief and the other guys she was with. "There's only one thing they could want in there."

"The necklace," she agreed.

North remembered the first time he'd gone through the Cairo exhibit and had seen the necklace. He'd thought the five artifacts were nothing but myth, just as he'd doubted the Thief's existence before he saw her, but there one was, real as anything else. He'd known it wasn't a fake because he'd felt its power. Like the watch he had tucked in his pocket, there was an energy around it—an energy that was eminently compelling. But unlike his watch, the necklace had felt like so much more. He figured that every Sundren in that room felt it, even if they didn't know why they were all enthralled by the display.

There was no way the Society or any of the Brotherhoods could be allowed to have power like that. Ruth had planned to take the necklace in the confusion of the deed, but maybe that couldn't wait. "Everything depends upon us having that necklace when the smoke clears," North said. Without it, there would be little chance of uniting the Antistasi and leading them. Without the necklace and the power it could impart, the deed wouldn't change who was in control—the members of the

Brotherhoods were all rich men, living in a country where money could buy anything at all, especially power. No, the Antistasi needed the necklace so they could stand above the rest with power of their own. "We can't let her get it first."

"No . . ." But Maggie was still frowning, her gaze distant like she was thinking through all the implications of this most recent development. Then she blinked and looked up at him. "Or maybe we just can't let her *keep* it."

INVISIBLE ENERGY
ALL AROUND

1904—St. Louis

T he heat of the day had waned some by the time Jack Grew finally
pulled himself out of bed, popped two more morphine cubes
into his mouth, and made his way to the Exposition. St. Louis
was a dump compared to the grandeur of New York, no matter how
glorious the Society believed their little fair was. They'd never reach the
status of the Order, now that he had transformed it, and their city would
always be a backwater town wishing it were something more.

Still, begrudgingly, he had to admit that the lights were something to
behold. They covered every surface of the fair, reflecting in the enormous
lagoon and shining brightly, late into the night. The crowds had started
to dwindle, and the Streets of Cairo were nearly empty. They were also
nothing more than a second-rate attempt at resurrecting the splendor of
a long-lost civilization. It was nothing compared to what Khafre Hall had
been, or what the Order's new headquarters would be when they were
complete. They didn't even have an authentic obelisk, he thought with
some disdain, not like Manhattan, where one was planted in Central Park
for everyone to see.

But none of that stopped Corwin Spenser and David Francis from
preening about their Society's offering at the fair—a singular stone set
into an exquisite collar of platinum and polished so that it seemed to
gleam from within.

An artifact that had once belonged in the Order's vaults.

Do they know what they have? Jack wondered as he stared at the necklace in the velvet-lined case before him. Could these two men—and the rest of their ridiculous Society—know that the stone was one of the treasures taken from Khafre Hall? Were they gloating because they thought he cared about the Order's power? Or did they truly believe they'd discovered some new object of power? He couldn't be sure.

He didn't actually care. The Order and its business only interested Jack insomuch as he could use them. He had already proven how easily the Inner Circle's leadership could be made inconsequential back at the Conclave nearly two years ago. Impotent old men, all of them.

What Spenser and Francis didn't realize while they boasted about the Society's power was that the Order was simply a means to an end, a convenient tool for gaining Jack access to the right people and the right places. Places like this chamber, which had been closed for the night to the public but which Jack now had free access to, without the worry of being watched.

"Where did you say you found this piece?" he asked, keeping his voice casual and easy.

"Oh, we couldn't reveal our contacts," Spenser said, sheer satisfaction on his face.

"With the number of people coming through, it must be difficult making sure that you secure a treasure like this," Jack mused. "Quite the feat, really."

They took the bait. "Not difficult at all," Francis boasted. "This chamber is fitted with the most modern security conveniences around. The walls are two feet of steel-reinforced concrete, impervious to bombs or bullets, and should anyone try to disturb the case, the doors seal over with vaults thicker than the bank downtown."

Inconvenient, but not impossible.

"We've also protected against any . . . less desirable elements," Francis added, his chest puffed out. "The ventilation system in this chamber is equipped with a machine that distributes a low level of suppressant for anyone who might think to use illegal powers to access it. Any disturbance and it increases the dosage tenfold, incapacitating the miscreant before they can cause any trouble."

"And the Antistasi?" Jack asked. "I hear your city has had trouble controlling that element of late."

Spenser bristled at that. "The Antistasi are not a threat to this city. The Society and their Guard have dealt with that problem, and should any other troubles arise, they too will be dealt with, swiftly and judiciously."

"Perhaps, but you failed to deal with the Devil's Thief, did you not?" Jack asked, keeping his tone mild and enjoying the way their faces flushed in consternation.

"We have it under control," Francis insisted.

"Do you?" Jack asked. "Because she *will* come for this piece, gentlemen. You must know that?" He paused, letting his implication sink in. "But you must have everything in hand, because it would be quite the embarrassment to have her take it from you before the ball, especially after all you've promised. I know my brothers at the Order are well familiar with the sting of *that* particular humiliation," he said, clearly implying that they'd enjoy witnessing the same thing happening to others. "And they're eager to see if the necklace is all that you've promised."

Spenser looked uneasy. "I'm sure you'll be able to tell them that it is," he said.

"Of course," Jack said. "Most definitely. Congratulations, gentlemen." He offered his hand to Spenser first. "You've outdone even the Order, I think."

Spenser still looked somewhat uneasy as he took Jack's hand. *Perfect.* Let them worry. It would keep the necklace safe from Darrigan and the girl until Jack could get his hands on it.

Across the room, Hendricks—the Guardsman from the hotel—was watching the group. Jack said his good-byes and motioned for Hendricks to follow him as he headed for the exit.

Outside, the Pike was as overcrowded as it was gauche. Jack led Hendricks away from the scene until they came to the building that housed displays of electricity. Inside the templelike structure, the De Forest Wireless Telegraphy Tower was sending messages through the air to Chicago and back. From what he understood, a similar technology combined with the hermetical arts was responsible for the Jefferson Guard's ability to communicate so effectively and efficiently. According to Hendricks, the Guardsmen each wore a small medallion that could be activated to alert the others when a danger was spotted. It was, he reluctantly admitted, ingenious.

It was also a development that had captured Jack's attention, since it wasn't all that long ago that he himself had been interested in building his own machine. He'd nearly forgotten about how close he'd been those years ago, but this exhibit made him want to revisit the idea. The Book, after all, held answers he could only imagine, and a secret within its pages that might make his machine finally possible.

"Is there something you needed, sir?" Hendricks said. If he had any concerns about their excursion, he didn't show it.

"I want to know where the Society found the piece they've displayed in the Streets of Cairo," he said. "The necklace that everyone comes to gawk at."

Hendricks' brows went up, a question in his eyes.

"I'm hoping they might help me find another," Jack said easily. "I'm a bit of a collector myself." He slipped the Guardsman a large bill.

"I'm sure I could look into it," Hendricks said, tucking the bill into his dark-coated uniform.

"There's much more where that came from if you do. I want to know everything about the necklace—where they store it, when it will be moved, *everything*. I need a good man to help me, Hendricks. I'm hoping that good man will be you."

"Of course, sir," Hendricks said, his eyes shining with avarice. "Happy to be of service."

"Excellent, Hendricks," Jack said, thumping him roughly on the back and leaving him there, with invisible energy all around.

THE VEILED PROPHET

1904—St. Louis

J ulien Eltinge was trying to catch his breath from the exertion of his final number as he walked to his dressing room, his heart still pounding from the excitement of the ovation he'd just received. It had almost been enough to erase the stress of earlier that day. When Darrigan and Esta had announced their plans to steal the necklace, Julien had seen his future crumbling. All his work, all his careful plans, destroyed on a whim. As though anyone could steal something from a place like the Exposition or from an organization as powerful as the Society. But his performance had recentered him, and the roar of the applause had eased the tension that had been building behind his eyes and the worry he'd been carrying in his limbs, just as it always did.

He still remembered the first time he'd understood what applause meant to him. Not the sound of it or even the way people looked standing and cheering, but the way it *felt*. How it had hit some essential part of him, deep down in the very marrow of who he was. That first round of applause had broken open something in him, and it had sent him on a chase to find more. For a long time, he chased it high and low, as eager and determined as a terrier after a rat. Now he knew better. Now he let the applause come to him.

All that he'd worked for, the success he'd dreamed of for so long, was almost within his reach. Every night he took the stage, the applause was louder. Every night, more and more people came to see his act, his *artistry*. And they understood.

His parents had scoffed at him when he'd tried to explain it, but they hadn't stopped him when he'd gotten on the train, his dreams packed in his suitcase next to the costumes he'd made for his act. They probably thought he would fail so miserably that he would be forced to crawl back to them and admit they were right.

He had vowed that would never happen, and he'd kept that vow. He'd fought tooth and nail—and often with his fists—but in the end, he'd won. St. Louis wasn't New York, but he was a star here, and that star was rising, and rising fast. Why, just that night he'd caught sight of Mr. Albee in the box to the left of the stage. It was a good sign that he'd come all this way to take in Julien's act. He was one of the most powerful vaudeville promoters around, and Julien had a feeling he'd come to make good on his promise.

An entire show of his own—a musical revue starring him, Julien Eltinge—in one of the biggest and most luxurious houses on Broadway. That could still come to pass, he told himself. Darrigan would keep his promise and retrieve that damned necklace before anyone realized Julien's connection to it. Things would work out. He and his career would be *fine*.

Julien closed the dressing room door soundly behind him and took the wig from his head, relishing the coolness of the air as it hit his sweat-damp hair and the solitude. Carefully, he arranged the curls on the dummy, making sure not to rumple any of them—it was more of a pain to fix them later than to take the time now. Then he grabbed his customary cigar from the dressing table and lit it, letting the richness of the tobacco coat his mouth and fill his senses. A reward for a job well done, as always.

In the mirror, the sight of the thick cigar held between his painted lips made him chuckle to himself. With her dark lashes and brightly painted lips, her blushing cheeks and the way he'd used makeup to sculpt her features into something more delicate, a woman looked back at him. It was the transformation—not the femininity—that gratified him, not the corset that was currently cutting into his rib cage or the gowns with their heavy beading and ruffles that scratched at his skin or even the way women would cut their eyes in his direction, their jealousy proof of his success. No. It was the performance itself. It was the artistry of making one thing into something else entirely. The impossible magic of it.

A sharp knock came at his dressing room door, and Julien called to see who it was.

"You got visitors," Sal said, poking his head into the dressing room.

After the day he'd had, Julien simply wasn't in the mood. "Tell them I'm not available."

The stage manager shook his head. "Not these visitors."

"Then tell them I've already gone," Julien said, turning back to his reflection in the mirror.

"I'm afraid it's too late for that," a voice behind Sal said.

In the mirror, Julien watched as the door opened wider to reveal a tall figure, its face shielded by a white veil of lace. The stage manager gave Julien a half shrug and moved out of the way to allow the Veiled Prophet to enter the dressing room. The figure closed the door behind him, and the sound of the latch engaging was as loud and resolute as a gunshot.

"Mr. Eltinge," the figure said.

"Mr. . . ." Julien trailed off, unsure of how to address the man who was taking up all the air in what had been a sanctuary moments before. He was suddenly aware of his in-between state. Without his wig, he wasn't completely one version of himself or another, and without either role to fall back on, he was at a loss.

The night that the Veiled Prophet had come to demand the necklace, he'd made it clear that the Society had kept careful tabs on Julien from the moment he'd arrived in town. They'd believed his act to be a danger at first, a corruption of the true values of the esteemed people of the city. They didn't need any of the tawdriness of the East, and if he mis-stepped, if he thought to bring any depravity to their town, they would act. They would end his career.

He knew then that they hadn't understood the first thing about him, and because of that, Julien had given in to their demands. He'd sold them the necklace for a song and everything had been fine—at least until Harte Darrigan and the girl had shown up and dragged him into this mess.

The Veiled Prophet, whoever it was behind the screen of lace, didn't bother to answer. "We have a proposition for you, Mr. Eltinge."

"A proposition?" Julien said, hating the way his voice cracked.

They can't know. . . .

"A job," the figure said. "One that would make good use of your talents."

Julien didn't miss the scorn in the Prophet's voice, but he wasn't a clown to be paraded out and made fun of. "And if I'm too busy for any extra employment at the moment?" he asked, taking another puff of the cigar, just to prove he couldn't be bullied.

The figure inclined its head, making the heavy lace in front of his face wave. "You know how far our influence reaches, Mr. Eltinge. We saw that Mr. Albee was at the theater this evening. He is a *particular* friend of ours."

Julien's stomach clenched. They could destroy all that he'd worked for if they had the ear of Mr. Albee. His show, his dreams, his future—all gone. "I suppose I could make a little time to hear you out," he said. "I've got a busy schedule with the show. Tomorrow evening, maybe? We're dark then."

"Tonight, Mr. Eltinge. Now, in fact."

"Now?" he asked, looking down at the gown he was still wearing.

"We'll give you time to make yourself more . . . presentable." His tone rang with distaste. "Our carriage will be waiting," the Prophet said before he took his leave.

Julien had a very bad feeling about this whole situation. He looked at himself in the mirror, but it was Darrigan and the girl he cursed. If the necklace was so dangerous, Harte should never have sent it to him in the first place. At the very least, Darrigan should have had the courtesy to stay dead.

PART

IV

THE MEMORY OF HER NAME

1904—St. Louis

T he late-June day was warm, and the sky was a bright, clear blue. All around Esta, the pristine white buildings of the fair were a marked contrast to the dirt and grime of the rest of the city. The couples who walked arm in arm and the families who held tightly to the small hands of their children could not have imagined that the well-dressed gentleman waiting at the water's edge was actually a woman, or that she was about to commit a crime.

There was something about the moments before a job began that made Esta's skin tingle—not with dread or apprehension, but anticipation and the sheer satisfaction of doing what she was born to do. Maybe it was just adrenaline, but Esta always felt like it had to be more than some random chemical reaction that made her body feel like it was singing, that made her mind feel clear and ready. It had to be a sign—a good omen of sorts. There had been very few moments in her life when everything felt completely right—when the pieces fell into their places—and most of them had been in the moments before a job. As she waited next to the railing near the large lagoon that anchored the Exposition, Esta was fairly certain that *this* was another of those times.

Maybe nighttime would have been a more expected choice, but after a few days of planning and after the information Julien had given them, she and Harte had decided that it would be easier to lift the necklace during the day rather than waiting until the fair closed. For one, they could use the crowds to their advantage, but more important, they knew what the Exposition was like during its open hours. They'd spent the last few days walking the grounds and pretending to be tourists as they cased the areas around the Streets of Cairo and the Pike. They knew how many Guardsmen were stationed there and when their shifts changed.

On the other hand, night was a black box. They didn't know what kind of security there might be or even how the necklace was housed at night. But during the day? The fine folks who ran the fair were even kind enough to draw them up a schedule so they knew when everything was happening—and what the best times were to create distractions.

According to the schedule, there were always at least two parades—one at midday and one later in the evening. They'd considered using the evening parade, since the darkness could give them some cover, but in the end they had decided that the safest and easiest plan required exposure.

Esta saw Harte approaching before he noticed her, and she allowed herself to take a moment to watch him as he walked through the crowd. In the last few days, they'd settled into a steady, if not completely comfortable, equilibrium. It was as though, without uttering a word, they'd come to the agreement that they wouldn't speak about the night they'd arrived—the kiss or the argument. It didn't mean that she felt any less hurt, but after what had happened during the boat ride, she didn't press. He would tell her everything eventually or he wouldn't—she couldn't force him to trust her or to see her as someone to depend on any more than she could stop the way her heart clenched a little each time she saw him—each time she remembered what it had felt like to have his lips against hers.

He was dressed in trim, olive-green pants paired with a matching waistcoat and lighter-colored jacket. With the straw boater shading his face and the easy way his arms swung relaxed at his sides, he looked fresh and crisp, like the portrait of a summer day. She knew the moment he saw her waiting—his mouth flattened and his eyes went tight, like he was preparing himself for something. But then his expression relaxed, and it was as though the tightness from a moment before had never existed.

As he approached, she had the oddest vision of his face lighting with a smile and him offering her the crook of his arm. She could almost see them, walking arm in arm, taking in the sights and sounds like anyone else. For a moment she wished they could let go of everything hanging over them and make that vision come to life. For a moment she wished that they could forget what they were about to do and pretend that they were just two people enjoying a sunny day at the fair.

But wishes were for suckers, and Esta didn't plan on being one of those, not ever again. Especially not when it came to Harte Darrigan.

"I don't think I'll ever get over this place," Harte said, pausing long enough to look at the water. The lagoon itself extended into the heart of the fair, and at the far end stood a pristinely white domed building—the Festival Hall. It glimmered with lights, even at noon. All along the tree-lined edges of the water, fountains sent cascading arcs of water into the air, while the cool white marble statuary stood as silent guards.

"The world isn't really like this," she said, her mood suddenly darker. She leaned against the railing and pretended to take in the scenery, but her attention was elsewhere. The stone beneath her hand looked like carved marble, but it was just painted concrete. *Fake, just like everything else in this place.* "Half these buildings are just shells. They'll come down in a few months, and it'll be like none of this had ever been here."

"I know . . ." His voice was wistful, and she glanced over to see him watching the gondolas gliding across the smooth, clear surface of the water. "Still. They put on a damn good show."

He wasn't wrong. The fairground itself was a marvel, even to Esta's jaded eyes. The buildings flanking the wide lagoon looked like they were made from marble and granite. They reminded Esta of buildings she'd seen in pictures of the great cities of Europe. But even with all the grandeur of the Exposition, compared to New York, St. Louis itself looked half-formed. Outside the walls of the fairground, the city was still a city on the edge of the frontier and worlds away from the crowded streets of New York. Beyond the city, the world waited.

"Did you take care of it?" he asked.

"Of course," she told him, pretending to look at the scenery while she made sure that no one was watching them. It hadn't been very difficult to pick the lock on one of the maintenance gates not far from the Pike. She'd left it closed, so it looked secure, but it would provide them an easy exit once everything happened. "You?"

He nodded. "No one was watching the armory. I replaced all the bullets I could find, but I'm not sure if it'll be enough."

"It'll have to be," she told him. "This will work." *It has to.*

But it wouldn't be easy.

The trickiest part about the entire job wasn't that it would happen in the bright light of day or in the midst of a crowded midway. It wasn't even that it was just the two of them. Julien wouldn't be there—they'd picked a day with a matinee show to ensure that he had an airtight alibi. He'd done what he could to help them, and now they would do what they could to keep him out of the rest. No, the trickiest part was that they would have to do almost everything without magic. With the Jefferson Guard on high alert, they couldn't chance using either one of their affinities—not unless they absolutely had to. They'd have to go in straight and use sheer skill. And, thanks to both Harte and Julien, a bit of showmanship.

"The parade starts in about fifteen minutes. We need to both be in Cairo by that time. You'll have to move fast. You have the charges?"

"I've got it, Harte," she said, annoyed with how quickly he'd shifted from enjoying the day to fussing at her. It reminded her a little of the way Logan used to, and suddenly she couldn't help but wonder what had happened to him. Had Jianyu found him? Or had Logan been able to reach Nibsy? But there would be time to consider that later. For now, she had to focus.

Theirs wasn't an elegant plan, but it was workable. They had smoke charges that they'd placed on fuses at various places along the Pike, and she would set them off right before she and Harte went into the Nile ride—just before the parade arrived at the area in front of the Streets of Cairo.

There was only one way in and out of the chamber where the necklace was displayed, and if they'd timed the fuses right, the charges should go off, flooding the Pike with strange-colored smoke that would, hopefully, be taken as an Antistasi attack. They were betting on the Guard rushing to the area and leaving the stone less guarded than it otherwise might have been.

If the schedule was accurate—and so far, it had been—before the smoke completely dissipated and the crowd realized there was no danger, the veterans of the Boer War, who reenacted their skirmishes twice a day, would be starting their first assault. Since Harte had replaced the blanks they usually used with more smoke charges, all hell should break loose again as soon as they fired their first volley of shots.

Between the people flooding out of the Boer War demonstration and the confusion on the Pike, the Guard should be nicely tied up. She and Harte should be able to slip the necklace out of its case and be on their way.

"If anything is off by even a few minutes, we could be stuck," Harte reminded her as he checked the pocket watches they each had to make sure the times were the same.

"I *know*." She was itching to get started. "We've gone over this a million times."

She snatched one of the watches from his hand as a family came up to the railing to look at the water. The parents were young—about the same age that Dolph had been. The father had by the hand a small golden-haired boy who looked like his miniature. When the boy started to cry, the father lifted him up gently so the boy could see the fountains just beyond the railing, while the mother fussed with the little boy's hair.

Esta didn't even realize she was watching them until Harte cleared his throat next to her, drawing her attention back to him.

"You need to focus." His voice was gentle, but the reprimand stung nonetheless.

"I *am* focused," she said, trying to ignore the way the little boy squealed in delight at the view of the water.

"You know that everything has to go perfectly for this to work, and we aren't even in control of most of the pieces. It isn't going to be easy."

"It never is." She glanced one last time at the family.

Maybe it was the brightness of the day or the sweetness of the vanilla and caramel wafting through the air, but as she watched the family go about their day—their lives—without a care in the world, Esta's hands curled into fists. She let her nails dig into her palms, accepting the flash of pain so that she could hold back the spike of anger that had caused her blood to go hot. *They have everything, and they have no idea.* And she would fight and scrabble and scheme . . . and in the end, she would get nothing at all. *And no one would even know.*

Or maybe they would, she thought with a spark of hope. Maybe these Antistasi, whoever they were, would keep the memory of her name and what she had done—or tried to do—alive, just as they had for the past two years.

"Hey, Slim." Harte's voice came to her from a distance. "Did you hear what I said? Are you okay there?"

"Yeah." She blinked, confused for a moment by the direction of her thoughts. "I'm fine."

It was the truth.

Who cared if she couldn't have everything? Who cared if the man who had been a father to her was a lie and her actual father was lost to her before she ever knew? Whatever pain lay in her past could just stay there. Her past had given her skills and talents she might not have otherwise had, and whatever the lies that had forged her, they didn't determine her future. She would be what she had chosen to become. And if she didn't make it through? Perhaps she would live on in some other way.

She straightened her spine and gave Harte the cockiest smile she could dredge up. "Let's go steal us the fair."

ON THE EDGE OF THE WEST

1904—St. Louis

Harte would have paid almost any price to be able to reach across the distance between them, pull Esta close, and kiss the smile off her face. But he didn't trust himself—or the power inside of him—to be able to stop. Instead, he stood with his hands tucked into his pockets so he wouldn't do any of the idiotic things running through his head.

As quickly as she gave him the smile, Esta was turning away, heading toward the Pike to set their plan in motion. His gaze followed her trim silhouette until she disappeared into the crowd. Inside his mind, the voice shifted and rumbled, clearly frustrated with his decision to let her walk away from him—again. He was getting fairly good at ignoring it, probably in the same way a person learns to ignore a chronic cough or a bad knee. You simply lived around it. But he couldn't ignore the fact that the power was getting stronger and the voice that spoke through it was getting clearer every day.

Still, despite the warmth of the afternoon, ice inched down his spine. A premonition. Or perhaps it was simply rational, levelheaded fear. They were about to steal a well-guarded necklace from the middle of a crowded fair in broad daylight.

This is never going to work.

Too bad that it had to. Julien's best chance of evading the Order's notice was for them to get the Djinni's Star and get out of town fast.

Harte pulled his cap down and checked his watch for the umpteenth time before he started walking. He didn't go in the direction of the Pike, as Esta had. Instead, he followed the waterways east, past the ornate palace-like buildings that held the exhibitions on electricity and industry, and then farther, past the Palace of Transportation, with its six identical sculptures bearing shields to guard the high arched entrance.

Everything is a palace, he thought. Even here, on the edge of the West, where the whole country was possible, Americans still wanted to be royalty. It was why people like Jack Grew and the rest of the Order could do what they did—the ordinary person allowed it. The average citizen liked the idea of a future where they might be as rich as a king or as powerful as an emperor. They might have talked about democracy, but what they wanted was the spectacle of royalty.

He continued past the building and entered the Pike close to Cairo, checking his watch again as he found a place near the Cliff Dwellers exhibition. *Perfect.* Already, he could hear the noise of the parade approaching.

But there was no sign of Esta.

A NEW ERA IN THE BOWERY

1902—New York

James Lorcan would have paid handsomely to have just one answer to any of his questions. There were too many variables at play, too much at risk. It had been five days since Mock Duck had brought Jianyu to the Strega and traded him for a handful of dollars and a notebook of secrets he could use against Tom Lee. Five days since James had had Jianyu in his hands, and five days since the damnable turncoat had somehow managed to escape.

At least the fire had been minor, and Paul Kelly's connections with Tammany meant that the brigades did more than just watch the building burn. Because of their help, James was able to sit at the back of the barroom and survey his domain.

At least Viola was taken care of. The image of Dolph's favorite assassin, bruised and bleeding from her brother's fists, still served to comfort— and amuse—him. As far as James was concerned, it proved that Dolph had always thought too highly of her. Viola had always been moody and temperamental—a liability. She'd never liked James, that much he knew. From the look of pure hate in her eyes the other day, she still didn't, but at least she wouldn't be a problem. She'd overplayed her hand when she'd gone back to her brother's protection, and all evidence so far indicated that Kelly would be able to control her. That much, at least, was a comfort. It made for one less thing to worry about.

The future was still too unsettled for his liking, though. James could not make heads or tails of the variables that seemed to waver in the

Aether, the paths rising up and then disappearing like ghosts. But he knew one thing for sure. Something was coming. Something that promised to change *everything*.

At the front of the Strega, the door opened, letting in a burst of cool air that James could feel even from the back of the room. It seemed that his thoughts of Paul Kelly had summoned the devil himself. All at once the atmosphere in the barroom changed as the people realized that the notorious leader of the Five Pointers had just arrived.

A few weeks ago Kelly's appearance there in the saloon that Dolph Saunders had ruled his empire from would have been unheard of. Before Dolph's death Kelly never would have dared to confront the Devil's Own on their own turf. But this was a new city, a new world. And all James could think was *Finally*.

Kelly was followed by two of his Five Pointers, broad men with the same ruthless expression that Kelly himself wore. Between them, they held a towheaded fellow James didn't recognize. The unlucky captive looked to be slightly older than James, but he had a softness to his features that almost made him seem younger. His left eye had been blackened and was already swollen shut, no doubt the effect of tangling with Kelly's men.

Sensing trouble, the patrons in the barroom murmured uneasily as Kelly and his men stopped just inside the doorway and surveyed the saloon. Most kept their eyes down, studying their cups as though the liquid within them might burst into flames at any moment. A few drained their glasses and left, giving Kelly and his men a wide berth as they departed.

Seemingly pleased with the reaction his entrance had caused, Paul Kelly made his way through the unusually quiet room. As he approached, James rubbed his thumb along the silver topper of his cane—a gorgon head with the face of an angel. *Leena's face.* The silver snakes that coiled beneath his thumb felt unnaturally cool, a reminder that whatever strength the Five Pointers might have in the streets, James and those he now controlled had power that Paul Kelly could only dream of.

But the coolness was also a reminder of how much was at stake. There was power locked within the silver gorgon head—the part of her affinity that Dolph had taken from Leena and used to ensure his control over the Devil's Own. But that power was useless to James, who didn't have the affinity to reach it . . . not until he had the Book to unlock it.

Kelly was nearly across the barroom, and James was still sitting. He refused to be seen as weak—not there on his turf and in front of his own people—so, ignoring the pain in his wounded leg, he stood up and steadied himself with the cane.

Sundren as he was, Paul Kelly could not have felt the way the magic in the room flared as he walked through the saloon. The air filled with the nervous warmth of affinities on the verge of becoming, as each Mageus present watched, wary and ready, for whatever would happen. To James Lorcan, it felt in that moment as though the whole world was no bigger than that particular smoky barroom and the people within it, each of them holding their breath and waiting.

"Paul," James said, greeting Kelly like they were old friends. "What brings you to the Strega tonight?" He glanced beyond Paul Kelly to the boy the Five Pointers was holding. "Or maybe I should ask what you've brought me?"

Kelly smirked. "My guys picked him up down on Broome Street. He's got a pretty enough face," he said, giving the blond a couple of sharp smacks on the cheek that had the boy wincing. "But not too many brains. He demanded I bring him to you."

"Did he?" James asked, ignoring the unsettled energy that permeated the barroom as he examined the blond.

"He did," Kelly said. "Which causes a problem for me. We need to get something clear, Lorcan—whatever mutually beneficial understanding we might have between us, I don't take orders from you or yours. Got it?"

"He's not one of mine," James said, turning his attention back to Kelly and assessing the danger in the air.

"He says otherwise."

The blond was breathing heavily, as though he were in pain, and staring at James from his one good eye. James ignored his face and focused on the Aether around him. It was hazy, indistinct, but it didn't seem to indicate that the stranger posed any threat. If anything, the way it was already fusing with the set patterns was a positive sign. He stepped toward the trio, the tap of his cane punctuating the uneasy silence in the bar.

"Who are you?" James asked the blond when they were face-to-face. There was definitely something to the boy—the warmth of magic hung around him, clear to anyone who shared it.

"Logan," the boy told him, never once flinching under James' steady stare. "Logan Sullivan."

"Who sent you, Logan Sullivan?" James asked.

The guy's expression never flickered. The Aether around him never wavered. "You did."

"*I* did?" James said, studying the stranger for some sign of deception.

"That's what he kept telling my guys," Kelly said.

"He's lying," James told Kelly as he continued to eye this new entity. "I don't know any Logan Sullivan, and I certainly don't know him."

"You do, and I can prove it," the boy said.

James got the sense this Logan Sullivan, whoever he was, wasn't lying. At least *he* didn't believe he was lying. Which wasn't going to help James' position with Kelly. He had to neutralize this danger quickly, before everything he'd so carefully positioned started to fall apart.

"I'm not interested in listening to your lies," James said, starting to turn away.

"Maybe you'd be interested in the Delphi's Tear," Logan said. "It's here, you know. In the city . . ."

James turned back to Logan. "What are you talking about?"

"You know exactly what I'm talking about," Logan told him, his expression never wavering. "You want the ring? I can find it for you. It's not far from here, but it's moving even as we speak."

"What's this?" Kelly asked, his voice dark and suspicious.

It was a delicate thing, to lead Kelly on without giving him too much. Information was power, and knowledge was the noose that could be slipped around a neck. But James didn't hesitate in his answer.

"It's one of the jewels I told you about—the ones that Darrigan and the girl made off with."

"The ones I sent my guys after?" Kelly narrowed his eyes in suspicion. "You'd better not have sent me on a chase, Lorcan."

"I didn't," James said, ignoring the threat. "Darrigan and the girl are out there, and when you find them and the things they stole, the Order will reward you handsomely."

Or they would if I wasn't planning on taking them first.

James considered Logan. "Where's this proof you claim to have?"

"Left inside jacket pocket," Logan told him.

Again James was struck by the stranger's steadiness, but he didn't read any danger here . . . quite the opposite.

James approached Logan again. "If I may?" The Five Pointers looked to Kelly, who gave them a subtle nod, and then James reached into Logan's jacket and fished out a small, paper-wrapped package. "What is it?" he asked.

"Open it," Logan said, his gaze calm and sure.

Too sure.

James tucked the cane under his arm and made quick work of the wrapping. His eyes told him what he was holding before his brain could accept it. "Where did you get this?" he asked.

"Like I said, you gave it to me."

It wasn't possible. The small notebook he was holding in his hand was instantly recognizable. After all, he had an identical one in his own jacket pocket.

"I didn't give you any—" His words were lost as he flipped through the book to find his own cramped, familiar handwriting on its pages. He stopped and went back to the beginning. . . . It was *definitely* his notes.

And his own notebook was *definitely* still in his pocket. Even now he felt the comforting weight of it.

Flipping forward, James stopped at the page he'd written earlier that morning. But *this* notebook continued on, still all in his own hand.

"What is it?" Kelly asked, clearly impatient to know what James saw in the notebook.

"It's nothing," James said, closing the notebook. "He's lying. This doesn't tell me anything at all."

Kelly frowned at James as though considering whether to believe him. Finally, he seemed to relent. "What should we do with him, then? I can have my guys take care of it if you want."

"Leave him to me," James told him.

"You?" Kelly seemed surprised, and more than a little disappointed.

"He's dragging my name through the mud. I think I should be the one to deal with him," James told him. Kelly wouldn't have respected him otherwise. "He won't bother you or yours again."

Kelly studied James for a long moment, and the unease permeating the room around them seemed to swell in the silence. But then he gave his two men another nod, and they dropped the boy, who crumpled to his knees, clearly injured.

"Mooch," James said. "Would you escort our guest to the cellar? Tie him up and make sure he's quiet until I get there. With force, if need be."

"No—" Logan tried to scramble to his feet, but Mooch and one of the other boys were on him before he could get far. With his soft features, he didn't stand much of a chance.

James waited until they were gone before he gestured to the table he'd been sitting at a few minutes before. "Have a drink with me? I owe you for bringing that bit of trouble to my attention."

Kelly studied him for another long moment before agreeing. "What could it hurt?" he said with a shrug. "Let's see what kind of swill Saunders stocked this place with."

"Better than you might imagine," he told Kelly, well aware of the nervous energy around them as he thumped the other man on the back.

James knew that every person in that barroom feared Kelly and the damage his Five Pointers could do. Even Dolph hadn't been able to protect them from the Five Pointers' viciousness in those final days.

Let them see, James thought. *Let them all see and understand exactly who I am and what influence I have.*

He poured two fingers of the house's best whiskey for each of them and raised his glass in a salute. Kelly watched him toss back the liquid before drinking his own.

"So," James said as he poured another glass for each of them. "How is your delightful sister these days . . . still raising hell?"

Kelly smirked. "Viola?" He laughed softly into his glass. "She doesn't raise anything unless I tell her to."

Perfect, James thought. *Exactly what I wanted to hear.*

A LAND SOAKED IN BLOOD

1902—New York

Barefoot and wearing nightclothes that were too large for him, Jianyu took a moment to test his balance while he had the bedpost to hold on to. The movement still made his vision waver, like he was looking through a fog, but he took a deep breath and forced himself to stay upright. It had been too long. *Far too long.*

By now, certainly, the boy Esta had warned him about would have arrived. By now the boy would have made contact with Nibsy. Which meant that he'd failed. *Again.*

He was not completely sure where he was, and he could not be sure how long he had been there. The times he had woken, he found that he could barely hold on to consciousness before the ground fell out from beneath him and he drifted back into the heavy darkness. But finally he had managed to claw free. The sun was slanting in through the thin curtains covering the single window in the room, and the air was warm and heavy with the smell of something laden with spices that were unfamiliar to his nose. But then he realized that he could pick out the sweetness of clove and the pungency of garlic, scents that reminded him of a home he would not see again.

Spurred on by that thought, he forced himself to take a step, pausing to make sure that the earth remained steady beneath him, unlike a day— or was it two?—before. Then, his desperation to find the boy Esta had warned him about had been so urgent, he had pushed too far and instead collapsed to the floor, jarring his already tender head again.

He took slow, tentative steps at first, testing himself, and when he was satisfied that his legs were steady, he followed the sound of voices through the door of the small bedroom and down a short hallway to a narrow living area, where he found three women sitting and stitching piles of men's pants. Cela was one of the three, but where the other two were engrossed in conversation with each other, she was working with her head bowed, concentrating on the task in front of her. She seemed separate from them somehow. Where the other two wore simple dark skirts and faded shirtwaists, Cela was wearing a gown the same shade of pink as a tea flower. It was a simple day dress, like any might wear, but again he was struck by the cut of it, the sharp tailoring that made it seem like something more. Her nimble fingers finished the cuff of one leg and moved on to the next, but her expression seemed far away—more sad than thoughtful.

He had spent only a few moments in her workshop at the theater, but that space had been neat and organized, the bolts of fabric stacked in straight lines and the bowls of beads and crystals arranged without even a spangle out of place. But nothing in this room sparkled. There was no silk or satin, and Cela herself looked tired.

The older of the other two glanced up and noticed Jianyu standing there, leaning against the doorway to keep himself upright. She cleared her throat, causing Cela to look up as well.

"You're awake," Cela said, the low tones of her voice making it sound like an accusation. "You shouldn't be up."

She was right, of course. The words were no sooner spoken than Jianyu felt himself swaying, and Cela was on her feet in an instant, helping him to the chair she had just been sitting in.

He thanked her, but along with gratitude, he felt the burn of shame. To be so weak here in front of these women. To be unable to fulfill his promises . . .

"You okay?" Cela asked, settling herself on the floor and taking up the pants she had been working on a moment ago.

He nodded rather than speaking, but the movement of his head caused his newly shorn hair to brush against his cheek, reminding him of all that had happened.

The older woman was watching him as she stitched, while the other one, a woman just a few years older than Cela, kept sliding glances his way as well. But it was the older woman who was the first to speak. "So, Mr. Jianyu . . . how long will you be staying with us, now that you're up?"

"Auntie—" Cela said, a note of warning in her voice. But the words that came next, Jianyu could not follow. They seemed to be in English, or some of them did, but Jianyu had trouble making sense of them. His head, perhaps . . .

But Cela's aunt seemed to understand. She answered back using the same unfamiliar tongue. The two women spoke for a minute, trading words, and Jianyu did not need to know the language they were speaking to discern their meaning, especially when the older woman's eyes kept cutting to Jianyu as the two spoke. After a moment, the older woman put down her sewing and motioned for the other to come with her, leaving Jianyu and Cela alone in the suddenly quiet apartment.

Cela made a few more stitches, but then her hands went still and she let out a long breath. Jianyu could see the tears turning her dark eyes glassy, but he had nothing to offer her.

"If I have caused you trouble with your family—"

Cela shook her head and wiped her eyes with the back of her hands. "My auntie is just like that sometimes. My cousin Neola is a bit easier to abide."

"The other girl?" Jianyu asked.

Cela nodded. Then she put aside the sewing she'd been doing. "How are you?"

"Well," he said, feeling that it was not a lie so long as he remained sitting.

"You look better," she told him. "That knock to the head you took was something awful. For a couple of days, I wasn't sure that you'd wake up."

There was something in her voice that sounded broken and brittle, but Jianyu felt he had no right to ask. "Thank you," he told her, his voice stiff. "You did not need to trouble yourself for me."

She gave him a doubtful look. "You're right about that, but seeing as how you got me out of the theater and away from Evelyn, I couldn't just leave you half-dead on the streetcar. And don't worry about my family," she said.

"Your aunt . . . she seemed angry," he told her.

"She usually is, around me," Cela said, waving away his concerns, but at his questioning look, she let out a sigh and began to explain. "My mama's family came from the Windward Islands. They always did think they were better than the people who've lived here for generations— definitely thought they were better than my daddy, who came from down South and whose parents weren't even born free. She's probably happy to see me sitting here stitching pants. They all told me I was a fool for trying to find a job in the white theaters. Said I didn't know my place, and if I just listened to Mr. Washington, I'd know I need to cast down my bucket where I was, not go looking for other oceans." She shrugged. "I always thought they were jealous because they didn't make half as much money as I did. Maybe my mama didn't give me her light skin, but she did give me her skill with a needle and her backbone. . . ." She hesitated, her gaze sliding away. "But maybe they were right all along."

Her words stoked something inside of him, some small ember of frustration he had carried over an ocean. He didn't understand her situation, but he understood the note of disappointment in her voice. "I doubt that," he told her, hoping that it was true for him as well.

"I don't know," she said with another deep sigh. Her eyes were shining again with the wetness of unshed tears. "Maybe I should have just been happy with the lot I'd been given rather than searching out greener fields. I got that from my daddy, though. He was never happy with good enough—and neither am I. But all his wanting cost him his life in the end, and all mine cost me everything I had. My home. My brother." Her voice broke, and she paused for a second as though trying to collect herself. "Now I'm back here, stitching some old pants, just like they said I would be. And the one person who understood me no matter what is gone."

"It seems, then, that I am doubly in your debt," he told her.

She shook her head. "We're even now, as far as I'm concerned."

"Darrigan sent me to protect you and the ring," Jianyu told her. "I have done neither."

"I didn't ask for no protecting," she told him, her expression tight.

"That matters little," Jianyu said. "It was not well done of him to give you the burden of the ring, to put you in such danger without warning you of what might come. But it was I who failed to protect you."

"That stupid ring," Cela said, pulling herself from the floor. "I wish I'd never laid eyes on it, or Harte Darrigan."

"I'm sure there are more than a few people who feel that way about the magician," Jianyu said dryly.

She looked at him, a question in her eyes. "Does that include you?"

He inclined his head. "Most definitely. Although, if I had not known him, I would also not have met you, and it seems to me more than a fair trade to know that someone with your strength and kindness is a part of this world."

She looked away, her cheeks flushing with what could have been embarrassment or pleasure, but at least the sadness in her expression had eased, if only a little. "You know," she said after an almost comfortable moment of silence between them, "I could help you with that hair of yours."

His hands went to the shorn strands that hung around his face. *There cannot be any help for this.*

"I'm pretty good with a pair of shears, and I used to cut my brother, Abel's—" She lifted her fist to her mouth, as though she was trying to keep the pain inside instead of letting it out. After a moment, she spoke again, her voice softer this time. "I used to cut Abel's hair all the time after our mother died. I can't put things back the way they were, but I can clean up the edges for you."

This was an offering he had not expected. It was also a gift he did not deserve, but somehow he could not stop himself from accepting it.

They sat in the small kitchen, a worn towel around Jianyu's shoulders to catch the clippings. At first, Cela was tentative, as though she was afraid even to touch him. But eventually the shyness and reluctance between them dissolved, and her fingers were strong and sure. The scissors whispered their steady tale as she worked.

"So, tell me about this ring," she said, letting her voice trail off, giving him the space to speak.

He told her what he could of the ring and of the rest of the artifacts, and once he started speaking, he found that he could not stop. He had often sat with Dolph in the evenings, speaking of any number of things—news of the city and hopes for the future and even thoughts about power and magic and its role in the world. But in the days before Khafre Hall, Dolph had been too busy plugging leaks on the bursting dam that was the Devil's Own to sit and visit, and after Khafre Hall they had all been alone in their grief—Jianyu, maybe, most of all. He had been so silent for days now that just having Cela's ear felt like a balm.

Cela listened without interrupting, her fingers and the scissors moving steadily over his head.

"So I must find the ring and keep it from those who would do harm with it," he finished.

She was silent for a moment as she worked, snipping at the hair along the nape of his neck. "You know, all this fuss over magic. People are so busy trying to keep it and control it that they're willing to do all sorts of evil for it." Her hands went still, and she stepped back to look him over. "But maybe nobody's meant to have it. Maybe it's just meant to fade away." She tilted her head to the side and then trimmed another piece of his hair.

"If you ask me," she continued, "it's because there's something wrong with this land. The people who were here first—the ones who truly belong here—got killed off or pushed aside, and that does something to a place, all that death and violence. Magic can't take root in blood-soaked earth. If you ask me, maybe it's a good thing. Maybe nobody should have that kind of power over anyone else." She brushed off his shoulders. "Go on. See what you think."

There was a small square mirror hanging on the other side of the room. Jianyu stepped toward it tentatively, in part because he was already unsteady on his feet, and in part because he was afraid to see the person who would greet him in the cloudy glass.

He didn't really look like himself. The hair that he'd once worn pulled back now framed his face. It wasn't his father's son that looked back, but some new version of himself. American and unrecognizable. He felt a thrill of something that might have been fear . . . or maybe it was simple readiness.

Cela was safe. He would find the ring. He had not yet failed, and he would not allow himself to.

THE MAP OF THE WORLD

1902—New York

J ames felt the map of the world shift as he finished reading the final
page in the notebook he'd taken from Logan Sullivan. He wanted to
believe that it was a hoax because the alternative was too impossible. He
wanted it to be a fabrication meant to lead him astray, but his senses told
him that the notebook and all that it held was nothing short of the truth.

He placed the notebook on the worn desk in front of him, next to
its twin.

Taking his glasses from his nose, he polished the lenses and considered
the possibilities. Every victory and every mistake he would ever make
were contained in the book Logan had brought him. With the strength
of his affinity and the knowledge in those notebooks, he could remake
his future. He could rewrite his own history—and more.

But first James had to be sure—*absolutely* sure—of who this Logan
Sullivan was. He'd spoken of the Delphi's Tear, and so James would give
him an opportunity to retrieve it. If Logan proved unable to do what he'd
promised, James doubted it would be much of a loss to dispose of him.

He considered the identical notebooks before finally taking up the
one Logan had brought him and tucking it into his pocket. Until he
knew for sure whether to trust the stranger, he would keep it close. After
all, since it possibly held a record of his life, it wouldn't do for anyone
else to find it. Then he grabbed his jacket and pulled on his cap, locking the door securely behind him as he left, and he went to talk to the
newcomer—the boy who would change his future.

411

THE PIKE

1904—St. Louis

The Pike was its usual circus of noise and confusion as Esta entered it, prepared to carry out her part of the plan. She had about ten minutes to get from the entrance, next to the huge monstrosity that was the fake Alps, to where she would meet Harte just outside Cairo. He'd take a different path—around the back of the Pike and entering from the east side of the boulevard—so that there was no chance of them being seen together.

In her pocket she had packets of smoking powder rigged with fuses. They were nothing more than some harmless stage props that Harte and Julien had made in preparation for the day, but it would take a while for the people who saw the smoke to realize that.

She passed the concessions for Asia and Japan and continued toward the enormous domed building that was the Creation attraction. Like the Nile boats in Cairo, it was also a ride. Like everything else, it was brash and too bright and overdone. She stopped near a vendor selling huge salted pretzels and checked the pocket watch she'd taken from Harte. Five minutes to go. She had at least two more to wait. In the distance, faintly, she heard the stirrings of the parade, the rumble of drums that told her the time was close.

She checked her watch again, and as she did, she had the strangest feeling she was being watched. Glancing up, she realized her instincts were right. Across the street, close to the entrance of the Incubator building, was the cowboy she'd seen disappear that first day at the theater. And he was looking straight at her.

There was no way she could do what she needed to do as long as he was watching her. Taking a breath, she pushed aside the panic and used a play from the cowboy's own book. She gave him a wink, and then she darted into the crowds of the Creation attraction, making herself as unnoticeable as she could while she pushed her way deeper into them. She looked back only once and saw that the cowboy was following her, so she shoved on until she found a small alcove to the right of the ticket window, where she pulled time slow.

Releasing a breath, she relaxed a little as the world went silent around her. Only a couple of days had passed since she'd tested her affinity when Harte left her at the boardinghouse, but during those days they'd been extra careful not to use their magic, just in case the Guard was nearby. It felt like it had been *so long* since she'd been able to flex her affinity, and now the sureness of her magic gave her the impetus to get on with it. She dodged through the crowd, until she was face-to-face with the cowboy who'd been following her. This close, she saw that he had eyes as green as a cat's, but one was flecked with brown enough that it looked like they were two different colors.

This should keep him busy. Lighting the fuse on the first packet, she tucked it into the outer pocket of his coat. Then she darted away, releasing time as she went.

She let her feet carry her toward Cairo, watching for marks. Pausing next to a trash bin, she pulled on time just long enough to light another fuse and place the packet into the bin. Then she moved on, releasing time once she was safely away. She had eight packets, which meant she needed to place six more before she reached Cairo. Working her way up the Pike, she found an empty baby carriage here, a half-drunken man there. Each time she approached, she used her affinity just long enough to place the packet.

It was working. Already she could see the Guards, who were stationed at odd intervals around the Pike, coming to attention as they sensed the magic in the air, but she was always far away from the location by the time they detected it.

When she reached the Cliff Dwellers attraction, where she and Harte were to meet, Esta knew she was later than they'd planned. The parade was too close, and she could tell by the thin set of Harte's mouth that he was trying not to be too obvious as his eyes searched the crowd for her. But his features relaxed and his mouth parted slightly in relief when he saw her.

"You're late," he said by way of greeting.

"I had a little trouble."

His brows went up. "What kind of trouble?"

"The cowboy from the other day? He saw me."

Harte frowned. "Maybe we shouldn't—"

"It's fine," she told him before he could finish his statement. "I took care of it—made sure that he didn't see me. And I left him a little surprise."

"I see," Harte said, but he still had that nervous, worried expression on his face.

"Let's go," she told him. "The parade's almost here."

She didn't give him time to argue before she started across the wide boulevard, toward Cairo and the necklace.

THE WEIGHT OF BELONGING

1902—New York

Leaving under the cover of darkness without so much as a good-bye was hardly any way to repay the kindness Cela's family had shown him over the past six days as he had healed, but Jianyu had already allowed too much time to pass since the ring had gone missing from her possession. He had been delaying the inevitable, but now he had another promise to keep. A wider world to protect.

Jianyu told himself that Cela would be fine, even if the tension in the house was thick enough for him to swim through. He saw the way they looked at her, but they were her family. She would be safe now that the stone was no longer in her possession, and they would take care of her until she was on her feet.

Perhaps he was a coward for not telling Cela that he was leaving, but if anyone came looking for him, she would be *safer* for not knowing.

He could have used his affinity to conceal himself, but his head still ached occasionally, and using the bronze disks would be too much of an effort. Besides, he was still unsteady, and he needed to save his strength for what was to come.

When he reached the corner of Amsterdam Avenue, a familiar figure stepped from the entrance of one of the saloons. He could have opened the light to hide himself, but it was too late. She had seen him. To run now would be disrespectful and insulting.

"I had a feeling you'd leave tonight," Cela said when he finally came to where she was waiting for him, her hands crossed over her chest. "That's it, then? You were just gonna go without so much as a good-bye?"

He did not respond. What was there to say? She was correct in her words and in the anger stirring behind them.

"After all I did for you? After I made my family take you in?"

"I owe you all a debt of gratitude—" he started, but Cela's temper snapped.

"This don't look anything like gratitude." She glared at him. "Where are you going, anyway?"

"It is better that you do not know," he said softly, hating the emotion in her eyes. Suspicion. Disgust. It was the emotion he regularly saw mirrored back to him in the eyes of those he met, the eyes of those who looked at him and saw not the person he was or the heart he carried, but the skin he wore. "You will be safer," he tried to explain.

"Safer?" she asked, a bark of ridicule in her tone. Then her brows beaded together. "You're going after that ring, aren't you?"

He did not respond, but from the way her expression shifted, she understood.

"Why? After all the trouble it's caused for everyone, why not just leave the blasted thing be?"

He gave her the only answer he could: "Because I have to."

"Why?" she pressed.

"I made a promise," he told her. "I gave Darrigan my word that I would see you safe and protect the ring. I have done the first, and now I must turn to the other."

"You don't owe Darrigan anything," she said, more softly now, a frown tugging at her full lips. "Neither of us owe him a single thing more."

"Perhaps," he conceded. "But I explained to you what the ring could do, did I not? In unworthy hands, it could have devastating effects. I cannot allow that to happen. I cannot allow the Order or anyone else who might do harm with the stone to obtain it."

Cela stared at him for a moment, her dark eyes sharp in their intensity as she considered his words. Then she let out a jagged breath that was as much frustration as it was understanding. "I'm coming with you, then."

"No—"

"I'm the one who lost that ring, so I'll help you find it."

"This is not your fight." Jianyu shook his head. "You will stay here, with your family, where you belong."

She gave him an exasperated look. "Were you in that house with me? I don't *belong* there."

He had seen, had felt the tension between them, but . . . "They are family. Your *blood*."

"They might be my mama's people, but they've never *really* been mine, blood or not." Her jaw was set and determined. "My grandparents didn't ever approve of the choice my mama made when she married my daddy for lots of reasons, but mostly it boiled down to his skin being too dark. Didn't matter that he worked his knuckles to the bone to give us a good life: a roof over our heads and shoes on our feet. According to them, he was low class, and when we came out with skin every bit as dark as his, so were we," she told him. "They never said it outright, but we knew."

Her shoulders seemed to sag with the weight of her confession. "My mama's people put up with us for her sake, but they never were any sort of safe harbor, even when she was alive. They blamed my daddy when she died a few years back from consumption, and now they're blaming me for Abel's death. I can see it in their eyes. They heard the whispers about how I ran from the house, and maybe they don't say it outright, but they're sure as hell thinking I had something to do with it. So no, I don't belong there. If you're leaving, I'm coming with you."

Jianyu understood the expression Cela wore as she lifted her chin, daring him to contradict her. It was the same as the mask he often wore himself, the steely armor that served as protection from the never-ending menace of a world that did not welcome him. But because he recognized it, he also knew what was beneath—the soft, essential parts of the soul that could be damaged beyond repair.

He frowned. "This is my burden to carry."

She let out a long sigh, and she looked suddenly fragile. "That's where you're wrong. The moment they came and took my brother, it became mine, too."

"But—"

She cut him off. "Tell me, did you have a plan for finding Evelyn?" She paused for his answer, and when it did not come, she shook her head. "What were you gonna do, wander around until you ran into her? It's a big city. At least I know where she lives."

NOT AS PLANNED

1902—New York

Nothing had gone the way Logan Sullivan had expected. When he'd left Professor Lachlan's building that morning, he hadn't planned to end the day tied up in the dark, dank cellar of some rotting building, guarded by two guys who looked like they'd started shaving when they were eight.

The redheaded one was especially worrisome. He kept rubbing his fingertips together, causing flames to dance at the tips of them, all the while leering at Logan. It was like he was just waiting for Logan to make a wrong move.

Which wasn't going to happen.

Maybe things hadn't gone that smoothly. Maybe Professor Lachlan had been wrong about how easy it would be—about how his younger self would *certainly* be able to tell that everything Logan said was the truth. It would have been a hell of a lot easier if those big goons hadn't caught him first, and it *definitely* would have been better if Esta hadn't made off with the package Professor Lachlan had entrusted Logan to deliver; the Book and the stones would have gone a long way toward smoothing things over.

But he'd still had the notebook, Logan reminded himself. Once the Professor read about himself, he'd know that Logan was telling the truth. He'd know exactly how helpful Logan had been to his future self, and he would believe him now. Maybe he'd even be able to help him get back to his own time. Although Logan had a sinking feeling that without Esta, that was going to be impossible.

Shit.

Footsteps echoed on the staircase that descended steeply into the cellar, an uneven gait that Logan recognized immediately. *There.* He'd been right all along.

Logan gave the redheaded guy—Firebug McGee, or whatever his name was—a smug look. It was only a matter of moments before Logan would be vindicated.

It was still a shock to see just how young the Professor was here, in this time. He couldn't be more than fifteen, close to the age Logan himself had been when he'd received a ticket and an invitation to fly across an ocean and start a new life. His uncle, a low-level fencer of stolen goods, had been one of the Professor's contacts in England, and he hadn't given Logan a choice in the matter. To the thirteen-year-old Logan, the whole thing had seemed almost too good to be true: He got out from under the constant threat of his uncle's fists, and the professor paid for his mother to have the house in the country, like she'd always wanted. And if Logan had to deal with a life behind the Brink or the headache of traveling through time or Esta's smart-ass tendencies, it had been worth it for the comfortable life and for the respect the Professor had given him.

But this boy wasn't yet the man the Professor would become. The Professor's younger face didn't even have a shadow of hair on it, and the eyes behind his gold-rimmed glasses, while familiar, were clear of the cloudy cataracts that would haunt him in the future. Still, there was the same uncanny knowledge in his eyes, the spark of intelligence that had let Logan know the very first time they'd met that the old man wasn't to be messed with.

It will be fine.

"Leave us." The boy who would one day become the Professor made it to the bottom of the stairs and stood in front of Logan, eyeing him with a familiar expression.

"You sure, Nibs?" the redhead asked, snapping the fire between his fingers as he watched Logan uneasily. "I can stay, just in case."

The Professor turned on the redhead. "You think I can't handle myself?" he asked in a voice like acid.

The fire on the redhead's fingertips went out. "I just thought—"

"We'd be in trouble if I depended on you to do the thinking, Mooch. But I don't. I depend on you to do what I ask, when I ask it. And I'm asking you to leave me with our prisoner. I'll deal with him myself."

"Right, Nibs. Sorry." Mooch cut Logan another threatening look, but he took himself up the steps, leaving Logan with the younger version of his friend and mentor.

"So," Logan said after a long beat of uneasy silence. He was unsure of where to start. The man this boy would become had been like a father to Logan. He'd taken Logan under his wing and taught him everything he knew, but the boy in front of him was a stranger. "They call you Nibs?"

"Only those who don't know better." The Professor's nostrils flared slightly, just as they had every time Logan or Esta had managed to do something to piss him off. It was eerie to see the action on this younger boy's face. "You can call me James, since I assume we know each other."

"Then you read the notebook," Logan asked, still too nervous to feel relief.

"I did." The Professor—James—leaned on the silver-topped cane. "It's quite an object you brought me. Too fantastical to be true, really."

"You don't believe it?" Logan asked. Unease prickled at the nape of his neck. *He has to believe.* Logan was royally screwed if he didn't.

"I don't believe anything without proof," James said, pushing his glasses farther up his nose. "You spoke of the Delphi's Tear?"

"It's here, in the city," Logan told him. Apparently, the notebook hadn't informed him about the package of other stones. Probably a good thing.

"You know this how?"

"It's what I do," Logan said, and when James narrowed his eyes, he explained further. "I mean, I can find things. Or, I guess I should say that

I can find things that are imbued with magic. I can find other things too," he said quickly, when James frowned at him, "but I'm most accurate when there's some kind of power involved."

"What about the rest of the artifacts? The stones and the Book?"

Logan felt his chest go tight. "The rest of them?" he hedged.

"You were supposed to deliver them to me, according to the notebooks. If the notes in those pages are to be believed, you should have a package for me. If you don't have the package . . ."

"I had it," Logan pleaded. "I swear I did."

"But you don't now," James said, looking more than ever like the disappointed professor Logan had known.

"Esta took them," he explained. "She knows how I am right after we slip through time, and she took advantage of it."

"Esta?" James had gone very, very still. When he spoke again, his voice was urgent. "*She* has the Book and the artifacts. You're sure of this?"

Logan nodded. "She left me here without them, and then those big guys picked me up before I could get to you."

"Kelly's boys," James murmured, but he wasn't looking at Logan. He was staring into the dark corner of the cellar, clearly thinking through something. Then, all at once, he seemed to come to a decision. "It's an interesting story."

"It's the *truth*."

"So you say. And I'm inclined to believe you, but I have no way of knowing for sure. You could have used the Book to deceive me."

"I didn't," Logan said, feeling again the itch of panic. "You have to believe me."

"Actually, I don't. Which presents a problem—for you, at least." He adjusted his grip on the head of his cane, a movement that was as much a threat as his words.

"Let me prove it to you," Logan begged.

"How?" James asked. "What more proof could you possibly offer?"

"Let me find the Delphi's Tear—the ring. It's close. I *know* it is. I'll find it and give it to you, and then you'll know I'm not hiding anything."

The boy's expression didn't betray even a flicker of interest. "You're sure that you know where it is?"

"Not exactly," Logan said. "But I could take you to it."

James considered the offer. "Mooch!" he shouted, his voice bellowing louder than Logan would have expected from such a slightly built boy.

"Yeah, Nibs?" The redhead appeared at the top of the steps with a speed that told Logan he'd been waiting.

"Bring Jacob and Werner and come down here."

That wasn't the reaction Logan wanted. While James watched the steps expectantly, Logan tested the ropes on his hands. If he could loosen them, maybe he could wiggle free. But the ropes were as tight now as they had been when Mooch first tied them, and before he could do anything, the three larger boys had come down the steps and were waiting for further orders.

"You wanted our help?" the sandy-haired one asked, and Logan gasped as he felt the air pressed from his chest.

"Not yet, Werner," James said, his gaze on Logan. "We need him alive . . . for now."

BREAKING AND ENTERING

1902—New York

When they finally arrived at the building, Jianyu looked up and found the darkened windows of the apartment where Cela said Evelyn lived and wondered—not for the first time—if the path he had placed himself on was the right one. As a child, he had never intended to become a thief. And now, because of the choices he'd made, he was without country or home, far from his family and in a situation beyond his imagining or his control. For a moment he looked up at the darkened sky above him, the sweep of stars that were the same constellations of his youth.

He found the stars that were the Cowherd and the Weaver Girl, as he often did on clear nights. In the tale, the two were banished from each other, divided by the band of the Silver River, just as he was divided by a continent and a sea from his boyhood home. But Jianyu's own choices had led him from his first home, and there would be no magpies to carry him magically back, and even if there were, he couldn't go. Not without the queue that was prescribed by Manchu law.

The future to come was unknown. His path was surely here now, in this land, but what might he do with it? Where might he go or what might he become if he were not bound by the Brink, now that he could not return to his homeland? And if the Brink was to remain, how would he choose to live in this world, where he was?

But the questions were premature. No future would be possible if the stone fell into the wrong hands. So he would make the choice to become a bandit—a thief—once more, to have a chance at some other future.

"You're sure she lives here?" Jianyu asked.

Cela nodded. "I had to fit her wardrobe a few months back when she was too busy or lazy to come in when the theater was dark. We should have plenty of time."

"We?" Jianyu said, turning to her as panic inched up his spine. He couldn't get the stone and keep her safe. "You're not coming," he said, his tone more clipped and short than he had intended.

"Like hell—"

"I need you *here*," he told Cela, trying to calm her temper before it erupted. There was not time for an argument. "To watch for any trouble."

"And just what am I supposed to do if I see some?" Cela asked doubtfully.

"Warn me." Before she could argue further, Jianyu added, "Can you make a birdcall of some sort? The window is open." He pointed to the way the curtain fluttered from the open window.

He knew she was angry, but he could not linger. Before she could stop him, he had opened the strands of light, pulled them around himself, and started for the building.

It was a simple thing to find Evelyn's rooms, but when he let himself in, the apartment was not what Jianyu had expected. The woman herself was like the ostentatious kingfisher in her dress and adornments, but the rooms were cold and barely furnished, with clothes heaped about in haphazard piles. It was the kind of place someone came to sleep off the effects of too much Nitewein or because they had no other option—not because it bore any resemblance at all to a home. Jianyu almost pitied her for living in such a place, but then he reminded himself that her actions did not lend themselves to pity. Evelyn had made her choices, and now she would bear the consequences of them.

There was enough moonlight coming through the open window that he could navigate easily enough, searching through boxes and under beds. He worked methodically, lifting silken stockings and then replacing them as carefully as he could, so it would appear that no one had been there. Better not to warn her.

He was sorting through the piles on her bed when he heard the sound of an owl.

Not an owl, he realized when the sound came a second time . . . and then a third. *Cela.*

Placing the piles of clothing back the way he had found them, Jianyu was already heading toward the door when he heard the click of the lock releasing. With nowhere to go, he pulled the bronze disks from his pocket and used them to open the wan moonlight and wrap it around himself. Certainly, Evelyn would be able to sense him, but if he was quick, she would not be able to catch him.

Positioning himself next to the door, he waited. But the person who came through was not Evelyn after all.

SESHAT

1904—St. Louis

The excitement of the parade had done its job, pulling people out into the wide boulevard and leaving the winding streets of Cairo nearly empty. Harte followed Esta as they made their way through the various bazaars selling their cheap trinkets and past the restaurant that left the air perfumed with the scent of heavy spices and roasting meats. His stomach rumbled at they passed, but he kept his focus on the back of Esta's narrow shoulders and the constant hum of energy from the power inside of him.

When they came to the replica of the Egyptian temple that housed the boat ride, Harte nearly stumbled from the way the power inside of him lurched, letting its presence be known. There was something about this particular attraction that agitated the voice, but there was only one way in and out of the chamber that held the necklace, and that was through the Nile River. He did his best to ignore the power as he slipped the attendant a few extra coins for a private boat and then followed Esta into it.

A moment later their oarsman pushed off, and they were entering the darkness of the first tunnel. The world of the fair fell away, and there was only the gentle sound of the water being parted by the oar and the stale mustiness of the canal. Harte didn't need to see Esta to know exactly where she was in the darkness. Even with the odor of the water, he could sense her next to him. Since she'd decided on the ridiculous ploy to dress like a boy, she'd given up the soft floral soap she'd used before. Instead, she had been using something simple and clean, and when the scent of it came to him in the darkness, the image of her in the morning, damp from washing and freshly scrubbed, rose in his mind.

It was a mistake—the power vibrated against the shell of who he was, pressing at the delicate barrier. Harte was intimately familiar with that boundary, because he often breached it himself when he let his affinity reach into a person to read their thoughts or shape their actions. Having his own threatened like this was an uncomfortable reminder of just how dangerous his affinity could be.

The oarsman was reciting his script in a monotone, but Harte could barely pay attention—all his focus was on keeping the power inside of him from bursting out. They passed through scenes depicting life in ancient Egypt—the building of the pyramids and the flooding of the Nile, with its resulting harvest. Faintly, the names of gods and goddesses registered, but as the boat progressed, the power grew stronger, and it became harder and harder to hold it back.

Esta was sitting next to him, her back straight and her attention forward—preparing, probably, for what they needed to do—but Harte could barely see straight. His hands felt clammy. His head swirled and the edges of his vision wavered as the voice echoed in his ears, screaming words he didn't understand in a language he did not know.

When they neared the end of the ride, the voice went silent and the power stilled, both falling away and leaving only a hollowed-out emptiness behind. Panting now, Harte forced himself to take a deep, steadying breath. They were nearly there. Two more chambers and then they would disembark and walk the so-called Path of Righteousness to the Temple of Khorassan, where the Djinni's Star waited. But the moment the boat began to enter the chamber filled with parchments and scrolls, the power lurched once again.

If Harte had thought it strong, or if he had thought himself able to control it, he realized that he'd been wrong. *So wrong.* Everything he'd experienced before had been nothing but a shadow of its true power. It had been hiding itself, perhaps waiting for this moment.

The boat, the false Nile, and the room of scrolls transformed itself into a different time, another place. The walls were rounded up to a ceiling that had been painted gold, and in the center of the room stood an altarlike table that held a book. A woman stood over it, her coiled hair hung around her lean face. Her kohl-rimmed eyes were focused on the parchment in front of her, and the very air seemed to tremble with the urgency she felt. There was magic here, warm and thick and stronger than Harte had ever felt before.

The woman's mouth was forming words that he could not hear, but he understood their meaning because he could feel their power vibrating through the air, brushing against him with an unmistakable threat. It reminded him of what it had felt like when Esta pulled him through time, awful and dangerous and *wrong*. As though the world were collapsing and breaking apart all at once. He watched with dread as she took a knife and sliced open her fingertip, dripping the dark blood into a small cup.

She picked up a reed and dipped it into the cup, mixing it before she touched it to the parchment. With each stroke, the energy in the air increased, whipping about with an impossible fury. Hot. Angry. Pure. Her face was a mask of concentration, her darkly ringed eyes tight and her jaw clenched as the power in the air began to stir the hair framing her face. She made another stroke with her reed and then another, until finally, her hand trembling, she finished.

The woman looked up at him as though she could see to the very heart of what he was. Every mistake he'd made. Every regret he bore day in and day out. Every fear. Every want. She looked into him and she knew them all.

And then, without warning, the woman dropped the reed and screamed as though she were being torn apart. The power swirling through the room swelled until there was only a furious roaring that felt as though it were bubbling up from the very heart of who Harte was. As though he had become her.

As she made the final stroke, the screaming was coming from deep within her and it was coming from outside of her as well. The world was roaring its warning, but she could not listen. She would not listen. She would finish what she had started, even as she felt herself flying apart, a sacrifice and an offering to the power that was the heart of all magic.

An offering that would transform her into something so much more.

Even as she felt the very core of who and what she was shattering, even as she felt the spaces within her swelling and splintering, she screamed again, clinging to the table as the power of the spell—her greatest and most awful creation—coursed through her.

He was coming. But it did not matter. He was too late.

Too late to stop her.

Too late to take the power that was held within the parchment and ink, the skins and blood that she had created. He had tried to steal this magic and make it his own, tried to dole it out for favor and power, to give it to those who had no right to touch it.

He was coming, and she would destroy him. She would rip the very stars from the sky if need be, but he would not triumph.

Traitor. Thief. He would die this night, and her masterwork would be safe.

But first . . . She took up one of the polished gems on the altar in front of her—a lapis lazuli—and focused her magic, pushing a part of herself into the stone. And then she took up another—malachite—and another, breaking herself apart so that she could become something more.

She took up the last of the five and felt herself splinter once more, divided and broken for some greater goal. As the stones began to glow, all at once the pain she had felt—the horror of unbecoming—ceased. She slumped over, catching herself on the table in front of her.

There was no time to rest. She moved quickly on unsteady legs as she placed the stones on the floor around the table. One by one, she positioned them around the outline of a perfect circle that had been drawn, even and balanced, to ring the table that held the Book.

She heard the sound of footsteps approaching and she turned. There was someone waiting in the shadows.

A man. An unseen face.

"Thoth," she said, her vision red with hatred.

The man stepped from the darkness and into the light. His head was bare, the brown skin of his scalp shaved clean of any hair.

"I knew you would come." Her voice was brittle in its accusation.

"Ah, Seshat . . ." He shook his head sadly. "Of course I came. I came to stop you from making a terrible mistake."

Her lip curled. "Do you think you can? You're nothing but a man."

"They call me a god now," he said with a soft smile.

"They'll see the error in their judgment soon enough," she said, coming around the table so that she was between the altar and the man.

"You can't destroy the pages you've created, Seshat. You would be damning all of us."

Her eyes were bright with anticipation. The fear, if it had been there to start with, was gone now. "Who said I want to destroy them?"

The air, hot and dry from the arid desert day, began to move, swirling around the altar, and the stones began to glow.

"Stop," Thoth commanded.

But she wasn't listening. The stones had become bright points of light, like stars that had fallen to the ground, and between them, the threads of being—the parts of the world that held chaos at bay—began to glow in strange, eerie colors.

"You tried to take what was not yours to have," she said, laughing a high, strange laugh. She sounded manic, unhinged, even to her own ears. Hysterical in her glee, she walked toward him. "You thought that you could wield power, you who were not born to it? You will never again touch the heart of magic. And your followers will turn on you. They will tear you to shreds. And I will dance over your bones as they dry in the sun."

The man, who had been wearing a look of horror, lunged for her, his face contorted now in rage.

She wasn't ready for his attack. She clawed at him, her nails raking red trails across his face, but he was stronger, and in the end she tumbled back, through the swirling colors and glowing threads that formed a boundary line around the altar, screaming as she went.

"Demon bitch," Thoth said, sneering at her as he wiped the blood dripping from his cheek. He looked at it with disgust and then he stepped toward her, approaching the line of glowing air but not coming close enough to touch it.

Inside the circle, her eyes were wide with panic. She was trapped, just as she'd intended to trap the secrets of magic. "What have you done?"

"I've used your own evil against you," he said. "You thought you could take all the power in that book for yourself?" He shook his head as he took the sword from his back, its blade curved like a scythe.

Inside the circle, Seshat raged and shrieked like the demon he'd called her.

"You know my weapon, Seshat, don't you? A knife made from the stars. Iron that fell from the sky." He walked over to the first of the stones and lifted the blade. "Capable of severing anything."

"No," she screeched, her voice ripping through the chamber.

But there was nothing she could do. Thoth brought the curved blade down and the stone split in two, its separate halves going dark. In response, Seshat released a keening wail that contained all the pain—the fear—that she felt.

Thoth walked to the next stone. "You won't be able to cause any more trouble," he told her, bringing the blade down again. "You won't be able to collect power for yourself any longer," he said, destroying the third stone.

By now she'd crumpled to the floor and was trying to pull herself to the altar where the book waited. When she looked up, her vision was going black. The darkness seemed to be consuming her, consuming the world.

Thoth walked to the fourth stone, and when he destroyed it, her spine arched and she fell backward onto the floor. It was darkness now pouring from her mouth, filling the room along with her wailing. But she pulled herself up again and looked at Thoth, the darkness in her eyes a living thing.

"There is nowhere you can hide from me," she told him. "I will find you, and I will tear apart the world to make you pay."

When Thoth drove the blade into the fifth and final stone, Seshat screamed one last time, the darkness pouring out of her until there was nothing left. No body. No blood. No bones. Only the empty echo of her screams.

THE UNMAKING

1904—St. Louis

Even as he came back to himself, Harte still felt like he was flying apart. He was haunted by the memory of the woman giving way to nothingness, could still feel the woman's panic and her dread and frustration at being bested. At being *unmade*. In a flash of understanding, he felt her longing and fury. An eternity of being trapped within the pages of the Book, waiting and planning and growing more and more angry.

The power inside of him had a name.

Seshat. A demon who would destroy the world to take her revenge.

She had lived and walked and tried to take magic for herself, had tried to keep it from the world. She had been stopped. She had been destroyed . . . except that she hadn't. A part of her had lived on in the very essence of the words she'd inscribed using her own blood. That part of her, the only part left after the rest had been destroyed with the stones, had waited in the pages of the Book, weak and broken and angry—*so angry.* But now it was ready—*she* was ready—to be reborn. To rip the world apart in retribution.

Harte was shaking with residual pain and trembling from the anger seething within him. Even as he surfaced from the vision, the shadows of a different time still hung around him, a haze through which his own world lay. He felt the dull smack of a hand across his cheek, and the shadows began to melt until only reality was left.

"What the hell, Harte?" Esta asked, and though her voice sounded angry, he was vaguely aware that there was a very different emotion in her whiskey-colored eyes. *Fear.*

He didn't want her to be afraid. Without thinking, he raised his head and pressed his lips against hers, but she didn't kiss him back. Instead she jerked away, with a look of absolute horror on her face. Her movement set the floor swaying.

Not the floor . . .

They were still in the boat, on the fake Nile in the heart of a fake Cairo, and they were supposed to be stealing a necklace. Behind him, he heard the oarsman make a shocked and disapproving sound. *And Esta's still dressed like a boy.*

"We need to go," she whispered through clenched teeth. "*Now.* Before he calls someone."

Harte wasn't sure if he could stand, but there wasn't really a choice. Using the railing to steady himself as he disembarked, he forced his legs to move, even as his head pounded dully and his vision was still wavering.

"We need to call this off," he told Esta as they joined the stream of other riders moving toward the exit. His legs felt unsteady beneath him as they started down the silvery path toward the chamber.

"It's too late for that. And we're too close," she hissed. "What is wrong with you, anyway?"

"I think it's more of a who than a what," he said, remembering the heat and the pain and the feeling of himself bursting apart. *And the betrayal.* The ache of it was still so real, so palpable, it had left him reeling.

She cut him a frustrated look. "You *are* going to explain to me what that was back there—if we manage to get out of here, that is. For right now you are going to pull yourself together. You have the packet, right?" she asked.

He patted his coat and felt the final smoke packet beneath his hand. "Yeah . . ."

They were already nearing the end of the silver path, where it opened into the larger chamber. All that was left to do was set off this final packet and use the smoke as a way to clear the room of other people and as a cover to escape with the necklace. It wasn't elegant, but it was workable.

But something wasn't right. Unlike the previous days, when the crowd in the room was five or six people deep to take a look at the necklace, the chamber was empty except for the handful of other riders who had disembarked with them. There were so few people that they had a clear view to where the glass cabinet stood, holding the Djinni's Star.

"No . . ." Esta's voice came to him the same instant Harte saw it. "It can't be gone," she said, walking toward the clearly empty display case in the center of the room.

The power inside of him lurched, and for a moment Harte felt as though the entire world was spinning on, very far away from her, and he was stuck, unable to reach it. The necklace was gone.

"It can't be—" he started, but on the far end of the room, a pair of Jefferson Guardsmen were watching the two of them. The other people had continued on through the chamber, because there wasn't anything to see or draw their attention, so the Guardsmen had noticed Esta and Harte's hesitation. But it was already too late. The Guardsmen traded glances, and one touched the gold medallion pinned to his lapel.

"It's a trap," he whispered, and the tone of his voice was enough to have her eyes going wide with understanding. "Come on."

They ran for the exit, but Guardsmen were already moving as well. Ahead of them, the door to the Pike was a bright beacon, urging them onward, but even as they closed the distance, Harte heard the metallic scraping of the gate starting to close. The exit was only a few feet away, but they would never make it. Already, the bars were descending over the door, and he could feel the cold warning of corrupted magic, a power that felt too much like the Brink.

The power inside of him churned as it realized they would be trapped, and Harte stumbled from the intensity of its anger—*her* anger. But Esta was there, catching him before he could fall. All at once, the room went silent and the bars paused. He turned to her and could see the concentration on

Esta's face. Around them, the dust swirled in the air and the light slanted toward them from the Pike, calling to them, urging them to run. Faster. The power inside of him—Seshat—roared in triumph and pushed toward the surface, pressing at the already weak barriers he'd tried to keep up between her and the world.

In an instant, he saw what she saw, understood what she understood— the terrible power that was the beating heart of magic, the threat of chaos overtaking the world.

Magic lived in the spaces between all things, but if it ever escaped, it could destroy the very bonds that held the world together. In that instant he could *see* it, the dark emptiness that lived in the spaces—the same emptiness he'd seen in the woman's eyes when she'd been consumed by it . . . The emptiness that had bled out of *Esta's* eyes like a horrible nightmare of what was to come. It stretched and grew, tearing apart the pieces of the world. It wasn't just destruction. It was an *unmaking*.

His new understanding was sharp and vivid and *so* real. If Seshat took Esta, if she used Esta's power, she could destroy the world. He could see it—the world dissolving into nothing—but the clarity didn't last for long. The moment they slipped through the gates, Esta released his hand and the world spun back into motion.

Outside the exhibit, the sun was blindingly bright and the Pike was in chaos, just as they'd planned it to be, but the Guardsmen from inside the exhibit were on their heels. Even before the two from inside could get out of the building, others were coming, pushing through the crowd to rush toward Cairo. Harte's head was still pounding and his legs felt as though they would give way with every step, but he grabbed Esta's hand, not caring how it might look, and pulled her onward.

The power inside of him surged toward her, but Harte didn't bother to shove it back down. All his strength was focused on pulling Esta through the frantic crowd and escaping from the Guard. He found the passageway that led back into the rest of the Exposition, just as they'd planned, and as soon as they were free from the confusion of the Pike, they ran.

DISCOVERED

Jianyu pulled himself far back in the corner as he watched the stranger enter the apartment. The man was young—tall, but more of a boy, really—with blond hair and a worried expression on his face. He closed the door behind him softly as he stepped into the apartment, and then Jianyu felt magic fill the room. The tendrils that brushed against him were warm, familiar, and the guy turned to stare into the corner with a confused expression.

Jianyu held his breath, certain that the boy had found him when the blond took a step toward the place Jianyu was standing. The boy's eyes narrowed, as though he were squinting to see through Jianyu's concealment, and took another step toward him, his hand raised.

But then, suddenly, the guy turned back toward the darkened room. He waited, silent, as though he were listening for something. Then he went to the window and knelt beside it.

Jianyu considered his options: If he left, the door would open and the blond would know someone else had been there. If he stayed, it might be just as dangerous—the blond was clearly Mageus, and the more Jianyu pulled on his own affinity, the more likely he would be found. Either way, he chanced being discovered, and caught.

Then the blond did something that made Jianyu's mind up for him— the boy began to tug at the windowsill. A moment later, the wooden trim came loose and he set it aside.

Again Jianyu heard the owl crying outside the window.

Too late.

But the boy was already pulling something from the space behind the window frame—a small package wrapped in cloth. Jianyu didn't need to see what was inside the package to know that it was the ring. He could feel it, somehow, its energy sifting through the air, cool and hot all at once. Strange and yet also compelling.

Logan. With his light hair and the decisiveness with which he found the ring, it could be no one else. Why Logan had come here was a question that would need to be answered, but Jianyu set aside that question for the time being and focused on the opportunity the boy's appearance afforded. This was more than a second chance—the ring and the boy here, together. The blond had located the ring, and now Jianyu would relieve him of it. And then, he would keep this Logan from causing any more trouble.

Slowly, he stepped closer as the boy began replacing the loosened piece of wood on the window. Carefully, so as not to make a sound, Jianyu moved toward the boy. A few feet more and the ring would be his.

Behind him, the door opened and the bare overhead bulb flickered on. Jianyu turned to see Evelyn in the doorway, her mouth as red as her hair and her eyes filled with fury.

"Well, what do we have here?" she asked with a smile that looked sharp enough to cut.

Jianyu backed out of Evelyn's path as she sauntered toward Logan, who looked even younger and more unseasoned than he had appeared when the room was dark. The boy's light eyes widened at the sight of her, and he tucked the package he had found in the windowsill behind his back.

"Now, now," she said softly. "What do you have there, handsome?"

Jianyu felt Evelyn's affinity flood the room. It was a soft, enticing magic that made him want to lean in and be seduced, and he could see that Logan felt the same when the boy's eyes went glassy. He brought the package out and showed it to her.

"That's better, isn't it?" Evelyn's mouth curved up as she took it from

LISA MAXWELL

him and unwrapped it. Then she slid the ring onto her finger, and when she did, Jianyu felt her affinity swell. She reached out to caress the boy's cheek, running her fingers through his light hair. He leaned into her hand, like a cat purring with contentment, but just as his eyes closed in satisfaction, she grabbed a handful of hair and, without warning, wrenched the boy to his knees. His eyes were still soft, submissive, as they stared sightlessly into the room, the effect of whatever Evelyn had done to him.

"Come out, come out, wherever you are," she trilled in her singsong voice. Her eyes were bright with power and her teeth were bared beneath her bloodred lips. "I know he's not alone. I can *feel* you here."

Jianyu went still, glancing toward the open door as he felt the warmth of her affinity increase, the tendrils of it curling under his chin like fingers caressing him. He struggled to resist it.

He could run now, but to run meant leaving the ring behind and leaving Logan to her mercy. Jianyu knew he could do neither.

"Let's make this easy," Evelyn said to the apparently empty room. It was clear from the way her eyes tracked without focusing on him that she had not yet found him. "You show yourself, and I'll let this one go. Or leave now if you'd like. You'll never get the ring, and I'll keep this handsome boy here as a pet." She stroked the boy's cheek with her free hand, then slapped his cheek sharply to punctuate her point.

Evelyn's magic was filling the room, already teasing at Jianyu's will. He could stay. He could give himself over to Evelyn and—

No. Jianyu gave himself a mental shake and wrapped his affinity around himself more tightly, like armor against her onslaught. Perhaps he could still retrieve the ring. If he moved quickly, it could be his, but he would not be able to save the boy. Not with the magic floating through the air, calling to him even now.

He took a step toward them, but he could not tell whether he was stepping toward the ring or Evelyn's call. He could not have stopped himself either way.

"That's it," Evelyn purred. "Why bother to fight?"

ONLY EMPTINESS

1904—St. Louis

E ven as she ran, her lungs burning and her heart pumping, Esta could feel the heat from the power of the Book creeping along her skin where her hand was clasped in Harte's. It felt as though it were testing her, a snakelike thing slithering alongside her own power, licking at her to probe for a weakness in her armor, for a way in. It was so much worse than back at the train station in New Jersey. Stronger. More dangerous—and also more enticing in a way it hadn't been before.

But her mind was too full with the crushing disappointment of not getting the Djinni's Star to really be tempted. The necklace wasn't there. *It was a trap.* Which meant that someone knew they wanted it. Someone knew they would try to steal it. And if the Guard caught them now, they might never have another chance to find it.

Esta refused to let that happen.

Together, she and Harte ran past the transportation building and then cut deeper into the fair, where the paths were narrower and the landscaping provided more cover. They dodged a cluster of families watching a puppet show and then weaved through a group of young men who were taking in the sights. All the while, the Guard was gaining on them, but when she heard hoofbeats, she knew that they couldn't outrun a horse.

Harte glanced back over his shoulder. "We need to get out of here," he told her. "*You* need to get us out of here. We need time."

He was right, but she was still reeling from a few minutes before when she'd gotten them out of the chamber. The darkness had been so immediate, so *strong* when she'd pulled the seconds apart to stop the gate from closing.

"I'll control it," he told her as though he understood her hesitation. "You have to—"

The riders were gaining on them. She could practically feel the thunderous pace of the horses telescoping each hoofbeat through the ground beneath her feet, like the earth had a heartbeat all its own. They rounded a bend and past the clock made of flowers that was the size of a carriage before they headed toward a smaller lagoon, but the horses were gaining on them. Their hoofbeats were like thunder, and she could practically smell the sweat of horseflesh and angry human.

"Now, Esta . . . *Now!*"

Never slowing, she clenched her jaw and found the spaces between the seconds, pushing her magic into them, pulling them apart so that the noise of the fair died away. They didn't stop running as the birds in the trees went silent and everyone around them went still, suspended in the moment. She glanced over her shoulder to find the horses frozen in an impossible tableau, like the statues that dotted the fairgrounds. Their mouths were open, pulled back violently by the bits between their teeth, and their manes looked like fingertips grasping at the air. And above the whole scene, a darkness was seeping into the world like a trail of black ink splattered across the page of reality, following them.

Following *her.*

The power sliding against her skin went hot as a brand, and the darkness lurched, growing until it blotted out everything. For a moment there was only the darkness, only emptiness, and at the sight of it—the *feel* of it—she ripped her hand from Harte's. The world slammed back into motion without warning, and the darkness that had threatened to obliterate everything just a second before faded, like a fog burned off by the sun.

"Esta?" Harte was reaching back for her, but his eyes lifted to something behind her, and from the fear in his expression, she felt suddenly wary.

She turned back, expecting to see the Guard, but instead she saw madness. A deep chasm had opened in the ground, like an enormous sinkhole. It almost looked as though the path they'd just come down had been ripped in two. The horses stopped short at the gaping wound in the earth, tossing the riders from their backs.

Esta let out a strangled sound and her feet started to slow, but Harte took her hand again and tugged her onward. She ran blindly, until she realized they'd stopped because they'd made it to the wall of the fair, where the exit she'd unlocked earlier waited. Her mind raced with the implications of what had just happened. It was the Book—there was no question of that. When Harte touched her, she could feel it as clear and true as she could feel the warmth of his skin. But what was it doing to her? To her affinity? The train and the elevator at the hotel, and now this gaping hole she'd—*they'd*—somehow created here at the fair . . . Her affinity was for time, not for the inert, so why was the Book having such an effect?

She was dazed from the reality of what had happened as she stumbled through the doorway, so she didn't see the people waiting on the other side until it was too late. Harte came through a moment later, and at the sight of them, his eyes met hers, and she thought she saw the colors flash in them.

The cowboy from before stepped out of the shadow of a waiting wagon and pushed his broad-brimmed hat back a bit as he came toward them. He had a gun in one hand, and the click of its hammer was clear as the peal of a bell, even over the distant noise of the fair.

Together Esta and Harte lifted their hands in surrender. If it had just been her, she could have pulled time still and ran, but Harte and the number of their opponents complicated things.

"Well, well . . . We meet at last," the cowboy said with a self-satisfied expression. "The Devil's Thief, in the flesh."

He knew. "Who are you?" Esta asked, lifting her chin as though *she* had cornered them and not the other way around.

"You can think of us as the cavalry," the cowboy said, touching the brim of his hat. "Unless you'd rather take your chances with the Guard."

Esta exchanged a silent, questioning look with Harte, but he only gave a small shake of his head.

"What do you want with us?" Harte asked.

"Me? I personally don't want anything at all," the cowboy said. "But there's someone who does want to make your acquaintance, and it's my job to make that happen. We can do this the easy way or the hard way, but either way, it's gonna happen. So what will it be?"

"You're not exactly giving us much of a choice," Harte said.

"There's always a choice to make," the cowboy drawled. "There's always a side to take. At the moment we're taking yours." He shrugged. "We could have just as easily not have. Give us a reason, and we're liable to change our mind."

Esta glanced at Harte, whose expression had gone flinty, but whose skin still had an unhealthy-looking pallor from whatever had happened in the Nile. Behind them the noise of the fair was growing closer. They had to get out of there. *Now.*

When she looked back to the cowboy, she straightened her spine and cocked her head to one side, making a show of confidence. "I suppose we could use a ride if you're offering."

"That's what I thought." The cowboy's mouth twitched as he lowered the gun and stepped aside to open the back of the wagon. As she approached to climb in, he held out a limp burlap sack. "I'm sure you'll understand that we need to take certain precautions?"

"I thought you were taking our side," Harte challenged. "We're not a threat to you."

"With all due respect, I have a hole in my pocket from one of your smoke devices that says otherwise," the cowboy told him. "If you're not a threat, then you shouldn't mind proving it."

They were wasting time. Without waiting for Harte's reply, Esta took the sack from the cowboy and shot Harte a determined look before she put it over her own head. A moment later her hands were being secured, and she felt herself being lifted as strong hands tossed her into the wagon. Not long after she heard Harte land next to her—he gave a small groan as the air went out of him—and then the door slammed shut.

The wagon lurched, and they were moving.

"Are you okay?" Harte asked, the hood over his head muffling his voice. She could hear him moving, probably already maneuvering his wrists and working at the ropes like this situation wasn't anything more than one of his magic tricks.

"I think so," she said, relieved that he'd made the choice to follow her without a fight.

"I'll be out of this in a second," Harte told her as the wagon lurched around a bend. "I can't imagine what you were thinking."

"I was thinking we needed a quick getaway, and they were offering. They're Antistasi," she added, as though that wasn't painfully obvious.

"Clearly. And they knew who you were," he said, his voice a combination of frustration and smugness.

"I know. I figured we can use that to our advantage," she said, hoping that she was right.

"They've certainly used you enough," he muttered. She could hear Harte still struggling against his own restraints. "Almost got it . . ."

Suddenly she heard the pop and the hiss of something close by.

"What was that?" Harte asked just as she began to smell something musty and sweet.

Esta didn't even have time to answer him before everything went dark.

THE PRESIDENT'S MAN

1904—St. Louis

Jack choked down the bland, overcooked chicken and sipped at a watery cocktail as he pretended to be interested in the plans Francis and Spenser were detailing about the ball that would occur at the end of the month. It was to be the first meeting of the Brotherhoods since the Conclave of 1902, an event that had gone a long way to solidifying the Order's power among its brethren and to coalescing Jack's own power as well. He would have gladly left before the second course had even been served, but he wasn't there on his own behalf. He was there on behalf of Roosevelt, so he called for another glass of scotch and pretended to be interested in the plans their committee was making for the president's visit.

Francis and Spenser were still tripping over themselves to impress Jack. It was pointless, really, considering that their suits were at least a season out of date and the food they'd selected had been out of fashion in Manhattan since before Jack left for his grand tour. But Jack understood. The men who populated the Veiled Prophet Society, including these two, believed that their little parade and subsequent ball would change things for their city. They thought that if they kissed Roosevelt's ass, they could bend his ear and accumulate the same power and influence the Order enjoyed.

What they didn't seem to understand was that Roosevelt was a New Yorker first and foremost, and the men of St. Louis would always be nothing more than merchant stock in fancy shoes. And they couldn't comprehend the future that was flying down the tracks to greet them at the speed of a steam train. What would matter in the years to come wasn't the squabbles among regions, but the country as a whole, and Jack would put himself in position to elicit any advantage he could when that time came.

He was finishing his drink when the door of their private dining room opened and a figure appeared in the doorway wearing a white lace veil over its face. Jack nearly snorted scotch through his nose at the sight of it, but the other men at the table went silent and stood in a respectful welcome, so he choked back the laugh that had almost erupted and followed suit.

The veiled figure—it must have been this Prophet the Society was always going on about—had another man with him, a dark-haired fellow who didn't look any happier to be there than Jack himself felt. Behind them came two Guardsmen, one of whom was Hendricks.

"Good evening, gentlemen," the Prophet said, directing them all to take their seats. "I'd like to introduce you to Mr. Julien Eltinge. Some of you might be aware that he's been gracing the stage down at the Hippodrome for a few months now. He's graciously agreed to help us with the parade by wearing the necklace until it arrives at the ball."

Jack set the glass he was holding back onto the table, his interest piqued. He'd been considering the easiest way to get to the necklace, and this presented a possibility. Whatever the men from the Society thought of this Julien Eltinge, the man didn't look all that impressive. In fact, he looked damn uncomfortable about the whole situation, which was just fine with Jack. Discomfort was something he could certainly exploit.

THE RETURN

Cela called again from her hiding place in the alleyway across from Evelyn's building, hooting into the night like some sort of deranged owl to warn Jianyu about the boy who'd gone into the building looking like all kinds of trouble. But the building across the street was dark and quiet. There was still no sign of Jianyu.

Maybe the boy was simply going home. Maybe he wasn't a danger after all. But Cela had been around long enough to know that her feeling about him was probably right. He was with a small group of other boys, a ragtag bunch that looked like they belonged on the streets of the Bowery—their brightly colored outfits and cocky strutting were out of place in the neighborhood where Evelyn lived.

Cela waited a moment longer and then made up her mind. She didn't want to return to her uncle's apartment with its cramped rooms and the family in it looking at her as though Abel's death had been her fault. Just the thought of the way they traded glances when they didn't think she was looking made her chest feel hollow, but it was nothing compared to the twisting vines of grief around her heart. If that boy was trouble, as she suspected, it might mean danger for Jianyu. She wasn't going to let the people who killed Abe have even one more victory.

Resolute, she took a breath and started out from her hiding place, but she hadn't even made it to the halo of the streetlight's glow before she was grabbed from behind and pulled back into the shadows.

Cela tried to scream, but a broad hand was clamped over her mouth, just as tight and unyielding as the one that was wrapped around her waist.

"Shhhhh," a voice hissed, close to her ear. "It's me."

If she hadn't been supported by the strength of the arm that held her, Cela would have been on the ground. Her legs went liquid beneath her, because she *recognized* that voice. And it was impossible.

"I'm gonna let you go now, but keep quiet, okay?"

She nodded, tears pricking her eyes. A moment later, the hand came away from her mouth and she spun to find her brother, Abel, standing there behind her, alive and whole and every bit as real as he'd ever been. For the first time in days, it felt like she could actually breathe.

Her arms were around his neck in an instant, and she couldn't stop the sob that welled up from inside of her.

"Shhhh," he repeated, his strong hands patting her back. "I told you, you have to keep quiet."

She pulled back and looked at him again, just to be sure he wasn't some terrible trick her mind was playing on her. Her hands cupped his cheeks. "Abe. You're dead."

"Do I look dead?" he asked, giving her the same doubtful look he'd given her a hundred times before when she'd tried to follow him and his friends through the city, nothing but a tiny girl tagging after boys who didn't want her.

"But *how*?" Her head was spinning and the vines around her heart were trading thorns for blooms. "They shot you."

Abe gave her a look like she should have known better. "Nobody shot me, Rabbit."

Her heart nearly broke to hear that stupid nickname on his lips again. "But I heard them," she said, her voice cracking without her permission. "I heard the gunshot, and then your body hit the floor."

"They tried awful hard, but I wasn't the one who got himself killed," he said, his expression going dark.

Abe isn't dead. Which meant . . . for the last week, he *hadn't* been dead. "Then where have you *been*?" she asked, realization hitting her. She'd been at her uncle's for nearly a week, and he'd never once come for her. He'd left her to think the worst. He'd left her to deal with their family on her own. He'd left *her*. She smacked at his chest. "I thought you were *dead*. I've been crying myself to sleep every night over you." She slapped his chest again. "And every morning I woke up not remembering for a second, and every morning I had to *re-remember*," she said, her voice breaking. And then, because it hadn't felt half as good as she'd wanted it to, she raised her hand to slap him again.

He caught her wrist gently. "I'm sorry I couldn't come, but I didn't want to lead the people who were after me to Desmond's place," he said, taking her by the hand. "I've been watching, though. Waiting for you to get far enough away for me to talk to."

"What do you mean, the people after *you*?" she asked, hesitating. "They were after *me*. Because of Darrigan's mother." *And the ring.*

Abe shook his head. "They were from the railroad."

"Why would the railroad come after you?" she asked.

"They were just trying to scare me off. A few of us guys have been talking with the Knights of Labor about unionizing the Pullman porters so they'd have to pay us a better wage and give us better shifts. That's about the last thing the company wants, so they thought they could convince me to stop, but their convincing looked an awful lot like forcing."

"So you *shot* them?" she asked, not understanding how the person in front of her could also be the brother she knew would never have hurt anyone intentionally.

"Things got heated, and they threatened you," he told her, his voice as dark as the shadows around them. "Look, I have a safe place uptown to stay with some guys from the *Freeman*. It'll be okay. We can talk about all the rest later."

"Abe—"

"I promise I'll tell you everything, but right now we have to go," he said, starting to tug her back toward the alley.

She took three steps before she stopped and pulled her hand out of his. "But Jianyu is still in there."

Abe nodded. "Which is why we need to go now, before he comes back."

He reached for her again, but she held her hand out of reach. "You don't understand. He's a friend of mine, and—"

A carriage had just rattled to a stop across from the alley, and with a sinking weight in her stomach, Cela recognized the woman who got out of it. She walked to the mouth of the alley as Evelyn started toward the building.

No. As soon as Evelyn had closed the entry door behind her, Cela stepped out of the alleyway and started hooting again. Abe tried to pull her back, but she shrugged him off.

"What are you doing?" he asked, looking at her like she had lost her mind.

"If that woman who just got out of the carriage finds him, there's gonna be trouble. I'm not going to just leave him."

"His trouble doesn't concern us," Abe said, putting his arm around her.

"It concerns *me*," she said, allowing herself a moment to enjoy her brother's warmth and strength. *Abe. Alive.* "Jianyu saved my life when you were off hiding without sending me so much as a word," she told him, her voice clipped and her nerves feeling like live wires. *Abe is alive.* He was into more than she'd understood, but he was alive.

He was quiet a moment before he let out a long-suffering sigh. "Then I guess we'd better go in after him."

Cela let Abe take the lead, since she knew they'd waste time arguing about it otherwise. They didn't run into anyone or any trouble in the building, but they stopped just down the hallway from Cela's open apartment door. She could hear someone talking, but she couldn't make out what was being said. From the voices, she knew that Evelyn and Jianyu were still in there, and that Evelyn wasn't happy.

"Let me go first," Cela whispered.

"No—" Her brother was adamant.

"Evelyn *knows* me," Cela explained. She didn't tell Abe how the bitch had also locked her in a room and stolen the one thing of value Cela had left. "I can distract her long enough to get an advantage."

"I'm not letting you—"

But Cela was already walking away from him. She didn't really have a plan, except that she'd lost her brother once that week. She'd lived through that pain, that horrible knowledge that he was gone, and she'd do whatever she could to make sure she never had to feel that again—even if it meant putting herself between Abe and that red-haired she-devil.

She didn't bother to knock or make any sound to introduce herself—the bigger the distraction, the better as far as Cela was concerned—but when she stepped into the open doorway and took in the scene unfolding, she realized she was in over her head. Evelyn's eyes were lit with some unholy light and she was holding a handful of the blond boy's hair as he knelt next to her, but across from her Jianyu had a knife to his own neck. The strain on his face was clear and his hands were shaking, like he was fighting to keep himself from pressing the blade into the soft skin of his throat.

Magic, she realized. Evelyn was one of them too. Her whole life she'd lived in the city and thought that the old magic had never touched her. She'd known it to be a dangerous force, a fearsome thing that the ordinary person had to be protected from, so it had come as an unsettling realization to know that she'd been living side by side with it all along. First Jianyu and Darrigan and now Evelyn. And while Evelyn was a dangerous hussy, Cela didn't figure it was the magic that made her that way.

Evelyn glanced up and saw Cela standing in the doorway, and her expression turned dark and thunderous. "Ah, Cela, I'd wondered where you'd scurried off to, and here you are." The corners of Evelyn's painted mouth curled up to reveal her teeth. "What an unpleasant surprise. But since you're here, do come in."

Cela felt herself softening, wanting to move into the room even though she knew it was a bad idea. She took a step toward them without meaning to, and then she fought against taking another.

"I was just entertaining a couple of unexpected guests," Evelyn told her. "Or rather, I should say, I was just teaching a couple of thieves a lesson. Perhaps you'd like to join us?"

"I'm just here for my friend. And what you took from me," Cela said, gritting her teeth against the strange pull she felt. Even though she knew what Evelyn was, what the woman was capable of, Cela felt drawn to her, enticed by her.

"You mean this?" Evelyn lifted her hand, and the ring that Darrigan had gifted Cela flashed in the light. "You're welcome to try to take it from me." She laughed. "Though I doubt a Sundren like you could manage."

Cela's feet were inching toward Evelyn. One and then the other, no matter how she fought. *Abe. I need Abe.*

She got the burst of a gunshot in answer.

The sound echoed through the cramped room as Evelyn crumpled to the floor with a gasp, grabbing her right arm. At the same moment, Jianyu dropped the knife he'd been holding and collapsed to his knees, his breathing heavy, and the boy Evelyn had been holding by the hair fell to the floor. He seemed too dazed to get himself up.

Abe was standing in the doorway, a pistol sure in his hand. "Let's go," he said.

"You *shot* her," Cela said, the shock of it still fresh and numbing as she watched Evelyn grab her arm, writhing in pain. The brother she'd known wouldn't have hurt a fly. *Who is this man who looks so much like him?*

She'd been content to see him through little-girl eyes for so long that she hadn't realized how strong and certain he'd become. But she *should* have. For two years Abel had taken care of her and protected her after their father had been killed. For two years he'd been her rock. She should have known that he would have had their father's sureness and their mother's stubborn strength inside of him, just as she did.

Cela turned back to the scene behind her. The blond boy lay there, not moving, as Jianyu climbed to his feet and went to Evelyn. He took her hand and tried to pull the ring from it, but even with her injured arm, she lashed out at him. He drew back, out of her reach.

"We have to go," Cela told him.

Jianyu glanced at her, his expression still slightly dazed and his forehead damp with the exertion of what he'd been through. "We can't leave without the ring."

"Then you'd better get it fast," Abel said. "Somebody will have heard the shot." He had Cela by the hand, but if her feet had moved on their own a moment before, it seemed like she couldn't move them at all now.

Evelyn was struggling up from the floor, her eyes glowing again with that strange, unholy light. "Come and get it," she purred, taunting Jianyu. "If you can . . ."

But Jianyu's face had gone slack, and his body was suddenly deathly still.

"Jianyu?" Cela asked, ignoring how her brother was trying to pull her from the room.

Jianyu was on his feet and his eyes were open, but he didn't seem to hear her.

Even as blood pooled beneath her, Evelyn was laughing, a deeply maniacal cackling that twisted into the pit of Cela's stomach. She took a step back.

"That's right," Evelyn said to Cela. "Run away. Run far, far away, little Cela." She laughed again, her face pale and her voice ragged. "The boys are mine."

"We can't leave them here." She ripped herself away from Abel and went to Jianyu, whose gaze was on some unseen thing in the distance. He wasn't listening to her, but she could tug him along. "Get the other one."

With a ragged grumble, Abe released Cela's hand long enough to scoop up the blond boy from the floor. "*Now* can we go?" he asked. "Or is there anyone else you want me to collect and carry for you?"

Evelyn was on the floor, trying to pull herself up as she grabbed her bleeding arm, and everything was chaos, but Cela felt a laugh bubbling up. With all the mess they were in, Abe was alive. As long as she had him, the rest didn't matter.

By the time they were in the stairwell, Jianyu had come back to himself and was walking under his own power. "The ring," he said, when they reached the bottom of the steps. He started to turn back.

"No." Cela tugged at him.

"We can't let her have it," he argued, trying to break loose from her grip, but she could feel how gently he treated her.

"You go back there now, you're going to be arrested for trying to kill a white woman," Abe told him.

From the expression on Jianyu's face, he wanted to argue.

"Can you get back in without her knowing?" Cela asked.

Jianyu met her gaze, and she saw the calculations play out in his mind. Finally he shook his head. "Even if she can't see me, she could sense me."

"Then you can't go back," she told him. "Not now."

"But the ring—"

"It won't do anyone any good if you're dead," Cela said. "We'll come back for it. I promise."

"Don't make promises you can't keep," Abe snapped. "We can't be here when the police arrive."

The blond didn't stir, so Abe didn't put him down. They ran into the night, leaving Evelyn howling behind them.

THE BREWERY

Esta came to slowly, reaching toward consciousness like a swimmer struggling up to the surface of a cold, deep lake. Her head pounded as she lay in the darkness and breathed in the dusty scent of the burlap sack still over her head. She didn't know where she was or how long she'd been out, but she remembered who had taken her.

The Antistasi.

Her breath hitched at the memory of everything that had happened at the fair—the missing necklace, the way the darkness had descended stark and empty and absolute when her affinity touched the power of the Book. The ground splitting open . . . *The ground* split *open.*

She pulled herself upright, but nearly toppled over again from the dizziness brought on by whatever they'd used to knock her out. Opium, maybe, from the way her affinity felt dull and numb, but not *only* opium. This was different from anything she'd experienced before—there was something about whatever they'd given her that made her feel untethered, like she wasn't quite attached to the earth but was floating free, even as she could feel the solid floor beneath her.

She called for Harte, but there was no answer.

After a while she thought she heard voices, and moments later the door opened. "Come on," a voice said. Since she didn't recognize it, she figured it must not be the cowboy. Rough hands grabbed her by the arms and dragged her from where she was lying. The moment they took her by the arms, she realized that her cuff was missing. Panic seized her as she realized what that meant, but she kept that emotion locked down. She would have a better chance of getting it back if they didn't know how important it was to her.

Once she was outside the wagon, Esta could hear buzzing insects and the soft rustling of trees. *Not the city.* She wobbled at first but recovered before anyone had to support her. Whatever was about to happen, she'd walk on her own two feet. But her head ached worse now that she was upright.

"Where are we?" she asked. Her tongue still felt clumsy and thick in her dry mouth, but her voice sounded strong. At least she *thought* it did.

"You'll see soon enough, but I'm going to warn you before we go in." It was the cowboy this time. "I'll give you the same warning I gave to your friend. If either of you even thinks about causing a lick of trouble, there ain't a person here what would think twice about taking care of you for good—no matter who you think you are. You got that?"

"Understood," she told him, even as she was already considering all the possible options for freeing herself and Harte if things went downhill.

"That's fine. Come on, now. This way . . ."

With her head pounding from the drug and her whole body feeling like her joints had come loose, it was a challenge to stay on her feet as she was led blindly through what felt like an obstacle course of ramps and steps. Finally, they entered a building—she knew, because the insects went quiet. From the way their footsteps echoed, it had to be a larger room, and from the other voices, they weren't alone. There were two, maybe three others already there.

They pushed her into a chair, and she felt them secure her to it with more rope. Then, without any warning, the sack they'd put over her head to blind her was pulled off. She blinked. Dim as the lighting was, it caused even more pain to shoot through her already throbbing head.

Esta ignored the pain as she squinted, trying to get her eyes to adjust. She'd been right. They were standing in something that looked like a large warehouse. On one side of the room, enormous silver tanks lined the wall. On the other side, a series of long tables held wooden crates filled with glass bottles. The stools in front of the tables stood empty. *A factory of some sort.* The people were gathered in a smaller, open space between the tanks and the tables. In addition to the cowboy, there was a handful of people—men and women of various ages. They seemed to be waiting for something.

Across from where Esta was sitting, two other guys in workman's clothes flanked a chair that held one last person—Harte. He still had the burlap sack covering his face, but that didn't seem to matter. Even with his face covered, she knew that he understood she was there—his head turned in her direction, and his entire body seemed to come to attention, straining against the ropes that held him to the chair.

"Is that you, Slim?" he asked. "They didn't hurt you, did they?"

"I'm fine," she told him, keeping her voice low and clipped. "You okay?"

"I'd be better if I could see something," he said, shaking his head a little, as if to shake off the bag.

"You'll see soon enough, when Ruth decides what to do with you," the cowboy told him. He frowned at Esta, but before he could say anything else, they heard a door opening from somewhere deep within the factory. The group turned toward the sound of the approaching footsteps, making it clear that someone important was arriving.

A moment later a woman appeared on the walkway above. She looked over the gathering below for a moment, before descending the steps to the factory floor. She was maybe in her early forties, but her hair was already shot through with gray, and she wore an expression that labeled her as the person in charge.

The woman—clearly the Ruth the cowboy had mentioned—gave a silent nod, and at her order, one of the men flanking Harte drew the sack off. He'd lost the hat he'd been wearing earlier, and his dark hair was a mess, sticking up in all directions. His eyes found hers, but they were too wide, too wild, and she narrowed hers at him in warning. If he wasn't careful, he was going to give away too much.

Stop it, she tried to tell him silently. But she wasn't sure if he understood. The cords of his neck were tense, and they didn't relax at the sight of her.

Without any introduction, Ruth turned to Esta, her voice unyielding as she asked a single question: "Where is it?"

Esta blinked. "Where is what?"

"The necklace," Ruth said, stalking toward the chair where Esta was tied.

"I don't have any necklace," Esta said, well aware of *exactly* what necklace Ruth was referring to. And if they knew about the necklace, it was possible they'd also realized what her cuff was.

Ruth pursed her lips, clearly not believing her. "There is only one thing you could have wanted in the Streets of Cairo—it's the same thing we want. We know you intended to steal the necklace, and we know that you went to the Exposition today to do just that. I allowed this particular farce to run to its conclusion because it suited my purposes, but the time has come. I'm out of patience." She leaned down until she was close enough that Esta could see the fine lines that had already started to carve themselves into her face. "I'll ask you this question only one more time: What have you done with the necklace?"

"We couldn't steal what wasn't there," Esta told her. "It was a trap. When we got to the chamber, there was nothing in the case, and the Guard was ready for us."

Ruth's expression faltered. "You're sure of this?" When Esta nodded, Ruth turned to the cowboy, but he only shrugged and gave a slight shake of his head. "I knew this would never work," she told him. "We should have stopped them days ago and gone after the necklace ourselves."

"Days ago?" Esta asked.

"A haircut and a suit might be enough to fool the Guard, but I'm not half so simple," Ruth said. "Esta Filosik. The Devil's Thief. I've had people watching you ever since North here saw you outside the theater."

Esta kept her expression from betraying even a flicker of the anxiety she felt at the woman's words. The fact that Harte had been right about her disguise barely even registered over the sudden and unpleasant realization that they'd been watched for days, and Esta hadn't even suspected. She was either getting rusty, or these people—these Antistasi—were more formidable than she'd expected.

"If you knew who I was, I can't imagine why you'd waste your time having me followed," she said, trying to affect a haughty indifference. "You'd know already that we're on the same side."

"Are we?" Ruth said.

"Of course," Esta insisted, refusing to show even a hint of her apprehension. She'd bluffed her way out of more difficult spots than this. If they thought she was the Devil's Thief, then she would use every bit of that title to her advantage. "That *is* that why you use my name so freely, isn't it?"

The woman's nostrils flared in irritation, but she didn't deny it.

"Yes, I know all about that," Esta said, going on the offensive. "I've seen the masks and gowns. I know how your little group pretends to be the Devil's Thief—to be *me*." She watches Ruth's expression go dark. "I know all about the Antistasi."

The woman let out a hollow laugh. "We are no more the Antistasi than a drop of water is the sea."

"But you're part of them," Esta pressed, testing the mood in the room as she spoke. Whatever doubts Ruth might have about her, the rest of the Antistasi in the room felt more tentative, supportive even—except maybe for the guy they called North. It seemed that even if Ruth didn't much care whether Esta was the Devil's Thief, the others in the room *did*. If she could use that to keep Harte safe, she would. "Or did you steal their name as well?"

"I've stolen nothing. We have *earned* the right to call ourselves Antistasi," Ruth admitted, her tone dripping with acid.

"So I've heard," Esta said, keeping her tone detached, aloof. She kept her eyes focused on Ruth, even as she wanted to look at Harte.

Ruth considered her. "Have you?"

Esta nodded. "You have quite the reputation in this town. It's impressive what you've accomplished," she said, playing to the woman's ego.

But the ploy didn't work. Ruth's eyes narrowed. "Then you know already that we are not to be trifled with. If you knew anything at all about us, you would know that we don't hesitate to destroy those we consider enemies."

"Of course," Esta said easily. "But I'm not your enemy. From what I hear? Seems like I'm more like your muse."

"You?" Ruth laughed again before her mouth drew into a flat, mocking line. "You're just a *girl*. The Devil's Thief is bigger than any single person—she's certainly bigger than *you*. You're unnecessary at best. At worst, you are a problem that needs to be dealt with."

"I'm not a problem," Esta told her. But then she considered her words and gave Ruth a careless shrug, refusing to be intimidated. "Then again, maybe I am, but I'm definitely not *your* problem."

"No?" Ruth mused. "From where I stand, you are a liability to myself and to the Antistasi."

Esta gave a cold laugh, using the motion to glance at Harte, who was watching the conversation with a tense expression of concentration. "How do you figure?"

Ruth stepped toward her. "The police and the Guard have been looking for you ever since the night we helped you slipped past them at the Jefferson Hotel. For a week they've been on high alert, searching everywhere for some sign of you, which has been more than a simple inconvenience for me. Your presence in my town has made it nearly impossible for my people to do their jobs and has put every one of us in danger of being discovered. All because the authorities believe you to be something special, something *dangerous*. The Devil's Thief," she said, but there was a hint of scorn in her voice. "But here you sit, at my mercy. Barely a woman and too soft for anyone with eyes in their head to mistake you for a man. You are nothing but a liability."

Esta let her mouth curve. "If you really believed that, you wouldn't have tied us up and drugged us just to have this little conversation."

"I don't take unnecessary risks," Ruth said, visibly bristling. "Not when the safety of my people is at stake."

"I haven't done anything to your people," Esta countered. "There's no reason to think I would."

Ruth tipped her head to the side. "You didn't plant a smoking device on my man?"

"He was following me," Esta said, unapologetic. "And it's not like he bothered to introduce himself. I didn't know who he was or that he was one of yours at the time, and I had to distract him. Besides, he seems to be just fine."

Ruth's brows drew together. "While I'll admit that I'm inclined to be impressed by anyone who's able to get the better of North, I'm *less* inclined to be forgiving of your attempt to incriminate us with your reckless display at the fair."

North. That must be the cowboy, Esta thought, and the way he was glaring at her only confirmed it.

"Do you know what would have happened if you were caught today?" Ruth continued. "Do you realize what it would have done to us?"

"I can't see how me being caught would have affected you in the least," Esta said.

"Which only shows how foolish you are," Ruth said. "I don't know who you really are, and I don't know if you have done even one of the many things that have been attributed to you, but I do know this— the Guard catching you would have been a victory for the Society and the other Brotherhoods. It would have been a fatal blow to the Antistasi movement *everywhere*. To catch you would have meant an end to the legend of the Thief. That legend is what keeps us safe even as it inspires fear in our enemies. Without it, we'd be exposed."

She hadn't even considered that. Esta had seen the women in the ballroom, she'd heard Julien talk about the exploits of the Antistasi, and she had admired them. She hadn't realized that she might be putting them in danger just by *actually* existing.

"It wasn't my intention to put any of you in danger," Esta said, trying to make her voice sound contrite. "I don't want to be a liability. I'd much rather be an asset."

"But you're not an asset, and without the necklace, what can you offer me?"

"Besides my name?" Esta asked, trying to come up with something that would be convincing enough to assuage Ruth's doubts.

"We already have that," Ruth told her. "Even without you, we can continue to use it."

"But you don't have a way into the Society," Harte said from across the room.

Ruth's brows drew together and she turned away from Esta to focus on Harte. His expression was strained, but he had a look of sheer determination in his eyes.

"Why would you imagine we need that?"

"Because we know that you have big plans," Harte said, drawing Ruth's attention toward him. "And we know what you're still missing."

BENEDICT O'DOHERTY

1904—St. Louis

Harte's head was still pounding from whatever they'd used on him in the wagon, and inside, the power of the Book was churning uneasily. It didn't like whatever that drug had been—and, to be fair, neither did Harte. His affinity felt hazy and indistinct, like the magic that was his usual companion was too far for him to reach.

Fine, then. Harte might be a magician by trade, but he was a con man at heart.

"If you know so much, perhaps we should dispose of you now," Ruth said, stalking toward him. She had a combination of fear and fury in her eyes—a combination that might prove dangerous—but at least she wasn't so focused on Esta any longer.

"That would be a mistake."

"Unlike you," Ruth said, "we do not make mistakes."

"Maybe not yet," Harte said, not so much as blinking. "But not taking advantage of what we can offer you? *Definitely* a mistake."

"Why do you think we need entry into the Society?" Ruth asked.

"The necklace wasn't at the fair. If you don't have it, that means the Society has moved it. How are you planning to get the necklace if you don't even know where it is?" He paused, letting his question hang in the air before he spoke again. "You're already running short on time."

Ruth straightened, and Harte could tell from the way her expression shifted that her actions were a show for everyone in the room. "You don't know what you're talking about."

"No?" Harte asked easily, relying on the impressions he'd gotten from when his captors had touched him without realizing the danger. "Your guys are spooked because they know you're not quite ready. They're thinking that maybe it's too big a risk, especially that one." Harte nodded toward the one who had held his hands behind his back—the one he'd managed to read just before he was tossed into the wagon. "Frank, right? He's got a sister up in Chicago. Figures that he could take off and go live with her instead of getting himself killed."

Ruth turned to the guy, whose face had gone pale. "Is this true? You doubt our undertaking?"

The guy shook his head dumbly for a second or two before he found words. "He's lying, Ruth. He's just trying to confuse us." But the fear in the guy's expression told a different story.

"Cowardice will kill you, Frank. Not my plans." Ruth nodded to one of the others. "Take him downstairs and make sure he's secured. There isn't room for misgivings and fear. Not now." Then she turned on Harte. "I know who she is, but who are you?"

"Someone just like you," he said simply. "I hate the Society and everything it stands for. We heard about what you did last fall—the attack on the construction of the Exposition. It was brilliant. Masterful, even."

Ruth considered him. "What is your name?"

"Benedict O'Doherty," Harte told her, the name slipping from his lips before he could consider it. "I'm called Ben for short." *Or I was, once.* It seemed he'd been resurrected twice now, he thought darkly.

"I don't trust either one of you," Ruth told him.

"That only proves you're not stupid," he said simply. "But not accepting our help—that *would* be stupid. Especially when we could help you be more successful than you've even dreamed. Give us a chance to prove ourselves. The one you just had taken away was worried about a job you had for him. Let us do it instead."

Her eyes narrowed as she thought it over. Then her expression cleared. "Fine," she said, her lips curling. "I'll give you this one chance to prove yourselves." She glanced at the cowboy. "Take him away and make sure he doesn't cause any problems."

"But the job—" Harte said.

"I think we'll let the Thief do it. If she's so powerful and so anxious to work with us, she shouldn't have a problem. And if she does anything at all to betray us, you'll be the one to pay."

JUST A GIRL

Maggie watched as her sister's people led the Thief and her companion away. They went calmly, though clearly reluctantly, and the way that the guy—Benedict—looked at the Thief, as though he would do anything at all to keep what was about to happen from occurring, nudged at something deep inside of her.

"Was that really necessary?" she asked Ruth, who was standing, impassive as always, watching as well.

Her oldest sister, the only mother she'd ever known, glanced over at her with impatience shimmering in her gaze. "Are you questioning my judgment?"

Maggie shook her head. "No, Mother Ruth. Just wondering . . ." But secretly, she *was* questioning her sister. She'd been questioning Ruth and her tactics for some time, but right now, she knew this was where she had to be. "If Lipscomb's people catch her—"

"Then they take care of a problem for me," Ruth said in a tone that brooked no argument. "She's not the Devil's Thief, Maggie. She's just a girl, same as you. Same as I once was. The Devil's Thief is bigger—it's something *we* created through our actions. If she's so stupid as to get herself caught by Caleb Lipscomb and his half-witted socialists, then it's what she'll deserve."

"And if she doesn't?"

Her sister's expression brightened. "Then she'll already be part of this. Think of it, Margaret. If she delivers the device, there won't be any way for her to change her mind. She'll be responsible for the explosion and for everything that happens after. If it goes well, as you've assured me it will, that means that she will have a hand in the effects of the serum. Not only will she understand the power it contains, but she will have the pride of knowing that she was part of it. She'll understand and be one of us for good. More important, everyone who might stand against us will know she's *ours*. When the other Antistasi groups know that the Thief chose *us*, it will go that much further toward solidifying our leadership."

Maggie couldn't help but frown. "You don't think you should tell her what we're doing?"

"Why should I?" Ruth asked. "This will be a test of her resolve—of her *loyalty* to our cause . . . and to me. If she's truly for us, she'll be willing to kill for us. And if she's not, we'll know now, before she has the chance to harm more important plans."

OUTMATCHED

1902—New York

Jack hadn't been backstage at Wallack's Theatre for weeks, not since he'd visited Darrigan, believing the magician to be an ally instead of an enemy. He would have gladly avoided the theater for the rest of his days, except that he was more certain Evelyn had something he wanted—and something that someone else was willing to kill her for.

It galled him that he still didn't know what it was.

The day after she'd come to his town house, ready and willing, he'd awoken to find her gone and his head pounding from all the sherry they'd had together. Because he'd overindulged, the memory of that night was still hazy and indistinct. Clearly, she hadn't been all that memorable, so he'd dismissed her. But then he'd read in the *Herald* about how she had been attacked. Intruders had broken into her home to rob her and shot her instead. Of course, she was using the attack for publicity, but that didn't change the fact that she must have had something of value. Which had reminded him of her earlier teasing.

The promise of discovering what she had was worth overcoming his disgust and the anger he felt simply walking through the maze that lurked behind the stage. No one stopped him months ago, and they didn't bother to now, either. Tucking the bouquet of roses beneath his arm, he knocked twice on Evelyn's dressing room door and entered when he heard her voice answer.

Her dressing room was nothing like Darrigan's. It was slightly larger, and the walls were draped with swaths of silks and satins, giving it a feeling of being both exotic and sensual. But Jack wasn't taken in by it. This time he would remain in control of the evening's progress.

Evelyn was draped across a chaise lounge, arranged like a painting in her silken robe. He couldn't see her injury, but clearly it hadn't been life threatening. Her red mouth curved up when she saw him. "Hello, darling," she purred. "Are those for me?" She lifted herself from the couch to accept the flowers from him, and when she did, he noticed the glint of gold on her finger.

The ring was enormous. Its golden filigreed setting held a stone far too large for a common trollop like Evelyn, and he knew in that moment that it was what the thieves had been after and what he'd come for.

"What is it, Jack?" Evelyn asked, arranging the flowers in the vase on her dressing table. "You look like you've seen a ghost."

"Not a ghost," he told her, his voice heavy with anticipation. "An *angel*."

Her eyes glowed, and she went to him, willing and warm and ready.

Later, when he was riding in the carriage back to his town house, he came out of the fog of desire and realized that he'd forgotten completely about the ring—*again*. He'd been right there, and he'd never even touched it. And he couldn't remember why. He couldn't even remember what had happened between them.

His hands clenched into fists. This time he couldn't blame it on the drink.

He should have known better. Something like this had happened to him before, in Greece, when he would wake without any idea of what had transpired in the hours before morning. He'd joked then that the girl he'd fallen for was a siren, tempting him to the rocks that would be his death, but he hadn't known how right he'd been. How devious the girl had actually been.

With sudden understanding, he realized that Evelyn was the same. Like the girl in Greece who had nearly ruined him, Evelyn was a witch—maggot scum who thought she could best him at his own game. But Jack wasn't the green youth he'd been then. Greece had changed him, and the Book that he had locked away safely in his rooms had made him into something new. Evelyn might have feral magic, she might even have a ring that amplified her powers, but she didn't have the Book. She couldn't begin to predict how outmatched she was.

THE SECRET ON
ORCHARD STREET

1902—New York

J ames Lorcan had a feeling that things would become more interesting not long after he'd watched Logan Sullivan enter the apartment building and heard the hoot of something that wasn't an owl nearby. He sent the others back to the Strega, except for Mooch, whom he kept nearby. He didn't need the muscle; whatever was about to happen, tonight wasn't the place for a fight. That would come later.

He kept to the shadows and watched the entrance of the building, until he saw the group of people appear. A sturdy-looking man with deep brown skin had Logan looped over his shoulder, and a girl James didn't recognize kept close by Jianyu. An unexpected development, to be sure, but it answered one question. And at least his companions were Sundren. Uninteresting, except for the way they now had two people who should have been his prisoners.

Mooch took a step toward the group of them already scurrying down the sidewalk, putting distance between themselves and the building, but James caught his arm.

"Just follow them. Find out where they're going, but don't do anything else. Then come back to the Strega."

Mooch looked like he wanted to argue, but James narrowed his eyes at the boy, and he seemed to decide against it.

Jianyu had Logan, but really, it didn't matter. The boy was as much a liability as he was an asset. Besides, James still had all the secrets he needed on the shelves of Dolph's bookcases, and now in the notebook tucked into his coat.

Jianyu's appearance here, at this apartment where he had no real cause to be, told James one very important thing—Logan hadn't been lying about who he was or what he could do. Which meant that the notebook he'd delivered wasn't a trap or a trick. It was nothing more or less than the truth.

It was late—nearly midnight—but there was another stop James needed to make now that he knew he could trust the words tucked near his chest, the words he would himself someday write.

The lights in the building on Orchard Street were out when he finally arrived, but that didn't concern him. He paid the woman on the third floor more than enough for the inconvenience of waking her.

She wasn't happy, but she didn't complain as she let James in and led the way down the narrow hall to the small room where the girl slept. He dismissed the woman and went to the girl's bedside, kneeling beside it so that he could wake her. The small face scrunched at the interruption, but eventually she reluctantly opened her sleep-crusted eyes to squint at him.

It used to be hard to look at the girl without seeing Leena looking back at him, judging him for the choices he'd made and the path he'd chosen. It had gotten easier, in time, to see past Leena's features—the golden eyes, the wide mouth that the girl would someday grow into—to the child beneath them. The promise in her.

Once he had thought that he could save her from Leena's faults. Dolph's partner, his wife, really, in everything but name, had been too soft when she should have been steel, too generous when she should have kept her cards close to her chest. It had been a surprise—a delightful one, but a surprise nonetheless—when Leena had decided to hide the child from Dolph. But in the end it had been her undoing.

He had hoped to mold the girl, to use her for his own bidding. Now James knew that in the end it would never work. He was raising a viper who would one day threaten everything he'd built, everything he was destined to become.

He could kill the girl now, but time was a funny thing, tangled as a knot and woven into a pattern that even he could not yet see. If he killed her, what might that change? What might he lose that her appearance had helped him to gain?

He couldn't kill her. Not yet. But he could use her to send a message.

He took Viola's blade from his jacket.

"Come, Carina, we're going to play a little game." He would send Esta a message through time and space and the impossible world. He would tell her he was waiting.

Using the blade named for the goddess of funerals, he began to cut.

THE DROP

1904—St. Louis

The carriage rattled onward through the night, carrying Esta toward some unknown destination. On the bench across from her, sprawled with a lazy confidence, North took up too much room. He had a revolver in his hand, a clear threat that she shouldn't try anything.

"Best not jostle that too much," he said, when she shifted the notebook that was resting on her lap. It looked like an average-size leather-bound notebook that anyone might carry with them, but it weighed more than an ordinary book should. Whatever was between the pages was dense and heavy—and dangerous. "We don't want it going off before you deliver it."

His warning made her sit a little straighter. "Where are we going, anyway?"

"You'll see," North said.

"I think I have a right to know who I'm going to kill," she told him, trying to affect a bored indifference. In reality, her hands were damp with nervous sweat as she tried to keep the book as still as she could while the carriage bumped along. Considering the roughness of the roads that led from the edges of town, where the brewery was, into the center of St. Louis, it had been a challenge.

"Who said anything about killing anyone?" North asked. His eyes were shadowed by the brim of his hat, but his thin mouth hitched up in the moonlight that shone through the carriage's window.

"It's a bomb, isn't it?" she asked, not yet allowing herself to feel any relief.

North's lips flattened, a thin scar at the edge of them flashing white with his annoyance. "Bombs are for Sundren. They're messy and sloppy. Nobody's gonna die tonight," he told her. "Except maybe you, if that package doesn't get to where it needs to be. And definitely your friend, back at Mother Ruth's, if you do anything to cause a problem."

Esta frowned, ignoring his bluster. If the Antistasi wanted her and Harte dead, they would have already tried to kill them. "If it's not a bomb, what is it?"

"It's a gift," he told her. Then he turned to watch out the window, signaling the end of the conversation.

A gift? Like hell.

The woman she'd heard the others call Mother Ruth had made it clear that whatever was in the parcel was dangerous. None of the Antistasi wanted to be anywhere near it when she handed it over to Esta with the warning not to open it until she was ready to make the drop. Ruth's instructions had been simple: Don't leave it anywhere but the center of the building, as close to the target as she could. And don't do anything to betray the mission, or Harte will die.

If Esta got caught? Well, that wasn't Ruth's problem. The people she was delivering the book to wouldn't take kindly to an intruder. Esta would be on her own and at their mercy, but no one had told her who the target was.

"At least tell me who I'm up against," she said, trying to draw North's attention back to her. The open road had given way to the stacked buildings of the outskirts of town, the factories and warehouses that lined the river.

"Does it matter?" he asked with a mocking smile. "You're the Devil's Thief, aren't you?"

"I like to be prepared," she said with a shrug in her tone. "And I like to be the one who decides whether the risk to my life is really worth the cost of theirs."

North looked at her, his odd, uneven-colored eyes piercing her unease.

LISA MAXWELL

"Who are *you* to make that judgment?" he said softly. "This isn't the first deed done in your name, and it certainly won't be the last. Now's not exactly the time to be getting all high and mighty about things."

His words rattled something inside of her. He was right. The Antistasi had used her name who knew how many times before. It didn't matter that she hadn't been the one to perpetrate any of the attacks; a choice she had made had set all of this into motion.

"That's what I thought." North turned to the window, scratching at the scruff on his jawline as he watched the passing city. Eventually, the carriage rumbled to a stop and North checked the window to see where they were. "We're here." He pushed his hat back so he could look her dead in the eye. "Unless you've changed your mind?"

Esta considered the options before her. She didn't doubt that the notebook she was carrying, whatever North said, was something dangerous. She could still say no. She could drop the notebook here, pull time around her, and run.

But then what?

Mother Ruth and the rest of the Antistasi back at the brewery still had Harte. They'd taken him away not long after he'd opened his big mouth, and Esta had no idea where they'd put him. By the time she figured it out, he might already be dead—she couldn't hold on to time *that* long, especially lately.

And even if she found Harte before they hurt him, she had no idea what they'd done with Ishtar's Key. She hadn't asked, because she didn't want to alert them to its importance if they hadn't already realized. But if they *had* already realized what kind of power the stone had . . .

She couldn't worry about that. For now she had a job to do. And if her choice was between Harte and the person this delivery was set for, there wasn't really a choice. Dakari, Dolph . . . Esta had lost too many people to lose another.

But there was one other thing, a point that kept niggling at her like an itch she couldn't reach. She knew she was being used. Esta's name had been thrown around for nearly two years now without her ever knowing, and if Ruth had her way, the Antistasi would continue to use it. But she'd had enough of being a pawn in someone else's game. She'd been led like a marionette on a string her entire life by Professor Lachlan. She wasn't about to allow Ruth the same power over her now.

No, Esta had seen the mood in the building when Ruth talked, and she'd heard the fear in Frank's voice when Ruth accused him of coward-ice. The Antistasi might follow Ruth, but that didn't mean that they liked her or trusted her. Which gave Esta an opening. But to gain their trust, she had to start by proving that she was one of them—beginning with North. Which meant that she had to go through with this.

"I'm not going to change my mind," she told North. "Who's my mark?"

He studied her for a second or two, as if trying to figure out whether this was just another trick. "Just remember, you're not the only one who can pull a disappearing act. If you try anything, your friend dies."

"I'm aware." She gave him a bored look. "Are we going to sit here all night," she asked when he continued to stare at her, "or are you going to tell me who this package is meant for?"

"Just making sure we're clear," he said. "You're looking for Caleb Lipscomb. You can find him at number four thirty-two. It's just down this row of warehouses and then to the right. Once you're inside, go up to the second floor."

Caleb Lipscomb. She'd never heard of him, but that didn't necessarily mean much. "How will I find him?"

North's strange eyes flashed with amusement. "You'll know him when you see him. He likes to be in the center of things. Off you go now," he said, unlatching the door.

Outside the carriage, the air was cooler, but it carried the scent of the river, a muddy, earthy smell layered over with the heaviness of machine oil and coal from the factories that lined its banks. Esta readjusted the parcel under her arm, making sure to keep it steady and the pages tightly closed. They'd told her that the fuse inside would activate when she pulled a loose sheet out of the center, and she didn't need that happening before she found the person it was intended for.

Her chest felt tight. She didn't believe North's claim that it wasn't a bomb, and even as she walked toward her destination, she had her doubts about whether she could go through with it. It was one thing in theory, but it was another when her feet were steadily moving her toward the moment she'd have to decide.

True, she's been ready to kill Jack back at the station. She'd had the gun in her hands and the resolve to end him—because he'd *deserved* it. Because she knew that he would hurt countless people if she'd let him live. And she'd been right. From what she'd learned, Jack had been one of the proponents of the Act. He was the reason that magic was now illegal and that Mageus could be hunted openly, oppressed legally. But this felt different somehow. Esta didn't know this Caleb Lipscomb, whoever he was. He was a faceless name, an unknown who had done nothing to her.

Still, she couldn't see a way out of the situation, not unless she wanted the Antistasi as another enemy. And not unless she was willing to risk Harte's life.

The building labeled 432 was a long warehouse that ran the length of a block—a factory or machine shop of some sort. A single dull yellow bulb lit the door. Everything about it felt like a trap. She looked back, considering her options, and saw that North was still watching her.

He gave a nod. *Go on,* the motion seemed to say, and she took the final steps into the sallow light of the bulb. Opening the door of the building as silently as she could, she stepped inside.

THE BETHESDA FOUNTAIN

1902—New York

Viola pulled the shawl up over her head and tucked it around her chin, keeping her face turned away from the other people riding the streetcar as it traveled north, toward Central Park. Paul thought she was going to the fish market over on Fulton Street, so she'd have to be sure to stop there—or somewhere—before she returned. She couldn't chance him becoming any more suspicious than he already was. Not when she was getting so close to the information she needed.

She got off the streetcar near Madison Avenue and walked along East Drive through the park until she came to the large open piazza where the enormous fountain stood, topped by a winged angel. She didn't come to the park much on her own—there wasn't really a need to. Most days, seeing people lounging about in the grass and enjoying a stroll through the wooded pathways only served to remind her of what she would never have. But on the occasions that she did pass through it, she made sure to take a path that would bring her past this fountain. It depicted the story in the Bible of an angel healing people with the waters of Bethesda.

In a family of Sundren, Viola had been an anomaly. The magic she'd been born with had felt like a mark that meant her life had been damned from the very beginning. So the story of the angel who healed with nothing but some water had always struck something inside of her, as though there were a chance her own soul might be cleaned someday, just the same.

But Viola was not a dreamer. She'd learned long ago that fairy tales were for other people. She lived in the body she'd been given and was gratified with the life she'd made for herself. She didn't imagine other lives, and she didn't yearn for impossible things, so it was doubly troubling when her chest felt tight at the sight of the pink muslin and ivory lace on the girl sitting by the fountain.

Ruby was waiting where her note had promised she would be. Next to her was a pile of packages all tied up with string and her fiancé, Theo. He was leaning back on the bench, his hands cradling his head as though he owned the world, and Ruby was writing in a small tablet, her face bunched in concentration. Gone were the sleek dark skirt and high-buttoned shirt finished with a tie, as she'd worn the day Viola had taken the pointless ride in their carriage. Today Ruby's gown looked like something designed for an innocent debutante. It was the palest pink, with softly puffed sleeves and a delicate flounce of lace at her throat. She looked like a picture, sitting there by the water. She looked untouchable. *Impossible.*

Some days it seemed as though the pearls Ruby had been wearing the night of Delmonico's—the delicate strand of ivory beads, and the way they had lain perfectly against the dip at the base of her throat—were seared into Viola's memory. She had a feeling that this moment would join that memory.

Bah! She shook off the thought and the heat she felt. The weather was changing—that was all. The sun was high and bright, and the warmth she felt brushing against the skin beneath her blouse had nothing to do with the stupid, *stupid* little rich girl who had been brainless enough to send a note by messenger to the New Brighton—right under Paul's nose. Ruby was going to get them both killed, but then, what did the rich care about a little thing like dying? They probably thought they could give the angel of death a few dollars and send a servant instead.

Theo saw Viola first and nudged Ruby, who looked up from her writing and squinted across the piazza. The girl's entire expression brightened the moment she saw Viola coming toward them, and she put the tablet of paper and pencil back into the embroidered clutch hanging from her wrist.

"You came!" Ruby said, and before Viola knew what was happening, she found herself enveloped in the rich girl's arms and in a cloud of flowers and amber and warmth.

When Ruby released her, Viola's legs felt weak, and she stumbled backward, her shawl falling from her head as she caught herself. At the sound of Ruby's gasp, she pulled the fabric back up, covering her head and the side of her face. But Ruby wouldn't let well enough alone. Silently, her delicate features twisting in concern, she reached up to move it away from Viola's face.

"Who did this?" Ruby asked, her voice so soft that Viola could barely hear it over the rushing of the fountain's water.

"No one. It's nothing," Viola said, hitching the shawl back up. She knew what Ruby was seeing—the purple-green bruise on the side of her jaw, the cost of slipping out to take the carriage ride without telling Paul where she was going. She'd missed saying good-bye to her mother, and he'd decided to beat some manners into her.

She could have killed him, but instead she'd taken the punishment without fighting. It had seemed to appease him well enough. What else could she do? She couldn't very well have told him where she'd been. But every time she spoke or took a bite of food, the bruise throbbed, and every time it ached, she promised herself that she'd pay him back tenfold.

Still, Viola felt somehow wrong for being here, with these people. They would hurt Paul if they could—especially the girl. They would break him, destroy him. She should want that—she *did* want that—and yet, he was still family. Still her blood. She didn't know anymore if that word meant anything, or if it was just another lie, like happiness and freedom.

"That is *not* nothing," Ruby said, reaching for her. "Someone hurt you."

"It doesn't matter," Viola said, brushing away her concern. People hurt other people all the time. Why should she be exempt?

Ruby's manicured fingertips reached to touch her cheek. "We can help you, you know. You don't have to—"

"Basta!" She pushed away Ruby's hand again. "What are you going to do? Take me home like some stray dog?"

Ruby blinked, clearly surprised at the tone of Viola's voice. Probably because no one else had ever dared talk to her in such a way. Ruby Reynolds was the type of girl who'd grown up without hearing the word "no," and Viola had been born with the taste of it in her mouth.

"Don't pretend you understand my life," Viola said, a warning and a plea. "Don't pretend you can do a thing to change it. And don't imagine that I want you to." She raised her chin. "I'll take care of it myself." It was a declaration and a promise all at once. "I don't need some little rich girl's charity."

She saw Ruby flinch, but the girl didn't back down. "I didn't mean it that way. I just wanted to help."

"I came like you asked," Viola said, ignoring the hurt in Ruby's voice. "Now, what is it that you wanted?"

"I thought we could talk." Ruby worried her pink lower lip with the edge of one of her straight white teeth.

"So talk," Viola told her.

"Maybe we could go somewhere more private," Ruby said, glancing around as though she were worried someone might see her talking to a woman as common as Viola.

Viola's chest felt tight, like when she'd been trussed up in stays that night at Delmonico's. She shouldn't have come.

She could still leave. She should, before she allowed this bit of rich fluff to make her start doubting herself or the life she'd chosen. But leaving would mean that Ruby had won, and Viola couldn't have that, either.

"Fine," she said, the word coming out even sharper than she'd intended. "Where do you want to go?"

"Perhaps we could take out one of the boats?" Theo said. "It's a pleasant enough day, and I could use the exercise."

Viola swallowed the sigh that had been building inside of her. She couldn't imagine a life so easy, so filled with luxury, that Theo needed to find work. Pointless work, rowing in circles and getting nowhere at all. *Ridiculous.* But the sooner they were done with it, the better. "Fine," she said, not quite looking at Ruby. "Let's go."

A BIDDABLE GIRL

1902—New York

V iola was mad at her for sending the note. Viola hadn't said anything specifically, but Ruby knew that the fire in the other girl's eyes had everything to do with being summoned. It wasn't what Ruby had intended to do, and yet now she could see that it was what she'd done just the same. She'd summoned Viola, the way she might call for her maid or ring for the cook to make her some tea. And somehow Theo had just made it worse by suggesting that they take one of the rowboats out onto the lake.

But Ruby found that no matter how quick her brain or how smart her tongue might be in any other situation, whenever she was around Viola, they both failed her. With Viola's violet eyes glaring at her, she hadn't been able to do much more than nod weakly.

"This is a terrible idea," she whispered as she walked next to Theo, with Viola trailing behind them.

"Why's that?" Theo asked, glancing over at her.

"Because she hates me," Ruby said, soft enough that Viola couldn't hear.

"She's a source, Ruby. Treat her like any other source. She doesn't need to like you. She needs to *help* you."

He was right, of course, but it certainly didn't *feel* that way.

Things didn't improve when the attendant who prepared the rowboat for them suggested that their servant could wait on the bench near the boat shed.

"No," Ruby said, her cheeks heating with absolute mortification. "She's coming with us." From the corner of her eye, she saw Viola's head whip around at her. "I mean to say, she's not my servant—our servant. She's our . . ." What, exactly, was Viola?

"Our friend will be coming along," Theo said, breaking in to rescue her.

Not that it stopped the heat that had already climbed up Ruby's neck and into her cheeks. Her skin would be blotchy and red. It was mortifying. Really, it was.

Viola was silent as they clambered into the boat and the attendant pushed them off into the water. Theo began rowing in long, slow pulls, causing the boat to glide away from the shore and into the center of the lake.

It *was* a beautiful day, just as Theo had said. Any other time, Ruby might have enjoyed the outing, floating on the water far from the worries and responsibilities that she usually carried with her. Weightless and serene. When she was just a girl, she had positively loved it when her father would bring her and her sisters down to the park, especially on early spring days like this one, when it seemed like the city would be in bloom at any moment.

But that was before everything happened. Theo had brought her a couple of times last summer, trying to cheer her up, but nothing worked for that better than work itself.

This *was* work, she reminded herself. But with Viola glaring at her, Ruby found it decidedly uncomfortable.

Viola was just so . . . *much.* It wasn't that she was large. She was even shorter than Ruby herself, and she certainly wasn't fat or even plump. But Viola's body had the curves and softness that Ruby's did not. She wasn't any older than Ruby, but somehow she looked like a woman rather than a girl. There was experience in her eyes. Knowledge.

Oh, but her poor face.

Viola noticed Ruby staring again and hitched her shawl up farther to cover her bruise.

Someone had hit her. Someone had *hurt* her, and it made Ruby want to destroy them in return.

Theo was whistling some unnameable melody as he moved them in slow, looping circles around the lake.

"Yes, well . . ." It was an inane thing to say. "We should talk."

Viola didn't reply. She simply waited expectantly, and Ruby, who always knew what to say, didn't know where to begin. It was vexing the way Viola stared at her as though she could see right through her, down to the parts that she hid from everyone except Theo—to the parts she hid *even* from Theo. In all the ballrooms she'd been in, swirled about in the arms of countless beaus, Ruby had never felt half as unsure of herself as she did with Viola's eyes on her.

Ruby took out her small tablet and pencil. It was a simple enough action, but it helped to center her a bit. "What do you know of your brother's association with John Torrio, Miss Vaccarelli?"

"Torrio is one of his guys," Viola said. "Paolo, he's grooming Torrio to take a stake in his businesses. He likes him," she said with no little disgust. Her nose wrinkled, a clear indication that she thought differently.

"And your brother," Ruby said, focusing the notes she was writing so she wouldn't have to look into Viola's eyes again. "What can you tell me about his businesses?"

"He has the New Brighton and the Little Naples Cafe, which are the ones our mother knows of, and then he has the Five Pointers." She listed out a few more things, a couple of brothels and other connections that Paul Kelly had, but they weren't anything Ruby didn't already know. "My brother is un coglione . . . how do you say? He's not a nice man. A bastard not by birth, but by choice."

Ruby believed every word of what Viola was telling her, but other newspapers had already dealt with Paul Kelly's connections to the underbelly of the city. It wasn't what Ruby was interested in.

"He sent John Torrio to kill me, didn't he?" Ruby asked, finally looking up from her paper. But this time it was Viola who wouldn't look at her. "It's okay," she told Viola. "I know you were there, but I know you didn't want to hurt me." She laid her hand on the other girl's knee.

Viola's eyes flashed up to meet hers, and, embarrassed and suddenly too warm, Ruby drew her hand away.

"Do you know why Torrio was sent to kill me, Miss Vaccarelli?"

Viola shook her head. "You wrote something they didn't like so much."

"Exactly. I wrote a story about a train accident, and it had nothing at all to do with Paul Kelly or any of his Five Pointers." Viola's brows had drawn together, but she didn't speak. Her eyes instead seemed to urge Ruby on. "The story was about a derailment outside the city, nine days ago. There was a man on that train, a friend of Theo's from school—"

"I wouldn't exactly call him a friend," Theo said dryly. "Especially not now . . ."

"They were acquaintances," Ruby corrected, trying to keep her own temper from erupting. "He told the medics who rescued him that he saw a man on the train who should have already been dead. When they pulled him out, he'd hit his head pretty badly, but he was talking about Mageus—about a magician named Harte Darrigan and a girl."

Viola's eyes widened slightly. "Harte Darrigan?"

Viola knows that name. But Ruby didn't know what that meant. "And a girl," she repeated. "I talked Theo into getting me access to this man, Jack Grew. He either didn't know who I was or he didn't care, because he told me everything that happened. It was a *monumental* scoop. And the Order did everything they could to kill it, up to and including trying to have me killed. So you see, I have a very personal stake in all of this. I will not be silenced, Miss Vaccarelli. I will not go be the good, biddable girl that they want me to be. I will expose them, and I will do everything I can to destroy the Order's power in this city." She paused, forcing her anger and impatience back down. "But this is bigger than the Order."

"It is?" Viola asked, her expression thoughtful and serious.

Ruby nodded. "If Jack Grew was right—and I think he was, considering the lengths the Order has gone to, all to shut me up—that train derailment wasn't an accident. It was an *attack*. And it was done with magic."

THE SWP

1904—St. Louis

When Esta went inside the building, it was dark, but she could see a light coming from a hallway to the right. In the distance she heard something like the murmuring of a crowd. Because Harte wasn't there, she took the risk of pulling her affinity around her and followed the source of the light until she found that it was coming from a set of stairs.

Keeping her hold on time, she went up the steps slowly, careful to keep the notebook balanced under her arm. At the top, there was another hallway, but at the far end of it, she saw a glow coming from beneath a door. As she walked toward it, the sound of her footsteps echoed into the silence that had been created by her magic. She found it unlocked, and with time still motionless, she slipped through.

On the other side was a large room filled with people. The high-ceilinged space stretched the entire width of the building, and the men and women within it were caught in the web of time gone slow, their mouths open and their expressions rapt as they listened to a speaker standing in the center. Though some sat on benches at the edges of the room, most were on their feet, crowded around the man elevated on the small platform of a stage. The speaker was dressed in shirtsleeves, which had been pulled back to reveal the broad forearms of a workman, but it was clear that his working days were behind him. His balding hair was nearly white, and his face was partially obscured by a full beard. His hand was raised, and his face was rapturous, his mouth opened and his eyes wild.

Esta had a sense that this man in the middle of the crowd was Lipscomb. She could leave the device here and go, but if she was wrong, it could mean trouble. She needed to make sure she had the right target.

Making her way through the crowd, Esta was careful not to touch anyone or bobble the parcel under her arm. She found a spot in the back corner, far from anyone who might notice her sudden appearance, and then she let go of her hold on time. The room spun back into life. The noise of the crowd was deafening, and the air suddenly held an electricity that had nothing to do with magic.

In the center of the room, the man's voice boomed over the crowd. "The bourgeois care nothing for the workers," he shouted. "They would print their money with the blood of our children. While our families work themselves to death in factories, the rich men of this city plan parties and balls. They feast while we starve! Look at the excesses of the Exposition," he shouted, pounding his fist against his hand to punctuate his words. "Instead of celebrating the worker—the true spirit of this country—the Exposition celebrates a feudal past that cannot be allowed to rise again. They've built palaces and temples in our city, a city where native-born sons die without a roof over their heads.

"Look at the Society, with its heathenish ways. They look to magic, to the *occult*, because they understand that the workers of this country will not be silenced. They know that only the heathen power can subdue the power of the workers when they unite. But we will show them that not even their sorcery will be enough to extinguish the fire lit here, in this place, tonight." He paused, looking around the room with satisfaction. "The Society has planned a parade—"

The room rumbled with disgusted murmurs, punctuated by low boos. The man's voice didn't carry with it any hint of magic, but there was power there nonetheless. Esta could feel him stirring the souls in the room all around her with nothing more than his words. The people around him were leaning in toward the platform on which he stood, their minds open and willing to accept what he was saying.

"Yes. Their parade is an abomination. Their prophet is a false one, an idol of profit and power created to suppress the voice of the proletariat. You all know this. You have seen it for yourselves every year since the brave porters stood up and demanded a living wage and were crushed by the powers of the bourgeois pigs. Every year the bourgeoisie remind us that they hold our lives in their hands—hands that have never known the weight of a hammer or the sting of labor—but not this year.

"This year we will rise up. This year, with the world watching, with the president himself viewing the spectacle, we *must* rise up and say *enough*. We must demand what is ours—with force, if necessary."

The crowd erupted around Esta, and she lifted her hands in half-hearted applause, so she wouldn't be noticed. But his words, along with the anger and hatred in his tone, made her uneasy. The room felt like a powder keg about to ignite.

"This your first meeting?" A girl had come up next to her and was examining her with an appraising look in her eyes.

"What?" Esta asked, unnerved at how easily she'd missed the girl's approach. She was wearing a dress of slate gray that was buttoned up to her chin. The color seemed too severe for how young she was, but the plain cut of it seemed to suit the girl's stern expression.

"You're a new face," the girl said, a question in her eyes.

Esta's mind raced. "I heard about this . . . this meeting," she said, improvising as she went. "And thought I'd see for myself what it was all about."

"Who'd you hear from?" the girl asked. Her voice was soft but determined. And her eyes were suspicious.

"Oh, one of the guys at the brewery told me. Said I might find it interesting."

The girl studied Esta a long moment more, like she wasn't sure if she believed the story, but then she relented. "I'm Greta, and you are?"

"John," Esta said, picking the plainest, most forgettable name she could think of.

"We're glad to have you, John," Greta told her as she handed Esta a sheet of paper. "Our movement needs more able bodies willing to stand firm."

Keeping the notebook clamped steadily beneath her arm, she accepted it without reading it. "Thanks," she said. "Who's that speaking now?"

The girl's eyes narrowed a little. "Your friend, the one at the brewery, he didn't tell you?"

Esta's throat felt tight. "He just said I'd be interested . . . didn't say much else."

"Where is he?" the girl asked. "This friend of yours?"

"Who knows?" Esta said, and when she sensed that it wasn't the right answer, she added, "Probably working overtime." She gave a shrug that she hoped looked tired and frustrated. "You know how it is—when the foreman says stay, you stay."

The girl's expression relaxed slightly. "Yes. We all know how it is." She looked to the speaker and then back at Esta. "That's Caleb Lipscomb. He's the current secretary of the SWP. He's brilliant."

"What's this parade he's talking about?"

"The Veiled Prophet Parade?" the girl asked, and the suspicion was back in her eyes. "They have it every year. . . ." Her voice trailed off like this was something Esta should have known.

"I'm new in town," Esta told her. "Came because my cousin said there was work, what with the Exposition and all. Only been here about two months."

The girl's expression didn't relax. "Where did you say you worked again?"

Esta felt as though the stiff collar of her shirt were strangling her, but she'd been in tighter situations than this. "The Feltz Brewery," she said, giving the name of Ruth's place, since it was the only place she knew of.

The girl made a sound in the back of her throat. "He's talking about the Veiled Prophet Parade that's set for Independence Day."

"This parade . . . It's a big deal?" Esta asked, trying to get a sense of what the girl thought of it.

"That depends on who you are. A lot of people in town like the spectacle of it, but there's plenty of us who know the truth." Greta shrugged. "It's just a show of power. The Society started the parade back in seventy-eight, after a railroad strike threatened to shut down the city. They couldn't let a bunch of simple workmen get away with an action like that, especially not ones with skin darker than their own, so they invented the Prophet and the Parade. They use the threat of magic to keep the workers in their places all the year through, and the parade is a reminder of their power—a reminder of who is truly free in this country." The girl's expression lit with determination. "We never make it easy for them, and this year's parade won't be any exception."

"I see," Esta said, glancing at the sheet in her hand. The bold, dark type only accented the anger in the words printed on the page.

"Well, enjoy the rest of the evening," the girl said. "If you have any questions at all, any of us with the broadsheets can answer them."

"Thanks," Esta told her, and turned her eyes back to the man speaking in the center of the room.

Go away, she thought as she felt the girl's eyes on her.

She pretended to pay attention to what Lipscomb was saying. After a few minutes, she glanced over her shoulder to find the girl still watching her. Inwardly she cursed. As long as the girl was there, Esta was stuck—she couldn't disappear, and she couldn't drop the package, not without giving away either what she was or what she was doing. Magic would make what she had to do easier, but with the girl, she couldn't risk it.

An opening parted in the crowd in front of her, and Esta took the opportunity it presented to slip through, little by little making her way closer to the small platform that Caleb Lipscomb was standing on. Every so often she paused, as though considering his words, and then would take the opportunity some shifting in the crowd offered to slip closer yet. She didn't doubt that the girl was still watching her, but there wasn't anything she could do about that.

When she was standing right in front of him, she stopped, keeping the notebook in her hands secure. She'd give it a minute or two before she made her move.

"But we must be vigilant," Lipscomb was bellowing. "We know there are those who would corrupt our purpose. Undesirable elements that bring with them the feudal superstitions of the old countries: the Catholics with their papist loyalty and those who refuse to set aside their feral magic to join the true proletariat. You know what I speak of," he shouted, his voice rising in a feverish pitch.

"Maggots!" shouted someone deep in the crowd.

Esta saw the curve of Lipscomb's mouth at the sound of the slur. "Yes. Why do they come here? Why do they seek to take the jobs we've worked so hard for? To disrupt the country we are trying to build with their dangerous ways?" Lipscomb shook his head dramatically. "We must guard against those who would pervert the true proletariat with their shadowy powers."

She pretended interest, hiding her disgust beneath a placid expression. *No honor among thieves, and no solidarity among the downtrodden, apparently.* Maybe she didn't know this Caleb Lipscomb, but she knew those like him and felt some of the guilt she'd been carrying about what she was supposed to do lift from her.

He would do the same to me, she thought as she pressed even closer to the platform. *He would do worse.*

When someone bumped into her, Esta let the sheet of paper the girl had given her drop to the floor. She waited until it landed at her feet before she stooped to retrieve it, and in a subtle movement perfected during her years of training, she placed the parcel on the floor and held on to the edge of the loose sheet within it. Then she slid the notebook forward, until the loose sheet came free and the device was directly under the platform.

The Antistasi had explained that she had less than five minutes once she removed the fuse, but when she got back up to her feet, she realized that she was penned in, trapped by the crowd that was on its feet, shouting with the fervor of true converts. There was no opening, so Esta made one, throwing an elbow sharply into the stomach of the man behind her. The man groaned and tumbled backward into the people behind him, and the crowd, already whipped into an excited frenzy, responded by pushing him back. In a matter of seconds, someone threw a punch, and the room erupted into chaos.

Esta ducked, keeping herself low as she shoved her way to the edges of the madness, and when she reached the other side, she pulled time around her and ran.

She didn't let go of time until she was outside the building and at the carriage where North was waiting. The sounds of the night returned as she opened the door and climbed in.

"Go!" she told him, looking back out the window.

He didn't look up from picking at his fingernails with the blade of a knife.

"Go!" she said again. "We need to get out of here."

"Let's just give it a minute or two to be sure."

He's insane.

Her breathing was still ragged from running out of the building and down the block, and her heart felt as though it would pound its way straight out of her chest. When you did a job, you didn't just wait around to get caught. "We need to get out of here before the police come."

"We have time," he said again, putting the knife away in his back pocket. He took out the pocket watch from inside his vest and considered it. "I'd say we got at least two more minutes to go."

Because she'd used her affinity to escape, it took nearly four.

North had just picked up the revolver when they heard the echo of a small explosion.

Esta's stomach dropped. "You said it wasn't a bomb," she told him, her mouth dry as she thought of all the people who had been in that room—workers, laborers, all who had come to listen because they needed hope. She'd been so angered by Lipscomb's words that she hadn't considered the other people when she set the device for him.

"No," he said, meeting her eyes. "I said nobody was going to die, and they won't. The explosives in that package won't do more than take a leg or an arm—just enough to put Lipscomb into the hospital and keep him out of our way." He twisted the knob on the side of his watch as the first of the people began to pour from the doorway of the building. With them came a dense, cloudlike fog, and even from more than a block away, Esta could feel the strange, icy-hot magic in the air.

"What did you do to them?" she asked.

"It's not what we did *to* them," he told her, glancing up from the watch. "It's what *you* did *for* them."

He clicked the watch closed, and Esta didn't have time to contemplate the meaning of his words before she felt her veins turn to ice and the world went white.

THE LAKE

1902—New York

Viola felt as though she couldn't breathe. "What do you mean, it was done with magic?" she asked Ruby. The girl's skin had gone from the palest cream to a high pink as she spoke, moved by the furor of her convictions. It didn't make her any less attractive.

"Jack was clear. The train didn't just derail. There wasn't a bomb. The two of them—Harte Darrigan, who was supposed to have died on the Brooklyn Bridge the day before the accident, and this Esta Filosik—used magic to destroy the train." Ruby leaned forward. "They used magic *beyond* the Brink."

"That isn't possible," she told Ruby. Not unless Darrigan had the Book. And for Esta to be with him? *No.*

"If it wasn't true, why would the Order go to such lengths to stop me from telling people?" Ruby asked.

But all Viola could do was shake her head numbly.

"The very fact that they were willing to hire your brother to kill me shows just how true it is. There are Mageus outside the city, and there's more," Ruby added. "Jack told me what really happened at Khafre Hall the night it burned."

Viola's stomach suddenly felt like it was filled with molten lead. "He did?" she said, trying to keep her voice steady, even as she wondered how deep the water around her might be. Had this all been a trap?

"They were robbed," Ruby told her, satisfaction shining in her eyes.

"A group of Mageus walked into their headquarters and took all their precious treasures."

"Oh?" Viola's voice sounded weak, even to herself.

Ruby nodded, her midnight eyes shining. "Yes, but the Order is still trying to cover it up. No one has let anything slip about who the thieves were or what they stole. As long as the people in this city believe that the Order is all powerful, they'll keep supporting them. That's why I need you. I need to know what happened in Khafre Hall."

"I don't know anything about what you're talking about," Viola said, forgetting where she was for a second. She almost lurched to her feet, but the rocking of the boat reminded her. "Take me back," she told Theo. "I'm done with this. With all of this."

"What is it?" Ruby asked, legitimately confused. "If you're worried about being attacked, we can protect you."

"You?" Viola laughed at the ridiculousness of the girl's statement. "*You* are going to protect *me*?"

"We can make sure you're safe from Paul Kelly when the story comes out—"

"Paul?" Viola asked, surprised.

"Don't you see?" Ruby said, lowering her voice. "It all makes sense. Kelly has Torrio—a Mageus—working for him at the same time that Khafre Hall is robbed? Paul Kelly, who is already known to be a notorious criminal—no offense," she added, her cheeks going pinker still.

Viola waved away her apology. "You think my *brother* is the one who broke into Khafre Hall?" she asked, astounded. It was better than Ruby knowing about Viola's own involvement, but not much better.

"I don't know for sure, but that's how you could help me. If we could prove that he did it, we could take down a crime boss and the Order all at once. Tammany would have to turn against Kelly, because they're interested in the Order's favor, and everyone would know that the Order is weak and pointless. And if we can find out what Kelly's guys took from them, maybe we could even track the objects down and make sure they don't fall into the wrong hands."

Ruby's mind was a marvel, but it was a dangerous marvel. If the girl insisted on investigating this, it was more than possible that she'd eventually discover the connection to Dolph, and to Viola herself. But if Ruby depended upon Viola for the information, Viola could direct it the way that she wanted. And if she was very smart, she could destroy Nibsy Lorcan in the process.

She'd been wavering about what she would do, but the idea of seeing Nibsy brought low made up her mind. Yes, her brother might be her own blood, but he'd chosen his path. Viola took a packet from the basket she was carrying and held it out to Ruby.

"What is this?" Ruby's eyes widened as she held out her hands.

Viola hesitated. "Receipts for the last few months," she told her. "I don't know what's in it, or if it will even help, but Paul, he has big plans. In the last week alone, he's already sent four of his Five Pointers out of the city."

"For what?" Ruby asked.

Viola shrugged. "I'm not sure, but he wants a bigger piece of the world than the streets of this city can offer, and I know my brother. The wide world doesn't need him meddling in it."

Ruby's brows drew together as she flipped through the receipts, studying them. "Is there anything more?"

"There's more, but Paul keeps them close. I haven't been able to get to them." Viola frowned at the thought of how closely her brother and his boys watched her. "But I will."

"When?" Ruby pressed, holding the package close to her.

"When I can," Viola said, irritated at the note of insistence in Ruby's tone.

"That isn't good enough," Ruby told Viola, her voice rising in volume as she hugged the parcel of documents even closer. "I need to know a date."

"Ruby," Theo said gently. He'd been rowing them steadily back to the edge of the lake.

"I'm not your servant," Viola huffed. "You don't get to tell me what to do or when."

"I never said you were," Ruby said, her pale cheeks flaming red. "I just meant—"

"You meant *nothing*, principessa," Viola snapped. The stress of being trapped so close to Ruby, of being cornered in so many ways, broke over the dams she'd built and poured out of her in a fiery tirade. "That is your problem. The risks you take, the dangers you put yourself in, all while dragging this one along with you like a puppy to heel—"

"Hey," Theo interjected, but Viola ignored him and continued.

"In your pretty little world, you're too safe to know what danger is. You give your commands, and you don't even bother to watch people jump. But you can't make me jump."

"I never—" Ruby started. "That is ... You're just—" And then she sputtered a bit more before she made an exasperated sound and turned away.

Viola pretended that she hadn't seen the way Ruby's eyes had gone glassy or the way her voice shook. Instead, she too turned away, ignoring both of them.

For the next few minutes, Theo continued to row them back. The moment they docked, Ruby was on her feet, being helped out of the boat by the attendant. She stomped off without another word, spoiled rich girl that she was.

Theo hopped out first and then helped Viola, who hated the feeling of the boat lurching beneath her, onto the dock. For a moment they stood in an uneasy silence, as though neither of them wanted to be the first to leave.

"I'm not going to apologize, if that's what you're waiting for," she said to Theo, who was watching her with too-steady eyes.

His mouth curved up, but his expression was sad. "I wasn't waiting for anything of the sort."

She glared at him. "Then why are you still here?"

"I'm thinking. . . ." He tapped his chin, his eyes squinting against the sun. "She means well, you know."

Viola just glared at him.

"I know what she looks like to you, but I've known Ruby since we were both knee-high. She's had a rough time of it, first with her father and then with everything that's happened to her family since. She really does want to help. In her own way, she's trying to do something worthy." But when Viola continued to glare at him, he let out a sigh. "This isn't going to end well, is it?"

The sincerity in his eyes had the fight draining right out of her. "Paul Kelly, he's not one to mess with—"

"That's not what I meant," he said, shaking his head. "But you're probably right about that, too. It was good seeing you again, Viola."

She reached out and caught him by his sleeve. "Is there any way to talk her out of this crazy plan?" she asked, somehow unable to keep an unintended urgency from her voice.

He laughed. "I've yet to be able to talk Ruby out of anything. She has more lives than the proverbial cat." Then his face softened. "Be careful with her, won't you?"

Viola frowned. "I don't know what you mean. . . ."

"I imagine you do," he said, giving her the funny, wobbly grin that would have looked half-drunken on anyone else. On Theo, it simply looked innocent and . . . well, too damn *nice*. "I think you know, and despite your bluster—which I quite enjoy, by the way—you will take care with her. If not, you'll answer to me."

He tipped his hat at her, and then he turned to gather Ruby's parcels before he ran to catch up with Ruby, leaving Viola alone at the edge of the lake with her mouth hanging open in confusion and feeling like somehow she'd just lost an argument she hadn't known she was having.

THE DIFFERENCE BETWEEN

1904—St. Louis

Harte didn't have any idea where the Antistasi had put him, but it had the subterranean feel of a coal cellar or a basement. They hadn't taken any chances, because not long after they'd dumped him on the floor, he'd heard the same *pop-hiss* he'd heard earlier, in the back of the wagon. A moment later he smelled the same thick odor that made his head feel like it was floating and his affinity go dull. Whatever it was had evaporated some time ago, but his affinity still felt like it was miles away.

The ropes on his wrist were too tight for him to wriggle out of, so he just sat there in the darkness they'd forced upon him and waited. The only positive development was that whatever the drug was, it shut the voice up inside of him. He figured it had to be something more than opium for it to have that kind of effect.

By the time he heard a door open, his arms had gone completely numb from being tied behind him. He scrambled to his feet, ready. If Esta had failed, they wouldn't be coming to celebrate.

"Come on, then," a familiar voice said. It was the cowboy—North.

The hands that took him by the arm weren't exactly gentle, but they didn't do anything more than lead him along.

Finally, they stopped, and when the sack was removed from his head again, he blinked past the sudden brightness to see that he was in a small office. And he wasn't alone. The woman was there—Mother Ruth, North, another girl with silver spectacles perched on her nose, who'd been there earlier, and Esta. She had a tired, worried look on her face, and even once she saw him, it didn't change. But they didn't have her tied up, and he wasn't dead yet, so he figured that meant something.

Even in that ridiculous suit with her hair chopped close around her face, she looked damned near perfect.

His eyes met hers. *You okay?*

She gave him the smallest of nods, but then her gaze shot to Ruth. "I did what you wanted, just like I promised. You can untie him now," Esta said. There was something in her voice that bothered him, but she looked unharmed.

"We'll untie him when we're ready," the cowboy said, his mouth hitching a bit on one side.

"She did everything you asked, North." It was the girl this time. She was a mousy-looking thing, especially with those glasses, but he didn't let that sway him. The last time he'd underestimated a person wearing glasses it had been a mistake.

"Maggie's right," Ruth said. "The girl has proven herself . . . for now. You can untie him."

In a single, fluid movement, the cowboy took out a thin knife and flicked it open. *Show-off.* But Harte kept his feelings to himself and masked his irritation with a look of utter boredom.

"Considering what you had me do, I think we've earned your trust, period," Esta told the woman.

"You delivered a package," Ruth said. "That's hardly grounds for you to make demands."

"I nearly killed a man," Esta said, her voice steady. "I set off some sort of magical bomb that did who knows what to all those people—people who never did anything to me."

The power inside Harte lurched at her words, stirred up with something that felt too close to pleasure for his liking. He must have made a sound, because North glanced at him. But Harte gritted his teeth and forced himself to remain composed.

Ruth gave Esta a pitying look. "Any one of those people would have done the same to you had they been given the opportunity."

"You don't know that," Esta said, but she didn't sound convinced.

"Do you know what the SWP is?" Ruth asked.

"They're socialists," Esta answered. "Workers who want a better life." But there was something unsettled in her voice. Something that made the power inside Harte pause and take notice.

"They do, but at what cost?" Ruth asked, stepping toward Esta. "I know those workers as well as I know the Society. They're the people who look up and dream of one day being tapped by the Veiled Prophet himself. Year after year they elect those who would erase magic from these shores. Year after year they buy into the fears of rich men; they lift up those fears and carry them on their shoulders, all because it's not they who will be harmed. The Act, the Guard, even the Society itself—none of it affects them.

"Perhaps they *were* innocents," Ruth continued. "Perhaps they simply wanted a better wage and more food on the table for their families. But Caleb Lipscomb knows exactly what he's doing. He uses them for his own advantage. Who do you think those workers are truly angry at? The capitalists who live in the fancy houses on McPherson Avenue?" She let out a derisive laugh. "*No.* Every man in that warehouse listening to Lipscomb speak wants to *become* those men. They picture themselves in those same fine houses, their children in silken pinafores and their wives dripping with jewels bought with the blood of the common worker. The people who follow SWP aren't really angry at the men who run this city. They're angry at those beneath them—the freshly arrived immigrants who are willing to work for a fraction of the wages they themselves demand. And they're angry at Mageus, who did nothing at all to achieve power they can't even begin to imagine."

She gave a shrug that also managed to broadcast her irritation. "Lipscomb knows that. His people were the cause of a riot three weeks ago over in Dutchtown. Three people died because Lipscomb started a rumor that the people who lived there were harboring Mageus who would use their power to take food from the mouths of the ordinary worker. He sees our kind as a threat because he knows that our power means we have a loyalty to something bigger than his group of angry men. He uses the people's anger because he can, because they fear what they don't know and won't understand. Do you know what Caleb Lipscomb is planning?"

"Something with the Veiled Prophet Parade," Esta told her.

"He was planning to place bombs on the parade route. You did the world a favor by putting him in the hospital, where he won't be able to stir up his followers."

"Why would you care about saving the Veiled Prophet Parade?" Harte asked.

Ruth turned to him. "I *don't* care about the parade, but every time there's an action by some group like the SWP, the Society turns the people's hatred toward the old magic. It helps them shore up their power, preying on the people's fears and prejudices. The loss of innocent lives would have been blamed on *us*."

"Then why the attack last night?" Esta asked. "It wasn't just a bomb that went off. I know there was magic involved. Won't those people blame you too?"

"Blame us?" Ruth laughed. "They'll *thank* us. But you're right. That wasn't a bomb. It was something infinitely more powerful—a gift of sorts that Maggie created." Ruth walked over and tipped the girl's chin up affectionately. "The Society and those like them might think they understand alchemy, but my sister has a talent for it they can only dream of."

"It's what you used in the attack last fall," Harte realized. And in the fog that they used to keep him and Esta subdued. It wasn't just opium and it wasn't simple magic. It was some combination of the two, some new thing altogether. At this realization, the power inside of him swelled, and he heard a voice echoing in his mind. *See?* It seemed to whisper. *See what they are capable of? The damage they will continue to do?*

But he shoved the voice aside, even as part of him realized that it was right. It was bad enough that men like those in the Order would pervert magic to claim power, but for Mageus to do it as well . . . ?

"No," Ruth said, releasing Maggie's chin. "Not *quite* like last fall."

Maggie turned to them. "Then, we were simply trying to slow down their progress," she told them. "My serum wasn't ready quite yet, and we needed more time."

"Serum?" Esta asked. She met Harte's eyes, but he didn't have an answer to the question.

A knock sounded at the door, and Ruth called for the person to enter. It was one of the guys from before—one who had been close to the wagon.

"You have news?" Ruth asked, her expression rapt.

"It worked," the guy said, beaming at Ruth. "They just brought in the first case to City Hospital. A girl who causes flowers to sprout from everything she touches."

Ruth let out a small breath, and Harte could see the relief—the victory—flash across her features. "Good. Have Marcus keep track of them and let me know if anything changes." Then she turned to Maggie. "*You did it.* This time, you finally did it."

"Did what?" Harte asked, frustration getting the best of him.

"She solved the problem that has been plaguing our kind for centuries." Ruth's eyes were practically glowing with satisfaction.

Harte shook his head, not understanding.

"Why do the Sundren hate what we are? Why do they cut us off and round us up and force us to suppress what we are until we become shells of ourselves? Until generations pass and the power in our veins passes with it?"

"Because we have an affinity for the old magic," Esta said, her voice oddly hollow. "Because we're different, and they know we have power they can't ever equal."

"Yes. Because they've *forgotten*," Ruth said fervently. "There was once magic throughout the world. Everyone had the ability to call to old magic. But through the ages, people have moved from where their power took root, and they left their memories behind them. Those who had forgotten what they might have been began to fear and to hunt those who kept the old magic close. Do you know what it means to be Sundren?" she asked. "It means to be broken apart, to be split from. Those who have let the magic in their bloodlines die are separated from an essential part of themselves. They're wounded and broken, and they have no idea what lies dormant deep inside. It's why they claw at the world, destroying anything in their path to get some relief from the ache they cannot name, the hollow inside themselves." Ruth paused. "But what if we could awaken that magic? What if we could heal that break? What if we were no longer different, because *everyone* had the magic that they fear in us?"

"The fog—" Esta's brows drew together.

"Don't you see?" Maggie asked, her expression hopeful. "We *cured* them."

But Harte wasn't so sure. He knew the difference between the warm, welcoming natural power that Mageus could touch and the cool warning of ritual magic. Everything he'd seen and experienced in his short life had told him that unnatural magic was a corruption. A danger. Dolph had believed he could use it, and he'd died instead. He'd taken Leena along with him.

"You mean you infected them," Harte said. "You didn't ask their permission or give them a chance to refuse." He couldn't see how that would turn out well.

North took a step toward him, but Ruth held up her hand. "What we did goes far beyond the individual people in that building tonight." Her voice carried the tremulous surety of a true believer. "We proved tonight that those ancient connections to the old magic are still there, waiting and latent. We simply woke them up and reminded them of what this world was supposed to be."

"According to whom?" he wondered. Harte had known people like Ruth, people who were so certain of the path before them. Dolph Saunders, with all his plotting and planning, willing to hurt even those he loved for what he thought was best. Nibsy Lorcan, who saw a different vision but believed it to be no less valid. Even the Order and men like Jack, who thought they knew exactly what the world should be. It was clear to him that Ruth and her Antistasi weren't so very different.

The mood in the room shifted as Ruth's eyes went cold. "You think this is my plight alone?" she asked. "The Antistasi are as old as the fear and hatred of magic. Their mission is one that has come down through the centuries. The Thief has proven herself admirably tonight as an ally to that cause. I wonder . . . will you?"

Esta's expression was pleading with him to keep quiet, but with the unsettled power inside of him, he couldn't help himself. "I make my own choices. I'm not a pawn, and I won't be used," he said, and the moment the words were out. Esta's jaw went tight, and her gaze dropped to the floor.

Ruth's mouth curved, but her expression was devoid of any amusement. "Well, then, if I were you, I'd choose quickly, Mr. O'Doherty."

THE OPPORTUNE MOMENT

1904—St. Louis

Jack had been standing at Roosevelt's side earlier that evening when word came of the attack. The president had just arrived on the morning train, and they'd gone straight to the fair, where he was presiding over an event in the Agricultural Building of the Exposition. Roosevelt had been examining a bust of his own likeness carved entirely out of butter, of all things, and as he posed for a photograph with his buttery image, Hendricks had come up next to Jack.

"There was an event last night," the Guardsman whispered into Jack's ear. "We have it under control now, but I thought you—and the president—would want to know right away."

"What happened?" Jack asked, leading Hendricks away from where anyone could hear. This could be exactly what he'd been waiting for. He'd known all along that sooner or later, the maggots would go too far and he would be able to use their mistakes against them.

"One of the factories down by the river, sir," the Guardsman told him. "A group of socialists were having a meeting. Lipscomb was injured in the explosion."

"Lipscomb?" Jack asked, not really that interested.

"He's one of ours, from here in St. Louis. A socialist rabble-rouser who works for the SWP. From the evidence we found, it looks as though his group was planning an attack on the parade next week."

"Did the explosion kill them?"

Hendricks shook his head. "No, sir. But there were . . . other injuries."

Roosevelt was already looking over at Jack and indicating that it was time to go. "What do I care about the injuries of a few damn socialists?" he asked, impatient at the apparent pointlessness of the interruption.

The Guardsman lowered his voice. "The attack used magic, sir, and the people who were injured, they have very . . . *peculiar* ailments."

"Peculiar how?" Jack asked.

"They've isolated the ones who've been brought into the hospital, but they're exhibiting some strange symptoms. One keeps setting fire to his bedclothes with nothing but his fingertips. Another makes it rain every time she cries. They reported a cloud of mist after the bomb went off, and the ones who've come in so far have said that they started experiencing their symptoms after it touched them." He hesitated. "They seem to be infected, sir."

Jack searched Hendricks' expression for any sign that he might be exaggerating. "Infected?"

The Guardsman's expression was grave, but there was a look of distaste in his features, like he'd just smelled something rotten. "By magic."

Roosevelt and his party had left the Exposition immediately, of course. No one was willing to take the chance of another attack until the perpetrators were rounded up and dealt with. Jack had overseen that, too. Roosevelt had left it to him, as he usually did. The president didn't understand, not really. His politics were nearly as popular as he was. He'd supported the Defense Against Magic Act in private, but he never made a fuss about it publicly. There were still too many who thought the old magic was nothing but a superstition, those who saw the maggots as ordinary people just trying to get by.

But Jack could already sense that the wind was shifting. These attacks were new, different, and infinitely more dangerous. If things kept up like this, the maggots would dig their own graves. And Jack would be there to bury them.

THE CUFF

1904—St. Louis

R uth looked out over the floor of her brewery and watched the final few women clean up for the night. A total of fifteen had been brought to the hospital showing signs of magic. Fifteen Sundren whose affinities had been awakened—it should have felt like more of a victory, but there certainly had been far more than fifteen people present at Lipscomb's meeting.

Perhaps others would appear tomorrow. Perhaps even now some were keeping themselves concealed because they knew what their symptoms meant. Because they knew what the world thought of the powers that were growing within them. If not, the serum would need to be adjusted further, and they were running out of time to get it right.

On the Fourth, dignitaries from all over the country would pour into the city for the Veiled Prophet Parade and Annual Ball, and her Antistasi needed to be ready. This year marked an opportunity unlike any other— with the Exposition, the Society was hosting more than their usual ball for the rich men of St. Louis. Instead, this year's ball was an attempt by the Society to wrest control of the country from the Order. A desperate bid to move the center of power from the east to the west. The list of attendees included not only the members of the Society and the usual dignitaries, who made an impressive enough target on their own, but also representatives from the various Brotherhoods across the country. Everyone of any importance would be there—politicians and titans of industry, oil barons and railroad tycoons—and most important of all, Roosevelt himself.

The boyish president was popular, but Ruth knew the truth: He was a friend only to those who could help him consolidate his power, which meant he cared nothing at all for those like her. He'd allowed the Defense Against Magic Act to pass without so much as a word against it, and now he would know the cost of that decision. If the Antistasi could unlock within him the magic that others feared, *everything* would change. A new civilization would be born, with the old magic as the equalizer between them all. But if the serum didn't work, or if it did not affect the most important targets, they would not have another chance.

Maggie was a smart girl—this early evidence of their success was proof of that. If need be, she would make the adjustments and her serum would work as it was intended. Ruth would accept no other alternative.

She turned away from her workers and went back into the solitude of her office, closing the door against the sounds of the storeroom below. In the top drawer of her desk, wrapped in a piece of flannel, was the bracelet they'd taken from the Thief when her men had searched the girl for weapons. It was an elegant silver cuff with an enormous dark gemstone that seemed to hold the colors of the rainbow within its depths.

The stone was too heavy for something so small. And it stank of magic. . . .

It wasn't the old magic, not completely. But it also wasn't the same as the objects she'd run across before, pieces like North's watch, which had been infused with freely given power to augment an affinity. The trade in those objects was cutthroat, but this piece was different. Older and more powerful.

Objects like the cuff she was holding took more than a simple ritual to create. Objects with power so deep and heavy took a life sacrifice, and they took a very special, a very rare sort of affinity.

Ruth knew that all Mageus had a unique connection to the very essence of existence. Most had an affinity that aligned with either the living, the inert, or the spirit. Affinities were as unique as people and might show up as strong or weak, as highly specialized or relatively vague.

Over time and across distance, they tended to wane. All Mageus knew that.

Once, though, there had been another kind.

Mageus with the power to affect the bonds of magic itself had always been rare. Most thought that such an affinity was nothing but a myth, like the tales of gods and goddesses of old. But every story held a kernel of truth deep within its heart, and the fear that this particular kernel would find root had been enough to spark the violent frenzy that was the Disenchantment. Those with an affinity for the very essence of magic had been eradicated, and thousands of others had become collateral damage as well.

Magic had suffered in those dark years, but it had not died, as its enemies had hoped. And it would not die now. Instead, with Ruth's plan and the help of Maggie's serum, it would flourish once more. But the appearance of this cuff was an unexpected windfall. Both the necklace and this cuff were powerful objects, capable of giving their holders power beyond the pale. Both would be essential in consolidating the Antistasi's power once magic was awoken, or at least they would once she had the necklace, too.

North appeared in the doorway of her office. "We got the two new ones set up. The girl's in with Maggie, and I locked the other one in a separate bunk. He won't be any trouble until morning, at least."

"Make sure the others know to watch him," she told him. "I want to know if there's any sign he's going to prove troublesome."

"Will do," he said, going off again into the darkened building.

Ruth wrapped the stone back in the flannel and then, for good measure, she locked it in her safe. She would keep it close, but she would keep the girl who had carried it closer. It wouldn't take much—the right words, a gentle push, and Ruth could mold the Thief into a weapon for her own use. And if the other one caused trouble? She would take care of it, just as she took care of all the problems that crossed her path.

PART

IT'S QUIET UPTOWN

1902—New York

There were too many men around, taking up the air in the place, Cela thought as she watched her brother and Jianyu eye each other from across the room. At the rate they were going, someone was going to draw first blood before morning. If the boys kept up their preening and posturing, it was going to be her.

"Would you two quit it already?" she said as she handed Abel a cup of the strong coffee she'd just brewed.

"I'm not doing anything," her brother said, still giving Jianyu an appraising glance.

"You're trying to lay him low with nothing but a look," she told him, her heart easing a bit at the very idea that he could give such a look. *Abel is alive.* "I should know, since you've tried to do it to me often enough."

"I just want to make sure we haven't made a mistake by bringing them here," her brother told her, gesturing to Jianyu and the boy they'd taken from Evelyn's apartment. "I didn't exactly ask Mr. Fortune's permission to have any more."

Abel had brought them to the house he'd been staying at ever since the fire, a nondescript building on 112th Street, in a part of town called Harlem. The building belonged to one of the publishers of the *New York Freeman*, the most important newspaper for the black community in the city. They'd apparently taken a recent interest in the labor issues that Abel had gotten wrapped up in.

"Jianyu is fine," Cela told him. "I told you already, he's a friend."

"Maybe he is, but what about that other one?" Abe asked, nodding to the white boy. He'd still been unconscious when they'd arrived uptown and was lying on his side, dead to the world.

"He's my responsibility," Jianyu said. He'd been quiet and watchful ever since they'd arrived at the building, cramped full of too many people. "I am in your debt for all that you have done for me tonight, and I will not impose on that generosity any further. I will take the boy and go."

"That's fine," Abe said, but Cela was shaking her head.

She knew what it was like to walk into Wallack's every day, the only brown face in a sea of white. It didn't matter that they wanted her there for her talent and skill. She was always separate from the rest, from the basement workroom they gave her to the way the performers acted around her. She wondered if Jianyu felt that way as well when he walked through the streets of this city that would always see him as an outsider, and whether he felt that way now, in a too-tight room filled with people he didn't know. But her brother's friends were all huddled together, turned away from the newcomers and talking among themselves.

"No," she told them. "You don't need to leave. Tell him, Abe. Tell him he's welcome to stay."

Her brother hesitated, and her irritation spiked.

"*Tell* him," she demanded. "You left me alone for nearly a week, Abel Johnson. I was at Uncle Desmond's most of that time, and you never once came for me, but Jianyu did. He got me out of that theater where that harpy actress had locked me up, so I'd say we're about equal in owing debts, wouldn't you?"

Abel frowned. "This isn't our fight, Cela," he said softly. "We have our own worries right now, our own battles to wage."

"Maybe it's not," she told him, "but have you ever considered *why* it's not?"

"Because we have enough problems without worrying about Mageus, too."

"That's what they want us to do, isn't it, though?" She was pacing now. "You don't see what Tammany is doing, offering black saloons their protection so long as we vote their way? They're not helping us. They're *using* us, same as politicians have ever done. You're fighting for better wages, aren't you? But who are you fighting? Who owns the railroads?" she asked, but she didn't give him time to answer. "I'll tell you who— they're all in the Order."

Her brother was considering her words, but he wasn't looking at her. He was staring at Jianyu like he was trying to make up his mind.

"You don't think that there are Mageus who look like us?" she asked. "Don't you remember the stories Daddy used to tell us? There were Africans who could *fly*, Abel."

"Those were just tales."

"Were they?" she asked softly. "Because he told those tales like they were the truth."

"Cela—"

"No," she said, shaking her head before he could use that condescending older-brother tone with her. "When I thought you were dead, when I was alone this last week, it changed me. I can't go back now. Maybe this isn't *your* fight, but Jianyu's my friend, so it's become *my* fight."

Jianyu was watching them, his expression unreadable. "You do not have to take on my fight," he told her. "You never should have been brought into this. Darrigan never should have involved you."

"But he did," she told him. Then she looked back at Abe. "If he goes, I go with him. I can't just hide forever, Abel. Not when I know that Evelyn has the stone, and not when I know how powerful it is. If the wrong people get that ring, who do you think they'll come after next? We won't be safe just because we don't have any magic."

Abel looked like he wanted to argue, but he was just silent for a long, heavy minute. When she saw his mouth hitch upward, she knew she'd won.

"You're worse than Mama, you know that?"

She smiled full-on then, her eyes damp with tears that she'd been holding back. "Why, Abel Johnson, that may be the nicest thing you've ever said to me."

"Don't let it go to your head, Rabbit." Then her brother's expression faltered. "What do we do with the other one?"

Cela glanced over to where the white boy had been lying. Her stomach sank. "Well, we'd have to find him before we can do anything with him," she said. Because the white boy was gone.

NIGHT WALKING

1904—St. Louis

T he room Ruth had assigned to Esta was still draped in darkness when she finally gave up trying to sleep. Too much had
happened—the missing necklace, being taken in by the Antistasi,
and the choice she'd made in that warehouse. Her thoughts felt like birds
taking flight, but she couldn't tell if they were flying toward some new
freedom or away from some unseen danger.

When Esta had dropped the package at the warehouse, she'd been
acting out of anger and desperation. Lipscomb's words had stroked that
part of her that still hurt from everything she'd lost and that craved
retribution. But the moment she'd heard the explosion, she'd realized
how far she'd gone. It was only when news had come of what the bomb
really was—what the Antistasi had truly done—that she felt as though she
could breathe again.

Ruth had awakened magic in Sundren. The idea was almost too fantastical to be true.

Except that it made a certain sense. Hadn't Professor Lachlan revealed
to her how the Order had once been Mageus? Rich men, they had come
to a new land, hiding what they were in plain sight and hoping to start
anew, without the threat of the Disenchantment and the fear of who they
were. As their magic began to fade over time, they worried that the newer
arrivals would be stronger and more powerful, so they'd built the Brink
to protect their own power. But they'd made a mistake—the Brink had
become a trap instead of a shield, and as their magic continued to fade

through the following generations, the Order themselves had eventually forgotten who they once were. Or maybe they simply refused to remember.

It was logical to think that those lost affinities could still be there, waiting below the surface to be awoken. And if that was possible, it meant that a different future was possible as well—one without the threat of divisions or the death of magic. In the version of the future that Esta had grown up in, a hundred years to come, most people believed magic was a fiction and Mageus were all but extinct. But if the Antistasi could resuscitate magic for everyone now, the future could be different. Maybe even better.

Clearly, Harte hadn't felt the same promise that Esta had at hearing the news. It wasn't long after he made his opinion known that North had escorted him from the room. Esta hadn't been able to go after him—not without losing the ground she'd gained with Ruth—but she needed to see him. Something had happened to him in the Nile, and she had a feeling it had something to do with the way he'd acted in Ruth's office.

She wasn't surprised to find the door to the room they'd put her in locked, especially after Harte's little display. She didn't blame Ruth and the rest of the Antistasi for not trusting her, despite what she'd done for them—she probably would have done the same. But a locked door had never been a problem for her, so she pulled her affinity around her and made quick work of picking the lock. She stepped over the Antistasi who'd fallen asleep at his post in the hall outside and started her search for where they'd put Harte.

She found him on the floor below, and she slipped inside the small, closet-like room before releasing her hold on time. There was a canister on the floor like the one from the wagon, probably used to make sure that he didn't cause any trouble.

Harte was sleeping on a narrow pallet, his breathing soft and even. She knelt next to him and pushed his hair back from his forehead as she whispered his name. When he didn't respond, she gave him a gentle shake until his eyes opened.

He blinked and turned toward her, finding her in the darkness of the room. "Esta?" he whispered, her name soft with sleep on his lips. His hands lifted to cup her face, his thumb brushing across her cheek and sending jolts of warmth through her.

"Are you okay?" she whispered, keeping her voice low so they wouldn't alert the guard outside his room.

He nodded as he pulled her toward him, slow and tentative, testing the moment. Lifting his head, he touched his lips against hers, so softly that her throat went tight. She felt another jolt of heat against her skin and an answering desire, and she didn't pull away. For the first time since that night they'd kissed at the boardinghouse, she felt like she could finally breathe.

Esta barely had time to register that the warmth she felt against her mouth wasn't brought on by the heat in their kiss. Just as she realized that it was the power inside Harte seeping into her, his entire body went suddenly rigid, as though all his muscles were contracting, and he jerked away from her. Scrambling upright, he retreated.

"You've come," Harte said, but it wasn't his voice she heard. There was something else to it, some other power layered over it. Impossible colors flashed in the depths of his eyes, and it wasn't completely Harte she saw looking out at her.

"What—" Her voice broke in a combination of fear and betrayal.

"I knew you would," the voice that was not Harte purred. The colors in his eyes faded, and the darkness that replaced them was pure in its emptiness, devastatingly cold and impossibly ancient. "You see the world as it is, fractured and terrible, and you have come to me, just as I predicted. I feel your anger, the rage that pulses clean and true. I can be the blade that lets you cleave the world in two."

Harte gasped, a horrible clutching sound, and then doubled over.

"Harte?" She wanted to reach for him and to back away all at the same time.

"Stay there," he rasped, breathing heavily. His jaw clenched as he fought whatever was inside of him.

She couldn't do anything more than watch and wait until, eventually, his breathing slowed and his body relaxed. When he looked at her again, it was only Harte she saw.

"What were you thinking?" he asked. "You can't just sneak up on me like that."

The sharpness in his voice cut straight through the already frayed leash that was holding her temper at bay. "What the hell, Harte? Were you there for *any* of that?" she asked, afraid to know the answer.

"You mean, do I remember kissing you?" he asked shakily. He raked his hand through his hair and looked miserable enough that she could almost forgive him for snapping at her. "I thought I was dreaming, and by the time I realized I wasn't, she'd already taken hold."

Her instincts prickled. "She?"

He let out an exhausted-sounding breath. "This *thing* inside me. I think it's a she." Then he told her everything that he'd seen when he'd lost it in the Nile—about the woman and the Book, about Thoth and the circle of stones. "Her name's Seshat. I think she's some kind of demon or something. Thoth was trying to stop her, but he didn't. And she didn't die. Part of her was trapped in the Book."

"You saw all of that?" she asked.

"More like I felt it. Like I was there, experiencing what she experienced," he said, shuddering a little at the memory. "She had stones—not the ones that the Order had, but ones like them. When Thoth destroyed them, it damaged her. I think it's what we need to do to contain her again. If we can connect the stones, we could trap that power again. We just have to figure out how to connect them."

But Esta already knew the answer to that. *She* could connect them. It was what Professor Lachlan had tried to do to her, and it was what she'd already known she would have to do if she wanted to end this madness once and for all. "We have to connect the stones through the Aether," she told him. "We'll need the Book, but once we have that, I can do it."

She reminded Harte about what had happened when she'd returned to her own time, and now she saw the moment when he realized what she meant. "No." He was shaking his head. "Absolutely not."

"It's the only way," she told him.

"I refuse to believe that," he said. "We will find another way. We'll get the Book back and there *will be* another way."

He looked so horrified and determined and ridiculously stubborn that she just nodded. "Sure," she said. Because what was the use of arguing? She wasn't there to save her own life. She was there to make sure that Nibsy couldn't win, to make sure that the Order and others like them couldn't destroy even one more future. And maybe, even to make sure that Harte could someday be free, like he'd dreamed.

"We need to go," he said, pulling himself to his feet. "We've already lost time, but if we can get back to Julien, we can figure out what the Society did with the necklace and get out of this town, just like we planned."

She was already shaking her head as he spoke. "We can't."

"We *can*," he told her, his eyes shadowed.

"The Antistasi—"

"The Antistasi aren't our problem," he said, dismissing her words before he even heard them. "The sooner we can find the Book, the sooner we can find a solution to how to control whatever this is inside me, and the sooner we can go back and stop Nibsy."

She was still shaking her head. "They have Ishtar's Key."

A CHOICE IN THE MATTER

1904—St. Louis

Harte went very still. "They have your cuff?"

Esta nodded, her expression tight. "I think they took it while we were unconscious in the wagon."

"Why didn't you say something?" he asked, feeling a bolt of panic. Without the cuff, they were stuck in 1904. Without the cuff, they couldn't control the Book, and if it got into the wrong hands . . .

"When was I supposed to tell you—while I was unconscious, or in the middle of the room while everyone was listening?" she asked, narrowing her eyes at him.

She was right. Between being captured and being separated while the Antistasi forced her to run their errands, there hadn't been any time to talk. "It's fine," he said, but he felt like he was trying to convince himself as much as her. "We'll get it back."

At first she only frowned, as though she were considering another option.

"You can steal it back," he insisted, because that much should have been readily apparent.

"I don't know if we should," she told him. "Not yet, at least."

"Of *course* we should. You're a thief, and a damn good one at that," he said, trying to figure out what she was thinking. "Why wouldn't you want to take it back?"

"I do," she insisted. "I'm just thinking . . . maybe we should wait. Hear me out," she protested, before he could argue. "We don't know where the necklace is right now."

"Julien can get that information," he reminded her. But they couldn't get to Julien as long as they were stuck here with the Antistasi.

"Sure. But what if we need more than the two of us to get it? Ruth and the Antistasi want the necklace, right? Why not use them like they're using us?"

He gave her a doubtful look. "They don't exactly seem like easy marks."

"Neither was Dolph," she argued. "But that didn't stop you from trying. Why not keep them as allies? Once they get the necklace, I can take both, and we can be gone."

Harte shook his head. "This plan of theirs—to infect people with magic—I don't like it. People should have a choice in the matter. Besides, it's dangerous, and if we get caught up in their mess, we might not get the opportunity to find the other stones."

But Esta brushed off his concern. "We won't have to get caught if we *help* them," she said.

"They're *attacking* people, Esta."

"They're *giving* them magic," she argued. "They're trying to make a difference."

Harte shook his head. *How can she not see it?* "Those people in the meeting didn't do anything to deserve what happened to them. What if they didn't *want* magic? What if they were happy with their lives as they were?"

Esta crossed her arms. "You heard what Ruth said about them—"

"Yeah," he told her before she could go on. "I heard what *Ruth* said. But we don't know those people. We don't know anything about who they are or what they've done. You're taking her word for it, when she's basically kidnapped us?"

Even in the dim light, he could see the determination in her expression, and at the sight of it, the power inside of him lurched with excitement.

"I heard the socialists talking," Esta told him. "I heard what they said about us."

Harte let out a breath. "You don't think that Ruth's attack might have just proven them right?"

Esta lifted her chin, her eyes blazing. "Maybe it was worth it if it changes things," she said.

"Esta—"

"No, Harte. Listen, we don't know where Jack or the Book are. We don't have *any* of the artifacts at this point. We are worse off than when we started," she pointed out. "The only way we know of to stop the power inside you from taking over is if I use my affinity. If it takes over—"

"It *won't*," he said, his voice hard. He would *not* allow her to sacrifice herself for him.

"*If that happens*," she repeated, "I won't be able to take you back. You'll be stuck here in 1904. If that's the case, the Antistasi might be the only chance we have left to fix the things we've changed. If their plan works, if they can really restore magic, you'll have a future. Every Mageus will. And neither Nibsy nor the Order will be in control of that future."

He shook his head, refusing to agree. "I can't believe that is our only option."

"Maybe it's not, but we have to at least consider that it might be."

"No—"

"Let's just give it a day or two," she pleaded. "We still don't know where the necklace is, and until we figure that out, we don't know if we'll need the Antistasi to get it. There's no sense burning bridges. Not until we have to."

He didn't like it. He didn't like this Mother Ruth or her Antistasi. And he didn't like how the power purred at seeing Esta so set on this path. There was something about its approval that told him this path wasn't the right choice.

But he knew Esta, and he knew that with her jaw set as stubbornly as it was now, there was no sense in arguing any further with her. Not at that moment, at least.

"Fine," Harte told her. "But at the first sign of a problem, at the first indication that things are going too far or spinning out of control, we are *gone*. We leave and we don't look back. Promise me that much, at least."

But before she could, the door to his closet-like room swung open, and North stood eyeing the two of them, his expression like flint. He stared at them for a moment, suspicion clear on his face.

How much did he overhear?

"Come on," North said, his voice as cool and flat as a penny. "The both of you."

Every one of his instincts told Harte that they should run. Now. Take the cuff and get the hell out before they were any more entangled with these Antistasi. Their fight wasn't his fight. The future they saw wasn't one he needed. But Esta gave him a pleading look, and he found himself unable to refuse.

THE AFTERMATH

1904—St. Louis

Esta glanced back to make sure that Harte was coming with her as she followed North. Somewhere deeper in the building, she heard a noise that she couldn't place until they came to a large, brightly lit room. Inside, Maggie and a couple of other women were trying to settle nearly a dozen children, most of whom were crying inconsolably.

"Thank god for more hands," Maggie said, handing the baby she was holding to Esta, who was too shocked by the whole situation to refuse the armful of squalling infant. Her arms tightened around the squirming baby, which only made the thing scream more, but at least she didn't drop it.

"Where did they all come from?" Esta asked as Maggie walked over to a toddler huddled in the corner and crouched down to brush the small girl's hair from her eyes.

At hearing footsteps behind her, Esta turned to see Ruth darkening the doorway they'd just come through.

"It seems our attack on Lipscomb struck an unexpected nerve," Ruth said. "The Guard just raided Dutchtown, probably looking for whoever carried out the attack. One of ours brought the children here. They know Maggie has a soft spot for little ones."

"But why the raid?" Maggie said as she scooped the girl into her arms. "The meeting was for the SWP. The Society should have been glad to be rid of that lot."

"I'm not sure why they retaliated," Ruth said, "but this is the effect."

"What happened to their parents?" Esta asked, adjusting the warm—maybe wet?—bundle in her arms. *Definitely wet.*

"Arrested," Ruth said. "They'll be charged and probably found guilty, which means either jail or deportation."

"But they didn't do anything," Maggie said, rocking the girl until her cries died to whimpering.

The one in Esta's arms didn't seem interested in being consoled.

"When has that ever mattered?" Ruth asked.

Esta looked around the room at the cheeks and red eyes of so many children. They should have been in the arms of their mothers or fathers, and she knew that they would always remember this moment, when the people who were supposed to protect them were torn away.

She remembered the day Dolph had taken her around the tenements of the Bowery. There she'd seen children no older than these kept indoors and away from sight so their powers wouldn't be exposed. He'd wanted to make a better life for them by destroying the Order and bringing down the Brink. He'd wanted a new future, and instead all he'd gotten was a bullet in the back. She wondered what had happened to the children he'd once protected in the two years since his death.

One thing was clear: The Society was no better than the Order. They used their Jefferson Guard to rule the city, the same as the Order used their power. It didn't matter that they were outside the Brink, on the far side of the Mississippi and on the edge of the West. Even away from the prison that was Manhattan, there wasn't any freedom here, not for Mageus. Not when the very magic that ran in their veins—the magic that was an intrinsic part of who they were—was despised and feared and hunted. Nothing would change. *Not until it was forced to.*

"North?" Ruth turned to him. "I want you to take some of our men and go round up the injured at the hospital."

"The socialists?" North asked, clearly surprised.

"The Society's retaliation was unexpected. I don't trust the Guard to look after the injured. Better to have the newly woken on our side than to have them against us," she said. Then she gave Harte and Esta appraising looks. "Take Ben with you. We'll need to get them out before dawn, and he can help you with any who prove difficult."

Harte met Esta's eyes from across the room, and she understood what he was thinking. This was exactly the type of danger he'd been worried about them getting caught up in, but standing there with an armful of squirming, screaming child, she felt even more strongly that she had to stay.

She had seen the terrible thing that lived inside Harte, and she knew now, more than ever, that she would give up herself to keep that power from breaking free. If she didn't make it, she needed to do whatever she could now to make a better future for him. She would help to ensure that neither the Order nor the Society could use the old magic against any Mageus ever again.

FERRARA'S

1902—New York

It was late morning when Viola made her excuses and left New Brighton to head south, toward the streets of the Bowery she'd once called home. Already the sidewalks were teeming with vendors selling their carts full of wares and the shoppers who were haggling for the best price. Groups of children littered the streets, playing with whatever they could find and minding themselves, since most of their parents would be working at one of the factories or sweatshops in the neighborhood. Viola remembered those days, when she'd just arrived and the streets of the city seemed like a strange and dangerous new world. She'd learned her English on those street corners, and she'd learned how different she was as well.

Putting those memories aside, Viola turned onto Grand Street, toward the gleaming glass windows and gilded sign of Ferrara's. When she stepped through the swinging door, the toasted bitterness of coffee and the sweetness of anise tickled her nose as she was enveloped in the warmth of the bakery. It smelled like her mother's kitchen at Christmas, when, even though her parents had hardly enough to pay for the roof over their heads, her mother would spend the days baking biscotti to gift to their neighbors. She'd picked this place because of the familiarity of it, because it was on her turf rather than theirs. But she'd forgotten what a powerful poison nostalgia could be. With a pang, it pulled her under and she was there again, a small girl with wild hair and a wilder heart, who had no idea how the world would try to press her small and demand things that she did not have to give.

But she wasn't that girl anymore. She understood too well now the dangers of the world, the hardness of hearts that learned early to hate.

In the back of the bakery, Ruby and Theo were already waiting for her. Ruby was dressed in another frock that made her look like a rose about to bloom, but her eyes were wide as she took everything in. On the table in front of them, a plate of pastries and three small cups of espresso sat untouched.

Viola was nearly to their table when Ruby finally saw her. Theo stood in greeting, but Viola waved him off as she slid into the seat. She was here on business, not pleasure.

"This place is a marvel," Ruby told Viola, giving her a stiff sort of smile that looked like she was trying too hard. "Thank you for sending the note," she said, taking one of the sfogliatelle from the plate of pastries. "You have news?" She took a bite of the pastry as she waited for Viola's answer.

Viola had barely opened her mouth to get to business when her words left her at the sight of the sudden rapture on Ruby's face as she ate the pastry. Her pink tongue darted out to catch the flakes of the delicate sfogliatella as she made a sound of pure satisfaction. And all Viola could do was watch, frozen with a strange combination of desire and hopelessness, as Ruby took another bite.

"Well?" Ruby glanced up at Viola, and as their eyes met, Ruby's widened just slightly and her cheeks turned a pink to outshine even the ridiculously feminine dress she was wearing.

"I think what she means to say," Theo interjected as he slid the plate closer to Viola, "is that you should try one, please, while you tell us your news."

"I know what they taste like," Viola told him, her mouth too dry to eat anyway. She gave herself a mental shake and focused on Theo, who was easier to look at. "I can tell you what they stole from the Order," she said, forging onward.

Ruby set the pastry down and leaned forward. "You can?"

Viola nodded. She still wasn't completely sure that she should reveal everything, but giving Ruby this much would be evidence that the Order's attempt to cover up the robbery was a lie. It would be one step closer in chipping away at their power. And it was that thought that spurred her into telling them about the Book and the five artifacts. "I don't know what they were," she lied, "but they were part of the Order's power."

Ruby's eyes shone. "Do you have proof?"

Only my memories, she thought as she remembered the strange chamber, the bodies they'd found there, and Darrigan's betrayal. "No, but I brought you some papers." Taking the packet from the pocket of her skirts, she slid it across the table. Within the package was evidence that connected her brother to Nibsy and the Five Pointers to the Devil's Own. "It's not enough," she told them. "But it's a start."

She almost didn't want to let the package go. It felt like the worst sort of betrayal of Dolph to point attention to the Devil's Own and the Strega. But he wasn't there anymore, she reminded herself, and if she could turn the Order on Nibsy and her brother both, they could help with the work of destroying them.

Ruby tucked the packet of papers away without so much as looking at them. "Thank you for this," she told Viola, reaching across the table and taking her hand. Ruby's cheeks went pink the moment that her gloved hand rested upon Viola's bare one, and she pulled back.

Viola glanced at Theo, and she saw him watching, his usually playful eyes serious. Which was a problem. That one, he looked like a puppy, but he saw too much, and Viola had been around long enough to know that she couldn't underestimate him.

"I think Paul has more," she told them. "There's something he's planning, something big that he keeps sending people out of the city for. I think it's connected to the Order and the items that were stolen." She frowned. Family or not, she couldn't imagine allowing her brother to ever have access to the power that the Order once had.

At the front of the bakery someone had come in and was talking in excited tones, loudly enough that it drew Theo's attention.

Ruby, realizing that he was listening, put down her pastry. "What is it?" she asked. "What are they saying?"

"Something about a fire," Viola said, translating the Italian for them. "One of the engine companies seems to be burning."

"An engine company?" Theo asked, frowning. "That's odd."

Viola listened again, following the conversation and understanding the fear in the voices. "Not so odd," she told them. "Do you know how many buildings have burned in the last week alone, all while the fire-fighters do nothing at all?"

"Why wouldn't they stop the flames?" Ruby asked, frowning at her.

"The Order has a point to make," Viola said with a shrug. She hadn't wanted to touch the offered food, because she didn't need them to buy her a thing, but Ruby still had a dusting of sugar at the corner of her mouth and Viola had to do *something* to distract herself. So she took the tazza of espresso sitting on the table in front of her and downed it in a single swallow, letting the hot bitterness of it steel her against her own stupidity.

"I don't understand," Theo said.

"Tammany controls most of the police and fire departments in this part of town," Viola explained. "The Order has been using Tammany's influence in the Bowery for revenge against what they lost for almost two weeks now."

"They're looking for the artifacts?" Ruby asked.

"And sending a message." Viola frowned as she listened to the man's voice rise in volume.

"Now what's he saying?" Ruby asked, leaning forward.

Viola wanted to reach across the table and brush the sugar from the corner of the other girl's mouth, but she wrapped her fingers in her skirts and held herself back instead. "It seems that things are turning," Viola said. Ruby was watching her again with those eyes the color of the ocean. They would pull her under if she wasn't careful.

"What do you mean?"

She didn't need to tell them any more. They didn't have to know. But there was something about the way Ruby was looking at her, so earnestly—as though maybe she saw Viola as a friend, as an equal—and Viola spoke before she could stop herself. "According to those men, water isn't even touching the fire," she told them. "The flames are being fed by magic."

THE NEWLY WOKEN

1904—St. Louis

N orth didn't really care what Maggie said about giving the new guy a chance, and he didn't care that the Thief had managed to deliver the device like she was supposed to. He'd found them too late to hear much of what they'd been talking about. But he still didn't trust either one of them, even if Ruth was starting to. Which was why he found himself sitting next to the one who called himself Ben as they drove the brewery's wagon toward the hospital to collect their new brothers-in-arms before the Guard could get to them. After the rounding up of the Mageus over in Dutchtown, Mother Ruth wasn't taking any chances. Considering that Ben looked like a born liar, North wasn't taking any chances either.

The hospital was on the north end of town, far from the excitement of the Exposition. It was still the dead of night, so they didn't pass more than one or two other travelers on the road. Rescuing the newly awoken should be an easy enough job, considering that they had one of their own on the inside working as a night charge.

He gave the horses another gentle flick of the reins to urge them on. Easy or not, the faster it was over with, the better. Next to him, Ben was silent, but North could feel the weight of his stare as he drove. After a couple of miles, he'd had about enough.

"You have a problem?" he asked, glaring at Ben. "Something you want to say?"

At first North didn't think he would answer, but then he spoke.

"Your tattoo . . . ," Ben said, and there was something funny about his voice.

North had heard enough about the mark he chose to wear on his arm in the years since he'd gotten it, which was why he usually kept the tattoo covered. But he hadn't bothered to button the sleeves of the shirt he'd tossed on when he'd been woken about the kids, and as he'd driven the horses, his sleeves had fallen back to reveal the dark circle that ringed his left wrist.

"What about it?" North asked, lifting his chin and daring him to say something.

"I knew someone who had a tattoo something like that," Ben said.

"I doubt that." He rotated his wrist to reveal the bracelet of ink formed by a skeletal snake eating its own tail. "Not unless he was Antistasi."

"It was *something* like that," Ben said, frowning down at it. "Is that what the symbol is—the mark of the Antistasi?"

"This symbol?" North said. "It's an ouroboros, which goes back way before the Antistasi. But, yeah, the Antistasi adopted it, probably sometime during the Disenchantment. They used it as a sign so they could identify each other," he said, pulling his sleeve back down. This time he fastened the cuff to hide the mark from view.

"You had to accept it, then, to be part of Ruth's organization?" Ben asked. North could tell he was trying to keep his tone light, but he was failing miserably.

"I didn't *have* to do anything," North said. He'd had the tattoo since he was sixteen, a promise to himself and to the father he'd lost. It was sheer luck that he'd run into Mother Ruth and her people not long after that, and even better luck that she'd taken him in. "Nobody is forced to take the sign. It's not the Middle Ages anymore."

"But you *did* take it."

"Because I liked what it stood for," North explained, answering the implied question. "The snake eating its own tail is an ancient symbol for eternity. Infinity." *Rebirth.* He'd been a different person before, and the serpent on his wrist reminded him he'd be a different person yet again someday.

"The serpent separates the world from the chaos and disorder it was formed from," Ben said, as if he knew something about it. "Life and death, two sides to the same coin, as my friend used to say. You can't have one without the other."

North frowned, not sure what to make of Ben's statement. He'd never thought of it like that, and he wasn't sure he cared to. "The Antistasi use it because it represents magic itself. Because everything in the world—the sun and the stars and even time itself—it all begins and ends with magic."

"And if magic ends," Ben said, his voice low and solemn, "so does the world."

North huffed out his disagreement. "Magic can't end," he said. "That's what the symbol shows. Magic has no beginning and no end. Since the Disenchantment, they've tried to snuff us out and kill us off, but they haven't been able to. We learn and bend, and then we change."

"You believe that?" Ben asked, looking at North with curious eyes.

"You don't?" North tossed back.

But Ben didn't answer, and it was too late anyway, because they'd arrived.

North pulled the wagon around back, just like they'd agreed to, and gave the signal—a couple of sharp whistles that were returned in kind. A few minutes later the back gates of the hospital opened and their work started in truth.

There were about a dozen people to move. One had his hands wrapped in gauze, and they all had a sleepy, docile quality to them.

"What's wrong with them?" Ben asked. "Did the serum do this?"

North shook his head. "This isn't the serum. The hospital doped them up to make sure they can't do anything. Morphine, probably." He understood why the nurses had drugged them. The newly made Mageus had caused too many problems because they didn't know how to control their powers.

He'd understood what Ruth's goal was in giving these people magic, but seeing it up close like this—it wasn't what he'd expected. Ruth had talked about freeing something inside these people, but they didn't look free. They looked worn and tired and like they'd been dragged through the mud and back. And they looked scared.

The last one out was a young woman who couldn't have been more than eighteen. Her blond hair hung limp around her face, and the smattering of freckles across her nose gave her the look of someone much younger. Like the rest, she had a stunned look to her, but unlike the others, she stopped to speak to North.

"Who are you?" she asked. "Where are you taking us?"

"We're friends," North assured her. "And we're here to take you somewhere safe."

She frowned at him, her eyes still glassy from the drug. "The hospital isn't safe?"

North sighed, feeling every minute of the sleep he was missing. He didn't have time to explain the reality of the girl's new world to her. "What's your name?" he asked instead.

"Greta," the girl said, frowning sleepily at him.

"Do you know what's happening to you, Greta?"

She shook her head. Her eyes shone with unshed tears. "I don't mean to do it, but I can't stop it. . . ."

"It's okay, sweetheart. Something inside you's woken up, that's all. The old magic is yours now." He tried to infuse his voice with the same reverence that Ruth used, but it didn't come out right, and the girl only frowned at him more.

"Mr. Lipscomb—Caleb. There was an explosion. Is he—"

"He'll be just fine," North assured her.

"They wouldn't tell us anything. They kept us locked up but wouldn't tell us what was going on."

Of course. Now that these poor souls had the old magic, they'd be treated like the pariahs they'd become. "We're here to free you," he said gently.

But her chin trembled, and the next thing North knew, the girl's cheeks were wet. He thought it was from tears, but a moment later North realized his cheeks were wet too.

"It's raining," Ben said, looking up. "There's not a cloud in the sky, and it's raining."

"I'm sorry." Greta sniffed. "I don't know why that keeps happening. I don't know how to make it stop."

North didn't know what to tell her. He'd imagined the people they'd given magic to as reborn, but these poor souls looked more like they were ready to curl up and die. He didn't have the words to comfort that kind of sorrow, and he wondered if he had any right, considering what his part in it had been. Without another word, he helped Greta into the back of the wagon. Before closing the door, he popped the fuse on a bottle of Maggie's Quellant and tossed it in with them.

"Is that really necessary?" Ben asked. "They could barely walk as it is. I doubt they're going to cause any trouble."

"They're like children," North explained. "They don't know how to control what they have. We got one in there who sets fire to his own hands because he can't stop it and another one who leaves a trail of growing vines on everything she touches. It's a long ride back to the brewery, and we can't risk them not being able to hold themselves together until they're safely back and we can show them how to control it." He glanced over at Ben. "You remember what it was like, don't you? When you were just a kid and you didn't realize everything you could do?"

"Yeah . . ." Ben's voice held the ghost of some past regret in it. "I remember."

"There you go," North said, climbing up into the driver's seat of the wagon and knowing without a doubt that he wasn't the only one with ghosts following his footsteps through life.

Bringing up his childhood apparently was enough to shut Ben up good and tight, which was fine by North. He didn't care to deal with any talking when he had thinking to do.

They rode in silence back through town to the brewery, with the first light of dawn setting the horizon aglow. But it was Ben who saw the smoke first.

"What's that?" he asked, pointing in the direction of a glowing place on the horizon, where a plume of black rose up like a nightmare, blocking the stars in the sky.

The brewery was on fire.

LIBITINA

1902—New York

By the time Viola made sure that Theo and Ruby were headed toward the safety of their own part of town and she made her way back to the New Brighton, Paul had already heard about the fire. He was pacing and shouting at his men, while the one they called Razor stood nervous and waiting nearby.

"Where have you been?" Paul asked, turning on her the second she was through the door. His face was mottled an ugly, angry red.

"Out," she told him, pretending that she didn't notice his agitation.

"Out?"

She shrugged. "I needed air." After the meeting with Ruby, she *still* felt like she needed air, not that Paul had to know about that.

"I needed you here," he snapped. "Station thirty-three, she's on fire, and it isn't any normal fire." He glared at her as though it were somehow her fault.

"You think *I* did this?" She glared at him in return.

"You were, as you said, *out.*"

She frowned, realizing that all of the Five Pointers were now watching her with a question in their eyes. "Fire is not my style, Paolo. You know that."

"If that station burns, Tammany is not gonna be happy," Razor said. "We have to do something."

Paul let out a frustrated growl and took Viola by the arm. "These are your people, so you're going to help me."

By the time they got over to the station, the air was heavy with smoke. Flames were tearing from the arching windows, and the front of the brick building was black with soot as the fire brigade pumped water toward the blaze. The steady stream from the pump truck didn't seem to be doing anything to stop the fire, probably because the heat of the flames wasn't the only warmth in the air.

Someone with an affinity for fire had to be nearby, feeding the flames, but where? She scanned the crowd, searching for some sign. The old magic was about connecting with the larger world, so it required focus and often needed contact—a sight line or direct touch. Whoever was at fault would be close.

"Find the maggot doing this or don't bother coming back to the New Brighton," Paul said.

Viola shrugged off the slur on her brother's lips. He'd called her worse. "And what am I supposed to do when I find him?"

"You're my blade, aren't you?" Paul glared at her.

"I don't have a knife," she told him. "You made sure of that."

"How many times do I have to tell you, you don't need one?" he said, his meaning clear. "Go on. Before it's too late."

She thought about arguing, but before she could, she heard the shattering of glass as a window cracked and flames poured out of it. If this station was destroyed by someone with the old magic, Tammany would retaliate. Innocent people would be at risk of being caught in the cross fire.

Without much choice, Viola ducked into the crowd, her eyes sharp for some sign of the perpetrator as she focused the warm energy that had nothing to do with the flames. She was halfway through the crowd when she saw a familiar figure standing on the steps of a building about half a block away. *Nibsy Lorcan.*

The boy's gold-rimmed spectacles flashed in the light from the blaze, and next to him was a boy with hair the color of flame focusing all his attention on the burning fire station.

She sent her affinity out, searching for the heat of the boy's affinity, the beating of his heart, and when she founded it, she tugged, just a little. Not enough to kill him, but more than enough to make him collapse to the ground.

Nibsy watched him go down, and then he began to scan the crowd. A moment later he found her, and his mouth curved up, as though he knew exactly how useless she'd become.

Too soft, an assassin who couldn't properly kill.

But that boy—he'd been one of Dolph's once. What was his name? She couldn't remember, but she knew that he wasn't the one who needed killing. That honor belonged to Nibsy, who was smiling at her as though he knew what she was thinking—and didn't care.

What she would give to wipe that smile from his face.

Viola let her affinity find the steady pulsing of the blood in his veins and reveled in the understanding that she held Nibsy's life. It would be so easy to end him. She could trade what was left of her soul for vengeance for Dolph's murder. Her soul, tarnished as it was, was hardly a worthy trade, but in that moment she felt as though it might do.

Better. She would kill him with her own hands.

Around her the street was in chaos. The crowd, who had gathered to watch a fire that could not be quenched, jeered their disappointment as the water began to have an effect on the flames. But Viola barely heard the noise, and though her eyes watered from the smoke, she didn't care as she walked toward Nibsy.

He started down from his perch, to meet her halfway. The nearer she came, the more amusement shone in his eyes.

"I hope you've made peace with your god, Nibsy," she said as she approached him. "I've come for you."

He didn't so much as flinch. "If I believed in a god, I would have lost faith in him years ago. You don't scare me, Viola. If you wanted to kill me, I've no doubt I would already be dead."

She curled her mouth into a deadly smile. "Perhaps, in your case, I prefer to play with my prey."

"I see that spending time with your family has only improved your delightful personality," Nibsy said, rocking back on his heels a bit.

"Bastardo," she spat. She would wipe the smugness from his face, and she would do it with her bare hands.

"I'm not your enemy, Viola," he said softly.

"Funny," she said. "You look just like him. I know what you did, how you betrayed Dolph. How you betrayed all of us."

"I never betrayed you. Dolph Saunders was a danger to himself and to our kind. He would have started a war that we couldn't have won. I protected the Devil's Own—and all of those like us," he said, sounding like he actually believed it.

"I never needed your protection," she sneered.

"No?" he asked, his tone mocking. "You're enjoying your time with your brother, then?" When she only glared at him, he spoke again. "You were meant for more than being Paul Kelly's scullery maid, Viola. Yes, I know how he uses you. He brags about it to me. *His blade.* His sister, who has learned her place." Nibsy shook his head. "Some blade—sharp enough to cut his potatoes and not much else these days, from what I hear."

"I could cut *you*," she told him.

"With what?" he asked, taunting her. "You miss her, don't you?" he asked, the glint in his eyes mocking her as much as his words.

Libitina. "You aren't man enough to wield her. But don't worry. I'll take her from you soon, and then I'll cut your heart out and leave it on Dolph's grave as a tribute."

"So bloodthirsty," he said, a laugh in his eyes. Then his face grew serious. "You're welcome to try to take your knife, but I'd rather *give* her to you."

She narrowed her eyes. It was a trick. This one, he was slippery as an eel, and just as treacherous. "Why would you? A boy as smart as you pretend to be should know I would only turn around and sink her into your heart."

"Because, despite everything that's passed between us, I think we could be friends."

A FINAL GAMBIT

James Lorcan watched the disbelief flash in Viola's eyes and then harden into hatred.

"Never," she said, practically spitting the word.

It was no more than he'd expected, but it wasn't enough to dissuade him. He inclined his head, conceding her point. "Then allies, perhaps."

She shook her head, and he knew she wanted to argue—she *always* wanted to argue—but he continued before she could deny it.

"We want the same thing, don't we?" he asked, measuring her mood. True, she could kill him in a blink, knife or no, but he knew her weakness, the secret that Dolph had hidden from everyone else—a misplaced sense of morality that kept her from killing with her affinity. Besides, if there had been any indication that she might strike, he would have known long before she did. So he pressed on. "We both want the end of the Order. Freedom for our kind."

"Dolph wanted those things as well, but you killed him," she pointed out.

"*Is* that what he wanted? Truly?" James paused, letting his words penetrate. He'd watched Dolph and Viola in the days before everything fell apart. Dolph's preoccupations had made this particular play more than easy for him. "Did Dolph tell you that himself? I don't think he did. He never told any of us the entirety of his plans. He didn't tell you what might happen at Khafre Hall, did he? He let you walk into a trap set by Darrigan without bothering to warn you."

He watched as her jaw tensed, but she didn't deny it—she couldn't.

"I would wager the Strega itself that he didn't tell you how he drove Leena to her grave."

"Lies," she hissed. "He did no such thing. He would never have hurt her."

James forced himself to keep his expression doleful and to hide every ounce of satisfaction this conversation was giving him. "You wear his mark, don't you, Viola? How do you think he found the power to make them into weapons against us?" he asked. "He took it from her. Why else would she have been taken so easily by the Order?"

She shook her head, as though refusing these truths, but he could tell that his words were worming their way beneath her skin, wriggling into her thoughts. Eating away at her sureness.

"You don't have to take my word for it," James said, pulling a package from his coat. "Here—" He offered it to her.

The moment she took the paper-wrapped parcel in her hands, he could tell she knew what it was. Her eyes narrowed at him, as though waiting for the trick. She wasn't stupid, after all. But that didn't mean that she was any match for *his* cunning.

"It's just a little gift, to show that I mean you no harm. You'll find everything you need to know within it," he told her. Thanks to the notebooks in the apartment, he could offer her proof in Dolph's own hand that everything he'd told her was true . . . or at least it would appear so. "Unlike Dolph, I don't keep secrets from my friends."

"We are *not* friends, and I don't need your tricks," she told him, but he didn't miss the way she held the package close to her. "But I will keep my knife."

"No tricks, Viola." He took a step back and started to go. He took three steps toward where Mooch was still lying unconscious—but not dead—on the ground. He gave her those three steps to think about all that had just happened, to let her doubts start to grow, before he turned back to her. "One thing, though. Why are you so sure that *I'm* the traitor?

What of Jianyu? He wasn't with us on the bridge. He's never returned to the Strega. I'm convinced he was working with Darrigan."

"Why would he?" she asked.

"Why not?" James said. "He wasn't ever really one of us, was he? I always told Dolph he was too soft for trusting one of them. But if you don't believe me, perhaps you can ask Jianyu yourself. I'd put good odds on him being at the Order's big gala. Word is that one of the artifacts might turn up there—a ring that has the power to amplify an affinity. Jianyu has already tried to get it for himself once. I imagine he'll try again."

And when the two of them faced off against each other, James would be the one left standing.

A BLIND RUSH OF FEAR

1904—St. Louis

In the driver's seat beside Harte, North urged the horses on as they raced toward the burning brewery, but the tired team barely picked up any speed. Or at least that was how it felt to Harte, who watched the flames grow in ferocity as they approached.

By the time they pulled into the driveway, at least half the brewery's warehouse—where the kegs of prepared ale and lager were stored—was completely in flames. The main building, with the offices and bunk rooms, wasn't burning, but Harte wouldn't feel better until he saw Esta for himself, safe and whole.

At the thought of losing Esta, it wasn't only Harte who felt the blind rush of fear. The demon inside of him, Seshat, was also afraid. He could feel her pawing and clawing at him, urging him on with a desperation that let him know exactly how important Esta was to both of them.

He jumped from the moving wagon as North slowed and ran toward Ruth, who was standing in a small clutch of people with her hands on her hips and murder in her eyes.

"What happened?" North gasped.

The flickering light of the flames only served to highlight the furious expression on Ruth's face. "We've been accused of aiding criminals," Ruth said, her voice jagged with anger. Her eyes darted to a line of men in dark coats with familiar armbands. *The Guard.*

"Criminals?" Harte asked.

"It doesn't matter," Ruth told him. "They've drummed up some false charge, and now they're making their point because we dared to help the children."

"The Guard started the fire?" Harte asked.

"Not that there'll be any proof of it," Ruth told him. "They have people who can start fires without touching a match, same as us. They've just chosen the other side."

"Where's Esta?" Harte asked, looking around the group that had gathered and not finding her.

"She's with Maggie and a couple of the others," Ruth said. "They're getting the children out the back, so the Guard doesn't notice."

"I'll help," Harte said, and took off toward the building.

"They won't let you through," Ruth called, but Harte wasn't listening. All he could think about was finding Esta and making sure that she was safe.

He had just reached the line of Guardsmen when an explosion erupted, and windows on one side of the main building shattered as flames burst from them. Harte picked up his pace, but Ruth had been right. He hadn't taken more than a few steps before the Guards were on him, roughly wrestling him back.

"No one crosses," the tallest of them said. His mouth hitched up. "For safety reasons."

"There could be people in there," Harte said, lunging toward them again in an attempt to get past, but there were five of them, and it was easy enough for them to push him back.

There was dark smoke pouring from the doors of the main building, where the large vats of lager were fermenting. Flames had already started eating the roof, but in front of them, a line of Guards was preventing anyone from doing anything to stop the fire.

A moment later, North was at his side.

"Maggie's in there," North told him, and Harte heard his own fear echoed in North's voice.

"Ruth said there was a back entrance?" The fire hadn't reached the end of the building that housed the living quarters, but the smoke would be a problem. "Maybe they're already out."

"There is a back entrance, but there's also a dozen babies to get out of there." North looked at the burning warehouse, where the flames had grown to consume even more of the building. "If that fire starts to spread—"

"Is there a way around back?" Harte asked.

North gave him a tense nod. "But if we go now, we might draw their attention. They'd have Maggie and the kids."

"So we split up," Harte told him. "I'll distract them, and you go around back."

North's brows drew together, and Harte knew North was considering how much to trust him.

"Go on," Harte said. "You can hate me later."

He didn't wait for North's agreement but went charging into the line of Guards, pulling at his affinity as he went. He had time to land one punch before the others were on him, but one punch was enough—fist to face—to change the Guardsman's intent. The Guardsman turned on his brothers and attacked. In the confusion, Harte managed to get his hands on two of the others, and in moments, they were fighting each other instead of him. He took the opportunity the confusion offered and slipped past, running as fast as he could toward the now-burning main building.

The front doors were open, and Harte could already feel the heat coming from inside the building, but he didn't stop to think about that. All he could think was that without Esta, he was lost. But what that meant—whether it was him or the power that spurred him on—he didn't bother to analyze too closely.

The fire seemed contained to the east side of the building. If he hurried, he could make sure Esta and the kids got out the back. He darted inside, pulling his shirt up over his mouth and nose to ward off the smoke that already hung heavy in the air. The main brewing chamber was a mess. The heat from the flames had already caused one of the giant vats of beer to explode, and Harte didn't want to be around if another one blew. He took the steps up to the offices quickly, breathing only sporadically, to avoid the smoke. The bunk rooms were empty, so he moved on to the nursery, calling Esta's name and not caring who heard him.

When he got to the nursery, the room was—thankfully—empty. *They must have gotten out.* Which meant that he had to get himself out.

Harte was halfway down the hall when another explosion hit, throwing him from his feet and knocking him into the wall. He staggered to his knees, steadying himself as he heard a crackling and another explosion. And then the ceiling broke open above him.

INTO THE FIRE

1904—St. Louis

Esta was helping lift one of the children into a wagon that had been waiting in the yard behind the warehouse when she heard the explosion and turned to see the main building go up in flames behind her.

We were just in there. A matter of a few moments and they would have *still* been in there.

Maggie gasped, her hand to her mouth as she adjusted the toddler on her hip. "No," she whispered. "No, no, no . . ."

Esta set the child she was holding into the wagon and turned to take the one from Maggie, who let go of it reluctantly. Her eyes were wide and glassy as she watched her family's business burn.

"We're safe," she told Maggie. "The kids are safe too. You can rebuild anything else."

But Maggie was shaking her head, and Esta couldn't tell if she was disagreeing or if she simply couldn't even hear her from the shock of it. North was there a moment later, taking Maggie in his arms like he didn't care who saw. His face relaxed in relief as he held on to her, whispering into her hair.

The last child had just been loaded into the wagon along with the dozen or so patients they'd rescued from the hospital when Mother Ruth came around the side of the building with a small group of people.

"Where's Har—Ben?" Esta said, correcting herself before she uttered the wrong name. He wasn't with the rest of the group.

"He's not with you?" North said, turning to Ruth.

Another explosion echoed from within the building.

Ruth shook her head. "Last I saw him, the crazy fool was running into the building."

"He thought you all might still be in there," North said, his voice sounding as hollow and shocked as Esta felt at the idea of Harte being inside of that building.

"He's inside?" Esta asked, the words clawing themselves free from the tightness in her throat. Above them, the roof of the main building crackled and shifted. As if reading her mind, Maggie grabbed her wrist.

"You can't—"

Esta tore her arm away and started running.

As soon as she was close, she pulled time slow and stepped through the doorway of the burning building without looking back.

She had no idea where Harte would be, but she'd start at the nursery. If he'd come in looking for her, that was where he would have gone.

The heat of the fire radiated in the passageways around her, but the flames themselves had gone still, like brilliant flowers blooming on the walls and ceilings. She couldn't stop time completely, so she couldn't stop the process of oxygen consumed by the fire. The heat was a constant, and the air hung heavy with deadly smoke, but she wouldn't stop. She *couldn't*. Not until she found Harte.

Esta's chest clenched when she turned into the hallway where the nursery waited and saw the pile of burning rubble. She nearly lost her hold on her affinity when she saw the shoe peeking out of it.

She didn't waste any time in starting to move the pieces of ceiling that had fallen on Harte, but it was taking too long. She uncovered his face and saw that his eyes were open—he wasn't dead, but he also wasn't any help, nearly frozen as he was. Considering her options, she let go of the seconds. The flames crackled to life in a roaring blaze, and Harte gasped as more pieces of the ceiling fell.

His eyes met hers, his face blanching when he saw her standing there above him.

"Help me," she said, trying to pull more of the rubble off him.

She could hear the building creaking as they worked, until finally he was free of the large piece that had pinned his legs down. "Can you walk?" she asked, coughing from the heat and the smoke.

"I think so," he told her, getting to his feet but tottering a little. She caught him before he could fall.

"Can't you . . . ?" He meant that he wanted her to stop time.

"No," she said. "Not with you. The building's too unstable." She could tell he wanted to argue, but she didn't give him the chance. With her shirt up over her nose and mouth, they moved as fast as they could through the hallway, toward the back of the building.

They were almost out when Esta stopped.

"What are you doing?" Harte asked, pushing her onward.

"My cuff. Ishtar's Key is in here," she said.

"Do you know for sure?" He coughed.

She shook her head. "But if it is . . ." The fire had started unexpectedly, and Ruth had been too busy arguing with the Guard—distracting them, so Maggie could get the children out—to do anything else. Maybe it wasn't in here, but she couldn't take that chance. "I can't leave without it," she said, turning back into the fire. Without it, they would be trapped there with no way back. And no way to set things right.

"No, Esta—" He grabbed at her hand.

"Let go," she told him, trying to shake him loose. But he was too stubborn, and already she could feel the heat of the power within him creeping against her skin, as stark and real as the fire.

"I'm not leaving you here. It's not worth dying for."

But hadn't she already made that decision? "I'm dead either way."

He shook his head and was about to argue with her, but she cut him off.

"I need that stone, but I can't do this with you, Harte. Not with whatever is inside you. Let me go, and I can at least try. I got *you* out, didn't

I?" She could tell he wanted to disagree, but he couldn't argue with that point. "I'll be back outside before you even notice."

"No, Esta," he said, tightening his hold on her arm until his fingers were digging painfully into her skin. There was something dark in his expression, a desperation that was stark and pure. In that moment, she couldn't tell what it was moving behind his eyes—whether it was he himself who cared that desperately or if it was something else. Seshat. The demon-like power inside of him—did Seshat know that the stones would be her undoing?

That thought made up her mind for her. "I'm sorry," she said, as she wrenched his arm to the side and laid him flat on his back. The moment his hand released her, she pulled time slow and dodged back into the flames once more.

A PEONY IN A TOMATO PATCH

*L*ies. Viola knew that the words coming from Nibsy's mouth were as foul and polluted as the muck that flowed in the sewer, and now that she had Libitina in her hands once more, she would show him what she thought of his lies. She began to unwrap the comforting weight of the knife when, from the corner of her eye, she saw a flash of pink that was utterly out of place in the dreary, sooty air of the Bowery.

She should have known that the girl wasn't going to listen to her and go back uptown, where she belonged. She shouldn't have been surprised to find Ruby there, craning her neck to see what was happening with the fire and looking every bit like a peony in a tomato patch.

Ruby was too engrossed in trying to see what was happening, but from the look of concentration and worry on Theo's face, he had realized that the crowd's mood was turning now that the steady stream of water was beginning to extinguish the blaze. With their source of entertainment dying, they were beginning to grow restless and rowdy.

Viola's instinct was to go to them. Neither of them belonged in the rough world of lower Manhattan, not like she did. But there was Nibsy to think of, and her revenge was so close she could taste the sweetness of it in the back of her throat.

Torn, Viola turned back to Nibsy, only to find that the rat was no longer there. She saw him, already a ways off, disappearing into the crowd and leaving the red-haired boy prone on the ground. *Dolph would never have done such a thing.*

But the boy wasn't her concern. He'd cast his lot when he'd started the fire.

Instead of going for him, she headed toward where Ruby and Theo were being jostled by the increasingly restless crowd. She was nearly to them when she saw that just beyond Ruby, her brother was heading in her direction. And he had John Torrio with him.

Viola could see what would happen—Torrio would catch sight of Theo, thinking he was Reynolds, and he would know that she had not killed the reporter. It would not matter that Theo hadn't ever been the target. All that would matter was that he would be proof that Viola had betrayed her charge, and more, she'd stopped Torrio from completing the job. If Torrio saw Theo and Ruby, if he realized what Viola had—or rather, had *not*—done, she'd be dead. And what's more, Theo and Ruby would both be dead, as well.

Waving her arms, Viola ran toward her brother and Torrio, trying to draw their attention so they would not turn slightly to the left and notice Ruby, pink and petaled as a flower. Because they would not fail to see her, not with how polished and delicate she looked amid the toughs of the Bowery.

"Paolo!" she called, desperate to reach him, but they were both searching the crowd, not hearing her. She shouted again, her voice clawing from her throat as he moved closer to where Ruby and Theo stood watching the fire.

Finally, Paul noticed her, and then Torrio did as well. When they saw Viola, they turned away from their original path—the one that would have taken them to Ruby—and came toward Viola instead.

"What is it?" Paul asked, his expression conveying his disappointment that she didn't have the culprit in hand.

"The one who did this, he's there, on the ground," she told him, pointing to the spot where the boy still lay, unconscious from her magic. "A red-haired boy, maybe fifteen years old. One of Nibsy Lorcan's boys."

"One of Lorcan's?" Paul asked, his expression filled with suspicion. "Are you sure?"

Viola nodded, keeping her expression steady even as she let her affinity unfurl to find Ruby's now-familiar heartbeat in the crowd. When she found it, steady and calm, she knew the girl was still safe—for the moment, at least.

Paul glanced at Torrio, sharing some unspoken communication between them before he turned back to her. "Did you take care of him?"

"Better," she told Paul. "I left him for you. A gift for Tammany," she explained.

"That wasn't what you were told to do," Paul said. "I told you to kill him."

"Killing him is no good. Think of it," she argued, before he could interrupt again. "If I killed him, what proof do you have that you've caught the one responsible? You can't tell if a dead man is Mageus. You can't ask him why he attacked or who he worked for. This way, you have the boy—you have *evidence*," she said. *Which means that you have proof that Nibsy is not to be trusted.* "Take him to Tammany and give them the favor of dealing with him themselves. They'll thank you for it."

Torrio was eyeing her suspiciously, but she didn't give him so much as a glance. Whatever Paul might want for the two of them, Viola wasn't interested.

Before Paul could agree or argue, Viola sensed the fluttering of Ruby's heart. The steady rhythm gave way to a more rapid beat, and Viola knew something was happening. "Quickly!" she shouted, pointing in the direction she'd left the boy.

Her actions had their intended effect. Paul and Torrio turned, almost as one, and the second their attention was diverted, she darted into the crowd to look for the birdbrained girl who was about to get herself killed.

DRAGGED UNDER

1902—New York

Even from her place far back in the crowd, Ruby Reynolds could feel the heat of the strange flames that were consuming the engine house. Now that she was standing amid the rabble and the crowd, she could tell for herself that what was happening had everything to do with magic. A moment before something had changed, and the water that had been streaming from the hoses began to have an effect on the flames.

The crowd had not liked that, not *at all*.

"We need to go," Theo said, using his body as a shield against the restlessness of the crowd.

"Just a minute more," she pleaded. "If we could only get a little closer . . ."

"We're *not* going any closer," he told her in a tone he rarely used on her.

"But, Theo—"

She barely had his name on her tongue when the crowd surged and she stumbled with it to the left. Suddenly, she was aware that what had been avid interest colored by excitement when she and Theo arrived had quickly turned to frustration, maybe even anger. Once, when she was younger, her father had taken her and her sisters to Coney Island to play in the surf, and she had ventured too far into the waves and had been dragged under. Being caught up in the suddenly raucous crowd reminded her of that moment, and she felt the same pang of betrayal she'd felt as a child when the water had turned against her.

At the time, her father had caught her up under the arms and set her back on her feet as though nothing had happened. Now Theo did what he could to shield her from the other bodies that were pressing and shoving against them, the dear, but it was all she could do to stay on her feet.

It was unbearably exciting.

From the look on his face, Theo didn't feel the same. *The poor dear.* He always had been so buttoned up and careful. But he'd also been her truest friend, through everything—her father's breakdown and the embarrassment it had caused her family and her mother's meddling to get all her daughters married off after his death. And then there was society's constant judgment. Not that she cared a fig for their judgment, but society made things so much harder than they needed to be. And through all of it, Theo had been there.

She was the worst sort of person to put him through this, and yet, if she could just figure out how the fire started—

"Ruby!" The voice cut through the noise around them. "Theo!"

Ruby turned and realized it was Viola, her violet eyes blazing with something that looked incredibly like fear. "Viola?"

She barely had time to recognize a warmth flush through her that had nothing to do with the fire before the crowd surged, pushing them to the left. Ruby staggered away from Theo, losing her balance, and fell into Viola. She had a moment to appreciate the other girl's strength. Viola was shorter than Ruby herself, but beneath the softness of her curves, her body was sturdy and strong enough to keep Ruby on her feet.

For a moment the connection between them felt absolutely undeniable. Her stomach fluttered as her chest went tight, and she felt the entire world narrow down to the piercing violet of Viola's darkly lashed eyes.

Viola froze, her arms going rigid around Ruby, and in that moment, the crowd fell away and there was a roaring in her ears as she was sure, *sure* that Viola had felt the same energy between them. But Viola simply set Ruby upright again and stepped back.

"Come on," Viola told them, taking hold of Ruby's wrist. "You need to get out of here. This way."

The warmth that had coursed through Ruby just a moment before cooled, but her skin was still hot where Viola's fingers circled her wrist. She tried to jerk away, but Viola held firm and turned to her.

"We need to go. *Now*," Viola commanded, glancing to Theo for support.

"She's right," he told her, his expression apologetic. "It's not safe here."

Safe? What was safety but a cage? Her whole life had been designed to keep her safe—away from trouble, away from harm—away from anything real or important. *No.* She'd made the decision that she wasn't interested in "safe" the day they found her father in his study, driven mad by his own obsession with safety. He'd tried to master magic, just as the men in the Order had instructed, and it had mastered him instead. No, not just mastered him, *destroyed* him—and it had nearly destroyed her entire family along with him.

Now Ruby was interested only in *truth*, and the truth was that no male journalist in her position would run because of a little scuffle.

"I can't leave now," she told her. "I need to find out what happened. The story—"

"It's not safe here for you," Viola said, pulling at her arm.

"I don't care," Ruby said, her face creased in frustration.

"Ruby—" Theo tried.

"No, Theo. We came to see the fire, and I'm going to see the fire." She turned to Viola, her veins warming with her determination. "If the flames weren't natural, I need to know. Don't you see how important this is?"

"It won't be important if you're dead," Viola said, struggling to stay upright in the tumultuous crowd.

There were worse things than dying, Ruby thought, thinking of her father in the sanitarium upstate before he died finally and her sisters, who sometimes loved their husbands but often did not. And of herself, forced to live stuck in a narrow slice of a life that should be so much bigger, so much *wider*.

"I think we should listen to Miss Vaccarelli," Theo told her. *The traitor.*

LISA MAXWELL

But Ruby shook her head and pushed her way farther into the crowd.

She hadn't gone more than three steps when a man nearby threw a punch that transformed the crowd into a cascading wave of violence. The people around her shoved, some diving into the fray and others desperately trying to retreat, and in that moment, she had the first inkling of fear. She stumbled back, and Theo was there, just as he always was.

Please, his familiar eyes pleaded, and as much as she wanted to be stronger, as much as she wanted to stand firm, she couldn't deny him. She gave him a nod, and together they followed the path that Viola was cutting through the crowd.

They were nearly there, nearly to the edge of the madness. A few steps more, Ruby thought, and they would be safe. But they'd barely reached the edge of the crush of bodies when the sound of sirens erupted through the air—the police were coming. In response, the crowd surged again, and as Ruby tried to regain her balance, a gunshot exploded over the noise and Theo's hand let go of hers.

She looked back in time to see him falling, the brightness of his blood blooming like a carnation tucked into his lapel.

HELPLESS

1902—New York

The sound of Ruby's scream cut through the noise and hit Viola like a dagger to the gut. She turned in time to see Ruby trying to catch Theo as he fell to the ground.

The crowd was scattering now, no longer bothering to fight each other as they tried to get away from the threat. Another gunshot erupted, and then another, as the street descended into madness.

Viola looked around, searching for her brother and Torrio even as she lunged back into the mess of the crowd for Ruby and Theo, but instead of finding the Five Pointers, she realized that the gunshots had come from a different source—two groups of the Chinese tongs were facing off in the midst of the madness. It was as though the entire Bowery had completely lost its mind.

Theo was on the ground, the fine wool of his suit already marred by the dirt of the streets and the blood that was seeping from his chest, and Ruby was there with him, cradling him. The girl's rosy complexion had gone an almost ghostly white, and her mouth was moving without any words coming out. But Theo was still breathing. His eyes were open, and he looked at Viola. "Get her out of here," he said, his voice racked with pain.

"No." Ruby glared at Viola. "I'm not leaving without him."

All around them was violence, but from the seriousness in Ruby's expression, Viola knew it would be pointless to argue. "Then you'd best help me get him up," she told Ruby.

With a sure nod, Ruby helped Viola hoist Theo upright as he groaned in agony. If Viola had expected the willowy-looking girl to falter beneath the weight of him, she was wrong. Ruby's face was creased with the effort of supporting Theo's weight as he dropped an arm over each of their shoulders, but Viola admired the girl all the more for her determination.

Even as her heart clenched to see the way Ruby looked at Theo.

By the time they moved him far enough away from the fighting to be safe, Theo was all but deadweight. Still, Viola urged them to go a little farther, until they found the relative safety of a doorway to a tenement that she recognized. Once, the people inside had been loyal to Dolph. She could only hope that they would recognize her as a friend instead of a traitor.

They pulled Theo inside, where the noise of the street was blocked out by the door. One tenant opened his door long enough to determine he wanted nothing to do with whatever was happening in the hallway.

Ruby cradled Theo against herself, patting his cheek softly, but Theo was fading. His eyes were half-open, but Viola could tell by their glassiness that he wasn't focusing on either one of them. His skin had gone pale as death, and his lips were already tinged with blue.

"No," Ruby said, her voice nearly breaking when he didn't respond. "You stay with me, Theodore Barclay. Do you hear me?" There were already tears on her cheeks. "Don't you dare leave me here alone."

But Theo didn't respond. His breathing was shallow, and there was a rattling sound coming from his chest that Viola knew too well. All at once she was in Tilly's apartment again, helpless to do anything as she watched her friend die.

Except she wasn't helpless this time.

"Please," Ruby said, leaning her forehead against Theo's. Over and over she pleaded, her voice trembling. But Theo didn't respond.

"Move," Viola said. Her voice sounded as empty and hopeless as she felt inside, but she could do this one thing, even if it meant exposing what she was. *"Move,"* she repeated, pushing gently at Ruby.

Ruby looked up at Viola, her eyes filled with tears, and opened her mouth to refuse, but Viola cut her off.

"I can help him," she said more gently. "But you need to let me."

Reluctantly, Ruby backed away from Theo, who was still bleeding. He was alive, though. Viola could tell from the blood that continued to flow from the wound in his chest.

She didn't want to touch him. She didn't need to touch him, but she knew it would be easier and would work faster if she did, so she placed her hand on his chest, over the wetness of the fabric. His blood was hot and slick beneath her fingers, but she ignored how clearly it spoke to her of dying as she pressed her affinity into him.

Little by little, she found the source of the damage and used her magic to knit him back together, until his body forced the bullet from the wound and into her hand. She didn't stop or allow herself to look up at Ruby, but continued to direct her affinity toward him, into him, pulling together the spaces that had been ripped apart by the violence of the bullet.

Pulling the life back into him.

He gasped suddenly, and she waited until he opened his eyes to back away. Her hands were sticky with his blood and holding what was left of the bullet. But he would live. He would be *fine*. And so would Ruby.

Viola looked up, drained but satisfied with what she had managed, only to find shock and horror in Ruby's eyes.

"It was *you*," Ruby whispered before Viola could so much as explain. "It was never John Torrio who was Mageus, was it?"

Viola's head was shaking of its own accord, even as she wanted to explain, to tell Ruby everything—how she had been ordered to kill her and how she had refused. But something in Ruby's tone stopped her, a coolness that Viola hadn't expected.

"You lied to me," Ruby said. "All this time, you were lying to me." There was something new in Ruby's eyes now. "You're *one of them*."

Confusion swamped her. "I—" She didn't know what she was supposed

566   LISA MAXWELL

to say. "But you told me you wanted to destroy the Order," Viola pleaded.

"Because they depend on magic for their power." Ruby's expression was a well of disgust. "Because this city will never be safe as long as unnatural power remains a threat. It destroyed my father—my entire family was nearly destroyed as well because of it," she said.

"I thought—"

"I can't believe I didn't see what you were." Ruby's eyes were filled with angry tears. "I should have known, but I let you get close to us. I actually *begged* you for help," she said, her words crumbling into a fit of hysterical laughter that broke into a sob. "And look what happened."

Something about the accusation in Ruby's voice had Viola's temper snapping. "I never asked you to come after me. I told you to stay away. I tried to warn you, didn't I?"

But Ruby wasn't backing down. "Theo nearly died because of *you.*"

Theo made a soft sound, but Ruby couldn't see that he was already improving, not through the haze of hate that shone in her eyes.

Viola staggered to her feet. "I'm not the one who dragged him into that mess today. I'm not the one who refused to leave." She lashed out at Ruby with all the hurt and anger she felt burning inside of her. It was a flame that would consume her. "That was *you,* Miss Reynolds. You can blame me all you want. You can hate me for what I am, for something I had no choice in and no ability to refuse, but while you're telling yourself stories about who and what is evil, you should remember that Theo getting shot is *your fault*," Viola said, her voice breaking. "I'm the one who *saved* him."

"Get away from me," Ruby told her, shielding Theo with her body. "From both of us."

The look in Ruby's eyes was one Viola had seen too many times before. The combination of loathing and fear struck her clear to the bone. She had spent too long trying to be what she wasn't, so this time she didn't fight. She honored Ruby's demand, and without another word, she turned and left. And she didn't look back.

DENIAL

1902—New York

Ruby could barely see from the tears in her eyes, but she wasn't sorry to see the back of Viola Vaccarelli. She *wasn't*.

She barely noticed that Theo was moving in her arms until he was already pulling himself upright, rubbing at the place on his chest that was still damp with blood.

"Theo?" His name came out in a rushing gasp as she threw her arms around him.

But he shook her off. "I'm fine," he told her, his voice still weak. "That was rather harsh, though, don't you think?" He cocked one brow in her direction, and her heart flipped to see the familiar, endearing look.

"What was?" she asked, already knowing exactly what he was talking about.

He only stared at her.

"She's one of them, Theo. What did you want me to do?"

"You could have thanked her," he said gently.

He was right, of course. *But she's one of* them.

"She lied to us," she said instead. She brushed his hair back from his face. "Are you truly all right?"

Taking a deep breath, as though testing out his lungs, he nodded. "I think I am, actually. Are you?" he said, his voice softening.

"I'm fine," she told him. "I'm not the one who was shot."

"That isn't what I mean. You *liked* her," he pressed.

568

"I didn't—"

"Don't," he said gently. "You lie to the whole world, but you've never needed to lie to me."

Ruby felt the burn of tears threatening again, but she shook her head, trying to will them away. "It doesn't matter," she told him. "She is one of them, and you *know* how I feel about magic. You know what it did to my family."

Theo didn't speak for a moment, but then he took her chin and turned her toward him. "Ruby . . ."

"*Don't*, Theo." She shook her head again, not wanting to think about any of it.

"No," he said, cupping her face. "You are my dearest friend, and because I love you as well as I've ever loved anyone, I'm going to tell you something that I should have told you months ago—before you started this quest of yours: Your father made his own choices, love."

She started to argue, but he stopped her with a single look. They'd been friends since they were both babes in leading strings. No one understood her as he did because no one had ever felt as safe as he had. But now he didn't look safe. Now he looked like the truth staring at her and forcing her to accept it.

"Yes, the Order might have driven your father deeper into an already unhealthy obsession, but he knew what he was doing when he started, and it had nothing to do with the good of your family or the good of the city. Magic didn't drive him to his breaking point. Perhaps it helped, but he did that on his own."

She was shaking her head and wishing that she could block his words, but in her heart—in that place where she had always understood unspoken things—she'd known this all along. She had been so young when her father had lost his mind and tried to attack a friend over some supposed magical object. He'd nearly murdered someone over a *trinket*, and it had been so much easier for her—for *all of them*—to blame the magic itself, that thing outside and apart from him. It had been so much more satisfying to hate and fight against *that* than to accept that her father had been the cause of her family's misfortunes.

Perhaps he'd dabbled in alchemy and other occult studies because of the Order. But Ruby knew the truth. Her father had always been the sort of man who wanted to be bigger and more important than he was. His membership in the Order wasn't separate from that. When she was a girl, his boasting and posturing had made it seem as though he were some paragon of manliness . . . like he was untouchable.

But she wasn't a girl any longer.

"She's never going to forgive me," Ruby whispered, remembering every awful word she'd spoken to Viola.

"Do you want her to?" Theo asked gently.

"I don't know," Ruby said, knowing the words were a lie even as she spoke them. But she was still so angry and felt so betrayed that she would never, *ever* admit it.

CLOSE TO THE SURFACE

1904—St. Louis

Harte hit the ground before he knew what was happening, the force of Esta's blow and his fall knocking the air from his chest. By the time he shook himself off and sat up, Esta was already running into the burning building again. He saw her silhouetted by the fire, and then she was gone.

At the sight of her disappearing, the power inside Harte rose up with a violence he wasn't ready for. All at once he was pulled under into darkness, where all he could feel was the pain of being torn apart, the rage at being betrayed, and the unbearable longing that had built over centuries of being imprisoned.

He didn't realize that he was trying to run toward the fire himself until he came to with North and one of the other brewery workers holding him back as he tried to tear himself away from them. *I will rip them apart to find her.*

But in a blink, his vision focused and he saw Esta appear again, walking toward them whole and unharmed. She met his eyes with a frown, and he could tell that she hadn't found the cuff.

He was grateful in that moment that the two guys had hold of his arms. Seshat was so close to the surface that he couldn't have stopped himself from going to Esta. He couldn't have stopped Seshat from taking her.

And Esta wouldn't have been prepared. She wouldn't have known until it was too late.

As his body started to relax, North and the other guy slowly released him. Concern was etched across Esta's features, but he didn't go to her. The power was still pressing itself at his boundaries, testing him.

He didn't trust himself to even be near Esta, let alone touch her, so he shook his head, warning her off.

Hurt flickered in her eyes, but he turned away from it, knowing that if he went to her now, the demon-like power inside of him would win.

"We need to go, before the Guard decides to do anything more," Ruth told the group.

Harte wanted to go to Esta, to wrap her in his arms and convince himself that she was still safe and whole, to convince her to leave these Antistasi and all the danger they presented, but Esta's hurt had turned to hardness. She was already walking away from him, helping Ruth and Maggie and the rest climb into the remaining wagon. And all Harte could do was follow.

THREATS AND PROMISES

1904—St. Louis

It was close to midnight by the time Julien Eltinge let himself out through the stage door and cut back through the alley behind the theater. The humid warmth of the night felt oppressive without so much as a breeze to cut through it. Still, it was quiet, a more than adequate respite from the exhausting day he'd had.

The morning had started with a meeting with Corwin Spenser, who had wanted to go over the plans the Society had been making to ensure security at the parade. Not everyone in town appreciated the Veiled Prophet's celebrations. The Society always expected trouble, rabble who would do anything to disrupt what should have been an evening of entertainment, but with the president in town, nothing could be allowed to go wrong—especially when it came to the necklace. Julien had assured the old man yet again that he was more than capable of taking care of anyone who might try anything during the parade. That meeting had been followed by back-to-back shows, where the house had been full but lackluster. The heat was affecting everyone.

He'd just turned the corner toward his own apartment when he realized that the carriage on the street behind him seemed to be following him. Slowing his steps, Julien waited for it to pass, but instead it pulled up alongside him and the door opened. Inside was a man he'd seen before—at a dinner the Veiled Prophet had required him to attend earlier that week. He wasn't one of the Society, but was a representative from one of the other Brotherhoods. Which had it been?

"Mr. Eltinge?" the man called. "Could I offer you a ride?"

New York, he thought suddenly, recognizing the clipped accent of the man's speech. Which meant he was from the Order.

"Thanks," Julien called, too aware of the sweat that was dripping down his back. "But I think I'll walk. It's a lovely night for it." He waved and continued on, hoping that would be the end of it.

It wasn't, of course. The carriage pulled up alongside him again.

"Oh, I think you'll want to come for a ride with me, Julien." He leaned forward so the streetlamp lit the planes of his face. "Unless you want me to explain to the Order where you *really* found that necklace."

The night felt sultry against his skin, but Julien's veins had turned to ice. "I'm not sure what you're referring to." He considered his options, but he doubted outrunning a horse was one of the better ones.

"I think you do," the man told him. "So I'm going to give you a choice—you can get into this carriage, and tell me everything you know about the Society's plans for the necklace on the night of the parade. If you do, I can protect you. I can make sure the Order never knows about your connection to Harte Darrigan or the theft of their most precious treasures. Or you can keep walking and count me as one of your enemies."

The man wasn't old, but he was soft, bloated from too much drinking and too little exercise. In a ring, Julien could flatten him, but life wasn't a boxing ring. Life was more of a chess game, and Julien was not about to find himself in check because of Harte Darrigan. "You know," Julien said, trying to keep his tone easy, "I think I could use a ride after all."

DISILLUSIONED

1902—New York

Viola didn't even know where she was walking. She was blocks away, nearly to the edge of the island, when her feet finally slowed and the haze that she was blindly walking through lifted. Suddenly exhausted, she stepped into the safe cover of a recessed doorway and sank to the ground, her legs collapsing beneath her. Realizing that the bullet was still in her hand, she tossed it away in disgust.

Then she took the package that Nibsy had given her from the pocket of her skirt. Viola paused a moment to allow the comforting weight to rest in her hands before she began to open the wrappings. Finally, she felt balanced. Grounded. *Ready.*

To hell with all her plans. Why should she wait for some future retribution? Why should she allow the Order to destroy Nibsy Lorcan when she could have the honor herself? She would carve him from the world, and then she would go for her brother. And when she had finished with them, she would go for the Order. The silvery blade flashed as soon as she tore the paper away, and she held it up, examining it. Reveling in its power.

She pulled herself up, letting the wrapping fall to the ground, but the markings on the paper caught her eye as it fell. Leaning over, she picked it up and examined the clear, familiar hand. She knew that writing, the way the letters slanted precisely to the right and the bold, confident stroke of the pen.

Dolph.

Her chest ached at the memory of her friend and at the loss of him, but as she let her eyes scan over the lines of writing, the ache turned into something else. Disbelief. Denial.

It can't be. Dolph wouldn't have written these words. He couldn't have harmed Leena this way. But there, stark as the letters on the page, was every step he'd taken and every intention he'd had—to take her power, to *use* her. The woman he'd claimed to love.

It must be a trick, she thought. Another of Nibsy's deceptions, because if it wasn't, everything she had known about Dolph Saunders had been a lie.

PART

VI

THE RIVER

1904—St. Louis

With the brewery in ashes, the Antistasi moved farther out the day after the fire, to a small camp on the banks of the Mississippi just south of town. Without really talking it over or deciding, Esta had gone with them. Harte had followed, but he wouldn't even look at her. He was keeping his distance and making excuses to be anywhere that she wasn't. Not that she completely blamed him, after the way she'd attacked him. Even now, while everyone else was trying to help the newly woken focus on their affinities, Harte was sitting on the bank of the river, his back to her and the rest.

Fine, then. He could sulk all he wanted to. When he got over himself, maybe he would realize that she'd had to at least *attempt* to get her cuff back. She tried not to think about what it meant that she hadn't found it.

Had she simply missed it? Or did Ruth still have it?

But letting her thoughts wander while she tried to help the new Mageus wasn't the safest thing to do, so she forced herself to forget about Harte's clear disapproval and to focus on the task in front of her. Most of the people from the hospital were still processing the reality of their new lives. Born Mageus learned how to use their connection to the old magic as children, and by the time they were grown, it was second nature. But Ruth's attack had been on adults. Learning how to focus their affinities—discovering what power they actually held—was proving to be challenging and frustrating for them.

It wasn't much more comfortable for Esta. The whole thing reminded her of her own childhood—the days she'd spent training with Professor Lachlan. She hated him. She *needed* to hate him, for all the ways he'd betrayed her. But helping the newly woken, she wondered if she didn't also owe him. He'd taught her how to find the spaces between the seconds and had coached her until she could pull them slow with hardly any effort at all. He'd given her Ishtar's Key and the secrets of slipping through time, a fact she didn't want to admit—even to herself. It was as he'd said—he'd made her.

Of course, she reminded herself, the man she'd known as the Professor wouldn't have *had* to do any of that if the boy she'd known as Nibsy hadn't stolen her entire life. Who would she have been if Nibsy Lorcan hadn't killed her parents?

Shaking off the questions of the past, she tried to focus on the man in front of her. Arnie was middle-aged, with a patch of hair on each side of his head and a ragged mustache tinged yellow on the edges. He kept losing focus, and when that happened, flames would burst from his fingertips, startling him and causing him to flail about until he found the pail of water to squelch the fire. If he wasn't fast enough—and he often wasn't—Esta would call one of the bottlers who worked at the brewery, and who was also a healer, to help with the burns.

"Think of it as a connection," Esta tried to explain as he soaked his hands in a bucket of water for the tenth time. "The whole world and everything in it is connected. Magic lives in the spaces between those connections. When you use your affinity, you're pressing at the spaces—reshaping them and manipulating them."

He frowned at her. "How does that help me with the fire? It's just *hot.*"

Honestly, she didn't know. Using her affinity, even when she was younger, had always felt intuitive, never dangerous.

"I barely blink and the flames erupt," he complained. "There's no spaces. It just *hurts.*"

"Maybe stop thinking of the fire as outside yourself?" she suggested. Fire, since it was a chemical reaction, was aligned with the inert, but time was different. It was Aether. It was everything.

She was a miserable teacher.

"I know you," a soft voice said from behind her.

Esta turned to see the girl from the warehouse staring at her. She looked younger now that she wasn't wearing the stiff, high-necked gray. Her nose was smattered with freckles, and her eyes held an accusation. "No," Esta lied, turning away from her. "You must be mistaken."

But the girl didn't give up. "John. Your name is John," she insisted. "You were there that night."

"No," Esta said, turning back in time to see the moment the girl's understanding clicked.

"You're one of them, and you were there that night," the girl said, her eyes widening. "I saw you. I *talked* to you."

The day was clear and sunny, warm with the heat of summer, but suddenly, there was a burst of icy air, like a blast of winter sweeping through. The tree above them shook with the force of it, and Esta looked up to find the green faces of the leaves crawling with frost.

"You did this to us," the girl said, stepping toward Esta. "I knew it was you. I knew it all along."

"No," Esta said, backing away. But she didn't have the nerve to lie to this girl who looked so scared and broken and angry. "I just—" How could she answer the hate in the girl's eyes? It didn't seem enough to explain that she was just a tool. That she hadn't intended anything, because the truth was that she had. She'd entered the warehouse that night knowing that others might be hurt. She'd chosen Harte and their mission to get the necklace over these people's lives, and it was a choice she would make again.

At least, she *thought* she would.

"Greta, that's enough." It was Ruth, who'd come up behind the girl.

"But he's the one—"

"I said enough. You're one of us now," Ruth admonished. "Calm yourself."

The icy wind died off, replaced by the normal warmth of the day.

Above, frost turned liquid dripped from the leaves, but their faces had gone brown from the cold.

"Come with me," Ruth said to Esta.

Glad to be away from Greta and her accusations, Esta followed Ruth. "She hates us."

"She doesn't yet understand the gift she's been given," Ruth said. "She will."

"What if she doesn't?" Esta asked before she thought better of it.

Ruth tilted her head and gave her the sort of look that Esta imagined only a mother would be able to give. "Would you give up your own affinity?"

"No, but I was born with it," Esta told her. "It's who I am. Greta didn't have any choice in the matter," she said, thinking of Harte's objections.

"Neither did you. Your affinity was bestowed upon you by fate, and yet you've come to see it as essential. In time, Greta will too. They all will," Ruth said.

It was clear that Ruth believed what she said, and her voice was so sure, so filled with emotion, that Esta could almost believe it too. Maybe she had just been a tool, but in the end, no one had forced her to attack Lipscomb and the warehouse full of people. She could have tried to find a better way, but she hadn't. She'd heard Lipscomb talk and she'd judged his life to be worth less than Harte's.

Maybe his life *had* been worth less than Harte's. But watching these newly woken Mageus struggle and seeing the fear in their eyes every time their affinities burst forth uncontrolled, she wasn't sure that she'd had any right to make that decision.

Taking a deep breath, Esta shoved away her doubts. "Did you want something?"

"You've acquitted yourself admirably this past night," Ruth said. "What you did for Maggie and the children during the fire, and here, with the newly woken."

"We told you that we weren't your enemy," Esta pointed out, trying to keep any trace of smugness from her voice.

"Yes, well . . ." Ruth paused, her nostrils flaring slightly, as though admitting as much had been an effort. "With all that's happened, it seems that I must count you as an ally after all," she said, not sounding all that happy about the situation. "With the damage to the brewery and the responsibility here with the newly woken, I need your help."

The words settled something inside of her. *This is it.* "What's your plan?"

"The Society," Ruth said. "I want to make them pay for what they've done to us. I want them to crawl."

"The feeling is definitely mutual," Esta told her. Whatever her doubts, that was one sentiment she could get behind one hundred percent.

"But crawling isn't enough. We need to be sure that they have no recourse left," Ruth said, glancing at Esta from the side of her eye. "The Society cannot be allowed to keep the necklace. I need a thief."

"Then you're in luck. Because I happen to be a damn good one." She gave a little bow. "But I have one condition. If I help you with this, I want what you took from me. I want my cuff."

Ruth was silent for a long moment. "If I don't agree?"

"I'll take it anyway," she said. "I could take the necklace too, before you even get close to touching it. But I'd prefer to work with you. I hope that the fact that I've stayed this long shows you that I'd rather help you than fight you." As she spoke, she realized that she wasn't sure how much of what she said was a lie—and how much was the truth.

"Fine," Ruth said, her jaw tight. "You help us destroy the Society and get me the necklace and the cuff is yours."

But then what? Would she simply steal the necklace too and leave Ruth and the Antistasi behind, as though she hadn't been part of this at all? Or was there a different way forward, a way where she and Harte didn't have to fight alone? The more Ruth talked and explained the Antistasi's plan, the more Esta wondered.

UNTIL THE END

1904—St. Louis

Harte saw Esta coming toward him too late to avoid her. It had been the better part of a day, and as far as he could tell, the power inside of him had settled itself down to a low rumble of discontent, but he didn't trust it. He'd kept his distance, all while keeping her in sight, because he didn't trust the Antistasi, either.

There was no doubt that Ruth was charismatic. She believed in the righteousness of what she was doing. But in Harte's experience, the line between belief and zealotry was often a fragile one, indistinct and prone to crumble when examined too closely. Her idea to give Sundren magic might have been noble had her victims been given any choice in the matter. But Ruth had forced it upon them, had infected them with a power that they neither wanted nor had any ability to control.

He couldn't quite see how that was much different from what the Sundren did by forcing Mageus to hide their affinities. Both sides were driven by desperation and fear, and they seemed to him two halves of the same coin.

As Esta sat next to him, he made sure to focus on locking down the power and was ready in case it decided to lurch toward the surface. It seemed quiet, but that could be just another of its tricks.

She didn't speak to him at first. Instead, Esta picked up a rock and lobbed it into the murky water beyond. The sun glinted off the surface, illuminating the ripples as they grew. For a second he could almost imagine that they were in another place, another situation. His whole life, he'd wanted only to be free from the city. But now that he was, he'd been so consumed with everything else, he'd barely had time to breathe.

"It's bigger than I imagined it would be," he said softly.

He felt her eyes on him. "The river?"

"All of it." He turned to her. "I knew it would be big, but I didn't realize."

She worried her lip with her teeth as she let out a tired breath. "I know what you mean. Bigger and . . . *different* than I thought." She paused, letting their mutual appreciation for the place they'd found themselves in stretch between them. "I'm sorry about flattening you," she told him. "I was just desperate to find the—"

"It's fine," he said, meaning it.

Esta gave him a small nod and turned to look back at the river.

"Ruth asked for our help," she said, finally breaking the heavy silence between them. "She wants to destroy the Society, and to do that, she needs to make sure they don't have the necklace."

Her voice was so hopeful, so determined, but something about it made the power inside of him feel like it was starting to wake again.

"We're not here to destroy the Society, Esta," he told her, his voice coming out more clipped than he'd intended because his attention was focused on Seshat, in case the demon decided to make another play for Esta. "We're here to get the necklace and get out, remember? The rest of this isn't our fight."

"Why isn't it?" she pressed. "We can do something here to *help* people."

"Or we could just make everything worse," he told her. At her agitation, the power seemed to pulse with excitement, swelling and growing. "Look what happened after Ruth attacked that meeting. Look at the people we rescued from the hospital."

"She gave them their power back," Esta said, remembering what Ruth had told her. "She *helped* them."

"She *attacked* them. *Look* at them," he said, turning her back to face the group of ragged-looking victims from the Antistasi's attack. Half were still dressed only in what they'd worn in the hospital. "Really look at them. Do any of those people look happy right now?"

She shrugged away from him. "They will be. Aren't you?"

He laughed. "Happy?" Shaking his head, he tried to figure out how to make her understand. His affinity had driven his father away and destroyed his mother. It gave him power over people, true, but it had also kept him apart. He was always wary, always afraid of getting too close or letting anyone know too much about him. "Nothing about my affinity has made me happy, Esta."

She frowned at him. "That can't be true."

"Let's just go," he said. "*Please.* We still have Julien. He can help us figure out where the necklace is, and then we can get it and get out of this town. We don't need the Antistasi or their grand schemes."

Esta gestured to her arm. "Ruth still has Ishtar's Key, remember? We can't leave without it."

He ran his hands through his hair, trying to keep his frustration in check, so that he could keep the demon inside of him locked away. "She doesn't exactly have a safe nearby, does she? We're in the middle of nowhere. How hard could it be to steal it from her and go? We don't need the rest of this. We don't need to attack the Society—"

"You would just walk away?" Her expression was unreadable, and when she spoke again, her voice came out as barely a whisper. "Even though they burned the brewery?" She met his eyes. "They could have killed *children*, Harte. The Guard knew there were children inside, and they didn't care. They wanted them to die. Because they're Mageus. Because one less Mageus is fine with the Society and the Guard, no matter how old or young."

He couldn't argue with anything she'd said. The fire was nothing short of evil, but the Society was no different from the Order. Now that he was outside the confines of the Brink, it was clearer than ever how pointless it was to think that they would ever defeat them. Crush one roach or one hundred, and there were still a thousand more you never saw, ready to swarm as soon as the lights went out.

Sure, they could help the Antistasi, and then what? The risks were too great, and the good that they might do? He wasn't sure if it was enough to make up for the damage they could cause in the process. "We can't," Harte said finally.

Esta's expression hardened. "It's too late to back out now."

He glanced at her. "What do you mean?"

She met his gaze and lifted her chin, stubborn as she ever was. "I already volunteered our connection with Julien."

Harte's stomach twisted. "You didn't . . ." They'd done enough to his old friend, mixing him up in this mess to start with.

"You already told Ruth we had a way into the Society," she pointed out.

"I didn't give her Julien."

"I know, but . . ." She let out a sigh, and when she glanced over at him, he could see the regret in her expression, but it wasn't as bright as the hope. "He *could* get us in, Harte."

"And then what?" He felt his temper spiking and the power growing alongside it. "We leave, and Julien has a target on his back. I can't do that to him."

"We won't be doing anything to him. Once the Antistasi release the serum, everything will be different. Think about it, Harte. The ball will be filled with dignitaries—representatives from all the Occult Brotherhoods. Anyone with any power at all will be there," she explained. "After the Antistasi set off the serum, the people who make the laws won't be interested in prosecuting magic if they have it them-selves. And this year, the ball has a very special guest—one that Ruth is specifically interested in. . . ."

"They're going to attack the president," he realized, his stomach twisting.

"That's the plan."

"It's a terrible plan, Esta. Can't you see that?"

The spark of defiance was back in her expression. "It might just work, Harte. People love Roosevelt. Someday they're going to carve his face into a mountain."

A mountain? He blinked. "How is that even—" He was getting sidetracked.

But Esta was determined. "No one is going to turn on Roosevelt, even if his affinity is awoken. He could be the solution—"

She'd lost her mind. She was so blinded by the fantasy that she was forgetting the possible cost. "No, Esta. We *cannot* let this happen."

"Why not?" she asked. "It's what Dolph would have wanted. For us to keep fighting. For us to try to actually change things."

"You don't know what Dolph wanted," Harte exclaimed. "*I* don't know what he wanted. No one did. He played everything too close to the vest. Look what he did to Leena."

She was shaking her head. "Maybe I don't know what all of his plans were, but I owe it to him to try to finish what he started."

"You're not Dolph, Esta."

"I know that," she snapped. But she was trembling with emotion.

"And you don't owe him anything," he said, more gently. "You can choose your own path, a different path."

"You just want me to run."

"I want us to *survive*," he corrected. "I want you to be able to look at yourself in the mirror and not loathe the reflection staring back," he told her. "Did you ever stop to think that maybe there was a reason your mother hid you from Dolph? I *knew* your mother. Leena wasn't okay with some of the things Dolph did. She wouldn't have hidden you from him otherwise. She must have wanted something more for you than the endless fighting and violence and death that he would have insisted you be part of."

"He wanted to change things—"

LISA MAXWELL

"Dolph might have been my friend once, but he wasn't the saint you're making him out to be. He hurt Leena because it was what he thought was best for her. For magic. For *everyone*. After he took her power, she never completely forgave him. How is what the Antistasi are doing any different?"

She was looking at him with an expression he'd never seen on her before, an expression that worried him, because he didn't know what it meant.

"We have a long road ahead of us," he said, more gently now. "Or have you forgotten what we're supposed to be doing? Nibsy is still out there somewhere, waiting."

"I *know*," she told him, pulling back the sleeve of her shirt.

"What is that?" On her arm were a series of scars that looked like letters. But she pulled away before he could make them out.

"I didn't have it before. We're changing things, and I'm well aware that Nibsy's still out there, waiting. But he's waiting for *me*, Harte."

He hated the sound of pain and worry in her voice, but it wasn't a good enough reason to do the Antistasi's bidding. "We need to get out of this town alive. If we do that, we can go back and fix things. We can make it so none of this—the Act, the Antistasi, none of it—ever happened. We can save people *that* way."

"And what if we can't?" she asked, her voice dark. "What if I *can't* get us back to 1902? What if I can't make any of this right?"

"You will—"

"You don't know that," she snapped. "And neither do I. I need to do this. In case . . ." But she didn't finish.

He started to reach for her. "Esta—"

"No, Harte," she said, standing and taking a step back from him. "I won't force you to help me, but I won't let you stop me either. You're either with me, or I do this alone."

He let out a tired breath. "You know I'm with you," he said.

His words seemed to relax something in her. She gave him a small smile and a satisfied nod before she went off to tell Ruth the news. He watched her as she left, her straight back and her arms swinging as she walked. Strong. Confident. So completely herself. "Until the end," he murmured, but he wasn't sure who he was speaking to as the wind carried away his words.

TABLEAUX VIVANTS

1902—New York

As the carriage rattled onward, Jack crunched two more cubes of morphine between his molars to deaden the pain throbbing in his head and to clear his mind. With the drug coursing through him, he felt like he could breathe again, and as the world came into sharper focus, he took the Book from the inside of his jacket. He used those final few minutes before he arrived at the Morgan mansion to pore over its pages—especially the notations that were in his hand, despite his having no memory of making them. He'd stopped worrying about that particular issue, though, and had decided to take it as a sign that the Book had chosen to reveal itself to him. A sign that he was not only worthy, but *destined*.

That knowledge had buoyed his confidence and made him *that* much surer of his path. He wasn't meant to be meek and obedient. With some help from the Book, he'd managed to take control of planning the Order's little gala so that he could direct the drama of the evening. But with the event only days away, Jack still had one aggravation that he hadn't quite managed to deal with, and her name was Evelyn DeMure.

He knew that the ring the actress wore was something more than it appeared. With the smooth perfection of the stone and the sizzle of power that he swore filled the air when it was near, he would have realized as much even without the details that the Book had revealed to him. The Inner Circle had always kept the contents of the Mysterium a closely guarded secret, known only to the very highest levels of the

Order, but during his nights of study, the Book had handed those secrets over to Jack. So he knew that the ring must be the Delphi's Tear, a stone created by Newton himself. He knew, too, how it had been created—by sacrifice—and what he could do with its power.

That night at the theater, he'd realized what Evelyn was and why she'd been able to defend herself—and the ring—from his advances. But now he had the answer to the problem she posed. The pieces were all coming together, and everything would be revealed at the gala, where Jack would take the ring and deal with Evelyn once and for all.

When the carriage finally stopped at the front door of his uncle's house on Madison Avenue, Jack tucked the Book back into his jacket. There, close to his chest, he could practically feel the power in it, a twin heartbeat pulsing in time with his own. He alighted from the carriage, ignoring the faint throbbing in his head. The morphine had helped with that. So did the knowledge that soon he would have everything he needed—everything he'd ever wanted. He directed the driver to bring in the crate that was strapped to the back of the carriage, a piece Jack had prepared himself for the spectacle of the gala.

He watched as one of his uncle's servants helped the driver carry the crate into the house, and then he followed, feeling more and more sure about what was to come. There was a new maid at the door waiting, a brown-skinned girl who wasn't to Jack's tastes at all. He gave her his coat and hat without a second thought and went to find out how the preparations were going.

In the ballroom, things had progressed nicely from two days before. Curtains of wine-colored velvet cascaded around the large pillars that skirted the room, transforming the open dance floor into four distinct stages, where the tableaux would be displayed.

Tableaux vivants were all the rage in the city. All the most exclusive events seemed to be featuring the often-scintillating displays of art come to life. Even the stuffiest members of society were drawn to the voyeurism of gazing upon their peers in any number of poses reproducing the scenes of classical art. Rumors were already scuttling through the city about which artworks the participants might be creating at the gala. To his aunt's infinite delight, the papers were abuzz about which of the year's debutantes would be involved, and what they might—or might not—be wearing. Reporters at every paper were practically frothing at the mouth for an invite. Just as the Order had hoped.

The Order might have planned the event to consolidate their standing in the city, but Jack would use it to his advantage. He would demonstrate his importance, his *consequence*, once and for all—not only to his family, but to the Order. To the entire city as well.

Evelyn was already there. She was standing on a small stool surrounded by seamstresses who were fitting her in the diaphanous bit of chiffon that she would be wearing in the tableau he had planned for her. She waved at him, and he felt the usual answering burst of lust deep in his gut that he now knew for the feral power that it was. Thanks to a talisman he'd inscribed on his chest that morning, a secret he'd found in the Book, her influence no longer had the effect on him that it had before. At least not from a distance—he still didn't trust her to get close.

He waved back, feigning more interest than he felt as he examined the costume. It was nearly perfect—Evelyn would be portraying the unconscious beauty in Henry Fuseli's enigmatic painting *The Nightmare*. By the end of the gala, Jack had the suspicion that she would find the image she portrayed more than apt.

He turned his attention to the other stages and preparations. He was discussing the best positioning for the Circe tableau with one of the other Order members when he was summoned into his uncle's office.

Jack had only once before visited Morgan's private study, when he'd returned from Greece, weak and broken and an embarrassment to himself and his family. He didn't relish being called back there, but he kept his head high as he entered, remembering that he had the Book and the favor it had conferred upon him.

Morgan's office was an ostentatious place, with burnished wood and vaulted ceilings barreling overhead. It was the sort of place meant for a prince of business, an emperor of commerce, but with the Book's warmth radiating against his chest, Jack barely noticed the grandeur.

Morgan turned when he entered, a look of disgust clear on the old man's face. "How are the preparations?"

"Nearly there," Jack said, confident.

"They should be finished," Morgan told him. "We're only two days away."

He allowed the sneering quality of Morgan's tone to roll off his back. In a matter of days, his uncle would be eating those words and begging Jack to share the knowledge and power he had with the rest of them. And Jack would happily laugh in his face.

He shrugged, hiding his true emotions. "They'll be done in plenty of time."

Morgan's bulbous nose twitched a bit. "They'd better be perfect," he demanded. "Have you seen this?" He thrust a newspaper at Jack.

"Seen what?" Jack asked, trying to discover the source of his uncle's agitation in the equally titillating headlines.

"The one about the fire," Morgan said, leaning over the desk to jab his thick finger at the newsprint. "The damn animals burned one of the stations down on Great Jones Street. That's Charlie Murphy's district—Tammany Hall's territory."

"I don't see how this matters to you—or to me, for that matter," Jack said. Tammany Hall was filled with upstarts, crooked Irish politicians who thought they had a chance at becoming something more than they were destined to be.

"It matters because we have an understanding with Tammany. They've been helping us put pressure on the maggots downtown."

"It's just a fire—"

"It's *not* just a fire," Morgan said, his voice dangerous. "It was intentional arson, and the flames weren't normal flames. For more than an hour, the hoses didn't touch them. The whole thing stank of feral magic."

"So?" Jack asked, not seeing how some decrepit engine company had any impact on him whatsoever. The whole Bowery could burn for all he cared.

"Do you know how bad this makes us look?" Morgan demanded, thumping at his desk. "How *ineffective*?"

Jack wondered how he'd ever been afraid of the old man. With all his bluster, it was clear how weak he was. True power didn't need to rage. It could quietly burn, consuming a place from the inside out.

"It only makes the Order look weak if you and the rest of the Inner Circle fail to answer it," he said. With the morphine in his veins, he was relaxed, his brain clear and sure. "If anything, this only helps our cause. It gives the Order the ammunition it needs to move against the maggots once and for all."

"Maybe, but if Tammany starts making trouble, it could mean problems for the Conclave. They're already starting to make overtures about how powerful they've become in the city," Morgan said. "The other day, Barclay said he heard one of them bragging about how, by the end of the year, the Order would be a nonentity."

"Who cares what one of them said—"

"*I* care," Morgan roared. "The Inner Circle cares. We have three other Brotherhoods coming into the city later this year for the Conclave, and I will not allow the Order to be seen as weak. The Conclave is just the beginning. It will determine who has power in the century to come—and who *doesn't*. It's bad enough that those damn thieves took the artifacts and the Ars Arcana. It's worse that because of *you*, others suspect that we've been weakened. If the Order doesn't claim our spot at the head of the united Brotherhoods now, New York will lose in stature and in *power*. Right now we have the president's ear. If we master the Conclave, we could have the entire country in the palm of our hands."

"I understand," Jack said. Because he *did* understand. He simply didn't have any intention of allowing the old farts that ruled the Inner Circle to be the ones who held that power.

"I doubt you do," Morgan snapped, "but if you screw this up, you will. Some of Tammany's people are coming to this gala, so it's essential that we show them exactly how powerful we are."

"We will," Jack told him, suppressing the amusement that he felt stirring inside of him. At the gala, the entire city would know *exactly* how powerful each of them was, and Jack would be the one on top.

ONCE MORE

1902—New York

With a knife in her hand, Viola could pierce a man's heart from forty paces. Because he wasn't an idiot, Paul didn't often allow her to have knives. Still, as she listened to her brother drone on about her most recent failings, she wondered what damage she would be able to do with the wooden spoon she was currently holding. Certainly, she should be able to do *something* to shut him up.

"I *know*, Paolo," she said, her hands on her hips. "But I don't want to go with John Torrio."

"Why not?" Paul asked, his brows bunching. "You think you're too good for him? Or is there some other reason, some other person I should know about?"

"I don't *like* him, that's why," she said, practically spitting the words.

He lifted his hand to slap her, but she only smiled. "No," he said, gritting his teeth as he lowered his hand. "We can't have you bruised for the gala."

"I still don't see why I should get trussed up for that maiale to drool over. I don't trust him, Paolo, and neither should you. He'll cut you in the back the second he can."

"You think I don't know that?" her brother asked. "Why do you think I want you to go with him?"

"I *know* why you want me to go with him. You don't trust me still."

"I don't trust *anyone*, including Torrio. I need my blade at my side walking into that gala, looking polished and sharp. You'll go with the Fox, and you'll do your duty to me and to the family, or you won't have a place here anymore." His mouth drew up on one side, exposing his crooked eyetooth. "But don't forget, it's not just Tammany's patrols or the boys in the neighborhood you have to watch your back for. I have friends in higher places now too. I'm sure my friend Mr. Grew would like to know where one of the thieves who stole the Order's treasures could be found. I'm sure they'd be even more grateful if I handed her over myself."

She spit on the floor at his feet. "You wouldn't dare," she said. "You'd be dead before you could open your mouth."

"So many threats, sister. And yet here I stand. Still holding your life in my hands." He stalked toward her. "I took you back into the protection of the family because Mamma asked me. Because she doesn't see you for what you are. She never did. You don't think I remember the way she and Papà used to coddle you, leaving me to clean up your messes? All because you were born a monster—a freak. You always thought you were better than the rest of us, as though the rules of this world didn't matter to you. But now you see. Now the rules are *my* rules. The city is *my* city."

She let out a bark of laughter. "Those men *use* you, Paolo. Tammany and the men in the Order both. They don't respect you or your money. It's too new. And it's too dirty for their liking."

His expression was thunderous. "Maybe they *think* they use me, but my money's as good as anyone's, and the country is changing, sister. Soon the age of their purses won't matter as much as what they contain, and I aim to have more."

"Paolo—"

"You go with Torrio, or you don't go at all, capisce?"

Viola clenched her teeth to keep from saying all the things she was feeling. If she didn't need a way into the gala, she would have tried her luck with the spoon. "I understand," she said, turning back to the pot she had been stirring before he'd interrupted her.

"I'll have a dress sent to you. Be ready by six, eh?"

LISA MAXWELL

She nodded, not trusting herself to say more, but the minute he was out of the kitchen, she launched the spoon across the room, right at the place where his head had been moments before. She'd do his bidding just one more time and put up with John Torrio's wandering eyes and too-free hands. But only because she needed her brother and his men to get close to the Order. After that, all bets were off.

MAROONED

L ogan Sullivan was cold, hungry, and in desperate need of a shower, but at least he was free. In the days since he'd been taken off guard in that woman's apartment, he'd been following her. Rather, he'd been following the stone, and he'd been collecting information.

Now, standing across from the Bella Strega, the witch on the sign stared down at him, as though daring him to run.

Maybe he should. The person Professor Lachlan was in the past wasn't the man Logan had known and come to think of as a mentor—as a father figure of sorts. The kid was barely sixteen and as cagey and dangerous as a feral cat. Going back to him now might be the worst idea he'd ever had.

But what were his other options? He didn't know anyone else in this version of the city, and at least he knew what the boy who called himself James Lorcan would become. If anyone could find Esta and force her to take Logan back to his own time, he would bet money it was the boy who ruled over the Bella Strega saloon.

Besides, now that he knew more about the stone—including where and *when* it would be—Logan had something to barter with. He'd never really paid all that much attention when Professor Lachlan had tried to teach him about the different parts of magic, but Logan hoped that if they could get ahold of that stone, then maybe—just maybe—it would be enough to get him home.

PREPARATIONS

1904—St. Louis

The brush felt cool as Julien dabbed the tip of it against Esta's eyelids, putting the finishing touches on her makeup for the evening. "Just a bit more," he said, his tobacco-laced breath fanning over her face as he dabbed once . . . twice . . . "There. Finished."

She blinked open her eyes and found him looking at her with a satisfied expression. Harte was standing nearby, frowning. "Well?" she asked.

"Perfection," Julien declared, and then he turned to the mirror to do his own makeup.

Esta came up next to him to check her reflection, and her mouth dropped open. Her skin was too pale, and her lips, which were already big enough, looked enormous painted in the orangey-scarlet that Julien had used. He'd lined her eyes with dramatic sweeps of kohl and had painted the lids with turquoise and gold. *Gold.*

"I look like a clown," she told Julien, pushing the long braids of the dark wig she was wearing out of her face.

Actually, she looked like one of the stylized paintings on the Streets of Cairo, but the effect was basically the same. They weren't any more authentic than she was.

Julien glanced at her in the mirror. "That is entirely the point."

"To look like some kind of circus freak?" she asked. Her mouth still felt sticky from the paint as she spoke.

"Don't smear your lips until they're dry," he said, ignoring her outrage as he lined his own with a softer shade of red.

"Why do you get to look like a woman while I have to look like a clown?" she asked. He'd done something to make her features look stronger and more angular than usual, while his own makeup had the opposite effect, transforming the masculine lines of his face into something softly feminine.

He glared at her in the mirror. "Because you *are* a woman. Trust me. No one is going to notice that little fact with your face looking like it is. You look exactly the way you need to look—just like every one of the other men who will be riding on the floats tonight."

She frowned at herself again and then caught Harte's eyes in the mirror. He had an expression on his face that looked like a combination of horror and pain. Which meant that the makeup was every bit as bad as she thought.

He hadn't talked to her since the other day, when they'd argued after the fire, but he was here now. He was going through with things as planned, so she'd won. Somehow, the victory didn't feel as gratifying as she'd thought it would. She'd say it was just nerves, but she made it a practice not to do nerves, especially not before a job as important and as dangerous as this one.

Letting out a frustrated breath, Esta took some more of the cotton batting and shoved it into the overly large corset she was wearing beneath the flowing white dress. It was ridiculous, flattening herself out only to stuff herself back up again just so she could fill out one of Julien's gowns. All because women weren't allowed to actually ride on the parade floats—it was unbecoming or immoral or something. She still didn't understand how a bunch of half-drunk men dressed as women was any better, but at least their hypocritical morality gave her a way into the parade and, even more important, a way to get close to the necklace.

A knock came on the dressing room door. "Your ride is here," Sal called.

"Tell them we'll be there in five," Julien shouted. Then he pulled on his own wig—a black bob that made him look like Cleopatra—and turned to Esta and Harte. "Well," he said. "This is it." He looked nervous. Too nervous.

"Relax, Jules," Harte said, patting him on the arm. "This is no different from any other show. It's all a bit of flash and sparkle, and then it'll be over."

"That's what I'm afraid of," Julien muttered.

He hadn't been happy to see them when they'd gone to him to tell him that they needed his help again. If they hadn't been in a crowded restaurant, Esta thought Julien probably would have laid Harte flat out just to get away. But in the end they'd explained their dilemma the best they could—without telling him anything about the Antistasi. If things went to plan, he'd never have to know—and he wouldn't be in any more danger.

"No one is going to pin this on you, Jules. I promise," Harte said, his voice as steady as his expression. "Ready, Slim?"

"You can stop with that name anytime now," Esta said, but the truth was that it helped. The little spark of irritation it inspired grounded her. "See you at the parade." She tried to give him a smile. Instead of replying, he gave her a terse nod, but his eyes were shaded and his expression was unreadable.

It had been a night not much different from this—and not that long ago—when she and Harte had ridden in an awkward silence to Khafre Hall. Then, she'd planned to betray everyone she had come to admire in New York. She'd had no idea that Harte had plans of his own. He'd been distant that night too, but somehow Harte felt farther from her now than he ever had before—even on that night back in New York when he'd believed her to be the worst kind of traitor.

He'd been pulling back for days now, she admitted to herself. Even before their argument, he'd been holding himself back, and any time they touched or she thought he might move toward her, a look came over him as though it was a mistake—all of it, an enormous mistake. But after the argument they'd had on the banks of the river? The tension between them had been worse.

Esta knew what Harte still thought—that the Antistasi were wrong. That this wasn't her fight. That she would come to regret her actions. But she didn't have time for softness or second-guessing, not with so much on the line. Look what had happened by leaving Jack alive. She'd listened to Harte, allowed him to sway her, and the future had changed for the worse. Mageus had suffered for it. *No.* She wouldn't be weak. Not now.

Dammit. She let out an angry breath and steeled herself for what was to come. In a matter of a little more than an hour, they would have the necklace and the world would be a different place. They would *make* it a different place. Or she would die trying.

She gave Harte a sure nod before she followed Julien through the theater and then out to meet the waiting cab. Guardsmen flanked the doors, so she pulled her magic in, clamping down on it as she climbed into the back of the carriage.

But the carriage wasn't empty as she'd expected. The Veiled Prophet was waiting for them, there in the dark velvety interior, and next to him was Jack.

THE DEVIL INSIDE

1904—St. Louis

After Esta and Julien left the dressing room, with the door closed solidly behind them, Harte had to fight to keep himself from following her. She'd looked up at him in the mirror a moment before, her face painted so that even he couldn't recognize her, and he'd seen more than Esta—he'd seen the woman in his visions, the one with eyes that turned black as night and who screamed and screamed and—

It was a coincidence. Except he didn't believe in coincidences.

He scrubbed his hand over his face and then, with a violence that even he didn't expect, he kicked over the chair next to the dressing table before he swept the rows of makeup and paint to the floor. Porcelain pots shattered and the colors from the different powders splattered in a haphazard mess.

He should have stopped her. He should have tried harder to talk her out of this mess of a plan. She'd been taken in by Ruth and the Antistasi, romanced by their fantasy of a world remade, but Harte didn't have the same stars in his eyes. He couldn't see a world remade and free, not when the voice inside of him promised nothing but destruction and death.

Magic was nothing more than a trap. A *trick*.

Or maybe he should have let her go, as he did. Maybe he *had* to. Who was he to judge Ruth and her Antistasi? Especially not with the power inside Harte trying to make him doubt himself until he was so tied up with fear and indecision that it could break through the final defenses he'd managed to keep up.

Breathing heavily, he stared at himself in the mirror—the dark circles under his eyes, the two days' growth of beard shadowing his jaw. If he looked close enough, he thought he could see the creature inside of him peering out from the depths of his own eyes.

Even now, his fingertips digging into the dressing table, Harte felt like he might fly away if he didn't hold tightly enough. Every day that passed was a day Seshat grew stronger. Every day he had a harder time completely pushing down the voice that was rumbling and gathering its power. She was clearer now—anger and sadness and destruction and chaos was her song, and Esta was the melody she sang to.

She would rip apart the world.

No. He wouldn't let that happen. Harte would do whatever he needed to in order to keep the Book from getting Esta—from *using her.* His visions, whatever they were, would not be his future.

Taking another deep breath, he pried his hands from the tabletop and stepped back. He closed his eyes and breathed deeply, using every last bit of himself to control the power inside of him. Then he moved the panel from the wall long enough to go through it and made his way out the back of the building.

North was waiting for him at the end of the alley in one of the brewery's wagons, which had been painted over to obscure the name. Ever since the fire, things had been easier between Harte and the cowboy, but North's only salutation was a tip of his hat as Harte climbed up onto the driver's bench.

"Your costume's there," North said, pointing toward the burlap sack on the floor.

As they drove, Harte pulled out a cape out and a matching mask. It was a grotesque-looking thing made of papier-mâché, with a snakelike face and straw to cover his hair.

When Harte was done dressing, North handed him a small flannel bag. He looked inside and found the necklace. If he hadn't known it was a fake, he never would have been able to tell. Ruth's people were good—damned good. The metal shone like the platinum of the real Djinni's Star, and the stone in the center of the collar had nearly the same otherworldly depth as the original. "It's perfect."

"Of course it is," North said. "Now, remember, when you switch it with the real necklace, fastening it will prime the activator. When they take it off, that should trigger the mechanism within it. This Julien fellow'll have maybe ten minutes before the acid burns through and the serum vaporizes."

"That shouldn't be a problem." Once Harte switched it off Julien on the float, the next person to touch it would be the Veiled Prophet himself, when he transferred the necklace to the girl who would wear it at the actual ball. According to the plan, that should happen just before the Veiled Prophet escorted the unlucky debutante and presented her to the rest of the attendees of the gala. Julien wasn't invited into that, so he'd be safe. "Everyone should be well on their way back to the meeting place when that happens. You have the bracelet Ruth took?"

"Maggie has it," North told him. "She'll give it to you at the Water Tower once it's all done."

"And then we'll be out of your hair for good."

North pulled the wagon to the side of the street and jumped down from the driver's perch to hitch the horses to a post as Harte opened the back. Inside, more than a dozen Antistasi were waiting solemnly, each dressed in the same costume Harte himself was wearing.

They filed out in silence, one by one, until they were all gathered around North.

"You'll need to make sure you get the right float," North instructed, going over the plan one more time. Distraction was what they needed. Distraction and confusion so that Harte could slip up onto the float and make the switch.

"The Prophet will be near the end of the parade," Harte told them, information Julien had been able to gather. "That's where we need to cause the most fuss."

"We'll do just fine at causing a fuss," one of the snake-people said, and the rest tittered in agreement.

"Remember," North told them, cutting into their laughter, "when the lights go out, you all need to scatter. Ditch the costumes wherever you can, and then get yourself back to camp. Don't go off together, either. Split up. If you get caught, do whatever you have to, but don't betray the rest of us. We'll get you out as soon as we can."

There was a murmuring of assent through the group as Harte pulled on his own mask, leaving it propped up on the top of his head.

"Good luck," North said, reaching out his hand.

Harte accepted the handshake. For a moment he considered pushing his affinity into North, just to be sure that Ruth hadn't made any other plans, but he couldn't afford North suspecting anything just yet. If they wanted to get both the necklace and Esta's cuff away from a pack of other Mageus, they needed the element of surprise.

They studied each other for a second or two, neither one of them willing to be the first to surrender, until Harte decided to let North win.

He released the cowboy's hand and gave him a silent salute as he pulled his mask down over his face. Then he joined the crowd of serpents and went to find the Veiled Prophet, the necklace, and the girl he would never deserve.

THE GALA

1902—New York

J ack Grew stood in the corner of his uncle's ballroom and surveyed all that he had created. Around him, candles glowed and crystal clinked. The low murmur of anticipation wrapped around him like a mantle, fortifying him for what was to come. Everyone who was anyone in New York society was there, including all the members of the Order and a handpicked selection of the press who were most likely to cover the event in the best possible light. In one corner, Sam Watson was chatting with the younger Vanderbilt. Across the room, his aunt was preening over the state of the ballroom. Everyone was happy, content. Including Jack.

He was close. So very, very close.

Watson had noticed him and was approaching from across the room, but Jack pretended not to see. Instead, he ducked behind the nearest curtain that separated the guests from the area behind the temporary stages that circled one side of the ballroom. The mood there wasn't the relaxed, champagne-tinged atmosphere of the crowd. Backstage, the nervous energy of the performers made the air feel almost electric. Anticipation flooding through him, Jack took the vial from his jacket and crunched two more of the morphine cubes. Then he slipped the vial back into his vest, next to the warmth of the Book, and made his way through the preoccupied performers to find Evelyn.

By the time he reached her, she was already wearing the gossamer gown that had been commissioned for her tableau. All the tableaux had been selected for specific reasons, but mostly to portray the strength of science and alchemy over the dangerous feral magic that had once nearly destroyed civilization. *The Nightmare* was to be the final tableau, the finale of sorts. In the painting, a fair-haired woman lay unconscious, draped over a low couch, with her head and hand hanging toward the floor. The way Fuseli depicted her, the sleeping woman might well be dead except for the faint blush of pink across her lips, and on her chest sat a gargoyle-like figure, a succubus that represented the idea of the nightmare, pressing down upon her, holding her in the deathly sleep.

Evelyn had already powdered herself even paler than usual for the tableau. Her skin was so white it practically glowed and was barely different from the ivory gown she wore. She touched up the pale pink paint on her lips in a small mirror, the gown hiding very little. It might as well have been transparent from the way it clung to her curves, and because it was so close to her powdered skin, at first glance it almost did seem transparent. That was all part of the fun, of course. Tableaux vivants were known for being titillating and risqué and for skirting the very edges of propriety.

But tableaux got away with being so provocative because of their subject matter—classical art. The gown Evelyn wore might have been enough to have her jailed on the streets, but for the tableau it was perfect. When she was reclining on the divan, the gown would look very much like the one in the painting, giving the impression of both a nightgown and a burial shroud, to heighten the similarities between the depths of sleep and death itself.

Of course, if Jack's plans came to fruition, those similarities would be one and the same tonight.

On her finger, the ring glinted in the low light. *Soon,* he promised himself as her eyes found him in the mirror and she turned to greet him. *Very soon.*

"Jack, darling," Evelyn purred. "How do I look?" She twirled, allowing the gown to spin.

By now the warm desire she elicited had become familiar to Jack, and with the ritual he'd performed earlier from the pages of the book, it was little more than an annoyance. But Evelyn wasn't the only actor that night. He put on a good show of softening his gaze and stepping toward her as though he wanted to kiss her, rather than wring her neck.

"Ravishing, as always," he said, counting the seconds until the satisfaction on her face turned to fear. "Did you find the wig I sent over?" Fuseli's sleeper was a pale blonde, and Evelyn's violently red hair would disturb the reality of the scene.

"I did," she told him. "I was just about to put it on." She peeked at him from under her lashes. "I also saw the nightmare. You've outdone yourself, Jack. He's marvelous."

"Isn't he?" Near the platform where Evelyn would eventually prostrate herself stood the misshapen figure that would be perched on her chest.

Evelyn walked over to it and ran her hand seductively over the top of the creature's head. "The expression on his face, it's so vital and *alive*. You can almost imagine him haunting your dreams, can't you?" she asked with a sly, seditious smile he'd come to recognize as her trying to manipulate him.

"I can more than imagine it," he said, examining the creature he'd created with his own hands. It had taken more than a few errors to get it just right, light enough to sit on her chest and with enough heft that it would hold up when the time came.

"The audience will be thrilled," she purred.

"Yes. Yes, they most definitely will be," he told her, biting back his anticipation. "Well, if you'll excuse me, I have to check on some other preparations. It's nearly time to begin."

BEFORE THE STORM

1902—New York

Cela tugged at the starched uniform she was wearing. She hadn't been born to wait on tables or clean up after people who thought they owned the world just because their daddies were rich. But she'd promised Jianyu that she would help him get the ring back. It had been a trying week, though, working as a domestic in the Morgan mansion. Every day she watched the preparations for this gala, she'd come to understand that none of these people needed any more power than they already had. They certainly didn't need some magic ring that could cause things to end badly for more than just people with magic. She believed Jianyu when he said that in the wrong hands, the stone in the ring could bring the entire world to its knees.

Cela wasn't built for kneeling.

She straightened her back and got ready. They had a little while longer to wait. The plan seemed simple enough—wait until Evelyn's scene was revealed, and then Jianyu could slide in and take the ring from her finger. If she tried any of her hocus-pocus, she'd have to use it on the whole place or risk exposing herself in the middle of a room full of men whose goal in life, other than making money, was destroying her kind.

Too bad Cela didn't believe anything could go that simply, no matter what Jianyu thought.

But she wasn't alone. Even if he didn't necessarily agree with her, Abe had decided to help. It might have been just to keep her from getting herself into more trouble than she could handle, but she wasn't going to complain. Across the room, he was carrying a tray of champagne. His eyes met hers and he gave a slight shake of his head. No sign of Evelyn yet.

She nodded to let him know that she was okay, and then she went to pick up some more dirty glasses. It was all about to begin.

AN OLD ENEMY

1904—St. Louis

When Esta saw Jack sitting in the gloom of the waiting carriage, she had to force herself to finish climbing aboard. Julien took the seat next to Jack, so she was forced to sit across from him. She swallowed down her nerves and followed Julien's example, leaning back and letting her legs flop wide beneath her skirts—mimicking the man she was supposed to be—and prayed that between the makeup Julien had painted her with and the dim lighting of the carriage, Jack wouldn't recognize her.

"Ah, Mr. Eltinge, and . . ." Jack's voice was expectant as he glanced sideways in her direction.

"This is Martin," Julien said, as though that explained it all. "Martin Mull."

"We weren't expecting anyone else," the man behind the gauzy lace veil told him.

Esta could feel Jack's interest in her, but she kept her face forward and forced herself to *keep breathing* as she met his gaze unflinchingly.

"Martin often serves as extra security for me," Julien explained easily. "Tonight of all nights, I assumed that extra security would be more than welcome. Especially considering what you're having me wear through the streets of the city."

There was a moment of long, tense silence before the Prophet inclined his head, the veil in front of his face waving with the motion. Esta could practically feel Jack's interest in her fade when the Prophet dismissed her.

Unconcerned, he removed a vial from inside his coat, took a couple of small cubes from it and placed them in his mouth, and then, considering it, he took a couple more before tucking the vial away.

It had been only a few weeks, but for Jack it had been longer, and the years showed on his face. He looked older than he had before, and his skin had a sallow and unhealthy puffiness to it. Maybe it was the effects of drinking, but somehow Esta didn't think so. His fingertips were drumming on his leg, and the nervous energy of their soft rhythm vibrated through the air in the small space.

He had the Book. He might even have it with him. He was sitting there, so close, and if she just risked using her affinity, she might be able to lift it from him.

But if she tried—if she managed to get the Book—Jack would know it was missing. His response to that discovery could throw all of their careful plans into chaos—including the plan to get the necklace. Her mind raced, but Esta couldn't see any way to get both the Book and the necklace. Not without putting everyone and everything else at risk. And not before the carriage rumbled to a stop and the door opened.

Outside, strings of electric bulbs lit a staging area that was swarming with people clad in outlandish costumes. Around one float, a band of people with their bodies painted in garish colors were dressed in feathers and buckskin. They stood talking with others dressed in Confederate gray. Around another float, men dressed like sultans, their faces darkened with paint and long false beards glued to their chins, stood laughing and drinking from a shared flask. On top of a miniature replica of one of the steamboats that crawled down the river, people stood in blackface and top hats, waiting for the parade to start.

Esta hadn't been expecting anything enlightened, but her stomach turned at the display around her. It was like the Klan had decided to throw a costume party, she thought, trying to affect bland indifference. She couldn't afford for anyone to notice her disgust. "They do this every year?" she asked Julien.

He nodded.

"Is it always this . . . ?" She was lost for words.

"It's my first year," he told her, frowning at a trio of men who were making lewd gestures to a fourth, dressed as a woman and laughing his fool head off. "But yes. I suppose it is."

They found the float that they were set to ride on—the Veiled Prophet's own. It was designed to look like a larger version of the boats in the Streets of Cairo. It had been built on the back of a large wagon, its sides painted in the same shimmering gold and bright indigo blue that adorned the attraction at the Exposition. On either side of the float, five men waited, oars in hand, for the parade to start. From the fact that they looked completely sober—unlike most of the revelers—Esta suspected they were the Jefferson Guard, added security for the Prophet and the necklace. In the center of the boat, a small raised dais held two golden thrones topped with an ornate canopy of jeweled silk.

A pair of uniformed Guardsmen approached, one of them carrying a small valise.

"Everything go as planned, Hendricks?" the Prophet asked.

The Guardsman holding the case nodded. "It's ready for you," he told the Prophet, offering the case for inspection.

The Prophet took a key from within his robes and opened the lock to reveal a glint of platinum and turquoise blue within. *The Djinni's Star.*

Esta clenched her hands into fists to keep herself from taking it now. It would be easy. Simple. She could get the Book and the necklace both. All she had to do was pull time still, take the necklace, and go. . . .

And Julien will be left holding the blame. He'd brought her, after all. They'd look to him for answers when she disappeared, and when he didn't have any, Esta doubted that it would matter. He'd be ruined.

He'd be lucky if he was *only* ruined.

Never mind that Ruth's people were waiting, ready to put themselves at risk in front of the entire city, most of whom had turned out to watch the parade. And Ruth still had Ishtar's Key. If Esta did anything to put the

Antistasi at risk, it would make it that much harder to get her cuff back.

There wasn't any good option. She'd have to just carry on as planned, even if all she wanted was to reach for the necklace now.

It was too late, anyway. The Prophet was already fastening it around Julien's neck.

"Now, Mr. Eltinge, just as we discussed," the Prophet said. "If anything happens to this during the parade—"

"No one will get past me, sir," Julien told him, his jaw clenching. He glanced at Esta, who glanced away. For an actor, he was a terrible con.

The Prophet nodded, his veil fluttering like an old woman's lacy curtains. "Then I believe it's time," he said, gesturing to the dais.

Julien climbed up first, unaided, and then the Prophet followed. Esta went after them, taking her spot close to Julien. In the confusion, she lost track of where Jack went, but the Djinni's Star was so, so close. And it was still completely out of her reach.

Little by little, the men who'd been milling around in half-drunk groups began to organize themselves, and the staging area grew less and less crowded as the individual floats departed. Esta could hear the thunder of drums as the bands began to move out and then, after what felt like an eternity, the boat lurched beneath her and they were moving.

The parade route was packed with people, each straining to get a better glimpse of the brightly lit floats that traveled through the city. Above them, each float was attached to the electric trolley car lines, the source of power for the electric bulbs that glowed like small suns, hot and dangerous, around the papier-mâché decorations.

As they rounded the corner of Linden and began the slow, steady progression toward the fairgrounds, Esta felt something sharp strike her cheek. She was rubbing the soreness when she was hit again, this time on the arm. "Ow," she said, rubbing at the newly tender place.

"It's just some of the usual trash," Esta heard the Prophet say. "Ignore it."

But the volley of projectiles assaulting them was only increasing.

Two of the men dressed as Egyptian sentries came to attention, moving to the side of the float, where they searched the crowds on the sidewalk below them. A moment later they were pointing to someone, and Esta saw the police who had been lining the route turn into the crowd to find the culprits.

"See," the Prophet said. "A simple nuisance."

The parade continued, and in the distance, Esta saw the arched entrance to the fair. *Soon,* she thought, keeping her eyes peeled for any other sign of trouble. *Harte will be here soon. And then it will be over.*

Or maybe, it will just be beginning?

They were about a block away from the entrance to the fairgrounds when Esta heard a commotion from the crowd. A wild scream split the air, and suddenly masked men emerged from the faceless spectators. They were dressed in dark cloaks, and their masks were made to look like the faces of snakes.

The Antistasi, Esta thought, her whole body feeling warm and ready at the sight of them. Just as they'd planned, and right on time. The men—and women, Esta knew—used the flash powder that Julien had supplied from the theater to distract and blind the line of police before they sprinted for the Veiled Prophet's float. Esta backed up to Julien, pretending to be the security she was posing as, and watched as more than a dozen of the snake-people climbed aboard.

The air was thick with unnatural magic, hot and icy together, as the Antistasi attacked, pulling the oarsmen from their perches and tossing them aside.

"Protect the queen," the Prophet shouted, and the remaining sentries formed a wall around them as the masked Antistasi attacked.

Esta found herself surrounded by chaos as she pretended to fight off the snake-people. But then one of them was immediately behind her, attacking Julien. *Harte.* She launched into the fray, executing the choreography they'd practiced so that their fighting provided the misdirection Harte needed to slip the necklace from Julien's throat and replace it with the replica. He gave her the signal, meeting her eyes with a look of sheer determination—and something else she couldn't quite read—and she did what they'd practiced, fighting him off Julien and pushing him from the float, where dark-suited policemen waited.

She didn't have time to worry about whether he landed safely. She was being pulled back herself suddenly, and before she understood what was happening, the floor of the dais was dropping down and she found herself trapped with Julien in a small cell. The floor above them closed over the top of the opening, and everything went dark.

COLLATERAL DAMAGE

1904—St. Louis

Harte fought against the hold the two police officers had on his arms, but it wasn't long before he was being shoved inside the back of a long, dark wagon with a handful of the other Antistasi. The door shut behind them, and the carriage rumbled on as Harte checked to make sure that the necklace was still tucked into the secret pocket sewn into his shirt.

During the fight, it had taken nearly all of his strength to keep himself from winning the mock battle he'd staged with Esta. The voice inside of him had rallied, urging him on—to take her down, to take everything she was. But that voice was quiet now.

It was a quiet he didn't quite trust. Maybe the power was pulling away from the stone tucked in his pocket, just as it had pulled away from the Book. But it could just as easily be lying in wait, preparing itself for its next onslaught.

Someone lit a match as Harte was pulling off the mask, and the other people in the back of the carriage all looked at each other for a moment. Then someone laughed. "Damn, that was fun," a man with a missing side tooth said as he wiped sweat from his brows and pulled off the gloves he'd been wearing.

Harte couldn't quite agree, not yet, at least. He'd relax when they were free.

When the carriage stopped, he waited, his skin prickling with awareness, until the door opened to reveal a policeman standing there, his

620

mouth twisted in disgust. "Looks like we got us a bunch of Antistasi snakes." Then his expression broke into amusement, and he stepped back to let them out.

Harte released the breath he'd been holding, and he felt the power shift inside of him. It didn't feel half as weak as he did.

He let the other guys go first. His nerves were still jangling from the adrenaline of what they'd just done, and he wasn't in a hurry to get moving, but once he stepped out, he was relieved to be outside the close, stale air of the carriage and into the warmth of the night. Ruth was standing next to the spot where the carriage had stopped, waiting with some of the other Antistasi.

"You made the switch?" she asked when she saw Harte alight.

Harte nodded. "It's done," he said.

Though he still didn't like it. If they couldn't manage to get back to 1902 and to stop all of this from happening—if they were stuck going forward from here, now—who knew what the repercussions could be of an all-out attack on the president?

He pulled out the necklace to show Ruth. "Now your part of the deal. I'll take Esta's bracelet."

"You'll have to wait," Ruth told him, reaching for the necklace.

He pulled it back. "Like hell—"

"Maggie hasn't arrived yet," Ruth said, cutting him off before he could get too worked up. "She should be here any minute."

"Then we'll talk about you getting the necklace once she arrives with the bracelet," Harte said, tucking the necklace into his jacket. Once Esta arrived, Ruth wouldn't get either of the artifacts.

They waited awhile as other people arrived, each breathing heavily and looking absolutely delighted with what they'd just done. Ten minutes passed and then twenty, and with each additional second, Harte grew more and more impatient. *They should be here by now.*

But before too long, the sounds of wagon wheels and hoofbeats quickly approaching signaled an arrival.

Not Maggie . . . *Esta*.

The power inside Harte lurched at the sight of the smaller carriage pulling up next to the brewery's wagon and swelled with need when Esta clambered out of the back before the wagon was even completely still.

But Esta's face wasn't the picture of satisfaction he'd been expecting. "Do you have it?" she asked. When Harte nodded, her expression didn't ease. "They have Julien," she said grimly.

"What do you mean?" Harte asked, stepping toward her and wanting more than anything to wrap his arms around her and pull her to him. But when the voice inside of him rose at that idea, he stopped short.

The plan had been straightforward. Dangerous, but easy enough once the necklaces were switched. The Prophet would take the decoy necklace from Julien and place it on the neck of the debutante who had been chosen as that year's Queen of Love and Beauty, and then the two of them—Esta *and* Julien—would leave.

"They took the Prophet's float off to the side street as soon as the attack happened. They had us in this small holding cell under the wagon's bed, and when we got to the Festival Hall, they let us out. But they took Julien right off—necklace and all. Jack was there waiting for him," she told Harte.

Harte froze. "*Jack Grew* is here?"

She nodded. "I tried to follow them, but the Guards wouldn't let me. Said it was for the artifact's security or something."

Harte didn't like any of it. There was no reason for Jack to go with Julien, unless Jack somehow knew. "Was Julien okay?"

"I don't think the Guards suspected anything," Esta told him. "They seemed more worried about the necklace than about Julien being any kind of threat. I think as long as he stays calm and keeps with the plan, we can go back and get him after they make the necklace switch."

He didn't like it, but things could have been worse. They could retrieve Julien, and maybe in the process, they could get the Book from Jack as well.

Soon they heard more hoofbeats approaching.

"Maggie has the cuff," Harte murmured to Esta as Maggie came into view. She nodded to him, letting him know she understood.

"Tell me you didn't do it," Maggie said to Ruth even before she slipped down from the horse. Then she ran to her sister and grabbed Ruth by the arms. "Tell me it isn't done. That it didn't work, or—"

"Everything went as planned," Ruth told her, frowning.

But Maggie was shaking her head like she didn't believe it.

"It's fine," Ruth told her, gentling her voice in a way Harte had never heard it. "Everyone's safe, and the necklace was switched. All is well."

"No," Maggie said. "*No.* We have to stop it."

"There's nothing to stop," Ruth told her.

"But the serum—it doesn't work."

Ruth frowned. "Of course it works. We saw with our own eyes—"

"They're *dying,*" Maggie said, her voice nearly hysterical. "I thought it was just that Arnie's burns were too much for him this morning, but then this evening it was Greta. She's gone already, and the rest are following, dying by their own magic. There's nothing I could do for them. Even Isobel couldn't do a thing to heal them. It's *killing* them."

Ruth's jaw tightened, and her eyes went hard. "That's unfortunate."

"It's not *unfortunate.* It's a catastrophe. They're all dying, and it's our fault. If that necklace detonates, we'll be responsible for the deaths of everyone at the ball. All those people—"

"So they'll die," Ruth said, pulling away. "How many of ours have they killed with their laws and their Guard and their hate?"

"We can't—*I* can't just let this happen," Maggie said, horrified. "This isn't what I intended. This isn't—"

"There's nothing we can do now," Ruth said. "It's already done."

"We can stop it," Maggie told her. "We can disrupt the ball—we can do something to get them out of the building before it's too late."

"I won't risk any of mine for the Society."

"It's not just the Society in there, Ruth. It's their wives and daughters, too," Maggie persisted, not noticing how close to her Esta had gotten.

"Who live off the benefits of the evil their husbands and fathers commit."

Maggie took an actual step back from Ruth and nearly ran into Esta. From the look of horror on Maggie's face, Harte suspected that she'd never quite seen this side of her older sister before. "Ruth," she pleaded.

They had the necklace, and from the look Esta was giving Harte, he knew she'd just lifted the cuff from Maggie. They could go now, before they got caught up in the fallout that was sure to come.

Except that he couldn't. "We can't leave Julien in there," Harte told Esta. Her horrified expression told him that she agreed.

"We can't leave any of them in there," she said, her voice shaking.

"How do you plan to get into the ball?" Ruth asked. "There will be Jefferson Guards at every entrance. Even if you could get past them, you would have to contend with more inside and the president's security on top of it."

"We'll figure something out," Harte said. But short of charging the doors and hoping for the best, Ruth was right. Trying to save the people in the ball was a suicide mission. With all the dignitaries that were attending, they'd never be able to get past the security, and if they did, they'd never get back out again. It was the whole the reason they'd taken the necklace from the parade.

"I can help with that," North said softly.

"I won't allow it," Ruth said. "It's a fool's errand. And you're not going anywhere until I get that necklace," she told Harte.

"You'll have to take it from me," Harte said.

"North," Ruth commanded. "Take care of this."

"With all due respect, ma'am, I'd rather not." North stepped between them.

"What are you waiting for?" Ruth asked the others.

But the men and women who'd dressed themselves as serpents to disrupt the parade didn't make a move to attack. Most of them studied the ground at their feet, their jaws tense and their shoulders hunched against the weight of what they had just helped to do.

"Then I'm done with the lot of you," Ruth said as she reached for her sister's hand. "Come, Maggie. Let's go before we're seen."

"I'm going with them," Maggie told her. She ignored her sister's protests and stepped forward to slip her hand into North's. The cowboy's eyes shone with satisfaction.

Ruth's face had turned a blotchy red, and her expression was a mixture of anger and shock. "Maggie, you'll come now as you're told." Even Harte could feel Ruth's impatience simmering in the air as thick and real as magic itself.

But Maggie looked over her shoulder at her sister and shook her head. "I haven't been a child for a long time, Ruth. I've caused this, and I'm going to do something to stop it."

NOTHING TO FORGIVE

1902—New York

Ruby took another look at herself in the long, mirrored panel of the ballroom's back wall and frowned.

"You don't have to do this," Theo said, frowning at the outfit she was wearing—or perhaps he was frowning at the lack of it.

He had a point. The peach-colored garment she wore beneath the gown might have covered her from neck to toes, but it left nothing to the imagination. She was portraying Circe, from the John William Waterhouse painting of the witch offering a cup of her potion to Ulysses. Over the nearly nude garment, Ruby's diaphanous gown was the color of the sea on a cloudy day. It hung loose over one shoulder, exposing more of her than she would ever have chosen to reveal on her own.

She glanced over her shoulder. "Of course I have to do this," she told him, steeling herself for what was to come. "Being back here gives me access I wouldn't otherwise have."

"I don't like it," Theo grumbled. "It's one thing to pass information on in the hopes of seeing what gets stirred up, but it's another thing altogether to put yourself in the middle of the very storm you've created."

"How am I supposed to know the truth if I'm not in the middle?" she asked, lifting the front of the gown in a vain attempt to get it to cover more. Frustrated, she gave up and let it fall again.

"Last time you insisted on getting in the middle of things, I distinctly remember being shot," he told her, his tone more dry than truly angry.

Still, Ruby felt guilt flood through her. "I don't think I'll ever be able to forgive myself for that," she told him, her voice barely more than a whisper.

His expression softened. "There's nothing to forgive," he said. "I'm alive and well. I just don't want to see you hurt."

Especially since Viola is no longer in our lives. The words hung unspoken between them.

But she wasn't going to think about Viola, not tonight. She'd wasted too much time not writing and not reporting in the last two weeks, and she was practically desperate to get a story that would make her editor look twice at her again.

She'd been rash, maybe, in passing along to Jack the information Viola had given her about Paul Kelly, even if she had sent it to him anonymously. She had thought to stir up the hornet's nest that was the Order to see what happened, but in truth, she'd been acting out of hurt and anger and spite. And maybe she had been impetuous to have Theo talk Jack into allowing her to be part of the tableaux. At the time, though, the Order's gala had seemed like a lifeline, a way back to the person she'd been before she let a pair of violet eyes sway her. But now, it felt like everything she'd once thought she had under control was slipping from her grasp.

She shook off that thought. It was nothing but nerves. Maybe she hadn't completely thought everything through, but at least she was there, as close as anyone could possibly get to the Order's biggest event since Khafre Hall had burned. Tonight, R. A. Reynolds would get a story like no one else's.

Still, the dress was ridiculous. She had never shied away from a little bit of scandal, but now she worried what her wearing it—and wearing it in front of anyone who mattered in her mother's circle—would do to Theo's reputation.

"If you don't want me to—"

Before she could finish, Jack Grew had come around the curtain. He eyed her for a second, looking far too pleased with himself, before he turned to Theo. "Barclay, you're going to have to go. We're about to begin."

Theo gave her a long, unreadable look, and in that instant she thought about changing out of the gown and going with him. But before she could, he was gone.

"You look like perfection, Miss . . ." He frowned. "I'm sorry. I know Theo has introduced us before, but your name seems to have slipped away from me." He gave her a smile that would have been charming had his eyes not been so calculating. "Product of the accident, I suppose—head injuries will wreak havoc, won't they?"

"Reynolds," she told him, wanting more than anything to get away from him and his leering. "Ruby Reynolds."

"Reynolds?" he asked, his expression darkening.

It was the same thing that had happened a thousand times before. If someone didn't already know whose daughter she was, their face would transform itself once they found out. But this was different. Jack's expression was more one of fury than pity, and Ruby realized her misstep.

It had been an Order member who'd ordered her death. *It could have been Jack.*

"Well, then," he said, his face still carefully blank. "You have everything you need?"

She nodded, trying to hide her fear with the brilliant smile she'd learned for her debut. "Yes, thank you."

"Excellent. It should be *quite* the show." He gave her an appraising look, and then he was gone, off to the next set of performers.

Ruby prided herself on being an intelligent woman, one whose intuition had gotten her out of countless scrapes over the years, so she knew she'd made a mistake. She needed to find Theo and get out of Morgan's mansion before anything else could go wrong. She put down the cup and the wand she'd been preparing to carry and started to pull her cloak over the scrap of fabric she was wearing.

"What are you doing, miss?" The costumer was there with a look of horror on her face. "You don't have time for that." The woman was already taking off the cloak and tucking it over her arm before Ruby could argue. "Up you go," she said, leading Ruby to the thronelike seat and handing her the cup and the wand she'd just discarded.

"I need to go," Ruby tried to tell her, but the woman just gave her an impatient *tut-tut*.

"Everybody has nerves. It'll be just fine. You'll see."

The music was already starting on the other side of the curtains, a trilling run of a harp and the soft sounds of a violin, and the woman was leaving with her cloak. And it was too late for Ruby to do anything more than carry on and hope that she was wrong about how badly things were about to go.

BASTA

1902—New York

It was only the weight of Libitina that kept Viola anchored as she took one step and then another into J. P. Morgan's ballroom. She was on the arm of John Torrio and surrounded by people who hated her, people who would just as soon see her dead or deported as anything else, and it took every bit of her determination to keep the hate from her eyes as she followed Paul through the crowd, nodding and introducing himself to people as they went.

They'd trussed her up again in a corset and a gown covered in silken flounces. A ridiculous thing that did nothing to disguise what she was. Worse, it seemed only to encourage the Fox, who kept sliding glances at the slope of her cleavage above the neckline of her dress. His arm would occasionally rub against the side of her tette, and she knew from the leering look in his eyes that the small brushes were no accident. Had she not needed him—and needed to keep attention *away* from herself—she would have gladly introduced him to her most deadly accessory, the blade strapped to the side of her thigh.

Paul and Torrio made their way through the room, dragging Viola along with them, and as they went, the glittering jewels and perfectly tailored silks of the women all around her only served to remind her of who she was—and who she *wasn't*. She'd never be one of these perfectly coiffed debutantes, so demure that they seemed able to blush on command. She didn't want to be one of them. Even if one of them had a sharp tongue and a nose that crinkled when she smiled.

Basta. She tried to take a breath, but the boning of the corset reminded her that in this world, women were not even supposed to breathe. *Focus.* She needed to figure out which of these preening pigeons had the ring.

The quartet of musicians in the corner were starting to warm up and the other attendees were beginning to find their seats when Viola noticed a familiar silhouette that had her nearly stumbling. Theo was there, talking to an older man who had his eyes. If Theo was there, and Torrio noticed . . .

He wouldn't do anything, she tried to tell herself. Not here, not in the midst of all the men they were trying to impress.

But if Theo was there, Ruby might be as well.

So what? She was done with them, finished. Wasn't she?

She was about to turn away, to settle herself between Paul and Torrio, when she saw Theo give the older man that sad, lopsided grin he'd given at the park. He'd warned her then that it wouldn't turn out well, and she hadn't listened.

None of this was his fault. Ruby had dragged him into this mess and had nearly gotten him killed. But Viola had risked everything to save him once. To simply hand him over to Paul and Torrio now? It would mean that all the hurt and the anger Viola had lived with since Ruby had looked at her with hate in her blue eyes had been for nothing.

Besides, Ruby loved him.

Viola would save Theo for that reason alone. If it was her lot in life to always want and never have, so be it. She was strong and smart and could make her own way. And there were worse things than loneliness. There were the long hours in the dead of night when you had to live with the choices you made.

She excused herself to follow Theo as he headed toward the back of the ballroom. Paul gave her a curious look, but the musicians were starting in earnest now, and he couldn't do much without creating a scene.

It wasn't that difficult to get ahead of Theo before he started back toward a side hall. When he rounded the corner, she pulled him into an unseen alcove.

He startled, but almost seemed unsurprised to see her. "Viola?"

"Shhh—" She pulled him farther into the alcove, away from prying eyes.

"I didn't really think I was your type," he said, giving her that lopsided smile again.

She opened her mouth to refute his words, her instinct after a lifetime of hiding and denying and refusing. But he wasn't looking at her with the same disgust that Paul or her mother had when they noticed how captivated she'd been with her English teacher years ago. "You're not," she told him, which was as close to an acknowledgment as she'd ever given anyone except Esta.

"Where's Ruby?" she asked, brushing past the moment because dwelling in it was far too dangerous. "Tell me she's not here."

"Of course she's here," he said. "Can you really imagine her missing something like this?"

No. "She has to go. Now."

He looked suddenly confused. "That's not possible. She's playing Circe tonight, and everything is about to—"

The music suddenly went silent, and a man's voice boomed over the crowd to welcome the attendees.

It's too late.

A REUNION OF SORTS

1902—New York

From his place concealed in the corner of the ballroom, Jianyu watched Viola follow the light-haired boy into a side hallway. It had been nearly two weeks since that day on the bridge when he'd last seen her. But in everything that happened, she'd disappeared, and he'd been unable to search. Now he wasn't sure what to make of the fact that she'd arrived with Paul Kelly.

Torn, he considered his options. He didn't know when he'd get another opportunity to speak with her—to explain all that she did not yet know—but he would have only one chance to get to Evelyn while she was at the center of attention and less able to retaliate. On the far side of the room, positioned close to an exit, Cela and her brother were watching the High Princept of the Order introduce the evening's honoree.

Jack Grew.

Jack stepped onto the stage and shook the High Princept's hand, and then he took command of the stage. Harte Darrigan had told Jianyu all about the upstart nephew of J. P. Morgan. He was reckless and dangerous. And he could not be allowed to get the stone.

But even knowing what he knew about Jack Grew, even with the mission before him, Jianyu could think of only one essential thing: *Viola is here.*

THE RIGHT TIME

1904—St. Louis

While North drove them toward the fairgrounds, Esta finished stripping off the Egyptian gown to the men's pants and shirt she was wearing beneath it. She was grateful that she hadn't given in to Julien's pleas for her to leave off the clothing beneath the costume. Using the strips of white linen she tore from the gown, she scrubbed as much of the makeup as she could from her face as the carriage rattled on.

North parked one street over from the fair's entrance and tied up the horses as Esta and Harte climbed out the back.

Maggie, who had ridden up front with North, was frowning, her eyes worried.

"Are you okay?" North asked, looking like he wanted to reach for her.

"Just thinking about Ruth—about how she looked when I walked away."

North's expression softened. "You did the right thing, Mags."

"She's my *sister*, Jericho," Maggie said, her tone dull and hollow. "She's my family, my flesh and blood, and what's more, she raised me like her own daughter."

"She's *used* you," North said, lowering his voice as he took Maggie's chin gently in his hand.

Harte glanced at Esta, his expression impatient as the two talked, but Esta could only shrug. If Maggie didn't make up her mind now, she'd be a liability inside.

"I know," Maggie was saying to North. "I know all that, but it doesn't change what we are to each other."

North took Maggie into his arms for a moment. "Sometimes blood's not enough, Mags."

Maggie's face crumpled. "I know."

Esta understood the emotion in Maggie's voice—the hurt that simmered below the confidence in the words. A betrayal like Maggie's sister's was one that would haunt her, just as Professor Lachlan's betrayal haunted Esta, following her with dogged footsteps. But it had also urged her on— to be better, smarter . . . *stronger*.

"Let's go," Harte told them, apparently done with waiting. "We need to get in there. We don't know how much time we have left. There's no telling when the Prophet is going to switch the necklaces."

But in the distance, the wailing of a siren erupted. The night was suddenly alive with sounds as bells clanged and more sirens droned.

"We're too late," Esta said, as the four of them paused to listen.

"The Festival Hall is on the other side of the fair," North told them. "Even without the crowds, it's nearly a mile from here. But maybe, if we hurry, we can still get some people out—"

"Once the acid hits the serum and the vapor forms, there will be no way in," Maggie said, her voice a strangled whisper.

Esta thought about her cuff and how useless it was in that moment. She couldn't risk using it now, because going back to stop everything meant crossing Ishtar's Key with itself. If it were only her life in the balance, she could have done it to make up for her part in all of this, but it *wasn't* only her life. She'd been so blinded by her own anger, so determined to be strong that she hadn't realized how far she'd veered from what they were supposed to be doing.

Harte had been right—about Ruth and about the Antistasi. They should have stuck with their own plan. They should have grabbed the cuff from Ruth and found the necklace on their own instead of getting tied up into the Antistasi's plot for vengeance. Maybe if she hadn't been so set on being strong—on being *ruthless*—the Antistasi would have had more trouble with their attack. Maybe the innocent people in the ball wouldn't be suffering right now.

She would carry the guilt of her part in the attack with her always, but she would not risk her cuff to change it. Not now. She *couldn't*—Nibsy was still out there, and if they didn't collect the stones, he would. She needed Ishtar's Key, not just for herself, but to stop him from controlling the Book's power.

But North was already taking out his pocket watch. "It's not too late yet," he told them, opening the cover and adjusting it. "They'll have guards all over the place during the ball, but before it starts, we might have better luck. I don't like to go back, myself. Nothing good usually comes from trying to fix what already happened. But I think this warrants it."

"Go back?" Harte asked.

"In time. My mama always used to say I had a knack for being in the right place at the right time," North told him. "I could be out in the streets running wild with the other kids and somehow know that dinner was on. In a blink, I'd be there at the table, right where I was supposed to be, before she'd even called me. If trouble was coming, I'd be out of the way before it ever arrived. Of course, I learned later on that it wasn't just a knack. It was a touch of magic. But I never could control it until I got this." North showed the two of them the watch.

It looked like any pocket watch: brass casing with a scratched crystal cover over the face. The minute and hour hands might once have been painted black, but the paint had rubbed away where North had touched them to change the time. The second hand stood still, and the watch itself didn't make so much as a tick, but Esta could feel the pull of it—the tug in the energy around her that marked it as having an unseen power.

Harte frowned at the watch. "Ritual magic?"

"I don't know about any ritual, but magic it's got," North told him. "I'll just adjust this back a bit. An hour maybe?"

"They might already have the Guard in place by then," Maggie said, worrying her lip.

"Right. Let's go back a few then. Once we're in, I can set us to the time we need," he told her. "If we can get into the building while it's still daylight, we can go forward again, until just before the Prophet arrives. That way, we can be ready for them."

Esta caught Harte's eye. "It will be fine," she said, understanding his reluctance.

But his jaw was tense and his eyes wary. "What about the stones we have?" he asked in a low voice so the others couldn't hear.

"I'll have to leave them here. In the wagon?" she asked.

"You really think that's wise?"

She didn't. It felt like abandoning part of herself to think about leaving the stones behind. But if North could take them back without her risking the cuff . . . "I don't see that we have any choice if we want to save Julien. We have to try to stop this if we can."

"What about in the wall?" he asked. "They'll be less likely to be found if Ruth comes for the wagon."

He was right. While Maggie was gathering her supplies from the back of the wagon, Harte and Esta found a place close to the wall of the fair-grounds to hide the stones. They buried them, and then Harte used one of Maggie's devices to set a trap. Anyone who might disturb it would get an unpleasant surprise.

"Come on over here." North motioned them around the corner from the gates. "Now hold on." Maggie reached out to take his arm first, and then Esta did the same. Harte hesitated, clearly dreading the thought of traveling through time again.

"If you're afraid . . . ," North teased.

Harte took hold of North, who only smirked as he clicked the watch shut.

THE ALCHEMIST

1902—New York

Jack took a minute to accept the applause as his due. It rolled over him, a benediction for all he'd suffered and all the plans he'd worked so diligently to put in place. The lights of the ballroom twinkled and shone, winking at him as the morphine coursed through his veins, clearing his mind. Opening him to the possibilities this moment held.

He lifted his hands, gratified to see the crowd follow his directive as he took control of the room and began the evening's festivities.

"Ladies and gentlemen, I cannot tell you what it means to me to be here tonight, honoring the Order's essential work and marking our commitment to the city we love so dearly. I know that for some of us, the past weeks have been a trial. Our newspapers have not always been kind to our esteemed organization or the work that we do to keep our city safe. But tonight we prove the naysayers wrong. *Tonight* we show that the power of logic and science, the enlightened study of hermetic arts, will always be far superior to the craven wildness of the old magic, which once threatened the very essence of civilization.

"Tonight, on behalf of the Order and their Inner Circle, I am honored to present our tableaux vivants."

The orchestra started into their first series of chords, a minor-key piece that sounded as dangerous as Jack himself felt, and the attention of the audience only bolstered him more.

"Without further ado, our first tableau, a painting by the esteemed Joseph Wright, *The Alchemist Discovering Phosphorous*."

With a flourish of his arms, the curtains on the first of the stages pulled back, revealing the dimly lit scene. Two men sat in the background, leaning over a desk as though doing calculations. In the foreground, J. P. Morgan himself played Wright's alchemist. His uncle was wearing a false beard and his expression was enraptured over the enormous glass flask held on an iron pedestal. Genuflecting before the altar of science, Morgan was dressed in an ancient-looking robe, tied with a sash.

The audience applauded politely, murmuring with amusement to see who was in the first tableau.

"A charming scene, to be sure," Jack told them, anticipation racing alongside the morphine in his blood. "But we can do better, don't you think?"

The crowd murmured and rustled, but he ignored them as he walked over to the tableau. His uncle and the other actors kept their positions, frozen as though they were living, breathing statues. He hadn't warned them, hadn't told them what he would do, because he wanted their shock as well.

"Those who live in the shadows of our city, like rats infesting the very structure of the society we have built here, depend upon feral magic. Weak, unruly power. But see what an enlightened study of the occult arts can accomplish." He lifted his hands and sank into the looseness of the morphine in his veins, and the words he'd practiced in the privacy of his room came from his lips as though he had been born to say them.

The orchestra went silent and the crowd tittered, but Jack barely heard them. He was calling to something bigger, something deeper. Against his chest, the Book felt positively hot.

Suddenly, the chandeliers flickered and the lights wavered. Then, as though they were some sort of fairy creatures, the light from the

THE DEVIL'S THIEF   639 chandeliers flew toward the dark liquid in the flask his uncle knelt before and set it aglow.

The audience went completely silent as the room went dark except for the glowing flask in the tableau, and then, all at once, they burst into thunderous applause. His blood thrummed, hot and sure. And he had only just begun.

A BRUSH OF MAGIC

1902—New York

The lights flickered back on, and Viola felt the chill of the unnatural magic seep out of the air. She shuddered slightly. "We need to get her now," she repeated to Theo.

He didn't need to tell her that it was impossible. She could see for herself that there was no way to get through the crowd and behind the curtain without everyone seeing her, including Paul and Torrio. When the curtain opened, Ruby would be exposed. Torrio would know the truth of Viola's duplicity, and neither of them would ever be safe again.

Vaguely, she felt the warm brush of magic nearby. At first she dismissed it as more of Jack's tricks, but when it didn't immediately dissipate with the cold power that had flooded the room, she had another thought. Her hand went instinctively to the slit she'd made in her skirts, to take her knife from its sheath and, in a single fluid motion, she held it up to the empty air. "Show yourself."

"Viola?" Theo sounded as though he thought she'd lost her mind, but she ignored him and moved toward the warm energy until it grew denser.

She pressed her knife forward, and in an instant Jianyu was there.

"Viola," he said, his voice every bit as nervous as he should have been.

She didn't lower her blade. Nibsy had indicated that Jianyu could have been one of the traitors, and while she didn't trust the conniving rat, she also didn't trust Dolph's spy, who'd been suspiciously absent for these long weeks. "So you return. Where have you been?"

Jianyu glanced down at the blade at the same time that Theo stepped toward her. But she glared at Theo and then turned her attention back to Jianyu. "You were there on the bridge," she said.

"I was—"

"You weren't any help at all then." She moved the blade closer.

"I was with Darriga—"

The blade went to his throat. "That traitor?"

"He's not the traitor you believe him to be," Jianyu told her.

But she only huffed out a sound of disbelief. She'd been in the Mysterium. She'd been the victim of his treachery. "You expect me to believe that? Where is he now? I'll kill him myself."

Theo made a worried sound, but she ignored him.

"He's with Esta—"

"Esta?" She'd helped the girl escape. Had she been wrong in trusting her, too?

"It is a very long tale, and not one I have time for now," Jianyu said. "One of the artifacts is here."

"I know—the ring. Nibsy told me you would be after it."

Jianyu frowned. "We cannot let him have it."

"I have no intention of letting either of you have it." She lifted Libitina's blade until it was squarely under Jianyu's chin. "Where is it?"

"I know who has it—she is backstage. I was on my way to get it when I saw you and—"

"Backstage?" *Where Ruby is.* "You'll take me." It was not a request.

"As long as you promise that you will listen to reason when this is all through. There is much I need to tell you."

"You'll take me," she repeated. She wouldn't make promises or submit to Jianyu's demands. But she would get the stone, and she would see Ruby safe—whatever it took.

THE VEILED PROPHET'S BALL

1904—St. Louis

Esta's vision went white, but she kept hold of North's arm until she could see again. Her legs felt unsteady beneath her, and her skin was clammy from the magic of the watch.

When the brightness faded, the night had turned to day. In the distance, the sirens had been replaced with the echoes of the Exposition—the hum of the crowd and the far-off melody of a brass band.

Harte let go of North first and shuddered as he stumbled and tried to keep himself upright. "That just feels *wrong*."

"What does?" North asked, putting the watch back into his pocket.

"You don't feel it?" Harte shivered again. When North shook his head, Harte tried to explain. "Magic usually feels warm, like something you'd want to blanket yourself with. But that? It feels like a shard of ice went straight through me."

"I've never felt anything warm," North said with frown. "And I don't feel any ice either. You, Maggie?"

The girl shook her head.

Esta caught Harte's gaze. North was Mageus—she could feel the warmth of his affinity mingled with the prickling iciness of the watch's magic—but he didn't seem as attuned to his affinity as she and Harte were. Maybe it was because, without the watch, his affinity wasn't all that strong. Or maybe there *was* something to the stories of the Brink—the stories of how it worked to keep magic whole. If she really thought about it, all the power she'd felt on this side of the Brink had been off, mixed with that strange, cold warning that spoke of ritual and decay.

Done with the conversation, North gave a nod, and they were moving. The four of them entered the fair without any problem and then made their way back toward the lagoon. It was still midafternoon and the fair was open, filled with visitors who were there to take in the sights. Boats trailed in lazy paths across the calm waters, unaware that in the span of a few hours everything would change. The lights would turn the water into a glimmering mirror of stars, the white marble of the buildings would glow, and if they couldn't fix this—if they couldn't stop the necklace from detonating or the people from being at the ball when it did—people would die, including the president. Esta shuddered at the thought of what a change like that could do to the future.

The ball was being held in the Festival Hall, the white domed building at the head of the enormous lagoon. Other than the boats, which would have taken too long, there was no direct route there. They had to cut around the buildings that held exhibitions of metallurgy and liberal arts, following the broad paths filled with people until they came to the Festival Hall.

From the gilded dome to the lavish curlicues of marble and plaster, the Festival Hall was a testament to excess. In a city where many of the streets remained unpaved and workers gathered in warehouses to plan their rise, it was unnecessary, this impractical bit of beauty. Everywhere, lush flowers bloomed in perfectly manicured gardens, fountains threw water into the air in elegant looping patterns, and ornate gazebos provided shade from the afternoon sun. It was beautiful and frivolous with its sculptures and carvings. It should have seemed utterly charming and beautiful and feminine, but it was also imposing.

The building stood two stories above the fair on its man-made hilltop like a citadel, with a double row of columns that ringed it like the bars of a cage. Blocking the main entrance was an enormous fountain, THE TRIUMPH OF LIBERTY carved into its base, and on three of its sides were smaller but no less ornate fountains, LIBERTY, JUSTICE, and TRUTH, which all cascaded down to the main lagoon below. And on the top of its gilded dome, the goddess Victory had been wrought in the image of a man. *Of course she had*. Esta wasn't even surprised. The entire building was a statement of the city's power, as though St. Louis could claim its place in the country with marble and water. It was also a statement of the men who'd commissioned it—the Society, filled with the city fathers who ruled from their mahogany boardrooms and marbled halls.

But inside, the hall was mostly a hollow, cavernous space. Though the Guard was everywhere around the grounds of the Exposition, it was too early in the day for them to have taken up their posts for the night, so Esta and the others were able to enter the rotunda of the building, blending in with the other tourists who gazed up to where the daylight streamed in through spotless windows as an enormous pipe organ played a hymn.

They didn't waste time listening the way the other visitors did, though. Esta took stock of the building—hiding places and weak points. The Guard would do the same, and so would the president's security, but it didn't hurt to be aware of the exits in a place.

North led them through the rotunda and then to a small service hallway near the far side of the building. The door to the service hall was almost unnoticeable because it blended in with the ornate details and the scrollwork of the rest of the building. Once they were in the safety of the hall, they were able to snake through the building unseen.

"The ball will be held in the main rotunda out there," North said, leading the way. He must have seen plans for the building to have such a clear sense of his direction.

"They'll be bringing the parade down the avenue and then around the back, past the Palace of Fine Arts," Esta told them, remembering where the Prophet's float had stopped long enough for the Guard to pull Julien out of the hidden chamber beneath it and lead him away.

"That's just on the other side of this wall here," North said. "When the Prophet's float arrived, did you see where they took Julien?"

Esta shook her head. "They grabbed him and left me behind. By the time I climbed out of the float, he was gone. They made the rest of us leave the fairgrounds from the back entrance, and then I came straight to you all. I don't know where they took Julien."

North considered the question, his eyes unfocused for a second. "The east wing of the building is mostly maintenance and workers, but on the west side, there are some rooms for offices and meetings. They'll want privacy, so I expect that they'll set up for the Prophet there."

With a nod, North pulled them into a broom closet barely big enough to hold them. "The ball starts at ten, when the parade arrives, so we'll need to be a little early to get into position." He adjusted the dial of his watch, moving the minute hand ahead so that it dragged the hours along with it. Then he looked up at them, meeting each of their eyes in turn. "Ready?"

They each took hold of his arm, and once again, the world flashed white.

HUNGRY

1904—St. Louis

If Harte never again had to feel the creeping sense of unease he got when North used that magical watch of his, it would be too soon. He'd thought it was bad when Esta had pulled him through the years, but North's magic was worse. When the world went white, he felt like it disappeared completely and like a shard of ice had stabbed him in the chest. Even once he got his vision back, the cold ache in his chest was still there, like the shard was still melting in the center of his heart.

The voice inside of him didn't like it any better than he did. He could hear it screeching in the hollows of his head, blocking out everything for a moment and reminding him of the vision he'd had of the woman—the demon—in the temple.

But he pushed that voice down until it was a low, constant rumble in the back of his mind and shook off the lingering discomfort of the ice in his chest as he tried to focus.

"We'll need clothes," North was telling them. "Uniforms or something. We don't want anyone to notice us, if we can help it."

"We just need to get Julien and cause a big enough disturbance to get everyone out," Harte argued. "The faster we do this the better."

"We can create a disturbance," Maggie said, taking North's hands.

"Are you sure?" Esta asked her.

Maggie patted the pockets of her dress. "I've got some things with me. Nothing that will do any real harm. Just some smoke and flares to put on a little show, but everyone's already going to be on edge after the attack on the parade. It shouldn't be a problem to clear the ballroom before they get into it. You two get that friend of yours."

North opened the door, and the sounds of the evening came through the crack—the murmuring of voices, the clattering of plates and silver being set, and farther off in the distance, the music of an orchestra. "We'll meet back at the wagon," North told them. "Good luck."

Once they were gone, Harte was alone in the narrow space with Esta. If it had been a challenge before to keep the power inside of him in check, it felt impossible now. Beneath the scent of dust and the sharp bite of some cleaning solvent, he could smell her—the soft scent of sweat, clean and pure on her skin, and the power she carried within.

The thought startled him. It wasn't he who could smell her power. Magic didn't have a smell . . . *did it*?

Her eyes found his in the gloom of the closet, and the power surged again.

"We need to get going," he said, his voice sounding almost unhinged. She heard it too. Her brows bunched over her whiskey-colored eyes.

"Are you okay, Harte?"

He wanted to shake his head. He wanted to tell her to run. But he could only stare numbly at her for a moment, his voice silenced by the effort of keeping the power inside of him in check.

North was right. "We'll need clothes," he said finally, choking the words out like a man drowning. "Something that doesn't stand out."

She studied him a moment longer, a question in her eyes. But she didn't ask it. "Leave it to me," she said.

He didn't argue for once. He didn't want her to go alone, but he needed to get away from her to get the power inside of him back under his control. But a moment was all that he had. She was no sooner out the door than she was coming back, her arms filled with two sets of dark suits and crisp white shirts.

"Do I even want to know?" he asked, trying to make light of the moment. But his voice was too tight, and the words came out as a reprimand he didn't intend.

She cut him a sharp look. "It's not half as exciting as you're thinking. They have a rack of uniforms for the waitstaff tonight." She gave him a shrug as she started unbuttoning the rough-spun shirt she'd been wearing. Beneath, her breasts were bound with wide strips of linen that contrasted with the expanse of tawny skin that was the color of the desert sand at twilight.

He shuddered, knowing exactly where that image had come from. Seshat was hungry. She was tired of his hesitation and his refusal to take what he wanted.

What she *wanted.*

It was easier to turn away from her, to not watch her long, lithe arms disappear beneath the cover of the new clothing. But he could still feel her. Every particle of his being was attuned to her—to the warm magic that was wound into the very center of her being.

Soon, the voice hummed. *So very, very soon.*

They finished dressing, and when he turned back to her, she was wearing a look of determination so quintessentially Esta that he could barely breathe. He wanted to touch her. He wanted to pull her to him and press his lips against hers, but he knew that he'd grown too weak beneath the constant onslaught of the power that dwelled inside of him. If he touched her now, he would not be able to stop, and they would both be done.

"Esta—" Her name came from his lips like a plea, and he could not tell if he was warning her or calling for her or simply girding himself against the power inside with the talisman of her name.

"Not now," she said, her eyes dark with understanding. "Not until we're out of here."

They left the safety of the broom closet and followed the hallway back to where the guests were already gathered in the rotunda. The orchestra was still playing its soft melody from the loft where the enormous organ loomed above them. On the far side of the room, a group of people had crowded around a mustached man with a pair of pince-nez perched on his nose. *Roosevelt.* The dark-suited men near him must have been part of his security detail.

Everywhere Harte looked, he saw the life he would never have. The silks and the jewels, the tinkling laughter. The champagne and the stiff upper lips and the freedom these men had to walk through the world as though they owned it.

He could not even bring himself to hate them for it, because he didn't know, if the tables were turned, that he would be any better. They were, all of them, only what life had carved them out to be.

"I don't think the parade has arrived yet," he told Esta.

"We should figure out which doors they'll use," she said.

"Not those main ones." He nodded to where they had come in earlier and where a steady stream of elegantly clothed people was arriving.

"Maybe in that maintenance hall?" she asked. "There's got to be some kind of delivery door, where they brought all of this in earlier."

"There's only one way to find out."

He straightened his shoulders to match the posture of the other servers, and then the two of them started across the center of the rotunda. At the edge of his vision, movement caught his eye, and he glanced up to see Maggie on the catwalk high above them. *At least that much will work.*

They found they were right. In the east wing, there was a door where various workers came and went. "They'll probably bring them through there," Harte figured. The Prophet still had to make the switch from Julien, who'd worn the necklace in the parade, to the real debutante, whose reputation depended on her *not* displaying herself so publicly in the city streets. The transfer had to be seamless, though. When the Queen of Love and Beauty was introduced to the ball in the rotunda, she would already be wearing the Djinni's Star.

They found a cart laden with stemmed champagne bowls just across from the doorway, and they each took up one of the cloths and pretended to polish the crystal as they watched for the Prophet's arrival. They didn't have to wait long. A few minutes later, the staff around them seemed to noticeably adjust themselves, picking up their pace and attentiveness, and not long after that, the Veiled Prophet came through the door. Behind him, two of the Jefferson Guard had Julien—one holding each of his arms.

Harte ducked his head, pretending to study the glasses, but he used the motion to watch as the group entered one of the unmarked doors in the hallway. Other Guardsmen took up posts on either side of the door.

"You there!" a voice said from behind Harte. "What are you doing? Those have already been polished."

Harte glanced up to find one of the waiters staring at them, his hands filled with a tray of canapés and a scowl on his face.

"Water spots," Esta told him, holding up one of the glasses.

The waiter scowled even more. "You don't both need to take care of water spots," he grumbled. "We need more men on the floor." He came over and thrust the tray toward her. "Take this out there. Roosevelt wanted some of the pâté."

Esta glanced at him. She didn't have much choice but to take the offered tray and head into the rotunda.

"Finish that up and get out there," the man snapped at Harte before he hustled off to reprimand someone else.

Harte kept his head down and polished the spotless champagne bowl in his hand, keeping his eye on the door where the Veiled Prophet had Julien. A few minutes later the door opened and the veiled man exited with a girl on his arm.

No. The debutante must have been waiting in the room. She was already wearing the decoy necklace, and now she was being escorted into the rotunda.

He would get Julien out of there, and then he would go after them.

Harte put the crystal back on the cart and started toward the Guardsmen. He moved fast, pushing his affinity outward as he grabbed one. The other attacked, but not fast enough. A moment later they were both staring, dazed, and making their way like sleepwalkers toward the exit of the building.

Carefully, Harte eased the door open and saw that there was one Guardsman left, looming over Julien.

"I told you, I had nothing to do with the attack." Julien's voice was filled with more irritation than fear, so that was something, at least. "Those barbarians came after me, too. Do you see this? Does this eye like something I did to myself?"

Harte slipped into the room and used the element of surprise to his advantage. He launched himself at the Guardsman and in a matter of moments had wrangled him to the floor. Pushing his affinity through the tenuous layers of skin and soul, he sent the Guardsman a single command. The man went limp beneath him, his eyes open, looking to the ceiling above.

"We need to go," Harte told Julien. "Now."

But Julien was staring between Harte and the incapacitated Guardsman. "You're . . . Dammit, Darrigan. You're one of them," he said, shaking his head as if he couldn't believe it.

"You can hate me later if it means that much to you," Harte told him. "If you don't move now, you can stay here and deal with the Prophet on your own. But I'm leaving."

Indecision flickered in Julien's expression. Finally, he sighed and stepped over the prone Guardsman. "You should have stayed dead," he muttered, but there was no hatred and no heat in the words.

"There are days I feel the same way, Jules." And today, with Seshat already clamoring inside of him, was definitely one of them.

The hallway was empty now, and they had a clear path to the door. They were nearly there when Harte heard the laughter behind him. He turned to find Jack Grew leaning against the wall, his eyes bright with hatred.

"Harte Darrigan," he said, stepping toward them. "Back from the dead . . . again."

Harte stepped in front of Julien, shielding him from Jack. "Go," he urged. "Get out of here, *now.*"

"But—"

Harte turned and pushed him through the exit, thankful for the gown Julien was in as he pressed a command into the bare skin of Julien's exposed back. *Leave. Now,* he ordered. *Don't look back.*

Then he turned to Jack.

"I knew you would come to me," Jack said, his voice rough.

Harte frowned. "I didn't come for you."

"Didn't you?" Jack stepped toward him.

"No, I—" But his words died in his throat. There was something shifting in Jack's eyes. Something dark that was looking out at him from inside. The skin on Jack's face flinched, twitching like he'd been struck, and then something beneath it rolled, creeping under the surface like a snake.

Harte reached for the cart of crystal and pushed it over, sending the glasses crashing to the floor as he turned and ran.

The voice inside of him was screeching, and it was all he could do to keep his feet moving as his shoes slipped on the broken glass coating the hallway. He was nearly to the rotunda when Jack spoke again.

"Did you think you could evade me forever, *Seshat?*"

At the sound of the name, the voice unleashed itself, rising in its force until Harte could not fight it. Until he was nothing more than a shell of skin and bone, directed and moved by some unseen power.

THE CURTAIN PULLED BACK

1902—New York

Under the warm blanket of Jianyu's affinity, Viola watched as a second curtain opened, revealing a scene with a boat and sailors, their faces a picture of horror as they tried to escape from three watery maidens dressed in flowing robes who seemed set on capsizing them.

"Hurry," she told Jianyu as he carried her on his back around the edges of the crowd, careful not to disturb anyone and give away his position.

Jack Grew was droning on as they walked, and as much as she would have liked to shut him up, Viola prayed he would keep talking. Four scenes had been on the program, which meant that Ruby could be revealed at any moment.

"Evil creatures, designed and forged to bring men to their knees. Their feral power was once a danger, once unchecked in the face of helpless man. But as time passed, as man learned and cultivated an enlightened view of magic, their time came to an end."

They were at the curtains, and while the audience was enraptured by the sight before them, Viola followed Jianyu as he slipped through the curtain to the area backstage. Jianyu released his hold on the light, and she felt the warmth of his affinity recede as she slid down from his back. "It will be easier this way," he said, before she could argue.

"If you leave with the ring, I'll find you," Viola promised. "And when I find you, it will not be to talk."

Her words didn't seem to have the desired effect, though. Jianyu's mouth curved up at the corners. "We leave here together," he promised. "As Dolph would have wanted."

It didn't take long for Viola to find Ruby, who was sitting on a mirrored throne in front of the closed velvet curtains, wearing a long, dark wig and looking for all the world like she was terrified of what was about to happen. She was dressed in a bit of nothing: a garment that was almost the exact color of her flesh and a scrap of material draped around her that matched the deep blue of her eyes.

For a moment Viola froze. It seemed that her feet wouldn't move and her voice wouldn't make a sound, because all she could do was stare at Ruby, who looked so forlorn and lost and absolutely perfect that Viola could barely breathe. But her hesitation was a mistake. By the time she'd pulled herself together, the curtain was already opening.

CIRCE

R uby lifted the chalice and the wand and raised her chin as the curtain opened, revealing her—*so much of her*—to the audience of Morgan's ballroom.

There was a sudden hush that made her want to drop the objects and run, but she kept herself still, frozen as a statue, just as she was supposed to. Her eyes were straight ahead, searching for some sign of Theo, but she didn't see him anywhere.

"The Order is proud to present to you John William Waterhouse's masterpiece, *Circe Offering the Cup to Ulysses*. Behold the mother of witches, she who would lure men to her cup only to transform them into swine."

To Ruby, he sounded positively angry about the whole thing, as though it were her and not some mythic being that had done the dastardly deed. The tone of his voice sent a chill through her, but she kept her hands lifted, just as the painting depicted, and counted the seconds until it was over.

Without warning, though, the cup she was holding suddenly turned cold, and the bowl of it, which had been empty only moments before, began to froth with a bloodred liquid that dribbled over the rim of the chalice and dripped onto her dress. She glanced over at Jack for some sign that this was supposed to happen, but all she saw was the fury in his eyes.

Before Ruby could figure out what was happening or how she could get away, the curtains closed and she nearly collapsed with relief. She could hear the applause on the other side of the velvet, but she didn't care. She set the bloody-looking cup on the floor and looked at her stained hand. For a moment she was back in that dirty tenement, trying to keep the life from seeping out of Theo. And then Viola was there.

"Come," Viola said, without any sort of preface. "We have to go. *You* have to go."

Viola. Here.

It was so unexpected, so completely unbelievable, that Ruby couldn't quite understand what she was seeing, much less follow the order Viola had just given her.

"Are you okay?" Viola asked when she realized that Ruby wasn't doing anything but staring at her.

Ruby was shaking her head and stepping toward Viola before she knew what her feet were doing. *Viola is here.* The relief of seeing her there was almost too much.

Her hand was still sticky with whatever had burst forth from the cup, but Ruby couldn't stop herself from reaching out to touch Viola's cheek, just to be sure it was really her. The creature in front of her was wearing a silken gown that could have fit in at the opera, along with Viola's usual scowl.

At her touch, Viola went very, very still. "What happened? Did they hurt you?"

But Ruby only shook her head and leaned forward, pressing her lips to Viola's.

The moment her lips touched Viola's, she realized what she'd just done. She started to pull away, horrified that she'd overstepped, when Viola's mouth went soft beneath hers. Ruby nearly collapsed from the combination of relief and exhilaration she felt pooling in her body, heavy and warm and—

Viola pulled away, her violet eyes wide. "Why did you do that?" she asked, her fingertips touching her lips. Her cheek was marred with the red from Ruby's hand.

"I don't know," Ruby told her. "I saw you and . . . I wanted to."

It was the wrong thing to say. Viola took a step back. "This is all a game to you, isn't it?"

Ruby's stomach dropped. Viola had misunderstood. "No—" She stepped toward Viola, but the look on Viola's face had her hesitating.

"What about Theo?" Viola asked, her voice dark.

Theo? "He wouldn't care," she said, knowing it was the truth. The poor dear would probably be relieved.

Viola was shaking her head. "You treat him like your plaything too." Her voice was low and rough. "The whole world, nothing but toys for you because you have nothing to lose. *Nothing.*"

But Viola was wrong. She didn't know, *couldn't* have known that Ruby had already lost everything and had decided that it wasn't worth living life like a mouse, always running. Always afraid. "That's not why—"

Viola's eyes were shining with angry tears. "You play with people's lives because you can and then you walk away and go back to your fancy bedroom—to your maids and your servants."

"No, you don't understand," Ruby pleaded. She wanted to apologize, to explain, but her throat was too tight, and she didn't have the words.

"I understand too much," Viola said dully, taking yet another step back. "I've lived in this world too long not to know how this will turn out. You have to go. *Now.*"

The pain in the other girl's tone pierced Ruby. She took a step forward, her hand raised. "Viola, we can figure this out. It will be okay—"

"It wasn't Torrio they sent to kill you," Viola said, her voice like the knife she'd been holding the first time they met. "It was *me.* I risked too much to save your life then, and I'm risking everything now. So whatever that was, whatever you think is between us, do this for me and leave. Because my brother is out there, and so is Torrio. If they realize who you are—if they see *Theo*—they're going to know. And we will both pay the price for that."

For Viola she would have stayed, she would have risked everything, but for Theo? Steady, innocent, wonderful Theo, who had always been her rock. Who never told her no? She couldn't sacrifice him.

"This isn't over between us," Ruby promised.

"Yes, it is," Viola said, but the shine of tears in her eyes gave away the lie of her words.

In the fraught silence that stretched like a chasm between them, a woman screamed, and on the other side of the curtain, the gala erupted into chaos.

WHAT LIVED INSIDE

1904—St. Louis

The morphine he'd taken earlier was making Jack feel unbearably light, as though his feet were no longer moored to the ground. As though he had already become the god he'd intended to be.

"I knew you'd come for me," he said, and the voice that came from within him was the one he often heard in his mind. That other version of himself that he'd found in Greece, when he'd come to understand what power was and what he might do with it. That other self had guided him, kept him on the straight and narrow, and had unlocked the secrets in the Book tucked close to his chest. It seemed only fitting that his two selves would merge now, that he would become what he'd always intended to be.

The magician no longer interested him. No . . . He desired what lived *inside* the magician. The power that had slipped from his fingertips those many years ago. The demon bitch who had evaded him too many times over the years and centuries. He would have her now. He would take every bit of her power for himself.

Darrigan's eyes had gone dark, and Jack—and the other voice that lived inside Jack—knew it was because the magician was no more than a shell. And Jack would have his revenge. He would destroy Darrigan once and for all.

"Thoth . . ." The words came from Darrigan's mouth, but they were not spoken by his voice.

"Seshat," Jack said, letting the syllables hiss from his mouth, soft as a snake. "You can't win this time. Without the protection of the Book, your power will be mine."

"Protection?" Darrigan's lips curled into a disgusted sneer. "The Book was my *prison*, and now that I am free, I will destroy you."

"You can't destroy me, Seshat. I have become power itself. I have become a god."

"Even gods need a home, Thoth. I will destroy *everything* to ensure that you never again walk free."

SESHAT'S RETURN

1904—St. Louis

Esta was offering the tray of canapés to Teddy Roosevelt himself when the first of Maggie's devices popped, showering sparks over the entire rotunda and spewing forth a fog that wove through the air like a living snake. The security pulled Roosevelt away, making a solid wall between him and any of the other attendees. A woman in the crowd screamed, and the crowd in the rotunda began a panicked stampede toward the doors.

Esta ran in the other direction. She'd heard the crash of shattering glass from the distant hallway, where she'd left Harte, and she'd known somehow that something had gone wrong. But she hadn't expected anything like what she saw when she arrived. Jack Grew was there, and Harte was speaking to him, but their voices were off, eerily inhuman. And Harte's eyes were completely black, with not even the whites showing.

"You had everything," Jack said in that strange, otherworldly voice. "You had the key to all power at your fingertips, the heart of magic at your command. It was yours to control—and instead you tried to destroy it."

"I tried to *save* it," Harte shrieked, his face contorted. "I created the words and the writing of them because I thought it would be enough to stop the eventual death of magic. But I was wrong. The Book was a mistake."

"The Book was a gift," Jack said, stepping toward Harte.

"You had no right to it," Harte spat. "You stole what was not yours to take. I counted you as a friend, and you betrayed me. I revealed my failures to you, and you abused my trust by giving power—broken and debased as it was—to the undeserving who could not appreciate it—all for something as vulgar as fame."

"Why should magic have belonged only to those like you?" Jack asked. "Once, all people could touch the power that threads itself through all of creation. Who were you to keep it from them?"

"Who were you to give it only to the sycophants who favored you?" Harte threw back. "You don't think I know what was behind your rise?" Harte laughed, and it was the high, manic laugh of a woman who had come unhinged. "You don't think I know how you stole the secrets I inscribed and doled them out only to those who could pay, those who could bestow power upon you?"

"I gave them to the worthy," Jack said. "And I was rewarded. You ... *You* were forgotten."

"Because of *you*," Harte spat. "Because of how you tried to destroy me. But you failed in that, didn't you? You didn't expect that, did you? If you had realized how I had been bound to the Book, you would have destroyed it—and me. But you didn't, and because of your shortsightedness, I bided my time, waiting for someone to release me. Waiting for *this* moment."

Harte lunged at Jack, pushing him backward into the rotunda. Above them, the air was filled with the living plumes of dark smoke caused by Maggie's devices—the distraction she'd promised. Within the depths of it, lights flickered like lightning flashing. Esta could feel the rumble of cold power mixing with the warmth of the old magic, the two battling and warring overhead like some alchemical thunderstorm about to break.

Beneath it, Harte and Jack were grappling with each other, their hands clawing and punching as they rolled across the ground. And the power that came off them was overwhelming, hot as the flames that had consumed the brewery and icy as the Brink all at once, clashing and warring as the two fought. For a moment Esta was sure that Harte would win.

But then something shifted inside Jack and roared up, pinning Harte to the floor. Harte had gone limp beneath him, like he'd lost consciousness completely.

Esta acted on instinct, pulling her affinity close and making time go still as she sprinted to where the two of them were. Shoving Jack off Harte with the bottom of her shoe, she went to Harte and placed her hands on his face. "Wake up," she pleaded. "Come on . . ." She tapped at his cheeks and urged him again.

Without warning, his eyes flew open. But before she could feel the shudder of relief, she realized that it wasn't Harte looking out at her. It was something dark and ancient peering from the coal-black depths of his eyes.

Harte's hand snaked out and gripped her by the wrist before she could even think to back away, and the intensity of the power she felt rise between them shook her so profoundly that she lost hold of her affinity. The world spun back into motion, and Jack moaned softly from where he'd toppled over on the floor.

But Esta didn't notice. The moment Harte had touched her, the moment the power within him had connected with hers, she'd been overwhelmed. And then, the world fell away. . . .

There was a chamber made of stone and clay and the sand of the desert. And there was a woman with eyes of amber, just like her own, and the woman had made a mistake. She leaned over an altar that held the open pages of a book, and her pain and frustration hung heavy in the air. But the woman looked up suddenly and her eyes met Esta's.

"You've come." The woman's voice echoed through the chamber in a language Esta did not know but could understand even so. And though she could hear the woman speaking, her mouth never moved. "The one who can release me. The one who can fulfill my destiny. I knew you would come. I knew you would give yourself over to me."

Esta was frozen in place, moored in time and Aether. She could not move as the woman looked into her very heart.

"I see you so clearly. I see what you desire. The end of this pain and struggle."

Esta wanted to deny it, but she could not so much as shake her head. No, she thought. I don't want this.

"I tried to save it. Magic. Power. The energy that flows between all things. It was dying. It was fading even in my time, as people forgot, divided themselves from each other and from the unity of all things. So I tried to preserve what I could by creating the writing. I thought I could save the heart of magic within the permanence of words." The woman's eyes flashed with fury. "But I was wrong. Creating the power of ritual through writing only weakened magic further. Magic isn't order—it's the possibility held within chaos. Ritual limited the wild freedom inherent in power, broke it apart and kept it fractured. But it also made it controllable, even for those who were without an affinity for it.

"I shared what I'd done with Thoth, because I believed him to be a friend. But he never was. He'd been born weak, and he wanted the power I was fated with. He saw what I'd done, and instead of helping me try to fix my errors, as he'd promised, he took the power for his own. He made a devil's bargain, trading everything we could have been for everything he wanted to be.

"When I realized, I made the stones. I broke magic apart to protect the last pure bit of it. To form a barrier against any who would try to take it.

"But Thoth was never an ibis. He was always a snake, stealing other people's eggs."

Esta saw then everything that happened—the way Thoth had trapped Seshat and then destroyed the stones. He took the Book, but he was a vain and fearful man, so he never stopped running. He never ceased collecting more and more power. More souls and more secrets.

"I put myself in the pages he wanted so badly, but I was trapped by the parchment and vellum I'd written upon in my attempt to preserve magic's true power. Once, I was almost freed again. A man . . . a great magician tried. But he was a coward, unable to contain my power. Now . . . Now I walk in a new body. Now you have come for me, and together we will end him."

How? Esta wanted to ask, but her mouth would not form the words.

"With you, my dear child. With the power inside you, we will end everything."

No . . . *Frozen though she was, the word echoed in her mind.* No. No. No.

But Seshat only laughed, the rich rolling sound echoing around the chamber. *"What did you think you were, child?*

"They hunted your kind—our kind—across eons. Across continents and centuries. They tried to wipe us from the world because they feared us. They were right to. You can touch the strands of time—the very material that carves order from chaos—just as I once could. And like I once could, you can tear them apart.

"Come—" The woman at the altar held out her hand. "Join me. Release me."

Looking into the woman's eyes as she pleaded, Esta realized that Harte had been wrong. Seshat wasn't a monster. She wasn't a demon, either. She was just a woman. A woman, like Esta, who had power. A woman who had believed in the possibility of the world and had been betrayed by it . . . And now she wanted revenge for that betrayal. The hurt inside of her, the pain of it was like the same flint that sparked inside Esta. She understood. It burned inside of her, how deeply she understood.

Why not *burn it all down and begin again?*

Because innocent people would die. She knew it as well as she knew that Seshat had started just as innocent. She knew too, because she herself had been taken in by the anger and vengeance of the Antistasi. It wasn't a mistake she would make again. Esta recoiled at the idea of accepting, even as she felt herself stepping toward the woman.

"Thoth cannot be allowed to continue," the woman said.

Seshat would unmake the world to destroy Thoth. She would sacrifice everyone—everything—to ensure that Thoth, the true Devil's Thief, would die.

"Don't act as though you're so righteous," Seshat chided her. "You forget that I have already seen the truth of your heart. I have already seen the yearning for retribution. The desire for revenge. The hate that burns brightly inside you can remake the world, my child."

Yes, Esta had wanted revenge. She'd wanted to make so many pay. But she'd been wrong.

It was too late. Seshat was already pulling her forward, and Esta felt her affinity drawn toward the ancient priestess. She felt Seshat's power vining around her, but this time it was purer than it had been in the station or in the hotel. This time there was no fighting.

The world felt like it would fly apart. The darkness, Esta realized, wasn't something that had appeared in the world. It was the world. It was the spaces between, opening and flooding. It was the unmaking of reality.

And there was nothing Esta could do to stop it.

THE NIGHTMARE
COME TO LIFE

1902—New York

The moment that Jack had planned for weeks had finally arrived. The first three tableaux had captivated the audience, enraptured them with the demonstrations of his and the Book's power—not that they realized that was what they were seeing. He was well aware that they thought the feats he'd accomplished were nothing more than parlor tricks. They were, compared to what was coming.

As the third set of curtains closed, Jack slipped two more cubes of morphine into his mouth before he stepped in front of the final set of curtains. He looked out at the audience as he waited for the room to grow silent. There were the men of the Inner Circle, the High Princept, and the rest of society. Men from Tammany were there as well, and another face, a particular friend he'd invited himself—Paul Kelly, who had turned out to be another disappointment. But Kelly would get his soon enough.

He waited until every pair of eyes was looking only at him—seeing him for what he *truly* was. And then he waited a moment longer, just because he could.

"Ladies and gentlemen, we come to our final tableau. Tonight the Order has presented a veritable bounty of beauty and wonder. You have been transported to the alchemist's laboratory and witnessed the moment when man began to take control of the dangerous powers that surround us. You have seen art come to life, revealing the long and tortured history of feral magic, of those unwilling to control the dangerous power inside themselves for the good of a just and enlightened society. But now our evening is nearly at an end."

He paused, let the anticipation grow in the room until he could practically feel their desperation for the curtain to be pulled back . . . until he had them in the palm of his hand.

"I present to you Henry Fuseli's *The Nightmare*. . . ." With another flourish of his hands, the curtains opened and the final tableau of the night was revealed.

Evelyn, clad in a blond wig and a wisp of a gown, was splayed out on a low couch, just as the woman in Fuseli's famed painting. Her arms arched gracefully to the floor and her eyes were closed in a semblance of sleep. Just as in the painting, sitting on her chest was a creature meant to represent the embodiment of nightmares. Jack had created the figure himself, a gargoyle-like incubus that looked like the image of the one in the painting.

The audience rustled in wonder and in fear. He could tell it was fear from the way the air seemed to go out of the room. It was the most exquisite of the tableaux, the most horrible and beautiful all at once, and it was about to be more so.

"Those who cling to the old ways, who lurk in the shadows of our streets, are a mark upon the perfection of our union. They represent a danger. Like the darkness that creeps into our dreams, those with feral magic lie in wait until we are at our weakest. Like nightmares come to life."

At his words, the incubus began to move, turning its head to stare out at the crowded ballroom, and Jack was more than gratified to hear the audience gasp. The incubus was, of course, no ordinary carving. It was a sort of golem, an impressive piece of magic that had been revealed to Jack during one of the long, morphine-filled nights when he woke with no memory of parsing the Book's secrets. That he'd been given this particular secret was a gift, and he considered it nothing less than a divine sign of what he was meant to do. Evelyn's feral power might affect the flesh and blood, but he doubted it would do much to the misshapen creature he'd fashioned out of clay.

"But nightmares are meant to be tamed, just as those who cling to the old ways must be tamed."

He could feel Evelyn's fear even from where he stood, and that along with the singing of the morphine in his blood only emboldened him.

"Tonight you have seen the wonders of the alchemist's discovery, sirens, and witches, but now I present a *true* siren. A witch who would try to destroy the Order."

At his words Evelyn seemed to sense the danger she was in. She tried to sit up, but the moment she began to move, the incubus caged her with its arms and pressed her back to the couch. Even as she screamed, he could feel the heat of her magic brushing at him, trying to tempt him and sway him from his path, but it didn't touch him. *She* couldn't touch him. He'd learned too much since that girl in Greece. He'd learned too much from the Book.

"Evelyn DeMure pretends to be a simple actress. Perhaps you've seen her at Wallack's Theatre?" From the rustling among the men, Jack assumed that some had more than seen her. "But she, like so many of their kind, is not what she pretends to be. She intended to fell us all. She was there the night that Khafre Hall burned. She thought she could enrapture me with her evil ways, but as you can see, her power is weak compared to the secrets of enlightened study."

He was close—so close—he thought as he lifted his hand, and the clay figure did the same. He brought his fingers together in a fist, and the creature mirrored his action over the tender skin of Evelyn's throat.

By now people were starting to come to their feet. Some were calling for him to stop, but Jack was calm. Allowing the golem to do his bidding, he turned back to the crowd. "But Miss DeMure, as charming as she pretended to be, isn't the only snake in our midst tonight. There is another, one who pretended to be an ally but in truth was doing the bidding of the very people we are trying to protect ourselves from."

He found Paul Kelly in the audience, the low-life bit of Bowery trash who had pretended to befriend him. Kelly had not only allowed Jack's enemy to live but had also aligned himself with one of the people responsible for Jack's greatest embarrassment.

"You all might have noticed that Mr. Kelly is here with us tonight. I'm sure you wondered why someone of his ilk had been invited to besmirch our event," Jack said, watching Kelly's eyes narrow at him. But he dismissed the threat.

This was his room, his moment.

"Officers," Jack called. "If you would be so kind, please escort Mr. Kelly and his colleagues to a more appropriate venue, where they can be dealt with."

A scream went up in the crowd, and Jack turned to see that some of the waitstaff had dropped their trays and were pulling pistols from their dark dinner jackets and taking hostages. Kelly's men. *No. They can't— They are ruining* everything, he thought with a burst of rage.

The Book felt warm against his chest as Jack watched victory slip through his fingers. Kelly simply smirked and darted into the crowd, which had broken down into complete madness.

THE FLASH OF A KNIFE

1902—New York

The room around Jianyu had churned into chaos at the sight of the Five Pointers in their midst. It did not take magic, it seemed, to drive fear into the Order's hearts. A few snub-nosed pistols did the trick just as well. The crowds of the ballroom were trying to shove through a single, narrow exit in an attempt to flee, but Jianyu had his sights set on one thing: the ring.

It was still on Evelyn's finger, but Evelyn was being guarded by the strange beast. From his own vantage point, the cold magic that surrounded the creature was telling. It was not natural, but that was no surprise coming from Jack Grew and the Order.

With light opened around him, Jianyu ignored the noise and the confusion and crept steadily closer to the beast sitting on top of Evelyn. She no longer seemed to be breathing, but the beast still had its clawed fingers gripped around her throat, her sightless eyes staring off into the room beyond.

He was nearly there when he saw Cela moving through the crowd with a single-minded determination. While everyone else was trying to flee, she looked like a koi struggling upstream as she worked her way toward the stage and Evelyn. With his affinity, she had not realized that he was already there.

Before he could warn her, he noticed a flash of dark hair and plum silk and saw Viola coming in the same direction. From the look of fury in her eyes, Viola had seen Cela too.

He had not taken the time to explain earlier, when he could have, he realized with a sick sense of dread. Viola would not know who Cela was. She would only see a stranger after the treasure she had told Jianyu not to take.

It felt as though the moment was suspended in amber and he was viewing everything from outside of it. The flash of Viola's knife coming from the folds of her skirt, the fury in her expression as she screamed at Cela to get away from Evelyn—to leave the ring.

Cela glanced over her shoulder, but she ignored the warning.

Because she did not understand who Viola was. Because she could not have known what would happen.

But Jianyu did—he could see it playing out before it occurred. Viola would launch her knife through the air. She would aim for Cela, and she would not miss.

Letting go of the light, Jianyu did the only thing he could do. Without considering the consequences to himself, he leaped in front of Cela, just as the knife slipped from Viola's fingertips.

The room narrowed to that moment, but even knowing he had been hit, Jianyu did not feel any pain when the knife cut through his tunic and pierced his skin, tearing past sinew and bone to lodge in his shoulder. He felt nothing at all but relief when he landed hard on the floor at Cela's feet.

She was there, standing over him with an expression that told him just how bad it was. Her hands were on his face and her mouth was moving, but he could not hear the words she spoke. When he looked up at Viola, he saw only horror in her eyes. They were rimmed in red as though she had already been crying for him.

Pulling himself up, he took the handle of the knife and pulled it from his arm.

Finally, he felt the pain, the sharp stinging of the blade as it slid from the place it made through his skin. Even with Cela holding a part of her skirt to his wound, trying to stop the blood, he knew that he had to reach Viola . . . had to make her understand.

"We have to get out of here," Cela told him, trying to get him to his feet, but he had to speak to Viola. He had to tell her one, essential thing.

"Come with us," he said, offering her the knife, which was still coated with his blood. His voice sounded far away, even to himself, but he repeated the offer again. "We need you."

But Viola was shaking her head and backing away.

And then Abel was there, hoisting him up to carry him out.

Jianyu didn't know where the ring was, or who had it, but in that moment he knew that it didn't matter as much as making Viola understand. "Come with us," he repeated, knowing that nothing would be possible as long as they were divided.

A MONSTROUS CHAOS

1904—St. Louis

J ulien ran from the Festival Hall without looking back. Outside, the crowd that had once been milling about the rotunda was gathered, the women holding one another and the men blustering like fat capons. The Prophet was there, as were others from the Society, all standing and watching as the lights flashed within the Festival Hall and the eerie smoke began to creep from beneath the doors.

He was standing apart from them, unsure of how he got there or what he was supposed to do now that he was outside. He wasn't onstage, so the gown he was wearing and the weight of the wig felt uncomfortable and out of place. Part of him thought that he was supposed to stay, to make sure that Darrigan and Esta were okay, but there was a deeper impulse to slink off into the night. He began to back toward the darkened fairgrounds, out of sight from anyone who might be looking for someone to blame, when an earsplitting scream erupted from the center of the crowd.

It was the debutante he'd met just moments before, the one who'd been selected as the Queen of Love and Beauty. They'd taken the decoy necklace from him and had given it to her, but now a thick, dark cloud of smoke was pouring from where the necklace still perched around her neck. She was tearing at it, trying to get it off, but it was clearly stuck.

I did this, he thought, horrified. He'd only wanted to clear his name, to get Darrigan out of town before anyone knew, and instead, he'd helped them create this monstrous chaos.

People were backing away from the poor girl, terrified of the darkness blooming from the jeweled collar, but Julien found himself walking toward her—toward the danger.

He was there before he could fully think through the consequences. Taking hold of the necklace, he wrenched his arms apart and broke it in two. The girl ran, probably back into the arms of her mother, and Julien hurled the necklace as far as he could, to spew its poison far, far away from the crowd.

But not before he'd breathed in some of the dark fog himself.

NEVER ENOUGH

Margaret Jane Feltz had done quite a lot of things in her life that she wasn't proud of at the moment. Most of those she'd done because she'd believed at the time it was the right thing to do, because *Ruth* had told her that it was, and because she'd wanted Ruth's warm approval more than she wanted the discomfort of standing against her sister.

Maggie might have had an uncanny knack for mixing chemicals and powders—a gift of the kitchen magic that seemed to run in her family—but she hated it just the same. Still, she was grateful for the one incendiary she'd held back just in case. When she saw Ben grab Esta by the throat, she felt the air in the rotunda go electric, hot and bright like she'd never in her life felt it. She pulled the small canister from her satchel and activated the fuse before she rolled it toward them, placing it between the angry blond man in the tuxedo and the two she'd come to think of as friends.

It popped with a violent burst of light, throwing Ben from Esta and knocking him unconscious to the floor.

She ran to where Esta was lying, prone and still on the polished marble floor, and a moment later North was there. They gathered the two of them, and then with a click of North's watch, they were gone.

Between the crowds from the parade and the news that was beginning to spread about the attack on the ball, the streets were in chaos. All of the Antistasi's planning, and for what? The Mageus would now be even

677

worse off than before. Ruth had been wrong—about everything. Maggie had suspected all along, but now she understood.

As they made their way through town to reach the train station, Maggie tried not to think about the fact that she was leaving behind her sister and the Antistasi, who had become her family. But she knew that she'd done all she could here, and now there was somewhere else she was needed more.

She'd tried so hard to do one small bit of good. But it hadn't been enough. It wasn't ever enough. This time, she vowed, it would be.

THE DAGGER

1904—St. Louis

Jack woke sometime in the depths of the night with only a hazy memory of everything that had happened at the ball. Darrigan and Esta had managed to get away. They'd taken the necklace, but they had not been able to retrieve the Book. Instead, they'd exposed themselves, and now the entire country knew about their evil intent. Those mistakes would only help him in the future.

After he'd returned to his room, he'd pored over the Book, looking for some answer, but he didn't recall the words he'd read or how the pages had begun to glow or how he had reached through them, knowing that they would open for him, knowing that his fingers would be able to sink through the paper itself to find the object he'd placed there some months before.

He turned to the vial of morphine and instead found something more. On the table next to the bedside was an ancient artifact—the same one he had hidden inside the pages of the Book for safekeeping so many months ago. He picked it up and turned it in the light, marveling at its appearance as he reveled in the weight of the stone it contained, a sign of the power held within it.

Jack had obtained the artifact itself ages ago—not long after he'd taken the Book from Darrigan. After the Conclave, he'd begun to worry that someone might find it. He'd used one of the spells in the Book to conceal the object within its pages, turning the Book itself into a container for the artifact so that he could carry both with him at all times.

But once concealed, the Book had not willingly given the artifact back. For more than a year now, he'd nearly driven himself mad with the work of trying to force the Book to reveal its contents, all to no avail.

Now, it seemed, his luck had turned. It was as though the Book understood the crossroads he was at, as though it knew that he would need all the power he could harness in the days and weeks to come, and it had given up its contents like an offering. A benediction for the journey ahead—a journey that he was well aware would be difficult but that was his very destiny to fulfill.

SLEEPWALKING

1904—St. Louis

sta didn't know how they got away from the fair. She remembered pain and a chilling burst of power, and then, little by little, she surfaced from the fog of what had happened. Seshat. Thoth. And the dangerous reality of her own affinity. By then North had taken them forward in time, to long after the fair had cleared out and everyone had gone back to the safety of their own homes.

She moved like a sleepwalker, barely seeing or hearing as Maggie and North led them through the fairgrounds back to the waiting wagon. She almost didn't remember to retrieve her stones—the cuff and the necklace—but Maggie helped with that. Then it was a dash to the station, and before she could process everything, she found herself in a Pullman car, resting next to Harte on the narrow bottom bunk.

Even with everything that had happened, even with her world feeling like it had fallen apart, the sun still managed to come up the next day. It warmed Esta's face through the window of the train, waking her. There was a moment just as she came out of sleep when she forgot where she was—*what* she was. In that moment between sleep and waking, she did not yet remember the night before. She did not think of the mistakes she'd made or the lives those mistakes had taken. She did not yet remember the terrible truths that had been revealed and the heartbreaking reality of what lay before her. Instead, she thought that she heard a woman's voice singing to her, and she thought she could almost remember the words of the song. It must have been a memory from somewhere long ago, when she was nothing but a child with no guilt, only innocence. With the world in front of her, wide and open as a promise.

But the softness and safety of the state between sleep and waking lasted only a moment. The ache in her bones and the pain echoing in her skull returned soon after, reminding her of what she'd been through. She felt soiled and wrung out, like an old rag not worth cleaning to keep. Even her bones felt like they would shatter if she moved the wrong way.

Distantly, she heard the soft snoring of the people in the small berth with her. North, propped awkwardly in a chair, and Maggie in the bunk above her. She remembered lying down next to Harte. The power he carried within him was quiet as she nestled next to him, trying to warm him and waiting for him to wake as she fought her own exhaustion.

But now the bed was cold and empty beside her.

She pulled herself up and looked around the small Pullman compartment, but there was no sign of Harte. After what had happened in the rotunda, North hadn't trusted Harte not to do something rash. He'd lashed Harte to the post of the bunk, but the rope North had used was now hanging empty.

Worse, her cuff—the one that held Ishtar's Key—was gone. In its place was a simple bracelet made of beads: the one he'd bought that first day at the fair. She reached for it, about to tear it from her wrist, but the moment she touched it, a jumble of images rose in her mind, and she felt an impulse so sure and clear that she knew it was a message he'd left for her, deep in her unconscious mind. He'd used his affinity on her, she realized. Rather than leave a note that could have been found or read by prying eyes, he left her a hope and a plea that only she could know.

He hadn't left her completely, then. But he also hadn't trusted himself enough to take her with him.

Cursing Harte for his heavy-handedness and herself for falling asleep, Esta stepped outside into the passage and then out onto the platform, where the prairie grass extended as far as the eye could see.

Harte was gone, but she wasn't alone. There was a long, unknown road ahead of them, one that led to another ocean, a distant shore. She would do what Harte had asked of her, and then, when she found him, she would make sure he regretted leaving her behind.

There was work left to do. A demigod to destroy. There were still stones to gather, a future to make.

And on the inside of her wrist was a scar—a single word in the Latin she'd learned as a child. A command calling her back, to New York and to the past.

Redi.

DISCEDO

1904—St. Louis

As the train marched along the landscape he'd only ever thought to see in dreams, Harte Darrigan watched the horizon turn from the impenetrable blanket of night to a soft lavender glow as the stars disappeared one by one in the creeping light of dawn. He'd dreamed of this his whole life, the impossible open plains and the shadow of the mountains in the distance and the freedom of it all. But now that it was his, he was every bit as trapped—as imprisoned—as he'd ever been, only this time it was a prison he carried with him.

He'd woken in the dead of night when the other train shuddered to a stop at some unknown station. Esta had been curled next to him, her arm thrown over him in the narrow bunk and her face still tense despite being deeply asleep. He could hear the soft, steady breathing of others close by, and for a moment he didn't know where he was or what had happened. Inside, the voice he carried was silent, but he could feel her there, breathing and licking her wounds.

And waiting.

It would have been easier, perhaps, to allow his eyes to close again, to allow sleep to pull him under. It certainly would have been more pleasant to stay there, close to Esta's warmth, breathing in her familiar scent. Letting himself lean on her. But even at the thought of it, the power within him started to rouse itself.

For a moment he allowed himself to nuzzle against Esta's neck and breathe. For a moment he allowed himself to wonder what it could have been like to stay with her like this, as though they were two ordinary people with their lives ahead of them and their whole future as a possibility. But though Harte was a liar and a con, he wasn't good enough to fool himself.

If he stayed, Seshat would do everything she could to take Esta.

If he stayed, Esta would give herself to try to save him.

He couldn't stay. But he would do what he could to save her. To save all of them.

REDITE

1904—New York

James Lorcan held the telegram between his fingertips and read it again, just to be sure of its meaning. Around him, the Aether bunched and shifted, the future remaking itself into the pattern of his design.

His agent in the West had two of the artifacts in their possession, and best of all, they had the girl. It was only a matter of time before everything fell into place.

He lit a match with one hand and ignited the corner of the telegram, watching it combust and transform into a pile of ash. Then he turned himself to the business of the day before him—the business of leading the Antistasi.

AUTHOR'S NOTE

~

I've tried to depict the 1904 Louisiana Purchase Exposition as accurately as possible in this book. With the exception of the fictitious Nile River ride, everything from the statue on the top of the Festival Hall to the exhibits and layout of the Pike is based on historical maps, original guidebooks, and pictures I found during my research. While the Nile River ride is an invention of my own, I based it on the research I did, especially about the problematic ways the fair represented race and culture. Because the 1904 characters experiencing the fair can't possibly be aware of the future repercussions of the event, I wanted to give readers a better understanding of the Exposition's complexities and contradictions and how they still remain with us today.

The fair had an enormous impact on St. Louis, the Midwest, and the country as a whole. Between April 30 and December 1 of 1904 nearly twenty million people visited the 1,200-acre fairgrounds, which included seventy-five miles of roads and walkways, fifteen hundred buildings, and exhibits from more than fifty countries and forty-three states. A visitor to the fair could have experienced wireless telegraphy, observed fragile infants being kept alive by incubators, watched the first public dirigible flight, or perused 140 different models of personal automobile. Theodore Roosevelt visited, Helen Keller gave a lecture, Scott Joplin wrote a song, and John Philip Sousa's band performed.

From its sheer size, the fair billed itself as the largest and most impressive display of man's greatest achievements. But as I showed in the story, alongside some of the most astounding scientific and technological breakthroughs of the age, the fair also displayed people. In doing so, the fair became part of the larger history of race, culture, and social evolution in America. This was not accidental. The planning committee curated anthropological displays that worked specifically in the service of imperialism and Western exceptionalism.

It's important to note that in 1904 most Americans didn't have access to foreign travel. The Exposition presented a solution—an opportunity to experience the world in miniature. However, the fair presented a very specific version of the world, one seen through the lens of the West. The organizers of the fair did try to separate the serious and "educational" exhibits that were brought by individual nations from the more scintillating and exotic "entertainment" attractions on the Pike, but the average fairgoer regularly confused the two. The effect was that the fair presented a world in which ethnicity and exoticism became a form of entertainment. People and cultures became objects to consume.

As I show in the story, the representation of different nationalities on the Pike was highly problematic, but the rest of the fair wasn't much better. The educational exhibits were purposely selected by the planners as scientific evidence of the natural progress of human history. Fairgoers could understand the superiority of their own culture in contrast to the so-called "primitivism" of foreign cultures. In 1904, anthropology was still a fledgling discipline of study, but the Exposition and other world's fairs like it demonstrated anthropology's usefulness in ordering people. Specifically, the fair helped to justify the dominance of the West and the usefulness of imperialism in scientific terms.

For example, the large Igorot Village exhibit was the direct product of America's recent victory—and acquisition of territories—in the Spanish-American War. Fair organizers brought people from the Philippine archipelago and displayed them as a sort of human zoo. Fashionably dressed fairgoers who observed the villagers' dress and customs saw the Igorots as less modern—and therefore *inferior*.

Another example of anthropology used in the service of Western imperialism was the appearance of Native Americans and First Nations

AUTHOR'S NOTE

peoples as exhibits at the fair. The fair itself was a celebration of the Louisiana Purchase, the very event that permitted westward expansion and spurred on the ideals of manifest destiny that led to the slaughter and decimation of Native peoples. Harte and Esta see the Cliff Dwellers concession, but those weren't the only Native Americans at the fair. Apache, Cocopah, Pueblo, and Tlingit peoples were also present as attractions. Attendees could purchase an autographed photo from Geronimo himself, who was then still the American government's prisoner of war, or view an operational model Indian School, where children maintained a routine for the viewing pleasure of tourists.

While the fair provided some, like Geronimo, a chance to be entrepreneurs, it also exploited them with unsanitary living conditions and poor compensation. Moreover, the Exposition's display of Native peoples depended on nostalgia and perpetuated the stereotype of a once-heroic and noble people, now defeated and dying. These stereotypes have persisted to this day and continue to cause harm to Native peoples.

Finally, it's also important to note that while the fair displayed diverse people, it was primarily attended by white Americans. When a planned Negro Day to celebrate emancipation was canceled, the chair of the local committee revoked Booker T. Washington's invitation and told him that "the negro is not wanted at the world's fair." W. E. B. DuBois, whose landmark book, *The Souls of Black Folk*, had been published to critical acclaim the year before, was not invited. The Eighth Illinois Regiment, an African American regiment, made an encampment at the fair but were prohibited from using the commissary by white soldiers, who refused to share. In short, the fairgrounds were not a welcoming space for people of color.

Perhaps it shouldn't be a surprise that the Exposition had such a problematic and often offensive relationship to race and culture. It was a product of its time, after all, but it was also a product of larger social forces. Eleven of the twelve committee members who organized and planned the fair were members of the Veiled Prophet Society, including the president of the committee, David Francis. As I reveal in the story, the VP Society's formation was a reaction to the Great Railroad Strike of 1877, a strike that involved large numbers of African Americans and immigrants. The creation of the VP Society and parade was a direct attempt by white city fathers to reclaim racial and class superiority in the city, and much of the design and experience of the fair—both historically and in my book—echoes that same agenda.

For all it might have done to bring technological advances and exposure to foreign nations, at its heart the Louisiana Purchase Exposition cannot be seen outside the larger system of white supremacy and Western imperialism that it helped to perpetuate. It wasn't alone in this project, however. The Exposition and other fairs like it were common around the turn of the century. Their mixture of exoticism as entertainment and cultural exploitation taught white Americans a version of the world steeped in Western superiority. That understanding had far-reaching effects that continue to impact Americans' understanding of race and culture even today.

For further reading:

Whose Fair? Experience, Memory, and the History of the Great St. Louis Exposition by James Gilbert

From the Palaces to the Pike: Visions of the 1904 World's Fair by Timothy J. Fox and Duane R. Sneddeker

"'The Overlord of the Savage World': Anthropology, the Media, and the American Indian Experience at the 1904 Louisiana Purchase Exposition" by John William Troutman

A World on Display: Photographs from the St. Louis World's Fair, 1904 by Eric Breitbart

ACKNOWLEDGMENTS

~

A book this big doesn't happen without help from a lot of people.

First and foremost, to my brilliant editor at Simon Pulse, Sarah McCabe, who dealt with missed deadlines and more unfinished drafts than any person should have to read. Her patience and confidence made this book possible, and her keen insights made this book immeasurably better. Thanks for pushing me and for always having the answer. I'm so glad your brain works better than mine.

To the entire team at Simon Pulse, who have been so amazing and shown this series (and me) so much support: Mara Anastas, Chriscynethia Floyd, Liesa Abrams, Katherine Devendorf, Chelsea Morgan, Sara Berko, Julie Doebler, and Bernadette Flinn. Many thanks to Tricia Lin, who read early drafts; and to Penina Lopez, Valerie Shea, Elizabeth Mims, and Kayley Hoffman, whose astute copyedits, proofread, and cold reads made the sentences shine. My heartfelt gratitude to Audrey Gibbons, Lauren Hoffman, Caitlin Sweeny, Alissa Nigro, Anna Jarzab, Christian Vega, Michelle Leo and her team, Nicole Russo, Vanessa DeJesus, and Christina Pecorale and the rest of the S&S sales and marketing teams, who've done so much for the success of this series. Thanks to Russell Gordon and Mike Rosamilia for making the book beautiful, inside and out. And special thanks to Craig Howell, who somehow managed to create art for the cover that outdid his previous work on *The Last Magician*.

I'm grateful to have Kathleen Rushall in my corner. She's a rock star of an agent, and her unwavering support made the whole process of writing this book almost bearable. Thank you for the check-in emails and pep talks. I'm so lucky that I get to work with her and all the wonderful agents at Andrea Brown.

Many thanks to all the wonderful readers, reviewers, bloggers, booksellers, and librarians who put *The Last Magician* on the *New York Times* list last year and who kept me going with their excitement and questions about this sequel. Special thanks go out to the Devil's Own, especially Joy Konarske, Cody Smith-Candelaria, Agustina Zanelli, Patrick Peek, Kim McCarty, Jennifer Donsky, Kim Mackay, Rachel Barckhaus, Ashley Martinez, and Alyssa Caayao, who went above and beyond to spread their love for the series. Thank you for helping to make TLM a success!

Writer friends are the best type of friends. Thanks to all my favorites, especially the amazing women who listened to me complain about *not* writing and then complain *about* writing, who read drafts or helped me brainstorm my way out of corners, and who make the world better with their beautiful words: Olivia Hinebaugh, Danielle Stinson, Kristen Lippert-Martin, Helene Dunbar, Flavia Brunetti, Christina June, Sarah Raasch, Jaye Robin Brown, Shanna Beasley, Shannon Doleski, Peternelle van Arsdale, Julie Dao, Angele McQuade, Risikat Okedeyi, and Janet Taylor.

And last but never least, my family. This book was a beast to finish, and my guys put up with me basically being not present in their lives for three entire months. I know how hard my working so much was on them, but they gave me the time and space and support I can't possibly deserve (but I'll gladly take anyway). To X and H, who are light and joy, and to J, who is everything. Thank you.

LISA MAXWELL is the author of *The Last Magician* and *Unhooked*. She grew up in Akron, Ohio, and has a PhD in English. She's worked as a teacher, scholar, bookseller, editor, and writer. When she's not writing books, she's a professor at a local college. She now lives near Washington, DC, with her husband and two sons. You can follow her on Twitter @LisaMaxwellYA and Instagram @LisaMaxwell13 or learn more about her upcoming books at Lisa-Maxwell.com.

THE SHATTERED CITY

THE SHATTERED CITY

BOOK FOUR IN THE LAST MAGICIAN SERIES

BY LISA MAXWELL

MARGARET K. McELDERRY BOOKS

NEW YORK   LONDON   TORONTO   SYDNEY   NEW DELHI

MARGARET K. McELDERRY BOOKS
An imprint of Simon & Schuster Children's Publishing Division
1230 Avenue of the Americas, New York, New York 10020

Text © 2022 by Lisa Maxwell
Jacket photo-illustration © 2022 by Craig Howell
Series design by Russell Gordon
Jacket design by Greg Stadnyk © 2022 by Simon & Schuster, Inc.

For information about special discounts for bulk purchases, please contact Simon & Schuster Special Sales at 1-866-506-1949 or business@simonandschuster.com.
The Simon & Schuster Speakers Bureau can bring authors to your live event. For more information or to book an event, contact the Simon & Schuster Speakers Bureau at 1-866-248-3049 or visit our website at www.simonspeakers.com.
Interior design by Brad Mead and Mike Rosamilia.
The text for this book was set in Bembo Std.
Manufactured in the United States of America
First Edition
2 4 6 8 10 9 7 5 3 1
Library of Congress Cataloging-in-Publication Data
Names: Maxwell, Lisa, 1979– author.
Title: The shattered city / Lisa Maxwell.
Description: First edition. | New York : Margaret K. McElderry Books, [2022] | Series: The last magician ; book 4 | Summary: Hunted by an ancient evil, Esta and Harte have raced through time and across a continent to track down the artifacts needed to bind the mystical Book's devastating power, and now, with only one artifact left, they must find a way to end the threat they have created or the very heart of magic will die.
Identifiers: LCCN 2022012214 (print) | LCCN 2022012215 (ebook)
ISBN 9781534432512 (hardcover) | ISBN 9781534432543 (ebook)
Subjects: CYAC: Magic—Fiction. | Time travel—Fiction. | BISAC: YOUNG ADULT FICTION / Fantasy / Historical | YOUNG ADULT FICTION / Social Themes / Prejudice & Racism | LCGFT: Fantasy fiction. | Time-travel fiction.
Classification: LCC PZ7.M44656 Sh 2022 (print) | LCC PZ7.M44656 (ebook) | DDC [Fic]—dc23
LC record available at https://lccn.loc.gov/2022012214
LC ebook record available at https://lccn.loc.gov/2022012215

This one is for the readers—
Those who have found their home
And those who are still searching.

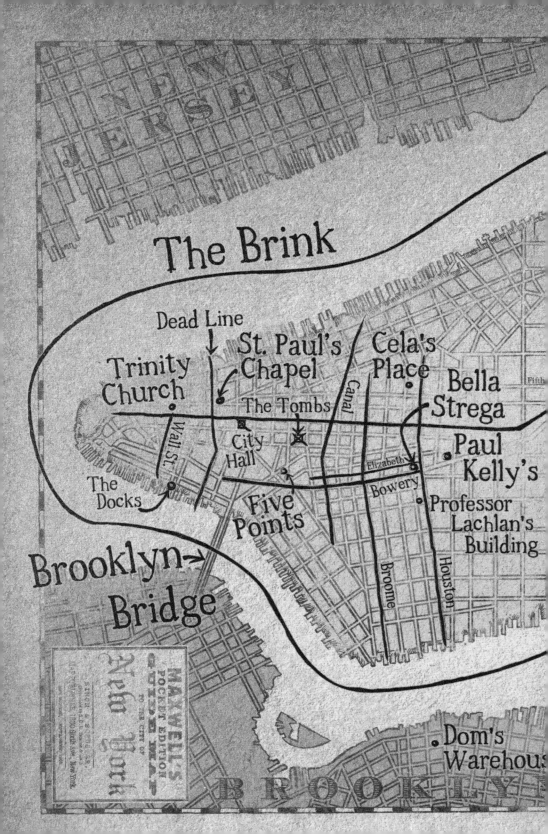

HUDSON RIVER

Schwab Mansion

Haymarket

Satan's
Circus

Broadway

CENTRAL
PARK

J.P.

Algonquin

organ Mansion

Madison
Square Garden

Third

BLACKWELL'S ISLAND

EAST RIVER

QUEENS

THE CITY

The city stirred as the sun dipped below the horizon and night began to rise. With a shuddering sigh, it felt the cool, timeless waters lapping at its shores, heard the endless wailing of children hungry within closed-off rooms. It tasted the fears of the women and men who wandered through the narrow channels of its streets, staking everything they had—everything they were—for a dream they often could not even name.

Far beneath the present, beneath the constant disappointment and the regret, the land remembered what natives and newcomers alike had long since forgotten. It remembered that once it had been a true place, before the land had been carved and flattened and pressed into order.

The city could not forget, because in the darkness, the past was always there. The future too. Alongside what was, the city could see the glimmer of what had been and what could *still* become, especially at night, when the past and future and all the possibilities in between seemed one and the same.

The city had watched itself change many times before and knew it would change again. But on that night, the deepest night in the darkest part of the year, it sensed something that felt like a beginning.

Or perhaps it felt like an end.

That night a dangerous new magic began to stir. Beneath the indifferent stars, cold fires smudged their heavy incense into the sky, and chaos flared. The streets that carved order into bedrock began to burn, and the city felt itself beginning to come undone.

But there were those who would stand and fight for an impossible future.

The city had barely noticed them when they'd first arrived on its banks days or weeks or years before: one with fire in her eyes and a knife in her hand, one who could fold the light but could not uncrease his own heart. They had been no different from any of the other desperate souls who came day after day, year after year, all hoping to carve a life from the unfeeling streets. That night they stood apart, and the city wondered. . . .

And there were others: those held no power at all—at least none that could be remembered. They had been born in the city's own cradle, but now the city took their measure.

Great beasts of smoke and fog rose from the cold fires as a demon raged, and the city watched her children fight. It watched them fall one by one. The assassin, the spy, and those who would help them. Broken and bleeding on a rooftop filled with angry men. A knife to the heart. A bullet to the brain.

And then there were the two. The Magician and the Thief. And the city stirred with interest once more. But in the end, they were too late, and their blood mingled with the rest.

The demon laughed, and the men who dreamed of greatness fled like the rats that tickled the city's ribs day and night. All except one, who stayed tucked into the shadows, eyes glinting at the sight of the broken bodies before him.

The city watched as the Serpent smiled. Like the city, he knew already that time was a circle, unending and infinite until shattered against desire. His hands tightened around a gorgon's head, and his lip curled.

Time went still. The night held its breath. But then, the world spun on.

The city shook off its disappointment. And it began to dream.

PART

I

ONLY A DREAM

Esta stared down at the small book in front of her. If not for the power radiating from it, the Ars Arcana would have been unimpressive. Unremarkable, even. It was smaller than one might expect of such a fabled object, bound in worn leather that had long since cracked and peeled from age. But the design carved into its cover was astounding. Clear and crisp, the geometric shapes were layered and woven into one another to form a complex sigil. The lines were so entangled that it was impossible to tell where one ended and the next began.

So much was riding on what the Book of Mysteries contained—the information *and* the magic within its pages—that Esta hadn't been able to fall asleep. She knew she should probably wait for Harte, but impatience made her a little reckless. She hadn't been able to stop herself from taking the Book from the satchel and running her finger along the intricate design carved into the leather of the cover. At the soft brush of her touch, the Book shuddered. The Aether around her trembled in response. Even the very quintessence of existence seemed to understand that the piece of pure, untouched magic within those pages could remake the world. Or destroy it.

For what was Aether but time, the very substance that carved order from chaos? And what was magic but the promise of power within chaos? Time and magic. Order and chaos. Once, the two had existed in a fragile equilibrium. Like the ouroboros, the ancient image of a serpent fated to forever devour its own tail, time kept magic in check, and the wild chaos of magic spurred time onward. But a mistake—an act of hubris, however well meaning—had changed everything. Now, deep within the Ars Arcana, a piece of the beating heart of magic waited. Severed and separated from time by an act of ritual, it was impossibly potent and dangerous. In the wrong hands, its power could cause unthinkable destruction.

Esta glanced over her shoulder to where Harte was still sleeping on the low sofa. On a makeshift pallet nearby, North's boy, Everett, snored softly as well. Even in sleep, he looked so much like his father. But North wasn't with them any longer. He had sacrificed himself for Everett—for the hope of a better future for all Mageus—in Chicago. And Esta would not allow that sacrifice to go wasted. She would do everything she could to claim them a different fate.

The enigmatic owner of the Nitemarket, Dominic Fusilli, had dropped them off at one of his warehouses in Brooklyn and told them to get some rest. As far as Esta knew, she was alone with the Book in the stillness of the night.

She could wake Harte—she probably *should* wake him—but it had been nearly two days since he'd had any real sleep, and he was still weak from being sick in California. He needed the rest. And also, she wasn't ready to tell him yet—not about what Seshat had revealed back in Chicago nor about what Esta had done to save his life. She'd promised to finish the ritual Seshat had started eons before, a ritual to place that severed piece of magic back into the whole of creation. It was a promise she had no idea how to keep.

The Book trembled again, beckoned. The answers were within those pages.

They have to be.

Her finger had barely made contact with the ancient cover when, suddenly, the Ars Arcana threw itself open, and the most terrible wailing split the silence of the night as the pages began flipping in a seemingly endless wave. Which shouldn't have been possible. The Book wasn't *that* big. There shouldn't have been *that* many pages. Then, just as suddenly as the Book had opened, its pages burst with a blinding flash of light so bright, Esta had to flinch away, shielding her eyes from its brilliance. When the light dimmed and her eyes readjusted, she was no longer in the warehouse in Brooklyn but back on the stage of the Chicago Coliseum. The Book was gone.

In her hand was the hilt of the dagger that held the Pharaoh's Heart, and beneath her, Jack writhed, his eyes open in rage and fear. She lifted the dagger, knowing what she must do—what she *had* done. What she would do a thousand times over. She knew what would happen next, the sickening crunch of bone. The terrible sinking of the ancient dagger's blade as it sucked itself deep into Jack's chest.

You would be so willing to kill for the power in these pages?

A voice echoed inside her head—it was her own voice and not her own at the same time. Startled, she stopped with the dagger over her head. All around, the crowd in the massive arena had gone silent.

Of course she would kill for the Book. She already had.

And now? Will you take the beating heart of magic as your own . . . ? Or will you give it over to the one who thinks herself a goddess?

The voice was no longer her own but Thoth's—the same voice that had spoken to her before, in Denver. In Chicago as well.

Will you sacrifice yourself for Seshat's mistakes? Do you trust in her promises so absolutely?

Esta shook her head, trying to shake off the voice. It couldn't be Thoth. She'd destroyed him and the danger he posed along with him, but the memory of him was so strong, and his words were already worming into her mind, poking at her misgivings and fears.

She will not save you, the voice whispered. *Given the chance, Seshat will destroy you and the world itself. For what? For simple vengeance.*

It was no less than Seshat had threatened for months now. But they'd made a bargain. Harte's life for Esta's promise . . .

You will die to keep that promise, the voice threatened. *But there is another way. Give your affinity over willingly, like so many have before you. You need not* die. *With your affinity, I could control Seshat's power. Your magic could remove Seshat from the Magician without destroying the boy who holds your heart. You could live beyond the reach of time, and your magician with you.*

She wanted to deny the temptation in those words, but she couldn't. *How?*

With the beating heart of magic.

The voice spoke again, a crooning caress along the inside of her mind. *Think of all you could do if only you would have the courage to take what I offer. Think of the chaos* you *brought into the world. Think of those you could save: Your friend who tumbled from the sky . . . All those who have died because of you . . . Your parents . . . Your magician, who is destined to be consumed by the demon within him.*

Seshat will not save them. She will not save you.

It *was* a temptation. It would have been a lie not to admit that to herself. To save Mari and North. To save Dolph and Leena, the mother she'd never met. To know that Harte would be safe.

Think of what you could do with the power in these pages, the voice tempted. It was her voice now, and Thoth's as well. Both together. Terrible and enticing all the same. *The demon bitch was too weak to truly take it as her own. But you, girl . . . you are more than Seshat could ever be. With the power in these pages, you could become* infinite. *Think of it,* the voice whispered. *Think of what you could accomplish if magic—pure magic,* true magic—*answered only to you.*

No. Esta recoiled from the idea. She'd seen what the quest for power had done to Seshat. To Jack. To Thoth. She didn't want the power in the Book; she only wanted to replace it into the whole of creation, where it belonged. She only wanted to complete the ritual that Seshat had started so long ago, as she'd promised she would.

I don't want that power, she told the Book. Told herself as well. *I only want to finish what Seshat started. I only want to set things right.*

Ancient laughter bubbled up from within the pages, from within herself.

Ah, the voice said, its amusement surrounding her. *You would reunite the piece of magic that Seshat stole. You would place the beating heart of magic back into balance with the marching of time. But will you be willing to do what is required?*

I'll do whatever it takes, she said.

But what of the cost?

No matter the cost. She'd already blackened her soul with Jack's death, hadn't she? She would pay again and again if she had to. To save the world. To save *Harte.*

The hilt of the dagger felt unnaturally cold in Esta's hand, and the energy of the Pharaoh's Heart pulsed through the Aether around her. She ignored the icy burn and plunged the blade down. The sickening grinding of bone vibrated through her arms as Jack's watery blue eyes widened in pain and surprise. As though he could not believe she could have bested him. As though he could not believe it was possible for him to lose.

And then Thoth was there, rising up, cold and terrible in his fury, and she did not hesitate to reach for her own terrible power, the affinity that was as much a part of her as her own skin. Without hesitation, she pulled at the Aether, the substance that held together all things. Time. Magic and its opposite. And she did not stop until the darkness that lived in the spaces between all things flooded into Thoth and tore him from this world.

That darkness poured from Jack and, as before, his screams and Thoth's mixed. It became a living thing—as alive and prescient as Thoth himself—as it gathered into a malevolent cloud swirling above. When Jack slumped back to the ground, emptied, the dark cloud broke, shattering itself into a million tiny shards. They fell like needles of cold energy onto the crowd—onto Esta—slicing through her too tender skin. It felt like the Brink crashing over her.

And then, all at once, it was over.

Esta was still gripping the hilt of the dagger, still pressing it into Jack's chest, but suddenly she felt the warmth of Jack's hands covering hers. She startled, because this *hadn't* happened before. It wasn't part of the memory. She looked down, but it *wasn't* Jack's hand that had gripped hers. Now it was Harte who lay beneath her. Harte whose lips were frothing with blood and whose hands were wrapped around hers, trying to pull the dagger from his chest. At the sight of his stormy eyes wide and empty, filled with an inky darkness, Esta scrambled away—

And fell off the edge of the world.

Her eyes flew open the second she landed, and it took more than a few seconds before the dream began to burn away and she realized where she was. Not in Chicago. Not in the presence of Thoth. No longer trapped in the nightmare that had felt like truth itself.

Moonlight filtered through the high, clouded windows of Dom's warehouse. *Brooklyn.* They were in Brooklyn now, she told herself, still trying to calm her breathing. Jack was dead and Thoth was gone, and it had been a dream. *Only* a dream.

But it felt too real. Even now, she felt the voice inside her, brushing at the fears deep within her.

Her mouth tasted foul, and her skin felt like ice. She'd fallen off the ratty couch she and Harte had curled themselves up on once they'd arrived. Harte was still asleep there. He shifted, moving into the space she'd just vacated, and though his face was calm and peaceful, Esta couldn't shake the image from her dream: his lips frothing with blood, his beautiful eyes clouded over by an inky black emptiness that obscured their usual stormy gray. There was a part of her that wanted to climb back up next to him, to tuck herself into his warmth and pretend for just a little while longer that everything was okay. But the dream was still too thick, too close.

Instead, Esta pulled herself up from the cold, filthy floor and eased the satchel from beneath Harte's head. She looked down at him, peaceful as he was, and forced the remaining vision of the dream away. Until it was only Harte as he truly was, his dark hair mussed from sleep, his cheekbones still too sharp from nearly dying of plague.

Unable to stop herself, she leaned down until her face was close to his. Even in his sleep, Harte seemed to sense her there and lifted his chin until their lips met. It was the barest brush of a kiss, nothing more than the whisper of their mouths meeting, but Esta felt the last bit of coldness from the dream drain away, and some of the tension she was carrying eased.

Harte was safe. *She* was safe. So what if she'd made a promise to Seshat that she didn't know how to keep? She'd figure it out. She would find a way to finish the ritual Seshat had started centuries before and bring time and magic back into balance. They had the Book now, and with it, all the secrets and spells that Thoth had collected through the years. And they had four of the five artifacts. The fifth waited a few decades before, just beyond the bridge, where Harte had left it with a friend. Seshat, magic, time—Esta would figure out a way to save Harte and in turn save them all.

And if she heard the voice of her dream echoing again in her waking, mocking her certainty? She shrugged it off. Pushed that voice back down deep and ignored it. Just as she tried to ignore the memory of the dream, of Harte bloodied and dead by her own hand.

There was light spilling from beneath a doorway at the other end of the hall. Everett was up, it seemed. She could use the company, especially now. She suspected that he could as well. After all, he'd lost his father just hours ago. He shouldn't be alone.

Clutching the satchel to her chest, she started down the hallway, leaving Harte peaceful and sleeping for a little while longer. The sooner Esta figured out what would need to be done, the better for everyone. But her hand had barely reached for the handle of the door when a sharp pain erupted along the underside of her arm, and she could not stop herself from screaming.

CLAVIS

1920—Brooklyn

The sound of Esta's screaming ripped Harte from sleep. There was no transition from unconsciousness to waking. The effect was instant. One second he was dead to the world, and the next he was on his feet, already moving before his brain could register where he was.

He was running down an endless hallway, sure that he was already too late—sure that Esta was already gone—when he saw her there in the light spilling from an open doorway, with Everett kneeling next to her.

No. No no no—

Shoving Everett aside, he took Esta in his arms, and it was only when she hissed in pain that he breathed. *Not dead. Not gone.* But she was hurt. Her face was etched with pain, and she was cradling her left arm, which was a bloody mess.

Everett was still there, crouched over them both. "What did she do to her arm?"

"*She* didn't do anything," Harte told him, hearing the fury in his own voice. "I'll kill him for this."

"You'll have to get in line." Esta sucked air through her gritted teeth as she tried to pull away from him to stand up.

He didn't let her go. Couldn't. Not when his sleep-muddled brain still hadn't quite accepted that she wasn't dead, wasn't gone.

"Who?" Everett asked, frowning as he watched Harte help Esta to her feet.

"Nibsy Lorcan." They said it together, because they both knew what the wounds on Esta's arm meant. They both knew who was to blame.

"The *Professor*?" Everett asked, frowning. "What does he have to do with anything?"

"He's the one who did this," Esta told Everett.

The other boy frowned. "How? He's trapped behind the Brink."

On her feet now, Esta winced as she looked over the bloodied mess of her arm. "That never stopped him from touching me before."

Her face was too pale, and Harte wanted to punch something. But he knew that wouldn't help anything—not yet at least. First he had to take care of Esta. "Could you go get some cool water? A clean towel or some gauze?"

"Alcohol if you can find any," Esta added, wincing. "I don't need this getting infected."

While Everett disappeared into the cavernous depths of the warehouse, Harte guided Esta into the warmly lit room. "What the hell did he do to you?"

"I think it's a burn," she told him through gritted teeth. "It feels like my skin's still on fire."

She was probably right. The skin on her forearm was raw and angry, puckered and bleeding. There were already welts forming, but the damage wasn't haphazard. Even with the ragged, swollen flesh, anyone could see the marks were purposeful. It looked like she'd been branded by some invisible iron. The smell of it—burned flesh, *her* flesh—was strong enough to make Harte's stomach turn.

"It's another message," she told him. "But I don't know what it—"

She gasped again, and Harte looked down to see her skin opening again. It looked like an invisible scalpel was slicing through her in thin, neat lines, just below the burn. A second later Harte realized what was happening. They were letters. The bastard was carving letters into her.

C-L-A

There was no way for him to stop what was happening. All Harte could do was cradle her arm, impotent with rage, as blood welled and dripped from Esta's wrist and the lurid letters continued to appear.

V-I-S

"Key," she whispered, her voice unsteady as she spoke in short, staccato breaths. "It means key. In Latin. It's just like before."

"It's nothing like before," Harte snapped, anger lashing through his tone so sharply that Esta flinched. He forced himself to calm his voice. He was still furious but not at her. He was angry that Nibsy had touched her again and that he couldn't do anything to stop it. "Last time, you woke up and discovered a scar that was already healed over. That's not what this is."

"No," she admitted. "But I think the difference is that *this* just happened."

"Clearly," Harte said, frowning.

Esta shook her head. "Last time, the scar appeared because he did something to the girl in the past. It was 1904 when that scar appeared, but he could have cut her—me—anytime after we left the city in 1902. Only the effects of it would have appeared. But I think these new marks are still bleeding because this literally *just* happened. It *is* happening. Here and now, in 1920."

Harte's mouth pressed together. It made sense, but the violence of it? "He's turned into a fucking butcher."

"He always has been," Esta said softly.

She was right. Nibsy had left a trail of broken lives in his wake.

"But why this? Why now?" Harte asked.

"Because he knows we're here. What happened back in Chicago has to be all over the news by now. This," she said, holding up her still-bloodied arm, "is his way of letting us know he hasn't given up. That he won't give up."

Everett had returned with a pitcher of water and some rags that looked nearly clean. "I found—" He stopped short, his face draining of color when he saw the newest injury—and the blood. "Oh god . . ."

"I'm fine," Esta said automatically.

"You're bleeding all over the place," Harte told her. "You're definitely not fine. Bring those over here," he ordered Everett, who was still too shocked to do anything more than obey.

"It's all I could find," Everett said, making the words sound more like an apology than an explanation.

"It's great," Esta said gently as she winced again.

Harte was still too angry—too terrified—to do anything more than make a half-formed grunt of thanks. His hands could manipulate cards right beneath a person's nose or pick a lock in the darkness of an underwater tank, but he could not seem to keep them steady as he dabbed the water over Esta's mangled skin.

"It's okay, Harte," she said, touching his wrist softly to stop him. To steady the shaking that even she must have been able to see. "I can clean my own arm."

"I have it," he said.

"Harte—"

"Just let me look at it, would you?" He could hear the tightness in his own voice. He stopped, closed his eyes, and tried to calm himself. "Let me do this for you," he said, opening his eyes again and meeting her gaze. He knew why she wanted to do this herself—why she felt like she had to do everything on her own—but he couldn't let it go. "Let me help you, Esta." He paused, and when he spoke again, he made his voice softer. "I need to make sure you're okay." He swallowed hard, hating how helpless he felt. "Please."

Any other time, Esta probably would have argued. Even now he could see that she wanted to. But she seemed to understand. Resigned, she offered up her hand.

Everett stood close by, watching as Harte worked as gently as he could to clean and bandage her wounds. His expression was creased with grief and worry, and Esta knew that it was more than her injuries that had put the hollowness in his eyes.

The burns were puckered and nearly indecipherable, but though the cuts were still seeping blood, the word was clear. *Clavis.*

"What does it mean?" Everett asked, frowning. "Is it a name or—"

"It's Latin for key," Esta said softly. "But I don't know what that's supposed to signify."

"Maybe he wants your cuff," Harte said as he covered the burns with some ointment from the kit before moving on to the cuts.

"Ishtar's Key?" Everett asked. "That makes sense."

"It's possible," Esta admitted. "But I can't help feeling like there's more to it. He had the cuff for ages and never did anything with it."

"We'll figure it out," Harte told her, trying to sound more confident than he felt. Hating that there was nothing he could do to protect her— except take care of Nibsy Lorcan once and for all.

"Well, well, well," a voice said from the doorway.

The three of them jumped at the sound of it, turning as one to find Dominic Fusilli, the owner of the Nitemarket and their erstwhile rescuer, standing in the darkened doorway. He had the satchel that had once been secured under Harte's head. Esta must have taken it when she'd woken up, but they'd all forgotten about it in the rush to help her. Dom had already opened it, already removed the small, worn book from within. It was too late to stop him.

The interest that lit Dom's face had Harte's instincts prickling in warning. "What do we have here?"

SACRIFICE AND POWER

1920—Brooklyn

Esta considered her options as she watched Dom flip through the pages of the Ars Arcana. They'd all been so distracted by the mess on her arm that none of them had heard Dom's footsteps approaching, and he'd found the satchel she'd dropped before they could pick it up. Now he had the Book and the artifacts, and Esta wasn't sure how to get them back without upsetting the one ally they seemed to have. It was too late to slip through the seconds and take it from him. He'd already seen the Book, and they were in his warehouse, under his protection. For now they were safe. And the Book wasn't going anywhere—she wouldn't let it.

Maybe she was wrong to be so uneasy. After all, Dom *had* saved them from an impossible situation in Chicago. Whatever magic he'd used on the van to transport them to Brooklyn in the blink of an eye had certainly allowed them to get far, far away from where the authorities would be searching. But Maggie didn't like Dominic Fusilli, so Esta figured that was a good enough reason not to trust him.

One look at Harte told Esta that he felt as uneasy as she did.

If Dom noticed their mood, he didn't show it. He was taking his time, studying the page he was on before turning to the next. "I still can't believe I'm looking at this," he said. "The Book of Mysteries. Here. In my hands. And the lost artifacts—or some of them. When I think of what these would sell for . . ." He let out a low whistle. "I'd be set for life."

"They're not for sale," Harte said flatly.

"Everything's for sale," Dom told them with a shrug. He glanced up at Esta. "Everyone has their price."

"Not us," Harte said, stepping toward Dom. "Not for these."

Esta placed her hand on Harte's arm. Starting a fight with Dom wasn't going to help anything. Better to convince him, to make him think that giving back the Book and the artifacts would help him in some way. "What Harte means to say," Esta told Dom, "is that we can't sell them *yet*. We have to use them first . . . to bring down the Brink."

Dom's brows lifted. "*This* is why you were in Chicago?"

She nodded. "The sooner we figure out how to use those artifacts to control the power in the Book, the sooner we can take care of the Brink. The sooner *you* could expand the Nitemarket like you wanted."

Dom's eyes shifted from the page he was reading back to Esta. "The answers are in here?"

"I don't know where else they'd be," she told him, and it wasn't even a lie. "The Order used that Book to create the Brink. It must describe how they did it and explain how we can end it."

"Maybe, but you'd have to figure out what any of this means first." Dom gestured to the markings on the page.

"I might be able to help with that," Everett said. "I've been studying the Order and their type of magic since I was just a kid."

"You're *still* just a kid," Dom said.

"Everett's the one who knew how to disable the tower in Chicago *and* how to reverse its power," Esta reminded Dom. But at the mention of Chicago, Everett's mouth went tight. She gentled her tone when she continued. "If he says he can figure it out, I believe him. If you're sure? You don't have to do this."

"I do," Everett told her. "I can't have it mean nothing. I need to help. I need to do whatever I can."

She knew he was talking about North, about the way he'd died so tragically the night before. "Okay," she said. "Thank you."

Dom still seemed reluctant to part with the objects in his possession.

"The sooner we know what's in those pages, the sooner you get your New York market. It's just 'good business,'" Esta told him, echoing the very words he'd used the night before.

Dom considered Everett, and Esta felt danger stir in the silence that fell as he thought about his options.

So many people had betrayed them for less, and now Dom held the Book and the artifacts in his literal hands. Esta waited, ready for whatever decision he made. She wouldn't allow him to take the Book, but attacking too early would mean turning their one possible ally into an enemy.

Finally, he made up his mind and slid the Book across the table. "It doesn't leave this room." Then he shot a warning look at Esta and Harte. "I'm gonna make some coffee. You two want some?"

Hours later, the burnt and bitter coffee had long since gone cold, but Everett hadn't made much progress. Harte was clearly getting impatient, but he didn't move far from her side. He'd taken to pacing within arm's reach. Dom seemed less concerned about how long things were taking. He still had the satchel and was examining the stones in each of the artifacts with the same sort of small magnifying glass that jewelers used.

"Amazing," he murmured, setting the Dragon's Eye back onto the table next to the other two. "There isn't anything about these stones that makes them physically different, but the power coming from them is something else." Dom set the crown back on the table and picked up the necklace, turning it over in the light and watching the stone flash and glimmer. "I haven't come across anything like them before. And I've seen plenty."

"That's probably because of how they were made," Everett said. It was the first he'd spoken since he'd started examining the Book.

"You found something?" Esta asked, leaning over the table to look at the page Everett had open. Harte moved closer.

"I think so," Everett told them. "Look at this."

There on the page was a series of sketches that clearly showed the five stones surrounded by detailed notes written in faded ink. On the facing page was a detailed drawing of the hand of the philosopher.

"*Is. Newton*," Esta read, running her finger along the inscription there. "Isaac Newton. This is how he did it, isn't it? This is how he made the stones."

"I think so," Everett confirmed.

Esta had already known that Isaac Newton was the one responsible for infusing artifacts he'd collected from ancient dynasties with the affinities of five powerful Mageus in an attempt to control and use the Book's magic. But the attempt had nearly driven him mad. In Chicago, she'd learned that Newton had been under Thoth's control all along. Somehow, Newton had managed to fight off Thoth before the ritual could be completed. He'd given the stones and the Book to the Order for safekeeping, back when the Order still had magic themselves. Years later, the Order had brought the artifacts across an ocean and tried to replicate Newton's work. They'd used them to create the Brink in an attempt to protect their magic and to keep the Book—and Seshat—under control. But the ritual had never been right—like Seshat's ritual, the Order's had never been finished, and the Order's protective barrier had turned into a trap. And then it had become a weapon.

"It doesn't look that different from the ritual that people still use to make magical objects," Dom said.

"What do you mean?" Esta asked.

"It takes a ritual like this to break part of someone's affinity away from them and infuse it into an object. This here . . ." Dom tapped on an elaborate design that looked strikingly like the one carved into the front cover of the Book. "Writing, like this design here, makes the ritual material."

"Sigils are the earliest forms of ritual magic," Everett told them. "The most common, too."

"I wouldn't be in business without them," Dom said. "But I've never seen one quite this complicated. You can't even really look at it straight, can you?"

"It's definitely ancient," Everett agreed. "Powerful, too. But this is different from the rituals used to make objects nowadays." He glanced at Dom. "My understanding is that most magical objects only contain a part of someone's affinity."

"Sure," Dom said. "That's usually how it works."

"Why would anyone willingly give up even a *part* of their affinity?" Harte asked.

Dom shrugged. "It's not always willing," he told them. "But desperate people do desperate things."

"It sounds like what Dolph did to Leena," Esta said, glancing at Harte.

He was frowning thoughtfully as he stared down at the Book. "Or like what Seshat did to herself by placing parts of her magic into the original stones." He glanced up and met Esta's eyes.

They were onto something here. She could feel it, and the expression Harte wore told Esta that he felt the same.

"This ritual is different, though," Everett said, pointing to a block of text on the page. "It's not meant to take part of an affinity. It's designed to take *everything*. All of a person's magic. And their life along with it."

Dom frowned. *"Everything?"*

Everett nodded. "The people who Newton used to power those stones didn't survive. They weren't supposed to."

This wasn't news. Esta learned that months ago, when the Professor had revealed himself and what he intended to do. But she couldn't help thinking of the Nitemarket and all the objects she'd seen for sale there. She thought, too, of what Dolph had done to Leena. "Why not just take part of their magic?"

"Because a life sacrificed is stronger," Everett told them, and when they all turned to him, he shrugged. "A life is singular. And taking a life can create a rare form of power."

But Esta wasn't sure that made sense. She looked down at the bandage on her arm. If a life was singular, how could there be two of her—the person she was and the other version of herself who was growing up under the thumb of Nibsy?

Because you are nothing. An abomination.

She shivered a little at the memory of Thoth's words back in Denver. She wasn't *nothing*. She couldn't be. She was herself. She wasn't some mistake in the time line.

Harte was staring at her—she could feel the intensity of his gaze—but she didn't look at him. She couldn't let Dom know how important this was, or she worried that he'd never give up the Book.

"Does it say what he planned on doing with the stones?" she asked.

Everett frowned and turned back to the Book. "It looks like his plan was to connect them using the Aether."

"That's what Seshat did," Harte murmured. "When she created the Book. She connected the stones she made with her affinity through the Aether."

"But Seshat was trying to save the old magic," Esta reminded him. "What was Newton trying to do?"

"He was trying to create the philosopher's stone," Everett said. When they all looked at him, he only shrugged. "Isn't that the goal of all the old alchemists? Create the substance that can transmute matter and let you live forever?"

Dom swore softly under his breath. "Did he succeed?"

"No," Esta told them.

Everett looked up at her, frowning.

"Newton never went through with the ritual," she reminded them. "He gave the stones and the Book to the Order for safekeeping instead. They're the ones who finally tried the ritual. But it didn't work the way they expected. It's what created the Brink."

"But the Brink didn't work," Dom said. "The Order doesn't have the philosopher's stone. If they did, we'd all know about it."

"Because the ritual went wrong," Harte told him.

"And also because the philosopher's stone isn't a *thing*," Everett said. "Not according to this . . ." He paused, studying the page.

"Well, go on," Dom directed, leaning forward to look over the page where Everett was reading. "What is it?"

"I don't know, exactly," Everett told them. "Alchemical recipes are more like poems than recipes. They're symbolic. Alchemists used them to obscure as much as to record their work. But it doesn't seem like Newton thinks the philosopher's stone is a thing so much as a state of being. A place. It's what he was trying to create by connecting the stones through the Aether."

"Aether is time," Esta said softly. Newton was creating a boundary made of time—or made from manipulating time. Just like Seshat was trying to do.

"That doesn't explain anything," Dom said, clearly growing impatient.

"Give me a second," Everett said, focusing more intently on the pages. "He united the artifacts to control the power in the Book and then . . ." As Everett turned the page, Esta saw that the next one was torn. The bottom half was gone.

"Then *what*?" Dom demanded.

"I don't know. It's missing." Everett frowned down at the missing page. "Whatever ritual he used, it's gone."

"Your arm, Esta." Harte's voice was soft, but there was a thread of fury in it that she didn't immediately understand.

"My arm?" He was already reaching for her, already pulling back her sleeve and unwinding the gauze. When the burned flesh was exposed, Esta understood. The strange markings there matched the ones on the page. But on the page, one line of markings included a row of Greek letters beneath it.

"It's not gone. It's a cipher," Dom told her, flipping back a few pages to where the images of Newton's gems were. The odd symbols were on that page as well.

"A cipher?" She was still too shocked to see the symbols on her arm replicated on the pages of the Book.

"Newton was hiding the ritual with code," Dom explained. "But half the key is missing."

"Maybe Newton didn't want anyone else to be able to replicate his process," Everett said.

But Esta was already shaking her head. That wasn't it at all.

"Clavis," Esta said, thinking of the newest word cut into her wrist. "Nibsy doesn't want my cuff—I mean, I don't doubt he does. But that's not why he carved 'Clavis' into the girl's arm. He knows we have the Book. He's telling us he has the other half of this page."

"It could be a trick," Harte argued. "Maybe he doesn't have anything."

"No," Esta said. "He tried the ritual before. He has the missing piece. He has the key to this cipher and the answer to how we can complete the ritual. He must have kept a piece of the Book separate when he sent me back with Logan. He must have known he'd need some kind of insurance in case I got away or took the Book from him. How else would he have been able to do this?" She pointed to the burns on her arm, the perfect match to the symbols on the page.

"He's forcing you back," Everett realized.

"Well, you're not going," Harte told her. "It's a trap."

"I know it's a trap," Esta said with a sinking feeling. "But he knows it's one that will work. The answers to controlling Seshat—to controlling the Book's power—are on the other half of this page. We have to get it back from him."

"That's *exactly* what he wants," Harte said. "We don't stand a chance if he's expecting us."

Harte was right, but that didn't change anything.

"We don't have a choice," she told him.

"Maybe not, but we have *time*," he reminded her.

"*No*, we don't," she said, lifting her raw arm to remind him. "I'm not going to sit around while Nibsy keeps carving me up."

His eyes narrowed, and he opened his mouth to argue with her, but before he could get a word out, a pounding sounded from somewhere in the bowels of the building.

Dom came alert instantly, and his eyes shifted to the Book and the artifacts still lying on the table. "Shit. They're early." Dom reached for the satchel and started loading the artifacts back into the canvas bag. "You all have to get out of here."

"Who's early?" Esta asked, already reaching for her affinity.

At first Dom didn't answer. He was too busy securing the Book back into the satchel.

Clearly done with being patient, Harte grabbed Dom, spun him around, took him by the collar, and shook. "*Who* is early?"

Dom licked his lips. His eyes darted from Esta to Everett, as though either would help him. Harte tightened his grip and gave Dom another shake. "Razor Riley and his lot," Dom said finally.

Harte went still, but he didn't release Dom. "From the Five Pointers, Razor Riley?"

"Where else would he be from?" Dom said, jerking away from Harte's grasp. He clutched the satchel close to his chest and turned to go, but Everett stood in his way, blocking the door.

"Why would Razor Riley be out there?" Harte demanded.

"Because he's working for Lorcan," Dom said, not bothering to look back at Harte. He spoke to Everett then, lowering his voice and softening his tone. "Let me go, kid. Lorcan doesn't know about you. Far as I'm concerned, he doesn't need to know. You can walk away now without getting mixed up in this."

"I'm already mixed up," Everett said, squaring his shoulders.

"Look, we don't have time for this." Dom turned back to Harte. "Razor's here to take the two of you to Lorcan, and I don't have any plans to get caught up in that mess. We can stand here arguing about things, or you can let me go, and maybe you get away. Maybe the kid here can even get out clean without the Professor ever knowing he was involved."

"You sold us out," Esta accused, unable to stop the stupid note of disappointment from her voice.

"I saved you from the mess you were in back in Chicago," Dom said, clearly affronted that anyone would be upset. "There's no way you were getting out of there without my help."

"But you were working for Nibsy the whole time," Harte growled.

"I don't work for anyone. I'm an independent businessman," Dom said. "The Professor made me an offer that sounded like a good deal at the time. If it makes you feel any better, I thought I would be helping you. I never intended to—"

"How much?" Harte demanded. "How much were our lives worth?"

"It doesn't matter," Dom said. "I'm not going to be able to collect, not if Razor doesn't get you." He gave them a devilish grin and clutched the satchel holding the Book and the artifacts tighter to his chest. "It's a fair trade, don't you think? You get to walk out of here alive and whole, and I get the payday I was promised."

Harte lunged for Dom, but Esta was already in motion. She didn't wait to warn Harte or make any heroic declarations. She simply took hold of her magic and pulled.

NEVER ENOUGH

1920—Brooklyn

Harte saw red as he lunged for Dom, but Esta had already caught him before he could even take a swing. The world went silent around them as she pulled him back, and it was only her sharp intake of breath, a sign that she was still in pain, that stopped him from breaking away from her and doing everything he could to pummel the conniving bastard who'd betrayed them.

He should have known that getting out of Chicago had been too easy. They should have left Dom's warehouse last night. *He* should have insisted that they go rather than collapsing into sleep on that filthy couch. Instead, he'd let himself believe that fate or chance or whatever higher power there might be had given him a handful of minutes to just breathe and hold Esta in safety. As though fate had been anything but a fickle bitch since he was born.

Esta glanced meaningfully at Harte, and he knew what she was asking: whether Seshat was still quiet. He gave her a small nod. Thanks to the Quellant, there wasn't so much as a rumble from the goddess trapped beneath his skin.

"Come on," she said, pulling him toward the door, where Everett was standing frozen in time. "We have to go. We don't have time for him."

"It wouldn't take long," he growled, thinking about the satisfaction he would feel when his fist landed square on Dominic Fusilli's nose. "And we're not going anywhere without the Book."

"I already have it," Esta told him, patting the satchel she'd slung across her chest. "The Book and the artifacts, too."

Harte took another look at the rat who'd betrayed them, longing to leave Dom with a broken nose to remember him by, but eventually he relented, and they moved together so she could pull Everett into her net of time as well.

Everett gasped, startled for a minute, but he recovered quickly. "If there was a way to bottle what you can do—"

Esta shot Everett a look that shut him up. "We go together. Whatever you do, don't either of you let go of me."

"Not a chance," Harte told her, squeezing her hand slightly. *Not ever again.*

"Let's go," Esta directed, nodding toward the open doorway.

Harte didn't argue this time. Together they moved toward the rear of the building, where they'd parked the truck in a gated yard late the night before. Esta and Everett started toward the vehicle, but Harte pulled them both back.

"What is it?" Esta asked.

The truck was still in the same place. The back loading area seemed to be empty as well.

"This feels too easy," Harte said. They'd slipped away from Dom without any trouble, and now they were just going to walk away? "If Nibsy is behind this, we need to be ready for anything. He knows you. He'll be prepared for what you can do."

"How?" she asked.

"I don't know," he admitted. "But if he knew somehow that we would eventually need that half-torn page in the Book, he certainly could predict that you would try to use your affinity to get away."

"Maybe . . . But his goons can't catch what they can't see," she said.

He admired her confidence, but then he'd always admired that part of her. Still, he couldn't shake his unease. "But what about what happened in Chicago? In the Nitemarket and at the convention, the Order used something that interfered with our affinities."

"He has a point," Everett said.

"If the Order has something to null the Quellant, like they did in Chicago, the Professor might, too," Harte told her.

Esta frowned. "We don't have much of a choice, though. We can't sit here and wait for whatever Nibsy might have planned. Our best chance is to move and hope we're faster than he is."

Harte hated that she was right, even if every instinct he had was screaming at him that this was a trap. "Fine. But we need to think this through. We need a plan."

She considered the truck before turning to Everett. "Can you drive that thing?"

It took a bit of doing, but they got themselves into the truck, with Esta between the two of them. She had her hand wrapped around the bare skin of Everett's wrist, so he could still maneuver the vehicle, and Harte had his fingers tangled with Esta's, so they could all stay within the net of her magic. When Everett turned the key, the sound of the enormous engine cranking to life was the only noise in the otherwise silent day.

Everett put the truck into gear and turned it around, but they'd barely pulled out of the gated area when Harte told Everett to stop. The back part of the building was accessible by a narrow alley that turned sharply left before emptying out onto one of the main streets of Brooklyn. But when they'd turned the corner, Harte saw that his earlier instincts had been right. They definitely had a problem.

Esta swore softly beside him.

"What *is* that?" Everett asked.

Ahead of the truck, the alley was filled with some kind of a thick, fog-like substance. It was dense enough that Harte couldn't make out anything beyond it. There was no way to see what waited for them within the soupy murk—or on the other side of it. Worse, it seemed to be *moving*. With every passing second, it filled more of the alley, approaching them and swelling in size despite the rest of the world being caught and held in Esta's power.

"Whatever that is, it shouldn't be moving," Esta told them, sounding every bit as uneasy as Harte felt.

"I knew this was a mistake," Harte said.

"We could go back?" Everett suggested. "Or, if they're expecting us to take the truck, we could go on foot. Or find another way out of this place."

Esta shook her head. "Nibsy would have accounted for the other exits too. At least the truck gives us a little protection, and it moves a lot faster than we could on foot."

"You're thinking we charge through," Harte said, knowing already it was the only real option.

"I think we have to go for it," she said. "Maybe if we expect the worst . . ." She didn't finish.

At first, none of them spoke. The world hung in the stillness of her magic, and there was no sound except for the nearly deafening rumble of the truck's engine. They all knew what the worst meant: they had the Book and four of the artifacts. If they didn't get through that fog, Nibsy would have almost everything he needed.

"If that fog is anything like what happened in Chicago, we need to worry about Seshat." He looked down at their joined hands. Whatever agreement or truce Esta might have made, he didn't trust the goddess not to take advantage of any opportunity she could. "If that fog destroys the Quellant, I won't be able to stop her."

Harte started to release her hand, but Esta caught his fingers more tightly and didn't let him go.

"He'll be expecting us to use my affinity," Esta said, considering the problem. "So maybe I shouldn't use it. Maybe I should let go of time, and we floor it and see what happens. You can have more Quellant ready, just in case, and once we're on the other side, I'll pull time slow again."

"If you can," Harte said.

"If I can't, at least we'll be in the truck. We'll have the benefit of speed. Maybe we'll be able to lose them."

LISA MAXWELL

"It sounds like our best option," Everett said.

"It sounds like our *only* option," Harte muttered, hating everything about the plan.

Ahead of them, the fog was closer still. It seemed to have grown denser, darker since they'd stopped.

"Get the extra Quellant ready," Esta told him. "Just in case." As he pulled the packet of tablets out of the leather satchel, she glanced at Everett. "Ready?"

Everett tightened his grip on the shifter and gave Esta a tight-mouthed nod.

"I'll release time as soon as we're moving." She gave Harte's hand a small squeeze, but before she could pull away, he caught her.

"Wait." He leaned in and pressed his lips against hers, allowing himself one more moment of hope, of *her*, in case everything went wrong, as it probably would. In case the Quellant didn't work again. In case Nibsy got the best of them this time.

Harte wanted to stay there, his mouth against hers, their breath intermingling, and pretend that their life could be easy. But he knew it wasn't possible—wouldn't *ever* be possible as long as Nibsy was chasing them and Seshat lived beneath his skin. The fog was still growing, still creeping malevolently toward them, so he pulled away, but he was glad to see that Esta's expression had turned as soft and dazed as he felt.

Her tongue darted out, licking her lips, and he felt a pull low in his gut. And he knew it didn't matter if they had a thousand years—it wouldn't ever be enough.

When she spoke again, her voice was rough with emotion. "Okay, Everett. Floor it."

GONE

Even with their lives hanging in the balance, Esta could only focus on the feeling of Harte's kiss still on her lips. Her arm might have been aching from the cuts and burns beneath the bandage before, but she barely felt those wounds now. She hardly felt the pain or the fear or even the weight of what was before them—because suddenly, everything felt *right*.

They'd been running for so long—too long—and even now they were running straight into danger, but when he'd stopped to kiss her, the weight of the world had lifted. Everything narrowed to nothing more than the two of them together. And if that was all she could ever have, she would take the memory, tuck it away, and keep it with her.

But there was no more time. There was only action, because the strange fog was now at the nose of the truck, and in a matter of seconds, they would be covered by it.

Everett threw the truck into gear, and the second it lurched forward, Esta released time and Harte. As the truck punched into the dense soup of the fog, she could feel a cold energy surrounding her. She couldn't see a foot in front of the truck, but she knew the second Seshat had awoken because she felt Harte flinch away like he was suddenly afraid to touch her. It took only a matter of seconds—barely time to take a breath or blink—and they were coming out through the other side. The fog grew thinner, and then daylight broke through.

Esta reached almost immediately for Everett, for her affinity, ready to pull time slow once she was sure they were free of whatever that trap had been, but as the murky light of the overcast day found them, her affinity slipped from her, and gunfire erupted.

"Go!" she screamed, but Everett was already shifting the truck into a higher gear and pushing the heavy vehicle's engine as hard as he could.

Harte's instincts had been right. As they breached the fog, they ran straight into an ambush. The alleyway was blocked by a line of men— Five Pointers, from the looks of it. The sharp, rapid retort of their guns echoed off the brick walls, as the glass of the windshield shattered.

"Get down!" she yelled to Harte as she ducked below the level of the dashboard and tried to shield herself from the shards of glass. She grabbed for Everett's wrist and tried again to pull the seconds slow, but Esta could feel the cold tendrils of the fog's energy still clinging to her. It felt like she'd walked through a particularly thick spiderweb. The sticky coolness of the corrupted magic clung to her skin, making it impossible to get a good grasp on her affinity. She would find the seconds and the world would almost go still, but then they'd slip away from her.

The truck swerved, and the sound of the shots followed them. Then suddenly the truck lurched to the left as they were hit from the side. Horns sounded as Everett steered the truck back into their lane, barely avoiding other traffic.

"You need to do your thing," Everett said, his voice tight and pained. "I don't know if I can shake them."

"I'm trying," she said. She almost had it, though. The cold wisps of the fog's unnatural energy were almost gone. "Just keep them off our tail a little longer."

Next to her on the floor, Harte was drawn and pale. His hands shook as he struggled to bring the tablets of Quellant to his mouth. She wanted to help him, but she knew that Seshat made touching him too dangerous.

"Esta—" Everett's voice was strained. "Please. You have to—"

The truck lurched again, and suddenly her affinity was whole again. Without hesitating, she grabbed the seconds and pulled them slow, but the world had barely gone quiet when Everett's hand fell from the shifter. She looked up to find Everett slumped over the steering wheel. His foot was still on the gas pedal, but he wasn't conscious. She grabbed the wheel and swerved around the stopped car they'd been about to slam into.

The world was silent now except for the roar of the truck. Everett's foot was still wedged on the gas pedal, and the truck was still careening through the Brooklyn streets, but Everett wasn't steering it.

"Everett . . ." She tried to pull him back off the wheel, tried to shake him to get some response, but he slumped back into the seat, his head lolling to one side as he let out a weak groan. That's when she saw the blood.

He'd been hit. She couldn't tell where the blood was coming from, but there was so much of it. His eyes were partially opened, unfocused, but he was still breathing—and still bleeding.

"Everett. You have to hold on, okay?" She let go of his wrist to freeze him in time and keep him from bleeding any more as she swerved the wheel and barely missed a milk truck. His foot was still wedged on the gas pedal, and it was all she could do to guide the truck around the traffic. She knew that if she pushed his leg aside and moved his foot off the gas without depressing the clutch at the same time, the truck would stall. Maybe she should do that. She could switch places with him and drive. But her affinity still felt off, and she didn't know how much longer she could hold the seconds at bay. They were still too close to the Five Pointers—or whoever it was that Nibsy had sent after them—to risk wasting any time. The farther away they could get, the better.

Esta looked down to find Harte frozen and pained-looking on the floor of the passenger side. The Quellant was still in his hands, but he didn't look like he'd been otherwise harmed. He couldn't do anything to help as long as Seshat was freed from the Quellant's effects, and she couldn't let go of time for that to happen as long as they were so close to the warehouse. She was on her own. She had to hold on to everything a little bit longer until she could lose Nibsy's guys and get them somewhere safe. So she left Everett's foot where it was, left the truck in gear, and tried to steer them through the silent, stopped Brooklyn traffic without killing anyone. But she had no idea where she was going.

When she turned down one of the side streets, Esta realized she'd made a mistake. The street dead-ended into a strip of land, and beyond that lay the river. At that speed, they would end up in the water. Without much choice, she pushed Everett's foot aside and felt the truck shudder as the engine stalled out. She barely managed to reach the brake before the truck hit the curb of the street and its front tires reached the edge of the grass.

As the engine hissed and shuddered, Esta simply sat there, trying to catch her breath. Unsure of what to do. She had no idea if they'd been followed. Pulling back Everett's jacket without touching any of his skin, she looked for the wound and saw that he'd been hit twice—once in the side and once in the upper thigh. Stuck in her net of time, his wounds weren't bleeding, but the instant she released her hold on the seconds, they would.

In the distance, the city waited beneath a heavy sky. The bridge rose from the water, a pathway toward her eventual fate, summoning her onward, but for now, the world was silent.

She had to release time. She knew that. She needed Harte to help Everett, and Harte needed the Quellant to be any use at all. But she didn't know just how far Nibsy's plans had gone. She had no idea what might happen when she released the seconds. For sure, Everett would start bleeding again. Seshat would likely rise up and fight. And there could be more of the Five Pointers, more of Nibsy's men waiting, ready for when they appeared.

But hesitation wasn't going to help her. She couldn't sit there, stuck in the abeyance of time forever. The minutes had to continue on, and so did she.

Esta let herself take one more breath in the silence, one more breath before everything might explode again, and then she let go of the seconds and watched the world spin back into motion.

Immediately, Harte gasped.

"Get that Quellant in your mouth," she told him as she reached for Everett, trying to put pressure on his wounds. "Everett . . . can you hear me? Can you talk?"

She sensed Harte's struggle, sensed him shuddering from the Quellant, and knew Seshat had receded, because suddenly he was there with her.

"What the hell happened?" Harte asked.

"You were right," she said, tapping lightly at Everett's cheek, willing him to focus on her. Waiting for the attack that didn't come. "It was an ambush. He's hit. We need to get him help."

Everett groaned. "No . . . have to go on."

She ignored him. "Come on, Harte. Help me move him over so I can drive. We need to get him to a hospital or—"

"No." Everett's eyes were open now. "Go."

"We are *not* leaving you here," Esta said, determined to ignore the grayish pallor of his skin, the way his eyes weren't quite focused on her. She ignored, too, the way her own hands were trembling. The way her heart felt unsteady and her throat felt tight. This couldn't be happening, not after North. Not after all they'd learned and all that had happened. "We're going to get you help."

"Too late," he said, flinching. "Have to go back . . . Make this right."

Esta's eyes were burning. She wanted to deny his request, but she couldn't find the words because she knew he was right. They probably wouldn't be able to find a hospital in time, and even if they did, in 1920 he likely wouldn't make it. But in the future . . . "I can take you forward. We can go where there's help."

She took Everett's hand as she held out her other hand to Harte. But he didn't immediately take hold.

"Esta," Harte said, his voice annoyingly gentle.

She bristled. "Take my hand, Harte."

But Everett was pulling away from her. "Make a good future for us . . . for my parents," he whispered, his voice barely a breath. *"Go."*

His chest didn't rise again.

"No," she said, shaking him slightly. His blood was still on her hands, and his eyes remained unfocused, glassy.

"He's gone, Esta." Harte was pulling her away, or at least he was trying to. But she didn't want to admit what had just happened, couldn't make herself move. "We have to go before the people who were after us catch up. We have to put as much space between us and Nibsy Lorcan as we can right now. We have to leave him."

"There's no getting away from Nibsy," she said dully, realizing the truth. Everett was gone, another person lost because of her actions.

But there was a way to fix this—there was a way to put everything to right.

She reached forward and closed Everett's eyes. "Being on this side of the Brink isn't going to keep us safe, and you know he's not going to stop coming after us. We have to go back into the city."

"Esta," Harte said. "Let's think this through."

"I have," she said. "It was always the plan to go back. We have to find the ring, and now we also need to get the missing piece of the Book from Nibsy. Without it, we can't end all of this."

"That doesn't mean we have to walk right into another one of his traps," Harte argued. "There has to be another way."

"There isn't. I'm not going to run from this, Harte." She took his hand in hers, belatedly realizing that hers was still marked with Everett's blood. "We're going to make him pay."

THE BRIDGE

1920—Brooklyn

The bridge to Brooklyn had always loomed larger than life in Harte Darrigan's mind. It was an enormous thing, a marvel of modern engineering that was about as old as he was. When he was a boy, he'd dreamed of walking across it, a free man escaping the prison of the city. Later, its wide span and the waters below had offered an answer to the problem of the power that he'd unwittingly accepted by touching the Book. It had always represented freedom to Harte, but now he was on the other side, preparing to cross back into the city he'd worked so hard to escape.

In the distance another bridge loomed, a marvel of steel. But it seemed appropriate somehow that they were there, on the same bridge that had led them out of the city months before. Now that span of steel and stone represented nothing more and nothing less than his fate.

Harte looked over at Esta when she paused at the foot of the long expanse that would lead them up and over the water. She was wearing a shapeless pair of workman's overalls, the only thing she could find in Dom's warehouse to replace her bloodstained dress from Chicago. Her hair was short now, but the humidity hanging in the air had it curling around her face in a way that almost suited her better than the long locks she'd had when they'd first met. Her mouth was set in its familiar determined line. He'd kissed that mouth—though not nearly enough—knew what her lips felt like when they molded against his, what she tasted like when their breath intermingled. Suddenly he felt more helpless than he ever had before, more helpless even than when he was lying in that filthy hole back in San Francisco, barely able to breathe. Barely able to do anything more than hope for death.

The angles of her face had become more than familiar to him—they'd become essential. *She'd* become essential. Maybe she'd always been that for him, though. His life had changed completely from the first moment he'd seen her on the dance floor of the Haymarket.

"What if it doesn't work?" he pressed. "What if we go after Nibsy and it isn't enough? What if he still wins?"

"He won't," Esta said, her jaw going tight. "I'll die before I let that happen."

"That's exactly what I'm afraid of," he told her softly. Because he knew that when Esta set her mind to something, there was no stopping her. And Harte didn't know how he'd keep her safe.

The sky above was growing heavier and more threatening as they started across the span of the bridge. Behind them, Brooklyn lay quiet and still. Ahead, Manhattan promised nothing but danger. His entire life, all he'd wanted was to escape from that very city. He'd plotted and planned, lied and betrayed, all to be on *this* side of the Brink. And he'd made it. Now he found himself in the unbelievable position of preparing to return to the prison he'd been born into.

There was no question that he would return. Esta was right; they had no choice but to cross back into the city, to go after Nibsy Lorcan, and to find the missing part of the Book. And there was nowhere he wanted to be but at her side.

"We need a plan," Harte said. "Once Nibsy realizes we've escaped, he'll be expecting us to come for him and the key. We've already seen what he's capable of. If we want any chance of walking out of this alive, we're going to have to think *around* him. But with all he's capable of, I don't know how to get past his talent."

"There might be a way," Esta said, glancing over at him. "But you're not going to like it."

Harte had a feeling he was going to *hate* it. But he squeezed her hand gently and waited for her to speak.

"We don't have to cross the Brink now," she told him. "We could choose any time to arrive."

"You think we should go back?" he asked, considering the possibilities. "It's where we have to go eventually. We can use the Book to hold the stones and—"

"He'll be expecting that too," she said. "He knows I have to take the cuff back. He's probably been ready for us to return all along—and we have to expect that he *will be* ready, whenever we finally do return." Her expression was thoughtful. "I think we should go forward."

"Forward?" It wasn't really a question of what she meant—Harte *knew* what she meant. But there was a part of him that needed her to say it.

"If we go back to 1902, we play right into his plans. We still don't have any answers about how to control Seshat's power or to use the piece of magic in the Ars Arcana to make things right. We haven't even figured out how to use the Book to take the stones back. But if we go forward in time?" She shrugged. "Professor Lachlan might still be waiting. He probably will be. But half a century is a long time to stay on high alert."

"But it's not impossible," Harte reminded her. "Not when it's Nibsy."

"No, not impossible," she admitted. "But before, there were *decades* when Professor Lachlan was waiting for me to reappear. During that time, he wasn't powerful. He wasn't the leader of the Devil's Own or any gang. He was a college professor, quietly biding his time and trying to keep his unnatural longevity from being noticed. He was alone for a long time before he put together the team I grew up with. At some point, he'd have to start lying low. If he's still using healers, he wouldn't want to draw attention to himself."

"You don't know that for sure," Harte said. "He isn't the same Professor that you grew up with. If he has that fog, he's liable to have more tricks."

"Probably," she admitted. "But we can expect that. We can be ready."

LISA MAXWELL

"We can't be ready for everything, Esta. We have no idea what kind of a future we'd be walking into," Harte argued.

"That's true, but right now? Nibsy is a grown man solidly in his prime. That attack back there tells us that he's strong and surrounded by allies. Maybe if we go far enough ahead, he won't be. When he's old, maybe he'll be weaker. Maybe he'll be alone. Maybe we'll have a better shot at getting the piece of the Book back from him."

"Or maybe he would have had even longer to plan," Harte said darkly. "Who knows what we've changed, Esta. He could have surrounded himself with more protection. It might be even harder to get to him. And with his affinity, we have to assume he'll know that we're coming the second we arrive in the city—*whenever* that is."

"Maybe," she said. "But we can plan for that. We know what power he has now. If we go forward, though?" She shrugged. "That's a future that *none* of us can predict. We have a real chance to take advantage of his surprise. We can't be ready for everything, but then, neither can he."

Harte hated the idea every bit as much as he'd expected to, but he couldn't deny that Esta had a point. If they crossed the bridge now, Nibsy would *definitely* be waiting for them on the other side of the bridge. He'd be waiting for them no matter when they came for the missing page, but slipping ahead—dealing with an old man instead of one in his prime— might at least give them the *possibility* of victory.

"Fine. We'll do it your way," Harte said, wishing there were some other option that didn't require multiple trips through time. She'd slipped him through time before, and it was always awful. Worse, once they were . . . *whenever* they were going, he'd be working blind. It wouldn't be the New York he knew. "When will you take us forward? Before we cross or . . . ?"

"Before makes sense," Esta said. "It's likely that Nibsy will have bigger numbers on the other side waiting for us now. And if we slip forward now, we'll still be outside the Brink. In case anything goes wrong. But I think we should get closer—maybe on the bridge. Maybe right before the Brink?"

He gave her a small, resigned nod. "Then I guess we better get going."

They walked on together, hand in hand, and as they approached the midpoint of the enormous span, Harte began to feel the telltale ice of the Brink's energy cutting through the heat of the summer day.

Esta looked up at him, her golden eyes calm and steady. "I'm going to have to release time to slip us forward. Are you ready?"

"Not even a little," he told her. But there wasn't really a choice. There was no way to run from this, no way around what they had to do. All roads had always led here, to this place—this city. The ring waited for them somewhere across the river in the years that had already gone by, and now they knew the key to stopping Seshat—to fixing the Brink—waited there as well, with Nibsy.

In the distance, the world had once more launched back into motion. He could hear the steady clattering rumble of traffic, the far-off wailing of a train's whistle, and over the sound of the wind, the water.

Esta squeezed his hand, and a second later Harte felt the beginning of the same nauseating push-pull he'd felt before. It was like being torn apart, like he was shattering into a million pieces, and then, suddenly, gunfire erupted from the foot of the bridge behind them.

He'd barely had time to look back and see the pair of men shooting at him when in the next second, they were falling. Endlessly tumbling until, all at once, it was over. Day had turned to night, and the summer's heat had transformed itself into the bitter bite of winter.

Harte's vision swirling, he fell to his knees and found himself sinking into the snow. Esta was there, cursing as she knelt beside him and rubbed his back.

"Are you okay?" she asked.

He nodded as he tried to pull himself together. His stomach was still rolling as he got to his feet.

"They threw me off," she told him, shivering when the wind gusted off the frozen river. "I should have expected an attack, but I didn't." She shivered again.

He tried to give her his jacket. She started to shrug him off, but he wrapped it around her anyway.

"We need to get going," she told him.

She was right. Even now, Nibsy might know they had arrived.

Harte noticed, then, just how much the world had changed. The city skyline in 1920 had been a marvel to him, but this? *This* city was nearly impossible to take in. Its buildings towered over the river, and they were lit so dazzlingly bright against the night sky that for a second he couldn't breathe. He'd seen glimpses of this city the time he'd used his affinity on Esta those many months ago, but to her, it had seemed ordinary. He hadn't really understood.

The bridge below vibrated with a steady stream of motorcars. The road was filled with enormous trucks and boxy automobiles that were all square angles and rumbling engines. The buildings on the other side of the river glowed like torches, and in the sky above, there were no stars. There was a scent in the air, heavy like coal smoke but different somehow.

"This is where you're from?" he asked.

"Not exactly," she said, frowning as she looked at the skyline. "But it's close." Esta took in the skyline for another long minute before she let out a long, weary-sounding breath and turned to him, her expression creased with worry and something too close to pain for Harte's liking. "I know what this means for you, Harte. I know what you did to get out of New York, and now you're willingly going to walk back into the prison of the Brink. Maybe you don't have to. You could wait here and—"

"I'm coming with you, Esta." And if part of him almost didn't mind? If he looked up at those soaring buildings, the sheer audacity of late-century Manhattan, and felt a small spark of . . . wonder? For *this* prison of a city? Because it was still a prison. Time hadn't changed that.

He'd have time to consider that later.

"Harte—"

Before she could argue with him any more, he leaned in and kissed her. Again. Because he could and because he wanted to. And because he wasn't stupid enough to take any time they might have together for granted, not *ever* again. He felt her surprise, her annoyance at the way he'd silenced her argument. As he pulled away from her, she was frowning.

Her shoulders sagged a little. "I just wish this could be different. I wish you didn't have to give up everything you wanted just to help me."

He wanted to tell her that he wasn't *only* helping her, that he wasn't giving up everything. He wanted to tell her that before she'd walked into his life, he hadn't had a clue about what he'd *truly* wanted. But he didn't say any of those things. Instead, he cocked his mouth into the wry grin he'd perfected years ago and gave her a wink. "But it's so much more fun when you owe me."

She rolled her eyes at him, but the breathy laugh that came with it was real. It broke the tension between them. "Keep telling yourself that, Darrigan."

He took her hand again, brushed his thumb across her soft skin, and watched with satisfaction as she shivered from something other than the bitter cold. Then all at once, the world went still as Esta pulled time to a stop. There were no more words. Nothing that needed to be said. In silence, together, they walked onward toward the city, with only the sound of their own footsteps to accompany them.

At first it was impossible to tell where the cold of the winter night ended and the power of the Brink began. They were so similar, the bite in the air and the dangerous energy that seemed to be reaching for them. It was still a ways off, but with each step they took, the night deepened. The winter wrapped more firmly around them. And the Brink warned them of what was to come.

When they reached the midpoint of the bridge, Harte felt a sudden change. There was a shifting, a pulse of energy, as the icy magic of the Brink flew toward them, wrapped around them, tried to pull them under.

Everything after that happened too fast, and later, he would never really be able to remember what came first and what followed. One minute they were walking toward the city, forcing themselves forward, step by step, and the next they were running as though their lives depended on it. They hadn't decided to run or even discussed it, but they seemed to know at the same time that they had to go *now*, and quickly, or they'd never make it through.

They were nearly to the other side of the bridge, but not close enough, when a new bolt of cold stabbed through Harte like a jagged, icy blade. And then everything began to fall apart.

THE DELPHI'S TEAR

1902—Bella Strega

J ames Lorcan twisted the ring on his finger, reveling in the power that
seemed to radiate from the crystalline stone. He smiled to himself as
the Aether vibrated with possibility. The Delphi's Tear was every bit as
powerful as he'd hoped.

Suddenly, though, the Aether shifted, and James came to attention.
Something was happening. Something was changing. He'd hoped that
with the Delphi's Tear, the Aether would more than suggest. But even
with the ring upon his finger, the Aether revealed no more than it had
before. It thrummed again, directing him onward with its usual vague
urgency.

He made his way down the back staircase to the Strega's barroom,
all the while following the wild fluctuations of the Aether. It was early
evening, too early for the usual crowd, but when he entered the saloon,
he found it louder than usual. The energy felt unsettled and more than a
little dangerous, and James saw the cause almost immediately.

Near the zinc bar, a drunken Mooch was speaking loudly enough to
be heard over the din. He was gesticulating as he spoke, railing to anyone
who would listen, as Werner tried—and failed—to quiet him. Quite a
crowd had amassed around the pair, and as Mooch continued to speak,
the feeling in the air grew more and more electric. Certain that this was
the cause of the disturbance, James paused, biding his time before he
made his presence known.

He'd been listening to the whispers filtering through the ranks of the

Devil's Own ever since he'd returned from the Flatiron Building with the Delphi's Tear on his hand—and without Mooch and Werner—two nights before. After Logan had described how the two had left with Viola, how they'd run to save themselves instead of finishing the mission he'd sent them on, James had assumed that he would not see them in the Bowery again—at least not alive. Yet there they were, disrupting his evening and threatening everything he was on the verge of building.

Gripping the cane tighter, he felt the magic within it flare stronger than ever as he took a step into the low-ceilinged room. Even those around the periphery were quiet, trying to listen to Mooch, so at first one noticed James enter. But as he walked through the crowd, an awareness rippled, and slowly people began to move out of his way, giving him room to pass freely.

He was nearly to the bar before he could hear clearly what Mooch was saying.

"It was an impossible job," the redheaded firebrand slurred, waving his glass of Nitewein around so wildly that the contents sloshed over his hand. "A suicide mission."

According to Mooch, they'd been sent into the Order's lair like lambs to the slaughter.

"Dolph Saunders wouldn't never have asked us to do it," Mooch railed, even as Werner tried to shush him. "Dolph would've had our backs."

"Nibsy *does* have our backs," Werner said, trying to take the glass away from his friend.

Mooch jerked his hand back, spilling the remained contents. "Nibsy Lorcan ain't more than a boy. People are following him like he's somebody, but he ain't nothing compared to the man Dolph—"

It was the final statement that had James stepping forward. The thump of his cane shouldn't have been audible over the noise of the saloon, but somehow it was enough for people to turn. The crowd went silent, because everyone understood that a line had been crossed. Everyone seemed to be holding their collective breath, waiting for what would happen next.

When Mooch realized that James had appeared, there was no flash of fear or misgiving. Instead, Mooch lifted his chin, his expression bleary-eyed and smugly indifferent. Next to him, Werner's expression had shifted into an alert wariness. Werner, at least, understood.

Stopping a few feet from Mooch, James leaned on the cane and again reveled in the feel of its power beneath his palm and the way it sang to the nervous energy careening through the room. As the room buzzed, he simply stared at the two boys without speaking.

Because he could. Because the Strega was his to command.

Mooch was a few inches taller than James and older as well. He was mean as a snake and could turn his fire on anyone—and did, often without provocation. But it didn't take a reading of the Aether to know that he wouldn't threaten James. Not here in the heart of the Strega. And not with his fire, at least. Because Mooch wasn't a leader. He was a coward.

"So," James said softly, knowing that nevertheless his voice carried through the room. "I see you have returned to us at last."

"Didn't expect that, did you?" Mooch demanded, too drunk to be nervous and too cocky to be smart.

"What is that supposed to mean?" James asked, his voice deadly calm.

"Don't listen to him none," Werner said, trying to push Mooch behind him. "Look, we would've come back sooner. We meant to. But the Order . . . they're everywhere. They're picking up anyone they suspect of having the old magic." Werner shifted nervously.

"I'm aware." James leaned into the cane, kept his expression free of any emotion. Beneath his hand, the power within the silver top—Leena's power and Dolph's—sizzled against his skin. "The rest of us are *all* aware of the danger we're currently in, no thanks to the two of you. And yet here you stand, blaming others for your own failures."

"Just take back what you said," Werner hissed into Mooch's ear. "Apologize."

But Mooch only lifted his chin higher.

Werner's eyes darted to James. "He's been drinking too much tonight,

Nibs. Nerves, you know. He's just talking shit, but he don't mean nothing by it."

"James," he corrected. "I've asked you to call me James."

"Right. *James*. Sorry." Werner ran a hand through his dark blond hair. "Like I said, Mooch here, he don't mean nothin.' Do ya, Mooch?" He elbowed his drunken friend. *"Tell him."*

Even inebriated as he was, Mooch's confidence suddenly faltered. There was a flicker of misgiving in his expression as he seemed to realize the gravity of the situation.

The smugness drained from his expression. "Yeah, I didn't mean nothing," he muttered half-heartedly. But he looked down, unable or unwilling to meet James' eyes.

"I see." James stepped closer. "But I wonder . . . why would you say something you didn't mean?" he asked, pretending confusion. "You said quite a lot just now."

"I was just talking, is all," Mooch told him. A soft belch highlighted his drunkenness and punctuated his confession.

James cocked his head slightly. "Were you?"

"Sure . . ." Mooch looked more nervous now. "I was just talking."

"You do that often, don't you?" James asked. He kept his voice soft and even.

The entire barroom had gone silent to listen. It felt like the Aether itself was holding its breath and waiting for what would come, and then James felt the shift, the telltale nudge that told him it was time.

"What?" Mooch seemed confused now.

"You often say things you don't mean," James clarified, allowing a bit more menace to color his tone. "You lie."

"I don't—"

"For instance," James continued, not allowing Mooch to explain. "When you told the others just now that you did everything possible to retrieve the ring, you were lying, weren't you?" He took another step forward.

"No. I wasn't lying about that," Mooch said. "Werner was there. He can tell you. There wasn't any way to get the ring out of that place."

Werner was backing away now. Another coward. But there would be time enough to deal with him later.

"You've lied to me before, Mooch. Do you think I don't know? When you told me that the police had released you from the Tombs, it was a lie," James said. "Wasn't it?"

"I don't know what you're talking about," Mooch said, but his voice cracked as he spoke, and his face was drained of color. "They released me, just like I said they did."

"No, Mooch. You had help. And you repaid your saviors by helping them break into my rooms," James said softly. "You allowed them to steal from me."

"No, Nibs—I mean, James," Mooch said, correcting himself as he stumbled over his words and his lies. "I *wouldn't*."

"But you did. Would you like to tell everyone here who it was that you let into the Strega that day back in May, or would you rather I told them?" James asked.

The silence around them now was deafening, but the Aether, it was dancing. Urging him on.

"You see," James said—and he was speaking to the room now, not only to Mooch. "It would be so much easier to believe that you'd done everything you could to bring me the ring if you hadn't let Viola Vaccarelli come into our home, our sanctuary. You helped her—a traitor to the Devil's Own—steal from me. From *us*."

"No, I—"

"Save your lies, Mooch." He leaned forward a bit, ignoring the boy's protest. "No one here believes them, just as no one believes you did everything you could at the Flatiron Building."

"But we *did*," Mooch said. "It was impossible to get the artifact like you wanted." Mooch looked to Werner, who wasn't by his side any longer. The other boy had already pressed himself back into the crowd.

"Another lie," James said. He held up his hand, the one bearing the ring, and allowed himself a to feel the satisfaction of seeing the color drain from Mooch's face. "Logan didn't walk away from his duty to the Devil's Own. But *you* did. Maybe you never wanted us to have this artifact." He lowered his voice. "Maybe you were working with Viola—and against *us*—all along."

"No way, Nib—James. That ain't it at all," Mooch said, backing away. But he was blocked by the bar behind him. "That ain't how it happened at all. Tell 'em, Werner. Explain what it was like up there."

Werner's eyes met James', and they widened slightly. But Werner didn't speak to help his friend. He just shook his head slightly and then looked away.

James took in every detail of the crowded saloon. There was not a soul there who hadn't been listening. He stepped toward Mooch. "It seems to me that while the rest of us risked ourselves for what Dolph Saunders built, you were off making nice with those who have betrayed Dolph and the Devil's Own."

"No, Nibs—*James. No.*" He sounded more sober now. "That ain't how it—"

"I think," James said, cutting him off before he could finish his protest, "that those of us who are loyal to Dolph's memory—may his soul rest in peace—should not stand for another lie from the mouth of a traitor."

He turned to the room and sensed that they were with him, every one of them. And why shouldn't they be? Hadn't he led them after Dolph had fallen? Hadn't he protected them from the Five Pointers and the threat of Tammany's police?

Jerking up his sleeve far enough to expose the intertwined snakes on his own arm, James looked around the room and met the eyes of those watching. "We all took this mark when we pledged ourselves to the Devil's Own, but this was never Dolph's mark alone. These intertwined serpents, life and death, were a promise to something larger than

Dolph Saunders. They were a promise to what he believed in. They were a promise of *loyalty*. Not to a man, but to an idea."

James turned back to Mooch now. He allowed his affinity to swell through the power in the cane just a little, testing it. Mooch reacted exactly as James had hoped, immediately grabbing his neck where the edge of a snake barely peeked out over the collar of his shirt. He grimaced and rubbed at the tattoo as though he were trying to rub off the ink inscribed into his skin.

"What the hell, Nibs?" Mooch whimpered.

Around them, the saloon rustled with uneasiness. James understood why. He could sense them all there, sense the marks that connected them to the cane he was holding, and he knew they could sense him as well. The Delphi's Tear might not have revealed the future to him, but the power in the artifact, along with his own connection to the Aether, made the cane he leaned against more powerful—and more dangerous—than it had ever been in Dolph Saunders' hand.

"Does it speak to you, Mooch?" James asked, swallowing the amusement that threatened to show in his expression.

"Please," Mooch said, his eyes filled with the kind of panic that could only be described as satisfying.

"Does your mark know of your betrayal?" James asked, taking another step closer.

"I didn't mean nothing by it," Mooch whined. "Maybe Viola and her rich toff did come and get me out of the Tombs. I know it was wrong to let them in, but she told me she just wanted to get something from her old room. You gotta believe me, Nibs—*James*. You gotta know I wouldn't do nothing to hurt the gang."

"But you did," James said. "Maybe you didn't mean anything by your actions, but they were a betrayal nonetheless. You think to compare me to Dolph Saunders? We all know one thing Dolph never tolerated"—he leaned closer until his face was a breath away from Mooch's—"*disloyalty*."

Before Mooch could so much as flinch away, James lifted the cane, and in a swift, impossible-to-stop motion, he placed the Medusa's head against the tattoo on Mooch's neck. She might have been kissing the dark ink on his skin, but at the touch of her cold silver lips, Mooch's scream tore through the saloon.

As the mark turned bloody, James began to draw on the power of the stone as well. He'd been experimenting with the cane for weeks now, had determined that his connection to the Aether gave him more flexibility to use the marks than Dolph ever had. Dolph had needed to touch someone—skin to skin—to borrow their affinity, but James could feel the marks through the Aether that surrounded a person. Until now, it hadn't been strong enough to do more than send a tingling bit of ice as a subtle warning to a single person. It had been enough to throw Viola off, but not enough to do any real damage.

With the power in the ring now on his finger, though? Things had changed.

Focusing through the Delphi's Tear, connecting it to the power in the Medusa's head, suddenly James could sense *every* person within his sight who wore the mark of the Devil's Own. He felt their link to the magic trapped in the cane head, felt the oaths they had given, and he used that connection to send a warning to everyone in that room. A promise. A threat.

The men and women in the barroom, the dangerous cutthroats, brawlers, and thieves who had once pledged themselves to Dolph Saunders, began to shuffle uncertainly. He could feel their panic rising, sensed that they all understood a new order had begun. And then he watched as, one by one, they began to kneel.

A DIFFERENT CITY

1902—The Bowery

Viola Vaccarelli eyed the darkened entrance to the stables from the mouth of the alleyway where she stood waiting in the shadows with Jianyu. Though she itched to charge in and just begin already, they couldn't risk being reckless. Ever since the events at the Flatiron Building a few weeks before, the city had been simmering. It seemed that every faction in the city had used the night of the Manhattan Solstice to tighten their control or increase their power.

Tammany had taken the Five Pointers' open warfare on the Order and the deadly attack on the plaza near Madison Square as a sign of the Order's weakness. In response, they'd increased the police presence throughout the city, and especially in the Bowery, to show who was truly in charge. The city might not be burning, as it had after Khafre Hall, but Tammany's police patrolled the poorest streets in the city with impunity, looking for any reason to bust open heads.

Having lost Tammany's previous support and help, the Order hadn't simply sat back to lick their wounds, as maybe they should have. Instead, they'd created patrols of their own and filled them with the roughest native-born men they could find. Viola knew their kind. She'd grown up with men like this all her life. Stronzi, tutti. The patrols were more than willing to turn their anger and hatred for the newest waves of immigrants into violence. When they weren't making trouble with the police, they prowled through the poorest tenements, searching for the Order's lost artifacts. It didn't matter if some of the people they injured in their searches weren't actually Mageus.

But the power struggle between Tammany and the Order wasn't the only danger in the city. With Paolo's absence, every gang was out for more territory . . . and for the blood of its rivals. The hole that Dolph Saunders' death had left in the power structure of the Bowery back in March had become the center of a building hurricane. Rival gangs didn't hesitate to take up weapons over the smallest slight. They were making ready for war.

To Viola's irritation, Nibsy had managed to maintain his hold on the Strega and the Devil's Own through his alignment with the Five Pointers. But as more of Dolph's rivals circled, there was no telling who would finally claim the Bella Strega and the territory that came with it.

Something was coming, of that Viola was certain. She'd seen the streets churn with riots enough times before that she knew they would soon erupt again. It was only a matter of when and a question of what might set them off. But this deep into the night, the city was almost quiet. Its ever-present noise was now little more than a gentle hum in the background, and it was almost possible to imagine a different city. *Almost.* But not quite, not when she knew that there was still violence stirring beneath. That violence had brought them to this part of town in the depth of the night.

The stables themselves were on the eastern edge of the Bowery, a little ways from the docks and nestled between buildings that held factories and sweatshops—far enough away from the nearest tenement that no residents milled around the streets. Viola didn't mistake the emptiness for safety, though.

"You're sure they've brought him here?" she whispered, glancing at Jianyu.

He gave her a single, nearly imperceptible nod. "Earlier this evening, but long after the horses were all in for the night."

Another Mageus had been taken up by the Order's patrols. Another soul that would have otherwise been lost.

For the last few weeks, word of abductions had been finding their way to Jianyu. A father taken from his pushcart. A brother who never returned home from his shift at the factory. One of the worried family members would appear on the street corner near the basement apartment where the two of them were currently staying, out of place in the neighborhood and desperate enough to turn to the very people they considered traitors. Jianyu never hesitated to offer his help, and Viola never bothered to argue against it. To her thinking, there was enough pain and suffering in the city without her adding more.

She watched for another long minute, waiting for some evidence of what was happening inside the stables, listening for any sound that might tell them when to make their move. Impatience grated against her already raw nerves. But too early, and they'd all be in danger. Too late, and . . .

They couldn't be too late.

Jianyu was already removing the bronze mirrors from his pockets, small disklike objects that helped him to focus his affinity and pull even the smallest strands of light out of the darkness. And it *was* dark. In this part of town, the shadows fell heavier than normal across the streets. Near the stables, the lamps hadn't been lit for the evening. Another sign that Jianyu's information wasn't incorrect. The Order always preferred to do their dirty work under the cover of night.

"If you are ready?" Jianyu asked, his expression tense with the effort of holding on to the light.

Viola nodded and stepped closer to him, looping one of her arms around his lean waist so he could wrap her in his cloak of magic. Then, hidden from any who might be looking, the two of them moved quickly toward the stables. Using Libitina, Viola made short work of the lock, and once the door was open, they let themselves silently into the building.

The air inside was even warmer than the balmy summer night, thick and moist with the breath of horses and the scent of hay. At first the only sound inside the stable was the soft shuffling of hooves and the occasional snort from a nearby stall. But then she heard it, muffled in the distance— the low moaning of someone in pain.

She exchanged a silent, knowing glance with Jianyu, and he nodded. Together they moved through the stables, past sleeping horses, until they came to another door. Not the stables then, but the next building over.

Surprisingly, this doorway wasn't secured. A bit of luck, but Viola did not relax. She kept her wits about her as she followed Jianyu into the narrow passage that ran between the two buildings. Another moan echoed in the darkness, but it was closer now. Jianyu sent her a silent look and nodded, before picking up their pace.

Finally, they came to the place where the passageway opened into a larger chamber. It was a factory of sorts. Large machines lurked in the shadowy gloom. In the center of the factory floor, four men stood above a boy who had been tied to a chair. Bruised and bloodied, Josef Salzer was barely recognizable from the beating, but the men—cowards that they were—clearly weren't finished with him. Three looked to be common day laborers, and were nothing more than hired muscle. But the other was dressed in an expensive-looking suit.

Because the Order doesn't trust their hired help. There was always one of their lower-level leccapiedi present, supervising without actually dirtying his hands. The Order's men always asked the questions, and the hired muscle delivered the answers.

"Again," the man in the suit said, his voice filled with bored indifference.

One of the larger men stepped forward and slammed his fist into the boy's face, and Josef's head ricocheted backward with such force that Viola nearly gasped. The Order's man didn't so much as flinch.

Viola sent her affinity out, sensing the heartbeats of every person in the room. Ready.

"Not yet," Jianyu whispered close to her ear. "It has to look as though they've killed him."

She swallowed down her hatred and her impatience. Jianyu was right. The Order could not know that Josef had survived. He looked a mess, but so far, the boy's heart was still beating. He'd lost a lot of blood, but they weren't yet close to killing him. He had a long way to go before death would offer any relief.

Josef let out a keening moan as his head rolled forward. Blood poured from his nose, staining the front of his torn shirt.

"It's very simple, boy. You give us a name, and we let you walk out of here tonight," the man in the suit said. He stood a few feet away, far enough not to be splattered. "Any name will do."

"I told you . . . I don't know anything," Josef said slowly, haltingly through broken teeth and a blood-filled mouth.

"You worked for a man named Dolph Saunders," the suited man said. "A gang boss who was responsible for attacking the Khafre Hall. Word is, you acted as a runner for him, delivering messages. You must know *something.*"

"Dolph's dead," Josef gasped, his chest heaving with the effort. "He's been dead for months."

"So you say," the suited man said. He shrugged, as though it didn't really matter. "Give us another name, then. You must know someone who was involved with the attacks. You must know who was loyal to him, who might have helped him. You give us their names, and we let you go. It's as easy as that."

It was never so easy, and from their previous experience with these late-night rescues, Viola knew that there was no chance of the boy ever walking away from this without Jianyu's and her help. But still they waited. She kept her affinity close, ready to stop the boy's words if it became necessary.

Josef's chest heaved with the effort to draw breath. He could have ended his misery by now. He could have given a name—any name, whether real or fake, involved or innocent. Instead, he lifted his head and glared at the man in the suit through swollen eyes. Then, every line of his broken and battered body defiant, he spit a wad of blood and phlegm at the man. But it fell short of him, landing at his feet.

Incensed, the Order's man lifted his fist.

"Now," Jianyu whispered.

Viola didn't have to be told twice. Without hesitation, she let her affinity flare and found the beating of Josef's heart, the blood thundering erratically through his veins. She slowed the rush nearly to a stop.

The boy's head flopped forward. His body went limp in the chair.

"What the—" The man in the suit froze, his fist still raised. When he realized the boy wasn't moving, his arm fell and he let out a curse. Then he turned on the stocky men with bloodied fists. "I told you that I needed him alive."

One of the larger, rough men thumbed at his nose. "You told us to make him bleed, and that's what we did."

"It ain't our fault if he can't hold his blood," another of the bruisers laughed.

The laugh set the suited man on a tear. Suddenly, they were all arguing, shouting about payment and orders, but Viola didn't care to listen. Her concentration was on the feel of her magic and the roaring in her ears as she focused on Josef's blood, on the beating of his heart. Slowly, she allowed it to beat once more. Twice. Enough to keep him alive. Enough to make the men believe he was dead.

"Shit," the suited man said. "We were close to breaking him. I could feel it."

He was wrong, of course. They hadn't been close, not when Josef Salzer had chosen to use what little strength he had to curse the men who could kill him. Now they wouldn't have the chance.

"Dump him out back," the suited man ordered. He tossed a pile of bills on the floor at the other men's feet, and then, with another disgusted string of curses, he turned and left.

The men lunged for the money. When they'd sorted out their shares, they passed around a flask and laughed about how easily they'd broken the boy. But eventually they got to work dealing with the body. There were saloons to visit and women to find waiting for them in the night.

Only when the men finally cut Josef from the chair and carried him,

THE SHATTERED CITY

still unconcious, out the back of the factory did she and Jianyu move, following silently as one. Hidden in the threads of Jianyu's affinity.

The men dumped Josef in the alleyway behind the factory. They didn't even bother to hide the body or cover their tracks. Why should they? No one would care about another piece of the Bowery's trash, dead in the gutter. And for those who did care? Josef's body only served as a warning for what could come for them as well.

Viola's jaw ached from clenching it all evening. She thought for sure her molars would crack from the pressure one of these nights, from the strength it took to keep her temper in check. The willpower it took not to let her affinity unfurl and kill them all.

When the coast was clear, she and Jianyu moved quickly. By the time they reached the boy, he was already sitting up, groggy and disoriented from the beating and from her magic. He wouldn't be able to walk on his own, she realized. One of his legs had been broken. She could help with that, once they were safe, once he was back in the arms of his mother, Golde.

But when Josef saw who was standing over him, it wasn't relief that crossed his face. It never was. His eyes widened, and he tried to back away. Thanks to the poisonous lies Nibsy had spread throughout the Bowery, Josef Salzer believed *they* were the traitors.

With a sigh, Viola sent out her affinity again, pulled on his heartbeat softly, just enough that he passed out once more.

"It's always the same," she muttered, helping Jianyu to support the boy's weight between the two of them. "Always the hate."

"The understanding comes later," Jianyu reminded her. "Golde will explain. She will make him understand."

"She'd better," Viola muttered. The summer's sultry heat had her sweating through her dress from the effort of dragging the boy through the streets. They had not expected a second building, so they had farther to go than they had planned.

"She will," Jianyu assured her.

"And then what?" Viola asked. She stopped short, suddenly exhausted beyond reason. It had already been weeks of this. Weeks and weeks of midnight rescues to save the lives of those who believed them to be villains. Weeks of never knowing when the Order and their men would come for them as well. All in the midst of a city on the verge of exploding.

And who would rescue her if that happened? Who would rescue Jianyu? After all they'd done, after all the lives they'd tried to save, who among the Devil's Own would risk their lives to save the two of them?

No one. She and Jianyu were on their own. Even with souls under their protection, even with life upon life owed to them, they were alone.

With Josef slung between them and the danger of the Conclave marching closer, Viola finally voiced the fear that she knew they both held silently in their hearts: "What if they never return?"

Jianyu didn't bother to ask who she was referring to. They did not often speak of Esta and Harte, but the Thief and the Magician were always there, a silent absence between them. "Then it becomes even more important to carry on," Jianyu said. "We do what we have always intended. We protect those we can protect. And we stop Nibsy and the Order from building any more power."

"*How?*" Viola asked, glancing at him. "Each week brings a new riot in the streets, a new victim to rescue. The Order will not stop searching for their treasures. They will not stop until every Mageus in this city has been damaged by their violence. And we don't even have an artifact to show for all the danger we're in."

"We have the silver discs," Jianyu said, urging her on. They still had quite a distance to cover before they reached the wagon waiting for them.

"Useless trinkets," she grumbled.

"You know that is not true," Jianyu told her. "You would not have taken them if they had not called to you with their power. Perhaps it is time to stop waiting for Darrigan and Esta to rescue us from our future. Perhaps it is time to begin searching for answers of our own."

But the Order had just left the discs sitting there, out in the open.

Unguarded. Unwatched. They could not possibly be so important. "What if there are no answers?"

In the distance, a dog barked, and then they heard the sound of shouting. The clattering of wagon wheels was growing closer. But between them, Josef Salzer was a deadweight, holding them down.

"Cela," Viola said. She was waiting for them around the corner, without any protection.

"We have to go," Jianyu told her. "We must get to her," he said, pulling Josef and Viola onward. "And we must go now."

ANOTHER MANHATTAN

1983—The Bridge

E sta felt her affinity waver as the icy warning of the Brink crashed over them, swelling until it had engulfed them both like a wave cresting over a seawall. The seconds suddenly felt sharp and dangerous, but she gripped them tighter, determined not to let them fly away from her as she dragged Harte onward.

She ran on instinct, their hands still clasped tightly and her breath coming hard, as she pushed through a thick wall of cold energy that seemed endless. The other enormous limestone tower of the Brooklyn Bridge was still fifty yards or more away, but it might as well have been fifty miles. Every step brought a fresh burst of pain as the seconds in the grasp of her affinity sharpened, twisting savagely to be free. Time felt like a live wire.

Suddenly, Esta felt Harte jerk out of the grip of her magic. She turned back to find him frozen with the rest of the world, his face contorted in a kind of desperate agony. This time she allowed the seconds to slip away from her, and as the world slammed back into motion and Harte was free, a wailing moan of sheer pain tore from his chest. She reached for him, but he pulled away.

"No!" His features contorted with another moan. "Don't touch me!"

"Seshat?" she asked.

A grimace was her only answer.

Separate now, they ran. Dimly, Esta was aware of sirens screaming in the distance as they burst through the last few yards of dangerous energy. When they finally broke free of the Brink's power, Harte tumbled to his knees, shivering in the shadows of the bridge's towers. His chest heaved from the exertion of the run, and Esta understood he was shivering from something more than the cold. His hands were pressed over his ears, holding his head, as though trying desperately to keep himself together.

"The Quellant?" she asked, needing to touch him but knowing she couldn't.

"Gone," he said through gritted teeth. "She's . . ." He groaned again, flinching from some unseen torture. "So angry. Can't—" He doubled over again.

Desperate to help him, Esta pulled out the leather pouch Maggie had gifted her so many weeks before, the one filled with various magical concoctions. With half-frozen fingers, she fumbled open the clasp, but when she looked inside, she suddenly couldn't breathe.

It's gone. It's all gone.

Everything inside the pouch had turned to powdery ash. The wind gusted, as if on cue, and she tried to clasp the pouch closed again to protect what was left. But she knew already that it was pointless. The incendiaries and Flash and Bangs—and most important of all, the Quellant—were gone. The Brink had taken everything. Incinerated all of it with its terrible power.

On her arm, her cuff felt icy hot, and she grasped the satchel that was slung diagonally against her chest. To her relief, the Book and the artifacts were still there. But without the Quellant . . .

Esta realized then that the sirens she'd been hearing for the last couple of minutes weren't in the distance any longer. They were coming closer. Behind them on the bridge, she could still feel the warning of the Brink, a devastating cold over the chill of the winter air. Before her, the streets seemed more dangerous than they had been before. The air felt suddenly alive, as though the city itself knew they'd entered. As though it was angry with their trespass.

"We need to go," she told Harte, her instincts prickling. The sirens were even louder now. They couldn't be found there, trapped on the bridge with the Brink behind them and no way to retreat. "Can you walk?"

Harte nodded, but from the agony in his eyes and the way he held himself stiff and hunched against the pain, she wasn't sure she believed him. But she couldn't help him, either. She couldn't even touch him without the Quellant to hold back Seshat.

Luckily, he was able to pull himself to his feet, and on unsteady legs he moved, lurching and stumbling next to her as they hurried along the remaining span of the bridge. They slipped and slid through the filthy slush covering the long, sloping walkway that led to the park where City Hall waited, white and sepulchral, in the snowy night. Even wearing the jacket Harte had given her, she wasn't dressed for the cold, and with the thin leather of her soles already soaked through, she could no longer feel her toes. But the cold that chilled her to the core was more than the weather. The echoing reminder of the Brink's energy still vibrated through her, a warning of what would happen to her affinity—to her very self—if ever she tried to leave the city again.

But somehow none of that mattered—not the slushy snow nor the ache in her frozen toes. Not even the unsettled fear that clung to her bones as sirens drew closer. All that mattered was Harte. Stumbling along beside her, he gasped and shook with each step, but he hadn't given up.

She had to get them somewhere safe. Off the bridge. Out of sight.

Esta led the way around the park that skirted City Hall, trying to make sense of the way this version of the city was different from the one she had known as a child. So much was the same—the height of the buildings and the lights and the speed and the noise of it—but this New York, modern though it seemed, wasn't hers. This city was somehow louder and dirtier. The scent of diesel smoke was heavy in the air, and trash and debris lined the streets, piled up alongside the homeless who'd made their beds beneath makeshift tents in the snowy park.

Harte tried to keep pace beside her, but he was struggling. By the time they reached the sidewalk in front of City Hall, he was breathing hard through clenched teeth. Without warning, he stopped and curled over, grabbing his head again. His whole expression twisted in pain.

"Harte?" Esta stepped toward him, but he flinched away, and when he finally uncurled himself, finally looked up at her, she saw a too-familiar darkness bleeding into the gray of his irises.

She'd made an agreement with Seshat. She'd killed Jack and destroyed Thoth along with him in exchange for Harte's life, but it was clear the goddess had decided not to uphold her side of their bargain.

"Just hold on a little longer," Esta told him, wishing she could do more as she tried to decide where to go. She wanted more than anything to put her arms around him, to keep him from flying apart, but she knew that without the Quellant, she couldn't take the risk.

The flashing red of police lights lit the buildings around them now as the squeal of tires tore through the night. A half dozen bright blue cars with glinting chrome fenders skidded to a stop near the mouth of the bridge, blocking the entrance to the walkway where they had just been.

"We have to keep moving," she told Harte. The police showing up like they had couldn't be a coincidence, even if she didn't understand how they could have known about their arrival. The Brink hadn't ever been monitored as far as she knew. But who was to say how much their movements through the past had changed this present? Who was to say what dangers waited in this version of the time line?

Harte was still huddled over, doubled into himself.

"We have to go. *Now*." In a few minutes those cops would be out of those cars and would start to fan out. They were clearly looking for something—for someone—and they would see the path the two of them had made through the snow. If they didn't get away before then, there would be no way to explain what she and Harte were doing in the nearly empty park in the middle of the night, coatless and dressed in clothing decades out of style.

The two of them scuttled along behind a row of newspaper boxes covered in graffiti, careful to avoid being seen. Half the windows had been busted out of the few boxes that were still standing. They had to keep moving, but with the police surrounding the area now, their only real choice was to go underground.

The Brooklyn Bridge subway station didn't look that different from the way it had looked in her own time. It still welcomed them with the same mechanical staleness the air underground always carried, that dust-laced scent of machines layered with the strong ammonia reek of urine. But at least the platform was protected from the icy wind and free from snow. At least they were out of sight.

Luckily, the station was mostly empty. A group of three guys in heavy coats huddled together on the far end of the platform. Even from a distance they looked completely strung out.

When Harte groaned again, grabbing at his head, they glanced up from whatever they were dealing, but a second later they turned back to their huddle. Uninterested.

She couldn't hear the sirens anymore, but that didn't put her at ease. She had no idea what was happening aboveground. Still, no one had followed them. At least not yet. Eventually someone would track them down. They had to get on a train, and fast.

Esta looked up. The station clock had been busted open, its hands removed, and its face obscured by graffiti, so she wasn't even sure what time it was. Late, by the emptiness of the streets and the platform, but this wasn't her New York. There were no digital readouts to tell her the schedule. There was nothing they could do but wait and hope that the next train would arrive before the police found them.

Harte crouched down, hunching against the peeling paint of the iron column in the center of the narrow cement platform. He was rocking a little, still moaning to himself, but at least the guys at the other end of the station didn't seem to notice or care. Just another junkie, as far as they knew.

"Is there anything I can do?" She crouched down next to him, wanting more than anything to brush the hair back from his pale, damp forehead. "Anything that would help?"

He shook his head, his teeth still gritted. "Stay back." His lips pressed together, like he was steeling himself against the next wave of whatever pain Seshat was inflicting. "Please. It makes it worse . . . when you're close. She's so angry. Wants you. So *badly*." He grimaced again. "She keeps screaming about Thoth. How she wants to destroy him."

It didn't make sense. "Thoth's gone. I took care of him when I killed Jack."

"Tell that to Seshat," Harte groaned. He looked even more wan in the yellowish glow from the fluorescent lights overhead.

The squeal of an arriving train echoed through the tunnels before Esta could reply.

Harte flinched, clamping his hands more tightly over his ears at the sound of screeching brakes as the train slid into the station. The litter along the edges of the platform fluttered in the gust of air the train brought with it.

The cars were boxier than the ones Esta had grown up riding, and the entire train was covered completely in graffiti, including the windows, so she couldn't see inside. She had no idea how many people might be riding or what might be waiting, but when the doors lurched open, no one exited. A disembodied voice echoed through the dimly lit station, instructing everyone to disembark. It was the last stop on the line.

Esta clenched her jaw in frustration at the worthless train. They couldn't just sit here waiting. Soon, the cops outside would start searching farther from the bridge. Soon enough, they'd search the station. But considering how late it was? She didn't know how long it would be before another train came along—

And then she realized which train it was.

"Come on," she told Harte, pulling him up by his sleeve-covered arm.

Clearly in too much pain to argue and too weak to pull away, he allowed her to drag him onto the train, but the second they were aboard, he seemed to realize how close she was and pulled away again. She understood why, but the rejection still stung as she took a seat in the row closest to the back door of the car. Harte took the bench opposite, making sure to keep his distance.

He flinched again, like another volley of pain had just shot through him. "I can't . . . ," he whispered. "Too much . . ." He rocked as he spoke to himself—or to Seshat. She couldn't hear him enough to be sure.

Esta willed the doors to close before anyone else arrived or tried to board, but she didn't let go of the breath she was holding until the train started to lurch forward slowly, not gathering much speed as it left the station. Harte didn't seem to notice. The rocking had stopped, and now he seemed suddenly too still, hunched as he was against the filthy wall of the train, his eyes closed and his mouth in a pained line.

"Just a little longer," she told him.

He grimaced in response, turning away from her.

The inside of the subway car was as covered in graffiti as the outside, and there was trash collecting beneath the seats. Subway cars in general weren't exactly the cleanest places in the city even in her own time, but this was something else. She'd seen pictures of the city before it was cleaned up back in the 1990s, but she hadn't spent much time in the eighties. The oddness of a city so similar to her own—and yet so different—was unsettling. As the train began to move, a bent syringe rolled to a stop against Esta's foot. She kicked it away.

The train swayed as it started to curve around the next bend, and Esta realized they needed to move. If they missed their chance, she was out of ideas. It was this or nothing.

She stood, bracing herself against the movement in the same way she had her whole life. It steadied her a little, the familiarity of the train's movement beneath her, lurching and swaying. Harte was huddled against the filthy window, his hands over his ears, as if he were trying to hold his head together.

"Let's go, Harte," she said as the train lurched again. She stood and made her way to the door at the end of the car and flung it open, but when she turned back, Esta realized Harte hadn't followed her. He was still curled in the corner of the seat, still grimacing and half-delirious from the pain.

JUST A LITTLE LONGER

1983—Lower Manhattan

Harte heard Esta calling him as if from a distance. It was hard to hear anything over the storm raging inside him. The instant they'd crossed the Brink and the Quellant burned away, Seshat had begun railing against him, swelling and clawing and pushing at the boundary between them. It felt as though his skin might split open if he didn't concentrate on keeping himself together.

He thought he had understood. He thought he'd felt the true extent of Seshat's affinity before. But this was different. Now he understood exactly why Thoth had wanted her magic. She was a force. *More than a force.* She was power and its antithesis. Even ancient and disembodied and half-broken by Thoth's betrayal, Seshat's magic was a living, breathing thing. Her power was astounding, *impossible.* Holding her back felt like he was trying to hold on to lightning.

Worse, Seshat wanted Esta more than ever.

Harte was only half-aware of where they were, and he had no idea where they were going. But he didn't think he could last much longer against Seshat's onslaught, not when he felt utterly decimated by her wrath.

You cannot stop me. I will take all that she is, all that she contains, and tear it from the world.

"No," he said, struggling to hold himself back—to hold Seshat back.

"Harte?" Esta was standing in an open doorway. Her short hair was a wild riot around her face in the gusting wind.

He could hear and see her, but he couldn't respond. All of his focus was on Seshat, pushing her back. On holding her down. *Just a little longer.*

Yes. Go to her, Seshat commanded, her power swelling within until he was on his feet. He couldn't stop his back from arching as she pressed and clawed at him. He could not stop himself from moving steadily toward the open door, toward Esta.

She had no idea the danger she was in.

Esta let the door slide closed and approached him, grabbing him by his sleeve. Seshat roared in triumph as Harte tried to pull away, but Esta was determined.

"We have to go. It's time," she told him, dragging him toward the door of the train again. "I just need you to hold on for a little longer."

Just a little longer. But Harte wasn't sure that he could. The pain of Seshat's power churned within him. The agony of what she was doing inside his skin. She was raging about Thoth. Screaming with a voice that could shatter his sanity.

Oh god, it's too much. He couldn't hold on. Needed it to end. Because this power, the immenseness of all that Seshat was and all that she could do wasn't something he could live through much longer.

He had to protect Esta. He had to keep her safe from the terror beneath his skin.

They were on the platform at the back of the train car now, but the wind whipping at his hair was nothing compared to Seshat's fury, and the darkness of the tunnel was nothing compared to the living, terrifying darkness roiling inside him. The walls of the tunnel slid past at a dizzying speed, and he understood what he had to do. He saw how easily he could end everything. The train was certainly going fast enough, and Esta wouldn't be able to stop him—she knew that she couldn't touch him while Seshat writhed beneath his skin.

Esta was still talking, but Harte could not understand what she was saying. He was too focused on keeping Seshat back. Too focused on the agony of feeling the goddess raging within him. She could not be allowed to touch Esta. He would keep Esta safe. If he could do nothing else, he'd keep Seshat from destroying her. And from destroying the world.

Esta was holding on to the metal railing, unhooking the metal chains that kept people safely on the platform at the end of the car. Then she turned back to him, and he saw the fear in her expression and knew what she must see in his own.

"Harte," she said, her voice coming to him from a distance. It felt as though he were locked tight in a watery box, with the noise of the audience far off. "It's going to be okay. You can do this."

She understands. The relief was almost enough to break Seshat's hold on him.

He'd been *fighting* for so long because he couldn't bear to leave Esta, but now the time had come. He saw it in her eyes, that she knew what had to happen, what needed to be done. He moved toward the edge of the platform as Seshat raged more violently. He wouldn't have thought that was possible, but he should have known better. Every time he thought he understood what she was capable of, the ancient power surprised him with still more.

His hands curled on the railing, wishing there were some other answer. But there wasn't. Even Esta understood that now.

The air around him felt warmer than it should have somehow, thicker too, like the dust and mold and smoke from the ages of trains passing through had lingered on.

Esta was talking again, and Harte watched her mouth move without hearing her. He wanted to kiss her just once more, but that was impossible—far too much a risk when Seshat was so close to the surface now. But while Harte couldn't make out what she was saying, he understood. This was the end.

He held up a hand, wishing he could touch her. With the goddess railing inside him, it took every ounce of his strength to force out the words he needed her to hear. "You . . . are not negotiable. Never have been." He grimaced against the power thrashing inside him. "Not for me."

Her eyes went wide, and the sudden terror there surprised him, but only distantly. Even as he backed away from her, she was trying to tell him something, her mouth moving excitedly and her eyes bright with fear.

"It's okay," he said, taking another step toward the edge of the small platform on the rear of the car. "I'll be okay."

"No!" He didn't need to hear her voice to know what she was saying, but he was already turning, already preparing himself, even as Seshat roared and wailed.

He closed his eyes, wishing he were braver, wishing he could go to his death without so many regrets. He took one last deep breath, hating that it reeked of the filth in the tunnel, and then he released his hold on the train rail and fell.

NOT EVER AGAIN

1983—Under the City

As the train screamed around the bend in the tunnel, Esta held on to the cold metal railing at the back of the car and promised herself that if they made it through the next few minutes, she would kill Harte Darrigan herself.

It was clear Harte wasn't listening to her. He was standing next to her on the edge of the train car's back platform, but his eyes were an inky black. His features were twisted in pain and fear, and his expression looked haunted . . . and determined. She understood exactly what he was preparing to do, and she wasn't about to let him. He'd promised that he would give up the idea of destroying himself to save her. He'd promised that they were in this together. And now she was going to make sure he kept that promise.

Just as the idiot released his hold on the railing, Esta slammed into him, pulling them both off the car and hoping it was enough momentum to get them across the gap. Because she had a hold on Harte, she couldn't stop herself from landing hard on the unforgiving concrete of the abandoned station's platform. Pain lanced through her arm where the skin was still tender and mangled beneath the bandage, but she ignored it and used all her strength to twist, rolling them both back from the edge as the train picked up speed to round the curve and exit the station. They weren't even touching skin to skin, but Esta could practically feel Seshat's power lancing through their brief connection. She moved quickly enough that it wasn't much more than a brush of darkness in her vision and sizzling heat across her skin.

Once she'd put some distance between them, Esta let herself lie there on the cold cement as she tried to catch her breath. Her arm was throbbing from holding on to Harte and from landing so hard, and her pulse felt erratic from the adrenaline still jangling through her. But at least they were safe. Silence surrounded them in the emptiness of the station. No red police lights flashed. No sirens screamed. No one seemed to have seen or followed them.

Above, nearly pristine green and gold tiles lined the vaulted ceilings of the old City Hall station, framing the dark glass of large, snow-covered skylights. The station was dark except for the eerie yellowish glow of emergency lamps that revealed the pedestrian exit.

Harte groaned nearby, and Esta turned her head to see him curled up on the ground a few feet away from her. She pushed herself upright, ignoring the aching in her arm as she listened to the last sounds of the train they'd just been on moving off into the distance on its northward route along the 6 line.

He moaned again, and Esta scooted closer to look at him. She wanted to touch him, to help him in some way, but she knew exactly how dangerous that would be. She let out an unsteady breath as she inched closer. *You are nonnegotiable.* The second Harte had given her those words, she'd understood what he was about to do. If the train hadn't reached the platform when it did, he would have jumped. He would have already been gone.

"You're a complete idiot, you know that?" she said softly, hating the way her voice hitched around the words. She didn't really mean it. She understood why he would have thrown himself from the subway car. Wouldn't she have done the same to keep the world safe? To keep *him* safe?

But she wasn't even sure that Harte could hear her. His eyes opened, wide and unseeing, but he didn't look in her direction. His gray irises had turned completely black, and the inky darkness was spreading to the whites as well. He grimaced, his face contorting, and she understood that he was still fighting Seshat.

Esta was going to make sure he won.

"Go." His mouth was drawn, pained, but his words made it clear he knew she was there. That *he* was still there. "She wants to *destroy* you."

"I don't have any plans to die today, Harte." She wanted to move closer and reassure him, but the air around him was charged and unsettled. "And you'd better not, either."

The City Hall subway station had been closed for nearly forty years. They'd shut it down in the forties, when the subway cars had grown too long and too large to fit into the curved station without creating an unsafe gap between the train and the curve of the platform. It had been empty and abandoned since then, and it wasn't exactly legal to visit it, so there was no one around. No vagrants sleeping in the corners, no junkies dealing on the stairwell, and no graffiti marring the shining ceramic tiles on the walls. Trapped in time, the station platform was silent and lonely. And almost clean. In short, it was exactly what they needed.

"This is where the very first subway train ever departed," she told him, speaking out loud because she had to prove to herself that her voice wouldn't shake.

Professor Lachlan had shown her this secret place when she was a girl. It had been a crisp fall day, and they'd ridden the 6 until the end of the line. They'd remained on the train as it made the loop in the station to turn around and head north, and she'd peered through the scratched windows to see this place, dimly lit but still shining like new. He'd wanted her to know everything about the city. Every nook and every secret.

An unpleasant thought occurred to her: Could he have known she would need this place one day?

She wasn't sure how to feel about that—the idea that even with the tangled knot of time, so much of her training could have been intended to lead her there, right where Professor Lachlan wanted her. Was it possible that despite everything, despite all they'd changed and all she'd thought they'd been able to do to avoid his grasp, he had known all along that this was where she would end up? How was she ever supposed to beat him if, in both the past and the future, he could still move her around like a pawn on a board? Despite the passing of time—despite the *changing* of history?

Harte had curled tightly into a ball, trying to protect himself against Seshat's fury and anger.

Esta looked around, considering her options—*their* options. She wasn't sure how long Harte could last like this, and without the Quellant . . . They needed the missing part of the Book. She needed to stop Seshat from destroying Harte.

"I have to get the key," she said, more to herself than to Harte. But this time he seemed to hear her.

"Esta, no." When he opened his eyes, he looked almost lucid . . . almost like himself. "You know Nibsy's waiting for you. He wants you to come for it, and I can't—" A groan tore from his throat that made her ache.

Without hesitating, she pulled time still, and the world went silent. "You're right, Harte," she said softly, her throat tight with emotion. "You can't."

The station had already been quiet, but now the far-off sounds of trains traveling along the tracks and the creaking of the pipes drained away into complete silence.

Esta took one last look at Harte and hoped that Seshat's powers couldn't harm him while he was held in the grip of her affinity's net. Or at least she hoped he wouldn't be aware and wouldn't remember the minutes that passed until she returned. She wished she could touch him just once before she left him, but she didn't dare. She couldn't risk it.

She'd been a fool for trusting Seshat to keep her word.

Esta had *killed* a man to keep her promise. She'd destroyed Thoth, eliminated the threat he posed, and *this* was how the bitch of a goddess repaid her? By driving Harte to nearly end everything by throwing himself from the train?

No. Esta wasn't going to sit there and hope that Seshat came to her senses. She wouldn't allow Seshat to destroy Harte or to hurt anyone or anything else. *Not ever again.* She'd get the key to Newton's cipher from Professor Lachlan, and then she would take care of Seshat herself. Even if it was the last thing she did.

Esta took the Book from the satchel and considered her options. She might be able to steal time, but she couldn't put off the inevitable. She was going back to Orchard Street.

Considering her options, Esta placed the Book on the floor and gave it a small push, sliding it closer to Harte. She lifted the satchel from her shoulder and slid it toward him as well. It could be a mistake to leave the Book and the artifacts, but it would be a worse mistake to let them fall into Nibsy's hands. The last thing she wanted to do was deliver the Ars Arcana directly to him. Then she took one more look at Harte—his too-sharp cheekbones, his rumpled dark hair. But when she reached his eyes, she saw the hold Seshat had on him.

She hated the blackness there, the dark power already overwhelming him. And she would do anything to destroy it. As she turned away and headed toward the tunnel that led up to the emergency exit, she vowed she'd see his eyes flash storm-gray at her once more.

UNEXPECTED ANSWERS

1902—The Bowery

Jianyu and Viola had barely made it around the corner before the police wagon tore down the street they had just been on. Hanging from its sides were uniformed men, off to round up whatever the disturbance in the distance happened to be.

Jianyu exchanged a look with Viola, and in silent agreement, they began to move faster.

It was not only Josef Salzer's unconscious body that weighed on Jianyu as they worked to get the boy to safety. Viola's words worried him as well.

What if there are no answers?

It had been months since that day on the bridge when Harte and Esta had left him to defend the ring and hold everything together. Months of chaos. Months of failure. He had lost the Delphi's Tear and any chance to reclaim a place in the Devil's Own along with it. And with each day that passed, he could not help but wonder what would become of them if Harte and Esta never returned. But Jianyu forced himself to push aside his worries for the future. They would still be there once Josef was safely in his family's keeping.

Finally they arrived at the side street where Cela waited with the wagon they had borrowed from Mr. Fortune and his newspaper the *New York Age*.

Cela was in the driver's perch behind a single mangy-looking nag. She was dressed in the rough-spun clothes of a common working man, trousers and a jacket that she had tailored to hide her true form. A man's broad-brimmed hat was pulled down low over her brow, shielding her face, but Jianyu did not miss the tightness of her fingers around the worn leather of the reins.

When they neared, he let out a low, soft whistle, the signal that they had arrived.

Cela straightened, the hat tipping back enough for him to see the soft curve of her cheek and the sharp line of her hairless jaw. Only a fool would not notice she was a woman beneath the clothes, but the city was filled with fools.

Her eyes were sharp as they searched the night, but it was only when they were standing at the foot of the wagon that Jianyu finally released his affinity enough to allow her to find him in the darkness.

"You made it in time?" she whispered, climbing down from her perch.

"Barely," Viola told her.

Cela had accompanied them on each of these trips over the last weeks, but even with all she had seen, she gasped when Josef Salzer's head tipped back and she saw his broken and bloodied face. She rushed over to help them.

"Barely is better than not at all," Jianyu told them.

Together they lifted Josef into the back of the covered wagon, and then Viola climbed in with the boy. She would need to stay close to keep his heart beating and his moans quiet until they arrived at the safe house far, far uptown.

When Jianyu lifted the gate of the wagon and secured it, Viola turned back, frowning at him. "You aren't coming with us?"

"I have to tell his mother," Jianyu told her. "Golde will be waiting for news, and she should not have to see the sun rise without it."

"We can wait," Cela said as she climbed back into the driver's perch.

He considered her offer, but when a shout went up in the distance, he shook his head. It was not worth it to risk more than one life. "Not tonight."

LISA MAXWELL

Cela did not look pleased, but she also did not argue. "Get back to us safe."

The note of concern in her voice settled deep within him, a reminder that he was not alone—that *they* were not alone—as he pulled his affinity close, opened what little moonlight found its way through the clouds above, and wrapped his magic around himself once more.

With so many police officers patrolling the streets, it took longer than usual for Jianyu to reach Golde Salzer's home. Josef's family lived in a pair of small, lightless rooms on the fourth floor of a tenement not far from the Bella Strega. The building was deep within territory under the control of the Devil's Own and, consequently, territory currently held by Nibsy Lorcan, so Jianyu kept his affinity close as he walked through the part of the city he'd once called home. No good would come of Nibsy knowing that he had been there.

The building where Golde and her children lived was mostly dark. Its inhabitants had no doubt already turned in for the night to prepare for the long day of work that would greet them when the sun rose. But he knew Golde would be up, waiting for word of her son. When Jianyu reached her door, he tapped the softest of rhythms and waited. When the door inched open, Golde's drawn, shadowed face appeared. Only then did he allow the light to recede a little, exposing himself. With a small jerk of his head, he motioned that she should follow, and then, wordlessly, made his way to the stairs and then up toward the roof. He did not look back to see if she was behind him.

Luckily, the roof was empty. All around, the Lower East Side fanned out in a jumbled mess of streets. The city felt quieter here. In the distance, he could almost make out the towers of the bridge in the hazy summer night. This close to the stars, the rot of the gutter and the stench of the streets below were barely detectable. Here, he could almost imagine the city was a different place, a better one.

Perhaps one day it would be.

A few minutes later, Golde stepped out onto the roof. She had a shawl pulled up over her hair, another wrapped around her. In her eyes, she carried the same distrust and the same wariness he regularly saw in the eyes of those who had been turned by Nibsy's honeyed lies. Even when she had come to him for help, she had not quite trusted him.

Golde glanced back at the stairwell once more, as though making sure she had not been followed.

Jianyu understood her nervousness. Golde had told him already that her husband did not approve of her seeking help to find their oldest son. The older man had been injured in a factory accident months before, back when Dolph was still running the Bowery, but the man's leg still had not healed enough to find work. He depended on his children and his wife to keep a roof over their heads and food on their table. They all depended on Josef, who had once worked for Dolph. Which meant that they now depended upon the generosity of Nibsy Lorcan. None of them could risk Nibsy finding out about Jianyu's involvement.

"You found him, my Josef?" she asked, her voice barely a whisper.

Jianyu nodded.

"Truly?" she asked, stepping toward him. The mistrust and hesitation all but vanished. "Where is he? I want to see him. Take me to my boy."

"Golde—" He stopped when her eyes flashed. "*Mrs.* Salzer. You know I cannot."

Her expression hardened. "I want to see my child. I want to see him with my own eyes."

Josef was no more a child than Jianyu himself was. The boy had been hardened by the streets like so many others. Still, he understood a mother's care, even if it had been a lifetime since he had felt it himself.

"Soon," Jianyu promised softly, hoping to calm her. "When we know for sure that it is safe."

"When it's safe," she said, cursing in German that Jianyu could not understand. "When has life for our kind ever been safe here in this blighted city?"

Jianyu could not disagree, but he did not mistake Golde's words as including himself in the sentiment. She meant Mageus, to be sure. But that did not necessarily mean that she considered the two of them as anything alike.

Golde looked up at him, her small face lined beyond its years. But that was what came of rooms full of children and only empty cupboards to feed them. "What do you want? Money? I told you already that I couldn't offer you much."

"Keep your coin," Jianyu said, trying to hide his frustration. "I told you before, there is no need. But your son is not the only one we protect. When we know for sure that the Order no longer searches for him, I can bring you to him."

She frowned. "There must be something I could give you. Something you want. Why else would you risk so much?"

It was a question Jianyu asked himself often. "I know what it is to need rescuing," he told her. "I had a friend once who risked everything for me. I am only repaying his kindness."

"You mean Dolph Saunders," Golde said.

Jianyu nodded.

"They say you betrayed him," Golde told him. "They say you betrayed the Devil's Own, you and that Italian girl. And yet here you are, saving my son, the same as Dolph himself would have."

Jianyu did not speak. He understood that Golde was not really talking to him, but to her own conscience.

"They knew him by name," Jianyu said. "The men who took your boy. It was no accident. They knew he worked for Dolph. Do you have any idea who might have betrayed him?"

Golde's brows drew together thoughtfully, but then she shook her head. "It could have been anyone. After I stopped Josef from taking the mark, a lot of the boys turned away from him."

"What mark?" Jianyu asked, suddenly alert. "Dolph's?"

"It's not his any longer," Golde said dourly. "That *boy* offered it to

Josef, the one who thinks he has the eggs to step into the shoes Dolph Saunders left behind."

"Nibsy Lorcan offered your son protection in exchange for taking the mark?" Jianyu considered the implications of this.

She nodded. "Josef had been running messages for him, the same as he had for Saunders, until about a week ago. The boy wanted him to take the mark. Josef would have, but I stopped him because Dolph Saunders promised me that it wasn't required for the job. If it was good enough for Saunders, it should have been good enough for the one who followed him," she said sourly. "So I said no. I told him that his god was more important than loyalty to any one man, and he's a good boy, my Josef. He listened. He honored me. And he lost the job because of it.

"When those men took him, I went to Lorcan. I told him how they'd taken my Josef—a boy who had always been loyal to the Strega and to the Devil's Own. I told him that Dolph had promised protection. . . ." She shook her head. "Lorcan told me that he wasn't Dolph Saunders, and Josef wasn't one of his. It's the only reason I sent word to you. I would have never sunk so low otherwise."

Jianyu was not surprised. He and Viola were never the first choice of those who the Order had taken. They were always the choice of the desperate. But the news that Nibsy had offered Josef a mark . . . None that they had rescued wore the mark of the Devil's Own.

"I'm sorry for it now," Golde said, surprising him. "I'm sorry for thinking of you so poorly. I shouldn't have listened to the whispers and gossip."

Her words unsettled something in him. How many times had Jianyu rescued someone from the Order's men only to have his actions thrown in his face? "There is no need to apologize," he said, feeling unspeakably awkward. "I will send word as Josef heals, and when it is safe, I will bring you to him."

Golde reached out and touched his arm. "Thank you," she told him, and then, pulling her shawl around her, she turned to go back into the building.

LISA MAXWELL

At first Jianyu did not follow. He stayed on the roof, under the sweep of stars with the city breathing around him, struck by what had just happened. Golde's words—her gratitude—were unsettling enough, but the news that Nibsy Lorcan might be building his ranks was more so. Especially if he was culling those who refused to take the mark.

It should not have been so surprising. In these unsettled times, it made sense that Nibsy would want to increase his numbers. With the leadership of the Five Pointers currently sitting in a cell on Blackwell's Island, with Tammany and the Order at odds, and with the gangs of the Bowery at one another's throats, Nibsy would want an army of supporters around him. *Of course* he would demand loyalty as well. The only question was what his next move would be once he'd amassed that army.

It was a question that was answered sooner than Jianyu expected. As he exited the front door of Golde's building, there was the boy himself— Nibsy Lorcan—waiting for him in the pallid shaft of a streetlamp's glow.

Before Jianyu had time to reach for his bronze mirrors or his magic, Werner stepped from the shadows, and he felt the breath being pressed from his chest.

THE LIBRARY'S SECRETS

1983—City Hall Station

W hen she reached the top of the stairs leading out of the subway, Esta made quick work of the locked emergency exit door and then carefully secured it again so it wouldn't look disturbed. She didn't have any plans to let go of time, but just in case . . . There was no use taking any chances.

Finally aboveground and in the icy night air, she turned her back on the steady red glow of the police lights that surrounded the bridge and started walking through the park that skirted the white stone buildings of City Hall. She tucked her hands into her pockets and hunched against the cold, glad that the wind was now as still as the rest of the world, and then she started trudging through the drifting snow in the park toward the redbrick building that had defined her childhood.

Esta hadn't gone very far when something made her pause. She looked back over her shoulder and saw the lights of two unfamiliar towers standing like twin sentinels in the winter night behind her. She'd never seen them before. In all her trips through time, there had never been a reason to. Professor Lachlan had kept her focused and on a tight leash. But the looming presence of the Twin Towers was yet another reminder that while this city might look similar to her own, it wasn't. She was a stranger here, and with all the changes she and Harte might have created to the time line, she could be standing on quicksand.

Turning north, she cut through the park, but before she reached Centre Street, she noticed a statue gracing the intersection that hadn't been there before. The body of a man gleamed almost golden in the dim light, but covered in snow, she couldn't tell who it depicted. There was something about it that sent a chill through her, though, even more than the night air. It was enough to make her pause and see what else had changed, but other than the statue, the area around City Hall seemed the same—past and future, almost identical.

She couldn't help but remember the day not so long ago when she'd first found herself in the past. Viola had still hated her and had brought her downtown to test her mettle on the Dead Line. It had been only a few months ago, but it felt longer. It felt like an eternity.

Esta shook off the past and kept walking, weaving her way through once-familiar streets. Caught in her magic, the cloudy windows of a graffiti-covered bus revealed the single passenger it carried on its late-night run. She wished she could grab the bus or hail a cab, but the city remained caught in her affinity, and it needed to stay that way—for Harte. To protect him for as long as she could.

Though her thin-soled shoes were soaked, the cold hardly touched her now. With each step, determination heated her blood. She would find the fragment of the Book and then—

And then what? As far as she knew, she couldn't do anything without all five of the artifacts—but the ring was in 1902, and Harte was stuck *here.* She couldn't leave him, not without releasing time and leaving him to Seshat's mercy. . . .

Or maybe she could, she thought as she trudged onward through the slush-covered sidewalks. Maybe she *could* slip back and get the ring from this Cela Johnson. If she timed it right, she could return before Harte could give in to Seshat's power or do anything stupid. It would be difficult but not impossible.

With time pulled slow, the streets of lower Manhattan felt like a graveyard. Light glowed from windows, but held in the net of her power, no one and nothing moved. She was alone in a crowded city, a solitary traveler on an impossible quest.

When she reached the Bowery, she couldn't stop herself from cutting down toward where the Bella Strega had been. She could almost see the city as it had once been, still inscribed there beneath the layers of graffiti and grit. But the Strega was lost to the past, and if she didn't succeed in retrieving the key to the cipher from Nibsy, her friends would be as well.

The Bowery was lined with the kind of heavy, boxy cars ladened with chrome that were popular in the 1980s. She passed one with its window busted out, another that was missing a front tire. It was no wonder people had called this part of the city Skid Row. Along the streets, the metal gates sealed off shop entrances for the night, but many of the buildings were boarded up and abandoned. She imagined that even if she released time, this part of the city would feel like a ghost town compared to the other versions of the Bowery she had known.

She reached the place where she thought the Strega should have been, but all she found there was a burned-out building. Something clenched inside her at the sight of it. Her eyes stung as she thought of the last time she'd been inside, but she steeled herself against those memories and turned her grief to resolve. Pulling her determination around her like a cloak, she turned her back on the parts of the past that could not be changed. She had to focus, to keep moving, because there was so much that could be different—so much that she might still change. As long as she didn't fail.

Cutting through the narrow stretch of Roosevelt Park, she finally arrived at Orchard Street. A few blocks more and she found herself standing in front of the building that had once been her home. The storefront on the first floor was still boarded up with plywood covered with layers of graffiti. Someone was curled up in a nearby stairwell with his battered, gloved hands curled around a bag-covered bottle. The building almost looked abandoned, like many of its neighbors, but above, on the topmost floor, a light shone like a beacon.

Esta went to the rear of the building, where a service entrance opened on the staircase that went up the back. She picked the lock in a matter of seconds and then let herself in. She paused, waiting for . . .

She wasn't sure what she was waiting for. An alarm? Some indication that the Professor—that *Nibsy*—knew she'd arrived? But nothing happened. The city remained silent. Time stood still. The air around her stirred only with her movement.

It smelled the same. It was such a strange thing to realize, but the second Esta was out of the cold air, memories of the past overwhelmed her. The back staircase had always had a kind of strange odor that she couldn't place, but now she recognized it as the smell of the tenements, the scent of the past rising up through to the present. Layers of mold and dust that no amount of paint could cover. Even in her childhood, the ghost of this smell had been there, ready to greet her anytime she came home.

But this was no homecoming, she reminded herself as she started up the narrow back staircase. She was there for only one reason—to retrieve the key to the cipher so she could stop Seshat from destroying the world. So she could save Harte.

Professor Lachlan owned the entire building—or he had when she'd been growing up twenty or more years from now. In her own time line, he'd owned the building since the middle of the century or earlier, so she assumed that in *this* version of the time line, things wouldn't be that different, especially considering the power he seemed to have wielded in 1920. The slip of paper she was looking for—the missing fragment of a single page—was somewhere within these walls. It had to be. She could search from the bottom up, but she knew she'd be wasting her time. The key to the cipher would be where Professor Lachlan kept all his treasures, secure in the safe on the top floor of the building.

Esta was almost warm by the time she reached the top of the staircase. It wasn't surprising to find the access door there locked, but she'd been picking locks since she could remember. As the lock gave the satisfying *click* to signal it had surrendered, she couldn't help but feel it was almost too easy. She slowly pushed the door open, making sure to keep her wits about her and time firmly in her grasp. So far, her affinity felt strong and sure.

On the other side of the heavy fire door, the entire floor had been converted into an enormous library. By the time she'd left to go back to 1902, Esta had helped Professor Lachlan turn it into the finest, most extensive collection of documents about New York City that no one had ever heard of. Now the library wasn't quite so full of the city's secrets. But Esta needed only one secret. It had to be there.

The library was lit by a single desk lamp that sat on an enormous oak table at the center of the room. It had been only a few weeks ago—years from now in the future—that Professor Lachlan had used that same table to show her all five of the Order's artifacts. That had been the moment she finally understood what he had been working toward and the first time she'd seen them all together.

The wide table was covered with the usual stacks of newspapers and books. It wouldn't change much, Esta realized. It was like he didn't care about hiding the treasures he'd collected. But then . . . *maybe he doesn't.* Maybe Professor Lachlan didn't care what she saw because he had always been waiting for her to return for the one thing he knew she would need. Or maybe he was just a sloppy old man who never learned how to take care of his own house.

Either way, the sheer amount of stuff to look through felt overwhelming. If the fragment she was looking for wasn't in the safe, she'd have to search the whole library. And if it wasn't there, she'd have to search the rest of the building as well.

It will be in the safe. There was nowhere else Professor Lachlan would keep it. Other than maybe on his own person. Would he have risked carrying around a tiny scrap of fragile paper for decade after decade when he could keep it securely locked away? She doubted it.

On the far side of the library, a painting hung on the wall where the safe should be. It hadn't been there during her childhood, but Esta recognized it. Depicted in finely swirling brushstrokes, Isaac Newton sat beneath a tree with the fabled Book in his hand and two moons above him in the sky. She made her way past the precarious stacks of books and papers until she was standing in front of the painting. The last time she'd seen the painting, it had been hanging in Dolph Saunders' apartment. She'd helped steal it from the Met for Dolph—for her *real* father—but it wasn't the painting she was interested in. It was what lay behind it.

Esta removed the painting carefully and set it aside, but her spirits sank when she saw what waited for her. She'd hoped it was still too early for Professor Lachlan to have installed the biometric safe he'd had when she was growing up. She'd hoped it would be a simpler mechanism, and one she could easily crack, but the flat panel on the front of the safe glared back at her instead. There was no tumbler, no lock for a key. No clear way into the safe.

Then something caught her eye—hanging on the wall nearby were two shadowbox frames, one holding a pair of bronze mirrors inscribed with Chinese characters and another with a glinting silver dagger that had once been Viola's.

Esta's heart lurched. It didn't matter that her two friends would have likely been long dead anyway. Professor Lachlan had no right to these items. He didn't deserve them. Worse, she knew that he hadn't come by them accidentally. Jianyu and Viola's belongings would never have found their way into Professor Lachlan's possession if he hadn't somehow been involved with their deaths.

She took a paperweight from the table and used it to break the glass in one of the frames. Then, careful not to get her finger anywhere close to the blade, Esta lifted Viola's knife from the velvet backing. Its handle was strangely cool to the touch and too heavy for something so delicate, but it was exactly what she needed. She thought Viola would more than approve.

Returning to the safe, Esta jammed the tip of the thin blade into the hairline seam of the safe, and then carefully, she began to cut. The knife sliced through the iron safe as easily as it had once sunk itself into a zinc bar. Methodically, she worked the blade around the door of the safe, tracing the opening until . . . *there*.

The instant the door fell away, something popped, and a second later smoke began to seep from within the safe. *Opium*. Or something like it, from the scent. She didn't have Harte's ability to hold her breath for endless minutes, but she had a little time. Looking at the thick stack of papers and notebooks within the safe, her stomach sank. She'd have to hurry.

OLD FRIENDS

1902—Bella Strega

James dismissed Werner and Logan once they had deposited Jianyu on the low couch in his apartment. It was well past dawn now, and the light from the early morning was enough to see by without using an oil lamp. Thanks to Werner, Jianyu was still unconscious, but in a matter of seconds—his breath finally returned to him—he woke. James watched, unconcerned and unmoved, as Jianyu gasped, lurching upright so violently he nearly fell off the couch. It gave him more than a small satisfaction to see the confusion in Jianyu's eyes and then the fear when he realized where he was.

"Sit down," James commanded at the first glimmer of warmth from Jianyu's magic. "And don't bother with that disappearing trick of yours. There's nowhere you can go in this city that Logan won't be able to find you again, unless, of course, you're willing to part with those mirrors of yours."

Jianyu's hands went immediately to the deep pockets hidden in his tunic to check that his bronze mirrors were still there. Relief swept across the sharp features of his face, making him appear every bit as weak as he truly was. It was exactly as James had expected: Jianyu would never go anywhere without them. Depending on the trinkets made him vulnerable, just as depending on Dolph Saunders to protect him had made him a fool.

"If you try to leave, Werner's outside to ensure that you stay," James told him. "So sit. We have things to discuss."

"I have nothing to discuss with you." The words were spoken through clenched teeth.

"Ah, but I think you do," James told him.

Delightful, really, the anger thrumming through Jianyu. He showed it so rarely, but James had always known it was there, hidden behind the careful facade. Few realized what Jianyu was capable of. They thought him quiet and still, but James had understood the truth almost immediately. He'd used it when it suited him before, and he'd use it again. After all, anger was such a helpful emotion—so easy to use against the one who carried it.

Standing, James made his way to the small kitchen area at the rear of the apartment, unconcerned with whether Jianyu would stay or attack. He already knew that Dolph's old spy would do neither. The Aether had felt off since the day he took care of Mooch. Now it shivered and bunched, anticipating a new path, but James understood that Jianyu was no danger. *Not yet.* He poured two cups of whiskey and brought them back to the sitting area, where Jianyu waited, still strung tight as a bow.

He offered one of the cups. "Take it," he commanded, when Jianyu at first refused. Then, after he'd pushed one glass into Jianyu's reluctant hands, he dragged a chair over, turning it so he could straddle the spindly back. He took his time drinking from his own cup.

"Not thirsty?" he asked when it was clear Jianyu had no intention of drinking. He shrugged. "Suit yourself." He drained his own glass and set it aside, enjoying the way it burned a little, warming his chest and urging him onward.

"What do you want?" Jianyu asked, setting the cup of untouched liquor aside.

"I thought I'd already made that clear. I'd like to talk," James said with a guileless smile. "Can't a couple of old friends have a simple conversation?"

"I am no longer your friend," Jianyu told him coldly. "I think perhaps I never was. And I am not interested in this conversation. I have nothing to say to you."

"Well, I imagine that's a lie," James said, keeping his voice affable, light. "I'm sure there are any number of things you wish to say to me."

Jianyu only glared at him.

"We don't have to be enemies, you know," James said, taking a sip and trying to call up the old version of himself, the boy that no one suspected. "We could work with each other. Fight the Order. Take control of the streets of this city. *Together.* As Dolph would have wanted."

"You killed Dolph," Jianyu said simply.

"You know that I had to," James told him.

"I know no such thing."

"He would have destroyed the Brink," James explained, though in truth, he didn't *need* to explain anything. He could have simply commanded. But for now the Aether whispered patience, and so he spoke gently, attempting logic and persuasion . . . and saved his final cards for later.

Jianyu's brows drew together, and James could see when the truth registered.

"You've talked to Esta," James said. "You know Dolph was wrong. The Brink can't come down, not without destroying magic. Dolph never would have accepted that answer. He was *obsessed* with destroying the Brink, because he thought that was the only way to destroy the Order. He was so convinced the Book was the solution that he never even considered the danger. How could he know more about the old magic than any of us and never realize that it's all connected? How could he not understand that to destroy even one part of it would have doomed us all?"

"That is not why you killed him," Jianyu said.

James let his mouth curl, just a little. "Don't paint him as some kind of saint, my friend. You know he wasn't. None of us is."

Jianyu didn't speak. He simply regarded James with his usual stony, unreadable stare. But all around them the Aether trembled and bunched, and he knew that Jianyu was calculating his chances of escape.

"I have no intention of keeping you here indefinitely," James told him truthfully. Why should he keep Jianyu a prisoner when he was so much more useful out in the city, stirring trouble and the Aether along with it. "Once we've finished our little discussion, you'll be free to go."

Jianyu snorted his disbelief.

"I'll find you again if I have more to discuss," James assured him. Then he finished his drink and set the cup aside. "Or Logan will."

"So talk," Jianyu said. "What is it that you want from me?"

James did smile then. Jianyu might have had more of a backbone than most suspected, but he wasn't a formidable opponent. He was barely even amusing.

"I want what you stole from the Order."

Jianyu's gaze fell, briefly, to the ring glittering on James' right hand. "You already wear the Delphi's Tear, there on your finger."

"Oh, come now," James said, growing impatient. He stood then, leaning on his cane as he drew himself up to loom over Jianyu, who remained seated. "There's no sense in denying it. Werner told me that Viola found something—silver discs. Logan confirmed that she took them." When Jianyu's expression betrayed his surprise, James only smiled. "I may be willing to offer a trade."

"You have nothing I want," Jianyu said.

"Lie," James countered. "I have *exactly* what you want. I have the Strega and the Devil's Own." He watched Jianyu's expression close up, like a house before a storm, and he knew he'd hit his mark. "You want your home. Your family. I can make that happen, Jianyu. I can convince them all it was a simple misunderstanding. I can make sure they welcome you back like the prodigal son."

Jianyu's mouth tightened, but he didn't respond. He also couldn't quite hide the longing in his eyes. And nothing could disguise the way the Aether danced.

"I could also offer you protection," James added.

"As you protected Josef Salzer?" Jianyu asked.

"He wasn't my concern."

"The boy was one of Dolph's," Jianyu charged. "If you believe yourself worthy of taking Dolph Saunders' place, he should have been yours to protect."

"I protect those who are *loyal*," he told Jianyu. "I offered the boy the mark, but Josef refused it. He made his own choices, and he suffered the consequences of them."

"Did he?" Jianyu asked, tilting his head. "Or was he offered up? It strikes me as damning that none of those we have saved from the Order wore the mark."

James didn't so much as blink, despite Jianyu's astuteness. "Josef Salzer was never my concern. None of them were. My only concern is the road that lies ahead. Destroying the Order. Reclaiming the power that once belonged only to those with the old magic." *Taking my place as their leader.*

"Your concern has only ever been for yourself," Jianyu charged, as though it were a failing—a sin of some sort—to survive.

James had had enough. Whatever the Aether signaled, his patience was at an end. "I want the sigils. I'm willing to offer you protection in exchange for them," he told Jianyu. "I'm willing to offer you an alliance."

Jianyu stood. "We are finished here." He started for the door, had his hand on the knob and was already pulling it open before James spoke again.

"The Order's already searching for what you stole," James said. "It's the reason for the patrols."

Jianyu stopped, one foot nearly out the door. He hesitated, his hand still on the doorknob, but eventually he turned back, just as James knew he would.

"I've kept them from you," James said. "I've offered up others to give you time to see reason, but I'm running out of patience. Soon they'll find someone who's willing to talk, and then the Order will come for you and your little crew." He paused, letting this information settle. "What will you do then? How will you protect your Sundren friends? You're alone. Without support or backup . . .

"Oh, I know you have each other," he said, waving away the silent argument he saw shimmering in Jianyu's expression. "But a lone Chinaman and an Italian girl against the Order? It's laughable. Outsiders, all of you.

Mageus on top of that. Face it, Jianyu. Alone, you don't stand a chance against what the richest men in the city are capable of. But under my protection? Under the protection of the Devil's Own?" He shrugged.

Jianyu did not speak at first. It was not hesitation—James understood this—but care. He'd never been rash before, and he would not start now. "What, *exactly*, are you offering?"

"Come back," James said softly. "Repledge yourself to the organization that your dearly departed Dolph Saunders built. Pledge yourself to *me*. Give Newton's Sigils into my keeping, and in turn, I will protect you and yours. Your Sundren will be safe."

"And what of Viola?"

James shrugged. "That depends upon Viola."

"You would take her back willingly after the injury she gave you?" Jianyu asked, eyeing the cane.

"She made a mistake," he said with another affable-looking shrug. "We could come to an arrangement."

The edge of Jianyu's mouth twitched, but he did not smile. "Those discs must be very valuable for you to make such a generous offer."

"They are," James said. He was sure of it.

A long, fraught moment passed between them as the Aether vibrated and danced. But with the strange vibrations that had plagued him for weeks, James could not read the message within it. He could not tell what answer Jianyu might give until he spoke.

"After what you have done, you cannot actually imagine we would simply hand over anything so powerful?" Jianyu said. "You cannot truly believe we would trust you?"

"But I would," James said easily. "In fact, I've imagined much, much more than that." James let the affability slide from his expression. In its place, James revealed the reality of who—of *what*—he had become. His hand caressed the coils on the Medusa's head, felt the cold energy there answering to him, and sent it out into the air. "You see, my old friend. You no longer have a choice."

THE PROFESSOR

1983—Orchard Street

Esta didn't waste time. Still holding her breath, she took the contents from the opened safe and started shuffling through, searching for some sign of the key. Already, her lungs were starting to ache. Soon they would begin to burn. She didn't have much time.

The safe was filled mostly with papers. A stack of ledgers seemed to list the contents of bank accounts—or some kind of accounts. A quick look told her that Nibsy's business holdings went quite a ways into the past. There was also an accordion folder filled with loose-leaf papers—notes, it looked like. As she flipped through the sheets of paper, she realized it was research. Spells. Rituals. There were answers here, she thought, her skin prickling with awareness.

The next item was a small, unremarkable notebook. She almost set it aside, but when she riffled through the pages, she noticed that something was wrong with the writing. The words written on the paper weren't steady or stable. After a certain date, the letters vibrated and changed, rotating through any number of combinations. It looked like the news clipping she'd taken back to the past originally had looked when she changed the past.

It was some kind of diary, she realized from the few stable entries. *Nibsy's diary.* The dates on the pages—nearly a century of them—remained steady, even as the entries blurred and shifted. Occasionally a name she recognized would shimmer to the surface, along with a few words. A phrase here. A sentence there. But before she could finish reading what the words said, they would blur again. Erasing and changing over themselves.

Professor Lachlan had kept a record of everything he'd done. But why were the entries so unstable? Hadn't the past already happened?

She flipped back to one of the few stable entries and allowed her eyes to scan over the contents. *I left him in the cemetery, bleeding into Leena's grave. The great Dolph Saunders. Finally facedown in the dirt. Exactly where he belonged.*

Esta felt grief twist in her chest. She'd never doubted Harte when he'd told her how Dolph had died, how Nibsy had betrayed them all and took more than Dolph's life—took everything he'd worked so long and so hard to build. But to see it there, stark and clear in the too-familiar writing she recognized from her childhood lessons?

She blinked back tears and turned the page.

The last stable entry detailed something about a gala at Morgan's mansion in May of 1902. Every page after was unsettled. Every entry remained indeterminate.

She realized immediately what the notebook meant. History could still be rewritten.

Esta flipped forward through the notebook, taking in page after page of entries that continued to shift and morph, until she found another that wasn't completely impossible to read: December 21, 1902. *The Conclave.*

As she watched, portions of the handwriting grew less erratic, the words solidifying into a clear description of what happened at the Conclave. The entry looked old, with the ink faded from the years, but there were places where words held steady. There on the page were names that she recognized: Viola. Jianyu.

They're dead. There, clear and solid and steady in the middle of the notebook's otherwise chaotic pages, was the description of how they died. They'd turned on each other. *Nibsy* had somehow turned them on each other. The words only grew steadier and more legible as she read, as though her being there, her knowing about their deaths, was somehow stabilizing that version of the past and making it absolute.

Her head spun, and she flipped the pages backward and then ahead, urgently searching for some other outcome. They could go back. They would go back and stop this—

A new line wrote itself into the notebook, an impossible future that couldn't be. The shock of seeing her name there on the page alongside Harte's made her nearly drop the diary. She gasped, trying to catch it, and accidentally inhaled some of the strange fog that had filled the library. Suddenly, she felt off-kilter, but she couldn't tell if it was from the terrible future the notebook had just revealed or from the opium-laced fog. With shaking hands, she picked up the notebook again by the edge of its cover. As it flopped open, a page came loose.

No. Not a page—a *piece* of a page.

The fog was already working on her affinity as she reached for it. Her magic was growing more slippery, but she knew before her fingers grasped the small piece of parchment that *this* was what she had come for.

Time was slipping away from her, but she had to know. Flipping the diary open again, she read the steady lines in the bold, neat hand, and her head spun with a combination of the opium in the air and her complete horror at the knowledge of what was coming—of what she couldn't stop. Viola's death. Jianyu's. And now, added to theirs, her own. And Nibsy Lorcan the victor.

No. She wouldn't let it happen. She knew now, didn't she? Knowing meant she could prepare. Knowing meant she could avoid that particular future. That *had* to change things, didn't it? But the names on the page remained maddeningly steady and clear.

Her head was still spinning, and her lungs were burning with the effort not to take another breath, but the power floating through the air in the strange fog had already done its work. Her affinity wavered, and then she lost hold of the seconds completely.

Esta tried to pull time slow again, but it was pointless. She tucked the notebook into her dress, knowing already that she was out of time. Professor Lachlan had been expecting her to come for the key, and he probably already knew she was there. She had to get outside. She had to get away before he caught her.

She sprinted for the back stairwell and took the steps two at a time, holding the handrails as she went. At the bottom, she reached for the dead bolt she'd resecured, but now the lock wouldn't turn.

Probably another security feature—a trap to keep her in.

It didn't matter, because Esta knew the building like the back of her hand. She knew every corner and niche to hide in, every twist of every hallway. She'd slipped out enough times as a child. Professor Lachlan couldn't keep her there. And besides, she still had Viola's knife.

But she'd barely started to slip it into the space between the door and the jamb when she felt more than heard the presence behind her on the stairs. When she turned, Professor Lachlan was standing on the landing above her, watching. He stepped into the light, allowing the hazy, yellow glow to illuminate him, casting his features in shadows.

On instinct, Esta reached for her affinity, but it was still deadened. Glancing at the hallway and then to the door that led out to the back of the building, she tried to decide which was her better chance for an escape. Neither was ideal.

Again, she pulled at the seconds, but again and again, they slipped through her fingers. She needed to stall.

The man on the steps looked younger than the one who had raised her, but he was dressed in the usual tweed he'd worn through her entire childhood. Even looming above her as he was, the Professor was a small man. He was more than a hundred years old, but he barely looked sixty. Still, Esta wasn't fooled into believing that he was frail, not with his hand resting softly on a familiar cane.

The Professor began to move easily down the steps toward her, and she noticed that he didn't limp anymore. The cane was more an affectation now than a requirement.

"You're looking good, Nibsy," she said, doing her best to conceal her apprehension. "You know, considering that you should be dead."

He ignored her taunting. "I knew you'd come," he told her. "It's a shame you have no hope at all of leaving. Not with your affinity intact."

Esta didn't respond. It wouldn't do any good to engage with him. She couldn't panic or do anything rash. She had to *think*.

She still had the knife. Maybe she'd never be as good an aim as Viola had once been, but her lack of skills wouldn't stop the magic in the blade from cutting. This man had killed so many: Dolph, Leena, Dakari.

No—he hadn't yet killed Dakari. But he would if she allowed him to live. He would hurt so many others.

And yet Esta *had* to allow him to live. There had to be someone waiting here to raise the girl she had once been. Someone had to forge her into the woman she needed to become. Or time would take its due, and it would take Harte with it.

Outside the building, the city beyond had come back to life. Sirens screamed in the distance, and the winter wind howled against the back door, but Esta's complete focus was on the man in front of her. She lifted Viola's knife.

"Will you kill me the same as you killed Jack Grew?" Professor Lachlan asked. He lifted his hands as if in surrender, but there was amusement in his old eyes.

She kept the knife raised, a silent threat. Nothing good could come from a long-winded discussion. Not with this snake of a man. She thought she might almost be able to feel her affinity coming back. A little longer and she'd be able to slip free of him.

His expression was as unreadable as it had ever been. "You made quite the impression on the entire country, you know. The pictures were everywhere—your face twisted in rage with your knife plunging into that poor man's chest. The blood splattered on your dress." His mouth twitched then as he looked her over—her ill-fitting overalls and inappropriate shoes. "How long has it been for you since that day? Have you lived with what you've done for weeks or years . . . or is the memory still fresh? Tell me, do you remember what it felt like as the blade pressed through bone? Do you still think about the life fading from his eyes?"

Esta refused to take the bait. She couldn't let herself think about Jack's death, not when it had barely been hours and not when the horror of what she had done was still too fresh. She couldn't let herself remember the way it had felt for the knife to slip past the bone and breath in Jack's chest. It would be with her, haunt her, always. And it didn't matter that Jack had deserved it. It didn't matter that Thoth would have destroyed everything with Seshat's power. Killing Jack had changed her, just as Harte had warned weeks before in the New Jersey train station.

Professor Lachlan's mouth curved, as though he understood that her thoughts had taken her back there. He took another step down toward her. "Did you enjoy it? It's a heady feeling to take a life."

"You should know," she said, keeping her voice calm. Easy. *Don't let him know.*

"It's true I've taken my share," the old man admitted. "It's something to watch the final breath, to see the light dim from the eyes. It's my one regret that I didn't stay to watch Dolph die. There was too much danger in waiting in the cemetery to stay, to enjoy my final victory." He tilted his head slightly, as though considering her. "You turned Jack Grew into a martyr, you know. By killing him there, in front of the crowded convention, you made him into a saint, not only for the Brotherhoods, but for the *country.* You have no idea what's followed—the gilded statues they've raised in his honor, the horrors they've committed in his name—or you would have come far sooner than now."

Esta remained silent. She wouldn't ask. She would *not* give him that satisfaction, even as dread crept down her spine.

"But you've arrived, as I knew you would. As I *planned* for you to," he said, adjusting his grip on the cane. She could see the silver of the Medusa's face peeking out between his fingers, and on his hand, flashing in the dimly lit stairwell, was the Delphi's Tear.

The last artifact—it was *here*. With that ring, they would have all five artifacts and the Book. They could stop Seshat. They had everything they needed—if only she could get it from him.

Esta schooled her expression. She couldn't let him know how much she wanted the ring. She couldn't broadcast what she was about to do . . . *especially* if he likely already knew. The effects of the opium fog were starting to ebb, but even if she could pull time around her, she'd have to touch the Professor to get the ring. It would draw him into the net of her affinity.

"I'm not here because you planned for me," she told him. *Stall. Keep him talking.* He loved to talk.

Her mind raced for a plan that would work. She spun through ideas, immediately discarding them as she took a step forward. If anyone died today, she would make sure it was him. Even if she had to kill him herself, that ring was what she needed to save Harte. She wasn't leaving without it.

"You know you can't kill me," Professor Lachlan said.

Esta, undeterred, gave him a smile that was all teeth. "I can try."

"You could," he admitted. "But you won't succeed. You should know by now that already I've planned for every possibility. Even this one."

A door to Esta's left opened then, spilling light into the dark vestibule, and when she turned to see what danger was approaching, her breath seized in her chest, and the world seemed to freeze.

Horror jolted through her as she came face-to-face with a ghost from her past.

MISSING

1902—Little Africa

C ela Johnson still felt the exhaustion of the night before, but she thought she was covering it well enough. Crossing her arms over her chest, she faced her brother, Abel, as confidently as she ever had. But even as they talked, she kept one ear alert for any indication that Viola or Jianyu might be returning to the small basement rooms they all shared.

Jianyu had not returned the night before. It wasn't unusual for him to deliver news of their midnight rescues to the waiting families, but he always returned before dawn. As the minutes ticked by and night turned to morning, Cela and Viola had both finally admitted something must have gone wrong.

Viola had gone out to find him. It wasn't any safer for her to be out alone, but at least she could defend herself in ways Cela couldn't. She'd left just after dawn, but it was nearly noon now, and she still hadn't returned. So Cela had more on her mind than Abel's too-familiar argument about why she needed to get out of the city. In the past few weeks, the conversation had become one she was beyond tired of having, especially since it was clear that neither she nor her older brother was going to change their mind.

"You're taking too many risks, Rabbit," Abel said. "One of these times, I'm going to come home and you're not going to be waiting for me."

"I know you're worried, and you're right to be," Cela told him, trying to keep the annoyance out of her voice. He meant well, and she understood his fear. She would have felt the same, would have been worried for his safety just as much if their situations were reversed. And he would have been every bit as determined as she was to stay. "But you know I can't leave now. I promised to help our friends, and I'm going to keep that promise."

Abel's mouth tightened, and the shift in his features made her brother look suddenly even more tired than usual. The dark circles beneath his eyes were deeper today, and the lines bracketing his mouth were grimmer. "You can still help them when things clear up a little. But until then, it's not safe here."

"It's never safe here, Abe."

He rubbed the growth of beard on his chin. "You know what I'm saying, Cela. Things are dangerous now. Police on every corner. Patrols hunting through buildings like they own them. What if you get caught up in that while I'm gone?"

"I'll be okay," she said gently. "I know how to watch out for myself. I've been doing it for long enough."

"What if you don't think of it as leaving? Maybe you could just take a trip," he pressed. "You could go stay with our uncle down on the coast. Get out of the heat of the city for a while."

"Abel Johnson, they don't want me there. You *know* that. And even if they did, I wouldn't want to bring my troubles to their doorstep. If I'm in so much danger, I'm going to stay right here and keep that danger from touching anyone else," she told him. "You need to stop worrying about me and get yourself ready to go. Doesn't your train leave in an hour?"

"I feel like I just got back," he grumbled. "Maybe I could get one of the other fellas to take this route. I'd feel better if you weren't alone."

"*Abel . . .*" She met his exasperated expression with one of her own. "I'm not alone here. I got people to watch over me," she said, trying not to think of what had happened to Jianyu or why Viola hadn't returned yet.

Her brother ran his hand over the dark, short-cropped curls that covered his head. "Too bad they're also the ones who got you into this mess."

She nodded. "And I trust them to get me out of it."

Abel cocked a brow in her direction, a question and a challenge. She wasn't stupid—she understood his worry and his point.

"They're not going to let anything happen to me," she assured him. Hadn't Viola killed Kelly's men just by looking at them? Cela knew exactly how much that single action had cost Viola. The Italian girl seemed perfectly content to kill with a knife but had some kind of strange moral code against using her magic to do the same. The fact that Viola had chosen to save Cela and Abel over her own soul by using her power? That was more than enough for Cela. Even if she was still prickly as a pincushion.

"Please, Cela—"

"I'm done talking about this, Abe." She let out a tired breath. "You trusted me to take care of myself when you went off hiding from those union busters, so you'll just have to trust me now. I'm not running off to the country like some scared mouse. This city is my home, and I'm not leaving it. I'm certainly not leaving my *friends*." She softened her expression and her voice as she stepped toward her brother and took his familiar face gently in her hands. He looked *so* much like their father. Acted like him too, sometimes, come to think of it. "I've lost everything else—our family's home, my job at the theater, the life I had before. I can't leave my city, too. I won't be chased off or sent away for my own good."

"Rabbit—"

"You have to go, so you'll go," she told him, stepping back. "You'll be gone two, maybe three weeks, and I'll be here waiting when you come back. I'll be *fine*, just like I always am. But if you lose this job—"

"I *know,* dammit. I know." He closed his eyes, and she knew he was begging patience and strength. But they both understood what would happen if he lost his position. It wasn't as though jobs that paid as well as working on the Pullman cars were just lying around like overripe fruit. It was thankless and exhausting work, but on good runs with the right kind of passengers, the gratuities he earned more than made up for the money he had to put into buying the bootblack and other supplies he needed just to *do* the job. With the money he earned, they could rebuild their home and their lives.

"I'll be fine. I promise," she said, giving him a brisk, tight hug before letting him go.

"Make sure you keep that promise," Abe said, his shoulders falling a little—a signal she'd won the argument. At least for the time being.

She stepped forward and wrapped her arms around her brother. "I know how to take care of myself, Abe."

He pulled back. "I know you do, Rabbit. But I can't stop myself from worrying. You're my sister, aren't you?"

She gave him another squeeze. "Always."

A whistle came from the street outside, and the two of them froze, listening as it sounded again. In the days that had passed since the Order's solstice ritual, they'd stayed out of sight as much as they could, lying low in the small basement room. They couldn't be sure who might know about their involvement with the theft of the Order's treasures, so they weren't taking any chances.

"That'll be Joshua," Abel said, pulling back. "Hopefully, he'll have some news about a better place."

"You asked him to find one?" she asked, surprised.

"I had a feeling you weren't going to bend any," he said, chucking her gently under the chin. There was still a sadness in his eyes that he couldn't quite hide.

"And you still bothered me with your arguing?" she asked, feigning irritation but feeling nothing but love and pride.

He shrugged. "I had to try, but if you're set on staying like I figured you'd be, I wanted to get you settled somewhere better than this place before I go."

Cela's throat went tight as she gave a small nod, grateful for her brother in every way a person could be grateful. "You better go on and talk to Joshua, then. Make sure he got us one of those big places up on Madison Avenue."

Abel shook his head, and it was clear he was more amused than truly exasperated when he left.

A few seconds after her brother went out to talk to their friend, Viola slipped into the room soundlessly. And alone.

Cela's skin prickled with dread. "You didn't find him?"

"Golde said he left not long after we saw him," Viola told her. "There's no sign of him after then."

"He wouldn't stay away like this on purpose," Cela said.

"I know," Viola agreed. "Something's happened."

"The Order?"

Viola frowned. "Maybe, but we have other enemies. Some closer to home."

"Nibsy," Cela said, thinking of who else might want to harm them. "Or the Five Pointers?"

"It could be any of them," Viola admitted. She stepped forward and laid her hand on Cela's arm. "We'll find him."

The door opened, and Abel entered in a rush. "Get your things," he said, not even noticing the somber mood of the room. "Take only what you can carry." When Cela didn't move fast enough for his liking, he started throwing some of her sewing supplies into a bag himself.

"Abel, what are you doing?" Cela asked, confused by the sudden change in her brother. "What's going on?"

Abel paused long enough to meet her eyes. "There's a group of men checking apartments one building over. And they're headed this way."

TRUST AND LIES

1983—City Hall Station

The last thing Harte remembered, he'd been tumbling from the moving train and landing hard—so hard that Seshat had been shaken into silence. But she hadn't remained silent for long. He'd barely had time to breathe before she'd started up again, her banshee's voice tearing at him from the inside as her rage bubbled and churned within, threatening to rip the very essence of him to shreds.

Then Esta had appeared above him. She'd been telling him something. Or trying to.

He couldn't hear her over Seshat's terrible noise, but he'd understood her intention. Even with all that had gone wrong, she wouldn't give up. Esta would walk straight into the trap Nibsy Lorcan had set for her, and there was nothing he could do to stop her.

And then, all at once, she was gone. *Gone.* Like she'd never been there at all.

In the distance, Harte heard the rumble of one of the underground trains and understood what must have happened. Esta had used her affinity. She'd left him to go after Nibsy by herself.

Looking around, he tried to get his bearings. The station was a dark, cavernous space. In his own time, they'd already started building the subway system. He'd walked by the opened streets many times, marveling at the audacity of the plan, but he hadn't imagined what it would actually be like to be completely underground. To feel so . . . entombed.

But then, he never could have imagined that the city would become the marvel that it was now. The piles of trash everywhere weren't that different, but the *height* of the skyline. Even through the haze of Seshat's fury, he'd been struck by the wonder of it all. The dizzying brightness of the buildings lit from within and the speed of cars streaming by.

He needed to figure out what to do next, but it was all he could do to keep himself from flying apart. He had to *think*. Esta had gone to deal with Nibsy on her own, but she never would have let go of her hold on time. Not unless something had gone terribly wrong. The fact that he was even aware that she'd left—and the fact that she hadn't returned—meant that she was in trouble.

Harte thought of the fog back in Brooklyn, the strange energy that had blasted through the Nitemarket and the convention in Chicago, and the Quellant that Maggie had invented. Even something as simple as the opium the Veiled Prophet Society had used in St. Louis to protect the necklace. There were so many ways to deaden an affinity and strip someone of their magic, and Nibsy Lorcan likely knew all of them.

Bracing himself against the onslaught from within, Harte tried to get to his feet. He had to find a way out of the station. He had to find Esta.

At the thought of her, Seshat's power slammed against the thin barrier that held her back, and Harte stumbled from the force of it, falling over again. His skin felt both feverishly hot and sickly cold at the same time, and his limbs were trembling. The ancient goddess had been quiet until they'd crossed back into the city. The second they'd breached the Brink, she'd become erratic. Desperate. *Terrified*. And her fear made her power feel even more dangerous.

Seshat screamed and raged as she railed against the bars of her cage, and Harte understood her intentions too clearly. She would destroy Esta and the world itself to keep Thoth from touching her power.

"He's gone. Thoth is dead." His unsteady voice was barely audible in the huge, vaulted chamber, even to himself. "He can't touch you."

Fool, she wailed. *Thoth is not gone. As long as he is anywhere, he is* everywhere. *And if he succeeds in controlling my power, nothing will stop him from claiming the beating heart of magic as his own. He will be unstoppable. Infinite. There will be no time, no place safe from his destruction.*

Harte pulled himself to his knees. Nothing Seshat was telling him was new, but none of it mattered. Not until he found Esta.

Toward the back of the station, there was a tunnel that glowed with a faint light. Possibly the exit? As he inched along, Seshat fought him. She didn't want him to leave the station, and the closer he came to the tunnel, the more erratic her fear became. But he was almost there. He'd nearly made it to the first of the steps that led upward into the darkened staircase.

And then, suddenly, Esta appeared. He'd been alone with Seshat's wailing, and then a heartbeat later she was *there*. She was *safe*.

Seshat froze, her wailing suddenly going silent as she retracted deep within him, and the reprieve was almost enough to make him weep with relief. He was too exhausted from her onslaught to wonder why. All he could do was collapse against the cold, hard wall, trying to catch his breath. He had to gather what strength he could, because he knew Seshat wouldn't stay quiet for long.

When he looked up, Esta's face was drawn and serious. Her eyes were hard, determined, and he knew instinctively that something had happened to her. It was there in her expression. Something had put a distance in her eyes like he'd never seen before.

"Are you okay?" he asked, still leaning against the tiled wall. "Did Nibsy harm you? Because if he touched you—"

"I'm fine." Her voice was strong and sure, but there was a stiffness in her tone that he didn't recognize.

"Esta?" he asked gently. "You can tell me."

"I don't want to talk about it," she told him. "Not right now. *Please.* Don't make me relive it."

The stern set of her usually soft mouth and the hardness in her eyes told the story clearly enough. *Fine then.* He wouldn't ask more of her than she could give, wouldn't drag the details from her. *Not now, at least.* But he desperately wanted to touch her. She'd done too much, taken on too much in the last few days, and there was nothing he could do to help her, to comfort her. Not with the threat of Seshat within him.

"The Book," she said, her gaze finding the scarred leather tome where it lay on the platform. He hadn't even noticed it there. She must have left it with him, and he'd been so distracted by Seshat's rage—so desperate to reach Esta before Nibsy could hurt her—that he hadn't protected it. He'd walked *away* from it.

"I'm sorry," he said. "I didn't—"

Esta wasn't listening. She hurried over to the Ars Arcana and stopped. Standing over it, she paused, clenching her fists at her sides, before she finally picked it up from the ground.

Seshat was still quiet, but Harte realized that it wasn't an easy quiet. The emptiness within him was somehow almost more terrible than her raging. Then, from somewhere deep within him, Harte felt Seshat's fear. It was as though she understood what was coming, what would happen next.

On unsteady legs, Harte made his way to where Esta was standing, paging through the Book. She was looking for something, and then she found it—the page that was half-torn and missing. With the Ars Arcana propped open in one hand, she pulled a small scrap of parchment from her pocket and held it up to the page. The pieces matched exactly, and the second the torn halves touched, Harte felt a jolt of power wash over him as the fragment fused itself back onto the page in a burst of molten light.

"You did it," Harte said, still barely believing it. "You got the key from Nibsy."

Her mouth went tight, but she nodded in a way that made him wonder what it had cost her. Because something had changed. Something had changed *her.*

"Now we'll be able to get the demon's power out of you, and once we have control over it, we'll finally be able to use the piece of pure magic in the Book." She was still looking at the newly complete page rather than him when she spoke. "We'll be able to change *everything*."

Harte felt a wave of panic rush through him. It was all happening too fast. "We still need the Delphi's Tear. We don't have the ring yet."

Esta peered up through her dark lashes, then pulled something from her other pocket. "This ring?"

She was holding the Delphi's Tear. Weeks ago—decades ago now—Harte had given it to Cela Johnson as payment for taking care of his mother. The ring should have been in 1902, waiting for them to retrieve it. Nibsy shouldn't have had possession of it. "How—"

"I'm a thief," Esta said without any irony or humor.

Harte didn't want to think about what it meant that Nibsy Lorcan had come to possess the ring. What had happened to Cela? Had Jianyu not reached her in time to protect her? Or had they both been unable to protect themselves?

"You have the others?" she asked.

He noticed the satchel lying on the ground and scooped it up, ignoring the way Seshat shivered within him. "They're right here, where you left them."

Esta nodded and took a thick piece of charcoal from the same pocket that had been holding the ring. "Go ahead and take them out." She crouched down and started drawing a circle on the ground.

"Wait." He stepped toward her. "Esta, we can't just rush into this. We don't know what this ritual will do to you."

She didn't give any indication that she'd heard him. Ignoring his worry, she continued her tracing, making steady progress on the circle that was quickly forming around her. It was maybe six or seven feet in diameter. Not enormous, but more than large enough for a person to stand in the center and hold out their arms.

"*Esta*," he said again, more forcefully. He stepped toward the line, but Seshat lurched within him, and he stopped short before crossing it. "Would you stop for a second? We have to talk about this."

"There's nothing to talk about." She looked up at him, pausing only long enough to speak. "We don't have time to argue. The police are searching for us. They know we crossed the Brink." Her expression was as brittle as her voice, and there was something of a warning in her words. As though she'd been pushed as far as anyone could be pushed before breaking. "If they find us, they'll take the Book and the artifacts, and everything will have been for *nothing*. I have to finish this *now*."

Harte took an instinctive step back at the forcefulness of her tone. Something terrible must have happened at Nibsy's place for her to be so closed off and distant. She'd faced something, done something, and now she *needed* this. Danger or not.

Seshat started to wail as Esta rolled up her sleeve, slipped the cuff from her arm, and set it along the dark circle she'd drawn on the ground. A little farther along the line, she placed the ring.

When Harte didn't immediately move, impatience flashed in Esta's expression. "I need the others."

"What if the ritual kills you?" he asked softly.

"It won't," she said, lifting her chin. Confident as she ever was.

"How can you know that?" Harte asked.

"I made the old man tell me everything when I took the key from him," she said.

"You can't believe anything Nibsy tells you." Harte shook his head. "You *know* that."

"I believe *this*." She pointed to the page of the Book. "It's all here. See . . . when you put the page together, these symbols aren't some secret code. They're just an older version of Greek. Professor Lachlan taught me to read this years ago." Her mouth formed strange syllables the likes of which Harte had never heard before. "*To catch the serpent with the hand of the philosopher: With power willingly given, mercury ignites. Elements unite. The serpent catches its tail, severs time, consumes. Transforms power to power's like . . .* It's all right here."

None of that was clear enough for him. "Esta—" But before he could say anything else, Seshat wailed and thrashed, causing him to nearly collapse with the effort of holding her back.

"Look at you," Esta said. "We need to get that demon out of *you* and back into the *Book.*"

"Not if it means losing you." He grimaced against Seshat again. "Nibsy nearly killed you before, trying to do this same ritual."

"I wasn't willing then, but I am now." Her jaw was set, and her eyes flashed. "My affinity, *willingly* given, will ignite the Aether and unify the artifacts. With them, we can control the demon goddess and use her power. Only the goddess can touch the piece of pure magic in the Ars Arcana, which means we need to get her out of *you* and back into the *Book* where she belongs. Where she can be controlled. I can do this. I know I can."

Lies, Seshat screamed. *You cannot allow her to do this. The only way to unite the stones is through sacrifice. Total and complete sacrifice of her affinity. She will die, willing or no, and whoever possesses the Book will possess my power as well.*

So that's it, he thought. If Seshat was fighting so hard against this, it meant that the ritual would work. *You expect me to believe you care about her at all?*

I'm not your enemy, Seshat said. *I never was. . . .*

But Harte was already shoving her down, back into the recesses of his soul.

"I need the artifacts," Esta said. She'd already placed the Book on the ground in the center of the circle.

His hands were shaking as he took out the crown, the necklace, and the dagger. In the dim lighting of the station, the pieces looked dull, almost ordinary, but he could feel their power thickening the air. He hadn't seen the five of them all in one place since he'd stolen them from the Order's Mysterium. Then he'd had the same foreboding. Now Seshat railed from somewhere deep, deep inside him, but he ignored her protests. If she didn't want this ritual to happen, there had to be a reason.

He stepped into the circle, but he didn't hand over the other three artifacts, not yet. "I can't lose you to this. We need to be sure. This isn't worth dying for."

A soft breath escaped from her lips. A sign that was as much exhaustion as frustration. "I know, Harte. I love you, too."

The shock of hearing those words from her bolted through him. How many times had he wondered, had he wanted to say those words only for them to stick in his throat? And now, after all they'd been through, she was giving them to him here? Just when she was about to take an incalculable risk? "You . . ." He couldn't seem to choke it out.

"Love you." The words still sounded stiff, like the creaking of a gate that needed oiling or the cracking of a lock that rusted shut.

He shook his head, feeling an unexpected dread. This wasn't how it was supposed to happen. "You don't have to say that."

"But I do." She gave him a small, brittle smile. "Now, if you could hand me the satchel? I'll need the other stones."

He was still too shocked, too overwhelmed to move. "Esta, I— Don't. *Please.*" Why wouldn't she look at him? "Don't you dare say your good-byes."

She blinked as though surprised by his assumption. "No. Not a good-bye. I just thought—" Her jaw went tight, and her expression became unreadable once again. "This *will* work," she said, cutting him off before he could say anything more. "It will be fine. Everything is going to turn out the way it's supposed to." She looked at him, her golden eyes pleading. "You *do* trust me, don't you?"

The sharpness in her voice threw him off, but he pulled himself together when she glared at him, and he had the sense again that something was wrong. That there was something she wasn't telling him. "Of course . . ." It was Seshat he didn't trust. Nibsy. *Himself.*

"This is going to work," she repeated, but he wasn't sure that she was talking to him anymore. She held out her hands and looked at him, clearly waiting for the artifacts. "I need you to believe in me." There was a spark of impatience in her eyes, an urgency that reminded him that something must have happened while she was away. There was a flinty determination in her expression he hadn't seen for months. "I thought you loved me?"

He did. After all they'd been through, how could she not know that he loved her? Which meant that, whatever misgivings he might have, he couldn't take the choice from her. It meant that he *had* to trust her. Afraid to get too close, he placed the satchel on the ground at her feet. Her eyes lit as she picked it up.

"Thank you," she whispered, relief softening her expression.

The unease he was feeling dissipated a little. She would be okay. *They* would be okay.

She got to work almost immediately. Completely focused on her task now, Esta placed the artifacts at separate points, evenly spaced along the circle on the floor. Before she placed the dagger that held the Pharaoh's Heart in its place, she used the ancient knife to slice open the tip of her finger.

It took everything Harte had not to stop her when he saw the bright red blood welling. *I trust her*, he reminded himself. More than he'd ever trusted anyone. So he held his tongue and prayed that they weren't wrong.

Back in the center of the circle, Esta knelt before the open Book again. Then slowly, carefully, she used her bleeding fingertip to trace over the design on the page as again she spoke words he couldn't understand, syllables that rattled strangely in his ears. As she worked, Harte could feel the power beginning to swirl around them. Beneath his feet, the space within the circle Esta had sketched onto the floor started to glow, faintly at first and then brighter.

On instinct, Harte took a step back from the Book. He had to get out of the circle, away from the enormous power flowing from the Ars Arcana, but at the edge of the circle, he ran into an invisible wall. Cold, deadly energy sizzled in warning, holding him in place. Stuck within the circle, he watched as light continued to pour from the page of the Book, lifting the short hair around Esta's face and illuminating her.

Another empty train slid into the station, its wheels screaming as it slowed and rounded the bend. But Harte barely noticed it. By now there was a wild energy growing in the cavernous space, a dangerous magic building. Within his skin, Seshat was screaming and wailing, more desperate and terrified than she'd ever been.

As the energy increased, there was a roaring in his ears that grew and grew until it blocked any other noise—the train, the far-off tracks, his own shouting. Even Seshat's screams eventually were drowned out by the ancient and indescribable cacophony that was filling his mind. Something was coming to life—a magic like chaos blooming. He could feel it tearing through the air, and the enormity of it took his breath away.

There was too much magic, too much *power*. But the energy, the chaotic wildness of it, had pinned him in place. He couldn't even begin to stop Esta from finishing the ritual.

He had to stop her. He knew suddenly that she had been wrong. This power? There was no surviving this. There was only sacrifice.

Harte knew what would happen next because he'd seen Seshat start this ritual before in the visions that had assaulted him back in St. Louis. Esta and Seshat, the reality and the memory—he could see them both, superimposed and simultaneous. What had been. What was. What would be.

"Esta," he screamed, but his voice was lost in the noise. She didn't look up. She couldn't hear him. Or if she could, she was too far into the ritual, too far gone into the totality of the magic swirling around her.

One by one the artifacts around him began to lift themselves into the air, floating in the invisible net of Aether that held all of creation together. One by one they began to glow with a strange, ethereal light, and Harte felt another power join the first—a familiar brush of magic that could only be Esta's. She was using her affinity to unite the stones, just as Seshat had eons ago. Just as the Book had instructed her.

There was nothing he could do. He couldn't stop her from sending her affinity outward, into the stones, or from connecting all she was to the artifacts and, with them, to the magic trapped in the Book. They joined together in a swirling eddy of power and light, like a Brink made visible.

Sweat was beading at Esta's temples, and her expression was strained. The power that could only be the piece of original magic trapped in the Book—the portion of the beating heart of magic that Seshat had trapped ages ago—was flowing through Esta now, consuming her. Linking her very self to the stones and to the Book. When she finally raised her eyes to meet his, their usual golden warmth was gone. In its place were bright hollows, empty sockets lit from within.

All at once a terrible bolt of energy coursed through the room, and then through Harte himself.

From somewhere deep, deep within the recesses of his very being, Seshat let out a soul-shattering scream that was anger and pain and terror made real. Harte felt the goddess's anguish as though it were his own. The power tore through him, and suddenly Harte could feel everything: the net of time and Aether that held the whole world together, the individual affinities and lives that had been stolen to power the artifacts, and the thin thread of Esta's own affinity connecting it all. Seshat clawed at him in a last, desperate attempt to stop her inevitable end. And then Harte felt the sureness of what would come, the absolute horror of knowing that he could be destroyed by the very magic that made him whole.

There were tears of blood streaming down Esta's face now, and Harte knew—knew absolutely and without doubt—that she had been wrong. The fear in her eyes—the pure surprised terror there—cracked his heart in two. She'd believed that this would work, and she'd been wrong. This ritual was killing her, *would* kill her. But Harte still couldn't move. He was rooted in place by the terrible beating heart of magic that surrounded him.

Then he, too, was being pulled apart.

When Seshat lost her grip within him, Harte felt himself shattering as the goddess' power drained from him. The pulsing power around him swirled, glowing ever brighter and hotter as Seshat's power joined it, growing like a storm about to crash over them both.

And then it did break. The light trembled and the power shattered, and Harte felt the sucking of some unseen wind drawing him toward the Book. With a flash of light, the Book pulled it all inward, slammed itself shut, and suddenly went dark.

The screaming stopped. Silence filled the station as Esta collapsed to the floor, her body limp over the now-closed Book.

Harte, finally able to move, ran to her. Sliding on his knees, he scooped her up and cupped her face. Begged her to stay with him. Begged any power listening to save her.

Esta's eyes fluttered open, but he wasn't sure if she could see him. She wasn't there, not really.

"He lied," she whispered, the surprise of this fact flashing through her expression. And then she was gone.

1902—Little Africa

Cela took one look at her brother's expression, saw the fear etched in his features, and knew he wasn't exaggerating the danger.

"Police?" Viola asked, already reaching for her knife.

Joshua shook his head. "Whoever they are, they're nobody official. They're trying not to be noticed, but they're not from the neighborhood."

Cela understood immediately what he meant. *White men.*

They'd picked the basement rooms in Little Africa on purpose. Just south of the Village and not far from Washington Square, the neighborhood had historically been the place where African-descended people lived, going way back to when the Dutch thought they were doing enslaved people a favor by giving them a little land to farm. Recently, the neighborhood had grown more mixed and was known for the black-and-tan dives on Thompson Street that kept the social reformers in a tizzy. But the buildings on those blocks were still predominantly populated by Negroes. Abel and Joshua had enough friends and contacts in the nearby buildings that it had felt like the safest place to stay. Since neither the Order nor the police bothered to recruit Negroes, their patrols couldn't get close without drawing attention to themselves as outsiders.

"The Order," Viola said.

Joshua nodded. "Most likely. They're making their way through the building next door," Joshua told them. "But word is they're looking for two specific Mageus." He looked at Viola. "A Chinese man and an Italian girl."

"That seems awful specific," Abel said, cutting his eyes in Cela's direction. She knew what he was thinking: *So much for your protection.*

"You have to go," Cela told Viola. She didn't know how the Order knew to look for them, but she wasn't going to sit around letting her friend get caught. She was already tossing their few belongings into a sack.

"We *all* have to go," Abel said, firmer than ever now.

"If those men are searching for Jianyu, we can't just up and leave without him," Cela explained as she shoved the last few items into the satchel. "What if he runs straight into that patrol? Even if he manages to get around them, he won't know where we've gone if we just disappear."

"Where *is* Jianyu?" Abel asked, his hands on his hips.

Cela glanced at Viola. "We don't exactly know," Cela said finally, unwilling to lie to her brother. "He didn't come back last night like we expected him to."

"What happened last night?" Abel frowned, and when Cela exchanged another silent look with Viola, it was enough to have him scrubbing his hands over his face. "No . . . Tell me you weren't out in the middle of the night *again*, pressing your luck. Not after you promised you'd be more careful."

"I only waited in the wagon," Cela said, knowing it wasn't really an answer.

"You only waited . . ." Abel looked to be at the end of his patience.

"Nothing happened," she said. "I got back fine."

"Jianyu didn't," Abel pointed out. "And now there are men out there searching for the two of them. It's only a matter of time before someone starts looking for you, too." He shook his head, and Cela could see the temper building. "We're not waiting."

"Abel—"

"Jianyu is grown," Abe told her. "He's going to have to take care of himself. My job is to keep *you* safe."

"I'll wait for you out front," Joshua said, clearly uncomfortable with the tension mounting in the small room. "You'll hear the signal if any-thing else happens."

"Thanks," Abel said, relief roughening the tone of the word. "I owe you."

"You sure do," Joshua told him without an ounce of humor. "Hattie would have me by the short hairs if she knew I was wrapped up in another one of your messes."

Once his friend was gone, Abel turned back to Cela and Viola.

"We're leaving in the next two minutes."

"Abel—"

"*Two minutes.* I'll give you two minutes to gather whatever you can carry, but if Jianyu doesn't show up by then, we're not waiting a second longer."

"Abe—"

"He's right," Jianyu said, appearing out of thin air like some kind of ghost. "You have to go."

No matter how many times she'd seen him do it, Cela was still thrown off by the unexpectedness of Jianyu's affinity. She'd known about magic since before she could remember, but seeing it? Feeling it right there in your presence? That was something else altogether. Something like *wonder.* But this time? Seeing him appear out of thin air, she felt nothing but relief.

Except he didn't look right. His expression was tight, and his color was off. He looked wan and unsteady on his feet.

"Where have you been?" Viola demanded, her voice sharp with the kind of frustration that grows from fear.

"There is no time for explanations," Jianyu said. "We have to leave, now."

"Finally," Abe said, throwing up his hands. "Someone's talking sense."

Cela glared at her brother, but Jianyu was still issuing orders.

"You especially have to go, Cela."

His words felt like a slap. A betrayal. "No," she said, ready to fight him every bit as much as she'd fought her brother on this point. "The patrol isn't looking for me," she told him.

"What patrol?" His brows creased.

"The one in the next building," Abel explained. "They're looking for Mageus that sound an awful lot like you and Viola here."

Jianyu let out a soft string of words she couldn't understand. "He works faster than I expected." He looked up at her. "You need to leave the city."

She started to argue, but Jianyu stepped forward and took her hands. "There is no time for argument," he said, gripping her fingers even more tightly. "You must leave. You must get outside of the Brink, where Nibsy Lorcan cannot touch you. And you must take the silver discs with you."

MERCURY IGNITES

1983—City Hall Station

The air was still warm, thick with the magic that had just exploded through the station. The artifacts were still glowing with their eerie luminescence, and Harte still felt the presence of a boundary around him, trapping him within the circle that Esta had drawn on the ground. Beneath Harte, Esta wasn't moving. He couldn't tell if she was breathing.

"Come on," he pleaded, jostling her softly. "Please, Esta. I can't—" His voice broke, and he swallowed hard against the horror rising in his throat. "*Please*. You have to wake up. You *have* to."

Because I can't do this without you.

But Esta didn't respond. She remained quiet and still, her body limp in his arms.

He lied. Those had been her final words to him, and she'd said them as though she couldn't believe they were true. Who had lied? Nibsy?

Of course Nibsy Lorcan would have lied. Why would she have thought otherwise?

Careful not to touch the Book beneath her, Harte maneuvered Esta to cradle her head on his lap, then brushed her hair back from her too-pale face. Still, she didn't stir. Her skin had gone a sickly gray, and her lips looked pale and bloodless. Her eyes were open, but their amber irises gazed unseeing at the dark skylights above.

He couldn't lose her. *Not like this.* He'd never even told her—

Esta blinked then and took a small, shuddering breath, and relief nearly knocked Harte over. He could tell she wasn't aware of him. He wasn't sure whether she could see or focus on anything at all. But if he leaned down, he could now feel the faintest whisper of breath coming from her mouth.

She was alive, and it was enough. It was *everything*. Esta was alive, and Seshat was trapped back in the Book, and Harte would do anything to make sure Esta kept breathing.

Suddenly there were footsteps coming from the corridor at the back of the station, and suddenly a group of men flooded out of the tunnel, surrounding the circle on the floor and the two of them inside it. They weren't police—at least Harte didn't think they were. Dressed in boxy coats with white sashes, the men wore a familiar silver medallion on their lapel. They looked like a version of the Jefferson Guard, but there was something off about them. It wasn't only the strange cut of their coats. It was their eyes—every single one of them had nothing but endless darkness where their eyes should have been. Pupils and whites together had been obscured, and in their place was a familiar, fathomless black.

"Thoth," Harte whispered, understanding suddenly without understanding anything at all. Seshat had said he was everywhere, but Harte hadn't believed her.

The men's mouths curved up in eerie synchronicity. "Yes," they all said, their voices chanting in unison, but it wasn't human voices that came from their mouths.

Harte had heard that voice before, in visions and in dreams. He still didn't understand how this could be, but he knew that Seshat had been right. Her anger and rage and especially her *terror* made horrible sense now. Esta might have killed Jack back in Chicago, but she hadn't managed to destroy Thoth. He'd escaped somehow, and now he was here, within these men. Years in the future. Controlling them as he'd once controlled Jack.

What did Esta do?

"She freed me," the men said, addressing Harte's unspoken thought in that singular, inhuman voice. "She *unleashed* me. Made me *more* than even I dreamed of being." The men laughed in eerie unison, a dark, mirthless scraping sound.

"No," he said, not willing to believe she had sacrificed so much for *this*.

"She's a mere child," the voices said, echoing through the cavernous chamber. "She never had the power to defeat me. But she released me, allowed me to become *infinite*. And now it seems she has helped me further. She has made it possible for me to take what is and was always destined to be mine." Together, all the men moving as one, they stepped toward the Book.

"No." The word was nothing more than a husk of breath, but the relief Harte felt at the sound of Esta speaking threatened to overwhelm him. She looked up at him then, and though her golden eyes were now rimmed in blood, he knew she wasn't gone—not completely. She could see him.

Suddenly, Harte felt another blast of magic. Power poured from the Ars Arcana, and because it was still connected to the circle and to Esta herself, it began to lift her from his arms as it coursed through her. As he held on to her, energy poured from her eyes and mouth, flooding the station with a magic more intense than anything Harte had ever felt before. He was trying to keep hold of her, but he could feel the heat of the magic vibrating through her. The sheer immensity of it.

Esta's skin grew feverish, and the artifacts began to glow again, now with an *impossible* brightness. The Aether connecting them was a wall of light, a swirling mass of energy and magic that threatened to destroy everything it could touch. The stones lit as though burning from within. The power in the air swirled, filling the entire space with the terrible chaos of pure magic.

It lasted for ages.

It lasted for mere moments.

Time lost meaning as the men who had surrounded the circle screamed and grabbed their heads. One by one, the darkness was pushed from their eyes, replaced with a blinding flash of light, and as their eyes went dark, the men fell to the ground. When the last one fell, the power drained from the air, and Esta collapsed back to the floor.

She was breathing. Barely. But she was unconscious again. Her eyes had closed, and she looked even paler and more lifeless than before. Around them, the men lay dead on the station platform. The circle remained aglow, and the artifacts and the Book were still hovering in the air, floating just above the ground.

Harte was so focused on Esta that at first he didn't hear the shuffling footsteps approaching or the odd tapping sound that punctuated them. He didn't realize that a new danger was approaching until it had already arrived. An old man with a cane stepped from the darkened tunnel into the dim station. Harte might have dismissed the old man, but he immediately recognized the cane—the polished silver of the gorgon's head was visible even from across the platform.

"Nibsy." Harte said the name like a curse.

But the old man only smiled. His eyes were focused on the Ars Arcana, abandoned on the station floor.

THE DEVIL'S MARKS

1902—Little Africa

Jianyu's words had Viola reaching on instinct for the pocket in her skirts, the one Cela had stitched for her to conceal the silver discs. Their now-familiar weight seemed almost a balance to Libitina's heft.

"Che pazzo?" she asked, incredulous. "You cannot send her off, unprotected, with the only leverage we have. Assolutamente nò. I took the sigils from the Order's rooms, and so *I* will be the one to keep them here, close by, where I can protect them."

Cela stepped away from Jianyu. "I don't want to take them anywhere, and I'm not leaving my city." Her mouth had gone tight and her eyes thunderous. "I'm not running like some scared rabbit."

"Bene," Viola said, nodding. "Cela, at least, talks sense."

"It is the only way," Jianyu said, looking more desperate than Viola had ever seen him. There was something in his expression that she had not noticed before when he looked at Cela. Something that reminded Viola too much of how she felt when she looked at Ruby Reynolds. A wonder, but a fear as well.

Abel had stepped forward. "We're *all* leaving. That patrol in the next building is going to be here any minute now."

"You must go, but we cannot go with you," Jianyu told him. "Not so long as Nibsy can track us. We cannot risk it."

"What are you talking about?" Viola asked, stepping forward.

"Logan did not die that night," he told her. "He delivered the ring to Nibsy."

She could not stop the curse that slipped from her lips, but the filthy words offered no comfort or relief. When they had seen the body falling from the tower, they had worried that Nibsy might have obtained the Delphi's Tear. They'd suspected *someone* had, considering the desperation of the Order over the past few weeks. But they hadn't known, not for sure. Now they did.

It didn't change their current situation. "Let them come. Nibsy Lorcan can be taken care of easily enough." She had already slipped her blade out, imagining the pleasure it would be to skewer him with it again. "We'll see how long he keeps the ring."

Jianyu turned on her with more emotion in his expression than she'd ever seen there before. "He has the marks, Viola. He can use them."

Viola froze, silenced by this news. *No. It can't be.*

"What marks?" Cela asked. "What are you talking about?"

But Viola understood too well the implications of Jianyu's words. Once, the tattoos had been a simple statement of loyalty, but they were not an oath without consequences. Everyone who took the marks pledged not only themselves, but their affinity, and anyone who broke that oath could be unmade by them.

Everyone. Including Jianyu and herself.

Viola pressed her lips together. "But the cane, it belonged to Dolph."

"Maybe once, but Nibsy has the cane." Jianyu's jaw went tight. "And he does not require the Medusa's kiss to use it."

"No . . ." But then a memory came back to her of a moment in a stairwell weeks before, when Nibsy had threatened her. "I didn't think . . . Madonna," Viola whispered, crossing herself. "I thought I'd been imagining it."

"You knew?" Jianyu asked.

She was shaking her head, unable to admit it even to herself.

"How long have you known this might be a danger to us?"

"I didn't know," she told him. "Not for sure."

"When?" Jianyu demand.

She flinched at the rare fury in his words. "The night of the solstice."

LISA MAXWELL

"You kept this information from me?" Jianyu asked. "I thought we were together in this. I thought—"

"I didn't believe it!" Viola snapped, fear warring with the anger she felt at herself for not listening to her instincts. Then her shoulders sagged. "When it happened, I told myself it was nothing. I didn't want to believe it could be possible, but . . ." She shook her head again, as though the motion could shake away the truth. "When we were coming down from the roof that night, before Paolo was taken, Nibsy made another of his stupid threats, and I thought I felt something. But it shouldn't have been possible."

"Perhaps not, but it is," Jianyu told her, reaching behind himself, so he could rub at his own back, where the tattoo of an ouroboros that matched hers lay beneath his tunic.

"No," Viola said, her mouth tight. "I cannot believe this. I *won't*. It must be a trick. If he could truly use the marks as you say, you would not have escaped."

"He *allowed* me to leave," Jianyu told her. "Cat and mouse. He is only toying with us, but when his patience runs out, he will come after the discs. And as long as we wear the marks, he can unmake us."

Viola tightened her grip on the dagger. "He can't use the marks if he's dead."

"Even if you could get close enough to kill him, it is no answer," Jianyu said. "Not when the Devil's Own all still believe in his forked tongue. We cannot fight them all," Jianyu told her. "And I know you, Viola. You do not want to kill those we once counted as friends."

Viola cursed softly, a string of Italian that would have made any of her brother's men blush. But Jianyu had already turned back to Cela, pleading.

"That is why you have to go," Jianyu said, turning to look at Cela. It was there again, that expression of longing in his eyes when he looked at her. The one that made Viola feel bereft.

"He's right," Viola told Cela and Abel. "As long as this danger exists, we cannot protect you." They could not even protect themselves.

"It's what I've been telling her for weeks now," Abel said.

"We don't even know what the discs do yet," Cela argued. "You could be sending me away for no good reason at all."

"If Nibsy Lorcan wants them, it is essential that he never gets them. You are the only one who can do this. You are the only one of us who can cross the Brink and take the discs where Nibsy Lorcan cannot reach them." Jianyu paused. "Where he cannot reach *you*."

A shrill whistle sounded from outside the small, high window in the wall.

"That's Joshua's signal," Abel told them. "It's time to go."

Jianyu felt the mood of the room shift as everyone went silent. From somewhere just outside the building came the sound of shouting.

"We're leaving," Abel told Cela. "And we're leaving right n*ow.*"

But before they could get out the door, Joshua was there, launching himself into the room and shutting it firmly behind him. "They're here!" he said, panting with the exertion of his sprint. "Five men. They saw me before I could get in here."

Through the thin wooden door, the sound of pounding and shouting came from the other end of the hallway.

"I can take care of this," Viola said, stepping toward the door, but Jianyu caught her gently by the arm.

"You cannot touch them," he said. "If they are looking for you, they likely know your affinity. If you harm them here, the Order will know. You will put everyone in this building in the Order's sights."

"He's right," Abel said, his jaw going tight. "If the Order knows Mageus were being hidden here, it would make the entire community look complicit."

Joshua swore. "This is exactly what we were worried about."

"We won't allow that to happen," Viola promised them, looking at Jianyu.

He understood immediately and offered her his hand as the pounding and shouting drew closer. "Take hold. Quickly, and they will not find any of us."

THE SERPENT'S JAWS

1983—City Hall Station

Harte watched as an older version of Nibsy Lorcan stepped into the dimly lit space of the station. He was acutely aware of how bad the current situation was. The artifacts and the Book were exposed and vulnerable, and Esta was still unconscious. He couldn't protect the artifacts or the Book without letting go of Esta, and he couldn't bring himself to do that.

"You know, Darrigan, I haven't been called that name in decades," Nibsy said with a disgusted squint. He wasn't as old as Harte would have expected him to be; the healers he used must have been absurdly talented. However much his appearance had changed, his eyes were the same, as small and as beady as a rat's behind the thick glass of his spectacles' lenses. "I didn't much like it way back when. I find I still don't."

Harte didn't care much what Nibsy Lorcan did or didn't like, but he needed time to think, to get Esta, the Book, and the artifacts out of there. He maneuvered so that his body was between her and Nibsy, protecting her and shielding the Book from Nibsy's view until he figured out a plan.

Nibsy took a small step forward, and when Harte wrapped himself more protectively around Esta, the old man only shook his head. "I'm the least of your worries right now. There'll be more of them coming any minute now." He nodded toward the bodies on the floor. "The amount of power the two of you set off will have every Guard in the city on their way. And there you are, trapped. Easy pickings."

Harte didn't respond. He wouldn't give Nibsy the satisfaction or the ammunition.

"I might not be able to cross that line, but the Guard won't have any issue with it, Sundren as they are. And she's too weak to fight more of them off. They'll drag you both away, and when you break that ritual spell and cross the boundary, it will kill you both as surely as anything."

"There shouldn't *be* any Guards," Harte said, trying to stall.

"Why? Because Esta killed Jack Grew?" the old man asked, amused. "Murdered him in the middle of a crowded arena in front of all the press. There were pictures in every paper. Newsreels played in every cinema for weeks after. Did you really think that would end the Guard and the Brotherhoods? Jack's death showed every Sundren in this country *exactly* how dangerous our kind are. It galvanized the Brotherhoods' cause and handed them popularity and power they never dreamed of wielding." His eyes narrowed. "She made him into a *martyr*, and the idiots in this land turned him into a saint."

Harte thought of the familiar darkness in the dead men's eyes and knew Nibsy was telling the truth, but he wondered whether Nibsy understood that more than Jack Grew's hatred had survived that night in Chicago. Thoth had as well.

"She doesn't have much time, you know, especially after what she's done to these fellows." The old man nudged one of the fallen bodies with his toe. "Even now, her connection to the artifacts and the Book is draining her. They want what they're owed. *Magic* wants what is owed."

The serpent catches its tail, severs time, consumes.

Harte had a million questions, but he didn't voice any of them. He remained silent and considered his options. From the way Nibsy was waiting at the edge of the sigil, Harte had a sense that, unlike the Guard, he couldn't cross the boundary Esta had created. Which meant that he'd been telling the truth. It also meant they had time. But he knew he didn't have *much* time.

"She has to finish what she started. It's the only way." Nibsy used the cane to point at the swirling energy around the sigil. "This is only the beginning of the ritual. Just like the Brink, if you try to leave, the power that she's awoken will take your affinity—both of your affinities. Unless she gives the spell what it desires, what she promised the whole of magic by beginning it, she'll die from what it's taking. That's the only way to end the ritual."

"What she promised?"

"Her power," Nibsy said, his eyes flashing with anticipation. "Her *magic*. It was the mistake the Order made in creating the Brink—believing they could use the power in the Book without offering something in return. They wanted power without the price. Without true sacrifice."

"You lied to her," Harte said, his jaw tight. "You said it wouldn't kill her."

"Of *course* I lied," the old man told him, impatience coloring his words. "About any number of things. The girl shouldn't have been fool-ish enough to believe me. But she's not dead, as far as I can see. The ritual hasn't killed her. Not yet. Now she has to finish what she started. It's the only way out for you. More, it's the only way to stop the Brotherhoods from having the key to infinite power." He took another step forward. "Think of the damage the Order did with the Book and the artifacts *before*. The atrocity of the Brink happened because they didn't understand how to control the demon bitch within those pages. But now that the girl has united the artifacts and reimprisoned Seshat? Think of what the Brotherhoods could do. They could touch the very heart of magic. Her sacrifice would be for nothing if the Brotherhoods gain control of the Book now."

Harte didn't believe for a second that Nibsy cared. He wanted the Book and the power it contained. But Nibsy was right about one thing—if the Brotherhoods got the Book, everything that had happened to them would have been for nothing. But if Esta died there—in that time before she could return the cuff to her younger self—none of it would matter.

"If she dies, we both lose," Harte reminded him.

"Not if she completes the ritual," Nibsy said, amusement glinting in his eyes.

Harte examined the open page that Esta had read before. *The serpent catches its tail, severs time.*

Harte considered those words. Could there be a chance . . . ?

"How can she finish anything?" Harte asked, the words tearing from his throat. "She isn't even conscious."

"You can help her," Nibsy said simply. "Use your affinity. Command her. She has to sacrifice her power. She has to finish what she began."

Harte took Esta's hand. He understood what Nibsy wanted him to do, but accepting it meant admitting defeat. His thumb traced along the rough, scarred skin on her wrist. "You want me to betray her," he said. "You want me to *kill* her."

The old man huffed an impatient breath. "Let's not pretend you're so noble, Darrigan. We've known each other too long to have lies between us. I know what you are."

"You don't know anything about me," he said.

"You expect me to believe that you've changed so much?" Nibsy scoffed. "*You,* the boy who sacrificed your own *mother* to escape this prison of a city. You've betrayed everyone who trusted you. No, Darrigan. People like us never change. We are who and what we are. So why delay the inevitable? Why this ridiculous charade? The girl has served her purpose. For both of us. She has to give her power to the stones. It's your only way out of the cage she's created for you. Unless you want to die at the hands of the Guard. Because once the Brotherhoods get the Book, you're dead either way."

Esta's breath shuddered, and Harte felt the energy in the room waver. He understood that she wouldn't last much longer.

"If she dies before the ritual is completed, you'll never leave that circle alive," the old man said. "When the Guard comes and they drag you across that line, the ritual will take your power and your life as surely as the Brink."

Desperately, Harte tried to remember the vision Seshat had shown him of that original ritual. What had she done? What had she been trying to do? He remembered how Thoth had shattered the stones, how that had doomed Seshat, causing her to flee into the Book. But what would Seshat have done to complete the ritual if Thoth hadn't arrived? Harte couldn't be sure. Seshat had never shared that piece of the puzzle with him. He didn't know what she'd intended to do.

"Help her do what must be done," Nibsy coaxed, looking suddenly more like the fifteen-year-old boy Harte remembered. "Save yourself, Darrigan. The Guard will be here soon. It's the girl's power or both your lives. And you and I both know that you are no martyr."

Beneath him, Esta's breathing was growing shallow. The energy in the room felt increasingly unstable. Harte looked down at her, at the face he knew every soft curve and sharp angle of. His heart twisted at the mess of silvery scars on her arm, awareness prickling at the nape of his neck.

Carefully, he cupped her cheek, considering his options, but she didn't respond. Her skin felt too cool to the touch.

Closing his eyes, Harte opened his affinity and broke the promise he'd made to Esta weeks before. It felt like a betrayal to cross the boundary between them, but he needed to be sure. But instead of Esta, he found nothing but darkness and pain. She was so consumed by the Book and its power, he couldn't sense anything of what she had been. He couldn't sense *her*.

"I'm so sorry," he whispered. "If there were any other way . . ." He kissed her then, brushing his lips against her forehead, and as his lips touched her skin, he sent out a single command.

Her eyes flew open as the power in the room went electric, but Harte didn't let go.

Nibsy was screaming. The cane he'd been holding clattered to the ground, and the old man fell to his knees beside it, writhing in pain.

"No!" Nibsy's face contorted in rage. But there was confusion in his expression as well. "How—"

Harte sent another command through their connection and watched as Seshat's power—the *Book's* power—ripped the affinity from Nibsy Lorcan. Or, most of it. Not enough to kill him, but enough to break him. The old man fell over, unconscious and without the magic that had guided him for so long.

By then the energy in the room felt erratic, and the air was suddenly charged, hot and dangerous. The energy coursing through her felt like fire against his skin, and Harte felt as though he would be burned alive if he kept holding on. He looked down at their joined hands, and he knew what had to be done. There wasn't a choice. Not any longer.

He sent another command through their connection, and the air around him came alive with magic. The artifacts glowed hot and bright before they flickered and then suddenly went dark. Slowly, the circle faded, until it was no more than a dark line on the station floor.

The platform was painfully silent, like the sound of the world had drained away. Esta's body had collapsed back onto the ground, but she wasn't moving. Carefully, Harte edged closer to her. He hesitated— knowing already but not wanting to accept the truth—before he finally reached out and touched her. She didn't respond, didn't move.

She wasn't breathing.

He tried to tell himself that he'd done what he had to do. That it was the only choice he'd had—for both of them. Otherwise, they would have both been trapped here for the Guard to find. Along with the Book. And the artifacts. They would have been sitting ducks, an offering of untold power for whoever found them.

There had been no other way, but he'd hoped . . .

Harte's throat was tight as he looked at the still and lifeless body. The reality of what just happened crashed through him, and panic clawed at his skin. But there was already a numbness settling over him, as absolute as the silence in the cavernous station. He should have felt bowled over. He should have felt destroyed. Instead, he felt . . . nothing. An endless emptiness had hollowed him out.

She was gone. There was no going back, no reversing the choices he'd made. He could only hope he'd chosen right.

A few yards away, the old man wasn't moving either, but he wasn't dead. Harte had made sure of it. He'd left Nibsy Lorcan just enough magic to survive, because he wanted the bastard to live long enough to know life without his affinity. The Guard could deal with him.

Nearby, the Book lay open and inert on the ground. It looked so unimpressive, a tattered old journal, just as it had appeared the first time he'd seen it deep in the bowels of Khafre Hall. But now he knew what waited inside those pages. And he knew what he had to do.

Slowly, Harte pulled himself to his feet. He felt severed from himself, as though he were walking through a terrible dream. The world around him hung unreal, unsteady. His head felt as though it were filled with cotton, but his hearing was slowly returning. Distantly, he heard the squealing of a train. If Nibsy was right, Thoth was still loose in the world. The Book and the artifacts needed his protection now more than ever.

He had to go. *For Esta.*

Harte felt like he was watching himself from a distance as he scooped up the artifacts and then, using the sleeve of his shirt so his skin didn't make contact, took the Book from where it rested on the floor. He put them all into the satchel and slung the canvas bag across his body.

A train was screaming into the station now. It was time.

He took one more look at the bodies, Nibsy and Esta, both lying still on the station platform. Seeing her like that, he felt something crack inside him. But he couldn't stay. If there was any chance for a future, any chance that the girl on the platform hadn't given her life for nothing, he had to go—to stop the Brotherhoods, to stop Thoth—and he had to go *now*.

The train slid into the station, and as it slowed through the curve, he leapt onto the platform of the back car. As it sped away into the darkness of the tunnel, Harte didn't look away from the carnage he was leaving behind. He kept his eyes on the body of the girl he loved until he couldn't see her any longer and hoped he hadn't made a terrible mistake.

LIKE LIGHTNING

1902—Little Africa

Cela understood immediately what Jianyu intended. Relief rocketed through her as she grabbed hold of his outstretched hand. Viola followed a half second later, but Abel and Joshua didn't move.

"Come," Jianyu said. "I can get you past them."

But Abel only shook his head. "You get my sister out of here. Make sure she's safe. Joshua and I will stay back and distract them. We'll meet you at the new place."

"No, Abe." Cela started to release Jianyu, but his fingers tightened around hers.

"They aren't looking for us," Abel told her, and the determination in her brother's expression made her pause. "Don't worry, Rabbit. We'll be right behind you."

But it wasn't enough. The Order's patrols wouldn't care if Abel and Joshua belonged there. She couldn't just leave him behind, not when it was her fault that they were still there. If she hadn't argued so much about waiting for Jianyu, they'd already be gone, and Abel wouldn't be in danger.

"Abe—" She started to plead with him, but a violent pounding shook the door and silenced her.

"Open up!" a man shouted from the other side.

The patrol didn't wait. A second later, the door flew open, the latch splintering at the force of the booted foot that had kicked it down.

Cela felt the world tilt suddenly, and her vision shifted, like she was looking through wobbly old glass. Before the men entering the room could careen into them, Jianyu pulled Cela and Viola back along the wall. Just barely out of reach.

Joshua and her brother were standing shoulder to shoulder, looking every bit as formidable as the light-haired white men who had just destroyed the entrance.

"Can we help you gentlemen?" Joshua said. He kept his voice contrite, almost humble. It was a dance he'd done too many times before. But Cela didn't miss the way he lifted his chin.

Don't start anything, Abe.

Cela felt Jianyu nudging her to the side, but she couldn't just leave them there.

Just hold your temper and get out alive, she pleaded silently.

"We're looking for a couple of maggots who were rumored to be seen in this neighborhood," one of the other men said.

"Maggots?" Abel shot Joshua a doubtful kind of look. "Haven't seen any maggots around here." He paused, giving the men a steady glare. "Haven't seen any Mageus, either."

One of the men stepped forward. His expression was twisted into a sneer of distaste. "Same thing, ain't it, boy?"

A muscle clenched in Abel's jaw, but to Cela's relief, he didn't take the bait. Joshua was silent next to him, but he crossed his arms over his chest in defiance. How many times had they done this, faced men who refused to recognize their manhood? Too many. She knew it wore on him—it wore on her, as well—but it hadn't broken him. It wouldn't. Abel Johnson was too damn strong.

Cela felt Jianyu nudge her again, this time tugging gently at her arm, but she didn't move. She couldn't leave her brother there with those men. Not until she knew he was safe.

"Search the place," the first man commanded. He was still glaring at Abe with open disgust, and he kept his gaze steady as the other two started tearing the meager furnishings apart.

Abel's gaze shifted slightly to glance past the man confronting him, ignoring the pair who were already tearing apart the room. His eyes seemed to find the place she was standing, invisible though she was, as though pulled by magnets. Or maybe like magic.

Go, he told her without saying a word. *Go.* It was a command that she couldn't refuse. Because it would only make it worse to stay—for him, and for them all.

This time she allowed Jianyu to pull her along. Together, they inched into the hallway, where they saw another two doors had been busted open by the other pair of mercenaries. She heard crying and felt Jianyu tug at Viola—a reminder that she could not use her magic here, not without harming the very innocents they were trying to protect.

In a matter of seconds they were out the back of the building in the rank-smelling alley where outhouses stood leaning unevenly in a row. Like every tenement, refuse from the residents was piled along the curb. But the area wasn't empty. There was a single white boy standing there like the whole place belonged to him. Cela had heard enough about Nibsy Lorcan that it took only one glance at the boy's gold-rimmed glasses and silver-topped cane for her to know who the kid was.

Jianyu skidded to a halt. Cela heard his sharp intake of breath, and the world went back into focus as he released her hand and reached for his chest. The boy blocking the way out of the alley only smiled softly as both Jianyu and Viola crumpled to the ground, like marionettes being cut from their strings.

"It's good to see you again, Cela," the boy said, his voice soft and almost conversational.

"Again?" Her skin was crawling with warning. Her friends were on their hands and knees now, struggling against whatever magic this boy was spinning, but she didn't dare look away from him. It was like coming face-to-face with a snake. Any sudden movement, and she didn't doubt he'd bite.

"We've never been formally introduced," the boy said. "But I've been watching." He gave her a small, dangerous smile that sent a skittering of unease down her spine. "You seem like a smart enough girl, but you have dangerous taste in friends."

She sensed Jianyu collapse, and Viola followed quickly after. She wanted to stop whatever was happening to them, but she had the sense that showing how much she cared would be a mistake. Besides, she wasn't about to kneel in front of this kid, not even to tend to her friends. Instead, she kept her eyes focused on the bespectacled boy and pretended that Jianyu and Viola weren't gasping for life at her feet.

"Nibsy Lorcan," she said, squaring her shoulders. "I've heard plenty about you, too."

His eyes flashed at that. "I'm sure you have."

"Wasn't anything good," she told him, proud of herself for keeping her voice from betraying her fear.

"There's usually more than one side to any story," the boy said.

"Looks pretty one-sided to me," she pressed, nodding toward her friends, who were too still now for her liking.

"I'll let them go in a minute," he told her. "But I wanted a chance to meet you first. A chance to talk. You see, we both want the same thing, Cela."

"I doubt that very much," she told him.

"You want your friends to be safe," he said. "I don't want to harm them."

She choked out a nervous burst of laughter. "I'm not sure this is the best way to show it."

"I didn't think their interference would be . . . *productive.*" He shrugged. "They don't understand."

Cela clenched her teeth to keep herself from saying all the things she wanted to. But she knew anything she said could be used against them. Talking to this boy was nothing but a trap.

The soft curve of Nibsy's mouth went flat. "Soon, Cela, the Order is going to fall, and power is going to shift in this city. You could be on the winning side. Think of what it would mean for your family—your brother. Think of what it could do for your people."

She kept her expression steady, knowing already that this boy was no more going to help her "people" than any other fool who wanted power. It was probably the first time he'd ever even ventured into this neighborhood.

She was tired of his games, his doublespeak. "Are you planning on telling me what you want?"

"I want to win," Nibsy told her. "I want to make those who've held us down and pushed us back pay. I think you might want that too. The police killed your father, didn't they? Just because of the color of his skin? Think of a world where they don't have the power to hurt you or yours. A city safe for people like us."

There was no "like us," not as far as Cela was concerned. "And you think *you* can make that happen?" she wondered. *Like some kind of white savior come to rescue the poor darker brother.*

"I know I can," he said. "But not alone. I'll need them to help—Jianyu and Viola both. I need my spy and my assassin. With them, I can't fail."

"You would trust them?" she asked.

"No, but in exchange for Newton's Sigils, I might be persuaded." The lenses of his glasses flashed in the sunlight.

The creeping feeling up her spine told Cela that, whatever happened, this boy should never, ever get ahold of those discs.

"We don't have them," Cela bluffed. "Viola dropped them on her way out of the building."

Fury flashed across the boy's face. It was there and gone in an instant, like lightning across the summer sky, but Cela wasn't so foolish as to pretend she hadn't seen it.

"Let's not waste our time with lies, Cela Johnson. I know you have them. I know they're here, close by. I could kill both of your friends and you as well to take them, if I wanted. But I meant what I told you. I'd rather do this with Jianyu's and Viola's help. So give them this message for me: Your friends should come back to the Strega and the Devil's Own. They should pledge themselves to me and to my cause. If they do, I'll welcome them with open arms. I can and will protect them from the dangers of this city." He nodded toward the building. "I'll offer my protection to you and your brother as well. Because it would be quite the tragedy if something happened to you. Or to your dear, *dear* brother. It would be a shame, for instance, if those men in there decide that you or Abel had something to do with the theft at the Flatiron Building."

"You sent them," she realized.

His mouth curved up. "Think of this as a warning. Tell your friends that there's no sense in trying to fight the inevitable. They can give over the sigils willingly, or next time I'll be sure to send someone more suited to finish the job."

"Go to hell," Cela spat.

She'd barely gotten the words out when she suddenly felt a sharpness in her chest as her breath rushed from her. She couldn't breathe. She couldn't do anything but feel the burning of her lungs. It was worse than simply holding her breath. It was like having the air and the life pressed out of her.

Her vision was already going dark around the edges, and her legs felt suddenly weak. She couldn't stop her legs from collapsing beneath her until she found herself kneeling on the ground in front of him. If she fell now, he could take the discs. She couldn't let that happen, but she also couldn't fight him.

"That," the boy said, as her chest burned, "was a mistake."

She was gasping for breath, but she still couldn't draw any air into her lungs. The world was spinning now, as she tried to stay up on her hands and knees, and then she collapsed completely. Above her, the sky was a bright, impossible blue. She blinked up, not understanding how things could have gotten so far out of her control so quickly.

The boy came and stood above her, a dark shadow blocking the beauty of the summer day. "First Darrigan and now these two. You really should pick your friends with more care, Cela Johnson. For your brother's sake, and your own."

A NEW IMPOSSIBLE

1983—The Bowery

As the subway train rounded the corner, the abandoned station platform slipped away, and along with it, Harte's final glimpse of the carnage it held. The new Guard, crumpled on the station platform. Nibsy, old and frail and unconscious.

And Esta's body. *Dead.*

The train continued onward, screaming and clattering as it swayed and shook down the track, but Harte felt like he was sleepwalking. The train's movement and noise were just another part of the nightmare. He didn't know how he managed it, but somehow he released the latch of the door and let himself into the empty train car.

Inside, lights were a glaring, unnatural bluish-white, and as the door slid closed behind him, the noise of the tracks was dampened, leaving him alone, not in silence, but in a muffled quiet that was no relief. Before, Seshat's earsplitting screams had overwhelmed him, and her wailing had drowned out nearly everything—the sounds of the city, Esta's words, his own thoughts. But now his mind was painfully quiet. After weeks of being possessed, occupied by a being that was not himself, Harte felt strangely empty. Or he would have, if he could have felt anything but the frantic clawing of grief.

He'd left her there. How could he have *left* her there?

His chest felt gripped in a vise, and his throat was closing up. He couldn't breathe, not deeply enough to keep his head from swirling. He felt as though he might never breathe again.

He couldn't stop remembering how Esta's eyes had gone white, lit from within by some unbelievable power. He couldn't stop seeing her cheeks stained with bloody tears. Her body, still and lifeless, on the platform. Her wide mouth gone slack and her whiskey-colored eyes dull and empty. He would never stop seeing her like that. As long as he drew breath, that image would be with him, stark and clear and *impossible*. He would *never* be able to forget.

He didn't want to forget. He would carry the memory with him, use it to fuel him and drive him onward.

The train squealed around another curve, nearly throwing Harte over. He couldn't go back, but he wasn't sure what to do next. He had no idea where the train was headed, but Harte knew where he had to go. *For Esta.*

A little while later, the train slowed into a station, and Harte prepared for . . . He had no idea what he was preparing for. An attack? More of the Guard? His hands reflexively tightened around the strap of the satchel that held the Book and the artifacts. Whatever happened next, he couldn't lose them. He *definitely* couldn't allow the Brotherhoods to get control of them. He couldn't let all that had happened have been for nothing.

When the train doors slid open, the noise of an alarm tore through the quiet of the empty car. A disembodied voice blared with a garbled warning to keep a watch for suspicious travelers.

They were searching for unregistered Mageus—for *him.*

He slouched in his seat, peering through a break in the graffiti that covered the window. On the platform, a pair of Guards had surrounded an old man. Another set of Guards stood nearby, blocking the station exit, their silver medallions glinting at their lapels. A group of three guys about his age stepped on board, seemingly unconcerned by the alarm or the Guards. They played at punching one another as their half-drunken laughter filled the silence of the car. When they looked in his direction, Harte turned toward the window, pulling up his collar to obscure his face.

It felt like an eternity before the doors slid shut again, but finally the train lurched onward. Harte kept his head turned away from the other passengers, but he couldn't relax. He had no idea what the next station would bring. Probably more of the Guard.

He couldn't just stay there, stuck on the train like a fish in a barrel. Easy pickings.

As the train sped down the track, Harte glanced back toward the rear of the car, where the new arrivals were standing, their bodies swaying as they held the overhead poles. Their voices were a low rumble, barely audible over the noise of the train, but a single look told him they weren't there for him. They weren't even looking in his direction.

When the train rattled to its next stop, the alarm once again split through the quiet of the car, but there weren't any Guards waiting on the platform. He considered leaving, but he had no idea where he was— or what might be waiting for him on the streets above. The signs were unreadable beneath the mess of graffiti, and he felt frozen with indecision. Once he got off the train, he knew what he needed to do next. But *next* seemed impossible when the memory of Esta's broken body was all he could think about.

The doors slid shut, and he was once again trapped. The train was moving again, but he still couldn't breathe. What if he'd made the wrong choice?

He didn't *want* to breathe. He didn't *deserve* to breathe. Not when he'd killed her. It hadn't been the ritual or Seshat or Nibsy. It had been *him*, the choice *he'd* made to use his affinity, to do what Nibsy had suggested. He'd forced her to give her affinity to the ritual and give magic what it demanded. He'd done it knowing that it would kill her, knowing that she wouldn't survive losing her magic.

Who could?

Maybe Nibsy had been right. Maybe people never changed. Harte had been a conman and a liar his entire life. He did what he did to save himself, knowing the cost.

Harte's skin turned hot at the thought. His head was throbbing as the blood in his veins churned and pounded in his ears. He felt himself break out in a cold sweat. *What if she didn't have to die?* His vision swam, started going dark around the edges as his stomach twisted, heaved.

When the doors opened, Harte lurched out of his seat, nearly falling as he scrambled to get off the train. He had to get out of the tomb-like car, had to get out of the oppressiveness of being underground.

Harte was barely on to the station platform when he heard a shout, and he knew he'd been seen. The guys who had boarded the train had suddenly turned their interest on him and were yelling after him. They'd already started to move toward the exit of the car, but they were too slow. The doors of the car closed on them before they could follow, and the train had started moving, taking the danger they posed along with it.

Even with the noise of the train receding into the distant tunnel, Harte didn't feel any relief. Leaning against one of the filthy, graffiti-covered pillars, he tried to keep himself upright under the burden of his guilt and regret. He had to keep moving, had to make whatever sins he'd committed worth it in the end. *For Esta.* He forced himself to take a breath and was rewarded with the fetid reek of urine and something unmistakably rotten. It turned his stomach. It reminded him of home.

There was a person huddled in the corner, wrapped so deeply in ragged blankets that Harte couldn't tell if they were alive. But he didn't have time to check on some stranger. He had to keep moving. If the other riders had suspected him, they would alert the authorities when they reached the next stop. The Guard would know where he'd disembarked. They'd come for him. But he couldn't be taken. Not yet. He had to keep going, had to make the sacrifice worth it. He forced himself to take one step and then the next. *For Esta.*

Everything he did from that moment forward would be for Esta.

HOLLOW

1902—Little Africa

B reath and air burst back into Viola's lungs as she came to consciousness in a rush of nausea and dread. Only one person she knew of
could attack like that—*Werner*. The coniglio. After what she had
done to get him to safety? *This* was his repayment? She never should have
let him go running off after the mess at the Flatiron Building. She should
have made sure he wasn't a liability.

Her cheek was pressed against the filth of the street, but she didn't
move. Not right away. Jianyu was lying next to her, and Cela just
beyond. Both were starting to stir, but Viola hesitated, sending out her
affinity instead. She found their two heartbeats, but not a third. Nibsy
was gone.

Her head still swirling, Viola pulled herself up, cursing herself silently
for letting down her guard. Cursing Nibsy as well for managing to get
the upper hand.

Jianyu was already on his feet, checking Cela for injuries.

"They're gone," Viola told him as she pulled herself up and brushed
herself off, trying not to think about the grime that had pressed against
her cheek. She turned on Jianyu, furious. "How could you be so stupid?
How could you lead him to us? You should have been more careful. You
should have—"

"I *was* careful," Jianyu said, frustration flashing in his expression. His
voice was sharper than Viola had ever heard it. "I would never put either
of you in danger."

"You didn't," Cela said. "He'd already sent the patrols. You didn't lead them here."

"What?" Viola turned to her.

"We had a nice conversation before he knocked me out. It's not just the sigils he wants. It's the two of you as well," Cela told them, her voice filled with unease. "He promised that he could protect me and my brother if you joined him again." She had wrapped her arms around herself as though she'd caught a chill, but there was an edge to her voice that Viola approved of.

"He can go to the devil," Viola snarled. "Nibsy Lorcan is a snake. You can't believe a single word that drops from his mouth." But even her bravado couldn't dispel her unease. She looked to Jianyu. "How could he find us?"

"He did not have to follow me, not when he can *track* us," Jianyu said. "Or, rather, he can track the sigils."

Viola didn't understand his meaning at first . . . and then, all at once, she did. "*Logan*," she said, spitting his name like a curse. She remembered what the boy had told her when they were trapped at the top of that building. "He can find objects infused with magic. Objects like the sigils." *And like my blade.* "But Nibsy, he didn't take the discs?"

Cela shook her head. "He could have. I don't know why he didn't."

"Knowing Nibsy, he has his reasons, and none of them portend well for us." Jianyu turned to Cela. "Can you understand now why I said you must take the sigils out of the city, beyond the Brink? Eventually, he will decide the time has come for him to take them from us. So long as the discs remain here, Nibsy will be able to find them. With Werner's help and control of the marks, he will be able to take them. There is nowhere in the city we can hide them, so you must take them out of his reach."

Viola saw then the reason for the wildness in his eyes, the cause for his desperation to get Cela to safety. He felt something for her. It was no less than she would do to protect the person she loved.

Suddenly, she could not stop herself from thinking of Ruby, who was far across the seas and living a life that Viola could hardly imagine. She could never be a part of that life, but at least Ruby was safe from Nibsy Lorcan and the Order.

"It's not enough," Viola said, her voice heavy with the truth of the matter. She was already reaching through the hidden slit in her skirt for Libitina. "The sigils are not the only objects that put us at risk. What of my knife? Your mirrors? If, as you say, Nibsy has the marks, we cannot allow him to find us so easily again. Libitina, she is a liability now. So are your mirrors." She turned and offered the blade to Cela. "You must take this as well. She will protect you, whenever you need protection."

"I don't want it," Cela said, stepping back, but she ran into Jianyu and couldn't retreat any farther. "He wants the two of you, and he's not going to stop just because I leave the city. I can't just run and leave you two behind to deal with the danger he poses."

"Then don't run," Viola said, offering her blade again, determined. "Help to protect us. Nibsy Lorcan already has the ring and control over the Devil's Own. He cannot be allowed to have any other power."

"The sigils must be kept from him," Jianyu agreed.

Viola took a step forward and gently placed Libitina in Cela's palm. "We trust you, Cela. Not to run, but to fight with us. By keeping them safe, you keep *us* safe. And many more as well."

Finally, Cela's fingers wrapped around the handle of the blade. "Fine," she said, her jaw tight. "I'll go. I'll take them outside the Brink and keep them away from Nibsy. But I'm not staying away forever. This is my city, *my* home. I won't be forced away. I'm going to come back," she vowed. "I'm going to return this to you."

How many times had Viola let her dagger sail through the air, willing it to hit some target or another? But this, *this* was terrifying. To simply hand it over? To watch it disappear into Cela's bag. It did not matter that Viola trusted Cela and Abel, nor that she knew this was the only real choice. Cela needed all the protection they could provide, but giving up Libitina meant she would have only herself, only her affinity, for protection.

"Certo," Viola said, trying not to show how much she wanted to grab her blade and take it back. "Even the Brink could not stop me if you tried to keep her from me." She pulled out the sigils and handed them over as well and watched as Jianyu gave her the bronze mirrors he kept always at his side.

Cela had barely managed to secure them in her bag when the door of the building burst open. Two of the patrolmen came bursting out. "There they are!" one shouted.

"Go," Viola said, turning to face the men.

"But Abel," Cela protested.

"Get her to the bridge," Viola told Jianyu, knowing that they'd been seen. Knowing, too, what that meant not only for Cela and Abel but for everyone in that building. "Va via! I will take care of this and make sure Abel is safe. Go!"

In a blink, Jianyu had taken Cela's hand and wrapped her in light, protecting them from the patrol's view. The men from the patrol were already running toward her and the place where Jianyu and Cela had just vanished from sight.

For so long, Viola had tried to avoid using her magic to kill. She had believed it was the worst sort of sin to use her gift to take life rather than save it, but the past few weeks had shown her how foolish she had been. Even with Libitina, she had been using her affinity all along, channeling her connection to blood through the intention of the blade. Dolph had given her the knife because he'd understood that she needed to have that measure of distance. Now she had come to accept that, affinity or blade, each death on her soul had been a choice she had made.

Once, she had cared for the state of her soul. She had wished for a different future. She had dreamed, perhaps, of being worthy of a different sort of life. But Ruby had wiped away that hope and replaced it with the understanding that the other life she'd imagined would never be.

She let her affinity fly free, and the first man fell. She relished the look of fear in his partner's eyes before she finished him as well.

When the area went silent, when the only sound was the constant hum of the ever-present city beyond, she waited for the regret that always came, the heaviness of remorse that so often weighed down her soul after she took a life. But this time, it did not arrive. In its place was a sort of empty ache, a hollowness that felt neither like salvation nor sin. It felt like the beginning of something she could not name.

Looking over her shoulder, Viola searched for some sign that Jianyu and Cela were still there. But nothing stirred. No one appeared.

Viola knew that she was completely alone in the strange silence of that back alley. She allowed herself a moment of grief to mourn the girl she had once wanted to be—the girl she never would become. Then she pulled herself together. There were still men in the building who hunted them, men who might be doing harm to Abel and Joshua. If it came to the choice between her and them, her soul was already too heavily marked for hesitation or regret.

OMFUG

1983—The Bowery

Harte's skin was still damp with sweat and his legs were unsteady as he carried his worry and regret up the trash-strewn steps of the subway exit into the cold, slush-covered night. When he reached the street above, he stopped short, overwhelmed by the changed city around him. Everything seemed brighter here. But then, beneath the changed facade, he was struck by how familiar it all felt. The low-slung buildings. The people milling about in groups on wide sidewalks. The way the city pulsed in the night. But above him, the sky was starless.

The sign on the corner read BLEECKER STREET. He *knew* that name.

Tucking his arms around himself against the bitter cold, Harte adjusted the strap of the satchel to secure it and started to walk. His shoes slipped on the ice-covered walk as he passed a group of people huddled against the cold, wreaths of smoke and breath circling them. In the distance, he heard the screaming of sirens. It was only a matter of time before someone started looking for him, and he didn't want to give himself away by looking back—or by looking guilty. As he traversed the short blocks of Bleecker, the sirens grew closer, so he picked up his pace.

He turned a corner, and then suddenly he knew where he was. Before him was the broad boulevard that was the Bowery.

The elevated trains were gone. Once, the tracks had shadowed the wide sidewalks, showering coal and ash on the people below. Now, when he looked up, all he could see was the heaviness of the sky. The street, once cobblestone and brick, was now a smooth stretch of dark ribbon marred only by the filthy, drifting snow and the occasional water-filled pothole. The lights lining the street were blindingly bright, turning the night into a false day. It reminded him of how the area around the Haymarket had once been in his own time. That part of the city had been called the Satan's Circus, and rightly so, but this version of the Bowery could likely wear that name just as well.

As he walked along, he saw men sleeping curled beneath old newspapers in freezing doorways. Many buildings in the area were caged or boarded, but the sidewalks weren't empty. Groups of people, young and old, milled about, ignoring the approaching sirens.

Everything had changed, but the city Harte had once known was still there. The names of shops and saloons were different now, but the buildings remained. The bones of the Bowery were the same, and he could almost see the ghost of his own time beneath the strange, new surface.

Still, the changes were disorienting, and he wasn't fooled into confidence by this glimpse of the past. The sirens were even louder now, and he understood it was only a matter of time before the Guard would arrive at the station he'd just exited and begin tracking him on foot. With the tracks he was leaving in the snow, he would be easy enough to find.

He couldn't keep running, and he couldn't chance leading them to the place he was headed. Instead, he needed to find somewhere to hide away until the danger passed and he could continue on.

Across the Bowery, there was a crowd of people gathered beneath a dirty white canopy emblazoned with a series of letters that didn't make sense as any kind of word. He couldn't tell what the place was, exactly—a saloon, maybe? The people seemed to be waiting for something at the entrance. Or perhaps they were just waiting. A perpetual cloud of smoke hung around them, and their laughter and voices carried through the cold night air.

The sirens were nearly there. In the distance came the barking of dogs and shouting, and Harte knew his time was up. The crowd under the awning would give him some cover at least, and if he could get inside . . .

He tried not to hurry across the street, because he didn't want to draw attention to himself. It took everything he had to keep his steps slow and measured, and the wide stretch of even road felt like an endless chasm between him and possible safety. Finally, he reached the building. Keeping his head down and his shoulders hunched, he inched behind a cluster of people waiting in line just as three vehicles emblazoned with the word "police" careened into the nearby intersection. One bore another symbol—Harte didn't need to see the details to recognize it as the Philosopher's Hand.

The same symbol had been proudly displayed on a banner back in Chicago at the Coliseum, where Jack nearly had become the vice presidential nominee. The Hand's appearance here had a chill running down Harte's neck that had nothing to do with the weather.

The sirens had finally drawn the crowd's attention, and the people in line around Harte started craning their necks, peering around one another to see what the commotion was about. Meanwhile, shards of red and blue light chased along the nearby storefronts, glinting off gated windows as uniformed men exited the vehicles. Two of the men were dressed in the boxy coats of the Guard, and their familiar silver medallions glinted in the brightness of the streetlights.

The pair of Guards said something to the others before heading toward the crowd. Harte slipped behind the person nearest to him and then began making his way to the door, using the distracted queue as cover. No one bothered to look at him. They were all too busy watching the action in the street to care that he was bypassing them in the line.

At the entrance, a bouncer sat on a stool, his head also turned toward the commotion in the streets. He was dressed in a dark leather duster and had his hands crossed over a barrel-shaped chest. Harte was nearly past when the guy put out his arm suddenly, blocking his way as he scowled.

"The cover's three." He held out his hand, waiting.

"Three?" Harte didn't know what the man was referring to.

"Dollars," the bouncer said, irritation growing in his expression.

Three dollars? It was an exorbitant sum. More than a day's wage for most working people. Harte couldn't imagine giving over that much money just to enter some sort of saloon. Not that the price mattered. Three dollars or three cents, he didn't have a penny to his name.

But he couldn't simply stand there waiting to be found.

With the Guards and their medallions so close, using his affinity would be dangerous, but he didn't have much choice. Not when the police and the Guards were already searching the groups of people in line on the sidewalk behind him.

Dipping his hand into his coat pocket, Harte pretended to retrieve the money, but instead of handing over the required entrance fee, he touched the guy's hand, sending a small charge of magic toward him. It was the second time in months that he'd used his affinity, and this time he couldn't ignore the thrill of satisfaction that went through him.

He had carried Seshat within his skin for so long. During that time, he hadn't used his affinity more than once or twice because he hadn't wanted to risk hurting anyone with the goddess's angry power. Now Harte realized just how much he'd been closed off from an essential part of himself. He'd always been ambivalent about his magic—at least since using it had been the cause of his mother's pain—but feeling the connection to the old magic again settled something in him. Perhaps his affinity was neither good nor bad. Perhaps it was simply a part of him, as intrinsic as his gray eyes or sharp chin. As essential as Esta was. He could no more deny his magic than he could deny his connection to her.

The bouncer blinked and dropped his hand, looking momentarily confused before waving Harte through. Without hesitating, Harte opened the scarred wood and glass door and plunged headfirst into the darkness and the noise of the saloon.

It was the volume that registered first. Before the filthy floors or graffiti-covered walls, before the smell of stale cigarettes and old liquor, a wall of sound overwhelmed him. The intensity of it, the *absoluteness* of the noise hit him with the force of something like magic. For a second he considered retreating and taking his chances with the police, but he quickly regained his footing and rejected that idea. He'd already used his affinity; the Guards' medallions would certainly have alerted them to his magic by now.

Lifting his hands to his ears, he pressed on through the crowd, who seemed unbothered by the sound, and headed deeper into the heart of the noise. The chaos inside the saloon—as unpleasant as it might be—was his best chance at evading the Guards. At least with the crowded tangle of bodies making it nearly impossible to press through, the police would have trouble finding him.

But the *racket*. He couldn't imagine *anyone* calling it music, but there seemed to be a stage. Performers. A sort of rhythm.

He pushed his way deeper into the crowd, careful to protect both the satchel he was wearing and himself as he was jostled and pummeled by the writhing, thrashing bodies around him. He tried to circle the edge of the room, heading toward the bar on the far side, but as he moved, he found himself caught in the crowd and pulled into the mass of bodies careening around him. There, in the center of the chaos, the noise was even louder. The rumbling of the rhythm thumped through his chest, rubbed up against the emptiness there, and pounded away at the aching grief. He felt utterly lost. All he could do was keep himself upright. Completely adrift in a turbulent, churning sea of bodies.

Harte thought of Esta suddenly. He wondered if she knew of this place or if she'd experienced anything like it before in her own time. Strangely, he imagined she would like it.

No. She would *love* it—the noise and anger and energy that filled the room, terrible and hypnotizing just the same. She would love the possibilities, the careless pockets ripe for picking and the anonymity of the throbbing crowd.

But thinking of Esta immediately brought up the stark memory of her body, crumpled and still on the station platform, and a wave of guilt and regret nearly brought him to his knees. *My fault. All my fault.*

The scream of the singer filled the room, tearing through the hollowness in his chest, echoing the grief there. Echoing, too, the rage. Overcome, he stopped trying to push through the crowd. Instead he gave himself over to it, allowed himself to be carried along by it.

The singer was screaming again, and it no longer mattered that he could not understand the words. He felt the truth in them. The ragged emotion in the voice spoke to him, and suddenly something within him broke and he found himself shouting back. He was screaming with the rest of them because, for some reason, he felt that he *had* to. There was no choice. He could let out the pain or be torn apart by regret.

Minutes or seconds or hours later, something shuddered through the crowd. A cold energy flooded the space, jolting him from the trance-like stupor he'd been in. His clothes were plastered to his skin by sweat beneath his light jacket, and his throat felt raw from screaming, but it took only a second to find the source of the disturbance. There, amid the still-writhing violence of the bodies on the dance floor, were members of the Guard.

Harte had known they would track him. He'd expected it. But he'd gotten so caught up in the crowd and whatever strange magic the music had spun to hold him in its grasp, he'd forgotten himself. He should have been gone already, but now he was trapped.

LIKE TO LIKE

1902—The Bowery

The Bella Strega was usually mostly empty in the afternoons, and that day was no different. When James returned from his errand over in Little Africa, there was only a handful of people curled around cups of Nitewein in the mostly silent bar. The new girl behind the bar, Anna, turned to the opening door and, when she saw who it was, gave him a welcoming smile.

"The usual?" she called.

He nodded before making his way to his regular table, moving slowly to keep his limp from being too obvious as he crossed the barroom. His leg was aching from his trek across the city and from standing on it for so long, but it wouldn't do to let the others know what a weakness it had become. Werner trailed behind like some kind of half-lost pup, but James could sense the hesitation in him. He'd been pliable enough since he'd returned empty-handed from the Flatiron Building with his tail between his legs, but he'd also been uneasy after James had dispensed with Mooch.

Even if Mooch's death hadn't stopped the Aether from rumbling, James did not doubt his decision. Mooch had been a problem for far too long. It was simply a lucky coincidence that the boy had made himself a convenient target for the necessary demonstration of James' power. Thanks to Mooch, no one would dare doubt his control over the Devil's Own now. And no one would dare move against him.

At least, no one who wore the mark.

Dropping into his usual chair, he tested the Aether as he waited for his drink. There was still something there, an indeterminacy that the day's activities had done nothing to calm. The vibration he felt, churning somewhere deep in the Aether, might have been a warning. Or it might have been the promise of more power. He couldn't quite tell. Not yet. And the diary was no help. It remained stubbornly unreadable since the gala. Useless as ever.

He needed something to change. He needed a victory of sorts to buoy him on.

The girl—Anna—approached the table with his usual glass of ale and gave him a flirtatious smile as she placed it on the table before him. When she retreated to the bar, she tossed a blushing glance over her shoulder in his direction. It was as direct an invitation as anything he'd ever seen.

As he drank, he watched Anna move behind the bar, more and more sure that his instincts had been correct. He'd hired her for a reason, and it wasn't just that she was easy to look at with her strawberry hair and milk-white skin. It also wasn't the fact that she'd accepted the position because she was clearly interested in him. After all, she wasn't the first who had tried to catch his eye with a coy smile since he'd taken over the Strega and the Devil's Own. She certainly wouldn't be the last. And he wasn't so desperate to fall for a seductive glance or an airy giggle.

Her willingness might have drawn his attention, but it hadn't been the most beguiling thing about her. The affinity that lived beneath her skin was far more interesting to James. From the first time he'd set eyes on her, he'd sensed the girl's connection to the old magic was a powerful one— and more, it was an affinity that could be of some use to him. He'd had enough of hobbling through the city on his injured leg. It was time to act.

He watched a bit longer, amused at how easily she entranced the men who leaned against the bar, hoping to catch her eye. They didn't see through her act: how she smiled sweetly at those who paid her attention and slipped her extra coins. She could blush on command when she wanted to, dipping her chin and preening when it suited her.

Yes, she was the one. It was time to test his theories about the Delphi's

Tear. What was the worst that might happen? Barmaids were easy enough to find. And James couldn't simply sit around waiting for Logan to return with news. Perhaps it would have been more efficient to simply take the sigils earlier, but the Aether had made it clear that it wasn't the best way forward. He needed Viola and Jianyu for what was coming. Of that, he was certain, even if he still could not completely see why.

He nodded to Werner, who jumped and came scurrying over. Again James noted that the boy was too nervous these days. If he got any jumpier, he might become a liability. Even if his affinity had its uses.

"Have Anna bring a growler of the new ale up to my rooms."

"Your rooms?" Werner looked surprised. "You want her to go to your rooms?"

James glared up at him. "Did I stutter?"

"No." Werner shook his head. "No, Nib—James. Sorry, it's just that I—"

"You *what?*" James asked, glancing up over the rim of his spectacles. He could almost imagine what Werner was thinking, comparing James to the poor, sainted Dolph Saunders, who never took a woman to his room, not even after Leena died.

But James wasn't Dolph, thank god. He was a hell of a lot smarter. And soon he'd be stronger, as well.

"Well?" he pressed. "Did you have something to say?"

Werner frowned as though he wanted to say more, but coward that he was, he kept his mouth shut. "No. I'll have her come right up."

"Give me five minutes," he said. "Then send her."

He didn't wait to see Werner's reaction. It took longer than he liked to climb the steps to the set of rooms above. He honestly didn't understand how Dolph could have stood it for so long, limping along through the city with such a weakness visible to anyone who might count themselves as an enemy. But then, Dolph Saunders hadn't had the benefit of the Delphi's Tear.

The ring was heavy on his finger, and its potent energy was a constant reminder of its potential. James had only to concentrate on his connection to the old magic and he could sense the answering power within the glasslike stone. But he couldn't *quite* join with that power, at least not as he'd hoped to.

Perhaps he should have known. The notebook from his future self had already told him that the stones worked best when they were aligned with affinities closest to the elements the stones were infused with. He could tap into some of the ring's power, but not all of it. Not truly. It hadn't given him any clearer view of the future, not like he'd hoped, but it would give him a more *certain* future . . . as long as Anna was as willing as he expected her to be.

By the time he reached his rooms, he was exhausted from the climb, hopefully for the last time. He had barely sunk into the worn cushions of the low couch when a knock came at the door.

"Come!" he called. "It's open."

Anna entered without any shyness at all. She was young, maybe a year older than himself, but the years without her family for protection had left their mark. Or perhaps that was simply the hunger she'd been born with to have more, to *be* more. It was a hunger he identified with and understood. It was one he could use.

"Where would you like this?" she asked, lifting the growler of ale she'd perched on her hip.

"In a glass," he told her, nodding toward the far corner of the room, where a cast-iron stove anchored the kitchen area. "Pour one for yourself as well and join me."

He didn't miss the flash of satisfaction in her eyes. *Blue. Like my sister Janie's.*

But he brushed away that thought and the sentimentality that came along with it. Janie was gone, along with his mother and father and everyone else. All he had now was himself and the future he could create.

"Oh, I shouldn't," Anna said, giving him a small smile that told him she knew already that she would.

"You definitely should," he encouraged. "Anna, isn't it?" Of course he knew it was.

She nodded, her bow-shaped mouth curving with the pleasure of being known, of being seen. It was almost too easy. She was almost too predictable. It would have been boring if he weren't so tired and in so much pain.

"Well . . . maybe just a wee nip," she said softly, pretending a sudden shyness he didn't buy for one instant. But the sound of her words brushed against memories. She was new enough, fresh enough, that she still sounded like the land of his childhood. His mother had said that—*a wee nip*. It was a reminder of all he'd lost. Of what he must become.

After she poured the ale, she took the seat he offered close to him on the couch without protest. The Aether trembled in response, and he knew that his plan would work.

They talked for a while, or rather she did. She chattered on about how grateful she was to have a place at the Strega, about her family and how they'd been taken by a bout of influenza the previous winter. As they drank one cup of ale after another, she prattled on, becoming bolder with each drink. When he placed his hand upon her knee, she didn't stop him. She only moved closer, practically onto his lap, but the pressure of her body made him wince.

"What is it?" She backed away, wide-eyed. "Oh, lord. It's your hip, isn't it? That injury—" Her hands came up over her mouth. "Oh, I *am* sorry. I shouldn't have—"

"It's fine," he told her. "It's not your fault that it hasn't healed properly. You know what happened, I'm sure . . . when Viola attacked me back in March on the bridge."

"I did hear a bit of something about that," she said. "But I can't imagine it. After all you've done, for her to attack you like that? And to leave you hurting so?" A combination of pity and hope flickered in her expression. "You know, James, after all you've done for me . . . maybe I can help?"

He feigned confusion. "What do you mean? Help how?"

Her mouth quirked. "I've done a fair bit of healing in my days," she said. "Perhaps I could have a go of it? Try to make things a little better for you?"

"You'd do that?" He blinked, waited for her to take the bait.

"Of course!" She moved closer, until her leg was pressed against his, and then rested her hand on his thigh. "You've given me a home, *safety* in a dangerous city. It's the very least I could do."

"I would be indebted to you," he said, and it even sounded as though he meant it.

"No! Never." She shook her head, but he knew it was a lie. It was what she wanted, to harness herself to his growing power. She wasn't even good at hiding it.

Too bad she'd never get what she desired most.

He waited a beat and then another before covering her hand with his and giving her a look that was pure sadness. "It wouldn't work anyway. The injury was made with Viola's knife—a bespelled blade. Natural magic alone wouldn't be enough. . . ." He glanced at her out of the corner of her eye. "But perhaps . . ."

"Yes?" Her voice was breathy as she inched closer yet.

"It's possible that you could focus your affinity through an object of ritual magic," he told her. "It would have to be powerful. . . ."

She took her other hand and ran a single finger over the surface of the ring he was wearing. "What about this?" Her eyes glinted, and he knew in an instant he'd been right.

It was a shame, really. She was so clearly drawn to power, so willing to do whatever it took. They might have been good together. At the very least, she might have been amusing for a while.

"The Delphi's Tear?" He lifted his brows.

She brushed her finger over it again, and this time she shuddered from the power radiating from it. "Maybe it would help?"

"It could be dangerous," he warned. "Channeling that much power. I'm not sure if you should . . ."

"I'd be willing to try. After all you've done for me." Her teeth scraped at her full lower lip, innocence and temptation all at once, but he didn't fall for it. And he certainly didn't have time to be interested. At least not until he was whole again.

He hesitated, only for a heartbeat. Only enough to make her think he was actually concerned for her safety. Then he took the ring, twisted it so it faced down, and grasped her hand so her palm was pressed to the ring between them. "Only if you're sure," he said.

She scooted closer until her whole body was pressed against him and squeezed his hand. Then she closed her eyes.

Almost immediately, energy crackled in the air, and James could feel Anna's affinity brush against the power in the ring. She was stronger than he'd realized. Her affinity swelled, and he felt an echoing call in his hip. He could feel himself knitting back together as the stone in the ring surged with heat. The gold suddenly felt like a brand against his skin.

Anna's eyes flew open. There was pain in her expression. And fear. She started to pull away, but James locked his hand around hers.

"Keep going," he commanded as he tightened his fingers, keeping her trapped with her skin pressed to the ring.

She was shaking her head, and there were tears streaming down her cheeks, but he only reached for the cane. A reminder of the promise she'd made a week ago when she'd allowed the intertwined serpents to be inked onto the skin just above her heart. Even now he could see the very edge of a tail curving up from the neckline of her dress.

"Finish it," he commanded, sensing the power in the silver gorgon's head surge against him.

He could feel everything—the knitting of bone and sinew and muscle healing, the pulsing power of the Delphi's Tear, and the fear coursing through the girl as she obeyed his command. Until the ache burned away to nothing. Until, spent, she slumped unconscious across his lap.

James could hardly breathe. The air was filled with the wild energy of their magic, with the power of the stone. It was only a knock at the door that sent him moving again. He pushed the girl to the side and stood, without pain. And without the aid of the cane.

But the Aether was still thrumming its indecipherable message. Healing his leg had been *an* answer, but it wasn't the one he was looking for.

Werner was waiting on the other side of the door. His eyes shifted to the room behind James, where the girl was lying on the couch. "Sorry," he said, blinking. "I didn't mean to interrupt. . . ."

"You didn't," he said honestly. "What is it?"

"Torrio just arrived," Werner told him. "Something about Eastman's guys roughing up some of the Five Pointers. He's waiting downstairs."

Perhaps that was the cause for the Aether's message.

James looked back over his shoulder and nodded toward the girl. He couldn't tell if she was breathing. He felt a pang of something like regret. She might have been amusing. But the ring was still warm on his finger, and his leg felt sure and steady beneath him, so he couldn't quite bring himself to care. "Take care of that, would you? I'll deal with Torrio myself."

FAMILIAR MAGIC

1983—The Bowery

With the music still pounding through the air and the bodies in the saloon still pulsing along with its rhythm, Harte quickly realized that the Guards weren't making much progress. They were trying to press through the crowded dance floor to search, but no one seemed to care about their authority. If anything, they reacted against their presence, and suddenly Harte felt magic hot and thick in the air. Familiar magic. *Old magic.* It felt like walking into the Strega, and he knew immediately that there were others like him there. The Guards' silver medallions were glowing, but the men who wore them didn't seem to know where to begin looking.

Without hesitating now, Harte touched the person in front of him, sending a small jolt of his affinity into them—just enough to move them aside. Again and again, he repeated the action, moving away from the police and toward—

He didn't know what he was moving toward. He only knew he had to get as far from the Guard as possible.

Before he could touch the next person, a hand grabbed his arm. Flinching away, he turned, ready to fight, but it wasn't a Guard. It was a girl. She barely came up to his chin, but the set of her shoulders and the spark in her eyes made her seem larger somehow. Her hair was a riot of spikes and fringy layers around her face, straw-blond streaked with an unnatural black, and a row of safety pins glinted up the side of her ear.

She jerked her head in the opposite direction from the way he'd been heading and started to lead him. But he pulled away.

Turning back, she glared at him. "They're here for *you*," she shouted, pointing to be clear what she meant over the volume of the music.

"How do you—"

"Just *look* at you," she shouted, glaring at him. "It's clear you don't belong. I don't know what your deal is, but you're going to put everyone in danger standing there like an idiot. Come on. There's a back way out."

Harte hesitated, but then he felt another wash of warm energy— cinnamon and vanilla cut through the reek of smoke.

"You can trust me," the girl said. "We're the same. I'm not letting those bastards win."

This time when she turned, he followed her through the bodies, away from the police searching, and toward a narrow hallway filled with groups of people—couples wrapped around each other and men with their heads together, turned away from the rest.

"Through there." She pointed down the gauntlet of bodies. A group of three men nearby turned to look at the two of them, their eyes like knives. But the girl narrowed her eyes at them, and they turned away.

From where he was standing, Harte couldn't see a door on the other end of the corridor. There were no signs of where the hallway led, but when he turned back to ask, the girl was gone. Behind him, the saloon was still pulsing with the same angry rhythm, and the Guards were still searching for him. Remembering the warmth and the cinnamon of the girl's magic, Harte plunged through the crowded hallway until he reached the end, where he found a door.

It could be a trap. He had no idea who the girl had been, and he'd had enough experience with Mageus who were more than willing to turn against their own kind for the right price to know that he couldn't trust her just because of their shared connection to the old magic. But there was no going back. He couldn't let the Book or the artifacts fall into the wrong hands, especially if Nibsy had told him the truth. If the stones were now unified, the Brotherhoods could use them to control Seshat, and through her, to control the power in the Book. There wasn't really a choice. He'd deal with whatever was on the other side of the door once he was through it.

For Esta.

The alley behind the bar wasn't empty, but to Harte's relief, there weren't any police, either. A few feet from the back door, a group of men laughed as they smoked. They barely noticed him as he walked past. Somewhere close by, sirens wailed their warning, urging him to keep moving.

The icy night air hit his cheeks like a slap, sharp and unexpected after the humid warmth of the saloon, but it was enough to remind him to be on guard. Without delaying any longer, he started walking, but he kept the hot anger of the noise and the crowd wrapped around him like a shield against the night.

Walking through the lower part of Manhattan was like walking through a dreamscape. Although the city he had once known was still there, enormous buildings now rose in the distance. The streets were devoid of horses and carriages, and the automobiles that occasionally passed weren't the slick fishlike sculptures he'd taken in with a kind of awed wonder in San Francisco. These vehicles were enormous, hulking beasts made of angles and shining silver. The city looked as though time had taken its claws to it, leaving it scraped and torn. Shattered. And more dangerous than it had once been.

Harte turned onto First Street and kept walking until he found Houston right where he expected it to be. He crossed the broad street, then cut southeast through the part of the city that had once been his home. East of Bowery, the landscape changed, and he discovered the neighborhood was now divided by a park that hadn't been there before. Where tenements had once tumbled atop one another, a wide stretch of snow-covered darkness now waited, broken only by the halos of an occasional lamp along the walkways. Even this late at night, there were people in the park. Some gathered in small clusters, while others slept on benches and alongside fences. They were likely harmless, but he decided on a longer route, taking Delancey Street instead of walking through the unknown park.

Finally, he turned south onto Orchard, and a few blocks later, he found the place he was looking for, the building where Esta had grown up. The bottom floors had once been a shop of some kind, but they were boarded up now. The tenements on either side looked empty. Their windows were covered with plywood and graffiti.

Actually, the whole building would have seemed abandoned to anyone not paying attention, Harte thought. But to someone looking carefully, the trappings of life were there, even with the windows dark and covered over. If there were answers to be found, they would be inside.

After considering his options, he went around the back. He wasn't expecting Nibsy to return anytime soon—if ever—but Harte wasn't sure who else might be inside. Esta had talked of a man named Dakari, of other team members and healers that Nibsy had used over the years. He'd have to be prepared for anything.

In a matter of seconds, he'd picked the lock and had the back entrance open. He waited, but nothing happened—no alarms sounded, and no one came running—so he stepped carefully across the threshold. Not even a second later, a cold blast of energy crashed over him, and a strange, dense fog began filling the space from the floor up. As it rose, he felt his affinity go dead. Cursing, Harte ran for the stairs, trying to get above the dangerous cloud.

Like most tenements, the building had a narrow, steep staircase running up through the back. The grime of the past had been washed away, and the worn wooden steps that should have been there were now sleek metal risers. The original gas lamps had been replaced with electric, but the lights were dark. He decided against turning them on. If the blast of cold was anything to go by, the entire building was likely set up like a trap.

When he reached the second-floor landing, Harte found that the space where a hallway should have been was now sealed over by a large steel plate. There wasn't a lock to pick or a doorknob to turn, but there was a cold energy radiating from it that indicated some kind of ritual magic at work. He would need to search that floor.

He continued upward to the next floor, searching. The third level had been converted to a series of living spaces. A large room at the front of the house contained couches and a larger version of the television set he'd enjoyed back in San Francisco. There was a comfortable bedchamber with thick velvet draperies and silk paper on the walls. Leather armchairs flanked the fireplace, and over the mantel hung a portrait of Nibsy, older than Harte had known him but younger than the man he'd met in the subway station.

There were two other bedchambers on that floor. One that had clearly been empty and unused for years and another that felt more recently used, but without any of the personality or luxury of Nibsy's own rooms. He made short work of searching the rooms, but there was nothing—and no one—there.

The fourth level had been left untouched and was clearly just storage. Nothing on that floor had changed in nearly a hundred years. The grime from oil lamps still crowned the ceiling and the walls were scraped and scarred from the families who had passed through them over the years. The individual apartments were filled with dusty boxes, but with the windows boarded up, it was too dark to see much more.

At the top of the building, Harte found another locked door. The dead bolt was surprisingly complex, but Harte managed to crack it after a few tries. When the door swung open, he found himself in an open space filled with shelf after shelf of books.

Nibsy's library.

He'd seen this room before, back when he still hadn't trusted Esta and had used his affinity to breach her defenses. Later, she'd told him more about the collection in that room, a collection she'd helped to gather for the man she'd called Professor Lachlan. She'd told him, too, about what the Professor had tried to do to her in that very room after Harte had sent her back to her own time, thinking she would be safer there.

All of Nibsy's secrets were in that library. The answers he needed were hidden there, and in the end, he'd find them all. But before he began searching, a large table in the center of the room covered with piles of newspapers and books caught his attention. Alongside the piles was a familiar glint of steel.

Harte took Viola's knife from the table and turned the stiletto blade over in his hand as he thought about the steel door on the second floor. He started to head back toward the stairs when he noticed the doors of an elevator on the far side of the room. There hadn't been elevator doors on the other floors he'd searched. Intrigued, he went to press the button to call the elevator, and a second later he heard the groaning growl of cables as the elevator approached. When the doors opened, he entered the cage carefully, ready for another trap. When nothing happened, he examined a row of numbered buttons. He pressed one, testing it, but realized it had been stabilized somehow. He pressed another, and it was the same. The only button that actually depressed was the one for the second floor. He depressed the "2," and the elevator shuddered as it began to descend.

When the doors opened, Harte found himself in a windowless vestibule lit by a flickering yellowish bulb. On one side was a row of four closed doors. Across from the doors, a long, broad desk faced a windowless wall. Black-and-white television screens had been stacked on the desk, four across and three high. He stepped closer to examine the pictures flickering on them and realized he was looking at the empty rooms of the building. There was the back entryway, still filled with the fog that had attacked the second he'd entered. The library. The interior of the empty elevator. The living quarters on the third floor.

Someone could have been watching him the entire time.

There was one other screen that depicted a room he had not yet found—a dark cell with a single cot illuminated by a thin beam of light.

Someone was huddled there. He couldn't tell from the flickering footage who the person was or whether they were breathing.

His hands felt damp and unsteady as he took hold of Viola's blade again and moved toward the first of the locked doors. Again, he felt the telltale brush of ritual magic. Cold emanated from the steel doorways. None had knobs or handles or locks, but Harte didn't need them. He didn't care who knew he'd been there.

Jamming the knife into the first one, he wrenched it open and found himself looking into an empty room. It wasn't the room on the screen, though. He tried the next and found a room of boxes. The next was a room that looked a little like the hospital in San Francisco. It held a narrow hospital bed with a bare, stained mattress and a metal stand draped with the same odd tubing that had been attached to his arm. It also wasn't the room on the screen.

There was one door left.

Glancing back at the screens, he saw the lump on the bed hadn't moved. He'd been making enough noise that it should've woken whoever that was. Unless they were already too far gone to move.

His hands shook as he placed the tip of the blade between the door and the jamb and wrenched the final door open.

The room was larger than it looked on the screen. Deeper. Darker, too. There was only a single source of light—a spotlight that illuminated the cot on the other side of the space. The figure lying there didn't move or stir at all.

Harte's breath felt tight in his chest as he took a step into the room. And then another. He waited, trying to listen for any sign of breathing or life.

The attack came from behind. Before he realized what was happening, something had been thrown over his head, blinding him, and arms like vises clamped around his neck. They squeezed. Tighter. Tighter still. He grabbed for his attacker, clawed at the strong arms that held him, but weak and unsteady after weeks of illness in California and days of not sleeping, Harte was barely able to stay on his feet, much less throw off his attacker. Before he could fight them off, his vision started to blur. He dropped the knife in a last attempt to pull away his attacker's arms.

Growling in rage, he tried to free himself. But he knew it was too late. He'd been caught by surprise. He'd failed Esta once again. It was the last thing Harte thought before everything went black.

PART

II

STEALING SECRETS

It had been nearly three months since Jianyu had sent Cela to safety outside the city, and he was no closer to discovering what Newton's Sigils could do or why Nibsy wanted them. Each day that passed felt like a wasted opportunity, and with each week, the situation in the city grew more tenuous. Over the summer, the Order had only grown more desperate to find their lost objects, and as their desperation grew, so too did their violence.

Perhaps it was good that Cela was outside the city, Jianyu thought. But it had been weeks since he and Viola had received word from her. Abel usually brought news, but with the demands of his job as a porter during the busy summer travel season, his trips into the city had become less frequent. Jianyu knew that Abel had people checking on her, watching over her, but she wouldn't be able to send word if she needed help.

And, even if she could, there would be no way for him to help if word ever came.

He tried to put thoughts of Cela out of his mind and focus on the task before him. Across the street, J. P. Morgan's Madison Avenue mansion loomed. Sweat slid down his back despite the hint of a chill in the late-September afternoon. After weeks of searching, he had narrowed his focus to Morgan himself. That day in the Flatiron Building, it had been Morgan who had immediately recognized the importance of the missing discs. Morgan had been the one to discover they were missing, and he had also been the one to name them—Newton's Sigils—and to explain that without them, the Order could lose control of the Brink.

If Jianyu had stayed a little longer, perhaps he would have already had the information he needed. But that night Jianyu had been too concerned about Cela and Abel, about whether Viola had reached them in time, to tarry for long. The details had not seemed important, not when his friends' lives were in danger.

Now that information had become essential.

It had been years since Jianyu had thought of himself as a thief. There might have been a danger in gathering the city's secrets, but he had always considered the work done for Dolph Saunders as something more than simple theft. After all, secrets could not be *stolen*, not truly. Not when they were given away by those careless enough to speak them aloud. What might be told in the ear of one man could travel for a hundred miles, and whose fault was it if he happened to catch a whisper on the wind?

Thievery, *true* thievery, was different, and Jianyu had enough experience with it in his youth to know the difference. The cracking of a lock, the lifting of an object precious to its owner—precious as well to someone who would pay. The heaviness of guilt and the breathless thrill of danger that came alongside the action. He knew these well. He had learned them young, and they had cost him everything.

The act of breaking into a local merchant's house back in Gwóng-dūng had been the event that had forced him to leave his homeland and come to this wretched country. Or rather, it had been the fact that he had been *caught* that had set his life on its current path. If not for that one fateful night, he likely would still be raiding homes along the Zyū Gōng.

In truth, he would likely have been long dead. Young thieves did not last long in his province.

Jianyu had been in Morgan's house before, at least three separate times, and he had come to understand the rhythm of the servants as they went about their tasks for the day. He was familiar with the wide hallways and towering ceilings, could navigate easily through the maze of rooms to Morgan's personal library. He was ready.

With the sun high overhead, wrapping his affinity around himself was as easy and natural as breathing, but he paused to make certain the light was secure, to be sure that no one could detect even a glimmer of his form. When a carriage pulled up in front of the house, he knew it was time. He crossed the street and mounted the front steps just as the enormous door opened and Morgan's wife stepped out. As she descended to the waiting carriage, he slid into the interior of the home.

The halls were empty, and so nothing stopped him from reaching Morgan's library quickly and without incident. Pausing long enough to be sure no one was near, he opened the door and slipped inside.

Immediately, he felt swallowed by the enormous, masculine space. This was no cozy room for contemplation. It was a room designed to impress, and he easily could imagine Morgan holding court behind the large mahogany desk, directing his empire from the comfort and luxury of the plush leather chair. Floor-to-ceiling shelves lined the walls, and the gilding on the spines of finely made books winked in the soft filtered light. The air smelled of wealth, of tobacco and wood polish, of amber and leather. Beneath his feet, the boldly colored Persian carpet was plush enough to swallow the sound of his steps, so he did not worry about being detected as he moved across the space, invisible as a ghost to any prying eyes.

The mansion was enormous, but Jianyu had decided to focus first on the library, Morgan's personal sanctuary. It seemed the likeliest place for the tycoon to keep his most important pieces—and his most important secrets. During his previous visits, he had made his way through two walls of shelves with no luck. He had opened book after book, but he had not yet found the answer to the question of the strange silver discs Viola had taken from the Order's new headquarters.

They needed those answers. Until they understood how to use Newton's Sigils, Cela had to remain outside the city.

Jianyu turned to the next section of shelving and, tilting his head from side to side to loosen the tightness in his neck and shoulders, he got to work. His fingers grazed the edges of the spines one by one, scanning the letters there. He searched for words that spoke of magic and science or told the tale of ancient lands and terrible power. The first shelf was Shakespeare. Dickens and Thackeray. Goethe and Dostoevsky. Literature and philosophy that Jianyu remembered from Dolph's collection. But not what he was looking for. In the next section over, however, a name shimmered from the spines that sent Jianyu's heart racing: Newton.

With light fingers, he tried to tip the first book toward him but found that it did not move. Not a book, he realized. An entire shelf that appeared to be volumes of Newton's work was actually a single, solid stretch of faux volumes, and with a bit of effort, he was able to fold the entire piece down. Behind it, he found a mechanism that could only be a strange type of combination lock. Its tumblers were cylindrical and inscribed with odd icons rather than the arabic numerals typical in the West.

Jianyu stepped back, considering the problem. There was no clear hinge on the hidden panel behind the false books. Whatever the lock kept safe was larger than the single shelf. Carefully he traced his fingertips along the edges of the section of shelving that he had been searching and realized that there was something more to the molding there than in other places in the library. Perhaps the lock protected a larger chamber, and the entire section of shelf would swing out? But then, this was not an exterior wall. It was more likely a compartment of some sort.

Carefully, he rotated the tumblers, but the images on their surface were nonsense. Hieroglyphs or some sort of cipher, he could not be sure. He could detect the faint rubbing of metal against stone when he moved them, but this was not the sort of thievery he had any experience with. He wished again that Esta or Darrigan had returned. He had no talent with locks.

He was still considering the problem, sure that the answers they needed must wait within, when he became aware of a noise. It came softly at first, barely audible through the thick walls of the mansion, but soon the rumble of male voices was on the other side of the door.

The door swung open suddenly, and J. P. Morgan entered the room, along with three other men. The same men who had been with him in the Mysterium that night—the High Princept and others from the Order's Inner Circle. Morgan stood in the doorway, ushering the men in, and before Jianyu could slip out, he pulled the door closed behind him, twisted the key in the lock, and pocketed it.

INTRUDERS

1983—Orchard Street

Esta still felt unsteady from whatever Professor Lachlan and the girl had drugged her with, but she was free. She couldn't believe her plan had worked. She hadn't really expected it to. Not when she was sure Professor Lachlan had been watching her every move. Not when the girl who was her exact image had somehow been an even better fighter than she had *ever* been. But she'd managed to outwit them in the end. The body beneath the bedsheet wasn't moving—at least for now—and the door to the cell was wide open.

Glancing up at the camera in the corner, Esta flipped off the red light that had been glowing at her like an all-seeing eye. She didn't care if it—if *they*—were still watching. The door was *open*. She was free.

On the floor at her feet, the person beneath the sheet started to move. It wouldn't take long before he was conscious again. She started to step over his body when she saw the knife that had fallen from his hand. Viola's knife. Frowning, she scooped it up. Professor Lachlan didn't deserve to keep it.

The figure on the floor was already pushing himself up, and she knew it was time to go. He'd be disoriented for a minute or two, but not long enough to waste time. She had just started to pull time slow when the man beneath the sheet moaned.

She stopped in her tracks. She knew the sound of that voice.

"Harte?" Esta turned and pulled the sheet from the body. There, trapped in her hold on time, was Harte.

She hadn't even considered that he'd come for her—how could he have known? If she had pressed a little differently, a little harder, she could have killed him. "Oh, god. *Harte.*"

In an instant Esta was on her knees next to him. She started to reach for him, to bring him into the net of her affinity, but then pulled back when she remembered they'd lost the Quellant and that Seshat was still a danger.

How is he here?

She released time, and with another wincing groan, he wobbled a little, rubbing at his eyes. He'd have a hell of a headache from what she'd done, but he was there. However he'd managed it, he'd come for her. He'd *found* her.

It was only a second, maybe two, before he blinked at her, but that time felt unbearably slow and sticky until his confusion cleared and he really looked at her. She saw as he recognized her—the flash of relief and some other deeper emotion in the depths of his stormy eyes.

"Esta?" He bolted upright then, his hands coming to frame her face. They were trembling a little, and his eyes were searching her face like he barely recognized her. "Tell me it's really you."

She pulled back on instinct from the frenzy in his voice and the wildness in his eyes, but he'd already grabbed her wrist. Without any thought of gentleness, he tore the bandage off. She gasped as the red, angry wounds burned in the open air. He seemed frozen as he stared down at the raw skin on her arm, and then his face split into a smile. He started *laughing.* He sounded like some kind of lunatic.

And then suddenly he wasn't laughing any longer. He was kissing her. His hands framed her face before she could stop him, but she realized that there was no sizzle of Seshat's power, no darkness threatening. He was kissing her, and she kissed him back. All that had happened fell away, and there was only Harte—his lips against hers, claiming her, as his strong fingers threaded through her hair. Pinned her to him.

Breathless, she pulled back. "How—"

"I *knew* it," he said, leaning his forehead against hers. His breathing was still heavy. His hands were still trembling, but then, so was she. "I knew it couldn't be—I didn't want it to be you."

"The girl," she said, understanding what must have happened. She'd hardly been able to believe it when she'd turned in the stairwell and found the other version of herself—the one that should have been an eighty-year-old woman. But the girl hadn't been old. She'd been like looking into a mirror. "He used her to get to you, didn't he?"

Harte nodded, closing his eyes.

She tried to pull back. "Is it safe? Seshat—"

"She's gone," he told her, not allowing her to retreat from him. "Locked back into the Book."

"The girl did the ritual?" The girl—the one who had looked so much like her, the one who had once *been* her in another time line, another reality.

Harte pulled back from her, and his stormy eyes were filled with pain so stark, so *clear*, it took her breath away.

"It killed her," Esta realized. "The ritual killed her."

He nodded. "I couldn't save her. And then I left her there." Closing his eyes, he pressed his forehead against hers. "I didn't mean—" His voice broke, and she felt him shudder.

The ritual killed her. That other girl. That other version of who Esta might have become. Dead. Gone.

She didn't understand how she could still be there, alive and whole, when the injuries on her arm proved that she and the girl shared a connection. Unless it was because the past remained malleable. It was still possible to save the girl—to save herself—by going back and giving her the stone. By putting history on a different path.

Esta had been so confident, so willing to take on the responsibility of removing Seshat from Harte's skin. She'd been ready to make the sacrifice—more than willing—but she knew now that it had only been because, secretly, she'd hoped there was a way to survive it. Now that it was over, now that she was still here and the truth of the ritual's consequences were irrefutable, Esta realized she'd been wrong. She hadn't been anywhere near ready to make the sacrifice that had been required. And she was damn grateful to be there, alive and with Harte.

Esta took Harte's face gently in her hands, her heart aching for him. She'd never forget finding him in that hellish hole in San Francisco, a hair's breadth from death, so she understood what he must be feeling. She knew what it was like to almost lose him. Even if he'd hoped it wasn't actually her who had returned to him in the subway station, he couldn't have known for sure. Not really. She and the girl were identical. Nibsy had made certain of it.

He'd been so damn proud of what he'd done. Because he'd had the ring, a change from her original time line, Nibsy had been able to augment the power of the healers he used. He'd been able to slow the girl's aging because he had known that Esta would come for him eventually. He'd ensured it by keeping that scrap from the Book, and he'd been ready.

And so had the girl, that other version of herself. It had been like fighting a better, tougher, and more prepared version of herself—and Esta had lost in the end.

Could Nibsy know so much? Predict *so much*?

"It wasn't me," Esta said, trying to push away her fear along with Harte's. Softly, she brushed Harte's hair from where it had fallen over his forehead. "I'm here. We're both here. We're both *alive*. You did what you had to do, and now we have a chance, Harte. Now that Seshat's no longer a threat to you, we have a *real* chance."

"I know. I keep telling myself that, but I just watched you die, Esta." His expression was bleak, empty. He let out another shuddering breath, as though expelling all the grief he was carrying. "I watched you die, and I *left* you there."

"You didn't leave me, Harte." She leaned forward and kissed him softly. "That wasn't me. I'm still here. You *came* for me."

"Knowing that doesn't seem to matter. I'm not going to be able to forget . . ." He looked at her, his expression fathomless and filled with grief. "The ritual didn't kill her, Esta. *I* did."

"No, Harte—"

"She'd trapped us in a circle of power—a ritual like the one Seshat did," he explained. "And then Nibsy came. The only way out of that circle was for her to finish the ritual by giving her affinity to the stones. But she couldn't do it on her own, not after what it had done to her already . . ."

"You used your magic," she said, understanding what had happened.

"We were trapped there, in that ritual circle, and the Guard was coming. If they'd found us . . . If they'd pulled us across that boundary . . ." He shook his head.

"The Guard?" Esta frowned. "The Jefferson Guard?" That couldn't be right. She'd killed Jack. She'd taken care of Thoth.

Harte nodded. "The power of the ritual must have drawn them into the station," he explained. "He told me it was the only way, but what if it wasn't? She looked so much like you."

From the vestibule outside the cell, a buzzing alarm blared, startling them both.

"Something's happening," Esta said, filing away all that Harte had just told her. She pulled herself to her feet and offered Harte a hand.

Scanning the monitors of the control room, they found the issue— men had entered through the back door. More through the front. Harte had been right. "Those aren't police," she said, noticing the familiar cut of the uniform and the glint of metal at their lapels. "The Guard is here."

The squad of Guardsmen was already climbing the back staircase. In the flickering black-and-white of the screens, the staircase light seemed filtered, like they were walking through a fog. There was a trio outside the door to the second floor—close to where they were currently standing—trying to figure out how to open it, while their comrades continued upward.

"I left Nibsy on the platform too," Harte told her. "It was only a matter of time before they traced him to this place."

Esta watched as a Guard took a small pen-like device from his coat and shot a beam of light toward the space between the door and the jamb. A few seconds later she heard an echoing noise coming from the room beyond that made it clear they were trying to cut through the door.

"You're sure the ritual took care of Seshat?" she asked Harte.

He nodded. "She's back in the Book. I felt her there, through you—through the girl. When I used my affinity to command her, I knew what she'd done to Seshat."

Esta wasn't sure what that meant, exactly, but there would be plenty of time for explanations later, once they were safe. First they had to get out of that building and away from the danger they were currently in.

She took his hand and pulled her affinity around her, silencing the buzzing alarm and the faint hissing from whatever the Guards were doing to the door. The screens stopped flickering, leaving the intruders all frozen in their tracks, caught in her net of time. Still, she didn't move. Not immediately. She waited for the telltale brush of Seshat's energy, the sizzling power that threatened to pull her under. And only after a stretch of seconds, only when she didn't feel Seshat's power, did she breathe again.

"She's really gone," Esta whispered, still only barely believing it.

Harte's mouth went tight. "Not gone but contained."

"I'll take it." Contained was fine. Contained she could work with. Especially since she hadn't been the one to die in the ritual. They still had a chance. As long as they got through the next few minutes.

"My cuff," she said. "Tell me you have it?"

Harte lifted his sleeve and slid it from his forearm.

"You have the rest?" She frowned as she took it and slid the silver cuff over her arm, felt the rightness of the stone's energy against her skin.

He patted the satchel. "They're all here. The Book, too."

But he'd kept her cuff, the artifact that meant the most to her, closer. He'd worn it on his own arm, against his own skin.

She leaned in and kissed him, quickly. Fiercely. Because she understood. And since they weren't dead yet, because she could.

INCONSEQUENTIAL

1902—East Thirty-Sixth Street and Madison Avenue

Jianyu pressed himself into the corner of the room to avoid detection as Morgan took his place behind the enormous desk, opened a box of inlaid wood, and offered cigars to the others as they took their seats.

"Has there been any news at all?" Morgan clipped the end from his cigar and lit the tip. He took a couple of deep puffs, then offered the heavy brass lighter to the older man across from him, a man Jianyu recognized as the High Princept.

"There have been some . . . developments," the old man said, examining the end of his cigar before lighting it.

"What developments?" Morgan asked, the cigar still clenched between his teeth. "Why is this the first I'm hearing of it?"

The other two men exchanged glances, but the High Princept ignored Morgan's outburst as he finished lighting his cigar. He took his time savoring the first few drags on the tobacco before finally licking his thin, papery lips and focusing on Morgan. "We felt it was unnecessary to involve your family any further."

"My family . . ." Morgan's eyes widened slightly.

The Princept took another puff and then settled back into the cushioning of the leather chair, as though this were his room, his meeting.

"You aren't actually considering freezing me out because of my stupid upstart moron of a nephew?" Morgan asked, clearly incredulous. "He's not even a Morgan. He's my wife's problem."

"He became your problem as well when we allowed him membership at your suggestion," one of the other men said. "He's been nothing but a menace ever since."

"I've taken care of that. Jack won't be a menace to anyone out in Cleveland," Morgan said, his temper clearly rising.

"Maybe you did your duty by sending him away, but Barclay's right," the Princept told him. "Because of Jack, we lost Khafre Hall. Because of the fiasco at the Fuller Building, the alliance we were building with Tammany is all but destroyed. We had the Delphi's Tear, and now it's gone. Newton's Sigils are gone as well."

"There's no evidence that was Jack's doing," Morgan said. "Barclay's grandson was named as well."

"Theodore was already on a ship bound for the Continent," the other man—Barclay—said. "And unlike you, I've made sure that he won't cause any problems in the future. How much more do we need to lose?"

Jianyu studied the man closer, startled to recognize the lines of Theo's profile in the older man's face. But where Theo was all affable kindness, the elder Barclay was stone and flint. He had no doubt that anyone who pressed the man was sure to catch his spark.

The nostrils of Morgan's large, bulbous nose flared. He was growing more frustrated by the second, but so far he was smart enough not to lose control of himself, or of the situation.

"This is preposterous," Morgan said, stabbing his cigar into a crystal bowl. "You wouldn't have even realized Newton's Sigils were missing if I hadn't noticed. You clearly didn't understand their importance, or they would have been locked into the Mysterium as they should have been."

"Locking them away would have done little good, considering that the Delphi's Tear managed to escape from that chamber." The Princept leveled a cold glare at Morgan. "Your dear nephew wasn't so lucky. Strange that he was even there."

"I'm not going to sit here and defend Jack," Morgan said. "He's a constant embarrassment to me and to the entire family. But if he had the ring, we would have found it."

"Perhaps," the Princept said.

Morgan stood. "What *exactly* are you implying?"

"We're not implying anything," the last man, who had so far been silent, said. "But it does seem strange that you are so focused on finding the sigils and not on the Delphi's Tear, as the rest of us have been."

"I've been focused on Newton's Sigils because none of you fools seem to realize how important they are to the Order's control over the city."

"So you've told us," the Princept drawled.

By now Morgan's face had turned an alarming shade of red. He stalked over to the bookshelf that Jianyu had just vacated and slammed open the secret compartment. Then, from a chain within his chest, he withdrew a small cylindrical piece of gold. Placing it in the center of the series of icons, he twisted, and the tumblers moved with a soft clicking sound, arranging themselves. With a *click*, they landed on their final combination, and the *snick* of a latch echoed through the waiting room. The other men all leaned forward, clearly curious to see what was about to happen.

From within the safe, Morgan drew out a thick leather envelope. He returned to his place behind his desk and opened the package, riffling through the contents until he drew out a piece of parchment and slipped it across the desk, facing the men.

The room was submersed in silence as the three men pored over the fragile scrap. Jianyu inched forward, trying to get a look at the document without being detected. The parchment was covered with a narrow, pinched script, but there were also diagrams—and the sigils were clear in the faded ink of the sketches.

"What is this?" the Princept demanded. "Where did you get it?"

"I came across it in a bundle of papers I purchased a few years ago," Morgan said.

"And you didn't think it was important to share this with the Inner Circle?" Barclay asked.

"Not particularly," Morgan told them. "As far as I knew at the time, the sigils were being used in the Mysterium to control the Ars Arcana's power. I never expected that anyone would be able to break into that chamber, much less take the Book of Mysteries. Moreover, I never dreamed that the Inner Circle was unaware of what they were capable of. You were using them. I assumed you understood."

"Of course we understood," the Princept huffed. "They old Mysterium used the sigils to protect the Book's power. But with the Ars Arcana missing . . ." There was an uneasiness in his tone now.

"Clearly you understand very little," Morgan told them. "These manuscripts show what our Founders knew and what the rest of you have forgotten. The sigils weren't only to protect the Book's power; they were protection *from* the Book's power." He poked a manicured finger at the diagram. "The Founders used them in the early days to keep the Book's magic under control. They can create a barrier of sorts to neutralize magic. Not unlike the Brink, but more its inverse."

"They form a key," Barclay murmured as he studied the document. "In the wrong hands . . . Maggots could use these to get through the Brink."

"Yes. In the wrong hands, Newton's Sigils could make the Brink inconsequential," Morgan said. "*That* is why I've been so interested in finding them. *That* is why I've personally funded the search for the sigils. Should the wrong person get ahold of them, they would control access in and out of the city. With it, they could undercut our power—with or without the artifacts."

Jianyu leaned closer, but he still could not make out what was written on the document.

"Newton devised the sigils when he discovered how powerful the Book was," Morgan explained, lifting the parchment from the desktop as he spoke and making it clear that it belonged to him. "He was terrified of what the Book could do, and so he gave the Founders of the Order a tool to contain its power."

"If this is true, we would have *known*," the Princept blustered.

"You *should* have known," Morgan sneered. "This history is no secret

to the oldest families in the Order. Those of us whose forefathers established this city and this Order and whose families have been here since
the beginning remember that there was a time when the Brink was not
a weapon but a mistake. The Founders did not realize the danger in the
power it contained until it was far too late. It was only through our
fathers' and grandfathers' dedication to the occult sciences that the Order
was able to use these sigils and transform the Brink into their greatest
strength.

"But in recent years, the Inner Circle has become complacent with
whom they offer membership to, and newer members, like yourself,
never bothered to learn our true history. You thought membership in our
hallowed organization would finally wash away the taint of new money
that clings to you like manure." Morgan huffed. "You may have managed
to claim leadership, but you never really understood the history of our
esteemed Order. You never bothered to learn of the struggles that forged
us, and so you cannot understand our true greatness. If you had, you
never would have allowed Newton's Sigils to go unguarded."

The High Princept had visibly stiffened under the onslaught of
Morgan's words. The old man's face had gone a mottled red, and it was
clear his temper was about to snap, but before he could open his mouth
to speak, a knock sounded at the door. The men froze, their protests
and anger silenced, as Morgan set the parchment on the desk again and
moved to answer the door.

"What is it?" Morgan barely opened the door, but the maid's voice
carried clearly enough.

"Sir." One of the staff was at the door. "You and your friends need to
get outside immediately. There's a fire started in the coal cellar and—"

"A fire?" the Princept asked. He was on his feet already, and Barclay
quickly followed.

Jianyu looked at the sheet of parchment sitting on the desk, the leather
folder filled with other secrets as well, and he waited. Too soon and he
might be caught. Too late and the chance would slip away.

"Yes, sir," the maid said, still not entering the room. "In the coal cellar."

"We should go, Morgan." Barclay stepped forward.

"My people will take care of the fire," Morgan growled. "This house is built like a fort. We're not in any real danger."

"I'm not waiting to find out," Barclay said, already pushing past Morgan.

Morgan tried to block his way. "You can't leave yet. You haven't told me what you've heard. You said there was news."

"The news can wait, John. I'm not going to leave my wife a widow because you're too thick-skulled to take the appropriate precautions," Barclay said, pushing past. The other man and the Princept started to follow.

Jianyu saw his opportunity, and without further hesitation, he scooped up the parchment, and the leather envelope as well, tucking them beneath his tunic and obscuring them with the light, just before Morgan turned back to the room and saw the now-empty desk.

Morgan lurched for the desk, giving Jianyu just enough room to slip past him and out the door, dodging around the retreating men of the Inner Circle and harried servants as he went. Behind him, he could hear Morgan cursing.

He slipped out of the mansion with a group of servants, hidden from their sight by the power of his affinity. There was smoke in the air, but there was something else as well—the telltale warmth of magic sizzled through the heat of the summer night. It brushed against Jianyu's neck, lifting the short hair there in warning. He did not have to wait long to figure out where it was coming from. Across the street, Nibsy Lorcan waited, concealed by the crowd of people who had gathered to watch dark smoke pour from Morgan's coal cellar.

Alarms clanged in the distance, growing ever closer, as Jianyu turned away. But he had not taken more than two steps when he felt ice creeping along the ink on his back. His steps froze as the pain intensified and his panic grew.

When he turned, Nibsy was watching him—or, rather, he was watching the spot where Jianyu was standing since Jianyu had not yet released the light. Tentatively, he took a step toward Nibsy, and the ice in his chest eased just a little.

So this is his game. He took another step, and then another, slowly moving toward the crowd of people where Nibsy waited. With each step he took, the icy warning in his skin eased a little. When he was nearly an arm's reach away, Nibsy spoke.

"We need to talk." Nibsy kept his eyes on the column of dark smoke coming from the mansion. He did not bother to look over at the spot where Jianyu stood. Why should he? Jianyu knew he could sense him through the marks. "Come," he said, turning away, back into the crowd.

He hesitated, but as soon as Nibsy began walking away, Jianyu felt the mark etched into his skin surge with a cold energy that turned his blood to ice and his knees weak with fear. Wordlessly he followed. Because he did not have a choice.

LISA MAXWELL

NO ONE IS SAFE

1983—Orchard Street

When Esta finally drew back from Harte, the warmth of his mouth remained imprinted upon her lips. With the seconds hanging in the net of time and the world silent around them, she paused to catch her breath, to marvel that he was there at all. While she'd been plotting her escape, he'd come for her. Somehow, Harte had known the other Esta wasn't her. Even after he'd watched her die, he'd come to Professor Lachlan's building—to find her. To save her.

Esta Filosik had never been the type to want or need saving, but now, looking into Harte's stormy gray eyes, she wasn't about to complain.

"As nice as that was . . . ," Harte started.

"Nice?" she asked, pretending to be insulted. "You think that was *nice*?"

His eyes softened. "There aren't words for what that was," he said, lifting her hand to his lips and placing a kiss on the center of her palm.

She felt her cheeks go warm. She felt *everything* go warm.

"But we should get going." He lowered their joined hands. "If my experience getting in here is anything to go by, we should expect anything trying to get out."

Together, they moved to the bank of now-frozen monitors, looking for the best path of escape. It was clear that the Guardsmen had already fanned out through the building. Knowing where the Guards were would help in avoiding them, but Esta wasn't ready to leave. Not yet.

"We need to go back up to the library," she told Harte.

"Esta, no." He shook his head. "We have to get out of the building. Now. While we still can."

"Harte, every secret Nibsy ever wanted to hide is up there," she said.

His brows drew together. "We'll come back."

"What if the Guard takes everything before we can? We don't have to go back blind," she said, remembering how fat the file in the safe was. And there was Nibsy's diary as well. "It's more than just knowing what happened in the past, Harte. Nibsy knew how to complete the ritual to neutralize Seshat, didn't he? He wouldn't have bothered if he didn't also know how to use the Book's power. He's been studying and planning for nearly a century, and the information upstairs is our best chance for understanding how to fix everything without making any more mistakes," she told him. "The answers we need are up there. But we're not the only ones who could use that information." She tapped at the image on the screen, the men mounting the staircase. "We have to get his notebooks and files, and we have to get them now. Before they do."

He wanted to argue. Esta could see it there in the sharp lines of his face, the set determination of his expression.

"You know I'm right about this," she told him.

"We have the Book and the artifacts, and thanks to what the girl did, Seshat's trapped within its pages," he argued. "She's not a danger anymore."

"She's not the only danger," Esta told him.

He frowned. "What are you talking about?"

She hadn't had time to tell him—not with all that had happened. Or maybe she'd been avoiding it. "It isn't over, Harte."

"Seshat isn't a threat anymore, Esta."

"But the Book is," she told him. "As long as there's a piece of pure magic in that Book, someone could use it. As long as it remains apart from the whole of magic and vulnerable to time, everything is at risk. Whoever controls it could control time itself. It isn't enough to put Seshat back into the Book. We have to fix the ritual Seshat began."

"We don't—"

"We *do*," she argued. "Until it's done, no one is safe. The world isn't safe. We need to return the piece of magic to the whole. *I* need to, Harte."

"It isn't your job," he said, looking panicked. "You can't save the world. You shouldn't have to."

"Seshat thought I could. And if I can—*because* I can—I *do* have to," she countered. "And what about the Brink? What about the city? We could fix the Brink and free the Mageus trapped here. I could free *you*. Those answers are up there. I *know* they are."

Harte was silent at first, but finally he gave in. "Fine," he said, not sounding like he meant it. "But quickly. And if *anything* else happens, we leave. No arguments."

"But—"

"I've lost you once today, Esta," he told her, his voice breaking around the words. "Don't ask me to do it again."

Her heart clenched. "You're not going to lose me, Harte—"

"I can't," he said. His eyes were determined. "I *won't*. Promise me. If I say we leave, we leave. No questions. No arguments."

She bristled at the command in his tone, but there were too many shadows flickering in the depths of his eyes for her to be truly angry.

"At the first sign of trouble, we're gone," she told him. "I swear."

He didn't look convinced, but his shoulders relaxed a little. "So what's the plan?"

She considered their options. "The elevator," she told him, realizing it wasn't included in any of the images on the monitor screens. "I'll have to let go of time to use it—"

"No—"

"We'll be at risk until it opens," she said, ignoring his protest. "But they haven't entered the library yet. As long as we can get to the top floor before they get through the door, they'll never see us."

He studied the glowing screens. "This is a terrible idea."

"There's no other door, Harte." She pointed to the end of the room, where the doorway had been sealed off by something more than a simple steel plate. "There's only one way in and out of this floor—through the elevator. We might as well go to the library."

His jaw was set, and he still looked unconvinced, but he allowed her to pull him toward the elevator doors.

"Ready?" she asked, hoping that they weren't making a mistake.

He didn't look ready at all. "There has to be a better way."

"There isn't. Not as far as I can see." She gave his hand a sure squeeze.

Not bothering to wait for Harte's next argument, Esta took one more breath before she let go of her affinity and allowed the seconds to spool out. Immediately, the buzzing alarm was back, and so was the sizzling noise from the doorway. Without wasting any time, she pushed the call button. They waited, their hands still clasped tightly together—ready for anything—as they listened to the groaning climb of the lift. The noise of it echoed through the building, louder than it had ever been in her child-hood, and she knew the Guardsmen could likely hear it too.

The elevator came to a lumbering stop, and as the doors began to open, she pulled Harte back at the last second. Just before one of the Guard rushed out.

Without hesitating, she pulled at her affinity, cursing as she slammed the seconds to a stop. But the Guard had already seen them. "Shit. Shit. *Shit.*"

The door was open, and the man was caught mid-lunge. Behind him were two others. Harte pulled her back, putting himself between them.

Almost too frustrated to be annoyed with Harte's protectiveness, Esta stepped to his side and considered the situation. She'd hoped to get out of the building without being seen, but it was too late to worry about that now.

"I'm going to have to touch them. To get them out of there," she explained. "They'll see us. Unless you can make it so they don't remember?"

He shook his head, his frustration palpable. "The entrance was booby-trapped. More of that fog. I still can't reach my affinity."

"Okay then." There was nothing they could do about the Guard seeing them. They just had to keep moving. Determined, she nodded, but she knew she was trying to convince herself as much as him. "We can do this." When it looked like he was about to argue—again—she cut him off. "It's the only way out, Harte." Then she stopped the rest of his arguments by grabbing the arm of the Guard closest to them and yanking the man into the room.

The Guard barely had time to register what was happening—and to see them both—before he stumbled forward and froze once again, caught back in the net of time she'd spun around them.

"I'm going to need your help on the next two," she told him.

This time, thankfully, he didn't bother to argue with her. Together, they managed to get the other two men out of the elevator. With each dazed, shocked look, she knew they were backing themselves into a corner. The Brotherhoods—or whoever was now in control of the Guard— would know they'd been there. They'd never stop hunting them.

But that was a worry for later. First they needed to get out of the building, preferably with all of Nibsy's secrets.

Once the elevator was empty, the two of them stepped inside, and Esta released her hold on the seconds. She pushed violently at the button for the top floor, even as the rattled men were pulling themselves to their feet and starting toward the closing door. The door slid shut just before the men reached it, but Esta couldn't feel any relief. They had no idea what might be waiting for them in the library.

Holding tight to Harte's hand, they watched the dial move as the elevator inched upward. They passed the third floor and then the fourth, and she knew with each second that the Guard back in the control room could have already alerted the others. Even now, they could be waiting in the library for them to arrive.

But when they reached the top floor and the door slid open, the library was empty. Without waiting, Esta reached for her magic and pulled time still. The buzzing alarm ceased, and the world fell silent again.

"The door," Harte said, pulling her toward the staircase door that was standing open. But even once the door was secured, even with time pulled close around her, she didn't feel any relief. Not in that room. The lack of Guards wasn't enough. She wouldn't feel any relief until they were out of the building, until she could walk away and never have to look back.

"The papers will be in the safe," she told him, shaking off her apprehension as she pulled him toward the painting on the other side of the room.

When they removed the picture of Newton, she saw that the safe had been repaired from where she'd mangled it earlier with Viola's dagger. Not surprising. She wouldn't have expected anything less of Professor Lachlan. This library was his citadel, and the safe had always been its inner sanctum.

Once more, she pressed Viola's dagger into the seam around the edge of the safe, and the magic-infused blade again sank into the metal. She was nearly through when she heard something from the other side of the library's door.

"That's impossible," she whispered, turning to look over her shoulder. There shouldn't have been *any* noise as long as she held the seconds in her grip.

But a sizzling hiss, like the sound of the Guards trying to cut through the door on the floor below, was coming from the far side of the room.

"Thoth," Harte whispered, and when she turned to him, his expression didn't contain the confusion she felt. It held only fear.

"He's gone," she told him. "I destroyed him in Chicago, when I killed Jack."

"You didn't," Harte said, his expression bleak. He didn't bother to explain. Instead, he took the knife from her and, wrenching it, pried the safe open. He grabbed everything inside. "We have to go."

"Wait, Harte—" The hissing had turned into a pounding now. "What are you talking about?"

"Later." He tugged her toward the elevator.

"We don't even know if we got everything," she said, looking back toward the mess of papers and books scattered around the room. "We have to make sure—"

"You promised, Esta," he said, turning on her. He nodded toward the pounding on the other side of the door. "That is the definition of trouble."

He was right. The stack of ledgers and folders in his arms would have to be enough.

They weren't quite into the elevator when the door fell forward, completely severed from its lock and hinges. Even before she could let go of time, before they could close the elevator and try to escape, two Guards lurched into the room. Their eyes were completely black, and Esta knew for certain that Harte hadn't been wrong.

Thoth wasn't gone.

As the Guard advanced, they spoke in unison. "The Book," they said, Thoth's voice echoing from their lips. "Give me the Book, girl. Or you will both die."

But she'd had enough death for one day—hell, for an entire lifetime. And Esta had no intention of giving *anyone* the Book. Instead, she focused on the seconds, searching for what she needed, and when she found an empty space, she pulled them both through.

The world lurched, and time pressed at her, threatening to tear Harte from her grasp, but Esta held tight, until suddenly, night turned to day and the blaring alarm faded to silence. They were alone in the closed elevator now, with no Guard and no threat of Thoth. Ishtar's Key was warm against her skin, and Harte's hand was still squeezing hers tightly. But he was leaning against the slick metal wall of the lift.

"You okay?" she asked as he let out a small groan. "You aren't going to be sick?"

He shook his head. "I don't think so." But he didn't sound sure. He looked pale and unsteady on his feet.

They needed some air and time to catch their breath and consider what their next step should be. Slipping through time had always been miserable for Logan. Clearly, it was bad for Harte as well. Especially considering what he'd been through in the previous weeks.

She pushed the button for the library, and when the doors slid open, she pulled him into the room. She didn't notice the figure sitting behind the broad desk until it was already too late.

Suddenly, icy fog blasted through them from all sides. Before Esta could grab for her magic, before she could even finish the thought that *the elevator was a trap*, her affinity slid away from her. Dead and cold and empty.

THE CHURCHYARD

As he walked away from the Morgan mansion, James smiled to himself at the fear that he'd seen in Jianyu's eyes. After the girl whose affinity healed him, he had not been able to practice much with the ring and with what he could do to the connections between the marks. He couldn't show such a display around the Devil's Own. Not yet, at least. He wasn't ready to draw their suspicion, or worse, invoke unnecessary fear, because he knew that his control over Dolph's people was still tenuous and in its earliest stages. The wrong move could tip the balance against him. Until he knew for sure what power the Delphi's Tear could truly afford him, until he'd *mastered* that power, he didn't want anyone to suspect what he might be capable of. Jianyu's compliance was an excellent sign, perhaps even a promise of the possibilities to come.

Since the last time they'd talked, Jianyu and Viola had been busy. They'd saved more of his castoffs from the Order's patrols, and they'd been searching for answers. For a while, he'd let them have their small victories, but now he was finished waiting.

With a simple tilt of his head, James signaled that Jianyu should come with him, and then he turned south, toward the Bowery, certain Jianyu would follow.

Neither of them spoke as they walked, not even when Jianyu finally released the light and appeared next to him. In stony, uneasy silence, they traversed the city in tandem as the sun sank lower on the horizon.

It was nearly dusk by the time they reached the church, and neither had uttered a single word. Jianyu remained silent as James opened the graveyard gate and let himself into the churchyard and walked among the weathered monuments until he came to a stop over the small, flat stone that held Leena Rahal's name. He felt Jianyu's frustration—his fear and his impatience—but though the Aether vibrated with that same unreadable tension, there was no other indication of any immediate danger. So James simply waited.

It took him longer to break than James expected, but eventually Jianyu showed himself to be the weaker of the two.

"I assume there is something you want? Some reason you led me on this chase?" Jianyu asked, his voice low and surprisingly unconcerned.

James didn't bother to turn or guard himself, because he knew Jianyu wouldn't strike. *Couldn't strike.* The Devil's Own belonged to him now, and Jianyu and Viola both understood *exactly* how quickly the Devil's Own would turn on them should he come to any harm. In the eyes of those who had once followed and trusted Dolph Saunders, it was Jianyu and Viola who were the traitors. And the remaining members of the gang would be more than happy to make either of them pay.

And if anyone else at the Strega suspected who the real architect of Dolph's demise was? It barely signified. He'd already made it abundantly clear what would happen to anyone who crossed him. Jianyu understood the danger as well.

James tossed a careless glance over his shoulder. "I wanted to pay my respects to an old friend."

"You were no friend to Leena." He took one menacing step toward James.

At the same time, James gripped the gorgon's head and sent a warning pulse through its connection to Jianyu's marks. The cane itself was no more than an affectation now, but he carried it with him anyway. It still had its uses, after all.

Jianyu stopped, his back arching against the place where Dolph's mark lay beneath his clothing, and James held the pulse of energy a second longer before releasing it and Jianyu both.

"I hope you've given serious thought to my offer," James said. "You're running out of time. Soon you'll need my protection."

"I seem to have done well enough on my own these past weeks," Jianyu told him.

"Have you?" James mused. "You can't still really believe you've been able to avoid my notice, not when I found you so easily today."

Jianyu's jaw clenched, but he didn't refute the claim.

"You didn't truly think you were so good at hiding, did you?" James asked, amused despite himself. *How could he have not known?* "This city isn't so big, really. I could have come for you at any time. I could have sent any number of factions after you had I wanted you out of my way. You and Viola have been safe because *I* willed it. It was a gift. And now you'll repay me for my generosity."

Jianyu's eyes were as sharp as any blade Viola had ever wielded. "I would rather die."

Tightening his hold on the Medusa's head, James focused on the Aether, on his connection to it, *through* it. He watched as Jianyu grimaced and went rigid again, fighting against the pain that he'd sent thrumming through the mark. "That can be arranged."

James took a step forward, indifferent to Jianyu's pain. Interested only in what he carried. "I want what you took from Morgan's house."

"What makes you think I took anything?" Jianyu gasped.

"I know you did," James told him. "Thanks to the distraction I helped to provide."

"You—" Jianyu's brows furrowed. "The fire."

"Of course," James said. "You didn't realize I'd been following you, but I had the sense that today could be important for you. For *us.*"

"Never for *us,*" Jianyu promised, but his words were empty when he could barely remain on his feet.

James tightened his grip on the cane, and Jianyu crumpled to the ground.

A few seconds later, he started to struggle up. The fury in his eyes made it clear he wanted a fight, so James depressed a small lever to release the hidden blade in the tip of the cane. Jianyu froze at the sound, clearly remembering the poisoned blade hidden there, and he remained still as James used it to slice open his tunic, revealing the leather envelope tucked within.

"I'll be taking this," he said, scooping up the package while Jianyu writhed in pain.

The Aether trembled, but the strange hum did not stop.

"They'll come for you," he assured Jianyu. "The Order is already searching for you, but without my protection, the rest will come as well. And when they do, you'll return to me. You'll beg for my protection."

Jianyu's expression was tinged with such fury, such glorious hatred . . . it was almost amusing.

"Oh, I know you'd never come to me to save yourself," James assured him. "You're far too noble and self-sacrificing for that. But you'd beg for those you care for. Those you've promised to protect."

He loosened his grip on the cane and released the connection he'd been holding through it. With a shuddering gasp, Jianyu pulled himself up onto his hands and knees. Then, slowly, he got to his feet.

"You don't want me as your enemy, Jianyu," James said softly, but the threat in his words was clear. "It would be *much* better for everyone involved if you counted me as a friend."

"I will never count you as a friend," Jianyu vowed.

James could practically *taste* his anger, his barely leashed temper. *Delicious.* Jianyu losing hold of his careful control would be more than entertaining. It would be perfect.

"You wound me," he said with a mocking smile. "Never is such a long time, you know. Just like being dead." Then he let his expression go cold. "I'll have the sigils one way or the other. Better to hand them over while you still can."

"You will never get them," Jianyu promised. "They are in a place where you cannot reach them. And they will remain there, far outside your grasp."

"Are they?" Nibsy asked, allowing his lip to curl as he clutched the Medusa's silver-coiled head. The ring's energy urged him on, but he held back. It wasn't time. Not yet. "Tell me, Jianyu . . . is Cela Johnson enjoying her time as a chambermaid in Atlantic City?"

Jianyu's face drained of color. His hands clenched into fists at his sides, but he seemed frozen. Unable to decide whether to attack or flee.

James didn't bother to hide his amusement now as he took another step further. "Did you really think I couldn't reach her simply because she was beyond the Brink? Did you forget that Kelly's men are mine now?" He gave Jianyu a pat on the cheek too sharp to be playful, and when Jianyu flinched, James couldn't help but laugh. "I'll be sure to have Razor Riley give Cela your regards."

"We are finished here," Jianyu said, nostrils flaring. He turned on his heels and slipped into the night.

"No," James said, more to himself than to Jianyu. "We're only just beginning."

TICK-TOCK

1983—Orchard Street

Esta lunged for the elevator buttons, even as she felt her magic hollowing out. But the lift was as dead as her affinity. No matter how violently she pressed, the elevator didn't respond.

"You're not going to be leaving that way." The old man's voice was soft and calm, and Esta knew he was speaking the truth. Somehow, he had known to be there in the library waiting for them.

Harte's hand tightened around hers, and when she looked over at him, they didn't have to speak to understand each other. The cold blast had affected both of them, and with the elevator dead, there was no choice. They'd have to go through the library and down the steps to escape, which meant they'd have to play the old man's game. At least until their affinities returned. She gave Harte a sure nod. They'd face this head-on.

Together, they stepped out of the elevator. Professor Lachlan was there at the other end of the large room, sitting beneath the portrait of Newton and the Book, behind the large table he'd always used as a desk. He had a pistol—the same gun he'd used to kill Dakari—sitting within reach on the tabletop.

"I wondered when you'd show up again," the old man said. "After you disappeared on the Guard a few days ago, I knew I only had to wait. But I suspected you wouldn't risk going too far ahead, because I taught you better than that. It looks like I was right. As usual."

Esta bristled at the presumptive ownership in his tone. "*You* didn't teach me anything." That had been a different version of Professor

Lachlan, one who had been every bit as duplicitous. But the old man sitting before them had lived a different life in a far different world.

I don't know this man, she thought. *Not really.* Though she did know what he was capable of. She'd seen that other version of herself, frozen unnaturally in time, and she understood exactly what he was willing to do in order to win.

But the man sitting at the far end of the library looked different. She hadn't taken them that far forward, but the slumped, wizened creature behind the large, scarred table looked nothing like the man who'd managed to get the best of her. Something had happened to him in the hours since he'd surprised her with the other version of herself and left her locked in the prison cell of a room. One thing was clear—physically at least, he was no longer a threat. She doubted he could even stand. But then, who needed to stand when they had a weapon that could do the job from a distance?

"How the hell did you get out of there?" Harte asked. "I left you for dead."

"Yes," the Professor said, his expression the portrait of mock sadness. "Isn't it terrible that an unregistered Mageus attacked one of the preeminent experts on the occult arts? Even without my affinity, I knew exactly where you would go. How else do you think the Guard found you so quickly?"

"I should've killed you when I had the chance," Harte growled.

"There's a part of me that wishes you had," Nibsy said. "Until you showed up just now, I would have welcomed death."

"Don't worry," Harte told him. "I can rectify that mistake." He started forward, but Esta held him steady. Even in the old man's current state, he could reach the gun before Harte could reach the desk.

Professor Lachlan coughed out something that might have been a laugh. "You always were a smart girl, in whichever life you led." He leaned forward a little. "Not ever as smart as you believed you were. But you did well enough for my purposes."

"I'm not doing anything for your purposes," she told him.

His pale, dry lips twitched at that. "As I said, you're not *nearly* as smart as you think you are. I'm not finished with you yet, girl."

"That's where you're wrong," Esta said. It was a bluff. With the gun in the Professor's reach and her magic cold and dead from whatever had just happened in the elevator, they didn't have the upper hand. But she pulled confidence around herself anyway, the last bit of magic she had left. "We're leaving, and you're not going to do a thing to stop us."

Esta gave Harte another small, sure nod and then turned away from the Professor. Hand in hand, they walked toward the staircase, and neither of them looked back.

"You would leave the answers you need and simply walk away?" the old man asked when they were halfway to the door. There was amusement in his tone, even though his voice sounded like the crackling of leaves.

She froze, hating herself for pausing.

"You have no idea how to use the power in the Book, do you?" the old man asked. "The beating heart of magic . . . Do you have any idea what it's even *capable* of?"

"Esta," Harte murmured, tugging gently on her hand. "He's not going to help us. You can't trust anything he says."

"I got you out of that ritual circle, didn't I?" Nibsy said. "I could have just as easily left you to die."

"Only because you needed the ritual to end so you could get the Book. There was nothing noble about you helping me. You killed that girl," Harte said, anger lashing in his words.

"No," the old man murmured. "*You* did that. I simply handed you the weapon. You're the one who chose to pull the trigger. You chose your life and your freedom over hers." He nodded to Esta.

"I knew it wasn't really Esta," Harte said.

"Did you?" Nibsy murmured, amusement glinting behind the thick lenses of his spectacles. "But you're wrong. It *was* Esta. Just not the version you're used to. That girl was simply another possibility of what could be."

"Then why let her die?" Esta asked. "You groomed her, kept her ageless over *decades*, and for what? She would have been far more willing to help you than I'll ever be."

"She served her purpose," the old man said. "She was an anomaly. An impossibility, and yet she still fulfilled her fate. With her sacrifice, the stones have been unified. Now they can be used to control the goddess and unlock the power in the Book."

"Not by you," Esta said. "You don't have the Book or the artifacts."

"But I will, when you take them back." The old man did smile then. "You see, *this* version of the time line was never my destiny." He turned to focus his cloudy eyes on Esta. "Just as dying in that ritual circle was not supposed to be yours. The girl doesn't matter—not her life, not her death—not so long as you return as you must."

"Or her life will become mine," Esta realized. "Her time line will become the only possibility."

"And the effects on history you created—the chaos and evil you unleashed—will become permanent." Professor Lachlan nodded. He adjusted himself in his seat to reach for a stack of papers, grimacing at the movement. "Your duplicity turned into a gift," he said. "Had you taken the Book directly back to my younger self, I would not have realized the possibilities the Book holds for time itself. Because of you, because you tried to betray me, I had another lifetime to learn. I had another lifetime to prepare."

"It won't matter," Esta promised.

"Oh, but it will," he told her. "Didn't I teach you that time was like a book and history merely the words on the pages? Tear out one page. Write over another. I believed the essence beneath would remain the same." He shrugged. "When you slipped away from Logan, when you saved the Magician from his fate and broke through the Brink, you created another story, a time line written overtop the first. But you didn't change the *essence* of the thing. You never changed time itself. But *I* will.

"The original time line is still there. Like a palimpsest. The life I was meant to have is waiting beneath the surface of *this* lifetime, beneath time and memory. So is yours. It's why you have to return, why you have to send Ishtar's Key forward with the other girl. Your very existence depends upon it. But you know this already. You have the Book and the goddess within it. You have the stones. And when you return to your past, as you must, you'll deliver me my victory."

"We won't deliver you anything," Esta promised.

The old man's expression didn't so much as flicker. "Tell yourself whatever stories you must, but the truth is this—you *will* return to the past. You've already decided, or you wouldn't still be here. Time would have already taken you. You will go back because you know that returning is the only way to save your friends, and now it's also the only way to erase the chaos *you* unleashed on the world. You will return, and when you do, I'll be waiting. You'll bring me everything I need to change time and magic and the world itself."

"We're done here," Esta said, trying to ignore the creeping dread that had started to sink its hooked fingers into her. He wasn't wrong about her returning to the past, but they would never let Nibsy win.

"We're not even close to done." The old man lifted the pistol, pulled back the hammer.

Without hesitating, she turned and placed herself between the old man and Harte.

"Esta, no," Harte said, trying to push her aside.

But she wouldn't budge. Harte was expendable, but she knew the Professor needed her. "He's not going to shoot at me," she said. "He needs me alive."

"She's right," the old man said. He hadn't yet aimed the gun.

"Put the gun down," she demanded, keeping herself in front of Harte. "I'm done with your games, old man."

"No," the Professor said. "You'll play a little longer. I'll even give you a fighting chance—it'll make things that much more interesting. You have a world to save, don't you?" He looked up from the dark body of the pistol. "I have the answers you need to save it. Think of what you could do if you knew how to unlock the secrets of the Book. You could fix the Brink. Free the city. Complete the ritual that the goddess started."

Harte cursed. "He's not going to give you anything real. He's never going to help us."

Esta knew that. But she felt rooted to the spot, like she was under some kind of spell. Because what if this old man *wasn't* lying? True, Nibsy would never help them. He would never willingly hand them the key to his defeat. But if he needed her to take this knowledge back? Games upon games. Those papers might be nothing, or they might hold the answers she needed. Without her affinity, though, she couldn't reach them.

"Come on, Esta," Harte urged, tugging at her gently.

"Tick-tock, girl." The old man lifted the gun. "Your time is running out."

She didn't think or hesitate. Esta simply moved on instinct, shoving Harte down and covering him with her body as the crack of the gunshot rang out.

There was only one. A single shot. And then silence.

Harte was already pushing her aside, checking her for injuries, but the silence in the room was more deafening than the shot itself.

"I'm fine," she told him, taking his face in her hands. Meeting his eyes until he knew it was true.

His gaze shifted behind her, and the color drained from his face. But she didn't need to turn to know what she'd see. Professor Lachlan slumped over a blood-splattered desk, the gun still resting in his lifeless hand.

ONE OF OUR OWN

1902—Atlantic City

Cela Johnson hated scrubbing floors. She hated the acrid smell of the cheap soap powder and the way the water and grime made her fingers prune and crack. She hated spending the day on her hands and knees when she was born to rise. She hated it almost as much as she hated hiding.

Once, her talent with a needle and thread had kept her from the housekeeping that most Negro women were forced into just to survive. Instead, she'd worked her way into the costume shop of a white theater, where the hours were good and the pay was even better. With her skills, she should have been able to find a position with any modiste in New Jersey, but that would be the first place anyone would come looking for her. People knew who she was, which meant she couldn't use her skills now to make her living, not without the possibility of someone taking notice. Her only real choice had been a position as a maid in one of the enormous new Atlantic City hotels that drew crowds away from the heat and stink of the sweltering Manhattan streets. She hated the work, but it paid for her room in a clean and safe boardinghouse, and at least with all the people who came through, she could keep her ears open for any news from the city.

And if the middle-class tourists acted as though she wasn't even good enough to breathe the same air as them? At least they tipped well. Sometimes. After nearly three months of work, she'd been able to save enough that, with what Abel earned as a porter, they would be able to start rebuilding their parents' home come fall.

If I'm back in the city by then.

Pushing aside that thought, Cela lifted herself from the damp and soapy floor. She would be back in the city by then, one way or another. It was her home, wasn't it? And she trusted Jianyu and Viola to figure out what the Order's discs could do, didn't she?

But it had been longer than she'd expected already. *Eighty-seven days.* It couldn't possibly be much longer. At some point, she was going to be done waiting.

She wiped her raw hands on her apron before taking up the bucket of filthy water and starting toward the back hallway, the tucked-away corridor where the hotel staff kept the whole place running. Her shift was nearly over, and she wanted nothing more than to take off the constricting uniform, unpin her hair, and have a nice long soak in a cool bath. Abel's train would be coming in later, and when he arrived, maybe they could grab dinner. It would be nice not to be so alone.

Turning the corner, she twisted just in time to avoid two young boys nearly careening into her and the bucket of dirty water. The water inside sloshed over, splattering on the clean floor, and with a sigh, she bent down to wipe it up before anyone could slip.

"Watch where you're going, girl," the father snapped as he passed. His wife simply lifted her nose, which looked like an overripe tomato from the sun, and gave a disdainful sniff.

Cela didn't say a word, but she ducked her head and kept her eyes focused on the floor until they were gone. She couldn't hide her loathing, and it wouldn't do anyone any good to let them see it. She wished—and not for the first time—that Viola were there. Over the past few weeks, she'd found herself missing the prickly Italian, and for more reason than her ability to stop a heartbeat from ten paces.

She didn't let herself think too much about Jianyu—not about his quiet strength or the way he managed to lead without trying at all. She certainly didn't think about what it meant that he'd come running down the street to find them after the mess of the Flatiron Building. It was easier to believe that she'd imagined the way he'd looked at her, as though she were something rare and precious, especially because he hadn't made any move in the months since then. His notes were terse and impersonal, without any indication that deeper feeling ran through his words. So maybe she'd only seen what she'd wanted to. It was easier not to think about it at all.

She was too busy imagining what Viola could do to the bratty little boys and their awful parents to notice the men who didn't belong when she first stepped into the chambermaids' workroom. But the sound of the flat, guttural New York accents broke through her daydreaming, and she pulled up short just before she could be seen.

"You sure you haven't seen her around?" the man was asking. He and his partner were talking to a trio of maids, their backs turned to the door that Cela had just entered. "She might be going by a different name."

"A Negro girl who can sew?" Flora said, giving the men a doubtful look. "That description could match a dozen of the girls who work here."

"This one's on the darker side," the other man said, turning to examine the other women, as though sizing them up by the color of their skin.

Cela pulled back, ducking into one of the alcoves where the mops and brushes were usually stored, but not before she recognized one of the men. She'd seen him before—at the Morgans' gala and in the saloon she almost hadn't escaped from the night of the Manhattan Solstice. Razor Riley. A Five Pointer. And he was there in Atlantic City. Looking for *her*.

She didn't know whether to be relieved that she didn't have Newton's Sigils on her or worried about how safe they were hidden in the floorboard of the boardinghouse's fruit cellar.

He isn't magic, she reminded herself. He might be close, but he couldn't track her or the discs, not like Logan Sullivan could. And anyway, she had been waiting for something like this to happen for weeks now. She'd known all along it was only a matter of time before someone came looking for her.

From across the room, Hazel caught her eye and lifted a single, arched brow. Cela realized then it had been a mistake to keep to herself so much over the last couple of months. She shouldn't have been so standoffish.

The chambermaids were a group of women she should've fallen in with easily. She could have had friends, support. But at first she'd been convinced that Jianyu and Viola would call her back to the city in a matter of days. And then later, when she realized it was going to take longer than she'd expected, Cela hadn't wanted to put anyone else in danger. Now her fate was in Hazel's hands.

"There's a reward," the other man said. "Our employer would be most generous to anyone who might be able to help us locate her."

"Why'd you say you needed to talk to her?" Hazel asked.

"For a business opportunity," Razor said easily. "Our boss's wife needs some new dresses, and this woman can sew them better than most."

Cela couldn't do anything more than shake her head at Hazel, silently pleading for the other woman not to give her away.

Hazel considered the situation before she finally spoke. "There isn't a woman worth her salt that don't know how to sew, mister," Hazel told him. "If your boss needs someone to stitch up a gown for his wife, I'm sure I could manage."

"I could too," another of the women said. "Or my sister's even better. You should see how delicate her stitching is."

The other women spoke up, one at a time and then all at once, clamoring about their own prowess with a needle until Razor and his partner, realizing they wouldn't get any help from that lot, turned without a word, clearly disgusted, and left.

Cela pulled back into the alcove, ducking away to avoid their notice. She didn't breathe again until she heard the door close behind them.

"You can come out now," Hazel called, her voice tinted with the soft cadence of the South.

Slowly, Cela emerged from the shadows of the cubby. The women were all waiting, expectant.

"Thank you," she said softly.

None of them spoke at first, but Hazel held Cela's stare. She was a little taller than Cela, with skin that some would have called "high yella" and hair that didn't so much as curl out of place around her heart-shaped face.

"I appreciate you not saying anything," Cela told them, suddenly uncomfortable. She'd been stupid not to make friends with these women. "I know I haven't been overly friendly—"

"No," Cecily said, placing her hands on ample hips. "You haven't."

"There isn't a one of us who doesn't have something we're trying to leave behind," Hazel said, cutting Cecily a sharp look. "Doesn't matter who you are or why they were asking for you. Those peckerwoods weren't getting a thing from us anyway. But you could have known that already if you hadn't been keeping to yourself so much."

"I'm sorry," Cela said. "I'm just—I'm grateful, that's all. Those men . . ." What could she possibly say about Razor Riley that wouldn't give away too much? That wouldn't put these women in danger?

"Those men are nothing but common trash from the city," Cecily said dismissively. "We see their type around here all the time. Acting like big-timers because they can afford a night at the Brighton. Maybe they mean something up in Manhattan, but down here?" She waved her hand.

"We gotta stick up for our own," Hazel added. "Don't we?"

Cela's throat felt too thick for words. Eighty-seven days she'd been alone, except for the brief stops Abel made in New Jersey. Eighty-seven days without anyone else to share her life—her joy or her worry. Pressing her lips together to ward off the threat of tears, she nodded.

"You off now?" Hazel asked, her expression softening a little.

Cela nodded again. "Just about."

"Some of us girls go over to Chicken Bone Beach on Friday nights," she said, making the invitation clear.

"I—" It was on her tongue to say no. She had to send word to Jianyu and Viola that the Five Pointers were getting close. But it had been an exhausting day of backbreaking work. It was late September, but the thick summer heat was still hanging around, and the idea of a dip in the cool ocean sounded better than a cramped bath in the shared boarding-house tub. Besides, these women were right. She'd been wrong to hold herself back. There was a sort of safety here in their community. A sort of acceptance and welcome, too. She'd forgotten that somehow. "I'd love to come out for a while. Thank you."

"No thanks needed," Hazel said. Her mouth curled into a wry grin. "But you might could get Chef to make up a little something from what's left of the lunch service for the rest of us to share. You know he's sweet on you."

Cela felt her cheeks heat. She hadn't been unaware of the way one of the sous chefs watched her when she was near the kitchen. He was handsome, to be sure. Tall with a sharp jaw and skin the color of deep mahogany, he spoke with an accent that hinted of islands and reminded her of her mother's people. Considering her situation, she hadn't let herself imagine there could be anything between them. But now that these women had reminded her she still had a life to live while she waited for the future to unfold, she couldn't help but wonder . . .

"I think I can manage that," she said, unable to tuck back her smile.

Abel's train wouldn't be in until close to nine, she told herself as she changed out of the soiled uniform and back into her regular clothes. Abel was in contact with Joshua, who was keeping track of Jianyu's and Viola's whereabouts in the city, so it's not like she could do anything much until he arrived. She had plenty of time to venture to the beach for a quick swim and maybe even to flirt with the handsome chef. And if she happened to make some allies while she was there? So much the better.

The kitchens were in the basement at the rear of the hotel, far from where the guests could hear the noise or feel the heat of the ovens. The scent of yeasty bread and the brininess of seafood met her as she turned into the service hall. Her stomach growled in response, and she realized it had been hours since her small lunch of sturdy bread and stale cheese. She hoped Chef was in a generous mood.

She never had a chance to find out. As she started to turn the corner into the passageway of the kitchen, strong arms grabbed her from behind, and a wide hand covered her mouth.

TOGETHER OR NOT AT ALL

1983—Orchard Street

Harte could feel Esta starting to shake. Her eyes were fixed on the far side of the room, where the old man who had once been Nibsy Lorcan had turned the gun on himself.

"Dammit," she whispered. "Why did he—"

"Come on," he said, lifting Esta to her feet. The old man was dead. It didn't matter why he did it, because it didn't change anything. "We have to get moving, in case someone heard that gunshot and comes to investigate."

"It's New York in the 1980s, Harte. Nobody is going to investigate a gunshot." But she slipped her hand into his. "You're okay?" she asked, checking him over again.

"There was only one shot," he reminded her.

"Right." She looked back over her shoulder, hesitating.

He squeezed her hand softly, rubbing his thumb across her cool skin. "He's not worth your pity, Esta."

"I know," she said, but the look in her eyes told a different story. Then he watched as she visibly pulled herself together. "We should take the papers. We should take anything that might help us."

"Nothing he was willing to give us is going to help," Harte told her. "You know Nibsy. It's just more lies."

"You're probably right, but that doesn't mean we should leave it here for someone else to find." She released his hand, and Harte felt suddenly adrift. "You heard him. He thought we would take this back and hand it over to his younger self. Maybe he was willing to risk helping us if he thought it was the way to help himself."

"Or maybe it's another trap."

"Probably," she admitted. "But can you really walk away from the possibility of answers? He knew how to do the ritual that got Seshat out of you, Harte. What if he really did figure out how to use the power in the Book? What if those papers could help us finish this?"

He wanted to reach for her because he felt like she might slip away for good if he wasn't touching her. But he curled his fingers and tucked them at his side instead.

"Fine. But let's make it quick." Thanks to whatever that bit of magic was in the elevator, they were without their affinities. He'd feel better when they were out of the building.

Esta approached the desk slowly, but once there, she hesitated for only a second before taking the stack of papers trapped beneath the old man's lifeless arm. When she made it back to Harte's side, he could see that the edges of some of them were stained red with Nibsy's blood. He took them from her and tucked them into the satchel with everything else.

Together they descended the back stairs. All around them, the building was muffled in an almost oppressive silence, but once they stepped out the back and into the bright chill of the winter day, the noise of the city hit them like a wall.

"This way," Esta said, taking him by the hand again and heading toward the busier thoroughfare of Delancey Street, but they hadn't gone more than a block before Harte felt the clear sense that someone was watching.

Tossing a glance over his shoulder, he cursed softly when he saw two men walking a few hundred feet behind them. They weren't obviously police or Guardsmen, but something about them made Harte think of the authorities. Maybe it was the inky black filling their eyes. "I think we have company."

Esta paused long enough to pretend to look at the wares in a large shop window. But her eyes were focused on the reflection in the glass. "Cops," she said softly, pulling him onward.

"Worse than cops," Harte told her. "Did you see their eyes?" Her jaw tensed, and he knew she had.

"There's a subway station up ahead," she told him. "We have to get away from this neighborhood."

The thought of going back into the subway tunnels made him nearly stumble. "If we go underground, we'll be trapped."

"Not if we keep moving," she said. But he didn't miss the soft "I hope" that she muttered under her breath. "We need a distraction."

The nearest subway entrance was at the end of the next block. Harte didn't have to look back to know the men were still following them, but when they came to the entrance, Esta cut straight through the crowd of people standing nearby, huddled around a barrel of something that was burning. When they were in the middle of the crowd, Harte stopped abruptly and shoved himself backward into one of the men warming his hands over the fire, knocking the guy into someone else. The effect was instantaneous, but he was ready for it. By the time the man caught himself, Harte was already pulling Esta through the crowd, leaving the men to turn on one another.

She gave him a bright, sharp smile and tugged him onward down the slush-covered steps.

Like the other stations, this one reeked of urine and trash, but in a stroke of brilliant luck, a train was already there, waiting. Together, they hopped the turnstiles and slid in just as the doors closed. Harte looked back through the graffiti-covered windows in time to see that the two black-eyed men had arrived at the station, but the train was already pulling away before the men could reach it.

The car was packed. The air was humid and warmer than the cold winter streets above, filled with the combined scents of too many bodies, cologne, stale smoke, and something mechanical. But the crowd wasn't enough to keep them safe.

Harte braced himself against one of the metal poles as the train picked up speed and leaned in to whisper into Esta's ear. "They saw us." The Guard or police—whoever the men were—knew what train they were on and which direction they were traveling.

Their faces were close, and even with the thick, fetid air around them, the light floral scent of the soap she'd been using back in Chicago tickled his nose.

"It doesn't matter," she said. "We're not staying here. Follow me."

Harte held tightly to Esta's hand as she dragged him through the press of bodies toward the rear of the car. When they arrived, she slid the door open, letting in a burst of air and noise. Harte turned to make sure no one was following. But if he'd worried at all that someone was watching and might try to stop them, he quickly realized no one cared. The other passengers kept their eyes forward or down, resolutely ignoring whatever was happening at the back of the train. This New York, for all its changes, wasn't so different from his own time, it seemed.

Quickly they moved across the swinging platform and then through the next car. It was packed, but slightly less so, and they made better time passing through the crowd and out the back end of the car. The train rounded a bend, its wheels squealing, as they arrived at the final car on the line. The crowd was lighter there, and Esta led them through the car and out the rear doors until they were standing on the platform at the back. There was nowhere else to go.

"We need to get off before it enters the station," she told him. "It'll slow when it approaches the next stop, but you have to watch out for the third rail when you jump."

She couldn't be serious. "The what?" He could barely hear her over the noise of the tunnel.

"Third. Rail," she shouted, pointing to the right side of the track. "There. It's electrified. You touch it, and you die."

He looked up at her but saw in less than a heartbeat that she was serious. This time, there was no hidden station, no platform to land on. She wanted him to jump from the train? Only a few hours before, he'd been planning on doing the same thing without any hope of surviving, and now she expected them to not only survive but to land without hitting an electrified part of the track? "Esta, no. This is insane. We can't—"

"How's your affinity? Because mine is dead right now," she said, her expression bunching with frustration. "The men following us back there—*whoever* they were—are going to know there are only two directions heading out of the last station. They'll have people waiting at both stops for us. This is our only chance, Harte." She was already climbing over the back railing of the car. "We can do this."

He wasn't so sure, but there was no choice except to follow her. Once they were both hanging from the back of the car, he looked over to find her staring out into the darkness of the tunnel behind them. Her short hair was whipping around her face, and her jaw was set.

She's afraid. For all her bluster and bravado, he knew by the way she was holding herself—stiff and apart from him—that she wasn't sure this would work.

"There has to be another way," he shouted, willing her to turn to him. To hear him.

She only shook her head. "It's slowing," she said. Finally, she looked at him, and her golden eyes were glinting with determination. "When I say go, you jump first."

"No," he said, moving his hand over so it covered hers. "We go together or not at all."

Her mouth pressed into a tight line, but she nodded. "Together, then. Ready?"

"Not even a little—"

"Now!" she shouted, and together they released the car and tumbled down onto the track.

TRUTH AND LIES

1983—Beneath the City

The instant Esta released the subway car and began to fall, she realized that maybe she'd made a mistake. The tracks were farther down than she'd expected, and she had plenty of time to regret her choices before she hit the unyielding ground below. She landed hard enough to knock the breath from her lungs and make her teeth rattle. Ignoring the pain, she wrenched herself into a ball and rolled away from the deadly third rail.

As the train traveled off to the station, the sound of its squealing brakes receded along with it, but it took a few seconds until she could breathe again.

Nearby, Harte groaned, and she forced herself to sit up, despite the sharp ache coming from the side she'd landed on. "Are you okay?" she asked, pulling herself to her feet and looking back in the direction the train had come from.

The tunnel wasn't completely pitch-black. Every hundred feet or so a fluorescent emergency light projected an unhealthy glow on the tunnel walls. The pattern of dark and light created a trail leading off into the distance.

"We have to get moving before another train comes," she told him, reaching for her magic and still finding it dead. "I think I saw a service tunnel that branched off a little ways back."

Together they stumbled down the track, listening for the telltale rumble of an approaching train. Finally, they found the tunnel. The jaundice-yellow lights lining its walls barely cut through the gloom.

"You don't think they'll search the tunnels once they realize we're not on the train?" Harte asked as they paused in the narrow opening.

"Let's hope we're out of here before they find us," she told him. "Come on."

They made their way into the gloom of the smaller service tunnel until the fluorescent glow of the main tunnel was no longer visible. A train passed by in the distance, making the ground shiver.

"Hopefully we can avoid the Guard, at least until our affinities return."

"What if they don't return completely?" Harte asked, voicing the question that had been worrying Esta since the blast of ice had drained her power. "What if Nibsy's done something to corrupt our magic?"

"They will." *They have to.* Without her affinity, they couldn't return to the past. "Nibsy needs us in 1902," she reminded him. "We're no good to him here—especially now. He wouldn't have done anything to jeopardize our ability to go back."

Harte grunted. She didn't need to see his face to know he wasn't feeling nearly as confident as she had just sounded.

She wished that *she* were as confident as she'd just sounded.

But Esta had to believe that she was right. The old man had only turned the gun on himself to make a point: *This* life didn't matter. This version of history was nothing to him.

"I can practically hear you thinking over there," Harte said. He spoke softly, but the darkness amplified his voice.

She stopped, suddenly overwhelmed by everything, and after a second she felt him step closer, felt him reach for her. His fingers brushed along her neck, finding her face in the darkness. He cupped her cheek gently with one hand, and she stepped into him as he pulled her closer with his free arm.

"Are *you* okay?" he asked, giving her words back to him.

"I will be." It wasn't a lie, but she was glad for the darkness. It was easier to pretend to be strong when he couldn't see the doubt on her face.

LISA MAXWELL

"We don't need our affinities," she told him, but it felt like she was really trying to convince herself.

He huffed his disagreement.

"I'm not saying they wouldn't be helpful," she said. "But we're more than our magic, Harte. We always have been. For now we just need to keep moving."

He didn't respond, neither to argue nor to agree.

"For example, we don't need magic to get out of these tunnels," she said, trying to remember one of the many lessons of her youth. She'd studied everything about the city, including the tunnels and rivers that lay beneath the modern streets. Professor Lachlan had prepared her for everything—maybe even for this.

"We don't?"

She stepped back from him. "No, we don't," she said, finally getting her bearings. "This way."

They walked for what felt like an eternity, stopping so Esta could consider their options any time they came to another place where the tunnels branched off. But her knowledge of the tunnels was more theoretical than practical. She couldn't be sure she was taking the right turns.

For a while they didn't speak. It had been only a few hours since they'd crossed the bridge back into the city, but enough had happened to fill entire days. The darkness of the tunnels and the comforting silence between them gave Esta time to think, to realize exactly how much they'd just been through. But one thought—one question—kept rising to the surface.

"How did you know?" she asked. Esta didn't specify what she meant, but Harte seemed to understand immediately.

"You mean, how did I know that it wasn't you?" He let out a long breath. "There were a lot of reasons. The fact that her arm was scarred and healed over was the thing that confirmed it. But that wasn't what made me suspect at first."

"What was?"

He didn't immediately answer. Instead, the crunch of gravel beneath their feet filled the space of words. When he finally spoke, his voice was softer and, despite still having her hand in his, he sounded farther away. "She told me that she loved me."

"And you didn't believe her," Esta said, her stomach twisting with some emotion that she didn't want to name.

"No," Harte said. "I didn't."

"Because . . . you don't believe that I do?"

Harte stopped suddenly. For a long, terrible moment, he didn't speak. But then he took her other hand in his. It was so dark in that part of the tunnel that even with her eyes acclimated to the lack of light, Esta could barely make out the features of his face. But she felt him breathing, steady and slow. Felt the warmth of his hands around hers, sure and steady. "No," he said. "That isn't it at all."

"Then what?" she asked, suddenly uneasy. "You didn't want her— me—to say it, or . . . ?" She tried to pull away, but he didn't let her go.

He let out an amused breath, and she felt the warmth flutter across her face. "That's not it either." There was a smile in the words that had impatience lashing at her.

"Then *what*?"

"She only said those words to prove herself to me," he told her. "But I *know* you, Esta. You've never used what we have between us to prove anything. You've *never* thrown love at me as a weapon."

She frowned, thinking of how they'd first met. Thinking too of the nights in the theater, when she had tried to seduce him for Dolph's cause. "I don't know that we're remembering things the same way."

"I'm not saying you didn't try to tempt me, especially back when we were still at odds," he said wryly, the humor in his words coming clearly through the darkness. "But I knew all along that it was nothing more than simple misdirection."

"Not *so* simple," she argued. But there was no heat in her words, because he was right. Esta might have tried to lure him in, but she never would have toyed with something as serious as love. Especially not once she really knew him. She might be a thief, but she had grown up feeling unwanted. So had he. She never would have used their connection as a weapon against him.

"You've never lied to me about anything that really mattered, especially not when it came to what this is between us." He lifted her hand to his lips, and she felt the warmth of his mouth brushing her knuckles. "Even then, even though Nibsy raised you to be ruthless and effective, you had far too much integrity for those kinds of games. And now?" He kissed her knuckles again. "You know you don't need to prove anything to me, especially not about how you feel. We've been through too much together. You are not negotiable. *We* are not negotiable. That's all there is to it."

His words warmed her. But suddenly his belief in her—in *them*—felt like an overwhelming weight. When had anyone given her that sort of trust so blindly?

Never.

And he was wrong. She had lied, and recently, too. It had been such a stupid, seemingly insignificant lie, but now, with his words wrapping around her, it felt like a wound between them. After everything that had just happened? She couldn't leave it there to fester.

"There's something I have to tell you." She bit her lip, feeling embarrassed and stupid and awful all at once. Harte didn't respond, so she had no choice but to go on. "Back in Chicago . . ." She paused, not knowing how to start.

"Esta?" he asked when she hesitated long enough that the silence had made it too difficult to start again.

"Back in Chicago, I told you something that wasn't completely true." She let out a breath, not knowing why it felt so hard to just say it. "I told you there hadn't been any"—she used his word for it—"*consequences*. To what happened on the train."

Harte didn't respond immediately, and the silence between them had weight now. There was distance within that silence too. "I don't understa—"

"I won't know for a week at least," she blurted.

Again, the silence. The distance. She couldn't quite draw breath, and it had nothing to do with the ache in her ribs. The tightness in her chest went deeper than that.

"You lied," he said—it wasn't a question. "About *that*?"

She wished she could see his face. Why had she thought that darkness would make this confession easier? "Only about knowing," she told him. "I still don't think anything happened. The timing was wrong, and the chances are so slim, and—" She was doing this all wrong. "I didn't think you'd let me do what I needed to do if you were worried about . . . *that*."

"You thought I would want to protect the child, if there was one." He was standing right next to her, but he sounded so far away.

She nodded, then realized he couldn't see her. "I was worried, but I was wrong. I never should have told you anything until I knew for sure. I don't want that lie between us. I want what you said just now to be true. I don't want *any* more lies between us, especially not about things that matter. And what we have, Harte?" She gave his hands a squeeze. "*This*? It matters."

He pulled away from her, leaving her hands cold. She suddenly wasn't sure what to do with them.

"I'm sorry," she said, wishing it were enough.

He didn't speak. In the distance, the tunnels vibrated, and suddenly she wished she had just swallowed the secret. Or maybe the city could just swallow her up.

"As soon as I told you, I regretted lying. I was going to tell you the truth, but then everything went south and—" She stopped. "I just needed you to see me as an equal, and not like some soft, pointless creature you needed to protect. It's not an excuse. It's not meant as one. But you deserve an explanation. I knew how dangerous it was going into the convention, and I needed you to know I could do whatever it took. I didn't want you to stop me."

"You really think I could have?" he asked. "I know you can do anything."

"After what happened on the train . . ." She felt her cheeks warm with the thought of his hands on her skin, the way they fit together. "When we were together, it was more than just physical. It wasn't something I could laugh off or walk away from, and you bringing up the possibility that it was a mistake?"

"Not a mistake," he said, brushing his fingers against hers again. "Not ever a mistake."

"No," she agreed. "Not a mistake. But you were acting like I was a problem to be solved, and I hated it."

"It was more than just physical for me too, Esta."

His words lifted a little of the weight she'd been carrying. "Things are different where I'm from, Harte. I don't need you to take care of me like that, and I didn't want anything to change between us because of it. From the way you were talking back in Chicago, I was afraid things already had."

Silence sprang up between them again, and Esta had to stop herself from filling it with her own words. She'd said enough. The ball was in his court now.

"I hate that you lied to me," he told her softly. "Especially about that."

"I know," she said. "I'm sorry, Harte. I—"

"But I understand why you did," he said. "I was an idiot."

She couldn't stop the bark of surprised laughter from escaping, but he was still talking.

"I see that now," he told her. "I was so overwhelmed by what had happened between us, and I didn't know what to do with any of it. I know things are different where you came from. I've seen glimpses of that world in the past few weeks. But it's not the world I grew up in, and after everything that happened, I just couldn't let myself become my father."

"You're *not*," she said fiercely, wishing she could see him. "You never would be."

"I know," he said with a small, humorless laugh. "I realized that back in San Francisco, but it didn't stop me from reacting on instinct. I made a mess of things."

"It wasn't just you," she admitted.

He kissed her then without warning and with an urgency that felt almost desperate, and she responded in kind. When their lips met, the last of the weight lifted, and suddenly she was flying. Harte's breath mixed with hers, the only air she needed. His hands were in her hair, angling her closer to deepen the kiss, and as she opened for him—with him—the heat of their mouths, the taste of him, overwhelmed her.

This kiss was a claiming, a homecoming. A match of wills and a promise of more. His hands framed her face, glided down the heated skin of her neck to her shoulders. One hand went to her waist, anchoring her to him, while the other traced the angle of her collarbone so softly that she thought she might die from wanting. They were trapped in an uncertain future, stuck in the muck and darkness of the underground, and it didn't matter. All she needed was this—Harte's mouth tangling with hers, his arms around her, and his hands on her skin. The friction of his fingertips brushing against her skin was perfect.

It was un*bearable*.

His teeth nipped at her lip, and she suddenly couldn't be close enough to him. She needed more. She didn't want anything between them any longer—no lies or regrets or even wanting. Covering his hand with her own, she showed him, helped him along by guiding him lower, until his hand was tracing down over her chest, to the curve of her breast beneath the rough overalls she was wearing, and she felt him deepen the kiss on a groan. But there was too much damn fabric between them. His hands were on her, but it wasn't enough. He was already working at the buttons at her neck and finally he slipped beneath the fabric. The rough pads of his fingers felt like flames tracing across her skin, and she could not stop herself from gasping.

Harte went still. "God, Esta." His voice broke as he pulled his hand away, leaving her feeling suddenly bereft. But his chest was heaving the same as hers. "We shouldn't be doing this."

"Yes," she said, stepping toward him. "Yes, we should."

But the moment had broken already. "I watched you *die.*"

"Not me," she said softly, her heart aching a little at the pain in his voice. "You knew it wasn't me." That fact alone felt miraculous, more precious than any treasure she could steal.

"I knew it wasn't you," he agreed. "Deep down, I knew. If I truly thought that girl was you, I would have died in that ritual circle with you. But, Esta, she looked *so* much like you." He reached for her then, framed her face with his hands so gently it brought tears to her eyes. "All I wanted in Chicago was for you to survive. I would have done anything—*said anything*—to make you want to go on, even if I wasn't with you. I never meant to bring up what happened on the train as a way to make you feel smaller. I know I can't protect you—that you don't *need* me to. And it destroys me. But the thought of you still in this world, surviving? That's all I need. That's all I want."

She kissed him then, rising just slightly on her toes to press her mouth against his once more. She meant for the kiss to be brief, but he leaned into it. Deepened it in a way that made her heart race again. It didn't matter that the tunnel smelled of dampness and rot or that she could hear something scurrying in the distance. There was only Harte. Only a perfect new under-standing between them.

Breathless again but settled now in a way she hadn't been before, she pulled away. "You're right. We shouldn't do this," she told him, fastening the buttons again with a small smile. "At least not here." She slipped her hands into his. "If I didn't make a wrong turn, the exit should be just around the next bend."

He pulled her closer and pressed another small kiss on the sensitive skin of her neck, just below her ear, and then together they continued on, her head spinning a little from the kiss.

They turned a corner and saw the access door ahead, bathed in the yellowish glow of an emergency light. "Ready to get out of here?" She pulled out Viola's dagger. "You want to do the honors?" she asked, offering it to Harte.

He gave her a small smile, but he'd barely reached for it when that smile slid from his face. He didn't take the blade. "Where are you hurt?"

"What?" she asked, confused at his meaning. But his words seemed to shake something free in her. All at once, she felt the throbbing ache in her side again from where she'd landed after jumping off the train. "I'm fine," she said, refusing to acknowledge the pain.

"You're not fine, Esta," he said, holding up his hand so she could see the dark smear of blood that stained his fingers and palm. "You're bleeding."

TO SKIN A FOX

1902—Uptown

Viola paced around the parlor of the small apartment above the *New York Age*'s offices and print shop, where she and Jianyu had been staying since they'd sent Cela away. She tried not to think of the minutes that had already passed. Jianyu should have been back by long before now.

She hated waiting in the cramped set of rooms while Jianyu went out to search for answers to the question of Newton's Sigils. She would rather have gone with him. With Nibsy in control of the marks, it wouldn't do for them both to be caught. This way, at least, should one of them be found by Nibsy or the Order—or any of the factions that might be hunting for them—the other could go on. Because someone needed to warn the Johnsons and wait for Harte and Esta. Someone would remain to continue fighting.

The door swung open suddenly, and Viola startled to her feet, a knife already in her hand, before she realized it wasn't an attack. The soft warmth of the old magic brushed against her skin as Jianyu appeared in the open doorway.

"Where have you been?" she demanded.

"We need to find Joshua," he said at the same time. "We need to send word to Cela as well. To anyone who could keep her safe."

His words brushed away whatever comforting warmth his magic had just created and replaced it with an icy feeling of dread. Viola lowered the knife that had already been aimed at Jianyu's heart at the same time she registered the panic and fear in his eyes. "What are you talking about?"

"Nibsy knows where Cela is," Jianyu said, his voice tight with a fury that Viola had rarely heard there. He closed the door solidly behind him and latched it for good measure. He was breathing heavily, as though he'd run across the city, and he leaned now against the back of a chair, trying to catch his breath.

"No," she told him, unwilling to believe what he was telling her. "That's not possible."

Jianyu's expression grew grim. "We have to send word to Joshua. She must be warned."

Viola shook her head. "Joshua, he left yesterday, remember? He'll be gone for three weeks."

"Then we must find another messenger," Jianyu said. She'd never seen him so frantic.

"Jianyu, slow down," she told him gently. "How could Nibsy have found Cela?"

"Your brother's men," Jianyu told her, looking more than a little disgusted. "He used the Five Pointers. He's sending them after her."

She knew that Nibsy and the Five Pointers had an alliance, but Johnny the Fox hadn't worked to claim command over Paul Kelly's gang only to hand his power to a boy. Especially not when the Fox hated Mageus every bit as much as her brother. "Why would Torrio follow Nibsy Lorcan's orders?"

"I do not know," Jianyu said, looking more shaken than Viola had ever seen him.

Because he cares for Cela.

"Are you sure Nibsy knows? Are you sure he isn't bluffing?" she asked

Jianyu raked his hand through already disheveled hair and shook his head. "He would not lie about such a thing."

"Of *course* he would," Viola told him. "Nibsy would lie about anything if he thought it would help him get his way."

"He knows she is in Atlantic City, Viola."

Dread curled in her stomach. If Nibsy knew that, he already knew too much.

"What if this is nothing more than a trap?" Viola asked, trying desperately for some other explanation. "Atlantic City, it's a big place, no? Maybe he don't know so much as he says. Maybe he wants us to run like scared rabbits and warn her, so his men, they can follow."

"We cannot take that chance," he told her, worry coloring his sharp features.

She understood what he was feeling. *Madonna*, did she understand. Hadn't she felt the same way when she saw Ruby being attacked by that terrible stone beast at Morgan's gala? She'd felt so helpless, so *desperate*, that she'd acted on impulse and skewered Jianyu with her blade by accident. She wouldn't let him rush in and make the same kind of foolish mistake now.

"Abel will be back soon," she reminded him. "We expect him tomorrow with news."

"Tomorrow may be too late." Jianyu ran a hand through his short hair, making himself look even more disheveled and harried. "I found the information about using the sigils. I had it in my hands. And then Nibsy . . ."

She understood immediately. Nibsy had the marks. "What could you have done? What can any of us do against the marks?"

Jianyu's mouth went tight. "I should have died to defend it."

"If Nibsy Lorcan wanted you dead, he would have made it so," Viola said, trying not to let her own fear show through her words. "He's up to something." Nibsy never would have let Jianyu go if he truly had everything he needed. "We must be careful not to rush and fall into his traps. We must think. *Plan*."

"Cela's safety cannot wait for that," Jianyu said, shoving aside the chair he'd been leaning on. "Not when the sigils can be used to open a doorway—a passage—out of the Brink."

"No. Non é possibile." She shook her head, refusing to believe something so preposterous. "Dolph, he would have known this. He would have wanted them, along with the Book of Mysteries."

Jianyu leaned against the door, his head tipped back. "Dolph was focused only on the Book," he reminded her. "You saw his journal, just as I did. There was no mention of Newton's Sigils. If he had known about them, the information would have been there."

A pounding came at the door, causing Jianyu and Viola both to jump. She reached for Libitina—an instinct she couldn't quite quit—before she realized the voice calling on the other side was familiar. A friend.

"Viola? Jianyu? You all in there?" Abel called, as the pounding came again.

Jianyu let out a breath at the sound of Abel's voice, and Viola heard her own relief echoed in it. Abel was back earlier than they'd expected him. He could get to Cela. Her brother was not trapped, as they were. He could protect her.

"Thank god," Viola said, dizzy with relief as Jianyu opened the door.

But when Abel stepped into the room, the look on his face turned Viola's relief to dread.

"She's gone." His voice broke as he stumbled into the room. "Her landlady said Cela didn't come home last night, and her room looked like it had been ransacked."

She met Jianyu's eyes again, and they exchanged a silent look of understanding before she turned back to Abel. "We'll get your sister back," she vowed.

"We cannot go after Nibsy," Jianyu told her. "Not with the marks—"

"I'm not going after that snake," Viola said. "Not yet. First, I'm going to go skin myself a fox."

MORE THAN MAGIC

1983—Times Square

H arte looked down at Esta's blood coating his hand and cursed himself for not realizing that she was hurt. Just seconds ago, that same hand had been touching her in places that, once, he'd only dared dream of. He'd forgotten that they were trapped underground in the filthy darkness of a foul-smelling tunnel filled with who knew what kind of vermin. Once his mouth had touched hers, once his hands had found the soft curve of her waist, none of that had mattered. Nothing had mattered but Esta.

Now he felt like the worst kind of ass. Because she was clearly hurt, and badly, from the amount of blood.

"I'll be okay, Harte." She tugged at her clothes to see where the blood was coming from, but when she twisted, she couldn't stop herself from sucking in a sharp breath.

"Come on," he told her, taking her by the hand and moving toward the doorway that promised to be an exit. He didn't even care what—or *who*—might be waiting as he forced Viola's dagger into the jamb and wrenched the lock in two.

On the other side of the door, they found a small, windowless room with another door. He made quick work of that lock as well, and then they were out. Free. Or, maybe not free, exactly. It was another of the subterranean stations, and there were people *everywhere*. Luckily, no one seemed to care that they'd just emerged from some kind of service door. One or two people might have tossed disinterested looks their way, but for the most part, no one paid them any attention at all.

Harte blinked at the sudden brightness, trying to make sense of the chaotic crowd around him, as Esta took charge.

"This way," she told him, apparently not thrown off by the noise and crush of the people around him. "It's rush hour. That should give us some cover." She tugged him onward through the crowd.

There was a battered mosaic on the wall that told Harte where they were: *Times Sq-42nd St.* Forty-Second Street, he understood, even if the crowds in the subway station didn't make sense this far uptown. That area had been mostly train tracks leading to the Grand Central Depot in the city he had known. And he didn't have any idea what a Times Square was.

But he didn't have long to ponder it before they emerged from the closeness of the subway station into the impossible brightness of enormous buildings covered in lights. Gone was the Forty-Second Street he had known. Gone were the brick streets and carriages of his own time. In their place, a strange new city had erupted. Buildings soared stories above him, and traffic poured by in a constant stream of boxy vehicles, many of which were painted a garish yellow.

He hadn't realized his feet had stopped and that he was standing in the middle of the crowded sidewalk until he felt Esta tugging on his hand.

"I know it's a lot, but keep moving," she told him gently.

She was right. If no one had paid any attention when the two of them had emerged from a maintenance tunnel in the station, people were noticing now. An older man in a heavy overcoat and a sharply brimmed hat glared at him and muttered something about *tourists* as he shoved by.

They joined the river of people moving along the sidewalks beneath the lit canopies of what seemed like a million marquees. There had always been theaters in New York, but not like this. Even Satan's Circus hadn't had lights like this . . . or *shows* like this, Harte thought, feeling his cheeks heat as he read the flashing lights advertising peep shows and barely clad girls, twenty-four-hour theaters and "burlesk." A large silver bus rumbled past, its graffiti-marred windows mostly concealing the tired-looking people within as it spewed a cloud of dark exhaust to mingle with the cigarette smoke already hanging in the air.

Harte coughed, his eyes watering from the bus's noxious fumes as he tried to keep pace with Esta. They crossed one street, then another, and then she stopped suddenly.

"No," she told him, looking completely rattled. "This isn't right."

They were standing in a wedge-shaped plaza in the middle of traffic. Vehicles streamed around them, and now that they paused, Harte could see that the small lit signs on top of the yellow automobiles said "taxi." Standing there in the middle of traffic felt a little like standing in the middle of a stampede, but Esta was unmoved by the bustle and speed around them. She was too busy looking up at a statue that glinted warmly in the setting sun.

Jack.

It wasn't the best likeness of him, but even with the too-broad shoulders, the too-strong jaw, and even without needing to read the placard below, Harte recognized the attempt to represent Jack Grew.

"This should be George M. Cohen," Esta said, horror clear in her voice.

"One of the Vaudeville troupe?" Harte asked, confused. The Cohen family had been a staple on the circuit, but none of them had been famous or important enough to warrant a statue. Especially not one this large or prominent.

Esta didn't answer. She was still staring up at Jack's image cast in something that looked suspiciously like gold. Then, slowly, she turned her head from side to side, taking in the city around her. Her hand tightened on Harte's as she let out a curse that would have made a sailor blush.

He turned and found what she was looking at. There was a wedge-shaped building across the street from them emblazoned with the directive to "Drink Coca-Cola." It was twice the size of any billboard he'd ever seen, far larger even than the one Wallack's had put up for his show.

But Harte understood that the advertisement wasn't what made Esta curse. Twenty or so feet above the street, words made from light chased around the building. They moved like magic, though he suspected it was a simple matter of electricity.

They weren't the only ones who were watching the words scroll past. Around them, others had paused to watch, reading what seemed to be the news of the day. And the news of the day was them.

Escaped unregistereds. Last seen in Bowery Station. Considered extremely dangerous.

"They're looking for us," he said.

Her jaw was set as she nodded. "I knew they would be, but . . . this isn't right," she told him. But he had the sense that she wasn't talking about the risqué signage all around him. "That statue of Jack—" She glanced over at him. "It's not supposed to be like this. He's not supposed to be anyone."

The sign above the words changed suddenly, like magic.

No, not magic, Harte realized. It was a sign made from slats of wood that had rotated to evolve into a new image. Now, instead of Coca-Cola, it displayed an image that looked unmistakably like the banner that had flown from the Coliseum back in Chicago: the Philosopher's Hand. The image shifted again, but this time not from any mechanical manipulation. Like the banner in Chicago, the image *was* enchanted somehow.

Esta cursed again as their faces looked down on the bustling streets from above. The whole street seemed to pause, holding its breath. Excited murmuring whipped through the crowd around them. Suddenly Harte was acutely aware of the dark-suited police officers standing on a corner nearby.

"We have to go," Esta said. She pulled him through the crowd and across the street, dodging the traffic that was slowly inching around the square, but Harte felt more than one set of eyes upon them as they left.

He glanced down at her, saw her skin pale in the bright daylight and noticed the tear in the heavy overalls she was wearing and the dark stain spreading around it. "We can't just keep running. You're still bleeding, Esta."

"I know." She swallowed hard, and he could instantly see the pain she'd been hiding from him. "We need supplies. And we need to find a place to lie low until we figure things out." When she looked up at him, her golden eyes were tight. "But I don't know where to go. I can't quite feel my affinity yet. I don't know what to do other than to keep moving."

Harte reached for his magic, but he couldn't *quite* sense anything more than the faraway feeling that his affinity was still there. Just out of reach. "Me neither. But it's like you said, we're more than our magic."

Her lips pressed tightly together, and he could practically hear her thinking. Finally, she came to some conclusion. "You're right. We'll just have to do this the hard way."

When the light changed, she tugged him across the street through the press of suited bodies that smelled of cologne and sweat. They followed the crowd along the sidewalk, moving with the tide of pedestrians uptown for a block or two as Harte tried not to run into any of the peddlers selling handbags and trinkets on the edge of the sidewalks.

Esta handed him something that seemed to be a hat declaring that he loved NY. "Put it on. The bill goes in the front."

He did as she instructed, pulling the broad brim low over his forehead as she slipped on a pair of dark glasses she hadn't possessed a second before.

"Where did you—"

"Thief. Remember?" she said, tossing him a sharp-toothed smile. If he didn't know her so well, he might have missed the pain and tightness bracketing her mouth. "Come on. I think I see a pharmacy up there. It'll have what we need."

The shop was like nothing he'd ever seen before—not even in 1950s San Francisco. The lights felt brighter. The products more garishly colorful. The whole store smelled of bleach or some other sort of astringent and stale air.

Grabbing a brightly colored basket from a stack by the door, Esta dragged him past row after row of metal shelving filled with a dizzying array of products. Occasionally, she would toss something into the basket. When they reached an aisle with packages emblazoned with red crosses, she grabbed even more, tossing items into the basket without seeming to consider her choices.

Harte followed wordlessly, overwhelmed by the abundance and astounded at the lack of shopkeepers. One surly-looking woman glared at them as she stocked shelves at a slow, plodding pace, but she didn't offer to help. She glanced away just as quickly as she'd noticed them. He'd never seen a pharmacy where you could simply walk through and select your own merchandise. But he barely had time to marvel at the system before they'd reached the clerk at the front of the store. Esta placed the basket filled with supplies on the counter to be tallied up, and while the old man pushed buttons on a strange contraption that must have been a cash register, she tossed a couple of chocolate bars onto the counter. Somehow, he wasn't even a little surprised to see Esta pull out a leather wallet filled with cash as she waited for him to finish ringing them up.

The man looked up at his machine and started to read the total, but he paused. His eyes narrowed and then focused on something behind them. "Hey, wait a minute. . . ."

Harte turned and found himself face-to-face with . . . himself. The shelf behind him held newspapers, and he and Esta were there, right on the front page.

"You're them," the man said. "The maggots they're looking for." He backed away, fumbling for something under the counter, and somewhere in the distance, a siren started to wail.

THE ALGONQUIN

1980—Times Square

Ever since Harte had noticed that she was bleeding, the wound in Esta's side had been aching more and more, but when the clerk behind the counter recognized them, that pain fell away. From the way he was searching blindly under the counter, he'd probably already triggered a silent alert. She had to get them out of there, but her affinity was still fuzzy, and they needed the supplies.

"We're not—" she started, but the old man pulled out a gun before she could finish. It was a small snub-nosed pistol, but the size didn't matter much in such close quarters. He was already pointing it in their direction.

"Put your hands up," he demanded. "The reward for the two of you is dead or alive, so I don't care if I have to shoot you."

Esta felt Harte go still next to her, freezing at the sight of the gun, just as she had. She reached for her magic again, and she could *almost* grasp her affinity. But it still felt slippery and just beyond her reach.

"We don't want any trouble," Harte said as he lifted his hands. He was using his most charming voice, the one he'd used onstage when he wanted to entrance an audience.

"Then you should have stayed the hell out of our city," the old man sneered. All the while the sirens were drawing closer.

"We'll leave," she told him, wondering if she could still grab the basket as she backed away slowly. "We're going now."

"Like hell you are," the old man said, drawing back the hammer on the pistol as he aimed it toward Harte. "You're not getting away again.

Not after you kidnapped that poor girl and murdered her in the subway."

Esta knew what was about to happen. There was too much anger and hatred radiating from the clerk for him to stand down. Even without her affinity, time seemed to go slow. His thumb had already cocked the hammer of the gun. His finger was on the trigger, was easing it back.

On instinct, she leaped in front of Harte, pushing him aside as she reached once more for her affinity, and . . . *there*. This time her fingertips brushed along her magic, and she managed to pull the seconds slow just as she careened into Harte and knocked him to the floor.

Heat erupted through her arm. Her connection to the old magic already felt unsteady, but now it felt like holding a live wire. But she gritted her teeth against the discomfort and held tight.

With the world frozen around them, the sound of the gunshot echoed like a far-off cannon, long and low, and there was an icy energy coursing through her arm. Her affinity still felt too unsteady—too dangerous—to focus on anything but holding tight to the seconds. She closed her eyes and focused on her connection to the old magic, but it slipped from her fingers as another shot rang out. The linoleum tile shattered next to where they'd fallen.

"We have to go. *Now*," she told Harte through gritted teeth as she reached for the seconds again.

Her affinity was there, but the cold that had rocketed through her when the bullet grazed her was getting worse. The icy throbbing in her arm felt like it was radiating from the wound, numbing her and wreaking havoc on what little of her affinity she could sense. The seconds still felt slippery and wild, and she didn't know how long she could keep hold of them.

As Harte pulled her to her feet, he saw that the bullet had grazed her arm. "You're hit."

"I'm fine," she told him, brushing off the fear in his stormy eyes. It wasn't completely a lie. She'd been grazed by a bullet before, so she knew this one hadn't done any real damage to her body, but she couldn't shake

LISA MAXWELL

the feeling that it had done something to her magic. Her arm burned like hell, if ice could burn, and the pain seemed to be spreading. She couldn't think too much about what that might mean, though—not until they were safe. "Get the basket of supplies."

Harte grabbed the plastic shopping basket, and then he ripped the gun from the clerk's hand for good measure. Together, they ran. Her arm screamed as she pushed open the heavy glass shop door, but she managed to keep hold of the seconds this time, despite the pain.

Outside, the streets around Times Square were frozen. People were halted mid-stride across busy intersections. The yellow flash of unmoving taxicabs dotted the crowded streets. Lights gleamed steadily, no longer flashing or twinkling. The persistent drone of the city, with its blaring horns and constant noise, was silent.

It was almost a comfort. Esta had done this so many times before. When things had gotten to be too much for her, when she needed a break—when she'd needed to feel in control of *something* in her life—she'd come to Times Square to watch the tourists take photos of everything and get swindled on fake Rolexes. She'd been just a kid then, but it had felt miraculous every time. Then, her magic had felt like a lifeline, the only thing that made sense. Now, with the tenuous grasp she had on the seconds, her affinity felt like a liability. They had to get moving.

She started walking without any idea about where they should go. There was a whole city they could hide in, but thanks to whatever tale Nibsy told the Guard, everyone was searching for them. Esta's mind raced, trying to think about where she was. *When* she was.

The subway wasn't an option, and neither was a taxi, so getting away from Times Square would be tricky. But there had to be somewhere they could hide for a while and regroup without anyone seeing them.

When they rounded the corner, they nearly ran into a trio of policemen frozen in time, and at the sight of them, Esta's magic slipped for just a second, and the world slammed back into motion. The noise of Times Square—squealing breaks and blaring horns and the drone of traffic and people—assaulted her. She saw the instant the police recognized them, but she couldn't quite grasp her magic.

"Run," she told Harte, ignoring her arm as she pulled him away from the police.

She could hear the cops behind her, shouting for the two of them to stop, but she plunged on, darting down the crowded sidewalks, dodging around pedestrians until—*there*—she finally managed to grasp the seconds.

The world went silent again, but she didn't stop tugging Harte onward through the tableau of now-frozen pedestrians. Her connection to the old magic felt even more unsteady than it had a moment before, and the ice in her arm was definitely spreading.

Then Esta realized where they could go. It was perfect. Times Square had changed dramatically since 1902, and most of the buildings that rose around them now hadn't been there at the beginning of the century. But she knew one that had. They could even slip back into the past without ever leaving, if they needed to.

"This way," she said, pulling Harte farther east along Forty-Fifth Street. They'd gone only a few yards when her magic slipped again, but this time no one seemed to notice that the two of them had basically just appeared out of nowhere. With the injury to her arm, she decided to let time spin on for a little while. She'd need her strength for what was coming next.

When they reached Sixth Avenue, they turned south and went one more block until she saw the cream stone and hunter-green awnings of the Algonquin Hotel. Despite all the changes in this part of town, the Algonquin had been a constant.

"Don't you think we should get away from this area?" Harte asked, frowning a little when she slowed to a stop in front of the hotel. He tossed a nervous look behind them.

"Probably," she admitted. "But running ourselves to exhaustion isn't going to help anything. It'll be safe enough here if we can get into a room without being seen."

Harte looked unsure until his gaze fell to her torn sleeve and the blood staining the side of the overalls. "Okay, then," he said. "If that's what you think."

She didn't want to know how bad she must look that he'd given in so easily. "How's your affinity?" she asked.

He shook his head. "Nothing but whispers. Not enough to risk anything."

It would have been nice to know that they could depend on Harte's magic to take care of any unexpected problems they might run into. If she could just keep hold of time, she could get them to safety, but her whole upper arm felt encased by ice now. Unsure what that meant, she worried instead about focusing on her affinity. Her connection to the old magic felt tenuous as the world when silent, and she had to grit her teeth to not lose hold of it. "Let's go."

They'd barely made it through the large, heavy doors when the seconds slipped from her grip and the soft sounds of the hotel wrapped around them. She reached for time again, but it took two tries before she was able to make the world go still.

Once they were through the entryway, the lobby of the Algonquin was all gleaming dark wood and luxury. Dark pillars flanked the space, reaching up to the ornately coffered ceiling above. Giant palms softened the overall impression of the room, creating cozy nooks around deep leather sofas and plush carpets. Esta would have given pretty much anything to collapse into one of those chairs and rest, but there wasn't time. Her connection to the old magic was still too unstable. She'd rest once they were in a room.

On one side of the space, golden elevator doors waited to take them up to safety, but Esta steered them to the other side of the lobby instead. There, the main check-in desk was staffed by two men in dark suits, and a yellow tiger cat sat on the counter, an unexpected sentinel sightlessly watching the still, silent room. She couldn't stop the seconds from slipping again as they approached the front desk, and she was sure the cat saw them before she could pull time tight.

Behind the counter, she found a small office. On one side, luggage was stacked and tagged, waiting for its owners, on the other side, the wall was covered by a large board with rows of metal pockets, like a filing system. Each of the pockets was labeled with numbers that corresponded to the floors of the hotel and the rooms they contained. A little of her worry eased. It would be easier to steal a room this way—like plucking that wallet filled with cash in Times Square had been easier. New York in the eighties might be gritty and dangerous, but it was also a city before computers had taken over. Before cameras watched the subway and credit cards were the most common currency. Cash, at least, was untraceable. Just as their use of a room would be.

"What are we doing back here, Esta?" Harte asked, frowning.

"We're getting a room," she told him.

He frowned. "We could have just picked a lock."

"Maybe," she agreed. "But this way no one will bother us."

It took her a minute to figure out the system, but once she did, it was easy enough to locate a room that still had a key hanging on the corresponding holder. She slipped the white notecard from the metal pocket, and with a pen she found on the counter, she wrote a false name on the card before placing it back into the corresponding room's slot. It looked like someone had been officially checked in now, so there wouldn't be any worry about an unexpected arrival. A Do Not Disturb sign on the door would take care of the rest.

She held up the key, feeling almost hopeful. But they were barely across the lobby when her head spun unexpectedly. Her connection to the old magic pulsed, sending a shock of heat through her, and she stumbled as she lost her grip on time again. She teetered on unsteady legs, but Harte was there to catch her. She didn't want to admit that his arms were the only thing holding her upright. Even once he set her back on her feet, she couldn't stop herself from leaning on him.

"Elevator," he growled, wrapping her closer to him and leading them both to the bank of golden doors.

EVERY WEAKNESS

1902—Bella Strega

James riffled through the stack of papers that Jianyu had been so generous to liberate from Morgan's mansion, but he couldn't quite believe what he was reading. He'd known J. P. Morgan was a collector, known as well that the Morgan mansion must have contained numerous secrets—he never would have maneuvered Dolph and Leena into infiltrating it otherwise. But he hadn't really expected *this*.

Never underestimate the ambition of men to dig their own graves.

He flipped over another sheet of paper and marveled at the secrets it contained. Line after line told the story of the men of the city, both past and present. Every weakness. Every possible indiscretion. Morgan, clearly, had been angling for more power for some time now. With this information at his disposal? He should have been able to claim the highest position in the Inner Circle. Had it not been for the bumbling mistakes of his nephew, perhaps he would have.

The collected scraps and bits of parchment told a history of the Order that was unlike any James had ever encountered. Here was evidence of their every victory and failure. It was a *true* accounting, rather than the narrative of half-truths and myths they currently wrapped themselves in.

The Aether danced when he picked up one of the sheets of parchment, an overlarge document compared to the others. Its ink had long ago browned and faded with age, but he knew at once that it was the most exciting—and perhaps the most important—of them all.

Newton's Sigils. There they were, clearly sketched on the page, just as

Werner and Logan had described them. According to the document, the thin discs were made of mercury, not silver. The Sigil of Ameth had been carved into their surface, just as it appeared in the painting of Newton with the Book that currently hung over the bookcase.

Here at last were the answers he had been searching for: the sigils could be used as a key. They could be used to get through the Brink.

It wasn't their original intent. Newton had designed them to neutralize the power of the Book. He'd infused them with some of his own power, because *Newton had been Mageus.*

He hadn't been a Sundren searching for power that wasn't his to claim, as the story went. No, he'd had a connection to the old magic already, but genius that he was, he'd learned that he could harness *more.* Just as alchemists sought to transform lead into gold, Newton understood that the Ars Arcana contained a piece of old magic, a shard so pure that it could transform *him.*

Myth and legend called what he was attempting to do to the philosopher's stone, the key to eternal life. But these documents made it clear that the philosopher's stone wasn't an object. It was a ritual that gave victory over *time* itself. But Newton had never finished that ritual. Something had happened. He hadn't been strong enough to look into the fire and live. He'd nearly gone mad from what the ritual had done to his affinity, so he'd fashioned the sigils to contain and neutralize the power in the Book.

With them, he created a space where the Book's power could be constrained.

Newton had given the Book of Mysteries and the artifacts to the men who would form the Order. He'd given them the sigils as well, a safeguard against the Book's power.

A hundred years later and those men had forgotten the danger in those pages. They had only remembered the promise. They either forgot the risk or believed themselves stronger than Newton, and they'd used the Book and the artifacts. They too failed in completing the ritual and created the Brink instead. Too late, the forefathers of the Order realized their error and found themselves trapped within a boundary of their own making. But they still had the sigils. And they found a way to use them.

He'd known that Cela Johnson's location would be important—the Aether had pushed him toward her and the objects she was hiding. But James hadn't imagined how essential the sigils could be.

With them, he could control the Brink.

More importantly, with them, he could control *Esta*—and with her affinity, he could finally claim the power of the Book for his own.

A knock came at the door, but the clock on the shelf told James that it was far too early for news of the sigils' location. Tucking the papers back into the leather envelope, he called for whoever it was on the other side to wait. Then, after Morgan's papers were secured, he opened the door to find Logan on the other side.

"Razor Riley is downstairs in the Strega," Logan said, looking clearly uncomfortable about this news. "He's asking for you."

"Why?" James sensed the Aether bunching somewhere far off, but the vibrations were steadily growing. Something was coming. Something new was happening, and whatever it was, it left him feeling uneasy.

Logan shrugged. "He wouldn't say. He wants to talk to you."

"Fine." He locked up the apartment and led the way down to the saloon.

Just as Logan had said, Razor Riley was waiting near the bar along with one of the other Five Pointers, Itsky Joe. Razor always looked like he was on the edge of exploding, but Joe looked uncomfortable. The shifty way their eyes took in the barroom, the defensive hunch to their shoulders, told him that the premonition he'd felt earlier hadn't been wrong.

Catching their attention from across the room, James gave a jerk of his head for them to follow him to his usual table. He sat with his back safely against the wall while they stood before him. He didn't bother to invite them to sit.

"I hope you're bringing me good news from Atlantic City?" He cocked a brow in their general direction expectantly.

Razor Riley was older than James by at least a decade, probably more. He had an ugly face made worse by a nose that had been broken one too many times. He might have been a large guy, a bruiser as good with a knife as he was with his fists, but he wasn't all that bright, not like Johnny the Fox. Yet next to Itsky Joe, Riley seemed like an actual genius.

Neither of them spoke at first, and James watched as they exchanged nervous looks. "You were stationed there, weren't you, Joe? I thought Torrio told me he'd sent you personally to watch the Johnson girl?"

Joe glanced at Razor Riley, but it was Itsky Joe who spoke. "Look, Lorcan, I'm gonna cut to the chase. Joe here'd been watching the girl for the last week, just like he was supposed to, but today she didn't come out of the hotel after her normal shift. We looked everywhere for her. She's gone."

"What do you mean she's gone?" James demanded, trying to keep his voice cold and level as he stared at the two men across from him.

"He means she's gone. She wasn't in the hotel, and she never went back to her rooms. I know because we searched them," Razor told him. "Somebody got to her before we did."

"Did you find anything in her rooms?" James demanded.

"No," Razor said. "All her things were like she'd left them. Seemed like she was planning on coming back. We tore the place apart looking, though. Even cut open the mattress and checked the floorboards. We didn't find any silver plates."

The Aether seemed to be laughing at him now.

"Someone has to know where she went," James said.

"The maids won't talk," Joe said. "Razor here spooked them, and now they're shut up tight as clams."

James cursed, low and vicious, as the Aether bunched around him again, the uncomfortable murmuring louder now than before.

"Get back to Atlantic City and keep your eyes open," he told the two of them. "People don't just disappear."

"We don't take orders from you," Razor told him.

James stood, gripping the silver gorgon and taking comfort in her cool sharpness. "Don't you?"

"No," Joe Itsky said with a sneer. "We don't."

"It would be a shame if our alliance shattered over something so terribly . . . *stupid.*" James glared at them as he grasped the cane topper, as he felt for the link to the marks through the silver Medusa's coiling hair.

All at once, the entire saloon seemed to change. Like a wind rustling through trees, a tremor of unease rippled through the people in the barroom, causing them to go strangely silent. As one, they turned toward the two men, and the air felt suddenly frantic with magic.

"Find her," James said once more.

This time the two Five Pointers weren't idiotic enough to refuse.

A WARNING

1902—Little Naples Cafe

By the time Viola made her way from Little Africa over to the Bowery, night had long since fallen. Her brother's place, the Little Naples Cafe, looked oddly quiet. When Paolo had been running things, raucous noise would have spilled out through the open windows and doors late into the night. But Paul was sitting in the Tombs waiting for a trial, and the lights of the Little Naples had remained low, its doors closed to those who weren't Five Pointers ever since.

With Paul still in prison, Johnny the Fox had stepped effortlessly into her brother's position as head of the Five Pointers. But her brother had made his bed, and now he could lie in it as far as Viola was concerned.

But Torrio had made a mistake. By aligning himself with Nibsy Lorcan, he'd chosen his side in the ever-churning battleground that was the Bowery. And by sending the Five Pointers after Cela? He'd made himself *her* enemy as well. If any harm at all came to Cela Johnson, Viola would make him regret it.

She watched a little longer as Razor Riley and another man scurried toward the Little Naples like the rats they were and disappeared inside. It didn't worry her none that they were there. Better to make it clear to all of them at once that she was done with their games.

Gathering herself, she crossed the street and gave the door a vicious kick. A knife was already in her hand as she stepped into the room, and without hesitation, she let it fly at the first of the Five Pointers dumb enough to charge her, pinning him to the wall through the meaty part of his arm. Then she let her affinity unfurl, felt the beating of every heart in the sparsely filled space, and brought them all down. Pulling at her affinity, she slowed their hearts until they fell unconscious, one by one, until it was only Torrio staring at her with undisguised hatred from across the room.

He stood to attack, but she sent a pulse of her magic through his blood until he too stumbled and fell back into his seat, clutching at his chest.

"Where is she?" Viola demanded as she stalked across the room. "Where have you taken her?"

"Who?" Torrio gasped, grimacing against the hold Viola had on him.

"Cela Johnson." She took a step forward, increasing the pressure slightly until Torrio's eyes widened. "I know you have her. You can tell me where you've taken her, or we can finish this now."

"I don't have the girl," he told her.

"Lies." She tightened her hold on his blood, not caring that his lips were turning blue. "I know you have her. And I do not care if I have to kill every one of your men before you give her up."

"I told you, I don't have her," Torrio said, his eyes desperate and his hands still grasping his chest as he spoke through gritted teeth.

"You were watching her for Nibsy Lorcan."

"I *was*," Torrio agreed. "But these two idiots let her slip away." He nodded toward Razor and another man.

Viola eased her grasp on Razor Riley's heartbeat until he groaned. She kicked his leg as she drew another knife from her skirts and commanded him to get up. Razor staggered to a sitting position and then to his feet slowly, leaning on the table for support.

"Where is Cela Johnson?" she demanded.

Razor glared at her, but he didn't speak, so she pushed more of her affinity into Torrio.

"Tell her," Torrio growled, his voice rough with the strain of what she was doing to him.

"Gone," Razor said, hatred burning in his eyes. "I told Lorcan already, someone else got to her first."

"I don't believe you," she told them. She *couldn't* believe them. Because Cela had to be with them. They *had* to know where she was. The alternative was unthinkable. "If you can't tell me the truth, you're useless to me."

Torrio groaned as she tightened her hold on him, but he sneered up at her. His face was colored with the same hatred as Razor's. The same disgust that her own brother often turned on her. "You can't kill me."

She pulled his blood slower, pressed at his heartbeat. "Certo?"

He gave her a leering smile. "You won't. Not if you ever want to see your mother again."

Viola's hold on her affinity slipped a little as the meaning of his words hit her, and she heard another moan come from the men who'd fallen. She had not thought of her mother in the weeks after the Flatiron Building. Pasqualina Vaccarelli had made it quite clear that she preferred her son and would side with him no matter what he had done. But Viola had not considered what that might mean with Paolo in jail. She'd simply assumed that with Paolo in prison, her mother would remain in her apartment close to the Italian community on Mulberry Street and that her mother's life would go on as always, the daily cycle of mass and market and martyrdom that characterized the lives of so many women in the Bowery.

She'd been shortsighted not to consider that Torrio would see their mother as a pawn in his play for power. She should have expected that he would take their mother into his keeping. Not to protect Pasqualina, though that's how he would make it appear. But as insurance. In case Paolo was freed from the Tombs and in case Viola herself had any thoughts to meddle with his affairs. Because Torrio knew that neither of them would put Pasqualina's life in danger.

"Paolo would gut you if you laid a single finger on her," Viola said.

"Your brother's currently indisposed," Torrio told her. "And if you kill me—if you touch any one of my men, nothing will protect her from what I can do."

Her heart was pounding, and panic was churning through her as Torrio pushed himself up to his feet, struggling against the power of her affinity. "I told you: I don't know where Cela Johnson is, and frankly, I'm finished taking orders from maggots."

"Are you?" Nibsy Lorcan stepped through the still-open doorway. "Viola," he said with a nod. "It's been a long time."

"Not long enough," she said, trying not to let her fear show. Already, she could feel the creeping ice of the mark's warning on the skin between her shoulder blades.

"Perhaps not," he agreed. "I'm going to need you to step away from my associate. We have things to discuss."

"Like hell," she said, taking a step toward Nibsy. She was already directing her affinity toward him, already sensing his blood and heart with her magic.

But Nibsy was faster. Pain shot through the ink that was inscribed in her skin, pain so sharp it brought her to her knees. She couldn't hold on to her affinity any longer, not when she felt it slipping away from her—being *ripped* from her.

"I don't want to hurt you, Viola." Nibsy continued to approach as she struggled to keep from writhing against the mark's magic that was tearing at her skin. "You could be an asset to the Devil's Own. To *me*. Just as you were to Dolph."

She was shaking her head, trying to find the strength to refuse him even as she felt herself flying apart.

"This is just a warning, Vee. It's just a small taste of what I'm capable of now." He crouched down before her. "In a moment I'm going to release you, and you're going to turn around and walk out of here. Because if you don't, that will be the end of you."

Tears were streaming down her cheeks, but she couldn't speak. "And if you die here, now, who will protect your friends? Who will protect your dear, *dear* mother?" He stood then, looming over her. It did not matter that his build was slight or that she could have easily beaten him in an actual fight, not when he had the marks.

All at once, the pain in her back ebbed, and she gasped with the relief of it.

"It's time for you to go, Viola," Nibsy commanded. "Get out of here and think about what I said. Soon you'll need to make your choice."

But she'd already made her choice—hadn't she? Then why couldn't she bring herself to say it? She felt frozen, caught in a way she never had before. Cela. Her mother. Jianyu. The Devil's Own. Dolph. The responsibility of far too many souls made it impossible to stand.

"Go," he commanded. "Before I change my mind."

Once again, the warning flared beneath her skin, and this time Viola did what he commanded. She ran.

SAFE ENOUGH

1983—Times Square

By the time the elevator opened onto the eighth floor, Harte was practically holding Esta upright. To his relief, when the doors slid open, the hallway was empty.

The wall across from the elevators was lined with mirrors, and he paused, shocked for a second to see just how bad the two of them looked. He still looked gaunt and pale from his illness in California. There were heavy, dark circles under his eyes, and his hair was standing up at all angles. With his jacket covered in filth from the subway tunnels, he looked like he'd just tumbled out of an opium den and was in need of his next hit on the pipe.

Esta's eyes met his in the mirror. She was tired-looking and dirty as well.

And wonderful. Because she was there, safe and alive and still his Esta. It didn't matter that her hair was a dark riot around her face or that her overalls were torn and dirty. But his eyes found the gash in her sleeve and the other dark patch of dampness at her side where her clothes had been ripped during her fall from the train.

"This way," Esta said, pulling away from his examination and ignoring her reflection in the mirrored wall. "We need to get into the room before someone notices us."

Beyond the bank of elevator doors, the hall split in either direction. Softly glowing lights hung overhead, and plush Oriental carpeting muffled their footsteps. Distant music drifted through the air from some unseen source. Harte kept his arm under Esta's, just to be sure, until they were finally standing in front of room 803. She used the key she'd taken from the office in the lobby without any problem, and once they were both inside, she bolted the door securely behind them.

The room reminded Harte a little of the hotel they'd stayed in back in San Francisco, where he'd recovered from the worst of his bout with the plague. That room had felt miraculous with its modern bed piled with goose-down pillows, unlimited hot water, and flickering television. This room was smaller—definitely cramped in size—but somehow it still felt like *more*.

The space was decorated with the same gleaming dark wood, richly colored carpeting, and golden accents as the lobby, but where the lobby had been grand, the room itself felt intensely intimate. Peaceful, even. On the left wall stood a single, enormous bed covered with a heavy burgundy jacquard quilt.

Esta went to the windows on the far end of the small room, where gauzy white curtains covered the bowed panes of glass. The same rich, burgundy jacquard framed the view beyond. She pushed back the filmy curtains to look at the street below. "No sign of trouble yet," she said, letting the curtains fall back into place. "I think we're safe enough for now. If anything changes, we'll be able to see from here—the entrance is below."

Harte nodded, but the lack of immediate trouble wasn't overly reassuring. He still couldn't quite reach his affinity, but the muffled silence and soft luxury of the space caused the tension in his chest to unwind a little.

He lifted the strap of the satchel over his head and, for the first time since he'd left the body that looked so much like Esta in the underground station, he set the Book and the artifacts down. They weren't really all that heavy, but he hadn't realized the weight of them—of what they meant, of what they could do—until he was no longer carrying the burden.

Taking Esta's arms gently, he turned her to see the tear in the side of her overalls. The fabric there had long since turned dark with her blood, and from the look of it, she was still bleeding. "We should take care of this."

Esta grimaced. "I need a shower first," she said, pulling away from him. "I feel like I've rolled through half the sewers in the city."

He had to force himself to let her go, to turn toward the window and focus on the steady traffic of Forty-Fourth Street to give her some privacy. But Esta didn't even bother to close the bathroom door. A minute or two later Harte heard the water starting, and he was instantly reminded of another time—it felt like a lifetime ago—when she'd installed herself in his apartment at Dolph Saunders' bidding. She'd been damn near euphoric to discover the hot running water and the porcelain tub.

He'd barely slept at all that night just from the thought of her soaking in the steaming water of that tub.

So much had changed between them since then. Perhaps there was no need, but Harte forced himself to stay at the window. Still, he couldn't stop thinking about Esta behind that door. Removing the mangled overalls. Stepping beneath the steaming spray of the modern shower.

With an exhausted sigh, he slipped off his soaked shoes and filthy jacket before sinking into the velvet club chair in the corner. He still felt far too filthy to lie on the bed, but the chair was deep and plush. He couldn't help but rest his eyes—just for a minute or two. Just until he could help Esta with her wounds.

When he opened his eyes again, he wasn't sure how much time had passed. Outside, day had turned to night, and the city lights seemed brighter than ever. Esta was standing over him, touching his arm gently to wake him.

"Harte?" She was frowning at him like she was worried.

"I'm fine," he said, trying to shake off the sleep that had overtaken him so soundly. "Sorry. I didn't mean to drift off."

Esta had wrapped herself in a thick white robe. As she moved, the front gaped a little, exposing flashes of her smooth, tawny skin. Her dark hair tumbled about her face, only barely damp from her shower.

"I waited as long as I could to wake you," she told him, lowering the sleeve of her robe to expose the soft curve of her shoulder.

He felt his gut go tight at the sight of her bare skin, clean and flushed from the heat of the shower. Without thinking, he stepped toward her, but he stopped short when she lowered the robe farther to expose the angry gash on her arm where the bullet had torn away skin. The wound had already started to fester and rot. Its ragged edges were a worrying shade of nearly black, and the skin around it was turning an unnatural gray. He didn't miss the brush of cold energy that sifted through the air when the wound was exposed.

He took her arm and examined the puckered, darkened skin. "You shouldn't have waited to wake me up."

"You needed the sleep," she said with a shrug.

He only glared at her, because he didn't trust himself to say anything else.

"My whole upper arm is starting to feel almost numb," she admitted. "It's like my blood and skin are turning to ice. And I think it's affecting my magic."

He looked over at the desk, where he'd placed the gun he'd taken from the clerk. "It must have been the bullet." His chest tightened at the thought of how much worse it would have been if the bullet had done more than simply graze her. What if it had actually gone through her arm?

"You're going to have to cut it out," she told him.

Releasing her arm, Harte stepped back. "There has to be some other answer. Maybe the Book—"

"It's spreading, Harte. I can feel it. Every second that passes, it gets worse," she said with a small shudder. "I could try to do it myself, but I'm not sure I could get everything."

"Esta, no—"

She'd already pulled the sleeve of the robe back up and turned to the pile of things he'd left on the table. When she found Viola's knife, she pressed it into his hands. "Please, Harte. You have to. Before it gets any worse."

Harte stared down at the glinting blade, horrified at the thought. "You know what this is capable of."

"I do," she said, turning her attention to the basket of supplies they'd taken from the store earlier.

"I could cut too deep," he argued. "What if I hurt you, Esta?"

"You won't," she argued. But she wasn't paying attention to him. She was too busy laying out clean towels and supplies. Gauze and some kind of ointment. A small sewing kit with the name of the hotel emblazoned on the case.

"You don't know that." He was staring down at the silvery blade, but all he could see was Esta broken and lifeless on the station floor. And then that was replaced with the thought of Esta bleeding to death there in that room. "I can't. I can't hurt you again—" His voice broke as the memory of her dying crashed through him, and he looked away, focusing on the swirling design in the carpet at his feet.

He sensed Esta stepping toward him, and when she was standing in front of him, he finally forced himself to look up from the floor. To meet her eyes. The fear and pain that had been in her expression a moment before had softened. She brushed the hair back from his forehead, but guilt turned his entire body cold. He tried to look away again, but she gently took his face in her hands, forcing him to look at her. "You *didn't* hurt me. She wasn't me, Harte."

He tried to pull away, but she stopped him.

"*She wasn't me,*" she repeated, more forcefully this time. "You *knew* that."

"Did I?" he whispered as doubt took the place of certainty.

"Of course you did," she told him.

"I didn't even try to find another solution." Nibsy had offered him an out, and he'd taken it. Had he really known it wasn't Esta? Now that they were out of danger, now that he could really think, he wondered if he'd been lying to himself. Maybe he'd just wanted to escape, like he always did.

"Whatever stupid thing you're thinking right now, you need to stop," Esta told him. "You did what you had to do to keep going, to come find me. You're not going to hurt me now."

He wished he could believe her, wished that he were half as certain as she sounded.

"I'm *already* hurt, Harte." Gently, she pressed a small, encouraging kiss to his mouth. "I trust you."

"You shouldn't," he told her, unable to stop himself from kissing her back. Softly. A brush of lips that made him want to lean in and take whatever she offered.

But she was injured, and he was a bastard for wanting more. He forced himself to pull back, to keep his hands clenched at his sides instead of pulling her closer like he wanted.

She stepped away, but she tossed an impish smile in his direction, as though she knew the direction his thoughts had taken. As though she maybe even approved. But she didn't move back toward him. She left him holding the knife, stuck in indecision, as she searched through a case of small bottles provided by the hotel. She found what looked like whiskey and downed the whole bottle, along with a handful of aspirin. Then she grabbed another bottle of something clear and downed it as well, wincing at the taste.

The knife in his hands felt cool, an impossible weight, as he watched her prepare the chair he'd just been sitting in, covering its arm with towels. "It'll be easier if I have something to support me," she told him, rolling the sleeve of her robe completely off before she took her place on the chair.

This time, not even the bare expanse of skin was enough to distract him. She was right. Even now he could see that the rot in her arm was spreading. Something had to be done. There was no other choice. As much as he couldn't imagine ever wanting to hurt her, he was going to have to do this. He was going to have to spill her blood and hope that Viola's blade didn't do worse.

"You'll tell me if I'm hurting you," he told her, a command more than a question.

"You can't hurt me any worse than this already is," she said.

Harte wasn't so sure. He'd seen Viola's dagger slice through solid wood and skewer a man's heart. He knew how badly it could cut Esta if he wasn't careful. Even once everything was ready, it took Harte a long couple of minutes to finally gather the courage to press the deadly blade into her skin.

ONE WAY OR ANOTHER

1902—Mott Street

When Viola returned with news that neither the Five Pointers nor Nibsy had Cela—or knew where she was—Jianyu knew of only one place he could turn. But as he navigated unseen through the city toward the mansion-like building at 20 Mott Street, he could not help but wonder whether he was making a mistake.

Once, he had been a regular visitor to Tom Lee's home. Once, he had been so favored by Lee and the On Leong Tong that most people in the Bowery had believed him to be Lee's nephew. But he had not stepped across the threshold of Lee's home since he had pledged his loyalty to Dolph Saunders the year before. His leaving was the ultimate betrayal, because he had left not only Lee's organization but also the closely knit community of his own people. In doing so, he had made an enemy of the self-proclaimed mayor of Chinatown. To Lee, Dolph Saunders had been yet another gwáilóu determined to keep the Chinese people in the city from claiming the success they rightly deserved, and the Devil's Own was simply another gang intent on stopping him from expanding their community and his prosperity by preventing Lee from claiming any more territory in the Bowery.

At the time, leaving the tong had been worth the risk. Lee might have helped to smuggle Jianyu into the country, and the On Leongs might have provided safety and employment once he had arrived in the city, but Jianyu had grown increasingly discontented with his role as Lee's most powerful weapon. Fleecing small family businesses was not the sort of job that had allowed him to sleep at night. At least with Dolph, Jianyu had felt like something more than a common criminal. He had felt as though he could make some small difference for Mageus in this terrible city and, hopefully, for his own people as well.

But the Bella Strega was no longer his home, and Dolph Saunders was no longer around to provide him protection. Now, Jianyu's only concern was for Cela's safety—and to keep Nibsy Lorcan from gaining any more power before Esta and Darrigan returned with the Book. He could no longer sit by and wait, willingly allowing the players in the city's game to continue without him. It was time to draw his own alliance.

With the threads of light pulled open around him, it had been easy enough to slip unseen down the busy thoroughfare that was Mott Street, the heart of Chinese life in the city. There, Jianyu was immediately surrounded by the sights and smells of his first days in New York. A wave of nostalgia swept through him, and he felt almost as though he were coming home. But with the amount of real estate Lee himself owned on the street, it was perhaps the most dangerous place he could be.

Jianyu passed 14 Mott Street, the headquarters of the tong, where Lee ruled with an iron fist. Next door, at 16 Mott Street, was the Chung Hwa Gong Shaw, or Chinatown's unofficial City Hall. There, Lee's influence was perhaps less violent but no less subtle. Lee had established himself as the leading Chinese figure in the city years before, when he aligned himself with Tammany and the police. Since then, he had acted as their deputy sheriff. It was only recently that Mock Duck and his Hip Sings had threatened that power.

Finally Jianyu reached 20 Mott Street, where Lee lived in an enormous three-story home. Its tall windows flashed in the morning sun, while balconies of fanciful wrought iron clung to its brick facade. There was not another family in the Chinese quarter that could afford three floors of luxury, and only a few of those who depended upon Lee for protection and support had ever been inside. Far fewer of the ordinary working poor could ever hope to amass even a fraction of Lee's prosperity.

In front of the building, a trio of highbinders stood guard in plain sight. In the past weeks, the Hip Sing Tong had grown bolder with its attacks on Lee and his territory. It was no doubt the result of the packet of information Nibsy Lorcan had given Mock Duck weeks before as payment for Jianyu's capture.

The rest of the city often dismissed Chinese men with their long queues and decidedly non-Western dress, viewing them as effeminate. As not *truly* masculine or virile. Few newspapers paid attention to the squabbling between the tongs, and even fewer citizens understood that these young men were every bit as deadly and dangerous as the Italian Mafia or Black Hand.

Jianyu knew better. The trio of Guards waited, sharp eyed and alert, ready to protect their employer from any danger. Well armed with knives and guns, they would shoot to kill any who might threaten their territory.

With his affinity strong and sure, Jianyu slipped easily past the high-binders. He waited a little longer until a peddler's cart clattered by, and then, using the noise to disguise the opening of the door, he let himself into Lee's mansion.

Inside, very little had changed since the last time Jianyu had been there. J. P. Morgan himself would have felt at home in the opulent space, with its plush carpets and gleaming furniture. There was even a grand piano holding court in one corner. The style of the large porcelain vases and colorful Chinese paintings gracing the walls were the one difference between the splendor of Morgan's mansion and the luxury of Lee's. But each piece of Lee's collection was particularly astounding in their beauty and rarity. Even a Westerner would easily be able to appreciate their value. Every detail of the home sent a message: Here was prestige. Here was *power*.

Perhaps once Jianyu had been swayed by the gleaming luxury of Lee's house—the promise that such prosperity could one day be his as well. Now he understood the truth. Lee had built his power and collected his riches in the same way Morgan and the other men of the Order did—on the backs of those who had no power to stand against them. On the backs of peasants who had no other choice.

LISA MAXWELL

Jianyu found Lee exactly where he expected him to be at this time of day, alone in his chambers. It was a simple thing to slip in undetected, but once he closed the door behind him, Lee knew he was no longer alone.

"I wondered when you would come back to me." The older man spoke in the Cantonese they shared. Turning in the direction of the door, Lee was almost uncanny in his ability to find the exact spot where Jianyu waited. But then, he had always been able to sense when Jianyu was near, even when he was wrapped in the light. "That is, I assume you are returning. Otherwise, you should have killed me already."

The old man looked the same. His full goatee was white with age, though the hair he had pulled back into a queue was still dark. Even now, after so many years of success and power in this new land, Lee still wore his hair long, in deference to a dynasty that currently held little power over his life. But the queue also meant that he could return to his place in Chinese society. It meant a way out should Lee ever desire one—an escape no longer available to Jianyu.

Under the cover of his magic, Jianyu lifted his hand to his own shorn hair, remembering the night a group of men had surrounded him in the Bowery, beat him, and cut his queue. But that terrible memory brought up another—the night Cela had trimmed the ragged ends of his hair, shaping them into a Western style. Her fingers soft but sure against his scalp.

He had to find her. He would do anything—even if it meant submitting to Lee—to ensure her safety.

Lee lifted one dark brow, his hooded eyes calm and sharp as he waited, ever unflappable. Ever sure in his command of the situation.

Releasing his affinity and allowing the light to close, Jianyu stepped forward, visible now. "I did not come to kill you."

"That, I think, is only the first of your many mistakes." Lee's mouth flattened.

"I do not fear your threats any longer," Jianyu said, perhaps foolishly. But he had lost his adopted home and mentor. He had lost the Delphi's Tear. And now he had lost Cela as well. What more did he have to lose?

"Perhaps you should," Lee said, his eyes flashing as brightly as the diamond stickpin in his lapel.

Jianyu inclined his head as though to agree. But he did not voice the sentiment. He would not give Lee so much this early in the negotiation. "I have not come to fight."

"I have nothing else to offer," Lee told him. "You cannot imagine you would be welcomed back with open arms."

No, Jianyu had not expected a warm welcome. In truth, he had no wish to be counted as one of Tom Lee's men again. But he needed them. And so he would do what must be done.

"I know of your problems with the Hip Sings," he said softly.

"You know nothing," Lee told him.

"Then the whispers I hear in the air are incorrect? Your men have not been picked off by Mock Duck's highbinders, while Tammany's police do nothing? Your fan-tan parlors have not been raided by the very police that promised to protect them, all because they believe that Sai Wing Mock can offer them more?" He paused, letting this information resonate. "People throughout the city are talking. They fear a new tong now, a new leader in the Bowery, one who threatens the rule of Mott Street."

Lee's cheeks were turning an angry red. "People are fools. Sai Wing Mock has no standing with Tammany. He can offer no protection to the Chinese people in this city, and his men are nothing but common criminals."

Jianyu nodded. "And yet his name is whispered from mouth to willing ear."

"Idle chatter."

"Perhaps, but people will believe it nonetheless. And bloodshed is not so idle," Jianyu said. "People grow wary of the war that is brewing."

"You tell me nothing I do not already know," Lee said. His eyes narrowed. "Why are you here?"

"I have a proposition for you. One that could be beneficial to both of us."

Lee laughed. "What good is your proposition when your word means nothing? You broke a blood oath already," he said. "And for what? A dead man cannot protect you."

"Then listen not to my words, but my actions." He took a rumpled package of papers from where he had tucked them inside his tunic and tossed them onto the table that stood between them.

Tom Lee's expression never shifted, but Jianyu could see the interest in his eyes.

"What is that?" Lee asked, making no move to pick up the packet of papers.

"Information," Jianyu said simply. "Perhaps the most powerful currency in the Bowery. You wish to know how the Hip Sings seem to anticipate your every move? You wish to know which bosses have their sights on Mott Street?"

"Everyone has their sights on Mott Street," Lee said, waving a hand dismissively. "I know this already."

"But do you know which enemies might strike, or when?" Jianyu nodded toward the package. "Once I was your eyes and ears in Chinatown, but for Dolph Saunders I did much more. I helped him build his territory and his power with the secrets I collected, and I could do the same for you."

"I have men enough for that," Lee said, sneering. "Did you believe you were so irreplaceable?"

"Can your men make Tammany bend to your will?"

Lee didn't bother to hide his interest. "Explain."

"You have long had an understanding with Tammany, and yet how many fan-tan parlors have their police raided this month?" Jianyu asked. But he did not wait for Lee to answer. "Why do you think their officers no longer honor your alliance? Because they seek more power. They see Mock Duck as the future of Chinatown. Tammany does as well. You must show them they are wrong."

There was doubt etched into Lee's features, but he was interested.

"Even now, Tammany is struggling to reassert themselves as the leaders in the city in opposition to the rich men who run the Order. But how can Tammany establish their power when the Order's patrols of mercenaries continue to stir chaos in the streets? The police have been unable to stop them. They sweep up Mageus and Sundren alike, and they make Tammany look weak. But if someone could provide information to stop these patrols? If the police knew where and when they might strike, would Tammany not be grateful?"

Lee was silent at first, considering the proposal. "I am to believe you can provide this information?"

"And more," Jianyu promised. "Think of it. With me as your eyes and ears, you will no longer be at the mercy of the Hip Sings' violence. You can reassert your place with Tammany as well."

"And in return? What do you expect?"

"Very little," Jianyu said.

"I doubt that," Tom Lee said, cutting his eyes in Jianyu's direction.

Jianyu inclined his head. "I need assistance in locating someone beyond the reach of the city," Jianyu explained. "A friend who is missing and likely in danger. I cannot leave the city, but your men could."

Tom Lee considered this, but his eyes were steady, and his expression gave nothing away. Finally, he spoke. "How can I be sure of your loyalty?"

"Name your price," Jianyu said.

"I want the Devil's Own," Lee said simply. "I want them all, and the territory now held by the Bella Strega along with them."

Jianyu fought to keep his expression from showing even a flicker of the horror he felt. "You cannot truly believe it is possible for me to deliver you the loyalty of so many."

Lee's brows rose. "Do you not think I understand that Nibsy Lorcan is aligned with Mock Duck? He has chosen a side, and in doing so, he has entered the war."

"I would happily make Nibsy pay for all he has done," Jianyu said. "But the Devil's Own, they are too vast, too diverse for me to guarantee their loyalty to you."

"You are not the only one who hears whispers in the streets," Lee said with a dark smile. "Nibsy Lorcan has a cane that once belonged to Saunders. I hear it has a certain power over the marks the Devil's Own have inscribed in their skin. I will find your friend and offer my protection, and in return, you will deliver me that cane. This is the price of the alliance you propose."

Jianyu thought of the mark on his own back and knew exactly what it would mean to hand Dolph's cane over to Tom Lee. He would be handing over his life and the life of every person who had ever trusted Dolph.

But Cela was missing. Somewhere beyond the city, beyond his ability to help her, she was in trouble, and it was in large part his fault. He had sent her away unprotected, too shortsighted to consider that Nibsy could reach far beyond the Brink. He would buy her safety now, whatever the cost. And he would see to the safety of the others later. "I will take your bargain."

"I thought you might," Lee said. He went to a tall rosewood cabinet that stood on the far side of the room. From it, he took a black braided silk band and, unfastening the ends, he turned to Jianyu.

"What is that?" Jianyu said, suddenly uneasy. The thin piece of cord looked like nothing at all, and yet his skin crawled with the cold energy coming from its clasp.

"You are not the only one with access to magic," Lee said. "I cannot trust your word, but I can trust this. You will wear this to seal our agreement. I will have command over you and your affinity . . ." Lee's expression was cold, hard. "One way or the other."

HIDDEN DEPTHS

1983—Times Square

At first Esta didn't feel the cut, but then all at once, she felt the cold magic of Viola's knife as the blade sank into her arm. She couldn't stop herself from gasping. It hurt worse than she'd expected, and she'd expected it to hurt a lot. Harte stopped with her sharp intake of breath, but she told him to keep going.

"The faster this is over with, the better," she told him. "The liquor's already helping."

It wasn't, really. Not nearly enough. But the thing about pain, really bad pain, is that there's a point at which it all starts to blend together. There's a point where the body almost stops feeling it.

Almost.

Gritting her teeth, Esta refused to so much as whimper again as Harte methodically ran the tip of the knife around the gash in her arm. He would stop again if he knew how much it *actually* hurt, and he couldn't stop. There was no way she could do this to herself.

She hadn't allowed herself to think about what the wound had meant until they'd made it safely into the hotel room. She'd known immediately that the wound had felt wrong. But when she'd taken off the ruined overalls in the bathroom, she'd still been surprised. The gash in her side was simple enough to deal with, but the festering edges of the skin where the bullet had grazed her told a truth she couldn't deny—it wasn't a natural injury. The bullet had contained some kind of ritual magic that hadn't existed in her version of the future. Even after she'd showered off the filth and scrubbed her arm clean, it looked like the infection had gotten worse. The cold still felt like it was spreading.

Harte worked slowly and carefully, his face tense with the concentration of slicing the tip of the knife through her skin without cutting too deeply. It was excruciating, but slowly, the cold magic of the wound was replaced by the warmth of her own blood. And then, finally, only the normal burning ache of a fresh cut remained.

When Harte was finished, blood welled, but there was no sign of the rotten magic that had drained the color from her skin and the affinity from her fingertips. When she reached for her affinity, it felt almost normal. The net of time hung around her, ready to be taken in hand, and only the barest whisper of Nibsy's trap remained.

"You're going to need stitches," he told her, examining the bloody wound.

"I can probably manage that," she said.

But he reached for the sewing kit and got to work.

The needle repeatedly piercing her skin hurt, but compared to the knife, the poking was almost bearable. By the time Harte had finished a row of six surprisingly neat stitches, the alcohol she'd gulped down had truly taken hold. The whole world felt softer, despite the throbbing pain in her arm.

"Not bad," she said, glancing up at him. "Who knew you were an expert tailor?"

He ran a hand through his hair and let out a ragged breath. "I couldn't afford a seamstress when I first started my act," he told her. "I had to figure things out until I could hire Cela."

Hidden depths. Sometimes she forgot how solitary he'd been for so long, living alone in the city with only his wits and charm and magic to get by. *Not alone anymore, though.* Not ever again.

After he dabbed ointment onto the stitches and wrapped her arm in gauze, Harte glanced up at her, his stormy eyes fringed with dark lashes. They'd been through so much together, but she suddenly understood what it must have been like for him back in San Francisco to be so help-less and dependent on her.

But his eyes on her—the serious way he was studying her, the care he had taken with her—made her skin feel warm. It made her *everything* feel warm. They were in a gorgeous hotel room, and now that the danger of the bullet had been taken care of, they were maybe even safe. At least for the time being. It didn't matter that her arm ached and that her side still needed to be tended to. Harte was standing there, shirtless and deter-mined, and she couldn't stop her thoughts from turning to that moment in the tunnels, when he'd touched her. She couldn't stop thinking about how she wanted him to touch her again.

"I wonder what happened to Cela," Esta said, trying to distract herself from the direction of her thoughts.

She'd met the seamstress from Wallack's during those weeks when she'd been working as Harte's assistant at the theater, back when she had been trying to con him for Dolph. Cela had been more than happy to make a costume to help Esta get back at Harte for his heavy-handedness. She'd been so brilliant with a needle and thread that Esta had barely been able to believe how stunning the finished piece had been.

Harte frowned as he secured the end of the gauze. "What do you mean?"

"Nibsy shouldn't have had the Delphi's Tear, Harte. I didn't steal that ring for him until well into the twenty-first century. I was thirteen when I took it from a party in the 1960s. But that other girl—the version of me that died—she never had Ishtar's Key. She wouldn't have been able to slip through time. Which means that Nibsy shouldn't have had the ring."

"You think he got to Cela," Harte said.

"I think it's possible," she admitted. "Something certainly changed."

"Maybe Nibsy got the ring later. We sent Jianyu to protect her. . . ."

"Maybe Jianyu wasn't enough." Esta pulled her robe back up around herself. The gash in her side still needed to be taken care of, but she could deal with that on her own.

Esta's mind was spinning furiously, trying to pull the pieces together. The answer was there; she could nearly see it. And then she did. "The diary."

"What diary?"

She ignored the question until she'd located the small notebook in the pile of papers they'd taken from the library on Orchard Street, the same one that the scrap of the Book had fallen out of earlier. The one that showed their fate. She curled her leg beneath her as she sat on the bed and opened the diary.

"What is that?" Harte asked, tilting his head to get a better view of the indecipherable writing. "And why can't we read it?"

"I think this is a record of Nibsy's life," she told him. "But for some reason, those events aren't certain anymore." Flipping through a few of the pages, she watched as the words morphed into new letters, new arrangements, bubbling up and then disappearing back into the page in a never-ending dance. "I've seen this before, or something like it. When I first came back, I brought a news clipping with me, and when I changed the events, the print did this. I used it to keep myself on track."

"You're thinking that Nibsy had access to this in the past?" His gaze shifted from the diary to her. "That he used it to find Cela?"

"I think we have to consider the possibility. The Nibsy you knew— the one I met back in 1902—wouldn't have known how to actually use the Book or the artifacts," she told him. "The Professor that I grew up with would have had to send his younger self something so he'd know what his older version knew. It makes sense that he'd send himself *every-thing*. He'd want to give himself every opportunity to avoid any possible pitfall and ensure his victory."

Harte took the diary and thumbed through it, his brows bunched together the whole time. "So at some point, something happened to change the course of his life."

"Or *he* changed something," Esta told him. "Like getting the ring from Cela."

"We can't know that for sure," he argued. "It's completely unreadable."

"But we don't know *when* it became unreadable," she said. "We don't know how long Nibsy might have had clear knowledge of his own future."

"If that's true, he would have known everything that happened," Harte realized. "Every victory. He could have avoided every past failure. He could have used this to change fate."

She took the diary from him. "I think that's exactly what he did," she said, flipping to the entry for December 21, 1902—the night of the Conclave. She handed it back to him and waited as he read. She knew when he'd reached the relevant part.

He looked up at her and then turned back to the page as though reading it again would change the words. "That can't be right," he told her, adamant. "I *refuse* to believe that *this* is what happens."

She understood his reaction. Hers had been similar, and the shock of it had nearly cost her everything. "When I first found the diary, it was only Viola and Jianyu, but the second I thought about going back to save them, it changed to that."

"No," he said, adamant. "It's wrong. Or it's another of Nibsy's tricks. Now that we know—now that *I* know—how can *that* still be the future when we know to stop it?" He closed the diary and tossed it onto the bed. "I don't believe it," he told her. "I refuse to believe that's just *it*. We have to be able to change it."

"There has to be a way to," she told him. "With the newspaper clipping, I changed things—or I changed the possibility of things. Nothing else about the past has been set in stone. Why should this be?"

"Or maybe we don't go back," Harte told her.

"That isn't an option," she reminded him. "We have to set things right. For North and Everett and Sammy. For everyone. And Ishtar's Key has to go back. Even if there were a way to keep time from unraveling, look what happens if I *don't* send the girl I was forward. You saw the girl I might have been. To Nibsy, she was nothing more than a sacrifice waiting to be made. Can you even imagine what her life must have been like to have been kept endlessly ageless, all for the sake of catching me? Despite what he did to her, she believed in him enough to risk everything for him. He broke her somehow, worse than he ever broke me."

"He never broke you, Esta," Harte told her, his voice dark with emotion. There was a rawness in his stormy eyes that made Esta feel strangely vulnerable—more exposed than she'd felt just a few minutes before when she'd been basically bared to him.

She thought at first that he might reach for her. The seconds stretched, and time felt as though it was holding its breath. She waited, wanting something she couldn't define. Needing him to touch her again.

But Harte stepped back instead.

"I'm going to wash up," he told her, his posture suddenly distant and his voice stiff.

He was avoiding her and avoiding the question of their future as well, but she let him go. She waited until she heard the bathroom door close, and when she heard the muffled sound of the water running, she finally let out a breath, wincing a little at the ache in her side, a reminder that she needed to get it bandaged.

Everything was a mess. They were stuck in a time line where Thoth hadn't been destroyed and Jack Grew had become a saint. They had an entire city hunting them—their faces were in every newspaper, on every news report. They could take a few hours to rest and regroup, but they couldn't stay in the soft, quiet luxury of that room indefinitely. Outside, the world waited. In the past, their likely deaths waited as well. Time held its breath, watching for what would come.

ENEMIES AND ALLIANCES

1902—The Bowery

The church smelled of incense. Once, the cloying sweetness of frankincense and myrrh had been a comfort to Viola. Now it reminded her of a tomb. On the altar, the priest murmured in Latin, his low voice rolling through familiar litanies as the people dotting the hard wooden pews mumbled their responses.

Viola's mother was among them. Pasqualina Vaccarelli sat in her usual position on the left side of the aisle, where she could face the Blessed Mother. Like the other women in attendance, her head was covered by a heavy mantle, and Viola knew that wooden beads turned dark by age would be spilling through her mother's fingers as Pasqualina moved silently through the prayers of the rosary. The beads had been her grandmother's, carried like a treasure across the ocean. Now they would never be Viola's.

From her own pew at the back of the church, Viola kept her veil pulled close around her face and her head bowed. She lifted her eyes only enough to take stock of the situation. There were at least three of her brother's men stationed at various points around the nave. The Five Pointers were familiar enough with the mass that they were virtually indistinguishable from the other worshippers as they stood and knelt, their hands clasped in prayer as they sang the appropriate responses to the priest's call. But the early weekday mass was populated mostly by women or those too old to work. Young and hardened by the streets as they were, Paul Kelly's men stood out.

Not Paolo's, Viola reminded herself. They were Torrio's now.

Mass ended, and the worshippers began stirring to leave. If her mother knew the men were there, she did not show it. Despite the stifling heat of the church, Pasqualina pulled her shawl around her as she left the pew, genuflected to the altar, and then turned to go. She passed Viola without seeing her.

The men began to stir, preparing to follow the older woman.

Viola allowed her magic to unfurl, but only a little. Her soul might be forever marked, but there were certain lines she would never cross. Killing here in the presence of god himself was one of those. She slowed their blood just a little, enough to have the men sinking back into their pews. Enough so she could follow her mother into the vestibule without them seeing.

"Mamma?" Viola whispered, catching her attention before Pasqualina could leave the church.

Her mother turned, dark eyes wide and a look of shock—of fear—on her wrinkled face. But the expression quickly softened to something more like confusion. "What are you doing here?" she asked in the Sicilian of her childhood. The language wrapped around her, but the harshness in her mother's tone grated against Viola's already frayed nerves.

"We have to go, Mamma," she urged. She took her mother gently by the arm and started to lead her toward the open door. Outside, the streets bustled, and freedom waited.

Her mother frowned and pulled away. "What are you talking about?"

"We need to go. Away from here," she said. "You're not safe, not without Paolo."

At her brother's name, Viola's mother's face turned hard. "You speak his name to me after what you have done?"

Unease skittered through Viola. "What *I've* done?"

"It's your fault that my Paolo, that my boy, is in that terrible place," her mother said. "Mr. Torrio, he told me everything. He told me how you betrayed your brother."

Viola took a step back. "*Torrio* is the one who betrayed Paolo, Mamma. Not me."

Pasqualina glared at her. "You think I believe this? After so little care you have for your own blood?"

"Mamma, Paolo is a dangerous man. He's made many enemies in this city," Viola explained. Enemies who had already threatened to use Pasqualina against both Viola and her brother. "And Torrio, he is one of them."

"Bah!" her mother said, throwing down the rag. "If you had any salt in that gourd of yours, you could have caught the Fox. He would have made you a fine husband, but no—"

Their time was up. Two of the Five Pointers from the church entered the vestibule. The taller of the two spoke to Viola's mother. "Signora Vaccarelli, is this girl bothering you?" He glared at Viola with a hardened expression that told her the man knew *exactly* who she was.

"Mamma," Viola pleaded. "Please. You have to believe me."

"Mr. Torrio sent us to see you safely home," the other scagnozzo said easily. "He worried that something like this might happen."

"Please," Viola pleaded. "Please come with me."

Her mother glanced at the two men looming over them, but when she turned back to Viola, her expression was as cold and unfeeling as the marble icons in the church. "Paolo, he gave you a home, gave you his protection, and what did you do in return? You chose sconosciuti over your own blood. *You* are the reason Paolo is in jail, not Mr. Torrio. You—"

"Torrio is a *rat*, Mamma. He'll use you against Paolo," she said, wishing she had more time to explain. "Johnny Torrio won't keep you safe. Neither will his men here."

"And you will?" Her mother's mouth pinched in disgust. "What? Will you take me to your melanzane?"

"Don't call them that," Viola said. Her voice was sharper than she intended it to be, but she didn't apologize, and she wouldn't retract her words.

LISA MAXWELL

Her mother pointed at her, jabbing at her chest to punctuate her words. "*There* is the truth. You could be here, working to help your brother until he returns, but still you choose others over your own blood."

"I haven't—"

"Now who lies?" Pasqualina shook her head. "I tried, Viola. I tried to be a good mother to you. I tried to make you into a good, god-fearing woman and to teach you what is right, to teach you the importance of the family. But I've failed. *Madonna*, how I've failed. Look at you. At your age I was already a wife, a *mother*. Instead, you run around the city like a crazy woman, come una *puttana*. I am finished trying." She turned to the men. "It was kind of Signore Torrio to think of me. Please, I would like to go now."

"Mamma—" She stepped toward her mother. "You can't go with them." It was the exact thing she'd come there to prevent. "You would choose Johnny Torrio over your own daughter?"

Pasqualina blinked, unmoved by the emotion in Viola's voice. She lifted a hand, as though brushing the past—and Viola with it—aside. "I have no daughter. Not anymore." Then Pasqualina Vaccarelli lifted her chin, proud and resolute, and brushed past Viola as though she were a stranger. The Five Pointers followed, and as the third passed, he gave her a rough shove with his shoulder.

Before she could even consider what to do, they were gone, leaving Viola alone in the stream of worshippers departing the church. At first, she could not move. The finality of her mother's words had turned her feet to lead. Strangely, it wasn't grief or regret that overwhelmed her now but a hollow sort of relief.

It was over. There was no returning from this, no way back into her family's arms. Not ever again.

Viola wasn't sure how she got herself back to the apartment. Navigating the bustling streets of the city felt like walking through a terrible dream.

Jianyu was already there when Viola arrived. He was sitting on the lone bench in the room, his shoulders hunched and his finger running along the underside of a black silken bracelet secured around his wrist. He was examining it so intently that he didn't notice her come in. There was an unsteady buzzing cold in the air, unnatural magic.

"What is *that*?" she asked, closing the door behind her.

Finally, he looked up at her. "It is done," he said, his voice sounding strangely hollow. When he looked up at her finally, there was a quiet desperation in his features. There was determination as well, though. "Tom Lee has agreed to our alliance. I will once more become his spy, and in return, his men already have been sent to seek out Cela."

"And that," she asked, nodding to the bit of unnatural magic tied around his wrist. "It is his price?"

"It is *part* of his price." Jianyu grimaced. "He will have my loyalty, or he will take my magic."

Viola frowned. "Only part of his price? What else does he want?" she asked, knowing already that she wouldn't like the answer.

Jianyu looked more miserable than she'd ever seen him. "He knows of Dolph's cane. I am to retrieve it for him."

Understanding settled through her. There could be only one reason Tom Lee would want the cane Dolph Saunders had carried—the same reason Nibsy Lorcan wanted it. "He wants the Devil's Own." *He* wants *us*.

Jianyu nodded.

"You can't have agreed to such a thing," she said, horrified. It was bad enough to have discovered that Nibsy Lorcan had the cane, and with it, the marks. But for Tom Lee, a Sundren who wanted only territory and wealth to have it? *No.*

"I had no choice," Jianyu said. "Cela is missing, and the fault for that lies with us. With *me*. We need Lee and his men. They can go beyond the Brink where we cannot. They can keep Nibsy too busy to cause trouble as well."

"But the marks . . ." She shook her head, unable to imagine a world where Tom Lee controlled the most powerful Mageus in the city.

LISA MAXWELL

"I have no intention of giving Tom Lee any more power than he already has," Jianyu told her. "Until his men find Cela, I have some time."

Viola nodded. "If they find her?"

"*When* they find her," he corrected. "I will do what I must. But I will not hand over the Strega or anyone who was loyal to Dolph. I will die first."

This was exactly what she feared.

It was a terrible plan. With his connections to Tammany, Tom Lee was far too powerful a force to toy with for long. Then another thought struck.

"We will figure this out," Viola promised. There had to be a way to remove that cord around his wrist without handing over every Mageus who had ever been loyal to Dolph. "Once I get Libitina back—"

"He assured me that he would know if I tried to remove it. If I do, he will enact the charm and take my magic . . . and my life." Jianyu gave her a weak smile, but the resignation in his eyes told the truth of the situation. There would be no easy way out of this. But he was right. He could have made no other choice, not when she had already failed so spectacularly to put pressure on Torrio. Trapped as they were behind the Brink, they needed help. They needed allies, even dangerous ones.

A knock sounded at the door, disrupting the heavy silence that had fallen over them. Together they turned in unison, hearts in their throats. No one but Joshua and Abel should know where they were, and both should have been in Atlantic City searching for Cela. But both would have known the rhythm to signal their identity.

Viola exchanged a look with Jianyu, a silent conversation that had both of them nodding. She readied her affinity as he eased toward the door, opening it just a crack to see who waited on the other side. And then suddenly he was flinging it open.

In the doorway stood Theo Barclay, and with him was Cela Johnson.

DISTRACTION

1983—Times Square

Harte soaked until the bathwater had gone nearly cold, but still he remained in the tub, not yet ready to face Esta again. How could he when he'd read Nibsy's diary, when he'd seen with his own eyes what their fates held?

No . . . He wouldn't let that be the future that waited for them. He'd do whatever it took to make certain of it.

His vows didn't help his conscience, though. He felt like the worst kind of ass. He'd just sliced her open and stitched her up. He'd just seen her death, there on the page of Nibsy's diary, and all he could think about was how soft her skin had felt beneath his hands. How much he wanted to touch her again.

But he was delaying the inevitable. He couldn't hide in the bathroom indefinitely. On the other side of the door, Esta was waiting. They had decisions to make, work to do.

Pulling himself from the tepid bath, he dried off and wrapped himself in a robe like the one Esta had been wearing. His reflection caught his attention, and under the bright garish glow of the modern electric lights, he was struck by how much he had changed in the last few weeks. His hair was too long. He'd always kept it neatly cut, and now it curled over the collar of the robe and fell into his face. Beneath his eyes, dark hollows told the story of too many days with no real sleep, and his once-sharp features now verged on gaunt. He looked like someone who had been sick recently, which . . . he *had* been. But he didn't want to see that weakness staring back at him. He didn't want to remember how completely *helpless* he'd been back in San Francisco.

He definitely didn't want Esta to remember that, either.

Pulling his shoulders back, he lifted his chin. *Better.* Or if it didn't make him look any better, it was as good as he was going to get.

Esta was sitting cross-legged on the bed. The robe she was wearing had come loose a little, and now it gaped, exposing the skin at the base of her throat. Maybe it was the graceful curve of her neck or maybe it was the smooth, exposed stretch of her leg that did him in, but suddenly it took everything he had not to go to her. He wanted to untie the robe and let it fall aside. He wanted to run his hands across the soft expanse of her skin. He wanted to see every inch of her. He wanted to take his time.

Touching her in the tunnels hadn't been nearly enough. Then again, Harte had a feeling that nothing would ever be enough when it came to Esta. But he forced himself to stay still. She'd been through enough in the last few hours. She'd been burned and bloodied, and now she needed time to heal. He was going to keep his hands off her.

He was going to try to, at least.

At first she didn't notice him. She was too deep in concentration, gnawing absently on her thumbnail as she studied the Ars Arcana, which was open on her lap. Stacks of Nibsy's papers were lined up around her on the bed. It looked like she'd been sorting them. When he took another step into the room, she finally looked up. He couldn't quite read the emotion in her whiskey-colored eyes.

"You didn't waste any time," he said, trying to keep the note of disappointment from his words. He knew they had to deal with what lay ahead, but he'd hoped they could set it aside—at least for the night. He wasn't ready to face the truth of what had to be done. Esta was right. They had to go back—he *knew* that—but that didn't mean he was ready to accept the possible future that Nibsy's diary had shown them.

When she frowned at him, frustration and maybe even hurt flashing through her eyes, he felt like an ass.

"I'm sorry," he told her. "That isn't what I meant. It's only that—"
How was he supposed to put everything he felt into words.

Her expression softened. "I know."

He took another step toward the bed. "Well, did you find any answers
yet?"

"Maybe." She swallowed hard enough that he could see the column of
her throat move, and then she turned back to the pages open before her.
"Jack's made our job easier with all the translations and notes he's left. I think
I found the ritual we need to use the Book as a container for the stones."

It should have been a victory, but Esta didn't seem happy or even
relieved. Her eyes were still too serious. "That bad?"

"No, that one is simple enough," she said. "Mostly because of what
the piece of magic in the Book can do." She closed the Book and stared
down at the cover.

There was more. He could see it there, on her face.

"What else did you find, Esta?"

She didn't answer at first, but when she finally looked up at him again,
he knew he wasn't going to like what she said.

"We need to talk, Harte. There are things I need to tell you. About
Chicago."

"You already told me—"

She shook her head. "Not about that. About what happened on the
stage when Jack was about to kill you. About what the piece of magic in
this Book can do and about the promise I made."

Unease slid cold down the back of his neck. "*What* promise?"

"You might want to sit down."

He took a seat on the other edge of the bed, away from the papers
and definitely away from the danger inside the Book. Then Esta told him
everything she hadn't yet—about the conversation she'd had with Seshat,
the danger of having a piece of magic held outside of time—how it
threatened the world and reality itself if it were controlled by the wrong
person or, worse, exposed to the killing power of time. Because if that

piece of magic died, everything died with it. She told him, too, about the vow she'd made to finish what Seshat started. The promise to complete the ritual and place the piece of magic back into the whole.

"Why would you promise such a thing?" he asked, horrified at the implications of what she was saying.

"You were about to die," she told him. "I would have promised *anything* to stop that from happening."

"Esta, no—"

"You would have done the same, Harte. But it wasn't only that," she told him. "I believed her. What she told me about the danger that piece of magic poses to the world—she wasn't lying. She was desperate. She just wanted to fix her mistakes."

"She wanted to destroy *you*," Harte reminded her. "She wanted to use you to destroy the entire world. I know because I *felt* it. Her anger. Her absolute desperation."

"Only because she believed there wasn't any other way," Esta argued. "She truly believed that her unmaking the world would be a kindness compared to what would happen if that piece of pure magic escaped. I offered her another way, and she accepted."

He started to argue, but she cut him off before he could form words.

"Seshat didn't have to accept the bargain, Harte. She already had me. She could have done whatever she wanted. She could have pulled me apart, taken my affinity, and *finished* it. But she didn't."

She had a point, but he didn't want to admit it. "It doesn't matter anymore. Seshat isn't a danger now, Esta. She's trapped in the Book again. We're safe."

"What if we're not?" Esta asked. "What if she wasn't lying? Seshat damaged magic. By taking it out of time, she put everything at risk. If we don't finish the ritual, if we don't place that piece of magic back into time, anyone could touch it. Especially now, with the artifacts united. If the ritual remains uncompleted, magic will die, and when it does, it will take everything with it."

"But, Esta, Seshat might have still been lying. Think about it—you grew up in a time even farther beyond the one we're currently in, and magic hadn't died yet. The world hasn't collapsed. Nearly a hundred years passed from the time I first stood on that bridge until the time you came back, and magic was *fine*."

"It wasn't fine, Harte." Esta was frowning at him, and he could sense her frustration. "Magic was basically extinct. Hardly anyone had an affinity. No one remembered what their families had even been. No one remembered what *magic* had been."

"But the world spun on," he argued, unable to stop the desperation he was feeling from seeping into his words.

"Maybe. But how much longer would it have lasted?" Esta's eyes softened. "She let me save you, Harte. She gave me another chance. I have to honor that. I have to try to complete the ritual she started."

Esta wasn't going to be swayed. He could tell by the set of her mouth and the determination in her eyes.

"Did she tell you *how* to finish the ritual, by any chance?" Harte asked sardonically, because anger was easier than fear. Safer, too.

Esta didn't take the bait. "No, but I think *you* know." She looked down at the open page and read words he'd heard not that long before. "*To catch the serpent with the hand of the philosopher*—"

"No." He tried to stop the memories of what had happened on the subway platform from flooding back. "No, Esta. Not that. You can't be serious. That ritual *killed* the girl."

"I know," she told him. "I need you to tell me what happened, Harte. I need to know what happened with the other girl—the other version of me."

"Esta, I can't—"

Moving aside a stack of papers, she scooted across the bed to where he was sitting. She was close enough now that he could smell the flowery scent of the soap on her skin, close enough that her leg rested against his. Gently, she took his hand. "Please, Harte," she said softly. "I need every detail. It's important."

He couldn't deny her. Slowly, he forced out the words. One by one, he handed his memories over to her and described everything he could remember: the ritual of drawing the circle on the floor, how she'd sliced open her finger and pressed it to the Book while she spoke words he couldn't understand. How he'd felt her affinity linking the stones, uniting them and using them to pull Seshat out of him.

"After that—you were still trapped inside the circle?" she asked. "Kind of like we're trapped inside the city by the Brink."

"And the same as Seshat was trapped when Thoth betrayed her," Harte said, drawing the connections between the rituals, between the memories.

"But you got out." Esta tilted her head, her brows drawing together. "Seshat couldn't get out of the circle Thoth trapped her in, and no one can get through the Brink."

Shame flooded through him. "I told you—I used my affinity. I forced her to give the rest of her magic over to the ritual. It drained her, and when her magic was gone, so was she."

Esta touched his cheek, pulled his face gently to hers, and kissed him softly. "It's okay," she said, kissing him again. "You did what you had to do. You *survived*."

He pulled away from her then, willed her to understand. "I had a choice, Esta. I didn't have to kill her."

"You knew she wasn't me," Esta said.

"I'm not sure that it matters," he said.

She considered that. "I think it does. If you hadn't done it, you both would have died, and that would have been terrible. Because this isn't over, Harte. There's so much more to do, so much more to make right. There's still so much at risk," she told him, and he heard the honesty in her words. "But I think what the girl did is the answer to how we fix magic. I think we need to replicate the ritual she used, but instead of putting Seshat into the Book, we need to put the beating heart of magic back into time."

Suddenly, he understood. She was talking about giving herself to it, just as the girl had done. And for what? For a half-mad demon who would have used her and tossed her aside.

"No." He was shaking his head. "I watched you die once already. I can't go through that again."

"Maybe I don't have to die. Maybe there's another way," she said. "You lived with Seshat inside of you for months. Do you really think she did the original ritual intending to die?"

"No," he admitted.

"With power *willingly given*, mercury ignites. Elements unite," she read. She tapped the page thoughtfully, and then looked up at him. "Power willingly given . . . Maybe it isn't a matter of living or dying. The girl in the station didn't give her affinity, not willingly. You *forced* her. Maybe that made the difference. Maybe if I'm willing to give up my affinity, I can finish the ritual without giving up my life."

She looked up at him through dark lashes. "Maybe I can fix everything, Harte. The Brink. The old magic. *Everything.*"

But for Harte, "maybe" wasn't good enough. "The promise you made to Seshat was to protect me—to protect the *world* from her insane desire to tear it apart. But Seshat isn't a danger anymore, Esta. Not to me, and not to the world. She's trapped in the Book again, like she was before we disrupted the flow of history. There isn't any reason to take that kind of a risk."

"Harte—"

"No, Esta," he said, refusing to listen to even one more word about the topic. "I won't allow it."

"You won't allow *what?*" she asked, and from the ice in her tone, he knew he'd said the wrong thing.

But he didn't have the strength or energy to fight her. *"Please—"*

"The answers are here, Harte. I *know* they are."

He let out a long, exhausted breath. "Maybe they are. But what if you're wrong? People don't walk away from losing their magic, Esta. My mother didn't. The girl today didn't, either."

"I think there's another way," she told him. "Seshat's trapped in the Book now, isn't she? We can use her power. Think about it. You used that other Esta's affinity to give the ritual what it wanted—the magic it demanded—and you walked out of that subway station alive. What if we use Seshat the same way? She's the one who started all of this. With the artifacts united, we can control her. We can use *her* affinity to complete the ritual in the Brink, and maybe we can walk away from that the same as you did?"

"How are we supposed to use the artifacts while they're inside the Book, Esta?" His brows were creased with worry. "If we remove them in the past, we're liable to lose them because they'll cross with themselves."

"There has to be a way," she pressed. "I've only scraped the surface of this, Harte. With all the power Thoth collected—all the knowledge and rituals—there *has* to be an answer in the Book. We can't have come this far only to stop now."

"What if you're wrong?" he asked.

"I don't think I am," she told him, far too certain for his liking.

"Are you really willing to risk everything without knowing for sure?" He moved toward her. "What about *us*, Esta? What about the future we could have together? Seshat isn't a risk. She's trapped in the Book. We don't have to do *anything*. We can go back and stop Jack and just be together."

"But the Brink—"

"The Brink is still out there," he told her, pointing toward the strange, modern city beyond. "It's terrible, but it doesn't mean we couldn't be together. The Brink isn't the thing holding us back."

"It's holding *you* back," she told him softly. "I really think that we could use Seshat to complete it. I don't think I have to give my life to do that. But more than that, Harte, could you really live in a future knowing you could have changed everything for the better but you didn't?"

He cupped her face gently. "*You* are my better," he said, letting his hands drift down her neck, down to her shoulders. He pulled her close. "I could live in any world as long as you're there with me."

"Harte . . ." Her voice was softer now.

He could not listen to any more of her arguments because he couldn't bear even one second of thinking of a world without her in it. Damn the Brink, and damn magic as well. Nothing mattered but her. So he kissed her. Fiercely. Ardently. He put everything he had, everything he was into the kiss. Because he had to stop this disastrous line of thinking. He had to convince her that this could be enough, that *they* were enough. They could go back and stop Nibsy. They could even stop Thoth. But she didn't have to die.

He couldn't lose her again.

She pulled back from him. "I know what you're doing, Darrigan."

"What?" He kissed her again, this time on that delicate skin where her jaw met her neck.

"You're trying to distract me," she said, her voice going breathy.

"Is it working?" he asked as he nuzzled into her neck.

"Maybe," she said with a sigh.

He nipped down to where her neck met her collarbone. "Then what's the problem?"

"I'm not exactly sure." She tipped her head to the side. "I just wouldn't want you to think you're getting away with it."

Drawing back, he gave her his most charming grin. "Noted."

Harte leaned in again, and this time she met him halfway, her lips parting for him. This time she was the one who deepened the kiss, who pulled him under. It wasn't her magic that made time feel like it was standing still. The whole world narrowed to her mouth against his, her fingers threading through his hair, her body moving closer to him.

Her hands slid under his robe, her palms brushing against the flat planes of his chest. Pushing his robe off his shoulders, she leaned toward him, practically climbing into his lap to get closer still.

His hands were already beginning to untie the belt of her robe when he realized what he was doing. It took every ounce of his strength to pull away from her. To stop.

LISA MAXWELL

"We can't do this," he said, barely able to catch his breath. She was looking at him with a dreamy expression that made him only want to lean in again.

"I think the train to Chicago proved that we absolutely can, Harte." She smiled as she kissed him again, and he couldn't resist the happiness of her mouth against his. But when she started to lower her robe, he stopped her.

"You're hurt, Esta."

"I'm fine," she said, lowering the robe a bit more, until her shoulders were bare to him and he could just see the gentle slope of her chest.

He tried to give her a stern look. "I just stitched you up."

She shrugged, looking down at the bandage on her arm. "You did." She glanced up through her lashes at him. "And I haven't properly thanked you."

Her hand was on his leg beneath his robe, and he couldn't stop from trembling at her touch. But when she started to inch her fingers upward, he pushed her away.

"We can't," he said. "There's too much of a risk. Until you're married to me, and—"

She pulled back, her brows snapping together. *"Married?"*

"Of course," he said, uneasy with her sudden stillness.

"I'm way too young to think about getting married," she told him.

He frowned. "You're older than half the brides in the Bowery."

"Maybe in 1902," she told him. "In my own time? People don't just run off and get married at seventeen. I can't even vote."

"Women can vote?" he asked.

She blinked, as though thrown off by his question. "Yes, but that's beside the point. You don't have to marry me, Harte. I don't need you to make an honest woman of me."

"I know I don't *have* to marry you, Esta." He suddenly felt a sinking sense of dread. "And I don't think *anyone* could make an honest woman of you."

She smacked him playfully. "I mean it. We can be together without all of that. Marriage is so . . . permanent."

"What if I *want* to marry you?" he asked. "What if I want permanent?"

Esta stared at him without speaking. Her silence was unreadable. He'd just assumed . . . After all they'd been through, he thought she felt the same.

"Unless that isn't what you want?" he asked. "I would never want you to feel any pressure—"

The corner of her mouth had twitched in amusement at that sentiment, as though to say *Good luck trying to make me do anything I don't want to do.* Some of his fear eased at the sight of it.

She was close enough that he could smell the soap from her hair, the mint on her breath. The entire world had narrowed to Esta. "I'm just saying that maybe that was a really shitty proposal, Darrigan."

He felt almost dizzy. "You'll marry me, then?"

She did smile then, satisfied like a cat who'd managed to drink all the cream. "One day. When this is all over." She leaned in and kissed him, softly at first and then more deeply, until he thought he'd never be able to come up for air. She was pushing down his robe now.

He pulled back. "We shouldn't, Esta. You're injured, and there's still the risk of a child. We can't do this."

She let out a long-suffering sigh. "Yes, Harte, we can." She climbed off the bed to go sort through the basket they'd taken from the pharmacy. When she found what she was looking for, she tossed him a package.

It took him a second to figure out what he was looking at, and then he realized. *Prophylactics.*

"I'm not going to pressure you," she told him. "But if you don't want this, I'm going to need you to tell me right now."

He looked up at her, afraid to say yes. Unwilling to say no. Knowing he wasn't anywhere near worthy of her, he felt himself nodding.

She smiled and untied her belt, and then she dropped her robe to the floor.

BOUND

1902—Uptown

Cela Johnson had barely stepped into the room before she found herself wrapped in Jianyu's ironlike embrace. She was aware of Theo closing the door behind them, of Viola's rapid spurt of Italian, but only barely. She'd been awake for nearly two days now and had already started to feel that slightly off-kilter dizziness that comes from exhaustion mixed with fear, but the second Jianyu's arms were around her, everything fell away. The fear. The worry. The room itself. For a moment it was only the strength of him, solid and secure, towering over her and the scent of him, cedar and sage, wrapping around her. Blocking out all that had happened.

But before she could register how easily they fit together, how perfectly his body aligned with the softness of hers, and how much returning to him felt like coming home, Jianyu was releasing her. Stepping back. He looked as shocked by his actions as she felt. Adorably, color pinkened the sharp lines of his cheeks and the tips of his ears.

"Cela," he said, his voice rough. "Where—" He shook his head, looking between her and Theo as though he could not believe either of them were real.

"Where have you been?" Viola demanded, cutting off Jianyu's attempt to form questions. "We thought you'd been taken."

"I nearly was," Cela told them. "But Theo found me first."

Viola turned on him, her eyes flashing. "*You?* Abel found her room torn to pieces. He is beside himself with worry. We all were! We thought Nibsy had gotten to you, or worse."

Shame flashed through Cela. "I'm sorry. I told Theo we should send word, but he thought it was too dangerous." She glanced at Theo, silently willing him to explain.

"We couldn't contact anyone," Theo told them. "Not until I was sure it was safe."

"Until *you* were sure?" Viola asked, stepping toward Theo, her finger jabbing in his direction as violently as any blade she'd ever held. "What are you even doing here? After all we did to get you out of that building, away from the Order's suspicions? You should still be in France."

"I was, but—"

"But *what*?" Viola let out a string of angry—and probably filthy— Italian curses. "Explain yourself."

"He is trying to, Viola." Jianyu placed what he probably intended as a calming hand on her arm, but she jerked away.

"I arrived back from the Continent two weeks ago," Theo said.

"You didn't send word," Viola said, frowning. She looked shocked by the news, and maybe even disappointed.

"There hasn't been time," Theo told her. "They've been watching me since I've returned. My family and the Order as well."

"You are not safe from the Order's suspicions?" Jianyu asked.

Theo shook his head. "Not completely. Thanks to you, they couldn't prove anything, and with how everything turned out back in June, they're angrier at Jack than anyone else. But Jack said enough about my involvement that they're still unsure. They don't exactly trust me."

"Still." Viola pouted. "You could have sent word. You should have let us know."

"I haven't had a minute to myself since my father summoned me back," Theo explained. "I barely had time to gather my things before my ship left. And from the minute we docked in the harbor, they've kept me busy. My father found me a position at his bank, and I started immediately upon my return. In the evenings, when I'm not working, I've been doing translations for Morgan. The Order is pretending that everything is fine, but they made it clear that I'm being tested. They've been keeping their eye on me. I couldn't risk trying to contact you, not when they were still so suspicious. I could have led them right to you."

"Yet you are here now," Jianyu said, pointing out the contradiction.

"Something happened that made it necessary," he explained. "When I was working on Morgan's papers, I overheard a meeting the Inner Circle was having. I don't think they realized the venting between the rooms was so connected, or they likely wouldn't have spoken so freely. But it was clear that the Order had information about Cela. Someone had tipped them off about her involvement with what happened at the Flatiron. They knew she was working at the hotel in Atlantic City, and they were planning on bringing her in for questioning. I had to get to her first."

Cela looked to Viola. "Once he got me out of the hotel, we had to get Newton's Sigils from where I'd stashed them at my boardinghouse. But there were men watching it. It took two days for them to give up so that we could get close."

"Two days and you could not send word?" Viola demanded.

"The last thing we wanted was to lead them back here," Theo repeated.

Cela lifted the satchel from where it was secured across her body and handed it to Jianyu. "They tore apart my room, but I had these some-where safer—the floor of the boardinghouse's root cellar. They didn't find them."

Viola snatched the bag from Jianyu. In a matter of seconds, she'd pulled her dagger from it. Her attention only on her blade, she handed the satchel back to Jianyu.

"I'm sorry I brought them back here," Cela said, feeling like she'd failed. "I've put you all at risk by coming back, but I didn't know what else to do."

Jianyu's expression softened. "You did well. Exactly as you should have."

"But Nibsy will be able to track you now," Cela said.

"He already can." Jianyu said darkly. "Better to have our weapons here. Better to meet him on our own ground than leave ourselves exposed and unprotected."

Cela bristled a little at this. "I can take care of myself, you know. Thanks to you and my brother's heavy-handedness, I have for months now." But when she saw the guilt that flashed in Jianyu's eyes, her frustration faded. "But you're right. I'm glad to be back. This city is my home. I won't let Nibsy Lorcan or the Order chase me from it again. This is where I want to stand and fight."

"It isn't only the Order and Nibsy we have to worry about now," Viola said, looking to Jianyu with an unreadable expression. "Not with Tom Lee's noose around your wrist."

Cela turned to him, confused. Her gaze dropped to his wrist and, just as Viola had said, there was a braided bit of silken cord tied there. "What is that?" She looked up at him and saw the frustration—the fear—in his eyes.

"We thought Nibsy had taken you," he explained. "We needed an ally who could move outside the city."

"But my brother could," Cela said, her stomach already flipping.

"He was already searching," Jianyu said. "We—I—could not leave it all upon Abel's shoulders."

"You went to Tom Lee for help?" Cela asked. He'd told her before how Tom Lee had treated him before he'd left the On Leongs for Dolph Saunders gang. "Why would you do that?"

"Because you were missing," Jianyu told her, the words infused with so much emotion that Cela took an actual step back.

"Well, call it off," Cela said. "You don't need him now."

Jianyu shook his head. "It is not so easy."

"It's *exactly* that easy," she told him, unnamed panic already creeping along her spine.

Jianyu only shook his head.

"But I'm *here*," Cela argued. "There's no one to look for any longer."

LISA MAXWELL

"He made an agreement that he cannot break," Viola said. "Not so long as that bit of dangerous magic lives on his arm."

Cela didn't have to ask to know the answer to her next question. There was no way Tom Lee would simply remove that bracelet of thread, not if he'd managed to trap a Mageus as powerful as Jianyu with a little bit of string.

THE CHOICE OF FATE

1983—Times Square

The throbbing in her side and arm woke Esta sometime in the deep hours of the very early morning. Still hazy with sleep, she heard the sounds of the modern city coming to her through the closed windows. The far-off honking of horns and the steady hum of traffic punctuated by the rumble of a heavy truck had been the lullaby of her childhood, the background noise of her entire life, and for a second she thought she was back in the room she'd grown up in on Orchard Street with the Professor. Her brain registered the weight of an arm thrown across her waist and the heat of the body pressed against her back. Then she remembered.

She smiled to herself in the darkness as Harte's breath fluttered against her neck. Other than her injuries, her body felt warm and relaxed. Her skin felt alive, buzzing with the memory of how Harte had touched her. Like she was something important. Valuable. Like she was *his*.

Her whole life, Esta had never felt like she fit—not with the crew she'd grown up with on Orchard Street. Not with the Devil's Own. Maybe Dakari had been different, but that hadn't stopped her from feeling the constant need to prove herself worthy. Of respect. Of love. With the Professor, she'd always needed to earn her place, and she had. But there, with Harte, Esta felt a kind of calm that she hadn't before. He'd seen the worst of who she was. He'd seen her at her weakest, and somehow it didn't matter. Somehow, he was still hers.

But then he shifted behind her, moving his arm so it pressed on the bandage at her side. A sharp burst of pain shot through the injury on her torso, and she had to clench her teeth to keep from making any noise. Once the worst of the pain had passed, she gently lifted his arm and slipped out from under it.

Wrapping the discarded robe around herself, she found the bottle of aspirin and took a couple more to dull the ache. Even with the noise she'd made, Harte still hadn't moved. He was sprawled beneath the mountain of bedcovers, his face slack with sleep. The sharpness of his cheekbones was a reminder that it hadn't been that long ago that he'd nearly died. As if she could ever forget.

Now that she was awake, she was too restless and unsettled to fall asleep again. Rather than climbing back into the bed, she grabbed the satchel that held the Book and Nibsy's papers, along with a package of Oreos from the minibar. She took everything into the bathroom, where she could turn on a light without waking Harte. The second she popped a cookie into her mouth, she realized how ravenous she was. And how much she'd missed junk food. The hit of sugar and hydrogenated oil tasted like a miracle. Maybe before, she would have barely thought about the ordinary, packaged snack, but after months of living in the past, the sweetness—the *normality*—of it felt like coming home.

She ate another as she opened the Book. The Ars Arcana was a marvel. It wasn't a single volume, as she'd always believed. Instead, it was a collection, which made sense considering that Thoth had used it as a record of the power he'd collected over the years. There were places where new pages had been added or sheets of parchment had been pasted in.

The pages were written in every language imaginable, including some that Esta didn't recognize. It was a record of Thoth's many lives over the ages. Symbols and diagrams littered most of the time-worn pages, but occasionally she came across an image painted in brilliant colors that seemed to defy its age. The Book was a startling repository of ritual magic from all corners of the world. Here were spells from the Far East, others from the southernmost tip of the Americas. Some of the writing looked to be done in Egyptian hieroglyphs. Jack had somehow translated some of the unfamiliar languages, but the parts written in more modern languages were—thanks to her training—easy enough for Esta to read.

Esta stopped at the pages she'd been studying earlier, especially the one that seemed to depict the ritual Newton had tried to perform ages ago. It was the same ritual used to create the Brink, and from what Harte had described, also the one the other version of herself had used to unite the stones and force Seshat back into the Book.

On one page, the image of the Philosopher's Hand shimmered in ink flecked with gold. The symbols above each of the fingers seemed to float within the page. The crown glinted and the star and moon almost appeared to glow. In the center of the palm, a fish sat within living flames that looked so real, she wondered how the Book didn't burn itself from within.

She'd seen this image before. It was a fairly common symbol traded among alchemists. Those who studied the occult sciences or who practiced the type of ritual magic of the Order understood the picture of the Philosopher's Hand as a recipe. In legend, it depicted the key to the transmutation of elements. With it, alchemists believed they could turn lead to gold or transform a simple mortal life into godlike immortality.

It was what Thoth wanted. To be infinite—and to be infinitely powerful.

You could have that power as well.

She frowned to herself, wondering where the thought had come from. She didn't want that power. She'd *never* wanted that power.

Running her finger over the gilded page, Esta could feel the grooves carved into the parchment by a desperate pen. The various objects represented the classical elements, and the flames represented mercury, which could unite them. But another name for mercury was Aether. *Time.* She thought of what Everett had said about Newton's quest for the philosopher's stone—how he was trying to form a boundary out of time—and she thought of what Seshat had been trying to do as well. Maybe myth and history had it wrong. Maybe the philosopher's stone wasn't an object but a place—a *space*—carved out of time. After all, Seshat had never intended to live forever. She'd wanted to make the old magic infinite—both outside of time and *part* of all time at once.

On the opposite page, Esta found markings that mirrored the burned wounds on her arm. The page was complete now—the other version of herself must have put the two together. The cipher was also complete, and she could see that what had appeared as symbols when torn in two were actually some kind of Greek. It was archaic, to be sure, but readable.

The answers are here. You need only be strong enough to take them.

Her hands trembled as she grabbed a pen and some of the hotel stationery and started to work.

Time dissolved around her—or it felt like it did. By the time she was done decoding the page, her hand was cramping, but Esta barely noticed. She finally understood.

Running a finger over the intricate sketch of the Philosopher's Hand, she wondered how she'd missed it before. The icons on the hand were connected by the element of mercury—*Aether*—just as the stones had been, both in Seshat's ritual *and* in the ritual that created the Brink.

And in the ritual the girl completed.

The boundaries formed by uniting the stones were made from time—or rather, Esta realized—they were made from time's *opposite*.

Her own affinity didn't *control* the seconds; it simply found the spaces between them and pulled them apart. Because magic lived in those spaces. It waited there, ready to unfurl, as time kept it constrained and ordered. In perfect balance. When Esta reached for her connection to the old magic, when she used her affinity to slow the seconds, she pulled those spaces apart, and in doing so she asserted power over the order imposed by time.

It was the same when she slipped through the years using Ishtar's Key. Esta didn't *control* the years. All she did was pull the layers of time, *apart*. She found the spaces and used her affinity to open them so she could slip through. After all, what was magic but the possibility of power contained within chaos? Her slipping through time had done nothing but insert chaos into the time line.

Nibsy had been wrong. Aether wasn't time itself. Aether was so much *more* than that. It was the indefinable quality of the spaces between, the substance that kept everything in balance. Her affinity wasn't for time but for its opposite. For the chaos inherent in magic itself.

That was why Seshat had been able to remove a piece of the old magic from the whole. It was the reason she could put its beating heart into the book she'd created. Not because she could touch the threads of time but because she could move them and manipulate them by controlling *magic itself.* That was also why Thoth needed Seshat, why he had *hunted* her over the ages. Without her power, he couldn't reach the pure piece of old magic trapped within the Book, and he certainly couldn't control it.

But *with* her power . . .

It was why Nibsy had used the girl to put Seshat back into the Ars Arcana. He needed Seshat's power as well.

Esta thought again of the night of the convention, of all that Seshat had told her and shown her. That night so long ago, she'd been trying to rectify her mistake. She had tried to correct the imbalance that she'd created by inventing ritualized magic.

She'd removed a piece of pure magic from the whole and infused it into the Book. But the power in those pages wasn't *inscribed.* It wasn't the stable writing of ritual. It was chaos, still pure in its possibility. A piece of magic that transcended the ordering of time.

It was why the Book could hold the stones. The magic within it was outside of time, beyond time's reach. It was also what made the Book so dangerous. If that power was released, it could destroy time and reality itself.

Esta placed her hand over the inscription of the Philosopher's Hand so that the symbols there floated above her own fingers. She turned her hand over, inspected her palm, and considered the burning fish in the drawing. *Aether.* Within herself. Outside as well.

Seshat had a similar affinity. She'd used her power to unite the stones, just as the palm united the fingers of the hand. Whole and complete, unite through the Aether that connected all things. A perfect circuit.

Had Thoth not interrupted and stopped her, Seshat would have reinserted that piece of magic back into time. But how?

She would have given up that piece of magic and the power that came with it, Esta realized. *By giving* everything *up.*

She read Newton's inscription again: *With power willingly given, mercury ignites. Elements unite. The serpent catches its tail, severs time, consumes. Transforms power to power's like.*

Power willingly given. Seshat had given nearly everything to perform the ritual. She'd placed almost all of her own affinity into the stones. *Would she have given the rest?* The girl had. That other version of herself had given up her entire connection to the old magic—or she'd been forced to.

Would it have turned out differently if the girl had been willing rather than coerced? Would the girl have survived, as Seshat would have survived? Or had Seshat always intended to die?

Somehow, Esta doubted it. Seshat believed that she would become something more by completing the ritual. The goddess didn't seem like the type to martyr herself.

But Seshat had never been able to finish the ritual. Thoth had stopped her before she could reinsert that piece of pure magic in the Book to the whole of creation, and for centuries, he'd been trying to use her power to replicate the ritual she'd never finished.

Not to save magic, as Seshat had been attempting to do. But to capture and control it.

Because maybe that's what the ritual does. "Transforms power to power's like," Esta read, puzzling over the words.

Seshat never would have just given up, and nothing about the goddess had ever struck Esta as purely altruistic. She wouldn't have sacrificed her power unless she thought she'd receive something in return. Seshat must have believed she would get something from the ritual—something more than simply saving the old magic—the same as Thoth.

Esta flipped to another page and reexamined the way the old alchemist's writing had gone from the straight, steady script to something more erratic that bordered on madness. Newton had believed the ritual was the key to the Philosopher's Stone—the answer to endless riches and eternal life. Thoth had likely used that desire for fortune and immortality to control him, the same way he'd used Jack's hatred.

Newton had been willing to *kill* for the power in the Book. He'd created the stones by sacrificing the lives and affinities of the most powerful Mageus he could find. But something had stopped him from finishing the ritual. *What was it?* Maybe he hadn't been strong enough, or maybe he hadn't been willing to give up everything—not his power and not the beating heart of magic, either.

Maybe that was the answer. Seshat had never intended to keep the magic in the Book for herself. She'd been ready to reinsert the piece of pure magic back into the whole once it was protected. She would have given it up, and in doing so, power would be transformed.

But maybe Newton had been unwilling to do that. The Order certainly had been unwilling to. They'd used the artifacts to create the Brink to *keep* their magic, but they never completed the ritual. Either because they weren't able or they refused to do what Seshat had been willing to do—to give her own power over to the ritual to complete it. To give up the power of the Book as well. *Power willingly given.*

Maybe that was why the Brink continued to take the power of Mageus who tried to cross out of the city—because it was still waiting for the final piece of the ritual. Thoth had told Esta that *time will always take what it is owed.* So too, it seemed, would magic.

But it would never be enough, Esta realized. The Brink was waiting for a power that no single Mageus could contain. It was waiting for the beating heart of magic.

That was how Seshat's ritual could still be completed. The Brink was created by the same ritual that Seshat had performed eons ago—a ritual formed by Seshat's power to touch the strands of time, just like Esta herself could. They could use that ritual. The piece of magic in the Book could be returned to the whole, and with it the Brink could be transformed into what Seshat had always intended for the ritual to create—a space where magic could not die. *Part for the whole. Like to like.* Magic could be saved.

But only if someone was willing to pay the ultimate price.

But it doesn't have *to be you. The demon goddess could be used . . .*

There *was* a way to control Seshat's power—through the stones—as Thoth had always intended. If Thoth could use the artifacts, so could Esta. She could help the goddess finish what had been started eons ago without giving up her own life.

Esta pressed her hand to the pages of the Book, as she had done in her dream, but nothing happened. She closed her eyes and tried to sense some indication of Seshat's power or her presence, but she wasn't Harte. The pages told her nothing of the life within them.

Running her fingers over the tightly bunched symbols on the page, she almost felt bad for Seshat. Maybe the ancient being *had* tried to kill her—and tried to destroy the world along with her—but once she'd been a woman who had only been trying to do the right thing.

How was Seshat any different from Esta herself? Hadn't Esta also tried to do right by magic and failed? Hadn't she, too, tried to change the course of history and made things immeasurably worse? Being trapped within lifeless pages had to be nothing short of misery. Why did Seshat deserve that fate when Esta herself now had a chance to walk free?

Whatever pity Esta might have felt, one fact remained: now that they had the Book and the artifacts, they could do what Thoth had planned all along—they could use Seshat's power to complete the ritual. They could go back and put history on the course it should have been on all along. With Seshat's power, they could fix the Brink, and by reinserting that piece of magic back into the whole, they could fix *everything*.

The problem was Nibsy.

He wanted her to return to the past. That much had been clear, even if his reason wasn't. There must be something he still needed from her. Maybe her power? Maybe he still needed to use her to control the Book.

It would be so much easier if they could just eliminate the threat he posed.

But they couldn't kill him. Otherwise, who would be waiting in the future to find the girl and to raise her? Who would send her back, so that she could remain on *this* path? It meant dooming that girl to a life being raised by a monster.

Esta had seen what this version of Nibsy had done to the girl. With her own eyes, she'd witnessed what she could have become in another life under his control. Could she really doom that other girl to that fate, just so she could claim a future with Harte for herself?

FUTURES PAST

1983—Algonquin Hotel

Harte woke from a deep sleep with a jolt. All at once he remembered what had happened in the subway station. Remembered Esta, broken and dead, and his own magic the reason it had happened.

Panicked, he struggled to free himself from the mess of blankets and sheets, but they felt like a serpent wrapped around him. Strangling him.

"Harte?" The mattress sank with Esta's weight as she sat next to him. "Are you okay?"

Not dead. The rest came back to him then as well. The rush through the city, the night they'd shared. Finally, he managed to free himself from the covers enough that he could sit up. Esta was there—*alive*—looking at him with concern.

"Fine," he told her, trying to wake himself fully. The nightmare of what had happened in that subway station still felt too close, too real. "I'm fine. Just a dream."

They were in the hotel, safe from the forces hunting them. Daylight streamed through the gauzy curtains, and he could hear the rumble of the city beyond.

He realized then that he wasn't wearing anything beneath the sheets, and though his cheeks heated at the memory of the night before, he felt desire pull low and sweet in his gut. He wanted to tumble her back into the bed and forget about everything else.

But Esta clearly had other ideas. She was already dressed—not in the robe she'd wrapped herself in the night before but in an outfit he'd never seen. A soft, oversized sweater in seafoam green concealed her shape, and pale denim pants covered the legs that had been bare just hours before. The clothing looked warm and comfortable. And he hated it.

"Where'd you get the clothes?"

"I raided the luggage in the bellhop's office," she told him. "Don't worry. I didn't let anyone see me. I got you some things too."

"Later," he said, and reached out his hand. She took it, and he tugged her toward him until she'd fallen into bed. Once she was situated across his lap, he took his time kissing her.

She hummed happily and leaned into the kiss, opening her mouth against his as she tangled her fingers in his hair.

Better. He ran his hands beneath the sweater, careful not to disturb the bandage on her side, and found the strap of her undergarments. His thumb was poised to unhook the fasteners when she went still. "Harte, wait . . ."

He did what she asked, but he left his fingers splayed across her back. Her skin was so warm beneath the thick clothing. "Do you really want me to stop?" He rubbed his thumb along the pearls of her spine until she shuddered.

"No, but—"

He kissed her before she could finish the thought, and by the time she pulled away breathless, he'd managed to unfasten the undergarment.

"Harte—" Her voice turned to a whisper as his hand ran across her skin and his thumb brushed the underside of her breast.

"Yes?" He paused, waiting for her. Dying a little with every second he didn't touch more of her.

Her head fell to his shoulder, and he felt the warmth of her breath against his skin. "I wish I could stop time forever," she whispered. "I wish we could live here in this room and this moment. Then we would never have to face what comes next. I want you—"

She leaned back to look at him, and he let her go. Let his hand fall away.

"But," he said softly, echoing her earlier statement.

"But," she agreed with a sigh.

It was only the wanting he saw there in her golden eyes that kept him from shattering completely.

For a long beat, he wondered if she would reconsider, but eventually she reached back beneath her sweater and refastened her underthings. Then she retrieved a small notepad from the chair where she must have been sitting before he woke.

"While you were sleeping, I've been working," she told him. "I think I've figured out some things."

His stomach sank. She was talking about going back, about returning the piece of magic to the whole. She was talking about risking everything for an ancient goddess who would give nothing but death and destruction in return. He'd wanted to forget about those problems—he'd wanted *Esta* to forget as well.

"I think I'm going to need to put on some pants before I hear about them," he told her.

He wrapped a sheet around himself and, taking the trousers she offered, retreated into the bathroom, where there wasn't enough cold water in the world to wash away the morning's desire.

When he could finally fasten the pants comfortably, he reemerged and found her sitting curled in the velvet armchair, deep in concentration as she read through a stack of Nibsy's papers. She noticed his entrance immediately this time, and when she looked up, her eyes raked over his body, taking in his shirtless torso and the soft woolen trousers. A part of him thrilled at seeing the heat in her gaze, but he needed her to stop looking at him like that if they were going to talk.

"Shirt?" he asked, his voice coming out more strained than he'd expected.

She blinked, and her cheeks flushed a damn delicious shade of pink.

"There are a couple to choose from," she said, visibly pulling herself together. She nodded at a pile of clothes near the television. "I wasn't sure what you'd like."

Once he was dressed, he took the chair at the desk, not trusting himself near the bed. Not when Esta kept looking at him like *that*. It took everything he had to listen to all she'd managed to puzzle out. But as she talked, some of the tightness in his chest eased.

"You really think that's the answer?" he wondered. "To use Seshat as Newton would have?"

"I do," she told him. "We have the Book, and with the artifacts, we can control Seshat. We can go back and use her power to fix the Brink. We can stop Jack before he causes any damage. We can save our friends."

The diary. Harte reached for the small book and skimmed through it until he found the date of the Conclave. He read the part of the entry that was still legible. Most of it was obscured, the details hidden by the strange changing letters, but one point was clear. "If we go back to save them, you die at the Conclave." He showed her the entry. "I *kill* you, Esta."

"*No* . . . ," she told him, as though the words weren't there, stark and accusing. And the truth. "I trust you with my life, Harte. You wouldn't hurt me."

"Maybe you shouldn't, because according to this, I already did," he said. "It's already done." He scrubbed his hand over his face, wishing he could erase the words from his memory. When he spoke again, he softened his voice. "What I don't understand is how. How the diary can be so sure—when we're here now? Years after this supposedly already happened."

Esta took the diary from him, frowning down at the page. "It didn't change to this scenario until I found it in Nibsy's library. I think the diary is certain because we are. We *will* go back. We've decided it, and one way or another, we'll change the past. We'll change it to *this*."

"But we know now," Harte pressed. "Shouldn't that fact change *everything*? Shouldn't we be able to avoid it?"

Esta's brows bunched as she considered the diary. "Maybe," she told him. "The details are still indistinct. They're still unsettled, so maybe the outcome is still undetermined."

"Except *that*," he said, pointing to their names, stark on the page.

"Except that," she repeated softly, staring down at the words as they undulated on the open page. Neither of them seemed to know what to say at first. "Maybe Nibsy knows too much. He must have had this diary in the past along with his affinity. Maybe he's seeing what we're seeing. If he has this diary, he'll always see us coming. He'll be able to outmaneuver us." She looked up at him then, a spark of determination in her golden eyes. "But he doesn't win."

"It sure as hell looks like he does."

She shook her head. "No. He *doesn't*. If he won—if he was able to get the Book and artifacts—the rest of this diary wouldn't be unreadable. History would have already settled itself into something more certain than this. And if he had won? Nibsy wouldn't have been the weak old man we just met. He would have used the Book and taken its power, and the world would already be unrecognizable." She flipped through the unreadable pages. "I think this means that there's still a way to beat him. There *has* to be."

"If we could kill Nibsy before the Conclave—"

"We can't," she told him. "We can't kill him at all."

"Why the hell not?" Harte asked.

"Once the Brink is fixed, we have to send Ishtar's Key forward with the girl. That fact hasn't changed. She still needs to be raised by the Professor, so he can send her back to find the Magician and search for the Book. Otherwise, none of *this* can happen." Her expression bunched in concentration. "I can't exist as I am now—*this* can never be—unless that happens," she told him, frowning. "Even though I die in this scenario, someone must have given the girl the stone and sent her forward. Otherwise—"

"It would have unraveled everything," Harte realized. But then another thought occurred to him. "If someone else could give the girl Ishtar's Key, maybe someone else could raise her too?"

The words in the diary wavered a little, as though suddenly the past was no longer set in stone.

"What do you mean?" she asked.

"Maybe it doesn't have to be Nibsy that raises you," Harte said, watching as the entry became more unsteady. Esta's name was still there alongside Viola and Jianyu's, but the ink almost seemed to vibrate with a new possibility. It had to mean that he was onto something.

"What if someone else could find her when she jumps forward and raise her to do what you did?" Harte pressed, thinking it through. "If there was someone else there in the future, waiting for her, we could eliminate Nibsy before *this past* becomes the truth."

Esta's expression was unreadable. "It would be such a risk to change the time line that much," she told him, chewing thoughtfully on her lower lip. "And even if we were willing to take that risk, who would we choose? Who could we trust?"

But they didn't have time to find the answer. Outside their window, a siren started to wail.

Esta leaned over and looked out through the gauzy curtains. The curse that came out of her mouth would have made a longshoreman blush.

"What is it?" Harte asked, but in truth, he already knew.

"They've found us."

PART

III

ALLIANCES

1902—The Bowery

Keeping the early-afternoon light wrapped around him, Jianyu made his way down Prince Street toward the heart of the Bowery and the stretch of the boulevard that held the Bella Strega. His pockets were weighed down with the coins he had collected from two opium dens and a fan-tan parlor, payment from the owners of each for Tom Lee's protection. The coins jangling in a pocket against his leg were a constant reminder that he was no longer his own man—that he had not been for weeks now. The circle of silk on his wrist was another reminder. One that was becoming more urgent.

Since he had accepted the piece of ritual magic in exchange for Tom Lee's help to locate Cela, the silken cord around his wrist had been easy enough to ignore. As long as Jianyu spent most of his days serving as lapdog to Lee, the tong leader had been happy enough and had not pushed the arrangement. Week after week, Jianyu had supplied information about the Order's patrols to Lee, who passed it on to the men at Tammany Hall. As the number of abductions and disappearances decreased, the police took the credit for calming the chaos in the Bowery, and Lee's standing with Big Tim Sullivan and Charlie Murphy had grown more secure.

But the Order had pulled back in the past two weeks. Without information to deliver to Tammany, Lee was becoming impatient. And with the On Leong's established ties to the political machine, things were growing more tense in Chinatown. Mock Duck's Hip Sings were becoming more brazen and violent in their attacks. Two days before, they had ransacked a gambling parlor that Lee protected and sent one of Lee's men to the hospital with numerous knife wounds. The attack was a reminder to Lee that control over the Bowery was still anyone's game, and Jianyu had not yet fulfilled his promise to deliver the Strega.

That morning, Jianyu had noticed that the bit of silk seemed to be tightening around his wrist. It was growing colder as well, like the blade of a knife poised and ready to slice. It was a message—of that Jianyu was certain. Tom Lee would not wait indefinitely for results. It did not matter if Cela was safe. As long as the silken cord tied him to Lee, their agreement stood. There was no breaking it, not even with Viola's blade. If he did not give Lee Dolph's cane—and control over the Devil's Own—he had no doubt that the braided silk would rip his affinity from him. But handing over Dolph's cane and his people to Tom Lee was an impossibility.

He would not betray the Strega or the Devil's Own, but to appease Lee, Jianyu had to make a show of his efforts to retrieve the cane. And so he had set his course toward the Strega.

Turning east, Jianyu pulled the light more securely around himself and kept a brisk pace through the nearly deserted streets. It was late in November, and the air was already starting to turn cold. Soon, winter would arrive, and with it, the punishing cold that Jianyu hated perhaps more than any other part of this terrible land. He missed the humid heat of his homeland on those cold, dark days. But there was no going back, no escape from the city, and no retreat from the course he was on.

Now that summer had closed its final pages, now that he was staring into the promise of winter's wrath, Jianyu did not know what was to come. Darrigan and Esta still had not returned. Nibsy wore the Delphi's Tear securely on his finger. And the Order's Conclave was ever closer on the horizon.

We have Newton's Sigils, he reminded himself. For reasons he could not guess, Nibsy had not tried to retrieve them again. If they could get the papers back from Nibsy, they might be able to figure out how to use the silvery discs. Because if he had to die, he would make sure his friends were safe.

LISA MAXWELL

As he made his way through the Bowery, the city seemed to be holding its breath. Throughout the dirty streets and shadowed alleyways, a strange, uneasy silence had simmered all through the summer. But the recent calm of the streets was only a mask for the chaos that waited beneath. It was only a matter of time before a spark would ignite the tinder of the city, and the streets would erupt once again.

How could it be otherwise? The danger of what was to come crept like a warning against his skin.

When Jianyu finally arrived at the Bella Strega, he paused, overwhelmed by a sense of loss he had not expected to feel. From across the street, he watched the entrance of the building that had once been his home, making note of people who came and went through the familiar, heavy door. Nibsy was likely inside, sitting in Dolph's seat in the saloon as though it had been his all along. Jianyu could picture him clearly: the boy's slight build, the glint of his thick spectacles, and the coldness in his eyes. How had none of them recognized the ice in him? How had none of them seen the snake in their midst?

And how could they hope to defeat him, when Nibsy held the power of the marks in his hands?

Finally, the person Jianyu had been waiting for emerged from the saloon. Werner Knopf had once worked for Edward Corey, the owner of the Haymarket. Before Bridget Malone had died in a fire there, Werner had helped her keep control over the often-rowdy dance floor. He had a particular affinity, one able to stop the air in a person's lungs. It made him dangerous in his own right, but Werner had never been a leader. He had always been content to take orders—first from Corey, then Dolph, and now from Nibsy.

Jianyu still was not quite sure how Dolph had managed to lure the boy to the Devil's Own or whether collecting Werner had been a good idea. But Jianyu had seen Werner's fear in the Flatiron. That night the boy had been willing to ignore Nibsy's orders to save himself. Perhaps he would be willing to do so again.

Once more, Jianyu pulled the light around himself, and then he began to follow Werner north along the Bowery, matching the other boy's pace. It was a risk, following him like this, because it was possible Werner would be able to sense him there, but it was a risk he had to take.

He followed Werner down one street and then another, until he realized the other boy's final destination was the Little Naples. When he disappeared into Paul Kelly's cafe, Jianyu found a place that was out of sight, and he settled down to wait.

It was nearly dark before Werner emerged, looking more than a little harried. Jianyu released his affinity and took one step from the shadows of the doorway he had been waiting in. Werner quickly noticed him waiting there, but to Jianyu's relief, the other boy did not take his breath. Not immediately at least. Werner's eyes shifted, right to left, as though he felt he was being watched, and then he gave a small jerk of his head, which Jianyu took to mean he should follow.

When they rounded the next corner, Werner turned on him. It was almost a relief when Werner slammed him up against the wall, placing his hand against Jianyu's throat.

"What are you doing here?" Werner demanded. "How did you find me?"

Jianyu did not even bother to shake him off. If Werner had wanted him dead, he already would be. "I followed you from the Strega."

"You can't be here," Werner told him, looking more panicked now. "If Nibsy knew I was talking to you—You're gonna get us both killed."

"I need to speak with you."

"*You* need to speak with *me*?" Werner repeated, incredulous.

"I understand that Nibsy has the marks," Jianyu said.

"Then you should've known better than to come here," Werner snapped. "What if the Fox had seen you? What if one of his men tells Nibsy?"

Jianyu tilted his head. "You fear Johnny the Fox? A Sundren you have sworn no oath to?"

Werner's mouth twisted in disgust. "Yeah, well, we all swore an oath to the Devil's Own, didn't we? You included."

"I have not broken that oath," Jianyu told him.

"No?" Werner asked. "Then what are you doing here, lurking in doorways instead of joining the rest of us in the Strega?"

"My loyalty is to Dolph, not to the one who murdered him."

Werner could not quite hide the surprise in his expression. But it quickly shifted to doubt and distrust. "Says the one who ran off and sided with Darrigan after he stabbed us in the back. Everyone knows the Five Pointers took out Dolph."

"And yet you walked out of their lair unharmed," Jianyu said. "Strange, is it not, how quickly Nibsy made allies of Dolph's supposed murderers? And now you run between them, an errand boy doing the devil's bidding."

"You don't understand nothing," Werner said. But he released him.

"Nibsy Lorcan is the one who killed Dolph," Jianyu said. "And now he uses all that Dolph built—the people Dolph once protected—for his own interests."

Werner looked unsettled, but his jaw was tight. Denial was clearly more comfortable than truth. "So what if he did kill Dolph?" Werner asked finally. "It's done, ain't it? He has the marks now. He runs the Strega. Anyone who tried to stand against him would be a fool."

"I have been called far worse," Jianyu assured him.

"You'd fight him?" Werner laughed. "What? You think you could take over the Strega and lead the Devil's Own?"

"I think that what Dolph Saunders worked for is worthy," Jianyu said. "I believe the Devil's Own should be more than Nibsy Lorcan's puppets."

"What do you want from me, Jianyu?" Werner said, sounding almost exhausted now.

"Your help."

Werner shook his head. "No, thanks."

"Not even if I can offer you a way out?" Jianyu asked.

Werner's eyes shifted. "A way out of what?"

"Everything. You would no longer have to fear Nibsy's control if you could leave the city," Jianyu told him. "Help me, and you could have your freedom from Nibsy Lorcan. You could have the entire world beyond the borders of this island."

Werner huffed out a laugh. "You're as mad as everyone says."

"Nibsy knows how to get out of the city," Jianyu told him. "Or has he not shared that information with the rest of the gang?"

That seemed to get Werner's attention, but suspicion clouded his eyes. "There ain't no way out of the city for Mageus like us."

"There is," Jianyu said. "There is a key to the Brink—a way for Mageus to pass through it without being destroyed. I have the tools. You saw the sigils Viola stole from the Order? We can use them to create a doorway. A safe passage for our kind."

Werner shook his head. "That ain't possible. People would know."

"People *did* know," Jianyu said. "The Order's Inner Circle knew. Once, long ago, it was information that the highest members protected, even from their own."

"So if you know so much, why are you sitting here talking to me?" Werner's eyes narrowed, but his interest was still keen.

"Because I do not yet have the ritual needed to use them," Jianyu admitted. "Nibsy took some papers from me a few weeks ago, papers I had stolen from J. P. Morgan's office. In them were the instructions. With those papers, the sigils could become a key to the Brink."

"You want me to get the papers," Werner realized. "You really think I'm going to stand against Nibsy for *you*?" He shook his head, a look of utter disgust on his face. "Maybe I should help *him*. Maybe I should get those discs back from you."

"Nibsy will never let you go, Werner," Jianyu said. "Your affinity is far too useful. Even if he had the discs, he has you by the mark you accepted. You are his. Unless you leave. Unless you go far beyond where he can reach. Help me get what I need, and I will make sure you are free. I can make sure anyone who has the mark can be free of Nibsy's control."

LISA MAXWELL

Werner was shaking his head, ready to reject the offer.

"Take your time," Jianyu said. "Ask Mooch what he thinks. Both of you could be gone before Nibsy Lorcan even understood what had happened. We can keep the both of you safe."

"Mooch is dead," Werner said, his voice hollow.

That news made Jianyu pause. "The Order?"

"He ran his mouth about what happened the night of the solstice, and Nibsy had enough." Werner rubbed his hand on the back of his neck. "He made an example of him."

The marks. Nibsy had used them in a show of power.

"I am sorry. But you cannot let yourself be next," Jianyu told him. "Nibsy Lorcan must be stopped, but Viola and I, we cannot do it alone. We need your help. We need the Devil's Own to remember what they once stood for, to stand again for what Dolph believed in. Think of it, Werner. Freedom from the Brink. Freedom from this city."

Werner shook his head. "I saw what Nibsy can do with those marks. I can't cross him."

"That is probably the smartest thing you've said since I met you." Logan Sullivan stepped out from around the corner then. His hands were tucked in his pockets, but the expression on his face was anything but relaxed.

Color drained from Werner's face. "You can't tell him, Logan. Please."

"Think about my offer," Jianyu said.

"He doesn't need to," Logan told Jianyu. Then he turned to Werner. "Take care of this. It's time to go."

But Jianyu had already pulled the light around himself. Before Werner had time to reach for his affinity, before he could attack, Jianyu was already gone.

A DIFFERENT LIFE

1902—Chelsea Piers

Ruby Reynolds ignored the brisk chill of the late-November breeze tearing at her hair as she studied the Manhattan skyline from the upper deck of the SS *Oceanic*. It would be a while still before they docked in Manhattan and disembarked. First the ship had to wait at the quarantine checkpoint for smaller boats to pull up alongside and transfer the new immigrants in steerage to Ellis Island.

Looking at the city in the distance, she could hardly believe it had been more than five months since she'd been sent to Europe, exiled by her own family because of what had happened at the Order's gala in the spring. Not because of the danger she'd been in, but because someone had seen her kissing Viola. Now she'd been summoned home, back to the life she'd trapped herself into. The life she'd trapped Theo into as well. But she was returning a different woman than she had been before.

When her family had decided to send her away early in the spring, Ruby had been furious. But as her sister Clara grew bored with shopping for a bridal trousseau, she'd given Ruby more and more time to herself. Time to write and to think. Time for Paris to change her.

She hadn't been looking for anything in particular when she'd wandered into the small, cluttered bookseller's shop on the left bank of the Seine, but behind its leaded glass doors, she'd found another world. Week after week, she'd met women who were permitted to have minds of their own. Women who had made entire *lives* on their own. While her sister went off to discuss the gossip from back home, Ruby was transfixed by a world where women cared more for art and politics than whose ball was the crush of the season. There Ruby saw that a different future was possible. In Paris, something was beginning, and in those rooms, she had begun to dream.

But as summer eased into fall, her mother had begun to suspect that Ruby was simply avoiding what waited when she returned to the city. Marriage. Duty. And then the endless march of days as a wife.

Theo's wife, she reminded herself. Dear, sweet Theo. Now trapped as she was in the situation *she* had created.

Their engagement had been her idea. When the first of her group found happiness in church bells and white lace, Ruby had turned to Theo, because she knew that if she *had* to marry—and really, there was little choice in her world—he, at least, would be comfortable. He, at least, would not try to press her into the mold that society had provided for a wife and mother. Theo understood her as no one else did. He would allow her to breathe, as much as anyone could breathe in her world.

She could not deny that meeting Viola had changed everything. Marriage to Theo had become less a solution than another weight to bear. But in Paris, Ruby had started to see that if she and Theo must marry, they could still make a life together that suited them.

They would return to the Continent, far from the prying eyes of New York society. Ruby could see herself in Paris, perhaps writing as Mrs. Wharton did. She could see herself establishing a salon, like Miss Stein's on the rue de Fleurus, and continuing to send her missives about life abroad to be published back in the States, as she'd been doing all summer. She could see Theo there in Paris as well, spending his mornings studying endless art in the many museums and his afternoons discussing his findings in the many salons. Theirs did not have to be a life of misery. It did not even have to be a life of regret.

And if Ruby often thought of a pair of violet eyes and the way her entire world had come into focus at the press of a single pair of soft lips? It did not matter. It *could* not matter. Viola had made that point quite clear. If Viola was not an option, Ruby would fill her life—and her heart—with other things.

Or at least, that was what she was telling herself as she pasted on a bright smile and prepared to follow Clara and Henry down the gangplank.

As she disembarked, she found Theo waiting in the crowd of the docks. It had been weeks since she'd seen him—almost as long since she'd had a letter from him—and she felt her whole self brighten at the sight of him there. She began to wave before she noticed his expression. He looked so very lost standing there in the midst of the smiling crowd that her stomach had turned itself into knots by the time she finally reached him.

"Hello," she said, feeling suddenly and unbearably awkward as she looked up at his familiar handsome face.

He leaned down and placed a chaste kiss on her cheek, as he'd done a hundred times before. "I've missed you," he said, and Ruby felt the truth of his words. But she knew implicitly that something was wrong.

"I've missed you too," she told him, meaning it. "I haven't heard from you in so long, I almost feared you'd forgotten me."

He frowned at her. "I wrote to you," he said. "Every week."

"I haven't received any letters." She turned to Clara with a silent question and saw immediately the brazen satisfaction in her sister's expression. "You *took* his *letters?*"

Clara raised her nose, imperious as ever. "We thought it best."

"Then you don't know?" Theo said before turning to Clara and Henry. "Tell me you've at least told her?"

"Told me what?" Ruby asked as her confusion grew.

"Everything's been prepared," Clara said. "What was there for her to know?"

"What was there for her to—" Theo rubbed his hand across his mouth. He looked at Ruby. "We're to be married."

"I know that," she told him, confused at the frustration in his tone.

His mouth drew itself into a flat line. "We're to be married on *Thursday.*"

"Thursday?" That couldn't be right. She was supposed to have time—to plan, to prepare. She needed time to tell Theo about the life she dreamed they might have one day.

Theo was glaring at Clara. "I can't believe you kept this from her." He ran a hand through his usually perfect hair, mussing it in a way that was distinctly un-Theo. "What else doesn't she know?"

Clara lifted her chin. "It isn't the business of a wife to question."

"What else is there?" Ruby demanded.

Her sister's mouth grew grim. "I've only done what was necessary. It's for your own good."

"Her own good," Theo mocked. He was well and truly angry now. "If you were stopping my letters, you should have prepared her."

"Prepared me for *what*?"

Theo let out a ragged breath as he turned his attention back to Ruby. "We leave for my new post with the bank the day after our wedding. There won't even be time for a wedding trip."

Ruby looked at her sister, who was still tight-lipped and unrepentant, but she barely cared about Clara's betrayal or secrecy. Even as she tried to understand what Theo was telling her, she knew. They were being sent away, exiled again. This was the Order's doing. She was sure of it.

"Where are they sending us?" Ruby asked, trying to keep her voice steady.

He grimaced. "I can't believe Clara took my letters. I'd already explained all of this. . . ."

"*Where*, Theo?"

His shoulders sank. "Kansas City."

"*Kansas City?*" It might as well have been on another planet entirely. From the look of utter misery on Theo's face, she knew he wasn't any happier about the situation than she was.

"I'm sorry, Ruby. I've tried to fight this, but there's nothing more I can do. If I don't take the post, Grandfather will cut me off. I would have no way to support us."

Because she sensed that Clara was still watching, Ruby forced herself to be calm. She tried to give Theo a brave look, but she could not manage any words of comfort. Not when they both knew the truth. They were still being punished for what had happened in May.

Half-numb, she allowed Theo to lead her farther and farther away from the ship as they followed Clara and Henry through the boisterous crowd that lined the docks. *Married*. Before the week's end, if their families had their way.

"I *am* sorry," Theo said as they walked a few paces behind her sister. "I had no idea they were keeping this from you."

"It's not your fault," she told him, looking up into his eyes. "We'll make do. We'll be together at least."

"I read your last column in the *Post*," Theo murmured a little while later.

"The one about Pompeii?"

He nodded. "It was beautifully done."

"I *was* happy with that one," she said, feeling suddenly wistful for those days in the Mediterranean sun. "It seemed somehow more important than the usual drivel I'd been writing about the width of women's skirts."

"The emotion you put into it," he told her. "The beauty of the land and the people. It's all there, clear as day on the page how you feel."

Ruby looked out over the water. She knew exactly what had made that particular article different. She'd been to Italy before, but this time she'd seen Viola everywhere she looked.

"I'm not sure if Viola saw it, but if she had . . . I think she would have understood," Theo said.

"I don't know what you're—" Her footsteps stopped along with her words. She and Theo had always had honesty between them. "It doesn't matter if she saw the piece," Ruby told him with a sigh.

"No?" he asked.

She shook her head, but she couldn't quite look him in the eye.

"I have an aunt in Edinburgh who would be happy for company," he told her. "I could get you a ticket on the very next steamer available. You could leave as early as tomorrow. She'd have you as long as you'd like."

Clara tossed a look back at them, looking more than a little disgruntled that they'd stopped. Theo pulled her along gently.

Ruby understood what he was offering, but she knew that Theo's aunt was no real answer. Edinburgh was far too cold and gray and damp. Agnes Barclay was a lovely old woman, even if she did smell of the mothballs she used to store her furs, but she wasn't a solution.

"Are you truly encouraging me to jilt you by sailing away to your spinster aunt mere days before our wedding?" Ruby lifted her hand to her chest in mock horror. "Society would never allow you to forget. The tale would follow you for years."

"Perhaps . . . Though it would have to travel across a few hundred miles to find me on the edge of the prairie," he joked.

"Perhaps you would find some strapping young pioneer woman to bear you sons," she said, trying to make light of the situation they'd found themselves in.

But her words fell flat. Instead of a joke, the statement sounded more like an accusation. It was unfair and awful of her. It was she who had roped Theo into their agreement and then turned around and kissed another. She was the one who had fallen desperately for someone else. Did he not also deserve the same?

Theo simply looked at her with his usual calm, unflappable kindness.

"Is that what *you* want?" Ruby asked, surprised to hear her voice breaking.

"What I want is for neither of us to settle," he told her, his words heartbreakingly kind. "For *neither* of us to be unhappy."

She placed her hand on his arm. "I could never be unhappy with you, Theo. A life with you wouldn't be settling."

He gave her a knowing look. "Darling . . ."

Ruby shook her head. "It's not a lie. The whole idea for the two of us to marry, it was never about *settling*. It was a way for us to somehow escape from—" *From what?* From the only lives they'd ever known? Lives that so many would give *anything* for.

She let out a long, tired breath and released his arm. "What happened to us, Theo? We had such dreams. You with your art and me with . . . *everything*."

"Everything is exactly what I want for you," Theo told her simply.

"But everything isn't possible, is it?" Ruby asked. "Maybe it never was. Perhaps we were kidding ourselves all along, and this is all that life was ever supposed to be—one long march of expectations and meaningless social responsibilities."

"We can still have adventures, darling." He gave her a small smile that barely lit his face before he grew serious again. "You know I've always loved you."

"Like a sister," she said dryly.

He wouldn't quite meet her eyes.

"Like a sister, Theo?" Ruby frowned at him, confused at the way his cheeks had gone pink. "Isn't that what you've always said?"

He took her hand in his then, but he didn't answer her question. "You're my best friend in all the world, Ruby. There isn't anything I wouldn't do for you. Be my bride. Walk away now. Whatever you want, I'll stand beside you and weather whatever storms may come our way."

She could leave. She knew in that instant that he was giving her permission to upend their lives and follow a different path. She could jilt this sweet man and return to the Continent to find her freedom. She could become a stranger in her own family, the lost spinster aunt. She might even find happiness.

Before, she likely would have taken the lifeline he'd just tossed her. Even now, if there were any chance at all that Viola could leave the city, that Viola might go with her out into the world, Ruby might have risked all. But if she could not have Viola—and she could *not*—then she would do whatever she must to make Theo's life one that he deserved.

LISA MAXWELL

Dear Theo. She took his face between her gloved hands.

"Ruby?" His cheeks went pink. "People are watching."

"Let them." It wouldn't be the first time one of her kisses created a stir. She pulled him to her. Softly, she pressed a kiss against his lips. They were warm, and he was so familiar, but she did not feel the fluttering kick of her heartbeat racing as she had when she'd kissed Viola.

"My jilting you is not a possibility," she told him.

"You're sure?"

She nodded, blinking away the tears that threatened to fall, and gave him a brave smile. "I'm sorry for what your family is doing to you, but together we will find a way through."

WHAT LIVES INSIDE

1983—Times Square

Esta's mind raced as she counted the dark vans on the street out-side the hotel. *Seven.* They completely blocked Forty-Fourth Street. Surrounding them were men and women in the same boxy coats they'd encountered back near Orchard Street—more of the Guard. One spoke into a walkie-talkie while others stood ready near the vans.

It was clear: they'd been tracked somehow. The Order or the Brotherhoods or whoever it was that the Guard now worked for had found them. They didn't have any more time to plan or consider. They needed to move. Now.

"There are some shoes that should fit you," she told him, nodding toward the pile of clothing she'd stolen from the luggage room as she gathered Nibsy's papers, the Book, and the artifacts. "They'll start search-ing the rooms soon. We probably don't have much time."

As soon as they were clothed and had gathered everything they needed, Esta took Harte's hand and pulled time slow. Her affinity felt sure and strong, as it had earlier. That, at least, was a relief.

When they slipped out into the hallway, a pair of Guards were fro-zen with their fists raised to pound on another of the doors. It was only luck that had them starting at the other end of the hall. A bleary-eyed businessman stood in one of the doorways, clad in nothing but boxers and a scowl, watching.

They took the steps down to the lobby, darting past more of the dark-suited Guards. The hotel was crawling with them, and when they reached the lobby, others were stationed at the exits and near the elevators, clearly trying to block any escape. The leader—a man with an extra set of medals across his chest—was speaking with the person behind the desk while the same yellow tiger cat stood silently by.

"They know we're here. We need to expect anything."

"Maybe we should go a different way," Harte said. "Is there a kitchen or—"

"It doesn't matter," she told him. "They would have blocked all the exits. At least this way, we have a straight shot to the street. It's gotta be close to the morning rush hour. We'll find a crowd and disappear."

Esta kept hold of time easily enough as they darted past the Guards in the lobby. As she suspected, there were Guards at the front doors as well. Through the glass, she could see more waiting outside.

"Do you think it's safe?" Harte asked.

"I don't think we have a choice," she told him.

He lifted her hand to his lips and kissed the back of it. "Then let's go."

She gave him a sure nod, and they went for it, bursting through the front doors as though every Guard in the hotel had been chasing them. She'd forgotten it was winter, and the burst of cold once she was through the door felt like a slap. For a second she thought she felt her affinity waver, but she'd barely taken another step before it was fine again. The world stayed frozen in time.

Then, all at once, the Guard waiting near one of the black vans turned toward them, and when he spoke, a familiar voice, dry as ancient parchment, came out of his mouth.

"I have waited a long time for you, Esta Filosik," the Guard said, stepping toward them with the jerky motions of a marionette dangling from strings.

"Thoth," Esta said, her voice barely a whisper. Her hand tightened on Harte's as she checked her affinity. The entire world stood still and waiting except for this one Guard. Except for Thoth.

Harte tugged at her, but she felt frozen in place. More, she had the sense that it was pointless to run. If Thoth could be anywhere, he could find her again and again.

"How are you here?" she asked. "I killed you back in Chicago."

The man-thing laughed in Thoth's eerie voice. "You killed the shell, girl. You *freed* what was inside."

"Esta," Harte said, his voice an admonition as he tried to pull her away. "We have to go."

The Guard's impossible eyes, black as an endless night, turned on Harte. "Where will you run?" the man mocked in a voice that was no longer human. "The city is mine." He spread his arms wide. "The whole *world* belongs to me."

"Not for long."

Before Esta realized what he was doing, Harte had already drawn the snub-nosed pistol he'd taken from the clerk at the pharmacy, aimed it at the man's chest, and fired.

"Oh god . . ." She looked at Harte. Then back at the man, who was already slumping to the ground. "Harte—"

The Guard was clutching his wounded stomach, and blood was already dripping from between his fingers. The darkness that had consumed his eyes was receding, and as it did, the man's face contorted in agony. But when the man looked up at the two of them, Harte saw something ancient shift across the man's features. "You cannot run," Thoth said. The Guard's teeth were red with blood, and when he coughed, more bubbled from his mouth. "You cannot hide."

"Watch us," he said.

This time Harte wasn't gentle. With a vicious jerk of her arm, he pulled Esta away from the dying man and into the crowded city beyond.

THE PRODIGAL

1902—The Docks

Jack Grew shoved his way through the crowd at the ferry docks, his stomach turning at the stink of humanity that surrounded him. He was glad to be back, even if it was without invitation. He'd been born in New York, and now that he'd seen much of the country, he was sure there was no place better. But as much as he'd missed Manhattan's finer points—the food and fashion and especially the women—he hadn't forgotten the impoverished urchins that tainted everything. He hadn't missed that at all.

The docks were littered with ragged, worn-out men and women freshly off the boat from whatever hellhole they'd left. The air stank of garlic and unwashed bodies. It seemed as though a steamer ship had skipped Ellis Island completely. Old women in babushkas and men with beards far too long and bedraggled to be fashionable waited for the next step in their journey. With any luck, they would continue on to some other place, but he wished they would just go back to wherever it was they'd come from.

Jack shoved his way past a group that might have been a family or might have been a pack of vagrants for all he knew. He kept moving until the crowded docks were finally behind him, past the line of dark carriages that waited for hire, and on to the private carriages beyond, where he found his mother's coachman, Adam—or was it Aaron?—waiting.

"Good afternoon, sir," Adam—or Aaron—said, taking Jack's bags and opening the door for him. "Did you have a pleasant holiday?"

"Holiday?" Jack asked. "Is that what the family has been calling my absence?"

Adam—or Aaron—blinked, but he didn't have a response. He turned to deal with the bags with a mumbled apology.

Jack hadn't been given a choice when he'd been shipped off to Cleveland to do inventory at one of his uncle's offices last summer. However his family had explained his absence to the rest of the world, Jack knew the truth: The position had been his uncle's way of getting him out of the city—and out of the Order's way.

But those long weeks of exile in the wilds of the Midwest had only served to convince Jack that there was no longer any use in trying to play the Order's game. Not when he could make plans of his own.

His mood darkened further the second he opened the carriage and saw his cousin J. P. Morgan Jr. waiting inside.

"Hello, Jack," Junior said without an ounce of warmth in his voice.

"How delightful. A welcoming committee of one," Jack drolled. There wasn't much choice but to take his seat on the bench across from Junior. Their knees practically touched in the cramped interior. "I assume your father sent you." He waved a dismissive hand, unwilling to allow Junior's unexpected appearance to throw him. "You might as well say whatever it is you've come to say, so we can both get on with our lives."

Junior frowned. "Come now, Jack. Can't one welcome his cousin home without so much animosity?"

"Perhaps . . . if the one offering the welcome wasn't completely full of bullshit." Jack waited, relaxed and completely at ease. Why shouldn't he be? He had the Book tucked securely against his chest, and now he had even more.

"I come on behalf of the family, of course," Junior began.

"Of course," Jack echoed, as though he cared a fig for what the rest of the family had to say.

"It worried us all when we received news that you'd relinquished your post in Cleveland," Junior began.

Jack shrugged, keeping his expression bland. "I found that the work didn't appeal to me. I gave notice, as required."

Junior frowned at Jack's impertinence. "You *disappeared*. For most of the summer, the family had no idea whether you were even still alive."

"I sent Mother a postcard. . . ." Jack gave him an indifferent smile.

"That was back in *August*," Junior sputtered, his tone every bit as imperious as the expression he wore. "It's nearly the end of November now."

"I also sent notice that I was returning," he pointed out, as though that fact should be obvious, considering Junior's current presence.

Junior bristled. "Jack, you aren't a boy anymore—"

"I'm *well* aware of that fact, even if the rest of the family regularly overlooks it."

"Be reasonable—"

"I am. More than," he said, cutting Junior off. "Your father stuck me in an insufferable position in an insufferable city. I did my duty, taking orders from the most ridiculous little man who smelled of onions and wore suits four seasons out of style, but after more than a month, I'd heard nothing from the family. I had no idea how long I was to waste out in the middle of nowhere, so I decided to take control of my life."

"You've been gone for *months*," Junior exclaimed. "Where on earth have you been?"

"I traveled around the country a bit, took in the sights." *Found what you could not.* "A grown man needs more of the world than the four walls of an ugly, cramped office, you know."

"The last time you tried to see more of the world, it ended rather badly," Junior said dryly. "Or have you forgotten what happened in Greece?"

Jack clenched his teeth and refused to give his cousin even a glimmer of temper. He wouldn't allow him the satisfaction. "Why, exactly, are you here, Junior?"

Junior let out a heavy breath, as though everything about the situation exhausted him. "The city isn't quite as it was when you left us."

"You mean when I was sent away."

His cousin glared. "The fact of the matter remains that things are . . . unsettled."

Jack lifted a single brow, inquiring. "That sounds rather unfortunate."

"After the solstice, the Inner Circle has done everything possible to silence any talk of what happened at the consecration ceremony. But the Order's alliance with the upstarts at Tammany is in tatters. We have been searching for those involved in the thefts, but with Tammany actively working against us, it's been impossible."

"You mean they won't allow you to ransack their wards as they did last winter?" Jack said, not bothering to hide his amusement. The richest men in the city, and they couldn't even manage to take in hand the filthy immigrant upstarts that ran Tammany Hall. So much for their hallowed institutions. So much for their supposed *power*.

Junior bristled. "The situation is delicate, and the family—the Inner Circle as well—has sent me to remind you of how much is at stake in the coming weeks. The Inner Circle has decided that you will remain uninvolved."

Jack didn't bother to cover his surprise. "What do you mean?"

"You'll receive this news officially soon enough, but Father believed it was important to prepare you. To avoid any unbecoming scenes," Junior said.

"What are you talking about?"

"The High Princept and the rest have decided that you should not attend the Conclave," Junior told him. "You are no longer invited to the gathering."

"Have they revoked my membership, then?" Jack asked, feeling a cold anger wash over him. In his front pocket, the Book seemed to tremble, understanding his fury.

"Not yet," his cousin told him. "But everyone involved believes it would be best if you are not present the night of the solstice. There is far too much at stake."

"Is that so?" Jack asked, forcing his voice to remain level.

"For the moment, yes. They've made their decision."

The carriage stopped at the Morgan mansion, and Junior alighted. When Jack didn't immediately follow, Junior turned to him. "The members of the Inner Circle are inside, along with the Princept. They require your presence."

"Consider their message already delivered. I'm afraid I have other plans," Jack said, keeping his voice pleasant.

Junior gave an exasperated sigh. "Come, Jack. Meeting with them now is the first step toward regaining their confidence."

"To be perfectly honest, I don't particularly care whether the old goats of the Inner Circle have confidence in me or not," Jack told him truthfully. "I actually *do* have another engagement—one I'd arranged before my arrival, as I wasn't expecting company on my ride into the city."

"Jack—"

"I'm finished dancing to their tune, Junior." Jack pulled the door shut and knocked on the roof of the carriage, leaving Junior to deal with the Inner Circle and the rest of the Morgan clan without him.

As the carriage rattled on through the city, Jack took two cubes of morphine and crushed them between his teeth simultaneously. *Finally.* Little by little, the tension in his head eased, and as the morphine lit his blood, the Book grew warmer, like a brand against his chest.

Fifteen minutes later the carriage stopped again, and Jack descended into the grime of the seaport. The area around the docks was lined with weather-beaten warehouses and teemed with longshoremen and other laborers, who looked at Jack from the corner of their eyes as he made his way through the maze of buildings.

He'd been away for months, but the warehouse he rented stood as it ever had, far at the end of the line of other low-slung structures. Making quick work of the lock, he entered the dark, dust-filled building.

Looming in the center of the space, the remains of his once-glorious machine waited. Before he'd left for Cleveland, he'd managed to rebuild the base and had been working on one of the circular arms, but he hadn't gotten much further. Now his progress was coated in dust.

He took the valise that had not left his side for the last few days and set it on the dusty tabletop. He didn't even care that the fine leather was being marred by the grime, because the contents were far more important. He opened it and took out an object he'd obtained only a few days before. *This* was what had drawn Jack away from the post where his family had deposited him and out into the wilds of the country.

With satisfaction, he held the piece up in the flickering lamplight. The ornate dagger gleamed, and the unpolished garnet in the hilt seemed almost to glow from within. He thought he might understand why legend called it the Pharaoh's Heart, because even now he could almost sense the throbbing power coming from the stone.

In a single, fluid motion, Jack brought the blade down, lodging it into the wood of the table. The stone in its hilt pulsed, blood red in the dim light of the warehouse, and Jack finally allowed himself to smile.

Let the Inner Circle believe what they wanted of him. They could try to push him out and keep him away, but they would inevitably fail. With the Book's knowledge and the power caught inside the stone, he would finish what he'd started so many months before.

Whatever the Inner Circle said, he would be at the Conclave. They could try to push him out and keep him away, but they would inevitably fail. It was time to show them all *exactly* what he was capable of. He would build his machine and harness the power of the Book, and then, when the time was right, Jack Grew would show the Brotherhoods what true power was.

All he needed was a maggot strong enough to bring all his plans to life. Fortunately, he knew how to find one.

THOSE WHO ARE LEFT

1983—Grand Central Terminal

The icy winter air nipped at Harte's cheeks, but he barely felt the cold. All around him, the world had frozen in time, caught in Esta's magic. He had no idea where he was going as he tugged Esta along. All he knew was that they needed to get away.

"How was he able to do that?" Harte asked.

"I don't know," she told him. "He always could."

The sidewalk was crowded with early-morning commuters, and Harte expected each person they passed to blink with night-dark eyes or break free from the hold Esta had on time. But no one did, and he didn't slow until they'd gone two blocks. Finally, Esta stopped him.

"We have to keep moving," he said.

"I know, but we can't just run ourselves to exhaustion. We need a plan," she told him, looking around as though to get her bearings. "I need to *think*."

"How are we going to plan when Thoth could be anywhere?" he reminded her. "He can be *anyone*. And your affinity doesn't touch him."

"So we need to go somewhere there's not a lot of people," she murmured. Suddenly her expression shifted. "I know where we can go."

She didn't explain as she took the lead, guiding him through the maze of enormous buildings that had grown up since the early century. They dodged across streets, winding through stalled traffic, until suddenly they came to a building that looked like something from the past. The cream-colored stone facade was dingy with pollution and age, but unlike the boxy, window-covered structures around it, this particular building featured towering columns and arched windows. It was crowned with a large, ornately gilded clock. Above, winged statues watched over the streets below.

"Where are we going?" he asked, trying to get his bearings in a much-changed city. All around him, skyscrapers towered. The crown of one flashed a brilliant silver in the winter sun.

"Grand Central," she told him.

On the other side of the doors, Harte found himself standing in a cavernous room topped with an arched ceiling. A train terminal. It was strangely gloomy for such a huge place, but perhaps that was because one wall of windows had been covered by a large advertisement for Kodak. Or maybe it was because the ceiling had been painted a dark cerulean blue. He thought he could almost make out the shape of constellations in the murkiness of the false sky, but he couldn't tell beneath the soot and the age of the paint. On the far end of the station, crowning what must have been the entrance to the trains, a large illuminated clock waited in vain to advance the next second forward.

Around them, crowds of travelers were caught in Esta's magic. Groups of suited men and women were clumped throughout the cavernous space mid-stride. Most had the determined expressions of people on their way to somewhere else.

"There are too many eyes here, Esta," Harte said, warily searching the crowd for any sign of movement. He wasn't going to be caught off guard again.

"I know, but it'll be faster this way," she told him. "He can't control everyone."

Harte shot her a doubtful look, because they actually *didn't* know what Thoth could do. But Esta didn't notice. She was too busy looking up at the large board on one wall.

"I'll have to let go of time," she said as she studied the tracks and the arrival times.

"No—"

"The train can't get here if it can't move, Harte. The next 6 train should be arriving in a few minutes. Until then, we can use the crowd for cover."

"Why do we need another train when we could go on foot?" he asked, not liking the idea of her letting time go.

"We could," she admitted. "But the place I have in mind is a good distance from here. Probably over an hour's walk."

That *was* a long time to risk being seen. And Thoth didn't seem to be bound by Esta's affinity, so it didn't much matter whether time was still. Better to get wherever she had in mind quickly. "Fine," he told her with a nod. "I trust you."

Warmth lit her golden eyes, and suddenly the station sprang to life. The sepulchral silence of the terminal was instantly replaced by the droning murmurs of the hundreds of people filling the large hall.

"The trains are over there," she said, pointing toward the doorway capped by the large glowing clock. Its seconds hand was steadily inching around the dial now. "We should try to time it so that we get to the platform right about the same time as the train. In case we've been spotted, we won't tip anyone off to the direction we're going until it's too late."

"I'm not jumping off any more trains," Harte told her, remembering the grime of the tunnel the day before.

"We shouldn't have to." Her eyes cut to him. "As long as your affinity's working?"

He reached for his affinity and felt the connection to the old magic that had been with him his entire life, sure and strong. He nodded.

Having his affinity back didn't make him feel any more confident. It was a sign that Esta had been right. Nibsy intended for them to return to the past. But Harte wasn't in any hurry to meet the fate waiting for him in the pages of that diary.

Looping her arm through his, Esta pressed her body close to his. "Let's go."

The tunnel that led to the trains was even more crowded than the large hall they'd just left. Dim chandeliers that might once have been ornate had too many lights missing to truly illuminate the passageway. Esta seemed unbothered by the crush of people that jostled them as they pushed their way through, but every bump and brush with a stranger put Harte more and more on edge. Along the passage, a few police officers in crisp dark-blue uniforms watched the crowd, but thankfully, there wasn't any sign of Guardsmen. And there was no sign of Thoth.

When they arrived at the platform, they still had three minutes until the train they were waiting for arrived. Esta led them over to a place by one of the steel pillars that lined the tracks and curled into him, tucking her face close to his neck. His heart raced at the scent of her so close to him before he realized what she was doing—hiding her face from the crowd. Following her lead, he dipped his head toward hers, blocking the view of their faces with the bill of his hat. It was a ridiculous-looking thing with "I ♥ NY" scrawled across the front, as though anyone could love this trap of a city.

"Just a few minutes more," she whispered, her breath warm against his neck.

"I don't mind the wait," he said honestly. Especially when she was so close to him.

She'd only just smiled up at him when he heard a commotion coming from the tunnel that led to the platform they were currently standing on. The shrillness of a whistle cut through the noise, and Harte sensed the people around them shifting. It didn't matter that the squealing of the approaching train was already echoing into the station. No one cared about its arrival, because everyone was craning their heads to look back and see what was happening. Esta stepped back from Harte, and her expression conveyed the same thing he was thinking—trouble had just arrived.

Somehow neither of them noticed that a small older woman had sidled up next to them until she was too close to avoid. She moved faster than anyone at that age had any right to, and before either of them could step back, she'd latched on to Esta's wrist.

"Let her go," Harte growled, but the old lady ignored him.

She was a tiny thing, but she must have been stronger than she looked, because Esta couldn't seem to shake her off. Or maybe she wasn't trying to? The old woman's eyes were clouded with age, but there was no inky blackness staining them.

"Gram, let that lady go," a woman with curly blond hair said. She looked at Harte with an apologetic expression. "I'm sorry about this. She doesn't mean anything."

"I know what I mean, Ella," the old lady said. "Go make yourself useful and keep them occupied."

"Gram—"

"Go!" the old woman told her. "You know what to do."

"But the Guard . . ." The frenetic energy of whatever was coming toward the platform was growing.

"Did I raise you to be a coward?" the old lady asked, which caused the younger woman to blink. "Take care of it."

The woman looked like she wanted to refuse but then thought better of it and darted off into the crowd.

The old lady turned to Esta. "We don't have much time. They're coming for you."

Esta seemed transfixed by the woman's hand around her wrist. "Who are you?"

"Someone old enough to remember," the old lady told her with a wry curve of her mouth. "I was just a girl when the Devil's Thief nearly destroyed the Order. We *all* remember."

Panic flashed through Esta's expression. "I'm not—"

"Don't play games, girl," the old lady snapped. "There isn't time. The Guard are coming, and you're injured. Worse, you're marked."

"Marked?" Harte asked, still not sure what was going on. "What are you talking about?"

The train was sliding into the station, but the wind Harte felt lifting his hair was somehow stronger than its arrival should have created. Warm energy coursed through the air, reminding Harte of the noisy music hall he'd found in the Bowery. There had been magic there as well.

"It's how they'll find you," she said. "It's how they find all of us not smart enough to keep hidden. Hold still now, and I'll do what I can."

Esta gasped, and Harte felt magic surge again. Behind them, the doors of the subway car were sliding open, and people were beginning to pour out onto the platform.

"We have to go," Harte told them, desperate to get Esta away from whatever was coming, and away from the woman as well.

Esta glanced at him, startled confusion in her expression, but she didn't seem afraid. Whatever the old lady was doing didn't seem to be harming her.

Suddenly, the old lady gasped and released her, stumbling a little. Esta reached for her, catching her before she could crumple. "Go," the woman said, trying to push Esta away. "I did what I could, but I couldn't remove the trace. Not completely. They'll be able to track you through your magic, so be careful. We can buy you some time, but if you don't go now, it'll be for nothing." She pushed Esta away as the wind on the platform increased. "Go!"

Esta was staring at the woman as though she didn't know what to do, so Harte made the decision for her. "Come on," Harte said, trying to drag Esta toward the train.

"We can't just leave her there," Esta told him.

"I'll be fine," the old lady said. She was leaning against the column now, her eyes closed. "We'll do what we can to protect you."

"Who will?" Esta asked.

The old woman's eyes opened. "All of us, dear. All of us who are left."

RESTLESS

1902—Uptown

As she waited for the water to heat, Cela heard the bells of the grandfather clock chime in the offices of the *New York Age* below. They marked another hour gone by without word from Jianyu.

Maybe she should have been used to his absences. He was up most days before dawn and rarely returned until long after dark. They didn't usually hear much from him while he was off to do the bidding of Tom Lee, working to fulfill the bargain he'd made with the tong boss to save her life. It didn't matter that she was safe. Lee had his spy, and he kept Jianyu busy from morning until night doing his bidding.

But that day, Jianyu *wasn't* working for Lee. He should have been back.

Both she and Viola had been against the idea of Jianyu going to find Werner Knopf. Viola didn't believe that the Devil's Own could be swayed to turn against Nibsy so long as he had possession of the marks, and Cela, who'd had her own experience with Werner's particular brand of magic, didn't think it was worth the risk. But neither had been able to dissuade him. Jianyu had been growing increasingly restless over the past few weeks. More and more often, he talked of the Strega and the people there, because he still believed that they could turn back to the path Dolph had set them on.

He had too much faith. Viola thought it was a fool's errand, and to a lesser extent, so did Cela. But she understood. Each day without answers meant another with Tom Lee's shackle on his wrist.

The last few months had been difficult. It had been a long, frustrating stretch, filled with days trapped in the small apartment and nights trying to save Nibsy Lorcan's castoffs. Danger was always imminent, but nothing ever seemed to happen. As summer eased into fall, hopeful patience had been replaced by consternation and desperation. No wonder Jianyu had gone. She likely would've done the same.

Finally, the sputtering from the percolator stopped, and she removed the coffee from the stovetop and took the pot to where Viola and Abel were sitting. Cela's brother had come by for an early dinner before he had to go. His train left at eight.

She'd been distracted by thoughts of Jianyu, but now she realized that Abel had been telling Viola of his plans to help them by spying on passengers.

"You can't be serious," Cela said. "If anyone suspects what you're doing, you'll be lucky if all you lose is your position. And then what?"

"I'll be fine. And there will always be another position," he told her, nodding his thanks as she poured him a cup of the freshly made coffee.

"Abel—" Cela started.

But he didn't let her finish. "The Order knows who you are, Rabbit. They wouldn't have been looking for you if they didn't think you were involved with that mess back in June. But you won't run, so I'm going to do whatever I can to protect you. I can't be here every day, but there are things I can do out there, beyond this city. There are men who would love to see the Order brought low—cattlemen and ranchers, businessmen and bankers, who are all tired of New York being the only place that matters. The other Brotherhoods are hungry, Cela. They want a piece of the power that the Order has held for too long."

Her nerves were already on edge waiting for Jianyu, but now fear and guilt churned in her as well. There was no way she could let him put himself into that kind of danger for her. "What, exactly, do you think *you* can do about it?" she asked, her voice sharper than she'd intended.

"The people who can afford Pullman berths aren't your average travelers," Abel reminded her. "They're people like the men in the Order. They don't even bother to hide their secret insignia or conversations from me. I'm just the porter." He shrugged as he took another forkful of food. "To them, I barely signify. But I hear things. A lot of people wonder just exactly how ready the Order is for the Conclave. They've heard whispers about some of the things that have happened—the fire in Khafre Hall, the move to a new set of headquarters—and they wonder if the Order is hiding something. Maybe they don't need to wonder anymore."

"They wouldn't listen to you," Cela pointed out.

Abel frowned. "Probably not, but they'd listen to one another. All it would take is a telegram or two delivered to the right people."

"How would you know the right people?" Viola wondered.

"We listen and watch," Abel said. "Me and Joshua, we know plenty of other porters who would be willing to gather some information. We know people on different lines who could send messages from the right locations. With their help, we can make it believable. If the other Brotherhoods think the Order is weak, they're more likely to cause trouble. Maybe if we cause enough problems for the Order, they'll be too busy to think about Cela here and start worrying about their own selves."

"It's too dangerous," Cela argued.

"It's no more dangerous than you staying here in the city." He shrugged, taking a careful sip from the steaming cup. "You know how white people are. They talk around the help. Listening isn't going to do anyone any harm."

"You're not talking about just listening, though," Cela said. "You're talking about forging telegrams. You're talking about involving yourself in ways that could get you killed."

"Rescuing the Order's castoffs every other week could get *you* killed, and I can't seem to stop you," he pointed out. "It's bad enough you won't leave the city. You don't have to keep risking everything in these midnight rescues."

Guilt washed over her. "I do, Abel."

"No, you don't." He put his fork down and took the napkin from his lap. "You don't owe them a thing. Certainly not your life."

"It's not because I owe them," she argued. How was she supposed to explain to him why she went with Viola and Jianyu on those midnight runs? It wasn't because she didn't understand the danger. And it was more than the rush of excitement she felt when she put on the trousers and the vest she wore to disguise herself. She'd spent her whole life living in a city where the haves could take whatever they wanted from the have-nots. But on those nights that she rode in the box of the wagon and steered them all to safety, she helped to right that imbalance—if only a little. "I owe it to myself, Abe."

When he frowned in confusion, she took his hand.

"Could you live with yourself knowing you could have saved a life, but you sat by instead?"

His mouth tightened, but he shook his head.

"Then how do you expect me to?" She gave his hand a squeeze, knowing that he would go through with his plan. Knowing that she would let him. "We're both cut from the same cloth, Abel Johnson. You and me. We aren't built to sit by."

"I'm going to go outside and wait for Jianyu," Viola said softly, excusing herself from the table. "This is a conversation for family."

Even once Viola was gone, Abel still didn't speak.

"I'm sorry I dragged you into this, Abe," Cela said finally.

He wrapped his other hand around hers. "You didn't drag me anywhere, Rabbit. I've thought this through, you know. It's going to work, and when it does, we'll have a whole network in place of people working together. Think of what we can build with that. Not just for your friends but for *our* people too. The world's changing, Cela. Pretty soon it's not going to be this place or that. This Conclave that the Order is throwing is just one example. The country's coming together, one way or another. We have to be ready too."

THE INVITATION

The bite of the late-November air was exactly what Viola needed to shake off the mood that Cela and Abel's bickering had put her in. She had already been on edge, waiting as they were for Jianyu to return from his foolish attempt to convince Werner to join them, but to see the siblings' love for each other—their mutual respect and concern, so starkly different from her own family—was too much.

It had been a long summer and a longer fall waiting for something to happen, but nothing had. Darrigan and Esta had not yet returned. Nibsy seemed content to let them suffer as they waited for him to make his move. Even the Order seemed more restrained of late—or perhaps they'd just run short of victims.

Meanwhile, Viola had been mostly confined to the small apartment they all shared above the offices of Abel's friend's newspaper. Nibsy had the marks and control over much of the Bowery, and John Torrio had the Five Pointers and control over the rest of it. Her mother no longer had a daughter. Even if she could walk the streets freely, even if she hadn't been worried that one of their enemies might follow her back and harm Cela and Abel, where would she go?

Theo seemed to be keeping his distance as well. It was necessary, she knew. His family still didn't quite trust him, and he didn't want to risk leading anyone from the Order to their location. But he was Viola's only real link to Ruby. Without his steady, sunny presence to remind her of how good he was, it was too easy for Viola to allow herself to imagine a different world, where Ruby might be hers.

Pushing away her maudlin thoughts, Viola wrapped her thin shawl around herself more tightly to ward off the chill. Luckily, the *Age* building was far enough uptown that it had a small garden in the back, if one could call a plot of dirt patched with scrubby weeds a garden. At least there, she could be under the sky. She could pretend she wasn't trapped like a rat.

She'd been out in the yard honing her blade for no more than fifteen minutes when Jianyu opened the gate. At the sight of him, some of the tension drained from her shoulders.

She lifted her hand in greeting, but the expression Jianyu wore made her pause.

"I take it that your meeting didn't go as well as you hoped?" she asked.

Without answering, Jianyu lowered himself to sit on the stoop next to Viola. "I suppose it went well enough. He did not kill me where I stood."

"Small blessings," she said dryly. "He won't join us."

"No," Jianyu said, sounding utterly deflated. "Werner's fear is too great. So long as Nibsy has Dolph's cane, he has the Devil's Own. So long as Nibsy has the Strega, the Devil's Own will suffer."

Viola frowned. "Why is their fate so important to you? Most of them never truly accepted you even when Dolph was alive. Saving them won't change that."

"It is not about their acceptance," he said, turning to her. "I had that and more with the On Leongs."

"Then what?" she asked, truly curious. They'd lived and fought side by side for so long, but she'd never really understood the strange clockworks that drove him. "Dolph is gone. You can't keep fighting for him."

"I have never fought only for him, Viola." His mouth curved grimly. "When I left the tong, it was not for Dolph. It was for myself, because I wished for something more. Dolph believed in a vision of what the world could be—for magic. For everyone. I believed in that vision."

"He was no saint, Jianyu," she said, remembering the truth of her old friend. "He hurt many people in his quest for this world he believed in."

Jianyu nodded. "He did. He helped many as well." He paused then, and the seconds stretched in silence as the city hummed around him. "I came to a point in my life when I made a choice between the man I was and the man I wanted to be. And the man I want to be would not allow innocents to suffer under Nibsy Lorcan's rule. Not the Devil's Own. Not anyone."

She looped her arm through his and leaned over to rest her head on his shoulder. "You're a good man, Jianyu," she told him. "But the world doesn't care for goodness. Only for strength."

He patted her arm. "Then I shall be strong as well."

They sat in companionable silence as the wind whipped through their hair and made their cheeks turn cold. When Jianyu spoke, his voice was serious.

"I cannot help but feel that something is starting, Viola. Beneath the peace in the streets, danger is churning. With every passing day, the Conclave grows closer, and Nibsy grows more certain of his power."

"And Darrigan hasn't returned," she acknowledged, speaking the truth that they'd both been avoiding. "You expected him by now. Esta, too."

"We are running out of time," Jianyu said. "If they do not return before the Conclave . . ." He shook his head.

Viola laid a hand upon his knee. "If they do not return, we will do what we must." But though her words were filled with confidence, the dread within her had been growing every day. They had no artifact, no allies. No idea what was coming next.

"Cela is inside?" Jianyu asked, pulling himself to his feet.

Viola nodded. "Abel as well. He has a plan to help," she said, unable to hold back her smile at the thought. Strange allies, indeed. "But he leaves on the eight o'clock train."

Jianyu was staring at the back door, not bothering to hide the concern in his eyes. Or the wanting.

"She won't go with him," Viola said. "Ask her as many times as you want, but her answer will be the same."

Jianyu let out an exhausted-sounding breath. "I know."

"At least here we can watch over her while Abel's gone."

"Perhaps." Jianyu frowned at Viola. "It is the one thing I blame Darrigan for, putting Cela at risk when he had no right."

"Only one? I have an entire list," Viola said, moving her hands far apart as though to show just how long it was.

Jianyu shook his head, amusement chasing some of the shadows from his eyes. "Perhaps I do as well."

"You should tell her how you feel," Viola said softly.

He turned to her, his expression guarded.

"I see it whenever you look at her. Anyone could," Viola told him with a shrug.

"Cela Johnson is not for me," Jianyu said stiffly. The easy companionship they'd had between them before was now replaced by formality.

"Perhaps you should give her a say in that decision," Viola suggested. "Perhaps she would feel otherwise."

But Jianyu only frowned at her a moment longer before jogging up the steps into the building.

Viola remained on the porch, thinking of bottle-green eyes and curling blond hair as she watched twilight cast shadows and the night cool to a chill. She understood Jianyu's reluctance, his fear.

She can never be mine. But how Viola wished it were otherwise.

The sky was growing deeper now, a lavender-gray that felt as somber as Viola's own mood. She wasn't ready to go in quite yet, so she stood and took her knife from its sheath. With a fluid motion, she sent it sailing toward the fence. Some of the tension in her eased a little at the sound Libitina made as her blade found a home in the weathered wood.

She went to retrieve it and then returned to the spot and threw it again. And again. And again, until she felt her muscles aching and her back beading with sweat despite the coolness of the night air. With the feel of the knife leaving her hand and the sureness of her aim, she could breathe again. She could almost forget.

Suddenly, a sound came from behind her, and she turned, her knife already raised and poised to be launched. Theo Barclay stood there in the shadows, as though her thoughts had somehow summoned him. His hands went up as if in surrender, and he stepped into the light just as Viola managed to stop herself from turning him into a pincushion. Her hands shook a little as she sheathed her knife.

"Why do you people never use a front door?" Viola asked, embarrassment and heartache turning to temper. "I could have killed you just now."

Theo smiled. "I appreciate your restraint." Then his smile faltered. "Ruby arrived today," he said, rocking back a little on his heels. "Her ship came in just this afternoon."

"You must be happy to have her back," Viola said. She itched to throw the knife again. To send it sailing through the air. To feel the burn in her muscles and the satisfaction of it landing in the wood.

Theo nodded, and silence stretched between them.

"Is there something else you wanted?" Viola asked, wishing that she had any right to ask after Ruby. Wishing for all the world that she didn't care how the pampered heiress was.

"I came to bring you an invitation." Theo stepped toward her, extending an envelope in his well-manicured hand.

"An invitation for what?" Viola looked at the parcel suspiciously before she finally, reluctantly, took it from him. Immediately she was struck by the softness of the paper, the thickness of it. Her name was written in a wild flourish of ink across the front.

"For the wedding," he told her, looking down at his feet as he spoke. "Ruby and I are finally going through with the ceremony we've been putting off for so long."

Viola's eyes snapped up in surprise. "When will it be?"

Theo gave her a small smile that looked more like a grimace. "Thursday."

"So soon," Viola murmured, her throat growing tight.

"I'm sorry I didn't come sooner, to tell you. This is the first I've been able to get away." Theo let out a long breath. "There's more. After the wedding, I'm starting a new position. In Kansas City."

"You're not leaving?" It had never occurred to her that Theo or Ruby would simply *leave*. But then, she'd forgotten that, unlike her, they could.

"It's more that we're being sent away," Theo said sourly. "The Order clearly wanted to be sure that neither of us would be in the city for the Conclave. While we were away, everything was arranged for us."

Viola was still staring at the looping scrawl on the invitation. "Who is it that's inviting me?" she asked, her traitorous heart clenching a little.

"I am," Theo said softly.

She should have known that it wouldn't be Ruby. After everything Viola had said at the gala when Ruby had taken the chance and kissed her? Viola had no right to expect anything more.

"No." Viola handed the envelope back, pushing it toward him when he wouldn't take it. "I'm sorry. I wish you happiness, but this, I cannot accept it."

But Theo only tucked his hands into his pockets. "Keep it," he told her. "Please. I hope that perhaps you'll even consider coming."

To see Ruby Reynolds married? Her head seemed to be shaking of its own volition. "I can't—"

"If not for me, come for Ruby," he told her. "She'd want to see you there."

"You can't ask this of me," Viola told him, studying the flowing script of her own name once more, because she could not quite manage to meet his eyes.

"It *is* rather selfish of me, isn't it? Especially after you went and saved my life not once but twice." Without even looking, Viola could hear the smile in his voice. "But sometimes I find myself an exceedingly selfish and completely preposterous creature."

It was a lie. Of all the many qualities that Theo Barclay possessed, not one of them was selfishness. There was a reason Ruby had chosen him, a reason Ruby *loved* him. It was the reason that he—and maybe *only* he—was deserving of her.

But Viola's traitorous heart wanted to deserve Ruby too.

Theo turned to go then, but he hadn't quite made it ten paces when he turned back. "I've been Ruby's friend since we were still in the cradle. She's often difficult, you know. When she sets her mind to something, it's nearly impossible to sway her—even if a better option is standing right in front of her. Still, I want you to know that I'll do anything necessary to keep her safe and make her happy."

Viola pressed her lips together, swallowing the emotion that had caught in her throat before she spoke. "Why do you tell me this?"

"Because I think you feel the same," he said gently. "Because you're maybe the only other person I'd trust her to—her safety and her happiness together." He tipped his finger to the brim of his hat and then stepped into the shadows.

Viola realized her hands were trembling as they held the invitation. She'd never seen or felt paper half so fine. Theo's words swirled through her mind with memories of the girl she should not want. Ruby Reynolds was a frivolous piece of fluff with her pink cheeks and silken dresses.

Except that she isn't. Beneath the silk and lace, Ruby had a spine of steel and courage like a lion. She was rich and protected and disgustingly perfect. Viola hated her and wanted her just the same, and Viola didn't need to open the envelope to know that she had no place in Ruby Reynolds' life. Or at her wedding.

OTHER PASTS,
OTHER FUTURES

1983—Grand Central Terminal

Esta allowed Harte to lead her into the waiting subway car just before the doors slid shut, but her arm was still buzzing with warmth from the old lady's magic. From between the various graffiti tags that covered the windows, she watched the woman droop to the floor while the people on the station tried to hold on to their hats or held their hands up to ward off the swirling wind.

There was still magic in the city, maybe even more than when she had grown up. There were still *Mageus* there, too, despite Thoth and the Order and everything Esta herself had done to the course of history. Maybe the Brink was still standing, and maybe the Order had more of a presence, but she remembered the old lady's words and wondered if what she'd done in Chicago had helped others like her. Maybe instead of forgetting, instead of simply allowing magic to die, more had decided to *fight*.

"What was she doing to you?" Harte asked as they found two empty seats. His voice was barely audible over the clacking of the car.

Esta rotated her arm and tested her injured side. "I think she was healing me?"

He frowned, as though he didn't quite believe anything could be that simple. She wasn't sure that she believed it either, but her side no longer ached. The wounds on her arm no longer felt tight and sore.

"But what was all that about being marked?" he asked.

"I don't know," she told him. "I've never heard of any kind of trace or mark before—not in any time. But who knows what Thoth has been capable of since I freed him."

"You tried to stop him," Harte reminded her.

"It doesn't matter what I *tried* to do," she argued. "Not when the results hurt people."

"I know," he told her, and there was a pang of regret in his words. She didn't have to ask to know he was thinking about Sammy.

She leaned into Harte, resting her head against his shoulder, and he wrapped his arm around her, nestling her into his embrace. They didn't need to say anything else, not when they both understood each other so perfectly. She wished she could let herself imagine that they were any young couple on their way uptown together. Safe. Content. Normal.

But Esta had never been normal, whatever that meant, and there wasn't time for playing pretend. She had no idea what the trace was that the old woman said they'd been marked with, but she suspected that it was the reason the Guard had found them at the Algonquin. She'd used her affinity to get them the clothes and likely had set off some sort of magical alarm. It meant they couldn't use their affinities or any magic without summoning the Order. It meant they likely wouldn't be safe as long as they were in that time, in *that* version of the city.

"We have to go back, Harte. And we have to go soon."

Harte let out a tired-sounding sigh. "I know." Those two words carried every ounce of the fear and regret that she felt herself. "So what's the plan? Where are we going right now?"

"North," she told him. "We need a safe place to secure the artifacts in the Book, and I know a place in Central Park that should work."

The twenty-minute trip felt like it took ages. It was a miracle that they didn't run into any other problems, but every time the car's doors closed without an attack, Esta didn't relax. They weren't truly out of danger. If what the old woman said about them being marked was true, the second they started the ritual to keep the stones safe, the Guard would likely know.

They disembarked at the 110th Street Station. Luck was on their side, and the small, dark platform was mostly empty. When they reached the street above, they walked for a few blocks until they came to the northern edge of Central Park.

As they approached the entrance to the park, Esta noticed the changes. The bricks lining the sidewalk were buckled, and half of them were missing. Trash lined the low stone wall that circled the park, and the path leading into it was cracked and uneven. Someone covered with a heap of filthy blankets was lying on one of the benches flanking the entrance. Beneath the sleeping figure, a paper-wrapped bottle had fallen over, spilling its contents onto the slush-covered walk.

Inside, Esta didn't find the park she'd grown up exploring. The grassy areas were riddled with sparse bare spots beneath the melting snow, and the pathways looked like they hadn't been repaved in years. She pulled Harte to the side before he could step on a bent syringe, but there was no avoiding the trash littering the area.

At least there weren't many people around. The farther into the park they ventured, the quieter it became, and soon the sounds of the city were no more than a gentle buzz in the background. Above, the trees caged them in with craggy, bare branches. It took her a second to remember the way, especially with how different everything looked, but eventually she found the path that led to the Blockhouse.

"This place looks older than I am," Harte said, peering up at the stone structure.

"It is." While she might have preferred the comfort of a hotel, there were too many people there. Too many exits to be blocked. Too many passages to be trapped. "You've never been here?"

He shook his head. "What is it?"

"An old Revolutionary War fort," she said. "The war ended before it ever saw any action, but we should be safe enough inside to get the artifacts secured." Or if not safe, at least they'd be able to see danger coming.

She shivered when a cold gust blew through the trees. "I should've found us warmer coats."

Harte cocked a brow in her direction. "Are we planning on staying long?"

"No," she said. The old woman's words made it clear that they didn't have time to get comfortable. They needed to secure the artifacts and get out of there. It was time to go back.

"Good," he told her, frowning up at the structure. "I've never really been one for the outdoors."

She thought of his apartment, of the enormous white tub and the hot running water that would have been a luxury at the time, and she laughed. "I think that's probably an understatement." Then she grew serious. "We should get started. The sooner we get the stones secured, the better."

They used Viola's blade to cut the rusted padlock off the barred door, and then they climbed through the low-hanging entrance. From the trash lining the small, stone-walled space, Esta could tell that they hadn't been the only ones with the idea of using the fort recently. She nudged aside a used condom with her foot and shuddered.

"Let's set up over there." She pointed to a spot near one of the openings in the block. "You can keep a lookout while I take care of the artifacts."

Harte took the satchel from where he'd slung it across his body and handed it to her, and in the matter of a few minutes, she had everything ready—the Book of Mysteries was open to the page that described the ritual, and the artifacts were arranged nearby. Viola's knife was in her hand. But she hesitated.

"What is it?" Harte was frowning down at her from where he stood a few feet away.

"I thought we'd have more time," she admitted. "Back in the hotel, I thought we were safe. It felt like we could stay there for a while. Just the two of us. I wouldn't have stopped you if I had known—" She pressed her lips together and fought back the tears burning at her eyes. She wanted too much, and she was afraid she couldn't have any of it.

He came over to where she was and wrapped her in his arms. "It's okay," he said.

"What if it's not?" she asked. "What if that was our chance, and I wasted it?"

His hands were rubbing her back gently as if to warm her, but there was a cold fear lodged deep within her that she couldn't quite shake.

"I keep thinking about what you said back at the hotel," she told him. "About someone else raising me. And the more I think about it, the more I realize how selfish I'm being. Even if we figure out a way for me to survive the Conclave, can I really send that girl forward in time to be raised by Nibsy now that I know what he's truly capable of?"

Harte's hands went still.

"You saw what he did to her," Esta continued. "He's worse now than he was before. He's more dangerous because he knows everything. Even if I'm willing to sacrifice her like that, even if I'm willing to send her forward, it means I have to let Nibsy live. And if I let him live, he's never going to stop hunting us. He's never going to give up trying to get the power in the Book."

"What are you saying?" Harte asked. "If you don't send her forward with the stone, you'll disappear. It'll be like you never existed."

She stepped back from him, because it was too hard to think when he was touching her. It was too hard to want something that maybe never should have been hers.

"Maybe I shouldn't have," Esta told him.

"No, Esta—"

"Think about it, Harte. You heard what Everett said: *A life is singular.* But mine isn't. It hasn't been since Nibsy mistakenly sent me forward in time as a toddler. I'm myself, and I'm that other version as well." She showed him her wrist with the scars of injuries she shared with another person. "We're separate, but the same. We're connected in a way I don't understand. Maybe that's not supposed to happen. Maybe I *am* an abomination," she told him, repeating what Jack—Thoth—had told her weeks ago in Colorado.

"I don't believe that," he said. "I *refuse* to believe that."

She smiled softly at the vehemence in his tone. "Maybe abomination is too strong a word. But I'm certainly an anomaly. I've introduced chaos into the time line just by existing." Her smile faded. "Maybe the only answer is for me to set that right. Maybe I'm supposed to go back and fix the mistakes I made. I can finish the ritual and make the Brink whole. Without the Brink, the Order would be powerless, and maybe magic could go on. But what does that matter if Nibsy is still a liability, more dangerous now than ever? If I wasn't worried about surviving, we could eliminate him and the danger he poses."

"You'd really kill him?" Harte asked. "I know what killing Jack did to you, Esta. You can't tell me you're really willing to take another life so easily."

"It wouldn't be easy," she said honestly. It had been terrible, and for the rest of her days, she would have to live with the memory of Jack's life seeping out beneath her hands. But if it meant ending all of this? If it meant saving someone else from carrying that burden? "But I saw what he did to that other version of me, Harte. He tortured her and twisted her into something I never want to be. How can I send a child forward to him, knowing that? How can we let him live, knowing that if he survives, no one will ever be safe? He won't stop, Harte."

"What about the girl?" Harte asked. "What happens to her if you sacrifice yourself and kill Nibsy?"

She'd been thinking about that problem ever since she realized that she could end the madness. She'd be dead, but that other version of her could go on. The girl could have the life that Esta should have lived, one not tainted by manipulation. One where she felt like she belonged.

"You could raise her," Esta told him. "You could give her the life I never had."

"No," he told her, adamant. "Absolutely not."

"Think about it, Harte," she told him.

"I won't," said. "I *can't*." He threw up his hands. "Esta, even if I was willing—and I'm *not*—it wouldn't work. Or have you forgotten? If you don't send the girl forward, then you never come back to find the Magician—and that's the end of me as well."

Esta froze. She *had* forgotten. She'd been so wrapped up in the horror of what Nibsy had done to that other version of herself that she'd nearly forgotten that Harte's destiny and hers were interlocked.

"You're right," she said, feeling more defeated than ever before. To choose between the girl—herself—and Harte? She couldn't. She *wouldn't*. "I don't know what I was thinking."

Harte sighed and took her in his arms, holding her tightly in the familiar comfort of his embrace.

"It's going to be okay," Harte said. "We have time, and if we don't, you'll steal us more. We'll figure out a way to deal with Nibsy Lorcan, but you have to promise me that you won't give up and do something rash."

"I just don't see how we can beat him," she whispered. Not when he knew so much.

Harte leaned forward until their foreheads were touching. "Hey," he said gently. "You're a thief, aren't you? And I'm nothing but a very talented con. We'll steal a future for ourselves, one way or the other."

"You're right," she said, still feeling unsettled.

"Promise me you won't do anything rash," he said. "Whatever happens, we do this together."

"I promise," she told him, meaning the words.

Then he kissed her. His lips were cold, rough from the dry winter air, and she felt his relief in the kiss. But she did not allow herself to get lost in it.

"Okay," she told him, pulling back. "We'll figure it out."

He stepped away, and she took a deep, steadying breath as she lifted the tip of Viola's knife to her finger once more.

"Be careful," Harte said, retreating farther.

We'll figure it out. She had to believe that. She had to think that this hadn't all been for nothing.

Gently, she pressed the blade into her finger, making the smallest cut possible. Blood welled at once, and without hesitating, she did what the ritual required and began to trace the symbol on the page open in front of her. Almost immediately, she felt something shift. Cold and hot energy climbed her arm as the page began to glow and the dark line of blood sank into the page. Three times she traced the figure, and then suddenly the page burst with light. A strange, humming energy brushed her cheeks, and she knew it was time.

She took the necklace first. The Djinni's Star gleamed in the wan winter sunlight, the turquoise stone sparkling with silvery flecks that looked like a hundred universes. It seemed only fitting she take this one first, since it was the first she'd ever stolen, years before. Maybe it was superstitious of her, but she had the sense that there was some power to the repetition. She lifted it over the glowing pages and then, remembering how Jack—how *Thoth*—had used the Book, she lowered it and watched as it disappeared into the pages with another flash.

It had no sooner disappeared than she heard a far-off sound—a steady, pulsing whir that second by second grew closer. They were coming. She reached for the Delphi's Tear and hoped there would be enough time to finish what she'd started.

INEVITABLE

1983—Central Park

When Esta had explained how they could use the Book to hold the artifacts, Harte had trusted her, but he hadn't understood. The idea that the Book could serve as some kind of magical container outside of time had seemed impossible and too good to be true. But as he watched the heavy glittering necklace sink into pages that certainly weren't thick enough to hold them, he began to believe that their plan might actually work.

The ring went next. The Delphi's Tear with its heavy, clear stone and ornate golden setting disappeared into the page, the same as the necklace had. Then Esta reached for the Dragon's Eye and was careful to keep the blood welling from her fingertip off the piece. The fantastical golden crown had cost his brother Sammie his life, and as Harte watched it disappear into the Book, he was reminded that, whatever the diary might prognosticate, he had no choice but to return to the past. It was the only way to give his brother a different future—a different fate. And he would find a way to save Sammie without sacrificing Esta's life.

The Pharaoh's Heart glowed blood red as Esta took it and began to feed the dagger into the Book, and when it had disappeared, the Ars Arcana pulsed with light as though it was hungry for more. Esta closed it securely instead. Ishtar's Key would remain where it belonged, snug in the silvery setting against her upper arm.

"We need to go," she said, looking up at the heavy winter sky. "They know we're here." She was already rewrapping the Ars Arcana in one of the Algonquin's fluffy white towels.

Harte realized then that the far-off droning hum of the city had changed. It was getting louder, growing closer.

Esta looked up at the sky above at the roofless room where they were standing. Then she tucked the covered Book back into the satchel and slung it over her shoulder. "We have to get out of here and find some cover."

The sound was even louder now, a steady mechanical chuffing that pulsed ominously as it grew in volume. Harte wasn't sure what the sound was, but he sensed that he didn't want to find out. Without hesitating, he took her hand, and together they hurried out of the fort and down the uneven stone steps into the park.

"This way," Esta told him, leading him onward.

"Why don't you use your magic?" he asked as the sound grew louder.

"I can't. Not if it's the way that they're tracking us." She picked up her pace. "And slowing time has never stopped Thoth. If we get far enough away, maybe we can lose them in the park."

He had no idea where they were going. He'd been to Central Park plenty of times, but never this far north. And even if he had, everything looked different now.

Esta led them from the path into more dense overgrowth, but the bare trees provided little cover. Their empty branches exposed them to the heavy gray winter sky above. They were moving as quickly as they could through the drifting snow on the forest floor, but they didn't get far before the source of the sound was upon them.

Harte felt the wind picking up as it had in the station, but this time it had nothing to do with magic. When he looked up, he saw an enormous beetle-like creature hovering over them.

No, not a creature. A machine.

He'd known that people had discovered flight. In San Francisco, he'd seen the silvery bodies of what Esta had called airplanes swimming through the sky, like minnows in a pond. But this was different. More horrifying and immediate. The dark metal insect loomed over them, and the sound it made was deafening. Thunderous. The pulsing, thumping beat echoed the frantic rhythm of his own heart as he and Esta raced along.

As though there was any chance of escape.

It happened so quickly. They were running hand in hand. Harte took one step, trying to navigate the snow-covered forest, and the next, the ground was gone. Suddenly, the world was turning itself inside out. Harte was falling. He felt himself torn apart, shattered into a million pieces, and then pressed back together. His head spun and he stumbled, barely catching himself before he went down.

Everything had changed. The snow was gone, and the forest was carpeted with moss and vines. The sky above was a brilliant blue, and the trees were green with fresh growth. The air no longer held the bite of winter. It hadn't yet warmed to the sweltering heat of summer, but the promise was there.

But they weren't far enough back. In the distance, he heard the blasting of a horn and the rumble of engines. Through the branches of the trees, he could see that the future city still loomed, enormous and impossible.

"When are we?" he asked, as Esta's steps slowed.

"I don't know?" She looked as shocked as he was.

"You didn't take us back?"

"I was going to," she told him. "I started to, but—I don't know. I hesitated. And then I saw this moment, and I just thought—" Her eyes were wide. "I didn't mean to . . . But I couldn't. Not yet." Her voice broke.

He understood. How could he not? She didn't want to face the choices that were coming any more than he did. Neither of them wanted to face the fate that waited for them in the pages of that damnable diary.

"It's okay," he told her, wrapping his arms around her. Because he could. Because the future hadn't unfurled yet in all of its terrible inevitability. His stomach still felt as though it had been turned inside out, but at least they weren't dead. "You stole us some time."

"I screwed up," she told him, trying to pull away. But he didn't let her. "I meant to go back. We're ready—"

"We're not." He brushed a piece of hair back from her face. She looked tired. Exhausted really. More worried than before. "We might have the stones tucked away, but simply having the Book and the artifacts doesn't mean we need to rush into whatever traps Nibsy has waiting for us. You made the right choice. You gave us time so that we don't have to run back unprepared."

She looked up at him, and the emotion swimming in her golden eyes felt like a punch to his gut.

"I know it's selfish of me," she told him. "But I want more time."

"So do I," he told her. "I want forever."

The glimmer of a smile tugged at her full mouth. "Me too, but I think we should probably settle for a day or two. We can find another room, rest, and make a plan."

"If we find another room, I'm not sure a day or two is going to work for me."

She did smile then, clearly amused despite herself. "We'd just be delaying the inevitable, Harte."

"Maybe." He wrapped an arm around her. "But I don't think anyone would blame us."

"*Harte*—"

"The past will still be there waiting for us, Esta," he reminded her. "It isn't going anywhere. We'll go back, but on our terms. Because we're ready, not because we're on the run."

She nodded. "You're right. We'll need clothes and supplies. We can't go back wearing this stuff. We'll need money, too." She looked out at the waiting city as though formulating a plan. But then she glanced at him from the corner of her eye. "You know, I *have* always wanted to stay at the Plaza."

"I have no idea what that is, but it sounds promising."

Her expression faltered as she stepped away from him. "I don't know how this trace thing works, but we should get moving. Maybe they can only track us if they know to be looking for it, but I don't think we should count on that. I took us back a few years. Not very far. Our arrival might have already triggered something."

He slipped his hand into hers. "Then by all means, let's go find this Plaza you spoke of before they arrive."

A TANGLED KNOT

1980—Central Park

Esta wasn't sure if her slipping them through time had triggered any sort of alarm. The old lady at Grand Central said she had a trace, but if her magic had activated it, no Guard arrived before she and Harte had left the area.

When the helicopter had been chasing them, she'd had every intention to take them all the way back, but as she'd sifted through the layers of time, she'd lost her nerve. And something about the moment—the soft green of spring or the calm peace of the undisturbed park, maybe—had called to her.

Or maybe that was her own cowardice. Because the truth was, she wasn't ready. One night with Harte wasn't enough before they rushed back and launched themselves into the final endgame. She accepted that Nibsy's diary might show her fate, but she wasn't ready to charge headlong toward it. Not yet. Not if there was *any* other way.

Once they were fairly certain that there wouldn't be any more helicopters coming after them, they left the underbrush and kept mostly to the paths. But the farther south they went, the harder it became to avoid people. Central Park in the early 1980s wasn't the park she knew. It looked worn out and run down, and most of the people they passed had hungry eyes. There were too many lumps of blankets and bags being guarded by bedraggled-looking souls. At the sight of them, Esta straightened her shoulders and walked a little faster.

"Don't look at them," she told Harte when she sensed him gawking.

She kept her own eyes straight ahead. "I'm not in any mood to fight off a junkie who might think we're dumb tourists and easy targets."

"I know this place," Harte told her when they came to the Reservoir. And as they continued on, he mentioned features of the park that he recognized from his own time, marveling at how much they'd changed.

"I knew the eighties were rough, but this place is a mess," Esta told him as they passed through a large open field with patchy grass and the frames of what might have once been fencing. In her own childhood, these fields had been manicured baseball diamonds. Now the grass between them was spotty, with bare earth showing through most of the field. Trash was strewn everywhere. "This is nothing like the park I grew up in."

They walked a little farther, and Harte noticed a building beyond the edge of the trees that he recognized. "There used to be a reservoir here."

Esta nodded. "They covered that over in the thirties."

"The sheep are gone," he noticed.

"Not a lot of room for sheep in the city these days," she told him, amused at his surprise. "Still plenty of rats, though," she said, as one scurried across the path a few feet in front of them.

"What else did they change?" he wondered. "Is the obelisk still there?"

"Cleopatra's Needle?" she said. "It's still there, over by the Met. You can't see it from here, though." And there wouldn't be time to go later. They could take a few days to plan, but they couldn't risk much more, no matter how much she might want to.

As they drew closer to the edge of the park, the noise of the city grew, and soon enough they came to where the park butted up against Fifty-Ninth Street.

"The Plaza's just there," she told him. "We'll need more cash to get a room without magic. For the clothing, too, but that should be easy enough. Tourists line up a couple of blocks over for carriage rides. We can head that way now. It shouldn't take long to find a few marks."

He followed her down the uneven, buckled sidewalk, toward where white carriages stood waiting with sad-looking mares. But her feet came to an abrupt stop before they were even close. Suddenly, her heart was in her throat.

"Esta?"

She heard Harte speaking to her, felt him move closer to make sure she was okay, but she couldn't respond.

"What is it?" he asked, gently guiding her to the side of the pathway.

"Dakari." She smiled through the burn of tears as she watched a young Dakari whisper something to his horse and pat it gently.

"Your friend Dakari?"

She nodded. She'd told Harte about him—about the kindness he'd showed her as a child. About how Nibsy had murdered him in cold blood to force her to return to the past with the Book.

"He's here?" Harte asked, now searching the line of carriages.

"There," she told him. "The white carriage with the gray horse."

Dakari's was the second in line. He was younger than Esta had ever known him. He was still tall and broad-shouldered, but he wasn't much older than a teenager. His deep brown skin wasn't yet creased in the lines that would come later, and he hadn't yet filled out. But his expressions were the same as he worked on brushing down the gray mare, his lips moving steadily as though he were speaking to the beast.

"Is he supposed to be here?" Harte wondered. "Or is this something else we've changed?"

"He's supposed to be here," she told him. But in all of the chaos of the previous days, she'd nearly forgotten that Dakari's existence was a possibility. "He arrived in the city in the early eighties. But Professor Lachlan didn't find him right away. He worked here for a few years before the Professor brought him on board." She wiped the tears from her cheek and choked back a laugh. "He looks so young—he can't be that much older than we are."

When she was a child, Dakari had been such an imposing figure, so sure of himself. His steady presence had been so much a part of her childhood, and he'd helped to make her who she was. She'd never imagined him like this, on the cusp of adulthood with his whole future in front of him. But now that she saw him, young and unmarked by Professor Lachlan, her heart ached for the man who died in the library that night. What might he have been if Nibsy hadn't gotten ahold of him? What else might he have done?

"Do you want to speak to him?" Harte asked.

She shook her head. "I couldn't." She felt another tear slide down her cheek, and she dashed it away. "What would I even say? 'Hi! You don't know me, but eventually you'll change my diapers?'" The thought made her feel ridiculous. "I just . . . I never thought I'd see him again."

Harte stilled. "You said that he knew you as a baby?"

She sniffled a little as she nodded. "Well, as a toddler. He was already working with the Professor when I showed up. He was older then. He'd been with Professor Lachlan for a while by then."

"Esta . . ." Harte's voice was barely a whisper when he spoke, as though he were afraid of time or fate or whatever powers existed hearing him. "What if Dakari is the answer?"

Confusion shadowed her expression. "The answer to what? Don't you remember? It's my fault that he's going to die."

"*Is* he going to die now?" Harte wondered. "Think about it. We just left Nibsy. He took his own life. How can he kill Dakari?"

Esta frowned. "Maybe he won't. Or maybe it's still a possibility. If we go back and set history on the course it should have been, then the Professor who just killed himself would never have happened."

"I don't know," Harte told her, scrubbing his hand through his hair until it stood on end. "How can *any* of this work? Time doesn't exactly seem to flow in straight lines."

"Doesn't it?" she wondered. "We created the Devil's Thief, and we saw the effects of that action on history." But it wasn't really that simple. If it were, Esta would have already been an impossibility.

"If that's true, why go back?" Harte asked. "Wouldn't the past remain unchangeable?"

"Because it's the only way to make a better future," she told him, her mind whirring as she considered something new. "I'd always imagined that we'd created a break somehow, that history veered off course. But maybe I was wrong. Maybe time isn't a line."

"What is it, if not a line?" Harte asked.

"It's something more complicated," she told him. "It's a tangle. A knot."

But that didn't quite fit either, not when she could sift so easily through the layers of minutes to reach a different time.

"Professor Lachlan said that time was more like a book," she told Harte. "Maybe he was right. Maybe you can change some of the words, but the basic story stays the same. Even if you removed whole pages, the book itself remained. The story is still there."

"But he believed the ending could be changed, Esta." Harte was frowning at her. "He wouldn't have sent you back to find me, to find the Book, if he hadn't believed that it could change his future in some substantial way."

"You're right," she told him. "He believed it would take something monumental to change time. Something that would be the equivalent of destroying the metaphorical book completely." She considered the implications of that, the way the Professor's metaphor aligned with the existence of the Book itself. He never would have destroyed the Book. He wanted its power too badly.

"Maybe we can write *over* the pages," she said, still thinking the idea through. "Maybe that's what we've been doing all along. We aren't erasing anything. Maybe the other versions *are* still there, waiting, and all the possibilities still remain somehow. At least until something happens to make them impossible."

"What if Dakari is the answer to rewriting *your* story?" Harte asked.

She stared at him, not understanding.

"You told me he was a mentor to you," Harte reminded her. "You told me how he basically raised you. What if he was the one who *actually* raised you?"

"You mean we could send him to find me?" Esta told him. "Maybe that's why time hasn't taken me yet, because *someone* can still be there."

Harte nodded. "You need to send the girl forward," Harte said. "And she needs to be sent back. But why should it matter who raises her?"

Maybe he was onto something. Maybe she was still living and breathing and part of the world because *someone* was still there to raise her. It could still be Nibsy. When they went back, they might still do something to make it possible for Nibsy to survive. But what if they didn't? What if it could be someone else who found the girl? Who raised her, and protected her, and sent her back?

"I don't know, Harte." Esta worried her lower lip with her teeth. "That's changing so much. Anything could go wrong. It could change *everything*. We could destroy Dakari's future."

"Or we could *give* him a future," Harte insisted. "He could be his own man, free from the Professor. And if we do it right, nothing else has to change."

"There are too many variables," she argued.

"Are there?" He drew her hands into his, and she felt the warmth of his magic sizzle across her skin. "Give me your past, Esta, and I can make sure Dakari keeps it on track."

Realization hit. "Your affinity."

He nodded.

"But that would take away his choice, his free will." She shook her head. "I can't do that to him."

"He's going to end up dead on Nibsy's floor, Esta." Harte's grip around her hands tightened. "We can give him a future. We can make sure that even if Nibsy makes it through alive, Dakari knows what's coming. We can make sure he survives."

She could protect him. She could make sure Dakari wasn't time's victim.

"It might not work," she said, chewing her lip as she watched the line of carriages.

Harte leaned in close to her until he could smell the soft scent of her hair. "But what if it does?"

SOMETHING BORROWED

1902—St. Paul's Chapel

As her mother adjusted the gauzy tulle around her face, Ruby couldn't help but think about how strange it was to be both solidly in your own body and somehow apart from it. She felt quite numb. The past three days had been a blur, and now that she was there at the church, dressed in the confection of silk and lace that Clara had selected, it all seemed so very absurd.

How quickly her life had changed, but not only in the last three days and not only because of the impending ceremony. If she were being truly honest with herself, her life had changed in the span of a single *second*. When her lips had touched Viola's at the gala, everything had come into focus. For the first time in her life, Ruby had the strangest sense that she could finally *breathe*.

But then it had all been ripped away.

Maybe if she had never kissed Viola. No . . . perhaps if she had never *met* Viola, there would not be this sinking feeling of regret. But there was no going back, no way to rewrite the past and make other choices. Now there was only the aisle before her, leading to a future that would not be terrible. She *knew* that. She was not marching toward her death or even toward a future filled with pain or suffering. She was simply walking toward Theo.

Somehow, though, that didn't seem to matter.

There she was, standing in the narthex of St. Paul's chapel, waiting for her own wedding to begin, and she would have rather been anywhere else. With her veil casting a white haze over her vision, Ruby could suddenly see more clearly than she ever had before. She'd never really intended to marry Theo. She'd always assumed *something* would come up to get them both out of their promises.

But nothing had. Now there was no escaping the path she'd put them both upon. Soon the organ would trill its opening notes and announce that any possibility of claiming the life she had once hoped for was officially at an end.

Her mother lifted the tulle over Ruby's face long enough to place a cool kiss on her cheek before she went to take her seat in the church, and then it was only Ruby and Clara's humorless husband, Henry. Because *of course* there would be a man. She was not even permitted to give herself into this new future.

The organ began to trill the familiar tune, and Henry offered his arm.

Ruby looked down at it and truly considered running. But she had never been one to run *from* something—only toward. And with her life suddenly unrecognizable, where would she even go?

"I don't believe I have to tell you how happy it makes all of us to know you'll finally be taken in hand," Henry said softly as they stepped into the open door and waited for the crowd in the church to rise. "Although I often have my doubts that Barclay will ever be man enough for that particular job."

Ruby swallowed down her anger and turned to him with what she hoped would look like a blinding smile to anyone close enough to see. "Dearest brother," she said through her clenched teeth. "Isn't it funny? We had the same fears about you on Clara's wedding day. But I doubt Theo will be half the disappointment to my family as you have been."

She could feel his arm tighten as her barb hit its mark, but Ruby stepped forward, starting down the aisle and forcing Henry to follow.

St. Paul's was a beautiful old chapel, with its white columns and arched vaulted ceilings overhead. At the other end of the aisle, waiting on the marble steps that led up to the great altar, was Theo, looking impossibly handsome in his morning coat—and impossibly nervous as well. He loved her. She *knew* that. He loved her enough to go through with this mad plan of hers, but what they were about to do here before god and these witnesses would end all other possibilities. Headstrong as Ruby might be, she was not fickle. Nor was Theo. They would take their vows seriously, and once they were wed, neither of them would be untrue.

They would not be miserable, but Ruby also suspected they would neither be truly happy—not as they might have otherwise been.

When Ruby had taken the first step into the church, the aisle seemed endless, but in no time at all she found herself standing at the altar next to Theo. He wore a smile, but his eyes betrayed the more complicated truth of how he felt. She imagined hers did the same. She understood the sadness in his expression—a bittersweet mix of affection and pain—because she felt the same echoing emotions. Before she realized it was time, Henry was already taking her hand and placing it upon Theo's. The rector was beginning to speak.

She met Theo's eyes through the haze of ivory tulle. *We don't have to do this*, she wanted to say. You *don't have to do this.*

But he only squeezed her hand in return. *It seems we do.*

On and on, the rector droned through the well-worn prayers, but Ruby heard none of it. All she could think was that this was a mistake. All she could feel was the enormity of her own guilt for forcing them to this point.

It will be okay, Theo's expression seemed to say. And Ruby knew he wasn't wrong. It *would* be okay. They would make a fine life with each other, but it would only ever be the shadow of the life she had dreamed of before she'd even known what to dream.

". . . speak now or forever hold your peace," the rector was saying. He paused then, waiting for someone to speak as the silence of the church threatened to crush her.

Theo turned to the few friends and family who had come to witness their union. His eyes searched the small group of their guests, but then something suspiciously like hope lit in his expression. It was enough to make Ruby turn as well, to see what it was.

In the rear of the chapel, sitting far off from anyone else, a pair of violet eyes met Ruby's. Ruby turned back to Theo, unsure of what was happening even as the rector continued with the ceremony, completely unaware that anything had just changed.

"What is she doing here?" Ruby whispered.

"I think she came for you," Theo told her, which was about the most preposterous thing he could have said.

"I require and charge you both, here in the presence of God," the rector droned, "that if either of you know any reason why you may not be united in marriage lawfully, and in accordance with God's Word, you do now confess it."

Theo's eyes suddenly didn't look quite so sad. "You can throw me over right here and now," he whispered, a small smile playing about his lips. "I wouldn't blame you one bit."

Ruby's heart felt as though it would burst in her chest. "It's impossible," she told him, feeling so many eyes upon them. The weight of expectations and promises not yet kept. But Ruby was already turning back once more to where Viola was sitting.

Viola looked like a woman carved from stone.

The rector was asking whether Ruby would take Theo as her husband, forsaking all others, but she wasn't listening. She was still looking at Viola. *Could she? Could they?* She had seen the women in Paris, the women who lived lives that she'd once thought impossible. . . .

But Viola could never go to Paris, Ruby realized. Not so long as the Order controlled the Brink.

". . . as long as you both shall live?" the rector asked.

The church was draped in silence, and it seemed that everyone—everything—was hanging on her answer. Past and future together meeting here in this one instant. This one *impossible* moment.

Ruby glanced back at the people in the church once more. But Viola

LISA MAXWELL

was no longer sitting there. She was making her way out of the church. She was leaving.

"It's okay, darling," Theo told Ruby, giving her hand a soft squeeze before releasing it.

"Miss Reynolds?" the rector said, clearly growing impatient.

Ruby opened her mouth, her throat tight with fear and hope. But in the end . . .

"I do," she said, her voice cracking.

She couldn't decipher the look Theo gave her as he slid his ring upon her finger, but it didn't matter. It was done.

The priest lifted his arms. "Those whom God has joined together, let no one put asunder."

The congregation murmured amen, and it was over. Her fate was forever sealed to his.

"You may kiss your bride," the priest told Theo, who looked just as shocked as she did that they'd actually gone through with it.

His cheeks went pink, and she gave him a small nod to let him know it was okay. Slowly, he stepped toward her, reached for her veil, and lifted it.

But his lips had barely brushed hers when she felt her bouquet start to vibrate. Surprised, she drew back. Something was happening to her flowers. They were moving and quivering as though they were alive, and then they began *melting*.

"What the—" Theo took an instinctive step back.

The people in the pews were murmuring, and Ruby was frozen with shock as her once lush bouquet began to melt, liquefying down the front of her full white skirts. As the flowers dissolved into a lurid mess, they began to release a strange green fog-like substance.

Horrified, Ruby finally managed to toss the bundle of flowers—and the strange fog—away from her, but the instant it landed, the entire bouquet exploded in a burst of cold flames. They crackled as they grew, flashing with peculiar colors.

Fear rippled like a wave through the wedding guests, as row by row they realized that something was happening—and then they all seemed to realize the danger. The flames climbed quickly, spreading as though the entire church had been doused in kerosene, and despite the lack of heat, a dark smoke began to fill the space. Within it, energy crackled like lightning about to strike. The smoke churned and gathered, moving as though directed and molded by unseen hands. By the time the terrible roaring began, the congregation had already dissolved into chaos. But Viola had long since gone.

LISA MAXWELL

TO CHOOSE OR COMMAND

1980—East Fifty-Ninth Street and Fifth Avenue

Esta watched Dakari from down the block, still unsure about whether she could really do what they were planning to do to him. Could she take away his free will by imposing a future upon him that wasn't of his choosing? How did that make her any better than Nibsy?

Over the past few days, they'd looked at every possibility from every angle, and they hadn't been able to come up with anything else. Maybe Harte was right. Maybe it was the only way to *give* Dakari a future. He hadn't been all that old when Professor Lachlan killed him. Once he raised the girl and sent her back to 1902 to find the Magician, once he completed the time loop, he could go on and have the life he deserved.

But it still wouldn't be the life he'd chosen for himself.

She thought of the last few days with Harte. They'd spent them gathering the clothing and supplies they needed without any real trouble and making their plans. They'd spent them *together*. It had been a reprieve, but nothing they did had yet changed the writing in the diary. No plans they made swayed the future inscribed there in Nibsy's own hand. Still, she'd been happy, even knowing that it was all about to end—even knowing that she could be returning to the past to face an unavoidable fate.

Maybe there was a chance they could outsmart Nibsy and change the entry in the diary. But was that possibility of a chance enough to do this to Dakari? Could she really choose her own life, her own happiness, over his?

No. She couldn't.

"Harte . . ." Esta turned toward him so that she didn't have to look at the line of horses and carriages. "I can't take his free will from him."

"Esta, we've been over this a thousand times," Harte told her, looking suddenly panicked.

"I know, but that doesn't change the fact that Dakari was under Professor Lachlan's control the whole time I knew him. I can't make him into my puppet. I can't do that to the one person who was *always* there for me."

"Esta—" Harte reached for her.

"No," she said, stepping back. "I can't. I'm sorry, but I just *can't*."

"Please," he said, taking her hand. "We can talk about this."

But she only shook her head, knowing there was nothing more to say.

"He's more important to you than I am?"

She saw the frustration cloud his face and the anger sparking in his stormy eyes, and she wished it were otherwise.

"Don't do that, Harte. You know this isn't about the choice between you or Dakari. It's about *me*. It's about what I can live with and what I'll live to regret. And having *this* regret? Even if everything works—if we survive the Conclave and manage to fix the Brink and neutralize the danger of the Book—even if we do all of that and succeed, knowing we'd hurt Dakari would poison everything between us."

He scrubbed his hand over his face. "What if it's not forced?"

"What do you mean?"

"What if I don't compel him?" Harte told her. "Maybe I could just suggest?"

"And what? Dakari just goes through life making choices without knowing why he's making them?" She shook her head. "No, Harte. I can't—" Then another idea occurred to her. "But if he agreed to it . . . It would be different if we could talk to him and if he understood what he was undertaking. Maybe if he had the *choice*."

Harte stared at her, dumbfounded. "What are you planning to do? Walk up to him and say, 'Hello. You don't know me yet, but you will. And, by the way, could you raise the baby that I used to be twenty years from now?'" He shook his head. "He'll think you're mad, Esta. Hell, *I* think you're mad, and this was mostly my idea."

"Maybe," she said. "But what if he doesn't? What if he agrees to help us?"

Harte shook his head, and she knew he wanted to argue.

"I want a future with you, Harte, but I can't have that—not even if everything else goes right. Not if I'm dragging the past along behind me."

"Fine," he said, drawing her close to him. "We'll try it your way."

"There's only one problem," she told him.

"There's a lot more than one," he said with a sigh. But he sounded more amused than exhausted. A few nights of uninterrupted sleep and a couple of good meals had done wonders for him. For *both* of them. The gauntness of his cheeks was nearly gone, and his eyes were no longer shadowed by the heavy hollows that had haunted him since San Francisco.

"If you're not compelling him, we won't have any way of knowing what choice he makes," she said. "We won't know if it's safe to eliminate Nibsy or not."

Harte considered the problem. "Maybe there is a way. . . ."

"Well?" She looked back at him. His mouth was so close to hers, and his gray eyes were smiling at her. "You're not going to tell me?"

"No. I don't think I will." He kissed her softly.

"Harte—"

"You'll have to trust me on this one, Esta." He kissed her again. "If it works, you'll know."

"We won't be able to touch Nibsy until—unless—it does," she told him. "If I can help—"

"You can't," he told her. "We'll have to leave it up to fate."

Too bad fate was a fickle bitch.

She took one more opportunity to lean into Harte, to allow herself to enjoy the way he touched her now like they'd always been together. The way her heart raced, even with the familiarity of him. They were going back, and for her, it would likely be the last time. If they made it through the Conclave alive, she'd have to give up Ishtar's Key, and maybe even her affinity. If they didn't . . . well, she wasn't going to think about that.

Still, the modern city—even this version of it, dirty and broken as it was—had always been her home, and even if everything went right, she'd miss the towering buildings of Midtown that felt like walking through a cavern. She'd miss the spacious hotel where they'd burrowed and planned. She'd miss all of it. But if they could get Dakari's help, if they could bend time and fate to their will, she'd have Harte.

"Are you ready?" he asked.

"Not even a little," she said, throwing one of his standard lines back at him.

It wasn't a lie, because before they could go back, she had to face her past. She had to face Dakari.

Esta swallowed against the tightness in her throat and willed herself not to start crying like a fool as they approached. Instead, she focused on what needed to be done and pasted on the kind of smile that could hide the emotion beneath. It was the smile she'd learned as a child, the one that had let her pretend everything was fine when all she'd wanted was for someone to gather her up and tell her she was enough.

They walked toward the line of carriages, arm in arm. To anyone they passed, she would appear to be nothing more than a girl with her boyfriend, madly in love. And because it was New York, hardly anyone looked twice at their clothes, styled for nearly a century before.

They were there too soon, standing in front of Dakari's rig, with the old gray mare that she knew was named Maude. He was wearing a ridiculous suit meant to mirror the clothes of old New York. But its thin fabric was stretched across his broad shoulders, and the cheap top hat appeared to be every bit the prop it was.

"You folks looking for a tour?" he asked when he noticed they'd approached.

"Possibly," Esta said, suddenly nervous. Suddenly unsure about their plan.

What had she been thinking? Now that she was standing in front of Dakari, facing him as a stranger, she couldn't seem to form words.

She stalled by distracting herself with the mare. Tentatively, she put her hand out and brushed her palm across its smooth coat. "She's a pretty horse."

"She's the best you'll find in the city," Dakari said with a smile. He looked so young. So fresh and unbothered. She wondered again who he could have been if Nibsy had never gotten his claws into him.

"The cars don't bother her?" Esta asked, knowing the question was completely inane but wanting to draw the time she had with him out a little longer.

"Nah," Dakari said. "Old Maude here is as steady as they come. She never spooks. She'd be happy to take you both for a tour of the park. Thirty even for half an hour."

Harte's brows shot up. "Dollars?"

"He still isn't used to the big-city prices," Esta said, laughing at the look on Harte's face despite herself. It was enough to remind her why she was doing this and what was at stake.

She wasn't ready to give him up.

"Actually," she said, trying to keep her voice steady. "We didn't come looking for a ride. We came looking for you, Dakari."

Dakari's brows rose, and he took a step back toward his horse with wariness clouding his expression. "Who are you? Who told you my name?"

"It's a long story," she said. When Harte squeezed her hand encouragingly, she continued. "But if you have a few minutes, it's one I think you should hear." She reached into the inner pocket of her jacket and took out a small object wrapped in a piece of flannel. She'd carried it with her everywhere—had managed to protect it through every danger of the last few months—because it was a connection to her own, true past. And to the one person she'd always loved.

Unwrapping the small knife, she offered it to him.

"Where the hell did you get that?" he asked, already reaching for his own jacket pocket.

"You gave it to me." She met his eyes. "More than thirty years from now."

Dakari took the same knife from his own pocket, a twin to the one he'd given her—the one she'd lost in the past and then found again. He looked down at the two matching blades. "My father carved this knife," he told her. "There shouldn't be another one like it."

"I know," she said, feeling a little more certain. "He gave it to you when you left for New York."

Dakari let out an uneasy breath and looked at her with a mixture of wonder and fear. "I think I'd like to hear that story of yours now."

MALOCCHIO

1902—St. Paul's Chapel

Viola had known that she was a fool three times over for venturing to St. Paul's the day of Ruby Reynolds' wedding. What business did she have at the church where Ruby would be wed? What had she hoped to accomplish by putting herself through such a thing? She'd gone out that morning with the purpose of trying to forget the event was even happening, and somehow her feet had directed her to the chapel just the same.

At first she hadn't gone in. Before the ceremony, Viola had watched from across the street as the guests began to arrive, all dressed in silk and lace. Then came the carriage decorated with swags of flowers and greenery, and within it, the bride. Viola had seen Ruby only from the back, a blur of ivory silk and tulle, but as she mounted the steps of the church, Viola felt her dark heart twist.

Suddenly, she hated Theo. She hated Ruby as well. Or she tried to.

She should have left. If Viola had even a little bit of anything at all between her ears, she would have. But her feet would not seem to go any direction but closer. When the bells had called out the hour and the organ had summoned the bride down the aisle, Viola could not stop herself from slipping into the back of the chapel. She waited until Ruby had finished her journey and had been given over to Theo's keeping before she took a seat at the back of the church, far from the rest of the guests. But she still felt too close.

At the altar, Ruby stood next to Theo, hand in hand. Fair and slender and perfectly matched. But when Ruby turned to the guests sitting in the church, there was no joy in her expression. Then Ruby's eyes found Viola's, and the sadness turned to surprise. Perhaps even hope?

Viola's heart had risen into her throat—but almost as soon as the moment had arrived, it was gone. Ruby turned back to the priest, who was asking for her intentions, and Viola realized it had all been a mistake. Her coming there. Her ever having hoped. *A terrible mistake.*

She didn't remember standing, didn't realize her feet were carrying her away from the church until she was nearly hit by a carriage when she stepped into the street. She'd pulled back just in time not to be flattened by hooves. Standing on the sidewalk, she ignored the curious looks of passersby as she tried to catch her breath. As she tried to keep her heart from crumbling to dust in her chest.

Finally, she forced herself to leave. She crossed the road without any care for her own safety. Darting between the carriages, she knew only that she had to get away—to escape—and she was nearly to the other side when the sound of an explosion drew her attention back toward the chapel.

Smoke was pouring from the church she'd just left, and the wedding guests were all fleeing, coughing and shouting as they fled from whatever was happening inside the sanctuary.

Viola didn't hesitate. She ran toward the church, only barely conscious of the cold energy that flowed from within it. Without stopping, she plunged headfirst into the fleeing crowd, shoving past women clad in silk and men in crisply pressed wool as she pushed her way back to Ruby.

Inside, she could barely see through the thick smoke. The flames climbing up the walls behind the altar had started to spread. They were a strange greenish blue, but despite their brightness, they gave off no heat. Instead, they continued to produce more of the thick, pea-soup fog that had filled the sanctuary. It crackled with an unmistakable cold energy. But however much the fleeing guests were shouting about Mageus, Viola understood the truth. This was the work of corrupt magic, debased by ritual and controlled by someone without any affinity.

Which didn't make it any less dangerous.

There was something else in the air as well—the sickening sweetness of opium. Its presence was cloying and heavy in the dense fog. Whoever had done this had come prepared.

From the front of the church, Viola heard a woman's scream, and sending her affinity out into the chaos, she found the familiar pulse of Ruby's heartbeat. It raced along, erratic, but alive just the same.

Viola took a shallow breath, trying to avoid the threat of the opium as she struggled through the fog until she'd reached the altar. She stopped short when she saw Ruby near the front of the church, not far from where she'd taken her vows with Theo at the altar.

At first Viola couldn't understand what she was seeing. There was an enormous creature lurking over the altar. It was shaped something like a man—impossibly broad, *impossibly* tall. But the arms were too long and the neck too short for any human, and when it opened its mouth to roar, the strange flames burst forth from its open jaws, and more of the dark smoke flooded out. It looked as though it had been taken from a nightmare. It seemed to be made of darkness, or perhaps it had been formed from something like the strange fog that filled so much of the sanctuary. But Viola knew it was solid and alive because it was holding Ruby over its shoulder like she was no heavier than a rag doll.

Theo was trying to free Ruby by attacking the creature with the blunt end of a tall candelabra, but the heavy base sliced through the monster without so much as touching it. Its fog-formed body simply rippled, even as its enormous arms continued to hold Ruby tight. When Ruby screamed a warning to Theo, a ribbon of fog slid across her face, obscuring her mouth as completely as any gag.

Suddenly, Jianyu was there next to Viola, gasping for breath.

"I followed you," he said simply, before she could even ask. He gave no more explanation but wore a look that said she should be thankful he had.

"It reminds me of the gala," she told him. This creature wasn't made from stone, but it seemed very much the same. Like that other creature, she could not sense a heartbeat. It contained no true life, no true magic.

Jianyu nodded his agreement. "If it is false magic, its master must be here, close. Rituals such as this cannot work without someone to direct them."

"Jack Grew," Viola said. He had wanted to frame Theo for stealing the ring, and he'd wanted Ruby dead long before this. Who else could it be?

"Possibly," Jianyu agreed.

"He must be cloaked in some kind of magic. I can't sense him," Viola said, frowning. There was no sign of any additional heartbeat. "We need to find him." But she couldn't bring herself to leave Ruby or Theo alone with this monstrous thing.

"You stay. Help them," Jianyu said, as though reading the direction of her thoughts. "I will find Jack."

"The opium—"

"Will not kill me. And I do not need my affinity to deal with Jack Grew," Jianyu reminded her with a steely expression. He plunged into the fog, leaving Viola to help Theo and Ruby on her own.

Viola stepped toward them, drawing Theo's attention. When he saw her, relief briefly flashed across his face, but then the creature swiped at him, drawing his focus back.

Theo swung the candelabra again, but the brass base barely left a mark on the rocklike hide of the beast. "I can't get her free. It's like fighting a ghost."

In the beast's grip, Ruby had gone limp and was no longer struggling to get away. Her skin was turning an ashen gray, and her eyes had fluttered shut. The creature was crushing her. Even now, her affinity already beginning to go numb from the opium, Viola could sense Ruby's heartbeat slowing.

Only a few minutes before, Viola had felt herself cracking in two because she had believed that Ruby had been lost to her. She realized now how very wrong she had been. *This* was something far worse. Viola would see Ruby married a hundred times over before she'd accept her death.

"We have to hurry, or it will kill her," Viola said. "Can you draw its attention toward you?" She was already reaching for Libitina, sending up the desperate prayer of a sinner to her god. "If you keep it busy, I will carve her out."

False magic for false magic. Please let this work.

Theo looked doubtful, but he did what she said and doubled around the creature before launching another attack from its other side. Swinging the heavy base of the candelabra once more, he sliced through the fog that formed its legs, again and again, until the creature turned on him.

It was all the entrance Viola needed. In a flash, she lunged for the billowing body of the thing, plunging her blade into the fog that formed its arm as she focused her intentions through the dagger and sliced downward. The blade tore through the smoke, ripping it apart as easily as if the creature had been made of paper. As the dismembered arm evaporated into nothing, Viola barely had time to try to catch Ruby and break her fall as she tumbled free.

The creature itself went suddenly still before exploding into a burst of flame and dark smoke. Viola braced herself over Ruby to protect the still unconscious girl from the icy blast. She murmured another desperate prayer as she touched Ruby's too-pale cheek.

"Please," she whispered, urging Ruby to wake up. She tapped Ruby's cheek gently.

Ruby gasped, drawing air back into her lungs, and opened her eyes. Immediately she jerked away from Viola as though she were still struggling against the creature that had held her. It was only when Viola backed up, her hands raised in surrender, that Ruby finally calmed herself enough to truly see who had hold of her.

"Viola?" Confusion flashed through her expression, but then her eyes fluttered shut again.

Theo had already come over to where Viola was cradling Ruby on the cold marble floor of the altar. "Is she—"

"She'll be okay," Viola said before Theo could so much as speak the words. "But we must go," Viola told him. "This smoke, it's too much. . . ."

Her affinity felt so far from her now that she could no longer feel Ruby's heartbeat. Nor could she sense anything or anyone else. The cold flames were still climbing, the strange murky smoke still billowing. She had no idea whether Jianyu had found Jack and managed to stop him.

"We need to get her into the air," Viola told Theo. And then she would return and put a stop to this madness alongside Jianyu.

Theo helped to lift Ruby, supporting her with his arm around her waist, as Viola stood.

"Theo?" Ruby was waking now, coming back to herself. She blinked, then saw Viola standing there. "Viola? You came back. . . ."

"Come," Viola commanded, looking away. It was too painful to see the warmth there in Ruby's bottle-green eyes, too painful to hope. "We must go. While we still can."

"I'm afraid it's too late for that," a voice said.

Jack Grew stepped from the smoke as another enormous creature began forming itself from the smoke that billowed behind him.

Theo ran for Jack, but he didn't notice the beast forming from smoke and fog until it was too late and he was already caught up in the monster's clutches.

Jack was murmuring something, some strange gibberish as the whites of his eyes began to go black as the night. It looked as though light and life had flooded out, leaving only emptiness.

Malocchio. As dangerous as the devil, and Viola knew that no cornicello would protect them from this perversion. This dark, adulterated magic had no place in this world.

Viola kept her blade raised and ready—it seemed enough to keep the deadly fog away—keeping one eye on the large figure as it formed behind Jack and another on the creature who held tight to Theo. She

LISA MAXWELL

could not risk throwing her only weapon, but if she could get past Jack, she could slice through the demon and free Theo by destroying it. If she could only slow Jack's heart, it would have been easy enough. She would not even regret it, taking his life here on the altar consecrated to god. But her affinity was dead to her by now, an effect of the opium that was thick and sweetly cloying in the smoke around them.

She had no idea where Jianyu was—or if Jack had gotten to him first. She could attack maybe one of the creatures, or she could attack Jack himself, but any attack would leave Ruby unguarded.

She lifted her knife, aiming for Jack.

"Kill me if you think you can," he told her, a sneering laugh in his voice. "But it won't stop my creations from ending you."

Viola froze. When she threw her knife at Jack, she would be completely defenseless. If Jack Grew wasn't lying, if these creatures somehow could exist without his direction, she'd be weaponless and without a way to defend Ruby or to rescue Theo. She could attack him herself, but it meant leaving Ruby without protection. Torn, she kept her knife poised, when she heard a voice whisper close to her ear.

"Give me your knife."

OUT OF TIME

1980—Central Park

Harte could practically feel Esta's nervousness as they rode in Dakari's carriage into the park. He hadn't said no or called her a madwoman, but that was a long way from him agreeing to help them. It was one thing to listen to a fantastical story. It was another completely to say yes to what they would be asking him.

As Dakari steered the carriage into the park, away from the crowds on Fifth Avenue, Harte wrapped his arm around Esta's shoulders and rubbed his thumb against her arm, trying to calm her. With the clothes they were wearing and steady clippity-clop of the horse's hooves, Harte could almost imagine they were already back, that they were already living another life. He and Esta, together.

But there was so much that needed to happen for that future to become real, and Dakari was the key. Even if Esta thought she had everything figured out with the Book and the Brink, there was no future for them as long as Nibsy's diary remained stubbornly unchanging. They had to take Nibsy out of the picture, and they needed Dakari's help to make that possible.

The diary still seemed like some kind of a trick Harte couldn't quite figure out. He would never hurt Esta on purpose, much less *kill* her. That fact alone should have made the words on the page impossible. And yet the entry had remained stubbornly consistent. The only thing that had affected it at all was their current idea to involve Dakari, but even that hadn't changed the words. It only made the ink on the page seem less sure of itself.

Dakari steered the carriage into an out-of-the-way corner of the park, and they alighted while he secured the horse and gave it an apple.

"You can do this," Harte whispered, urging Esta on. Then he listened to her spin the story of her life.

She started from the beginning. Or maybe it was the end. She told Dakari everything—everything except his own death. And when she was done, when she had lain out everything they needed of him, he frowned for a long, uncomfortable minute.

"And you think *I* can help you with this?" Dakari asked, his voice filled with doubt.

"You're the only one who can," Esta said. "I know it's asking a lot . . ."

Dakari shook his head. "That's an understatement. I don't know, man."

Harte had the sudden sense, then, that Dakari would refuse.

"You don't have to decide now," she told him. "It's your choice, completely."

"You're telling me I could change everything?" He didn't seem as though he believed her.

She nodded. "The Guard. The Order. The way they hunt our kind now? It's not supposed to be like this. You could live in a different world. You were *supposed* to live in a different world."

He looked down at the two pocketknives that rested in the palm of his hand. The knife his father had carved. The knife there should have only been one of. "Dammit."

"I know," she said. "I always was a pain in your ass."

He smiled a little at that. "I can't promise you anything," he told them.

"You don't have to," Harte said. "I can give you everything you need."

"And nothing you don't," Esta reminded Harte, cutting her eyes in his direction.

"The choice will be yours," Harte told him. But he wondered if he could really walk away, knowing Dakari was likely their only chance.

Dakari thought for a long stretch of minutes while the wind whistled in the trees above them. The horse nickered softly, tired of waiting for its next destination.

Esta suddenly slipped her hand into Harte's, and the world went silent around them.

"What are you doing?" he asked, panic rising. She was risking the Guard finding them by using their magic.

"He's going to say no," she told him.

"Maybe not," he said, but he didn't sound convincing even to himself.

"He is." She sounded certain. "And when he says no, you're not going to do anything."

Harte's brows drew together. "You're sure?"

She nodded.

"You know what that might mean, Esta." He had to clench his jaw from saying more, from begging her to reconsider. But she was right. If he forced Dakari—if he coerced the one person who had always loved her—it would always be between them.

"When he refuses, we're going to let him go," she told him. "You're not going to use your affinity to take away his free will."

"Even if it means the entry in the diary might come to pass?" he asked.

"You would never hurt me, Harte." She was pressing her lips together, and he could tell she was fighting back tears. "I will take every single second I have with you. But I won't steal any more than I deserve." She kissed him softly. "I love you too much to do that to either of us."

She released time before he could react and before he could respond. The city was humming around them again, but the world had narrowed down to Esta. Her whiskey-colored eyes drinking him in, her hands warm and sure in his.

"I know," he told her.

"What?" Dakari frowned for a second, confused. But then his expression cleared. "Fine," he said. "I'll do it."

"You will?" Harte asked, hope shooting through him.

"I can't promise things are going to work out like you want, but I'm willing to try," Dakari told them, looking down at the pocketknives. "I don't have any other way to explain this. And I think my father would have wanted me to try. He always did say my traveling here was for a reason. Maybe this is it."

"Thank you," Esta said softly, her eyes shining with tears.

"Don't thank me yet. We're not anywhere near done." He looked to Harte. "So, how do we do this?"

Harte held out his hand. "It's simple."

Dakari hesitated for a second, but then he took Harte's outstretched hand, and the second their skin connected, Harte focused on his affinity and sent everything through the bond between them. Dakari's eyes widened as though he sensed the intrusion, but then a calm, dazed expression fell over him.

"Don't forget—" Esta started, but Harte shook his head to shush her. He had one chance to get this right. He needed to concentrate on what he was trying to do.

The change happened almost immediately. It was as though they could feel the echo of something shattering in the atmosphere. Just like when they'd crossed back into the city, the air seemed to shift, and then the sirens began. Harte thought of the trace they'd been marked with, but he didn't allow himself to panic. There was more he needed to give Dakari. Unspoken instructions that might mean the difference between defeating Nibsy or the fate in that diary. He wasn't finished yet. . . .

"Hurry," she told Harte.

He shook his head slightly, as if to say, *Not yet,* but the sirens were getting louder, closer.

They were out of time.

TOO LATE

1902—St. Paul's Chapel

Jianyu coughed as the smoke from the strange flames clawed at his throat. Because of the opium in the air, he had all but lost his hold on the light. He had found Jack and followed him to the front of the church, where Viola was struggling to hold back the bride. Theo Barclay was there as well, struggling against one of the creatures formed from the strange, unnatural smoke. Even as Viola tried to keep the girl from danger, she had her knife raised and aimed for Jack Grew. But behind Jack loomed another of the monsters.

Viola's eyes went a little wide at Jianyu's request, and at first she did not relinquish her blade.

"*Now*, Viola!" he insisted. "With your blade, I can free him. Allow me to try."

She never turned away from Jack or the creature, but tucking her knife behind her back, she relinquished her dagger into Jianyu's hands.

"Please, Jack," the bride pleaded, her voice ragged with fear. "Theo's done nothing—"

"Nothing?" Jack asked, his voice suddenly hollow and cold. "He helped the maggots attack the Order. He helped them take the Delphi's Tear and Newton's Sigils. He tried to *ruin* me." Jack's eyes glowed unnaturally bright with glee. "Now he'll pay for daring to cross me."

"You're insane," the bride said, going suddenly still. It was as though she had only just realized Jack Grew's madness.

Jack simply laughed. "I'm far from insane, Ruby. I am simply more than your feeble, utterly *female* mind could ever begin to imagine." Jack gave the girl a cold smile. "I have taken possession of magic far more powerful than you—or your maggot friends—could ever hope to understand."

Jianyu used the cover provided by their conversation to edge his way ever closer. Hidden by the light and the fog, he positioned himself near the creature. Desperately, he considered the way it was built, searching for some weakness. He understood he had only one attempt to bring it down before Jack realized and turned it on him as well.

"I don't need to understand your pathetic false magic to destroy it," Viola said, drawing Jack's attention back to her.

Jianyu did not hesitate. Though he felt his affinity slipping away from him, he lunged. With a flash of steel, he plunged Viola's knife into the smoke and tore the creature open. Where the slice of the blade created a gash, blue-gray flames erupted, immolating the beast with a burst of otherworldly fire.

At the same time, the last bit of his hold on the light slipped from him, and he knew he was exposed.

Jack Grew turned on Jianyu, and when he realized what had happened, his expression turned murderous. He charged at Jianyu as the other creature began to move toward Viola and the bride.

"Get Ruby out of here," Theo shouted to Viola.

"I won't go without you," Ruby told him, struggling again against the hold Viola had on her.

As the two argued, Jianyu's focus was on the creature that was moving steadily toward them. He could cut it easily with Viola's blade, but with his affinity numb and impossible to reach, he no longer had the element of surprise.

By now the girl had torn herself away from Viola, but the other creature was already coming for her. Jianyu could see what would happen— the beast would reach her, and she would not be able to fight it off.

Jianyu leapt, trying to reach the figure of smoke, but Theo was faster. He put himself directly in the creature's path, using a candelabra to try to fend it off. The creature only billowed larger, rippling with something that might have been laughter if the roaring noise it made had been anything remotely human. It towered now, fifteen or more feet in the air. Three times the size of a normal man.

Theo was not dissuaded. He batted at it again, trying to force it back, but the candelabra sliced through the fog of its body without touching it. In an instant, the creature had grabbed him by the neck and lifted him into the air.

"Theo!" the bride screamed.

"Take her," Theo shouted, his face turning a sickening purplish red. "Viola! Get her out of—"

His words went silent as the creature tightened its grip, and the man's body jerked, a terrible, lurching convulsion, before he went completely limp.

Jianyu felt as though the entire world had focused down to the image of Theo hanging lifeless from the monster of smoke that towered over them.

"*Theo!*" The bride was screaming and tugging against Viola's hold on her, her face a mask of grief and horror that Jianyu felt echoed deep in his own bones.

The bride turned on Viola suddenly, clutching her by the shoulders as though she would shake the very life out of the assassin, who looked every bit as horrified as Jianyu felt. "You have to save him," she begged Viola. "It's not too late. Not for you. You can save him."

Jack took a slow step forward, as though there was no urgency at all. As though the sanctuary around him was not swirling with chaos and terror.

"Oh, it was too late for Theo Barclay the second he aligned himself with maggots who would try to destroy the Order," Jack said. "Or rather, I suppose it was too late for him the second his antics affected me."

"No . . ." The bride's moaning wail tore through the noise and confusion.

Jack looked almost amused. "He interfered where he should not have, and because of it, he nearly destroyed *everything*."

"You're a monster," the bride said, her voice angry and hollow. "You won't get away with this. I'll make sure everyone knows what you are."

"Take her," Jianyu commanded, finally breaking through Viola's shock.

She did not move, but simply stared at him, wide-eyed, as though she was unsure of what to do.

"You must take her from this place," he told her. The girl would only get herself killed if she stayed making threats she could not keep, and Jianyu owed Theo Barclay too much to allow his intended to die like this. "Now. Go!"

"I won't go!" Ruby screamed, tearing at Viola like a hellcat bent on escape as she tried to reach the creature still holding Theo's limp body. Her face was stained with tears, and her voice was raw with grief and fury. "Not without him."

"I wasn't planning on allowing you to anyway," Jack said, and as he lifted an arm, the beast lurched forward again. "Such a shame, isn't it, that the *maggots* chose today of all days to attack your wedding? What a *tragedy* that both the bride *and* the groom were killed by their dangerous, *feral* power. Something really should be done about it."

As Jack Grew's words dissolved into laughter, Jianyu leapt for the monstrous smoke, slicing at the body with Viola's knife. This beast was larger than the others by far, and this time it did not immediately burst into flames. Instead, it reared back as if in pain, trying to dislodge Jianyu. In the process, it dropped Theo to the floor, and his body hit the hard marble below with a sickening thud.

"We have to help him. You have to *help* him!" Ruby cried to Viola.

But it was already too late. There was nothing Viola would be able to do for Theo, not anymore.

"You must go," Jianyu ordered as he tried to wrestle the beast back with the dagger. "Would you deny Theo the last thing he asked for?" Jianyu asked Ruby as the monster stalked ever closer.

With his words, the fight seemed to drain out of the bride, and the girl fell into Viola's arms.

"Your knife," Jianyu shouted, ready to toss it back to Viola. She would need something for protection.

"Keep it," Viola said. "I *will* come back for you."

"I know," Jianyu told her simply. "Go."

As Viola tugged the bride away, disappearing through the dense fog, Jianyu turned back to Jack Grew.

Jack Grew had gone completely still and was examining Jianyu with narrowed eyes. "I've been looking for one like you," he said. Suddenly the fog around Jianyu began to swirl. Anticipation lit Jack's eyes. "The things I'll do with the power that lives within you."

"You are certainly most welcome to try," Jianyu said as he prepared for the attack, hoping that Viola would be swift.

THE DIARY

1980—Central Park

The wailing sirens were growing closer, but Harte wasn't done yet.

"Hurry," Esta told him, but his eyes were still closed, and his hand was still wrapped around Dakari's. He shook his head slightly, as if to say, *Not yet*.

She considered using her affinity. Maybe she could grab the two of them and hold them in the net of time until Harte was finished, but her power over the seconds had never stopped Thoth.

They needed to go, and they needed to go *now*. They had to lead the Guard and Thoth away from Dakari before anyone saw him. He'd already died once because of her. She wouldn't put a target on his back by letting the Guard find them together. Even if it meant dooming herself to an unknown future.

Esta jerked Harte away, breaking his hold on Dakari's hand, hoping he'd done enough. Dakari gasped as though surfacing from water, and Harte shuddered, stumbling a little before he caught himself.

"What happened?" Dakari asked. "Did it work?"

"They know we're here," she told him, as another siren cut through the air. "But we're not going to let them find you."

Dakari blinked in confusion. He looked almost drunk, and she didn't want to leave him there unprotected. But in the distance she heard the rhythmic thumping of a helicopter. They were out of time. They couldn't take him with them, and there wouldn't be a chance to come back to see him again. Once she was in the past, there would be no returning, not if she sent the child forward with Ishtar's Key. But somehow saying goodbye felt impossible.

It didn't matter that this rangy-looking teen wasn't really *her* Dakari. She launched herself at him anyway and wrapped him in a hug. For a second he just stood shocked, and then his arms were around her.

"Is that all really going to happen?" he asked, whispering close to her ear.

She nodded. "But it doesn't have to. You can change things, but it will be your choice." She squeezed a little tighter, wishing she could tell him everything she'd never said. "Whatever you choose, there aren't any regrets. You made my life bearable. You made it everything."

He looked shaken. "It's a lot to take in."

"I know. I'm sorry." She thought about that night she went back, about the night he died. "Whatever you do, don't trust the Professor," she told him. "He'll use you until he doesn't need you anymore. It doesn't matter what he promises. He's never going to put you before his own interests."

Releasing him, she stepped back, wishing she could stay. She would have liked to know him now, before he'd been trained by the Professor and honed into the weapon he'd later become. But there wasn't time. There were Guards in the park. She could see the black of their boxy coats through the thick foliage and hear the confused exclamations from the people they were searching.

"You're going to need this," Harte told him, handing over the small diary.

"What are you doing?" Esta asked. This wasn't part of the plan.

Harte glanced at her. "You're going to have to trust me on this." Then he turned back to Dakari. "You'll know what to do with it when the time comes." He held out his hand, and Dakari took it, pulling him in for a rough hug.

There was some unspoken conversation between the two of them, but eventually Dakari stepped back and climbed into his rig. With a flick of the reins, he spurred the horse onward, and then he was gone.

"Good-bye," Esta murmured, watching the carriage disappear around the corner. Then she turned to Harte. "Promise me that you didn't—"

"I wouldn't betray you like that, Esta." He slipped his hand into hers. "I promise."

"You really didn't, did you?"

Harte shook his head, and suddenly Esta wondered if she'd made a mistake. They could have known what Dakari would do. They could have been sure.

And she would have hated herself every day because of it.

"It's in fate's hands now," Harte told her.

"No," she said. She swallowed down her fear. "It's in Dakari's. We have to give him a chance, though. We need to lead the Guard the other way."

They started to run back toward the entrance to the park, until they came face-to-face with a squad of Guard. When they were sure that the men had seen them, Esta squeezed Harte's hand. She reached for her affinity and slowed time as she stepped toward him, and as the world hung silent around them, she kissed him. She only meant to hold on to the seconds long enough to capture the Guard's attention, but the second their lips met, Harte pulled her into the kiss.

He kissed her fiercely, like she was something precious. He kissed her like he was saying good-bye.

She was left breathless and wanting and without any idea of what she was supposed to say.

"This is going to work, Esta."

But they didn't know that. Dakari was one of the best men she knew, but time was a tricky beast, and the past was waiting. "You gave him the diary," she said. "We won't know what we're walking into."

"It doesn't matter," Harte told her. "I am never going to do anything to hurt you. I don't care what that page says. I'd die myself before I took your life."

THE SHATTERED CITY

"If we don't get out of here, it's not going to matter," she told him, trying to brush away her fear.

"Ready?" Harte asked, releasing her.

"Let's go," he said, and the second she let go of time, they ran, leading the squad of Guard down the winding path away from the direction Dakari had gone. When they reached the pond, they followed the path around rock formations covered in graffiti that rose out of the bedrock. And when she thought they were far enough away for Dakari to be safely out of range, Esta slowed time around her again.

The city went silent as they slowed, trying to catch their breath. Their pace was slower as they rounded a corner and headed toward one of the arching tunnels that carried one path over another. They were halfway through the tunnel when something changed. The world was still silent, caught in the web of time and Aether, but a line of Guard stepped into the opening on the other end to block their way. Their eyes were an inky black.

She cursed, but when they turned back to retreat, the path they'd just taken was blocked as well. More Guard had filed into the tunnel opening behind them. Their eyes were also empty of light and color.

Around them, the wind shifted unnaturally, and she thought she heard laughter.

"It's time, Esta," Harte said, his hand firm around hers. "We're ready."

One of the men lifted something that looked like a large fire extinguisher and aimed it in their direction. Harte jerked her back as the device began spraying a thick, bluish fog. They couldn't retreat too far, though, because on the other side, the other line of Guard was approaching.

But it didn't matter. They *were* ready, and it was time for them to go.

Esta was already focusing on her affinity, already riffling through the layers of time and history, until *there*. She had just reached the layer she needed when the fog began to swirl. She pulled them both through just as a cold wave of energy blasted over her. She felt her hold on time slipping, but she gritted her teeth and forced herself back, back, back.

But her magic lurched, and her hold on time went erratic.

It didn't feel like when she'd been shot by that bespelled bullet. Her affinity didn't seem to be slipping from her or draining away like before. Instead, her connection to the old magic felt like something wild and alive. The power flowing through her and tethering her to this time, to *this* place, went simultaneously hot and cold, and her grip on time—on *Harte*—began to slip.

All at once, time itself began to change. The layers of history, those years piled one atop the other, began to blur. She could no longer see the distinct layers of time, each minute anchored to this one, singular place. Now she saw *everything*. The minutes and seconds multiplied, twisted, until each minute contained *all* minutes. Each second held the promise of every possible second. And she saw, suddenly, what she had missed before—the possibilities inherent in the Aether, the way it connected *everything*.

The spaces between things weren't empty. They were filled with all that had been and all that might ever be.

The city flashed and blurred around her, and time became a living thing. There, within the layers—within the promise of each second—she saw every possibility, all at once. Simultaneously present and past and future.

There was the city as an untouched place, infinite in what it might become. There was *her* city as it had once been before she saved the Magician or became the Devil's Thief. Before she'd changed the flow of time. That past was still there, a ghost or memory within the layers of time. She couldn't reach it, but it wasn't gone. Because it was still *possible*.

One possibility among infinite possibilities.

Her affinity felt like a separate thing. No longer only a part of her, but a part of *everything*.

You could have all of this. The thought came unbidden, stark and absolute, and she knew somehow it was true. With the power in the Book, she could remake the world. *You could remake time itself.* She could reclaim all that she thought was lost.

Because it *wasn't* lost. Every time line, every change she'd created, it was still *there*. Within the seconds. Waiting.

It could be yours. The life you never got to have. Any life you might claim.

Her affinity flared, and she saw into the spaces between. For a blinding instant, she saw all that the city could have become had it taken a different course, had the Brink never severed it from its place in creation. But then she saw a different future. She saw *every* future, the beautiful and the terrible all at once. She saw futures where they won and the old magic grew and futures where they lost everything.

And then she saw the Brink fall, felt the terror of time turning to nothing—of the world and existence ceasing to be. And she understood *that* future, *that* possibility, was there waiting as well. Reality came undone as the city became an aching maw that was not time or place. It was only emptiness and lack.

Esta didn't realize at first that she'd begun slipping there into the nothingness of that unmade city, unmoored from time. But then she felt the familiar pull of time, the same terrifying sensation she'd felt back in Colorado of flying apart and being unmade. In a panic, she reached for her connection to the old magic, but whatever the Guard had doused her with was doing its worst. Her affinity was cold now. Distant. The seconds felt slippery, and the layers were flashing by too quickly for her to see any single time or place.

With all her strength, she reached for the city she had known, struggling against everything to find a layer where the city still stood and where she could still exist. But she'd only barely glimpsed it, had just started to grasp those seconds, when everything went dark.

DANGEROUS MAGIC

1902—St. Paul's Chapel

Viola struggled to drag Ruby from the church without harming her. She understood why Ruby was fighting her; she didn't want to leave Theo or Jianyu with Jack and his creatures, either. But Ruby was a liability. She was fragile and devastated, and Viola could not both protect her and help Jianyu at the same time.

"We can't leave him there," Ruby wailed, again trying to turn back.

"He wanted you safe," Viola reminded Ruby. Fear coursed through her even as she felt the crack in her heart growing, expanding so wide and deep that it felt like soon it would spread through her entire body. With one more heartbreak, she might shatter completely.

"You can save him," Ruby said with a desperation that only made the crack in Viola's heart ache all the more. "If we go back, you can save him."

"I can't." Viola shook her head as she fought back tears, wishing it were otherwise. She had seen the way Theo had jerked and gone still in the monster's grasp. She'd heard the sickening sound of his body when it hit the floor, and she knew that he was no longer with them. She could mend a wound or rend a heart in two, but she had no power over death. Though she would have perhaps traded whatever was left of her very soul if she could have only stopped Ruby's keening grief.

"You did it before. I watched you remove a bullet from his body. You saved him before," Ruby charged, her eyes wide and half-delirious from the shock of what had happened. Then she released Viola and stepped back. "Or is it that you won't?" Her voice had become cold and hollow, and her eyes were as hard as the diamond band that now sparkled on her finger.

Viola's throat was so tight she could barely speak. "I would if I could, but not if he's—" She couldn't say the word. She could not be the one to make this real for either of them. "Please. You must come with me now. Come, and I'll return for Theo," she promised. "I'll bring him back to you."

She could not tell Ruby the truth. She could not explain to Ruby that each second she wasted could be the moment that one of those creatures did to Jianyu what they'd done to Theo. Viola *had* to go back. She had to return to the dangers within the church, but only for Jianyu, because Theo's life was beyond her reach now.

Her promise to return for Theo worked, though. It was enough to allow Ruby to relent, and Viola was able to pull her through the side door of the chapel, where they found themselves in a graveyard. Viola led Ruby past the worn stones and uneven ground, breathing as deeply as she could. She willed the effects of the opium to wane enough that she might be able to again grasp the edges of her affinity. She needed something more than a single knife when she returned to the battle.

Compared to the chaos within the church, the graveyard was starkly silent. The day itself was unbearably bright. Despite the cold in the air, the sky above was an indecent blue, clear and absurdly serene. Viola hurried Ruby to the side of a mausoleum and found a place shielded from view.

"You must stay here," she told Ruby. "Keep yourself out of sight. Please." Viola's affinity had not yet returned to her, but that didn't matter. Even without her magic, she could certainly destroy a man who had become a monster. "Promise me that you'll stay here."

Ruby nodded. "I promise. I'll wait right here, out of sight. Please, Viola. Save him for me."

Unable to lie, Viola turned without answering and started to move toward the door, but she hadn't even gone four steps when flames erupted once more, blocking the exit they'd just used. A blast of cold energy, every bit as dangerous as the Brink had ever been, careened through the churchyard, nearly bowling Viola over with its power.

Ruby was on her feet, already charging back toward the chapel, but Viola snagged her and held her back. Flames were now completely blocking the door they'd just come from. There was no way to retrace their steps, no way to reach Jianyu.

"The front," Viola commanded Ruby, hoping against hope that Jianyu had managed to escape before the fire engulfed the building.

Together, they dashed through the graveyard, stumbling over ancient headstones, until they reached the front of the church. A crowd had already gathered on the sidewalk, barely far enough from the building for safety. Viola held Ruby back as the front doors of the church flew open and Jack Grew appeared with Theo draped over his shoulder.

All at once the flames that had been crackling in the doorway died down and the smoke began to dissipate. The crowd went completely silent as Jack descended the steps of the chapel slowly, like a hero returning from battle.

When Ruby recognized who was draped over Jack's shoulder, she moaned. It was a broken sound, filled with pain and devastation. She lurched forward to run toward the front of the church—to run to Theo—but Viola kept hold of Ruby by the waist and didn't let her go. Together, they watched in horror as Jack reached the bottom of the chapel's steps. The crowd parted just enough to make room for him to lay Theo's body on the gravel walkway.

Theo's body was limp and lifeless, and his head lolled back at an unnatural angle.

Ruby whimpered, still struggling to break free of Viola's grip.

"Shhh," Viola told her gently, tugging her back farther from view. Her instincts were prickling, and she cursed the opium that was still thick in her system. She did not have her blade, and she could not grasp her affinity.

"We have to find the bride!" Jack shouted. "Ruby Reynolds. They took her. Mageus did this. They killed Theo Barclay. I tried to stop them from killing his bride as well, but I was too late." His voice rose in near hysteria. "They're *monsters*. Look at what they've done to this hallowed building. *Look* at what they've done to my friend."

"Lies!" Ruby screamed, but Viola clamped her hand over Ruby's mouth before she could draw attention their way.

"We have to go," Viola said, but Ruby was still fighting her.

"We can't let him lie," Ruby told her, desperate with her grief. "Let me go, and I'll tell them I'm fine. I'll tell them Jack is lying. That he's the one who did this." She struggled to get away from Viola, scratching and clawing to be free. "Let me go, Viola."

Viola didn't listen. "Jack won't let you live, not after what you've seen. He would never allow you to speak against him. If you go out there, if you show yourself now, you're dead. He'll kill you as he killed Theo."

"Then let him kill me," Ruby sobbed, still trying to push away from Viola. "Let him show everyone the monster he is. It's no worse than I deserve."

Viola could feel her affinity starting to return to her—*too late*—and found Ruby's heartbeat, wild and erratic. Viola let her magic flare, only a little, just until Ruby went limp in her arms.

FRAGILE

1902—Uptown

ela heard the carriage approaching right about the same time she got a sort of chill down her spine. She put down the trousers she was stitching and stepped out onto the front stoop of the building as Viola was helping another white lady down from a hired carriage. The other lady was dressed for a wedding—her own, it looked like—and her face was nearly as pale as the lace that was framing it. She didn't seem to be completely conscious, but she leaned on Viola in a dazed sort of way.

If Viola was bringing home the bride, something had gone terribly wrong.

"Where's Jianyu?" Cela asked, coming down the steps to help Viola with the girl.

Viola didn't so much as look at her when she answered. "I don't know," she said, her voice tighter than usual. "Help me get her inside?"

"Who is she?" Cela asked.

"Theo's," Viola said simply, and the way her eyes welled up was all Cela needed to know before she took the bride's other arm and helped Viola get her up the steps of the front stoop.

Abel was off on a Pullman run. He wouldn't be back for two weeks, but his friend Joshua was there, hanging around to keep an eye on her like he usually did when her brother was away. He looked up from his papers and gave Cela a questioning look as she helped the white girl into the room. All Cela could do was shrug.

They got the girl situated on a cot in the back room, but she just sort of sat there, slumped—as much as anyone could slump in a corset—and stared into the distance.

"Looks like she can't hardly breathe in that thing," Cela said, frowning at the way the girl didn't seem to respond to anything they did. "Help me loosen it up, would you?"

Together, they unfastened the endless row of buttons that secured the dress in the back and then undid the laces of the girl's corset to loosen the boning. Beneath, her pale skin was marked with angry red lines. The girl didn't so much as stir. She just sat there like some sort of fancy porcelain doll, but when the corset was finally off, the girl took a deep, shuddering breath. And then she began to cry.

Good lord, Cela thought. Abel was going to kill her if he came back to yet another problem.

"Shhh . . ." Viola eased the girl back down onto the cot and tucked her beneath a heavy blanket. As quickly as the girl's tears had started, they stopped. Her eyes fluttered closed, and she began breathing more softly, all peaceful-like.

Viola didn't say a word about anything until she and Cela were back in the kitchen, and even then, she didn't settle. Instead, she propped her hands on the sink and stared out the window.

Cela traded looks with Joshua, who was watching Viola warily now. She understood. Viola was being so unusually quiet that it was starting to make Cela nervous too.

"Come on now," Cela said, putting a light hand on Viola's shoulders. "Whatever happened out there, it's gonna be okay."

When Viola turned to her, there was nothing but raw pain in her strange violet eyes. She looked so completely vulnerable—so *unlike* herself—that Cela let out a small sigh.

"Come sit down here," Cela told her, offering her a chair. "And when you're ready, you can tell me everything."

"I'm going to head back down to the office," Joshua told Cela, giving her a meaningful look that she knew meant he'd be close if she needed him.

Cela drew some water from the pump at the sink and filled two cups. Then she took the seat across from Viola and offered her the drink. "You look like you could use something stronger, but I think we better start with this."

Viola took a sip, reluctantly, but once she started drinking, she didn't stop until the cup was drained. Then she let out a sigh that telegraphed exhaustion and pain.

"I should have stayed away," Viola said, staring into the cup without lifting it to her lips. "I had no business there, but . . . Oh lord, if I hadn't been there." She buried her face in her hands. "If Jianyu hadn't followed to help . . ."

"What happened?"

Viola only shook her head. "There was an attack at the church." She looked up at Cela then. "Jack Grew came for them—Theo and Ruby both. He wanted to punish Theo for what happened on the solstice."

"Where's Theo now?" Cela asked, already knowing by the grief in Viola's eyes what the answer was.

"Jack killed him," Viola said, her voice as hollow as her expression. "There was nothing I could do." She said the words like an apology.

Cela's chest felt so tight at the realization that Theo was gone, she could barely draw breath. She reached across the table, to take Viola's hand. "Viola . . . Where is Jianyu?"

Viola only stared at their interlocked hands, and Cela had the same twisting, sinking feeling of dread as when she had thought Abel had been killed. *No . . .*

Viola looked up and met Cela's eyes. "I don't know."

She told Cela then what had happened in the church, what Jack Grew had done.

"And you left Jianyu to deal with Jack and those creatures on his own?" Cela asked, panic warring with anger.

"He told me to go," Viola said numbly, as though she couldn't believe the words she was saying. "Why did I *listen* to him? I saw what those creatures, what that *madman* could do, and left him there."

Cela's heart felt like it was in a vise. There was an ache in her chest and one behind her eyes as well. She wanted to rail at Viola for leaving Jianyu behind, but she understood immediately that blaming her would do no good. Panicking would do no good.

Jianyu will be fine. He'd slip out of there and be back to them in no time. *He has to be.*

"I failed them," Viola murmured, utterly bereft. "I left them both behind."

Cela wanted to agree, but instead she squeezed Viola's hand firmly. "You saved that girl's life, just like Jianyu told you to."

Later, they sent Joshua out to see if he could gather any news, and then they sat together for a long while after that, not so much talking as just holding a silent vigil until the world outside turned to night. Cela finally stood to light the lamps, so they wouldn't have to sit around in the dark. She was just finishing when the bride appeared in the doorway to the kitchen.

Cela knew good work when she saw it, and whoever had made the girl's gown was a talented seamstress. An expensive one too, from the look of it. The frock must have been truly stunning earlier that morning, with all the lace and embroidery still crisply pressed. But now the hem of the white satin was marred with the grime of the city, and the lace flounces hung limp from her shoulders.

Viola stood immediately, but she seemed frozen, like she suddenly didn't know what to do. Cela took one look at her, the way she was looking at Ruby Reynolds with her heart in her eyes, and suddenly everything became clear.

They stood there for a long stretch, stuck in the moment and unable to shake themselves free. Cela thought that maybe they each understood just exactly what the others were feeling, that mixture of longing and loss

LISA MAXWELL

that made her throat feel tight. That made her want to scream and cry and tear at her skin all at once.

Jianyu will come back, she told herself, not quite understanding why that point seemed so essential. But Theo Barclay would not, and beyond the tremor of fear that Cela felt in the pit of her stomach, she felt the ache of loss. Still, she knew that it was nothing compared to what this poor girl must feel.

"I see you're awake, Miss Reynolds." She paused, regretting her mistake. "Or should I call you Mrs. Barclay?"

The girl stared at her for a long second, like maybe Cela hadn't spoken the English she was born with.

"Ruby," she said finally, not answering the unspoken question. "Just Ruby."

Cela nodded. "Well, Ruby, let's get you something else to wear." She went around the table, took the girl by the arm, and guided her up the stairs.

"I'm going out." Viola was practically vibrating, and Cela knew that she wasn't thinking straight. She was overwhelmed with grief and anger, and she was likely to do something stupid if she went out alone.

"That's a bad idea, Vee," Cela told her. Nothing good could come from running on fury and grief. "Just sit back down and wait with us."

She was shaking her head. "I can't."

"Of course," Ruby said, her voice tinged with something too close to spite for Cela's liking. "You pretend to be so strong and powerful, but when you're up against anything, what do you do? You *run.* You ran at the gala, and you ran back at that church. You're a coward, Viola Vaccarelli. It's your fault Theo's dead."

Viola's expression turned unbearably bleak.

"Shhhh," Cela said. "You don't mean that."

The white girl turned on her. "I *do.* I mean it." She looked at Viola. "Theo was only mixed up with the Order because of *you.* Because you and your friends needed to steal some stupid artifact from them. I know all about what you did. He told me how he helped you, how he put himself at risk for you."

"I tried to stop him," Viola said, her voice breaking. "I never wanted him to risk himself for us."

"But he did, didn't he?" The girl's voice turned hollow. "He saw what you were doing as some silly adventure. He thought he was helping his friends. But you were never his friend. You never should have let him put himself at risk. *That's* why Jack Grew came after us today, because of what happened last June. All because of you and your friends. And you don't even have the Delphi's Tear to show for it. The Order still wins. *Jack* still wins. Theo would be alive right now if he'd never gotten mixed up with the likes of *you*. Theo died for *nothing*."

The viciousness in the girl's voice nearly had Cela leaving her to fend for herself. But Ruby was leaning on her too much to let her go, and Cela understood what grief could do to a person's tongue.

But it was too late to defuse the situation. She watched the color drain from Viola's face and her violet eyes go glassy with tears. There wasn't time to step forward and comfort Viola. She rushed from the room before Cela could take one step to stop her.

Before Cela could go after Viola, the girl collapsed. Her legs went right out from under her like the porcelain doll she appeared to be. Cela slid down with her, wrapping her arms around the girl, who was quivering now like a leaf in the wind.

"I didn't mean it," Ruby whispered, and then she burst into tears.

"Hush," Cela soothed. "It's going to be okay."

The girl let out a shuddering sob. "No, it's not. She's going to hate me."

"Viola doesn't hate you," Cela said, thinking of the pain and especially of the longing in Viola's eyes every time she'd looked Ruby's way. "Viola's been nothing but nerves since she dragged you in here, all because she's *worried* about you. She'll be back soon enough, once she cools off. And then you two can make nice. You'll see."

She finally got the girl calmed down and helped her out of the wilted white dress. For a long time, they waited together in the halo thrown by the oil lamps all night for some kind of news, but when the first rooster crowed, neither Viola nor Jianyu had returned.

IV

ADRIFT

1902—Central Park

One second, Harte had been stuck in the tunnel, trapped between two lines of the Guard that had pinned them in, and the next, he was falling through time. At the same instant he'd felt a blast of icy energy from the Guards' fog, the heat of Esta's magic flashed through him. The ground disappeared beneath them, and he felt himself tumbling into nothing. Time tore at him until he thought there was no way he would survive it. He knew this was it. Time would rip him apart. And then the pain grew so great that he *wished* it would.

He didn't even realize Esta's hand was no longer in his, not at first. He landed hard, unable to stop himself from slamming into the unforgiving ground. His head was still spinning, and his stomach felt as though it would turn itself inside out.

It felt worse every damn time it happened, and this time he couldn't stop himself from retching. After his stomach was completely emptied and his mouth tasted like a Bowery gutter, he finally began to catch his breath. Only then did he realize he was alone.

Harte scrambled to his feet, nearly falling over because of the dizziness still plaguing him, but Esta was nowhere to be seen. The Guards were gone, but so was she.

Beyond the trees, the city had changed. The enormous buildings that had swept the clouds had now disappeared. In their place, the city of the past had returned. It looked like his city. It sounded like his city as well— there was no squealing of sirens, and the steady rumble of automobiles had drowned away to nothing. The clip-clop of horse hooves had him scrambling to the edge of the tunnel.

Dakari.

But it wasn't Dakari's white open carriage on the road that ran over the tunnel. Instead, a wooden coal wagon plodded along, pulled by a mismatched pair of old nags. Harte realized then that the trees were nearly bare. The last of late autumn's gold clung to a few of their branches instead of the lush spring greens he'd been expecting.

This wasn't the plan.

They'd intended to slip back as close as possible to when they'd left— not long after Khafre Hall and the events on the bridge. They knew they would need time to use the Book and fix the Brink, to discover if their plan with Dakari had worked, and to try to stop both Jack and Nibsy. They knew, too, that they had to stop the rumors of the Devil's Thief. It should have still been late spring. The air should have been warm with the promise of the sweltering summer to come. But it wasn't. The wind kicked up, and a clutch of dried leaves swirled around his feet, thickening the air with the scent of their rot. The coolness in the breeze spoke of winter and snow.

He didn't know *when* this was, but he knew Esta was gone. If he happened to find himself in a time she couldn't reach—

No. It wasn't possible that he'd lost her. As soon as Ishtar's Key cooled enough to travel again and as soon as whatever was in that fog wore off, she would come. She *had* to come.

He waited late into the night. At some point, he drifted off to sleep, and he woke the next morning chilled to the bone and shivering from the overnight frost. But he still didn't leave, because leaving meant accepting, and he wasn't ready to do that. Not yet. *Not ever.* He kept watch all through the day. Waiting. Knowing the world would right itself. That Esta would appear.

Near twilight, he realized he had an audience—a small newsboy who'd stopped to stare.

"You okay, mister?" The boy's hat was askew, and he had a bruise beneath his eye that had turned a yellow-green.

"No," Harte told him. Because the truth of what had happened was beginning to become undeniable. "Not even a little."

"Buy a pape'?" The boy lifted the stack of newspapers he had slung under his arms, unconcerned with Harte's answer or mood.

"No," Harte said, waving him away. "I don't want a damn paper— Wait. *Yes.* Yes, I do." He stood, shaking off the stiffness in his joints as he took a bill from his pocket. He didn't care what the denomination was—anything but a coin would have been far too much. He just wanted a paper. He needed to know.

"Mister?" The newsie sounded confused.

"Just take it," Harte said, shoving the money toward the boy. "I don't need any change."

Wide-eyed, the newsie took the bill from him and handed over the whole stack of papers. He darted away before Harte could change his mind.

Harte barely noticed him go. His eyes were already scanning the header of the newspaper for the date, and when he found it, he nearly collapsed with relief.

December 1, 1902.

Feeling suddenly light-headed, he leaned against a nearby tree to keep himself upright as he let all but the one newspaper he was holding flutter to the ground. It was okay. He might not be in the right month, but Esta had gotten him to the right year. She *could* still reach him, and they hadn't missed the Conclave. They weren't too late. She might already be here.

And if she doesn't come?

Harte hated the voice in his head, hated the question as well. But he knew the answer. He'd fight for her. He'd carry on. He was in his city now, and he had allies waiting. He had only to find them.

He turned back to the tunnel, still empty. Still without any sign that Esta would appear. There was a part of him that wanted to stay, in case she arrived. But he couldn't live in that tunnel, waiting for endless hours and days like some kind of vagrant. The police swept through the park regularly enough that they'd notice him, and that was only if one of the gangs didn't get to him first.

They had a plan, didn't they? Whenever she arrived, they'd find each other, and then they would set things right.

Harte took one last look, and then he started walking toward the Bowery. He had been away only a matter of months, but his travels had changed him. After San Francisco and Chicago, after seeing a New York that towered and rushed around him, this city felt different, and he felt different within it. He'd seen what it would become, and he could almost see that promise now, waiting like a sleeping beast ready to rouse itself. The world felt like it was holding its breath, waiting for the future to arrive.

Or maybe it was waiting for something else. . . . There was an atmosphere in the streets he couldn't quite place. An uneasy hum of something about to begin.

He headed south. Cela Johnson would be waiting. So, too, would Jianyu and Viola. He would need allies in the weeks ahead if there was to be any chance of them stopping Jack or Nibsy, of using the Book or stabilizing the Brink. Hopefully, Esta would arrive before the Conclave. Or maybe he hoped she was late. Maybe he hoped the terrible future written in the diary would never happen if she simply missed it.

Either way, Harte had to find the others. He would have to prepare them for what was coming, because he knew he'd need their help.

But when he turned down the street where Cela lived, he found only the burned-out remains of what had once been her home. He couldn't tell how long ago the fire had occurred—trash and other detritus had accumulated in the corners of what was left of the building—but there had been no move to rebuild.

In the distance, he heard the clanging of a fire bell. The whining of hand-cranked sirens.

LISA MAXWELL

He'd left his mother with Cela at the house that had once stood on that lot. He assumed his mother was gone. She'd been in bad shape when he'd left her to Cela's care. But had his mother passed from the opium Nibsy had doused her with before the fire? Or had she been trapped in the flames that had consumed the home?

Had Cela made it out?

He looked around at the buildings that were still standing, silent and uninterested in his distress. He had to find Cela, or he'd never know. Which meant he had to find Jianyu.

But Jianyu could be anywhere in the city.

With one last look at the burned remains of Cela's home, he turned his feet toward the Bowery, toward the one place that might have the information he needed. He only hoped he wasn't already too late.

HELLCAT

Bella Strega

James Lorcan had almost grown used to the strange rumbling under-current in the Aether that had plagued him since not long after the summer solstice, but when the Aether shifted violently that night, he knew immediately that something was coming. Still, he felt no fear at the trembling that signaled an approaching danger. He felt only anticipation. He'd long since placed the players on the board, and finally the game would begin.

When the doors to the Bella Strega burst open with a gust of cold, he wasn't surprised to see that it was Viola. He'd been expecting her for so long, she was practically late. With a knife in her hand and her eyes flash-ing fury, she entered the barroom ready to fight like the hellcat she was. Everyone in the saloon went silent, because everyone in that barroom knew what she could do—with the blade *and* with her magic.

Werner stepped forward, but James gave a subtle shake of his head to stop him. Viola had none of her usual cold, calculating calm. Something had unhinged her, and because of it, she'd made a mistake by coming here unprotected. It would make what was to come that much more entertaining. So he'd let the game play out. When Viola finally came to her inevitable end, it would be his hand that ended her. Not Werner's.

"Bastardo!" she hissed, finally spotting James from across the dimly lit space. The people standing between them parted like water as she stalked toward him.

"Viola," he drawled, keeping his voice easy and unconcerned despite her rapid approach. "How nice of you to visit. I see you haven't lost a bit of your charm."

"I'll show you my charm," she said, lifting the knife and pointing the tip at his throat.

It wasn't *her* knife, which was interesting. And she didn't skewer him. Nor did she touch him with her magic. He knew she wouldn't. She was there for blood, but for some reason, she wasn't ready to draw it quite yet.

"To what do I owe this delightful visit?" he asked. He leaned forward a little, unafraid of her blade, but he kept one hand tight around the cane at his side.

Her eyes shifted to the silver Medusa, and he understood that she knew what he was capable of. He saw fear flicker in her expression—just a glimmer—before she shook it away and narrowed her eyes.

"I hope you're here to accept my offer," he said, knowing already that she wasn't. "Perhaps you've come to repent of your sins and rejoin your family?"

"You are no family of mine," she said through clenched teeth. "And I have nothing to repent, other than letting you live for so long. But I think that's a mistake I maybe can be correcting. *Adesso.*"

He didn't bother to conceal his amusement. "Don't you think you have that backward? After all, I'm the one with control of the marks. You live by my mercy alone."

"You aren't worthy of the oath I made," she sneered. She let her gaze travel around the room, and she spoke to the Strega now, to the Devil's Own. "This one, this *snake*, he's not worthy of *any* of your lives. He's done nothing but take and take."

She found Werner in the crowd and focused on him. "Tell them," she commanded. "Tell them all how he sent you to die on a fool's errand. Dolph would never have done such a thing."

"Dolph did far worse," James drawled. "I assure you."

"I *know* what Dolph did," she said, turning on him, as vicious as she ever was.

"And you forgive him?" James wondered. "He took Leena's affinity, stole it without her knowledge or her permission, and in doing so, he destroyed her."

His words had the effect he intended. The crowded barroom rustled as people murmured about this new information. Saint Dolph, the martyr. Not so saintlike anymore.

"All because he wanted power," James added. "Power over us. Over you as well." He stood then, bringing himself to his full height. He no longer needed the cane, but he kept it in his hand just the same. Sent a flash of energy through the silver Medusa until Viola visibly flinched. "He wasn't worthy of this power."

"And you think you are?" she mocked, still grimacing against the slight pressure he was sending through the mark.

Not enough to kill. But enough to distract her. Enough to remind her who was truly in charge.

She straightened. "Tell them what you do, Nibsy. Tell them how many of those who don't wear the mark you've sacrificed to the Order's patrols." She turned to the barroom. "Dolph Saunders protected those who couldn't protect themselves. But this one, he uses the weakest among us. How many are missing today because of *him*?"

Her voice broke on the last word as he sent another bolt of warning through the magic that connected her tattoo to the cane.

"Why did you come here, Viola?" James asked. "Clearly you didn't come to make amends."

She stepped toward him. Her shoulders were back, but he knew the stiffness in her step was because of the steady pain he was sending into her mark. Her ability to ignore it would have been admirable if she weren't such a nuisance.

"I came for the ring."

"You can't imagine that I'd ever give it to you." He laughed softly, amused despite himself.

"Then I'll take it," she growled. "Dead men don't put up so much of a fight." She lifted her blade, preparing to hurl it toward his heart.

Before she could, his eyes shifted to Werner. And Viola went down.

SHATTERING

Viola came back to consciousness racked with unspeakable pain. Terrible energy was flooding through her body, turning her blood to ice and making her feel as though she were about to fly apart. The pain went on and on, until suddenly it stopped and everything went dark.

She wasn't dead. Not yet. But her body felt as though it had been run through with electricity, and she could imagine very easily wanting to die. She could imagine giving herself over to death without any regrets if that pain came again.

She was tied to some table. Her eyes were closed, because it was too much effort to force them open, but her lack of sight made all her other senses more aware. Her body ached against the unforgiving table, the smell of stale beer and tobacco made her stomach turn, and her mouth tasted of coppery blood.

Maybe it would have been easier to just simply give in. To relent and be dragged under by death. The end would have been a comfort compared to the terror and pain she currently felt. But she forced herself to draw in another shallow breath that made her ribs feel like they were being cracked open. And then another.

"Ah," a familiar voice said. "I see you're still with us . . . for now."

Viola didn't respond. She didn't so much as stir. It was taking every bit of energy and strength she had just to live.

She'd been a *fool*.

It had been a volatile mixture of grief and desperation combined with the truth in Ruby's words that had pushed Viola onward through the city, determined to end Nibsy Lorcan's life once and for all. Theo was dead, and Ruby would hate her forever because of it. What did she have to lose? She had been determined to get the ring back from that traitorous snake. If Theo was dead, she'd wanted to make sure his death hadn't been for nothing.

She opened her eyes a little and tried to make them focus. There, at the level of her gaze, was Leena's likeness. The silver Medusa with her friend's face stared blankly, unseeing. Mocking her.

Had she been thinking clearly when she left the *New York Age*'s building, maybe she would have made a plan. Maybe she would have waited until her anger had eased before charging into a pit of vipers. Instead, she'd gone to the Bella Strega convinced that she didn't care what happened—not to herself, not to any of them. If the Devil's Own broke apart, if they were devoured by the snakes who ran the Bowery, then so be it. It would be their own fault since they were standing by and allowing Nibsy to pervert what Dolph had built.

When she had marched into the Strega, she'd been desperate. She had already lost her home, her family, her . . . hope. She had nothing left to lose.

Oh, but she had been wrong about that, she thought as Nibsy's hand adjusted itself on the silver topper of the cane. The ring was right there, secure on his finger, and the clear stone seemed to wink at her, taunting her.

He crouched down, until they were eye to eye. Through the thick lenses of his spectacles, he looked her over, amusement shining in his light eyes.

"It doesn't have to be like this, Viola." Nibsy's voice was gentle, coaxing, but she knew it was all an act. His cloudy blue eyes glowed with amusement behind the thick lenses of his gold-rimmed glasses. "You can still repent. Renew your oath and join me. Come back to the Devil's Own. Come *home*. Be my blade, and I'll let you live."

She reached for her affinity to show him exactly what he could do with his false promises, but her magic slipped through her fingers. Her blood felt heavy and slow, like she'd been doused with opium or Nitewein.

"*Tsk-tsk*," he said, amusement curling in his voice. "Always so vicious."

The mark on her back flared with icy energy again, and she felt herself jerking up off the table she'd been tied to. Pain shot through her, *unspeakable* pain, and she felt that essential part of herself—her connection to the old magic—starting to crumble.

Just when she thought it was the end, the pain ceased, and her body slumped back to the table. She felt the energy in the barroom shift. The people had not left. They were watching, murmuring and waiting. They were allowing it to happen. *Because it wasn't happening to them.* But there was a thread of discontent in their nervous heartbeats. There was a fear growing that had not been there before.

Viola knew that Nibsy was playing with her, just as she understood that he was nowhere close to done. Her suffering amused him, certainly, but it served a purpose. She'd allowed herself to become an example to those standing around the barroom—of his power, of what happened to anyone who crossed him.

And still, no one stepped forward to help her. Theo was dead, and Ruby hated her. Cela would not know where she was, and Jianyu would be too late, if he wasn't dead himself. She had always felt apart, but now she understood what it felt like to be truly alone.

"Have you learned your lesson, Viola?" Nibsy asked. "It's not too late. Even now I would welcome you back, if only you give me your oath."

"I'd rather die," she told him.

"That," he said without any emotion at all, "can be arranged."

Suddenly, she felt hands upon her, and then the coolness of air on her back as someone tore her blouse in two, exposing the tattoo inked between her shoulder blades. It had nearly gone numb from the icy-hot ache of Nibsy's previous attempts to break her, but now the ink was boiling in her skin. It screamed of the danger she was in.

"Good-bye, Viola," Nibsy said, lifting the cane.

Her skin already hurt too much to feel the Medusa's kiss. She barely sensed the pressure, but then all at once, cold and unnatural magic shot through her. If the pain she'd experienced before was terrible, *this* was worse. She could not stop the scream that tore from her throat.

She would not survive this.

Viola knew with the same certainty that she had felt every time she reached for her blade that she would not live to see the next day. She would never be able to tell Jianyu how much she valued his friendship or to thank Cela for forgiving her. She would not live to see the Order destroyed or Nibsy Lorcan struck down. And she would never be able to tell Ruby how she truly felt.

That was the biggest regret of all. The Order could go hang. Nibsy Lorcan could as well. But she'd lied that night at the gala when Ruby had opened her heart and Viola had rejected it. She'd lied to Ruby, and she'd lied to herself about what she was willing to risk.

How foolish she'd been to be afraid of love, when this terror—this *pain*—she now felt existed in the world. How stupid of her to reject such a gift.

Viola's eyes flew open, and she searched the crowd surrounding her for some sign of pity, of mercy. Werner was standing there, white as a sheet. Unmoving.

Please—she mouthed, her voice no longer working. He could stop Nibsy. He could stop all of this. *Please.*

But she saw the fear in his eyes, and she understood he would not stand against his new boss. Not now. Likely not ever.

Viola was flying apart, her body separating from her soul. She was being ripped to shreds right along with her magic. She felt herself shattering, felt her magic crumbling away, and her life with it.

And then, suddenly, everything exploded.

TAINTED MAGIC

arte took out Werner first. It was the only choice, considering what Werner's affinity could do. The single shot did exactly what he'd expected and launched the people in the Bella Strega into chaos. It wasn't exactly the most elegant form of misdirection, but it served his purpose.

After finding Cela's house destroyed by fire, there was only one place he could think of to go where he was sure to find some answers—the Strega. He hadn't known what to expect, not after all they'd done to change the course of time and history. But when he'd reached the saloon, he realized that even his worst fears hadn't come close to the reality of the scene he found there. Viola was tied to the table that Dolph once favored—the one where he'd once gathered his closest friends—and Nibsy Lorcan was using Dolph's cane to unmake her.

If Viola was there, somehow trapped and under Nibsy's control, where was Jianyu? What could have possibly happened over the past months to make *this* scene a possibility?

If he didn't save Viola, he'd never find out.

Harte hadn't even paused. There wasn't time to worry about whether Werner deserved to die, because Harte had seen a similar scene play out before. He'd watched when Dolph had destroyed a man in this same way years before—it was the reason he'd never taken the mark himself. He refused to let that fate happen to Viola, not when he was there to stop it. When he'd lifted the snub-nosed pistol he'd taken from the future, he hadn't aimed to injure. He needed Werner to stay down, because he knew he'd have only one attempt to get Viola out of there alive.

As Harte stalked through the frantic crowd, he touched an exposed wrist here, a bare neck there. He hadn't used his affinity so much in months. Hell, he'd never used his affinity that much at all, but he didn't hesitate now. Wrapping his magic around him, he reached through the shells of humanity and commanded as many as he could. He had only so many bullets left in the gun, after all. By the time he reached the other side of the barroom, he already had the pistol aimed at Nibsy's chest. No one moved against him.

Instead, the barroom descended into an unsettled quiet. A couple of the Devil's Own were trying to save Werner, but most had realized that something else was happening. No one stepped forward to help Nibsy or stop Harte. But the whole room turned to watch the drama that was about to play out.

"I wondered when you might show up again, Darrigan," Nibsy said, glancing over Harte's shoulder to the door he'd just come through. "But you seem to be missing something. Or will Esta be joining us later?"

Harte ignored the taunting calmness in Nibsy's voice. The knowing glint in his eye. "Let her go, Nibs."

Viola's dark hair had fallen from its pins and now covered her face, so Harte could not tell if she was conscious. Her shirt had been torn open, from neck to waist, and her corset had been cut away to expose the skin on her back. There between her shoulder blades, something that might have once been Dolph Saunders' mark had been transformed into a bloody mess. Her skin looked blistered and torn, and the once-black tattoo had turned the color of blood. The mark itself—or what was left of it—was glowing, as though there were a fire beneath her skin, burning her from within.

"I don't see why I should." Nibsy touched the silver head of the cane to her back again, and cold energy flashed through the room.

Harte felt the hair on his arms and neck rise as Viola screamed. The skin on her back bubbled and blistered as the snakes inscribed into her skin began to move. As they rippled and pulsed, the ink turned bloody, and Harte knew that if he didn't stop Nibsy, she wouldn't last much longer.

He drew the hammer back on the pistol. "I'm not going to ask you again, Nibs. Let Viola go, or I'll pull the trigger right now."

"You can't kill me," Nibsy said, not making any move to release Viola from the Medusa's kiss.

"Try me," Harte challenged.

"If I die, Esta dies as well," Nibsy said with an amused shrug. "I'm necessary to her very existence. And she's necessary to *yours*."

He was right. Harte had no way of knowing where Esta even was—or *when* she was—but if Dakari didn't follow through, then Esta's existence depended on Nibsy Lorcan's life. He couldn't risk killing him. *Not yet.* Not until he got the sign he was waiting for. But that sign had not yet appeared.

"I don't have to kill you to make you regret hurting her," Harte warned. "The bullet in this gun doesn't need to take your life to destroy your magic. Tell me, Nibsy, what do you think your life would be like without your affinity?"

Nibsy's expression faltered a little, and Harte could see him calculating. Reading the room or the Aether—or whatever it was that he did to get three steps ahead of everyone. The cold power swirling through the room eased a bit, even if Nibsy didn't move the cane from Viola's blistered and bloodied back.

"This gun happens to be a little gift from the future," Harte explained, taking another step forward. "The bullets in it are tainted with ritual magic made to destroy Mageus. I've seen up close what it's capable of. One strike and your affinity will be virtually useless. And if you don't manage to cut out the rot in time? The damage will spread. It won't kill you right away, but you'll wish it had. Now step away from her, or I'll be more than happy to demonstrate."

Nibsy hesitated, calculating still, but then suddenly he seemed to have a change of heart. He lifted his hands, raising the cane above his head as well. "Fine," he said. "Take her, for all the good it will do you."

"Back up," Harte said. "And tell your guys there to stay back as well.

Anyone moves, anyone tries *anything*, and you're the one who'll get the bullet."

Nibsy spread his hands wide, but Harte didn't accept his cooperation as a given. He kept the gun leveled at him the whole time, waiting for the trick.

"Tell that one to untie her," Harte commanded, nodding toward an unfamiliar blond boy about his own age. He'd noticed the interest in the blond's expression the second Nibsy mentioned Esta's name, and he had the sense he knew who the guy might be.

"Logan," Nibsy said, confirming Harte's suspicions about the boy's identity. "Go ahead and cut Viola free."

Logan had been one of Professor Lachlan's. He'd grown up with Esta, but Harte didn't know whether it was loyalty or desperation that had made him Nibsy's.

As Logan was working on cutting the ropes securing Viola's legs, Harte sidled up behind him, brushing the back of his fingers along the boy's neck. He sent a quick pulse of magic through him, a command to ensure his complicity. When Logan was done cutting the ropes from Viola's wrist, he lifted her gently in his arms without being told and brought her over to where Harte was waiting. All the while, Harte kept the gun aimed at Nibsy's chest.

Viola let out a moan in response to being moved, but she didn't seem to be conscious. Her head hung back over Logan's arms, her limbs loose and limp.

"Are you taking him as well?" Nibsy asked. He'd lowered his hands by now and had them resting on the silver Medusa's head.

"For now," Harte said.

"Keep him." Nibsy shrugged. "He's too soft to be of much use anyway."

Harte wasn't sure he trusted Nibsy's appraisal of Logan, who had once been loyal enough to the Professor to bring Esta back as his prisoner. But for now, under the thrall of Harte's affinity, Logan had his uses.

He considered the cane resting beneath Nibsy's hands, but it would have to wait. He had to get Viola somewhere safe before the uneasy interest in the barroom turned to something else. At that moment, he couldn't risk anything more than surviving.

Harte nodded to Logan. "Let's go," he said, never lowering the gun as they backed out of the Strega.

A dozen or more pairs of eyes watched as they retraced his steps, leaving through the front door of the saloon. No one made any move to stop them, though it would have been easy enough to block their path and make things more difficult. He hadn't charmed *that* many people. Maybe it was shock, or maybe it was simply unwillingness to involve themselves in dangers that didn't directly affect them. Whatever the case, it never would have happened under Dolph. Had someone attacked the Strega as he just had, the Devil's Own wouldn't have stood for it.

Whatever the reason for their silence, Harte hoped that it held. There were only a couple of bullets left in the gun, and if the Devil's Own did decide to attack, he couldn't shoot them all.

He didn't want to, either.

Once they were outside, Harte kept the gun firmly in his grasp, but he reached out to grab Viola's wrist. It took only a second to discover the information he needed.

A block over, they found a covered carriage for hire, and with a quick shake of the driver's hand, he made sure that the fellow wouldn't remember them once he dropped them at the address he gave. They didn't seem to have been followed from the Strega, not that it made Harte relax any. If Nibsy let them go, there was a reason.

Viola was still unconscious when they finally arrived at the address Harte had taken from her memories. It was a brick building, three stories tall, with a large sign that pronounced the offices of the *New York Age* across the front door.

He alighted from the carriage and then took Viola from Logan before the other boy jumped out as well. She was barely breathing, and her skin was a ghastly gray.

Logan stood there, still half in a daze under the control of Harte's affinity. "Go knock on the door. See if Jianyu is in there," he commanded.

But Logan hadn't even crossed half the distance to the building when the front door of the building flew open and Cela Johnson emerged.

"Harte Darrigan?" she said, her eyes as wide as if she'd seen a ghost. Then she realized who he was holding. "Oh, god. Viola."

Another woman had emerged from the building as well. Tall and lithe, the blonde took one look at the scene in the street, focused on Viola hanging unconscious and unmoving in Harte's arms, and shoved past Cela. "No," she said, brushing the hair back from Viola's face. "She can't be—"

With the girl tugging at Viola, Harte could barely keep hold of her.

He struggled to adjust his grip so he didn't drop Viola. "Cela, if you could—"

Cela was already taking the blond girl by the shoulder and pulling her back.

"She's not dead," Cela told the girl.

Harte knew Cela understood. The worry in her eyes spoke more loudly and clearly than even her words could.

At least not yet.

FOR SPORT OR SLAUGHTER

The Docks

Jianyu opened his eyes to darkness. The floor was cold and hard beneath him. It smelled of dirt and dampness, and when he tried to lift himself from it, he found that one of his ankles had been secured. The shackle felt unnaturally smooth—unnaturally cold as well. And though he could not see what held him, he knew it was no simple piece of metal. When he stood, he could take no more than two or three steps in either direction. He had been chained in place, like some kind of animal. But whether he was being kept for sport or for slaughter, he could not tell.

He did not know where he was. In the distance, he could detect a gentle murmuring that he could not quite discern; it was too far off. In the space around him there was only silence. The air was thick and close, choked with dust and the scent of something heavy and metallic—and also with the cloying sweetness of opium. All around him, he felt the cold energy of counterfeit magic. He reached for his affinity, but with the sweetness of the opium, he was not surprised to find a numb hollowness where his connection to the old magic should have been.

Jack Grew knew what Jianyu was, and it seemed that he was taking no chances.

He had been so close to escaping. After Viola had taken Theo's bride to safety, Jianyu had nearly slipped away himself. But before he could make it to the back of the church, another of the beasts had formed itself from the thick smoke, billowing up as unexpectedly as a nightmare. It happened so quickly—far more quickly than before—and before he could react, Jianyu had been caught up by the throat. He rubbed at the soreness that ringed his neck now, remembering what it had felt like to struggle . . . and to lose.

He was not sure how long he sat there, waiting for whatever would come, but the darkness was severed suddenly and unexpectedly by a flash of light not so very far away. The block of brightness might well have been a doorway opening to another world. Jianyu's eyes ached as he squinted against the glare, but he knew immediately who the figure silhouetted against the brightness was.

"I see you're not dead," Jack Grew said, lighting a lantern and then another until the space was completely illuminated.

Jianyu did not bother to respond. While Jack busied himself with the lamps, Jianyu took stock of his situation. They were in a warehouse, and in the center of the space was a large metal structure that could only be the terrible machine Darrigan had described to him. The machine that had killed Tilly. The machine that could destroy all magic for a hundred miles. The Magician had destroyed the machine, but there it was. Whole once again.

As Jianyu had suspected, his ankle was chained to a stake cemented into the ground, but the shackle was a single, unbroken piece of dark steel without any hinge or latch. There was no keyhole—no lock to pick— and the cold energy of the corrupted magic was strong enough that it made the dangerous piece of silk wrapped around his wrist feel like no more than a whisper. A few feet away was a broad table piled with papers and tools. Among the clutter was Libitina, too far away to be of any use on the shackle.

Jack carried with him a burlap sack and a ceramic growler. As he approached Jianyu, he took a small paper-wrapped parcel from the bag and tossed it at Jianyu's feet, just within reach of the end of the chain. Then he set the growler beside it, before unpacking the rest. The bag contained another of the paper-wrapped parcels, some notebooks, and a flask of something that smelled strongly of whiskey when it was opened.

Jack took a sip from the flask and then set it aside on the makeshift table before he began to unwrap what appeared to be a sandwich.

Jianyu only watched. He did not move to inspect the package Jack had dropped on the floor at his feet. Nor did he try to reach for the growler. His thirst was of less concern than understanding Jack's plans.

"It's not poisoned, if that's what you're worried about," Jack said, glancing at Jianyu as he chewed. "If I wanted you dead, you already would be."

Considering his current predicament, that particular reassurance meant very little. It guaranteed even less.

"I know full well you can understand me. You might as well eat," Jack said, and then took another long drink from the flask. "You'll want to keep up your strength for the escape I know you're already planning."

Jianyu's stomach rumbled at the thought. Reluctantly, he opened the parcel to find a hard-crusted roll filled with odd-smelling meat. His nose wrinkled, but Jack was right—he did need to preserve his strength, because he was not planning on remaining a prisoner for long. He took a bite, but it was nearly impossible to choke down the terrible food, and the water in the growler was little help. It was overly warm and tasted bitterly of sulfur. He set both aside, disgusted with the food and with himself.

"I'm sure you're wondering why I haven't killed you," Jack said after he'd finished his own lunch.

He had, actually, but Jianyu simply stared at Jack. There was little to be gained by conversing with a madman.

"Or perhaps you'd prefer to enjoy the surprise of what's to come?" Jack asked pleasantly.

Jianyu remained silent. He *would* prefer to know, but he had no interest in playing these games. Better to watch. Better to wait. Eventually someone as volatile as Jack would misstep.

Jack removed an object from within the jacket he wore. He held it up and showed it to Jianyu. "Do you know what this is?"

Even if Jianyu had not known anything at all about the Ars Arcana, the strange energy coming from the small leather book in Jack's hands—the heady warmth of the old magic and the cold warning of counterfeit magic mixed together—would have told Jianyu that the book was more than it appeared. But Jianyu knew the Book. He had seen it before in Esta's possession. Jianyu also knew that Esta and Darrigan had taken the Book with them when they left the city. They had used its power to pass through the Brink, so they could search for artifacts and retrieve them before Nibsy did. For Jack to have the Book now . . .

Jianyu's mind was racing. If Darrigan and Esta had died on the train, as the news reports had suggested, it meant they were not searching for the artifacts—*had not been searching all this time.* If they were gone, they would not be returning at all.

There was no one coming to save them.

Jack had already opened the Book. His mouth was forming the shape of strange words, and his voice rose so that the droning sound of the unknown syllables filled the air in the warehouse. As he spoke, Jack's eyes had gone impossibly black. It looked as though the pupil had grown, consuming the iris and the white as well, until there was nothing but darkness, nothing but emptiness within.

Except, when Jack turned to him, he realized that the darkness was not empty. He thought he saw something shift there in that void. Something apart from the man seemed to lurk within.

Jianyu noticed the circle then. How had he missed it? Someone had traced it into the dirt of the floor, just beyond the reach of his chain, but now it was beginning to glow with a dangerous energy that brushed against his skin in warning. The air around him went thick with magic, and suddenly his arms and legs felt as though unseen hands were jerking him upward until he was floating above the ground, splayed out and helpless to fight against it. Around his wrist, the silken band had gone as cold as ice.

THE POWER WITHIN

J ack Grew felt more than the warmth of the morphine in his blood. The power within him had taken over and was whispering the ancient words that caused potent magic to begin swirling through the warehouse. He gave himself over to that power, reveled in it, as the very Aether lit around him.

The maggot was hanging, caught in the Aether, his arms and legs stretched as though pinned to some invisible rack. He was grimacing as he tried to free himself, but he'd give up soon enough. He should have realized that it was pointless to fight against the Book's power.

Jack took the Pharaoh's Heart from the sack and noticed the maggot's interest.

"Do you recognize this?" Jack asked. "No, don't try to pretend otherwise. I see it there in your eyes. You know what it is. Perhaps you've seen it before? Maybe you were there in Khafre Hall that night when your friends destroyed it." He held the blade up a little, noticing how the bloodred garnet in the hilt seemed to glow in response to the magic coursing through the air. "The Pharaoh's Heart. An apt enough name, I suppose, since I will be using it to cleave the magic from your heart."

The Chinaman remained silent, but he could not completely guard his emotions. There was fear in his narrow eyes.

Jack took the rest of the supplies from his satchel, including the large onyx he'd found out west. He turned the crystal back and forth in the lamplight, admiring the way it gleamed. He'd been right. It would be perfect for what he planned to do.

"What will you do with me?" the Chinaman asked through clenched teeth.

"You aren't really in any position to be asking questions," Jack mused. "But since you've so little time left, I'll have pity. You see, you're about to become a part of history."

He took the dagger in hand and walked toward the maggot, relishing the brush of power as he stepped over the boundary line of the ritual.

"That doesn't appeal to you?" he asked when the Chinaman didn't react. "Think of it, a filthy immigrant like yourself, destined to always be other, and now your feral magic will help me change the world."

"Are you so sure the world can be changed?" the maggot asked quietly.

"I *know* it can be changed," Jack said, snapping with temper at the Chinaman's impertinence. "And I am the one who will finally accomplish what the others could not. I will be the one to finally rid this city—this *country*—of the threat from maggots like you."

He stalked forward, feeling sureness of his purpose heat his blood. Or perhaps that was the morphine.

"The old men who rule over the Order are convinced that the Brink is the solution to protecting the city from feral magic. They believe that the maggots who have sullied our streets can be contained." Jack knew otherwise. If it were possible simply to *contain* undesirables, the Chinese vermin overrunning Mott Street with their violence and filth would never have even entered the city. They, at least, were easy enough to spot. But maggots in general? They hid too easily among the refuse of the city's streets.

And they were still coming, more each day. The Brink did nothing to dissuade them. It certainly didn't *stop* them.

It was the central problem that the old goats like his uncle failed to recognize—*refused* to see. The Brink could never be a solution to the dangers of feral magic because it *depended* on the power it harnessed from the maggots who dared to cross it. It *needed* them. It allowed them to live, to *exist*, because it had to.

"The Inner Circle refuses to understand. Vermin cannot be contained. Like the rats that plague our streets, they must be *eliminated*. And it must be now, before the danger grows any greater.

"Perhaps before, they could have bought themselves a few more years by strengthening the Brink. Perhaps with the Delphi's Tear they could have even managed to convince the Brotherhoods of their continued importance. But now?" He reached up and gave the maggot a couple of quick, sharp slaps on his cheeks. "Thanks to you and your friends, the Order has nothing. No artifacts. No Book of Mysteries. No hope to regain their footing." He smiled at the thought of their demise. Of his inevitable victory. "Soon they will have even less, and I will be the one to step forward and remake them."

Jack walked over to the machine and ran his hand over the curve of one of the heavy metal arms. He gave it a gentle push and watched as the entire contraption lurched into a slow, graceful movement. The arms orbited around the center console, dodging past one another like an enormous gyroscope.

"We live in a modern age, an age of wonders. Why should we depend on antiquated magic when science can augment our understanding of the occult?" He stopped the swinging arms. "This machine is powered like every other machine—with electricity. It only requires something to harness the energy it harvests, so that energy can be used. Think of it—I will be able to protect the country from the feral power of maggots like you while providing enough energy to power a bright new future. All I needed was something like this," he said, gesturing to the dagger.

The Chinaman remained silent, but Jack could tell he was impressed. He could see the utter fear in the maggot's expression.

"There is the problem of scale," Jack said, frowning. "A single machine can do only so much. With this one stone and the machine installed in Tesla's tower, I could reach a hundred miles, more than enough to exterminate the vermin in this city. But what good would that do for the *country*? One machine doesn't solve the problems we face, not when maggots are now pouring in through other ports as well."

"You would make five machines," the Chinaman murmured, his eyes wide with terror.

Jack only laughed. "You're thinking of the other artifacts." Which only confirmed his likely involvement with their theft. "No. I will make enough of them to cover the entire country. From sea to shining sea, as it were."

He smiled at the confusion on the maggot's face. "You seem to be making the same error in logic as the old fools of the Inner Circle have made," Jack told him. "They believe their artifacts are so precious, so utterly unique."

The Chinaman's dark brows drew together. He seemed interested despite himself. "Are they not?" he asked.

"Oh, the Order's artifacts are precious. They're ancient pieces taken from the ancient dynasties. They're powerful as well. But they are not *singular*. Once, they were the same as this." Jack took the glittering black stone and lifted it to the level of the Chinaman's eyes. "Nothing more than a gem, beautiful and pure. They were symbolic, but otherwise powerless until they were transformed by the Ars Arcana. It's all here, in these pages. The ritual is complex, but not impossible to re-create. It only requires a maggot powerful enough to complete it."

He placed the stone on the floor directly beneath the man's body. "Luckily, Barclay and his bitch of a fiancée provided the perfect opportunity to find one."

"The attack on their wedding was a trap," the maggot realized.

"Well, it wasn't *only* a trap," Jack told him. "Barclay caused me enough trouble last June that he deserved his fate. I won't mourn him in the least. But yes . . . I had hoped to ensnare more than Theo and his blushing bride. I knew that he must have had help to escape from the Flatiron Building, and I assumed that whoever saved him once would be willing to rescue him again. I was right. As I expected, you and your maggot friends came running to his defense. But you were too late, and you weren't strong enough. Feral magic never is.

"Now I have everything I need. The power in the Book. The feral magic beneath your skin. And an enchanted blade to cut that magic from you," Jack told him. "With the Pharaoh's Heart, I'll use you to transform this hunk of stone into something more."

"You'll create another artifact," the Chinaman realized.

"Nothing so precious as an *artifact*," Jack corrected. "I'll create something more common, an object that can be reproduced as long as there are gemstones to mine and feral magic to harvest. With it, I'll finally be able to balance the power of this machine. And with my machine, I'll be able to destroy those who threaten our land. I'll change *everything*. And the old men of the Order will have no choice but to step aside. What little power they've built over the last century will be mine to wield, and I will do even more than those old goats ever dreamed."

"The Order cannot want you to take their power. . . ." The Chinaman couldn't hide his confusion.

Jack scoffed. "Perhaps, but they'll be too busy to realize what's happening until it's already done," he said. "You see, the Conclave is destined to be attacked by dangerous maggots desperate to destroy the Order, just as they destroyed poor Theo Barclay. In the chaos, the Brotherhoods will be tossed into disarray. But I'll be ready. The Order will finally recognize my greatness, as will the other Brotherhoods. And I will claim my rightful place as their leader. It's a shame you won't last long enough to see my victory."

"You would attack your own?" the Chinaman dared to ask.

"I would *save* my own," Jack corrected. "The entire city is already awash with fear after what happened at St. Paul's. They will blame your kind for the terrible tragedy at the Conclave, just as they already blame you for Theo Barclay's death. Imagine their fear when the richest and most powerful men of our time fall. The entire city—no, the *country*— will understand the threat that maggots like you pose.

"And in the wake of that tragedy, I will be the one to lead the Brotherhoods into a world built free from the dangers of feral magic. When the Brink falls, my machines will take its place, and with them, I will build a country clean of the maggots who would bring us low—a new century free of the dangers of feral magic." Jack paused, cocking his head slightly as he considered the man. "And to make all this happen, all I require is a small sacrifice."

The Chinaman suddenly seemed to realize the true danger he was in and began thrashing impotently against his invisible bonds.

"Now, now . . ." Jack smiled. "There's no use fighting the inevitable, is there?"

He lifted the dagger and sliced the shirt from the man's chest. There was more than the warmth of morphine in his blood now. The power within him, that voice that urged him on and guided him, was thrumming with anticipation. It was further proof of his worthiness, further evidence that victory must soon be his.

The maggot was shaking now, fighting against a power he could not hope to defeat. Jack ignored his protests, reveled in his fear, and pressed the point of the dagger to his chest. The bloodred garnet in the hilt grew brighter, and Jack could feel the power within it calling to him.

His hands almost did not feel like his own as they began to guide the blade, slicing into the Chinaman's chest to create the intricate pattern from the front of the Ars Arcana. Blood welled from the maggot's skin, and Jack felt the beginnings of feral power stirring in the air as the Aether around him vibrated. He finished his first cut and continued on, carefully replicating the symbol from the Book on the Chinaman's bare chest. As he cut, the maggot tried to keep himself from crying out. His face twisted with the effort of holding back evidence of the pain, but in the end, he broke. A ragged, guttural moan tore from his throat as the sigil was nearly complete.

Energy pulsed wildly around him, like a small storm building in the otherwise silent warehouse, but the magic seemed erratic. It wasn't as powerful or sure as he would have expected.

He was nearly done—there were only a few more lines to connect—when someone started pounding on the warehouse door. At first Jack thought to ignore the intrusion. But the pounding grew more urgent, and in the end, he lowered the dagger. He'd waited too long to rush this and miss the moment of completion. He'd get rid of the intruder, and then he would *savor* it.

It wasn't like the maggot was going anywhere.

On the other side of the door, his mother's coachman, Adam—or was it Aaron?—waited, looking uneasy.

"You aren't supposed to be here yet." He'd paid the man handsomely to do what he asked and to keep quiet about it.

"Sorry, sir, but I didn't have a choice," the driver said, looking nervous. "It wasn't your mother that sent me. Mr. Morgan himself wants to see you."

Jack cursed. "You didn't tell them where I was?"

"No," the driver said. "They didn't ask. Just told me to go fetch you and make it quick."

"Give me a minute," he told the man, and then slammed the door in his face.

He considered the body of the maggot suspended a few yards away and cursed again. The rest of the ritual would have to wait. It was too delicate a procedure to rush and risk a mistake, especially when he couldn't be certain that he could find another maggot with so much power again before the Conclave. And he couldn't make his uncle wait. Not now, when he was so close. If the Order suspected what he was doing, they might realize what he had in his possession, and they'd certainly try to take it for their own.

He couldn't allow that to happen. His plan to unseat the Inner Circle from power depended on the element of surprise.

Jack tucked the dagger beneath his jacket and then secured the Book of Mysteries in its usual hidden pocket, close to his heart. He left the maggot where he was, suspended in the Aether. Once he dealt with his uncle and whatever demands Morgan felt like issuing, he'd return and finish the job. By the time tomorrow dawned, he would have the stone he needed, and the machine would be complete.

LONGING

Uptown

Cela still couldn't quite believe that Harte Darrigan was standing there, alive and in the flesh. She didn't *want* to believe that it was Viola in his arms, bloody and unconscious and looking like she was two steps from the grave. But denial wouldn't keep her friend alive.

"What happened to her?" she asked.

"Nibsy Lorcan," Harte told her. "She's hurt pretty badly."

At this declaration, Ruby wailed and tried to break free of Cela's hold. But holding the near-hysterical heiress back, Cela waved Harte inside.

"Take her upstairs," she told him. "Third floor. The room she's been using is the second door on the left."

Harte turned to the blond boy that Cela recognized from the night at Evelyn DeMure's apartment. Logan was his name, or at least that's what Jianyu had told her. He'd been with Nibsy Lorcan before, but now he was standing next to Darrigan with a dazed expression on his face.

"You listen to Cela," he told the boy. "Any order she gives, you do it. And you don't talk to anyone else until I come back. Understand?"

Logan blinked with a far-off look and nodded.

Seemingly satisfied, Darrigan headed toward the house with Viola still draped in his arms. Cela watched him go, far too aware of just how bad off Viola must be to not even stir when he jostled her as he mounted the steps.

Cela looked at Logan. She didn't have any idea what she was supposed to do with him. The last thing Mr. Fortune would want messing around with his newspaper business was another white boy. "Go on upstairs to the kitchen. Have a seat at the table and don't go nosing off anywhere."

"Yes, ma'am," the boy said, and then followed Harte into the building.

Ruby was still making a sort of terrible keening sound as she sobbed in Cela's arms. Any second now, she was going to break completely, but Cela didn't have time for that. Not with the two white boys making trouble in Mr. Fortune's building. She took the white girl by the shoulders and, pushing her back a little, gave her a firm but gentle shake. "You gotta stop that noise," she told her. "Hush, now. Your tears aren't helping anyone."

"My fault," the girl moaned.

Maybe it was and maybe it wasn't, but Cela didn't have the energy to deal with Ruby's hysterics. She'd worked in theaters with less drama. "Then do something about it," she snapped, realizing too late how sharp her tone had become. She let out an exhausted breath, knowing she wasn't really upset at Ruby. She was scared for Viola, same as the girl.

"I'm going to need some supplies," Cela told Ruby, trying to make her voice a little gentler. "We'll need some hot water to clean her wounds. Find whatever clean towels and blankets you can, and you'd best grab my sewing basket, just in case."

Ruby simply stared at her.

"You can do that, can't you?" Cela asked, her voice sharpening again. "I know you've probably had women like me running your baths since you were a baby, but if you want to take responsibility for what happened to Viola, then you'll get yourself together. She needs us."

The girl wiped the wetness from her eyes. "You're right," she said with an undignified snuffle. "I can do it. Towels and water. I'll fetch them for you."

Cela didn't know who Ruby was trying to convince, but if it stopped the other girl from wailing, she didn't much care.

"Good. I'm going up to check on them," Cela said, releasing her shoulders. "Make sure that other boy is in the kitchen where I sent him, and then bring everything to Viola's room when you have it."

She gave the girl a quick, sure embrace. "She's going to be okay, Ruby."

Ruby wrapped her arms around her in return, and for a second they just stood there in the open air of the street, an unlikely pair brought together by even more unlikely circumstances.

"She has to be," Ruby whispered.

By the time Cela reached the doorway of the small room where Viola slept, Harte had already laid her facedown on the narrow bed. Cela stopped short when she saw Viola's back. "Jesus," she whispered, lifting her hand to her mouth. She'd never seen anything like it.

"I don't know how Nibsy got a hold of her," Harte said. He was kneeling by the edge of the bed, peeling the blood-soaked fabric away from Viola's skin with the long, noble fingers that had once manipulated locks. "The Viola I knew would've killed him before she let him touch her."

"She'd just watched a friend of hers get murdered, so I don't think she was exactly thinking straight," Cela said softly.

Taking a breath to fortify herself, she stepped into the room and pushed Harte aside gently so she could see what needed to be done. Viola's back was a bloodied mess. A dark tattoo of two intertwined snakes lay between her shoulder blades. Had it not been split open and bleeding, it would have looked like the one Jianyu also had etched into the skin of his back.

"I've never seen damage like this," she murmured, almost afraid to start. "I can't even begin to picture the weapon that caused it."

"He used the mark against her." Harte's voice sounded hollow. "When I found her, he already had the silver cane top pressed against her."

Cela's brows bunched in concern. "This is what happened because he tried to take her affinity?"

Harte nodded. "He started to. It looked like he was ripping the magic out through her skin. If I'd been a few minutes later . . ."

Jianyu and Viola had tried to explain about the marks and the control that Nibsy had over them, but Cela hadn't realized. Not really. She knew their magic was a part of them, but now she could see exactly what that meant. It looked like her skin had burst open, like her body had turned on itself.

There was a gasp from the doorway behind her, and Cela knew Ruby had arrived with the supplies.

"If you're not going to be able to handle yourself, just leave the stuff there and go," Cela told her, tossing a stern look over her shoulder.

Ruby looked like a ghost, but the edge in Cela's voice must have shaken some sense into her. Cela watched something harden in Ruby's expression as she drew herself up. If she'd thought the girl nothing but a porcelain doll, she now started to revise her judgment. There was steel in Ruby's eyes. Determination likely born from getting whatever you wanted for an entire life.

Cela nudged Harte away, and together with Ruby, they began the terrible, painstaking process of working on Viola's back. Once the crusted-over blood was washed clean, Cela could see the true extent of the damage. It was worse, somehow, than she'd expected. Viola's back looked like a piece of shredded silk, but luckily Cela had plenty of experience with mending far more delicate things.

"How does it look?" Harte asked.

"She's going to need stitches," Cela said, stretching her neck. With all the damage, it would take a while to put her back together. "But she's still breathing, and I'm not sensing any infection yet. I think she might come through."

"Do you know where Jianyu is?" Harte asked. "I expected to find him here with you."

Cela couldn't stop her cheeks from heating, though she knew that wasn't what Darrigan meant. She shook her head. "He's not here," she told him, not sure how she managed to keep her voice steady. Darrigan's unexpected appearance and Viola's injuries had been enough to distract her, but now the worry returned like a wave crashing over her.

LISA MAXWELL

She couldn't keep the emotion from her voice as she told him how Jianyu had followed Viola to Ruby's wedding and how he hadn't returned. And when she glanced back, the expression on Darrigan's face—the pity in his eyes—let her know that he saw the truth of her feelings.

"So the two of you are . . . ?" he asked awkwardly. His ears had gone red.

"We're friends," she told him stiffly. "Nothing more."

Darrigan only frowned silently as he studied her. She wasn't sure what he saw in her eyes or in her expression, but when he spoke, his voice had softened. "Does he know?"

Cela thought about denying what Darrigan's words implied. She could have pretended that she didn't understand or that he was out of place in his asking, but all she could think about was the way Jianyu had taken her in his arms when Theo had brought her back to the city. The strength and sureness of his embrace had made her think that he might feel as she did. But he was always so careful, and it was only sometimes that she caught him looking at her when he thought she didn't notice.

She could have brushed off Darrigan's question, but whether prayers or curses or ritual spells, there could be power in words. With Jianyu missing, with Viola bloodied and bruised before her, Cela couldn't bring herself to lie.

"Sometimes I think he does," she whispered. "Sometimes I think he maybe even feels the same." She turned back to working on Viola's back, though her hands didn't move. "But he has ideas about who he is and what he deserves."

"We all do," Harte told her. "And we're nearly always wrong." He paused, and Cela wondered what he was thinking. She didn't need to wonder *who* he was thinking about. "Jianyu's a good man."

"One of the best," Cela agreed with a small, terrified smile.

"I'll see about looking for him while you're finishing up here," Harte told her.

She hadn't realized how tense she was until the worry coiling within her eased a little at Darrigan's words. "You think you know where he might be?"

"Not yet," Harte said. "But maybe Logan can help with that."

"Be careful, Darrigan," Cela warned. "This isn't the same city you left. A lot has happened while you've been away."

He gave her an unreadable look. "You have *no idea* how true that is."

Once he was gone, Cela turned back to Viola and reached for her needle and thread. With the first poke and pull of the thread, Viola released a ragged, whimpering moan. Cela took that as a sign that she wasn't dead yet and kept stitching.

SECOND CHANCES

Harte had complete confidence that Cela would be able to close up the ragged skin on Viola's back, but he wasn't sure if that would be enough. Dolph's cane touched more than the surface of a person. The power within that silver gorgon's head went far below the skin to destroy the person's connection to old magic, but that connection—that part of any Mageus, no matter how strong or weak their power might be—was an essential part of them. Intrinsic and interwoven. Removing it, or even attempting to, usually meant death.

The fact that Viola wasn't already dead made her damn lucky. She'd be even luckier if she walked away with her magic intact.

Logan was sitting at the kitchen table, right where Harte had told him to wait. He was staring off absently in the direction of the sink, or maybe he wasn't looking at anything at all. He looked lost, like he was unsure of where he was or what he was supposed to be doing. But when he saw Harte enter the kitchen, he got to his feet. He opened his mouth like he wanted to say something but then thought better of it.

Finally, when he did speak, Logan didn't ask any of the questions Harte had expected.

"Back at the Strega, James made it sound like he expected Esta to be with you." Logan took a step toward Harte. "Do you know where she is? I need to find her. I have to talk with her."

Harte eyed the other boy, sizing him up. He tried to see what Esta might have seen and wondered if this guy had meant something to her once. "What do you want with her?"

The guy shook his head, lifting his hands a little. "No, it's not like that. She's like a sister to me."

Harte only glared at him. "You brought her back here at gunpoint," he reminded Logan. "Not exactly very brotherly of you."

Logan at least had the grace to look embarrassed. "Look, man, I'm sorry about that, but I can't undo it now. I just want to get back to my own time, back to my old life. Esta's the only one that can do that for me, so if you know where she is, you gotta tell me. Please. I'm *begging* you."

Harte knew Logan wasn't anywhere close to begging, and for a second or two he considered reaching forward and grabbing Logan's wrist. It would be so easy to let his affinity flare, to issue another series of commands. They could use a spy in the Bella Strega, one they could depend on. It might be worth the risk, even if Nibsy would likely expect it. But Esta's voice was in his ears, brushing against his conscience about taking Logan's free will.

It didn't seem to matter that he'd already killed a boy today. He hadn't hesitated in ending Werner's life to save Viola's. But he hesitated now. He wasn't sure if that meant he was getting better or just getting soft.

It wasn't that he trusted Logan, not after what he'd done to Esta. Not after he'd been standing there, healthy and unharmed and clearly part of Nibsy's crew in the Strega. But Logan seemed sincere enough, and Harte Darrigan knew better than anyone that everyone deserved a second chance. And if he could use Logan? All the better.

"I don't know where Esta is right now," he told Logan honestly. "But she'll find us eventually. In the meantime, I need your help to find a friend of ours."

Logan crossed his arms over his chest, and the expression he wore gave his answer before his words did. "Why would I want to help you?"

"Because Esta will be here soon enough, and when she arrives, she's not going to have a lot of incentive to help you, not after what you've done." Harte shrugged. "But maybe if you helped a friend of hers, *maybe* she'd be more willing to listen to your sob story about how Nibsy made you do it."

Logan's nostrils flared with frustration.

"We can do this the easy way, or we can do this the easier way," Harte told him, ready to use his magic if he needed to.

"What's that even supposed to mean?" Logan asked, his face screwed up in confusion.

"It means I want to give you the choice, but I don't have the patience to wait forever." He'd lost too much time already.

Logan considered him. "Fine," he said. "I'll help you find your friend, but when Esta arrives, you're going to convince her to help me."

"I'll do my best," Harte said, clapping Logan on the shoulder. "But if you know Esta at all, you'd already know there's no convincing her of *anything*."

Logan exhaled. "Yeah. I know." He glanced at Harte. "I take it I'm looking for the Chinese guy?"

"Jianyu," Harte corrected. "He has a name."

Logan lifted his hands again. "Sorry."

Harte glared in warning. "You should be able to find him if you track the bronze mirrors he carries."

"I know," Logan said. "But I'm not some kind of oracle. I'm more like a metal detector. I need to get close enough for a read to find someone. And Jianyu could be anywhere in this city."

"Maybe," Harte agreed. "But I know a couple of places where we can start."

An hour later, they parked the wagon they'd borrowed from the *New York Age* at the edge of the warehouses that lined the dockyards. They'd already driven by Jack's town house near Washington Square without any luck.

"Well?" Harte asked, but he already knew the answer from the way Logan's expression had gone tight.

"The mirrors are here somewhere," Logan told him. Apparently, he was smart enough not to lie.

Across the street from where they were parked, the warehouses blocked the view of the water, but Harte could feel the Brink in the distance, waiting. He'd been down to this area near the docks before, but that was months ago, and in the gloom of the early evening, the low-slung structures all looked the same. He wasn't sure which one had been Jack's.

"You're coming with me," Harte said, hopping down and securing the horse to a nearby hitch.

The day had already been cold, but now that the sun had gone down, the temperature had dropped even further. The chill in the air made Harte wish he'd thought to bring a coat. A gust of wind came in off the river and brought with it another brush of icy energy. A warning and a promise of what the Brink would do to any who crossed it.

Esta could change that. The thought rose sudden and unwanted. Harte tried to push it aside but found that he couldn't. Esta *could* change it. She had the Book and the artifacts, and she had an affinity for Aether. Esta believed she could do the ritual and use Seshat as the sacrifice to complete it. She believed that being willing to give up everything would be enough to let her live, but Harte wasn't so sure. He'd seen that other version of her perform the same ritual. *And I watched her die.*

He refused to watch her die again.

But standing so close to the shore, he wondered if it was his choice to make, even if he could find a way to stop her. It had been easy enough to forget about how terrible it was to live there, trapped in the city, once he'd been beyond it. But now that he was there, close enough to the Brink that he felt the edges of fear creep along his skin, he wondered if he had any right to doom countless others for his own selfish happiness.

Maybe he had to trust her. Maybe he had to let her try.

"Are we doing this or what?" Logan asked, rubbing his arms and looking every bit as uneasy as Harte felt.

"Yeah," he said, mentally shaking himself free of the direction his thoughts had taken. "Let's go."

Logan grabbed him by the sleeve and nodded in the opposite direction from the way Harte had turned. "It's this way."

THE MYSTERIUM

The Flatiron Building

Jack Grew bristled with impatience as he sat in the visitors' gallery of the Order's headquarters high above Madison Square Park. Two floors above, the new Mysterium stood empty, as powerless as the feeble old goats who had summoned him like a dog to heel. The city glittered below, waiting for its future to unfold—a future he was determined to take for his own.

Soon, he promised himself. The Book echoed the sentiment by pulsing twice softly in the breast pocket where it rested against his heart. He heard the whispered encouragement rise within him. Soon he'd show them the dog had teeth.

It was all a game to the Inner Circle. The summons. The waiting. But they had entered a game board they did not truly understand, and they were playing a match they had no hope to win.

When the doors finally opened behind him, Jack turned from the window, putting the city to his back. He arranged his face in an expression of bland curiosity as the High Princept entered.

"Sir," he said with a small deferential nod.

The old man barely blinked. "If you'll come this way?"

It wasn't like he had much choice.

Jack followed the High Princept from the sterile quiet of the visitors' waiting room into the lush inner sanctum of the Order. As they traversed the winding passageways designed to disorient any would-be attackers, Jack could not help but wonder why they had summoned him. He'd remained quiet and out of the way these past weeks, just as they'd requested. What could have possibly drawn their attention? And why was the Princept himself acting as escort?

Finally they came to the library where everything had gone to shit on the solstice. The doorway to the Mysterium stood open in the ceiling above.

"After you," the Princept insisted, waving his hand in the direction of the steep metal staircase that led upward.

Interested despite himself, Jack accepted the invitation. When he emerged into the room above, it wasn't empty. His uncle was there, as were the other members of the Inner Circle. They were draped in ceremonial sashes, and each wore a golden medallion with the Philosopher's Hand hanging from a cord around their necks. Only his uncle betrayed any irritation that Jack had arrived.

Like the library below, the Mysterium felt hollow and somehow less impressive than it had the night of the solstice. In the center of the room, a sculpture of iron and gold meant to represent the Tree of Life waited, its branches empty of the artifacts that should have lived in the spaces designed to house them. During the solstice, the tree had glowed with an otherworldly light, protection for the one artifact that had slipped away. Now its gilded branches stood cold and powerless.

But as interesting as it was to be summoned by the Inner Circle and escorted personally by the High Princept, his patience was at an end. The Chinaman waited with all the promise of his feral magic. Jack didn't have time for these games.

"I assume that eventually you'll get around to telling me why you've called me here tonight," Jack said, enjoying the way his uncle visibly bristled at his irreverent tone.

"Watch yourself, boy," Morgan growled. "You stand in a sacred place."

"Not by my own choice," he reminded them. "I was told that your summons couldn't wait."

"What could you possibly have to be so busy with?" Morgan asked, sneering down his large nose. "More of your chorus girl trollops? Do the family a favor and keep the next one alive."

Jack felt his blood go hot, but the High Princept stepped between them.

"Enough," the Princept said, lifting a hand. "We called you here because of the events that transpired earlier today."

Jack waited, barely breathing, as the Book seemed to pulse in warning against him. *They can't know.* He'd been so careful to make sure that no one would suspect that the events at St. Paul's had been his doing.

"It seems that we've underestimated you," the Princept said, glancing at Morgan.

His uncle wore a look as though he smelled something rotten, but he didn't reply.

"What you did at Barclay's wedding was . . . admirable," the Princept continued.

"It would have been more admirable had Barclay's grandson not ended up dead," Morgan muttered.

Jack realized then that the older Barclay was missing from the meeting. "I'm sorry I couldn't do more," Jack murmured. "Theo's death was a true tragedy."

"It was murder." Morgan's nose twitched as he narrowed his eyes at Jack as though he suspected. "The Barclay boy didn't even get his wedding night, and the bride is gone. Vanished without a trace. Likely dead, and if not dead, then ruined beyond saving."

Jack remained silent. There was nothing to be gained by speaking.

"But those beasts," the Princept said. "You cannot deny that Jack was instrumental in helping to quell the danger."

Quell . . . Inspire. It was all of a piece, really.

"It's put us in a damned impossible position," Morgan bristled.

"I'm sorry my actions today inconvenienced you," Jack said, refusing to show even a glimmer of the amusement—or the temper—he felt stirring. "Perhaps next time I should stand aside when maggots attack our people."

"There was nothing wrong with what you did today, my boy," the Princept told him. "You likely saved the chapel with your quick thinking. But news has spread quickly, and the events that transpired today are unfortunate for more reasons than the tragic loss of Theo Barclay." He stepped over to the windows that faced out over the city, turning his back to Jack as he spoke. "As of late, we've heard murmurings throughout the Brotherhoods, concerns about our ability to remain in control of the maggots in this city."

"Somehow word has spread that we may no longer be in possession of those objects that gave us our power so long ago," his uncle added, glaring at Jack.

"If you are implying that I told others—"

"No," the Princept said. "That isn't what we're saying."

His uncle was staring at Jack as though he disagreed.

"But things between the Brotherhoods are . . . delicate. Until today, we have managed to deflect the rumors about the missing artifacts," the Princept told him. "But what happened at the chapel is already making its way around to the various organizations. I've already heard from the Veiled Prophet. They want to know what is happening in this city. They have questions about their own safety and about whether the Order of Ortus Aurea is fit to lead. Which is why we've called you here tonight."

Jack waited, impatience buzzing along his skin.

"The other Brotherhoods will surely learn of your actions today, if they do not already know. It is essential that we present a united front when they arrive in this city." The Princept turned back to him. "You'll be attending the Conclave after all, it seems." It wasn't a request, but Jack wouldn't have refused it anyway.

"I see." Satisfaction simmered within him.

"This is a mistake," Morgan said to the Princept. "You can't possibly imagine that his attendance at the Conclave will end any differently than the other travesties he's been involved with."

"We don't have a choice," the Princept told Morgan. "If he isn't there, standing beside us as one Order, what do you think Gunter and Cooke and the rest will think? The hero of St. Paul's, not invited? It will only make the rumors seem plausible. We cannot allow anyone to think that the Order itself is fractured. No, we must stand united. We must make them believe that nothing has changed, that there is no distress from within our ranks. It's our only chance to make it through that night and retain the power we currently hold."

He turned back to Jack. "But make no mistake, boy. Every one of the men from the other Brotherhoods will come to the Conclave hoping to find our weakness. They've been talking to one another—trading telegrams and stirring discord. They're waiting for an opening to take the seat of power from New York, and you aren't going to do anything that gives it to them."

Jack clenched his teeth, but he could not stop himself from speaking. "Did you call me here only to berate me like some unruly schoolboy? After all I've done, all you've witnessed me—"

"Shut up, Jack," Morgan snapped. "You haven't done anything but screw up since you went off on your Grand Tour. First that mess with the girl in Greece, and then you were duped by the maggots who destroyed Khafre Hall. And still that wasn't enough. In these very rooms, you let the Delphi's Tear slip away. Now Barclay is dead and his bride is gone, and the entire country is whispering about the Order of Ortus Aurea's failure. Because of *you*. All the parlor tricks in the world wouldn't give you the right to speak to us as equals."

"That's enough, Morgan," the Princept said. Then he turned to Jack. "We can't rewrite the past, but we can make sure to claim the future. You'll come to the Conclave, as I said, and you'll stay out of trouble. We cannot afford one of your spectacular disasters. Too much is riding on that night. The Conclave is more than a gathering of the Brotherhoods. It's the anniversary of our Order's founding, the anniversary of our greatest achievement." The Princept pointed toward the windows, where a dark ribbon of water divided the island from the rest of the country. "But if we are unsuccessful in reconsecrating the Brink, everything will be lost."

On the evening of the solstice, the power of the sun had illuminated that boundary through the crystal of the windows. Then, he had been able to see it, wavering and unstable already.

The Princept looked out into the darkness beyond the city. "The world is changing, Jack, and the Brotherhoods are becoming impatient to claim power of their own. Other cities are growing in wealth, and every day more and more of those with feral magic come to our shores and threaten what we have built. The other Brotherhoods see themselves as worthy of partnership rather than fealty. They want a seat at the table, and they want the power that comes with it."

"But we have no interest in sharing," Morgan added.

"None whatsoever." The Princept turned back to him. "We will welcome the Brotherhoods, but we have no intention of divesting ourselves of our place as their leaders. Before the destruction of Khafre Hall and the theft of our treasures, it would have been easier. We had already fortified the powers in the stones, and with them, we would have transformed the Brink—and the city with it.

"This city was carved out by magic," the Princept explained. "Its very design was intended to augment the power of those who had mastery of the occult sciences. We would have used what our forefathers created here—the Brink, the streets and hidden rivers, all mapped onto the power that runs through everything—to demonstrate our power to the other Brotherhoods. To show them that Manhattan was *truly* singular, and with it the Order. Every Mageus who dwelled in these streets would have had their magic ripped from them, and the Brotherhoods would have understood what was possible."

"Quite impressive," Jack murmured, trying not to show his true reaction. He hadn't realized their plans went beyond the Brink itself. He had never thought the old men of the Inner Circle capable of such imagination. He'd assumed them to be relics of the past, naive to the threats of the modern world.

"It's more than impressive," Morgan sputtered. "It was to be the future of the Order, the future, perhaps, of the world."

No, Jack thought to himself. He refused to believe or accept that. Not when the Book urged him on and promised a future that these old men could only begin to imagine. Not when the voice inside him whispered that the future belonged only to *him.*

"What will you do now?" Jack wondered. They had no artifacts, and he had possession of the Ars Arcana.

"We'll do what must be done to preserve our power," the Princept told him. "We are not without resources. The city itself will provide the answer. We may not have the artifacts, but we still have the power built into this land."

"The grid," he realized. The city hadn't been built along the traditional measures of longitude and latitude, but in alignment with ley lines infused with power. All connected to the Brink itself.

The Princept could not stop himself from gloating. "Yes. The artifacts would have made things easier, but the modern age has given us *other* tools to provide the power we need to reconsecrate the Brink and maintain our power over the other Brotherhoods and the city. *Electricity.* Lightning made by man. The modern and the ancient brought together."

It was an impressive idea, possibly even a plan that would work, except for one small issue. "And the Brink? I thought Newton's stones were necessary to stabilize it."

The Princept and his uncle exchanged an uncomfortable look, and Jack knew in an instant that whatever they said, this plan would not fix the problems with the Brink. Without the artifacts, they could not hope to reconsecrate it, and this plan would not make it stronger. It would not protect the city.

"We're confident that the increased energy will provide the Brink the power it needs until we are able to locate the stones," the Princept said.

They weren't confident of anything, but they were clearly willing to lie to him and to the other Brotherhoods. Worst of all, they were willing to lie to themselves.

"What we require is that you refrain from mucking it up," Morgan said. "The other Brotherhoods will expect you to be present, but you will stay out of the way. And if you do anything at all to put the Order or our power in jeopardy, I will make sure that you are sent so far from this city that you never return."

Jack watched his uncle, gratified at least to see that Morgan was unhappy about this entire situation. "You have nothing to worry about, gentlemen. I'm grateful for the opportunity to witness the Order's rebirth, and I would never dream of doing anything to put our city or our hallowed organization at risk."

Morgan muttered something under his breath, but Jack ignored him. His uncle had never believed in him. He'd done nothing but hold him back, probably because he was threatened by his promise. But in the end, he'd see. They all would.

Jack had no intention of coming to heel. This new information helped to bring his plans more clearly into focus. Let them believe that he was penitent and docile. They'd learn otherwise soon enough. In fact, the Inner Circle would have ringside seats to witness the birth of Jack's power. And J. P. Morgan would be the first one to fall.

ANOTHER STONE

The Docks

Harte and Logan passed three buildings before Logan finally stopped, and Harte recognized where he was. It looked like the others, but there was a marking on the door and a padlock too expensive and shiny for the filth of the docks.

The building was secured, but Harte made quick work of the lock, and in a matter of seconds they were inside. Lamps weren't necessary because the far side of the warehouse was already aglow. There, in the light of the ritual circle, Jianyu was suspended in midair, his arms and legs stretched out as though held by invisible cords. His tunic had been torn open, exposing the bloodied skin of his bare chest.

Harte rushed across the room, only barely registering the lurking metal structure in the center. He knew what it meant—Jack had rebuilt the machine—but it was pointless to waste time destroying it again. He'd just build another and another until they stopped him for good.

"Jianyu?" Harte stayed outside the ritual circle, not sure what would happen if he crossed over it.

Jianyu opened his eyes slowly, lifting his head with clear difficulty to try to find the source of his name. When he saw Harte standing there on the other side of the glowing circle, his brows drew together. "*Darrigan?* You returned."

Harte didn't love the note of disbelief in Jianyu's voice. "I told you I would."

"You seem to have taken your time about it," Jianyu said, giving him a droll look that turned into a grimace of pain.

"Hold tight," Harte said, taking stock of the situation. "We're going to get you out of there."

"We?" Jianyu grimaced again.

Looking back over his shoulder, Harte saw that Jianyu was right. Logan was gone.

He should have gone further and used his affinity. At least then he'd have some help. And he could have been sure that Logan wouldn't become yet another weapon in Nibsy's arsenal.

Cursing softly at his soft-hearted stupidity, he thought about going after Logan, but he dismissed the idea almost immediately. It was more important to get Jianyu out of the mess he was in.

"I don't think I should cross that line," Harte said, examining the ritual circle. He'd seen circles like it trap Mageus enough times before. The last thing he wanted was for Jack to return to the warehouse and find *him* stuck inside it as well, like some kind of early Christmas present.

He searched the room for some answer to getting Jianyu out of that circle and considered a couple of different ideas before his gaze snagged on a familiar flash of silver resting on a nearby table. He pushed a pile of Jack's notes and diagrams aside and found Viola's knife sitting there.

"How did *you* get here?" he wondered, taking up the blade. The last time he'd seen it, Esta had secured it in the satchel before they'd talked to Dakari. Of course, that was a later version of this knife. Not the one in his hand.

"Viola," Jianyu groaned, gasping in pain. "Did she—"

"She's with Cela," Harte told him. No sense in making him worry until they knew anything for sure. There would be time enough for him to tell Jianyu everything. But first . . .

Harte crept closer to the circle, feeling the brush of cold energy as he approached. He didn't really know what he was doing or whether it would work, but if the blade could cut through pretty much anything, maybe it could cut through ritual magic as well. Like answered to like, after all.

Edging the tip closer, he held his breath, and with a quick, sharp push, he sliced through the dirt floor of the warehouse, severing the circle. The line went dark where the blade had cut it, and Harte released a relieved breath at the sight. Once more he edged the tip closer and pushed, and as the cold energy licked dangerously against his skin, a portion of the circle went dark. He did it twice more, widening the opening until there was a space large enough for him to step through.

He considered the situation—the ritual circle, the missing piece, and his friend suspended on invisible bindings, hanging in the air. And the strange dark crystal sitting beneath him. Suddenly he understood.

Jack's making another stone. Which would give him all the power he needed to make the machine functional. There wasn't time to wait. He had to get Jianyu out of there, and he had to get him out *now*.

He stepped through the opening in the circle and hoped he wasn't making a mistake. Then, on instinct, he drove the tip of the knife through the black crystal, and as the blade sank through the stone, it cracked in two, and a burst of icy magic passed over him like an explosion. His magic flashed hot in response, and Jianyu fell to the ground.

Harte helped him up, looping Jianyu's arm over his shoulder and pulling him out of the now-dead circle.

"Jack has the Book," Jianyu told him.

"I know," Harte said.

"What happened?" Jianyu asked. "Where is Esta?"

"She's coming," he said, because it was the only thing that could be true. "Right now we have to get out of here before Jack comes back."

They'd nearly made it across the warehouse when he heard a carriage approaching.

Harte looked around the warehouse for some other exit or somewhere to hide, but the open space offered no cover. "If that's Jack—"

There wasn't any other exit. All they could do was run for it and hope it wasn't Jack, but Harte's hopes were dashed when he eased his head out and saw Jack Grew's familiar figure alighting from the carriage. He was giving some kind of order to his driver, who looked more than a little tired of taking them, and Harte and Jianyu took the distraction as an opportunity to slip out of the warehouse and ease around the corner.

Once they were out of sight, they started to run.

STRENGTH

Uptown

Viola didn't know how long she'd been unconscious. Pain made time unsteady, and at some point she'd lost track of the hours and minutes. When she finally woke, it was to the sound of weeping. She wasn't the one crying, though she probably had every right to be, considering the pain she was currently feeling. She opened her eyes but didn't have the strength to turn her head and find the source of the sniffling sobs. Still, even with only the wall in front of her, she recognized where she was. She'd stared at this wall often enough in the last few weeks.

But how? She remembered the Strega, remembered the flash of temper and grief that had spread through her, and then remembered hearing an explosion. Werner. Nibsy. The Medusa's kiss. They were all mixed up in her memory. Who had come for her? How had they saved her when Nibsy had been so determined to destroy her?

She shuddered a little at the memory of what that had been like—to be captured and helpless. To be unmade by Leena's magic.

The pain had been terrible, but more unbearable was the knowledge that she'd done it to herself. She'd known what Nibsy was capable of and what power he had at his disposal, and she'd gone anyway.

Perhaps she had died.

But no, hell would not be so soft as the bed beneath her, and heaven certainly wouldn't hurt so much. She wasn't dead, as much as she might have preferred it right then.

Gathering her strength, she tried to turn her head, and suddenly the sniffling sobs stopped.

"Viola?"

It took everything she had to push through the pain of moving, but when she turned, there was Ruby Reynolds, sitting in the lamplight. Her eyes were red and her nose swollen and pink from tears, but she was not looking at Viola with hatred.

"No," Ruby said, rushing over to her. "You shouldn't move. You'll tear the stitches."

Viola realized then that her back was covered with some kind of cloth that had been wrapped around her torso. A bandage of some sort.

"I need to sit," Viola told her. "I've been in this position so long, my neck feels like it'll never be straight again." But Ruby didn't owe her anything. Not after all that had happened—not after Theo. "Is Cela here? She can maybe help me up."

"Let me," Ruby said softly.

Viola wanted to say yes. She wanted to accept Ruby's help, to feel Ruby's hands upon her skin. But yes seemed a dangerous word. It was too much to believe that Ruby was real and whole and here. Too much to hope that Ruby would want to help her, to *touch* her.

"Please?" Ruby asked, mistaking Viola's silence for some other emotion.

Viola nodded, trying to keep the tears from welling over.

Gently, Ruby took her by the arm and helped to ease her upright. She understood then what Ruby had meant by tearing the stitches—every movement brought fresh bursts of pain to the skin on her back. It felt tight and hot with the aching.

"Water?" Ruby asked, offering a tin cup to Viola.

She shook her head. "Why are you here? Why are you helping me?" She could not stop herself from asking. "After all I did to you, to Theo . . ."

"You didn't do anything to Theo," Ruby said with a soft sob. "You tried to save him."

"But I didn't," Viola said, closing her eyes against the memory of Theo's broken body falling from the monster's grasp. "I couldn't," she whispered. "It's my fault he's dead."

"No, Viola." Ruby took her hand. Her skin was soft and warm, but Viola could feel her trembling. "I never should have said those things to you. I never should have blamed you. I was so sad, so angry at myself."

"You did nothing," Viola said, not understanding.

"What happened to Theo was my fault, Viola. It wasn't yours."

Viola ignored the pain she felt when she moved her hand and did it anyway, to brush the tears from Ruby's face. "No—"

"Theo was only marrying me so I wouldn't have to marry someone else," Ruby told her.

Viola's brows drew together. "He loved you."

Ruby nodded. "He did, but he never should have married me." She withdrew her hand from Viola's. "We were just children when I forced him into the engagement."

"Forced?" Viola frowned.

"Well, maybe not *forced*," Ruby admitted. "But I pushed and pushed until he agreed, and I always told myself that he could back out at any time. Except I realize now that Theo never would have." She shoved back the hair that had fallen into her face and looked at Viola. "He gave me an opportunity to jilt him," she admitted. "When I arrived a few days ago, he offered to help me run off to stay with an elderly aunt of his in Scotland."

"You didn't go," Viola said, wondering what that meant.

"No," Ruby told her. "But if I had been brave enough to free him from our childish agreement, he wouldn't have been there at the church. He wouldn't be—" She stopped suddenly, and the tears started again.

Viola laid her hand on Ruby's arm. "I didn't know Theo so long, but the time I did know him? Theo wasn't the type of man you could force."

Ruby was looking at her through watery green eyes.

"I tried to talk him out of helping us. I threatened him, too, maybe a little, but no." She shook her head. "It didn't matter the danger. Theo made up his mind, and that was that. That one, he was stronger than most."

"He was, wasn't he?" Ruby said, wiping a tear away.

Viola took her hand again and squeezed it. "He wouldn't want you to do this, to blame yourself. If he was at that altar, he was there by his own choosing."

Ruby's lips pressed together as she nodded, but at first she didn't speak.

"I wanted someone to stop it," Ruby whispered finally, as though this confession was almost too terrible to make. She was staring at their two hands. "I was standing there before god and our families, with Theo's hand in mine, and the rector had just asked my intentions, and all I could think was that I wished that something would make it stop. *Anything.*"

Viola's heart felt like it was being squeezed in a vise. She wanted to tell Ruby that what happened wasn't her fault, that her wanting and wishing didn't make evil grow there in that holy place. Not when the evil was inside Jack Grew. But she couldn't find the words to say anything. She was too afraid to break the moment hanging between them.

Ruby looked at Viola through her lashes. "I wanted it to be you."

MORE THAN ENOUGH

Ruby watched Viola's reaction to the words that had just escaped from her mouth—the slight widening of her eyes, the panic that shifted in those violet depths—and she wondered if she had made a mistake.

She hadn't planned on saying any of the things she'd just said to Viola. She wasn't even sure that she'd known the truth of those words until they were already tumbling out of her mouth, changing her life and her world just by their existence.

She hadn't wanted to marry Theo. Truth.

She'd trapped him because of her own selfishness. Another truth.

She'd stood on that holy altar, pledging her life to him before god and the world, but she'd been thinking about another. She could not deny it.

Maybe if Ruby had never been sent off to Europe, things would have been different. Maybe if she hadn't spent months watching women who had built lives with one another, who were happy together. Not content. Not settling. Fulfilled. *Together*. Maybe then she could have forgotten about Viola. Perhaps she might have finally accepted Viola's rejection back at the gala and moved on toward a happy future with Theo Barclay. But Paris had changed everything. It had shown her what was possible. It had whispered to her that Viola's rejection had been nothing but fear.

As a journalist, her lodestar was the truth, and so she had to admit that truth now, most of all, to herself. The truth was simply this: She would have given anything right then to stop the world from spinning, to stop her life from being forced down a path she could never return from. *Anything*. She would have even given Theo.

Of course, desperate bargains were easy enough to stomach when they seemed impossible. It was a far different thing to face the reality. Theo was gone. She was, at least, in part to blame.

"You didn't cause this," Viola told her. "Nothing you did, nothing you wished for. You aren't the reason Theo died."

Ruby closed her eyes to hold back the tears. "I wish I could believe that."

"Do you know how many times I've sat in a church, pleading?" Viola asked. "Bargaining with and begging whoever might be listening?"

Ruby shook her head. She had no idea what a girl as strong and brave as Viola would ever need to beg or bargain for.

"Too many times," Viola said, glancing away. "My whole life I've spent sitting in churches just like that one, promising anything—offering *anything*—to be free from this connection to the old magic that lives in my skin, that beats with my blood. My whole life, no one has answered those prayers. Because god, he don't work like that. He's not gli folletti, flitting through the air to grant our wishes."

Surprised, Ruby looked up. Why would Viola want to give up that essential part of her, that piece of light that made her so uniquely herself? "But your affinity, it's part of you. Why would you ever wish it away?"

"Bah," Viola exclaimed with disgust. "It's nothing but a curse."

"No," Ruby said, squeezing her hand. When Viola wouldn't look at her, she scooted closer on the bed, took Viola's face in her hands, and turned her head. So that she would have to see, have to understand. "It's part of you, Viola. It's nothing to be ashamed of."

But Viola backed away from her. "I don't understand you. You know what I am, what I've done. The lives I've taken. The people I've killed." She shook her head. "Why do you not see?"

"See what?" Ruby asked.

"The truth," Viola said.

Ruby realized then what she hadn't understood before. It was so easy to look at Viola, all brash temper and headstrong fire, and think that nothing could touch her. Maybe she should have seen it sooner—maybe it was what had drawn her to Viola in the first place—how similar they were. Neither one of them fitting in the world they were given. Both of them wanting more. But someone had hurt her.

"Who was it?" Ruby asked.

Confused, Viola looked back at her. "What do you mean?"

"Who convinced you that you're not enough just as you are?"

This time it wasn't panic Ruby saw but pain. Shadows darkened Viola's violet irises, and she tried to turn away again.

But Ruby wouldn't allow it. She shifted so Viola had to look at her. "You can't see yourself clearly at all, can you?"

"I know what I am," Viola whispered.

"Do you?" Ruby wondered. "I've seen you with your friends. I've seen your heart, Viola Vacarrelli. You can't hide it from me."

Viola tried to shrug off her words, but Ruby would not allow her to.

"*You* can't hide from me," she said. "I don't know who convinced you that your affinity was evil, but they were wrong. Maybe you're brash, with a temper to go along with it. But you're strong because of it. You're *good*, Viola. Clear to the center of who you are." A lock of hair had fallen from Viola's usual low chignon, and Ruby tucked it behind her ear as a tear escaped from Viola's eyes. "Beautiful, too."

She leaned forward, slowly, so that there was every opportunity for Viola to escape, and when she didn't, Ruby kissed her. Gently at first, a question. And then, all at once, Viola leaned into her, and the whole world focused down to the truth of Viola's mouth, the feel of her lips against hers, the *taste* of her. When Viola lifted her hands, threaded them through Ruby's hair, and brought her closer, she was lost.

It was too easy to forget that earlier that morning she had been some-one else's bride. Too easy to forget where she was, *who* she was, and what had just happened.

But suddenly Ruby felt something between them shift, and Viola stopped.

"We shouldn't be doing this," Viola said, nearly breathless.

"Why?" Ruby challenged. "Because some crusty old men told us it isn't possible to live a life without them?"

Viola blinked. "That's not—"

"They're wrong," Ruby told her. "I've seen how wrong they are." She saw the confusion, the interest in Viola's expression. "In Paris, I saw the lives women can lead. *Together.* In the open. Happy."

Viola shook her head. "That's not what I meant. But don't you see? It doesn't matter, because I'll never go to Paris. I'll never leave this city."

Because of the Brink. How stupid she'd been to forget. "Then we'll make our Paris here."

Viola only stared at her, and Ruby began to think that maybe she'd been wrong about what was between them. She'd just assumed that Viola felt the same, and with that kiss—

"And what of Theo?"

Theo. She waited for the guilt and shame to wash over her . . . but it never came. When she thought of Theo, when she thought of what had happened to him today, grief creased her heart. But not shame. He'd wanted this for her. He alone had understood. And because of what he gave—for her, for them—he would always be a part of the bond she felt with Viola. He would never truly be gone.

"I think he'd approve," she told Viola. "You know, he talked about you and your friends when he came to visit me this past summer. He told me everything about what you'd done, what he was helping you with. He admired all of you so much, but I think he loved you most of all."

"He's the one who invited me to your wedding," Viola said, her eyes glittering with unshed tears.

"Maybe he knew what both of us needed," Ruby told her.

Viola leaned forward, rested her forehead against Ruby's. "Sei pazza. You know that?"

"Maybe a little," Ruby told her with a shrug. "But I've been called far worse."

Viola choked out a surprised laugh.

"I want this, Viola. Whatever it is between us," Ruby confessed.

"Ruby—"

"No," she said, unwilling to allow Viola to brush aside what she knew was there. She'd tried this once before, but she'd made a complete mess of it. She would get it right this time. "I'll mourn Theo for the rest of my life. His death will always be a regret that I carry with me, but not telling you how I felt? Not making you understand? What I feel—all of *this*—it's not some silly whim of some silly rich girl. I understand what might lie ahead if we choose this—if we choose each other. I understand how hard all of it might be, but it doesn't matter."

"It matters," Viola argued. "Do you think I could ask that of you, to drag you down to my level?"

"Why can't you see?" Ruby shook her head. "Viola, I lost *everything* today—my family, my best friend, and the life I once had—and none of it mattered compared to how I felt when they brought you in earlier, broken and bleeding. You're better than all of them put together, and you would never drag me down. Whoever it was that made you believe you weren't enough, they were fools, and I won't let them get between us now. Let me stand next to you. Choose me, choose *us*, and the rest will figure itself out."

Viola stared at her for a long beat, and the world began to tilt. Ruby was certain her life was destined to be colored by loss and disappointment. But then Viola leaned in and kissed her.

"Pazza," Viola whispered. But she kissed Ruby again.

Someone cleared their throat in the doorway.

"Glad to see you're still with us," Cela said to Viola.

Viola started to move away from Ruby, but Ruby caught her hand, held tight, and looked Cela right in the eye.

Cela's mouth quirked a bit. "I'll give the two of you a minute, but Darrigan's back with Jianyu. And you're probably going to want to hear their news."

THE BLACK CORD

Jianyu hissed in pain as Cela tended to the wound that had been caused by the silk cord around his wrist. He had not told anyone how the cord had grown smaller in recent weeks, but when he had removed his shirt so that Viola could take care of the wounds on his chest, there had been no way to hide it. Not when the black silk was so tight, it had practically embedded itself into his skin. Viola had healed the cuts Jack had made with a small burst of her magic, but her affinity had not touched the corrupt power in the shackle around his wrist.

"Sorry," Cela whispered, grimacing a little at the pain she was causing him. But she did not stop her examination.

There was no denying it any longer. The black cord had been growing progressively smaller, but when Jack Grew had tried to harvest his magic, the bracelet had become like a garrote. The more power Jack had pressed into Jianyu's body with the tip of the dagger, the tighter the braided silk had become.

"I don't think there's anything I can do," Cela told him with a frustrated sigh. "Why didn't you tell us it was getting so bad?"

"There was nothing you could have done," Jianyu said, pulling away and immediately regretting the loss of the comforting warmth of Cela's hands. "The bargain was mine to make. So too are the consequences."

"Che cassata!" Viola snapped. "You should have told us. We aren't any of us alone in this. Not anymore."

She was right. But he had not wanted them to worry about things that could not be changed.

"It was not so tight as this until Jack Grew touched me with the

494

dagger." He did not know how to explain that the cold ritual magic it contained seemed stronger now, too. It radiated up his arm and down through all his fingers. He opened his hand and closed it, wincing at the stiffness there.

When he noticed Cela watching him with a worried frown, he stopped and clasped his hands together.

"Maybe Lee already had a claim to your affinity," Darrigan said, eyeing the black silk on Jianyu's wrist. He was leaning against the counter, slightly apart from those sitting around the table, as he had been the entire time Viola and Cela had tended to Jianyu's wounds.

Jianyu frowned, remembering the way he had felt nearly torn in two as the dagger and the silk had warred for control over his affinity. "You think this cord might have offered protection?"

Harte shrugged. "It's possible. When I found you, it looked like Jack was nearly done with the ritual. But you walked away with your magic intact. Maybe that bit of thread saved you."

"He doesn't look saved to me," Cela told Harte. "He looks like he's about to lose a hand if we don't figure out how to get this off him."

"Only Tom Lee has the power to remove it," Jianyu said. "And he will not until I deliver what I have promised him."

"You've done nothing *but* deliver," Cela said sourly. "He keeps you running day and night. Nothing is ever enough."

"Perhaps, but I have not yet given him what he wants most," Jianyu reminded her.

"I know. And after seeing what that cane did to Viola's back, I understand," Cela said with a sigh. "Even if you could get it from Nibsy Lorcan, you wouldn't hand it over to Lee—or anyone else."

Jianyu was not sure why a part of him uncoiled at the realization that Cela knew him so well. When had he ever been seen so clearly? Perhaps not since Dolph. Perhaps not even then.

"Maybe another solution will present itself," Jianyu told them, not at all believing that such a fantasy would come to be.

The truth was that Tom Lee would never let him go. The truth was also that Jianyu would never offer up the Devil's Own.

"But you don't believe it will," Cela said, her voice hollow with understanding. "You've already made up your mind, haven't you?"

"Nothing is certain," he told her, wishing that he felt the truth of his own words. "But this piece of thread is the least of our problems."

"That piece of thread will *kill* you," Cela argued.

"If Jack Grew destroys the Brink, it will kill us all," Jianyu reminded her. He had already explained what Jack had revealed to him.

"I still don't understand," Ruby said. "Wouldn't that solve your problem? Without the Brink, anyone with the old magic could leave the city. None of you would be trapped here." She turned to Viola. "You could leave. We could go anywhere."

"It's not that easy," Harte said. He stepped toward the table. "Jianyu's right. If Jack brings down the Brink, it doesn't mean freedom for Mageus. It means the end."

"Of magic?" Ruby asked.

"Of *everything*," Jianyu told her.

Ruby frowned. "How can that be?"

"Because everything is connected," Harte said. "All of the magic the Brink has taken over the years is still linked to all of the old magic in the world *and* to all Mageus who still carry an affinity for it. If the Brink is destroyed, it would destroy everyone who has a connection to the old magic."

"That would kill hundreds—maybe thousands—just in this city alone," Cela said, her eyes meeting Jianyu's.

"It would destroy magic itself," Viola corrected.

"You would all die?" Ruby asked, her eyes wide with new fear.

"Not only us," Jianyu said softly. "The old magic is not some spell to cast or control. It lives in the spaces of all things."

"End magic, end the world," Viola said.

"Doesn't Jack know that?" Cela asked, clearly horrified. "How could he not?"

"I'm sure you could fill whole libraries with all that Jack Grew doesn't know," Ruby said wryly. "If what you're saying is true, we have to stop him."

"We?" Viola looked at her.

"I'm with you now," Ruby said, taking her hand.

Jianyu watched as color rose in Viola's cheeks and the two women shared a secret look, a silent conversation between them. He glanced at Cela, who was watching as well, and then suddenly she looked up at him, and he felt his world shift.

He looked away first, unwilling to consider the warmth building inside his chest. Unwilling to let himself hope. Cela Johnson was not for him. Who was he but an outsider to this land? Trapped in the city, trapped now too in a country that did not want his kind. She deserved far more than he could ever offer.

But he did not have to look to know that Cela was watching him still.

"He's not going to bring down the Brink," Harte said. "Or, at least, he didn't before."

Darrigan told them then about the future he and Esta had seen in St. Louis and the years beyond.

"In the future we saw, the Conclave is the turning point. Because of the attack on the Conclave, the entire country will turn against the old magic," Darrigan said. "People who live far from Manhattan, people who maybe haven't ever thought about Mageus, will learn to fear those with the old magic. The whole country will come to see the old magic as a threat, and they'll outlaw it. The Defense Against Magic Act will make magic and anyone with a connection to it illegal. After the DAM Act, every Mageus on these shores will be in constant danger of being discovered and rounded up.

"But now we know—it isn't Mageus who attack the Conclave." He turned to Jianyu. "If what Jack told you is true, it's going to be Jack himself who attacks."

"Just as it was he who attacked the church yesterday," Jianyu confirmed.

"That's not surprising. He's done this sort of thing before—or he will," Harte told him. "He'll use the power he's gained from the Book to make it appear that Mageus are at fault, and then he'll swoop in as the hero of the day."

"We have to reveal what he's doing," Ruby told them. "People need to know that Jack's the one who attacked the church and killed Theo. They need to know he's planning another attack."

"Who will tell them?" Viola asked.

"I can," Ruby said. "I can go back, write article after article. Do you know how many papers my firsthand account will sell? Someone will publish it. They won't be able to resist."

"No one will believe it," Viola said. "When do they ever believe a woman's words? They won't want to believe what you write, no matter the truth. I saw the crowd outside of St. Paul's when Jack brought Theo's broken body like a trophy to lay at their feet. They never questioned him because they *wanted* to believe the tale he told. It only confirms the hate and fear that live in their hearts about our kind."

"Viola's right," Darrigan said. "It's not enough to reveal Jack's plan and hope the authorities step in. Hell, the authorities are probably on his side."

"So we kill him," Viola said, her eyes flashing.

"That will only confirm the public's beliefs," Jianyu told her.

"We can't kill Jack," Darrigan told them. "Remember? Esta tried that, and it only released the demon inside him. It made things worse."

Jianyu believed the tale Darrigan had spun about ancient beings and cursed souls. He'd seen the living blackness take over Jack Grew, had he not? And the danger of the goddess that inhabited the Book matched too closely to what he'd overheard in Morgan's mansion.

"Perhaps there is a way to control the danger that lives within Jack Grew's skin so we can eliminate the threat of them both," Jianyu told Darrigan. "We have Newton's Sigils."

Darrigan frowned in confusion.

"If what Morgan said is to be believed, the sigils were created to control the power in the Book—a power you say might have been this goddess, Seshat," Jianyu explained. "Could they not also control the power in Jack?"

"But we have no idea how to use them," Viola reminded him.

"Nibsy has Morgan's papers, which means he has the answers we need," Jianyu said. "If we retrieve those documents, perhaps we could use the sigils and eliminate the threat within Jack before the Conclave."

"It's worth a try," Darrigan told them. "Since I never took the mark, I should be the one to go. Dolph's cane can't touch me."

"You cannot go alone. You have not seen the papers we require," Jianyu said.

"No, Jianyu," Cela said. "I saw what that boy did to Viola. You can't go running into danger as well. Not as long as you're wearing the mark."

The worry in her voice warmed him and terrified him just the same.

"I do not fear Nibsy Lorcan," Jianyu told her. "This twist of magic around my wrist is no less dangerous than anything he can do. One way or another, my life is marked."

"You're talking like you've given up," Cela said, her brows drawing together.

"No," Jianyu corrected. "But fate has thrown its dagger. Perhaps if I reach for the handle, I will not be caught by the blade."

"Or maybe you'll be sliced to bits," Cela said darkly.

He inclined his head, acknowledging her point. "But the danger in the Strega might prove useful in other ways," he told her as he considered the dangerously tight cord around his wrist. "Tom Lee may have more patience if he believes I am still seeking the cane. Perhaps I might buy myself some time."

"We need to act, and we need to do it before the Conclave." Darrigan looked suddenly lost and unsure as he scrubbed his hand through his hair. "So much has happened, and the Conclave is only a couple of weeks away. I thought we'd have more time. We were supposed to have more time. If Esta doesn't arrive before then—"

Darrigan stopped as though he'd said too much.

"I think," Jianyu said carefully, "it is far past time for you tell us where Esta is."

BAIT

They waited a week for Esta to arrive before they made their move on the Bella Strega, and during that week, Harte grew less and less sure in his belief that she would find him. How could she not have appeared by now? His affinity had long since returned from the substance the Guard had doused them with. It only stood to reason that Esta's should have as well.

Each day that passed made him worry that something more was keeping her. Perhaps something had happened to Ishtar's Key, or perhaps she had landed in some danger that they hadn't expected and was trapped by one of their enemies.

He worried too that he was the cause of her absence. They couldn't eliminate Nibsy unless they were certain that Dakari would do what he'd promised. Harte had believed he found a way. He had hoped to return to 1902 and find evidence of that possibility, but the sign he was looking for had not materialized. Now he began to worry that what he had done—the minute change he'd inserted into Esta's history—had some larger effect that he hadn't intended.

Without the diary, he was flying blind, and without Esta, he was growing desperate.

He kept those worries to himself, just as he kept his knowledge of what would happen to his friends should they not take care of Jack before the Conclave. He told himself that the future could still be changed. He told himself that what had been written in Nibsy's diary need never come to be. But he wondered if they didn't deserve some right to their own fate.

They had waited long enough. Each day that passed was one day less they had until the Conclave was upon them—one day less to plan, to prepare, and to neutralize the threat that Jack posed to the march of history and the future of all magic. They needed the instructions for using Newton's Sigils. Until they had those documents, they could not be sure that the strange silvery discs could do what Jianyu believed.

Harte still had trouble believing that Newton's Sigils could be the answer to dealing with Jack. But the day had arrived for them to find out.

"She will come," Jianyu said as though sensing the direction of Harte's thoughts.

They were heading toward the Bowery and were both wrapped in Jianyu's affinity, protection against any who might be searching for them.

Harte could have denied his worry, but he found that he no longer had the energy to pretend. "What if she went too far?" Harte asked, voicing the one fear that had haunted him through the days and nights without Esta. "If she was thrown off course by the Guard's attack, anything could have happened. If she went too far—or not far enough—if she landed at a time when Ishtar's Key already existed—if it crossed with itself—she'd be stuck. Trapped. Maybe for good."

And if that happened, if it became impossible to give the cuff to her younger self . . . she'd be gone.

"I might not ever know," he whispered, his greatest fear of all.

Jianyu stopped and clapped him on the shoulder. His grip felt sure and strong. "She *will* come, Darrigan."

"How can you be so sure?" he asked.

Jianyu released him with a small shrug. "I have no other choice."

In the days since the attack on the wedding, the mood in the Bowery had shifted. The increased police presence was enough to have the various gangs drawing inward. But the factions in the Bowery were chafing under this new control. Each day Jianyu brought word from the On Leongs that Lee was growing impatient to act. It was the perfect situation to stir into a distraction so they could get to the papers Nibsy had stolen.

They left the park and headed south once more, the sky heavy and gray above them. As they walked, snow began to fall, coating the world and erasing the grime and filth of the city. In moments like this, Harte could almost believe that a different life was possible. He could almost fall in love with the city that had born him and raised him and made him who he was. *Almost.*

Without Esta, the city was nothing but a prison once again. But with her . . .

They went to the Little Naples Cafe first and then to find Sai Wing Mock and the Hip Sings. With Jianyu's help to keep them unseen, it was simple enough for Harte to use his affinity and put their plan into action before they headed back toward the Bowery. Back to the Strega.

Under the cover of Jianyu's affinity, they watched the door of the saloon from under the cover of a shop awning farther down the block. The sign over the entrance bore the likeness of a golden-eyed witch— Leena, the woman Dolph had loved. But now, the more Harte looked, he saw Esta in those features too.

His heart clenched.

"This will work," Jianyu promised as they waited for some sign that their morning's work had borne fruit. "Nibsy will be forced to deal with the problems we have created for him. It will give us time."

It was the best distraction they could think of. Both the Five Pointers and the Hip Sings had formed tenuous alliances with the Devil's Own because of what they believed Nibsy could do for them. But as of that morning, the leaders of those two organizations would begin having second thoughts about the trust they placed in Nibsy Lorcan. The commotion caused when they both showed up at the Bella Strega at the same time would, with luck, be enough of a distraction to allow Harte and Jianyu to steal back the documents Nibsy had.

But Harte knew how slippery Nibsy could be. He wished he felt half as sure as Jianyu.

"Maybe we should have told the others," he said, watching the street for some sign that their plan was working.

It didn't take long before John Torrio arrived with a large group of Five Pointers, including Razor Riley. Torrio and Riley went into the Strega, leaving their men to stand guard outside. When the group of Hip Sings arrived not long after, they found their way blocked by Torrio's men. The mood on the streets changed quickly as the two factions began to circle each other, with Sai Wing Mock demanding entrance into the saloon.

Harte and Jianyu didn't wait to see who won that particular argument. They hurried around to Elizabeth Street, where the back entrance of the Strega waited, unguarded. But just before they were inside, Harte paused.

"I'm sorry about this," he said, and sent a pulse of magic into his friend. "But it's better this way."

Jianyu's gaze went a little fuzzy, but he did not release his hold on the light. "What?"

"Wait outside and don't let anyone see you," Harte told him. "If I'm not back in ten minutes, it means something's gone wrong, and you can let the others know what I've done. But don't you dare come back for me alone."

Then he released Jianyu and started up the steps to the apartment that had once belonged to Dolph Saunders.

The lock was a surprise, though perhaps it shouldn't have been considering what he knew of Nibsy. It was easy enough to pick, and in a matter of seconds, he was inside.

He didn't waste any time, did he? Harte thought, looking at the changes Nibsy had made in the once-familiar space. His gaze snagged on the painting above it. The one he'd seen just days before in the Professor's office. It was another reminder of the future that might unfold if they didn't manage to change the course of history.

It wouldn't take Nibsy long to realize that the simultaneous arrival of both Johnny Torrio and Mock Duck was nothing more than a distraction, so Harte didn't hesitate. He went to the bookcase, searching for the leather folder Jianyu had described. He'd sorted through one of the shelves when he heard the door open behind him.

He turned at the same time he heard a metallic *snick*. Nibsy already had a pistol primed and aimed directly at his chest.

Nibsy stepped into the apartment, not bothering to close the door behind him. "I wondered when I'd see you again, Darrigan. I have to say, I expected you sooner than this."

Harte lifted his hands slowly, keeping his attention on the gun. But he didn't miss what Nibsy was holding in his other hand.

"I assume you're looking for these?" Nibsy lifted the leather portfolio and then tossed it onto a nearby table. "Well, there it is. Not that it'll do you any good."

"Don't you think you should be downstairs with your guests?" Harte asked. "Careful, or you might lose your saloon."

Nibsy only smiled, his eyes flashing with amusement behind his thick spectacles. "Your care is touching, Darrigan, but my people are far too loyal and too powerful to let anyone get the best of them. They'll handle the problem. It's not like they have a choice. Torrio and Sai Wing Mock should know better than to come into my territory making threats. And their alliance means nothing, not in the grand scheme of things."

Harte realized that they'd made a tactical mistake. Both he and Jianyu had assumed Nibsy would protect his troops since they were all that stood between him and losing everything. They'd been wrong. It was clear now that Nibsy would sacrifice everyone in the barroom if it meant he might get his hands on the Book.

"I should have killed you," Harte said, realizing that without Jianyu's help, he had no way out.

"Such a shame you didn't. Now you'll never have the chance," Nibsy told him with a small, amused smile.

He kept the gun on Harte as he poured a glass of Nitewein.

"Here." Nibsy set the glass on the floor between them. "Drink it. I don't want any unfortunate incidents with that affinity of yours."

Harte stared at the glass and then looked back at the gun. He could try to lunge for him. He still had his affinity. But Nibsy's skin was covered almost completely, and the gun would likely go off before he could use his magic.

"It's the wine or a bullet, Darrigan," Nibsy said. "I don't need you alive, but it would make things so much more entertaining."

Stay alive. It was the only thing that mattered.

He reached for the glass slowly, but at first he wouldn't do more than look at the dark liquid inside. He had to delay a bit longer, until his command wore off and Jianyu realized he was gone.

What had he said? Had he commanded him to leave? He suddenly couldn't remember.

Delay, he thought as he stared at the Nitewein. *Someone will come.*

Someone *had* to come. It wasn't possible that he'd been so stupid to step right into Nibsy's trap again.

"Oh, don't worry so much, Darrigan," Nibsy said as Harte considered the Nitewein. "You aren't the one I want. You're only the bait."

THE MESSAGE

Central Park

Esta opened her eyes, and the darkness that she'd fallen through transformed itself back into the tunnel. She felt unsteady from all that had just happened—all she'd just seen—but the second she realized that the weather was bitterly cold and snow covered the ground beyond the tunnel's entrance, she sprang to her feet. Her head swirled at the sudden movement, but she tried not to panic. Though it was damn hard to stay calm when her affinity was dead, the city was covered in snow, and Harte was nowhere to be seen—*and* when the memory of the unmade world was still clinging to her like old cobwebs.

Against her arm, the stone in her cuff thrummed with an unsteady warmth. At least she still had Ishtar's Key. It meant that she hadn't gone too far off course. She hadn't crossed herself and the stone. Even though it wasn't spring, as they'd planned, it meant that she still had a chance to sift back through the layers of years to Harte and to get things on track. Once the stone cooled, she could get back to where she'd intended to go. She could find Harte. Once her affinity returned.

If it returns.

Esta let out an uneasy breath at the thought. She couldn't let herself go there. Not yet. *Not ever.*

Rubbing her arms for warmth, she considered her situation. It was snowing. Large, white flakes tumbled from the heavy gray sky. From the shelter of the tunnel, she could see the city clearly through the bare branches of the trees. Gone were the soaring skyscrapers of mirrored glass and steel. Brick and stone structures lined the park. It looked similar to the city as it had been in 1902. Maybe she was close to the right time.

Her gaze caught on a set of markings low on the wall of the tunnel. Her name. Someone had written her name in chalk. Along with the words "New York" and "age."

She crouched down, ran her fingers along the letters, wondering what they meant, wishing she could understand what they signified by simply touching them. She tried to tell herself that there was any number of reasons that her name would be there, but she knew the only reason was if Harte had been there as well.

But how long ago did he write this?

There wasn't anything she could do as long as her affinity was dead, so she figured she might as well figure out what the words meant. And whether Harte was here as well.

The words turned out to be a newspaper, and through a little investigation, she finally found the large brick building that held the paper's offices. It was far uptown, away from the Bowery and the areas their friends would have frequented.

She studied the front entrance for a long while before realizing that she had no other real options. As long as her affinity still felt cold and empty, there was nothing to do but try to find someone she knew, someone who could tell her what might have become of Harte.

Inside the main vestibule, Esta shook the snow from her hair and shoulders before knocking on the heavy office door. A middle-aged man with light brown skin and a pair of pince-nez spectacles on his nose opened it and gave her a look somewhere between irritation and resignation.

"You'll be looking for Abel and his folks," the man said before Esta could even open her mouth to speak. "Upstairs."

He shut the door in her face.

Esta didn't know any Abel, but the man had been confident enough that she figured it would be worth trying the apartment upstairs. When she knocked on that door, she heard shuffling from within, and then suddenly the door was thrown open and Cela Johnson was standing there, a look of absolute shock on her face.

"Who is it?" Viola's voice called from somewhere in the apartment.

But Cela didn't answer. "Is it really you?" she asked Esta in a voice close to a whisper.

Esta nodded. "Is Harte here?"

Before Cela could answer, Viola was pushing her aside.

"Chi é—" Viola froze, her violet eyes wide, and then suddenly the prickly assassin launched herself at Esta and wrapped her in a fierce embrace.

Esta felt the burn of tears as she returned Viola's embrace. She wasn't too late. They weren't gone. *Not yet.* She could save them. "Where's Harte?" she asked. "Is he here?"

Viola nodded as she looked her over. "I can't believe it. Darrigan, he said you'd come, but after a week, we weren't so sure."

"So Harte *is* here?" Esta asked, her stomach flipping. She hadn't lost him. "What's today's date?"

"The eighth of December," Cela said.

"But what *year*?" Esta asked.

Cela frowned. "It's 1902. What other year would it be?"

Relief washed over her. They weren't where they intended to be, but at least they were together. And they could always go back if they needed more time.

Once they were inside, Cela introduced Esta to Joshua, who seemed to be a friend of her brother's, and a blond girl, who seemed to be Viola's. But there was no one else there.

Confused, she turned to them. "Where's Harte?"

Then she saw the uncomfortable look Cela and Viola were exchanging.

"What?" Esta asked. Her mind spun with a thousand scenarios for a thousand things that could have happened to him. The Order. Nibsy. Jack. "He's okay, isn't he?"

"Yes, of course," Cela told her. "He's out with Jianyu."

Again, the uncomfortable silent exchange between the other women.

"What's going on?" Esta said.

"We thought they were checking for you," Viola told her. "Every day he goes to see if you've come. To make sure that his message is clear."

"It was clear," she told them with a wobbly smile. "He must have missed me."

Viola cursed under her breath as she cut her gaze to Cela. "You know where they went, no?"

"They wouldn't . . ." Cela's brows drew together. "Not without telling us."

"They're men, aren't they?" Viola asked. "Of course they would!" Then she turned back to Esta. "They've gone to the Strega to get back what Nibsy took from Jianyu."

"They've been gone all day. Even if they went to do something as stupid as that, they should have been back by now," Cela said. Again the silent look exchanged with Viola.

Viola was already reaching for her shawl and her knives. "After we rescue them, I'm going to murder them myself."

PREDICTABLE

The Bowery

Though Cela urged the tired nag onward through the city, the small delivery wagon they'd borrowed from the *Age* could not move fast enough for Esta. Winged horses wouldn't have been fast enough, not when she knew that Harte had been brash and reckless enough to go after Nibsy on his own.

She told herself that it must mean his affinity had returned, because he couldn't have possibly been so stupid to go to the Strega with nothing but his wits for protection. It should have given her some hope, because it meant that whatever the Guard had used on them was only temporary. But it was hard to hope when her own affinity remained cold and empty. No matter how hard she concentrated, she couldn't reach it.

As the wagon navigated the cluttered confusion of the early-century streets, Viola and Cela tried to fill Esta in on what happened since she and Harte had left in May. Ruby sat in the back of the wagon, listening as well. She'd been unwilling to be left behind. Speaking in stops and starts, they weaved the tale that made clear how much she'd missed—and how much had happened because Jack had possession of the Book.

But the Conclave was still two weeks away, she reminded herself. They could still stop Jack and Nibsy, both. And if Cela and Viola were to be believed, there might be a way to control Thoth long enough to unmake him completely. She was determined to save her friends from the fate she'd seen in the Professor's diary—to change the fate written on those pages and to save them all.

511

When they came down Elizabeth Street, Viola ordered Cela to stop the wagon after she noticed Jianyu waiting outside the Strega's back door. He looked lost, like he was in some kind of a daze, staring at the door without seeming to see it. Esta barely waited for the wagon to stop before she leaped down and was already trying to shake Jianyu from whatever stupor he was in before Cela could tie off the reins.

"Jianyu, where's Harte?" She shook him again when he didn't respond. "Was he with you? Is he inside?"

Jianyu finally blinked away the daze he was in and focused on her. Shock and surprise flashed through his expression. "Esta?" He lifted a hand like he was about to touch her and make sure she was really there, but then thought better of it. "You have finally returned to us?"

"I have," she told him. "But I need to find Harte. Do you know where he is?"

Jianyu didn't immediately answer. He had the telltale glassy look to his eyes and the docile confusion that often came with having your consciousness invaded. "Where is he, Jianyu? I need you to *think*. What was the last thing you remember?"

"The Five Pointers and Hip Sings had just arrived, as we planned," he told her, his focus already growing sharper. "We sent them—Darrigan sent them—as a distraction. We were going to find Morgan's papers." He took a sharp breath, like something had just startled him. "Darrigan was not supposed to go in alone. This was not the plan."

"But it sounds like something he'd do," she said, looking up at the silent windows of the building. *Dammit, Harte.*

"I'll need your help," she told him. "My affinity's not quite steady right now. Can you get me inside?"

"Certainly," he told her, looking more settled and alert now.

"You can't go in there again," Cela said, catching Jianyu's arm before he could reach for Esta. "You know what could happen." Cela turned to Esta. "Please. You can't ask him to do this. That boy has the marks. He nearly took Viola apart."

"It does not matter," Jianyu said, pulling away from Cela.

"You saw what he did to Viola," Cela told him, her voice breaking with emotion. "Don't ask me to piece you back together too."

He lifted his hand, touching her cheek with a tenderness that surprised Esta. It seemed that so much had happened while they were gone.

"Jack attempted to destroy me with the Pharaoh's Heart and the power of the Book, and he could not," Jianyu told Cela. "Let Nibsy try."

"Why would you give him the chance?" Cela asked. "There has to be another way."

"There is no time," Jianyu told her.

"I'm coming too," Viola said, her knife already in hand.

"No." Jianyu held up his hand as though to stay her, and to Esta's surprise, Viola actually paused. "Please. I need you here. Watch over Cela and make sure no harm comes to her."

Viola looked like she wanted to argue, but one look at Cela had her changing her mind. She nodded instead. "Hurry. And come back safe."

"I don't need watching over," Cela argued, bristling in frustration.

"Then let me stand by you instead," Viola told her.

Jianyu offered his hand. "If you are ready?"

"Let's go save Harte from his own stupid bravery," Esta told him, taking it.

Almost immediately, she felt the buzz of warm magic wrapping around her as the world went wobbly.

"Come back to us safe," Cela told them, but she was looking at Jianyu when she spoke.

Esta saw his expression soften, but he didn't respond. Instead, they turned and pushed into the back entrance of the Strega, leaving the noise of the streets behind.

It had been only a few months since Esta had been there, but it might as well have been an eternity. Once, the scent of Tilly's bread would have warmed the air, but now only the smell of stale ale and tobacco smoke welcomed them. A racket was coming from the direction of the barroom, but she ignored it and followed Jianyu up the back stairs, invisible in the cloak of his affinity.

"So, you and Cela?" she asked as they climbed.

"Cela has been a true friend in these weeks," he answered, and it was only the bit of pink that warmed the tips of his ears that gave anything away.

"She's pretty great," Esta told him.

"Cela Johnson is not for me," Jianyu said.

She glanced at him from the corner of her eye. "She sure looks at you like she wants to be for you."

He turned to her like he would argue. But instead, his mouth went tight, and he continued onward without speaking.

Soon enough they were at the doorway of Dolph's apartment, and Esta stopped. She couldn't seem to make herself take that next step and walk through the door.

Jianyu gave her a questioning look, but she only shook her head to tell him she was okay.

She had to be okay. She had to focus, because Harte was likely on the other side. She would not think about the time she'd spent in that apartment with Dolph, never suspecting her true connection to him. It was too late to go back, too late to grasp those minutes like the treasures they had been. Now there was only forward, to Harte. To whatever the future held.

The door to the apartment was ajar, and a familiar voice carried through the gap.

Nibsy.

Silently, they slipped into the apartment.

Harte was standing on the other side of the room with his hands raised. He was wearing a sleepy, almost drunk look, and he was smiling despite the gun Nibsy had aimed at his chest. On the table next to Nibsy was a leather folder. In the hand not holding the gun, Nibsy leaned upon Dolph's cane.

They'd barely gotten through the door when Nibsy visibly stiffened, like a predator catching the scent of prey. Suddenly, Esta heard Jianyu gasp. She felt the warmth of his magic dissipate as a shock of ice burst around them.

Jianyu let go of her hand as he went rigid. His back arched, and he fell to his knees, writhing against some invisible torture. She wanted to help him, but she didn't dare move as long as Nibsy had Harte held at gunpoint. She couldn't save them both, and now that Jianyu's affinity was no longer cloaking them, she might not be able to save anyone.

Even drugged as he seemed to be, Harte's expression sharpened the second he realized she had come for him. His stormy eyes were dark with emotion—hope and fear and love all at once. He started to get up, but Nibsy lifted the gun as a reminder and gestured for him to remain where he was.

I'm okay, she wanted to say to soothe the fury and the terror in his eyes. *We'll be okay.*

Nibsy stepped to one side, keeping the gun on Harte as he turned to face her. "I thought you might join us," he said pleasantly. "Jianyu as well, I see." Esta saw Nibsy's fingers tighten on the cane, and Jianyu jerked in pain.

"Let them go, Nibsy," Esta said.

He pretended to consider her request. "No," he said after a thoughtful beat. "I don't think I will."

Jianyu cried out again, his face contorting in agony. He'd gone nearly white with the pain of what was happening to him.

Harte's expression turned murderous, but he didn't move. He didn't dare to with Nibsy's gun still aimed at his chest.

"You don't really want them." Esta lifted the strap of the satchel over her head. "You want this."

Nibsy stilled, and even without her affinity, time felt like it were standing still. "You brought it? Just as I always knew you would."

She nodded. "The Book and the artifacts, too. But you need me to work the ritual. I'm willing to make a bargain. You let those two go, and it's yours. Take me instead of them."

Harte's expression turned to horror. "No, Esta. Don't—"

"Hush," Nibsy said, easing back the hammer of the pistol. "I've heard about enough from you."

She didn't look at Harte. She couldn't risk it, not so long as Nibsy held the gun that could end his life. "If you hurt him—"

"You'll what?" Nibsy said. "You aren't in the position to be making any demands."

She took Viola's knife and placed it at her own throat. "Aren't I?"

Nibsy considered her offering, his eyes narrowing in suspicion. She knew he didn't trust her or believe her, but he didn't have to. He just had to take his attention off Harte long enough so they could get away.

"You can have one," Nibsy said finally. "And I'll see the contents first."

Esta pretended to consider this offer and then, slowly, she lowered the knife.

"Fine." She allowed herself a quick glance at Harte, who was still shaking his head, trying to deny the bargain she seemed to have struck. Even through his half-drunken stupor, she hoped that he already understood what she intended to do. "I'll take Jianyu."

"Interesting choice." Nibsy's mouth twitched with amusement.

Jianyu screamed, his body twisting in pain.

"I'll take Jianyu alive and *whole*," she said. "If you hurt him or kill him, the deal is off."

"Show me what's in the satchel," Nibsy demanded. "Open it."

Esta saw the doubt in his expression, but there was hope as well. Yearning. She moved slowly, carefully unlatching one buckle and then the other. She looked at Harte once more. Willed him to understand.

"No, Esta—"

But she was already moving. With a violent twist, she swung the bag toward Nibsy's face. He reacted on instinct, reaching for it and taking his attention off Harte just long enough to give them a chance.

In that fraction of a second, Harte lunged. One shot went off, but it flew wide, shattering a window without hitting anyone. Before Nibsy could fire again, Harte was on top of him, pinning him to the floor and trying to wrestle the pistol from Nibsy's grasp.

Esta went to Jianyu. His wrist was bleeding, and his hand was already coated in his own blood. It was coming from a black bracelet of some sort cutting into his wrist, and the cold energy coming from it told her that ritual magic was involved. But there wasn't any way to stop it. She couldn't figure out how to get it off him.

Out of the corner of her eye, she saw Harte punch Nibsy—once, twice—until blood was pouring from his nose, and he only barely tried to get away. The fight seemed to have been beaten out of him, but he was laughing like some kind of lunatic.

"So predictable," Nibsy said, blood dripping from his nose into his mouth. "Always so predictable."

Harte tore the gun from Nibsy's hand and pointed it at his chest. "Am I predictable now?"

"Eminently," Nibsy said with a leering smile.

Cocking back the hammer, Harte aimed at Nibsy's chest. "You don't deserve to live. You don't deserve to take even one more breath."

"You won't kill me," Nibsy said, suddenly deadly calm. "You can't. You *need* me."

"No—"

"He's right," Esta said. "You can't kill him now." *Not without dooming me.* "Unless you know?"

Harte kept the gun still aimed squarely at Nibsy's chest, but his mouth went tight. He shook his head.

"Then you can't," she said. "As much as he might deserve it."

Harte's features hardened, and Esta watched as he waged a battle within himself that she understood too well. Deciding, Harte tossed the gun to the side and punched Nibsy once more, viciously, squarely in the nose.

Nibsy wasn't laughing anymore. He wasn't even moving. But considering she was still there, Esta figured he'd survive. Harte's stormy eyes were burning with fury as he drew back his fist again.

"Leave him," Esta said.

But Harte didn't move off Nibsy's still body. He seemed frozen, his hand clenched into a fist, ready to strike.

"He's not worth it." She was trying to help Jianyu up from the floor, but with the agony of the bracelet cutting into his wrist, he wasn't exactly steady on his feet. "I need your help."

That seemed to be enough to have Harte hesitate and lower his fist. He climbed off Nibsy slowly, reluctantly, and got to his feet. He started to move toward her, but Jianyu held up his hand.

"The cane," Jianyu said through clenched teeth. "The papers as well."

Harte pried the cane from Nibsy's hands and then scooped the leather folder from the table, tucking it securely inside his coat. Then he helped Esta get Jianyu up from the floor.

Harte hesitated at the door, turning back to look at Nibsy's unconscious body. "It's a mistake to leave him."

"Probably," she said.

"He's not going to stop, Esta."

"I know." But there was nothing they could do. *Not yet.* First, they needed to get out of the Strega without any more problems. They needed to save their friend. "Jianyu is more important right now. He's bleeding pretty badly, Harte. And I can't get him down the steps alone."

Harte cursed when he finally noticed the blood dripping down Jianyu's hand. "It's worse," he said softly, and the worry was clear in his expression.

"What is it?" she asked.

He shot her a dark look. "Later."

As they descended the steps, they heard voices growing louder, closer.

By the time they reached the bottom of the staircase, Jianyu was no longer writhing. He was almost able to walk on his own. But at the bottom of the stairs, a familiar face stepped into their path, blocking their escape.

Bella Strega

When Logan Sullivan had realized that James wasn't going to do anything about John Torrio and Mock Duck brawling in the Bella Strega, he'd done what any sane person would do. He'd hidden behind the bar and waited for the goons who followed James to deal with the threat.

It took longer than he expected. As the barroom had erupted into chaos, people seemed to realize that James had already left. It hadn't taken long before they started leaving as well. Marked and unmarked alike, few seemed willing to be drawn into a Bowery brawl that didn't benefit them, and in a matter of minutes the only people left were the Five Pointers and the Hip Sings, tearing the whole place apart.

Which worried Logan. He hated the damn saloon, but it was the one safe place he'd found in that godforsaken version of the city, and James was the one shield Logan had against the dangers of this stupid time. But if James wasn't going to stick around, neither was he. The first chance he had to get the hell out of there, he did.

But if the arrival of Torrio and Mock Duck had been a surprise, finding Esta descending the back stairs was a complete shock.

"Logan?" Her mouth parted. She didn't exactly look happy to see him.

"Esta." Her dark brown hair was shorter than he'd ever seen it, and there was a sharpness to her features that he didn't remember her having before. She'd always been confident and brash, reckless and impertinent, but now there was also a calmness beneath it all. A sureness that went beyond simple confidence. He wasn't sure he liked it one bit.

For a second, though, he was too surprised to do anything but stand there like a complete moron, staring at the group of intruders who had clearly just come down the back steps. Along with her was Darrigan, the damned magician who had twisted Esta's loyalty and made her betray the Professor and their team. They were helping the Chinese guy, who didn't look so good, down the steps.

"What are you doing here?" Then he saw James' cane in Darrigan's hands, and everything started to come together. "It was you, wasn't it? The fight in the saloon. *You* made it happen, didn't you?"

Esta's eyes went wide. "Please, Logan. You don't understand—"

He stepped more squarely into their path. "What the hell have you done, Esta? Do you have any idea what's happening in there? They're destroying the place." Then another thought occurred to him. "Where's James? What did you do to him?"

Her features hardened. "Get out of our way, Logan."

"*That's* all you have to say to me?" he demanded. "After the mess you made? After you *left* me here?"

"Please, just step aside and let us go," she told him. "I don't want to fight you."

"I don't particularly care what you want." He crossed his arms. "I'm not moving an inch until you agree to take me back."

"Back?" Her brows drew together.

"Yes, back," he said, then considered. "Or forward. Whatever you want to call it. The bottom line is that I want out of here. I want to go back to my normal life in the normal world. You have no idea— You can't understand how terrible it's been for me here." She was frowning at him, but he didn't care. "I miss reality. I miss television and iPhones and reliable running water. I miss penicillin. Hell, I even miss the streets only smelling like piss and garbage instead of like horse shit on top of that. You want to get out of here? Fine. But I'm going with you, and the only place we're going is back to where we belong."

Esta glanced at Darrigan, who still looked murderous. They seemed to exchange a silent conversation between them.

"I *am* where I belong, Logan," she told him. "Here, with my friends. Fighting with them for what's right."

Panic inched along his skin. He'd practiced this conversation a million times in his head. He'd thought of every possible variation, but he hadn't considered that she'd want to stay here in this hellhole of a time. "These aren't your friends, Esta. And you don't want to stay here. There's nothing for us here."

The pity in her eyes made his skin crawl. "I can't take you back," she said.

"Can't?" he asked. "Or *won't?*"

"Does it really matter?" she asked. "Either way, it's not happening. I don't have time for this right now, Logan."

"Really?" he said, feeling suddenly furious. "*You* don't have time for it? You have all the time in the world, Esta."

"Not now I don't," she said. Her jaw went tight, and he knew she would dig her heels in harder.

"Esta, you have to listen to me—"

"No, Logan," she snapped. "*You* need to listen. The world you knew doesn't exist anymore. When you brought me back here? That changed *everything.*"

He ignored the tremor of unease he felt at her words. They had to be lies. She'd been turned by the Magician, and now she'd say anything to keep Professor Lachlan from winning.

"I don't believe you, and I also don't care," he told her. "So what if it's a different world? As long as there's indoor toilets and the internet, it's where I want to be."

"You don't get it," she snapped. "I've been back—or close to it—and no amount of indoor plumbing can make up for what it's like. It's not the world you left. You're safer here."

He thought of the battle raging in the saloon and knew she was insane.

His heart was pounding in his ears. "You just don't want to help me. He's twisted you, *changed* you."

"She's not lying," Darrigan said, as though anyone could believe a con man like him.

"Get out of our way, Logan." Esta adjusted her grip on Jianyu. Her gaze shifted to the door behind him and then back. "I'm warning you. Step aside. You don't need to get hurt."

"No," he said. "You're not going anywhere." He squared his shoulders and prepared to do whatever he had to so she couldn't slip away again.

COLLATERAL

Viola did not kill the boy, though Jianyu could tell from the fury in her violet eyes that she wanted to. But she did use her magic to remove him from their path. One minute, Logan Sullivan was standing against them and issuing demands, and the next, the warmth of old magic coursed around them, and Logan was on the floor.

"Come," she commanded, beckoning them forward, toward the open door. "Cela is waiting with the wagon."

At the mention of Cela's name, Jianyu felt a flash of panic. "She should not be here."

"Neither should you," Viola scolded. "We're a team, no? You and Darrigan should have included us. Maybe *this*"—she gestured toward his clear injuries—"wouldn't have happened."

Or perhaps it would have been worse, Jianyu thought. But he knew better than to start a pointless argument when Viola was snapping with temper.

In the distance, Jianyu could hear shouting coming from the saloon. It sounded like an argument or brawl. The voices were louder, and the uproar far more violent than he had expected. Something crashed, like glass shattering.

What had they done?

Jianyu had never intended to put the Devil's Own in danger, only to keep Nibsy occupied. Which clearly had not worked. Nibsy had not been distracted, and now the Strega sounded as though it were at war.

He thought to go, started to turn in the direction of the noise. They needed to stop the madness that Darrigan's affinity had inspired, but he was only upright because Darrigan and Esta were supporting him.

"Whoa," Esta said gently. "Wrong direction."

"But the Strega—"

"We don't have time," Darrigan told him.

They were already dragging him out the back door of the building before he could argue any further.

Outside, snow swirled in the air. The clouds had grown heavier above, making the daylight seem slanted. Everything looked softer somehow, cleaner and quieter than it had before. Or maybe that was the loss of blood and the pain making him delirious.

They were barely out the door when he saw the familiar wagon from the *New York Age* waiting across the street. There was Cela sitting on the driver's perch, watching the building, her long legs clad in trousers and a man's cap pulled low over her brow. There was nothing about her that looked remotely like the boy she was playing at being, especially not once she noticed they'd emerged. The instant her eyes locked on him and saw that he was injured, she was moving.

But the change in her expression—the fear in her eyes—had warmth blooming inside him, pushing away the pain despite the icy wind and the cold energy radiating through his arm. That warmth felt too close to joy. Too close to wanting.

He could not allow himself to believe that the concern he had seen flash across Cela's features was for him alone. She would have felt the same no matter who was injured. He would not start thinking that he had any right to her care. He *could not* begin hoping for that.

Cela opened the gate of the wagon, her expression still painted with fear, and she watched as they helped Jianyu into the back. He felt like a fool—weak as a child—as Cela helped Darrigan and Esta get him into the wagon, but he did not have the strength to bat them away. He kept his jaw clenched tight, though, so he wouldn't cry out and betray the amount of pain he was currently in.

Once everyone had climbed into the back, Cela hesitated. Her gaze had caught on the bloody mess of his hand, and when she lifted her eyes to meet his, he could not read the emotion there. It was not pity. It was not even fear any longer. She closed the door, securing them, before Jianyu could begin to understand why the look she had given him made him feel so very . . . unsettled.

The jerk of the wagon starting off shot a fresh burst of pain through him. He could not quite stop the grunt of pain that escaped. At least the others were too busy with each other to notice how badly he was hurt. Harte was looking at Esta as though he had just unearthed a rare treasure, taking her face in his hands and examining her for any sign of injury. Viola was checking that Ruby was unharmed as well.

"I don't know why you're worried about me when Jianyu's the one who's *actually* hurt," Ruby said, brushing her aside.

Viola turned then, as though she had forgotten, and from the way her expression shifted and the color drained from her cheeks, Jianyu understood exactly how bad he must look.

"Madonna," she whispered, looking down at his arm. "What happened in there?"

"Nibsy," Darrigan said darkly, which seemed to be all the explanation that any of them needed.

"What did he do to your arm?" Esta asked, gesturing at the place where the black cord had embedded itself into Jianyu's skin.

It was worse than it had been. There was no denying that fact. Before, the piece of braided silk thread had been cutting into his skin, which had been bad enough. Now, the bit of thread had changed, transformed by the corrupt magic it contained. It no longer appeared to be a solid, braided cord. It seemed to be transforming, as though the silk had been liquefied by the magic within it and was melting into him, fusing with his skin. The braided threads appeared to be separating as well, and now some had begun to vine up his arm, like deadly tendrils seeking out the affinity that lay within him. More crept down beneath the blood coating his hand, and they were still moving, slowly but steadily creeping and spreading their terrible cold energy with every passing second.

"That isn't Nibsy's work," Viola told Esta. "It's part of the bargain this one made with Tom Lee." As the carriage bumped and rattled and Jianyu tried to keep himself from crying out in pain, Viola explained the situation that had driven him to make his foolish alliance. "He wanted protection for Cela, but that bit of evil was the price of the agreement."

"It was necessary," Jianyu argued. He would not regret the choice he had made. It did not matter that Cela had been safe all along. She had been in danger, and if Theo Barclay had not reached her first, his bargain might have been the only thing to protect her. It was worth it, mistake though it might have been. Cela's life would always be worth it, whatever the price might be.

"You could have waited," Viola argued.

"Would you have?" he asked, glancing from Viola to Ruby and back.

She understood his silent message, and at least she was honest enough not to say anything more.

"He put his affinity up as collateral for Lee's help?" Esta said.

"And Lee seems to be ready to call in the deal," Darrigan said. He lifted Jianyu's wrist to examine it, eliciting a fresh grunt of pain from Jianyu.

"Enough." Jianyu drew his arm back to cradle it against his chest and protect it from the rattling of the carriage.

"But I don't understand," Esta said. "If that thread is linked to Tom Lee, how was Nibsy able to tap into it?"

"I do not think he was," Jianyu told her.

"I saw what happened," Esta argued. "Your arm didn't start bleeding until we were there with Nibsy. He did something to you, and whatever that thread is doing now, he was the cause of it."

Jianyu grimaced. "Only because he was trying to use the mark against me."

"It happened again?" Viola asked, frowning.

"I believe so," Jianyu told her. "It felt much like when Jack tried to perform his ritual. This bit of corrupted magic asserted its previous claim over my magic once more. This is the result."

"It protected you again," Harte told him.

"Protection? *This* you call protection?" Viola asked, horrified. "*Guarda!* Even now it's growing. This is no protection. This is a curse, and if you don't remove it, you're going to lose your hand."

Jianyu wished it were so easy. The pain radiating through his arm was from more than a simple wound. The silk cord's icy magic felt as though it was seeping into his bones. "From the way this feels? I worry I will lose more than my hand."

"There has to be something we can do," Esta said. "There has to be some way to get out of your bargain."

"There is no way to remove the charm without Lee knowing and taking his payment in full," Jianyu said with a grimace.

Viola eyed the cane. "You have what you need," she told him, nodding toward the silver Medusa's head. "Take it to Lee. Get that piece of evil off you while you still can."

"No, Viola." Jianyu hissed in pain when the carriage hit another rut in the road. "No. I will not do that. I *cannot.* Whatever happens to me, Tom Lee cannot have possession of the cane. He cannot be given that kind of power or control over the Devil's Own. No one should have that sort of control over another."

"Be reasonable, Jianyu," Viola begged, eyeing the black vines crawling up his arm. "Lee won't wait forever, and you won't last if this continues."

He could not stop himself from groaning as the wagon hit another bump and a fresh bolt of pain lanced through him. She was right, but he did not see what there was to do about it.

"See?" she told him. "If you allow this to continue, it will kill you."

"You would let Lee control you?" he asked. "Because if I give him this cane, that is what will happen. He will control everyone who was once loyal to what Dolph tried to build. He would have you, Viola. He would use you and your magic for whatever purposes he desired."

Viola lifted her chin. "He could try."

Jianyu bit back a smile at his friend's fire, but this was bigger than either him or Viola. "Even if you were willing to risk it, could you truly hand over the lives of all of those who were once our friends? All those we once vowed to help Dolph protect?"

She had no answer to that.

"Giving Lee the cane is not the answer," he told her, sure of this if nothing else. "I pledged my loyalty to the Devil's Own, and I will not betray them. I will not betray *you*, either, my friend."

"They wouldn't do the same for you," she told him.

"But you would. You already have," he said, thinking of all they had been through.

Viola did not seem to agree. She was not going to let the issue go. "Jianyu—"

"I have no plans to be a martyr, Viola."

"What is your plan?" Esta asked.

"These past weeks, I have been considering the issue, and I believe there may be a way, at least to buy more time." He looked at Darrigan. "You retrieved the papers?"

Harte nodded, patting the front of his shirt.

"Perhaps they hold the key," Jianyu said, hoping that his reasoning was correct. "Morgan believed that Newton's Sigils could create a protective barrier. Perhaps we can use them as protection from the magic Lee is using against me."

Viola's eyes widened. "Why would you not tell us this?" Viola asked. "We could have retrieved those papers *weeks* ago."

"What was there to tell?" Jianyu shrugged. "It was a theory only, not enough to put anyone at risk."

"Your *life* was worth that risk," Viola told him.

Her fierce belief warmed him, even if she was wrong. "We have the documents now. Perhaps the answers we need are there."

Viola shook her head. "Even if Newton's Sigils work, even if we can figure out how to use them, that doesn't stop this," she told him. "Only Lee can do that. You must go to him. You must take the cane and be done with this."

"That's not quite true," Esta told them, her expression thoughtful. "I could do it."

"How?" Jianyu asked.

"My affinity," she told him. "It's more than just slowing down time. I can touch the Aether that holds everything together, which means I can also pull it apart. I could unmake the ritual magic for you."

Jianyu did not understand how that helped. "But if Lee realizes you are trying to tamper with the cord, the magic in it grows more powerful. Every time we have tried to remove it, it has only made things worse."

"If Newton's Sigils do what you believe, they'll cut Lee off from his connection to that thread, right?" she asked. "Without that connection, he can't hurt you. If the sigils work, if you're right, I can unmake that cord while you're within the sigil's protection. At least, I think I can."

She was looking at Harte now, and there was some silent conversation happening between them. He nodded, and Jianyu understood that something more was happening. Something more had been decided.

"It might work," Harte said before Jianyu could ask what else they planned to do. "You just need to hold on until we can get back."

The cart lurched suddenly to the left, and they all scrambled to find something to hold on to. Pain lanced through Jianyu's arm, and Viola cursed as she tumbled over. They'd barely had time to right themselves when the wagon lurched again.

"Che diavolo?" Viola said, trying to steady herself and Ruby.

The sliding window at the front of the wagon opened, and Cela's face appeared in the small opening.

LISA MAXWELL

"We're being followed," Cela told them.

"Who is it?" Jianyu asked.

Viola was already moving toward the back gate, where she could take care of their pursuers.

"I'm not sure," Cela said. "Hold on, though. I'm going to try to lose them."

CASTOFFS

Esta barely had time to comprehend what Jianyu had just revealed—that Newton's Sigils could be the answer to stopping Thoth—before the delivery wagon rounded another corner, throwing her into Harte. He caught her solidly in his arms, but she didn't have time to appreciate the strength of his arms around her or the relief of knowing that she hadn't lost him, not when they were being followed.

"Can you tell who's chasing us?" she asked Viola, who had opened the back gate just enough to look out at the traffic behind them.

"I don't know," Viola said, cursing when the carriage lurched as it took a turn to the right. "I can't tell for sure."

Jianyu was holding his arm, trying to keep himself steady, but she could tell the effort was costing him.

The wagon swerved again, and Harte looked at Esta. "Newton's Sigils aren't going to help anyone if we don't get out of this mess."

"My affinity—" She stopped, felt it stirring there. *Maybe.* She kissed him soundly and felt her world click into place at the feel of his mouth on hers. "I'll be right back."

Esta crawled through the small doorway that opened into the driver's cab. There, Cela was urging the exhausted-looking horse onward, dodging through the traffic as they climbed northward through the city. She had no idea if her affinity was strong enough yet or if what she planned to do would even work.

"We're going to try something," she said, offering her hand to Cela, who didn't hesitate to grasp it. Focusing everything she had on her connection to the old magic, Esta forced the seconds to a stop. Everything went still—the world, the horse, and the wagon as well.

It wasn't the same as a car, she realized with a sinking sense of dread. The horse was a living thing, caught in the spell of her affinity along with everything else.

As Esta released time, Cela stared at her, completely unaware that anything had happened. "Well?" she demanded.

"I'm going to need you to drive as straight as you can. And whatever you do, don't let me go," Esta told her.

Cela blinked at her in confusion. "What are you—"

But Esta was already leaning far over the front lip of the driver's perch. She tightened her grip on Cela's hand and leaned forward to touch the back flank of the horse. As soon as her fingers brushed the coarse hair of the animal, she reached for time. Using all her concentration and strength, she slowed the seconds.

Cela gasped, and the wagon started to slow.

"No!" Esta shouted. "Keep driving. Steady as you can."

Her hand was damp with sweat, and her skin felt warm with the effort of holding on to Cela and the seconds, all while keeping a precarious balance over the front of the wagon. When they hit a pothole and slid a little through the snow-covered street, Esta nearly lost her grip, but she fought hard to keep them all—herself and Cela and the horse—in the net of her power. By the time they'd put entire blocks between them and whoever was following them, Esta was damp with sweat. The icy winter air lashed at her face, but she ignored the sting of it.

As they rounded another corner, she realized they were close to Washington Square. The arch wouldn't be built there for years to come, but it was easy enough to recognize with its stately homes and manicured pathways. Exhausted, she pushed away from the horse and fell backward onto the driver's perch as the world slammed into motion around her.

Cela tossed a disconcerted look in her direction. "What *was* that?"

"Hopefully enough to get us away," Esta said, looking back around the side of the wagon. The streets held the occasional carriage or wagon, but they seemed to have lost whoever had been chasing them.

"Well? Any sign of them?" Cela asked.

Esta looked again, and this time she noticed the logo of the newspaper emblazoned on the side of the wagon. "We can't go back to the *Age*," she told Cela. "If they saw the name on the wagon, they'll know where to find us."

Cela's eyes widened. "We have to go back. We can't just leave Joshua and the rest to fend for themselves," Cela said. "They need to know that trouble is coming. We have to warn them."

"We will," Esta promised. "But first we have to get Jianyu somewhere safe."

Fear tightened Cela's features, and she looked torn between two terrible options. "It's bad, isn't it?" she whispered.

"Really bad," Esta told her gently. "I want to make sure your friends at the newspaper are safe, but that bracelet Tom Lee put on him is still changing. I think it's going to kill him if we don't get it off."

Cela's mouth pressed into a thin line. She looked like a woman at war with herself. "*Can* we get it off?"

"I think there's a way, but we can't do it in the back of this wagon," Esta told her. "Is there somewhere else we could go? Somewhere safe?"

Cela nodded. "There's a safe house we've been using for the people we've rescued from the Order." She still looked torn in two, but she turned the wagon west and headed toward the water.

The building they stopped next to looked like any other tenement in the city—drab brick with uneven steps, fire escapes cluttered with clothing despite the freezing weather, and windows covered by white curtains. But there was something about the place that set Esta's teeth on edge, something that made her want to turn around and go the other direction.

LISA MAXWELL

"Where are we?" Esta asked, following Cela down from the driver's perch.

Cela busied herself with securing the horse and wagon. "You'll see soon enough."

When they opened the back of the wagon, Jianyu looked worse than he had a few minutes before. The blood was nothing now compared to the veining darkness that was creeping steadily up his arm. Climbing ever closer to his heart.

Esta sensed Cela coming up behind her, and she felt fear in the other girl's sharp intake of breath at the sight of Jianyu and his arm.

They helped him down, but when Jianyu saw where they were, he began to panic. "No, Cela. We have to leave. This is far too dangerous," he argued. "We can't risk leading our enemies here. If the Order or Nibsy or anyone knew of this place—"

"It's the only place I could think of," Cela told him. "It's been safe for months now."

"I cannot risk them—"

"You're going to have to," Cela snapped. "You don't have a choice."

Esta wasn't sure what the subtext of their conversation was, but they didn't have time to argue, not with how much worse Jianyu's arm currently looked. "She's right. We need to get that thing off you, and it needs to happen now."

Jianyu was still trying to argue and fight against Harte's support, but the pain he was in was making it difficult.

"It will be safe here," Viola said. "There's no reason to think otherwise. But that wagon, it will give us away."

"You'll need to move it," Esta told her. She was aware of Harte watching her as though she might disappear, but there would be time for that later.

"I need to take it back," Cela told her. "It belongs to my brother's friend. I can't risk anything happening to it, and I need to warn the others," Cela said. She looked like she didn't want to leave them. "Whoever was after us will have seen the newspaper's name. If they can't find us, they'll go after the *Age*. I can't leave Joshua unprepared."

"And Abel," Jianyu said. "Is he not expected tonight as well?"

Cela nodded. "I need to warn him, too."

"You cannot go alone," Jianyu argued. "We should all—" The words were barely out before his whole body contorted in pain and nearly collapsed to the snow-covered ground.

They all rushed toward him to keep him upright, but Cela moved fastest of all.

"We need to get him inside," Esta said, looking up at the building and feeling that same creeping unease. "If you're sure it's safe."

"No," Jianyu said.

"It's fine," Cela told her at the same time. She turned to Jianyu. "You need to stay here and let your friends take care of you."

"I need to protect those inside," he whispered.

"You already have." She kissed his cheek softly. "It's your turn now."

When she stepped back, Cela had tears in her eyes.

"Maybe Harte could take the wagon," Esta suggested, knowing that Cela wanted to stay.

She could tell that Harte hated the idea—and she didn't blame him—but Cela shook her head before Harte could even start to refuse. "It wouldn't be right for anyone but me to go."

As the others helped Jianyu into the building, she watched Cela climb back into the wagon.

"Be safe," she told Cela.

"You take care of him, okay?"

Before Esta could do more than nod, Viola shouted for her to wait. She was already handing Jianyu over to Esta and Harte.

"I'm going with her," Viola told them.

"I'll come too," Ruby said.

But Viola shook her head. "You'll be safer here with them," she told Ruby. "And I'll be back soon." She looked at both Esta and Harte. "Jianyu will show you the way."

"You should stay," Cela said as Viola climbed into the wagon. "They'll need your protection."

"They have plenty inside to keep them safe," Viola told her. *"Andiamo."*

Cela hesitated a second longer more before she snapped the reins and launched the wagon into motion. In a matter of seconds, the wagon disappeared into the falling snow.

Almost as soon as they were gone, Jianyu's legs nearly went out from under him. Esta caught him up, supporting him with Harte's help. "We need to get him inside."

She looked back up at the building, and despite all her misgivings, she helped Harte keep Jianyu upright as they made their way through the darkened entryway.

Inside, the building was strangely quiet. The tenement houses Esta had been in before were always noisy. They were crowded with homes and places where people lived out loud, because it was pointless to try to go unheard. The walls were too thin, and the rooms were too crowded for any hope of privacy. But the hallways of this building didn't echo with voices. There was an uneasy silence that filled them, like all sound had been sucked away. It was cold as well, and the hallway was filled with the chill of corrupted magic.

Jianyu directed them through the main hall, and Ruby led the way as they took the back staircase up three floors.

"What *is* this place?" Esta whispered as she helped him up the steep stairs. It felt almost dangerous to speak out loud.

"A safe house that Dolph used." Jianyu groaned. "He showed it to me before he died."

"It feels . . . *wrong*," Esta said with a shudder.

"You get used to that," he told her. "It's the magic."

"Not natural magic," Ruby said with a shiver. It seemed that she could feel the wrongness of the place too.

"No," Jianyu agreed. "Not natural magic. Dolph had it charmed somehow to keep the uninvited from entering." He paused, though whether gathering his strength or remembering the past, Esta couldn't tell. "I never understood why he showed me this place. It was as though he knew somehow that we would need it."

"He trusted you," Harte said softly. "He knew he could rely on you if anything happened to him."

Finally, they arrived at their destination, an apartment on the third floor. With some difficulty, Jianyu managed to rap his knuckles in a rhythmic pattern on the door. There was rustling from within, a pause, and then the clicking of locks being unlatched.

An older woman poked her head out of the opening, and when she saw Jianyu, she opened the door, but her eyes went wide when they stepped from the dark hallway into the light of the apartment. "What happened to him?"

"Nibsy," Harte said, which was apparently all the answer the woman needed.

Immediately, her expression changed from horror to determination. "Well, what are you waiting there for? Bring him in and let's take a look—" Then her eyes lifted to Ruby, standing behind them in the doorway, and she frowned, looking suddenly anxious. "Wait . . . I know her." She took a step toward Ruby, fear suddenly shadowing her features. "She's the one they're looking for. The heiress bride. What is she doing here? If the Order discovers her here—"

"She's with us," Jianyu said simply.

"But not one of us," the woman said, still looking horrified.

Esta realized then that she recognized the woman. Months before, Dolph had taken her on his rounds and introduced her to the families in his keeping. Golde and her children were one of many stops on the tour.

"Golde?" Esta said, trying to remember if that was her name.

The woman frowned at Esta, but then her eyes widened. "I remember you," she told Esta. "You came that day, with Saunders."

Esta nodded. "How are you? What are you doing here?"

"Later," Jianyu told them with a groan. "Please. I cannot—" But he grimaced again before he could finish.

Golde gave one more nervous look at Ruby but then ushered them all inside. As they followed her through the apartment, Esta realized it had not been divided up into small, cramped rooms like most tenements, and it felt larger than it should have been inside. The entry parlor was larger than most New York apartments. Beyond it was a wide corridor lined with doors, and as they passed by, people began to emerge from the closed rooms, curious to see who had arrived. The warm buzz of magic in the air told her they were Mageus.

"Go on, the lot of you," Golde said, turning to shoo back the growing crowd. "There's nothing for you to see here."

They stayed back, but they didn't retreat.

"Who are they?" Esta asked. She was aware of them still watching from a distance.

"They're Dolph's," Jianyu told her. "They were in trouble and needed a safe place."

Golde grumbled. "Maybe they were Saunders' before, but they're my trouble now."

"No one forced you to live here," Jianyu said with a groan. But humor laced his words.

"Who else was going to?" Golde sniffed disdainfully. "It's not like you know how to cook or clean, and I wasn't going to let my Josef go without good food in his stomach or a strong hand to keep him in check." The woman's mouth wobbled a little.

"He still has not spoken to you?" Jianyu asked softly.

She shook her head. "Not yet," she whispered.

"He will come around," Jianyu told her. "It is not you that he is angry with."

"You don't deserve his anger," she said with a sigh. Golde turned to Esta. "It's thanks to this one that my boy is even alive."

"I don't understand," Esta said.

Golde's expression was serious. "My boy, Josef, and the others, they're all hiding from the Order's patrols. If not for Jianyu and Viola—"

"We can tell this tale later," Jianyu said as they finally settled him into a chair. He looked at Harte. "The papers. I do not think I have much more time."

A DECLARATION OF WAR

Cela's heart was in her throat as she guided the wagon through the slick streets of the city. Snow was still falling, heavy and constant, but she didn't have time to notice its beauty. If the people pursuing them had seen the name emblazoned on the side of the wagon, they might already be on their way to the offices of the *Age*. Joshua might already be in danger. And if any of the people looking for them saw the wagon she was currently in? She'd be in trouble too.

Viola was next to her in the driver's seat, silent and stoic as a statue. She seemed to understand that Cela wasn't in any mood for talking. Not when it was taking all her concentration to keep the wagon steady in the quickly accumulating snow.

They smelled the smoke a half mile away, but Cela knew before they were close enough to see the dark smoke pouring from windows that the *New York Age* building was on fire.

Her first instinct was to push the exhausted nag even faster, but Viola grabbed the reins before Cela could snap them again.

"Stop," Viola told her. "Park the wagon over there before someone sees."

She was right. The people who had been pursuing them would be watching for the wagon. They needed to stay out of sight for their own safety. But Cela needed to find Joshua and the others.

They parked the wagon in an alley so the name of the paper would be hidden from anyone who might be looking, and then, on foot, they started toward the crowd that had gathered near the burning building.

It was worse than she'd thought. Now, less than a half block away, Cela could see clearly that the entire building was already engulfed. The snow continued to tumble down, indifferent to the tragedy unfolding, but even from so far, she could feel the warmth of the flames brushing against her skin.

She felt someone tall creeping up behind her, too close. Before she could turn, she heard a male grunt of pain as Viola spun to confront their attacker.

"Abel?"

Her brother was clutching at his chest, his features bunched in clear pain.

"Let him go, Viola," Cela said, slapping at her friend, but Viola had already released him.

Abel gasped for breath and looked more than a little unsettled as he pulled himself together.

"What are you doing here?" Cela asked. "I didn't expect your train to get in until later this afternoon."

"It's nearly five," he told her.

She realized then that the darkening sky was from more than the snow flurries or the black smoke pouring from the *Age*'s building. It was later than she'd realized.

"When I got here, there were already white men surrounding the place," he told her. "Order patrols from the looks of it. They've rounded up the people inside."

"Joshua?" Cela asked.

Abel's jaw went tight. "Mr. Fortune, too."

"Then let's go and get them," Viola said, already moving toward the building.

Abel caught Cela's arm before she could follow Viola. "You can't go back there, Rabbit. It's too dangerous."

"We have to stop her from doing something stupid," Cela told her brother. "She's going to make everything worse."

As soon as they reached the spot where Viola had stopped, Cela realized that it *couldn't* get any worse. Just beyond the edge of the crowd, a group of men with guns had Joshua and some of the other employees of the *Age* on their knees. Along with them was Mr. Fortune.

Joshua saw them in the crowd. He met Cela's eyes and then Abel's, shaking his head a little as though to warn them away. But he looked terrified.

Rightly so. The men who had them hostage were too bold, too confident, considering the crowd that had gathered.

Cela recognized their type easily enough. The rough-cut clothing, grease-stained hands, and the excitement that sparked in their light eyes at the power they'd been handed marked them as men the Order had hired. Cela and her friends had been trying to stop those patrols all summer, but there was always an endless supply of white men angry enough to be used as weapons.

One had Ruby's wedding gown in his hand. He was holding it high enough for the crowd to see and explaining that the men were all guilty of aiding the abduction.

Another placed a gun to Joshua's back.

He never had a chance to fire. The man went down unexpectedly, crumpling like a puppet whose strings had been cut. The others turned, startled by the man's collapse, but they didn't have time to act. One by one they fell.

Cela didn't have to see the look of determination and fury in Viola's eyes to know the cause. She grabbed her arm. "You have to stop this."

Viola only shook her off. Two more men went down.

"Tell me you're not killing them, at least," Cela said. It would only cause more problems.

Viola turned to her. "Tell me you don't want me to."

Cela couldn't. "It won't help."

The final man went down, freeing the *New York Age*'s employees. Joshua was up first. He tossed a grateful, nervous look in their direction before turning to help Mr. Fortune up from the snow-covered ground. All around them, the crowd had already surged forward to help.

"What have you done?" Cela asked, her mind spinning with the implications of what had just happened. "They'll know for sure now that the *Age* was helping Mageus."

"They already knew," Viola said, regret clear in her violet eyes. "They had Ruby's dress."

"She's right," Abel said softly. "That was evidence enough to prove our involvement. It's all the excuse they needed."

"But she didn't need to confirm it," Cela told him. She turned on Viola because she didn't know where else to put her fear. "You put a target on the back of everyone at the paper, maybe everyone in this neighborhood with what you just did here!"

"You think those men cared about your friends helping us?" Viola asked darkly. "You know as well as I do that the payment they get from the Order is only an excuse. It's permission to do what they want to do anyway. Do you think that they would have stopped at this building?" She shook her head. "This was the opening shot. Those men, small, pathetic creatures that they are, wouldn't have stopped here. They would have continued on, terrorizing this entire neighborhood because of the license the Order's payment gave them."

"But what you just did will confirm to the entire city that Mageus did take Ruby."

"Maybe so," Viola told her. "But now those men who were forced to kneel, their families, and all these people, they will know we did not just stand by and allow others to be harmed. They will know we stand with them. That we are not their enemy, and from us they have nothing to fear."

LISA MAXWELL

CIRCLE OF LIGHT

The Safe House

Esta wanted nothing more than to take five minutes alone with Harte—to make sure he was okay—but she knew they were running out of time to help Jianyu. Their reunion would have to wait. The package of papers Harte and Jianyu had reclaimed from Nibsy had so much information—about the Order and their history and the Brink—but it had taken too long to sort through it all. They started to worry that maybe the instructions for using the sigils weren't even there. Nibsy could have ferreted them away somewhere separate.

"There," Jianyu said. He was doubled over now, and his skin too pale and slick with sweat. He pointed to a piece of parchment that had been folded in thirds, and Esta realized that his hand was nearly completely black now. But the cord around his wrist was clearly affecting more than his arm.

Esta looked at the page Jianyu pointed to and recognized the cramped, uneven scrawl almost immediately. It looked the same as the pages that Newton had written in the Book. "This is it," she whispered to herself and to Harte, but it took another few minutes for them to figure out what they were seeing.

The diagram on the parchment seemed to depict four discs—the sigils—connected through the Aether. "It should create a kind of force field," she explained.

"A what?" Harte asked.

"A kind of barrier," she said, trying to explain.

"Like the Brink?" He was frowning. "Or like the ritual circle the girl used?"

"I don't think so," she said, reading a note scrawled sideways in Latin. "It's not opening the spaces the way the Brink does. It's not doing anything with the Aether at all other than directing it around an area. Like a magical fence. It's easy enough, except that I think it would work best with four people. The ritual would be more stable."

"I'll help if I can," Ruby said.

Esta frowned down at the page. "I'm not sure if that'll work. It looks like it takes some kind of energy to activate the sigils. I think we need people who have a connection to the old magic."

Golde stepped forward. "He saved my boy," she told them. "I'll help with whatever you need."

"It might work with two," Esta said, considering. "You and Harte could each hold two of the sigils."

A man stepped into the room from where he'd clearly been listening in the hallway.

"What do you want, Yonatan?" Golde asked. "Here to make trouble again? Because we don't have time for your complaints."

The man was middle-aged, with thinning hair and a round stomach that strained the buttons of his shirt. "I'll help," he said.

"You?" Golde frowned at him.

"He saved my life too, didn't he?" The man seemed almost uncomfortable admitting this. "I'll help."

"Good," Esta said, before Golde could change the man's mind. "That's three." She looked past Yonatan, to the others waiting in the hallway. "It shouldn't be dangerous. You just have to be willing to try."

At first none of them moved.

"Cowards, all of you," Golde said, stalking over to them. "You stand and gawk, but none of you are man—or woman—enough to help the one who keeps you safe."

The people watching from the hallway remained silent. A few looked uneasily down at their feet, while a few looked defiant.

"We didn't ask to be brought here, Golde," a woman with curling blond hair said. "We didn't ask him to keep us here away from our work and our families."

"Neither did you ask the Order to hunt you for sport," Golde said, her anger simmering through her words.

"Maybe he saved us from the Order, but he sure didn't save Dolph." The speaker was a boy Esta recognized from her days at the Strega. He was a tall, rangy kid with acne shadowing his jaw who might have been named Henry or Harry.

Another stepped forward. "From what I hear, he's the one who got Dolph killed."

"That's not true," Esta said, frustrated and at the end of her patience. "Jianyu had nothing to do with Dolph's death. Neither did Viola."

"That ain't the way Nibsy tells it," the first kid said.

"Nibsy Lorcan is a liar and a traitor," Harte said. His voice had a dangerous edge to it. "He's the one who killed Dolph, and he's the one who sold every one of you over to the Order."

"And we should believe you?" the kid asked, narrowing his eyes. "You were never one of us."

"You don't have to believe him. Not when Nibsy told me himself," Esta said. "He killed Dolph, just like he killed Leena. He arranged everything so he could take the Strega and the Devil's Own."

Golde stepped forward. "Do you think I don't understand how you feel? Do you think it was any easier for me to accept that a boy like Lorcan could bring down the great Dolph Saunders?" She shook her head. "But I know what happened with my Josef. I went to Nibsy and asked him to save my boy, but he wouldn't. He refused because my son hadn't taken his mark. He laughed at my fear. Jianyu," she said, turning back to where Jianyu was struggling to stay upright. "He helped with no question of payment or price. He helped with no promises."

A door opened in the hallway, and a ripple went through the crowd as a younger teenager stepped forward. He was short, small even for his fourteen or fifteen years, with Golde's same ashy brown hair and hazel eyes.

"Josef?" Golde's heart was in her eyes.

"I'll be the fourth," the boy said, glancing at his mother before turning his attention back to Esta. "Tell me what I need to do."

They didn't waste any more time. Esta arranged them in a circle with Jianyu in the center. He looked worse than ever, but she couldn't let herself worry about that—only about the ritual ahead.

The silvery discs felt strangely cool to the touch, a mark of the corrupted magic within them. On the surface was a design similar to the one on the Book—it wasn't exactly the same, more like a blurred version of the original. Like a copy of a copy. She took the first of the sigils and had Harte hold out his hands. Gripping the sigil on the edges like a vinyl record, she used her thumb to send it spinning, with her two middle fingers as the pivot.

It spun slowly at first, but just when she feared it might stop, the silvery surface began to glow, as though it had caught fire, and the sigil began rotating faster and faster. When it was spinning fast enough that the disc looked like a ball of light, she placed it over Harte's outstretched hand. It hung there, suspended in the Aether, above his palm.

"Focus your affinity through this," she told him. "You need to try to connect with the part of yourself that can speak to the old magic."

He nodded, and she could see the concentration on his face. When she was sure he had it, she took her hands away, and the disc remained floating in the air, a shimmering sphere of light.

She'd never done ritual magic herself, so she wasn't prepared for the way it tingled across her skin and lifted the hairs on her neck. She wasn't prepared for the brush of power that felt exhilarating—like flying and falling all at once. It was nothing like the comfort of her own affinity. That was warm and soft, like an old friend. But this? She wasn't prepared for how much she wanted *more*.

LISA MAXWELL

Esta repeated the same process with Golde next, and then with Yonatan. Finally, she placed the last of the glowing spheres over Josef's outstretched hands. The boy flinched when the sigil flashed even brighter. All at once, cold magic swept through the room as the four sigils connected in a blinding flash of light.

Almost immediately, Jianyu's entire body went limp. He was no longer contorted in pain, but Esta wasn't sure if it was because he was protected from Lee's connection to the black thread, or if it was because—

"He's still breathing," Harte said, as though reading the direction of her thoughts.

She looked at him, his face aglow with the strange power of the sphere of light he held in his hands, and he nodded encouragingly. *You can do this.*

"Let's get that thing off his arm," Esta said, and she stepped across the boundary and into the circle.

QUESTIONS OF AETHER

Bella Strega

J ames Lorcan didn't know how much time had passed between when
Darrigan had managed to escape and when Logan found him unconscious and bloody on his own living room floor. He immediately
noticed what was missing: the portfolio from Morgan's mansion and the
cane.

"Did the boys take care of the problem in the Strega?" James asked
as he sat himself upright. He gingerly dabbed his battered nose, wincing
at the slight pressure. Then he tilted his head back, so the blood could
run down his throat instead of all over his rug. He'd have to find another
healer to fix it, and soon. Preferably before he showed himself in the
saloon.

"I don't know," Logan told him, looking distinctly more uneasy than
usual. "I didn't stick around to find out."

"You didn't stay?" James glared at him.

"The others were leaving," Logan said, feeling suddenly uneasy. "If
your own people aren't going to fight, I'm not getting my head busted in
for some stupid saloon."

"Who left?" James asked.

"I didn't take down their names," Logan told him. The boy was jangling with nervous energy, coward that he was. "But Marcus and Arnie
for sure."

James frowned. Marcus and Arnie were old blood. They wore the
mark, but they hadn't stood and fought for the Strega?

The Aether shuddered around him. That stupid, constant droning seemed louder now, more perverse in its insistence that something was coming and more determined to hide it from his view.

He shoved over the small table, shattering the glass that had been sitting atop it and splattering Nitewein on the Persian carpet. The way it marred the ornate pattern in the weave, like drops of blood on fabric, settled something in him. Any time he chipped away at the perfection of Dolph's life gave him a thrill of satisfaction.

"Come," he ordered, and without waiting to see if Logan would follow—of *course* he would—James took the steps down to the bottom floor and entered the barroom.

It was a disaster. Chairs lay broken in heaps and glass littered the floor. There were a handful of his people there, looking morose and dejected as they stared at the mess. But Logan had been right. The majority of the Devil's Own were nowhere to be found. They'd fled like rats from a sinking ship. Not even the fear of the marks had been enough to have them stand and fight for the place that served as their home.

The few who remained stood when he entered, but they didn't make any move to explain.

He called over Murphy, one of the new boys he'd recruited in the weeks after the Flatiron, when the heat of a city summer stirred tempers and made men volatile. Murphy, like other new faces that had come to call the Strega their own, had gladly accepted the mark. He, like so many others, had yearned to be part of something. James' possession of the ring, along with his new alliance with the Five Pointers, had been enough to convince them that *this* was what they were willing to die for.

Unlike those who had followed Dolph, the new boys never asked inconvenient questions, never pressed. The newer ones, like Murphy, were easier to control without their inconvenient memories and misplaced loyalty to Saunders and with the freshly inked snakes entwined on their skin.

"Find the others," he told them. Then he turned to the bar to see if any of the whiskey had survived.

When John Torrio and Razor Riley had entered the Strega a few hours earlier, no one had paid them any attention. Maybe it was because the two had become regulars since Torrio had made the alliance with the Devil's Own as payment for the help James had given him to wrestle control of the Five Pointers from Paul Kelly. Or maybe there was another reason why none of the Devil's Own noticed the pistols carried by the two as they stalked through the crowded bar toward the table where James usually held court. Not until Torrio had it pointed directly at James' head.

It seemed that the stupid dago was tired of waiting. He wanted the territory he'd been promised, and he wanted it immediately.

James had managed to talk him down, but who knows what might have happened if Mock Duck hadn't arrived a few minutes later, shoving into the Strega like he and his highbinders belonged there.

But it wasn't a coincidence that his two newest allies had both shown up that day at the same time, both primed for a fight and ready to brawl.

"The attack was a distraction," he said.

Logan blinked at him.

"Esta's back," he told Logan, cataloging the guilt he saw flash through the other boy's eyes. "But you already knew that, didn't you?"

At least Logan had the good sense to look away. "I tried to stop her, but . . . I don't know what happened, James. One second I was blocking their way, and the next . . ." He looked more than a little unsettled by it. "I woke up on the floor, and they were already gone."

"Viola, if I had to guess," James said. Though it could have just as easily been Logan's own incompetence or cowardice. "But it doesn't matter. If Esta's back, it means the Book is back as well. She wouldn't come without it."

Logan frowned, his brows drawing together in confusion. "I didn't sense it."

The Aether lurched uneasily.

"That's impossible. Esta wouldn't leave it unguarded. She'd have it with her." He focused and felt the Aether, trembling and uncertain. Something wasn't right. Something hadn't gone according to plan.

"If it's still in the city, I can find it for you," Logan said, ever earnest.

"I know," James told him. "It's why I've kept you around despite your complete ineptitude. Esta and Darrigan aren't going anywhere. For now I want you to find me someone to take care of this broken nose. You can track the Book for me after."

There was one bottle of whiskey left unbroken. After taking two long swigs to help with the pain in his broken face, James went to the sink and pumped some cold water into the basin. Carefully, he washed away the blood that had already started clotting around his nose and lips. The shirt was ruined, but he took it off and soaked it anyway.

There was a part of him, an impatient boy deep inside, who cursed himself for not going after Newton's Sigils weeks ago. He'd wanted to. He'd thought of nothing else ever since he'd taken Morgan's papers and realized what they could do, what he could use them for. But every time he tried to form a plan, the Aether counseled patience. Any scheme, any attack that he began to map out sent uneasy vibrations through the ethereal substance around him and dread down his spine.

He needed to wait. He trusted his magic, and the Aether had never led him wrong, but he could not understand why. *Especially* now that Darrigan and Esta had bested him.

There had to be a reason.

He left the mess of the Strega in the hands of the people who hadn't run at the first sign of struggle and headed back up to his apartment, dabbing at his still-bleeding nose as he went.

Once inside he took stock. They'd taken Morgan's papers, but he already knew the contents of those. They'd taken the cane as well, which would make things more delicate. But he still had the Aether, and he still had the Devil's Own.

Settling himself on the couch while he waited for Logan's return, he took the small diary from his pocket and flipped through the entries. Most of it remained unreadable except for one page. But something there had changed. The future was becoming more certain.

Esta was back, and now the entry about the Conclave was settling itself.

Perhaps there was a reason he wasn't supposed to have the sigils yet. Words rose up on the page, hints of a future that could become. Perhaps he didn't need them *quite* yet.

They had taken the papers and had Newton's Sigils as well. Neither were weapons that could be used against him. The sigils were strange, powerful occult magic with the ability to protect Mageus from the Brink and to control a power as dangerous as the Book. He'd let them take the risks, and then, when the time was right, he'd step in and claim the rewards.

Let Esta and Darrigan believe they'd won this round. James knew the truth. Closer and closer, the final gambit was coming, and if the Aether was true and the words in the diary were correct, they were positioning themselves exactly where he wanted them.

Until then, he had work to do. He could not allow the alliances he'd made to crumble, not so long as they were useful. And he could not lose his hold on the Devil's Own.

GHOSTS OF THE PAST

Uptown

Viola refused to apologize for killing the bastardi that had destroyed the building that belonged to Cela's friends. She had not acted in a fit of rage. *No.* She had acted to save the lives of those who had stood by her, and she had sent a message in the process. This is who she would stand beside. This is who she would fight for. And if the Order and their scagnozzi came for Cela's friends, they would have to come through her.

And if she dreaded having to tell Jianyu what she had done? She would deal with it when she saw him. When he was well.

If he was well.

"Can't this thing go no faster?" she growled as the streetcar plodded steadily south.

Cela shushed her, while the other riders pretended they hadn't heard.

"We'll be there soon enough," Cela told her, but Viola could hear the fear in her friend's voice.

It took too long, that trek back down to Dolph's safe house near the river. She still couldn't quite believe that her old friend had been able to hide such a thing from her. She did not have any trouble understanding why Dolph had confided in Jianyu, but she still wondered why he hadn't told her as well.

Finally they arrived, Abel along with them, and it was Cela who was first through the cold warning of the front doors and led the way up to the third floor, where the apartment waited. Viola and Abel followed closely behind, but Viola paused before she entered. She hated visiting this place. She knew how they saw her—they thought her a murderer at best, and they feared her when she was around. It didn't matter that she'd helped to save every life within those walls. Somehow it still wasn't enough to erase the distrust in those they'd rescued.

She closed her eyes, girding herself for the judgment that was sure to come, and took a deep breath. The hallway was silent, peaceful, and she wished she could just wait there until it was over. Her attention snagged on a movement at the other end of the corridor, where a doorway to the back stairs stood open, but when she looked, nothing and no one was there.

Still . . . With all the dangers that surrounded them, it wouldn't hurt to be careful. And she was in no hurry to go inside. She wasn't yet ready to know whether their mad plan to save Jianyu had worked . . . or had failed.

At the end of the hallway, Viola found the staircase empty. She listened, just to be sure, and considered checking the other floors. But she knew she was being stupid. No one else could enter the safe house—Dolph had made sure of it. She was only delaying the inevitable. She took another deep, steadying breath, and along with the dust, she breathed in the scent of old books—aged leather and parchment and the acrid scent of drying ink—that reminded her somehow of her old friend.

She wished Dolph were still there. She wished he had lived to see the leader Jianyu was becoming and the peace that she herself had found. She wished most of all that they hadn't failed him so utterly and completely.

A shout came from the open apartment door that shook Viola out of her melancholy. *Ruby.* Forgetting the ghosts of the past, she ran.

Her knife was already in her hand when she reached the large back gathering room. She found Ruby immediately, huddled in the corner of the room with her face turned away from the scene.

"Are you okay?" Viola asked, touching her face, her neck, her arms. "Where are you hurt?"

"I'm fine," Ruby said, her eyes squinting against the brightness in the room. "I was only startled. It's just so much—"

Cold magic crackled through the air as Viola turned to take in the scene playing out in the center of the room. Darrigan and Golde along with Golde's son and one of the others were holding blinding orbs. A visible wall of energy connected them to form a curtain of light, and behind that boundary, Esta was bent over Jianyu's body. His eyes were open and the muscles of his neck were corded with his screaming, but she couldn't hear anything other than the low roar of counterfeit magic swirling around them.

On the other side of the circle, Abel was holding Cela back.

Viola stepped closer, trying to see beyond the boundary of energy and light. Esta looked like a girl made of fire. Her eyes were closed as she gripped Jianyu's arm, and as Viola watched, she felt a wave of warm magic swirl around them, warring with the cold energy in the air.

Then the blackness that had sunk into Jianyu's skin began to ripple.

GONE

The Safe House

Esta had felt the difference the second she'd stepped into the circle of light. It was like the atmosphere within the boundary created by the sigils was different somehow. Her ears had crackled, threatening to pop from the pressure, and her skin had gone hot and cold all at once as the corrupt magic brushed against her. Sound had drained away, leaving only silence, and when she'd reached for her affinity, she had found it strong and sure.

She knelt next to Jianyu, who was no longer conscious. He was still breathing, just as Harte said, but time was running out. Examining his wrist, she suddenly wasn't sure what she was supposed to do. It had seemed so simple before, but now that she was standing at the threshold, she hesitated.

What did you think you were, child? Seshat had purred. Esta was like Seshat. The same as Seshat.

Esta hadn't wanted that knowledge then, but she'd felt the truth of it in Chicago. She'd been so close to just *destroying* every bit of hatred in that arena. *You can touch the strands of time. . . . You can tear them apart.*

Esta had tried with Thoth, but she had failed. She'd only made things worse.

But you didn't have the sigils, she reminded herself.

Shoving her misgivings aside, Esta closed her eyes as she reached for time, that indelible net of creation within which all things were suspended. It hung clear and distinct around them, but she noticed that the time inside the circle was somehow different from the rest. It was as though it had been severed, set aside as a space beyond.

She filed that information away, and this time when she pulled, she focused on Jianyu—on the silken cord that had woven its way into him. Little by little, she called on the spaces between things, pulled and tugged, until . . . *there*. She could feel the very molecules that made the thread—the protein and carbon and every atom within it. The silken thread was breaking apart as chaos rushed in. She reached in, grabbed hold of the very essence of the thread.

And then she tore it from the world.

She unmade it completely by allowing the spaces between—the chaotic power of the old magic—to swallow the thread whole, like a snake devouring its prey.

Suddenly, Jianyu gasped, and his arm jerked awkwardly.

Esta jolted as her connection to the piece of silk evaporated as though it had never been, and when she looked down, the silk was gone. Jianyu's wrist was bleeding, but there was no sign of the dark veining magic that had threatened his life.

She turned to Harte, who had been watching, and the smile on his face matched her own. But when she stepped toward him, she realized she couldn't get close. Whatever boundary the sigils created kept her in just the same as it kept Tom Lee's connection out.

"You have to break the ritual," she shouted, but the flash of confusion on Harte's face told her that he couldn't hear anything. She pointed to the spinning ball of light and mimed breaking a stick in two.

Harte immediately understood. He lowered his hands and stopped the sigil from spinning, and with a burst of icy energy, the chain of magic that had formed the boundary around them broke. Then he caught her up in his arms and held her tight.

"You did it," he whispered. Then he kissed her, long and full. When he drew back, there was no mistaking the pride in his eyes, or the heat. "I knew you could, but . . . You know what this means?"

She did. The world tilted a little as the effort—and the importance—of what she'd just done nearly knocked her over.

Cela was there—Esta hadn't even noticed her return, but she was kneeling beside Jianyu, who was already coming to. Abel was standing close by and helped them both up from the floor.

Esta let herself lean into Harte's body. It wasn't just that she was exhausted—or it wasn't only that. *This* was the answer they'd been looking for.

She'd tried to kill Thoth once before by killing Jack, but it hadn't worked. She thought she'd unmade Thoth then, but now she felt the difference. Now she understood. Maybe if they could trap Jack using Newton's Sigils, they could contain Thoth until she could rip him from the world in truth this time. They could make sure he never walked the earth again in *any* body, in any form. Maybe they could destroy Jack *without* killing him.

"We can finish this," she told him, feeling more certain with every passing second. "We have everything we need. We have the Book and the artifacts. We'll use the sigils to take care of Thoth, and once we do, we can stop Jack as well. There are still two weeks before the Conclave. And then we can use Seshat's power to take care of the Brink."

She saw the doubt in Harte's eyes, the worry. "The stones, Esta. How are we supposed to touch them here? Nibsy has the ring, and Jack has the dagger. That's at least two that we know for sure will disappear the second they're out of the Book."

"Don't you see?" She kissed him again, unable to stop the joy from bubbling up within her. "The sigils are the answer—to finishing Thoth *and* to using Seshat's power. I felt it, Harte. The boundary they make cuts off everything, even *time*. We can use them to take the artifacts out of the Book, and then we can complete the ritual. We can unite magic and time, and we can finish this once and for all."

Harte still looked unmoved. "We don't have to rush anything."

"You know that isn't true," she whispered. "This has to be done. *Before* the Conclave."

He didn't have an argument for that. He knew what the diary she'd taken from Nibsy foretold: the deaths of Jianyu and Viola. Esta's as well. He refused to let *that* particular future come to be.

"If we find Jack before the Conclave, we can use the sigils to trap Thoth within them, and I can eliminate the threat he poses."

"And once we trap the demon?" Viola asked. "Then can I kill the bastardo who murdered Theo?"

Ruby took Viola's hand and gave her a watery-eyed look of approval.

"I'm not sure it's going to be that easy," Esta told her as she remembered the sickening suck of the dagger sliding into Jack's chest and the way he'd looked at her—him, not Thoth—right before he died in Chicago. They couldn't risk making him a martyr as she had before. "If we're the ones who kill Jack, it's only going to reinforce how dangerous people with the old magic are."

"What do I care what people think?" Viola asked. "I care only that Jack would be dead."

Ruby murmured her agreement, but Esta knew she was right about this. "Jack's the least of our problems. We can take care of Thoth, but the Brink is more important. If I'm right, these sigils could be the answer. We could do what Dolph always wanted to do. If we use the Book, we can stabilize the Brink *before* the Conclave. We cut the Order off at the knees and take away the danger Jack presents at the same time."

"It's true, then?" Jianyu said. "You have the Book and the artifacts within it?"

Esta nodded. "We have everything. We can end this." She walked over to where she'd left the satchel on a chair in the corner and brought it to the large kitchen table as the others gathered around. She unfastened the satchel and took out the first-aid kit and other supplies so she could remove the thick white towel they'd wrapped the Book in early that morning before they left the Plaza.

Even before she touched it, she had the sense that something was wrong. Her hands began shaking as she removed the towel from the bag.

The second she grabbed it, she knew there was nothing inside, but her brain refused to accept it. Even once she unwrapped the folded towel, she didn't want to believe it. But there was no denying the truth. Inside the towel, there was nothing but dark ash.

Everything was gone. The Book, the artifacts within it, and any hope they had of ending this.

Esta shook out the towel, certain that it would reveal the Ars Arcana if she just willed it hard enough, like a magician revealing a trick. Nothing but ash tumbled out.

"Well?" Viola demanded. "Where is it? Where's the Book of Mysteries?"

A feeling of unbelievable dread was coursing through Esta as she looked at the empty towel. "We should have realized," Esta whispered, still too struck by the horror of what had happened to fully process it.

They had been so careful. They had planned and schemed and found the answers they needed. They had known not to cross the stones, but why hadn't they considered that the Book itself might follow the same rules?

Why would they have considered *that*? They couldn't have known, because unlike the stones in the artifacts, the Book had never crossed with itself through time. *Not until now.*

"It's gone," she said, her voice hollow with defeat. "It was here. We had it. We had *everything*, but now it's gone. And the artifacts are gone with it."

They had no Book and no artifacts, save the cuff around Esta's arm. And there was no guarantee that Dakari would take on what they'd asked of him—no guarantee he'd even made it out of the park before the Guards found him. They might never know if they could take Nibsy out of the equation.

No, it wasn't *exactly* where they'd started. Somehow, it felt worse.

"The Book isn't gone," Jianyu told her. "It's here, in the city. With Jack. I saw it not even a week ago."

"Jianyu's right," Harte said. "If Jack is here, then the Book is as well.

We can still get it back from him. We can still stop him, Esta. And now that we have the sigils, we can destroy Thoth."

That thought buoyed her spirits, but only a little. Because it wasn't enough. The version of the Book with Jack wasn't *their* Book. It wouldn't contain the artifacts or the angry goddess who had been trapped within the pages of that other Book.

"But what about the artifacts?" she asked. "They're still out there. Without them, there's no chance of stabilizing the Brink. Even if we had them, Seshat's gone."

Her eyes met Harte's, and she knew that he understood exactly what she meant.

Without Seshat, there was no way to fix the Brink—not without sacrificing herself.

PART

V

HARTE

The Docks

As Harte Darrigan waited, tucked back into the shadows of one of the long warehouses that lined the docks, he thought of another night not so long ago. For him, it hadn't been that long since those terrible, lonely nights after the job at Khafre Hall, when he was an enemy to everyone—the Devil's Own, the Order, and Esta as well. He'd been utterly alone as he had executed his careful plans, but being alone had been necessary—it had been the best chance of slipping past Nibsy's defenses and to protect Esta and the others as well.

Then, the city had felt like his inevitable tomb. He'd had no hope of escaping. He had not expected to live beyond the following day, much less escape the Brink and travel across a continent and through time itself.

After all he'd been through, he suddenly found there was a strange comfort in the familiarity of the city—of *his* city. He'd seen Manhattan soaring to impossible heights, had seen the speed of the world by train and automobile, had seen another sea as well. None of it had brought him the peace he'd been searching for. None of it had been enough.

Esta's profile was clear against the softness of twilight, and as he looked at her, something in him settled, as it always did.

"What?" she asked, noticing his attention.

He shook his head as though to say, *Nothing*, but when she continued to frown, he attempted to explain. "I was considering how strange it feels to be back."

Her expression softened then. Sadness eased the tension around her eyes. "I'm sorry, Harte," she whispered, misunderstanding his meaning.

"Don't be," he told her. "I'm exactly where I want to be." He leaned down and kissed her.

"Me too," she told him. "But I wish it could have been different. We were so close. . . ." She let out a long sigh. "We wasted so much time when we should have just come back and taken the Book from Jack here and now. So many people got hurt because of it."

"There's still time to change that," he told her. "We'll figure it out soon enough, but right now it's time to pay Jack a visit."

Jianyu appeared suddenly. "He is inside, just as we expected. Viola is waiting nearby, close to the building, to make sure he cannot leave."

"It's time," Esta said, sounding suddenly nervous. Her breath hung in a cloud around her.

"This is going to work," Harte told her, slipping his hand into hers. "We have everything we need. Jianyu will get us in, Viola will slow Jack down, and before he even knows what's happening, we'll have him trapped with the sigils. Once we take care of Thoth, we'll worry about the Book and the artifacts with one less enemy at our throats."

"But what if I can't destroy Thoth?" she asked. "It was challenging enough to take care of a piece of silk, but that bit of counterfeit magic was nothing compared to what Thoth has been able to accumulate over the centuries."

"You can do this," Harte told her. "And this time, Thoth won't be able to get away."

Esta nodded, but she wasn't wearing her usual brash confidence, so he drew her close again and gave her the kind of kiss that told her everything he felt. *You can do this. We can do this. It will be okay, because I believe in you.*

"You *can* do this," he told her, in case she hadn't received the message, and then kissed her once more.

"If the two of you are finished?" Jianyu looked vaguely uncomfortable to be witnessing their show of affection.

LISA MAXWELL

Harte gave his old friend a grin. "I don't think I'll ever be finished with that particular activity, but we're ready enough."

Esta smacked him softly, but he could see the tension had eased from her a little. A small, secret smile had replaced the worry that had been bracketing her mouth.

They took Jianyu's hands, and Harte felt the world wobble, as it had on the bridge that day so many months ago, when Jianyu had saved him from the death he'd originally planned for himself. Around them, the city shivered and breathed, and for once, the familiarity of it felt like a comfort. He knew this city. He'd mastered it once, and he would reclaim it.

They were nearly there when Viola came flying out of the darkness. "He's leaving," she said, pointing toward the narrow alleyway between the warehouses.

Harte could just make out the silhouette of a man running in the opposite direction.

"I couldn't stop him," Viola told them. "There's something blocking my magic. I can't even hear his blood."

"Thoth," Esta told her, as they saw Jack turn toward the water.

The four of them took off after him, but as they rounded the corner, Jack was already getting into a boat. Harte knew they'd never be able to reach him if he was able to pull away from the shore.

Esta must have had the same thought, because they'd barely taken another step when the world went silent around them. After grabbing Harte's hand, she reached for Jianyu's as well and brought him into the circle of her affinity. Together, they ran toward the water's edge and the waiting boat, but with their hands joined they couldn't go half as quickly as any one of them might have alone.

They were nearly to the boat when Jack emerged from the small pilot's house and tossed off the lines attaching the craft to the dock.

Not only Jack, Harte thought. *Thoth.*

The Brink's icy power was a cold warning the closer they came to the dock, but they pushed through, desperate to reach the boat and Jack.

But it was too late. Jack was already moving away from the dock, steering the craft out into the water, away from the shoreline.

They couldn't let him escape, not when he was so determined to destroy the Brink. Esta knew what it would mean if he succeeded. She'd seen that future as she fell through the years, and she could not allow that to happen.

Esta started to leap for the boat, but Harte held tight to her.

"You can't," he told her. "Not with the Brink."

Jack stood on the back of the craft, his eyes as black as the night itself, watching them. As the boat drifted silently out into the East River, toward the Brink and away from any chance of catching him, Harte heard a laugh carrying across the water to him. Not Jack's, but someone far more ancient and powerful.

THE GAME OF FATE

The Safe House

Esta paced in front of the windows, occasionally glancing out to the snow-covered street outside Dolph's safe house. She could tell it was beginning to annoy her friends, who must have felt every bit as frustrated and disappointed as she did, but she needed to move. She should've been out there, doing *something*.

But what could she do? Jack was gone, beyond the Brink. And he'd taken the Book and any sign of his machine with him. All they could do was wait for word from Abel and his friends, who had left the city in an attempt to track Jack. But none of them were good at waiting.

She still couldn't quite believe that she was there, back in the past. She couldn't believe that everything had gone so very wrong. And it had happened so quickly.

Back in the future, before they had talked with Dakari and before the Guards' attack had thrown everything off, Esta had felt certain they could succeed. They'd had the Book and the stones, and because of that, they had Seshat's power to control. But in a matter of seconds, she'd managed to screw everything up. If she could have just held on a little tighter as they slipped through time, maybe they would have had longer to plan. If she had only been a little stronger, maybe things would be different. Maybe even without the Book, they could have changed more.

By arriving so late in the year, they'd missed their opportunity to stop any of the events that happened after they'd handed Jack the Book months before. The Order's gala, the heist at the Flatiron Building, even the attack on Ruby's wedding—those events couldn't be changed now, unless she was willing to change the lives of the people she cared about.

Esta couldn't do that—*wouldn't* do that—especially not now that she'd met Ruby and Cela. Not once she'd understood the bonds that her friends had formed with those women because of what they'd been through together while she and Harte were gone. She couldn't take that from them, especially when there wasn't any guarantee that going back farther would make anything better. Because even if they went back, they still wouldn't have the Book or the artifacts.

The only real choice was to stay, to go forward from this point and fight with all they had. But while they all understood that their failure to catch Jack before he slipped away meant that they may not have another chance to stop him until the Conclave, Esta and Harte more than the others knew the additional dangers that event held.

"Would you sit down already?" Viola barked with a frustrated huff. "Back and forth all day—you've been wearing a hole in the floor, and I can't watch you no more. It's driving me mad."

Esta's feet came to a stop as she realized everyone was looking at her. "I'm sorry," she told them, feeling suddenly awkward. "I just—I don't know what to do next, and I've never been good at waiting."

"Come and sit," Jianyu said gently. "We all feel the same."

Harte slid the chair next to him back from the table, and she took it, grateful for his presence. At least she still had him. At least they had this time together.

Cela came in a few minutes later, brushing the snow from where it had settled in the curls of her dark hair as she took off her heavy coat and hat and set them aside.

"Any news?" Esta asked, even though she knew Cela would have led with the information if there had been any.

She shook her head. "Abel's got people on almost every line running out from New Jersey. If Jack shows up, we'll know. But so far there hasn't been any sign of him."

"He's staying close," Harte said, his voice heavy with the same regret they were all feeling. "He's not going to run. He's just finalizing his plans."

"I can't believe we let him go," Viola said, temper lashing her words. "I should have killed him when we first found him, before he had the chance to run. That should have been the plan." She paused then, her expression heavy with regret. "But I couldn't even stop him from running."

"Because he's more than Jack," Esta told her. "He's been able to slip past my magic as well."

"Jack will return," Jianyu assured them. "He was too determined to take power from the Order, too certain of his victory to turn away from it. Now we must put aside our regrets and begin to plan. Jack will attack the Conclave and attempt to destroy the Brink. We must find a way to stop him there."

But at the mention of the Conclave, the memory of Nibsy's diary sent a bolt of fear through Esta. *If they stand with you, they're sure to die. You've seen their future. You know their fate.*

She couldn't allow that to happen. She couldn't allow them to die there. But she'd seen that vision of what a future without the Brink could be. She'd felt the emptiness, the hollow nothingness of a world unmade, and she could not allow that to happen. Still . . .

"The Conclave is too dangerous," Esta said. "There has to be some other way, some option we haven't considered."

"What other option is there?" Jianyu asked. "Jack told me of his plans. We cannot allow the Brink to fall. What is it that you haven't told us?"

Esta looked at Harte, who knew the truth, but he only shook his head.

"We have to tell them," she said.

"Tell us what?" Viola asked.

"Esta, nothing good can come from this," Harte warned.

"We tried to avoid it, but we're here now. They have a right to know." She turned to her friends, who were watching her with barely leashed frustration, and she told them about Nibsy's diary, about what it had shown. "If we try to stop Jack at the Conclave, there's a good chance you'll die."

"You kept this from us?" Jianyu asked Harte.

"Because I didn't believe it." Harte closed his eyes as though gathering strength. "I *don't* believe it."

"Did you not read it with your own eyes?" Jianyu pressed.

"The diary also said that I'll end up killing Esta," Harte said, his voice like a lash. Everyone went silent at the outburst.

"This is true?" Viola asked.

"Yes," Esta told her.

At the same time Harte said, "No." He gave her a sharp look. "I refuse to let some dumb book that belonged to Nibsy Lorcan determine my fate."

Esta tried to slip her hand into his. "It's okay, Harte."

"Nothing about this is okay," he said. He was practically vibrating.

"Where is the diary now?" Ruby asked.

"We left it," Esta said, glancing at Harte. "We gave it to a friend."

"You *left* it?" Cela asked. "It told the future, and you didn't think to bring it?"

Viola threw up her arms. "Why would you do something so stupid?"

"*I* left it," Harte told them. "Esta didn't have anything to do with it, and I didn't give her a choice."

Esta looked at Harte and wondered for the hundredth time what he'd done. He still wouldn't tell her why he'd left the diary with Dakari. She knew it had something to do with Nibsy, but whatever Harte's reason, it apparently hadn't worked.

"The diary does not matter," Jianyu said finally. "Whatever it might have shown us does not signify in our decisions."

"How can you say that?" Cela demanded. "If it says you're going to die, of *course* it signifies."

"Jack *must* be stopped," Jianyu said, as though the point were as simple as that. "Should he bring down the Brink, it will mean the end of everything." He gave a small shrug. "We are the only ones who know of his plans, and so we must be the ones who stand in his way."

"I can't ask you to do that," Esta said. "I can't ask you to walk into that danger knowing that it likely won't work, knowing that you probably won't walk away."

"You are not asking it of us," Jianyu told her. "I nearly died under Jack Grew's hand. I know what he is capable of, and I will choose my own path. No matter what the consequences for my life may be."

"Jianyu is right," Viola said. "Whatever the diary might have said, Jack cannot be allowed to create this future you described where the old magic is hunted. He cannot be allowed to keep the Book."

"What we read weeks ago doesn't mean anything," Harte told them. "The Conclave is still two weeks away. We still have time to learn more. We still have time to improve our chances."

"I might be able to help with that," Ruby said. The entire table of people turned to her, waiting.

"What do you mean?" Esta asked.

"My family has been tangled up in the Order's business for years," she explained. "Do you know how many secrets my uncle and my sisters' husbands have let slip in front of me? They don't even bother to hold back, probably because they assume women are too vapid to pay attention, much less understand. If I go back after escaping from the terrible Mageus who attacked my wedding, they're likely to trust me. I could get the information you need."

"Assolutamente *no*," Viola told her. "It's too dangerous. I won't allow it."

Ruby gave her a pitying smile. "It's better for our future if you understand now that there's very little you can do to stop me when I put my mind to something."

"Please," Viola begged. "Don't ask me to stand by while you walk into that sort of danger."

Ruby stepped toward Viola and took her hand. "I can do this—I'm certain of it. It won't even be an act to play the distraught widow. They won't suspect."

"Jack might," Viola argued. "He's not so stupid as everyone thinks."

"He'd have to come back to the city to find out," Esta pointed out. "And if he returns before the Conclave, even better. We can take care of him then."

"Jack Grew killed Theo. He destroyed one of the kindest souls I've ever known. He took my best friend from me." Ruby's eyes were glassy with tears, but her voice was filled with steel. "I will do anything—risk *anything*—to make him pay for that."

"We could use her help, Viola," Esta said, earning herself a dangerous look from the assassin. But she ignored it because she understood her friend's fear. In Viola's position, she'd likely do the same. "If we have more information, we're less likely to run into trouble. Maybe we can avoid the fate that was written in those pages."

"She has a point," Cela said. "Ruby could go places and get information that none of the rest of us could even dream of getting close to."

"I'll be okay, Vee," Ruby said. "I can handle myself. You *know* that."

"Fine," Viola said eventually. "But I don't like this one bit."

"None of us do," Jianyu said, laying his hand on Viola's arm. "But the die has been cast, and the game has already begun. We have no choice but to play the positions we hold on the board." He turned to Esta. "Whatever that diary might have said, whatever our fate, we will remain beside you and do what we must. Not because you ask it of us. But because we choose it for ourselves."

Esta looked at the faces of the people sitting around the table—people who had once been strangers and now had become her dearest friends. Viola and Jianyu, Cela, and now Ruby as well. And Harte. *Always Harte.*

They were all still there, standing next to her and ready to face any danger. Unquestioning. Loyal.

For her entire life, Esta had wanted this. Friends. *Family*. People who would stand by her without question. Now they were here. Hers for the claiming. Without question or payment. She didn't deserve any of them.

But maybe one day she would.

INTO THE LION'S DEN

Madison Square Park

"How do I look?" Ruby asked, trying to ignore the way her stomach was flipping with nerves. It was one thing to propose going back to spy on the Order in theory, but now that she was once again wearing her stained wedding gown, things had grown much, much more real. She hadn't considered what it would be like to wear it, but once she slipped the dress on, she could only think of Theo. She hoped he was with her as she climbed into the carriage that would take her back to her own world and her old life—because she'd never really lived in that world without Theo there by her side.

"You know how you look," Viola told her. She was trying not to show her fear, and her worry came out as temper instead.

"That bad?" Ruby joked, earning her another sharp look from Viola that made her want to smile and cry all at once.

"What do you want me to say?" Viola asked, sounding suddenly tired. But she turned to Ruby, let her eyes drift over her face, her body, and her gown. "You look like you always look. Beautiful. You're a vision, even with the torn satin and the dirt on your hem. Like an angel come down in the night."

She felt her skin go warm at Viola's appraisal. "I guess that's a decent enough compliment for a start," Ruby told her, trying to keep their banter from turning too serious.

Viola must have noticed the nervous tremor in Ruby's voice, because her expression softened. "You come back alive and unharmed, and I'll praise your beauty and fashion until you can't stand it no more." She squeezed Ruby's hand.

"I'll come back just fine," Ruby promised. "I'm not afraid of Jack or the Order—any of them."

"You should be," Viola said. Then she shook her head. "Don't underestimate them, cara."

"I know what they're capable of," Ruby told her. "I won't let my guard down. I can do this."

"I know you can," Viola agreed. "But that don't mean I have to like it. If anything happens, I won't know. I won't be able to help you."

"Nothing is going to happen," Ruby reassured her. "Everything is going to be fine."

"But Jack, he knows—"

"For Jack to say anything against me, he's going to have to return to the city first. *Then* he's going to have to admit that he lied the day Theo died," she reminded Viola. "He's not going to do that. He has too much riding on his attempt to be some kind of hero."

The wagon stopped at the dark edge of Madison Park. "This is it," Ruby said. "I'll come to the park as soon as I can get away, just like we planned. Wait for me by the fountain. If I'm not there by two, I'm not coming. But please, don't come for me, and don't worry. I'll be fine. I'll see you as soon as I can get away."

"Two days," Viola demanded. "No more."

She couldn't stop her mouth from curving at Viola's determined insistence. "I thought you wanted me to be safe?"

"I want you here, with me," Viola told her. "Where I can kill anyone who thinks to hurt you."

"As soon as I can get away without drawing suspicion, I'll come. I *promise.*" She leaned forward and kissed Viola, sighing a little as Viola responded without hesitation, lifting her hands to frame Ruby's face and gently deepening the kiss.

Ruby could have stayed there in that dark, dirty little wagon forever as long as Viola's mouth was pressed against hers. With their lips touching and their breath intermingled, she could almost forget what lay ahead. The danger she was placing herself in and the importance of the information she needed to get fell away. There was only Viola. Only *now*. In that impossible moment, the Order didn't matter, and neither did the city beyond.

She didn't notice at first when the carriage rattled to a stop, but Viola drew back. Her violet eyes glowed with a need that Ruby felt too keenly. One day, they would have hours to explore each other, hours to ignore the world. But to have those hours—to imagine that future together—they had to stop Jack. And to stop Jack, they needed information that only Ruby could attain.

Then the wagon's back gate opened, and Jianyu was there, waiting. It was time.

He helped Ruby down from the back of the wagon's bed, and then she felt the world go a little wobbly as he wrapped her in magic. It felt a bit like looking through old-fashioned glass.

"Take care of her," Viola demanded, but her eyes searched the darkness, and Ruby understood that she could not see them any longer.

She stepped forward for one last kiss, but Jianyu held her back.

"Come," he whispered.

Reluctantly, Ruby complied. With her arm tucked through Jianyu's, they set out through the darkened park hidden by his affinity. She did not allow herself to look back even once—she couldn't. If she turned back, she might lose her nerve or change her mind. So she walked onward, her head high, promising herself that she would do everything she could to create a future for them. A future where the Order and the Brink and Jack Grew had no power.

And if she could make Jack suffer for what he did to Theo? *All the better.*

It wasn't long before they were standing beneath the soaring blade of the Fuller Building—the Flatiron, as the city had taken to calling it for its strange shape.

"You do not have to do this," Jianyu said when Ruby paused, looking up at the building. "If you are unsure—"

"No," Ruby said. "I *need* to do this. I'll be fine."

"Do not underestimate the danger," he warned.

She gave him a weak smile. "I won't, but I've been pretending for these fools my whole life, and they've never suspected. What's another few days?"

She released Jianyu's arm and stepped out of the safety of his magic. When she turned back, she couldn't see him any longer, but she knew he was there. She could sense him waiting. Watching.

Her dress was a puddle of silk and taffeta chiffon, but suddenly it felt like armor. She'd worn this gown for Theo, and she felt him now by her side. Terrified though she might be, Ruby would do this in his memory. She would get the information they needed to destroy the man who had killed her dearest friend. And then she would help bring the entire Order to their knees.

Looking up, she gathered her courage beneath the star-swept night, and then, with a blood-curdling scream, she shoved her way into the building.

"Help!" she cried, bursting through the doors. "Someone, please help me!" And then she collapsed into a sobbing heap on the floor.

NEWS FROM THE CITY

New Jersey

T he warehouse space he'd rented in New Jersey was not much warmer than the chill winter air outside, but though Jack Grew was in nothing more than shirtsleeves, he didn't feel the cold. Not even now, in the dead of night. How could the cold touch him when there was a fire burning within him and a voice urging him onward and onward?

His machine was nearly done, and it was *magnificent*. The gleaming steel of the curved arms glinted in the light of the lamps. He'd redesigned it for his new purposes, and sometimes the sheer magnificence of what he'd created left him breathless.

Jack hadn't succeeded in finding a maggot to power a new stone. It was his singular regret. But he had the Pharaoh's Heart, and if he failed to locate a maggot before the Conclave arrived, it would serve his purposes well enough. It was worth the risk of losing the stone to claim his new future.

A knock sounded at the door on the far side of the warehouse. That would be Aaron, he thought, wiping the grime from his hands and putting on his jacket, where the Book was tucked safely into the hidden pocket against his chest. *Right on time.*

The coachman looked half-frozen by the time Jack opened the door and let him in. While the sniveling little man shivered, Jack barely felt the burst of winter that followed in with him.

It hadn't taken much—a few extra dollars thrown his way and the help of a fairly simple spell—to ensure Aaron's loyalty. With the coachman's position in his mother's house, he traveled between the Grews and the various Morgans often enough to be useful. Servants knew more about their employers than anyone ever wanted to think about, and more, they talked to one another behind closed doors. Aaron had been more than helpful with making Jack privy to those conversations.

"What news do you have for me?" he asked, securing the door behind them.

"David Francis has been giving the Inner Circle fits," Aaron said, rubbing his hands together to warm himself.

"From the Society?" Jack asked.

Aaron nodded. "Word is that the other Brotherhoods are coming for blood. The Inner Circle is nervous. They're not sure that the Conclave will be enough to maintain their power."

"Did you get the plans yet?" Jack asked.

Aaron took a paper-wrapped package from within his coat. "One of the maids at the Vanderbilts knows a girl who works for the High Princept at the Flatiron. One of those harem girls they keep for their ceremony. She managed to get me these." He started to offer the parcel, then withdrew it before Jack could take it. "She's risking a whole lot by taking these, though. She's going to expect something in return."

Glowering, Jack turned to his things and took a handful of bills from his wallet. "Will this suffice?" He tossed them on the table for Aaron, whose eyes lit at the sight.

"That should do," the coachman said, greed coloring his features. "At least to start." He tossed the parcel on the table and took up the pile of money, counting it before he tucked it into his jacket. "It should all be there, the plans for the Garden and the Conclave. They're doing something with the electric grid, too. Wiring it up for some kind of big exhibition."

Jack left the parcel where it was. There would be time enough to go through its contents later. "Anything else?"

"Your mother is still beside herself because you ran off again," he said. "And your uncle keeps showing up to the house demanding that she tell him where you went. Oh . . . and one other thing. The Reynolds girl, they found her."

Jack's instincts prickled. "They found Ruby?"

Aaron blew into his hands. "Yeah. She came running right to the Order. Said she managed to escape from her kidnappers."

"Has she said anything about what happened to her?" Jack asked.

"Not much," Aaron told him with a shrug. "Says she doesn't remember anything. Whoever took her must have drugged her up pretty bad. But she'll tell anyone who listens that it wasn't maggots that did it. Which makes sense, I guess. If it were maggots that took her, how would she have gotten away?"

"How indeed," Jack said, considering this new piece of information.

He ushered Aaron out and bolted the door behind him again before turning to the information the coachman had delivered. But he had trouble concentrating on the plans, detailed and revealing though they were. He hadn't expected Ruby to return. If she had any brains in that pretty head, she would have run far, far away from him.

But if she was back and telling tales about her experience, she was up to something. It meant his plans would have to change. He'd intended to arrive back in the city the day of the Conclave, early enough to make his preparations but not so early as to get caught up in the Order's drama or his family's expectations. Or to put himself at risk of being found by Darrigan and his band of maggot filth. Now he'd have to return sooner. Because he could not allow Ruby Reynolds to interfere. He was so close to victory. He would not let some stupid girl get in the way of his plans.

MORNING'S LIGHT

The Safe House

Harte woke early in the morning and reached for Esta only to find her side of the bed cold. It was still dark, long before dawn. Pushing himself upright, he rubbed his eyes and tried to wake himself. Moonlight lit the window, but the room was empty.

He wrapped a blanket around his shoulders to ward off the chill in the air and padded barefoot down the hall, knowing already where he'd find her. She hadn't been sleeping well the last few nights, and this wasn't the first night he'd awoken to find her gone.

She was where he expected, sleeping on a well-worn couch in the front parlor. It reminded him of the time he'd returned home to find her in his apartment, courtesy of Dolph. How many weeks ago had that been? He wasn't sure any longer. He'd been through years and years, back and forth through time, and the experience of it had left him turned inside out and unmoored. But the sight of Esta, sleeping there in the moonlight, settled him. Terrified him.

The Conclave was coming, and with it, the threat of the future he'd read in Nibsy's diary. It was a future he'd do damn near anything to prevent.

Esta shivered in her sleep and curled into herself more tightly.

With a sigh, Harte took the blanket from his shoulders and wrapped her in it before lifting her gently. She didn't wake as he carried her back to the room they shared or when he settled her into bed. She only sighed and moved her body closer to his warmth when he climbed in with her.

But he didn't sleep any more that night. He couldn't stop thinking about what might happen if they couldn't stop Jack before the Conclave. He couldn't stop regretting his decision to give Dakari the diary. With it, at least they might have known what was coming. For the rest of the night, he lay awake, watching Esta's fitful sleep and listening to the building settle and sigh.

It was a strange place, perhaps because of how it was bespelled or perhaps in spite of it. Dolph's building. Another secret he'd kept. Harte had to admit he was grateful, even if the building felt alive sometimes. As though the walls themselves were listening to their conversations.

He must have finally drifted off to sleep sometime around dawn. When he finally woke, the slant of the winter sun told him it was later in the morning than he usually slept. Esta was still in the bed next to him, but she was sitting up and reading the stack of Nibsy's papers that had survived their trip back into the past. She set them aside when she saw he was stirring.

"Good morning," she said, snuggling into him.

"What time is it?" he asked, maneuvering her closer, so she was tucked into his side, their bodies fitting perfectly together.

"Around ten." She kissed his neck, nuzzling into the tender skin just beneath his ear. He felt her smile against his skin. "I don't remember coming back to bed. Again. Thank you." She gave him another soft kiss that shot a bolt of heat straight through him.

He pulled her over him and kissed her until they were both lost.

They had so little time left. The Conclave was coming, and with it the possibility of fate.

"Stop thinking," she murmured against his mouth. Then she deepened the kiss and slid her hand down his body until he could not think at all.

Later, they curled together skin against skin, warm beneath the covers, and watched the light change in the room. The minutes ticked by, one by one, but even the peace of being there with her was not enough to make him forget what lay ahead.

"I can't lose you," he told her.

Esta let out a deep sigh and turned to him. "You're not going to lose me, Harte."

But he didn't believe that could be true. He'd ruined everything he'd ever loved—his mother, his brother. He couldn't let that happen to Esta, too.

When he didn't immediately respond, she took his face in her hands. "You aren't going to lose me. I don't care what that diary said. You aren't going to hurt me."

"I know." He looked into her whiskey-colored eyes and saw the determination there, the fierceness that he'd fallen for almost at once. "I'd die before I'd do anything to hurt you."

"You aren't going to die, either."

He couldn't stop himself from smiling softly at her determination. She spoke as though she could take fate and destiny in her hands and bend it to her will. But then, she was Esta. Maybe she could.

"I've been thinking," she told him.

"A dangerous proposition to be sure."

She smacked him playfully, but then the amusement drained. "We have to consider Nibsy."

"He's the last thing I want to think about right now," he told her, brushing his lips over the tender skin of her neck. He's the last thing Harte wanted to deal with *period*.

"Harte, be serious," she said, trying to pull away. When he didn't let her go, she let out a not-unsatisfied sigh and allowed him to work his way along her neck, trailing his lips against her jaw and then finally kissing her.

She was breathless and flushed again by the time she managed to unentangle herself. "Seriously, Harte."

"I don't want to think about Nibsy," he repeated.

"But we have to," she said. This time he let her go, because he knew she was right. They were only delaying the inevitable, and it wasn't going to help anyone to ignore the fact that Nibsy Lorcan was likely already three steps ahead of them. "He might have the diary here, in this time. If he does, he's going to be able to predict what we do. We need to do everything we can to stop him."

What if there's no way to stop him?

Harte pushed the thought aside. Just because his idea hadn't worked didn't mean that another couldn't. "What do you have in mind?" he asked.

"We should get the others," she told him. She was already sitting up, already getting out of the bed.

He rolled on his side and watched her reach for her clothes. He let his eyes take in every inch of her, memorizing the curve of her back. The golden expanse of her skin. He wanted to touch her again. "Do we have to?"

She smiled back at him. "We do."

"But maybe it could wait." He was trying for playful, but the words had come out strained.

Esta's smile faltered. "I don't think it can."

He rolled onto his back and stared up at the ceiling. There was a crack in the plaster that traversed the entire room, dark against the dingy white of the paint. "The Conclave is coming too soon," he told her. "I feel like we have so little time left."

The bed dipped next to him, and Esta was there. She'd put on a large sweater, but her legs were bare. "We're going to have time, Harte. I have to believe that."

He tried to give her a sure smile, but he couldn't quite make his mouth curve. "If anyone can steal it for us—"

"I will," she promised. "Now get dressed. We have work to do."

AN ARRIVAL

Esta threw on her clothes quickly and left Harte still lying in bed because she knew if she didn't keep moving, she'd be back there with him. As much as she wanted to laze the day away, the truth of the matter was that they *were* running out of time. It had been days since Ruby had gone back to be their spy, and they hadn't heard anything. Every day Viola went to the park to wait for her, and every day she'd been disappointed.

There was still no sign of Jack, despite Abel's best efforts, and there had been no further word from Nibsy.

It didn't feel right, the silence from the Bowery. Esta couldn't believe that Nibsy had simply let them walk away with Morgan's papers. If he wasn't coming after them, he must have a reason, and whatever that reason was, it was likely linked to the future they'd seen in his diary.

That was, in large part, what had been keeping her awake at night. Nibsy's silence—his inaction—was like a splinter festering beneath her skin. But last night she'd had an idea.

She and Harte had taken one of the empty rooms on the fourth floor, away from the people who'd already made the safe house into their home, and she took her time descending to the floor below, thinking through the ideas she'd come up with in the dead of night.

At the landing of the third floor, she hesitated. In the distance, she could hear the soft murmur of voices, but there in the stairwell, it was quiet. It seemed impossible that Dolph had somehow managed this, an entire building that no one knew existed. It was another secret about her father discovered too late. Another piece of the puzzle that might have been her life if things had gone differently.

She wondered if Leena had known about this place. Maybe she and Dolph had come here before Esta was born. Had her parents spent time in these rooms together, planning their future or helping those in the city that needed to be hidden? Or had this been a place Dolph had kept from Leena, just as he'd hidden his intentions and plan to use her magic to fuel the cane?

What a lonely existence that must have been. So many secrets and so many lies. He'd been so afraid to trust that he'd left himself isolated. Maybe if he hadn't, Nibsy wouldn't have been able to strike.

Esta forced herself to push those thoughts aside. That part of the past was a page that could not be unwritten. Leena was gone, dead long before Esta had arrived in the past—far beyond where she could go and impossible to save. Dolph was gone too. Not even Viola could bring people back from the dead. It was time to focus on the future and on what could be done to try to change it.

The building was bustling when she finally made her way to the large communal area in the back of the third floor, where everyone usually gathered. Viola and Jianyu were already there. Cela was too, along with some of the other occupants who had warmed to them.

Not everyone had. Some still held suspicions about Jianyu and Viola, because of their skin or their gender, or because of the lies Nibsy had spread. But that morning the gathering room seemed like a friendly place. The mood was light, and the sun was shining in through the opened drapes.

"You slept awful late this morning," Cela said with a knowing grin. She glanced at Esta as she sipped from her mug. "Long night?"

Esta ignored the heat in her cheeks and poured herself some coffee. "I refuse to dignify that question with an answer."

Viola laughed knowingly. "I think you just did."

Cela lifted her mug in a salute, and Viola returned the gesture. Jianyu pretended he wasn't listening.

"Where's Darrigan this fine morning?" Cela asked, still smiling. "Too worn out to join us for breakfast . . . or is it lunch?"

"Darrigan is right here," Harte said from the doorway. "And he's fine this morning, thank you very much."

"You always did have such a high opinion of yourself, Harte," Cela murmured into her cup. But her eyes were smiling when she glanced at Esta. "But is it well founded, I wonder?"

Esta's cheeks were burning, and as much as she was enjoying the gentle ribbing—the camaraderie and friendship of these women—she had little experience with either and had no idea what to do with it.

"You'd think that the lot of you would have more to do than sit around and gossip like a bunch of chickens," he muttered. But he came up behind Esta and, wrapping her in his arms, nuzzled into her neck. "I told you we should have stayed in bed." He kissed her softly before letting her go.

Esta couldn't exactly argue. The heat of his mouth on her sensitive skin brought with it memories of his mouth on other places, and she had to focus much harder than anyone should just to slice herself a piece of the brown bread Viola had baked earlier. She took her time and only turned back to the room after she'd composed herself.

But from the knowing looks on the other women's faces, she'd failed miserably.

"Esta had something she wanted to discuss," Harte told them, thankfully drawing the attention away from her. "Something to do with Nibsy."

Grateful for the opening, Esta brought her breakfast over to the table. "I've been thinking—"

"Is that what they're calling it these days?" Viola asked, her mouth twitching.

It was only Jianyu's steady, encouraging expression that let Esta shake off the teasing and get to her point.

"I think it's a bad sign that Nibsy hasn't come after us yet," she told them. "He's not the type that just lets someone beat him."

"We have been here," Jianyu reminded her. "Hidden by the magic of this place."

"Sure," she agreed. "But we've been out there, too. There's no sign that he's even looking for us."

"Maybe he already knows where we are," Viola told her. "He has Logan. He's been able to find us before, even when we thought we were well hidden."

"That's one possibility," Esta admitted. "But I worry he's not looking because he already knows where we'll end up. If he has the diary—his version of it—it's likely he knows we'll go to the Conclave. He might simply be waiting to make his move there. Especially if he's being guided by the messages from his future self."

Silence descended as they all considered this.

"It feels likely," Jianyu agreed. "But it changes little. Regardless of the threat Nibsy poses, the Conclave is where Jack will try to take power, and we must be there to stand in his way."

"I know," Esta said. "But we should do everything in our power to make it harder for Nibsy to do that."

"What are you thinking?" Harte asked.

"I'm thinking that we have to start with the cane," she told them. "If we could use the sigils to destroy Tom Lee's bracelet, we can do the same with Dolph's cane. We can't chance it falling back into Nibsy's possession."

"You would unmake it," Jianyu said, considering the proposal.

Esta nodded. "And once it's been destroyed, we make sure that people know. We make sure that the Devil's Own understands that they're free."

"You'd take his army," Viola said approvingly.

"No," she told them. "We'd *free* them."

"They may not want to be freed," Jianyu said finally.

Esta acknowledged that he had a point. "But at least they'd have the choice."

Golde had stepped into the room. "I'm sorry to interrupt, but there's someone outside. I think it's the boy who was hanging around with Lorcan. He's looking up at the building like he knows that we're here."

Everyone around the table went still, and she knew what they were likely thinking. Maybe she'd spoken too soon about Nibsy coming for them.

"Is he with anyone?" Esta asked.

The woman shook her head. "He's just standing there alone. But he shouldn't be. He's making the others nervous."

Esta went to the window that looked over the front of the building and peered down. "It's Logan," she said, then turned back to the others. "I'll go out and talk to him."

"Not alone you won't," Harte said.

Viola was already standing as well. "I'm coming, too."

PLAYING THE ANGLES

It took real effort for Logan Sullivan to stay where he was, standing in the drifting snow in front of the building. Something about the place made him want to turn and walk away, and the longer he stood there, the more painfully desperate that urge became. There was no chance of him going up to the front door, even though he wanted to. Even though he knew Esta was inside. Even staying there on the sidewalk was a struggle.

He'd been searching the city for days to find the Book, just like he'd been commanded, but every day that he couldn't find it was another day closer to James finally losing his patience. Logan couldn't risk that. Since he'd let Esta and Darrigan slip away that day the Strega got trashed, James had been nothing but fury. He had a group of new boys who were still standing by him—big, rough, bruising types who took the mark happily and displayed it where it could be seen. Guys like Murphy, whose cold eyes gave Logan the creeps.

James had made it well known that anyone who'd abandoned the Strega the day of the attack was no longer welcome. If they couldn't stand and fight for the Devil's Own, they were on their own, mark or no mark, without protection from the Hip Sings or the Five Pointers. But Logan had been around enough meetings that he knew the truth. It wasn't only that James would no longer protect the people who'd left that day. He was using the deserters to shore up his alliances by handing over their names and locations. Between the new boys and his allies, he'd declared open season. And Logan knew it was only a matter of time before he was next.

He wasn't going to let that happen.

Maybe he hadn't found any trace of the Book within the city's borders, but could sense Ishtar's Key, and that was enough to keep his feet bolted to the sidewalk, no matter how unpleasant the sensation of staying was. He was going to talk to Esta. He was going to demand that she take him back. If he just waited long enough, he knew she'd be forced to appear.

He wasn't wrong. It took longer than he'd expected, but finally the front door of the building opened, and Esta came out, alive and in the flesh. Following close behind her was Darrigan. Viola was with them as well, looking more alive than Logan had expected her to be considering that he'd watched James nearly tear her to pieces with that cane of his. When Darrigan had carried her out of the Strega, Logan had assumed she was a goner. Especially considering the lack of medical care available in this godforsaken time.

But he didn't want to think about that. He'd probably never get over the sight of her naked back or the way her affinity had bubbled up in blood and fire straight from within her skin. He didn't want to remember, and he'd resisted taking the mark himself because he didn't want to be next.

"Esta," he said. "Thank god I found you."

She was frowning at him. "What are you doing here, Logan?" Her eyes were sharp, narrowed in suspicion.

"Look, I'm sorry about the other day," he told her. It was almost the truth.

"Are you?" she asked, her voice flat and angry. "You nearly got us killed."

He ran a nervous hand through his hair and started having second thoughts about this plan. Or maybe they were third thoughts, since he'd already second-guessed himself a few times.

"Look, I didn't mean to be so difficult back at the Strega," he told her. "I wasn't thinking straight, you know? You surprised me."

"Enough with the bullshit, Logan," she said. "I know you meant everything you said back there. You would have stopped us from leaving if it hadn't been for Viola, so cut to the chase. Why are you really here, Logan? I've already told you I can't take you back."

He had the sudden insight that this wasn't *his* Esta. She might have looked like the girl he'd practically grown up with, but there was something fundamentally different about her now. It felt like he didn't know her, like maybe he had never really known her.

"Well?" She crossed her arms over her chest.

"I'm here because I'm done with James," Logan told her. "He's not the guy we knew."

"He is," Esta disagreed. "He's *exactly* the man we knew. We just never saw it because we didn't want to."

She wasn't exactly wrong. This younger version of Professor Lachlan at first had seemed like a completely different person, but the longer Logan had been with him at the Strega, the more he'd seen the seeds of the man their Professor would become.

"Look, the bottom line is that I can't stay there anymore, Esta," Logan told her. "He's going after anyone he thinks isn't completely loyal. Or he's sending his allies after them. And the thing is, he gave me one job—to find the Book—and I already know it's impossible. You don't have it."

Viola had a knife in her hand, and she lifted it in his direction. "I should have killed you then before you could cause us any more problems," she told him.

"Wait, Viola," Esta said, staying the Italian girl with a silent look. Then she turned back to Logan, her expression as implacable and unreadable as ever. "You're sure I don't have it?"

"I don't sense it, and I've known you long enough to know you wouldn't leave it somewhere. You'd keep it on you so you could protect it."

Esta glanced at Darrigan, and some indecipherable conversation happened silently between them.

"You still haven't told us what you want," Esta said, turning back to him.

"I can't go back to the Strega without the Book," he told her. "If I walk in there and tell James you don't have it, that it's nowhere? I'm dead. I need to get out of here. You have to help me."

"I can't," she said, frowning.

"I know you, Esta," he said, leaning into his plea now. "You can snap me back in an instant. It wouldn't be anything for you."

"You don't understand, Logan." Her expression was intractable. "There's nothing to 'snap' back to. The life you led, the world you knew? You changed all of that when you dragged me back here at gunpoint and handed Nibsy the diary."

"You know about that?" he asked.

"I didn't for sure," she admitted. "But I do now."

"Please," he begged. "I'll do anything you want."

Esta considered his plea for long enough that he started to get nervous. She wouldn't really say no to him, would she? No one ever really said no to him.

"There's only one thing you can help us with," she told him.

"Anything," he promised.

"Get us the diary," she said. "You do that, and I'll take you back after the Conclave."

"That's impossible," he told them. "He never puts it down."

"That's the deal," Darrigan told him.

"Even if I could get it without getting myself killed, it's not enough. I can't just wait around for you to finish playing with fate. If I get the diary, you take me back. *Immediately*."

"I can't," Esta said. "There's too much at stake. It's after the Conclave or not at all."

Logan felt like tearing out his own hair. "That's more than a week away. Do you know what he could do to me in that time?"

"You'd have a place here," Esta said. "We'd keep you safe."

"No," Logan said. "It has to be now."

"You're not listening, Logan." Esta looked like she was about to lose her temper. "There is no *back* if we don't stop Jack from attacking the Conclave. If he does, he could bring down the Brink. But if we stop him, we can get the Book, and then maybe—just *maybe*—there will be a future for you to go back to."

"Jack has the Ars Arcana?" Logan asked. It didn't explain why he couldn't sense it, though.

Esta nodded. "He does, and if we don't take it from him, then everything changes. Everything about *your* future depends on what happens at the Conclave, Logan. You think things were hard in the world we grew up in? They'll be worse in a country where magic itself—and those with a connection to it—is made illegal. But Nibsy's going to try to stop us, and as long as he has that diary, he might be able to. Get the diary, and maybe we can stop Jack. If that happens, you get to go home."

But what if James wins?

Logan knew better than to voice the question aloud. "You're sure I'd be safe here?"

"I swear it," Esta told him.

He considered his options, but finally he decided. All he wanted was to go back to his normal life. He wanted to go home. If Esta was offering him a chance, he'd take it.

Esta exchanged a long, silent look with Darrigan, and when they'd finished whatever conversation they'd just had, they turned to him.

"There's no going back once you're with us, Logan," Esta told him. "If James kills me, it's game over for your dreams of getting back to your own life. And if he kills any one of my friends? I won't be feeling generous enough to take you back."

"I know that." He wouldn't let them see his nerves. *I just want to go home.*

"You're sure we can trust him?" Darrigan asked.

"No," Esta told Darrigan, never once looking away from Logan. "But if he turns on us, Viola will take care of him."

"Happily," Viola said, her violet eyes as sharp as her knife.

Esta did look at Darrigan then. "It's our best shot."

He didn't look happy about it, but eventually, the Magician held out his hand. "I don't like this, but I trust Esta. So welcome to the team."

UNSETTLED

Once Logan had disappeared around the corner, Jianyu released his hold on the light. It was a dangerous gamble to send Logan back to Nibsy as a spy and even more dangerous to let him carry the knowledge that they wanted the diary.

"Do you believe you can trust him?" he asked Esta.

"No," she said sadly. "That isn't the Logan I knew. When I went back to the future the first time, my world had already changed. Logan and even Dakari were different from the people I'd grown up with. So I don't know anything about this Logan, but it doesn't matter. Harte took care of that."

Harte nodded. "Even if he's not for us, he won't be able to betray us."

"Do you think there is any truth to what he said?" Jianyu wondered. "What he told us about what Nibsy is doing with the Devil's Own."

"Probably," she said. "It sounds like something he would do."

They turned together to go back into the warmth of the building, and as they climbed the stairs to the rooms on the third floor, the problem of the Devil's Own pressed at him.

It had been his idea to play the Hip Sings and the Five Pointers against one another to distract Nibsy. But the idea had not worked. Nibsy had sensed that the distraction was a ploy, and he had left the Devil's Own to protect the Strega. When they had run—as any sane person would—he had viewed their actions as a betrayal.

Because Nibsy Lorcan did not view those who wore the mark as friends or partners, not in the way Dolph had. James viewed them as expendable.

When they reached the door to the apartment, Jianyu stopped them just inside the parlor. What he had to say was for his friends alone.

"You need to destroy the cane," he told Esta. "You were right. Nibsy Lorcan can never be allowed to hold that power again. But as long as it exists, someone can use those connected to it as weapons. As cannon fodder for their own selfish desires."

"He's right," Viola agreed. "We need to make sure it's not a liability."

"It needs to be done today," Jianyu told them.

"We can do it right now," Esta said.

They started toward the back room, but when they reached the larger gathering space where the cane rested under the watchful eye of Golde Salzer, he stopped before entering the room. Cela was there too. Her eyes met his, and he understood the silent question she was asking.

Is everything okay?

He nodded. *All is well.*

Good, her eyes seemed to say. *Come get warmed up.*

The ease of their silent conversation was a comfort, but he took a step back. What right did he have for comfort when people were being hunted for Nibsy's sport because of him, because of the events he had set into motion?

There, sitting around the corner, were a handful of the people he had helped to free from the Order's patrols. Some seemed content enough to while away their days with menial tasks to keep them entertained. But he had already started to hear the whispering. Many were growing tired of being away from their lives. It did not matter that without the protection of the building, they might not have lives to return to.

They were safe, but what good was safety when they were trapped? How was this building, with all its protections, any better than the Brink?

All that he had tried to do, and none of it was enough.

"What is it?" Viola asked when she sensed Jianyu's hesitation.

"Why do we wait?" he asked, stepping into the room. "We have the sigils, and we have Newton's diagrams. We have the Order's records as well. We know what the silver discs are capable of. We could free people and release them from this city."

"We've been over this," Esta told him. "We can't risk losing the sigils. Not until we use them on Thoth."

"There's a way out?" A boy stepped forward—Golde's son, Josef. "You could help us escape from the Order and Nibsy Lorcan both, but instead, you're keeping us here?"

The others had gone quiet, and he knew they were listening.

"We're not keeping you here," Darrigan said, but his voice was too tight. "You can leave anytime you want."

"No, we can't," Josef argued. "Out there, the Order knows who I am. So does Nibsy. What do you think he would do if we left? He'd find us, and he'd use whatever he could to force us into telling him about this place. But if we could get out of the city—"

"Can we?" another of the tenants asked. "Is it really possible?"

"It is," Jianyu told them.

"We *think* it is," Esta corrected. She turned to the gathering crowd. "It's true that the Order used the sigils to get through the Brink more than a hundred years ago, but we don't have any idea what they would do now. We can't risk them, and we can't risk *any* of you to test some theory written a century ago."

"We saw what happened with Jianyu's wrist," Josef pressed. "I *felt* it. You know they'll work."

"*Josef,*" Golde said, stepping toward her son.

"No, Mutter," he snapped, stepping back. "They're *lying* to us. Can't you see that? They're no better than Lorcan or Dolph Saunders or anyone who would control us."

"They saved you," Golde said. "They risked their lives, and then they gave you a roof over your head and a safe place to sleep, and what have they asked for? *Nothing.*"

"There's always something," Josef said. "Besides, I wouldn't have needed saving if I had taken the mark like I wanted to."

His mother reached for him again, but he jerked away and stormed off. A few seconds later, they heard a door slam.

"I am sorry, Golde," Jianyu said.

"You have nothing to be sorry for," she said with an apologetic shrug. "He's young. He doesn't understand."

Jianyu turned to Esta. "We cannot keep people here forever."

"We won't," she told him. Then she turned to the others. "I know it's hard," she said. "I know it's difficult to believe, but I've seen the world that this will become if we don't stop Jack Grew. I wish we didn't need to wait. I wish we could take every one of you outside the Brink right now, but if we lose the sigils, we lose everything."

"If we keep people trapped here, against their will, perhaps we already have," Jianyu argued.

"You can't think that," Cela said.

"No?" he asked, feeling suddenly uncomfortable with the intensity in her expression and the fire in her dark eyes.

"No." It was Yonatan who spoke now. He'd helped with the ritual to remove the cord from Jianyu's wrist, but he mostly kept to himself. "The boy is wrong. He's too young to know how wrong he is, but I see what you've done here. The lives you've saved." The man shrugged. "Maybe it's hard not to be free, but when has our kind ever been truly free in this city? You've given us safety, and now we'll give you our patience. And we'll trust that you'll keep your word."

"We will," Esta told them. "I promise. After the Conclave."

It seemed to settle the mood of the building, but Jianyu was still bothered by what Logan had said. There were still people in danger because of what he and Darrigan set into motion.

"Darrigan, could I have a word?"

Harte glanced to Esta, who nodded, before following Jianyu out to the front parlor, where they would be less likely to be overheard.

"What is it?" Darrigan asked once they were alone.

"I cannot help but think about what Logan told us—about the

destruction we caused and the people we have put in unnecessary danger."

The Magician frowned, but his expression held interest. "What are you thinking?"

"It will not be enough to destroy Nibsy's cane if he has others to command," Jianyu said. "I think it is time we pay another call on John Torrio and Sai Wing Mock."

He considered the proposal. "I think you're right. Let me just go tell Esta and the others what we're doing. They should be able to handle the cane while we're gone."

"I'll wait for you outside."

The air was warmer than it had been all week, but it still chapped Jianyu's nose and lips as he waited for Darrigan.

"So you're leaving, just like that?" When Jianyu turned back around, Cela was standing in the doorway at the top of the stoop. "Running off to save the world without so much as a good-bye?" she asked, descending the steps slowly toward him.

He felt caught in her gaze as she approached him and tipped her head up to look at him. Her brown eyes seemed even deeper, and now he could see the flecks of green near their irises. He was not sure at first what to say. "There is something I must do."

Her expression softened. "There always is."

Confused by her words, he started to move back, to put the distance between them that he always maintained. But she caught his hand.

"Not this time," she said. "Where are you going, anyway?"

"To make amends for a problem I caused," he told her.

"You know you didn't make Torrio and Mock Duck mean as snakes, don't you?" She was closer now, and he could smell the scent of her, floral and tropical, with a note of something woodsy and clean. "You've done more than anyone could have asked."

He did not respond to that statement. He had no idea how.

Cela looked up at him. "Tell me something."

LISA MAXWELL

"Yes?"

"You keep yourself so busy being good, proving that you're worthy of a dead man's approval, but are you ever going to deal with this?" she asked, waving her hands between them. "Are you ever going to address what there is between you and me?"

Panic froze his tongue.

Cela let out a tired-sounding sigh. "I can practically see that brain of yours churning through all the reasons there shouldn't be a you and me. But while you're thinking, consider this, too."

She rose onto her toes and pressed her mouth against his. Soft and sweet. He closed his eyes, unable to resist her, and suddenly he could no longer feel the cold.

But the kiss was over before it began. She looked up at him, smug satisfaction shining in her expression.

"That's what I thought." And with a small smile, she turned on her heel and left him standing there in the bright cold of a winter's day.

Jianyu didn't even hear Darrigan approach until the Magician let out a long, amused whistle. "You're going to need to breathe there, sport. And just a suggestion, but maybe next time? Kiss her back."

VAGUE PROMISES

From his usual table at the back of the Bella Strega, James Lorcan watched over the crowd. They were quieter than usual and had been since Torrio and Sai Wing Mock's boys made matchsticks of the furniture and tore the barroom apart. But in the days since then, he'd put things back together—his alliances, his saloon, and his control over the Devil's Own.

And if there were those who had disappeared into the Bowery despite wearing the mark? He would not let that concern him. There were others who would replace them, others who already had.

It was nearly midnight when Logan entered the saloon and looked around warily. The boy was always nervous, jittery, and unsure of himself, but for the last few days, he'd been different. Every time he entered James' presence, the Aether shifted and bunched. Unlike the others in the Devil's Own, Logan had no loyalty to the Strega or to James other than what was inspired by desperation and fear. But desperation pushed people to do things they otherwise wouldn't, and fear had the nasty habit of making them stupid.

In the days since Esta had slipped away from them, James had been allowing Logan some freedom—enough rope to either help him catch a thief or to hang himself. But tonight the vibrations had grown more insistent about Logan's possible duplicity.

It was time to ensure he wasn't a risk.

He called out and waved the boy over. When he saw the summons, Logan hesitated. He looked suddenly ill, and when he finally started to move, he came slowly, with his eyes shifting around the barroom the entire time.

"Well?" James asked, rubbing his thumb across the Medusa's coiling hair. "What have you discovered for me?"

"I found her," Logan told him. "I tracked Ishtar's Key to a building north of Washington Square. But she doesn't have the Book. Or if she does, she's not keeping it there," Logan told him, unable to meet his eyes.

It was no more and no less than what he'd suspected. The Aether had been whispering of missed opportunities for days, but now it seemed to whisper of deception as well. Logan, it seemed, had made a choice. A rather unfortunate one.

"That certainly is terrible news," he said. "For you especially."

Logan looked up then, fear in his expression. "For me?"

"Yes," James agreed. "You have no connections to this city, no talents other than to find magical objects, and you've failed to do that. You've refused my offer of the mark again and again. Because you believe that you're destined for other places . . . or because you aren't truly loyal?"

"No, James," Logan said, his eyes growing wider. "That isn't it at all."

"Isn't it?" James pretended to consider the situation.

"No," Logan said. "I wouldn't do anything against you, James. You have to know that."

"Do I?" He nodded to Murphy, indicating that he should come over as well. "Maybe you're right. You haven't given me any real reason to doubt your intentions—not yet, at least. But I can't help but wonder . . . What use are you to me if you can't accomplish the task I've kept you around for?"

By now Logan had noticed Murphy's approach and understood he wasn't safe. Fear shivered through him, coward that he was.

"Unless you *do* know something more?" James asked, glancing over his spectacles. "Something you wish to share?"

Logan looked distinctly uncomfortable, and James watched as the war played out within him.

"She's never going to take you back, Logan. Whatever Esta might promise you, whatever she might have told you, she's lying." James shrugged. "It's what she does. She was trained to deceive. But she will not win. When everything is settled and when the dust clears, Esta Filosik will meet the fate intended for her. If you trust her, if you take her side against me, then you'll share her fate as well."

"She doesn't have the Book," Logan said again. He glanced up at Murphy. "I wasn't lying about that. I wouldn't lie to you, James."

"If she doesn't have the Book, then where is it?"

Logan shook his head, his eyes wide. "I don't know. Maybe it's not in the city."

But it would be. The diary had assured him of as much.

"What aren't you telling me?" he asked, testing the Aether as he spoke. "What are you trying to hide?"

"I wouldn't—" He stopped when Murphy's hands landed on his shoulders. His eyes went wide. "Esta knows where the Book is going to be. She's making plans."

"Sit down, Logan." James nodded to Murphy, who pressed Logan forcibly into the empty chair on the other side of the table. "I want to know what you found out. And this time you'll tell me everything."

He listened to the Aether as Logan evaded his questions, and the more he struggled, the more convinced James became that someone had gotten to him. He'd been compromised, likely by Darrigan. But the question was how—had he submitted to Darrigan's magic of his own free will, or had he been trapped?

And could he still be used?

James considered him as he tested the Aether around him. The humming was insistent today, more unsettled than the usually buzzing unease he'd almost grown accustomed to.

The Conclave was coming, but he was no closer to understanding the directions fate would push him. And all the while, that incessant vibration in the Aether taunted him. He'd figure out soon what it meant and silence it once and for all.

LISA MAXWELL

"Do you trust me, Logan?" he asked.

"Sure, I trust you, James. You made me what I am—or you will."

"I sincerely hope that isn't true," he said. "But I'm willing to give you another chance. Maybe you can make up for your failings."

Logan licked his lips nervously. "Whatever you want, James."

"Since you claim that you can't bring me the Book and that you don't know any of the traitors' plans, maybe it's time for you to make a statement of who you stand with and who you're against."

"You want me to take the mark." The color drained from Logan's face. "I don't know . . ."

"That is the heart of the problem." He leaned forward. "You *don't* know. You're unsure of where your loyalties lie."

"No. That's not it—"

"But it is," he said sympathetically. "And I'm afraid I can only offer protection to those who are loyal to the Devil's Own—those who are loyal to me alone. What are you afraid of, Logan? Darrigan stole the cane. The mark is nothing more than your promise to me and to those whom I protect."

Logan swallowed hard, clearly understanding the threat. "Give me some time to think about it, would you? A day or two."

If he gave Logan a day or two, he'd run straight to Esta. The truth was there, clear on his face.

James got to his feet. "You can have the night." He gave Murphy another small nod, the indication that perhaps Logan would be more amenable to making that choice with a little encouragement.

He didn't stay to watch what happened next. He didn't particularly care. Logan would take the mark, or Murphy would take care of him. Either way, it didn't seem to have solved anything. Despite pinning Logan into a corner, the Aether still hummed uncertainly.

Back in his own apartment, James took out the diary that Logan had brought him from his future self and again looked over the impossible pages, cursing their refusal to reveal everything as they once had. The future was his to make, to bend and form to his will, but for weeks now the diary had refused to show him the path.

Now something seemed to be changing. The future was coming into focus.

The Ars Arcana would soon come back into the city—this diary made that fact clear, and Logan had confirmed the truth of it. When it did, Esta and Darrigan would go after it. They and the other traitors would risk everything to try to take it back from Jack Grew, and James would let them.

The Aether vibrated with encouragement at this decision, and he knew it was the right path. He would let them fight, and then, when the risk was over, he would make them fall.

In the end, the Book would be his.

THE BIND

The Safe House

Esta was sitting next to Harte around the table in the back room of the safe house with Cela and Abel, waiting for the others to arrive. Jianyu and Viola would be along in a while as well, and then they could go over everything together. Until then, they had the news Abel brought them. The pressure he'd been helping apply to the Order seemed to be working, and he could get firsthand news outside the Brink that they could trust.

"The delegation from California won't be in until the day of," Abel told them, running through the list of names in front of him. "Their trains are set to arrive the afternoon of the twenty-first. But the men from out west—the Ranchers' Syndicate—and the ones from St. Louis are planning to be here the night before."

"You mean the Veiled Prophet Society," Harte said darkly, glancing at Esta.

She had a sense of what he was thinking about. The regret in his eyes was for Julian, who hadn't deserved any of what happened to him.

"They don't really wear veils, do they?" Cela wrinkled her nose.

"Just the head guy," Esta told her, remembering the ridiculous costume and the fateful fear that the men hid beneath it.

"Veils or hoods, it doesn't make much difference when the marrow's all the same," Abel said.

"So they're Klan?" Cela asked.

"Not exactly, but they're all part of the same family tree," Abel explained. "The Society got their start busting up railroad strikers about twenty years or so ago. The city fathers in St. Louis didn't like the way all the workers were coming together, Negro and white alike, so they made sure to stop that before it got anywhere at all."

"Of all the Brotherhoods, they're probably the most organized," Darrigan told them. "They're likely the closest to making a play for power. If we can stir up something there, it might put more pressure on the Order."

"I'll let Mr. Fortune know," Abel told him. "He's familiar with the Veiled Prophet nonsense, and after what Viola did to save him and his men, he's more interested than ever to go after the Order and their like any way he can."

"I can't imagine there's a Negro in this city that won't have something to say about the Order welcoming Klansmen right out in the open, no matter what they might call themselves," Cela told her brother.

"Probably not," he said. "And I'm sure that the men involved with the Order wouldn't want the publicity if the other papers pick up the story. There's a reason the Klan wears hoods, and here in the north? People like to pretend they're not as low as all that."

Esta wasn't sure that involving more innocent people in their current mess was the answer. "I don't want anyone else getting hurt. Especially not Mr. Fortune. If the Order retaliates—"

"He's not worried right now," Abel told her. "With the fire, there was no proof at all that he was housing Mageus, much less the missing Reynolds girl. And then when she showed up *wearing* the wedding gown that the patrol supposedly found?" He shrugged. "Everyone's backing away from the story. The Order's pretending they didn't have anything to do with it."

"What about Jack?" Harte asked. "Any sign of him yet?"

Abel shook his head. "Sorry. No one's caught word of anything that might point to where he could be. It's like he's some kind of ghost."

Jianyu was there suddenly, appearing in the doorway. His eyes found Cela first, as usual, and Esta watched whatever was going on between them play out silently. She wondered if Abel noticed as well. She wondered if he was as tired of the simmering emotion between the two as the rest of them were.

"You're back early," Esta said, pretending she hadn't noticed the way that they were looking at each other.

"Did you have any luck?" Cela asked.

Jianyu took a folded bundle of papers from his sleeve and placed them on the table. "The Inner Circle are keeping to themselves. Outside of their new headquarters, they do not say much about the arrangements of the Conclave. But the Garden does not seem to have the same concerns about secrecy. I found these in their offices."

"Seating charts?" Darrigan asked, frowning. "Not sure what kind of help those will be."

"It's always good to know the players on the board," Esta told him, giving Jianyu an encouraging smile.

"I have the floor plan as well," Jianyu said, pointing to the sketches he had made from the originals. "The Order will hold events throughout the building. From what I gather, they will start here, with speeches in the main arena, but the ritual will take place in the open air. Here . . . on the roof. There's more. . . . Timetables for the catering and staff."

"So Jack could strike anywhere," Esta realized.

"But he is most likely to strike during the ritual," Jianyu told them.

"Which means we should focus our attention on the roof," Harte said.

"Any word from the Bowery?" Esta asked.

Jianyu's expression grew more serious. "There is still no sign of Logan. Nibsy seems to be keeping him close."

Esta's stomach sank. It had been a risk to draw Logan into this. She should have just turned him away. Despite what he'd done to her, she hadn't wanted to see him hurt. He was a pawn as much as anyone.

"And what about Nibsy?" Harte asked.

"He remains within, safely surrounded by those who still stand by him," Jianyu told them. "He seems in no hurry to make any move."

"That doesn't mean anything," Esta said, thinking of the diary. "He knows what's coming. He just has to wait."

She hated that Nibsy had that luxury while they were scurrying around like rats. The truth of the matter was, they were running out of time. The Conclave was mere days away now, and they weren't anywhere close to ready.

A COMPLETE FOOL

Jack Grew didn't tell anyone when he returned to the city. He kept his movements to himself, electing to stay at a hotel instead of his own, more comfortable town house. He hadn't contacted his family or the old fools in the Order. He'd been watching and listening, waiting for the perfect time to make his presence known.

When he arrived at a banquet the Order held the night before the Conclave, he wasn't surprised to find Ruby Reynolds there, dressed completely in black and whispering into the High Princept's ear as though they were old confidants.

"Jack . . . What a surprise. We weren't sure we'd see you here tonight." His cousin, Junior, sidled up next to him. A crystal glass of something light and sparkling dangled between his fingers.

"I was invited," he said stiffly, his eyes still on the Reynolds bitch. "The High Princept issued the invitation himself."

"I see," Junior said. But his tone made it clear it was a decision the family hadn't been consulted about.

He turned to his cousin. "Is there something you wanted, Junior?"

Junior's eyes narrowed, and his almost affable expression turned more severe. "My father wanted me to remind you that you aren't to do anything that would put the family at risk."

"I would never," Jack said dryly.

"And yet . . ." Junior shrugged. But the expression he wore didn't match the bored indifference in his voice. "You're on your last bit of goodwill, Jack."

"Goodwill?" He tilted his head. "Is that what this is? How delightful," he said flatly. Then, before his cousin could even sputter a response, Jack cut him off. "You and your father—the family—have nothing to worry about. I'm here only because I was summoned. I'd rather be anywhere else than this gathering of overstuffed old men. I will be on my very best behavior."

Junior blinked at the severity in Jack's tone. "Well . . . see that you are."

Before Junior could drift back to the crowd, Jack caught him by the sleeve. "The Reynolds girl's back, is she?"

"I believe she's officially Mrs. Barclay now, despite the tragedy," Junior said. He was frowning in her direction. "She turned up a week ago, ranting and raving at the Order's headquarters."

"It's good to see she survived her ordeal," Jack said, infusing his tone with sincerity. "The High Princept seems quite taken by her, but then, beautiful young women often do have that effect on old men."

His cousin sneered at him. "In this case, I think his interest goes far beyond her beauty."

Jack lifted his brows and gave his cousin a questioning look.

"He still believes it was maggots who captured her," Junior explained. "He believes he can get information about them and their plans if he keeps her close."

Jack was sure that the Princept believed a lot of things, old fool that he was. But Jack would discover the truth. And if the situation worked to his own benefit? All the better.

He waited until Ruby had wandered away from the Princept's side not long after the meal, and he followed her. She went to the coatroom first, and Jack waited behind one of the large columns that anchored the entryway to see what she would do. Instead of leaving once her cloak was wrapped around her shoulders, she turned back into the mansion. With no more than a glance in the direction of the party, she continued toward one of the unused hallways that led deeper into the heart of the mansion.

Jack followed far enough behind that she couldn't detect him and watched as she let herself into a locked room using a hairpin.

Apparently her new friends had taught her all manner of skills.

He gave her time to get into the room before he followed, and she turned in surprise, knowing already that she was cornered. He looked around the room and realized that it was Vanderbilt's private temple. There was an altar in the center and a Tree of Life painted on the wall. Ruby, it seemed, had been helping herself to the cloaks that had been folded there in preparation for the Conclave.

"Miss Reynolds," he said, placing himself between Ruby and her only chance for escape. "You seem to have lost your way."

She straightened. "It's Mrs. Barclay now," she corrected, her mouth going tight. She lifted her chin, regal as a queen, but her eyes betrayed her nerves.

So she isn't a complete fool.

"You were a wife for so short a time," he said mockingly. "I'd forgotten."

"I haven't," she told him. "I remember my wedding day like it was yesterday. I remember *everything.*"

"Such a tragedy," he said, not bothering to hide his amusement. The evening was becoming far more entertaining than he'd expected. "My condolences on your loss." He waited a beat, allowing her nerves to tighten.

"What do you want, Jack?"

"As I said, you seem to have lost your way," he told her. "Or perhaps you haven't. You don't have them fooled, you know."

Ruby's mouth was still pressed tight. "I've no idea what you're talking about," she said, moving forward. The items she was taking were still tucked beneath her cloak. But he stopped her, catching her by the arm.

Fear flashed through her bottle-green eyes, and Jack smiled, tightening his grip until he saw pain join it. "Your family really shouldn't allow you to wander about unescorted," he told her, keeping his tone easy.

"You're a bastard, you know that?"

"Such language from a lady," he mocked. "But I'd rather be a bastard than a corpse."

She backed away from him then, and this time he allowed her. But as she passed him, he whispered a string of ancient syllables into the air. He felt the words, strange though the language was, bubble up from within him, wrap around them, and settle over the room.

Ruby stopped, and he saw her eyes go glassy.

"You seem a bit confused, Mrs. Barclay," he said pleasantly, looping her arm through his again. "Please, do allow me to escort you."

He allowed her to take the cloaks, because it suited his plan even better than he could have imagined, and then he led her quietly back the way they came. He left her standing in the entryway. "I assume you can see yourself out," he told her, snapping his fingers and then walking away.

ANOTHER SUNSET

Viola waited under the cover of trees in the Grand Army Plaza, the portion of Central Park directly across from the Vanderbilt mansion. It was a ridiculous structure, all peaked rooflines and decorative gables, dark brick and smooth stone that glowed in the lamplight. At this time of night, the traffic on Fifty-Seventh Street was practically nonexistent, but it didn't calm her any. She wouldn't feel like she could breathe until the girl she loved was no longer in that nest of vipers.

Finally, she saw Ruby emerge from the front doors of the mansion, her blond curls glinting in the moonlight. She stopped just outside the door and waited beneath the enormous portico, her icy breath wreathing her head, until her carriage was brought around. Viola forced herself to be patient, and then, when the carriage departed, pulling up alongside the park, she made her move, using her affinity to make the driver drowse just enough that he wouldn't notice her opening the door and slipping inside.

"What's wrong?" Viola asked, her stomach turning at the expression Ruby wore. "What happened in there?"

"I'm not sure . . ." Ruby blinked at her, but there was a fuzziness in her eyes, like she was walking through a dream. "I got the robes." She took the pile of fabric out from the folds of her thick velvet cloak and looked down at them as though she had never seen them before. "The members and their wives will all be wearing them. It should get everyone in safely."

Viola took them and set them aside before squeezing onto the cushioned bench next to Ruby. She hated the way the black widow's weeds made Ruby look drawn and pale, but tonight it was worse.

"Something happened," Viola said, taking Ruby's hands in hers.

"Your fingers are freezing," Ruby told her, blinking away the last of whatever daze she'd been in.

"It's winter," Viola said with a shrug.

"You aren't wearing nearly enough." Ruby unfastened the neck of her cloak and opened it, adjusting herself so Viola could wrap it around herself as well.

Ruby's hair smelled of flowers and her clothes of cigar smoke. On her breath, Viola could detect the sweetness of champagne. All of it, scents from a life she could not imagine.

But it didn't seem to matter. With a contented sigh, Ruby settled into Viola. "I've missed you," she said.

Glad for the darkness of the carriage, Viola felt her cheeks go warm. "I'm sure that big, soft bed of yours and all the servants have been a trial," she told her.

Ruby chuckled. "Truly. They're just awful." Then her voice grew more serious. "It really is awful, Vee. I don't belong there anymore. Maybe I never did."

"This will be over tomorrow, and you can leave," Viola told her. "You can go wherever you want."

"I don't think I'll be leaving the city," Ruby said, leaning her head into Viola's.

Viola closed her eyes and savored the feel of the other girl against her. How easy it was to sit like this, together. How *right*. "Theo would want you to live your life," she said finally, speaking through the tightness in her throat. "He told me about how happy you were in Paris. You should go."

"I'm not leaving unless you come with me," Ruby told her. She took Viola's face softly between her hands.

"You know I can't." And nothing had ever hurt so much as that simple, undeniable truth. "Not so long as the Brink keeps me here."

Ruby kissed her softly. "Then I suppose we'll have to find a place uptown."

"Ruby—"

"You're right about one thing, Viola. Theo would want me to live my life," Ruby said. "*My* life. The one I choose. I will miss him every single day I have left to live. I will mourn him just as long. But I'll bless his memory as well, because by marrying me, he gave me freedom I never expected. Our families tried to tie him to me with my dowry, but since we officially married before he died, that money is mine alone now. No one can tell me how to use it. And when this is over, we'll be together."

Viola knew she should argue. It was impossible, what Ruby was proposing. To stay here beneath the watch of Ruby's family, in the city where her magic would only ever be a liability? But she couldn't bring herself to. For this one, small moment, she wanted to dream.

But the truth of Nibsy's diary waited to reveal itself, and dreams were dangerous distractions.

"The cloaks should get you in without any trouble," Ruby repeated. Then she explained what she'd gleaned of the Order's plan. The streets would turn deadly, and the Brink would be recharged. "They're going to be using electricity," Ruby said. "They're so proud of themselves harnessing the power of science to fuel their magic that they couldn't keep it a secret. If Jack's going after the Brink, he'll likely do it there. It's his best chance to have the biggest impact on their ritual."

The carriage was rolling to a stop, and Viola knew their time was nearly up. Another sunrise, another sunset, and the die would be cast. Their fates would be known.

Unable to help herself, she leaned forward and kissed Ruby until the other girl melted and opened for her. Until she could taste the expensive champagne on Ruby's lips.

"You shouldn't be there tomorrow," Viola said, feeling more than a little breathless. "It's too dangerous."

"I'll be there," Ruby said. "For you, and for Theo. For the end of the Order and Jack Grew. We'll finish this, and then we'll start the life we both deserve."

PLENTY OF TIME

It had been six days since Cela had acted a fool and kissed Jianyu. Six days of wondering what was going on in that head of his. He'd been avoiding her. But she was done with waiting. The Conclave was tomorrow, and she wasn't about to let him go running off headlong into his possible doom without forcing him to confront the truth about the feelings between them. If he didn't reciprocate them, fine. But she wasn't going to spend the rest of her life wondering.

She found him up on the roof of the building, right where she'd expected him to be. Ever since the dustup a few days before with Golde's boy, he'd been avoiding the other occupants in the safe house every bit as much as he'd been avoiding her.

The second she opened the door onto the roof, he turned. If he was surprised to see her, it didn't register. He watched her walk toward him with the same measured calm he always wore.

Armor. It had taken a while for her to understand, but now she thought she might. He kept himself closed up, calm and steady no matter what, as a kind of disguise. It meant that people were less likely to notice him, despite the color of his skin or the magic that ran in his veins. It kept him safe.

"Tomorrow's the day," she said, trying for lightness. But her voice betrayed the fear she'd been trying to hide.

He nodded, still looking at her with those fathomless eyes of his. She suspected he saw everything as well.

Then he surprised her. She'd expected him to do any number of things, including to pretend he didn't know why she was there or to deny the connection that felt undeniable between them. She hadn't expected him to touch her. But that's exactly what he did.

Slowly, he lifted his hand to her cheek, and despite the promises she'd made to herself to stay stoic and strong, her traitorous body responded by leaning into the warmth of his hand.

"Your skin is freezing," he said, frowning, as though he'd just noticed she wasn't wearing more than a shawl.

"I'm fine." And she was. She didn't even feel the bite of the wind with him touching her.

With an exasperated huff, he stepped back to remove his heavy over-coat and draped it around her shoulders. All at once, she was engulfed in the scent of him—the warm amber and sage and the not unpleasant musk of his sweat.

"Now you're going to be the one freezing," she told him, unable to hold back the smile that threatened.

"You did not come here to talk about the weather," he said. His expression was unreadable.

"No," she admitted. "I didn't."

"You came to talk about our earlier discussion," he said. He looked out over the city, as though he could no longer hold her gaze. "You gave me quite a lot to think about."

"Have you?" she wondered. "Thought about it?"

A long beat passed, and she heard his soft exhale of breath. "Every second of every day."

Cela hadn't realized how nervous she'd been until those words unlocked a wave of relief. "And?" She turned toward him. He was still looking out over the city, toward the river beyond. The lines of his face were sharp against the hazy blush of twilight, and while he studied the city, she studied him. "What did you come up with?" she asked finally when she couldn't stand to wait anymore.

"I will never leave this city," he told her, "but I still cannot claim it as my home." He turned to her then, looked deeply into her eyes as though willing her to understand. "Even if tomorrow goes well, even if the fate inscribed in Nibsy's diary can be changed, I have no future to offer you."

Unease inched up her spine, made her heart feel unsteady in her chest. "Jianyu—"

"No," he said gently. "You must understand this. In this land, I will never belong. But even if I could go back, even if I could pass through the Brink unharmed, even if I wanted to travel back across the seas to the land of my birth, I could not."

"Is that what you want?" she asked. She'd never considered it before, never even imagined that he might want to return. "To go back to your homeland?"

"No," he told her. "I also do not belong there any longer. I find myself a man between worlds, with no home in either."

She slipped her hand into his. "So make your home with me."

The city settled around them. The low, steady hum that had rocked her as a baby and guided her days seemed to wrap around Cela now as she waited for his decision.

He kissed her then, and though his mouth was firm and resolute against hers, it felt more like a question than an answer. "You make me want things I cannot have."

"Why can't you have them?" she asked, her mouth so close to his that she could taste the jasmine tea on his breath.

"Sometimes I forget the reasons," he told her, and he kissed her again. But this time was no question. He wrapped her in his arms and claimed her mouth as his own.

She allowed him to, offering herself up and giving everything over to him, to what lay between them. Because tomorrow was another day, another danger. Because today was all they ever had. Here, this beautiful, terrible, impossible now.

They were both breathless when they broke away from each other.

"There is nothing I can offer you," he told her. "I cannot even promise you tomorrow."

"So give me today," she said, slipping her hand into his. "Give me tomorrow as it comes."

He pulled her into a tight embrace, resting his face against her neck. "It would be a difficult life. I would make you regret my choices."

She laughed then. "Have you ever been able to make me do anything?"

"Your brother will want to murder me," he murmured.

"Let me handle Abel," she told him, but then she thought about his point.

"Cela—"

"No," she said before he could go and ruin what they'd just shared. "Don't you dare say another word." She kissed him again, softly this time, so he couldn't change his mind.

"Tomorrow is going to be fine," she told him. "We're going to stop Jack, and we're going to get the Book, and then the two of us are going to have plenty of time to figure everything out. But until then, I have an idea that might help with your problem in the Bowery."

A CHANCE

Esta Filosik was a thief, and a damn good one at that. She'd slipped out of a thousand impossible situations, had evaded her enemies countless times. But nothing in her life—no failure or mistake—had prepared her for the situation she currently found herself in. There was no slipping out of this, no evading her destiny, and there was no time left to steal.

Thanks to Ruby, they had an idea of what the Order's plans were. They were going to use the street grid to charge the Brink with electricity in an attempt to display their power for the Brotherhoods. Thanks to Abel and his friends, the Order was running into the Conclave on the defensive. But they still didn't know what Jack had planned, and they didn't know how to evade Nibsy—or if they even could. And the time for planning was up. In just a few hours, the Conclave would begin, and one way or another their fates would be sealed.

"Once we're inside, we need to find Jack," Esta said, trying to focus on what they could still control. "If we can corner him before he does anything, maybe we'll get to him before he can start the attack."

"I still say we should just kill him and be done with it," Viola told them.

Esta felt the same. But she knew it wouldn't work.

"It's not enough to kill Jack," Esta reminded her. "If Thoth gets free, then he can find someone else to do his bidding, and we haven't solved anything. And if he gets free *tonight*? There's a few hundred likely options for him, each one of them every bit as willing as Jack was. We need to trap Jack first, so I can destroy Thoth before he can get free."

"*Then* I can kill him," Viola told them.

"No, Viola. You can't," Esta said, wishing it were otherwise. But she remembered the sickening suck of the dagger sliding into Jack's chest, the way he'd looked at her—him, not Thoth—right before he'd died in Chicago, and she knew it wasn't the answer. Not for her, and not for Viola, either.

"If we kill him, we prove the Order right. We make those with the old magic into the villains, the same as what happened before. That's what caused the DAM Act and everything else that followed. You're going to have to trust us. The last thing we want to happen is to turn him into some kind of martyr."

She thought of the first time she'd seen Jack, when he was a middle-aged man at Schwab's mansion, back in the twenties. *That's* the future they needed for him. One where he wasn't important or even respected.

"We don't need to kill him, but we need to make sure he loses all credibility after tonight. He has to look like such a fool that no one will ever listen to him or take him seriously again."

"I like him better dead," Viola said with a pout.

"I'm not disagreeing," Esta said. "But if Jack dies, it can't be by our hand."

"We must take his victory from him," Jianyu said. "We must protect the Brink."

"Not just the Brink," Esta told them. "The Order as well."

Viola cursed her displeasure, but Esta had already explained this to them. "If Jack succeeds, people will die tonight. Rich people—*important* people. Not the kind of people that let things go."

"The Inner Circle," Jianyu said. "We should begin there. He would destroy them all if he could."

"The High Princept?" Harte wondered.

"Maybe," she said, wishing they'd taken the time to learn more while they were in the future. "Ruby will try to stay close to him and signal us if there's anything happening, and Viola will stay close to Ruby," Esta said before Viola could interrupt.

Viola huffed her agreement. "Finally you talk some sense."

"The most important thing is to keep the attack from happening, and if it does happen, we have to protect the Order. The fate of every Mageus in this country for another century depends on that."

"So it has come to this," Jianyu said. "Our only chance is to help the very people who would destroy us or risk being destroyed ourselves."

Viola cursed. "First you want us to save the Brink, the terrible magic that can rip our very lives apart, and now we must save the men who would kill us where we stand? So much risk, and for what? If we succeed, everything will go back to how it was. The Brink will stand. The Order will survive. And those of us who have the old magic will be no better off."

Esta hated that she was right. "We can still stop Jack," she reminded Viola. "Harte and I saw what happened when he had power. I know this isn't the situation we hoped for, but we can still change things. We can stop that other future from happening."

"The Conclave isn't the end," Harte said. "We still have the sigils."

"You mean if we don't all end up dead," Viola said darkly.

"That's not going to happen," Harte told them.

"It might. We don't know what Nibsy has planned," Viola argued.

"Thanks to Yonatan and some of the others, Nibsy will likely be too busy dealing with a minor uprising tonight to bother with us," Jianyu said.

"They agreed?" Cela asked.

"You were right," he told her. "They were more than willing to help."

"What are you talking about?" Esta asked.

"It was Cela's idea," Jianyu said.

"I only suggested that maybe you all should include the others in this," Cela told them.

Esta's stomach sank. "It's too dangerous."

"They live with danger every day, Esta." Cela shook her head. "I've spent enough time here listening to conversations and learning who these people are that I understand why they want to help. Nibsy Lorcan took everything from them, and they're ready to take some of that back. They've never been cowards. Isn't that why you saved them?" she asked Viola.

Viola was forced to admit that it was.

"The people living in this building, the ones you've been so good to protect, are the ones who *didn't* break," Cela reminded them. "They didn't break then, and they won't now."

"They might not wear the mark," Jianyu told her. "But they are still loyal to what the Devil's Own was supposed to stand for. Not to a man or a building, but to an ideal."

"They're going to wage war on the Strega?" Esta asked.

"No. They're going to demand an end to Nibsy Lorcan's rule," Jianyu told them. "Even if Nibsy himself is not distracted, they will occupy the people he has left. They will do what they can to give us a chance."

A chance. It almost seemed like too much to hope for, but Esta would take it.

Eliminating Thoth and taking the Book back from Jack wouldn't solve the problem of the Order's control over the city or the danger of the Brink, but it would give those who had the old magic a chance. At least Jack wouldn't be a threat. At least the path of history could come closer to what should have been: There would be no DAM Act without Jack's attack on the Conclave, no Reticulum without his possession of the Book. No President Grew. And maybe one day they could do more.

"If we can get the Book from Jack, a different future is still possible," Esta said. "As long as we stop Jack tonight, we can start again. We know where the artifacts are waiting. We know how to use the Book. And we have Morgan's papers, along with all the secrets the men in the Order might want to hide. The Conclave is just the beginning."

She could feel Harte looking at her, and she knew what he was thinking—about the Book and the artifacts. About what it would cost her to use them to destroy the Brink.

Golde knocked on the doorframe to announce her arrival. "I'm sorry to interrupt," she told them. "I know you're busy, but there's something that's happened. Something you should know. My Josef—he's gone."

AN UNEXPECTED VISITOR

Bella Strega

Josef Salzer was a coward. The boy was so terrified of the choice he'd made that he was shaking like he had a palsy. He's been a coward to let his mother keep him from taking the mark months ago, and he was a coward now. But at least he had turned out to be a useful one.

"And Esta believes they can use the sigils to trap this demon?" he asked the boy.

Josef nodded. "That's their plan. They're going to go to the Conclave and try to find Jack Grew before he can attack anyone. Once they unmake the monster that's inside him, they'll take the Book."

"You've seen this ritual?" James asked. "With your own eyes?"

"She took care of the curse on that Chinaman's arm," Josef told him. "I was one who helped. I held one of those magic discs they have while it was spinning like a ball of light. And then Esta stepped inside to work on that curse. She broke it too. Healed him up fine. Then we all stopped our discs so they could both get free."

James' interest peaked. "She was trapped?"

"I don't know," Josef said, looking suddenly even more frightened—if that were even possible. "I suppose she was."

James considered this news and felt the Aether lurch around him in ways that made his blood race. That wretched hum still pulsed in the background, but it was barely noticeable now. Barely a nuisance.

With a small nod, he let Murphy know to dispose of the kid, and he made his way back to the privacy of his apartments, where he could study the diary.

It remained mostly unreadable, but more had been revealed—enough that he could tell the Salzer kid hadn't been lying. The sigils were part of it.

He leaned back in his chair and considered the problem in front of him. He'd known since the beginning that he would need someone with an affinity like Esta's to touch the power in the Book. If the sigils could trap a demon, perhaps they could trap her power as well.

No wonder the Aether had urged patience for so long.

He'd let Esta and the others take all the risks. Once Jack Grew had been taken care of and the demon had been destroyed, James would make his move.

One by one he'd let her watch as he destroyed her friends, plucking away her layers of protection. He'd enjoy seeing the end of those who should have been following him all along. He'd make them regret their choices. Jianyu, Viola, and the Sundren trash that trailed behind them.

His only regret was that there wouldn't be time to savor Darrigan's end. After all that damned magician had done to him, after all he'd put James through . . . But obtaining the Book was more important than enjoying Darrigan's pain. His own *future* was more important.

And then, when Esta was at her weakest, when she had no one to step in and save her, he'd take *everything*.

He took the silver gorgon's head from where he kept it beneath his shirt. It wasn't exactly comfortable to walk around with the hard metal tucked under his arm, but it was necessary. He'd had the replica made not long after he'd taken it from Saunders. From the very beginning he'd known that possessing the cane would unlock control over the Devil's Own, but he'd expected it to put a target on his back as well. Just as it had for his old boss. Unlike Dolph, however, James was smart enough to protect what was his.

If Dolph could take Leena's affinity and place it into that bit of silver,

LISA MAXWELL

why couldn't he do the same with Esta's? Once he had her magic, he could use it at will. And once he had the Book, he was one step closer to unlocking its power.

Parts of the future might still be undetermined, but the diary showed him what was certain: Esta would attempt to regain the Book. He'd allow her to, just as he'd allow her to take care of the unfortunate issue of whatever it was living within Jack Grew.

And then Esta Filosik would die.

THE INFINITE NOW

As the carriage carrying them toward the Conclave rattled on through the city, Esta could not help but think of a night not so long ago when she'd sat in another carriage next to Harte. That night, she'd planned to betray him. It hadn't mattered that she'd felt a connection to him like she'd never felt with anyone else. That night she'd forced herself to see him only as the Magician, as her opponent and enemy. Because she'd believed that the future of magic had been riding on her choices.

She hadn't exactly been wrong. Everything *had* been riding on that night. But Esta hadn't understood *anything*. Because she believed the Professor, because she'd trusted him to guide her—because she wanted to be worthy of his approval—she'd made the wrong decision.

Tonight would be different. The world, again, was hanging in the balance, but this time she knew who she was fighting for. She knew who she was fighting *with*. Tonight she and Harte would stand together against the Order, against Nibsy as well. And with any luck, together, they would change the course of time.

"Do you remember the night we took the artifacts from Khafre Hall?" Harte asked as though reading the direction of her thoughts.

"*We?*" She turned toward him all mock offense. "If memory serves, *you* were the one who took them. And you left *me* sitting onstage in a room full of people who would have cheerfully murdered me if they had the chance." There was no anger in her tone, though. Only distant amusement. She nestled into him more. "Or am I thinking of someone else?"

"Definitely someone else," Harte agreed, all false innocence. "I would never—"

"You would," she corrected, slipping her arm through his. She tilted her face up to his. Their lips were inches apart, and she could smell the mint on his breath, the soft scent of his skin, clean and warm, and that indefinable scent that was only Harte. "You *definitely* would. Apparently I go for that sort of thing."

"Thank god for that," he said, his stormy eyes dancing.

Her smile slipped from her face. "It was raining that night."

"Better than this insidious cold," Harte told her, rubbing his hands to warm them. "In the middle of the summer's heat, I always think I want winter to come, until it actually arrives."

"I didn't want to leave," she said, still remembering that night. "I didn't want to betray you or to leave you behind."

She'd gone back through time to stop the Magician, but instead she'd found a home. She'd hated every second of the drive to Khafre Hall, because she had known what was coming. Once she had her cuff—along with the Book—she had known she had to betray him. And she'd believed that there was no coming back. By then she'd come to love the city as it had been and the people she'd met there. If she were honest, by then she'd come to love Harte.

But then, maybe she'd loved him from the beginning, just as she'd always loved the city.

In all its seasons. Through all its years and ages, she'd never wanted to live anywhere else. While Harte had always wanted to escape, this island of Manhattan had been Esta's only home, and even when she'd been able to leave, nowhere else had ever quite fit her the way these streets did. Nothing except for Harte had felt as right to her as choosing to come back.

"I never should have chosen anyone but you," she told him.

He lifted their interlocked hands to his mouth and placed a soft kiss on the back of hers. His stormy eyes never left hers. "You never have to choose again. Tonight it's both of us together. Or it's nothing at all."

But she wasn't sure he was right.

She hadn't told Harte about all the things she'd seen as she fell through time to find him. At first, it had been hard enough to remember or to know whether any of it was real. But in the past weeks, those memories had grown more certain, more insistent. The more she'd thought about what she'd seen when she was caught in time, the more she'd started to wonder if those visions held the answer to the final, unthinkable fate that Nibsy's diary had revealed.

They were nearly there. Outside the carriage window, Esta could see the blade of the Flatiron Building. At its base, Madison Square Park was lit by hundreds of glowing luminaries, and beyond that the enormous structure of the Garden was lit like a temple.

In her own time, Madison Square Garden was in a completely different location. It had been moved in the 1920s and then rebuilt again in the 1960s. The Garden she'd grown up with was the longest-standing and perhaps the most iconic. But the enormous, round arena that stood atop Penn Station wasn't nearly as beautiful or striking as the ornate building that stood on the corner of Thirty-Sixth Street and Madison Avenue in 1902. This version of the Garden was barely a decade old, and it would be a few years still before its famed architect would be murdered on the rooftop he'd designed by the jealous husband of a showgirl he'd been sleeping with. It had the look of a Moorish palace, with its roof lined with towers that looked like minarets.

The tallest of the towers soared over the park, rising like a finger pointing toward the heavens. It was only *barely* smaller than the Flatiron Building itself. At the top of the tower, Augustus Saint-Gaudens' *Diana* glistened in gold, her naked body caught in an elegant arabesque as she held her bow aloft, ready for the hunt.

Esta could see why the Order had chosen this location for their Conclave. The beauty and size of the building, and the grandeur of it as well, lent an immediate air of power and importance. The Flatiron Building nearby was a statement of the city's innovation, a preview of the modern era to come. The entire area around Madison Square was awash with light. Electric bulbs had been strung along the walkways of the parks, and enormous columns of light shot up from the rooftops of nearby buildings. The roof of the Garden was perhaps the brightest spot of all.

That was where it would happen. Thanks to Ruby, they knew for sure that the final ritual would be held on the rooftop of the Garden. There, with the grid of the city visible below, the Order would use an electrical current to replicate the power of the stones and the Book. If Jack was to attack, he would do it *there* high above the city streets, at the apex of the Conclave, during that final, essential ritual. If they wanted to stop him, if they wanted to take back the Book and eliminate Thoth, they had to do it before that final ritual.

The cold energy coming from the silvery disks Esta carried beneath her cloak gave her a chill that had nothing to do with the wintery night air. Their plan could work. If they found Jack in time, they could corner him and use the sigils to trap him—to contain Thoth so that she could destroy the creature he'd become. Once that was done, they could stop whatever attack he intended.

It was a simple enough plan, but so much could go wrong. If the words in Nibsy's diary had any truth to them, a lot likely would.

As traffic inched along, bringing them ever closer to the building and their awaiting fate, Esta turned to Harte. "There's something I need you to promise me."

"Anything," he told her without any hesitation. But there was a question in his storm-colored eyes.

"There's a distinct possibility this won't end well," she told him.

"Esta—"

"No, Harte, listen. I saw what was written in that diary, the same as you. And as much as I want to ignore it, we can't."

"I'm not going to kill you," he told her. "I *couldn't*."

"You could," she said softly. "The words on that diary page prove it's a possibility, however unlikely it might feel."

His brows snapped together in frustration. "I'm not having this discussion. We are going to make it out of this tonight, and we're to make it out together."

"I hope so," she told him. The sureness in his voice had brushed away some of the icy dread clinging to her. "But I trust you, Harte. I know that you wouldn't hurt me. If you killed me in some version of tonight, you must have had a reason, and that reason must have been an outcome worse than my death."

"There is no worse outcome for me than your death," he told her.

He was wrong. She'd seen it herself, hadn't she? She'd seen futures more terrible than death, and she'd felt a terrifying nothingness that waited as a possibility lodged in time.

Esta fought back the tears that threatened. "I feel the exact same way, Harte. But whatever happens in there, I need you to promise me that you'll do whatever you have to in order to keep Nibsy from winning. Especially if he tries to take my affinity."

Harte went very still. "How could he?"

"If he got hold of the sigils—" She stopped. It felt too dangerous even to utter it out loud. But she'd seen the world as it would be if the Brink fell.

"We have Viola," Harte reminded her. "Nibsy won't get anywhere near you or those discs."

Esta leaned her head on his shoulder. "All I'm saying is that if everything goes wrong and if there is no other option, you should do whatever you need to do to keep him from winning."

"He can't win if he's dead," Harte said.

"But you can't kill him," Esta reminded him. "Even if I'm about to die. Even if everything else is falling apart. If there's any chance at all that you or the others can get away, there has to be someone to send the girl forward to. Or it will doom everyone." She glanced at him. "Unless you know?"

Harte was frowning at her. He shook his head slightly.

It meant that there was a good chance that the fate they'd read in Nibsy's diary would be realized tonight. It felt impossible. How could she believe Harte would ever hurt her, much less kill her outright? Unless . . .

A thought occurred to her then, one that she'd been trying to ignore ever since she'd read those words written in Nibsy's own hand. There *were* fates worse than dying. She'd seen the possibility of a world torn apart. She also remembered the pain and terror of nearly being torn apart herself when she'd originally brought the Book to Professor Lachlan and he'd tried to take her affinity to control it.

There had been a reason Professor Lachlan had wanted them to return to the past. Maybe it was because the diary had shown him how to win.

"There might not be a choice," she whispered, horrified at the thought of it. "If we're not successful tonight, if Nibsy somehow gets the upper hand . . ." She couldn't bring herself to finish that statement. "It might be the only way to stop him."

Confusion shadowed Harte's expression. "What, exactly, are you saying, Esta?"

"The diary," she told him. "Maybe it doesn't show the worst-case scenario. If he managed to get control of the Book, or worse . . . control over my power? Maybe it isn't Nibsy who has to die tonight. Maybe it's me."

"*No*," Harte said. "I refuse to believe that's possible. It's not going to happen. I won't *allow* that to happen."

"Harte . . ." She closed her eyes, because she couldn't look at him, not when she asked *this* of him. "If Nibsy is about to win—if the worst has happened and he somehow manages to get control of my affinity—you have to take me out of the equation."

"No, Esta—"

"We *cannot* allow Nibsy to control the Book," she said, her mind spinning furiously. "Ever since that day in the library, I've been trying to figure out why the Professor would have wanted us to come back here. I knew there had to be a trap of some sort. I knew he had to have some bigger plan. Maybe it's been right in front of us the whole time. He needs my power to control the Book. It's possible he'll find a way to get it."

"I would kill him first," Harte vowed.

"But you *can't*. The girl has to go forward, or everything we've been through—all that we've done and all that we've lost—will have been for nothing. If she goes forward, we still have a chance to start again. If she goes forward, maybe in another time line there's some other possibility where we *do* win. But if that girl doesn't go forward, or if there's no one waiting to send her back, then it's over."

A heavy silence filled the carriage before Harte responded.

"You're not actually asking me to kill you, Esta?" he asked, his voice straining with emotion. He pulled away from her. "Absolutely not."

"If everything is falling apart, you might have to, Harte," she told him. "Nibsy *cannot* be allowed to control the Book with my affinity. He cannot be allowed to have that kind of power. If he has me, if I'm going to die anyway, then take the possibility of victory away from him. It would be a mercy."

"I can't," Harte said, his voice breaking a little. "It's not possible."

"But it is. You've already done it," she told him. "Don't you see? We found that book eighty years from now. It's already happened. There is a time line where you do kill me, and because you do, Nibsy doesn't win. He ends up a bitter old man, waiting for a future that never comes."

"Please, don't ask this of me," he told her, his voice breaking. "Even if the world is cracking in two. Even if the Brink is about to erupt and everything will end because of it. I can't be the one."

"You're the *only* one who can, Harte. You're the only one I would trust with this." She cupped his face gently and forced him to look at her. "My life isn't worth the entire world."

"*Yes*, it is," he told her, taking her hand from his face and clasping it in both of his. "It *absolutely* is." His eyes were shadowed with pain, their stormy depths like the wave-tossed sea. "Don't you understand? Everything I've done since I decided to stay in the city, since I met you on the bridge that day, has been for you. To me, you're the only thing that matters. The world can go to hell if you're not here in it."

His words made her feel like she would break into a million pieces, but she couldn't let them sway her. "You don't really mean that," she told him.

"I do," he said softly.

"Promise me, Harte," she whispered, begging him. "Please. I need to walk in there knowing that there is no possibility of Nibsy winning. *Please.*"

"Fine," he told her. "I'll promise. But only because I'm not going to ever need to make good on it. We're going to do this, Esta. We have our way in, and we know how to stop Jack. Nibsy is not going to touch you. It's going to be okay." He kissed her then with an ardent fierceness that let her know just how terrified he was. And just how determined as well.

The carriage came to a stop in front of the entrance to the Garden, and before she could say anything more, it was time to face their fates. They lifted the hoods of the cloaks Ruby had stolen for them up over their heads until they shadowed their faces and hid their identities. Then Harte alighted first, reaching back to help Esta down as well.

The walls of the Garden were aglow with electric lamps that cut through the depth of the night. Flanking the door were enormous cauldrons burning with multicolored flames. She looked back only once to see Cela on top of the driver's perch, dressed in a top hat and cloak. They nodded up at her silently, and she tipped her hat at them before steering the carriage away.

Harte offered Esta his arm, and knowing that the time for argument was over, Esta accepted it. Together, they followed the line of robed figures up a path that glowed with electrical lights toward the Garden.

As they stepped up to the entrance and handed over their stolen tickets without any trouble at all, Esta thought that maybe she'd been wrong to demand his promise. She'd asked too much, but not because she was afraid. Tonight, fear could not drive them. Only certainty. Tonight, the future could be anything they made it. Arm in arm, they pressed into the crowd of the Conclave, walking steadily onward toward their destiny.

WHAT LAY AHEAD

On the night of the Conclave, Jack Grew didn't particularly mind being one of the faceless masses seated in the Garden. As far as he was concerned, it was better if his uncle and the rest of the Inner Circle believed he had accepted their edict to keep out of trouble. Let them assume that he was no better than one of the sheep sitting around him. At least there in the crowd, no one was paying him any attention. It would make it that much easier to step forward when the time came and accept his place as their savior.

He could not deny there was a sense of anticipation in the air that night that went beyond his own. The grand arena was filled with men from around the country, along with their wives or consorts. Many, clearly, had never been outside their own backwater towns before. Jack had enjoyed watching them as they descended from their carriages, craning their necks to look up at the buildings around the park. They marveled at the size of the Garden and at its beauty.

Perhaps some had come with the idea to wrestle control from the Order. They all had come ready to judge whether the Order still had any right to claim supremacy over the Brotherhoods. But none had any idea at all of what lay ahead. By the end of the night, the tides would have changed, and Jack himself would be the one to bring their boats to shore.

The first half of the evening's event was filled with endless speeches and posturing. He'd expected that. Planned for it. It gave him time to settle himself, to take another of the morphine cubes and let its bitter warmth fortify him. He barely paid attention as, one by one, the leaders of each of the Brotherhoods stepped forward to present themselves and their platforms to the Conclave as a whole. They spoke of their growing numbers, of the burgeoning cities, and of their plans for the future. They exposed their craven desperation for power and importance and their distinct lack of good breeding.

Jack saw the threat they posed, but unlike the Inner Circle, he understood that you couldn't simply bat them away like the annoying insects they were. They'd only come back for another try. No, the only way to deal with men like this was by giving them what they wanted—a sense that they were equals to the titans of New York. Only then could the Brotherhoods be brought together under one banner—but it wouldn't be the Inner Circle who led them.

By the time the night was over, *his* era would begin.

Eventually, the time for talking finally, *blessedly*, came to an end. The High Princept called for a brief recess to allow the group to move from the general assembly hall to the rooftop, and Jack followed along amiably, a wolf among sheep. The Book pulsed against his chest in anticipation, urging him on toward a future that could only be glorious. And within, the voice that had become his second conscience purred its approval.

The rooftop of the Garden was usually closed in the winter, but the ritual ahead required open air and a sense of drama that the vaulted hall below could not provide. Jack couldn't deny that the setting was an excellent choice. In addition to the space it afforded and the grandeur of the star-swept sky above, it provided an extraordinary view of the city beyond. The buildings already climbing toward the clouds. The electric lights turning night into day. The promise of it all. The *power* held within its streets.

The Flatiron Building, like the prow of a ship, was impressive, but it was only the newest feature of a larger, far older design. New York itself was a city made for magic, elegantly planned and meticulously designed. Now it was on the cusp of unimaginable greatness. Only here could the men from the other Brotherhoods—those from the middle and far west, who had neither polish nor cultural refinement—see that *this* city was the center of everything. Only here would they understand that a new century was just beginning, one that would carve itself out from the chaos of feral magic. A new world.

The sharpness of the icy December night was a welcome relief after the hot air that had been spouted in the preceding hours. The night sky was clear enough to view the steady progress of the constellations that watched over their proceedings. All around the roof, the towers of the Garden loomed like sentinels, dark fingers against the light of the city beyond. At the top of the highest tower, a naked Diana was illuminated from below, her arrow pointing southward toward the Bowery, as though she, too, were interested in hunting the vermin in their midst.

Along the outer perimeter of the roof, large iron cauldrons churned with flames that sent plumes of incense-laden smoke into the air. Other than alchemical lamps that had been positioned along the aisles of seats and the stars above, the cauldrons provided the only light. It gave the whole area an ancient, mystical atmosphere that it never had during the summer months, when the small stage was used for reviews featuring long-legged chorines and singers in spangled gowns. It was impressive, even to Jack's jaded eyes, but it was also perfect for his own uses. The shadows cast by the flames were exactly what he needed.

As the robed men of the various Brotherhoods began to settle themselves into seats that had been arranged in a half circle, facing the direction of the park, Jack found the person he'd been watching for all evening. He made his way through the crowd to where Ruby Reynolds stood not far from the High Princept. He saw her stiffen when she realized he was approaching and felt pure satisfaction when he saw she understood that there was no way to avoid him without drawing attention.

"Miss Reynolds," he said, inclining his head slightly.

"Mrs. Barclay," she corrected primly, lifting her chin. She was still studying the crowd, her eyes searching for something or someone.

"I wasn't aware you'd had a wedding night," he said, amused at the way her head snapped around and by the fire in her eyes. It would be gratifying to see that fire go out. "I wonder," he drawled. "*Is* a marriage that remains unconsummated *truly* a marriage?"

"You're a pig, Jack," she told him. "And tonight you're going to get *exactly* what you deserve."

"One can hope," he told her pleasantly, and when she turned to leave, he caught her by the arm. "Best if you watch yourself tonight, Ruby. It would be a tragedy if you joined your dearly departed husband sooner rather than later."

She tried to free herself from his grasp, but before she could storm off, Jack whispered a single, ancient word.

"What did you say?" she asked, looking suddenly unsteady.

"I simply said to enjoy your evening." Then, before she could escape, he jerked her close and whispered the word again while slipping a small pistol into her hand. It was a delicate little thing with a pearl handle. Exactly the type of weapon a woman would select for herself. When he released her, Ruby had a dazed look in her eyes, and she stumbled off without a word, taking the gun along with her.

He watched her go until her hooded figure had disappeared into the crowd.

"I thought we made it clear that you weren't to make any sort of scene."

Jack turned to find his uncle and cousin standing behind him, looking sour as old women. "What were you doing with the Reynolds girl?"

"I believe she's a Barclay now," Jack said, amused despite himself. "And it wasn't I who was making the scene. She doesn't seem quite stable."

"You had your hands on her," Morgan accused.

"Yes, Uncle," Jack said. "I admit that I did take her by the arm. Gentle as a child. You might thank me for stopping her."

"Stopping her from what?" Morgan asked, his large nose twitching.

"I don't know *exactly*," Jack said, feigning confusion. "But she seemed a bit hysterical. All the talk of feral magic must have brought up terrible memories. Someone might want to check on her. I don't trust that she wouldn't do something desperate. I could go, if you'd like?"

"You're not going anywhere," Morgan said, which was the exact answer Jack had planned for. "Junior can go after the chit. You sit down and try not to get in the way. Things have gone too well so far for you to make any sort of trouble."

Jack opened his hands as if in surrender. "As you wish."

Smiling secretly to himself, he went to find a seat in the center of the audience. In his pocket, the Book felt nearly alive. It pulsed in time with the steady beating of his own heart.

An intricate piece of metalwork grew up from the rear of the stage, providing a backdrop for the Order's next act. It was a larger and more intricate version of the Tree of Life that stood in the Mysterium, high across the park. In its branches, hundreds of tiny alchemical candles threw their otherworldly glow across each of the filigreed leaves. Above those topmost branches, the upper floors of the Flatiron Building were just visible. Below, beneath the platform of the stage, his machine lay hidden. Ready and waiting to rise into a new future.

Across the park, the upper floors that comprised the Order's new headquarters were alight, a crown on the bladelike building. The windows of the ceremonial library and the new Mysterium glowed with a brilliant amber that no simple gas lamp or electric bulb could have produced. It looked much like the golden light that had been visible on the solstice so many months before—molten and powerful, created by the sort of practiced and controlled magic that could bring the country into a new future. But Jack knew the truth. It wasn't magic alone that created the effect. The Order was channeling modern electricity through the ritual there, increasing its potential exponentially.

The Mysterium would be where the evening's display began. There, a group of men from the Inner Circle would be waiting to initiate the ritual that would demonstrate their continued relevance.

Too bad Jack had gotten to those men first. Too bad the Order's great gambit was destined to fail.

The wind gusted across the rooftop, causing the people around him to shuffle slightly, shuddering from the cold, but Jack Grew barely felt the ice in the air. He placed another of the morphine cubes between his teeth and let the bitterness fortify him, allowed its heat to invigorate him.

Soon it would begin. Jack had only to watch and wait. With the Book in his pocket, with fate on his side, he would be the one to direct his destiny and bring about the Order's end.

UPRISING

Bella Strega

On the winter solstice, night came early, covering the city with a blanket of darkness that would remain undisturbed for hours to come. The longest night in the coldest part of the year marked the turning from winter toward spring. For James Lorcan, it would mark the turning of his destiny.

Far uptown, the Order would be beginning their Conclave. Men from all across the land had arrived to do what countless civilizations had done for centuries, to keep watch for the dawning of a new day. To mark a moment of rebirth. They were dressed in their finery and jewels, wrapped in the confidence of their wealth, but they could not predict what was coming.

In the Bowery, it wasn't spirits who roamed the streets that night, but men. The anger and frustration that had been slowly simmering for months beneath the uneasy peace of the surface was beginning to boil over.

James heard the shots fired in the distance, the clanging of bells, and the shouts in the streets below, but he ignored them and turned the page of the small diary. The words on the page shimmered, coming ever clearer into focus.

Tonight, all would be revealed. Tonight, his destiny would be known.

Around him, the Aether felt frantic. The buzzing drone that had plagued him for months was barely noticeable now. It bunched and lurched, stirring his anticipation. Pushing him, guiding him, as it had always done before.

A pounding sounded at his apartment door, and when he opened it, Logan was waiting on the other side. "There's a problem in the saloon."

"What kind of problem?" James asked.

Logan grimaced, as fearful and uncomfortable as ever, despite the new ink he wore on the underside of his wrist. "It's hard to explain."

The Aether lurched, murmuring its uncertainty.

"Torrio?" James asked. The damned Five Pointer had been unsettled ever since he and his men had torn the Strega to pieces fighting the Hip Sing highbinders.

"It's not Torrio or the Chinese guys," Logan told him. "I don't know who they are, but there's a lot of them. There's hardly a place to stand. They're screaming and chanting. They're shouting for *you*."

The Aether trembled then, urging him on. "It's nothing but a distraction."

"It's an *uprising*," Logan argued. "They're demanding to speak to you tonight, or they're threatening to tear the place apart. You need to go down there before everything blows up."

"What do I care?" James told him. The Strega had always been a means to an end. After tonight, he'd have far more to rule over than a sordid saloon on the Bowery. "Let them have it."

Logan stared at him, incredulous. But then, how could he possibly understand?

The Aether leaped and danced in anticipation. The vibrations were so frantic now he could no longer hear the buzzing that had bothered him for months.

"It's starting," he told Logan. And when the night was over, he would hold the key to controlling far more than a simple Bowery barroom. Soon he would have the Book of Mysteries and everything he needed to unlock its power.

He'd have the world itself in the palm of his hand.

"Get your coat," he told Logan. "I need you to come with me."

DEVIATIONS

Madison Square Garden

J ianyu was growing impatient. He and Viola were waiting on the main level of the Garden for some sign of Ruby Reynolds, who should have been along before now. He looked up at the grand clock at the end of the cavernous hall and wondered what was keeping her—and how much longer they could afford to wait.

It was not that he had any fear of being discovered. Both of them were still wrapped in his affinity, hidden from sight within the strands of light, just as they had been since the beginning of the evening. They had slipped into the hall with the rest of the attendees, rich men and women who had come from across the continent to celebrate the solstice and decide the fate of their Brotherhoods. While men who were boiling with fear and raging with hate had given speech after speech, he and Viola had stolen away from the crowd and taken the opportunity to search the building for some sign of what Jack was planning.

In the end, their search had turned up nothing. The corridors and back rooms were clear of any obvious danger, and nothing seemed amiss on the roof either. It would have been easier had they found some small hint as to what Jack had in store. Without any clues, all they could do was watch and wait.

But first they had to find Ruby.

"She'll be here," Viola said, but Jianyu wondered who she was trying to convince—him or herself. She was vibrating with her usual impatience, but tonight there was an edge to it.

Ruby should have already arrived. She was supposed to have slipped away from her escorts while the crowd found their seats on the roof above, long before the ritual was to begin. Jianyu alone could have ferried her out to the carriage where Cela and Abel would be waiting to take her back to the safe house, but Viola had insisted on being involved.

"We cannot wait much longer," Jianyu told her. Cela and her brother would not be able to circle the block very many times before someone noticed their carriage.

There were many reasons that Jianyu had fought to keep the Johnsons outside the Garden that night. After the attack on the *New York Age*'s offices and Viola's subsequent decision to end the men who had perpetrated it, the Order clearly suspected a connection between the Mageus and the Negro Community. They would not have requested a staff of only white workers for the evening's festivities otherwise. Because there would have been no way for the Johnsons to blend in without discovery, Jianyu had refused to put either Cela or her brother at any more risk than they already were.

She had been livid, but it was better this way. With Cela safely outside, he could focus on the dangers ahead without worrying about which of them might touch her. He would get through the night—he would *live* through the night—and when it was over, only then would he allow himself to consider what they had spoken about earlier. Only then would he let himself remember the feel of her lips against his.

"There," Viola said, pointing toward a single robed figure descending the back staircase. The woman's hood had flopped back as though Ruby did not care who saw that she was not where she was supposed to be. "See? I told you she would come."

But Ruby did not immediately head for the place where they had agreed to meet. Instead, she paused at the base of the stairs and considered her options. When she reached the midpoint of the room, she stopped and looked around as though she did not know where she was supposed to be.

Jianyu hesitated.

"*Andiamo,*" Viola said, impatient as ever. "You wanted her to come, and now you hesitate. What are you waiting for?"

Jianyu frowned, unsure of the reason. But he waited longer still, until Ruby began moving in their direction. She stopped short of their meeting place.

"Hello?" Ruby whispered, searching the empty room for some sign.

Only then did Jianyu release the light, making them both visible once more.

Ruby let out a relieved breath at their appearance. "Thank heavens," she said in a hurried breath. "You have to come with me."

"No," he told her. "Cela has already been waiting too long. Harte and Esta will have expected us by now."

But Ruby was taking Viola's hand. "Please, you must come. You have to see this."

"Viola," Jianyu warned, because he could see that she was already softening. "This is not the plan. We are supposed to get her outside, remember? The whole point was to get her to safety."

"You must come," Ruby urged again. "Please. Come this way, and I can show you . . ." She was already leading Viola in the opposite direction of the exit.

"Stop," he said. "We need to get you outside. Cela cannot wait forever, not without drawing attention."

"But this is important," Ruby said, pleading to Viola. "It's the machine. Jack's machine. It's here."

Jianyu went very still. "Are you certain?" There were very few things that could have turned his feet from the path they had decided upon, but the mention of the machine, the terrible contraption that Jack had designed to eliminate those with the old magic, was one.

How could they have missed something so large? "We checked the entire building," he told her. "We found no sign of the machine."

"You didn't check everywhere," she said. "Hurry. We don't have time to waste. He's going to use it tonight. And if that happens, everyone within a hundred miles with the old magic will die."

Jianyu looked back toward the entrance of the Garden and then again at the large clock hanging over the main floor. Cela would be waiting for Ruby. There was no time to tell her of any change in their plans, not before the final events of the evening began. But if the machine was there, somewhere in that building, they needed to find it.

They needed to destroy it.

"Fine," he told Ruby and Viola both. "Take us to the machine, but be quick. There is no time to waste."

They hurried through the empty arena to a door hidden by the fabric that had been draped to cover the bare brick of the walls. It was a door that he had not discovered in all his trips to map the floor plan of the arena.

"This way." Ruby moved back the fabric so they could enter. "It's just down here."

The hallway beyond was narrow and dark, lit only by the flickering of the occasional dim bulb. They followed the hall along the length of the arena, and when they turned a corner and found another doorway, he felt the cold warning and stopped.

"Quickly," Ruby urged again.

Hair rose along the nape of his neck. "The machine is down there?"

Ruby nodded. "It's just a little farther."

"Well?" Viola asked, looking as uncomfortable about the cold energy emanating from the door as he felt.

"Can you sense anything?" he asked.

"No one," Viola told him. "But then, I couldn't sense Jack before. So why should I now?" Her mouth tightened. "We could get the others?"

They'd already wasted too much time. Esta and Darrigan were waiting on the rooftop above, and Cela was expecting him, but if the machine was there, it could not wait. Not if Jack planned to use it that night.

He shook his head. "There is no time for the others."

"Wait here," Viola told Ruby. She handed her the copy of Libitina that Esta had brought back from another time. "If anyone comes, you use this." Then she turned to Jianyu. "Let's go."

Opening the light, he wrapped Viola in his magic, and they stepped inside. But the second he crossed the threshold, he felt a shift. Cold pulsed around him, and he heard a grinding of metal as a barred gate began to descend across the entrance of the chamber.

Instantly, he released his affinity and lunged for the opening they had just passed through, but when his hands hit the bars, he pulled back. They were cold as ice, charmed or infused with some dangerous, corrupted magic.

"Ruby," Viola said. "Quickly. My knife."

Ruby's eyes were wide and unseeing. She stood, staring into nothing, the knife dangling from her fingertips.

"*Ruby*," Viola called again.

But Ruby showed no signs of hearing her. She continued to stare, and her pupils were so dilated that they nearly overwhelmed the green. The knife dropped, clanging to the floor.

Without another word, Ruby turned and left them there, even as Viola called to her.

They were alone. Trapped in the dark, where no one would think to look for them.

Somewhere in the distance, a thunderous crack echoed, and the building began to quake.

CONSECRATION

Harte stood next to Esta at the edge of the crowded rooftop, waiting for Jianyu and Viola amid the crush of robed men. He knew their types. He'd met men like them in St. Louis and San Francisco, and he'd heard about Esta's brushes with their brothers in Colorado. He knew what each of them was capable of, but he paid them little attention. Jack was the true danger that night.

Jack, however, didn't seem to be in any hurry. He'd been careful to keep himself in the middle of the crowd, where it was impossible to get him alone and corner him with the sigils. He also didn't seem to be planning or plotting anything.

"Why is he just sitting there?" Esta whispered, pulling her cloak low over her forehead to keep from being seen. "Shouldn't he be *doing* something by now? Preparing or . . . *something*?"

"I don't know," Harte said. He didn't particularly *want* Jack to do anything, but the lack of action didn't make him feel any safer.

She frowned. "So far he looks as bored as we are."

"Maybe that's the point?" Harte studied Jack. He looked far too relaxed, too confident. Like he was already sure that he would succeed.

Harte looked around the rooftop again, but other than the strange alchemical torches and flickering cauldrons, nothing seemed capable of causing the kind of destruction Jack had to have been planning.

"I'd feel better if Viola and Jianyu were here," Esta whispered. "What do you think is keeping them?"

"They had to wait for Ruby," he reminded her. "It's likely she couldn't slip away as quickly as she'd planned. She knew how important it was not to call attention to her departure."

"Well, they'd better hurry."

Suddenly, a drumroll interrupted the softly murmured conversations. The robed men who were still standing and milling about began to shuffle quickly toward their seats, while those already sitting straightened a little taller to see what was happening as the lights around the rooftop flickered and dimmed.

"It's starting," Esta whispered.

And Jack still hadn't made any move. He was still just sitting there in the middle of the row, just to the left of the stage, shoulder to shoulder with the men next to him. It would have been impossible for him to do *anything* without drawing attention to himself.

The drumroll continued, swelling in volume and intensity, until the crack of a rim shot ended in a flash of light that revealed a line of barely clad women at the back of the seating.

"Figures," Esta muttered, sounding annoyed with the whole scene.

Harte knew it had been nothing more than simple stage magic. There was no burst of hot or cold energy, but the illusion was effective enough to have the crowd gasping and murmuring with excitement. Or perhaps that was caused by the lack of clothing on the women. They were dressed in nothing more than glimmering silk sarongs, and their bodies had been painted the same gold as the Diana that balanced above them. Around their necks hung cut crystals, each to symbolize a digit of the Philosopher's Hand: the key, the crown, the lantern, the star, and the moon.

Another drumroll began, and the women parted to reveal five robed men.

"That must be the Inner Circle," Esta whispered.

The group followed the women who were silently processing down the middle aisle, toward the stage that had been erected on the side of the roof facing the park and the Flatiron Building. Slowly they walked, with every eye on the roof watching the sway of their hips as they continued up to the stage and then began to climb.

On the stage, an iron tree glimmered with a hundred lights. It was large enough for the women to sit within its branches, Harte realized. Like gilded birds, they took their places, lounging in positions to best display their impressive. . . assets. And the crystals that hung around their necks.

The Inner Circle mounted the stage not far behind them. Unlike the dark robes worn by the other Brotherhoods, the old men of the Inner Circle were dressed in ceremonial robes made of golden silk. The High Princept was easily recognizable in silk so white it seemed almost to reflect the light of the moon. Harte supposed that the outfit was meant to give him a regal appearance, but the winter wind made the fabric of his robe billow and made the old man look small and almost shriveled in comparison.

The Princept raised his arms, and the crowd grew silent.

"We welcome to our city our fellow brothers of the occult sciences. To the steadfast men of the Veiled Prophet Society, we bid welcome. As above . . ."

An entire section that could only have been the delegates from St. Louis responded, droning, "So below."

"To the courageous settlers of the west, the Syndicate, we bid welcome. As above . . ."

Again a portion of the rooftop erupted in answer: "So below."

"And finally, our newest brothers, those who guard our westernmost shores, the Vigilance Committee. We bid you welcome. As above . . ."

"So below" came the echoing reply.

"As above, so below, and so we bid all welcome to our city, to this bastion of hope and prosperity," the Princept said. "From its earliest days, this island has been a shining light. Centuries ago, it served as a foothold in the wilderness, and the men who carved civilization out of chaos became exemplars of what was possible for the worthy in this great and noble land. And so, on this darkest night in the deepest part of the year, we commemorate their work and bind ourselves to the mission of the Brotherhoods. We gather to reconsecrate ourselves to the power of the occult sciences as we look onward into the new century."

The crowd erupted into applause, and the Princept basked in their adulation. Harte watched the muscle in Jack's jaw twitch as he clapped slowly along with the rest. The Princept raised his hands to quiet the crowd before he continued.

"For decades now, the Order of Ortus Aurea has protected this great city from the darkness threatened by feral magic. During that time, we have led all those worthy of the occult sciences into a new, golden dawn. For more than a century, our work here has protected this city, and the country beyond."

Again came a smattering of applause, but this time it seemed contained to the portion of the roof where the Order sat.

Harte sighed. "They do love droning on about nothing, don't they?"

Esta nodded, biting back a smile. "Endlessly."

"Our Founders saw the threat to these shores, the creeping danger of feral magic, and were not satisfied to allow the danger to go unchecked. They were determined to protect this land of opportunity and plenty, and they used their great skills—their sacred artifacts—to protect the innocent. Their fortifications have stood steadfast, and tonight we reconfirm our commitment to this noble calling and our commitment to this nation and its people. Tonight we reconsecrate the power that has been at the heart of our country's safety for so long. Tonight we reaffirm our commitment to these streets and to the land beyond."

"Where are they?" Esta wondered again, looking back over her shoulder to the entrance of the roof. "They should *definitely* have been here by now."

"They will be," Harte told her, hoping he was right.

Esta frowned, searching the crowd on the rooftop. "They'd better be. We can't do this alone."

Out of nowhere, a thunderous crack echoed through the air, and the top of the Flatiron Building flashed, bursting with light. Harte watched as the light grew into a churning ball of otherworldly flame, and then, suddenly, a bolt of something that looked like amber-colored lightning shot out through the crystalline windows of the Mysterium to the fountain at the center of Madison Square Park.

The crowd on the roof gasped in appreciation and applauded again.

Worth Square was barely big enough to be considered a park, and its obelisk—a tombstone for some long-dead general—was a modern piece, not anything as large or authentic as the Egyptian obelisk that stood in Central Park. Now, though, everyone's eyes were being drawn to that small plot of land. The monument had started to glow from within, the gray stone turning brighter and brighter, until another thunderous crack echoed through the air and another bolt of light erupted from its tip and shot across the park, meeting the bolt from the Mysterium.

As the two lines of energy intersected in the center of the park, it formed a ball of light that started to swell. As it expanded, the alchemical flames that had illuminated the park leaped and danced, and the cement pathways of the night-dark park began to glow.

Harte realized then what he maybe should have realized before: The walkways of the park formed another symbol. Another *sigil*. Perhaps it wasn't as ornate or intricate as the one on the Book or the ones carved into the silver discs, but as those pathways turned to shimmering, he couldn't deny the cold power that was rising into the air.

Hadn't Ruby told them that the Order built the city—designed the very grid of streets—to channel occult power? Hadn't Jianyu and Viola explained how the Manhattan Solstice had transformed those streets during the Golden Hour? Harte hadn't quite understood, but now he did.

The Order no longer had its artifacts or the Book of Mysteries. They'd lost Newton's Sigils as well. But they had this, the city itself. The power that had somehow been built into it as part of the design. This was how the Order would convince the other Brotherhoods of their supremacy.

LISA MAXWELL

This was how they would attempt to recharge the Brink . . . and this would be where Jack would attack. He'd use this display somehow in his attempt to bring everything down around them.

But as the sidewalks of Madison Square Park burned bright, the pathways like carpets of undulating flame, Jack did not make a move.

"Why isn't he *doing* anything?" Esta asked. "And where are Viola and Jianyu?"

Harte didn't have answers to either of those questions. He was too busy trying to predict what might happen next.

"Something's wrong," Esta told him. "We need to find them."

"No," he said, touching her arm softly to steady her. "We need to stay here with Jack. We have to trust them."

There was something stirring in the air, a strange energy that had his hair rising and his instincts sparking.

"My brothers," the Princept called out. "Behold the mastery we have attained. Behold our city alive with power, ready to accept the future fate has held in store."

Another crack sounded, this time closer yet, and Harte jerked Esta back to protect her, ducking like everyone else on that roof as sparks flew from the tallest of the Garden's towers. High above, the goddess Diana began to glow as energy coursed through her body. She was a woman aflame, and then, just when she had turned nearly incandescent, the energy being channeled through her bolted out from the tip of her arrow and careened through the air to join the other currents in the park below.

The crowd murmured in appreciation as the cauldrons flashed, their colored flames rising into the night, and the pathways of the park pulsed with light. And then, little by little, the light from the park began to move. To *spread*. The bright energy might have been magic or electric or something between, but it moved like molten molasses creeping toward the pathways of the streets, and little by little, it began to light the city from within.

OVERCHARGED

Jack watched as the three bolts of light came together as one in the center of the park and reveled in the feel of electricity and power thick in the air. Everything was going exactly to plan. The Order had no idea that it had already initiated its own inevitable end.

Already, the electrical charges were coursing into the center of the park, hitting the precise location where multiple ley lines came together. The Order had believed themselves to be so clever, using the ley lines to carry the charge to the Brink. They'd believed it would be enough to simply give the magic surrounding the city a bit more energy, creating a visual demonstration that would keep their would-be usurpers quiet. What they *didn't* realize was that the amplification of the ley lines, focused as they were through the grid of the city, could do more than illuminate the Brink. It could destroy it.

The Order hadn't considered what would happen if the Brink were to be *overcharged*. They never suspected that the trustworthy minions they'd put in charge of starting the ritual might fail to stop it at the appropriate time. They had no idea how easily the Brink could shatter and fall, and with it, their control over the city.

But Jack would never allow the danger of feral magic once contained by the Brink to escape and pollute the country beyond. Once the Brink had fallen, Jack himself would step forward with the answer. With the push of a lever, he would show the Brotherhoods what the future could be. Not an antiquated boundary, limited by the magic of a bygone world, but a glorious machine. He would make them believe in what was possible—a world filled with machines capable of cleansing the entire continent.

Jack reached into his pocket and let his fingertips stroke the cracked and aged leather of the Ars Arcana. A voice inside him whispered of a promised future, of a glorious rise, and he thought he could *almost* feel the power within those pages crackle and pulse. Ever since he'd set himself on this path, as his plans had begun to come together over the past few weeks, the Book had seemed different somehow. Stronger. The power in those pages felt as though it was ready to awaken, and the voice inside him whispered that if he were brave enough, he could grasp it. *Use it.* Bend it to his will.

Murmuring a string of ancient syllables under his breath, Jack traced the symbol on the cover, and he felt the Book shudder. The cauldrons around the edges of the roof had been burning steadily with undulating flames of every color, but now, called forth by his words, they began to smoke. Unnoticed by those on the rooftop too interested in the pyro-technics lighting the park below, a dark greenish-gray fog began to creep and grow.

By now the pathways of the park were molten with energy. Like lava, it flowed outward, following the grid that had been designed so many years ago to channel the power deep within the city's core. Steadily, the light flowed and spread toward the land's end, where the dark strip of water—and the Brink—was waiting.

OUT OF SIGHT

Cela was still near livid at Jianyu for keeping her out of their plans. She wasn't much happier with her brother, who'd agreed without hesitation that it was better for her to stay *outside* and wait.

Outside. As though anything was going to happen *outside*. She huffed to herself, annoyed at the heavy-handedness of the men in her life.

"I know you're not happy, but those noises you're making aren't going to convince me it's a good idea to go in there," Abel said from his seat on the driver's perch.

"Ruby should've been out by now," Cela told him. They'd been circling the blocks around Madison Square for the better part of an hour, waiting for some sign that things were progressing as planned inside, but none had come. The blond heiress was long overdue.

"There's still time," Abel said, steady as ever. "The final ritual doesn't even start until after midnight."

"Still," she said. "There should have been some sign by now."

"If something has gone wrong, we'd know."

"How?" she asked.

"We just would," Abel told her. But she realized he was sounding less sure by the minute.

"I still don't see why we couldn't help."

"We are helping," he told her. "Someone has to be the getaway driver."

"Some help," she muttered.

Abel had a point, as much as she refused to admit it. Whatever was going to happen tonight wasn't likely to be something her friends could just stroll away from. Someone had to be ready with a fresh horse and a good, solid carriage.

"Look, Rabbit, just because Mr. Fortune isn't nervous about the Order these days doesn't mean I'm going to take any chances with you," Abel said. "Maybe they've backed off publicly, but those men aren't stupid. They know that the patrols they sent to burn down the paper's building didn't die natural deaths. They know that Fortune and his people had protection, and they'll be looking for any excuse to come after not only us but the whole community."

She let out a resigned sigh. He was right. It wasn't just their lives on the line. Cela might have been willing to risk that. But she knew what could happen when a whole community got blamed for a single man's actions. It had cost her father his life, and others right along with him. She wouldn't be the cause of that, no matter how much she might be worried about her friends.

When the first thunderous crack reverberated across the sky, Abel cursed and had to fight to keep the horses from bolting.

"I told you she should have been here by now," she said, climbing into the driver's perch with him. "It's starting."

When the second bolt crashed, they both knew something had gone wrong.

"We can't just sit here," she told her brother.

He didn't respond, but she could see the worry lining his face.

When the third thunderous crack reverberated across the sky, she looked up to see the goddess of the tower's bow lit and a bolt of light like an arrow's path coursing down to the park, and she decided.

Abel was too busy looking up to notice her climbing down until she was already standing on the street.

"What the hell do you think you're doing, Cela?"

"I'm going in there, Abe," she told him.

"Like hell—"

"You can either come with me or you can wait here," she said, but she was already turning and running toward the entrance.

Abel caught up with her before she'd reached the main entrance and directed her off to the side. "Are you crazy?"

"I have to get in there," she told him, trying to pull away.

"Not that way." He jerked his head, nodding toward an unmarked employee entrance down the block a little farther.

For a second, she didn't think she was hearing him right.

"Let's go," he told her. "Before I change my mind."

They made it into the building without any trouble. Nobody was around to see them slipping through the service hallways. Thanks to the work Jianyu had done to map out the building, they found their way to the arena without any trouble.

They arrived just in time to see Ruby emerging from a split in the heavy, draping fabric that covered the walls.

Relief bolted through her, but Cela barely took a step in Ruby's direction before Abel caught her arm.

"Wait a second," he whispered.

"Where's she going?" Cela asked as she watched Ruby turn away from the exit.

"Looks like she's headed up to the roof."

Ruby looked back, as though checking to make sure she hadn't been followed, before turning toward the stairs.

"Did you see her eyes?" Cela asked. Ruby'd had a blank, dazed look to her. "Something's not right."

They watched as Ruby took the steps up toward the ritual on the roof.

"We need to get out of here, Rabbit," Abe told her.

"Where did she come from?" Cela asked, studying the place where Ruby had emerged from the curtains. "There shouldn't be any kind of passage back there."

"Maybe Jianyu missed something," Abe said. "We're not staying to find out. If the rich white girl wants to go play with her rich white friends, I say we let her."

But Cela's instincts prickled. She'd gotten to know Ruby over the past weeks, and nothing about what she'd just seen felt right. Something had gone terribly wrong.

They could go after Ruby and make sure she was okay, but that meant going up to the roof. It meant being seen by any number of people who might connect her or Abel to the *New York Age* just by the color of their skin.

Or she could find out where Ruby had just come from.

One or the other.

"I'm not leaving yet."

"I will carry you out of here," Abel threatened.

"You can try," she said. "But it'd be a lot easier if you just came with me. Something's back there. I got a feeling we need to go check it out."

Abel looked like he about wanted to murder her. "You're sure about this feeling?"

"I wish I wasn't."

The hallway was a long, narrow passage with barely any light, but she didn't let the darkness bother her. The second she saw it, she knew that there was no legitimate reason Ruby should have been back there. Her instincts buzzed again, and they pushed onward.

When they rounded the corner and saw the bars blocking her path, Cela thought for a second she'd been wrong. Abel was already taking her by the hand, starting to turn back, when Jianyu shifted out of nothingness and appeared. Viola was there beside him suddenly as well.

"Cela," he said, stepping toward the bars. But he came short of touching them. "Why are you here?"

"It seems like I'm rescuing the two of you," she said, pointing out what should have been obvious.

"You should not be here," he told her. She would have been angry at his greeting if his voice hadn't been ragged with fear. He turned on Abel. "How could you let her come?"

"She had a feeling," Abel told Jianyu with a resigned shrug.

"How did you find us?" Viola asked.

"I saw Ruby leaving this hall," Cela told them.

"Was she alone?" Viola's expression was a study of worry. "Where did she go?"

Cela nodded. "There wasn't anyone with her, far as I could tell. But she was heading up to the roof."

"Jack," Jianyu said softly. "He is the only one who could be behind this."

"You have to go after her," Viola pleaded. "If Jack has her . . ."

Cela noticed Viola's blade on the ground not far from the bars. "We're not going alone."

ANTICIPATION

The sky hung dark and heavy above as James walked through the city with Logan following like a dog a few steps behind. He hadn't bothered to check on the saloon. Why should he? His destiny lay north, where the Order stirred corrupted magic and where the possibilities he'd seen flash across the diary's pages waited.

His cheeks burned with the cold of the winter air, but he craved the bite of pain and the way the frosty air focused him. Block by block they marched, past brawling in the streets. Past homes closed off from the dangers of the night. He could have taken a cart or a streetcar, but this felt right somehow, his feet meeting the solid earth beneath him. Steady as he traversed the city that would soon be his.

A few miles north, the Order would be beginning their evening's festivities. He could imagine them, the men who would one day bow to him. He could practically see them there, not knowing the future he was about to create.

Finally, they made it to the part of town where the Flatiron Building sliced through the night. The park was lit with hundreds of luminaries lining the walks with an ethereal glow that could only be the result of corrupted magic. Beyond the park, the Garden was awash with light. The sky above them glowed so brightly, it nearly blocked out the stars.

"Where are we going?" Logan asked, breaking what had been a more preferable silence.

"To the Conclave," he said, as though that should have been clear enough.

They cut through the park, and as they walked, James felt the brush of cold energy on his cheeks. He thought he felt vibration beneath his feet, a steady pulsing like the city itself had a heartbeat. With each step, he fell in time with that ancient rhythm. With each step, the Aether stirred, joined the song, and pushed him onward. Something trilled suddenly within the Aether, and he paused, waiting.

"What is it?"

"Shhh—" He held up his hand to silence Logan.

The buzzing was back. Clearer now. Like a hive of bees growing closer.

He thought something moved in the shadows, but when he turned, nothing was there.

"Do you sense anything?" he asked. "I need to know if any of Esta's friends are close by."

Logan frowned but shook his head. "I don't think so. Not here."

"You're sure?" The buzzing throbbed now, a warning that inched across his skin. "There's nothing?" He took Logan by the lapels. "Be *sure*."

"No—" Logan's eyes had gone wide. "There's nothing here but those lamps."

All at once, the buzzing ceased. Faded.

The Aether pulsed softly again, returning to its previous order, but James didn't feel any relief. He wouldn't until the Book was in his hands and Esta's power was under his control.

"Come on," he told Logan, and set off toward the Garden once more.

Outside the entrance, he looked up toward the rooftops. If Josef Salzer's information was right, the ritual would be held there. His own destiny would unfold there as well.

The Aether seemed to approve.

"Is Esta inside?" he asked. He needed to be sure.

Logan hesitated before confirming she was. "She's in there. I can feel Ishtar's Key." He frowned. "They're close, and . . . something else. Another of the artifacts?"

The Pharaoh's Heart. Right where he'd wanted it to be.

"And the Book of Mysteries?"

Logan looked up to the roofline, where otherworldly flames sent their fragrant smoke into the air. "It's there."

The Aether danced in anticipation, pushing him on. He tested the possibilities and found the one that assured his victory. And if the faint unsettled hum was still present? It no longer signified. It was time.

Suddenly a crack of thunder split the night, and an impossible light flashed through the darkness. James lifted his hand to shade his eyes as he squinted against the glare of the brightness. Magic crackled and cold power brushed along his skin, beckoned and threatened all at once.

He felt the Aether lurch, and he turned to see that Logan was walking away from him. He was heading toward the entrance of the building.

Because Logan believed Esta could still save him. James had sensed this possibility for days now. But he'd come prepared for this eventuality, even if he had hoped Logan would have been smart enough to choose otherwise.

It was a shame, really. The boy could have been so useful.

Taking the silver gorgon from within his shirt, he focused his affinity through the ring on his finger and pushed them both through to the magic that lay within. He could feel its connection to the newly inked mark on Logan's wrist, and he sent a small pulse of power through.

Logan froze, but James could sense the boy struggling against his hold.

"What were you planning to do, Logan?" James stepped toward him slowly. He pressed his affinity through the ring, through the silvery topper, and Logan turned. He tried not to. He struggled against the hold that James had on him, despite the pain he must have been feeling, but he turned just the same.

"Did you think you would run to her?" James asked, tightening his hold on Logan's mark—on his *will*. "Did you think she would save you from me?" He laughed softly.

"You think I don't know what you want? Do you think I'm not aware of what you've been planning for, even as you pledged yourself to me and took the mark? Esta was never going to take you back," James told him truthfully. "That possibility has never existed. It was never an option."

He pushed more of his affinity through the silvery snakes, shoved his power through the mark, and Logan screamed. He was still frozen, unmoving, but blood was beginning to drip from his wrist.

"Please—"

James was unmoved by the desperation in Logan's eyes. Desperation made people weak, and there was no place for weakness in the world he would build.

"I gave you a chance to choose differently," he told Logan. "Even after I knew you went to Esta and Darrigan, even after I knew you'd promised to betray me, I gave you the opportunity to turn from that path. I tried to make you see the truth."

The boy was clearly straining from the effort of fighting against the hold of the mark. But there was no possibility of fighting against that magic, not when the Delphi's Tear was snug on James' hand. He focused his affinity through that ancient stone and sent another command through the Aether that had been his guide for so long.

Logan struggled against the compulsion, but he never had a chance. Bloody tears streaming down his cheeks, he knelt there before James.

"You could have been so much more," James said, feeling only the hint of regret. *Such a useful tool.*

Then, with another sure push, he used the mark to tear the magic from Logan's very soul.

Logan collapsed, a bloodied heap on the ground as another crack sounded and another arc of light shot through the sky overhead.

James looked up to see the flames in the cauldrons rising and great beasts beginning to form themselves from the smoke.

With the Aether jangling in anticipation, James stepped into the Garden to claim the glorious future that was his and his alone.

THE LADY ON THE TOWER

Esta watched as the bolts of electricity and magic that had illuminated the park crept through the city. The streets lit one after another, until finally the strange light met the water that encircled the island. She knew when that energy hit the Brink, because suddenly a flash of blinding light turned the midnight sky into day.

The robed figures on the rooftop gasped in awe and then applauded the spectacle, but Esta had a sinking sense that something was wrong.

"Here, in the depths of darkest night, we bring to the world a brilliant new dawn," the Princept called from his place on the stage. "From our ritual this night will come a new era. Golden in promise. Powered through the mastery of the occult sciences and the modern world."

In the distance, a wall of light shimmered against the star-draped sky. Colors of every type wove through the glistening curtain of power as the Brink became visible, magic made real. It wrapped around the island, as far as the eye could see, throwing up enough light that it wiped the stars from the sky.

But Jack still hadn't made a move. He was sitting in the same place, placidly watching the proceedings with only the barest hint of interest in his expression. If they hadn't known he was going to attack, if they hadn't been sure of it, Esta would never have suspected him.

"Why isn't he doing anything?" Esta asked.

"I don't know," Harte said. "But he will."

"What if he doesn't?" she wondered. "What if we're wrong?"

"It's Jack, Esta." Harte took her hand. "He's completely predictable, and this isn't the first time he's tried to frame Mageus by attacking. He's done this before. There's no reason to think we're wrong."

In the distance, the Brink pulsed and shivered. The colors within it flashed, twisting and twirling.

"Our forefathers brought the Brink into being through the force of their will," the Princept continued. "Through the powers bestowed by angels and demons, they carved from the Aether protection for these shores, for this world. But there are those among us tonight who would question our glorious Order. There are those who came here tonight not in the bounds of brotherhood."

The crowd felt suddenly unsettled at the change in the Princept's tone, but he continued, undeterred.

"There are those who have come here this hallowed night because they believed the Order of Ortus Aurea to be weak and feeble. There are those who came not as brothers, not to join with us in the good and noble quest to eradicate feral magic from our shores, but as enemies from within."

A rustling erupted through the gathering as men from the various Brotherhoods began murmuring among themselves. The sounds of their voices grew as they voiced denials and accusations.

But the Princept didn't pay them any mind. He simply held his hands aloft, and the hundreds of alchemical flames contained within the branches of the tree behind flared from soft green to a blinding gold. The women perched there glistened, and the cut crystals around their necks flickered with the reflection of the flames.

Drawn by the spectacle like moths to flame, the crowd went quiet again.

"Do not come here with lies on your tongues," the Princept said, his expression furious. "Come instead ready to kneel in penitence for your hubris and greed. *Kneel!*" he commanded, his voice rising above the din of the night.

Beyond, the city was awash with energy, and the Brink flashed again, as if in warning. But on the rooftop, the robed men went still, as though caught in the spell of his words. Slowly, one by one, they did what he commanded and began to kneel.

Jianyu and Viola were there suddenly, appearing out of nothing next to them.

"Where have the two of you been?" Esta asked, searching them for some sign of injury. But they seemed whole and well.

"Jack," Jianyu replied darkly.

"But he's been here the whole time," Harte told them. "He's never once left his seat there."

Jianyu frowned as though he wanted to argue, but he looked beyond Esta to where Jack was sitting in the crowd. "You're sure?"

"Positive," Esta told him.

"Have you seen Ruby?" Viola asked.

Esta shook her head. "She didn't come find you?"

"She did," Jianyu said, but before he could explain, an earsplitting scream tore through the crowd.

Esta turned to find the crowd rippling with fear, but at first she couldn't figure out what was happening. Jack was still there in his seat, serene and unbothered as he'd been all night.

"There!" someone shouted.

The crowd rippled again as hundreds of faces turned, looked upward to the highest tower of the Garden.

"That explains where Ruby went," Harte murmured darkly.

"What is she doing?" Viola asked. She gripped Esta's arm, and there was no mistaking the fear that cut through her voice.

"I don't know," Esta told her.

Ruby was standing on the topmost ledge of the tower, far above them. Her hood had been pushed back, and with her brilliant blond hair shining in the night, everyone below could see who it was. But she wasn't alone. In her hand was a small silver gun, and she had it pointed directly at her companion's head.

"She has your boy, Morgan," someone shouted. "Isn't that Junior?"

It was clear from the way his face had drained of color that he was terrified. His hands were raised, and he was pleading for his life as Ruby nudged him toward the edge.

"No," Viola said. "This can't be. She wouldn't—"

"She's not," Esta said, glancing back at Jack, who was watching the events unfold with amusement glinting in his watery blue eyes. As she watched, she saw his pupils expand and his eyes darken. "He has her under some kind of spell or charm. She's not in control right now."

"I'm going," Viola said.

"No!" Esta grabbed Viola's arm and grimaced as she felt the lash of her affinity. "Viola, no. We have to get to Jack. That's how we'll stop this. *That's* what will save Ruby."

"I can't leave her there," Viola said.

"If you go running up there now, who knows what will happen," Harte told her. "You're likely to startle her into doing something that can't be undone. We need to take care of Jack. Now, while the crowd is distracted."

"What if she falls?" Viola asked. Her violet eyes were glassy with tears.

"We cannot leave her there," Jianyu said. "I will go. I can approach without her knowing. I can stop her from this course." His mouth went tight. "I can try."

Esta considered the situation. "Okay." Even if she knew it was a distraction. "We can't let her fall, and if Ruby kills Morgan's son, it'll create a new problem."

"I will not allow that to happen," Jianyu said, but his gaze drifted to a spot just over Esta's shoulder. "There is more trouble coming. You need to get to Jack before it arrives."

Jianyu was gone before he could explain, but when Esta looked back over her shoulder in the direction Jianyu had been looking, she understood.

"Madonna," Viola said, crossing herself. "These ones are bad news."

The cauldrons that had been burning with fantastical fires all night were now smoking, and as Esta watched, the green-gray fog-like smoke began to swell and grow until they were not columns of smoke at all but enormous beasts made of fog.

AS ABOVE

Jianyu opened the light around himself and, beneath the cover of his affinity, he dashed for the tallest tower at the far end of the rooftop, hoping he would not be too late. Taking the steps two at a time, he ran up toward the tower where Ruby Reynolds was holding J. P. Morgan's eldest son at the end of a gun.

She must have been bespelled earlier. It was the only explanation for why she had led them into that trap of a chamber. It was the only explanation as well for why she would threaten the life of one of the most powerful men in the city—possibly even the country.

Jianyu was nearly to the top of the tower when he heard someone let out a bloodcurdling scream. And then came another.

Picking up his speed, he pushed himself until his lungs ached and his legs burned with the effort. Finally, he reached the top and saw that both Ruby and the Morgan heir were still there. No one had fallen. No one had died.

But the rooftop below was awash with chaos.

They should have expected this. They should have predicted that Jack would use the same tricks as before. Jianyu watched with a sense of too-familiar horror as three enormous beasts hewn from fog and smoke began to attack the crowd. But he could not help those people now. Not when the Morgan heir was pleading for his life.

Jianyu considered the problem. Any move he made to reveal himself might cause Ruby to jump or fall or fire the gun. He could not do anything to startle her, especially since he had no idea what kind of charm she was under. He had no idea what might trigger a reaction.

The only solution was to stop her before she understood what was happening. He could only hope that whatever corrupted magic had her in its grasp would not sense him before he could get to her.

Without hesitating any longer, he reached for her, and in one swift and sure movement he swiped at her, hitting the point on the side of her neck that would stun her into unconsciousness. When Ruby began to collapse, he released his hold on the light and reached for her, catching her before she could fall. The pistol she'd been holding tumbled from her hand and landed in the middle of the chaos below.

The man she had been holding at gunpoint startled but caught himself on the edge of the building before he fell. As Jianyu pulled Ruby to safety, Morgan's son managed to climb back inside the tower. He froze when he saw Jianyu crouched over Ruby, trying to wake her, and there was such hatred in his eyes that it felt like an actual slap.

"Filthy maggot," the Morgan heir said, glaring at the two of them. He inched around the top of the tower, avoiding Jianyu.

It did not matter that he had just saved this man's life. Morgan's son, like his father before him, would never believe that there was any good in those with the old magic.

"I give you your life, and still you hate us?" he wondered.

Morgan's son did not answer. He stayed silent, cowering in the corner.

Beyond, the city looked like it was aflame. From that height, Jianyu could see the entire expanse of streets. The neatly laid-out lines looked like a grid of molten gold, and beyond, the Brink had become a wall of power and light. It was shuddering with the power being channeled into it, and Jianyu realized that the streets themselves were answering in reply.

He felt something more then. The building beneath him was quaking, and the tower was beginning to sway.

This is how he will do it. The realization was both immediate and terrible.

"Why have they not stopped the ritual?" Jianyu demanded.

"I bet that's exactly why you're here, isn't it? To stop the ritual. To watch the Brink fall," Junior sneered.

"I do not want the Brink to fall this night," Jianyu said. "You must tell me how it works. Where is the power coming from? Why has it not stopped?"

"Lies," Junior said. "I won't fall for your tricks. I'm not telling you anything."

"You do not understand," Jianyu said, pointing out over the city toward the wavering wall of power beyond. "Look at the streets. They are near to breaking apart. This cannot be what you intended."

Junior did look, and his expression clouded.

"The Brink *cannot* fall," Jianyu told him. "If it does, so too does the city. So too does all of creation."

"You're lying," Junior told him, but there was fear in his eyes now— more fear than there had been a second before. "I know your type. This is some kind of trickery. You and the Reynolds chit are in this together. You're trying to confuse me. Well, I won't be confused. I won't be distracted."

Distraction. How had they not seen it? The attack was nothing more than misdirection.

They had been trying to discover what Jack would do to destroy the Brink. They had imagined he might use some ritual, perhaps even his great machine, but the truth was there—clear as the night sky above. He would destroy the Order with its own weapon. Ruby's attack on Junior had afforded the necessary distraction, and now, as energy continued to pour into the streets, Jack would simply allow it to become overloaded.

It happened all the time in the city. The fragile electrical grid would overload with energy, and the lights would flicker and dim from the excess. The same would happen to the Brink if they did not stop it.

"Do you not see what is happening?" Jianyu asked. "We must stop the ritual."

The ground was rumbling unsteadily beneath them, but Junior's eyes

LISA MAXWELL

hardened. "*There's* the truth. You want me to stop the ritual because you want to destroy us. I won't. I won't have any part of this."

"You are a fool," Jianyu said, knowing their time was running out.

Below, another of the smoke beasts emerged, climbing up over the edge of the building from the street below. Thrown over its shoulder was Cela. She dangled unconscious, not fighting her captor.

She was not supposed to be there. Abel was supposed to take her back to the wagon to wait. . . . Unless the beasts had found them before they made it. He had to get to them, to get to *her*.

He took Ruby into his arms and wrapped his affinity around himself. He realized quickly that her weight would only slow him down, and Cela could not wait. Instead of carrying Ruby down to the rooftop, he found an alcove to tuck her into far enough back from the ledge that she would be safe. Then he ran. Junior could fend for himself. Below, the beasts of smoke were still raging, and his friends needed help.

WHERE MAGIC LIVES

Esta could do no more than watch as the smoke from the cauldrons transformed itself into beasts. Viola and Jianyu both had
tried to describe these monsters, but watching the fog gather
itself into solid, tangible creatures was something altogether different. All
around her, the rooftop was awash in confusion as the Order and their
guests attempted to escape. The robed men and women of the various
Brotherhoods pushed and shoved, trampling over one another in a desperate attempt to reach the steps first.

But not everyone was lucky enough to get out. The beasts weren't
attacking haphazardly, Esta realized. They were specifically going after the
men on the stage. Jack was attacking the leaders of the Order—the men
known as the Inner Circle—just as they'd predicted. One of the larger of
the monsters had cornered J. P. Morgan and was herding him toward the
edge of the roof. Morgan was attempting to use a folding chair to fend
off the attack, but it was useless against the creatures. With each swing,
the chair cut through the smoke, and the monster re-formed. With each
swing, he stepped back, closer to the edge.

Another of the beasts had the High Princept. It had lifted the old man
over its shoulder and was carrying him across the roof like a rag doll.

Viola handed Esta a blade. It was the knife she'd brought back from
the Professor's library, the twin to Libitina. "Those beasts are nothing but
corrupt magic made by corrupt men," Viola told her. "And like men,
they can die."

But Esta knew that a knife, even one as deadly as Viola's, would never
be enough. There were too many of them.

"We'll never get to them all in time," she said, watching Morgan being pushed ever closer to the edge of the roof.

"We need to go after Jack," Harte told them. "Attacking those things individually will take too much time, and it will force us to split up. Which is likely exactly what Jack wants."

"Harte's right," Esta told Viola. "If we get to Jack, maybe we can stop this. We just need to find him."

Suddenly, the building shook violently, like an earthquake had just rippled through the bedrock below. Esta grabbed hold of Harte in time to stay upright, and they clung to each other until the worst of the shaking stopped.

Viola cursed, crossing herself as she looked beyond the place where they were standing.

Esta turned to find a mass of greenish-gray smoke billowing up over the ledge of the building. The smoke continued to creep up over the edge of the roofline, rising around them as it coalesced again into another one of the beasts. Tendrils of smoke transformed into an enormous arm, and as it reached for them, Viola let out a vicious scream and sent her knife flying through the air.

It struck true, and as it disappeared into the smoke, the beast roared. Its chest split, bursting open as the creature was obliterated, but as the fog dissipated, a figure fell to the ground. It had been carrying someone within itself.

Cela, Esta realized in horror as the monster fell, releasing its victim. The knife had gone clear through its fog-formed body and had found purchase in Cela's side.

Abel screamed his sister's name and ran for where she'd fallen.

Viola started to follow, but Esta grabbed her. "We need to get to Jack."

"No," Viola said, trying to tear away from Esta. "I can save her. I can—"

Esta looked over to where Cela had fallen. Abel was there with her, holding her head in his lap. Her eyes were open, and though her face was bunched in pain, she was speaking to him.

"We *will* save her," Esta promised. "But we have to stop Jack. If we don't, more of those will attack. Until we destroy Thoth, none of this stops."

Viola's brows drew together, and Esta knew she wanted to argue. She tried to pull away, but Esta held her fast.

"You have to trust me on this, Viola," she pleaded. She'd seen a future where Jack won, where the destruction of the Brink ended everything. She could *not* let that happen. "If Jack gets away, the Brink could fall, and then everything will have been for nothing. No one will make it out. Please help me. For Cela. For Theo."

Certainty settled over Viola's features. "Fine. Show me where the bastardo is. It's time to end this."

"There," Esta told Viola, pointing to the stage, where Jack watched with amusement as his uncle and the others were being pressed back toward the edge of the roof. Soon, they'd run out of room and have nowhere else to go.

As the monsters herded the Inner Circle toward their inevitable end, Jack pressed a lever in the base of the Tree of Life, which had long since been emptied of its bare-chested birds. With a grinding of metal and gears, the branches slowly began to fold down and away, and in their place an enormous machine rose from within the stage.

Jack turned to them as his machine ascended into place. His eyes were already flooded with the inky blackness that signified Thoth's presence. "Esta Filosik," he purred in a voice older than the city. "I've been waiting for you."

Esta glanced at Harte and then at Viola, giving each of them a subtle nod to make sure they were ready. She could only hope that Jianyu had been successful in the tower and was in place as well.

She knew from the blackness that filled Jack's eyes it would be pointless to use her affinity. To capture Thoth, they had to surround him, and they had to do it without depending on their magic. But they'd planned for this very eventuality, and she trusted her friends.

"I see you've decided to join us as well," Jack said to Viola. "Convenient, though you and the Chinaman were supposed to wait for me downstairs." His mouth curled. "No matter. I can harvest your power here as well as anywhere."

Jack took the Pharaoh's Heart from within his robes and slid the ornate blade into the machine. As it locked into place, Esta felt a burst of warning cold, and when the enormous orbital arms of the machine started to rotate, the building shivered. As they rotated, dodging in and out around one another like an enormous gyroscope, the arms picked up speed, and the dangerous energy snapping through the air started to build. She felt the Aether lurch as that icy energy coursed around them, like a whirlwind of power circling through the air.

There was no sign of Jianyu, but Esta knew they were out of time.

This was the same type of machine that had killed Tilly. And if they didn't stop Jack, one like it would kill Sammie's mother and countless others in San Francisco. If they didn't stop him there and then, he'd *never* stop. Not until the old magic and everyone who had an affinity for it was wiped from this land.

Esta looked at Harte and saw the determination in his stormy eyes. Saw, too, everything he felt for her. Everything that lay between them. And she vowed that their story would not end there on that desolate rooftop at the hands of a madman. She would steal them a tomorrow. She would bring a different possibility into being.

Viola came up beside Esta, shoulder to shoulder. She straightened her spine and lifted her chin as she gave Esta a sure nod. *Now or never.*

Time seemed to hold its breath as Esta looked around the rooftop—at the chaos Jack had caused, at the steadfastness of her friends. There was no sign of Jianyu, but they couldn't wait. She had to trust that he was in place.

"Now!" she screamed, and just as they'd planned, Esta ran directly for Jack.

As she'd hoped, her attack drew his attention, distracting him long enough for Harte and Viola to get in position. They already had their sigils, were already setting them spinning, when suddenly Jianyu was there as well—appearing from the night behind Jack. He was holding two of the sigils and with his position, completed the circle with her and Jack inside.

Not only Jack.

When Esta had lunged for Jack, Thoth had surged. But she'd expected him to. She'd been ready, and he'd been so focused on attacking her that it was already too late for Thoth or Jack to stop the others from trapping them within the boundary of the sigils. Already, Esta could feel the strange, cold energy as the discs transformed into golden orbs of light and power. Harte shouted the command, and she felt the Aether shift as a boundary erupted, connecting the sigils, trapping her and Thoth within.

She barely had time to appreciate the silence within that circle, the way that she felt suddenly severed from everything around her, because in an instant, Jack was on her and it was clear that he wasn't going to go easy on her because was a woman.

But she'd expected that as well.

With a vicious twist of her arm, Esta tore herself out of Jack's grip and, letting her body move on instinct that had been drilled into her for her entire childhood, she maneuvered around him, swept his legs out from under him, and then pinned him to the ground. Her knee was across his throat, holding him in place, as she pushed her hands against Jack's chest.

"Where is your weapon, girl?" Jack—or the thing inside him—said in an ancient voice.

She gave him a cold smile. "I'm the weapon." Who needed a knife when the power within her could slice through creation? She focused on her connection to the old magic, and as her affinity swelled, she pressed her magic into Jack.

Jack suddenly looked nervous. When he spoke again, it was Jack's true voice that came from his mouth. "Please, Esta," he said, his voice breaking. "Please. I don't want to die."

She felt a pang of pity for the fear in his eyes—for the humanity he'd thrown aside. But there wasn't time for pity. Not when the world was at stake.

She pressed her affinity into him further and found Thoth's power waiting there.

"You cannot win, girl." The thing inside Jack began to laugh. And when he spoke again, the voice that came out of Jack's mouth was her own. "You cannot free the world of me, Esta Filosik. Not without destroying yourself."

She would not be distracted.

Reaching for her magic again, Esta forced the spaces apart. Tearing at time and existence and the substance that held Thoth to this world.

Jack's eyes went inky black again, and Esta could sense Thoth's fear. She felt his anger as well, but she didn't pause or hesitate. She concentrated harder, focused all her magic—that connection to the spaces between all things—into Jack, into Thoth, and then she began to slowly tear them apart.

She felt Thoth—all that he had ever been—struggle against her hold on him. She heard his laughter somehow echoing deep within herself, a wild and hysterical cackling that would have been terrifying if she didn't have his very existence in the palm of her hand.

With everything she had, she took hold once more, but Thoth reared up suddenly, blasting her with the strength of power he'd collected over centuries. The force of it jangled along the connection between them, and she felt her affinity begin to waver.

POWER CONTAINED

Harte felt the strange, unnatural energy of the barrier created by Newton's Sigils course through him like icy dread as Esta battled alone against both Jack and Thoth together. As she fought, the power within the sigils surged and pulsed more wildly than they ever had before.

The building quaked beneath his feet, and the city shuddered while darkness swirled within the confines of the sigils like some malevolent storm about to break. Esta was clearly straining now, and her expression was twisted with the determination to keep Thoth from breaking free. He felt the warmth of her magic waver and prayed to any angel or demon who might hear that her affinity would be enough.

Around the circle, he saw his friends struggle to keep hold. Viola cursed and gritted her teeth. Her expression was tense with the strain of fighting against the magic that whipped through the air around them. Jianyu's neck was corded with the effort of holding on.

"We can't let him out," Harte yelled, reminding them all of what was at stake.

He sensed the boundary they'd created was growing fragile and unsteady, and he had the sinking sense that it was too much. *Thoth* was too much. But Harte had walked through a world where Thoth's power wasn't contained by any one man, and he refused to let that happen again.

The darkness billowed within the confines of the sigils, pushing and pawing like some demon sent to destroy. But Thoth was neither god nor demon. He'd once been nothing more than a simple man who, like Jack, had tried to claim far more than he'd had any right to. The centuries might have twisted him into something more, but at heart, he was human, the same as Seshat had been. Not even Mageus. And a man could be moved.

"Take this," Harte said, gesturing to Viola that she should take the sigil he held. "Esta needs help. *Take it!*"

Viola hesitated, momentarily confused at his command, before she realized what he intended. Carefully, she inched closer, until he could set the spinning ball of power in her hand. With it, she could take his place and keep the boundary unbroken.

"Whatever you do, don't let go," he told the two of them. "*Everything* depends on it."

"We won't," Jianyu shouted. "Go!"

Without hesitation, Harte stepped into the storm.

Inside the boundary formed by the silver discs, the air felt heavier. Magic crackled and cold power lashed at his skin. Esta was in the center, wrestling with Jack. She'd managed to pin him down, but her face was contorted in agony with the effort of holding him and Thoth. Darkness was beginning to pour from Jack's mouth, but it remained within the narrow boundary they'd created. With every passing second, it swirled faster and faster as Thoth tried to escape.

Harte knelt across from Esta, with Jack between them. Her eyes widened when she saw him there. He couldn't hear anything over the roaring that filled the circle, but he knew what she was trying to tell him. She wanted him to go, to save himself and the others, but he only shook his head.

"Together!" he shouted, and then he pressed one hand over hers and one to Jack's chest and focused everything he was into both of them. He sent the command out, felt it hit against the wall of Thoth's consciousness, and pressed onward.

Just a man.

Beneath his knees, the building quaked again, and Harte felt the blistering heat of Esta's magic sizzling along his skin.

He'd known from the beginning that she was powerful. He'd known all along that her affinity was unique. But Harte hadn't truly realized what Esta could do. Until that moment, when he felt the full force of her affinity coursing around him, he'd never *truly* understood what she was capable of. Beneath his hands, he felt Thoth's pain and fear. He sensed the ancient being's absolute terror at what was happening to him, and Harte finally understood then what Esta could do—what she was.

Like Seshat. The same.

It was why the goddess had wanted her from the beginning. Because with her affinity, she could unmake the world if she wanted to. She could tear at the threads of creation and spread wide the spaces between what was and wasn't. She could destroy *everything,* and in the midst of that swirling storm of magic and darkness, he wondered if maybe she would.

Esta gave another wrenching groan, and Harte felt her magic snapping and sizzling around him as she called to the Aether and commanded the quintessence of existence. He could feel the heat of her power, the strength of it.

The malevolent cloud around them began to churn until suddenly it broke. Not into hundreds of pieces, as it had in Chicago, but into *nothing.* He felt the instant Thoth was torn from creation, because suddenly Harte's connection to the man within was gone. At the same instant, Esta pulled her hands away from Jack and nearly collapsed.

Jack wasn't moving, but he was still breathing—not that Harte was overly concerned.

Esta started to fall over, and Harte lurched to catch her. He moved around Jack, so he could better position her in his arms. She was breathing heavily, and her skin was clammy and damp with sweat.

"Is he gone?" She trembled a little, her body exhausted from all she'd just done. "Did we do it?"

Harte nodded. "You did."

Relief flickered across her face, but then all at once her features contorted in agony, and she let out a shout of pain. Her mouth opened in a silent scream.

"Esta?" Harte brushed her hair back, tried to get her to look at him, but her eyes were opened, focused on the midnight sky above. "What's happening? What's wrong?"

She looked at him then, terror in her golden eyes.

Suddenly, Viola screamed, and Harte felt the boundary around them, the wall of energy created by the sigils, become dangerously fragile. Viola's body had gone rigid. Her head was thrown back, and her spine was arched. Jianyu was the same. They looked like they were being tortured.

Something moved on the edge of the roof. Harte turned in time to see Nibsy Lorcan approaching.

Harte adjusted his hold on Esta and helped her to her feet. He'd be damned if they'd face Nibsy on their knees. The boundary around them felt suddenly dangerous, and Esta whimpered. Her knees seemed to go out from beneath her, but Harte caught her up against him again.

They had to get out of the boundary.

"Drop the sigils," Harte told Viola. "Just let them go. You have to break their connection so we can get out of here." He pulled Esta toward the edge of the circle, but the cold energy surged again, pushing him back into the center.

Viola let out a keening moan, but she didn't drop the balls of light in her hand.

"Now, now," Nibsy said, mocking. "It's far too soon for you to be leaving. After all, I've just barely arrived. And we have so much to do."

Harte looked at Jianyu and Viola, but they were clearly struggling against some unseen force.

"They can't help you," Nibsy told him, taking a silvery object out of his pocket. "Not so long as I have this."

The Medusa's head from Dolph's cane. Harte stared in disbelief. "We took that," he said, his mind spinning. How had Nibsy gotten it back? "We unmade it."

"You don't really think I'd walk around carrying the real one? Unlike Dolph, I'm not some dumb mark, Darrigan," he told Harte. "But it seems you are. And with the ring to amplify my affinity, I can do so much more with this beauty than Dolph ever dreamed."

He kissed the gorgon's mouth. Viola cried out, and Jianyu groaned in pain. Esta had gone stiff in his arms. Somehow Nibsy was using his control over Viola and Jianyu to control the area within the sigils, and Esta with it.

Nibsy only smiled.

"You see, Dolph might be able to take magic through the marks they wear, but I can take their will. Thanks to the Delphi's Tear, I can make them dance like puppets on a string," Nibsy told him. And to Harte's horror, both Jianyu and Viola began to shake. "I can make them *kneel*." The second the words were out, they collapsed to their knees.

Viola gasped, and it was clear from the way her features were twisted in agony that she was fighting something, but the cold power around them surged, and a terrible scream tore from Esta's throat.

"Your friends might try to fight me, but they'll only be hurting themselves." He stepped forward. "Convenient, isn't it, that you figured out the sigils could control a demon? Just think of what they can do to a *girl*. Thanks to your friends here and their willingness to wear Dolph's mark, I'll be able to take Esta's power just as you took that demon's. But I have no plans to unmake that power. Not when I can use it."

Esta was struggling against whatever magic Nibsy had her wrapped in, but she wasn't succeeding. Tears streamed down her face, and when she looked up at him, there was terror in her eyes.

"Such a valiant effort. But in the end, she'll succumb. They all will." He took a step forward. "You never really had a chance, you know, Darrigan. It was always going to end here, like this. I was always going to win. But then, you knew that already, didn't you?"

"Harte—"

Esta jerked from his arms, her head thrown back at an awkward angle. "You can't— You can't let him . . . Please—" She gasped in pain as her golden eyes found his. "You promised."

"No—" He knew what she was asking for, but he couldn't. The gun he'd taken from the man in the future was tucked into his jacket. There was one last bullet, and she wanted him to take her out of the equation. But he couldn't. *Wouldn't.*

Drawing the gun, he turned to Nibsy.

But the bespectacled boy only smiled. "You can't kill me, Darrigan. Not without dooming her as well." He shrugged. "I suppose she's doomed either way, but at least I will make her end mean something. With her affinity, I'll change the world."

"She's not dying, Nibsy," Harte said, lifting the gun. Taking aim. "Not today."

ONE IMPOSSIBILITY

Esta was caught up in a power she didn't understand. The sigils had been turned against her, just as she had used them against Thoth, and there was nothing she could do. As long as Viola and Jianyu wore Dolph's mark, they couldn't break free of Nibsy's hold.

The boundary around them pulsed and shivered, and she felt her own affinity drawing away from her. Nibsy was standing outside the boundary, with the Delphi's Tear on his finger and the top of Dolph's cane in his hand.

She'd read pieces of this future on the page of the diary. She'd seen glimpses of it when she tumbled back through the past. She'd known there was a chance that Nibsy could best them, but she'd convinced herself they could get around him somehow. She'd convinced herself they could avoid the fate that stupid diary had foretold.

She should have guessed he'd be as slippery as a snake. She should have known he'd find a way around them.

Now it was too late. They'd played into his hand—or he'd directed them there, pushing and maneuvering until they were right where he wanted them, just as the Professor had promised. Harte was lifting the gun, taking aim at Nibsy, and there was nothing she would have liked better than to see the traitorous bastard fall. But he couldn't. Not if there was any chance for the rest of them. Not if there was any chance for the girl to do things better the next time around.

"No!" she shouted, her voice clawing out of her throat as she struggled against the draw of Nibsy's power. She had to fight. If Thoth could, then so could she. Because she refused to succumb. She refused to let him win.

"You can't," she shouted, but her voice was barely a whisper over the roaring power around her.

He turned to her, panic and pain shadowing his eyes. "He has to die. This has to end."

"If you end him, you end me as well. You promised, Harte," she reminded him. "If you end him, there's no one for the girl to go to. It will erase everything—all that we've had together. All that we've been together. It can't happen without him."

"I can't, Esta." His voice shook, but the gun in his hand was steady. "You can't ask me to do this."

"You have to." She felt tears streaming down her face, but she struggled on. "Do it, Harte. Now. Before it's too late. Give that girl the future that can lead to us. Give her a chance to do what we couldn't. To change what we couldn't."

His jaw clenched as he refused her pleas. In his hand, the gun shook, but it was still aimed at Nibsy. "I can't. I won't lose you."

"You won't," she told him, willing him to understand. "It's the only way." Time was a twisting knot, unknowable and unforgiving. "This is only one possibility. One of infinite possibilities, but if you kill him instead of me, you end them all."

He was shaking his head. "What good are infinite possibilities if they always come to this? If this is our fate, I refuse to accept it."

Then he turned resolute toward Nibsy and lifted the gun.

Esta tried to reach for her affinity, tried to stop the seconds, but she was still caught in the buzzing power of the sigil's energy. Her power wasn't her own. "No—" she pleaded.

Viola cried suddenly, and a shot rang out. But the bullet went wide and ricocheted off a wall. It wasn't Nibsy who went down.

Suddenly Harte gasped and clutched his chest as he collapsed to the floor.

"Viola, no!" Esta screamed when she realized what was happening. "Please. No. You can't do this. You have to fight him."

"Oh, she is. For what little good it will do her." Nibsy smiled then, a slow, satisfied curve of his thin lips. "You didn't really think I'd take the chance of letting him shoot me?"

"Please, Viola." Tears clouded Esta's vision as she watched Harte struggle against Viola's power. His face was draining of color, but the gun was still in his hand. He struggled to lift it, his arm shaking as he took aim.

Nibsy only laughed, but when the shot went off, his laughter died as his body lurched. He staggered forward.

"No," Esta said as Nibsy clutched his chest like his fingers alone could keep the blood in his body.

"No," she said again, waiting for what she knew would come next. She'd felt time tear her apart before, that horrifying feeling of being unmade.

Nibsy looked up at her, but Esta couldn't see his eyes past the glare of the light glinting off his glasses to tell whether it was surprise or fear that colored his expression. And then he fell to the ground like a puppet whose strings had been cut.

The cold energy around her drained away, and she felt herself flying back together. She lunged for Harte just in time for him to lurch upward, gasping for air.

"You shouldn't have done that," she told him through her tears, because what he'd done couldn't be taken back. She didn't know how long she had before time would take what it was owed. "I told you not to kill him."

"He didn't."

Esta froze at the voice, her heart thundering in her ears as she turned to see an impossibility step out of the shadows of the roof. He wore a murderous expression, and in one hand, he held a gun.

Dolph Saunders glared down at Nibsy's body. "That shot has always belonged to me."

ONE HUNDRED TIMES OVER

Jianyu thought he knew what it meant to be trapped. How many times before had he felt imprisoned—by his own poor choices, by this jail of a city, by fate itself? But none of those struggles had prepared him for what it would mean to be truly controlled. When he felt the mark on his back flare and his will recede, when he felt Nibsy Lorcan hold his every possibility through the power in the ring, he understood what desperation truly meant.

Esta and Darrigan had been trapped in the boundary of the sigils, and he could do nothing to free them. Struggle though he might, he could not fight against the hold Nibsy had on him. There was a terrible roaring in his ears, and his back had begun to burn and blister with the effort of fighting the compulsion of the mark, but it was no good.

This hell was what the future would be if Nibsy took Esta's magic, if he used it to control the Book. And there was nothing Jianyu could do to stop it.

When the shot rang out, he barely heard it. At first he did not know what it meant. But as Nibsy stumbled and fell, the power coursing through the mark went warm and then dead. The leash that had been holding him snapped, and he fell back with the sudden absence of its pressure. In the space between him and Viola, Esta rushed to Darrigan, and from the shadows of the roof stepped a ghost.

Not a ghost, Jianyu realized.

Dolph Saunders was dead. For months now, he had believed that Dolph was dead. But . . . there had been no body. No proof except Nibsy Lorcan's word.

They had all believed that word. *Jianyu* had believed, because he could not have imagined a world in which Dolph Saunders allowed Nibsy to take all that he had built and bend it to breaking. But this was no ghost, for there was no spirit that killed with a gun. His skin was perhaps more colorless than it had been before, and his cheeks were sunken from the weight he had lost, but with the shock of white in his hair and the icy blue of his eyes, there was no mistaking that his friend was alive.

Dolph threw the gun aside as he limped to where Nibsy lay. The boy's body was motionless. No breath stirred in his chest, and even from that distance, it was clear that his magic was dead. The look in Dolph's eyes was as cold and as dangerous as the Brink itself as he glared down at the boy. Then he crouched and took the silver gorgon from his hand.

As he turned the piece over in his hand, Dolph's expression was unfathomable, a mixture of fury and regret, of loss and love. After the length of a heartbeat, he tucked it into his coat and stood.

Before Jianyu could gather his wits, Viola had already launched herself across the distance. She stopped short, just before she reached Dolph.

"Is it really you?" she whispered, slowly lifting her hand as though to touch him.

Dolph lifted a single brow. "Disappointed?" he asked wryly. But Jianyu could hear the exhaustion and the *worry* in his tone.

She smacked him. "Where have you been?" Viola demanded. "We thought you were dead. Nibsy *told* us you were dead." She smacked him again, and Dolph allowed it, taking the punishment as his due.

"I'm sorry, Vee," he told her once her fury was spent. "If there had been any other way—"

She threw her arms around him then, silencing his excuses. "You *idiot*."

Dolph seemed to melt into her embrace. Slowly, his arms came around her. "It's good to see you, too."

She drew back from him again. "You didn't need to wait so long, you know," she said tartly. "You didn't have to let him get so far."

"I did," Dolph told her. "I couldn't risk doing it any other way."

"Jianyu!" Abel was shouting from the other side of the roof, where Abel was leaning over Cela.

The sound of his name jolted him from the shock of seeing Dolph. "Viola," he called. "I need your help. Cela—"

Viola turned away from Dolph and was moving before Jianyu even finished.

Abel had Cela's face cupped in his broad hands. "Come on, Cela. Stay with me," her brother begged. "Look at me. Right here. Just keep your eyes on mine."

But Cela's eyes were wide with pain and fear. Her hands were clutching her side, where Viola's knife protruded, covered in her blood.

"Get out of my way," Viola said, but Abel wouldn't be moved. He tried to shake Viola off.

Jianyu knew it would take more than a simple touch to heal the wound made by that knife. Gently, he took Abel by the shoulders as Viola removed the small, carved seal from her pocket. "Let her work."

He held Abel firmly as Viola wrenched her blade from Cela's side. Cela cried out in pain, and Abel flinched under Jianyu's hands as blood began pouring from the wound.

Cela looked up at them, her eyes first finding her brother but then looking beyond Abel to lock on Jianyu as Viola began to work.

He had been a fool.

Jianyu had told himself that he could not burden her with the sort of life the two of them might share. He had told himself that she was not strong enough to bear such a weight, that eventually she would break and come to hate him. But as her eyes remained on his, steady and clear, he knew himself for a liar. His fear had never been for her but for himself. Because losing her would break him in a way that nothing else had been able to.

She had not asked for tomorrow but only today, and he had been reluctant to give her even that. He would not be so stupid again. He remembered being healed by that seal, the small artifact they had stolen from Morgan's collection at the Metropolitan months ago and knew that the next few minutes would not be easy for her. As the cold energy of the seal filtered through the air, he promised her silently that he would give her every tomorrow, a hundred times over. As he watched her skin knit itself together, he vowed that he would start today.

THE FUTURE'S PAST

Dolph Saunders knew he was a bastard and a fool as well. All the good that had come to him in his life—his Leena, his friends, his people at the Bella Strega—he hadn't appreciated any of it. Not truly. Not until he'd been forced to live alone, hidden away in the unused upper floors of the safe house he'd charmed, guarding against any contact with his previous life. He hadn't known what regret was until he had to stand by and watch Nibsy Lorcan destroy everything he'd built.

Because it was the only way to change everything.

But when Viola and Jianyu turned from him to help their fallen friend, he felt the bone-deep knowledge that his actions had changed more than he'd expected. He'd heard their voices these past weeks as they came up through the ceiling of the floor below. He'd watched from a distance as Jianyu had stepped forward to become the leader Dolph had always believed he could be, as Viola stood by his side without shame or regret, and he'd been glad for it. He'd been gratified that, for all his mistakes, he had somehow managed to set the foundation for something larger—something better—than he could have ever built himself. And they had done it without him. *Despite* him.

And if he felt the loss of something he could not quite name as he watched his friends, their heads bent close together across the roof, he did not regret it.

The rooftop was a disaster. It would have been so much easier if he could have stepped in an hour ago. Hell, months ago would have been preferable. But Dolph had done the hardest thing he'd *ever* had to do— he'd bided his time and *waited*. Even when he saw Nibsy in the park not an hour earlier, when he could have struck the traitorous snake down and ended the danger, he had held himself back.

While everything went to hell, he'd done nothing but watch, impotent and pointless, because he had believed it was the only way they might claim the chance to make a different world.

In one corner, a clutch of men in shining robes were huddled, fearful as children. Chairs and tables had been overturned as people scattered from the danger. One of the large cauldrons had been tipped over, and now its fiery contents were smoldering on the tiles. The rest of the Order had fled like the cowards they were.

Darrigan and the girl were getting up, and the way Darrigan was looking at Esta—the way he held her face in his hands like she was something infinitely precious—told Dolph everything he needed to know about the state of things between the two. The Magician and the Thief had become something larger and more complete together than either of them had ever been apart.

"It's good to see you, old man," Darrigan said, slinging his arm protectively around Esta. "I wondered if I would. But I should have known you'd want to make an entrance."

Dolph shrugged. "Turns out I'm a hard man to kill."

"*You* did this?" Esta asked Harte, glancing between the two of them. "You should have told me."

"You know I couldn't," Harte said. "The fewer people who knew, the more likely it was to have a chance of working. Keeping secrets is the only way I'd ever gotten around Nibsy before."

"I don't understand," she told Dolph. "If Nibsy didn't kill you, why did you wait until now to show yourself?"

"I had to," Dolph explained. He took from his jacket the small notebook that had been the bane of his existence these past months. Every time he had wanted to act, it had counseled caution, so he had waited until the words on those pages pushed him to this time and place, to this singular chance to bring the Brink's power to an end.

"That's why you gave Dakari the diary," Esta said, looking up at Harte. Her expression shifted suddenly, and tears made her eyes glassy. "He did it," she whispered to Harte. "He chose to help us. He *saved* us. But why the diary? How could you have predicted that would work?"

"I didn't, exactly. But I knew Dolph well enough to know he would've needed some kind of proof," Harte told her.

"He wasn't wrong about that," Dolph admitted. He likely would have ignored the warnings and premonitions if it hadn't been for the diary—the way the pages changed and adjusted themselves to the path time took.

"But how did it get here?" she asked.

"You gave it to me," Dolph told her, confused.

"I didn't," Esta said. "I never had that until a few weeks ago. I couldn't have brought it to you."

Dolph's brows rose at her insistence. "And yet you did."

She'd brought it to him with a warning and with an ingenious garment that kept Nibsy's bullet from piercing his skin. It had been a leap of faith to believe the girl when she'd first arrived, but after she'd saved his life, he'd had little choice.

Darrigan took her hand to calm her. "I didn't know if it would work, but I figured that if you could exist simply because the possibility remained that you'd go back—if the diary could tell us about our deaths, even though we still lived—then maybe other possibilities could exist as well. I took a chance with Dakari, because I hoped that if he helped us, maybe we could use the loop in time that you have to create by sending the girl back to our advantage."

Esta had gone silent, her eyes wide and unblinking. And then wonder broke over her features. "You played the possibilities," she whispered to Darrigan. "You changed a past that had already happened from a future that might never be. Nibsy wouldn't have been able to see the threat coming. Even if he'd been using the diary, he would have believed the entry there."

Darrigan nodded. "Exactly. I'd hoped to keep everything close enough that the diary wouldn't change so Nibsy wouldn't realize what I'd done."

"You're a genius!" She kissed him.

And she didn't stop.

Unaccountably uncomfortable by the display, Dolph cleared his throat.

"I hate to interrupt your moment," Dolph said, stepping closer to the edge of the roof. "But this isn't over yet." He nodded toward the city beyond. "Something is happening to the streets."

Jianyu and Viola had come over to where they stood by then, along with their friends.

"The Order was using the grid to channel power to the Brink," Jianyu explained.

"It's more than that," Dolph told his old friend as he watched the streets below vibrate uneasily with the glow of an otherworldly power. Cold energy corrupted by ritual magic was thick in the air. The whole city seemed on the verge of breaking apart. "Something has gone wrong."

"The attack on the ritual and on the men of the Order was nothing more than a distraction," Jianyu told them. "This was Jack's plan, for the ritual to run out of control. If it is not stopped, the electric power it is channeling will overwhelm magic built deep within the city, and when it reaches the Brink . . ."

"It will short it out like an overblown fuse," Dolph said. "Like half the electricity in the city does."

He'd wanted the Brink to fall. That one hope—even more than his desire for revenge—had been the reason he'd remained in hiding these past months. But he didn't want it to fall like this.

It wasn't just the building beneath his feet. The entire city was awash with terrible power. Manhattan had become a city of fire. Its streets were lit with magic that crackled and swelled, and beyond it, the Brink wavered, pulsing with the energy that was coursing into it.

"We have to cut off the power," Esta said.

She was right. If they didn't stop this madness, the grid of the streets wouldn't be able to hold the flow of electricity much longer. Even now the streets threatened to shatter.

"There isn't time," Harte told her. "We don't even know where to begin."

"With the statue," Jianyu told them, pointing up toward the gilded Diana glowing with light. "We can start there."

But when Dolph looked up to the towers, it was not only Diana who stood against the night. A girl clad in one of the Order's robes stood with her arms wide. Her golden hair glinted in the light.

"No—"Viola screamed as the girl began to fall.

FURY AND VENGEANCE

Harte watched in horror as Ruby tumbled from the tower, her dark robes like a leaf carried in the breeze, and then suddenly he felt the brush of Esta's magic, and Ruby Reynolds was there, steady and alive, standing on her own two feet.

As the others rushed forward in relief and confusion, something drew his attention across the rooftop. *Jack.*

In the shock of Dolph's appearance and the concern over Cela's injury, everyone had forgotten about Jack. They'd left him lying unconscious where he'd fallen, but in the meantime, he'd come to. Ruby's little leap must have been his doing—a distraction to ensure he could sneak off back to the machine.

Before Harte could do anything, Jack pressed the lever, and the large orbital arms started to move. Jack looked up, watching with a maniacal glee as the machine picked up speed. He was so engrossed with his victory that Jack didn't notice Harte run for him until he was nearly across the stage.

Harte crashed into Jack, pummeling him as he pushed him down, and Jack fought back, laughing like a madman as he lashed out.

"It's too late," Jack said, taking a wild swing and nearly connecting with the side of Harte's head. "Every maggot in this city is about to die."

Harte drew back his fist, and when he connected with the side of Jack's face, he gathered his affinity and pushed all of his magic toward Jack. Then he drew back his fist again. And again.

He wasn't aware that the others had arrived or that already Viola was using her dagger to slice the Pharaoh's Heart out of where it had been locked into the machine. He didn't notice the arms stuttering and slowing. All he could see was the blood spurting from Jack Grew's nose. All he could feel was the crunch of bone beneath his fist.

"Harte—" He heard Esta's voice as though from far away.

He realized he was still punching an unconscious man. Jack's face was a bloody mess, and his own knuckles were raw from hitting him. But he drew his arm back again.

"We can't kill him, Harte," Esta said softly, holding his arm so he couldn't strike Jack again. "Not like this."

She was right. Jack Grew might deserve to die, but Harte wouldn't be the one to make him into a martyr.

He let Esta tug him back, but then he saw the shape of the Book outlined beneath Jack's robes. Breathing heavily, his blood singing with adrenaline, he pushed the fabric away and opened Jack's coat. There, secured in a specially made inner pocket, was the Ars Arcana.

Harte reached for the Book without thinking. Why should he have worried? The version of the Book that had contained Seshat was gone, burned to ash when Esta had brought it back and crossed it with itself. There shouldn't have been any goddess in those pages. There shouldn't have been any danger in touching *this* Book, here in *this* past. But the second his fingers touched the worn leather cover, Harte realized his mistake.

All at once, he felt a familiar ancient power flooding through him. It wasn't like before. What had happened the first time he'd touched the Book, back in Khafre Hall, was a pale imitation of pain compared to this. Then Seshat had been too broken, too fractured to do anything more than wail. Now she attacked.

Harte screamed as Seshat breached the boundary between himself and the nothingness she threatened. He was barely able to throw up enough defenses in time to keep her from ripping him apart. The Book tumbled from his hands, falling open on the rooftop, where its pages lay open, pulsing with light.

He saw the confusion in Esta's expression, saw that she would step toward him, and he threw up his hands to warn her off. "No," he shouted, backing away.

"Harte?" Esta's brows were drawn together in concern. Her golden eyes were wide with fear, but when she looked down at the Book, he knew she understood.

Within his skin, the goddess raged.

"Seshat," he said, grimacing against another of her onslaughts.

"That isn't possible." Esta scooped up the Ars Arcana from where he'd dropped it. The pages seemed to riffle of their own free will, and the power within it lit the lines of her face. "She isn't in *this* version of the Book, Harte."

"Somehow she was," he groaned, struggling to push down the goddess's power.

Seshat was screaming, her ancient voice wailing sentences that didn't make any sense.

Esta took another step toward him, but he threw up his hands again. "Keep her back," he told the others. "Keep her away from me."

Whatever Seshat may have been trying to tell him, all Harte could sense was her anger. Her hunger. She wanted. *Desperately*. Fury. Vengeance. Her emotions made clear what her incoherent raging could not.

"Harte, Seshat was in the Book that we *lost*," Esta reminded him, as though he could have forgotten. As though that wasn't the very reason he'd been so careless. "She can't be in this one."

"There's only one Book of Mysteries," Dolph told her. His icy eyes met Harte's. "The Ars Arcana is unique, made exceptional by the piece of pure magic it contains."

Esta's expression lit, and she looked at Harte with hope in her eyes. "If that's true, it means we might still have a chance."

EVER ONE

Esta's mind raced with the implications of what Dolph Saunders was telling her. She had believed that they'd lost their chance to complete the ritual and stabilize the Brink when the Book had disappeared as they'd slipped back into the past. But maybe they hadn't. The Ars Arcana that Harte had just touched was not the Ars Arcana they had possession of . . . and yet Seshat had been waiting in those pages.

"The Ars Arcana isn't some normal artifact," Dolph explained. "Its power isn't something that can be replicated. Its singularity is the reason it has been so revered and hunted over the centuries. There are a thousand legends, a hundred myths, but one thing is always clear: There is always and ever *one* Book."

"Within time and beyond it all at once," Esta murmured, thinking of what Seshat had told her, what she'd seen with her own eyes. "Because it not only contains a piece of magic outside of time. It *is* a piece of magic outside of time." She pressed her hand to the open page, wishing it were like the Book in her dream. Wishing it would tell her what to do next.

"What does that mean?" Jianyu asked.

She thought about all she knew of time and its opposite, all she'd seen falling through the years when time had revealed its truth. If the spaces between time could contain every possibility at once, then maybe the Book could as well.

"It means we might still have a chance to fix the Brink," she told them as she flipped through the Book, searching.

When she reached a slip of paper, she stopped, and hope flared bright in her chest. It was a piece of stationery with the Algonquin Hotel's name emblazoned across the top. She held it up and showed them. "I put this in the *other* Book. But time doesn't matter in these pages."

She turned to Harte, willing him to understand. "When the Professor trapped Seshat in that other version of the Book, he trapped her in *all* versions of the Book. If we use the sigils, we can remove the other artifacts from *this* Book. We can use them and complete the ritual that will stabilize the Brink. Everything we need is right here. The Book, the artifacts . . . and me. We can get her out of you. We can still use her power to complete the ritual—to fix the Brink and place the piece of magic within this Book back into the whole—just like we planned. With the Book and the artifacts, with *Seshat*, we can end this once and for all."

The building beneath them shook again, and in the distance the Brink quivered, its bright boundary illuminating the night.

He shook his head. "You'd still have to give up your affinity," he reminded her, remembering the girl who died on the subway platform. "It's the only way to use the stones and control Seshat. I watched you do that once before. You won't walk away. There's no surviving that, Esta."

But she didn't believe that. "With power willingly given," she said, reminding him of what Newton had written. "That other girl wasn't willing, Harte. You forced her to give up her affinity. Maybe if she'd done it on her own, maybe if she'd been strong enough—"

"You can't risk your life for *maybe*," he told her.

"Maybe's all we've ever really had." She stepped toward him, wishing she could touch him now. Determined that she would soon enough.

The building quaked again, but it wasn't only the building. The entire city could barely contain the power coursing through its streets. In the distance, the Brink was a wall of wavering light. But even now she could see the dark lines beginning to creep through the brilliance of it.

"We can still cut the power," he pleaded. "There's still time. You can *steal* us more time."

But she understood the truth. All the time in the world wouldn't change the choice before her. Everything had led here, and now she had to choose. The fate of the world or herself.

She'd seen the fate of the world if she chose wrong.

"I don't know if it's possible to change the future, but I do know that I can't sit by and let the Brink fall or the Order continue to rule over the old magic in this city. I can't watch Seshat destroy you, and I can't walk away from this, not when I know I can fix it. All of it. The Brink, the Order, the future I saw—I can stop all of it."

"What are we waiting for?" Viola asked. "If Esta says it will work, it will work."

She met Viola's steady violet gaze and was surprised at the trust there.

For her entire life she'd made a point of never needing anyone. It had always been easier that way. Safer. *Lonelier, too.* She'd never depended on anyone—not until Harte. Not until she'd learned to trust the people who were standing around her now. She looked at them now, one by one. Viola and Jianyu. Cela and Ruby. And, impossibly, Dolph, the father she had never known. All of them with her.

And Harte.

"I need you to trust me, Harte. We can do this," she told him, correcting her earlier words. "But only together . . . Please. Because I can't do it by myself."

Seshat was raging inside Harte, but everything fell away except for Esta. Proud and determined and beautiful in her conviction. She believed she could complete the ritual. She believed she could use Seshat's power and give her own without dying, but if she was wrong . . .

"I do trust you." *Of course* he did. "But what if you're misunderstanding what Newton wrote? When you give up your magic, what if that's the end?"

"I'm not wrong, Harte," she told him with that same brash confidence that had attracted him to her from the very first. "But it doesn't matter. We have to try. And if this *is* the end?" Her eyes were glassy with unshed tears. "You've given me more in the past few months than anyone could deserve in a lifetime."

"*You* deserve a lifetime, Esta." He wanted to touch her. *Needed* to touch her. But he couldn't. Not with the demon goddess in his skin.

"All I've ever wanted was for someone to see me the way you do," Esta told him, a sad smile tugging at her mouth. "For myself. Without qualification. Without having to earn it. You gave me that. Now let me give what *I* can give. Let me do what I was born to do, Harte. Stand with me. *Please*. Don't make me walk into this with any regrets."

The building quaked beneath them again. In the distance the electric power had turned the Brink into a wall of light, but that wall was cracking. Even now Harte could see the black veining through it, threatening to break it apart.

Esta was right. They were out of time.

He glanced at Abel and Cela. "We're going to need to borrow Mr. Fortune's carriage one more time."

"No way in hell," Abel said. "We're coming with you."

"We're coming, too," Jianyu said, stepping forward with Viola. "You'll need us to hold the boundary steady and keep watch."

"I can't ask that of you," Esta told them, looking suddenly panicked at the idea.

"You didn't," Viola said. She glanced up at Ruby, who laced her arm more securely through Viola's as though to indicate that she was coming as well.

Dolph walked over to Nibsy's still body and pried the ring off his finger. He tossed it to Darrigan. "We're going to need this."

"We?" Harte asked.

"Do you really think I tortured myself these last few months for something so simple as vengeance?" Dolph asked. "This is it—the one chance to finish what the Order began. I was the one who went after the Book and released this mess into the world, so I'll help to finish what I started. I owe it to those who have fallen." He looked at Viola. Jianyu. "And to those I've disappointed and betrayed. If we can stop the Brink from taking one more life, then I can go to my grave knowing I've done all I could to make up for my failings."

He'd no sooner spoke than they heard a thunderous crack. In the distance, the Brink lurched, and a wave of energy snapped through the streets, rippling through the city and threatening to shatter it.

"We need to go," Jianyu told them. "We need to get to the Brink."

Esta turned to him then, and in her golden eyes was everything they hadn't yet said. But he understood. He'd always understood.

"Let's go end this, Harte."

He wouldn't be able to touch her once more before they leapt into the unknown. He wished he could. He wanted to wrap his arms around her and keep her safe. *Forever.* But maybe all they'd ever had was the moment before them, stark and beautiful in its wonder and terror.

He could no more stop Esta from this path than he could stop magic itself. And whatever happened, he'd be with her.

"Together," he said finally. Because he knew in that instant that it didn't matter. If they died today or a thousand years from now, whatever time he had with her would never be enough.

IN BROOKLYN

Viola's fingers were laced through Ruby's as the wagon careened toward the bridge, urged on by Abel's steady hand and caught in the web of Esta's power. Beneath its wheels, the streets had been turned into buckled bits of cobblestone and concrete from the energy coursing through the city's grid.

She'd been there the night of the Manhattan Solstice. Viola had watched the sun's light transform the streets into rivers of gold, shimmering with power. She'd felt the danger and the wonder as well, but this? *This* was far worse. The three bolts of electric power, amplified by whatever corrupt ritual the Order had performed, had not stopped pouring their energy into the center of the park. The sigil in Madison Square was a beacon of light, and from it, that dangerous power flowed, feeding into the grid of streets and lighting the city from within, threatening everything.

Beneath the wagon, the streets quaked under the strain of the power charging into them. They wouldn't hold. But the bridge was ahead, just there in the distance, growing ever larger as they approached. So too was the Brink.

Viola believed Esta, trusted her as well. But that didn't mean she wasn't afraid of what was to come. Though the thought of approaching that terrible barrier willingly—of breaching it? The very idea made her recoil. Since she'd come to those shores, since her family had crossed into the city, not caring what it meant for her power, Viola had known, bone-deep, that the Brink was the deadly limit of her existence. Now she would test that limit with nothing but flimsy silver discs, ritual objects created by a simple man.

It would be worth it, she thought as she looped her arm through

Ruby's and drew her closer. If it worked, perhaps they would have a chance.

If the city didn't end them first.

"Once we get there," she told Ruby softly, "you should go. You and Cela and Abel. Get yourselves across the bridge and away from the danger."

"No," Ruby said, her fair brows knitting themselves together. "I'm staying."

"There's nothing you can do," Viola said.

"I'm not running off," Ruby argued. "I'm not leaving you to whatever fate you're about to walk into. The Brink can't touch me."

"Do you see these streets?" she asked. "Do you see what's happening all around us? It's not the Brink you have to fear right now. It's the island itself. If we can't stop this—"

"You'll stop it," Cela said from her place across the wagon. She was sitting shoulder to shoulder with Jianyu, their bodies pressed close together despite the room they had around them.

"Viola is right," Jianyu said. "You and your brother, and Ruby as well, you must get to the other side. It will be safer in Brooklyn, where the city's grid does not reach."

"It won't be safer anywhere if the Brink comes down," Cela reminded him. "Isn't that what you told us?"

"End magic, end the world," Ruby said, giving Viola's words back to her.

"We're not going anywhere," Cela told them. "None of us."

It happened too quickly and not quickly enough. The streets were shuddering with the power coursing through them. The long span of the bridge was already beginning to sway when Abel urged the wagon up over the dark waters to the wall of flame that waited.

When the wagon came to a stop, Viola turned to Ruby again, pleading. "Please," she said. "It will be better if I know you're safe. If anything happened to you—"

Ruby's eyes were glistening with tears as she leaned forward and kissed her, silencing her words. "I feel the same," she whispered. "I'm not going anywhere. I'll be here waiting, and when this is over, we're going to cross that bridge together."

Viola looked up at the Brink, visible now. Icy energy mixed with sizzling heat, and the corrupt magic and natural power it had harvested for over a century pulsed and shivered, undulating slowly. Beyond the span, in the east, the edge of the world was beginning to glow with the promise of another day.

She kissed Ruby once more and vowed that day would arrive.

BETTER MEN

Jianyu helped Cela down from the bed of the wagon despite his misgivings. He would have rather she remained aboard and left with Abel, as Viola had suggested. They would have been safe in Brooklyn, whatever happened. But he saw the set of her jaw, the sharp determination in her eyes, and knew better than to waste his words with arguing. The truth of the matter was they would succeed or the world itself would die. Safety was an illusion that none of them could afford.

He released his hold on her waist and immediately regretted the loss. As her brother looked on from his perch on the wagon, he was unsure of what to say.

"Cela . . . I—"

But she shook her head. "Don't you dare start telling me your good-byes," she said. She had pulled her bravery around her, but he did not miss the way her lips trembled or the shine of tears in her eyes. "We have things to discuss, you and I. We've got plenty of time."

"Cela," he started again. She needed to understand. "If anything happens—"

"I'll be right here," she said. "Where I belong."

He did not answer, but simply looked at her, trying to memorize every curve and angle of her face. He could not quite make himself move forward, but neither could he turn away.

She turned her face up to him and kissed him softly, there with her brother in plain view.

With his heart in his throat, Jianyu glanced up at where Abel sat, watching, but if Cela's brother had any feelings about what he had just witnessed, they did not show.

Without another word, Jianyu joined his friends. Dolph was standing not six feet from the fiery wall of the Brink, gazing up with a sort of terrible wonder.

"You could have sent word," Jianyu said as he came up next to his friend.

"No," Dolph told him, glancing in his direction. "I couldn't have. And you did well enough on your own."

Jianyu huffed. He had let Nibsy Lorcan destroy everything Dolph had built—everything they had built together.

"You held it together," Dolph told him as though reading his thoughts.

"Not enough," he said with true regret. "The Devil's Own will be glad to have you back at the head."

"I'm not coming back," Dolph told him. He turned to Jianyu. "If this works, I'm leaving. And if it doesn't . . ." He shrugged. "There's nothing in the city for me now."

"But the Strega," Jianyu said. "Everything you built?"

"It will be in good hands," Dolph told him. He took the cane topper from within his coat and examined it. His jaw tightened, and without any warning, he lobbed the silvery head out over the edge of the bridge to the waiting water below. Then he turned back to Jianyu. "Well? What do you say? They'll need someone to lead them. A better man than I've ever been."

Realization dawned as Jianyu understood what he meant. "I could never," he argued, taking a step back from the Brink and Dolph and everything that his offer entailed.

"You could," Dolph told him. "It's yours if you want it. It's yours already, if you'll only take it."

"We have to get moving," Esta said. "Something's happening."

Jianyu noticed then that the vibrations beneath their feet were growing in intensity. The streets of the city had grown even brighter and more frenzied.

"It's the sunrise," Viola said.

He understood immediately what she meant. At the solstice, the setting sun had charged the streets with power. Now the rising sun was doing the same. If it reached the correct angle . . .

"Quickly," Jianyu shouted, already taking one of the sigils he had been carrying and offering it to Dolph. "We do not have much time."

ELEMENTS UNITE

The fear in Jianyu's voice had Esta turning back to look over her shoulder at the city. With every passing second, things were growing worse. Viola was right. The sunrise seemed to be adding to the energy that was already too much for the streets to contain. A thunderous rumble split the air, and she watched in horror as the bridge swayed. At the base of the long span, the part closest to the land, an enormous crack crawled across the pavement, severing them from the city and trapping them up against the Brink. But Esta didn't trust that they'd be safe in that no-man's-land between the city they'd come from and the line that could destroy them. She remembered what had happened when she and Harte had crossed back into the city. If the Brink lurched as it had then, everything would be over.

She turned to Harte, panicked suddenly at how quickly everything was moving. They were out of time. "Whatever happens, I need you to know—"

"Don't," he said, his jaw tight. The gray of his irises was a storm-tossed sea. "Not now."

"Then when?" she asked.

His jaw tensed. "After. You can tell me whatever you have to say after."

"Harte—" Her throat was tight, and she wanted to step into his arms, wanted nothing more than to touch him.

"I can't walk into this without any hope at all," he said.

She wanted to kiss him. She needed the feel of his mouth on her lips as she walked into the flames, but Seshat still waited within his skin.

Dolph took the ring from his finger and held it out to her. "I believe you'll need this."

Esta looked up at him, the man who had fathered the child she had once been. Despite the stripe of white in his dark hair, he wasn't an old man—no more than five or six years older than she was herself. She knew then that if they made it through this, she would never be able to tell him who she was.

She couldn't tell him any of it, she realized. Because if he knew about the child, she knew he would never let her go.

There was no more time for words or hesitation. They moved together as one, as though they had always known somewhere deep within the cells of their very being that this was their purpose and their fate. Viola, Jianyu, Dolph, and Harte positioned themselves in a circle with Esta and the Book of Mysteries in its center. They each held one of Newton's Sigils, the paper-thin discs covered in mercury and inscribed with a ritual that could protect them from the Brink's claim.

One by one they set the discs to spinning. One by one the flat bits of metal flashed, transforming themselves into orbs of light. Cold energy rose around them, and the atmosphere shifted as they suddenly connected, one to another. The bridge was unsteady beneath them, and the Brink shook, pulsing threateningly in the sky above them, but inside the circle of light there was only silence.

Harte's eyes were on her, determined and steadfast, and suddenly everything seemed to drain away but the two of them. She did not say, *I love you*. She did not say that she was afraid or that she wished there had been more time. She did not say any of the things she should have. She offered none of the words she'd kept inside for so long because it had felt too dangerous to release them.

But he gave her a small nod and mouthed the words *I know*.

The bridge shook again, and one of the enormous stones tumbled from the tower above them.

"No!" Harte shouted when the boundary wavered. "Hold it steady. We move together, on my count . . ." Then he began to lead them slowly, carefully into the swirling power of the Brink.

As they walked, energy snapped around them. She could feel it threatening the boundary they had created with the sigils. Her hair lifted, stirred against her cheeks at the cold magnetic energy, and she felt her affinity lurch. Beyond the protection of the sigils, the Brink was still there—calling, *demanding*.

She didn't waste any more time. She flipped open the Book, and once she had found the page she needed, she placed the Ars Arcana on the ground open-faced.

With Viola's knife, Esta made a small, careful cut along the same scar from before, and then—hoping she was right, hoping she hadn't just led them all to certain death—she pressed her bleeding fingertip to the open page. As her blood disappeared into the parchment, a cold power blasted up from the pages and washed over her. The Book seemed to quiver beneath her hands.

If there was only ever one Book, if it was made of a piece of pure magic—within time and beyond it all at once—it meant that the Book they'd had in 1980—the one they'd used to secure the artifacts—was also *this* Book. Which meant . . .

Carefully, she touched the page. It felt like ice and fire all at once, but the second her fingertips brushed against the parchment, she felt a burst of energy—the crackle of something like an electric shock—and her finger dipped *into* the page. She pressed farther, until her hand disappeared up to the wrist, and then she went farther still. She couldn't see her hand any longer, but she could feel the substance it pushed through, cold and alive and strangely like it had felt when time tried to unmake her back in Colorado.

When she took her hand from the page, she had an ornate dagger in her hand.

With a shaking breath, she reached for the next.

The necklace and the crown, the dagger and the ring.

One by one, she put them on, tucking the dagger into her waistband so it could press against her skin. The stones immediately grew warm, as though they understood what was to come, and the Brink shuddered in response. Outside the circle of the sigils, wind began to swirl, tearing at her friends' clothing and hair. All around them, the icy energy of the Brink pressed in on the fragile protection of the sigils' boundary.

"Hurry," Jianyu told her, his voice strained.

Quickly, Esta turned back to the Book and turned to the page she needed.

"To catch the serpent with the hand of the philosopher . . . ," she read, whispering the words to herself like a prayer. But was the serpent time? Or was magic itself?

She hesitated with a sudden unease. What if she *had* misunderstood?

No . . . The recipe was clear enough, at least to her. She'd been raised on Latin and the occult sciences—trained and honed for this. Because the Professor had believed he could use her to do this very ritual.

Professor Lachlan had thought he could use her affinity to take this power. He had stolen her life so that he could take control of the beating heart of magic for himself. But now she would be the one to claim the ritual.

What else will you claim? The thought was as unexpected as it was unwelcome.

The stones were hot against her skin, and the wind beyond the boundary had picked up speed. But within the space that her friends were holding, there was only silence.

What else could she claim? What had Thoth told her?

You could transform time. Make the world anew.

But she didn't want a world remade. She wanted *this* world, with all its uncertainty. True, there was hate and fear, but as she looked at her friends risking everything, she knew there was beauty, too. And there was Harte.

Outside the silence of the circle, the storm was increasing. She felt the boundary grow more tenuous, and she turned back to the page open before her. The Philosopher's Hand—the recipe for the mythic substance known to change lead into gold and men into gods. Five fingers of the

hand, linked to one of the five elements, aligned with the five artifacts she now wore.

"With power willingly given, mercury ignites," she read. "Elements unite."

Newton's writing seemed to writhe on the page, like the Book itself knew the moment was near. The individual letters shivered, glowing with a sudden luminescence as the Brink began to crumble.

She focused her affinity and poured it into the stones that lay against her skin. At first she wasn't sure what she was supposed to do, but then she felt it. The spaces between the stones and the magic within them, the possibility of the chaos it held. She continued, giving herself over to it—giving her affinity to the old magic willingly—and she felt the instant the stones joined, twining with her magic as they were connected by Aether. In a single, staggering burst of cold power, they united as one, and at the center, burning like the fish in the Philosopher's Hand, she felt her magic catch fire.

Caught in the thrall of that power, she could do nothing more than marvel at first. She understood why men had craved it—*killed* for it—over the eons. This wasn't only the old magic, with its warm assurance and steady strength. This was something more. *Ritual magic.* Power beyond the spaces between. Power that could be multiplied and molded.

Power that you could claim.

Sound drained away, and Esta could no longer hear the wind whipping around her or her friends' screams for her to hurry. She understood suddenly what Newton must have felt centuries ago when he'd attempted this very ritual, when he'd held the power of those stones in the net of his own affinity and saw what he could become. The awe of it. The fear as well.

But there was more. She wasn't finished, not when the Book still held the beating heart of magic, not when Seshat still raged within Harte's skin. It was time to finish what Seshat had started so long ago.

It was time to place the beating heart of magic back into the whole.

Esta felt power dance along her skin, as cool as silk and as sharp as a blade as she turned back to the page before her. The letters were glowing now in earnest, urging her on.

"The serpent catches its tail," she whispered. "Severs time, consumes. Transforms power to power's like."

The most obscure of all the lines—the most difficult and the most important. Some myths believed the serpent was time. Others, like the Antistasi, saw the ouroboros as magic itself.

Time and magic, two halves to the balanced whole that *everything* depended upon. Within the Book was a piece of pure magic, held outside the threat of time. Outside the circle of the sigils was the Brink, a boundary made from the Aether—made from *time*. One would be consumed. The other transformed.

It wasn't enough to just let the Book's power go within the Brink. That wouldn't do anything but overload the already-overwhelmed boundary. *That* much power? The Brink would shatter and fall—and it would take *everything* along with it. But there was a way to complete the ritual. There *had* to be.

If she got this wrong . . .

Her skin was singing, and her blood felt alive as she laid her hand on the open page of the Book. Focusing her affinity through the stones, she reached for the spaces between all the Book was and all it had ever been. Just as she'd found the curse sunk into Jianyu's skin, she felt it there—the piece of old magic—pure and alive and wild in its infinite possibilities. She sent her affinity into the spaces between that magic and the world, and she tore them apart.

THE SERPENT
CATCHES ITS TAIL

The stones burned against Esta's skin as she tore the piece of pure, untouched magic from within the pages Seshat had used to hide it eons before. She ignored the sizzle of energy that felt like lightning about to strike and swallowed down the taste of blood on her tongue. It took everything she had to hold on to that power.

She understood then what Seshat had tried to do—how powerful Seshat truly must have been to accomplish such a thing as removing a piece of magic from the whole. It was like holding infinity and nothingness all at once.

The Book fell away, crumbling to ash, and the space within the sigil was transformed. She'd felt something like this sense of terrifying possibility before, when she'd slipped back to this time, but that had been nothing compared to what the Book had concealed. She could feel everything— sense *everything*—the world and time and the spaces between.

The area within the boundary of the sigils became filled with the power that had been in the Book and was transformed by it. Chaos bloomed with all its beauty and its terror. It felt like stepping into the heart of an atom, like standing in the middle of an emptiness that held within it an infinite number of possibilities.

Magic lives in the spaces. That's what Esta had been taught. It was what she had always believed, but now she understood that *living* was too tame a word for what magic contained.

No wonder Newton had panicked. No wonder he had stopped the ritual before it was complete.

But it was too late for Esta to turn back. The Book was ash at her feet, and released from its bonds, the beating heart of magic swelled, growing to fill the boundary delineated by the sigils.

Viola was screaming, and Jianyu was telling them to hold tight. Harte looked back over his shoulder at her. Esta saw the desperation in his eyes as she felt the boundary waver and began to realize how far over her head she was.

The serpent catches its tail . . . severs time . . . consumes.

If the beating heart of magic broke free of the boundary, it would destroy time—and in doing so, destroy *reality* itself. After all, what was time but that substance that kept the spaces ordered and magic's power in check? But because of what Seshat had done, the power she'd taken from the Book was beyond time's reach. If it escaped from the boundary of the sigils, it would do more than simply destroy the Brink. It would consume *everything*.

Swirling around her was chaos itself. Pure and filled with possibility. But possibility meant *everything*, not only the good. Possibility included the end.

Esta knew she had to hurry. She had to finish the ritual before the ritual could finish her.

The Brink had been made the same way Seshat had created a boundary for the Book those eons ago—the same way the other version of herself had created a ritual circle in the subway—through Aether. *Through time.* By pulling at the spaces within time, between time, Seshat and the Order had created a space that craved magic.

Esta would give the Brink what it craved. She would take the beating heart of magic, that piece of power protected from time, and push it back into the spaces left by the ritual, completing the ritual that the Order had left undone. And she would use Seshat to do it.

As the power welled, stronger and more urgent, she heard Viola curse and Dolph laugh in what could only have been amazement. But Harte was watching her as though if he looked away, she might disappear.

She had to get to Harte—*to Seshat.*

Slowly, Esta pushed through the nearly solid wall of chaotic power surrounding her. It felt like swimming through concrete, but eventually she was within an arm's length of him.

"It's time," she shouted, and then reached out her hand.

But Harte only shook his head. He was saying something, but she couldn't hear him.

"It's *time*, Harte." She held her hand out again as the boundary line continued to waver, trembling as her friends struggled to hold it steady.

"I hate this," he told her. The gray of his eyes mirrored the storm around them. She could see herself reflected there. She could see everything they might be, if only they could make it to the other side.

"I know," she said, and before he could stop her, she grabbed his wrist.

Immediately she felt Seshat lurch, and Esta threw herself—her affinity and her life—into the space between them. But the goddess would not go easily. Esta hadn't expected her to. She focused her affinity through the stones of the artifacts and pressed her magic into Harte. There, she found the places where Harte ended and Seshat began. She let her magic flare within those spaces.

She felt the goddess's power sizzling up her arm, felt the darkness beginning to swell as a desert night rose up around her. A woman whose eyes were lined with kohl stepped from the spaces into time, and as fire flashed in Seshat's ancient gaze, Esta realized her mistake.

It wouldn't work. Esta couldn't force Seshat. She couldn't use the goddess's power like so many had tried to. Doing so would make her no better than Jack or Newton or Thoth. She could try all she wanted to control Seshat—to *use* her—but Esta understood in a sudden, terrible epiphany that it wouldn't work.

With power willingly given.

That's why Newton had failed. That's why the Order had failed as well. The power sacrificed to balance magic and time, to make the two into one, had to be freely given. It couldn't be stolen, as ritual magic had stolen power for so long.

But with the horror of that discovery came new understanding. Esta could see how to fix it—the Brink, the Book, all of it. Not by forcing Seshat, but by giving *herself*—her magic—in *place* of Seshat's.

There was only one answer. She had to *free* Seshat. Even if it meant dooming herself.

Darkness was bleeding into the world, filtering through the spaces and starting to claw at her, but Esta wrenched her magic back. Focusing her affinity through the stones, she pushed Seshat away. Seshat lunged for Esta, tearing at her eyes and face with razor-tipped nails, but with the artifacts hot against her skin, Esta held her back. Held her caught in the Aether.

"I won't use you as the others would have," she told the goddess—the woman—struggling against her.

"*Lies!*" Seshat screamed. Her kohl-rimmed eyes were bright with a hatred that took Esta's breath away. "But it will not work. You seek power for yourself, but you will unmake all."

"I never wanted power," Esta told her. "I just wanted Harte, but if I can't have him, then I'll leave the world safe."

You could make the world anew.

Esta shook her head and shoved the thought aside.

"Tricks upon tricks," Seshat said, still struggling against Esta's hold. "I see the desire in you. I see the duplicity as well."

Against her skin, the artifacts burned hot, but Esta held tight to their power. Through the haze of Seshat's illusion, she could see her friends on the bridge struggling. Their faces were twisted as if in agony as they fought with everything they had to keep the sigils steady. Just behind the illusion of Seshat's face, she could see Harte's features.

Outside the safety of their circle, the Brink was wavering and threatening to fall. They didn't have much time.

Under Esta's feet the desert sand rippled, just as it had once before in dreams. A desert serpent set to devour.

Maybe this was always how it was supposed to be. Maybe everything had led her to this. What was it Thoth had told her? That she was an abomination? That time would take what it was owed.

She'd been trying so hard to find a way to keep what she had—the life she knew—but she'd ignored the possibility that maybe it was never supposed to have been hers. Time wouldn't have to take her. She'd give herself. Willingly. She'd end this, once and for all.

"Why do you hesitate?" Seshat mocked. "Now that you have me, now that you have all that you have dreamed about for centuries, can it be that you are afraid?"

"I'm not afraid," Esta said. It wasn't a lie. Afraid didn't begin to describe what she felt. She was terrified and devastated and emboldened all at once. She looked at the people surrounding her, and she would not let them down.

Esta stepped toward Seshat, and she saw the fear in the ancient woman's eyes. But caught in the power of the artifacts, Seshat could not move, much less escape. Esta held tight to the goddess and tore her from Harte. Freeing her.

The desert night evaporated, and the roaring warning of the Brink rose again. Harte was breathing heavily, and the others were screaming for her to hurry. To finish it.

Harte's gaze shifted behind her to where Esta knew Seshat was still held, caught in her affinity, and then back. He blinked in confusion, like he couldn't quite understand what he was seeing. Stepping toward him, Esta sent her affinity out into the stones, giving herself to them fully. Emptying herself of her magic and her power as she pressed a kiss against his mouth.

"Be happy, Harte," she told him. "Be *free*."

His mouth was moving, and she knew what he was saying. But she could not hear the words.

"I love you," she told him as the world shuddered. Her legs fell out from under her as the last of her magic began to draw away. Beneath her body, the bridge was quaking, and all around her the beating heart of magic threatened her affinity. Threatened to consume. But this time she didn't fight it. This time she let it go and gave herself over to it.

Above her the Brink surged. Color and light, like the beginning and end of creation. Chaos and the possibility within it. Time twisted in on itself, a devouring serpent, but as she felt herself flying apart, familiar ancient laughter rose from within her.

"Did you think you could destroy me, girl?" Thoth whispered from the deepest recesses of her soul. "How could you hope to destroy that which you carried inside you all along?"

TIME, CONSUMES

As Esta collapsed like a broken doll, Harte did not hear the low, dark laughter rolling through the silence. At first he heard nothing but the terrible beating of his own heart.

With the sigil held aloft in his outstretched hand, he could not have stopped her from kissing him, even when he knew she was saying good-bye. She was there—*right there*—her mouth against his, her breath in his lungs, and he couldn't do anything to stop her from doing what she intended to do.

He felt her magic, the same power he'd only recently come to under-stand on the rooftop when she'd torn Thoth from this world. And he knew that something had happened—something had changed. It wasn't Seshat that Esta was using to complete the ritual. She was doing it *herself*, and the terror of that realization had him almost dropping the glowing sigil he held in his hand. He felt the burn of magic, hot and bright and real, and he knew that Esta was giving herself to the Brink. Sacrificing herself for all of them.

At first he didn't hear the laughter. At first he could only hear the roaring in his ears as he looked at the vision of Seshat standing over Esta's unmoving body. She was there—a woman dressed in linen and silk, with hair dark as a desert night—and yet she was not. But it wasn't victory on Seshat's face but fear.

Seshat lifted her ancient eyes to look at Harte. "Why would she do that?" the goddess asked. "She had my power there in her hand, and she let me go."

Harte didn't know what had led her to change her mind about the plan. He only knew that Esta must have had a reason, but he didn't have time to discover the answer before everything began to fall apart.

Suddenly, Esta's spine arched and her head jerked back so she was looking up at the starless sky. Her body began to rise from the ground until it hung, suspended by nothing but the Aether she had once commanded. Her mouth was open in a silent scream. But as long as he held the sigils to keep the boundary intact, Harte could do nothing but watch as darkness flooded from Esta's eyes and mouth.

Viola cursed, threatening and railing against what she was witnessing, but she was no more able to help than Harte was. Around the circle, they all shouted for her to fight whatever power had overtaken her, but they could not drop the sigils—could not break the boundary.

Harte heard the laughter then, the dark, rolling mirth that he'd heard before in the Festival Hall when Thoth had found him—and Seshat within him—and had tried to tear her from his skin. The others were struggling against the dangerous energy of the Brink and the magic from the Book, but Harte shouted for them to hold steady. He knew that everything depended on it. They couldn't let the power of the Book loose into the world, especially not there in the center of the Brink, and they couldn't release the demon that had come to claim it.

Harte watched, powerless and horrified, as the darkness that flooded from Esta coalesced before him, a shadowy figure like a man shaped from nightmares. The shadow-man turned to him, transforming slowly into a familiar figure. As his features sharpened, Harte recognized him—the man with the head shaved bare who had doomed Seshat to centuries of misery within the pages of the Book.

Thoth.

It couldn't be. It wasn't *possible.* They'd destroyed Thoth—*unmade* him on the roof of the Garden. Harte had been there. He'd felt the full force of Esta's power as she'd ripped Thoth from this world.

"Not completely," the shadow-man whispered in a voice cast from the darkest hours of night. "Not when she had a shard of me within

LISA MAXWELL

her own skin." He smiled his serpent's smile. "Not when she carried me with her. Once she damaged her soul by murdering that fool, it was easy enough to find a place deep in the recesses of all that she was. It was easy enough to wait for her to carry me with her until it was time to claim my final victory."

"The convention," Harte realized. When Esta had tried to destroy Thoth the first time, back in Chicago, he'd infected everyone there—including, apparently, Esta herself.

Suddenly the desert night fell around him. Gone were the Brink and the city. Gone was everything but the circle of power that contained the two ancient beings and Esta's body. The stones in the artifacts she wore were bright points of light, burning with the power she'd infused them with.

"How delightful that she's prepared herself for me," Thoth purred. "With the stones and her magic, I'll finally be able to grasp the Book's power for myself." Thoth circled closer to where Esta floated, caught in the Aether and the magic around her. "The beating heart of magic, here in the palm of my hand. With it I will remake the world anew. An infinite world that bends to my will."

"That power will *never* be yours," Seshat told him, circling closer. "I will tear you from the world, from history and memory together. And there will be no one to remember your name."

"It's too late, Seshat." Thoth laughed softly. "The game is up. The final move has been played, and I've waited too long for my victory to wait any longer."

The shadowy figure looked more corporeal now, as though he'd been gathering strength as he spoke. He began to murmur then, unintelligible syllables to form ancient words, but as his voice rose, Esta's body arched back again. Harte watched as the scars on her arm opened as though being traced by a blade of light, and power vibrated through the air as her blood began to drip.

Seshat screamed.

"Did you think I hadn't prepared for every possibility?" Thoth asked. "Thanks to the ritual magic carved into the girl's arm, her power—and the stones—are mine. And with them, I'll take yours. And then I'll take the world."

"We have to do something," Viola shouted. "We have to help her!"

"We must hold the boundary," Jianyu said.

"It won't matter if the Brink falls," Viola argued.

She was right. Already, Harte could see the darkness starting to over-take the wall of light, and within that darkness was nothing. With that darkness would come the end of everything.

"If he's using the stones, it means there's still connection there," Dolph shouted. "Use it, Dare."

Harte understood what Dolph was telling him. "Take this," Harte shouted, gesturing that Dolph should grab hold of Harte's glowing orb in his other hand. "Whatever you do, don't break the barrier. You can't let any of this get out. Especially not those two."

As soon as Harte stepped into the circle, Thoth noticed and turned to him immediately. The ancient man's eyes were voids, deep as coldest midnight.

"You've come," he said, his smile filled with anticipation. "How entertaining."

"Not for you," Harte told him. Then he lunged for Esta and pushed all of his affinity into her, just as he had done with the other version of her.

He could feel Thoth's power tearing at him, but he held on until—
there—the last bit of Esta's affinity, still connected to the power in the stones. Without hesitation, he pushed his magic toward the united stones, just as he had in the subway tunnel weeks before.

It wasn't enough to stop Thoth. It wasn't enough to control him. But it was enough to make him stumble, and in that instant, Seshat made her move.

She lunged for Thoth and clawed at his face. Her eyes flashed brilliantly white, and Harte felt the heat of her power swirling around him. Seshat held tight to Thoth's face, and as her nails dug into his skin, there was a roaring like nothing Harte had yet heard. His ears felt like they would bleed from the sound of it as the shadowy figure began to come undone. All at once, Thoth broke apart, until there was nothing left.

The others were struggling now, Harte could tell. With only the three of them, the boundary was less even, less sure.

"Finish this," he told Seshat.

But the goddess—now no more than the shadow of a woman—only shook her head. "I cannot."

"*Finish* it," Harte demanded again. "You started this. It's time to end it."

"I cannot!" Seshat shouted, her kohl-rimmed eyes wild with fear and regret. "Once, perhaps. Ages ago, I would have given everything. My life for the world's. I would have finished the ritual. I would have created a space in this world apart from the rest. Of the world and separate from it, where magic could be cut off from the ravages of time. But that was long ago, years before I'd been reduced to a shadow of myself. Centuries before I was trapped as a spirit within the pages of the Book. Now my connection to the old magic is not strong enough. I cannot finish what I began, not alone. It must be the girl."

"No!" Harte raged. "She's already given enough."

"She must give more," Seshat told him, her eyes wild and bright. "You must help her."

Harte was shaking his head. He wouldn't. He *couldn't*. "You did this," he accused. "You tricked her into giving up her magic—"

"It was her choice," Seshat said. "Her choice alone. But she must finish what she started. Help her. Help her finish the ritual."

"No," Harte said. He refused to do that again, to listen to lies. "If I compel her, she won't be willing. I can't do that again. I won't kill her. I *won't*."

"She must finish what we started," Seshat told him. "I am no longer strong enough to finish this ritual, but she is. It's the only way. Save the world, save the girl. Save the girl, save us all. If she gives her power, there is enough of me left to help keep her alive."

"How am I supposed to believe you when I've seen your heart?" he accused.

The woman shrugged. Beneath their feet the bridge began to crack and crumble. The towers were starting to fall, block by block. Dolph shouted for the others to hold steady, even as he ducked from the flying debris.

"You don't have a choice," Seshat told him. "She knows what she had to give, and she chose it willingly. Sacrifice cannot be taken, you see. Not like those terrible stones. Sacrifice freely given is far more powerful."

"But *what* does she have to give?" Harte demanded.

Seshat smiled softly. Sadly. "Only all that she is."

"No," Harte said, refusing. He tried to shove Seshat away, but she stilled his hand.

"Look," she told him. "*Look*." She took his hand, held it in hers, and he knew what she intended.

He sent his affinity out, into the part of Seshat that remained in this world. And he understood. There was a way to end this, to complete the ritual of the Brink. To put the beating heart of magic back into the whole.

And there was a way for Esta to live. To go on.

"She'd be a prisoner," he said. "She'd never be able to leave the city."

"I know of prisons," Seshat told him. "Hers would be a palace."

But even palaces could chafe, could constrict. Harte Darrigan knew of prisons as well. He couldn't damn Esta to this one. "I won't do that to her," Harte said, refusing.

"She has already made the choice," Seshat said. "There is no going back, and it is not for you to take this from her."

The Brink was breaking apart. Dolph and Jianyu and Viola were using every bit of their strength to hold the boundary tight, but it didn't matter. One side of the enormous stone tower began to crumble, and as it fell, the ground beneath his feet buckled and tilted. The entire span of the bridge moved, undulating like the waves in the river below. The span of road beneath her feet moved slowly at first, but soon became a terrifying rise and fall that signified the collapse that was coming.

Esta's eyes fluttered open, but she didn't see him there. Not at first. Though her mouth was moving, no sound came from her lips. But he saw what she was saying. He understood that she was still there—still alive—and she was not giving up.

The bridge was moving faster now, more violently.

"Help me," she whispered. Her golden eyes met his, and they burned with the fire he'd seen that first night they'd met. She did not blink or look away, and he knew he could not deny her. Not this. Not anything.

Tears burning in his eyes, he took her hand. "Together," he whispered.

Her eyes closed as though in relief, and he did not wait for them to open again before sending his affinity through her. The Brink flashed in a terrible brilliance, and he felt the Book's power shudder through him as the world was torn in two.

POWER TO POWER'S LIKE

First, there was pain. There was the endless ache of emptying herself until she was nothing but the shell of a memory.

The world shuddered, quaked, and Esta felt the future she had seen—that nightmare of nothingness—begin to open around her. Magic flared, hot and hungry, as it pushed the spaces wide. Consumed time. Transformed the very pieces of reality into their opposite. Magic bloomed. Time came undone. And the world began to be unmade.

She saw the bridge begin to fall, the enormous stone towers collapsing in on themselves, one at a time. The great span of steel and concrete rippling like a wave. She saw her friends fighting to keep the fragile boundary intact—fighting to keep the beating heart of magic from destroying the world.

The bridge shifted and buckled, and she felt the pull of something terrifyingly familiar. Though her affinity was all but gone now—pushed into the stones and into the ritual that hungered for it—Esta felt almost like she was falling through time. There was the bridge, about to crash into the river below. There it was, whole. There was the empty river, in the time before men had ever dared to build across such a length. Just as had happened in Colorado, she felt time flicker around her. Just as when she'd lost Harte in the trip back to this time, she felt all of the possibilities of each second. The city as it was, as it could be, as it would never be again.

And then there was nothing at all. There was only the city unmade. The world forgotten.

Esta felt herself flying apart. It was a pain she'd felt before, this terror of being ripped from the very fabric of time. Time flexed and rose around her, pulsing with a strange energy. Unsteady. Unwieldy. And it felt *hungry*. Just as it had before, when it threatened to unmake her.

A hand snagged her wrist, and Esta's first thought was for Harte. But it wasn't Harte. It wasn't any of those who stood with her that day.

"You must give the rest," Seshat told her in a voice that sounded like chaos and light. The woman was gone, and the goddess had returned. Her kohl-rimmed eyes were bright beacons. "You must give *everything*. You can keep none of what you are. Power willingly given. It is the only way to sever time, the only way to save what was."

Esta realized then that she could feel the stones—barely, but they were there. She was still tethered to them, still clinging to a thread of her own affinity. To Seshat.

"You would have given your life," Esta realized.

"My magic, my life. Time and chaos. Two sides to singular coins. I would have given everything, and in doing so, I could have created a place, a pocket within time where time could not touch the beating heart of magic," Seshat told her. "By severing time, power would have been transformed, and both time and magic could have thrived together."

A place.

Suddenly, it made sense in a way it hadn't before. Time had *always* been linked to place, Esta realized. It was how she'd slipped through the layers. Seshat would have anchored the pure, protected piece of magic to a space—a literal place in the world—to keep the whole from dying.

Wasn't that what the Order had been trying to do as well? It was why they'd originally built the Brink—not as a weapon, but as an attempt to keep what they knew they were losing. Because their magic had never taken root in this land.

"The Brink," Esta told her. "If I give my affinity to finish the ritual, the Brink will become that place, won't it? The entire city will be a space where the old magic cannot die."

Seshat nodded. "A space severed from time's power over magic. Give time what it is owed—give it your power and your life—and watch power be transformed. Within the boundaries of that space, time will have no power over the old magic or those who have an affinity for it."

"The girl," Esta realized. "If I do this, if I give everything—"

"Time's terrible power will no longer be able to touch her," Seshat said. "The space within the boundary you create will stand apart, cut from the chaos you have introduced into the world with your very existence. History can be remade. Time can be reclaimed."

"I don't understand—"

"What is history but a kind of magic?" Seshat asked. "A story written to create a truth, like ritual magic carves power with time. Make your choice, girl—your affinity or the world?—for I am no longer strong enough to complete the ritual. But perhaps *we* can. Give up all that you are, and I will help you complete the ritual I began. Together we can seal the beating heart of magic back into its place, protected in time. But it must be now, and it must be all."

Esta knew what her choice would be. There was no hesitation, no regret. She would give up her power willingly. And she would die. But there was no other choice. Not for the world. Not for her friends—or for Harte.

Esta let go of the final piece of her affinity and felt herself flying apart, but despite the fear and pain of feeling herself being unmade, she gave everything over to time. Seshat was there as well, their powers locked together in the endless void that threatened everything. Together they pushed the swirling, beating heart of magic into the spaces of the Brink and made it one with time.

And then there was nothing at all.

Not darkness. Not light. Not pain or relief. There was only silence for the span of a minute or a lifetime.

Time shuddered, and suddenly it was a desert night that surrounded her. There was Seshat, goddess and woman. Her ancient eyes were aglow with power. Within their irises, Esta saw the Brink reflected. Every color that existed and some that she could not name swirled and churned, ribbons of power. Seshat smiled then, soft and sad, and Esta knew what she was giving.

"Why?" Esta asked, screaming into the void.

"You could have taken my power, but you were not like the others. You gave me my freedom, so I will give you your life." Seshat flickered suddenly, like the room back in Colorado. There was a woman with hair like night, a goddess with eyes of fire, the image of her flashing through all the possibilities of what she could have once been—what she would never be again. "It was always my ritual to finish," Seshat told her. "This is the price. Your magic for all of magic. Your life for the world. You must remain within the space we have created here, and you will not have your affinity for the old magic. But you will have a new world. A new beginning, without time's claws to tear you from your fate. Power transforms . . ." Then she released Esta's hand, and in a swirling of light and heat, she was gone.

Esta felt the loss keen and terrible and final, but as Seshat gave herself over, Esta felt a spark. A thread of connection between them broke, and the vision of the desert fell. The world around her struggled against its unmaking, as the beating heart of magic began to fill the spaces, remaking them anew. Transforming the Brink. She felt time and magic fuse, and she felt, too, her connection to it. Her affinity as part of that completeness.

She understood Seshat's words then. She would never be able to leave. Not without severing that connection to the Brink. Not without undoing what had been done.

With a terrible crash, like the shattering of glass, she saw the Brink burst with light, and the city within its arms was suddenly separate from time. She closed her eyes, turning away and shielding her face, because she could not look into the searing brightness, not without coming undone herself.

When she opened her eyes again, the bridge had gone still. The soft light of morning was beginning to warm the sky to a lavender blush. Above her, the great towers of the bridge had been remade.

Then Harte was there.

She looked up into the stormy gray of his eyes and saw how her future could begin.

EPILOGUE

I t was New Year's Eve, and the barroom of the Bella Strega was filled with the pleasant murmuring of people celebrating and the warmth of the old magic. Esta remembered the first time she'd ever visited, a night when the power had flickered and the strength of magic had felt electric in the air. She hadn't known then that the saloon would become a home to her and the people in it the family she'd always wanted.

She sat with Harte, curled into a booth tucked into the corner, and watched her friends. Viola stood in her familiar place behind the bar, serving drinks with a surly pout. Jianyu sat next to Dolph at the table in the back, with Cela talking animatedly at his side. Dolph laughed at something she said and adjusted the toddler on his knee.

"You're really not going to tell him?" Harte wondered.

She nestled into the crook of his arm. "What's there to tell? He has a daughter, doesn't he?" Tomorrow they were leaving, Dolph and the girl who would never have to be sent forward—the girl who would never have to become a thief and a con. "He has a fresh start, and she has a future."

"And what about you?" he asked.

She kissed him. "I have a future too."

"Stuck here in this trap of a city forever," he said, frowning at her.

It was the price she'd been willing to pay. Her affinity for a world. It felt like a bargain. No . . . it felt like she'd gotten away with the perfect crime.

Ruby burst in through the front door a few minutes later, bringing a gust of winter and snow with her. She had a stack of newspapers in her hand, and she waved them brightly to get Viola's attention. "It's here!"

Viola stopped in the middle of pouring a customer's ale and abandoned the bar altogether as every eye in the saloon turned toward the blonde.

"Well, come on, you two," Ruby said, her eyes as bright as her smile as she waved Harte and Esta over. "Don't you want to see?"

"She's not going to let us be, is she?" Harte whispered.

"Not usually," Esta said, smiling at the way Ruby's sunshine complemented Viola's dark moods so well. "We'd better go before she has Viola drag us over."

They made their way through the crowded barroom to where Ruby was already distributing copies of the *New York Sun*, which contained her latest article. She proudly handed Esta a copy.

"Look there." Ruby beamed. "We made the front page!"

The headline told of the Brink's demise and the Order's disintegration. The Brotherhoods had scattered after the attack on the Conclave. The effects of that attack had been too broad and sweeping for the Order to try to hide. The city had been thrown into disarray, its citizens terrorized by the magic that had threatened to bring everything down. And thanks to Ruby's articles, everyone knew that it had been ritual magic, like that practiced by the Brotherhoods, that had been the danger. With popular opinion turned against them, it seemed unlikely that the Brotherhoods would be making noise anytime soon.

Beneath the headline was a byline by R. A. Reynolds. Esta scanned the story, appreciating Ruby's ability to convey drama without turning it into a farce. "I still can't believe Morgan gave you that quote about Jack," Esta told her.

"It's not like he had much choice," Ruby said. "Not after what Jack did to me and to Morgan's own son. There were too many witnesses to deny it." She shrugged. "They had to do something to save face. It was easy enough to pin everything on his nephew."

"It helps that a dead man isn't likely to argue," Harte murmured.

The authorities had found Jack's body on the sidewalk beneath the Garden once everything was over. He'd fallen—or jumped—to his death after they'd left him, and the whole Morgan clan had denounced him immediately. They, along with the Order, had been happy to blame the chaos of the night on Jack's actions, conveniently forgetting their own roles.

"They paid three times my previous rate," she told Viola, wrapping her arm around Viola's waist. "With this and the rest of my dowry, we have more than enough for a place in Paris come spring." Her smile faltered. "If you still want to go?"

"Certo," Viola said, her violet eyes filled with an uncharacteristic tenderness. "With you, I'd go anywhere."

"And now you truly can," Ruby said, smiling down at her again. Then she looked at Esta. "It's because of you. Because of what you did and what you sacrificed that we can have a life together away from here. Everyone can choose."

Esta returned her smile. *Not everyone.*

Before emotion could overtake her, Esta turned to Dolph. "What time is your train?"

"We leave for Chicago at noon," he said. After all he'd built, he was leaving the city behind. Not because he was running from his past, but because he was heading toward a new future.

"Abel's on that route," Cela told him. "He'll be sure to watch out for you."

"I still can't quite believe I'm leaving," he said, his eyes taking in the saloon.

"You do not have to go," Jianyu told him.

But Dolph only wrapped his hands more securely around the small girl on his lap. "Ah, but I do, my friend," he said. "I've made too many enemies in this city to ever be truly safe here. And there are too many ghosts haunting this place. We need a fresh start. She deserves one." He kissed the top of the girl's head, and the girl giggled and looked up at him adoringly.

Esta felt her heart ache at the sight—at the tenderness of a father and daughter reunited—but she had no regrets. The girl on Dolph's lap wasn't her, and thanks to Seshat and all they did to transform the Brink, the girl would never have to *become* her. She wouldn't have to carry the burden of time. She'd have a life of her own. A real future. And a father who would protect her without question or price.

"You'll look up the fellow I told you about?" she asked Dolph, reminding him of an earlier conversation they'd had once she knew he was leaving.

"Jericho Northwood?" Dolph said.

"He goes by North sometimes," she said. "Redhead who thinks he's a cowboy. With his mismatched eyes, you won't be able to miss him. I know it's a lot to ask, but it's important. I made a promise, and you finding him would go a long way in helping me to keep it."

"I have the letter you gave me," Dolph told her. "I'll be sure to deliver it."

With any luck, the letter would set North on the path to Maggie and put him on course to the life he deserved to live. A life without the problems of the Devil's Thief or the dangers of the Antistasi. A life with Maggie and their kids. There were others they still needed to help, like Harte's brother, but this was a first step.

"It's the least I can do after what you've done for me—for all of us," Dolph told her. He paused, considering her as he sometimes did. As though he wanted to ask, as though maybe he knew. But the moment passed, as it always did when the girl on his lap squirmed and demanded another cookie. He smiled as he indulged her, but then he grew serious. "I've done nothing to deserve this second chance, but I'll gladly take it."

"What will you do about the Strega?" Harte wondered.

"I've made Jianyu my partner," Dolph told them. "He'll be running things from now on."

"Only until you return," Jianyu reminded him.

"*If* I return." Dolph laughed. "Maybe I'll discover that Chicago suits me. Or maybe, if it doesn't, we'll head farther west."

"Bah," Viola told him. "You'll be back. You couldn't stay away from this place, from this city." *From us*, her eyes seemed to say.

"Maybe," Dolph admitted. "But until then, the Bella Strega will be in good hands, and the Devil's Own along with it."

"You couldn't have made a better choice," Esta told him truthfully. It wouldn't be easy, but if anyone was up for the work of bringing together the various factions in the Bowery, it was certainly Jianyu. Especially now that he had Cela by his side.

"Enough," Dolph said. "There will be time for good-byes tomorrow. Tonight we drink to friends who have become family." He lifted his glass, and the others all responded in kind.

Family. It was what Esta had wanted since she was a girl, and now she had it. At least for this one brief, shining instant. They settled in for the evening, talking and drinking and simply being together one last time before everything changed. Together they welcomed the new year, and with it, a chance for new beginnings.

It was nearly morning when Esta felt herself nodding off and Harte nudged her. "We should go," he whispered.

They said their good-byes and promised to see Dolph and his daughter off at the station later that morning.

Outside the Strega, snow was falling on the Bowery. The soft, frozen blossoms of snow continued to tumble down, covering the trash-lined gutters and broken cobbles and turning the world around them white. A lonely milk wagon rattled by, its wheels cutting a fresh path through the snow.

"I think they'll like Chicago," Esta said, nestling into Harte for warmth as they made the long trek uptown to the apartment that had once been his alone. "I'm not sure they'll ever come back. And Viola—she and Ruby will be happy in Paris. They can start a new life."

Harte didn't respond more than to nod in agreement.

But as they walked, the thought of new beginnings made Esta's mind turn to her own future—to theirs. And when they reached Washington Square, Esta stopped. Harte pulled up beside her, but he didn't speak. He seemed to sense that she needed to say something, and he gave her patience as he waited for her words.

"I've been thinking a lot," she told him. "About everything that's happened. About the future that lies ahead." She took a step away from him, felt the quiet hush of winter in the city wrap around her. "You aren't trapped anymore, Harte. The Brink is no longer a threat to our kind. Dolph is leaving. Viola is as well. You could go too. Anytime you wanted."

"What about you?" he asked, his expression unreadable.

"You know I can't leave." It had been the price she had to pay—a price she would have happily paid a million times over.

"Does that bother you?" he asked, brushing the snow from her hair.

"No," she told him honestly. "Everything I've ever wanted is here. This city, it's home. It always has been. I never wanted to escape this place, not like you did." Her throat felt tight.

"And you would have me leave you here?" he asked, frowning.

She didn't want him to, but . . . "I don't want you to feel trapped, Harte. I know how hard you fought to be free of this place, and I don't want you to ever feel trapped again. There's a whole world out there waiting for you. You don't have to stay because of me."

"What if I want to?" He stepped closer, wrapped her in the warmth of his arms.

"You'll change your mind," she told him. "I need you to know that it's okay if you do. I don't want to be the chain keeping you here. You can go. Whenever you need to go. It won't change anything between us."

He considered her in silence as the moon hung heavy in the darkened sky and the snow swirled around them in its light. "I've already seen the world, Esta. I saw the entire country, from one side to the other. I saw a future that was bigger and more unbelievable than even I could have dreamed." He let out a soft sigh. "Everything I ever did to get out of this city—every lie I ever told, every person I ever betrayed—I was only looking for a way to be free."

"You *should* be free," she told him, meaning it. "You deserve to be."

He shook his head. His stormy eyes were serious now. "Don't you see? No matter how far I traveled, no matter when we were, the only place I ever felt anything close to free was with you."

He kissed her then, tipping her chin up so their lips could press together, and Esta felt something ease inside her that she hadn't realized was wound so tight. Ever since she'd survived what happened on the bridge, ever since she'd found herself without magic and trapped in the city that Harte had always hated, Esta hadn't been able to stop from wondering what would happen between them. She knew it was only a matter of time before Harte would decide he wanted to leave the city.

"I'm not going anywhere, Esta." His breath was warm on her face. "Not now, not *ever*."

"I don't want you to regret it," she whispered.

"I could never regret choosing you," he told her. Then he kissed her again, slow and deep, and as she lost herself in the feel of his lips, the strength of his arms, and the warmth of him, her worries began to ease.

He pulled away and broke the kiss only when a passing carriage clattered by. "Let's go home, Esta."

Home. The word meant more than their small apartment just north of Washington Square. It meant Harte and the future they could build together. It meant everything.

She looped her arm through his, and with their bodies pressed close together, they continued through the snow. They'd gone only a little more than a block when he spoke again.

"Do you miss it?" he asked. "Your affinity, I mean? I know what it was like to take the Quellant, but at least I knew that it would wear off eventually. What you did, what you sacrificed . . ."

"I wouldn't change anything." She'd be lying to say that it had been easy to adjust, but she didn't regret the choice she'd made. "I'm still not used to not having a connection to the old magic. It feels a little like losing a limb must. Like my affinity should be there. Like it *is* there, and I've just forgotten how to reach it."

"You'll never go back to your own time again," Harte said softly.

"I know." She'd made peace with that. Mostly.

They turned north to cut through the park. Gas lamps flickered, throwing their soft light on the shimmering snow. Esta looked up at the sweep of stars overhead and knew she'd be okay. With Harte next to her, with her friends safe, she would be grateful for every day that lay ahead of her. They would make their own magic. And if she would never again see a speeding car or enjoy the luxuries of her own time? It did not matter. What she'd received in return was so much more.

But in the depth of the night, it was easy to see what the city would become. It was so easy to remember the towering height, the speed and the noise. She looked up, where one day there would be a great arch anchoring Washington Square, and beyond, uptown, where one day buildings would scrape the clouds. She thought she saw the shape of something glimmering there in the night sky, the familiar peak of the Empire State Building. And she wondered . . .

The night eased around them, and her steps slowed to stopping.

"Esta?"

She slipped her hand into Harte's and watched with wonder as the glimmering tower became more clear, more *real*. Her heart began to race.

"I think . . ." But it seemed too dangerous to say the words aloud.

"What is it?" he asked.

She could not stop smiling. It couldn't be. *And yet . . .*

The city settled around her, welcoming her home. Embracing her as its own. Urging her on. There in the darkness she could see the infinite.

LISA MAXWELL

She'd sacrificed everything willingly. She'd given up her magic in its entirety. But it wasn't *gone*. Instead of being within her, it was all *around* her, anchoring her to the city. Connecting her to time itself. Her magic was still there in the spaces of the night, ready and waiting for her to reach for it. To *grasp* it.

"Come with me," Esta said, and together she stepped with Harte into the darkness, through time, to that other city waiting beyond.

ACKNOWLEDGMENTS

~

When I came up with the idea for a badass girl thief who could see in bullet time about ten years ago, I knew it felt like a big idea. But I had no way of knowing what it would become. There are so many people to thank and acknowledge for all they've done in making this book and the entire series a success. Even a book as big as this one couldn't possibly contain my gratitude. But here goes . . .

To Jason, who I usually save for last in the acknowledgments. There is no way I could write books and keep my sanity without having a true partner in my life. Thanks for letting me talk about made-up people with you any time of day or night, and thanks for always being my person. None of this is possible without you.

To my boys, Max and Harry, who absolutely *are* amazing. Thanks for supporting me through every deadline and for letting me be your mom. You're a million times cooler than I will ever be, and I can't wait to see the incredible things you'll do.

To my brilliant editor, Sarah McCabe, who has been the lifeline for these books. Her intelligence, patience, and ability to spot any time-travel paradox is unparalleled, and I'm damn lucky to have her.

To my agent, Kathleen Rushall, who has always had my back, even when I didn't. I can't imagine wanting anyone else in my corner. Thank you. For all the things.

To everyone at Simon & Schuster who has touched this book and this series. There isn't a word in this book that hasn't been made better by the intrepid copyeditors, readers, designers, and publicists who have worked on this series. I couldn't ask for a better publishing team.

To the fierce and fiery women writers I'm lucky to call friends: Abbie Fine, Christina June, Danielle Stinson, Helene Dunbar, Jaye Robin Brown, Kristen Lippert-Martin, Olivia Hinebaugh, Sara Raasch, and Scarlett Rose. Thank you for every lunch date and group text and email. A special shout-out to Danielle, who read this monster as a draft and gave me the best advice. Go buy all of their books. Seriously. Their words will make your life better.

And last but not least, thank you to the readers who have lived in this story for the last few years. Thank you for your patience and your support. I'm so glad that you love these characters as much as I do, and I'm so grateful for all you've done to promote and support the series. I hope this final chapter was everything you wanted it to be and more.

LISA MAXWELL is the *New York Times* bestselling author of young adult fantasy, including the Last Magician series and *Unhooked*. She's worked around words all her life and is currently a professor at a local college. She has strong opinions about pasta and a soft spot for loud music and fast cars. When she's not writing books, you can usually find her going on adventures with her husband and two amazing boys. Though she grew up in Akron, Ohio, she now calls Northern Virginia home. Follow her on Instagram @LisaMaxwellYA, or sign up for her newsletter to learn more about her upcoming books at Lisa-Maxwell.com.

THE LAST MAGICIAN

ALSO BY LISA MAXWELL

Gathering Deep
Sweet Unrest
Unhooked

THE LAST MAGICIAN

BY LISA MAXWELL

SIMON PULSE

NEW YORK   LONDON   TORONTO   SYDNEY   NEW DELHI

SIMON PULSE

An imprint of Simon & Schuster Children's Publishing Division

1230 Avenue of the Americas, New York, New York 10020

First Simon Pulse hardcover edition July 2017

Text copyright © 2017 by Lisa Maxwell

Front jacket title typography and front jacket and case photo-illustration
copyright © 2017 by Craig Howell

Back jacket photo-illustration copyright © 2017 by Cliff Nielsen

For information about special discounts for bulk purchases, please contact
Simon & Schuster Special Sales at 1-866-506-1949 or business@simonandschuster.com.

The Simon & Schuster Speakers Bureau can bring authors to your live event.
For more information or to book an event contact the Simon & Schuster Speakers
Bureau at 1-866-248-3049 or visit our website at www.simonspeakers.com.

Jacket designed by Russell Gordon

Interior designed by Brad Mead

The text of this book was set in Bembo Std.

Manufactured in the United States of America

8 10 9 7

This book has been cataloged with the Library of Congress.

ISBN 978-1-4814-3207-8 (hc)

ISBN 978-1-4814-3209-2 (eBook)

For Harry, who is proof that magic is real

THE MAGICIAN

March 1902—The Brooklyn Bridge

The Magician stood at the edge of his world and took one last look at the city. The spires of churches rose like jagged teeth, and the sightless windows of tumbled buildings flashed in the rising sun. He'd loved it once. In those lawless streets, a boy could become anything—and he had. But in the end, the city had been nothing but a prison. It had borne him and made him and now it would kill him just the same.

The bridge was empty so early in the morning, a lonely span reaching between two shores. Its soaring cables were lit by the soft light of dawn, and the only sounds came from the waves below and the creaking of the wooden planks beneath his feet. For a moment he let himself imagine that a crowd had started to gather. He could almost see their tense faces as they stood in the shuffling silence and waited for his latest attempt to cheat death. Raising one arm in the air, he saluted the invisible audience, and in his mind, they erupted into cheers. He forced his face into the smile he always wore onstage—the one that was little more than a lie.

But then, liars do make the best magicians, and he happened to be exceptional.

As he lowered his arm, the silence and emptiness of the bridge wrapped around him, and his stark reality came into focus. His life might have been built on illusions, but his death would be his greatest trick. Because for once there would be no deception. For once it would be only the truth. His ultimate escape.

He shivered at the thought. Or perhaps that shiver was simply from the icy wind cutting through the fine material of his dress jacket. A few weeks later and there wouldn't have been any chill to the air at all.

It's better this way. Springtime was all fine and good, but the rank stink of the streets and the sweltering, airless buildings in the summer were another thing. The feeling of sweat always dripping down his back. The way the city went a little mad because of the heat. He wouldn't miss *that* at all.

Which was, of course, another lie.

Add it to the pile. Let them sort out his truths once he was gone.

He could still leave, he thought with a sudden desperation. He could walk across the remaining span of the bridge and take his chances with the Brink.

Maybe he *would* make it to the other side. Some did, after all. Maybe he would simply end up like his mother had. It wouldn't be any worse than he deserved.

There was a small chance he would survive, and if he did, maybe he could start over again. He had enough tricks at his disposal. He'd changed his life and his name before, and he could do it again. He could *try*.

But he knew already that it would never work. Leaving was just a different kind of death. And the Order, not bound by the Brink as he was, would never stop hunting him. Not now, at least. Destroying the Book wouldn't be enough. When they found him—and they would—they'd never let him go. They'd use him and use him, until there was nothing left of who he'd once been.

He'd take his chances with the water.

Pulling himself up onto the railing, he had to grip the cable tightly to keep balanced against those gusting spring winds. Far off in the direction of the city, he heard the rumble of carriages, the cry of wild, angry voices signaling that the moment for indecision had passed.

A single step is such a small thing. He'd taken countless steps every day without ever noticing, but this step . . .

LISA MAXWELL

The noise at the mouth of the bridge grew louder, closer, and he knew the time had come. If they caught him, no amount of magic or tricks or lies would help. So before they could reach him, he released his hold on the cable, took that final step, and put himself—*and the Book*—in the one place the Order could never follow.

The last thing he heard was the Book's wailing defiance. Or maybe that was the sound tearing from his own throat as he gave himself over to the air.

PART

I

THE THIEF

December 1926—Upper West Side

It wasn't magic that allowed Esta to slip out of the party unseen, the bright notes from the piano dimming as she left the ballroom. No matter the year, no one ever really looks at the help, so no one had noticed her leave. And no one had noticed the way her shapeless black dress sagged a bit on one side, the telltale sign of the knife she had concealed in her skirts.

But then, people usually do miss what's right in front of them.

Even through the heavy doors, she could still faintly hear the notes from the quartet's ragtime melody. The ghost of the too-cheery song followed her through the entry hall, where carved woodwork and polished stone towered three stories above her. The grandeur didn't overwhelm her, though. She was barely impressed and definitely not intimidated. Instead, she moved with confidence—its own sort of magic, she supposed. People trusted confidence, even when they shouldn't. Maybe *especially* when they shouldn't.

The enormous crystal chandelier might have thrown shards of electric light around the cavernous hall, but the corners of the room and the high, coffered ceiling remained dark. Beneath the palms that stretched two stories up the walls, more shadows waited. The hall might have appeared empty, but there were too many places to hide in the mansion, too many chances someone could be watching. She kept moving.

When she came to the elaborate grand staircase, she glanced up to the landing, where an enormous pipe organ stood. On the floor above, the private areas of the house held rooms filled with art, jewels, priceless vases, and countless antiques—easy pickings with everyone distracted by the loud, drunken party in the ballroom. But Esta wasn't there for those treasures, however tempting they might have been.

And they were *definitely* tempting.

She paused for a second, but then the clock chimed the hour, confirming that she was later than she'd meant to be. Tossing one more careful glance over her shoulder, she slipped past the staircase and into a hall that led deeper into the mansion.

It was quiet there. Still. The noise of the party no longer followed her, and she finally let her shoulders sag a bit, expelling a sigh as she relaxed the muscles in her back from the ramrod-straight posture of the serving girl she'd been pretending to be. Tipping her head to one side, she started to stretch her neck, but before she could feel the welcome release, someone grabbed her by the arm and pulled her into the shadows.

On instinct, she twisted, holding tight to her attacker's wrist and pulling it forward and down with all her weight, until he let out a strangled yelp, his elbow close to popping.

"Dammit, Esta, it's me," a familiar voice hissed. It was an octave or two higher than usual, probably because of the pressure she was still exerting on his arm.

With a whispered curse, she released Logan's arm and shook him off, disgusted. "You should know better than to grab me like that." Her heart was still pounding, so she couldn't manage to dredge up any remorse for the way he was rubbing his arm. "What's your deal, anyway?"

"You're late," Logan snapped, his too-handsome face close to hers.

With golden hair and the kind of blue eyes that girls who don't know better write poems about, Logan Sullivan was a master of using his looks to his advantage. Women wanted him and men wanted to be him, but he didn't try to charm Esta. Not anymore.

"Well, I'm here now."

"You were supposed to be here ten minutes ago. Where have you been?" he demanded.

She didn't have to answer him. It would have pissed him off more to keep her secrets, but she couldn't suppress a satisfied grin as she held up the diamond stickpin she'd lifted from an old man in the ballroom who'd had trouble keeping his hands to himself.

"Seriously?" Logan glared at Esta. "You risked the job for *that?*"

"It was either this or punch him." She glanced up at him to emphasize her point. "I don't do handsy, Logan." It hadn't even been a decision, really, to bump into him as he moved on to grab some young maid, to pretend to clean the champagne off his coat while she slipped the pin from his silken tie. Maybe she should have walked away, but she hadn't. She *couldn't.*

Logan continued to glower at her, but Esta refused to regret her choices. Regret was for people who dragged their past along with them everywhere, and Esta had never been able to afford that kind of deadweight. Besides, who could regret a diamond? Even in the dimly lit corridor, the stone was a beauty—all fire and ice. It also looked like security to Esta, not only because of what it was worth but also for the reminder that whatever happened, she could survive. The heady rush of adrenaline from that knowledge was still jangling through her blood, and not even Logan's irritation could dampen it.

"You do whatever the job requires." He narrowed his eyes at her.

"Yeah, I do," she said, her voice low and not at all intimidated. "Always have. Always will. The Professor knows that, so I'd have thought you would have figured it out by now too." She glared at him a second longer before taking another satisfied look at the diamond, just to irritate him. Definitely closer to four carats than she'd originally thought.

"We can't afford any unnecessary risks tonight," he said, still all business. Still clearly believing he had some sort of authority over their situation.

She shrugged off his accusation as she pocketed the diamond. "Not so much of a risk," she told him truthfully. "We'll be long gone before the old goat even notices it's missing. And you *know* there's no way he saw me take it." Her marks never did. She leveled a defiant look in his direction.

Logan opened his mouth like he was going to argue, but she beat him to it.

"Did you find it, or what?" Esta asked.

She already knew what the answer would be—*of course* he'd found it. Logan could find anything. It was his whole reason for being—at least it was his whole reason for being on the Professor's team. But Esta allowed him his triumph because she needed to get him off the topic of the diamond. They didn't have time for one of his tantrums, and much as she hated to admit it, she *had* been later than they'd planned.

Logan's mouth went flat, like he was fighting the urge to continue harping about the diamond, but his ego won out—as it usually did—and he nodded. "It's in the billiards room, like we expected."

"Lead the way," she said with what she hoped was a sweet enough expression. She knew the floor plan of the mansion as well as he did, but she also knew from experience that it was best to let Logan feel helpful, and maybe even a little like he was in charge. At the very least, it kept him off her ass.

He hesitated for a moment longer but finally gave a jerk of his head. She followed him silently, and more than a little smugly, through the dim hall.

All around them, the walls dripped with paintings of dour noblemen from some bankrupt European estate or another. Charles Schwab, the mansion's owner, wasn't any more royal than Esta herself, though. He'd come from a family of German immigrants, and everyone in town knew it. The house hadn't helped—built on the wrong side of Central Park, it was an entire city block of overdecorated gilding and crystal. Its contents might have been worth a fortune, but in New York, even a fortune wasn't enough to buy your way into the most exclusive circles.

Too bad it wouldn't last long. In a handful of years, Black Friday would hit and all the art lining those walls, along with every bit of the furnishings, would be sold off to pay Schwab's debts. The mansion itself would sit empty until a decade later, when it would be torn down to make way for another uninspired apartment building. If the place weren't so obviously tacky, it might have been sad.

But that was still a few years off, and Esta didn't have time to worry about the future of steel tycoons. Not when she had a job to do and less time than she'd planned.

The two turned down another hallway, which ended at a heavy wooden door. Logan listened carefully before pushing it open. For a second Esta worried he would step into the room with her.

Instead, he gave her a serious nod. "I'll keep watch."

Grateful that she wouldn't have Logan breathing down her neck while she worked, she slipped into the scent of wood polish and cigars. A thoroughly masculine space, the billiards room wasn't filled with the over-fussy gilding and crystal that adorned the rest of the house. Instead, tufted leather chairs were arranged in small seating groups and an enormous billiards table anchored the space like an altar.

The room was stuffy from the fire in the hearth, and Esta pulled at the high neckline of her dress, weighing the risks of unbuttoning the collar or rolling up her sleeves. She needed to be comfortable when she worked, and no one was there but Logan—

"Get a move on it," he demanded. "Schwab's going to start the auction soon, and we need to be gone by then."

Her back still to Logan, she searched the space as she forced herself to take a deep breath so she wouldn't kill him. "Did you figure out where the safe is?"

"Bookcase," he said before closing the door and sealing her into the stifling room. The silence surrounding her was broken only by the steady ticking of a grandfather clock—*tick . . . tick . . . tick*—a reminder that each second passing was one closer to the moment they might be discovered. And if they were seen—

But she put that fear out of her mind and focused on what she had come to do. The wall opposite the massive fireplace was lined with shelves filled with matching leather volumes. Esta admired them as she ran her fingers lightly over the pristine spines.

"Where are you?" she whispered.

The titles glimmered softly in the low light, keeping their secrets as she felt along the underside of the shelves. It wasn't long before she found what she was looking for—a small button sunk into the wood, where none of the servants would hit it accidentally and where no one but a thief would think to look. When she depressed it, a mechanism within the shelves released with a solid, satisfying *click,* and a quarter of the wall swung out enough for her to pull the hinged shelves forward.

Exactly as she'd expected—a Herring-Hall-Marvin combination floor safe. Three-inch-thick cast steel and large enough for a man to sit comfortably inside, it was the most sophisticated vault you could buy in 1923. She'd never seen one so new before. This particular model was gleaming in hunter-green lacquer with Schwab's name emblazoned in an ornate script on the surface. A beautiful vault for the things a very rich man held most dear. Luckily, Esta had been able to crack more challenging locks when she was eight.

Her fingers flexed in anticipation. All night she'd felt outside of herself—the stiff dress she was wearing, the way she had to cast her eyes to the floor when spoken to, it was like playing a role she wasn't suited for. But standing before the safe, she finally felt comfortable in her own skin again.

Pressing her ear against the door, she started to rotate the dial. One click . . . two . . . the sound of metal rubbing against metal in the inner cylinders as she listened for the lock's heartbeat.

The seconds ticked by with fatal certainty, but the longer she worked, the more relaxed she felt. She could read a lock better than she could read a person. Locks didn't change on a whim or because of the weather, and there wasn't a lock yet made that could hide its secrets from her. In a matter of minutes, she had three of the four numbers. She turned the dial again, on her way to the fourth—

"Esta?" Logan hissed, disrupting her concentration. "Are you finished yet?"

The last number lost, she glared over her shoulder at him. "I might be if you'd leave me alone."

"Hurry up," he snapped, and then ducked back into the hall, closing the door behind him.

"Hurry up," she muttered, mimicking his imperious tone as she leaned in again to listen. Like the art of safecracking could be rushed. Like Logan had any idea how to do it himself.

When the final cylinder clicked into place, she felt an echoing satisfaction. Now to try the combinations. Only a minute more and the contents would be open to her. A minute after that and she and Logan would be gone. And Schwab would never know.

"Esta?"

She cursed. "Now what?" She didn't look at Logan this time, keeping her focus on the second, incorrect, combination.

"Someone's coming." He glanced behind him. "I'm going to distract them."

She turned to him then, saw the anxiety tightening his features. "Logan—" But he was already gone.

She thought about helping him, but dismissed that idea and instead turned back to the safe. Logan could take care of himself. Logan would take care of both of them, because that was what they did. That was how they worked. She needed to do her job and leave him to his.

Two more incorrect combinations, and the heat of the room was creeping against her skin, the scent of tobacco and wood smoke burning her throat. She wiped her forehead with the back of her sleeve and tried to ignore the way her dress felt as though it would strangle her.

She tried again, dismissing the trickle of sweat easing its way down her back beneath the layers of fabric. Eight. Twenty-one. Thirteen. Twenty-five. She gave the handle a tug, and to her relief, the heavy door of the safe opened.

Outside the room, she heard the low rumble of male voices, but she was too busy scanning the vault's contents to pay much attention. The various shelves and compartments were packed with canvas envelopes filled with stock certificates and bonds, file folders stuffed with papers, stacks of neatly bound, oversize bills. She eyed the money, disappointed that she couldn't take even a dollar of the odd-looking money. For their plan to work, Schwab couldn't know that anyone had been there.

She found what she was looking for on a lower shelf.

"Hello, beautiful," she crooned, reaching for the long black box. She barely had it in her hands when the voices erupted in the hallway.

"This is an outrage! I could ruin you with a single telegram," Logan bellowed, his voice carrying through the heavy door. "When I tell my uncle—no, my *grandfather*—how abysmally I've been treated here," he continued, "you won't get another contract on this side of the Mississippi. Possibly not on the other, either. No one of any account will speak to you after I—"

It must be Schwab, Esta thought, pulling a pin from her hair and starting to work on the locked box. Schwab had been trying to make his mark on the city for years. The house was one part of that, but the contents of the box were an even more important part. And it was the contents of the box that Esta needed.

"Be reasonable, Jack." Another voice—probably Schwab's. "I'm sure this is a simple misunderstanding—"

Panic inched along her skin as her mind caught up with the man's words. *Jack?* So Schwab wasn't the only one out there.

However good Logan might be, it was never optimal to be outnumbered. In and out fast, with minimal contact. That was the rule that kept them alive.

She wiggled the hairpin in the lock for a few seconds, until she felt the latch give way and the box popped open.

"Get your filthy hands off me!" Logan shouted, loud enough for Esta to hear. It was a sign that things were escalating too quickly for him to contain.

She set the box back on a shelf so she could lift her skirts and remove the knife hidden there. Even with the scuffle in the hall, Esta felt a flash of admiration for Mari's handiwork as she compared the knife from her skirts to the jewel-encrusted dagger lying in the black velvet of the box. Her friend had done it again—not that she was surprised.

Mariana Cestero could replicate anything—any material from any time period, including Logan's engraved invitation for the party that night and the six-inch dagger Esta had been carrying in the folds of her skirt. The only thing Mari couldn't completely replicate was the stone in the dagger's hilt, the Pharaoh's Heart, because the stone was more than it appeared to be.

An uncut garnet rumored to be taken from one of the tombs in the Valley of the Kings, the stone was believed to contain the power of fire, the most difficult of all elements to manipulate. Fire, water, earth, sky, and spirit, the five elements that the Order of Ortus Aurea was obsessed with understanding and using to build its power.

They were wrong, of course. Elemental magic wasn't anything but a fairy tale created by those without magic—the Sundren—to explain things they didn't understand. But misunderstanding magic didn't make the Order any less dangerous. Just because the stone didn't control fire didn't mean there wasn't *something* special about the Pharaoh's Heart. Professor Lachlan wouldn't have wanted it otherwise.

Even in the soft light thrown by the fire, the garnet was polished so smoothly it almost glowed. Without trying, Esta could feel the pull of the stone, sensed herself drawn to it, not like she'd been drawn to the diamond stickpin, but on a deeper, more innate level.

After all, elemental magic might be a fairy tale, but magic itself was real enough.

Organizations like the Order of Ortus Aurea had been trying to claim magic as their own for centuries. Schwab had purchased the dagger and arranged the night's auction in the hopes of buying his way into the Order, but since the only magic the Order possessed was artificial and corrupt ceremonial magic—pseudoscientific practices like alchemy and theurgy— they wouldn't be able to sense what Esta could. They wouldn't know that Mari's stone was a fake until much later, when they were running their experiments and trying to harness the stone's power. Even then they would assume it was Schwab who had cheated them . . . or that Schwab couldn't tell the difference to start with. Schwab himself would believe that the antiquities dealer who'd sold him the dagger had swindled him. No one would realize the truth—the real Pharaoh's Heart had been taken right out from under them.

Esta made the switch, placing the counterfeit dagger into the velvet-lined box and tucking the real dagger back into the hidden pocket of her skirt. It was heavier than the one she'd been carrying all night, like the Pharaoh's Heart had an unexpected weight and density that Mari hadn't predicted. For a moment Esta worried that maybe Schwab *would* notice the difference. Then she thought of the house—his overdone attempt to display the number in his bank account—and she shook off her fears. Schwab wasn't exactly the type to understand which details mattered.

Outside the room, something crashed as an unfamiliar voice shouted. More quickly now, Esta locked the box, careful to put it back on the shelf exactly as it had been, and closed the safe. She was securing the bookcase when she heard Logan shout—an inarticulate grunt of pain.

And then a gunshot shattered the night.

No! Esta thought as she sprinted for the door, the crack of gunfire still ringing in her ears. She needed to get to Logan. He might be a pain in the ass, but he was *their* pain in the ass. And it was her job to get them *both* out.

At the other end of the hall, Logan lay on the floor, trying to pull himself up, while Schwab attempted to wrestle the gun away from a balding blond man in a tuxedo that bulged around his thick middle. Struggling against Schwab, the blond leveled the gun at Logan again.

Esta comprehended the entire scene in an instant and immediately took a deep, steadying breath, forcing herself to ignore the chaos in front of her. She focused instead on the steady beating of her own heart.

Thump. Tha-thump.

As regular as the cylinders of a lock tumbling into place.

Thump. Tha-thump.

In the next beat, time went thick for her, like the world around her had nearly frozen: Schwab's wobbling jowls stilled. The angry sweat dripping from the blond man's temple seemed to be suspended in midair as it fell in excruciatingly slow motion toward the floor.

It was as though someone were advancing the entire world like a movie, frame by painstaking frame. And *she* was that someone.

Find the gaps between what is and isn't, Professor Lachlan had taught her.

Because magic wasn't in the elements. Magic lived in the spaces, in the emptiness between all things, connecting them. It waited there for those who knew how to find it, for those who had the born ability to grasp those connections—the Mageus.

For those like Esta.

She hadn't needed magic earlier that night, not to escape the party or to pick the lock, but she needed it now, so she let herself open to its possibilities. It was almost as natural as breathing for her to find the spaces between the seconds and the beating of hearts. She rushed toward Logan, stealing time as she darted through the nearly frozen tableau.

But she couldn't stop time completely. She couldn't reverse the moment to stop the blond's finger from pressing the trigger again.

She wasn't quite to Logan when the sound of the gun shattered her concentration. She lost her hold on time, and the world slammed back into motion. For Esta, it felt like an eternity between the door of the billiards room to where she was standing, exposed, in the hallway, but for the two men, her appearance would have been instantaneous. For members of the Order, it would have been immediately recognizable as the effect of magic.

The men froze for a moment, their eyes almost comically wide. But then the blond seemed to gather his wits about him. He jerked away from Schwab, lifted the dark pistol, and took aim.

ON THE BRINK

Dolph Saunders was born for the night. The quiet hours when the city went dark and the streets emptied of the daylight rabble were his favorite time. Though they might have been criminals or cutthroats, those out after the lamps were lit were his people—the dispossessed and disavowed who lived in the shadows, carving out their meager lives at the edge of society. Those who understood that the only rule that counted was to not get caught.

That night, though, the shadows weren't a comfort to him. Tucked out of sight, across the street from J. P. Morgan's mansion, he cursed himself for not being able to do more. His crew was late, and there was an uneasiness in the air—it felt too much like the night was waiting for something to happen. Dolph didn't like it one bit. Not after so many had already disappeared, and especially not when Leena's life was at stake.

It wasn't unusual for people to go missing in his part of the city. Cross the wrong street and you could cross the wrong gang. Cross the wrong boss, and you might never be heard from again. But those with the old magic, especially those under Dolph's protection, knew how to avoid most trouble. A handful of his own people disappearing in the span of a month? It couldn't be an accident.

Dolph didn't doubt the Order was to blame, but they'd been quiet recently. There hadn't been a raid in the Bowery for weeks, which was unusual on its own. But even with their Conclave coming up at the end of the year, his people hadn't heard a whisper to hint at the Order's plans.

Dolph didn't trust the quiet, and he wasn't the type to let those loyal to him go without answers. So Leena, Dolph's partner in absolutely everything, had gotten herself hired as a maid in Morgan's house. Morgan was one of the Order's highest officials, and they'd hoped someone in the household would let something slip.

For the past couple of weeks, she'd polished and scrubbed . . . and hadn't found out anything about the missing Mageus. Then, two nights ago, she didn't come home.

He should have gone himself. They were his people, his responsibility. If anything happened to her . . .

He forced himself to put that thought aside. *She'll be fine.* Leena was smart, strong, and more stubbornly determined than anyone he knew. She could handle herself in any situation. But her magic only worked on the affinities of other Mageus. It would be useless against the Order.

As though in answer to his dark thoughts, a hired carriage pulled up to the side of the house. They weren't expecting a delivery that night, and the arrival only heightened Dolph's apprehension. With the carriage obscuring his view, he wouldn't be able to see if there was trouble.

Before he could move into a different position, angry male voices spilled out into the night. A moment later, the door of the carriage slammed shut and the driver cracked his whip to send the horses galloping off.

Dolph watched it disappear, his senses prickling in foreboding as the sound of fast footsteps approached. He gripped his cane, ready for whatever came.

"Dolph?"

It was Nibsy Lorcan. A castoff from the boys' mission, he had shown up in Dolph's barroom a few years back. Slight and unassuming, he would have been easy enough to overlook, but Dolph could sense the strength and tenor of a person's affinity from ten paces. He'd thought Nibsy would be a valuable addition to his crew, and he'd been right. With Nibsy's soft-spoken demeanor and sharp wit, the boy managed to win the respect of even the surliest of Dolph's crew, and with his affinity for predicting how different decisions might pan out, he'd quickly earned a place at Dolph's right hand.

As Nibsy came into sight, the lenses of his thick spectacles glinted in the moonlight. "Dolph? Where are you?"

Dolph stepped out of shadows, revealing himself. Despite the heat of the night, his skin felt like ice. "Did you find her?"

Nibs nodded, trying to catch his breath so he could speak.

"Where is she, then?" Dolph asked, his throat going tight as he searched the house again for some sign. "What happened?"

"The Order must have been expecting us," he said, still wheezing for breath. "They got Spot first, right off. Knife to the gut without any questions. And then Appo."

"Jianyu?"

"I don't know," Nibsy gasped. "Didn't see where he went. I found Leena, though. Morgan had her in the cellar, but . . . I couldn't get to her. They'd created some kind of barrier. There was this foglike cloud hanging in the air. When I got close, it felt like I was dying." Nibsy shuddered and took another gulping breath. "She's pretty weak. I couldn't have dragged her out of there. But she tossed this to me," he said, holding out a small object wrapped in muslin. "Told me to leave her. And there was more of them coming, so . . . I did. I'm sorry. I shouldn't have—" His voice cracked. "They took her."

Dolph took the object from Nibs. A bit of cloth had been wrapped around a brass button—one Dolph recognized from the maid's uniform Leena had worn. The scrap weighed no more than a breath between his fingertips. It was ragged on one side. It must have been torn from one of her petticoats. She'd used what looked like blood to scrawl two words in Latin across its surface. *Her blood*, he realized. The message had been important enough to bleed for. But at the sight of the smeared letters, already drying to a dark rusty brown, a feeling of cold dread sank into his very bones.

"We'll get her back." Dolph refused to imagine any other outcome.

He rubbed his thumb across the scrap, feeling its softness along with the familiar echo of Leena's energy. He pressed his own magic into the scrap, into the traces of her blood, trying to feel more and understand what had happened. While he could sense a person's affinity if they had one, could even tap into it and borrow it if he touched them, reading objects hadn't ever been his strength.

Still, Nibs was right—what little trace of Leena he sensed felt off, weak. He tossed the button aside but tucked the scrap of fabric into his inner coat pocket, the one closest to his heart.

"There's still time," he said, already heading toward the place where their carriage waited.

With the streets empty of traffic, they caught up to the other coach quickly. But as they followed it south through the city, he had a sinking feeling about where the carriage was headed. When they finally turned onto Park Row, Dolph knew for sure.

He directed their carriage to stop at the edge of the park that surrounded City Hall. Beyond the night-darkened gardens stood the great, hulking terminal that blocked the view of the bridge to Brooklyn. Steel and glass, it loomed almost like a warning in the night. Beyond it stood the first bridge of its kind to cross such a great span of water. And bisecting the bridge was the Brink, the invisible boundary that kept the Mageus from leaving the city with their magic intact. From corrupting the lands and the country beyond with what the Order—and most of the population— believed was feral, dangerous power.

Leena, like Dolph himself, had been born to the old magic. For the Order to bring her to the bridge meant only one thing—they knew what she was. And they were going to use the Brink to destroy her affinity. To destroy *her*.

He wouldn't let that happen.

Dolph watched as the hired cab carrying Leena turned beyond the terminal, toward the entrance for vehicles crossing the bridge. "I'll go on foot," he said. "You stay here. To keep watch."

"You sure?" Nibs asked.

"We can't chance alerting them." There would be no way to hide if they followed by carriage, but on the walkway above they might be able to surprise them, maybe have a chance to save Leena. "They'll have to wait to pay their toll. It will be easy enough for me to catch up."

"But with your leg," Nibs said. "I could—"

He cut Nibs a deadly look. "My leg's never stopped me from doing what needs done. You'll stay here, as I said. If I'm not back before their carriage appears again, go warn the others. If this goes badly, the Order may be coming for them all." He stared at Nibs, trying to convey the weight of the moment.

Nibsy's eyes widened a bit. "You'll be back," Nibs told him. "You'll bring Leena back."

Dolph was glad for the assurance, but he wasn't going to depend on it. Pulling his cap low over his eyes, he began to walk in the direction of the terminal. He ignored the stiffness in his leg, as he always did, and lifted himself up the wide steps that led to the entrance of the bridge. Once he was above, he kept away from the thin columns of lamplight on the planks of the walkway. Using the shadows for cover, he moved quickly despite his uneven gait—he'd lived with it for so long now that it was part of him.

The hired carriage was pulled to a stop before the first tower of the bridge—just beyond the shoreline. Below, three figures emerged. One reached back to pull out the fourth. Even from that distance, he knew it was Leena. He sensed her affinity—familiar, warm, *his*. But she was hanging limply between her captors. He felt the weakness of her magic, too, and when he got closer, he saw what they had done to her, saw her bruised face and bloodied lip. Saw her flinch with a ragged exhale and struggle against the men as they started to pull her toward the tower, toward the Brink.

His blood went hot.

Dolph, like every other Mageus in the city, knew what would happen when a person with the old magic crossed that line. Once they stepped across the Brink, it drained them. If the person was lucky and their affinity was weak—closer to a talent than a true power—they might survive, but they'd be left permanently broken from that missing part of themselves and would spend the rest of their life suffering the loss.

But for most, the Brink left them hollowed out, destroyed. Often, dead. So he understood what it would do to Leena, who was one of the most powerful Mageus he'd ever known.

Keeping to the shadows, he calculated his chances of getting Leena away from the men. He could take one down easily enough, even with his leg as it was, and the poisoned blade in his cane could do well enough on the other, but the third? There wasn't time to go back for Nibs, not that the boy would be much help in a fight.

"Hold her up, boys," the leader of the three said. "I want to see the fear in her eyes—filthy maggot."

The two men pulled Leena upright and one gave her a sharp smack across the cheek.

Dolph's blood pulsed, his anger barely leashed. But he forced himself to stay still, to not rush in and ruin his one chance of freeing her.

Still, seeing another man touch her, harm her . . . His knuckles ached from his grip on his cane. *To hell with destroying the Brink.* He would destroy them all.

He crept through the shadows until he was almost directly above them. Already he could feel the cold energy of the Brink. Unlike natural magic, which felt warm and alive, the Brink felt like ice. Like desolation and rot. It was perverse magic, power corrupted by ritual and amplified by the energy it drained. And like all unnatural magic, it came with a cost.

This close, every ounce of his being wanted to turn and flee. This close, he could feel how easily everything he was could be taken from him. But he wouldn't let anyone touch her like that again.

The man who spoke lifted Leena's head by her hair. "There you are," he said with a laugh when she opened her left eye to look at him. Her right eye was swollen shut. "Do you know what's about to happen to you, pigeon? I bet you do. I bet you can feel it, can't you?" The man laughed. "It's what maggots like you and your kind deserve."

Leena's eye closed. Not a betrayal of weakness, Dolph knew, but to gather her strength.

That's my girl, Dolph thought as Leena muttered a foul curse. Then she opened her unbruised eye and spit in the man's face.

The man reacted instantly. His hand flew out, and Leena's head snapped backward at the force of the blow.

Dolph was already moving. He hoisted himself up onto the railing and busted the streetlamp with the end of his cane. Like prey that sensed a hunter nearby, the men below went still as the light went out, listening intently for the source of the disturbance.

"What are you waiting for?" the leader shouted, breaking their wary silence, but his voice had an edge of nerves to it that wasn't there before. "Drag her over."

The men didn't immediately obey. As they hesitated, their eyes still adjusting, Dolph switched his patch, so he could see with the eye already accustomed to darkness. The bridge below now clear and visible to him, he dropped soundlessly from the walkway above. He ignored the sharp ache in his leg as he landed on the leader, knocking him to the ground and plunging the sharp blade concealed in the end of his cane into the man's calf. The man let out a scream like he was being burned alive.

That particular poison did have a tendency to sting.

As the leader continued to scream, Dolph turned to the next man, but he was already struggling against some unseen assailant. With a sudden jerk, he went still, his eyes wide as he slumped to the ground. Jianyu appeared, seemingly materializing out of the night, and gave Dolph a nod of acknowledgment as they turned together to face the third man.

The only one left seemed too paralyzed by fear to realize he'd be better off running. He was holding Leena in front of him like a shield.

"Leave me be or I'll kill her," he said, his voice cracking as he blinked into the dark.

Dolph stepped steadily toward them as Jianyu circled around the man's other side.

"You were already dead the moment you touched her," Dolph murmured when he was barely an arm's reach away.

The man stumbled back, and Leena took the opportunity to struggle away from him. But he was too off-balance and his hold was too secure. Instead of letting her go, the man pulled her with him as he stumbled back, away from Dolph and toward the cold power of the Brink.

Without thought for his own safety, Dolph reached for them, but his fingers barely grasped the sleeve of the man's coat. The fabric ripped, and the man—and Leena—fell backward into the Brink.

Dolph knew the moment she crossed it, because he felt her surprise and pain and desperation as keenly as if it were his own. The night around them lit from the magic coursing through her, draining from her. She screamed and writhed, her back arching at a painful-looking angle. Her arms and legs went stiff and shook with the terrible power that held her.

The man holding her screamed as well, but not from the Brink. When she began convulsing, he dropped her and ran, disappearing into the night of that other shore, where Dolph couldn't follow.

But Dolph's eyes were only for Leena. He watched in helpless horror as her body shook with the pain of her magic being ripped from her. He moved toward her, pushing past his own bone-deep fear of the Brink, but when his fingers brushed against the icy energy of it, he couldn't make himself reach any farther.

"Leena!" he shouted. "Look at me!"

She slumped to the ground, drained but still moaning and twitching with pain. He could no longer feel her affinity.

"Leena!" he screamed, fury and terror mingling in his voice.

It was enough to distract her for a moment, and even as her face contorted, she tried to turn toward the sound of his voice.

"That's it," he said when their eyes finally met.

Her expression was wild with the pain and shock of the Brink's devastating effect, but she wasn't dead yet. As long as her heart beat, there was a chance, Dolph told himself, pushing away the truth.

People didn't come back from the Brink.

Still, Leena was different, he told himself as she tried to focus on him. Dolph thought for a moment he saw her there, his own Leena, somewhere behind the agony twisting her features.

"I need you to come to me, *Streghina*. I need you to try," he pleaded.

And because she was the strongest person he'd ever known, she *did* try. She forced herself to move, reaching for him, her limbs trembling with effort as she pulled herself back to safety.

"That's it, my love. Just a little more," he told her, struggling to keep his voice from breaking into the animal-like wail he felt building within him.

With the last of her strength, she inched along. Her face was drawn tight, but she kept going. His Leena. His own heart.

"You can make it. Just a little farther."

But she looked up at him, her once-beautiful eyes now a lurid bloodred. Her expression was determined as she tried to whisper something, but before she could finish, she collapsed beyond his reach.

"No!" he screamed. "You can't leave us. You can't give up now." He knelt as close to the Brink as he dared get, willing her to keep moving.

But Leena only blinked up at him, barely able to focus with her unbruised eye.

No, he thought wildly. He wouldn't accept her fate. *Couldn't* accept it. Not his Leena, who had stood by his side since they were children. Not the woman who had been his partner in every way, despite all the mistakes he had made. He couldn't leave her there. No matter what it meant for him.

Dolph forced himself to reach out to Leena, to press through the searing cold bit by bit. To ignore the excruciating pain. Breaching the Brink was like putting your hand through glass and feeling the shards tear through skin and tendon. Or like dipping yourself in molten metal, if liquid steel could be colder than ice.

But even that pain didn't compare to the thought of losing her.

Finally, he grabbed Leena's hand. She blinked slowly, vacantly, at the pressure of his grasp, but with his fingers now wrapped securely around hers, he found that he didn't have the strength to pull her back. The Brink was already wrapping its icy energy around his wrist, burrowing deep beneath his skin to seek out the heart of who and what he was.

Then, suddenly, he was moving. Jianyu had taken him by the legs and was pulling him and Leena both back, away from the invisible boundary. With the strength he had left, Dolph took Leena into his arms and settled her across his lap, barely aware of the numbness inside his own chest.

"I wasn't fast enough," Jianyu said. "I tried to get her before they took her, but . . ."

Dolph wasn't even hearing him.

"No," Dolph whispered, tracing the lines of her face. Her breath rattled weakly from her lungs as he clutched her to him, rocking and pleading for her to stay with him. "I can't do this without you."

But she didn't respond.

"No!" he screamed when he realized her body had gone limp in his arms. "No!" Again and again, he wailed into the night, hatred and anguish hardening him, sealing him over, like a fossil of the man he'd once been.

A SLIP THROUGH TIME

December 1926—The Upper West Side

E sta froze as the blond trained the gun on her. His expression was a mixture of disgust and anticipation as he shifted his aim between her and Logan.

"I told you," he growled at Schwab. "I *warned* you something like this would happen."

"Jack!" Schwab yelled, grabbing for the man's arm again. "Put that gun down!"

Jack shook him off. "You have no idea what they are, what they're capable of." He turned to Esta and Logan. "Who sent you? Tell me!" he screamed, his face red with fury as he continued to swing the gun back and forth, alternating between the two of them.

Esta glanced at Logan and noticed the dark stain creeping across the white shirt beneath his tuxedo jacket. His eyes flickered open and met hers. He didn't look so cocky anymore.

"I won't be ruined again," the blond said as he cocked the hammer back again and steadied his aim at Logan. "Not this time."

Never reveal what you can do. It was one of their most important rules. Because if the Order knew what she was capable of, they would never stop hunting her. But they'd already seen her. And the stain creeping across Logan's shirt was growing at an alarming rate. She had to get him out, to get him back.

It seemed to happen all at once—

She heard the click of the gun being cocked, but she was already pulling time around her.

"Noooooo!" Logan shouted, his voice as thick and slow as the moment itself had become.

The echoing boom of the pistol.

Esta rushing across the remaining length of the hallway, putting herself between Logan and the gun.

Grabbing Logan tightly around the torso, she reached for safety . . . focusing all of her strength and power to reach further . . . and pulled them both into an empty version of the same hallway.

Daylight now filtered in through an unwashed window at the far end of the hall, lighting the dust motes they'd disturbed in the stale air of the completely silent house.

Logan moaned and shifted himself off her. "What the hell did you do?"

She ignored her own unease and took in the changed hallway, the silent, unoccupied house. "I got us out of there."

"In front of *them*?" His skin was pale, and he was shaking.

"They'd already seen me."

"You didn't have to come barging in like that," he rasped, grimacing as he shifted his weight. "I had it under control."

She should have been irritated that he'd reverted to his usual pain-in-the-ass demeanor so quickly, but Esta was almost too relieved to care. It meant his injury probably wasn't killing him. Yet.

Esta nodded toward his bloody shirt. "Yeah. You were doing great."

"Don't put this on me. If you hadn't gone after a diamond, you wouldn't have been late meeting me. We could have already been gone before Schwab showed up," he argued. "None of this would have happened."

She glared back at him, not giving an inch. But she knew—and hated—that he was right. "I got you out, didn't I? Or maybe you'd prefer being dead?"

"They're going to know."

"I *know*," she said through gritted teeth.

To Schwab and the other man, Esta and Logan would have seemed to disappear, and people *didn't* just disappear. Not without magic—*natural* magic. Old magic. Even Schwab would have understood that much.

"The Order will have heard about it," Logan said, belaboring his point. "Who knows what that will do. . . ."

"Maybe it won't matter," she said, trying to will away her uncertainty. "We've never changed anything before."

"No one has ever seen us before," he pressed.

"Well, we don't live in the 1920s. It's not like they're going to keep looking for a couple of teenagers for the next hundred years."

"The Order has a long memory." Logan glared at her, or he tried to, but his eyes still weren't quite focusing, and the dizziness that usually hit him after slipping through time was having a clear effect. He fell back on his elbows. "When are we, anyway?"

Esta looked around the musty stillness of the hallway. All at once she felt less confident about her choices. "I'm not sure," she admitted.

"How can you not be sure?" He sounded too arrogant for someone who was probably bleeding to death. "Weren't you the one who brought us here?"

"Yeah, but I'm not sure *exactly* what year it is. I was just trying to get us out of there, and then the gun went off and . . ." She trailed off as she felt a sharp pain in her shoulder, reminding her of what had happened. She touched the damp, torn fabric gingerly.

Logan's unfocused gaze raked over her. "You're hit?"

"I'm fine," she said, frustrated that she'd hesitated and ended up in the bullet's path. "It's barely a scratch, which is more than I can say for you." She pulled herself off the floor and offered Logan her hand.

He allowed her to help him up, but he swayed, unsteady on his feet, and put all his weight on her to stay upright.

"We're not any later than forty-eight. Probably sometime in the thirties, by the look of the house. Can you walk at all?" she asked before he could complain any more.

"I think so," he said, grimacing as he clutched his side. The effort it had taken to stand had drained him of almost all color.

"Good. Whenever this is, I can't get us back from in here." Pain throbbed in her shoulder, but the bullet really had only grazed her. She'd heal, but if she didn't get Logan back to Professor Lachlan's soon, she wasn't sure if he would. "We need to get outside."

The fact was, Esta's ability to manipulate time had certain limitations, mainly that time was attached to place. Sites bore the imprint of their whole history, all layered one moment on top of the other—past, present, and future. She could move vertically between those layers, but the location had to exist during the moment she wanted to reach. Schwab's mansion had been torn down in 1948. It *didn't* exist during her own time, so she couldn't get them back from inside the house. But the streets of the Upper West Side were still basically the same.

Logan stumbled a little, but for the most part, they made it through the empty house without much problem. As they reached the front door, though, Esta heard sounds from deep within the house.

"What's that?" Logan lifted his head to listen.

"I don't know," she said, pulling him along.

"If it's the Order—"

"We have to get out of here. *Now*," she said, cutting him off.

Esta opened the front door as a pair of deep voices carried to her through the empty halls. She tugged Logan out into the icy chill of the day, and they stumbled toward the front gates of the mansion.

Traveling through the layers of time wasn't as easy as pulling on the gaps between moments to slow the seconds. It took a lot more energy, and it also took something to focus that energy and augment her own affinity—a stone not unlike the Pharaoh's Heart that she wore in a silver cuff hidden beneath the sleeve of her maid's uniform.

Against her arm, her own stone still felt warm from slipping through time a few minutes before. The pain of her injury and everything else that had happened had left her drained, so trying to find the right layer of time was more of a struggle than usual. The harder she tried, the warmer the stone became, until it was almost uncomfortably hot against her skin.

Esta had never made two trips so close together before. She and the stone both probably needed more time to recover, but time, ironically enough, was the one thing that neither of them had if she wanted to avoid being seen again.

The voices were closer now.

She forced herself to ignore the searing bite of the stone's heat against her arm, and with every last ounce of determination she had left, she finally found the layer of time she needed and dragged them both through.

The snow around them disappeared as Esta felt the familiar push-pull sensation of being outside the normal rules of time. Schwab's castlelike mansion faded into the brownish-red brick of a flat-faced apartment building, and the city—*her* city—appeared. The sleek, modern cars and the trees full with summer leaves and other structures on the streets around them materialized out of nothing. It was early in the morning, only moments after they'd originally departed, and the streets were empty and quiet.

She let out a relieved laugh as she collapsed under Logan's weight onto the warm sidewalk. "We made it," she told him, looking around for some sign of Dakari, Professor Lachlan's bodyguard and their ride.

But Logan didn't reply. His skin was ashen, and his eyes stared blankly through half-closed lids as the modern city buzzed with life around them.

LIBERO LIBRO

November 1900—The Bowery

Dolph Saunders sat in his darkened office and ran his finger across the fragile scrap of material he was holding. He didn't need light to see what was written on it. He'd memorized the single line months ago: *libero Libro.*

Freedom from the Book.

At least, that's what he thought it said—the *e* was smudged. Perhaps it was better translated, *from the Book, freedom?*

"Dolph?" A sliver of light cracked open the gloom of his self-imposed cell.

"Leave me be, Nibs," Dolph growled. He set the scrap on the desktop in front of him and drained the last of the whiskey in the bottle he'd been nursing all morning.

The door opened farther, spilling light into the room, and Dolph raised his hand to ward off the brightness.

"You can't stay in here all the time. You got a business to run." Nibs walked over to the window and opened the shades. "People who depend on you."

"You don't value your life much, do you, boy?" he growled as the brightness shot a bolt of pain through his head.

Nibs gave him a scathing look. "I'm almost sixteen, you know."

Dolph gave a halfhearted grunt of disapproval but didn't bother to look up at him. "If you keep using that mouth of yours, you won't make it that far."

"If you drink yourself to death, I'm not gonna last the month anyway," Nibs said calmly, ignoring the threat. "None of us will. Not with Paul Kelly and his gang breathing down our necks. Monk Eastman's boys have been making noise too. If you don't get back to work and show them you're still strong enough to hold what's yours, they're going to make their move. You'll lose everything you've built."

Dolph thumped the bottle onto the desk. "Let them come."

"And the people who'll get hurt in the process?"

"I can't save them all," he said with a pang of guilt. He'd sent Spot and Appo to their graves, hadn't he? And he hadn't even been able to protect Leena, the one person he would have given anything—*everything*—to protect.

"Leena wouldn't have stood for you acting like this," Nibs told him, taking the risk to come closer to the desk.

"Don't," Dolph warned, meaning so many things all at once. *Don't speak of her. Don't remind me of what I've lost. Don't push me to be the man I'm not any longer. Don't . . .*

But Nibs didn't so much as blink at his tone. "That's the message she gave me that night, isn't it? You're still trying to figure it out?"

Instinctively, Dolph picked up the fabric and rubbed his fingers across the faded letters. "Leena would have wanted me to."

"Can I see?" Reluctantly, Dolph handed the fragile scrap over to Nibs, who studied it through the thick lenses of his spectacles, his face serious with concentration as he tried to decipher the Latin. "Have you figured it out? What book do you think she means?"

"I can't be sure, but I think she means *the* Book."

Nibs glanced up at him over the rims of his spectacles, confusion and curiosity lighting his eyes. "*The* Book?"

Dolph nodded. "The Ars Arcana."

Surprise flashed across Nibsy's face. "The Book of Mysteries?" He handed the scrap back with a frown. "That's only a myth. A legend."

"Maybe it is, but there are too many stories about a book that holds the secrets of magic for there not to be some truth to them," Dolph said, accepting the scrap with careful fingers.

"There are?"

Dolph nodded. "Some stories claim the Ars Arcana might be the Book of Thoth, an ancient tome created and used by the Egyptian god of wisdom and magic, lost when the dynasties fell. Others say it was a record of the beginning of magic, stolen from a temple in Babylon before the city crumbled. They all end with the Book's disappearance." Dolph shrugged. "What's to say that someone didn't find it? What's to say the stories aren't true? If the Ars Arcana is real, what's to say the Order doesn't have it? Look at the devastation the Brink has wrought. . . ."

"But the Order—"

"The Order's power had to come from something," Dolph said irritably. "They aren't Mageus. They don't have a natural affinity for magic, so how did they come to have the power they wield now, even defiled as it is?"

Nibs shook his head. "I've never really thought about it."

"I have. Who's to say that this book isn't *the* Book? What else would Leena have been willing to sacrifice herself for?"

Nibs hesitated. "What will you do?"

"I don't know." Dolph let out a tired breath and placed the scrap on the desk before him. "Leena was no green girl. If anyone could handle themselves against the Order, it would have been her. Even you didn't see how badly it would turn out."

"I'm sorry. . . ."

"I don't blame you. It was her choice, and mine. But I don't know if I can make that choice for anyone else."

"But Leena's message . . ." Nibs frowned. "What if this book—the Ars Arcana, or whatever it is—what if it *is* the key to our freedom?"

"I don't know if I can ask anyone else to put themselves at that kind of risk for a hunch."

"They're already at risk," Nibs said. "Every day more come to this city, believing they've found a haven only to find themselves in a prison instead. Every day, more and more Mageus arrive and become trapped by the Brink—by the Order."

"You think I don't know that?" Dolph grumbled, tipping the bottle up again and frowning when he found it empty.

"They need someone to protect them. To lead them." Nibs took the bottle from Dolph.

It can't be me.

Dolph rubbed his chin, and the growth of whiskers there surprised him. Leena would have hated it. She liked his face clean and smooth and often ran her fingers over his skin, leaving trails of warmth behind.

She *used to* run her fingers over his skin, he corrected himself. But she'd been gone for months now, and Dolph hadn't felt anything since then except for the ice lodged in his chest. And the emptiness that filled his very soul.

"I can't lead them, Nibs. Not anymore."

The boy cocked his head, expectant, but didn't push.

"It's gone."

An uneasy silence grew between them as Dolph wondered if he'd ever been so young. By the time he was sixteen, he'd already put together his own crew. He'd already started on this mistake of a journey to change their fortunes. He had just over a decade on Nibs, but those years had aged him. And the past few months had hardened him more than an entire lifetime of regrets could have.

"*Everything* is gone?" the boy asked carefully.

Dolph licked his dry lips. "Not everything, no. But when I reached through to get Leena, the Brink took enough."

"The marks?"

"I can't feel them anymore. I won't be able to control them either." He met Nibs' questioning eyes. "They won't fear me if they know."

"So we don't let them know." Nibs gave him a long, hard look. "Control doesn't have anything to do with fear. Control is all about making them think following you is their idea."

"If they find out, they'll turn, and without Leena—"

"Even without Leena, you still have Viola for protection. You're not defenseless."

Nibs was right. Leena's ability to defuse the affinities of anyone around him who meant to do them harm had helped him build his holdings, but Viola could kill a man without touching him. He was making excuses, running scared, and that was something he'd never done before.

"Do it for her," Nibs urged. "If she sent you this message, it's what she wanted. Going after the Book, going after the Order, don't you think it's what she intended for you to do?"

"Fine. Put some people on it—people we trust. But I don't want word getting out about what we're looking for. If anyone else found out that the Ars Arcana exists . . ." He didn't finish the thought, but they both understood how dangerous it could be if others knew that he was after it. A book that could hold the secrets of magic? Whoever had it could be as unstoppable as the Order.

Which meant that Dolph had to be sure to get it first.

"I'll get on it," Nibs said, "but would you do me a favor?"

"What now?" Dolph asked, furrowing his brow in irritation.

"Get yourself a bath or something. The gutter out back smells better than you do."

ISHTAR'S KEY

Present Day—Orchard Street

The first indication that something was wrong was the entrance to Professor Lachlan's Orchard Street building. When Dakari got them back, the building looked the same from the outside, but inside, things had changed. There was a new, ultramodern lobby, complete with a security desk and a guard she'd never seen before. And extra security measures on every floor, at every door.

The building had always been something of a fortress, an odd place to call home, but now its austerity made the unseen threats outside its walls seem that much more foreboding.

But that wasn't the worst of it.

The brightly lit workroom in the basement of their building, where Mari once had produced everything the team needed, was nothing more than a dusty storage closet. Esta had returned from 1926 to find Mari was gone.

It wasn't just that Mari was no longer part of their team. Mari no longer even *existed*.

Esta had used every skill she'd learned over the years from Professor Lachlan to look for her friend. She'd searched immigration records and ancestry registries for some sign of Mari or her family, but instead Esta had found the unsettling evidence that her world had somehow changed.

It was more than Mari's disappearance. Small shifts and subtle differences told Esta the Order of Ortus Aurea had grown stronger and become emboldened in the late twenties and beyond, when they hadn't before. Waves of deportations. Riots that hadn't existed before. A change in who had been president here and there. All the evidence showed that the Order was more powerful now than they had been before Esta and Logan went to steal the Pharaoh's Heart.

With shaking hands, Esta did the one search she'd been dreading—the night of the heist. She had to know if that had been the source of the changes. She had to be sure.

She wasn't surprised to find herself inserted in the historical record where she never should have been. Not by name, of course. No one there that night could have known who she was. But she found a small article that talked about the break-in and the theft of the Pharaoh's Heart.

They knew she'd taken the real dagger.

And from the sparse two inches of print, it was clear they knew that Mageus were behind it.

She'd underestimated the danger they faced. She'd been raised to defeat the Order, trained since she was a young girl in all the skills necessary to do just that. Esta had read the history—public and private—and spent her childhood learning about the devastating effects the Order had on Mageus in the past. She trained daily with Dakari so that she could fight and defend herself against any attack, and still she hadn't truly understood. Maybe it was because the Order of Ortus Aurea and all they'd done so long ago seemed more like myth than reality. The stories had been so monstrous, but in actuality, the Order itself had always been little more than a shadow haunting the periphery of Esta's vision, the boogeyman in her unopened closet. It had been so easy to slip through time, to take things from right under their noses, that she'd never understood . . . not really.

Yes, the Order had created the Brink, and yes, that invisible barrier had effectively stripped the country of magic—and Mageus—over the years. Maybe there had once been a time when everyone knew magic existed, and certainly there was a time when people feared and persecuted those who had it, but by the end of the twentieth century, old magic—*natural* magic—had been mostly forgotten. A fairy tale. And as the public forgot magic, they forgot their fears. The Order had gone underground. It was still a threat to those few Mageus left, of course, but without public support, it operated in secret and its strikes were limited.

The changes in the Professor's building, the small differences in the history books, and, most personally, the erasure of Mari's very existence made Esta think that might no longer be the case.

She had caused this.

In the choices she'd made, she had somehow traded Logan's life for Mari's, traded the relative safety that had been her life for this other, unknown future. She hadn't even realized that was possible.

She had known that traveling to other times carried risks, but Professor Lachlan had taught her that time was something like a book: You could remove a page, scratch out a word here and there, and the story remained the same except for the small gaps. He had always believed it would take something monumental to change the ending.

Apparently exposing her powers to save Logan had been enough.

Three days after she brought Logan back, Esta found herself sitting at the end of his bed, watching his slow, steady breathing. He'd lost a lot of blood, and Dakari's affinity for healing hadn't been strong enough to stave off the infection his body was fighting. He still hadn't come to.

It wasn't that she'd ever been particularly close to Logan, but he was a part of the Professor's team. They needed him. And seeing him pale and so very still shook her more than she would have expected.

She knew the moment Professor Lachlan entered the room, his soft steps punctuated by the click of the crutch he used. Esta didn't turn to greet him, though, not even when he took a few steps through the door and paused as he often did when he had something to discuss with her.

"Don't say it. Please—don't even say it."

"Perhaps I was going to thank you for saving him."

"Bull." She did turn then. Professor Lachlan hadn't moved from the doorway. He was leaning, as usual, on his silver crutch.

She wasn't sure exactly how old he was, but despite his advanced years, the Professor was still fit and slender. He was dressed in the same uniform of tweed pants and a rumpled oxford shirt he'd worn when lecturing to scores of undergraduates at Columbia over the years. He was a small man, not much taller than Esta herself when he straightened, and at first glance most people overlooked him, often dismissing him as too old to be worth worrying about.

Most people were idiots.

The cataracts that had plagued him for years clouded his eyes, but even so, they were astute, alert. Three days ago, when she'd told him what had happened and tried to explain about Mari, he'd simply listened with the same impassive expression he usually wore, and then he'd dismissed her. They hadn't talked since.

"You were going to tell me I broke the most important rule," Esta said. She'd been waiting for this lecture for three days now. "I put us all at risk by blowing our cover and exposing what we were to the Order. I already know that," she said, feeling the pang of Mari's loss more sharply.

"Well, then. It's good of you to save me the trouble." He didn't smile. "We need to talk," he said after a moment. "Come with me."

He didn't wait for her agreement, so Esta didn't have much choice but to leave Logan and follow the Professor down the hall to the elevator. They rode the ancient machine in silence, the cage vibrating and rattling as it made its way to the top of the building he owned. It had once been filled with individual apartments, but now Professor Lachlan owned all of it. She'd grown up in those narrow hallways, and it was the only home she could remember. It had been a strange childhood filled with adults and secrets—at least until Logan arrived.

When the doors opened, they stepped directly into the Professor's library, its walls lined floor-to-ceiling with books. These weren't like the unread, gilded spines of Schwab's books, though. Professor Lachlan's shelves were packed with volumes covered in faded leather or worn cloth, most cracked and broken from years of use.

No one had a collection like his. He'd purchased most of the volumes in his personal library under false names. Others, he'd had Esta liberate from reluctant owners over the years. Many of his colleagues knew his collection was large, but no one knew how extensive it was, how deep its secrets went—not even the members of his own team. In truth, no one dead or alive knew as much about the secrets New York held as James Lachlan did. Esta had spent almost every day of her childhood in that room, studying for hours, learning everything she needed to blend in during any time in the city's history.

She'd hated those hours. It was time she would have rather spent on one of their daily walks, the long, winding strolls that Professor Lachlan used to teach her the city, street by street. Or better, prowling through the city herself, practicing her skills at lifting a wallet, or sparring with Dakari in the training room. The long hours she'd spent learning in that room had served her well, though. That knowledge had gotten her and Logan out of more than one tough spot.

But it hadn't helped at Schwab's mansion. She made a mental note to do more research on the blond—Jack—whoever he was. If their paths crossed again, she'd be ready.

Professor Lachlan made his way slowly into the room, straightening a pile of papers and books as he went. Clearly, he was in no hurry to get to his point.

It was a test, she knew. A familiar test, and one she was destined to fail.

"You said we needed to talk?" she asked, unable to stand his silence any longer.

The Professor regarded her with the expression he often wore, the one that kept even the people closest to him from knowing his thoughts. He might have made an excellent poker player, if he'd ever cared to gamble. But he never did anything unless he was already sure how it would turn out.

"Patience, girl," he told her, his usual rebuke when he thought she'd acted impulsively—which was all too often, in his opinion.

He took a few more labored steps toward his desk, his lined face creasing with the effort. When his cane slipped and he stumbled, she was at his arm in an instant.

"You should sit," she said, but he waved her off with a look that had her stepping back.

He hated it when anyone fussed. He never wanted to admit that he might *need* some fussing every so often.

Never expose your weaknesses, he'd taught her. *The minute someone knows where you're soft, they can drive in the knife.*

"I don't have time to sit." He leveled an unreadable stare in her direction. "You allowed a member of the Order to see you." His tone made it clear that the words were meant to scold as much as to inform.

"What was I supposed to do?" she asked, lifting her chin. "Leave Logan? I saved his life. I brought him back to you. I kept our team together."

Professor Lachlan's expression didn't so much as flicker, but something in the air between them changed. "You lost sight of your assignment."

"I got the dagger."

His mouth went tight. "Yes, but that wasn't the only thing you took, was it?"

"I tried to give you the diamond."

"I didn't send you to steal diamonds. If you had been on time, as was planned, none of this would have happened."

"I can't say that I'm sorry," she told him, forcing herself to meet his eyes. "I saw an opportunity, and I took it. Just like you taught me."

"You did, didn't you?" He studied her. "You've always been a good student, possibly even better than Logan—though not as disciplined—but your impulsiveness had consequences this time."

She'd learned long ago not to flinch under the weight and expectation of the Professor's stare, so she didn't now. But the reminder of her mistakes hit its mark.

Her throat went tight. "What do you want me to do? I can go back, fix it."

"What would you do? Try to stop yourself?" Professor Lachlan shook his head. "I don't know if it's even possible. And I won't risk any more damage to the stone for a fool's errand." He pinned Esta with his steady, patient stare just as he'd done since she was a small girl. "What's done is done. We go on from here. As always."

"But the Order," she reminded him. "You said yourself, they've seen me now." She looked up at him, forcing herself to meet his eyes the way he had taught her when she was a girl. "The whole point of stealing from the past is so the Order can't see me coming, but now they'll know. They might even be waiting for me." *I'm useless to you,* she couldn't stop herself from thinking.

And if that were true, what role could she play in the Professor's world? If she couldn't do the job he had groomed her for, where would she belong?

"They saw you in 1926, true. But that only means they'll know who and what you are *after* that point." He gave her a look that said she should have figured that much out on her own.

Understanding hit. "But not *before,*" she whispered.

"No, not before," he agreed.

"There *has* to be plenty to take from the years before the twenties."

Professor Lachlan leveled another indecipherable look in her direction that had her falling silent as he made his way steadily past the stacks of old newspapers and books to the large wall safe at the far side of his office.

He placed his hand against the sensor, and when the lock released, he took a large box from the recesses of the vault. Esta kept quiet and didn't bother to ask him if he needed help with it, not even when it was clear he did. Finally, he managed to make his way to the large desk that stood at the midpoint of the room.

The heavy oak table was covered in piles of papers and stacks of books. Setting the box on one of the smaller piles, he sank into a straight-backed chair and set the crutch aside before he bothered to speak.

"Back when I found you wandering alone in Seward Park, I wasn't in the market for a child. But when I discovered what you could do—your affinity for time—I realized you could be the key to my plans," he said, leaning forward in his chair. "It's why I've spent the last twelve years training you, teaching you everything you would need to know to go to any point in the city's past and take care of yourself.

"I didn't adopt you because I wanted to steal shiny baubles and old journals," he said, his voice twisting with his annoyance. He stopped short then, as though realizing he'd let his emotions get away from him, and then started again, more measured this time. "This has never been about getting rich, girl. Each of the jobs you've done has had a purpose." He opened the box. "I needed information, and that information led me to the various treasures you've managed to bring me."

One by one he took the objects out of the box.

"You're familiar with the Pharaoh's Heart," he said as he removed the newly stolen dagger from the bag. "But your first real piece was the Djinni's Star."

He took out a heavy necklace that Esta remembered taking from an Upper East Side jeweler four or five years back. In the platinum settings was a rare turquoise that seemed to hold an entire galaxy within its blue depths.

"And I'm sure you'll remember the Delphi's Tear," he said, holding out an agate ring with a stone so clear and pure it looked almost liquid.

Of course she remembered. She was barely thirteen when she'd slipped it off the finger of a socialite sometime in the 1960s. It had been the first of the pieces she'd taken from the past and the first piece she'd stolen with Logan's help. He'd been an unexpected—and not altogether welcome—addition to the Professor's crew. Esta hadn't been happy when Professor Lachlan had introduced Logan, the nephew of one of his contacts. She'd seen it as a sign that she wasn't trusted enough, that Professor Lachlan didn't think she was ready to go out on her own. She'd been even less happy when they'd all gone together, with each of them taking one of her hands to slip back through to the midcentury city. Logan had found the ring, and she'd taken it. And she'd hated him a little for being so necessary.

He'd won her over, though—too fast. She'd been young and didn't have much experience with anyone outside the Professor's small circle, so she didn't know at first to look beyond his charm. She'd fallen for it, until she realized that everything was a game to Logan. It wasn't that he was heartless or uncaring. He was as dedicated and loyal to the team—and to Professor Lachlan—as she was. But whether it was a shiny jewel or a never-been-kissed girl, he was only interested in the chase. And once the chase was over . . .

"Then there's the Dragon's Eye," Professor Lachlan said, bringing Esta's attention back to the present moment as he removed a glittering tiara from the box. At its center was a large piece of amber so flecked with gold that it practically glowed.

She'd found that piece in Chinatown sometime in the forties. She'd been fourteen, and it was the first big job they'd done without Professor Lachlan escorting them. By then she'd accepted what Logan was and had forgiven him for making her think he was something more. She'd even formed a begrudging friendship with him. Professor Lachlan needed and trusted Logan, and she trusted Professor Lachlan. So that was that.

"And then there's the Key." Finally, he pulled out the most familiar treasure of all—Ishtar's Key. The rock was a strange, dark, opal-like stone that glimmered with a deep rainbow of colors. Set into an arm cuff that fit perfectly against Esta's own biceps, it was the stone that allowed her to slip vertically through the layers of time. Her stomach sank when she saw the jagged line bisecting its smooth surface, the reminder of yet another consequence of her mistakes.

When they'd finally gotten back to their building on Orchard Street, Esta had discovered the crack. The only explanation was that she'd used it too much without giving it time to cool, but they didn't know what it might mean for the stone's power. She hoped it was a positive sign that even from across the room, its familiar warmth and energy still called to her.

Looking at the objects on the table was like looking at her own history, but she understood that there was more to the display than a walk down memory lane. Seeing the five objects there on his desk, she could tell there was a pattern she hadn't previously understood.

Professor Lachlan ran his finger over the crack in Ishtar's Key, pausing thoughtfully before he spoke. "These five stones were once in the possession of the Ortus Aurea. Back when the Order was at the very pinnacle of its strength, it kept them in a secure room called the Mysterium, a vault deep within their headquarters in Khafre Hall. Only the highest circles ever had access to them, but their existence was the very source of the Order's power, until they were stolen."

She looked up at him. "Stolen?"

Professor Lachlan opened one of his notebooks and flipped through it until he found a page with a yellowed piece of newsprint taped onto it. He turned the book so Esta could read the story.

"Back in 1902, a group of Mageus attempted to take down the Order," he explained, pointing at the clipping. "They broke into the Mysterium and stole the Order's most important treasures. But one of the crew double-crossed the rest, and the job went off the rails. The crew scattered, and the artifacts disappeared."

She scanned over the faded column of print. "This is a story about a fire," she said, confused. There was no mention of a robbery.

"Of course it is. The Order couldn't let anyone know what had really happened. If word got out that they'd been robbed of such important treasures—by the very people they were trying to control, no less—they would have looked weak. It would have put them at risk for more groups to try retaliating. They hid their losses. They hid their failures. They pretended nothing had happened, that everything was the same.

"It worked, for a while at least. I've already taught you about the early years of the last century. You know how dangerous this city was for anyone with the old magic—the fires, the raids disguised as simple policing to protect the city. And there was always the Brink. Stealing the Order's artifacts didn't change any of that. But as the years passed, the old magic began to fade and be forgotten. New generations were weaker than the ones who had come before, and the city began to forget its fear.

"The Order never forgot, though. For years the highest members of the Order tried to find these pieces and bring them back together, but because of the work we've done, they've never managed to. Occasionally a piece would pop up at an auction, like the one at Schwab's mansion, or rumors of another would surface, but since that original theft, these pieces have never been in the same room." The Professor smiled, his old eyes sparking. "Until now."

He didn't have to tell Esta that there was something about the various stones that made them more than they appeared. Just as Ishtar's Key called to her, the artifacts together seemed to saturate the entire space with a warm, heady energy.

"You see," he continued, "there has been a method to what we've done these past years. One by one, I discovered the fate of the stones. One by one, I've collected them and kept them safe. But it's not enough. Everything we've done has only been a prelude to one item, the last of the artifacts." He leaned forward. "I've been more than careful, or haven't you noticed? Each job has been a little farther back, each one a little more challenging. I was getting you ready for the one job that means everything."

Esta straightened a bit. Professor Lachlan was still willing to trust her. He still *needed* her.

"What's the mark?" she asked, her voice filled with a bone-deep desire to prove herself to him.

He smiled then. "We need the final item that was stolen that day. A book."

Esta couldn't hide her disappointment. She'd stolen plenty of books for him over the years. "You want me to get another book?"

"No, not *another* book." His old eyes gleamed. "You're going to get *the* Book—the Ars Arcana."

Even with all her training and the many, *many* hours she'd spent learning about the city and about the Order, Esta had never heard that particular term before. Her confusion must have shown.

"It's a legendary book, a text rumored to be as old as magic itself," he explained with a twist of impatience. "For years it was under the Order's control, and I believe it can tell me how to use these stones to topple the Order once and for all. Imagine it, girl—the few Mageus left wouldn't have to hide who we are anymore. We'd be *free*."

Free. Esta wasn't sure what that word even meant. She loved her city, had never really thought about or yearned for a life outside it. But Professor Lachlan was looking at her with an expression of hope and warmth. "Tell me where it is, and it's yours," Esta said.

"Well, that's where it gets tricky." Professor Lachlan's expression darkened. "The Book was lost. Probably destroyed."

"Destroyed?"

Professor Lachlan nodded. "One of the team double-crossed the rest. He took the Book and disappeared. If the Book still existed, I would have found it by now. Or Logan would have." His eyes lit again. "That's why you have to stop the traitor before he can disappear. If you can save the Book and bring it back here, it would change *everything*."

Anticipation singing in her blood, Esta kept herself calm, determined. "Who is he? Where do I find him?"

Studying her a moment longer, Professor Lachlan's mouth turned up ever so slightly. It wasn't a real smile, but it was enough to tell her that she'd started to win back a measure of his approval. "The spring of 1902, when the heist happened," he said, tapping the news clipping. "You're going to have to go back further than you've ever gone before. The city was a different place then."

"I can handle it," she said.

"You don't understand. . . . *Magic* was different back then. Now the city is practically empty of magic. Now people think magic is a myth. But back then the streets would have felt electric. People knew that the old magic existed, and they feared those who held it. Back then there was still the feeling in the air that something was about to start. Everyone was picking sides."

"I know," she told him. "You've taught me all of this."

"Maybe I did." He sighed as he lifted Esta's cuff from the table and examined it, frowning as he studied the crack in the stone. "But I'm still not sure you're ready. This last job makes me wonder . . ."

Esta wanted to reach for the cuff, but she held back. It wasn't exactly hers—the Professor only permitted her to wear it when he needed something from the past. Otherwise, he kept it safe in his vault. Still, the cuff had always *felt* like hers, ever since the first time he'd slipped it onto her arm a little more than six years ago, when she was eleven years old, and shown her that she was meant for more than lifting fat wallets out of tourists' pockets.

"I won't disappoint you again," she promised.

He didn't offer her the cuff, though. He was still punishing her, however gently. Teasing her with the promise of the stone but reminding her who Ishtar's Key—and the power that came with it—really belonged to.

"We can't afford to wait for Logan to heal. You'll go after the Book now, and you'll go alone."

"Alone?" Esta asked. "But without Logan, how will I find it?"

"You'll get yourself on the team that steals it."

Confused at the change in their usual way of working, Esta frowned. "But if we waited for Logan to heal, we could get there before them. In and out quick, like you've always said. We don't have to take the risk of it disappearing."

"No," Professor Lachlan said sharply. "It won't work."

"But with my affinity—" she started.

"It isn't enough," he snapped, cutting her off. "Do you think you could simply waltz into the Order's stronghold and lift the Book? You're a gifted thief, but it took a team to get in, to get past their levels of security. And the person who eventually double-crossed them was essential to that."

"There has to be another, easier way," she argued.

"Even if there were . . ." Professor Lachlan shook his head. "Every one of our jobs has been carefully designed so that the Order never knew when they were actually robbed. Every time you've taken an artifact, I've planned it so the theft was invisible, so they couldn't trace it to us. I did that for a reason. But look what happened this last time—you *changed* something by being exposed. How much more of our present might be affected if you mess with the events of the past?"

He tapped again on the news clipping. "The heist has to happen *exactly* as it happened then. You can't risk changing anything. Think about it—if the heist doesn't occur or if the Order knows who was behind it, there's no telling what that might do to the future. To *our present*. The only difference can be who gets the Book. Otherwise, think of what repercussions there might be."

She thought of Mari and knew too well what the effects might be.

"Besides," he said, examining the crack in the surface of the stone, "I'm not sure that Ishtar's Key could handle taking two through time again. You put a lot of pressure on the stone with what you did at Schwab's mansion. You'll have to do this alone." He still wasn't smiling as he held out the silver cuff. "Unless you don't feel up to the challenge?"

Esta hesitated before she reached for it. This, too, seemed like a test, but if she failed this time, how much more damage could she do? How many more lives might she be putting in danger?

But if she succeeded . . . Maybe by getting the Book, she could make everything right again. Maybe she could get Mari back.

She thought of the uncounted others who might still live in the shadows of the city, their affinities weak and broken from years of disuse and generations of forgetting. If one mistake in the past could have caused so many changes to her present, what might destroying the Order do?

If she succeeded, she could do more than simply fix the mistakes she'd made and make her present right again. Maybe she could rewrite her own future. Reclaim magic.

There would be no more hiding—for any of them.

She took the cuff. The silver was still cold from being in the vault, but she slid it onto her arm without so much as a shiver. Again, she felt the pull of the stone, like something was warming her from within. Something that felt like possibility . . . and the promise of power. "Tell me who betrayed them," she said, determined. "Who is it I need to stop?"

Professor Lachlan's mouth curved into a smile, but his eyes held nothing but cold hate. "Find the Magician," he told her. "And stop him before he destroys our future."

THE DEVIL'S OWN

Harte Darrigan cursed himself ten times over as he pushed his way through the crowd of The Devil's Own, a smoke-filled boxing saloon on the Lower East Side named for the gang that ran it. The sound of bones crunching as fist met face caused the crowd to surge with an eagerness that made Harte's pulse race and turned his resolve to mush.

The dive was filled with the type of people Harte had done everything he could to avoid becoming. They represented the most dangerous parts of humanity—if you could even call it that—south of Houston Street, the wide avenue that divided the haves from the have-nots and probably-never-wills. Harte himself might have been a liar and a con man, but at least he was an honest one. Or so he told himself. He'd risked everything to get out of Paul Kelly's gang three years ago, and he didn't want the life he'd managed to build for himself since then to get muddied by the never-ending war between the different factions that ruled lower Manhattan.

Yet there he was.

He shouldn't have come. He was an idiot for agreeing to this meeting, a complete idiot to let Dolph Saunders goad him into being drawn back into this world with an impossible promise—freedom. A way out of the city. It was fool's dream.

Harte must be a fool, because he knew what Dolph Saunders was capable of and, still, he had agreed to meet him. He'd seen Dolph's cruelty with his own eyes, and if Harte were smarter, he'd turn tail and leave before it was too late. . . .

But then a familiar voice was calling his name over the crowd, and he knew his chance had passed.

The kid approaching him was probably the skinniest, shortest guy in the room. He wore a pair of spectacles on the tip of his straight nose, and unlike most of the crowd that populated The Devil's Own, he wasn't dressed in the bright colors or flamboyant style that characterized the swells of the Bowery. Instead, the kid wore suspenders over a simple collarless shirt, which made him look like an overgrown newsboy. Unlike the barrel-chested men curled around their drinks after a long day of hard labor, Nibsy Lorcan had the air of someone who spent most of his time indoors poring over books.

"Harte Darrigan," Nibsy said, giving a sharp nod of his head in greeting. "It's good to see you again."

"I wish I could say the same, Nibs."

The kid tucked his hands into his pockets. "We were beginning to think you wouldn't show."

"Your boss made it sound like I'd be an idiot not to come and at least listen to what he had to say."

Nibsy smiled genially. "No one could take you for an idiot, Darrigan."

"Not sure I agree with you, Nibs, seeing as I'm here and all. Where's Dolph anyway? Or did he send you to do his dirty work for him like usual?"

"He's in back, waiting." Nibsy's eyes flickered over the barroom. "You know how he is."

"Yeah," Harte said. "I know exactly how he is. Just like I should have known better than to come here."

He turned to go, but Nibs caught him by the arm. "You're already here. Might as well listen to what he has to say." He gave an aw-shucks shrug that Harte didn't buy. "At least have a drink. Can't argue with a free drink, now, can you?"

He glanced at the doors at the back of the barroom.

Harte might have been an idiot, but he was a curious idiot. He couldn't imagine what would have made Dolph desperate enough to ask for his help after the falling-out they'd had. And he wanted to know what would possess Dolph—a man much more likely to hold his secrets close—to make such wild promises.

"I'll listen to what he has to say, but I don't want any drink."

Nibs shifted uneasily before recovering his affable-looking smile. "This way," he said, leading Harte toward the back of the bar and through double saloon doors to a quieter private room.

It might have been years since Harte had seen him, but Dolph didn't look all that different. Same lean, hard face anchored by a nose as sharp as a knife. Same shock of white in the front of his hair that he'd had since they were kids. Same calculating gleam in his icy eyes. Or at least in the eye Harte could see—the other was capped by a leather patch.

There were four others in the room. Harte recognized Viola Vaccarelli and Jianyu Lee, Dolph's assassin and spy, respectively. The other two guys were unknowns. From their loud pants and tipped bowler hats, Harte guessed they were hired muscle, there in case things went south. Which meant that Dolph trusted Harte about as much as Harte trusted Dolph.

Fine. Maybe they'd been friends once, but it was better this way.

"Good to see you again, Dare," Dolph said, using an old nickname Harte had long since given up. Harte didn't miss that Dolph hadn't offered his hand in greeting, only gripped the silver gorgon head on the top of his cane more tightly.

"Can't say the feeling's mutual."

The two peacocks in the corner scowled, but Viola's mouth only twitched. She didn't reach for her knives and he wasn't dead yet, so he must be safe for the moment.

"You want something to drink?" Dolph asked, settling himself back in his chair but not offering a seat to Harte.

"Let's cut the bullshit, Dolph. Why'd you want to see me? You know I'm out of the game."

"Not from what I've heard. Whatever freedom you pretend, Paul Kelly's still got you on a leash, doesn't he?"

"I'm not on anybody's leash," Harte said, his voice a warning. But he wasn't surprised that Dolph knew the truth. He always did manage to find out the very things a person wanted to keep hidden. "And I know there's no way you can do what you hinted at. Getting out of the city? I wasn't born yesterday."

"Then why *did* you come?" Dolph asked.

"Hell if I know," Harte said. He realized he was crushing the brim of his hat and forced himself to relax his fist.

Dolph's eye gleamed. "You never could resist a challenge, could you?"

"Maybe I wanted to see if the rumors about you were true," he said coldly. "If you'd really lost it after Leena, like everybody said."

"I don't talk about that." Dolph's expression went fierce, even as his face went a little gray. "*Nobody* talks about that if they want to keep breathing."

"I bet they don't," Harte said. He shook his head. "This was a mistake." He turned to go, but Jianyu stepped in front of the door, blocking his way. "Call him off, Dolph."

"I've got a proposition for you," Dolph said, ignoring Harte's command.

"I'm not interested." He turned his attention to Jianyu. "I bet your uncle's real proud of you right about now, isn't he? He must love you being a lapdog for that one there."

Everyone knew that Jianyu Lee was the nephew of Tom Lee, the leader of the On Leong Tong over in Chinatown. The kid could have had his own turf, maybe even run his own crew, but here he was working for Dolph. That was the thing about Dolph Saunders—he had this way of pulling people in. Even people who should've had some brains.

Jianyu just smiled darkly, an expression that warned Harte not to push.

"I said *call him off*, Dolph," Harte said again, trying not to let his nerves show. He might be a fool, but he wasn't stupid enough not to realize how dangerous his position was.

"I think you'd be interested if you gave me five minutes," Dolph said. "Or I can always have one of my boys convince you."

"Threats?" Harte glanced up at the two rough-looking boys still looming behind Dolph. "That isn't usually your style, old man."

Dolph couldn't have been older than his midtwenties. But with the streak of white hair and the way he'd been born to lead, Dolph had always seemed even older. Once, "old man" had been a term of endearment between friends. Not anymore. Now Harte slung the nickname like an insult.

Dolph's mouth curved to acknowledge the slight, but he didn't otherwise react. "Never used to be," he admitted. "But it turns out you *can* teach an old dog new tricks." His mouth went flat. "Sit. Give me five minutes before you go off half-cocked. Or haven't you grown out of your temper yet?"

The two puffed peacocks behind Dolph shifted, like they were getting ready for their boss's next order. Harte eyed them warily and measured the inconvenience of a black eye if he left against the sting of his wounded pride if he gave in. It was damn hard to charm an audience when you looked like a common thug, so he went back to the table and took a seat.

"Five minutes. But I'll tell you straight off, I'm not interested in any of your scheming. Never was."

"I won't call you on that particular lie, but getting out of the city isn't a scheme," Dolph said, signaling to Nibsy to pour Harte a glass of whiskey. "It's a real possibility."

The fine hairs at the nape of Harte's neck rose in warning. There was only one way out of the city—through the Brink—and it was a trip Harte had no interest in taking. Not by choice. Not by force, either.

He shifted in his seat. "More threats?" he asked, cautious.

"Not a threat. A proposition. A way out."

"None of us can get out of the city," Harte said carefully, wondering what Dolph was up to. "Not without paying the price. Every Mageus in town knows that."

Dolph took a long, slow drink from the glass in front of him and then motioned for Nibsy to pour another before he spoke. "The Brink hasn't always been there, Darrigan. Did you ever stop to think that if the Order was able to make it, then there has to be a way to *unmake* it?"

"Now I *know* you're wasting my time." Harte shook his head. "If you knew how to punch a hole out of this rattrap of a city, you'd have already done it and then started charging admission for the crossing." He started to push his chair back to go, but Jianyu had moved behind him and pressed his shoulders down. Jianyu's thumb was firm against a tender spot at the crook of Harte's neck, keeping him in his seat. "Get your lackey off me, Dolph. I have somewhere else to be."

"The Ortus Aurea doesn't have any real magic," Dolph continued. "Everything they have, everything they can do—it's counterfeit power. It all comes at a cost. The Brink isn't real magic, but it's destroying real magic just the same."

"It seemed real enough when it took everything my mother was and left her a shell of what she used to be."

"I'm not saying the Order isn't powerful. What I *am* saying is that they can be stopped," Dolph said. "The men in the Order see magic as some kind of mark of the divine. They can't bring themselves to believe that the poor, wretched masses who come to these shores could possibly have a stronger connection to divinity than they themselves do. But we both know that magic isn't anything to do with angels or demons. Old magic, the kind you and I know intimately, is a connection with the world itself. You can't split affinities into neat categories or elements any more than you can separate fire and air. One needs the other. When the Order tries to divide up the elements and control them through their rituals and so-called science, there's a cost. It weakens magic as a whole."

"Funny for you of all people to say that," Harte said flatly, without so much as blinking. He tested the pressure against his shoulder and found he still couldn't move.

Dolph frowned, but he didn't respond to Harte's implied challenge. "You know I'm right. The power they wield isn't a natural part of the world, like ours is, and I believe the Brink can be destroyed if we take away the source of their power."

"You're talking about taking them head-on," Harte said. That was a stretch, even for Dolph.

"I'm talking about destroying the one tool they have to control us."

"You're talking about a fairy tale."

Dolph didn't blink. "Every day people come to this country—to this city—because they believe their children will be safer here than in the places they're from. They're lured by the promise of a life away from the superstition and hate in their own countries. All lies. Any Mageus that enters this city is snared like a fish in a net. Once they land on these shores, they can't leave without giving up the very thing that defines them, and trapped on this island as they are, they're at the mercy of the Order. Held down, held back, always kept in their place by those in power."

"I know all that already, Dolph," Harte said. His stomach churned. Of course he knew. "But there *are* ways to make a life here, even in this city."

Dolph gave him a mocking look. "You mean like you have?"

"I've done well enough for myself."

"Sure you have. You've managed to get yourself some smart new clothes, a safe apartment in the good part of town, and money in your pocket. You've even managed to find yourself some well-connected friends. But do you think you'd last a day in your new life if those new friends of yours knew who you actually are?" Dolph leaned forward. "*What* you are?"

Harte refused to so much as flinch. "You plan on outing me and destroying the life I've built for myself? I've lived through worse."

"No, Darrigan," Dolph said. "I'd prefer to use that new life of yours to our advantage."

"I'm not interested in helping your advantage."

Dolph ignored his rebuff. "It's good you've managed to do what you have, but you always were scrappier than most. There's plenty who aren't. And even scrappy as you are, you can only get so far in this city. You and I were friends once, so I know how it must chafe to always have to hide what you are. As long as the Order has power over our kind, it will always be a liability. But if the Order's main tool for controlling us was destroyed, you could have a different life. The Brink *can* be undone, I'm convinced of it."

"You can't know that," Harte challenged. "And I like my life well enough. I'm not about to get myself killed over one of your mad theories."

"It's not a theory." Dolph nodded to Jianyu, and the pressure on Harte's shoulders eased. Then he pulled a small scrap from his pocket and set it on the table so Harte could read the faded writing on its surface. "Leena died getting that to me."

Harte read the smeared letters on the scrap and then glanced up at Dolph. "I don't speak Italian."

"It's Latin," Dolph corrected.

"What's it mean?"

"Libero Libro. It means that the Order has a book—"

"I'm sure they have lots of books."

"Probably," Dolph said, not taking the bait. "But there's one book in particular they protect more than any other, and getting this book means freeing our kind."

Harte gave him a doubtful look. "A single book couldn't do all of that."

"The Ars Arcana could."

This gave Harte pause. "You think the Order has the Ars Arcana?"

Dolph tapped his finger against the scrap of fabric. "I do."

Harte shook his head. "Even if you're right, even if the Order has the Book of Mysteries, you'll never be able to get it. Everyone knows that Khafre Hall is built like a fortress. You couldn't even get through the front door, much less get your hands on any book—Ars Arcana or otherwise."

"I think you're wrong," Dolph said. "With the right team, we can get in *and* get the Book. Think of it, Dare. . . . We could change *everything*. No more slums. No more scraping by. Without the Brink standing in your way, you could walk out of this city a free man to go make your fortune. You could do *anything*, go *anywhere*, and keep your affinity all the while."

Harte ignored the lure of that promise. "The only people who can get into the front door of Khafre Hall are members of Ortus."

"So we'll have a member let us in," Nibs said.

For a moment all Harte could do was gape at the boy. "*You're* insane too," he said. "Did you forget that they *hate* us? There's no way one of their members is going to help one of us."

Dolph pinned Harte with a knowing glare. "That life you've made for yourself has introduced you to some interesting people. Word is you've been seen with Jack Grew, one of J. P. Morgan's nephews, I believe?"

"So what of it?" Harte said, even more wary than before.

"Morgan's one of the highest-ranking members of the Order."

"No," Harte said, shaking his head as he pushed away from the table and stood. "No way in hell. *No.*"

But Jianyu's strong hands sat him back down roughly and held him in his seat.

"It's like you said, you've managed to make a whole new life for yourself. New name. New suit. New address on the right side of town. If you keep rubbing elbows with the right people, you could get us in."

Harte choked out a hollow laugh. "I'm not in the market for suicide. Besides, even if what you're proposing is possible, even if you and your crew could get in and get this book, the Order wouldn't simply accept defeat. They'd hunt down every Mageus in this town. You'd get hundreds of innocent people killed. Thousands, maybe. No one with magic—or with connections to people with magic—would be safe."

"We're *already* not safe," Dolph countered. "We already live like rats, fighting each other for whatever the Order leaves us. Everyone's so worried about getting a little bit more for themselves, they don't even realize they're killing one another over the garbage.

"The Order of Ortus Aurea *depends* on that, Harte. They want us lining up along old divisions, clinging to what we know so that we can't imagine a bigger future. But I've already imagined it. Look at the people in this room right now—Viola, Jianyu. I've started putting together a team that could take down the Order once and for all. I need someone to get us in, though. Someone with the right talent for it." His jaw tightened. "Someone like you."

Harte knew what it must have cost Dolph to say those words, but it wasn't enough. Not considering how dangerous the Ortus Aurea was and how much he had to lose.

"You've had your five minutes."

Dolph studied Harte a long minute before lifting his hand and gesturing vaguely for Jianyu to release him. "I'm not taking your answer now," Dolph said, dismissing him. "You listened and maybe you'll think about it. We'll talk again."

The pressure no longer on his shoulders, Harte stood. "No, we won't. I'm not interested now, and I won't be interested ten days from now, so you can just leave me the hell alone."

He maneuvered through the still-crowded barroom, cursing himself again for his own curiosity, his stupidity for coming in the first place. Because damn if Dolph wasn't right—he had listened, and now he *was* thinking. He was thinking about the possibility of getting out of that godforsaken city. Of being free once and for all.

Dolph Saunders might need him, but Harte certainly didn't need Dolph. He'd find a way to do it on his own.

Harte pushed his way through the crowd and out into the night. He never once looked back, so he didn't see the knowing smile curve at Dolph Saunders' mouth.

BENEATH THE EPHEMERAL MOMENT OF NOW

Present Day—Orchard Street

The next evening, Esta sat on the edge of her bed reading over the yellowed news clipping yet again, as though the century-old scrap could tell her something more about what had happened the night of the heist. She probably shouldn't have taken it from Professor Lachlan's office, but she hadn't been able to help herself. He was sending her back, alone this time and for longer than she'd ever been in the past before, and it was all happening too fast. She didn't feel nearly as confident as she wanted to.

Someone rapped on the door to her room, and she jumped at the sound of it.

"Just a minute!" Her fingers shook as she folded the clipping into a small waxen envelope and shoved the packet as far down into her corset as she could manage.

The knock came again. "Esta?" The voice was muffled by the heavy door.

Relieved that it wasn't Professor Lachlan, she opened the door to reveal Dakari on the other side. She looked up into his familiar face. "Is it time?"

"Not quite. I came to check your arm again." Dakari had been with Professor Lachlan longer than any of them. The Professor had found him in an illegal fighting club more than twenty years ago. After he made his share of the pot by winning his fights, he'd charge his opponents for the privilege of being doctored by him, so they could go back to their lives without the bruises he'd left on their bodies.

It wasn't work he would have otherwise chosen for himself, so when the Professor offered him a position, he took it. Part bodyguard, part healer, Dakari was over six feet of pure muscle, but when he smiled—and he often smiled at Esta—he looked exactly like the kind soul he was.

"It's fine," Esta said, not letting him into the room. He'd already checked it that morning anyway.

"Humor me." He gave the door a gentle push and stepped into her room.

With a dramatic sigh, she unbuttoned the neckline of her dress enough to show him her shoulder. She'd taken off the bandage the day before, and now the wound from the bullet wasn't anything more than a spot of new pink skin that would one day barely be a scar.

Dakari took her arm in his hands and pressed his thumb over the spot as he studied it with careful concentration. Her own skin wasn't exactly pale, but his was darker. His palms were rough from years of fighting, but his magic came as a soft pulse, the warmth that characterized most of her childhood. Those hands could kill a man in 532 different ways, but they had also healed every one of her scrapes and bruises—mostly after he'd put her through a punishing training session. Because of Dakari, she could take care of herself, and because of him, she'd always felt like she had someone to take care of her.

If she'd lost him the way she'd lost Mari . . .

"You'll do," he said after he was done examining her. "It's healed well enough that you won't have to worry about infection. You ready?"

She nodded.

"Then why do you look so unsure?" He frowned at her. "You're never unsure before a job."

"I'm fine," she said, turning away, but he took his hand and lifted her chin, forcing her to look him in the eye.

"Tell me. Before your worries become the distraction that gets you killed."

Esta hesitated, but finally she said, "You really don't remember Mari?"

Dakari frowned. "That's what's bothering you?"

She nodded. "Messing up the way I did, it changed things. She was my friend, and she doesn't even exist now."

"You can't know that your actions were what erased her life."

"What if they were? What if I make another mistake? What if, when I come back, other people are gone? Other lives are erased?"

He thought for a minute before reaching into his boot and pulling out a small pocketknife with an ornately carved bone handle. He offered it to her, and when she took it, he gave her a serious look. "That was my father's. He gave it to me before I left my country. I would only give that to someone I trusted. Whatever happens, I trust you with my life."

The knife was warm from having been snug against Dakari's leg, and though it was small, its weight was reassuring.

"Thank you," she said, her throat tight with emotion as she tucked the knife safely into her own button-up boots. "I'll bring it back to you. No matter what."

"I know you will," he said, and gave her a wink. "And I'll be here waiting for you."

Esta took a deep breath. "Let's get this over with."

By the time Esta was in the back of Dakari's car and heading toward their destination, it was nearly four in the morning on a Tuesday, long after most of the bars had closed. People should have been home, asleep in their tiny apartments, but even this deep in the night, the city glowed. The streets still teemed with life as the car crawled upward, past the low-slung buildings of the village, toward the towers of Midtown.

Esta rolled down the window, letting the hot breath of summer rustle across her face. With it came the familiar smells of the city, stale and heavy with the metallic choke of exhaust and the ripeness of too many people sharing one tiny piece of land. But it was also enticing—the scent of danger and possibility that lived and breathed in the crowded streets. Dirty and frantic though it was, the city—*this* city—was home. She'd never wanted to be anywhere else.

Dakari turned onto Twenty-Eighth Street and then pulled into a narrow parking lot that spanned the block between two streets. The lot had been an alleyway a century before, one of the countless places in the city that hadn't been built over and changed beyond recognition. A place where she could slip into the past without being seen.

He stopped just inside the lot and shut off the engine before turning to her. Draping his large forearm across the passenger seat, he looked at her. "You ready?"

She gave him what she hoped was a sure nod, and they both got out of the car. He leaned against the back of it, eyeing her. "See you in a few?" he asked, turning his usual farewell into a question.

Despite the heat of the summer night and her layers of linen and velveteen, Esta felt a sudden chill. She made herself shake it off. This was only a job, she reminded herself. It was *her* job.

"You always do," Esta told him, giving her usual wink. She didn't let the confidence fall from her face until her back was turned.

Dakari's voice came to her as a whisper: "Keep yourself safe, E."

She glanced over her shoulder. "You doubting me?"

"Never in a million." His eyes were still solemn as he raised his chin in a silent salute.

For a heartbeat, Esta imagined getting back in the car and telling him to drive. *Just drive.* Dakari had always had enough of a soft spot for her. He'd probably do it, too, no questions asked.

It wasn't that she wanted to run from the responsibility the Professor had given her. She didn't even need that long . . . just another jog around the block to settle her nerves. Another few minutes with the bright lights and the hurried pace of *this* city. *Her* city.

But she didn't want Dakari to know she was nervous. It was bad enough admitting it to herself. Wrapping her hand more securely around the smooth handle of her carpetbag, Esta started walking toward the center of the lot, away from the car and from Dakari's reassuring presence.

She didn't let herself look back again.

The parking lot was quiet, and it smelled like that combination of piss, garbage, and exhaust that only New York could smell like in the summertime. Something scuttled beneath one of the sleeping cars, but Esta ignored the noise, and as she walked, she let her doubt fall away.

Or, rather, she shoved it away.

Trying to find the right layer of time was a little like riffling through the pages of a book. Sometimes she could catch glimpses of what each layer held—the flash of chrome, a bright swirl of skirts. It took all her concentration to find a single image to latch on to, a single date to focus on, before she could slip through to it. And, of course, it took the power held in Ishtar's Key.

As she looked past the present moment, the stone in the cuff answered by warming itself, almost humming against her already-heated skin. The tumble of trash and debris along the edges of the buildings, the pallid glow of a yellow security light over a door—all of it went blurry as she searched down through the layered moments of the past. Back, back, back . . . until she found what she was looking for.

A single day. A single moment waiting beneath her modern world.

She reached for it, preparing herself for the unsettling feeling of slipping out of her own time. Her destination was there, well within her ability to reach it, but just as she started to feel the energy of her own magic tingling along her skin, her foot froze in midair and her breath went tight in her chest as an unexpected feeling of absolute dread rocketed through her.

The image in her mind faltered, and her own world came into focus again.

"Shit." Esta dropped her bag and took an actual step backward, away from the glimmer of the past and from what she had to do. Her fingers felt clammy and damp inside the smooth leather of her gloves, but the stone was hot against her skin.

Above her, the brightly lit top of the Empire State Building looked down, mocking her inability to erase it. To find a time before it had defined the skies of the city.

Esta didn't do nerves, but there she was, struggling to shake off her trepidation, forcing herself to gather the courage to do what she'd done a hundred times before. She knew the city, its streets and secrets. Its people, and especially its past. Professor Lachlan had made sure that every minute of her childhood had been devoted to preparing her for this. She was ready.

So why did it feel so impossible?

"You okay?" Dakari called.

She took a breath to steady herself but didn't look back at him. "I'm fine," she lied.

She had to focus. *This* was what Professor Lachlan had saved her for. *This* was why he'd rescued her, kept her out of the system, and had given her the only home she remembered. If she couldn't do this one thing he asked of her, where would she go? Who would she be?

Esta picked up her bag again and, teeth clenched in determination, expelled another a deep breath through her nose. Her head was pounding, but she adjusted the smooth handle of the bag in her gloved grip and started again.

There . . .

The time she was seeking was there, just beneath the ephemeral moment of now. She found the date Professor Lachlan had directed her to waiting for her beneath the layers of years and memories. In that moment, her fear receded a little, and the rightness of what she was about to do wrapped around her.

Lifting her foot to take a step, Esta could feel the familiar push-pull sensation of simultaneously flying apart and collapsing in on herself. But then the bewildering dread spiked through her again like a warning.

Something's wrong.

But Esta didn't do nerves. She forced herself through the feeling, through to the past.

Every cell in her body was on fire as the brick walls on either side of her began to blur and the cars around her began to disappear. The lights of the city dimmed, the tip of the Empire State Building started to fade, and as she began to feel the cold blast of winter from that other time, a barrage of shouts came from the mouth of the lot where Dakari's car waited.

Esta hesitated, her body screaming with the effort of keeping hold of her present as the past pulled at her. Her vision cleared, and she saw Dakari struggling against a trio of hooded figures, his expression determined as he fought free of them.

I have to help him. . . .

"Dakari!"

"Go!" he shouted, looking at her with such determination that her hold of the present slipped.

"Dakari!" she screamed again as gunfire erupted and she watched his large body jerk and slump to the ground. The shock of it knocked her backward, far past the place where the dirty pavement should have caught her.

Esta couldn't stop. She lost her grip on her own city, her own time, and was falling into light itself, barely catching herself before she landed hard, in a deep drift of snow.

PART

II

SIREN'S CALL

February 1902—Wallack's Theatre

Harte Darrigan brushed a piece of lint from the front of his crimson waistcoat before checking his appearance once more in the cloudy dressing room mirror. Lifting his chin, he examined the edge of his jawline for any place the barber might have missed during his regular afternoon shave, and then he ran his fingertips over the dark, shortly cropped hair above his ears to ensure it was smooth and in place. Stepping away from the footlights didn't mean he'd stepped offstage. His whole life had become a performance, one long con that was the closest thing to freedom he could ever have.

A knock sounded at his dressing room door, and he frowned. "Yes?"

The stage manager, Shorty, opened the door. "You got a minute?"

"I'm heading out to meet someone in a few—"

"Good. Good," Shorty said, closing the door behind him. He had the nub of a thick cigar between his teeth, and as he talked, ash from the still-smoldering tip fluttered to the floor. "Here's the thing—the management has been talking lately, and—"

"This again?" Harte let out an impatient breath to hide his nerves. He knew what was coming, because they'd had a similar conversation last week. And the week before. There were too many theaters in the city, and it didn't matter how good your act was; people got bored too quickly.

"Yes, this again." Shorty took the cigar from between his teeth and used it to punctuate his point, jabbing it into the air and sending more ash floating to the floor. "They run a thee-ate-er here, Darrigan," he said, snapping out the word to emphasize the second syllable. "This is a business, and a business has to make money."

"They make plenty of money, and you know it," Harte said, shrugging off the complaint as he turned to fix the knot in his cravat. "The house was decent this afternoon, and even pretty good tonight."

"I know. I know. But decent and pretty good ain't enough anymore. The owners have been talking about maybe switching some things up . . . changing the acts a little." Shorty gave him a meaningful look.

His fingers stilled and the silk around his neck suddenly felt too tight. "What are you trying to say?"

"I ain't *trying* to say nothing. What I *am* saying is that you've gotta do something to get more people in the seats. Something new."

Harte turned back to Shorty. "I did add something new, or weren't they watching? The escape I did tonight was new. Two sets of handcuffs, shackles, and ten feet of iron chains—"

"Yeah, yeah. You got yourself out of a locked box. Big deal. Houdini's been breaking out of things for years now. Nobody cares anymore. You want top billing? You need something bigger. Something with some more flash." Shorty put the cigar back between his teeth.

Harte clenched his jaw to keep from saying something he'd regret. "Is that all?"

"Yeah, kid. I guess that's it. Just wanted to tell you what's what. Thought you'd want to know."

Harte didn't thank him. He stood silent and expressionless as Shorty shrugged and took his leave. Once the door was closed and he was alone, he cleaned up the fallen ash.

Still unsettled, he turned to the mirror and took a deep breath before giving himself a smile, his clear gray eyes searching his reflection for any indication that his old life was showing through. There wasn't room for a misstep or a crack in the carefully cultivated facade he presented to the world. That night, nothing could be left to chance.

Finally satisfied, he let the smile fall from his face, as heavy and sure as a curtain falling between acts. He pulled on his gloves and coat and took up his hat from where it rested on the dressing table before extinguishing the lamp and letting himself out of his dressing room.

It was barely past midnight, and already the theater was empty and silent. Playing this house was nothing like the rough-and-tumble theaters of the Bowery, which remained open at all hours of the night, their drunken audiences roaring for more—more skin, more laughter, more of the brittle pieces of self-respect Harte had tried to hold on to night after night.

Harte had escaped those beer-stained halls well over a year ago, but Shorty's warning was one more reminder that it wouldn't take much for him to find himself back there again. With nowhere to go but farther down.

He wouldn't let that happen.

Far-off sounds echoing through the cavernous building told him there were still a few stragglers left. No doubt they were gathered in the chorus girls' dressing room, drinking Nitewein to burn off the excess energy brought on by the crowd. Or to numb the constant ache of hiding what they were.

The theater world was filled with Mageus. The stage was a good place for those with magic to hide in plain sight, but for many in the business, using their affinity onstage made them crave it that much more. The rumbling approval of the crowd only amplified that yearning to answer the old call of magic, to embrace what they really were. Many resorted to using the opium-laced liquor to stop the resulting ache. Usually it was enough to get them through to the next performance.

For Harte it was exactly the opposite—the applause was the only thing that made the ache any better.

He'd been invited to their after-hours gatherings plenty of times before, but he hadn't been invited that night. Actually, he hadn't been invited for quite a while, come to think of it. At some point the others must have given up on their well-meaning attempts to bring him into their circle.

It was probably for the best, he thought, brushing aside any regret like the lint from his coat. He had too many secrets to risk entanglements. Especially now.

"Sneaking off without even a good-bye?" The voice came to him through the darkness, smoky and warm.

His hand tightened on the brim of his new silk hat. He was already on edge from Shorty's warning, but he pasted on his usual charming smile. "Would I ever sneak away from you, Evelyn?" he asked as he turned to face her.

"You're always sneaking away from me," she purred, "but I can never tell why."

The woman stepped forward into a beam of light, her ruby mouth pulled into a sultry pout and her eyes glassy from the drink. It didn't matter that every night he passed within inches of her when he exited the stage and turned the spotlight over to her. Familiarity did nothing to mute the effect of Evelyn DeMure because every ounce of her attraction was calculated, manipulated, and most of all, imbued with magic.

In her act, she and her two "sisters" wore flesh-colored bodysuits beneath Grecian-inspired gowns that barely covered their most scandalous parts. With their legs visible almost to the thigh and the risk that at any moment the gowns might unravel completely, the three performed a series of songs filled with double entendres and bawdy jokes that kept the audience—male and female alike—on edge, hoping for more.

Evelyn wasn't wearing the bodysuit now. Her eyes were still ringed in kohl and her lips were stained by bold paint, but her embroidered emerald robe hung low to reveal one creamy, bare shoulder and the slope of her full chest. Her henna-tinted hair, a red too vibrant to be real, was soft and untamed around her face.

An effective display altogether, he admitted. Even with her age showing at the corners of her eyes, she would have brought any man to his knees.

But Harte wasn't one of those who filled the theater eager for a glimpse of thigh—or something more—and who fell at her feet at the stage door. He knew her appeal came from something more than simple beauty. Even drunk as she was on Nitewein, whispers of magic betrayed her attempt to entangle him.

Ignoring the tightening in his gut, he gave her a formal nod. He wouldn't be taken in, especially not by the tricks of a siren like Evelyn.

"Where *are* you running off to so fast?" she crooned, taking another few steps toward him. Cat and mouse.

Desire coiled in his gut, but he held his ground, pretending his usual indifference to her many charms. "Urgent business, I'm afraid." He gave her a roguish grin that promised his destination was anything but.

Evelyn's expression flickered, and Harte thought he saw the hurt behind the pride she wore like armor. But for all he knew, that was also part of her act, another effect perfectly calculated to slay him.

He could find out, of course. It would be easy enough to strip off a glove, pretend that he was lured into her too-obvious seduction. It would only take a touch. . . . Harte took a step back instead, placing his hat on his head at a rakish angle and touching the brim in a silent farewell.

"You're really not going to tell me where you're going?" She crossed her arms, hitching the robe back up over her bare shoulder as her mouth went tight.

He'd upset her, not hurt her. "Sorry, love. I never kiss and tell." And with a wink, he left her standing in the back of the empty stage as he stepped out into the night.

For a moment he permitted himself the luxury of letting go. There, in the shadows of the stage door, he allowed himself to breathe, imagining a future when he could be more than his starched lapels and expertly tied cravat. More than this mask he wore.

Just how much more, he wasn't sure. . . . That depended on how well the evening went.

Adjusting his hat again, he tucked his cane beneath his arm and checked his pocket watch to see how much later he was than planned. *It could be worse,* he thought, glad to be away from the pull of Evelyn's magic and the weight of Shorty's warning.

Tonight things would start to change. Tonight he'd finally take his first steps toward true freedom. He started walking, making his way toward the part of the city called Satan's Circus, and his certain destiny.

A STAR-BRUSHED SKY

Twenty-Eighth Street near Fifth Avenue

Esta stumbled to her feet, stark fear coursing through her. She didn't notice the icy shock of the snowbank or the searing pain on her upper forearm where the silver cuff burned against her skin. The echo of the gunshot still rang in her ears.

Dakari.

She turned to where the entrance of the parking lot had once been, open and waiting, but now the street beyond was lit softly by an antique streetlamp. Unsteady on her feet, Esta took a tentative step forward, knocking the wet snow off her skirt as she went. Above, the sky was empty, completely devoid of the skyscraper that had been there moments before.

No . . .

Even with the snow drifting around her skirts, she staggered toward the street. Her muscles and bones ached as they always did after slipping through time. *No*, she thought as she came to the entrance of the alley.

But no amount of denial could change what was.

She stepped onto the wide, cobbled sidewalk and took in the changed city. A few minutes before, the tall shoulders and flat faces of uninspired, boxlike buildings had lined the streets. Now the structures were shorter, squat with rows of windows like watching eyes. A couple of the buildings hadn't changed that much, but now their street-level shops were capped with faded awnings rolled back to protect them from the heavy weight of the snow. Where a canyon of buildings once stood, now barely a gully of shops remained, as though life in the city was the reverse of nature, time building up instead of washing away.

She took it all in, the silence of the streets and the swath of stars—she could see *actual stars*—above her. Marveling at how different and familiar everything looked all at once, she barely heard the muffled clattering of hooves. It was a sound so rare in her own city that it didn't register as a danger, and she glanced back barely in time to avoid being run down by a horse-drawn carriage.

The driver gestured angrily and cursed her as he passed, and the wheels of the carriage caught at her skirts, making her stumble back. The heel of her boot slipped on the icy road, and she went down hard, landing in the slush-filled gutter.

Shaking from the adrenaline still pulsing through her, she stood up and brushed herself off—again.

A high-pitched whistle sounded, and Esta looked up to search for the danger. Instead, she found a red-faced old man, his filthy shirt open at the collar to expose the hairs climbing up from his chest. He was leaning far over a second-story fire escape, his eyes squinting at her like he was having trouble focusing.

"Süsse!" he called, grabbing at the front of his unbelted pants as he leaned drunkenly over the edge of the rickety railing. "You're missing your brains tonight, ja, Süsse? I can help you to find them." His words were slurred, his German oddly accented to Esta's ears.

Some things never change, she thought as disgust swept away her panic. She made a rude gesture and cursed back at him in his own language. The man doubled over laughing and almost fell from the fire escape. By the time he'd caught himself, Esta had already retreated to the relative safety of the alley.

But her bag was gone. The only evidence that remained were the footprints in the snow leading off to the other end of the street.

"No," she whispered. It was a stupid, rookie mistake that she never would have made if she hadn't been so distracted by the attack and so shaken by the memory of Dakari's body jerking and falling. The bag had contained everything she needed—

Except none of that mattered anymore. She had to get back. She had to help Dakari. To make sure he wasn't . . .

She couldn't even think the word.

Blinking back tears, she took a breath and focused on finding her own time—layers marked by brighter lights, blaring car horns, and the glow of the city stretching far above her.

But nothing was there.

No shimmers of past or future. Nothing at all but that present moment in an unfamiliar city filled with the cold scent of winter and a night so quiet it chafed.

Her chest was tight, her whole body shivering as she worked to unfasten the tiny buttons at her wrist. Finally, the last one came free. The icy air bit against her exposed skin as she pulled her sleeve up as far as it could go and reached beneath it.

As she pulled the cuff off, she let out a hiss of pain. She hadn't noticed the injury before, but now her upper arm throbbed and ached where the top layer of skin had peeled away with the metal. But the shock of the pain was nothing compared to the shock of what she saw when she examined the cuff.

The burnished silver had turned black and the iridescent stone was covered in what looked like black soot. Confused by its appearance, she touched it gently with her fingertip, and the stone crumbled on contact, disintegrating like ash until only the empty, burned-out setting was left.

Ishtar's Key was gone.

At first she couldn't process what she was seeing. Her stone couldn't be gone.

Had it burned up because she'd hesitated between present and past? Had she put too much pressure on it, cracked as it had already been?

As the reality of its disappearance began to set in, the loss hit her like the ache of a missing limb. Or maybe like something even more vital, like her heart. Without the stone, she couldn't find the layers of time. Without the stone, she wasn't anything more than an exceptionally good thief stuck in a city that wasn't her own.

Panic emptied out her chest, leaving her breathless and panting.

She was trapped. In the past.

She would never again argue with Logan about who was in charge on a job or enjoy the surprise in Dakari's eyes when she bested him on the mat. She would never again see the city she knew and loved, with its dizzying speed and clattering rush and brilliant buildings that erased the stars. She would die *here*, in this other city, not even a footnote in the history books. Alone and out of time.

She sank to her knees in the snow, laid low by the truth of her situation. But as the cold dampness began to seep through the layers of her skirts, a thought occurred to her: *Her* stone was gone, yes. But *the* stone wasn't gone. Ishtar's Key was still here, in this time, with all the other artifacts. With the Book she'd been sent to retrieve.

Was that it, then? Had Professor Lachlan been right about the stone's properties? He said they were unique—*singular*. Maybe Ishtar's Key had disintegrated because it was already there, waiting for her in the past.

But if that were the case, had he known this would happen, that she might be trapped here? And if he had, why hadn't he warned her?

The whole situation felt like another one of the Professor's tests, which meant it was another chance to prove herself to him. Only this time, her life—her very future—was at stake.

The thought only made her that much more resolved. If she could get the Book, she could get the earlier version of the stone as well. Once she had it in her possession, she could return to her own time. She could make sure Dakari was okay.

Another wagon clattered past the open mouth of the alley, the wooden wheels rattling and the muffled *clip-clop* of hooves disrupting the stillness of the night. In theory, she had been trained with all she needed to fit into the past, to blend with the people there and do what she was meant to do. But theory and reality felt like such different things from where she stood now, alone in a dark alley, listening to horse-drawn carriages clattering down streets that should have held the soft rumble of engines and blaring horns of automobiles.

But worrying about her fate wasn't doing anyone any good. The city might have changed dramatically, but she hadn't. She could still put the plan into action. She would make her way to the Haymarket and find Bridget Malone, as Professor Lachlan had instructed. She helped girls with magic find places to use their skills, places that weren't the back rooms of brothels. If the rumors were right, the madam worked for Saunders specifically. Esta just had to get Bridget's attention.

The only way to go was forward, as always.

Looking up and down the street, Esta got her bearings. Even though the streets looked so different, her own city was still there, pulling her in the direction she had to go and, with a little luck, toward Bridget Malone.

A SMART MOUTH

The Haymarket

By the time Harte turned onto Sixth Avenue, he could see the glow of the Haymarket ahead. It was the best-known—and most notorious—dance hall in the city. Inside, those who lived above Houston Street rubbed elbows with waiter girls from the slums, music played long into the night, and for the right price, the private stalls on the upper floors could be used for any entertainment a paying customer wanted.

Not that he needed any diversions of that type. He knew well enough what attachments like that could do to people. He'd seen what it did to his mother and knew firsthand how love and infatuation had made her desperate enough to throw everything away—including him.

He wasn't that little boy anymore, though. If the evening went to plan, he might be able to leave all those memories and regrets far behind him.

Stepping out from the shadow of the elevated tracks that ran above the entrance of the dance hall, he climbed the three steps and passed through the narrow entryway. Even before Harte was completely inside, the bright notes of a newly popular ragtime tune and the discordant buzz of the crowd assaulted him.

The moment he stepped through the door, a girl with white-blond hair took his overcoat. She was so young, not even the paint on her face could cover her greenness. She was eager—new, perhaps. But he knew the innocence beneath the powder and paint wouldn't last for long. Not in a place like the Haymarket.

Harte gave a tug to straighten his sleeves. "Mr. Jack Grew is expecting me," he said, imbuing his soft voice with the same compelling tone that made his audiences lean forward to listen. He gave over his hat—but not his gloves. Those he tucked into his jacket.

"He's not arrived yet," the girl told him, her cheeks burning scarlet. Another mark of her doomed innocence.

"Let him know I'm at the bar when he does?" He slipped the girl a few coins.

He made his way through the crush of bodies, hating the too-potent spice of perfumes that were barely able to hide the stale odor of sweat beneath. It reminded him too much of how far he'd come, of those mornings his mother would stumble home smelling the same.

Shaking off the memories, he found a space at the crowded bar and ordered, tipping the woman who poured his drink more than necessary when she served him. Her eyes lit, but he turned from her, making it clear he wasn't interested.

The first floor of the dance hall was already crowded. Women in brightly colored silk gowns with painted smiles clung too closely to the men who led them across the floor. The minutes ticked by as he nursed his drink. When it was gone, he didn't order another. Half an hour past when they were to meet, Jack Grew still hadn't shown.

The hell with it.

He wasn't staying. He probably shouldn't have come in the first place. Ever since Shorty had given him the warning, nothing about the night felt right, and Harte hadn't survived so long by ignoring his instincts. He'd go back to his apartment, run a steaming-hot bath in the blessed silence, and wash off the grime of the day. He could deal with Jack some other time.

Harte placed the empty glass back on the bar, but as he made to leave, he felt the unmistakable warmth of magic nearby.

Impossible. No one would be stupid enough to use their affinity in the Haymarket, not when many in the room had ties to the Ortus Aurea.

Not when the entire hall was monitored by the watchful eyes of Edward Corey's security guards. Corey, the owner of the Haymarket, played both sides. He had close ties to the Order, but it was rumored that he also used Mageus as guards, people who were willing to rat out their own in exchange for a fat paycheck each week.

But there it was again—the rustling of magic calling out to him and anyone else nearby with an affinity.

Harte scanned the crowd. On the edges of the room, it was clear Corey's men had sensed it as well. Already, they were on the move, searching for the person who'd brought the contraband power into the ballroom.

In the periphery of Harte's vision, a flash of deep green caught his eye at the same time that he felt another flare of warmth. He turned and found the source of it—a girl smiling up at her much older dance partner, while her fingers dipped nimbly into his pocket.

Harte was halfway across the dance floor before he realized she didn't look like the other girls. She was young, which wasn't unusual in her line of work, but her face wasn't covered in the usual powder and paint, and her eyes didn't have the weariness of a woman who'd already given up. Her clothes, a gown in deep hunter velvet, fit her slender figure too well to have been ready-made. Clearly, she came from money, but from the way she was maneuvering her right hand into her dance partner's pocket without him noticing, she was no novice dip. It was an intriguing combination.

By the time her partner looked up at him, Harte had already taken hold of the girl's wrist, effectively drawing it out of the man's pocket and stopping the couple's dance.

"May I help you?" the old man sneered.

Harte smiled pleasantly, letting his eyes go a little glassy and soft as he turned to the girl. She tried to pull away, but he had her secure. "I've been looking for you, darling," he said, allowing the words to slur together a little.

"I'm sorry, but this one is already taken," the old man said, attempting to wrestle the girl back from Harte. "Go find one of the others."

"But I *love* her," Harte told him, refusing to relinquish control. He swayed a bit on his feet for effect.

The old man's thick brows bunched in a scowl. "Then perhaps you should have kept better watch of her."

"You're right," Harte told him, turning his attention to the girl, who was glaring at him with eyes the color of whiskey and with just as much fire. He gave her a besotted smile. "I should have never let you go, not after you *stole* my heart," he said, enjoying the way the girl's eyes widened slightly when he emphasized the word.

"I don't believe I know you," the girl said, her voice shaking a little. Her words were well formed, her voice soft, cultured, but then, so was his. Considering his own beginnings, her lack of accent didn't mean much. The more interesting question was where she'd learned to pick pockets. And why her teacher hadn't warned her about using her magic in the Haymarket.

"You couldn't have forgotten so soon." Keeping in character, Harte lifted his free hand to his chest dramatically, as though struck. "Why, it was only last Friday we met here. The band was playing this very song when your eyes found mine across the room. I was reluctant, but you were"—he lowered his voice conspiratorially— *"convincing."* He gave her a teasing wink before he turned to her partner.

"It was nothing at all to overlook her little affliction for such beauty." Harte leered at the girl, who was still trying to pull away from him. He felt a pang of conscience at the fear lurking behind the anger in her golden eyes, but Corey's men were too close. Better she fear him than meet with them.

Why he had decided to help her was beyond him, though. He was no white knight, no one's protector.

"Yes, well . . ." The old man looked uneasily at the girl as he relinquished her to Harte. "Who am I to stand in the way of young love?"

Harte pulled her closer to him as the old man backed away into the crowd. "Easy now," he whispered, his head close to hers. She smelled faintly of flowers and something soft and musky, like sandalwood. It was what a summer day should smell like, he decided, instead of the stink of the streets.

She was still struggling to get away from him, but he tightened his hold, a subtle adjustment that to any other dancer would look like an embrace. "Go along with me and don't make a scene."

"I'll show you a scene," she hissed.

She wasn't small. She was nearly as tall as he was, and her features were more interesting than classically pretty. On anyone else, the wide mouth with such a sharp nose might not have worked, but on her it was striking. Her eyes were bright with fury, and damn if it didn't make her that much more attractive.

Or maybe that was the whiskey talking. . . .

The girl wriggled again, settling into his arms, and then suddenly, she twisted, trying to knock him off-balance. But Harte had been in his share of dirty fights. He countered her attack easily, wrapping her in his arms to secure her again as he drew them both into the swirl of men and their women on the dance floor.

"Impressive," he murmured, leading them into the first turn of a waltz.

The girl's golden eyes narrowed at him, her cheeks flushed from the exertion of trying to get away. He'd been right—her skin was clean of paint. Unlined, it looked smooth and soft as a petal.

I should let her go. . . .

Over the girl's shoulder, he saw one of Corey's men prowling the dance floor, still searching for the source of the magic. The man turned, looking in the girl's direction.

"Dance with me," Harte told her, leading her away from the man and toward the center of the crowded dance floor.

Energy spiked around her again as she struggled to get free from him. "I wouldn't dance with you if—"

Corey's men were getting closer. Without thinking through the consequences, Harte covered her mouth with his own, locking her in his arms as he brought her close.

The kiss did exactly what he'd intended—the warmth of her magic went cold as she stiffened, pressing against his shoulders with her hands. Corey's men were right next to him now, so he deepened the kiss and pulled her against him, away from them.

She smelled clean as a prayer beneath the soft scent of her soap, and it had been so long since he'd been that close to a girl—to anyone, really—that it took everything he had to keep his own wits about him. He was barely able to keep track of the two guards as they began to move away.

Without warning, her body went pliant in his arms, and he reacted instinctively. He couldn't have stopped himself if he had tried. But he didn't try. Instead, he drew her closer, the velvet of her gown soft beneath his fingertips, as she kissed him back.

Maybe he'd been wrong, he thought as her mouth moved in heady rhythm with his. Maybe she wasn't so innocent after all.

His brain felt heavy, numb, and he didn't know what to make of her. . . .

But even that thought was distant and obscure as her lips slid against his. He wasn't thinking at all when he parted his lips slightly, seeking to taste her. He wasn't considering how bad an idea it was when she opened her mouth for him. He was simply lost.

In that moment, the danger Corey's men posed didn't exist. Nor did the crush of bodies around them. He couldn't think of anything at all but the feel of her mouth against his, the scent of her filling his senses . . . until her sharp teeth bit down hard enough on his tongue to draw blood.

He released her and grabbed his mouth with a surprised yelp. *You bit me,* he wanted to say, but by the time he opened his eyes the girl was already gone. The only trace she left was the tingling energy from her sudden burst of magic and the taste of blood in his mouth.

It wasn't that she'd ducked away into the crowd. *No.* She'd been there one second and in a blink—in *less than a blink*—she had simply vanished.

He'd spent years working on illusions, and he'd never seen anything quite like it before.

He needed to go before Corey's men returned.

Instead, he stood stupidly in the middle of the swirling bodies, his tongue smarting, his head muddled by the whiskey, and his entire body electrified by the memory of her mouth against his. Impressed by her in spite of himself.

"Darrigan?" A voice was calling his name through the haze. "Harte Darrigan, is that you?"

His mind still spinning, Harte turned to find Jack Grew making his way across the dance floor. Too late to make his escape, he swallowed the blood that had pooled in his mouth and waved a greeting to Jack. He hardly felt any satisfaction at Jack's appearance. All he could think of was the girl.

"I thought that was you," Jack said with a smile that told Harte he'd already been drinking. "Well, come on, then. I have a table in the corner." Jack pointed across the crowded room.

"Lead the way," Harte said amiably. He tentatively checked his still-tender tongue as he forced himself to forget about the girl and focus on the situation before him. She wasn't his problem anymore, but Jack Grew might be his solution.

A WASTE OF GOOD BOOTS

Esta ducked farther back into an alcove on the second floor and tried to force herself to calm down. She unfastened the top two buttons of the heavy velvet dress to dispel the heat that had climbed up her neck.

He'd kissed her.

She could still feel him on her lips, still taste the whiskey that had been on his breath. She didn't know who he was or why he'd picked her, but she hated him for it.

First he'd ruined her chance at lifting the old man's wallet—and her chance of getting Bridget Malone's attention right along with it—and then, of all things, he'd kissed her like he had a right to.

As his head had bent toward her, it felt like time had gone slow, like the room had dimmed around them and she was frozen. It wasn't that he had any power to *actually* stop time, not like she had. It was simply that she—who had spent her whole life training for attacks, who was an expert at getting out of tough situations—knew what was about to happen and somehow *still* couldn't make herself move away or put a stop to it.

Worse, she'd kissed him back. *Like an idiot.*

When his lips finally touched hers, she'd been braced for an attack, so she was too surprised by how gentle he was to even think. She'd felt the warmth of his mouth, the scent of him, like soap and fresh linen and citrus, and something inside of her had split open. It wasn't that she'd never been kissed before. Of course she'd been kissed. By Logan, by men she'd needed to distract on various jobs. She might have even gone as far as saying she liked it, the tangle of breath, the push-pull excitement of desire.

But she hadn't realized how much she craved gentleness. How susceptible she still was to a yearning for human contact that was more than the physicality of her sparring matches with Dakari. For *warmth*.

His mouth had offered her that, and for a moment she'd fallen into the kiss as easily as breathing. She hadn't even tried to stop herself. It was like the mistakes she'd made with Logan all over again.

If she was honest, that bothered her more than the kiss itself.

Luckily, she didn't have time to be honest with herself any more than she had time to think too much about the kiss. *Or* how stupid she'd been. Thank god she'd finally come to her senses and given it all back to him, and then some.

Too bad that only made her feel marginally better.

From her vantage point in the alcove, she could see the entire ballroom, including the boy. He'd been so commanding on the dance floor, she'd assumed he was older, but now that she looked closer at him, she realized he didn't have any more than a couple of years on her.

She couldn't help but watch him. It was important to understand your enemy, she told herself. It didn't hurt that he was nice enough to look at. His suit fit perfectly over his broad shoulders. She knew firsthand that there wasn't any padding in his coat—she'd felt his strength as he'd gripped her wrist and held her in his arms. Still, there was something about him that bothered her. Something more, that is, than the way he kissed.

Maybe it was simply that the old adage was true—you really can't con a con—but after a few minutes of studying him, she realized all his confidence and swagger was an act. Or at least part of one. Just like Logan's easy charm was a way to manipulate and Dakari's fierce features were only a cover for the softness beneath.

The longer she watched, the more she noticed how uncomfortable he was. He fidgeted. The small tugs at his sleeves, the way he touched his temples to make sure every hair was in place, the way he arranged the gloves on the table, lining up the fingertips so they matched—he couldn't seem to stop checking himself. The longer she watched, the more she wondered what he was hiding. Or what he was hiding from.

Then something struck her—the other man at the table was familiar. It took her a second to place him, but once she realized that he'd been older the last time she'd seen him, she easily recognized the blond as the man who'd shot Logan in Schwab's mansion.

She pulled herself back from the railing. She wouldn't steal the Pharaoh's Heart for another twenty years or more, and in that past, he hadn't known her. She was probably safe enough now, but it was too much of a coincidence that the man who had ruined everything at Schwab's mansion was here as well.

She needed to find Bridget Malone before anything else happened. . . .

"Well, what have we here?" a voice said from behind her.

Esta jumped and turned to find a large man with whiskers like a goat leering at her, his belly preceding him into the small alcove. With him came the stale reek of sweat and beer and too much cologne.

"Corey said he had a treat for me tonight." His heavy gold signet ring flashed as he flexed his fingers in what was clear anticipation. "I see you've anticipated my arrival," he said, gesturing to her open collar.

At first Esta thought the man had made a mistake or had confused her for someone else, but his eyes traveled over her, lingering on her chest, her corseted waist and hips. She remembered suddenly where she was, in one of the semiprivate areas the girls who worked the hall used to entertain their clients. The man clearly thought she was there waiting for him on purpose, and before she had a chance to correct him, he'd already moved closer, blocking her in with his wide body.

She *really* hadn't wanted to injure anyone else tonight, she thought, as the man took another step forward. Backing up until she was pressed against the railing, she considered her options.

"Now, now," the man slurred, stumbling toward her. The smile curving his lip exposed his yellowed teeth when she lifted her hands, preparing for his attack. "None of that," he said, the excitement clear in his voice.

The man grabbed for her, and he was lighter and faster on his feet than Esta expected. She barely had a chance to focus on the moment, to find the spaces between the seconds, so she could create a path through it and away from him. The room stilled, the bright cawing laughter and tinny notes of the band dimmed to a low drone, and the man went almost comically slow, as though he were moving through air as thick and solid as sand.

Relief flooded through her like quicksilver. It was almost too easy to slip past the man's massive body. She caught the laugh bubbling up in her chest at the confusion in his eyes as she slipped out of the alcove, beyond his grasp. The second she let go of time, the world slammed back to life, and the man stumbled heavily to the floor with a groan.

In her relief, she didn't realize how alert he actually was. Before she could get away completely, he caught her by the ankle.

"Let me go!" Esta growled under her breath. She didn't want to draw attention to herself, not here in the middle of this overcrowded room. She had to get away and find Bridget. She needed to get back to what was important—the Book, the stone. The job she had been sent to do.

But the man seemed to be enjoying himself. "That how it's to be, is it?" He laughed, tugging on her with his ironlike grip, and hauled her along the floorboards, back toward the alcove.

In that moment, what she wouldn't have given to be able to do anything else—to be able to call up a wind or send a jolting shock. But all she could do was manipulate the present. A powerful-enough affinity when she was nicking a diamond stickpin, it was useless if someone had ahold of her, unless she wanted to slow time for them as well.

"I'm not here for you," she hissed at him again, trying to pull away.

"You were waiting for me," the man said, his eyes bright with the chase.

"Corey, whoever he is, didn't send me." She gave him a few sharp kicks as she tried to get her ankle free.

The man simply laughed and dug his fingers into her ankle. His eyes were alert and more clear than they had been seconds ago, and before she could brace herself, he gave a sharp, unexpected jerk that brought her to the floor. Nearby, a group of people glanced over their shoulders at her struggle and then promptly averted their eyes.

The man laughed and kept tugging, causing Esta's skirts to climb higher as he dragged her, exposing her legs as she fought against him. But it was no use. He had one ankle and was reaching his sausagelike fingers up her skirts, pinching her bare thigh above her petticoats, up farther. . . .

Not caring who saw her now, she let out a vicious kick that caught the man directly in the face. She felt the crunch of bone collapsing through the thin sole of her boot, and then blood spurted from the man's broken nose. He roared like an injured bear but still didn't let go of her ankle. His fingers tightened as he twisted her leg painfully, his eyes bright with some lurid excitement, and she felt her own bones ache under the pressure.

Desperate, she kicked him again. And again. Exactly like Dakari had taught her. Until the heels of her button-up boots were coated with the man's blood. Finally, his fingers released their grip, and he slumped unconscious to the floor.

Esta scurried away from him, vaguely aware of the group of people who had surrounded her. The man's face was a broken mess as he lay sprawled on the floor, but he was still breathing. For now, at least.

The group around her had grown silent. She met the eyes of one girl with too-pink cheeks whose skin had gone an ashy gray beneath the paint.

"I didn't mean . . . ," Esta started, but her words died as the girl let out a ragged scream at the same time that two men from the crowd took a step toward Esta.

She could tell by their expressions that pleading would get her nowhere.

Esta stood on shaking legs. She would try to find Bridget later. For now she needed to get as far away from the crowded hall and the snub-nosed bouncers as she could. But suddenly she couldn't breathe. Her lungs seized, her chest went tight, like the oxygen had drained from the room. In a panic, she searched the still life around her for some sign of an attack, but her vision was already going fuzzy around the edges. Desperately, she struggled to pull in air that seemed to be missing from the room.

Before she could even begin to focus on the seconds ticking past her, before she could find the spaces between them to escape, a sharp pain erupted across the back of her head. And then everything went black.

THE APPROACH

Jack glanced up at the commotion in the balcony, but he dismissed it without another look. Harte, though, had felt the spike of magic, the telltale energy jolting through the room that only someone who had an affinity to the old magic would recognize. He wondered what the source of it had been, and whether the girl had been the unlucky recipient of the attention from Corey's security.

If so, it was partially his fault for chasing her away. He should never have kissed her. He should have found a different way. His stomach tightened with guilt, but there wasn't anything he could do for her now.

He turned his attention back to Jack, who was taking two glasses of whiskey from a waiter girl's tray. The prodigal nephew of J. P. Morgan, Jack Grew was one of the sons of the city. His family was deep into the political machine and were known members of the Order of Ortus Aurea, so no one was more surprised than Harte when Jack had shown up at his dressing room after a show months ago, wildly excited about the act and desperate to know everything about Harte's skills.

Harte had kept Jack at arm's length . . . until the night Dolph Saunders summoned him to propose that suicide mission of a job. After that, Harte saw Jack in a different light and had started cultivating a careful friendship with him, all the while figuring out how he could best use him. And how he could keep Jack away from Dolph.

"It's been a few weeks since I've seen you," Harte said, accepting one of the glasses. "I was surprised to get your message earlier."

"Sorry about that." Jack grimaced. "I haven't had time to do anything lately," he said before taking a long swallow of his drink. "My uncle's been on my case all week to help with a reception for an exhibition he's planning at the Metropolitan. Opens Friday, though, so at least it'll be over with at the end of the week."

"Oh? I hadn't heard about it. . . ." Harte let his voice trail off, as though his not hearing was some mark against the reception itself.

"Some big fund-raiser," Jack said sourly into his nearly empty glass. "It's a waste of everyone's time."

Harte gave him a wry smile. "Kind of you to help with it."

Jack snorted at the joke. "Kindness has nothing to do with it. I would have found a way to get out of it, but there are a couple of things I wanted the chance to examine."

"Oh?" Harte asked, his voice breezy and his expression disinterested, because he'd learned over the past few months that it was the easiest way to egg Jack on. At first Jack had been careful and closed off in their conversations when it came to his family or the Order, but Harte knew how to work an audience. It wasn't long before Jack was willingly handing over information in an attempt to prove his own importance and win Harte over.

"He's got quite the collection of art from the Ottoman Empire, but some of these pieces are fairly unique. He tends to keep his most valuable and rare pieces to himself, but with the Conclave at the end of the year, he couldn't resist showing off."

"Anything I'd be interested in?" Harte asked, careful to keep his tone easy and light.

Jack nodded. "Maybe. A couple of the seals and tablets go back to ancient Babylon, and there's at least one manuscript owned by Newton himself." Jack smiled. "It won't exactly be a burden to take a close look at those. Especially since they haven't granted me access to the collections at Khafre Hall."

"Still holding you off, are they?" Harte asked with a disapproving shake of his head.

"Of course," Jack grumbled. "Only the Inner Circle has access to the records, and until I prove myself, my uncle's not going to sponsor me. If this event goes well, though, maybe I'll be a step closer. It's not as if they can hold me off forever." He glanced at Harte. "They know as well as I do that they're all basically fossils. They don't want to face facts—it's only a matter of time before they're completely obsolete. The world's changing too fast to stay in the past."

"It's a damn disgrace," Harte murmured, pretending to take another drink. "And they're damn fools to underestimate you, Jack. You're the best of the lot of them." He raised his glass. "Here's to it being over quickly, so you can get back to more important endeavors."

"I'll drink to that." Jack lifted his glass, but he stopped before he could return the toast. "Speaking of damn fools," he muttered as a trio of young men in well-tailored coats approached.

When they stopped at the table, three pairs of eyes appraised Harte with the kind of bored indifference that only the truly rich could affect.

"Gentlemen," Jack said, reluctance tingeing his voice as he stood to greet them.

Harte followed suit. He recognized the three easily. Considering how often they were in the society columns, anyone would. One was a Vanderbilt, another was Robert Winthrop Chandler, who was a cousin of the Astors, and the last was the younger J. P. Morgan, Jack's own cousin. These men were the sons of the city, kings of their world—or they would be when their fathers finally decided either to hand over the reins of their empires or die.

"Fancy meeting you here, Jack," Chandler said with a cold gleam to his eyes. "Though I can't say I know your friend."

Jack made the introductions, but if any of the three recognized Harte's name, they didn't show it. They also didn't bother to extend their hands in welcome.

"It's an honor to meet you all," Harte said, not letting his pleasant, impassive expression falter as he gave them a small bow, an answer to the insult of them not greeting him properly.

"Aren't you going to invite us to join you?" J. P. Morgan, Jr. said, lifting one brow in challenge.

Harte could practically feel the reluctance rolling off Jack, but there was nothing for it.

"Please," Jack said, waving at the empty chairs at the table. "Why don't you join us?"

The men traded cool glances with each other and then, seemingly in amused agreement, took the offered seats. The three men were all older than Jack, closer to thirty than twenty. Harte immediately understood that they viewed Jack as a joke and Harte himself as an intrusion.

Not that they would say anything outright. Jack wasn't the richest or the most powerful person at the table, but he was still one of them— even if his family had recently dragged him back home, humiliated, after he'd almost married a Greek fisherman's daughter on his grand tour.

But their good breeding would only get him so far.

A waiter girl brought an extra chair for the table. She gave Jack a drunken smile and draped herself over his shoulders to whisper something close to his ear that made him roar with laughter. Her appearance only reminded Harte of how unique the other girl had been, the one responsible for his aching tongue. The one who had made him lose all sense before she disappeared.

He gave himself a mental shake. He couldn't afford to let his mind wander back to the girl now. Not surrounded by these men—every one of them members of the Order. Every one of them more powerful than Jack himself.

Harte was careful to keep his face pleasant as they all waited for Jack to finish with the girl, who was now sitting squarely on his lap. The one sitting directly across from him was J. P. Morgan, Jr., the heir to Morgan's fortune and his standing in the Order. The younger Morgan wore a knowing expression, as though he understood exactly how uncomfortable Harte felt.

Morgan lifted a neatly rolled cigarette to his mouth and took a long, squinting drag, exhaling the smoke through his nose as he spoke. "Jack's mentioned you before. Says you're quite the man to see perform."

Harte inclined his head as though he hadn't noticed the way Jack's cousin sneered the word "perform." Like he was no better than an organ grinder's monkey. "I'm happy to hear that he's spoken so well of me."

Morgan, still squinting, gave a shrug. "He's mostly mentioned how you're wasting yourself—your talents—on the stage."

Harte let his mouth curve up ever so slightly. "My talents were made for the stage. And the stage has done well enough by me in turn." He gave his left sleeve another small tug, well aware that he was drawing attention to the jeweled cuff link that glinted there.

Vanderbilt leaned forward. "You're quite the enigma, Mr. Darrigan," he said. "What is that, Irish? Or is Darrigan simply your stage name?"

"I'm afraid it's the only name I lay claim to," Harte answered, his voice dangerously even.

"A man of mystery, are you?" Jack's cousin drawled. "I've heard about you. A classic tale—come from nowhere and here you are, the toast of Broadway. Why, even my mother has seen your performance. She swears you gave the most amazing demonstration." He gave a humorless laugh. "Insisted that you must have some sort of real power."

"Your mother is too kind."

"Is she? I've often thought she was rather flighty," Morgan said with an indifferent shrug. "She was nervous, but I told her, of course, that it was impossible. We all know that if you were that sort of filth, you would have already been taken care of, don't we?" The threat was clear. "The Order would have heard about it. So, it must be mere tricks you do, I told her. Illusions. Not true magic at all."

Harte kept his face in that careful, pleasant mask that had been his ticket out of the slums and into the footlights. "I'm sure the Order would have already taken care of any threat if I posed one. I have the utmost respect for the work they do to keep us safe from those who would threaten our way of life. But I assure you, there's nothing simple about my tricks," he said easily, while dread inched along his skin. He was in too deep. There were many variables he hadn't prepared for—first the girl, now this circling around magic.

Damn Jack for throwing me into this.

"No?" the younger Morgan challenged, a smirk creeping at the corners of his mouth.

Harte didn't react to it. "If Jack's spoken of me, then I'm sure he's told you—I've made a careful study of the hermetic arts," Harte said, inclining his head. "Alchemy, astronomy, theurgy. The usual branches of the occult sciences. I don't perform *tricks.*" He forced himself not to glance over at Jack for help, keeping his focus steady on Jack's cousin. "I present demonstrations of my *skill* and the knowledge I've acquired through my many years of study."

"Yes. He might have mentioned something like that," Morgan said.

"You didn't believe him." It wasn't a question. The smug certainty in his own superiority was clear as day on Morgan's face. As was the disbelief that anyone not of their own class could have mastered any sort of power. It took a considerable amount of effort on Harte's part not to smile at the irony of it.

"I make my own decisions," Jack's cousin told him, squinting through another deep drag on his cigarette before he snubbed it, violently, on the marble tabletop. "Though when it comes to Irish filth"—he raked his eyes over Harte's pristine, perfectly tailored clothes—"or whatever it is you are, there's rarely anything to decide." He leaned forward, malice glinting in his eyes. "What was that rumor I heard about you? Oh, yes . . . the bastard son of a Chinaman."

The other men at the table shifted. Even if Jack was the wastrel of the family, good breeding and manners went deep.

Luckily, Harte didn't have the problem of good breeding. His mouth curved wickedly, the barbing response already loaded on his tongue, but before he could speak, he felt the familiar brush of magic and the unsettling feeling that someone was watching him. His words were forgotten, and he went on alert.

He was on his feet instantly, searching.

Morgan laughed. "Going somewhere, Darrigan?"

The others chuckled, but Jack was still too busy with the waiter girl to even notice how badly things were progressing at the table.

Harte couldn't find any sign of the girl's green velvet dress or whiskey-colored eyes. *Maybe it was Corey's security,* he thought, which wasn't any better. There had already been too much magic in the air, and magic was something Harte Darrigan couldn't risk being associated with. Not with these men, members of the Order who posed an even greater threat than Corey's security.

Morgan smirked over his glass of champagne. "Feeling out of your depth, are you?"

Jack finally looked up from the bit of silk and muslin on his lap. "You can't be leaving already," he said, sputtering in confusion. "You . . . you haven't even finished your drink." As if that was the point that truly mattered.

Harte ignored Morgan and gave Jack a wry look. "I'm not really thirsty anymore."

"But—"

"Jack, gentlemen, the one thing my many years onstage have taught me is when to make an exit." He gave the other men a nod, allowing his cold gaze to linger on Morgan, to send the message that he wasn't afraid of him. "I'll see you later, Jack."

Truth be told, Morgan's barbs hadn't hurt nearly as much as Harte's swollen tongue.

A moment later, he was pushing through the crowd toward the door, but he couldn't shake the feeling that someone was watching, tracking him, as he moved steadily into the cool freedom of the night beyond.

IN THE DEAD OF NIGHT

He'd barely made it to the end of the block when Harte heard Jack's voice calling him through the din of the crowded sidewalks. He didn't stop at first, just continued barreling down the sidewalk—away from the Haymarket. Away from the whole mess of a night. But Jack was determined.

With a sigh, Harte stopped and turned, giving Jack a chance to catch up. He might as well get this over with. . . .

Jack had the kind of patrician good looks most of his class sported: straight, narrow nose; light eyes; strong, square forehead. He wasn't that much older than Harte himself, but the humiliation in Greece had done a number on him. Away from the glittering lights of the dance hall, he looked worn, run-down. His face was flushed and damp from the exertion caused by his sprint. It made his puffy skin and the shadows beneath his eyes look that much worse.

"What is it, Jack? Coming back for another round? Was there some insult you forgot to get in yourself?"

"You left," Jack said, ignoring Harte's sarcasm and his anger. His bloodshot eyes betrayed his sincere confusion. As though no one had ever walked out on him before.

It was probably the truth. Even if Jack was his family's current black sheep, few would have risked word of an insult getting back to his famous uncle. Harte probably couldn't afford it either, not if he wanted Jack to trust him, but he was too on edge to care. Morgan Jr. and the rest had come too close to the truth, and in that instant he'd seen all his careful plans crumbling between his fingers.

"Look, Jack, I only came tonight because you invited me. I wasn't expecting to be the evening's entertainment. Usually my audience pays for that particular pleasure."

"It's not like that, Darrigan—"

"It was *exactly* like that, Jack."

"I didn't expect them to be there, and then . . ." Jack took a deep breath, as though he was trying to steady himself.

"And then you sat there with your hand down a girl's dress and let your cousin insult me."

Jack had the decency to look the slightest bit uneasy at this charge. "I'm sorry, Darrigan, but—"

"But nothing, Jack. Aren't those the same ones you're constantly complaining about? *They* don't understand your genius. *They* don't understand the dangers we face," Harte mimicked. Then he pinned Jack with a caustic glare. "I thought we understood one another—"

"We do!" Jack protested.

"But tonight you tossed me to the wolves," Harte continued.

He took a breath and stepped back from Jack. It was too easy to call up the old indignation, the bitterness he thought he'd long ago put to rest. It was too easy to still let their words affect him. Which wouldn't do, not in a situation as delicate as this one.

He needed to keep his wits about him and his head cool. He needed to make sure he—and not his emotions—were in control. He'd been working on earning Jack's trust for too long to screw it all up now.

"Look, let's go somewhere and talk," Jack offered. "I'll buy you a drink and make it up to you. We can talk. Without them."

"I don't know . . . ," Harte hedged, making a show of checking his watch. *Let Jack be the eager one,* he told himself, mentally pulling back. You couldn't force a con. The mark had to believe it was his own idea.

Jack was already stepping to the curb. "Let me get us a cab. There's a quiet bar over on Fortieth—"

"It's getting late, and I have an early show tomorrow," Harte said, staying where he was.

Because the last thing he wanted was another smoky barroom. He needed to walk, to clear his head. He needed some space away from Jack Grew and all the feelings the evening had stirred up.

He needed Jack to want it.

"Anyway, I'm more than finished with this evening." Harte pulled his overcoat around him against the brisk winter air.

Jack let his arm fall to his side, and for a moment he looked like he wasn't sure what to do. Then he straightened, his eyes wide and his expression suddenly eager.

"You know," Jack said, "you should come."

"Come where?" Harte asked. He kept his tone flat, so Jack wouldn't guess at how the invitation affected him, how his heart had kicked up in his chest and how it felt suddenly too much even to breathe.

"Come to the gallery opening. As my guest."

I'm close. So very close. "I have the eight o'clock show . . . ," he started.

"Oh, right," Jack said, his shoulders sinking.

"But I'm not on until well after nine," Harte continued. "I'm sure I could swing by for a little while."

"You should," Jack insisted, looking relieved.

"I'll think about it," Harte said, the thrill of this small victory coursing through him. But he forced himself to keep his expression noncommittal, placid.

"I'll send you over an invitation, just in case."

"Sure, Jack. You do that." Harte gave a small salute. "I'll see you around," he said, and without another word, he turned and left Jack Grew behind with the noise of Satan's Circus.

As he walked, the elevated train thundered by overhead, coughing its coal-fired way to its final destination, and the city grew quiet. The crowded sidewalks gave way to streets lined with serene townhomes, but in that silence he felt a chill, and he knew danger of some sort had followed him.

Keeping his gait steady, he turned right, following to where the street opened onto Madison Square. Then he slipped into the quiet of the gardens and waited.

It didn't take long before he saw his stalker pause at the gates of the park. Harte recognized him immediately. Cursing under his breath, he considered his options. Finally, he decided that the direct route would be best.

"Why are you following me, Nibsy?" he asked, stepping out from the shadows.

The lenses of the boy's spectacles flashed in the moonlight. "Harte Darrigan? Is that you?" Nibs called, like he hadn't been following Harte all the time. Like it was a surprise to run into an old friend in an empty park in the dead of night.

"You know damn well it's me. You've been following me for three blocks." He walked toward the boy until they were nearly toe-to-toe. "Were you at the Haymarket, too?" he demanded, wondering if the sense of unease that had driven him to his feet might have been Nibsy and not the girl after all.

"The Haymarket?" The boy sounded confused, but Harte didn't believe the act for a second. People tended to overlook Nibsy Lorcan because he didn't have any discernible affinity, but then, neither did Harte. Nibs kept his secrets close to the vest, but Harte knew that anyone Dolph Saunders trusted as much as he trusted the boy had to have something to him. It should have been easy enough to find out for sure, but Nibs had a way of staying just out of reach—a defense mechanism, Harte supposed. One that seemed to serve him well.

Even now Nibsy took a step back.

"Don't try to tell me you didn't know I was at the Haymarket," Harte said, too tired to deal anything else that night.

Behind his glasses, the boy's eyes were unreadable, but Harte got the sense they were taking everything in.

"Yeah, you got me all right," Nibsy said affably enough. "Bridget told me you were meeting with Jack Grew."

So they were finally coming to it. New York might have been one of the biggest cities in the world, but Harte should have known he couldn't do anything without everyone knowing his business. "Yeah, I met with him, all right. With Vanderbilt and Chandler and a couple of others, too. What business is that of yours? And why were you waiting for me to start with?"

"I needed to talk with you. They won't let me backstage anymore." There was a tone of reproach in his voice.

"It's a new policy," Harte said, skirting the truth. In fact, it was *his* new policy. A few weeks before, Nibsy had started showing up and pestering him about Dolph's proposal again. It got so bad Harte could barely think straight, much less get ready for his next performance.

Besides, he had plans of his own, and he couldn't chance Nibsy running into Jack.

The boy frowned, like he understood this wasn't exactly a lie, but it also wasn't exactly the truth. Which was what worried Harte about the kid—he always seemed to know a little too much when he shouldn't have known anything at all. "Does your meeting with Jack Grew mean you've thought about Dolph's proposition?"

"Not a chance," Harte said, shaking his head.

In truth, Harte had done little else *but* think about Dolph's proposition. It was the reason he'd been getting friendlier with Jack. Harte wasn't about to join the ragtag crew Dolph Saunders was assembling. He'd had enough of working for other people to last him a lifetime. But he'd thought a lot about *why* Dolph was assembling them—and about how he could do the same job, but better, and on his own.

"Dolph's still eager to have you on board," Nibsy said, rubbing his hands a little for warmth. "He needs you to make a go of it."

While Harte could appreciate a bit of theater as well as the next person, he wasn't buying the meek-and-humble routine Nibs was playing for him. "Why's that? Far as I can tell, Dolph isn't hurting any for talent. All I can do is make some rabbits disappear."

Nibsy didn't react, and he didn't call Harte on the lie, which made him wonder how much Dolph had shared with Nibs. "Dolph still thinks you're our way in. With you on board, the job would be a certain bet," Nibsy said, ducking his head to look over the rims of his glasses. "You gotta at least consider it."

"It's been a long day, Nibs. I had two curtains today, and three more tomorrow. The only thing I'm considering is the way my bed's going to feel when I finally sink into it." Harte clapped the boy on the shoulder, squeezing gently. It wasn't the kid's fault that Dolph had put him up to this, but Harte wasn't soft enough to care. "Take care, and stop following me, will you?" he said as he walked past Nibs.

"So what do I tell Dolph?" Nibsy called.

Harte turned, walking backward for a few steps. "Tell him I'm still not interested in the suicide mission he's cooked up." Not when he had plans of his own.

BRIDGET MALONE, I PRESUME

The Haymarket

The first thing Esta noticed when she came to was that she wasn't alone. Her head still ached from the blow, and she was slumped against a damp wall in a room that smelled dank and old, the way basements do.

She kept her breathing steady, her body still as she slowly moved her hand down her leg. Her fingers finally found the edge of her boot, but Dakari's knife was gone.

All at once the air went out of her lungs. Her eyes opened as her chest constricted in a desperate attempt to breathe.

"Ah, so I was right," a rasping voice crowed. "You *are* awake."

Esta's vision struggled to adjust to the sudden brightness, and when it did, she saw that the light in the room wasn't coming from a lamp, but from a person holding a dancing flame in the palm of her hands.

"That's enough, Werner," the woman said, nodding to the boy standing next to her. He glared at Esta, but a moment later she could breathe again.

"You're maybe wondering where you are?" the woman said with a sly, satisfied smile. She was small and surprisingly willowy, considering the rasping tenor of her voice. With her coppery hair and fair skin, she might have once been pretty, but now she only looked worn. The boy was about Esta's own age with a squint-eyed glare and a smirk on his face.

Esta didn't particularly care where she was, because she wasn't going to be there for very long. She focused on the seconds that ticked by, but her head felt wobbly and unclear, and when she tried to slow time, she felt a splitting pain behind her eyes. She couldn't keep the panicked gasp from escaping her throat when time slipped out of her grasp, eluding her.

"That would be the opium," the woman said as Esta tried to pull herself back up against the wall. "We couldn't have you leaving us too soon, could we now? You'll find it impossible to call on your affinity so long as the poppy remains in your blood, so it's best you resign yourself to being our guest for a while longer. Until we decide what your fate will be."

"Please," Esta said, forcing herself to make her voice small. She noticed the sticky sweetness hanging in the air now, the fuzziness in her head.

"You've caused me quite the problem, girl," the woman cut in, her voice barely above a whispering growl. "The man you laid low is Mr. Murphy, and he happens to be one of Mr. Corey's best customers and one of the most powerful men in the city. There's few daft enough to cross him as you did. He'll not rest until he finds the girl who broke his ugly gob, and he'll not be satisfied until he pays someone back in kind. That someone isn't going to be me. He's a right nasty one. The type to enjoy every second of your pain, if you understand what I'm saying?"

Esta made no move, but the woman gave a wan smile nevertheless.

"Ah. You *do* understand, then." The smile fell from the woman's face, and her eyes went cold. "So you'll understand that you don't have much time before Mr. Corey turns you over to him. Unless you give me a good reason not to, of course."

Esta schooled her expression to give nothing away. Not a blink to tell the woman that the idea of being at the large man's mercy was more than repulsive. Not a twitch to give away the panic of not being able to call on her magic.

"You think you're so brave? That you can protect yourself from the likes of him?" the woman scoffed. "Here, let me show you. . . ." The fire in her outstretched hand grew, danced, as she brought the flame up closer to her face and pulled down the high collar of her dress with her other hand. Beneath the lace, her skin was scarred in a gnarled mass.

Esta couldn't stop from wincing.

"I was pretty once, like you. You go on with your determined eyes and stiff spine, but the strongest spine will snap easily with a boot pressing down on it. Murphy has eyes everywhere in this city. Magic or no, you'd not last two days without help or protection."

"You can give me protection from Murphy?"

The woman nodded. "If you can make it worth my while. You've caused a right mess for Mr. Corey, and his messes always become mine. I hate messes, girl, so if you're not worth more than the problem you've caused, I'll hand you over to Mr. Murphy wrapped in lace and tied with a bow of the finest silk. And I won't think twice about whether you ever see daylight again."

Esta started to protest, but the woman raised her hand. There was no sign of burns or scarring from where she had held the fire, and Esta's skin tingled again from the magic that seemed to saturate the air in the room.

"However . . . Murphy isn't one of *us*. And I'd just as soon he go hang than get one bit of pleasure he hasn't rightly paid me for. If you prove to be a smart girl, *perhaps* I know of someone who could protect you . . . so long as you *remain* useful, that is." The woman stepped closer. "Tell me, why did you come to be in my ballroom when you clearly weren't looking for the company of a man?"

"I came to find Bridget Malone."

The woman didn't react, save for a small muscle that ticked near her eye. She studied Esta a little longer, and then she exchanged a glance with Werner, who gave a subtle shrug.

"Bridget Malone, you say?" the woman asked. Her voice, if it was possible, had gone even rougher.

"I was told that she finds places for people with certain . . . abilities," Esta said, never once breaking the stare with the woman. "People like us."

"And what *abilities* do you claim?"

Esta tried to focus again. The cloud of opium was already starting to dissipate, and its power over her was starting to wane. "I'm a thief," she said simply, sticking as close to the truth as was possible.

"A thief?" Even through the rasp of the woman's voice, Esta could hear her doubt. "There's already enough of those in the city to fill all the cells in the Tombs thrice over. Why would anyone have use of another?"

"Because I'm the best of them. I can steal a diamond, an elephant, or anything in between. No one can stop me"—Esta leaned forward as though sharing a secret—"because no one can *see* me."

Werner laughed, but the woman simply watched Esta, searching her face for some signs of the lie.

The woman's mouth made a pinched shape of disbelief. "You can prove this?"

Esta took a breath, closed her eyes, and in the split second it took for Werner and the woman to exchange another, more doubtful glance, Esta had pulled time to a stop, crossed the room, and plucked the brooch from the neckline of the woman's dress. Before the woman's suspicious eyes returned to where Esta had been sitting, she was gone.

When Werner came barreling through the door, the woman wide-eyed behind him, Esta was waiting, leaning against the wall outside the room with a bored look on her face. Using her affinity through the remaining haze of the opium had all but drained her. She couldn't have done anything more to escape if she had wanted to, even if Werner hadn't immediately gone on the attack.

The second Werner saw her, she felt her chest go tight and her throat begin to close, but this time she was ready for the unsettling feeling of being suffocated. She'd never felt magic quite so powerful before, which was worrisome enough. But worse, from the way he was taking orders, Esta understood that he probably wasn't all *that* powerful, not relative to others. Professor Lachlan had tried to warn her, but now she understood—magic *was* different there. Like nothing she'd ever experienced.

But she didn't have time to worry about that fact. If the two knew how little strength she had left, Esta would lose her upper hand, so she pretended a calm confidence she didn't feel. When the woman saw she hadn't escaped—hadn't even tried to get away—she slapped Werner's arm. A heartbeat later, Esta could draw air into her lungs once more.

"A fair trick," the woman said, her face not betraying any hint of surprise or anger or even interest. "But you wouldn't have gotten very far. Not with Mr. Murphy looking for you."

"Who said I was trying to leave?" Esta said, holding up the brooch so the fake stones glinted in the light thrown by the ball of fire in the woman's hand. "I was only proving how useful I could be. Besides, why would I run from the very person I'm looking for? Miss Malone, I presume?"

The woman blanched a little, but managed to hold on to her composure as she reached out and took the brooch Esta was holding. "Please," Esta said. "I need a place to stay. I'm a hard worker, and I will be loyal to any who help me."

"The city doesn't need any more thieves."

"I can make it worth your while." Esta ran her fingers along the edge of her bodice until she found the small pocket sewn into the lining. Relieved that they hadn't found it, as they had her knife, she pulled out the diamond she'd taken in Schwab's mansion. "Here," she said, offering Bridget the stone. "This is all I have."

After a long moment, Bridget took the stone and examined it, then eyed Esta again as she tucked the diamond into her pocket. "Maybe I know somewhere you could go. . . . Where are your people?"

Relief coursed through her, but she tamped it down. It was too soon to celebrate. "Dead. There was a fire. . . ." She let her voice trail off, and she glanced away, sinking the hook into the lie.

Werner shifted uneasily on his feet at the mention of the word. No doubt he'd had his own experiences with the fires that were so were common in this city. She'd learned from Professor Lachlan about the "accidental" blazes that consumed whole buildings filled with magical refugees while the fire brigades—controlled by and dependent on the Order—stayed away.

Bridget's eyes narrowed. "There's no one to come looking for you?"

"No one except your Mr. Murphy," Esta told her.

In the long moment that followed, it took every bit of strength Esta had left not to falter. If Bridget refused to help now, she wasn't sure what she would do. The Professor's plan hinged on Esta exposing herself and Bridget seeing something of interest in Esta's talent, but they hadn't planned on Esta making an enemy of Bridget. If the madam turned her away, or worse, turned her over to Murphy, Esta had already used every ounce of her strength on the desperate bid to prove herself. She had nothing left, not even the diamond. And if they drugged her any more, she'd be beyond helpless.

"How did you know who I was?" Bridget asked.

"I'm good at recognizing a tell," she explained with a shrug. "A good thief knows how to read a mark."

Bridget's features registered her understanding of what Esta's words implied—that *she* had been the mark—but she didn't address the insult.

"You hesitated when I said your name."

Bridget frowned. "I didn't—"

"It wasn't much. And then there was the tiniest tick of a muscle in your cheek. If I hadn't been looking, I wouldn't have seen it at all." Esta conveniently left out the fact that she was always looking, always aware. Professor Lachlan had trained her too well not to be.

Bridget's mouth went tight. Then she spoke to Werner. "Take her to Dolph Saunders. He should be at the Strega this time of night."

At the mention of the name, Esta felt a surge of victory, but she tamped it down. She wouldn't get ahead of herself. Not yet.

"Please . . . ," she said, hesitating when Bridget's eyes narrowed. "Can I have my knife back?"

"What knife?" Bridget asked, her face impassive as flint.

"The one that was in my boot. The one you took."

Bridget's expression never wavered. "After I've saved you from Mr. Corey, after I've offered to help you find protection, you accuse me of stealing from you?"

Esta met Bridget's steady gaze and weighed her options. She needed the knife—the safety and assurance it represented, the link that it was to her own time. But she also needed Bridget Malone to give her an introduction to Dolph Saunders.

Dakari would understand, she told herself.

She'd come back later. There would be time enough to get the knife back.

When she didn't argue any more, Bridget gave her a smug look before addressing Werner again. "If Saunders isn't pleased with her abilities, bring her back here and we'll give her to Mr. Corey." She glanced at Esta, a warning in her expression. "If she tries anything at all, kill her."

A NEW AGE

The Docks

Jack Grew closed his eyes against the throbbing in his head as the carriage rattled onward. Perhaps that last round of drinks had been a mistake. Actually, the entire night had been a mistake, from the beginning to the end . . . though the bit of silk who'd managed to walk away with the contents of his wallet had been worth it, he thought with a small smile. It wasn't like she got away with much anyway. He knew not to bring a heavy wallet to a place like the Haymarket, no matter what the rest of the family currently thought of him.

He'd show them how wrong they were, eventually. It was only a matter of time before his project would be complete, and then his uncle and his cousins and the rest would forget about that unpleasantness in Greece with the girl and recognize his vision. He'd be back in the Order's good graces, and they would have no choice but to give him the respect he deserved.

It wasn't as though he would have *really* married the girl. She'd bespelled him. Tricked him with her power.

Then she'd made off with his grandmother's ring, proving his entire family—including Junior—right. Which, truly, was the one sin he could never forgive her for.

Most days he tried not to think of her—or of the whole mess—but as the carriage rattled on, he couldn't stop the direction of his thoughts. Maybe it was the last round of whiskey, or maybe it was the disaster of the evening, but the memory of his mistakes pulled at him, and he couldn't help but wallow in the past.

He'd gone on his grand tour so naive, so full of expectations. He'd thought he would find great secrets in Europe's hallowed libraries and laboratories to help the work of the Order, but he found a girl instead.

She'd made him believe she was different from the others. For a while he'd been taken in by the sun in her smile and the glimmering promise in her eyes, and he'd started to think that perhaps the Order had misunderstood the threat Mageus posed to the country. But in the end she showed herself to be a miscreant, a criminal like all the others. In the end her betrayal proved that the Order had been right all along. If left unchecked, those with the old magic would take advantage of good people, *normal* people. If left to go free, they would destroy everything in their path.

But, egad, she'd been beautiful. With curves in all the right places and a mouth—

The carriage came to a clattering stop, and Jack grabbed hold to keep from being thrown forward. That last round had *definitely* been a mistake.

"Wait for me," he commanded the driver as he alighted. "I'll be just a minute."

Despite the cold, the air smelled of fish and the heavy metallic tang of oil and machinery. The wind cut harder there, close to the water, so Jack pulled his fur-lined collar up around his neck to ward off the chill as he walked toward his destination, a long, low-slung building nearly indistinguishable from the others. He used his key on the heavy lock and let himself in.

Inside, it wasn't much warmer, but a small stove glowed in the corner where an old man sat hunched over his work, his back to the entrance. Sparks from a welding torch flew up around the man, silhouetting him like a living gargoyle. When the man heard the door slam, he switched off the torch and turned to greet Jack.

"How's it coming?" Jack asked.

The man lifted the heavy welding mask, revealing a face lined by age and scarred by some earlier mishap. "It comes," he said with a shrug.

"How much longer?"

The man considered the question. "A week, maybe more. But you'll need to find a way to stabilize the power it generates before it'll work properly."

Jack frowned. A week wasn't so long, and the Conclave wasn't until the end of the year. He still had time to get it right. Still, with the failures of the night still fresh, impatience scraped at him.

"Let's see how she runs."

The old man frowned. "I haven't connected the receptors. It won't build up a sustained charge—"

"That doesn't matter. I want to see the progress you've made."

Jack walked to the center of the room, where a cloth was draped over a large object. He took the corner and snapped the cloth away, imagining himself in that moment not so long from now when he would make this same movement, revealing his creation, his greatest triumph, to the Order. No one would be laughing at him then.

A large machine gleamed dully in the oil lamp's wavering glow. Wide, orbital arms surrounded its central globe, like a giant gyroscope. Like a gyroscope, it would bring balance.

The body wasn't complete—there were unconnected wires and plugs sprouting from its missing panels—but eventually the machine's inner workings would be covered with sleek, polished steel. A beautiful piece of machinery for a new age. A modern age, free from the threat of the feral and uncontrolled magic of the Mageus.

Jack had been thinking about bringing Harte Darrigan along with him that night to show him the progress he'd made. He had a feeling Darrigan would understand, might even be impressed by what Jack had managed to accomplish in so short a time.

It wasn't enough, though. Jack still hadn't figured out how to contain the energy the machine generated. The Brink could do it, but that was such old, outdated magic. If he could only figure out *how* the Brink did it, Jack could solve his problem, could apply the old methods to his new project.

But the Order kept its secrets close, even from its own members. Until he proved himself, they wouldn't let him into the Mysterium to search for the answers he needed. So he would have to find them for himself.

Jack thought Darrigan might be able to help with that. Considering the amazing feats he'd seen Darrigan do onstage—things that only someone with a deep knowledge and understanding of magic could do—the man must know something that could help Jack solve this last problem.

And Darrigan understood the importance of an audience. Of a little drama. It was what the Ortus Aurea needed—secrecy and small strikes weren't enough. Not anymore. Not with the ever-increasing hordes coming to their shores, and Mageus hidden among them.

What was needed for this new century was a statement of power to prevent the maggots from seeing the city as a haven for their feral magic in the first place. No more simply containing the threat. No more trying to keep them out. It was clear enough that Ellis Island had been a failure. Despite the inspectors, Mageus were still getting in.

No. They had to be eliminated.

He had a feeling that Harte Darrigan would understand that as well, but his cousin had chased him off.

Junior always had been a veritable horse's ass, Jack thought bitterly. So full of his own importance.

"Go on," he told the old man. "Fire it up."

He circled the machine, admiring the metalwork and modernity of it. If it worked—and eventually it *would* work, Jack had no doubt—it would change everything. He would show them all, and then he would be the one to lead the Order into the future.

THE BELLA STREGA

As Werner led her south through the city, the wind whipped like knives tearing at her skirts, but Esta barely felt it. Bridget had told Werner to take her to Dolph Saunders, which meant she was one step closer to her goal.

There weren't many traces of Saunders in the historical records—a journal entry here, a newspaper clipping there. Only whispered rumors had made their way through the years. He was described as a ghost. A madman. A genius. At some point, he'd simply disappeared.

Unlike the other gang bosses, who were only interested in amassing their fellow countrymen and using ties to the old country as a way to recruit, Saunders collected Mageus the way some people collect old coins. But none of the records gave any real answers to how the man managed to bring so many disparate people together under his protection and control—individuals who, by all rights, should have been enemies.

In short, Dolph Saunders had been as powerful as he was mysterious. But whatever he might have been—or might *be*, Esta reminded herself— she needed him. He was the one who'd organized the team to steal the Ortus Aurea's treasures. With Bridget Malone's introduction, Dolph Saunders would be more likely to trust her. But from that point, it would be up to Esta herself to earn a place on that team. From there, she would be working blind.

They continued past theaters with their glittering marquees and restaurants with gilded lettering on their windows. As they walked, she could see the echoes of a future that had not yet arrived—the grids of streets that would remain unchanged through the years, the familiar shapes of buildings that would survive for a century more—but it wasn't a future she could access. She had no way to reach forward through the layers of time and grab hold of the world where she belonged.

As they walked, Werner's posture changed. The comfortable, loping gait he'd had when they'd left the Haymarket went stiff, cautious, and by the time they turned onto the Bowery, the wide street that glowed even more brightly than Broadway, everything about his bearing said he was on guard. Which put Esta on guard as well.

Even in her own time, the Bowery was lined by the shorter buildings characteristic of most of lower Manhattan. Now, elevated train tracks partially obscured them, casting shadows over the people bustling along on the packed sidewalks below. As Werner led her through the crowds, the nearly deafening rumble of a small steam engine shook the heavy metal girders overhead, showering the pedestrians below with soot and filling the air with a cloud of acrid smoke.

They made their way through a crowd gathered around a makeshift table of wooden crates set up beneath the glow of an electric streetlamp. Behind the crates, a boy in a thick scarf and fingerless gloves shuffled cards with the dexterity of a Vegas dealer. Three-card monte, Esta realized, and she couldn't help but smile as she noticed another young boy making his way through the crowd, lifting coins and watches from the spectators as their attention was focused on the sucker losing his money at the table.

Her fingers twitched. It would be so easy to make a living without the countless cameras that watched from every street corner and the wallets filled with plastic cards that could be traced. If she were stuck here for good, maybe it would be okay—

No. She wouldn't let herself even entertain that possibility. She was going to get on Dolph Saunders' team, get the Book *and* Ishtar's Key, and get back to her own city. She wasn't going to be distracted by the promise of a fat wallet. People were depending on her.

Eventually, they reached a corner saloon with an ornate marquee. Brilliant red and white lights spelled out the words BELLA STREGA, and the sign above depicted a woman in black with a waspish waist and dark, cascading hair. Her back was to the street, and she looked over her shoulder, her golden eyes glowing as a smile curved her scarlet lips.

"This is it," Werner said, and Esta thought that he sounded almost nervous about entering.

She followed him through the double doors and practically sighed when the blast of warmth from within hit her frozen face. Cigar smoke hung heavy in the air, and the smell of sweat and old beer was stronger than it had been at the Haymarket.

Along with the stale reek of too many bodies and the cloud of smoke, there was something else about the saloon—a frisson of energy that whispered along her skin and warmed her every bit as much as the coal stove in the corner of the room. It was that same sizzling sensation she'd felt right before Werner had taken the breath from her lungs. Yet another reminder that in this time, magic was different. In her own city, she'd never encountered magic like this, affinities so strong they stirred the very air.

The electric energy was a warning of sorts, but the warmth running across her skin was also a comfort. She had always struggled to feel like she belonged with Professor Lachlan and his team, but as she stepped into Dolph Saunders' lair, Esta felt strangely at home.

Werner pushed Esta ahead of him, toward the back of the saloon, where a man who could only be Dolph held court. He was younger than Esta had expected—he couldn't have been much more than his midtwenties, but his dark hair sported a shock of white that made him seem older at first glance.

Or maybe it was that he carried his authority with an ease that the overdressed boys around him didn't. Dolph was dressed simply, the sleeves of his shirt rolled to expose his strong forearms. One bore the tattoo of a snake that wound around his wrist and crawled up into the arm of his shirt. His hair wasn't slicked back like the other boys, but curled around his lean face, and he wore a patch over one eye that made him look a little like a pirate. Lying across the table in front of him was an ebony cane topped with what looked to be a silver replica of a screaming Medusa.

He wasn't a handsome man. He didn't have the polished charm that Logan cultivated to disarm his marks, but even from across the room Esta could tell Dolph Saunders didn't need something as ordinary as charm to get his way.

"Go on," Werner urged, pushing her forward through the parted crowd.

Esta didn't miss the nervousness in Werner's voice, and she didn't blame him. Though Dolph sat with a slouching indifference, the power he held over the room was obvious from the way everyone seemed oriented toward him. Even those not close to his table tossed furtive glances his way.

Noticing that someone was approaching, Saunders looked up from the conversation he had been having with a light-haired boy sitting next to him. The eye free from the patch was a clear blue, but at their approach, his expression went tight. Her instincts urged her to run, but Esta knew she wouldn't get a second chance, so she stepped forward. Toward the danger he embodied, and toward her only possibility of getting home.

AMBITION AND DESIRE

Dolph Saunders had never liked surprises. He valued the ears and eyes he had around the city, and he paid well for the lips that whispered the secrets many would rather keep silent. So he was less than pleased to see Werner Knopf, Edward Corey's latest lackey, walk into his saloon without so much as a warning.

Dolph glanced at Nibs, who was sitting next to him, but the boy shook his head, an indication that he didn't know the cause for the visit.

Someone was going to pay for this particular surprise. Especially since Werner wasn't alone.

Dolph squinted through the haze of smoke to make out the girl's face. Even with his weakened affinity, he could sense she was powerful. *Another unwelcome surprise.* It was the last thing he needed. Especially now, when he didn't have Leena by his side to neutralize the threat of the girl's magic and when the streets were filled with murmurings about how he had been unable to protect Leena from the Order's power.

There were always murmurings, of course. The new arrivals already carried with them the fears passed down by parents and grandparents who had survived the Disenchantment—the witch hunts and inquisitions that marred Europe's history. In the span of a century, the Mageus had gone from being revered as healers and leaders to being feared by those without affinities. In the span of a century, science and the quest for enlightenment had turned the old magic into a dangerous superstition and the Mageus into pariahs.

Forced to live on the margins of society, they taught their children to hide what they were. Their descendants, desperate for a chance at a different life, believed in the tales told about this city, the promise that magic was protected here. They carried their fears across the seas with them, right alongside their meager parcels, and found themselves trapped.

The girl was new to Dolph, which meant she was new to the city as well, but she didn't seem to be afraid. She didn't vibrate with that same worry and fear of being found out that marked most new arrivals. *Interesting,* he thought, testing the air for some sign of her intentions and finding only desire and ambition. Both admirable qualities—but also dangerous, depending on who wielded them.

He tightened his grip on his cane and, making certain a scowl was firmly in place, he leaned forward to greet Werner and his guest.

"Who's this?" he asked in the boy's native German.

"Bridget found her," Werner replied with a nod to the girl. "Thought you might be interested."

The girl was tall and stood with a straightness that indicated an internal strength he looked for in members of his crew. She had chestnut-brown hair that framed a heart-shaped face and a straight nose that was a bit too long to be called delicate, but that suited her. Her dark brows winged over honey-colored eyes that looked like they knew too much. But those eyes were innocent just the same. A mark against her—innocence didn't do well in his world.

He motioned for Werner to come forward and bent his head so the boy could whisper in his ear about the girl—about how she'd nearly killed Charlie Murphy, a fellow so deep in Tammany's pocket, he'd never find his way out. About how the girl hadn't confessed what her affinity was, but that she'd stolen the brooch from right beneath Bridget Malone's chin and the madam hadn't been able to lift a finger to stop her. Hadn't even seen her take it.

All interesting enough. But again, dangerous considering the fragile state of his own affinity these days.

"Do you know who I am?" he asked, watching every minute flicker of her expression.

The girl was silent before she spoke, but when she did, her voice was clear, deferent but not cowed. "Miss Malone said you were someone who could offer protection."

Once he might have been able to read her as easily as an open book, but even with his weakened affinity, he could taste the lie in her words. She knew exactly who he was but wasn't trying to sway him with overblown praise, as many would have.

"Why would I waste my time doing a thing like that?" he asked, curious about how her voice seemed to suggest fear but not own it. She was either a brilliant actress or someone had taught her—and taught her well.

"I'm a good worker. I'd be loyal to you," she pressed.

"You'd have to be damn near a miracle considering the trouble you'd cause me if I took you on. Charlie Murphy wouldn't be pleased, and the last thing I want right now is Tammany Hall after me."

In truth, Charles Murphy and everyone like him could go sit on his own thumb as far as Dolph was concerned. Those stuffed pigeons at Tammany thought they ran the city. Let them keep thinking it, Dolph had always said to any who worried. The truth would always out. Tammany could chase paper and manufacture votes—he had other plans.

"I can make it worth your while," the girl said, straightening her spine. She was nearly as tall as Werner when she stood at her full height.

"I have more than enough dips right now," he said after weighing his choices. He glanced to Werner. "Send her back to Corey."

"*No,*" the girl said as she twisted violently and freed herself from Werner. "You don't have any like me."

The crowd around him went still and watchful at the commotion as she managed to evade the boy's attempt to grab her again.

Dolph raised a hand for him to wait, and the girl stepped closer to his table.

"I can steal anything," she said. "My marks never see me coming or going. I've never once been caught. *Never.*"

It didn't take any magic to see there was no lie in her words this time.

Again, Dolph tried to sense the flavor of her affinity. Before that night on the bridge, it would have been an easy enough thing to accomplish, but not anymore. The barroom was too full of magic for him to separate the girl's from the others.

"You *need* me," she added, pushing a loose piece of hair out of her eyes.

He huffed out a breath, amused. She must have known that he could take everything she held dear and twist it to breaking, but still she wasn't afraid. It took quite a bit to impress him, but Dolph Saunders thought this girl might have enough backbone to do just that. Maybe if things weren't so precarious.

Nibs cleared his throat.

Dolph frowned at the interruption. He would have made an example of anyone else, but Nibsy was rarely wrong about his impulses. And at the moment Nibs was eyeing the girl thoughtfully.

"You think we should keep her?" Dolph asked.

"What could it hurt to see what she can do?" He glanced over at Dolph. "She might have her uses."

Dolph turned to the girl. "I doubt you're anything special," he said, a bold-faced lie. But best make sure the girl didn't know he was too interested. "Still . . . if Bridget thinks you might be of help—"

Before he could finish speaking, the lights in the barroom surged, glowing so brightly that many of those drinking at the bar and at tables around the room squinted, raising their arms to shield themselves from the glow. The lights pulsed twice, the energy in the room flickering and crackling, and then the electric in the barroom went out completely.

The city was used to the power surges and outages that came with the ever-growing expansion of the electrical grid, but this had been something more. The second the room had plunged into darkness, he felt like what little remaining magic he had was gone.

For a moment he felt the shock of being hollowed out. *Empty*. Like a living death.

It had lasted less than a minute, but the stark terror he'd experienced when his magic was briefly torn from him left a coldness behind that went clear to the bone. Even after the lamps were lit and the room was aglow, his skin still felt chilled despite the stuffy warmth of the saloon.

A BAD BUSINESS

Viola Vaccarelli watched as the lamps around the edges of the saloon were lit, illuminating the apprehensive expressions of the patrons. She understood the nervous glances they traded with one another, because she'd felt it too. The blackout had been something more than the usual inconvenience.

Dolph caught her eye from across the room. He was already making his way through the uneasy crowd to where she stood behind the bar.

Leaning on the bar for support, he spoke in low tones, as though he didn't want anyone else to hear. "You felt that?"

Viola made a pretense of polishing a glass, but gave him a subtle nod as she kept her attention on the room, alert for any sign of attack. "What was it?" she murmured low enough so the patrons at the bar couldn't hear.

Behind her, a man called for another drink, but she ignored him and set a glass in front of Dolph instead.

"No idea."

But she didn't miss the way his hand tightened on the cane. Ever since the night on the bridge, the night they lost Leena, Dolph had been changed. She knew the loss had been a blow, but there had to be something more to have made him so different. Where once he never betrayed his worries, now he was often on edge.

The customer down the bar was whistling now, hooting to get Viola's attention as he thumped his glass on the counter. "Hey! You hear me or what, puttana?" the man called.

Dolph glanced over and began to push himself away from the bar, but Viola tapped his arm and shook her head slightly. She didn't need protection, at least not from some drunken stronzo making a nuisance of himself.

"Scusa," she said, her other hand already finding the familiar cool weight of the knife she had tucked into her skirts. "I'll be right back."

"Try not to kill him too badly," Dolph said, pulling away from her and smiling softly into his glass.

Viola made sure she had the man's attention before she gave him a slow, warm smile. He elbowed the customer sitting next to him, gloating at his success, as she began to approach him. She let him think she was interested, amused even at his antics, and with the smile still on her face, she drew the knife and with a flick of her wrist sent it sailing through the air.

The satisfying *thunk* of it finding a sheath in the cast zinc vibrated down the length of the bar, and she didn't hide her laugh at the look of surprised horror that flashed across the man's face. She took her time closing the distance between them to retrieve her blade, and when she finally made it to the end of the bar, she leaned across to whisper a warning into his ear.

When she pulled back, away from the rank stink of his body and the beer on his breath, she saw that the man's face had all but drained of color. *Va bene.* Good.

"Thank you for not skewering him," Dolph said with a hint of humor when she returned.

Viola made a throaty sound of disapproval under her breath. "You've told me it's a bad business to kill the customers, no?" she said tartly. She had trouble controlling her accent when she was angry, and for a moment she heard her mother in her own voice and felt a fierce pang of longing.

"I appreciate you watching out for my bottom line," Dolph mused. "Perhaps you could also watch out for my property? I'll have to pay to repair what you've done to my bar." He frowned thoughtfully. "I'm not even sure I *can* repair the mark that knife of yours left."

Viola shrugged off his concern. "Leave it as a warning," she said, picking up another glass to distract herself.

"I might," he said after a second.

She could practically feel him watching her, as he often did when he was trying to press her into opening up to him. But she didn't have anything to say. What was done was done. She'd made her choices, and if she had regrets, she'd save them for Father McGean.

"What sort of game was that trick with the lights?" At first the voice seemed to come out of nowhere, but then Jianyu materialized next to Dolph, his elbows resting on the bar as though he'd been there all along.

He probably had been, Viola thought with some irritation. Jianyu's ability to disappear was a skill that came in handy when Dolph needed to know things, but it was less opportune for the rest of them. In Dolph's crew, it was nearly impossible to keep secrets—no matter how personal they might be.

Jianyu had been with them only a little over a year. Maybe Dolph trusted the boy after so short a time, but Viola was still uneasy around him. Especially when he looked as humorless as he did then.

Dolph lowered his voice and slipped into Cantonese, and the two went back and forth for a moment in tense, low tones, effectively keeping Viola from their conversation. As her frustration—and temper—began to grow, she thumped the glass down to get their attention, but they were too engrossed in their argument to notice.

Just as she'd finally had enough and was about to say something, Jianyu's posture changed. "You really think it could have been the Order?" he asked, doubt thick in his voice. "It doesn't seem their style to strike so broadly. Too much risk that it would affect more than our kind."

Viola hated to admit it, but . . . "He's right. The Order usually prefers to strike in secret."

"I don't know what else it could have been," Dolph admitted. "There's been no word on the streets?"

Jianyu shook his head. "Not even a whisper."

"I don't like it," Viola said. "Nothing good happens when the rats all go to ground."

"I agree," Jianyu said, giving Viola an appreciative glance. Then he tilted his head to gesture across the room. "Who's the girl? I saw her come in with Werner. She moves like a cat about to pounce."

Viola couldn't keep herself from smiling at the aptness of the description.

"Bridget sent her." Dolph downed the rest of the ale and passed the glass back to Viola. "Tells me she's a thief."

"You have enough of those already," Viola said, dismissing the idea as easily as Dolph had.

"Bridget doesn't usually waste my time. Nibs thinks she might be of use."

"You will try her?" Jianyu asked.

Dolph squinted across the room to where Werner and the girl stood. "Yes. I think I will," he said. "Profits have been down lately, especially with the last raid. If she can work the Dead Line undetected, she could be an asset."

The girl didn't look like much. She was tall, yes, and she held herself with a calmness that Werner certainly didn't have. But her clothes were too fine, her skin too fresh and soft. It took strength to last in Dolph Saunders' world, and from across the room, Viola wasn't sure the girl had it.

"And if she can't?" Viola asked, almost feeling sorry for her.

"It won't be my loss, now, will it?"

No, it wouldn't be, Viola thought. Dolph was good to his people and did what he could to protect them. Certainly he'd feel regret about her loss, as he did about Spot and Appo . . . and certainly he mourned Leena still. But he valued those who could take care of themselves.

In that way he wasn't that different from the other bosses. In the Bowery it wasn't always a matter of good and evil. Often it was a matter of what you could live with. What—or who—you were willing to sacrifice to survive. It was a lesson she'd learned well enough herself.

THE LAST MAGICIAN   133

Dolph clapped Jianyu on the shoulder. "I need information. If it was the Order, they'll be celebrating. Someone will slip up."

Jianyu finished his drink. "I will look into it myself."

Dolph tilted his head toward Viola, who came closer. "That girl—I want you to keep an eye on her for me tonight, eh? She'll have no second chance here."

TO STEAL THE NIGHT

Esta watched Dolph Saunders make his way back across the sawdust-covered floor of the saloon to where she and Werner waited. He walked unevenly, putting his weight on the cane he held in his left hand, but Esta didn't mistake that for a weakness. Not with the way patrons parted for him without a word as he passed.

And not with the way the two at the bar had followed his every move, like he was the center of their universe. The girl behind the bar didn't look much older than Esta herself, maybe seventeen. Then there was the boy who had appeared, it seemed, out of nowhere. One minute the space next to Dolph had been empty, and then in a blink, the boy had materialized.

He wore his black hair in a long braid down his back in an older style she'd seen in Chinatown when she'd stolen the Dragon's Eye. He was dressed in the style of the day: close-fitting vest and trim pants, but his black shirt was made of silk and had a mandarin collar. Like the girl, he clearly had talents of his own, but even from across the barroom, Esta could tell from his posture that he held a wary respect for Dolph.

"My apologies," Dolph said, taking his seat at the small round table once more and pinning them with his one-eyed stare.

"The lights—" Werner shifted into anxious German, as though to keep Esta from understanding.

"It happens," Dolph said, cutting him off.

But Esta understood it was a lie. The flare of the lights had been something more than an outage. It wasn't that Dolph Saunders had any visible tell—he kept his voice calm, his posture easy and still—but with the unease permeating the barroom, the man's stillness spoke volumes.

He turned to Esta and shifted back into the unaccented English he'd originally spoken in. "I've decided to give you a trial."

She bobbed her head in acknowledgment and thanks, keeping all trace of the victory she was feeling from her expression. She was one step closer to her goal.

"Don't be so pleased with yourself. Not yet, at least," he growled. "It's been a slow night, and I've seen at least fifteen leave already because of that trick of the lights. Nobody else is going to come in this late, especially with the power still out. If you're going to work for me, the thing you need to know before we begin is that I hate to lose and I can't stand waste. Tonight will be both—a loss of profit and a waste of my employees' talents. Rectify that. You've got twenty minutes to turn me a profit for this evening." He leaned forward, a gleam in his eye. "Steal me the night, girl."

Esta couldn't help but smile. *Steal me the night*, like it was an impossible task. Like she hadn't been born to do exactly that.

Her limbs might have still felt drained, and the back of her head still ached from whatever they'd hit her with earlier, but her blood was free of the opium's effects now, so without a word she turned and lost herself in the crowd. Even with the electric lights still out, there was barely room to step between the bleary-eyed men and women who stared morosely into their cups. Easy pickings, really.

But these weren't the sort of marks Esta usually gravitated to. They had a desperation hanging about them, an air of exhaustion and hope and regret all mingled with the warmth of their magic. They probably worked long hours to afford what little relaxation an evening at the Strega could give them. She wouldn't steal from them. Not even for Dolph Saunders.

Besides, she had the sense it wouldn't be enough to bring him a pile of their coins. To earn his respect and a place in his world, it would take more than money.

From behind the bar, the girl watched, tracking her through the barroom with subtle adjustments but never actually looking in Esta's direction. No doubt Dolph had instructed her to keep an eye on her . . . which gave Esta an idea.

It didn't take her twenty minutes, but the opium had drained her more than she'd expected, and it took every bit of her energy to slip through time undetected as she made her way around the saloon, selecting her prizes. It was barely twelve minutes later when she faced Dolph Saunders once again.

"You've got more time," he said, barely glancing up at her. "I told you, I can't abide waste."

In reply, she tossed a fat leather wallet onto the table, the money within spilling out of the unlocked clasp. The eyes of the man standing behind Dolph went wide in recognition, and he reached into his coat, searching for the wallet that was sitting in front of him.

Dolph watched as the man picked up the wallet and counted the bills inside. Then he turned back to Esta, unimpressed. "With more time, you could have brought me twice as much."

"I can only bring you what they're carrying, and in this crowd, that isn't much," she told him easily. "If I take all of it, what will they have left to buy your drinks with?"

Dolph Saunders frowned before glancing up at Werner. "Tell Bridget I can't use her."

Esta ignored him. She pulled out a brightly polished brass disk she'd taken from the guy who'd appeared at the bar and set it on the table. It turned out he wasn't actually invisible. When she slowed time, she could see that he'd simply been manipulating the light and shadows of the room, bending them around him to make it seem like he'd disappeared.

Dolph Saunders stared at the disk. "Impressive. Though you can buy these anywhere over on Mott Street these days."

"I haven't been to Mott Street today. Do they sell these there as well?" She tossed a gleaming silver knife with a thin stiletto blade onto the table before he could finish. It slid across the scarred wooden surface and came to a rest in front of him, the sharp point aimed directly at him. The bare tang of the knife had a series of arrowlike marks like the letter *V* cut into the metal.

Dolph Saunders looked up at Esta then, piercing her with that too-steady gaze of his. "You must not value your life to steal from Viola."

"On the contrary—I value myself too much to do anything less." She leaned forward, propping herself on the table so they were eye to eye. "I can steal you all the coins you want. Even if I'd taken every penny from every pocket here tonight, there would have still been room for you to doubt my value. But I can do more for you than steal a few dollars. Like I said . . ." She pulled out her final coup and held it up so the entire table could see. "I can steal anything. No one can catch me. Not your crew . . ." With that, she gently set the silver gorgon head in front of Dolph. "Not even you."

Dolph Saunders picked up the piece that had, moments before, been securely attached to the top of his cane. His features were unreadable as he examined it and confirmed that, indeed, she'd managed to steal the carved silver face from right under his nose. Right out from his hands, to be exact. Then he looked up at her with that cold, single-eyed stare.

Esta shifted uneasily. For the first time all evening, she thought maybe she had gone too far. Maybe she should have stopped with the barmaid's knife. A strange circle of silence surrounded Dolph Saunders' table, as though everyone who'd remained could sense that something in the air had changed—and not for the better.

But then Dolph huffed out an almost amused breath, and his hard mouth turned up slightly into what might have been a smile. It changed something in his face—not that it made him look less intimidating. A smile on Dolph Saunders was like one on a tiger: surprising, unsettling, and most of all, a reminder that the cat had teeth.

He took his time refitting the knob onto his case, shaking his head again as he examined the completed piece. Then he glanced over at the boy next to him, who gave a barely perceptible nod. "Thank Bridget for me," Dolph said finally. "I'll take the girl on. For now, at least."

Werner backed away from the table, but any relief she might have felt was quickly erased by the realization that she was now alone with Dolph Saunders and the rough-looking boys standing behind his table. They were all built like boxers, and their tailored vests were cut to emphasize their trim waists and wide shoulders. Each boy wore a common uniform of an outlandishly bright shirt and a derby hat cocked to the left over his slicked-back hair.

Not boys, Esta reminded herself. In this city, even boys no older than fifteen would have been men for years. Each would have earned their swagger by surviving childhood, and then by finding and keeping a place in an organization like the Devil's Own. She'd be an idiot to mistake their youth for innocence. Or to forget how dangerous their world had made them.

"What's your name, girl?" Dolph said, peering up at her.

"Esta. Esta Filosik."

"Filosik? I don't know that name. Where are your people?"

"I don't know," she said, giving him the truth. "I never knew them."

Dolph clenched his jaw and studied her. "If you bring me any trouble—"

"I won't," she interrupted.

He waited a second longer, and the whole barroom seemed to be holding its breath, waiting for his final pronouncement.

Dolph motioned for one of the boys to come forward, a ginger-haired guy who was dressed in a red shirt that clashed with his pale, freckled skin. The boy's tightly fitted vest emphasized his broad, stocky shoulders, and a ridiculous-looking cravat was tied in a complicated knot at his throat. His outfit made him look like he was playing at being a gentleman, but a winding tattoo barely visible at the top edge of his collar contradicted the look. The mark on his neck looked like the top of a circle—a wide, ornate arc that clearly had more to it—but Esta couldn't make out any detail in the dimly lit barroom.

"Mooch here'll show you to your room," Dolph informed her when he was done speaking to the boy. "Tomorrow you start working the Dead Line. Don't make me regret it."

THE DEAD LINE

The next morning Esta was already awake and dressed in the same green velvet she'd worn the day before—the only clothing she had left—when the dull *thump* sounded at the door. She opened it to find a familiar silver knife sunk into the wood and the girl with dark hair—and an even darker expression—waiting in the hall.

The barmaid from the night before stepped forward and pried her knife from the door. She was about a head shorter than Esta and dressed in a simple skirt and plain-fronted blouse instead of the low-cut gown she'd been wearing when Esta had stolen her stiletto. Her eyes were the most startling shade of deep violet, and a mass of wavy hair was pinned into a loose knot at the nape of her neck. Her wide, soft mouth was pulled down into a disapproving frown.

"My name is Viola," she said with a low, throaty voice that still carried the faintest hint of her native Italian. She made a show of cleaning the tip of her blade and didn't bother to look at Esta when she spoke. "I don't like you. Dolph, he tells me not to kill you for taking my knife, so I won't. *This* time." She finally lifted her violet gaze, pointing the razor-sharp tip of the blade at Esta as she spoke. "But don't test me again. Capisce?"

Esta raised her hands to signal her understanding.

Viola slid the knife back into the slit in the side of her skirt before handing her a worn wool cloak and giving a jerk of her head. "Come. We'll get you something to fill your belly. Today you work the Dead Line."

Viola took her downstairs to the Strega's kitchen and introduced her to Tilly Malkov, a girl with mouse-brown hair. Tilly offered Esta a hunk of hard, crusty bread, a cup of burnt coffee swimming with cream, and a welcoming smile that crinkled the corners of her soft green eyes.

Esta took the seat at the large kitchen table that Tilly offered her, but as she picked at her bread, she kept a watchful eye on Viola.

After a few minutes, Tilly surprised Esta by touching her hand. "Don't worry so much," she said. As she spoke, a tingling warmth spread like sunshine on a summer's day over Esta's skin. She gave an amused nod toward Viola. "That one isn't so bad. She's all honey and no sting," she said with a wink.

Esta pulled her hand away, feeling unaccountably better, more relaxed, but also more on edge.

"Don't listen to her. Libitina here stings just fine," Viola told her, spinning the point of her stiletto knife on the tabletop with a menacing look in her eyes.

"You named your knife," Esta said, amused even as Viola glared. "*Of course* you named your knife."

The mouse-haired girl only smiled and shook her head, dismissing them both as she wiped her hands on her apron and went back to work at the stove. Viola continued to scowl as she polished her blade, but Esta didn't miss the way Viola's eyes followed Tilly's every move. Or the way her cheeks flushed anytime Tilly glanced up with a warm smile.

When they were finished eating, Viola led Esta out the back entrance of the saloon, onto Elizabeth Street. The snow from the day before was starting to melt, leaving the streets and sidewalks a murky mess that already smelled of the manure and garbage the banks of snow had covered.

"So . . . ," Esta began, in an attempt to break their awkward silence. She pulled the borrowed cloak around her, glad for its warmth. "You and Tilly . . . ?"

Viola turned on her sharply, her expression fierce.

"Sorry," Esta said, realizing her misstep. "It's just . . . the way you watched her," she tried to explain. "I thought maybe——"

"We're friends," Viola snapped, but her cheeks had gone pink again, and Viola wasn't the type of girl who wore a blush well.

"Of course you are," Esta corrected. "My mistake," she said, feeling a sudden ambivalence. She knew better than to let her own modern sensibilities affect her on a job. It was sloppy of her, dangerous. But behind the censure in Viola's eyes was fear . . . maybe even sadness?

Viola stomped off again without another word on the matter.

It was easy enough to keep up with Viola's shorter strides, but harder to let it go. After a block of walking in silence except for the crunch of the snow beneath their feet, Esta couldn't stand the rigid set of Viola's shoulders anymore. "For what it's worth," she said softly without slowing their pace, "she seems wonderful."

Viola stopped short. "Yes," Viola agreed, tossing a wary look toward Esta. "She is." She waited another two heartbeats, as if daring Esta to push again, before she turned and continued down the bustling sidewalk. But this time her steps were softer and her expression didn't have the same wariness as it had moments before.

Unlike the wide boulevard that was the Bowery, Elizabeth Street was a narrow jumble of redbrick buildings all butted up against one another. The shops were opening for the day, and the shopkeepers had already started rolling carts of merchandise out to the sidewalks. Above their cluttered display windows, fire escapes clung to the sides of the buildings. Long underwear and shirts fluttered from them like invisible people who had decided to stop to lean against the railings and watch the scene below.

"The first rule," Viola said, drawing herself up as though the whole conversation about Tilly had never happened, "is you don't take from our own. You work the cars or the streets north of Houston. You work the Line and the banks, but you don't dip into pockets Dolph protects. The second rule, you don't cross any of the other bosses. Dolph works hard to keep Paul Kelly and Monk Eastman off his people. He don't need you messing that up."

"How will I know who's who?"

Viola gave her an impatient scowl. "You'll figure it out. One way or another."

The two went a couple of blocks farther and then cut over a block to where a horse-drawn streetcar rattled to a stop at a curb nearby. Viola opened the door at the back of the bus-shaped vehicle and directed Esta inside. After Viola placed a couple of coins into a battered metal box at the front of the car, they found seats on the two narrow wooden benches along the length of the smudged windows. With the windows closed against the cold, the car smelled strongly of the tobacco spit that stained the floor and the sharp, metallic reek of motor oil.

Outside, the bright signs of the dance halls and glittering windows of cheap jewelry stores gave way to more sedate shops, each piled with canned goods and household items. Then they turned onto Canal Street, past the legendary prison built to look like an Egyptian tomb.

"Have you been with Dolph long?" Esta asked.

Viola glanced at her out of the corner of her eye. "Long enough," she said, turning her attention back to the street passing outside the window.

"And you like working for him?" Esta tried again.

At first Viola seemed to ignore the question, but then, just when Esta thought she wouldn't answer, she turned. "Look. We're probably not gonna be friends, you and me. I don't need any more friends. I don't need the chitchat the ladies make with each other over the weather or the price of meat. I work for Dolph because I want to work, and he lets me. Do I like it?" she said with a shrug. "I'm not married to some fat idiota, having his babies one after another, am I? I work hard, maybe, but I'm good at what I do. Dolph gives me that much. What else is there to like?"

"Nothing," Esta murmured her understanding. She knew what it was to need to feel useful. If Professor Lachlan hadn't found her, she'd probably be unaware of what she was, what she could do. She couldn't imagine what it would be like to never feel the deep, echoing satisfaction of a job well done. To simply be ordinary—or worse, a freak in her world, where magic was nothing more than a bedtime story. Maybe Professor Lachlan had never been what anyone would call an affectionate father, but he'd given her that much.

About fifteen minutes into the jarring ride, the streetcar slowed next to a curb, and Viola gestured for Esta to get out.

"We're at City Hall," Esta said, recognizing the building.

Viola made a dismissive sound in her throat. "We gonna walk a little farther, and then you go on your own."

"On my own?" Esta blinked, surprised at this pronouncement. She'd assumed Viola had been sent to watch her.

"You told Dolph you're a good thief, no?"

"Yes . . . ," Esta said slowly, not liking where this was going.

"The tricks you did last night don't prove nothing. You want Dolph's protection? Then you earn it by working the Line." Viola pointed down the street they were walking. "It used to be good pickings down on Wall Street with all the bankers. Fat wallets. Lots of gold and jewels. Easy items to fence. But a few years back, Inspector Byrnes drew the Dead Line.

"Byrnes is gone, but the Line's still there. Downtown, they pick up any known pickpocket on sight. Dolph loses a lot of his boys that way. But you're new, and you say you can steal anything?" She shrugged. "So you'll work the Dead Line. Maybe you won't get caught."

"And if I do?"

Viola glanced at her, indifferent. "My advice? You don't get caught. The Tombs isn't a place for a girl, not even a big girl like you," Viola said, cocking a mocking brow toward Esta.

They walked on down Park Row, past the towering double turrets of a castlelike building looming above them, and then on past a lonely-looking cemetery, its tombstones like broken teeth sticking out from the remaining snow. When they rounded the corner, Esta found herself staring up at the brownish-gray exterior of St. Paul's.

"This is as far as I go," Viola said, coming to a stop near the deep covered portico of the chapel. "They know me there, but you keep walking, three, maybe four blocks thataway, and you'll find the bankers. Should be easy to make your quota if you're half as good as you claim. If you don't come back . . ." She shrugged. "You'll find your way, or we won't have to worry about you no more."

AS ABOVE, SO BELOW

Viola was right. South of Fulton Street, the city's financial district was heaven for a thief. Bankers and lawyers with fat wallets and jeweled pins. Women with purses filled with coins. Easy pickings.

And a complete waste of time.

Even without using her affinity, it didn't take her long to get her quota and then some. Less than an hour later, she'd found her way back to a streetcar heading north and was on her way uptown.

She still wore the empty silver cuff under the sleeve of her gown, a reminder of what was at stake, of what she had to do. All night, she'd tossed and turned in the narrow, musty-smelling bed—if you could even call it that—thinking about her missing stone. Planning her next move.

Professor Lachlan had warned her it was too much of a risk to change anything about the heist, but he hadn't known—or hadn't warned her— that Ishtar's Key would basically incinerate. She hadn't planned on being trapped in the past.

She was already working blind when it came to Dolph Saunders. She needed more information, more options in case things didn't go as planned, because *nothing* could stop her from getting Ishtar's Key. Not when the future held Dakari, shot and possibly dying. No one would come looking for him, not until he didn't return and it was too late.

According to the clipping she'd lifted from Professor Lachlan's notebook, Khafre Hall was located on Park Avenue. In her own time, that part of Park Avenue was an elevated road leading into Grand Central, but in 1902, the gleaming white facade of the terminal didn't exist. If the world of lower Manhattan felt eerily familiar earlier that morning, the streets of Midtown looked like a completely different world. The soaring skyscrapers that would one day box in the sky weren't even a dream yet. Instead, the avenue was lined by shorter, ornately decorated buildings— stately homes and large hotels, and just north of Forty-First Street, the enormous edifice that was Khafre Hall.

The Order's headquarters might have been named for one of the great pyramids, but with its four stories of white marble, it looked more like a transplanted villa from the Italian Renaissance. Esta didn't have any doubt she'd found the right place, though. High atop the roof, gold statues of various gods glinted beneath the winter's sun. Above the building's main entrance, the cornice was carved with the words AS ABOVE, SO BELOW, a phrase supposedly coined by Hermes Trismegistus, the mythic combination of the Greek god Hermes and the Egyptian Thoth that the Order saw as its precursor. The heavy bronze doors were inscribed with a symbol Esta recognized easily as the Philosopher's Hand—an alchemical recipe depicting the secrets of unlocking occult powers.

Professor Lachlan had taught her all this as part of her training. He'd shown her the different representations of the hand to teach her about the theories of alchemy, to explain how the Order misunderstood and perverted the very notion of magic by trying to divide existence into neat parts in their efforts to control it.

The building was impressive, a declaration of the Order's beliefs and a demonstration of their power in this city. The fact that they never rebuilt after the theft of the artifacts was evidence of how much they'd been weakened. But the building as it was now served as a reminder of all she would have to face. Of all she still had left to lose. Even from her vantage point across the street, it looked impenetrable.

The street was quiet, so she took the clipping from its hidden pocket to look over it again for some clue of what had happened. But when she unfolded the delicate paper, the once-clear type looked blurred, smudged. The individual letters seemed to wriggle and writhe on the page, like they were trying to transform themselves into other letters, to rearrange themselves into other words.

Esta blinked hard and rubbed at her tired eyes, sure that she must be seeing things, but when she looked back, the words remained stubbornly unreadable. It was as though the future that had once been an established fact was no longer clear or determined. The heist was no longer an established fact.

"No," she whispered to herself as she brought the paper closer to her eyes. Like she didn't have perfect eyesight. Like getting closer would do something to stop the words from swirling and shifting on the page.

She hadn't done anything wrong . . . had she?

"You!" The voice came from so close that she barely had time to turn before the man from the night before had ahold of her wrist. His face was blackened and bruised from her brutal attempt to escape, but now a hideously gleeful expression lit his features. "I thought that was you."

She tried to jerk away, using her erratic motions as a cover for the way she crumpled the clipping and slipped it into her sleeve. "Let me go," she demanded, struggling against him. "I don't want to hurt you again." And the last thing she wanted was to draw attention from anyone inside Khafre Hall.

Charlie Murphy only laughed and started tugging her across the street. "You won't have the chance to hurt me again, not when I'm through with you." He laughed again, and his grip on her wrist tightened as he wrenched her arm painfully, pulling her close enough that she could smell the sourness of his breath.

"Let me go," she said, refusing to plead.

"I know what you are. I recognized what you did at the Haymarket," he said with an almost unholy anticipation lighting his face. "I'd planned to hunt for you. I was looking forward to seeing the fear in your eyes when we found you."

"So sorry to disappoint," she snarled, grabbing the arm he held her wrist with. Calling on every one of the techniques Dakari had taught her, she twisted violently. The move caught him by surprise, as she'd intended, and he released her with a yelp of pain.

But it only slowed him for a moment. The look of anticipation he'd worn moments ago was now transformed to seething hate. She needed to get away, but before she could pull time to a slow, Murphy's eyes went wide. He went completely rigid before collapsing hard and motionless to the ground.

The way his body had jerked and then fallen had jarred her enough that she'd lost her hold on time, and before she could regain it, her arms were pinned to her sides and she was surrounded by an earthy, spicy scent that reminded her of patchouli. A soft, disembodied voice whispered in her ear to be still, and Esta realized that maybe Dolph hadn't let her go off alone after all.

THE CURRENCY OF SECRETS

Dolph had been right to be suspicious of the new girl. What business could she possibly have here at Khafre Hall?

With her arms wrapped around her, pinning her in place, Jianyu could practically hear her thinking. Her whole body had gone tense and ready to fight, and he was not so stupid as to underestimate her. He'd seen the way she'd dispensed of Murphy, and he didn't doubt she had something equally unpleasant in mind for him. She was no innocent, fresh off the boat and adrift in a dangerous city. She was too well trained.

"Unless you want Dolph to know of this, be still," he whispered.

The girl hesitated, but a moment later the fight went out of her, enough that he could guide her down the street, away from the watching eyes of Khafre Hall. The moment they were around the corner, he let go of the light and revealed himself.

He didn't release her arm, though.

"You followed me?" she asked, eyeing him.

"Did you expect you wouldn't be watched? Dolph Saunders doesn't trust easily, and for good reason, it appears. Why did you come here?"

"I was going for a walk," she said flatly. "It's a beautiful day."

"So you took a stroll in front of Khafre Hall?" he asked, amused.

Her mouth went tight, but she didn't answer. Yes, she was well trained indeed to keep so composed when she'd clearly been caught red-handed. She had to know that lies would be pointless now.

"Why aren't you still working? The sun is barely at midday."

"I'm done," she said.

It didn't seem to be a lie, but she hadn't been downtown long enough to be finished. Especially without magic. He'd followed her, concealing himself carefully, and he hadn't so much as sensed a whisper of her affinity. "Your quota was thirty-five dollars. That's more than most men make in a month," he said.

"I can show you my purse if you don't believe me. But you'll have to let me go so I can get to it." She glanced up at him, a sly look in her eyes. "It's under my skirts."

"It doesn't explain why you're here, at the Order's hall," he said, not taking the bait.

Her expression was steady. "I wanted to see it for myself."

"Why?" he pressed, not yet sensing a lie.

"Don't you want to know your enemy?" she asked.

"The Order, you see them as your enemy?"

"You don't?" She threw the question back at him.

But Jianyu didn't answer. He didn't owe her his story. "I'm going to release you, and then we are going to return to the Bella Strega."

"You'll tell Dolph about what happened, won't you?" she asked, frowning.

"Not if you come quietly." When surprise bunched her expression, he explained. "I find it to be more beneficial at this moment to have you in my debt."

"I'm not sure I want to be in your debt."

He inclined his head. "An astute observation. Feel free to tell Dolph yourself, then, about how you wandered off from your assigned post and were almost caught by a member of the Order outside Khafre Hall."

From the look on her face, he knew it would never happen.

"Of course, you could try to fight me, or you could attempt to run off. In that case, I will tell Dolph everything. You will not be in my debt, but you will also never be safe in this city again. Not with Dolph Saunders and his people looking for you."

She frowned. "I don't like being threatened."

"No one does," he told her. "Though if you truly mean us no harm, my words pose no threat."

Her expression was still shuttered and angry, but also intelligent. He could tell the moment she understood she had very little choice. "Fine," she said sourly. "I'm Esta, by the way. You should probably know my name if you plan on blackmailing me."

He let go of her arm. "I am Jianyu Lee. And I already knew your name."

Esta frowned, looking down at her wrist as though she expected to find some mark. "Great. Glad we got that cleared up," she muttered. Glancing up at him, she made a small flourish with her hand. "Well, what are we waiting for? Lead the way."

When they arrived back at the Strega, Dolph Saunders was sitting in his usual place in the back of a full barroom. Jianyu knew the crowd wasn't there to drink, though.

He sensed the girl's curiosity as she watched the men and women approach Dolph's table, one by one.

It wasn't an unfamiliar scene in the poorest neighborhoods. All of the gang bosses traded in favors and kept their people in line through their debts. Jianyu's uncle, at least in name, often held court in a similar way. On Mott Street, Tom Lee collected bribe money to keep the police away from fan-tan dealers and to provide protection from the Hip Sing highbinders. It was only a small part of the life of Chinatown, but it was one Jianyu knew too well. And one he hated.

He'd come to this country, to this city, because Lee promised him a better future than he'd had in his own country, but he'd arrived to find that Lee had smuggled him into the country not to help him but to use him. With his affinity for light, he could make himself impossible to see, which meant he could strike without warning. But he hadn't left his home, his mother, and everything else behind to be a mercenary for a common criminal like Tom Lee.

Jianyu still didn't know how much he approved of Dolph Saunders' methods, but it was clear that he was different from Tom Lee. The people filling the Strega weren't like those his uncle exploited. They came hat in hand, each with the same stoop to their shoulders that made them look as though they were perpetually carrying some invisible burden. Each would speak with Dolph for a few moments, usually some plea to find a son or for help with their rent or for relief from some other burden.

Debts came due, certainly, but at least Jianyu was never asked to collect on them.

After a minute Dolph looked up and saw them standing at the back of the room. He said something to Nibs, who got up and started making his way through the crowded barroom.

Nibs nodded a silent greeting to Jianyu before turning his attention to the girl.

"You're done already?" he asked, doubtful.

The girl maneuvered her hand through a concealed slit in her skirts and pulled out a small purse. Nibs opened the parcel and thumbed through its contents before lifting his gaze to Dolph and giving him a slight nod.

"I'll take her from here," Nibs told Jianyu.

He bristled at the dismissal but didn't argue. Let them believe him to be obedient. It made it that much easier to know where each of Dolph's crew stood, to know whom to trust. And to file away their secrets for when he might need them.

FOUNDATION WORK

The boy who had dismissed Jianyu was young, with light hair and thick, round spectacles perched on the tip of his thin nose. "They call me Nibs," he said, extending his hand. "Nibsy Lorcan."

Esta eyed him before finally taking it. His ink-stained fingers were firm, but his weren't the rough hands of a fighter, and that fact put her somewhat at ease.

He smiled then, a boyish grin that seemed out of place in the barroom. "They're all still talking about you. The way you stole the top from Dolph's cane. Everyone's surprised Viola didn't try to skewer you after that stunt you pulled with her knife. No one is allowed to touch her knives—not unless it's the sharp end first, if you know what I mean."

"Delightful," Esta said, feeling suddenly uneasy with so much attention.

The boy peered at her. "I'm not gonna ask you how you managed it. That's your business. For now, at least. But I'll warn you, if Dolph decides you aren't worth the trouble, there won't be anything that anybody can do for you."

"Understood," she said, wondering where Jianyu had gone. She was still on edge after confronting Murphy and then being bested by Jianyu, and she didn't like the idea that he could use her little visit to Khafre Hall against her at any time. "I only want to earn my place here. If there's anything else I can do, any way to be helpful to Dolph—"

"I'll let you know," Nibs said, cutting off the conversation with a gentle smile.

Taking his cue, she changed the subject. "What's happening here?" she said with a jerk of her head.

"It's the weekly gathering," Nibs told her. "People with debts due come to pay them, or to ask for more time. Others come requesting favors."

"Looks lucrative," she mused.

"Oh, Dolph doesn't charge," Nibs said. When she looked at him, surprised, he clarified: "He trades in secrets." The boy shrugged. "Which I guess is lucrative in its own right."

"I bet." She glanced at him. "What secret does he know about you?"

Nibs didn't even blink. "Who says it isn't the other way around?"

She laughed, amused by his unexpected bravado.

The doors to the bar banged open then, a loud clattering burst that had everyone inside looking toward the three figures silhouetted by the light of the afternoon. The boy let out a soft whistle.

"Dolph Saunders!" the middle figure bellowed. "I want the girl."

The barroom went eerily silent as the three men lumbered into the barroom of the Strega. Esta recognized the one on the left as Werner, and at the sight of him, she shifted uneasily, turning away from the center of the room and tipping her head down, to hide her profile.

"Who is that?" she whispered.

The boy's face didn't betray any emotion. "That would be Edward Corey, the owner of the Haymarket. He seems to know who you are. . . ."

Esta's stomach twisted.

Dolph Saunders took his time looking over one last contract, signing his name, and blowing on the ink to dry it. He didn't bother to look up when he finally did answer; he simply picked up the next bunch of papers. "What are you doing here, Corey?" he said, irritation coloring his words. "This isn't your side of town."

"You heard me, Saunders. I'm here for the girl. I know Bridget sent her to you."

The entire room seemed to hold its breath as Dolph considered Corey's statement. "I'm not sure what girl you're referring to. Unlike you, I don't run that sort of business."

"Are you telling me the girl isn't here?" Corey said, taking a few more menacing steps forward. "Or are you telling me that you're protecting her?"

Dolph did look up then. "Anyone here know the girl he's looking for?" he said flatly.

Esta started to move slowly, getting ready to pull time around her and make her escape, but Nibsy's hand snaked out and held her in place. She was stuck. She couldn't do anything without drawing attention to herself, and she couldn't slow time without giving away what she could actually do to Nibs.

"Give it a moment," Nibs whispered, barely moving his mouth.

A loud scraping noise tore through the silence of the barroom as Dolph Saunders stood, his chair tumbling behind him. "I think you were mistaken, Corey. There's no girl here for you."

"Don't play with me, Saunders. Charlie Murphy wants the girl, and if he doesn't get her, he's going to come after me. I'm not about to let that happen. I'll send him straight to your doorstep. You know he's got friends you can only imagine. They'd pull your license, close this shithole down, and destroy everything you've built for yourself—your entire life—at the snap of my fingers."

"Now, there you've made a mistake," Dolph said softly.

"No mistake. If they find out what you are, they'll take everything you have."

"That would only matter if there was anything I cared about losing," Dolph told him. "But you . . . You have quite a lot to lose, don't you, Corey? You like to play the big man with the boys over at Tammany, don't you?" Dolph shook his head. "I know you're also trying to get yourself in with the Order. You're playing too many sides at once, and if any of them find out what *you* are . . ."

Corey sputtered for a second. "You don't know—"

"I know *everything* about you, Corey," Dolph said, his voice like sandpaper. "I know about the little rendezvous you had with the woman on Broome Street, though I'm guessing her husband doesn't. I know what you had for lunch and what you're thinking about having for dinner. I know who your family is—*what* your family is—so I know you might be weak enough to pass, but I wonder what your friends in the Order would think if they knew the truth?" Dolph paused for a moment, letting the words hang in the air.

"Are you threatening me?"

"Of course not. We're all friends here. We're all in this together . . . unless you turn on us first. But if you don't want everyone else in this city to know as well, you'll get the hell out of my saloon and take yourself back uptown where you belong. You'll deal with Murphy and get him to forget there was ever any girl to find."

Esta began to relax a little as she saw Corey hesitating. His narrow face was becoming an alarming shade of red. "You . . . You . . ." But his words foundered.

"Yes. That's right. Now you're understanding." He glanced at Werner. "I think it's best if you don't show your face here again, don't you?"

Werner nodded weakly, his expression grim as Dolph picked up his chair and sat at the table again, dismissing them all without another word.

Dolph didn't look up again, but four of his larger boys stepped forward, their thick arms crossed over broad chests and a gleam in their eyes that anyone could see was them itching for a good brawl. Corey seemed to get the message, and with a jerk of his head, he left, followed by Werner and the other man.

Esta let out a relieved breath, and the room started cautiously to come back to life.

"Let's go," Nibs whispered to Esta, never letting go of her wrist.

"Go where?"

"Somewhere else," he said. He handed the purse off and tugged her along. "Anywhere else. Trust me. He's going to be in a rotten mood after all that."

They slipped out into the brisk afternoon air. It would be light for a while, but already the Bowery was coming to life for the evening.

"Will Corey really keep Murphy away?"

Nibs shrugged. "He has a good enough reason to. If Murphy found out that Corey was lying to him and the rest of the Order, he'd lose everything. But people don't always act in their own best interest." Nibs peered at her a few seconds longer. "You know, maybe there is something you could do for me—and for Dolph. It would go a long way toward thanking him for protecting you."

"Sure. Anything."

"I'd like you to come see a show with me."

Esta studied him, confused at the odd request. Then, realizing what he was asking, what he intended, her frustration grew. "Look, you seem nice enough," she said as gently as she could, "but I'm not interested."

The boy smiled softly, as though he were amused. "I didn't think you would be. Still, I'd like you to come with me." His tone was sincere enough that she almost believed him.

"I'm only here to work."

"Humor me," he said, tucking his hands into his pockets as he rocked back on his heels. "Consider it part of the job."

Esta narrowed her eyes at him. His position with Dolph made it nearly impossible for her to say no, and he seemed to know it. "Just a show?"

He chuckled. "Okay, fine. There's someone I'd like you to meet." An odd look crossed his face. "But I'm serious about it being part of the job. Dolph's been trying to get this particular guy on the crew for months now, but so far he hasn't been moved by any of my appeals. Maybe you'll have more luck."

"I don't know why I would," she countered

"I got a feeling about you," Nibs said. "Darrigan just might go for a pretty face."

CLASSIC MISDIRECTION

Wallack's Theatre

"T ough crowd tonight," Evelyn said from behind Harte's shoulder as he watched Julius Tannen's monologue fall flat.

He didn't bother to look back at her. He was too busy counting the empty seats in the house. Shorty was right. Things weren't looking good.

At first, the audiences had poured in to see his act. The entire city had been talking about the miracles he'd accomplished on that stage. But the city was only so big. It didn't matter how amazing the effects he presented were—after a while, everyone had seen them. He needed something new.

Better, he needed to get out.

"Any second now they're going to start throwing fruit," he muttered, disgusted.

"I bet you thought you'd escaped from all that when you moved uptown." A smile curved in Evelyn's voice, but there wasn't any warmth. "Just goes to show, even the polish of the upper crust only goes skin deep." She moved closer and lowered her voice. "We missed you last night, after the show."

Harte doubted that very much. Twenty minutes in, they all would have been too numbed by the Nitewein to care about anything but the next pour.

"Still won't tell me who you ran off to see?" she purred, resting her hands on his shoulders and looking up at him. Her eyes were soft, the pupils large and unfocused.

Frowning down at her, Harte wondered suddenly what had made her start drinking so early in the day. But then he realized he didn't really care. It wasn't his place to care. He knew where caring got you.

Harte shrugged off her hands. "No one important."

He didn't need anyone asking questions about his meeting with Jack Grew. It was bad enough that Nibsy Lorcan was following him again. And cornering him like that in the park? It didn't bode well. If Dolph Saunders had an idea of what he was up to . . .

But there couldn't be any way for Dolph to know. Harte had been too careful. Or so he hoped.

He tilted his head, stretching his neck as he tried to loosen himself up. The city had felt almost claustrophobic lately, and the events of the night before hadn't helped things. And not being able to have a proper meal since the girl had assaulted him . . . well, that had only made things worse.

The act onstage was getting the signal from the stage manager to wrap things up, so Harte took one final look at himself in the small mirror on the wall and fixed a smudge in the kohl beneath his right eye as the orchestra trilled the notes that cued his entrance.

Beyond the glare of the footlights, the sparse crowd rustled discontentedly in their seats as he took the stage. The faces in the audience were frowning and clearly impatient to see something worth the price of their fifty-cent ticket. He hadn't planned anything new, but it was too late to do anything about that now.

"Ladies and gentlemen," he called, letting his voice boom over the theater as he settled into the persona he'd perfected for the stage. "I have traveled far and wide to learn the occult arts, the hermetical sciences. Today I bring you evidence that we mere humans might converse with the divine. And that the divine," he said, flourishing his hand to ignite the flare palmed there, "might converse with us in turn."

The ball of fire burst from his palm, hovered for a second in the air, and then vanished. It was a simple enough trick, but it did its job. An interested murmuring rustled through the house as a stagehand rolled out a table filled with props.

"Do not be alarmed," he said, taking up a pair of steel hoops large enough to fit over his head. "This is not the magic of old, wild and untamed, capable of seduction and destruction. There is no danger here," he called, manipulating the rings so that they locked together, came apart. "For my powers come not from the accident of birth, but from careful scientific study and practiced skill. Because I have devoted myself to the mastery of the occult sciences, the powers I demonstrate have no command over me." With a flourish, the hoops seemed to vanish. "Instead, I bend them to my will," he finished, plucking a hoop out of thin air, making it materialize before the audience's very eyes.

The house was silent now, all eyes watching and waiting for what he would do next. Rich or poor, every audience was the same. Some might dismiss tales of the old magic as nothing more than legend. Some might fear its existence still. Most had been taught to hate the people with affinities for it. But like the Order, they all desperately wanted magic to be real. They wanted to believe that something was out there bigger than they were—as long as that something could be controlled by the right sort of people.

He wasn't sorry for using their fears and their hopes, their prejudices and their sense of righteousness against them. For distracting them from the truth. He was simply surviving in a world that hated what he was.

Once the audience was on his side, he felt himself relax into his act. He stripped off his jacket and rolled up his shirtsleeves to show nothing was hidden beneath them before he ran through a series of his usual, seemingly impossible card manipulations and sleight-of-hand tricks. All the while, he drew the audience in with tales of his travels. He told them how he had been a guest in a maharaja's court as he swallowed a dozen single needles and thread, and insisted it was the court's sorcerer who'd taught him to bring the needles back up, threaded neatly at even intervals along the silken string. He'd studied the mysteries of science and alchemy under the most learned men in Europe, and discovered many secrets of the universe in the shadow of the great pyramids.

All lies, of course. He'd never stepped foot off the island of Manhattan, had never even dreamed it was possible until Dolph Saunders had put the idea into his head.

"Ladies and gentlemen," Harte said, drawing the moment out dramatically before he launched into his final effect. "Now I will demonstrate my sovereignty over the forces of life and death. In this, my most daring demonstration, I will require a volunteer. Someone with the strength of will to withstand the lure of the Otherworld and the courage to face what lies beyond the veil of our understanding."

He stepped downstage so that he could see beyond the glare of the footlights, searching for a mark. Usually, he liked to find a man for this effect, preferably a large one who was clearly doubtful or scowling. Someone the audience would believe to be uncertain, skeptical. But as he screened the crowd, he found someone else in the audience—the girl from the Haymarket.

At first he thought she'd come for him. His gut went tight and his whole body felt warm, and for a moment he couldn't move. He could only stare at her, like she was some strange apparition he'd imagined into being.

Then he saw she was sitting next to Nibsy Lorcan, and every last bit of his anticipation went cold.

It couldn't be a coincidence that they were both in the theater, that they had both accosted him the night before. But any of Dolph's people should have known how stupid it was to use magic in the Haymarket. Had the whole thing been some sort of setup? Another way for Dolph to entangle him?

He'd see about that.

Harte made his way down the short flight of steps to the audience, pretending to still be searching for a suitable volunteer. By the time he'd made it to their row, the girl had found something interesting to examine in the stitching of her gloves. Her jaw was tight, and her cheeks were flushed.

Good, Harte thought. *Let her be nervous.* His tongue still throbbed, but damn if the pain didn't also remind him of how it had felt to have her mouth against his. How for a moment—when she had seemed willing to return the kiss—he'd felt a kind of dizzying freedom that part of him itched to have again.

Which just went to show how dangerous she was.

"Miss?" he said, offering her his ungloved hand. "If you would be so kind?"

She glanced up, fear warring with the violence in those strange tawny eyes. "Oh, I'm never kind." She waved him off.

He offered his hand again, but even as she started to refuse, Nibsy was already pushing her to her feet.

"She'd love to," he told Harte. There was a spark of something like anticipation in the boy's eyes.

Seeing Nibsy excited should have put him on guard, but Harte couldn't bring himself to care.

"Don't make a fuss," he murmured when she tried to pull away. Harte was already firmly tucking her arm under his. "You'll only look like a fool." He tightened his arm over hers, pinning her in place at his side.

"I suppose you would know best about that"—she gave him a smile that was all teeth—"seeing how you've made an art of it." Her expression was murderous, but for some insane reason that only made him more curious about her.

Because of his success, girls had been only too happy to smile and fawn on him, but none of them really wanted the person beneath the name. They wanted the polished magician, the showman who could wine and dine them and fulfill their dreams of being onstage themselves. This girl didn't want any of that. She didn't want him at all, at least not that she would admit.

He liked that about her.

Maybe his mother had been right after all—there was clearly something wrong with him.

"Why are you here?" he whispered, focusing on what was important as he led her down the aisle to the stage.

"I was told there'd be entertainment," she said, not caring who heard.

Then she leaned in, as though to tell him a secret, but spoke loudly enough for the front rows to hear. "I think my escort might have overpromised."

Harte swallowed his amusement and schooled his features as the audience tittered. "I see," he said, handing her up the first of the steps to the stage. He followed close behind, and when he got to the top step, he leaned forward and whispered in her ear, "And last night, is that the kind of . . . *entertainment* you prefer?"

She whipped around, outrage sparking in those honey-colored eyes of hers, but he only gave her a wink before addressing the audience.

"Ladies and gentlemen, this lovely creature has been so kind as to grace us with her beauty and courage this fine evening. What is your name, miss?"

The girl scowled at him silently until he cocked an expectant brow. "Esta," she said, apparently realizing that the fastest way off the stage was to cooperate.

"Dear Esta—named for the stars—has graciously volunteered to assist me in one of the most perilous demonstrations of my connection to the powers of the Otherworld." He ignored the girl's snort and motioned to a stagehand, who rolled out a large wooden crate that had been painted to look like an ornate wardrobe.

"If you would examine this wardrobe for any inconsistencies, any false backs . . ." He gestured to the crate. When Esta didn't immediately move, he urged her again. "Please, do remove your gloves and give it a thorough examination." He held out his hands, as though to take her gloves.

The girl gave him another tart look, but she removed her gloves and handed them over to him. The leather was smooth as a petal, and he wondered again where she'd come from and who she was to have such finely made gloves when she was clearly taking orders from Nibsy.

She began inspecting the box, her pert mouth still scowling, and Harte had the sudden, unwelcome memory of the night before, of how her lips had gone soft and almost welcoming for—

"She's a ringer!" a drunken voice called out from the audience, a welcome interruption from the direction his thoughts had taken.

"No, I'm not," the girl called. Then, before he could stop her, she shouted, "You should come up here, too, and see for yourself." She batted her eyes at Harte. "He can come, can't he? You don't have anything to hide . . . do you?"

The audience tittered with laughter.

"Well?" she asked, all mock innocence.

She had him in a corner. *Fine. He'd deal with it, and then he'd deal with her.* He pasted on his most charming smile, as though he were in on the joke, and turned back to the audience. "Of course not."

The heckler turned out to be a large man whose coat was pulled tight across his stomach. While he checked over the cabinet, a nervous and excited energy ran through the audience. But Harte Darrigan didn't make mistakes. Not anymore, and not on *his* stage, where he felt most at home and most in control. No girl was going to change that, no matter how much the sight of her full mouth twisting in amusement reminded him of the night before and how her lips had felt against his. He pressed his still-sore tongue against the sharp point of one of his teeth, to remind himself of what had happened the last time he lost his head over her.

When they both were done, he held out his bare hand to help her into the box, bracing himself for the warmth of her fingers. "If you're satisfied?"

"Oh, I don't know. . . ." There was a vicious gleam in her eyes. "I'm not sure that you have the skills to satisfy," she said loud enough for the audience to hear.

The audience rustled again with more laughter, and someone in the back whistled.

He leaned very close, until he could feel the warmth of her and detect the light, sweet scent from her hair. "No one's ever complained before," he said, offering his bare hand to her again. "Unless you're afraid?"

To the audience, her momentary reluctance probably appeared to be more of her toying with him, but Harte was close enough to see the reason she hesitated before taking his hand. He saw in her golden eyes the inner battle the girl was waging with herself between the choice to meet his challenge or to admit she was nervous. And he saw the moment her pride won.

She gave the audience another dazzling smile, goading them on as she made him wait a moment longer. When she finally slid her long, slender fingers into the palm of his hand, the shock of her warmth was almost enough to distract him from his relief. If he'd had his wits about him, maybe he would have found a way to take better advantage of that moment. But at first he could only look at their two hands joined in the glare of the spotlights—hers soft and surprisingly small against his.

"Well?" she asked, glancing again at the audience she now held in the palm of her hand. "You did promise . . . satisfaction, did you not?"

The heckler, who was still onstage with them, let out a loud, braying laugh, and the audience rustled again, but this time, he fed on their amusement, used it for what came next.

He lifted her hand, presenting her to his public. "The lady will now put herself at my mercy. At the mercy of the powers of the universe around us . . . powers that I control," he said dramatically, as he led her toward the open cabinet. "On my command, she will disappear from this world and travel to the Otherworld beyond until I call her back."

He looked at the girl then, and her tawny eyes were still laughing at him. But when he squeezed her hand gently, pushing his own power through himself, through the fine softness of her skin, those eyes went wide.

She looked down at their joined hands and whispered a single word. It was the kind of curse that most well-bred ladies had never even heard, much less used.

"Maybe later," he whispered as he squeezed her hand again and sent another pulse of energy through his fingertips. He helped her up into the cabinet, relishing the way her brow furrowed in confusion. "Enjoy your trip," he whispered, so the audience couldn't hear.

Harte had to work to keep his face fixed in the serious mask he'd perfected for the stage as he closed the door in her face and latched it securely. He'd enjoyed sparring with her . . . too much. But he didn't have time for her, not on his stage and not in his life. He took the corner of the cabinet and pushed, rotating it like a top. It moved faster and faster, spinning of its own volition, until it was floating inches and then feet off the stage. The audience went silent watching.

Lifting his hands in a dramatic gesture, he made the revolving cabinet stop. Then, all at once, the sides flapped down, so all that remained was a steel-framed box, empty and open. The audience could clearly see the curtain behind it.

A few people in the audience gave some halfhearted applause, but most of the faces remained bored. Unimpressed.

"Perhaps you think this is a matter of mirrors or optical tricks?" He pulled a small, snub-nosed pistol from his jacket, and the audience grew attentive, suddenly interested in what would come next.

"Perhaps you could help me again, sir?" He gestured to his heckler to come forward, then handed him the pistol and a single bullet.

"If you would do the honors of loading this gun?" He turned to his audience. "To guarantee that this is no trick of mirrors, that the girl has well and truly disappeared, I will fire the bullet into that target," he said, gesturing to a large padded mat behind the empty frame of the cabinet.

Harte found Nibsy in the audience and met the boy's eyes. Nibsy's expression was impassive, apparently unconcerned with the girl's safety.

When the man was done with the pistol, Harte took it from him, leveled his arm, and took aim. A drumroll began, low and ominous.

"No!" a female voice called out from the audience.

Harte didn't react. His finger tightened, and the bullet exploded out of the gun, through the empty box, and into the padded target behind.

Scattered applause grew, but the audience was still quiet, waiting. Just the way he liked them. It was never enough to make the volunteer disappear. The real trick was bringing her back.

"Never fear," he said, letting his voice carry over the crowd. "Though the fair Esta is no longer in our world, I will summon her to return.

Behold—" With another wave of his hand, the walls of the cabinet began to rise, like a flower closing, and the cabinet began spinning again, more slowly now as it sank back down to the stage floor.

He approached it and gave it one more spin, making sure the front door was facing the audience, and then opened it with a triumphant flourish.

The audience went completely silent, and then after a moment, laughter began to erupt.

Harte turned to see the cabinet, empty. The girl wasn't there.

He cursed under his breath and tried not to look as frantic as he felt. He turned back to the audience. "Ladies and gentlemen, if you allow me to—"

"Are you looking for me?" a now-familiar voice called.

His skin felt suddenly hot. He could hear his own heartbeat in his ears, as his entire career flashed before his eyes. The audience shuffled, turning and craning their necks to see the source of the voice.

The girl stood and waved. "I'm over here," she called from one of the center rows of the theater.

The people around her startled. She might as well have been a ghost the way she'd appeared in their midst. Their mouths hung open as she excused herself, climbing past two people who sat gaping as she moved toward the center aisle.

At first the audience was too shocked to do anything more than stare, and a deafening silence filled the cavernous house. Even Harte couldn't do much more than stare. She'd managed to seat herself in the middle of a row without anyone noticing her. As he gaped, dumbfounded at how she'd outmaneuvered him again, the applause started slowly and then grew until the audience began coming to their feet, whistling and calling for more.

The girl was already half gone before he came to his senses and realized he needed to go after her. She blew him a kiss and gave a wave from the back of the theater before ducking through the doors to the lobby. Harte found Nibs sitting in the middle of the standing ovation. He gave Harte a smirking salute, then got up and started pushing his way through the frenzied crowd, following the girl.

MASTER OF THE OTHERWORLD

Esta let her feet carry her out of the theater—and far, far away from Harte Darrigan. She barely noticed that night had already fallen over the city; the icy chill in the air didn't even touch her. She couldn't feel anything but the shock of finding herself no longer inside the cabinet onstage but out in the audience.

Pushing her way through the crowd gathered on the sidewalk outside the box office, she didn't bother to apologize or slow her steps, not even when she careened into a large man helping a woman out of their carriage. She had to get away.

She had to figure out what the hell had just happened.

She remembered getting into the cabinet, remembered feeling the sizzling heat of his magic against her palm and knowing he'd done something to her. She remembered the wink he'd given her—the one that promised trouble—before he locked her into the wardrobe. But after that . . .

Nothing.

Nothing at all until she found herself watching Harte Darrigan from the audience again. Not until the audience's laughter at seeing the cabinet empty shook her from her stupor.

She didn't know how she'd come to find herself in the middle of the theater—much less in the middle of the row—but she could guess. From his clear agitation when he realized he was alone on an empty stage, Esta understood that she was still supposed to have been inside that cabinet. She must have decided to leave, to use her own magic and get herself into the audience without any of them realizing. But she couldn't remember actually doing it.

From the moment Nibsy had said Harte Darrigan's name, Esta knew she was about to meet the person she'd been sent to stop—the Magician. The moment he'd walked onstage, she'd also recognized him immediately as the boy from the Haymarket. At first she'd been uneasy, but after watching him for a few minutes, her worry turned to relief. With his overblown drama and tacky stage magic, she couldn't believe that this was the Magician. Stopping him would be easy, she thought.

But sitting in the audience, shocked and without any understanding of how she'd gotten there, she realized the Magician was more than he appeared to be. That he would be a formidable opponent.

Luckily, it had taken her only a second to gather her wits and retake control of the situation. The surprise at seeing her in the middle of the audience had transformed his entire face. He'd looked so disarmed that she almost felt guilty for the laughter her little disappearing act caused. *Almost.*

But then the look on his face changed from surprise to something else, and she knew she had to get out of there—fast.

"Esta!"

She barely heard the voice calling her name as she darted through the crowd, faster now as she tried to outpace her panic. The Magician must have erased her memory or manipulated her in some other way. It was magic, clearly, and not the half-baked stage magic that made up the rest of his tricks. But what was his affinity, and how far did it reach? Could he still affect her now—still control her?

The thought made Esta shudder for reasons that had nothing to do with the cold. Professor Lachlan was depending on her to stop the Magician, but he already had the upper hand. And now he had her on the run.

Esta pulled up short, coming to a dead stop that forced the people behind her to dodge around her. *No.* She wasn't going to let him chase her off. That wasn't going to happen again.

She turned back to find the street sign of the intersection she'd crossed, but lurking above her, as though she'd conjured him in her thoughts, was the Magician.

Larger than life, Harte Darrigan looked down with stormy gray eyes from the huge billboard that took up most of the theater wall behind her.

"Esta! Wait!" Nibs finally caught up to her. He was panting, but his face was glowing with excitement as he caught her arm. "That was excellent. I couldn't have planned it better myself. How'd you manage it?"

"I don't know," she murmured, pulling away from him. She was quickly growing aware of the cold now, of how it cut through the velvet of her dress, and she rubbed her arms, trying to ward off the chill.

Nibs handed her the cloak she'd left behind. "You don't know?" he asked, surprised.

She shook her head as she pulled the cloak around her, but it did nothing to dispel the cold. "I can't remember how I got out of that box or how I ended up sitting in the theater."

"Interesting." Nibs glanced over his spectacles at her.

"You could have warned me about what he could do," she said, turning on him.

He didn't so much as flinch at the heat in her words. "I thought it would be better for you to go in without expectations. Anyway, you played it brilliantly. You threw him off, which is something I've never managed," he said, admiration clear in his voice. "Dolph'll be pleased."

She couldn't quite feel buoyed by that news. Not at that moment.

"I wanted to see what you could do. And you weren't ever in any *real* danger. I was only trying to get his attention." His expression was smug behind the thick lenses. "And you certainly did that. Dolph was right to keep you," he said.

She glared at him. "What's that supposed to mean?"

"Just what I said. He made a good choice in not giving you back to Corey. You're a damn good thief, but there's more to you than that, isn't there?" he asked, squinting through his lenses at her.

"There's only one way to find out," she challenged, making sure to meet his eyes. Daring him to accept it. "Give me something to do other than stealing purses."

He studied her a long, tense moment, and she could practically hear the calculations he was making in that mind of his. "Maybe we will," he said.

They walked in silence for a while before they found a streetcar heading in the right direction, but all the time, she swore she could feel the eyes of the Magician following her home.

OLD FRIENDS

Harte took his bow quickly, barely hearing the applause and not bothering with his usual flourishes. His whole body jangled from the surge of adrenaline he'd felt at seeing the girl—*Esta*, she'd said her name was—materialize across the room. His mind was already racing with the possibilities. He had to find her. He *had* to know how she did it.

He pushed past Shorty, who was shouting at him to get back onstage and finish his act. He just needed to duck into his dressing room to grab his overcoat and keys, but when he pushed open the door, he found that the room was already occupied.

"John," Harte said, covering his surprise at finding Paul Kelly's second-in-command sitting in the chair near his dressing table. John Torrio was about nineteen, not much older than Harte. Torrio had the same swarthy skin and hard-nosed looks, but not the polish or the style of his boss, and Harte's *ex*-boss, the leader of the Five Point Gang.

Pat Riley, better known in certain circles as Razor, was examining a set of handcuffs that were dangling from the mirror. Harte had been dodging Kelly and his boys for months now—ever since Dolph had told him about the Book—so having these two appear unannounced and unexpected could only mean their boss was done being patient.

He reached beyond the depths of his unease and pulled up what he hoped was an affable, confident smile. "Gentlemen, what do I owe this pleasure?"

"Kelly sent us," Torrio said, straightening the sharp lapels of his suit as he spoke. "But I'm sure you know that, seeing as how you've been avoiding us. The boss needs your services again."

"I'm not in the game anymore," Harte said, keeping a wary eye on Riley. "Kelly knows that. The last time was supposed to be the last time. We had an agreement."

Riley dropped the cuffs so they clattered onto the table and turned to look squarely at Harte. "The agreement's changed."

It always does, Harte thought, fighting the urge to scream in frustration.

John Torrio slouched comfortably in Harte's dressing chair, his eyes projecting the lazy confidence of someone who had Paul Kelly's full authority behind him. "You know Kelly's got eyes everywhere, Darrigan. You telling me you thought you could be rubbing elbows with J. P. Morgan's people and nobody wouldn't notice?"

"You're here because I had a drink with Jack Grew?" Harte asked.

"And Morgan's son."

"I don't know Morgan's son. And he doesn't want to know me," Harte said, eyeing his coat over Torrio's shoulder. He shouldn't have bothered to come back for it. He could have caught up with the girl *and* managed to miss these two.

Though, now that he stopped to think, maybe he should let her go. She was involved with Nibsy somehow, which meant she had to be tangled up with Dolph Saunders as well. The last thing Harte needed was that particular complication, especially with Kelly's men sitting in his dressing room.

Still, that trick of materializing across the theater in a fraction of the time it would have taken anyone else to do it—the crowd had gone wild. If he could replicate it, he wouldn't have to worry about ticket sales for a long time. Even if she was wrapped up with Nibsy Lorcan, Harte wanted to know how she'd done it. But first he had to get rid of the two men standing in his way.

"But you *do* know Jack?" Razor insisted.

Torrio nodded. "That's enough for the boss."

"Jack's only an admirer of my work," Harte said easily, which was true enough. "He thought I could teach him how to pull coins out of his ear. Make him as rich as his uncle."

Torrio snorted, half-amused. "I bet he did. But like I said, your new friendship interests Mr. Kelly. Greatly."

Harte made a show of unrolling the sleeves back down his arms, all the while keeping part of his awareness on the two men. "I meet lots of people," he told them. "I wasn't aware I had to check with Kelly every time I had a drink with someone."

Razor Riley growled in answer. "Watch yourself, Darrigan. Kelly told us to talk to you. He didn't say we had to be nice."

Harte ignored Razor and kept his focus on Torrio. "What interest does Kelly have in Jack Grew, anyway?"

"You know the boss," Torrio said with a shrug. "He's always interested in growing his connections. Jack Grew's pretty high up in the world."

Harte couldn't hide his surprise. "Jack's a nonstarter," he said truthfully. "From what I hear, he was this close to being shackled to some fisherman's daughter in Greece, because all his brains are in the wrong head. The boy wouldn't be able to tell his ass from his armpit without Daddy to help him, and the whole family knows it. Kelly wouldn't be able to get within ten feet of him before Morgan's people got wind of it."

"Such little faith you have," Torrio drawled, picking at his nails before he lifted his eyes to meet Harte's. "You really think Mr. Kelly don't know what he's doing?"

"Kelly wants you to work on Grew," Razor clarified.

"Work on him?" Harte repeated, feeling a cold twist of understanding in his gut.

"You know what he wants," Torrio said, taking his hat from Harte's dressing table.

It was one thing to use his affinity on shady politicians from Tammany or on the boys in the neighborhood, but tangling with the Order of Ortus Aurea? It was too risky, or Harte would have already done it. With magic, he could have wrapped Jack around his finger a lot easier. But he knew that if the Order got wind of it, they'd end him. Or worse.

"I don't have any sway over Jack Grew," Harte hedged.

"That ain't the way I hear it. The way I hear it, you got the *touch* with difficult people." Torrio's mouth twisted into something that might have been a smirk. "Kelly wants an introduction."

"I can't understand why."

"Not that it's any of your business, but the word around town is that the Order's having an important get-together soon. Word is that anyone of any importance in the city will be there. Kelly don't want to be stuck in the slums forever, Darrigan. He wants an invitation to that gathering. He wants an invitation to the Order. And he's confident you can make that happen. . . . After all, you already have an in with Jack."

"Jack Grew and his like, they're from a different world than us," Harte said with a shrug. "They could barely stand to have me at their table, and—"

"I'm sure you'll figure something out," Torrio interrupted. He gave Harte's cheek a not-so-gentle pat.

"If I don't want to figure something out?" Harte asked.

"You know Kelly has ways of persuading. It would be a shame if anyone found out about any of your little secrets, now, wouldn't it? Never know what might happen to you."

There were any number of secrets Paul Kelly knew about Harte Darrigan, any number of things that could ruin him if his old boss decided to expose him.

"I see," Harte said slowly.

"I thought you might," Torrio said as Razor Riley sat stone-faced behind him.

"I need time to think about it. Figure out the best way in."

"Mr. Kelly thought you might say that. He has the utmost faith that you'll make the right choice. Me? I ain't so sure. I think you might need a push in the right direction." Torrio shrugged. "I'm more than happy to give you that push."

"Well, this has been most enlightening, boys." Harte held out his hand, a last-ditch attempt to take control of the situation. "Give Kelly my regards, won't you?"

Torrio looked at the outstretched hand but didn't offer his own. "You put on a good show, Darrigan, but your time's running out to make good." He gave a jerk of his head before leading the way out of the dressing room. Razor gave Harte a look that said he wouldn't mind if Harte screwed up, and then he followed Torrio, shutting the door behind him.

Harte threw the lock on the door before he sank into the chair near his dressing table. It was still warm from Torrio's body, which only served to remind him how much trouble he was in. Paul Kelly, a member of the Order? He couldn't fathom it. But if it came to pass . . . Harte couldn't help but shudder.

He still remembered the first time he'd ever met Paul Kelly, about five, maybe six years ago. Back then Dolph Saunders had taken him under his wing, and he'd felt like the world was his. So when he found out his mother was back in the city—someone had seen her in one of Paul Kelly's cathouses—he didn't ask Dolph for help. He went to see for himself.

He'd gone to curse her for leaving him, but once he'd realized what she'd become, he understood what his actions had done. He couldn't leave her there. It had been easy enough to get her out. But of course Paul Kelly heard about it and came after him.

Back then Kelly was beginning to make a name for himself. Mostly, his gang was made up of rough-looking Italian boys who didn't need the evil eye to give someone a bad day, and they had Harte before Dolph even found out about it. But Kelly saw something valuable in Harte's abilities, so he gave Harte a choice that day, which was more than he gave most: work for the Five Pointers, or end his short life in the Hudson. Harte picked the Five Pointers. Despite everything he'd been through, he'd still been too naive to know the Hudson might have been a better bet. He was wearing the Five Pointer's brand before Dolph could do anything to help him.

A few years after that, when he'd collected enough of Kelly's secrets, he'd negotiated an exit from the gang. He'd renamed himself, made a whole new life, and started working theaters and dime museums in the

Bowery, learning his craft from some of the old guys. He thought he'd made it out, but it wasn't even six months later when Kelly called on him for a "favor." *For an old friend.* But one more led to another and another.

He'd tried not to think too much about the way his favors for Kelly often lined up with his lucky breaks in the theater business. He told himself that it was his skill more than Kelly's pressure that had gotten him the first gig north of Houston or his first appearance in a Broadway house. But Torrio and Razor's appearance only underscored the truth—Dolph Saunders had been right about Kelly having him on a leash. The only way to get away from Kelly's influence was to get out of the godforsaken trap of a city.

And the only way to do that was to get the Book before anyone else did.

Harte picked up the handcuffs Razor Riley had moved. They were the first cuffs he'd ever cracked, back when he was a stupid kid from Mott Street who'd gotten picked up for lifting a half-rotten orange from a peddler's cart. Breaking those cuffs and getting out of the Black Maria wagon bound for the boys' mission had been his first taste of what it might feel like to choose his own destiny. He'd kept them as a reminder of how far he'd come, and of how far he still had left to go.

Sure, Dolph Saunders and Paul Kelly were both breathing down his neck, but he had something neither of them had and both of them wanted—a willing contact in the Ortus Aurea. It would still be tricky, convincing Jack to trust him enough to get him into Khafre Hall. It would be damn risky going against an organization that snuffed out Mageus for sport. But those cuffs were a reminder that he'd been in tough spots before.

He hung the cuffs back on their hook where he'd be able to see them. His entire life had been one big escape act. Getting out of that prison of a city wouldn't be any different.

CHANGING FEATHERS

Esta spent the next few days working the Dead Line without complaint—and staying far away from Harte Darrigan. The letters and words in the news clipping she kept tucked against her skin had not stopped shifting. The future, the heist that needed to happen, was still undetermined, a fact that made her nervous, anxious. If the heist didn't happen, she'd never get back.

On Wednesday, she worked on Wall Street, fleecing unsuspecting bankers in the sleeting rain. With the rotten weather, it took longer than the day before to meet her quota, especially since she was relying on her skill rather than her magic whenever possible. She understood that in *this* city, magic was as much a liability as a tool, a mark for an unknown enemy to track her or find her.

Despite the rain, it was still early when she made it back to the warmth of Tilly's kitchen, exhausted and hungry. The kitchen wasn't empty. At the end of the long, heavy table, Dolph sat huddled with Viola, Jianyu, and Nibs. They didn't pay any attention to her arrival, but when Tilly heard the door open, she turned from what she was doing at the sink. Seeing it was Esta, she wiped her hands on the apron covering her dress and grabbed a covered plate to bring over to her.

"You're back early," Tilly said. She set the plate on the end of the counter and took the cloth off the top to reveal sliced hard cheese, salami, and some grapes that had already been picked over.

Leaning a hip against the counter, Esta selected one of the remaining grapes. "The streets are a mess," she said. "I got my quota, so I came back. I didn't feel like melting today."

Tilly gave her a quizzical look. "Melting?"

"Nothing," Esta said, realizing her slip.

"Another new dress?" Tilly asked, teasing.

Esta shrugged as she popped a grape into her mouth. "Change your feathers often enough, and the mark won't recognize the bird." The words came naturally, without thought, but the moment they were out, the grape suddenly tasted bitter. They were Professor Lachlan's words, lessons she'd been taught until they were a part of her. And she was failing him.

That close to the stove's warmth, she unwrapped herself from the damp cloak she'd been wearing. She nodded to the table where Dolph sat with Viola, Jianyu, and Nibs, their heads all bent close together and their voices low. "What's going on there?"

Sliding a cup of milk toward Esta, Tilly gave her a wry look. "Big plans, like always."

Dolph thumped the table with his fist, and Viola said something vicious in Italian as she gestured wildly with her hands.

"They don't seem to be going too well."

"They're not, from what I can tell," Tilly said, turning back to the sinkful of dishes.

Esta picked up a towel and took one of the wet plates from where Tilly had set them on the counter. Wiping at the plate, she kept an ear toward the group at the table. "What are they trying to do?" she said, keeping her voice low.

Tilly glanced over at her out of the corner of her eye. "Something that will probably get one of them killed," she murmured. She shook her head, obviously disgusted with the whole idea.

"It's not possible," Viola snapped. "You want that we walk into a crowded room, take everything right from under their noses, and get away without being caught. All while cleaning out everyone in the room *at the same time*? Sei pazzo!"

"We've been over this. Jianyu can slip in undetected," Dolph started.

"And then what?" Nibs asked gently. "He's no thief, Dolph."

"He steals secrets well enough," Dolph insisted.

"Secrets don't have *weight*," Viola said, punctuating her words with her hands. "This is different. You want him to take everything? To rob a room filled with members of the Order *while* we take the exhibit? It's too much for one person."

"Maybe we don't need to take all of it?" Jianyu offered. "Taking a prized piece or two should be more than enough."

"No!" Dolph thumped again. "It's not. They can't know what we're after. If we take everything, they're less likely to know why they were robbed."

"Then what do you suggest we do?" Viola asked.

"We'll send you," Dolph said.

"Bah! Be serious. I'm no thief, and you don't want them dead, do you?"

Esta took a sip from the cup of milk, using the excuse of the movement to glance over at the tense group around the table, but she practically choked when she found Nibs watching her.

"What about her?" Nibs said as she was turning away.

"What?" Dolph snapped.

"Esta, the new girl. She's lasted nearly a week downtown, hasn't she? You know she's talented—you couldn't even stop her." He shrugged. "Why not have her fleece the crowd? Jianyu can focus on the art."

Dolph turned to look at her with his icy stare. He studied her a second, his features tense. "No," he said after a moment, and turned back to the table.

"She does have light fingers," Jianyu pressed, his eyes sliding over to her. He gave her an unreadable look, a reminder of what he had over her.

"*No,*" Dolph said again, as though that was the end of that.

"I agree," Viola said, glaring at her. "Not the girl."

For some reason it was Viola's dismissal that rankled. "Why not 'the girl'?" Esta asked. She took a step toward them, never letting her gaze drop from Viola's. "You need something taken, and it's what I do. I managed to take that knife right out of your pocket, didn't I?"

"You haven't managed it since," Viola snapped, her eyes narrowing.

"Haven't bothered to try."

"Enough," Dolph said before Viola could come back at her.

Esta looked to Dolph. "You know I'm more than capable."

"But I don't know if I can trust you."

"Only one way to find out," Esta challenged.

Dolph didn't speak at first, simply stared at her, his cold blue eye serious.

"You're all worse than a couple of tomcats fighting over an alley," Tilly said, bringing a plate of food to the table. "Esta's fine, Dolph. I have a good feeling about her, and if you were honest with yourself, you'd know you trust her."

"You don't know that," he said, glancing at Tilly.

"I know she'd already be gone if you didn't." She gave him a stern look. "Use her. Maybe you'll be less likely to get somebody killed that way."

"Tilly's right," Nibs said. "We can use the girl."

"The girl has a name," Esta muttered.

"Fine," Dolph said, taking one of the biscuits Tilly had brought over. "Take a seat," he said to Esta. "But know this—if you even think to cross us—"

"You'll be dead before you lift a finger," Viola finished.

Jianyu was silent, not adding his own warning, but his eyes were steady, watchful.

Luckily, she wasn't planning to cross them. Not yet, at least.

THE CORE OF MAGIC

I t was long after the Strega had closed its doors for the night when Dolph finally made his way back to his lonely apartment. Once, it had been filled with warmth and life, but now the silence served as penance. He settled himself at the table by the fire to look over the floor plans for the Metropolitan and the notes he'd collected about the exhibition so far, as well as Jianyu's latest report.

Sometime later, a sharp knock at the door stirred him from his solitude. He glanced up at the clock and saw that he'd worked well past midnight, far too late for someone to disturb him if it wasn't important. "Come," he barked, stepping in front of the table to block the view of the paperwork.

Viola entered, and Dolph relaxed a measure, taking his chair again as he motioned for Viola to close the door behind her. Her unease permeated the air around them.

"What is it?" he asked, gesturing to the empty chair across from him.

Viola shook her head. "I won't stay long." But she didn't immediately speak.

"It's been a long day, so if you have something to say, you'd best get to it."

Her eyes found the sheets of papers and notes on the table, and then she glanced up at him. "You really think it's wise to include the girl in this?" she said finally.

"That seems to be the current consensus," Dolph said, sinking back into his own chair.

Viola scowled. "I don't trust her."

"You don't trust anyone, Vi. Except maybe Tilly, and even then . . ."

He gave a tired shrug. What was there to say about that, if Viola wouldn't say it herself?

Not that he blamed Viola for being so wary. She'd trusted her family, hadn't she? Raised as the dutiful daughter, she'd done everything they'd asked of her—became her brother's weapon when he began making enemies that came with the reputation he was building in the neighborhood. But when they'd heard whispers that she was getting too close to one of the teachers at the night classes she attended, they'd made the woman—and any hint of an affair—disappear and tried to sell Viola off to the highest bidder. For her own good, of course.

As young as she had been and with the family she came from, she'd risked her life leaving their house, and she'd risked everything else in trading her loyalty to him for protection. Not that she had trusted him enough to tell him everything that had happened. But he'd found out on his own. He always did.

Still, he'd never forget the day Viola arrived at the Strega, her lip split and crusted over, the skin around her left eye as purple as the iris. She'd walked through the saloon doors with her chin up, her shoulders back, and had promised him that she would do anything he asked of her if he would keep her family from dragging her back. Because if they tried, she would kill them rather than live under their control, and she didn't know if she could live with that.

Viola had kept her promise to him for more than three years now, and he'd come to depend on her. Come to almost enjoy her flashes of temper and to respect her intractable will. But he didn't have the patience for any of it that night.

Viola was silent at first as she took the seat opposite. Then, after a thoughtful moment, she leaned forward and spoke in low, halting tones. "We could wait awhile, you know. There's no reason to rush. Or we could do as Jianyu suggested and only take the art. It would be enough to embarrass Morgan without risking everyone to a green girl we still don't know."

Any other time, Viola's point would have been well taken. Usually, he'd spend months watching and waiting before he'd even consider taking someone new into his confidence. But this time . . .

"We can't wait." He'd been searching for answers for too long now, and he was still missing an important piece of the puzzle. He pushed a sheet of paper that held a list of names.

"What's this?"

"More have gone missing."

Viola studied the list, her eyes squinting and her mouth moving soundlessly as she tried to make out the names. "People always go miss—" She stopped short and looked up at him in surprise. "Krzysztof Zeranski?"

Dolph nodded. The city had a tendency to swallow the weak, but Mageus with stronger affinities, like Krzysztof, were usually better at avoiding that fate. Lately, though, it seemed that some of the most talented—and most powerful—were disappearing again, exactly as they had last year. "He helped with a fire on Hester Street last week. It's possible he was seen."

Viola handed him back the list. "What does this have to do with the job at the Metropolitan?"

"The Order is up to something. Look at that list, Viola. Krzysztof has a talent for calling to water. Eidelman grows nearly impossible blooms at his flower shop over near Washington Square, and anyone knows you talk to Frieda Weber if you want the sun to shine on your wedding day. They all could be confused for elementals."

Viola shook her head. "But they're not. Water, air, earth—they all are part of one another. To call to one is to call on the very core of magic itself."

"I know that and you know that. Hell, every Mageus was born with that knowledge deep in their bones, but the Order and their like—people who've never felt the call to connect with the world around them—fall back on the myth that you can separate the parts of magic to make it more manageable. Look at the Brink itself—as though you can separate the affinity from the Mageus without damaging both? It's impossible. No Mageus can fully recover from what it does to them, and every time one of our rank is laid low by it, magic as a whole is weakened.

"Maybe I'm wrong about this. Maybe I'm seeing patterns that aren't there, but I don't think so. This happened before, when we lost Leena. These names suggest that it's starting again. I can't ignore that fact, just as I can't forget that every day we wait is a day closer to the Conclave. They're planning something—something bigger than we've seen before—and we're running out of time to figure out what it is. We need the Ars Arcana."

"This is about the Book again?" she asked, clearly irritated.

"It is," he said.

"You really think a simple book is so important?"

"Leena never would have sacrificed herself for a *simple* book, Viola. Not unless it was *exactly* that important. I trusted her in life, and I'll trust her in this. I'm convinced the Order has the Ars Arcana, and I'm convinced we need it to beat them."

Viola's violet eyes were still unsure. "If we were truly brave, we could take on the Order without worrying about some stupid book. What chance could they stand against us? Conigli, all of us, for not fighting them."

Dolph shook his head. "Maybe once that would have been true, but now? Magic is dying, and it has been for some time. Away from the old countries, every generation forgets a little more. You've seen it yourself, haven't you? How each generation is a little weaker than the one before it. Maybe one hundred—even fifty—years ago, we might have stood a chance, but I wouldn't risk a stand now. No one with any sense would."

"So we wait until we're ready. We build our power," she argued. "We could take our time, chip away at the Order's power until they're weak enough to defeat."

"You don't understand. . . ." He leaned forward a bit. "What I'm trying to do is about more than simply bringing down the Order. If I'm right about the Ars Arcana, it contains the very secrets of magic itself."

"We *have* the secrets of magic." She tapped her chest. "It flows in our very blood."

"True, but we've forgotten. We could be *so* much more. The Order wouldn't be able to stop *any* Mageus from fulfilling their destiny ever again. We could make this whole country a haven for our kind." When she continued frowning, he pressed on. "This has become bigger than me, bigger than what I lost when the Order took Leena from me."

"What does any of this have to do with the museum? The Book isn't there."

"The Morgan exhibit has pieces I need to examine," he said, sliding the exhibition program toward her. Jianyu had managed to lift one from the printer where it was being made, so Dolph knew exactly what Morgan had. He knew exactly what he needed.

She glanced up at him, a question in her eyes.

"Getting into Khafre Hall won't be enough—the Order will have the Mysterium protected by more than a locked door. I'm expecting something like what they kept Leena in before they killed her—something that would hurt any Mageus who tried to come close. We'll need to break through that protection," he said, taking the program back from her and pointing to one entry in particular. "I think this might work."

She studied the entry doubtfully. "Morgan wouldn't put anything so dangerous—so important—on display," she challenged.

"He might if he didn't realize what he had," Dolph argued.

"You can't know that for sure."

No, of course he didn't know for sure. But it wasn't as though he could simply walk into the museum and examine the piece himself without raising suspicions. "I know enough, and Nibs is optimistic."

Viola studied him with narrowed eyes. "No . . . There's something more. Something you're not telling us."

"If I'm not telling you, then it's not your business to know," Dolph said, his impatience seeping into his words.

But Viola didn't seem to heed the warning in his voice. "You used to trust me, you know."

He let out an exasperated sigh. "I *still* trust you, Vi."

"You keep secrets from us." She shook her head. "You've always kept secrets from us, I suppose, but now I think there's something more. If you aren't careful, you're going to get us all killed."

"Are you saying you want out?" he asked tightly.

She studied him with eyes as sharp as the knives she had hidden in her skirts. The clock *tick-tick-ticked* out the seconds as they passed, each moment feeling like one closer to everything unraveling.

Leena would have known what to say to soothe Viola. She would have told him if this whole gambit was a mistake. But would he have listened?

"Are you saying I have a choice in the matter now?" Viola asked, her eyes never leaving his.

"You've always had a choice," he said, keeping his voice level, his expression placid. "But when you pledged your loyalty and took my mark, you understood the consequences of making it."

Her expression didn't so much as flicker. "I don't need your threats, Dolph. Mark or no mark, I keep my word."

"I know that, Viola," he told her. "If you don't want in on the Metropolitan job, I don't want you there. Too much is at stake for anyone not to be all in." He paused, lowered his voice. "We could use your help on it, though."

"Fine," she said after another long moment. "But if the girl crosses us—"

"I don't think she will."

"Will you give her your mark before?" she asked.

He should. Anyone he let close enough to do a job like this should have been made to take his mark, but with his affinity hollowed out and weak, the marks were pointless. He wasn't sure what would happen— what he would reveal—by marking the girl without his magic intact.

Viola frowned at his hesitation. "You're too soft on her."

"I'm not."

"You admire her," she insisted.

"She's a talented thief, but—"

"I can see why," Viola continued, ignoring him. "She's stubborn and too bold. She reminds me a bit of Leena in that way. But you're letting your sympathy cloud your judgment. I worry you trust her for the wrong reasons."

"I worry you dislike her for the wrong reasons," Dolph said softly.

"What are the right reasons, Dolph?"

But when he went to answer, he found that he didn't know anymore.

THE METROPOLITAN

Central Park East

E sta checked her reflection in the glass covering an eighteenth-century watercolor. The disdainful eyes of the wigged man in the portrait stared back at her, and she had the sudden, uneasy sense that he could see right through her. She only hoped no one else could.

Ignoring his disapproving gaze, she craned her neck from right to left to make sure that every stray hair was still tucked up into the silk tarboosh, the fezlike hat that all the servers were wearing that night. It was lucky, she supposed, that they were wearing them. She was nearly as tall as most men, and it was easy enough to wrap her chest to hide her curves, but without the hat, it would have been harder to hide her hair and pass as one of the male servers. Otherwise, she didn't doubt Viola would have made an argument for cutting it.

The silken pants and long tuniclike coats—all part of the exhibition's general theme—were a bonus too. To finally be out of the long skirts she'd been wearing made her feel freer than she had in weeks. Not that the serving uniforms or any of the decorations were even remotely authentic. With the shine of the silk and beaded details that glittered as she moved, the outfit looked more like something from a Vegas show.

To her own eyes, she still looked too feminine. There was no disguising the soft skin on her face or her thick, dark lashes, but she knew enough about people by now to know that they only ever saw what they expected. If they even looked at the help at all.

"You—boy," a voice shouted from the end of the hall. "Get away from there!"

Esta startled at the voice, and turned to find a large, broad-shouldered man in a dark suit coming her way. One of the museum's guards. She stepped away from the portrait and lowered her eyes.

"Don't you have somewhere to be?"

"On my way now, sir," she said, coughing out the words in a tone lower than her usual voice. She kept her head down and tried to put some swagger in her step as she moved past him.

Steady, she told herself. *Not much farther now . . .*

But as she passed, she felt tendrils of energy reach out and brush against her. Her skin tingled with awareness, and she nearly stumbled from the surprise of it.

He's using magic.

There shouldn't have been any other Mageus in the museum—Morgan was part of the Order, and the exhibition would be filled with its members—but the flicker of magic came again as she continued to walk away.

She kept her eyes down and moved as fast as she could without looking suspicious, but she didn't relax until she turned out of that gallery, into the quiet emptiness of a wide hall filled with statuary.

When she was well out of earshot, she cursed to herself and broke into a jog. She rounded the corner and took the steps in a far stairway two at a time. At the bottom, she turned into a larger sculpture gallery and kept her pace up as she rushed through it.

"Leaving so soon?" A shadow stepped out from behind a large urn.

Esta stopped dead, her heart in her throat, and turned to find Nibs. "What are you doing in here?" He was supposed to be outside, waiting to orchestrate their getaway.

"I could ask you the same," he said with a frown. "You should be upstairs with the other servers. I vouched for you."

"I wasn't trying to leave," she said. "I was coming to find you."

He gave her a doubtful look.

"We have a problem with the guards—they're Mageus."

His brows bunched over his round glasses as he studied her. "You're sure?" he asked, suspicious.

"Of course I'm sure. I know magic when I feel it, and the guy who saw me upstairs? He was using it." She glanced over her shoulder to make sure he hadn't followed. "I think he might have been checking me somehow."

Nibs frowned. He didn't seem half as concerned as Esta thought he should be. "If he was checking for your affinity, he must not be strong enough to find it unless you use it."

"How can you possibly know that?"

"You're still standing here."

The fact that he was right didn't make her feel any better. "I thought Morgan was a member of the Order."

"He's in the Inner Circle, their highest council."

"Then don't you think Mageus are the *last* people who should be here tonight?"

"You're here," Nibs pointed out. "I'm here."

"Yeah, to take the art. Not to guard it."

Nibs considered that. "It could be another team." His brow furrowed again, and he stared off in that half-vacant way he did when he was thinking. "But that doesn't feel right."

"They're working for Morgan?"

"Or the museum. But seeing as how Morgan's on the main board of directors here, it amounts to the same thing."

"That doesn't make sense," she told him. "The Order hates us."

"True, but it wouldn't be the first time they used us against each other. There are plenty in this city desperate enough to do nearly anything, including working for the Order." He glanced at her. "Look at the Haymarket. Corey might not be in the Order yet, but he's trying to get in. He might not be all that powerful, but he's a Mageus, same as the guards he employs. Even if he keeps his own identity a secret, his people all know who he rubs elbows with, but they think they're protected because they work for him. They're willing to rat out other Mageus, even though the unlucky ones get handed over to the Order."

Esta realized then how much danger she'd really been in that night. "That's horrible."

"Maybe, but you can't really blame them. Corey pays, and he pays well. Bad enough that the Order forces us to live in the worst parts of the city and uses their influence with the public to keep us in our place, but that's not enough for them. No, they still have one weakness—they can't sense magic like we can. But if they turn us against each other, it solves the problem."

"We didn't plan for this," Esta said. "We have to call it off and get out of here. *Now*. We can come back when we've figured out a different way in—"

But Nibs wasn't listening. He glanced down the hall toward where the guests were beginning to arrive, his eyes soft and unfocused. Then, all at once, he seemed to come to some decision. "No."

"No?" She gaped at him.

"Jianyu's already inside the gallery."

Esta went very still. "It's already locked?"

Nibs nodded. "And the room is half-full of Morgan's guests."

"We won't be able to warn him," she said, as the realization of how tight a spot they were in sank heavy in her stomach. "The second the doors open, he's done."

It had seemed simple enough when they'd laid it all out earlier. Without motion sensors or cameras, it should have been an easy job of evading a few guards. Morgan was set to inspect the gallery and his exhibition before the show. Concealed, Jianyu would slip in with him and wait until they'd secured the room. There were no windows, no other doors—no way in or out except through the locked and guarded entrance to the next gallery where the reception would happen.

At eight o'clock, Morgan would give a speech, and then the doors to his exhibition would be opened to his guests. By then Jianyu would have cleaned out the room and hidden himself along with the loot. The guests—all the leaders of the city and newspapermen reporting on the event—would be the first to see that Morgan's so-called great exhibition was nothing more than some empty frames and glass cases. All that would be left was for Jianyu to sneak out in the confusion. Easy.

All the while, Esta would be using the distraction of the robbery to clean out the rest of the guests—jewels, cash, anything that would embarrass Morgan further.

"We have to get him out of there," she told Nibs.

Except that now Jianyu was locked in a room, blocked by a crowd that contained Mageus playing for the enemy, watching for any sign of magic. When the doors opened, the walls would be bare and the guards would find Jianyu, who would be using his affinity to conceal himself. Once they found him, everything could be traced back to Dolph and the rest of his people.

"Even if you could get him out, you can't call off this job," Nibs said. "Dolph wants this done, and he wants it done tonight."

There has to be a way. "So we'll have to do it without magic, which means we'll need a distraction," she said, thinking through the plan and imagining what the Professor would have done, how he'd taught her to use what was available. "The best we can hope for is to throw them off, to point them away from Jianyu and away from Dolph. And we'll need backup if everything goes wrong."

"What are you thinking?" Nibs said, curious now. Interested.

"I think we need Viola," she told him, hoping that the half-baked idea she was formulating on the fly would work. And hoping that Viola wouldn't kill her for what she was about to ask her to do.

CLEVER THIEF

Harte made his way through an empty gallery toward the sound of voices ahead. He'd been to the museum before, countless mornings on the free-entry days, when he stared at paintings that promised a world beyond the narrow strip of land he was trapped on. Usually, on those days, the rooms would be filled with the chattering of women more interested in discussing the fashions of the other visitors than looking at the art. So that night, the silence felt like a gift. It transformed the whole place into his own private gallery, allowing him to imagine—just for a moment—that he'd attained the life he'd dreamed for himself.

He stopped in front of a landscape, a dramatic vista of glimmering rivers and sky-capped mountains in the distance. Places like that existed. Places that were clean and open, free from the stink of the city with its coal-laden air and trash-filled gutters. He had to believe that someday he would see them for himself. He took a moment more to let the image fortify him, and then he continued on toward his destination.

Eventually, the voices grew louder, and he came to the large, airy gallery that held a series of medieval altarpieces. It was currently serving as a space for less spiritual concerns—the cocktail party for J. P. Morgan's many guests. Servers in brightly colored tunics carried trays of champagne to Morgan's guests, who glittered in their jewels and silk.

Harte handed his invitation to a doorman, who gave it only a cursory glance before handing him a program and nodding for him to continue. But as Harte passed through the entryway, he felt the warning warmth that signaled magic in the air. It crawled across his skin, tousling his hair as it inspected him.

The guards are Mageus. It was an unexpected and unsettling development, to say the least, but Harte forced himself to keep walking into the crowded room as though he hadn't felt anything. People without affinities could rarely feel magic the way Mageus could, so Harte didn't allow himself to so much as pause. Instead, he pulled everything he was inward, locking down his own power with a speed that made his skin go cold.

The guards weren't the only challenge he faced in that room. The gallery was filled with a veritable who's who of New York society—bankers from Wall Street and politicians from Tammany, and many of the millionaires who'd built their houses along Madison or Fifth. A few well-known reporters lurked by the far wall, making notes with stubby pencils in their palm-size tablets as they watched the crowd with sharp, perceptive eyes. Harte recognized Sam Watson, the *Sun* reporter who'd done a feature on his act the previous summer. The story had helped ticket sales, but Harte hated how it had made him feel like an insect on display.

He also hated that at least a small measure of his success was owed to the same man who'd made it his mission to write so regularly—and viciously—about the dangerous Mageus that might be lurking among the newly arrived immigrants. Seeing Watson that night wasn't all that surprising, but the last thing Harte needed was for Watson to start dropping hints about his pedigree—or lack of one—in front of Jack.

Before Harte could turn away, Watson spotted him and began making his way across the room. "Harte Darrigan," he called, extending his hand with a slick grin. "I'm surprised to see *you* here."

"Oh?" he said, shaking Watson's hand. It would have been easy enough to get rid of the reporter, but with the guards, Harte was forced to deal with him.

"Doesn't seem like your usual crowd." Watson nodded toward the full room. "Or maybe you're here as the floor show?" he suggested with a less-than-friendly smirk.

"I think you're mistaking me for one of the chorus girls you like so much," Harte said breezily, but he clutched his hands behind his back to keep himself from punching the ass. "Evelyn sends her regards, by the way."

"Really?" Watson said a little too eagerly, but when he realized Harte was only toying with him, his expression went dark.

"How're things in the newspaper business?" Harte asked before Watson could needle him any more.

While Watson was prattling on about his latest editorial, something drew Harte's attention to the far side of the gallery. One of the servers stumbled, nearly running into a man in tails in an attempt not to drop a tray of empty glasses. The man reached out to steady the boy, and when he did, the server's hand dipped quickly into the man's pocket.

He watched with interest as the server used the confusion as a distraction, nimbly slipping whatever he'd taken into his tunic.

No, not his . . . *hers.*

Harte almost laughed out loud. With the shapeless tunic and her dark hair tucked beneath her cap, the girl blended in with the rest of the staff well enough. No one—him included, until that moment—was paying any real attention to the people bearing trays of drinks and canapés. But he was paying attention now.

"Would you excuse me?" Harte asked Watson. He didn't wait for a reply.

He was almost halfway to her when he heard his name over the din of the crowded room. "Darrigan!" Jack's voice called again, unmistakable this time.

Harte turned to find Jack pushing his way through the crowd and lifted his hand in greeting. If he went for the girl now, Jack would probably follow him, so he gave Jack a short nod and gestured toward a server carrying a tray of champagne. After retrieving a glass for himself and a second for Jack, he made his way back through the crush of the room.

"Good man," Jack said, accepting the drink.

"Thanks for having me." Harte lifted the glass in a silent toast as he scanned the room, looking for the girl. "This is quite the event."

Jack downed the champagne, set the empty goblet on a passing server's tray, and picked up another one. "Same as always, but my uncle seems pleased. Might even be happy enough to get him off my back for a while."

"Best of luck with that," Harte said, barely sipping at the drink as he looked again for some sign of the girl. He didn't see her, which didn't make him feel any better, but he ignored his nerves and pulled on the mask he always wore for Jack. "Have you had a chance to look at the exhibit yet?"

"I have." Jack's eyes lit. "There's at least one piece that looked interesting—one of the Babylonian seals he collects."

"A seal?" Harte asked, trying to picture it.

"A small cylindrical piece about so big." Jack held up his thumb and forefinger two inches apart. "It makes an imprint when rolled across wet clay or rubbed with ink. They were often used as signatures, but my uncle tends to be more interested in the ones used as amulets. Most are made from ceramic or stone, but I believe the one I was examining was carved from unpolished ruby . . . astounding, really, considering the size of it. But my uncle interrupted me before I could find out for sure." He scowled. "Now it's under glass for the foreseeable future."

Before Harte could ask anything else, a drumroll sounded through the room, ending with a sudden *crack*. A shout of *"Aiiiieeee!"* went up, and the crowd turned, almost as one, to see what was happening.

"I believe that's the entertainment. It'll probably be the only redeeming thing about this bore of an evening," he murmured. "Shall we?"

"After you," Harte said affably, following Jack through the press of bodies to a space where the crowd had moved aside to allow the performers room.

A procession was coming through the grand arched entrance of the gallery. First came two men in the same sort of billowing pants the servers wore, but their outfits were more extravagant, with heavy embroidery and intricate details on their vests and shoes. They carried wide, flat drums on their hips and were followed by another musician plucking a driving tune made up of minor chords and melodies on a pear-shaped guitar.

A figure wrapped in gauzy silken veils appeared in the doorway, and then she was spinning, dropping the veils as she undulated across the floor, until she was in the center of the room. The curves of her stomach and chest were exposed in flashes of skin and then hidden again by the gossamer fabric she whipped around her, and her fingers tapped tiny cymbals to the rhythm of the drums as her hips twisted and snaked.

"Egad," Jack said with a laugh as he elbowed Harte hard enough to nearly spill the champagne Harte was holding. "It's a damn good thing the old man left me in charge of the entertainment, isn't it?" He tossed back the last of his champagne, licking his lips as he watched the girl dance.

Harte couldn't blame him. He was also finding it difficult to take his eyes off the dancing girl. Her costume seemed to hide as much as it revealed, teasing the audience as her hips moved in an almost indecent rhythm. She was the embodiment of a mystery, especially with the bottom of her face covered by a veil that fluttered beneath her strange violet eyes—

Viola?

Harte looked more closely, awareness prickling. It *was* Viola. First the girl, and now this? It had Dolph Saunders written all over it, and Harte didn't want to be anywhere close when whatever they were planning happened.

But how was he supposed to leave so early without making Jack suspicious?

In the center of the room, Viola was still dancing. Harte was going to start backing away, using Jack's interest in the performance to his advantage, but when the music changed, she dropped her finger cymbals and, in a dramatic motion, reached behind her back and withdrew a brace of thin, silver knives that glistened in the brilliant electric light of the gallery.

Harte stopped short, watching warily as Viola danced with the knives splayed between her fingers. He'd heard about what Viola could do with a knife, the way she could hit any target from any distance. Whoever her target was that night didn't stand a chance, but then again, neither did she. The second she used her affinity, she'd be found out.

Without warning, the drum snapped out a rim shot, and Viola let a knife fly. *Swiiip*, it sailed through the air and took a cap off a server's head, pinning it to the wall behind. The room erupted into wild applause, and Jack elbowed him, absolutely delighted at the show.

But there had been no spike of energy, no telltale warmth to give away her magic. *Maybe her skill with the knives is simply that—a skill,* he thought, when none of the guards moved to stop her.

As she spun, all eyes in the room were on her, waiting for her next move with the kind of nervous excitement Harte had seen before dogfights or before bare-knuckle matches. It was the desire to see violence done to someone else, to be close to the blade of danger without ever being cut.

It wasn't anything Harte himself was interested in anymore. He'd had too much violence and danger in his life already. The only thing that interested him now was what the girl was doing. He saw her then, the only one moving across the room instead of watching the entertainment, inching her way toward the door to the gallery beyond.

So that's her game, he thought with sudden uneasiness.

In the middle of the floor, Viola was still dancing, now weaving through the room, pulling one of the dour-looking guards into the dance with her gossamer scarf. The other guards laughed, slapping each other as they watched her draw their friend into the center of the room. Away from the door he was supposed to be guarding.

Misdirection, Harte understood. It was the heart of any illusion, and Viola's was particularly effective.

Swiiip. Another knife sailed through the air, pinning the sleeve of another guard to the wall. More laughter erupted as he tried to free himself.

Harte began to move toward the closed gallery, to where the girl was standing with her back to the door, her hands behind her. Again, there was no betraying energy, no sign that she was using any affinity.

Clever thief. Talented, too, if she could pick that lock without looking *and* without magic. Luckily, she was too busy concentrating on her task to notice him approaching her, but she went completely still when he sidled up next to her.

"Fancy meeting you here," he said, dipping his head low so that no one else would hear. He was ready this time for the effect she had on him, the talent she had for distracting him when he should most be paying attention.

Her eyes widened, but that was the only indication of her surprise. "Go away," she told him, her hands still working behind her.

He had to admire the backbone in her. "You know, you can't use magic in here—they have Mageus watching for it."

"I'm aware," she said, glancing at him.

He frowned. "If you're doing what I think you're doing, you'll never get out of here without it."

"It's sweet of you to think I need saving, but I'll be fine. If you'd be a dear and leave me alone, that is."

"Save *you*?" he said, widening his eyes dramatically. "Is that what you think I'm doing?" He inched closer. "I'm only interested in saving myself. You do what I think you're about to do, and I might get caught in the crossfire."

"Then maybe you should get out of the way."

He moved closer, lowering his voice so only she could hear. "Maybe those men in the dark suits would be interested in meeting you. I'm sure they'd have a few questions about why you're dressed like that."

"I'd be happy to give them some answers," she said too sweetly, batting her eyes at him innocently. "I'm sure they'd love to hear all about a certain magician who has more magic than they realize up his sleeves."

"You wouldn't," he said, almost amused in spite of himself.

"I might," she said, but her eyes were laughing at him. "I've decided I kind of hate you, you know."

He found himself smiling. "I assure you, sweetheart, the feeling is mutual."

"Well, then . . . Since we seem to understand each other now, you might want to move."

The smile fell from his face. "Mo—"

The word was only halfway out when he felt the breath of air as a silver knife flashed between them. It was enough to make him step back.

Then the lights went out.

A CHANGE IN PLANS

Her heart was still pounding from the surprise of having Harte Darrigan materialize out of nowhere. She'd been so busy focusing on the feel of the lock, letting the vibrations from the pick guide her, that she hadn't even seen him until it was too late.

Thank god for Viola. Or thank god Viola had only distracted him, when Esta was pretty sure Dolph's assassin would have been just as happy to skewer them both. She'd definitely wanted to earlier, when Esta had explained her plan for Viola to create a distraction by replacing the troupe's dancer. She had a feeling Viola didn't forgive easily.

Not that she had time to worry about that. The second the lights went out, Esta slipped into the next gallery, leaving behind the gasping, buzzing crowd in the antechamber.

"Jianyu?" she whispered. "Are you here?"

"Where else would I be?" His voice came out of the darkness. "What is happening? This was not the plan."

"Plan's changed," she said, sparking a small flame and lighting the nub of a candle she'd carried in her sleeve. Then she lifted her tunic and removed the clothing she'd hidden there. "They have Mageus for guards. If you use your affinity, you'll never get out. Here—" She tossed him the gauzy pants and scarf. "Loosen your hair and put these on. And be quick about it."

Jianyu rubbed the silky fabric between his fingers. "These are for a woman."

"Yeah. Get moving." She took the bundle of objects Jianyu had collected and began fastening them beneath her clothes. She wrapped a rolled canvas around her upper thigh and tucked a couple of small carved cylinders into the fabric binding her breasts.

Jianyu wasn't changing. He simply glared at her. "You want me to dress as a *woman*?"

"That's the basic idea," she said, sliding a smaller canvas around her other ankle, fastening it in place with the garter for her socks.

"No," Jianyu said, dropping the sapphire silk into a pile at his feet.

Esta turned on him. "We have *maybe* two minutes left before the lights come back on. That means we have less than two minutes to get you out of here before we can't. In about ninety seconds, I'll be on the other side of that door and on my way to the carriage out back, and you'll be on your own. You can either get over your fragile masculine pride and put on the damn skirt or deal with the Order yourself."

After a moment of stony silence, he began unbraiding his hair, glaring at her all the while. He looked like he wanted to kill someone, and Esta knew he probably could, but he didn't argue as he made quick work of the rest, covering his head and face with the gauzy scarf. It didn't do much to hide his masculinity. If anyone bothered to really look, they would know he was a man dressed in women's clothing.

Not that they had any other choice at that point. She'd just have to hope that people would only see what they expected to, or that they wouldn't bother looking at all.

"Very pretty," she taunted as she slipped the last item into her waistband. "Ready?"

Jianyu glared at her.

"Maybe relax your shoulders a bit?" she suggested. "If you want to get out of here, you need to at least *try*."

"I *am* trying," he snapped, pulling himself up even taller and broader than before.

We are so screwed.

"Okay, well, try harder," she said, adjusting the scarf over his face to cover his scowl. "When you get out there, you need to pretend like you've been there the whole time. Follow Viola's lead." She snuffed the candle with her fingertips.

On the other side of the door, the crowd had grown frantic, which was convenient because their noise covered the sound of the latch as they entered the outer room. She made sure the lock caught, so it would look like the gallery had never been breached.

"Go," she whispered, pushing Jianyu into the crowd as the lights came back on.

There was a moment of shocked silence, before the crowd's voices rose again, louder than they'd been before. Men barked for someone to explain what had happened, and women gasped, grabbing at their jewels to make sure they were all in place.

"If you could give me your attention—" A voice came from somewhere on the other side of the room, low and male and full of its own importance, but it took a few more tries before the crowd would quiet enough to listen to the man speaking.

Nearby, Harte Darrigan blinked at the brightness, squinting as his eyes adjusted to the sudden return of the light. Esta feigned confusion like everyone else as she sidled away from his reach. In the far corner, J. P. Morgan had found something to stand on and was telling the crowd to stay calm, that it had simply been a problem with the power, but it had been solved and there was no reason to worry. The evening would go on as planned.

Not quite as planned, Esta thought as she lifted a tray from a nearby cart and made her way through the crowd. Afraid to jostle the items beneath her clothing, she walked cautiously.

In the center of the room, Morgan was commanding the musicians to begin playing again, and they immediately launched into another driving tune that was all drums and cymbals. Esta cringed as she saw that Jianyu was standing stiffly, his arms crossed over his chest, instead of making an effort to blend in. But no one seemed to notice. A few more minutes— another pass around the room for Viola and the boys, a careful exit for herself—and they'd all be safe.

Esta kept her pace steady as she moved ever closer to the arched entrance of the gallery, accepting empty glasses from people who seemed willing enough to forget the momentary darkness now that the lights were back on. From across the room, Viola caught her gaze and gave a subtle nod before she led the troupe—including Jianyu—beneath the arched entry, out into the museum. Their music faded as they moved away, until it stopped altogether.

They were out.

Now it was up to her to get their haul—and herself—out safely as well. Because if she was caught, there would be no one left to help her.

She was already halfway to the entry, only a few yards more to freedom, when Morgan began his speech about the collection. His voice boomed through the room as he declared his deep affection for the Ottoman Empire, for their great discoveries and mystical art.

Almost there, Esta thought, closing the final few feet between her and the exit. *A little farther*—

Then someone snagged her arm, and she startled, nearly dropping the tray of glasses. She looked over her shoulder to find Harte Darrigan's stormy eyes boring into hers. With the tray of stemware balanced precariously in her other hand, she couldn't shake him off. If his hand moved a few inches up her arm, he'd definitely feel the roll of stolen parchment she'd wrapped there, and especially after that little stunt she'd pulled on his stage, she didn't know what he would do.

"Let me go," she whispered furiously.

He studied her a moment longer with eyes that seemed far older than his years. Then he took the glass he was holding and placed it on her tray. "You missed one," he said. He still didn't release her arm.

She was trapped.

Panic seized the breath in her chest, made her feel as though every heartbeat was a step toward her inevitable end. Morgan's voice was still droning on, but he sounded very far away—like she was listening to him through a long tunnel. It felt like she was stuck in the spaces between seconds, unable to go back and make another choice. Unable to do anything to change what was about to happen without putting herself—and everyone else—in more danger.

But the sudden eruption of applause brought her back to herself. The room snapped into focus, and the panic that had strangled her receded to a dull ache. Her mind raced.

They were about to open the doors to the other gallery. In a moment they would see that the collection was gone. Once that happened, the museum would be locked down. She'd be trapped, strapped from head to toe with pieces of priceless art. She had to get out before that happened.

But he didn't release her. "Don't you want to see the exhibition?" he asked, his voice steady.

He knows. And now he was toying with her.

She glared at him and tried to tug away again, but it was too late. The *click* of the lock echoed through the room and the gallery doors opened with everyone watching, waiting to see Morgan's jewel of a collection.

A gasp rang out in the crowd as the gallery doors stood open, exposing the ransacked room, the missing collection.

The Magician glanced over as the news of the theft filtered through the crowd, and then he looked back at Esta. His eyes were curious and, if she wasn't mistaken, more than a little appreciative.

She could *not* be caught. Not now, before she had saved the Book and retrieved her stone. And not there, in a room filled with members of the Order.

With a quick motion, she flipped her tray toward him.

Instinctively, his whole body sprang into action. He released her and lunged for the tray to catch it before the glasses fell. But though he'd let her go, the racket of the glasses crashing to the floor caused the people around him to turn. Already another server was coming to help.

The mouth of the room was only a few feet away, but dark-suited men were moving to block any exit. She'd never make it, unless . . .

Esta knew it was a risk, but she couldn't be trapped. She had to get the art out. She had to get *herself* out. There wasn't a choice. So she pulled time around her and ran for it.

She didn't bother to see whether the guards sensed her magic as she slipped past them and into the hall. She didn't stop for anything, just ran as fast as her feet would carry her, down the winding staircase and back through the statue gallery to the service entrance. Barreling past another guard, who was frozen in midrun toward the gallery, she made it out of the museum, into the quiet night, but she didn't release her hold on time. She moved effortlessly through the silent, still world. The bare fingers of the park's trees, so much smaller than in her own time, were dark shadows against the star-filled sky as she passed the knifelike point of Cleopatra's Needle. They waved her on as she made her way down the lane to where the carriage was waiting.

The others would be gone, she knew. If everything had gone to plan. She didn't release time until she reached the dark body of the carriage. The horses nickered when she knocked, using the rhythm of beats she'd been taught. To her relief, the door opened.

But that relief changed to caution when she saw that Dolph sat concealed in the shadows, waiting. "You have the items?" he asked as she took the seat opposite him.

She gave a nod, and he rapped on the roof twice with his silver-topped cane to signal the driver. With a lurch, the carriage started off, rattling down the cobbled road.

The small, dark space felt too close, too confined with Dolph's long legs taking up most of the room between them. She pulled her legs as far from his as she could and tried to shake off her nerves. He'd taken a risk in allowing her to help them, and everything had gone wrong.

"Well?" His voice was low, expectant.

She began unfastening the items, taking them from their hiding places beneath her clothes. Dolph took them from her, one at a time, but his expression lit at the sight of a small, carved stone cylinder. He tucked it away in the inner pocket of his coat, like it was something more important than the rest.

After a few long moments of silence punctuated only by the rattling of the wheels and the strained squeak of the seat beneath her, Dolph spoke. "Nibs told me what happened tonight."

"He did?" Her mouth went dry.

"You took quite a risk, going through with things," Dolph said. "You could have gotten yourself out and left Jianyu to his own fate."

She relaxed a little. He wasn't talking about her use of magic. "That's true," she admitted. "I could have."

"You thought about it," he challenged, his expression unreadable in the dappled shadows of the coach.

"No, actually. Once I knew Jianyu was trapped, it never crossed my mind."

"I find that difficult to believe," Dolph said.

Esta leaned forward until her face was lit by the flickering light coming through the small window. She wanted him to see the truth of her words, the sincerity of her intention. Dolph Saunders needed to trust her if she was ever going to get into Khafre Hall. She needed to be on that crew if she was ever going to get close enough to stop the Magician and get her hands on the Book . . . or her stone. Her only way back was through Dolph.

"I never considered getting myself out," she told him. "You trusted me with this, and I was not going to betray that trust. My only thought was to find a way to get *everyone* out safely. I did my job, like I promised I would."

He considered that for a moment, but his expression didn't change. Instead, he leaned back in his seat lazily, his fingertips drumming against the silver Medusa that topped his cane. "Your job was to fleece the crowd," he said, his lean face grim in the shadows of the coach.

"Who said I didn't?" She pulled out a necklace studded with enormous diamonds and emeralds. The stones glimmered as they dangled from her fingertip. "Mrs. Morgan sent this along with her compliments."

Dolph's finger stopped moving. "Did she?"

Esta did let her mouth curve then. "Well, maybe she would have, if she had known it was gone."

As Dolph took the necklace from her, his expression grudgingly appreciative, Esta didn't feel any sense of victory. Dolph might be pleased, but she couldn't help worrying about what it meant that the Magician had seen her. Harte Darrigan would know Dolph was behind the robbery, and she didn't know what he might do with that knowledge.

And she couldn't help but worry that her use of magic to escape might come back to haunt her. To haunt them all.

A DAMN GOOD TRICK

I t had been a damn good trick, making all that art disappear in a matter of the two minutes or so the lights had gone out, and with none of them using their affinities. But the girl had left a mess in her wake, the least of which was the mixture of leftover champagne Harte was covered in and the crystal goblets shattered on the floor around him.

She seemed to have a way of quite literally disappearing every time they met. It was something to do with her affinity, he knew. He should have been annoyed by her habit of leaving him empty-handed and look- ing like an idiot, but that, too, was a damn fine trick, and he couldn't stop himself from admiring her for it. Even if this time she'd left him in a precarious place.

There had been no way around talking to the squat police captain. He stood, dripping and smelling like a cheap clip joint, as he relayed a version of what he'd seen.

He could have handed the girl and Dolph and the rest of them over, which would have certainly improved his standing with Jack, but that would've come with certain risks. Considering that the girl knew enough about him to make her dangerous, he hadn't been sure that telling the police everything was the best idea.

Better not to be caught in his own net. Better to have something up his sleeve against Dolph Saunders—and the girl—just in case.

If he'd been smarter, he would have left the minute he saw the girl. He had known something was about to happen, and he should have left instead of trying to find out what she was up to. Now he'd missed his curtain, which wouldn't go over well, considering the talk Shorty had given him the other day. He'd have to do damage control when he got back.

"The papers are going to have a field day with this," Jack said dully as he came up next to Harte. "The whole family is going to blame me, you know. So much for getting them off my back."

"It's damn unfair," Harte agreed, pretending more sympathy than he actually felt. "How much did they get away with?"

"Nearly everything of any real value." Jack glanced across the room to where J. P. Morgan and his son were still in tense discussions with the police chief. "At least three canvases were cut from their frames. Even if they're returned, they'll be irreparably damaged. And all the seals are gone, including the one I told you about." Then he noticed Darrigan's shirtfront and jacket were a mess—stained and damp. "What the hell happened to you?"

Harte made a show of examining his damp lapels. "Accident with one of the servers."

"Accident, you say?" Jack frowned, looking over the ruined jacket. "Which one was it? I'll look into it, make sure they're taken care of for you."

"Oh, don't bother," Harte said, waving it off. The last thing he wanted was for Morgan—or anyone else—to look too closely at him. Especially not when they were investigating a crime. "It happened when the lights went out. I don't think it could have been helped."

"Damn mess," Jack muttered. He glanced over at Harte, lowering his voice so no one would hear. "The head of security told my uncle there were definitely Mageus involved."

"Oh?" Harte said, trying to mask his surprise with bored indifference. "They know that for sure, do they?"

Jack glanced back at his uncle again and then pulled Harte away, steering him toward a quiet part of the room. "It's something new the director was trying. Employing people with, shall we say, *special* qualities. My uncle—and the Order—approved of it, if you can believe that. They didn't bother telling me, or I would have told them it was a mistake. As though they'd ever willingly give up one of their own."

"Thick as thieves," Harte agreed, eyeing the guards, who were still watching the room.

He reminded himself that the guards' affinities couldn't be *that* strong—they would have caught the girl, otherwise. Still, it wouldn't do to linger. It wasn't worth the chance. "Well," he said, clapping Jack sympathetically on the shoulder, "I've already missed my curtain, and I need to get back to explain things."

"I *am* sorry about that," Jack said with a frown.

Darrigan pasted an easy smile on his face. "I'm sure when the story hits the papers tomorrow, I'll be able to talk my way out of it," he said.

Jack snagged his arm. "You don't know how they did it, do you?"

Harte froze. "Excuse me?"

"How did they get everything out of that locked room? I watched them secure it earlier myself. No one was in there, and no one could *get* in there, not with this gallery filled with people. The lights weren't out for more than a minute or two." Jack hesitated, eyeing Harte. "It was a little like one of your tricks."

Cold unease trickled down Harte's spine. "I don't do tricks," he said carefully.

"You know what I mean . . . onstage?"

"Those are *effects*, Jack. Demonstrations of skill. Whatever magic might have been involved tonight isn't any I'm familiar with, and I'm a victim here as much as anyone—someone managed to take my watch in the confusion." He held up the empty chain to display the missing pocket watch.

"I know that." Jack rubbed his hand over his mouth. He looked tired and hungover, and it wasn't even past midnight. He looked *vulnerable*. "I'm sorry for dragging you into all of this."

"You know," Harte said carefully, taking advantage of the moment. "Maybe you're right. Maybe I *could* help you with this."

Jack looked up. "You could?"

"Of course, Jack. That's what friends do. They help each other. I don't know anything about the old magic, of course . . . but you're right. I know how to make things disappear better than anyone. Maybe I could figure out how they did it. I'm not making any promises, but I'd be more than willing to look into the matter."

A desperate hope lit Jack's eyes. "I'd appreciate it, Darrigan. I really would."

"And if we happened to figure it out, your uncle would appreciate it too, wouldn't he?"

"I'm sure he would."

"He'd have no reason to keep you out of the Inner Circle, would he?" Jack shook his head.

"And once you're one of them . . . you could put in a good word for your friend, couldn't you?"

"Of course," Jack said, understanding. He gave Harte a knowing smile. "It's what friends do."

Harte nodded. "Let me think about it and see what I can come up with," he told Jack. "I'll let you know."

"Thank you," Jack said, grasping his hand to shake it.

"But let's not tell anyone yet, okay? I wouldn't want to get their hopes up." *Or their suspicions,* Harte thought as he took the risk to send a small pulse of his power against Jack's hand.

When he released Harte's hand, Jack stared at him for a moment, a little dazed. "I'll talk to you soon, then," he said, before he turned away, heading toward the ransacked gallery.

Harte watched him go, the mixture of the pull of his affinity and adrenaline singing in his veins. He was closer than he'd ever been to hooking Jack and gaining the entry to the Order that he needed if he wanted to get the Book. If he wanted to get out of the city. But he had to be careful and take his time. There was no room for a single misstep. The girl knew too much. Dolph was too powerful. And if Harte wasn't careful, he and all his dreams could end up as shattered and pointless as the shards of crystal still littering the floor.

Bella Strega

Sitting cross-legged on her small cot of a bed, Esta chewed at her lip as she read Professor Lachlan's news clipping again. Once they'd returned to the Strega the night before, Dolph had thanked her again and left her to herself. But Esta hadn't been able to sleep much, not after she checked the clipping. She kept checking it throughout the night, hoping that something would be different. Yes, the letters had stopped wavering and the words had finally resolved themselves into clear sentences, but that hadn't improved things.

The story had changed.

No fire. No destruction of Khafre Hall. Instead, the article was a bland piece about a party the Order had thrown to thank their newest member, Harte Darrigan, for apprehending the mastermind behind the Metropolitan Museum robbery, a saloon keeper named Dolph Saunders. Some items were still missing, but the article said that because Saunders died on his way to the prison on Blackwell Island, authorities didn't have high hopes for recovering them. Especially since Saunders' crew had scattered, abandoning his saloon and other holdings, which were being confiscated by the city.

Of course he'd died, Esta thought as her stomach twisted. To get to the island, they would have taken him out of Manhattan . . . right through the Brink. Dolph wouldn't have stood a chance. None of them would have.

Somehow the future had changed. Most likely, her being there had changed it. The Magician's treachery was even worse now, and she didn't know what other implications that might have. She had to fix it, but she had no idea how.

A knock sounded at the door, startling her. "Coming," she called as she tucked the clipping back into its protective wax sleeve with shaking fingers and then slid the small packet down the front of her corset.

When she opened the door, Jianyu was waiting on the other side.

"Can I help you?"

His expression was unreadable. "Dolph wants to see you."

Her chest went tight. "What for?" she asked, glad that her voice didn't sound as shaky as she felt. She thought he'd been pleased with her when they arrived back in the Bowery late the night before, but with her unsettling discovery of the changes in the news clipping, she wasn't taking anything lightly.

"It was not my place to ask," Jianyu said evenly. "He's waiting in his apartment downstairs."

"Okay," she told him, smoothing her rumpled skirt. "Give me a minute?"

Jianyu nodded, but just as he turned to leave, he seemed to change his mind. "You dressed me as a woman."

"I did," Esta admitted, feeling more uneasy with every moment that passed beneath Jianyu's watchful gaze.

"It was insulting."

Esta frowned. "Only if you think women are somehow less than men."

"Are they not?" Jianyu asked, sincerely surprised and confused.

Frustration spiked. This was a different time, she reminded herself, and yet . . . "A woman saved you, so you tell me."

Jianyu seemed to consider this. "It is true that things would have been difficult for me without your help."

Esta snorted. "More like impossible."

"Then I suppose I am in your debt."

"Or we could just call things even," Esta said.

Jianyu studied her for a moment, and then he gave the barest nod and left without another word.

Esta watched him go, wondering what exactly had just happened between them. She wasn't sure, but she thought maybe she'd found another ally. That fact made her feel somewhat better as she made her way down to the door of Dolph Saunders' apartment. She hesitated for a moment, calming herself and gathering her wits about her, before she knocked.

"Come," a familiar voice called from inside.

The door was unlocked, so she eased her way into his rooms and was greeted with a welcome breath of warmth. A coal stove burned in the corner, and near it, Dolph sat at a small desk, making notes in his ledger. He didn't bother to look up when she came in, but the sight of him so soon after she'd read about his death shook her. If she didn't fix things, she was looking at a dead man.

"Jianyu said you wanted to see me?"

He must not have noticed the way her voice broke, because he never took his concentration from his ledger as he gestured for her to come in. "Give me a second," he said.

"Of course," she told him, finally taking a look around his home.

Dolph was a man of few words. He never dressed in anything but black or dark grays, which gave the impression that he was perennially waiting for a funeral to begin. With all his glowering, she didn't expect his apartment to feel so comfortable.

A faded floral carpet covered most of the bare floorboards, and the room had a softness that her own didn't have. The furnishings were worn and well used, but the delicate spindles of the straight-backed chairs against the wall and the graceful camelback arch of the small divan were the selections of someone with an eye for decorating. In all, it had a distinctly feminine feel, which was only underscored by the wispy lace panels over the windows on the back wall of the front parlor.

Above a small shelf lined with books hung a painting that Esta recognized. It was one of the larger oil paintings they'd liberated from Morgan's collection the night before. In it, a young man reclined beneath an apple tree, a dog at his feet and a wide book open in his hands as he pondered a fallen apple. Dolph had, apparently, wasted no time in making it his own.

The news clipping had mentioned the painting as part of the evidence they had against him, so seeing it hanging on his wall was another reminder of his new fate. She wanted to tell him to get rid of it, to get rid of all the evidence he might have, but she wouldn't be able to explain herself. She needed him to continue to trust her if she was going to fix things, so instead she gestured to the newly framed canvas.

"Is that supposed to be Isaac Newton?" she asked as she studied the scene. With the apple resting on the ground by his feet, it could have been depicting him discovering gravity, but it was a strange painting, otherwise. A crescent moon hung opposite a bright sun, and the book the figure held in his hands bore odd symbols that looked like a series of interlocking circles and parallelograms, with a star in the center. It wasn't any math or science she'd ever seen.

Across the room, Dolph's pencil stilled and he looked up, his pale eye taking her measure for a long moment. "It is."

"But this looks so . . . mystical. I thought he was a scientist."

Dolph's brow furrowed. "There never was much of a line between science and magic, especially not that far back. Early sciences—alchemy or theurgy, for instance—were just ways for those without affinities to try to do what Mageus could do. Newton wasn't any different, but Newton's the least interesting thing about that piece."

Then Dolph turned back to his ledger, making it clear he wasn't interested in further conversation on the topic.

Esta was about to ask him what the most interesting thing was, when she heard Professor Lachlan's voice in her head—*Patience, girl*. How many times had he reminded her to take her time, to avoid whatever impulse drove her forward until she thought the situation through and considered all the possible outcomes?

Too many times. And there was even more at risk now.

So she bit back the question and occupied herself instead by look-ing over the books in his small collection—Voltaire, Rousseau, and Kierkegaard, all in their original languages. She wasn't surprised, somehow.

Eventually, Dolph finished whatever he was doing in the ledger and closed it. "Tell me what you know of Harte Darrigan," he said finally.

"The Magician?" she asked, suddenly wary. *He can't know,* she reminded herself. "Not much," she hedged. "Nibs took me to see his show the other night."

"I'm aware. He told me that Darrigan was quite taken with you."

Esta frowned. "I don't know that I'd use those words, exactly."

"Really?" Dolph leaned back in the chair a little, crossing his arms over his chest and giving her the full weight of his stare. "What words would you use?"

Pain in my ass, thought Esta, trying not to let her nervousness show. *A pain in yours, too, if I don't stop him.* Not that she could tell him what she knew, how things might have changed. Dolph had no reason to believe her, and without her stone, she had no way to prove it.

"I don't know." She shrugged. "He seems talented enough, but I was onstage with him for less than five minutes."

"You talked with him again at the museum."

Her stomach twisted again. "I didn't plan that—"

"I never said you did," Dolph murmured. "But as I said, he seems taken with you."

"I'm not interested in him, if that's what you're worried about."

"And if I want you to be interested?" Dolph asked.

"I'm still not interested," Esta told him, firm.

He didn't say anything else at first as she stood there, growing increas-ingly uncomfortable.

"Was there something you needed from me?" she asked, breaking the silence when she couldn't stand it anymore. "I still have my quota to bring in today, and it's pointless to steal wallets if the money's already been spent."

LISA MAXWELL

"You won't need to worry about that today," he told her.

"Why?" she asked, her throat tight. "Did I do something wrong?"

He lifted himself from the chair without answering and took his time about rinsing his teacup and saucer in the long enameled sink in the attached kitchen. Esta shifted, trying not to let her impatience get the best of her as he set the cup aside to dry and crossed the room to fetch his coat. He'd already stepped past her and opened the door before he spoke again.

"Walk with me," he said, a command if ever there was one.

Curious and more than a little worried about her position with him, she didn't argue. They walked in a wordless, companionable silence through the dimly lit hallway, down the narrow stairs, and out onto Elizabeth Street.

"Am I allowed to ask where we're going?" she said once they'd gone more than a block without Dolph saying anything.

He glanced at her. "If I said no, would that stop you?"

"Probably not," she admitted.

"And if I don't want to tell you?"

"I'd probably be curious enough to follow you anyway."

"Fair enough," Dolph said. "We're going to be making some calls today."

"On who?" she asked.

He gave her an unreadable look and didn't answer as he continued on.

Two blocks later, they arrived at a building that looked like all the other tenements in the neighborhood: same worn redbrick walls, same cluttered fire escapes, same small children playing out on the walk, watched over by a tired-looking woman with a scarf wrapped around her head for warmth. Inside, it smelled of coal smoke and garlic, of onions cooked days before and too many bodies. The halls were narrow, like the ones above the Strega, and the walls were stained with the residue of the lamps burning softly in the windowless space.

On the fourth floor, Dolph knocked at a door and was let into an apartment by an older woman wearing a shapeless dress and an apron.

Inside the apartment, the air was filled with a sharp chemical scent. The furniture had been pushed up against the walls, and five children—none older than ten or eleven—sat in the center of the floor around a pile of silk flowers. They barely looked up at the visitors, quickly turning their small faces back to the task before them as they glued the tiny silk petals onto wire stems one by one.

"How are you, Golde?" When the woman gave an inarticulate shrug, Dolph went on. "I came to see about your husband," Dolph said, switching into German.

The woman shook her head. "He won't see anyone."

Dolph seemed to accept this and didn't press. "How is he?"

The woman twisted her hands in her apron as she sat at the table and began gluing her own flowers. "The doctors say he'll heal."

"His position?"

She shrugged, a small movement that broadcast her fear and worry without a single word. "Filled, I suppose. He'll find another. We'll get by."

Esta crouched down to watch the children at work as Dolph talked to the woman about the state of their affairs—the rent that needed to be paid, the groceries she could barely afford. The little ones looked at Esta with the same tired, cautious eyes as their mother, but the youngest held up one of the silk flowers as an offering, her fingers red and raw from her work.

Esta took the delicate bloom carefully and pretended to give it a sniff. The girl smiled softly. Suddenly Esta felt the warm pulse of magic, and the flower petals began to move, fluttering open and closed.

The girl grinned, proud of the demonstration, and Esta pulled a coin from her pocket and presented it to the child, whose eyes widened. "Go on," she whispered, but the child didn't seem to understand, so Esta placed the coin in the small hand and closed it.

"Where's your oldest, Josef?" Dolph asked, nodding to where Esta kneeled with the children.

"Out," the woman said, her tone bleak. "Sometimes he collects coal for us during the day. Keeps us in warmth at least."

"And the other times?"

"With his father sick, he runs with a group of boys from the street." The woman shrugged, defeated. "I don't like them, but what can I do? He's nearly fourteen. I'm lucky he hasn't left altogether."

"Send him to me when he gets home. I have some work I can give him." When the woman frowned, Dolph spoke again to reassure her. "Nothing dangerous. I need someone to make small deliveries. He's welcome to collect your coal while he's out."

"My husband won't want any of your bargains," the woman said warily.

"No bargain required, and I won't ask your son for his oath, if that's what worries you. He's too young to be making those decisions, but he needs to be kept busy. Kelly or Eastman won't be so understanding if he gets mixed up with them. The boy can keep the position even once your husband's well, so long as he spends his nights at home with you."

The woman didn't argue the point any further, simply nodded her head and turned back to the flower she was piecing together.

Dolph glanced at Esta. "We've other stops to make."

At the next building, they visited a girl who couldn't have been any older than Esta herself. The baby on her hip fussed and a toddler played at her feet as Dolph accepted her cup of coffee and sat to talk with her.

"Dzień dobry, Marta. I came because I heard about Krzysztof.... There's been no sign of him? No news?" he asked in Polish.

The girl shook her head as she stood to stomp out the paper doll the toddler had just set on fire with nothing but his will and his affinity. "Nie," she said sharply, cracking the child across the hand, which caused him to begin wailing and set the baby off as well.

Dolph bent down to look at the little boy and placed his finger against his lip. The little boy seemed startled at the sudden attention and went quiet, his small lip still quivering as he tried to catch his breath. Taking a handkerchief from his pocket, Dolph wiped the snot that was running from the boy's nose, then ruffled his hair and offered him a wax-wrapped piece of caramel before turning back to the boy's mother.

The little boy remained silent, watching Dolph talk to his mother as he jawed at the candy. In the course of their conversation, Dolph promised the woman that someone would deliver laundry to be done from the Strega. They settled on a generous price, and he assured her he'd look into her husband's whereabouts himself.

The whole time Dolph spoke to the boy's mother, Esta couldn't help but picture him shackled in a prison boat, heading toward the Brink.

She'd been six when Professor Lachlan first explained the Brink to her. Until then, she hadn't understood they were trapped in the city. He'd taken her to the Brooklyn Bridge and told her about the Order. The farther they had walked along the bridge, the colder the summer day felt. Even before they came to the soaring arches of the towers, Esta had become so scared that she'd cried. Tourists eyed them both suspiciously as Professor Lachlan had picked her up and carried her back to where they'd started. If it had been terrifying to simply be close to the Brink, she couldn't imagine the horror of crossing.

Dolph didn't deserve that. *No one* did.

The morning wore on, with Esta pretending not to listen to the discussions Dolph had with one family after another. Each apartment was more cramped than the last, each family more desperate. Most of them had children who were wild to be outdoors but who clearly had affinities they couldn't control yet. And without control, the children had to be kept hidden.

By the time it was past noon, the sun had burned away the hazy clouds and the air was teasing them with the promise of spring.

"You hungry?" Dolph asked.

"I could eat," she told him as her stomach growled in response. She still didn't understand what his purpose had been in taking her with him, showing her all he had.

She followed him back through the neighborhood. Despite relying on his cane, Dolph walked at a quick pace through the crowded streets. He had a way of moving that made his limp seem more like a strut. A confidence that fooled you into thinking there was nothing wrong with his leg.

When they came to Houston Street, Esta was surprised to see she recognized their destination. In her own time, Schimmel's Bakery was on the other side of Houston, but when she stepped up into the tiny storefront, the smell of bread and onions wrapped around her and squeezed her with nostalgia. All at once, she was a small girl again, remembering the times Dakari had taken her out for a snack after their training session, an apology and reward all at once. And they'd often gone to Schimmel's for a knish.

She let the memory of her other life wash over her for a moment. Dakari's kind, crooked smile. Mari's tart comebacks to every one of her complaints. Even Logan's condescension. And Professor Lachlan . . . trusting her to get this job done, one way or another.

They were all unreachable to her. With the changes in the news clipping still tucked against her skin, she wasn't sure if she'd ever be able to reach them again.

In all her trips, all the jobs she had done, she had never felt so untethered from her own history, which she could only hope still lay somewhere, unreachable, in the future. Esta never wallowed, but she allowed herself a moment to miss it—the indoor plumbing and the speed of cars and the streets that weren't filled with shit. And the people she cared about.

"What will you have?" Dolph asked, eyeing her as though he understood her mind had been elsewhere. But he didn't call her on it and he didn't press, and she found herself unspeakably grateful for that.

They took their order to go, shifting the warm, heavy pastries between their fingers to keep from being burned as they walked and ate.

It tasted the same, Esta thought. A hundred years, and the way the starchy filling of the knish melted in her mouth, dense and warm with just enough salt, took her right back to being ten years old. To the fall days when she would sit with Dakari on a bus bench, trying to eat the whole thing before it went cold as he reviewed the day's lesson, her progress and her mistakes.

She'd been nearly eleven before she could finish a whole one on her own, but now, with her hunger gnawing at her, one didn't seem nearly enough.

"Exactly how many languages *do* you know?" Dolph asked.

The knish suddenly tasted like ash in her mouth. Esta swallowed the bite she'd just taken, choking it down as her stomach flipped nervously, and then regarded him as blankly as she could manage. "I'm not sure what you mean."

Dolph gave her an impatient look. "I watched you today as we made the calls. You were listening."

"I wasn't—"

But he shot her a look that made her swallow her protest. "How many?" he pressed.

"Several," she admitted finally. It had been a major part of her training, and luckily she picked them up quickly.

Dolph took another mouthful of his knish. "You didn't think that relevant information to mention before?"

She shrugged, choosing her words carefully. "Not everyone appreciates the skill. Like you said, I *was* listening today. A lot of people see that as more of a liability than an advantage."

He nodded. "Lucky for you, I'm not one of them."

She blinked up at him, relieved. "You're not?"

He shook his head. "But don't think you can hide things from me without it costing you my trust."

"I won't make that mistake again," she assured him, ducking her head and hoping he couldn't read the lie in her words.

"See that you don't."

After that, they walked in silence for a while before she felt brave enough to ask the one question that had been bothering her all morning. "Why did you bring me along today?"

"In part, I wanted to see how you would react to the people I protect. There are too many who believe we should keep to our own, and they're not willing to cross new lines. A lot of people never talk to anyone who isn't from the village they grew up in. A lot of people are only interested in protecting their own. That's what the Order wants. They don't want Mageus to realize we have more in common than we have differences, because keeping us divided means their own power stays secure.

"But I also wanted you to see with your own eyes what I'm trying to do and what's at stake if we fail." He popped the last of his knish into his mouth and finished it before he continued. "Golde's daughter took a liking to you." He gestured to the flower Esta still had tucked into her hair.

"She was sweet," Esta said, feeling suddenly defensive.

"She is. But what life does she have to look forward to? She'll live out her days in those rooms, or other rooms like them, without any chance for something more. All because she can make a silken flower bloom. If she's lucky, the Order will never touch her directly, never let her building burn down around her or cart off her father or husband for crimes they didn't commit. She probably won't be lucky. Few are. Marta wasn't so lucky. Her husband disappeared a little over a week ago. She has no other family here. If I didn't step in, what would become of her and her children without him?"

"And that's it?" she asked, still trying to figure out what made this man tick. If everyone had a weakness, everyone also had an angle. She didn't believe that Dolph Saunders was any different. "You just help them, with no expectation of reward? No conditions?"

He considered her question for a moment before he spoke, and when he finally did, his words were measured. "I'm no saint, Esta. I'm a businessman with multiple properties, with employees who depend on me, with people in this neighborhood whose respect I've earned. I'd like to continue being that man. I've always been ambitious, maybe too ambitious for the life I was born into. If the Order falls, that's good for me, for my businesses. For my future prospects in this city. If I'm the one to bring the Order down, people will be grateful and I will reap the benefits. There's no doubt of that, and I'd be lying not to admit it.

"But I also know what it means to starve. I've slept on the streets and I learned how to escape from those who would hunt me. I know the strength of will it takes to fight back from the bottom, and I know that not everyone has that strength. So, yes, I have my own interests, but I'm not completely without a heart, whatever the rumors about me say."

Esta studied him for some sign of the lie in his words. Professor Lachlan had taught her everything he could, had trained her to bring down the Order that pressed them into narrow lives. But he'd never concerned himself with the world beyond their small crew. To free themselves was enough. But here was Dolph Saunders, a man who had every reason to be out for himself, for the power he could grab, telling her something different. "And you trust them? You trust all the people you help not to give you up to the Order?"

"What choice do I have?" he asked wryly. "No one can survive on their own. Not even me.

"Do you have any other questions?" he asked, but in his tone was a clear indication that he was done answering them.

She shook her head. She already had too much to think about.

"You handled yourself well last night. Jianyu probably owes you his life."

"I did my job."

"So humble?" Dolph's mouth curved slightly. "I think you have depths you're still hiding from me, Esta Filosik. I'm not sure I like that about you."

She frowned, worried by the sureness in his voice. "I would never do anything to hurt you or anyone you protect." It was a lie, but she managed to choke it out with admirable ease. She'd been trained well, after all.

Yet all her training couldn't stop the twist of guilt she felt now that she knew Dolph and the rest. There was no way to do what Professor Lachlan had asked her without hurting them all in the end. And if she hurt Dolph, she was hurting every person he helped in turn.

"But how far would you go for them?"

Esta didn't answer at first. She understood he was appraising every move she made, every word she spoke. Agreeing too readily would mark her as a fool, or worse. When she finally answered, she spoke only the truth: "If it was to stop the Order? I'd risk everything."

"So would I," he told her. He hesitated briefly before he spoke again. "I have plans for the Order," he explained. "Perhaps you could help me with those plans. Nibs seems to think you might be able to."

Licking her lips, Esta considered her next words carefully. "I . . . I'm not sure if Nibs is right, but I'd be willing to do whatever I can."

"I'm glad to hear that," he said, though his expression didn't soften. "Then I have a job for you. We can call it a test to see how serious you are and how much I can depend upon you. My plans depend on someone joining us. Someone who has been quite reluctant to do so."

"Harte Darrigan," she said, putting the pieces together.

"He saw you at the museum, and he knows you work for me. That makes him a liability."

"I'll make sure he's not," she promised. She'd put to rights whatever she'd done and put Harte Darrigan back in his place.

Dolph chuckled. "If I wanted him dead, I'd send Viola," he joked. "My plan *depends* upon Darrigan's help. I want you to get him for me."

SPARKS OF POWER

The Docks

The old fool was never going to finish with his tinkering. Jack paced the dirt floor of the warehouse as the sound of metal on metal and the blast of the welding torch grated at his raw nerves. Ever since the robbery at the museum, he'd paid the old man double to work around the clock to finish the machine. It should have been done by now.

Finally, the old man backed away from the machine and gave it one more look. "That should do it."

"Have you made the adjustments I sent you?" Jack asked, holding up the roughly cut diamond. There would be hell to pay when his father found out how much he'd spent on the stone, but if this worked, it wouldn't matter. If this worked, they would thank him. He'd be a goddamn hero.

He didn't know why he hadn't thought of it before, but something had clicked when he'd learned that his aunt had lost a family heirloom at the museum—a priceless necklace filled with rare emeralds and diamonds. They were singular, irreplaceable . . . and they had given him an idea.

Of course he couldn't simply generate power with a machine, no matter how complex and modern it might be. He needed an object for the power to be focused into.

Didn't the Order depend on their artifacts to keep the protections secure in the Mysterium? He'd never seen them himself, but he'd heard about them—five gemstones that one of the most powerful alchemists to have ever lived had collected from five ancient civilizations steeped in magic. That alchemist had found a way to imbue the artifacts with power through complex rituals, power that the Order could draw on still. True, only the Inner Circle understood the secrets of the artifacts, but Jack was no idiot. He'd spent the last year learning everything he could—everything his uncle and the others would permit him to. If those stones could hold magical power, why couldn't this one?

It had cost him everything he had—and some that wasn't actually his to give—to convince the antiquities dealer to part with the stone. But he needed something more than a simple jewel. This diamond had been found in the tomb of Thutmose III, the same pharaoh who had erected the very obelisk that now stood in Central Park. There was a symmetry to it that buoyed Jack's confidence. It could work.

"I've made the changes," the old man said with a less-than-hopeful look as he took the stone and examined it. "But I don't see how a bit of rock will be enough to defuse the power buildup this thing generates."

"It's not your job to see. Just follow instructions," Jack ground out. "You *have* followed my instructions, haven't you?"

The old man nodded.

"Then there shouldn't be any problem," Jack snapped. "Get this installed in the central globe, and then start her up. Let's see if you're going to disappoint me again."

The old man gave a worried nod and then went back to the wiring. A few minutes later, he connected the power and a buzzing roar began from somewhere deep within the heart of the machine. Then the large, orbital arms began to rotate, slowly at first and then faster, until the center globe began to glow.

"It won't hold," the old man said, shielding himself behind a large metal toolbox as he started to pull on the wires.

But Jack was confident, or if not confident, desperate enough to give it a chance. "No! We'll wait. See what she can do."

Egad, it's a thing of beauty. Sleek and modern, powerful in its promise. The arms spun, crossing each other in a blur of motion, like erratic rings of Saturn. Bolts of energy—of magic—leaped between the twin poles of the sphere. A perfectly contained universe. Only this was a cosmos *he* would control.

Let the Order laugh about his other failures. They would eat their words in the end. With this machine, he would do what they had only ever dreamed of doing. He would put a stop to the ever-encroaching threat of the Mageus. He would end them, once and for all. And when they were gone, when the city was clean and free from their corruption, the Order would recognize his brilliance, would reward him as they moved into the future, returning the city—the entire country—to the promise it had once held.

"Mr. Jack," the old man shouted.

"I said to wait!" he yelled, barely able to hear himself over the noise the machine made. His eyes were wide and his hair whipped at his face, lifted by the wind the machine created in the center of the room. It felt as though he were standing on the edge of a precipice between the past and the future, and the violent charges of energy that licked at his skin only made him want to move closer to the edge.

His machinist pulled himself farther behind the metal box, but Jack stood in the open, daring fate to contradict him again. If the blasted thing exploded, let it take him with it. That would be easier than admitting he'd failed again. Or having to explain to his father where the money in his trust fund had gone.

But the machine didn't explode. It picked up steam, the bolts of energy dancing around the central globe, chilling the air that whipped around them. Sparks of life, of power.

"It's holding!" he said, unable to contain the laugh as the wonder and a dangerous hope grew in his chest. "It's working!"

The old man peered out from behind the toolbox, his eyes wide.

Jack laughed again, relief and excitement mixing in a heady cocktail that had his blood humming. *It worked.* "This is only the beginning," he said, more to himself than to the man who had built the machine.

It would be *his* beginning. No one else's.

He walked to the controls and made a few adjustments, levering the machine until its power was focused exactly where he wanted it. He pointed that power toward the part of the city that was no better than a rat's nest, considering the vermin that hid themselves there. He would take back his city.

Jack smiled. *Balance, indeed.*

"Send word if anything changes," Jack called, fitting his hat on his head as he made his way out into the cold. His machine worked. He'd been right about the diamond. Everything would work out. He needed a drink to celebrate.

A DIFFERENT KIND
OF DANGER

Wallack's Theatre

After the week he'd had, Harte needed a good night. He'd managed to talk his way out of missing the performance when he got caught up at the Metropolitan—the front-page spread in the *Sun* had helped with that. But because it had mentioned him by name, Paul Kelly's boys had been back. Kelly hadn't been happy to see that Harte had been making progress with Jack and not cutting him in on the action.

Harte thought he'd managed to convince Torrio and Razor that he needed a little more time, but then he'd spent the rest of the week waiting for the other shoe to drop. And avoiding Jack, because he still had no idea how he was going to explain the museum robbery without putting himself at risk.

It didn't help much that the audience had been cold so far, barely impressed with his sleight of hand and only somewhat amused as he made the impossible seem possible. But they hadn't turned on him yet. The almost full house had everything to do with what was about to happen—they were waiting with growing impatience for the debut of his newest, most death-defying escape.

The man he'd selected from the audience to secure his handcuffs and chains had already returned to his seat with the smug assurance that there was no way Harte could get out. He made a show of wriggling and writhing to demonstrate how secure they were, because it never hurt to add a bit of drama. When two stagehands lowered him into the clear tank of tepid water, bound in chains and wearing nothing more than a pair of bathing shorts, the audience went gratifyingly silent as he sank to the bottom.

The screen hadn't yet been lowered in front of the tank when the theater lights surged, pulsing like a heartbeat for a moment, and then went completely dark.

Even under the water, he could hear the frantic murmuring of the crowd, and he felt an answering panic. He knew it was impossible, but he swore the flare of the lights before they went out had pulled at his affinity, had made him feel a hollow ache that darkened the edges of his vision and caused his head to swirl.

But when he gasped, the mouthful of water he took in reminded him of where he was and what was at stake. He forced himself to let go of his panic and to focus on taking advantage of the unexpected drama of the situation.

Working quickly, he slipped the metal pin from its hiding place under a false fingertip, and contorting himself as he'd practiced hundreds of times before, he wedged it into the locks on the cuffs. By the time the stagehands lit the kerosene lanterns at the foot of the stage a few minutes later, Harte was already out of the tank, dripping wet and holding the heavy chains in his outstretched hands.

The crowd went wild. Even in the dim light, he could see the amazement on their faces as wonder replaced fear. He'd not only escaped the water—this time, he'd also defeated the utter darkness that had alarmed even the most cynical men in the audience.

He gave the house his most dazzling smile and took his bow, letting the rumble of the crowd's approval roll over him. But their thunderous applause did nothing to alleviate the unease that clung to him, as cold and uncomfortable as his wet drawers. He gave his audience one last grateful salute before he ceded the stage to Evelyn and her so-called sisters.

As the first of the three girls sashayed into the spotlights, the crowd erupted again, this time in hoots and whistles. Apparently, a pair of legs was all it took for the audience to forget their amazement. The realization dulled the usual shot of adrenaline he got from being onstage, leaving him feeling jittery and nervous, aching to flex his affinity again.

Harte handed the unlocked chains to one of the stagehands and pulled a robe around himself as he navigated the maze of ropes and pulleys back-stage and made his way back to his dressing room.

He wasn't surprised, somehow, to see the girl waiting for him. He'd been expecting something like this for days now, ever since he'd almost ruined her chance to escape at the museum. Still, her appearance, a burst of color and fire in his drab little dressing room, made him pause.

"I'm guessing Dolph sent you," he said, closing the door behind him.

She was dressed in a deep-plum-colored skirt and a creamy blouse that draped over her curves without hiding them. Her dark hair was pulled back from her face and gathered loosely at the nape of her neck. Delicately carved jade combs accented the burnished-chestnut curls. Dressed as she was, she could have passed for one of the ladies on Park Avenue, but the wicked spark in her eyes was at odds with the polish of her clothes.

It wasn't that long ago that John Torrio had been sitting in that same place, and Harte had the sudden thought that he wasn't sure which of the chair's occupants might be more of a threat to his own well-being.

"Back to assault me again?" He tucked his hands into the pockets of the robe and wished like hell she hadn't come.

Most of all, he wished there wasn't a part of him that was glad to see her again, safe and whole. And in his dressing room.

"Unfortunately," she said, leaning toward him almost conspiratorially, "I'm under strict orders not to. This time, at least."

"How disappointing that must be for you," he drawled, relaxing a little into her humor.

"You have no idea." She sighed dramatically and leaned back in his dressing chair. Shadows thrown by the lamp flickered across her face, and he had the distinct feeling she was laughing at him, despite the serious expression on her face. "I did want to thank you, though," she said, and he could tell that the words cost her.

Amused despite himself, he crossed the room to where his clothes were waiting for him on the radiator. "For?"

"For not telling anyone what you saw the other night," she said.

He glanced back at her. "Who says I haven't?"

She frowned, her dark brows pulling together. "Morgan looked pretty upset in that picture on the front page. I doubt I'd be here if he had any idea who was involved."

"He was," Harte admitted. "Very upset. I wouldn't thank me just yet, though."

"No?" She tilted her head slightly, an almost imperceptible shift, but enough to tell him she was worried.

Good. Let her worry. She kept him on his toes every time they met, so it was only fair he got to do the same. Never mind how much he was growing to like their games.

"You never know when I might happen to remember something." He gave her a meaningful look. "Something that the police might find interesting."

"Are you trying to blackmail me?" she asked.

"Not trying, no. Not yet, at least." He smiled pleasantly, because he had the sense it would irritate her even more. "But give me time, and I might find something I want from you."

She let out a derisive laugh. "In your dreams."

He winked. "Every night, sweetheart."

"Look, as much fun as this has been, I'm only here because Dolph needs a favor from you."

"I'm well aware of what Dolph wants from me. I'm also pretty sure I've already made my answer clear about that particular topic."

"I'm supposed to change your mind," she said, fluttering her thick lashes in his direction.

Understanding the ruse for what it was, he laughed. "Seeing as there isn't any shortage of beautiful women in my business, even a figure as fine as yours probably won't be enough to turn my head." He gave her a wry look as he stripped off his robe and hung it over the dressing screen. "No offense, of course," he said as an afterthought.

"None taken."

If he'd been hoping to make her uncomfortable, it didn't work. She didn't seem the least bit concerned now that he was standing in little more than a pair of sodden shorts. Or that she was in a mostly darkened room alone with him. She didn't even look away. If anything, she seemed to be enjoying herself. Her expression was one he recognized too well—the anticipation of the game. Which only served to irritate him more.

"Considering I have information that could make Dolph's life much more uncomfortable, it seems like I'm the one who should be asking for favors," he said.

"What sort of favor would you like?" she asked, her gaze unwavering.

He'd just stood on a stage in front of three hundred people, but he felt suddenly, inexplicably bare. Like she'd turned his own state of undress against him.

"I'd have to put some thought into it," he said.

"Be careful you don't hurt yourself," she said, her eyes wide in mock concern.

He shook his head at her cheek and stepped behind the dressing screen to shuck off his wet shorts and pull on dry ones. And to give himself some space so he could think.

It was unnerving, the way she looked at him so directly, without a blush to her cheeks or any sign of discomfort at all. But he also admired her for it . . . not that he had any plans to let her best him again.

"There's got to be something you want," she said. "Something Dolph can do for you to change your mind."

"Dolph Saunders doesn't have anything I want," he said truthfully as he pulled on his warm pants. From the other side of the screen, he heard the sound of metal on metal, and he looked to see what she was doing.

"There's no key for those," he warned when he saw her playing with the handcuffs that hung from his dressing table.

"Really? Then I suppose I should be extra careful." With a flick, she locked one of the iron cuffs around her wrist. "Oops." She brought her gloved hands to her mouth, which only drew attention to how pink her lips were. How soft they looked. How they'd felt against his.

He remembered those lips. . . . He also remembered the teeth behind them. Some things weren't worth the trouble.

"Guess I'm stuck." Her eyes never left his. "I'll just have to hang around here for a while . . . until you see things my way."

"Like I said, I'm not interested in whatever Dolph wants from me." Which wasn't the complete truth. He was more interested than ever in getting himself out of town, especially with Paul Kelly's boys breathing down his neck. It just wasn't enough to make him interested in getting caught in Dolph Saunders' web. Whatever Dolph had planned, it would be dangerous and reckless, like it always was. Now that Dolph didn't have Leena to ground him, it would probably be even more so. "I've never really had a taste for suicide."

"Your act indicates otherwise," she drawled, the handcuff still dangling from her wrist like a bracelet. "You were dying out there."

"Funny." He gave her a dark look.

"It's a bit stale, don't you think?" She stepped toward him slowly, a challenge if ever there was one. "Houdini already has the market on escape acts. You need something"—she waved her hand vaguely, letting the cuff swing loose on her wrist—"you know, to spice things up. I'd be happy to give you some pointers, if you'd like."

If she hadn't been so bad at seduction, he would have been more irritated about the Houdini comment. She would have been better to come at him straight, not that he'd be telling her that anytime soon.

"*You're* going to give me pointers?" He wanted to laugh, but then she leaned close, and the scent of her strangled his senses and made his throat go tight.

"Don't you remember?" she whispered in his ear. "The crowd loved us."

"Did they?" He turned his head so their faces were barely a breath apart, and he sensed that she had to steady herself.

Interesting. She didn't want him to touch her, but she also didn't want him to know she was avoiding it. He could use that.

"Well, they loved *me*," she said, her pink lips twitching in amusement. "They were simply tolerating you."

He could feel the warmth radiating from her, and she smelled like sunshine. Like fresh laundry and soap. That close, her eyes looked even more like dark honey, but they also held a challenge, and he never could refuse a dare. He leaned closer still, enjoying the way she tensed as she stopped herself from backing away. Enjoying turning her game back on her.

"Tolerating me, you say?" He stopped short of touching his lips to her neck.

"Mm-hmm," she murmured, suddenly sounding awfully breathless.

"What if what I want is you?" he asked.

"I'd say you couldn't have me."

"No?" And then he latched the other handcuff around her wrist.

Her eyes widened, and she backed away from him, but to his surprise, she didn't panic or curse him for seeing through her ruse, as he'd expected. She didn't look thrown at all, just examined her locked wrists and did the one thing he didn't expect: She *laughed*. Delight sparked in those glittering eyes of hers.

"You said there's no key?" She didn't seem the least bit worried.

"I lost it years ago," he told her with a shrug. He turned away from her to take his shirt from the radiator and slip his arms into its warmth, satisfied with the spot he'd managed to maneuver her into. Until he remembered the lock she'd picked at the museum.

But by the time he turned back around, her wrists were already free, and she was dangling the unlocked handcuffs from her fingertip.

YOU CAN'T CON A CON

"I'm afraid it's going to be harder than that to get rid of me," Esta said, enjoying the look on Harte Darrigan's face at how quickly she'd managed to escape.

It was a pretty enough face, she supposed. He had rough, brooding good looks at odds with the refined act he put on, both of which were only improved by the smudges of kohl beneath his eyes. But she knew from her experience with Logan that charm and good looks often only went skin deep. Darrigan was too good of a performer to reveal whatever was beneath that charm of his, and she was too smart to be taken in by the charm itself—or whatever was beneath, come to think of it.

Still, she had to admit, she'd enjoyed the view when he'd taken off the robe to expose the wet shorts he was wearing. Who wouldn't? They'd clung to his well-muscled thighs, which only complemented his flat stomach and broad, defined shoulders. He had an angry-looking, angular welt on his right shoulder, like a brand or a scar, which was at odds with the uptown act he put on. An injury from some past life, she suspected. Otherwise, his body was damn near perfect—definitely the result of a lot of hard work.

She couldn't help but admire that, and not only because he was nice to look at. It meant he knew what it was to work at something, to master it. He knew what it meant to not *only* depend on magic.

It was a lesson she'd learned as a girl. When Professor Lachlan first taught her how to dip into a pocket for a fat purse, he never let her use her affinity. Only once she could lift a wallet without tipping off the mark did he show her how magic could amplify and augment her already developed skills.

Admiration or not, she wouldn't let herself be distracted. Not by the magician's corded arms or by his teasing smile, which was probably another mask. According to the news clipping, the Khafre Hall job *wasn't* a fact anymore. She had to get Harte Darrigan on board, to make sure he was part of the team *and* to make sure he wasn't the one who gave up Dolph. She didn't have time to swoon over some boy, no matter how pretty he was.

He took the cuffs from her, frowning as he examined them.

"I didn't break them, if that's what you're wondering," she said when his brows drew together in a puzzled expression. She held up the hairpin she'd used. It was the only useful thing about the elaborate style that one of Dolph's people had done for her earlier that day.

Esta had tried to tell them that Harte Darrigan wasn't going to be impressed by a new outfit or hair, but they'd insisted. *Seduce him,* they'd said, but a con only works if the mark wants what you're selling.

The handcuff trick *did* seem to impress him, though. For a moment at least.

But a second later, he shrugged indifferently and pulled his armor back into place as he hung the cuffs from the hook where she'd found them. "An easy enough trick to manage with some practice, I suppose. It's not a secret that I keep those here."

"Try another pair," she challenged. "There's not a lock that's ever stopped me before."

"After that trick at the museum, I don't doubt it. But I know how to pick a lock too, sweetheart."

"Bet you I'm faster."

As he studied her, she could see the internal struggle. A part of him, she knew, itched to test her, to show her that *he* was better. But the other part eventually won out. "Like I said, I'm not interested in your games, and I'm still not interested in whatever Dolph Saunders has planned."

"Maybe you should be." She took another step toward him. "How long do you think this gig is going to last for you?" she asked.

"As long as I want it to." He gave her a smug look and then set to fastening the buttons on his shirt.

"The same tired tricks can only work for so long."

"They're not tricks," he corrected. "They're *effects*. And I can always come up with new ones."

"Same tired audience, though. Eventually they're going to want something new. *Someone* new."

"You have no idea what you're talking about," he said, but his expression wasn't so sure.

"But if the Brink came down," she continued, ignoring his outburst, "you could get out of this town."

"Who says I want to?"

She couldn't help but laugh at that. The yearning in his expression was so stark, it was unmistakable. "If you could leave New York, you could have a new town whenever you wanted one. A new audience every night. The whole world would be open to you."

A strange expression crossed his face for the briefest of moments, transforming it. But then he seemed to collect himself, and his usual mask of pleasant indifference snapped back into place. "Who says I need Dolph Saunders to get out of this town?" He finished straightening his collar in the mirror before taking a black silk tie from the hook nearby.

She didn't like this newfound confidence of his. "He can offer you protection," Esta said, grasping for some other angle to disarm him. She reached for the information she'd been armed with. "You *and* your mother."

Harte went very still. "I don't take threats lightly."

"It wasn't meant to be a threat," Esta told him, confused at his reaction.

"Considering that very few know I even *have* a mother, I'm not sure how I could take it as anything else." He was still tense.

"Everybody has a mother," Esta said with a halfhearted laugh, trying to appear more relaxed than she felt. Something had changed when she mentioned his mother. Apparently, Dolph and Nibs had given her just enough information to hang herself. Any ground she might have gained had slipped away, taking more with it.

Harte was silent for another long, uncomfortable moment, studying her as though he was looking for some hint at what her game was. In that moment, he looked every bit the Magician she'd expected to encounter. Cold. Ruthless. And completely capable of double-crossing anyone.

After a moment, he spoke. "I'll consider Dolph's proposal if you tell me something."

"What's that?" she asked, wary.

"What, exactly, does Dolph have on you?" He took a step toward her, his head cocked to the side in a question.

"Nothing," she lied. He was too close and the room felt suddenly too small. She lifted her chin. "I'm useful to him."

"Is that all you are?" Harte asked, studying her more intently. "Useful? It seems so . . . *pedestrian*."

She couldn't stop the image of Charlie Murphy, red-faced in the street, from flashing through her mind. And she couldn't help but think of Dolph, sailing to the prison on Blackwell Island, helpless against the Brink.

"Ah, so he *does* have something on you," he said, satisfied. "I figured as much."

"You figure wrong," she said, but the game had already changed. She'd managed to hold her own at first, maybe even caught him off guard with the handcuffs, but now he was on the offensive.

Harte Darrigan shook his head. "No, I don't think so. Dolph has never been one for charity cases," he told her. "Whatever help or promises he's made you, he'll take it out of you in kind. That's how all the bosses downtown work, and he's no different. Once you're in, it's impossible to get away."

"You don't know what you're talking about," she said, lifting her chin. Hadn't she seen with her own eyes what Dolph was doing, how he was helping the weakest among them?

He ignored her protests. "Tell me, do you already wear his mark?"

"His mark?" she asked before she could stop herself.

She cursed inwardly when Darrigan smiled, because she knew she'd just revealed that there were other things about Dolph Saunders she didn't understand, things that Harte Darrigan knew about, which gave him an edge she couldn't afford.

"I'm sure you've seen the tattoo he gives those in his crew. It's always been the price of admission for his protection." He turned from her then and took a vest from a hook on the wall. "It's not one I'm willing to pay." His storm-cloud eyes were steady on her, determined. "Ever."

She hadn't been around long, but she had noticed the tattoos that some of those around the Strega wore. She just hadn't understood what they were. "He may be willing to negotiate that point," she told him, a bluff if there ever was one.

He tossed a disbelieving look in her direction as he buttoned the vest. "I can't imagine he would. No mark, no way to control me."

Just then, his dressing room door opened, and Esta turned to see a woman with aggressively red hair peek her painted face in. "Harte, dear," she started to coo, but when she saw Esta, her eyes narrowed. "Oh. So sorry," the woman said, not at all sounding like she was. "I didn't realize you were entertaining."

"I wasn't," Harte told the woman, who stepped into the room without being invited. "She was just—"

"Having the most delightful chat with a dear old friend," Esta interrupted, using the woman's unexpected appearance to her advantage and taking back control. She infused her words with the notes of an Eastern European accent as she offered her hand to the woman. "It's so lovely to meet one of his *leetle* theater friends," she said with a smile that was all smug condescension. "I am Esta von Filosik, of course."

The woman's eyes went cold. "You say you're a friend of his?"

"No—" Harte started to say, but not before Esta spoke over him.

"Of course!" she lied easily. "We met ages ago, in Rastenburg, when he studied under my father. We were but children then, but we became"—she paused dramatically and slid a warm look to Harte—"quite *close*. Did we not, *darling*?"

"So this is what you've been running off to?" The woman's mouth went tight.

To Esta's immense satisfaction, Harte Darrigan—for once—seemed at a loss for words.

"He left to continue his studies, but now we are reunited," Esta told the woman, sidling up to Harte and slipping her arm through his in a proprietary way. He started to pull away, but she held him tight. "And you are?"

"Evelyn DeMure," the woman said, making an obvious show of looking Esta over from head to toe.

As she did so, Esta felt the warm energy of Evelyn's magic wrap around her, and she had the sudden feeling of being drawn to her, the sudden desire to release Harte. She couldn't seem to stop her arms from falling away. . . .

"Evelyn," Harte warned.

A moment later, the warmth faded, but Esta had already released her hold on his arm.

"Is there something you needed?" Frustration simmered in his voice.

Evelyn gave Esta a smile that was mostly teeth before she turned to Harte. "A letter was delivered for you just now," she said, holding out a crumpled envelope. "Next time get someone else to take your messages, would you? I'm not your errand boy."

"No one could confuse you for a boy, Evelyn," he said with a grin obviously meant to charm, but the woman didn't soften. His smile faltered as he took the letter from her outstretched hand. He tore the edge of the envelope, but even once he pulled out the folded sheet of paper, Evelyn didn't seem in any hurry to leave.

"I thought you weren't allowing visitors backstage anymore?" she said, glancing again at Esta with a look as sharp as one of Viola's knives.

Harte didn't seem to hear her. He was too busy reading the note, his brows furrowing over narrowed eyes. Then, all at once, he balled the paper in his closed fist, and when he looked up, the fury in his eyes had Esta wanting to take a step back.

"Usually I wouldn't," he said, looking at her with a stony, unreadable expression. "But for an *old friend*, I had to make an exception."

Everything in her went on alert. Esta had no idea what was in that note, but something had changed in him. All playfulness was gone. She didn't know what this new game was, and she had a feeling that she shouldn't stick around to find out.

"I was actually about to leave," she told Evelyn. "It was lovely to see you again, Harte. Do think about my proposition?"

He stared at her, his mouth tight. "Perhaps we could discuss it in more detail?" he said flatly. "Soon."

It was a victory, but she couldn't help feeling like there was something else happening that she didn't understand and wasn't in control of.

"Tomorrow, perhaps?" she asked, hopeful and wary all at once. "We could continue our discussion?"

His gray eyes bored into her. "I'm not sure about tomorrow—I've got some things to clear up. It might take a few days," he told her. His voice carried a curious note of determination.

"I'll look forward to it," she told him, trying not to show her unease. Then she pasted on a smile. "Until then? It was lovely to meet you," she told Evelyn, before turning to take her leave.

Just as she was opening the door, he grabbed her wrist and tugged her back toward him.

"That isn't any way for old friends to part, now, is it?" he asked softly, almost playfully, but the look on his face didn't match his tone.

He was already pulling her toward him. "As you said, we were once so very . . . *close*."

She had to force herself not to pull away. Esta needed Evelyn, who was still watching with ice in her eyes, to believe that she was who she claimed to be. Within the hour, the entire theater would know about the curious visitor in Harte Darrigan's dressing room. You couldn't *buy* gossip as effective as that. He'd be stuck with her.

But before she could find a way out of his grasp, she was in his arms. All at once she was back in the Haymarket. His eyes held no warmth or seduction, but her stomach flipped just the same at the intensity she saw there.

He gave her a moment to pull away, to refuse him and what she knew was about to happen. But pulling away would mean destroying the cover she was trying to establish. Instead, she looked up at him, met the challenge head-on. Dared him to go through with it.

It's an act, she told herself, when amusement sparked behind those gray eyes of his, when they softened just a little. Professor Lachlan had warned her about the Magician. *Don't be taken in by him. Get the Book before he does and stop the—*

Then his lips were on hers and she felt the warm energy of his affinity wrap around her, sink into her skin, violating the boundaries between them in a way she didn't have time to prepare herself for and couldn't protect herself from. His energy was hot, electric, and there was something about it that pulled her in even as she knew that it was a trap.

Despite the heat of his magic, the kiss itself held no passion or warmth. It was over before it had barely begun, but something had happened. He'd gained something more than her embarrassment.

"Until later, then, sweetheart?" he murmured as he released her. His expression was impassive, even as his eyes glittered with victory.

"I'll look forward to it," she said, and was glad to hear that her voice trembled only the tiniest bit. It wasn't fear but fury that jangled through her—fury at him for laying a hand on her, fury at herself for not being ready. Then she let herself out of the dressing room and pulled time around her so that she could get out of the theater without anyone seeing her shake.

THE MESSAGE

Harte stared at the open door, trying to figure out what he'd just heard and seen. The wild thoughts and images twisting through the girl's mind didn't make any sense at all.

"Well," Evelyn drawled, her rouged lips pursed. "That was instructional."

"Yeah," he said, more to himself than her. "It was." And yet he couldn't help but think he knew even less now than before.

"You two are old friends?" She gave an indelicate snort. "And I'm the Virgin Mary."

Her words shook him from his thoughts, and he finally realized Evelyn was still watching him. Her bright hair and painted face looked tired and garish in the dim light of his dressing room lamp. It wasn't only the shadows that it cast over her face that made her seem older, a worn-out shell of who she might have once been. It was that he was looking at her now compared to the girl—to *Esta*—and seeing their intrinsic difference.

The kiss had left him with more questions than answers, and it had shaken him in a way he couldn't think too closely about.

From the way she ran out of there, he had a feeling that it had shaken her, too. Rightly so, he supposed. After all, when he took her off guard and pushed past her defenses, he'd sensed that while the girl might have come with a message from Dolph, she'd also come for herself.

"So the note . . . Was it important, or what?" Evelyn asked, nodding toward it.

"Just something I have to take care of," he told her. He tucked the crumpled paper into his pocket and grabbed his jacket. "I have somewhere I need to be."

He left Evelyn in his dressing room and headed out with the sinking feeling that he might already be too late.

The paper had been monogrammed with the familiar symbol of the Five Point Gang—a cross with an extra arm that mirrored the legendary intersection of Orange Street, Cross Street, and Anthony Street, which was now the turf of Paul Kelly. It was the same symbol they'd branded into the skin on his shoulder when he'd made the choice to take Kelly's offer. Seeing it would have been enough to set him on edge, but the address written in a strong, slanting hand—Kelly's own—was only a block from the apartment he'd rented for his mother last May.

He knew at once the note was a warning about how much Paul Kelly could still control Harte's future. Certain it would be pointless to go to his mother's apartment, he went off in search of the address in the message instead.

The toffs who went slumming south of Houston might have thought that Chinatown was where the opium dens in the city were, but in reality, joints were hidden all over town. Knowing his mother, it wasn't a surprise that the address on the paper led to one of the worst he'd ever seen.

When he found her on a low platform in a dingy basement on Broome Street, he was already too late. She was barely conscious, her head supported awkwardly by a small wooden stool and her hand loosely clutching the long pipe. Scattered on the floor nearby were three shells, their curved bowls containing the dark evidence of her latest binge.

He had his suspicions about how she'd obtained so much of the sickly sweet drug, but he didn't really want to know. It was bad enough that he had to see her like this. And to realize he still cared enough to be disappointed.

Still, even as her cracked lips moved in some silent conversation within her drug-induced dream, she was alive and mostly safe. Whatever she'd done to him—what he'd driven her to do—pieces of the woman he'd once known remained beneath the years of disappointment and madness. Part of her would always be the fairylike creature who had spun tales of a distant land for the small boy he'd once been.

It was his own fault she'd chosen to leave him. His own fault for driving her away.

Her hair was gray now, and he couldn't stop himself from cringing as he pushed the greasy strands away from her face. "Ma," he said gently, trying to rouse her. "Come on. It's time to go."

She opened her drowsy eyes. Her light irises were glassy, her pupils large and vacant-looking from the effects of the drug, but she smiled at him before her eyes drifted shut again.

"No, Ma," he told her through gritted teeth. "You have to wake up. We have to go." He had to get her out of there. He needed to get her somewhere safe before Kelly or his men found her again. Or before she ran up an even bigger bill he would end up paying.

A soft moan gurgled from her throat in response, but her face remained slack, her breath shallow. Then she opened her eyes again, and for a moment they focused on him. "No," she whispered. "Please, no . . ."

"I'm not going to hurt you, Ma," he said, pulling his hand back from her.

"Leave me alone," she told him, her voice ragged with fear and disgust. "Unnatural boy. *You* made him go. You took him from me."

"I know," he said tightly, because it was easier to agree than to argue. "It's all my fault." Which was the only truth that mattered anymore.

He'd only been a boy. He hadn't known what he was capable of or how to control what he could do. When she found out he'd made his father, a drunk who'd rather use his hands to beat them than to make a living, leave, his mother had turned on him. She'd risked everything to try crossing the Brink to find his father.

She didn't get through it, though. Even her desperation to find the man she loved wasn't enough to push her past the terrible boundary. But she'd tried. She'd touched its power, and it had certainly changed her. There were days Harte wondered if death wouldn't have been a kinder fate. When he found her again, years later, she wasn't the woman she'd once been. Instead, she spent her days chasing anything that would take away the ache of the emptiness the Brink and his lout of a father had left behind.

Maybe Harte should have hated her for abandoning him. Maybe there was a small part of him that did. But in the end, he reserved his true hatred for the father who had deserted them long before he'd actually left.

And for *himself*. For driving her away.

She raised her hands slowly and gazed at them with unfocused eyes, as if noticing them for the first time. "These used to work miracles. The women used to come to me even when I was a girl," she said, her voice still carrying the soft notes of his childhood. Then her expression turned sour. "But you took it from me."

His jaw tensed. "You can blame me later. Right now we need to get you home."

She looked up at him, her pale green eyes lost in her own memories. "Little Molly O'Doherty can make you pretty enough to win any man, they'd say. I can't anymore, and it hurts—" Her voice broke, and she closed her eyes again. "It aches so terribly, and I wanted it to stop, if only for a little while. I needed—"

"You don't have to explain it to me," he told her, his throat tight with regret and shame for what she'd become. What *he'd* pushed her to. "Can you get up?"

He didn't want to have to touch her again. The rank sweat—or worse—was overpowering enough from where he was. It reminded him too much of what her leaving had cost him—of nights spent in trash heaps trying to get warm, the stink of unwashed bodies that had hunted him because they could.

Because no one had been there to stop them.

Because deep down, he had known he deserved it all.

He cursed when his mother wouldn't move, and wondered if maybe he could pay the man at the door to keep her until the drug wore off. He could collect her then—or maybe send someone else for her.

He needed to go. He'd moderated his breathing, but he was still starting to feel the haze of the poppy's smoke wrap around him, leaching out the frantic energy that the girl and Kelly's note had left him with, and he hated it. Hated the way it dulled who and what he was. Hated the way that part of him wanted to stay for a while and allow the quiet emptiness to fill him up. Just for a little while . . .

"I'm going now, Ma," he said, shaking off the temptation. "I'll be back in the morning, when you're feeling better."

Standing to leave, he looked at her one last time, hating her and loving her just the same. She was yet another thing tying him to the city, his duty to her like a straitjacket holding him against his will. A locked box he couldn't find a way out of.

He was barely out the door when he heard frantic shouts and realized that a crowd had gathered down the block. The smell of wood smoke and something else, something harsher and more chemical, hung in the air, and he saw that buildings nearby were on fire. On either end of the block, the blaze raged toward the center—toward the building where his mother was.

It couldn't have been an accident, two buildings burning like that. Two buildings bookending the room where his mother lay half unconscious. Not with the note he had still crumpled in his pocket.

The note, it seemed, wasn't the only message Paul Kelly had sent him.

Cursing the whole way, he ran back down the short flight of steps into the basement den, shouting for the sleepy-eyed guard to rouse the others. He grabbed his mother, his stomach turning and his throat tightening as the stink of her unwashed hair and clothes assaulted him. The smoke-filled night would be a reprieve compared to what she smelled of, but he pushed through his revulsion and got her out of the building, through the crowd, and into the waiting taxi at the curb. He gave the driver her address, and tried to keep her upright as the carriage rattled to a start across the uneven pavers.

When he leaned out the window, away from the smell of her, he saw Paul Kelly's men watching him from the shadows.

THE CENTER WON'T HOLD

Bella Strega

Usually, the noise of the crowded barroom was enough to settle Dolph's nerves on even the most frustrating of days. He always sat against the back wall, in part because he only had to watch one direction for an attack, and in part because he could watch the events of the night without being involved in them. From his usual table, he could observe everything he'd built, test the mood of the Bowery, and plan for all he still wanted to accomplish without anyone bothering him.

Though the room was already nearly filled with people drinking and laughing, Dolph found himself restless. There had been reports of a fire down on Broome Street. He'd sent some of his people to help stop the flames and get the innocent out, but there was only so much they could do without alerting suspicion. People would be hurt, and he was impotent to do anything about it.

Tilly had gone out on some errand, or he would have been in her kitchen, allowing her easy way to soothe him. He needed some of her soup, its heady, golden broth laden with matzo balls, or some of her fresh bread that tasted like life itself.

He needed the *Book*. But to get the Book, he needed Harte Darrigan's help.

The girl wasn't his last chance to hook Harte Darrigan—he *knew* that—but she was close to it. And she'd been gone a long time.

It rankled, still not knowing what she was capable of. A thief for certain. Most likely trustworthy, based on her performance at the museum. But she was still hiding something from him, and since he didn't know how her affinity worked, he couldn't predict how she might move against him. And he couldn't ask, not without revealing his own lost affinity. His crew expected him to already know.

Not that long ago, he wouldn't have worried at all. Leena, with her calm strength, would have been able to neutralize the girl if she attacked with her magic. And before the Brink, he would have been ready, would have known the flavor of that magic from the moment they'd met.

Before the Brink, he would have been able to do so much more. With a shake of her hand, he could have used her affinity for himself for a time, without harming her, just as he could with any Mageus. Once, his talent had made him seem limitless. Now he had to settle for pretending, for running a long con on those who trusted him.

He wasn't so green as to think that the game could last forever. Someone would eventually realize his weakness . . . and take advantage of it. The only question was who—and when the betrayal would come.

As though spurred on by his dark thoughts, a commotion erupted from the front of the building. He went on alert, ready for the danger, as the double doors of the barroom sailed open, clanging against the wall from the force. The crowd turned almost as one to see who had arrived. And then murmuring began, sweeping through the saloon like the fires that often tore through the Bowery's most dilapidated tenements. Like the one earlier that night had.

Dolph was nearly halfway across the room when he saw it wasn't any danger at all, but Jianyu, standing in the open doorway. The look of distress on the boy's face had Dolph's neck prickling in alarm, but he moved faster when he saw who Jianyu carried.

"We're closed," Dolph shouted. "Viola! Shut it down. Mooch, Sean—get everyone out of here."

His crew was well trained. They didn't ask questions or hesitate, but snapped into motion like a well-oiled machine. His employees were already gently guiding the other patrons toward the exit, but everyone was craning their necks to see what had caused the confusion.

"He's killing her!" someone shouted, and Dolph felt the anger and fear of the crowd turn, almost as a single unit, toward Jianyu. Their once-unsettled murmurs grew into an angry, noisy jumble of languages. Energy spiked throughout the room as each person drew their affinity around them—whether for protection or to attack, Dolph didn't know. A moment later, the first slur tore through the room, its guttural sound as vicious and ugly as the hatred behind the word, and the tenor of the crowd changed, transforming into something more dangerous.

Dolph raised his cane and brought its silver cap down with a vicious crack against the last-call bell with an earsplitting clang. "I said we're closed! Out! All of you!" He took a step forward, swinging his cane in front of him and not caring who it hit, as he helped to herd the crowd out into the night.

"Push those out of the way," Dolph called, pointing to a pair of shorter, square tables that lined the wall as he latched the door. "Put her over there on the floor, where she won't hurt herself."

WHAT HAPPENED ON
FULTON STREET

Jianyu carried Tilly, writhing and moaning in his arms, toward the spot that had been cleared for them. Around him, Dolph's people drew closer. He could feel their wariness, their distrust.

Before he could settle her, Viola pushed her way to the front, wiping her hands on her apron.

"Che cos'è?" she started to say, but the words died on her tongue when she saw who he had, and she went dangerously still. "What did you do to her?" Viola growled.

Jianyu felt her magic before she had even drawn her knives. Hot, angry, it assaulted him like a blast from a furnace, and the pain that gripped his entire body had him gasping for breath. His blood felt like fire, his lungs like dried cement. He struggled to stay upright, to keep from dropping Tilly, whose writhing made her difficult to hold.

"Viola! Enough," Dolph barked, catching him by the elbow before he toppled over. "Unless you want him to drop her, leave him be. Someone get Nibs in here. Now!"

Viola's eyes were sharp and bright, but a moment later, the heat receded from his blood, and Jianyu drew in a deep, heaving breath. Suddenly aware of the grip Dolph had on his arm, he pulled away and took the final few steps on his own to settle Tilly on the floor.

"Hold her legs for me, Vi," Dolph directed, as he took hold of Tilly's upper arms to keep her from scratching at her face and neck. Already the skin there was red with raised welts from her own nails.

She was still thrashing about as she moaned in agony, but her color had all but drained on the long walk back—she looked deathly pale.

"What happened?" Dolph demanded, his expression cold.

Jianyu went on alert at the suspicion in Dolph's voice. He'd been stupid to let his guard down, to believe that he could make a life for himself away from his own people. To believe that he could be accepted outside the streets of Chinatown, when he was barely accepted within their boundaries.

Of course he'd heard the same slurs hurled at him before, and at others on the streets of the city. He should have been used to it, but the surprise at hearing it *here*, in the place he thought of now as his home? To be accused of killing the girl he was trying to save? It shouldn't have been any more than he expected. But then Viola turned on him as well. And now Dolph was looking at him with ice in his pale eyes.

He expected at any moment to feel the burn of the tattoo on his back, but to his surprise—and relief—it never came. Which meant Dolph must trust him still. The knowledge was enough to unclog his throat and allow the words to break free. But he wasn't sure it was enough to heal the rift he felt in the room.

"I cannot say for sure. . . ."

"Try," Dolph commanded, his temper flaring. "What was she doing near the Brink?"

"She wasn't at the Brink," Jianyu told him. "This happened on Fulton Street."

SOMETHING NEW

B y the time Esta made it back to the Bowery, the shock of whatever Harte Darrigan had done when he kissed her had mostly faded, but she didn't feel any better about her situation. On the streetcar ride downtown, she couldn't help herself from checking the clipping. It still hadn't changed back. Whatever success she'd had with Harte Darrigan, it hadn't been enough. She wasn't sure what *would* be enough.

She carried that worry with her back to the Bowery, and the moment she stepped into the Strega, it swelled. Something was very, *very* wrong. It was late, well into the time when the bar should have been packed with throngs of Mageus drinking away their sorrows and stress, but the saloon was nearly empty.

"We're closed!" one of the bowler-hat boys grunted, standing to block her way. His name was Sam or Sean—something with an *S*—but she was new enough that he didn't recognize her.

Luckily, before she had to really argue her point, Nibs came and waved her in.

"What's going on?" she asked, taking in the small crowd at the back of the room. The energy in the air was hot, erratic. Even from across the barroom, she sensed that everyone was on the edge of using whatever magic they had, and their fear snaked through the space like a living thing.

"Dolph shut us down about an hour ago," Nibs said, his expression more uncertain than she'd ever seen him. "It's Tilly."

When Nibs finally pushed them through the gathered crowd, she saw Dolph talking in low tones to Jianyu, while Viola held Tilly's legs to the ground to keep her from thrashing about. The mouse-haired girl was writhing like she was on fire. Her eyes were wide, staring at the ceiling, and her throat and face were red from where it looked like she'd raked her own nails down her skin.

"What happened to her?" Esta asked, watching as Tilly grimaced, moaning and trying desperately to get free.

"We don't know," Nibs told her.

"Bring me some Nitewein," Dolph told Jianyu. "Double the poppy."

Jianyu looked grim as he nodded. He pushed his way past the group and returned a few minutes later with a bottle of inky liquid. Dolph told a few others to help Viola hold Tilly, and then, kneeling over her, he coaxed the liquor down her throat himself.

Tilly took one halting sip at a time, choking on the liquid at first and then gulping it desperately. Little by little the writhing stopped, and Tilly's arms went limp at her sides, her eyes glassy and vacant.

Dolph waited to make sure Tilly was calm before pulling himself stiffly to his feet. His skin was flushed, and a sheen of perspiration glistened on his upper lip as he ran a hand through his wavy hair.

"Take her upstairs," Dolph told a pair of the bowler-hatted boys, one of whom scooped the girl up into his arms. "Go on and be with her," he said to Viola as he handed her the bottle of Nitewein. "Let me know if there's any change."

Nibs spoke to Esta in a hushed tone, as if he didn't want anyone else to hear. "Dolph thought it was the Brink, but Jianyu said it happened down on Fulton Street, near the Dead Line."

"What was she doing on Fulton Street?" Esta asked.

"Trying to help someone," Dolph said, approaching them. "Golde's son, Josef. You remember her?" he asked Esta. "We visited their home just the other day. He was with a group of boys. They were playing some game, daring each other to go farther downtown, when something went wrong. One came back here for help. Everyone else was out dealing with a fire over on Broome Street, so Tilly went. Found Jianyu on the way."

"I felt the cold energy in the air, warning us away," Jianyu told them. "But she insisted on helping the child. She'd barely reached for him when she went straight as a rod and fell backward." He closed his eyes for a moment, as if remembering what he'd seen. "Then she began shaking and moaning, as though being flayed by a thousand whips. She could not hear me when I called to her, so I pulled her back, away from the boy's fallen body. I brought her back here."

"What about the boy?" Nibs asked.

"I could not carry both, and I could not risk being struck down if I wanted to get her back safely. She was still breathing, and I thought maybe . . ."

"You did fine," Dolph told him, clapping Jianyu on the shoulder. "You could have left her—plenty would have. I'm grateful you brought her back, and I'm grateful you came back to us as well."

Jianyu's cheeks flushed, but he didn't look as though he agreed. From his wary, unsure expression, it was clear he thought he had failed in some way.

Dolph didn't seem to notice.

"We'll need to send someone down to check and see if the boy's still there," Dolph said to Nibs. "If he is, I don't want anyone getting close enough to end up like Tilly. Jianyu said it felt like the Brink, so until we know more, that's how we'll treat it. Be sure to take someone who won't be at risk with you."

"What about his mother, Golde?" Nibs asked.

"I'll go tell her myself."

Nibs frowned. "You don't think it could be the entire Dead Line?" he asked Jianyu.

"I don't know," Jianyu said.

"We better hope it's not," Dolph said. "It would cut the city in half. Still, something as big as this . . . Someone has to know something." Dolph glanced at Jianyu. "I need information. Someone will have talked."

Jianyu gave a serious nod. "I'll go myself," he said.

"Do that," Dolph murmured.

After Jianyu bowed slightly and headed out into the night, Dolph turned his attention to Nibs. "After you take care of the boy, people will need to be warned. We'll need to be vigilant, at least until we figure out what's causing this."

"I'm on it," Nibs said, and hurried off in the direction of the Bowery, taking a group of the bowler-hat boys with him.

Dolph waited until they were gone before he looked to Esta. "Well?" he asked, dispensing with any pleasantries.

She knew what he was asking. "I think he'll talk," she told him, wishing that alone was enough to fix the future. To save Dolph from that fate. "He said he had something to take care of, but he should send word to you soon."

"What else?" he asked, eyeing her as though he knew there was more.

She hesitated. "He won't take your mark." When Dolph was silent, she continued. "I told him it was negotiable."

Dolph's expression creased. "That wasn't for you to say."

"I didn't have much choice if I wanted to keep him interested. Maybe if you'd warned me, or if I even knew what the mark was, I could have come up with something else." She leveled a frustrated glare in his direction, ignoring the danger he posed. "He's willing to talk now. From what I understand, that's more than anyone else has managed to get from him."

Dolph glared back at her, but he didn't argue any further. After a long, tense moment, he turned to glance back at the door where they'd taken Tilly up to the apartments above. It stood empty and silent.

"How bad is it?" Esta asked. But Dolph didn't have to answer for her to know the truth. She could see it in his anguished expression, in the tightness of his posture.

"For Tilly, it's as bad as it can be," he said. "For the rest of us? It's something new, and that rarely bodes well for our kind."

THE WEIGHT OF NIGHT

Dolph waited until the Strega was completely clear before he locked the doors and ventured out to discover what he could. Pulling his cloak around him and the brim of his cap low over his face, he headed south, toward Fulton Street and the notorious Dead Line. When the lights of the Bowery grew dim and the streets grew darker still, he switched the patch over his eye, so that he could navigate the night without falling into a coal cellar or some other trap laid for unsuspecting marks.

Rats rustled in the gutters as he passed, and the wind cut through his heavy cloak, but the cold March winds barely touched him. How could they, when everyone already said ice ran in his veins?

Let them say it, he thought bitterly. Ice or no, his ways had saved enough that he wouldn't apologize for them. He'd carved out a life for himself, hadn't he? He'd battled against all odds to achieve what he had. His own family had seen him as a liability, had tossed him out when he couldn't work anymore at the factory that had mangled him as a child. To them, he was another mouth they couldn't feed, so they had sent him away to save the others.

He couldn't blame them, really. Desperation and fear could make anyone do nearly anything, and sometimes a single sacrifice was necessary to save many.

Back then, Dolph had been so angry, full of vinegar and bile. He'd been too stubborn to accept death or the boys' workhouse as his life, lame foot or not. And he'd been too smart to follow anyone else. While the other urchins begged for bread or stole coins from fat pockets, the secrets Dolph stole helped to make him who he was. Those secrets would either save him—or kill him—in the end.

Let the others fight over ragged strips of land they could never own. He knew the truth—there was a whole land made for him and his kind. Or there would be soon, if he had anything to do with it. Once the Brink came down, the Mageus could be free to do whatever they would. Once the old magic was restored, no one would be able to stop them. Without the Order of Ortus Aurea holding them back, they could remake the whole country as a land for magic. Those without it could learn for themselves what it was to live narrow, hen-scratched lives.

They were close now, closer than he'd ever been. Soon he would have Darrigan, and then he would have Jack Grew, and then the Order would be in his sights. But first he needed to deal with this new danger that had risen up in their midst.

He walked on, not bothered by any of the shadowy figures who huddled in doorways, their cigarettes flickering like fireflies in the bitter night air. Before he was within a block of Fulton Street, Dolph could already sense something wasn't right. There was a cold energy sizzling in the air like a live current, a warning to any with magic to stay away.

He pushed on, closer still, until he could force himself to go no farther. At the corner of Fulton and Nassau, he turned east and followed the icy energy along the length of Fulton. It felt almost as though he were walking along the perimeter of a high-voltage fence that was invisible to the eye. *Like the Dead Line has come to life.*

Dolph continued to walk, feeling his way along the Line as it ran down Fulton. As he walked, he fought the strangest urge to reach out and run his fingers through the energy beyond the sidewalk's edge, to stir its power.

Maybe it was some new trap. Or maybe it was because he'd been touched already by the Brink, that its power was now a part of him.

Magic was like that. Whether natural, like that of the Mageus, or corrupted, like the power the Order was able to wield, like called to like. Magic, whatever its form, could tempt the weak with its promise of power. Which was part of what the Sundren were afraid of—that magic was a drug, like the opium that trapped so many. Those without an affinity for it feared that magic was a compulsion. Those who had touched power knew it wasn't a completely unfounded fear.

In the old countries, there were stories of magic—and Mageus—run rampant. Plagues and deaths blamed on the same people who had once been asked to heal and guide. But that was before the Disenchantment, before the Ortus Aurea and other Sundren like them began hunting his kind and penning them in, destroying even the memory of a world permeated by the old magic as they took power for themselves.

The Order believed themselves to be men of reason. They called themselves enlightened, but in the end they were merely human, wanting what they didn't have and taking what wasn't theirs because they could.

This new danger was definitely man-made. Unnatural. The power it radiated felt broken, as though a part of the world had become unmoored from itself. Whatever had happened to the Dead Line, like the Brink, it had been designed to control. To punish.

He had no idea how this new threat worked. He wasn't sure if it was simply a line or if its power had engulfed the entire southern end of Manhattan, and he wasn't sure if it was like the Brink—which would allow entry into the city but not escape—or if it would destroy any who crossed in either direction.

But if this new line *was* the Brink, if it marked a constriction of their territory, who was to say it wouldn't move again? If it continued to creep north, they would have nowhere to go.

Across the street, Jianyu materialized out of the night and began to walk toward him.

"What news did you find?"

Jianyu shook his head. "No one's talking. Khafre Hall is dark. If this is the Order's doing, they are very quiet."

"It couldn't be anything *but* the Order's doing," Dolph argued. "Things are changing, and I can't say they're changing for the better." He glanced over to Jianyu, read the stiffness in the boy's spine, the closed expression on his face. "About earlier . . . I'm sorry for what Viola did."

Jianyu's expression didn't change. "She was afraid. People do all manner of things when fear drives their hearts."

"Still. You're one of us, and I don't want you to ever doubt that. The people in the bar, the things they said earlier? They don't speak for me, and they won't be allowed to darken my doorway again."

Jianyu inclined his head, but he didn't respond, and Dolph couldn't tell if he believed the sincerity of his apology or not.

Dolph couldn't blame him. After all Jianyu had been through, after all the city and the country had done to his people, why would he trust anyone, much less Dolph, who made it his business to remain as mysterious and unknowable as he could?

"You'll keep looking?" Dolph asked. "For Tilly?" he added, knowing that whatever Jianyu might think of him, he would do what he could for the girl.

"Of course," he said, and with another small bow, he disappeared into the night.

The weight of the night on his shoulders, Dolph turned back toward the Bowery, back toward Golde's apartment and the empty place at her table. Back to his streets, his own home, and all the people he was no longer sure he could protect.

A ROOM FILLED WITH FEAR

As the sky started to lighten outside Viola's window, Esta rubbed her eyes and stretched out the kinks in her back. She had finally convinced Viola to give Tilly more Nitewein a few hours before dawn. The first person who had offered her kindness in this city was now slumped on her side in the bed, her thin shift damp with sweat, her eyes glassy and unfocused. She looked three feet from death's doorstep, but at least she wasn't screaming anymore.

Esta dipped the rag back into the bucket of murky water and placed it against Tilly's feverish forehead once again. At the feel of the cool cloth, Tilly moaned.

Viola paused until Tilly settled again, but then continued to pace in the corner of the small room.

"You can sit down anytime now," Esta told her. So much for the cold, fearless assassin—Viola had been wearing a hole in the floor for most of the night.

"I still don't like it. Tilly, she never had the Nitewein. She would have hated to be like this," Viola said, her voice trembling as she gestured vaguely toward the girl in the bed.

"She wasn't exactly having the time of her life with all the screaming and moaning," Esta muttered. If she thought Viola would accept sympathy, Esta would have offered it. Instead, she gave Viola something to strike back at, a distraction from her worry.

"What did you say?" Viola demanded.

"Nothing. Never mind." Esta dipped the rag and placed it against Tilly's feverish brow again. Neither of them spoke for a long while, but Viola's fear filled the room as she resumed her pacing.

"Does she know how you feel?" Esta asked softly, not looking at Viola.

Viola's footsteps went still and a long, uncomfortable moment passed during which Esta wondered if she'd gone too far. But then . . .

"No," Viola said, her voice barely a breath but containing more heartbreak than a single word should be able to hold.

Esta met Viola's eyes. "You never told her?"

Viola let out a ragged breath and looked at the bed where Tilly lay. She shook her head. "It doesn't matter. Her friendship is enough."

Esta took the cloth and dipped it back into the water, not knowing what to say, what comfort to offer. She didn't know if Tilly had known or understood how Viola felt, but from the warm smiles she'd seen the two share, Esta couldn't help but think that maybe she did. And Esta knew Tilly cared for Viola, even if it wasn't in quite the same way. Still, she wasn't sure whether saying anything would help Viola or make things worse, so she kept her thoughts to herself.

But she stayed.

The morning passed slowly into afternoon, the streets outside the window growing noisy with the business of the day, but nothing inside the room had changed. Tilly had not improved . . . if anything, she seemed to be more pale and her cries more desperate every time the Nitewein began to wear off.

Tilly's cries had Viola strung tight as a garrote wire, and when Viola's temper snapped each time they had to give Tilly more Nitewein, Esta's was the only exposed throat in the room. Which would have been an easier burden to shoulder if Esta wasn't aware of just how deadly Viola could be. By the afternoon, Esta's shoulders were tight and her eyes felt like someone had thrown sand into them from the lack of sleep. She couldn't remember the last time she'd eaten, and as much as she wanted to help Tilly, she wished someone—anyone—would come and relieve her.

As if in answer, the door to the room opened, its uneven hinges creaking, and Dolph Saunders limped into the room. His hair was a riot of waves around his face, and his eyes were ringed with dark circles.

When she saw him, Viola stepped forward, putting herself between Dolph and Tilly.

"Stand down, Vi. I'm not here for that," Dolph told her, sounding tired and drawn. "And despite your impressive skills, you know well enough that you couldn't stop me if I were."

Viola's jaw clenched, but she didn't argue.

Dolph turned to Esta. "Have you slept any?" he asked, his voice gruff.

"About as much as you did, from the looks of it," Esta told him.

"You've been here all day?" He seemed surprised.

"Most of the night, too. It's not like I could sleep with the noise she was making." She nodded toward Tilly.

"Noise?" Dolph asked, looking at Viola.

"Mostly it was the screaming that kept me up," Esta told him. She shrugged, willing away her own exhaustion. "I thought I might as well help since I wasn't getting any sleep."

"She should have been sedated." Dolph glared at Viola.

Viola crossed her arms. "She is now, if that makes you happy."

"Immensely," he drawled. Then he turned back to Esta. "How is she faring?"

"I don't have any idea. She's quiet now, though."

Viola stepped forward. "She'll come through. Don't you worry none."

With an impatient glare, Dolph turned to Viola. "I'll worry when I'm ready to, and not a second before." Then his tired expression seemed to soften as he leaned into his cane. "We'll give her a bit more time. Keep her sedated this time," he told Viola sternly.

"She'd hate this," Viola said softly, her worried eyes locked on the pale girl in the bed.

"Hate it or not, it's necessary. Keeping her calm is the most we can do for her now. Her affinity is still there, but it's been broken somehow. It'll be up to her to decide whether she's strong enough to go on without it."

"Of course she'll be strong enough," Viola told Dolph, her jaw set determinedly. "She always was."

"I don't disagree, but surviving this will require a different sort of strength than she's had to draw on before. Time will tell." Dolph turned to Esta. "Come with me." He didn't wait for her to follow.

Just before Esta made it to the door, Viola grabbed her wrist.

The girl's strange violet eyes bored into her. "Thank you. For what you did for her," she said, her voice breaking. "And for me."

"It was nothing," Esta told her, an easy enough truth.

But Viola only squeezed her wrist more tightly. "No one else came," she said simply, before she let Esta go.

Esta slipped out of the room and found Nibs and Dolph waiting for her in the hall.

"Should I make the arrangements?" Nibs was asking.

Dolph shook his head. "Not yet. There's a small chance she could still pull through. We'll give her some time."

Nibs frowned. "She's a talented healer."

"I'm well aware of that," Dolph said as he led the way down to the staircase at the end of the narrow hall. "But Tilly's always been stronger than most. And her magic isn't completely gone. She's been loyal to me, so we'll give her—and Viola—time before I decide."

"Decide what?" Esta couldn't help asking.

"I won't let her suffer," Dolph said shortly. "And I can't allow her to become a liability."

A dark understanding rose in Esta. "So you'll—"

"I'll do what needs to be done to protect those who depend upon me," he growled, pulling himself to his full height as though daring Esta to cross him. When she didn't, he spoke again. "Darrigan sent me a note today, as you said he would. He'll meet with me in two days' time. With both Viola and Tilly otherwise occupied, I'd like you to be around—in case I need your help with him."

Esta nodded. "Anything else?"

"Yes," Dolph said, looking her over. "Go get some sleep. You look like something dragged from the gutter."

A HOMECOMING OF SORTS

Wallack's Theatre

Harte looked at the bottle of Nitewein someone had left on his dressing room table and considered his options. Going to Dolph Saunders for protection would be bad enough as a last resort. It was worse to be forced into it.

He picked up the bottle and tipped it side to side, watching the dark, viscous liquid coat the sides of the green glass. Removing the stopper, he took a sniff. Flowers and something sweet cut through with the bite of cheap wine. It smelled like an opium den and a saloon all mixed together, revolting and beguiling just the same.

How bad could it be if it made him forget what he had to do?

After pouring himself a glass, he sat staring at his reflection. He had his mother's chin, and his hair waved like hers, but he saw too much of his father looking back at him for his liking.

His nerves were jangling as he slowly lifted the glass.

The smell hit him, sweet and floral and sickening, and all at once a memory rose from that time after he'd rescued his mother from Paul Kelly's brothel. She never could stay sober for long, and every time she went missing, he'd have to hunt through smoke-filled basements to find her and keep her from any more trouble. He would try not to look as he pulled her clothes around her and dragged her back home, but she'd only hate him in the morning anyway. For seeing her like that. And for taking her away from the only thing she'd let herself love other than his father.

Unnatural boy.

He put the glass down and resealed the bottle. In the mirror, his reflection stared back at him, doubtful. After he was done cataloging his faults and putting away his regrets, he reached for his pocket watch before he remembered it had been stolen.

Not that he really cared if he was late.

Harte hated everything about the world below Houston—its rotten, trash-lined streets, the tumbled rows of tenements teeming with desperation and despair. Even the air, which was permeated by the stench coming from the outhouses behind them. So he hated what he was about to do even more.

He didn't have to go in, he thought, as he came to The Devil's Own Boxing Club. He should have stayed away months ago—maybe none of this would have ever happened. Nothing was stopping him from turning around and going right back to where he belonged, to his uptown theater and his clean, airy set of rooms. To his porcelain tub and a bath of boiling-hot water. To the life he'd built out of nothing. A life that *could* still be enough.

But the fire said otherwise.

He'd managed to get his mother sober enough to leave her at a new address, but how long would it be before Kelly and his boys found her again? And they *would* find her, because Harte had no intention of letting Paul Kelly anywhere near Jack. He couldn't imagine what Kelly wanted with the Order of the Ortus Aurea, but if he ever managed to get their power behind him, it wouldn't mean anything good for his kind, and especially not for Harte himself.

Much as he hated admitting it, Dolph Saunders was the only way he saw to get around that possibility. After all, Dolph had a reputation for protecting outcasts from the wrath of the other gang bosses downtown, including Kelly's own sister, Viola. Let them fight each other while Harte made his move. If Dolph was right about what the Book contained, he'd be out of the city and safely on the other side of the Brink before any of them realized what had happened. They would be stuck inside, unable to reach him, and he'd be free.

He ignored the twinge of guilt he felt when he thought of the other Mageus who would still be trapped. *But they're already trapped.* If anything, he told himself, their lives might be better if the Order didn't have their Book.

When he gave the kid on the other side of the door his name, he was let through to a long, familiar hallway to the back of the building. The closer he got to the end of it, the stronger the scent of sweat and blood and the more vivid the memories.

He'd spent the year after his mother had abandoned him—and before he was forced into Paul Kelly's gang—hanging around The Devil's Own. Back then, Dolph had still been a lanky teenager. He'd seemed larger than life to twelve-year-old Harte. Even with his limp, Dolph had commanded the respect of anyone who knew him in the Bowery, and of anyone who dared cross him. It was the kind of respect Harte himself craved, and Dolph had become something of an older brother, the mentor and protector his own father had never been. The boxing club had become a safe space for him—or at least it had been safer than the streets where he'd spent too many nights. He'd learned to fight there, to protect himself in ways that had nothing to do with magic. And he'd spent more nights than he could count eating at Dolph and Leena's table in their rooms above the Bella Strega.

After he'd gotten caught up in Kelly's gang, he'd stayed away from them both. It had been more than three years since Harte had even talked to Leena, but the ache of her loss hit him then, suddenly and far too late. She'd been only a handful of years older than him, but she'd mothered him in ways his own mother had never been able to. Still, even after he'd heard she lost a baby, Harte hadn't risked crossing Kelly—or Dolph—to visit her. But now that he was back, surrounded by memories he thought he'd put aside, he was overwhelmed by the thought of her being gone. Leena had been too stubborn and determined to do anything she didn't want to do, but Dolph should have never put her in a position to be harmed by the Order.

Leena had meant everything to Dolph, so Harte didn't have any illusions about how disposable *he* would be. And he didn't feel all that much remorse for what he planned to do in the end. The Book would be his, and Dolph Saunders could go hang for all he cared.

When he reached the main practice room, he found Dolph in the same place he'd seen him so many times before—perched on a low stool, his chin resting against his silver-tipped cane as he watched two of his boxers pummel each other in the ring above him. They were both bare-chested, their skin already slick with sweat and their chests heaving with exertion. They couldn't have been more than fifteen or sixteen, but already, each sported the tattoo that marked them as Dolph's—a double ouroboros that featured a skeletal snake intertwined with a living one.

Life and death, Dolph had once told him, back when they'd still been friends. Survival was about balance. The threat of death could inspire you to carve out a life worth having.

Once, Harte had been eager to take Dolph's mark, but Dolph had said that, at twelve, he was too young to make that decision. He'd considered it again when he'd wanted to get out of Kelly's gang. Dolph could have easily given him the secrets he needed to buy his freedom.

He'd thought that trading one mark for another was something he could live with, and he'd come to the boxing club to do just that. But because he'd been early that day, Harte had seen what happened to those who crossed Dolph Saunders. He understood then what the mark was capable of, what *Dolph* was capable of.

He would never forget it—the way the man who was years older than Dolph had cowered and begged for another chance. The cold look in Dolph's eyes as he rejected the pathetic appeals. Dolph had motioned for two of his boys to hold the man still, and then he'd simply touched him with the head of his cane. The second the silver Medusa touched the tattoo, the mark came to life. The two snakes began moving, and the man's skin rippled as the ink turned the color of blood.

And then it did become blood. The man screamed like a banshee until the two boys dropped him, and he fell unconscious to the floor. By then, the air in the room had gone cold and energy crackled, but Dolph had barely seemed to notice. He'd given a curt nod, and the two boys had dragged the man away—unconscious or dead, Harte couldn't tell.

Harte had turned around and left that day, and he had vowed to never take another's brand again. He would do everything on his own, trust no one but himself. Even if it meant never *truly* getting away from Kelly's reach.

Except now he might have a way. Stealing the Ars Arcana from the Order—from Dolph—might be a crazy, impossible death wish of a way, but Harte was about desperate enough to take it.

"You're late," Dolph said with his usual brusqueness. He didn't bother to turn around. "I don't like to be kept waiting."

"Last I checked, I'm not one of your lackeys."

"Not yet," Dolph said, finally glancing over his shoulder to pin Harte with his blue-eyed stare.

"Don't get ahead of yourself, old man."

Dolph didn't react to the nickname the way he usually did. Instead, he let out a tired breath and gave Harte an unreadable look. "I'm glad you've come."

Suspicious, Harte crossed the room to where Dolph was sitting. "I'm only here because that skirt of yours conned me into it." It wasn't the truth, of course, but it was better if Dolph thought he still had the upper hand.

One of the boys nailed the other with a right hook that sent blood splattering. A few drops landed on Harte's polished black boots, and it took everything he had not to wipe it away in disgust.

"That's enough for today," Dolph told the two bloodied boys. "You're losing your touch if you were taken in by a pretty face, Darrigan."

"What can I say? She was persuasive. But she's not your usual type," Harte said as he watched the boys leave. "Though she does remind me a little of Leena, too much of a hellcat to fall in line easily . . . So maybe she is your type after all. My mistake."

"Don't," Dolph growled.

"Where'd you find her?" Harte pushed, ignoring the tension that had risen between them at his mention of Leena. He knew it was a low blow, one she'd have taken him to task for, but he would use whatever advantage he could. And he'd hold Dolph accountable for what he'd done to her.

"You're not here because of her." Dolph eyed him. "You think I don't know that Kelly's men have been breathing down your neck lately?"

Harte went still.

"Oh, come off it," Dolph said. "I have eyes in every part of this city. I heard about the fire the other day, and I know that Razor Riley helped to set it."

Harte held up his hands. "You know what? I was wrong. Turns out I can't do this," he said, taking a step backward, preparing to leave. "I'd say it was good to see you again, Dolph, but you don't deserve the effort it would take to lie." He turned and let his feet take him toward the door, but he hadn't finished crossing the room when Dolph spoke.

"You know I can protect you from Paul Kelly. Your mother, too. I would have done it years ago if you weren't so damn stubborn and proud."

Harte stopped where he was, but he hated Dolph that much more for knowing the one thing that would keep him listening. "I'm still not willing to pay the price for your help. I'm not taking your mark," he said. He kept his eyes focused in front of him.

"I haven't offered it," Dolph said, his voice tight.

"You did once." He turned back to look at Dolph and let his old friend see that he wouldn't be swayed. "I came that day, you know. I saw what you did to that man—what *your mark* did to him." It had taken him two years more to gather enough of Kelly's secrets to negotiate his exit from the gang, but he'd solved his own problems then. He'd do it again if he had to.

"I didn't realize . . ."

"Did Leena know?" Harte asked. "Did she have any idea what you were playing at?" Back then Harte had left because he was afraid, but now he knew enough to understand that what Dolph's mark had done stank of ritual magic.

Dolph's jaw went tight. "That's none of your—"

"Leena never would have been okay with it."

"She didn't know how dangerous things were," Dolph snapped, "or how precarious our position was." He took a breath as though trying to calm himself. "Leena was too good for this world," Dolph said softly.

"Your Leena?" Harte laughed. "Maybe she *was* a saint—she must have been, to put up with you—but she was also tough as nails and smarter than anyone. I bet she was livid when she found out you were dabbling in ritual magic. I would have bought tickets to watch that fight."

From the flush in Dolph's cheeks, Harte knew he was right. "She understood."

"I bet she did," Harte mocked, shaking his head.

"Do you really think I'm the first Mageus to try strengthening my power?" Dolph asked.

"Of course not." Stories of Mageus trying to make themselves stronger by using ceremonies or ritual objects were as old as magic itself. They were the source of legends about witches and shamans, magical creatures the Sundren feared.

No, Dolph wasn't the first to try to claim more than he was born with, and he wouldn't be the last.

"Weren't *you* the one who taught me the cost of what the Order was doing, the way they damaged magic itself each time they manipulated the elements and claimed power that wasn't theirs?"

Dolph scowled at him. "You weren't around then. You don't know what it was like—I didn't know who I could trust or who I could depend on. So, yes, I did what I had to do to protect mine. How else was I supposed to fight against the Order?"

"I don't know." Harte shook his head. Dolph couldn't even see how many lines he'd crossed to get what he wanted. "But you weren't supposed to *become* them."

"I'm *nothing* like the Order," Dolph snapped.

"No?" Harte pressed. "The Order thinks what they're doing is right, that they're only protecting what's theirs—their land, their people, their country. That's how everyone else sees it too. The whole city believes them, believes Mageus are something to be feared and lets the Order have their way. Your mark could destroy a person—*did* destroy a person. How is that *any* different from what the Order does? How will you be any different if you get this book you're after?"

The muscle in Dolph's jaw jumped, and his whole body radiated tension. "Considering how cozy you've been getting with Jack Grew, I can't imagine you really care."

"You're right. I don't." The Order, the Bowery, the city itself. It was all the same to Harte. Each one was holding him down, holding him back. He'd throw them off one by one, until he was free, or he'd die trying.

Dolph glared at him. "Did you come because you're finally willing to join us, or only to remind me of my failures?"

They'd finally come to it. He wasn't sure he could do it until the words were already out: "You want my help," Harte told Dolph. "I'm willing to give it in exchange for protection. I want Kelly off my back—for good—and I want my mother safe. But you'll have to take my word for a guarantee. I won't be branded by you. Not for anything."

It was a gamble. If Dolph rejected his offer, he'd have to deal with Kelly on his own. If Dolph demanded that Harte take his mark, he'd be as shackled to Dolph as he'd been to Paul Kelly, and Harte wouldn't—couldn't—let that happen.

A long minute passed, the two of them standing in stony silence, waiting to see who would break first.

"Fine," Dolph said. His hand was gripping his cane so tightly his knuckles were white. "I'll take your word. But if you go back on it, I'll destroy the life you've built for yourself one piece at a time. I'll make sure the entire city knows what you truly are. If the Order doesn't finish you off, Viola will."

"Fine with me," Harte said. If everything went to plan, he wouldn't be in the city to care. And if things went as badly as they could go, he'd gladly take a quick death at Viola's hand over whatever Paul Kelly or the Order would dish out. "I have to say, I'm a little surprised you agreed."

"Things have changed," Dolph said. "We can't afford to wait for the Order's next move."

He told Harte about what had happened to Tilly, about how she'd had her magic stripped from her. How at that very moment, she was fighting for her life.

"You think the Brink has moved?" Harte asked, chilled by the idea.

"I don't know, but this latest attack makes me more sure than ever— we have to take the Order down. To do that, I need the Book. To get the Book, we need a way into Khafre Hall as well as a way *out* that doesn't involve getting everyone killed."

Harte gave a hollow laugh. "Is that all?"

"Probably not, but it's the minimum. If you don't have Jack Grew on the hook already, you will. It's only a matter of time. I've heard about him: brash, quick-tempered, and has something to prove. He's the perfect mark."

"That's the problem. *Everyone's* heard about him, and he knows it. He's skittish," Harte said. "Unpredictable. His family knows it, and they watch him pretty closely. I'm not one of them, no matter how well I shine up. If they warn him off, he'll listen, because he has too much to lose with them right now." He gave Dolph a knowing look. "Especially after that mess at the Metropolitan."

"So make him think he can't lose." Dolph gave him an impatient glare.

"I've been trying, but it's not so easy. He wants me to find out what happened at the museum." He paused, never blinking, as he sent the clear message that he knew Dolph had been behind the robbery. "I'm assuming you don't want him to discover the truth."

"So give him something better."

"What are you proposing?"

"Use the girl," Dolph said. "She can help you hook him. She's already established her cover, hasn't she?"

"The long-lost-lover angle," Harte said, realizing exactly how deep her game had been the day before. She'd penned him more ways than one.

"The daughter of one of your illustrious teachers. I bet she would have secrets Jack Grew would love to learn," Dolph said with a satisfied smile. "Secrets that could make him a huge success in the Order. *That's* what he really wants."

He hated the fact that Dolph was right.

"I already told her, I work alone," Harte said.

"Not anymore. And not if you want my protection," Dolph told him. "You won't take my mark, but you *will* agree to work with Esta. Otherwise, you're welcome to take your chances with Kelly and his boys. Your mother, too. I won't make this offer twice."

Harte's jaw was so tight his temple ached. "It's not much of a choice when you put it like that."

Dolph shrugged. "There's always a choice. The question is which one you're willing to live with."

"You or Kelly," Harte said, his voice as threatening as his mood. "Why do I feel like I'm only getting to pick my poison?"

"It's still a choice," Dolph drawled.

Harte shook his head. "You always were a bastard."

"Takes one to know one." There was the hint of amusement in Dolph's expression.

"Fine. We'll do it your way. But when this is over, you don't bother me again. You don't contact me or try to find me. If we're all not already dead, you don't even know me. Period."

The amusement faded from Dolph's face. "Agreed. But if I get any hint of you going against me or mine, I won't hesitate to end you. My mark or no, I will strip you of everything you hold dear."

"You should have gone on the stage," Harte said dryly. "You've developed quite the flair for the dramatic. If that's all?"

"That's all." Dolph nodded. Then he softened his voice. "It really is good to see you again."

"I can't say the feeling is mutual," Harte said, but he couldn't stop his mouth from curving up. "Keep my mother out of Paul Kelly's grasp, and you won't have anything to worry about on my end. I'll get what you need." Harte extended his hand to shake on the deal they'd made.

Dolph shook his head. "I wasn't born yesterday, Dare. I have a few things to take care of, but I'll be sending Esta to you in a couple of days."

"What do you mean?" Harte asked. His hand dropped to his side.

"She'll be staying with you and keeping an eye on things while the two of you work together."

"She can't stay with me." He shook his head. "I don't want her there."

Dolph laughed. "I won't call you on that lie, but you're going to have to take her."

"You know it'll ruin her," Harte argued, unexpected anger curling in his stomach at the thought. "Her reputation won't recover."

"That won't matter if the Order kills us first." Dolph pulled himself to his feet. "You worry about keeping your end of our agreement. She'll let me know of any unwanted developments."

Harte could only stand there, his frustration rising as he watched Dolph limp off in the same direction the two boys had gone, dismissing him without so much as a good-bye. The reek of the sour, coppery dried blood wrapped around his throat, choking him. He wasn't sure if he'd managed to negotiate a good deal or simply tied a noose around his own neck.

"That's it?" he called out. "You're going to send me the girl, and I'm supposed to figure out the rest? I take on all the risk, and you sit, safe in your castle."

"I've already given you everything you need." Dolph turned to look at him over his shoulder. "But—"

"Yeah?" he snapped, his frustration mounting.

"The girl's currently under my protection," Dolph said softly, "so if you actually *do* ruin her, you'll answer to me."

PART

III

RUINED

The Docks

The machine was in ruins. Metal fragments were lodged in the wood of the walls and in the chest of the old man. The hulking globe in the center looked like it had melted.

Jack nudged the body with his toe. *Dammit.*

All of his work had been for nothing. Months of work. Months of waiting. Wasted.

"Get this cleaned up," he told the boy who'd brought him the news. He tossed him a coin. "Then put out word that I need a machinist. Now."

"And the old man?" the boy asked, eyeing the body warily.

"Dump him in the river."

Jack didn't stay to make sure the work was done. The warehouse, even with all its square footage, felt claustrophobic. Like the walls were pressing in on him, squeezing him until there wasn't a drop of blood left for him to give. He'd risked everything, gambled everything, and he had been *so* close. *Dammit.*

He kicked over a barrel and sent a pair of rats skittering away.

There was still something he was missing. Some key to making the machine work. There had to be, because he wouldn't let himself believe that *they* were more powerful.

Reason and logic would prevail.

He would prevail.

The machine should have been perfectly functional. The problem would have been easy enough to figure out if the High Princept would just let him consult the Ars Arcana. Certainly, the Order's most important artifact, their most sacred text, would have the answers he needed. But there were parts of Khafre Hall only the Inner Circle had access to, and the Mysterium, with all its secrets, was one of them. So unless something changed, he was on his own.

Tugging at the collar of his shirt, Jack stomped back out to the carriage. When his father found out what had happened to the money in his trust fund . . . when his uncle and the rest of the Inner Circle found out . . .

Jesus. They'd never let him in. Worse, he'd never be able to set foot in society again.

Dammit.

He needed more information. He needed the Order to trust him enough to let him into the Mysterium, because he knew the answer was there. Solving the Metropolitan robbery would go a long way toward getting into their good graces, but Harte Darrigan had been avoiding him the last few days. He was trying to be patient, trying to give the magician a chance to work on the problem, but at this rate, the machine would never be done in time for the Conclave.

He needed to figured out what he was missing, and fast, or he'd be ruined.

But most of all, he needed a drink.

DREAMS FROM WAKING

Bella Strega

Something had happened. It had come suddenly and absolutely, as a wave might overtake a small boat out to sea, leaving Viola struggling to stay afloat. For three days she'd watched her friend suffer, writhing and moaning despite the laudanum in the wine. For three days she had paced the floor in Tilly's room or sat on the edge of her narrow bed, holding her hand and whispering everything she'd wanted to say for so long.

Night and day she'd stayed. Tilly couldn't hear her, but night and day Viola continued whispering, using her mother tongue, because the words felt right in that language. Her meaning felt somehow more suited for the soft melodic rhythm of the country that had made her.

But her words and prayers had not been enough.

Neither had her power.

She was an assassin, but only because that was what the world had made her into. Because her brother had needed a black hand of death to smite his enemies, and his life was the one her family valued. His success was all that had mattered to them. She might have been made an assassin, but her affinity had never been intended for death. And nothing they did, nothing anyone could do, had changed that.

But it wasn't enough. *She* wasn't enough.

Even now she could sense Tilly's blood, the beating of her fragile heart, the energy that was the very signal of life within a body. Even now she pushed everything she was, every ounce of power she had, into her friend. She had been doing it for days, but no matter what she did, the broken part wouldn't heal.

Because Viola could only command flesh, and what was broken in Tilly was something more.

Around dawn, something had changed. The wave had come over them, cold as the lonely sea she had once crossed, and the fight had gone out of her friend. That spark of energy that signaled a life began to waver, and for the first time since Viola had seen Tilly writhing in Jianyu's arms, she truly worried that Tilly might not pull through.

Since then, Tilly's skin had gone even more ashen, and now she lay still, her chest rising and falling in uneven, ragged breaths that rattled in her throat. Viola had heard that sound before, but now she could not— would not—allow herself to believe its message.

She barely noticed when Esta went to find Dolph, or when he arrived. Even when the room began to fill with the people from his crew who had loved Tilly, who had depended on her calm, steady presence in the Strega's kitchen, Viola was scarcely aware of them, she whose every day was filled with the rushing thrum of rivers of blood, the beating drum-beats of a world filled with hearts.

The crowd in the room might as well have been made of stone that morning for all she noticed them as she fought against the truth lying in Tilly's bed. As she willfully ignored the way her friend's hands had turned cool, the way her fingertips and nails had lost all color.

Dolph stepped forward from his vigil at the foot of the bed. "You know what needs to be done, Vi. You know it's time to let her go."

Viola shook her head, pressing her lips together. "She'll be better tomorrow. I know she will."

Dolph rested his hand on Viola's shoulder. "I understand," he said softly. "I know exactly what it's like to watch someone you care for slide away from you. To watch your own heart cease to beat."

Viola swallowed down the hard stone she felt in her throat and turned to him. "She is not dying."

"Her magic's gone," Dolph told her. "It has been for days. Now she's going too. It's time we let her. It's time *you* let her."

"She will not die," Viola repeated, her voice barely a whisper. "She will fight. She will be better. I just need to give her more time."

"You know that's not true," Dolph said gently. "Yes, she did fight. You've helped her, and she fought hard, but what's happened is too much. It would have been too much for any of us. Think of what it would be like, what it would mean to lose your power. Can you imagine not being able to reach a part of yourself? To feel it stripped away?" His voice broke, and he paused for a moment to compose himself. "To live without it."

Viola grimaced. "No," she whispered. All at once she realized what he must have felt watching Leena die. No wonder he had seemed so changed after.

"Tilly's fought hard enough. Allow her the rest she's earned."

Anger spiked through her, drowning the pain with a sense of righteous fury. She would not be commanded. She would *not* be the instrument of death. Not this time. She would use her affinity to keep Tilly's heart beating and in doing so atone for all those other hearts she'd stopped. And no one would stop her. Not Dolph Saunders. Not even with the threat of his mark.

Dolph staggered a bit, his lean face twisting with pain as she let her power fill the room, as she found all the parts of him that made him a living man and started to pull them apart one by one. Slowly, so he could feel what she felt. She was so focused, she didn't notice the way the others rustled in fear, backed away.

"You know I'm right," Dolph gasped, gripping his cane as he tried to stay upright. "Do this last thing for her."

Viola shook her head, her vision blurry with tears as her power crackled through the room.

"Free her," Dolph said, barely able to stand. The veins in his cheeks had turned dark, like tiny rivers floating to the surface of his skin. "Kill me if you must, but let her go," he rasped.

Yes. She would kill him for even suggesting it. She'd killed before, and for lesser reasons. But despite what people believed, she did not often kill like this. Years ago, she had learned to throw knives, to carve out a life with the sharp tip of a blade, because she knew her god damned her for using her gift to take lives, as her brother wanted, rather than to save them, as she could. But she would use everything she was now. She would risk the fires of hell and everything that came with them for Tilly. For herself.

Dolph staggered to his knees as she pushed her affinity toward him, felt the pulse, the light . . . and the broken pieces that even she couldn't heal.

She realized then what he'd been carrying since that night they lost Leena. The secret he'd been hiding from them all.

The fight went out of her. She released her affinity, let go of her hold on Dolph, and crumpled against Tilly's barely moving chest, unable to stop the sob that tore from her throat. She stayed there, emptying herself of pain and grief, for who knew how long.

Until she had nothing left.

Until she finally felt the warm, steady hand on her shoulder.

She shrugged Dolph off and wiped the wetness from her cheeks.

"It's time," Dolph said. "Allow her to go in peace."

Viola turned to the crowded room, her eyes burning from the tears she'd shed. Who were these people? Not the family she'd been raised by, when blood was supposed to be thicker than anything. No, that family had turned from her. They'd wanted her to be what she could never be, and she had chosen again. She saw now in that motley group that she had chosen well. And so had Tilly.

"She wouldn't want them here for this," she told Dolph. "She wouldn't want them to see." Because it would be hard for them to watch, and Tilly would have hated their suffering. And because Viola knew somehow that Tilly wouldn't want them to understand what she could actually do.

Tilly had seen through the mask she wore, had never believed her to be the coldhearted assassin the rest saw. One person knowing her truth had been enough. It had to be, because Viola's role was her shield. It allowed her to survive in a world that would rather see her dead. Tilly had understood that as well, and she had given Viola friendship, even when she could not give more.

Dolph nodded, and one by one the silent crowd in the room began to depart. A few were brave enough to come forward and touch Viola gently on the back or the shoulder before they went. Then the new girl, Esta, came forward to take her turn as well.

Esta touched her shoulder gently, like a bird landing on a branch. "I think she must have known how you felt for her," she whispered.

Viola shook her head, wondering as she had before how this strange girl could see her so clearly. "She would have despised me," Viola whispered.

"I don't think she would have. Tilly understood people." Esta gave her shoulder a gentle squeeze. "She loved you. Anyone could see that, even if it wasn't in the way you hoped."

Viola looked up, wanting to believe those words, and found Esta's eyes glassy with tears but free from lies. Free, too, from the judgment she expected there. "I still don't know that I like you," she said. "But Tilly did. And you're right. She *did* understand people. Better than I ever could. You'll stay?"

"Yes," she whispered to Viola. "Of course."

Viola's throat was too tight to do more than nod her thanks, and then she turned her attention back to Tilly. She was afraid to look away, afraid that the moment she blinked or stopped watching, she'd miss Tilly's last breath. Or that she would cause it.

A suffocating silence blanketed the room, broken only by Tilly's rasping, uneven breath.

"Viola . . . ," Dolph whispered gently. "It's time."

Viola ignored him and took Tilly's hand in hers, rubbing her thumb over the pallid skin as her whole body trembled with the effort not to let her grief spill out and drown her. She lifted the limp hand to her cheek, closing her eyes and imagining for a moment that she was strong enough to save her friend. That this was all a horrible dream.

But Viola knew dreams from waking. She knew the thick scent in the air and the rasping sound in Tilly's throat, and she'd never looked away from death before. She wouldn't look away now.

Viola opened her eyes and took a long, deep breath as she placed Tilly's hand gently across the girl's own stomach. Then she whispered one last thing into her ear.

Tilly blinked, turning her eyes ever so slightly to look up at Viola. For a moment her gaze was focused, as though she had come back to herself long enough to see who it was who stood above her—just long enough to say good-bye.

Tears blurring her vision, Viola pulled her hand away, and with it, she pulled away her affinity, that fragile thread holding Tilly to this world.

Life and death, two sides to the same coin. Her family saw her as a killer, and so she had become one. Everyone else believed her to be a killer, because they forgot that death is simply the other side of life. But Viola never forgot. She couldn't. She'd tried to save her friend, and she'd failed.

Tilly's chest heaved in a final, ragged breath. And then her body sank motionless back to the bed, her empty green eyes staring sightlessly above.

THE TREE OF KNOWLEDGE

Esta felt the room go cold, the magic draining from the space like air sucked from a vacuum. Viola reached over, her always-steady hands shaking, and gently traced her fingertips over Tilly's face, closing the girl's eyes. Then she stared, mute and tearless, at the girl's still body.

As Esta watched, she remembered suddenly what Logan had looked like, pale and unconscious in the narrow bed after the mess at Schwab's mansion. How was it possible that she hadn't thought about him for days now? Had life in this city been so all-consuming that she'd lost sight of why she was there? Then she thought of the clipping, still tucked safely against her skin—if the heist didn't happen, if she changed too much just by being here, what would happen to all the people she'd left behind?

"Come," Dolph whispered, nodding toward the door. "We'll give her the space she needs to grieve."

In the hall, he gave a silent jerk of his head to indicate that she should follow him. When they reached his rooms a floor below, he opened the door and ushered her through it. He gestured for her to take a seat in one of the chairs near the bookcases, and then he poured himself a drink.

Esta was almost grateful to see that he seemed as shaken as she felt with what they'd witnessed. After downing the first glass of whiskey, Dolph poured himself another and then sat in the armchair across from her. He didn't speak at first. Instead, he swirled the liquid in the chipped cup he held in his broad, calloused hands before taking another long swallow. Finally, he looked up at her.

"Thank you for staying," he said, his voice no more than a whisper. His jaw was tight, and in his eyes she could see the pain of losing Tilly, and if she wasn't mistaken, maybe the pain of something more.

"It was nothing," she told him, still unsteady from the rush of Viola's magic.

"No, that's not exactly true." His eyes were shadowed with the evidence of sleepless nights and worry. "Most aren't willing to bear witness to pain that can't be remedied. Most find it easier to simply turn away. On behalf of Viola—and Tilly—I thank you for not doing that."

They sat there for a long while, an impromptu wake. Dolph took a drink every so often from his glass of whiskey, while Esta waited for him to speak or to dismiss her so she could escape the heavy silence.

He set his drink aside. "Harte Darrigan visited me yesterday. We've come to an understanding. I have you to thank for that."

"Good," Esta said. "I'm glad I could help."

"I'm sending you to him."

"What?" She sat up straighter.

"You'll need to pack your things."

"Wait. . . . You *gave* me to him?" she asked, incredulous.

"Of course not," Dolph said. "I want a pair of eyes I trust on Darrigan at all times. What you did at the museum for Jianyu and the rest of the crew, what you did today for Viola . . . You're one of us now. I'm trusting you can keep him on task."

Esta felt the instinctive need to argue. She didn't want to leave the Strega, didn't want to go stay with Harte Darrigan. But she stopped herself. This was what she'd been hoping for all along, wasn't it? Dolph was handing her the perfect situation—a chance to get close to the Magician. A chance to stop him before he ruined all their futures. She wouldn't waste it. "What do you need from him?"

"Darrigan hasn't always been the polished magician he is now. Once, he wasn't any different from any of the boys in the Bowery. But he's managed to carve out a new life for himself, and that new life comes with some very powerful friends."

"He knows people in the Order?"

Dolph nodded. "Specifically, he's become friends with a fellow named Jack Grew, who happens to be J. P. Morgan's nephew. I don't need to explain to you how important a contact like that is, not with what's happened to Tilly. I need information, and Darrigan is our best chance to get it. His connections are our best opportunity to get a crew into Khafre Hall."

She feigned surprised. "You're not planning to rob them?"

Dolph nodded.

"That's a bigger risk than the Metropolitan," she said, pretending to be more concerned than she actually was.

"It is, but if we do it right, the rewards are bigger too. I want to end their reign over this city, over our kind." Dolph leaned over to take a book from the shelf. "I want to make this land safe for magic."

He opened the volume—a ledger or journal of some sort. Its pages were filled with the same strong, even hand. He took a small envelope from between the pages and pulled out a worn scrap of fabric, which he handed to Esta.

She looked closely at the faded and smeared letters. "That's *blood.*"

Dolph nodded. "Someone died getting that message to me. A woman named Leena Rahal, a woman I trusted with my life."

"What does it say?" She frowned, playing dumb to lead him on. She didn't need him to know that she knew Latin as well as any of her other languages. "Something about a book?"

"Have you ever heard of the Ars Arcana?"

Esta shook her head, keeping her eyes on the bloodied words so the lie wouldn't show.

Dolph flipped through the pages of the journal, and finding the place he wanted, he held it out to her. On the page was an image that she recognized easily enough from her many lessons with Professor Lachlan— the Tree of Knowledge. This image was different from others she'd seen, though. Usually, the tree's wide branches held symbols representing the ancient mysteries, alchemical notations that were attempts to explain the interworkings of heaven and earth. In this version, though, the tree was aflame, and at the source of those flames was a book. Like the bush Moses found, like the fish in the center of the Philosopher's Hand, the book wasn't being destroyed by the fire.

"There are stories passed down through time of a book that holds the secrets of the old magic—the Ars Arcana, or the Book of Mysteries. Some believe it contains the very beginnings of magic. Others believe its pages hold the history of Mageus, but legend has it that whoever possesses the Book also can wield the power it contains. Of course, like the Golden Fleece or the philosopher's stone, the Book is supposed to be nothing more than a story—a myth," Dolph told her. "But I believe the Ars Arcana is real, and I believe the Ortus Aurea has it."

"Because of this?" she asked, holding up the scrap.

"In part, but the more I've looked into it, the more sure I've become. That image isn't a simple picture. It's a complex arrangement of symbols—the book aflame, the moon and stars circling. It should look familiar to you." He gestured toward the painting hanging over his shelves, the one she'd helped to steal.

"Newton is holding the same book, with the same symbols on its pages," she realized, looking between the two.

"The circular symbol there is called the Sigil of Ameth, the Seal of Truth. The Order believes an initiated magician could use it to unlock power over all creatures below the heavens—and some above as well. The Ars Arcana is supposed to contain the one true sigil. I don't think it's any coincidence that J. P. Morgan, one of the highest-ranking members of the Order, owned that painting. I think Morgan couldn't help himself from bragging about his knowledge. The Order has the Ars Arcana. I *know* it."

"You want to steal the Book," she said, letting her excitement show.

"We could use the knowledge it contains to destroy the Brink. Without the Brink and the Book, the Order would be finished. More than that, I believe we could let magic—old magic, *true* magic—grow free again. *Libero libro.* The Book will free us."

"Does Harte know all of this?"

"He knows what I'm after," Dolph admitted, "and he knows the Book could bring down the Brink."

Which is why he took it, Esta realized. *He wanted it for himself.*

But then . . . why had he disappeared? Why had *the Book* disappeared? It didn't make any sense. There had to be something more to what happened, and she would have to be smart—and more patient than she'd ever been—to figure it out. Or risk disrupting the future even more.

"Why are you telling me all of this now?" Esta asked.

"Because I need you to understand the importance of what we are undertaking. It will be difficult to do what I'm planning. Khafre Hall is a fortress. Without someone on the inside, the job will be impossible. Jack Grew's our way in, and Harte Darrigan is our way to him. So you'll go to Darrigan and you'll make sure he gets Jack on the hook."

Before she could ask anything else, they were interrupted by a sharp knock at the door.

"Come," Dolph said, his eyes never leaving Esta's.

Nibs opened the door. "There's news."

"Well, get in here and tell me about it," Dolph barked.

With a nod, he stepped into the room and closed the door softly behind himself. "Whatever happened to the Dead Line," Nibs said, "it's done. Gone."

Dolph's brows drew together. "What do you mean, gone?"

"The crew you had patrolling over on Fulton said that it just disappeared. One minute it was there, and the next, there was a flare of energy and they couldn't sense it anymore."

"When was this?"

"A couple hours ago," Nibs said. "I went down to check for myself before I came to you. I wanted to make sure. But it's gone, all right."

"That was right about when Tilly got worse," Esta realized.

"It was," Dolph said, his expression stony. He finished his drink before he spoke again. "Gather your things and get yourself to Darrigan's. I want Grew on the hook, and I want it to happen before anyone else has to die."

EVEN KITTENS HAVE CLAWS

Harte's Apartment

Knowing how Dolph Saunders worked, Harte had half expected the girl to be waiting for him when he got back to the theater. Actually, he'd planned on it. He'd spent the long walk back from The Devil's Own thinking of all the things he wanted to say to her—the rules he'd establish to put her in her place and keep her there. When she didn't appear, he couldn't help feeling almost disappointed. And when she *still* hadn't made an appearance by the end of the night's second show, he could only wonder what Dolph was up to and whether he'd keep the bargain they'd made.

Even prepared as he was, the last thing he expected to find when he let himself into his apartment late the next night was the girl, curled up like an overgrown kitten on the narrow couch in his front parlor. She was fast asleep, her head resting on her arm and her breathing soft and even. At first he simply stood there staring. In sleep, her features looked different—softer, somehow.

Not that he was fooled into thinking she was harmless—even kittens had claws, after all. And he'd had enough experience with this one to know hers were sharper than most.

He wondered how long she'd been there. She looked uncomfortable with her neck tipped to the side at such an awkward angle. Her dress was a shade of blue that reminded him of the spring sky, but the hem was marred with the grime of the winter streets. He cringed at the sight of her damp boots up on the clean chintz upholstery. They would leave a mark if she stayed that way.

With a sigh, he went over to the sofa. "Esta," he whispered. "Come on. Wake up." She didn't seem to hear him, so he reached down to shake her arm gently. "I said wake—"

The next thing he knew, he was flat on his back on the carpet, staring up at the ceiling. He had no idea how she'd managed to move so quickly out of a dead sleep, but it had taken less than a second for her to sweep his legs out from under him with her ankle and twist his arms around to pin him to the floor. Her eyes were wide and furious, but they weren't really lucid until she blinked away the sleepiness in them and saw him beneath her.

"Oh," she said, confusion flashing across her otherwise intense expression.

"Off?" he choked, barely able to breathe.

"Sorry," she murmured, her voice still rough and drowsy as she shifted off him. "But you shouldn't grab me like that," she said sourly, as though her nearly breaking his neck had somehow been *his* fault.

"You shouldn't break into people's homes if you don't want to be grabbed." He lifted himself to his feet and went to turn on another light. "And I *didn't* grab you. I was trying to wake you. Your boots are ruining the furniture."

She blinked, her face wrinkling in confusion as she looked at her feet. "They're clean," she argued, but she reached down and began unbuttoning them anyway. When she'd pulled off both boots, she left them in a heap on the floor and didn't bother to cover her slender ankles.

"How did you even get in here?" he demanded, trying to gather his wits. There was something he was supposed to be telling her right now, something he was supposed to say. "I was expecting you at the theater yesterday not in my very locked, very secure apartment. Not in the middle of the night."

"No *so* very secure," she argued. "And it's barely past midnight. I didn't mean to fall asleep," she said, fighting off a soft yawn.

Her hair was a mess, half tumbled down from sleep, but Harte focused on what was important . . . if he could just remember what that was.

She gave in to the yawn. All the action did was call attention to her mouth, which made him remember other things that weren't exactly helpful at that moment.

He'd made a mistake. A tactical error. This was never going to work if he couldn't focus long enough to take control.

"So, am I going to be taking the couch, or are you going to be a gentleman and give me your bed?" she asked, batting her eyes innocently.

"The only way you're getting into my bed is if I'm in there with you," he told her.

"Not likely," she drawled.

"Then I guess you're taking the couch," he told her. "Best you learn now, I'm no gentleman."

"Figured as much," she said, pulling herself up and tossing him a pillow as she walked toward the back of the apartment.

"Where are you going?" he asked.

"I need to use the facilities," she told him. But she walked right past the open bathroom and into his bedroom, and before what she was doing completely registered, she'd shut his bedroom door and clicked the latch in place, leaving him holding the pillow.

It took a second for him to process what had just happened, but once he did, he stormed across the apartment and pounded on the door. "Open this door, Esta."

"No, thanks," she called from within. "I'm good here."

"I mean it. I'll bust it down if I have to."

There was a rustling sound from within that he refused to think about too closely. It couldn't be the sound of petticoats falling to the floor or her gown being unlaced. He would *not* allow himself to imagine her disrobing on the other side of the door. And even if she were, he would not let himself care.

"Feel free. It's your apartment," she said, and he could practically hear the shrug in her voice.

He ran his hands through his hair in exasperation. "What are you doing in there?"

"What do you think I'm doing?" she called.

He had a sudden vision of what she would look like in his bed, her dark hair spilled out across his pillow, but he locked that image down and threw away the key. "I think you're trying to take my bed," he said, inwardly groaning at his bad luck.

"I don't think I'm trying at this point." Her voice came from closer to the door now.

His bed was going to smell like her if she slept there, and then he'd never be able to sleep soundly again. He pounded again and then eyed the door. He could probably break it down. "I want my bed, Esta."

The door cracked open and her face appeared. Her shoulders were bare except for the lacy straps of her chemise, and she'd taken her hair down so it fell around her shoulders in loose waves. "Think of this as me helping you better yourself," she said, as she tossed a small object at him.

He grabbed for it out of instinct, giving her the time she needed to slam the door in his face and click the lock in place once more.

"Better myself?" He looked down at the object he was holding—the pocket watch he'd lost at the Metropolitan exhibition. "What's that supposed to mean?"

"Just what I said, Darrigan," she called through the closed door. "By the time I'm through with you, you'll be a real live gentleman."

The next morning when he woke, his neck was stiff from sleeping on the couch. He pulled himself up and ran a hand over his face, trying to rub away his grogginess and to will away the dreams of dark, silken hair and lacy chemises that left him feeling restless and unhinged. He was still in his clothes, since Esta had locked him out of his own room, but now, across the apartment, the door to his bedroom stood open.

Approaching the door warily, he saw that his bed was rumpled and unmade. The blankets were thrown back, and in the center of the bed, the mattress sagged where someone had slept, but the girl wasn't there. She wasn't in his tiny closet of a kitchen, either. As he pulled on a fresh shirt, he had the brief, impossible hope that maybe the night before had all been part of the same awful dream. Then he heard the off-key singing coming from his bathroom.

He knocked on the bathroom door. "Esta?"

The singing went suddenly silent. "You didn't tell me you had a bath-tub," she called.

"I didn't invite you to use it, either," he said, trying not to think of her soaking in the white porcelain tub. It didn't matter if it was his sanctuary—the mark of how different *this* life was from his old one. He didn't need the image of her tawny limbs, or any other part of her, naked in the warm water. In *his* warm water.

He heard the sounds of sloshing, and a moment later the door opened. Esta was standing with one of his large towels wrapped around her. Her shoulders were bare again, and wisps of her hair that had fallen from where she'd piled it on her head were stuck to her damp skin. Water was still dripping down her neck and her legs, leaving puddles on his tiled floor.

For a moment he couldn't think, much less speak.

"You have a *bathtub*," she said again, and she made the word sound like something miraculous. Her face was scrubbed clean, pink from the heat of the water, and she was smiling at him as though he'd just saved her life. "I'm never leaving."

Then she shut the door in his face. *Again*.

His hands clenched into fists at his sides, and for a minute he had to focus on breathing. He had to remind himself that this would be worth it in the end. It would all be worth it when he walked out of the city a free man and left all of this behind him.

He turned without a word, grabbed an orange from the bowl on his kitchen counter, threw on his hat and coat from the stand by the door, and left, slamming the door behind him. He'd go to the theater. People there might eat knives, dance with bears, and shimmy across the stage half-naked, but at least they didn't make him feel insane.

THE SCENT OF BETRAYAL

Paul Kelly's

There was something about the warming weather that drove the desperate a little wild. With spring came more boats, and with those boats, more immigrants hoping to carve out their own piece of the rotten fruit that was the city. And as spring teased the promise of summer, tempers began to flare. Always with something to prove, the new crop of boys would try their luck with knives or guns as they worked to claim meager pieces of territory. Street corners. Back alleys. Nothing worth dying over, but they did just the same.

With his cane and uneven gait, it was nearly impossible for Dolph to go unnoticed by those who might not know any better. It would have been easier to use the cover of night to do what needed to be done, but some business required the stark light of day—to send a message that he didn't fear anyone in the city. Not the Order of Ortus Aurea, whose constant presence kept his kind crawling in the gutters. Not the men at Tammany, who'd clawed themselves to the top of the city only to forget they'd been born in the slums. And not Paul Kelly, who seemed to be planning a move to establish himself as a true rival.

Kelly fashioned himself as a nob, and if it weren't for that crooked nose of his, evidence of his days as a boxer, he probably could have blended in at the Opera. He sure spent enough to dress the part. But at heart, Kelly—whatever his adopted moniker might suggest—was a paisan. The fancy clothes, the well-heeled style, it was all a cover so he could pretend he was different from every other dago fresh off the boat, crawling through the muck of the city to make something of themselves.

When Dolph entered, Kelly's men came to attention, their hands reaching for the guns they kept beneath their coats, but Kelly waved them off. "Dolph Saunders. Quel est votre plaisir?" he asked, slipping into perfect French.

So, he doesn't want his boys to hear us, Dolph understood. "Il est temps de rappeler vos hommes." *It's time to call off your men.*

Kelly's wide mouth turned down. "I'm not sure I can. My boys have been having a good time of it," he said, nodding to John Torrio, who sat at the table across the room.

"They went too far setting that fire," Dolph growled. "Six people died in those blazes, four of them children."

Kelly gave a careless shrug. "You said you wanted pressure on Darrigan."

"On Darrigan, yes," Dolph said. "But killing innocents wasn't the deal."

"There aren't any innocents in this town," Kelly told him. He pulled a silver case from his inside jacket pocket and took his time selecting one of the thin, perfectly rolled cigarettes inside.

He had style, Dolph admitted, feeling tired and older than his own twenty-six years. Kelly was only a couple years younger than Dolph, but he had something that felt new. Kelly had a different style, one that drew the boys who filled the barroom around them. One that could be dangerous if it ever found a wider audience.

Dolph took the seat across from Kelly without waiting for an invitation. "That may be, but I have Darrigan now. Our deal's done."

Kelly took two long drags on the cigarette and let the smoke curl out of his wide nostrils. "You know, I got to thinking. . . . Why would Dolph Saunders need Harte Darrigan? And why would Harte Darrigan be sniffing around with Jack Grew, especially when Jack's a member of the Order? I thought to myself, those two things can't be coincidences." He squinted a little as he took another drag. "So I asked myself, what do they know that I don't?"

"I don't know what you're talking about," Dolph said easily. "Harte was mine first, that's all. I wanted him back."

"That's a nice story." Kelly smiled around the cigarette. "But I don't buy it. You're no stranger to taking what isn't yours. Speaking of which, how is my dear sister these days?"

Dolph allowed himself a cold smile. "She sends her love. It comes with a blade and a handful of curses I couldn't repeat in mixed company. Might offend the delicate sensibilities of your boys there."

"Sounds like Viola." He gave Dolph a challenging look. "She'll betray you eventually, you know, and return to me. I'm family, and she knows the importance of family. Il sangue non é acqua."

"I'm not sure *she* knows the truth of that."

"She will," he said, and the threat was clear.

"She's under my protection."

"For now," Kelly said smoothly, and then shifted onto a new topic. "I've been hearing things around town about this big shindig the boys in the Order have planned—this Conclave at the end of the year. Word is, anyone who's anyone will be there."

"Only if you're a member of the Order," Dolph said.

Kelly's expression never changed. "So maybe I'll become a member."

Dolph let out a surprised laugh before he realized Kelly was serious.

Kelly leaned forward, his expression determined. "I'm not like you, Saunders. I aim to be someone someday."

"You're already someone," Dolph argued. "You control half the blocks south of Houston right now. You didn't need the Order for that."

"No, I didn't need them, but it wouldn't hurt to have that kind of power on my side, now, would it?" He smiled, a leering sort of grin that had all of Dolph's instincts on alert.

"It's a pipe dream, Kelly. The Order only takes their own kind. You might have power and you might even have enough money, but it will never be the *right* kind of money to get in with the blue bloods uptown."

Kelly took another long drag on the cigarette and eyed Dolph like he was weighing the pros and cons of giving anything away. Then he stubbed it out in the crystal bowl sitting on the table next to him, twisting the slender butt between his meaty fingers. "Maybe you're right. But like I said, I was curious, so I started asking around. And I started listening. And what I hear is that you're after some book the Order has."

Dolph felt suddenly paralyzed. *Someone had talked.* Someone he'd trusted had said too much, given too much away. There was a weak link in his organization, maybe even a rat.

"So I said to myself, Dolph Saunders and I, we are smart men, well read and erudite and all that. But there's no book worth risking the wrath of the mayor's precious little boys' club unless it's some powerful book."

"If those rumors were true, I'd deserve whatever I got for my stupidity," Dolph said, leaning back in his chair and making a show of his amusement.

Kelly smiled like he could see right through him. "Playing dumb doesn't suit you, Rudolpho."

Dolph remained silent. He didn't let his expression so much as flicker. "I don't know what you're talking about."

"So that's how it's to be?" Kelly shrugged as he lit another cigarette. "Fine. This isn't a tea party. You want me to call my boys off Darrigan, I'm going to need something more from you, something Darrigan can't give me. You and I both know he can do an awful lot. And this book . . . From the sound of things, *it* can do an awful lot too. Maybe more than even you can."

"A deal's a deal, Kelly." Dolph stood to take his leave. "I already gave you what you needed on the mayor, and Darrigan's playing nice now."

Paul Kelly laughed, the smoke from the cigarette spilling from his nose, like he was some sort of demonic beast. "I'm not your dog, Saunders. I won't be brought to heel. As far as I'm concerned, Darrigan's still mine. You want him outright, it's gonna cost you."

Even as Kelly spoke those words, Dolph was already planning how to deal with this new development. His grip tightened on his cane. "Name your price."

"I want the Strega."

Dolph laughed. "I'll see you in hell first."

"Your words, not mine," Kelly said easily.

"You're going to regret the day you crossed me," he said, standing.

Paul Kelly gave him a smile that was all teeth. "I doubt that, Saunders. I doubt that *very*, very much."

Dolph didn't say anything as he turned to go. If he were honest with himself, he would have admitted that he'd sensed betrayal growing thicker in the air for weeks now—the uneasy energy of a lie being told, the heady anticipation that marked the casting of rigged dice.

But Dolph hadn't been honest on the day he was born, and he certainly wasn't any better now. Not when he'd lost so much. And not when everything depended on keeping those losses a secret.

TEMPTATION COMES IN MANY FORMS

Wallack's Theatre

The bottle of Nitewein was still sitting on Harte's dressing room table. He swore he could hear it calling to him ever since the girl had taken up residence in his small apartment.

It was bad enough that she'd blown through his neat, orderly life with her very presence—the off-key singing that carried through the bathroom door as she soaked in his porcelain tub, the silk stockings draped over the parlor furniture. The smell of the floral soap she used that didn't seem to match the hard-nosed stance she took on absolutely everything, but suited her just the same. It had permeated the air in his apartment, and he had the feeling that the scent of it would remain even after she was gone.

And she *would* be gone. As soon as the job was over, she'd leave. Just like everyone left. Just like he would leave as soon as he could.

Well, good riddance, then.

He wanted her gone.

He wanted his life back.

He wanted a way out of this mess he'd found himself wrapped up in. He picked up the bottle of Nitewein and rolled the liquid around inside it.

Evelyn appeared in his open door. "You look horrible," she said.

"Thanks." She wasn't wrong. He had deep circles under his eyes from not sleeping. But how was he supposed to sleep on that lumpy couch that barely held him, especially when he knew *she* was less than ten feet away? Maybe it really had been too long since he'd been with a girl. That had to be all it was.

He eyed Evelyn.

She seemed to read his mind. "What?" she said with a sly smile.

"Nothing," he told her, dismissing the idea. It would be a mistake far worse than a glass of Nitewein.

But Evelyn seemed to have read his thoughts and was already sauntering across the room. He felt the caress of her magic. He should have stopped her—*really, he should*—but the warmth that rubbed against him soothed something inside him. That part of him that had started pacing and prowling the first day the girl opened his bathroom door dressed in nothing but a towel. *A towel, for god's sake.* Like any man in his right mind could have resisted that.

Harte *had* resisted, though. It had taken a good long walk and two stiff drinks before the show that day, but he hadn't gone back to his apartment, not until he knew Esta was asleep. And he'd resist Evelyn, too. Because nothing good could come from leading on a siren.

"Did you need something?" he asked, studying himself in the mirror. He took the pot of kohl and the small brush and started to dab it under his eyes, but his hands were shaking and he smudged it. Harte cursed under his breath.

"Let me," Evelyn said, taking the brush from his fingertips. She settled herself on his lap, and before he could stop her, she was brushing at the smudged kohl with her fingertip. At each gentle *tap, tap, tap,* tiny sparks of warmth began to relax him.

This close, he realized her eyes were the most amazing shade of blue. Like the open seas. Like freedom and possibility.

Her red mouth pulled up as she took the brush and gently applied the kohl to the edges of his eyes. As she worked, he felt more relaxed than he had in days. In *weeks.* The soft weight of her on his lap felt like an anchor in a stormy port.

When she was done, she gave his left eye one last smudge with the pad of her thumb, and he couldn't have stopped himself if he wanted to. A moment later, their mouths tangled. She tasted like wine, he thought vaguely as he pulled her closer, desperate for more of her. And more, as their mouths mashed in a fit of heat and impatient fury.

It was like he was drowning and she was air. And he couldn't get enough of it, of her. He barely heard the door open. He was only faintly conscious of someone entering the room.

"Well, this is a pretty picture," a voice said somewhere on the edges of his consciousness, but he ignored it and dived deeper into Evelyn's kiss.

It wasn't until Evelyn was ripped from his lap and he sat gasping for air that he comprehended it was Esta who'd come in. She had Evelyn by the hair and was dragging her out of the room, and all Harte could seem to do was sit and stare mutely.

"Bitch," she said, tossing Evelyn out of the room. "You come near him again, and it'll be your last time."

"You and what army is going to stop me?" Evelyn sneered.

"I'll leave that to Dolph Saunders."

"Dolph Saunders?" Evelyn looked suddenly uneasy.

"We understand each other, then," Esta said, laying on her false accent thick.

"I understand fine," Evelyn sneered. "You're going to regret this."

Esta didn't bother to respond, simply slammed the door in Evelyn's face. Then she turned to Harte, her golden eyes on fire. "You have something on your face," she said, taking the glass of water on his dressing table and, without any warning, tossing it directly in his face.

He sputtered in surprise. "What——?"

"Oh, save it. You're lucky I came when I did." She crossed her arms. "I can't believe you fell for her."

"I don't answer to you," he snapped, feeling more uneasy than angry. But inside, he was a ball of panic and fury. *What the hell just happened?*

"After that little display, maybe you should. Lord knows you can't take care of yourself." She shook her head. "There's enough magic in the air here to suffocate a person."

"Magic?" he asked, stunned. His mind still hadn't caught up to what was happening . . . what *had* happened.

Esta stared at him like she was waiting for him to put the pieces together.

Then he felt it—Evelyn's affinity was still snaking through the room like opium smoke, curling about him. Still calling to him. *Shit.* Right when he most needed to keep his wits about him, he was losing his damn mind instead.

Turning back to the mirror, he saw for the first time the mess he was—the dark streaks running beneath his eyes from the water, the red ringing his mouth like one of Barnum's clowns. No wonder Esta looked like she wanted to kill him. He wanted to kill himself when he thought about how stupid he'd been to let Evelyn touch him.

"You're welcome," she said.

"What are you doing here, anyway?" he asked, taking out his frustration on her.

"You've been avoiding me," she said, a furrow between her eyes. "You never came back to your apartment last night."

"You were already asleep." Harte tried wiping the red from his mouth.

"You weren't there this morning," she pressed.

"I left early."

"Like I said, you're avoiding me. You promised Dolph you'd help get Jack," she pressed. "You made a deal."

But he'd had enough of women for one day. "Dolph can go hang."

"You don't get it, do you?" she snapped. "People are disappearing. Tilly is *dead.*" Her voice broke at the admission.

"Dead?" He hadn't realized. "I knew she was hurt, but—"

"She's gone." Esta's shoulders sagged, and it seemed like all the fire in her had faded.

"When?"

"A couple of days ago—before Dolph sent me."

"I'm sorry," he said softly.

"Are you really?" she asked, her voice flat, cold. He didn't have an answer for that. "This thing we're doing? It's bigger than Dolph—bigger than either of us. I don't care what you think about me or how angry you are that you're stuck with me. This isn't exactly a picnic for me, either, you know. But you need to pull yourself together and get over it. We need to get to work before you lose Jack Grew completely." She softened her voice. "Or before anyone else has to die."

Her words hit him like a slap, but he shoved away the pang of guilt he felt when he saw the sadness in her eyes. She wasn't some innocent in this, whatever she might pretend. She was there because Dolph Saunders had penned him into a corner, but he knew that wasn't the only reason.

"That's a nice speech. But tell me something, Esta. Why are you really here?"

Her eyes went suddenly wary. "I don't know what you mean. Dolph sent me to watch you. Why else would I be here?"

"You tell me. Who's the old man?" he asked, taking a step toward her.

"What?" The color drained from her face. "I don't know what you're talking about." She turned to go, but he grabbed her wrist.

He remembered the images he'd seen when he kissed her the last time she was in his dressing room. "I know about the old man with the crutch, in the room lined with books."

"How could you possibly know that?" she whispered, not bothering to deny it. Her golden eyes were wide with disbelief.

"I know you're not *only* here because of Dolph," he pressed, ignoring her question. "You're here for yourself—because the old man told you to find the Magician."

"Please," she said, trying to get away from him. "You're hurting me."

He saw then how tightly he was grasping her wrist and released her immediately. "I'm sorry," he said, shaken by the sight of the red mark he'd left on her delicate skin. He took a step back from her as she rubbed her wrist, hating himself for how easily his temper had spiked. How easily he'd become his father's son.

When he turned back, her eyes were steady on him, calculating. "You were in my head." She took a step toward him, closing the distance he'd put between them. "Is that what you do? Climb into people's heads and violate their most private thoughts? Do you have any idea how *wrong* that is?"

He ignored the familiar wave of shame. "You cornered me in my dressing room and lied to Evelyn about who you were. So, yeah . . . I took a look. I needed to protect myself. I needed to see exactly what your game was."

"When you kissed me," she realized, raising her fingers to her lips. "Then you should have your answers already." She lifted her chin, her eyes filled with disgust. And if he wasn't mistaken, with fear.

"It doesn't work like that," he snapped, hating his own limitations. And hating that what he'd done—what he *was*—had made her afraid. . . . Just as it had his mother.

She huffed out a laugh. "You really expect me to believe that?" she asked, but her voice shook, at odds with her show of confidence.

"It's the truth. I only get impressions unless I focus pretty intently, and if you remember, I was a little too distracted to really focus." He tucked his hands into his pockets. "I saw the old man, the library, and I heard him say 'Find the Magician.' That's it. That's all I know." He didn't look away, wouldn't back down from this. "Who *is* he, Esta? I need to know why you came for me. I need to know why you're *really* here."

Her mouth went tight, and for a moment he thought she would continue to lie to him. Finally, she spoke. "He's my father." Her eyes were steady, even as her voice shook. "Or, rather, he's as close to a father as I ever had. He raised me. Trained me to pick locks and lift wallets. He made me who I am."

He studied her, searching for a sign of the lie, but all he found was a sharp pain in her expression that he recognized too well. "Where is he now?"

"He's dead," she told him, her voice hitching. "Gone."

Even through the haze Evelyn had left behind, he felt like a veritable ass. "I'm sorry. I didn't know."

"Yeah, well . . ." Her mouth went tight. "Some affinity you have, isn't it?"

Harte ignored the insult. "If he's dead, why did you still come to find the Magician?"

Esta licked her lips. "Because he told me to. He could see things. He had an affinity for knowing about things that would happen."

"And why did you need to find me?"

She took a breath, still wrestling with herself, but then she met his eyes. "He said that you were going to disappear with the Book that Dolph's after. And if you do that, the Book will never be recovered. You're going to destroy any chance we *ever* have of defeating the Order."

"And you believed him?" Harte said, suddenly cold.

"He'd never led me wrong before," she said. And that much, at least, sounded like the honest truth.

"For what it's worth, I don't have any plans to destroy the Book."

"For what it's worth, I wouldn't let you." She shook her head and let herself out.

The room felt strangely empty once Esta was gone, as though she'd taken something vital with her. He looked at his reflection again, the smudges under his eyes, the stain of red that left his lips looking bloodied.

Who knew how far Evelyn would have taken things if Esta hadn't interrupted? He owed her for that, even if she'd only done it because Dolph needed him. But he didn't know how he'd ever pay her back with anything but betrayal.

THE GLASS CASKET

Harte was still avoiding her. He always came back to the apartment late, long after she was asleep, and he would be gone before she awoke every morning. After she'd given everything away in his dressing room, maybe that was safer. She'd been cornered, and she'd acted on instinct. Too bad her instincts tended to get her in trouble. *Like what happened with Logan.*

But with every day that passed, the news clipping remained stubborn in its insistence that Dolph Saunders was going to die.

Enough was enough. She had a job to do—she needed that book and she needed Ishtar's Key. And Dolph was sure they couldn't do anything without Harte, which meant she needed him, too. He couldn't avoid her forever.

After breakfast, she set off for the theater to confront him, but it wasn't Harte she found when she arrived. The first person she ran into was the red-haired harpy.

"You're back," Evelyn said, sounding like she meant, *Go away.*

"Of course. I'll be around quite a lot from now on," Esta said in her falsely accented voice as she headed toward Harte's dressing room.

"He isn't there," the woman called, a mocking note in her voice. "He's down below."

Straightening her spine, Esta gave Evelyn a cold smile before she turned and made her way through the maze of the backstage hallways and then down a staircase to a damp-smelling room beneath the theater. She thought she heard water and wondered if the theater wasn't built over one of the hidden rivers in the city. Just ahead, there was a light, and as she moved toward it, she heard a familiar voice letting out a string of curses.

"Harte?" she called, navigating through the cluttered storage area until she came to where he was working.

The Magician had pulled a vanishing act, because the boy before her could have been any factory worker, any laborer in the city. He was dressed in worn brown pants held up only by a pair of suspenders. They sagged low on his narrow hips, and his shoulders and arms were bare beneath his sleeveless shirt, which was damp with sweat. He looked more unbuttoned and human than she'd ever seen him.

Then he flipped the visor up on the welding mask and ruined the effect.

"Get in," he said, pointing to the table where the strange, coffinlike tank he'd been working on was sitting. His eyes were a little wild.

She took a step back.

"I mean it. Get in. I need to see if this will fit you."

"Why?" she asked suspiciously. "Looking for new and inventive ways to dispose of my body?"

"The thought did cross my mind once or twice," he said dryly.

She bit back a laugh. "Nice of you to spring for a glass coffin. Wood is so 1899."

He glared at her, scratching his chin. "It's not a coffin. It's a—wait. Maybe you're right."

"I usually am."

However hard his eyes were, Esta sensed that he was too excited to really be mad. "We *could* go with the defying-death angle. The Glass Casket has a nice ring to it, don't you think?"

Esta eyed him. "What do you mean, *we*?"

"You and me. If I'm stuck with you, I'm going to make use of the situation."

"I thought you'd decided on avoiding me," she said, crossing her arms.

"Didn't you say we had to get to work?" he said, frowning at her. "I've been getting things ready."

She narrowed her eyes at him, not trusting the excitement in his expression. "Ready for what?"

"We're going to run the lost heir on Jack."

"Am I supposed to know what that means?"

He frowned. "It's a con game. If it works, Jack's going to believe that we have something he'd do anything to get. *You're* going to be the lost heir."

"What, exactly, am I the heir *of*?" she asked, walking over to run the tips of her gloved fingers against the smooth glass.

"You, sweetheart, just happen to be the long-lost illegitimate daughter of Baron Franz von Filosik, who was rumored to have found the secret to the transmutation of basic elements before his untimely death."

"Is that an actual person?"

"Of course it is." He paused. "Wasn't that all part of Dolph's plan? I figured that's why you introduced yourself to Evelyn with that name."

She glanced up from the glass box, trying to hide her surprise. After all, she'd been improvising about who she was that day in the dressing room. She'd given her own name, not one Dolph had invented. Not that Harte needed to know that.

"Of course it was the plan," she said, trying to stay in control of the situation. "Who was he, this Baron von Filosik? What did he do?"

"Dolph didn't explain it?"

"He just gave me the name," she lied.

Harte gave her a knowing look. "Yeah, that sounds exactly like something he'd do."

Esta relaxed a little with his acceptance of her story, but she couldn't help but wonder if the Professor had known somehow that the name he'd picked after he found her in the park would come in handy one day.

"Well?" she pressed. "If this con is going to work, I should know my own fictional father."

"You will, but for now all you need to know is that the transmutation of the elements is basically the Holy Grail for most alchemists. The good baron died in a fire some years back, along with all his secrets. Or so people thought." He waggled his eyebrows at her. "But now his secret daughter has returned to continue her father's work. And she's lonely and afraid and could use a protector."

She rolled her eyes at him. "And *that's* supposed to be me?" she asked, doubtful.

"If you can pull it off? Yes," he told her. "As far as Jack Grew's concerned, you've recently shown up in town in need of help from an old friend—that would be me. We just have to make him believe that it would be better if *he* were the one you relied on. After all, you'd be very grateful to such a person, wouldn't you? You might even be willing to share your father's secrets with that person."

"So we make Jack believe that I have my fake father's secret files?"

"And we make him think you're vulnerable enough to give them up with the right *encouragement*. In this case, an introduction at Khafre Hall."

"You really think that will work?"

"It's what we have."

"Which is *such* a ringing endorsement."

"Look, Jack's been interested in my act for months now, but he's like the rest of them—he believes that his family's money and status makes us fundamentally different. That's what will catch him—he won't be able to accept that you would choose me over him if you had the option."

"He's going to rescue me from you," she realized, appreciating the simplicity of trapping Jack with his own greed and narrow-mindedness.

"That's the basic idea. He'll have to prove himself to you somehow, and that's what will trap him."

"But what does this death trap have to do with me being the daughter of some dead baron?"

"You have to earn your keep somehow," he told her, the corner of his mouth kicking up wryly. "So you're helping me with my demonstrations."

"I don't know," she hedged, eyeing the box. "That doesn't really seem necessary."

"It's all part of the con." He ran a hand over the glass case. "That disappearing thing you did was a great effect. We're going to build on it to hook Jack into believing that you have secrets that could help him with some experiments he's been doing."

"What kind of experiments?"

"No idea," Harte admitted. "I haven't been able to get him to tell me yet. Like I said, he still doesn't completely trust me. He's been using me for information, but he's still keeping me at arm's length." He glanced back in the direction of the stairwell, as though checking to make sure no one else could hear. "So how did you do it?" he whispered. "The disappearing thing. I'm going to need to know what I'm working with."

"I'd be happy to." She leaned in. "Right after you tell me what you're really planning to do with the Book. Because I don't believe for a second you really plan to hand it over to Dolph."

He pulled back, his eyes wary. "Or we can work around it."

She gave him a shrug. "If you insist."

They stared at each other for a moment, neither wanting to be the first to flinch. Neither wanting to be the one who gave up any ground. To Esta's relief, his excitement to show her the glass casket won out.

"Okay, then . . . Come take a look at what I've done here. I want you to see how it works." He closed the hinged lid and then opened it, to show her how smoothly it moved. When he depressed a hidden lever at the end of the case, the glass lid slid silently free of the frame, like a car window rolling down. "I've been working on this for a while, but I finally figured it out." Then he grinned.

Esta's stomach did an unexpected—and definitely unwanted—flip. When his mouth turned up like that, into a real smile instead of the one he pasted onto that smug face of his onstage, he looked almost boyish. Almost like someone she'd like to know . . . if she wasn't who she was and he wasn't who he was. If he hadn't just all but admitted he was making his own plans.

But they *were* who they were, and she couldn't let herself forget that *he* was the one she was supposed to stop. If he betrayed the team, it would mean more than the loss of the Book. But now, it might also mean the death of Dolph Saunders. What would happen to his crew—to all the people who depended on him—if he were gone? What chance would any of them have against the viciousness of the city and the Order that controlled it without Dolph to lead them and to protect them?

"You made this?" she asked, stepping around so that the glass box was between them.

"Yeah. I've been working on the idea for a while. I was going to do it myself, but with your . . . whatever it is you do, I think it'll be better." He slid the glass back into place and closed the lid. "Most people do this effect behind a screen or with a box, where no one can see what the girl is doing. But with you, we can do something new." He ran his hand over the glass coffin. "The girl—that'll be you—will disappear right before the audience's eyes. No mirrors or screens, no capes or hiding. *Poof.* You'll be gone." He eyed her. "Assuming, of course, you can manage it."

"I can manage it," she said, "but don't you think it's a little risky to have me disappear like that? It'll raise suspicions about how I did it. Maybe about what I am."

"No, it won't," he said, his gray eyes dancing. "That's the beautiful thing about it. No one will believe you *actually* disappeared, because no one will expect you to have real magic. They expect that everything I do onstage is a trick, an illusion. Half the audience will be telling the other half that they knew how it was done."

Even though she knew he was still up to something, *this* version of Harte Darrigan was disarming. His face was smudged and his hair was standing up in a riot of loose waves. His clothes were rumpled, and although he was attempting to play things cool, he was practically vibrating with anticipation. It was all a hundred times more compelling than anything she'd seen him do onstage. It seemed so authentic. This Harte Darrigan seemed so *real.*

All part of his game, she reminded herself. For all she knew, it was just another con.

"Are you going to get in, or what?"

Esta hesitated. "You aren't going to trap me in there?"

"I'm not promising anything," he joked, but when she gave him a doubtful look, he let out an impatient huff. "You saw how the mechanism works, didn't you?" Then he held out his hand, a challenge in his eyes.

Frowning, Esta took his hand and allowed him to help her step up onto the table and into the glass box. It was a tight fit with the bulk of her skirts.

"Good," he said, looking her over. "Now lie down, would you? I need to make sure it's not too long or too short."

She barely had enough room for her hands to be at her sides.

"There's a small lever by your right toe. It'll take some practice to find—"

She hit the lever, and he had to jump to catch the glass top from sliding too quickly. "You were saying?"

He scowled at her. "And *now* we close it."

"But—"

Before she could protest, he was already pulling the top down and locking it with a bronze padlock. Fog from her breath started to build on the glass, inches from her nose. Suddenly, the air felt too warm, too close.

"There aren't any air holes," he shouted, his voice muffled by the glass. "You'll have to work fast."

No air holes? She was going to kill him.

Her foot fumbled for the latch but missed the first time.

If he doesn't finish me off first, that is.

"We'll have a cue or something," he was shouting, motioning to the lever near her foot. "Some sort of hand motion or signal to . . ."

She pulled time around her, slowed the seconds, and depressed the latch. The glass released, and she slid it away from her face, taking a moment to breathe in the cool, musty air of the basement and allowing the prickle of panic to recede from her skin before she climbed out. Composing herself, she wiped her sweaty palms on her skirts and then slid the glass back into place before examining Harte. Nearly frozen mid-word, his eyes gleamed.

He loves this.

Whatever else he pretended, whatever he'd done or was going to do, she could see that he wasn't pretending his excitement for this new trick—effect. *Whatever.* The point was that he loved it as much as she loved the rush from lifting a fat wallet or hearing the tumblers of a lock click into place.

She felt that strange lurch in her stomach, one that she didn't like at all, so she released time and watched Harte sputter midsentence.

"... let you know—*oh.*" His face split into a surprised smile. His stormy eyes lit, unguarded and unaware that he was showing her some-thing new about himself. "Yes! That's it exactly." Then he seemed to realize he'd revealed too much. "You'll have to wait for my cue, of course," he said, back to his usual arrogance. "You don't want to come out too soon and ruin everything. We'll have to—"

"You locked me in an airtight box," she said flatly, interrupting him.

His brow furrowed. "That's kind of the point. If there's no sense of danger, the audience won't care."

"You. Locked. Me. In. An. *Airtight.* Box," she said again, enunciating each word through her clenched teeth.

"Maybe we should add something more," he said, not paying any attention to her outrage.

"You could have warned me before you locked me in. You *should* have warned me."

He ran a hand through his already mussed hair. "You got out," he said, looking at her as though he didn't understand her point.

"You could have killed me!"

"I didn't—" he started to say, but when she stepped toward him, he put his hands up defensively. "Okay, you're right. I'm sorry. I should have warned you."

"Dolph isn't going like it if I end up dead."

"You're probably right about that, too." He ducked his head and unlatched the bronze padlock. "But other than the almost dying, what do you think?"

She shrugged, reluctant to give him any credit at all. "It'll be okay."

"Okay?" He laughed. "No. This will be like nothing anyone has *ever* seen. If this doesn't convince Jack that you have something he wants, nothing will. This has to work."

"It will," she said, looking over the glass coffin again. "We'll make it work. Together."

"We just might," he said, his expression changing. "Here's to bringing down the Order." He held out his hand, his eyes serious. Esta considered all the reasons she shouldn't let him touch her, but in the end she placed her gloved hand in his. He squeezed gently, but the warmth she felt thrum through her had nothing to do with the peculiar energy left behind by magic.

The atmosphere between them grew thick, charged. She pulled her hand away.

"Esta . . . ," he started, but hesitated as though he didn't quite know what he wanted to say.

Before he could figure it out, a voice called from close by. "Harte?" Evelyn said, stepping into the light thrown by his work lamp.

The moment broken, he took a step back from Esta, looking suddenly embarrassed. Or guilty. "Yeah?" He wiped the hand that had just shaken hers on his pants.

"Shorty wanted me to let you know you're on in twenty."

"He sent you down here?" he asked, a frown tugging at his mouth.

Evelyn put her hands on her hips. "Is that a problem?"

"No. Sorry. Thanks for letting me know. I'll be up in a minute."

"I'll see you upstairs," she said sweetly, before giving Esta a pointed glance and then slinking back from wherever she'd come.

Esta watched her go, wondering how long Evelyn had been standing in the shadows. And how much she'd heard. But if Harte was concerned, he didn't show it.

"Look, I've got to get ready for the show, but stick around, would you?"

She glanced up at him, surprised. He'd never invited her to stay and watch his show, or to wait for him after.

"So we can practice again," he finished, tugging at one of his suspenders. "I'm thinking once we work on the timing, I can get ahold of Jack. It shouldn't take us that long to get it right."

"Oh, right," she said, feeling suddenly stupid. *Of course.* "Dolph would want us to get this going. We've taken long enough."

"So you'll wait?"

"Yeah," she said, pasting on an encouraging smile. "Absolutely."

After he'd disappeared up the steps, she let the smile fall from her face and ran her hands along the smooth glass of the box. It was a good idea, a good effect, she had to admit. It *might* even be enough to convince Jack Grew that she had something he wanted, but they couldn't take any chances. The trick needed to be better than good—it needed to be spectacular.

IMPROVISING

Harte had never seen Esta so on edge. After he'd explained how they would run the lost heir on Jack, they'd settled into a steady—if not quite comfortable—rhythm as they prepared for the Friday-night performance. Everything he'd thrown at her—and it had been plenty—she'd given back to him in turn, and with a smirk on her face that told him she was enjoying herself. But standing in the wings, her apple-green silk gown glinting in the lights from the stage, she was going to chew a hole in her lip while she watched the act before him.

"You'll be fine," he said, resting his hands on her bare shoulders. He felt her stiffen, but she didn't pull away, even when he rubbed his thumb gently over the pink scar on her arm. She wouldn't tell him what it was from, but the angry pucker of skin had drawn his attention and his concern.

"Don't," she whispered, turning her head back to look at him with a frown. Her honey-colored eyes were serious, and if he wasn't mistaken, scared.

"I wasn't," he told her. "I wouldn't."

She snorted her disbelief at his words, but she didn't pull away, and he realized that he liked the way her skin felt under his fingertips. Soft, when there had been so little softness in his life for so long. He knew enough not to depend on it, though, because it couldn't last. Not with so much standing between them. He had to get out of the city, and for that he had to remember that she was just another thing standing in his way.

He dropped his hands from her shoulders.

"Do you think he's out there?" she asked, peering past the stage into the theater.

"Second box to the right," he told her. "There's no need to be nervous. This is going to work."

"I'm not nervous," she said, tilting her head to the side. "Just ready."

"You'll come on when I give the cue, just as we rehearsed."

"I know. I know," she said. "You've gone over this a hundred times. *Two* hundred times." But her voice didn't have the usual bite.

"Don't forget to—" The organ trilled his introduction, and it was too late for any more instructions. "*Just* like we practiced. You'll be fine."

She nodded, but there was something in her eyes that worried him. "Esta—"

"What are you waiting for?" Shorty hissed. "That was your cue!"

Unable to wait any longer, he gave her what he hoped was a stern but encouraging look, and took the stage.

Word that he was debuting a new effect had gotten out, and the seats were nearly full. The audience went gratifyingly silent when he stepped into the spotlight, and when he lifted his arms to salute the crowd, a rumble of applause rolled over him, settling his nerves and steeling his resolve. He worked through his usual bits, and the audience seemed willing enough to watch, because they knew something bigger, better was coming.

"Ladies and gentlemen." The words came as easily as the prayers his mother had taught him when he was a boy, but this time, much more was riding on his performance than a good night onstage. "I have a special treat for you this evening. A new demonstration and a new beauty for you to feast your eyes upon." He held out his hand, as they'd practiced, and Esta glided onto the stage.

If she'd been nervous before, there was no sign of it now. She walked like a debutante, like she'd been born to tread the boards. But then maybe she had. After watching Esta the past few days, he'd come to understand that she was one of the best grifters he'd ever seen. Maybe even better than him.

"May I present to you Miss Esta von Filosik of Rastenburg. I studied under her father, the foremost expert on the transmutation of the elements. He made great breakthroughs in the hermetic sciences before his untimely death, and now Miss Filosik has come to these shores to share her father's secrets with all of you. Tonight she will demonstrate her mastery over the powers of the Otherworld by cheating death"—he paused dramatically, letting the crowd's anticipation grow—"in the Glass Casket."

Excited murmurs rustled through the crowd. As the assistant rolled the box onto the stage, he chanced a glance in the direction of Jack's box and was relieved to see him leaning forward against the railing of the balcony, watching with clear interest.

"If you would?" he said, offering Esta his hand, as they'd practiced.

She hesitated, though, and didn't take it as she was supposed to.

"My dear," he said, offering his hand again.

"Oh, I don't know." She shook her head and took a step back.

He offered his hand again and forced the smile to stay put on his face. *This can't be happening. Not again. Not now.* "Come, my dear. It's perfectly safe."

A slow smile curved her lips, and he had the sudden feeling that he wasn't going to like what happened next.

"Oh, I bet you say that to all the girls," Esta told the audience in her throaty accented voice as she crossed the stage, ignoring his outstretched hand and turning all his careful planning on its head.

He could practically feel the audience's confusion and their amusement. Hushed whispers rustled through the room as they waited to see what the girl would do next, and whether he would be able to regain control.

Harte Darrigan had survived his mother leaving him, a childhood in the streets he'd rather forget, and working for a boss who thought it was easier to kill people than to talk things over. He'd made a life from keeping his cool in sticky situations, but none of that had managed to prepare him for being in the spotlight—*his* spotlight—with Jack Grew in the audience and himself completely at her mercy.

He was afraid to look in Jack's direction, afraid to see what his reaction would be. This whole con depended on Jack feeling like Harte was real competition, feeling like he had something to prove and someone to beat.

She could ruin everything.

He'd let himself believe that he'd taken control of the situation, but he'd been as easily conned as any mark, taken in by a pair of honeyed eyes and pink lips and the soft, clean scent of flowers. He had known she was up to something. Worse, he'd let himself forget that anyone working for Dolph Saunders had to be a snake. And he had the sinking feeling he'd just been bitten.

Then something shifted in the audience. The murmuring died a bit, as though they wanted to see what would happen next.

He hadn't lost them yet. He could still save this.

"Please, if you would simply step into the casket, we can continue our demonstration." He held out his hand. *"As we planned,"* he said through clenched teeth.

She let out a dramatic sigh, raising her hand to the curve of her chest—a move he had no doubt was intentional. "Oh, all right, *darling*," she said with a wink to the audience. "But there *are* easier ways to get rid of me."

Someone in the audience chuckled.

"My father always said a handsome face would be the death of me," Esta said dramatically. Then she shrugged. "I hate when he's right." Finally, she took his hand and climbed the steps to sit in the glass box.

"What are you doing?" he whispered, as he made a show of helping her arrange her skirts.

"I'm improvising," she told him through her smile.

Improvising? He'd show her improvising.

Her eyes went wide when she understood what he was about to do, but she didn't have time to stop him before he closed the lid.

It was wrong of him, maybe even a little cruel. He knew she hated to be in there. Through all their practicing, he'd gathered that there was something about being in that small, confined, airless space that made her jittery like nothing else could. They'd worked it out so he closed the lid at the last possible second.

That was before she went off script. He couldn't afford any more of her *improvising*, so he shut the lid tight, latched on the padlock, and tossed the key into the audience with a flourish. Esta made a good show of it, frantically pounding at the glass to get out. At least, he thought with a twinge of guilt, he hoped it was only a show.

He gave the signal for the stagehands to bring out the second part of the trick—a contraption that suspended an iron weight over the glass box by a piece of rope.

"Fire. The most volatile of all the elements," he told the audience as he set off a flare in his hand and used it to light a candle beneath the rope. "If I am not able to call upon my mastery of the Otherworld's powers, the flame will burn through this rope and the weight will fall, crushing the casket . . . and Miss Filosik with it."

The theater was on the edge of their seats, watching the girl struggle against the glass box, watching the candle eat away at the fragile rope. Waiting with violent glee to see whether she'd live or die.

He picked up his scarlet cape and twirled it over his head. *One . . .*

Over the casket where the girl writhed and slapped at the glass. *Two . . .*

He closed his eyes and sent up a quick prayer to the god he'd long given up on that he hadn't overplayed his hand. Then he twirled the cape in front of him, obscuring the audience's view for less than a second, as the candle ate through the final bit of rope.

Just as the weight fell, shattering the glass.

Three.

A MISSTEP

She took a moment to enjoy Harte's dazed look of relief before she gave the shocked audience her most dazzling smile.

"I guess Papa was wrong," she said, and the audience went wild.

She took her time raising one arm, like he'd taught her, to take her bow. The thrill of the crowd's rolling applause sank into her, warming something deep within her.

In that moment, she understood Harte a little better.

He was staring at her, and for once, he was speechless. Not that she blamed him. She hadn't exactly warned him about the costume change she'd orchestrated. She'd paid the theater's seamstress, Cela, to create the scrap of a costume she was now wearing, because she'd been watching in the wings for days now, and all that watching had taught her something—it wasn't only wonder and awe that sold an act. A little skin didn't hurt either.

Evelyn and her sisters, if that was what they really were, had about as much talent as a trio of alley cats in heat, but they knew when to show a little leg and to give a little tease. And they got the audience's attention every single night.

Harte's face was turning an alarming shade of red as she made one last curtsy and took herself off, stage left. She was barely out of the footlights when he came charging behind her. He ripped the robe from the stage-hand's grasp and wrapped it around her.

"What the hell was that?" he asked. "And what are you wearing?"

"Do you like it?" She opened the robe to give him a better look.

In her own time, the outfit—a corseted top with off-the-shoulder sleeves and a pair of bloomers that came to midthigh—would have been laughably modest. The entire thing was made from a gorgeous midnight-blue silk and was studded with crystals that glittered in the dim light of the wings like a field of stars. Old-fashioned as it might be, she loved it. Not only was it beautifully made, but after the long skirts and layers of fabric she'd been wearing for weeks now, she felt lighter. More like herself.

Harte opened his mouth, but all that came out was a choked sound. He tied the robe back around her again.

She decided to take it as a compliment.

He was still sputtering in anger when Evelyn came up to them and wiped at Harte's cheek with her fingertip. "You got something on your face, there." Then she laughed at him and walked off.

He reached up, still wordless, and rubbed where she'd touched. His brows furrowed as he saw the red stain on his fingertips, and when he looked in the small mirror on the wall, he turned an even deeper shade of red.

"You kissed me?"

Esta shrugged. "I thought it would be a nice touch."

She hadn't planned it, but when she had pulled the seconds around her and made time go slow, it seemed too easy to simply get herself out of the box and slip the green gown off. He'd been so bossy all afternoon, she couldn't resist playing with him a little—giving him back some of what he'd given her—so she'd left the bright red imprint of her lips on his cheek before she let go of her hold on time.

To the audience, it all happened at once—the amazing escape, her metamorphosis into the new outfit, and the mark on his cheek. For them, she'd gone from seconds-away-from-death to victory in a blink.

"You should have cleared it with me," he said, rubbing at the red spot and making it worse as he smeared it.

"Funny. I've thought that every time you've kissed *me*. Besides, it worked, didn't it?"

"It doesn't matter if it worked," he told her, turning to her with an expression so angry, she took a step back.

Esta pulled the robe tighter around herself and headed toward Harte's dressing room. She didn't bother to check if he was following her. She didn't need to—she could practically feel him breathing down her neck.

She tossed off the robe as she walked into the room. Before she had time to turn around, he'd slammed the door, closing them into the small space alone and away from the prying eyes of the other performers. She turned, her arms crossed, and propped herself against his dressing table, refusing to be intimidated. "What is your problem? Tonight went well. Better than well. They loved it."

"This is *my* act," he said, stalking toward her. "It's *my* call what happens out there. You don't get to change it without my say-so."

She'd known he'd be a little annoyed, maybe even upset by her not telling him, but she truly hadn't predicted that her little addition to the act would make him so *furious*. Their almost-easy partnership for the last few days had made her forget her position, and she'd miscalculated, forgotten how different things were between men and women in this time. Harte might have acted more enlightened than most, but he was still a product of his time. Of course he'd take any adjustment to his act personally. She should have realized.

Not that she was going to apologize. The risk had worked, and he was going to have to deal with it. She turned her back to him so that she could use the mirror to take off her stage makeup.

His face appeared in the mirror behind her, looming over her shoulder. "I thought after this week—"

"Darrigan!" Shorty poked his head through the door before she could finish. "Good job, kid. That was a helluva trick you two did out there," he said as he came into the room, a cigar clamped between his teeth. He gave Harte a rough thump on the back that seemed to shut him up and then handed him a slip of paper. "Message for you," he said with another thump on the shoulder before backing out and closing the door behind him.

"What is it?" Esta tried to peer at the message while Harte used his shoulder and his height to keep its contents away from her.

"It's from Jack," Harte said. "He wants to have dinner with us tomorrow night."

She tried not to gloat—*really* she did—but she couldn't help smiling. "You're welcome."

"Don't," he growled, his expression hard. "This didn't happen because of what you did out there. It happened *in spite* of it." He waved the paper at her. "You could have ruined everything."

"But . . ." Her smile faltered.

"Did you even consider that your little improvisation might not have worked? We hadn't rehearsed it. I've been working for months to get Jack to believe that I am what I say I am. We had *one* chance for Jack to see you for the first time. *One.* Any misstep could have ruined all of that."

"I'm sorry," she said, suddenly struck by how impulsive she'd been. How thoughtless.

"You're lucky I don't call this whole thing off," he told her. "I could tell Jack everything I know about you and the Met. I could wash my hands of Dolph Saunders and this whole mess of his."

"No!" She stepped toward him and grabbed his arm. "Please, don't."

"Why shouldn't I?" he said. "Why shouldn't I wash my hands of the lot of you?"

Shame burned her cheeks, and she might as well have been standing in Professor Lachlan's office, listening to him tell her the exact same thing. "Because it's not their fault," she said softly. "Don't punish them for what I did."

He studied her, and she could barely breathe while she waited for his answer. "This is the Order we're talking about, Esta. If they find out what we are—if *Jack* finds out what I am—it's not going to end well. I won't let your carelessness take me down with you. If we're going to do this, I have to be able to trust you to do what you say you're going to do. Otherwise, I'm done. I'm out for good. Damn Dolph and the lot of you."

"You don't have to worry," she promised. "It won't happen again." She forced herself to meet his eyes, hoping that he didn't see the lie there.

"You're sure?"

"Yes," she insisted, praying he would believe her. "You can trust me." *At least until the very end.*

A NEW PARTNERSHIP

The Haymarket

Ever since he'd confronted her after their performance, Harte had noticed that Esta was more subdued. Not cowed, by any means, but watchful, like she was waiting for something. But as the hack pulled up to their destination, she looked downright nervous.

"I'm not going in there," Esta said, when she realized where the carriage had stopped. "You should have warned me. I never would have come."

"I thought you'd appreciate the surprise," he said, confused by her reaction. "After all, this *is* where we first met."

"You don't understand," she said, trying again to tug away from him. "People in there . . ." She hesitated as though searching for the right word. "They might recognize me. It could ruin everything."

Ignoring the stiffness in her posture, he held her out at arm's length and took a moment to look her over. She was wearing the dress he'd picked from the ones she'd bought—or taken. He never knew for sure with her. It was a golden color with beads that caught the light no matter how she moved. Strings of more beads were all that covered her shoulders, and the neckline dipped dramatically to showcase the gentle slope of her chest and the garnet collar that sat around her throat. She looked like a living flame.

She'd argued that something more inconspicuous would be better. In the end, though, she'd agreed with him that Jack needed to be impressed by her and had worn the dress. But seeing it in his apartment was different from seeing the gown in the moonlight. And knowing that he'd picked it for her, that she'd willingly worn it for him, was another thing altogether.

And he didn't want to think too much about how that made him feel.

"They won't recognize you," he said, giving her a smoldering look meant to tease as much as to assure her. "No one would—not looking like that."

The compliment had the effect he'd intended, and she snorted, crossing her arms over her chest. "I know a line when I hear one, Darrigan."

He met her gaze before he spoke. "Then you should know that wasn't a line."

She gave him her usual scowl, but her shoulders relaxed a little and she looked more like herself.

He took her hand and tucked it through his arm. "Are you ready?"

"I don't think—"

"This will work. Just stay close, and you'll be fine." He started to lead her toward the Haymarket, but when they were almost to the door, he stopped, remembering something. "If anything should happen tonight—"

"You just told me everything would be fine."

"It will be," he assured her. "Whatever you do, though, no magic once we're inside. Corey's security is trained to detect it, and they won't hesitate to act if they sense you using it. You're lucky you got out without them catching you last time."

Esta stopped in her tracks and looked up at him. Her mouth was slightly open, and she was looking at him as though she'd never seen him before.

"You were trying to help me," she said. "That night when we first met. You had a reason for manhandling me, didn't you?"

"I have no idea what you're talking about," he told her, and before she could press him about it any more, he led them toward the dance hall's entrance.

Inside, the band was playing a ballad—Harte recognized the melody as one of the songs Evelyn belted out onstage each night. He led Esta through the crush of people and around the main floor of the ballroom. "I want a table upstairs, where we can see the whole floor. I don't want to miss Jack when he comes in."

Fastening an aura of ease and charm around him like armor, Harte made his way through the room slowly, knowing exactly how uncomfortable she was with being paraded around and introduced to various people they encountered. She smiled and said all the right things, but every time he stopped to chat with someone, her posture grew more rigid and her smile more strained. He'd been around her long enough now that he was starting to learn the subtle shifts in her mood. Esta might always act as though nothing touched her, but tonight her eyes were giving her away. She was still on edge.

Eventually he found them an empty table at the balcony railing with a clear view of the first floor. Below, the Haymarket was alive with color. Women in brightly colored gowns swirled around the dance floor, while pink-faced men leaned against the central bar, laughing too loud as they held their tumblers of whiskey. Across the table from him, Esta was quiet, watching the room with guarded eyes.

After a few minutes of silence, she spoke, startling him from his thoughts. "You love all of this, don't you?"

"What?" He took his eyes from the door to look at her.

She was sitting with her elbows propped on the table, her chin against her folded hands, a question in her eyes. "The attention. The way so many people know who you are and want to talk with you. You pretend to be indifferent, but underneath you're like a cat with cream."

He shrugged off his discomfort at how clearly she'd seen through him. "I'm not going to complain," he said. "There are a lot worse ways to spend an evening." *Like starving in a gutter. Or trying to stay clean when the whole world is determined to make you filthy.*

"What were you thinking about just now?" she asked, sitting up a little straighter, her eyes focused completely on him now. "Your whole expression just . . . closed up."

She was too perceptive by half. "Nothing," he told her, feigning ignorance about her concern.

It was clear she didn't believe him. She was still staring at him as though he'd give up all his secrets if she were patient enough. But that couldn't happen. He called over a server and ordered a bottle of champagne, avoiding her eyes and her expectations as the waiter poured two glasses.

"To our new partnership," he said with his practiced, pleasant smile as he raised a glass to toast her.

She only watched him with those serious eyes of hers, and didn't bother to lift her glass or take a drink. "It's an impressive mask you wear," she said. "Even knowing it's there, I can barely see a crack."

He placed his glass on the table, untouched as well. "I'm not sure what you mean," he said stiffly. "I am exactly what I appear to be."

"That's probably more true than you know." Still not taking the champagne, she turned to watch the room below.

After a few minutes, he missed her attention and wanted her to turn back, if only to spark at him again. That, at least, was more amusing than this sullen silence. But Esta's attention was on the floor below. She drummed her fingertips softly against the base of her champagne flute as if waiting for something to happen.

Or maybe she was waiting for *someone*, he thought with a sudden unsettling jolt of unwelcome jealousy.

It all served to remind him that they weren't *really* there together by choice. She wasn't really his or even on his side. They were sitting on opposite sides of the board, playing each other in hopes of gaining the same prize. But he had so much more at stake, and if push came to shove, he wouldn't let her be the victor.

He stood and held his hand out to her. "Dance with me," he said, not allowing himself to think about the motivation behind his impulse.

She looked up at him, her eyes betraying her surprise. But she didn't make any move to accept his invitation.

Now that he was standing, he felt like an idiot. "I think our mark arrived," he lied, when he started to fear that she would refuse him and he'd be forced to sit down, humiliated.

"Oh?" Still, she didn't reach for his hand.

His neck felt hot. The people at the table next to them laughed at something—probably him—and he had to fight the urge to tug at his collar and adjust the cuff links at his wrists. "We should make sure Jack sees us," he pressed.

"Of course," she murmured, but there was no pleasure or anticipation in her eyes as she *finally* took his hand and allowed him to lead her down to the dance floor.

Harte recognized his mistake almost immediately. He'd never been one for waltzing, usually preferring instead to work the edges of the room or the men near the bar. So he'd forgotten how it felt to take a girl by the waist, to hold her smaller hand in his and pull her close as he spun her around the room. He'd forgotten the way his head could spin as the music wrapped the couples in its hypnotizing rhythm, the way the entire world could narrow to one pair of golden eyes.

He felt drunk, suddenly, even though he hadn't touched the champagne either. Off-balance. Inexplicably swept away by the song, by the moment, and against all his better judgment, by *her*.

One glance at her face showed that she didn't feel the same. She moved gracefully, allowing him to lead her across the floor, but she wasn't really *with* him. Her concentration was on the room around them, not on the small, private world they were creating within the span of their arms and the rhythm of their steps. The realization was like water on a fire, and by the time the song wound down to its close, Harte had sobered. Convenient, because as Esta made her final curtsy to him, he caught sight of Jack Grew over the top of her head.

He offered his arm to escort her off the floor, and when she accepted it, he bent his head toward hers. "Are you ready?"

She gave a small nod as she met his eyes. He wasn't sure what he saw there now—determination? Resignation? It worried him that he couldn't read her, didn't know what she was thinking. Not without using his affinity, and doing that would mean losing the one ally—however tenous that might be—that he had. But the time for delaying was over. They had work to do.

TO SINK THE HOOK

The orchestra at the Haymarket had just finished a cloyingly senti-mental waltz that had grated against Jack's already-raw nerves. He was at the end of his rope. He'd put everything he had left—and a lot that wasn't his to take—into rebuilding his machine. The new machin-ists had been working day and night to restore the hunk of metal and wire, and it was nearly ready to try again. But trying it again was pointless unless he could figure out how to stop the blasted thing from exploding.

He was running out of time—his father's ship would leave from London in another week. When he arrived in New York, his men of business would tell him about the emptied accounts, and Jack would be on a one-way train to Cleveland, or some other godforsaken uncivil-ized place in the wilds of the Midwest. He wouldn't be around for the Conclave, much less to make his triumphant return to the Order's good graces.

But at least the Haymarket stocked passable scotch.

He raised the glass to his lips, anxious for the numbing burn and the taste of smoke and fire, but when he tilted it back, he found it empty. He peered down, wondering when he'd finished the drink. Then he lifted the empty glass to signal the barmaid to bring him another while he waited for Darrigan and his doxy to show up.

The thought of them arriving buoyed him a bit. The demonstration they'd done the night before had been remarkable. Impossible. He could use a little of the impossible on his side right now.

Over the racket of the crowd, he heard his name and lifted his head to find Harte Darrigan walking toward him. On his arm was the girl from the night before. Tall and lean, she could have been an Amazon in another life, but in this one she was a vision in a gown spun from gold. If the dress wasn't enough to convince him that she was different from the usual theater types, the jewels at her neck would have been. No chorus girl had jewels like that.

"Thanks for the invitation tonight," Darrigan said as he closed the distance between them, offering Jack his hand as he approached with the girl.

"I'm glad you could make it," Jack said, taking Darrigan's hand. *Damn if it isn't good to see him again,* he thought suddenly. *Everything is going to be fine.*

Darrigan made a small flourish with his hand as he brought the girl forward. "May I present Miss Esta von Filosik." Harte smiled warmly at the girl. "Esta, this is a good friend of mine. A *very* important man in our city, Mr. Jack Grew."

Jack couldn't help but preen a bit under the praise. "Miss Filosik," he said, with a slight nod of his head. This close, he saw that his original impression had been right. Her face was free from any paint and her clothes were so well fitted that they must have been custom-made.

"You must call me Esta," she told him, offering her hand. She spoke with a foreign lilt to her voice, but it wasn't the gutteral sound that filled the saloons of lower Manhattan. Instead, it had the refinement of some-one well bred and educated. "Any friend of Harte's is one of mine."

"Esta it is, then." He took her hand and bowed low over it, lifting his eyes to take in the shapely bodice of her gown, the creamy expanse of her chest.

She gave him a slow smile, peering up at him through her lashes, but then her eyes went wide. Her mouth opened in a soft *oh.*

Well, well, he thought with anticipation as the girl stared at him as though she appreciated what she saw. . . .

"We arrived a bit early and were taking a turn around the floor. There's a table waiting upstairs," Harte told him. "If that's all right with you?"

Jack released the girl's hand. "That sounds fine."

"Wonderful." The girl gave him a slow, encouraging smile. "I believe the champagne should still be cold."

"Champagne, you say?" He looked down at his empty glass, feeling that much better about the days ahead. "That sounds as perfect as you look, my dear."

DÉJÀ VU

Esta cringed inwardly at Jack's obvious come-on. A hundred years, and men never figured out that lines like that didn't work.

As Harte led her back to their table, it took effort to keep her features relaxed. She was still unsettled from the premonition she'd had when Jack had looked up as he bowed over her gloved hand. She'd been overwhelmed by the memory of those same eyes in a darkened hallway, when he was pointing a gun at her before he turned it on Logan.

If Harte hadn't started talking again, she would probably still be frozen. But she reminded herself that there was no way Jack could know her or remember her: She'd first met him in 1926, some twenty-four years from now. She would be fine. She'd get through this.

Ten minutes later, though, she regretted having him at their table. Harte was a different person around him, condescending and dismissive of everyone, including her. It was a part of their plan, she told herself. He was only giving Jack an opening, using her—the mistreated mistress—as bait. But it was still an ordeal to sit through.

He was even worse than Logan, Esta thought as she listened to the two men bluster at each other. Logan had a sort of natural charm he used to disarm his victims, but Harte's was something more. Whatever charm he came by naturally had been cultivated and honed with the precision of an artist. It was so overwhelming that his mark had no choice but to be taken in by it.

She did know better, and she'd almost been taken in by it, she admitted, thinking of the warm fluttering in her belly as they'd danced. The moment he'd taken her in his arms, she'd felt trapped and protected all at once, and she hated herself for almost liking the feeling. Hated that she'd had to focus on something—*anything*—else during the dance, because he was looking at her with an intensity that made her cheeks warm.

The whole ordeal had made her feel things she didn't want to examine too closely. Unnerved. Unbalanced. And maybe most dangerous of all, *unsure.*

All part of his game, she reminded herself—a game she *had* to win.

As she kept half of her attention on the conversation at their table and the other half on the ballroom, she couldn't help but think that Dakari's knife might still be somewhere in that building. It grated at her, the knowledge that she was a thief who couldn't even steal back something that belonged to her. And it worried her, going back to her own time without that bit of proof about what once had been. After the way the clipping had changed, who knew what future she'd be going back to?

Jack was nearly through the first bottle of champagne when a flash of coppery hair caught her eye. Down on the floor, Bridget Malone was making her way along the edge of the room.

Esta was on her feet before she realized what she was doing.

"Sweetheart?" Harte asked, a warning threaded through the endearment.

She didn't care about his warnings, though. He had Jack well enough in hand. She *had* to try. "Would you gentlemen excuse me?"

"Where are you going?" Harte asked through his clenched teeth.

She could still make out Bridget's fiery hair moving through the crowd. "Just to powder my nose, *darling,*" she said with a shy smile. "It will only take a moment. . . . If one of you could direct me?"

"Back behind the bar," Grew told her as he reached for the bottle again. His face had turned blotchy and red from the warmth of the room and the amount of wine he'd consumed.

She could tell Harte wanted to protest, but she promised to return quickly before he could, and then made her way through the crowd.

At first she went in the direction Grew had pointed, but when she was out of view, she cut beneath the overhang of the balcony and headed in the direction Bridget Malone had taken.

When she reached the corner of the room, she found that Bridget had vanished. There wasn't a door or hallway for the madam to have gone through, but the woman was gone. Confusion settled over Esta as she searched for some answer to Bridget's disappearance.

She found it a moment later when a portion of the wall slid open and one of the waiter girls emerged carrying a tray of clean barware. Before the panel slid shut, Esta picked up her pace and slipped through the opening into the dark silence of an empty hallway.

At the end of the passageway, Esta could just make out the glow of the flame Bridget held in her hand. From the smell of roasting meat that filled the air, the passage was also connected to the kitchens, but Esta wondered where else it might lead and whether it was connected to the lower floors. The room Bridget had kept her in before was below, in the cellar of the building.

The light wavered, and then the woman turned a corner and the passageway fell into shadow. Beams of light filtered through small holes in the wall, and Esta went to one and peered through to find a private dining room. From the looks of it, the passage was lined with more openings, probably so the management could keep tabs on their patrons without their knowledge.

She peered through the next set of openings and found another room, this one filled with men smoking cigars and talking in voices amplified by alcohol and a sense of their own invincibility. Among them was the man who had assaulted her weeks ago, Charlie Murphy. His nose was still crooked, but the bruises on his face had healed. Not that it improved his looks any. She watched them, trying to follow the flow of their conversation. They were discussing some event—a gala to celebrate the spring equinox, from what she could understand. That was when it hit her— they were all members of the Order.

"It didn't last long enough," a bald man was arguing as he pounded on the surface of the table, causing the stemware to shake.

"Nearly a year," another said.

"In the past it was more like a decade. The stones are dying."

The stones?

"They aren't dying," the bald man insisted. "But I agree there's something fundamentally wrong. I can't believe it's the artifacts themselves, though. Maybe there was a problem with the ritual?"

"I'd like to see you tell the Inner Circle that." Murphy laughed. "More likely it's a problem with the maggots we've been able to find. My father used to say the Irish were bad, but these newest arrivals? Dirty and uneducated, and don't even get me started about the Jews and Catholics."

"You're probably right. What power could possibly be derived from rabble like that? I'll tell you what needs to happen—"

A waiter entered carrying trays of food, and the men seemed to take it as a signal to change the topic. Dolph had talked about people going missing. She wondered if this was connected to it in some way.

The end of the hallway beckoned as the server made a show of carving the roast. In his presence, the men turned their conversation to mundane topics. Sports and stocks and the damnable traffic that was growing every day. Anything but magic.

Esta was growing impatient. Too much time had passed already. If she was going to get Dakari's knife, she had to go now. If only she could use her affinity . . . If she could slow time, she could be done in a blink. But she couldn't chance that. She had to make a choice. Did she go for the knife or stay and see what more she could discover? Dakari or Dolph's crew? Her own past or her new present? There wasn't time for both.

She had one job—to get the Book and to get home. Nothing was more important than that, not even Dakari. But the men on the other side of the wall were talking like there was a problem, like the Order had a weakness. Which was a fact that could only help them. Dolph and Professor Lachlan—all the Mageus.

Dakari would understand.

She peered through the openings and listened again, but before she could catch the thread of their conversation, she heard a familiar voice.

"What are *you* doing here?" Bridget Malone was suddenly there, next to her in the darkness, and looking none too happy to see her.

A TRAP IN A TRAP

Harte glanced over the dance floor below, looking for some sign of Esta's return. She'd been gone too long. Had she run into trouble? Or was she up to something?

"So tell me, Darrigan, how did you *really* meet the lovely Miss Filosik?" Jack tipped what was left of the bottle into his glass. The champagne fizzed and foamed over the edge of the bowl, dampening the white cloth on the table. "Are you and she . . . ?" He waggled his eyebrows suggestively.

"We've been friends since we were children," Harte said, leaving his answer open enough for Jack to make his own assumptions.

"Really?" Jack smirked.

"Yes. Believe it or not, the story I told onstage was true. I know Esta from my travels abroad. Her father was one of my first teachers. Perhaps you've heard of him . . . Baron von Filosik?"

Jack's face bunched, and Harte could practically see his alcohol-soaked mind trying to place where he'd heard that name. It took a moment, but then Jack's bleary eyes widened a fraction. "Not the Baron *Franz* von Filosik?"

"The same," Harte said easily, relieved that Jack had finally made the first step toward entering his little game.

"*You* knew the baron?" Jack asked.

He pretended he didn't notice Jack's surprise. "I was lucky enough to have lived with the baron when I was just beginning my quest for knowledge about the mysteries of the elemental states. He saw some talent in me and admired my drive to understand the secrets of the occult arts. It was he who directed me to the Far East and provided me with the introductions I needed to finish my studies. This was all before his untimely death, of course."

Jack frowned, puzzled. "I didn't know he had any family."

"Few did. Franz never married Esta's mother. It's maybe the only thing that saved her when his estate burned to the ground. I'm sure you've heard about that, the great tragedy it was. All of his breakthroughs were lost. His vast knowledge, gone."

"It probably set us back fifty years, maybe more," Jack agreed.

Harte leaned forward, his voice low. "Except, I don't think everything was destroyed."

Jack's brows went up, and even though his eyes were barely focusing, Harte saw interest in them. He could practically feel Jack's willingness to be convinced, to believe. It wouldn't take much more to push him the rest of the way.

"Esta has a trunk she keeps under lock and key. Won't tell me what's in it, won't let me see what it contains." Harte glanced to the left and right, making sure it looked like he was worried about being overheard. He lowered his voice. "I think it might be some of her father's papers."

"You don't say?"

Harte nodded. "You know what he was working on when he died, don't you?"

Jack looked momentarily thrown off. "Oh, yes. Wasn't it the . . . ?" He hesitated. "The, um . . ." He snapped his fingers, as though the words were on the tip of his tongue.

"The transmutation of basic elements," Harte supplied helpfully.

"Of course," Jack agreed. Then he blinked through his alcoholic haze like someone just surfacing from sleep. "You're not saying he created the philosopher's stone?"

"Rumor had it that the good baron was *very* close to a breakthrough." Harte leaned forward. "In his last letters to me, he hinted that he'd been successful at isolating quintessence—"

"Aether?" Jack whispered, excitement clear despite the glassiness of his eyes.

Harte nodded. "But he died before he could answer any of my questions or tell me anything more."

"Right," Jack agreed. "Terrible tragedy."

"It was." Harte hesitated, like he wasn't sure if he should share a secret. "More so if, as Esta believes, his death wasn't the accident it appeared to be."

Jack blinked. "She believes it was foul play?"

Harted leaned closer. "She believes someone found out what the baron was doing, how close he was to unlocking the secrets of divine power. Imagine what might be possible with that information. You could make the elements bend to your will."

"Yes." Jack licked his lips. "Imagine that. . . . But who would want to stop him from such a great discovery?"

"When I studied with him, the baron had suspicions he was being watched. He confided in me once that he worried there were those in the local village—Mageus—who didn't want him to succeed. He'd made arrangements so his work wouldn't be lost in case anything happened. If that trunk of hers contains what I think it might, it would be a discovery of amazing importance, Jack."

"You think she could be convinced to share it with us?" Jack asked, his expression unabashedly hungry.

"That's my problem." Harte frowned. "We're old friends—more than friends, really," he said, imbuing his voice with a lecherous note, "but she hasn't let me see what's inside. I think she's still testing me to see if I can help her. She's tired of living on the edges of society. She's the daughter of a baron, and while her father was alive she lived like one. But with his death, she lost her income and any standing in her town. So she's come to this country, like so many come, to start again. She wants her old life back, to live like the daughter of a baron is entitled to live, and whatever's in that trunk, she believes it's enough to gain her entrance to the highest society." Again he glanced around and then lowered his voice. "She's been implying she wants to get the attention of the Order. Of course, I thought of you. With your help, with your connections, she might be willing to share her father's work with us."

"She might not have anything, though," Jack said, frowning. "She could be leading you on. It's in a female's nature to be manipulative and deceitful."

"It could be that she's lying," Harte acknowledged, "but she was the one who designed the effect you saw last night. It's quite extraordinary what she's able to do."

"Designed it *herself*?"

"As much as it pains me to admit it, she still won't tell me how she accomplished it. I think she's been teasing me, withholding that information to get what she wants."

"Well, we can't let her get away with that, can we?" Jack said with a roguish grin.

"You have an idea?"

"Maybe with the right enticements, I could soften her up, find out if she's being honest about what she has."

"You'd do that for me?" Harte said, pushing down an unexpected jolt of jealousy.

"Of course. We're friends, aren't we, Darrigan?" Jack took another long drink. "And it's not as though it would be a chore to breach her defenses."

Harte's hands clenched into fists beneath the table, but he kept his expression the picture of eager appreciation. "I'd be awful grateful. I'd hate to be made a fool of, but if she does have her father's secrets, she could be very useful to me."

"To both of us. Miss Filosik and her secrets don't stand a chance," Jack said, raising his glass.

"Not a chance at all," Harte agreed pleasantly as he watched Jack finish off the last of the champagne. He couldn't have scripted the evening any better himself. Jack had fallen for the bait just as they'd planned for him to, but Harte couldn't shake the feeling that he'd made a misstep somehow. He just wasn't sure what it was, or how it might come back to bite him later.

Still, successes should be celebrated, so he pasted on his most charming smile and was about to call for another bottle when a shadow fell over his table. Harte looked up to find Paul Kelly standing over him.

"Hello, Darrigan," Kelly said genially. He was dressed impeccably, as usual, in a crisp suit, but his eyes held a warning. "Fancy meeting you here."

A moment of silence passed, where Harte was too shocked by Kelly's appearance to utter a word. It was as if he'd awoken to discover all those months of freedom had been nothing but a dream. He was thirteen years old again, looking at his certain death.

"Aren't you going to introduce us?" Kelly asked expectantly, shaking Harte from his stupor.

Jack glanced at Kelly and then looked to Harte. "Do you know this gentleman?" he asked, and Harte could see the confusion in Jack's bleary gaze as he took in Kelly's well-cut clothes and his long-ago broken nose.

He was stuck. Kelly was making enough of a name for himself that Jack might recognize it, and if he did, it might destroy all the work Harte had done to make himself seem respectable. But if he refused, Kelly was sure to make a scene.

"This is an old acquaintance of mine, Jack. Paul Kelly, Jack Grew. Jack, allow me to introduce you to Mr. Kelly."

Jack, who thankfully showed no sign of recognizing the name, shook Kelly's hand, and then to Harte's horror, he asked Kelly to join them. "We were just celebrating a mutually beneficial opportunity we stumbled upon," he told them.

"Were you?" Kelly asked, taking the seat Esta had left open. He eyed the waiting glass of champagne. "I'm a bit of a businessman myself," Kelly told him.

Jack sputtered a bit, making some excuses and trying not to reveal what they'd been talking about as Paul Kelly sat on the other side of the table with his usual cold-eyed stare.

Harte felt as though he couldn't breathe. He'd risked everything—including his mother's life—to keep Kelly away from Jack, and now they were sitting at a table together. He needed to get out of there, he thought as he glanced again to the floor below, hoping for some sign of Esta's return.

"You have somewhere to be?" Kelly said as he took a slim cigarette from a silver case.

"No," he lied. "Nowhere at all."

Before Kelly could call him on his lie, a whistle sounded from the floor below. Harte turned in time to see a squad of helmeted policemen making their way into the ballroom, the beginning of a raid on the prostitutes that strolled the floor and the illegal gambling that often took place in the back rooms.

"Well, gentlemen," said Kelly, who didn't seem the least bit surprised at the raid. "I think it's time we make our exit."

THE MISSING KNIFE

B ridget's face was shadowed, but Esta could still make out the remains of a purplish bruise across the side of Bridget's cheek.

"I came for my knife," Esta said, realizing as the words tumbled from her mouth how absolutely stupid they sounded.

"What knife?" Bridget asked, looking both harried and confused at the same time.

"The one you took from my boot," Esta insisted.

"I didn't take anything," Bridget said, glancing beyond Esta, toward the entrance of the passageway. "You're mad if you think I did, and you're mad for coming back here after I went to the trouble to get you away."

"There was a knife," Esta said as ice settled into her veins. There had to be. *Because if there was no knife, there might be no Dakari.* But Bridget didn't seem to be lying.

"I'm not a thief . . . unlike some," Bridget snapped. "You need to get out of here. Do you have any idea what will happen to you if Corey sees you here?"

She took hold of Esta's wrist and tugged her toward the ballroom. But when she eased the panel open to enter the barroom again, the room on the other side had erupted into a riot. Women screamed and men tumbled over each other to avoid the clubs that the police were using on the heads of anyone who struggled to get away. "We have to go," Bridget said. "Come on. If they see us without escorts, they'll assume we're working girls. It's the whole point of the raid. They'll arrest us for sure."

But Esta had an escort. She looked up toward the balcony, but with the mess of people tearing at one another to get away, she couldn't tell if Harte was still there.

"Where are you going?" Bridget shouted as Esta pulled away and began shoving her way through the crowd, pushing against the flow of people. She was so intent on searching for Harte that she didn't notice the policeman behind her until she heard the shrill scream of his whistle. And she didn't notice the baton he held until it came down on her head.

THE WATER'S EDGE

The ballroom was in chaos. As soon as the whistle sounded, Harte felt paralyzed by the memories crashing into him. He was eleven again, cornered in the alley where he'd made his bed that night, unable to escape.

"Darrigan!" Jack was pulling at him, saying something.

But the sound of the whistles and shouts drowned out everything but the memory of being dragged from his sleep and into a Black Maria packed so tightly with filthy men and women that he couldn't move. Couldn't get away from the stink of them. Couldn't get away from their hands. Grabbing at him, pulling at him . . .

He couldn't breathe.

Jack's voice came to him from somewhere far off. "This way, Darrigan."

Harte let himself be led, panicked confusion keeping him from processing what was happening until they stepped out into an alley that reeked of rotten meat and piss, the smells of his childhood. It took everything he had not to retch.

When the cool night air hit his face, he gasped, sucking the air into his lungs. He was barely aware of Jack shaking Paul Kelly's hand, thanking him for the help getting out of the hall.

"Good seeing you again, Darrigan," Kelly said with a rough slap on his back, before he hailed a cab and disappeared into the night.

As he came back to himself, Harte had the sudden—and delayed—realization that he was no longer inside the Haymarket.

"What are we doing out here, Jack?"

"We're not getting swept up in the raid, that's what," Jack said. His hair was sticking up at an odd angle and the shoulder of his jacket was torn, but he looked pleased with himself. Almost exhilarated from their escape. "Damn nice of Kelly to help us out of that mess."

"We can't leave without Esta," Harte said, starting to go back.

Jack caught him by the arm. "Are you insane? The girl will be fine. All those jewels? They'll let her go. Hell, they'll probably escort her home. Come on. I can't be caught up in this, and I can't imagine you'd want to spend a night in the Tombs either."

He pulled his arm away from Jack, but Harte didn't move. He couldn't be taken to the Tombs, he thought as the wave of panic crested over him again. *Not again.*

"Are you coming or not?" Jack asked, tugging at him.

Harte looked back at the rear door of the Haymarket. "But Esta—"

"She'll be fine."

He turned on Jack. "You can't know that."

Jack gave him a shrug. "You're right. I can't. Think of it this way: If she gets caught up in the mess, at least she won't be keeping the baron's journals from us anymore." He elbowed Harte as he laughed at his own joke.

Harte's fingers closed into a fist and it took everything he had not to drive it into Jack's pretty white teeth. But to do that would destroy the con and any chance of ever getting the Book.

"Come on," Jack insisted. "There's something I want to show you."

He couldn't leave Esta, but he also couldn't let Jack get away. Not when he was so damn close.

"Well?" Jack asked, impatient.

She was probably already outside, halfway back to their apartment—*his* apartment, he corrected. She'd be fine, he told himself. If the tables were turned, she would probably do the same. She'd *improvise*, wouldn't she? She was good at that.

"Fine," he told Jack, looking back at the door one last time. "Let's go."

They walked a block west, avoiding the noise coming from Sixth Avenue, where some of the Haymarket's customers and waiter girls had tried to avoid the police but ran right into them instead. If Esta had gone that way—

If she went that way, she can get out of it. Whatever magic it was that allowed her to move like lightning, disappearing and reappearing in barely a blink, she'd be fine. He needed to stay with Jack. They were too close to let him off the hook now.

The cab they found smelled like someone had been sick in it earlier, but Jack didn't give any indication that he noticed. Instead, he slouched back in his seat with his eyes half-closed as the carriage started off.

After a while, though, it became clear that Jack wasn't taking them toward the mansions on Fifth Avenue, as Harte had expected. When he saw the spires of Trinity Church, a landmark well below the safety of Canal Street, he started to worry.

"Where are we going?" Harte asked as the carriage rattled on.

Jack opened his eyes enough to squint at him. "You'll see," he said with a self-satisfied smile. Then he closed his eyes again and, a few seconds later, let out a soft snore.

As they rode, Jack dozed drunkenly while Harte considered his options. But the carriage never stopped as it followed a route that cut deeper and deeper into the poorly lit neighborhood streets, each progressively darker and quieter than the last.

When they approached the eastern edge of the island, Jack snorted and came awake with a jerk. When he saw where they were, he looked excited, anxious, and suddenly more sober than he had all night. But as they followed the shoreline, the closer they came to the towering span of the bridge, and the more uneasy Harte became.

He couldn't cross that bridge, but he also couldn't stop the carriage without risking all the work he'd done to get Jack this comfortable. More important, Harte couldn't let Jack realize the *real* reason he couldn't cross the bridge.

Every block they passed brought the bridge closer still. Harte glanced at Jack's wrist, noticing the sliver of exposed skin between his cuff and his gloves. He'd wait until they turned toward the bridge, just to be sure. Until the danger of the Brink was worth the risk—

But then Jack rapped on the driver's window, and the carriage came to a shuddering stop. "We're here," he said, excitement and anticipation shining in his eyes despite the effects of the champagne.

Harte took a breath, relieved that the carriage had finally stopped, but he didn't let his guard down.

The docks that bordered the river in that part of town were a forest of ships' masts and a maze of warehouses crouched close to the ground. Harte wasn't familiar with the area. The river's edge was the domain of the longshoremen and the river rats who raided the cargo. Most people were smart enough to stay away from the docks, where the roughnecks often looked away if a body was dumped into the river. And most Mageus would have never chanced coming that close to the Brink that silently circled the island somewhere just offshore. Even now, even with the water still some distance away, Harte could swear that he felt the chill of it.

Jack gave the driver orders to wait and then led them through the uneven grid of buildings bathed in moonlight, swinging his arms at his sides and whistling the occasional off-key tune like they were walking through Central Park and not one of the dodgiest parts of the city. Harte never had trusted that sort of blind confidence. Usually, it was a mask for ignorance, and in his experience, both were dangerous.

Everywhere, shadows lurked, rustling in doorways and curling against the walls of the buildings. Occasionally, one of the shadows would bring fire to its fingertips. A flicker of flame would come to life, the puff of smoke enwreathing a briefly illuminated face, and then the night would go dark again.

It isn't magic, Harte reminded himself. Just a simple flare of a match, the mundane glow from the flickering tip of a cigarette.

This close to the river, Harte could almost detect the scent of the water. On the other side lay everything he'd never been able to reach, an entire land that was more than the stinking streets and the day-after-day scrambling urgency of the city. A world where he could be something more than a rat in a trap.

But in the next breath, the scent of water was covered by the heaviness of axle grease and soot, the ripeness of days-old fish and oyster shells. A reminder that he still had a long way to go before he could be making plans about a different future.

Finally, they came to a long, unremarkable warehouse. Jack took a ring of keys from his coat and made quick work of the heavy padlocks on the wooden door. But before the last one clicked open, he turned to Harte. "You probably wouldn't even need a key, would you?" he asked, cocking his head to the side. Jack's face was covered by shadows, but his body had gone rigid, like he'd finally sobered up enough to comprehend what he was doing. To have second thoughts.

"I'm not a thief, Jack."

"I know that." Jack shifted uneasily. "But I'm taking a risk in showing you this. I think you'll understand, and I'm going to trust it'll interest you enough that I won't have to worry."

"Whether I'm interested or not, you don't have to worry about me. I don't want any trouble."

Jack frowned like he was puzzling over something. For a second Harte thought Jack would change his mind, so he pulled on a look of boredom and moderate impatience. "Look, I didn't ask you to bring me here, but can we get on with it already? I need to get back and check on Esta, so if we're not going in—"

"No," Jack said, giving himself a visible shake. "You've come all this way, you should see it. I want you to." He pushed the door inward. Beyond it, blank darkness waited, but Jack quickly lit a kerosene lamp near the door. "After you," he said.

In the center of the room, there was a large misshapen object covered by a cloth. With a smile lighting his face as much as the lamp, Jack drew the heavy tarp off and revealed something that could have been pulled from the pages of Jules Verne. The machine clearly wasn't complete yet, but Harte could make out the gist of it: a large central globe made from what looked like glass, which was surrounded by three concentrically ringed arms that glinted in the light.

It looked harmless enough, quiet and still as it was, but there was something about the machine that made Harte nervous.

"Amazing, isn't it?" Jack said, giving one of the great orbiting arms a push, which made all the others glide slowly through their separate rotations as well.

"What the hell is it?" Harte asked, trying to shake the sense of apprehension he had standing next to it.

"*This* is the future, Darrigan," Jack said, beaming.

"The future?" Harte eyed him doubtfully.

"Come here and take a look." Jack walked past Harte to a long work-table on the left side of the room. Various blueprints and maps were laid out in haphazard piles, anchored in place by drafting tools and angles. He motioned for Harte to join him.

Reluctant to get too close to the strange machine, Harte made his way around the outer edge of the room, to the table where Jack was standing. At the far end of it was a model, a small rectangular building with a single tower growing from its center. The tower was capped with an odd, onion-shaped roof that reminded Harte of a picture he'd seen once of a Russian church.

"What is all this?" Harte asked.

Jack pointed to the model of the building. "My uncle's building a larger version of this out on Long Island. It's going to be a wireless transmitter—Tesla's doing the design. When it's done, it will transmit telegraphs, maybe even pictures, through the air. My uncle believes it's going to revolutionize the world of business."

"You don't think it will?" Harte asked, responding to the tone in Jack's words.

"I think he's thinking too small and missing the point entirely," Jack said as he began shuffling through a pile of papers. "Here, look."

Jack smoothed out one of the crumpled sheets for Harte to inspect.

"It's the Philosopher's Hand," he said, glancing up at Jack before returning his focus to the paper. The image was familiar to Harte—he'd studied enough alchemy to recognize the symbol and knew what it stood for.

"Exactly. I knew you'd understand," Jack said, excitement lighting his eyes. "Five fingers for five distinct elements, the basis of all we know and understand about otherworldly power. Everyone who studies the occult arts knows that the elements are the key to unlocking the secrets of magic. If you isolate the individual elements, you can harness their energy and command them to bend to your will. But look what holds them together."

The image depicted a hand with its fingers spread wide, each tipped with a different symbol—a key, a crown, a lantern, a star, and the moon. In the open palm, the fish and the flame, the symbols for . . .

"Mercury," Harte said, tapping the center of the palm. "The element that transcends all others. Sometimes known as quicksilver."

"Or Aether," Jack added. "The same substance the baron was able to isolate, if you're right."

"What's your point, Jack?" Harte asked, unease crawling down his spine. Perhaps he'd played his game a little too well: Jack had not only taken the hook, he now seemed to be dragging him out to sea. "And what does this have to do with that machine? Or with the future?"

"Everything." Jack stopped short. "It has *everything* to do with the future. Every day, the world sends more and more of its filth to our shores. Among them, Mageus sneak into our city. Filthy. Uncivilized. *Dangerous.* Their very existence threatens our civilization and, as we've seen for ourselves, the safety of our property and our citizens. But this machine will change everything, Darrigan." He ran his finger over the tip of the tower's roofline. "It will put a stop to that threat once and for all."

"The Brink already keeps the Mageus in their place."

"Maybe that was true during a simpler time," Jack said. "When the Brink was created, there were far fewer coming here. It was enough to simply trap them on the island. But the numbers have been steadily increasing. There have been attempts to meet the growing threat, of course. Ellis Island, for instance, was supposed to keep Mageus from ever setting foot on our shores, but those measures haven't been enough. Devious as they are, more maggots slip through the inspectors every day. There are even reports that some have made it off the island and onto the mainland. That cannot stand. The Order knows something has to be done. They've been working on a plan to increase the Brink's reach, but what they're doing won't work."

"No?" Harte kept his eyes trained on the model of the building, feigning interest to cover his fear.

"Not as long as they're using old-fashioned ideas—old-fashioned magic—instead of modern science. And so long as they're thinking too small."

"The Brink is small?" Harte asked, trying to keep his voice even.

Grew nodded. "But my machine won't be. Consider this, Darrigan. Tesla's tower will revolutionize wireless transmission, true, but it's only the *beginning* of what could be done with it. With the kind of power this receiver can generate, it could make the Brink obsolete." He smoothed out the rumpled paper bearing the Philosopher's Hand again. "The Brink was created more than a century ago by a ritual manipulation of the elements through the Aether. It's old-fashioned alchemy: Five artifacts, each imbued with the power of one of the basic elements, were used to complete the ritual. Like this hand—all the elements are connected through the Aether, the palm. It creates a circuit of sorts. When a Mageus passes through it, their power unbalances that circuit, and whatever magic they possess is drawn toward the elemental energies of the Brink as it attempts to balance itself.

"The whole system is self-perpetuating, powered by the very feral magic it takes, which is why it's lasted for so long with very little maintenance. But the Aether is the key," Jack said eagerly. "There are two problems with the Brink, though. First, the power taken from any Mageus who tries to cross the Brink becomes part of the circuit, but we can't do anything more with that power. For all intents and purposes, it's lost. We can't *use* it." Jack eyed him. "That's a waste, don't you think?"

"Yes," Harte forced out, his stomach turning. "Quite."

"This machine would put an end to that. Instead of redistributing the power it harvests, it collects it and holds it separately."

"And the other problem?"

"The Brink is limited by its size. When it was first created, no one knew how quickly the city would grow or that the wilds of Brooklyn and beyond would become what they have. No one could have imagined how many people would come to our shores. No one imagined that they would come *despite* the Brink."

"Desperate people will do desperate things," Harte murmured. They would chance the Brink and commit themselves to living in a rattrap of a city because it was still better than the places they came from, places still ravaged by the hate spurred on during the Disenchantment. Because the hope for a different future was *that* powerful.

"It's not desperation, Darrigan. It's a complete disregard for our way of life. The Order is aware of this problem, of course. They were hoping to unveil their grand plan at the upcoming Conclave, when the entire Order gathers, but it isn't working. The original artifacts aren't powerful enough to expand the size of the Brink without making it unstable. Now they're trying to replicate the original creation of the Brink, all in the hope that perhaps they might be able to re-create it in other places, trap any Mageus that manage to avoid New York. That hasn't worked either." He shook his head, a mocking expression on his face. "But will the Inner Circle listen to me?"

"No?" Harte asked, trying to hide his hopefulness.

"Of course not. They're stuck in the past, and its weight is dragging them under. It will drag us *all* under." With a violent motion, Jack swept the papers off the table, causing them to flutter into the air and then settle onto the ground at Harte's feet. "They're so focused on containing the maggots, they don't realize it has never worked. They're like rats, the way their numbers seem to be growing. Like rats, they need to be *exterminated*, and when I get my machine working, that's exactly what we'll do." He walked over to it and ran his hand over the shining metal of one of the orbital arms. "Once this machine is installed in Tesla's single tower, it will have enough energy to clean a one-hundred-mile radius of any feral magic. *Much* more efficient than the old rituals. Imagine one of these in every major city. It would send a message—a warning—to any who would come to this country and try to turn us from our destiny."

"One hundred miles?" Harte asked, feeling almost faint. "You're sure?"

"The last time we tested it, the field it generated reached as far as Fulton Street, and that was only at a fraction of its capacity." Jack smiled slyly.

"Quite impressive," Harte said, but he thought of Tilly as he said it and felt sick. He hadn't realized what Jack was capable of. He'd been goading him on, encouraging him, when he should have been paying more attention.

"It is, isn't it?" Jack agreed. "When I multiply what this machine is capable of by the power of Tesla's transmitter, we can easily wipe out all the feral magic in Manhattan, maybe even reach as far as Philadelphia and Boston. But unlike the Brink, the power this machine will generate once it's installed in Tesla's tower would be *usable*. Imagine it—feral magic eradicated, transformed into civilized power that could be used to guide and shape the future of this new century. Or . . . it could become a weapon unlike any the world has ever seen. This country could become even greater than the empires of Europe after the Disenchantment."

Harte didn't have any idea how to respond without giving away his true feelings. He hadn't realized that the Brink kept the power it took from Mageus, but to increase that danger?

If Jack succeeded, if the Order ever controlled such a machine, magic would be doomed *everywhere*, as would every single person with an affinity. If Jack was right about the machine's possibilities, Harte's plan to leave the city was pointless. If he didn't find a way to stop Jack, to destroy the machine, there wouldn't be anywhere to hide.

"You said the machine doesn't work?" he asked.

"No." Jack scraped his hand through his hair, frustrated. "Not yet, at least. I haven't found a way to stabilize the power that it collects. There's something about feral magic that isn't stable. The last one I built didn't last a week before it blew up and killed my machinist." His eyes were a little wild as they searched the silent metal, as though it would whisper its secrets if he waited long enough. "All the power it generated was lost."

Just like Tilly. The existence of the machine explained the strange boundary on Fulton Street, but if Tilly had died when the machine exploded . . . what did that mean about Dolph's plan to destroy the Brink?

"It's not the machine," Jack continued, not noticing Harte's dismay. "The design is flawless—I did it myself. The mechanism works perfectly when it's in motion. But after meeting your Miss Filosik, I've realized what I'm missing."

"You have?" Harte asked, not liking the sound of that one bit.

"It's the *Aether* I've been forgetting about."

"The Aether?" He could barely make himself say the word.

"Yes, of course! I don't know why it didn't occur to me before." Jack ran a trembling hand through his hair again, making himself look even more disheveled and unhinged. "Without isolating the Aether, the power would be unstable, unpredictable. In the Philosopher's Hand, Aether is what stabilizes the elements, so it might also stabilize the power this machine harvests. The problem is no one since the Last Magician has been able to isolate or produce it."

"The Last Magician?" Harte's head was still spinning. "I'm afraid I'm not sure who that is."

"No?" Jack's brows wrinkled in surprise, and an unwelcome wariness flashed in his eyes.

"At least not by that particular name," Harte amended. It felt as though everything were spinning out of control.

LISA MAXWELL

Jack studied him a moment longer. "The Last Magician was someone like us, devoted to studying the hermetic arts many centuries ago. It's rumored that he succeeded in ways others haven't since. Some of his breakthroughs helped to create the Brink."

"He was a member of the Order?"

"Not exactly, but the Order built upon his work. We have his journal, a record of all he'd learned and all he accomplished—a tome called the Ars Arcana. Arcanum, of course, being another name for the philosopher's stone."

"That can't be a coincidence," Harte said knowing that Jack could never, *never* get the Book. "You think this book will help you isolate Aether?"

"I do, but the Order keeps it under lock and key. Only the highest ranking members have access to it. I've been trying to take a look for months now, but I'm not a member of the Inner Circle. Now, that no longer matters." Jack smiled, an unholy excitement lighting his face. "If you're right about your Miss Filosik, I might not need to see those records. Not if we can get her to share her father's secrets with us."

Harte's mind raced to stay ahead of Jack. The machine changed everything....

Harte suddenly remembered the old man's prediction, that he would somehow destroy the Book. He hadn't completely believed Esta, hadn't believed in the prediction. But now he understood, because he could see clearly what he had to do.

He needed the Book, now more than ever.

"You'd have to get her to trust you," Harte said as an idea struck him: If Jack was interested in Esta, if he was still on the hook, they could still run their game. If they could hold off Jack *and* get the Book, maybe he could still get out of the city. As soon as he was out, he would destroy the Book and any chance Jack or the Order had of finishing this machine.

He wouldn't be able to tell Esta until it was over. She didn't understand what was at stake, if not now with Jack, then someday with someone. And he knew that with her faith in the old man's words, he would never convince her that the Book was too dangerous to exist.

But that didn't mean she couldn't still help him.

When everything was done, when they were safe, maybe he'd be able to explain. Maybe she'd even forgive him.

And if she didn't?

He'd lived with worse.

"I'm sure that won't be a problem," Jack said with a devilish smile. "It's possible my machine could be working before the Conclave, as I planned."

"The Order won't have any choice but to recognize your genius," Harte told him, hiding his true feelings behind his most dazzling smile. Inside, he felt like he could barely breathe.

"And the maggots won't have a chance."

Harte nodded his agreement and clapped Jack on the back, but silently he vowed to do everything in his power to make sure that future never came to be.

A CHANGE OF HEART

It was nearly three in the morning before Harte finally got rid of Jack and made his way back home. He let himself into the apartment, expecting to find Esta already locked in his room. Or, more likely, wide-eyed and ready to throttle him for leaving her. After what Jack had shown him, though, he'd be happy to take his chances with her anger. He couldn't get away from the docks, and from that nightmare of a machine, fast enough. But when he lit the lamps, there was no sign she'd even been there.

He told himself he'd wait an hour and forced himself to sit, watching the clock on the side table as the seconds ticked by. By the time thirty-seven minutes had passed, he'd had enough. Grabbing his coat and hat, he headed out again to find her.

The streets had been long since cleared by the time he made it back to the Haymarket. Police barriers were up, and the front door of the dance hall had been boarded over. The smell of smoke still hung in the air. The sidewalks were mostly empty, but a boy was asleep in one of the doorways nearby, curled against the street. Harte tapped him gently to wake him. When the boy's eyes blinked open, angry at the disruption, Harte held up a dollar and watched the boy's eyes go wide.

"Did you see a woman in a gold-colored gown tonight?"

"I've seen lots of women," the boy said, straightening his soft cap and reaching for the money.

Harte pulled it away. "She was wearing a necklace with garnets and diamonds that looked like a collar. And black feathers in her hair."

"I might have seen her," the boy said, eyeing him.

"Where?"

"I think she was with everyone else they took off to the Tombs." The boy pulled the money from Harte's grip. "But they all looked the same, so maybe it wasn't her." He tucked the money into his shirt and turned back over.

The Tombs? A memory of a damp floor and a crowded room filled with rough hands rose to strangle him. It was his fault. He'd been so angry with her after her little stunt onstage that he'd purposely pushed her. He'd let her wander off. Then he'd left her behind.

He had to tell Dolph. They had to get Esta out before something happened to her. Because there were plenty of ways to die that didn't require being put six feet under. He should know.

The Strega was nearly empty by the time Harte got to the Bowery. Viola was wiping down the bar top when Harte walked in.

"We're closing," she said as he came through the door. When she recognized him, "Oh, it's you." She gave him a stern look. "Where's Esta?"

He looked around the barroom before waving her over. "I need to see Dolph," he said.

"He's not here."

"Where the hell is he?"

Viola shrugged. "He sometimes gets restless this time of night. He went out."

"Well, when will he be back? I need to talk to him."

"Who knows? He's been in a mood lately." She narrowed her eyes at him. "Where is our girl?"

Harte frowned. "That's what I need to talk with Dolph about."

In a flash, her knife was out and at his throat. He could feel the sharp bite of its tip pressing against his neck.

"What have you done with her?" Viola demanded.

"I haven't done anything with her," he said keeping his eyes steady on her, so she would know he wasn't lying. "But there was a raid on the Haymarket tonight. She might have been taken."

The tip of the knife pressed more firmly against his skin. "What do you mean, taken?"

"We were separated in the confusion, and she didn't come back to my apartment. She might have been taken to the Tombs. I need help to find out for sure, and to get her out if that's what happened."

"I *knew* I didn't like your too-pretty face." He felt the prick of the knife and then the heat of his own blood as a drop trickled down his neck.

Harte remained motionless, because he didn't want Viola to know exactly how nervous he was. Or for her knife to slice any deeper. "If you're going to kill me, get it over with already," he told her, all false bravado. "Otherwise, tell me where Dolph went so I can get her back."

She scowled at him a moment longer. "I really don't know," she said, pulling the knife back and wiping its bloody tip on her skirt. "The boy might. Dolph tells him things sometimes." She frowned as she glanced in Nibsy's direction. Then she eyed Harte. "You *will* get her back." It wasn't a question.

"That's the plan," he said, moving toward the place where Nibs sat, working out something in a notebook at one of the back tables.

"I need to find Dolph," he said, without any other greeting. "Now."

"He's out." The boy didn't bother to look up. "Should be back in a few hours."

"I don't have a few hours."

Nibs looked up then, but there wasn't any concern on his face. Only curiosity.

"It's Esta," Harte explained. "She got caught up in a raid. I think she's been taken to the Tombs."

The boy cocked his head to the side and peered through the thick lenses of his glasses. "Dolph did say you were meeting with Jack Grew tonight. Did you manage to hook him?"

Harte ran his fingers through his hair, frustration spiking in him. "Yeah, nearly."

"Nearly? Or for sure?"

"It doesn't matter," Harte snapped. "Jack can wait."

"Got under your skin, did she?" Nibs looked entirely too pleased with himself. "I thought she might."

"It's not that," he denied. But even as he said the words, he knew they were a lie.

"No?" Nibs asked, curious.

"No," Harte said, refusing to admit that Nibs was right. "We need her is all. We can't get the Book without her."

"Sure we can," Nibs told him with a shrug. "Pickpockets and thieves are a dime a dozen."

"Not like her they're not," he said, not realizing until the words were out that he actually *meant* them. "We have to get her out of there before something happens to her." Because he needed her, he told himself. Not for any other reason.

"Playing the white knight now, Darrigan? The role doesn't exactly suit you," he mocked. "Forget about the girl. Right now your job is to focus on Jack Grew. Esta will get out when she gets out. Or she won't. It doesn't really matter now."

"Of course it matters," Harte growled.

Nibs shook his head. "She already did what we needed her to do," he said. A taunting smile erased the innocent, guileless expression he usually wore as something shifted in his eyes. "She hooked you, didn't she?"

He had known all along that he'd been played, but somehow hearing it straight from Nibs, understanding that Esta was nothing more than a pawn for Dolph, had Harte's temper snapping. In an instant he had the boy out of his chair, pinned against the wall. He sensed Viola's watchfulness from across the room, but he didn't care.

Nibs didn't even blink.

"I'm not some stupid mark," Harte growled.

"That right there is your biggest weakness, Darrigan. You think you can't be played. But Esta proved you wrong, didn't she? I knew she would, almost from the second I saw her. She played you *beautifully*."

In that moment Harte didn't want anything but to make the boy pay for his words. All he saw was fire and blood and anger as he drove his fist into Nibsy's face. He heard the crack of bone and felt the sickening crunch. At the same time his magic flared, and he pushed every bit of his affinity at Nibs, digging deep below the boy's innocent-looking surface.

The shock of what he saw plowed into him like a prizefighter's fist. Harte had always known there had to be something more to the boy than his innocent-looking smile and soft-spoken temperament, but he'd never expected *this*. Dolph was too smart, too powerful—how had the boy tricked him? Tricked them all?

Shaken by what he'd seen, Harte released Nibsy's collar and let the boy fall to the floor. A moment later, though, he felt another jolt—the shocking impact of Viola's magic slamming against him. Gasping, he stumbled toward the wall, barely able to keep himself upright.

"We're fine," Nibs called, as he pulled himself to his feet. "Let him go, Vi. It was a simple misunderstanding."

Harte couldn't focus enough to see Viola's reaction, but a second later the hot power she'd shoved toward him dissipated, and he could breathe again. He kept one hand on the wall at first, because his legs were still shaking. Across the room, Viola was watching him with careful eyes.

"I would have let Viola kill you if I didn't still need you," Nibs said. "Don't ever forget that. When you stop being of use to me, you're a dead man."

Harte ignored the threat and lowered his voice so Viola couldn't hear. "You can't actually think what you're planning will work?"

Nibs dabbed at his nose with the back of his hand. "I think it already is."

"You'd betray your own kind? For what?" Harte said, his mind racing. "Dolph would *free* you. Hell, he has some do-gooder notion of freeing everyone."

"You don't actually believe that." Nibs shook his head, disgust shadowing his features. "Dolph is no saint—you know that. You've seen what he's capable of. You've seen what he'll do for power. He loved Leena more than he loved anyone, and he managed to use her, to break her."

"What the Order did to her wasn't his fault," Harte said, finally accepting that truth. Harte might have wanted to blame him still, but Dolph hadn't created the Brink. He hadn't been the one to push Leena over it.

"No, but the marks were." Nibs nodded. "How do you think the marks worked, Darrigan?"

"Ritual magic. You're not telling me anything I don't already know," Harte sneered, refusing to let Nibs goad him into attacking again. Not with Viola watching.

"So you know he used Leena's affinity to create them?" Nibsy's eyes were dancing. "Of course you didn't know that. No one knew that particular fact."

"Dolph never would have done that to Leena," Harte said, trying to sound more confident than he felt.

"Don't kid yourself. Leena had always been his protection. Her ability to block any Mageus within her sight from using their affinity against Dolph or his people kept him safe. But everything they worked together to build wasn't enough for him. So he did a ritual to bring the marks to life, but he used *her* affinity in it. It weakened her. It made her angry, too. She said she forgave him, but I'm not sure that was completely true." He tilted his head, thoughtful. "Maybe if he hadn't taken so much from her, she could have fought the Order. Maybe she wouldn't have died on the Brink."

"Everyone dies on the Brink," he said, not taking the bait.

Nibs inclined his head. "So I wonder why you would want to keep it up?"

"I've agreed to help Dolph, haven't I?" Harte said, unease creeping through him. *He couldn't know.* "We have a deal. You know that."

"I know what you've *told* Dolph. But I also know you're a talented liar, Darrigan." Nibs shook his head. "I know a lot of things. About you.

About Dolph. About how people work and the choices they'll make. You might say I have an affinity for it."

So that was his talent? The absolute sureness the kid seemed to have made his skin crawl. "You don't know shit."

"I know that Dolph is blinded by his need to put things to rights for Leena. To avenge her. But bringing down the Brink won't destroy the hate and suspicion that feeds the Order's power. It'll only be the opening shot of a war he's not ready to fight. Do you really think he'll simply give the power of the Book away when he realizes what we're truly up against? He couldn't even leave Leena what she already had."

Harte shifted uneasily. He didn't trust Nibs—not after what he'd seen in the boy's heart and mind—but what he was saying made a sick sort of sense. Still, he knew what Nibs intended. . . .

"So you'd take it upon yourself to undercut him? You'd take the Book's power for yourself? Use it to rule the Mageus who are left?"

"Saw that, did you?"

"I saw everything, Nibs."

"Then you know that you and I aren't so very different, Darrigan. We're both working against Dolph. Neither of us has any desire to destroy the Brink. Which is why we're going to keep working together. And in exchange, I'll give you what you want most—a way out of the city."

"Are you forgetting that you pledged Dolph your loyalty? When he finds out what you're planning, you're as good as dead."

"You mean because of the mark?" the boy asked, ripping back his sleeve to show the tattoo below the crook of his elbow. "I'll let you in on a little secret, Darrigan. When Dolph tried to save Leena, the Brink took his ability to control us. The marks are useless now."

It couldn't be true—and yet Dolph *had* agreed almost too easily to Harte's demand to refuse his mark. "Even if that's true, you're under-estimating him."

"No, I think my estimates have been perfect. My estimations are *always* perfect." He gave a shrug that couldn't hide his smugness.

"Not so perfect. I bet you weren't estimating that you'd have a broken nose tonight."

Nibs frowned, but he didn't argue. "All that matters is that Dolph's done everything I've expected him to do so far. And so have you."

"Not anymore. I'm out," Harte said, backing away. "I don't want any part in what you're planning. You might need me, but I don't need you."

Nibs laughed. Blood dripped down his lips and chin as he talked, but he didn't seem to notice it. "You don't understand, do you? There *isn't* any way out for you, Darrigan. You're in this to the end."

"Like hell I am."

Nibs took a step toward him. "What do you think you're going to do? I know what you've been planning all along. You think you'll take the Book and run, don't you? Leave us all trapped in here while you find freedom. But let me ask you one question—do you have any idea where your mother is right now?"

Harte froze. "What does that matter?"

"You tell me."

"After what she did to me, she can rot for all I care," Harte said stiffly, but panic was already roiling in his stomach.

"Oh, that's good," Nibs said, clapping slowly. "Quite the performance. If you hadn't asked Dolph to hide her from Kelly, I might even have believed you just now. But she's your soft spot, Darrigan. Always has been. Dolph knew that. It's why he sent Kelly after you."

"Dolph wouldn't work with Kelly."

"To get you, he would. He *did*. It was my suggestion, and it's worked out *beautifully*. They made a little trade—Dolph's secrets for Kelly's lackey. And you reacted exactly as he expected you to." He licked his lips. "Dolph's still too tied up with Kelly to bother giving me any trouble, but you ran right into his snare. The fact is you *do* care what happens to that mother of yours, and as long as you won't cut her loose, the string she has you on is always going to be your noose."

"You have no idea what you're talking about," Harte spat. If he could just get close enough to Nibs to touch him again without Viola noticing . . .

But she was still watching, and he had a feeling that if he did anything else to Nibs, she'd be in the mood to kill first and ask questions later.

"You know, Dolph had me take care of getting her situated. She likes opium, doesn't she, your mother?" Nibs stepped closer to Harte and smiled, his teeth stained red from the blood. "You're not out. And you won't breathe a word of our little conversation here to anyone. Not unless you want me to make sure your mother's out too. I can make sure she gets all the poppy she wants. Not to kill her. Not right away, at least. But there are worse things than dying, aren't there?"

Harte reached for him again, but this time the boy dodged away. "No, I don't think so. I know you can do more than read minds, Darrigan. I don't think I want you to touch me again."

"The only reason I'd touch you is to kill you," he growled.

"You're welcome to try. No one's been able to yet. I'm always three steps ahead of them, and I always will be." Nibs gave him a threatening look. "Go get Morgan's nephew. I want that book, or I'll make sure that everything you hold dear is destroyed. Your name. Your mother. Even your girl."

"I don't care."

"Let's not waste our time with lies, Darrigan. Get out of here before I tell Viola you need to be taken out." He smiled, satisfied. "She'll believe me, you know. They all will, because I'm one of them. And you *never* will be."

Harte took a step back, a war rioting inside him. All of his careful plans were crumbling around him. But then he thought of Esta, stuck in that dank, vermin-infested prison. Esta, who could steal anything. He could never tell her all of what he planned, but with her help, it just might work.

"You've overplayed your hand, Nibs."

"No," the boy said with a lurid smile. "You only think I have."

THE THREAD UNRAVELS

Viola was still washing glasses behind the bar when Dolph returned, tired and frustrated. He walked over to the bar, and she poured him two fingers of whiskey without his asking.

"You look worse than when you left."

Dolph stared at the drink, but he didn't take it. "I wasn't out for my health. Kelly's up to something. His boys cut up three of ours tonight."

"I thought you'd worked out something with him," Viola said with a frown.

He ignored the implied question. "He has some bigger game going. Even Jianyu is having trouble figuring out what it is." He took the glass in his hand and rubbed his thumb over its smooth surface.

"I could try to find out for you?"

"No," he said, and when she scowled at him, he explained, "It's not that I don't trust you to handle yourself, but I don't need Kelly to know we're worried." She continued to frown down at where her blades were resting on the bar top. He'd upset her, but she didn't argue.

That silence almost bothered him more. She'd been too quiet ever since Tilly's death. He told himself it was natural, expected, but with everything else going on, he wasn't sure if maybe there was something more happening with her.

"Jianyu return yet?" he asked.

"No, but Darrigan came in not long ago. Said that Esta had been picked up at the Haymarket. He was looking for you, but he had words with Nibs and then went storming off."

"Is that right?" Dolph eyed the boy at the back of the barroom. "About what?"

"You'd need to talk to Nibs."

The boy was sitting at his usual table in the back of the bar, poring over the nightly ledgers. His glasses were perched over a swollen nose and his right eye had already turned a painful-looking purple-green.

"I didn't know you were taking up prizefighting," Dolph said, easing himself into his usual chair.

"Not on purpose," Nibs said, glancing up. "Darrigan did it."

"Oh?"

"I might have pushed him too far when I reminded him that the Book was more important than the girl."

"Viola mentioned something about Esta getting herself arrested in the raid tonight. Do we need to send someone?"

"Darrigan will get her out," Nibs said. "He seems to be even more tied up with her than we planned."

"That's good, isn't it?" Dolph asked. "It's exactly what I wanted. Maybe if he's attached to her, he won't do anything stupid."

"Unless she's tied up with him, too." Nibs made another mark in his book.

"That would be a problem?"

"It would be if they started getting ideas," Nibs said with a frown. "We wouldn't want them going off on their own and cutting us out."

The boy was always figuring, always planning. It was a skill that Dolph had prized, back when he'd had the means to control Nibs. Back when taking his mark meant taking an oath of loyalty. But now that the marks were dead and useless, and Nibsy knew, Dolph was starting to wonder how much faith he should put in the boy whose plans rarely went awry.

Looking at Nibsy's broken nose and battered face, though, Dolph dismissed that thought almost as quickly as it had come to him. He was getting too paranoid. After all, the boy had taken a hit from Darrigan for him—a direct one, from the looks of it. That had to mean something.

He'd talk to the girl and make sure things were progressing. It wouldn't hurt to remind her what she stood to lose.

"Any news yet about what caused the raid?" Dolph asked. "It's too much of a coincidence that after months of quiet, the police pick tonight of all nights."

"I haven't heard from Bridget yet, if that's what you're asking." Nibs glanced up at him. "It's strange, now that I think of it. Usually she sends word by now. You don't think she was the one to tip them off, do you?"

"I doubt it." Dolph frowned. "Bridget hates the Order and pretty much everyone else. She wouldn't have anything to gain by helping them."

"Then where did she disappear to?"

"I don't know," Dolph said, uneasy.

He understood what Nibs was suggesting, but Bridget Malone owed him too much to cross him. After all, Dolph had freed her from her violent drunk of a husband. He'd given Bridget a second chance and the freedom to build a new life, and she repaid him by sending him new talent before the other bosses found them. Most of their kind knew of the arrangement, and if a girl found herself in a bad situation, she knew to go to Bridget. He couldn't see what she would have to gain by starting the raid.

"Did you finish with your business?" Nibs asked, turning back to his ledgers. "I expected you back a while ago."

"There were problems with Kelly tonight. A gang of his attacked three of our boys. Beat them to a pulp—it'll be lucky if Higgins can walk after he heals."

Nibs peered up over the wire rims of his spectacles. "Did they cross into Kelly's turf?"

"Of course not," Dolph said. His people knew to be careful. "It happened on Elizabeth Street, not two blocks from here. Kelly's boys shouldn't have even been there."

"You sure it was Kelly's that did it?" Nibs asked.

LISA MAXWELL

Dolph nodded. "They carved the Five Pointer's mark into each of their cheeks. Even if they recover from the other wounds, that will leave a scar. They'll be marked now for life."

"I thought you said he was under control," Nibs said.

Dolph frowned. Things were changing, he thought to himself. *Too fast.* And for the first time since he'd started down this road, he wondered if he would be able to keep up. "I'll send Viola. She can take care of the ones who did it without any evidence."

Nibsy's brows went up. "Wouldn't it be better to let Kelly know? It might put him back in his place."

"No. Let him wonder. Let him worry about his weaknesses and who his enemies might be. The more uneasy he is, the more vulnerable he'll be," Dolph said, but even as he spoke, he couldn't help wondering how much he was talking about Paul Kelly and how much the words were a warning to himself.

THE TOMBS

Halls of Justice

The city's Halls of Justice, better known as the Tombs, were a layer cake of depravity. The top floors housed the petty criminals—pickpockets, green game runners, and other less violent offenders. The farther down you went into the building, the worse the prisoners became. By the time you reached the second floor, you were among robbers and murders, and the ground floor held the worst of all—runners for the local games, shyster lawyers, phony bondsmen, and of course the city's police, who were so deep in the pockets of Tammany that justice was only a word they tossed around like the latest dirty joke.

Harte had spent a night there not long after his mother left him. Locked in a cell with grown men, he'd been helpless to do more than survive the night huddled in the corner, fending off unwanted advances the only way he knew how—with magic. For that to work, though, he'd let them touch him, skin to skin.

He'd made it through that night, but he hadn't left unaffected. After that night, he'd understood *exactly* what people were capable of.

Even now, safe as he was, staring up at the ornately carved columns and window lintels designed to look like some ancient Egyptian burial chamber, he felt as soiled as the building's once-white facade. He could only imagine what was happening to Esta.

My fault. He'd pushed her to go into the dance hall, even when she'd clearly been worried. He'd goaded her over dinner—an act for Jack, but one he'd enjoyed a little too much because of what she'd done during

380

the performance. And then he'd left her behind. Now, because of him, she was in the prison that still haunted his dreams. And he had no idea how to get her out.

But he needed her out. If he was going to stop Jack from finishing his machine, avoid the future Nibs had planned, *and* get around Dolph, he was going to need her help.

The night he'd spent behind the walls of the Tombs, he'd sworn to himself that he would never be put in a position where he was that helpless ever again, and for the most part he'd held himself to that. Until now. Somehow, in the span of one night, everything had gone ass over elbow.

He let out a string of curses under his breath that would have embarrassed a prison guard.

"I knew you had a rougher side underneath all that polish," an amused voice said from behind him.

Harte turned to find Esta dressed with a ragged coat covering her evening gown. Her hair had mostly fallen and the black feathers that had adorned it the night before were broken or tilted at haphazard angles. The shock of seeing her there, safe and whole, sent such a wave of relief crashing through him that, before he thought better of it, he had his arms around her, crushing her to him, barely conscious of how she was pushing away.

It was only the smell of the coat that brought him back to his senses. It reeked of sweat and onions and stale tobacco. As he let her go and took a step back so he could breathe, he felt suddenly aware of how impulsively he'd reacted to seeing her. How dangerous it would be to let himself forget everything that was at stake.

"What are you doing here?" she asked.

"I'm rescuing you," he said, knowing exactly how absurd the words were even as he spoke them. She was standing there, right in front of him. And now she was smiling. She clearly didn't need to be rescued. "How did you get out?"

"I told you that day you tried to lock me up with those stupid hand-cuffs of yours—there isn't a lock I can't crack."

He frowned, trying desperately to regain his footing. "That was a risk, using your affinity in there. Someone might have noticed," he said, cring-ing inwardly at how stupid he sounded.

"I didn't. Use my affinity, I mean. I'm good enough without it. Once I got out of the cell, I traded the necklace for this coat and then lifted this." She held up a visitor's pass. "They're not exactly the brightest bunch, you know?"

"Desperate people rarely are."

She wrinkled her nose slightly as she pulled the filthy coat tighter around her, completely hiding her dress. "Did you make any progress with Jack?"

That's all she has to say? "You aren't going to ask why I left you?"

She blinked at him, her brows bunching. "I didn't know you did."

"Yeah." Harte squared his shoulders, daring her to complain about his choice. "I went with Jack when the police raided the ballroom. He was interested, and I didn't want to lose him. I left you," he challenged.

Her brow furrowed, but only slightly. "That's good, if you got some-thing from him."

It wasn't the response he expected. "It is?" She should have been angrier. She should have been furious with him for leaving her. He would have been.

But she never reacted in any predictable way. It was maddening.

She rolled her eyes. "I'm not some wilting violet, Harte. You should know that much about me by now. If the situation was reversed, I prob-ably would have done the same."

"You would have, wouldn't you?" he said, reminding himself of all the reasons he shouldn't trust her.

"What?" she asked warily.

"Where did you go last night?" he asked. "When you left me with Jack."

"I told you, I had to powder my nose."

She played you beautifully. That was what Nibs had said. How much was she still playing him?

"You were gone long enough to powder your entire body," he said, crossing his arms over his chest. "Try again. And this time, try without the lies."

"You don't trust me? I thought we were past this."

He huffed out a sound of disbelief. "You don't trust me, either, or you'd tell me what took you so long to get back to us. Were you meeting someone?"

"I don't know what you're talking about," she said, and she turned to walk away, but he snagged her wrist and pulled her back.

"There's too much at stake for any more lies between us. I came here to rescue you today," he said softly, trying a different approach.

Her expression was closed off, distant. "I didn't need you to rescue me."

Frustration had him wanting to lash out at her, but he held it in. Kept himself calm. This was too important to make any misstep because of his ego. "That isn't the point. *I came.*"

"But why? You've been trying to get rid of me since Dolph sent me. This would have been a perfect opportunity."

"Because I can't do this without you. I need you to hook Jack, but I need to know whose side you're on."

"I'm with Dolph," she told him, her brows furrowing. "Just like you're supposed to be."

"Are you? Or are you with Nibsy?"

Her brow wrinkled. "He works for Dolph," she said. "Isn't that the same thing?"

"Sure." He rubbed his hand over his mouth, scratching at the growth of whiskers that were already beginning to itch. "You're right."

"Are you okay?"

"If we're going to pull this off, we need to be able to trust each other."

"You really came back for me?" she asked, tilting her head to one side, so that a single lock of her hair fell over her forehead and into her eyes.

"Yeah. I did," he said, keeping his hands tucked into his pockets so that he wouldn't reach for her, wouldn't brush that lock of hair aside just so he could feel it slip between his fingers.

He was still uneasy. But if he was going to get the Book and keep it away from Jack and Nibsy, he needed her. Especially now that he couldn't depend on anyone else. He just had to keep his heart locked up and his head on straight.

ANGLES AND EDGES

Harte's Apartment

Esta sat on the edge of Harte's porcelain tub, looking at the news clipping. She'd changed something, or she'd started to. The story of Dolph's arrest and death was still there, but it kept blurring, as though the words couldn't decide which future to pick. She thought she could *almost* make out another story floating just beneath the surface of the page, like another time waiting for her to slip through to it. But then she'd blink, and it would be gone.

In truth, she was only delaying the inevitable moment when she'd have to face Harte again. He'd come back for her, and she had no idea what to do with that.

Maybe she'd been going about things all wrong. Professor Lachlan said she had to stop the Magician, and she'd assumed that meant working against him. But her actual goal was to get the Book, and maybe to do that, it would be easier to work *with* him. Maybe they didn't have to be enemies.

Except in the end, she would still betray him, just as she would betray the rest.

There was nothing for it, though. No way around it. To finish her job, she needed the Book. If she took the Book, the rest of them would lose. It didn't—*couldn't*—matter that she'd come to think of them as friends. She already had friends—Dakari and Mari, even Logan. But Mari was gone because of a mistake she had made. And if she didn't do what she'd been sent here for, she could be sacrificing Dakari and Logan's futures as well as her own. There wasn't a way to save them all.

But she wasn't there to save them all, she reminded herself, even as she felt her throat go tight. She had a future to get back to, and as much as she had grown fond of this time, grown to respect and admire the people in it, she refused to regret what she had to do.

She pulled the plug and watched the grime of the night before swirl down the drain, right along with most of the confidence she'd managed to summon. *Suck it up,* she told herself as she pulled Harte's robe around her. What was done was done. A minute past too late wasn't the time to start having regrets.

When she stepped out of the steamy bathroom, Harte was on the sofa, waiting with a sullen expression. On the table next to him, a neat pile of orange peelings sat atop a handkerchief. She could practically hear him think, the way he was sitting there—his hand scratching at the day-old scruff on the edge of his jawline as his eyes stared off into space.

He was so deep in thought that he didn't seem to notice her until she settled herself next to him.

"Feel better?" he asked, looking up.

"Yes. Much." She tucked her legs up under her.

"Wouldn't you rather get dressed?" He looked troubled when his gaze drifted over the robe she was wearing. Almost nervous.

Fine with her. She'd take any advantage she could get.

"No, I'm good," she said, leaning back comfortably. "It feels *amazing* to be out of that corset."

He gave her another uneasy look but didn't say anything more. It felt to Esta like he was on the edge of making some decision but wasn't sure whether to jump.

So maybe she'd give him a little push.

"Thanks for coming back for me," she said softly, touching his hand.

Harte looked momentarily surprised, but then he pulled away from her and composed himself. "Don't think it means more than it does." He picked up the newspaper and made a pretense of looking over the front page. But his motions were stiff and it was clear his eyes weren't focusing on any headline. "I need you to get Jack. Otherwise, I would have happily let you rot in there."

"Then I guess it's a good thing I didn't need your help after all," she drawled, frustrated with his moodiness. This approach clearly wasn't working, so she got up from the couch. She'd regroup and figure out another way.

He caught her by the hand, gently this time. She could have pulled away, but instead she turned to look at him. There was an unreadable expression on his face that made her pause.

"Don't start telling yourself stories about me, Esta. I'm not some knight in shining armor."

"I never said you were."

"I don't have some hidden heart of gold. I'm a bastard, in every sense of the word."

He seemed to be trying to convince himself as much as her. "I never thought otherwise."

"I know how women are," he muttered.

She looked at him and saw him anew—the sadness in his eyes. The way he held himself as though he were bracing for a slap. "You don't know half of what you think you do," she said softly.

"I know more than you can imagine. I saw where believing too much in a man got my mother." His mouth went tight.

"I'm sorry—"

"Don't be. I should've died in a gutter somewhere before my twelfth birthday. I would have deserved it after what I did."

She couldn't stop herself from taking a step toward him. "What could you have possibly done to deserve that at only eleven years old?"

"I sent my father away," he said. He lifted his chin, like he was waiting for her judgment.

She shook her head, not understanding. "You were a child. How could you send a grown man anywhere he didn't want to go?"

He looked at her, his stormy eyes dark with some unspoken emotion.

"I can do more than get into your head to see what's there. Do you remember that day onstage? When Nibsy brought you to the theater the first time? I put a suggestion into your mind. I told you what I needed for you to do to make the effect work. I gave you a command, and you obeyed."

She frowned. "That's not how I remember things ending up."

His mouth turned down. "Yeah, well . . . you weren't in the cabinet at the end, like you were supposed to be, but you did everything else. And you forgot everything the second the door of the cabinet opened, just like I told you to."

It felt right to her, answered one question that had been looming. But it raised so many more. "You really ordered your father away?"

He nodded. "The only thing he spent more time doing than beating me and my mother was drinking. I wanted a break. I just wanted her to be happy again, so I told him to leave. He did."

"You tried to save her."

"He never came back. He left the city, or he tried to. But he didn't get much farther than the Brink." His eyes were flat, emotionless.

"You were only a child. You couldn't have known," she said, thinking about her own inability to control her affinity at that age. She'd always been too impulsive, but then it had been worse. Like the time she was with Dakari and saw a tourist with an open backpack in Central Park. He'd warned her against it, but she thought she could lift the wallet inside before anyone noticed. But she hadn't quite known how to hold the seconds for very long, and they caught her with her hand in the bag. It was only Dakari's quick thinking that got her away, but he was a black man in a city where stop and frisk was the rule of law. He ended up flat on the pavement, his arms wrenched behind him while she couldn't do more than stand by and watch, tears clogging her vision.

He ended up spending the night in a holding cell. She'd never forgotten that day. Dakari had lived to forgive her, but from the sound of things, Harte's father hadn't been so lucky.

"My mother didn't care. When she found out what I had done, what

I *could* do, she was horrified. She went after him. She *hated* me for what I'd done. She risked the Brink to find him."

"Oh, Harte . . ."

"She didn't get very far, but even getting that close changed her," he said, his voice flat and almost emotionless, like he was telling her someone else's story instead of his own.

"I *am* sorry."

"Don't be," he told her. "It made me stronger. It made me who I am."

They weren't so different, the two of them. They'd both been abandoned by their parents, but at least she'd had the Professor. He'd seen something in her worth saving, but Harte never had that. She still might not trust him, but she understood him. The drive that made him who he was, the determination to prove himself—the bone-deep need to belong somewhere—those were all things she knew very well.

She understood the hurt, too. The fear that there was something intrinsically wrong with you to make the people who were supposed to love you leave. The way that fear either hardened you or destroyed you. It had turned into a sort of armor for her, another weapon in her arsenal, and she suspected the same was true of Harte.

"Don't look at me like that." He narrowed his eyes.

"Like what?"

"Like you know something about me. It'll be easier for both of us if you can get it through your head right now that I don't need some girl to come along and fix me. Life's carved away any softness I might have had, and all that's left now are hard edges. That's all I'll ever be. That's all I ever *want* to be."

She studied him—the stiff shoulders, the tight jaw, and the stormy eyes that dared her to judge him, and she had the sudden urge to ruffle his feathers again. She wanted to see the boy she'd met in the basement of the theater, the rumpled boy whose eyes glowed with possibility instead of desperation. She wanted to throw him off so he'd lose that distant look, just for a moment. She wanted to see if she could.

"I'm not here to save you." She sat next to him again and felt a surge of satisfaction when his brows furrowed.

"No, you're not, are you?" he asked, looking at her with the strangest expression.

"Nope," she said truthfully, reaching up to run her fingers through his hair. "I wouldn't bother trying."

"You wouldn't?" He looked wary now, but he didn't retreat. He seemed frozen, almost mesmerized.

"Who said I want you to be anything but what you are? I like your angles and your edges," she told him, hoping he could hear the truth in her words. "I have plenty of my own, you know."

"I know," he said, his voice soft with a hint of hope and desperation.

She smiled at the nervousness in his eyes. "I'd slice right through anyone softer."

He stared at her for what felt like a lifetime, as though he was afraid to move. As though he was afraid not to. "You would, wouldn't you?"

She nodded. He smelled of oranges, and she could imagine what it would be like to close the distance between them and have a taste of his lips. Kissing Harte on purpose would be like everything else between them—a battle of wills. A clash of temper. An unspoken understanding that neither would back away or back down.

And then what?

The thought was like cold water. In the end, she'd have to take the Book from him, from Dolph as well, and leave them all here in this past to face their fates alone.

"This is a terrible idea," she murmured.

"I know," he said, leaning closer.

Nothing is more important than the job. Professor Lachlan's words echoed in her mind, reminding her of the last time she'd lost sight of what was important. Reminding her that she had another life, another set of responsibilities, waiting for her. Maybe she didn't need to fight Harte, but she couldn't let herself start believing there was any future possible for them. At least no future that didn't end in betrayal.

She pulled back, ignoring the way her throat had gone tight with something that felt too close to longing. But what she longed for—for him, for a rest from constantly being on guard, for a place to call her own—she wasn't sure. "We have too much at stake to muck everything up with this." She motioned between them.

The urgency had drained from his eyes, and she could no longer read the expression on his face as he pulled farther back from her. The space between them, which was no more than the length of her arms, suddenly felt impossible. "You're right."

"I'm sorry, Harte. I—"

"No," he said. "Don't. There's no need. We were caught up in a moment, that's all. I'm the one who should be apologizing. But we can't get caught up like that again." He got up from the couch and headed into the kitchen.

Still unnerved, she followed him. "So you said that last night went well with Jack?" she asked, her voice a bit higher than usual. Desperate to get things back on track.

"It did," he told her, pouring himself a glass of water. He seemed to want to keep the table between them. That was fine with her.

"And?"

He took a long drink of the water before he spoke. "The good news is that you were brilliant last night. Jack absolutely believes you're the lost heir. It'll be up to you to reel him in, but it shouldn't be hard. He's itching to prove himself, so he's primed to make mistakes.

"Jack will be at the show again tonight," Harte continued. "It's all arranged. All you have to do is pretend you're interested in him when he comes backstage after. Stroke his ego a little and let him dig his own grave. Just lead him on enough to get us an invitation to Khafre Hall. We'll need a reason for him to want us there, though."

She remembered the men behind the wall at the Haymarket. "I think I have an idea of how to do that."

"You do?"

She nodded. "I heard something at the Haymarket that might help us." He gave her a quizzical look, but she ignored the question in his eyes. "The Order has a big party coming up for the equinox. It would be a shame if their entertainment canceled on them, don't you think?"

His expression shifted. "That should be easy enough. I'll talk to Dolph—it'll keep him happy to be in on the action." Something like relief flashed in his usually stormy eyes, softening them. Suddenly he looked like the boy in the basement of the theater, the boy she'd wanted to know better.

The boy she'd eventually betray.

Her heart twisted, but she ignored it. The deception was necessary. It was like Professor Lachlan had taught her: Emotions were a trap. Nothing was more important than the job.

THE BALANCE OF POWER

N early a week later, Dolph Saunders watched from the window of Harte Darrigan's apartment as Jack Grew helped Esta out of an unremarkable carriage. The girl smiled up at Jack and allowed herself to be walked to the door, but once the pair was close to the building, Dolph could no longer see them.

"Are they back yet?" Nibs asked from the doorway to the kitchen.

"Esta is. She'll be up soon."

The rooms were large and airy, clean and comfortably furnished. The boy had done well, and he'd done it on his own. Dolph himself had never had the chance to create a life like this, but for a moment he imagined what it might have been like if he'd chosen another path. If Leena had married him, they could have built a life on lies, moving uptown and pretending to be a normal couple, a normal family.

But they had started down this path together, and now he wouldn't turn from it.

A few minutes later the girl let herself in. She startled—but only a little—when she saw him and Nibs waiting.

She took her time about removing her hat and cloak, placing them neatly on the rack by the door. "What are you two doing here?" she asked, turning back to him.

"Waiting for one of you to return," he said flatly. "We came to check on you."

"I didn't know you were into personal service," she said dryly. There was something brittle in her voice, and her expression was hard as flint. He had the unwelcome sense that something had changed for her, and he wasn't sure why that bothered him. But he hadn't survived so long by ignoring his instincts.

"I'm not usually, but when I feel that people are hiding something from me, I'm willing to make exceptions."

"I'm not hiding anything. I've told him everything since you sent me over here," she said, nodding toward Nibs. "You could call him off, you know. I don't need him checking every day. Every other day might be a nice change."

Nibs gave her a wry grin. "And here I thought you were starting to like me."

"Enough," Dolph said before Esta could respond. He'd already seen the table in the kitchen piled with papers and maps, drawings and diagrams. They were farther than he'd suspected. "You're sure you've told him *everything*?" he asked, eyeing her.

"Yes, of course." She met his eyes, her expression calm and determined.

He waited for the lie, but he didn't sense it. Perhaps she was simply better at concealing her thoughts. She had the same straight-backed sense of her own abilities that she'd had the first night, and the air around her still tasted of desire and ambition. Dolph liked that about her, but it still worried him.

"Well?" he asked, dispensing with the pleasantries. "Show me."

"Everything's in the kitchen."

They followed her into the small room. Nibs took an orange from the bowl on the table as Esta leaned over a diagram of Khafre Hall and made a note on the western side of the building. Then she walked them both through everything—the four dinners she'd had with Jack, the way he seemed intent on boasting about his knowledge of the Order. It was clear he was trying to use his status to impress her and to take advantage of her, just as they'd expected.

"He's been bragging to Harte about how easily swayed I am by his pretty face and deep pockets," she told Dolph. "As if I don't know all his money comes from his family. I'd almost feel bad about the position he's going to be in when we're through with him if he weren't so insufferable."

"You've done well," Dolph said, glancing at Nibs. He'd left much of the details about their progress out of his reports. Someone was lying, but to his frustration, Dolph couldn't have said who it was. He'd trusted Nibs for so long, but the girl seemed sincere as well.

"The Mysterium has to be below this room," she said, pointing to a spot on the map.

"I thought the boiler room was there," Nibs said, turning the paper to get a better view.

"It is. But Jack mentioned something tonight that I think we can use." Her excitement was palpable. "The building goes deeper here than we thought." She pointed to a spot on the plans beneath Khafre Hall's central meeting room.

"You know that for sure?" Dolph asked.

"Pretty sure. Apparently, they picked this particular location for their headquarters on purpose. Something to do with the congruence of the elements." She glanced up at him with a puzzled look. "I don't really understand half of what Jack said, but the main point is that the whole place is built over one of the city's lost rivers. Something about making sure the elemental powers were balanced."

"You're sure about this?" Dolph felt some of his earlier concern about the girl receding.

"I'm positive. Jack was so anxious to make sure that I knew *he* understood all about the importance of aligning the elements, he practically drew me a map." She smiled up at him, and for a moment he had a thought of Leena.

Ridiculous. Esta looked nothing like her. But there was something in the way she carried herself, something about her confidence that tugged at memories best left buried. Maybe Viola had been right—he was too soft on her. He could only hope he wouldn't live to regret that.

"Does that change anything?" he asked Nibs.

The boy considered it. "If there's a river under there, we would have a second way in—or out. We'd have to account for that."

"Have you told Darrigan about this?" he asked Esta.

"Yes," a voice said from behind them. "*Have* you told Darrigan about this?"

AN INVITATION

"Harte—" Esta looked momentarily surprised—maybe even a little guilty—when she turned to find him watching from the doorway. It was the guilt in her expression that made him wary. "This is cozy," he said, stepping into his kitchen. He hadn't planned on her being back from her date with Jack yet. She'd been staying out later and later every night, but he'd come home to spend some time in his apartment alone for once. He hadn't been prepared to find her bent over their notes with Dolph. And Nibs. Seeing the boy there, in his own apartment, made his vision go red and his every instinct go on high alert. But he kept himself under control. "Having a little meeting without me, are you?"

Her brows drew together. "We wouldn't be having it without you if you'd been here when I got back."

Maybe she was telling the truth. Maybe he could trust her—after all, Dolph was there too. But the way she'd managed to edge him out little by little had already been bothering him. And now to find her with Nibs . . . "You haven't been home this early in over a week. What am I supposed to do, sit around waiting? I had things to attend to at the theater," he said, his jaw tight.

She gave a derisive huff. "I'm sure you did."

"What's that supposed to mean?" he asked, stepping toward her.

"Nothing." She glared at him. "But you're not the one fending off Jack's constant pawing. I swear he's part octopus."

"You wouldn't have to fend him off if you'd let me come along." But for the last two nights, she'd insisted that Jack wanted to see her alone.

Esta thought they could get further if Jack believed he was getting the best of Harte by stealing his girl. Harte had agreed, reluctantly, but he couldn't help worrying that Esta had the advantage while he wasn't there. Whatever truce they might have come to, he had to remember that he couldn't fully trust her. No matter how much he might want to.

He smirked. "How far did he manage to get with you tonight?"

"You ass—" Her cheeks flushed.

"If you two are finished?" Dolph asked, impatience simmering behind his words.

"I'm not even close to finished," Harte told him, his eyes still steady on Esta. "What are you doing here anyway?"

"I came to check up on you," Dolph said, and there was a note of something in his voice that Harte had never heard before. That usual thread of confidence seemed to be worn away, near to breaking.

He looked at Dolph. "You don't need to check up on me," he said as he removed his coat and slung it on the back of a chair. "I'm keeping my word, like I said I would." He purposely ignored Nibs. There was no way he'd be able to keep up the ruse if he acknowledged the boy.

Dolph's icy gaze met his. "Are you?"

"Yes." Harte yanked his cravat loose and pulled at the collar of his starched shirt.

"Jianyu tells me that Paul Kelly was seen having drinks with Jack Grew. You wouldn't have had anything to do with that, would you?"

Nibs shifted, as though listening more intently to his answer.

Panic laced its fingers around Harte's throat, but he fought through it. "I'm not going back on my word," he said, answering the implied question rather than the stated one. But when Dolph didn't respond, only continued to pin him with that all-knowing stare of his, Harte added, "Kelly managed to get to Jack without my help."

"When was this?"

"The night of the Haymarket fiasco. I came to the Strega to tell you, but you were out."

"Yes," Dolph said. "I saw that you'd *talked* to Nibs."

"I didn't do anything he didn't have coming to him."

"There's no hard feelings, Darrigan. I shouldn't have goaded you when you were all worked up over Esta being arrested." Nibs gave Esta a small, almost-embarrassed smile that had Harte wanting to punch him again.

"You were worked up over me?" Esta asked, puzzled.

"Gave me quite the shiner," Nibs told her, the challenge clear in his tone.

"You punched him?"

"No one mentioned a meeting with Kelly," Dolph said with a low growl.

Harte ignored the other two and focused on Dolph. "The meeting with Kelly must have slipped my mind," he drawled. "Had to get your girl here out of jail since this one wasn't any help."

It was a gamble to throw that fact out there. . . . He probably shouldn't be poking at Nibs. If only he'd had more luck finding his mother. Once she was safe, it would be easy enough to tell Dolph everything he'd seen that night when his fist met Nibsy's face. But until he knew Nibs couldn't hurt her, he was basically muzzled.

"And after?" Dolph asked, his expression grim. "You had plenty of time to tell me."

"I've been a little busy since then," he said, gesturing to the evidence on the table between them. "Besides, didn't you tell me you'd taken care of Paul Kelly? I didn't think he was a problem anymore."

Dolph's jaw tensed, but he didn't respond. *Not a good sign.*

Harte took the momentary reprieve to change the course of the conversation. "What haven't you told me?" he asked Esta.

"Except for what I learned tonight, I've told you everything," she snapped.

"And when were you planning to tell me that?"

"As soon as I saw you, of course. But you got your knickers all in a twist over Dolph and Nibs being here and—"

"What was I supposed to think?" Seeing her with Dolph, not being included in whatever their conversation was—it had emphasized even more starkly how precarious his position was. He was playing them against each other, and if he wasn't careful, he'd end up trapped in the middle.

Esta glared at him. "You were supposed to shut up for a minute and put away that fragile male ego of yours so I could tell you what happened tonight."

"Fine." She was right, not that he'd admit it to her, especially not in front of Dolph, who seemed far too amused with the whole exchange. "So talk."

"As I was about to tell them—and would have told *you*, if you'd given me a second—remember how the Order is having something of a soiree to celebrate the spring equinox? It's in a week, and it seems their usual entertainment has become suddenly unavailable."

"A pity," Dolph said dramatically.

She glanced at Dolph. "Isn't it? But they've found themselves in need of someone at rather short notice. I suggested you, of course," she told Harte, pausing for dramatic effect and enjoying the anticipation in the boy's eyes.

"And?"

She pulled an embossed card from the handbag dangling from her wrist. "We've been invited to perform at Khafre Hall."

PART

IV

THE HISTORY OF NOW

Esta could feel Harte's eyes on her in the darkness of the carriage. Outside the window, the rain-drenched city passed by at a slow, steady pace. *I'll miss this,* she thought with a sudden pang of longing. This city was so different from hers, but it had become home just the same. She loved how it seemed to know it was on the cusp of greatness, as though it were simply waiting for the years to pass and reveal what it would become. Now that she had spent so many weeks walking those cobbled streets, she would always see *this* city there, beneath her own. At night, especially, she would never again need the help of Ishtar's Key to sense this time, this place, sitting just below the present. Just beyond her grasp.

Because there would be no returning. Once she had her stone, she *could* come back, but she knew already that once she left, she never would. There would be no reason to. She could look back on newspapers and reports like the clipping tucked securely in her bodice, but so many of the people she'd come to respect were invisible and unimportant to the men behind desks who wrote history.

She could not let that distract her, though. Against her skin, the waxen envelope with the news clipping reminded her that she had other responsibilities and another place to be. Whatever fondness Esta might have felt for this time, for this city, the news clipping reminded her that she had a duty to the future. She had to make sure that the past remained just as it should have been, or else who knew what her future might hold?

And the only way to do that was to make sure Harte didn't take the Book. To betray him—to betray all of them.

"Are you ready?" he asked, his voice soft.

"Of course," she told him, but she wasn't sure how much of a lie it was.

Not that it mattered anymore. Before the night was over, the Book and the stone would be hers, and she would be gone.

"It'll be fine," he said, his eyes steady. "Just like we practiced." He reached over and ran his fingers over her shoulders, rubbing lightly at the stiff muscles in her neck.

For a moment she felt only a strange, sudden wash of relief, as though all the tension between them, all the distrust and anger drained away with the tension in her muscles. And for a moment she allowed herself to feel real regret for what she was about to do. But no sooner did she let herself relax against the warmth of his fingertips than she also felt the heat of his magic.

She jerked away, her heart pounding in her chest. *I am such an idiot.* "Stay out of my head, Harte."

He stared at her, his expression unreadable until she turned away, wondering what he'd managed to see that had put that look on his face. Wondering what it meant for her careful plans.

They rode the rest of the way in a dangerous silence. She kept her eyes focused out the window, resolutely ignoring him and using the time to gather her thoughts. She could practically feel him watching her, but she refused to turn and give him anything else. There was too much riding on this night. Too much he could have discovered with that single touch.

The carriage came to a clattering stop. "We're here," he said, as though she couldn't see that for herself.

Harte got out of the carriage first and opened a large black umbrella before handing her down as well. Esta glanced up at the driver, Nibsy, who looked wet and miserable sitting in the drizzling rain. She gave him a nod that she hoped seemed confident. She wished she could apologize. After all, in the next two hours she'd betray him as well.

"It's time," Harte said.

She straightened her back and strengthened her resolve. Everything that had happened to her, everything she was, came down to this night. She knew that both Dolph and Harte wanted the Book. Both would try to take it for themselves.

And both would have to lose.

IN THE VIPER PIT

Khafre Hall

❝It's time," Harte said, sensing that Jack was already watching them from the covered portico, but Esta only stared at him with an unreadable expression. He would have been more comfortable to see rage in her eyes, but she was looking at him now with an emotion he couldn't place, and that worried him more than fury would have.

Maybe it had been a mistake to use his affinity on her one more time, but he had to know what he was in for. She'd been so reserved ever since Dolph had shown up unannounced at his apartment, doing everything by the book but never once letting him see what she was thinking. He'd hated it, the tiptoeing around each other. There had always been tension between them, a sense that they were both on different sides of the same game, but he felt like the game had been slipping away from him. And now he knew the truth.

He wished . . . He didn't know what he wished. That he hadn't seen the intentions behind those honey-colored eyes of hers? That he hadn't predicted her duplicity so easily? Or maybe, stupid as he was, he wished that he could stop himself from the inevitability of hurting her? But wishes were for children, and he'd grown up a long time ago. Only one of them could win this game, and it *had* to be him.

"You're going to have to talk to me eventually," he said. "Jack's going to notice if you don't. He'll suspect that something is wrong."

"Don't worry about me." Her expression was devoid of emotion. "I'll do my job. You just make sure to do yours."

Harte glanced back at Nibsy. The boy looked like a drowned rat sitting up in the driver's seat, but his eyes were steady and he wore an expression that warned not to cross him. Harte gave him a nod and pulled Esta's arm through his. She was stiff, clearly not wanting him to touch her. She looked afraid, not like someone who was planning to double-cross him before the night was through.

Looks could be deceiving, he thought to himself, ignoring the pang of regret he felt. *Let the games begin.*

Jack was waiting, nervous and jittery, with a glass of what was probably his usual whiskey already in his hand. He downed it and came to greet them. "Hell of a night, isn't it?" he said, sweat beading at his temples.

Harte extended his hand. "It was good of you to have us, Jack."

Next to him, Harte felt Esta transform. "Jack, *darling* . . ." She pulled herself away from him and held out both of her hands to greet Jack in her rolling accent. "I am *so* looking forward to meeting your friends."

Jack gave her a leering smile that made Harte clench his hands into fists. *She isn't for me,* he reminded himself.

"They're looking forward to meeting you as well," Jack told her, his voice carrying a note of something like lechery. Esta only smiled up at him.

Harte cleared his throat. "Did the equipment for our demonstration arrive?"

Jack didn't take his eyes from Esta. "This afternoon. It's all set up and ready for you."

"Good, good," Harte said, clapping Jack on the shoulder and giving him a bit of a shake. "Should we go in?"

Jack looked suddenly less sure, but he nodded and then led them through a short antechamber lit by torchlike sconces mounted to the wall. There, he gave their names to a man sitting in a caged room that reminded Harte of the ticket booth at the theater. After the man checked over his list and was satisfied, the click of a latch echoed and the wall directly in front of them began to part, allowing the golden glow of the room beyond to spill into the small space.

On the other side of the wall, the building was transformed. Gone were the wood-paneled walls and marble floors of the typical gentleman's club. Instead, walking through the opening in the wall was like stepping into an ancient Egyptian tomb. Gold glinted on the walls, highlighting borders of bright indigo and aquamarine symbols carved into sandstone pillars. Even with the size of the building, Harte hadn't expected anything like this. It was a room meant to inspire, to overwhelm, and Harte hated to admit that it had worked.

"Impressive, isn't it?" Jack said to Esta, who nodded and looked fairly awed herself.

She smiled at Jack, a secret smile that had Harte's stomach going sour. "It's as beautiful as you told me," she murmured.

"This way. We have your demonstration set up in the amphitheater."

They followed Jack to another receiving room. With jewel-toned silks capping the high ceiling, the room was reminiscent of Arabia. Palm trees claimed the walls, and a woman in a sparkling veiled dress performed a dance, gyrating her hips and torso as she snaked her way through the room. As they passed, her violet eyes met Harte's.

Good, he thought. At least that much was in place and going to plan.

The next hour was an interminable parade of the richest men in the city. They each took their turns looking him over as they greeted Esta. As they made their way through the room, Harte was well aware that everyone was watching, expecting him to make a mistake and betray his lack of breeding. He wouldn't give them the satisfaction. Tonight was his, and his alone.

"Well, well," a familiar voice said from just behind him. "Harte Darrigan. You have quite the busy social schedule these days, don't you?"

He stopped midstep, closing his eyes long enough to gather his wits—and his patience—as he forced his mouth into a smile. "Sam Watson," he began, turning to greet the reporter with his usual smile, but he stopped short when he saw who was on Sam's arm. "Evelyn?"

She was draped in black silk and had a satisfied gleam in her eye.

"Harte," she said, her voice smug. "What a lovely surprise." The way her mouth curled up told him to be on his guard. She wasn't any more surprised than she was a natural redhead.

"What are *you* doing here?" Harte asked. The room felt like it was spinning. Evelyn and Esta. Evelyn *here* with Sam Watson. At Khafre Hall. On the night when nothing could go wrong.

Looking him up and down, she smiled. "I could ask the same of you."

"I invited her," Sam said, wrapping an arm around her bare shoulder. "I'm covering the celebration tonight for the *Sun*."

"Are you?" Harte said. "First the Gala at the Met and now this? Why, Watson . . . you've turned into a society columnist."

Fury flashed through the reporter's eyes, but he managed to keep himself controlled. "I don't know, Darrigan. I have a feeling that, like the museum debacle, I'll get a better story than my editors were expecting tonight. Don't you?"

"I'm sure I wouldn't know," Harte said flatly, refusing to react to the clear challenge. "I'm just the floor show. Speaking of which, we should probably go prepare. If you'd excuse us?"

"Of course," Sam said pleasantly enough. "I'm looking forward to seeing what you can pull off tonight." He gave Harte a smile that was all teeth. "Until later?"

Harte gave him a noncommittal nod and then escorted Esta away, toward the doors of the amphitheater.

"What is she doing here?" Esta whispered, once they were far enough away.

"I don't know." But whatever Evelyn was doing, it was nothing good.

"We need to get out of here."

"She's a friend, Esta. She wouldn't do anything—"

Esta grabbed his arm, the first time she'd willingly touched him since the carriage ride. "She *knows*, Harte."

"What?" He shook his head in confusion.

"That day in the theater . . . when you were showing me the glass casket and she came to find you? I'd bet anything she heard you talking about the lost heir, about our plan with Jack."

His mouth felt suddenly dry. "You can't know that for sure. And besides, she's one of us. What would she have to gain by helping Jack?"

Esta pressed her lips together, impatience flashing in her eyes. "I don't know, but why is she *here*? Why tonight? You had to see that look of satisfaction in her eyes. She should be nervous being in a room filled with the Order—we are, and we have a team backing us up. No . . . She's planning something. Who's the man she's with?"

"Sam Watson. He's a reporter for the *New York Sun*."

"Sam Watson?" Her face drained of color.

"She and Sam go way back," Harte explained, making a show of smiling at the people passing with questioning eyes. "It's possible he looked her up because I teased him at the museum." But his instincts were screaming that Esta was right—Evelyn was up to something. And if she *did* know about the lost heir . . . After all the times he'd turned her down, and then after Esta humiliated her that day in his dressing room, she'd have plenty of reasons to hurt them. Especially if she got something out of it herself.

"You don't actually believe that, do you?"

"No," he admitted. "But she must be mad to come here tonight."

"But the payoff would be enormous," Esta said. "She wouldn't be the first Mageus to betray her kind in the hopes of a better life," she added, her expression unreadable. She seemed lost in thought and very, very far away from him.

"Are you okay?"

She blinked and, pressing her lips together, gave him a sure nod. "We should go. I can fake sick, and we'll keep Jack on the hook and try again some other time. It's too much of a risk with her here, *especially* if Evelyn knows."

They probably could get away with calling the whole thing off, but the Order wasn't the only thing Harte had to worry about. If they didn't go through with this, he didn't doubt that Nibs would take it as a reason to retaliate. Harte might be able to save himself tonight, but that would mean damning his mother . . . again.

"We've already tossed the dice," he said numbly. "And now we're just going to deal with where they've fallen."

"But—"

"Come on." He tucked her arm securely through his and led her into the cavernous space of the theater, all the while feeling like he was walking toward his certain doom.

A GOLDEN DAWN

The auditorium looked like one of the old movie palaces that people in Esta's own time were always trying to preserve. It was designed to look like an outdoor Roman amphitheater set under a canopy of sapphire blue. Long-limbed nude statues graced marble railings and towering columns. Above, instead of a ceiling, wisps of enchanted clouds plodded in a steady path across a star-studded sky.

Jack waved to them from the front of the room, near the stage, his expression anxious.

"Are you ready?" Harte murmured.

"Not even a little."

Evelyn knew what they were planning—Esta would stake her life on it—and nothing good could come from that. Especially with how she'd treated the other woman.

She could still fake sick or create some kind of diversion to get out of there. They didn't have to go through with this. They could leave, regroup. Try again when things were safer or more certain . . . But she knew instinctively it was too late for that. There was the news clipping tucked against her skin—the one with Sam Watson's name in the byline—to remind her what was at stake. If she ran now, she might never have another shot at the stone, so she allowed Harte to lead her through the crowd toward where Jack waited near the stage.

At least everyone was in a mood for celebration. The members of the Order and their bejeweled wives were floating on the rivers of champagne they'd been drinking during the cocktail hour, and laughter punctuated conversations all around them.

It's a good sign, she told herself. *It has to be.*

But she couldn't shake the feeling that she was hours, minutes away from knowing once and for all whether everything she'd done was enough. She would either succeed and be back in her own city by daybreak, or she'd—

No. She wouldn't even think about the alternative.

Jack seemed to have relaxed a little, though that might have had something to do with the glass of amber liquid in his hand. He led them backstage, where they would wait for their cue, and then he left them to take his own place in the audience.

From their vantage point, they could see the entire crowd as they took their seats and turned their pale faces to the man on the stage.

The men and the women in the audience didn't look like monsters. None of the crews of rough boys who patrolled the Bowery looking for Mageus were sitting in those seats. The silk-clad women, the tuxedoed men . . . she would wager that none had ever gotten their hands dirty in that way. Maybe they didn't know what the effects of the Order were. Maybe they didn't realize the pain and suffering the Order of Ortus Aurea caused for the people in the streets of lower Manhattan.

But the moment the High Princept—one of the highest-ranking members—stepped forward to speak, any charitable thought she might have been entertaining evaporated.

"As above," the High Princept called out, and the audience responded as one with the rest of the phrase, "so below."

"We gather tonight to celebrate the equinox, that time of balancing, of new birth, a reminder of our solemn duty to our people, to our way of life."

"I think I'm going to be sick," Esta whispered.

Harte shushed her, but his jaw was tight, his hands clenched in fists at his sides, so she had a feeling he felt the same.

"We gather together this night, brothers who have dedicated themselves to the principles of Reason and the project begun by our forefathers, pillars of the Enlightenment," the High Princept droned on. His tone and cadence made clear that this was a well-worn speech. "We stand on the shoulders of giants, and we build on what the founders of this great nation have accomplished. As the great thinker John Locke reminds us, no man's knowledge can go beyond his experience, and so we have made it our duty to immerse ourselves in experience, to push the boundaries of what is known about the Great Chain of Being, unlocking its secrets with our dedication and work."

The audience erupted into applause, and the speaker waited for it to subside, a small smile threatening at the corners of his mouth. The energy in the room was electric, but it wasn't the warmth of magic. Instead, the room was filled with the pulse of excitement that often runs through a mob before they explode into action: the sizzle of electrons, the tang of ozone, and the heady sense of righteousness that can only come from belief in purpose, no matter how insidious that belief may be. No matter the hate that might sustain itself from that darkly beating heart.

The Princept went on, buoyed by the crowd: "We have worked tirelessly for more than a century now to increase our knowledge for the good of our land, and this land owes our Order a great debt. Since its beginning, the Order of Ortus Aurea has continued the project of Enlightenment on these shores. But now we face an ever-growing threat. Hidden among those who would come to our shores with an innocent willingness to become part of our great nation is an undesirable element."

Someone in the crowd shouted out a slur, as the rest of the audience rustled. But the High Princept merely smiled benevolently.

"Yes. These Mageus come not with open hearts, willing to throw off the superstitions of their past, but with insidious intent. They hide in the shadows of our society, using their powers to take advantage of the innocent, set on the degradation of our standard of living and the debasement of our citizenry. It is against this element that we have worked tirelessly, for there is no cause more important than the character of our citizenship and the standard of living of our people.

"So let us join together to reaffirm our purpose and our dedication to this great land. Let us welcome all those who come to our shores willing to take up the mantle of democracy and Reason. But let us be always aware that there are those who pose a threat to our very way of life. For their power, uncontrolled and based not upon study and Reason but from uneducated impulse, is the antithesis of the foundations of democracy. Should their power be allowed to take root in this land, it would leave the once fertile soil of our nation barren and drained of promise.

"Let us recommit this day to our divine calling and prepare for a new dawn, a golden dawn of Reason and Science to balance against this danger in our midst. . . ."

"I'm definitely going to be sick," Esta whispered to Harte as the High Princept finished his speech to a thunderous round of applause from the audience. She'd known—of *course* she'd known—what the Order stood for, but to have to stand and face it, to pretend that the words weren't about her, about everyone she knew and cared for?

"Just focus on what we have to do," Harte told her. "Nothing else matters." He turned to her. "Block all of that out. You can't let them get into your head, especially not right now."

The High Princept raised his arms until the crowded amphitheater went quiet. "In celebration of this night, we have for your enjoyment a demonstration of the power of Reason . . . the very power our hallowed organization champions. May I present Mr. Darrigan, who has pulled himself up from obscurity through the study of the occult sciences, and his assistant, Miss von Filosik, daughter of the late baron, to whom the study of alchemy owes so much."

It was time. There was nowhere to go but out onto the stage. Harte offered his hand, and she placed her gloved palm in his as she pasted a brilliant smile on her face and allowed him to lead her onward into the glow of the footlights.

THE CARD SWITCH

I f he hadn't spent so many years learning the delicate art of pretending, Harte might have hesitated. He might have felt weakened by the onslaught of the Princept's speech, by the ragged anger simmering in the room. But he'd lived on the edge of survival for so long that he simply relied on the skills that had become instinct and took the stage with his usual practiced flair. Esta, he could tell, was nervous. He could sense the tension in her posture, and he could see the fear in her eyes. He only hoped the footlights were too bright for the audience to see it as well.

He launched into some of his better effects—the Indian needle trick and a daring manipulation of fire, to start with. Then he gestured offstage for their final demonstration of the evening, and the stagehands rolled out a large, gleaming vault.

Esta looked at Harte, her eyes wide. Confused.

He knew what she was thinking. They had prepared all week for her to perform the Glass Casket. They'd prepared for *her* to be the one who stole the Book and the artifacts. But after what he'd learned from Nibsy, he hadn't trusted her not to fall for the boy's innocent act like everyone else. While they'd practiced, he'd made his own plans—a card switch on a much larger scale. At first he had thought to protect her so she couldn't be implicated when Dolph or Nibs found out what he'd done. But now that he knew what she'd planned, he was glad he'd kept his secrets.

He gave her a wink that would look like little more than a playful exchange to the audience, but he knew she would understand. *I'm a step ahead of you.* Because he'd worked too long and had come too far to be stopped by something as cliché as a pretty face now. And with the threat of Jack's machine, there was too much at risk.

Stepping to the front of the stage, Harte lifted his arm and saluted the audience. Never before had there been so much at stake in a performance. Never before had an audience been so dangerous. But having the odds stacked against him had never stopped him before, and it wouldn't stop him from doing what needed to be done now.

"Gentlemen . . . ?" He turned to the Princept who'd introduced him and the other high-ranking man at his side. "If you would come up and inspect this vault? Be thorough. Leave no doubt as to its durability."

"Actually," the Princept said, "we've arranged a little surprise for you." He gave a nod to someone offstage, and Sam Watson appeared with a set of chains and cuffs. Evelyn walked beside him, eating up the spotlight as she came closer to them.

Harte's throat went tight as Sam gave him a sharp-toothed smile that promised nothing good. But he kept his expression calm, indifferent, even as his mind raced with all the possibilities about how everything was about to go sour.

"We've all heard what you're capable of, Mr. Darrigan, so we hope you'll agree to a little challenge. Instead of using your own chains, I'm sure you wouldn't mind testing your abilities against the locks *we* provide. These cuffs were brought straight from the Halls of Justice, and all the locks and chains have been kept under my supervision until this moment to ensure they haven't been tampered with in any way. I trust that won't be a problem?"

"Of course not." Harte gave Sam his most charming smile, relieved. Handcuffs and chains were nothing to him. He'd made an art of escaping his whole life. If this was all they could throw at him, he could take it.

Esta, however, looked considerably less sure.

As they clapped him in the handcuffs and wrapped him in chains, the Princept checked over the safe, and when he was satisfied, he confirmed its integrity to the waiting crowd.

When they were finished securing him, Harte turned to the audience. "This safe is two-inch-thick steel with a double-bolt mechanism," he told the waiting crowd. "Once inside, a person would have ten minutes to escape before the air begins to thin. After twenty minutes, they would become light-headed and lose all sense of reason. At thirty minutes, they would begin to lose consciousness. At forty-five minutes, the air would run out." He paused dramatically, allowing the silence to settle over the audience. "To remain trapped so long would mean certain death . . . unless, of course, a person could manipulate the very matter of these bonds and free himself before that happens. Unless a person could command the very air to sustain him."

An interested murmuring rustled through the audience.

He ignored the unfamiliar weight of the handcuffs. "Gentlemen," he said, addressing the men who had chained him. "If you would be so kind as to lock me in?"

CHECKMATE

D olph Saunders stepped from the noise of The Devil's Own into the blessed, blessed silence of the night. He didn't waste time, but made his way swiftly along the empty street, sticking to the shadows. He had one more stop to make before he returned to the Strega to wait for news.

The cemetery was bathed in the wan light of the moon. He was only twenty-six, but he felt the aches of a much older man. He was weary, wrung out. Tired of the constant games. The constant need to be two steps ahead of the danger dogging at his heels.

If all went well tonight, those games would be at an end. One way or another.

"It's finished, Streghina. Tonight it will be done. *And you will be avenged*," he added softly. Though he wasn't sure why, for surely the dead could hear what was in the deepest recesses of his worn and fractured heart.

He knelt at the foot of the grave Leena now shared with their child, the one she'd lost because of what he'd done, and prayed for her forgiveness. He prayed that what he was doing—his attempt to get the Book and to bring down the Brink and the Order once and for all—would make up for all he had done, but before he was finished, Dolph sensed that someone had entered the cemetery.

The intruder waited in the shadows near the gate, allowing Dolph the privacy of his audience with the dead, but Dolph could feel his impatience.

"What is it, Nibsy?" he said, speaking into the night. He didn't take

419

his eyes from the grave as the boy approached him. "It can't already be done?" he asked, knowing that no good news would have come so soon.

"No, it's not. Not yet," Nibsy said.

The shot went off, shattering the night before Dolph even realized the boy was holding a gun, before he could turn and fight.

"But you are."

As Dolph slumped onto Leena's grave, everything fell into place.

In that instant, Dolph knew what he should have figured out long before but had been too willingly blind to see. Of course it had been Nibs, the very person who had guided his every decision after he lost Leena. The one who had known what the Brink took from him, who had suggested that he use Paul Kelly to pressure Harte.

Even before all of that, it was Nibs who had assured him that Leena would be safe. How deep had the boy's game gone? How blind had Dolph been in his willingness to trust?

He'd wanted an ace in his pocket and had chosen a serpent instead.

But the knowledge had come too late. He felt his heart beat once, twice more, and then the cold night faded as the world around him went dark.

A SECRET TOLD

Khafre Hall

The click of the heavy safe door swinging open echoed through the room. Esta could only watch as the men began to wrestle Harte into the massive safe. They'd rehearsed for this moment, and every single time, the rehearsal involved *her* getting into the Glass Casket. *Her* making her way into the Mysterium. *Her* finding the Book and the stone, and then *her* taking them, sifting through the layers of time and giving them to Professor Lachlan, where they belonged.

She'd been so stupid not to be prepared for him doing something like this, but she wouldn't go down without a fight.

"Wait!" she shouted, drawing the attention of the men to her. "A kiss for luck?"

The men exchanged glances before shrugging and stepping aside.

"She could have a key," Evelyn said. "You should check her to be sure."

But if Evelyn had thought to expose her, it didn't work. It took only a moment for Esta to open her mouth and demonstrate that she hadn't hidden a key or pick there, and then they let her by.

Harte's expression was stony as she approached him.

"Good luck, darling," she said, loud enough for anyone onstage to hear as she slid her arms around his neck and tilted her face toward him. As her lips came closer to his, she saw the question—the challenge—in his eye. And she pulled time still.

He gasped as the world went slow around him, his eyes wide with confusion, and then, with wonder. "So this is what you do," he murmured. "This is your affinity?"

"Shut up and focus," she snapped. "We don't have much time."

"It looks like we have all the time in the world," he said wryly as he nodded to the nearly frozen room around them.

"It's only slowed, not stopped completely. I won't be able to hold it indefinitely." She shook him a little. "What the *hell* are you doing?"

"I could ask the same of you," he said coldly. "But I already know."

Her stomach sank at the memory of his touch in the carriage. "I'm not the one switching the act up." But the words sounded weak, even to her.

"No?" he asked. "You weren't planning to take everything and leave us all holding the bag?

"You don't understand—"

"You told me the old man—your father—was dead, but that's not true, is it? You were going to take him the Book," he said, confirming her worst fears. "I'd started to trust you. *Everyone* trusted you."

"Maybe they shouldn't have." Her voice came out so much flatter, so much less confident than she'd intended.

Suddenly, she was painfully aware of the way the light slanted, the way the motes of dust hung suspended and unmoving around them in the beams of the footlights, like stars come to earth. She wanted to explain everything, tell him exactly why she needed the Book, but he was right. She'd take the Book back to Professor Lachlan like she was supposed to, but she couldn't lie to herself about what it meant for the people here.

"Nothing's more important than the job I have to do," she whispered, willing him to understand.

"I sure hope that's true." Harte's expression shuttered. "Because they'll go after Dolph, you know. They'll go after all those friends of yours."

"They'll go after them anyway. I *have to* take the Book. To protect it. *To protect them.* If I don't do this, they're dead—Dolph, Nibsy. Who knows who else."

His eyes went cold. "Is that all Nibsy gets out of your duplicity?"

"This doesn't have anything to do with him."

Harte laughed, a derisive huff of air that sounded as cracked and broken as the trust between them. "This has *everything* to do with him."

He wasn't making any sense, but she had to make him understand. She had to convince him. "If you take the Book now, every Mageus in this city will be lost."

"They're lost if I don't take the Book," he said, and he told her about the machine that Jack had built.

"Why didn't you tell me that morning?"

"Probably for the same reason you didn't you tell me the truth about the old man you called your father. You've never trusted me."

"And for good reason. Look at what you are doing! You're leaving me at the Order's mercy while you make off with the Book."

"You don't get it, do you? Nothing about this is meant to hurt you," he said, regret thick in his voice. "This was all just supposed to be misdirection, to take the suspicion away from you. I was going to come back for you. We were going to get out of the city together. Destroy the Book together. . . . Before I saw what I saw. Before I understood what you're planning."

Her chest tightened. "That's easy for you to say now."

"No, it's not. It's the hardest thing in the world to admit to what you gave up." He leaned his head toward her until their foreheads touched. "Unless you've changed your mind? Come with me. Help me destroy the Book. It's the only way to ensure the Mageus are safe from Jack and all those like him."

"I can't," she said, hating herself a little for how much she wanted to say yes. "Even if I wanted to, it would never work."

He pulled away from her, his expression stony from her rejection.

She ignored the hurt in his eyes, the anger in his expression. "This isn't about me," she whispered to him. "This is so much bigger than the two of us. Your life won't mean anything if you go through with this. If you take the Book, maybe you will keep Jack away from it, but you'll also condemn all of our kind to another century of the Order's control. You will condemn magic—and all Mageus with it—to a weakened half-life of existence. And it will *never* recover," she told him. "*We* will never recover. There is no walking away from this."

"You can't know that."

"I *do*. I've seen it. I've *lived* it. I know firsthand what the effect of your choices will do to our kind and to our world if you go through with this. But if you stop this now, maybe we can still fix things. Maybe we can change *everything*."

He looked at her, his stormy eyes testing her for the truth in her words. She knew they were unbelievable, but this was her only chance to finish what she'd started by coming here.

"You have to believe me." Esta took his face in her hands, feeling the cleanly shaven cheeks and the warmth of his skin beneath her fingers. "And *you* know how to see if I'm telling you the truth."

Someday, maybe she would share a kiss that was more than deception and manipulation. Someday, maybe she would press her lips against someone else's for no other reason than desire or aching want. *Maybe*.

But today was not that day.

She closed the distance between them, and at the very moment she pressed her lips against his, she let go of her hold on time. As the world spun back into motion, she put every piece of herself into the kiss, pulling him toward her, tangling her mouth against his, willing him to take what he would as she opened her mind to him. Because if he got the stone, if he took the Book and destroyed it, she would be lost. *Everything* would be lost.

His lips were impassive at first, and her stomach twisted with the understanding that he wouldn't take what she was offering. But then she felt the pulse of his magic, warm and now more familiar than it should have been. She didn't pull back or flinch away this time. Instead she bade him take all he would. His magic wrapped around her as his lips opened against hers, and she allowed herself to be laid bare, to risk everything for the chance that he wouldn't pursue this course he had set them on.

It was only when a smattering of applause came from the audience that she remembered where she was and what they were doing. She stepped back from him, her cheeks hot, but Harte's expression was impassive. Unreadable.

It doesn't matter if he believes me, she told herself. *All I have to do is slow time and I can get away—*

"Why don't you come stand with me, sweetheart?" Sam Watson said, taking her by the arm and pulling her away from the safe before she could do anything. He didn't release her arm, but he gave her a wink. "Best to make sure there's no question that your Mr. Darrigan doesn't have any assistance."

"Of course," she murmured, eyeing his hold on her arm. As long as he was touching her, she couldn't use her affinity, not without bringing him with her. She couldn't do anything about Harte or what he might have planned for the Book. All she could do was watch as they locked him into the safe and wait. And hope that what she'd told him had been enough.

THE MYSTERIUM

Still stunned by what Esta had shown him, Harte moved by instinct, pushing against the back of the vault to loosen the bolts there, adjusting his arms to slip free from the chains, all the while struggling to understand what he'd just seen.

What he'd found when he pushed into her mind was too unbelievable. Like something out of H. G. Wells. *She had to be lying.*

But he knew he would have been able to see the lie in her intentions, and no matter how he searched, there hadn't been one there. His head swirled with the strange images as he let himself out of the back of the safe, where Jianyu was already waiting, obscuring the view of anyone who might be watching. Together they moved to the back of the stage. When Harte saw the coast was clear for him to slip out into the hallway beyond, he gave Jianyu a nod to let him know he was good.

What he'd seen in Esta's mind changed nothing.

It changed everything.

As he came around the corner, he almost ran directly into Viola, who was hiding in the shadows. She was now dressed in black, looking every inch the assassin.

"Where's Esta?"

"On the stage, where she's supposed to be."

"This was not the plan."

He felt the searing energy of her magic a second before his head felt like it was being pressed in a vise. His vision started to blur, and he had the sense that at any moment everything could go black. "Dolph didn't tell you the whole plan," Harte said, fighting past the urge to scream from the pressure behind his eyes.

Viola raised a single arched brow in his direction, and a spike of pain shot through his chest. "Dolph trusts me."

"Dolph doesn't trust anyone right now," he gasped. "No one had the entire plan except me and him." Another bolt of pain rocketed through his chest, nearly making his legs give out. "It's better this way. They won't be able to accuse her of anything as long as she's standing on the stage with them. If they can't accuse her, they won't be able to trace it back to Dolph," he said, and the pressure eased a little. "Besides, she's not alone. Jianyu is there, isn't he? He'll make sure she gets out."

She lifted one of her knives to his throat. "I don't like this."

He met her glare head-on, fighting past the remaining pain. "We can argue about this, or we can finish what we came to do and get out of here."

Viola glared at him a moment longer, and then the pressure in his head eased completely, and he almost collapsed from the relief of it. "If you're lying to me, you won't make it out of this place alive."

She gave him a jerk of her head, and he followed her silently back through the Egyptian room. They stayed to the edges of the chamber, using the shadows of the great Egyptian gods to conceal themselves, until they came to the other side.

Gilded double doors carved with elaborate renderings of the tree of life marked the entrance to the Mysterium. If Jack had been correct, the passage behind those doors was available only to the Inner Circle, the highest and most exclusive members of the Order. Jack himself had never seen what lay beyond those doors, and if Harte had any say in it, he never would.

Viola dispatched the guard on the other side of the door before he could so much as lift a finger to sound an alarm. Once they were through, they found a wide hall that slanted downward, like a ramp. The floor was made of a polished black granite that reflected the light of the greenish lamps that hung from the walls, which were carved with gilded alchemical symbols. From where they were standing, they couldn't see the end of the hall. It passed downward, into the earth, and then cut to the right around a sharp corner.

Harte and Viola moved quickly, following the passage until it ended at a brass cage.

"Come on," Harte said, pulling the grated door of the elevator aside.

Viola hesitated. "You want me to get into that?"

"Unless you'd rather wait here." He climbed into the elevator's cage, and Viola, scowling at him, stepped warily into the small boxlike room.

Once she was in, he secured the gate and pressed the lever to make the elevator start its slow descent. The smooth granite turned to concrete and then bedrock as they continued down, rumbling into the depths of the building—into the very heart of the island itself.

"We should be ready for anything," he said, but when he glanced over, Viola already had her knives out.

When the elevator finally rattled to a stop at the bottom, Harte could hear water running nearby. The air was cool and damp. No one was waiting for them as they exited the elevator, but when they stepped out, they found another set of double doors, this time cast in iron and carved with mirror images of the Philosopher's Hand.

The closer they got to the doors, though, the more he could feel the cold energy that permeated them. Jack hadn't mentioned anything about protection on the Mysterium itself, but now that they were faced with entering it, Harte wasn't sure if they could.

"There's no way through that," he told Viola, feeling the sudden overwhelming reality that every risk he'd taken that night had been for nothing. "This isn't going to work. I need to get back onstage before—"

But Viola didn't seem bothered. She took a small item from an inner pocket and gestured toward the doors. "Dolph had a feeling we would find something like this."

"What is that?" he asked, eyeing the piece of pinkish stone she was holding. There was something carved on its surface, writing he couldn't make out.

"It's what we took from the museum—an amulet in the form of a seal. If Dolph's right, the inscription should break whatever protection this is."

As he motioned her forward, he wondered if it was the same piece Jack had been interested in. She held the object loosely between her index finger and thumb, and then she began rolling it over the door.

"To break false magic," Viola said, "you need to use false magic." She drew an intricate design of circles and concentric shapes onto the door, and as she worked, the seal left a glowing imprint of the markings from its surface. The markings began to swell and bleed over, until the entire door was alight with energy. All at once, the light broke, and the cold drained away from the space, until only the door was left.

Harte found himself immediately grateful that he hadn't turned Dolph over to the police as he'd considered after the Metropolitan burglary. Without the seal, they never would have gotten past those doors.

He gave a silent jerk of his head, and together he and Viola slipped cautiously into the Mysterium. On the other side of the doors, they found themselves in a cathedral-like chamber with a huge dome. The whole space was lit by the same otherworldly flames as the hallway above. A chemical reaction of some sort, he supposed.

They stepped farther into the room, toward a tall, square table in the middle. Its four legs stood atop round silver discs. On the center of it, a low golden bowl held a crystalline substance that looked neither liquid nor solid but seemed to glow from within. Next to the bowl lay a necklace with an enormous turquoise gem and a silver cuff he'd seen before—in the images Esta had given to him just minutes ago when she'd kissed him onstage.

It was yet another sign that he couldn't simply dismiss what she'd shown him. She couldn't have known what the cuff looked like unless everything she'd shown him was true.

Around the circumference of the room, five greenish lamps threw their eerie light up the curved stone walls, and three of the lamps had bodies lying in the pallid beam of their light, suspended in air as though on an invisible table.

"Madonna," Viola whispered, crossing herself. "I know these." She walked toward the nearest body, a man with graying hair and a thick beard. He was dressed in a white robe, his hands were crossed over his chest, and on his left index finger was a ring with a huge stone so clear it looked almost liquid. "This is Krzysztof Zeranski. He went missing a few weeks ago." She walked to the next body, a woman with light hair capped by a golden crown. She too was dressed in a white robe, and she too was unconscious. "Frieda Weber."

The final body was on the other side of the room, but even in the dim light, even from that distance, they could make out the vivid copper of Bridget Malone's curling hair. Viola walked over, her hand extended as though she could stop what had already happened. "No," she whispered, glancing back at Harte. "She disappeared the night of the Haymarket raid."

Bridget wasn't wearing a jewel, as the other two were. The blade of a dagger was plunged into her middle. "She's still breathing," Harte said, even as he knew that such a thing couldn't be. Not skewered by the knife as she was.

"But not bleeding."

"Should we help them?" Harte wondered out loud.

Viola shook her head. "I don't think there's anything to be done. We need to find the Book and get out of here." She walked over and examined the table. "I've seen these signs before," she said, pointing to the four discs the legs of the table rested on.

Harte frowned as he studied them. They were complex geometric designs—a pentagram inside of other shapes, all ringed by concentric circles. "I haven't."

"Dolph has a painting, one he took from the museum. This symbol is depicted there." She glanced up at him, her expression determined. "This is it."

As he looked around for some sign of the Book, he noticed that the entire floor of the chamber was a dazzlingly vivid mosaic of the tree of life made from precious stones. The branches sprouted from the central trunk, and at the end of each of the five limbs were five empty indentations in the floor. It was something of a puzzle, he realized—an enormous lock with a five-part key.

"I think we need to unlock it," he told her.

"Unlock what?"

"This image. The tree of life is an alchemical recipe. In alchemy, the pictures are symbols of elements or chemical reactions. I think the floor is a larger version of one. If we want to find the Book, I think we have to complete the formula." He looked around the room for some answer, and then he realized. "The cuff and the necklace—bring them over here."

He tried to fit the necklace and then the cuff into one of the indentations, but neither fit, so he moved on to the next and then the next, until he found the one that worked for the necklace. As the turquoise stone slid into place, its entire branch began to glow, as if the gemstones that formed it were lit from within. Then he repeated the process to find the spot for the cuff.

When the stone in the cuff clicked into place, he turned to Viola, who had been watching with a wary crease between her brows. "We need to get those as well," he said, meaning the jewels on the bodies at the edge of the room.

She frowned, but gave him a nod.

They approached Krzysztof first, but when Viola reached for the ring, she drew her hand back. "It feels like death. How are we supposed to get them?"

"As quickly as we can," he told her. "You still have that seal?"

She nodded and, understanding, traced it over Krzysztof's fingers and the ring.

"Let's give it a try," he said when the entire hand was aglow with the imprints from the seal. His fingers twitched as he readied himself. He could have used Esta right then, with her ability to lift any object in a blink, and for a heartbeat he regretted leaving her behind on that stage. But then he steadied himself and focused on what he needed to do.

The moment his finger touched the ring, he felt cold energy prickle along his fingertips, but he pulled it off as quickly as he could. As soon as it slipped free of Krzysztof's finger, the man's body fell lifeless to the floor. Viola cursed and crossed herself again, but Harte forced himself to keep moving. They were taking too long already.

"I'll work on this one. You do Frieda."

He found the location for the ring and then together they found the indent where the crown fit, before they turned to Bridget.

"We'll have to take out the knife," he realized. His stomach turned with the very thought of it. "You're better with knives than I am."

Viola only glared at him, so he traced the seal around the place where the knife was protruding from Bridget's stomach, and when he couldn't delay any longer, he grasped its garnet-encrusted hilt and pulled hard. He felt the resistance of flesh and muscle against the knife, heard the suck of her body as it released the metal. Bridget fell, deadweight, to the floor, and blood began to ooze from the wound.

Harte turned away before his stomach revolted and focused on the task at hand. There was one space left, and he had to insert the knife vertically, so its blade sank into the glittering floor. When the stone in its hilt finally clicked into place, the last branch lit and the entire floor began to shake. And then it began to move.

The altar in the center began to rise, floating on the silvery discs. Beneath it, a portion of the floor lifted as well, and as the thick column of the floor rose, Harte saw that the altar was actually the top of a much larger cabinet, and within the cabinet was a book.

They approached slowly, watchful in case the table above them was some kind of trap. The Book didn't look like anything special—it was small, no bigger than any of the ledgers Shorty used at the theater to keep track of ticket sales. The cover was crackled and dark with age, and it bore the same geometric design as the silver disks on the floor. Its pages hung out unevenly, as if the book had been added to over the years.

"That's it?" Viola asked, her voice laced with disgust. "All of this mess, all of this waste, and it's an ugly little thing?"

Harte reached his hand out slowly, waiting for some other trap. The moment his fingertips made contact with the cover, the green flames on the walls rose, flashing in a bright explosion of color that both he and Viola backed away from. Smoke filled the air, sickening and sweet and too familiar. *Opium.*

"We need to go," she said, reaching for the Book.

But Harte had not come so far to lose now. Before she could get the Book, he grabbed it.

The moment his fingers were around its cover, a hot, searing energy shot up his arm and into his chest, and his head was filled with the sounds of hundreds of voices. *Thousands of voices.* The noise lasted only a few seconds, but to Harte it felt like a never-ending barrage of screams and chants and voices in languages he didn't have words to describe. It felt as if time were standing still as they assaulted him, and then, just as quickly as they came, they were gone.

Or if not gone, they quieted. He could feel them still, inside of his head. Inside of *him.* They felt hungry.

He shook himself, trying to dismiss the last of the noise still whispering at the edges of his mind. He shouldn't have been able to understand the strange languages, but he understood what they were trying to tell him. Touching the Book felt like reading a person—all impressions and images—but stronger, clearer.

All at once he understood how wrong he had been about everything. How shortsighted they all had been to misunderstand so thoroughly. All at once he knew what had to be done.

"What is it?" Viola asked when he just stood there with the Book in his hands.

"Nothing," he said as he placed the Book in a bag and then went around the room to collect the other artifacts. "Let's go." He tucked the bag under his coat as the table began descending again. "I need to get back into the safe before they realize I'm gone or the whole thing is blown."

"I'll take that first," she said, holding him at knifepoint. He began to feel a sharp driving pressure inside his skull, Viola's way of warning him not to push.

He hesitated for a moment. But with voices still haunting his mind, urging him on, he knew what he was meant to do.

The opium smoke was growing thick in the room, but he wasn't sure how much it had affected her. He'd have to take his chances that it had weakened her enough for him to get away. Before she could make the pain in his head any worse, he threw the bag into the air, and when her eyes followed it, he attacked.

THE REVEAL

The minutes ticked by.
    Ten.
    Fifteen.

What's taking so long? Esta didn't doubt that Harte had a way out of the safe. She'd seen him do more difficult escapes before—at least the safe wasn't filled with water—but he wasn't a thief. Once Harte was out, she had no idea how he would be able to manage the rest on his own before the Order realized what was happening.

Twenty minutes.

The audience began to murmur expectantly. Esta forced herself to keep a pleasant, unworried smile pasted on her face, but she felt every pair of eyes in the audience focused on her.

"It's taking him quite a while," the High Princept said, his expression unsure.

She knew he was worried. It was one thing to play a harmless prank on a performer, but it was another to watch a man possibly dying onstage while you stood by doing nothing to help.

Sam Watson looked a little too pleased. He leaned over as though to whisper but spoke loud enough that anyone onstage could have heard him. "Perhaps the great Harte Darrigan isn't quite the master of the elements he claims to be?"

Across the stage, Evelyn smirked.

"I'm sure you're mistaken," Esta said, trying to pull away without much luck. "I have every faith he will succeed. He has command over forces far beyond your understanding."

But as the seconds ticked by, that faith began to falter.

At half an hour, the audience was shouting for them to open the safe and let the magician out, but Esta told them to wait. If there was any hope that giving up all her secrets had worked, she needed to give Harte time—to get the Book and the artifacts and to get back into the safe, so they could both escape together.

Across the stage, the High Princept was growing more agitated, and Evelyn was watching with her red mouth drawn into a smirk and her eyes bright with anticipation. A moment later she touched the High Princept on the arm and leaned over to whisper something into his ear.

The old man's eyes went curiously blank, and though he seemed completely calm, he barked for the vault to be opened. *Evelyn's doing.*

The audience went quiet as the combination was given and the large tumbler of the lock was rotated carefully. Esta tried to pull herself away from Sam Watson, who seemed to have a grip of steel. If she could just get away, she could slow time and find Harte. She could maybe even get him back into that safe before anyone understood what was happening.

But before she could find a way to disentangle herself from the reporter, the door swung open.

A gasp swept over the theater when the audience realized Harte was no longer in the safe.

"It's the girl!" Evelyn said, pointing at Esta as she came across the stage to where Sam still held on to her. "I told you, didn't I? I warned you they were up to something."

"So you did," Sam Watson said as he gripped her arm even more tightly and jerked her around to face the High Princept.

"This is all part of the effect . . . part of the act," Esta tried to tell them, but she couldn't keep the tremor out of her voice. "You simply have to close the safe and give him a chance to reappear."

"She's lying," Evelyn said, walking across the stage to where Sam Watson held Esta. "Harte Darrigan makes other people disappear. He never gives up the stage on his own. He's up to something, and she's helping him, just like I told you. She's no baron's daughter. It's all a con. I heard them myself. 'Here's to bringing down the Order.' Isn't that what you said?"

Esta shook her head, but she couldn't force out the words.

"Where's the magician?" the Princept snarled, so close to her face that she could smell the alcohol on his breath. "Where is Darrigan?"

"I don't know," she said honestly. Not that he would believe her. Not that *any* of them would believe her.

"Lock the entire building down," the High Princept shouted, his aged face turning an alarming shade of red. "I want every inch of this place searched until he's found. And you—" He pointed at Jack Grew, who was sitting white-faced and wide-eyed in the front row. "This is *your* fault. I won't forget that *you* were the one who brought them here." Then he turned to Sam Watson. "Take her to the safe room, and if you ever want a chance at full membership, do *not* let her get away."

The Princept stormed off down the steps, into the chaotic crowd, leaving Esta trapped by Sam Watson's strong grip. The theater had erupted into chaos.

She tried to shake off Watson, but every time she tried to maneuver, he countered it easily. Finally, he had her pinned, so she couldn't move.

"Please . . . this is a simple misunderstanding. I had nothing to do with him disappearing."

"Shut your lying mouth," Watson said, pulling her arms back until her joints screamed in pain. "You don't think I know you were a part of this too? I know you're one of them—" Before he could finish, Watson went stiff and released his hold on her. Suddenly, his head snapped backward, and then he buckled forward, doubling over and falling to the floor.

Esta stared, shocked. "Jianyu?" She didn't have time to react before Jianyu materialized before her.

"Come," he said, gesturing toward the back of the theater, where a large man stood in their way.

Jianyu put his arms up, ready, but she grabbed his hand instead and pulled at time. All around them, the movement in the room went slow. The frantic activity stilled. Men in tuxedos halted midstep as they tried to climb over one another, their faces portraits of rage and fear. Evelyn's overly painted face froze in its look of shocked surprise as she reached for Sam, who was now lying on the floor.

Jianyu's eyes went wide, and then he gave her a slow smile. "I see," he said, nodding with appreciation. "Come. We'll go together." She watched as he maneuvered the small disks in his hand and saw the shadow fall around them. "It's safer this way." Then he started to lead her in the direction of the rear of the stage.

"We have to stop Harte," she told him, pulling in the opposite direction. "He changed the act. He's going after the Book."

"I know," Jianyu said, refusing to go.

"You know?"

"It was all part of the plan." Jianyu gave her another tug, and she was confused enough that she let herself be pulled toward the room styled like an Egyptian tomb. When they found themselves back in that ornate chamber, she pulled him to a stop.

"I don't understand." All around them the building was silent, and the eyes of the enormous figures lining the walls seemed to watch them. "You *knew* he was going to switch the act on me?"

Jianyu nodded. "He came to Dolph with the idea a couple of days ago. He said he wanted to draw suspicion away from you."

"No, that's not right. It's another trick," she said, sure that it was only one more level of Harte Darrigan's game. It had to be.

"If it's a trick, Viola will dispense with him soon enough. Come."

She didn't trust Harte, but she knew what Viola could do, so Esta allowed Jianyu to lead her through the chaos of the building and out into the street.

Outside, the night was alive with confusion. Already she could hear the clanging sound of the fire brigades rushing toward them. There were flames lighting the western edge of the building, the dark smoke pouring out of broken windows. They used the confusion to dart away, toward the place where Dolph's carriage was waiting.

When they made it to the carriage, Nibs looked down at them from the driver's seat.

"Where's Darrigan?"

"He's not out yet?" Jianyu asked.

Nibs shook his head.

Esta's chest felt too tight to draw breath. All she'd shown him, and it hadn't been enough.

She heard the sound of footsteps coming toward them, and they all turned as one. For a heartbeat, hope flared in Esta's chest. For the space of a second, she expected to see Harte.

But it was Viola, dressed all in black and running toward them. "Go!" she shouted as a group of men stormed out the door behind her. She turned long enough to throw a knife back at them, hitting one in the throat so he crumpled to the street.

"But Darrigan—" Nibs said as Viola climbed into the cab.

"It doesn't matter. I have the Book," Viola told him.

"You're sure?" Nibs asked, his eyes flashing up to the building.

"I took care of him."

"What do you mean?" Esta asked, not wanting to really understand. But understanding just the same.

"He's gone, capisce?" She held up the bag. "We have what we came for." Viola slammed the door of the carriage.

Nibsy whipped the horses into action, and the carriage leaped away, leaving Harte Darrigan behind them.

Viola's eyes met Esta's. "I'm sorry," she said, and there was real regret, real pain in them. "I know the two of you had grown close, but I couldn't let him take this." Viola reached across the carriage and touched Esta's knee gently. "If there was another way—"

"I know," Esta told her truthfully. But she couldn't stop the burn of tears behind her eyes.

"You truly killed him?" Jianyu asked.

"He attacked me first."

Jianyu frowned. "Dolph trusted him."

Viola's eyes met his. "He shouldn't have."

Esta turned away from them both, pretending to stare out of the window of the carriage. Instead, she removed the clipping from the bodice of her dress. Despite everything that had gone wrong, it gave her some relief to see that it had returned to its original form.

No, Dolph never should have trusted Harte Darrigan, but at least he hadn't won. The past seemed to have been returned to its original path, and the Book was safe in Viola's care, which meant Esta still had a chance to complete the job she'd been sent to do.

She'd stolen from Viola and Dolph before. She could do it again.

She should have felt relieved, satisfied the job had been salvaged, so she didn't understand why the ache in her chest when she thought of Harte dead felt as though the night would swallow her whole.

MADNESS IN THE STREETS

Bella Strega

When they made it back to the Strega, Dolph was nowhere to be found.

"We should wait for him," Viola said when Nibs tried to take the bag she had carried from Khafre Hall. He tugged a bit harder, but Viola refused to relinquish it. "I give this to Dolph and no one else."

Nibs frowned. "Then I suppose we should send someone to fetch him."

No one expected that the bowler-hatted boys would return bearing his body instead.

They'd found Dolph shot in the back and already dead, lying across Leena's grave. The boys carried him in with a quiet solemnity that seemed at odds with the garish shirts and vests, and they placed him on the zinc bar top. Even in death, his skin nearly as pale as the flash of white in his hair, Dolph's very presence commanded the room.

The motley bunch of men and women he'd unified under his mark stood in an uneasy silence. There was no sign of the usual warmth of magic in the barroom. It had all but drained from the air, as though Dolph had taken it with him as he took his last breath, as though each of them understood that the one thing that had linked them was now gone, and in his absence—in the absence of the power of his mark—a new consensus would have to be negotiated.

"He'd want us to go on," Nibs said, his voice grave. "He'd want us to finish what we'd started."

Dolph's closest crew gathered around his usual table—Viola, Jianyu, and Nibs. Esta hung back at first, but Viola took her by the arm and escorted her back with the rest. Jianyu gave Nibs an encouraging look, and Nibs opened the bag and looked inside.

Esta knew from the way his expression changed that something was wrong. With shaking hands, he dumped the contents on the table. A few misshapen rocks. A small ledger bearing the theater's logo. And the dried peelings from an orange.

They all stared at the items in a horrified silence.

"No . . ." Nibsy shook his head as he pawed through the items, turning them over, examining them. "No!" he shouted, pushing them from the table with a vicious swipe of his arm. He turned on Viola. "This is *your* fault," he said. He had his finger in her face, and his expression was murderous. "You let this happen!"

Viola stared at the now empty table, shaking her head as though denying what they were all seeing. "*No.* I took the bag from him. I *killed* him."

"Are you sure about that?" Nibs' brows drew together.

"Certo! I know when I kill someone," she snarled, looking every bit like Nibs would be her next victim.

"Did he touch you?" Nibs asked.

"What? What are you talking about?"

"Did he *touch* you?" Nibs shouted. His face had turned a violent shade of red, and he was up in her face, so close that she could have bitten him.

Viola pushed him back and wiped his spittle from her face. "He fought me for the Book, so yes. He touched me. But he was dead a moment later."

"If he touched you, he could have altered your mind."

"What are you talking about? I *killed* him."

"It's what Darrigan does," Nibs sneered, shaking his head at her. "He can read minds, and he can put ideas into them as well. All it takes is a single touch, skin to skin. You probably wouldn't have even noticed."

"He's right," Esta said, numb with disbelief.

Viola shook her head. "No. It's not possible. There was opium—or something like it—a cloud of it filled the room when we took the Book from its place. There was no way Darrigan could have done anything, not before I killed him. My knives don't need magic to work."

"Where's the knife you used?" Nibs asked.

Viola pulled out Libitina, her favorite stiletto blade, and held it up.

"Where's his blood?"

"There should have been blood," Viola whispered.

"Darrigan was a stage magician, you imbecile. He trained himself to hold his breath longer than anyone should be able to. The opium wouldn't have affected him if he didn't breathe it."

"No . . . ," Viola whispered, shaking her head. As though she refused to believe that he'd tricked her so easily, that he'd destroyed everything.

Dolph was dead and the Order would hunt them, and they didn't have the Book.

Nibs only glared at her. "Then where's the Book? Where are the artifacts?"

Viola didn't have an answer.

But for Esta, the news was *that* much more devastating. She'd failed. Harte Darrigan—the *Magician*—had the Book, and he was gone.

So were the artifacts. So was her stone.

And so was any chance of her ever getting home.

It wasn't long after that things started to fall apart.

Before dawn broke the next day, an entire block of tenement buildings went up in flames. The fire brigades stayed away, but boys who wore the Five Point Gang's mark were seen at the edges of the crowd. Watching. Stopping any who tried to douse the fires or rescue their belongings. Their alliance with the mayor—and with the Order—seemed to be growing more complete.

Under Tammany Hall's protection, the members of Kelly's gang didn't hesitate to attack anyone they thought might be a threat. Fights broke out over innocent glances. Gunfire rained in the streets, catching anyone nearby in the crossfire.

No one in the Bowery was safe. Not as long as the Order was set on vengeance.

Of course, all the unrest was reported as more evidence of the threat the incoming masses of immigrants posed. After he wrote about the fire at Khafre Hall, Sam Watson turned his daily columns to denouncing the Mageus for the threat they posed to the city. Criminals, degenerates, and thieves were pouring across the borders, he argued, and nothing was being done. If they could destroy an institution as old and important as Khafre Hall, he reminded everyone, they could also threaten the country's very way of life.

Near Herald Square, ladies in feathered caps and gentlemen in white gloves pursed their lips and shook their heads as they *tsk-tsk*ed the plight of the mayor having to control such a threat. Above Houston, the people of Manhattan went on about their lives as usual, willfully ignoring the madness that raged in the streets below.

But the citizens of the areas around Five Points and the Bowery lived on the knifepoint of fear. They knew the madness wasn't their own doing. Everyone was running scared.

Everyone, it seemed, except Nibsy Lorcan, who had somehow stepped into the space left by Dolph Saunders with an ease that surprised Esta. No one had questioned it when Nibs began issuing orders while Dolph's body was still cooling on the bar. While everyone else had turned inward, becoming silent and wary with the irrevocable evidence of Dolph's death, Nibs seemed to have grown six inches overnight. He sat in Dolph's old seat like it had always been meant for him.

Too soon, she thought. And she couldn't help but remember Harte's words—*this has* everything *to do with him.*

No one else seemed to question Nibsy's rise, though. Or if they did, they were still too dazed with the shock of what had happened to care.

A week later, they were huddled in the kitchen of the Strega, away from the rest of Dolph's gang, when a trio of bowler-hatted boys came through the door. The four of them—Nibs, Viola, Jianyu, and Esta—turned as one, already bracing for something worse. The tallest of the three boys stepped forward to where Nibs was sitting and then gave a jerk of his head, like he wanted to speak to Nibs alone.

Nibs took the boy aside and listened intently, his nostrils flaring and his features going hard as the boy talked.

"What do you mean his mother's gone?" Nibs hissed loudly enough for the rest of the room to turn and watch.

"Just what I told you. They says you ordered her to be moved."

"To where?" Nibs asked, his face furious.

"They says they didn't know," the boy said with a shrug.

"Well, who took her?"

The boy hesitated, a look of confusion on his face. "They says *you* did."

Viola sent Esta a questioning look from across the table where they were sitting, but Esta shook her head. She didn't know what the boys were talking about. She glanced at Jianyu, but he was too busy watching Nibsy and the other boy with a quiet intensity.

"I didn't do any such thing," Nibs seethed, barely able to control the volume of his voice now.

"There's one more thing," the boy said. He held himself on guard, like he was about to dodge a punch.

"What?" Nibs' chest was heaving.

The boy held out a folded piece of paper. "They says I was supposed to give you this."

Nibs took the paper with a vicious swipe that had the boy startling back. "Get out," he barked, and he waited until the three boys left before he opened the message and read it. When he was done, he glanced up at Esta.

Both Jianyu and Viola straightened in their chairs.

"What?" she asked, not at all liking the look on Nibsy's face.

He handed her the paper without a word.

It was an advertising flyer. On it, the bold block letters proclaimed that the great Harte Darrigan would attempt the impossible by cheating death with a jump from the Brooklyn Bridge. And across the image of the bridge was a message scrawled in a familiar script: *If you want the Book, bring me the girl.*

"Harte Darrigan, it seems, isn't dead after all. Not yet, at least," Nibs said, meeting her eyes when she looked up from reading. "There's something I'm missing," he said, staring blindly into space. Thinking, no doubt. Making connections. Then his eyes rested on Esta. "I can't believe he didn't give you any indication of what he had planned."

Esta went on alert. Nibs had been watching her for two days now, and every time she caught him looking, it gave her an uneasy feeling. Like he saw something in her that he didn't like. "He used me the same as everyone," she said carefully. "If it looked like we were close, it was another part of his game."

"No . . ." Nibs stared at her, the expression in his eyes unreadable. "I don't think that's the case at all. You meant something to him."

She laughed, a cold, hard expulsion of air that she filled with every bit of her disdain. "I assure you, I meant nothing to him. Or maybe you forgot how he left me on that stage without any warning."

"So *you* say," Nibs said softly.

"So I know," she told him. "He left me in a room full of the Order's members. If it hadn't been for Jianyu, I'd still be there."

Nibs huffed out a laugh.

"She speaks truly," Jianyu said. "He left her without any protection. He had no way of knowing that I would be there, waiting. That was something Dolph had arranged."

Esta hesitated only a moment at the lie that had slipped so easily from Jianyu's lips. "See?" she snapped. It took everything she had in her not to glance at Jianyu. "Harte Darrigan can go to hell for all I care."

That much was true.

He'd left her. He'd betrayed them all, but he'd left *her*. And she hated herself for caring about that, for forgetting—even for a moment—why she was there, in that city. But it wasn't over yet. She would have one more chance to stop him from destroying the Book—one more chance to save them all.

She would not fail again.

ONE FINAL NIGHT

The Docks

O nce night had cloaked the city, Harte watched the boat carrying the Order's artifacts glide from the docks, its engines off. When it was out of reach of the shoreline, the great boilers fired up, and the squat craft began to move faster, cutting a path through the starlight reflected in the dark water. He stayed where he was until the boat was no more than a dot on the horizon, knowing for certain now that he would never have the chance to make that trip, would never know what those other shores held in store.

Nibs Lorcan had overplayed his hand by warning Harte. It had taken some doing—late nights and secrets kept from Esta—but in the days leading up to the heist, Harte had managed to grease the right palms for word of where his mother might be. In the end it had been easy enough, especially with the right kind of touch.

Once he discovered she'd been stashed in a rank basement of a brothel near the docks, it had been hell to wait, but he knew he couldn't simply take her out of there without Nibs knowing. If Nibs had realized that he'd lost his leverage, he would never have let Harte near Khafre Hall or the Book. So he'd waited, unwilling to chance anything until the night of the heist, when it would be too late for Nibs to do anything to stop him.

But by the time Harte finally got to his mother, she'd been fed so much opium that it would be a miracle if she recovered at all. Still, he got her out, as he'd promised. As he gave the old couple who ran the brothel a stack of bills for their trouble, all he had to do was let his finger brush against their palms. It would have been hardly noticeable to them, especially with the way they were focused on the money, but a moment later they didn't remember him at all.

His mother was safe now, or as safe as she could be. Now he needed to turn himself to other things.

He'd been watching Jack's warehouse for two days. There'd been no sign of Jack, or anyone else, and Harte was finally confident that it was safe enough to chance approaching it. He couldn't finish things until he destroyed the machine and the plans to build another. After all, Harte Darrigan might be a bastard, he might be a double-crossing low-life scoundrel, but he wasn't so low as to leave a machine like that whole before he made his escape. Not when he knew the danger it posed to hundreds—maybe thousands—of innocent people.

It wouldn't be enough to stop Jack indefinitely, he knew, but it would set him back for a while. It would maybe even give the rest of them a fighting chance. Especially once Harte—and the Book with him—were gone.

First the machine. The wrench weighing down the pocket of his overcoat should do the trick. He'd destroy Jack's creation and send the whole damn place up in flames.

Then he'd go after Esta. He'd explain everything.

A shadow stirred near one of the low buildings at his back, and his every instinct came alert. No one could have known he was there. He'd taken every precaution, hidden his tracks twice over. There was no mistaking it, though—the feeling he had of being hunted.

"Who's there?" he called, but the soft lapping of the water was all he heard in reply. "I know someone's out there."

He waited, listening, but the feeling of being watched didn't go away.

"If you're thinking of killing me, I'd advise against it. If I'm dead, you'll never find out where I've put the things you're looking for," he said, not knowing if it was one of Dolph's crew or someone from the Order, and not really caring. Let them do the job for him for all he cared.

He hadn't lied—they'd never find the Book or the strange artifacts, not where he'd put them.

"Show yourself!" he called, his hand already wrapped around the wrench in his coat pocket. As though that would offer much protection.

Jianyu stepped into a shaft of moonlight. Maybe he should have been relieved that it wasn't Viola, but Harte still felt a tremor of fear run through him.

Let me explain, he wanted to say. But he didn't. Standing in the darkness near the water's edge was no place for pleading. He stood a little straighter instead.

"Did Dolph send you?" he asked, pretending a confidence he didn't feel.

"Dolph's dead," Jianyu told him, the flatness in his voice confirming his words.

"That's what I'd heard." He hadn't wanted to believe it, though.

"Shot in the back over Leena's grave," Jianyu said, even though Harte hadn't asked. He could almost feel the anger—and the anguish—in Jianyu's usually calm voice. "The night you betrayed us."

"I didn't betray Dolph," Harte said. "We had an arrangement, and I kept my word to him." But he knew when he'd heard whispers of Dolph's death that everything had gone south.

"Then where is the Book?"

"Safe," he said.

Jianyu's mouth turned down. "It would be safer with me."

"If it were with you, Nibs would have it, and we'd all be screwed."

Jianyu didn't say anything, simply continued to study him across the narrow stretch between them.

"I didn't kill Dolph," he said finally.

"If I thought you did, you'd be dead already."

He didn't trust Jianyu's too-calm demeanor. "If you didn't come to kill me, why *are* you here?"

"I'm here because Dolph is dead." He gave Harte an unreadable look and took a step closer. "But what we do from here . . . that is up to you."

FOOL ME ONCE

Jack's Apartment

J ack Grew was packing the last of his suitcases when the message came. An hour later, he would have been on a train bound to Cleveland and his new position as an assistant to the undersecretary of a refinery on the shores of Lake Erie. The message changed all that. Or at least put it on hold for the time being.

Jack held on to the folded slip of paper like a lifeline.

Not that he trusted Darrigan. No, he wouldn't be taken in by that charlatan again.

Daughter of Baron von Filosik? Like hell she was. He'd had people search Darrigan's apartment while the pair were putting on their little show at Khafre Hall, and they didn't find any sign of a trunk, or anything else that would indicate that the girl was who they said she was. The redhead had been right. They'd played him, and now Darrigan was going to pay.

I have the Book for you. Come alone, the message said.

Not a chance.

When Jack's carriage came to a stop at the foot of the bridge early the next day, he found a steady stream of people heading in the same direction. It looked as though the entire bridge had been closed down to the usual streetcar and carriage traffic, so he stopped a man to ask where they were headed. The man didn't seem to understand what Jack was saying, but he handed him a crumpled flyer.

Beneath the grease stains and wrinkles, Jack saw the image of the bridge and the smirking face of Harte Darrigan.

It shouldn't have surprised him that he was walking into a virtual circus, considering who he was dealing with. But if Darrigan thought to throw Jack off with this crowd, he was wrong. He'd learned his lesson, and now Darrigan would learn *his*.

He told his uncle—who had of course told the High Princept—about the note. The Order had taken everything from there.

Jack looked over his shoulder at the row of buildings lining the waterfront. He could just barely make out the glint of the sharpshooter's sight in a fourth-floor window. If anything went wrong, the Order wouldn't allow Darrigan to get away. If he tried to come back into the city, he was a dead man. If he tried to make it to the wilds of Brooklyn, Order patrols were already waiting. And if Jack himself happened to be in the line of fire . . . the High Princept had already made it clear that no one would care.

A suppressed shudder ran through him.

That wasn't going to happen. If anyone was going to kill that piece-of-shit magician, it was going to be him.

So Jack made his way with the rest of the crowd, following the long incline that led out over the shoreline and toward the soaring towers of the bridge. He took the entrance to the far right, one usually taken up by streetcars and trains. The farther he walked, the denser the crowd became, but this wasn't the refined crowd of Broadway. All around him, the clamoring of too many languages assaulted his ears. Guttural and brash, the voices were a noisy babble that made him feel as if *he* were the one who didn't belong.

It only served to make him angrier. After all, his family had practically built this city.

Still, the crowd would make it that much more difficult for the Order to deal with Darrigan. He pulled the brim of his hat low on his forehead and started on his way toward the arches of the first tower. The crowd had come to a stop there, a motley throng of humanity dressed in the gaudy satins and bright taffetas of people who didn't know better, people who bought their goods ready-made and three seasons out of fashion. And in the center of the teeming mass, as still as a rock in a current, was the magician.

ENDGAME

The Brooklyn Bridge

It was hard to even pretend confidence with a gun pressing into the small of her back, but Esta did what she could. She couldn't use her affinity, not with the grip the large boy had on her arm, but she could use the other magic Professor Lachlan had taught her when she was a girl. *Confidence is the key to any con. If they see you sweat, you're dead.*

The morning wind had kicked up by the time they made their way across the span of the bridge to the arches of the first tower that held the monstrous suspension cables aloft. With every step, she sensed what remained of Dolph's crew becoming more nervous, and who could blame them? Though the day was warm, there was a chill in the air. A cold, malicious energy that whispered of danger. A reminder that ahead was the end of the world for anyone with magic.

She hadn't been on this bridge since she was a child.

Now, the closer they got to that tower, the more she felt like the girl she'd once been. But Professor Lachlan wasn't there to help her, and she had a sinking feeling that if anyone carried her off the bridge this time, it would be because she was dead.

She straightened her spine, ignoring the kiss of the gun. She would get the Book and the stone from Darrigan, or she would die trying.

The boy pushed through the crowd, dragging her along, with Nibs following close behind. Viola was there too, somewhere, ready to step in if need be, as were Jianyu and a handful of Dolph's crew. All there to make sure that everything went their way, and to be certain that Harte Darrigan never came back into the city.

They made their way toward the front of the crowd. Each step was one closer to the cold currents of energy warning them of disaster and death. Eventually, they reached the point where she could see Harte, already warming the crowd up with some minor sleight of hand. When he looked up and saw her, an emotion she couldn't read—and one she didn't want to think too much about—flashed behind his eyes.

"Ladies and gentlemen," he announced. "I see my assistant has arrived." He held out his hand, as though nothing had happened between them. As though he'd never betrayed her, never left her for dead in a theater filled with the Ortus Aurea. "Esta, my dear?" When she didn't move, he asked the crowd to encourage her.

Applause surrounded them, and when she glanced at Nibs, for some indication of what she should do, she saw his indecision. His eyes were narrowed as he considered Harte, but then he gave a nod of his head. "If you try anything at all, you're dead," he told her.

She was sick of that particular threat. With a frustrated huff, she stepped toward Harte.

"I've missed you, sweetheart," he said, as he took her hand and made a show of kissing it for the audience.

"Funny," she replied, her eyes stinging with tears that had nothing to do with the breeze. "I haven't thought about you at all."

The audience close enough to hear roared their approval.

Harte had already removed his cloak. He handed it to her, and then he proceeded to remove his waistcoat as well. Before he could finish unbuttoning his vest, there was a disruption from deep within their numbers, and an uneasy murmuring rose within the crowd as a man made his way forward, gun drawn.

Harte's expression faltered just a little as he gave Jack Grew his most charming smile. "Jack! How good of you to make it."

"Give me the Book, Darrigan," Jack said, pointing the gun directly at his chest. "And the artifacts as well."

"You'll get them soon enough—"

"The Book!" he screamed, cocking back the hammer. "I will not allow you to make a fool of me again."

Harte's face went serious. "You're going to have to be patient, Jack. If you shoot me now, you'll never get what you came here for. So if you'd just lower that thing and—"

It felt like it all happened at once. She was on the bridge, and she was also standing in the hallway of Schwab's mansion. She was watching Harte about to be shot, and she was seeing Logan bleeding on the floor. Two moments, two places in time, but the same gunman. The same deadly weapon set to stop a beating heart.

She grabbed Harte and pulled time slow at the same moment that the gun went off, at the same moment that the bullet began traveling in its deadly path. And when she looked up, the bullet inched past them, so close they could feel its heat.

"I thought you hadn't missed me?" Harte said, close to her ear.

She realized that she was holding on to him maybe more tightly than she needed to. "Where's the Book?" she asked, not letting go as she backed away from him and the smell of oranges and Ivory soap.

"It's in my cloak." He indicated that she already held the cloak in her arms. "Along with your cuff."

"My cuff—" Her chest went tight.

"The one you showed me. The one you were after."

Around them, the world was silent. "And the rest?" she asked.

"Gone," he said, pushing a piece of hair out of her eye. "I sent them out of the city last night. By now they're on separate trains, heading to all the places I'll never go."

Her fingers tightened on the silky material of the cloak in her hands. "Why would you do that?"

"The Order can't have them, not with what Jack has planned. And I couldn't let Nibs get them either."

"Nibs?" He wasn't making any sense.

"He planned all of this from the beginning—Leena's death, Dolph going after the Book, even you—" He pressed his lips together. "He's the one who killed Dolph."

"No." She shook her head. "Dolph was shot the night of the heist. Nibs was with us."

"Was he?" Harte asked flatly. "Do you know for sure he was waiting outside Khafre Hall that entire time?"

"I can't believe he would . . . ," she started to say, but her words fell silent.

But it would explain so much about how tense the last couple of days had been at the Strega, about why Nibs had insisted on the gun against her back. "You were in the hall with us," she argued. "You can't know—"

"I know what he intended to do," Harte continued, his voice urgent. But he wouldn't look directly at her. "For all his ability to see how things will turn out, he wasn't expecting me to punch him that night you got taken to the Tombs."

She glanced back at Nibs, his face frozen in a sort of strangled fury, and she saw him suddenly in a different light. She'd been a fool not to see it all along.

"He's been pulling Dolph's strings the whole time. Dolph had no idea."

Esta shook her head again, wanting to deny everything he was telling her. It had to be more of his lies. "You should have warned Dolph."

"I couldn't," Harte said, not meeting her eyes. "Nibs had my mother, and I've already wronged her enough in my life. I couldn't do anything more to her. I thought I could work around Nibs. I thought I could get you out too, but things didn't go quite as I planned that night."

"You should have told me."

"I couldn't chance him finding out that you knew. The only way I could figure to get around him was to keep you working blind. There was too much at stake."

"You mean like Dolph's life?" she argued.

"I never meant for Dolph to die, but this was bigger than Dolph's life, Esta. He understood that. Nibs *cannot* get the Book. Do you understand me? He doesn't want to free the Mageus from the city. He wants to rule them. To use them—us—against the Sundren." His jaw clenched. "The Book's dangerous, Esta. It's not what you think—it's not what *any* of us thought. In the wrong hands, it would give someone devastating power. If Nibs were the one to control it, he'd be able to make himself more powerful than any Mageus who's ever lived. I can't imagine the devastation that would follow. No one would be safe."

"I can't . . ." The enormity of what he was saying felt unbelievable. "Why now? Why tell me all of this when it's too late to do anything?"

"Because it's not too late for you," he said. "I'm giving you a way out."

He took her hand and placed something heavy and smooth into her palm. *The cuff with her stone.* Immediately, she felt the warmth of it. The sureness of its power calling to her.

"Do what you need to do, but either way, get yourself out and take the Book with you. You can't let either Nibs or Jack get ahold of it. *Everything* depends upon that. Do you understand? Take it where they can't follow."

"But I—"

"Do you understand?" he demanded again.

"What about you?" she asked, still looking for the angle, the indication that this was all part of a larger game for him.

"I'm dead either way. The Book—it's not a normal book. It's like some sort of living thing." He grimaced, and then he met her eyes. The gray irises that had become so familiar to her were different now. She thought she could see something more than her own reflection in them, colors that she didn't have names for flashing in their depths. "When I touched it, I read it more easily than I can read a person. I've seen what's in there, and it's a part of me now. Even if you take the Book to where they can't reach it, the Order won't ever stop hunting me." He shook his head. "I can't risk that. If they see me jump and see me die, they won't have any reason to hunt you . . . or anyone else. You want to protect the people Dolph was protecting? This is the only way." He gave her a heartbreaking smile. "Whatever happens, the great Harte Darrigan won't soon be forgotten after what I do here today."

Her heart ached. *Yes, you will,* she knew. If he jumped from that bridge, no one would remember him in a week or a month, and definitely not over the years.

"So we bring down the Brink before that happens," she told him. "We free everyone right now and take the Order's power away from them." It wasn't the job she'd been sent to do, but it was what Professor Lachlan intended anyway, she reasoned.

"You don't understand. *None* of us do. The Brink isn't just a prison, Esta. It was built to *protect* magic. If it comes down, it won't free Mageus. Think about Tilly—when Jack's machine blew up, it took her life with it. Destroying the Brink would do the same thing. It would destroy any magic that it's taken, and when it does that, it would break everything connected to that magic. You, me, every Mageus who exists is connected to the old magic. When part of that dies, so will ours. And without our magic . . ." He couldn't finish.

She didn't have words to respond to him. It was too ridiculous and too big a lie to be believed. The Brink was what *killed* them, not what protected them.

"You can't expect me to believe that."

"I'm here, aren't I?" He swallowed hard, his mouth tight. "If the Book had offered me a way out of the city, don't you think I'd be gone? Do you really think I'd be here, in the middle of this circus otherwise? I *could* have used the Book to get through the Brink, but the magic in the Book is too powerful. The Brink itself might not have held. Jack told me how they made the Brink—connecting the elements through Aether. The Order has been trying to find a way to make it larger and more powerful, but Jack told me the connections through the Aether are too unstable. The Book might have been able to get me through, but that much magic could be enough to overload the circuit. And if that happens, it would be worse than any electrical outage."

"Because it would make magic go dark," she said, slowly putting the pieces together.

"Exactly. If I could have gotten out, I would have. I would have even taken you with me. But I can't risk destroying the circuit through the Aether. I'm still here because there's no way out without destroying the entire Brink, and to destroy it would be to threaten all magic. *All* Mageus. There's no way out for me, so I'm trusting you to help me finish this."

She stared at him, searching for the crack in the mask that would expose the lie in what he was telling her. But she did believe one thing—if there was a way out of the city, if there was a way through the Brink, Harte Darrigan *would* have taken it already.

But he hadn't.

Even now he was giving the Book to her and giving up the one thing he'd wanted from the beginning. If that wasn't enough to convince her, the fear in his stormy eyes was.

"Ready?" he asked.

"No," she said. There were a million other questions she needed to ask. There had to be another way. "I can't—"

He placed his fingers against her lips to stop her. "Let's finish this." He tore himself away from her grasp, and as he slipped away from her, she let go of time and the world began again.

When Harte didn't fall, Jack stood, too shocked to move, which gave the crowd time to wrestle the gun from his grasp. It took only a few moments more before he was arrested and dragged away, screaming and shouting all the while.

Once it was calm, Harte took his time removing his shirt. The muscles of his arms broadcast exactly how tense he was as he made a show of stripping for the public. The cool air raised gooseflesh on his bare shoulders, but his eyes were steady, calm.

"A kiss for luck, my dear?" he asked, his gray eyes determined.

When the crowd erupted with enthusiastic hoots, she couldn't deny him. She allowed him to put his mouth over hers, but this was not the kiss she'd wanted for herself that day in Harte's apartment. His lips were cool, as though he'd already been claimed by the water below, and there was nothing but a resigned determination in the quick brush of skin against skin, mouth against mouth.

She wasn't sure she trusted him, but to know he was about to die?

I can take him back with me, she thought in a sudden rush. To hell with everyone who might see them disappear.

Too soon, he pulled away from her, and the time for decisions had passed.

With a flourish, Harte mounted the railing. His eyes scanned the crowd, looked over them to the city beyond, and she thought she saw regret flash across his expression.

Nibs exploded from the crowd. "Stop him!"

Esta saw some of Dolph's boys move toward the railing where Harte stood, but before they could come any closer, police stormed the bridge. The crowd descended into confusion, surging in all directions to get away from the raised billy sticks and angry whistles of the police. In the confusion, she was pushed back from the railing, and from Harte.

There was no way to reach him. No way to turn him from what he meant to do. She'd saved the Book, but she couldn't save him.

Harte's eyes met hers. *Go!* he mouthed, and the air seemed to shimmer around him, the sun throwing up a glare as he let go of the cabled railing, and then he was gone.

Her heart seized. *Too late.*

She pushed through the crowd to the railing, where he'd disappeared. Below, there was no sign of him. She watched, waiting for him to surface or for some indication that he'd made it, but even as the crowd behind her was a riot of anger and confusion, the water was silent, holding its secrets as absolutely as a grave.

Esta didn't see Nibs coming for her through the crowd. She was too busy trying to breathe through the shock of what had just happened. But as she clung to Harte's cloak, she felt the hard outline of the Book. Her cuff was warm in her hand.

He hadn't betrayed her in the end. He'd given her exactly what she needed.

But before she could fully comprehend that he was well and truly gone, she felt someone grab her arm.

"Did he give it to you?" Nibs demanded, his pale face close to hers. "I know he told you where it is."

"What?" She tried to shake him off, but his hands gripped her arm painfully.

"Tell me," he said, pulling a snub-nosed pistol from his jacket and placing it under her chin. "Tell me or you can join him."

She couldn't breathe. She couldn't make sense of what was happening.

"Tell me what he did with the Book!" Nibsy said, his breath hot and sour on her face as the cool barrel of the gun pressed against her throat.

"I—" Esta knew in that moment that Harte had been right. She couldn't give it to him. She knew then that whatever happened, Nibs would never be worthy of the power it held. Her mind raced for some lie as she shifted the cloak against herself so he wouldn't feel the Book within its folds.

He clicked the hammer of the gun back, but before he could pull the trigger, his body went rigid and he gasped in pain. The gun fell from his hand, and he let go of his grip on Esta as he grabbed his leg.

Esta backed away from him and looked up to find Viola standing a few feet off, her face creased into a serious frown as she watched Nibs pull the silver knife from his thigh. She gave Esta a solemn nod, and then she was gone, melting into the crowd as though she'd never been there.

Only the feel of the cuff in her hand, warm and urgent and compelling, brought Esta to her senses. She gave in to the pull of Ishtar's Key, allowed the warmth of its energy to expand her until she could see the layers of time and history in that place—all the seconds to come that wouldn't have Harte Darrigan in them.

Nibs looked up at her, hate and anger twisting his features. He raised the gun, but it was too late. She'd found the layer of time she wanted, and she was gone.

A STARLESS SKY

Present Day—The Brooklyn Bridge

Esta barely had time to dodge the semitruck as it sped past her. Gasping, she clung to the side of the roadway. The gusting air from the passing traffic lifted the hair around her face and whipped her skirts around her legs. It was night, but the glow of the city—*her* city—shattered the darkness. The gentle hum of automobiles replaced the clattering racket of cobbled streets and wooden wheels, and above her, she couldn't make out the stars.

Everything felt too fast. After weeks in a city that moved at the speed of a plodding horse or a rumbling elevated train, the flurry of cars and people felt like too much.

Harte's cloak was still in her arms, the Book still heavy within its folds. And if she just ignored the fact that it smelled like him, that combination of Ivory soap and the faint scent of oranges, she'd be fine.

She had to be fine. She still had work left to do.

She kept her head down and made the long walk back to Midtown, to the parking lot she'd left from, beneath the crown of the Empire State Building. For her, weeks had passed, but for this city, everything felt exactly the same. The summer night was warmer than the day in late March she'd left behind, and by the time she reached her destination, she was sweating from the heavy skirts and the pace she'd set.

As she rounded the corner, she stopped short and then retreated. The street where Dakari's car had once been was now blocked off, and a small crowd had formed. Shards of red from the lights of police cars bounced off the darkened windows of the surrounding buildings. From her vantage point, she couldn't see the street where Dakari had fallen, and she couldn't tell if he was still there.

Esta had tried to return to a few minutes after she originally left, just as Professor Lachlan had taught her. But after the walk from the bridge, she was too late. If they had Dakari . . . If he were injured or worse . . .

She had to fix this. She had to go back and save him.

Forcing herself to ignore the sounds of the sirens and the lights flashing around her, Esta focused on finding the layers of time. The stone in the cuff on her arm grew warm, but she ignored its heat and sifted through the moments, peeling back the minutes and seconds until she thought she was close to the instant the gunfire had erupted. She could almost see it—the lights from the police cars began to dim, their sirens fading into the quiet of the night before her original departure.

But just as she found that moment, the same sense of foreboding came over her that had made her body feel as if it were burning all those weeks ago, the night she left. The stone felt hot, like a branded warning against her skin. Just as it had before.

Something is wrong.

She took a deep breath, fighting against her own panic, struggling to make herself slip back to the seconds before Dakari was attacked, but this time, her instincts worked against her. With a gasping sob, she lost her hold on time, and the present—with all its light and noise—came flooding back. She bent over to steady herself, her heart pounding and her skin cold despite the warmth of the summer night. Despite the heat of the stone against her skin.

"No," she whispered, as though hearing her own voice would help her overcome her fear. But her voice sounded scared, shaken. It was too much of a coincidence for her to feel this way twice, but whether it had something to do with this particular moment, with the stone, or with something else, she didn't know. What she did know was that Dakari's life depended on her. She needed to try again, for Dakari's sake, but before she could, a hand grasped her by the shoulder and pulled her back as another hand covered the yelp of surprise that she would have otherwise let out.

"Shhhhh," a familiar voice said, close to her ear. "I'm going to let you go, but you need to keep quiet."

She turned to find Dakari standing behind her, but she couldn't do much more than open and close her mouth numbly, searching for the words that wouldn't come. "How did you . . ." she said finally, but she trailed off. She couldn't make sense of what she was seeing even as she felt the relief of having him there, whole and alive, before her.

He tore open his shirt, showing her the marred bulletproof vest beneath. "I'm always prepared, E." He rubbed at his chest, grimacing. "Though those gunshots are going to leave a bruise," he said.

Esta noticed the blood on his pants. "Dakari, your leg."

"I know, but I had to wait for you to get back. Now that you are, we should get out of here." In the distance she could already hear the scream of another siren bouncing off the buildings. "Come on," he said, lifting himself from the pavement. "You drive."

She caught the keys he tossed her.

"Maybe you could do that time thing you do? Get me back faster?" he asked.

"Right," she said, still so relieved to see him that she could hardly breathe. *He's not gone,* she thought as she pulled the seconds slow. "I thought you were dead." She helped him to the car, the city silent around them.

"Nah. I'm damn hard to kill." He patted his bulletproof vest again, wincing as he slid into the backseat with his injured leg propped in front of him.

"Who were those guys?" she asked as she took the driver's seat and glanced back in the rearview mirror.

A shadow crossed his expression. "Who knows?" he told her, but he didn't quite meet her eyes as he said it. "How long were you away this time?" he asked, tending to his leg as she started the car and began navigating through the strange tableau of a city gone nearly still.

"Weeks," she said, suddenly overwhelmed by the knowledge that they were all dead. Whatever had happened on that bridge, it was more than a hundred years later. Jianyu, Viola, the rest of the crew at the Strega, they'd all be dust in the grave by now. And she would never have the chance to say good-bye.

"Did you get it?" he asked, watching her with careful eyes in the rear-view mirror.

She nodded, and the relief that flashed across his face was so stark, it surprised her. Had he thought she wouldn't?

"The Professor'll be pleased."

"Maybe," she told him.

"What do you mean?" he asked, his brows drawn together in concern.

"I don't think we can destroy the Brink," she said, remembering everything Harte had told her. "Even if we could . . . I don't know if we *should*."

Dakari's expression was stern. "You don't mean that."

"I don't know anymore. I need to talk with Professor Lachlan. He'll know what to do."

Dakari didn't speak for a long moment. "You're right, E. You've been through a lot. Maybe you're not thinking straight. Let's just get back and we'll work it all out then." He wouldn't say anything else, but he kept eyeing her uneasily as she drove the final blocks to Orchard Street.

The exterior of the building on Orchard Street didn't look any different than it had when she left weeks ago, but then, why would it? For the people in her own time, she'd been gone only a few minutes. She looked up at the dark brick, seeing it through new eyes. It was an old tenement, and in the moonlight, with the lights out all around and the neighborhood quiet, it could have been a hundred years in the past. She could almost imagine walking the four blocks to Elizabeth Street and letting herself in through the Strega's back door. For a moment she imagined that the people she'd met there and come to admire weren't all dead and gone.

Dakari opened the front door and let them into the empty foyer. To Esta's relief, the foyer looked like it had before her mistakes at the Schwab mansion. It was, she hoped, a good sign—a sign that maybe she'd managed to fix her mistakes.

But it didn't feel like home anymore.

There was a clean, almost sterile quality to the place that felt wrong to her now. A building like this one should be teeming with life. There should be the sounds of children in the halls and the smells of five different apartments cooking dinner. But there had never been the sound of children in those hallways while she lived in them.

The door of 1A opened to reveal the true entrance of the building. Logan was waiting on the other side.

"You're up," Esta said, surprised to see him whole and healthy. "You're feeling okay?"

He frowned. "Why wouldn't I be?"

"You were shot," she told him, confused.

He glanced at Dakari. "I'm not sure what you're talking about."

Her stomach sank. "You were shot on the Schwab job. When I left, you weren't even conscious yet. . . ." Her words trailed off. "You don't remember being shot by the blond—by Jack?"

"There wasn't any blond," Logan said, looking at her as though she'd lost her mind. "There was you trying to save some serving girl and almost getting thrown out, but I don't remember any blond guy. And I definitely would have remembered being shot."

"Well, I'm glad to see you're okay."

He gave her another doubtful look. "The Professor's upstairs. He's waiting."

Dakari followed her into the elevator and pushed the button for the top floor.

"There really was a blond," she told him, needing him to believe her.

"Logan almost died. I brought him back. Something changed. Somehow things are different."

"Am I different?"

She glanced up at him. "No. I don't think so. You're still here."

He seemed surprised at that. "Where else would I be?"

"Nowhere," she said. "What about Mari?"

"She's probably in her workshop. What about her?"

She didn't have time to explain about Mari. The elevator was already coming to a stop, and Dakari was pulling back the gate and opening the door for her to step through.

I must have done something right. But the victory felt hollow when she thought of all the mistakes she'd made. When she thought of Harte Darrigan standing on the edge of that railing and willing her to go.

The Professor's library seemed mostly the same, but the piles were neater and there was something different in the way chairs and tables were organized. At the other end of the room, Professor Lachlan sat, peering through a large magnifying glass at the pages of an open book. He didn't look up, even though he must have heard the elevator arrive, but finished the passage he was reading and made a note in a notebook.

When he finally looked up, his eyes narrowed. "Do you have it?"

She held up the cloak. "Right here," she said.

"Good." He held out his hand. "Give it to me."

Esta hesitated. He seemed different. More distant, more demanding.

He's always been demanding, she reminded herself. Still, something felt wrong. For a moment she thought about trying to remove the Book from the inner pocket of the cloak herself, so that she didn't have to hand over both. It seemed wrong, somehow, to give this piece of Harte to anyone else, since it was all that was left of him.

"Esta?" Professor Lachlan asked, his jaw tense. "Give me the Book."

Dakari stepped up behind her. "Come on, E. Give the Professor the Book," he said softly, but there was a thread of steel in his voice he'd never used on her before.

Confused by their mood, she handed the cloak over without any further argument.

It took the Professor a moment to find the secret pocket, but rather than bothering with figuring out how to access it, he took out a small knife. There was nothing she could do but watch as he tore open the material and pulled out the Book.

It was smaller than she'd expected from the weight of the cloak. "That's it?" she asked, looking at the small, dark volume.

But she knew it was. On the cover was the symbol she recognized from the painting in Dolph's apartment and the book he'd shown her. She had no doubt that this small, unremarkable tome was the Ars Arcana, the Book that so many people had wanted. That so many people had died for.

Professor Lachlan's eyes were bright, eager. He ignored her disappointment as he ran his fingers over the symbol on the cover. "After all this time."

"Esta was telling me she doesn't think we should destroy the Brink," Dakari said.

"That's not what I said. And I was going to tell him myself." Esta glanced up at Dakari's flinty expression, and the feeling of unease she'd had since she walked into the building grew.

"What, *exactly*, were you going to tell me?" Professor Lachlan asked.

"It's about destroying the Brink. I don't think we can, not even with the Book," she said, swaying a little on her feet. She wanted nothing more than to collapse into the ancient sofa and tell him everything, but she had the sense that this was too important to relax.

"And what makes you think that?"

"Harte . . . I mean the Magician told me when he gave me the Book. He said destroying the Brink could destroy magic."

The Professor didn't look pleased. "And you believed him?"

"I don't know," she said honestly. "But I think we should be careful with that, and with the Brink. I think we should make sure we understand what we're doing."

"It's not your job to think about these things."

"I know. It's just . . . I thought you should know before you do anything."

The second hand on a clock ticked, the only sound in the silent library. "He got to you."

"No, it's not that," she told him, but she wasn't sure if she spoke the truth.

"He turned you," Professor Lachlan said, his voice flat and filled with disgust.

"*No.* I brought you the Book. I did my job."

Another long silence strangled the room. "Of course you did," he said, but the Professor didn't sound pleased. "I'm sure you're simply tired," he told her. "Overwrought. After all, I imagine you've been through quite an ordeal. Perhaps you should return to your room and rest."

"Maybe," she said. "It's been a long day." She gave a weak laugh. "It's been a long month."

"We can talk more about this tomorrow," Professor Lachlan told her, but his attention was already on the Book in his hands.

Esta turned back toward the elevator. She was halfway across the room when something caught her eye—a flash of silver in a shadowbox frame she didn't remember seeing there before. For a moment she looked at the art, not understanding what she was seeing, but then, all at once, she understood. "Those were Viola's," she told Professor Lachlan. Her stomach twisted at the sight of the slim stiletto blades crossed and mounted in the frame. There was no mistaking the deep *V*s cut into the exposed tangs of each. "How did you get them?"

"Excuse me?" Professor Lachlan asked.

She went over to the wall, to look closer at the knives. "How could you possibly have these?"

Professor Lachlan glanced at her. "I've had them for ages," he said. "Or don't you remember?" He gave Dakari a nod. "Perhaps it would be best if you escort her to her room?"

"I'm fine," Esta started to say, but Dakari was already at her side again.

"I'm sorry," he told her, his soft, dark eyes pained.

"What?" she asked, confused by his words. Before she understood what was happening, his arm snaked out to cage her against him and she felt the sharp bite of something in her biceps. "Dakari?"

She looked down at the place where the syringe was sticking into her upper arm, but her words already felt thick and the edge of her vision was already going black.

AN OLD FRIEND

Esta came to slowly, her head throbbing as she opened her eyes to find herself on the floor in a windowless room. She was still wearing a corset and long skirts, her clothing from the past, so at first she thought it had all been a bad dream. That she was still back in her narrow room above the Strega, but she could hear a siren in the distance, a wailing reminder that she was no longer with Dolph and the rest. She was home, but the ache in her arm where Dakari had jabbed her with the needle and the foggy numbness that filled her head wasn't the welcome she'd expected. Everything felt upside down.

She wasn't sure where she was, or if she was even still in Professor Lachlan's building. Her head was spinning as she pulled herself up and felt around the walls of the room, trying to find the door. She made it around the three corners of the small space before she found two seams where a door should have been, but there was no handle and no lock, only a smooth plate of metal over where the locking mechanism should be.

No matter how much she searched, she couldn't find any place to pick a lock or jimmy a hinge. It was a prison built for a thief.

It was a prison he'd built for her.

It could have been minutes or hours that she sat there in the darkness before she finally heard voices coming from the other side of the wall. She scuttled back and tried to focus enough to pull the seconds slow. But time slipped away from her—she couldn't find the spaces. She felt like she had in the basement of the Haymarket, unable to call on her affinity and at the mercy of whoever was coming for her.

The wall split open, and she blinked, shielding her eyes from the light of the hall. "Come on, E."

"Dakari? Is that you?" She wanted it to be him, but she also didn't know if she could trust him anymore.

A moment later he had hoisted her up onto still-shaky legs and was leading her out of the room.

"What's going on?" she asked him, and when he didn't answer, she tried to pull away. "Where are we going?"

He kept a tight hold on her, though, refusing to answer her questions as he half led, half dragged her down the hall toward the elevator.

"Why are you acting like this, Dakari? It's *me*. You know me." If she only had his knife, maybe she could have gotten through to him. But the knife was lost to the past, and if things didn't improve, she didn't know what her future held in store. "*Please*," she tried again.

He wouldn't look at her as pushed her gently into the elevator, and he kept hold of her the entire time the cage made its slow, rattling climb to the top. "Just answer his questions and do what he asks. Prove yourself to him, and it'll be fine. Everything can go back to how it should be."

But she doubted anything could ever go back to the way it had been before. Too much had changed.

When the elevator stopped at the library, Dakari led her forward. "Come on."

It was night, but she had no idea how long she'd been out of it with the drug they'd given her and no idea how much time had passed in the windowless prison they'd kept her in. The lights in the library were off, except for the small desk lamp that illuminated the Professor's face as he bent, serious and focused, over the Ars Arcana. Near him on the table were the five artifacts laid out in a straight line.

When he heard them approaching, he glanced up. "Are you feeling better?"

"You drugged me and locked me in a doorless room," she said, well aware she was pushing him. "What did I do to deserve that? I brought you the Book."

"You were also talking nonsense about the Brink being indestructible."

"I was only trying to warn you."

"Yes, and where did you get the information?"

"From Harte," she said, knowing how damning that sounded.

"Of course you did. Because you came to trust him, didn't you? It was exactly what I was afraid of happening. It's exactly why I gave you some incentive to return."

"An incentive?"

Professor Lachlan didn't so much as blink. "You're impulsive, but you're also predictable. I knew that if you believed Dakari's life was in danger, you'd be sure to return, no matter how you might have come to feel about those in the past."

She felt numb from more than the drug they'd given her now as the image of Dakari's body jerking from the impact of the bullets rose in her mind. He'd been wearing a vest, but those bullets hadn't been blanks. They'd torn through his legs. "You could have killed him!"

"His life was never in danger," the Professor said, dismissing her.

Esta glanced up at Dakari, but her old friend's expression was unreadable, his features closed off and distant. If he was upset or surprised by this news, his face didn't show it.

"You risked Dakari's life because you didn't trust me?" she pressed.

"I wouldn't have trusted anyone that much, but especially not you, impulsive girl that you are. So, no. I didn't trust that you wouldn't be swayed by Dolph Saunders or even the Magician. I couldn't trust that you wouldn't take one look into Harte Darrigan's pretty gray eyes, listen to his poor-little-boy-lost sob story, and decide to give him a chance. I gave myself some insurance. I gave you an incentive to return." He stared at her, his nostrils flaring from the exertion of his tirade.

With those words, something inside her clicked, and apprehension wrapped around her. "How did you know he had gray eyes?"

"What?" Professor Lachlan's face bunched in irritation.

"Harte Darrigan. You couldn't know what color his eyes were. Pictures wouldn't have shown you that."

His expression went slack, as though he realized the slip, but then a smile curved softly at his lips. "You always have been too observant for your own good."

Unease slinked through her. "You always told me that it made me a good thief."

"It did. But it also makes you a problem." Professor Lachlan spoke to Dakari. "If you'd secure her, I'll take it from here."

She knew it was coming, but she could still hardly believe what was happening when Dakari wrestled her into a chair and secured her arms and legs with rope.

"Just tell him the truth, E. If you're still with us, everything's gonna be okay."

"Dakari?" she pleaded, but it fell on deaf ears. He was already heading toward the elevator.

"You know, you were never supposed to come back here. None of this had to happen if you'd have just done what you should have. If you'd only given me the Book that day on the bridge—"

Esta turned back to meet Professor Lachlan's gaze. "How could I have given *you* the Book? That was a hundred years ago."

Professor Lachlan didn't speak at first, but there was something in his expression that made Esta's skin crawl. "Maybe you're not so very observant, after all. You don't recognize me, do you?" He frowned. "Have I really changed so much?"

"You look exactly the same as the last time I saw you," she said, confused by his question.

"A few weeks, a lifetime. Strange how similar two spans of time can be. I was right about you then. I've been right about you all along."

She saw then what maybe she should have seen before. "No . . ." He'd changed over the years, but beneath the age spots and wrinkles, beneath the tuft of white, thinning hair and the frailness, she thought she could see the boy he'd been. "Nibs?" she said, her voice barely working.

"I always hated that name," he told her.

LISA MAXWELL

"It can't be. You *can't* be him. That's impossible."

"It's *improbable*, not impossible. What's a century when you can find healers like Dakari to keep you whole?" Professor Lachlan gave Esta a chastising look. "What's a century when you're waiting for the key to your plans? I'm a patient man, Esta. You must know that much by now."

"You killed Dolph," she said. "He trusted you, and you killed him." She shook her head. "I don't understand—Dolph wanted to destroy the Brink. He wanted to bring down the Order. You were on the *same side*. There wasn't any reason to kill him."

Professor Lachlan—Nibs—sneered. "Dolph had some grand plan to destroy the Brink and free the Mageus in the city. But what would that have done? Started a war with the Sundren, a war we were too weak to win . . . at least with the Book in *his* hands."

"They were better hands than yours."

"He thought we needed the Book to gain our freedom, as though the Book of Mysteries, the most ancient and hallowed record of magic, was some simple grimoire he could use to break a wicked spell," Professor Lachlan scoffed. "He always was shaky on his Latin tenses. He misunderstood the message Leena sent him before the Order took her. I know, because she explained it to me when she gave me the note. . . . Not that I bothered to correct him. As long as he wanted to keep pursuing the Book, it worked for me, but I knew all along that it wasn't that the Book could free us, but that we could free *the Book* . . . And now I plan to do just that."

"But the Brink—"

Professor Lachlan waved off her protest. "I never cared about destroying the Brink. It never stopped me from doing the things I wanted to do. It can stay up for all I care. It's a mere nuisance compared to what the Ars Arcana contains," he told her, tapping the Book. "This isn't just a record of the most important magical developments throughout history. It is an object infused with the very *source* of magic. Whoever can unlock it controls it. And whoever controls it will have the whole world in their hands."

Esta remembered then what Harte had told her on the bridge—that no one had really understood the Ars Arcana's true nature. He'd been wrong. Nibs had known. Nibs had *always* known, and he'd manipulated them all.

"And you think you should have that power?" she asked, urging him on as she tried to think of some way out of the mess she'd walked right into.

"Why not me? The Order could barely touch the power these pages contain. They knew what the Book was capable of, which is why they kept it under lock and key. But they were never brave enough to actually use it. They'd been warned by the last person brave enough to attempt unlocking the Book's secrets and wielding its power after it nearly drove him mad."

"One of the Order?" she asked, realizing that she could just begin to feel the drug they gave her wearing off. She didn't know how long it would take before she could be free of it, but she might be able to wait it out. She needed to keep him distracted, to keep him talking. A little longer, and she could try to escape.

"One of their earliest founders," Professor Lachlan told her. "Most don't realize Isaac Newton started his career as an alchemist. Before he sat under any tree, he searched for the philosopher's stone—for a way to isolate quintessence. I've had a long time to learn about the Ars Arcana, a long time to learn about Newton's secrets. He got as far as creating the five artifacts by imbuing ancient objects from the five mystical dynasties with the power of Mageus whose affinities happened to align with the elements. But he stopped before he ever managed to unite them and use them to control the power of the Book. Historians believe that he had a nervous breakdown in 1693, but that wasn't what happened at all. It was the Book, and his breakdown was the result of attempting to control its power. After he recovered, he gave up alchemy and entrusted the Book to the Order for safekeeping."

"You always told me that elemental magic wasn't real magic," she argued, still reeling. "Or was that a lie, too?"

"It's not. Elemental magic *isn't* real magic. It requires breaking up the pieces of creation, dividing them and weakening them in order to control them. Real magic is about controlling the whole of creation, the spaces between the elements that make up the very fabric of existence. Mageus don't need the elements, but we can use them. We've always been able to use them. With the right rituals, the elements can be quite useful to augment natural power. It's what made the Order what it is. It's what made you what you are," he told her, lifting the cuff and examining it in the light of the desk lamp.

"The Order doesn't have real magic," she argued. She was feeling stronger now, but she had to keep him talking until she figured out how to escape. So she pressed on, taunting him with her disbelief. "They aren't Mageus. All the power they have is stolen."

He placed the cuff back onto the table before he looked at her. "That may be true now, but it wasn't always. The Order of the Ortus Aurea began as a front. Like so many of those so-called occult societies, it was formed so the richest, most influential Mageus could hide in plain sight. The Order is one of the oldest, though, and they were able to maintain their power even as the Disenchantment destroyed magic."

That news contradicted everything she'd ever been taught, everything she'd ever believed. "You're telling me that the members of the Order were once Mageus?"

"Of course they were. There's always been magic in the world, and at one time most people could put their finger on it, until they allowed themselves to forget. The Disenchantment helped with that. When the climate on the Continent grew too dangerous, the Mageus who could leave, did. They brought their little society to the New World, because they thought they could start fresh and they believed the new land was one where magic could take root. It didn't work, of course. Away from their homelands, after a few generations, their power had faded. So they used the secrets in these pages to create the Brink as a way to protect their magic.

THE LAST MAGICIAN

"But they couldn't control it. What began as a way to build their power became a trap, and their magic continued to fade. A few generations more and the only magic they had left was the power they could steal through their experiments. The Brink was never intended as a weapon, but it became one well enough.

"By the time my family arrived in Manhattan, back in 1888, the Order had forgotten what they once were, what they'd come from. They feared the power that was coming to their shores, so they tried to eliminate it. They targeted the weak, the poor. Those who had no voice, no power to fight back. They killed my father because he tried to speak out, and then they hunted down my mother and brothers and sisters. I only got away because I was off working. An eleven-year-old, working at a factory just to put bread on the table.

"They had no idea what fear was, but they will. Newton knew that if anyone could finish what he started and control the Book's power, they'd be as powerful as a god, the last magician the world would ever know. Now that I have the Book and the stones, I can unlock the power of the Ars Arcana. I've been waiting a lifetime—more, really—for this moment."

"So do it already," she challenged. "You're standing here monologuing like some cartoon villain. If you have all the pieces, what are you waiting for?"

He smiled. A slow, creeping curve of his narrow lips. "I've been waiting for *you*, Esta."

"I won't help you."

"Oh, I think you will."

When he lifted himself from the chair and worked his way around the table to where she sat, she realized then that he didn't have his usual crutch. Instead, his hand rested on a cane topped with a silver Medusa head.

"That was Dolph's," she said through clenched teeth as anger flashed through her.

"Yes, it was. You might say he bequeathed it to me."

"More like you stole it."

"Mere semantics. All that matters now is that I've nearly won. Dolph Saunders didn't get the Book. Because of your work, Harte Darrigan didn't either."

Disgust rose in her throat. "I would *never* help you."

Professor Lachlan tipped his head to the side, his expression calm. "What makes you think you'll have any choice?"

THE IMPOSSIBLE CHOICE

Esta pulled against the ropes, desperate to loosen them enough to free herself. She wanted nothing more than to destroy the man in front of her. But the ropes holding her were too tight. They barely moved.

Professor Lachlan straightened. "You're only going to wear yourself out, and I'm nowhere near done with you."

"Funny, I'm more than finished with you," she spat.

He laughed as he made his way to the table that held the artifacts, scooping them up and bringing them to where she was still tied to the chair. "You certainly inherited your mother's fire, didn't you?"

Her voice sounded like gravel when she finally found it: "You knew my mother?"

Professor Lachlan took a moment to look her over, his cloudy eyes studying her. "Dressed like that, you look a bit like her, you know. Not much, but a little. Same eyes. Lighter hair." He placed the crown that held the Dragon's Eye on her head, so the cool metal lay snug against her forehead. "You're certainly impulsive like she was. Stubborn, too."

"You told me you found me in a park." Her own voice sounded very far away, and all around her, the room felt like a tunnel.

"I lied," he said, fastening the collar that held the Djinni's Star around her neck.

"Or maybe you're lying now."

"Am I?" He slid the ring with the clear agate called Delphi's Tear onto her left middle finger.

She could feel the warmth of the stones, but they didn't call to her, not like Ishtar's Key did. Professor Lachlan was still holding the cuff, and if he would just put it on her arm—if she could just fight past the drug in her system—maybe she could get away.

"You have to be lying." Because if he wasn't, then everything that Esta had ever believed about herself was also a lie.

"I'm surprised you didn't put it all together for yourself. You might be impulsive, maybe a bit overemotional, but I've never thought of you as stupid." He huffed out an amused laugh. "You didn't, though, did you?"

He studied her for a moment before he continued. "Actually, now that I look at you, you definitely have more of your father in you. I wonder why someone didn't notice the resemblance. Not that they would ever have put that together—not when everyone thought Dolph and Leena's child died at birth."

"Dolph?" she whispered.

"And Leena . . . who wasn't *quite* his wife." Professor Lachlan gave her a less-than-friendly pat on the cheek, but she didn't even feel the sting of his hand against her skin.

No.

Dolph Saunders couldn't be her father. She'd sat across from him countless times, had talked with him and argued with him. She would have known. When he bought her the knish from Schimmel's and told her what he wanted to do, wouldn't she have realized? When they brought his body in, pale and lifeless, and she had mourned with the others, wouldn't she have felt something—*anything*—that would have made her recognize who he was to her?

"That's not possible," she said through the tightness in her throat. "Dolph Saunders died more than a hundred years ago."

Professor Lachlan gave her a pitying look. "You *are* capable of traveling through time, aren't you?" He held up Ishtar's Key. "With the right equipment, that is."

"I would have remembered—"

"You were far too young to remember anything. You couldn't have been more than three when everything went wrong. After Darrigan took the Book and destroyed half of Khafre Hall, Tammany's patrols and the Order's influence made life a living hell in the Bowery—you know that now for yourself."

"No," she whispered, as though uttering that single syllable could change the truth that was staring her in the face. "I was there. He didn't have a child."

"He didn't *know* he had a child. Leena kept it from him after he betrayed her. He was so desperate back then to shore up his power that he didn't tell her he was dabbling in ritual magic. She didn't find out until it was too late that he'd taken some of her power and used it to turn his marks into weapons. The shock of it sent her into labor too early, and when you were born, she told everyone you'd died."

"How could she?"

"In those days, it was fairly easy. Fathers weren't all that involved. I think the real question you mean to ask is *why*." He shrugged. "Because it was clear from the beginning that you were something special, something rare and powerful, and she didn't trust that Dolph wouldn't use you as well."

"He never knew?" she asked, horrified that anyone could do such a thing.

"He never even saw you. She was desperate to protect you, and you should know well enough that desperate people are capable of terrible things. But they also make easy marks."

"She trusted you," Esta realized. It was the only way he could know.

Professor Lachlan nodded. "She needed an ally, and she believed in me. I don't think she ever intended to hide you for long, but lies have a tendency to take on lives of their own. We both knew your affinity was something different. Maybe once there had been others who could do what you can do, but they were hunted and eliminated during the Disenchantment. You were rare, even in 1902. An unexpected anomaly born from unexpected parents.

"It was easy enough to get her out of the way—Dolph believed me when I told him Leena would be fine going into Morgan's house. He was supposed to die that night as well, the stubborn bastard. But in the end it was easy enough to get rid of him, too."

"You killed them both," she whispered, still trying to process what he'd revealed. She was suddenly glad there was a chair holding her up, because she wouldn't have trusted her legs to do the job. "You lied to me about everything."

"I also saved you. Life is full of contradictions, isn't it?" All the amusement melted from his expression, and he leaned even closer. "By the end of the year, things had only gotten worse. Their Conclave was coming up, and the Order was growing increasingly desperate to find their artifacts. I knew if the raids got ahold of you, the Order would keep you. I couldn't risk losing you, so I did the only thing I could. I used Ishtar's Key to hide you."

He held up the cuff and examined the stone. This stone didn't have the crack bisecting its smooth surface. Even from that distance, Esta could feel its call.

"I'd experimented with it myself, and I knew it could be used to focus or amplify magical power, even if I wasn't completely sure what it would do for you. You were too small to have any control over your power, but I knew that if I got you scared enough, you'd use your affinity. So I locked you in a closet, and when you stopped crying, I opened the door to find you gone. Exactly as I'd hoped. Far out of the reach of the Order.

"They took me in, of course, and the interrogation wasn't an easy one. I didn't exactly walk away from it," he said, gesturing to his leg. "When I got back, the old woman I'd left watching the room said you'd never returned. I'd expected you to be back in minutes, maybe hours after the Order's men left." He frowned. "Ishtar's Key was more powerful than I'd realized, and you made me wait quite a while longer before you finally showed up. More than ninety years. But I was right in the end—it all worked out. I waited, and while I waited, I planned, and sure enough, you eventually appeared. As I knew you would."

"You *stole* me. You stole my entire life."

"I *made* you. I gave you a life you would never have had back then. And now you're going to repay the favor." He slipped the cuff onto her arm.

She could sense its heat, the call of its magic, but her blood still wasn't quite clear of whatever drug he'd given her, so she couldn't draw on it.

"Do you know what time is, Esta?" Professor Lachlan smiled when she didn't answer. "It's the substance that connects everything, the indefinable quality that transcends *everything*. It is the quintessence of existence—*Aether*. There was a reason I wanted you, a reason I saved you."

"Aether?" Esta asked, remembering Harte's words on the bridge.

He took the dagger, the one she'd stolen from Schwab's mansion that fateful night when everything had started to go wrong, and examined its tip. "It's a bit primitive, I know, but these things do tend to work better with a little blood."

Esta held herself steady, refusing to so much as flinch when the Professor approached her with the knife. Slowly, he traced it across her chest, just beneath her collarbone. She didn't even feel the bite of the blade. Her entire world had imploded—she'd betrayed her friends in the past and now she'd been betrayed by the only family she'd ever known. Everything she thought she knew about who she was or why she'd been saved was a lie. With everyone turned against her, she had no way out.

What was a little blood, a little pain in the face of all that?

When he was done, when her wound had started to feel hot, he tucked the knife into the bodice of her dress, so its blade was pointing down toward her belly and the Pharaoh's Heart lay flush against her skin.

"Aether connects all of the elements," he explained, "and so I will use your affinity to connect the stones. With them united, I'll be able to control the power of the Book."

"And what about me?" she said, hating the way her voice shook. "What happens to me?"

"I expect the same thing that happened to all the Mageus whose power was taken to create the original stones." He gave her an unreadable look. "You're just the vessel."

She tried to struggle against the ropes again, but with the dagger against her skin, she couldn't move without slicing herself to ribbons.

"Now, now. It'll only be a few more minutes." Professor Lachlan smiled softly then, and it wasn't the cold smile of Nibsy Lorcan, but instead was the smile Esta had grown up with, the smile she had craved so desperately as a child.

That betrayal sliced deeper than any wound the dagger could make.

But she lifted her chin. She would not let him know how afraid she was. The only thing she would allow him was her hate.

Professor Lachlan returned to the table and retrieved the Book. He ignored her as he flipped to a page he'd carefully marked, and then he began to read aloud.

At first it sounded like Latin, but as he droned on, the tenor of his voice changed, as though something had come over him, and she could no longer understand the individual words. As he chanted, the syllables grew more and more strange, until they no longer sounded like words, until his voice no longer sounded human, and as he chanted, the stones in the pieces of metal pressed against her skin began to grow warm. On and on he went, until time seemed to lose all meaning, until the heat from the stones felt as though it would burn straight through to her bones, until a strange wind had begun to swirl around the library, rustling the papers until it grew strong enough to send them into the air. Until the lights began to flicker. Until all at once, a terrible roaring filled her ears.

And then everything went dark.

The air in the room went still.

But Esta wasn't gone.

CONTINGENCIES

A flame flickered nearby, illuminating the deep wrinkles of Professor Lachlan's face as he approached her. "You're still alive," he said softly, like he was talking to himself more than her. "It didn't work."

"I can't say I'm all that sorry."

Professor Lachlan leaned close to her. "You will be." He used the intercom to tell Logan to check the breakers in the basement, and he began removing the artifacts from her one by one, beginning with her cuff. A moment later the lights flickered on again.

"Did you say one of the words wrong?" she asked, purposely poking at him.

"No. I said everything perfectly," he told her as he took the final artifact back. "I was afraid this might happen. I was afraid it had been too long."

"So your grand plan isn't going to work after all?" She didn't allow herself to hope. Not so long as she was still tied to the chair.

"Of course it will. There might not be enough magic left in the world for the ritual to work now, but there was before. So you'll take the Book back to the boy I once was, back to a world where magic still had power and I was still young enough to use it."

"Why would I ever do that?"

He studied her for a moment. "Because if you don't, you'll most likely disappear. If Ishtar's Key isn't in the past, I won't be able to give it to you as a child."

Her mind was racing. "Then I should have already disappeared," she challenged. "Me bringing Ishtar's Key back here, to this time, would have already changed my life. The date you gave me the stone would have already passed by now. Nibs—you—wouldn't have been able to give me the stone as a young girl, I wouldn't have grown up in this time, and we wouldn't be having this conversation."

"Unless you've already done it. I don't think this moment would change until you make the conscious decision to change the past." He smiled, clearly pleased with himself. "I've seen every connection, planned for every contingency. It's a particular *talent* of mine."

So that was Nibsy's power. No wonder he kept it such a secret.

Esta lifted her chin. "Maybe I'd rather disappear than let you win," she said. "Did you plan for that?"

"Actually, I did," he said. He walked to his desk and pressed a button. A moment later, the elevator rattled to life, the lift climbing toward them.

He pulled a gun from the drawer in his desk and aimed it directly at her. The barrel was tipped with a silencer.

"I won't help you unlock the power in that book," she said, pleased to hear that her voice didn't shake even if she did. "I'd rather die."

Professor Lachlan smiled. "I'm sure you would. But who would you be willing to sacrifice with you?"

The door to the elevator opened then. "You called, Professor?" Dakari said, stepping into the room.

"No!" she screamed, fighting against the ropes that held her. "Dakari, go—"

But it was too late. The gun went off, a soft clap followed by the louder sound of Dakari hitting the floor.

"No," she cried, and her eyes were already burning with tears. She was still fighting against the ropes, and against the truth of what had just happened.

Professor Lachlan walked to where she was sitting and jerked her chin up, forcing her to look at him. "It seems you have a choice after all. You can choose to fade away. Choose to disappear and never exist. Maybe it'll happen immediately. Maybe you'll have time to watch everyone you've ever cared for die, just as Dakari has. Logan. Mari. Her entire family you're so fond of. I'll bring them here for you, make sure you can see them plead for their lives before I kill them. So they can know it was you who signed their death warrant. Or you can do what I ask and take the Book back to my younger self."

"No," she whispered, shaking her head.

"You like to save people, don't you? Think of it—you could rewrite this future and give Dakari a new life in a world without the Order. A life that wouldn't end in a heap on my library floor. If you're very good, you might even convince my younger self to have mercy on Dolph's crew."

She couldn't stop the tears that ran down her face. She turned away from Professor Lachlan, unable to stomach him so close to her, and across the room Viola's knives glinted in the dim light.

Jianyu. Viola.

Maybe she couldn't save Dolph, but she could still save them. As long as she didn't give up, she could go back and try once more to change things.

"Fine," she said, keeping her eyes on Viola's knives, so Professor Lachlan wouldn't see the hate in her gaze. "I'll do it. But I will fight you every step of the way."

Professor Lachlan—Nibs—whoever he was—smiled. "I wouldn't expect anything less, girl, but know this: You're playing against a stacked deck. I've already considered everything you might do, and I've already accounted for all the outcomes. Fight all you want, but the future will be mine."

Professor Lachlan hadn't lied about being prepared. He'd accounted for what seemed like every contingency.

Logan had her by the arm to ensure she didn't use her affinity without taking him with her. The gun was just a precaution, they'd told her. In case she got any ideas. Not that she believed them. Once they were in the past, it would be easy enough for Logan to kill her.

They'd given her some sort of drug, timing it so that as they walked the six blocks to the park, it would wear off just enough to allow her to use Ishtar's Key to take Logan back to 1902. She wouldn't have a chance to get away before then, not without dealing with the gun.

She'd been given an exact date, one week after the day on the bridge. Once they were back, Logan had specific instructions about what to look for. If she tried to take him to any other time, he'd kill her. Or he'd injure her badly enough to make her want to cooperate.

Once they were back, the Strega would be an easy walk. There would be very little chance of her getting away, or for her to ruin Professor Lachlan's plans for them to deliver the Book and the stones. And once Nibs had them, there would be no stopping him.

To make things worse, she didn't really know Logan—not this version of Logan. She didn't have the same memories he did of their shared history, and all she could go on to predict how he would act was the hope that the intrinsic nature of a person was steady and stable no matter what trajectory their life took. He might have been a pain in the ass before, but he hadn't been evil. He wouldn't have purposely hurt someone. She could only hope that was still the case.

But she wasn't sure she believed it.

She kept her head down, her posture slouched, like the weight of the world—its past, present, and future—was on her shoulders. *Let them believe they've won,* she thought to herself. Let them think she was penned in. Even if she wasn't yet sure how she'd ever manage to get out.

The Professor looked at his watch, and when the time came that the medication would have been out of her system, he gave a stiff nod.

Logan jammed the gun harder into her back, a cue that she needed to start. But she still felt sluggish and numb from the lingering effects of the drug, so it was harder than usual to find the right moment, the exact time she was supposed to hit. She pushed down through the layers of years, until she felt the familiar pull of that time. Strange, she thought, for it to feel almost as if she were going home.

But Esta forced herself to ignore the sappy sentiment. It took everything she had to guide them to the moment she wanted. In the distance, the Freedom Tower—the city's one-fingered salute to the rest of the world—began to fade. The city dimmed around them and she felt that push-pull sensation, like she would fly apart and collapse in on herself all at once as she pulled them to the date she needed. The park receded and the city of yesterday began to materialize, and just as she was almost through, just before the present disappeared and the past was made real, Logan began to scream and tear at the bag he had strapped to his chest, the bag that contained the other artifacts and the Book.

Instinctively, she understood that this was the best chance she would have. She gave her arm a vicious twist, wrenching herself away from him, and Logan, who was still focused on the bag, let her go just as they landed hard on the damp cobbled streets of Old New York.

Her entire body was shaking with the effort it had taken to get away from him, and the cuff on her arm was warm. The neighborhood was eerily quiet for the middle of the day. In the distance, she heard the clanging of bells and smelled the heavy chemical smell of buildings burning.

Slipping through time always left Logan momentarily dizzied, and it did this time as well. He'd barely managed to pull the bag off and toss it away from himself when a group of darkly dressed boys came around the corner. *Five Pointers.*

Their eyes lit when they saw the two of them lying on the sidewalk, Logan still dazed from the trip, and their pace increased.

But before the boys could reach her, Esta pulled time slow and scooped the bag up. She brushed the grime of the streets from her dress, and with the world silent and still around her, she started to walk. She had somewhere she needed to be, a life she needed to save. She had to go back. She had to get to the bridge. Logan could fend for himself.

THE MAGICIAN

March 1902—The Brooklyn Bridge

The Magician stood at the edge of his world and took one last look at his city. Around him, chaos erupted on the bridge, but his eyes were on the only thing that mattered—Esta.

Go, he willed her. She had to take the Book where they would all be safe from it. She had to take *herself* there too, far away from Nibs or Jack or anyone else who might use her. *Including him.* If the Order ever found out what she was, what she could do . . .

Go.

But she wore the same stubborn expression he recognized from every other time he'd tried to get her to do something. *She wasn't leaving.* She wasn't getting away while she could. He'd expected her stubbornness, though, had known he would have to take the decision from her. It was only one step. A single step and it would all be over.

He closed his eyes and let himself feel the wind on his face one last time as he leaned into it—

And then he was falling, and the air around him pushed and pulled at him, pressing in on his body until he was so dizzy he thought he would vomit, his head pounding with an unnatural pressure. He fell and fell until he hit the ground in front of him, with something—someone—pinning him down.

He heard a soft, feminine moan, and the weight rolled off him.

"Jianyu?" Esta's voice came to him like a dream. "What are you doing here?"

It took him a second to find his voice, to make himself understand what he was seeing, but it was Esta. It was *really* Esta, not some dream of her. The bridge was empty and silent, and she was sprawled across Jianyu's back, looking more confused than he'd ever seen her. And he wasn't dead.

"He was helping me," Harte said, pulling himself up. He was still reeling from the shock of seeing her. The absolute wonder at being alive, when moments ago he'd thought Jianyu had decided to let him fall.

"Helping you?" She pulled herself off Jianyu, who lay unconscious on the ground. "Helping you do what?"

"Fake my own death." He swallowed uncomfortably when her expression seemed more angry than relieved.

Esta just stared at him with her eyes wide and a look of utter consternation on her face. It was maybe the first time he'd ever seen her at a loss for words.

"You're shaking," Harte said, touching her cheek with a trembling hand. Her skin was pale, her hair a mess around her face.

"I'm fine," she told him, but she didn't push him away. Then, all at once, her face crumpled. "You idiot," she said, slapping Harte. "You told me you were going to jump." Her voice was nearly manic, and her eyes were wild with unshed tears. "I thought you were dead," she cried, her voice cracking as her chin trembled.

"I'm not dead," he said softly, glad to hear his voice was so steady, considering how shaken he felt. He hadn't known for sure that Jianyu was going to be there, as they'd planned. When he'd leaned into the wind, Harte was forcing himself to put all his trust, his entire life, into someone else's hands.

She slapped him again, and he raised his arms to fend off the attack, but fell over instead, his head spinning from the motion. "Esta, stop!"

"You lied to me again!"

"I had to," he said, pulling himself upright again. He caught her hands, gently, so that she couldn't hit him again. "I needed you to get the Book away from Nibs and Jack, and I knew you wouldn't leave any other way."

But her expression didn't soften. Her golden eyes were still filled with fire. "You told me the Order would never stop hunting you."

"They won't."

Jianyu moaned nearby but hadn't yet come to.

"Then why?"

She seemed to have calmed down, so he released her hands. "I was going back to the city, to stop Nibs and the Order . . . to create a different future for you to return to."

Esta went still, her expression wary. "And I'm just supposed to believe you now?"

"He speaks truly," Jianyu added with a groan as he finally pulled himself upright. "We arranged everything after Dolph was found." He took a look around and seemed to realize finally that the bridge was empty. "What happened? Where did everyone go?" he asked, puzzled.

"They left hours ago," Esta explained.

"Hours?"

"For you, it would have felt like moments," Esta told him. "I thought I was just grabbing Harte. I didn't realize you were there too when I reached through."

Jianyu looked utterly perplexed. "Reached through?"

"Through time," she said. "I couldn't come all the way through. So I just kind of . . . pushed you past the moment you were in, to a different time." She rubbed at her arm, and pain flickered across her expression. "It's a long story."

Jianyu peered at Esta with confusion and no little amount of curiosity. "I would be most interested to hear your explanation."

"Later." Harte turned to Esta. "We had to make the Order and Nibs, *everyone*, believe that I was gone," he said, trying to explain. "Hell, you were supposed to believe it too. You were supposed to stay in your own time, when you'd be safe."

"There's no such thing as safe anymore," she said softly. Then she looked to Jianyu. "Does Viola know too? Was she in on this?"

"I thought the fewer who knew, the better. Easier to avoid suspicion around Nibs," Jianyu told her.

"Nibs," Esta said, her voice breaking.

Then she told them about Nibs and Professor Lachlan, about Dakari's death and Logan's betrayal.

"How did you ever get away?" Harte asked.

"I improvised." A small smile tugged at her lips. "And now I have this." She pulled the Book from the bag that she had slung across her body, but her eyes were still staring into its interior, and the color was draining from her face. "No."

"What?" he asked, wondering what could have put that look on her face after everything they'd been through.

She pulled out a charred piece of metal that looked strangely familiar. "Is that——?"

"They're gone," she whispered, dumping the contents of the bag onto the ground. The artifacts he'd stolen, all charred so badly they were nearly beyond recognition. "This happened before. When I came here the first time to find you. I showed you, remember?"

"Your cuff," Harte said, remembering the strange images that had flashed through his mind when she'd kissed him onstage. "What happened to them?"

"I don't know," she said. "But I wonder . . . I felt the same heat and pain when I reached to push you through as I'd felt the first time I came back. There must be something to the stones. They must not be able to exist in the same time as themselves."

Harte thought for a moment. "Nibs wouldn't have sent the stones back with this Logan character if he knew this would happen. He won't be able to get to them either. Not where I've put them. We're safe. It's over."

"It's not." She looked up at him, her expression unreadable. "Someday he will get them. He has before. We have to get the stones before he does."

"They seem to be beyond repair," Jianyu said, gesturing to the charred remains.

"Not these," Esta said. "The others." She met Harte's eyes. "The stones that should still be in *this* time."

"They're outside the city, and he's *inside*. He can't get out of the Brink."

"But they won't always be outside the city. Eventually they'll make their way back in. I know, because I've stolen every one of them before." She grabbed his arm. "And what's worse, Logan is here now. I left him lying on the sidewalk about a week from now. He's going to find Nibs, and he'll tell him everything that happens in the future. We can't let him have that information *and* the stones. We *have* to get to the stones before he does."

Harte frowned. "There's no way to get through the Brink without destroying it."

Her eyes were wide, her expression unreadable, but he could tell she was thinking, turning over ideas in her mind. And then something clicked, something shifted. "Maybe there is," she told him, sounding strangely calm.

"Esta, I've explained this . . ."

"I know. You told me that the Brink was like a circuit—that taking the Book through would short it out with the excess power. But there *are* ways to get through a circuit. There are ways to touch electricity. Look at the birds on the wires—you just can't be grounded."

He shook his head, not understanding. "Grounded?"

"Maybe grounded is the wrong word. But you're worried that the power of the Book would short out the Brink, right? We just need to keep the Book from disrupting the current of the Brink. Something Professor Lachlan—Nibs—told me might help. Aether and time are the same thing. Why can't we use my affinity for time to block the Book's power from disrupting the Aether of the Brink? Then it wouldn't over-load the circuit, and maybe there wouldn't be any magical blackout."

"That might work," Jianyu said, his voice thoughtful. "It is not so different from what I do with light to disappear. I bend it around myself. If she could direct the Aether of the Brink around the Book instead of through it—"

"You don't understand, Esta. That won't work."

"Why not? If it's a circuit, then all we have to do is—"

He rested his hand on her arm, stopping her words. "It won't work because all that power isn't in the Book anymore." He swallowed hard, finally forcing himself to accept what he'd known ever since the voices had crashed into him in the Mysterium. "All that power is in *me*."

Her mouth dropped open. "*In* you?"

He nodded, unable to speak. Because he wasn't sure how long he'd be able to live with it inside him, how long he'd be able to control it.

"So this is what you were hiding?" Jianyu asked, his voice dark.

He shifted, feeling vaguely guilty. Jianyu had risked so much to help him. "I told you everything I could."

"You should have told me *everything*," Jianyu said, his voice carrying a note of anger that Harte had never heard before, not even that night when Jianyu found him on the docks.

Esta shook her head. "It doesn't matter now. We need the stones."

He looked at her more closely then, with her hair falling down around her face and her clothes rumpled beyond repair. It was probably certain death for the both of them if he went along with her mad plan. But with the Book living inside of him, chipping away at him a little more every day, he already was a dead man. If her plan actually managed to work, maybe she could save them both. If not, he would happily take any number of minutes more he could in that crazy world, especially if they were minutes fighting with her.

"You'll need to find Viola and let her know what happened," she said to Jianyu. "We have some time before we catch up to when I left Logan. If you can keep him from getting to Nibs, that will buy us more. Because once Nibs knows that I'm back, he won't stop at anything to get the Book." She turned back to Harte, her eyes already shining with determination. "He won't know you didn't actually jump, and he won't know about the stones. That will give us an advantage, but even so, we're going to need every bit of luck to get this right."

"We're going to need a hell of a lot more than luck," he muttered, his head still swirling at everything that had happened, all that she wanted to do.

"I will find Viola, and together we can keep your friend from Nibs," Jianyu promised. "We'll give you all the time we can."

"But then what?" Harte said, still refusing to allow himself to hope.

"Then we unite the stones, take control of the Book's power," Esta said.

Harte frowned. "I'm not sure any one person should control it."

"I'm not either, but I'm not willing to let Nibs or the Order be the ones to make that decision," she said. "Are you?"

"I, for one, am not." Jianyu stood and offered his hand to help Harte to his feet. He handed Harte a parcel that he took from inside his own coat. "You go with Esta. I will see to things here."

Harte hesitated for a minute. "I owe you my thanks. For trusting me, even when I didn't deserve it. For helping me. You could have let me fall."

"I did it for Dolph," Jianyu said. "Do not forget your promise, and do not prove me a fool." And with a small bow of his head, he disappeared, leaving Harte and Esta alone on the bridge.

Harte watched the place where Jianyu had just been, and after a moment he unwrapped the parcel and put on the shirt that it contained.

"So you'll help me?" Esta asked as he buttoned the shirt. "You'll show me how to get through the Brink using the Book?"

It was no longer morning, Harte realized. The sun had just set and the whole skyline was aflame with the glow of twilight reflecting off the buildings. It looked like a city on fire, a dangerous and dazzling place.

He tucked in the shirt, straightened the sleeves. "You shouldn't have come back," he told her.

"I didn't have much of a choice," she said, and her golden eyes were clouded with pain.

"What you're asking me to do, what you're planning, it could be the death of us both."

"If we don't, it could be the death of *everyone*. Nibs cannot get those stones. The Order can't either."

"And what if we make everything worse?" The voices in his mind were louder now, humming their promises and threats. *They knew what she was. They wanted her.* He rubbed the back of his neck, a feeble attempt to subdue the thing that now lived inside of him.

"We still have to try."

He looked once more at that far side of the bridge, at the world he had come to believe he would never reach. *But Esta is back,* the voices whispered. So maybe, just maybe . . .

There was no talking her out of it, no turning her away from this course. And there was a part of him that didn't want to.

He held out his hand. "If you're ready?"

She looked up at his open palm and shook her head as she pulled herself to her feet. "Nice try."

But then she slipped her arm through his, and together they began walking toward the cold power of the Brink.

ACKNOWLEDGMENTS

This is a big book, and it took a lot of people to make it happen. Thanks go first and foremost to Michael Strother, who loved my pitch for this book and whose guidance made it so much better. I'm *so* grateful that Sarah McCabe was willing to adopt this behemoth and for her astute insights and support (even when the word count continued to grow). The entire team at Simon Pulse are my heroes for giving me the gift of more time to make it right and the gift of their support for this story. Craig Howell and Cliff Nielsen made *the most* amazing cover art, and I'm still blown away by the beautiful map Drew Willis designed. I could not be more indebted to the sharp eyes of Penina Lopez for her copyediting, to Valerie Shea for her proofreading, and to Clare McGlade for her cold read.

Thank you to all of the people who read early drafts: Kristen Lippert-Martin helped me solve a major plot issue and saved the book, Hope Cook's honest words helped me see mistakes I hadn't intended to make and saved the book, and Olivia Hinebaugh kept my spirits up when I felt like the whole project was pointless and saved the book. Kathryn Rose and Helene Dunbar also gave me essential insights to make this story stronger, and I'm grateful for their help.

Thanks to Flavia Brunetti, Guillaume Amphoux, and Christina Ketchum, who all assisted with some of the non-English phrases and words. Any mistakes are, of course, my own. The awesome people at the Lower East Side History Project were unbelievably helpful in walking me around the areas in this book and helping me find where everyone lived. They also give excellent dim sum recommendations.

I'm not sure what I would do without my rock star of an agent, Kathleen Rushall.

I should probably also thank Chris Cornell, who has no idea that his music was the soundtrack to writing this. Who knows why *Higher Truth* worked for 1902 New York, but it did.

To my family, who has lived with this book for as long as I have. It wasn't easy to write, which means there were times I wasn't easy to live with. To J, who makes it possible to run off to the city for research and never doubts that this is what I should be doing, and to H, and X, who are my hearts: I couldn't do any of this without their support, and I wouldn't want to.

Finally, like so many in this country, I'm the product of immigrants. A few years back I was looking at Ellis Island ship manifests, and I noticed that none of my great-grandmothers were listed as literate. I'm sure those women would have found me a strange creature with my fancy degrees and complete disinterest in housekeeping, but I hope they would be proud. After all, it was because of their sacrifices and determination that I find myself here, making a life out of the very words they came to this country unable to read. So for those women, and for all who came before, imperfect as they might have been, thank you.

LISA MAXWELL is the author of *Sweet Unrest, Gathering Deep,* and *Unhooked.* She grew up in Akron, Ohio, and has a PhD in English. She's worked as a teacher, scholar, bookseller, editor, and writer. When she's not writing books, she's a professor at a local college. She now lives near Washington, DC, with her husband and two sons. You can follow her on Twitter @LisaMaxwellYA or learn more about her upcoming books at Lisa-Maxwell.com.